USEFUL SUBJECT INDEX TERMS

Administration
  Agents
  Financial operations
    Accounting
    Funding
    Payroll
    Taxes
  Legal aspects
    Censorship
    Contracts
    Copyright
    Liabilities
    Regulations
  Personnel
    Labor relations
    Unions
  Planning/operation
    Producing
  Public relations
    Advertising
    Community relations
    Marketing
Audience
  Audience composition
  Audience-performer relationship
  Audience reactions/comments
Basic theatrical documents
  Choreographies
  Film treatments
  Librettos
  Miscellaneous texts
  Playtexts
  Promptbooks
  Scores
Design/technology
  Costuming
  Equipment
  Lighting
  Make-up
  Masks
  Projections
  Properties
  Puppets
  Scenery
  Sound
  Special effects
  Technicians/crews
  Wigs
Institutions
  Institutions, associations
  Institutions, producing
  Institutions, research
  Institutions, service
  Institutions, social
  Institutions, special
  Institutions, training
Performance/production
  Acting
  Acrobatics
  Aerialists
  Aquatics
  Animal acts
  Choreography
  Clowning
  Dancing
  Directing
  Equestrian acts
  Equilibrists
  Instrumentalists
  Juggling
  Magic
  Martial arts
  Puppeteers

  Singing
  Staging
Performance spaces
  Amphitheatres/arenas
  Fairgrounds
  Found spaces
  Halls
  Religious structures
  Show boats
  Theatres
    Auditorium
    Foyer
    Orchestra pit
    Stage,
      Adjustable
      Apron
      Arena
      Proscenium
    Support areas
Plays/librettos/scripts
  Adaptations
  Characters/roles
  Dramatic structure
  Editions
  Language
  Plot/subject/theme
Reference materials
  Bibliographies
  Catalogues
  Collected Materials
  Databanks
  Descriptions of resources
  Dictionaries
  Directories
  Discographies
  Encyclopedias
  Glossaries
  Guides
  Iconographies
  Indexes
  Lists
  Videographies
  Yearbooks
Relation to other fields
  Anthropology
  Economics
  Education
  Ethics
  Literature
  Figurative arts
  Philosophy
  Politics
  Psychology
  Religion
  Sociology
Research/historiography
  Methodology
  Research tools
Theory/criticism
  Aesthetics
  Deconstruction
  Dialectics
  Feminist criticism
  New historicism
  Phenomenology
  Reader response
  Reception
  Semiotics
Training
  Apprenticeship
  Teaching methods
    Training aids

Other frequent subjects
  AIDS
  Alternative theatre
  Amateur theatre
  Archives/libraries
  Avant-garde theatre
  Awards
  Black theatre
  Broadway theatre
  Burlesque
  Casting
  Children's theatre
  Community theatre
  Computers
  Conferences
  Creative drama
  Educational theatre
  Elizabethan theatre
  Experimental theatre
  Farce
  Feminist theatre
  Festivals
  Folklore
  Fundraising
  Gay/Lesbian theatre
  Gender studies
  Health/safety
  Hispanic theatre
  Improvisation
  Indigenous theatre
  Jacobean theatre
  Jewish theatre
  Liturgical drama
  Management, stage
  Medieval theatre
  Metadrama
  Minstrelsy
  Monodrama
  Movement
  Multiculturalism
  Music hall
  Mystery plays
  Mythology
  Neoclassicism
  Off Broadway theatre
  Off-off Broadway theatre
  Open-air theatre
  Parody
  Passion plays
  Performance spaces
  Playhouses
  Playwriting
  Political theatre
  Popular entertainment
  Press
  Radio drama
  Regional theatre
  Religious theatre
  Renaissance theatre
  Restoration theatre
  Ritual-ceremony
  Satire
  Story-telling
  Street theatre
  Summer theatre
  Touring companies
  Transvestism
  Vaudeville
  Voice
  Women in theatre
  Workshops
  Yiddish theatre

International Bibliography of Theatre: 1996

Published by the Theatre Research Data Center, Brooklyn College, City University of New York, NY 11210 USA.

© Theatre Research Data Center, 1998: ISBN 0-945419-07-4. All rights reserved.

This publication was made possible in part with in-kind support and services provided by Brooklyn College and the University Computing & Information Services of the City University of New York.

The paper used in this book complies with the Permanent Paper Standard issued by the National Information Standards Organization (Z39.48-1984).

THE THEATRE RESEARCH DATA CENTER

Rosabel Wang, Director

The Theatre Research Data Center at Brooklyn College houses, publishes and distributes the International Bibliography of Theatre. Inquiries about the bibliographies and the databank are welcome. Telephone (718) 951-5998; FAX (718) 951-4606; E-Mail RXWBC@CUNYVM.CUNY.EDU.

INTERNATIONAL BIBLIOGRAPHY OF THEATRE: 1996

Benito Ortolani, Editor

Catherine Hilton, Executive Editor   Margaret Loftus Ranald, Associate Editor

Rosabel Wang, Systems Analyst

Rose Bonczek, Managing Editor   Helen Huff, Online Editor

Mickey Ryan, Research Assistant

The University Consortium
for the
International Bibliography of Theatre

Brooklyn College City University of New York	Columbia University New York	Florida State University Tallahassee
University of California Santa Barbara	University of Guelph Ontario	University of Washington Seattle
	Université du Québec Montreal	

The International Bibliography of Theatre project is sponsored by the American Society for Theatre Research, the Theatre Library Association, and the International Association of Libraries and Museums of the Performing Arts in cooperation with the International Federation for Theatre Research.

Theatre Research Data Center
New York 1998

QUICK ACCESS GUIDE

GENERAL

The Classed Entries are equivalent to library shelf arrangements.

The Indexes are equivalent to a library card catalogue.

SEARCH METHODS

By subject:

Look in the alphabetically arranged Subject Index for the relevant term(s), topic(s) or name(s): e.g., Feminist criticism; *Macbeth*; Shakespeare, William; Gay theatre; etc.

Check the number at the end of each relevant précis.

Using that number, search the Classed Entries section to find full information.

By country:

Look in the Geographical-Chronological Index for the country related to the *content* of interest.

Note: Countries are arranged in alphabetical order and then subdivided chronologically.

Find the number at the end of each relevant précis.

Using that number, search the Classed Entries section to find full information.

By periods:

Determine the country of interest.

Look in the Geographical-Chronological Index, paying special attention to the chronological subdivisions.

Find the number at the end of each relevant précis.

Using that number, search the Classed Entries section to find full information.

By authors of listed books or articles:

Look in the alphabetically arranged Document Authors Index for the relevant names.

Using the number at the end of each Author Index entry, search the Classed Entries section to find full information.

SUGGESTIONS

Search a variety of possible subject headings.

Search the **most specific subject heading** first, e.g., if interested in acting in Ibsen plays, begin with Ibsen, Henrik, rather than the more generic Acting or Plays/librettos/scripts.

When dealing with large clusters of references under a single subject heading, note that items are listed in **alphabetical order of content geography** (Afghanistan to Zimbabwe). Under each country items are ordered alphabetically by author, following the same numerical sequence as that of the Classed Entries.

TABLE OF CONTENTS

ACKNOWLEDGMENTS

We are grateful to the many institutions and individuals who have helped us make this volume possible:

The participating officers, faculty and staff members of the University Consortium institutions:

Brooklyn College: President Vernon Lattin, Vice-President Patricia Hassett, Provost Christoph Kimmich; Professor Benito Ortolani;

Florida State University: Dean Gil Lazier, Professor John Degen;

University of California, Santa Barbara: Professor Simon Williams;

University of Guelph, Ontario: Professor Alan Filewod, Graduate Assistant Julie A. Moore;

Université du Québec à Montréal: Prof. Hélène Beauchamp, Graduate Assistant David Whiteley;

University of Washington, Seattle: Professor Barry Witham, Graduate Assistant Ron West;

Columbia University, New York: Professor Arnold Aronson;

Other University Consortium associates:

Professor Joseph Donohue, University of Massachusetts, Amherst, Chair of the Consortium Council Board;

Professor Emeritus Irving M. Brown, Brooklyn College, Consultant to the Consortium;

President Thomas Postlewait, ASTR;

President Noëlle Guibert, SIBMAS;

President Erika Fischer-Lichte and the University Commission of FIRT;

Hedvig Belitska-Scholtz, National Széchényi Library, Budapest;

Magnus Blomkvist, Stockholms Universitets Bibliotek;

Ole Bøgh, University of Copenhagen, Denmark;

Elaine Fadden, Countway Library, Harvard University, Boston;

Temple Hauptfleisch, University of Stellenbosch;

Veronica Kelly, University of Queensland, Brisbane;

Danuta Kuźnicka, Polska Akademia Nauk, Warsaw;

Tamara Il. Lapteva, Russian State Library, Moscow;

Nicole Leclercq, Archives et Musée de la Littérature, Brussels;

Shimon Lev-Ari, Tel-Aviv University;

Anna McMullan, Trinity College, Dublin;

Lindsay Newman, University of Lancaster Library, and SIBMAS of Great Britain;

Louis Rachow, International Theatre Institute, New York;

Michael Ribaudo and Pat Reber, CUNY/Computing & Information Services, New York;

Willem Rodenhuis, Universiteit van Amsterdam;

Francka Slivnik, National Theatre and Film Museum, Ljubljana;

Jarmila Svobodová, Theatre Institute, Prague;

Alessandro Tinterri, Museo Biblioteca dell'Attore di Genova;

And we thank our field bibliographers whose contributions have made this work a reality:

Jerry Bangham	Alcorn State Univ., Lorman, MS
Helen Bickerstaff	University of Sussex Library, UK
Maria Olga Bieńka	Polska Akademia Nauk, Warsaw
Rose Bonczek	Brooklyn College, City Univ. of New York
Magdolna Both	National Széchényi Library, Budapest
Sarah Corner-Walker	University of Copenhagen, Denmark
Ekaterina Danilova	State Library of Russia, Moscow
Clifford O. Davidson	Western Michigan Univ., Kalamazoo, MI
Krystyna Duniec	Polska Akademia Nauk, Warsaw
Jackline F. El	Brooklyn, New York
Jayne Fenwick-White	Glyndebourne Festival Opera, Lewes
Ramona Floyd	Sandbox Theatre Productions, New York, NY
Steven H. Gale	Kentucky State University, Frankfort, KY
Carol Goodger-Hill	University of Guelph, ON
James Hatch	Hatch-Billops Collection, New York, NY
Jane Hogan	TCI, Theatre Crafts International, New York, NY
Cherry Horwill	University Library, Univ. of Sussex
Helen Huff	Graduate Center, City Univ. of New York
Yvette Hutchinson	University of Stellenbosch
Valentina Jakushkina	State Library of Russia, Moscow
Toni Johnson-Woods	University of Queensland, Brisbane
Marija Kaufman	National Theatre and Film Museum, Ljubljana
Jarosław Komorowski	Polska Akademia Nauk, Warsaw
Joanna Krakowska-Narożniak	Polska Akademia Nauk, Warsaw
William L. Maiman	TCI, Theatre Crafts International, New York, NY
Margaret Majewska	Polish Centre of the International Theatre Institute, Warsaw;
Alenka Mihalič-Klemenčič	University of Maribor Library, Slovenia
Clair Myers	Elon College, Elon, NC
Maria Napiontkowa	Polska Akademia Nauk, Warsaw
Steve J. Nicholson	University of Huddersfield, UK
Danila Parodi	Museo Biblioteca dell'Attore di Genova
Michael Patterson	De Montfort University, UK
Margaret Loftus Ranald	Queens College, City Univ. of New York
Rosy Runciman	Cameron Mackintosh Ltd., London
Mickey Ryan	Synergy Ensemble Theatre Company, Islip, NY
Heike Stange	Freie Universität Berlin
Juan Villegas	GESTOS Revista de Teoria y Practica del Teatro Hispanico, Univ. of Cal.-Irvine
Rafał Wegrzyniak	Polska Akademia Nauk, Warsaw
David Whitton	University of Lancaster, UK

A GUIDE FOR USERS

SCOPE OF THE BIBLIOGRAPHY

Materials Included

The *International Bibliography of Theatre: 1996* lists theatre books, book articles, dissertations, journal articles and miscellaneous other theatre documents published during 1996. It also includes items from prior years received too late for inclusion in earlier volumes. Published works (with the exceptions noted below) are included without restrictions on the internal organization, format, or purpose of those works. Materials selected for the Bibliography deal with any aspect of theatre significant to research, without historical, cultural or geographical limitations. Entries are drawn from theatre histories, essays, studies, surveys, conference papers and proceedings, catalogues of theatrical holdings of any type, portfolios, handbooks and guides, dictionaries, bibliographies, and other reference works, records and production documents.

Materials Excluded

Reprints of previously published works are usually excluded unless they are major documents which have been unavailable for some time. In general only references to newly published works are included, though significantly revised editions of previously published works are treated as new works. Purely literary scholarship is generally excluded, since it is already listed in established bibliographical instruments. An exception is made for material published in journals completely indexed by *IBT*. Studies in theatre literature, textual studies, and dissertations are represented only when they contain significant components that examine or have relevance to theatrical performance.

Playtexts are excluded unless they are published with extensive or especially noteworthy introductory material, or when the text is the first translation or adaptation of a classic from an especially rare language into a major language. Book reviews and reviews of performances are not included, except for those reviews of sufficient scope to constitute a review article, or clusters of reviews published under one title.

Language

There is no restriction on language in which theatre documents appear, but English is the primary vehicle for compiling and abstracting the materials. The Subject Index gives primary importance to titles in their original languages, transliterated into the Roman Alphabet where necessary. Original language titles also appear in Classed Entries that refer to plays in translation and in the précis of Subject Index items.

CLASSED ENTRIES

Content

The **Classed Entries** section contains one entry for each document analyzed and provides the user with complete information on all material indexed in this volume. It is the only place where publication citations may be found and where detailed abstracts are furnished. Users are advised to familiarize themselves with the elements and structure of the Taxonomy to simplify the process of locating items indexed in the **classed entries** section.

Organization

Entries follow the order provided in Columns I, II and III of the Taxonomy.

Column I classifies theatre into nine categories beginning with Theatre in General and thereafter listed alphabetically from "Dance" to "Puppetry." Column II divides most of the nine Column I categories into a number of subsidiary components. Column III headings relate any of the previously selected Column I and Column II categories to specific elements of the theatre. A list of Useful Subject Index Terms is also given (see frontpapers). These terms are also sub-components of the Column III headings.

Examples:

> Items classified under "Theatre in General" appear in the Classed Entries before those classified under "Dance" in Column I, etc.

> Items classified under the Column II heading of "Musical theatre" appear before those classified under the Column II heading of "Opera," etc.

Items further classified under the Column III heading of "Administration" appear before those classified under "Design/technology," etc.

Every group of entries under any of the divisions of the **Classed Entries** is printed in alphabetical order according to its content geography: e.g., a cluster of items concerned with plays related to Spain, classified under "Drama" (Column I) and "Plays/librettos/scripts" (Column III) would be printed together after items concerned with plays related to South Africa and before those related to Sweden. Within these country clusters, each group of entries is arranged alphabetically by author.

Relation to Subject Index
When in doubt concerning the appropriate Taxonomy category for a **Classed Entry** search, the user should refer to the **Subject Index** for direction. The **Subject Index** provides several points of access for each entry in the **Classed Entries** section. In most cases it is advisable to use the **Subject Index** as the first and main way to locate the information contained in the **Classed Entries.**

TAXONOMY TERMS

The following descriptions have been established to clarify the terminology used in classifying entries according to the Taxonomy. They are used for clarification only, as a searching tool for users of the Bibliography. In cases where clarification has been deemed unnecessary (as in the case of "Ballet", "*Kabuki*", "Film", etc.) no further description appears below. Throughout the Classed Entries, the term "General" distinguishes miscellaneous items that cannot be more specifically classified by the remaining terms in the Column II category. Sufficient subject headings enable users to locate items regardless of their taxonomical classification.

THEATRE IN GENERAL: Only for items which cannot be properly classified by categories "Dance" through "Puppetry," or for items related to more than one theatrical category.

DANCE: Only for items published in theatre journals that are indexed by *IBT*, or for dance items with relevance to theatre.

DANCE-DRAMA: Items related to dramatic genres where dance is the dominant artistic element. Used primarily for specific forms of non-Western theatre, e.g., *Kathakali, Nō.*

DRAMA: Items related to playtexts and performances where the spoken word is traditionally considered the dominant element. (i.e., all Western dramatic literature and all spoken drama everywhere). An article on acting as a discipline will also fall into this category, as well as books about directing, unless these endeavors are more closely related to musical theatre forms or other genres.

MEDIA: Only for media related-items published in theatre journals completely indexed by *IBT*, or for media items with relevance to theatre.

MIME: Items related to performances where mime is the dominant element. This category comprises all forms of mime from every epoch and/or country.

PANTOMIME: Both Roman Pantomime and the performance form epitomized in modern times by Étienne Decroux and Marcel Marceau. English pantomime is indexed under "Mixed Entertainment."

MIXED ENTERTAINMENT: Items related either 1) to performances consisting of a variety of performance elements among which none is considered dominant, or 2) to performances where the element of spectacle and the function of broad audience appeal are dominant. Because of the great variety of terminology in different circumstances, times, and countries for similar types of spectacle, such items as café-concert, quadrille réaliste, one-person shows, night club acts, pleasure gardens, tavern concerts, night cellars, saloons, Spezialitätentheater, storytelling, divertissement, rivistina, etc., are classified under "General", "Variety acts", or "Cabaret", etc. depending on time period, circumstances, and/or country.

Variety acts: Items related to variety entertainment of mostly unconnected "numbers", including some forms of vaudeville, revue, petite revue, intimate revue, burlesque, etc.

PUPPETRY: Items related to all kinds of puppets, marionettes and mechanically operated figures.

N.B.: Notice that entries related to individuals are classified according to the Column III category describing the individual's primary field of activity: e.g., a manager under "Administration," a set designer under "Design/technology," an actor under "Performance/production," a playwright under "Plays/librettos/scripts," a teacher under "Training," etc.

CITATION FORMS

Basic bibliographical information

Each citation includes the standard bibliographical information: author(s), title, publisher, pages, and notes, preface, appendices, etc., when present. Journal titles are usually given in the form of an acronym, whose corresponding title may be found in the **List of Periodicals**. Pertinent publication information is also provided in this list.

Translation of original language

When the play title is not in English, a translation in parentheses follows the original title. Established English translations of play titles or names of institutions are used when they exist. Names of institutions, companies, buildings, etc., unless an English version is in common use, are as a rule left untranslated. Geographical names are given in standard English form as defined by *Webster's Geographical Dictionary* (3rd ed. 1997).

Time and place

An indication of the time and place to which a document pertains is included wherever appropriate and possible. The geographical information refers usually to a country, sometimes to a larger region such as Europe or English-speaking countries. The geographical designation is relative to the time of the content: Russia is used before 1917, USSR to 1991; East and West Germany 1945-1990; Roman Empire until its official demise, Italy thereafter. When appropriate, precise dates related to the content of the item are given. Otherwise the decade or century is indicated.

Abstract

Unless the content of a document is made sufficiently clear by the title, the classed entry provides a brief abstract. Titles of plays not in English are given in English translation in the abstract, except for most operas and titles that are widely known in their original language. If the original title does not appear in the document title, it is provided in the abstract.

Spelling

English form is used for transliterated personal names. In the **Subject Index** each English spelling refers the users to the international or transliterated spelling under which all relevant entries are listed.

Varia

Affiliation with a movement and influence by or on individuals or groups is indicated only when the document itself suggests such information.

When a document belongs to more than one Column I category of the Taxonomy, the other applicable Column I categories are cross-referenced in the **Subject Index**.

Document treatment

"Document treatment" indicates the type of scholarly approach used in the writing of the document. The following terms are used in the present bibliography:
   Bibliographical studies treat as their primary subject bibliographic material.
   Biographical studies are articles on part of the subject's life.
   Biographies are book-length treatments of entire lives.
   Critical studies present an evaluation resulting from the application of criteria.
   Empirical research identifies studies that incorporate as part of their design an experiment or series of experiments.
   Historical studies designate accounts of individual events, groups, movements, institutions, etc., whose primary purpose is to provide a historical record or evaluation.
   Histories-general cover the whole spectrum of theatre—or most of it—over a period of time and typically appear in one or several volumes.
   Histories-specific cover a particular genre, field, or component of theatre over a period of time and usually are published as a book.
   Histories-sources designate source materials that provide an internal evaluation or account of the treated subject: e.g. interviews with theatre professionals.
   Histories-reconstruction attempt to reconstruct some aspect of the theatre.
   Instructional materials include textbooks, manuals, guides or any other publication to be used in teaching.
   Reviews of performances examine one or several performances in the format of review articles, or clusters of several reviews published under one title.

Technical studies examine theatre from the point of view of the applied sciences or discuss particular theatrical techniques.
Textual studies examine the texts themselves for origins, accuracy, and publication data.

Example with diagram

Here follows an example (in this case a book article) of a **Classed Entries** item with explanation of its elements:

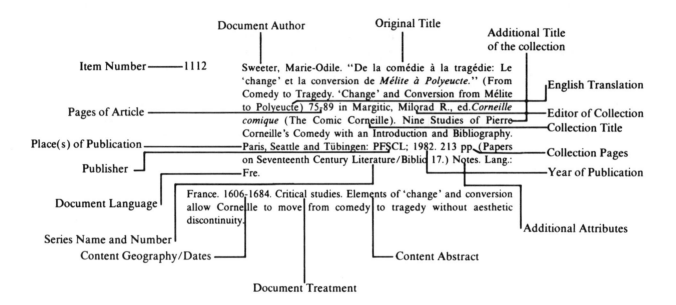

SUBJECT INDEX

Function

The **Subject Index** is a primary means of access to the major aspects of documents referenced by the **Classed Entries**.

Content

Each **Subject Index** item contains
- (a) subject headings, e.g., names of persons, names of institutions, forms and genres of theatre, elements of the theatre arts, titles of plays.
- (b) column III category indicating primary focus of the entry
- (c) short abstracts describing the items of the **Classed Entries** related to the subject heading
- (d) content country, city, time and language of document
- (e) the number of the **Classed Entry** from which each Subject Index item was generated.

Standards

Names of persons, including titles of address, are listed alphabetically by last names according to the standard established in *Anglo-American Cataloguing Rules* (Library of Congress, 2nd edition, 1978).

All names and terms originating in non-Roman alphabets, including Russian, Greek, Chinese and Japanese have been transliterated and are listed by the transliterated forms.

Geographical names are spelled according to *Webster's Geographical Dictionary* (3rd ed. 1997).

"SEE" references direct users from common English spellings or titles to names or terms indexed in a less familiar manner.

Example:

Chekhov, Anton
SEE
Čechov, Anton Pavlovič

Individuals are listed in the Subject Index when:

- (a) they are the primary or secondary focus of the document;
- (b) the document addresses aspects of their lives and/or work in a primary or supporting manner;
- (c) they are the author of the document, but only when their life and/or work is also the document's primary focus;
- (d) their lives have influenced, or have been influenced by, the primary subject of the document or the writing of it, as evidenced by explicit statement in the document.

This Subject Index is particularly useful when a listed individual is the subject of numerous citations. In such cases a search should not be limited only to the main subject heading (e.g., Shakespeare). A more relevant one (e.g., *Hamlet*) could bring more specific results.

"SEE" References

Institutions, groups, and social or theatrical movements appear as subject headings, following the above criteria. Names of theatre companies, theatre buildings, etc. are given in their original languages or transliterated. "See" references are provided for the generally used or literally translated English terms;

Example: "Moscow Art Theatre" directs users to the company's original title:

Moscow Art Theatre
SEE
Moskovskij Chudožestvennyj Akademičeskij Teat'r

No commonly used English term exists for "Comédie-Française," it therefore appears only under its title of origin. The same is true for *commedia dell'arte*, Burgtheater and other such terms.

Play titles appear in their original languages, with "SEE" references next to their English translations. Subject headings for plays in a third language may be provided if the translation in that language is of unusual importance.

Widely known opera titles are not translated.

Similar subject headings

Subject headings such as "Politics" and "Political theatre" are neither synonymous nor mutually exclusive. They aim to differentiate between a phenomenon and a theatrical genre. Likewise, such terms as "Feminism" refer to social and cultural movements and are not intended to be synonymous with "Women in theatre." The term "Ethnic theatre" is used to classify any type of theatrical literature or performance where the ethnicity of those concerned is of primary importance. Because of the number of items, and for reasons of accessibility, "African-American theatre," "Native American theatre" and the theatre of certain other ethnic groups are given separate subject headings.

Groups/movements, periods, etc.

Generic subject headings such as "Victorian theatre," "Expressionism," etc., are only complementary to other more specific groupings and do not list all items in the bibliography related to that period or generic subject: e.g., the subject heading "Elizabethan theatre" does not list a duplicate of all items related to Shakespeare, which are to be found under "Shakespeare," but lists materials explicitly related to the actual physical conditions or style of presentation typical of the Elizabethan theatre. For a complete search according to periods, use the **Geographical-Chronological Index**, searching by country and by the years related to the period.

Subdivision of Subject Headings

Each subject heading is subdivided into Column III categories that identify the primary focus of the cited entry. These subcategories are intended to facilitate the user when searching under such broad terms as "African-American theatre" or "*King Lear.*" The subcategory helps to identify the relevant cluster of entries. Thus, for instance, when the user is interested only in African-American theatre companies, the subheading "Institutions" groups all the relevant items together. Similarly, the subheading "Performance/production" groups together all the items dealing with production aspects of *King Lear.* It is, however, important to remember that these subheadings (i.e. Column III categories) are not subcategories of the subject heading itself, but of the main subject matter treated in the entry.

Printing order

Short abstracts under each subject heading are listed according to Column III categories. These categories are organized alphabetically. Short abstracts within each cluster, on the other hand, are arranged sequentially according to the item number they refer to in the Classed Entries. This enables the frequent user to recognize immediately the location and classification of the entry. If the user cannot find one specific subject heading, a related term may suffice, e.g., for Church dramas, see Religion. In some cases, a "SEE" reference is provided.

Example with diagram

Here follows an example of a **Subject Index** entry with explanation of its elements:

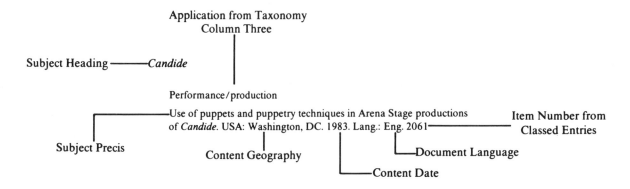

GEOGRAPHICAL-CHRONOLOGICAL INDEX

Organization

The **Geographical-Chronological Index** is arranged alphabetically by the country relevant to the subject or topic treated. The references under each country are then subdivided by date. References to articles with contents of the same date are then listed according to their category in the Taxonomy's Column III. The last item in each Geographical-Chronological Index listing is the number of the Classed Entry from which the listing was generated.

Example: For material on Drama in Italy between World Wars I and II, look under Italy, 1918-1939. In the example below, entries 2734, 2227 and 891 match this description.

Italy — cont'd		
1907-1984.	**Theory/criticism.**	
	Cruelty and sacredness in contemporary theatre poetics.	
	Germany. France. Lang.: Ita.	2734
1914.	**Plays/librettos/scripts.**	
	Comparative study of *Francesca da Rimini* by Riccardo Zandonai and *Tristan und Isolde* by Richard Wagner.	
	Lang.: Eng.	3441
1920-1936.	**Plays/librettos/scripts.**	
	Introductory analysis of twenty-one of Pirandello's plays	
	Lang.: Eng.	2227
1923-1936.	**Institutions.**	
	History of Teatro degli Indipendenti. Rome. Lang.; Ita.	891
1940-1984.	**Performance/production.**	
	Italian tenor Giuseppe Giacomini speaks of his career and	
	art. New York, NY. Lang.; Eng.	3324

Dates

Dates reflect the content period covered by the item, not the publication year. However, the publication year is used for theoretical writings and for assessments of old traditions, problems, etc. When precise dates cannot be established, the decade (e.g., 1970-1979) or the century (e.g., 1800-1899) is given.

Biographies and histories

In the case of biographies of people who are still alive, the year of birth of the subject and the year of publication of the biography are given. The same criterion is followed for histories of institutions such as theatres or companies which are still in existence. The founding date of such institutions and the date of publication of the entry are given—unless the entry explicitly covers only a specific period of the history of the institution.

Undatable content

No dates are given when the content is either theoretical or not meaningfully definable in time. Entries without date(s) print first.

DOCUMENT AUTHORS INDEX

The term "Document Author" means the author of the article or book cited in the **Classed Entries**. The author of the topic under discussion, e.g., Molière in an article about one of his plays, is *not* found in the **Document Authors Index**. (See Subject Index).

The **Document Authors Index** lists these authors alphabetically and in the Roman alphabet. The numbers given after each name direct the researcher to the full citations in the Classed Entries section.

N.B.: Users are urged to familiarize themselves with the Taxonomy and the indexes provided. The four-way access to research sources possible through consultation of the Classed Entries section, the Subject Index, the Geographical-Chronological Index and the Document Authors Index is intended to be sufficient to locate even the most highly specialized material.

CLASSED ENTRIES

THEATRE IN GENERAL

1   Lépine, Stéphane. "Théâtre et cinéma: les lieux du temps." (Theatre and Cinema: Scenes of Time.) *JCT*. 1996; 78: 174-179. Notes. Illus.: Dwg. Photo. B&W. 6. Lang.: Fre.
1995-1996. Critical studies. ∎Reflections on the differences between film and theatre, inspired by Youssef Ishaghpour's *Visconti. Le Sens et l'Image.*

2   Erenstein, Robert L. *Een theatergeschiedenis der Nederlanden. Tien eeuwen drama en theater in Nederland en Vlaanderen.* (A Theatre History of the Netherlands: Ten Centuries of Drama and Theatre in the Netherlands and Flanders.) Amsterdam: Amsterdam UP; 1996. 914 pp. Pref. Biblio. Index. Illus.: Design. Graphs. Pntg. Diagram. Plan. Dwg. Poster. Sketches. Photo. B&W. Color. Architec. Detail. Grd. Plan. 636. Lang.: Dut.
Netherlands. Belgium: Flanders. 990-1995. Histories-specific. ∎An extensive study that gives an overview of the great variety of theatre in the Low Countries.

3   Moore, Dick. "Drama Desk Discusses Future of Broadway." *EN*. 1996 June; 81(5): 5. Lang.: Eng.
USA: New York, NY. 1996. Historical studies. ∎Report of a luncheon meeting of the Drama Desk, the association of New York drama critics, editors and reporters. Topics included questions of the future audiences for serious theatre, new ideas on promotion and marketing, new producers and artistic leaders, and diversification.

4   Shenton, Mark. "Theatre on the Internet." *TheaterW*. 1996 Oct 21; 10(12): 32-36. Lang.: Eng.
USA: New York, NY. 1996. Technical studies. ∎Ways in which the internet can be used by theatre fans or practitioners. On-line services for *Playbill*, links to other web sites, production information.

Administration

5   Fritsch, Sibylle. "Der Mann im Hintergrund." (The Man in the Background.) *DB*. 1996; 9: 17-19. Illus.: Photo. B&W. 2. Lang.: Ger.
Austria: Vienna. 1974-1996. Historical studies. ∎Portrait of dramaturg Hermann Beil, Claus Peymann's closest collaborator at Burgtheater: their cooperation, division of labor, programs.

6   Bouchard, Michel Marc. "Assurer la relève et favoriser l'innovation." (Guaranteeing a New Generation and Favoring Innovation.) *JCT*. 1996; 78: 116-118. Illus.: Photo. B&W. 2. [Taken from a speech given at the Huitièmes entretiens du Centre Jacques-Cartier, Lyon, December 8, 1995.] Lang.: Fre.
Canada. 1970-1995. Critical studies. ∎Quebec theatre's crisis of the 1985-1995 decade and the need for support of new artists and new works from existing associations and theatres.

7   Bruyère, Marie-France. "Gestion et pratique: Un Lieu d'expérimentation." (Management and Practice: A Place for Experimentation.) *JCT*. 1989; 52: 147-150. Illus.: Dwg. 1. Lang.: Fre.
Canada: Montreal, PQ. 1989. Histories-sources. ∎Marie-France Bruyère, administrative director of Théâtre Petit à Petit, describes peculiarities of managing an experimental theatre.

8   Colbert, François; David, Gilbert; Lagueux, Denis. "Le Temps de l'art et le coût de l'art: Le Financement des théâtres institutionnels au Québec." (Time for Art and Cost of Art: The Financing of Institutional Theatres in Quebec.) *JCT*. 1989; 53: 21-26. Notes. Illus.: Dwg. Photo. B&W. 2. Lang.: Fre.
Canada. 1976-1988. Empirical studies. ∎Results of study *Les effets des contraintes financières sur les projets artistiques des compagnies membres de T.A.I. (Effects of fiscal constraints on artistic projects of Théâtres Associés Inc. member companies)*, comparing 1976-77 season with 1986-87 season.

9   Gruslin, Adrien. "Des Chiffres et des lettres." (Numbers and Letters.) *JCT*. 1989; 50: 91-93. Notes. Illus.: Dwg. 1. Lang.: Fre.
Canada. 1989. Histories-sources. ∎Supremacy of economics over art in contemporary Quebec theatre administration.

10   MacFarlane, Teri. "Sponsoring the Shaw." *PAC*. 1996; 30(2): 12. Lang.: Eng.
Canada: Niagara-on-the-Lake, ON. 1972-1996. Historical studies. ∎Bell Canada has struck a partnership with Shaw Festival which has resulted in funding for the festival, an interactive website, and a means to raise Bell's profile with customers.

11   Waytiuk, Judy. "Finding the Money." *PAC*. 1996; 30(3): 26-27. Illus.: Photo. B&W. 3. Lang.: Eng.
Canada. 1994-1996. Historical studies. ∎The responses of Shaw Festival, Manitoba Theatre Centre, and Prairie Theatre Exchange to governmental funding cuts.

12   Dose, Johannes. "Kulturhauptstadt Kopenhagen." (Copenhagen, Cultural Capital.) *DB*. 1996; 10: 20-23. Append. Illus.: Photo. B&W. 3. Lang.: Ger.
Denmark: Copenhagen. 1996. Historical studies. ∎Portrait of Copenhagen and its cultural programming, including financial problems and perspectives.

13   Finnbogadóttir, Vigdís. "An Optimistic Look at Theatre." *EN*. 1996 July/Aug.; 81(6): 3. Illus.: Photo. 1. Lang.: Eng.
Denmark: Copenhagen. 1996. Historical studies. ∎Text of the major speech at the sixteenth Congress of the International Federation of Actors (FIA) by Vigdís Finnbogadóttir, President of Iceland and a former stage director, on the importance of theatre in society and the central role actors play.

14   Moore, Dick. "Eisenberg Observes at Theatre Confab in Copenhagen." *EN*. 1996 July/Aug.; 81(6): 3. Illus.: Photo. 1. Lang.: Eng.
Denmark: Copenhagen. 1996. Historical studies. ∎Equity Executive President Alan Eisenberg attends the sixteenth Congress of the International Federation of Actors (FIA), an organization linking the unions of professional artists in more than 35 countries worldwide. This year's conference dealt with live theatre.

CLASSED ENTRIES

THEATRE IN GENERAL: —Administration

15   Kitching, Laurence P.A. "Die deutsche Wanderbühne in Reval zur Zeit der schwedisch Herrschaft." (The German Touring Troup in Reval in the Age of the Swedish Government.) *MuK.* 1996; 1: 17-45. Notes. Append. Illus.: Handbill. B&W. 2. Lang.: Ger.
Estonia: Tallinn. 1630-1692. Historical studies. ■Reconstructs a chronology of the group's activities through seventeen unpublished petitions (*Suppliken*) in the town archive.

16   Hodsoll, Frank. "Public Funding for the Arts—Past, Present, and Future." *JAML.* 1996 Sum; 26(2): 115-124. Lang.: Eng.
Europe. North America. 500 B.C.-1996 A.D. Historical studies. ■Overview of governmental patronage of the arts in Western culture from Periclean Athens to present day, with an eye toward the future.

17   Klaić, Dragan. "A Peek Out of Subsidy Land." *ThM.* 1996; 27(1): 75-82. Lang.: Eng.
Europe. 1996. Critical studies. ■Divining the future of subsidizing the arts in Europe, both public and private, as businesses merge and the European community moves closer to unifying.

18   Nouguès, Hélène; Chach, Maryann, ed. "Hélène Nouguès: Shubert's Oldest Employee." *PasShow.* 1995 Fall/Win; 18(2): 2-9. Illus.: Photo. B&W. 4.
France: Paris. USA: New York, NY. 1906-1995. Histories-sources. ■Career of Hélène Nouguès, Parisian representative of the Shuberts. Includes autobiographical sketch, and correspondence between the Shuberts and herself, with an introduction by the editor. Continued in *PasShow* 19:1 (1996 Spr/Sum), 2-14.

19   Bofinger, Jörg. "Travestie am runden Tisch." (Travesty at the Round Table.) *THeute.* 1996; 3: 34-37. Illus.: Photo. B&W. 3. Lang.: Ger.
Germany. 1995-1996. Historical studies. ■Lawyer's analysis of the results of a discussion of contracts initiated by Deutscher Bühnenverein and the problems of making decisions about new kinds of contracts.

20   Grund, Stefan. "Konzepte für ein Theater der Zukunft." (Concepts for a Theatre of the Future.) *TZ.* 1996; 1: 32-35. Illus.: Photo. B&W. 2. Lang.: Ger.
Germany: Schwerin. Austria: Graz. 1996. Histories-sources. ■Interviews with Ingo Waszerka, director of Mecklenburgisches Staatstheater, and Horst Gerhard Habert, director of Steirischer Herbst, about their efforts to renew their theatres from both the administrative and artistic point of view.

21   Herzog, Roman; Everding, August. "Dummes Sparen hilft nicht." (Foolish Saving Does Not Help.) *DB.* 1996; 7: 10-15. Illus.: Photo. B&W. 6. Lang.: Ger.
Germany. 1996. Histories-sources. ■Statements about current problems in theatre by Federal President Herzog and president of Deutscher Bühnenverein, August Everding. Published on the occasion of the 150th anniversary of Deutscher Bühnenverein.

22   Merck, Nikolaus. "Theaterreport Mecklenburg-Vorpommern." *TZ.* 1996; 6: 30-33. Illus.: Photo. B&W. 6. Lang.: Ger.
Germany: Mecklenburg-Vorpommern. 1996. Historical studies. ■The current state of theatres in the region and the diminished possibilities for development in the face of budget cuts.

23   Mihan, Jörg. "Junge Chefs." (Young Bosses.) *TZ.* 1996; 4: 35-39. Illus.: Photo. B&W. 4. Lang.: Ger.
Germany. 1996. Histories-sources. ■Conversations with East German theatre workers in different leading positions: Sven Schlöttche, Arne Retzlaff, Martin Fischer, and Hans-Peter Frings.

24   Möller, Karl-Hans. "Die Laus im Pelz." (Letting Somebody in for It.) *dRAMATURg.* 1996; 2: 11-17. Lang.: Ger.
Germany. 1996. Historical studies. ■Job description for dramaturgs, with emphasis on working with authors, productions and audiences.

25   Nix, Christoph. "Demokratie im Theater." (Democracy in Theatre.) *BGs.* 1996; 10: 12-15. Lang.: Ger.
Germany. 1996. Histories-sources. ■Theatre manager describes the necessity of democratic discourse in theatre, with discussion of organization, art, money, and democracy.

26   Roble, Wilhelm. "Frankfurter Zustände." (Conditions in Frankfurt.) *DB.* 1996; 8: 36-39. Illus.: Photo. B&W. 3. Lang.: Ger.
Germany: Frankfurt. 1996. Historical studies. ■Impressions from the latest season at Frankfurt, disputes among the theatres, omissions of the cultural administration and statements of the three directors Peter Eschberg of Frankfurter Schauspiel, Sylvain Cambreling of Oper Frankfurt, and Tom Stromberg of Theater am Turm.

27   Ruf, Wolfgang. "Landesbühnen als Modelle?" (Regional Theatres as Models?) *DB.* 1996; 6: 30-33. Illus.: Photo. B&W. 4. Lang.: Ger.
Germany. 1996. Histories-sources. ■Interview with Herbert Hauck, the theatre chief of Westfälisches Landestheater, about changing theatre structures and new perspectives for regional theatre.

28   Ruf, Wolfgang. "Ein Zipfel der Adlerschwinge." (An End of the Eagle Wing.) *DB.* 1996; 11: 38-40. Illus.: Photo. B&W. 4. Lang.: Ger.
Germany: Potsdam, Brandenburg. 1996. Historical studies. ■Reports the desolate politico-cultural situation of the theatres of Brandenburg (Brandenburger Theater GmbH) and Potsdam (Hans-Otto Theater), and the public debate over their proposed merger.

29   Stephan, Erika. "Wunder nach der Wende." (Miracles after Reunification.) *THeute.* 1996; 9: 30-34. Illus.: Photo. B&W. 6. Lang.: Ger.
Germany: Jena. 1991-1996. Historical studies. ■Description of new subsidy arrangements between Theaterhaus Jena and the local and regional governments, in which the theatre receives a subsidy of 1.3 million DM per season and is required to make half a million itself.

30   Stoll, Dieter. "Grosse Pläne, Schlichte Erkenntnis." (Huge Plans, Simple Insight.) *DB.* 1996; 5: 26-29. Illus.: Photo. B&W. 2. Lang.: Ger.
Germany: Kaiserslautern. 1996. Historical studies. ■Portrait of Wolfgang Quetes, artistic director-designate of Pfalztheater at Kaiserslautern, a typical German theatre with sections of opera and drama. Includes an interview about his career as an opera director.

31   Wenzel, Karl-Heinz. "Jugendtheaterarbeit." (The Work of Youth Theatre.) *SuT.* 1996; 158(2): 2-5. Illus.: Photo. B&W. 3. Lang.: Ger.
Germany. 1996. Historical studies. ■Starting conditions, aims, possibilities, and limitations of youth theatre, and the function of the principal of the group.

32   Gajdó, Tamás. "Tények és legendák. A Kelemen László-irodalom." (Facts and Legends: Literature on László Kelemen.) *SzSz.* 1996; 30/31: 56-62. Notes. Lang.: Hun.
Hungary. 1792-1990. Historical studies. ■Summary of Hungarian theatre historiography regarding László Kelemen (1762-1814), the first Hungarian theatre manager, also an actor and translator.

33   Márfi, Attila. "Színjátszás Pécsett, az abszolutizmus idején—a cenzúra intézkedései." (Acting at Pécs during the Period of Absolutism—Censorship.) *SzSz.* 1996; 30/31: 201-215. Notes. Lang.: Hun.
Hungary: Pécs. 1850-1863. Historical studies. ■Summary of theatrical operation at Pécs in the second half of the nineteenth century from the aspect of censorship.

34   Marx, József. "A struktúra rosszkedve—A budapesti színházak gazdálkodása." (The Moodiness of the Structure—Theatre Management in Budapest.) *Sz.* 1996; 29(9): 29-33. Illus.: Photo. B&W. Lang.: Hun.
Hungary. 1995-1996. Critical studies. ■Summary of the uncertainty and gloom of the Hungarian theatrical landscape, with suggestions for theatres and their funding sources, national, municipal or corporate.

35   Feinberg-Jütte, Anat. "Die Realität, aus der Theaterkonflikte gemacht sind." (The Reality of Which Theatre Conflicts Are Made.) *TZ.* 1996; 6: 14-17. Illus.: Photo. B&W. 4. Lang.: Ger.
Israel. 1996. Historical studies. ■The current situation of Israel's eleven public theatres, including plays, productions, audiences, and the uses of drama and theatre.

THEATRE IN GENERAL: —Administration

36 Kim, Soo-Jin. "Repertory, Ku Paramjikan Panghangeun?" (The Repertory System: Which Way Should It Go?)*KTR.* 1996 Feb.; 21 (2): 36-39. Illus.: Photo. B&W. 4. Lang.: Kor.
Korea: Seoul. 1996. Critical studies. ■The term 'repertory' is misused for a repetition or prolonged run of a certain play by a company. But a series of Oh Tae-Suk's plays by Mokwa Theatre Company can be called a desirable example of 'repertory system'.

37 Tesselaar, Suzanne. *Theatermarketing: met cases uit Proeftuinen.* (Marketing in the Theatre: With Case Studies of the Proeftuinen Project.) Delft: Eburon; 1996. 225 pp. Illus.: Graphs. Diagram. Photo. B&W. 50. Lang.: Dut.
Netherlands. 1990-1995. Historical studies. ■Account of a project concentrating on marketing strategies applied to Dutch theatre practice.

38 Ziębiński, Andrzej; Pászt, Patrícia, transl. "Színházmodellek." (Models of Theatre.) *Sz.* 1996; 29 (9): 21-28. Illus.: Photo. B&W. 8. Lang.: Hun.
North America. Poland. 1991-1996. Historical studies. ■Polish critic Andrzej Ziębiński analyzes the structures and operating methods of commercial and non-commercial theatres in the West, from the aspect of the profound changes already achieved and to be expected in Polish theatre.

39 Lenczowska, Joanna. "Programy teatralne w Krakowie do 1939 roku." (Cracow Theatre Programs up to 1939.) *PaT.* 1996; 45 (3-4): 324-399. Notes. Append. Illus.: Handbill. B&W. 36. Lang.: Pol.
Poland: Cracow. 1871-1939. Historical studies. ■Analysis of a collection of theatre programs.

40 Meissner, Krystyna. "The Need for a Cultural Policy." *TP.* 1995 Apr.; 37(2): 9-10. Illus.: Photo. B&W. 2. Lang.: Eng, Fre.
Poland. 1995. Critical studies. ■Discusses the need for new cultural initiatives in Polish theatre to meet the demands for a changing society.

41 Szetela, Maciej. "Krakowski afisz teatralny /1781-1893/." (Cracow Theatre Posters, 1781-1893.) *PaT.* 1996; 45(3-4): 247-323. Notes. Index. Biblio. Illus.: Poster. B&W. 30. Lang.: Pol.
Poland: Cracow. 1781-1893. Historical studies. ■Classification and analysis of theatre posters.

42 *Finansovye sredstva teatrov, koncertnych organizacij i kollektivov Ministerstva kul'tury Rossijskoj Federacii.* (Budgets for Theatres, Concert Organizations, and Other Groups under the Ministry of Culture of the Russian Federation.) Moscow: Ministerstvo Kul'tury RF; 1996. 100 pp. Lang.: Rus.
Russia. 1994-1995. Histories-sources. ■Information on the financial results of theatrical activity.

43 Jefremova, Jekaterina; Berger, Johannes, transl. "Ablösung." (Relief.) *TZ.* 1996; 5: 52-56. Illus.: Photo. B&W. 2. Lang.: Ger.
Russia: St. Petersburg. 1996. Historical studies. ■Theatre in St. Petersburg at the end of the millenium and possibilities for development, by a professional theatre critic.

44 Pervušin, B. "Delo o žetone." (The Case of the Token.) *MoskNab.* 1996; 1-2: 84-86. Lang.: Rus.
Russia: Moscow. 1990-1996. Historical studies. ■History of the Union of Theatre Makers (Sojuz teatral'nych dejatelej), with emphasis on one of the founders, Natalija Lavrova.

45 Smeljanskij, A.M. "Teat'r dlja vyživanija i vyživanie teatra." (Theatre for Survival and Survival of Theatre.) *TeatZ.* 1996; 6: 4-7. Lang.: Rus.
Russia. 1980-1996. Critical studies. ■The economic difficulties of theatres, predictions for the future, and role of theatre in contemporary society.

46 Bergman, Ingmar. "Vad vilja kulturbyråkraterna?" (What Do the Culture Bureaucrats Want?)*Dramat.* 1996; 4(1): 48. Illus.: Photo. Color. Lang.: Swe.
Sweden. 1996. Critical studies. ■A satirical presentation of the official report of culture *Kulturpolitikens inriktning (The Aim and Direction of the Cultural Policy)* which recommends decentralization.

47 Busk, Yvonne. "Mer teater för pengarna?" (More Theatre For the Money?)*Tningen.* 1996; 20(76-77): 7-9. Illus.: Photo. B&W. Lang.: Swe.
Sweden. 1987. Critical studies. ■A presentation of the different attitudes of regional theatres and independent groups toward performances given free to the schools by state-owned theatres.

48 Kristoffersson, Birgitta. "Inlevelse, lust och ett evigt sökande." (Feelings, Pleasures, and an Endless Search.) *Dramat.* 1996; 4(1): 36-39. Illus.: Photo. B&W. Lang.: Swe.
Sweden: Stockholm. 1980. Historical studies. ■Profile of director Peter Langdal, co-manager of Copenhagen's Betty Nansen Teatret and candidate for the position of manager at Dramaten, the Royal Dramatic Theatre of Sweden.

49 Nobling, Torsten; Edström, Per Simon; Blomquist, Kurt. "Kulturutredningen." (The Culture Report.) *ProScen.* 1996; 20 (1): 14-19. Lang.: Swe.
Sweden. 1996. Critical studies. ■The considerations of STTF on the cultural policy of the Swedish government.

50 Brown, Ian; Brannen, Rob. "When Theatre Was For All: the Cork Report, After Ten Years." *NTQ.* 1996 Nov.; 12(48): 367-383 . Tables. Lang.: Eng.
UK-England. 1985-1995. Historical studies. ■The Arts Council's independent enquiry into the needs of the publicly funded theatre and funding priorities, established under the chairmanship of Sir Kenneth Cork, provided a carefully constructed case for a funding increase. Article provides insight into its establishment, process, recommendations, and long-term impact.

51 Heiser, Mark. "The Martin-Harvey Letters." *TD&T.* 1996 Win; 32(1): 48-53. Notes. Illus.: Photo. B&W. 2. Lang.: Eng.
UK-England. 1920-1935. Historical studies. ■Case study of the history of theatre unionization. Emphasis on union boycotts arranged by prominent actor-manager Sir John Martin-Harvey. Excerpts from letters written by Martin-Harvey included.

52 Robson, Charles. "An Impressive Impresario." *PlPl.* 1996 June: 8-9. Illus.: Photo. B&W. 1. Lang.: Eng.
UK-England. 1996. Histories-sources. ■Interview with theatre producer Duncan Weldon discussing his position as the director of Chichester Theatre, his opinion of the British star system and rising production costs.

53 "Encore, Encore." *Econ.* 1996 Aug 10; 340(7978): 66. Illus.: Photo. B&W. 1. Lang.: Eng.
USA. 1937-1996. Critical studies. ■Broadway and film production of revivals: their appeal, successes and failures.

54 Berson, Misha. "Women at the Helm: In Leadership Posts Once Reserved for Men, They're Challenging Our Assumptions About Sex and Power." 61-80 in Martin, Carol, ed. *A Sourcebook of Feminist Theatre and Performance: On and Beyond the Stage.* London/New York, NY: Routledge; 1996. 311 pp. Notes. Index. Lang.: Eng.
USA. 1994-1996. Critical studies. ■Argues that women are breaking through the barriers engineered by the predominantly white male industry of theatre. Questions on new challenges at these higher levels are explored.

55 Brustein, Robert; Novak, Peter; Sellar, Tom; Malina, Judith; Field, Thalia; Acker, Kathy; Auslander, Philip; Dolan, Jill. "On Money." *ThM.* 1996; 27(1): 84-98. Lang.: Eng.
USA. 1996. Critical studies. ■Series of essays on the future of funding, new directions in raising money for the arts and criticism of government's indifference to its own culture.

56 Chach, Maryann; McNamara, Brooks, ed.; Swartz, Mark, ed. "An Industry Unto Himself: An Interview with George Fenmore, Part I." *PasShow.* 1996 Fall/Win; 19(2): 2-16. Illus.: Handbill. Photo. B&W. 10. Lang.: Eng.
USA: New York, NY. 1927-1996. Histories-sources. ■Interview with long-time theatre merchandiser George Fenmore.

57 Cobb, Nina Kressner. "Looking Ahead: Private Sector Giving to the Arts and the Humanities." *JAML.* 1996 Sum; 26(2): 125-160. Notes. Lang.: Eng.
USA. 1996. Histories-sources. ■Condensation of a report commissioned by the President's Committee on the Arts and Humanities regarding private sector funding.

THEATRE IN GENERAL: —Administration

58 Copilevitz, Errol. "The Potential Dilemma of Contingent Gifts." *FundM*. 1996 Feb.; 26(12): 34-38. Illus.: Photo. Color. B&W. 2. Lang.: Eng.
USA. 1996. Historical studies. ■Do's and don't's of dealing with donor-imposed restrictions to optimize an organization's funding capabilities.

59 De Shields, André. "Equity Celebrates Africanamerican Heritage Month 1996." *EN*. 1996 May; 81(4): 4, 7. Illus.: Photo. 4. Lang.: Eng.
USA: New York, NY. 1996. Historical studies. ■Three speakers relate their experience as African-American entertainers: Larry Leon Hamlin, founder of the National Black Theatre Festival in Winston-Salem, North Carolina, author/actress Norma Jean Darden, and television producer Gil Noble.

60 Dowd, Jim. "The Art of Making Art: Broadway Advertising." *TheaterW*. 1996 Aug 26; 10(4): 26-30. Illus.: Photo. Poster. Handbill. B&W. 10. Lang.: Eng.
USA: New York, NY. 1996. Historical studies. ■Commercial art for Broadway theatre. Trends, illustrations, images.

61 Erdman, Andrew L. "Edward Bernays and the 'Golden Jubilee of Light': Culture, Performance, Publicity." *TA*. 1996; 49: 49-64. Notes. Illus.: Photo. Handbill. B&W. 2. Lang.: Eng.
USA: Dearborn, MI. 1929. Historical studies. ■Edward Bernays' handling of the 'Golden Jubilee of Light' which included a reenactment of the invention of the light bulb with Thomas Edison himself, and how it ushered in a new era of public relations, performativity and manipulation.

62 Field, Derek C. "Gary McAvay: Let's Get this Show on the Road." *PerfM*. 1996 Fall; 22(1): 3. Illus.: Photo. B&W. 1. Lang.: Eng.
USA: New York, NY. 1996. Histories-sources. ■Interview with president of Columbia Artists Theatricals Corporation (CAMI Theatricals), Gary McAvay.

63 Filichia, Peter. "Stagestruck." *TheaterW*. 1996 Jan 29; 9(26): 11-14. Illus.: Photo. B&W. 1. Lang.: Eng.
USA: New York, NY. 1996. Histories-sources. ■Executive director of the League of American Theaters and Producers, Jed Bernstein, discusses plans for future of Broadway, including audience development, physical changes to environment, marketing.

64 Grizzard, Claude T., Jr. "The Ten Basic Commandments of Successful Fundraising." *FundM*. 1996 July; 27(5): 26-30. Lang.: Eng.
USA. 1996. Historical studies. ■Ten rules for any organization to follow in its pursuit of funding.

65 Hauser, Karen. "On the Future of Broadway Ticket Pricing." *TheaterW*. 1996 Jan 22; 9(25): 29-34. Lang.: Eng.
USA: New York, NY. 1996. Historical studies. ■Availability and demand for tickets, how to take advantage of discounts, audience response to prices. Producer Bernard Jacobs, president of Shubert Organization, discusses producers' approach to ticket pricing.

66 Kreidler, John. "Leverage Lost: The Nonprofit Arts in the Post-Ford Era." *JAML*. 1996 Sum; 26(2): 79-100. Notes. Lang.: Eng.
USA. 1957-1996. Historical studies. ■Examines the Ford Foundation's success as a patron of nonprofit arts groups, and what must be done, now that the Foundation's influence has lessened, regarding alternative funding initiatives.

67 Magruder, James. "The Image Thing: Making the Point with Posters." *AmTh*. 1996 Oct.; 13(8): 30-40. Illus.: Dwg. Sketches. Photo. B&W. Color. 29. Lang.: Eng.
USA. 1996. Historical studies. ■Graphic design and poster artwork used for theatre promotion nationwide. Impact of images, approaches to design, effectiveness of posters as advertising. Includes numerous examples of poster art from regional theatre.

68 Mitchell, Kimberly. "Theatreworks/USA and Touring: An Interview with Nancy Nagourney." *PerfM*. 1996 Fall; 22(1): 4-5. Lang.: Eng.
USA: New York, NY. 1996. Histories-sources. ■Interview with Theatreworks/USA business manager, Nancy Nagourney.

69 Moore, Dick. "LORT Negotiations Begin." *EN*. 1996 Jan/Feb.; 81(1): 8. Lang.: Eng.
USA: New York, NY. 1996. Historical studies. ■Current contract negotiations for LORT (League of Resident Theatres) theatres. Equity seeks significant improvements and is working hard to mobilize members.

70 Moore, Dick. "LORT Contract Extended: Negotiations to Continue in March." *EN*. 1996 Mar.; 81(2): 8. Lang.: Eng.
USA: New York, NY. 1996. Historical studies. ■The continuation of negotiations between the League of Resident Theatres (LORT) and Actors' Equity Association. Negotiations halt the risk of a strike in regional theatres.

71 Moore, Dick. "Equity Extends Self-Pay Health Coverage to Domestic Partners." *EN*. 1996 Mar.; 81(2): 1. Lang.: Eng.
USA: New York, NY. 1996. Historical studies. ■Actors' Equity extends health insurance benefits to domestic partners of participants on a self-pay basis. Qualifications for the benefits are included in article.

72 Moore, Dick. "Theatre Flourishing in Chicago." *EN*. 1996 Mar.; 81(2): 1, 8. Lang.: Eng.
USA: Chicago, IL. 1996. Historical studies. ■Production workweeks are on the rise in Chicago. Author attributes part of increase to new theatre, the Oriental, which had been dark since 1981.

73 Moore, Dick. "New LORT Contract Includes Separate Auditions for AEA Members." *EN*. 1996 Apr.; 81(3): 8. Lang.: Eng.
USA: New York, NY. 1996. Historical studies. ■Under the new contract, Equity and LORT have agreed to separate auditions for members and non-members. This decision continues a long-running dispute with the National Labor Relations Board on potential unfair procedures found in Equity's audition rules.

74 Moore, Dick. "Equity, LORT Reach New Three-Year Pact." *EN*. 1996 Apr.; 81(3): 8. Lang.: Eng.
USA: New York, NY. 1996. Historical studies. ■Negotiations have been concluded for a new three-year contract between the League of Resident Theatres and Actors' Equity Association. Includes highlights of the new changes.

75 Moore, Dick. "Contract Expiration Dates." *EN*. 1996 Apr.; 81(3): 7. Lang.: Eng.
USA: New York, NY. 1996. Histories-sources. ■List of expiration dates for twenty-eight Equity contracts all across the nation.

76 Moore, Dick. "AEA Exchanges with Great Britain." *EN*. 1996 Apr.; 81(3): 7. Lang.: Eng.
USA: New York, NY. 1995-1996. Historical studies. ■List of actor exchanges between American Actors' Equity Association and British Actors' Equity Association.

77 Moore, Dick. "LORT Ratification Vote Underway: More Than 7,000 Members Casting Ballots." *EN*. 1996 May; 81(4): 1, 2, 6. Chart. 1. Lang.: Eng.
USA: New York, NY. 1996. Historical studies. ■Actors' Equity overwhelmingly votes to ratify new LORT contract. Article relates specific information on contract negotiations, and reports on dire financial straits of LORT theatres in light of reduced government funding.

78 Moore, Dick. "Censorship Is Butt of Artists' Campaign." *EN*. 1996 June; 81(5): 1. Lang.: Eng.
USA: Los Angeles, CA. 1996. Historical studies. ■An innovative campaign, which protests censorship and cuts in the arts by sending Senator Jesse Helms packages of cigarette butts.

79 Moore, Dick. "The National Arts Endowment: Still Under Fire, Still Needs Your Support." *EN*. 1996 May; 81(4): 7. Lang.: Eng.
USA: New York, NY. 1996. Historical studies. ■The 1996 government appropriation for the National Endowment for the Arts. This status report reiterates that the Endowment is still under attack, with funding guaranteed only through October 1, 1996. The urgent need to contact members of Congress to object to cuts is outlined.

80 Moore, Dick. "Council Approves New Three-Year COST Agreement." *EN*. 1996 May; 81(4): 8. Lang.: Eng.
USA: New York, NY. 1996. Historical studies. ■Account of the new three-year Council of Stock Theatres agreement which features improve-

THEATRE IN GENERAL: —Administration

ments in housing, per diem, sick leave, and working conditions for stage managers.

81   Moore, Dick. "Three Withdraw from COST, Bargain Separately." *EN*. 1996 May; 81(4): 8. Lang.: Eng.
USA. 1996. Historical studies. ■Ogunquit Playhouse, Cape Playhouse, and Westport Country Playhouse withdraw from the Council of Stock Theatres bargaining unit to function as independent producers.

82   Moore, Dick. "Negotiations Set to Begin in July as Production Contract Expires." *EN*. 1996 June; 81(5): 8. Lang.: Eng.
USA: New York, NY. 1996. Historical studies. ■The Broadway production contract expires on June 30, but terms will continue to be in effect until September 2, 1996. Members will continue to work under the current terms and conditions until a new contract is ratified. Equity and the League of American Theatres and Producers will begin negotiations on the new contract on July 15.

83   Moore, Dick. "Agents Discuss 'The Business'." *EN*. 1996 July/Aug.; 81(6): 2. Lang.: Eng.
USA: New York, NY. 1996. Historical studies. ■A new series of seminars for members of Equity on 'the business.' Guests will include agents, casting directors, general managers, directors, choreographers, and other members of the theatre business community.

84   Moore, Dick. "Equity's Bonding Policy and How It Works." *EN*. 1996 June; 81(5): 1. Lang.: Eng.
USA: New York, NY. 1996. Historical studies. ■Procedures of Equity's bonding policy and reasons why it is important in light of changes in the Broadway production contract.

85   Moore, Dick. "ADlibs." *EN*. 1996 June; 81(5): 2. Illus.: Photo. 3. Lang.: Eng.
USA: New York, NY. 1996. Historical studies. ■Producer Robert Whitehead was honored at a benefit for the Theatre Development Fund, a tribute to producer Rosetta LeNoire was held to benefit the AMAS Musical Theatre Company, a multiracial company she founded in 1968, and singer Robert Merrill received the Lawrence Tibbett Award for a lifetime of professional achievement.

86   Moore, Dick. "Equity, League Exchange Proposals." *EN*. 1996 July/Aug.; 81(6): 8. Lang.: Eng.
USA: New York, NY. 1996. Historical studies. ■Equity and the League of American Theatres and Producers begin negotiations on production contract. Article outlines Equity's major proposals as well as the proposals of the League.

87   Moore, Dick. "Cross Border Transfers Discussed with Canadian AEA." *EN*. 1996 July/Aug.; 81(6): 1. Lang.: Eng.
USA: New York, NY. Canada. 1996. Historical studies. ■American Equity and Canadian Equity discuss cross-border transfer of actors in general and specifically jurisdiction over an upcoming tour of *Show Boat*, which will cover both Canada and the US.

88   Moore, Dick. "MSUA Pact Runs to Year 2000." *EN*. 1996 Sep.; 81(7): 1. Lang.: Eng.
USA: New York, NY. 1996. Historical studies. ■The new Musical Stock and Unit Attraction (MSUA) Agreement is ratified after difficult negotiations.

89   Moore, Dick. "Actors' Fund Clients Offer Gratitude, Praise." *EN*. 1996 July/Aug.; 81(6): 5. Lang.: Eng.
USA: New York, NY. 1996. Historical studies. ■The annual report of the Actors' Fund including testimonials from people who have benefited from the direct aid the Fund provides.

90   Moore, Dick. "Production Contract Negotiations in Recess." *EN*. 1996 Sep.; 81(7): 8. Lang.: Eng.
USA: New York, NY. 1996. Historical studies. ■Ongoing negotiations for the new Broadway production contract. Part of delay is due to death of Bernard B. Jacobs, president of the Shubert Organization. Many issues still unresolved.

91   Moore, Dick. "Equity Mourns Death of Bernard B. Jacobs." *EN*. 1996 Sep.; 81(7): 1. Illus.: Photo. 1. Lang.: Eng.
USA: New York, NY. 1916-1996. Historical studies. ■Tribute to recently deceased Bernard Jacobs, president of the Shubert Organization, a major producing organization on Broadway. Article includes details of death, as well as history of Jacobs with the Shubert Organization.

92   Moore, Dick. "Equity, League Reach New Four Year Agreement." *EN*. 1996 Oct.; 81(8): 8. Lang.: Eng.
USA: New York, NY. 1996. Historical studies. ■Equity and the League of American Theatres and Producers reach tentative agreement on a new four-year production contract covering Broadway, sit-down companies and touring productions.

93   Moore, Dick. "Players' Guide Discontinues Publication." *EN*. 1996 Oct.; 81(8): 8. Lang.: Eng.
USA: New York, NY. 1942-1996. Historical studies. ■*Players' Guide*, the talent directory that has been a mainstay of agents, casting directors and producers for 54 years, ends publication.

94   Moore, Dick. "Equity Negotiates Improved Severance Package for *Les Miserables* Company." *EN*. 1996 Dec.; 81(10): 1. Lang.: Eng.
USA: New York, NY. 1996. Historical studies. ■Equity negotiates an improved severance package for its members recently terminated from the Broadway production of *Les Misérables*.

95   Moore, Dick. "Council Approves Administrative Changes." *EN*. 1996 Dec.; 81(10): 1. Lang.: Eng.
USA: New York, NY. 1996. Historical studies. ■The Council of Actors' Equity approved a series of administrative changes affecting executive job descriptions and redefining the responsibilities of the executives in all offices.

96   Moore, Dick. "Eight Officers, 20 Councillors to Be Elected in 1997." *EN*. 1996 Dec.; 81(10): 1, 2. Lang.: Eng.
USA: New York, NY. 1996. Historical studies. ■Eight National Officer seats, fourteen Council seats in the Eastern Region, one in the Central Region and five in the Western Region are open in national elections.

97   Moore, Dick. "Actors' Work Program Awards Swire Scholarships." *EN*. 1996 Dec.; 81(10): 2. Lang.: Eng.
USA: New York, NY. 1996. Historical studies. ■The Actors' Work Program, sponsored by Actors' Equity, presents its annual Willard Swire Memorial Scholarships to four Equity members. The awards are named for a founding father and former director of AWP who died in 1991.

98   Moore, Dick. "Pensions Up, Assets Exceed $500 Million." *EN*. 1996 Dec.; 81(10): 7. Lang.: Eng.
USA: New York, NY. 1996. Historical studies. ■Equity releases its annual Pension and Health Trustees Report.

99   Moore, Dick. "Earle Hyman Enters Hall of Fame." *EN*. 1996 Dec.; 81(10): 8. Illus.: Photo. 1. Lang.: Eng.
USA: New York, NY. 1996. Historical studies. ■Actor Earle Hyman is inducted into the Theatre Hall of Fame along with Julie Andrews, Brian Bedford and Eileen Atkins, and costume designer Florence Klotz. Posthumous inductees are actor Nancy Walker, drama critic Richard L. Coe of the *Washington Post* and costume designer Irene Sharaff.

100   Moore, Dick. "NYC Agency Promotes, Trouble Shoots for Theatre Industry." *EN*. 1996 Dec.; 81(10): 9, 10. Illus.: Photo. 4. Lang.: Eng.
USA: New York, NY. 1996. Histories-sources. ■Interview with Patricia Reed Scott, Commissioner of the Mayor's Office of Film, Theatre and Broadcasting, and Wally Rubin, its Director of Theatre, on the development of Broadway Initiatives, a program that attempts to forge a closer alliance between the City of New York and theatre, labor, and manager to increase film and theatre production in New York City.

101   Moore, Dick. "Equity's Bonding Policy and How It Works." *EN*. 1996 Jan/Feb.; 81(1): 1. Lang.: Eng.
USA: New York, NY. 1996. Historical studies. ■Major provisions of Equity's bonding policy for seasonal theatres as well as year-round theatres.

102   Napoleon, Davi. "The Dodgers: Broadway's 'A' Team." *TheaterW*. 1996 Feb 5; 9(27): 16-23. Illus.: Photo. B&W. 6. Lang.: Eng.
USA: New York, NY. 1968-1996. Biographical studies. ■Profile of Broadway producers Michael David, Ed Strong, and Sherman Warner of Dodger productions. Past productions, goals, fundraising, and selection of properties.

103   Nunns, Stephen. "Reflections in the Mirror: Public Arts Funding in the United States." *JADT*. 1996 Fall; 8(3): 79-93. Notes. Lang.: Eng.

THEATRE IN GENERAL: —Administration

USA. 1994. Historical studies. ■The continuing debate on the state of arts funding in the United States.

104 Nunns, Stephen. "Is Congress Easing Up on the NEA?" *AmTh.* 1996 July/Aug.; 13(6): 58-59. Lang.: Eng.
USA: Washington, DC. 1996. Historical studies. ■Negative impact of Republican policy on the National Endowment for the Arts. Budget cuts, congressional support, and the hope that attacks on the NEA may be slowing down.

105 Nunns, Stephen. "Exemption Extinction?" *AmTh.* 1996 Sep.; 13(7): 63-65. Lang.: Eng.
USA: Washington, DC. 1996. Historical studies. ■Attacks on nonprofit institutions, financial abuses, amendments introduced to limit nonprofit organizations' participation in politics. Includes lists of do's and don'ts related to federal guidelines for nonprofits.

106 Pace, Guy. "1996 Annual Employment and Membership Report." *EN.* 1996 Dec.; 81(10): 3-7. Illus.: Graphs. Chart. 19. Lang.: Eng.
USA: New York, NY. 1996. Historical studies. ■Year-end reports of Equity's employment, membership and finances. These reports serve not only to discern patterns of major Equity activity and significant membership characteristics, but also provide guidance for policy making choices and future strategic planning.

107 Reis, George R. "The 1997 Non-Profit Software Directory." *FundM.* 1996 Oct.; 27(8): 12-22. Lang.: Eng.
USA. 1996. Historical studies. ■Directory, and description, of software useful to non-profit organizations.

108 Reiss, Alvin H. "As Art Presenters Confront Difficult Times, Quality Programming Remains High Priority." *FundM.* 1996 Mar.; 27(1): 52-53. Illus.: Photo. Color. 2. Lang.: Eng.
USA: New York, NY. 1996. Historical studies. ■Touches on two separate conferences held in New York City by the Association of Performing Arts Presenters and the International Society for the Performing Arts, relative to strategies for future funding.

109 Reiss, Alvin H. "On-Target Fundraising Campaign Helps Arts Center Win New Partners and New Life." *FundM.* 1996 Aug.; 27 (6): 36-37. Illus.: Photo. B&W. 1. Lang.: Eng.
USA: New Haven, CT. 1996. Historical studies. ■Success of the funding campaign for the Shubert Performing Arts Center.

110 Reiss, Alvin H. "Creative Strategies and New Partnerships Help Art Win Friends and Funds." *FundM.* 1996 Jan.; 26(11): 54-55. Illus.: Photo. B&W. 2. Lang.: Eng.
USA: New York, NY. 1996. Historical studies. ■Discusses creative partnerships between theatre groups such as the Gertrude Stein Repertory Theatre and Freestyle Repertory Theatre with business, relating to bartering talent and creative technology in exchange for funding.

111 Reiss, Alvin H. "Arts Activities: Key Aspect of Olympic Games." *FundM.* 1996 July; 27(5): 54-56. Illus.: Photo. B&W. 2. Lang.: Eng.
USA: Atlanta, GA. 1996. Historical studies. ■Corporate backing of art and theatre, and its relevance before and during Atlanta's hosting of the 1996 Olympic Games.

112 Reiss, Alvin H. "The Man Who Invented Grantsmanship." *FundM.* 1996 May; 27(3): 53-54. Lang.: Eng.
USA. 1996. Critical studies. ■Humorous piece about the fictitious Henry T. Grant—a satire of the American funding process.

113 Reiss, Alvin H. "States Are Key Funding Source for the Arts." *FundM.* 1996 Feb.; 26(12): 54-55. Illus.: Photo. Color. B&W. 2. Lang.: Eng.
USA. 1996. Historical studies. ■State arts councils as one of the strongest sources of funding in the USA, in spite of declining federal support.

114 Reiss, Alvin H. "Corporate Sponsorship of the Arts Growing Throughout the World." *FundM.* 1996 Nov.; 27(9): 30-31. Illus.: Photo. B&W. 1. Lang.: Eng.
USA. 1996. Historical studies. ■Overview of corporate sponsorship of the arts worldwide, and its gradual rise.

115 Samuels, Steven; Tonsic, Alisha. "Theatre Facts 1995." *AmTh.* 1996 Apr.; 13(4): 1-16. Illus.: Photo. Graphs. B&W. 26. [Supplement.] Lang.: Eng.

USA. 1995. Historical studies. ■A report on performance and potential in the American nonprofit theatre based on Theatre Communications Group's annual fiscal survey.

116 Snow, Leida. "Help! Public Arts Funding on a Respirator." *TheaterW.* 1996 Jan 8; 9(23): 11-17. Illus.: Photo. B&W. 1. Lang.: Eng.
USA. 1996. Historical studies. ■Impact of federal legislation and Republican policy on federal arts and humanities agencies. Focus on the National Endowment for the Arts and its funding.

117 Snow, Leida. "Congress Continues to Hobble the Arts." *TheaterW.* 1996 May 6; 9(40): 29-30. Lang.: Eng.
USA: New York, NY. 1996. Historical studies. ■Impact of Republican policy on the arts, particularly funding for the National Endowment for the Arts. Pending legislation, budgets.

118 Snow, Leida. "Funding For the Arts: You Can Make a Difference." *TheaterW.* 1996 July 22; 9(51): 35-37. Lang.: Eng.
USA: New York, NY. 1996. Critical studies. ■Local politicians discuss the impact of Republican policy on funding for the National Endowment for the Arts.

119 Stasio, Marilyn. "Merle Debuskey." *AmTh.* 1996 Apr.; 13(4): 26-27. Illus.: Photo. B&W. 1. Lang.: Eng.
USA: New York, NY. 1996. Biographical studies. ■The career of theatrical publicist Merle Debuskey, now retired.

120 Stevens, Louise K. "The Earnings Shift: The New Bottom Line Paradigm for the Arts Industry in a Market-Driven Era." *JAML.* 1996 Sum; 26(2): 101-113. Notes. Lang.: Eng.
USA. 1996. Critical studies. ■Focuses on the need to base funding on market economy strategies as private subsidies dry up or are not enough to cover costs.

121 Stockdale, Joe. "New Kid on the Block: Producer Julian Schlossberg." *TheaterW.* 1996 Dec 30; 10(22): 37-44. Illus.: Photo. B&W. 3. Lang.: Eng.
USA: New York, NY. 1962-1996. Histories-sources. ■Broadway producer discusses his approach to producing, budgets, past and current productions.

122 Sullivan, Jeanne English. "Copyright for Visual Art in the Digital Age: A Modern Adventure in Wonderland." *JAML.* 1996 Spr; 26(1): 41-59. Notes. Biblio. Lang.: Eng.
USA. 1996. Critical studies. ■Discusses legal challenges and approaches to copyright law presented to artists and their lawyers in the age of the internet.

123 Swartz, Mark. "In Memoriam: Bernard B. Jacobs." *Pas-Show.* 1996 Fall/Win; 19(2): 16-18. Illus.: Photo. B&W. 8. Lang.: Eng.
USA: New York, NY. 1996. Biographical studies. ■Brief memorial to deceased president and co-chief executive officer of the Shubert Organization and the Shubert Foundation.

124 Tiedemann, Kathrin. "Sale!" *TZ.* 1996; 1: 20-21. Illus.: Sketches. B&W. 6. Lang.: Ger.
USA. 1996. Historical studies. ■Report on radical cuts to state-subsidized culture passed by Congress. Includes an interview with Barbara Janowitz about the projected effects of the cuts.

125 Wasserstein, Wendy. "Let Them Eat Plays." *DGQ.* 1996 Win; 33(4): 4-6. Lang.: Eng.
USA: Washington, DC. 1995. Histories-sources. ■Playwright Wasserstein relates her experience lobbying on behalf of the NEA, her meeting with Speaker of the House Newt Gingrich, and expressing the importance of non-profit theatres as a wellspring of new playwrights and new ideas.

126 Wyszomirski, Margaret Jane. "Where Do We Go From Here? The Future of Support for the Arts and Humanities." *JAML.* 1996 Sum; 26(2): 75-77. Lang.: Eng.
USA. 1996. Critical studies. ■Introduction to the theme of this volume, the future of funding for the arts.

Audience

127 Leeker, Martina. "Die Zukunft des Theaters im Zeitalter technologisch implementierter Interaktivität." (The Future of Theatre in the Age of Technologically Implemented Interaction.) *dRAMATURg.* 1996; 1: 3-13. Lang.: Ger.

CLASSED ENTRIES

THEATRE IN GENERAL: —Audience

1996. Critical studies. ■Calls for a new definition of theatre in the context of increasing interaction with new mass technologies. Considers the strong separation between acting and looking.

128 Camerlain, Lorraine. "Jouer le jeu." (Playing the Game.) *JCT.* 1996; 80: 70-76. Notes. Illus.: Photo. B&W. 12. Lang.: Fre.
Canada: Montreal, PQ. 1976-1995. Histories-sources. ■Influence of twenty memorable Quebec productions on critic Lorraine Camerlain.

129 Larose, Jean. "Rire de la scène." (Laughing at the Stage.) *JCT.* 1989; 50: 39-42. Illus.: Photo. B&W. 2. Lang.: Fre.
Canada: Montreal, PQ. 1950-1989. Histories-sources. ■Unexpected reactions from audience at showing of Akira Kurosawa's film *Ran* and a staging of Paul Claudel's *Partage de midi (Break of Noon).*

130 Marcil-Lacoste, Louise. "Zébrures." (Stripes.) *JCT.* 1989; 50: 180-182. Illus.: Pntg. 1. Lang.: Fre.
Canada. 1989. Critical studies. ■Brief reflection on fleeting contact between actor and spectator, illustrated by poem *Zébrures.*

131 Michaud, Ginette. "Sortie." (Exit.) *JCT.* 1989; 50: 148-149. Notes. Illus.: Dwg. 1. Lang.: Fre.
Canada. 1989. Critical studies. ■Difficulties in provoking strong reactions with theatre, and need to shake spectators' perspective.

132 Pedneault, Hélène; Petrowski, Nathalie. "Correspondance." *JCT.* 1989; 50: 43-54. Illus.: Pntg. Dwg. Photo. B&W. 9. Lang.: Fre.
Canada. 1989. Histories-sources. ■Playwright Hélène Pedneault and critic Nathalie Petrowski exchange personal perceptions of theatre in relation to cinema and representation of women in dramatic arts.

133 Vaïs, Michel; Pavlovic, Diane; Lavoie, Pierre. "Quelle sorte de spectateur êtes-vous? Le jeu du test." (What Kind of Spectator Are You? The Test.) *JCT.* 1989; 50: 232-240. Illus.: Dwg. TA. Photo. B&W. 5. Lang.: Fre.
Canada. 1989. Empirical studies. ■Tongue-in-cheek multiple-choice test for Quebecois theatregoers and means of evaluating responses designed to measure theatrical assiduity, critical sense and star quality.

134 Baiardo, Enrico. *La platea e la scena.* (House and Stage.) Genoa: De Ferrari; 1996. 105 pp. Pref. Illus.: Dwg. B&W. Lang.: Ita.
Europe. 1100-1996. Critical studies. ■The evolution of the audience in relation to the great communicative revolutions: photography, radio, and television.

135 Kalisch, Eleonore. "Handeln in einer Gesellschaft von Zuschauern." (Acting in a Society of Spectators.) 79-137 in Fiebach, Joachim, ed. *Spektakel des Moderne.* Berlin: Humboldt-Universität: Institut für Theaterwissenschaft/Kulturelle Kommunikation; 1996. (Berliner Theaterwissenschaft 2.) Notes. Lang.: Ger.
Europe. 1700-1799. Historical studies. ■Adam Smith's thoughts on the relationship between actor and spectator and its consequences for a culture of performance.

136 Rendall, Steven. "Reading in the French Renaissance: Textual Communities, Boredom, Privacy." 35-43 in Hart, Jonathan, ed. *Reading the Renaissance: Culture, Poetics, and Drama.* New York, NY/London: Garland; 1996. 290 pp. (Garland Studies in the Renaissance.) Notes. Biblio. Index. Lang.: Eng.
France. 1500-1600. Critical studies. ■Reader response theories of community as reflected in Renaissance representations of scenes of storytelling (as oral performance) and their reception by audiences. Reference to Marguerite de Navarre's story cycle, *Heptaméron.*

137 Chiout, Hans. "Schultheater kommt selten an die 'grosse' Offentlichkeit, an das 'breite Publikum.' Braucht es sie?" (School Theatre Seldom Finds a 'Great' Public, a 'Wide Audience': Does It Need Them?)*SuT.* 1996; 157(1): 2-3. Illus.: Photo. B&W. 1. Lang.: Ger.
Germany. 1996. Historical studies. ■The importance of an appropriate understanding of the categories of audience and public for school theatres.

138 Simon, Zoltán; Koncz, Zsuzsa, photo. "Mit tudunk a közönségről? Egy felmérés tanulságai." (What Do We

Know About the Audience? Lessons of Research.) *Sz.* 1996; 29(2): 44-45. Illus.: Photo. B&W. 1. Lang.: Hun.
Hungary: Budapest. 1988-1995. Critical studies. ■Summarizing the results of a research (conducted in 1988 and 1995) concerned with the public of Budapest Radnóti Theatre.

139 Kaynar, Gad. "'Get Out of the Picture, Kid in a Cap': On the Interaction of the Israeli Drama and Reality Convention." 285-301 in Ben-Zvi, Linda, ed. *Theater In Israel.* Ann Arbor, MI: Univ. of Michigan P; 1996. 450 pp. Notes. Lang.: Eng.
Israel. 1990-1991. Critical studies. ■The relationship of the Israeli play and its audience, with analysis of Dudi Ma'ayan's *Arbeit macht frei (Work Makes You Free)* at the Akko Theatre Center, Danny Horowitz's *Cherli Ka Cherli,* an oratorio for speaking voices and chorus (Jerusalem Khan Theatre, 1978), and brief references to Holocaust drama.

140 Eversmann, Peter G.F. *De Ruimte van het Theater. Een studie naar de invloed van de theaterruimte op de beleving van voorstellingen door de toeschouwer.* (Theatre Space: A Study on the Influence of Theatre Space on Audience Experience of Performances.) Amsterdam: Univ. of Amsterdam; 1996. 411 pp. Pref. Biblio. Tables. Gloss. Illus.: Design. Photo. B&W. 40. [Summary in English.] Lang.: Dut.
Netherlands. 1650-1995. Empirical research. ■Dissertation on the influence of space on audience perception and appreciation. Uses case studies and interviews. Includes historical outline.

141 Ahrends, Günter. "Von der Kollusion zur Partizipation? Beispiele der Ritualisierung im experimentellen amerikanischen theater." (From Collusion to Participation? Examples of Ritualization in the American Experimental Theatre.) *FMT.* 1996; 1: 56-69. Notes. Lang.: Ger.
USA: New York, NY. 1960-1969. Historical studies. ■American avant-garde theatre's experiments with audience involvement and alternative spaces, with emphasis on Richard Schechner, Joseph Chaikin, and Jerzy Grotowski.

142 Reiss, Alvin H. "Arts Program Aims at Audience of Tomorrow—Today." *FundM.* 1996 Sep.; 27(7): 36-37. Illus.: Photo. B&W. 1. Lang.: Eng.
USA: New York, NY. 1996. Historical studies. ■The High 5 Tickets to the Arts program started by the American Symphony Orchestra to expand its audience base among 20-30 year olds in New York.

143 Saldaña, Johnny. "'Significant Differences' in Child Audience Response: Assertions from the ASU Longitudinal Study." *YTJ.* 1996; 10: 67-83. Biblio. Notes. Lang.: Eng.
USA: Tempe, AZ. 1984-1991. Empirical research. ■A seven-year study by Arizona State University of drama with and theatre for children followed thirty children from kindergarten to sixth grade. The study attempted to analyze how regularly scheduled classroom drama and frequent theatre viewing affected the way groups of children interpreted theatre.

Design/technology

144 Ruling, Karl G. "Entech." *TCI.* 1996 Aug/Sep.; 30(7): 50-56. Lang.: Eng.
Australia: Sydney. 1996. Historical studies. ■Report on the second Entech tradeshow, with list of awards given and products exhibited.

145 Tilles, Denise. "The Wizard from Oz." *LDim.* 1996 Sep.; 20(7): 56-61, 121-122. Illus.: Photo. Lighting. Color. 15. Lang.: Eng.
Australia: Adelaide. USA: New York, NY. 1996. Biographical studies. ■Career of Australian lighting designer Nigel Levings: his recent Tony award for designing *The King and I* on Broadway and equipment used, his work world-wide in musical theatre and opera. Includes selected designology list of his career.

146 Cordero, Carlos. "Hallazgos, encuentros y extravíos." (Discoveries, Encounters and Misconducts.) *Cjo.* 1996 July/Dec. ; 103: 18-19. Illus.: Photo. Sketches. 1. Lang.: Spa.
Bolivia. 1996. Historical studies. ■Theatre festivals in Bolivia in times of changing political climate. Covers the sixth annual Festival de Teatro de los Barrios from a design/technology perspective.

147 Belzil, Patricia. "Théâtre jeunes publics: La scène comme un livre d'images." (Theatre for Young Audiences: The Stage

CLASSED ENTRIES

THEATRE IN GENERAL: —Design/technology

as a Picture Book.) *JCT.* 1992; 63: 40-47. Notes. Illus.: Photo. B&W. 6. Lang.: Fre.
Canada: Montreal, PQ. 1989-1992. Technical studies. ■Scenic techniques used by Montreal children's theatre companies to get and maintain audience interest, and to assist children in understanding the story.

148 Fedoruk, Ron. "Challenges for the Future: Is There Much Future in Scenography?" *TD&T.* 1995 Spr; 31(2): 21-26. [Address to USITT conference in Beijing.] Lang.: Eng.
Canada. 1994-1995. Historical studies. ■Canadian scenographer reviews current Canadian theatre: huge, high-tech musicals and 'quirky' fringe theatre.

149 Goyette, Claude. "Le lieu théâtral: réflexions sur une pratique scénographique." (The Theatre Space: Reflections on a Scenographic Practice.) *JCT.* 1996; 79: 61-67. Notes. Illus.: Dwg. Plan. Grd.Plan. Fr.Elev. 4. Lang.: Fre.
Canada: Montreal, PQ. 1996. Histories-sources. ■Claude Goyette describes his approach to designing a set for a given theatre space.

150 Lépine, Stéphane. "Stéphane Roy: lieux de mémoire." (Stéphane Roy: Locations of Memory.) *JCT.* 1992; 63: 7-15. Illus.: Photo. B&W. 15. Lang.: Fre.
Canada: Montreal, PQ. 1988-1992. Technical studies. ■Emotional and mnemonic relationships between character and space set up by set designs of Stéphane Roy.

151 Noël, Lola; Vigeant, Louise. "Encadrements et pyramides: Pierre Granche chez UBU." (Frames and Pyramids: Pierre Granche at UBU.) *JCT.* 1992; 63: 31-39. Notes. Illus.: Photo. Dwg. B&W. 13. Lang.: Fre.
Canada: Montreal, PQ. 1982-1992. Histories-sources. ■Sculptor Pierre Granche's creative process as scenographer for *Luna-Park*, 1992 coproduction of Denis Marleau's Théâtre UBU and the Musée d'art contemporain.

152 Pavlovic, Diane. "Gilles Maheu: l'espace vital." (Gilles Maheu: The Living Space.) *JCT.* 1992; 63: 16-30. Notes. Illus.: Photo. B&W. 16. Lang.: Fre.
Canada: Montreal, PQ. 1980-1992. Technical studies. ■Contributions of scenery and use of space in creating theatrical discourse in the multidisciplinary creations of Gilles Maheu and his company, Carbone 14.

153 Rewa, Natalie. "Astrid Janson's Designs for Performance." *ADS.* 1996 Oct.; 29: 85-98. Notes. Illus.: Photo. B&W. 2. Lang.: Eng.
Canada. 1972-1996. Technical studies. ■Career of scene designer Janson, and her balance of sculptural attitude with the moving world.

154 Wickham, Philip. "Le chiffonnier prodigieux: Hommage à Jean-Yves Cadieux." (The Prodigious Ragman: Homage to Jean-Yves Cadieux.) *JCT.* 1996; 79: 112-119. Notes. Illus.: Design. Photo. B&W. 8. Lang.: Fre.
Canada: Montreal, PQ. 1985-1995. Biographical studies. ■Retraces the career of costume designer Jean-Yves Cadieux.

155 Durst, Richard. "The 1994 International Forum on Stage Design in Beijing." *TD&T.* 1995 Spr; 31(2): 9-12. Lang.: Eng.
China, People's Republic of: Beijing. 1995. Historical studies. ■USITT's President outlines major events and players at the International Exposition.

156 Pui-Man, Lam Tung 'Rosie'. "Challenges for the Future: The Performing Arts in Hong Kong." *TD&T.* 1995 Spr; 31(2): 27-30. [Address to USITT conference in Beijing.] Lang.: Eng.
China, People's Republic of: Hong Kong. 1993-1995. Historical studies. ■Hong Kong designer reviews recent developments in teaching and staging theatre in the Asian capital.

157 Berezkin, V. "Vozvraščajas' k Kvadriennale-95." (Return to Quadrennial '95.) *TeatZ.* 1996; 3: 8-12. Lang.: Rus.
Czech Republic: Prague. 1995. Historical studies. ■Account of the Prague Quadrennial.

158 Bílková, Marie. "Petr Nikl—Scholar in the Landscape of Dreams/explorateur des paysages du rêve." *DTh.* 1996; 12: 47-55. Illus.: Photo. B&W. 11. Lang.: Eng, Fre.

Czech Republic: Prague. 1987-1996. Critical studies. ■Young stage designer Petr Nikl and his work for the theatres.

159 Bílková, Marie. "The Rough World of Marta Roszkopfova/Le monde dur de Marta Roszkopfová." *DTh.* 1996; 11: 43-56. Illus.: Photo. B&W. Color. 26. Lang.: Eng, Fre.
Czech Republic. 1974-1996. Critical studies. ■Works of stage and costume designer Marta Roszkopfová.

160 Bőgel, József. "Prágai Quadriennálé '95 (Szcenográfiai szemszögből)." (The Prague Quadrennial '95: The Scenographic Aspect of the Exhibition.) *SFo.* 1995/1996; 22/23(3/4-1/2): 20-24. Illus.: Photo. B&W. 12. Lang.: Hun.
Czech Republic: Prague. 1995. Historical studies. ■Report on the programs and events of the world's largest show of scenery and costume designers, theatre architects and students.

161 Vigeant, Louise. "La Quadriennale de Prague: Les scénographes à l'honneur." (The Prague Quadrennial: In Honor of Scenographers.) *JCT.* 1996; 78: 145-151. Notes. Illus.: Photo. B&W. 15. Lang.: Fre.
Czech Republic: Prague. 1995. Historical studies. ■Prague Quadrennial exposition of scenic arts (architecture, set design and costume design) featured kiosks from forty countries.

162 Burian, Jarka M. "Two Women and Their Contribution to Contemporary Czech Scenography." *TD&T.* 1996 Fall; 32(5): 19-39. Notes. Illus.: Photo. Sketches. 18. Lang.: Eng.
Czechoslovakia. 1980-1995. Historical studies. ■The work of Marta Roszkopfová and Jana Zbořilová. Both prefer to do scenery and costumes together in a unified design. Examines their early training, aesthetic views on design, and production work.

163 Unruh, Delbert. "Speaking the Truth: The Stage Designs of Ján Zavarský." *TD&T.* 1996 Sum; 32(3): 23-30. Illus.: Photo. 22. Lang.: Eng.
Czechoslovakia. 1970-1990. Historical studies. ■The career of scenic designer Ján Zavarský as a colleague of Svoboda and a practitioner of Action Design scenography. Includes analysis of his theoretical work as well as his practical applications in production.

164 Hammershøy Nielsen, Benedikte. "At kommunikere en idé." (To Communicate an Idea.) *TE.* 1996 Dec.; 81-82: 12-14. Illus.: Pntg. Dwg. 4. Lang.: Dan.
Denmark: Copenhagen. 1995-1996. Histories-sources. ■An interview with Rolf Alme, leader of the set design department at Statens Teaterskole, and set designer Louise Beck about what skills are important to teach the new set designers.

165 Moles, Steve. "Brisk Business." *LDim.* 1996 Apr.; 20(3): 89-96. Lang.: Eng.
France: Paris. 1996. Technical studies. ■Report on European lighting trade show. Exhibitors, products.

166 Moles, Steven J. "SIEL 96." *TCI.* 1996 May; 30(5): 58-60. Lang.: Eng.
France: Paris. 1996. Historical studies. ■Survey of the 1996 SIEL trade show with a list of companies and products represented.

167 Sadowska-Guillon, Irène. "Transformer la poésie en matière: Entretien avec Guy-Claude François." (Transforming Poetry into Matter: Interview with Guy-Claude François.) *JCT.* 1992; 63: 48-54. Illus.: Photo. B&W. 5. Lang.: Fre.
France: Paris. 1961-1992. Histories-sources. ■Guy-Claude François discusses his concept of his functions as scenographer, technical director and theatre designer, and his work with Ariane Mnouchkine and Théâtre du Soleil.

168 Söderberg, Olle. "Underhållningsteknik på franska—SIEL 96." (The Technology of Entertainment in the French Way—SIEL 96.) *ProScen.* 1996; 20(1): 33-34. Lang.: Swe.
France: Paris. 1995. Historical studies. ■A report from the fair of technology, mostly on the sound equipments for discos.

169 Burkhardt, Peter. "Neue Mittel und Wege bei der Wiederverwendung von abgespielten Bühnendekorationen und Dekorationselementen." (New Methods and Ways of Re-using Worn Scenery and Scenic Elements.) *BtR.* 1996; 4: 25-28. Illus.: Design. Diagram. B&W. 8. Lang.: Ger.

THEATRE IN GENERAL: —Design/technology

Germany. 1996. Histories-sources. ■Suggests using the internet to facilitate the trade of used scenery or scenic elements among theatres.

170 Helm, Rebecca. "Branchentreffpunkt Elbflorenz." (Field Meeting in Florence on the Elbe.) *BtR.* 1996; 5: 64-74. Illus.: Photo. Color. 11. Lang.: Ger.
Germany: Dresden. 1996. Historical studies. ■Reports on and criticizes seminars, talks, workshops, and the fair of the 48th conference of stage hands.

171 Huneke, Walter. "Generalsanierung des Bühnen der Hansestadt Lübeck." (The Complete Restoration of the Stages of the Hanseatic Town Lübeck.) *BtR.* 1996; 5: 14-30. Illus.: Design. Photo. B&W. Color. 19. Lang.: Ger.
Germany: Lübeck. 1996. Historical studies. ■Technical equipment of Bühnen Lübeck.

172 Koch, Johann-Jürgen. "Die Erneuerung der tontechnischen Anlage in Staatstheater Darmstadt." (The Renewal of Sound Technology Equipment of Darmstadt Staatstheater.) *BtR.* 1996; 2: 48-52. Illus.: Photo. Color. 3. Lang.: Ger.
Germany: Darmstadt. 1996. Histories-sources. ■Director of the sound system describes possibilities and difficulties in getting funding for a top quality standard system during times of decreased financial support.

173 Kull, Gustaf. "Utbildningskommissionen i Dresden." (The Education Commission at Dresden.) *ProScen.* 1996; 20(3): 32. Lang.: Swe.
Germany: Dresden. 1996. Historical studies. ■Report from OISTAT's commission on education, which discussed a strategy for sharing teachers throughout all member countries.

174 Nobling, Torsten. "Hydralik och elektronik för scenteknik." (Hydraulics and Electronics for the Stage.) *ProScen.* 1996; 20(3): 17-28. Illus.: Photo. Dwg. B&W. Lang.: Swe.
Germany: Lohr am Main. 1996. Technical studies. ■Report from a conference on hydraulic and electronic stage technology, with discussions of the technology of Vienna's Burgtheater and Staatsoper, as well as the Kassel Opernhaus. Continued in *ProScen* 20:4 (1996), pp 26-32, with discussion of Warsaw's National Theatre, the Bayreuth Festspielhaus, and Göteborgs Operan.

175 Petschik, Volker. "Dimmer—ein neues Konzept." (Dimmer: A New Concept.) *BtR.* 1996; 6: 18-23. Illus.: Diagram. 6. Lang.: Ger.
Germany. 1888-1996. Historical studies. ■History and development of the dimmer, introducing a new dimmer.

176 Reinecke, Frank. "Erweiterung der Bühnenmalerei." (Enlarging Painted Scenery.) *BtR.* 1996; 4: 22-24. Illus.: Design. Photo. B&W. 5. Lang.: Ger.
Germany: Heidelberg. 1996. Histories-sources. ■Author describes his computer animation for a production of *The Second Mrs. Kong* by Harrison Birtwhistle, directed by Ralph Bridle at Theater der Stadt Heidelberg, and the creative power of computer animation for theatre artists.

177 Répászky, Ernő. "Showtech'95 Berlin 1995. május 30-június 1.—SIEL'96 Párizs 1996. február 12-14.—Európai színháztechnikai szaklapok szerkesztőinek és kiadóinak I. konferenciája, Párizs 1996. február 12-14." (Showtech'95, Berlin—SIEL'96, Paris—1st Convention of the Editors and Publishers of European Technical Journals, Paris.) *SFo.* 1995/1996; 22/23(3/4-1/2): 11-15. Illus.: Photo. B&W. 13. Lang.: Hun.
Germany: Berlin. France: Paris. 1995-1996. Technical studies. ■Reports on European theatre conferences and exhibitions.

178 Sykora, Peter. "Challenges for the Future: Tomorrow Becomes Today." *TD&T.* 1995 Spr; 31(2): 13-14. [Address to USITT conference in Beijing.] Lang.: Eng.
Germany. 1995. Historical studies. ■German scenographer maps out theatre for a wider humanity in the future.

179 Bőgel, József. "Kiállítás és könyv a 85 éves Varga Mátyásról." (Exhibition and Book on the 85-Year-Old Mátyás Varga.) *SFo.* 1995/1996; 22/23(3/4-1/2): 49-53. Illus.: Photo. Design. B&W. 20. Lang.: Hun.
Hungary: Budapest, Szeged. 1910-1995. Biographical studies. ■Life and career of the renowned Hungarian stage designer, graphic artist, as represented by an album.

180 Bőgel, József. "Egy szolgáltatóművész pályaképe—Bárdy Margit kiállítása." (Career of a Costume Designer—Margit Bárdy's Exhibition.) *Sz.* 1996; 29(4): 41-42. Illus.: Photo. B&W. 2. Lang.: Hun.
Hungary. Germany. 1929-1996. Biographical studies. ■Presenting the works of Margit Bárdy, Hungarian-born costume designer living in Germany since 1956 with an outline of the artist's career.

181 Bőgel, József. "A színjátszás katalizátora—Varga Mátyás: Egy életmű díszletei." (The Impetus of Acting—Mátyás Varga: Stage Designs of a Life-Work.) *Sz.* 1996; 29(8): 47-48. Illus.: Design. B&W. 3. Lang.: Hun.
Hungary. 1910-1995. Reviews of publications. ■An introduction to the exhibition of the life-work of scene designer Mátyás Varga, on his 85th birthday.

182 *Emanuele Luzzati: illustratore.* (Emanuele Luzzati, Illustrator.) Genoa: Tormena; 1996. 108 pp. Biblio. Filmography. Illus.: Sketches. Dwg. B&W. Lang.: Ita.
Italy: Genoa. 1921-1996. Histories-sources. ■Catalogue of an exhibition held in Genoa in December and January 1996-1997 about the illustration work of the scenographer Emanuele Luzzati.

183 Barbour, David; Boepple, Leanne. "SIB." *TCI.* 1996 Aug/Sep.; 30(7): 56-68. Lang.: Eng.
Italy: Rimini. 1996. Historical studies. ■Report on the International Exhibition of Equipment and Technology for Discotheques, Dance Halls and Rental Films, with list of companies and products represented.

184 Clark, Mike. "Stop Line." *LDim.* 1996 Jan/Feb.; 20(1): 51-55. Illus.: Photo. Lighting. B&W. Color. 9. Lang.: Eng.
Italy: Bergamo. 1996. Technical studies. ■Architectural, interior and stage lighting design for new multi-use facility called Stop Line. Special effects used, laser shows, equipment.

185 Clark, Mike. "Fantastic Voyage." *LDim.* 1996 Oct.; 20(8): 54-57, 94-96. Illus.: Photo. Color. 5. Lang.: Eng.
Italy. 1996. Technical studies. ■Designer Paolo Gualdi: his design and use of projections in concerts, operas and theatrical events, founding of his company Le Grande Immagini, equipment, use of slides and film.

186 Barbour, David. "The Circus Comes to Tokyo." *LDim.* 1996 June; 20(5): 30-34. Lang.: Eng.
Japan: Tokyo. 1996. Technical studies. ■Creation of Musical Circus, comprised of an international staff of over 175 directors and performers. Challenges for lighting designer Kurt Landisman working with unfamiliar equipment and power, importing of equipment.

187 Barrett, Patrick. "A Bench-Built XLR Cable Tester." *TechB.* 1996 Oct.: 1-3. Illus.: Diagram. 2. [TB 1288.] Lang.: Eng.
North America. 1996. Technical studies. ■Design, necessary parts, circuitry and use of lighting cable test system.

188 Coleman, Robert. "Spot-Welding Scrim with Sobo." *TechB.* 1996 Oct.: 1-3. Illus.: Photo. B&W. 6. [TB 1289.] Lang.: Eng.
North America. 1996. Technical studies. ■Materials and process for patching damaged scrim using glue instead of sewing.

189 Damoth, Douglas, ed. "96-97 Buyer's Guide." *LDim.* 1996 July/Aug.; 20(6): 10-226. Lang.: Eng.
North America. 1996. Technical studies. ■Annual *Lighting Dimensions* Buyers Guide: lighting products, manufacturers, hardware, related special materials.

190 Faulkner, Lee. "Simultaneous Realtime Control of Sound and Light with Midi." *TechB.* 1996 Oct.: 1-2. Illus.: Diagram. B&W. 1. [TB 1290.] Lang.: Eng.
North America. 1996. Technical studies. ■Creating special effect of onstage computer that has a 'personality' using an offstage actor, and synchronizing sound and pulses of light to create the illusion.

191 Francis, Tim. "The Steel-Framed Texas Triscuit." *TechB.* 1996 Apr.: 1-2. Illus.: Plan. Diagram. 2. [TB 1283.] Lang.: Eng.
North America. 1996. Technical studies. ■Instructions for construction and installation of triscuit steel framing, and its possibilities for use as a stock platform.

192 Holden, Alys. "A Frameless Turntable." *TechB.* 1996 Apr.: 1-3. Illus.: Diagram. 6. [TB 1287.] Lang.: Eng.

THEATRE IN GENERAL: —Design/technology

North America. 1996. Technical studies. ■Design, construction and installation of scenic turntable.

193 Knasiak, Chris. "A Recycled-Bike Rig for a 'Zinging' Puppet." *TechB.* 1996 Apr.: 1. Illus.: Diagram. 1. [TB 1285.] Lang.: Eng.
North America. 1996. Technical studies. ■Rigging a special effect for a 'flying' puppet figure on stage using aircraft cable and the rear part of a bike frame.

194 Mangrum, Barbara. "Extending the Life of Strip-Light Color Media." *TechB.* 1996 Apr.: 1. Illus.: Diagram. 2. [TB 1284.] Lang.: Eng.
North America. 1996. Technical studies. ■Adjusting form and distance of filters to increase longevity in strip lights.

195 Patterson, Michael. "A Pneumatic Tab Turner." *TechB.* 1996 Apr.: 1-3. Illus.: Diagram. 2. [TB 1286.] Lang.: Eng.
North America. 1996. Technical studies. ■Construction, installation, and cost of a pneumatic masking system and controls.

196 Sammler, Ben, ed.; Harvey, Don, ed. "Index." *TechB.* 1996 Apr.: 11-15: 1-5. [TB 1227-1286.] Lang.: Eng.
North America. 1996. Technical studies. ■Index of articles in *TechB* from Numbers 1227 to 1286, categorized by costumes, lighting, painting, props, rigging, safety, scenery, tools, sound and special effects.

197 Obracaj, Piotr. "Challenges for the Future: A Return to Tradition." *TD&T.* 1995 Spr; 31(2): 31-33. [Address to USITT conference in Beijing.] Lang.: Eng.
Poland. 1994-1995. Historical studies. ■Polish designer describes trends in his country's theatre—with a glance at the past.

198 Berezkin, V. "'Itogi sezona-96'." (Results of the Season, 1996.) *TeatZ.* 1996; 8: 26-30. Lang.: Rus.
Russia: Moscow. 1995-1996. Historical studies. ■Exhibit of theatrical painting at Dom Aktera.

199 Ignatieva, Maria. "Pasha Kaplevich: Portrait of a Contemporary Russian Designer." *TD&T.* 1994 Fall; 30(4): 31-36. Lang.: Eng.
Russia. 1948-1994. Historical studies. ■The work of Paša Kaplevič with directors Anatolij Vasiljév and Vladimir Mirzoev.

200 Koroleva, L.A. "Etničeskie kul'turnye tradicii pri sozdanii kollekcij teatral'noj i sovremennoj odeždy." (Ethnic Cultural Traditions in the Creation of a Collection of Contemporary and Theatrical Clothing.) 45-48 in *Problemy kul'tury gorodov Rossii.* Omsk: Rossijskij Institut kul'turologii; 1996. Lang.: Rus.
Russia. 1800-1996. Historical studies. ■The evolution of Western theatrical costumes.

201 Lobanov-Rostovskij, Nikita D. "Kollekcionirovanie russkich kostjumov i dekoracij." (Collecting Russian Costumes and Decorations.) *MA.* 1996; 1: 223-226. Lang.: Rus.
Russia. 1996. Histories-sources. ■Collector of theatre costumes and decorations describes his exhibitions.

202 Nikitin, V.R. *Dom oknami za zakat: Vospominanija.* (A House with Windows to the West: Memoirs.) Moscow: Intergraf Servis; 1996. 352 pp. Lang.: Rus.
Russia: Moscow. 1897-1976. Biographies. ■Scenic artist Leonid Aleksandrovič Nikitin, his life and work in the Malyj and Proletkult theatres.

203 Oves, L. "'Vozduch dolžen byt', i belye pjatna'." (One Must Have Air, and Blank Spaces.) *PTZ.* 1996; 10: 4-10. Lang.: Rus.
Russia: St. Petersburg. 1996. Histories-sources. ■Interview with theatre artist Mart Kitaev.

204 Savickaja, O. "Ol'ga Savarenskaja (igraem sebja)." (Ol'ga Savarenskaja: As Herself.) *PTZ.* 1996; 9: 62-65. Lang.: Rus.
Russia: St. Petersburg, Moscow. 1990-1996. Historical studies. ■Work of the scene designer Ol'ga Savarenskaja.

205 Selvinskaja, T. "Ljubov' moja—cecha." (My Love: Production Area.) *TeatZ.* 1996; 6: 42-44. Lang.: Rus.
Russia: Moscow. 1990-1996. Historical studies. ■Theatre artists of the Vachtangov Theatre: Aleksand'r P. Ozerov, Vladimir I. Konenkov, and Vladimir V. Kruglov.

206 Toporišič, Tomaž. *Slovenska scenografija in kostumografija.* (Slovene Scenography and Costume Design.) Ljubljana: Slovenian Designers Association; 1995. 34 pp. Illus.: Photo. Color. Lang.: Slo.
Slovenia. 1991-1994. Histories-sources. ■Catalogue of the exhibition of Slovene scenic and costume design which took place at the Prague Quadrenniale in 1995.

207 Edström, Per Simon. "Meddelande från stiftelsen Svenska Teatertekniska Samlingarna, STTS." (A Notice From the Swedish Foundation for Theatrical Technique Collections, STTS.) *ProScen.* 1996; 20(1): 30. Lang.: Swe, Eng.
Sweden: Värmdö. 1995. Historical studies. ■A presentation and call for contributions to the newly established STTS.

208 Edström, Per Simon. "Meddelande från stiftelsen Svenska Teatertekniska Institutet, STTI." (A Notice From the Swedish Institute of Technical Theatre.) *ProScen.* 1996; 20(1): 32. Lang.: Swe, Eng.
Sweden. 1995. Historical studies. ■A presentation of the Institute for the promotion of research and education within theatrical technique.

209 Edström, Per Simon; Forslund, Camille, transl. "Hur teatern lyftes upp i rymden." (How Theatre Was Blasted into Outer Space.) *ProScen.* 1996; 20(Extra): 10-11. Illus.: Photo. Color. Lang.: Swe, Eng.
Sweden. 1940-1970. Technical studies. ■Some thoughts about the development of the regulation of light up to the thyristor.

210 Flood, Kent; Ekvall, Anders; Dahlberg, Ralph. "Datoriserad ljussättning." (Computerized Lighting.) *ProScen.* 1996; 20(4): 23-25. Illus.: Photo. Color. Lang.: Swe.
Sweden. 1996. Technical studies. ■A presentation of AVAB's software Offstage for lighting a play in virtual reality, just using your own computer, without worrying about stage rehearsals.

211 Haglund, Birgitta. "En osynlig konstart?" (An Invisible Art?) *Thingen.* 1996; 20(76-77): 55-61. Illus.: Photo. B&W. Color. Lang.: Swe.
Sweden. 1980. Histories-sources. ■A survey of the artistic and professional status of the lighting designer, based on interviews with Claes Aller, Torkel Blomkvist, Ellen Ruge, Jens Sethzman and Hans-Åke Sjöquist.

212 Jonson, Lotta; Hammershøy Nielsen, Benedikte, transl. "Scene, rum, lys og farve." (Stage, Space, Light and Color.) *TE.* 1996 Dec.; 81-82: 8-11. Illus.: Photo. B&W. 7. [Originally published in *Form* 2 (1996).] Lang.: Dan.
Sweden. 1996. Critical studies. ■The partnership between stage designer Carouschka and lighting designer Jens Sethzman, including their work on *XXX* directed by Kenneth Kvarnström. Their use of space and light is illustrated with photos from *XXX*.

213 Kull, Gustaf. "Möte om utbildning på Södra Teatern, Caféteatern." (A Meeting About Training at Södra Teatern, Caféteatern.) *ProScen.* 1996; 20(2): 40-42. Lang.: Swe.
Sweden: Stockholm. 1996. Technical studies. ■A report from a discussion about the training of designers and technicians at theatres in Sweden.

214 Most, Henrik; Juellund, Rikke. "Om en scenografs sprog." (On the Language of the Set Designer.) *TE.* 1996 Dec.; 81-82: 28-30. Illus.: Photo. B&W. 3. Lang.: Dan.
Sweden. 1996. Histories-sources. ■An interview with the set designer and sculptor, Karin Lind, with emphasis on the effect of her background as a sculptor on her work as a set designer: use of materials such as plastics and metals.

215 Söderberg, Olle. "Bernt Thorell, STTF's hedersordförande." (Bernt Thorell, the Honorary Chairman of STTF.) *ProScen.* 1996; 20(2): 18. Lang.: Swe.
Sweden: Stockholm. 1976. Historical studies. ■A portrait of the chief technician of the Royal Dramatic Theatre, who has been the anchor of STTF.

216 Söderberg, Olle. "Succé är bara förnamnet." (Success Is Just the First Name.) *ProScen.* 1996; 20(3): 7-9 . Illus.: Photo. Color. Lang.: Swe.

THEATRE IN GENERAL: —Design/technology

Sweden: Stockholm, Värmdö. Finland: Helsinki. 1996. Historical studies. ■A report from OISTAT's section on history and theory of scenography, theatrical architecture and theatrical technology.

217   Thorell, Bernt. "20 år med STTF." (Twenty Years With STTF.) *ProScen.* 1996; 20(2): 8-11. Lang.: Swe.
Sweden. 1976. Historical studies. ■A short historical survey of STTF by the former chairman.

218   Kull, Gustaf. "Utbildning, OISTAT." (Education, OISTAT.) *ProScen.* 1996; 20(2): 38-40. Lang.: Swe.
Switzerland: Luzern. 1995. Technical studies. ■A report from the commission of education of OISTAT, with references to the training of technicians in the USA and Europe.

219   Bonds, Alexandra B. "Kuando 1991: A New Beginning, A Ritual Pilgrimage." 165-181 in Oliva, Judy Lee, ed. *New Theatre Vistas: Modern Movements in International Theatre.* New York, NY/London: Garland; 1996. 219 pp. (Studies in Modern Drama 7.) Notes. Lang.: Eng.
Taiwan: Taipei. 1990. Histories-sources. ■The author's experience as costumer, supervisor of faculty and students, and designer and builder of puppets for productions of traditional and new pieces on Taiwanese life and culture, as well as a pilgrimage parade using actors, banners, and larger-than-life puppets.

220   Parker, Ellie. "Ellie Parker Interviews William Dudley, May 13 1995." *STP.* 1996 June; 13: 83-91. Lang.: Eng.
UK. 1985-1995. Histories-sources. ■Scene designer discusses his work with directors and his preference for community plays in which actors and audience share the same space.

221   Parker, Ellie. "Talking About Theatre Design with Tim Albery, Maria Björnson, Tom Cairns, Stephen Daldry, William Dudley, Nettie Edwards, David Fielding, Ian MacNeil, Antony McDonald, Iona McLeish, David Pountney, Bruno Santini." *STP.* 1996 June; 13: 72-82. Notes. Biblio. Lang.: Eng.
UK. 1912-1995. Histories-sources. ■Based on informal interviews with directors and designers, seeks to define the ideal working relationship between the two. Includes discussion of Stanislavskij and Craig, Brecht and Neher.

222   Barbour, David; Lampert-Gréaux, Ellen; McHugh, Catherine. "The PLASA Parade." *LDim.* 1996 Nov.; 20(9): 116-145. Lang.: Eng.
UK-England: London. 1996. Technical studies. ■Comprehensive list of exhibitors at the Professional Lighting and Sound Association, equipment and products.

223   Barbour, David; Lampert-Gréaux, Ellen; McHugh, Catherine. "PLASA." *TCI.* 1996 Nov.; 30(9): 56-70. Lang.: Eng.
UK-England: London. 1996. Historical studies. ■Report on the Professional Lighting and Sound Association's international trade show in London.

224   Carver, Gavin. "Computer Aided Scenography: Some Observations on Procedures and Concepts." *STP.* 1996 Dec.; 14: 20-33. Notes. Biblio. Lang.: Eng.
UK-England. 1996. Technical studies. ■The advantages of computer-assisted scenography: it speeds up technical drafting and encourages visual experimentation. The ability to explore three-dimensional space, light and movement in ways not previously available to the designer is said to promote a collaborative and holistic approach to design.

225   Kristensen, Carsten. "Scenograferne tager initiativet." (The Set Designers Take the Initiative.) *TE.* 1996 Dec.; 81-82: 15. Lang.: Dan.
UK-England: London. 1996. Historical studies. ■Profile of the new training program for set designers, the MA in scenography at Central Saint Martin's College of Art and Design, created by Pamela Howard, which aims to produce set designers who will be creators, not just technicians, and who will have the initiative to launch projects.

226   Lampert-Gréaux, Ellen. "Maris Ensing." *TCI.* 1996 Oct.; 30(8): 39. Illus.: Photo. B&W. 1. Lang.: Eng.
UK-England: Kent. Netherlands: Rotterdam. 1984-1996. Biographical studies. ■Developer of software for lighting controllers, Maris Ensing.

227   Lampert-Gréaux, Ellen. "Irish Interrogation." *TCI.* 1996 Jan.; 30(1): 14. Illus.: Photo. Color. 1. Lang.: Eng.
UK-England: London. 1995. Technical studies. ■Lighting design Rick Fisher's efforts to light a non-traditional proscenium stage and his collaboration with scene designer William Dudley on Ron Hutchinson's play *Rat in the Skull* directed by Stephen Daldry at the Duke of York's Theatre.

228   McHugh, Catherine. "ETC to the Rescue." *TCI.* 1996 Apr.; 30(4): 11. Illus.: Photo. Color. 1. Lang.: Eng.
UK-England: London. 1995. Technical studies. ■Flaws in lighting design for pop performer Yanni's concert at the Royal Albert Hall.

229   Moles, Steve. "Abundant ABTT." *LDim.* 1996 June; 20(5): 60-64. Lang.: Eng.
UK-England. 1996. Technical studies. ■Trade show of the Association of British Theatre Technicians: exhibitors, equipment.

230   Moles, Steven J. "ABTT in London." *TCI.* 1996 Aug/Sep.; 30(7): 69-71. Lang.: Eng.
UK-England: London. 1996. Historical studies. ■Survey of the Association of British Theatre Technicians trade show, with a list of exhibitors and their products.

231   Sarver, Linda. "Challenges for the Future: Observations of an International Forum of Theatre Design." *TD&T.* 1995 Spr; 31(2): 34-42. [Address to USITT conference in Beijing.] Lang.: Eng.
UK-England: London. 1994-1995. Historical studies. ■US designer recounts experiences at the Scenofest event for the European Scenography Centre in London. Other centres are in Prague, Utrecht, and Barcelona.

232   Wengrow, Arnold. "Jocelyn Herbert: A Theatre Workbook." *TD&T.* 1994 Fall; 30(4): 12-30. Lang.: Eng.
UK-England: London. 1956-1994. Histories-sources. ■Interview with scenographer Jocelyn Herbert. Her work with the Royal Court, the National, and the English Stage Company.

233   "Special Membership Issue." *TD&T.* 1996 Special; 32(4): 2-152. Lang.: Eng.
USA. 1996. Historical studies. ■Special issue devoted to membership lists of the USITT.

234   "LDI95, Part I." *LDim.* 1996 Jan/Feb.; 20(1): 88-110. Illus.: Photo. Color. 10. Lang.: Eng.
USA: Miami, FL. 1996. Technical studies. ■Lighting Dimensions' largest trade show ever. LDI Awards, exhibitors, equipment, companies and products featured including fog machines, aerial rigging, and lasers. Continued in *LDim* 20:2 (1996 Mar), 78-113: 'Remembering Miami'.

235   "LDI 96 Exhibitors." *TCI.* 1996 Nov.; 30(9): 26-27. Lang.: Eng.
USA: Orlando, FL. 1996. Historical studies. ■List of exhibitors to be featured at the Lighting Dimensions International 96.

236   "John Alvin." *TCI.* 1996 Jan.; 30(1): 21. Illus.: Photo. Poster. B&W. Color. 3. Lang.: Eng.
USA. 1996. Technical studies. ■Profile of designer/illustrator John Alvin and his contributions to the posters of Broadway's *Victor/Victoria* and the film *Batman Forever.*

237   "Industry Resources 96/97." *TCI.* 1996 June/July; 30(6): 17-20. Index. Lang.: Eng.
USA. 1996. Instructional materials. ■Guide to industry resources in costuming, lighting, scenery, projections, special effects, properties and sound for the entertainment industry.

238   "1997 Buyers Guide." *TCI.* 1996 Dec.; 30(10): 20-224. Index. Lang.: Eng.
USA. 1996. Technical studies. ■Guide to manufacturers and equipment for lighting, scenery, sound, costuming, projections, make-up and special effects equipment.

239   "*The Wizard of Oz* on Ice." *TCI.* 1996 Apr.; 30(4): 28-33. Illus.: Photo. Dwg. Sketches. Color. 21. Lang.: Eng.
USA: New York, NY. 1996. Technical studies. ■Collaboration of production designer Mark Fisher, costume designer Frank Krenz and lighting designer LeRoy Bennett on *The Wizard of Oz* ice show.

240   "Industry Resources Issue." *LDim.* 1996 Dec.; 20(10): 31-268. Lang.: Eng.

CLASSED ENTRIES

THEATRE IN GENERAL: —Design/technology

USA. 1996. Technical studies. ▪Comprehensive list of contact information for manufacturing companies, service organizations, consultants, suppliers, and organizations relevant to lighting professionals.

241 Aveline, Joe. "Square Sektion Metal Tubes Importance for Scenography." *ProScen.* 1996; 20(Extra): 14-17. Illus.: Photo. B&W. Color. Lang.: Eng.
USA. 1950-1996. Technical studies. ▪Survey of the increasing use of square-section metal tubes for everyday scene-building.

242 Backalenick, Irene. "Building Dreams: Atlas Scenic Studio." *TheaterW.* 1996 Sep 23; 10(8): 36-41. Illus.: Photo. B&W. 3. Lang.: Eng.
USA: Bridgeport, CT. 1996. Historical studies. ▪Reconstruction of Atlas Scenic Studio after a fire. History of company, construction of Broadway and touring sets.

243 Barbour, David. "In Memoriam: Kenneth M. Yount." *TCI.* 1996 May; 30(5): 17-18. Lang.: Eng.
USA: New York, NY. 1996. Biographical studies. ▪Obituary for the costume designer and director of the Theatre Development Fund Costume Collection.

244 Barbour, David. "Reviving the Unrevivable." *LDim.* 1996 Jan/Feb.; 20(1): 64-68, 70, 72. Illus.: Photo. Lighting. B&W. Color. 7. Lang.: Eng.
USA: Millburn, NJ. 1996. Technical studies. ▪Timothy Hunter's lighting design for Paper Mill Playhouse revivals of Tom Eyen and Henry Krieger's *Dreamgirls* directed by Mark Hoebee and Arthur Kopit/ Maury Yeston's *Nine* directed by Robert Johanson. Challenges, equipment, lighting plot.

245 Barbour, David. "All That Glitters." *LDim.* 1996 Oct.; 20(8): 20-21. Illus.: Photo. Color. 1. Lang.: Eng.
USA: New York, NY. 1996. Technical studies. ▪Visual approaches of production designer Mark Wendland and lighting designer Mimi Jordan Sherin for New York Shakespeare Festival's production of *Timon of Athens* directed by Brian Kulick.

246 Barbour, David. "In Memoriam: Grace Miceli." *TCI.* 1996 Feb.; 30(2): 10. Lang.: Eng.
USA: New York, NY. 1995. Biographical studies. ▪Obituary for Grace Miceli, co-founder of Grace's Costumes, which built and rented costumes to all arts disciplines.

247 Barbour, David. "LDI 96: The Workshops." *TCI.* 1996 Oct.; 30(8): 43-44. Lang.: Eng.
USA: Orlando, FL. 1996. Historical studies. ▪An instructor's survey of the workshops presented at the 1996 Lighting Dimensions International.

248 Barbour, David. "Ed McCarthy, Chris Dallos." *TCI.* 1996 Feb.; 30(2): 28. Illus.: Photo. B&W. 2. Lang.: Eng.
USA: New York, NY. 1996. Biographical studies. ▪Profiles of two rising lighting designers, Ed McCarthy and Chris Dallos.

249 Barbour, David. "In Memoriam: Alan Owen and Carl Wilson." *TCI.* 1996 Mar.; 30(3): 10-11. Lang.: Eng.
USA: Plano, TX, New York, NY. 1995-1996. Biographical studies. ▪Obituaries for lighting designer Alan Owen and wig designer, make-up artist, costumer Carl Wilson.

250 Barbour, David. "Narelle Sissons." *TCI.* 1996 May; 30(5): 29-30. Illus.: Photo. B&W. 1. Lang.: Eng.
USA: New York, NY. 1996. Biographical studies. ▪Profile of scenic designer Narelle Sissons, with a look at her set for CSC's production of Joe Orton's *Entertaining Mr. Sloane.*

251 Barbour, David. "High End vs. Vari-Lite: The Story So Far." *TCI.* 1996 Aug/Sep.; 30(7): 16-17. Lang.: Eng.
USA. 1996. Technical studies. ▪Report on patent infringement suits between theatrical lighting companies Vari-Lite, Inc. and High End Systems.

252 Barbour, David. "In Memoriam: Peggy Clark." *TCI.* 1996 Oct.; 30(8): 19. Lang.: Eng.
USA: New York, NY. 1996. Biographical studies. ▪Obituary for lighting designer Peggy Clark, who started her designing career in 1938.

253 Bell, Gregory. "Air-Lift Casters: A Low-Cost Alternative." *TD&T.* 1996 Sum; 32(3): 12-16. Illus.: Photo. Sketches. 3. Lang.: Eng.

USA. 1996. Historical studies. ▪Air-lift casters as a low-cost alternative to pancake cylinders on scenic units.

254 Bell, Ken; Thomas, Richard K. "Sound in the Performing Arts: The Dramatic Auditory Space." *TD&T.* 1995 Sum; 31(1): 17-26 . Lang.: Eng.
USA. 1995. Technical studies. ▪A presentation on sound control and placement, and the relationships among space, audience, and production.

255 Bergen, Jim van. "Papal Visit 95." *TCI.* 1996 Jan.; 30(1): 43. Lang.: Eng.
USA. 1995. Technical studies. ▪Description of various sound equipment used during Pope John Paul II's USA visit.

256 Bergen, Jim van. "LDI 95 and AES." *TCI.* 1996 Jan.; 30(1): 46-58. Lang.: Eng.
USA: Miami Beach, FL, New York, NY. 1995. Technical studies. ▪Report on Lighting Dimension International trade show for lighting and sound professionals, and the Audio Engineering Society's 99th Convention for sound professionals, with a list of companies represented at both events. Continued in *TCI* 30:2 (1996 Feb), 50-68.

257 Bergen, Jim van. "Microphones: Some Unsung." *TCI.* 1996 Aug/Sep.; 30(7): 30-31. Illus.: Photo. Color. 3. Lang.: Eng.
USA: New York, NY. 1996. Technical studies. ▪Assessment of several high-quality microphones.

258 Boepple, Leanne. "The Learning Curve." *LDim.* 1996 Nov.; 20(9): 104-110. Illus.: Photo. Color. 2. Lang.: Eng.
USA: New Brunswick, NJ. 1996. Technical studies. ▪Training in lighting design and electrics at Rutgers University's Mason Gross School of the Arts. Supervisor Steven Hempel describes improvements to equipment and program, finding outside sponsors.

259 Boone, Steve. "Learning to Live with OSHA." *TD&T.* 1996 Spr; 32(2): 49-53. Notes. Biblio. Lang.: Eng.
USA. 1995. Historical studies. ▪Five steps that provide a framework for compliance with OSHA regulations regarding health and safety in the theatre workplace.

260 Brauner, Leon I. "Pittsburgh: 1997." *TD&T.* 1996 Fall; 32(5): 9-11. Illus.: Sketches. 2. Lang.: Eng.
USA: Pittsburgh, PA. 1996. Historical studies. ▪Looks forward to the 1997 USITT conference to be held in Pittsburgh.

261 Brauner, Leon I. "An Old Man's Dreams and a Young Man's Vision." *TD&T.* 1994 Sum; 30(3): 22-26. Lang.: Eng.
USA: Nashville, TN. 1994. Historical studies. ▪USITT Conference Fellows Address on a better world for artists and the art of theatre.

262 Calhoun, John; Cashill, Robert; Ruling, Karl G. "Snowed In at ShowBiz Expo New York." *TCI.* 1996 Mar.; 30(3): 11-12. Lang.: Eng.
USA: New York, NY. 1996. Technical studies. ▪Report on the ShowBiz Production Expo New York, and the effect of a blizzard on the proceedings.

263 Calhoun, John. "Showbiz Expo." *TCI.* 1996 Oct.; 30(8): 17-18. Lang.: Eng.
USA: Los Angeles, CA. 1996. Historical studies. ▪Survey of the ShowBiz Expo, pointing to the prominence of digital technology at this years show.

264 Calhoun, John; Cashill, Robert. "NAB." *TCI.* 1996 Aug/Sep.; 30(7): 68-69. Lang.: Eng.
USA: Las Vegas, NV. 1996. Historical studies. ▪Report and analysis on new and improved products at the 1996 National Association of Broadcasters trade show.

265 Cashill, Robert. "Reno Strikes Silver." *TCI.* 1996 Jan.; 30(1): 31-33. Illus.: Photo. Color. 4. Lang.: Eng.
USA: Reno, NV. 1995. Technical studies. ▪Technical elements contained within the new Silver Legacy Resort and Casino.

266 Cashill, Robert. "Jekyll & Hyde: Theatre Vets Cook Up Drop-Dead Manhattan Dining." *TCI.* 1996 Feb.; 30(2): 44-47. Illus.: Photo. Color. 9. Lang.: Eng.
USA: New York, NY. 1996. Technical studies. ▪Technology behind the horror-themed dining experience at Jekyll & Hyde, and theatrical set and lighting designer Dan Hoffman who was hired to make it work.

267 Cashill, Robert. "Electro-Voice Speaks Up." *TCI.* 1996 Feb.; 30(2): 48. Lang.: Eng.

THEATRE IN GENERAL: —Design/technology

USA: New York, NY, Buchanan, MI. 1996. Technical studies. ■Sound products for the Broadway theatre market, Electro-Voice.

268 Cashill, Robert. "BRC's Expanding Vision." *TCI.* 1996 Mar.; 30(3): 26-27. Illus.: Photo. Color. 2. Lang.: Eng.
USA: Burbank, CA. 1996. Technical studies. ■Profile of BRC Imagination Arts, a company that designs, creates, and manages educational attractions using live performance, holography, film, and stage scenery and lighting.

269 Cronin, Chris. "Sound Software." *TCI.* 1996 Aug/Sep.; 30(7): 22-25. Illus.: Photo. Diagram. Color. B&W. 10. Lang.: Eng.
USA. 1996. Histories-sources. ■Professional sound designers John Kilgore, Dan Moses Schreier, David Budries, John Gromada and Jon Gottlieb share what software they use when designing for a project.

270 Cummings, Scott T. "A Universe Askew." *AmTh.* 1996 Dec.; 13(10): 10-14. Illus.: Photo. B&W. 6. Lang.: Eng.
USA: New York, NY. 1996. Biographical studies. ■Life and career of set designer John Conklin: his national and international work, techniques and approach to design, postmoderist style. Includes list of his scenic designs for the past year.

271 Davis, Jeff. "High End's Studio Color." *TCI.* 1996 Aug/Sep.; 30(7): 16. Illus.: Photo. Color. 1. Lang.: Eng.
USA. 1996. Technical studies. ■Preview of High End's new Studio Color lighting unit, a wash luminaire to replace Mole-Richardson fresnels.

272 DiLorenzo, Valerie. "USITT Visits Nashville." *TD&T.* 1994 Sum; 30(3): 9-12. Lang.: Eng.
USA: Nashville, TN. 1994. Historical studies. ■Overview of Nashville USITT Conference.

273 Duerden, Bruce. "A Treadmill for Edwin Drood." *TD&T.* 1996 Fall; 32(5): 46-48. Illus.: Sketches. 3. Lang.: Eng.
USA. 1996. Historical studies. ■Building a scenic unit (a treadmill) for a university production of Rupert Graves's *The Mystery of Edwin Drood*, at Utah State University Theatre.

274 Dunham, Rich. "Distinguished Lighting Designer Ken Billington." *TD&T.* 1996 Win; 32(1): 27-35. Illus.: Photo. B&W. 2. Lang.: Eng.
USA: New York, NY. 1970-1996. Biographical studies. ■Profile of lighting designer Ken Billington with references to his training with Tharon Musser, Broadway productions he has designed, *Hello, Dolly!*, *Moon Over Buffalo* and *Buttons on Broadway* and his attitudes about technology and the importance of collaboration.

275 Faurant, Nicole; Pannell, Sylvia J. Hillyard. "Irene Corey and the Everyman Players: Observations on a Collaborative Theatre Ensemble." *TD&T.* 1996 Spr; 32(2): 44-48. Illus.: Photo. 3. Lang.: Eng.
USA: New Orleans, LA. 1980-1995. Historical studies. ■The work of costume designer Irene Corey and the Everyman Players, directed by her husband Orlin Corey.

276 Ferreira, Ted. "The Devil Made Me Do It." *TCI.* 1996 Feb.; 30(2): 11. Illus.: Photo. Color. 1. Lang.: Eng.
USA: La Jolla, CA. 1995. Technical studies. ■Jim Youmans' set design for *Randy Newman's Faust*, which premiered at La Jolla Playhouse under the direction of Michael Greif.

277 Ferreira, Ted. "Associate Design." *TCI.* 1996 Mar.; 30(3): 50-51. Lang.: Eng.
USA: New York, NY. 1996. Histories-sources. ■Associate designers Campbell Baird, Dawn Chiang, Dana Kenn, Michael Lincoln, Ted Mather, and Mark Nayden discuss the role of the associate and the working relationships with the principal designer, and other members of the production team.

278 Ferreira, Ted. "Casinos Royale." *LDim.* 1996 Sep.; 20(7): 72-75, 114. Illus.: Photo. Lighting. Color. 6. Lang.: Eng.
USA: Las Vegas, NV. 1996. Biographical studies. ■Theatrical lighting designer Marc Rosenberg's move to designing architectural lighting in Las Vegas. How his theatrical background prepared him for designing for casinos and malls, and founding his company MarCAD Design.

279 Frohnmayer, John. "The Art of Success and the Business of Art." *TD&T.* 1994 Sum; 30(3): 18-21. Lang.: Eng.

USA: Nashville, TN. 1994. Historical studies. ■USITT Conference keynote address by former NEA chairman John Frohnmayer covers links between design and contemporary business and politics.

280 Funicello, Ralph. "Challenges for the Future: The Theatre Voice." *TD&T.* 1995 Spr; 31(2): 15-16. [Address to USITT conference in Beijing.] Lang.: Eng.
USA. 1995. Historical studies. ■US designer stresses a stronger voice to keep American theatre vital.

281 Grayson, Phil. "Roomer for Windows: A Better Kind of CAD." *TCI.* 1996 Oct.; 30(8): 47-48. Illus.: Diagram. Color. 1. Lang.: Eng.
USA. 1996. Technical studies. ■Introduction to using Computer Assisted Design software ROOMER for Windows, an aid to the set designer which also gives the user the ability to use perspective.

282 Griego, R. Elisa. "Pinless (and Painless) Pipe Pockets." *TechB.* 1996 Jan.: 1-3. Illus.: Design. B&W. Detail. 4. [TB 1281.] Lang.: Eng.
USA. 1996. Technical studies. ■Time-saving method for sewing fabric is described: only tools needed are a fabric pencil, snap line, and a tape measure.

283 Haines, Chris. "Erasing the Distance." *AmTh.* 1996 July/Aug.; 13(6): 60-61. Lang.: Eng.
USA: Philadelphia, PA. 1996. Technical studies. ■Digital technology presented at Crosswaves, a new annual festival devoted to the developing relationship between performance and technology. Particular focus on digital imagery for plays, rock concerts and operas.

284 Hartung, Tim. "1996 USITT Architecture Awards Program." *TD&T.* 1996 Sum; 32(3): 17-22 ia. Illus.: Photo. 6. Lang.: Eng.
USA. 1996. Historical studies. ■Listing of the 1996 USITT Architecture Awards winners honoring theatre design projects worldwide.

285 Hartung, Tim. "The 1994 USITT Architecture Awards." *TD&T.* 1994 Sum; 30(3): 13-17. Lang.: Eng.
USA. 1994. Historical studies. ■USITT honors seven outstanding projects in the inaugural year of its architectural awards program: the Murray Theatre renovation in Highland Park, IL, the Cerritos Center for the Performing Arts in Cerritos, CA, the John Tishman Auditorium in New York City, the Fairfield Center for Creative Arts in Fairfield, CA, the Temple Hoyne Buell Theatre in Denver, Caroline's Comedy Theatre Club in New York City, and the Portland (Oregon) Center for the Performing Arts.

286 Hase, Thomas. "Technical Directors: US vs. Germany." *TCI.* 1996 Oct.; 30(8): 60-61. Lang.: Eng.
USA: Milwaukee, WI. Germany. 1996. Technical studies. ■Comparison of duties and approaches of Milwaukee Repertory Theatre's tech director Richard Rogers and Stadtheater Giessen's Helmut Stresemann.

287 Hills, James. "Modifying Kodak's Fun Flash for Theatrical Effects." *TechB.* 1996 Jan.: 1. Illus.: Photo. B&W. 1. [TB 1279.] Lang.: Eng.
USA. 1996. Technical studies. ■Lino Stavole's method for achieving many types of flash effects employing a Kodak flash camera, as exemplified in the Toledo University production of Christopher Durang's *The Actor's Nightmare*.

288 Hogan, Jane. "Chad McArver." *TCI.* 1996 Nov.; 30(9): 23-24. Illus.: Photo. B&W. 1. Lang.: Eng.
USA: New York, NY. 1985-1996. Biographical studies. ■Career of lighting designer Chad McArver.

289 Hogan, Jane. "Van Santvoord." *TCI.* 1996 Oct.; 30(8): 42. Illus.: Photo. B&W. 1. Lang.: Eng.
USA: New York, NY. 1980-1996. Biographical studies. ■Profile and career of set designer Van Santvoord.

290 Hogan, Jane. "1996-1997 Book Buyers Guide." *TCI.* 1996 Oct.; 30(8): 55-59. Lang.: Eng.
USA. 1996. Bibliographical studies. ■Book buyers guide compiled to appeal to those involved in the design and technological aspects of the entertainment industry.

291 Izenour, George C. "Thirty Years of Multiple-Use Concert Hall Theatre Design." *TD&T.* 1996 Fall; 32(5): 30-40. Illus.: Photo. Sketches. Chart. Grd.Plan. R.Elev. 27. Lang.: Eng.

CLASSED ENTRIES

THEATRE IN GENERAL: —Design/technology

USA. 1966-1996. Historical studies. ∎Shrinking budgets demand that facilities be engineered to accommodate many different uses. Author examines thirty years of the multiple-use design, beginning with the Jesse Jones Hall in Houston, Texas.

292 Jenkins, Paulie. "The Martin PAL 1200." *TCI.* 1996 Nov.; 30(9): 54. Illus.: Photo. Color. 1. Lang.: Eng.

USA. 1996. Technical studies. ∎The improved color-mixing system of the Martin PAL (profile automated luminaire) 1200.

293 Johnson, David. "Growing Up in Public." *LDim.* 1996 Mar.; 20(2): 32-33, 35-36, 39, 41. Illus.: Photo. Color. 6. Lang.: Eng.

USA: Austin, TX. 1996. Technical studies. ∎Profile of prominent lighting manufacturers High End Systems. Products and technology developed, personnel, company's expansion.

294 Johnson, David. "Mystic Scenic Studios." *TCI.* 1996 Oct.; 30(8): 22. Illus.: Photo. Color. 4. Lang.: Eng.

USA: Dedham, MA. 1996. Technical studies. ∎Profile of Mystic Scenic Studios whose shop handles projects ranging from museum installation to live Disney/MGM shows.

295 Johnson, David. "Electronic Theatre Controls (ETC)." *TCI.* 1996 Oct.; 30(8): 24-25. Illus.: Photo. Color. 3. Lang.: Eng.

USA: Madison, WI. 1996. Technical studies. ∎Profile of the lighting company Electronic Theatre Controls and its president Fred Foster: company produces the popular Source Four lighting instrument.

296 Johnson, David. "In Memoriam: Howard Crabtree." *TCI.* 1996 Aug/Sep.; 30(7): 12. Lang.: Eng.

USA. 1996. Biographical studies. ∎Obituary for playwright, actor and costume designer Howard Crabtree.

297 Kellerman, Lawrence; Pilbrow, Richard; Ruling, Karl G. "TCI Light Products of the Year." *TCI.* 1996 Mar.; 30(3): 32-33. Illus.: Photo. Dwg. B&W. 7. Lang.: Eng.

USA. 1995. Technical studies. ∎Review of new lighting products.

298 Korogodsky, Danila. "Dinosaurs: Searching for Inspiration Among Bones and Myths: A Designer's Sketchbook." *TD&T.* 1996 Spr; 32(2): 10-17. Illus.: Sketches. 9. Lang.: Eng.

USA: Milwaukee, WI. 1994-1995. Histories-sources. ∎Costume designer Danila Korogodsky recounts her experience designing dinosaur costumes for *Dinosaurs*, by Jim DeVita, directed by Rob Goodman, at First Stage Milwaukee, a children's theatre.

299 Krisl, Eric. "Heat Control and Lighting Systems Design." *LDim.* 1996 Oct.; 20(8): 66-75. Illus.: Photo. Diagram. Color. B&W. 7. Lang.: Eng.

USA. 1996. Technical studies. ∎Optical coatings to separate light from heat. Uses and limitations of these coatings, equipment.

300 Lampert-Gréaux, Ellen. "Transatlantic Lighting." *LDim.* 1996 Mar.; 20(2): 54-59, 115. Illus.: Photo. Color. B&W. 12. Lang.: Eng.

USA: New York, NY. UK-England: London. 1996. Technical studies. ∎Profile and career of lighting designer Mark Henderson. His work at the National Theatre and on Broadway, including *Hamlet*, *Indiscretions* and *Racing Demon*. Comparison of British and American style of design, his training, techniques, collaborations with directors.

301 Lampert-Gréaux, Ellen. "Parallel Careers." *LDim.* 1996 Apr.; 20(3): 52-57, 100. Illus.: Photo. Color. B&W. 9. Lang.: Eng.

USA: New York, NY. 1996. Technical studies. ∎Lighting designer Beverly Emmons and her work as artistic director at the Lincoln Center Institute. Productions designed on Broadway, collaboration with directors and other designers, her work on *The Heiress* for which she received a Tony nomination.

302 Lampert-Gréaux, Ellen. "BAM's Next Wave." *TCI.* 1996 Mar.; 30(3): 25. Illus.: Photo. Color. 2. Lang.: Eng.

USA: New York, NY. 1995. Technical studies. ∎Stylized design was the leitmotif for the 1995 Next Wave Festival at Brooklyn Academy of Music.

303 MacDuffie, M. Robin. "Pneumatic Debris Cannons." *TechB.* 1996 Jan.: 1-3. Illus.: Design. B&W. Detail. 1. [TB 1282.] Lang.: Eng.

USA. 1996. Technical studies. ∎Description of a pneumatic debris cannon designed by Chris Darland, used for explosion effects of flash and noise.

304 Maginnis, Tara. "Putting Personality in Your Portfolio and Resume." *TD&T.* 1996 Fall; 32(5): 49-57. Illus.: Sketches. Photo. 15. Lang.: Eng.

USA. 1996. Instructional materials. ∎Advice to costume designers on putting together portfolios and resumes, especially on using visual aids. Article includes a sample resume.

305 Nelson, Steve; Paulson, Rocky. "Fall Protection For Arena Shows." *TD&T.* 1996 Win; 32(1): 13-26. Lang.: Eng.

USA. 1996. Critical studies. ∎Discussion of appropriate fall protection for arena performances. Emphasis on fall protection equipment and training.

306 Parsons, Charles T. "Sound in the Performing Arts: Quick and Dirty Speaker Plots Using AutoCad." *TD&T.* 1995 Win; 31(1): 47-54. Lang.: Eng.

USA. 1995. Technical studies. ∎A tutorial for understanding and using AutoCad v 10 in the creation of sound speaker plots.

307 Payne, Darwin Reid. "Computer Rendering: Manual Rendering Scanned Images and Computer-Generated Models." *TD&T.* 1994 Sum ; 30(3): 30-37. Lang.: Eng.

USA: Nashville, TN. 1994. Technical studies. ∎Using computer modeling programs to produce scenographic drawings.

308 Porter, Lynne. "Virtual Lightlab." *TCI.* 1996 Oct.; 30(8): 45-46. Illus.: Photo. Color. 2. Lang.: Eng.

USA. 1996. Technical studies. ∎Critique of West Side Systems' Virtual Light Lab software as an aid for designers.

309 Raoul, Bill. "Olio On A Roll To Go, Please!" *TD&T.* 1996 Win; 32(1): 61-65. Illus.: Dwg. B&W. 3. Lang.: Eng.

USA. 1996. Technical studies. ∎Profile of the Olio Roll Drop. Emphasis on the process required to create the effect and work the Olio Roll Drop.

310 Reaney, Mark. "Virtual Scenography: The Actor, Audience, Computer Interface." *TD&T.* 1996 Win; 32(1): 36-43. Illus.: Photo. B&W. 13. Lang.: Eng.

USA: Lawrence, KS. 1996. Historical studies. ∎The use of virtual reality in the University of Kansas' production of Elmer Rice's *The Adding Machine*, emphasis on the effects with audience response.

311 Reiter, Amy. "Linda Buchanan: A Chicago-Based Designer Achieves National Recognition." *TCI.* 1996 Mar.; 30(3): 38-41. Illus.: Photo. Color. 7. Lang.: Eng.

USA: Chicago, IL. 1977-1996. Biographical studies. ∎Career of set designer Buchanan.

312 Ruling, Karl G. "The Jands Hog." *LDim.* 1996 Jan/Feb.; 20(1): 74, 76, 78, 80, 82. Illus.: Photo. Color. 1. Lang.: Eng.

USA. 1996. Technical studies. ∎Profile of the Jands Hog 250 and 600, a line of lighting control consoles with software developed by Flying Pig Systems. Comparison to other equipment, features, advantages.

313 Ruling, Karl G. "Strand Lekolite Zoom 25/50." *LDim.* 1996 Apr.; 20(3): 84-88. Illus.: Photo. Color. 2. Lang.: Eng.

USA: New York, NY. 1996. Technical studies. ∎Analysis of new lighting instrument: its contemporary technology, comparison to other equipment and models, advantages, capabilities.

314 Ruling, Karl G. "LAN Control." *TCI.* 1996 May; 30(5): 52-53. Discography. Illus.: Photo. B&W. 1. Lang.: Eng.

USA. 1996. Technical studies. ∎Development of a system protocol for control and monitoring allowing manipulation of parameters on audio objects.

315 Ruling, Karl G. "The Altman Shakespeare 600." *TCI.* 1996 Jan.; 30(1): 42. Illus.: Photo. Color. 1. Lang.: Eng.

USA. 1996. Technical studies. ∎The new Altman Shakespeare 600 lighting instrument, designed by Altman and comparable to the ETC Source Four.

316 Ruling, Karl G. "Rosco Light Shop V2.3." *TCI.* 1996 Jan.; 30(1): 45, 60. Lang.: Eng.

USA. 1996. Technical studies. ∎Windows program Light Shop V2.3 developed by Crescit Software that makes photometric calculations easier: marketed by Rosco.

THEATRE IN GENERAL: —Design/technology

317 Ruling, Karl G. "USITT." *TCI*. 1996 May; 30(5): 54-57. Lang.: Eng.
USA: Fort Worth, TX. 1996. Historical studies. ■Survey of the 1996 United States Institute for Theatre Technology Conference and stage expo with a selective listing of the companies and products represented there.

318 Ruling, Karl G. "Controlling the King." *TCI*. 1996 Aug/Sep.; 30(7): 31. Illus.: Photo. Color. 1. Lang.: Eng.
USA: New York, NY. 1996. Technical studies. ■Descriptions of the Hudson Motion Controller, a computerized theatrical motion control system used by Hudson Scenic to move scenic elements in Broadway shows.

319 Ruling, Karl G. "NSCA." *TCI*. 1996 Aug/Sep.; 30(7): 44-50. Illus.: Photo. Color. 3. Lang.: Eng.
USA: St. Louis, MO. 1996. Historical studies. ■Survey of the National System Contractors Association trade show, with list of products and companies represented.

320 Ruling, Karl G. "Shipboard Dimmers: Why Not Wye?" *TCI*. 1996 Oct.; 30(8): 62-64. Lang.: Eng.
USA. 1996. Technical studies. ■Advantages to using grounded neutral wye power systems.

321 Ruling, Karl G. "The Strand 430/530/550/630/650 Consoles." *TCI*. 1996 Mar.; 30(3): 48-49. Illus.: Photo. Color. 1. Lang.: Eng.
USA. 1996. Technical studies. ■Report on Strand lighting consoles.

322 Ruling, Karl G. "The Rise of Ethernet." *TCI*. 1996 Mar.; 30(3): 52-53. Lang.: Eng.
USA. 1996. Technical studies. ■Manufacturers use of Ethernet as a replacement for the DMX512 as a means of controlling moving lights, smoke machines and other devices.

323 Ruling, Karl G. "Clearing the Air About Fog." *TCI*. 1996 Apr.; 30(4): 45-48. Lang.: Eng.
USA. 1996. Technical studies. ■Health concerns related to the use of glycol-based fog in theatres and other venues, and a look at some studies done on the subject.

324 Ruling, Karl G. "City Theatrical Co." *TCI*. 1996 Apr.; 30(4): 44. Illus.: Photo. B&W. 1. Lang.: Eng.
USA: New York, NY. 1996. Technical studies. ■Profile of Gary Fails, president of City Theatricals Co., which provides lighting and special effects equipment for Broadway shows.

325 Ruling, Karl G. "Computer-Generated Scenic Design." *TCI*. 1996 Apr.; 30(4): 50-51. Illus.: Photo. Color. 1. Lang.: Eng.
USA. 1996. Technical studies. ■The technology behind computer-generated scene design and an affirmation of old ways as still relevant.

326 Salzer, Beeb. "Thoughts on Thinking." *TD&T*. 1996 Fall; 32(5): 12-18. Notes. Lang.: Eng.
USA. 1996. Historical studies. ■Essay on the need for theatre artists to pay attention to advancements in scientific discoveries.

327 Thomas, Richard K. "Sound in the Performing Arts: Using Computers to Create Sound Scores." *TD&T*. 1995 Sum; 31(1): 27-36 . Lang.: Eng.
USA. 1995. Technical studies. ■Using computers to create sound scores for theatrical productions.

328 Thomas, Richard K. "Sound in the Performing Arts: Theatre Sound Cue Sheets." *TD&T*. 1995 Win; 31(1): 37-46. Lang.: Eng.
USA. 1995. Technical studies. ■Introduction of basic principles of creating, maintaining, and using cue sheets for theatre sound scores.

329 Thomas, Richard K. "Mid-Size Recording and Playback Techniques: A New Frontier in Theatrical Sound Design." *TD&T*. 1996 Fall; 32(5): 41-45. Illus.: Sketches. 3. Lang.: Eng.
USA. 1996. Historical studies. ■A new recording technique known as M-S recording and its possibilities for theatrical sound design.

330 Tsu, Susan. "Challenges for the Future: Costume Designers, Misplaced Persons." *TD&T*. 1995 Spr; 31(2): 17-21. [Address to USITT conference in Beijing.] Lang.: Eng.
USA. 1995. Historical studies. ■American costume designer muses on an economic climate that is forcing theatre to make increasingly conservative choices.

331 Unruh, Delbert. "Virtual Reality in the Theatre." *TD&T*. 1996 Win; 32(1): 44-47. Lang.: Eng.
USA. 1996. Critical studies. ■The benefits of using virtual reality equipment in the theatre. Emphasis on improved sightlines, manipulation of environment and spatial perceptions and enhanced performance dynamics.

332 Waszut-Barrett, Wendy. "Theatre of the Fraternity: Staging the Ritual Space of the Scottish Rite of Freemasonry, 1896-1929." *TD&T*. 1996 Sum; 32(3): 46-49. Illus.: Photo. 11. Lang.: Eng.
USA. 1896-1929. Historical studies. ■Theatre design in the amateur performances of the Scottish Rite Freemasons, a male social fraternity popular in the late nineteenth and early twentieth centuries.

333 Weathersby, William, Jr.; Boepple, Leanne. "California Dreamin'." *LDim*. 1996 Sep.; 20(7): 94-108. Lang.: Eng.
USA: San Francisco, CA. 1996. Technical studies. ■Lightfair International trade exhibition sponsored by the Illuminating Engineering Society of North America: equipment, new technology, companies and their products.

334 Weathersby, William, Jr. "Rock & Roll Hall of Fame." *TCI*. 1996 Feb.; 30(2): 38-43. Illus.: Photo. Plan. Diagram. Color. 10. Lang.: Eng.
USA: Cleveland, OH. 1996. Technical studies. ■An inside look at the architectural lighting and structural design of the newly-opened museum for rock music.

335 Weaver, Arden. "USITT Design Exhibition, 1996." *TD&T*. 1996 Sum; 32(3): 31-45. Illus.: Photo. 37. Lang.: Eng.
USA. 1996. Historical studies. ■Examples of outstanding costume, scenery, and lighting designs by twelve members of USITT: Ursula Belden (scenery), Alexandra Bonds (costumes), Bruce Brockman (scenery), Marie Cloud (scenery), John Culbert (scenery), Larry Kaushansky (scenery), Margaret Mitchell (costumes), Michelle Nay (costumes/scenery), Tim Poertner (lighting), Rooth Varland (costumes), and John Wolf (lighting).

336 Wengrow, Arnold. "Christian Thee." *TCI*. 1996 Mar.; 30(3): 47. Lang.: Eng.
USA. 1996. Biographical studies. ■Description of *Behind the Curtain*, a cut-out book about a theatre performance of *Hansel and Gretel*, by children's book illustrator and former stage designer Christian Thee.

337 Willard, Helen. "Stage Expo: A Photo Roundup of the Texas-Big Stage Expo 1996." *TD&T*. 1996 Sum; 32(3): 8-11. Illus.: Photo. 17. Lang.: Eng.
USA: Fort Worth, TX. 1996. Historical studies. ■Photo essay on the 1996 Stage Expo.

Institutions

338 "Where and When." *AmTh*. 1996 May/June; 13(5): 30-35. Illus.: Photo. B&W. 3. Lang.: Eng.
1996. Histories-sources. ■List of theatre highlights from selected festivals worldwide. Productions, authors, directors, companies, venues, dates.

339 Lebedina, L. "'Kto vyderžit—tot i vydjužit'." (One Who Will Bear It Will Win.) *TeatZ*. 1996; 3: 24-26. Lang.: Rus.
Novosibirsk. 1995. Historical studies. ■Account of Novosibirsk's Christmas theatre festival.

340 Castillo, María. "Reapertura del Teatro del Pueblo: 'Unir la belleza con la resistencia'." (The Reopening of the Teatro del Pueblo: 'Uniting Beauty with Resistance'.) *LATR*. 1996 Fall; 30(1): 163-166. Lang.: Spa.
Argentina: Buenos Aires. 1996. Historical studies. ■The grand reopening of the Teatro del Pueblo, built in 1930.

341 D'cruz, Glenn. "Artists Into Academics Into Artists: The University of Melbourne Performance Drama Program 1975-94." *ADS*. 1996 Apr.; 28: 146-166. Notes. Append. Lang.: Eng.
Australia: Melbourne. 1975-1994. Critical studies. ■Critique of the last twenty years of academic in-fighting within the performance drama program of the University of Melbourne.

THEATRE IN GENERAL: —Institutions

342 Robertson, Tim. "Making Up, Breaking Down." *Overland.* 1995 Sum; 141: 45-50. Lang.: Eng.
Australia: Melbourne. 1968-1978. Histories-sources. ■Actor, director, writer Robertson's personal reminicences about working at the Pram Factory.

343 Löffler, Sigrid. "Die Ballade vom Wiener Kitzel." (The Ballad of the Viennese Thrill.) *THeute.* 1996; 5: 9-10. Illus.: Photo. B&W. 2. Lang.: Ger.
Austria: Vienna. 1996. Historical studies. ■Everyday life at the Burgtheater.

344 Reissinger, Marianne. "Salzburg, Zank und Zauber." (Salzburg, Quarrel and Magic.) *DB.* 1996; 9: 24-27. Append. Illus.: Photo. B&W. 2. Lang.: Ger.
Austria: Salzburg. 1996. Historical studies. ■Impressions from the Salzburger Festspiele, both administration and performances.

345 Wille, Franz. "Im Salzkammergut, da kamma gut lustig sein." (In Salzkammergut You Could Really Be Funny.) *THeute.* 1996; 9: 4-9. Illus.: Photo. B&W. 4. Lang.: Ger.
Austria: Salzburg. 1996. Reviews of performances. ■Impressions and reviews of the Salzburger Festspiele as Peter Stein gives up the directorship, with discussion of Raimund's *Der Alpenkönig und der Menschenfeind (The Alpen King and the Misanthrope)*, directed by Stein, Shakespeare's *A Midsummer Night's Dream* directed by Leander Haussmann.

346 "La rédaction au cours des âges." (The Editorial Team over the Years.) *JCT.* 1996; 80: 236. Illus.: Graphs. 1. Lang.: Fre.
Canada: Montreal, PQ. 1976-1996. Histories-sources. ■Lists founders, editors, guest editors, guest practitioners and editorial interns of Les Cahiers de théâtre *Jeu* and their years of editorial activity.

347 "Le Conseil d'administration au cours des âges." (The Administrative Council over the Years.) *JCT.* 1996; 80: 237. Illus.: Graphs. 1. Lang.: Fre.
Canada: Montreal, PQ. 1976-1996. Historical studies. ■Members of administrative council of Les Cahiers de théâtre *Jeu* and years on council of each.

348 Arrell, Doug. "The 1995 Winnipeg Fringe Festival." *NWR.* 1996 Jan.; 21(2): 30-31. Illus.: Dwg. B&W. 1. Lang.: Eng.
Canada: Winnipeg, MB. 1995. Critical studies. ■Overview of the 1995 Winnipeg Fringe Festival with references to *Ordinary Days* written and performed by Bruce McManus, *Unlovable You* by Dennis Trochim and *Tales of Sexual Deviance* by Mike Bell.

349 Belzil, Patricia. "Coups de théâtre: Le Rendez-vous international de théâtre jeune public." (The International Children's Theatre Festival.) *JCT.* 1990; 57: 103-111. Notes. Illus.: Photo. B&W. 8. Lang.: Fre.
Canada: Montreal, PQ. 1990. Historical studies. ■Diversity of styles and cultures at Rendez-vous international de théâtre jeune public (aka Coups de théâtre) and reviews of productions presented.

350 Bobjan, Raymond. "Defining Collaboration: On Attention and Collaboration." *CTR.* 1996 Fall; 88: 35-37. Illus.: Photo. B&W. 3. Lang.: Eng.
Canada. USA: Cleveland, OH. 1996. Histories-sources. ■Theatre Labyrinth's artistic director discusses his company's collaborative work practices. Emphasis on collective structures and collaborative workshops.

351 Brown, Lois. "Power in the Performer's Hands." *CTR.* 1996 Sum; 87: 28-30. Notes. Illus.: Photo. B&W. 2. Lang.: Eng.
Canada: St. John's, NF. 1996. Critical studies. ■Dramatic voice and cultural tradition in the collaborative works of the Resource Centre for the Arts. Emphasis on the Centre's *Time Before Thought*.

352 Craig, Alexander. "Hungry for Survival?" *PAC.* 1996; 30(2): 6-9. Illus.: Photo. B&W. 2. Lang.: Eng.
Canada. 1996. Historical studies. ■Quebec between the referendums is a difficult place for performing arts in either language.

353 Desperrier, Hélène. "Rêver à l'envers." (Dreaming Backwards.) *JCT.* 1996; 80: 111-113. Illus.: Photo. B&W. 2. Lang.: Fre.
Canada: Victoriaville, PQ. 1973-1996. Histories-sources. ■Anecdotes of Desperrier's twenty-three years experience with touring company Théâtre Parminou.

354 Dupuis, José. "À dos de métro ... : Le réseau des maisons de la culture." (Piggybacking the Metro: The Maisons de la Culture Network.) *JCT.* 1996; 79: 79-82. Notes. Illus.: Photo. B&W. 1. Lang.: Fre.
Canada: Montreal, PQ. 1996. Historical studies. ■Social functions of Montreal's network of 'maisons de la culture' (cultural centers) and physical properties of their performance spaces.

355 Farfan, Penny. "Survivors of the Ice Age Festival and Symposium." *CTR.* 1996 Fall; 80: 6-10. Notes. Illus.: Photo. B&W. 4. Lang.: Eng.
Canada: Winnipeg, MB. 1996. Critical studies. ■Profile of the Survivors of the Ice Age Festival and Symposium, hosted by PRIMUS Theatre. Emphasis on strategies for theatrical survival despite financial instability and a lack of government funding.

356 Fowler, Richard. "Epilogue: Why Did We Do It?" *CTR.* 1996 Fall; 88: 54-55. Illus.: Photo. B&W. 1. Lang.: Eng.
Canada: Winnipeg, MB. 1996. Histories-sources. ■A retrospective on the Survivors of the Ice Age Festival and Symposium by artistic director of PRIMUS Theatre.

357 Guay, Denis; Camerlain, Lorraine. "De la technologie à la 'pataphysique: Les 20 jours du théâtre à risque." (From Technology to 'Pataphysics: Les 20 Jours du Théâtre à Risque.) *JCT.* 1991; 59: 135-142. Notes. Illus.: Photo. B&W. 6. Lang.: Fre.
Canada: Montreal, PQ. 1990. Historical studies. ■Discusses nature and function of 'risk theatre' and reviews the productions of Montreal's 1990 Les 20 jours du théâtre à risque (The 20 Days of Risk Theatre) festival.

358 King-Odjig, Alanis. "To Keep the Seventh Fire Lit." *CTR.* 1996 Sum; 87: 17-18. Illus.: Photo. B&W. 3. Lang.: Eng.
Canada: Manitoulin Island, ON. 1996. Historical studies. ■Profile of script development and workshopping methods of the Anishinaable theatre group De-Ba-Jeh-Mu-Jig.

359 Lavergne, Jan-Marc. "La Ligue Nationale d'Improvisation: La Mecque du rire?" (The National Inprovisation League: The Mecca of Laughter?)*JCT.* 1990; 55: 108-111. Notes. Illus.: Photo. B&W. 3. Lang.: Fre.
Canada. 1988-1990. Critical studies. ■Pleasure of participating, not laughter, as defining principle of Ligue National d'Improvisation.

360 Lavoie, Pierre. "'Sur la corde raide'." ('On the Tightrope'.) *JCT.* 1990; 55: 44-47. Notes. Illus.: TA. 1. Lang.: Fre.
Canada: Montreal, PQ. 1985-1989. Historical studies. ■Latin-American productions in history of Festival de théâtre des Amériques and decision to allow European shows for the 1989 festival.

361 Lavoie, Pierre. "Les théâtres et le public de demain." (Theatres and the Audience of Tomorrow.) *JCT.* 1992; 65: 93-98. Illus.: Photo. B&W. 2. Lang.: Fre.
Canada: Montreal, PQ. 1992. Histories-sources. ■Artistic and general directors of Nouvelle Compagnie Théâtrale (Brigitte Haentjens, Jacques Vézina), Salle Fred-Barry (Paul Lefebvre), Théâtre de Quat'sous (Pierre Bernard) and Théâtre du Nouveau Monde (Lorraine Pintal) define their institutions' roles in education and the preparation of future audiences.

362 Lazaridès, Alexandre. "4e édition du Festival de théâtre des Amériques." (Fourth Edition of the Festival de Théâtre des Amériques.) *JCT.* 1991; 60: 35-53. Notes. Illus.: Photo. B&W. 14. Lang.: Fre.
Canada: Montreal, PQ. 1991. Historical studies. ■Festival de Théâtre des Amériques' internationalism includes Europe and plays in several languages. Review of many of the productions.

363 Lévesque, Solange. "De l'importance du terme..." (On the Importance of the Term...)*JCT.* 1989; 52: 39-44. Notes. Illus.: Dwg. Photo. B&W. 2. Lang.: Fre.
Canada. 1970-1989. Historical studies. ■Quebec companies that have emphasized experimental theatre, and changing importance of term 'experimental' over time.

364 Martineau, Maureen. "Le Théâtre expérimental peut-il être 'populaire?" (Can Experimental Theatre be 'Popular'?) *JCT.* 1989; 52: 116-119. Notes. Illus.: Photo. B&W. 2. Lang.: Fre.
Canada. 1978-1989. Histories-sources. ■Théâtre Parminou's work as experimentation in popular theatre.

CLASSED ENTRIES

THEATRE IN GENERAL: —Institutions

365 Roberts, Brynly. "Go West!" *PAC.* 1996; 30(3): 22-23. Illus.: Photo. B&W. 3. Lang.: Eng.
Canada: Lethbridge, AB. 1983-1996. Historical studies. ■Summer musical comedy has proved lucrative for the New West Theatre Company allowing them the financial freedom to produce more serious productions.

366 Rondeau, Jean-Léon. "Sans filet." (Without a Safety Net.) *JCT.* 1996; 80: 113-114. Illus.: Photo. B&W. 1. Lang.: Fre.
Canada. 1974-1993. Histories-sources. ■Jean-Léon Rondeau's memories of launching Théâtre Parminou in 1974 and Académie Québécoise de Théâtre in 1993.

367 Ronfard, Jean-Pierre. "Vous dites expérimental?" (Did You Say Experimental?)*JCT.* 1989; 52: 45-50. Notes. Illus.: Photo. B&W. 4. Lang.: Fre.
Canada: Montreal, PQ. 1975-1989. Histories-sources. ■Jean-Pierre Ronfard, founder of Théâtre Expérimental de Montréal (now Nouveau Théâtre Expérimental), defines intentions and ideals of experimental theatre.

368 Ronfard, Jean-Pierre. "Les Mots s'usent. Usage. Usure." (Words Get Used Up. Usage. Usury.) *JCT.* 1989; 52: 113-115. Lang.: Fre.
Canada: Montreal, PQ. 1989. Histories-sources. ■Systematic testing of theatrical principles as the goal of experimentation, as with work of Jean-Pierre Ronfard's Nouveau Théâtre Expérimental.

369 Shantz, Valerie. "Survival Lessons—Surviving 'Survivors': A Personal Assessment." *CTR.* 1996 Fall; 88: 49-53. Illus.: Photo. B&W. 6. Lang.: Eng.
Canada: Winnipeg, MB. 1996. Critical studies. ■Assessment of the impact and value of the symposium portion of Survivors of the Ice Age Festival and Symposium. References to company structures, training, and theatrical spaces.

370 Shiller, Romy. "Drag King Invasion: Taking Back the Throne." *CTR.* 1996 Spr; 86: 24-28. Biblio. Illus.: Photo. B&W. 4. Lang.: Eng.
Canada: Toronto, ON. 1996. Critical studies. ■Profile of the Greater Toronto Drag King Society with references to their performances *Strange Sisters* and *Tinsel and Trash.* Emphasis on the group's Butch-Femme aesthetic.

371 Tremblay, Jean-Louis. "4e Quinzaine internationale du théâtre de Québec: 'une fête de théâtre par tous et pour tous'." (Fourth International Quebec Theatre Festival: 'A Celebration of Theatre by All and for All'.) *JCT.* 1990; 57: 113-122. Illus.: Photo. B&W. 11. Lang.: Fre.
Canada: Quebec, PQ. 1990. Historical studies. ■Wide variety of styles and target audiences at Quinzaine internationale du théâtre de Québec, with descriptions of most productions. List of prizes awarded.

372 Vaïs, Michel. "Visibilité 1992: le 8e festival de théâtre amateur de Montréal: Notes d'un juré." (Visibility 1992: The 8th Festival of Amateur Theatre of Montréal: Notes of a Juror.) *JCT.* 1992; 65: 136-141. Illus.: Photo. B&W. 3. Lang.: Fre.
Canada: Montreal, PQ. 1992. Critical studies. ■The Festival de théâtre amateur de Montréal showcased local talent and demonstrated a predilection towards known texts and collective creations. Critiques each of the eleven entries.

373 Vaïs, Michel. "Le Phénomène des festivals fringe." (The Fringe Festival Phenomenon.) *JCT.* 1991; 60: 65-74. Notes. Illus.: Poster. Photo. B&W. 9. Lang.: Fre.
Canada. 1985-1991. Historical studies. ■Researcher Erika Patterson analyzes and reviews history of fringe festivals in Canada.

374 Vaïs, Michel. "Quand le théâtre va à l'école." (When Theatre Goes to School.) *JCT.* 1992; 65: 83-89. Notes. Illus.: Photo. B&W. 2. Lang.: Fre.
Canada. 1991. Critical studies. ■Conditions and difficulties of children's theatre companies touring schools in Quebec, based on a brainstorming session held at Théâtre du Sang Neuf in Sherbrooke, November 6, 1991.

375 Vaïs, Michel. "J comme *Jeu.*" (J as in *Jeu.*) *JCT.* 1996; 80: 158-163. Notes. Illus.: Photo. B&W. 5. Lang.: Fre.
Canada: Montreal, PQ. 1973-1996. Histories-sources. ■History of Michel Vaïs' involvement in periodical Cahiers de théâtre Jeu.

376 Vigeant, Louise. "Carrefour 92: de jeunes mais solides metteurs en scène." (Carrefour 92: Young but Solid Directors.) *JCT.* 1992; 65: 115-120. Notes. Illus.: Photo. B&W. 4. Lang.: Fre.
Canada: Quebec, PQ. 1992. Historical studies. ■Quebec's international festival Carrefour 92 featured works of young directors examining the present, questioning the past and projecting into the future with plays such as Atelier Sainte-Anne's *La Tragédie comique,* Takeshi Kawamura's *A Man Called Macbeth* and Ödön von Horváth's *Don Juan kommt aus dem Krieg* directed by Stéphane Braunschweig.

377 Vigeant, Louise. "Nous, l'humanité..." (We, Humanity...) *JCT.* 1996; 81: 20-31. Notes. Illus.: Poster. Photo. B&W. 9. Lang.: Fre.
Canada: Quebec, PQ. 1996. Historical studies. ■Diverse representations of the human condition and importance of freedom at Quebec's 1996 Carrefour international de théâtre, with reviews of productions, in particular Benno Besson's staging of Molière's *Tartuffe,* Robert Lepage's *Les Sept Branches de la rivière Ota (The Seven Streams of the River Ota)* and Serge Denoncourt's staging of Ariane Mnouchkine's *Méphisto.*

378 Walker, Craig Stewart. "Why Theatre? Questions and Answers." *CTR.* 1996 Spr; 86: 55-57. Lang.: Eng.
Canada: Toronto, ON. 1995. Critical studies. ■Overview of the 1995 Why Theatre Conference with references to the Theatre Passe Muraille production of John Mighton's *The Little Years* and Ronnie Burkett's marionette show *Tinka's New Dress.*

379 Walling, Savannah. "Survival Techniques: Forces on the Artists/Artists on the Forces." *CTR.* 1996 Fall; 88: 11-19. Notes. Illus.: Photo. B&W. 5. Lang.: Eng.
Canada: Vancouver, BC. 1996. Critical studies. ■Vancouver Moving Theatre artistic director Savannah Walling discusses the cultural obstacles threatening indigenous original art. Emphasis on economic restraints and competition with electronic media and international mega-musicals.

380 Walsh, Ce Anne; Peters, Helen; Chage, Robert; Draskoy, Andrew; Kieley, Jillian. "Training to Survive, III: PRIMUS Theatre: Workshops In Newfoundland." *CTR.* 1996 Fall; 88: 26-30. Notes. Illus.: Photo. B&W. 6. Lang.: Eng.
Canada: St. John's, NF. 1995. Historical studies. ■Description of acting workshops run by PRIMUS Theatre in St. John's, and their influence on the Newfoundland theatre community.

381 Wickham, Philip. "4e Festival québécois de théâtre universitaire." (Fourth Festival Québécois de Théâtre Universitaire.) *JCT.* 1991; 60: 75-82. Illus.: Photo. B&W. 5. Lang.: Fre.
Canada: Montreal, PQ. 1991. Historical studies. ■International participation and greater visibility of Fourth Festival québécois de théâtre universitaire. Reviews of the university-produced shows.

382 Wickham, Philip. "La cigogne est passée près du clocher: Création de *Théâtre—les Cahiers de la maîtrise* à l'UQAM." (The Stork Came Near the Belltower: Creation of *Théâtre—les Cahiers de la maîtrise* at the Université du Québec à Montréal.) *JCT.* 1996; 81: 143-146. Illus.: Photo. B&W. 1. Lang.: Fre.
Canada: Montreal, PQ. 1996. Historical studies. ■Université du Québec à Montréal's theatre master's program launches new journal: *Théâtre—les Cahiers de la maîtrise.*

383 Winston, Iris. "A Dream Come True: Kanata Theatre Moves Into its New Playhouse." *PAC.* 1996; 30(2): 20-22. Illus.: Photo. Diagram. B&W. 4. Lang.: Eng.
Canada: Kanata, ON. 1968-1996. Historical studies. ■Kanata local theatre groups which mount five productions each season, and their new performance space designed by award-winner Peter Smith.

384 Sentis, Verónica. "Santiago, Chile: Festival de nuevas tendencias teatrales." (Santiago, Chile: Festival of New Theatrical Trends.) *Gestos.* 1996 Nov.; 11(22): 177-184. Illus.: Photo. B&W. 3. Lang.: Spa.
Chile: Santiago. 1996. Historical studies. ■Report on the festival.

385 Garavito, Lucía. "V Festival Iberoamericano de Teatro de Bogotá." (Fifth Hispanic-American Theatre Festival in Bogotá.) *LATR.* 1996 Fall; 30(1): 111-122. Notes. Illus.: Photo. 9. Lang.: Spa.

CLASSED ENTRIES

THEATRE IN GENERAL: —Institutions

Colombia: Bogotá. 1996. Historical studies. ■Account of the fifth Hispanic-American Theatre Festival. Groups from all othe world reflected drama and theatre that involved Hispanic themes and issues.

386 Gutiérrez, Alfonso. "Festival Nacional de Teatro, Cali 1996: En busca de la identidad." (National Festival of Theatre, Cali 1996: In Search of an Identity.) *LATR*. 1996 Spr; 29(2): 191-194. Illus.: Photo. 2. Lang.: Spa.
Colombia: Cali. 1996. Historical studies. ■Festival gives evidence of a vital, growing theatre community in Colombia, including Casa del Teatro in Medellín and Ensamblaje Teatro Comunidad de Santafe in Bogotá.

387 Martínez Tabares, Vivian. "Cali 96: una puerta al teatro Colombiano." (Cali 96: A Doorway to the Colombian Theatre.) *Cjo*. 1996 Jan-June; 102: 84-89. Illus.: Photo. 6. Lang.: Spa.
Colombia: Cali. 1996. Critical studies. ■Performances at the National Festival of Theatre featuring the work of theatre groups such as Teatro Experimental de Cali, La Candelaria, El Local, and La Mama.

388 González Rodríguez, Rafael; Winks, Christopher, transl. "Teatro Escambray: Toward the Cuban's Inner Being." *TDR*. 1996 Spr; 40(1): 98-111. Biblio. Notes. Illus.: Photo. B&W. 7. Lang.: Eng.
Cuba: La Macagua. 1968-1996. Critical studies. ■Sociocultural investigation of Grupo Teatro Escambray's communication with its audience. Past productions and their themes, style of performance, political influences on choice of material and audience response.

389 Rudakoff, Judith. "R/Evolutionary Theatre in Contemporary Cuba: Grupo Teatro Escambray." *TDR*. 1996 Spr; 40(1): 77-97. Biblio. Notes. Illus.: Photo. B&W. 8. Lang.: Eng.
Cuba: La Macagua. 1959-1996. Historical studies. ■History of collective headed by Carlos Perez Peña. Influence of Cuban politics and censorship on their productions and development, performance styles, future goals, complete list of their production history, excerpt from play *La Paloma Negra (The Black Dove)* by Rafael González Rodríguez, directed by Peña, translated by Christopher Winks.

390 Csáki, Judit. "A szomszéd kertje—A cseh színház plzeňi fesztiválon." (The Neighbor's Garden—Czech Theatre at the Pilsen Festival.) *Sz*. 1996; 29(1): 45-48. Illus.: Photo. B&W. 3. Lang.: Hun.
Czech Republic: Pilsen. 1995. Reviews of performances. ■The program of the Pilsen theatre festival Divadlo '96.

391 Herman, Josef. "O historii zřizování divadel v Čechách." (The History of the Establishment of Theatres in Bohemia.) *Svet*. 1996; 7(5): 158-166. Lang.: Cze.
Czech Republic: Prague. 1700-1996. Historical studies. ■The establishment of theatres in Bohemia.

392 Kerbr, Jan. "Školní zkušenosti." (Experiences from School.) *Svet*. 1996; 7(3): 82-89. Lang.: Cze.
Czech Republic: Brno. 1996. Historical studies. ■Report on Setkání Brno '96, a festival of student theatre.

393 Petišková, Ladislava. "A Moveable Feast/Fête mouvante." *DTh*. 1996; 12: 56-64. Illus.: Photo. B&W. 9. Lang.: Eng, Fre.
Czech Republic: Kolín. 1996. Critical studies. ■The 3rd festival of movement 'Kašparův Kolínský memorial' which was dedicated to the 200th anniversary of the birth of mime artist Jean Gaspar Deburau.

394 Procházka, Vladimír. "Connections and Overlap/Dépassements et affinités." *DTh*. 1996; 12: 42-46. Illus.: Photo. B&W. 6. Lang.: Eng, Fre.
Czech Republic: Pilsen. 1996. Critical studies. ■The theatre festival Divadlo '96.

395 Beck, Dennis C. "Divadlo Husa na Provázku and the 'Absence' of Czech Community." *TJ*. 1996 Dec.; 48(4): 419-442. Notes. Biblio. Illus.: Photo. 1. Lang.: Eng.
Czechoslovakia. 1968-1995. Historical studies. ■History of Divadlo Husa na Provázku (Theatre Goose on a String) from its formation as a political entity allowing a 'free' voice under totalitarian rule, as well as its current role in a new democracy.

396 Vaïs, Michel. "*Le Théâtre Libéré de Prague. V. & W.*" (The Liberated Theatre of V and W.) *JCT*. 1993 ; 66: 110-112. Notes. Illus.: Dwg. Photo. B&W. 3. Lang.: Fre.
Czechoslovakia: Prague. 1925-1938. Historical studies. ■Profile of Osvobozené divadlo, founded by Jiří Voskovec and Jan Werich. Based on the book by Danièle Monmarte.

397 Barba, Eugenio. *Teatro. Solitudine, mestiere, rivolta*. (Theatre: Solitude, Profession, Rebellion.) Milan: Ubulibri; 1996. 319 pp. Append. Illus.: Photo. Sketches. B&W. Lang.: Ita.
Denmark: Holstebro. Norway: Oslo. 1964-1995. Histories-sources. ■Eugenio Barba, animator and director of the company Odin Teatret for more than thirty years, analyzes his theatre, the break with tradition, the importance of workshops and training.

398 Flarup, Jane. "Fest i fortidens univers." (A Party in the Universe of the Past.) *TE*. 1996 Dec.; 81-82: 44-46. Illus.: Photo. B&W. 3. Lang.: Dan.
Denmark: Århus. 1996. Historical studies. ■Account the Århus Theatre Festival, with emphasis on the trend toward innovative productions of plays from the past (such as those by Shakespeare or Wagner) or stagings of fairy tales.

399 Krøgholt, Ida. "ISTA—at skabe deltagerens blik." (ISTA—To Create the View of the Spectator.) *TE*. 1996 June; 79: 10-13. Illus.: Photo. B&W. 3. Lang.: Dan.
Denmark: Holstebro. 1996. Historical studies. ■Account of demonstrations of Grotowski's method at International School of Theatre Anthropology seminars, where Barba uses it to direct the attention of the spectators.

400 Malmborg, Ingvar von. "Från Helvede till Hamlet." (From Hell to Hamlet.) *Tningen*. 1996; 20(78): 6-9: ia. Illus.: Photo. B&W. Lang.: Swe.
Denmark: Vordingsborg. 1980-1996. Histories-sources. ■A presentation of the theatre group Teatret Cantabile 2, based on an interview with the actor and director Nullo Facchini.

401 Sierz, Aleks. "Experimental Theatre in Cairo." *NTQ*. 1996; 12(45): 86-87. [*NTQ* Reports and Announcements.] Lang.: Eng.
Egypt: Cairo. 1995. Historical studies. ■Reports on widely-ranging performances at the Seventh Cairo International Festival for Experimental Theatre, which included every kind of theatre in every kind of space.

402 Fredrikson, Hans. "Antropologin som ingång till teatern." (Anthropology As an Entrance to the Theatre.) *Tningen*. 1996; 20(78): 10-12. Illus.: Photo. B&W. Lang.: Swe.
Europe. Asia. 1996. Historical studies. ■A report from the 10th ISTA festival.

403 Schneider, Wolfgang. "Klein, aber fein." (Little But Nice.) *G&G*. 1996; 9: 43-51. Illus.: Poster. Photo. B&W. 3. Lang.: Ger.
Europe. 1996. Historical studies. ■Report on children's theatre productions: *Bilderschnur* by Hanne Trolle, *La plage oubliée 1&2* and *Enfin la Plage!* written and directed by Joelle Rouland at Théâtre de la Manicle, *Sterntaler* directed by N. Twum Nketia and played by the puppeteer Margrit Gysin, *Dinosaurier* by Roberto Frabetti performed by La Baracca at Testoni Ragazzi, *Waschtag* by Theaterwerkstatt Pilkentafel.

404 Söderberg, Olle. "OISTAT ett panoramafönster mot världen." (OISTAT, a Picture Window on the World.) *ProScen*. 1996; 20(2): 22, 26. Lang.: Swe.
Europe. North America. South America. 1968. Historical studies. ■A presentation of l'Organisation Internationale de Scénographes, Techniciens et Architectes de Théâtre, its history and purpose and its organization.

405 Drukman, Steven. "A Bracing Plunge into Finnish Diversity." *AmTh*. 1996 Nov.; 13(9): 24, 78. Illus.: Photo. B&W. 1. [Headed by Title: 5 Corners of our theatrical world.] Lang.: Eng.
Finland: Tampere. 1968-1996. Critical studies. ■History and current productions of Tampere International Theatre Festival.

406 Klett, Renate. "Nicht nur Starstunden in Samtnächten." (Not Only Starry Hours in Velvet Nights.) *THeute*. 1996; 9: 14-15, 17. Illus.: Photo. B&W. 2. Lang.: Ger.
France: Avignon. 1996. Reviews of performances. ■Review of the festival in Avignon.

THEATRE IN GENERAL: —Institutions

407 Kranz, Oliver. "Zwischen In und Off." (Between In and Off.) *DB.* 1996; 9: 28-31. Illus.: Photo. B&W. 3. Lang.: Ger.
France: Avignon. 1996. Reviews of performances. ■Report on the 550 performances of the fiftieth Avignon festival and Avignon-OFF. Includes commentary on the meaning of the festival.

408 Lamont, Rosette C. "Samuel Beckett at Ninety: The Strasbourg International Festival." *WES.* 1996 Fall; 8(3): 27-32. Illus.: Photo. 4. Lang.: Eng.
France: Strasbourg. 1996. Historical studies. ■Account of the month-long Beckett Festival (Strasbourg International Festival), including productions as well as lectures and discussions. Emphasis on productions of *Not I, That Time,* and *Ohio Impromptu* by Maryland Stage Company, directed by Xerxes Mehta, and a trio of short plays for television and video, *Eh, Joe, Ghost Trio,* and *Nacht und Traüme,* featuring American actor Alvin Epstein.

409 Lansman, Émile. "Quand les théâtreux font le zèbre à Limoges...!: 7e Festival international des Francophonies." (When Theatre-Types Make Zebra Stripes at Limoges...!: Seventh International Francophone Festival.) *JCT.* 1991; 58 : 127-135. Notes. Illus.: Poster. Photo. B&W. 7. Lang.: Fre.
France: Limoges. 1990. Historical studies. ■Confrontation of French and African cultures at Limoges' 1990 Festival international des Francophonies and reviews of plays presented.

410 Lansman, Émile. "Un lieu de rencontre, de défi et d'apprivoisement mutuel: 8e Festival international des Francophonies en Limousin (1991)." (A Space for Meetings and Challenges: Eighth International Francophone Festival in Limousin.) *JCT.* 1992; 63: 82-89. Notes. Illus.: Photo. B&W. 8. Lang.: Fre.
France. 1984-1991. Historical studies. ■Examines functions of the Festival international des Francophonies en Limousin, and director Monique Blin's policy of sustaining support for artists such as Werewere Liking and Michel Marc Bouchard over the course of several festivals.

411 Parola-Leconte, Nora. "III Festival Don Quijote de Teatro Hispano." (The Third Don Quixote Festival of Hispanic Theatre.) *LATR.* 1996 Spr; 29(2): 173-182. Illus.: Photo. 7. Lang.: Spa.
France: Paris. Spain. 1994. Historical studies. ■The third Don Quixote Festival of Hispanic theatre held in Paris featuring Spanish theatre groups from Andalusia, Madrid, and Catalonia.

412 Roy, Irène; Bédard, Anne. "'Pratiques spectaculaires et sciences de la vie'." (Staging Practices and Life Sciences.) *JCT.* 1990; 55: 40-42. Lang.: Fre.
France: Saintes. 1989. Historical studies. ■'Pratiques spectaculaires et sciences de la vie' conference united theatre artists and theorists with scientists in psychology, biology and ethology.

413 Sadowska-Guillon, Irène. "Le 44e Festival d'Avignon: Un Nouveau souffle." (The 44th Festival d'Avignon: A Second Wind.) *JCT.* 1990; 57: 128-134. Illus.: Photo. B&W. 4. Lang.: Fre.
France: Avignon. 1990. Historical studies. ■Renewal at the 1990 Festival d'Avignon with new theatre spaces and a return to written texts, with accounts of individual productions.

414 Sadowska-Guillon, Irène. "Le 46e Festival d'Avignon: un festival de transition." (The 46th Festival d'Avignon: A Festival of Transition.) *JCT.* 1992; 65: 133-135. Illus.: Handbill. 1. Lang.: Fre.
France: Avignon. 1992. Critical studies. ■Defense of evolution and current priorities of the Festival d'Avignon under Alain Crombecque and reviews of 1992 season.

415 Sadowska-Guillon, Irène. "45e Festival d'Avignon: Création à l'honneur." (Forty-fifth Festival d'Avignon: In Honor of New Works.) *JCT.* 1991; 60: 54-64. Illus.: Photo. B&W. 6. Lang.: Fre.
France: Avignon. 1991. Historical studies. ■Many anniversaries and a prominent place for new works mark 1991 Festival d'Avignon. Reviews of select productions.

416 Sadowska-Guillon, Irène. "Festival d'automnne à Paris: Hommage à Michel Guy." (The Paris Festival d'Automne: Homage to Michel Guy.) *JCT.* 1992; 65: 155-159. Illus.: Photo. B&W. 3. Lang.: Fre.
France: Paris. 1992. Critical studies. ■Alain Crombecque's artistic direction of the XXIe Festival d'automne offered guaranteed successes well within audience expectations.

417 Sljusarenko, Anatolij. "Ničejnyj ostrov." (Nobody's Island.) *TeatZ.* 1996; 11-12: 42-43. Lang.: Rus.
Georgia: Gelendjik. 1996. Historical studies. ■Profile of Torikos Theatre by its artistic director.

418 "'Die Schauspielkunst wird für gewöhnlich nicht in Büchern gelernt...' (B.B.)." ('Acting is not usually learned from books' [B.B.].) *TZ.* 1996; 5: 25-27. Illus.: Photo. B&W. 6. Lang.: Ger.
Germany: Hamburg. 1996. Historical studies. ■Musical and acting training at the Musikhochschule and University of Hamburg.

419 Asel, Harald. "Stabilität in der Provinz." (Stability in the Provinces.) *TZ.* 1996; 1: 44-45. Illus.: Photo. B&W. 1. Lang.: Ger.
Germany: Kaiserslautern. 1995. Historical studies. ■The opening of Pfalztheater and its prospects.

420 Barth, Claudia. "'Wenn wir schon nicht miteinander sprechen können, sollten wir wenigstens zusammen spielen'." (If We Cannot Talk to Each Other, We Should at Least Play Together.) *SuT.* 1996; 158(2): 14-17. Illus.: Photo. B&W. 2. Lang.: Ger.
Germany: Munich. 1989-1996. Histories-sources. ■Interview with Ursula Obers and Claus-Martin Kraft, directors of Initiativgruppe Förderung ausländischer Kinder, Jugendlicher und Familien, an institution dedicated to immigrant welfare, about its theatrical activities for children.

421 Benz, Stefan. "Das Glück im Keller." (Happiness in the Cellar.) *DB.* 1996; 12: 22-24. Illus.: Photo. B&W. 3. Lang.: Ger.
Germany: Wiesbaden, Mannheim. 1996. Historical studies. ■Two new children's theatres: Hessisches Staatstheater in Wiesbaden, directed by Dick Fröse and Nationaltheater, Schnawwl in Mannheim, directed by Brigitte Dethier.

422 Blöss, Cathrin. "Wir reden vom Leben, wenn wir vom Tod sprechen." (We Speak about Life when We Speak of Death.) *G&G.* 1996; 9: 35-37. Lang.: Ger.
Germany: Freiburg. 1995. Historical studies. ■Impressions from the international directors' seminar organized by ASSITEJ, on the theme of farewell, death, and dying.

423 Bochow, Jörg. "Ein russisch-deutsches Theater Laboratorium in Berlin." (A German-Russian Theatre Laboratory in Berlin.) *TZ.* 1996; 3: 34-36. Illus.: Photo. B&W. 8. Lang.: Ger.
Germany: Berlin. 1996. Histories-sources. ■Conversation with director and teacher Jurij Alšic, artistic director of AKT-ZENT, an international theatre center founded in 1995.

424 Brandenburg, Detlef. "Mast- und Schotbruch in Kiel." (Broken Mast and Torn Sails in Kiel.) *DB.* 1996; 8: 18-21. Illus.: Photo. B&W. 5. Lang.: Ger.
Germany: Kiel. 1996. Historical studies. ■Analyzes the crisis of the Bühnen der Landeshauptstadt theatre, which was initiated when a new team of directors (Kirsten Harms, Nikolaus Büchel, and Emmanuel Bohn) took over the management in 1995-96, resulting in decreased audiences and increased deficit. Includes discussion of the new, smaller program and attempts to win back the audience.

425 Brandt, Ellen. "Highlights in Berlin." *DB.* 1996; 7: 16-18. Illus.: Photo. B&W. 4. Lang.: Ger.
Germany: Berlin. 1996. Reviews of performances. ■The most important productions of the 33rd Theatertreffen.

426 Burkhardt, Werner. "Fast tot, jetzt sehr lebendig." (Nearly Dead, Now Very Much Alive.) *THeute.* 1996; 12: 25-27. Illus.: Photo. B&W. 3. Lang.: Ger.
Germany: Bremen. 1996. Historical studies. ■Profile of Bremner Theater personnel: Klaus Pierwoss' third season as administrative director, productions directed by Konstanze Lauterbach and Stefan Moskov.

CLASSED ENTRIES

THEATRE IN GENERAL: —Institutions

427 Csáki, Judit. "Színház a fal után—A német színházi találkozóról." (Theatre After the 'Wall'—German Theatre Festival.) *Sz.* 1996; 29(8): 33-35. Illus.: Photo. B&W. 3. Lang.: Hun.
Germany: Berlin. 1996. Reviews of performances. ▪Report on the meeting of German theatres, Theatertreffen.

428 Dermutz, Klaus. "Drama Europa." *THeute.* 1996; 8: 25-32. Illus.: Photo. B&W. 6. Lang.: Ger.
Germany: Bonn. 1996. Reviews of performances. ▪Impressions and reviews of the Bonner Biennale festival.

429 Guhr, Bernd; Neubauer, Gerhard; Poppe, Andreas. "Neuer Name, bewährtes Modell." (A New Name, a Proven Model.) *TZ.* 1996; 3: 24-25. Illus.: Photo. B&W. 5. Lang.: Ger.
Germany: Leipzig. 1996. Histories-sources. ▪A self-portrayal of Hochschule für Musik und Theater Felix Mendelssohn Bartholdy, formerly Theaterhochschule Hans Otto, by three of its teachers: its acting education and its traditions in Leipzig.

430 Jahnke, Manfred. "Von der Leichtigkeit des Spiels." (On the Lightness of Playing.) *DB.* 1996; 11: 44-46. Illus.: Photo. B&W. 4. Lang.: Ger.
Germany: Halle. 1996. Historical studies. ▪The Werkstatt-Tage for children's and youth theatre, with comparison of German-language and international productions. Includes an interview with festival director Tristan Berger.

431 Kranz, Dieter. "David Zeigt, was es kann." (David Shows What He Can Do.) *THeute.* 1996; 3: 31-33. Illus.: Photo. B&W. 7. Lang.: Ger.
Germany: Dresden. 1996. Historical studies. ▪Portrait of the youth theatre Theater der Jungen Generation.

432 Krug, Hartmut. "Aller-Welts-Theater." (All-World Theatre.) *DB.* 1996; 5: 14-17. Illus.: Photo. B&W. 4. Lang.: Ger.
Germany: Dresden. 1996. Histories-sources. ▪Interview with Hannah Hurtig, program manager of the Theater der Welt festival.

433 Kull, Gustaf. "Hochschule für Bildende Künste i Dresden." (The College of Art at Dresden.) *ProScen.* 1996; 20(3) : 34. Illus.: Photo. Color. Lang.: Swe.
Germany: Dresden. 1996. Historical studies. ▪A presentation of the most advanced of the German training schools of art, where five branches are theatre oriented: scenography, masks, stage painting, costuming and properties.

434 Laages, Michael; Lennartz, Knut. "Dresden und die Welt." (Dresden and the World.) *DB.* 1996; 8: 10-14. Illus.: Photo. B&W. 5. Lang.: Ger.
Germany: Dresden. 1996. Reviews of performances. ▪Alternative theatre dominated the Theater der Welt festival.

435 Laages, Michael. "Eigensinn seigt—aber wie lange?" (Obstinacy Wins Out: But for How Long?)*DB.* 1996; 10: 10-12. Illus.: Photo. B&W. 5. Lang.: Ger.
Germany: Bremen. 1996. Historical studies. ▪Discussion of the difficult second season of Bremer Theater, which produced *Die Dreigroschenoper (The Three Penny Opera), Iwona, Księzniczka Burgundia (Princess Yvonne),* and *Moses und Aron.*

436 Lennartz, Knut. "Zwischen Wein und Wasser." (Between Wine and Water.) *DB.* 1996; 1: 44-47. Illus.: Photo. B&W. 6. Lang.: Ger.
Germany: Rathen. 1946-1996. Historical studies. ▪Profile of the performing organization Landesbühne Sachsen, its three performance spaces for drama and opera, and its open-air stage Felsenbühne Rathen.

437 Lennartz, Knut. "Die Geschichte eines Vereins." (The History of an Association.) *DB.* 1996; 4: 36-41. Illus.: Photo. B&W. 9. Lang.: Ger.
Germany. 1828-1996. Historical studies. ▪Documentation of the Deutscher Bühnenverein, 1828-1918. Continued up to the present in *DB* 5 (1996), 36-41.

438 Linzer, Martin. "Eine Woche Frankfurt am Main." (A Week in Frankfurt am Main.) *TZ.* 1996; 1: 10-15. Illus.: Photo. B&W. 8. Lang.: Ger.

Germany: Frankfurt am Main. 1996. Historical studies. ▪The current status of Schauspielhaus Frankfurt (am Main) with respect to personnel, economics, and aesthetics.

439 Linzer, Martin. "Närrische Ermutigung." (Foolish Encouragement.) *TZ.* 1996; 3: 64-65. Illus.: Photo. B&W. 3. Lang.: Ger.
Germany: Cottbus. 1996. Historical studies. ▪Staatstheater Cottbus, near the Polish border, directed by Christoph Schroth: described as a positive example of German theatre.

440 Lüber, Klaus. "Spielen Sie bitte einen Misthaufen." (Please Play a Dungheap.) *TZ.* 1996; 3: 26-28. Append. Illus.: Photo. B&W. 4. Lang.: Ger.
Germany: Berlin. 1996. Histories-sources. ▪The experiences of students who audition for admission to a number of different drama schools.

441 Merschmeier, Michael; Wille, Franz. "Babylon an der Elbe?" (Babylon on the Elbe?)*THeute.* 1996; 5: 28-30. Illus.: Photo. B&W. 4. Lang.: Ger.
Germany: Dresden. 1996. Histories-sources. ▪Interview with Hannah Hurtzig, program manager of the Theater der Welt festival.

442 Merschmeier, Michael. "Mit neuen Stücken am Puls der Zeit." (With New Plays on the Pulse of the Age.) *THeute.* 1996; 5: 31-32. Illus.: Photo. B&W. 5. Lang.: Ger.
Germany: Bonn. 1996. Histories-sources. ▪Interview with Manfred Beilharz, director of the Bonner Biennale festival.

443 Petzold, Claudia. "Leichen im Keller, Blick voraus." (Bodies in the Basement: A Look Ahead.) *DB.* 1996; 1: 41-43. Illus.: Photo. B&W. 3. Lang.: Ger.
Germany: Berlin. 1995-1996. Historical studies. ▪Portrait of Horst H. Filohn, new director of the Renaissance Theater, and his plans for an animated theatre.

444 Pfister, Eva. "Orientierung an der Bühnenliteratur." (Orientation to Dramatic Literature.) *TZ.* 1996; 3: 20-23. Illus.: Photo. B&W. 10. Lang.: Ger.
Germany: Bochum. 1996. Histories-sources. ▪Portrait of the Westfälische Schauspielschule and a conversation with its director, actor Hans Schulze.

445 Pietsch, Ingeborg. "Und wo stehen wir?" (And Where Do We Stand?)*TZ.* 1996; 6: 56-59. Illus.: Photo. B&W. 4. Lang.: Ger.
Germany: Halle. 1996. Reviews of performances. ▪Groups, themes, and productions of the international *Werkstatt-Tage* of children's and youth theatre.

446 Pietsch, Ingeborg. "Theater im Schwimmbecken." (Theatre in the Pool.) *TZ.* 1996; 4: 62-64. Illus.: Photo. B&W. 4. Lang.: Ger.
Germany: Freiburg. 1996. Historical studies. ▪Profile of Theater im Marienbad, a children's theatre group.

447 Pössel, Christine. "Heute morgen in Augsburg." (This Morning in Augsburg.) *THeute.* 1996; 2: 63-65. Illus.: Photo. B&W. 3. Lang.: Ger.
Germany: Augsburg. 1995. Histories-sources. ▪Interview with Friderike Vielstich, new director of Städtische Bühne.

448 Répászky, Ernő; Vajda, Ferenc. "OISTAT Bizottságok ülései." (Sessions of Various OISTAT Commissions.) *SFo.* 1995/1996; 22/23(3/4-1/2): 17-19. Illus.: Photo. B&W. 2. Lang.: Hun.
Germany: Berlin. Israel: Tel-Aviv. Austria: Graz. 1995-1996. Historical studies. ▪Reports on the programs of different sections of OISTAT.

449 Ret, Angelika. "Der Sammlungsbereich documenta artistica im Stadtmuseum Berlin." (The 'documenta artistica' Collection in Berlin's Stadtmuseum.) *SIBMAS.* 1996; 11(2): 17-22. Lang.: Ger.
Germany: Berlin. 1979-1996. Historical studies. ▪Review of the extensive collection, its topics, exhibitions, archival practice.

450 Reuter, Ulrich. "Theater ist die Basis des Berufs." (Theatre Is the Basis of the Profession.) *TZ.* 1996; 3: 16-18. Illus.: Photo. Dwg. B&W. 5. Lang.: Ger.

THEATRE IN GENERAL: —Institutions

Germany: Essen. 1996. Histories-sources. ■Interview with Hanns-Dietrich Schmidt, dramaturg and dean of the drama section of Folkwang-Hochschule.

451 Reuter, Ulrich. "Methodenreform in den 70er Jahren." (Methodology Reform in the 1970s.) *TZ.* 1996; 3: 19. Illus.: Photo. B&W. 5. Lang.: Ger.

Germany: Essen. 1970-1979. Histories-sources. ■Conversation with actor and teacher Jakob Jenisch of Folkwang-Hochschule and the University of Essen about the changes of the 1970s.

452 Schenk, Dietmar. "Leopold Jessners Berliner Schauspielschule 1925-1931." (Leopold Jessner's Berlin Drama School, 1925-1931.) *SIBMAS.* 1996; 10(1): 13-16. Lang.: Ger.

Germany: Berlin. 1925-1931. Historical studies. ■Short history of acting studios at what is now the Hochschule der Künste and the tradition of the first drama school in Prussia.

453 Schulze-Reimpell, Werner. "50 Jahre und kein Ende." (Fifty Years and No End.) *THeute.* 1996; 8: 32-33. Illus.: Photo. B&W. 2. Lang.: Ger.

Germany: Recklinghausen. 1996. Reviews of performances. ■Impressions and reviews of the Ruhrfestspiele festival.

454 Schulze-Reimpell, Werner. "Das lästige Museum." (The Tiresome Museum.) *DB.* 1996; 10: 44-45. Illus.: Photo. B&W. 3. Lang.: Ger.

Germany: Düsseldorf. 1996. Historical studies. ■Current problems and tasks of theatre museums, based on the museum in Düsseldorf: exhibitions, research, reduced public support.

455 Stephan, Erika. "Ein Schuss Heimatgefühl." (A Touch of Home Emotion.) *DB.* 1996; 12: 18-21. Illus.: Photo. B&W. 5. Lang.: Ger.

Germany: Leipzig. 1946-1996. Historical studies. ■History of Leipzig's Theater der Jugend, the oldest professional children's theatre in Germany: its changes after reunification, interview with its director Hans Gallert.

456 Stoll, Dieter. "Zwischen Aufschwung und Abwicklung." (Between Boom and Unwinding.) *THeute.* 1996; 5: 35-38. Illus.: Photo. B&W. 8. Lang.: Ger.

Germany: Erlangen. 1996. Historical studies. ■Financial and artistic conflicts between the Stadttheater and the independent theatres in Erlangen.

457 Stoll, Dieter. "Nürnberger Wendungen." (Changes in Nuremberg.) *DB.* 1996; 12: 40-43. Append. Illus.: Photo. B&W. 5. Lang.: Ger.

Germany: Nuremberg. 1996. Historical studies. ■Portrait of Wulf Konold, new general director of Städtische Bühnen. Includes an interview with Konold.

458 Stumpfe, Mario. "Schauspielbildung in Berlin." (Acting Training in Berlin.) *TZ.* 1996; 3: 6-9. Illus.: Photo. B&W. 10. Lang.: Ger.

Germany: Berlin. 1996. Historical studies. ■Portrait of Hochschule der Schauspielkunst Ernst Busch, which follows the principles and practice of the Max Reinhardt school. Continued in *TZ* 5 (1996), 22-24, with discussion of Hochschule der Künste.

459 Szilágyi, Mária. "Régi témák új köntösben—Theatertreffen Berlin'96." (Plays in New Interpretations—Theatertreffen Berlin '96.) *Sz.* 1996; 29(8): 36-39. Illus.: Photo. B&W. 3. Lang.: Hun.

Germany: Berlin. 1996. Reviews of performances. ■A cross-section of this year's festival of German theatres.

460 Weinkauff, Gina. "Pflaumen am Donnerstag." (Plums on Thursday.) *TZ.* 1996; 4: 58-61. Illus.: Photo. B&W. 3. Lang.: Ger.

Germany: Esslingen. 1996. Reviews of performances. ■Impressions from the sixth children's theatre meeting in Esslingen/Baden-Württemberg.

461 Wille, Franz. "Mit der Giesskanne in Regen stehen." (Standing in the Rain with a Watering Can.) *THeute.* 1996; 8: 16-23. Illus.: Photo. B&W. 12. Lang.: Ger.

Germany: Dresden. 1996. Reviews of performances. ■Impressions and reviews of the Theater der Welt festival.

462 Wille, Franz. "Ein Wessi in Weimar?" (A 'Wessi' in Weimar?)*THeute.* 1996; 4: 28-31. Illus.: Photo. B&W. 5. Lang.: Ger.

Germany: Weimar. 1996. Histories-sources. ■Interview with Günther Beelitz, director of Deutsches Nationaltheater, about program, administration, everyday life, and the future of the theatre.

463 Wille, Franz. "Heute in Weimar." (Today in Weimar.) *THeute.* 1996; 4: 22-27. Illus.: Photo. B&W. 11. Lang.: Ger.

Germany: Weimar. 1996. Historical studies. ■Impressions of the cultural scene in Weimar, the 1999 'Cultural Capital of Europe', and the Deutsches Nationaltheater.

464 Barácius, Zoltán. *Megkésett rekviem: a megszüntetett vajdasági magyar színházak története.* (Late Requiem: History of the Dissolved Hungarian Theatres in Voivodship.) Subotica: Szabadegyetem; 1996. 225 pp. (Életjel könyvek 65.) Append. Biblio. Index. Illus.: Photo. Handbill. B&W. 52. Lang.: Hun.

Hungary. Yugoslavia. 1949-1959. Historical studies. ■History of Hungarian theatre in Voivodship (in former Yugoslavia) with a rich collection of data on companies and premieres.

465 Bérczes, László. "Másszínház Magyarországon (1945-89)." (The 'Other' Theatre in Hungary (1945-1989).) *Sz.* 1996; 29(3): 42-48. Notes. Illus.: Photo. B&W. 15. Lang.: Hun.

Hungary. 1945-1989. Historical studies. ■An exhaustive analysis of the 'other' (alternative, fringe or marginal) theatre in Hungary. Continued in *Sz* 29:4 (1996), 44-48, and 29:5 (1996), 43-48.

466 Bérczes, László; Koncz, Zsuzsa, photo.; Benda, Iván, photo.; Katkó, Tamás, photo. "Hét nap színház—Beszélgetés Nánay Istvánnal." (Theatre for Seven Days—An Interview with István Nánay.) *Sz.* 1996; 29(6): 24-27. Illus.: Photo. B&W. 3. Lang.: Hun.

Hungary: Debrecen. 1996. Histories-sources. ■Interview with the editor of *Színház* on his work organizing the annual Festival of Hungarian theatres for 1996.

467 Cenner, Mihály. "Kelemen László és az első magyar társulat emlékei." (László Kelemen and Memories of the First Hungarian Professional Theatrical Company.) *SzSz.* 1996; 30/31: 50-55. Lang.: Hun.

Hungary. 1790-1890. Historical studies. ■The early remains of the first professional theatrical company, Magyar Színjátszó Társaság, (operating 1790-1796) in museums, archives and memorial places.

468 Darvay Nagy, Adrienne. "A Kolozsvári Nemzeti Színház (1821. március 12-1919. szeptember 30.)." (The Kolozsvár National Theatre, March 12, 1821-September 30, 1919.) 33-46 in Kántor, Lajos, ed. *Kolozsvár magyar színháza 1792-1992.* Kolozsvár (Cluj-Napoca): Kolozsvári Állami Magyar Színház; 1992. 141 pp. Lang.: Hun.

Hungary: Kolozsvár. 1821-1919. Historical studies. ■Study in the history of Hungarian acting in Kolozsvár from the opening of the first permanent theatre to Transylvania's becoming part of Romania after World War I.

469 Föld, Ottó. *Bohémvilág.* ('Bohemia.') Budapest: Föld Ottó; 1996. 328 pp. Pref. Illus.: Photo. Dwg. B&W. Lang.: Hun.

Hungary: Budapest. 1849-1968. Histories-sources. ■Documents of the history of the Városligeti Színkör (the 'Light Muse' was founded by the Feld family), where the program was mainly operetta, farce and parody, but international stars also appeared on the stage including Eleonora Duse, Ernesto Rossi, Sarah Bernhardt, Gustavo Salvini.

470 Gergely, Géza. "Kollégiumtól a Nemzetiig—A vásárhelyi színjátszás története." (From the College to the National Theatre—The History of Theatre in Tîrgu Mureş.) *Sz.* 1996; 29(7): 2-5. Illus.: Photo. B&W. 7. Lang.: Hun.

Hungary: Marosvásárhely. Romania: Tîrgu Mureş. 1803-1962. Historical studies. ■History of the Hungarian theatricals in Marosvásárhely/Tîrgu Mureş from the beginnings, the school theatre in 1790s, to 1962.

471 Indig, Ottó. *A nagyváradi színészet másfél évszázada (1798-1944).* (A Century and a Half of Hungarian Theatre in Oradea, 1798-1944.) Bucharest: Kriterion; 1991. 398 pp. Append. Biblio. Index. Illus.: Dwg. Photo. B&W. 28. Lang.: Hun.

THEATRE IN GENERAL: —Institutions

Hungary: Nagyvárad. Romania: Oradea. 1798-1944. Histories-specific.
■A comprehensive study of Hungarian theatre operating in Nagyvárad
(now Oradea in Romania) with a collection of data on the program in
the period.

472   Kántor, Lajos. "Nemzeti Színház—modern színház (1944-
1992)." (National Theatre—Modern Theatre, 1944-1992.)
57-70 in Kántor, Lajos, ed. *Kolozsvár magyar színháza 1792-
1992*. Kolozsvár (Cluj-Napoca): Kolozsvári Állami Magyar
Színház; 1992. 141 pp. Lang.: Hun.
Hungary. Romania: Cluj-Napoca. 1944-1992. Historical studies.
■History of post-war Hungarian ethnic minority theatre in Romania:
focus on director György Harag's activity between 1973 and 1984.

473   Kántor, Lajos; Kötő, József. *Magyar színház Erdélyben
(1919-1992)*. (The Hungarian Theatre in Transylvania,
1919-1992.) Bucharest: Kriterion; 1994. 271 pp. Pref.
Append. Biblio. Lang.: Hun.
Hungary. Romania. 1919-1992. Historical studies. ■A comprehensive
theatre history of Hungarian ethnic minority theatre in Romania with a
rich collection of data on the programs of Transylvanian theatres in
Kolozsvár (Cluj-Napoca), Marosvásárhely (Tîrgu Mureş), Nagyvárad
(Oradea), Sepsiszentgyörgy (Sfintu-Gheorghe), Szatmárnémeti (Satu-
Mare) and Temesvár (Timişoara).

474   Karácsony, Ágnes, ed.-in-chief. *Színházi képregény'96: 100
év Kecskeméten*. (Theatre History in Pictures '96: 100 Years
in Kecskemét.) Kecskemét: Hírös Teátrum Alapítvány;
1996. 239 pp. Append. Pref. Illus.: Photo. Dwg. Handbill.
B&W. 403. Lang.: Hun.
Hungary: Kecskemét. 1896-1996. Histories-sources. ■A richly illustrated
jubilee album of the 100-year-old Katona József Theatre of Kecskemét.

475   Kerényi, Ferenc. "Az erdélyi és a magyarországi hivatásos
színjátszás kezdeteinek tipológiai egybevetése." (A Typolog-
ical Analysis of Early Professional Acting in Hungary and
Transylvania.) *SzSz*. 1996; 30/31: 5-10. Notes. Lang.: Hun.
Hungary. 1696-1809. Historical studies. ■The early development of professional acting in Hungary and Transylvania at Magyar Játszó Társaság
and Erdélyi Magyar Színjátszó.

476   Kötő, József. "Kolozsvár a színjátszás 'tanuló oskolája'
(1919-1944)." (Kolozsvár As the School of Acting, 1919-
1944.) 47-56 in Kántor, Lajos, ed. *Kolozsvár magyar
színháza 1792-1992*. Kolozsvár (Cluj-Napoca): Kolozsvári
Állami Magyar Színház; 1992. 141 pp. Lang.: Hun.
Hungary. Romania: Cluj-Napoca. 1919-1944. Historical studies.
■History of Hungarian ethnic minority theatre in Romania between the
World Wars.

477   Margitházi, Bela; Marx, József, photo.; Bérczes, László,
photo. "Tevékeny tanúk." (Active Witnesses.) *Sz*. 1996;
29(7): 6-12. Illus.: Photo. B&W. 8. Lang.: Hun.
Hungary. Romania: Tîrgu Mureş. 1946-1995. Histories-sources. ■Four
artists of the former Székely Színház: actors Irma Erdős, Lóránd Lohin-
szky, and László Tarr, and director Miklós Tompa.

478   Nánay, István; Bartha, László, photo. "Fél évszázad." (Half
a Century.) *Sz*. 1996; 29(7): 1. Illus.: Photo. B&W. 1. Lang.:
Hun.
Hungary. Romania: Tîrgu Mureş. 1946-1996. Historical studies.
■Celebrating the fiftieth anniversary of the permanent theatre in
Marosvásárhely/Tîrgu Mureş (Romania), originally operated by the
Hungarian minority under the name of Székely Színház, then as Hungar-
ian State Theatre and presently as the Hungarian-speaking division of
the Romanian theatre.

479   Nánay, István. "Az erdélyi színjátszás helyzete ma." (Hungarian Theatre in Transylvania Today.) *SzSz*. 1996; 30/31:
25-29. Lang.: Hun.
Hungary. Romania. 1945-1992. Historical studies. ■A brief summary of
today's Hungarian theatres operating in Romania.

480   Nánay, István; Ilovszky, Béla, photo. "Tíz év Gödöllőn—
Stúdiószínházi találkozók." (Ten Years in Gödöllő—
Meetings of Studio Theatres.) *Sz*. 1996; 29(2): 2-3. Illus.:
Photo. B&W. 1. Lang.: Hun.
Hungary: Gödöllő. 1986-1996. Historical studies. ■Ten-year history of
the annual festivals of studio theatres as seen by a critic.

481   Nánay, István; Koncz, Zsuzsa, photo. "Az örökös igazgató—
Beszélgetés Radó Vilmossal." (Manager for Life—An Interview with Vilmos Radó.) *Sz*. 1996; 29(10): 20-23. Illus.:
Photo. B&W. 5. Lang.: Hun.
Hungary: Kecskemét. 1949-1996. Histories-sources. ■A conversation
with the doyen of Hungarian theatre managers Vilmos Radó, who
devoted half a century to the theatrical life of Kecskemét, from 1958 to
file as the managing director of Katona József Theatre, which is celebrating its 100th anniversary in 1996.

482   Papp, János. *A békéscsabai műkedvelő színjátszás története,
1845-1944*. (History of the Amateur Theatre in Békéscsaba,
1845-1944.) Békéscsaba: Munkácsy M. Emlékház; 1996. 92
pp. (Csabai história 2.) Notes. Biblio. Append. Illus.: Photo.
Handbill. B&W. 20. Lang.: Hun.
Hungary: Békéscsaba. 1845-1944. Historical studies. ■A collection of
data on the 100-year history of amateur acting in Békéscsaba with an
introductory study.

483   Rajnai, Edit. "A Magyar Színház műsorpolitikájának
története (1907-1918)." (Program Policy of the Magyar
Színház, 1907-1918.) *SzSz*. 1996; 30/31: 172-195. Lang.:
Hun.
Hungary: Budapest. 1897-1918. Historical studies. ■Analysis of eleven
seasons' repertoire of the Magyar Színház under the management of
László Beöthy.

484   Róna, Katalin; Koncz, Zsuzsa, photo. "Szabadság és
merészség—Beszélgetés Szikora Jánossal." (Freedom and
Daring—An Interview with János Szikora.) *Sz*. 1996; 29(12):
37-39. Illus.: Photo. B&W. 4. Lang.: Hun.
Hungary. 1980-1996. Histories-sources. ■Meeting director János Szikora, newly appointed artistic director of Szeged National Theatre.

485   Szalczer, Eszter. "*Mr. Dead and Mrs. Free*: the History of
Squat Theatre—A Retrospective Exhibition at Artists Space
Gallery." *SEEP*. 1996 Spr; 16(2): 30-39. Notes. Illus.:
Photo. 4. Lang.: Eng.
Hungary: Budapest. USA: New York, NY. 1969-1981. Historical studies.
■Through the current exhibition, author recalls history of Squat Theatre:
from its birth in Budapest as Szobaszínház to the creation of its last per-
formance by the original group, *Mr. Dead and Mrs. Free*. Its develop-
ment as a political theatre, from being banned by the Hungarian
government in Budapest to the entire company emigrating to the United
States and setting up Squat in New York City in 1977.

486   Szántó, Judit. "A százéves Vígszínház." (The Hundred-Year
Old Comedy Theatre.) *Sz*. 1996; 29 (5): 1. Lang.: Hun.
Hungary: Budapest. 1896-1996. Historical studies. ■Editorial on the
Vígszínház.

487   Upor, László. "Zeppelin helyett." (Instead of a Zeppelin.)
Sz. 1996; 29(8): 1. Lang.: Hun.
Hungary: Debrecen. 1996. Critical studies. ■László Upor, one of Comedy Theatre's literary managers, summarizes his impressions of this
year's National Theatre Festival held in Debrecen.

488   Edling, Lars. "Grotowskis sidste fase." (Grotowski's Last
Stage.) *TE*. 1996 June; 79: 17-19. Illus.: Photo. B&W. 2.
Lang.: Dan.
Italy: Pontedera. 1996. Histories-sources. ■A visit to Jerzy Grotowski's
Centro per la Sperimentazione e la Ricerca Teatrale.

489   Nah, Véronique. "Transformer les choses." (Changing
Things.) *JCT*. 1989; 50: 31-32. Illus.: Photo. B&W. 2. Lang.:
Fre.
Italy: Florence. 1979-1989. Histories-sources. ■Poetics of children's the-
atre company Teatro dei Piccoli Principi according to collaborator
Véronique Nah.

490   Poggioli, Fabio. *Sulle orme della 'Compagnia dei Giovani'*.
(On the Footprints of the 'Young Company'.) Rome: Carte
Segrete; 1996. 251 pp. Biblio. Illus.: Photo. B&W. Lang.: Ita.
Italy. 1954-1973. Biographical studies. ■The activity of the Compagnia
dei Giovani, created by actors Giorgio De Lullo, Romolo Valli, Rossella
Falk, Anna Maria Guarnieri, and others, and its significance to Italian
theatre.

THEATRE IN GENERAL: —Institutions

491 Tiedemann, Kathrin. "Romeo und Claudia auf dem lande." (Romeo and Claudia in the Country.) *TZ*. 1996; 3: 46-48. Illus.: Photo. B&W. 5. Lang.: Ger.
Italy: Cesena. 1981-1996. Historical studies. ■Profile of Societas Raffaello Sanzio, described as subversive and avant-garde: its history, its work with amateurs.

492 Vaïs, Michel. "La remise du prix Europe ... et un théâtre carcéral exemplaire." (The Awarding of the Europe Prize ... and an Exemplary Prison Theatre.) *JCT*. 1996; 81: 79-86. Notes. Illus.: Photo. B&W. 5. Lang.: Fre.
Italy: Taormina. 1971-1996. Historical studies. ■Description of the Prix d'Europe award ceremonies and festival. Grand prize was awarded to Robert Wilson, second prizes for New Theatrical Realities to Théâtre de Complicité of London and Carte Blanche-la Compagnia della Fortezza, a prison theatre group from Sicily. Productions included Wilson's *Persephone*, Complicité's *Three Lives of Lucie Cabrol* by John Berger, and a videotape of Fortezza's *Les Nègres* by Jean Genet, directed by Armando Punzo.

493 Wolford, Lisa. "*Action*: The Unrepresentable Origin." *TDR*. 1996 Win; 40(4): 134-153. Notes. Illus.: Photo. B&W. 6. Lang.: Eng.
Italy: Pontedera. 1987-1996. Historical studies. ■Activities of the Workcenter of theatre artist and teacher Jerzy Grotowski: research, use of term *Action* as an indication of genre, referring to a full-length performance structure with a crafted, repeatable score. Description of newest work being developed by the group.

494 Kim, Soo-Jin. "Changdan Sipdolil Manun Urie Kukdandul." (Korean Theatre Companies Which Have Turned Ten Years Old.) *KTR*. 1996 Mar.; 21(3): 16-21. Illus.: Photo. B&W. 4. Lang.: Kor.
Korea: Seoul. 1986-1996. Historical studies. ■Profile of four theatre companies on the occasion of their tenth anniversaries: Michoo, Arirang, Yeonheedan Keoripae, and Jakunshinua. Describes unique characteristics of each company.

495 Mikey, Fanny. "El intercambio ha logrado lo que no ha logrado la política." (Interchange Has Achieved What Politics Has Not Achieved.) *Cjo*. 1996 July/Dec.; 103: 26-27. Illus.: Photo. 1. Lang.: Spa.
Latin America. 1988-1996. Historical studies. ■Benefits of cultural exchange among Latin American countries participating in international festivals. Emphasis on the annual festival in Bogota, which was founded in 1988.

496 Peixoto, Fernando. "Nuevos estímulos para neuvos caminos." (New Encouragement for New Ways.) *Cjo*. 1996 July/Dec.; 103: 29-31. Illus.: Photo. 1. Lang.: Spa.
Latin America. 1996. Critical studies. ■Argues that there is an element of competitiveness in the character of festivals that leads to prejudice and negates possibilities for critical debate and self-criticism.

497 Ramos-Perea, Roberto. "Los festivales no son una vía agotada." (Festivals Are Not A Dead End.) *Cjo*. 1996 July/Dec.; 103: 32-34. Illus.: Photo. 1. Lang.: Spa.
Latin America. 1996. Critical studies. ■A defense of festival theatre's objectivity and organization.

498 Karpova, N. "Mir vašemu domu." (Peace to Your Home.) *TeatZ*. 1996; 5: 9-11. Lang.: Rus.
Mari El Republic: Yoshkar-Ola. 1995. Historical studies. ■Account of festival of Russian theatres.

499 Žegin, N. "Festival' russkoj diaspory." (Festival of the Russian Diaspora.) *TeatZ*. 1996; 2: 44-48. Lang.: Rus.
Mari El Republic: Yoshkar-Ola. 1995. Historical studies. ■Account of the second international festival of Russian drama theatres.

500 Goulooze-Müller, Maud. "Sociëteit De Koepel. Sjieke concurrent van De Kring mislukte." (Club De Koepel: Classy Competitor of De Kring Failed.) *OnsA*. 1996; 48(5): 120-125. Illus.: Photo. B&W. 10. Lang.: Dut.
Netherlands: Amsterdam. 1945-1954. Historical studies. ■The artist club De Koepel, which went bankrupt after a few years, and its failure to attract a lively membership.

501 Vaïs, Michel. "Visite au Musée du théâtre d'Amsterdam." (Visit to Amsterdam's Theater Museum.) *JCT*. 1993 ; 67: 111-116. Notes. Lang.: Fre.
Netherlands: Amsterdam. 1949-1993. Historical studies. ■History, current functions, holdings of Amsterdam's Theater Museum and the Netherlands Theatre Institute, and their integration in a system of institutions for the lively arts.

502 Fiebach, Joachim. "Cultural Identities, Interculturalism, and Theatre: On the Popular Yoruba Travelling Theatre." *ThR*. 1996; 21(1): 52-58. Notes. Lang.: Eng.
Nigeria. 1944-1971. Historical studies. ■Describes the history, techniques and performances of Hubert Ogunde's Yoruba Travelling Theatre, highlighting the absorption of cultural borrowings in the construction of African cultural identity.

503 Pignataro, Jorge. "Verdaderas ventanas abiertas." (Truthful Open Windows.) *Cjo*. 1996 July/Dec.; 103: 31-32. Illus.: Photo. 1. Lang.: Spa.
Paraguay: Montevideo. 1995. Historical studies. ■Account of the Muestra Internacional Festival in Montevideo, which showcased theatre from all over the world.

504 Bulat, Mirosława. "Jung Teater i Naj Teater w Krakowie." (Jung Teater and Naj Teater in Cracow.) *PaT*. 1996; 45 (3-4): 511-539. Notes. Illus.: Handbill. Photo. B&W. 15. Lang.: Pol.
Poland: Cracow. 1935-1938. Histories-sources. ■Materials relating to Yiddish-language performances in Cracow by Michał Weichert's troupe, known as Jung Teater or Naj Teater.

505 Butkiewicz, Zenon. *Nasz Współczesny. Teatr Współczesny w Szczecinie 1976-1996.* (Our Contemporary: Teatr Współczesny in Szczecin, 1976-1996.) Szczecin: Wydawnictwo Promocyjne Albatus; 1996. 117 pp. Pref. Append. Illus.: Photo. 73. Lang.: Pol.
Poland: Szczecin. 1976-1996. Histories-specific. ■History of Teatr Współczesny (Contemporary Theatre) based on interviews with its artistic directors. Includes listings of the theatre's repertory and members.

506 Dion, Gregg. "From No Man's Land to No Man's Theater: The Theatre of the 8th Day Returns to Capitalist Poland." 185-205 in Reinelt, Janelle, ed. *Crucibles of Crisis: Performing Social Change*. Ann Arbor, MI: Univ of Michigan P; 1996. 250 pp. Notes. Illus.: Photo. 5. Lang.: Eng.
Poland: Poznań. 1989-1995. Critical studies. ■Teatr Ósmego Dnia's reception upon returning from exile to Poland, where the new capitalism has stripped the avant-garde of its former social functions and identity.

507 Juliusz, Tyszka. "Skąd się wzięła Kana?" (Where Does Kana Come From?) *DialogW*. 1996; 9: 157-165. Lang.: Pol.
Poland: Szczecin. 1996. Critical studies. ■Profile of the Kana alternative theatre group, winner of the Fringe First and Critics' Award at the Edinburgh Festival in 1993.

508 Mjagkova, I. "Torun'. Pervaja pjatiletka." (Torun: The First Five Years.) *TeatZ*. 1996; 3: 14-18. Lang.: Rus.
Poland: Torun. 1990-1995. Historical studies. ■History of the Contact theatre festival.

509 Moszkowicz, Jerzy; Rudziński, Zbigniew. "Where Are We?" *TP*. 1996 July; 38(3): 9-15. Illus.: Photo. Color. B&W. 5. Lang.: Eng, Fre.
Poland. 1996. Critical studies. ■Critique of the state-owned Polish institutions of children's theatre and puppetry, said to provide overwhelmingly conservative pap, and of the commercial Polish theatre's reluctance to offer more productions for youth.

510 Popiel, Jacek. *Krakowska Szkoła Teatralna. 50 lat PWST im. L. Solskiego w Krakowie.* (Theatre School in Cracow: Fifty Years of the Solski State Graduate Theatre School.) Cracow/Warsaw: PWST im. L. Solskiego/Presspublication; 1996. 184 pp. Pref. Index. Append. Illus.: Photo. 32. Lang.: Pol.
Poland: Cracow. 1945-1995. Histories-sources. ■Anniversary volume in which the history of Cracow Theatre School (PWST) is told by its professors and students.

511 Tyszka, Julius; Cynkutis, Jolanta, transl.; Randolph, Tom, transl. "Polish Alternative Theatre During the Period of

CLASSED ENTRIES

THEATRE IN GENERAL: —Institutions

Transition, 1989-94." *NTQ*. 1996; 12(45): 71-78. Notes. Illus.: Photo. B&W. 6. Lang.: Eng.

Poland. 1989-1994. Historical studies. ∎The new political and economic order liberated thousands of independent student and amateur theatre groups from their political duties, charging them to support new means of social communication. This article outlines the alternative theatre tradition, strategies for survival, and future prospects.

512 Zielińska, Maryla. "On the Centre for Contemporary Art." *TP*. 1996 Jan.; 38(1): 38-42. Lang.: Eng, Fre.

Poland: Warsaw. 1995. Histories-sources. ∎Interview with the director of the Centre for Contemporary Art, Wojciech Krukowski, regarding the place of theatre in the institution.

513 Zielińska, Maryla. "The Foundations Are Laid." *TP*. 1996 July; 38(3): 3-6. Illus.: Photo. B&W. 2. Lang.: Eng, Fre.

Poland: Warsaw. 1996. Histories-sources. ∎Interview with the chairwoman of the Polish ASSITEJ center, Halina Machulska, about the future of the institution and children's theatre in Poland.

514 Koltai, Tamás. "Bukaresti mozaik—Uniószínházak fesztiválja." (Bucharest Mosaic—Festival of the Union of European Theatres.) *Sz*. 1996; 29(2): 37-42. Illus.: Photo. B&W. 5. Lang.: Hun.

Romania: Bucharest. 1995. Reviews of performances. ∎Summing up the interesting productions at the 4th meeting of European theatres.

515 "Sjužety 'Baltiskogo Doma'." (Fragments from Baltiskij Dom.) *MoskNab*. 1996; 5-6: 20-22. Lang.: Rus.

Russia: St. Petersburg. 1995-1996. Historical studies. ∎Report from the Baltiskij Dom Baltic theatre festival.

516 Begunov, V. "Za okolicej, ili Vnutrennee zarubež'e." (Outside the Gate, or Abroad at Home.) *SovD*. 1996; 4: 170-178. Lang.: Rus.

Russia. 1990-1996. Historical studies. ∎Problems of youth theatres, including Petrozavodsk Youth Theatre, directed by Ol'ga Arifmetikova, and Teat'r Prichastije, directed by Pavel M. Konovalov, among others.

517 Dal'skaja, K. "Dom v centre Baltiki." (The House in the Baltic Center.) *TeatZ*. 1996; 10: 39-41. Lang.: Rus.

Russia: St. Petersburg. 1991-1996. Historical studies. ∎Six years of theatre festivals at Baltiskij Dom.

518 Dmitrevskaja, Marina. "S:t Petersburg." (St. Petersburg.) *Tningen*. 1996; 20(76-77): 51-54. Illus.: Photo. B&W. Lang.: Swe.

Russia: St. Petersburg. 1995-1996. Historical studies. ∎A survey of the theatres and their repertory in the free democratic St. Petersburg, with references to the directors Lev Dodin, Anatolij Praudin, and Temur Čcheidze.

519 Gromov, N. "Ermitažnyj teat'r." (The Hermitage Theatre.) *PTZ*. 1996; 10: 28-30. Lang.: Rus.

Russia: St. Petersburg. 1785-1996. Historical studies. ∎History of the founding and development of the theatre.

520 Korogodskij, Zinovyj. "Teat'r junych zavtra." (Theatre for Youth—Tomorrow.) *TeatZ*. 1996; 6: 12-14. Lang.: Rus.

Russia: St. Petersburg. 1990-1996. Histories-sources. ∎Profile of Teat'r pokolenyj (Theatre of Generations) by its director.

521 Lebedina, L. "'Schauspiel' po-russkij." ('Schauspiel' in Russian.) *TeatZ*. 1996; 3: 54-55. Lang.: Rus.

Russia: Novosibirsk. 1990-1996. Historical studies. ∎Profile of Novosibirsk's youth theatre Globus, directed by Grigorij Gobernik.

522 Maljutin, Jakov O. *Zvezdy i sozvezdija*. (Stars and Constellations.) St. Petersburg: Drama; 1996. 172 pp. Lang.: Rus.

Russia: St. Petersburg. 1940-1996. Histories-specific. ∎An actor of the Mariinskij on the history of the theatre's development.

523 Muchtarov, I. "Na ploščadi s bolšim fontanom." (On a Square with a Big Fountain.) *TeatZ*. 1996; 5: 22-25. Lang.: Rus.

Russia: Tashkent. 1990-1996. Historical studies. ∎Theatre life in Tashkent, with reference to Gorkij Russian Academic Theatre, Vladimir Šapiro, artistic director, among others.

524 Proskurnikova, Tatiana. "Vospominanija dlja buduščego." (Memories for the Future.) *TeatZ*. 1996; 3: 2-7. Lang.: Rus.

Russia: Moscow. 1994-1996. Historical studies. ∎The work of the Union of Theatre Makers of Russia.

525 Revjakina, M. "Iz žizni novosibirskogo molodežnogo teatra 'Globus'." (About the Novosibirsk Youth Theatre Globus.) *TeatZ*. 1996; 6: 9-11. Lang.: Rus.

Russia: Novosibirsk. 1990-1996. Histories-sources. ∎The theatre's manager describes the group's activity, including marketing and working with an audience.

526 Skoročkina, O. "Slovno celoe vojsko." (As a Full Army.) *TeatZ*. 1996; 10: 30-31. Lang.: Rus.

Russia: St. Petersburg. 1996. Critical studies. ∎Review of the repertoire of Akademičéskij Teat'r Comedii, Tatjana Kazakova, artistic director.

527 Starceva, N. "Pjesa na dvoich." (A Play for Two.) *TeatZ*. 1996; 6: 42-45. Lang.: Rus.

Russia: Rostov-na-Donu. 1996. Historical studies. ∎Profile of Rostov's Theatre for Youth (Teat'r Junogo Zritelja), Aleksand'r Kompanijcev, director.

528 Hizsnyan, Géza. "Színházi fesztivál Szlovákiában." (Theatre Festival in Slovakia.) *Sz*. 1996; 29 (1): 40-45. Illus.: Photo. B&W. 3. Lang.: Hun.

Slovakia: Nitra. 1990-1995. Reviews of performances. ∎Summing up the events of the festival in Nitra.

529 Nánay, István. "Nyitrai jegyzetek." (Festival Notes at Nitra.) *Sz*. 1996; 29(12): 1. Lang.: Hun.

Slovakia: Nitra. 1996. Reviews of performances. ∎An account of the Nitra Festival, an annual survey of Slovakian theatres, further enriched by guest appearances of several companies from abroad.

530 Inkret, Andrej, et al. *Akademija za gledališče, radio, film in televizijo*. (Academy of Theatre, Radio, Film and Television.) Ljubljana: AGRFT; 1996. 215 pp. Biblio. Illus.: Photo. Color. Lang.: Slo.

Slovenia: Ljubljana. 1946-1996. Historical studies. ∎History of the academy, which began as the Academy of Acting Arts and has now been incorporated into the University of Ljubljana.

531 Štaudohar, Irena. *Exodos—Festival sodobnih odrskih umetnosti*. (Exodos—Festival of Contemporary Performing Arts.) Ljubljana: Cankarjev dom; 1996. 60 pp. Illus.: Photo. B&W. Lang.: Slo.

Slovenia: Ljubljana. 1996. Historical studies. ∎The program of the international festival of contemporary performing arts held in Ljubljana.

532 Laws, Page. "South Africa Through the Prism: Festival in Grahamstown, 1996." *NTQ*. 1996 Nov.; 12(48): 390-393. Illus.: Photo. B&W. 1. [*NTQ* Reports and Announcements.] Lang.: Eng.

South Africa, Republic of: Grahamstown. 1996. Historical studies. ∎Overview of 500 events in drama, dance, music, opera, film and visual arts, with frequent references to their political relevance for South Africa. Mentions especially the productions of *Macbeth* by Marthinus Basson and the Afrikaans *Donkerland I and II* by Deon Opperman.

533 Odendaal, Louw; Schutte, Johan. "ATKV Toneel '95: 'n reenboog met spatsels goud." (ATKV Toneel '95: A Rainbow Spattered with Gold.) *SATJ*. 1995 May; 9(1): 100-110. Illus.: Photo. B&W. 7. Lang.: Afr.

South Africa, Republic of. 1995. Historical studies. ∎Account of the Afrikaans Language and Culture Organization's annual Campus Theatre Festival for newly commissioned plays produced by university drama departments.

534 Reverte Bernal, Concepción. "X Festival Iberoamericano de Teatro de Cádiz." (Tenth Spanish-American Festival of Theatre in Cádiz.) *LATR*. 1996 Spr; 29(2): 183-190. Lang.: Spa.

Spain: Cádiz. 1995. Historical studies. ∎Festival featuring Equipo Teatro Payro (Buenos Aires), Casa via Magia (Rio de Janeiro), La Máscara de Cali, Teatro Buendía (Havana), Teatro La Troppa de Santiago, Ur Teatro (Madrid), and Teatro del Sur (Granada).

535 Lane, Jill. "Albert Boadella and the Catalan Comedy of Cultural Politics." *JDTC*. 1996 Fall; 11(1): 81-100. Notes. Illus.: Photo. 2. Lang.: Eng.

CLASSED ENTRIES

THEATRE IN GENERAL: —Institutions

Spain-Catalonia. 1967-1985. Critical studies. ■Albert Boadella, founder of Catalan theatre company Els Joglars, and his struggles with the relationship of theatre to the development, maintenance, and representation of national community. Boadella has evolved a cultural political comedy form to resist conformity and censorship. Examines how comedy mechanisms and the mechanics of politically committed theatre inform and 'deform' each other in Boadella's practice.

536 Edling, Lars. "Ingen vanlig teaterutbildning." (Not an Ordinary Theatre Training.) *Tningen.* 1996; 20(79): 14-16. Illus.: Photo. B&W. Lang.: Swe.
Sweden: Sotenäs. 1995. Historical studies. ■A presentation of the Sotenäs Teateratelje, an independent actors' school with ambitions of cross research, with reference to the leader Michael Norlind.

537 Gerhardsson, Björn. "Nationalteater—för vilka?" (A National Theatre—For Whom?)*Dramat.* 1996; 4(1): 49. Lang.: Swe.
Sweden: Stockholm. 1996. Historical studies. ■A provincial's view of Dramaten, the Royal Dramatic Theatre, with emphasis on the opinion that more productions should be broadcast on television.

538 Hoogland, Rikard. "Historien om krisen på Östgötateatern." (History of the Crisis of Östgötateatern.) *Tningen.* 1996; 20(75): 9-10. Illus.: Photo. B&W. Lang.: Swe.
Sweden: Norrköping. 1995. Historical studies. ■Claes Peter Hellwig gives his version of the financial problems and the turbulences of the artists and the staff during his year as manager of Östgötateatern.

539 Hoogland, Rikard. "Ett teaterparaply?" (An Umbrella For the Theatres?)*Tningen.* 1996; 20(78): 13-14. Illus.: Photo. B&W. Lang.: Swe.
Sweden: Stockholm. 1993. Critical studies. ■Presentation of Teaterkollektivet Rex, or T Rex, a combination theatre company and producing agency that intends to produce new Swedish drama.

540 Hoogland, Rikard. "Mannen som ska göra det." (The Man Who Shall Do It.) *Tningen.* 1996; 20(79): 29-31. Illus.: Photo. B&W. Lang.: Swe.
Sweden: Gothenburg. 1996. Historical studies. ■A presentation of Ronny Danielsson, the new theatre manager of Göteborgs Stadsteater, and his plans for the repertory to save the financial situation.

541 Hoogland, Rikard. "Bastarder under jord." (Bastards Beneath the Earth.) *Tningen.* 1996; 20(79): 36-37. Illus.: Photo. B&W. Lang.: Swe.
Sweden: Gothenburg. 1995. Historical studies. ■A presentation of the independent group Teater Bastard and their new production of Pär Lagerkvist's *Bödeln (The Executioner).*

542 Hoogland, Rikard. "En återuppstånden teater." (A Resurrected Theatre.) *Tningen.* 1996; 20(79): 38-39. Illus.: Photo. B&W. Lang.: Swe.
Sweden: Gothenburg. 1996. Historical studies. ■A report from the new life of Atelierteatern after the burning of their building and their theatre plans for school children.

543 Söderberg, Olle. "Frisse, STTF's meste doldis." (Frisse, the Most Unknown Person of STTF.) *ProScen.* 1996; 20(2): 19-20. Illus.: Photo. Color. Lang.: Swe.
Sweden. 1970. Biographical studies. ■A portrait of the editor of *ProScen:* Karl-Gunnar Frisell.

544 Sörenson, Elisabeth. "Bortom nålsögat." (Beyond the Eye of the Needle.) *Dramat.* 1996; 4(4): 10-15. Illus.: Photo. B&W. Color. Lang.: Swe.
Sweden. 1965. Histories-sources. ■A presentation of the training of the actors in the five theatre schools of Sweden, with references to Stockholms Teaterhögskola, and interviews with the pupils or recently examined actors.

545 Tiselius, Henric. "En osannolik kraft." (An Unbelievable Force.) *Tningen.* 1996; 20(79): 44-46. Illus.: Photo. Color. Lang.: Swe.
Sweden: Gothenburg. 1995-1996. Historical studies. ■A survey of the independent group Teater Bhopa and its director Alexander Öberg, and their adaptation of Homer: *Det gudomliga kriget (The Divine War).*

546 Wigardt, Gaby. "Stockholms Parkteater, en unik företeelse." (The Stockholm Parkteater, a Unique Phenome-

non.) *Dramat.* 1996; 4(2): 27-28. Illus.: Photo. Color. Lang.: Swe.
Sweden: Stockholm. 1996. Histories-sources. ■An interview with the new artistic director of Stockholms Parkteater, Benny Fredriksson, about the aim of Parkteatern to give theatre, dance and music of good quality free to the people of Stockholm.

547 Blomquist, Kurt. "OISTAT—utvärdering av 'Lilla Kongressen och PQ-95'." (OISTAT—an Evaluation of 'The Small Conference and PQ-95'.) *ProScen.* 1996; 20(1): 22. Lang.: Swe.
Switzerland: Luzern. Czech Republic: Prague. 1960. Historical studies. ■A report from the conference of OISTAT and the Prague Quadrennial of 1995.

548 Feller, Elisabeth. "So viel Anfang war selten." (So Much Beginning Has Been Rare.) *DB.* 1996; 11: 20-23. Append. Illus.: Photo. B&W. 5. Lang.: Ger.
Switzerland: Basel. 1996. Historical studies. ■Portrait of Basler Theater and interview with Michael Schindhelm, the new artistic director.

549 Richard, Christine. "Erst zum Neger: Jetzt das Wetter." (First the Blacks, Now the Weather.) *THeute.* 1996; 10: 22-26. Illus.: Photo. B&W. 8. Lang.: Ger.
Switzerland: Basel. 1996. Reviews of performances. ■Productions of the Welt in Basel festival, including the festival's own production, *Lina Bögli* directed by Christoph Marthaler.

550 Wille, Franz. "Die Stimmung macht das Schauspiel." (Atmosphere Makes the Drama.) *THeute.* 1996; 9: 18-19. Illus.: Photo. B&W. 2. Lang.: Ger.
Switzerland: Basel. 1996. Histories-sources. ■Interview with Michael Schindhelm, new director of Basler Theater, about money, art, and plans.

551 Sorokina, N. "Esli posmotret', podumat', vspomnit'." (What If We Look, Think, Remember.) *TeatZ.* 1996; 8: 8-12. Lang.: Rus.
Tatarstan: Cheboksary. 1991-1996. Historical studies. ■Report on the 'Tuganlyk' theatre festivals.

552 Charles, Peter. "Home from Home: An Appreciation of Denville Hall." *PlPl.* 1996 Aug/Sep.; 507: 36-37. Lang.: Eng.
UK-England: Northwood. 1926-1996. Critical studies. ■The founding and history of Denville Hall, a retirement/nursing home for actors and actresses. Founded by actor-manager Alfred Denville in 1926, it is now run by The Actors' Charitable Trust.

553 Gandolfi, Roberta. "Cultura delle donne e ricerca teatrale agli inizi del Novecento. The Pioneer Players di Edy Craig." (Women's Culture and Theatre Research in the Early Twentieth Century: Edith Craig's Pioneer Players.) *TeatroS.* 1996; 11(18): 167-202. Notes. Lang.: Ita.
UK-England: London. 1911-1918. Historical studies. ■The history of the Pioneer Players, founded by Edith Craig: its artistic and political aims and its role as a platform for the blossoming women's culture.

554 Jacomino, Fernando J. León. "Parabêns Londrina." (Congratulations London.) *Cjo.* 1996 July/Dec.; 103: 55-62. Notes. Illus.: Photo. 6. Lang.: Spa.
UK-England: London. Latin America. 1968-1996. Historical studies. ■Latin American content of the London International Theatre Festival, with emphasis on performances by De La Guarda of Buenos Aires and the dance theatre of Wilson Pico.

555 Persson, Marie. "Ett paradis för teaterarbetare." (A Paradise For Theatre Artists.) *Tningen.* 1996; 20(76-77): 10-12 . Lang.: Swe.
UK-England: London. 1990. Historical studies. ■A presentation of the Royal National Theatre Studio under the directions of Sue Higgins.

556 Smythe, Eva. "Anniversary Time: Eva Smythe at the Unicorn Arts Theatre." *PlPl.* 1996 Oct.; 508: 24. Lang.: Eng.
UK-England: London. 1926-1996. Historical studies. ■On the 50th anniversary of the Unicorn Theatre, the oldest professional theatre company for children in England, founded by Caryl Jenner, and the 70th anniversary of the Arts Theatre, where the Unicorn has been located since 1962.

557 Wearing, J.P. "Nancy Price and the People's National Theatre." *THSt.* 1996 June; 16: 71-89. Notes. Append. Illus.: Photo. 6. Lang.: Eng.

CLASSED ENTRIES

THEATRE IN GENERAL: —Institutions

UK-England: London. 1930-1940. Historical studies. ∎The People's National Theatre, founded by Nancy Price and J.T. Grein, produced non-commercial theatre at popular prices, built a subscription audience, and offered different plays every week. Author reconstructs history of the group. Includes a list of eleven seasons of production.

558 Wilcock, Richard. "Meet the Neighbours." *PlPl.* 1996 June; 38: 38. Lang.: Eng.
UK-England: Leeds. 1996. Critical studies. ∎Profile of the European Directors School at the West Yorkshire Playhouse. Emphasis on the detailed training process, requirements for admission and the academic component of the program.

559 Di Cenzo, Maria. *The Politics of Alternative Theatre in Britain, 1968-1990: The Case of 7:84 (Scotland).* Cambridge/New York, NY: Cambridge UP; 1996. 261 pp. (Cambridge Studies in Modern Theatre.) Notes. Biblio. Index. Illus.: Photo. 14. Lang.: Eng.
UK-Scotland. 1968-1990. Histories-specific. ∎Critical performance history of 7:84 (Scotland), created after 7:84 Theatre Company split into English and Scottish groups.

560 Feuchtner, Bernd. "Richtig Klasse." (Real Class.) *THeute.* 1996; 10: 21. Illus.: Photo. B&W. 1. Lang.: Ger.
UK-Scotland: Edinburgh. 1996. Reviews of performances. ∎The atmosphere and highlights of the music program of the Edinburgh Festival.

561 Kranz, Oliver. "Hillary Strong verteidigt die Freiheit." (Hillary Strong Defends Freedom.) *THeute.* 1996; 10: 17-20. Illus.: Photo. B&W. 4. Lang.: Ger.
UK-Scotland: Edinburgh. 1996. Reviews of performances. ∎Impressions and reviews of the fiftieth Edinburgh Festival, with reference to *Orlando* by Virginia Woolf, directed by Robert Wilson, *Four Saints in Three Acts* by Virgil Thomson and Gertrude Stein, directed by Robert Wilson and produced by Houston Grand Opera, *Diadia Vania (Uncle Vania)* by Čechov, directed by Peter Stein, produced by Teatro di Roma and Teatro Stabile di Parma, *Iphigenie auf Tauris (Iphigenie in Tauris)* adapted to ballet by Pina Bausch after the opera by Christoph Willibald Gluck.

562 Loney, Glenn. "Dance Dominates Edinburgh Festival." *WES.* 1996 Fall; 8(3): 59-64. Illus.: Photo. 3. Lang.: Eng.
UK-Scotland: Edinburgh. 1996. Historical studies. ∎Examination of dance pieces in the current Edinburgh Festival including Mark Morris's Dance Group, The Nederlands Dans Theater, the Martha Graham Dance Company, as well as standard theatre pieces such as Traverse Theatre's *Shining Souls* by Chris Hannan and David Greig's *The Architect.*

563 Shenton, Mark. "An Insider's Guide to the Edinburgh Festival." *TheaterW.* 1996 Oct 7; 10(10): 26-33. Lang.: Eng.
UK-Scotland: Edinburgh. 1996. Historical studies. ∎Practical guide for lodging, ticket purchase, and viewing schedules for Edinburgh Fringe Festival.

564 Taxidou, Olga. "Making Theatre for the Festival Culture: Scenes from the Edinburgh Festival 1994." *STP.* 1994 Dec.; 10: 40-43. Lang.: Eng.
UK-Scotland: Edinburgh. 1994. Critical studies. ∎Considers productions of *Les Sept Branches de la Rivière Ota (The Seven Streams of the River Ota)* by Robert Lepage, and *Die Stunde da wir nichts voneinander wussten (The Hour We Knew Nothing of Each Other)* by Peter Handke, directed by Luc Bondy.

565 Lebedina, L. "V okružajuščem blagolepii niščety." (Surrounded by the Greatness of Poverty.) *TeatZ.* 1996; 11-12: 33-36. Lang.: Rus.
Ukraine: L'vov. 1995-1996. Historical studies. ∎Theatrical life in Ukraine, with emphasis on L'vov's Zolotov Lev festival.

566 "Gypsy of the Year." *TheaterW.* 1996 Dec 30; 10(22): 54-56. Illus.: Photo. B&W. 6. Lang.: Eng.
USA: New York, NY. 1996. Historical studies. ∎Broadway Cares/Equity Fights AIDS sponsors annual fundraiser featuring performances from artists currently appearing in Broadway productions.

567 Baldridge, Charlene. "Miracle in a Bean Field: South Coast Rep." *TheaterW.* 1996 July 1; 9(48): 32-35. Illus.: Photo. B&W. 2. Lang.: Eng.
USA: Costa Mesa, CA. 1996. Historical studies. ∎Artistic directors Martin Benson and David Emmes discuss South Coast Rep's past and future

seasons, impact of economy on their funding, improvements in theatre space, expansion of organization, awards received.

568 Barbour, David. "Turning 30 with the New York Public Library for the Performing Arts." *TCI.* 1996 Jan.; 30(1): 44. Lang.: Eng.
USA: New York, NY. 1966-1996. Historical studies. ∎Anniversary of TCI's publication coinciding with that of the New York Public Library for the Performing Arts.

569 Blaney, Retta. "Regional Theater Marketing." *TheaterW.* 1996 Jan 29; 9(26): 15-21. Illus.: Photo. B&W. 3. Lang.: Eng.
USA. 1996. Historical studies. ∎Funding, audience development and marketing plans for Pennsylvania Stage Company, Center Stage, Portland Stage Company and Milwaukee Repertory.

570 Blood, Melanie N. "Theatre in Settlement Houses: Hull-House Players, Neighborhood Playhouse, and Karamu Theatre." *THSt.* 1996 June; 16: 45-69. Notes. Illus.: Photo. 2. Lang.: Eng.
USA: Chicago, IL, Cleveland, OH, New York, NY. 1896-1930. Historical studies. ∎Study of three successful community-based theatre programs emerging from the reform movement and settlement houses, which influenced both social service and theatre practice in America. Each program enacted a sociopolitical philosophy in experimental theatrical practice, as well as encouraging women and African-Americans to participate in theatre.

571 Branth, Janicke. "En taenketank for kunstnere." (A Think Tank for Artists.) *TE.* 1996 Feb.; 77: 22-23. Illus.: Photo. B&W. 1. Lang.: Dan.
USA: New York, NY. 1992-1996. Histories-sources. ∎A visit to Robert Wilson's Watermill Center, a theatre/performance laboratory which also provides housing for visual artists, including painters, sculptors, and video artists. Emphasis on the annual summer workshops.

572 Brauner, Leon I. "Fort Worth Texas: Culture, Cadillacs & Cowgirls." *TD&T.* 1996 Win; 32(1): 8-12. Lang.: Eng.
USA: Fort Worth, TX. 1996. Critical studies. ∎Brief profile of the USITT Annual Conference and Stage Expo.

573 Brustein, Robert. "Subsidized Separatism." *AmTh.* 1996 Oct.; 13(8): 26-27, 100-107. Lang.: Eng.
USA. 1996. Histories-sources. ∎Response to playwright August Wilson's keynote address at the TCG Conference in which he advocated a separation of Black and white theatre to help emphasize the uniqueness of Black culture. Includes Wilson's response to Brustein's article.

574 Buckley, Michael. "Double Casting Coups: The Matrix Theater Company." *TheaterW.* 1996 July 1; 9(48): 20-25. Illus.: Photo. B&W. 3. Lang.: Eng.
USA: Los Angeles, CA. 1996. Historical studies. ∎Joseph Stern, artistic director for the company, discusses past and current seasons, high level of acting talent, strategy of double casting roles and its impact on the actors. Several company members give brief testimonials about their experiences in the company.

575 Dolan, Jill. "Producing Knowledges that Matter: Practicing Performance Studies through Theatre Studies." *TDR.* 1996 Win; 40(4): 9-19. Notes. Biblio. Lang.: Eng.
USA. 1996. Critical studies. ∎Transcript of speech given at 1996 Performance Studies Conference. How institutions enable or obstruct production of knowledge, observations, teaching, and institutionalization of performance studies.

576 Dolan, M. *Chicano Theatre in Transition: The Experience of El Teatro de la Esperanza.* Ph.D. thesis, *Index to theses,* 43-3231. Glasgow: Univ. of Glasgow; 1994. Notes. Biblio. Lang.: Eng.
USA: Santa Barbara, CA. 1965-1994. Historical studies. ∎Sets Chicano theatre in its historical, social and political context, from its emergence in the mid-60s in tandem with the U.S. civil rights movement, to its decline.

577 Fraden, Rena. *Blueprints for a Black Federal Theatre, 1935-1939.* Cambridge/New York, NY: Cambridge UP; 1996. 266 pp. (Cambridge Studies in American Literature and Culture 81.) Notes. Biblio. Index. Illus.: Photo. 18. Lang.: Eng.

THEATRE IN GENERAL: —Institutions

USA. 1935-1939. Histories-specific. ■The extensive plans for Black theatre under the Federal Theatre Project, in which satellite theatres were planned from Seattle to New York City.

578   Geer, Richard Owen. "Out of Control in Colquitt." *TDR*. 1996 Sum; 40(2): 103-130. Notes. Biblio. Illus.: Photo. B&W. 14. Lang.: Eng.

USA: Colquitt, GA. 1987-1996. Historical studies. ■Director discusses his development of community plays with theatre company Swamp Gravy through oral histories and folklore. Goals to revitalize the community, funding the project, relationship with community actors, audience response. Includes 'Some Thoughts on Direct Address and Oral Histories in Performance' by director Jo Carson and excerpt from play *Brown Dress* adapted by Jo Carson from story by Edith McDuffie.

579   Griffin, Gretchen. "Sharing What You've Got." *AmTh*. 1996 Oct.; 13(8): 85-86. Illus.: Photo. B&W. 1. Lang.: Eng.

USA: New York, NY. 1996. Historical studies. ■The Vineyard Theatre's program which provides temporary shelter for itinerant artists. Funding grants for artists who lack their own space, budget.

580   Hartigan, Patti. "The Morphing of Fort Ord." *AmTh*. 1996 Jan.; 13(1): 30-32. Illus.: Photo. B&W. 2. Lang.: Eng.

USA: Monterey Bay, CA. 1996. Historical studies. ■Conversion of a former military base into a university multi-use facility. Playwright and activist Luis Valdez discusses progressive curriculum, integrating the arts into the main course of studies, and use of current technology.

581   Horwitz, Simi. "Bidding for Broadway." *TheaterW*. 1996 Sep 23; 10(8): 30-34. Illus.: Photo. B&W. 3. Lang.: Eng.

USA: New York, NY. 1996. Historical studies. ■Auction sponsored by Broadway Cares/Equity Fights AIDS which raises money for AIDS through the sale of theatre memorabilia and 'walk on' roles in Broadway shows.

582   Horwitz, Simi. "Inside New Jersey Theater." *TheaterW*. 1996 Apr 1; 9(35): 31-37. Illus.: Photo. B&W. 5. Lang.: Eng.

USA: Madison, NJ. 1996. Historical studies. ■New Jersey Theatre Group executive director Laura Aden discusses theatre companies, productions, and funding of such in the state. Special focus on the New Jersey Shakespeare Festival and its success under new management, educational outreach programs.

583   Horwitz, Simi. "A New League." *TheaterW*. 1996 June 3; 9(44): 72-74. Lang.: Eng.

USA: New York, NY. 1930-1996. Historical studies. ■Executive director of the League of American Theatres and Producers Jed Bernstein describes advances and improvements within the League, future plans, projections for the future of Broadway.

584   Horwitz, Simi. "Behind the Scenes: MTC's Big Bash." *TheaterW*. 1996 July 15; 9(50): 36-44. Illus.: Photo. B&W. 4. Lang.: Eng.

USA: New York, NY. 1996. Historical studies. ■Annual gala fundraiser for Manhattan Theatre Club: planning, entertainment, personnel. Artistic director Lynne Meadow and managing director Barry Grove discuss preparations and challenges of event.

585   Hulbert, Dan. "Atlanta's Olympic Moment." *AmTh*. 1996 July/Aug.; 13(6): 51-52. Illus.: Photo. B&W. 1. Lang.: Eng.

USA: Atlanta, GA. 1990-1996. Historical studies. ■Work by local theatre companies highlight the Olympic Arts Festival: Actor's Express, 7 Stages, and Alliance Theatre.

586   Johnson, Ernie. "Vivian Robinson." *BlackM*. 1996 Nov/Dec.; 12(2): 9,18. Illus.: Photo. B&W. 1. Lang.: Eng.

USA: New York, NY. 1996. Biographical studies. ■Obituary for Vivian Robinson, executive director of AUDELCO, and producing angel of Black theatre.

587   Jones, Chris. "Monsters of Mainstay?" *AmTh*. 1996 Mar.; 13(3): 46-48. Illus.: Photo. B&W. 2. Lang.: Eng.

USA: Cleveland, OH. 1992-1996. Historical studies. ■Increase of non-profit multi-space arts centers in the U.S. and their role as presenting organizations. Focus on Playhouse Square Center: financial stability, touring Broadway productions.

588   Langworthy, Douglas. "Inside the Tent." *AmTh*. 1996 Sep.; 13(7): 17-22. Illus.: Photo. B&W. 15. Lang.: Eng.

USA: Princeton, NJ. 1996. Historical studies. ■Report on the 11th National Conference for Theatre Communications Group: addresses by authors August Wilson and John Ralston Saul, role theatre plays in the changing world, workshops and other guest speakers. Includes series of quotes from theatre figures responding to the issue of colorblind casting, and excerpts from Saul's speech.

589   Moore, Dick. "Broadway Cares/Equity Fights AIDS Week Is November 24-December 1, 1996." *EN*. 1996 Nov.; 81(9): 2. Illus.: Photo. 3. Lang.: Eng.

USA: New York, NY. 1996. Historical studies. ■Nation-wide effort by theatre company and Equity members to raise funds for the Tenth Annual Broadway Cares/Equity Fights AIDS effort.

590   Moore, Dick. "Actors' Fund's Aurora Residence Is Open in New York." *EN*. 1996 Mar.; 81(2): 1. Lang.: Eng.

USA: New York, NY. 1996. Historical studies. ■The Aurora Residence, sponsored by the Actors' Fund of America to provide affordable, supportive housing to special low-income groups including the elderly, working professionals and persons with AIDS, also houses the Frederick O'Neal Memorial Library, established in memory of a past Equity president by the Associated Actors and Artistes of America.

591   Moore, Dick. "Open Enrollment in Effect During May for Changes in Health Insurance." *EN*. 1996 Apr.; 81(3): 1. Lang.: Eng.

USA: New York, NY. 1996. Historical studies. ■During May, participants in the Health Fund may change health insurance coverage and/or add dependents to existing coverage. Domestic partners may be added at this time.

592   Moore, Dick. "Silver Reports at Eastern Meeting." *EN*. 1996 May; 81(4): 1, 6. Lang.: Eng.

USA: New York, NY. 1996. Historical studies. ■Actors' Equity President Ron Silver reports on a variety of issues for members: the Broadway Initiatives, the New York Theatre Trust, the current state of government arts funding, and ways to stimulate economic development.

593   Moore, Dick. "BC/EFA's Easter Bonnet Competition Raises $1,304,525: 25 Companies Present Bonnets, 43 Casts Raise Funds." *EN*. 1996 May; 81(4): 3. Illus.: Photo. 7. Lang.: Eng.

USA: New York, NY. 1996. Historical studies. ■The Tenth Annual Easter Bonnet Competition, the two-day Broadway and Off Broadway spectacular which features singing, dancing, and hats, raised over $1 million for Broadway Cares/Equity Fights AIDS. The event, held at the Palace Theatre, raised the most funds for any fundraising event by BC/EFA.

594   Moore, Dick. "Aurora Residence Opens in NY." *EN*. 1996 July/Aug.; 81(6): 1. Illus.: Photo. 1. Lang.: Eng.

USA: New York, NY. 1996. Historical studies. ■The official opening of the Actors' Fund's new Aurora Residence. A gift of $750,000 from Broadway Cares/Equity Fights AIDS will underwrite social and volunteer services the residence will provide.

595   Moore, Dick. "Annual Paul Robeson Award Goes to George C. Wolfe." *EN*. 1996 Nov.; 81(9): 1. Illus.: Photo. 1. Lang.: Eng.

USA: New York, NY. 1996. Historical studies. ■Account of the presentation of Equity's annual Paul Robeson Award to director/producer George C. Wolfe for his work bringing the African-American cultural tradition to theatre.

596   Moore, Dick. "Working Group Aims to Increase Jobs, Financing, Production on Broadway." *EN*. 1996 Nov.; 81(9): 1. Lang.: Eng.

USA: New York, NY. 1996. Historical studies. ■The Broadway Initiatives Working Group combines labor and management executives to develop long-term planning to spur new play production on Broadway and expand audiences.

597   Moore, Dick. "Broadway Cares/Equity Fights AIDS Flea Market, Auction Shatters Record: $468,500 Raised in New York at Annual Shubert Alley Event." *EN*. 1996 Nov.; 81(9): 4. Illus.: Photo. 3. Lang.: Eng.

USA: New York, NY. 1996. Historical studies. ■Account of Tenth Annual Broadway Cares/Equity Fights AIDS Flea Market and Grand Auction, featuring leading stars of Broadway, Off Broadway, and film appearing and donating time and personal items. Also auctioned were

THEATRE IN GENERAL: —Institutions

opportunities for high bidders to appear in Broadway shows and television comedies.

598 Moore, Dick. "Gypsy of the Year Competition Sets BC/EFA Record." *EN.* 1996 Jan/Feb.; 81(1): 4-5. Illus.: Photo. 5. Lang.: Eng.
USA: New York, NY. 1989-1996. Historical studies. ■The success of the seventh annual Gypsy of the Year Competition raised $1,213,000 for Broadway Cares/Equity Fights AIDS.

599 Napoleon, Davi. "Schoolbiz." *TheaterW.* 1996 Jan 15; 9(24): 9-11. Illus.: Photo. B&W. 1. Lang.: Eng.
USA: Cleveland, OH. 1996. Historical studies. ■Working relationship between Cleveland Play House, artistic director Peter Hackett, and Case Western Reserve University's theatre department, headed by John Orlock. Curriculum, actor training, advantages of training in a professional setting.

600 Portantiere, Michael. "Bare Necessities." *TheaterW.* 1996 Apr 29; 9(39): 26-27. Illus.: Photo. B&W. 1. Lang.: Eng.
USA: New York, NY. 1996. Histories-sources. ■Interview with actor Jerry Mitchell in which he describes *Broadway Bares*, an annual event which raises money for Broadway Cares/Equity Fights AIDS.

601 Reiss, Alvin H. "Unrestricted Corporate Donations Target of United Theatre Fund." *FundM.* 1996 Dec.; 27(10): 34-35. Lang.: Eng.
USA: New York, NY. 1996. Historical studies. ■History and goals of the National Corporate Theatre Fund, which focuses strictly on corporations as the source of donations to theatre enterprises.

602 Richardson, Kim Blaise. "C. Bernard Jackson." *BlackM.* 1996 Nov/Dec.; 12(2): 9. Illus.: Photo. B&W. 1. Lang.: Eng.
USA. 1996. Biographical studies. ■Obituary for C. Bernard Jackson, founder and director of the Inner City Cultural Center in Los Angeles.

603 Rogan, Mary Ellen; Winkler, Kevin. "The Impact of AIDS on Archival Collections in the Performing Arts." *PAR.* 1995; 19 (1): 17-24. Lang.: Eng.
USA: New York, NY. 1996. Historical studies. ■Method of acquisition of archival materials from performing artists afflicted with AIDS, and how an artist's death from AIDS affects the acquisitional and appraisal process.

604 Seyda, Barbara. "Divine Testimonies: Sydné Mahone and Crossroads Theatre Company." *TDR.* 1996 Spr; 40(1): 119-140. Notes. Biblio. Illus.: Photo. B&W. 6. Lang.: Eng.
USA: New Brunswick, NJ. 1980-1996. Histories-sources. ■Interview with director of play development for Crossroads Theatre which is dedicated to African-American theatre. Her background, artistic vision, and editorial work on plays found in the anthology *Moon Marked & Touched by Sun: Plays by African-American Women*, published by Theatre Communications Group.

605 Sundgaard, Arnold. "The Group Remembered." *JADT.* 1996 Spr; 8(2): 1-11. Notes. Lang.: Eng.
USA: Lake Grove, NY. 1939. Histories-sources. ■Playwright Arnold Sundgaard recalls his experiences during the last summer workshop of the Group Theatre.

606 Webb, Dorothy. "Nora Tully MacAlvay—Her Life in the Theatre." *YTJ.* 1996; 10: 84-95. Biblio. Notes. Lang.: Eng.
USA: Michigan City, MI. 1900-1986. Historical studies. ■Career and life of youth theatre artist Nora Tully MacAlvay, especially her work with and for young people in the Lake Michigan area and her life project, MacAlvay's Children's Theatre Workshop.

607 Wilson, August. "The Ground on Which I Stand." *AmTh.* 1996 Sep.; 13(7): 14-16, 71-74. Illus.: Photo. B&W. 2. Lang.: Eng.
USA: Princeton, NJ. 1996. Histories-sources. ■Transcript of playwright August Wilson's controversial address to Theatre Communications Group conference in which he discusses state of Black theatre in America and advocates separation of Black and white theatre.

608 Wolf, Matt. "Death Becalms Her." *AmTh.* 1996 May/June; 13(5): 28-29. Illus.: Photo. B&W. 1. Lang.: Eng.
USA. UK-England: London. 1990-1996. Critical studies. ■American debut of touring ensemble troupe, Théâtre de Complicité. Co-founder

Simon McBurney discusses their production of *The Three Lives of Lucie Cabrol*, performances, sources for the collaborative work.

609 Zesch, Lindy. "Miami's Theatrical Caché." *AmTh.* 1996 Nov.; 13(9): 26, 80. Illus.: Photo. B&W. 3. [Headed by Title: 5 Corners of our theatrical world.] Lang.: Eng.
USA: Miami, FL. 1979-1996. Critical studies. ■Highlight productions of the International Hispanic Theatre Festival founded by Mario Ernesto Sanchez. Budgets, performance spaces, struggle to attract national attention.

610 Kazimirovskaja, Natalia. "Baltiska huset." (The Baltic House.) *Tningen.* 1996; 20(78): 35-37. Illus.: Photo. B&W. Lang.: Swe.
USSR: St. Petersburg. 1987. Historical studies. ■A report from the Baltiskij Dom, with guest performances from all countries around the Baltic sea.

611 Šach-Azizova, T. "Spektakl' dlja minifesta." (Play for a Mini-Festivity.) *TeatZ.* 1996; 6: 31-35. Lang.: Rus.
USSR: Rostov-na-Donu. 1989. Histories-sources. ■Recollections of the international festival of plays for children and youth.

612 Vajl, M. "'Prošlo 200 let'." (Two Hundred Years Have Passed.) *TeatZ.* 1996; 4: 16-19. Lang.: Rus.
Uzbekistan: Tashkent. 1990-1996. Histories-sources. ■Description of Il'chom Theatre by its director Mark Vajl'.

613 Gutiérrez, Alfonso. "Rajatabla en sus 25 años." (Rajatabla at 25 Years Old.) *LATR.* 1996 Fall; 30(1): 151-153. Notes. Illus.: Photo. 1. Lang.: Spa.
Venezuela: Caracas. 1971-1996. Historical studies. ■History of Grupo Rajatabla.

614 Theissen, Hermann. "Goodbye Belgrad?" *THeute.* 1996; 12: 33-37. Illus.: Photo. B&W. 7. Lang.: Ger.
Yugoslavia: Belgrade. 1996. Reviews of performances. ■Impressions of off-theatre at the Bitef festival, the theme of which was Remembering the Future.

Performance spaces

615 Jordan, Robert. "Visualizing the Sydney Theatre, 1796." *ADS.* 1996 Apr.; 28: 30-52. Notes. Append. Illus.: Dwg. B&W. Chart. 3. Lang.: Eng.
Australia: Sydney. 1796. Histories-reconstruction. ■Speculation as to the size, whereabouts and appearance of the Sydney Theatre, a structure about which there is no factual information. Includes a chart in the appendix with possible dimensions.

616 Alfons, Gerd; Sinz, Pamela. "Erweiterung des Festspiel- und Kongresshauses Bregenz." (Enlargement of the Bregenz Festival and Congress Buildings.) *BtR.* 1996; 4: 29-31. Illus.: Design. Photo. B&W. Color. 5. Lang.: Ger.
Austria: Bregenz. 1995-1996. Historical studies. ■Report on the enlargement of the foyer, cloak rooms, and shops.

617 Lampert-Gréaux, Ellen. "São Paulo Opera House." *TCI.* 1996 May; 30(5): 48-51. Illus.: Plan. Dwg. Color. 5. Lang.: Eng.
Brazil: São Paulo. 1996. Historical studies. ■Plans for the 24,000 seat Novo Teatro de São Paulo, due to be completed in 1999.

618 Productions Recto-Verso. "Comme si la fonction du théâtre devait être thérapeutique ou libératrice." (As If the Function of Theatre Had to Be Therapeutic or Liberating.) *JCT.* 1989; 52: 124-128. Illus.: Photo. B&W. 8. Lang.: Fre.
Canada: Matane, PQ. 1984-1989. Histories-sources. ■Method of experimental creation based on found spaces by collective Productions Recto-Verso.

619 Beauchamp, Hélène. "Une recherche en cours: La carte et le territoire." (Research in Progress: The Map and The Territory.) *JCT.* 1996; 79: 72-78. Notes. Illus.: Photo. B&W. 4. Lang.: Fre.
Canada: Montreal, PQ. 1995-1996. Histories-sources. ■Report by one of the researchers on project aimed at mapping out Montreal's theatre territory and understanding inscription of theatre culture in architectural history.

THEATRE IN GENERAL: —Performance spaces

620   Charbonneau, François. "La Visibilité urbaine de la culture." (The Urban Visibility of Culture.) *JCT.* 1989; 50: 94-98. Notes. Illus.: Photo. B&W. 3. Lang.: Fre.
Canada: Montreal, PQ. 1989. Critical studies. ■Urban planner argues need to integrate rehearsal spaces and performance spaces into urban fabric in order to create visibility of cultural production.

621   Charest, Rémy. "Les antres de Méduse." (Medusa's Lairs.) *JCT.* 1996; 79: 70-71. Illus.: Photo. B&W. 1. Lang.: Fre.
Canada: Montreal, PQ. 1995-1996. Critical studies. ■Possibilities and actualities of multidisciplinary arts building Méduse and its performance spaces, Studio d'essai In Vitro and Salle Multi.

622   Goldberger, Anne. "Rencontre avec la Place des Arts: le regard d'une étrangère." (Encounter with the Place des Arts: A Foreigner's Perspective.) *JCT.* 1996; 79: 91-95. Notes. Illus.: Photo. B&W. 2. Lang.: Fre.
Canada: Montreal, PQ. 1996. Critical studies. ■Domination of commercial concerns at Place des Arts, billed as the largest multidisciplinary cultural complex in Canada.

623   Knowles, Richard Paul. "Survival Spaces: Space and the Politics of Dislocation." *CTR.* 1996 Fall; 88: 31-34. Illus.: Photo. B&W. 3. Lang.: Eng.
Canada. 1996. Critical studies. ■The politics of Canadian theatrical spaces. Emphasis on organizational spaces, performance spaces and the Canadian cultural landscape.

624   Laliberté, Martine. "Théâtres de la récupération." (Theatres of Recuperation.) *JCT.* 1996; 79: 87-90 . Notes. Illus.: Photo. B&W. 2. Lang.: Fre.
Canada: Montreal, PQ. 1985-1996. Historical studies. ■Tradition of transformation of buildings into theatrical spaces in Montreal's Plateau neighbourhood.

625   Lévesque, Solange. "L'espace et le spectateur." (Space and the Spectator.) *JCT.* 1996; 79: 56-60. Illus.: Photo. B&W. 5. Lang.: Fre.
Canada: Montreal, PQ. 1996. Critical studies. ■A spectator's impressions of recently refitted Montreal theatre buildings: Espace GO, Veillée, Rideau Vert, Théâtre d'Aujourd'hui, Usine C.

626   Raymond, Yves. "Espaces transformables, espaces problématiques." (Transformable Spaces, Problematic Spaces.) *JCT.* 1996; 79: 83-86. Notes. Illus.: Photo. B&W. 3. Lang.: Fre.
Canada: Montreal, PQ. 1996. Critical studies. ■Possibilites and limitations of Montreal's adjustable stage theatres for scenography and audience-performer relationships.

627   Vigeant, Louise. "Espaces culturels au coeur des villes." (Cultural Spaces at the Heart of Cities.) *JCT.* 1996; 81: 132-139. Notes. Illus.: Photo. B&W. 6. Lang.: Fre.
Canada: Montreal, PQ. France. 1996. Critical studies. ■Transforming buildings into theatres and multidisciplinary centers, and placing cultural centers in urban landscape.

628   Ölveczky, Miklos. "Entwurf für ein neues Nationaltheater in Kopenhagen." (Blueprint for a New National Theatre in Copenhagen.) *BtR.* 1996; 3: 28-33. Illus.: Design. B&W. 12. Lang.: Ger.
Denmark: Copenhagen. 1996. Historical studies. ■The possible rebuilding of the royal theatre and the enhanced flexibility of the performance spaces that would result.

629   Gurr, Andrew. "Some Reasons to Focus on the Globe and the Fortune: Stages and Stage Directions: Controls for the Evidence." *ThS.* 1996 May; 37(1): 23-34. Notes. Biblio. Lang.: Eng.
England: London. 1599-1622. Historical studies. ■The Fortune and the Globe Theatres were the first playhouses in London to be designed by and for the playing company that expected to use them. By examining the plays written for these theatres for stage directions and other features, author argues that more can be learned about their designs and their stages.

630   Rutter, Carol Chillington. "The Dyer's Hand: Philip Henslowe." *AtG.* 1996 Win: 17-19. Illus.: Photo. Pntg. 3. Lang.: Eng.
England: London. 1587-1603. Biographical studies. ■Profile of Henslowe, a London businessman who built the Rose Theatre.

631   Wright, I[an] R. "An Early Stage at Queens'." *STP.* 1996 June; 13: 62-71. Notes. Lang.: Eng.
England: Cambridge. 1541-1640. Historical studies. ■The discovery of a document, dating from 1640, about the instructions for assembling a stage in the dining-hall of Queens' College, Cambridge, yields insights into the staging of Elizabethan and Jacobean plays, in particular the use of a thrust stage, and suggests that the commercial theatres of London that followed were modeled on such stages as the Queens' theatre rather than on inn-yards.

632   Stribolt, Barbro; Forslund, Camille, transl. "Den stora förändringen eller från barock scen till tittskåpsteater." (The Great Reformation or From Baroque to Picture-Frame Theatres.) *ProScen.* 1996; 20(Extra): 4-5. Illus.: Photo. B&W. Lang.: Swe, Eng.
Europe. 1780-1850. Historical studies. ■A short historical survey of the changing ideals from the spectacular Baroque to the realistic Romanticism, as regards the actors' space in the scenery.

633   Brühl-Gerling, Wolfgang; Förster, Petra; Hänsch, Wolfgang; Jargosch, Gunter; Magirius, Heinrich; Schulz, Joachim; Thomsen, Walter; Zeiler, Wolfgang. "Das Schauspielhaus Dresden." *BtR.* 1996; Special issue: 8-24. Append. Illus.: Design. Dwg. Photo. B&W. Color. 18. Lang.: Ger.
Germany: Dresden. 1912-1995. Historical studies. ■History and architecture of the building, its reconstruction in 1995, and its technical equipment.

634   Dobritzsch, Elisabeth. "Das Ekhof-Theater in Gotha." (The Ekhof Theatre in Gotha.) *BtR.* 1996; 2: 8-14. Illus.: Pntg. Photo. Color. 6. Lang.: Ger.
Germany: Gotha. 1681-1996. Historical studies. ■Architectural history of the theatre from its beginnings as a ballroom to the contemporary reconstruction of the historical stage equipment.

635   Döring, Gerhard. "Theater im Schlossgarten Armstadt." (Theatre in the Castle Gardens of Armstadt.) *BtR.* 1996; 6: 8-11. Illus.: Photo. Color. 7. Lang.: Ger.
Germany: Armstadt. 1841-1995. Historical studies. ■History of the classical theatre building and its equipment, which has been renovated and modernized.

636   Fischer, Petra; Rösner, Peter. "Theater der Jungen Generation." (Young Generation Theatre.) *BtR.* 1996; Special issue: 62-70. Illus.: Design. Photo. B&W. Color. 20. Lang.: Ger.
Germany: Dresden. 1949. Historical studies. ■The origin and operation of the theatre, and the conversion of the building from a ballroom into a children's theatre.

637   Goden, Michael. "Vom Stadttheater zu den Bühnen Lübeck." (From Municipal Theatre to the Lübeck Stages.) *BtR.* 1996; 5: 8-12. Illus.: Design. Dwg. Photo. B&W. 8. Lang.: Ger.
Germany: Lübeck. 1908-1996. Historical studies. ■History of the building of Theater Lübeck, architect Martin Dülfer, and its recent restoration.

638   Grosser, Helmut. "Geschichte des Theaterspielens in Dresden." (History of Acting in Dresden.) *BtR.* 1996; Special issue: 33-45. Illus.: Design. Pntg. Dwg. Photo. 44. Lang.: Ger.
Germany: Dresden. 1800-1996. Historical studies. ■History of Dresden's performance spaces.

639   Jacob, Theo. "Die Felsenbühne Rathen." *BtR.* 1996; Special issue: 73-74. Illus.: Plan. Photo. B&W. Color. 6. Lang.: Ger.
Germany: Rathen. 1935-1996. Historical studies. ■History of the open-air theatre, located in a dramatic rocky landscape, and its reconstruction, which began in 1995.

640   Kümmel, Peter. "Die fantastische Fabrik." (The Fantastic Factory.) *THeute.* 1996; 6: 28-32. Illus.: Photo. B&W. 8. Lang.: Ger.
Germany: Stuttgart. 1985-1996. Historical studies. ■Portrait of Theaterhaus, a former factory, and its founder Werner Schretzmeier.

THEATRE IN GENERAL: —Performance spaces

641 Laages, Michael. "Bau im Nesselfeld." (Building in a Field of Nettles.) *DB*. 1996; 4: 22-23. Illus.: Photo. B&W. 2. Lang.: Ger.
Germany: Braunschweig. 1996. Historical studies. ■The architecture of the new playhouse Staatstheater, Kleines Haus, its use and chance for success in a city of conservative theatrical tastes.

642 Linzer, Martin. "Neuer Schwung durch neues Haus." (New Swing through a New House.) *TZ*. 1996; 3: 66-67. Illus.: Photo. B&W. 3. Lang.: Ger.
Germany: Braunschweig. 1996. Historical studies. ■The new small theatre of Staatstheater Braunschweig, and the plans of drama director Tatjana Rese to stage not only dramatic productions but music and dance theatre as well.

643 Peiseler, Christian. "Roter Sandstein vor vollem Haus." (Red Sandstone in Front of a Full House.) *THeute*. 1996; 5: 39-42. Illus.: Photo. B&W. 7. Lang.: Ger.
Germany: Kaiserslautern. 1996. Histories-sources. ■Interview with Pavel Fieber, director of the newly built Platztheater, about its architecture and artistic program.

644 Poppenhäger, Annette. "Bau-Boom." (Building Boom.) *DB*. 1996; 6: 42-45. Illus.: Dwg. Photo. B&W. 7. Lang.: Ger.
Germany. 1996. Histories-sources. ■Presents new building models for theatres to be built within the next few years, with discussion of financial planning for these buildings.

645 Weidner, Manfred. "Problematik Orchestergraben—Ein Orchestervorstand engagiert sich!" (Problematic Orchestra Pit: An Orchestra's Managing Director Gets Involved.) *BtR*. 1996; 1: 52-55. Illus.: Design. Color. 2. Lang.: Ger.
Germany: Kassel. 1996. Historical studies. ■Structural insufficiencies of the orchestra pit of the Staatstheater and the efforts of musicians and technicians to overcome the problem.

646 Lajtai, Zoltán. "Német színház épült Szekszárdon. A moziból lett színház." (A German Theatre in Szekszárd—A Cinema Transformed into a Theatre.) *SFo*. 1995/1996; 22/23(3/4-1/2): 35-38. Illus.: Photo. B&W. Fr.Elev. Grd.Plan. 11. Lang.: Hun.
Hungary: Szekszárd. 1913-1994. Technical studies. ■In 1994 the first theatre for a national minority in Hungary was opened in Szekszárd. The Art Nouveau style building had been used as a cinema between 1913 and 1986.

647 Ault, Tom. "The Queen's Cavern." *TD&T*. 1996 Win; 32(1): 54-60. Notes. Illus.: Photo. B&W. 12. Lang.: Eng.
India: Orissa. 1600-1996. Historical studies. ■Profile of the Queen's Cavern Theatre with emphasis on its preservation and audience seating arrangement.

648 Banu, Georges. "Les Rôles et le fantôme." (Roles and the Phantom.) *JCT*. 1989; 50: 208-210. Illus.: Photo. B&W. 2. Lang.: Fre.
Italy. 1989. Historical studies. ■Inscription of memories in the architecture of theatres, especially historic Italian theatres.

649 Åberg, Tommy. "Här har censorerna reserverade platser." (Here the Censors Have Reserved Seats.) *Tningen*. 1996; 20(76-77): 22. Illus.: Photo. B&W. Lang.: Swe.
Malta. 1741-1996. Historical studies. ■A report from the Manoel Theatre, which now is used only for guest performances, with emphasis on censorship.

650 Weathersby, William, Jr. "National Center of the Arts, Mexico City." *TCI*. 1996 May; 30(5): 34-43. Illus.: Photo. Plan. Color. 16. Lang.: Eng.
Mexico: Mexico City. 1996. Critical studies. ■Report on the recently finished Centro Nacional de los Artes, a collaboration of US consultants and Mexican architects.

651 Rooy, Max van. *Een circus van steen. De architectuur van een zeldzaam theater*. (A Circus of Brick: The Architecture of a Unique Theatre.) Amsterdam: E.M. Querido; 1996. 120 pp. Illus.: Graphs. Dwg. Sketches. Photo. B&W. Color. 184. Lang.: Dut.
Netherlands: Amsterdam. 1887-1995. Historical studies. ■The renovation and extension of Theater Carré, originally built as a winter circus. Includes historical background on theatre architecture.

652 Rooy, Max van. *De ongebouwde Theaters van Amsterdam*. (The Unbuilt Theatres of Amsterdam.) Amsterdam: Stichting Het Theaterfestival; 1996. 68 pp. Illus.: Design. Graphs. Plan. Dwg. Photo. B&W. Color. 124. Lang.: Dut.
Netherlands: Amsterdam. 1900-1990. Historical studies. ■A series of projects for theatres in Amsterdam. Designs, sketches, and models indicate the kind of theatre thought to be needed at various times throughout the century.

653 van Gelder, Henk. "Teloorgang van Theaters op het Rembrandtplein. Theaterplein veranderde in horecaplein." (The Disappearance of the Theatres in Rembrandt Square: The Square of the Theatres Becomes a Place of Restaurants.) *OnsA*. 1996; 48(7/8) : 188-193. Illus.: Photo. Color. B&W. 9. Lang.: Dut.
Netherlands: Amsterdam. 1890-1996. Historical studies. ■The transformation of Amsterdam's theatre district into a tourist area featuring bars, restaurants, and tourist attractions.

654 Jędrychowski, Zbigniew. "Budynki teatralne w Minsku Litewskim." (Theatre Buildings in Minsk.) *PaT*. 1996; 1-2(118): 118-128. Notes. Biblio. Illus.: Graphs. Pntg. Poster. B&W. 7. Lang.: Pol.
Russia: Minsk. 1801-1863. Historical studies. ■Minsk theatre buildings that housed Polish professional stages and their history.

655 Edström, Per Simon. "En ny gammal teater på Djurgården." (A New Old Theatre at Djurgården.) *ProScen*. 1996; 20(1): 24-26. Illus.: Dwg. B&W. Lang.: Swe.
Sweden: Stockholm. 1801. Historical studies. ■A proposal to reconstruct the old Djurgårdsteatern at Stockholm as an event of the European Capital of Culture of the year 1998, with references to some old descriptions of the theatre.

656 Edström, Per Simon. "Ordenhuset Biofästet på Skansen." (The House of the Order Biofästet at Skansen.) *ProScen*. 1996; 20(2): 28-30. Illus.: Photo. Dwg. B&W. Color. Lang.: Swe.
Sweden: Stockholm. 1920. Technical studies. ■A proposal to restore the original lighting equipment for a retirement home auditorium used for a variety of purposes including films and theatre.

657 Guillemaut, Alf. "Operan och Dramaten har fått nya verkstäder." (Operan and Dramaten Have New Workshops.) *ProScen*. 1996; 20(4): 17-22. Illus.: Photo. Color. Lang.: Swe.
Sweden: Stockholm. 1995-1996. Historical studies. ■A presentation of the new workshops for the Royal Dramatic Theatre and the Royal Swedish Opera at Kvarnholmen, just east of Stockholm, where every aspect of manufacturing for the stage and storage space is located under one roof.

658 Nobling, Torsten. "Teaterlada." (The Theatre Barn.) *ProScen*. 1996; 20(2): 12-17. Illus.: Dwg. B&W. Lang.: Swe.
Sweden: Gustavsberg. 1995. Critical studies. ■A presentation of ideas for a theatre building on an island of the Stockholm archipelago by students of the Royal Technical College.

659 Olzon, Janna. "The Globe återuppstår." (The Globe Resurrected.) *Tningen*. 1996; 20(76-77): 13-14. Illus.: Photo. B&W. Lang.: Swe.
UK-England: London. 1985-1996. Historical studies. ■The new Shakespeare's Globe Theatre and the International Shakespeare Globe Centre, with reference to the problem of reviving the Shakespearean audience.

660 Condee, William F. "Visualizing the Stage." *TD&T*. 1995 Sum; 31(1): 9-16. Lang.: Eng.
USA. 1995. Technical studies. ■A comparison of proscenium or illusionistic stage and the open or presentational stage.

661 Condee, William F. "du Pont's Fountains: Creating an Image of American Aristocracy." *TA*. 1996; 48: 30-40. Notes. Illus.: Dwg. B&W. 4. Lang.: Eng.
USA: Kennett Square, PA. 1798-1995. Historical studies. ■History of the development of Longwood Gardens with its fountains, topiary, and the open-air theatre which was sometimes used for public performances.

662 Epstein, Milton; Cohen-Stratyner, Barbara Naomi, ed. "The New York Hippodrome: A Complete Chronology of Perfor-

CLASSED ENTRIES

THEATRE IN GENERAL: —Performance spaces

mances, from 1905 to 1939." *PAR*. 1993; 17/18(1): 1-535. Index. Lang.: Eng.
USA: New York, NY. 1905-1939. Histories-sources. ■Complete chronology of performances at the New York Hippodrome with eight genre specific indices preceded by one 'master' index: all-star variety, concert, film, miscellaneous, opera, spectacle, sports and vaudeville.

663 Gallagher, John; Weathersby, William, Jr. "Fulton Opera House Returns to Grace in Lancaster, PA." *TCI*. 1996 May; 30(5): 23-24. Illus.: Photo. Color. 2. Lang.: Eng.
USA: Lancaster, PA. 1996. Historical studies. ■Report and review of the newly refurbished Fulton Opera House.

664 Harms, Carl. "The Great White Way Is Lighting Up—Again." *EN*. 1996 July/Aug.; 81(6): 5. Illus.: Photo. 5. Lang.: Eng.
USA: New York, NY. 1996. Historical studies. ■Author takes a 'photo' tour of the 42nd Street theatre district and reports on recent changes including the New Victory Theatre, Disney's restoration of the New Amsterdam Theatre. Also notes changes in other buildings on the street.

665 Horwitz, Simi. "The New 42nd Street." *TheaterW*. 1996 Jan 29; 9(26): 28-37. Illus.: Photo. Sketches. Grd.Plan. 5. Lang.: Eng.
USA: New York, NY. 1920-1996. Historical studies. ■Renovation plans for The New Victory, New Amsterdam, and other performance spaces in the Broadway district. Major corporations involved, history and architecture of buildings, financial and physical presence of Disney Corporation and its potential impact on the kinds of shows planned.

666 Loney, Glenn. "Southwestern Salvation." *TCI*. 1996 Dec.; 30(10): 14-17. Illus.: Photo. Color. 2. Lang.: Eng.
USA: Phoenix, AZ. 1991-1996. Technical studies. ■Report on the restoration of the Orpheum Theatre, an old vaudeville house.

667 Mohler, Frank. "Architecture: Drafty Appalachian Gymnatorium Renovated, Transformed into State-of-the-Art Theatre." *SoTh*. 1996 Fall; 37(4): 6-11. Illus.: Photo. B&W. Grd. Plan. 8. Lang.: Eng.
USA: Boone, NC. 1938-1994. Historical studies. ■An account of the 1992-1993 renovation of the 1938 Volberg Theatre at Appalachian State University in Boone, North Carolina, into a modern theatre, with a history of the theatre and specifications of design and equipment.

668 Weathersby, William, Jr. "The Geary Theatre." *TCI*. 1996 Oct.; 30(8): 34-37. Illus.: Photo. Color. 6. Lang.: Eng.
USA: San Francisco, CA. 1996. Historical studies. ■Restoration of American Conservatory Theatre's home, the Geary Theatre, with focus on its decor and technical upgrades.

669 Weathersby, William, Jr. "Roundabout's Second Stage." *TCI*. 1996 Jan.; 30(1): 15-16. Illus.: Photo. Color. 1. Lang.: Eng.
USA: New York, NY. 1994-1995. Technical studies. ■Physical description of the newly opened Roundabout Theatre Company's second stage, the Laura Pels Theatre.

670 Weathersby, William, Jr. "Hawaii Theatre Center Revived in Honolulu." *TCI*. 1996 Aug/Sep.; 30(7): 10-11. Illus.: Photo. Color. 2. Lang.: Eng.
USA: Honolulu, HI. 1996. Historical studies. ■Report on the restoration and technical upgrade of the 1,400-seat Hawaii Theatre Center.

671 Weathersby, William, Jr. "Aronoff and Running." *TCI*. 1996 Nov.; 30(9): 12-13. Illus.: Photo. Color. 1. Lang.: Eng.
USA: Cincinnati, OH. 1995-1996. Historical studies. ■Marks the first anniversary of the Aronoff Center for the Arts and reviews its physical attributes.

672 Weathersby, William, Jr. "Jordan Hall Revived." *TCI*. 1996 Mar.; 30(3): 22-24. Illus.: Photo. Color. 1. Lang.: Eng.
USA: Boston, MA. 1903-1996. Historical studies. ■Report on the Jordan Hall, a National Historic Landmark, its rehabilitation and re-opening to the public.

673 Weathersby, William, Jr. "Livent to Renovate 42nd St. Theatres." *TCI*. 1996 Mar.; 30(3): 24. Illus.: Plan. Color. 2. Lang.: Eng.

USA: New York, NY. 1996. Technical studies. ■Garth Drabinsky, CEO of Livent Realty, and his plan to create a 1,839-seat theatre within the shell of the dilapidated Lyric and Apollo theatres.

674 Weathersby, William, Jr. "The New Victory Theatre." *TCI*. 1996 Apr.; 30(4): 42-43. Illus.: Photo. Color. 8. Lang.: Eng.
USA: New York, NY. 1996. Technical studies. ■Tour and review of the newly restored New Victory Theatre as part of the 42nd Street revitalization plan.

Performance/production

675 Alonge, Roberto. *Scene perturbanti e rimosse. Interno ed esterno sulla scena teatrale.* (Remote and Upsetting Scenes: Inside and Outside on the Theatrical Stage.) Rome: La Nuova Italia Scientifica; 1996. 149 pp. (Studi Superiori NIS 282.) Pref. Notes. Illus.: Photo. B&W. Lang.: Ita.
500 B.C.-1996 A.D. Historical studies. ■The use of space and the meaning of scenic structure, with emphasis on the 'open' space of theatre through the Renaissance and the 'closed' space of later drama.

676 Risum, Janne. "The Crystal of Acting." *NTQ*. 1996 Nov.; 12(48): 340-355. Notes. Biblio. Lang.: Eng.
1901-1995. Critical studies. ■Analysis of a variety of metaphors and language for acting.

677 Wilcox, Dean. "What does Chaos Theory Have to do with Art?" *MD*. 1996 Win; 39(4): 698-711. Notes. Lang.: Eng.
1995. Critical studies. ■Connection between arts and physics and the relationship between contemporary scientific inquiry and contemporary performance techniques, with emphasis on chaos theory.

678 Wolford, Lisa. "Seminal Teachings—The Grotowski Influence: A Reassessment." *CTR*. 1996 Fall; 88: 38-43. Notes. Biblio. Illus.: Photo. B&W. 6. Lang.: Eng.
1968-1996. Historical studies. ■Examination of the teachings of Jerzy Grotowski. References to his influence on the artists and companies attending the Survivors of the Ice Age Festival and Symposium. Emphasis on his rejection of naturalistic performance style in favor of overt theatricality.

679 Godin, Jean Cléo. "Théâtres africains." (African Theatres.) *JCT*. 1991; 59: 109-113. Notes. Illus.: Photo. B&W. 5. Lang.: Fre.
Africa. 1980-1990. Historical studies. ■Overview of francophone theatre in Africa, with emphasis on its diversity and eclecticism. Summary of an issue of the French literary journal *Notre Librarie* 102.

680 Díaz, Jorge. "El vacío del Festival de Córdoba." (The Vacuum of the Cordoba Festival.) *Cjo*. 1996 July/Dec.; 103: 20-21. Lang.: Spa.
Argentina: Cordoba. 1996. Historical studies. ■Agues that the theatre festival in Cordoba concentrates so much on the political and economic meanings of the festival itself that it ignores the theatrical content of the individual productions.

681 Ferreyra, Halima Tahan. "Construir los propios diseños." (Building One's Own Design.) *Cjo*. 1996 July/Dec.; 103: 34-35. Lang.: Spa.
Argentina: Cordoba. 1996. Historical studies. ■The impact of different cultures on theatre festivals in Latin America. Article uses the Festival Latinoamericano de Teatro de Córdoba as a model.

682 Javier, Francisco; Rajotte, Suzanne, transl. "Renouveau du théâtre argentin des dernières années." (Renewal of Argentinian Theatre in Recent Years.) *JCT*. 1991; 59: 102-108. Notes. Illus.: Photo. B&W. 4. Lang.: Fre.
Argentina. 1975-1990. Historical studies. ■Identifies three principal movements in recent Argentinian theatre: dramatic realism, realist-based avant-garde and experimental theatre based on street theatre, collective creation and theatre of images.

683 Pellettieri, Osvaldo. "El teatro paródico al intertexto político en Buenos Aires (1970-72)." (The Political Intertexts of Parodic Theatre in Buenos Aires 1970-72.) *LATR*. 1996 Fall; 30(1): 33-43. Lang.: Spa.
Argentina: Buenos Aires. 1970-1972. Historical studies. ■Analyzes parodic theatre and its intertexts as a form of reflexive realism, and identifies its types.

CLASSED ENTRIES

THEATRE IN GENERAL: —Performance/production

684 Sikora, Marina F. "V Congreso Internacional de Teatro Iberoamericano y Argentino." (Fifth International Hispanic-American and Argentinian Theatre Congress.) *LATR.* 1996 Fall; 30(1): 155-160. Lang.: Spa.
Argentina: Buenos Aires. 1996. Historical studies. ■Account of the fifth International Hispanic-American and Argentinian Theatre Congress.

685 Fahey, Maryann; Mailman, Deborah; Parry, Lorae. "Laughing Women." *AFS.* 1995 Fall; 21: 69-77. Illus.: Photo. B&W. 3. Lang.: Eng.
Australia. 1992-1995. Histories-sources. ■Three comedy writers/performers at the International Women Plawrights Conference discuss their influences, creative process, elements of comedy, experiences as women in the field, character development.

686 Leahy, Kath. "Power and Presence in the Actor-Training Institution Audition." *ADS.* 1996 Apr.; 28: 133-139. Notes. Lang.: Eng.
Australia. 1993. Critical studies. ■Critique of the audition methods employed by Australia's institutions of theatrical training. Argues that cultural background has a great influence on how a potential student approaches the audition.

687 Paskos, Mick. "Deck Chairs on the Street." *FAR.* 1995 Sep 8: 12-13. Illus.: Photo. B&W. 3. Lang.: Eng.
Australia: Fremantle. 1995. Critical studies. ■Deckchair Theatre's *Cappucino Strip* and artistic director Angela Chaplin's reaction to the negative criticism of the environmental theatre production.

688 Stelarc. "From Psycho to Cyber Strategies: Prosthetics, Robotics and Remote Existence." *CTR.* 1996 Spr; 86: 19-23. Illus.: Photo. B&W. 4. Lang.: Eng.
Australia. 1996. Histories-sources. ■Australian performance artist Stelarc discusses the human body as moving from the biological zone in performance into the cyberzone of interface, extension and amplification. Emphasis on the reconfiguration of gender in cyberspace.

689 Tait, Peta. "Devouring Lesbian Bodies: Aerial Desire in Club Swing's *Appetite*." *TheatreF.* 1996 Sum/Fall; 9: 4-11. Biblio. Illus.: Photo. 8. Lang.: Eng.
Australia: Melbourne. 1996. Critical studies. ■Lesbian desire in *Appetite* by Club Swing, directed by Gail Kelly. Club Swing is a performance group that uses circus techniques as part of their aesthetic of 'physical theatre' and lesbian feminism.

690 Dermutz, Klaus. "'Ich kann wirklich Freude geben'." (I Can Really Give Joy.) *THeute.* 1996; YB: 24-33. Illus.: Photo. B&W. 6. Lang.: Ger.
Austria. 1996. Histories-sources. ■Actress of the year Angela Winkler, chosen by theatre critics from Germany, Switzerland, and Austria: profile and interview.

691 Klein, Holger. "Shakespeare auf österreichischen Bühnen." (Shakespeare on Austrian Stages.) *SJW.* 1996; 132: 195-200. Illus.: Photo. B&W. 2. Lang.: Ger.
Austria. 1994-1995. Reviews of performances. ■Productions of Shakespearean plays and operas, including *Romeo and Juliet* directed by Ludiv Kavin at Theaterbrett and by Karl-Heinz Hackl at Burgtheater, *As You Like It*, directed by Rosemarie Fendel at Theater in der Josefstadt, *Hamlet* by Ambroise Thomas, directed by Stephen Lawless at Volksoper, and *Die lustigen Weiber von Windsor*, composed by Otto Nicolai and directed by Robert Herzl at Volksoper and directed by Ernst Poettgen at Salzburger Landestheater.

692 Müry, Andres. "Wenn der Otto mit dem Otti ..." (When Otto with Otti ...)*THeute.* 1996; 9: 10-11. Illus.: Photo. B&W. 1. Lang.: Ger.
Austria: Salzburg. 1996. Histories-sources. ■Conversation between two comic actors, Otto Schenk and Otto Sander.

693 Thieringer, Thomas. "Die Wurst heisst Wurst, weil's Wurst ist oder Das Leben verliert dadurch, dass man's kennenlernt." (Sausage Means Sausage, Because It Is Sausage—or Life Loses Meaning When You Get to Know It.) *THeute.* 1996; 8: 41-44. Illus.: Photo. B&W. 5. Lang.: Ger.
Austria: Vienna. 1996. Historical studies. ■Actor, cabaret artist, and playwright Josef Hader and his play *Indien (India)*, which has been filmed.

694 Yates, W.E. *Theatre in Vienna: A Critical History, 1776-1995.* Cambridge/New York, NY: Cambridge UP; 1996. 348 pp. (Cambridge Studies in German.) Notes. Biblio. Index. Illus.: Photo. 33. Lang.: Eng.
Austria: Vienna. 1776-1995. Histories-specific. ■Covers major developments in genre, major theatres, actors, and playwrights.

695 Darvay Nagy, Adrienne. "Belarusz színházi esték." (Belorussian Theatre Evenings.) *Sz.* 1996; 29(2): 42-43. Illus.: Photo. B&W. 1. Lang.: Hun.
Belorus: Minsk. 1996. Reviews of performances. ■Report on a meeting as well as on some interesting performances by a participant of the discussion on 'Theatre at the End of the 20th Century—A Search for New Perspectives', organized by the Belorussian Centre of the International Theatre Institute (ITI).

696 Malpede, Karen. "Working with Dreams in Dubrovnik and Sarajevo." *NTQ.* 1996 Nov.; 12(48): 384-387. [NTQ Reports and Announcements.] Lang.: Eng.
Bosnia: Sarajevo, Dubrovnik. 1996. Histories-sources. ■Playwright's experiences with Bosnian acting students, including discussion of dreams.

697 Mendenhall, Marie. "Art Under the Gun in Sarajevo." *NWR.* 1996 Jan.; 21(2): 6-8. Illus.: Photo. B&W. 4. Lang.: Eng.
Bosnia: Sarajevo. 1992-1995. Critical studies. ■Profile of Croatian performers and refugees, Džemila and Savić Delić, discussing their experiences as actors in Sarajevo, their refugee status in Canada and theatrical aspirations.

698 Mogobe, T.T. *Theatre in Botswana: A Study of Traditional and Modern Forms.* Ph.D. thesis, *Index to theses*, 45-8895. Leeds: Univ. of Leeds; 1995. Notes. Biblio. Lang.: Eng.
Botswana. 1994. Historical studies. ■Analyzes theatre from a historical perspective, approaching it as a movement. Discusses traditional Setswana theatre, and modern drama.

699 George, David S. "Encenador Gerald Thomas's *Flash and Crash Days*: Nelson Rodrigues without Words." *LATR.* 1996 Fall; 30(1): 75-88. Notes. Biblio. Lang.: Eng.
Brazil. 1985-1996. Historical studies. ■Analysis of Thomas's production *Tempestade e Fúria*, which attracted large crowds and much critical attention.

700 Beaulne, Martine. "Toujours la même passion." (Still the Same Passion.) *JCT.* 1996; 80: 110-111. Illus.: Photo. B&W. 1. Lang.: Fre.
Canada. 1976-1996. Histories-sources. ■Memories of professional experiences of actor-director Martine Beaulne.

701 Bédard, Réjean; Martineau, Maureen; Desperrier, Hélène. "Face à Farce." (Face to Farce.) *JCT.* 1990; 55: 105. Illus.: Photo. B&W. 6. Lang.: Fre.
Canada. 1990. Histories-sources. ■Réjean Bédard, Hélène Desperrier and Maureen Martineau, actors from Théâtre Parminou, discuss humour and their stock comic characters.

702 Bélanger, Louis. "Spectacles, prise 2." (Shows, Take Two.) *JCT.* 1990; 55: 56-63. Illus.: Photo. B&W. 6. Lang.: Fre.
Canada: Montreal, PQ. 1989. Historical studies. ■Impressions of four successful productions at the 1989 Festival de théâtre des Amériques: *Suz o Suz* presented by La Fura dels Baus, *Terre promise/Terra promessa (Promised Land)* coproduced by Teatro Dell'Angolo and Théâtre de la Marmaille, The Wooster Group's *The Temptation of St. Antony* and *Six Characters in Search of an Author* directed by Anatolij Vasiljėv.

703 Belzil, Patricia; Burgoyne, Lynda; Massoutre, Guylaine. "Petits coups d'oeil sur un grand théâtre." (Little Glimpses of a Great Theatre.) *JCT.* 1996; 81: 32-49. Notes. Illus.: Photo. B&W. 19. Lang.: Fre.
Canada: Montreal, PQ. 1996. Critical studies. ■Nineteen children's theatre plays of Montreal's Coups de théâtre festival and qualities that made them effective.

704 Belzil, Patricia. "Sous le manteau d'Arlequin." (Under the Proscenium Arch.) *JCT.* 1996; 80: 46-48. Illus.: Photo. B&W. 5. Lang.: Fre.

THEATRE IN GENERAL: —Performance/production

Canada: Montreal, PQ. 1988-1995. Historical studies. ■Impressions of favorite Montreal theatre productions and qualities that made them memorable.

705 Bénard, Johanne. "'Stand up' ou 'Sit down': 'House' de Daniel MacIvor." (Stand-up or Sit-down: Daniel MacIvor's *House*.) *JCT*. 1992; 64: 106-111. Notes. Illus.: Photo. B&W. 1. Lang.: Fre.
Canada: Toronto, ON. 1992. Critical studies. ■Elements of stand-up comedy, performance art and theatre in Daniel MacIvor's *House*, directed by Daniel Brooks (Theatre Passe Muraille, 1992).

706 Boivin, Mario. "'Where no one has gone before'." *JCT*. 1989; 52: 129-131. Illus.: Photo. B&W. 1. Lang.: Fre.
Canada. 1982-1989. Histories-sources. ■Director Mario Boivin describes his approach to directing and its experimental nature.

707 Burgoyne, Lynda. "Les grandes dames de la scène." (The Great Ladies of the Stage.) *JCT*. 1996; 80: 37-41. Notes. Illus.: Photo. B&W. 6. Lang.: Fre.
Canada: Montreal, PQ. 1976-1996. Historical studies. ■Contributions of women to Québécois theatre productions, 1976-1996.

708 Camerlain, Lorraine. "Et si, un moment, le théâtre n'était que jeu..." (And If, Sometimes, Theatre Was Only Play...) *JCT*. 1989; 50: 170-177. Notes. Illus.: Photo. B&W. 5. Lang.: Fre.
Canada: Montreal, PQ. 1989. Critical studies. ■Tension between truthful interpretation and play in acting, and diversity of acting in contemporary Montreal theatre.

709 Caux-Hébert, Patrick. "Le Théâtre expérimental." (Experimental Theatre.) *JCT*. 1989; 52: 154-156. Notes. Illus.: Photo. B&W. 2. Lang.: Fre.
Canada: Quebec, PQ. 1989. Historical studies. ■Characteristics of experimental theatre, drawing on examples such as Théâtre Repère's *La Trilogie des dragons*.

710 Dansereau, Luc. "Méchant théâtre." (Mean Theatre.) *JCT*. 1992; 65: 112-114. Illus.: Photo. Handbill. B&W. 2. Lang.: Fre.
Canada: Montreal, PQ. 1992. Histories-sources. ■Mécanique Générale artistic director Luc Dansereau's frustrations and freedom creating *Méchant Motel* without financial support or external obligations.

711 De Decker, Jacques. "La Pose." (The Pose.) *JCT*. 1989; 50: 162-163. Illus.: Photo. B&W. 1. Lang.: Fre.
Canada. 1989. Critical studies. ■Trend in theatre, especially Quebec's théâtre d'images, to rely on slowed or frozen images. Desire of theatre artists to leave a lasting mark.

712 Denis, Jean-Luc. "Savoir préparer l'avenir ou des effets du manque de clairvoyance sur la régression du théâtre d'expérimentation au Québec: Première partie: Causes intrinsèques." (Knowing How to Prepare for the Future or the Effects of the Lack of Clairvoyance on the Regression of Experimental Theatre in Quebec: Part One: Intrinsic Causes.) *JCT*. 1989; 52: 176-184. Notes. Illus.: Photo. B&W. 4. Lang.: Fre.
Canada. USA. 1982-1989. Critical studies. ■Compares causes of decline of experimental theatre in Quebec with Richard Schechner's analysis of decline in American avant-garde.

713 Ducharme, André. "Rire à pleurer." (Tears of Laughter.) *JCT*. 1990; 55: 86-88. Illus.: Photo. B&W. 2. Lang.: Fre.
Canada. 1990. Critical studies. ■Reflection on what succeeds or fails to provoke laughter.

714 Faucher, Jean. "Libre, jeune et brouillon." (Free, Young and Messy.) *JCT*. 1989; 52: 157-158. Illus.: Photo. B&W. 1. Lang.: Fre.
Canada: Montreal, PQ. 1989. Histories-sources. ■Director Jean Faucher gives his view of experimental theatre and his hesitation to work in that genre.

715 Flaherty, Kathleen; Hurford, Deborah. "Journeys Without Maps." *CTR*. 1996 Sum; 87: 31-33. Illus.: Photo. B&W. 2. Lang.: Eng.

Canada. 1996. Critical studies. ■Examination of the dramaturgical process required of post-modern texts. Emphasis on Blake Brooker's *The Land, The Animals*.

716 Forsythe, James. "Spirituality In Actor Training." *TRC*. 1996; 17(1): 67-82. Notes. Biblio. Lang.: Eng.
Canada. 1996. Historical studies. ■Examination of the relationship between spirituality and actor training. Emphasis on the spiritual practices of Taoism and Zen Buddhism in Western conservatory acting programs.

717 Fournier, Alain. "Recherche appliquée." (Applied Research.) *JCT*. 1989; 52: 51-54. Notes. Illus.: Photo. B&W. 1. Lang.: Fre.
Canada. 1989. Historical studies. ■Experimental theatre as scientific research.

718 Fréchette, Richard. "Avec la bouille que j'ai." (With the Face I've Got.) *JCT*. 1990; 55: 93-95. Illus.: Photo. B&W. 1. Lang.: Fre.
Canada. 1990. Histories-sources. ■Actor Richard Fréchette gives two anecdotes on the impact of a comic face on casting.

719 Gerson, Christiane; Camerlain, Lorraine, ed. "Le regard de l'enfance: Entretien avec Serge Marois." (The Perspective of Childhood: Interview with Serge Marois.) *JCT*. 1993; 66: 68-75. Illus.: Photo. B&W. 4. Lang.: Fre.
Canada: Montreal, PQ. 1976-1993. Histories-sources. ■Writer-director Marois' highly visual approach to theatre for young audiences with his company Arrière-Scène, in productions such as *Boîtes* (1984) and *Train de nuit* (1987).

720 Gilbert, Reid. "(Re)visioned, Invisible, and Mute: Male Bodies in Rumble Productions' *Strains*." *MD*. 1996 Spr; 39(1): 160-176. Notes. Lang.: Eng.
Canada: Vancouver, BC. 1949-1996. Critical studies. ■Historical significance, representation of the gay male body, mise-en-scène in collaborative production directed by Chris Gerrard-Pinker and Norman Armour at Station Street Theatre.

721 Godin, Diane; Legault, Yannick; Lesage, Marie-Christine; Wickham, Philip. "Des désordres signifiants." (Meaningful Disorders.) *JCT*. 1996; 81: 50-63. Notes. Illus.: Photo. B&W. 14. Lang.: Fre.
Canada: Montreal, PQ. 1989-1996. Historical studies. ■The 1996 festival Vingt jours de théâtre à risque: reviews of some of the productions, history of the festival, discussion of the purpose of experimental theatre.

722 Godin, Diane. "Cet alliage si particulier." (This Peculiar Alloy.) *JCT*. 1996; 80: 82-83. Illus.: Photo. B&W. 4. Lang.: Fre.
Canada: Montreal, PQ. Switzerland: Geneva. 1985-1995. Critical studies. ■Alliance of text and acting in successes of Comédie de Genève's 1985 production *L'Oiseau vert* (*L'Augellino belverde*), Nouvelle Compagnie Théâtrale's 1993 production of Albert Camus' *Caligula* and Théâtre les Trois Arcs' 1995 production of *L'Ange et le Corbeau* (*The Angel and the Crow*) written by Francis Monmart.

723 Guay, Hervey. "À Propos de l'avant-garde nord-américaine." (On North American Avant-Garde.) *JCT*. 1989; 52: 81-84. Notes. Illus.: Photo. B&W. 2. Lang.: Fre.
Canada. USA. 1980-1989. Historical studies. ■Fragmentation of narrative and domination of visual in avant-garde theatre of Wooster Group, Robert Wilson and Gilles Maheu.

724 Hébert, Marie-Francine. "Changer le monde." (Changing the World.) *JCT*. 1996; 80: 134. Notes. Illus.: Photo. B&W. 1. Lang.: Fre.
Canada: Montreal, PQ. 1975. Histories-sources. ■Playwright Marie-Francine Hébert's memories of production conditions of Théâtre de la Marmaille (later Théâtre des Deux Mondes) children's theatre company during preparations of her *Ce tellement 'cute' des enfants*.

725 Lavoie, Pierre. "Spectacles, prise 1." (Shows, Take One.) *JCT*. 1990; 55: 48-55. Notes. Illus.: Photo. B&W. 10. Lang.: Fre.
Canada: Montreal, PQ. 1989. Critical studies. ■Impressions of productions at 1989 Festival de théâtre des Amériques, grouped by themes: 'I remember', 'crossing borders', 'foreign bodies'.

CLASSED ENTRIES

THEATRE IN GENERAL: —Performance/production

726 Lavoie, Pierre. "'Le pays de nos désirs...'." ('The Country of Our Desires'.) *JCT*. 1996; 80: 77-81. Notes. Illus.: Photo. B&W. 10. Lang.: Fre.
Canada: Montreal, PQ. 1976-1995. Biographical studies. ■Review of remarkable Montreal theatre productions with special focus on works of Robert Lepage.

727 Lefebvre, Paul. "Ce qui manque aux acteurs québécois." (What Quebecois Actors Lack.) *JCT*. 1989; 50: 130-132. Illus.: Photo. B&W. 1. Lang.: Fre.
Canada: Montreal, PQ. 1988. Histories-sources. ■Personal anecdote of teacher at Ecole Nationale de Théâtre illustrates spontaneous impulses of real life that fail to be captured on stage.

728 Lesage, Marie-Christine. "Renouveau et faux départs: La création théâtrale à Québec." (Renewal and False Starts: Theatrical Creation in Quebec.) *JCT*. 1993; 67: 106-110. Notes. Illus.: Photo. 2. Lang.: Fre.
Canada: Quebec, PQ. 1992-1993. Critical studies. ■Trends in theatre creation in Quebec City exemplified by Antoine Laprise's *Marchands de planètes* (Ô Délire), Lope de Vega's *Fuente ovejuna/Fontaine-aux-moutons*, (Théâtre Repère) and Michel Nadeau's *Bureautopsie* by Théâtre Niveau Parking. The creation of multidisciplinary project Méduse uniting Recto-Verso, Arbo Cyber, and PluraMuses.

729 Lévesque, Solange; Lefebvre, Paul. "Un Théâtre de la nuit: Entretien avec Pierre-A. Larocque." (A Theatre of the Night: Interview with Pierre-A. Larocque.) *JCT*. 1989; 52: 85-112. Notes. Illus.: Photo. B&W. 21. Lang.: Fre.
Canada: Montreal, PQ. 1971-1989. Histories-sources. ■Pierre-A. Larocque's influences, themes in his scenarios and characteristics of his scenic creations. Also, obituary for Larocque and theatrography.

730 Lévesque, Solange. "Envols et vertiges autour de Chagall." (Flights and Dizzy Spells around Chagall.) *JCT*. 1989; 51: 7-13. Illus.: Photo. B&W. 5. Lang.: Fre.
Canada: Montreal, PQ. 1988-1989. Critical studies. ■Influence of Marc Chagall's work in Cirque du Soleil's 1988 show and dance troupe O Vertige's *Chagall*.

731 Lévesque, Solange. "Les Sentiers du rire: Entretien avec Denise Filiatrault." (The Paths of Laughter: Interview with Denise Filiatrault.) *JCT*. 1990; 55: 81-86. Illus.: Photo. B&W. 3. Lang.: Fre.
Canada. 1970-1990. Histories-sources. ■Comedian Denise Filiatrault's impressions of the state of comedy and comedic forms in Quebec.

732 Lévesque, Solange. "Faire battre son coeur et celui des autres en même temps: Entretien avec Pascale Montpetit." (To Stir One's Own Heart and Those of Others: Interview with Pascale Montpetit.) *JCT*. 1991; 60: 83-92. Illus.: Photo. B&W. 4. Lang.: Fre.
Canada: Montreal, PQ. 1980-1991. Histories-sources. ■Actress Pascale Montpetit describes her career and her approach to acting.

733 Lévesque, Solange. "Au bout de l'art: Entretien avec Martine Beaulne." (At the Frontiers of Art: Interview with Martine Beaulne.) *JCT*. 1993; 67: 41-52. Illus.: Photo. B&W. 6. Lang.: Fre.
Canada. 1970-1993. Histories-sources. ■Director Martine Beaulne's concepts of the functions of theatre, and the influences that have shaped her directing methods. List of productions directed by Beaulne.

734 Lévesque, Solange. "Julie Vincent: Entre collectif et solo." (Julie Vincent: Between Collective and Solo.) *JCT*. 1991; 61: 44-45. Notes. Illus.: Photo. B&W. 1. Lang.: Fre.
Canada: Montreal, PQ. 1988-1991. Bibliographical studies. ■Recent acting, directing and writing work of Julie Vincent, with a description of her 1988 one-woman show *Noir de monde (Dark of the World)*.

735 Lévesque, Solange. "Mémoire." (Memory.) *JCT*. 1996; 80: 84-87. Illus.: Photo. B&W. 7. Lang.: Fre.
Canada: Montreal, PQ. 1981-1995. Historical studies. ■Notes on acting and direction of sixteen productions seen in Montreal.

736 Marois, Serge. "Une Question de nature, d'attitude face à la vie." (A Question of Nature, of an Attitude toward Life.) *JCT*. 1989; 52: 120-123. Illus.: Photo. B&W. 4. Lang.: Fre.
Canada: Montreal, PQ. 1967-1989. Histories-sources. ■Director Serge Marois describes extent to which his work can be described as 'experimental'.

737 Massoutre, Guylaine. "Terrain de jeu." (Play Ground.) *JCT*. 1996; 80: 25-32. Notes. Illus.: Dwg. 6. Lang.: Fre.
Canada. Europe. 1996. Critical studies. ■Acting and theatrical creation as play in space, considered from children's and adults' perspectives.

738 McIntosh, James. "Fred Davis Loved a 'Challenge'." *PAC*. 1996; 30(3): 17. Illus.: Photo. B&W. 1. Lang.: Eng.
Canada. 1921-1996. Historical studies. ■Obituary for Canada's foremost TV moderator and promoter of the performing arts.

739 Paventi, Eza. "L'année de l'ébranlement." (The Year of Agitation.) *JCT*. 1996; 81: 64-67. Notes. Illus.: Dwg. Photo. B&W. 5. Lang.: Fre.
Canada: Montreal, PQ. 1996. Historical studies. ■Creation of twelve experimental productions by Grand Théâtre Émotif, founded by Gabriel Sabourin, Louis Champagne and Stéphane Crête.

740 Poissant, Claude. "T'auras pas ta pomme ..." (You Won't Get Your Apple ...)*JCT*. 1989; 50: 160-161. Illus.: Dwg. 1. Lang.: Fre.
Canada: Montreal, PQ. 1989. Histories-sources. ■Director Claude Poissant describes theatre performance as an emotional parade for audience.

741 Rickerd, Julie Rekai. "Today's Japan." *TCI*. 1996 Jan.; 30(1): 12-13. Illus.: Photo. Color. 1. Lang.: Eng.
Canada: Toronto, ON. Japan. 1995. Critical studies. ■Report on Today's Japan, a multi-disciplinary exposition held in Toronto, October through November, 1995.

742 Robitaille, Pierrette. "La Comédie du comique." (The Comedy of the Comic.) *JCT*. 1990; 55: 89-90. Illus.: Photo. B&W. 1. Lang.: Fre.
Canada: Montreal, PQ. 1990. Histories-sources. ■Actress Pierrette Robitaille reflects on comedy and social function of laughter.

743 Roussel, Daniel. "En trois temps, en trois espaces et au-dessus de trois vertiges..." (In Three Times, in Three Spaces and above Three Vertigoes.) *JCT*. 1996; 80: 177-180. Illus.: Photo. B&W. 3. Lang.: Fre.
Canada. USA. 1996. Critical studies. ■Comparison of acting for theatre, television and film.

744 Roy, Lise. "Juste un?" (Just One?)*JCT*. 1996; 80: 144-145. Illus.: Photo. B&W. 1. Lang.: Fre.
Canada: Montreal, PQ, Quebec, PQ. 1976-1996. Histories-sources. ■Favorite memories of actress Lise Roy's work in theatre and television.

745 Roy, Milène; Michoue, Sylvain. "Un Téléphone sur la tête de Hamlet." (A Telephone on Hamlet's Head.) *JCT*. 1989; 52: 139-140. Illus.: Photo. B&W. 1. Lang.: Fre.
Canada: Montreal, PQ. 1989. Histories-sources. ■Milène Roy and Sylvain Michoue, co-founders of Voxtrot, contemplate describing their work as 'experimental'.

746 Saint-Pierre, Louise; Camerlain, Lorraine, ed. "L'art de dire les textes: Entretien avec Aline Caron." (The Art of Speaking Texts: Interview with Aline Caron.) *JCT*. 1991; 61: 115-119. Notes. Illus.: Photo. B&W. 2. Lang.: Fre.
Canada. 1960-1991. Histories-sources. ■Aline Caron's life as a voice teacher and her philosophy and techniques of teaching.

747 Vaillancourt, Pauline. "Le chant-acteur." (The Song-Actor.) *JCT*. 1996; 80: 172. Illus.: Photo. B&W. 1. Lang.: Fre.
Canada. USA. Europe. 1996. Technical studies. ■Potential uses of song in acting.

748 Vaïs, Michel. "Jeux de pose." (Playing a Pose.) *JCT*. 1989; 50: 152-158. Notes. Illus.: Photo. B&W. 6. Lang.: Fre.
Canada. 1989. Historical studies. ■Poses and pauses in theatre, both on stage and in the audience.

749 Vaïs, Michel. "NU: c'est du grec." (NU(de): It's Greek to Me.) *JCT*. 1996; 79: 98-104. Notes. Illus.: Dwg. Photo. B&W. 3. Lang.: Fre.
Canada: Montreal, PQ. 1996. Historical studies. ■Account of nudity among audience as well as cast of Grand Théâtre Émotif du Québec's production *Nudité (Nudity)* by Robert Gravel and Alexis Martin, and subsequent police ban.

THEATRE IN GENERAL: —Performance/production

750 Vaïs, Michel. "Ce théâtre qui a traversé ma carrière de critique." (The Theatre that Has Spanned My Career as a Critic.) *JCT*. 1996; 80: 49-57. Illus.: Photo. B&W. 13. Lang.: Fre.
Canada: Montreal, PQ. 1976-1995. Historical studies. ■Descriptions of twenty remarkable productions seen in Quebec, with emphasis on works of Gilles Maheu, Robert Lepage and Denis Marleau.

751 Vigeant, Louise. "Le Théâtre avec ou sans drame." (Theatre With or Without Drama.) *JCT*. 1989; 53: 27-31. Notes. Lang.: Fre.
Canada. 1989. Critical studies. ■Questions reasons for contemporary trend of producing theatre based on non-dramatic texts.

752 Vigeant, Louise. "Vingt ans sous le cerisier." (Twenty Years Under the Cherry Tree.) *JCT*. 1996; 80: 58-62. Illus.: Photo. B&W. 10. Lang.: Fre.
Canada: Montreal, PQ. 1976-1995. Historical studies. ■Memories of remarkable productions in twenty years of Quebec theatre.

753 Vigeant, Louise. "Robert Wilson: la mise en beauté de la futilité de l'être." (Robert Wilson: Beautifying the Futility of Being.) *JCT*. 1993; 67: 125-130. Notes. Illus.: Photo. B&W. 4. Lang.: Fre.
Canada: Montreal, PQ. 1980-1993. Biographical studies. ■The work of Robert Wilson, and the juxtaposition of beauty with death and senselessness in his two Montreal productions: *Le Regard du sourd* and Gertrude Stein's *Doctor Faustus Lights the Lights*.

754 Vincelette, Michèle. "Il était une fois." (Once Upon a Time.) *JCT*. 1996; 80: 173-176. Notes. Illus.: Photo. B&W. 2. Lang.: Fre.
Canada: Montreal, PQ. 1992. Historical studies. ■Techniques of storytelling and memories of Montreal's first Festival interculturel du conte.

755 Weiss, William. "Pour une voix mobile: Une nouvelle approche de la formation de la voix et de la parole." (For a Mobile Voice: A New Approach to Voice and Speech Training.) *JCT*. 1991; 61: 114. Notes. Illus.: Dwg. Diagram. Photo. B&W. 3. Lang.: Fre.
Canada. 1991. Historical studies. ■Identifies four types of vocal training and advocates an approach that aims at broadening the motor skills used in speaking.

756 Wickham, Philip. "L'âge de raison." (The Age of Reason.) *JCT*. 1993; 66: 135-140. Notes. Illus.: Dwg. Photo. B&W. 2. Lang.: Fre.
Canada. 1990-1993. Historical studies. ■Functions of the dramaturg and introduction of dramaturgs in Quebec theatre practice.

757 Wickham, Philip. "Une dégustation verticale." (A Vertical Tasting.) *JCT*. 1996; 80: 66-69. Illus.: Photo. B&W. 8. Lang.: Fre.
Canada: Montreal, PQ. 1988-1995. Critical studies. ■Analysis of author's reactions to a number of Montreal productions and the production elements that provoked them.

758 Linzer, Martin. "Von Santiago nach Cottbus." (From Santiago to Cottbus.) *TZ*. 1996; 6: 34-37. Illus.: Photo. B&W. 4. Lang.: Ger.
Chile. Germany. 1970-1996. Histories-sources. ■Profile and interview with director Alejandro Quintana, who emigrated from Chile to East Germany in the 1970s.

759 Salter, Denis. "China's Theatre of Dissent: A Conversation with Mou Sen and Wu Wenguang." *ATJ*. 1996 Fall; 13(2): 218-228. Notes. Illus.: Photo. B&W. 2. Lang.: Eng.
China, People's Republic of. 1996. Histories-sources. ■Interview with artistic director of Xi Ju Che Jian (Garage Theatre), Mou Sen, and actor Wu Wenguang: Mou's production of *File 0 (Ling Dang An)* based on poem of same title by Yu Jian, its world-wide tour, evolution of project, political and financial difficulties faced as dissident artists in a repressive culture.

760 "Un festival permanente: *Conjunto* entrevista a Octavio Arbeláez." (A Permanent Festival: *Conjunto* Interviews Octavio Arbeláez.) *Cjo*. 1996 July/Dec.; 103: 5-11. Illus.: Photo. 3. Lang.: Spa.
Colombia: Manizales. 1984-1996. Historical studies. ■Interview with Octavio Arbeláez, director of the current Manizales Festival, on the role of Latin-American theatre festivals since the first Festival de Teatro de Manizales in 1984.

761 Kershaw, Baz. "Cross-Cultural Performance in a Globalized World." *TheatreF*. 1996 Win/Spr; 8: 67-72. Biblio. Lang.: Eng.
Colombia: Bogotá. UK-Wales: Cardiff. 1995-1996. Historical studies. ■The cross-cultural theatre experience as seen in a production of Taller Investigación de la Imagen Teatral's production of a 'participatory installation' *The Labyrinth—Ariadne's Thread* at the Centre for Performance Research in Cardiff.

762 King, Roberto Enrique. "Colombia: Periplo Teatral." (Colombia: A Theatrical Journey.) *LATR*. 1996 Spr; 29(2): 195-202. Lang.: Spa.
Colombia. 1995. Historical studies. ■Theatrical activity on the literal and figurative margins of Colombia: in Cúcuta, near the border of Venezuela, in Santa Marta, and in Cartagena.

763 García Abreu, Eberto. "Quince años del Festival de Teatro de la Habana." (Fifteen Years of the Theatre Festival in Havana.) *Cjo*. 1996 July/Dec.; 103: 21-23. Illus.: Photo. 2. Lang.: Spa.
Cuba: Havana. 1981-1996. Historical studies. ■Concentrates on reconciliation and interchange between Latin American countries.

764 Lukeš, Milan. "Menzel a Werfel. Anatomie úspěšnosti." (Menzel and Werfel. The Anatomy of Success.) *Svet*. 1996; 7(1): 44-53. Illus.: Photo. B&W. 3. Lang.: Cze.
Czech Republic: Prague. 1996. Critical studies. ■A production of Franz Werfel's play *Jacobowsky und der Oberst (Jacobowsky and the Colonel)*, directed by Jiří Menzel at Divadlo na Vinohradech.

765 Závodský, Vít. "Eva Tálská. The Well Concealed Director/Un metteur en scène bien dissimulé." *DTh*. 1996; 11: 19-26. Illus.: Photo. B&W. 8. Lang.: Eng, Fre.
Czech Republic: Brno. 1996. Critical studies. ■The work of Eva Tálská, director and stage designer.

766 Christoffersen, Erik Exe. "Yoricks grimasse." (Yorick's Facial Expression.) *TE*. 1996 June; 79: 13-16. Illus.: Photo. B&W. 1. Lang.: Dan.
Denmark. 1996. Historical studies. ■Based on the tenth ISTA seminar (spring, 1996), describes the work demonstration as a means of understanding the magic of acting.

767 Garsdal, Lise. "Ordet under anklage." (The Word on Trial.) *TE*. 1996 Dec.; 81-82: 36-38. Illus.: Photo. B&W. 3. Lang.: Dan.
Denmark. 1996. Critical studies. ■Essay on the status of the word in theatre. Cites the opinion of Klaus Hoffmeyer, leader of the Royal Theatre, that theatre will return to large, powerful speech. Argues that the current appreciation of the monologue as a theatrical genre indicates that society is no longer based on two-way communication.

768 Søholm, Morten; Søholm, Anja. "Interview med Robert Lepage." (An Interview with Robert Lepage.) *TE*. 1996 Dec.; 81-82: 34-35. Illus.: Photo. B&W. 2. Lang.: Dan.
Denmark. Canada. 1996. Histories-sources. ■An interview with Robert Lepage on his work as a director of both plays and movies.

769 Robbins, Kenneth. "Vestiges of Control: Censorship and Society in Contemporary Egyptian Theatre." 105-118 in Oliva, Judy Lee, ed. *New Theatre Vistas: Modern Movements in International Theatre*. New York, NY/London: Garland; 1996. 219 pp. (Studies in Modern Drama 7.) Biblio. Lang.: Eng.
Egypt. 1993. Critical studies. ■Historical and critical overview of contemporary theatre in Egypt. Divided into three parts, the public, private and 'free,' theatre in Egypt is vital, but subject to censorship by the government.

770 Edmond, Mary. "Yeomen, Citizens, Gentlemen, and Players: The Burbages and Their Connections." 30-49 in Parker, R.B., ed.; Zitner, S.P., ed. *Elizabethan Theater: Essays in Honor of S. Schoenbaum*. Newark, DE/London: Univ of Delaware P; 1996. 324 pp. Notes. Lang.: Eng.
England. 1573-1677. Historical studies. ■Actor Richard Burbage, his father James and uncle Robert (who built The Theatre in 1576) and their descendants. Argues that the prestige given to people who associated

THEATRE IN GENERAL: —Performance/production

with the theatre made it possible for the Burbages to transform themselves from working class to gentlemen. Explores connections between people of the theatre and greater society.

771   Kinservik, Matthew J. "Benefit Play Selection at Drury Lane 1729-1769: The Cases of Mrs. Cibber, Mrs. Clive and Mrs. Pritchard." *TN.* 1996; 50(1): 15-28. Notes. Lang.: Eng.
England. 1729-1769. Historical studies. ■Discusses the reasons for the benefit choices of three actresses, and assesses their earnings.

772   Korda, Natasha. "Household Property/Stage Property: Henslowe as Pawnbroker." *TJ.* 1996 May; 48(2): 185-196. Notes. Biblio. Lang.: Eng.
England. 1592-1604. Historical studies. ■New historicist approach that questions assumption that women played no part in Elizabethan stage production and corresponding social and economic interdependencies. Examines Philip Henslowe's *Diary* for neglected evidence of the significant role women played in this network that supported Elizabethan stage production.

773   Mangan, Michael. "'... and so shall you seem to have cut your nose in sunder': Illusions of Power on the Elizabethan Stage and in the Elizabethan Market-Place." *PerfR.* 1996 Fall; 1(3): 46-57. Notes. Lang.: Eng.
England: London. 1590-1642. Critical studies. ■The use of magic in Elizabethan/Jacobean society and playhouses said to demonstrate an integration of 'serious art' and 'popular performance' in theatre of the period. An exploration of the implicit relationships of audiences to different aspects of the conjuring in *Doctor Faustus*.

774   Orgel, Stephen. *Impersonations: The Performance of Gender in Shakespeare's England.* Cambridge: Cambridge UP; 1996. 179 pp. Notes. Index. Pref. Illus.: Photo. Sketches. Dwg. 19. Lang.: Eng.
England. 1589-1613. Critical studies. ■Explores the phenomenon of the boy players' performance of women in Elizabethan England. Argues that the construction of gender and the nature of the desire engendered by it operates as a binary opposition that is central to a correct reading of the place of women, and thus their absence, in Elizabethan theatre.

775   Sorrell, Mark. "Edmund Kean and Richardson's Theatre." *TN.* 1996; 50(1): 29-38. Notes. Lang.: Eng.
England. 1800. Historical studies. ■Describes Richardson's traveling theatre and the appearance before the king of the young Edmund Kean.

776   Sutcliffe, Christopher. "Kempe and Armin: The Management of Change." *TN.* 1996; 50(3): 122-134. Notes. Lang.: Eng.
England: London. 1599. Historical studies. ■Discusses the policy decisions taken by the Lord Chamberlain's Men to replace Will Kempe with Robert Armin in order to appeal to a more socially and economically select audience.

777   Thomson, Peter. "Pearl and Mackarel." *STP.* 1993 Dec.; 8: 80. Lang.: Eng.
England: London. 1673-1864. Historical studies. ■Points out that the notorious appearance in 1864 on stage of a well-known prostitute, Cora Pearl, in Offenbach's *Orphée aux Enfers* was predated by the one performance of a well-known seventeenth-century prostitute, Betty Mackarel, in a burlesque in 1674.

778   Auslander, Philip. "Liveness: Performance and the Anxiety of Simulation." 196-213 in Diamond, Elin, ed. *Performance and Cultural Politics.* London/New York, NY: Routledge; 1996. 282 pp. Notes. Index. Lang.: Eng.
Europe. North America. 1995. Critical studies. ■The performativity of 'live' performance, including its marginality with respect to the encroachment of technologies of reproduction (such as video) on live performance.

779   Banfield, Chris; Crow, Brian. *An Introduction to Post-Colonial Theatre.* Cambridge: Cambridge UP; 1996. 186 pp. Notes. Biblio. Index. Lang.: Eng.
Europe. North America. Asia. Africa. 1880-1950. Critical studies. ■Examines postcolonialism as an indigenous response to colonialism, marked by resistance and strategies of opposition. Focuses on the work of Derek Walcott, August Wilson, Jack David, Wole Soyinka, Athol Fugard, and Badal Sircar, and Girish Karnad.

780   Becker, Peter von. "Schauspielerin, Sängerin, Tänzerin." (Actress, Singer, Dancer.) *THeute.* 1996; 5: 12-18. Illus.: Photo. B&W. 9. Lang.: Ger.
Europe. 1963-1996. Biographical studies. ■Portrait of actress Anne Bennent.

781   Berghaus, Günter. "The Ritual Core of Fascist Theatre: An Anthropological Perspective." 39-71 in Berghaus, Günter, ed. *Fascism and Theatre: Comparative Studies on the Aesthetics and Politics of Performance in Europe, 1925-1945.* Oxford: Berghahn Books; 1996. 315 pp. Biblio. Notes. Index. Illus.: Photo. 24. Lang.: Eng.
Europe. 1925-1945. Historical studies. ■Explores the dynamic and reciprocal relationship between the rulers and the ruled during the fascist era and analyzes ritualism as a form that was employed to foster the bond between them.

782   Brook, Peter; Stronina, M., transl. *Bluždajuščaja tocka: Stat'i. Vystuplenija. Intervju.* (Wandering Point: Articles, Performances, and Interviews.) Moscow/St. Petersburg: Artist. Režisser. Teat'r; 1996. 272 pp. Lang.: Rus.
Europe. 1946-1987. Histories-sources. ■Translation of *The Shifting Point, 1946-1987* (New York: Harper & Row, 1987): Brook describes his practices and experiments in theatre and film, his thoughts on the potential of theatre art.

783   Carlson, Marvin. *Performance: A Critical Introduction.* London/New York, NY: Routledge; 1996. 247 pp. Notes. Biblio. Index. Lang.: Eng.
Europe. North America. 1960-1995. Critical studies. ■Overview of the modern concept of performance, how it has developed in various fields, and ways in which its multiple applications overlap and interact. Using contemporary theatre history and theory, author examines relationships between performance, postmodernism, and the politics of identity.

784   Gosman, Martin; Walthaus, Rina. *European Theatre 1470-1600: Traditions and Transformations.* Groningen: Egbert Forsten; 1996. 173 pp. Illus.: Dwg. B&W. 8. Lang.: Eng.
Europe. 1470-1600. Critical studies. ■Proceedings of a festival of early drama held by the faculty of arts of the University of Groningen in 1991.

785   Griffin, Roger. "Staging the Nation's Rebirth: The Politics and Aesthetics of Performance in the Context of Fascist Studies." 11-29 in Berghaus, Günter, ed. *Fascism and Theatre: Comparative Studies on the Aesthetics and Politics of Performance in Europe, 1925-1945.* Oxford: Berghahn Books; 1996. 315 pp. Biblio. Notes. Index. Illus.: Photo. 24. Lang.: Eng.
Europe. 1925-1945. Historical studies. ■Fascism as a generic phenomenon, using theoretical perspectives drawn from the social sciences. Concentrates on the theatricality intrinsic to fascism as a political ideology.

786   Huxley, Michael, ed.; Witts, Noel, ed. *The Twentieth-Century Performance Reader.* London/New York, NY: Routledge; 1996. 421 pp. Notes. Biblio. Index. Lang.: Eng.
Europe. North America. 1915-1995. Critical studies. ■Compilation of interviews and essays from forty-two theatre artists on the practice of twentieth-century experimental performing arts. Focuses on both practice and theory.

787   Kazda, Jaromír. "Středověké divadlo: Představa světa a svět představ." (Medieval Theatre: The Idea of the World and the World of Ideas.) *Svet.* 1996; 7(4): 18-27. Lang.: Cze.
Europe. 1000-1500. Historical studies. ■Brief history of medieval theatre.

788   Kempinski, Tom. "Can Propaganda Be Art? Or Is Any Art NOT Propaganda?" *PlPl.* 1996 Nov/Dec.; 509: 28-30. Lang.: Eng.
Europe. 1996. Historical studies. ■Argues that all art is propagandistic, whether intentionally or not.

789   Kühnl, Reinhard. "The Cultural Politics of Fascist Governments." 30-38 in Berghaus, Günter, ed. *Fascism and Theatre: Comparative Studies on the Aesthetics and Politics of Performance in Europe, 1925-1945.* Oxford: Berghahn Books; 1996. 315 pp. Biblio. Notes. Index. Illus.: Photo. 24. Lang.: Eng.
Europe. 1925-1945. Historical studies. ■Key features of fascist cultural politics as part of an economic and social policy.

THEATRE IN GENERAL: —Performance/production

790 Marranca, Bonnie. *Ecologies of Theater: Essays at the Century Turning.* Baltimore, MD/London: Johns Hopkins UP; 1996. 289 pp. Illus.: Photo. 3. Lang.: Eng.
Europe. USA. 1980-1995. Critical studies. ■Essays on the work of Robert Wilson, Rachel Rosenthal, Heiner Müller, Maria Irene Fornes, and Meredith Monk, as well as contemporary performance events.

791 Ogden, Dunbar H. "Set Pieces and Special Effects in the Liturgical Drama." *EDAM.* 1996 Spr; 18(2): 76-88. Lang.: Eng.
Europe. 900-1600. Historical studies. ■Examination of the rubrics of the extant liturgical drama provides much more information than previously realized. These include the use of stage properties, machines for ascending and descending, special stage settings, sounds, lighting, appearances and disappearances. Continued in *EDAM* 19:1 (1996 Fall), 22-40.

792 Pavlovic, Diane. "Petite histoire de Don Juan." (Brief History of Don Juan.) *JCT.* 1989; 50: 18-26. Notes. Illus.: Dwg. Photo. B&W. 10. Lang.: Fre.
Europe. 1989. Historical studies. ■The seductive nature of theatre. Includes discussion of audience-performer relationship.

793 Tanitch, Robert. "Robert Tanitch Remembers: Beauty and the Beast." *PlPl.* 1996 Aug/Sep.; 507: 31. Lang.: Eng.
Europe. USA. Canada. 1946-1996. Critical studies. ■Recounts several versions of the *Beauty and the Beast* story, from Jean Cocteau's film version (*La Belle et la Bête*) starring Josette Day and Jean Marais, Nicholas Stuart Gray's 1950s stage version for children with Michael Bryant in the role of the Beast, and the current Disney film version (music by Alan Menken, lyrics by Howard Ashman and Tim Rice, book by Linda Wolverton) as well as a current stage production touring both Canada and the US, based on the current film, directed by Robert Jess Roth, starring Chuck Wagner as the Beast.

794 Albert, Pál. "Cirkusz-színház—Nagy József-bemutató Párizsban." (Circus Theatre—Josef Nadj Premiere in Paris.) *Sz.* 1996; 29(7): 36-37. Illus.: Photo. B&W. 1. Lang.: Hun.
France: Paris. 1996. Reviews of performances. ■Report on the production *Le Cri du Chaméléon (The Chameleon's Cry)* by the Hungarian-born Joseph Nadj and his company Théâtre du Signe.

795 Apter, Emily. "Acting Out Orientalism: Sapphic Theatricality in Turn-of-the-Century Paris." 15-34 in Diamond, Elin, ed. *Performance and Cultural Politics.* London/New York, NY: Routledge; 1996. 282 pp. Notes. Index. Illus.: Photo. 1. Lang.: Eng.
France: Paris. 1898-1905. Critical studies. ■French gay and lesbian sexual identity and its mediation by the culturally exotic stereotype, the Oriental female, in performance. Reference to *Scheherazade* by the Ballets Russes, performances of Ida Rubinstein, Sarah Bernhardt, and Cléo de Mérode.

796 Decock, Jean. "The Other Avignon." *WES.* 1996 Fall; 8(3): 17-20. Illus.: Photo. 2. Lang.: Eng.
France: Avignon. 1996. Historical studies. ■Account of the Avignon fringe festival including *Le Mât de Cocagne*, adapted from a novel by René Depestre, directed by Gérard Gélas and his Théâtre du Chêne Noir, Louis Calaferte's *Chez les Titch*, directed by Thierry Chantrel and performed by the Sortie de Route (Lyons), Marivaux's *Le Jeu de l'Amour et du hasard*, directed by by J.P. André and performed by his Théâtre du Triangle, and a rock version of Hugo's *Hernani*, directed by Christophe Thiry with the Attrappe Theatre Company.

797 Féral, Josette. "Pour une autre pédagogie du théâtre: Entretien avec Alain Knapp." (Towards an Alternative Theatre Pedagogy: Interview with Alain Knapp.) *JCT.* 1992; 63: 55-64. Illus.: Photo. B&W. 5. Lang.: Fre.
France: Paris. 1992. Histories-sources. ■Alain Knapp outlines his approach to teaching actors, calling for presence and an intimate connection to the character.

798 Féral, Josette. "Look. Festival de la mode." (Look. Fashion Festival.) *JCT.* 1996; 81: 87-88. Illus.: Poster. Photo. B&W. 2. Lang.: Fre.
France: Paris. 1996. Critical studies. ■Robert Wilson's *Look* on the border of fashion show and theatre.

799 Garcia Martinez, Manuel. "Interview with Anne Delbée." *WES.* 1996 Fall; 8(3): 13-15. Lang.: Eng.

France: Avignon. 1996. Histories-sources. ■Interview with French director Anne Delbée on her early career, influence of Antoine Vitez, the impact of her gender on her work, and her current views on staging.

800 Jeschke, Claudia. "Körper/Bühne/Bewegung. Dramaturgie und Choreographie als theatrale Strategien." (Body/Stage/Movement: Dramaturgy and Choreography as Theatrical Strategies.) *FMT.* 1996; 2: 197-213. Notes. Lang.: Ger.
France. 1700-1996. Critical studies. ■Theatrical representations of acting and dance analyzed through the typologies of the body in French dance since the sixteenth century (includes geometric, mechanistic, instrumental, structuring, hermeneutic, documenting, and subjective typologies).

801 Kennedy, Emmet; McGregor, James P.; Netter, Marie-Laurence; Olsen, Mark V. *Theatre, Opera, and Audiences in Revolutionary Paris: Analysis and Repertory.* Westport, CT/London: Greenwood P; 1996. 411 pp. (Contributions in Drama and Theatre Studies, 62.) Pref. Notes. Biblio. Index. Tables. Lang.: Eng.
France. 1789-1799. Histories-specific. ■Authors examined contemporary newspapers and other archival records to determine what theatregoers were actually viewing during the Revolution. Includes sections on the authors of the plays, the performances, the great successes for each year, the popular genres, the theatres and their directors, audiences, critics and the police, and extensive indices of statistical information.

802 Lassale, Jacques. "Elogio della maestria nel buio." (Praise of Mastery in the Darkness.) *TeatroS.* 1996; 11(18): 383-388 . Lang.: Ita.
France. 1995. Histories-sources. ■Director and acting teacher's thoughts on pedagogy and the transmission of knowledge, with quotations from his favorite artists.

803 Mustroph, Tom. "Theater der Gegenwart, Theater des Alltags." (Theatre of Today, Theatre of Everyday Life.) *TZ.* 1996; 5: 38-40. Illus.: Photo. B&W. 1. Lang.: Ger.
France: Paris. 1996. Reviews of performances. ■The intersection of life and theatre in four Paris productions: *Le jour et la nuit (Day and Night)* by Didier Bezace after three texts from *La misère du monde* by Pierre Bourdieu, directed by Bezace at Théâtre de L'Aquarium, *Banana* (Zulu music), a street performance, *Iphigénies* after *Iphigéneia he en Aulíde (Iphigenia in Aulis)* by Euripides, directed by Augusto Boal at Théâtre de L'Opprimé, and *La Controverse de Valladolid* after Jean Claude Carrière directed by Antonio Diaz-Florian at Théâtre de l'Epée de Bois.

804 Savarese, Nicola. "Artaud vede il teatro Balinese all'esposizione coloniale di Parigi del 1931." (Artaud Sees Balinese Theatre at the International Colonial Exhibition in Paris in 1931.) *TeatroS.* 1996; 11(18): 35-84. Notes. Lang.: Ita.
France: Paris. 1931. Critical studies. ■Artaud's encounter with the Balinese theatre in Paris: selection of reviews and essays written for the event by journalist and critics in that year and Artaud's own review as published in the *Nouvelle Revue Française* on October 1, 1931.

805 Wehle, Philippa. "The Avignon Festival's Fiftieth Birthday." *WES.* 1996 Fall; 8(3): 5-12. Illus.: Photo. 3. Lang.: Eng.
France: Avignon. 1996. Critical studies. ■Coverage of the fiftieth Avignon Festival, including an historical overview of the festival, Théâtre National de Dijon's production of Kafka's *The Trial*, directed by Dominique Pitoiset, Cechov's *The Cherry Orchard (Višněvyj sad)*, performed by Bulgaria's Sfumato company, Silviu Purcarete's adaptation of Aeschylus' *Suppliants (Hikétides)*, entitled *Danaïdes*, *Les Commentaires d'Habacuc*, a dance-theatre piece by Hungarian Josef Nadj, and the opening piece of the festival, *Edward II*, by Christopher Marlowe, directed by Alain Françon, and performed by his Théâtre de la Colline troupe.

806 "Was wir erwarten." (What We Expect.) *TZ.* 1996; 3: 30-33. Illus.: Photo. B&W. 14. Lang.: Ger.
Germany. 1996. Histories-sources. ■Directors Michael W. Schlicht, Christoph Schroth, Wolf Bunge, and Herbert Olschok explain what they expect from graduates of a drama school. Continued in *TZ* 5 (1996), 32-33, with the comments of Ralf-Günter Krolkiewicz, Tom Kühnel, and Robert Schuster.

THEATRE IN GENERAL: —Performance/production

807 Becker, Peter von. "Ein Poet—Von Pol zu Pol." (A Poet: From Pole to Pole.) *THeute.* 1996; 1: 16-22. Illus.: Photo. B&W. 8. Lang.: Ger.
Germany. 1969-1995. Biographical studies. ■Portrait of director and Kortner Award winner Klaus Michael Grüber.

808 Becker, Peter von. "'Ich liebe alle Leute, die keinen Stil haben!'." (I Love All Those Who Lack Style.) *THeute.* 1996; YB: 82-90. Illus.: Photo. B&W. 9. Lang.: Ger.
Germany. Austria. 1940-1996. Histories-sources. ■Portrait of actor Gert Voss, with an interview covering Heiner Müller, Peter Zadek, the East-West conflict, and mystery and enlightenment in theatre.

809 Benz, Stefan. "Mainzer Wechsel." (Change in Mainz.) *DB.* 1996; 6: 46-49. Illus.: Photo. B&W. 4. Lang.: Ger.
Germany: Mainz. Germany: Düsseldorf. 1953-1996. Biographical studies. ■Portrait of Michael Helle of the former East Germany, now leading director of Staatstheater Mainz GmbH, and Düsseldorfer Schauspielhaus.

810 Gound, Stefan. "Mit Schwung vom Stapel gelaufen." (Launched with Verve.) *TZ.* 1996; 2: 30-32. Illus.: Photo. B&W. 4. Lang.: Ger.
Germany: Kiel. 1995-1996. Historical studies. ■Directors Kirsten Harms, Emmanuel Bohn, and Nikolaus Büdel of Bühnen der Landeshauptstadt: their development of new structures and performances, use of new theatre spaces, and growing acceptance by their audience.

811 Grund, Stefan. "Va'yomer—Er aber sprach." (Thus He Spoke.) *TZ.* 1996; 6: 18-19. Illus.: Photo. B&W. 4. Lang.: Ger.
Germany: Hamburg. Israel: Tel Aviv. 1996. Reviews of performances. ■Productions by Itim and Batsheva Dance Company at the Hamburg summer theatre festival.

812 Hartmann, Gert. "Das selbstverständliche Recht auf Kunst." (The Natural Right of Access to Art.) *TZ.* 1996; 2: 40-45 . Illus.: Photo. B&W. 11. Lang.: Ger.
Germany. UK. 1980-1996. Historical studies. ■Theatre of and with handicapped people, including experimental theatre. Discusses Peter Radtke, Graeae Theatre Company of London, Theater Thikwa and RambaZamba of Berlin.

813 Hentschel, Anja. "Mobilitätsforschung und Theatergeschichte: Zur Mobilität von Schauspieleren im 18. Jahrhundert." (Mobility Research and Theatre History: About the Mobility of Nineteenth-Century Actors.) *KSGT.* 1996; YB: 55-72. Notes. Illus.: Diagram. Maps. B&W. 7. Lang.: Ger.
Germany. 1800-1899. Historical studies. ■Research on mobility of actors from Devrient's guest performances and its interaction with his engagement. Includes a quantitative analysis of guest performances.

814 Hesse, Ulrich. "Rudolf Mirbt wäre jetzt hundert." (Rudolf Mirbt Would Be One Hundred Now.) *SuT.* 1996; 158(2): 20-24 . Append. Illus.: Photo. B&W. 3. Lang.: Ger.
Germany. 1896-1974. Historical studies. ■Portrait of bookseller Rudolf Mirbt, a founder of the amateur theatre movement in Germany, and his importance to young people's, amateur, and school theatre.

815 Kahle, Ulrike. "'Der Micha kann allet'—oder vom Glück, sich verwandeln zu können." (Micha Can Do Anything: Or the Joy of Being Able to Change.) *THeute.* 1996; 3: 12-15. Illus.: Photo. B&W. 4. Lang.: Ger.
Germany. 1996. Biographical studies. ■Portrait of actor Michael Wittenborn.

816 Krusche, Friedemann. "Report: Rostock." *THeute.* 1996; 9: 23-29. Illus.: Photo. B&W. 6. Lang.: Ger.
Germany: Rostock. 1989-1996. Historical studies. ■Theatre in Rostock since reunification.

817 Linzer, Martin. "Ausbildungsmodell." (Training Model.) *TZ.* 1996; 3: 4-5. Illus.: Photo. B&W. 5. Lang.: Ger.
Germany. 1996. Histories-sources. ■Interview with Rolf Nagel, acting teacher and managing director of Europäische Theaterakademie Konrad Ekhof in Hamburg, about the present state of acting education in Germany, on the occasion of the theatre meeting of German-speaking drama students.

818 Mans, Michael. "Heilige und Narren, und ein Massenmörder." (Saints and Fools, and a Serial Killer.) *TZ.* 1996; 6: 43-47. Illus.: Photo. B&W. 4. Lang.: Ger.
Germany: Berlin. 1996. Reviews of performances. ■Impressions of the Berlin independent theatre scene during a two-week period, with discussion of venues, new concepts, and the attempts to define a new aesthetics.

819 Merschmeier, Michael. "'Wenn wir Jungen erwachen...'." (When We Youth Awaken.) *THeute.* 1996; YB: 40-53. Illus.: Photo. B&W. 5. Lang.: Ger.
Germany. Austria. Switzerland. 1996. Historical studies. ■The question of whether there is a generational change among directors of German-language theatres.

820 Panse, Barbara; Mumford, Meg, transl. "Censorship in Nazi Germany: The Influence of the Reich's Ministry of Propaganda on German Theatre and Drama, 1933-1945." 140-156 in Berghaus, Günter, ed. *Fascism and Theatre: Comparative Studies on the Aesthetics and Politics of Performance in Europe, 1925-1945.* Oxford: Berghahn Books; 1996. 315 pp. Biblio. Notes. Index. Illus.: Photo. 24. Lang.: Eng.
Germany. 1933-1945. Historical studies. ■The effect of censorship by the Nazi government on German theatrical traditions and practice.

821 Panse, Barbara. "Il Simposio de Teatro en Berlin." (Second Theatre Symposium in Berlin.) *LATR.* 1996 Fall; 30(1): 123-132. Lang.: Spa.
Germany: Berlin. Latin America. 1996. Historical studies. ■Second symposium on Modern Latin American Theatre, concentrating on collaboration between Latin America and Germany.

822 Permutz, Klaus. "Der dunkle Kontinent: Liebe." (The Dark Continent: Love.) *THeute.* 1996; 2: 58-62. Illus.: Photo. B&W. 5. Lang.: Ger.
Germany. 1957-1996. Histories-sources. ■Interview with actress Imogen Kogge.

823 Rehnitz, Alban. "Abenteuer pur." (Pure Adventure.) *TZ.* 1996; 5: 18-21. Illus.: Photo. B&W. 12. Lang.: Ger.
Germany: Rostock. 1996. Historical studies. ■Acting education at the Schauspielschule in Rostock and its cooperation with Volkstheater.

824 Rijnders, Gerardjan. "Fremder Blick." (Alien Sight.) *TZ.* 1996; 4: 28-31. Illus.: Photo. B&W. 2. Lang.: Ger.
Germany: Berlin. Netherlands: Amsterdam. 1996. Histories-sources. ■Excerpts from the diary of the author, who is a director, author, and artistic director of Toneelgroep Amsterdam, during a guest appearance at Deutsches Theater entitled *Moffenblues.*

825 Rischbieter, Henning. "Zur Geschichte der Dramaturgie." (Toward a History of Dramaturgy.) *dRAMATURg.* 1996; 2: 3-10. Lang.: Ger.
Germany. 1770-1996. Historical studies. ■Short history of the work of the dramaturg beginning with Lessing.

826 Schültke, Bettina; Berghaus, Günter, transl.; Tate, Laura, transl. "The Municipal Theatre in Frankfurt-on-the-Main: A Provincial Theatre under National Socialism." 157-171 in Berghaus, Günter, ed. *Fascism and Theatre: Comparative Studies on the Aesthetics and Politics of Performance in Europe, 1925-1945.* Oxford: Berghahn Books; 1996. 315 pp. Biblio. Notes. Index. Illus.: Photo. 24. Lang.: Eng.
Germany: Frankfurt am Main. 1925-1945. Historical studies. ■The legal and administrative framework of National Socialist theatre politics and its reflection in changes in German repertoire as seen at the Stadtheater (Frankfurt/Main).

827 Shafer, Yvonne. "Productions in Germany." *WES.* 1996 Fall; 8(3): 43-48. Illus.: Photo. 4. Lang.: Eng.
Germany. 1996. Historical studies. ■Current productions in Germany: Franz Werfel's *Goat Song (Bocksgesang)* at the Kleines Haus, directed by Tobias Wellemeyer, Strauss's opera *Arabella* at the Dresden Opera House, directed by Peter Konwitschny, the Vogtland Theater's production of Ionesco's *Rhinoceros.*

828 Shasa, Michael. "Verwandelt Natur in Kunst." (Transforms Nature into Art.) *THeute.* 1996; YB: 8-18. Illus.: Photo. B&W. 7. Lang.: Ger.

THEATRE IN GENERAL: —Performance/production

Germany. Austria. 1948-1996. Histories-sources. ■Actor of the year Josef Bierbichler, chosen by a group of theatre critics from Germany, Switzerland, and Austria: profile and interview.

829 Silberman, Marc. "The Actor's Medium: On Stage and in Film." *MD.* 1996 Win; 39(4): 558-565. Notes. Lang.: Eng.
Germany. 1918-1929. Historical studies. ■How acting changed as expressionist theatre became expressionist film.

830 Stein, Peter. "'Die Sprache ist unser leben'." (Language Is Our Life.) *THeute.* 1996; 12: 6. Illus.: Photo. B&W. 1. Lang.: Ger.
Germany: Hamburg. 1996. Histories-sources. ■Text of Stein's speech about Fritz Kortner's understanding of theatre on receiving the Kortner Prize.

831 Stumpfe, Mario. "Am Anfang fängst du immer wieder von vorne an (?)." (At First You Always Start from the Beginning.) *TZ.* 1996; 3: 10-12. Illus.: Photo. B&W. 9. Lang.: Ger.
Germany: Berlin. 1996. Historical studies. ■Portraits of two students of the Hochschule der Schauspielkunst Ernst Busch, with emphasis on the difficult transition from school to theatre practice.

832 Stumpfe, Mario. "Trügerische Bewegung." (Deceptive Movement.) *TZ.* 1996; 4: 54-57. Illus.: Photo. B&W. 6. Lang.: Ger.
Germany: Bremen. 1996. Historical studies. ■The current theatre situation in Bremen.

833 Thamer, Hans-Ulrich; Taylor, Ann, transl. "The Orchestration of the National Community: The Nuremberg Party Rallies of the NSDAP." 172-190 in Berghaus, Günter, ed. *Fascism and Theatre: Comparative Studies on the Aesthetics and Politics of Performance in Europe, 1925-1945.* Oxford: Berghahn Books; 1996. 315 pp. Biblio. Notes. Index. Illus.: Photo. 24. Lang.: Eng.
Germany: Nuremberg. 1935-1945. Historical studies. ■The mass orchestration and pseudo-religious nature of the National Socialist rallies in Nuremberg, used to symbolize the Third Reich's glory and power.

834 Wesemann, Arnd. "Eine Woche voller Hamburger." (A Week Full of Hamburger.) *TZ.* 1996; 2: 24-29. Illus.: Photo. B&W. 8. Lang.: Ger.
Germany: Hamburg. 1996. Historical studies. ■The Hamburg theatre scene at Thalia Theater, Kampnagel, Hamburger Kammerspiele, and Möbius Theaterkahn, and their productions, mostly music and entertainment.

835 Wille, Franz. "Wem die Stunde schlägt." (For Whom the Bell Tolls.) *THeute.* 1996; YB: 70-80. Illus.: Photo. B&W. 8. Lang.: Ger.
Germany. Switzerland. 1996. Critical studies. ■Director Christoph Marthaler's aesthetics and his experiment in bringing together theatre, physicality, and politics.

836 McDonald, Marianne. "Theodoros Terzopoulos: Theatre of the Body." *TheatreF.* 1996 Sum/Fall; 9: 19-25. Biblio. Illus.: Photo. 6. Lang.: Eng.
Greece: Athens. 1986-1996. Historical studies. ■Profile of Theodoros Terzopoulos, the director of Theatre Attis: his work with the plays of Heiner Müller, and his continuing work with Greek classical tragedy.

837 Fernández-Molina, Manuel. "La actividad teatral en Guatemala en la primera mitad del siglo XX." (Theatrical Activity in Guatemala in the First Half of the Twentieth Century.) *LATR.* 1996 Spr; 29(2): 131-146. Biblio. Lang.: Spa.
Guatemala: Guatemala City. 1900-1960. Historical studies. ■History of growth and change in Guatemalan theatre, including sections dealing with Teatro Colón, Jorge Ubico, and university theatre.

838 Albert, István. "Vámos László." (László Vámos.) *OperaL.* 1996; 5(2): 2. Lang.: Hun.
Hungary. 1928-1996. Biographical studies. ■Obituary for László Vámos, stage director and commissioned director of the Hungarian State Opera House.

839 Bene, Kálmán. "Egy érdekes epizód Szeged színháztörténetéből. Vajda János színházi tudósításai." (An Interesting Episode from Szeged's Theatre History: János

Vajda's Theatrical Reviews.) *SzSz.* 1996; 30/31: 217-221. Notes. Lang.: Hun.
Hungary: Szeged. 1855-1856. Reviews of performances. ■Poet János Vajda's reviews of performances by actor Kálmán Szerdahelyi and dancer Emília Aranyvári. The latter performance was cancelled due to the unsuitable performance space.

840 Bérczes, László; Lisztes, Edina, photo.; Szabó, Péter, photo. "Mese üres terekről." (A Tale About Empty Spaces.) *Sz.* 1996; 29(1): 30-31. Illus.: Photo. B&W. 3. Lang.: Hun.
Hungary: Budapest. 1995. Reviews of performances. ■Meditation on the manifold possibilities of new theatrical spaces inspired by a performance of Scottish author Irvine Welsh's *Trainspotting* directed by János Csányi.

841 Enyedi, Sándor. "A Kolozsvári Magyar Színház 1925-ös bukaresti vendégjátékai." (Guest Performances of the Kolozsvár Hungarian Theatre in Bucharest, 1925.) *SzSz.* 1996; 30/31: 19-24. Notes. Lang.: Hun.
Hungary. Romania: Bucharest. 1925. Historical studies. ■History of three Hungarian performances of the 1925 season at Teatrul Popular, Bucharest.

842 Enyedi, Sándor. "A kolozsvári magyar színészet hőskora (1792-1821)." (The Heroic Age of Hungarian Acting in Kolozsvár 1792-1821.) 19-31 in Kántor, Lajos, ed. *Kolozsvár magyar színháza 1792-1992.* Kolozsvár (Cluj-Napoca): Kolozsvári Állami Magyar Színház; 1992. 141 pp. Lang.: Hun.
Hungary: Kolozsvár. 1792-1821. Historical studies. ■The beginnings of professional acting in Transylvania from the first performance of theatrical company to the opening of the first permanent theatre building.

843 István, Mária. *Látványtervezés Németh Antal színpadán (1929-1944).* (Scenic Design on Antal Németh's Stage, 1929-1944.) Budapest: Akadémiai; 1996. 110 pp. (Művészettörténeti füzetek 24.) Append. Biblio. Index. Notes. Illus.: Design. Photo. B&W. 67. Lang.: Hun.
Hungary. 1929-1944. Historical studies. ■The work of director Antal Németh, with emphasis on the influence of the stage direction of the 1920s, his connections with the 'unofficial' side of Hungarian fine arts, and his reform of mainstream theatre at Nemzeti Színház Budapest, 1935-44, while maintaining his interest in the avant-garde. Includes discussion of his work with scene designers Álmos Jaschik, János Horváth, Mátyás Varga, and Zoltán Fábri.

844 Kerényi, Imre. "Búcsú." (Farewell.) *Sz.* 1996; 29(4): 2. Illus.: Photo. B&W. 1. Lang.: Hun.
Hungary. 1928-1996. Histories-sources. ■Tribute to László Vámos by a fellow director.

845 Koltai, Tamás. "Rekviem egy színházi emberért—Vámos László (1928-1996)." (Requiem for a Theatre Man—László Vámos (1928-1996).) *Sz.* 1996; 29(4): 1. Illus.: Photo. B&W. 1. Lang.: Hun.
Hungary. 1928-1996. Histories-sources. ■Memory of the director of plays, musicals and operas, by critic and editor-in-chief Tamás Koltai.

846 Koltai, Tamás. "A színikritikusok díja 1995/96." (Theatre Critics' Award 1995/96.) *Sz.* 1996; 29(10): 1-19. Illus.: Photo. B&W. 12. Lang.: Hun.
Hungary. 1995-1996. Reviews of performances. ■Individuals and productions voted the season's best by twenty-seven professional theatre critics: director Péter Gothár (for Albee's *Who's Afraid of Virginia Woolf?*), actors Mari Csomós, Iván Kamarás, Kati Lázár, and István Holl, designers Csaba Antal, Levente Bagossy, Györgyi Szakács, as well as Lajos Parti Nagy's *Mauzóleum (Mausoleum)* (best new Hungarian play), productions of *Klára Zách* by Stúdió K, *A dzsungel könyve (The Jungle Book)* adapted by László Dés, Péter Geszti and Pál Békés at Pesti Szinhaz, and Csaba Kiss, organizer of the experimental season of Győri Nemzeti Színház, Padlásszínház.

847 Koltai, Tamás. "Larger than Life." *HQ.* 1996 Spr; 37(141): 145-150. Lang.: Eng.
Hungary. 1995-1996. Reviews of performances. ■Review of ten productions of English or English-related plays on Hungarian stages: Shakespeare's *Macbeth* dir László Marton, Vígszínház, and *Othello* dir József Ruszt, Budapesti Kamaraszínház. Jonson's *Volpone* dir Péter Léner, József Attila Színház. Middleton and Rowley's *The Changeling* dir

THEATRE IN GENERAL: —Performance/production

Balázs Simon, Vígszínház. Webster's *The Duchess of Malfi* dir Péter Telihay, Miskolci Nemzeti Színház (compared to a later guest performance by Cheek by Jowl). Arden's *Live Like Pigs* dir Tamás Ascher, Katona József Színház. Osborne's *A Patriot for Me* dir Tibor Csizmadia, Thália Színház. Martin Sherman's *Bent* dir Róbert Alföldi, Budapesti Kamaraszínház. *A dzsungel könyve (The Jungle Book)*, adapt Pál Békés and László Dés, dir Géza D. Hegedűs, Pesti Színház. Péter Müller and László Tolcsvay's *Isten pénze (God's Money)* dir Viktor Nagy, Madách Színház.

848 Kovács, Zoltán, ed.; Tarnói, Gizella, ed.; Váradi, Zsuzsa, ed. *A színház csak ürügy. Keleti István utolsó ajándéka.* (Under Cover of Theatre: István Keleti's Last Gift.) Budapest: Irodalom Kft.-Journal Art Alapítvány; 1996. 329 pp. Append. Lang.: Hun.
Hungary: Budapest. 1950-1990. Histories-sources. ■Recollections of actor, director, teacher István Keleti and his involvement in amateur theatre by his colleagues and students.

849 Mészöly, Dezső; Ikládi, László, photo. "Mesterré lett tanítvány." (The Student Who Became a Master.) *Sz.* 1996; 29(4): 6-8. Illus.: Photo. B&W. 3. Lang.: Hun.
Hungary. 1949-1990. Histories-sources. ■The peculiar beginning of director László Vámos' career recalled by author-translator Dezső Mészöly.

850 Nagy, Viktor; Ikládi, László, photo. "Tanár úr." (The Teacher.) *Sz.* 1996; 29(4): 4-6. Illus.: Photo. B&W. 2. Lang.: Hun.
Hungary. 1928-1996. Histories-sources. ■Memories of a young director on his teacher László Vámos.

851 Petrovics, Emil. "Színházország díszpolgára." (Honorary Citizen of 'Theatre Land'.) *Sz.* 1996; 29(4): 3-4. Illus.: Photo. B&W. 2. Lang.: Hun.
Hungary. 1928-1996. Histories-sources. ■Recollections of composer Emil Petrovics on director László Vámos.

852 Tóth, Ferenc. "Kelemen László Csongrád megyei kötődései." (László Kelemen's Family Background in Csongrád County.) *SzSz.* 1996; 30/31: 63-65. Lang.: Hun.
Hungary. 1730-1812. Biographical studies. ■History of actor-director László Kelemen's family with reference to his diary.

853 Piper, Suzan; Day, Tony, transl.; Piper, Suzan, transl. "Performances for Fifty Years of Indonesian Independence." *RevIM.* 1995 Win/Sum; 29: 37-58. Notes. Illus.: Photo. B&W. 1. [Articles from the Indonesian press.] Lang.: Eng.
Indonesia. 1995. Historical studies. ■Collection of articles focusing on contemporary state and concerns of various forms of Indonesian performing arts including *dangdut*, pop and rock music, *wayang*, dance and film. Published to commemorate 50th anniversary of Indonesian independence.

854 Ben-Zvi, Linda. "Nola Chilton." 367-372 in Ben-Zvi, Linda, ed. *Theater In Israel.* Ann Arbor, MI: Univ. of Michigan P; 1996. 450 pp. Lang.: Eng.
Israel. 1960-1995. Histories-sources. ■Interview with director Nola Chilton on her work in documentary theatre.

855 Ben-Zvi, Linda. "Muhammad Bakri." 393-398 in Ben-Zvi, Linda, ed. *Theater In Israel.* Ann Arbor, MI: Univ. of Michigan P; 1996. 450 pp. Lang.: Eng.
Israel. 1963-1994. Histories-sources. ■Interview with Arab actor Muhammad Bakri on working in Israel and on relations between Arabs and Jews and theatre's relationship to both.

856 Cummings, Scott T. "Yossi Yzraely." 383-391 in Ben-Zvi, Linda, ed. *Theater In Israel.* Ann Arbor, MI: Univ. of Michigan P; 1996. 450 pp. Lang.: Eng.
Israel. 1938-1994. Histories-sources. ■Interview with director Yossi Yzraely on directing theatre in Israel and the place of theatre in Israeli culture.

857 Fridštejn, Ju. "Zigzagi sud'by Michajla Kazakova." (Twists and Turns of Michajl Kazakov's Career.) *TeatZ.* 1996; 11-12: 44-45. Lang.: Rus.
Israel: Tel Aviv. 1996. Biographical studies. ■The actors's work in Israel.

858 Urian, Dan, ed. "Perspectives on Palestinian Drama and Theater: A Symposium." 323-345 in Ben-Zvi, Linda, ed. *Theater In Israel.* Ann Arbor, MI: Univ. of Michigan P; 1996. 450 pp. Notes. Lang.: Eng.
Israel: Oranim. 1992. Historical studies. ■Report on series of conference papers presented at a symposium on Palestinian theatre in Israel and the Occupied Territories. Topics covered included: twentieth-century Palestinian drama and theatre until 1948, cultural background of Palestinian theatre, Arab theatre in Israel from 1948 to 1992, women in Palestinian theatre, working in two cultures (Israeli and Palestinian), and modern contemporary Palestinian theatre artists and companies.

859 "Questo strano teatro creato dagli attori artisti nel tempo della regia, che ha rigenerato l'avanguardi storica in sieme al teatro popolare. Come un editoriale." (The Strange Theatre Created by Actors at the Time of the Directors' Theatre, which Regenerated Both Historical Avant-garde and the Popular Theatre: Something of an Editorial.) *TeatroS.* 1996; 9(18): 9-24. Lang.: Ita.
Italy. 1900-1970. Historical studies. ■The two poles of twentieth-century theatre: on the one hand, popular theatre and directors' theatre, and on the other, the theatre of the artist-actor exemplified by Eleonora Duse and Antonin Artaud.

860 Barbina, Alfredo, ed. "Lettere a Silvio D'Amico." (Letters to Silvio D'Amico.) *Ariel.* 1996; 11(1): 189-195. Lang.: Ita.
Italy. 1899-1955. Histories-sources. ■Four letters written from Ettore Petrolini, Jacques Copeau and Orazio Costa to Silvio D'Amico. These letters belong to the collection of the archives of the Civico Museo Biblioteca dell'Attore di Genova.

861 Biagi, Enzo. *La bella vita. Marcello Mastroianni racconta.* (Marcello Mastroianni Tells about 'La bella vita'.) Rome/Milan: ERI Rizzoli; 1996. 190 pp. Index. Lang.: Ita.
Italy. 1924-1996. Histories-sources. ■Actor Marcello Mastroianni tells about his life, work and lovers in a biography-interview with the Italian journalist Enzo Biagi.

862 Gassman, Vittorio; Soavi, Giorgio. *Lettere d'amore sulla bellezza.* (Love Letters on Beauty.) Milan: Longanesi; 1996. 230 pp. Lang.: Ita.
Italy. 1995-1996. Histories-sources. ■A collection of letters on art, life and beauty written by the Italian actor Vittorio Gassman and the writer Giorgio Soavi.

863 Menza, Maddalena. *Bonaventura alla conquista del cinema.* (Bonaventura at the Conquest of Cinema.) Florence: Firenze Atheneum; 1996. 142 pp. Index. Biblio. Filmography. Illus.: Photo. Sketches. B&W. Lang.: Ita.
Italy. 1909-1973. Historical studies. ■Bonaventura is a character created by the Italian actor-author and cartoonist Sergio Tofano. A study of Tofano's activity as an actor for theatre and cinema and his direction of the films *Cenerentola e il signor Bonaventura (Cinderella and Mr. Bonaventura)* and *Giamburrasca.*

864 Micciché, Lino. *Luchino Visconti. Un profilo critico.* (Luchino Visconti: A Critical Profile.) Venice: Marsilio; 1996. 161 pp. Pref. Biblio. Append. Filmography. Illus.: Photo. B&W. Lang.: Ita.
Italy. 1936-1976. Biographies. ■The work of director Luchino Visconti.

865 Pretini, Armando. *La 'Signoria di madonna Finzione'. Teatro, attori e poetiche nel Rinascimento italiano.* (The 'Rule of Dame Pretense': Theatre, Actors and Poetics in the Italian Renaissance.) Genoa: Costa & Nolan; 1996. 159 pp. (Studi di storia del teatro e dello spettacolo.) Notes. Biblio. Lang.: Ita.
Italy. 1500-1600. Critical studies. ■Biographies of two of the most famous Italian actors of the period: Domenico Barlacchi called Barlacchia and Francesco de' Nobili called Cherea. The growing importance of the actor and the dramatic work which begins to be considered a literary work.

866 Schivo Lena, Alessandra. *Anna Fiorilli Pellandi. Una grande attrice veneziana tra Sette e Ottocento.* (Anna Fiorilli Pellandi, Great Venetian Actress of the Eighteenth and Nineteenth Centuries.) Venice: Il Cardo; 1996. 167 pp.

THEATRE IN GENERAL: —Performance/production

(Ricerche.) Pref. Notes. Biblio. Append. Illus.: Dwg. B&W.
1. Lang.: Ita.
Italy: Venice. 1772-1841. Biographies. ■Life and work of famous Venetian actress, including correspondence between the actress and her husband Antonio Pellandi (an actor himself) and the Venetian playwright Alessandro Zanchi.

867 Schnapp, Jeffrey T. *Staging Fascism: 18BL and the Theater of Masses for Masses.* Stanford, CA: Stanford UP; 1996. 234 pp. Index. Notes. Append. Illus.: Photo. 65. Lang.: Eng.
Italy: Florence. 1933. Histories-specific. ■The most extreme attempt within the Mussolini regime to produce a mass theatre. Concentrates on the first production to serve as a vehicle on the fascist subject, *18BL*, principally written by Alessandro Pavolini and Alessandro Blasetti. A colossal spectacle set outside Florence on a spectacle site and performed only once, *18BL* is examined as an exposition of fascist cultural politics.

868 Schnapp, Jeffrey T.; Dagnini Bray, Ilaria, transl. *18BL Mussolini e l'opera d'arte di massa.* (18BL: Mussolini and Art for the Masses.) Milan: Garzanti; 1996. 285 pp. (Collezione storica.) Lang.: Ita.
Italy. Historical studies. ■Translation of *Staging Fascism: 18BL and the Theater of Masses for Masses* (Stanford UP, 1996). Analysis of Fascist spectacle, including one organized in Florence by Alessandro Blasetti, using 3,000 actors and attracting 20,000 spectators, and 'starring' the Fiat 18BL van, which was used by the Italian army in World War I.

869 Thompson, Doug. "The Organisation, Fascistisation and Management of Theatre in Italy, 1925-1943." 94-112 in Berghaus, Günter, ed. *Fascism and Theatre: Comparative Studies on the Aesthetics and Politics of Performance in Europe, 1925-1945.* Oxford: Berghahn Books; 1996. 315 pp. Biblio. Notes. Index. Illus.: Photo. 24. Lang.: Eng.
Italy. 1925-1943. Historical studies. ■Attempt by Italian theatre practitioners to persuade the Fascist government to provide guaranteed financial support for 'good theatre' and for the creation of a National Theatre following the French, German and Russian models. The legacy of this organization in Italy today.

870 Verdone, Mario; Madia, Isabella, transl. "Mussolini's 'Theatre of the Masses'." 133-139 in Berghaus, Günter, ed. *Fascism and Theatre: Comparative Studies on the Aesthetics and Politics of Performance in Europe, 1925-1945.* Oxford: Berghahn Books; 1996. 315 pp. Biblio. Notes. Index. Illus.: Photo. 24. Lang.: Eng.
Italy. 1925-1943. Historical studies. ■Examines the *carri di tespi*, circus-like performing groups that sought to reach new audiences in smaller remote cities and in the lower strata of society by performing plays and operas. Argues that they fulfilled Fascist ideology's idea of theatre as a means of educating the masses.

871 Hall, Edward; Acton, David. "Japan, 2." *PlPl.* 1996 Mar.: 36-38. Lang.: Eng.
Japan: Tokyo. 1996. Histories-sources. ■Personal account, by director Edward Hall and actor David Acton, of their staging of *Richard III* at the Panasonic Globe Theatre in Tokyo. Emphasis on the demonstrative style of acting used in the production.

872 Kishida, Rio; Phelan, Peggy. "The Contemporary Body." *AFS.* 1995 Fall; 21: 21-30. Illus.: Photo. B&W. 3. Lang.: Eng.
Japan. USA: New York, NY. 1977-1995. Critical studies. ■Excerpts from Kishida's presentation at the International Women Playwrights Conference, on the significance of the physical body in ritual and contemporary theatre, and Phelan's paper on how effectual ritual transformation informs some contemporary women's performance art in the US.

873 O'Quinn, Jim. "Suzuki and Spring Snow." *AmTh.* 1996 Nov.; 13(9): 21-22. Illus.: Photo. B&W. 2. [Headed by Title: 5 Corners of our theatrical world.] Lang.: Eng.
Japan: Toga-Mura. 1960-1996. Critical studies. ■Director and acting teacher Tadashi Suzuki and his plan for an eight-nation Theatre Olympics and a festival of new writing and performance.

874 Poulton, Cody. "'Today's Japan' in Toronto: A Report." *ATJ.* 1996 Fall; 13(2): 192-217. Notes. Biblio. Illus.: Photo. Color. B&W. 16. Lang.: Eng.
Japan. Canada: Toronto, ON. 1996. Historical studies. ■Critical analysis of modern Japanese productions presented at Toronto Theatre Festival:

Dionysus by the Suzuki Company of Toga (SCOT), directed by Suzuki Tadashi, *pH* created by Furuhashi Teiji, performed by Dumb Type, *Forests, Gathering Honey of the Moon (Mori, tsuki no mitsu o toru)* by choreographer Yamada Setsuko, composed by Fujieda Mamoru, performed by dance company Biwa-kei, *A Cry from the City of Virgins (Shōjo toshi kara no yobigoe)* by Kara Jūrō, directed by Kim Sujin, performed by Shinjuku Ryōzanpaku company, *The Great Doctor Yabuhara (Yabuhara kengyō)* by Inoue Hisashi, performed by Chijinkai company, directed by Kimura Kōichi, *No No Miya*, a chamber opera by Rudolph Komorous, directed by Billie Bridgeman, performed by Tapestry Music Theatre, *Les Sept Branches de la Rivière Ota (The Seven Streams of the River Ota)* developed and directed by Robert Lepage, performed by Ex Machina. Comments on the vitality of contemporary Japanese artistic culture.

875 Salz, Jonah. "East Meets West Meets Hamlet: Get Thee to a Noh Master." 149-163 in Oliva, Judy Lee, ed. *New Theatre Vistas: Modern Movements in International Theatre.* New York, NY/London: Garland; 1996. 219 pp. (Studies in Modern Drama 7.) Notes. Lang.: Eng.
Japan: Kyoto. 1981-1994. Histories-sources. ■The work of the touring company Noho Theatre Group, founded by the author and Japanese actor Akira Shigeyama, which uses *nō* performance techniques in the production of Western texts. Productions examined include *Act Without Words I* and *II* by Samuel Beckett, Yeats's *At the Hawk's Well*, and Woody Allen's *Death Knocks*.

876 Azparren Jiménez, Leonardo. "Ha sido un gran crítico de los festivales." (He Has Been a Big Critic of Festivals.) *Cjo.* 1996 July/Dec.; 103: 14-18. Illus.: Photo. Sketches. 2. Lang.: Spa.
Latin America. 1936-1996. Histories-sources. ■Pepe Monleón, critic and advocate for Latin American theatre, reviews a sixty-year history of theatre festivals.

877 Harper, Roxana Avila. "El festival: una especie en vías de extinción." (The Festival: a Species on the Road to Extinction.) *Cjo.* 1996 July/Dec.; 103: 11-14. Illus.: Photo. 2. Lang.: Spa.
Latin America. 1936-1996. Historical studies. ■Defense of the festival as a valuable resource. Argues that there should be more festivals, especially outside university settings.

878 Joffré, Sara. "Entre ponerle y no ponerle." (To Put It On or Not To Put It On.) *Cjo.* 1996 July/Dec.; 103: 24-25. Illus.: Photo. Sketches. 2. Lang.: Spa.
Latin America. 1996. Historical studies. ■The author's experience of international theatre festivals in Latin America and her defense of festivals in general.

879 Risum, Janne. "La piedra preciosa de la actuación." (The Precious Stone of Performance.) *Cjo.* 1996 Jan-June; 102: 67-83. Notes. Illus.: Photo. Sketches. 11. Lang.: Spa.
Latin America. 1910-1995. Critical studies. ■The actor's performance in twentieth-century theatre historiography, including postmodernism and poststructuralism. Analysis of acting theories of Stanislavskij, Mejerchol'd, Barba, Decroux, Brecht, Piscator, Schechner, Grotowski, Artaud, and Mnouchkine.

880 Woodyard, George. "El contacto con el mundo que me interesa y fascina." (What Interests and Fascinates Me Is Contact with the World.) *Cjo.* 1996 July/Dec.; 103: 35-36. Illus.: Dwg. 1. Lang.: Spa.
Latin America. 1968-1996. Historical studies. ■Since the first Latin American theatre festival in 1968 in Manizales (Colombia), theatre festivals continue to interest because they reflect topical, current issues as well as larger cultural and political currents from a wide variety of world theatre.

881 Sorokina, N. "Kyrlja." *TeatZ.* 1996; 8: 21-23. Lang.: Rus.
Mari El Republic: Yoshkar-Ola. 1898-1942. Biographical studies. ■The work of actor Jyvan Kyrlja in the national theatre of Mari El.

882 Compton, Timothy G. "Mexico City Theatre: Summers 1995 and 1996." *LATR.* 1996 Fall; 30(1): 135-151. Notes. Illus.: Photo. 5. Lang.: Eng.
Mexico: Mexico City. 1995-1996. Historical studies. ■Account of the 1995 and 1996 summer seasons in Mexico City, reflecting work written by Mexicans as well as international classics.

THEATRE IN GENERAL: —Performance/production

883 Alkema, Hanny. *De Wondere Wereld van Cilly Wang.* (The Magical World of Cilly Wang.) Amsterdam: Theater Instituut Nederland; 1996. 147 pp. Pref. Illus.: Photo. B&W. 30. Lang.: Dut.

Netherlands. 1920-1970. Biographical studies. ■The work of Vienneseborn Cilly Wang in the Netherlands as an actress, dancer, and puppeteer.

884 Mason, Susan. "*On the Edge*: Utrecht, Netherlands 1993." 59-72 in Oliva, Judy Lee, ed. *New Theatre Vistas: Modern Movements in International Theatre.* New York, NY/ London: Garland; 1996. 219 pp. (Studies in Modern Drama 7.) Biblio. Lang.: Eng.

Netherlands: Utrecht. 1993. Histories-sources. ■Account of an international theatre project, *On the Edge*, designed and coordinated by Eugène van Erven and for which the author served as dramaturg. The subjects of the project were third-world immigrants in the Netherlands, and the project was an attempt to achieve a process-oriented workshop dealing with intercultural communication and aesthetic methods and values.

885 Schwartz, Gary. *Ritsaert ten Cate Now.* Maastricht: Stichting Sphinx Cultuurpirjs; 1996. 80 pp. Biblio. Illus.: Photo. B&W. 31. Lang.: Eng.

Netherlands. 1930-1995. Biographical studies. ■The life and work of the founder of the Mickery Theater and host of many touring avant-garde theatre groups since the 1960s.

886 Van Melle, Marius. "De Amsterdamse Familie Huf. Aankleding en verbeelding van het Leven." (The Huf Family of Amsterdam: Dressing and Imagination of Life.) *OnsA.* 1996; 48(5): 114-120. Illus.: Photo. Color. B&W. 7. Lang.: Dut.

Netherlands: Amsterdam. 1826-1996. Historical studies. ■The Huf family of actors, who moved to the Netherlands from Germany in the nineteenth century.

887 Diamond, Elin. "Performance and Cultural Politics: Introduction." 1-14 in Diamond, Elin, ed. *Performance and Cultural Politics.* London/New York, NY: Routledge; 1996. 282 pp. Notes. Index. Lang.: Eng.

North America. Europe. 1995. Critical studies. ■Introductory essay to volume on performance and cultural politics describing the themes of the volume: the ways in which performance has come to overrun and expand theatre from text to body and give dominance to the spectator, the relationship between performativity and performance, and the relationship between performance and cultural studies.

888 Gunnell, Terry. "'The Rights of the Player': Evidence of Mimi and Histriones in Early Medieval Scandinavia." *CompD.* 1996 Spr; 30(1): 1-31. Notes. Lang.: Eng.

Norway. Sweden. Iceland. 793-1400. Historical studies. ■Examination of medieval Scandinavian literature for evidence of active performers and styles of entertainment.

889 Diamond, Catherine. "Quest for the Elusive Self." *TDR.* 1996 Spr; 40(1): 141-169. Notes. Biblio. Illus.: Photo. B&W. 10. Lang.: Eng.

Philippines: Manila. 1565-1996. Historical studies. ■Role of contemporary Philippine theatre in the formation of cultural identity. Preservation of and Western and Asian influences on traditional art forms. Special focus on political theatre group Philippine Educational Theatre Association (PETA) and the Cultural Center of the Philippines and their productions.

890 Bablet, Denis; Pályi, András, transl.; Fodor, Géza, intro. "Színészi technika—Denis Bablet beszélgetése Jerzy Grotowskival." (Acting Technique—Denis Bablet's Interview with Jerzy Grotowski.) *Sz.* 1996; 29(3): 36-41. Illus.: Photo. B&W. 8. Lang.: Hun.

Poland: Wrocław. 1967. Histories-sources. ■Translation of French critic Denis Bablet's 1967 interview with Grotowski, with an introduction.

891 Budzik, Wojciech; Baron, Katarzyna, transl. "Alternatives Theater in Polen." (Alternative Theatre in Poland.) *TZ.* 1996; 4: 51-53. Illus.: Photo. B&W. 2. Lang.: Ger.

Poland. 1956-1996. Historical studies. ■Forty years of Polish alternative theatre and possibilities for development.

892 Cioffi, Kathleen. "Maybe Theatre Is Born: Directing Student Theatre in Communist and Post-Communist Poland." 73-88 in Oliva, Judy Lee, ed. *New Theatre Vistas: Modern Move-*

ments in International Theatre. New York, NY/London: Garland; 1996. 219 pp. (Studies in Modern Drama 7.) Biblio. Notes. Lang.: Eng.

Poland: Gdańsk. 1984-1988. Histories-sources. ■The author's four-year collaboration with the English Language Theatre Group of the University of Gdańsk where she directed three productions: Caryl Churchill's *Cloud Nine*, Christopher Durang's *The Actor's Nightmare*, and *The Varieties of Religious Experience* by William James (adapted by Frank Cioffi).

893 Skambraks, Jürgen; Schechner, Richard. "Terra Teatralis pro Societate." *Flamb.* 1996; 4: 35-53. Illus.: Graphs. Photo. B&W. 7. Lang.: Ger.

Poland: Gardzienice. 1977-1996. Histories-sources. ■Portrait of the avant-garde theatre group Gardzienice Theatre Association (Ośrodek Praktyk Teatralnych), with a statement by and interview with director Włodzimierz Staniewski.

894 Timoszewicz, Jerzy, ed. *Rozmowy z Leonem Schillerem 1923-1953.* (Conversations with Leon Schiller, 1923-1953.) Warszawa: Państwowy Instytut Wydawniczy; 1996. 366 pp. Pref. Notes. Index. Illus.: Sketches. Lang.: Pol.

Poland. 1923-1953. Histories-sources. ■Collection of interviews with theatre director Leon Schiller (1887-1954), presenting Schiller's artistic activity and political views.

895 Wesemann, Arnd. "Zurück zu den Wurzeln einer 'Grünenkunst'." (Back to the Roots of a 'Green Art'.) *TZ.* 1996; 4: 46-47. Illus.: Photo. B&W. 2. Lang.: Ger.

Poland: Cracow. 1996. Historical studies. ■Report on the present situation of Polish theatre in Cracow and its history.

896 Darvay Nagy, Adrienne. "Sorsüldözöttek—Román előadások." (People Pursued by Fate—Romanian Performances.) *Sz.* 1996; 29(8): 43-46. Illus.: Dwg. Photo. B&W. 3. Lang.: Hun.

Romania. 1994-1996. Reviews of performances. ■Notable and sometimes controversial Romanian productions by returned expatriate directors: Bulgakov's *Běg (Flight)* dir Cătălina Buzoianu, Teatrul de Comedia, Bucharest. Enescu's opera *Oedipe* dir Andrei Şerban, Teatrul de Operă şi Balet, Bucharest. *Danaïdes*, an adaptation of Aeschylus' *Hikétides*, directed by Silviu Purcărete, Teatrul Naţional, Craiova.

897 Nánay, István; Szabó, Péter, photo.; Zsila, Sándor, photo. "Határokon túlról." (Beyond the Borders.) *Sz.* 1996; 29(11): 25-27. Illus.: Photo. B&W. 3. Lang.: Hun.

Romania. Slovakia: Košice. Ukraine: Beregovo. 1995-1996. Reviews of performances. ■Overview of the season's productions of the Hungarian ethnic minority theatres in neighboring countries.

898 Savarese, Nicola, ed. *Teatri romani. Gli spettacoli nell'antica Roma.* (Roman Theatre: Entertainments in Ancient Rome.) Bologna: Il Mulino; 1996. lxxviii, 318 pp. (Polifonie. Musiche e spettacolo nella storia.) Biblio. Illus.: Sketches. B&W. Lang.: Ita.

Rome. 300 B.C.-500 A.D. Historical studies. ■Collection of essays on theatre in everyday life in ancient Rome: the Hellenistic and Roman theatre, Etruscan origin, athletic contests, gladiators, and playwrights including Plautus and Terence.

899 *Teatralnye problemy teoretičeskoj i praktičeskoj aprobacii sistemy pedagogičeskich vozdejstvij (Mežvuzovskij sbornik naučnych trudov). Vypusk II.* (Theatrical Problems in the Theoretical and Practical Implementation of Theatre Teaching: Collection of Articles, Volume II.) Tambov: n.p.; 1996. 140 pp. Lang.: Rus.

Russia. 1996. Critical studies. ■Problems of professional training of directors of amateur theatres.

900 Al'tšuller, A. "Djadja Ko (Konstantin Nikolajévič Deržavin)." (Uncle Ko: Konstantin Nikolajévič Deržavin.) *PTŽ.* 1996; 10: 54-47. Lang.: Rus.

Russia: St. Petersburg. 1903-1956. Biographical studies. ■The career of Deržavin, a director and theatre scholar, with emphasis on his work as a teacher.

901 Balykina, N. "'Dlja aktera samoe važnoe—éto umenie slyšat' režissera'." (For an Actor, the Most Important Thing Is the

CLASSED ENTRIES

THEATRE IN GENERAL: —Performance/production

Ability to Listen to the Director.) *ISK*. 1996; 8: 65-69. Lang.: Rus.

Russia: Moscow. 1990-1996. Histories-sources. ■Interview with actor Sergej Makoveckij about his work in film and at the Vachtangov Theatre.

902 Borev, Ju.B. *Iz žizni zvezd i meteoritov: Predanija i istoričeskie anekdoty o pisateljach, akterach, chudožnikach, učenych i drugich dejateljach kul'tury.* (From the Life of Stars and Meteors: Legends and Historical Anecdotes about Writers, Actors, Artists, Scientists and Other Cultural Figures.) Moscow: RIPOL; 996 . 552 pp. Lang.: Rus.

Russia. 1900-1938. Histories-sources. ■The theatrical figures included in the book are opera singer Fëdor Šaljapin and director V.E. Mejerchol'd.

903 Čubarova, Alena. "'Krasnorečivye miraži mysli...'." (Verbal Mirages of Thought.) *TeatZ*. 1996; 2: 16-17. Lang.: Rus.

Russia: Moscow. 1996. Histories-sources. ■Actress describes her work in Erotica Theatre, directed by Aleksand'r Demidov.

904 Fridštejn, Ju. "Uroki parallel'noj istorii." (Lessons of Parallel History.) *TeatZ*. 1996; 4: 6-8. Lang.: Rus.

Russia: Moscow. 1996. Historical studies. ■The work of director Kama Ginkas at Teat'r Junogo Zritelja.

905 Fridštejn, Ju. "Ja s nim obščajus' na ravnych." (I Address Him as an Equal.) *TeatZ*. 1996; 9: 48-49. Lang.: Rus.

Russia: Moscow. 1996. Histories-sources. ■Interview with actor Aleksand'r Jacko.

906 Garkalin, V. "Kak sygrat' v teatre muchu, a v kino smert'?" (How Do You Play a Fly in the Theatre and Death in a Movie?) *TeatZ*. 1996; 1: 34-35. Lang.: Rus.

Russia: Moscow. 1996. Histories-sources. ■Interview with actor Valerij Garkalin about his artistic principles and his views on the correlation between theatre and cinema.

907 Goldovskaja, M. "Stariki." (Old People.) *ISK*. 1996; 11: 170-185. Lang.: Rus.

Russia: Moscow. 1960-1996. Histories-sources. ■Interview with directors Iosif Hejfic and Leonid Trauberg and actor Georgij Milljar, who began in theatre and later worked in film.

908 Ivanov, V. *Mnemozina. Dokumenty i materialy po istorii russkogo teatra XX v.* (Mnemosyne: Documents and Materials on the History of Twentieth-Century Russian Theatre.) Moscow: GITIS; 1996. 288 pp. Lang.: Rus.

Russia. 1910-1929. Histories-sources. ■Publication of archival documents of Jévrejnov, Charms, and Foregger.

909 Kazakov, Michajl; Mordvinceva, N.B., ed. *Michajl Kazakov. Akterskaja kniga.* (Michajl Kazakov: Actor's Book.) Moscow: VAGRIUS; 1996. 432 pp. Lang.: Rus.

Russia: Moscow. 1934-1996. Histories-sources. ■Kazakov's acting career.

910 Kolesova, N. "V sporach s desjatoj muzoj." (In Arguments with the Tenth Muse.) *TeatZ*. 1996; 1: 39-42. Lang.: Rus.

Russia: Moscow. 1990-1996. Critical studies. ■Comparison of the work of actors and directors, with reference to Mark Zacharov, Nikolaj Karačencov, Aleksand'r Zbruev, and Aleksand'r Abdulov.

911 Korogodskij, Zinovyj. *Načalo.* (Beginning.) St. Petersburg: SPB GUP; 1996. 434 pp. Lang.: Rus.

Russia: St. Petersburg. 1980-1996. Histories-sources. ■Director and acting professor's views on the meaning of his teaching, problems of teaching theatre, and issues in contemporary theatre.

912 Krečetova, R. "Mutanty." (Mutants.) *TeatZ*. 1996; 4: 2-4, 26-29. Lang.: Rus.

Russia. 1990-1996. Critical studies. ■Theatre critic on problems of audience, criteria for reviews, contemporary theatre culture, and conflicts in the actor/director relationship.

913 Kuznecov, O. "Budem ljubit' ili 'make love?'." (Will We Love or Make Love?) *TeatZ*. 1996; 2: 3-5. Lang.: Rus.

Russia: Moscow. 1990-1996. Critical studies. ■Problems of portraying love on stage in contemporary theatre.

914 Lemon, Alaina. "Hot Blood and Black Pearls: Socialism, Society, and Authenticity at the Moscow Teatr Romen." *TJ*. 1996 Dec.; 48(4): 479-494. Notes. Biblio. Lang.: Eng.

Russia. 1930-1992. Historical studies. ■Portrayals of gypsies in performances at the Teat'r Romen: how tropes of performance reproduce marginal identity as authentic. This 'real' characterization of gypsies has a long tradition in Russian theatre and either positions them as standing apart from society, or standing in for society.

915 Lepskaja, L.A. *Repertuar krepostnogo teatra Šeremetjevych: Katalog pjes.* (The Repertoire of the Šeremetjev Serf Theatre: Catalog of Plays.) Moscow: Gosudarstvénnyj central'nyj teatral'nyj muzej A.A. Bachrušina; 1996. 176 pp. Lang.: Rus.

Russia. 1700-1800. Historical studies. ■Operas, comedies, and ballets of the serf theatre. Includes vocabulary, articles on lives of serf performers.

916 Litvin, M. "Oni byli odnoj gruppy krovi..." (They All Had the Same Blood Type.) *TeatZ*. 1996; 6: 8-9. Lang.: Rus.

Russia: Moscow. 1872-1922. Biographical studies. ■The influence of Leopold Suleržickij on the life and career of Jévgenij Vachtangov.

917 Litvinenko, N.G. "Teat'r." (Theatre.) 60-84 in *Russkaja chudožestvennaja kul'tura vtoroi polovin' XIX v.: Dialog c epochoi.* Moscow: Nauka; 1996. Lang.: Rus.

Russia. 1800-1896. Historical studies. ■History of theatre, analysis of acting schools, comparative analysis of urban and provincial theatre.

918 Ljubimov, B. "Ja ne aktera zrju...'." (I Am Not Looking at Actors.) *TeatZ*. 1996; 5: 7-8. Lang.: Rus.

Russia: Moscow. 1990-1996. Critical studies. ■Theatre critic and professor at Russian Art Academy on the problems of Russian theatrical training: the education of actors, meaning and audience, criteria for the professional level of theatre.

919 Maksimova, V. "'Vtoroj žizni ne budet...'." (There Will Be No Second Life.) *TeatZ*. 1996; 8: 39-42. Lang.: Rus.

Russia: Moscow. 1990-1996. Critical studies. ■Analysis of problems in contemporary theatre, including the actor-director relationship and the modernization of theatre.

920 Michalev, V. "Legko li kinorežisseru v teatre?" (Is It Easy for a Film Director in the Theatre?) *TeatZ*. 1996; 1: 25-27. Lang.: Rus.

Russia: Moscow. 1990-1996. Critical studies. ■Comparison of film and theatre directing by a film critic and professor at the State Institute of Cinematography, using as examples the work of Mark Zacharov and Andrej Tarkovskij.

921 Pavlova, I. "Antidjuring." *TeatZ*. 1996; 1: 29-32. Lang.: Rus.

Russia: Moscow. 1980-1996. Critical studies. ■Comparison of film and theatre acting with reference to the actors Aleksej Batalov, Nonna Mordjukova, Leonid Filatov, and Oleg Menšikov.

922 Piccon-Vallin, Beatrice. "Il lavoro dell'attore in Mejerchol'd. Studi e materiali." (The Actor's Work in Mejerchol'd: Studies and Materials.) *TeatroS*. 1996; 11(18): 85-140. Notes. Lang.: Ita.

Russia. 1874-1940. Critical studies. ■Mejerchold's pedagogical and research work on the actor, the importance of improvisation and music.

923 Popov, L. "Našego vremeni slučaj." (Chance of Our Time.) *TeatZ*. 1996; 10: 15-17. Lang.: Rus.

Russia: St. Petersburg. 1991-1996. Historical studies. ■Theatre life in St. Petersburg.

924 Rabinjanc, N. "Valerij D'jačenko." *PTZ*. 1996; 10: 41-44. Lang.: Rus.

Russia: St. Petersburg. 1980-1996. Biographical studies. ■The actor's work in Leningrad Young People's Theatre.

925 Rojtman, Jurij. "Vybor." (Choice.) *TeatZ*. 1996; 5: 39-42. Lang.: Rus.

Russia: Moscow. 1990-1996. Histories-sources. ■Interview with directors Jurij Tamer'jan of Vladikavkaz Drama Theatre, Boris Lucenko of Minsk Drama Theatre, Vladimir Konstantinov of Yoshkar-Ola, and Michajl Tumašov of the Russian theatre in Barnaul.

926 Ščeglov, Aleksej V. *Irina Vul'f i sovremenniki.* (Irina Vul'f and Her Contemporaries.) Jaroslavl: Jaroslavskij Poligrafkombinat; 1996. 112 pp. Lang.: Rus.

CLASSED ENTRIES

THEATRE IN GENERAL: —Performance/production

Russia: Moscow. 1900-1996. Histories-sources. ■Theatre architect recalls actors Irina Vul'f, Faina Ranevskaja, Rostislav Pljatt, Ljubov' Orlova, and others.

927 Sergeeva, T. "Golodnomu chočetsja poleta." (A Hungry Person Wants to Fly.) *TeatZ*. 1996; 11-12: 40-42. Lang.: Rus.

Russia: Moscow. 1960-1996. Historical studies. ■Profile of actors Oleg Striženov, Vladimir Korenev, and Gennadij Bortnikov.

928 Skoročkina, O. "'Probit'sja k živomu tetru'." (Get Through to Live Theatre.) *TeatZ*. 1996; 10: 28-29. Lang.: Rus.

Russia: St. Petersburg. 1996. Histories-sources. ■Interview with director Tatjana Kazakova of the Academic Comedy Theatre on theatre problems and the actor-director relationship.

929 Strongin, V. *Akterskie istorii: Obrečennyj Michoéls i drugie.* (Actors' Stories: Doomed Michoéls and Others.) Moscow: Kniga premjer; 1996. 112 pp. Lang.: Rus.

Russia: Moscow. 1996. Histories-sources. ■Creative portraits of Andrej Voznesénskij, Viktor Slavkin, Savelij Kramarov, Andrej Mironov, and others.

930 Ul'janov, Michajl Aleksandrovič. *Vozvraščajas' k samomu sebe.* (Returning to Myself.) Moscow: Centrpoligraf; 1996. 310 pp. Lang.: Rus.

Russia: Moscow. 1960-1996. Histories-sources. ■Russian actor on his profession and the specifics of the actor's trade.

931 Usatova, Nina. "'Ja v režisserov obyčno vljubljajus'." (I Usually Fall in Love with Directors.) *PTZ*. 1996; 10: 44-48. Lang.: Rus.

Russia: St. Petersburg. 1990-1996. Histories-sources. ■Actress describes her work with Fontanka Youth Theatre.

932 Višnevskaja, I. "Iskusstvo Kassandry." (The Art of Cassandra.) *TeatZ*. 1996; 6: 26-30. Lang.: Rus.

Russia: Moscow. 1894-1939. Biographical studies. ■Career portrait of actor Boris Ščukin.

933 Zabozlaeva, T. "Dejatel'." (Activist.) *TeatZ*. 1996; 10: 43-44. Lang.: Rus.

Russia. 1990-1996. Biographical studies. ■The career of actor Jurij Tomoševskij, formerly the director of Prijut Komedianta.

934 Zacharov, V. "Krepostnoj teat'r N.G. Cevlovskogo." (The Serf Theatre of N.G. Cevlovskij.) *Krajs*. 1996; 3-6: 30-53. Lang.: Rus.

Russia. 1600-1899. Historical studies. ■Russian serf theatre and ballet companies, with emphasis on founder Nikolaj G. Cevlovskij.

935 Zinčenko, O. "Mne kažetsja, gorodu nuzno ozit'." (It Seems to Me that the City Needs to Come Alive.) *TeatZ*. 1996; 10: 38-39. Lang.: Rus.

Russia: St. Petersburg. 1990-1996. Histories-sources. ■Interview with Vladislav Pazi, director and manager of Otkritij Teat'r (Open Theatre).

936 Marker, Frederick J.; Marker, Lise-Lone. *A History of Scandinavian Theatre.* Cambridge/New York, NY: Cambridge UP; 1996. 399 pp. Biblio. Notes. Index. Illus.: Photo. 75. Lang.: Eng.

Scandinavia. 1300-1990. Histories-specific. ■History and development of theatre in Scandinavia examining dominant styles and trends in various periods.

937 Stockenström, Göran. "Scandinavian Drama: Medieval and Modern." *CompD*. 1996 Spr; 30(1): 3-10. Notes. Lang.: Eng.

Scandinavia. 1996. Critical studies. ■Introduction to an issue devoted to Scandinavian drama and film.

938 Peterson, William. "Singapore's Festival of the Arts." *ATJ*. 1996 Spr; 13(1): 112-124. Notes. Biblio. Lang.: Eng.

Singapore. 1994-1996. Historical studies. ■Asian-oriented theatre festival designed to support local culture: experimental theatre and audience response, establishing cultural policies for a diverse society, conflict with government which imposes censorship.

939 Korošec, Helena. *Radost gledaliških delavnic.* (The Joy of Theatre Workshops.) Celje: H. Korošec; 1996. 51 pp. Lang.: Slo.

Slovenia. 1996. Instructional materials. ■A handbook with basic exercises on acting techniques for school teachers and children's theatre trainers.

940 Riccio, Thomas. "Politics, Slapstick, and Zulus on Tour." *TDR*. 1996 Win; 40(4): 94-117. Notes. Illus.: Photo. B&W. 14. Lang.: Eng.

South Africa, Republic of: Durban. 1993-1996. Critical studies. ■Author's personal experience creating street theatre in South Africa, impact of the legacy of apartheid and political violence on their work, use of traditional Zulu story-telling, focus on their piece *Makanda Mahlanu.*

941 Monleón, José. "Una vía agotada o aún insegura." (A Dead End or Still Uncertain Way.) *Cjo*. 1996 July/Dec.; 103: 27-28. Illus.: Photo. 2. Lang.: Spa.

South America. 1996. Critical studies. ■The distinct characters of theatre festivals, due to different circumstances, criteria, and programming. There is no one ideology for the festivals, all of them contribute to a number of disparate ideologies.

942 Linares, Francisco; MacCandless, R.I., transl. "Theatre and Falangism at the Beginning of the Franco Régime." 210-228 in Berghaus, Günter, ed. *Fascism and Theatre: Comparative Studies on the Aesthetics and Politics of Performance in Europe, 1925-1945.* Oxford: Berghahn Books; 1996. 315 pp. Notes. Index. Biblio. Illus.: Photo. 24. Lang.: Eng.

Spain. 1935-1945. Historical studies. ■Theatre as a tool of the Falangist movement to influence public opinion and to improve the standards of Spanish cultural production.

943 London, John. "Competing Together in Fascist Europe: Sport in Early Francoism." 229-246 in Berghaus, Günter, ed. *Fascism and Theatre: Comparative Studies on the Aesthetics and Politics of Performance in Europe, 1925-1945.* Oxford: Berghahn Books; 1996. 315 pp. Notes. Index. Biblio. Illus.: Photo. 24. Lang.: Eng.

Spain. 1935-1945. Historical studies. ■Sport as an integral part of the performative language of fascism, sporting politics and aesthetics in Spanish Falangist ideology and bureaucratic control of sport as seen in public ceremonies.

944 Barba, Eugenio; Szántó, Judit, transl. "Színházi antropológia—Első hipotézis." (Theatre Anthropology—First Hypothesis.) *Sz*. 1996; 29(7): 38-43. Illus.: Photo. B&W. 5. Lang.: Hun.

Sweden. 1974-1980. Histories-sources. ■Hungarian translation of an essay by theatre innovator Eugenio Barba concerning his theatre workshops based on his International School of Theatre Antropology.

945 Busk, Yvonne. "Musikaliska språk." (Musical Languages.) *Tningen*. 1996; 20(79): 11-13. Illus.: Photo. B&W. Lang.: Swe.

Sweden: Västerås. 1996. Historical studies. ■A report from the conference 'Teater i musiken och musiken i teater (The Theatre In Music and Music In the Theatre)' where composers, directors and playwrights discussed the importance of cooperation of musicians and actors, with references to the composer Rolf Enström and Pär Ahlbom.

946 Hallin, Ulrika. "Mitt fokus ligger på rytmen." (My Focus Stays on Rhythm.) *Tningen*. 1996; 20(75): 43-45. Illus.: Photo. B&W. Color. Lang.: Swe.

Sweden. 1970. Historical studies. ■The musician Ale Möller speaks about his career as theatre musician, and his works with the director Peter Oskarson, with references to Folkteatern i Gävleborg and *Hästen och tranan (The Horse and the Crane)* directed by Leif Sundberg at Orionteatern.

947 Hoogland, Rikard. "Energi och busighet." (Energy and Mischief.) *Tningen*. 1996; 20(78): 4-5. Illus.: Photo. Color. Lang.: Swe.

Sweden: Stockholm. 1983. Biographical studies. ■A presentation of the young actress Jessica Liedberg.

948 Hultén, Henrietta. "Integritet och intelligens." (Integrity and Intelligence.) *Tningen*. 1996; 20(75): 4-5. Illus.: Photo. Color. Lang.: Swe.

Sweden: Stockholm. Bosnia and Herzegovina: Sarajevo. 1993. Histories-sources. ■An interview with the young director Jasenko Selimović, with

THEATRE IN GENERAL: —Performance/production

references to his experiences of the Bosnian theatre compared to the established theatre life of Sweden.

949   Johansson, Ola. "Helheter på genomresa." (Totalities In Transit.) *ProScen.* 1996; 20(75): 11-14. Illus.: Photo. B&W. Lang.: Swe.

Sweden: Stockholm. 1994. Critical studies. ■Three guest performances have been a revival for the genuine physical theatre: the three-dimensional space, the here and now and the interaction with a live audience, with references to Robert Lepage's staging of *Ett drömspel (A Dream Play)* by Strindberg at the Royal Dramatic Theatre, Volksbühne with Christoph Marthaler's *Murx* and *The Three Lives of Lucie Cabrol* of Théâtre de Complicité, directed by Simon McBurney.

950   Lagercrantz, Ylva. "Röker känt folk Kent?" (Do Famous People Smoke Kents?)*Dramat.* 1996; 4(4): 42-45. Illus.: Photo. B&W. Color. Lang.: Swe.

Sweden. 1950. Critical studies. ■A discussion of well-known actors in advertising or PR campaigns with reference to Yvonne Lombard and Justine Kirk.

951   Lahger, Håkan. "En lektion i humor." (A Lesson of Humour.) *Dramat.* 1996; 4(2): 10-12. Illus.: Photo. Color. Lang.: Swe.

Sweden: Stockholm. 1996. Biographical studies. ■The actor Robert Gustafsson speaks about his comic figures on television shows, and theatres, and his upcoming debut at the Royal Dramatic Theatre in Ionesco's *La Leçon* staged by Hans Klinga.

952   Petersen, Nils Holger. "A Newly Discovered Fragment of a *Visitatio sepulchri* in Stockholm." *CompD.* 1996 Spr; 30(1): 32-40. Notes. MU. Illus.: Photo. B&W. 2. Lang.: Eng.

Sweden: Stockholm. 1201-1300. Historical studies. ■Attempts to find a context for a fragment of a *Visitatio sepulchri* recently located in Stockholm.

953   Sörenson, Margareta. "Kan barnteatern överleva?" (Can Children's Theatre Survive?)*Dramat.* 1996; 4(1): 46-47. Illus.: Photo. Color. Lang.: Swe.

Sweden. 1995. Critical studies. ■An appeal for a generous children's theatre, cheap and with quality in spite of the reductions in cultural funding.

954   Tiselius, Henric. "En kinesisk midsommarnattsdröm." (A Chinese Midsummer Night's Dream.) *Tningen.* 1996; 20(78): 39-44. Illus.: Photo. B&W. Color. Lang.: Swe.

Sweden: Stockholm. China, People's Republic of: Shanghai. 1996. Historical studies. ■A report from the Swedish guest performance of *A Midsummer Night's Dream* with the pupils of Teaterhögskolan, directed by Ma Ke, and what the Swedes learned from and about Chinese theatre.

955   Tiselius, Henric. "Pekingoperan en skatt." (Beijing Opera a Treasure.) *Tningen.* 1996; 20(78): 44-46. Illus.: Photo. B&W. Color. Lang.: Swe.

Sweden: Stockholm. China, People's Republic of. 1989. Critical studies. ■Director Peter Oskarson of Orionteatern on multiculturalism, Swedish people's theatre, and his collaboration with Chinese director Ma Ke on a production of *A Midsummer Night's Dream.*

956   Jauslin, Christian. "Shakespeare-Inszenierungen in der deutsch-sprachigen Schweiz." (Shakespearean Productions in German Switzerland.) *SJW.* 1996; 132: 200-203. Illus.: Photo. B&W. 1. Lang.: Ger.

Switzerland. 1994-1995. Reviews of performances. ■Productions of ballet and operatic adaptations of Shakespearean plays: *Macbeth* composed by Antonio Bibalo and directed by Kurt Horres at Stadttheater Bern, *Much Ado About Nothing* directed by Thomas Schulte-Michels at Basler Theater, *A Midsummer Night's Dream*, choreographed by Youri Vámos at Basler Theater, *Romeo and Juliet*, a guest appearance by the joint production of Jerusalem-Khan Theater and Al-Kasab-al-Quds at Theaterhaus Gessnerallee.

957   Koslowski, Stefan. "Bürgerturner spielen Theater. Zur Basler Theatergeschichte des 19. Jahrhunderts." (Citizen Gymnasts Play Theatre: Toward a History of Nineteenth-Century Theatre in Basel.) *KSGT.* 1996; YB: 219-239. Notes. Illus.: Photo. B&W. 4. Lang.: Ger.

Switzerland: Basel. 1870-1900. Historical studies. ■Traditions and influences of the gymnasts and how they regarded theatre and theatre practice.

958   Linzer, Martin. "'Seien wir realistich, versuchen wir das Unmögliche'." (Let's Be Realistic and Try the Impossible.) *TZ.* 1996; 5: 34-36. Illus.: Photo. B&W. 5. Lang.: Ger.

Switzerland: Bern. 1996. Histories-sources. ■Conversation with Leonie Stein, director-designate of the acting section of the Bern Conservatory.

959   Flockemann, Miki. "A Situated Perspective on Contemporary Feminist Theatres (Review article of Lizbeth Goodman's *Contemporary Feminist Theatres: To Each Her Own.* Routledge, London and New York, 1993)." *STP.* 1994 Dec.; 10: 31-38. Lang.: Eng.

UK. USA. South Africa, Republic of: Cape Town. 1968-1994. Critical studies. ■In a favorable review of Goodman's survey, which covers American and British feminist theatres from 1968, Flockemann emphasizes the importance of 'situatedness' and relates this to the emergent feminist theatre of South Africa, as exemplified in Fatima Dike's play *So What's New?*, performed in Cape Town in 1994.

960   Aston, Elaine. "Gender as Sign-System: The Feminist Spectator as Subject." 56-69 in Campbell, Patrick, ed. *Analysing Performance: A Critical Reader.* Manchester/New York, NY: Manchester UP; 1996. 307 pp. Notes. Biblio. Index. Lang.: Eng.

UK-England. 1990-1995. Critical studies. ■Examines how the feminist spectator, as subject, is addressed by theatrical sign-systems in mainstream and feminist performance contexts. Proposes a new methodology for theatrical reception which takes account of gender and may be used for play and production analysis.

961   Barker, Clive. "Tell Me When It Hurts: the 'Theatre of Cruelty' Season, Thirty Years On." *NTQ.* 1996; 12(46): 130-135. Notes. Lang.: Eng.

UK-England: London. 1964. Histories-sources. ■Summarizes personal response to performances presented by the RSC's Experimental Group, directed by Peter Brook with Charles Marowitz under the title 'Theatre of Cruelty'.

962   Bratton, J.S. "Miss Scott and Miss Macauley: 'Genius Comes in All Disguises'." *ThS.* 1996 May; 37(1): 59-74. Notes. Biblio. Lang.: Eng.

UK-England. 1800-1835. Historical studies. ■Two recovered histories of women in theatre: Elizabeth Macauley, a musician/singer/composer as well as actress and playwright, performed in her own one-person shows. Jane Scott built and financed the Adelphi Theatre where she wrote and performed in her own shows.

963   Campbell, Patrick. "Bodies Politic, Proscribed and Perverse: Censorship and the Performing Arts." 267-289 in Campbell, Patrick, ed. *Analysing Performance: A Critical Reader.* Manchester/New York, NY: Manchester UP; 1996. 307 pp. Index. Notes. Biblio. Lang.: Eng.

UK-England. 1994-1995. Critical studies. ■The opening up of performance representations, not just for female artists and their audiences but also for those 'others' whose activities in the past attracted censure.

964   Carklin, Michael. "Mediums of Change: The Arts in Africa '95 Conference." *SATJ.* 1996 May; 10(1): 89-93. Notes. Biblio. Lang.: Eng.

UK-England: London. 1995. Historical studies. ■Report on the Arts in Africa '95 Conference held in London, September 29-October 1.

965   Carlotti, Edoardo Giovanni. "La maschera e lo specchio. L'attore e le sue immagini nella cultura teatrale britannica fra Otto e Novecento." (The Mask and the Mirror: The Actor and his Image in British Theatrical Culture of the 19th and 20th Centuries.) *IlCast.* 1996; 9(25): 41-65. Notes. Lang.: Ita.

UK-England. 1800-1996. Critical studies. ■An outline of the main characteristics of English acting, relying heavily on writings of William Archer, G.H. Lewes and Henry James in the late nineteenth century.

966   Charles, Peter. "The Clergyman's Daughter: A Tribute to Margaret Rawlings." *PlPl.* 1996 Aug/Sep.; 507: 16. Lang.: Eng.

UK-England. 1906-1996. Historical studies. ■Tribute to actor Margaret Rawlings, concentrating on her career during the 1940s and 50s.

967   Charles, Peter. "Beryl Reid: The Glorious Eccentric." *PlPl.* 1996 Nov/Dec.; 509: 12-13. Lang.: Eng.

THEATRE IN GENERAL: —Performance/production

UK-England. 1919-1996. Historical studies. ▪Tribute to actor Beryl Reid, with emphasis on her performances in *The Killing of Sister George*, by Frank Marcus, both in the film version by Robert Aldrich and in the stage productions at the Duke of York's Theatre in London and the Belasco Theatre in New York, for which she won a Tony Award in 1967.

968   Charles, Peter. "Doing Her Job." *PlPl*. 1996 Feb.: 8-9. Lang.: Eng.

UK-England. 1927-1996. Biographical studies. ▪Tribute to actress Kathleen Harrison with references to her performances in *The Corn Is Green*, *Waters of the Moon* and in the television series *Mrs. Thursday*.

969   Cheesmond, Robert. "Bread and Circuses." *STP*. 1993 June; 7: 26-33. Notes. Lang.: Eng.

UK-England: Hull. 1891-1990. Critical studies. ▪Argues that the problem of casting for productions where the roles are predominantly male and the group of students is predominantly female rises from too great a reliance on text. Discusses how the author's own performance-oriented productions of Wedekind's *Spring Awakening* in 1972 and of Arthur Kopit's *Indians* in 1980 overcame this problem.

970   Cohen, Ed. "Posing the Question: Wilde, Wit, and the Ways of Man." 35-47 in Diamond, Elin, ed. *Performance and Cultural Politics*. London/New York, NY: Routledge; 1996. 282 pp. Notes. Index. Illus.: Photo. 1. Lang.: Eng.

UK-England: London. 1895-1896. Critical studies. ▪Victorian norms of masculinity as reflected in playwright Oscar Wilde's libel trial.

971   Davis, Jim. "The East End." 201-219 in Booth, Michael R., ed.; Kaplan, Joel H., ed. *The Edwardian Theatre: Essays on Performance and the Stage*. Cambridge: Cambridge UP; 1996. 243 pp. Notes. Index. Lang.: Eng.

UK-England: London. 1912-1914. Historical studies. ▪Records the theatrical life and theatrical change of London's East End before the first World War.

972   Davis, Tracy C. "Edwardian Management and the Structures of Industrial Capitalism." 111-129 in Booth, Michael R., ed.; Kaplan, Joel H., ed. *The Edwardian Theatre: Essays on Performance and the Stage*. Cambridge: Cambridge UP; 1996. 243 pp. Notes. Index. Lang.: Eng.

UK-England. 1890-1914. Historical studies. ▪Argues that the large-scale production and distribution of Edwardian theatre shut women out of management and financially significant ventures, and that this economic perspective helps to explain the girl heroines of musical comedy and the music halls' caricatures of suffragettes.

973   DiGaetani, John Louis. "Theatre in London: Winter 1996." *WES*. 1996 Spr; 8(2): 23-26. Illus.: Photo. 3. Lang.: Eng.

UK-England: London. 1996. Reviews of productions. ▪Theatre in London including Matthew Warchus's production of Jonson's *Volpone* at the National, Bertolt Brecht's *Mother Courage* directed by Jonathan Kent at the National, and Sean Matthias's production of Sondheim's *A Little Night Music*.

974   Donohue, Joseph. "What Is the Edwardian Theatre?" 10-35 in Booth, Michael R., ed.; Kaplan, Joel H., ed. *The Edwardian Theatre: Essays on Performance and the Stage*. Cambridge: Cambridge UP; 1996. 243 pp. Notes. Index. Lang.: Eng.

UK-England. 1890-1914. Historical studies. ▪Problems of approach and access in analyzing Edwardian theatre. Delineates differences between the Edwardian theatre and its predecessor, the Victorian theatre, and its descendant, early modern theatre.

975   Eagleton, Julie. "Eagleton's Angle." *PlPl*. 1996 Mar.: 18-19. Illus.: Photo. B&W. 2. Lang.: Eng.

UK-England. 1996. Histories-sources. ▪Interview with actor/dancer Jim Dale discussing his career as a stuntman and songwriter, and his performances in *The Taming of the Shrew*, *Oliver*, and *Me and My Girl* on Broadway.

976   Emeljanow, Victor. "Towards an Ideal Spectator: Theatregoing and the Ideal Critic." 148-165 in Booth, Michael R., ed.; Kaplan, Joel H., ed. *The Edwardian Theatre: Essays on Performance and the Stage*. Cambridge: Cambridge UP; 1996. 243 pp. Notes. Index. Illus.: Sketches. 2. Lang.: Eng.

UK-England. 1907-1912. Historical studies. ▪Mainstream theatre journalism from the formation of the Society of Dramatic Critics to its replacement by the more narrowly defined Critics' Circle.

977   Gale, Maggie B. *West End Women: Women and the London Stage, 1918-1962*. New York, NY: Routledge; 1996. 262 pp. Index. Notes. Biblio. Illus.: Photo. 9. Lang.: Eng.

UK-England: London. 1918-1962. Histories-specific. ▪Women playwrights and performers on the London stage from a cultural and theatrical perspective. Uses feminist and psychoanalytic theory to focus on issues of gender, power, and class.

978   Goodman, Lizbeth. *Contemporary Feminist Theatres: To Each Her Own*. Routledge: London; 1993. 313 pp. (Gender in Performance.) Illus.: Photo. B&W. 27. Lang.: Eng.

UK-England: London. 1970-1994. Historical studies. ▪The development of feminist theatre in Britain, with detailed discussion of the work of the Women's Theatre Group, Monstrous Regiment, Gay Sweatshop, and Siren. Includes lesbian and Black women's theatre.

979   Goodman, Lizbeth. "AIDS and Live Art." 203-218 in Campbell, Patrick, ed. *Analysing Performance: A Critical Reader*. Manchester/New York, NY: Manchester UP; 1996. 307 pp. Index. Notes. Biblio. Illus.: Photo. 5. Lang.: Eng.

UK-England. 1990-1995. Critical studies. ▪The impact of AIDS and performance work as it touches on issues of contemporary representation: sex and queer culture, the role of the audience in the mainstream and alternative performance of social issues, the theatricality of politics and the politics of theatricality, and the role of gender.

980   Hornby, Richard. "Actor Training in London." *TheaterW*. 1996 Feb 19; 9(29): 34-39. Illus.: Photo. B&W. 1. Lang.: Eng.

UK-England: London. 1963-1996. Historical studies. ▪British approaches to actor training, with particular focus on the Royal Academy of Dramatic Art (RADA) and The London Academy of Music and Dramatic Art (LAMDA). Comparison to American training, funding.

981   Jones, Jennifer. "The Face of Villainy on the Victorian Stage." *TN*. 1996; 50(2): 95-108. Notes. Lang.: Eng.

UK-England. 1830-1900. Historical studies. ▪The popular physiognomic sciences of the nineteenth century and their reflection in melodrama, in which villains were perceived to look 'foreign'.

982   Kaán, Zsuzsa; Cooper, Bill, photo.; Spatt, Leslie E., photo.; Clark, Nobby, photo. "A *Csipkerózsiká*-tól a *Starlight Express*-ig. Londoni jegyzetek—IV. rész." (From *Sleeping Beauty* to *Starlight Express*: Notes from London, Part 4.) *Tanc*. 1995; 26(7/9): 41-43. Illus.: Photo. B&W. 3. Lang.: Hun.

UK-England: London. 1992-1995. Reviews of performances. ▪Notes on some of the ballet and musical performances in London this summer.

983   Kemp, Sandra. "Reading Difficulties." 153-174 in Campbell, Patrick, ed. *Analysing Performance: A Critical Reader*. Manchester/New York, NY: Manchester UP; 1996. 307 pp. Lang.: Eng.

UK-England. 1994-1995. Critical studies. ▪The reader in postmodern performance: the nature and importance of interpretation, the use of multimedia and multiculturalism, and the stability of the reader. Author uses the avantgarde films of choreographer Yvonne Rainer to explore these issues.

984   Kempinski, Tom. "Creative and Interpretive Artists: The End of a Myth." *PlPl*. 1996 Aug/Sep.; 507: 28-30. Lang.: Eng.

UK-England. 1996. Critical studies. ▪Argues that there is no difference between the creative and the interpretive and that theatre artists—playwright, director, designer and actor—are both creative and interpretive in practice.

985   Kennedy, Dennis. "The New Drama and the New Audience." 130-147 in Booth, Michael R., ed.; Kaplan, Joel H., ed. *The Edwardian Theatre: Essays on Performance and the Stage*. Cambridge: Cambridge UP; 1996. 243 pp. Notes. Index. Illus.: Sketches. 2. Lang.: Eng.

UK-England. 1890-1914. Historical studies. ▪The demographics of Edwardian playgoing and attempts to regulate audience behavior. How

THEATRE IN GENERAL: —Performance/production

organizations like the Independent Theatre and Stage Society helped lay the groundwork for the Court Theatre's 'management' of its spectators.

986   Kranz, Oliver. "Im Zentrum nichts Neues." (Nothing New in the Center.) *TZ.* 1996; 5: 44-47. Illus.: Photo. B&W. 3. Lang.: Ger.

UK-England: London. 1996. Reviews of performances. ∎Observations of the past season of London theatre, mainstream and fringe, festivals and companies.

987   Metcalf, Margaret. "'Playing for Power': Text and Performance." *STP.* 1993 June; 7: 18-25. Notes. Lang.: Eng.

UK-England. 1908-1993. Histories-sources. ∎Account of the author's one-woman show *Playing for Power* based on drama created by the Actresses' Franchise League, founded in 1908, incorporating extracts from *The Prologue* by Israel Zangwill, *The Anti-Suffragist* by H.M. Paull, *Woman This, Woman That* by Laurence Houseman, *A Chat with Mrs. Chicky* by Evelyn Glover, performed in St. Albans and at the Edinburgh Festival.

988   Normington, Catherine. "Are the Mysteries Such a Mystery?" *STP.* 1996 June; 13: 54-61. Notes. Biblio. Lang.: Eng.

UK-England: Greenwich. 1433-1995. Critical studies. ∎Takes issue with Lesley Wade Soule's article *Demystifying the Mysteries* (*STP* 1995 Dec, 12: 99-116) by asserting that they are easily accessible to a contemporary audience without the need for adaptation, and exemplifies this by reference to her own staging of the Mystery plays with students at the University of Greenwich.

989   Paget, Derek. "Mirror Images: Rehearsal and Performance on Screen and Stage." *STP.* 1996 June; 13: 17-28. Biblio. Lang.: Eng.

UK-England. 1995-1996. Critical studies. ∎Differences between stage and television techniques of acting and directing, based on the recording of *Farewell, My Love*, a television drama-documentary about euthanasia by Peter Berry, directed by Richard Signy, and produced by Sita Williams. The TV director's role as 'co-ordinator' rather than interpreter, and the actors' need to 'miniaturize' their performances compared to stage acting.

990   Percival, G.W. *Developments Towards a Theatre of the Absurd in England, 1956-1964.* Ph.D. thesis, *Index to theses,* 45-3239. St. Andrews: Univ. of St. Andrews; 1995. Notes. Biblio. Lang.: Eng.

UK-England. 1956-1964. Historical studies. ∎Aims to demonstrate the existence of an indigenous expression of absurdism far broader and significantly more complex than that which has been recognized by theatrical reviewers during the past thirty years.

991   Preusser, Gerhard. "Ein Fräulein von Welt." (A Young Lady of the World.) *THeute.* 1996; 6: 25-27. Illus.: Photo. B&W. 7. Lang.: Ger.

UK-England: London. 1967-1996. Biographical studies. ∎Portrait of actress Jacqueline Macauley.

992   Seymour, Anna. "Cultural and Political Change: British Radical Theatre in Recent History." *ThR.* 1996; 21(1): 8-16. Notes. Illus.: Photo. B&W. 4. Lang.: Eng.

UK-England. 1960-1996. Historical studies. ∎Discussion of Banner Theatre Company's work (particularly their theatricalization of the miners' strike with the North Staffordshire Miners' Wives Action Group) as an example of cultural intervention in English alternative theatre of the 1980s.

993   Shank, Theodore. "Cultural Routes Across the Arab World." *TheatreF.* 1996 Sum/Fall; 9: 88-94. Illus.: Photo. 3. Lang.: Eng.

UK-England: London. Arabic countries. 1995. Histories-sources. ∎Transcript of the sessions of the International Festival of Theatre conference held in London at the Institute of Contemporary Arts. The talks focused on the means of production, both within and outside the state structures, in Arab countries, and the development of new aesthetics in response to changing Arab societies.

994   Shenton, Mark. "London News." *TheaterW.* 1996 Jan 22; 9(25): 35-39. Illus.: Photo. B&W. 1. Lang.: Eng.

UK-England: London. 1996. Histories-sources. ∎Preview of the 1996 season for legitimate theatre: productions and their authors, venues, actors, directors, performance dates.

995   Shields, Ronald E. "Nurturing a Festival Spirit: The London Speech Festival, 1928-1939." *TextPQ.* 1994 Oct.; 14(4): 321-329. Notes. Lang.: Eng.

UK-England. 1928-1939. Historical studies. ∎History of the festival, which presented and celebrated social, pedagogical, and artistic innovation.

996   Stokes, John. "'A Woman of Genius': Rebecca West at the Theatre." 185-200 in Booth, Michael R., ed.; Kaplan, Joel H., ed. *The Edwardian Theatre: Essays on Performance and the Stage.* Cambridge: Cambridge UP; 1996. 243 pp. Notes. Index. Lang.: Eng.

UK-England. 1912-1920. Historical studies. ∎Drama criticism by Rebecca West.

997   Tompsett, A. Ruth. "Changing Perspectives." 244-266 in Campbell, Patrick, ed. *Analysing Performance: A Critical Reader.* Manchester/New York, NY: Manchester UP; 1996. 307 pp. Index. Notes. Biblio. Lang.: Eng.

UK-England. 1994-1995. Critical studies. ∎Argument for broader representation by race, sex, age, and ability in the performing arts.

998   Verma, Jatinder. "The Challenge of Binglish: Analysing Multi-Cultural Productions." 193-202 in Campbell, Patrick, ed. *Analysing Performance: A Critical Reader.* Manchester/New York, NY: Manchester UP; 1996. 307 pp. Index. Notes. Biblio. Lang.: Eng.

UK-England. 1990-1995. Critical studies. ∎The work of Black and Asian theatres in England: Talawa Theatre Company, Tamasha Theatre Company, and Tara Arts.

999   Waters, Hazel. "'That astonishing clever child': Performers and Prodigies in the Early and Mid-Victorian Theatre." *TN.* 1996; 50(2): 78-94. Notes. Lang.: Eng.

UK-England. 1835-1865. Historical studies. ∎The child performer and the changing expectations of the Victorian theatre. Describes the aura of freshness a young person could bring to the heavily mannered gestural form of acting still in vogue.

1000   Ley, Graham. "'Past Masters': a Meyerhold Symposium." *NTQ.* 1996; 12(46): 192-193. [*NTQ* Reports and Announcements.] Lang.: Eng.

UK-Wales: Aberystwyth. 1995. Historical studies. ∎This symposium concluded a series of workshops on biomechanics and offered demonstrations of 'Throwing the Stone', 'The Bow', and 'The Slap'.

1001   Pearson, Mike. "The Dream in the Desert." *PerfR.* 1996 Spr; 1(1): 5-15. Notes. Illus.: Photo. Dwg. B&W. 14. Lang.: Eng.

UK-Wales. Argentina. 1991-1992. Histories-sources. ∎Extensive though fragmentary extracts documenting the content of the 1992 performance by Brith Grof entitled *Patagonia*, which focused on the experience of Welsh immigrants.

1002   Begunov, V. "Svoboda porchodit ... kakaja?" (Freedom Is Here: How Is It?) *SovD.* 1996; 2: 164-172. Lang.: Rus.

Ukraine. 1995-1996. Historical studies. ∎Problems of Ukrainian theatrical life, with emphasis on the repertoire of the Les' Kurbas Theatre, Vladimir Kučenskij, artistic director.

1003   Reznikovič, Michajl Ju. *Ot repeticii k repeticii.* (From Rehearsal to Rehearsal.) Kiev: Abris; 1996. 344 pp. Lang.: Rus.

Ukraine: Kiev. 1990-1996. Histories-sources. ∎Theatre director on problems of teaching theatre, contemporary trends in theatre, and the professions of director and actor.

1004   "Season 1996-97 Schedules." *AmTh.* 1996 Oct.; 13(8): 43-70. Illus.: Photo. B&W. 6. Lang.: Eng.

USA. 1996. Histories-sources. ∎Comprehensive list of upcoming season for regional theatres. Includes titles, authors, directors, companies, venues, dates.

1005   Allen, Norman. "Helen Hayes Awards." *TheaterW.* 1996 June 10; 9(45): 58-59. Illus.: Photo. B&W. 1. Lang.: Eng.

USA: Washington, DC. 1996. Histories-sources. ∎Highlights of awards show and winners of Washington DC's annual theatre honors.

THEATRE IN GENERAL: —Performance/production

1006 Babb, Roger. "Otrabanda Company and *The Fairground Booth*." *SEEP*. 1996 Fall; 16(3): 41-44. Illus.: Photo. 1. Lang.: Eng.
USA: New York, NY. 1996. Historical studies. ■Otrabanda's production of Aleksand'r Blok's *Balagančik* at La MaMa Experimental Theatre Club, inspired by Mejerchol'd's 1906 production.

1007 Backalenick, Irene. "The 1996 Season in the Berkshires." *TheaterW*. 1996 June 10; 9(45): 32-38. Illus.: Photo. B&W. 3. Lang.: Eng.
USA: Stockbridge, MA, Great Barrington, MA, Williamstown, MA. 1996. Histories-sources. ■Profile of 1996 seasons for regional theatres in the Berkshires: Shakespeare & Company (artistic director Tina Packer), Williamstown Theatre Festival (Michael Ritchie, producer), and Berkshire Theatre Festival (artistic director Arthur Storch). Includes productions, casting, directors.

1008 Barton, Robert. "Acting Access." *TTop*. 1996 Mar.; 6(1): 1-14. Notes. Biblio. Illus.: Photo. B&W. 2. Lang.: Eng.
USA. 1996. Critical studies. ■Myths surrounding physical disabilities, which limit and marginalize the disabled from acting and acting classes.

1009 Bernardo, Melissa Rose. "The 41st Annual *Village Voice* OBIE Awards." *TheaterW*. 1996 June 10; 9(45): 21-22. Lang.: Eng.
USA: New York, NY. 1996. Histories-sources. ■Highlights of Awards show, given by *Village Voice* newspaper, comprehensive list of winners in all categories.

1010 Blau, Herbert. "Flat-Out Vision." 177-195 in Diamond, Elin, ed. *Performance and Cultural Politics*. London/New York, NY: Routledge; 1996. 282 pp. Notes. Index. Illus.: Photo. 1. Lang.: Eng.
USA. 1995. Critical studies. ■The performativity of vision, photography, and systems of representation.

1011 Buckley, Michael. "50 Years of Tonys." *TheaterW*. 1996 June 3; 9(44): 30-40. Illus.: Photo. B&W. 4. Lang.: Eng.
USA: New York, NY. 1996. Historical studies. ■History of the Antoinette Perry Awards: past winners, artists, productions and producers, production of the awards ceremonies themselves.

1012 Buckley, Michael. "New Faces of '96." *TheaterW*. 1996 May 20; 9(42): 20-39. Illus.: Photo. B&W. 7. Lang.: Eng.
USA: New York, NY. 1996. Biographical studies. ■Biographies and careers of award-winning young performers on the Broadway scene: Daphne Rubin-Vega in Jonathan Larson's *Rent* directed by Michael Greif at the Nederlander, Jose Llana and Joohee Choi in Rodgers and Hammerstein's *The King and I* directed by Christopher Renshaw at the Neil Simon Theatre, Ben Wright in Rodgers and Hammerstein's *State Fair* directed by Randy Skinner at the Music Box, Jim Stanek and Jessica Boevers in Shevelove, Gelbart and Sondheim's *A Funny Thing Happened on the Way to the Forum* directed by Jerry Zaks at the St. James Theatre, Matt McGrath in Jon Robin Baitz' *A Fair Country* directed by Daniel Sullivan at the Mitzi E. Newhouse.

1013 Buckley, Michael. "A Celebrity Cornucopia." *TheaterW*. 1996 Nov 25; 10(17): 24-45. Illus.: Photo. B&W. 11. Lang.: Eng.
USA: New York, NY. 1996. Biographical studies. ■Personal holiday and performance memories of actors Lou Diamond Phillips, Donna Murphy, Daphne Rubin-Vega, Elaine Page, Kim Hunter, Ann Duquesnay, Christine Pedi, Mary Louise Wilson, Tracy Nelson, Ellen Muth, Cameron Boyd.

1014 Bufferd, Lauren. "Remembering *Resetting the Stage*: Collaboration and Conflicts of a Performing Arts Exhibition." *PAR*. 1995; 19(1): 1-15. Illus.: Photo. Handbill. B&W. 5. Lang.: Eng.
USA: Chicago, IL. 1960-1990. Critical studies. ■Difficulties faced by the coordinators of the performing arts exhibit 'Resetting the Stage: Theatre Beyond the Loop, 1960-1990' in mounting this celebration of 30 years of Chicago theatre at the Chicago Public Library.

1015 Campbell, Patrick. "Interpretations and Issues." 1-16 in Campbell, Patrick, ed. *Analysing Performance: A Critical Reader*. Manchester/New York, NY: Manchester UP; 1996. 307 pp. Notes. Biblio. Index. Lang.: Eng.
USA. UK-England. 1968-1995. Critical studies. ■Introductory essay on feminist performance and theory. Sets the framework for a series of essays on collaborations of postmodernism and feminism in music, dance, theatre, and multi-media performance.

1016 Canning, Charlotte. *Feminist Theaters in the USA: Staging Women's Experience*. London/New York, NY: Routledge; 1996. 272 pp. Index. Notes. Append. Biblio. Illus.: Photo. 9. Lang.: Eng.
USA. 1969-1986. Histories-specific. ■Uses different models of feminist critical and historical practice to examine early feminist theatre's emergence, its position within feminist politics and within feminist communities of women, and its theatrical production and reception in the specific context of the US.

1017 Canning, Charlotte. "Contiguous Autobiography: Feminist Performance in the 1970s." *TA*. 1996; 49: 65-75. Notes. Lang.: Eng.
USA. 1970-1979. Critical studies. ■Exploration of the meanings, representations, and definitions of women's lived experience, and how it challenged pre-existing perceptions in women's performance art and theatre of the 1970s.

1018 Cardeña, Etzel; Beard, Jane. "Truthful Trickery: Shamanism, Acting and Reality." *PerfR*. 1996 Fall; 1(3): 31-39. Notes. Illus.: Photo. B&W. 1. Lang.: Eng.
USA. 1959-1995. Critical studies. ■A comparative analysis of relationships between illusion and reality in shamanistic/ritual practices, and in Western acting traditions, from the perspectives both of performers and of audience. Proposes that the distinctions between the two practices are blurred, not absolute.

1019 Carlson, Marla. "*Sponsus* at The Cloisters." *EDAM*. 1996 Fall; 19(1): 62-64. Lang.: Eng.
USA: New York, NY. 1996. Historical studies. ■The interpolation of appropriate musical items contemporary with the play as a solution to the problem of physicalizing medieval theatre for contemporary audiences, with reference to a production of the St. Martial de Limoges *Sponsus* by the Ensemble for Early Music at the Cloisters, directed by Frederick Renz.

1020 Carlson, Marvin. "Autobiographical Performance: Performing the Self." *MD*. 1996 Win; 39(4): 599-608. Notes. Lang.: Eng.
USA. 1276-1995. Critical studies. ■Autobiographical performance and how it challenges traditional relationship between actor and character. History of solo performance, current rise in solo female performance artists, social and political content.

1021 Carter, Hilma. "Pavlovsky Festival." *LATR*. 1996 Fall; 30(1): 161-162. Lang.: Eng.
USA: Hollywood, CA. Argentina. 1995-1996. Historical studies. ■Account of a festival held by Stages Theatre Center of Eduardo Pavlovsky's plays. Plays by the Argentinian playwright include premieres of *Cerca (Close)* and *El señor Galindez (Mr. Galindez)*, both directed by Paul Verdier. Pavlovsky directed his signature piece *Potestad (Paternity)*, *El bocón (The Big Mouth)*, and *Paso de dos (Pas de deux)*.

1022 Chase, Tony. "Selected Florida Theater Listings." *TheaterW*. 1996 Jan 22; 9(25): 24-25. Illus.: Photo. B&W. 5. Lang.: Eng.
USA. 1996. Histories-sources. ■Listing of season offerings for regional and dinner theatres in state of Florida.

1023 Chase, Tony. "Producing in Florida." *TheaterW*. 1996 Jan 22; 9(25): 18-23. Illus.: Photo. B&W. 3. Lang.: Eng.
USA: Boca Raton, FL. 1977-1996. Historical studies. ■Producer McArt of Jan McArt Royal Palm Dinner Theater discusses past and current productions at her theatre. Also focus on Coconut Grove Playhouse production of *Ladies in Retirement* by Edward Percy and Reginald Denham, starring Julie Harris, directed by Charles Nelson Reilly. Harris and Reilly discuss reasons for performing in Florida.

1024 Chase, Tony. "Bea Arthur Onstage." *TheaterW*. 1996 July 1; 9(48): 26-31. Illus.: Photo. B&W. 2. Lang.: Eng.
USA: Beverly Hills, CA. 1996. Biographical studies. ■Television and Broadway career of actress Arthur. Past roles, training, collaborations, and current role in *Bermuda Avenue Triangle* by Joseph Bologna and Renee Taylor at the Canon Theatre in Beverly Hills.

THEATRE IN GENERAL: —Performance/production

1025 Chinoy, Helen Krich. "Art Versus Business: The Role of Women in American Theatre." 23-30 in Martin, Carol, ed. *A Sourcebook of Feminist Theatre and Performance: On and Beyond the Stage.* London/New York, NY: Routledge; 1996. 311 pp. Notes. Index. Lang.: Eng.
USA. 1750-1940. Historical studies. ■Essay on the early pioneers of women's work in theatre, including Mercy Otis Warren, Anna Cora Mowatt, Olive Logan, Ada Isaacs Menken, Eva Le Gallienne, Susan Glaspell, Edith Isaacs, Cheryl Crawford, Margaret Webster, and Hallie Flanagan.

1026 Church, L. Teresa. "NBTF: National Festival Celebrates Accomplishments of Black Theatre Groups, Artists." *SoTh.* 1996 Win; 37(1): 14-20. Illus.: Photo. B&W. 9. Lang.: Eng.
USA: Winston-Salem, NC. 1995. Historical studies. ■Account of the events and participants of the fourth biennial National Black Theatre Festival in Winston-Salem, NC, including a sidebar on performer/playwright Nick Stewart.

1027 Connor, Steven. "Postmodern Performance." 107-124 in Campbell, Patrick, ed. *Analysing Performance: A Critical Reader.* Manchester/New York, NY: Manchester UP; 1996. 307 pp. Lang.: Eng.
USA. Europe. 1990-1995. Critical studies. ■Postmodern elements in contemporary performance in theatre. Examines Tom Stoppard's play *Travesties*, the performance approach of director Richard Foreman, and Peter Handke's *Offending the Audience (Publikumsbeschimpfung).*

1028 Dicker/sun, Glenda. "Festivities and Jubilations on the Graves of the Dead: Sanctifying Sullied Space." 108-127 in Diamond, Elin, ed. *Performance and Cultural Politics.* London/New York, NY: Routledge; 1996. 282 pp. Notes. Index. Illus.: Photo. 2. Lang.: Eng.
USA. 1995. Histories-sources. ■Ruminations of the performativity of Blackness from the author's own experiences.

1029 Dolan, Jill. "Fathom Languages: Feminist Performance Theory, Pedagogy, and Practice." 1-22 in Martin, Carol, ed. *A Sourcebook of Feminist Theatre and Performance: On and Beyond the Stage.* London/New York, NY: Routledge; 1996. 311 pp. Notes. Index. Lang.: Eng.
USA. 1960-1995. Critical studies. ■Introductory essay on feminist performance and theatre: focus on intersections of theory and practice, as well as the pedagogical challenges and opportunities for feminist theatre.

1030 Dowd, Jim. "Regional Theater Preview: The East." *TheaterW.* 1996 Sep 16; 10(6): 21-37. Lang.: Eng.
USA. 1996. Histories-sources. ■Scheduled productions for the 1996-1997 season at regional theatres east of the Mississippi. Venues, dates.

1031 Dowd, Jim. "Regional Preview Part II: The West." *TheaterW.* 1996 Sep 30; 10(9): 36-41. Illus.: Photo. B&W. 2. Lang.: Eng.
USA. 1996. Histories-sources. ■List of scheduled productions for the 1996-1997 seasson at regional theatres west of the Mississippi. dates, venues, directors.

1032 Dubois, Lisa A. "Nashville Actresses' Scrapbook Sheds Light on the Beginnings of Modern Theatre." *EN.* 1996 Oct.; 81(8): 5. Illus.: Photo. 1. Lang.: Eng.
USA: New York, NY. 1895-1910. Historical studies. ■A scrapbook of two actresses, Lillian and Marjorie Shrewsbury, reveals life on the road. The scrapbook contains a contract that reveals the harsh conditions under which actors labored before Actors' Equity was established.

1033 Feldman, Alice E. "Dances with Diversity: American Indian Self-Representation Within the Re-Presentative Contexts of a Non-Indian Museum." *TextPQ.* 1994 July; 14(3): 210-221. Notes. Biblio. Lang.: Eng.
USA. 1994. Critical studies. ■Explores live performances of native songs and dances by American Indians for museum visitors as a part of museums' efforts to develop culturally diverse programming.

1034 Gagnon, Pauline. "Atlanta: Cultural Olympiad Links Theatre and Sport." *SoTh.* 1996 Sum; 37(3): 4-6. Illus.: Photo. B&W. 2. Lang.: Eng.
USA: Atlanta, GA. 1996. Historical studies. ■An account of the upcoming Cultural Olympiad at the 1996 Olympic Games in Atlanta, Georgia, with a list of scheduled events.

1035 Gatti, Armand. "Mon théâtre, mes films, qu'est-ce que c'est?" (My Theatre, My Films, What Is It?)*JCT.* 1996; 80: 137-139. Illus.: Photo. B&W. 1. [Extracts from an article in *Le Monde diplomatique,* Feb 1992.] Lang.: Fre.
USA: Rochester, NY. Histories-sources. ■Playwright-director Armand Gatti describes staging *Train 713* at the University of Rochester.

1036 Genard, Gary. "The Moscow Art Theatre's 1923 Season in Boston: A Visit From On High?" *THSt.* 1996 June; 16: 15-43. Notes. Biblio. Illus.: Photo. Sketches. 6. Lang.: Eng.
USA: Boston, MA. 1923. Historical studies. ■The American tour of the Moscow Art Theatre: America's influence on Stanislavskij's and Nemirovič-Dančenko's plans for the art theatre, and the dissemination and misinterpretation in the United States in succeeding decades of Stanislavsky's famous 'System' for training actors.

1037 Hall, Hazel. "Jory Urges Actors to 'Bring Yourself to the Table'." *SoTh.* 1996 Sum; 37(3): 12-14. Illus.: Photo. B&W. 1. Lang.: Eng.
USA. 1996. Histories-sources. ■An account of a speech by Actor's Theatre of Louisville artistic director Jon Jory to the All Convention Session of the Southeastern Theatre Conference on his view of the contemporary theatre, with extensive quotation from the speech and the question/answer session.

1038 Huston, Hollis. "Flavors of Physicality." *JDTC.* 1996 Fall; 11(1): 35-54. Notes. Lang.: Eng.
USA. 1996. Critical studies. ■Theoretical treatise on stage physicality in acting, including theories of Craig and Artaud.

1039 Istel, John. "Marcus Stern." *AmTh.* 1996 Nov.; 13(9): 56-57. Illus.: Photo. B&W. 1. Lang.: Eng.
USA: New York, NY. 1996. Biographical studies. ■Profile of opera and stage director Stern: productions, techniques, influences, use of music, current work on *The Chang Fragments* by Han Ong at the Public Theatre.

1040 Jones, Chris. "Edinburgh, U.S.A." *AmTh.* 1996 May/June; 13(5): 22-23. Illus.: Photo. B&W. 4. Lang.: Eng.
USA. 1996. Historical studies. ■Recent growth of fringe festivals in the U.S. Structures of festivals, types of acts and productions featured, includes listing and dates of fringe festivals for the year. Includes information on the Orlando, San Francisco, and Seattle fringe festivals.

1041 Landau, David. "Interactive Theatre (A Closer Look)." *DGQ.* 1996 Sum; 33(2): 20-24. Lang.: Eng.
USA. 1996. Critical studies. ■Playwright David Landau, himself the author of an interactive show *Ghost of a Chance*, debates with himself as to whether or not this form of entertainment should be considered theatre.

1042 Lansfeld, Gilbert. "The *TheaterWeek* 100: The Most Powerful People in the Theater in the Year of the Diva." *TheaterW.* 1996 Aug 26; 10(4): 16-25. Illus.: Photo. B&W. 10. Lang.: Eng.
USA: New York, NY. 1996. Histories-sources. ■Listing of influential actors, producers, directors, designers, playwrights, composers, and theatres in the 1996 Broadway theatre season.

1043 Lecure, Bruce. "Acting: Physical Choices Make Characters Memorable." *SoTh.* 1996 Win; 37(1): 6-10. Illus.: Photo. B&W. Chart. 4. Lang.: Eng.
USA. 1970-1996. Critical studies. ■Discussion of physical centers and their variable traits as an aspect of characterization, illustrated with reference to popular film performers' flexibility in manipulating their physical centers, ranging from Dustin Hoffman (flexible) to Kevin Costner (inflexible).

1044 Loney, Glenn. "Fabulous Invalid Rallies: Broadway, 1995-96." *NTQ.* 1996 Nov.; 12(48): 387-390. [*NTQ* Reports and Announcements.] Lang.: Eng.
USA: New York, NY. 1995-1996. Critical studies. ■Comprehensive survey of Broadway and Off Broadway plays, musicals, and solo performances reveals a marked improvement in range and quality in productions, albeit many of them limited to short runs, and without much encouragement to the experimental theatre.

1045 Martin, Jennifer. "The Period Movement Score: Embodying Style in Training and Performance." *TTop.* 1996 Mar.; 6(1): 31-41. Notes. Biblio. Illus.: Photo. B&W. 1. Lang.: Eng.

THEATRE IN GENERAL: —Performance/production

USA. 1996. Critical studies. ■The research and preparation of a period movement score, with emphasis on use by actors in rehearsal and as a framework in developing its character.

1046 McCain, Susan. "Anna Strasberg: Exploring the Real Method." *SoTh*. 1996 Sum; 37(3): 20. Illus.: Photo. B&W. 1. Lang.: Eng.
USA. 1995. Historical studies. ■A report on a seminar in which Lee Strasberg's widow, Anna, sought to clarify 'the Method' as taught by her husband, focusing on common misconceptions.

1047 McCauley, Robbie. "Thoughts on My Career, *The Other Weapon*, and Other Projects." 265-282 in Diamond, Elin, ed. *Performance and Cultural Politics*. London/New York, NY: Routledge; 1996. 282 pp. Notes. Index. Illus.: Photo. 2. Lang.: Eng.
USA. 1990-1995. Histories-sources. ■Performer Robbie McCauley on her career in performance and her current work in *The Other Weapon*.

1048 Meyer, Petra Maria. "Ästhetik des Gegenwartstheaters im technischen Zeitalter." (The Aesthetics of Contemporary Theatre in the Techological Age.) *FMT*. 1996; 1: 3-14. Notes. Lang.: Ger.
USA: New York, NY. 1990-1996. Critical studies. ■The use of television and computers in theatrical production: the artistic and theoretical relevance of the Wooster Group's *Fish Story*.

1049 Moore, Dick. "Joint Subcommittee Formed to Study Smoke and Fog." *EN*. 1996 Jan/Feb.; 81(1): 1. Lang.: Eng.
USA: New York, NY. 1996. Historical studies. ■Committee formed to address concerns about the adverse effects on performers of exposure to stage smoke and fog.

1050 Moore, Dick. "Women's Health Initiative Set to Launch with 'Nothing Like a Dame' on February 25." *EN*. 1996 Jan/Feb.; 81 (1): 1. Lang.: Eng.
USA: New York, NY. 1996. Historical studies. ■Broadway Cares/Equity Fights AIDS, the Herrick Foundation, and the Actors' Fund of America presents *Nothing Like a Dame*, directed by Susan Shulman, a celebration of women in theatre to launch the Phyllis Newman Women's Health Initiative of the Actors' Fund.

1051 Moore, Dick. "Theatre Hall of Fame Celebrates 25th Anniversary." *EN*. 1996 Jan/Feb.; 81(1): 2. Lang.: Eng.
USA: New York, NY. 1971-1996. Historical studies. ■The Theatre Hall of Fame, located in Broadway's Gershwin Theatre, celebrates its 25th anniversary.

1052 Moore, Dick. "Ninth Annual Broadway Cares/Equity Fights AIDS Holiday Appeal Raises $1,723,000." *EN*. 1996 Jan/Feb.; 81 (1): 4-5. Illus.: Photo. 3. Lang.: Eng.
USA: New York, NY. 1987-1996. Historical studies. ■Coverage of the 1995 fundraising year for Broadway Cares/Equity Fights AIDS, a nationwide effort to raise funds to care for Broadway's AIDS crisis.

1053 Moore, Dick. "NTCP Updates Artist Files." *EN*. 1996 June; 81(5): 8. Lang.: Eng.
USA: New York, NY. 1996. Historical studies. ■Call for actors to enroll in the Non-Traditional Casting Project's Artist Files/Artist Files Online, a national talent bank of artists of color, and artists who are disabled.

1054 Moore, Dick. "Derwent Awards Go to Santiago-Hudson, Hamilton." *EN*. 1996 June; 81(5): 1. Illus.: Photo. 2. Lang.: Eng.
USA: New York, NY. 1996. Historical studies. ■Ruben Santiago-Hudson and Lisa Gay Hamilton win the 51st annual Clarence Derwent Awards honoring the most promising male and female performers on the metropolitan scene.

1055 Moore, Dick. "Non-Traditional Casting Makes Strides." *EN*. 1996 Sep.; 81(7): 2. Illus.: Photo. 2. Lang.: Eng.
USA: New York, NY. 1996. Historical studies. ■Recent success stories in nontraditional casting in American theatres.

1056 Moore, Dick. "A Tale of Two Roles: Equity Member in Bid for Congressional Seat." *EN*. 1996 Dec.; 81(10): 11. Illus.: Photo. 1. Lang.: Eng.
USA: Orlando, FL. 1996. Historical studies. ■Actor Al Krulick, while appearing in *The Hunchback of Notre Dame* at Disney/MGM Studios, runs as a candidate for Congress from the 8th District in Orlando.

1057 Nachman, Gerald. "Broadway's Runaway Babies." *TheaterW*. 1996 June 3; 9(44): 66-68. Lang.: Eng.
USA: New York, NY. 1996. Historical studies. ■Stars who abandoned performing on Broadway for film and television. Focus on Julie Andrews, Barbra Streisand, and Liza Minnelli.

1058 Napoleon, Davi. "Teaching Actors to Fight." *TheaterW*. 1996 Feb 19; 9(29): 28-32. Illus.: Photo. B&W. 1. Lang.: Eng.
USA. 1996. Historical studies. ■Methods of teaching stage combat to actors at various universities in the US. Methods of approach, safety concerns, advantages for actors who train in it.

1059 Peterson, Deborah C. *Fredric March: Craftsman First, Star Second*. Westport, CT/London: Greenwood; 1996. 296 pp. (Contributions in Drama and Theatre Studies 65.) Biblio. Index. Append. Illus.: Photo. B&W. 5. Lang.: Eng.
USA. 1897-1975. Biographies. ■Biography of stage and film star Fredric March. Includes appendices with breakdowns of every play in which he appeared, his radio and television work, and his film work. Concentrates on his performance career and his emphasis on the craft of acting.

1060 Portantiere, Michael. "Jeff Trachta: From Seminary to Soaps to *Grease*." *TheaterW*. 1996 Feb 19; 9(29): 52-55. Illus.: Photo. B&W. 2. Lang.: Eng.
USA: New York, NY. 1994-1996. Histories-sources. ■Interview with actor Trachta discussing past roles, his career in soap operas, and current lead role in the Broadway musical *Grease*.

1061 Pourchot, Eric. "After Ceausescu: A Discussion of Romanian Arts Issues at the New York Public Library for the Performing Arts." *SEEP*. 1996 Spr; 16(2): 44-49. Notes. Lang.: Eng.
USA: New York, NY. Romania. 1989-1996. Historical studies. ■The discussion included prominent Romanians from the performing arts, including directors Liviu Ciulei and Andrei Serban, and addressed decreased government funding and the impact on the arts of the fall of the Ceauşescu government.

1062 Rea, Charlotte. "Women for Women." 31-41 in Martin, Carol, ed. *A Sourcebook of Feminist Theatre and Performance: On and Beyond the Stage*. London/New York, NY: Routledge; 1996. 311 pp. Notes. Index. Lang.: Eng.
USA. 1960-1975. Critical studies. ■1979 essay on women's theatre and the American women's movement, with discussion of the work of It's All Right To Be a Woman Theatre (Sue Perlgut), Women's Unit and Womanrite Theatre (Roberta Sklar), and the New York Feminist Theatre (Lucy Winer and Claudette Charbonneau).

1063 Roach, Joseph. "Kinship, Intelligence, and Memory as Improvisation: Culture and Performance in New Orleans." 217-236 in Diamond, Elin, ed. *Performance and Cultural Politics*. London/New York, NY: Routledge; 1996. 282 pp. Notes. Index. Illus.: Photo. 3. Lang.: Eng.
USA: New Orleans, LA. 1874-1995. Critical studies. ■Examines the rites and secular rituals of a performance-saturated interculture.

1064 Robinson, Amy. "Forms of Appearance of Value: Homer Plessy and the Politics of Privacy." 237-261 in Diamond, Elin, ed. *Performance and Cultural Politics*. London/New York, NY: Routledge; 1996. 282 pp. Notes. Index. Lang.: Eng.
USA: New Orleans, LA. 1896. Critical studies. ■The historical performance of racial 'passing,' as cultural performance. Author examines the case of Homer Plessy, a black man whose 'performance' as a white subject instigated 'separate but equal' provisions into American law.

1065 Rogoff, Gordon. "The Presence of Joe." *AmTh*. 1996 Nov.; 13(9): 16-20, 76. Illus.: Photo. B&W. 5. Lang.: Eng.
USA: New York, NY. 1969-1996. Biographical studies. ■Life and career of director/performer/author/teacher Joe Chaikin. Work with the Open Theatre, current and future projects. Includes sidebar article by Shawn-Marie Garrett on upcoming productions of *1969 Terminal 1996*, a re-working of the piece *Terminal* by Susan Yankowitz, originally developed with the Open Theatre. Also includes excerpt from revised script, and list of upcoming production work by Chaikin.

1066 Schachenmayr, Volker. "Thinking Originally." *TheatreF*. 1996 Win/Spr; 8: 73-74. Illus.: Dwg. 2. Lang.: Eng.

CLASSED ENTRIES

THEATRE IN GENERAL: —Performance/production

USA. 1995-1996. Histories-sources. ■Author discusses his collaboration with Laura Farabough on *Real Original Thinker* performed at Stanford University.

1067 Seeds, Dale E. "Trickster by Trade: Thomas Riccio on Indigenous Theatre." *TDR.* 1996 Win; 40(4): 118-133. Notes. Illus.: Photo. B&W. 11. Lang.: Eng.
USA. 1988-1996. Histories-sources. ■Interview with theatre artist Riccio on indigenous traditions, work with native peoples around the world, and adopting their traditions and voice into performance texts.

1068 Shank, Theodore. "George Coates Interviewed by His (Virtual) Audience." *TheatreF.* 1996 Sum/Fall; 9: 26-34. Illus.: Photo. 14. Lang.: Eng.
USA: San Francisco, CA. 1996. Histories-sources. ■Interactive Internet interview with George Coates on his latest stage production *Twisted Pairs*, a performance piece about the Internet. The production is continued on a web site, constructed so that audiences can continue the interactive performance experience. Coates speaks about the on-line future of theatre.

1069 Simons, Tad. "Wendy Knox." *AmTh.* 1996 Sep.; 13(7): 52-53. Illus.: Photo. B&W. 1. Lang.: Eng.
USA: Minneapolis, MN. 1996. Critical studies. ■Artistic director of the Frank Theatre discusses her vision for the theatre, productions, and her approach to directing.

1070 Sisley, Emily L. "Notes on Lesbian Theatre." 52-60 in Martin, Carol, ed. *A Sourcebook of Feminist Theatre and Performance: On and Beyond the Stage.* London/New York, NY: Routledge; 1996. 311 pp. Notes. Index. Lang.: Eng.
USA. 1970-1975. Historical studies. ■1981 essay on the place of lesbian theatre within the feminist theatre movement.

1071 Solomon, Alisa. "The WOW Cafe." 42-51 in Martin, Carol, ed. *A Sourcebook of Feminist Theatre and Performance: On and Beyond the Stage.* London/New York, NY: Routledge; 1996. 311 pp. Notes. Index. Lang.: Eng.
USA: New York, NY. 1980-1985. Critical studies. ■1985 essay on performance at WOW Cafe, a feminist performance space where Split Britches and Holly Hughes were first seen. Discusses the development of an aesthetics involving gay performance that ran counterculture to prevailing feminist culture.

1072 Swarbrick, Carol. "Curtain Up on Actors' Equity—Part III." *EN.* 1996 June; 81(5): 6. Illus.: Photo. 1. Lang.: Eng.
USA: New York, NY. 1919. Historical studies. ■Third in a series on the actors' strike of 1919 and Equity's fight for recognition. Includes accounts of various actors, playwrights, and producers supporting Equity, such as Ethel Barrymore appearing as the spirit of Equity in a benefit to support the Equity Strike Fund. Continued in *EN* 81:6 (1996 July/Aug), p. 6, with details on the strike and its resolution: Equity's right to represent professional actors.

1073 Watt, Eva Hodges. "In Search of Antoinette Perry." *TheaterW.* 1996 June 3; 9(44): 42-52. Illus.: Photo. B&W. 3. Lang.: Eng.
USA: New York, NY. 1889-1996. Biographical studies. ■Biography of actress and director Antoinette Perry, namesake of Broadway's Tony Awards. Her roles, personal life, productions directed, and her involvement in Stage Door Canteens during World War II.

1074 Wolf, Stacy. "The Queer Performances of Mary Martin as Woman and as Star." *WPerf.* 1996; 8(2): 225-239. Notes. Biblio. [Issue 16.] Lang.: Eng.
USA. 1922-1994. Critical studies. ■Argues that Martin deployed discourses of womanhood and stardom to produce a category of 'queer white wealthy theatrical womanhood,' as gendered performance.

1075 Wolford, Lisa. "Ta'wil of Action: the New World Performance Laboratory's Persian Cycle." *NTQ.* 1996; 12(46): 156-176. Notes. Illus.: Dwg. B&W. 7. Lang.: Eng.
USA: Cleveland, OH. 1987-1995. Historical studies. ■This experimental theatre company, founded in 1992 by artists who collaborated in Grotowski's Objective Drama Program, investigates traditional performance techniques of various cultures. Its Iranian director Massoud Saidpour uses Sufi teaching stories for presentation by a multi-cultural ensemble.

1076 Beniaminov, Aleksand'r D. *Artist bez grima: Vospominanija.* (Artist without Make-Up: Notes.) St. Petersburg: Chudožestvennaja literatura; 1996. 304 pp.. Lang.: Rus.
USSR: Leningrad. 1937-1969. Histories-sources. ■The author's work as an actor with Leningrad Comedy Theatre.

1077 Smyšljaev, Valentin S. *Pečal'no i nechorošo v našem teatre ... (Dnevnik 1927-1931 gg.).* (It's Sad and Not So Good in Our Theatre: Journal, 1927-1931.) Moscow: Intergraf Servis; 1996. 320 pp. Lang.: Rus.
USSR: Moscow. 1927-1931. Histories-sources. ■Actor and director V.S. Smyšljaev recalls his colleagues in Moscow theatre: actors and directors Boris Afonin, Andrej Žilinskij, Ivan Bersenev, Michajl Čechov.

1078 Tumašov, M. "Muzyka tela." (Body Music.) *TeatZ.* 1996; 5: 34-36. Lang.: Rus.
Uzbekistan: Tashkent. 1996. Historical studies. ■History of the Russian school of acting and the problems of actor's technique.

1079 Knežević, Dubravka. "Marked with Red Ink." *TJ.* 1996 Dec.; 48(4): 407-418. Notes. Biblio. Illus.: Photo. 1. Lang.: Eng.
Yugoslavia: Belgrade. 1978-1995. Historical studies. ■Political theatre activity in Belgrade featuring student activity, street theatre, and Dah Teatar, whose 'in the street' production *This Babylonian Confusion* blended political theatre, new performance techniques and songs.

1080 Riccio, Thomas. "In Zambia, Performing *The Spirits.*" *TheatreF.* 1996 Win/Spr; 8: 58-66. Biblio. Illus.: Photo. 7. Lang.: Eng.
Zambia. 1995-1996. Histories-sources. ■Author relates his experiences rehearsing, directing and performing *Imipashi (The Spirits)*, a puppet and mask performance piece created by the first national theatre project in Zambia, the Liitooma Project. *Imipashi* evolved from traditional myths and was given a four-week performance tour.

Plays/librettos/scripts

1081 Lazaridès, Alexandre. "Autour du mythe de Don Juan." (Of the Myth of Don Juan.) *JCT.* 1992; 63: 65-68. Notes. Lang.: Fre.
1630-1992. Critical studies. ■Functions of the myth of Don Juan, and their inscription and transformation in history from Tirso de Molina's *Burlador de Sevilla* to the present.

1082 Baxter, Virginia; Grant, Clare. "Talking Back: A Conversation." *AFS.* 1995 Fall; 21: 153-169. Notes. Illus.: Photo. B&W. 1. Lang.: Eng.
Australia. 1978-1995. Histories-sources. ■In a staged conversation at the International Women Playwrights Conference, performer/playwrights speak about their work and work of other women currently writing for *Performance and Performance Art* of Australia.

1083 Bobis, Merlinda; Cathcart, Sarah; Lemon, Andrea; Mills, June. "New Storytellers." *AFS.* 1995 Fall; 21: 39-54. Illus.: Photo. B&W. 2. Lang.: Eng.
Australia. USA. Philippines. 1981-1995. Histories-sources. ■Story-tellers at the International Women Playwrights Conference discuss their working processes, performance techniques, cultural influences on their work and their source material.

1084 Brand, Mona; O'Loughlin, Iris, ed. "Four Australian Women Playwrights." *AFS.* 1995 Fall; 21: 129-151. Illus.: Photo. B&W. 1. Lang.: Eng.
Australia. 1930-1970. Histories-sources. ■Dialogue between Brand and O'Loughlin at International Women Playwrights Conference discussing the lives and work of playwrights Betty Roland (*Vote 'No!'*), Oriel Gray (*The Torrents*), Nancy McMillan (Wills) (*Christmas Bridge* and *Here Under Heaven*). Includes excerpts from all plays.

1085 Glass, Jodie; Robertson, Matra; Chang, John, transl.; Nicholls, Christine Napurrurla, transl. "Ritual and the Body." *AFS.* 1995 Fall; 21: 13-20. Illus.: Photo. B&W. 2. Lang.: Eng.
Australia. Korea. 1970-1995. Histories-sources. ■Transcript of Glass's interview with Jeannie Nungarrayi Herbert, an Australian Aboriginal story-teller and visual artist, and Robertson's interview with Korean shaman Kim Kum hwa.

THEATRE IN GENERAL: —Plays/librettos/scripts

1086 Holledge, Julie; Tait, Peta. "Introduction." *AFS.* 1995 Fall; 21: 3-10. Illus.: Photo. B&W. 2. [Special issue: Third International Women Playwrights Conference.] Lang.: Eng.

Australia. 1995. Historical studies. ■Describes theme of conference: the relationship between traditional women's ritual or storytelling and contemporary women's performance. Combined elements of a theatre conference and an international performance festival. Lists countries represented, papers presented, conference activities.

1087 Belzil, Patricia. "Le Théâtre des Vampires." (Theatre of Vampires.) *JCT.* 1996; 80: 207-210. Illus.: Photo. B&W. 4. Lang.: Fre.

Canada. 1996. Critical studies. ■The absence of a theatrical horror genre, and the potential interest of horror themes, especially vampires.

1088 Mailhot, Laurent. "Ironie et humour dans la tradition théâtrale canadienne-française." (Irony and Humor in the French-Canadian Theatrical Tradition.) *JCT.* 1990; 55: 72-78. Notes. Illus.: Photo. B&W. 3. Lang.: Fre.

Canada. 1606-1990. Historical studies. ■Forms and formats of humor in French-Canadian and Quebecois theatrical practice.

1089 Nadeau, Carole. "'Chaos K.O. Chaos': Témoignage." ('Chaos K.O. Chaos': Witness.) *JCT.* 1992; 64: 102-105. Notes. Illus.: Photo. B&W. 1. Lang.: Fre.

Canada: Quebec, PQ. 1992. Histories-sources. ■Carole Nadeau identifies influences of Samuel Beckett in creation of her one-woman show *Chaos K.O. Chaos.*

1090 Raynauld, Isabelle. "Raymond Villeneuve: Des voix dans l'espace." (Raymond Villeneuve: Voices in Space.) *JCT.* 1991; 61: 39-41. Notes. Illus.: Photo. B&W. 2. Lang.: Fre.

Canada: Montreal, PQ. 1987-1991. Bibliographical studies. ■Raymond Villeneuve's radio and theatre scripts, such as *Jasmin, le héros* (*Jasmin the Hero*) and *Squat*, portray ruptured relations and dysfunctional communication.

1091 Ronfard, Jean-Pierre. "En Contrepoint." (In Counterpoint.) *JCT.* 1990; 54: 123-125. Illus.: Photo. B&W. 2. Lang.: Fre.

Canada: Montreal, PQ. 1970-1990. Historical studies. ■Observations on homosexuality in Quebec theatre.

1092 Vaïs, Michel. "L'édition théâtrale: Une année de remous." (Theatrical Publications: An Eventful Year.) *JCT.* 1991; 61: 89-93. Notes. Illus.: Photo. B&W. 8. Lang.: Fre.

Canada. 1990-1991. Historical studies. ■Current state of publication of playtexts and essays on theatre in Quebec.

1093 Leslie, Robert W. "Sienese Fools, Comic Captains, and Every Fop in His Humor." 146-169 in Davidson, Clifford, ed. *Fools and Folly.* Kalamazoo, MI: Medieval Institute Publications; 1996. 176 pp. (Early Drama, Art, and Music Monograph Series 22.) Notes. Lang.: Eng.

England. Italy. 1465-1601. Historical studies. ■Comparative study of the Sienese fool of early Italian burlesque and *commedia* and the fools of Ben Jonson's 'humors' plays. Focus on Antonfrancesco Grazzini's *La strega* (*The Witch*) and Jonson's *Every Man in His Humor.*

1094 Davidson, Clifford, ed. *Fools and Folly.* Kalamazoo, MI: Medieval Institute Publications; 1996. 176 pp. (Early Drama, Art, and Music Monograph Series 22.) Notes. Index. Append. Illus.: Dwg. Sketches. 12. Lang.: Eng.

Europe. 1047-1673. Historical studies. ■Collection of essays on the representation and symbolism of the fool character in literature and myth in the Middle Ages.

1095 Greene, Thomas M. "Ritual and Text in the Renaissance." 17-34 in Hart, Jonathan, ed. *Reading the Renaissance: Culture, Poetics, and Drama.* New York, NY/London: Garland; 1996. 290 pp. (Garland Studies in the Renaissance.) Notes. Biblio. Index. Lang.: Eng.

Europe. 1500-1600. Critical studies. ■The changing status of the symbolic act of ceremony and ritual, and the effects of this change on literary texts in the Renaissance. Author discusses a wide variety of rituals and ceremonies from liturgical masses to festivals, royal entries and processions, and court masques.

1096 Billington, Sandra. "The *Cheval fol* of Lyon and Other Asses." 9-33 in Davidson, Clifford, ed. *Fools and Folly.* Kalamazoo, MI: Medieval Institute Publications; 1996. 176 pp.

(Early Drama, Art, and Music Monograph Series 22.) Notes. Lang.: Eng.

France: Lyon. 1436-1547. Historical studies. ■The symbolism of the ass in plays, poetry, pageants and festivals of the Middle Ages and the inversion which, in Lyon, especially during the festival of *cheval fol*, asserts the folly of pretensions of the proud.

1097 Sadowska-Guillon, Irène. "Splendeurs et misères de l'édition du texte de théâtre." (Splendors and Miseries of Publishing Theatrical Texts.) *JCT.* 1991; 61: 94-101. Notes. Illus.: Photo. B&W. 9. Lang.: Fre.

France. 1949-1991. Historical studies. ■Recent history of publication of plays and theatre essays, especially in the bimonthly *L'Avant-Scène* and by Actes Sud.

1098 Hafner, Dorinda; Subasinghe, Somalatha; Tur, Mona Ngitji Ngitji. "Traditional Storytellers." *AFS.* 1995 Fall; 21: 33-38. Lang.: Eng.

Ghana. Australia. Sri Lanka. 1988-1995. Histories-sources. ■Excerpts from authors' presentations at the International Women Playwrights Conference in which they discuss story-telling traditions of their native countries and personal and cultural influences on their work.

1099 Chang, Lan-joo. "Minjokuk, ku Pyounhwalongwa Aproue Panghangeun." (The National Theatre, on Its Development and New Direction.) *KTR.* 1996 Mar.; 21(3): 22-24. Illus.: Photo. B&W. 3. Lang.: Kor.

Korea: Seoul. 1987-1996. Critical studies. ■Change of focus from ideological to individual issues in contemporary theatre of the nation. Also shifts in methods of acting, technical approaches due to change in performance spaces from outdoor to indoor theatre.

1100 Bramsjö, Henrik. "Marina Tsvetajeva, ogripbar och i rörelse." (Marina Cvetajeva, Intangible and in Movement.) *Dramat.* 1996; 4(4): 50-51. Illus.: Photo. B&W. Lang.: Swe.

Russia. 1892-1941. Historical studies. ■A short survey of the Russian poet Marina Cvetajeva and her life.

1101 Blumberg, Marcia. "Re-Evaluating Otherness, Building for Difference: South African Theatre Beyond the Interregnum." *SATJ.* 1995 Sep.; 9(2): 27-37. Biblio. Lang.: Eng.

South Africa, Republic of. 1991-1995. Critical studies. ■Reassessment of the contexts and theatrical texts of South Africa beyond the interregnum, with regard to the traditionally devalued of a society, emphasizing women in theatre, with a comparison of Fatima Dike's 1991 play *So What's New* with her 1995 *Street Walking and Company Valet Services.*

1102 Jenkins, Ron. "Ridere del razzismo in Sud Africa." (Laughing at Racism in South Africa.) *TeatroS.* 1996; 11(18): 335-358 . Lang.: Ita.

South Africa, Republic of. 1980-1990. Critical studies. ■The most popular comedies of the South African theatre of the 80s and 90s use laughter in the struggle against apartheid, to show racism's hypocrisies and to ask for real social change.

1103 Borup, Niels. "Broget og gyldent." (Variegated and Golden.) *TE.* 1996 Feb.; 77: 10-11. Lang.: Dan.

UK-England. Germany. Slovakia. 1996. Histories-sources. ■Impressions from a trip through the European theatre landscape. Includes brief mentions of *Taking Sides* by Ronald Harwood and *Das Dritte Rom* by Alexander Sepljarskij.

1104 Kempinski, Tom. "Creative & Interpretive Artists—the End of a Myth." *PlPl.* 1996 Aug/Sep.: 28-30. Illus.: Photo. B&W. 1. Lang.: Eng.

UK-England. 1996. Histories-sources. ■Playwright Tom Kempinski on the distinction between the creative and interpretive artist, with reference to his *Duet for One.*

1105 Levy, Deborah; Lipkin, Joan. "Identity, Sexuality and the Body." *AFS.* 1995 Fall; 21: 115-125. Notes. Illus.: Photo. B&W. 1. Lang.: Eng.

UK-England. USA. 1959-1995. Histories-sources. ■Excerpts from authors' papers presented at International Women Playwrights Conference: construction of identity in the work of playwrights and the perceptions of their audiences, representations of sex and sexuality. Discusses Levy's play *The B-File—An Erotic Interrogation of Five Female Personas.*

THEATRE IN GENERAL: —Plays/librettos/scripts

1106 Tanitch, Robert. "Beauty And The Beast." *PlPl*. 1996 Aug/
Sep.: 31. Lang.: Eng.
UK-England. 1945-1996. Critical studies. ∎The evolution of the Beast
character in four versions of *Beauty and the Beast*, including Cocteau's
La Belle et la Bête, a stage version by Nicholas Stuart Gray, and Disney's
cartoon and live musical versions.

1107 Tanitch, Robert. "Othello Black or White?" *PlPl*. 1996 Apr.:
31. Illus.: Photo. B&W. 1. Lang.: Eng.
UK-England. 1956-1996. Critical studies. ∎Debate over the casting of a
white or Black actor in the role of Othello. References to Laurence Fish-
burne in the film version of *Othello* and to the Old Vic's 1956 production
starring John Neville and Richard Burton.

1108 Safronova, L.A. *Starinnyj ukrainskij teat'r.* (Ancient Ukrainian Theatre.) Moscow: Rossijskaja politiceska i
énciklopedija; 1996. 352 pp. Lang.: Rus.
Ukraine. 1600-1799. Histories-specific. ∎Early Ukrainian theatre.

1109 Boney, Bradley. "The Lavender Brick Road: Paul Bonin-
Rodriguez and the Sissy Bo(d)y." *TJ*. 1996 Mar.; 48(1):
35-58. Notes. Biblio. Illus.: Photo. 3. Lang.: Eng.
USA. 1992-1994. Critical studies. ∎Critical essay on the 'dandy,' used as
a theatrical signifier for homosexuality in English-language plays
throughout the late nineteenth century and most of the twentieth century.
Queer and performance theories are used to examine the production of
the body in this context through the work of playwright/performer Paul
Bonin-Rodriguez including *Talk of the Town* (1992), *The Bible Belt and
Other Accessories* (1993), and *Love in the Time of College* (1994).

1110 DeDanan, Mary. "Sean San Jose Blackman." *AmTh*. 1996
Dec.; 13(10): 40-41. Illus.: Photo. B&W. 1. Lang.: Eng.
USA: San Francisco, CA. 1996. Historical studies. ∎Blackman's organization of the fundraising project *Pieces of the Quilt*, a collection of seventeen short plays about AIDS by established playwrights, that will tour
to various theatres with all proceeds donated to AIDS service organizations.

1111 Horwitz, Simi. "A Midsummer Playwright's Dream." *The-
aterW*. 1996 July 29; 9(52): 36-39. Illus.: Photo. B&W. 1.
Lang.: Eng.
USA: Poughkeepsie, NY. 1996. Historical studies. ∎Producer Peter
Manning of New York Stage and Film (in residence at Vassar College's
Powerhouse Theatre) discusses the company's mission of developing the
playwright and new works, and productions planned for current season.

1112 Miller, Jim. "Workers' Theatre and the 'War of Position' in
the 1930s." *MD*. 1996 Fall; 39(3): 421-435. Notes. Lang.:
Eng.
USA. 1929-1995. Historical studies. ∎Historical context of workers'
drama and evaluation of *Art as a Weapon* and *Newsboy* by Workers Laboratory Theatre, *15-Minute Red Revue* by John Bonn, and *Waiting for
Lefty* by Clifford Odets, arguing that *Newsboy* was most effective and
popular of the group.

1113 Rose, Brian A. *'Jekyll and Hyde' Adapted: Dramatizations of
Cultural Anxiety.* Westport, CT/London: Greenwood; 1996.
176 pp. (Contributions in Drama and Theatre Studies 66.)
Pref. Index. Biblio. Lang.: Eng.
USA. 1887-1990. Critical studies. ∎Using Robert Louis Stevenson's *The
Strange Case of Dr. Jekyll and Mr. Hyde* as an archetype, investigates
how ideas derived from adaptations of specific narrative sources create
motifs, and how these motifs assume importance in popular culture.
Examines adaptations of Stevenson's story from early theatrical endeav-
ors to films.

1114 Wein, Glenn. "The Writing on the Wall About Interactive
Theatre." *DGQ*. 1996 Sum; 33(2): 15-19. Illus.: Photo.
B&W. 1. Lang.: Eng.
USA: New York, NY. 1996. Histories-sources. ∎*Grandma Sylvia's
Funeral* co-creator Glenn Wein (with Amy Lord Blumensack) searches
for categorization for this interactive show, which is often compared to
Tony 'n' Tina's Wedding.

1115 Proskurnikova, Tatiana. "Le Théâtre soviétique en temps de
transition." (Soviet Theatre in Time of Transition.) *JCT*.
1991; 58: 71-76. Illus.: Photo. B&W. 2. Lang.: Fre.
USSR. 1960-1991. Historical studies. ∎Discovery of new source material
for Soviet theatre repertoire following political changes in USSR.

Reference materials

1116 Darvay Nagy, Adrienne. "WECT-Europe—A Kortárs
Színházi Világenciklopédia első kötetéről."
(WECT-Europe—First Volume of *World Encyclopedia of
Contemporary Theatre.*) *Sz*. 1996; 29(10): 36-38. Illus.:
Photo. B&W. 1. Lang.: Hun.
1945-1990. Critical studies. ∎Presenting the first volume of *WECT* published by several international theatre organizations and concerned with
world theatre after the second World War. In reviewing this volume centered on Europe, the author highlights the aspects related to Hungary.

1117 Patterson, Michael. *German Theatre: A Bibliography from
the Beginning to 1995.* Leicester: Motley P; 1996. 887 pp.
Biblio. Lang.: Eng.
1200-1995. ∎Bibliography of works on German-language theatre
throughout the world.

1118 Pottie, Lisa M.; Cameron, Rebecca; Costello, Charles.
"Modern Drama Studies: An Annual Bibliography." *MD*.
1996 Sum; 39 (2): 247-330. Lang.: Eng.
1995. Historical studies. ∎International bibliography of current scholarship, criticism and commentary in theatre from April 1995-March 1996.
Includes list of journals indexed with acronyms.

1119 Müller, Wiebke, ed. *Performing Arts Yearbook for Europe
97.* London: Arts Publishing International; 1996. 696 pp.
Pref. Index. [7th ed.] Lang.: Eng.
Europe. 1996-1997. Histories-sources. ∎Focuses on major and medium-
sized professional companies, with selected notable small subsidized and
young people's or children's theatre companies. Adds organizations, festivals, venues, promoters, agents, media, competitions, publications,
training, and services. Includes e-mail and world wide web addresses.

1120 Schumacher, Claude. *Naturalism and Symbolism in Euro-
pean Theatre: 1850-1918.* London/New York, NY: Cam-
bridge UP; 1996. 531 pp. (Theatre in Europe: A
Documentary History.) Notes. Index. Biblio. Pref. Illus.:
Photo. 67. Lang.: Eng.
Europe. 1850-1918. Histories-specific. ∎Primary source documents in
English on theatre in France, Germany, Russia, Scandinavia, England,
Italy, and Spain. Primarily concerned with actors and acting, dramatic
theory and criticism, theatre architecture, stage censorship, settings, cos-
tumes, and audiences.

1121 Söderberg, Olle. "Publikationskommissionen i Györ." (The
Commission of Publications at Györ.) *ProScen*. 1996 ; 20(4):
33-35. Illus.: Photo. Color. Lang.: Swe.
Hungary: Györ. 1996. Historical studies. ∎A report from OISTAT's
meeting about the plans for an expanded version of the dictionary *New
Theatre Words* with many more languages, to be published in four parts.

1122 Székely, György. "Német színjátszás Pest-Budán: 'Hedvig
Belitska-Scholtz-Olga Somorjai: Deutsche Theater in Pest
und Ofen, 1770-1850', Band 1-2." (German Theatre in Pest-
Buda: *Deutsche Theater in Pest und Ofen, 1770-1850, Band
1-2* by Hedvig Belitska-Scholtz and Olga Somorjai.) *SzSz*.
1996; 30/31: 250-251. Lang.: Hun.
Hungary. Germany. 1770-1850. Critical studies. ∎Review of the
catalogue (Budapest: Argumentum, 1995, 1300 pp) which includes data
on 7200 performances over eighty seasons.

1123 *Il Patalogo diciannove. Annuario 1996 dello spettacolo.
Teatro.* (The Patalogo 19: 1996 Entertainment Yearbook.
Theatre.) Milan: Ubulibri; 1996. 244 pp. Illus.: Photo. B&W.
Lang.: Ita.
Italy. 1996. Histories-sources. ∎1996 yearbook of the Italian theatre with
brief critical notations.

1124 Vigeant, Louise. "Les mots de l'humour." (Words about
Humour.) *JCT*. 1990; 55: 120-125. Illus.: Photo. B&W. 14.
Lang.: Fre.
North America. Europe. 1990. Instructional materials. ∎Twenty-five
word lexicon of vocabulary relating to comedic devices and forms.

1125 Lukan, Blaž. *Gledališki pojmovnik za mlade.* (The Theatre
Glossary for Young People.) Šentilj: Aristej; 1996. 109 pp.
Index. Biblio. Gloss. Illus.: Photo. Dwg. Color. B&W. Lang.:
Slo.

CLASSED ENTRIES

THEATRE IN GENERAL: —Reference materials

Slovenia. 1996. ■An introduction to theatre, performance, acting and stage technology for young people, including a short history of theatre and a glossary of theatre terms.

1126 Vevar, Štefan; Kaufman, Mojca. *Slovenski gledališki letopis: 1994/1995.* (Slovene Theatre Annual: 1994/1995.) Ljubljana: SGFM; 1996. 291 pp. (8th expanded edition of the Repertoire of Slovene Theatres 1867/1967.) Pref. Index. Lang.: Slo.
Slovenia. 1994-1995. Histories-sources. ■A list of the dramatic, opera, ballet and puppet productions in Slovene professional and some non-professional theatres of the 1994/1995 season. Includes a bibliography (books, magazines, theatre, programs) of the Slovene press on the Slovene theatre, productions and drama.

1127 Barbour, Sheena, ed. *British Performing Arts Yearbook 1997.* London: Rhinegold; 1996. viii, 583 pp. Pref. Index. [10th ed.] Lang.: Eng.
UK. 1996-1997. Histories-sources. ■Concentrates on venues, with a large section for companies and solo performers (dance, drama, community, puppets, mixed entertainment, opera and music). Other sections cover support organizations, supplies, arts festivals and education.

1128 Blair, Samantha, ed. *British Theatre Directory 1996.* London: Richmond House; 1996. 632 pp. Pref. Index. Illus.: Photo. B&W. 4. [24th ed..] Lang.: Eng.
UK. 1995-1996. Histories-sources. ■Emphasizes venues, with additional sections for local authority entertainment facilities, production (managements, companies, festivals, community theatre, mime, children's, circus, and puppets), agents, media, publishing, bookshops, training and educations, organizations, suppliers and services.

1129 McGillivray, David, ed. *Theatre Guide 1996-1997.* London: Rebecca; 1996. 437 pp. Pref. Index. Illus.: Photo. B&W. 70. [Formerly *McGillivray's Theatre Guide* and *British Alternative Theatre Directory*.] Lang.: Eng.
UK. USA: New York, NY. 1996. ■Useful guide to non-mainstream theatre companies and solo performers, including comedy, variety, circus, mime and street entertainment. Also lists selected venues, rehearsal rooms, training, organizations, festivals, services, and supplies.

Relation to other fields

1130 Kay, Floraine; Levy, Jonathan. "The Use of the Drama in the Jesuit Schools, 1551-1773." *YTJ.* 1996; 10: 56-66. Biblio. Notes. Lang.: Eng.
1551-1773. Historical studies. ■On five hundred stages around the world, over 100,000 plays were presented, most written, directed, and designed by Jesuit lay teachers. Author argues that theatre was crucial to Jesuit education and that it was, and remains, of educational value.

1131 Collins, Darryl. "Emperors and Musume: China and Japan 'On the Boards' in Australia, 1850s-1920s." *EAH.* 1994 June; 7: 67-92. Illus.: Handbill. Photo. Dwg. Sketches. Poster. 27. Lang.: Eng.
Australia. 1850-1993. Historical studies. ■Asian presence on the Victorian and Edwardian stage in Australia: includes discussion of stereotypes, the influence of political events, Asian performers, companies, plays, and authors, with excerpts from some plays.

1132 Gillot, Venetia; Lyssiotis, Tes. "Identity and Displacement." *AFS.* 1995 Fall; 21: 105-113. Illus.: Photo. B&W. 1. Lang.: Eng.
Australia. 1979-1995. Histories-sources. ■Excerpts from authors' papers presented at International Women Playwrights Conference discussing, in a performance forum, cultural displacement for writers from immigrant cultures who are working in Australia.

1133 Jordan, Robert. "Convict Performances in a Penal Colony: New South Wales, 1789-1830." *ThR.* 1996; 21(1): 33-40. Notes. Lang.: Eng.
Australia. 1789-1830. Historical studies. ■The role of theatre in the process of normalization of New South Wales penal colony, exemplified by the Sydney Theatre (1796-1804) and Emu Plains convict theatre.

1134 Sharman, Jim. "In the Realm of the Imagination: An Individual View of Theatre." *ADS.* 1996 Apr.; 28: 20-29. [Inaugural Rex Cramphorn Memorial Lecture, Belvoir Street Theatre, Sydney, 23 July 1995.] Lang.: Eng.

Australia: Sydney. 1995. Histories-sources. ■The political and social state of theatre in Australia.

1135 Stamberg, Ursula. "Der Bedeutungswandel des National-theaterbegriffs für das deutschsprachige Theater in Prag." (The Changing Importance of the Term 'National Theatre' for the German-Language Theatre of Prague.) *KSGT.* 1996; YB: 203-217. Notes. Lang.: Ger.
Bohemia: Prague. 1783-1938. Historical studies. ■The different forms of German *Nationaltheater* in the various political configurations of the city and its relationship to the various nationalities represented there.

1136 Arbour, Rose Marie. "Jouer des yeux." (Acting with the Eyes.) *JCT.* 1996; 80: 169-171. Illus.: Photo. B&W. 1. Lang.: Fre.
Canada. USA. 1950-1996. Critical studies. ■How postmodernism challenges formal conventions of theatre as well as figurative art, with analysis of art installations as performance in which the spectator moves rather than remaining still. Includes discussion of media art and computer simulation, in which both artist and audience remain still before a screen.

1137 Beauchamp, Hélène. "Une si belle passion." (Such a Beautiful Passion.) *JCT.* 1992; 65: 67-74. Notes. Illus.: Photo. B&W. 2. Lang.: Fre.
Canada. 1989-1990. Empirical research. ■Profiles and motivations of adolescent students active in theatre, based on a survey, of students and teachers from twenty-two schools across Quebec.

1138 Beausoleil, Claude. "Lumière!" (Light!) *JCT.* 1989; 50: 222-223. Notes. Illus.: Photo. B&W. 1. Lang.: Fre.
Canada. 1989. Histories-sources. ■Poet Claude Beausoleil offers poetic vision of place of memory in theatre faced with uncertainty of future.

1139 Camerlain, Lorraine. "Un mouvement irréversible." (An Irreversible Movement.) *JCT.* 1992; 66: 9-12. Notes. Illus.: Photo. B&W. 3. Lang.: Fre.
Canada. 1980-1993. Historical studies. ■Changes in the position of women in theatre in Quebec between 1980 and 1993.

1140 Camerlain, Lorraine. "Réflexions sur le scandale." (Reflections on Scandal.) *JCT.* 1996; 80: 182-184. Illus.: Photo. B&W. 1. Lang.: Fre.
Canada. 1996. Critical studies. ■Moral overtones of word 'scandal' and dangers of its over-use in theatre criticism.

1141 David, Gilbert. "L'Infini de la mémoire." (Infinity of Memory.) *JCT.* 1989; 50: 228-231. Illus.: Dwg. Photo. B&W. 3. Lang.: Fre.
Canada. 1989. Critical studies. ■Accumulation of collective memory in and about Quebecois theatre.

1142 Denis, Jean-Luc. "L'Ère du quant-à-soi." (The Era of Reserve.) *JCT.* 1989; 50: 137-138. Illus.: Dwg. 1. Lang.: Fre.
Canada. 1989. Critical studies. ■Argues prevailing modernist attitude is actually closed against truly innovative ideas and aesthetics.

1143 Féral, Josette. "Le Théâtre n'a pas de pouvoir, c'est là sa force." (The Theatre Has No Power, That Is Its Strength.) *JCT.* 1989; 50: 86-88. Illus.: Photo. B&W. 1. Lang.: Fre.
Canada. 1989. Critical studies. ■Argues that lack of social influence of theatre liberates it from socioeconomic constraints.

1144 Féral, Josette. "'Pouvoirs publics et politiques culturelles: enjeux nationaux'." (Public Powers and Cultural Policy: What Is at Stake.) *JCT.* 1992; 63: 95-101. Illus.: Dwg. 2. Lang.: Fre.
Canada: Montreal, PQ. 1991. Critical studies. ■The conference 'Pouvoirs publics et politiques culturelles', uniting representatives from several countries to discuss state cultural intervention and cultural policy, outlined problematics but not solutions. Outlines chief presentations of participants such as Jacques Rigaud and Michelle Rossignol.

1145 Fischer, Barbara. "A Cyclopean Evil Eye: On Performance, Gender and Photography." *CTR.* 1996 Spr; 86: 9-14. Illus.: Photo. B&W. 5. Lang.: Eng.
Canada. 1996. Critical studies. ■Discussion of the avant-garde representations of the human body in Michael Snow's pictorial *Venetian Blind* and Colette Whiten's sculpture *Casting No. 7, Structure No. 7.*

CLASSED ENTRIES

THEATRE IN GENERAL: —Relation to other fields

1146 Hundert, Debra. "Teacher Perceptions of the Value and Status of Drama in Education: A Study of One Ontario School Board." *YTJ*. 1996; 10: 25-35. Biblio. Append. Lang.: Eng.
Canada: St. Catharine's, ON. 1995-1996. Empirical research. ■Results of study that analyzes perceived differences between drama's educational value and status. Factors examined include gender, years (if any) of drama training, years of teaching, and aspects of drama's educational status. Includes statistical reports on study.

1147 Lapierre, Laurent. "La crise de l'art ou l'art de la crise?" (Crisis of Art or Art of Crisis?)*JCT*. 1996; 80: 33-36. Notes. Illus.: Photo. B&W. 3. Lang.: Fre.
Canada. USA.. 1966-1996. Critical studies. ■Importance and inevitability of crisis in performing arts.

1148 Latouche, Daniel. "Le Théâtre et la mémoire collective." (Theatre and Collective Memory.) *JCT*. 1989; 50: 206-207. Notes. Illus.: Photo. B&W. 1. Lang.: Fre.
Canada. 1989. Historical studies. ■Collective memory in Quebecois culture, and theatre in this memory.

1149 Lavoie, Pierre. "La Boîte à échos." (The Echo Box.) *JCT*. 1989; 50: 66-73. Notes. Illus.: Dwg. Photo. B&W. 6. Lang.: Fre.
Canada. 1970-1989. Historical studies. ■Tension between artists and political and religious powers in Quebec and elsewhere.

1150 Lazaridès, Alexandre. "Les hommes sauvages." (Savages.) *JCT*. 1996; 80: 185-190. Illus.: Dwg. Photo. B&W. 3. Lang.: Fre.
Canada. France. 1700-1996. Historical studies. ■Historic and contemporary functions of the theatre critic.

1151 Lizé, Claude. "Du théâtre au cégep: pour quoi faire?" (Theatre at the College: For What Purpose?)*JCT*. 1992; 65: 63-66. Notes. Illus.: Photo. B&W. 1. Lang.: Fre.
Canada: Rouyn, PQ. 1972-1992. Critical studies. ■Evolution of theatre education at the Abitibi-Témiscamingue CÉGEP (college) in Rouyn as reflection of changing ideologies and student priorities.

1152 Marier, Yves-Érick. "Le reflet s'attarde sous le pont." (The Reflection Lingers under the Bridge.) *JCT*. 1996; 80: 140-141. Illus.: Photo. B&W. 1. Lang.: Fre.
Canada: Quebec, PQ. 1950-1996. Histories-sources. ■Actor-teacher Yves-Érick Marier's concept of a social function for his theatre practice.

1153 Marois, Serge. "Les lectures-théâtre de l'Arrière-Scène." (The Theatre Lectures of Arrière-Scène.) *JCT*. 1992; 65: 90-92. Illus.: Photo. B&W. 1. Lang.: Fre.
Canada. 1972-1992. Historical studies. ■Profile of the school-touring company Arrière-Scène, its nontraditional productions, and its educational function as children's theatre moves away from didacticism.

1154 Noël, Lola; Camerlain, Lorraine. "Recherches de femmes." (Women's Research.) *JCT*. 1992; 66: 15-18. Notes. Illus.: Photo. B&W. 2. Lang.: Fre.
Canada. 1975-1993. Critical studies. ■Reconsiders articles from *JCT* 16 (1980), 'Théâtre-femmes' from a contemporary perspective.

1155 O'Sullivan, Dennis. "L'Expérimental au théâtre: Mutations d'une métaphore." (The Experimental in the Theatre: Mutations of a Metaphor.) *JCT*. 1989; 52: 73-80. Notes. Illus.: Photo. B&W. 5. Lang.: Fre.
Canada. France. 1880-1989. Historical studies. ■Changing nature of theatrical experimentation according to demands of social context.

1156 O'Sullivan, Dennis. "Le réveil d'Athéna." (Athena's Waking.) *JCT*. 1992; 66: 23-25. Illus.: Photo. B&W. 1. Lang.: Fre.
Canada. 1980-1993. Critical studies. ■Changes in the position of women in Québécois theatre since the publication of the 'Théâtre-femmes' issue, *JCT* 16 (1980).

1157 Smith, Mary Elizabeth. "On the Margins: Eastern Canadian Theatre as Post-Colonialist Discourse." *ThR*. 1996; 21(1): 41-51. Notes. Lang.: Eng.
Canada. 1860-1994. Historical studies. ■The interaction of national and regional cultural identities and their impact on theatre in Canada, principally during the period of Canadian Confederation, as seen in the formation of regional companies.

1158 Tompkins, Joanne. "Canadian Virtual Realities: Canadian Theatre and Australian Theatre Criticism." *ADS*. 1996 Oct.; 29: 4-6. Notes. Lang.: Eng.
Canada. Australia. 1996. Critical studies. ■Introduction to the special focus of this issue, Australian perspective of the Canadian theatrical identity.

1159 Vigeant, Louise. "Théâtre de la mémoire, mémoire du théâtre." (Theatre of Memory, Memory of Theatre.) *JCT*. 1989; 50: 200-205. Illus.: Photo. B&W. 4. Lang.: Fre.
Canada. 1989. Critical studies. ■Role of memory on perceptions of theatre artists, spectators and critics.

1160 Vigeant, Louise. "'Better if they think they are going to a farm': Entretien avec Melvin Charney." ('Better If They Think They Are Going to a Farm': Interview with Melvin Charney.) *JCT*. 1989; 50: 211-213. Illus.: Photo. B&W. 1. Lang.: Fre.
Canada. 1982-1989. Histories-sources. ■Interview with sculptor and architect Melvin Charney, with discussion of the theatrical nature of his works.

1161 Vigeant, Louise. "Au nom du plaisir et de l'intelligence: Pour une plus grande place du théâtre dans l'enseignement." (In the Name of Pleasure and Intelligence: For a Greater Place for Theatre in Teaching.) *JCT*. 1992; 65: 55-62. Notes. Illus.: Photo. B&W. 6. Lang.: Fre.
Canada. 1992. Critical studies. ■State of theatre education in Quebec's CÉGEPs (colleges), and the role of theatre education in forming citizens and a future public for theatre.

1162 Wickham, Philip. "Expériences: pour une approche non spécialisée de la formation théâtrale." (Experiences: Toward a Non-Specialized Approach to Theatrical Education.) *JCT*. 1992; 65: 75-82. Notes. Illus.: Photo. B&W. 2. Lang.: Fre.
Canada: Montreal, PQ, Outremont, PQ, Saint-Laurent, PQ. 1991-1992. Historical studies. ■Paul Gérin-Lajoie secondary school and Collège de Saint-Laurent's theatre programs as examples of integrated, general theatre education.

1163 Schumann, Peter B. "Theater in der Nebenrolle." (Theatre in a Supporting Role.) *DB*. 1996; 5: 44-47. Illus.: Photo. B&W. 2. Lang.: Ger.
Chile. Argentina. Uruguay. 1970-1996. Historical studies. ■The role of Chilean, Argentinian, and Uruguayan theatre in the resistance against military governments since the 1970s, when they played an important role as public spaces of social protest. Discusses aesthetic development and the struggle for new theatrical models. Includes discussion of Teatro Colón of Buenos Aires, Teatro Galpón and Alvaro Ahuanchain of Uruguay, and Teatro la Memoria and Alfredo Castro of Chile.

1164 Snow, Leida. "The Great Wall Stands: Reflections on China." *TheaterW*. 1996 Feb 26; 9(30): 42-45. Illus.: Photo. B&W. 3. Lang.: Eng.
China, People's Republic of. 1984-1996. Historical studies. ■Presentation of American musicals and plays in China. Societal differences, translation challenges, role of culture in Chinese society, political restrictions.

1165 Varley, Julia. "An Interview with Patricia Ariza: An Exercise of Pleasure." *PerfR*. 1996 Sum; 1(2): 75-82. Illus.: Photo. B&W. 2. Lang.: Eng.
Colombia: Bogotá. 1975-1995. Historical studies. ■Ariza's recent theatre work with the poor and dispossessed in Bogotá, including drug addicts, prostitutes, transvestites and potentially violent young people.

1166 Havel, Václav. "Politics, Theatre and Clownery/La politique, le théâtre et la clownerie." *DTh*. 1996; 12: 2-13. Illus.: Photo. B&W. 11. Lang.: Eng, Fre.
Czech Republic: Prague. 1996. Critical studies. ■Acceptance address by Václav Havel, President of the Czech Republic, on the occasion of the conferral of an honorary degree from the Academy of Performing Arts, Prague, 4 October 1996.

1167 Albertová, Helena; Vaïs, Michel, transl. "Un nouveau théâtre se cherche." (A New Theatre Seeks Its Identity.) *JCT*. 1993; 66: 88-95. Notes. Illus.: Dwg. 1. [Translation of a conference paper presented at the Département de théâtre

THEATRE IN GENERAL: —Relation to other fields

of l'Université du Québec à Montréal, March 13, 1992.] Lang.: Fre.

Czechoslovakia. 1989-1992. Historical studies. ▪Relates trends in Czech theatre to social conditions produced by the 1968 Soviet invasion and the 1989 revolution.

1168 Norgaard, Bjorn. "The New Europe." *PerAJ*. 1996 May; 18(2): 64-67. Illus.: Photo. B&W. 2. [Number 53.] Lang.: Eng.

Denmark: Copenhagen. 1996. Critical studies. ▪Review of the installation 'The New Europe—every morning we have to start over again' at the Galleri Susanne Ottesen, commemorating the fall of the Soviet empire.

1169 Ruyter, Nancy Lee. "The 10th Session of the International School of Theatre Anthropology." *Gestos*. 1996 Nov.; 11(22): 171-175. Notes. Lang.: Eng.

Denmark: Copenhagen. 1996. Historical studies. ▪Report on the symposium.

1170 Balme, Christopher B. "Pictured Passions: Zum Verhältnis von Malerei und Schauspieltheorie in England im 18. Jahrhundert." (Pictured Passions: The Relationship between Painting and Acting Theory in Eighteenth-Century England.) *KSGT*. 1996; YB: 147-165. Notes. Illus.: Pntg. 4. Lang.: Ger.

England. 1700-1799. Historical studies. ▪The interaction between paintings and the acting of David Garrick as evidence of a paradigm shift in theatre aesthetics, in which dominance passed from the text to the visual sign.

1171 Betcher, Gloria. "A Tempting Theory: What Early Cornish Mermaid Images Reveal about the First Doctor's Analogy in *Passio Domini*." *EDAM*. 1996 Spr; 18(2): 65-76. Illus.: Maps. B&W. 1. Lang.: Eng.

England: Cornwall. 1400-1600. Historical studies. ▪In the second part of the Cornish *Ordinalia*, the mermaid is used to demonstrate a theological point about the nature of Christ. While there are connections between drama and art in Cornwall, the theory that the visual artists were influenced by the drama cannot be sustained.

1172 Evans, Robert C. "Forgotten Fools: Alexander Barclay's *Ship of Fools*." 47-72 in Davidson, Clifford, ed. *Fools and Folly*. Kalamazoo, MI: Medieval Institute Publications; 1996. 176 pp. (Early Drama, Art, and Music Monograph Series 22.) Notes. Append. Lang.: Eng.

England. 1494-1570. Historical studies. ▪Analysis of the poem, its portrayal of the fool, its popularity and influence, and its value as an historical and cultural source.

1173 Walsh, Martin W. "The King His Own Fool: *Robert of Cicyle*." 34-46 in Davidson, Clifford, ed. *Fools and Folly*. Kalamazoo, MI: Medieval Institute Publications; 1996. 176 pp. (Early Drama, Art, and Music Monograph Series 22.) Notes. Lang.: Eng.

England. 1390-1505. Historical studies. ▪Analysis of the fool image and the character of the court fool in the romantic poem *Robert of Cicyle* which was dramatized several times in the Middle Ages.

1174 Chartrand, Harry Hillman. "Intellectual Property Rights in the Postmodern World." *JAML*. 1996 Win; 25(4): 236-319. Notes. Lang.: Eng.

Europe. North America. 1996. Critical studies. ▪The challenges faced by governments, artists, and society in general in protecting the intellectual diversity of all cultures.

1175 Kołdrzak, Elżbieta. "Inspiracje wschodnie we współczesnym teatrze poszukującym /Barba, Brook, Grotowski/." (Oriental Inspirations in the Modern Questing Theatre: Barba, Brook, Grotowski.) 92-104 in Wąchocka, Ewa, ed. *Od symbolizmu do post-teatru*. Warsaw: Fundacja Astronomii Polskiej; 1996. 256 pp. Lang.: Pol.

Europe. 1996. Historical studies. ▪Theatrical performance and ritual: Jerzy Grotowski's concept of the sacrificial act of the performer, Eugenio Barba's idea of the secular rite of the search for meaning, and Peter Brook's attempts to realize a third culture in *The Mahabharata*.

1176 König, Marianne. "Von der Aneignung fremder Kulturen im westlichen Theater." (The Appropriation of Alien Cultures in Western Theatre.) *MuK*. 1996; 1: 115-126. Notes. Lang.: Ger.

Europe. 1600-1996. Critical studies. ▪The background, structures, and problems of the reception of the alien.

1177 Larrue, Jean-Marc. "Le Théâtre expérimental et la fin de l'unique." (Experimental Theatre and the End of Uniqueness.) *JCT*. 1989; 52: 64-72. Notes. Illus.: Dwg. Photo. B&W. 3. Lang.: Fre.

France. 1850-1989. Historical studies. ▪Emergence of experimental theatre in context of modernist philosophy of scientific advancement and commercialization.

1178 Ruf, Wolfgang. "Viel Rhetorik, wenig Klarheit." (Much Rhetoric, Less Clarity.) *DB*. 1996; 9: 36-37. Lang.: Ger.

France: St. Etienne. 1996. Historical studies. ▪Report on the first European Theatre Forum, a meeting of theatre workers and politicians concerned with cultural policy for the discussion of the common interests of European theatres.

1179 Wagner, Kitte. "Imperialisme og teater." (Imperialism and Theatre.) *TE*. 1996 June; 79: 4-7. Illus.: Photo. B&W. 2. Lang.: Dan.

France. UK-England. 1970-1996. Historical studies. ▪The work of directors such as Ariane Mnouchkine and Peter Brook, which focuses on the meeting of cultures and seeks to heal cultural damage created by Western colonialism.

1180 "'11 Wochen lang ist Schule Theater'." (For Eleven Weeks, School Is Theatre.) *SuT*. 1996; 157(1): 18-20. Illus.: Photo. B&W. 1. Lang.: Ger.

Germany: Berlin. 1989-1996. Histories-sources. ▪Interview with Werner Schulte, theatre teacher at an integrative school, about his work with eleven-year-old pupils.

1181 Borello, Christine. "Échos germaniques du théâtre français." (Germanic Echoes of French Theatre.) *JCT*. 1996; 81: 71-78. Notes. Illus.: Poster. Photo. B&W. 4. Lang.: Fre.

Germany: Saarbrücken. 1995. Historical studies. ▪Saarbrücken's Perspectives festival introduces French theatre to German audiences. Descriptions of shows at 1995 festival.

1182 Freentschik, Klaus. "Theater im Tollhaus." (Theatre in Mental Institutions.) *MuK*. 1996; 1: 47-67. Notes. Lang.: Ger.

Germany. France. 1800-1966. Historical studies. ▪Theatre in mental institutions and its use as a psychological therapy.

1183 Grund, Stefan. "'Ich hab ja nicht die Faust in der Tasche...'." (I Don't Bottle Up My Anger.) *TZ*. 1996; 5: 4-7. Illus.: Photo. B&W. 3. Lang.: Ger.

Germany: Hamburg. 1996. Histories-sources. ▪Interview with Frank Baumbauer, director of Deutsches Schauspielhaus, about art as resistance.

1184 Herzog, Roman. "Ansprache vom Bundespräsidenten." (The President's Speech.) *BGs*. 1996; 8/9: 12-15. Lang.: Ger.

Germany. 1996. Histories-sources. ▪General statements about cultural policy on the occasion of the 150th anniversary of Deutscher Bühnenverein by the president of the Federal Republic of Germany.

1185 Just, Renate. "Eastside Story." *THeute*. 1996; 3: 24-30. Illus.: Photo. B&W. 15. Lang.: Ger.

Germany: Chemnitz. 1996. Histories-sources. ▪Impressions of everyday life in Chemnitz, in town and at the theatre.

1186 Kirsch, Mechthild. "Exiltheater und deutsche Klassiker." (Exile Theatre and the German Classics.) *KSGT*. 1996; YB: 241-250. Notes. Lang.: Ger.

Germany. 1933-1945. Historical studies. ▪Ideological uses of theatre during the National Socialist period. Includes both the appropriation of classic authors such as Goethe, Schiller, Kleist, Lessing, and Hölderlin, the work of theatre practitioners in exile such as Toller, Becher, and Brecht, and the attempts of directors such as Jessner and institutions such as Freie Bühne and Schauspielhaus Zürich to portray the 'true' Germany.

1187 Müller, Ulrike. "Verrechnet, Frau Kahrs!" (Miscalculated, Mrs. Kahrs!)*TZ*. 1996; 1: 4-5. Illus.: Photo. B&W. 2. Lang.: Ger.

THEATRE IN GENERAL: —Relation to other fields

Germany: Bremen. 1995. Historical studies. ■The announcement of the closure of a section of Theater der Freien Hansestadt, which was accompanied by protests and solidarity among theatre people.

1188 Nanowa, Elitza; Stumpfe, Mario. "Off oder Proff? Krisenmanagament im Freien Theater." (Off or 'Proff'? Crisis Management on the Independent Theatre Scene.) *TZ*. 1996; 6: 38-40. Illus.: Photo. B&W. 8. Lang.: Ger.

Germany: Berlin. 1996. Histories-sources. ■Discussion with directors Hans-Werner Kroesinger, Antje Borchardt, Jo Fabian, and Dirk Cieslak, and producers and managers Tom Till, Jochen Sandig, and Zebu Kluth about the crisis of the independent theatres, the mistakes of cultural policy, and possible solutions.

1189 Obermeier, Thomas. "Paradies und das." (Paradise and That.) *TZ*. 1996; 3: 50-59. Lang.: Ger.

Germany. 1968-1989. Historical studies. ■Analysis of the influence on theatrical structure and performances of social movements and changes in the former East Germany in 1989, and comparison of the situation with that of West Germany in 1968.

1190 Renkes, Ulrich. "'Es braucht einen Revisor'." (An Auditor Is Needed.) *TZ*. 1996; 5: 4-8. Illus.: Photo. B&W. 4. Lang.: Ger.

Germany: Bochum. 1996. Histories-sources. ■Conversation with Jürgen Kruse, director of Schauspielhaus Bochum, about art as resistance.

1191 Roms, Heike. "Time and Time Again." *PerfR*. 1996 Spr; 1(1): 59-62. Biblio. Illus.: Photo. B&W. 3. Lang.: Eng.

Germany. Israel. 1991-1995. Critical studies. ■Documents and analyzes the five-hour performance of *Arbeit macht frei (Work Makes You Free)* by Dudi Ma'ayan at the Akko Theatre Center, dealing with memories and reconstructions of aspects of the Holocaust, including detailed description of parts of the performance, which required audiences to travel to several locations, and discussion of the gap between conventional public commemoration in museums and the trauma of individual recollection.

1192 Salter, Chris. "Forgetting, Erasure, and the Cry of the Billy Goat: Berlin Theatre Five Years After." *PerAJ*. 1996 Jan.; 18(1): 18-28. [Number 52.] Lang.: Eng.

Germany: Berlin. 1991-1996. Critical studies. ■Post-wall position of Berlin theatre in the debate of the new intellectual reactionaries, and the increasing difficulties faced by more free-thinking directors in the face of a stagnating art form.

1193 Schaeffer, Renz. "Protestantische Kirchen und Theaterinterieurs des 18. Jahrhunderts als Ort bürgerlicher Emanzipation." (Eighteenth-Century Protestant Churches and Theatre Interiors as Places of Bourgeois Emancipation.) *KSGT*. 1996; YB : 167-176. Notes. Lang.: Ger.

Germany. 1700-1799. Historical studies. ■Comparison of architecture in Protestant churches and theatre buildings in northern Germany.

1194 Schelling, Franke. "Vom Jugendspiel zum Fronttheater." (From Youth Play to Vanguard Theatre.) *SuT*. 1996; 158(2): 25-28. Notes. Lang.: Ger.

Germany. 1900-1945. Historical studies. ■The development of the amateur play movement during the National Socialist period.

1195 Ulrich, Renate; Wiegand, Elke. "'Unsere Kunst musst Biss Haben. Sonst—wozu?'." (Our Art Must Be Sharp. Otherwise, What Is it For?)*dRAMATURg*. 1996; 1: 30-41. Lang.: Ger.

Germany, East: Berlin, East. 1990-1991. Historical studies. ■Analysis of twelve interviews with actresses from East Berlin, including Petra Kelling, Jutta Wachowiak, and Angelika Waller, regarding their experiences after German reunification, with emphasis on the specifically female reactions to social change.

1196 Timm, Mikael. "2400 år av missförstånd." (2400 Years of Misunderstanding.) *Dramat*. 1996; 4(3): 36-39. Illus.: Photo. Color. Lang.: Swe.

Greece: Athens. Sweden: Vetlanda. 404 B.C. Historical studies. ■A comparison between the agoras of Athens and a small square at Vetlanda with reference to why ancient Greek culture is still relevant to contemporary life.

1197 Bános, Tibor. *A Csárdáskirálynő vendégei.* (The Guests of the Czardas Queen.) Budapest: Cserépfalvi; 1996. 229 pp. Illus.: Photo. Dwg. B&W. 36. Lang.: Hun.

Hungary. 1910-1956. Historical studies. ■Collection of studies of actors, directors, theatres, and noteworthy productions of the 1950s, including Tamás Major of the National Theatre. Includes historical background of Budapest cabaret, the popularity of operetta in spite of changed circumstances.

1198 Enyedi, Sándor. "Dokumentumok a két világháború közötti romániai magyar színjátszás idejéből." (Documents from the History of Hungarian Theatre in Romania between the World Wars.) *SzSz*. 1996; 30/31: 222-232. Notes. Lang.: Hun.

Hungary. Romania. 1918-1940. Histories-sources. ■Texts of four important archive materials on Hungarian theatre in Romania with an introduction.

1199 Strasszenreiter, Erzsébet. "Dokumentumok az ötvenes évek színházi életéből." (Theatrical Documents from the 1950s.) *SzSz*. 1996; 30/31: 233-249. Notes. Lang.: Hun.

Hungary. 1950-1956. Histories-sources. ■Introducing Hungarian theatre of the fifties as reflected in ten archive materials.

1200 Bharucha, Rustom. "Under the Sign of the Onion: Intracultural Negotiations in Theatre." *NTQ*. 1996; 12(46): 116-129. Notes. Illus.: Photo. B&W. 5. Lang.: Eng.

India. 1977-1995. Histories-sources. ■Distinguishes between interculturalism and intraculturalism as experienced by the author when directing his *Guindegowdana Charitre*, an Indian version of *Peer Gynt*. Explores the implications of translating this text across and within cultures as well as from one language to another.

1201 Corey, Frederick C. "Performing Sexualities at an Irish Pub." *TextPQ*. 1996 Apr.; 16(2): 146-160. Notes. Biblio. Lang.: Eng.

Ireland: Dublin. 1996. Critical studies. ■Elements of performance in same-sex desire rituals in an Irish pub, now that a loosening of legal restrictions has led to a redefinition of sexuality in Ireland.

1202 Ben-Ami, Ilan. "Government Involvement in the Arts in Israel—Some Structural and Policy Characteristics." *JAML*. 1996 Fall; 26(3): 195-219. Biblio. Lang.: Eng.

Israel. 1920-1996. Historical studies. ■Historical review of public funding of the arts in both pre-state and contemporary Israel.

1203 Schonmann, Shifra. "Jewish-Arab Encounters in the Drama/Theatre Class Battlefield." *RDE*. 1996; 1(2): 175-188. Biblio. Lang.: Eng.

Israel. 1977-1995. Historical studies. ■Attempts to increase awareness of the role that drama and theatre play in everyday life, using three Jewish-Arab projects as a mode for reflections on the peace process in the Middle East.

1204 Vajda, Ferenc. "A színházi tér, mint a kommunikatív folyamat környezete." (Theatrical Space as Environment for Communicative Processes.) *SFo*. 1995/1996; 22/23(3/4-1/2): 33-34. Illus.: Diagram. B&W. 1. Lang.: Hun.

Israel: Tel Aviv. 1995. Historical studies. ■The lecture delivered at the Session of the OISTAT Commission for Theory and History, Tel Aviv, 1995.

1205 Cavallo, Pietro; Berghaus, Günter, transl.; Passannanti, Erminia, transl. "Theatre Politics of the Mussolini Régime and Their Influence on Fascist Drama." 113-132 in Berghaus, Günter, ed. *Fascism and Theatre: Comparative Studies on the Aesthetics and Politics of Performance in Europe, 1925-1945.* Oxford: Berghahn Books; 1996. 315 pp. Biblio. Notes. Index. Illus.: Photo. 24. Lang.: Eng.

Italy. 1925-1943. Historical studies. ■The Fascist aesthetic as articulated in the political manifestos and speeches of dictator Benito Mussolini.

1206 Dermutz, Klaus. "Die grosse Tragödie ist nicht der Tod, sondern das Vergessen." (The Great Tragedy Is Not Death But Oblivion.) *THeute*. 1996; 8: 1-5. Illus.: Photo. B&W. 2. Lang.: Ger.

Italy. 1996. Histories-sources. ■Interview with director and author Cesare Lievi about Italy after the elections and the possible change in cultural policy.

1207 Gentile, Emilio; Rickitt, Kate, transl. "The Theatre of Politics in Fascist Italy." 72-93 in Berghaus, Günter, ed. *Fascism and Theatre: Comparative Studies on the Aesthetics and Poli-*

THEATRE IN GENERAL: —Relation to other fields

tics of Performance in Europe, 1925-1945. Oxford: Berghahn Books; 1996. 315 pp. Biblio. Notes. Index. Illus.: Photo. 24. Lang.: Eng.

Italy. 1925-1945. Historical studies. ■The dramatization of myth by means of collective ceremonies as an essential element of the theatricalization of Fascist politics in Italy.

1208 Newbigin, Nerida. "Art and Drama in Fifteenth-Century Florence." *EDAM.* 1996 Fall; 19(1): 1-22. Illus.: Photo. B&W. 6. Lang.: Eng.

Italy: Florence. 1400-1600. Historical studies. ■The relation between art and drama in Florence, with reference to plays of the Annunciation and saint plays and their analogues in painting.

1209 Villegas, Juan. "De la teatralidad como estrategia multidisciplinaria." (Theatricality as a Multidisciplinary Strategy.) *Gestos.* 1996 Apr.; 11(21): 7-19. Notes. Biblio. Lang.: Eng.

Latin America. 1996. Historical studies. ■Theatricality and its historical impact in Latin America.

1210 Hoeane, M. *New Directions in Theatre-for-Development in Lesotho.* Ph.D. thesis, *Index to theses,* 45-8890. Leeds: Univ. of Leeds; 1995. Lang.: Eng.

Lesotho. 1970-1994. Historical studies. ■Identifies new developments in the methodology, i.e. innovations and adaptations developed on the ground to make the theatre approach work better. Also discusses its relation to theories of development.

1211 Versényi, Adam. "The Mexican Revolution: Religion, Politics, and Theater." 57-78 in Reinelt, Janelle, ed. *Crucibles of Crisis: Performing Social Change.* Ann Arbor, MI: Univ of Michigan P; 1996. 250 pp. Notes. Lang.: Eng.

Mexico. 1904-1994. Critical studies. ■The use of theatrical religious spectacle for sociopolitical communication and propaganda by Mexican revolutionaries past and present, especially in the Chiapas region.

1212 Stekelenburg, Liesbeth van. *'Het toont in kleen begrip al 's menschen ijdelheid': De portrettencollectie van de Stadsschouwburg Amsterdam.* ('It shows in a nutshell human vanity': The Portrait Collection of the Stadsschouwburg Amsterdam.) Amsterdam: International Theatre and Film Books; 1996. n.p. Illus.: Photo. B&W. 75. Lang.: Dut.

Netherlands: Amsterdam. 1895-1995. Histories-sources. ■Description of the portraits in the lobby of the Stadsschouwburg.

1213 Tjon Pian Gi, Walther; Dijk, Ilse van; Vries, Annette de. *Passen op het podium. Opstellen over theater in de multiculturele samenleving.* (Steps on Stage: Essays on Theatre in a Multicultural Society.) Amsterdam: Stichting Scarabes; 1996. 102 pp. Pref. Biblio. Append. Illus.: Photo. B&W. 7. Lang.: Dut.

Netherlands. 1988-1996. Critical studies. ■Essays by members of the former Scarabes Foundation, which was dedicated to the development of immigrant theatre, on multicultural approaches to regular theatre practice.

1214 Harple, Todd S. "Considering the Maori in the Nineteenth and Twentieth Centuries: The Negotiation of Social Identity in Exhibitory Cultures." *JAML.* 1996 Win; 25(4): 292-305. Notes. Biblio. Lang.: Eng.

New Zealand. UK-England. 1807-1996. Historical studies. ■William Jenkins' exhibit, *Hariru Wikitoria,* of living members of different Maori tribesmen and women, which toured Britain beginning 1863, with dance and facial tattoos, compared with current exhibit of traditional Maori art at the Metropolitan Museum of Art.

1215 Abah, Oga Steve. "Theatre for Development as a Non-Formal Method of Education in Nigeria." *RDE.* 1996; 1(2): 245-260. Biblio. Notes. Illus.: Photo. Maps. B&W. 3. Lang.: Eng.

Nigeria. 1972-1996. Critical studies. ■Theatre for Development as a people's theatre that allows communities to address their own social or political problems on their own terms through participation, analysis, and questioning.

1216 Pandey, Ranjana; Remotigue, Fe. "Cultural and Class Identity." *AFS.* 1995 Fall; 21: 95-103. Illus.: Photo. B&W. 2. Lang.: Eng.

Philippines: Mindanao. India: New Delhi. 1986-1995. Histories-sources. ■Remotigue, a leader in people's theatre movement and Pandey, founder/director of puppet company Jan Madhyam, discuss female identity as viewed through their culture and art at the International Women Playwrights Conference.

1217 Braun, Kazimierz. *A History of Polish Theater, 1939-1989: Spheres of Captivity and Freedom.* Westport, CT/London: Greenwood; 1996. 233 pp. (Contributions in Drama and Theatre Studies 64.) Index. Biblio. Pref. Lang.: Eng.

Poland. 1939-1989. Historical studies. ■Polish theatre in the context of political and cultural developments. Includes a historical narrative as well as discussion of various theatrical problems and selected theatre artists.

1218 Głowacka, Malwina. "Międzyepoka." (The Inter-Epoch.) *DialogW.* 1996; 11: 141-148. Lang.: Pol.

Poland. 1989-1996. Historical studies. ■The repertory of Polish theatre companies in the transitional period after the collapse of communism.

1219 Majcherek, Wojciech. "Większi niż scena." (Larger than the Stage.) *DialogW.* 1996; 1: 110-123. Lang.: Pol.

Poland. 1924. Biographical studies. ■Three theatre artists, all born in 1924, whose working life coincided with the period of Communist Poland: Kazimierz Dejmek, Adam Hanuszkiewicz, and Andrzej Łapicki.

1220 Repsch, Ewa Maria. "Theatre Education." *TP.* 1996 July; 38(3): 23-26. Illus.: Photo. Poster. B&W. 2. Lang.: Eng, Fre.

Poland. 1996. Critical studies. ■Essay on the importance of theatre education in Polish schools as a means of teaching children to develop their aesthetic sensitivity, and encourage cultural activity.

1221 Simpson, Peggy A. "Report from Poland: The Theatre in Economic Transition." *TA.* 1994; 47: 47-60. Notes. Lang.: Eng.

Poland. 1994. Critical studies. ■Financial difficulties faced by Polish theatres during the transition from socialism to capitalism.

1222 Zielińska, Maryla. "Towards Modern Theatrology." *TP.* 1995 July; 37(3): 17-21. Illus.: Photo. B&W. 5. Lang.: Eng, Fre.

Poland. 1995. Histories-sources. ■Interview with theatre anthropology proponent Zbigniew Osiński discussing its place in Polish society.

1223 Witts, Noel. "Negative Utopia: Reflections on Theatre in Romania after Ceaușescu." *PerfR.* 1996 Sum; 1(2): 35-39. Biblio. Illus.: Photo. B&W. 1. Lang.: Eng.

Romania. 1965-1995. Historical studies. ■Theatre in post-Ceaușescu Romania is said to have lost its confidence and become a commodity.

1224 Beuvič, L.P. "Teat'r v sovremennoj sociokul'turnoj situacii." (Theatre in the Contemporary Sociocultural Situation.) 75-78 in *Problemy kul'tury gorodov Rossii.* Omsk: Rossijskij Institut kul'turologii; 1996. Lang.: Rus.

Russia: Cheljabinsk. 1990-1996. Historical studies. ■Transformations of Cheljabinsk's theatrical life.

1225 Čudinovskich, Irina. "O prepodavanij teatra v obščeéstetičeskich klassach." (On Teaching Theatre in General Aesthetics Classes.) *Iskv.* 1996; 3: 15-20. Lang.: Rus.

Russia: Moscow. 1996. Histories-sources. ■Teaching methodology discussed by a teacher of play production using school children as performers.

1226 Dümcke, Cornelia. "Alte Krankheiten und neues Bücken." (Old Diseases and New Bending.) *TZ.* 1996; 5: 57-60. Illus.: Photo. B&W. 1. Lang.: Ger.

Russia. 1996. Historical studies. ■Russian theatre economy and current cultural policy and financing.

1227 Kuz'menko, O.D. "Metodologičeskie osnovy speckursa 'Teat'r i kino v Rossii'." (The Methodology of the Special Course 'Theatre and Film in Russia'.) 51-55 in *Kultura i tvorčestvo: Materialy konferencii.* Moscow: MGOPU; 1996. Lang.: Rus.

Russia. 1996. Historical studies. ■The correlation of theatre and film in the course, problems and controversies of the two genres, specifics of acting for theatre and for film.

1228 Quevillon, Michel. "Theatrum mundi." *JCT.* 1996; 80: 10-12. Notes. Illus.: Photo. B&W. 3. Lang.: Fre.

THEATRE IN GENERAL: —Relation to other fields

Russia. 1880. Critical studies. ■Theatricality and character portrayal in works of Fëdor Dostojévskij, particularly *The Brothers Karamazov*.

1229 Smol'jakov, A. "Bez vozrasta." (Ageless.) *TeatZ.* 1996; 7: 10-12. Lang.: Rus.

Russia: Moscow. 1918-1919. Historical studies. ■The influence on poet Marina Cvetajeva of Vachtangov's Third Studio, Moscow Art Theatre.

1230 Stepugina, T.V. *Gorod i iskusstvo: subjekty sociokul'turnogo dialoga.* (The City and Art: Subjects of Sociocultural Dialogue.) Moscow: Nauka; 1996. 286 pp. Lang.: Rus.

Russia. 1990-1996. Historical studies. ■Emphasis on the role of the theatre in metropolitan culture.

1231 Polic, Radko. "Living in Solitary Confinement." *PerAJ.* 1996 May; 18(2): 25-26. [Number 53.] Lang.: Eng.

Slovenia. 1995. Histories-sources. ■Excerpt of an interview with Slovenian actor Radko Polic who refuses to take sides in the conflict raging around him.

1232 Hodge, Polly J. "Photography of Theater: Reading Between the Spanish Scenes." *Gestos.* 1996 Nov.; 11(22): 35-58. Biblio. Illus.: Photo. B&W. 5. Lang.: Eng.

Spain. 1956-1996. Critical studies. ■Relation between photography and theatre as visual media, especially with respect to Spanish theatre.

1233 Soufas, C. Christopher. "Audience, Authority, and Theatricality in Velázquez's *Las meninas*." *Gestos.* 1996 Apr.; 11(21): 66-81. Notes. Biblio. Illus.: Photo. B&W. 1. Lang.: Eng.

Spain. 1400-1996. Critical studies. ■Analysis of Velasquez's painting *Las meninas*: the influences of history, theatre, and poetry. Emphasis on the interpretation of the painting as narrative, and the need for the viewer to adopt a theatrical point of view.

1234 Frank, Marion. "Theatre in the Service of Health Education: Case Studies from Uganda." *NTQ.* 1996; 12(46): 108-115. Notes. Lang.: Eng.

Uganda. 1989-1991. Critical studies. ■Examines structures and techniques inherent in applied theatre and analyzes two plays, one of them performed by the group J.K. Ebonita, the other *Give a Chance* by David Kateete, used to supplement AIDS education programs.

1235 "Checklist of Taught MA Courses in British Drama." *STP.* 1994 June; 9: 57-66. Lang.: Eng.

UK. 1994. Critical studies. ■A list of nineteen British universities offering Master of Arts degrees in Drama and Theatre Studies, with details of their courses. Continued in *STP* 10 (1994 Dec), p. 47.

1236 Oddey, Alison. "What Shall I Do With My Amstrad?" *STP.* 1996 June; 13: 105-110. Lang.: Eng.

UK. 1996. Critical studies. ■A parodistic complaint about the pressures on the contemporary theatre lecturer having to be familiar with ever-changing computer technology.

1237 Prentki, Tim. "The Empire Strikes Back: the Relevance of Theatre for Development in Africa and South-East Asia to Community Drama in the U.K." *RDE.* 1996; 1(1): 33-49. Biblio. Illus.: Photo. B&W. 1. Lang.: Eng.

UK. 1976-1995. Historical studies. ■Investigates possible gains, in terms of contemporary social relevance, for community theatre and drama from the foreign influence of Theatre for Development and considers the relative merits of different models of practice.

1238 Somers, John. "Theater und Drama im britischen Schulsystem." (Theatre and Drama in the British School System.) *SuT.* 1996; 157(1): 26-31. Illus.: Photo. B&W. 4. Lang.: Ger.

UK. 1965-1996. Historical studies. ■The history of Theatre-in-Education. Third part in a series.

1239 Verma, Jatinder. "Binglish: a Jungli Approach to Multi-Cultural Theatre." *STP.* 1996 June; 13: 92-98. Lang.: Eng.

UK. 1996. Histories-sources. ■The director of Tara Arts Centre argues for a multicultural approach to theatre that he calls 'Binglish' in an address to the Drama Lecturers' conference (April, 1996).

1240 Farfan, Penny. "Writing/Performing: Virginia Woolf *Between the Acts*." *TextPQ.* 1996 July; 16(3): 205-215. Notes. Biblio. Illus.: Photo. B&W. 1. Lang.: Eng.

UK-England. 1941. Critical studies. ■Woolf's use of the device of the play-within-the-novel and the metaphor of performance to conceptualize

the connection of art to lived experience: how performative acts of feminist artists might contribute to the transformation of gender norms.

1241 Franks, Anton. "Drama Education, the Body and Representation (or, The Mystery of the Missing Bodies)." *RDE.* 1996; 1(1): 105-119. Biblio. Lang.: Eng.

UK-England. 1979-1995. Historical studies. ■Explores ways in which bodies create meaning, how meanings are represented in and by bodies, and pursues some of the implications for drama education of considering the body as a form of representation.

1242 Merkin, R. *The Theatre of the Organized Working Class, 1830-1930.* Ph.D. thesis, *Index to theses*, 45-6144. Warwick: Univ. of Warwick; 1993. Notes. Biblio. Lang.: Eng.

UK-England. 1830-1930. Historical studies. ■Traces the history of working-class political organizations in theatrical performances, starting with the Chartists and ending with the Labour Party. Concludes by pointing to the wealth of undiscovered material, and also to the existence of political theatre prior to the emergence of the Worker's Theatre Movement in the 1920s.

1243 Nicholson, Helen. "Performing Sanity: The Case of Georgina Weldon." *TA.* 1996; 49: 35-48. Notes. Illus.: Photo. B&W. 1. Lang.: Eng.

UK-England: London. 1875-1885. Historical studies. ■The writer and actress's use of theatrical ability and publicity to resist attempts by her husband and doctor to have her committed.

1244 Phelan, Peggy. "Playing Dead in Stone, or, When Is a Rose Not a Rose?" 65-88 in Diamond, Elin, ed. *Performance and Cultural Politics.* London/New York, NY: Routledge; 1996. 282 pp. Notes. Index. Illus.: Photo. Dwg. Sketches. 4. Lang.: Eng.

UK-England: London. 1989. Critical studies. ■Using performance theory to argue that archaeological excavations, such as that of the Rose Theatre, are driven by cultural, political and economic considerations.

1245 Shaughnessy, Nicola. "Theatres of Absurdity: Pedagogy, Performance and Institutional Politics." *STP.* 1996 June; 13: 39-53. Lang.: Eng.

UK-England. 1996. Histories-sources. ■Personal account by a theatre teacher required to stage plays with student groups and having to respond to the conflicting needs of pedagogy, fair assessment, modularity, satisfying the expectations of an audience, inadequate resources and performance spaces.

1246 Thomson, Peter. "The Death of Difference: Malignity and the TQA." *STP.* 1996 Dec.; 14: 59-63. Lang.: Eng.

UK-England. 1996. Critical studies. ■Questions the methods and criteria of the Teaching Quality Assessment exercise, to which British university theatre departments are regularly subjected as an audit to justify government funding.

1247 Whybrow, Nicolas. "Turning Up the Volume at the Oasis: Invisible Theatre Exposed!" *RDE.* 1996; 1(2): 221-232. Biblio. Notes. Lang.: Eng.

UK-England. 1995. Historical studies. ■Reports on a project by the young people's theatre company Blah, Blah, Blah entitled *Turning Up the Volume*, which took place at the Oasis Youth Centre, Salford, and which attempted to fuse the techniques of a performance artist, Claire Thacker, with those of an educational theatre company.

1248 Widdows, Joy. "Drama as an Agent for Change: Drama, Behaviour, and Students with Emotional and Behavioural Difficulties." *RDE.* 1996; 1(1): 65-78. Biblio. Lang.: Eng.

UK-England. 1978-1995. Historical studies. ■A structured account of drama as an agent for changing behavior in the educational situation is followed by an innovative drama program which can be adapted for all age ranges.

1249 Kershaw, Baz. "The Politics of Performance in a Postmodern Age." 133-152 in Campbell, Patrick, ed. *Analysing Performance: A Critical Reader.* Manchester/New York, NY: Manchester UP; 1996. 307 pp. Lang.: Eng.

UK-Scotland: Glasgow. USA: New York, NY. 1994-1995. Critical studies. ■Uses the Wooster Group's *L.S.D. (...Just the High Points...)* and Welfare State International's *Glasgow All Lit Up!* to discuss the place of performance and theatre in the politics of postindustrial societies.

THEATRE IN GENERAL: —Relation to other fields

1250 Maguire, T.J. *Politics, Pleasure and the Popular Imagination: Aspects of Scottish Political Theatre, 1979-1990.* Ph.D. thesis, *Index to theses,* 45-8893. Glasgow: Univ. of Glasgow; 1992. Notes. Biblio. Lang.: Eng.
UK-Scotland. 1979-1990. Critical studies. ■Analyses the widening gap between Scots civil society and the British state under Thatcherism. Locates Scottish theatre within its own context, rather than as peripheral to the conventional Anglocentric model.

1251 Soule, Lesley Wade. "Magdalena 1995: Mothers of Invention." *NTQ.* 1996; 12(45): 85-86. [*NTQ* Reports and Announcements.] Lang.: Eng.
UK-Wales: Cardiff. 1995. Historical studies. ■Reports the events at a week-long workshop and symposium about mothers making theatre.

1252 Anderson, John D. "*As I Lay Dying:* Faulkner's Tour de Force One-Man Show." *TextPQ.* 1996 Apr.; 16(2): 109-130. Notes. Biblio. Lang.: Eng.
USA. 1930. Critical studies. ■Function and purpose of 'performing consciousness', and the shamanistic implications of the character Darl's roleplaying in William Faulkner's *As I Lay Dying,* a novel adapted for the stage a number of times.

1253 Butsch, Richard. "American Theatre Riots and Class Relations, 1754-1849." *TA.* 1995; 48: 41-59. Notes. Tables. Lang.: Eng.
USA. 1754-1849. Historical studies. ■Argues that theatre disturbances in America expressed working-class demands for an egalitarian culture and rejection of class privilege, as against upper-class defense of traditionally English theatre and actors.

1254 Cockrell, Dale. "Callithumpians, Mummers, Maskers, and Minstrels: Blackface in the Streets of Jacksonian America." *TA.* 1996; 49: 15-34. Notes. Lang.: Eng.
USA. 1800-1844. Historical studies. ■Examines the use of blackface during the early nineteenth century, its social meaning for both Black and white performers and audience.

1255 Etim, James S. "Bondage in Male and Female Authored Works: A Cross-Cultural Analysis." *WJBS.* 1996 Fall; 20(3): 158-163. Biblio. Notes. Lang.: Eng.
USA. Africa. 1996. Critical studies. ■The theme of bondage in recent Black works from Alice Walker's novel *The Color Purple* to Wole Soyinka's *The Lion and the Jewel.*

1256 Filicko, Therese. "In What Spirit Do Americans Cultivate the Arts? A Review of Survey Questions on the Arts." *JAML.* 1996 Fall; 26(3): 221-246. Notes. Lang.: Eng.
USA. 1996. Empirical research. ■Set of assumptions made from a series of surveys taken on Americans' attitudes on the arts.

1257 Fletcher, Reagan. "Lost and Found and Lost." *PasShow.* 1995 Fall/Win; 18(2): 9-11. Illus.: Photo. B&W. 5.
USA: New York, NY. 1925-1995. Historical studies. ■Rediscovery and identification of four pastel art works, by the artist Lyna Randel, that once hung in the lobby of the Shubert Theatre.

1258 Garcia, Lorenzo. "Images of Teaching and Classroom Drama." *YTJ.* 1996; 10: 1-15. Notes. Biblio. Lang.: Eng.
USA. 1996. Critical studies. ■How elementary school teachers carry out a drama curriculum. By examining 'images' teachers hold of their work in the classroom, interpretations of how they perceive, organize, and respond to their teaching situations can be gathered.

1259 Hayes, Steve. "Sideshow in San Diego." *AmTh.* 1996 Nov.; 13(9): 64-65. Illus.: Photo. B&W. 2. Lang.: Eng.
USA: San Diego, CA. 1996. Critical studies. ■Comparison of theatre productions being presented near the Republican National Convention. Focus on Mac Wellman's *7 Blowjobs* at San Diego Repertory and *FritzCon '96,* a comedic satire presented by the Fritz Theatre.

1260 Jackson, Shannon. "Civic Play-Housekeeping: Gender, Theatre, and American Reform." *TJ.* 1996 Oct.; 48(3): 337-362. Notes. Biblio. Illus.: Photo. Sketches. Handbill. 4. Lang.: Eng.
USA: Chicago, IL. 1890-1915. Historical studies. ■Connections among the Progressive reform movement, the woman's movement, and performance as seen in Edith de Nancrede's Marionette Club at the Hull-House Settlement.

1261 Lazarus, Joan. "Teaching Teachers: Eight Models of Professional Development in Theatre." *YTJ.* 1996; 10: 36-55. Biblio. Append. Notes. Lang.: Eng.
USA. 1994-1996. Historical studies. ■A review of eight successful programs of professional development in theatre for teachers and their relation to various educational reform efforts: Alliance Theatre (Atlanta), Creative Arts Team/Kaplan Center (NYC), Lincoln Center Institute (NYC), Metro Theatre Company (St. Louis), Mid-South California Arts Project (Northridge, CA), Southeast Institute for Education in Theatre (Chattanooga), Tennessee Arts Academy (Nashville), and Wolf Trap Institute for Early Learning through the Arts (Washington, DC).

1262 London, Todd. "The Importance of Staying Earnest." *AmTh.* 1996 Jan.; 13(1): 24-25. Illus.: Sketches. B&W. 2. Lang.: Eng.
USA. 1996. Critical studies. ■Exploring the need of artists-in-training to justify the desire to make art, and the political, financial and spiritual challenges faced by artists to continue their work.

1263 Mahone, Sydné. "Black Theatre Matters." *DGQ.* 1996 Fall; 33(3): 12-15. Lang.: Eng.
USA. 1996. Critical studies. ■Argues that individual success of African-American artists at 'mainstream' white theatres gives a distorted picture of the success of Black theatre. Author champions inclusion of Black artists in a white mainstream, but warns against the conclusion that Black theatres are doing well.

1264 Marra, Kim. "A Lesbian Marriage of Cultural Consequence: Elisabeth Marbury and Elsie de Wolfe, 1886-1933." *TA.* 1994; 47 : 71-96. Notes. Illus.: Photo. B&W. 1. Lang.: Eng.
USA: New York, NY. 1886-1933. Biographical studies. ■The relationship of theatrical agent Elsie de Wolfe and interior decorator and designer Elisabeth Marbury and their influence on American theatre.

1265 Moore, Dick. "World AIDS Day Observed." *EN.* 1996 Jan/ Feb.; 81(1): 2. Lang.: Eng.
USA: New York, NY. 1996. Historical studies. ■Equity celebrates World AIDS Day.

1266 Norflett, Linda Kerr. "Black Theatre Network Reflects on the 1995 National Black Theatre Festival." *BlackM.* 1996 Mar/Apr.; 11(5): 7-9,14. Illus.: Photo. B&W. 2. Lang.: Eng.
USA: Winston-Salem, NC. 1995. Historical studies. ■Overview of the extensive educational programming at the 1995 National Black Theatre Festival, revealing the Festival's desire to provide for the needs of scholars, practitioners, and youth.

1267 Nunns, Stephen. "The PG-Rated World of Candidate Bob Dole." *AmTh.* 1996 Oct.; 13(8): 97-99. Illus.: Photo. Sketches. B&W. 2. Lang.: Eng.
USA: Washington, DC. 1996. Critical studies. ■Examines presidential candidate's critical views of popular culture and his attacks on the art and entertainment industry.

1268 Nunns, Stephen. "A Capital Goodbye." *AmTh.* 1996 Dec.; 13(10): 52-53. Illus.: Photo. B&W. 1. Lang.: Eng.
USA: Washington, DC. 1996. Historical studies. ■American Arts Alliance salute to retiring members of Congress, and honoring their long support for the arts.

1269 Ouaknine, Serge. "Sources et perspectives du théâtre expérimental." (Sources and Prospects of Experimental Theatre.) *JCT.* 1989; 52: 55-63. Illus.: Photo. B&W. 5. Lang.: Fre.
USA. Canada. 1960-1989. Critical studies. ■Philosophical underpinnings shared by scientific research and experimental theatre.

1270 Park-Fuller, Linda M. "Performance as *Praxis:* The Intercollegiate Performance Festival." *TextPQ.* 1994 Oct.; 14(4): 330-333. Notes. Lang.: Eng.
USA. 1945-1994. Historical studies. ■Impact of intercollegiate interpretation/performance festivals on the organization of performance in American culture in the latter half of the twentieth-century.

1271 Patraka, Vivian M. "Spectacles of Suffering: Performing Presence, Absence, and Historical Memory at U.S. Holocaust Museums." 89-107 in Diamond, Elin, ed. *Performance and Cultural Politics.* London/New York, NY: Routledge; 1996. 282 pp. Notes. Index. Illus.: Photo. Dwg. Sketches. 4. Lang.: Eng.

THEATRE IN GENERAL: —Relation to other fields

USA: Washington, DC, Los Angeles, CA. 1994-1995. Critical studies. ■The public performance of the term 'Holocaust' in the U.S. Holocaust Memorial Museum in Washington and the Beit Hashoah Museum of Tolerance in Los Angeles.

1272   Reiss, Alvin H. "A Donor Reflects on an Arts Contribution." *FundM*. 1996 Oct.; 27(8): 36-37. Illus.: Photo. B&W. 1. Lang.: Eng.
USA: Columbus, OH. 1996. Histories-sources. ■Author's personal reflections on donating his collection of tapes, interviews and papers to Ohio State University's Fine Arts Library at the Wexner Center for the Performing Arts.

1273   Rodden, John. "A *TPQ* Interview: 'Improv is My Pedagogical Style': Camille Paglia on Teaching as Performance Art." *TextPQ*. 1996 Apr.; 16(2): 161-171. Notes. Lang.: Eng.
USA. 1996. Histories-sources. ■Interview with 'performing artist-intellectual' Camille Paglia regarding her view of teaching as performance art.

1274   Rodden, John. "A *TPQ* Interview: Gerald Stern." *TextPQ*. 1996 July; 16(3): 270-289. Notes. Lang.: Eng.
USA. 1925-1996. Histories-sources. ■Interview with poet Gerald Stern regarding his life and work, with emphasis on his public reading performance style, and his ease as a story-teller.

1275   Rogers, Richard A. "Rhythm and the Performance of Organization." *TextPQ*. 1994 July; 14(3): 222-237. Notes. Biblio. Lang.: Eng.
USA. 1994. Critical studies. ■Rhythm as a form of social discourse. Expands the understanding of what constitutes organization, calling for a greater accounting of the role of physiological structures in human social life and performance.

1276   Rose, Heidi M. "Stylistic Features in American Sign Language Theatre." *TextPQ*. 1994 Apr.; 14(2): 144-157. Notes. Biblio. Lang.: Eng.
USA. 1994. Critical studies. ■Explores the stylistic features of American Sign Language literature, focusing on how both referential and aesthetic components of bodily expression are used to create a textual performance.

1277   Schechner, Richard; Gerstle, Alan; X, Marion; Barnett, Douglas O. "Plowing August Wilson's 'Ground'." *AmTh*. 1996 Dec.; 13(10): 58-60. Lang.: Eng.
USA. 1996. Critical studies. ■Four responses to playwright Wilson's article 'The Ground on Which I Stand', *AmTh* 13:7 (1996 Sep), in which he addressed the state of Black theatre in America, multicultural casting, and funding.

1278   Schneider, Raymond J. "Tampa: A Tale of Two Cities." *TextPQ*. 1994 Oct.; 14(4): 334-341. Notes. Biblio. Lang.: Eng.
USA: Tampa, FL. 1990. Historical studies. ■How performance festivals can give participants a better sense of the host city's essence and history, and how attending a festival in Tampa affected the author's sense of the city.

1279   Sequeira, Debra–L. "Gifts of Tongues and Healing: The Performance of Charismatic Renewal." *TextPQ*. 1994 Apr.; 14(2): 126-143. Notes. Biblio. Lang.: Eng.
USA. 1994. Critical studies. ■Ritual performance as an enactment of the sacred and how it is reflected in the prayer rituals of the Charismatic movement.

1280   Storr, Anni V.F. "Audiences, Exhibitions, and Interpretive Labels." *PAR*. 1995; 19(1): 25-37. Lang.: Eng.
USA. 1996. Critical studies. ■The use of titles to broaden the appeal of artistic works for a non-specialist audience. Uses the example of John Singer Sargent's portrait of actress Ellen Terry, labeled as Lady Macbeth.

1281   Stratyner, Barbara. "The Museum Paradox: The Co-Existence of Narrative Structure and Audience Advocacy." *PAR*. 1995; 19 (1): 39-96. Notes. Biblio. Lang.: Eng.
USA. 1996. Critical studies. ■Pros and cons of narrative structure in museum exhibits, and whether it hinders or helps an audience's understanding, or imprints institutional authority and perspective on the culturally disadvantaged.

1282   Veder, Robin. "Tableaux Vivants: Performing Art, Purchasing Status." *TA*. 1996; 48: 4-29. Notes. Illus.: Dwg. B&W. 2. Lang.: Eng.
USA: New York, NY. 1850-1900. Historical studies. ■Popularity of *tableaux vivants*, usually based on a popular novel or historical event, and the status involved by performing in one.

1283   Villaseñor, Maria Christina. "The Witkin Carnival." *PerAJ*. 1996 May; 18(2): 77-82. Illus.: Photo. B&W. 2. [Number 53.] Lang.: Eng.
USA: New York, NY. 1996. Critical studies. ■Dramatic compositions within the work of photographer Roger Witkin, with a macabre sense of human mortality.

1284   Young, Lisa Jaye. "Spiritual Minimalism." *PerAJ*. 1996 May; 18(2): 44-52. Illus.: Photo. B&W. 4. [Number 53.] Lang.: Eng.
USA: Pittsburgh, PA. 1995. Histories-sources. ■Report on the 1995 Carnegie International Festival.

1285   Wosiek, Maria, ed. "Zeznania Witolda Wandurskiego w więzieniu GPU." (The Inquiry on Witold Wandurski in the GPU Prison.) *PaT*. 1996; 45(3-4): 487-510. Append. Notes. Illus.: Photo. B&W. 2. Lang.: Pol.
USSR. 1933. Histories-sources. ■Materials from the inquiry against the Polish writer, who was connected with the Communist Party and who directed the Polish theatre in Kiev from 1929 to 1931.

1286   Santaella, Cristina. "Ritual Practices in Venezuela: The Dynamics of Domination and Submission in the Cult of María Lionza." *Gestos*. 1996 Apr.; 11(21): 127-144. Notes. Lang.: Eng.
Venezuela: Yaracuy. 1996. Critical studies. ■Theatrical aspects of pagan rituals devoted to the spirit of María Lionza.

1287   Dohn, Irma. "Verbindet die Kultur oder trennt sie?" (Does Culture Unite or Does it Divide?)*dRAMATURg*. 1996; 2: 36-43. Illus.: Photo. B&W. 1. Lang.: Ger.
Yugoslavia. 1996. Histories-sources. ■Excerpt from a discussion at the Bonner Biennale with theatre people from the former Yugoslavia, including Kaca Celan, Dušan Jovanović, Rejan Dukovski, Dušan Kovačević, and Goran Stefanovski, about the influence of politics on producing art.

1288   Furlan, Mira. "A Letter to My Co-Citizens." *PerAJ*. 1996 May; 18(2): 20-24. Illus.: Dwg. B&W. 1. [Number 53.] Lang.: Eng.
Yugoslavia. 1991. Histories-sources. ■Furlan, a Croatian actress married to a Croatian Serb, describes leaving her native country as a result of death threats because she worked with artists on both sides.

1289   Kis, Danilo. "On Nationalism." *PerAJ*. 1996 May; 18(2): 13-16. Notes. [Number 53.] Lang.: Eng.
Yugoslavia. 1978. Critical studies. ■Novelist Danilo Kis' critique of nationalism as paranoia and its narrowing effect on those afflicted with it, including artists.

1290   Miocinovic, Mirjana. "The Other Serbia." *PerAJ*. 1996 May; 18(2): 27-29. [Number 53.] Lang.: Eng.
Yugoslavia: Belgrade. 1992-1995. Histories-sources. ■Excerpt of an interview with Serbian theatre expert focusing on her reason for giving up her professor's chair at the University of Belgrade.

1291   Panovski, Naum. "Prelude to a War." *PerAJ*. 1996 May; 18(2): 2-12. Notes. [Number 53.] Lang.: Eng.
Yugoslavia. 1996. Historical studies. ■The effect of the disintegration of Yugoslavia, after the fall of communism, on its theatres and theatre artists, many of whom now live in exile. Also discusses theatre's role in the process.

Research/historiography

1292   Graff, Bernd. "Theatergeschichte als Mediengeschichtsschreibung." (Theatre History as Media Historiography.) *KSGT*. 1996 ; YB: 5-23. Notes. Biblio. Lang.: Ger.
Critical studies. ■Critique of the branch of theatre studies that depends uniquely on theatrical texts and performances. Includes discussion of Luhmann's system theory and its relevance to theatre studies.

CLASSED ENTRIES

THEATRE IN GENERAL: —Research/historiography

1293 Kvam, Kela. "Omkring teater og tekst." (Concerning Theatre and Text.) *TE.* 1996 Sep.; 80: 8-9. Illus.: Photo. B&W. 1. Lang.: Dan.
1996. Historical studies. ■Account of a seminar organized by the Department of Art History and Theatre Research at Copenhagen University on the relationship between theatrical text and textual theatre in the 1990s. Includes the author's opinions on the coexistence of visual and textual theatre in the future.

1294 Pleśniarowicz, Krzysztof. *Przestrzenie deziluzji. Współczesne modele dzieła teatralnego.* (The Space of Disillusion: Models of Contemporary Theatre.) Cracow: Universitas; 1996. 393 pp. Pref. Index. Illus.: Diagram. Lang.: Pol.
1900-1995. Critical studies. ■A summary of contemporary understanding of the play and a reflection of present methodological capacities of theatre studies.

1295 Ulrich, Paul S. "Abonnement Suspendu der Unterirdischen Gedächtnisstützen." (Suspended Subscription of Underground Memory Aids.) *KSGT.* 1996; YB: 83-101. Notes. Lang.: Ger.
Europe. 1700-1899. Historical studies. ■Prompter journals and almanacs as sources of information on eighteenth- and nineteenth-century staging practices.

1296 Danig, Susanne. "Inspirationen fra Artaud." (The Inspiration of Artaud.) *TE.* 1996 Dec.; 81-82: 40-43. Illus.: Photo. Dwg. 3. Lang.: Dan.
France. Denmark. 1896-1996. Historical studies. ■Account of a seminar in honor of the one hundredth anniversary of the birth of Antonin Artaud at the Department of Theatre Studies, Copenhagen University. Includes a brief biography of Artaud.

1297 Koch, Rüdiger. "'Nicht von Pappe!'." (Not of Cardboard!) *SIBMAS.* 1996; 11(2): 22-28. Lang.: Ger.
Germany: Darmstadt. 1800-1996. Historical studies. ■The paper theatre collection of collector Walter Röhler, with a brief history of paper theatre and its importance for theatre studies and children's theatre.

1298 Meiszies, Winfried. "'Theaterstadt Düsseldorf?'." (Theatre City Düsseldorf?)*SIBMAS.* 1996; 10(1): 25-29. Lang.: Ger.
Germany: Düsseldorf. 1996. Critical studies. ■Notes on local theatre historiography, which has the advantage of describing everyday history and theatre on the basis of extensive collections.

1299 Enyedi, Sándor. "Ferenczi Zoltán erdélyi színháztörténete száz év után." (Zoltán Ferenczi's Transylvanian Theatre History after One Hundred Years.) *SzSz.* 1996; 30/31: 147-152. Notes. Lang.: Hun.
Hungary. 1892-1895. Historical studies. ■Essay on Zoltán Ferenczi's work on the 'History of Theatre of Kolozsvár' (published in 1897 on the occasion of the 100th anniversary of Hungarian theatre in Transylvania) including some documents.

1300 Kerényi, Ferenc. "Az első magyar színháztörténész: Endrődy János." (The First Hungarian Theatre Historian: János Endrődy.) *SzSz.* 1996; 30/31: 141-146. Notes. Lang.: Hun.
Hungary. 1790-1793. Historical studies. ■Source-criticism and historical analysis of the works of Piarist teacher, writer János Endrődy (1756-1824), author of the history of the first Hungarian professional theatrical company (as introductions to the playtexts from their program published in four volumes, 1792-3).

1301 Gough, Richard. "Archive Review: Cricoteka—Centre for the Documentation of the work of Tadeusz Kantor." *PerfR.* 1996 Fall; 1(3): 107-109. Notes. Lang.: Eng.
Poland: Cracow. 1996. Histories-sources. ■A review, celebration and analysis of the Cricoteka archive of Tadeusz Kantor, which has assembled his writings and drawings, photographs and videos of his work, and published and unpublished texts, in order to preserve Kantor's ideas in the minds of future generations. The archive is also a museum and exhibition space.

1302 Dalrymple, Lynn. "Researching Drama and Theatre in Education in South Africa." *SATJ.* 1995 Sep.; 9(2): 61-81. Notes. Biblio. Lang.: Eng.
South Africa, Republic of. 1995. Critical studies. ■Examination of some research paradigms, and discussion of methods and methodologies that may best yield answers in the context of drama and theatre in education.

1303 Dreier, Martin. "Theatersammlung und Theatergeschichte." (Theatre Collection and Theatre History.) *KSGT.* 1996; YB: 73-81. Lang.: Ger.
Switzerland. 1996. Historical studies. ■Director of the Schweizer Theatersammlung describes contradictions between the collections and theatre history and the cooperation of the Schweizer Theatersammlung and the Institut für Theaterwissenschaft.

1304 Kershaw, Baz. "No 2 in The Messy-stuff Dialogues." *STP.* 1996 June; 13: 99-104. Lang.: Eng.
UK. 1996. Critical studies. ■A parodistic proposal that in order to boost ratings in the British National Research Assessment Exercise (a survey which ranks British theatre research institutions) the works of Aristotle and Boal might be included.

1305 MacDonald, Claire. "Archive Review." *PerfR.* 1996 Spr; 1(1): 123-125. Illus.: Dwg. 1. Lang.: Eng.
UK-England: Totnes, Devon. 1920-1995. Historical studies. ■An account of the archives held by the Dartington Hall Trust, which contain primary and source material relating to artists who worked and lived in the utopian community founded in Dartington in the 1920s to foster links between the progressive arts and social change. Identifies sections of the archive relating to Michael Chekhov's Theatre Studio, Kurt Joos and the Ballet Joos, Rudolph Laban, Martha Graham, Merce Cunningham, Margaret Barr, Margaret Wallmann, Mary Wigman and Udy Shankar.

1306 Trussler, Simon. "John Harrop: New Renaissance Man." *NTQ.* 1996; 12(45): 89. [NTQ Reports and Announcements.] Lang.: Eng.
UK-England. USA. 1931-1995. Biographical studies. ■Obituary of John Harrop, an Englishman who taught, directed, and acted on the west coast of North America, and who was advisory editor of *Theatre Quarterly* and *New Theatre Quarterly* for over twenty years.

1307 Mandressi, Rafael. "La nación en escena: Notas sobre el nacionalismo teatral en la historiografía uruguaya del teatro." (The Nation on Stage: Notes on Theatrical Nationalism in Uruguayan Theatre Historiography.) *LATR.* 1996 Spr; 29(2): 147-164. Biblio. Notes. Lang.: Spa.
Uruguay. 1910-1990. Historical studies. ■Chronology of Uruguayan theatre history approached through nationalism and national theatre.

1308 Grady, Sharon. "Between Research Design and Practice: In Pursuit of 'Something Else'." *YTJ.* 1996; 10: 16-24. Biblio. Lang.: Eng.
USA. 1996. Critical studies. ■Ideological struggles over research methods reveal relationships between research design and practice. Author argues that these struggles can be resolved by combining empirical studies with ethnographic research and application.

1309 Hill, Philip G. "Doctoral Projects in Progress in Theatre Arts, 1996." *TJ.* 1996 May; 48(2): 209-214. Lang.: Eng.
USA. 1996. Bibliographical studies. ■List of doctoral projects in theatre arts in the United States, organized by topic.

1310 McConachie, Bruce. "Parlor Combat." *JADT.* 1996 Fall; 8(3): 94-102. Notes. Lang.: Eng.
USA. 1996. Critical studies. ■Essay on academic theatre historiography: conflict between the interdisciplinary approach, and the traditional 'provincialism' of the past.

Theory/criticism

1311 Fiebach, Joachim. "Theatralitätsstudien unter Kulturhistorisch-komparatistischen Aspekten." (Studies of Theatricality from Historico-Cultural and Comparative Aspects.) 9-67 in Fiebach, Joachim, ed.; Mühl-Benninghaus, Wolfgang, ed. *Spektakel des Moderne.* Berlin: Humboldt-Universität: Institut für Theaterwissenschaft/Kulturelle Kommunikation; 1996. 203 pp. (Berliner Theaterwissenschaft 2.) Notes. Lang.: Ger.
1996. Critical studies. ■Develops a theory of studies of theatricality that analyzes cultural and sociopolitical communication. Includes discussion of other theoretical methods such as cultural studies, cultural and social historiography, and ethnographic anthropology.

1312 Höfele, Andreas. "Jetzt-Theater: Zur Inszenierung der emphatischen Präsenz." (Now-Theatre: Toward Perfor-

THEATRE IN GENERAL: —Theory/criticism

mance of the Emphatic Presence.) *FMT.* 1996; 1: 45-55. Notes. Lang.: Ger.
1996. Critical studies. ■An aspect of ritual theatre that shifts the focus from re-enactment to enactment.

1313 Kirchmann, Kay. "Die Signatur des Anderen." (The Signature of the Other.) *Tanzd.* 1996; 35(4): 8-15. Illus.: Photo. B&W. 8. Lang.: Ger.
1996. Critical studies. ■The changing relationships between signs and bodies in the media age. Includes discussions of digital light projections on the body, tattooing and body piercing.

1314 Schermbeek, Mieke N. van. *Anders dan anders. De heldin als Ideaal in de ogen van de vrouwelijke recipiënt.* (The Other Way Around: The Heroine as Ideal through the Eyes of the Female Receiver.) Amsterdam: Univ. of Amsterdam; 1996. 318 pp. Pref. Index. Biblio. [Summary in English.] Lang.: Dut.
1996. Critical studies. ■Dissertation on feminist literary criticism, with reference to the work of Teresa de Lauretis as well as Propp, Souriau, Freud, Levi-Strauss, Althusser, and Lotman.

1315 Conradie, P.J. "Debates Surrounding an Approach to African Tragedy." *SATJ.* 1996 May; 10(1): 25-34. Biblio. Lang.: Eng.
Africa. 1996. Critical studies. ■Considers the debate as to the viability and desirability of a distinctively African concept of tragedy.

1316 Kerr, David. "African Theories of African Theatre." *SATJ.* 1996 May; 10(1): 3-23. Notes. Biblio. Lang.: Eng.
Africa. 1969-1996. Critical studies. ■Looks at various approaches, by both African and Western theorists, to African theory: debates include explorations of indigenous theatre's close association with religious ritual, and the various theories on the origins and functions of African drama.

1317 Ukpokodu, Peter. "'Lest One Good Custom Should Corrupt the World': African Theatre and the 'Holy' Canon." *SATJ.* 1995 Sep.; 9(2): 3-25. Notes. Biblio. Lang.: Eng.
Africa. Europe. 1995. Critical studies. ■Argues for theatrical experimentations, and for canonical flexibility and inclusiveness, to make theatre more relevant to the different cultures of the world.

1318 McAuley, Gay. "Theatre Practice and Critical Theory." *ADS.* 1996 Apr.; 28: 140-145. Notes. Lang.: Eng.
Australia. 1996. Critical studies. ■Defends text/character/narrative based theatre from the post-modernist contention that it has gone the way of the dinosaur.

1319 Williams, David; George, David. "Listening to Images: Pleasure and/in the Gift." *ADS.* 1996 Apr.; 28: 63-78. Notes. Illus.: Photo. B&W. 4. Lang.: Eng.
Australia. Perth. 1994. Histories-sources. ■Condensation of several recorded discussions between academics David Williams, an actor and director, and David George, a director of multicultural performances, focusing on the interaction of practitioners from different art-forms, and the ethics of collaborative performance making.

1320 Andrès, Bernard. "De la critique en action: Témoignage d'un transfuge." (Criticism in Action: Testimony of a Renegade.) *JCT.* 1989; 52: 168-174. Notes. Illus.: Photo. B&W. 4. Lang.: Fre.
Canada. 1968-1989. Historical studies. ■Aesthetic and ideological characteristics of experimental theatre.

1321 Beauchamp, Hélène. "D'Osmose et de proximité." (Of Osmosis and Proximity.) *JCT.* 1989; 50: 80-82. Illus.: Photo. B&W. 1. Lang.: Fre.
Canada. 1989. Critical studies. ■Subversive power of theatre to carry more meaning than can be accounted for in quantifiable analysis.

1322 Belzil, Patricia; Burgoyne, Lynda; Fréchette, Richard; Lavoie, Pierre; Lévesque, Solange; Raynauld, Isabelle; Vaïs, Michel; Vigeant, Louise; Denis, J.L. "La Critique à l'épreuve du rire: 'HA ha! ...' au T.N.M." (Criticism Put to the Test of Laughter: 'HA ha! ...' at the Théâtre du Nouveau Monde.) *JCT.* 1990; 55: 126-135. Illus.: Photo. B&W. 10. Lang.: Fre.
Canada: Montreal, PQ. 1990. Critical studies. ■A pastiche of the styles of Montreal-area theatre critics, reviewing the 1990 Théâtre du Nouveau Monde production of *HA ha!* by Réjean Ducharme.

1323 Burgoyne, Lynda. "Lettre d'une sorcière à un 'critique' de théâtre." (Letter from a Witch to a Theatre 'Critic'.) *JCT.* 1993; 67: 38-40. Notes. Illus.: Dwg. 1. Lang.: Fre.
Canada: Montreal, PQ. 1993. Critical studies. ■Open letter to Luc Boulanger, theatre critic for *Voir*, a Montreal weekly, analyzing the sexism in his reviews of plays by women.

1324 Ducharme, André. "Demandez au turban qui dort." (Ask the Sleeping Turban.) *JCT.* 1989; 50: 178-179. Notes. Illus.: Photo. B&W. 1. Lang.: Fre.
Canada. 1989. Critical studies. ■Theatre tradition and modernity in competition with contemporary media technology.

1325 Gélinas, Aline. "La 'Présence du critique'." (The 'Presence of the Critic'.) *JCT.* 1991; 59: 53-57. Notes. Illus.: Photo. B&W. 3. Lang.: Fre.
Canada. 1991. Critical studies. ■Compares arts critics to artists, working in medium of language to change world through refined perception.

1326 Lavoie, Pierre; Pavlovic, Diane. "Ouverture." (Overture.) *JCT.* 1989; 50: 7-13. Notes. Illus.: Dwg. TA. Photo. B&W. 6. Lang.: Fre.
Canada: Montreal, PQ. 1976-1989. Historical studies. ■Evolution of Les Cahiers de Théâtre *Jeu* from ideologically-oriented criticism to aesthetic reflections. Table listing membership in editorial committee.

1327 Lavoie, Pierre. "De la rigueur et de la susceptibilité." (Rigour and Touchiness.) *JCT.* 1993; 67: 131-135. Notes. Illus.: Photo. B&W. 1. Lang.: Fre.
Canada. 1993. Critical studies. ■Québécois anti-intellectualism in theatre criticism, as described by Danielle Zana in *Journal d'une nomade au pays de Jacques Cartier* and exemplified by comments of playwright Michel Marc Bouchard.

1328 Lavoie, Pierre. "Un festival hanté par l'absence." (A Festival Haunted by Absence.) *JCT.* 1996; 78: 132-144. Notes. Illus.: Photo. B&W. 9. Lang.: Fre.
Canada: Montreal, PQ. 1994-1995. Historical studies. ■Montreal press coverage of the sixth Festival de Théâtre des Amériques.

1329 Lévesque, Solange. "Magie, mage, image." (Magic, Mage, Image.) *JCT.* 1996; 80: 152-155. Notes. Illus.: Photo. B&W. 2. Lang.: Fre.
Canada. 1950-1996. Critical studies. ■Value of theatre depends on excitement it generates rather than production value. Memories of 'magic' theatre experiences.

1330 O'Sullivan, Dennis. "Question(s) de rencontre." (Question(s) of Encounter.) *JCT.* 1989; 50: 34-38. Notes. Illus.: TA. Photo. B&W. 5. Lang.: Fre.
Canada. 1989. Critical studies. ■Dennis O'Sullivan of Théâtre Zoopsie describes theatrical production as a convergence of theatre traditions, institutions, the audience, and conditions of production.

1331 Pedneault, Hélène. "J'aime la vie." (I Love Life.) *JCT.* 1989; 52: 151-153. Illus.: Photo. B&W. 2. Lang.: Fre.
Canada. 1989. Critical studies. ■Affirms that all theatre is necessarily experimental.

1332 Vaïs, Michel. "D'Atrides à Zilon." (From Atridae to Zilon.) *JCT.* 1993; 66: 114-117. Notes. Illus.: Dwg. 2. Lang.: Fre.
Canada: Montreal, PQ. 1993. Critical studies. ■Considers the propriety of Montreal daily *Le Devoir*'s criticism of director Alexandre Hausvater in two January articles.

1333 Wickham, Philip. "Le chat sort du sac." (Letting the Cat out of the Bag.) *JCT.* 1996; 80: 198-203. Illus.: Dwg. Photo. B&W. 4. Lang.: Fre.
Canada. 1996. Critical studies. ■Relation of critics to theatre artists, and evaluation of Les Cahiers de théâtre *Jeu* in form of (fictitious) roundtable discussion.

1334 Fearnow, Mark. "Theatre for an Angry God: Public Burnings and Hangings in Colonial New York, 1741." *TDR.* 1996 Sum; 40 (2): 15-36. Notes. Biblio. Illus.: Photo. Dwg. Sketches. B&W. 8. Lang.: Eng.
Colonial America: New York. 1741. Historical studies. ■Public punishment and execution as theatrical event and popular entertainment. Theory that increase of public executions of African population by white

THEATRE IN GENERAL: —Theory/criticism

Protestants was rooted in belief of sacrifice for purification and activated by their fears of minorities.

1335   Krečetova, R. "Čerep." (A Skull.) *TeatZ*. 1996; 9: 24-26. Lang.: Rus.
Estonia: Tallinn. 1970-1979. Histories-sources. ■Theatre critic on her work at the Ugala theatre, Jaak Allik, artistic director.

1336   "Unheavenly Lengths." *Econ*. 1996 Mar 9; 338(7956): 85-86. Illus.: Photo. B&W. 1. Lang.: Eng.
Europe. 1945-1996. Critical studies. ■Cultural examination of sometimes excessive length of European film, theatre, symphonies, operas and literature.

1337   George, David E.R. "Performance Epistemology." *PerfR*. 1996 Spr; 1(1): 16-25. Notes. Lang.: Eng.
Europe. 1995. Critical studies. ■Attempts to establish a model for analyzing the nature and practice of performance through a phenomenological methodology, and insists that other approaches have proved inadequate. Argues that Western theatre has been dominated by words and ideas, and that performance should be seen as primary and representing nothing but itself.

1338   Hiss, Guido. "Die metaphysische Maschine. Aspekte der symbolistischen Theaterreform." (The Metaphysical Machine: Aspects of Symbolist Theatre Reform.) *FMT*. 1996; 2: 137-155. Notes. Lang.: Ger.
Europe. 1900. Critical studies. ■The historical meaning of Symbolist theatre.

1339   Hoffmann, Eric Alexander. "Theater als System. Ein systemtheoretischer Versuch." (Theatre as System: A Theoretical/Systematical Attempt.) *KSGT*. 1996; YB: 25-39. Notes. Biblio. Lang.: Ger.
Europe. 1700-1799. Critical studies. ■The use and effect of the paradigms of systems theory in theatre research, with examples from eighteenth-century works of aesthetics and theatrical programming.

1340   Kotte, Andreas. "Simulation als Problem der Theatertheorie." (Simulation as a Problem of Theatre Theory.) *FMT*. 1996; 1: 33-44. Notes. Lang.: Ger.
Europe. 1000-1996. Critical studies. ■The complex relationship between theatre and life, with reference to Baudrillard, Debord, Tertullian, and dance as mass movement.

1341   Lazaridès, Alexandre. "La Deuxième larme d'émotion." (The Second Tear of Emotion.) *JCT*. 1989; 50: 119-122. Illus.: Photo. B&W. 2. Lang.: Fre.
Europe. 1791-1989. Critical studies. ■Pathos and kitsch, drawing on musical examples from European classical music.

1342   Pavis, Patrice; Gonzalez Díaz de Villegas, Carmen, transl. "¿Hacia una teoría sobre el interculturalismo en el teatro? Posibilidades y limitaciones del teatro intercultural." (Toward a Theory of Interculturalism in the Theatre? Possibilities and Limitations of Intercultural Theatre.) *Cjo*. 1996 July/Dec.; 103: 37-54. Notes. Biblio. Illus.: Dwg. 11. [Translated from the introduction to *A Reader in Intercultural Performance*, ed. Pavis (London/New York: Routledge, 1996).] Lang.: Spa.
Europe. 1978-1996. Critical studies. ■Intercultural theatre and theory as seen in works of Peter Brook, Eugenio Barba and Ariane Mnouchkine, as well as Tadashi Suzuki and Robert Wilson, reflecting the diversity of world culture. How theory intersects with interculturalism.

1343   Pavis, Patrice. "Toward a Theory of Interculturalism in Theatre? The Possibilities and Limitations of Intercultural Theatre." *Gestos*. 1996 Apr.; 11(21): 23-47. Notes. Biblio. [Introduction to *A Reader in Intercultural Performance*, Patrice Pavis, ed. (London/New Nork, NY: Routledge, 1996).] Lang.: Eng.
Europe. 1978-1996. Critical studies. ■Significance and future of intercultural theatre, reciprocal influence of theatrical practices. Multiple definitions of culture and their importance to the theatre experience using examples from the writing of Brook, Barba and Mnouchkine.

1344   Varsa, Mátyás. "A színész második természete." (The Second Nature of the Actor.) *Sz*. 1996; 29(7) : 45-48. Illus.: Photo. B&W. 4. Lang.: Hun.

Europe. 1800-1990. Critical studies. ■A theoretical analysis of acting as retraced in foreign and Hungarian writings by outstanding theatre men.

1345   Costaz, Gilles. "Robert Lepage à Paris." (Robert Lepage in Paris.) *JCT*. 1992; 65: 160-164. Illus.: Photo. B&W. 3. Lang.: Fre.
France: Paris. 1992. Historical studies. ■Critical reception of five Lepage productions at XXIe Festival d'automne à Paris: Shakespeare's *Macbeth*, *Coriolan* and *La Tempête* (Théâtre Repère, translated by Michel Garneau) and Lepage's own *Polygraphe* (written with Marie Brassard) and *Les Aiguilles et l'Opium*.

1346   Lehmann, Johannes. "Betrachter und Betrachtete: Überlegungen zu Diderots 'Paradoxe sur le comédien'." (The Observer and the Observed: Thoughts on Diderot's *Paradoxe sur le comédien*.) *KSGT*. 1996; YB: 41-54. Notes. Lang.: Ger.
France. 1773. Historical studies. ■Argues that Diderot's text implies a specific aesthetics as well as a dramatic theory.

1347   Pavis, Patrice. "Performance Analysis: Space, Time, Action." *Gestos*. 1996 Nov.; 11(22): 11-32. Notes. Illus.: Graphs. Diagram. B&W. 3. Lang.: Eng.
France. 1996. Critical studies. ■Interdependence of space, time and action, and its importance when analyzing performance.

1348   Freud, Sigmund; Szántó, Judit, transl.; Fodor, Géza, intro. "Pszichopata alakok a színpadon." (Psychopathological Characters on the Stage.) *Sz*. 1996; 29(1): 32-35. Notes. Illus.: Photo. B&W. 4. Lang.: Hun.
Germany. 1905-1906. Critical studies. ■Translation of Freud's essay with an introduction by a theatre researcher.

1349   Lazarowicz, Klaus. "Theaterwissenschaft als Goldmacherkunst?" (Theatre Research as Alchemy?)*BGs*. 1996; 8/9: 16-17. Notes. Lang.: Ger.
Germany. 1986-1996. Critical studies. ■Critique of the use of the word 'theatricality' in studies by Joachim Fiebach, Rolf Münz, Andreas Kotte, and Helmar Schramm.

1350   O'Toole, Fintan. "What are Critics For?" *Econ*. 1996 Oct 12; 340(7987): 91-92. Illus.: Photo. B&W. 1. Lang.: Eng.
Ireland. 1996. Critical studies. ■Analysis of the job of a theatre critic by a working professional: his power, aesthetic judgement, common complaints of actors and directors, and how serious criticism can aid a play.

1351   D'Amico, Silvio; Bricchetto, Enrica, ed. *La vigilia di Caporetto. Diario di guerra 1916-1917*. (The Eve of Caporetto: A War Diary, 1916-1917.) Florence: Giunti; 1996. 302 pp. (900 Italiano.) Notes. Lang.: Ita.
Italy. 1916-1917. Histories-sources. ■The war diary of critic and theatre historian Silvio D'Amico, founder of the actor's academy (Accademia d'Arte Drammatica) in Rome.

1352   De Marinis, Marco; Chaple, Amparo, transl. "Repensar el texto dramatico." (Reconsidering the Dramatic Text.) *Cjo*. 1996 Jan-June; 102: 4-8. Notes. Illus.: Photo. 2. Lang.: Spa.
Italy. 1995. Historical studies. ■Essay on writing about and criticizing dramatic texts.

1353   Marinetti, Filippo Tommaso; Magyarósi, Gizella, transl.; Fodor, Géza, intro. "A futurizmus kiskátéja." (The Manifesto of Futurism.) *Sz*. 1996; 29(9): 39-48. Illus.: Photo. Dwg. Design. B&W. 8. Lang.: Hun.
Italy. 1913-1921. Critical studies. ■Introduction and publication of Marinetti's most significant writings on Italian Futurism.

1354   Leuthold, Steven. "Is There Art in Indigenous Aesthetics?" *JAML*. 1996 Win; 25(4): 320-338. Notes. Lang.: Eng.
North America. 1996. Critical studies. ■Discusses what things are second nature in a culture, i.e., craft, religious ritual, entertainment, that make it art, or can be considered art.

1355   Ward, Cynthia. "Twins Separated at Birth? West African Vernacular and Western Avant-Garde Performativity in Theory and Practice." *TextPQ*. 1994 Oct.; 14(4): 269-288. Notes. Biblio. Lang.: Eng.
North America. Togo. Europe. 1970-1994. Critical studies. ■Similarities and divergences between African vernacular performance, such as Togolese concert party, and the western avant-garde movement.

THEATRE IN GENERAL: —Theory/criticism

1356 *Teat'r v zerkale kritiki: Sbornik statej.* (Theatre in the Mirror of Criticism: Collected Articles.) Ekaterinburg: Dom aktera; 1996. 192 pp. Lang.: Rus.
Russia. 1996. Critical studies. ■Articles on theory of theatre.

1357 Mackin, Aleksand'r P. *Po sledam uchodjaščesgo veka.* (In the Footsteps of the Expiring Century.) Moscow: Aslan; 1996. 272 pp. Lang.: Rus.
Russia. 1906-1996. Histories-sources. ■Theatre critic looks back over his life, and the importance of theatre and of Mejerchol'd in it.

1358 Pavlova, I. "Pochval'noe slovo rutine." (In Praise of Routine.) *TeatZ.* 1996; 1: 2-4. Lang.: Rus.
Russia. 1996. Critical studies. ■Problems in the correlation of theatre and contemporary cinematography.

1359 Zorin, S.M. "Optičeskij teat'r—novyj vid ispolnitel'skogo iskusstva." (Optical Theatre: A New Performing Art.) 83-86 in *Elektronika, muzyka, svet.* Kazan: FEN; 1996. 299 pp. Lang.: Rus.
Russia. 1990-1996. Historical studies. ■Account of an emerging theatrical form, optical theatre.

1360 Hutchison, Yvette. "'Access to Rather Than Ownership of': South African Theatre History and Theory at a Crossroads." *SATJ.* 1996 May; 10(1): 35-47. Notes. Biblio. Illus.: Diagram. B&W. 1. Lang.: Eng.
South Africa, Republic of. 1900-1996. Historical studies. ■South African theatre history and theory to date, with an evaluation of possible neglected areas and a consideration of present trends in theatre, both mainstream and community, within the context of the cultural debate in South Africa.

1361 Loots, Lliane. "Colonized Bodies: Overcoming Gender Constructions of Bodies in Dance and Movement Education in South Africa." *SATJ.* 1995 Sep.; 9(2): 51-59. Notes. Biblio. Lang.: Eng.
South Africa, Republic of. 1995. Critical studies. ■Body as receptor of cultural signs and symbols of the gender dynamic in South African society. Dance and movement education as a way of exposing these constructs, drawing on the philosophy of Michel Foucault, with the focus on sexuality as a locus of power.

1362 Sirayi, Mzo. "Oral African Drama in South Africa: The Xhosa Indigenous Drama Forms." *SATJ.* 1996 May; 10(1): 49-61. Notes. Biblio. Lang.: Eng.
South Africa, Republic of. Africa. 1700-1996. Critical studies. ■Seeks to define African drama by discussing its origin in precolonial Africa, particularly South Africa, examining hunting, circumcision ceremonies, and oral narratives as forms of oral African drama, and discussing its function.

1363 Wahnón, Sultana; MacCandless, R.I., transl. "The Theatre Aesthetics of the Falange." 191-209 in Berghaus, Günter, ed. *Fascism and Theatre: Comparative Studies on the Aesthetics and Politics of Performance in Europe, 1925-1945.* Oxford: Berghahn Books; 1996. 315 pp. Notes. Index. Biblio. Illus.: Photo. 24. Lang.: Eng.
Spain. 1935-1945. Historical studies. ■The Fascist aesthetics of Ernesto Giménez Caballero and Gonzalo Torrente Ballester.

1364 Goodman, Lizbeth. "Feminisms and Theatres: Canon Fodder and Cultural Change." 19-42 in Campbell, Patrick, ed. *Analysing Performance: A Critical Reader.* Manchester/New York, NY: Manchester UP; 1996. 307 pp. Notes. Biblio. Index. Illus.: Photo. 5. Lang.: Eng.
UK-England. 1980-1995. Critical studies. ■The implications of feminist theatre for academic study, as well as major theoretical concepts which help to situate feminist theatre alongside other areas of cultural representation and academic study.

1365 Hoy, Mikita. "Joyful Mayhem: Bakhtin, Football Songs, and the Carnivalesque." *TextPQ.* 1994 Oct.; 14(4): 289-304. Notes. Biblio. Lang.: Eng.
UK-England. 1994. Critical studies. ■Bakhtin's theories of carnival and the carnivalesque applied to British football songs, shedding new light on the relationship between lyric and performance, chants and challenges, and allegiances and enemies.

1366 Moody, Jane. "The Silence of New Historicism: A Mutinous Echo from 1830." *NCT.* 1996 Win; 24(2): 61-89. Notes. Illus.: Handbill. B&W. 2. Lang.: Eng.
UK-England. London. 1797-1830. Critical studies. ■An argument against the marginalizing of spectator and the blurring of the conventional boundaries between performances, texts and events in the theory of the 'New historicism' through an analysis of the text, marketing, and performance at the Royal Coburg of the nautical drama *The Mutiny at the Nore* by Douglas Jerrold.

1367 Rubidge, Sarah. "Does Authenticity Matter? The Case For and Against Authenticity in the Performing Arts." 219-233 in Campbell, Patrick, ed. *Analysing Performance: A Critical Reader.* Manchester/New York, NY: Manchester UP; 1996. 307 pp. Index. Notes. Biblio. Lang.: Eng.
UK-England. 1990-1995. Critical studies. ■The authenticity debate in the performing arts.

1368 Sanchez-Colberg, Ana. "Altered States and Subliminal Spaces: Charting the Road towards a Physical Theatre." *PerfR.* 1996 Sum; 1(2): 40-56. Notes. Biblio. Illus.: Photo. B&W. 4. Lang.: Eng.
UK-England. Germany. 1900-1996. Historical studies. ■Attempts to define the evolution of physically-based performance, without reductive classification. Argues that contextualizing physical theatre requires consideration of its locations within both avant-garde theatre and avant-garde dance. Includes consideration of the history of contemporary dance from Duncan to Bausch, and of movement as language in the legacy of German expressionism and Laban. Physical theatre is seen to have emerged as a hybrid since the early 1980s, and the performances and practices of DV8 and of Vandekeybus are analyzed in detail.

1369 Sheperd, Simon. "The Blind Leading the Blind." *NCT.* 1996 Win; 24(2): 90-107. Notes. Lang.: Eng.
UK-England: London. 1807-1809. Critical studies. ■A critique of the 'new historicism' through a study of the afterpiece *The Blind Boy*, in which the author seeks the identity of author, the reason for the play's popularity, and circumstances of performance.

1370 Stowell, Sheila. "Suffrage Critics and Political Action: A Feminist Agenda." 166-184 in Booth, Michael R., ed.; Kaplan, Joel H., ed. *The Edwardian Theatre: Essays on Performance and the Stage.* Cambridge: Cambridge UP; 1996. 243 pp. Notes. Index. Illus.: Photo. 2. Lang.: Eng.
UK-England. 1912-1914. Historical studies. ■Theatre criticism in suffrage newspapers. Includes discussion of political protests at theatres.

1371 Allison, John M., Jr. "Narrative and Time: A Phenomenological Reconsideration." *TextPQ.* 1994 Apr.; 14(2): 108-125. Notes. Lang.: Eng.
USA. 1994. Critical studies. ■Argues that human beings are best understood as story-*livers* rather than as story-tellers, and explores the implications of a broader understanding of time and narrative for the study of literary, dramatic, and natural narrative.

1372 Auslander, Philip. "Live Performance in a Mediatized Culture." *TA.* 1994; 47: 1-10. Notes. Lang.: Eng.
USA. 1994. Critical studies. ■Argues that the traditional assumption that mediatized representations are grounded in or preceded by live events no longer applies, that their status has been inverted.

1373 Bacon, Wallace A. "The Dangerous Shores—One Last Time." *TextPQ.* 1996 Oct.; 16(4): 356-358. Notes. Lang.: Eng.
USA. 1996. Critical studies. ■Essay on the necessary relationship between text and performance.

1374 Banks, Stephen P. "Performing Public Announcements: The Case of Flight Attendants' Discourse." *TextPQ.* 1994 July; 14(3): 253-267. Notes. Biblio. Lang.: Eng.
USA. 1994. Critical studies. ■Analysis of public announcements by flight attendants on nine flights of three US airlines, using Norman Fairclough's theoretical performance scheme of description, interpretation, and explanation.

1375 Birringer, Johannes. "Border Media: Performing Postcolonial History." *Gestos.* 1996 Apr.; 11(21): 49-65. Notes. Illus.: Photo. B&W. 1. Lang.: Eng.

THEATRE IN GENERAL: —Theory/criticism

USA. 1992-1996. Critical studies. ■Changing attitudes toward historical dogma in the post-colonial Third World as reflected in two performance pieces: *The Year of the White Bear/The New World (B)Order* and *Two Undiscovered Amerindians Visit the First World*, written and performed by Guillermo Gómez-Peña and Coco Fusco.

1376 Bredbeck, Gregory W. "The Ridiculous Sound of One Hand Clapping: Placing Ludlam's 'Gay' Theatre in Space and Time." *MD*. 1996 Spr; 39(1): 64-83. Notcs. Lang.: Eng.
USA: New York, NY. 1967-1987. Critical studies. ■Comparison of Ludlam's development of Ridiculous Theatre with the germination of gay and lesbian politics in New York. Includes excerpts from Ludlam's writing.

1377 Dolan, Jill. "Building a Theatrical Vernacular: Responsibility, Community, Ambivalence, and Queer Theatre." *MD*. 1996 Spr; 39(1): 1-15. Notes. Lang.: Eng.
USA: New York, NY. 1960-1996. Histories-sources. ■Keynote address from Queer Theatre Conference with new introduction and summary of panels and conference events by author. Discusses rise of gay and lesbian studies, performance and criticism.

1378 Gantar, Jure. "Catching the Wind in a Net: The Shortcomings of Existing Methods for the Analysis of Performance." *MD*. 1996 Win; 39(4): 537-546. Notes. Lang.: Eng.
USA. 1996. Critical studies. ■Division between academic and theatre practitioners in performance analysis, theoretical analysis of text vs. live performance.

1379 Gerland, Oliver. "Brecht and the Courtroom: Alienating Evidence in the 'Rodney King' Trials." *TextPQ*. 1994 Oct.; 14(4): 305-318. Notes. Lang.: Eng.
USA: Los Angeles, CA. 1991-1994. Critical studies. ■Applying Brecht's theory of alienation to the evidentiary approaches of the attorneys in the trials of the police officers who beat Rodney King.

1380 Horwitz, Simi. "John Lahr: Literary Lion." *TheaterW*. 1996 Feb 19; 9(29): 20-27. Illus.: Photo. B&W. 1. Lang.: Eng.
USA: New York, NY. 1929-1996. Histories-sources. ■*New Yorker* magazine theatre critic discusses his approach to theatrical criticism, current theatre scene, writing influences, and personal background.

1381 Jarmon, Leslie. "Performance as a Resource in the Practice of Conversation Analysis." *TextPQ*. 1996 Oct.; 16(4): 336-355 . Notes. Biblio. Illus.: Photo. B&W. 15. Lang.: Eng.
USA: Austin, TX. 1996. Empirical studies. ■Examination of embodied performance as an analytical tool when studying human interaction, as used in a study conducted in the speech department at the University of Texas.

1382 Lamont, Rosette C. "Towards an International Theatre." *MD*. 1996 Win; 39(4): 585-598. Notes. Lang.: Eng.
USA. 1950-1995. Critical studies. ■The participation of American artists in a physical and intellectual international theatre through images, language and movement. Examines Tadeusz Kantor's Cricot 2, Luc Bondy's performance of Peter Handke's *Die Stunde da wir nichts voneinander wussten (The Hour We Knew Nothing of Each Other)* at Le Châtelet, and *The Trojan Women: A Love Story* by Charles Mee, directed by Tina Landau.

1383 Moore, Dick. "Critic Talks of Criticism, Acting." *EN*. 1996 Nov.; 81(9): 2. Lang.: Eng.
USA: New York, NY. 1958. Histories-sources. ■Reprint of a 1958 interview with now deceased theatre critic Walter Kerr. Kerr discusses what constitutes quality acting, good criticism, and the obligations of the critic.

1384 Muñoz, José Esteban. "Ephemera as Evidence: Introductory Notes to Queer Acts." *WPerf*. 1996; 8(2): 5-17. Notes. Biblio. [Issue 16.] Lang.: Eng.
USA. 1996. Critical studies. ■Questions surrounding the issue of proof in performance studies. The ontological aspects of performance lead to accusations of a lack of historical grounding and conceptual staying power. Author argues that this ephemeral quality of performance acts as an alternative to presentation of evidence, especially in regards to queer performance.

1385 Nellhaus, Tobin. "Performance, Hegemony and Communication Practices: Toward a Cultural Materialist Analysis." *TA*. 1996; 49: 3-14. Notes. Lang.: Eng.

USA. 1996. Critical studies. ■Suggests a further investigation into the social use and organization of the modes of communication and how they govern performance strategies, and an examination of the role of performance in reproducing and/or transforming social relations.

1386 Nemser, Cindy. "Critical Decision: Theaters vs. Reviewers." *TheaterW*. 1996 Oct 7; 10(10): 34-37. Lang.: Eng.
USA. 1963-1996. Historical studies. ■History and current practice of the extended preview of a production to avoid receiving negative reviews. *New York Newsday* critic Linda Winer's role in aiding Consumer Affairs to create policy regarding previews, opinions of a selection of reviewers on the subject.

1387 Plum, Jay. "Pleasure, Politics, and the Performance of Community: Pomo Afro Homos's *Dark Fruit*." *MD*. 1996 Spr; 39(1): 117-131. Notes. Lang.: Eng.
USA: San Francisco, CA. 1990-1996. Critical studies. ■Relationship between identity and representation in Pomo Afro Homos' play and explores performance as a means of forging community. Pomo's founder Brian Freeman describes representation of lesbians and gay men of color.

1388 Rodden, John. "A *TPQ* Interview: The Performing Artist-Intellectual: The Personae and Personality of Camille Paglia." *TextPQ*. 1996 Jan.; 16(1): 62-82. Notes. Lang.: Eng.
USA. 1990-1996. Histories-sources. ■Interview with critic/academic Camille Paglia, discussing her theories on the dramatic versus the literary, and the critic as artist.

1389 Rosenberg, Tiina. "Klassisk teater, en dragshow?" (The Classical Theatre, a Drag Show?)*Tningen*. 1996; 20(76-77): 46-50. Illus.: Photo. B&W. Lang.: Swe.
USA. Europe. 1981. Critical studies. ■Feminist critic Sue-Ellen Case's work on the non-existence of women in theatre history, and Heiner Müller's plays.

1390 Sidnell, Michael J. "Performing Writing: Inscribing Theatre." *MD*. 1996 Win; 39(4): 547-557. Notes. Lang.: Eng.
USA. 1996. Critical studies. ■Difference in theatrical texts as pure literature and those performed. Complex relations between writing and performance of theatre.

1391 States, Bert O. "Performance and Metaphor." *TJ*. 1996 Mar.; 48(1): 1-26. Notes. Biblio. Lang.: Eng.
USA. 1996. Critical studies. ■Critical essay on the meaning and nature of performance. Author examines the current state of performance theory, using the danger of metaphorical analogy to illustrate the difficulty of defining performance. The theoretical writings of Erving Goffman, Victor Turner, Richard Schechner, and Peggy Phelan are used as illustration.

1392 Wallace, Robert. "Performance Anxiety: 'Identity,' 'Community,' and Tim Miller's *My Queer Body*." *MD*. 1996 Spr; 39(1): 97-116. Notes. Lang.: Eng.
USA. 1992-1996. Critical studies. ■Performance theories applied to Miller's one man show: representation of the human body in performance, critical response.

1393 Watson, Ian. "Theatre as Social Science: A Comparative Study of Eugenio Barba's Barter Performances and the 1992 Los Angeles Riots." *MD*. 1996 Win; 39(4): 574-584. Notes. Lang.: Eng.
USA: Los Angeles, CA. 1970-1992. Critical studies. ■Performance studies as an analytic tool for the understanding of social events. As an example, the 1992 Los Angeles riots are compared to the theatrical barter of Eugenio Barba.

Training

1394 Beauchamp, Hélène. "Training to Survive, I: The Making of Survivors: The Space Within." *CTR*. 1996 Fall; 88: 18-22. Notes. Illus.: Photo. B&W. 9. Lang.: Eng.
Canada. 1996. Critical studies. ■Training process for creative artists, spanning from initial training to production. Emphasis on personal space, instructional methods, creation and composition.

1395 Walling, Savannah. "Training to Survive, II: Training, Growth, and Healing: A Strategy for Living." *CTR*. 1996 Fall; 88: 23-25. Illus.: Photo. B&W. 3. Lang.: Eng.

THEATRE IN GENERAL: —Training

Canada: Vancouver, BC. 1996. Critical studies. ■Vancouver Moving Theatre's artistic director, Savannah Walling, discusses theatre training as a method of self discovery and development. Emphasis on personal growth and healing.

1396 Brown, John Russell. "Performance, Theatre Training, and Research." *NTQ.* 1996 Aug.; 12(47): 207-215. Notes. Lang.: Eng.

UK-England. USA. India. 1992-1995. Critical studies. ■Develops the articles on training for the theatre by Clive Barker (*NTQ* 1995, 11(42): 99-108) and Richard Schechner (*TDR* 1995: 39(2): 7-10), and makes alternative proposals.

1397 Lacey, Stephen; Pye, Doug. "Getting Started: an Approach to Relating Practical and Critical Work." *STP.* 1994 Dec.; 10: 20-30. Lang.: Eng.

UK-England: Reading. 1994. Histories-sources. ■Drama teachers at University of Reading discuss their use of practical drama to teach critical practice, which they believe should be central to a degree course in drama.

1398 Haedicke, Susan C. "'I Don't Have Time to Teach Writing': The Artist's Journal in Theatre Courses." *TTop.* 1996 Mar.; 6 (1): 43-50. Notes. Biblio. Illus.: Photo. B&W. 2. Lang.: Eng.

USA. 1996. Critical studies. ■Strategy for teaching writing in theatre courses. Emphasis on student creativity and artistic freedom.

1399 Istel, John. "Under the Influence: A Survey." *AmTh.* 1996 Jan.; 13(1): 38-42, 80-82. Illus.: Photo. Sketches. B&W. 4. Lang.: Eng.

USA. 1996. Histories-sources. ■Responses of theatre educators to survey that asked how influence of film, television and mass media on our culture has shaped their approach to training actors for the theatre.

1400 Napoleon, Davi. "Mixing Musicals and *Macbeth*." *TheaterW.* 1996 Oct 14; 10(11): 32-38. Illus.: Photo. B&W. 3. Lang.: Eng.

USA. 1996. Historical studies. ■Theatre programs at University of Arizona and Syracuse University which combine music and theatre.

DANCE
General

Administration

1401 Klingner, Norbert. "Zur urheberrechtlichen Schutzfähigkeit der Choreographie." (Toward a Copyright for Choreography.) *Tanzd.* 1996; 33(2): 12-14. Lang.: Ger.

Germany. 1996. Technical studies. ■Essential features of German copyright law for independent choreographers, including extent, imitation and adaptation, and payment.

1402 Ångström, Anna. "På tok för lång!" (Far Too Tall!) *Danst.* 1996; 6(3): 22-24. Illus.: Photo. B&W. Lang.: Swe.

Sweden: Stockholm. 1916. Historical studies. ■A survey of the careers of Bengt Häger as impresario to dance, director of dance schools, the Dancemuseum and the Carina Ari Library, as well as the Grand Prix International Video Dance, with references to Birgit Cullberg, Kurt Joos and Rolf de Maré.

Design/technology

1403 Schmidt, Jochen. "Happy-End, kurz vor Schluss." (Happy End, Just Before the End.) *DB.* 1996; 6: 14-18. Illus.: Photo. B&W. 5. Lang.: Ger.

Netherlands. 1946-1996. Historical studies. ■Set designer Keso Dekker and his collaboration with choreographer Hans von Manen.

Institutions

1404 Beaven, Pat. "Dancenet." *PAC.* 1996; 30(3): 18-19. Illus.: Photo. B&W. 2. Lang.: Eng.

Canada: Toronto, ON. 1996. Critical studies. ■Dancenet provides a stage for local dancers of all kinds to perform, as well as a networking opportunity for artists, agents and educators.

1405 Cossette, Claude. "Chronologie des oeuvres et des événements présentés par Tangente 1981-1991." (Chronol-

ogy of Works and Events Presented by Tangente 1981-1991.) *JCT.* 1991; 59: 59-91. Illus.: Photo. B&W. 8. Lang.: Fre.

Canada: Montreal, PQ. USA: New York, NY. 1981-1991. Histories-sources. ■Chronological list giving date, location, title, creator(s) and nature of event (dance, theatre, photo exhibit, etc.) for every event presented by Tangente dance company.

1406 Roepstorff, Sylvester. "Kaerlighed til gulvet og fordobling af kroppene." (A Love for the Floor and Doubling the Bodies.) *TE.* 1996 Dec.; 81-82: 48-51. Illus.: Photo. B&W. 4. Lang.: Dan.

Denmark: Copenhagen. 1996. Reviews of performances. ■Account of Dancin' City '96 festival, with reference to *Decodex* choreographed by Philippe Decouflé and to Merce Cunningham.

1407 Servos, Norbert. "Pas de deux mit Publikum." (Pas de deux with Audience.) *DB.* 1996; 3: 34-37. Illus.: Photo. B&W. 2. Lang.: Ger.

Germany: Berlin. 1996. Historical studies. ■Portrait of the dance company of the Komische Oper, directed by Marc Jonkers and Jan Linkens: program, audience, open working methods, slow changes.

1408 Stoll, Dieter. "Tanz im Dunkeln." (Dance in the Dark.) *DB.* 1996; 4: 30-31. Illus.: Photo. B&W. 2. Lang.: Ger.

Germany: Nuremberg. 1996. Historical studies. ■The effect of the political and cultural decision to subordinate the successful dance company Tanzwerk, directed by choreographer Amanda Miller, to the administration of the opera company, Opernhaus, of Städtische Bühnen.

1409 Hofsten, Ingela. "Norrland får mera dans på scen." (Norrland Will Have More Dance On Stage.) *Danst.* 1996; 6(1): 14-15. Illus.: Photo. B&W. Lang.: Swe.

Sweden: Sundsvall, Kiruna, Härnösand. 1995. Critical studies. ■A report from the new possibilites to enjoy all sorts of dance in the north of Sweden, with references to the young company Norrdans and the choreographer Jeanne Yasko.

1410 Schneider, Katja. "'Ich freue mich über jede Veränderung'." (I Am Glad about All Changes.) *Tanzd.* 1996; 35(4): 4-7. Illus.: Photo. B&W. 3. Lang.: Ger.

Switzerland: Basel. 1980-1996. Histories-sources. ■Conversation with Joachim Schlömer, artistic director of Tanztheater Basel: his aesthetic concepts and working methods.

Performance spaces

1411 Schneider, Detlev. "Das Festspielhaus Helleran." (The Helleran Festival Theatre.) *BtR.* 1996; Special issue: 46-50. Illus.: Design. Dwg. Photo. B&W. Color. 12. Lang.: Ger.

Germany: Dresden. 1910-1996. Historical studies. ■History of the dance theatre of the Helleran complex, and its use by the NS, the Red Army, and currently by the friends' association, Förderverein.

Performance/production

1412 Burgoyne, Lynda. "Milène Roy: le corps parlant." (Milène Roy: The Speaking Body.) *JCT.* 1996; 79: 108-111. Notes. Illus.: Photo. B&W. 3. Lang.: Fre.

Canada: Montreal, PQ. 1996. Biographical studies. ■Juxtaposition of text and movement in Milène Roy's one-woman show *Une cloche à vache suspendue à mon âme* (1996, Théâtre la Chapelle) and biographical information on Roy.

1413 Chouinard, Marie. "Le Don de kinesthésie universelle." (The Gift of Universal Kinaesthetics.) *JCT.* 1989; 50: 145-147. Illus.: Photo. B&W. 1. Lang.: Fre.

Canada: Montreal, PQ. 1989. Histories-sources. ■Dancer and choreographer Marie Chouinard's purpose in dancing as manifestation of impulses.

1414 Dussault, Geneviève. "Le Signe animé: Réflexions sur la notation de la danse." (The Animated Sign: Reflections on Dance Notation.) *JCT.* 1991; 59: 46-50. Biblio. Illus.: Photo. B&W. 6. Lang.: Fre.

Canada. USA. 1900-1991. Historical studies. ■Historic and contemporary forms and function of dance notation.

1415 Gélinas, Aline. "Le corps, l'espace." (Body, Space.) *JCT.* 1996; 80: 142-143. Illus.: Photo. B&W. 2. Lang.: Fre.

DANCE: General—Performance/production

Canada: Montreal, PQ. 1992. Histories-sources. ■Representation of body in Aline Gélinas' choreographies *La Consentante (The Willing Woman)* and *Tombeau de la soeur (Tomb of the Sister).*

1416 Lévesque, Solange. "Une étincelle dit: 'Lumière': Entretien avec Alain Populaire." (A Spark Says: 'Light': Interview with Alain Populaire.) *JCT.* 1996; 81: 90-98. Illus.: Photo. B&W. 3. Lang.: Fre.
Canada: Montreal, PQ. Belgium. 1996. Histories-sources. ■Alain Populaire's 1996 choreography *Equinoxes* and his views on creating dance in Belgium and Quebec.

1417 Maheu, Gilles. "Laisser une empreinte." (Leaving a Mark.) *JCT.* 1989; 50: 164-165. Illus.: Photo. B&W. 1. Lang.: Fre.
Canada: Montreal, PQ. 1989. Histories-sources. ■Director Gilles Maheu compares his technique of using frozen images to photography.

1418 Mirbt, Felix; Vaïs, Michel, transl. "Une anecdote?" (An anecdote?)*JCT.* 1996; 80: 126. Illus.: Photo. B&W. 1. Lang.: Fre.
Canada: Ottawa, ON. 1988. Histories-sources. ■Author describes how he staged Stravinskij's *L'Histoire du soldat* for the National Arts Centre.

1419 Panet-Raymond, Silvy. "Habiller et dévêtir le regard de la spectatrice." (Dressing and Undressing the Female Spectator's Gaze.) *JCT.* 1991; 59: 51-52. Illus.: Photo. B&W. 2. Lang.: Fre.
Canada. 1991. Histories-sources. ■Dancer Silvy Panet-Raymond's concept of communication through dance beyond language and stylistic codes.

1420 Vedel, Karen Arnfred. "De dansede Sydney og Øster Faelled Torv." (They Danced in Sydney and at Øster Faelled Torv.) *TE.* 1996 Dec.; 81-82: 52-55. Illus.: Photo. B&W. 4. Lang.: Dan.
Denmark: Copenhagen. Australia. 1996. Reviews of performances. ■*Compression 100*, created by Tess de Quincey, choreographer and dancer, and Stuart Lynch, sculptor and dancer. The piece has been staged in Sydney and in Copenhagen during the Dancin' City '96 festival.

1421 Niiniluoto, Maarit; Wirberg, Agneta, transl. "Den finska tangon till lyckan bär." (The Finnish Tango Leads to Happiness.) *Danst.* 1996; 6(6): 22-23. Illus.: Photo. B&W. Lang.: Swe.
Finland. 1917. Critical studies. ■A survey of how the tango became genuinely Finnish.

1422 Foster, Susan Leigh. "Pygmalion's No-Body and the Body of Dance." 131-154 in Diamond, Elin, ed. *Performance and Cultural Politics.* London/New York, NY: Routledge; 1996. 282 pp. Notes. Index. Lang.: Eng.
France. 1734-1847. Critical studies. ■Three different choreographic realizations of Pygmalion's story—by Marie Sallé in 1734, Louis Milon in 1799, and Arthur St. Léon in 1847, all staged at the Paris Opéra, with a paradigm for the narrativization of theatrical dance.

1423 Gallotta, Jean-Claude; Buffard, Claude-Henri. "Comme un cheval fou." (Like a Mad Horse.) *JCT.* 1989; 50: 140. Illus.: Dwg. 1. Lang.: Fre.
France: Grenoble. 1989. Histories-sources. ■Choreographer Jean-Claude Gallotta describes conditions necessary for him to work.

1424 "Else Lang." *Tanzd.* 1996; 35(4): 26-29. Illus.: Photo. B&W. 5. Lang.: Ger.
Germany: Cologne. 1905-1996. Biographical studies. ■Account in tabular form of Lang's work as a dancer, teacher, and choreographer.

1425 Möller, Ute. "Tanz kann im Gehirn glücklich machen." (Dance Can Make You Happy in the Brain.) *Tanzd.* 1996; 33 (2): 4-11. Illus.: Photo. B&W. 10. Lang.: Ger.
Germany. 1976-1996. Histories-sources. ■Interview with dance photographer Gert Weigelt.

1426 Schmidt, Jochen. "Ein Meister auf der Durchreise." (A Master Passing Through.) *DB.* 1996; 5: 22-24. Illus.: Photo. B&W. 2. Lang.: Ger.
Germany: Hagen. UK-England. 1958-1996. Biographical studies. ■English choreographer Richard Wheelock, focusing on his work in Hagen since 1991.

1427 Stöckemann, Patricia. "Ich möchte etwas über Menschen erzählen." (I Would Like to Tell Something about People.) *Tanzd.* 1996; 34(3): 4-9. Illus.: Photo. B&W. 4. Lang.: Ger.
Germany: Münster. 1980-1996. Histories-sources. ■Conversation with dancer and choreographer Daniel Goldin.

1428 Wolf, Dagmar. "Maja Lex. Tänzerin, Choreographin und Pädagogin der reinen Gesetze." (Maja Lex: Dancer, Choreographer, and Teacher of the Pure Rules.) *Tanzd.* 1996; 34(3): 15-23. Notes. Append. Illus.: Photo. B&W. 8. Lang.: Ger.
Germany. 1906-1986. Biographical studies. ■Describes Lex's life from an artistic and educational point of view, with regard to its political aspects.

1429 Jálics, Kinga; Becker-Rau, Christel, photo. "'Egyetlen ember változik át'—Találkozás M. Kecskés Andrással táncpantomim-művésszel." ('There Is One Single Man Changing'—Meeting M. András Kecskés, the Dance-Pantomime Artist.) *Tanc.* 1995; 26(7/9): 12-13. Illus.: Photo. B&W. 1. Lang.: Hun.
Hungary. 1974-1995. Histories-sources. ■A talk with an artist whose solo-performances are a kind of individual combination of classical pantomime, expressive dance and ballet.

1430 Jálics, Kinga; Szalay, Zoltán, photo.; Simara, László, photo. "Mai Odüsszeusz—Solymos Pál." (An Odyssey of Today—Pál Solymos.) *Tanc.* 1995; 26(4/6): 10-11. Illus.: Photo. B&W. 2. Lang.: Hun.
Hungary. 1972-1995. Histories-sources. ■Conversation with the 'senior' solo dancer of Pécs Ballet on the occasion of his performance of the title role of *Rock Odüsszeia (Rock Odyssey)* performed by the Rock Theatre in Budapest.

1431 Kaán, Zsuzsa. "Báli táncok reneszánsza: A palotás—A keringő." (Renaissance of Ballroom Dancing: The 'Palotás'—The Viennese Waltz.) *Tanc.* 1995; 26(10/12): 52-53. Illus.: Photo. Dwg. B&W. 2. Lang.: Hun.
Hungary. 1700-1990. Historical studies. ■Introduces two ballroom dances: 'Palotás' and the Viennese Waltz, as 'overture' to the ball season and the rebirth of the February opera-ball in 1995.

1432 Pór, Anna. "Fülöp Viktor és *A szarvaskirály* a Radnóti Színpadon." (Viktor Fülöp and *King Stag* on Radnóti Stage.) *Tanc.* 1995; 26(4/6): 50. Lang.: Hun.
Hungary: Budapest. 1995. Reviews of performances. ■Viktor Fülöp's choreography for *Il re cervo* by Carlo Gozzi, using movement reminiscent of *commedia dell' arte.*

1433 Ananya. "Training in Indian Classical Dance: A Case Study." *ATJ.* 1996 Spr; 13(1): 68-91. Biblio. Notes. Lang.: Eng.
India. 1949-1996. Critical studies. ■Teacher/disciple relationship in Indian classical dance training. Dedication to the teacher, requirements to be a guru, decline of the system in contrast with more modern dance training, traditional and modern teaching methods.

1434 Brakel-Papenhuijzen, Clara. *Classical Javanese Dance: The Surakarta Tradition and its Terminology.* Leiden: Koninklijk Instituut voor Taal-, Land- en Volkenkunde; 1995. 252 pp. Illus.: Photo. Dwg. B&W. 114. Lang.: Eng.
Indonesia. 1850-1990. Historical studies. ■Detailed study of the Surakarta tradition.

1435 Day, Tony. "In Search of Southeast Asian Performance." *RevIM.* 1995 Win/Sum; 29: 125-140. Notes. Biblio. Lang.: Eng.
Indonesia. 1880-1995. Critical studies. ■Explores Southeast Asian poetry and dance performance for cultural expressivity, meanings of tradition and modernity in the works, definition of performance and ritual, and ritual and spectacle in these forms.

1436 Lipp, Nele. "Metaphern unserer Epoche." (Metaphors of Our Age.) *Tanzd.* 1996; 33(2): 27-30. Illus.: Photo. B&W. 2. Lang.: Ger.
Italy. Belgium. 1989-1994. Histories-sources. ■Interview with visual artist Fabrizio Plessi about his collaboration with choreographer Frédéric Flamand on a dance piece called *Icare—Titanic—Ex-machine (Icarus—Titanic—Ex machina).*

DANCE: General—Performance/production

1437   Schino, Mirella; Sykes, Leo, transl. "Shankuntala Among the Olive Trees." *ATJ.* 1996 Spr; 13(1): 92-111. Notes. Biblio. Illus.: Photo. B&W. 3. Lang.: Eng.
Italy. Denmark: Holstebro. 1993-1996. Critical studies. ■Project in which thirty Western scholars, actors, directors worked with director Eugenio Barba and Sanjukta Panigrahi, a dance artist, exploring ways of expressing the Sanskrit drama *Shakuntala.* Developed in three stages at Fara Sabina and Holstebro under the auspices of the International School of Theatre Anthropology.

1438   Majorova, M. "Žukovskie sezony." (Žukovskij's Seasons.) *Balet.* 1996; 1: 29-31. Lang.: Rus.
Russia: Zhukovsky. 1990-1996. Historical studies. ■The school of the arts, Fantasija dance theatre, and children's dance theatre (Detskij Teat'r Tanca) of the city of Zhukovsky.

1439   Moisejév, Igor Aleksandrovič. *Ja vspominaju ... Gastrol' dlinoju v žizn'.* (I Remember Now: Long Tour of a Life.) Moscow: Soglasie; 1996. 224 pp. Lang.: Rus.
Russia: Moscow. 1924-1996. Histories-sources. ■The choreographer's memories of his work for the Bolšoj and folk dance group, as well as problems in the art of dance, and specifics of the choreographer's profession.

1440   Romaščuk, I. "...Ja veruju: Razmyšljaja o muzyke Michajla Bronnera." (I Believe: Thoughts on Michajl Bronner's Music.) *MA.* 1996; 1: 113-118. Lang.: Rus.
Russia: Moscow. 1990-1996. Critical studies. ■Dramatic elements in the music of Michajl Bronner and the use of dramatic choreography.

1441   Šeremetjevskaja, N. "Inostrannye kontrakty Valentina Manochina." (Valentin Manochin's International Contracts.) *Balet.* 1996; 2: 40, 44. Lang.: Rus.
Russia: Moscow. 1990-1996. Histories-sources. ■Interview with Manochin, a choreographer who has also worked in Israel.

1442   Hellström Sveningson, Lis. "Från en värld av dansande banktjänstemän." (From a World of Dancing Bank Employees.) *Danst.* 1996; 6(6): 3, 5. Illus.: Photo. B&W. Lang.: Swe.
Sweden. Indonesia. 1985. Histories-sources. ■Interview with choreographer Ulf Gadd about the attitudes toward dance in Sweden and Bali, and about his ballet *Tango Buenos Aires 1907.*

1443   Sörenson, Margareta. "Niklas Ek." *Danst.* 1996; 6(3): 16-17. Illus.: Photo. Color. Lang.: Swe.
Sweden: Stockholm. 1968. Biographical studies. ■A short presentation of the career of the dancer Niklas Ek, son of Birgit Cullberg, and his new career as an actor.

1444   Briginshaw, Valerie A. "Postmodern Dance and the Politics of Resistance." 125-132 in Campbell, Patrick, ed. *Analysing Performance: A Critical Reader.* Manchester/New York, NY: Manchester UP; 1996. 307 pp. Lang.: Eng.
UK-England: London. 1992. Critical studies. ■The political potential of postmodern dance and feminism as seen in *Perfect Moment,* directed by Margaret Williams, choreographed by Lea Anderson, performed by the Cholmondeleys and the Featherstonehaughs for a televised performance.

1445   Fleming, Louis K. "'I got here by sheer hard work!'." *PAC.* 1996; 30(2): 23-25. Illus.: Photo. B&W. 1. Lang.: Eng.
USA: New York, NY. 1995-1996. Biographical studies. ■Profile of Canadian-born Jean Freebury, member of the demanding Merce Cunningham Dance Company.

1446   Gener, Randy. "Graciela Daniele's Garden of Dancerly Delights." *AmTh.* 1996 Apr.; 13(4): 12-17. Illus.: Photo. B&W. 8. Lang.: Eng.
USA: New York, NY. 1981-1996. Critical studies. ■Director/choreographer Daniele's adaptation of Gabriel García Márquez's novella *Chronicle of a Death Foretold* for Broadway. Audience reception, Daniele's techniques and influences, personal history, past productions.

1447   Horwitz, Simi. "Pilobolus and the Theater of Dance." *TheaterW.* 1996 Aug 5; 10(1): 34-39. Illus.: Photo. B&W. 2. Lang.: Eng.
USA: New York, NY. 1971-1996. Historical studies. ■Artistic director Michael Tracy discusses history and productions of the artistic collective Pilobolus. Blend of dance and theatre, past productions, budget, techniques and training within the troupe.

1448   Krasner, David. "Rewriting the Body: Aida Overton Walker and the Social Formation of Cakewalking." *ThS.* 1996 Nov.; 37 (2): 67-92. Notes. Biblio. Illus.: Photo. 1. Lang.: Eng.
USA. 1900-1918. Historical studies. ■Musical actress Aida Overton Walker used race, gender, and class to transcend boundaries in extending the cakewalk dance into the larger society. By rewriting the bodily gestures of the dance, she constructed a new form that appealed to both elite whites and middle-class blacks.

1449   Ståhle, Anna-Greta. "Dansen som kamouflage." (Dance as Camouflage.) *Danst.* 1996; 6(1): 18-19. Illus.: Dwg. B&W. Lang.: Swe.
USA. 1819-1861. Biographical studies. ■A survey of the career of Lola Montez.

1450   Westerlund, Lennart. "Frank Manning." *Danst.* 1996; 6(6): 18-19, 24. Illus.: Photo. B&W. Lang.: Swe.
USA: New York, NY. 1926. Biographical studies. ■A presentation of the Lindy Hop dancer Frank Manning, his background and career, and now his new career as teacher for the young generations all around the Western world.

1451   Zalán, Magda; Marcus, Joan, photo. "A táncosnő arcképe—Twyla Tharp." (Portrait of a Dancer—Twyla Tharp.) *Tanc.* 1995; 26(1/3): 48-49. Illus.: Photo. B&W. 2. Lang.: Hun.
USA. 1973-1994. Biographical studies. ■Profile of the dancer and choreographer.

Reference materials

1452   Eszéki, Erzsébet, et al. *Magyar táncművészet 1990-1995.* (Hungarian Dance Art 1990-1995.) Budapest: Magyar Táncműv. Szöv.-Planétás; 1996. 159 pp. Pref. Append. Illus.: Photo. B&W. 103. Lang.: Hun.
Hungary. 1990-1995. ■An illustrated guide to the dance art of Hungary in the 90s summing up the companies, training schools, workshops, soloists, associations, archives with important data on the ensembles (introduction, premieres, guest performances, dancers, contact etc.) concerning professionals and amateurs as well.

Relation to other fields

1453   McMurray, Line. "Le MAC face à l'effervescence du milieu de la danse au Québec: Entretien avec Yvan Chevalier." (The Ministry of Cultural Affairs Faced with the Effervescence of Dance in Quebec: Interview with Yvan Chevalier.) *JCT.* 1991; 59: 23-26. Illus.: Photo. B&W. 3. Lang.: Fre.
Canada. 1991. Histories-sources. ■Contributions of Ministère des Affaires culturelles (Ministry of Cultural Affairs) to development of dance companies and independent choreographers.

1454   Servos, Norbert. "Wie man Tanz-Politik macht." (How Politics Are Made in the Dance World.) *DB.* 1996; 2: 50-52. Lang.: Ger.
Germany: Cologne. 1996. Historical studies. ■Summary of a meeting of 150 choreographers, teachers, directors, journalists, and scholars on dance and politics.

1455   Körtvélyes, Géza. "Szereti ön Antony Tudort, avagy kivel beszélhetünk itthon a táncról? Meditáció a művészi tánc szerepvállalásáról." (Do You Like Antony Tudor, or With Whom Can We Speak About Dance in Hungary? A Meditation on the Role of Artistic Dance.) *Tanc.* 1995; 26(7/9): 38. Lang.: Hun.
Hungary. 1900-1990. Critical studies. ■Contradictions between dance art and Hungarian cultural life. The lack of dance expertise and training.

1456   Engarås, Ingrid. "Dansvarning." (Beware of Dance.) *Danst.* 1996; 6(6): 10-12. Illus.: Handbill. B&W. Lang.: Swe.
Sweden. 1989. Critical studies. ■An appeal for a more balanced view on the now popular rave parties and drugs.

1457   Olsson, Irène. "Studion som en lekplats." (The Studio As a Play Ground.) *Danst.* 1996; 6(5): 10-11. Illus.: Photo. B&W. Lang.: Swe.

DANCE: General—Relation to other fields

Sweden: Stockholm. 1967. Biographical studies. ■A presentation of Karin Thulin, former dancer of the Cullbergbaletten, who has turned dance therapist, with special interest in psychosomatic patients.

1458 Sandberg, Helen. "Erna som tycker mycket om dans." (Erna Who Loves Dancing Very Much.) *Danst.* 1996; 6(5): 3-6. Illus.: Photo. B&W. Color. Lang.: Swe.
Sweden: Stockholm. 1942. Histories-sources. ■A presentation of Erna Grönlund, professor of dance therapy, including an interview about her career and her experiences of working with mentally disturbed children.

1459 Sjöberg, Henry. "Syndfull dans." (Sinful Dance.) *Danst.* 1996; 6(6): 8-9. Illus.: Photo. B&W. Lang.: Swe.
Sweden. 1785. Critical studies. ■Dance as an offense to good behavior: survey of Swedish attitudes.

1460 Hayes, Jill. "Dance Therapy: Process and Performance?" *STP.* 1996 June; 13: 29-38. Biblio. Lang.: Eng.
UK-England: Chichester. 1996. Historical studies. ■Account of a course in dance therapy at the Chichester Institute of Higher Education, in which students discovered free movement, explored group dynamics and gained insights into themselves.

1461 Schorn, Ursula. "Deutsch-jüdische Versöhnungsarbeit." (German-Jewish Work of Reconciliation.) *Tanzd.* 1996; 35 (4): 16-21. Notes. Lang.: Ger.
USA: San Francisco, CA. 1996. Histories-sources. ■The experiences of the author, a dance therapist and psychotherapist, conducting a workshop with American dance therapist Armand Volkes.

Research/historiography

1462 Fügedi, János. "Elmaradt interjú Szentpál Máriával, 1919-1995." (A Missed Interview with Mária Szentpál, 1919-1995.) *Tanc.* 1995; 26(4/6): 46-47. Illus.: Photo. B&W. 2. Lang.: Hun.
Hungary. 1919-1995. Biographical studies. ■Obituary for teacher and expert in Laban dance notation.

1463 Fügedi, János. "Tánclejegyzés és táncelemzés számítógéppel." (Dance Notation and Dance Analysis by Computer.) 173-197 in Szúdy, Eszter, ed. *Tánctudományi Tanulmányok 1994/1995.* Budapest: Magyar Táncművészek Szövetsége; 1995. 230 pp. Biblio. Notes. Illus.: Diagram. B&W. 23. Lang.: Hun.
USA. Hungary. 1976-1992. Technical studies. ■After a short review of dance technology and computer applications of Labanotation the study introduces a computer program called DanceStruct, developed by the author at the Institute for Musicology of the Hungarian Academy of Sciences.

Theory/criticism

1464 Klein, Gabriele. "Tanz—eine universelle Sprache?" (Dance: A Universal Language?)*Tanzd.* 1996; 34(3): 10-14. Notes. Lang.: Ger.
1996. Critical studies. ■The possibilities and limitations of intercultural communication in dance, the misconception that dance is a universal language, and the reality that dance consists of many different 'languages'.

1465 Lepecki, André. "As If Dance Was Visible." *PerfR.* 1996 Fall; 1(3): 71-76. Notes. Lang.: Eng.
North America. Europe. 1960-1996. Critical studies. ■A speculative analysis of the nature of dance and its relationship to written attempts to recreate and reconstruct it. Draws on Lacanian definitions for theoretical positions, and on the practice and philosophy of Martha Graham and Anna Halprin.

1466 Sokolov-Kaminskij, A. "Znamenatel'naja vstreča dvuch kul'tur." (A Significant Meeting of Two Cultures.) *Balet.* 1996 ; 6: 19-20, 38. Lang.: Rus.
Russia: St. Petersburg. 1995. Historical studies. ■Account of a symposium on Russian influence on early twentieth-century choreography (June 1995).

1467 Ståhle, Anna-Greta. "Birgit och pennan." (Birgit and the Pencil.) *Danst.* 1996; 6(3): 12-13. Illus.: Photo. B&W. Lang.: Swe.
Sweden. UK-England. France. 1946-1953. Critical studies. ■A presentation of the writings of Birgit Cullberg in the newspaper with reports from the European dance of the late 1940s and early 1950s.

1468 Carter, Alexandra. "Bodies of Knowledge: Dance and Feminist Analysis." 43-55 in Campbell, Patrick, ed. *Analysing Performance: A Critical Reader.* Manchester/New York, NY: Manchester UP; 1996. 307 pp. Notes. Biblio. Index. Lang.: Eng.
UK-England. 1980-1995. Critical studies. ■Examines the relationship of pertinent aspects of feminist theory to dance and outlines ways in which this approach can offer new readings of dance works.

Training

1469 Nenander, Fay. "För danselevens maximala utveckling." (For the Maximum Development of the Dance Pupil.) *Danst.* 1996 ; 6(4): 20-21. Illus.: Dwg. Color. Lang.: Swe.
Italy: Turin. 1996. Historical studies. ■A report from the seminar 'Towards Movement Efficency', with focuses on anatomy and how to correct the pupils correctly.

1470 Westman, Nancy. "Att öppna vägen till människans innersta." (To Open the Way to the Innermost Human Being.) *Danst.* 1996; 6(5): 6. Lang.: Swe.
Spain: Palma de Mallorca. 1980. Historical studies. ■A presentation of Compania Infantil de Danza and its leader Xavier Henry, with reference to the dance for disabled children.

1471 Grönlund, Erna. "Hur blir man dansterapeut?" (How Do You Become a Dance Therapist?)*Danst.* 1996; 6(5): 8. Lang.: Swe.
Sweden: Stockholm. Finland: Helsinki. 1991. Critical studies. ■A presentation of the new training of dance therapists in Sweden and Finland.

1472 Persson, Tommy. "Vacker ångest." (Beautiful Anguish.) *Danst.* 1996; 6(6): 6-7. Illus.: Photo. B&W. Lang.: Swe.
Sweden: Uppsala. 1996. Critical studies. ■A report from Juan Carlos Copes' tango class at the Swedish tango society Cambalache at Uppsala.

Ballet

Administration

1473 Kistrup, Eva. "At tilgodese eliten—såvel som bredden!" (To Consider the Interests of the Elite as Well as the More Ordinary Dancers.) *TE.* 1996 June; 79: 32-35. Illus.: Photo. B&W. 4. Lang.: Dan.
Denmark. 1951-1996. Critical studies. ■Critique of the way in which director Peter Schaufuss uses his dancers at Kongelige Danske Ballet: many good dancers go abroad, feeling that their talents are wasted in Denmark. Argues that the problem is not new.

1474 Meinertz, Alexander. "Den Kgl. Ballet—i internationalt selskab." (The Royal Danish Ballet and Its International Relations.) *TE.* 1996 Sep.; 80: 18-21. Illus.: Photo. B&W. 3. Lang.: Dan.
Denmark. 1992-1996. Historical studies. ■Maina Gielgud, the new ballet mistress of Kongelige Danske Ballet, hopes to bring new stability to the company, which has been through a number of ballet masters in recent years, and to strengthen the classical repertoire.

Design/technology

1475 Christensen, Charlotte. "De magiske scenebilleder—virkelighedsflugt og drømmerejser." (Magical Scenography: Escape from Reality and Dream Travel.) *TE.* 1996 Apr.; 78: 20-23. Illus.: Dwg. Pntg. 2. Lang.: Dan.
Denmark: Copenhagen. 1830-1871. Historical studies. ■Scenery at the Royal Danish Theatre in August Bournonville's time.

1476 Zeuthen, Lotte Ladegaard. "En romantisk minimalist." (A Romantic Minimalistic Painter.) *TE.* 1996 Dec.; 81-82: 24-26. Illus.: Pntg. Photo. B&W. 2. Lang.: Dan.
Denmark: Copenhagen. 1996. Histories-sources. ■An interview with the painter Per Kirkeby, who created the scenography for *Swan Lake* directed by Peter Martins at Kongelige Teater.

DANCE: Ballet

Institutions

1477 Maksov, A. "Ežegodno—v čest' Nurjeva." (Annually at Nureyev's.) *Balet*. 1996; 6: 26-27. Lang.: Rus.
Bashkiria: Ufa. 1995. Historical studies. ■Performances by French and Russian dancers at the third Nureyev ballet festival in Ufa.

1478 Bell, Karen. "A New Home." *PAC*. 1996; 30(2): 26-27. Illus.: Photo. B&W. Architec. 2. Lang.: Eng.
Canada: Toronto, ON. 1996. Historical studies. ■The National Ballet's new home, the Walter Carsen Centre, has many large studios as well as physiotherapy facilities, costume production workshops, offices and a library.

1479 Draeger, Volkmar. "Tanzlichter des Nordens." (Dance Lights of the North.) *TZ*. 1996; 2: 33-37. Illus.: Photo. B&W. 6. Lang.: Ger.
Germany. 1996. Historical studies. ■The ballet companies of the big theatres of northern Germany: Landestheater Mecklenburg, Deutsche Tanzkompanie, Theater Vorpommern, Mecklenburgisches Staatstheater, Volkstheater Rostock, and their different conditions, concepts, and perspectives.

1480 Viola, György. "Markó Iván Bayreuth-i jubileuma." (Iván Markó's Jubilee in Bayreuth.) *Tanc*. 1995; 26(7/9): 40. Illus.: Photo. B&W. 3. Lang.: Hun.
Germany: Bayreuth. Hungary. 1985-1995. Histories-sources. ■Interview with Iván Markó on the occasion of his 10-year-long activity in Bayreuth as choreographer and ballet-director of the festival.

1481 Körtvélyes, Géza. "Jegyzetek az Operaházi Balettegyüttes négy évadjáról (1988/89-1991/92)." (Notes from the Four Seasons of the Opera Ballet between 1988/89-1991/92.) 68-87 in Szúdy, Eszter, ed. *Tánctudományi Tanulmányok 1994/1995*. Budapest: Magyar Táncművészek Szövetsége; 1995. 230 pp. Append. Lang.: Hun.
Hungary: Budapest. 1988-1992. Critical studies. ■A period in the development of the Ballet Company of the Budapest Opera, characterized by features alien to the preceding decades.

1482 Uhrik, Dóra; Horvát, Éva, photo.; Hingyi, László, photo. "Levél Eck Imréhez." (Letter to Imre Eck.) *Tanc*. 1995; 26(10/12): 8-9. Illus.: Photo. B&W. 3. Lang.: Hun.
Hungary. 1930-1995. Histories-sources. ■In a friendly letter, Dóra Uhrik, former soloist of the Pécs Ballet, congratulates Imre Eck, their ex-director and choreographer. The artist is the recipient of the first Philip Morris Ballet Flower Award: 'for Life-work'.

1483 Kaán, Zsuzsa. "Madam Ohya balettversenye." (Madame Ohya's Ballet Competition.) *Tanc*. 1995; 26(10/12): 44-45. Illus.: Photo. B&W. 8. Lang.: Hun.
Japan: Osaka. 1995. Reviews of performances. ■Summary of the events of the 7th International Masako Ohya Ballet Competition in Osaka.

1484 Pudełek, Janina. "Balet Jana Cieplińskiego (1922-1925)." (The Ballet of Jan Ciepliński, 1922-1925.) *PaT*. 1996; 1-2(61): 61-87. Append. Illus.: Photo. Poster. B&W. Lang.: Pol.
Poland. 1922-1925. Historical studies. ■Origin and activity of the Balet Jana Cieplińskiego, which was inspired by French and Russian ballet as well as by Polish folklore.

1485 Pudełek, Janina. "Balet Polski Feliksa Parnella /1935-1939/." (The Polish Ballet of Feliks Parnell, 1935-1939.) *PaT*. 1996; 45(3-4): 540-559. Notes. Append. Illus.: Photo. B&W. 5. Lang.: Pol.
Poland: Warsaw. 1935-1939. Historical studies. ■History of the Polish ballet troupe and its guest performances throughout Europe.

1486 Demeneva, L. "Baletnaja truppa Permskogo teatra opery i baleta imeni P.I. Čajkovskogo." (The Ballet Troupe of Perm's Čajkovskij Opera and Ballet Theatre.) *Balet*. 1996; 6: 12-18. Lang.: Rus.
Russia: Perm. 1925-1996. Historical studies. ■History of the theatre, its founding and activity.

1487 Inozemceva, G. "Festival' junych tancovščikov iz škol iskusstv." (Festival of Young Dancers from Ballet Schools.) *Balet*. 1996; 6: 27-28. Lang.: Rus.
Russia: Moscow. 1995. Historical studies. ■Festival of choreography departments from children's ballet schools.

1488 Krylova, M. "'Vaganova-prix': vse, kaky u vzroslych." (The Vaganova Prize: Everything Just Like with Adults.) *Balet*. 1996; 6: 23-24. Lang.: Rus.
Russia: Moscow. 1995-1996. Historical studies. ■The third international 'Vaganova Prize' ballet competition and festival.

1489 Mariayer, Nina. "Vita nätter på Vaganova." (White Nights at Vaganova.) *Danst*. 1996; 6(1): 21-23. Illus.: Photo. B&W. Lang.: Swe.
Russia: St. Petersburg. 1988-1995. Critical studies. ■A report from the Vaganova School and the competition for young dancers with references to the difficult situations of the ballet schools in the former Soviet Union.

1490 Žadina, O.; Kuramšin, V. *Škola baleta Askol'da Makarova*. (The Ballet School of Askol'd Makarov.) St. Petersburg: Akropol'; 1996. 48 pp. Lang.: Rus.
Russia: St. Petersburg. 1994-1996. Historical studies. ■The teaching methods of Askol'd Makarov.

1491 Gajnullina, V. "Iz letopisi meždunarodnogo festivalja klassičeskogo baleta imeni Rudol'fa Nurjeva." (From the Records of the Rudolf Nureyev International Festival of Classical Ballet.) *Balet*. 1996; 2: 12-13. Lang.: Rus.
Tatarstan: Kazan. 1987-1996. Historical studies. ■The ten years of the festival's activity.

1492 Kaán, Zsuzsa; Cooper, Bill, photo.; Spatt, Leslie E., photo. "Kortárs művek a Royal Ballet repertoárján. Londoni jegyzetek—II. rész." (Contemporary Works in the Repertoire of the Royal Ballet: Notes from London, Part 2.) *Tanc*. 1995; 26(1/3): 46-47. Illus.: Photo. B&W. 3. Lang.: Hun.
UK-England: London. 1963-1994. Historical studies. ■The modern program of the company.

1493 Kaán, Zsuzsa; Crickmay, Antony, photo.; Cooper, Bill, photo. "Reflektorfényben az Angol Nemzeti Balett. Londoni jegyzetek—III. rész." (In the Limelight the English National Ballet: Notes from London, Part 3.) *Tanc*. 1995; 26(4/6): 37-39. Illus.: Photo. B&W. 2. Lang.: Hun.
UK-England: London. 1993-1995. Critical studies. ■Notes on productions of the Royal Ballet.

1494 Zalán, Magda; Pratt, Caroll, photo.; Elbers, Johan, photo. "Pezsegjen a halandó élet—Modern balettek a Kennedy Center 1995/96-os jubileumi évadjában." (Mortal Life Must be Teeming—Modern Ballet Performances at the Kennedy Center in the 1995/96 Jubilee Season.) *Tanc*. 1995; 26(10/12): 42-43. Illus.: Photo. B&W. 2. Lang.: Hun.
USA: Washington, DC. 1970-1995. Reviews of performances. ■The ballet program of the 25-year-old Kennedy Center, with emphasis on Martha Graham's ensemble, which gave a guest performance at the 1996 Spring Festival in Budapest.

Performance/production

1495 Dulova, E. "Élegičeskaja poézija poloneza." (The Elegiac Poetry of the Polonaise.) *Balet*. 1996; 6: 29-30, 38. Lang.: Rus.
Belorus: Minsk. 1995. Historical studies. ■The success of the ballet *Polonez (Polonaise)* choreographed by Galina Sinel'nikova to music by Michal Oginskij and produced by the Belorussian Bolšoj Opera and Ballet Theatre.

1496 Ladygina, A. "Strasti po Elizarjevu." (Lusting After Elizarjev.) *Balet*. 1996; 1: 20-22. Lang.: Rus.
Belorus: Minsk. 1995. Historical studies. ■The premiere of the ballet *Strasti (Rogneda)*, music by Andrej Mdivani, choreography by Valerij Elizarjev.

1497 MacFarlane, Teri. "Margaret Illmann." *PAC*. 1996; 30(1): 14-16. Illus.: Photo. B&W. 2. Lang.: Eng.
Canada. USA. 1989-1995. Historical studies. ■Australian Margaret Illmann's rise to principal dancer at the Canadian National Ballet. Chronicles her roles on Broadway and television.

1498 Rickerd, Julie Rekai. "A Canadian Nutcracker." *TCI*. 1996 Mar.; 30(3): 7. Illus.: Photo. Color. 2. Lang.: Eng.

DANCE: Ballet—Performance/production

Canada: Toronto, ON. 1995. Technical studies. ■Choreographer James Kudelka and designer Santo Loquasto's concept for new production of Čajkovskij's *The Nutcracker* by the National Ballet of Canada, done at the behest of the institution's artistic director Reid Anderson.

1499 Krasovskaja, V.M. *Zapadnojevropejskij baletnyj teat'r. Očerki istorii: Romantizm.* (Western European Ballet Theatre: Historical Articles on Romanticism.) Moscow: Artist. Režisser. Teat'r; 1996. 432 pp. Lang.: Rus.
Europe. 1800-1900. Historical studies. ■Articles on the works of outstanding dancers including Marie and Filippo Taglioni, Fanny Elssler, Carlotta Grisi, and Jules Perrot.

1500 Maácz, László. "Shakespeare a táncszínpadon II." (Shakespeare on the Ballet Stage—Part 2.) 5-22 in Szúdy, Eszter, ed. *Tánctudományi Tanulmányok 1994/1995.* Budapest: Magyar Táncművészek Szövetsége; 1995. 230 pp. Notes. Lang.: Hun.
Europe. 1809-1994. Critical studies. ■Analysis of choreographies with respect to different views on fidelity to Shakespeare and evolving different dance styles and dramaturgy.

1501 Hézső, István. "*Nijinska/Nijinski*—Jelentés Párizsból." (*Nijinska/Nijinski*—Report from Paris.) *Tanc.* 1995; 26(7/9): 39. Illus.: Photo. B&W. 1. Lang.: Hun.
France: Paris. 1913-1995. Reviews of performances. ■Review of a ballet evening presented by the Paris Opera Ballet at the Bastille Opera.

1502 Spångberg, Mårten. "Yvan Auzely." *Danst.* 1996; 6(1): 12-13. Illus.: Photo. B&W. Color. Lang.: Swe.
France. Sweden: Stockholm. 1965-1995. Histories-sources. ■Yvan Auzely speaks about his career as dancer, and now as actor in Swedish with references to Cullbergbaletten and Mats Ek.

1503 Géza, Körtvélyes; Mezey, Béla, photo. "Poézis és szenvedély ... Kún Zsuzsa köszöntése." (Poesy and Passion ... Compliments to Zsuzsa Kún.) *Tanc.* 1995; 26(1/3): 8-9. Illus.: Photo. B&W. 4. Lang.: Hun.
Hungary: Budapest. 1950-1994. Biographical studies. ■Greeting Zsuzsa Kún, ballet dancer of Budapest Opera House for 25 years and former director of the Hungarian Ballet Institute (1972-1979), on her 60th birthday.

1504 Hézső, István. "Aradi Mária." (Mária Aradi.) *Tanc.* 1995; 26(1/3): 20-21. Illus.: Photo. B&W. 2. Lang.: Hun.
Hungary: Budapest. Netherlands: Amsterdam. 1950-1994. Histories-sources. ■Interview with ballet dancer Mária Aradi on her life and career.

1505 Jálics, Kinga; Mezey, Béla, photo.; Schuch, József, photo. "Harangozó-díjas: Bombicz Barbara—'Visz a lendület, lehetetlen megállni!'." (Barbara Bombicz, Harangozó-Prize Winning Artist: 'I Am Carried by Impulse, It Is Impossible to Stop'.) *Tanc.* 1995; 26(7/9): 8-9. Illus.: Photo. B&W. 3. Lang.: Hun.
Hungary. 1978-1995. Histories-sources. ■Conversation with one of the founding members of the Győr Ballet, who has also gained a name as a choreographer.

1506 Kaán, Zsuzsa; Papp, Dezső, photo. "Markó Iván újra itthon." (Iván Markó Is Home Again.) *Tanc.* 1995; 26(1/3): 10-11. Illus.: Photo. B&W. 4. Lang.: Hun.
Hungary: Budapest. 1994-1995. Histories-sources. ■Interview with choreographer Iván Markó after returning from his 4-year stay abroad.

1507 Körtvélyes, Géza; Kanyó, Béla, photo. "Világsztárok az Operában—Jegyzetek a III. Nemzetközi Balettgálához." (World Stars in the Opera—Note on the 3rd International Ballet Gala.) *Tanc.* 1995; 26 (10/12): 34-35. Illus.: Photo. B&W. 5. Lang.: Hun.
Hungary: Budapest. 1995. Reviews of performances. ■Account of the gala, at which sixteen dancers presented works from a wide range of twentieth-century choreographers.

1508 Kővágó, Zsuzsa. "Milloss Aurél színházi koreográfiái III. (1938)—válogatás olaszországi leveleiből." (Theatre Choreographies by Aurél Milloss (1938)—Part 3, and His Selected Letters from Italy.) 55-67 in Szúdy, Eszter, ed. *Tánctudományi Tanulmányok 1994/1995.* Budapest: Magyar Táncművészek Szövetsége; 1995. 230 pp. Notes. Append. Lang.: Hun.
Hungary. Italy. 1935-1947. Historical studies. ■Theatre choreographies of Hungarian émigré Aurél Milloss and dance concerts with his partner Lya Karina in Hungary in the 1930s (quoting from contemporary press reports). Includes letters and excerpts from Milloss' correspondence with painter István Pekáry 1943-1947.

1509 Mátai, Györgyi; Kanyó, Béla, photo.; Tóth, László, photo. "A mandarinok állva halnak meg?! Születésnapi interjú Havas Ferenccel." (Do Mandarins Die Standing?! Birthday Interview with Ferenc Havas.) *Tanc.* 1995 ; 26(4/6): 8-9. Illus.: Photo. B&W. 2. Lang.: Hun.
Hungary. 1935-1995. Histories-sources. ■Congratulates 60-year old artist, who dances the title role of *A csodálatos mandarin (The Miraculous Mandarin)* by Béla Bartók (choreography: Gyula Harangozó).

1510 Nádasi, Myrtill; Kanyó, Béla, photo. "Solymosi és a Royal Ballet." (Zoltán Solymosi and the Royal Ballet.) *Tanc.* 1995; 26(10/12): 16-17. Illus.: Photo. B&W. 2. Lang.: Hun.
Hungary. UK-England: London. 1992-1995. Histories-sources. ■A conversation with the Hungarian dancer Zoltán Solymosi on his successes and recent break with the Royal Ballet.

1511 Rajk, András; Tóth, László, photo.; Bolla, Anna, photo. "A Fehér Rózsa lovagnője—Lakatos Gabriella, a Magyar Állami Operaház örökös tagja." (A Lady Knight of the White Rose—Gabriella Lakatos, Life Member of the Hungarian State Opera House.) *Tanc.* 1995; 26(10/12): 18-19. Illus.: Photo. B&W. 3. Lang.: Hun.
Hungary. 1927-1989. Biographical studies. ■A portrait of one of the best-known stars of Hungarian ballet.

1512 Uitman, Hans. *Toen de Parijse benen de Moerdijk passeerden! De invloed van de Parijse boulevardtheaters op het Amsterdamse ballet (1813-1868).* (When Parisian Legs Crossed the Moerdijk! The Influence of Parisian Vaudeville Theatre on the Amsterdam Ballet, 1813-1868.) The Hague: Pauper; 1996. 78 pp. Notes. Biblio. Illus.: Photo. B&W. 12. Lang.: Dut.
Netherlands: Amsterdam. 1813-1868. Historical studies. ■The ballet tradition of the Parisian boulevard theatre and its influence on Amsterdam ballet.

1513 *Memuary Marius Petipa.* (Memoirs of Marius Petipa.) St. Petersburg: Sojuz chudožnikov; 1996. 160 pp. Lang.: Rus.
Russia. 1822-1900. Histories-sources. ■Petipa's creation and production of ballets, work on opera dances, association with the Imperial Theatres.

1514 "Teat'r 'Kremlevskij balet'." (The Kremlin Ballet Theatre.) *Balet.* 1996; 1: 8-10. Lang.: Rus.
Russia: Moscow. 1990-1996. Biographical studies. ■The work of choreographer Andrej Petrov at the Kremlevskij Balet.

1515 Belova, E. "Prizračnoe sčastje pečal'nogo bala." (The Ghostly Happiness of a Sad Ball.) *Balet.* 1996; 6: 3-5 . Lang.: Rus.
Russia: St. Petersburg. 1995. Historical studies. ■Dmitrij Brjancev's production of Boris Marčello's ballet *Prizračnyj Bal (Ghostly Ball)* in St. Petersburg's Chamber Ballet Theatre (Teat'r Kamernogo Baleta).

1516 Burjakova, Ju. "Ne takoj balet—ljubov' moja." (My Love Is Not Ballet Like This.) *PTZ.* 1996; 9: 115-116. Lang.: Rus.
Russia: Moscow. 1996. Biographical studies. ■Artistic portrait of ballerina Ljubov' Kunakova.

1517 Gaevskij, V. "Dve sud'by." (Two Destinies.) *MoskNab.* 1996; 3-4: 23-30. Lang.: Rus.
Russia. 1990-1996. Historical studies. ■Profile of dancers and choreographers Kas'jan Golejzovskij and Fëdor Lopuchov.

1518 Gubskaja, I. "Faruch Ruzimatov." *PTZ.* 1996; 10: 33-36. Lang.: Rus.
Russia: St. Petersburg. 1990-1996. Biographical studies. ■The work of the ballet master of the Kirov Ballet compared to that of Rudolf Nureyev.

1519 Inozemceva, G. "Tri vozrasta Margarity Gotje." (Three Ages of Marguerite Gautier.) *Balet.* 1996; 2: 33-34. Lang.: Rus.
Russia: Moscow. 1995. Historical studies. ■Account of the ballet *Dama s kameljami (Camille)*, choreographed by Natalija Kasatkina and Vladi-

DANCE: Ballet—Performance/production

mir Vasiljév to the music of Verdi's *La Traviata* and performed at the Moscow Theatre of Classical Ballet.

1520 Južina, K. "'S pervogo šaga k vysokomu artistizmu'." (A First Step Toward Higher Artistry.) *Balet.* 1996; 1: 25-26. Lang.: Rus.

Russia: Moscow. 1996. Historical studies. ■The work of choreographer and ballet teacher Michajl Lavrovskij.

1521 Kurilenko, E.N. *Muzykal'nyj teat'r: nadeždy i dejstvitel'nost'.* (Musical Theatre: Hopes and Reality.) Moscow: Gosudarstvénnyj institut ilkusstvoznanija; 1996. 222 pp. Lang.: Rus.

Russia: Moscow. 1996. Critical studies. ■The role of music in contemporary ballet, ballet as seen on television or film, and the music theatre of Eino Tamberg.

1522 L'vov-Anochin, Boris. "Diapazon tancovščika." (The Dancer's Diapason.) *Balet.* 1996; 2: 2-3. Lang.: Rus.

Russia: Moscow. 1990-1996. Historical studies. ■Dancer Nikolaj Ciskaridze.

1523 Luckaja, E. "Rejting Ljudmily Sacharovoj." (Rating Ljudmila Sacharova.) *MuZizn.* 1996; 5-6: 16-18. Lang.: Rus.

Russia: Perm. 1970-1996. Biographical studies. ■Profile of Ljudmila P. Sacharova, artistic director of Perm's school of choreography.

1524 Messerer, Sulamif'; Vasiljév, A., ed. "Žizn' v teatre i vne ego." (Life In and Out of the Theatre.) *Balet.* 1996 ; 2: 5, 30-31, 48. Lang.: Rus.

Russia: Moscow. 1980-1989. Histories-sources. ■Ballerina Sulamif' Messerer recalls her work at the Bolšoj Theatre.

1525 Nechendzi, A. "Nikita Dolgušin: urok Taljoni." (Nikita Dolgušin: Taglioni's Lesson.) *Balet.* 1996; 1: 3-5. Lang.: Rus.

Russia. USA. 1995. Historical studies. ■Dolgušin's work in the performance of choreographic miniatures, with emphasis on a performance in California.

1526 Ragozina-Panova, G. "Sozdavaja buduščee baleta." (Creating the Future of Ballet.) *Balet.* 1996; 1: 18-19. Lang.: Rus.

Russia: Perm. 1970-1996. Historical studies. ■Work of choreographer Ljudmila P. Sacharova.

1527 Zozulina, N. "Baletnyj materik." (Ballet Continent.) *PTZ.* 1996; 9: 117-121. Lang.: Rus.

Russia: St. Petersburg. 1990-1996. Biographical studies. ■Creative portrait of Vera M. Krasovskaja, ballerina of the Mariinskij Theatre.

1528 Clinell, Bim. "Rädda Birgits baletter." (Save the Ballets of Birgit.) *Danst.* 1996; 6(3): 18. Illus.: Photo. B&W. Lang.: Swe.

Sweden. France: Paris. 1996. Histories-sources. ■A discussion with the former dancer Lena Wennergren-Juras about Cullbergbaletten, and the difficulties of reviving the ballets of Birgit Cullberg.

1529 Greider, Göran. "Modet att förenkla." (The Courage To Simplify.) *Danst.* 1996; 6(3): 15. Illus.: Photo. B&W. Lang.: Swe.

Sweden: Stockholm. 1977. Critical studies. ■An analysis of Birgit Cullberg's *Rapport*, based on the Seventh Symphony by Allan Pettersson.

1530 Hellström Sveningson, Lis. "Mia Johansson." *Danst.* 1996; 6(4): 12-13. Illus.: Photo. Color. Lang.: Swe.

Sweden: Gothenburg. 1988. Biographical studies. ■Mia Johansson speaks about her career so far as dancer at Göteborgs Operan, with reference to the choreographer Robert North.

1531 Näslund, Erik. "En kvinnas kropp i männens värld." (A Woman's Body in a Man's World.) *Danst.* 1996; 6(3): 5-9. Illus.: Photo. B&W. Lang.: Swe.

Sweden: Stockholm. 1920. Biographical studies. ■A survey of the long career of Birgit Cullberg, with references to *Fröken Julie*, her husband, the actor Anders Ek, and Martha Graham.

1532 Näslund, Erik. "Hur ska det gå med Birgit Cullbergs baletter?" (What Will Happen With Birgit Cullberg's Ballets?) *Danst.* 1996; 6(4): 23. Illus.: Photo. B&W. Lang.: Swe.

Sweden. 1967. Critical studies. ■An appeal for the restoration of Birgit Cullberg's ballets while there is still time to do so.

1533 Olsson, Irène. "1700-tal, svensk danshistoria är fotad i 1700-talet." (18th Century, the Swedish History of Dance Is Based

on the 18th Century.) *Danst.* 1996; 6(2): 8-11. Illus.: Photo. B&W. Lang.: Swe.

Sweden: Stockholm. 1773-1996. Historical studies. ■The ballet director Frank Andersen and the choreographers Ivo Cramér and Regina Beck-Friis speak about the importance of the eighteenth-century tradition for the Royal Swedish Ballet, and the responsibility to go on with the old technique, with references to Drottningholms Slottsteater.

1534 Olsson, Irène. "Madeleine Onne." *Danst.* 1996; 6(6): 20-21. Illus.: Photo. Color. Lang.: Swe.

Sweden: Stockholm. 1969. Histories-sources. ■An interview with the dancer Madeleine Onne about her career and her different roles.

1535 Sörenson, Margareta. "Birgit & teatern." (Birgit & the Theatre.) *Danst.* 1996; 6(3): 10-11. Illus.: Photo. B&W. Lang.: Swe.

Sweden: Stockholm. 1950-1987. Critical studies. ■A discussion on Birgit Cullberg's relation to theatre and dance, based on her writings as *Baletten och vi (The Ballet and Us)* and her choreographic works.

1536 Spångberg, Mårten. "Palle Dyrvall." *Danst.* 1996; 6(2): 18. Illus.: Photo. B&W. Lang.: Swe.

Sweden: Stockholm. 1990. Biographical studies. ■A presentation of the young dancer Palle Dyrvall, his background and future plans for choreography.

1537 Sadovskaja, N. "Ne teat'r dlja aktera, a akter dlja teatra." (Not Theatre for the Actor, but the Actor for Theatre.) *Balet.* 1996; 2: 8-10. Lang.: Rus.

Tatarstan: Kazan. 1996. Histories-sources. ■Interview with Vladimir Jakovlev, artistic director of Kazanskij Balet.

1538 Zalán, Magda; Freeman, Melanie, photo.; Swope, Martha, photo.; Jack, Robbie, photo. "Perpetuum mobile csontból és (kevés) húsból—Edward Villella, a Miami City Ballet igazgatója." (Perpetuum Mobile of Bone and (Little) Flesh—Edward Villella, the Director of Miami City Ballet.) *Tanc.* 1995; 26(7/9): 44-47. Illus.: Photo. B&W. 4. Lang.: Hun.

USA: Miami, FL. 1936-1995. Histories-sources. ■Balanchine-trained dancer Edward Villella's new career at Miami City Ballet.

1539 Liepa, Maris Éduardovič. *Ja choču tancevat' sto let.* (I Want to Dance for a Hundred Years.) Moscow: Vagrius; 1996. 240 pp. Lang.: Rus.

USSR: Moscow. 1936-1989. Histories-sources. ■Memoirs of the great dancer, his work at the Bolšoj and the Kremlin Palace Ballet Theatre and with Gennadij Abramov, Boris Akimov, Vadim Guljaév, and Ljudmila Gurčenko.

1540 Zalán, Magda; Mezey, Béla, photo. "'Jó éjt királyfi!' Emlékezés Aleksszandr Godunovra (1949-1995)." ('Good Night, Sweet Prince!' In Memory of Aleksand'r Godunov [1949-1995].) *Tanc.* 1995; 26(4/6): 41-43. Illus.: Photo. B&W. 2. Lang.: Hun.

USSR. USA. 1949-1995. Biographical studies. ■Obituary for the former star of the Bolšoj and American Ballet Theatre.

Training

1541 Gerševič, A.G. *Aleksand'r Puškin. Škola klassičeskogo tanca.* (Aleksand'r I. Puškin's School of Classical Dance.) Moscow: Artist. Režisser. Teat'r; 1996. 255 pp. Lang.: Rus.

Russia: St. Petersburg. 1932-1970. Historical studies. ■The work of Aleksand'r I. Puškin, a classical dance teacher, and his contribution to the methodology of ballet art.

1542 Hamera, Judith. "The Ambivalent, Knowing Male Body in the Pasadena Dance Theatre." *TextPQ.* 1994 July; 14(3): 197-209. Notes. Biblio. Lang.: Eng.

USA: Pasadena, CA. 1994. Critical studies. ■Classical ballet training, in the context of a semi-professional company such as the Pasadena Dance Theatre, serving as an initiatory vehicle for male participants.

Ethnic dance

Design/technology

1543 McCarl, David. "The Powwow Circle: Native American Dance and Dress." *TD&T.* 1996 Sum; 32(3): 50-58. Illus.: Photo. 10. Lang.: Eng.

DANCE: Ethnic dance—Design/technology

USA. 1850-1929. Historical studies. ■Examines the dress of Native American dancers during the ritual powwow dances. Author finds six major categories divided by gender and dance style.

Institutions

1544 Kováts, György. *A Miskolci Avas Táncegyüttes, 1951-1996.* (Avas Folk Dance Ensemble of Miskolc, 1951-1996.) Miskolc: Rónai Művel. Közp; 1996. 200 pp. Pref. Append. Illus.: Photo. B&W. 125. Lang.: Hun.
Hungary: Miskolc. 1951-1996. Historical studies. ■Chronicle of the 45-year old folk dance group.

Performance/production

1545 Zsuráfszki, Zoltán; Diósi, Imre, photo. "A mesternő arcképe–Gondolatok Györgyfalvay Katalinról." (The Portrait of the Master–Reflections of Katalin Györgyfalvay.) *Tanc.* 1995; 26(7/9): 10-11. Illus.: Photo. B&W. 3. Lang.: Hun.
Hungary. 1971-1995. Biographical studies. ■Profile of the choreographer by her student and colleague, now artistic director of Budapest Táncegyüttes.

1546 Ruyter, Nancy Lee. "Ancient Images: The Pre-Cortesian in 20th Century Dance Performance." *Gestos.* 1996 Apr.; 11(21): 145-155. Notes. Lang.: Eng.
Mexico: Mexico City. USA: Irvine, CA. 1996. Critical studies. ■Native precolonial influence on contemporary Mexican and Hispanic-American dance, including the Ballet Folklórico de México, the street dance group Conchero, and the Mexican-American troupe Azteca.

1547 Harding, Frances. "Actor and Character in African Masquerade Performance." *ThR.* 1996; 21(1): 59-71. Notes. Illus.: Photo. B&W. 10. Lang.: Eng.
Nigeria. Sierre Leone. 1968-1993. Critical studies. ■Analysis of contemporary traditional African masked performance, with emphasis on identity of the performer and the psycho-physical processes involved in use of mask.

1548 Eagleton, Julie. "Eagleton's Angle: Michael Flatley Talks to Julie Eagleton." *PlPl.* 1996 Oct.; 508: 8-9. Lang.: Eng.
USA: Chicago, IL. 1958-1996. Histories-sources. ■Interview with American-born Irish dancer/choreographer Michael Flatley. Flatley talks about his current hit production *Lord of the Dance*, directed by Arlene Phillips, now touring worldwide.

Theory/criticism

1549 Kaán, Zsuzsa. "Vitányi Iván." (Iván Vitányi.) *Tanc.* 1995; 26(7/9): 18-19. Illus.: Photo. B&W. 3. Lang.: Hun.
Hungary. 1943-1995. Histories-sources. ■Interview with Vitányi, a dance historian, aesthetician, and expert on cultural policy.

Modern dance

Administration

1550 Wisti, Toni. "An Interview with Nancy Umanoff." *PerfM.* 1996 Fall; 22(1): 5-6. Lang.: Eng.
USA. 1996. Histories-sources. ■Interview with managing director of the Mark Morris Dance Group, Nancy Umanoff.

Design/technology

1551 Slingerland, Amy L. "Mountain Languages." *LDim.* 1996 Jan.; 20(1): 20-21. Illus.: Photo. Color. 1. Lang.: Eng.
USA: New York, NY. 1995. Technical studies. ■Lighting designer Roma Flowers' image-oriented lighting for Via Theatre Company's dance theatre piece *i fell off the mountain and stubbed my toe on the thorny prick of your cold cold heart (or) bashing my head against a brick wall until i can taste blood.*

1552 Slingerland, Amy L. "Altogether Different." *TCI.* 1996 Apr.; 30(4): 26. Illus.: Photo. B&W. 2. Lang.: Eng.
USA: New York, NY. 1996. Technical studies. ■Reviews technical aspects of the annual Altogether Different dance series held at the Joyce Theatre.

Institutions

1553 Davida, Dena. "L'art itinérant: Qui hébergera la danse à Montréal? À l'intention du jury du programme indépendanse: Déclaration de la directrice artistique de Tangente 1991." (Itinerant Art: Who Will House Dance in Montreal? To the Jury of the Program Indépendanse: Declaration of the Artistic Director of Tangente 1991.) *JCT.* 1991; 59: 17-20. Illus.: Photo. B&W. 2. Lang.: Fre.
Canada: Montreal, PQ. 1977-1991. Histories-sources. ■Dena Davida, artistic director of Tangente, recounts her company's difficulty in finding a home and describes its role in creating new choreographies despite economic hardship.

1554 Lehmann, Valérie. "Tangente: Pourvu que ça dure..." (Tangente: Assuming It Lasts...)*JCT.* 1991; 59: 21-22. Illus.: Photo. B&W. 2. Lang.: Fre.
Canada: Montreal, PQ. 1980-1991. Critical studies. ■Remarks on dance company Tangente's tenacity and important contribution to experimental dance.

1555 Lévesque, Solange. "Festival international de nouvelle danse 1989." (1989 International Festival of New Dance.) *JCT.* 1990; 55: 7-21. Notes. Illus.: Photo. B&W. 23. Lang.: Fre.
Canada: Montreal, PQ. 1989. Historical studies. ■Diversity and significant Japanese presence characterize Montreal's 1989 Festival international de nouvelle danse. Brief reviews of many productions.

1556 Lévesque, Solange; Camerlain, Lorraine. "Depuis dix ans: Tangente: Entretien avec Dena Davida et Silvy Panet-Raymond." (For the Past Ten Years: Tangente: Interview with Dena Davida and Silvy Panet-Raymond.) *JCT.* 1991; 59: 7-16. Illus.: Photo. B&W. 6. Lang.: Fre.
Canada: Montreal, PQ. 1977-1991. Histories-sources. ■Dena Davida and Silvy Panet-Raymond, co-founders of dance company Tangente, review its history and give indications of future directions.

1557 Servos, Norbert. "Tanz zwischen Manier und Stil." (Dance Between Manner and Style.) *DB.* 1996; 10: 38-41. Illus.: Photo. B&W. 3. Lang.: Ger.
Germany: Berlin. 1996. Reviews of performances. ■Impressions of the Berlin international dance festival emphasizing the variety of techniques and styles, new forms of dance theatre.

1558 Wesemann, Arnd. "Ellipsen und Epilepsien." (Ellipses and Epilepsies.) *TZ.* 1996; 3: 44-45. Illus.: Photo. B&W. 1. Lang.: Ger.
Germany: Düsseldorf. 1992-1996. Historical studies. ■Profile of the new dance theatre group Neuer Tanz, directed by Wanda Golonka and V.A. Wölfl, on the occasion of the first performance of their *Wüst(e)xyz.*

1559 Korobkov, S. "Homo ekschibitionismes." (Homo Exhibitionismus.) *Balet.* 1996; 2: 14-15. Lang.: Rus.
Russia: Moscow. 1995. Historical studies. ■Report on the second international festival of modern dance at the Teat'r Nacij (Theatre of Nations).

1560 Kotychov, V. "Formula tanca: Zametki s Meždunarodnogo festivalja sovremennogo tanca." (Dance Formula: Notes from the International Festival of Modern Dance.) *MuZizn.* 1996; 3-4: 9-11. Lang.: Rus.
Russia: Moscow. 1995. Historical studies. ■Report on the second festival, held at Teat'r Nacij.

1561 Lindström, Sofia. "Skånes Dansteater–en bebis med stjärnpotential." (Skånes Dansteater–a Baby with Star Potential.) *MuD.* 1996; 18(3): 18-19. Illus.: Photo. B&W. Lang.: Swe.
Sweden: Malmö, Lund. 1995. Historical studies. ■A presentation of the new dance company in the south of Sweden, its artistic director Patrick King and all the problems to establish the dance in the new surroundings.

Performance/production

1562 Postrewka, Gabriele. "Iris Scaccheri–Tanz aus Argentinien." (Iris Scaccheri–Dance from Argentina.) *Tanzd.* 1996; 32(1): 24-25. Illus.: Photo. B&W. 1. Lang.: Ger.
Argentina. 1940-1995. Biographical studies. ■Portrait of the dancer and choreographer, her influences, performances at La Plata and Teatro Colón, and her independent productions.

CLASSED ENTRIES

DANCE: Modern dance—Performance/production

1563 Oberzaucher-Schüller, Gunhild. "'Auch das Neue hat die Wienerische Note'." (Innovation Also Has a Viennese Character.) *Tanzd.* 1996; 32(1): 8-15. Notes. Illus.: Photo. Dwg. B&W. 6. Lang.: Ger.
Austria: Vienna. 1890-1959. Biographical studies. ■The work of dancer and choreographer Gertrud Bodenwieser and its significance to the Austrian dance movement.

1564 Oberzaucher, Alfred; Oberzaucher-Schüller, Gunhild. "Wer waren die Lehrer von Gertrud Bodenwieser?" (Who Were Gertrud Bodenwieser's Teachers?)*Tanzd.* 1996; 33(2): 15-22. Notes. Illus.: Photo. Dwg. B&W. 10. Lang.: Ger.
Austria: Vienna. 1910. Biographical studies. ■Dance training and other dance activities in the early days of Viennese independent theatre.

1565 Dussault, Geneviève. "Le corps montréalais: Réflexions sur le Festival international de nouvelle danse 1992." (The Montreal Body: Reflections on the Festival International de Nouvelle Danse 1992.) *JCT.* 1992; 65: 142-146. Illus.: Photo. B&W. 4. Lang.: Fre.
Canada: Montreal, PQ. 1992. Critical studies. ■Montreal choreographies are characteristically fueled by personal experience inscribed in the body, compared to other choreographies presented at Festival international de nouvelle danse 1992.

1566 Faucher, Martin. "La Redécouverte de l'émotion." (The Rediscovery of Emotion.) *JCT.* 1991; 59: 36-37. Illus.: Photo. B&W. 1. Lang.: Fre.
Canada: Montreal, PQ. 1989. Histories-sources. ■Dancer Martin Faucher describes his experience creating *Les Traces 1* under choreographer Daniel Léveillé.

1567 Febvre, Michèle. "La Danse et l'effet-théâtre: Théâtralité?" (Dance and the Theatre Effect: Theatricality?)*JCT.* 1991; 59: 38-43. Notes. Illus.: Poster. Photo. B&W. 6. Lang.: Fre.
Canada: Montreal, PQ. 1960-1991. Critical studies. ■Tension between 'dancing quality' and theatricality (narrative structure, character, dramatic tension, mimetic reproduction of reality) in Montreal choreographies.

1568 Léveillé, Daniel. "La Nouvelle danse: Pièces d'identité." (The New Dance: Identity Pieces.) *JCT.* 1991; 59: 27-35. Illus.: Photo. B&W. 6. Lang.: Fre.
Canada: Montreal, PQ. 1976-1991. Critical studies. ■Approaches to character creation in modern dance, and analysis of character in choreographies by Edouard Lock, Jean-Pierre Perrault, Paul-André Fortier, Marie Chouinard and Ginette Laurin.

1569 Lévesque, Solange. "'Mon Meilleur professeur, c'est le quotidien: Entretien avec Jocelyne Montpetit." ('My Best Teacher Is Everyday Life': Interview with Jocelyne Montpetit.) *JCT.* 1990; 55: 22-27. Illus.: Photo. B&W. 4. Lang.: Fre.
Canada: Montreal, PQ. Japan. 1980-1990. Histories-sources. ■Influence of *butō* and Japanese teachers on practice of dancer Jocelyne Montpetit.

1570 Olsson-Forsberg, Marito. "Dans i Montreal." (Dance in Montreal.) *Danst.* 1996; 6(1): 2-5. Illus.: Photo. B&W. Color. Lang.: Swe.
Canada: Montreal, PQ. 1995. Historical studies. ■A survey of the importance of the modern dance in French-speaking Canada, with references to Le Groupe Nouvelle Aire, Edouard Lock, Marie Chouinard, Jean-Pierre Perrault and Paul-André Fortier.

1571 Härkönen, Birgitta. "Köpenhamn väcker tankar ur hjärtat." (Copenhagen Awakens Thoughts in the Heart.) *Danst.* 1996; 6(5): 21-22. Illus.: Photo. B&W. Lang.: Swe.
Denmark: Copenhagen. 1996. Historical studies. ■A report from the cultural capital of the year 1996, with references to the installations and dance events of Merce Cunningham's guest performance.

1572 Mollerup, Birgit; Michelsen, Gete; Graae, Irene; Lønqvist, Lisa; Espersen, Lizzie; Bircow Lassen, Tove; Winkel, Lasse. "Asta Mollerup—en pioner i dansk dansehistorie." (Asta Mollerup: A Pioneer in Danish Dance History.) *TE.* 1996 Feb.; 77: 26-29. Illus.: Photo. B&W. 5. Lang.: Dan.
Denmark: Copenhagen. 1881-1945. Historical studies. ■The life and work of Mollerup, who founded a school of dance in Copenhagen in 1933 and introduced modern dance into Denmark, by her former students. Her influences include Isadora Duncan and Mary Wigman.

1573 Wrange, Ann-Marie. "En magisk Pina." (A Magical Pina.) *Danst.* 1996; 6(4): 16-17. Illus.: Photo. B&W. Color. Lang.: Swe.
Denmark: Copenhagen. 1996. Critical studies. ■A report from the guest performance of Pina Bausch's Tanztheater Wupperthal, with references to *Nelken (Carnations)* and *Viktor.*

1574 Dienes, Gedeon. "Isadora Duncan Svédországban." (Isadora Duncan in Sweden.) 42-54 in Szúdy, Eszter, ed. *Tánctudományi Tanulmányok 1994/1995.* Budapest: Magyar Táncművészek Szövetsége; 1995. 230 pp. Biblio. Illus.: Photo. Dwg. B&W. 4. Lang.: Hun.
Europe. 1906-1907. Historical studies. ■History of Duncan's Swedish performances and reactions to them.

1575 Kluncker, Heinz. "Eine fliegende Holländerin." (A Flying Dutchwoman.) *TZ.* 1996; 3: 60-63. Illus.: Photo. B&W. 2. Lang.: Ger.
Germany: Konstanz. 1996. Biographical studies. ■Portrait of Yugoslavian-born dancer and choreographer Nada Kokotović and her work at Stadttheater Konstanz.

1576 Loney, Glenn. "Pina Bausch Meets the Press." *WES.* 1995-96 Win; 7(3): 67-70. Illus.: Photo. 1. Lang.: Eng.
Germany: Wuppertal. 1995. Histories-sources. ■General press conference/interview with dance director Pina Bausch at the Edinburgh Festival on her new work *Nelken (Carnations).*

1577 Scheier, Helmut. "Ausatmen, einatmen." (Breathe Out, Breathe In.) *DB.* 1996; 1: 30-32. Append. Illus.: Photo. B&W. 3. Lang.: Ger.
Germany. 1982-1996. Biographical studies. ■Portrait of choreographer Stephan Thoss, who works in the tradition of German free dance.

1578 Schmidt, Jochen; Kranz, Dieter. "Bausch, Ek, Schlömer." *DB.* 1996; 7: 20-24. Illus.: Photo. B&W. 4. Lang.: Ger.
Germany. 1996. Reviews of performances. ■The booming dance theatre scene, with reference to performances by Pina Bausch, Mats Ek, and Joachim Schlömer.

1579 Skånberg, Ami. "Dansteater i Tyskland och Sverige." (Dance Theatre in Germany and Sweden.) *Danst.* 1996; 6(5): 23-24 . Lang.: Swe.
Germany. Sweden. 1945. Historical studies. ■A report from a conference about the development of Tanztheater with references to Suzanne Linke, Mary Wigman, Kurt Joos and Folkwangschule, and the Swedish choreographers Birgit Cullberg and Birgit Åkesson.

1580 Sörenson, Margareta. "Gammal saga som ny." (Old Tale As New.) *Danst.* 1996; 6(4): 19. Illus.: Photo. B&W. Lang.: Swe.
Germany: Hamburg. 1996. Critical studies. ■A report from Mats Ek's new version of *The Sleeping Beauty (Dornröschen)* for the Hamburger Ballett Ensemble.

1581 Jálics, Kinga; Papp, Dezső, photo. "Egy igazi megszállott. Találkozás Bakó Gáborral." (A Real Fanatic. Meeting Gábor Bakó.) *Tanc.* 1995; 26(1/3): 16-17. Illus.: Photo. B&W. 2. Lang.: Hun.
Hungary. 1982-1994. Histories-sources. ■Portrait sketch of a young dancer-choreographer.

1582 Kaán, Zsuzsa; Mezey, Béla, photo. "Tatár György—'Európában művész lettem, Amerikában ember lettem!'." (György Tatár-'In Europe I Became an Artist, in America a Human!'.) *Tanc.* 1995; 26(4/6): 14-16. Illus.: Photo. B&W. 3. Lang.: Hun.
Hungary. USA. 1940-1995. Histories-sources. ■Interview with Tatár, a Hungarian-born dancer, formerly with the ballet of Budapest Opera House,who has lived in the U.S. with his wife and partner Kató Patócs since 1947.

1583 Roboz, Ágnes; Kanyó, Béla, photo. "Szentpál Olga, a magyar mozdulatművészet nagyasszonya. Emlékezés születésének 100. évfordulója alkalmából." (Olga Szentpál, the Hungarian Noble Lady of Eurhythmics—Commemorating Her 100th Birthday.) *Tanc.* 1995; 26(10/12): 50-51. Illus.: Photo. B&W. 5. Lang.: Hun.

DANCE: Modern dance—Performance/production

Hungary. 1895-1995. Biographical studies. ■Survey of the activity of a prominent representative of 20th-century Eurhythmics in Hungary by her last pupil on the occasion of her 100th birthday.

1584 Kaposi, Edit; Vass, Dániel, photo. "Lábán Rudolf nyomában a Monte Veritán—I. rész." (Following in the Footsteps of Rudolf Laban on Monte Verità—Part 1.) *Tanc.* 1995; 26(1/3): 52-53. Illus.: Photo. B&W. 2. Lang.: Hun.
Italy: Ascona. 1913-1918. Historical studies. ■The Hungarian-born dancer and scholar's spiritual experiences in the Italian alps. Continued in *Tanc* 26: 4/6 (1995), 51-53.

1585 Fuchs, Lívia. "Bevezetés az amerikai és európai modern tánc törénetébe." (Introduction to the History of the American and European Modern Dance.) 23-41 in Szúdy, Eszter, ed. *Tánctudományi Tanulmányok 1994/1995.* Budapest: Magyar Táncművészek Szövetsége; 1995. 230 pp. Notes. Lang.: Hun.
North America. Europe. 1890-1990. Historical studies. ■An exhaustive picture of the modern dance trends of the 20th century tracing the events in Western Europe and America from generation to generation, from the trail-blazers to the postmodern dancers.

1586 Frege, Ilona. "An Interview with Gary Gordon, Rhodes University, October 1994." *SATJ.* 1995 Sep.; 9(2): 97-102. Lang.: Eng.
South Africa, Republic of: Grahamstown. 1994. Histories-sources. ■Interview with choreographer Gary Gordon on the state of dance in South Africa.

1587 Swedberg, Jacob. "En gemensam vision." (A Joint Vision.) *Danst.* 1996; 6(4): 2-5. Illus.: Photo. B&W. Lang.: Swe.
Sweden: Norrköping. 1995. Histories-sources. ■An interview with the composer Michel van der Aa and the choreographer Philippe Blanchard about their joint *Staring at the Space* involving a symphony orchestra and dancers in the concert hall of Norrköping.

1588 Swedberg, Jacob. "Att känna in varandra." (To Come to Recognize Each Other.) *Danst.* 1996; 6(4): 4-6. Illus.: Photo. Color. Lang.: Swe.
Sweden: Stockholm. 1995. Histories-sources. ■An interview with percussionist Kjell Nordeson and dancer Nathalie Ruiz about their joint production *Relief* where both are on stage and occasionally dance together.

1589 Wrange, Ann-Marie. "Den skärpta blicken." (The Strained Gaze.) *Danst.* 1996; 6(2): 12-13. Illus.: Photo. Color. Lang.: Swe.
Sweden: Stockholm. 1996. Critical studies. ■Cristina Caprioli speaks about her *L'invisibile canto del camminare* with roots in the Italy of Monteverdi as well as Calvino.

1590 Wrange, Ann-Marie. "Scenisk alkemi." (Scenic Alchemy.) *Danst.* 1996; 6(2): 17. Illus.: Photo. Color. Lang.: Swe.
Sweden: Stockholm. 1996. Critical studies. ■Per Jonsson speaks about the importance of performance art for his choreographic imagination, with references to several performances during the 1980s.

1591 Wrange, Ann-Marie. "Mats Ek på TV." (Mats Ek On TV.) *Danst.* 1996; 6(2): 20. Illus.: Photo. Color. Lang.: Swe.
Sweden. 1976. Critical studies. ■A presentation of Mats Ek's several works for TV, with reference to his and the producer Gunilla Wallin's *Smoke.*

1592 Spångberg, Mårten. "Nya dansmodet." (The New Fashion of Dance.) *Danst.* 1996; 6(2): 16. Illus.: Photo. Color. Lang.: Swe.
UK-England: London. 1996. Historical studies. ■A report from *Spring Collection,* a festival of modern dance from Great Britain.

1593 Siegel, Marcia B. "Virtual Criticism and the Dance of Death." *TDR.* 1996 Sum; 40(2): 60-70. Notes. Biblio. Illus.: Photo. B&W. 3. Lang.: Eng.
USA. 1996. Critical studies. ■Defense of choreographer Bill T. Jones's AIDS-related work *Still/Here* against *New Yorker* dance critic Arlene Croce's charges.

1594 Wrange, Ann-Marie. "På dansens barrikader." (On the Barricades of Dance.) *Danst.* 1996; 6(2): 2-5. Illus.: Photo. B&W. Color. Lang.: Swe.

USA: New York, NY. Sweden: Stockholm. 1960. Histories-sources. ■Interview with Margaretha Åsberg on her years of study in New York and her later career in Sweden, and the new attitude toward dance as pure movement, with references to Moderna Dansteatern and Yvonne Rainer.

Relation to other fields

1595 Cardinal, Diane; Laflamme, Carole. "De la Danse à la société: Autour d"Affamée': Entretien avec Jo Lechay et Eugene Lion." (From Dance to Society: About 'Affamée (Starving)': Interview with Jo Lechay and Eugene Lion.) *JCT.* 1990; 56 : 127-129. Illus.: Photo. B&W. 1. Lang.: Fre.
Canada: Montreal, PQ. 1990. Histories-sources. ■Jo Lechay and Eugene Lion's visions of convergence of art and politics, and political content of their collaboration *Affamée (Starving).*

1596 Møller, Søren Friis. "Har vi tabt maelet?" (Have We Been Left Speechless?)*TE.* 1996 June; 79: 28-31. Illus.: Photo. B&W. 6. Lang.: Dan.
Denmark: Copenhagen. 1996. Historical studies. ■Account of an international dance festival in which Jérôme Bel from France, Alain Platel from Belgium, Sasha Waltz from Germany, Merce Cunningham from the USA and José Nanas from Venezuela participated. Focus on the reflections of society in modern dance.

1597 Odenthal, Johannes. "Tendencies in European Dance." *PerfR.* 1996 Spr; 1(1): 108-110. Notes. Biblio. Illus.: Photo. B&W. 1. Lang.: Eng.
Europe. 1995. Critical studies. ■Contemporary dance as a democratic counter-movement to classical ballet, which remains at the heart of European dance, described as reactionary.

1598 Ashford, John. "Choreography at the Crossroads." *PerfR.* 1996 Spr; 1(1): 110-113. Notes. Biblio. Lang.: Eng.
UK-England. 1995. Critical studies. ■Political, social, and aesthetic possibilities of dance in contemporary Britain, with emphasis on the diverse cultural influences available.

1599 Lepecki, André. "Embracing the Stain: Notes on the Time of Dance." *PerfR.* 1996 Spr; 1(1): 103-107. Notes. Biblio. Illus.: Photo. B&W. 2. Lang.: Eng.
UK-England. 1995. Critical studies. ■Possibilities and difficulties in creating dances of political resistance that might deny of the logic of the market or the exotic and facilitate a genuine encounter with the other.

1600 Conner, Lynne. "'What the Modern Dance Should Be': Socialist Agendas in the Modern Dance, 1931-38." 231-248 in Reinelt, Janelle, ed. *Crucibles of Crisis: Performing Social Change.* Ann Arbor, MI: Univ of Michigan P; 1996. 250 pp. Notes. Illus.: Photo. 1. Lang.: Eng.
USA. 1931-1938. Critical studies. ■The effect of the Socialist agenda on the work of two principal dance artists of the 1930s, Doris Humphrey and Martha Graham. Argues that social change brought about a short-lived but significant reconfiguration of modern dance.

Research/historiography

1601 Dienes, Valéria; Dienes, Gedeon, ed., intro. *Orkesztika—Mozdulatrendszer.* (Orchestics—Movement System.) Budapest: Planétás; 1996. 163 pp. Append. Biblio. Pref. Illus.: Photo. B&W. 93. Lang.: Hun.
France: Paris. Hungary: Budapest. 1908-1994. Histories-specific. ■Orchestics is a system of human movements derived from their scientific analysis by Valéria Dienes. The book consists of four parts: a detailed introduction, the description of the system (containing the four studies of space, time, force and meaning), the story of its development and a few important documents.

1602 Major, Rita. "Nyolcvan év a tánc szolgálatában. Születésnap utáni beszélgetés Dienes Gedeonnal." (Eighty Years in the Service of Dance: Meeting the 80-Year-Old Gedeon Dienes.) *Tanc.* 1995; 26(4/6): 12-13. Illus.: Photo. B&W. 3. Lang.: Hun.
Hungary. 1914-1995. Histories-sources. ■Interview with dance scholar Dienes about his research, and present status of dance.

DANCE: Modern dance

Theory/criticism

1603 Laliberté, Sylvie. "Fuira-t-il le futile." (Will He Flee the Futile.) *JCT*. 1991; 59: 44-45. Illus.: Photo. B&W. 2. Lang.: Fre.
Canada: Montreal, PQ. 1991. Histories-sources. ■Dancer Sylvie Laliberté's opinions on the aesthetics of postmodern dance.

1604 Wulff, Helena. "Att tolka tidens rörelse." (To Interpret the Movements of Time.) *Danst*. 1996; 6(2): 6-7. Illus.: Photo. B&W. Lang.: Swe.
USA: New York, NY. 1960. Historical studies. ■A survey of Sally Banes' career as a critic and researcher, with references to the postmodern dance in New York and the new interdisciplinary research.

DANCE-DRAMA

General

Institutions

1605 Schmidt, Jochen. "Aufruhr, Aufbruch, Anspruch." (Rebellion, Awakening, Demand.) *DB*. 1996; 10: 30-33. Illus.: Photo. Color. 3. Lang.: Ger.
Australia: Melbourne. Indonesia: Jakarta. 1996. Reviews of performances. ■Report on the congress and performances of the Asian festival organized by the World Dance Alliance in Melbourne and Jakarta.

Performance/production

1606 Chadzis, Athina. "Gegen den Strom." (Against the Tide.) *Tanzd*. 1996; 32(1): 16-23. Notes. Illus.: Design. Photo. Dwg. B&W. 12. Lang.: Ger.
Germany: Hamburg. 1918-1924. Biographical studies. ■The lives of unknown expressionist mask dancers Lavinia Schulz and Walter Holdt, and the archive devoted to them in Hamburg.

1607 Feuchtner, Bernd. "Echt ist schlecht." (Genuine Is Bad.) *THeute*. 1996; 12: 28-29. Illus.: Photo. B&W. 2. Lang.: Ger.
Germany: Cologne. 1996. Historical studies. ■Description of the dance-drama production *Riefenstahl* by Johann Kresnik at Schauspielhaus Köln.

Kathakali

Basic theatrical documents

1608 Tampura, Kottayam; Zarrilli, Phillip B., intro., transl.; Nayar, V. R. Prabodhachandran, transl.; Namboodiri, M.P. Sankaran, transl. "*Kalyānasaugandhikam (The Flower of Good Fortune)*: A *Kathakali* Drama by Kottayam Tampura." *ATJ*. 1996 Spr; 13(1): 1-25. Notes. Biblio. Illus.: Photo. B&W. 6. Lang.: Eng.
India. 1625-1996. ■Complete playtext with accompanying notes on *kathakali* dance-drama and list of terms used in performance text.

1609 Varman, Kulaśekhara; Sullivan, Bruce M., intro., transl.; Unni, N.P., transl. "*Tapatī-Samvaranam*: A Kūtiyāttam Drama by Kulaśekhara Varman." *ATJ*. 1996 Spr; 13(1): 26-53. Notes. Biblio. Illus.: Photo. B&W. 1. Lang.: Eng.
India: Kerala. 1100-1996. ■One complete act of the play focusing on the *kūtiyāttam* performance tradition, with introduction on characters, Hindu religious foundations, contemporary temple performances, three centers of instruction for the art form.

Performance/production

1610 Daugherty, Diane. "The Nangyār: Female Ritual Specialist of Kerala." *ATJ*. 1996 Spr; 13(1): 54-67. Biblio. Illus.: Photo. Color. B&W. 12. Lang.: Eng.
India: Kerala. 1300-1996. Critical studies. ■Female temple servants and their role as *kūtiyāttam* actresses. Religious tradition, initiation rites and their performance of the ritualistic *nangyār kūttu*.

Nō

Plays/librettos/scripts

1611 MacDuff, William. "Beautiful Boys in the *Nō* Drama: The Idealization of Homoerotic Desire." *ATJ*. 1996 Fall; 13(2): 248-258. Notes. Biblio. Lang.: Eng.
Japan. 1349-1996. Critical studies. ■Examines the *nō* theatre of Japan in order to explore homoerotic elements in the playtexts. Background of same-sex attachments in medieval Japan, and implications of such relationships for the understanding of *nō*.

1612 Tyler, Royall. "Korean Echoes in the *Nō* Play *Furu*." *EAH*. 1994 June; 7: 49-66. Notes. Illus.: Photo. Dwg. Sketches. B&W. 12. Lang.: Eng.
Japan. Korea. 1183-1420. Critical studies. ■Korean influence found in the *nō* play *Furu* which is widely held to be by Zeami.

DRAMA

Administration

1613 Lavoie, Pierre. "'From coast to coast, and in the U.S.A.': Diffusion et promotion du théâtre québécois au Canada anglais et aux États-Unis: Entretien avec Linda Gaboriau." ('From Coast to Coast, and in the U.S.A.': Spreading and Promoting Quebecois Theatre in English Canada and the United States: Interview with Linda Gaboriau.) *JCT*. 1991; 59: 118-125. Notes. Illus.: Photo. B&W. 2. Lang.: Fre.
Canada: Montreal, PQ, Toronto, ON. 1983-1988. Histories-sources. ■Translator Linda Gaboriau describes her experience at Montreal's Centre des Auteurs Dramatiques, organizing cultural exchanges and generating interest in Quebecois drama outside of Quebec.

1614 Vaïs, Michel. "Du Théâtre Expérimental des Femmes à l'Espace GO: Entretien avec Ginette Noiseux." (From the Théâtre Expérimental des Femmes to Espace GO: Interview with Ginette Noiseux.) *JCT*. 1990; 57: 51-62. Illus.: Photo. B&W. 6. Lang.: Fre.
Canada: Montreal, PQ. 1985-1990. Histories-sources. ■Artistic director Ginette Noiseux reviews past administration of Espace GO (formerly Théâtre Expérimental des Femmes), current status and future plans.

1615 Cekinovskij, B. "Paradoksy nekommerčeskogo teatra." (The Paradox of Non-Commercial Theatre.) *TeatZ*. 1996; 8: 18-20. Lang.: Rus.
Russia: Moscow. 1990-1996. Historical studies. ■'Independent' plays and commercialism in theatre art.

1616 Garon, Lana. "Pozicija." (Position.) *TeatZ*. 1996; 11-12: 20-21. Lang.: Rus.
Russia: Moscow. 1990-1996. Histories-sources. ■The literary manager of Stanislavskij Theatre discusses her work.

1617 Sosič, Marko. *Tisoč dni, dvesto noči*. (A Thousand Days, Two Hundred Nights.) Nova Gorica: Branko; 1996. 239 pp. Lang.: Slo.
Slovenia: Nova Gorica. 1991-1994. Histories-sources. ■Memoirs of the former director at the Primorsko dramsko gledališče.

1618 García Ruiz, Víctor. "Los mecanismos de censura teatral en el primer franquismo y *Los pájaros ciegos* de V. Ruiz Iriarte (1948)." (The Mechanisms of Theatrical Censorship in the Early Franco Era and *The Blind Birds* (1948) by Víctor Ruiz Iriarte.) *Gestos*. 1996 Nov.; 11(22): 59-85. Notes. Biblio. Lang.: Eng.
Spain. 1939-1975. Historical studies. ■Illustrates the methods of government censorship through a case study of Ruiz Iriarte's play.

1619 Kristoffersson, Birgitta. "Ingrid Dahlberg—ny dramatenchef." (Ingrid Dahlberg, the New Manager of Dramaten.) *Dramat*. 1996; 4(1): 16-18. Illus.: Photo. Color. Lang.: Swe.
Sweden: Stockholm. 1960-1996. Histories-sources. ■Interview with Ingrid Dahlberg, formerly a television journalist and the manager of the Drama Section of Svensk Television, who has now succeeded Lars Löfgren as manager of the Royal Dramatic Theatre.

DRAMA: —Administration

1620 Nicholson, Steve. "'Nobody Was Ready for That': The Gross Impertinence of Terence Gray and the Degradation of Drama." *ThR.* 1996; 21(2): 121-131. Notes. Lang.: Eng.

UK-England: Cambridge. 1926-1932. Biographical studies. ■Account of Terence Gray's relations with the Lord Chamberlain, and with English theatrical culture generally, in the 1920s. Attributes closure of Cambridge Festival Theatre, directed by Gray, to Gray's frustration at commercialism and debasement of public taste.

1621 Boyd, Julianne. "SSDC Speaks Out on Property Rights." *TheaterW.* 1996 Sep 9; 10(6): 31-32. Lang.: Eng.

USA: New York, NY. 1996. Historical studies. ■President of the Society of Stage Directors and Choreographers discusses property rights protection, focusing on case of Joe Mantello's direction of Terrence McNally's *Love! Valour! Compassion!,* which he claims was duplicated by a Florida theatre.

1622 Drukman, Steven. "A Standoff in Charlotte." *AmTh.* 1996 May/June; 13(5): 46-47. Illus.: Photo. B&W. 1. Lang.: Eng.

USA: Charlotte, NC. 1996. Historical studies. ■Legal action taken against Charlotte Repertory Theatre for presenting Tony Kushner's *Angels in America, Part I: Millennium Approaches* due to local laws regarding public nudity.

1623 Moore, Dick. "La Mama's Ellen Stewart Receives Rosetta Lenoire Award." *EN.* 1996 May; 81(4): 1. Illus.: Photo. 1. Lang.: Eng.

USA: New York, NY. 1996. Historical studies. ■Ellen Stewart, founder and artistic director of La MaMa Experimental Theatre Club, received the 1996 Rosetta LeNoire Award at the Eastern regional membership meeting April 12. This award honors outstanding achievements in multi-racial or nontraditional casting.

1624 Stockdale, Joe. "Directors' Property Rights." *TheaterW.* 1996 Aug 12; 10(2): 22-29. Illus.: Photo. B&W. 1. Lang.: Eng.

USA: New York, NY. 1996. Historical studies. ■Controversy over directors' rights to their artistic interpretive choices. Focus on director Joe Mantello and the Society of Stage Directors and Choreographers' (SSDC) lawsuit against director Michael Hall and the Caldwell Theatre for copying his work on the Broadway production of Terrence McNally's *Love! Valour! Compassion!.*

Audience

1625 Dussault, Louisette. "'Miracle! Miracle!'." *JCT.* 1996; 80: 135-136. Illus.: Photo. B&W. 1. Lang.: Fre.

Canada: Montreal, PQ. 1973. Histories-sources. ■Actor Louisette Dussault recalls spontaneous audience reaction to her performance of Michel Tremblay's *La Résurrection de Lazare (The Resurrection of Lazarus)* (adapted from Dario Fo's *Mistero Buffo*) at Théâtre du Nouveau Monde in 1973, directed by André Brassard.

1626 Fréchette, Carole. "Si peu." (So Little.) *JCT.* 1989; 50: 55-56. Illus.: Photo. B&W. 1. Lang.: Fre.

Canada. 1989. Critical studies. ■Incapacity of contemporary Quebec theatre to spark debate.

1627 Lefebvre, Paul. "Qui a peur du théâtre?" (Who's Afraid of Theatre?)*JCT.* 1990; 55: 78-80. Illus.: Photo. B&W. 2. Lang.: Fre.

Canada. 1990. Critical studies. ■Argues the importance of laughter in theatre's role of forming community among spectators. Postscript on spontaneous laughter on stage.

1628 Lévesque, Solange. "'À quelle heure on meurt?': Au-delà du théâtre." ('What Time Do We Die?' Beyond Theatre.) *JCT.* 1989; 51: 44-48. Illus.: Photo. B&W. 4. Lang.: Fre.

Canada: Montreal, PQ. 1988. Histories-sources. ■Spectator describes personal impressions of Martin Faucher's stage adaptation of Réjean Ducharme's novel *À quelle heure on meurt? (What Time Do We Die?).*

1629 Mendenhall, Marie. "*A North Side Story or Two.*" *NWR.* 1996 Jan.; 21(2): 28-29. Illus.: Photo. B&W. 4. Lang.: Eng.

Canada: Regina, SK. 1993-1995. Critical studies. ■The social and theatrical effects of the community play *A North Side Story or Two,* produced by Common Weal Productions, on Regina's North Central neighborhood and audience.

1630 Ronfard, Jean-Pierre. "La rumeur maligne." (The Vicious Rumor.) *JCT.* 1996; 80: 191-194. Illus.: Photo. B&W. 2. Lang.: Fre.

Canada: Quebec, PQ. 1996. Histories-sources. ■Director Jean-Pierre Ronfard contrasts his personal reaction as audience member with critical reception of Serge Denoncourt's 1996 production of Ariane Mnouchkine's *Méphisto.*

1631 Weller, Philip. "'Kill Claudio': A Laugh Almost Killed by the Critics." *JDTC.* 1996 Fall; 11(1): 101-110. Notes. Lang.: Eng.

England. 1599-1990. Critical studies. ■Analysis of audience reaction to a line spoken by Beatrice in Shakespeare's *Much Ado About Nothing,* with attention to critical disapproval of performances in which the line provokes laughter.

1632 Dallett, Athenaide. "Protest in the Playhouse: Two Twentieth-Century Audience Riots." *NTQ.* 1996 Nov.; 12(48): 323-332. Notes. Lang.: Eng.

Ireland: Dublin. USA: Berkeley, CA. 1907-1968. Historical studies. ■Argues that the riots at the opening of Synge's *The Playboy of the Western World* (Abbey Theatre) and at the Living Theatre's *Paradise Now* were provoked by a breach of the implicit contract between performers and audience.

1633 Komorowski, Jarosław. "Księcia Radziwiłła spotkanie z Shakespearem. 'Poskromienie złośnicy' w Królewcu w 1664 roku." (Prince Radziwill's Meeting with Shakespeare: *The Taming of the Shrew* in Königsberg in 1664.) *PaT.* 1996; 45(3-4): 423-434. Notes. Illus.: Pntg. Dwg. Photo. B&W. 5. Lang.: Pol.

Prussia: Königsberg. 1664. Historical studies. ■The first Polish spectator at a Shakespearean performance in the seventeenth century.

1634 Kljuev, V.G. "Čelovek v zritel'nom zale." (Person in the Audience.) 182-203 in *Iskusstvo i social'naja psichologija.* Moscow: Gosudarstvénnyj institut iskusstvoznanija; 1996. Lang.: Rus.

Russia: Moscow. Germany: Berlin. 1898-1956. Historical studies. ■Brecht's analysis of the problems of the actor-audience relationship.

1635 Garfinkel, Sharon. "The Chief Prosecutor." *PlPl.* 1996 Aug/Sep.: 21. Lang.: Eng.

UK-England: London. 1996. Histories-sources. ■Interview with the chief prosecuter of the Nuremberg trials, Lord Hartley Shawcross. Emphasis on the memories the play *Nuremberg: The War Crimes Trial* evoked, his personal memories of Nuremberg and his thoughts on the verdict.

1636 Logan, Stephen. "Shakespeare's Ears." *AtG.* 1996 Win: 10-11. Illus.: Sketches. B&W. 2. Lang.: Eng.

UK-England: London. 1996. Critical studies. ■Contends that an imaginative, modern audience at the open-air Shakespeare's Globe can get a true sense of the Elizabethan theatrical experience.

Basic theatrical documents

1637 Kelly, Katherine E. *Modern Drama by Women, 1880s-1930s: An International Anthology.* London/New York, NY: Routledge; 1996. 319 pp. Notes. Biblio. Illus.: Photo. 15. Lang.: Eng.

1880-1940. ■Plays on themes of politics, social policy, the professions, and the arts, translated into English where appropriate. *Sanna kvinnor (True Women)* by Anne Charlotte Leffler Edgren, *Anima (Her Soul)* by Amelia Rosselli, *Maria Arndt* by Elsa Bernstein (Ernst Rosmer), *Votes for Women* by Elizabeth Robins, *La Triomphatrice (Triumphant)* by Marie Lenéru, *El amo del mundo (The Master of the World)* by Alfonsina Storni, *Juurakon Hulda (Hulda Juurakko)* by Hella Wuolijoki, *Chōji midare (Wavering Traces)* by Hasegawa Shiguré, *L'Araignée de Cristal (The Crystal Spider)* by Rachilde (Marguerite Eymery), *Sviataia krov' (Sacred Blood)* by Zinaida Gippius, *The Dove* by Djuna Barnes, and *The Purple Flower* by Marita Bonner.

1638 Diament, Mario; Diament, Simone Zarmati, transl. "Interview." *MID.* 1996 Fall; 30(1): 103-127. Lang.: Eng.

Argentina. 1996. ■Translated text of *Interview.*

1639 Glickman, Nora, ed., transl.; Waldman, Gloria, F., ed., transl. *Argentine Jewish Theatre: A Critical Anthology.*

DRAMA: —Basic theatrical documents

Lewisburg, PA/London: Bucknell UP/Associated Univ Presses; 1996. 346 pp. Biblio. Notes. Lang.: Eng.
Argentina. 1926-1988. ■English translations *El cambalache de Petroff (Petroff's Junkshop)* by Alberto Novión (1937), César Tiempo's *La alfarda (The Tithe)* (1937), Samuel Eichelbaum's *El judío Aarón (Aarón the Jew)* (1926), Germán Rozenmacher's *Simón, Caballero de Indias (Simón Brumelstein, Knight of the Indies)* (1935), *Krinsky* by Jorge Goldenberg (1977), *Mil años, un día (A Thousand Years, One Day)* by Ricardo Halac (1986), Osvaldo Dragún's *Arriba Corazón (Forward, Heart)* (1987), and Diana Raznovich's *Objetos perdidos (Lost Belongings)* (1988). Also includes playwright biographies.

1640 *"A Dialogue Between a Stump Orator and a Noted Squatter."* ADS. 1996 Apr.; 28: 106-116. Lang.: Eng.
Australia: Melbourne. 1850. ■Complete text of play.

1641 Parr, Bruce, ed., intro. *Australian Gay and Lesbian Plays.* Paddington: Currency; 1996. 341 pp. Lang.: Eng.
Australia. 1970-1996. ■Includes *Mates* by Peter Kenna, *A Manual of Trench Warfare* by Clem Gorman, *Pinball* by Alison Lyssa, *What Do They Call Me?* by Eva Johnson, *Blood and Honour* by Alex Harding, *Is That You Nancy?* by Sandra Shotlander and *Furious* by Michael Gow. Introduction discusses pioneers of Australian gay theatre, early gay plays and histories of plays included.

1642 Radic, Thérèse. *The Emperor Regrets.* Sydney: Currency; 1994. 66 pp. Lang.: Eng.
Australia. 1994. ■Complete text of Radic's play.

1643 The Clichettes. *"Out for Blood."* CTR. 1996 Spr; 86: 32-48. Notes. Illus.: Photo. B&W. 15. Lang.: Eng.
Canada. 1996. ■Complete playtext with accompanying production notes.

1644 *"La dernière réplique du personnage."* (The Character's Last Line.) JCT. 1996; 80: 230-234. Illus.: Photo. B&W. 1. Lang.: Fre.
Canada. France. England. 1595-1996. ■Final lines of the principal characters of forty-five plays, chiefly by French, English and Quebecois playwrights.

1645 Dixon, Sean. *"The District of Centuries."* CTR. 1996 Sum; 87: 36-54. Notes. Lang.: Eng.
Canada. 1996. ■Complete playtext of *The District of Centuries* with accompanying production notes.

1646 PRIMUS Theatre. *"Far Away Home."* CTR. 1996 Fall; 88: 56-68. Notes. Illus.: Photo. B&W. 9. Lang.: Eng.
Canada. 1996. ■Complete playtext with accompanying production notes.

1647 Lill, Wendy; Tompkins, Joanne, ed. *"The Glace Bay Miners' Museum."* ADS. 1996 Oct.; 29: 115-154. Lang.: Eng.
Canada. 1996. ■Complete text of Lill's play with a brief introduction by Joanne Tompkins.

1648 Molivar, Carlo Felipe; Lefebvre, Paul, transl.; Douesnard, Chantal, transl. "Une pièce dont 'Jeu' ne parlerait probablement pas et pour moi c'est un problème: 'Viandes fraîches (Carnes frescas)' de Carlo-Felipe Molivar.'' (A Play which 'Jeu' Will Likely Not Discuss and for Me That's a Problem: 'Fresh Meat (Carnes frescas)' by Carlo-Felipe Molivar.) JCT. 1996; 80: 88-95. Notes. Illus.: Photo. B&W. 3. Lang.: Fre.
Canada: Montreal, PQ. Spain: Madrid. 1995-1996. ■French adaptation of act 2, scene 5 of *Carnes Frescas* by Molivar, with descriptions of the two characters in the scene.

1649 Nolan, Yvette. *"Child."* ADS. 1996 Oct.; 29: 112-114. Lang.: Eng.
Canada. 1996. ■Complete text of play.

1650 Nolan, Yvette, ed.; Quan, Betty, ed.; Seremba, George, ed. *Beyond the Pale: Dramatic Writing from First Nations Writers and Writers of Colour.* Toronto, ON: Playwrights Canada P; 1996. 234 pp. Index. Lang.: Eng.
Canada. 1995-1996. ■Twenty-five plays by Canadian natives and people of color. All plays are concerned with the theme of cultural identification in a pluralistic society. Plays and playwrights include *Body Blows* by Beverly Yhap, *Encore* by Dirk McLean, *Kyotopolis* by Daniel David

Moses, *Napoleon of the Nile* by George Bwanika Seremba, and *One Ocean* by Betty Quan.

1651 de la Parra, Marco Antonio. *"Ofelia o la pureza."* (Ophelia or Purity.) Cjo. 1996 Jan-June; 102: 37-57. Lang.: Spa.
Chile. 1996. ■Text of de la Parra's play.

1652 Mou, Sen; Cheung, Fai, transl. *"File 0: A Theatre Poem."* TheatreF. 1996 Win/Spr; 8: 11-21. Illus.: Photo. 6. Lang.: Eng.
China, People's Republic of: Beijing. 1995-1996. ■Text of *Ling Dang An (File 0)* conceived and directed by Mou Sen and Xi Ju Che Jian theatre group.

1653 Torriente, Alberto Pedro; Winks, Christopher, transl. *"Manteca."* TDR. 1996 Spr; 40(1): 19-43. Illus.: Photo. B&W. 4. Lang.: Eng.
Cuba. 1993. ■Complete playtext with notes from journal editor Richard Schechner discussing production of the play.

1654 Varela, Víctor. *"El Arca."* (The Ark.) Gestos. 1996 Nov.; 11(22): 133-160. Illus.: Photo. B&W. 2. Lang.: Spa.
Cuba. 1996. ■Complete text of Varela's play.

1655 Hoy, Cyrus, ed.; Turner, Robert Kean, ed.; Williams, George Walton, ed. *The Dramatic Works in the Beaumont and Fletcher Canon.* Cambridge/New York, NY: Cambridge UP; 1996. 752 pp. Notes. [Volume 10.] Lang.: Eng.
England. 1609-1613. ■Critical editions of plays in the Beaumont and Fletcher canon. Contains the texts of six plays written by Fletcher and his collaborators, Nathan Field, Philip Massinger, Ben Jonson, George Chapman, John Ford and John Webster: *The Honest Man's Fortune, Rollo, The Spanish Curate, The Lover's Progress, The Fair Maid of the Inn,* and *The Laws of Candy.*

1656 Zijlstra, A. Marcel J., transl. *"The Play of Daniel (Ludus Danielis)."* 87-126 in Ogden, Dunbar H., ed. *The Play of Daniel: Critical Essays.* Kalamazoo, MI: Medieval Institute Publications; 1996. 132 pp. (Early Drama, Art, and Music Monograph Series 24.) Notes. B&W. 26. Lang.: Eng.
France. 1140-1994. ■This transcription of the play was originally prepared for performance at the twenty-ninth International Congress on Medieval Studies at Kalamazoo. Includes notes on the musical transcription and translation of the Latin text.

1657 Bauer, Wolfgang Maria. *"Spät."* (Late.) THeute. 1996; YB: 91. Lang.: Ger.
Germany. 1996. ■Text of short play.

1658 Bukowski, Oliver. *"Lakoma. Ein kurzes Drama."* (Lakoma: A Brief Drama.) THeute. 1996; YB: 66-67. Lang.: Ger.
Germany. 1996. ■Text of brief play.

1659 Jonigk, Thomas. *"Triumph der Schauspielkunst."* (Triumph of Acting.) THeute. 1996; YB: 21-23. Lang.: Ger.
Germany. 1996. ■Complete playtext.

1660 Müller, Elfriede. *"Lupo. Ein Comic."* (Lupo: A Comic Strip.) THeute. 1996; YB: 34-35. Lang.: Ger.
Germany. 1996. ■Text of Müller's play.

1661 Scheller, Paul. *"Aschenputtels—eine Spielvorlage."* (Cinderellas: Project for Play.) SuT. 1996; 157(1): 5-12. Illus.: Photo. B&W. 6. Lang.: Ger.
Germany. 1996. ■A play of ideas developed by Theater-AG SZ Ronzenlenstrasse of Bremen.

1662 Euripides; Altena, Herman, transl., ed., annot. *Euripides Fenicische Vrouwen.* (Euripides' *Phoenician Women.*) Baarn/Antwerp: Ambo/Kritak; 1996. 102 pp. Pref. Notes. Biblio. Append. Lang.: Dut.
Greece. Netherlands. 409 B.C.-1996 A.D. ■Dutch translation of *Phoinissai (The Phoenician Women)* as produced by Hollandia. Includes textual annotations and an extended preface.

1663 Kampanéllis, Iákovos; Chambers, Marjorie, transl. *"The Four Legs of the Table."* MID. 1996 Spr; 29(2): 5-42. Lang.: Eng.
Greece. 1996. ■Complete text translation of Kampanéllis' play.

1664 Görgey, Gábor; Brogyáni, Eugene, transl. *"Public Bath."* MID. 1996 Fall; 30(1): 5-20. Lang.: Eng.
Hungary. 1996. ■Translation of *Népfürdö.*

DRAMA: —Basic theatrical documents

1665 Páskándi, Géza; Brogyáni, Eugene, transl. *"In Shadow."* *MID.* 1996 Spr; 29(2): 43-51. Lang.: Eng.
Hungary. 1996. ■Translation of *Árnyékban.*

1666 Páskándi, Géza; Brogyáni, Eugene, transl. *"No Conductor."* *MID.* 1996 Spr; 29(2): 53-74. Lang.: Eng.
Hungary. 1996. ■Translation of *Kalauz nélkül.*

1667 Taub, Michael, ed. *Israeli Holocaust Drama.* Syracuse, NY: Syracuse UP; 1996. 332 pp. Biblio. Lang.: Eng.
Israel. 1955-1989. ■Holocaust drama and the Israeli theatre tradition: *Lady of the Castle (Baalat Haarmon)* by Leah Goldberg (1955), *Hanna Senesh* by Aharon Megged (1958), *Children of the Shadow (Yaldei Hatzel)* by Ben-Zion Tomer (1962), *Kastner* by Motti Lerner (1985), and *Adam* by Joshua Sobol (1989).

1668 Loy, Mina. *"Two Plays."* *PerAJ.* 1996 Jan.; 18(1): 8-9. [Number 52.] Lang.: Eng.
Italy. 1915. ■Complete text of Mina Loy's brief *Two Plays*, consisting of *Collision* and *Cittàbapini.*

1669 Loy, Mina. *"The Pamperers."* *PerAJ.* 1996 Jan.; 18(1): 10-17. [Number 52.] Lang.: Eng.
Italy. 1916. ■Complete text of Loy's *The Pamperers.*

1670 Duyns, Don. *Toneel.* (Theatre.) Amsterdam: International Theatre and Film Books; 1996. 346 pp. Pref. Lang.: Dut.
Netherlands. 1989-1996. ■Collection of Duyns' plays.

1671 Kirchausen, Maritza. *"Con guitarra y sin cajón."* (*With a Guitar and Without a Case.*) *Cjo.* 1996 July/Dec.; 103: 63-93. Lang.: Spa.
Peru. 1996. ■Text of Kirchausen's *Con guitarra y sin cajón.*

1672 Cajal, Oana Hock. *"Berlin/Berlin."* *ThM.* 1996; 26(3): 53-84. Illus.: Dwg. B&W. 6. Lang.: Eng.
Romania. 1996. ■Text of Cajal's first English-language play *Berlin/Berlin.*

1673 Pippidi, Alina Mungiu; Taub, Michael, ed. *"The Evangelists."* *MID.* 1996 Fall; 30(1): 69-102. Lang.: Eng.
Romania. 1996. ■Alina Mungiu Pippidi's own translation of her play, *Evangheliști.*

1674 Viorel Urma, Sergiu. *"Chessgame."* *MID.* 1996 Fall; 30(1): 21-67. Lang.: Eng.
Romania. 1996. ■Viorel Urma's own translation of his play *Joc de șah.*

1675 Brodsky, Joseph. *"Democracy! Act II."* *PerAJ.* 1996 Sep.; 18(3): 92-122. [Number 54.] Lang.: Eng.
Russia. USA. 1996. ■Complete text of Act II of *Demokratija (Democracy!)*, includes revisions made by Brodsky to a previously printed version.

1676 Grdina, Igor. *Slovenska meščanska dramatika I.* (Slovene Bourgeois Drama I.) Ljubljana: Študentska organizacija Univerze; 1996. 124 pp. Lang.: Slo.
Slovenia. 1834-1932. Critical studies. ■Texts of *Doktor Dragan* by Josip Vošnjak and *Tekma (The Competition)* by Anton Funtek. Includes a presentation of these two forgotten playwrights.

1677 Brouwer, Ronald. *Teatro. Nieuwe teksten van drie Spaanse toneelschrijvers. Belbel, Cabal, Sanchis Sinisterra.* (Teatro: New Texts by Three Spanish Playwrights—Belbel, Cabal, Sanchis Sinisterra.) Amsterdam: International Theatre and Film Books; 1996. 198 pp. Pref. Lang.: Dut.
Spain. 1990-1995. ■Dutch translation of three recent Spanish plays: *Talem (Nuptial Bed)* by Sergi Belbel, *Castillos en el aire (Castles in the Air)* by Fermín Cabal, and *Valeria y los pájaros (Valeria and the Birds)* by José Sanchis Sinisterra.

1678 Díaz, Jorge. *"Historia de nadie."* (*Nobody's Story.*) Estreno. 1995; 21(1): 14-16. Lang.: Spa.
Spain. 1995. ■Complete text of play.

1679 García, Rodrigo. *"Obras cómicas."* (*Comic Works.*) *Gestos.* 1996 Apr.; 11(21): 157-175. Notes. Biblio. Illus.: Photo. B&W. 2. Lang.: Eng.
Spain: Madrid. 1996. ■Complete text of García's new comedy.

1680 Pineda, Concha Romero. *"Allá él: Monólogo original de Concha Romero Pineda."* (*It's Up to Him:* Original Monologue by Concha Romero Pineda.) Estreno. 1994; 20(1): 8-14. Illus.: Photo. B&W. 1. Lang.: Spa.

Spain. 1994. ■Complete text of play.

1681 Rodríguez Méndez, José María. *"Isabelita tiene Ángel."* (*Isabelita Has an Angel.*) Estreno. 1994; 20(1): 10-28. Illus.: Photo. B&W. 2. Lang.: Spa.
Spain. 1976. ■Complete text of play.

1682 Sanchis Sinisterra, José; London, John, transl. *"Ay, Carmela!."* *MID.* 1996 Spr; 29(2): 75-115. Lang.: Eng.
Spain. 1996. ■Translated text of *¡Ay, Carmela!.*

1683 Barnes, Peter. *"Democracy and Deconstruction."* *NTQ.* 1996 Aug.; 12(47): 203-206. Lang.: Eng.
UK-England: London. 1995. ■Introduces an unfinished piece *Luna Park Eclipses*, which was performed in the National Theatre Studio, and gives its text.

1684 Kane, Sarah. *"Blasted."* *ThM.* 1996; 27(1): 35-64. Illus.: Photo. B&W. 6. Lang.: Eng.
UK-England. 1994. ■Text of Sarah Kane's play *Blasted.*

1685 Case, Sue-Ellen, ed. *Split Britches: Lesbian Practice/Feminist Performance.* London/New York, NY: Routledge; 1996. 276 pp. Index. Biblio. Notes. Lang.: Eng.
USA. 1985-1995. ■Anthology of the work of Split Britches, a feminist/lesbian performance group. Includes five plays written with different degrees of collaboration by group members Deb Margolin, Peggy Shaw, and Lois Weaver: *Split Britches, Beauty and the Beast, Little Women: The Tragedy, Upwardly Mobile Home,* and *Lesbians Who Kill.* Also includes two plays written with collaborators: *Belle Reprieve* (a reworking of Williams's *A Streetcar Named Desire*) with the British group Bloolips, and *Lust and Comfort* with Gay Sweatshop.

1686 Cleage, Pearl. *"Blues for an Alabama Sky."* *AmTh.* 1996 July/Aug.; 13(6): 21-20, 62. Illus.: Photo. B&W. 6. Lang.: Eng.
USA. 1996. ■Complete playtext, includes interview with playwright conducted by Douglas Langworthy.

1687 Dixon, Michael Bigelow, ed.; Volansky, Michele, ed. *A Decade of New Comedy: Plays from the Humana Festival.* Portsmouth, NH: Heinemann; 1996. 313 pp., 268 pp. [2 vols.] Lang.: Eng.
USA. 1986-1995. ■Volume One includes *Astronauts* by Claudia Reilly (1986), *Some Things You Need to Know Before the World Ends (A Final Evening with the Illuminati)* by Larry Larson and Levi Lee (1986), *Road to Nirvana* by Arthur Kopit (1989), *Zara Spook and Other Lures* by Joan Ackermann (1990), and *In the Eye of the Hurricane* by Eduardo Machado (1991). Volume Two contains *The Death of Zukasky* by Richard Strand (1991), *Cementville* by Jane Martin (1991), *Watermelon Rinds* by Regina Taylor (1993), *Below the Belt* by Richard Dresser (1995), and *Trudy Blue* by Marsha Norman (1995).

1688 Dixon, Michael Bigelow, ed.; Volansky, Michele, ed. *By Southern Playwrights: Plays from Actors Theatre of Louisville.* Lexington, KY: UP of Kentucky; 1996. 240 pp. Lang.: Eng.
USA. 1984-1992. ■Includes *The Cool of the Day* by Wendell Berry (1984), *Five Ives Gets Named* (1983) and *That Dog Isn't Fifteen* by Roy Blount, Jr., *Blood Issue* by Harry Crews (1989), *Head On* by Elizabeth Dewberry (1995), *Digging In: The Farm Crisis in Kentucky* by Julie Crutcher and Vaughn McBride (1990), *Tent Meeting* by Larry Larson, Levi Lee and Rebecca Wackler (1986), *2* by Romulus Linney (1990), and *Loving Daniel Boone* by Marsha Norman (1992).

1689 Dove, Rita. *"From The Darker Face of the Earth."* *Callaloo.* 1994 Sum; 17(2): 374-380. Lang.: Eng.
USA. 1994. ■Text of the eleventh scene from Dove's verse play.

1690 Dove, Rita. *"The Darker Face of the Earth."* *AmTh.* 1996 Nov.; 13(9): 33-55. Illus.: Photo. B&W. 6. Lang.: Eng.
USA. 1996. ■Complete text of this play in verse including an interview with the playwright conducted by Misha Berson.

1691 Farabough, Laura; Schachenmayr, Volker. *"Real Original Thinker."* *TheatreF.* 1996 Win/Spr; 8: 75-88. Illus.: Photo. 9. Lang.: Eng.
USA. 1995-1996. ■Text of Laura Farabough and Volker Schachenmayr's *Real Original Thinker.*

DRAMA: —Basic theatrical documents

1692 Field, Thalia. "*Hey-Stop-That.*" *ThM.* 1996; 26(3): 11-24. Lang.: Eng.
USA. 1996. ■Complete text of Thalia Field's *Hey-Stop-That.*

1693 Gotanda, Philip Kan. "*Ballad of Yachiyo.*" *AmTh.* 1996 Feb.; 13(2): 25-42. Illus.: Photo. B&W. 6. Lang.: Eng.
USA. 1996. ■Complete playtext, including brief interview with playwright Gotanda conducted by Nina Siegal.

1694 Hamalian, Leo, ed.; Hatch, James V., ed. *Lost Plays of the Harlem Renaissance, 1920-1940.* Detroit, MI: Wayne State UP; 1996. 467 pp. (African American Life Series.) Append. Lang.: Eng.
USA: New York, NY. 1920-1940. ■Includes *On the Fields of France* by Joseph Seamon Cotter, Jr., *A Pillar of the Church* by Willis Richardson, *The Yellow Peril* by George S. Schuyler, *Son-boy* by Joseph S. Mitchell, *Mother Liked It* by Alvira Hazzard, *The Girl from Back Home* by Ralf M. Coleman, *Black Damp* by John Frederick Matheus, *You mus' be bo'n ag'in* by Andrew M. Burris, *Environment* by Mercedes Gilbert, *Run little chillun* by Francis Hall Johnson, *Darker Brother* by Conrad Seiler, *Scarlet Sister Barry, Young Black Joe* and *The em-Fuehrer Jones* by Langston Hughes, and *Track Thirteen* by Shirley Graham.

1695 Hwang, David Henry. "*Trying to Find Chinatown.*" *TheatreF.* 1996 Sum/Fall; 9: 83-87. Illus.: Photo. 2. Lang.: Eng.
USA. 1996. ■Text of David Henry Hwang's new play, commissioned by the Actors Theatre of Louisville as part of the Humana Festival.

1696 Iizuka, Naomi. "*Skin.*" *TheatreF.* 1996 Win/Spr; 8: 42-57. Illus.: Photo. 8. Lang.: Eng.
USA. 1995-1996. ■Text of the play, the major character of which is based on Georg Büchner.

1697 Kyle, Christopher. "*The Monogamist.*" *AmTh.* 1996 Mar.; 13(3): 23-39. Illus.: Photo. B&W. 5. Lang.: Eng.
USA. 1992-1996. ■Complete text of play, includes interview with playwright.

1698 McCord, Louisa Susannah Cheves; Lounsbury, Richard C., ed. *Louisa S. McCord: Poems, Drama, Biography, Letters.* Charlottesville, VA/London: UP of Virginia; 1996. 487 pp. Index. Biblio. Notes. Pref. Illus.: Photo. 1. Lang.: Eng.
USA: Charleston, SC. 1810-1879. Critical studies. ■The work of Louisa S. McCord, including her only drama, a five-act tragedy *Caius Gracchus*, written in 1851.

1699 Parks, Suzan-Lori. "*Venus.*" *TheatreF.* 1996 Sum/Fall; 9: 40-72. Lang.: Eng.
USA. 1996. ■Text of *Venus* by Suzan-Lori Parks.

1700 Reed, Ishmael. "*Savage Wilds.*" *Callaloo.* 1994 Fall; 17(4): 1158-1204. Lang.: Eng.
USA. 1988. ■Full playtext of Ishmael Reed's *Savage Wilds*, first performance at Julia Morgan Theatre in Berkeley, CA in 1988, directed by Ed Bullins.

1701 Rivera, José. "*Maricela de la Luz Lights the World.*" *AmTh.* 1996 Dec.; 13(10): 25-38. Illus.: Photo. Sketches. B&W. 7. Lang.: Eng.
USA. 1996. ■Complete playtext, includes interview with playwright by Stephanie Coen.

1702 Robbins, Kenneth; Elwell, Jeffery Scott. "*Atomic Field.*" *SoTh.* 1996 Fall; 37(4): 12-27. Illus.: Photo. B&W. 1. Lang.: Eng.
USA. 1996. ■Complete playtext of Kenneth Robbins' *Atomic Field*, preceded by an interview with the playwright by Jeffery Scott Elwell.

1703 Shepard, Sam. "*Buried Child.*" *AmTh.* 1996 Sep.; 13(7): 27-48. Illus.: Photo. B&W. 6. Lang.: Eng.
USA. 1978-1996. ■Complete playtext (rewritten from earlier version), including interview with playwright by Stephanie Coen.

1704 Skipitares, Theodora. "*Under the Knife.*" *PerAJ.* 1996 May; 18(2): 93-117. Illus.: Photo. B&W. 13. [Number 53.] Lang.: Eng.
USA: New York, NY. 1996. ■Complete text of *Under the Knife: A History of Medicine* with an introduction by the author.

Design/technology

1705 Rickerd, Julie Rekai. "Lights and the Man." *LDim.* 1996 Oct.; 20(8): 38-43. Illus.: Photo. Color. B&W. 13. Lang.: Eng.
Canada: Niagara-on-the-Lake, ON. 1996. Biographical studies. ■Lighting designer Kevin Lamotte's career with the Shaw Festival. Productions, training, awards.

1706 Rickerd, Julie Rekai. "A Motorized Merchant." *TCI.* 1996 Oct.; 30(8): 13-14. Illus.: Photo. Color. 1. Lang.: Eng.
Canada: Stratford, ON. 1996. Technical studies. ■Mechanized sets built for the Stratford Festival's production of *The Merchant of Venice* helped create the visual concept of director Marti Maraden and designer Phillip Silver.

1707 Wengrow, Arnold. "A Mandate for Design: Cameron Porteous and the Shaw Festival." *TD&T.* 1996 Spr; 32(2): 34-43. Illus.: Photo. 13. Lang.: Eng.
Canada: Niagara-on-the-Lake, ON. 1980-1995. Historical studies. ■The work of scenic designer Cameron Porteous in his fifteen years at the Shaw Festival. Concentrates on Porteous's work on Rostand's *Cyrano de Bergerac* directed by Derek Goldby, Shaw's *Saint Joan* directed by Neil Monroe, Coward's *Cavalcade* directed by Christopher Newton, and Shaw's *Pygmalion*, also directed by Newton.

1708 Kim, Soo-Jin. "Yeonkukwa Younghwa, Ku Kyouriggye Humulgi." (Breaking Down the Boundary Between Plays and Films.) *KTR.* 1996 Mar.; 21(3): 30-33. Illus.: Photo. B&W. 6. Lang.: Kor.
Korea: Seoul. 1996. Technical studies. ■Techniques of multi-media used in plays by three theatre companies: *Mulchong (The Water Gun)*, presented by Kinodrama, *Pyeokwagulinun Namja (The Man Painting on the Wall)* presented by Muitos, and *Kaspar* shown by Ulikukchong.

1709 Spalińska, Jagoda Henrik. "Stage Designer at Teatr Narodowy." *TP.* 1996 Oct.; 38(4): 17-23. Illus.: Sketches. Color. B&W. 3. Lang.: Eng, Fre.
Poland: Warsaw. 1949-1996. Histories-sources. ■Interview with scene and costume designer Łucja Kossakowska about her career at the Teatr Narodowy.

1710 Zielińska, Maryla. "French Memories: An Interview with Krystyna Zachwatowicz." *TP.* 1996 Apr.; 38(2): 19-22. Illus.: Dwg. B&W. 2. Lang.: Eng, Fre.
Poland. France. 1962-1996. Histories-sources. ■Interview with the Polish scene designer concerning her experiences designing for the stage in France.

1711 Edström, Per Simon; Forslund, Camille, transl. "Dramatikern och scenografen." (Dramatist and Scenographer.) *ProScen.* 1996; 20(Extra): 12-13. Illus.: Photo. Color. Lang.: Swe, Eng.
Sweden: Stockholm. 1907-1961. Critical studies. ■Comparison of Strindberg's vision for his play *Ett Drömspel (A Dream Play)* and that of today's playwrights, including Sven Olof Ehrén, who designed *Va nu då (What Now)* by Per Simon Edstrom, set in an ice stadium.

1712 Johnson, David. "VariLites in *Paradis.*" *LDim.* 1996 Apr.; 20(3): 24. Illus.: Photo. Color. 1. Lang.: Eng.
UK-England: London. 1996. Technical studies. ■Simon Corder's lighting design for Simon Callow's adaptation of *Les Enfants du Paradis* for the Royal Shakespeare Company.

1713 Karam, Edward. "A Patriot for Me." *TCI.* 1996 Feb.; 30(2): 9. Illus.: Photo. B&W. 1. Lang.: Eng.
UK-England: London. 1996. Technical studies. ■Description of designer Tom Piper's set for the RSC's production of John Osborne's *A Patriot for Me* at the Barbican, noting the lights by Andy Phillips and costumes by Pamela Howard.

1714 Lampert-Gréaux, Ellen. "An Ideal Fit." *TCI.* 1996 Aug/ Sep.; 30(7): 7. Illus.: Photo. Color. 1. Lang.: Eng.
UK-England: London. USA: New York, NY. 1993-1996. Technical studies. ■Variations in Carl Toms' costume designs for three versions of Peter Hall's production of *An Ideal Husband* by Oscar Wilde, two in London and one on Broaadway.

1715 Loney, Glenn. "Edinburgh Adventures." *TCI.* 1996 Jan.; 30(1): 18. Illus.: Photo. Color. 1. Lang.: Eng.

DRAMA: —Design/technology

UK-Scotland: Edinburgh. 1995. Technical studies. ■Report on the technical side of the 1995 Edinburgh Festival, with focus on production of Frank McGuinness's *Observe the Sons of Ulster Marching Towards the Somme* mounted by the Abbey Theatre, directed by Patrick Mason.

1716 Barbour, David. "Country Matters." *TCI.* 1996 Oct.; 30(8): 7. Illus.: Photo. Color. 1. Lang.: Eng.
USA: New York, NY. 1996. Technical studies. ■Designer Edward Gianfrancesco's country flavored set for Tom Ziegler's *Grace & Glorie*, Criterion Center's Laura Pels Theatre.

1717 Barbour, David. "Picasso at the Lapin Agile." *TCI.* 1996 Apr.; 30(4): 62. Illus.: Photo. Dwg. Color. 3. Lang.: Eng.
USA: New York, NY. 1996. Technical studies. ■Scott Bradley's set design for Steve Martin's *Picasso at the Lapin Agile* at Steppenwolf, Westwood Playhouse, and the Promenade Theatre.

1718 Barbour, David. "In Living Color." *TCI.* 1996 May; 30(5): 7-8. Illus.: Photo. Color. 2. Lang.: Eng.
USA: New York, NY. 1996. Technical studies. ■Lighting designer Peggy Eisenhauer's bold use of color for the Public Theatre's production of Nilo Cruz's fantasy play *Dancing on Her Knees*, directed by Graciela Daniel.

1719 Barbour, David. "Big Business." *TCI.* 1996 May; 30(5): 11-12. Illus.: Photo. Color. 1. Lang.: Eng.
USA: New York, NY. 1996. Technical studies. ■Stephen Olson's design concept for the set of Richard Dresser's *Below the Belt* at the John Houseman Theatre.

1720 Barbour, David. "Winter Wear." *TCI.* 1996 May; 30(5): 12-13. Illus.: Photo. Color. 1. Lang.: Eng.
USA: Ashland, OR. 1996. Technical studies. ■Costumer Marie Anne Chiment's designs for the Oregon Shakespeare Festival's *The Winter's Tale* directed by Fontaine Syer.

1721 Barbour, David. "Party Time." *LDim.* 1996 Apr.; 20(3): 10. Illus.: Photo. Color. 2. Lang.: Eng.
USA: New York, NY. 1996. Technical studies. ■Brian MacDevitt's lighting design for Manhattan Theatre Club's production of Craig Lucas' *Blue Window*.

1722 Barbour, David. "The Night Shift." *LDim.* 1996 Oct.; 20(8): 13. Illus.: Photo. Color. 2. Lang.: Eng.
USA: New York, NY, New Haven, CT. 1996. Technical studies. ■Lighting designer Don Holder and his work for the Circle in the Square production of Eugene O'Neill's *Hughie* starring and directed by Al Pacino. Challenges faced by moving the production from Long Wharf Theatre to Broadway.

1723 Barbour, David. "Private Lives." *TCI.* 1996 Jan.; 30(1): 10-11. Lang.: Eng.
USA: New York, NY. 1996. Technical studies. ■Costumer Elizabeth Fried's troubles in designing for a play set in the 1970s, Wendy Belden's *Crocodiles in the Potomac*.

1724 Barbour, David. "Family Affairs." *TCI.* 1996 Aug/Sep.; 30(7): 6. Illus.: Photo. Color. 1. Lang.: Eng.
USA: New York, NY. 1996. Technical studies. ■Scene designer Robert Brill's Broadway debut with Sam Shepard's *Buried Child* and his first collaboration with his wife, director Loretta Greco, on the New York Theatre Workshop production of Nilo Cruz's *A Park in Our Own House*.

1725 Barbour, David. "Hello, Dolly." *TCI.* 1996 Dec.; 30(10): 6. Illus.: Photo. Color. 2. Lang.: Eng.
USA: New York, NY. 1996. Technical studies. ■Appraisal of John Arnone's set design for Christopher Durang's *Sex and Longing*, directed by Garland Wright for Lincoln Center Theatre Company.

1726 Barbour, David. "Hoofing It." *TCI.* 1996 Dec.; 30(10): 7-8. Illus.: Photo. Color. 1. Lang.: Eng.
USA: New York, NY. 1996. Technical studies. ■Guy Sherman's sound design for the Valiant Theatre Company's production of Eugène Ionesco's *Rhinocéros*.

1727 Barbour, David. "Clothes Horse." *TCI.* 1996 Nov.; 30(9): 9-10. Illus.: Photo. Color. 1. Lang.: Eng.
USA: New York, NY. 1996. Technical studies. ■Designer Michael Krass' costumes for Mary Louise Wilson and Mark Hampton's play *Full Gallop.*

1728 Barbour, David. "Chekhov, Tennessee." *TCI.* 1996 Nov.; 30(9): 11. Illus.: Photo. Color. 1. Lang.: Eng.
USA: Cincinnati, OH. 1996. Technical studies. ■Critique of Candice Donnelly's costumes for Tennessee Williams' *The Notebook of Trigorin*, an adaptation of Čechov's *The Seagull (Čajka)*, at the Cincinnati Playhouse.

1729 Barbour, David. "Words Are Weapons." *TCI.* 1996 Apr.; 30(4): 10. Illus.: Photo. Color. 1. Lang.: Eng.
USA: Princeton, NJ. 1996. Technical studies. ■Robert Brill's set design, using projections by John Boesche, for Emily Mann's *Greensboro*, directed by Mark Wing-Davey at the McCarter Theatre.

1730 Barbour, David. "Peter Dervis." *TCI.* 1996 Apr.; 30(4): 24. Illus.: Photo. B&W. 1. Lang.: Eng.
USA: New York, NY. 1996. Technical studies. ■Spotlight on Peter Dervis, who has built a business out of providing both visual research and historical background to set and costume designers in theatre and film.

1731 Chase, Anthony. "Seven Guitars." *TCI.* 1996 May; 30(5): 6-7. Illus.: Sketches. Color. 1. Lang.: Eng.
USA: Pittsburgh, PA, New York, NY. 1996. Technical studies. ■Scott Bradley's set design for *Seven Guitars* by August Wilson, directed by Lloyd Richards: a co-production of American Conservatory Theatre, Huntington Theatre, and the Mark Taper Forum.

1732 Cleveland, Elbin. "Self-Taught Designer Finds Fulfillment in Theatre." *SoTh.* 1996 Sum; 37(3): 16-19. Illus.: Photo. B&W. 4. Lang.: Eng.
USA. 1957-1996. Historical studies. ■A profile of the career of scenic designer Paul Owen, currently lead designer at the Actors' Theatre of Louisville.

1733 Hogan, Jane. "Trojan Women Versus the Elements." *LDim.* 1996 Sep.; 20(7): 32. Illus.: Photo. Color. 2. Lang.: Eng.
USA: New York, NY. 1996. Technical studies. ■Challenges faced by lighting designer Blake Burba for En Garde Arts' outdoor production of *The Trojan Women: A Love Story* by Charles Mee, Jr., directed by Tina Landau, presented at an abandoned amphitheatre.

1734 Johnson, David. "A Public Service." *TCI.* 1996 Aug/Sep.; 30(7): 6-7. Illus.: Photo. Color. 1. Lang.: Eng.
USA: New York, NY. 1996. Technical studies. ■Sound designer John Gromada's incorporation and augmentation of the sounds of the Lexington Avenue subway into Caryl Churchill's *The Skriker* directed by Mark Wing-Davey at the Public Theatre.

1735 Karam, Edward. "Bleeding Hearts." *TCI.* 1996 May; 30(5): 16. Illus.: Photo. Color. 1. Lang.: Eng.
USA: Cambridge, MA. 1996. Technical studies. ■Use of color in the set and lights for the American Repertory Theatre's production of *Tartuffe*, and the collaboration of respective designers Robert Israel and Mimi Jordan Sherin and director François Rochaix.

1736 Kempf, Jim. "Rotating Doors." *TechB.* 1996 Jan.: 1-3. Illus.: Design. B&W. Detail. 3. [TB 1280.] Lang.: Eng.
USA. 1996. Technical studies. ■Description of rotating doors used in a traveling production of Shakespeare's *The Taming of the Shrew*.

1737 Lampert-Gréaux, Ellen. "Gallo's Magic." *LDim.* 1996 Jan/Feb.; 20(1): 34-36. Illus.: Photo. Color. 5. Lang.: Eng.
USA: New York, NY. 1996. Technical studies. ■Paul Gallo's lighting design for Shakespeare's *The Tempest* directed by George C. Wolfe, and challenges in transferring production from outdoor Delacorte Theatre to Broadway.

1738 Lampert-Gréaux, Ellen. "Jane Greenwood Goes Modern." *TCI.* 1996 Aug/Sep.; 30(7): 36-39. Illus.: Photo. Color. 12. Lang.: Eng.
USA: New York, NY. 1996. Technical studies. ■Jane Greenwood's mastery of contemporary costuming in such shows as McNally's *Master Class*, Albee's *A Delicate Balance*, Jon Robin Baitz' *A Fair Country* and Andrea Martin's *Nude Nude Totally Nude.*

1739 Langworthy, Douglas. "Riccardo Hernández." *AmTh.* 1996 Mar.; 13(3): 40-41. Illus.: Photo. B&W. 4. Lang.: Eng.
USA. 1996. Biographical studies. ■Profile of scene designer Hernández: style, directors he has collaborated with, techniques and influences.

1740 Napoleon, Davi. "Taking Liberties." *TCI.* 1996 May; 30(5): 9. Illus.: Photo. Color. 1. Lang.: Eng.

CLASSED ENTRIES

DRAMA: —Design/technology

USA: Chicago, IL. 1996. Technical studies. ■Technical aspects of Terry Johnson's Steppenwolf production of Stephen Jeffrey's *The Libertine.*

1741 Napoleon, Davi. "Schoolbiz." *TheaterW.* 1996 Feb 19; 9(29): 40-44. Lang.: Eng.

USA. 1996. Historical studies. ■Training programs for lighting designers in universities. Teaching methods, equipment, combining training with practical experience.

1742 Perkins, Kathy A. "Felix E. Cochren: Designing for the American Theatre." *BlackM.* 1996 Aug/Sep.; 12(1): 7-8,16. Illus.: Photo. Design. B&W. 2. Lang.: Eng.

USA: New York, NY. 1980-1996. Biographical studies. ■Career of costume and set designer Felix E. Cochren.

1743 Ruling, Karl G. "Sound with Feeling." *TCI.* 1996 Apr.; 30(4): 19. Lang.: Eng.

USA: Rochester, NY. 1996. Technical studies. ■Challenges faced by sound designer Jessica Murrow to develop a sound design for William Inge's *Picnic* at the National Technical Insitute of the Deaf, that would work for both hearing and hearing impaired audience.

1744 Ruling, Karl G. "VR Scenery Onstage." *TCI.* 1996 Apr.; 30(4): 49. Illus.: Photo. Color. 2. Lang.: Eng.

USA: Lawrence, KS. 1996. Technical studies. ■The use of computer generated, stereoscopically projected sets in a University of Kansas production of Elmer Rice's *The Adding Machine* by designer Mark Reaney with director Ronald Willis.

1745 Ruling, Karl G. "Lighting Denial." *TCI.* 1996 Mar.; 30(3): 9-10. Illus.: Photo. Color. 1. Lang.: Eng.

USA: New Haven, CT. 1996. Technical studies. ■Richard Nelson's lighting design for the Long Wharf Theatre's production of Peter Sagal's *Denial.*

1746 Ruling, Karl G. "Holiday in the Round." *TCI.* 1996 Feb.; 30(2): 7. Illus.: Lighting. B&W. 1. Lang.: Eng.

USA: New York, NY. 1996. Technical studies. ■Problems presented by doing Philip Barry's *Holiday* in the round at Circle in the Square, and how set designer Derek McLane and lighting designer Don Holder worked together to solve them.

1747 Schreiber, Loren. "Micro Programmable Logic Controllers: Low Cost Automation for the Stage: Or Learning to Love Ladder Logic." *TD&T.* 1996 Spr; 32(2): 18-24. Illus.: Diagram. Photo. 10. Lang.: Eng.

USA: San Diego, CA. 1990. Historical studies. ■Programmable logic controllers in the Lowell Davies Festival Stage/Simon Edison Center for the Performing Arts's production of Shakespeare's *As You Like It,* directed by David Jenkins.

Institutions

1748 Jones, Liz. "Filling the Silences: La Mama." *AWBR.* 1994 June; 6(2): 23-24. Illus.: Photo. B&W. 2. Lang.: Eng.

Australia: Melbourne. 1967-1994. Historical studies. ■Alternative performance, especially plays by women, at La Mama, named for La MaMa Experimental Theatre Company of New York. Includes discussion of Val Kirwan's *Mamalamur.*

1749 Stojanovski, Stefo. "The Australian-Macedonian Drama Group." 27-35 in Bivell, Victor, ed. *Macedonian Agenda.* Five Dock, NSW: Pollitecon Publications; 1995. 228 pp. Illus.: Photo. B&W. 2. Lang.: Eng.

Australia: Melbourne. 1983-1994. Historical studies. ■Discusses history, aims and present writings of the Australian-Macedonian Drama Group, and its impact on Australian society.

1750 Tait, Peta. *Original Women's Theatre: The Melbourne Women's Theatre Group, 1974-1977.* Parkdale: Artmoves; 1994. 94 pp. Notes. Biblio. Append. Lang.: Eng.

Australia: Melbourne. 1974-1977. Historical studies. ■History of the Melbourne Women's Theatre Group, and Australia's changing social landscape during the period 1974-1977.

1751 Fritsch, Sibylle. "Bilderträume im tiefen Keller." (Pictures of Dreams in the Sub-Basement.) *DB.* 1996; 3: 43-45. Illus.: Photo. B&W. 3. Lang.: Ger.

Austria: Vienna. 1980-1996. Historical studies. ■Portrait of Gruppe 80, directed by Helga Illich and Helmut Wiesner in a former cinema: its aesthetic and programmatic concept.

1752 Kralicek, Wolfgang. "Servus, Austria oder Der Tod ist nicht wirklich das Ende." (Goodbye, Austria, or Death Is Not Really the End.) *THeute.* 1996; 7: 12-21. Illus.: Photo. B&W. 17. Lang.: Ger.

Austria: Vienna. 1996. Reviews of performances. ■Impressions of the Wiener Festwochen, with descriptions of the highlights of the festival: *Das Mädchen aus der Feenwelt oder Der Bauer als Millionär (The Girl from Fairyland or The Farmer as Millionaire)* by Ferdinand Raimund directed by Ursel and Karl-Ernst Herrmann at Burgtheater. *Der gläserne Pantoffel (The Glass Slipper)* by Ferenc Molnár, directed by Jürgen Flimm, a coproduction with Thalia Theater. *Der Clarissa-Komplex (The Clarissa Complex)* by Hans Neuenfels after *Der Mann ohne Eigenschaften (The Man Without Qualities)* by Robert Musil, a coproduction with Bayerisches Staatsschauspiel, Residenztheater. *Alma* by Yehoshua Sobol, directed by Paulus Manker at Sanatorium Purkersdorf. *Hochschwab* by Martin Schwab, directed by Hans Gratzer.

1753 Löffler, Sigrid. "Deja-Vus im House Frankenstein." (Déjà Vu in the House of Frankenstein.) *THeute.* 1996; 11 : 38-39. Illus.: Photo. B&W. 1. Lang.: Ger.

Austria: Graz. 1996. Historical studies. ■The avant-garde character of the Steirischer Herbst Festival, with attention to Wolfgang Bauer's *Menschenfabrik (People Factory)*, directed by Thomas Thieme at Vereinigte Bühnen Graz.

1754 Injachin, A. "Ufimskij variant." (Ufa Variation.) *TeatZ.* 1996; 5: 17-19. Lang.: Rus.

Bashkiria: Ufa. 1990-1996. Historical studies. ■Profile of Respublikanskij Russkij Dramatičeskij Teatr, Michajl Rabinovič, senior director.

1755 Frederick, Rawle. "Stage One Bolsters Bermuda's Black Theatre." *BlackM.* 1996 May/June; 11(6): 9. Illus.: Photo. B&W. 1. Lang.: Eng.

Bermuda: Hamilton. 1996. Historical studies. ■A look at Stage One Productions as it prepares to stage Audley Haffenden's *A Buffalo Jumps the Moon* to be directed by Kensley McDowall.

1756 Ackerman, Marianne; Vaïs, Michel, transl. "Festival de Stratford: la fin d'un règne, le début d'un autre." (Stratford Festival: The End of One Reign, the Beginning of Another.) *JCT.* 1992; 65: 127-132. Illus.: Photo. B&W. 3. Lang.: Fre.

Canada: Stratford, ON. 1992. Critical studies. ■Problems with the Stratford Festival as it changes artistic directors from David William to Richard Monette, and reviews of its 1992 season.

1757 Brunner, Astrid. "Perfect Proportions." *ArtsAtl.* 1996; 14(4): 36-41. Illus.: Photo. B&W. 7. Lang.: Eng.

Canada: Wolfville, NS. 1991-1996. Critical studies. ■Profile of the new Atlantic Theatre Festival, directed by Michael Bawtree and Michael Langham: its new space, artistic vision, public support, sponsors and actors.

1758 Brunner, Astrid. "Astrid Brunner Interviews Walter Learning." *ArtsAtl.* 1996; 14(3): 44-47. Illus.: Photo. B&W. 6. Lang.: Eng.

Canada: Fredericton, NB. 1961-1996. Histories-sources. ■History of Theatre New Brunswick, and an examination of the role of that playwright and administrator Walter Learning played in its development.

1759 Campbell, Mark. "Creativity." *PAC.* 1996; 30(1): 26. Illus.: Photo. B&W. 1. Lang.: Eng.

Canada: Halifax, NS. 1995-1996. Historical studies. ■The Women's Theatre and Creativity Centre offers workshops in expression and creativity, and hopes to form a loose-knit ensemble of women to create occasional pieces.

1760 Coen, Stephanie. "Divisions in the Flesh." *AmTh.* 1996 Nov.; 13(9): 22-23. Illus.: Photo. B&W. 2. [Headed by Title: 5 Corners of our theatrical world.] Lang.: Eng.

Canada: Quebec, PQ. 1979-1996. Critical studies. ■Principal productions at the Carrefour festival including Ariane Mnouchkine's adaptation of Klaus Mann's *Méphisto* presented by Théâtre du Trident directed by Serge Denoncourt, Peter Brook's staging of Beckett's *Happy Days* for Théâtre Vidy-Lausanne and Robert Lepage's *Les Sept Branches de la Rivière Ota (The Seven Streams of the River Ota)* developed collectively by Ex Machina.

1761 Cottreau, Deborah. "Writing for a Playwright's Theatre." *CTR.* 1996 Sum; 87: 5-8. Lang.: Eng.

DRAMA: —Institutions

Canada: Toronto, ON. 1996. Histories-sources. ■Interview with Urjo Kareda discussing her dramaturgy at Tarragon Theatre.

1762 David, Gilbert; Lavoie, Pierre. "Vingt-cinq ans au service des auteurs: Le Centre des auteurs dramatiques: Entretien avec Hélène Dumas et Lorraine Hébert." (Twenty-five Years in the Service of Playwrights: The Centre des Auteurs Dramatiques: Interview with Hélène Dumas and Lorraine Hébert.) *JCT*. 1991; 58: 77. Notes. Illus.: Photo. B&W. 9. Lang.: Fre.
Canada: Montreal, PQ. 1965-1991. Histories-sources. ■Reviews history of Centre des Auteurs Dramatiques and its current methods of helping new and established playwrights develop new texts. Also offers perspectives on status of contemporary Québécois playwriting.

1763 Day, Moira. "Shakespeare on the Saskatchewan 1985-1990: 'The Stratford of the West' (NOT)." *ET*. 1996; 15(1): 69-90. Notes. Biblio. Illus.: Photo. B&W. 1. Lang.: Eng.
Canada: Saskatoon, SK. 1953-1996. Historical studies. ■Outlines the history of the Shakespearean summer festival in Saskatoon, how it was related to the festival in Ontario and the effect of the 1989 tour.

1764 Garebian, Keith. "Revisionism: The 1995 Shaw Festival." *JCNREC*. 1995; 30(4): 162-171. Illus.: Photo. B&W. 2. Lang.: Eng.
Canada: Niagara-on-the-Lake, ON. 1996. Critical studies. ■Examination of productions of the 1995 Shaw Festival season, with attention to the theatre's mandate to produce the plays of Shaw and his contemporaries in the light of modern experience.

1765 Garebian, Keith. "Revisionism (Part II): The 1995 Stratford Festival." *JCNREC*. 1996; 31(2): 166. Illus.: Photo. B&W. 2. Lang.: Eng.
Canada: Stratford, ON. 1995. Critical studies. ■Love in its many forms was the theme of the Stratford Festival's 1995 season under new artistic director Richard Monette.

1766 Gerson, Christiane; Camerlain, Lorraine. "Coups de théâtre 1992." *JCT*. 1992; 65: 147-154. Notes. Illus.: Photo. B&W. 5. Lang.: Fre.
Canada: Montreal, PQ. 1992. Historical studies. ■The Coups de théâtre 1992 series of the Rendez-vous international de théâtre jeune public gave artists and audiences the opportunity to experience creations and theatrical experiments featuring a transgression of theatrical codes and a borrowing from other disciplines.

1767 Gilbert, Sky. "Dramaturgy for Radical Theatre." *CTR*. 1996 Sum; 87: 25-27l cd. Lang.: Eng.
Canada: Toronto, ON. 1996. Critical studies. ■Examination of the dramaturgical approach at the Buddies in Bad Time theatre. Emphasis on responsive dramaturgy.

1768 Griffin, Leanne. "Saskatoon Fringe." *NWR*. 1996 Jan.; 21(2): 31-32. Illus.: Dwg. B&W. 2. Lang.: Eng.
Canada: Saskatoon, SK. 1995. Critical studies. ■Overview of the Saskatoon Fringe Festival with references to *Sunflowers* by Madeleine Dahlem, *Deirdre's Cause* by Pamela Rhae Ferguson and *Bed Language* by Susan Williamson.

1769 Love, Myron. "From Freelance to Full-Time: Prairie Theatre Exchange Has a New Artistic Director." *PAC*. 1996; 30(1): 20-22. Illus.: Photo. B&W. 1. Lang.: Eng.
Canada: Winnepeg, MB. 1970-1995. Historical studies. ■Profile of Prairie Theatre Exchange and the career of its new artistic director, Allen MacInnes.

1770 MacFarlane, Teri. "Diversity within Shavian Parameters." *PAC*. 1996; 30(2): 10-12. Illus.: Photo. B&W. 2. Lang.: Eng.
Canada: Niagara-on-the-Lake, ON. 1996. Critical studies. ■The Shaw Festival is programmed to reflect diverse tastes through its three theatres. Artistic director Christopher Newton has demonstrated integrity in partnering with sponsors.

1771 Munday, Jenny. "Brave New Words at Theatre New Brunswick." *CTR*. 1996 Sum; 87: 9-10. Lang.: Eng.
Canada: Fredericton, NB. 1996. Critical studies. ■Examination of Theatre New Brunswick's approach to developing new and regional plays.

1772 Potvin, Jacinthe. "Difficile de parler de soi: Témoignage." (Hard to Talk about Oneself: A Testimony.) *JCT*. 1993; 66: 53-57. Illus.: Photo. B&W. 2. Lang.: Fre.
Canada. 1969-1993. Histories-sources. ■Potvin recalls her work as actor and artistic director with the children's theatre company/commune Théâtre de Carton.

1773 Rewa, Natalie; Sidnell, Michael J. "FTA." *CTR*. 1996 Spr; 86: 51-54.
Canada: Montreal, PQ. 1996. Critical studies. ■Brief profile of the 1996 Festival de Théâtre des Amériques with references to *La Classe morte (The Dead Class)* by Cricot 2 and Anne-Marie Cadieux's *La Nuit (Night)* produced by La Vieille 17.

1774 Rickerd, Julie Rekai. "The Atlantic Theatre Festival." *TCI*. 1996 Oct.; 30(8): 14-15. Illus.: Photo. Color. 1. Lang.: Eng.
Canada: Wolfville, NS. 1993-1996. Historical studies. ■Profile of Atlantic Theatre Festival, founded by Christopher Plummer, Michael Langham and Michael Bawtree.

1775 Ritchie, Sherri. "Edmonton Fringe." *NWR*. 1996 Jan.; 21(2): 34-35. Illus.: Photo. B&W. 3. Lang.: Eng.
Canada: Edmonton, AB. 1995. Critical studies. ■Overview of the Edmonton Fringe Festival with references to the Noises in the Attic production of *Elephant Wake*, directed and written by Jonathon Christenson, *Pandora's Squeezebox* by Debbie Patterson and *Why Can't They Make a Pair of Pantyhose with the Crotch that Stays Where Yours Is?* by Zandra Bell.

1776 Smith, Peter; Johnson, Lise Ann. "240 Cups of Play Development." *CTR*. 1996 Sum; 87: 11-13. Illus.: Photo. B&W. 2. Lang.: Eng.
Canada: Montreal, PQ. 1996. Historical studies. ■Playwrights' Workshop methods, with emphasis on the extended workshop format and the importance of providing additional time and resources to playwrights.

1777 Springate, Michael. "A Deeper Questioning of Assumptions." *CTR*. 1996 Sum; 87: 34-35. Lang.: Eng.
Canada: Toronto, ON. 1996. Histories-sources. ■Factory Theatre artistic director and dramaturg Springate shares his thoughts on the function of dramaturgy in Canadian theatre and at the Factory Theatre.

1778 Vaïs, Michel. "Espace Libre hors les murs." (Espace Libre Beyond Its Walls.) *JCT*. 1989; 52: 164-167. Illus.: Photo. B&W. 3. Lang.: Fre.
Canada: Montreal, PQ. 1989. Critical studies. ■Aesthetic differences between productions of Carbone 14 and Nouveau Théâtre Expérimental explain why former tours while latter remains local.

1779 Wehle, Philippa. "Robert Lepage's *Seven Streams of the River Ota*: Process and Progress." *TheatreF*. 1996 Win/Spr; 8: 29-36. Biblio. Illus.: Photo. 6. Lang.: Eng.
Canada: Quebec, PQ. 1995. Historical studies. ■Public rehearsals of Lepage's latest epic theatre piece *Les Sept Branches de la Rivière Ota (The Seven Streams of the River Ota)*, performed by Lepage's company Ex Machina. First conceived in 1993 and performed at the Edinburgh Festival in 1994, it was changed and reexamined before appearing at the Vienna Festival in May 1995.

1780 White, Bob. "playRites: The ATP Experience." *CTR*. 1996 Sum; 87: 14-16. Illus.: Photo. B&W. 4. Lang.: Eng.
Canada: Edmonton, AB. 1996. Historical studies. ■Profile of the 1996 Alberta Theatre Projects festival playRites. Emphasis on Eugene Stickland's *Sitting on Paradise*.

1781 Wickham, Philip. "Pour opsiser le monde." (To Opsize the World.) *JCT*. 1993; 67: 141-147. Illus.: Photo. B&W. 4. Lang.: Fre.
Canada: Montreal, PQ. 1983-1993. Critical studies. ■Serge Denoncourt's approach to directing with Théâtre de l'Opsis, focusing on clear contemporary interpretations of classic plays.

1782 Fai, Cheung. "The New Stage of Chinese Theatre." *TheatreF*. 1996 Win/Spr; 8: 4-6. Illus.: Photo. 2. Lang.: Eng.
China, People's Republic of: Beijing. 1995-1996. Historical studies. ■Independent theatre in China, focusing on the work of Xi Ju Che Jian (Garage Theatre). The group creates new artistic works for contemporary Chinese theatre, such as *File 0 (Ling Dang An)* and *Things Related to AIDS*, directed by artistic director Mou Sen.

DRAMA: —Institutions

1783 Frank, Adam. "The Double Life of Shanghai Theatre." *AmTh.* 1996 Jan.; 13(1): 68-70. Illus.: Photo. B&W. 3. Lang.: Eng.
China, People's Republic of: Shanghai. 1930-1996. Historical studies. ■Brief history of theatre in Shanghai, the Shanghai Dramatic Arts Center directed by Yu Luo Sheng and their choices of productions, financial pressures, impact of censorship on theatre.

1784 Borup, Niels. "Hold Fast!" *TE.* 1996 Feb.; 77: 24-25. Illus.: Photo. B&W. 1. Lang.: Dan.
Denmark: Odense. 1995. Historical studies. ■Report from a festival for professional group theatres, with discussion of plays performed by thirteen different groups, including Bådteatret's *Fluen (The Fly)* and La Balance's *Galefyrsten (The Crazy Prince)*.

1785 Loney, Glenn. "Birgitte Price, Drama Chief of the Danish Royal Theatre." *WES.* 1995-96 Win; 7(3): 99-106. Illus.: Photo. 4. Lang.: Eng.
Denmark: Copenhagen. 1995. Histories-sources. ■Interview with Birgitte Price, artistic director of the Danish Royal Theatre's Drama Division. Price discusses her plans for the 1996 celebration of Danish culture, the role of her gender in her career, and the training of young actors.

1786 Bermel, Albert. "No More Playing Safe." *AmTh.* 1996 Oct.; 13(8): 22-24. Illus.: Photo. Sketches. B&W. 3. Lang.: Eng.
France: Paris. 1673-1996. Historical studies. ■Theatre company Comédie-Française: history of company, current innovations in productions and interpretations, organizational structure.

1787 Caillère, Anne. "Retour aux sources: Le Théâtre National de Strasbourg comme laboratoire dramatique entre 1975 et 1983." (Return to Sources: The Théâtre National de Strasbourg as Drama Laboratory from 1975 to 1983.) *JCT.* 1991; 58: 55-63. Notes. Illus.: Photo. B&W. 3. Lang.: Fre.
France: Strasbourg. 1975-1983. Historical studies. ■Explorations in individual and collective playwriting at the Théâtre National de Strasbourg under Jean-Pierre Vincent.

1788 Fréchette, Carole. "Dix jours en Avignon: Voir ou ne pas voir." (Ten Days in Avignon: To See or Not to See.) *JCT.* 1989; 51: 55-60. Notes. Illus.: Photo. B&W. 3. Lang.: Fre.
France: Avignon. 1988. Historical studies. ■Over-abundance of shows at 1988 Festival d'Avignon and remarks on select productions.

1789 Jacobs, Catrin. "'Teatern skall deltaga i verkligheten." (The Theatre Must Take Part in Reality.) *Dramat.* 1996; 4(3): 24-26. Illus.: Photo. Color. Lang.: Swe.
France: Paris. 1957-1995. Historical studies. ■A presentation of Ariane Mnouchkine and Théâtre du Soleil, with reference to their production of *Tartuffe*.

1790 Sadowska-Guillon, Irène. "Europe théâtrale: 1er festival de la Convention théâtrale européenne." (First Festival of the European Theatrical Convention.) *JCT.* 1990; 55: 35-39. Illus.: Photo. B&W. 4. Lang.: Fre.
France. 1989. Historical studies. ■Festival presented French plays interpreted by foreign companies, classic texts, and important new works.

1791 Sadowska-Guillon, Irène. "Le Nouveau visage du théâtre de l'Europe à Paris." (The New Face of Théâtre de l'Europe in Paris.) *JCT.* 1990; 57: 81-86. Notes. Illus.: Photo. B&W. 2. Lang.: Fre.
France: Paris. 1990. Historical studies. ■New directions for Théâtre de l'Europe as Lluís Pasqual takes over from Giorgio Strehler as artistic director.

1792 Wigardt, Gaby. "En lektion i uthållighet." (A Lesson in Stamina.) *Dramat.* 1996; 4(3): 40-41. Illus.: Photo. Color. Lang.: Swe.
France: Paris. 1950-1996. Historical studies. ■A presentation of Théâtre de la Huchette, and its long-running Ionesco plays *La Cantatrice chauve* staged by Nicolas Bataille and *La Leçon* staged by Marcel Cuvelier, including an interview with the leader Jacques Legré.

1793 Garon, L. "Sad." (A Garden.) *TeatZ.* 1996; 5: 46-49. Lang.: Rus.
Georgia: Tbilisi. 1995-1996. Historical studies. ■Profile of the A.S. Gribojédov Russian Drama Theatre, artistic director, Georgij Kavtaradze.

1794 Becker, Peter von. "Es muss auch mal den Kopf kosten können!" (Sometimes Even Somebody's Neck Can Be on the Line.) *THeute.* 1996; 9: 20-22. Illus.: Photo. B&W. 4. Lang.: Ger.
Germany: Düsseldorf. 1996. Histories-sources. ■Interview with Anna Badora, new director of Düsseldorfer Schauspielhaus, about plans and problems, fun and seriousness.

1795 Becker, Peter von. "Hell und Dunkel." (Bright and Dark.) *THeute.* 1996; 1: 30-31. Illus.: Photo. B&W. 4. Lang.: Ger.
Germany: Heidelberg. 1996. Historical studies. ■The departure of Peter Stoltzenberg and the arrival of Volkmar Clauss as managing director of Stadttheater Heidelberg. Plays produced include *Lulu* by Frank Wedekind, directed by Ralph Bridle, *Le retour au désert (Return to the Desert)* by Bernard-Marie Koltès, directed by Stephan Kimmig.

1796 Brendt, Ellen. "Ein Kind der Sonne." (A Child of the Sun.) *DB.* 1996; 3: 22-25. Illus.: Photo. B&W. 4. Lang.: Ger.
Germany: Berlin. 1996. Historical studies. ■Profile of Maxim Gorki Theater, Bernd Wilms, artistic director.

1797 Kift, Roy. "Fifty Years 'Ruhrfestspiele'—A European Festival in Germany." *WES.* 1996 Fall; 8(3): 37-42. Illus.: Photo. 4. Lang.: Eng.
Germany: Recklinghausen. 1996. Historical studies. ■The current state of contemporary European theatre as reflected in the festival. Productions include *Romeo and Juliet* by the Roma Theater Pralipe, directed by Rahim Burban, *Uncle Vanya (Diadia Vania)* by the Thalia Theater, directed by Jürgen Flimm, and Thomas Christoph Harlan's *Ich selbst und kein Engel*, directed by Brian Michaels, and performed by acting students at the Folkwang school in Essen.

1798 Manthei, Fred. "'Die ganze Welt ist eine Bühne'." (All the World's a Stage.) *TZ.* 1996; 6: 48-51. Illus.: Photo. B&W. 4. Lang.: Ger.
Germany: Bremen. 1996. Histories-sources. ■Interview with Norbert Kentrup, manager, actor, and director of the Bremer Shakespeare Company about its history, funding, and methods.

1799 Merschmeier, Michael; Wille, Franz. "Das Ende der Kinderstücke?" (The End of Children's Plays?) *THeute.* 1996; 1: 37-40. Illus.: Photo. B&W. 4. Lang.: Ger.
Germany: Berlin. 1996. Histories-sources. ■Interview with author and director Volker Ludwig about financial and conceptual problems of GRIPS Theater for children.

1800 Penter, Ulrich. "Herzkunst oder Kunstherz?" (Art from the Heart or Artificial Heart?) *TZ.* 1996; 1: 6-9. Illus.: Photo. B&W. 5. Lang.: Ger.
Germany: Bochum. 1995-1996. Historical studies. ■The success of Leander Haussmann, the new director at the Schauspielhaus Bochum, said to be less a result of his stage performances than of his methods of producing them.

1801 Pfister, Eva. "Die Ära Canaris." (The Age of Canaris.) *DB.* 1996; 7: 28-31. Illus.: Photo. B&W. 5. Lang.: Ger.
Germany: Düsseldorf. 1986-1996. Histories-sources. ■Interview with Volker Canaris, managing director of Düsseldorfer Schauspielhaus, about his administration, programming, relationship to critics and audience.

1802 Pfister, Eva; Ruf, Wolfgang. "Wo sind die Autoren?" (Where Are the Playwrights?) *DB.* 1996; 8: 22-26. Append. Illus.: Photo. B&W. 5. Lang.: Ger.
Germany: Bonn. 1996. Reviews of performances. ■Impressions of the Bonner Biennale festival, noting the preference for a fragmented dramatic structure.

1803 Pfister, Eva. "Gegen den Rest der Welt." (Against the Rest of the World.) *DB.* 1996; 11: 17-19. Illus.: Photo. B&W. 4. Lang.: Ger.
Germany: Düsseldorf. 1996. Critical studies. ■Portrait of Düsseldorfer Schauspielhaus, under the direction of Anna Badora: analysis of the first four performances: *Lulu* by Frank Wedekind, directed by Badora, *Der Film in Worten (The Film in Words)* by Rolf-Dieter Brinkmann, directed by Thirza Bruncken, *Bullets Over Broadway* by Woody Allen, adapted for the stage by Jürgen Fischer and directed by Sönke Wortmann, *Der Teufel kommt aus Düsseldorf (The Devil Comes from Düsseldorf)* by Daniel Call, directed by Dietrich Hilsdorf.

DRAMA: —Institutions

1804 Preusser, Gerhard. "Spass mit Mühe." (Fun with Trouble.) *THeute*. 1996; 8: 38-40. Illus.: Photo. B&W. 1. Lang.: Ger.
Germany: Bochum. 1995-1996. Historical studies. ■Profile of Bochumer Schauspielhaus under the directorship of Leander Haussmann.

1805 Reuter, Ulrich. "Pause in Europa." (Break in Europe.) *TZ*. 1996; 4: 40-43. Illus.: Photo. B&W. 7. Lang.: Ger.
Germany: Bonn. 1996. Reviews of performances. ■Report on the third Bonner Biennale focusing on new plays by European dramatists.

1806 Ruf, Wolfgang. "Die Tugenden des Realismus." (The Virtues of Realism.) *DB*. 1996; 2: 26-29. Illus.: Photo. B&W. 1. Lang.: Ger.
Germany: Osnabruck. 1990-1996. Histories-sources. ■Interview with Klaus Kusenberg, artistic director of Städische Bühnen, about aesthetic influences, working methods, and programs.

1807 Schulze-Reimpell, Werner. "Company versus Stadttheater?" *DB*. 1996; 4: 34-35. Illus.: Photo. B&W. 1. Lang.: Ger.
Germany: Bremen. 1986-1996. Historical studies. ■The increasing competition between Theater der Freien Hansestadt and Bremer Shakespeare Company in the face of funding cuts and a declining audience.

1808 Stephan, Erika. "Kein Leipziger Allerlei." (No Leipzig Medley.) *DB*. 1996; 3: 30-33. Illus.: Photo. B&W. 4. Lang.: Ger.
Germany: Leipzig. 1996. Historical studies. ■Portrait of the Schauspiel Leipzig, Wolfgang Engel, artistic director: its everyday life and financial problems.

1809 Tiedemann, Kathrin. "Die Transformation von Alltag in Kunst." (The Transformation of Everyday Life into Art.) *TZ*. 1996; 3: 38-39. Illus.: Photo. B&W. 3. Lang.: Ger.
Germany: Dresden. 1996. Histories-sources. ■Conversation with Hannah Hurtzig, program director of Theater der Welt.

1810 Wille, Franz. "Erbe der Zukunft." (Inheritance of the Future.) *THeute*. 1996; 2: 46-48. Illus.: Photo. B&W. 3. Lang.: Ger.
Germany: Berlin. 1996. Histories-sources. ■Interview with Peter Palitsch, Fritz Marquardt, and Peter Sauerbaum about the future administration of the Berliner Ensemble.

1811 Wille, Franz. "Einfach kompliziert." (Simply Complicated.) *THeute*. 1996; 3: 8-9. Illus.: Photo. B&W. 2. Lang.: Ger.
Germany: Berlin. 1996. Histories-sources. ■Interview with Martin Wuttke, new director of Berliner Ensemble.

1812 Zerull, Ludwig. "Durchgestartet." (Started Through.) *THeute*. 1996; 6: 33-35. Illus.: Photo. B&W. 4. Lang.: Ger.
Germany: Braunschweig. 1996. Historical studies. ■The new season at the Staatstheater, Kleines Haus, opening with a new program including Ibsen's *Peer Gynt*.

1813 Mickel, Karl. "Das Berliner Ensemble der Ruth Berghaus." (Ruth Berghaus' Berliner Ensemble.) *TZ*. 1996; 2: 50-51. Illus.: Photo. B&W. 1. Lang.: Ger.
Germany, East: Berlin, East. 1970-1974. Histories-sources. ■Her dramaturg describes Berghaus' artistic development at Berliner Ensemble, and the experiments and innovations that led to her dismissal.

1814 Trotter, Mary. "Women's Work: Inghinidhe na h'Eireann and the Irish Dramatic Movement." 37-56 in Reinelt, Janelle, ed. *Crucibles of Crisis: Performing Social Change*. Ann Arbor, MI: Univ of Michigan P; 1996. 250 pp. Notes. Illus.: Photo. Dwg. 3. Lang.: Eng.
Ireland: Dublin. 1900-1902. Critical studies. ■The Irish women's nationalist group Inghinidhe na h'Eireann (daughters of Erin), which produced *Deirdre* by AE (George Russell) and *Kathleen ni Houlihan* by W.B. Yeats with Lady Gregory. Their theatrical collaborations, intended to promote the nationalist cause, are said to cross lines of religion, class, and gender.

1815 Nir, Yael. "Israel's Rina Yerushalmi and Her Directorial Experiments in Spatial Interrelations." 183-196 in Oliva, Judy Lee, ed. *New Theatre Vistas: Modern Movements in International Theatre*. New York, NY/London: Garland; 1996. 219 pp. (Studies in Modern Drama 7.) Notes. Lang.: Eng.
Israel: Tel Aviv. 1990-1992. Critical studies. ■The work of Itim Theatre Ensemble and its artistic and founding director Rina Yerushalmi. Focuses on two productions: *Hamlet* and Büchner's *Woyzeck*. Analyzes Yerushalmi's theatrical philosophy and aesthetic approach to her work.

1816 Carlson, Marvin; Mason, Susan. "The 1996 Dutch Theatre Festival." *WES*. 1996 Fall; 8(3): 91-98. Illus.: Photo. 6. Lang.: Eng.
Netherlands: Amsterdam. 1996. Historical studies. ■Coverage of Het Festival including Djuna Barnes' *The Antiphon* performed by Toneelgroep Amsterdam, directed by Gerardjan Rijnders and co-produced with the Flemish company Blauwe Maandag Compagnie, Het Zuidilijk Toneel's production of Camus' *Caligula* directed by Ivo van Hove, and two youth theatre productions, Ghent's Speeltheater's *Alleen Alleen (Alone Alone)*, and Teneeter's *The Tempest*.

1817 Deuss, Bart; Wiersinga, Pim. *De verovering van het Bos. Tien jaar toneel in het Amsterdamse Bos.* (The Conquest of the Forest: Ten Years of Theatre in the Amsterdamse Bos.) Amsterdam: Theater Het Amsterdamse Bos; 1996. 48 pp. Illus.: Photo. B&W. 54. Lang.: Dut.
Netherlands: Amsterdam. 1986-1996. Historical studies. ■Open-air productions of the Amsterdam forest.

1818 Mason, Susan. "Werner Schwab's Feces Dramas and De Trust Theatre Company of Holland." *TheatreF*. 1996 Win/Spr; 8: 22-28. Biblio. Illus.: Photo. 6. Lang.: Eng.
Netherlands: Amsterdam. 1988-1996. Historical studies. ■The work of De Trust, founded in 1988 by Rik De Zaak and a group of actors, with emphasis on the 'feces dramas' created by Schwab at the collective, including *Overgewicht, ombelangrijk: Vormeloos (Overweight, Unimportant: Formless)*, *Volksvernietiging of mijn lever is zinloos (Genocide or My Liver Is Meaningless)*, *De Presidentes (The Women Presidents)*, and *Mijn Hondemond (My Dogmouth)*.

1819 Mol, Pauline; Pals, Mariëlle; Zonneveld, Loek. *Theater Artemis 1990-1995*. Amsterdam: International Theatre and Film Books; 1995. 96 pp. Illus.: Photo. B&W. 35. Lang.: Dut.
Netherlands: 's-Hertogenbosch. 1990-1995. Historical studies. ■History of the youth theatre Artemis.

1820 Krasiński, Edward. "The Teatr Narodowy of Warsaw." *TP*. 1996 Oct.; 38(4): 3-11. Illus.: Photo. Color. B&W. 9. Lang.: Eng, Fre.
Poland: Warsaw. 1765-1996. Historical studies. ■History of Poland's national theatre.

1821 Raszewska, Magdelena. "The Dreams of Directors of Teatr Narodowy." *TP*. 1996 Oct.; 38(4): 12-16. Illus.: Photo. B&W. 3. Lang.: Eng, Fre.
Poland: Warsaw. 1923-1996. Historical studies. ■Artistic agendas of the various directors of the Teatr Narodowy, focusing on Juliusz Osterwa, Wilam Horzyca and Kazimierz Dejmek.

1822 Čirva, Jurij. "Leonid Andrejév včera, segodnja, zavtra." (Leonid Andrejév Yesterday, Today, and Tomorrow.) *TeatZ*. 1996; 11-12: 52-55. Lang.: Rus.
Russia: Orel. 1996. Historical studies. ■Report on Russian classics festival in honor of Andrejév, with discussion of his plays.

1823 Gaevskaja, M. "Po sledam čechovskogo marafona." (Following the Čechov Marathon.) *SovD*. 1996; 4: 179-197. Lang.: Rus.
Russia: Moscow. 1995-1996. Historical studies. ■Report on the second international Čechov theatre festival.

1824 Gaevskij, V. "Vachtangovskoe." (Vachtangov's.) *TeatZ*. 1996; 6: 24-25. Lang.: Rus.
Russia: Moscow. 1921-1996. Historical studies. ■The founding and development of the Vachtangov Theatre.

1825 Kuchta, E. "Antigona, oborvancy i vochljaki." (Antigone, Paupers and Trash.) *TeatZ*. 1996; 10: 26-28. Lang.: Rus.
Russia: St. Petersburg. 1990-1996. Critical studies. ■The work of Bolšoj Dramatičeskij Teat'r im. G.A. Tovstonogova, Temur Čcheidze, director.

1826 L'vov-Anochin, Boris. "Ob akterach Novogo teatra." (About Novyj Teat'r Actors.) *TeatZ*. 1996; 4: 42-44. Lang.: Rus.

DRAMA: —Institutions

Russia: Moscow. 1980-1996. Histories-sources. ■History and activities of Novyj Teat'r by its director.

1827 Luckaja, E. "'Žanna d'Ark'. Versija." (*Jeanne d'Arc*: Version.) *MuZizn.* 1996; 5-6: 7-8. Lang.: Rus.

Russia: Moscow. 1995. Historical studies. ■The repertoire of the Stanislavkij Dramatic Theatre in the 1995 season.

1828 Pavlova, I. "Dom bez chozjaina." (A House without an Owner.) *TeatZ.* 1996; 10: 32-37. Lang.: Rus.

Russia: St. Petersburg. 1990-1996. Critical studies. ■The work of Bolšoj Dramatičeskij Teat'r im. G.A. Tovstonogova, with emphasis on the modern theatre process in its productions.

1829 Šach-Azizova, T. "Moskva, Rossija, Evropa." (Moscow, Russia, Europe.) *TeatZ.* 1996; 8: 2-7. Lang.: Rus.

Russia: Moscow. 1996. Historical studies. ■Report on the second international Čechov festival.

1830 Saščenko, Georgij A. "Večnyj beg bez finiša." (Endless Marathon.) *TeatZ.* 1996; 10: 7-9. Lang.: Rus.

Russia: St. Petersburg. 1990-1996. Histories-sources. ■The work of the Puškin Academic Drama Theatre (formerly the Aleksandrinskij Theatre), by its director.

1831 Sidorenko, L.N. "MXAT i russkaja kul'tura." (The Moscow Art Theatre and Russian Culture.) 117-124 in *Kultura i tvorčestvo: Materialy konferencii.* Moscow: MGOPU; 1996. Lang.: Rus.

Russia: Moscow. 1990-1996. Historical studies. ■Moscow Art Theatre's role in preserving and cultivating Russian traditions, with emphasis on the plays of Ostrovskij.

1832 Slavkin, Viktor. "Teatral'nje lamentacii." (Theatrical Lamentations.) *TeatZ.* 1996; 11-12: 11-12. Lang.: Rus.

Russia: Moscow. 1980-1996. Historical studies. ■The history of the Stanislavskij Theatre and its current problems.

1833 Stanco, Vladimir. *To byl moj teat'r.* (That Was My Theatre.) Moscow: GKCM V.S. Vygockogo; 1996. 252 pp. Lang.: Rus.

Russia: Moscow. 1964-1996. Histories-specific. ■The history and development of the Taganka Theatre, including the role of Vladimir Vysockij, by poet Vladimir Stanco.

1834 Starosel'skaja, N. "'My ne vrači, my—bol'." (We Are Not the Doctors, We're the Disease.) *TeatZ.* 1996; 11-12: 30-32. Lang.: Rus.

Russia: Moscow. 1996. Historical studies. ■Profile of Teat'r Okolo Doma Stanislavskogo, Jurij Pogrebničko, artistic director.

1835 Svobodin, A. "Teat'r ožil. Ostalos' čut-čut... (Iz dnevnika)." (Theatre Came to Life: A Little to the Left—From a Diary.) *TeatZ.* 1996; 10: 10-14. Lang.: Rus.

Russia: St. Petersburg. 1996. Critical studies. ■Theatre critic's notes on the 1996 repertoire of the former Aleksandrinskij, now known as the Puškin Academic Drama Theatre.

1836 Vasilinina, I. "Bud' sčastliva, Aleksandrinka!" (Be Happy, Aleksandrinka!)*TeatZ.* 1996; 10: 2-6. Lang.: Rus.

Russia: St. Petersburg. 1990-1996. Historical studies. ■Profile of the Puškin Academic Drama Theatre, Georgij A. Saščenko, artistic director.

1837 Vasilinina, I. "Larčik otkryvaetsja neprosto." (The Box Does Not Open Easily.) *TeatZ.* 1996; 11-12: 22-29. Lang.: Rus.

Russia: Moscow. 1996. Historical studies. ■The repertoire of the 1996 season of Stanislavskij Theatre, Vitalij Lanskoj, artistic director.

1838 Vdovenko, I. "Fobii: 'Otsvety' MDT." (Phobias: *Reflected Glare*, Malyj Drama Theatre.) *MoskNab.* 1996; 1-2: 42-44. Lang.: Rus.

Russia: St. Petersburg. 1990-1996. Historical studies. ■Productions of Malyj Drama Theatre, Lev Dodin, artistic director.

1839 Zabavskich, E. "Gennadij Čichačev: 'Nado ljubit' zritelej'." (Gennadij Čichačev: We Have to Love Our Audience.) *Selmol.* 1996; Feb: 37-39. Lang.: Rus.

Russia: Moscow. 1990-1996. Historical studies. ■Moskovskij Teat'r under the direction of Gennadij Čichačev.

1840 Zlobina, A. "Kogda by grek uvidel naši igry." (When Would a Greek See Our Plays.) *NovyjMir.* 1996; 11: 198-211. Lang.: Rus.

Russia: Moscow. 1995-1996. Historical studies. ■The season's repertoire of the Gorkij Academic Theatre (Moskovskij Chudožestvénnyj Akademičéskij Teat'r im. M. Gorkogo).

1841 *Zbornik Gledališča Toneta Čufarja Jesenice.* (The Survey of The Tone Čufar Theatre, Jesenice.) Jesenice: Gledališče Toneta Čufarja; 1995. 40 pp. Biblio. Illus.: Photo. B&W. Lang.: Slo.

Slovenia: Jesenice. 1945-1995. Historical studies. ■Survey of the productions and actors of Gledališče Toneta Čufarja.

1842 *Slovenski gledališki festival—31: Borštnikovo srečanje 1996.* (Slovene Theatre Festival: the 31st Borštnik's Meeting 1996.) Maribor: SNG; 1996. Illus.: Photo. B&W. Lang.: Slo.

Slovenia. 1996. Historical studies. ■The program of the 31st competitive meeting of Slovene theatres, Borštnikovo srečanje.

1843 Hartman, Bruno. *Slovensko dramsko gledališče v Mariboru do druge svetovne vojne.* (The Slovene Drama Theatre in Maribor until the Second World War.) Maribor: Obzorja; 1996. 290 pp. Illus.: Photo. B&W. Lang.: Slo.

Slovenia: Maribor. 1861-1941. Histories-specific. ■History of the theatre and its development from amateur and political beginnings to a professional theatre.

1844 Ovsec, Peter. *Šentjakobsko gledališče Ljubljana, leta ljubezni in dela 1921-1996.* (Šentjakob Theatre Ljubljana, Years of Love and Work, 1921-1996.) Ljubljana: Šentjakob gledališče; 1996. 207 pp. Illus.: Photo. B&W. Lang.: Slo.

Slovenia: Ljubljana. 1921-1996. Historical studies. ■Memories and photographic material of the amateur theatre Šentjakob.

1845 Predan, Vasja. *Slovenska dramska gledališča.* (The Slovene Drama Theatres.) Ljubljana: Mestno gledališče ljubljansko; 1996. 171 pp. (The Ljubljana City Theatre Library 122.) Lang.: Slo.

Slovenia. 1650-1996. Histories-specific. ■A concise history of Slovene dramatic theatre in general and of the institutions in particular.

1846 Guillemaut, Alf. "Market Theatret." (Market Theatre.) *ProScen.* 1996; 20(4): 6-11. Illus.: Photo. Color. Lang.: Swe.

South Africa, Republic of: Johannesburg. 1976. Historical studies. ■A presentation of the Market Theatre, both as an institution and a theatre building, including interviews with the technical manager Richard Barnes and the stage manager Toni Markel.

1847 Gray, Amlin. "Sunstruck in Spain." *AmTh.* 1996 Nov.; 13(9): 25. Illus.: Photo. B&W. 1. [Headed by Title: 5 Corners of our theatrical world.] Lang.: Eng.

Spain. 1996. Critical studies. ■Highlights of the Festival Internacional de Almagro. Performance spaces, audience response.

1848 Andersson, Bibi; Ekblad, Stina; Göranzon, Marie; Kalmér, Åsa; Weiss, Nadja; Åberg, Ulla. "Vi tar tempen på Dramaten." (We Take the Temperature of Dramaten.) *Tningen.* 196; 20(75): 6-8. Illus.: Photo. B&W. Lang.: Swe.

Sweden: Stockholm. 1985. Critical studies. ■Six women from the Royal Dramatic Theatre give their views of the repertory and regimen of the eleven years of Lars Löfgren as theatre manager.

1849 Hoogland, Rikard. "Jag har alltid hejat på Angeredsteatern." (I Have Always Cheered On Angeredsteatern.) *Tningen.* 1996; 20(79): 40-41. Illus.: Photo. Color. Lang.: Swe.

Sweden. 1996. Historical studies. ■The new theatre manager for Angeredsteatern, Niklas Hjulström, speaks about his plans with the theatre and its cultural place in Gothenburg.

1850 Kristoffersson, Birgitta. "Skillinge Teater—ett djärvt projekt." (Skillinge Teater—a Bold Project.) *Dramat.* 1996; 4 (2): 26-27. Illus.: Photo. Color. Lang.: Swe.

Sweden: Skillinge. 1995. Historical studies. ■A presentation of the summer theatre at Skillinge, a small village in the south of Sweden, where the actors Mikael Strandberg and Katarina Zell have successes with tragedies.

1851 Lahger, Håkan. "Vad ska vi med teater till?" (To What Use Do We Have the Theatre?)*Dramat.* 1996; 4(4): 26-29. Illus.: Photo. B&W. Lang.: Swe.

Sweden: Stockholm. 1960. Histories-sources. ■Interview with theatre critic Leif Zern about the Royal Dramatic Theatre: pro and con, and the

DRAMA: —Institutions

importance of keeping an ensemble of permanent actors (with reference to the work of Ingmar Bergman).

1852 Werkelid, Carl Otto. "Sista sommaren med Lars." (The Last Summer With Lars.) *Dramat.* 1996; 4(3): 18-21. Illus.: Photo. Color. Lang.: Swe.

Sweden: Stockholm. 1985-1996. Histories-sources. ▪An interview with Lars Löfgren about his ten years as theatre manager of the Royal Dramatic Theatre, with references to the return of Ingmar Bergman and how to manage the fundraising.

1853 Iljalova, I. *Artisty teatra im. G. Kamala: biobibliografičeskij spravočnik.* (The Actors of the Kamala Theatre: Biobibliographical Listing.) Kazan: Tatarskoje knižnoje izdatel'stvo; 1996. 250 pp. Lang.: Rus.

Tatarstan: Kazan. 1995. Histories-sources. ▪Information about Tatarskij Gosudarstvénnyj Akademičéskij Teat'r im. G. Kamala and its actors.

1854 Dungate, Rod. "Living in Hope." *PlPl.* 1996 Dec/1997 Jan.; 510: 38-39. Lang.: Eng.

UK-England: Worcester. 1994-1996. Histories-sources. ▪Interview with Jenny Stephens, artistic director of the Swan Theatre, one of England's forty-four regional theatres. Concentrates on her difficulties in being funded, how she selects a season, and challenges in directing.

1855 Dungate, Rod. "Stratford Upon Avon Programme 1996/97." *PlPl.* 1996 Aug/Sep.: 44. Lang.: Eng.

UK-England: Stratford. 1996. Histories-sources. ▪The Royal Shakespeare Company's new season with reference to the transfer of all Stratford productions to theatres in London, Newcastle, and Plymouth, as well as to other cities through touring productions.

1856 Dungate, Rod. "RSC Openings." *PlPl.* 1996 Aug/Sep.: 44-46. Lang.: Eng.

UK-England: London, Stratford. 1996. Critical studies. ▪Discussion of recent RSC openings. Emphasis on Shakespeare's *Troilus and Cressida* and *The General from America* by Richard Nelson.

1857 Raab, Michael. "Londoner Dramaturgie." (The Dramaturgy of London.) *DB.* 1996; 1: 22-25. Illus.: Photo. B&W. 4. Lang.: Ger.

UK-England: London. 1996. Historical studies. ▪Portraits of the Bush and Almeida theatres, their focus on contemporary playwrights, and their working methods.

1858 Winson, Alan. "Changes at the Royal Court." *WES.* 1996 Spr; 8(2): 27-30. Illus.: Photo. 2. Lang.: Eng.

UK-England: London. 1996. Historical studies. ▪As the Royal Court begins an architectural restructuring, its mission as a home for new playwrights continues. New works recently seen include Nick Grosso's *Sweetheart.* Includes specifics on architectural changes as the theatre shuts down and productions are moved to the Duke of York's and Ambassadors Theatres for the next two years.

1859 Trousdell, Richard. "Crossing Boundaries: Directing Gay, Lesbian, and Working-Class Theatre in Scotland." 3-24 in Oliva, Judy Lee, ed. *New Theatre Vistas: Modern Movements in International Theatre.* New York, NY/London: Garland; 1996. 219 pp. (Studies in Modern Drama 7.) Notes. Lang.: Eng.

UK-Scotland: Glasgow. 1986-1995. Critical studies. ▪Critical account of the work of Clyde Unity Theatre, founded by Aileen Ritchie and John Binnie to address a neglected audience. The company tours all over Scotland performing radical theatre, new plays dealing with social issues such as sexuality, health, race and the position of women in Scottish society. Notes on the collaborative nature of the creations.

1860 Blaney, Retta. "Big Dreams/Small Spaces." *TheaterW.* 1996 Mar 18; 9(33): 34-43. Illus.: Photo. B&W. 5. Lang.: Eng.

USA: New York, NY. 1996. Historical studies. ▪Efforts of theatre companies Third Eye Repertory, The Alpha and Omega Theater Company and Gilgamesh Theater, to renovate new theatre spaces and establish an artistic home for actors, playwrights and designers.

1861 Chase, Tony. "Josephine Abady to the Rescue." *TheaterW.* 1996 May 20; 9(42): 41-43. Illus.: Photo. B&W. 2. Lang.: Eng.

USA: New York, NY. 1991-1996. Historical studies. ▪Director Abady as new artistic director of Circle in the Square. Financial challenges, his-

tory of the company, proposed season, fundraising, strategies for revitalizing the company.

1862 Coe, Robert. "Steppenwolf Howls Again." *AmTh.* 1996 May/June; 13(5): 12-19, 60-61. Illus.: Photo. B&W. 12. Lang.: Eng.

USA: Chicago, IL. 1974-1996. Historical studies. ▪Profile of Steppenwolf Theatre Company: development and history, productions and playwrights (special focus on current production of Sam Shepard's *Buried Child*), future programming. Focus on former managing director Stephen Eich and acting members Gary Sinise, Jeff Perry, John Malkovich, former artistic director Randall Arney and current artistic director Martha Lavey.

1863 Croyden, Margaret. "Jon Jory: Louisville Legend." *TheaterW.* 1996 Sep 16; 10(6): 44-45. Lang.: Eng.

USA: Louisville, KY. 1996. Biographical studies. ▪Artistic director of Actors' Theater of Louisville Jory. Background, creation of the company, vision for company.

1864 Daniels, Jeff. "Circle Repertory Company: 1969-1996." *AmTh.* 1996 Dec.; 13(10): 48. Illus.: Photo. B&W. 1. Lang.: Eng.

USA: New York, NY. 1978-1996. Histories-sources. ▪Former acting company member relates personal experiences in Circle Rep's production *Fifth of July* by Lanford Wilson, directed by Marshall Mason, on the occasion of Circle Rep's closing operations.

1865 Gluck, David. "Over Hill and Dale with Gorilla Rep." *AmTh.* 1996 Dec.; 13(10): 55-57. Illus.: Photo. B&W. 2. Lang.: Eng.

USA: New York, NY. 1996. Historical studies. ▪Gorilla Rep's productions of free park performances of Shakespeare. Director Christopher Sanderson discusses their environmental and interactive style, and goals of the company.

1866 Gussow, Mel. "The Plays Tell the Tale." *AmTh.* 1996 July/Aug.; 13(6): 52-54. Illus.: Photo. B&W. 3. Lang.: Eng.

USA: Louisville, KY. 1979-1996. Historical studies. ▪Actors Theatre of Louisville and its dedication to the development and production of new works. Focus on the Humana Festival, artistic director Jon Jory.

1867 Horwitz, Simi. "David Hays: At the Helm on Ship and Stage." *TheaterW.* 1996 Feb 5; 9(27): 24-33. Illus.: Photo. B&W. 2. Lang.: Eng.

USA: Chester, CT. 1996. Historical studies. ▪Founder and CEO of National Theatre of the Deaf discusses financial crisis facing company, past productions and artists, its touring companies, educational outreach, and challenges faced by deaf artists.

1868 Horwitz, Simi. "Make Mine Manhattan: New York City's Most Successful Nonprofit Celebrates 25 Years." *TheaterW.* 1996 Dec 9; 10(19): 36-44. Illus.: Photo. B&W. 3. Lang.: Eng.

USA: New York, NY. 1972-1996. Historical studies. ▪Artistic director Lynne Meadow and managing director Barry Grove on Manhattan Theatre Club's history, mission, success, funding, commitment to playwrights, outreach programs.

1869 Klunzinger, T.E. "A Rose Grows in Chelsea: A Tale of Two Michigan Theatres." *DGQ.* 1996 Fall; 33(3): 40-44. Lang.: Eng.

USA: Chelsea, MI. 1966-1996. Historical studies. ▪The Purple Rose Theatre Company founded by actor Jeff Daniels and BoarsHead theatre founded by Richard Thomsen and John Peakes. Both companies dedicated to nurturing new playwrights.

1870 Kuftinec, Sonja. "A Cornerstone for Rethinking Community Theatre." *TTop.* 1996 Mar.; 6(1): 91-104. Notes. Biblio. Lang.: Eng.

USA. 1986-1996. Critical studies. ▪Examination of the touring Cornerstone Theatre with emphasis on their production and rehearsal process and their exploration of community-based work. References to a Cornerstone production, in Long Creek, Oregon, of *The Good Person of Setzuan.*

1871 Lamont, Rosette C. "I Remember La MaMa." *TheaterW.* 1996 Dec 16; 10(20): 43-49. Illus.: Photo. B&W. 1. Lang.: Eng.

DRAMA: —Institutions

USA: New York, NY. 1960-1996. Histories-sources. ■Interview with artistic director of La MaMa Ellen Stewart on the history of the company, their international programming, theatre companies and artists they have supported over the years.

1872 Miller, Stuart. "Master Builder Bram Lewis." *TheaterW.* 1996 Oct 7; 10(10): 38-45. Lang.: Eng.
USA: Purchase, NY. 1996. Historical studies. ■Artistic director of Phoenix Theatre discusses company's origins, mission, financial and management challenges in establishing a theatre in an area where other theatres had failed.

1873 Miller, Stuart. "Rattlestick: Mentoring the Unknown." *TheaterW.* 1996 Jan 15; 9(24): 31-34. Illus.: Photo. B&W. 1. Lang.: Eng.
USA: New York, NY. 1996. Historical studies. ■David Van Asselt's artistic direction of Rattlestick theatre company. Company's focus on developing playwrights, creating new works, and its playwright mentoring program which pairs new playwrights with professionals.

1874 Napoleon, Davi. "Family Values at the American Rep." *TheaterW.* 1996 Nov 4; 10(14): 35-37. Illus.: Photo. B&W. 1. Lang.: Eng.
USA: Cambridge, MA. 1996. Historical studies. ■Artists balancing personal family demands with rehearsal schedules and travel constraints. Focus on ART and their methods of keeping a resident company together.

1875 Newlin, Keith. "Uplifting the Stage: Hamlin Garland and the Chicago Theater Society." *JADT.* 1996 Win; 8(1): 1-17. Notes. Lang.: Eng.
USA: Chicago, IL. 1909-1915. Historical studies. ■Historical account of the Chicago Theatre Society, its founders, Hamlin Garland and Donald Robertson, and its acting troupe, the Drama Players. The Society's aim was to help educate audiences on the nature and function of avant-garde theatre, and it served as a model for the Little Theatre movement.

1876 Oliva, Judy Lee. "Diablomundo and the Royal Hunt: The Shadow and the Sun." 197-216 in Oliva, Judy Lee, ed. *New Theatre Vistas: Modern Movements in International Theatre.* New York, NY/London: Garland; 1996. 219 pp. (Studies in Modern Drama 7.) Notes. Lang.: Eng.
USA: Knoxville, TN. Argentina: Buenos Aires. 1994. Critical studies. ■Collaboration of the Clarence Brown Theatre Company and Diablomundo on Peter Shaffer's *The Royal Hunt of the Sun.* The production explored the clash of cultures in America from the sixteenth century to the present.

1877 Pesner, Ben. "The Alley Theatre: Approaching Fifty." *DGQ.* 1996 Spr; 33(1): 37-43. Lang.: Eng.
USA: Houston, TX. 1947-1996. Histories-sources. ■Brief history of the Alley Theatre, and an interview with present artistic director Gregory Boyd regarding the company's future.

1878 Ramach, Michael. "KSF Uses The Magic of Shakespeare To Open New Vistas for Students, Adults." *SoTh.* 1996 Spr; 37(2): 30-32. Illus.: Photo. B&W. 2. Lang.: Eng.
USA: Louisville, KY. 1960-1996. Historical studies. ■A brief profile of the Kentucky Shakespeare Festival, including educational outreach programs.

1879 Reiss, Alvin H. "New York Shakespeare Festival Reaches Out to Tap New Audiences, New Supporters." *FundM.* 1996 Apr.; 27 (2): 54-55. Illus.: Photo. B&W. 1. Lang.: Eng.
USA: New York, NY. 1996. Historical studies. ■The New York Shakespeare Festival's search for new funding possibilities, aside from the capital provided by profits from its production of *A Chorus Line*: cultivation of new business partners, new audiences, and also returns from shows produced by the Festival.

1880 Van Erven, Eugène. "When José Met Sally: Chicano Theatre in L.A. at Grassroots and Mainstream." *NTQ.* 1996 Nov.; 12(48): 356-366. Notes. Biblio. Illus.: Photo. B&W. 5. Lang.: Eng.
USA: Los Angeles, CA. 1986-1996. Historical studies. ■Outlines history of the Hispanic Playwrights Project, founded and directed by José Cruz González from the South Coast Repertory, and compares his work with that of Sally Gordon with the economically disadvantaged through her Teatro de la Realidad.

1881 West, Anthony James. "How Many First Folios Does the Folger Hold?" *SQ.* 1996 Sum; 47(2): 190-194. Notes. Tables. Lang.: Eng.
USA: Washington, DC. 1996. Bibliographical studies. ■Reports on still unsettled number of Shakespearean first folios held by the Folger Shakespeare Library.

1882 Wiese, Martha. "Roanoke's Mill Mountain Provides Setting for Playwrights to Fine Tune New Works." *SoTh.* Fall 1996; 37 (4): 28-32. Illus.: Photo. B&W. 3. Lang.: Eng.
USA: Roanoke, VA. 1964-1996. Historical studies. ■A brief profile of the Mill Mountain Theatre in Roanoke, Virginia.

1883 Zachary, Samuel. "Y.E.S.!: New Play Series at NKU Showcases Talent, Rejuvenates and Unites Theatre Department." *SoTh.* 1996 Spr; 37(2): 24-29. Illus.: Photo. B&W. 5. Lang.: Eng.
USA: Highland Heights, KY. 1983-1996. Historical studies. ■A history and description of Northern Kentucky University's 'Y.E.S.' Festival for new plays, with selection criteria and production process.

Performance spaces

1884 Vaïs, Michel. "Parcours architectural du Théâtre d'Aujourd'hui." (Architectural Odyssey of the Théâtre d'Aujourd'hui.) *JCT.* 1996; 79: 49-55. Notes. Illus.: Photo. Diagram. B&W. Architec. 4. Lang.: Fre.
Canada: Montreal, PQ. 1958-1996. Historical studies. ■History of theatre spaces and performance conditions of Théâtre d'Aujourd'hui, from its inception as the Apprentis-Sorciers to the present.

1885 Vigeant, Louise. "Le nouveau Nouveau Monde: un lieu ouvert, vivant et modeste: Entretien avec la directrice du Théâtre du Nouveau Monde, Lorraine Pintal, l'architecte Dan Hanganu et le scénographe Luc Plamondon, de chez Trizart." (The New Nouveau Monde: An Open, Lively and Modest Space: Interview with Théâtre du Nouveau Monde director Lorraine Pintal, architect Dan Hanganu and scenographer Luc Plamondon, of Trizart.) *JCT.* 1996; 79: 39-48. Illus.: Photo. B&W. 8. Lang.: Fre.
Canada: Montreal, PQ. 1996. Histories-sources. ■Conception team of Pintal, Hanganu and Plamondon discuss social, aesthetic, technical and financial aspects of reconstruction of Théâtre du Nouveau Monde's theatre building.

1886 Marsolais, Gilles. "Des théâtres et des hommes." (Of Theatres and Men.) *JCT.* 1996; 79: 32-38. Notes. Illus.: Diagram. Photo. B&W. Grd.Plan. 7. Lang.: Fre.
Europe. 600 B.C.-1996 A.D. Historical studies. ■Audience-performer relationships and implications for scenography of historic theatre structures (Greek, Elizabethan and Italian) and contemporary alternatives.

1887 Hughes, Alan. "Comic Stages in Magna Graecia: the Evidence of the Vases." *ThR.* 1996; 21(2): 95-107. Notes. Illus.: Photo. B&W. 11. Lang.: Eng.
Italy. 400-325 B.C. Historical studies. ■Examines iconographic evidence of fourth-century BC vases from southern Italy and Sicily and argues that wooden comic stages were not temporary and/or portable, as often claimed, but substantial constructions erected in permanent theatres. Also supports revisionist view that vase scenes depict Attic Old Comedy, not local Italiote forms.

1888 Pauli, Agneta. "Georg Pauli och skådespelarna." (Georg Pauli and the Actors.) *Dramat.* 1996; 4(2): 42-44. Illus.: Photo. B&W. Color. Lang.: Swe.
Sweden: Stockholm. 1907. Historical studies. ■The four mural paintings of Georg and Hanna Pauli in one of the foyers of the Royal Dramatic Theatre.

1889 "Gorgeous Palaces, Solemn Temples." *AtG.* 1996 Win: 2-3. Illus.: Photo. Color. 4. Lang.: Eng.
UK-England: London. 1996. Critical studies. ■Description of the temporary *frons scenae*, reconstructed from the original and built for the Globe's prologue season.

1890 Kiernan, Pauline. "The Star of the Show." *AtG.* 1996 Win: 4-6. Illus.: Photo. Color. B&W. 7. Lang.: Eng.
UK-England: London. 1996. Critical studies. ■Performance space as functioning character in the inaugural production in the new Globe of

CLASSED ENTRIES

DRAMA: —Performance spaces

Shakespeare's *The Two Gentlemen of Verona* directed by Gaynor Macfarlane.

1891 Pfister, Eva. "Shakespeare's Globe." *DB.* 1996; 10: 28-29. Illus.: Photo. B&W. 3. Lang.: Ger.
UK-England: London. 1996. Historical studies. ■Report on Shakespeare's Globe and its opening production, *The Two Gentlemen of Verona.*

1892 Seacat, James. "Architecture: Expansion at Actors' Theatre of Louisville Sets Stage for 21st Century." *SoTh.* 1996 Spr; 37(2): 10-17. Illus.: Plan. Photo. B&W. 9. Lang.: Eng.
USA: Louisville, KY. 1964-1995. Historical studies. ■A descriptive account of the Actors' Theatre of Louisville's $12.5 million renovation and expansion, with description of remodeled facilities and specifications of design and equipment.

Performance/production

1893 Gilbert, Helen; Tompkins, Joanne. *Post-Colonial Drama: Theory, Practice, Politics.* London/New York, NY: Routledge; 1996. 344 pp. Notes. Biblio. Index. Lang.: Eng.
1880-1950. Critical studies. ■Focuses on the breakdown and subversion of canons, historical narrative revisionism, the recuperation of the traditional and the carnivalesque, constructs of the physical body (and their subtexts of race and gender), and finally on the contradictions of neo-imperialism. Examines the work of John Coulter and Carol Bolt (Canada), Ebrahim Hussein (Tasmania), Percy Mtwa (South Africa), Roger Mais (Jamaica), Derek Walcott (St. Lucia), and Ngũgĩ wa Thiong'o (Kenya).

1894 Kennedy, Dennis. *Looking at Shakespeare: A Visual History of Twentieth-Century Performance.* Cambridge/New York, NY: Cambridge UP; 1996. 381 pp. Illus.: Photo. 171. Lang.: Eng.
1900-1995. Histories-specific. ■Pictorial history of twentieth-century Shakespeare productions around the world. Photos accompanied by text situating Shakespeare in theoretical and cultural contexts.

1895 Opel, Anna. "Inszenierte Anblicke—Rosalinde, Kunigunda und Moderne Frauen." (Directing Aspects: Rosalinde, Kunigunda, and Modern Women.) *dRAMATURg.* 1996; 1: 14-20. Lang.: Ger.
1996. Critical studies. ■A gendered view of the direction of aspects of a character, the organization of the visible and the invisible in the idea of a character, with reference to Rosalind in Shakespeare's *As You Like It*, Kunigunde in Kleist's *Käthchen von Heilbronn*, and the characters of Elfriede Jelinek's *Krankheit oder Moderne Frauen (Illness or Modern Women).*

1896 Ruffini, Franco. *I teatri di Artaud. Crudeltà, corpo-mente.* (Artaud's Theatres: Cruelty, Mind-Body.) Bologna: Il Mulino; 1996. 250 pp. (Quarderni di Teatro e Storia.) Index. Notes. Biblio. Append. Lang.: Ita.
1886-1948. Critical studies. ■Artaud's work as actor and director and his theatrical ideas as expressed in *Le Théâtre et son double.*

1897 Graham-Jones, Jean. "Productions of *Telarañas* by Eduardo Pavlovsky." *LATR.* 1996 Spr; 29(2): 61-70. Notes. Biblio. Lang.: Eng.
Argentina: Buenos Aires. 1976-1985. Historical studies. ■Changes in the sociopolitical and aesthetic climate of Buenos Aires and Argentinian theatre reflected in two productions of *Telarañas (Cobwebs)* by Eduardo Pavlovsky: directed by Alberto Ure as a family tragedy at Teatro Payró in 1977 and by Ricardo Bartis as a satire of totalitarianism at Teatro del Viejo Palermo in 1985.

1898 Budde, Autje. "Krieg der Landschaften." (War of Landscapes.) *TZ.* 1996; 4: 12-16. Illus.: Photo. B&W. 2. Lang.: Ger.
Australia: Sydney. 1996. Critical studies. ■Critical analysis of *The Aboriginal Protesters* by Mudrooroo (Colin Johnson), directed by Noel Tovey at The Performance Space. The play uses Heiner Müller's *Der Auftrag (The Mission)* to explain the situation of Australian aboriginals.

1899 Holledge, Julie; Rose, Phyllis Jane. "How Many Women Playwrights Can You Name?" *AWBR.* 1994 June; 6(2): 16-18. Lang.: Eng.

Australia. Asia. 1994. Historical studies. ■Celebration of women playwrights of the Pacific Rim in anticipation of the 3rd International Women Playwrights Conference in Adelaide. Career sketches of Shen Hong-Guang, Li Ying Ning, Ratna Sarumpaet, Koharu Kisaragi, Rio Kishida, Kim Kum hwa, Leow Puay Tin, Lorae Parry, Renée, Fe Remotigue, Stella Kon.

1900 Osborne, Tony. "Site Specific Performance as Theatre Regeneration." *FAR.* 1995 Sep 8: 16-17. Illus.: Photo. B&W. 2. Lang.: Eng.
Australia: Perth. 1994. Critical studies. ■Site specific staging as a way of reviving theatre, using the Big Idea production of *A Drive Thru Life*, a company created piece staged by group founder Mar Bucknell in an East Perth warehouse, as an example.

1901 Balvín, Josef. "Smrt, hudba a smích. Na okraj dramatického díla Thomase Bernharda." (Death, Music and Laughter: On the Border of Thomas Bernhard's Dramatic Work.) *Svet.* 1996; 7(6): 26-42. Illus.: Photo. B&W. 3. Lang.: Cze.
Austria. Czechoslovakia. 1931-1989. Critical studies. ■Analysis of Bernhard's drama and the first productions of his plays in Czech theatres.

1902 Becker, Peter von. "Abschied von gestern..." (Farewell to Yesterday.) *THeute.* 1996; YB: 4-7. Illus.: Photo. B&W. 6. Lang.: Ger.
Austria: Vienna. 1996. Historical studies. ■Peter Zadek's production of Čechov's *Višněvyj sad (The Cherry Orchard)* at Burgtheater, which was designated the production of the year by a group of critics from Germany, Switzerland, and Austria.

1903 Brink, André. "Seminar in Salzburg." *PlPl.* 1996 Dec/1997 Jan.; 510: 21. Lang.: Eng.
Austria: Salzburg. 1996. Historical studies. ■Account of theatre seminar in Salzburg. Addresses issues of artistry, entertainment, and social commentary. Concentrates on the opening day master acting class, taught by Arthur Miller and David Thacker, where scenes from Miller's *I Can't Remember Anything* and *Death of a Salesman* are enacted.

1904 Kubikowski, Tomasz. "The Salzburg Actors Speak About *The Wedding*." *TP.* 1995 Apr.; 37(2): 17-21. Illus.: Photo. B&W. 4. Lang.: Eng, Fre.
Austria: Salzburg. 1992. Historical studies. ■Reception of the first German translation of Stanisław Wyspiański's *Wesele (The Wedding)*, by Karl Dedecius, directed by Andrzej Wajda at the 1992 Salzburger Festspiele, and the actor response to performing it.

1905 Löffler, Sigrid. "Sieben Sirenen des Prä-Feminismus." (Seven Sirens of Pre-Feminism.) *THeute.* 1996; 1: 13-15. Illus.: Photo. B&W. Color. 3. Lang.: Ger.
Austria: Vienna. 1996. Historical studies. ■Claus Peymann's exploration of the writer Ingeborg Bachmann in a collage titled *Ingeborg Bachmann Wer? (Ingeborg Bachmann Who?)* at Burgtheater.

1906 Merschmeier, Michael. "Die Zeit der Kirschen ist vorbei." (The Time of Cherries Is Over.) *THeute.* 1996; 3: 4-7. Illus.: Photo. B&W. 3. Lang.: Ger.
Austria: Vienna. 1996. Historical studies. ■Analysis of the acting of Josef Bierbichler and Angela Winkler in Peter Zadek's production of *Višněvyj sad (The Cherry Orchard)* at Burgtheater.

1907 Ruf, Wolfgang. "Schnitzel-Jagd." (Paper Chase.) *DB.* 1996; 5: 10-13. Illus.: Photo. B&W. 2. Lang.: Ger.
Austria: Vienna. 1996. Historical studies. ■The first performance of *Die Ballade vom Wiener Schnitzel (The Ballad of the Wiener Schnitzel)*, written and director by George Tabori at Akademietheater. Includes an interview with Tabori by Sybille Fritsch about the closeness between humor and seriousness.

1908 Fried, István. "Primadonna-darab a primadonnáról. Herczeg Ferenc színműve Dérynéről." (Primadonna-Play on the Primadonna: Ferenc Herczeg's Play about Déry.) *SzSz.* 1996; 30/31: 44-49. Notes. Lang.: Hun.
Austria-Hungary. Hungary: Budapest. 1907-1928. Critical studies. ■The effect of the different political situation on the interpretation of *Déryné ifjasszony (Mrs. Déry)* by Ferenc Herczeg in productions by Sándor Goth (Vígszínház, 1907) and Jenő Horváth (Nemzeti Színház, 1928).

1909 Székely, György. "Történelmi sikersztori—Látványosság 173 előadásban." (Successful Story of a Historical Play—A Spec-

DRAMA: —Performance/production

tacle in 173 Performances.) *Sz.* 1996; 29(8): 2-5. Illus.: Photo. B&W. 4. Lang.: Hun.
Austria-Hungary: Budapest. 1896-1926. Historical studies. ■History of the stage career of György Verő's festive play *Ezer év (A Thousand Years)* presented on the occasion of the millennial celebrations of Hungary in 1896.

1910 Darvay Nagy, Adrienne. "Petőfi drámája a kolozsvári színpadon." (Petőfi's Drama at Kolozsvár's Theatre.) *SzSz.* 1996; 30/31: 11-16. Notes. Lang.: Hun.
Austro-Hungarian Empire: Kolozsvár. 1876-1883. Historical studies. ■Study of a staging, Sándor Petőfi's *Tigris és hiéna (Tiger and Hyena)* directed by Gyula Ecsedi Kovács at Kolozsvár (today: Cluj-Napoca, Romania) in 1883.

1911 Burgoyne, Suzanne. "Belgian/American Theatre Exchanges: Reflections and Bridges." 25-42 in Oliva, Judy Lee, ed. *New Theatre Vistas: Modern Movements in International Theatre.* New York, NY/London: Garland; 1996. 219 pp. (Studies in Modern Drama 7.) Notes. Biblio. Lang.: Eng.
Belgium: Brussels. USA: Omaha, NE. 1986-1987. Histories-sources. ■The author's return to the Institut National Supérieur des Arts du Spectacle et Techniques de Diffusion to work with Paul Anrieu and the INSAS directing students on Arthur Miller's *Death of a Salesman* and *The Crucible*, and her direction of her own students in Paul Willems's *Il pleut dans ma maison (It's Raining in My House).*

1912 Coleman, Malinda. "Nele Paxinou and Her Baladins du Miroir." *WES.* 1995-96 Win; 7(3): 77-80. Illus.: Photo. 2. Lang.: Eng.
Belgium. 1995. Historical studies. ■Nele Paxinou, founding director of Les Baladins du Miroir, and her production of *A Midsummer Night's Dream.* After touring France and Belgium, the production appeared at the August Festival de Théâtre in Spa.

1913 Kramer, Femke. "*Rederijkers* on Stage: A Closer Look at 'Metatheatrical' Sources." *RORD.* 1996; 35(1): 97-109. Notes. Lang.: Eng.
Belgium. Netherlands. 1500-1599. Historical studies. ■The need to use non-theatrical texts as well as the many extant rhetorical plays in any evaluation of the genre's staging norms.

1914 Baku, Shango. "The Making of *Zumbi.*" *TheatreF.* 1996 Win/Spr; 8: 89-95. Illus.: Photo. 5. Lang.: Eng.
Brazil: Salvador. UK-England: London. 1995-1996. Histories-sources. ■The coproduction of *Zumbi*, a play by Marcio Meirelles and Shango Baku about a Black Brazilian hero, by Black Theatre Co-operative and Bando de Teatro Olodum, directed by Meirelles, at Theatre Royal, Stratford East.

1915 Mason, Vivian K. "Year of Improvising in the Balkans." 119-134 in Oliva, Judy Lee, ed. *New Theatre Vistas: Modern Movements in International Theatre.* New York, NY/London: Garland; 1996. 219 pp. (Studies in Modern Drama 7.) Biblio. Lang.: Eng.
Bulgaria: Blagoevgrad. 1993. Histories-sources. ■A year of intercultural theatre exchange at the American University in Bulgaria, focusing on three productions the author directed: Arthur Miller's *The Crucible*, Tennessee Williams's *The Glass Menagerie*, and Tony Kushner's *Angels in America.*

1916 "'La Maison suspendue': Autoportrait d'une oeuvre." (*The House Among the Stars*: Self-Portrait of a Work.) *JCT.* 1991; 58: 99. Illus.: Diagram. Photo. B&W. 2. Lang.: Fre.
Canada: Montreal, PQ. 1990. Histories-sources. ■Production credits for Compagnie Jean-Duceppe's 1990 production of Michel Tremblay's *La Maison suspendue (The House Among the Stars)* and a genealogical chart showing relationships of the characters.

1917 Beauchamp, Hélène. "Of Desire, Freedom, Commitment and Mise-en-scène as a Very Fine Art: The Work of the Theatre Director." *ADS.* 1996 Oct; 29: 155-167. Notes. Illus.: Photo. B&W. 2. Lang.: Eng.
Canada: Montreal, PQ. 1996. Critical studies. ■Philosophies of two female directors working in Montreal, reflected in Martine Beaulne's production of Goldoni's *La Locandiera (The Mistress of the Inn)*, and Lorraine Pintal's production of Edward Bond's *Company of Men.*

1918 Bell, Karen. "Christopher Plummer as John Barrymore." *PAC.* 1996; 30(3): 13. Illus.: Photo. B&W. 1. Lang.: Eng.
Canada: Stratford, ON. 1996. Critical studies. ■Actor Plummer and his one-man show *Barrymore* by William Luce directed by Gene Saks.

1919 Bell, Karen. "Leslie Nielsen Gets Serious." *PAC.* 1996; 30(3): 16. Illus.: Photo. B&W. 1. Lang.: Eng.
Canada. 1996. Critical studies. ■Stage work of comic film actor Leslie Nielsen with his one-man touring show *Clarence Darrow for the Defense.*

1920 Bell, Karen. "Multiple Make-Overs." *PAC.* 1996; 30(2): 4-5. Illus.: Photo. B&W. 3. Lang.: Eng.
Canada. 1996. Historical studies. ■Actors Tom Wood and Nicola Cavendish play multiple roles in A.R. Gurney's *Later Life* at Vancouver Playhouse and Canadian Stage Company.

1921 Bénard, Johanne. "Tromper l'attente." (Whiling Away the Wait.) *JCT.* 1992; 64: 19-26. Notes. Illus.: Photo. B&W. 4. Lang.: Fre.
Canada: Montreal, PQ. 1988-1992. Critical studies. ■Activity and theatricality of André Brassard's 1992 version of Samuel Beckett's *En attendant Godot* (Théâtre du Nouveau Monde) constrasted with immobility and atemporality of Beckett's 1988 version, produced for television by Walter Asmus (published by Vision Seuil).

1922 Bergeron, Annick. "Vladimir et Estragon: Entretien avec Normand Chouinard et Rémy Girard." (Vladimir and Estragon: Interview with Normand Chouinard and Rémy Girard.) *JCT.* 1992; 64: 36-40. Illus.: Photo. B&W. 2. Lang.: Fre.
Canada: Montreal, PQ. 1992. Histories-sources. ■The actors discuss playing Vladimir and Estragon in André Brassard's 1992 production of Samuel Beckett's *En attendant Godot* (Théâtre du Nouveau Monde), and the portrayal of the duo as burlesque actors.

1923 Bergeron, Annick. "Pozzo et Lucky: Entretien avec Jean-Louis Millette et Alexis Martin." (Pozzo and Lucky: Interview with Jean-Louis Millette and Alexis Martin.) *JCT.* 1992; 64: 41-45. Illus.: Photo. B&W. 3. Lang.: Fre.
Canada: Montreal, PQ. 1992. Histories-sources. ■Millette and Martin discuss their interpretations of Pozzo and Lucky in André Brassard's 1992 production of Samuel Beckett's *En attendant Godot* (Théâtre du Nouveau Monde), and the portrayal of the duo in classical and serious styles, respectively.

1924 Brassard, Marie. "Credo." *JCT.* 1989; 50: 110-111. Illus.: Photo. B&W. 1. Lang.: Fre.
Canada: Quebec, PQ. 1985-1989. Histories-sources. ■Marie Brassard, collaborator with Théâtre Repère, prioritizes physical transmission of emotions over intellectual communication of ideas.

1925 Caton, Jacolyn. "Urban Issues: Welcome to the Hood." *PAC.* 1996; 30(1): 6-8. Illus.: Photo. Poster. B&W. 3. Lang.: Eng.
Canada: Regina, SK. 1995-1996. Historical studies. ■Account of the community play *A North Side Story or Two* by Common Weal Productions, which explored contemporary social problems in the north central area of Regina.

1926 Côté, Lorraine. "Un métier fait de choix et de paradoxes: Réflexions d'une ex-Zorro." (A Profession Made of Choices and Paradoxes: Reflexions of an ex-Zorro.) *JCT.* 1989; 52: 132-138. Notes. Illus.: Photo. B&W. 3. Lang.: Fre.
Canada: Quebec, PQ. 1978-1989. Histories-sources. ■Actress Lorraine Côté traces the choices that formed her career.

1927 Coursen, H.R. "Two Productions of *Hamlet*: Stratford and Ashland." *SQ.* 1996 Spr; 47(1): 61-72. Notes. Lang.: Eng.
Canada: Stratford, ON. USA: Ashland, OR. 1994. Critical studies. ■Comparison of Richard Monette's production at the Stratford Festival and the Oregon Shakespeare Festival production directed by Henry Woronicz, focusing on their intimate approaches.

1928 Crête, Jacques. "*India Song.*" *JCT.* 1996; 80: 127. Illus.: Photo. B&W. 1. Lang.: Fre.
Canada: Montreal, PQ. 1979. Histories-sources. ■Jacques Crête's memory of staging Marguerite Duras' *India Song* in 1979 with his company, Théâtre de l'Eskabel.

DRAMA: —Performance / production

1929 Dickman, Marta. "Le triomphe de la beauté." (The Triumph of Beauty.) *JCT*. 1992; 64: 126-130. Notes. Illus.: Photo. B&W. 2. Lang.: Fre.
Canada: Montreal, PQ. 1981-1992. Critical studies. ■Visual signs and representations of beauty in Alice Ronfard's staging of Normand Chaurette's *Provincetown Playhouse, juillet 1919, j'avais 19 ans* (Espace GO, 1992).

1930 Drainville, Martin. "Être un comique naturel, une expérience tragique pour un comédien?" (Being a Natural Comedian, a Tragic Experience for an Actor?)*JCT*. 1990; 55: 91-92. Illus.: Photo. B&W. 1. Lang.: Fre.
Canada. 1970-1990. Histories-sources. ■Actor Martin Drainville's apprenticeship in comedy and its importance to his acting career.

1931 Drapeau, Sylvie. "Le 'Sentiment'." ('Feelings'.) *JCT*. 1989; 50: 112. Illus.: Photo. B&W. 1. Lang.: Fre.
Canada: Montreal, PQ. 1989. Histories-sources. ■Actress Sylvie Drapeau reflects on contemporary pertinence of advice on acting given by Louis Jouvet.

1932 Drapeau, Sylvie; Wickham, Philip. "Jeune Winnie." (Young Winnie.) *JCT*. 1992; 64: 84-85. Illus.: Photo. B&W. 1. Lang.: Fre.
Canada: Montreal, PQ. 1990. Histories-sources. ■Sylvie Drapeau describes playing Winnie in Samuel Beckett's *Happy Days* at age 28 at Espace GO in 1990, directed by Brigitte Haentjens.

1933 Ducharme, André. "Pas le choix d'être: Entretien avec Anne Dorval." (No Choice but to Be: Interview with Anne Dorval.) *JCT*. 1990; 57: 25-30. Illus.: Photo. B&W. 4. Lang.: Fre.
Canada: Montreal, PQ. 1990. Histories-sources. ■Anne Dorval's instinct-based acting technique, and her performances in Théâtre du Nouveau Monde's 1990 production of Molière's *L'École des femmes (The School for Wives)* directed by René Richard Cyr, and Quat'sous' 1990 production of *Les Lettres de la religieuse portugaise (The Letters from the Portuguese Nun)* directed by Denys Arcand.

1934 Faucher, Françoise. "Winnie, comme une soeur." (Winnie, Like a Sister.) *JCT*. 1992; 64: 81-83. Illus.: Photo. B&W. 1. Lang.: Fre.
Canada: Montreal, PQ. 1981. Histories-sources. ■Françoise Faucher's memories of playing Winnie in Samuel Beckett's *Happy Days* in 1981 at the Café de la Place, directed by Jean Faucher.

1935 Féral, Josette. "Arrêter le mental: Entretien avec Pol Pelletier." (Stopping the Mental: Interview with Pol Pelletier.) *JCT*. 1992; 65: 35-45. Notes. Illus.: Photo. B&W. 4. Lang.: Fre.
Canada: Montreal, PQ. 1992. Histories-sources. ■Pelletier's theoretical basis for her actor training methods, oriented towards suppression of mental activity and augmentation of physical energy.

1936 Gauthier, Manon. "Souvenirs de comédienne." (Memories of an Actress.) *JCT*. 1989; 53: 69-71. Notes. Illus.: Photo. B&W. 2. Lang.: Fre.
Canada: Montreal, PQ. 1980-1986. Histories-sources. ■Actress Manon Gauthier recalls production history of her one-woman stage adaptation of Michel Tremblay's novel *C't'à ton tour, Laura Cadieux (It's Your Turn, Laura Cadieux)*.

1937 Hébert, Ginette. "Entre l'arbre et la patère: le doigt de Brassard." (Between the Tree and the Coat Tree: The Hand of Brassard.) *JCT*. 1992; 64: 9-18. Notes. Biblio. Illus.: Photo. B&W. 5. Lang.: Fre.
Canada: Montreal, PQ. 1992. Critical studies. ■André Brassard's production of Beckett's *En attendant Godot (Waiting for Godot)* for Théâtre du Nouveau Monde, with emphasis on the realization of Brassard's vision through the scenography of Stéphane Roy, costume designer Luc J. Béland, lighting designer Michel Beaulieu and properties designer Lucie Thériault.

1938 Hunt, Nigel; Denis, Jean-Luc. "Oui, non, peut-être." (Yes, No, Maybe.) *JCT*. 1989; 50: 190-191. Illus.: Photo. B&W. 1. Lang.: Fre.
Canada. USA. UK-England. 1989. Critical studies. ■Trend among anglophone actors to employ realist style founded in philosophy of rationalism.

1939 Jubinville, Yves. "La véritable sainte Cadieux: Notes intempestives à propos d'une actrice en chair et en os." (The True Saint Cadieux: Impetuous Notes on a Flesh and Blood Actress.) *JCT*. 1996; 79: 25-30. Notes. Illus.: Photo. B&W. 3. Lang.: Fre.
Canada: Montreal, PQ. 1996. Critical studies. ■Significance of stage presence in Anne-Marie Cadieux's interpretation of the Marquise de Merteuil in Brigitte Haentjen's staging of Heiner Müller's *Quartett* (Espace GO, 1996).

1940 Lamont, Rosette C. "Why Theater? An International Conference in Toronto." *TheaterW*. 1996 Jan 1; 9(22): 30-33. Illus.: Photo. B&W. 1. Lang.: Eng.
Canada: Toronto, ON. 1996. Critical studies. ■International conference and theatre festival hosted at Toronto's University College, organizer Professor Pia Kleber. Focus on Berlin Schaubühne's production of *Hedda Gabler* directed by Andrea Breth.

1941 Lavoie, Pierre. "'L'espoir est une poire'." ('Hope is a pear'.) *JCT*. 1992; 65: 24-29. Notes. Illus.: Photo. B&W. 4. Lang.: Fre.
Canada: Montreal, PQ. 1975-1992. Critical studies. ■Pol Pelletier's one-woman show *Joie* (Théâtre d'Aujourd'hui, 1992, directed by Gisèle Sallin) seen in light of her past work and training.

1942 Lazaridès, Alexandre. "Vision carnavalesque et théâtre gai." (Carnivalesque Vision and Gay Theatre.) *JCT*. 1990; 54: 82-90. Notes. Illus.: Dwg. Photo. B&W. 6. Lang.: Fre.
Canada. 1970-1990. Critical studies. ■Gay theatre in Quebec as Bakhtinian carnival.

1943 Le Coz, André. "'En attendant Godot'/N.C.T. 1971." *JCT*. 1992; 64: 47-56. Illus.: Photo. B&W. 14. Lang.: Fre.
Canada: Montreal, PQ. 1971. Histories-sources. ■Fourteen archival photos from a 1971 production of Samuel Beckett's *En attendant Godot* directed by André Brassard at the Nouvelle Compagnie Théâtrale.

1944 Lépine, Stéphane. "Dans les remous de l'*Indiana*." (In the Backwash of the *Indiana*.) *JCT*. 1996; 78: 96-103. Notes. Illus.: Dwg. Photo. B&W. 3. Lang.: Fre.
Canada: Montreal, PQ. 1996. Histories-sources. ■Dramaturgical consultant Stéphane Lépine explores the difficulty of staging Normand Chaurette's plays, in a production journal for Denis Marleau's 1996 production of Chaurette's *Le Passage de l'Indiana*.

1945 Lévesque, Solange. "Mettre en scène sa blessure: Entretien avec René Richard Cyr." (Putting One's Wound on Stage: Interview with René Richard Cyr.) *JCT*. 1990; 57: 8-24. Illus.: Photo. B&W. 9. Lang.: Fre.
Canada: Montreal, PQ. 1980-1990. Histories-sources. ■René Richard Cyr discusses his directing career and his approach to staging Molière's *L'École des femmes (The School for Wives)* at the Théâtre du Nouveau Monde, 1990.

1946 Lévesque, Solange. "L'ironie comme leçon: Entretien avec Hélène Loiselle." (Irony as Lesson: Interview with Hélène Loiselle.) *JCT*. 1993; 67: 13-22. Illus.: Photo. B&W. 8. Lang.: Fre.
Canada: Montreal, PQ. 1950-1992. Histories-sources. ■Loiselle's start in acting in the 1950s compared to conservatory training, and the creation of Larry Tremblay's one-woman show *Leçon d'anatomie (Anatomy Lesson)*.

1947 Lévesque, Solange. "Cinq Shakespeare, cinq visions." (Five Shakespeares, Five Visions.) *JCT*. 1993; 67: 136-140. Notes. Illus.: Photo. B&W. 5. Lang.: Fre.
Canada: Montreal, PQ, Quebec, PQ. Romania: Craiova. 1993. Critical studies. ■Five productions of Shakespeare plays demonstrate openness (of text and of directors) to radical stagings: Guillermo de Andrea's *La Nuit des rois (Twelfth Night)* at the Rideau Vert, Silviu Purcarete's *Titus Andronicus* with the Craiova National Theatre and Robert Lepage's *Coriolan, Macbeth*, and *La Tempête (The Tempest)* with Théâtre Repère.

1948 Lévesque, Solange. "D'un lieu à un autre: 'Arlequin, serviteur de deux maîtres' du Théâtre de la Bibliothèque à la Nouvelle Compagnie Théâtrale." (From One Space to Another: *The Servant of Two Masters* from the Théâtre de la Bibliothèque to the Nouvelle Compagnie Théâtrale.) *JCT*. 1996; 79: 68-69. Illus.: Photo. B&W. 1. Lang.: Fre.

DRAMA: —Performance/production

Canada: Montreal, PQ. 1995-1996. Critical studies. ■Comparison of Enfants de Bacchus' staging of Goldoni's *Il servitore di due padroni*, (Serge Denoncourt, director), at Théâtre de la Bibliothèque, with its restaging at Nouvelle Compagnie Théâtrale.

1949 MacGeachy, Patricia; Wickham, Philip, transl. "Une bouche, trois fois." (A Mouth, Three Times.) *JCT.* 1992; 64: 88-89. Illus.: Photo. B&W. 2. Lang.: Fre.

Canada: Montreal, PQ. 1991-1992. Histories-sources. ■Author describes performing in three versions of *Not I* by Samuel Beckett: twice with director Andrès Hausmann and Imago theatre company, and once in Louise Bourque's film *Just Words*.

1950 Magny, Michèle. "Des mots..." (Words...)*JCT.* 1996; 80: 148-149. Illus.: Photo. B&W. 1. Lang.: Fre.

Canada: Montreal, PQ. 1976-1995. Histories-sources. ■Favorite lines delivered by actor Michèle Magny.

1951 Melançon, Benoît. "Jouer Marivaux demain?" (Playing Marivaux Tomorrow?)*JCT.* 1996; 80: 204-206. Notes. Illus.: Photo. B&W. 1. Lang.: Fre.

Canada. 1996. Critical studies. ■Examines difficulties of staging Marivaux in Quebec, and offers suggestions for directors on how to mount his works effectively.

1952 Montmorency, André. "Entre le boulevard et la ruelle." (Between the Boulevard and the Alley.) *JCT.* 1989; 50: 196-198. Illus.: Photo. B&W. 2. Lang.: Fre.

Canada: Montreal, PQ. 1976. Histories-sources. ■Actor André Montmorency questions subterfuges employed by actors by evaluating his interpretation of Sandra in Michel Tremblay's *Damnée Manon, sacrée Sandrá (Damned Manon, Cursed Sandra)* at Théâtre de Quat'sous.

1953 Panneton, Danièle. "Bouche en délire." (Mouth in Delight.) *JCT.* 1992; 64: 86-87. Illus.: Photo. B&W. 1. Lang.: Fre.

Canada: Montreal, PQ. 1990. Histories-sources. ■Author recalls performing Samuel Beckett's *Pas moi (Not I)* in Denis Marleau's montage *Cantate grise* (Théâtre UBU, 1990).

1954 Pavlovic, Diane. "L'Acteur fasciné: Entretien avec Yves Jacques." (The Fascinated Actor: Interview with Yves Jacques.) *JCT.* 1989; 50: 28-30. Illus.: Photo. B&W. 1. Lang.: Fre.

Canada: Montreal, PQ. 1989. Histories-sources. ■Actor Yves Jacques describes seduction involved in playing a woman in Michel-Marc Bouchard's *Les Feluettes (Lilies)*.

1955 Pelletier, Pol. "Réflexions autour de 'Joie'." (Reflections about 'Joie'.) *JCT.* 1992; 65: 30-34. Illus.: Photo. B&W. 2. Lang.: Fre.

Canada: Montreal, PQ. 1990-1992. Histories-sources. ■Title of performer-author Pelletier's *Joie* expresses her attitude towards theatrical creation as popular art necessary for life.

1956 Pontaut, Alain. "C'est quoi, ça, le 'théâtre d'été'?" (Just What Is 'Summer Stock'?)*JCT.* 1990; 55: 114-115. Illus.: Photo. B&W. 2. Lang.: Fre.

Canada. 1990. Critical studies. ■Difficulties of defining the supposedly homogeneous genre of Quebec's French-language 'summer stock'.

1957 Robitaille, Jack. "Odeur de théâtre." (Scent of Theatre.) *JCT.* 1996; 80: 115. Illus.: Photo. B&W. 1. Lang.: Fre.

Canada: Quebec, PQ. 1994. Histories-sources. ■Anecdote of Jack Robitaille's death scene as Palmiro in Luigi Pirandello's *Questa sera si recita a soggetto (Tonight We Improvise)* at Théâtre du Trident.

1958 Sabourin, Jean-Guy. "Et pourtant elle tourne." (And Nevertheless It Turns.) *JCT.* 1996; 80: 149-150. Illus.: Photo. B&W. 1. Lang.: Fre.

Canada: Montreal, PQ. 1980. Histories-sources. ■Director Jean-Guy Sabourin recalls his 1980 staging of Brecht's *Leben des Galilei (The Life of Galileo)* with his company, Théâtre de la Grande Réplique.

1959 Sadowska-Guillon, Irène. "De Michel Garneau à Normand Chaurette: L'Aventure québécoise de Gabriel Garran." (From Michel Garneau to Normand Chaurette: The Quebecois Adventure of Gabriel Garran.) *JCT.* 1991; 59: 114-117. Illus.: Photo. B&W. 2. Lang.: Fre.

Canada. France: Paris. 1975-1990. Biographical studies. ■Director Gabriel Garran's work directing Quebecois playwrights such as Michel Garneau and Normand Chaurette in France.

1960 Soldevila, Philippe. "De l'architecture au théâtre: Entretien avec Jacques Lessard." (From Architecture to Theatre: Interview with Jacques Lessard.) *JCT.* 1989; 52: 31-38. Illus.: Diagram. Photo. B&W. 8. Lang.: Fre.

Canada: Quebec, PQ. 1968-1989. Histories-sources. ■The founder and co-artistic director of Théâtre Repère describes his use of architectural ideas in staging.

1961 Steinberg, Lola. "'L'École des femmes'." ('The School for Wives'.) *JCT.* 1990; 57: 30-34. Notes. Illus.: Photo. B&W. 1. Lang.: Fre.

Canada: Montreal, PQ. 1990. Critical studies. ■Misogyny in Molière's *L'École des femmes (The School for Wives)* and its treatment by director René Richard Cyr in Théâtre du Nouveau Monde's 1990 production.

1962 Vaïs, Michel. "Les Lectures de l'archipel: Entretien avec Alexandre Hausvater." (The Archipel Readings: Interview with Alexandre Hausvater.) *JCT.* 1991; 58: 90-94. Illus.: Photo. B&W. 3. Lang.: Fre.

Canada: Montreal, PQ. 1990-1991. Histories-sources. ■Director Alexandre Hausvater on the importance of translating and producing international contemporary drama, and his foreign play-reading series with Productions de l'Archipel.

1963 Vaïs, Michel. "Le poids de la tradition: Entretien avec André Brassard." (The Weight of Tradition: Interview with André Brassard.) *JCT.* 1992; 64: 27-35. Illus.: Photo. B&W. 4. Lang.: Fre.

Canada: Montreal, PQ. 1992. Histories-sources. ■André Brassard's use of burlesque and work with actors in creation of his 1992 version of Samuel Beckett's *En attendant Godot* (Théâtre du Nouveau Monde).

1964 Vaïs, Michel. "Construire un personnage: Entretien avec Marc Béland." (Building a Character: Interview with Marc Béland.) *JCT.* 1993; 66: 76-86. Notes. Illus.: Photo. B&W. 6. Lang.: Fre.

Canada: Montreal, PQ. 1992-1993. Histories-sources. ■Actor Marc Béland explains his process in creating the title role of Albert Camus' *Caligula* at the Nouvelle Compagnie Théâtrale, directed by Brigitte Haentjens.

1965 Vaïs, Michel. "L'R des *Repentirs* ou Trois metteurs en scène mis à nu." (*Pentimento* or Three Directors Stripped Bare.) *JCT.* 1996; 81: 128-131. Notes. Illus.: Dwg. 3. Lang.: Fre.

Canada: Montreal, PQ. 1996. Historical studies. ■Description of a theatrical experiment at Théâtre de l'Opsis in which three directors publicly prepared scenes from Racine's *Phèdre*, working with actors in half-hour segments. The directors were Gervais Gaudreault, Serge Denoncourt, and Jean-Luc Bastien.

1966 Vigeant, Louise. "Rendez-vous à Duhamel." (Encounter at Duhamel.) *JCT.* 1991; 58: 100-103. Illus.: Photo. B&W. 2. Lang.: Fre.

Canada: Montreal, PQ. 1990. Critical studies. ■Themes and dramatic structure of Michel Tremblay's *La Maison suspendue (The House Among the Stars)* and their treatment in André Brassard's 1990 staging by Compagnie Jean-Duceppe.

1967 Vigeant, Louise. "Les 'lunettes québécoises': élément de réflexion sur la mise en scène." ('Quebecois Glasses': Elements of Reflection on Directing Practice.) *JCT.* 1996; 80: 14-19. Notes. Illus.: Photo. B&W. 3. Lang.: Fre.

Canada: Montreal, PQ. 1993-1996. Critical studies. ■Individualism and sexuality as traits of a Quebecois directing style reflecting Quebecois ideology, with examples Denis Marleau's version of Georg Büchner's *Woyzeck* (Théâtre UBU, 1994), Claude Poissant's versions of Marivaux's *Le Triomphe de l'amour* and *Le Prince travesti* and Lorraine Pintal's *Jeanne Dark*, adapted from Brecht's *Die heilige Johanna der Schlachthöfe (Saint Joan of the Stockyards)*.

1968 Villeneuve, Rodrigue. "'Provincetown Playhouse, juillet 1919, j'avais 19 ans': À la lettre." ('Provincetown Playhouse, 1919, I Was Nineteen Years Old: To the Letter.) *JCT.* 1992; 64: 123-125. Notes. Illus.: Photo. B&W. 1. Lang.: Fre.

DRAMA: —Performance/production

Canada: Montreal, PQ. 1981-1992. Critical studies. ■Strategies of illustration and presentation versus respect for textual complexity in Alice Ronfard's staging of Normand Chaurette's *Provincetown Playhouse, juillet 1919, j'avais 19 ans* (Espace GO, 1992).

1969 Vincelette, Michèle. "Chronologie fragmentaire des pièces de Samuel Beckett produites et présentées au Québec et à Ottawa." (Fragmented Chronology of Plays by Samuel Beckett Produced and Presented in Quebec and Ottawa.) *JCT.* 1992; 64: 90-94. Illus.: Dwg. Photo. B&W. 7. Lang.: Fre.

Canada: Ottawa, ON, Montreal, PQ, Quebec, PQ. 1956-1992. Historical studies. ■Chronology of Quebec and Ottawa productions of Samuel Beckett, listing year, title, company and artists involved.

1970 Vingoe, Mary. "This Is Not My Curriculum Vitae." *CTR.* 1996 Sum; 87: 19-21. Lang.: Eng.

Canada. 1985-1996. Histories-sources. ■Playwright and dramaturg Vingoe discusses her development as a dramaturg and the function of the dramaturg in Canadian theatre.

1971 Zana, Danielle. "Naviguer entre deux continents." (Navigating between Two Continents.) *JCT.* 1989; 50: 183-185. Notes. Illus.: Photo. B&W. 1. Lang.: Fre.

Canada. 1989. Histories-sources. ■Actress-director Danielle Zana describes freedom and constraints of contemporary actors faced with classical texts.

1972 "The 1994 Shanghai International Shakespeare Festival." *SQ.* 1996 Spr; 47(1): 72-80. Notes. Lang.: Eng.

China, People's Republic of: Shanghai. 1994. Historical studies. ■Report on the 1994 Shanghai International Shakespeare Festival.

1973 Shank, Theodore; Cheung, Fai, transl. "Mou Sen on *File 0.*" *TheatreF.* 1996 Win/Spr; 8: 7-10. Illus.: Photo. 1. Lang.: Eng.

China, People's Republic of: Beijing. 1995-1996. Histories-sources. ■Interview with Mou Sen, artistic director of theatre group Xi Ju Che Jian, on his recent production *File 0 (Ling Dang An).*

1974 Varley, Julia. "Gocce di rap. Conversazione con Patricia Ariza del Teatro 'La Candelaria'." (Drops of Rap: Conversation with Patricia Ariza of Candelaria Theatre.) *TeatroS.* 1996; 11(18): 359-382. Lang.: Ita.

Colombia. 1994. Histories-sources. ■Julia Varley of Odin Teatret interviews Patricia Ariza of Teatro La Candelaria.

1975 Birringer, Johannes. "La Melancolía De La Jaula (The Melancholy of the Cage)." *PerAJ.* 1996 Jan.; 18(1): 103-128. Notes. Illus.: Photo. B&W. 4. [Number 52.] Lang.: Eng.

Cuba. Mexico. 1994. Historical studies. ■The effect of Latin American and Latino/Chicano productions on contemporary art and performance, with emphasis on Mexican and Cuban performers.

1976 Císař, Jan. "Metalingvistická funkce nonverbalních složek v inscenacích Petra Lébla." (The Metalinguistic Function of Nonverbal Features in the Productions of Petr Lébl.) *Loutkář.* 1996; 5: 99-101. Illus.: Photo. B&W. 1. Lang.: Cze.

Czech Republic: Prague. 1996. Critical studies. ■Aspects of puppetry in Lébl's productions at Divadlo na Zábradlí.

1977 Hořínek, Zdeněk. "Milan Uhde od ironie ke katarzi." (Milan Uhde from Irony to Catharsis.) *Svet.* 1996; 7(2): 152-168. Illus.: Photo. B&W. 2. Lang.: Cze.

Czech Republic: Prague. 1996. Critical studies. ■The dramatic work of Milan Uhde, followed by an interview with the playwright.

1978 Král, Karel. "Rakve se šlehačkou—kde domov můj. Abeceda Vladimíra Morávka." (Coffins with Cream—Where Is My Home. The Basics of Vladimír Morávek.) *Svet.* 1996; 7(4): 85-91. Illus.: Photo. B&W. 1. Lang.: Cze.

Czech Republic: Prague. 1996. Histories-sources. ■The theatre work of young director Vladimír Morávek.

1979 Reslová, Marie. "Všechny mé historky jsou trapné." (All My Stories Are Painful.) *Svet.* 1996; 7(4): 74-84. Illus.: Photo. B&W. 6. Lang.: Cze.

Czech Republic: Prague. 1996. Histories-sources. ■Interview with director Vladimír Morávek, the creator of some controversial productions. The interview also turns to the director-actor relationship.

1980 Sloupová, Jitka. "Angličané v Čechách. Mimo hlavní proud—zatim?" (Englishmen in Bohemia: Outside the Mainstream.) *Svet.* 1996; 7(3): 68-73. Illus.: Photo. B&W. 3. Lang.: Cze.

Czech Republic: Prague. 1996. Critical studies. ■The staging of American and British plays on the stages of Czech theatres.

1981 Sebesta, Juraj. "The Stoka Group of Bratislava and the Slovak Theatre." *SEEP.* 1996 Win; 16(1): 28-35. Illus.: Photo. 3. Lang.: Eng.

Czechoslovakia. 1968-1989. Historical studies. ■The ideological style of social criticism in Slovak theatre from the Soviet Invasion to the Velvet Revolution, with emphasis on the work of STOKA, directed by Blaho Uhlár.

1982 Loney, Glenn. "One Week of Copenhagen's Culture Year." *WES.* 1996 Fall; 8(3): 73-76. Illus.: Photo. 1. Lang.: Eng.

Denmark: Copenhagen. 1996. Historical studies. ■Account of Teatret Cantabile 2's production of *Hamlet* directed by Nullo Facchini, staged in abandoned shipyards, and other theatre events.

1983 Loney, Glenn. "Copenhagen as Europe's 1996 Culture Capital." *WES.* 1996 Spr; 8(2): 59-62. Illus.: Photo. 2. Lang.: Eng.

Denmark: Copenhagen. 1996. Historical studies. ■Performing arts events planned for Copenhagen in 1996 including dance, opera, and theatre. Theatre events concentrate on Det Kongelige Teater as well as a myriad of activities in environmental spaces throughout Copenhagen.

1984 Møller, Søren Friis. "Tidens fuga." (The Flight of Time.) *TE.* 1996 Dec.; 81-82: 32-33. Illus.: Photo. B&W. 1. Lang.: Dan.

Denmark. Canada. 1996. Reviews of performances. ■Robert Lepage's visit to Denmark with two performances, *Hiroshima* and *Elsineur (Elsinore).*

1985 Scharbau, Puk. "En rejse i stemmens energifelt og Shakespeares." (A Journey into the Power of the Human Voice and Shakespeare's Universe.) *TE.* 1996 Sep.; 80: 16-17. Illus.: Photo. B&W. 1. Lang.: Dan.

Denmark. UK-England. 1996. Histories-sources. ■Actress describes working with voice teacher Nadine George in London, with reference to a workshop on voice and the Shakespearean text.

1986 Bassnett, Susan; Booth, Michael R.; Stokes, John. *Three Tragic Actresses: Siddons, Rachel, Ristori.* Cambridge/New York, NY: Cambridge UP; 1996. 210 pp. Notes. Index. Biblio. Illus.: Photo. 25. Lang.: Eng.

England. France. Italy. 1755-1906. Critical studies. ■The work of actresses Sarah Siddons, Rachel, and Adelaide Ristori.

1987 Gurr, Andrew. "The Date and Expected Venue of *Romeo and Juliet.*" *ShS.* 1996; 49: 15-25. Notes. Lang.: Eng.

England: London. 1592-1599. Historical studies. ■Attempts to date the first staging of *Romeo and Juliet* by identifying spaces like the Rose Theatre as venues capable of handling the demanding stage directions, i.e. balcony, trap door, etc.

1988 Jones, Nesta. "Towards a Study of the English Acting Tradition." *NTQ.* 1996; 12(45): 6-20. Notes. Lang.: Eng.

England. 1590-1995. Historical studies. ■Outlines history and technique of the English acting tradition, the influence of the challenge of new playwriting, playwrights' response to specific companies or the personalities of particular actors, and the signs and manners of class distinction.

1989 Kinservik, Matthew J. "*Love à la Mode* and Macklin's Return to the London Stage in 1759." *ThS.* 1996 Nov.; 37(2): 1-22. Notes. Biblio. Tables. Chart. 2. Lang.: Eng.

England: London. 1753-1759. Historical studies. ■Biographical essay on incident in the life of actor/playwright Charles Macklin. Author cites new evidence to account for Macklin's disappearance from the stage (1753-1758), as well as the success of his 1759 farce *Love à la Mode*, presented at Drury Lane.

1990 Montrose, Louis. *The Purpose of Playing: Shakespeare and the Cultural Politics of the Elizabethan Theatre.* Chicago, IL: Univ of Chicago P; 1996. 227 pp. Index. Notes. Lang.: Eng.

England. 1590-1620. Historical studies. ■Shakespeare and his company's relationship to political and cultural authorities, with an extended

DRAMA: —Performance/production

analysis of gender, ideology, social status, and theatricality in *A Midsummer Night's Dream.*

1991 Phillips, Louis. "The Dramatic Critic at Elsinore." *DGQ.* 1996 Sum; 33(2): 30-32. Lang.: Eng.
England. 1600-1601. Critical studies. ■Fictional review of *The Murder of Gonzago,* as if the critic were present at the performance wherein Hamlet caught the conscience of the King.

1992 Sheperd, Simon; Womack, Peter. *English Drama: A Cultural History.* Oxford/Cambridge, MA: Blackwell; 1996. 412 pp. Index. Append. Biblio. Lang.: Eng.
England. 1500-1994. Histories-specific. ■English drama as both theatre history and cultural history. Considers medieval, Renaissance, and Restoration theatre, melodrama of the nineteenth century, naturalism of late nineteenth century and early twentieth century, and the post-war era up to 1994.

1993 Styan, J.L. *The English Stage: A History of Drama and Performance.* Cambridge/New York, NY: Cambridge UP; 1996. 448 pp. Notes. Biblio. Index. Illus.: Photo. 20. Lang.: Eng.
England. 1300-1990. Histories-specific. ■English drama through its changes in style and convention. Author analyzes the key features of staging, including early street theatre and public performance, the evolution of the playhouse and the private space, and the pairing of theory and stagecraft in the works of modern dramatists. Four playwrights are discussed in detail—Marlowe, Shakespeare, Jonson, and Shaw.

1994 Sutton, R.B. "Further Evidence of David Garrick's Portrayal of Hamlet from the Diary of Georg Christoph Lichtenberg." *TN.* 1996; 50(1): 8-14. Notes. Lang.: Eng.
England. 1755. Historical studies. ■David Garrick's interpretation of Hamlet in Shakespeare's play, as seen from Lichtenberg's journal.

1995 Viator, Timothy J. "Vanbrugh's Aesop." *TN.* 1996; 50(3): 135-145. Notes. Lang.: Eng.
England. 1696-1759. Historical studies. ■Synopsis of the play and analysis of cast lists, with special reference to the performance of the vignettes.

1996 Jančék, S. "Stepen' 'russkocti'." (The Level of 'Russian Influence'.) *TeatZ.* 1996; 5: 26-28. Lang.: Rus.
Estonia: Tallinn. 1996. Histories-sources. ■Interview with Éduard Toman, artistic director of Russian Drama Theatre.

1997 Krečetova, R. "Koška v džunglach." (Cat in a Jungle.) *TeatZ.* 1996; 3: 19-23. Lang.: Rus.
Estonia. 1996. Histories-sources. ■Interview with director Mati Unt of Tallinn Drama Theatre.

1998 Bennett, Susan. *Performing Nostalgia: Shifting Shakespeare and the Contemporary Past.* London/New York, NY: Routledge; 1996. 199 pp. Index. Biblio. Notes. Lang.: Eng.
Europe. North America. 1985-1995. Critical studies. ■Study of recent Shakespeare performances, films, and videos within a theoretical framework based on an analysis of postmodern 'nostalgia'.

1999 Engle, Ron. *Maxwell Anderson on the European Stage 1929-1992: A Production History and Annotated Bibliography of Source Materials in Foreign Translation.* Monroe, NY: Library Research Associates Inc.; 1996. 430 pp. Index. Pref. Lang.: Eng.
Europe. 1929-1992. Bibliographical studies. ■List of American playwright Maxwell Anderson's plays in translation, as well as production. Also covers his works in libraries, archives, theatre collections, and museums all over Europe.

2000 Harrington, John P. "Resentment, Relevance, and the Production History of *The Playboy of the Western World.*" 1-9 in Gonzalez, Alexander G., ed. *Assessing the Achievement of J.M. Synge.* Westport, CT/London: Greenwood; 1996. 197 pp. (Contributions in Drama and Theatre Studies 73.) Biblio. Index. Pref. Lang.: Eng.
Europe. North America. 1907-1995. Historical studies. ■The continuing interest in Synge's play as illustrated by ongoing productions worldwide, and its unclassifiability as a nationalist or romantic play. Discusses the question of whether the play fulfills Synge's pessimistic vision or celebrates Irish fortitude.

2001 Lux, Joachim. "Spurensuche." (Search for Traces.) *TZ.* 1996; 5: 28-30. Illus.: Photo. B&W. 5. Lang.: Ger.

Europe. 1995. Histories-sources. ■Dramaturg describes his visits to drama schools in Moscow, Budapest, Milan, and London with director Karin Beier, in search of an international acting team for a production of *A Midsummer Night's Dream.*

2002 Shaheen, Yousef. "The Production of Meaning in Shakespeare with Reference to *The Merchant of Venice.*" *STP.* 1996 Dec.; 14: 34-47. Notes. Lang.: Eng.
Europe. 1740-1987. Critical studies. ■Interpretations of *The Merchant of Venice* are described to illustrate variations in the production of meaning by the same text: Jonathan Miller's 1970 production with its emphasis on class divisions, Komissarževskij's surreal designs for his 1932 production, portrayals of Shylock by Edmund Kean, Charles Macklin, and Henry Irving, and Antony Sher's realization of the role in Bill Alexander's 1987 production, which used a stereotyped portrayal of Shylock to challenge the prejudices of the audience.

2003 Wright, Elizabeth. "Psychoanalysis and the Theatrical: Analysing Performance." 175-190 in Campbell, Patrick, ed. *Analysing Performance: A Critical Reader.* Manchester/New York, NY: Manchester UP; 1996. 307 pp. Index. Notes. Biblio. Lang.: Eng.
Europe. 1990-1995. Critical studies. ■The relation of psychoanalysis to theatricality and representation, with reference to Heiner Müller's *Hamletmaschine.*

2004 Koski, Pirkko. "Esa Kirkkopelto and Tragedy in Finland." *WES.* 1996 Spr; 8(2): 35-38. Illus.: Photo. 2. Lang.: Eng.
Finland. 1995-1996. Historical studies. ■Up and coming young director/playwright Esa Kirkkopelto and his recent productions in Finland including his own *Yrjö Kallisen valaistuminen (Yrjö Kallinen's Illumination).*

2005 Vuori, Suna. "The Intuitive Directing of Finland's Laura Jäntti." *WES.* 1995-96 Win; 7(3): 111-113. Illus.: Photo. 2. Lang.: Eng.
Finland: Turku. 1995. Historical studies. ■Finnish director Laura Jäntti and her award-winning production of *Punahilkka (Red Riding Hood),* adapted by Jäntti from a novel by Märta Tikkanen, at the Turku City Theatre.

2006 "Grzegorzewski in France." *TP.* 1996 Apr.; 38(2): 23-27. Illus.: Photo. Color. B&W. 3. Lang.: Eng, Fre.
France: Paris. 1994-1995. Historical studies. ■Critical reception of Jerzy Grzegorzewski's production of Molière's *Dom Juan,* which was staged at the Comédie de Saint-Etienne in 1994, and in 1995 at the Théâtre Silvia Montfort.

2007 Added, Serge; Slaughter, Robin, transl. "Jacques Copeau and 'Popular Theatre' in Vichy France." 247-259 in Berghaus, Günter, ed. *Fascism and Theatre: Comparative Studies on the Aesthetics and Politics of Performance in Europe, 1925-1945.* Oxford: Berghahn Books; 1996. 315 pp. Notes. Index. Biblio. Illus.: Photo. 24. Lang.: Eng.
France: Paris. 1940-1945. Historical studies. ■Jacques Copeau, director of Théâtre du Vieux-Colombier: his relationship with the Vichy régime, his adjustment to social and cultural changes, and possible political influences on his work.

2008 Albert, Pál. "Rítus a rozsdatemetőben—Gabily utolsó munkája." (A Rite in the Scrapyard—Gabily's Last Work.) *Sz.* 1996; 29(11): 45-46. Illus.: Photo. B&W. 2. Lang.: Hun.
France: Gennevilliers. 1996. Critical studies. ■Introducing *Gibiers du Temps (Spoils of Time),* the last work of the late French director, Didier-Georges Gabily. A trilogy based on the theme of Phaedra and Hippolytos.

2009 Alonge, Roberto. "Molière sulle scene di Parigi." (Molière on Paris Stages.) *IlCast.* 1996; 9(25): 87-102. Notes. Illus.: Photo. B&W. Lang.: Ita.
France: Paris. 1995. Reviews of performances. ■Jacques Weber's performance in his own production of *Tartuffe,* Ariane Mnouchkine's interpretation of the same play with allusions to religious fundamentalism, and Simon Eine's production of *Le Misanthrope* at the Comédie-Française.

2010 Barranger, Milly S. "*Les Atrides*: Ariane Mnouchkine's Dance of Death." *TextPQ.* 1994 Jan.; 14(1): 77-85. Notes. Lang.: Eng.

DRAMA: —Performance/production

France: Paris. 1992. Critical studies. ■Examination of the production of *Les Atrides*, Théâtre du Soleil's adaptation of Aeschylus' *Oresteia* combined with Euripides' *Iphigéneia he en Aulíde (Iphigenia in Aulis)*, under the direction of Ariane Mnouchkine.

2011 Becker, Peter von. "Kleine Hamletmaschine." (The Little Hamletmachine.) *THeute*. 1996; 2: 49-53. Illus.: Photo. B&W. 4. Lang.: Ger.

France: Paris. 1996. Historical studies. ■Peter Brook's production *Qui est là (Who Is There?)*, based on Shakespeare's *Hamlet* and theories of Gordon Craig, Bertolt Brecht, V.E. Mejerchol'd, and Antonin Artaud, at Théâtre aux Bouffes du Nord.

2012 Bíró, Yvette; Orzóy, Ágnes. "A Grotesque Fugue." *PerAJ*. 1996 Jan.; 18(1): 57-63. Illus.: Photo. B&W. 2. [Number 52.] Lang.: Eng.

France. 1994. Critical studies. ■Examines production of *Une Femme Douce* adapted by Robert Wilson and Wolfgang Wiens from *The Possessed (Besy)* by Dostojévskij, directed by Wilson in Paris.

2013 Bradby, David. "Staying Alive: An Interview with Patrice Chéreau." *TheatreF*. 1996 Sum/Fall; 9: 12-18. Illus.: Photo. 5. Lang.: Eng.

France. 1996. Histories-sources. ■Director Patrice Chéreau talks about his experiences working with playwright Bernard-Marie Koltès, especially his *Dans la solitude des champs de coton (In the Solitude of the Cotton Fields)*, first performed at the Théâtre des Amandiers in Nanterre. Chéreau is now working on a new production of the play for the 1995 Edinburgh Festival.

2014 Carlson, Marvin. "Doubled Myths by Mesguich." *WES*. 1996 Fall; 8(3): 21-25. Illus.: Photo. 3. Lang.: Eng.

France: Lille. 1996. Historical studies. ■Two productions by Daniel Mesguich and his company La Métaphore. Molière's *Dom Juan* is Mesguich's first production of this play, but he stages Shakespeare's *Hamlet* often. Article examines common themes and images Mesguich uses in both plays.

2015 Cloutier, Raymond. "Living Circus." *JCT*. 1996; 80: 122-123. Illus.: Photo. B&W. 1. Lang.: Fre.

France: Grenoble. Canada: Montreal, PQ. 1968. Histories-sources. ■Impact of seeing Living Theatre's staging of Sophocles' *Antigone* (1968 European tour) on subsequent work of Raymond Cloutier with Grand Cirque Ordinaire.

2016 Costaz, Gilles. "UBU et la presse française." (UBU and the French Press.) *JCT*. 1996; 81: 68-70. Illus.: Poster. Photo. B&W. 2. Lang.: Fre.

France: Avignon. 1996. Historical studies. ■Critical reception of Denis Marleau's stagings of Normand Chaurette's *Le Passage de l'Indiana (The Crossing of the Indiana)* and Thomas Bernhard's *Maîtres anciens (Old Masters)* with Théâtre UBU at the Festival d'Avignon.

2017 Féral, Josette. "'On n'invente plus de théôries du jeu': Entretien avec Ariane Mnouchkine." ('We No Longer Invent New Theories of Acting': Interview with Ariane Mnouchkine.) *JCT*. 1989; 52: 7-14. Illus.: Photo. B&W. 3. Lang.: Fre.

France: Paris. 1988. Histories-sources. ■Director Ariane Mnouchkine's theories of acting, character creation and casting.

2018 Féral, Josette. "Un Stage au Soleil: Une Extraordinaire leçon de théâtre." (A Workshop at Soleil: An Extraordinary Lesson in Theatre.) *JCT*. 1989; 52: 15-22. Illus.: Photo. B&W. 4. [English version of same text appeared in *The Drama Review*.] Lang.: Fre.

France: Paris. 1988. Historical studies. ■Advice on acting given by Ariane Mnouchkine in week-long workshop.

2019 Féral, Josette. "Un Second regard: Entretien avec Sophie Moscoso." (A Second Look: Interview with Sophie Moscoso.) *JCT*. 1989; 52: 23-30. Notes. Illus.: Photo. B&W. 3. Lang.: Fre.

France: Paris. 1988. Histories-sources. ■Sophie Moscoso describes being member of Théâtre du Soleil and its principles of acting.

2020 Finter, Helga. "Der Körper und seine Doubles: Zur (De-) Konstruktion von Weiblichkeit auf der Bühne." (The Body and Its Doubles: The (De)construction of Femininity on Stage.) *FMT*. 1996; 1: 15-32. Notes. Lang.: Ger.

France: Paris. Switzerland: Lausanne. Germany: Berlin. 1990-1996. Critical studies. ■The complexity of concepts of gender onstage, using performances of *Orlando* by Virginia Woolf, directed by Robert Wilson with Isabelle Huppert (Lausanne, Paris) and with Jutta Lampe at Schaubühne (Berlin).

2021 Fredette, Nathalie. "Dix conseils à l'usage des comédiens, des comédiennes et des metteurs en scène." (Ten Recommendations for Actors, Actresses and Directors.) *JCT*. 1996; 80: 195-197. Illus.: Photo. B&W. 3. Lang.: Fre.

France. 1950-1996. Histories-sources. ■Staging and acting indications by Jean Genet, taken from his plays and letters, and the challenges of following them.

2022 Galipeau, Jacques. "Les feux de la rampe." (The Footlights.) *JCT*. 1996; 80: 121-122. Illus.: Photo. B&W. 1. Lang.: Fre.

France: Paris. 1971. Histories-sources. ■Anecdote of Jacques Galipeau playing Orgon in Jean-Louis Roux's staging of Molière's *Tartuffe* (Théâtre du Nouveau Monde, 1971 European tour).

2023 Garcia Martinez, Manuel. "Grüber Directs Genet's Splendid's." *WES*. 1996 Spr; 8(2): 9-10. Illus.: Photo. 1. Lang.: Eng.

France: Paris. 1995. Reviews of productions. ■Klaus Michael Grüber's production of Genet's *Splendid's* at the Odéon, part of the Autumn Festival. The German text was by Peter Handke.

2024 Garcia Martinez, Manuel. "Interview with Brigitte Jaques." *WES*. 1995-96 Win; 7(3): 17-21. Lang.: Eng.

France. 1995. Histories-sources. ■Interview with director Brigitte Jaques on her career in the theatre, on being a female director, and her love of Corneille as seen in one of her latest productions, *Suréna*.

2025 Garcia Martinez, Manuel. "Interview with Claudia Stavisky." *WES*. 1995-96 Win; 7(3): 23-24. Illus.: Photo. 1. Lang.: Eng.

France. 1995. Histories-sources. ■Interview with actress/director Claudia Stavisky on her theatrical career, especially her latest work, Edward Bond's *Mardi*.

2026 Garcia Martinez, Manuel. "Interview with Ewa Lewinson." *WES*. 1995-96 Win; 7(3): 31-34. Lang.: Eng.

France. 1995. Histories-sources. ■Interview with director Ewa Lewinson on her theatre career.

2027 Happé, Peter. "Staging *L'Omme Pecheur* and *The Castle of Perseverance*." *CompD*. 1996 Fall; 30(3): 377-394. Notes. Lang.: Eng.

France. England. 1400-1600. Historical studies. ■Comparative study of the staging of the French mystère *L'Omme Pecheur* and the English mystery play *The Castle of Perseverance*.

2028 Lahaye, Louise. "Du théâtre Québécois à Paris." (Quebec Theatre in Paris.) *JCT*. 1989; 51: 61-63. Notes. Illus.: Photo. B&W. 1. Lang.: Fre.

France: Paris. 1988. Critical studies. ■Impact of three Quebec productions on Parisian public: Michel Tremblay's *Albertine en cinq temps (Albertine in Five Times)* directed by André Brassard, and Groupe de la Veillée's *Les Cahiers de Malte*, an adaptation of Rainer Maria Rilke's *Notebooks of Malte Laurids Brigge (Die Aufzeichnungen des Malte Laurids Brigge)*, and of Dostojévskij's *Idiot*.

2029 Lamont, Rosette C. "Letter from Paris: 1995-1996." *WES*. 1996 Spr; 8(2): 11-16. Illus.: Photo. 1. Lang.: Eng.

France: Paris. 1995-1996. Historical studies. ■Theatrical life in Paris, including the influence of President François Mitterrand's love of theatre and his recent death. Plays covered include Robert Badinter's play about Oscar Wilde, *C.3.3.*, directed by Jorge Lavelli at the Théâtre National de la Colline, Wilde's *The Importance of Being Earnest*, directed by Jérôme Savary at the Théâtre National de Chaillot, Hans Peter Cloos's production of Shakespeare's *Romeo and Juliet* at the Théâtre du Rond-Point (formerly the Théâtre Renaud-Barrault), and Deborah Warner's production of Shakespeare's *Richard II* at the Bobigny, with Fiona Shaw in the lead role.

2030 Lamont, Rosette C. "Tartuffe and the Imams." *WES*. 1995-96 Win; 7(3): 13-16. Illus.: Photo. 1. Lang.: Eng.

France. 1995. Historical studies. ■Account of Ariane Mnouchkine's latest production, Molière's *Tartuffe*. The rigidly moralistic Muslim world

DRAMA: —Performance/production

of the Middle East is seen in the production in its costumes, sets and music.

2031 Lamont, Rosette, C. "Agathe Alexis' Self-Creation." *WES.* 1995-96 Win; 7(3): 25-30. Illus.: Photo. 3. Lang.: Eng.
France. 1995. Historical studies. ■The work of actress/director Agathe Alexis at Théâtre National de la Colline, with attention to the plays of Francisco Nieva.

2032 McGee, Caroline. "The Opening of the Fall Season in Paris." *WES.* 1996 Fall; 8(3): 33-36. Illus.: Photo. 3. Lang.: Eng.
France: Paris. 1996. Historical studies. ■Account of the fall 1996 theatrical season, focusing on the Festival d'Automne de Paris, including Peter Brook's production of Beckett's *Happy Days*, the Comédie-Française's *Tite et Bérénice* by Corneille, performed at the Théâtre du Vieux Colombier, directed by Patrick Guinaud. Also covers playwright/director Olivier Py's *La Servante—Histoire sans fin*, performed in a former factory outside Paris, and La Comédie-Italienne's *Le Jardin des amours enchantées*, adapted and directed by Attilio Maggiulli from Goldoni's *Il genio buono e il genio cattivo* at the Théâtre Rue de la Gaité.

2033 Scholck, Georges. "Paris—klassisch." (Paris—Classical.) *DB.* 1996; 2: 47-49. Illus.: Photo. B&W. 2. Lang.: Ger.
France: Paris. 1996. Reviews of performances. ■Productions: *Richard III* by William Shakespeare, directed by Matthias Langhoff at Théâtre Gérard-Philippe, *Phèdre* by Racine directed by Anne Delbée at Comédie-Française, *Qui est là? (Who Is There?)* directed by Peter Brook at Bouffes du Nord, based on Shakespeare's *Hamlet*, and *Le Prince travesti (The Prince in Disguise)* by Marivaux, directed by Brigitte Jaques at Aubervilliers.

2034 Schultz, Uwe. "Die Macht ein Traum—Ein Machtverlust die Travestie." (Power a Dream—Loss of Power a Travesty.) *THeute.* 1996; 5: 23-25. Illus.: Photo. B&W. 2. Lang.: Ger.
France: Paris. 1996. Reviews of performances. ■Guest appearances by Robert Lepage in *Hamlet Solo, Elsineur,* and *Roi Lear*, directed by Georges Lavaudant at the Odéon.

2035 Shevtsova, Maria. "Interview with Ariane Mnouchkine." *WES.* 1995-96 Win; 7(3): 5-12. Illus.: Photo. 4. Lang.: Eng.
France. 1995. Histories-sources. ■Interview with director/playwright Ariane Mnouchkine on her hunger strike and her commitment to theatre for citizens.

2036 Singleton, Brian. "Body Politic(s): the Actor as Mask in the Théâtre du Soleil's *Les Atrides* and *La Ville Parjure*." *MD.* 1996 Win; 39(4): 618-625. Notes. Lang.: Eng.
France. 1990-1995. Critical studies. ■Political dimensions of the actor's body in Hélène Cixous' *La Ville parjure (The Perjured City)* and *Les Atrides* as performed by Théâtre du Soleil under the direction of Ariane Mnouchkine. Use of masks and gesture, full-body masks, politics of Mnouchkine's interculturalism.

2037 Stuber, Andrea. "Párizsi randevú—Nádas Péter: *Találkozás*." (Rendezvous in Paris—Péter Nádas: *The Encounter*.) *Sz.* 1996; 29(8): 40. Lang.: Hun.
France: Paris. Hungary. 1979-1996. Reviews of performances. ■A report on the third performance of Péter Nádas' play (1979) in France from the first production staged in Avignon in 1990 through a radio adaptation to the present first night at Théâtre du Rond-Point in Paris, with a brief survey of the international stage career of the drama.

2038 Vigeant, Louise. "Le théâtre et le monde, effets d'étrangeté: Entretien avec Stéphane Braunschweig." (Theatre and the World, Alienation: Interview with Stéphane Braunschweig.) *JCT.* 1992; 65: 121-126. Notes. Illus.: Photo. B&W. 4. Lang.: Fre.
France. 1980-1992. Histories-sources. ■Influence of Antoine Vitez and Bertolt Brecht on directing style of Stéphane Braunschweig.

2039 Vinter, Marie. "Det uvirkelige teater." (The Unreal Theatre.) *TE.* 1996 June; 79: 24-27. Illus.: Photo. Photo. B&W. 2. Lang.: Dan.
France. 1964-1996. Critical studies. ■Analysis of the plays of Bernard-Marie Koltès as staged by Patrice Chéreau, with emphasis on *Dans la solitude des champs de coton (In the Solitude of the Cotton Fields)* and *Le Retour au désert (Return to the Desert)*. Includes a brief survey of Chéreau's career and description of his minimalist staging.

2040 Urušadze, P. "Robert Sturua. Do i vo vremja potopa." (Robert Sturua: Before and After the Flood.) *TeatZ.* 1996; 9: 33-34. Lang.: Rus.
Georgia. 1980-1996. Critical studies. ■Creative portrait of director Robert Sturua, with emphasis on his productions of Shakespearean plays.

2041 Becker, Peter von. "Die gläsernen Masken." (The Glassy Masks.) *THeute.* 1996; 11: 14-19. Illus.: Photo. B&W. 11. Lang.: Ger.
Germany: Düsseldorf. 1996. Critical studies. ■Reviews of plays produced at Düsseldorfer Schauspielhaus under the direction of Anna Badora: Wedekind's *Lulu*, Woody Allen's *Bullets Over Broadway* adapted for the stage by Jürgen Fischer, and Rolf-Dieter Brinkmann's *Der Film in Worten (The Film in Words)*.

2042 Becker, Peter von. "Die unerträgliche Schwere des Scheins." (The Unbearable Heaviness of Appearance.) *THeute.* 1996; YB: 56-58. Illus.: Photo. B&W. 1. Lang.: Ger.
Germany: Berlin. 1996. Critical studies. ■Analysis of Einar Schleef's Berliner Ensemble production of Brecht's *Herr Puntila* in the context of Schleef's aesthetics.

2043 Carlson, Marvin. "Report from the Ruhr." *WES.* 1996 Spr; 8(2): 77-80. Illus.: Photo. 4. Lang.: Eng.
Germany. 1995. Historical studies. ■Current theatre in the Ruhr valley region of Germany including the Düsseldorfer Schauspielhaus and director Karin Beier, the Kleineshaus, the Theater an der Kö, Deutsche Oper, the Tonhalle (all in Düsseldorf). Also covers productions at the Schauspielhaus in Bochum under Leander Haussmann, Mulheim's Theater an der Ruhr, the Grillo Theater in Essen, and the Schauspielhaus in Dortmund.

2044 Carlson, Marvin. "Andrea Breth's Hedda Gabler." *WES.* 1995-96 Win; 7(3): 59-62. Illus.: Photo. 3. Lang.: Eng.
Germany: Berlin. 1995. Historical studies. ■Andrea Breth's production of Ibsen's *Hedda Gabler* at the Schaubühne am Lehniner Platz.

2045 Carlson, Marvin. "Karin Beier's Midsummer Night's Dream and The Chairs." *WES.* 1995-96 Win; 7(3): 71-76. Illus.: Photo. 3. Lang.: Eng.
Germany: Düsseldorf. 1995. Histories-sources. ■Director Karin Beier's theatre career, especially her latest productions at the Schauspielhaus, *A Midsummer Night's Dream* and *Les Chaises (The Chairs)*.

2046 Clemens, Claus. "International und lang." (International and Long.) *SJW.* 1996; 132: 180-187. Illus.: Photo. B&W. 2. Lang.: Ger.
Germany. 1994-1995. Reviews of performances. ■Productions of Shakespeare's *Romeo and Juliet*, directed by Rahim Burhan at Roma Theater Pralipe, and *Hamlet*, directed by Frank-Patrick Steckel at Schauspielhaus Bochum.

2047 Eckert, Nora. "In Memoriam Ruth Berghaus." *TZ.* 1996; 2: 49. Illus.: Photo. B&W. 1. Lang.: Ger.
Germany. 1928-1996. Biographical studies. ■The director's life in and understanding of theatre.

2048 Engel, Thomas. "Cash Registers and Kangaroos: Konstanze Lauterbach." *WES.* 1995-96 Win; 7(3): 63-66. Illus.: Photo. 3. Lang.: Eng.
Germany: Klagenfurt. 1995. Historical studies. ■Director Konstanze Lauterbach's staging of Brecht's *Der aufhaltsame Aufstieg des Arturo Ui (The Resistible Rise of Arturo Ui)* for the Vienna Theatre Festival. Article focuses on the production's clear political stance and symbolistic, musically accentuated scenes.

2049 Espinosa, Norge; Sandoval López, Orestes; Thomas, Gerald; Ulive, Ugo. "Heiner Müller: In Memoriam." *Cjo.* 1996 Jan-June; 102: 90-98. Notes. Illus.: Photo. Sketches. 6. Lang.: Spa.
Germany. Latin America. 1929-1994. Historical studies. ■Tribute to deceased theatre artist Heiner Müller.

2050 Franke, Eckhard. "Himmelsmacht und Menschenhölle." (Heavenly Power and Human Hell.) *THeute.* 1996; 12: 38-41. Illus.: Photo. B&W. 6. Lang.: Ger.
Germany: Mülheim, Frankfurt am Main. 1996. Critical studies. ■Political themes in *Schlangenhaut (Snakeskin)* by Slobodan Šnajder, directed by Roberto Ciulli at Theater an der Ruhr and directed by Alexander Brill with amateurs at Schauspielhaus Frankfurt. The play deals

DRAMA: —Performance/production

with the mass rapes and crimes of the war in Bosnia, and the difficulty of directing and acting these themes.

2051 Franke, Eckhard. "Fortüne fünf vor zwölf." (Good Fortune at the Eleventh Hour.) *THeute.* 1996; 1: 24-27. Illus.: Photo. B&W. 5. Lang.: Ger.
Germany: Frankfurt am Main. 1995. Reviews of performances. ■Analysis of three performances at Frankfurter Schauspielhaus in view of budgetary cutbacks: Brecht's *Baal* directed by Anselm Weber, Thomas Bernhard's *Heldenplatz (Heroes' Square),* directed by Peter Eschberg, and Julien Green's *The Enemy (L'ennemi),* directed by Hans Falár.

2052 Franke, Eckhard. "Vorsicht Ferienzeit!" (Attention! Holiday Period.) *THeute.* 1996; 11: 36-38. Illus.: Photo. B&W. 2. Lang.: Ger.
Germany: Saarbrücken, Mainz. 1996. Reviews of performances. ■Productions of two new plays: *Touristen (Tourists)* by Elfriede Müller directed by Reinhard Göber, at Saarländisches Staatstheater (Saarbrücken) *Dollmatch* by Jens Roselt, directed by Matthias Merkle at Staatstheater Mainz Gmbh.

2053 Ginters, Laura. "Georg Büchner's *Dantons Tod*: History and Her Story on the Stage." *MD.* 1996 Win; 39(4): 650-667. Notes. Lang.: Eng.
Germany. 1902-1994. Critical studies. ■Development of the portrayal of female characters in stagings of Büchner's play. Considers productions directed by Alexander Lang and Rudolf Noelte in 1981 and by Klaus Michael Grüber, Frank-Patrick Steckel, and Ruth Berghaus in 1989-90.

2054 Hamburger, Maik. "Regisseure aus Israel und England in Thüringen." (Directors from Israel and England in Thüringen.) *SJW.* 1996; 132: 174-179. Illus.: Photo. B&W. 2. Lang.: Ger.
Germany: Weimar, Erfurt. 1994-1995. Reviews of performances. ■Visiting Shakespearean productions in Germany: *The Merchant of Venice* directed by Hanan Snir of Israel and *Titus Andronicus* directed by Robin Telfer of England.

2055 Höfele, Andreas. "Planschbecken und Drehtür." (Wading Pool and Revolving Door.) *SJW.* 1996; 132: 169-174. Illus.: Photo. B&W. 1. Lang.: Ger.
Germany: Munich, Mannheim. 1994-1995. Reviews of performances. ■Performances of Shakespeare's plays in southern Germany: *Twelfth Night* directed by Matthias Fontheim at Residenztheater, and *Macbeth* directed by Hans-Ulrich Becker at Nationaltheater.

2056 Hörnigk, Frank. "Germania 3 Gespenster am toten Mann." (Germania 3 Ghosts after His Death.) *TZ.* 1996; 4: 4-7. Illus.: Photo. B&W. 3. Lang.: Ger.
Germany: Berlin, Bochum. 1996. Critical studies. ■Comparison of two productions of Heiner Müller's *Germania 3*: directed by Leander Haussmann at Schauspielhaus Bochum and by Martin Wuttke at Berliner Ensemble.

2057 Hostetter, Elisabeth Schulz. "Creating a New Voice: An Interview with Oliver Reese." *WES.* 1996 Spr; 8(2): 87-94. Illus.: Photo. 1. Lang.: Eng.
Germany: Berlin. 1995. Histories-sources. ■Interview with German director Oliver Reese, at the Maxim Gorki Theater.

2058 Hütter, Martina; Koslowski, Alexander; Manthei, Fred; Susemihl, Birgit. "(B)rave New Shakespeare." *SJW.* 1996; 132: 187-195. Illus.: Photo. B&W. 2. Lang.: Ger.
Germany. 1994-1995. Reviews of performances. ■*The Merchant of Venice* directed by Peter Sellars as a guest performance at Thalia Theater, *The Jew of Malta* by Christopher Marlowe and *Nathan der Weise* by Gotthold Ephraim Lessing, directed by Anselm Weber at Deutsches Schauspielhaus, *Nathan/Hamlet-Essenz '94*, directed by Markus Lachmann at Junges Theater Göttingen, *As You Like It* directed by Thomas Krupka at Deutsches Theater, *A Midsummer Night's Dream* directed by Jens Schmidl at Schauspielhaus Hannover, *Pericles* and *Cymbeline* directed by Pit Holzwarth at Bremer Shakespeare Company, and *Othello* directed by Frank Hoffmann at Bremer Schauspielhaus.

2059 Jörcher, Gerhard. "Kasse und Klasse: Freiburg spielt Theater-Bundesliga." (Box Office and Class: Freiburg Produces First League Theatre.) *THeute.* 1996; 1: 27-29. Illus.: Photo. B&W. 2. Lang.: Ger.
Germany: Freiburg. 1995. Reviews of performances. ■The third year of Hans J. Amman's administration of Freiburger Theater and Amman's involvement in financial and political matters. Refers to productions of Maria Irene Fornes' *Mud*, directed by Karsten Schiffler, Brecht's *Im Dickicht der Städte (In the Jungle of Cities),* directed by Wolf Seesemann, and Goethe's *Torquato Tasso* directed by Christoph Biedermeier.

2060 Kahle, Ulrike. "Viel Wind unter den Flügeln." (A Lot of Wind under the Wings.) *THeute.* 1996; 12: 20-24. Illus.: Photo. B&W. 6. Lang.: Ger.
Germany: Hamburg. 1957-1996. Biographical studies. ■Portrait of Sven-Eric Bechtolf, actor and director at Thalia Theater.

2061 King, Marna. "Leipzig: A City and Its Theatre Intersect." *WES.* 1996 Fall; 8(3): 65-72. Illus.: Photo. 4. Lang.: Eng.
Germany: Leipzig. 1996. Historical studies. ■The work of Wolfgang Engel in his first year as artistic director of Schauspiel Leipzig, with reference to Peter Handke's *Die Stunde da wir nichts voneinander wussten (The Hour We Knew Nothing of Each Other)* directed by Engel, Heiner Müller's *Der Auftrag (The Mission)* directed by Konstanze Lauterbach, Georg Kaiser's *Von Morgens bis Mitternachts (From Morn to Midnight)* directed by Engel, and Wedekind's *Frühlings Erwachen (Spring Awakening)* directed by Johanna Schall.

2062 Kluncker, Heinz. "Ach wie gut, dass niemand weiss..." (How Great Nobody Knows.) *DB.* 1996; 7: 25-27. Illus.: Photo. B&W. 3. Lang.: Ger.
Germany: Bochum. 1996. Critical studies. ■Leander Haussmann's production of Heiner Müller's last play *Germania 3* performed at Bochumer Schauspielhaus.

2063 Kranz, Dieter. "Friedhof der Lüste." (Cemetery of Pleasures.) *THeute.* 1996; 4: 14-17. Illus.: Photo. B&W. 4. Lang.: Ger.
Germany: Hamburg, Leipzig. 1996. Reviews of performances. ■Two new interpretations of Kroetz' *Der Drang (The Crowd)* directed by Wilfried Minks at Deutsches Schauspielhaus in Hamburg and by Christine Emig-Könning at Schauspiel Leipzig.

2064 Kranz, Dieter. "Prinzessin Aschenputtel im Wiederstand." (Princess Cinderella in the Resistance.) *THeute.* 1996; 7: 22-25. Illus.: Photo. B&W. 2. Lang.: Ger.
Germany: Hamburg, Leipzig. 1996. Critical studies. ■Comparison of productions of Gombrowicz's *Iwona, Księzniczka Burgundia (Princess Yvonne)* directed by Karin Beier at Deutsches Schauspielhaus in Hamburg and by Andrea Moses at Schauspiel Leipzig, Theater an der Fabrik.

2065 Kranz, Dieter. "Evangelisches Oberammergau?" (Protestant Oberammergau?) *THeute.* 1996; 9: 35-36. Illus.: Photo. B&W. 2. Lang.: Ger.
Germany: Wittenberg, Magdeburg. 1996. Critical studies. ■Comparing performances about Martin Luther: *Luther Rufen (Calling Luther)* by Harald Müller, directed by Peter Ries at the Open-air theatre in Wittenberg, *Luther* written and directed by Wolf Bunge, dramaturg Hans-Peter Frings and Norbert Pohlmann at Freie Kammerspiele in Magdeburg.

2066 Krusche, Friedemann. "Schützenfest und Schlachtplatte." (Shooting Match and Sausage Plate.) *DB.* 1996; 5: 42-43. Illus.: Photo. B&W. 1. Lang.: Ger.
Germany: Magdeburg. 1993-1996. Historical studies. ■Playwright Stefan Schütz and his two-year cooperation with Freie Kammerspiele, resulting in a performance of *Schlachteplatte (Sausage Plate).*

2067 Lennartz, Knut. "Die Schlacht um Strauss." (The Battle over Strauss.) *DB.* 1996; 9: 14-16. Illus.: Photo. B&W. 1. Lang.: Ger.
Germany: Munich. 1996. Historical studies. ■The first performance of *Ithaka* by Botho Strauss at Münchner Kammerspiele, directed by Dieter Dorn, with attention to public discussion about the author's politics.

2068 Lennartz, Knut. "Ein Stück—vom wem?" (A Play—From Whom?) *DB.* 1996; 12: 30-32. Illus.: Photo. B&W. 3. Lang.: Ger.
Germany: Berlin. 1996. Critical studies. ■Comparison of the text of Carl Zuckmayer's *Der Teufels General (The Devil's General)* with its production at Volksbühne by Frank Castorf. Focuses on the question of authorship.

DRAMA: —Performance/production

2069 Linzer, Martin. "Der Auftrag—nicht mehr erfüllbar?" (Is The Mission No Longer Accomplishable?)*TZ*. 1996; 4: 8-11. Illus.: Photo. B&W. 4. Lang.: Ger.
Germany: Leipzig, Berlin. 1996. Critical studies. ▪Comparison of productions of *Der Auftrag (The Mission)* by Heiner Müller, directed by Konstanze Lauterbach at Schauspiel Leipzig and by Frank Castorf for Berliner Ensemble.

2070 Ljubimov, Jurij Petrovič; Sidorina, S., ed. "'Kak ja stavil Gamleta'." (How I Staged *Hamlet*.) *TeatZ*. 1996; 3: 31-37. Lang.: Rus.
Germany: Berlin. 1988. Histories-sources. ▪Ljubimov describes his work in Berlin. Continued in *TeatZ* 9 (1996), 17-19.

2071 Meech, Tony. "Shakespeare unser Zeitgenosse: a Note on the Bremer Shakespearetheater Production of *Die lustigen Weiber von Windsor* to Celebrate the Dedication of the Globe Building Site on Shakespeare's Birthday 1993." *STP*. 1993 June; 7: 54-57. Lang.: Eng.
Germany: Bremen. UK-England: London. 1993. Critical studies. ▪Argues that there are two great advantages to performing Shakespeare in translation: the director has much greater freedom and the actors need not be trained in the speaking of Elizabethan blank-verse. Reference to a production in German of *The Merry Wives of Windsor*, directed by Pit Holzwarth, to inaugurate the Globe building site in London.

2072 Merschmeier, Michael. "Ich—ist ein anderer." (I—Is Another.) *THeute*. 1996; 10: 4-13. Illus.: Photo. B&W. 10. Lang.: Ger.
Germany. 1996. Biographical studies. ▪Portrait of actor Udo Samel.

2073 Pfister, Eva. "Shakespeares Schwester." (Shakespeare's Sister.) *DB*. 1996; 1: 18-21. Illus.: Photo. B&W. 4. Lang.: Ger.
Germany: Düsseldorf. 1990-1996. Biographical studies. ▪Portrait of director Karin Beier, her working method, and her productions of both Shakespeare and contemporary authors.

2074 Pfister, Eva. "Neonazis, umkäkelt." (Neo-Nazis, Change your Tune.) *DB*. 1996; 6: 10-13. Append. Illus.: Photo. B&W. 4. Lang.: Ger.
Germany: Hamburg. 1996. Historical studies. ▪Thirza Bruncken's production of *Stecken, Stab und Stangl (Stick, Rod, and Pole)* by Elfriede Jelinek, with discussion of the two women's preferred aesthetic working methods of editing, collage, and quotation.

2075 Preusser, Gerhard. "Blitzstart Stillstand Traumtanz." (Lightning Start Standstill Dream Dance.) *THeute*. 1996; 11: 20-25 . Illus.: Photo. B&W. 3. Lang.: Ger.
Germany: Bonn. 1996. Reviews of performances. ▪Schauspielhaus Bonn's season: *Hamlet* by Shakespeare, directed by Andras Fricsay Kali Son, *Lector (The Reader)* by Ariel Dorfman, directed by Frank Hoffmann, *Doña Rosita la soltera (Doña Rosita Remains Single)* by García Lorca, directed by David Mouchtar-Samorai, *Teeth 'n' Smiles* by David Hare.

2076 Ruckmann, Friedrich. "Wanderer über viele Bühnen." (Traveler on Many Stages.) *TZ*. 1996; 2: 4-7. Illus.: Photo. B&W. 5. Lang.: Ger.
Germany: Berlin. 1996. Historical studies. ▪The commemoration of the late Heiner Müller at Berliner Ensemble, and an analysis of Müller's East German productions.

2077 Ruf, Wolfgang. "Der besessene Spieler." (The Player Obsessed.) *DB*. 1996; 7: 40-43. Illus.: Photo. B&W. 5. Lang.: Ger.
Germany. Austria. 1979-1996. Biographical studies. ▪Portrait of actor Martin Schwab, a quick-change artist.

2078 Ruf, Wolfgang. "Berliner Bilderbogen." (Illustrated Broadsheet from Berlin.) *DB*. 1996; 1: 10-11. Illus.: Photo. B&W. 3. Lang.: Ger.
Germany: Berlin. 1996. Histories-sources. ▪Impressions of the theatre of the capital city, and the tension between Eastern nostalgia and Western commercial theatre.

2079 Schumacher, Ernst. "Puntila." *DB*. 1996; 2: 44-46. Illus.: Photo. B&W. 4. Lang.: Ger.
Germany: Hamburg, Halle. 1996. Reviews of performances. ▪Comparison of productions of Brecht's *Herr Puntila* as directed by

Manfred Wekwerth at Neues Theatre, Schauspiel Halle, and by Frank Castorf at Deutsches Schauspielhaus.

2080 Shafer, Yvonne. "Report from Germany: Berlin, Trier, Munich." *WES*. 1996 Spr; 8(2): 67-76. Illus.: Photo. 3. Lang.: Eng.
Germany: Berlin, Trier, Munich. 1995. Historical studies. ▪Current theatre in Germany as seen in Berlin at the Deutsches Theater, in Trier, and in Munich at the Kammerspiele, the Residenztheater, the Munich Staatsoper, and the Staatstheater am Gärtnerplatz.

2081 Stephan, Erika. "Zweimal—Ein Spiegel der Zeit." (Twice: A Mirror of the Age.) *THeute*. 1996; 4: 20-21. Illus.: Photo. B&W. 2. Lang.: Ger.
Germany: Seifenberg, Gera. 1996. Reviews of performances. ▪Two productions of Čechov's *Ivanov*, one directed by Heinz Klevenow at Neue Bühne, the other directed by Michael Jurgons at Schauspiel Bühnen der Stadt Gera.

2082 Stryk, Lydia. "A Tale of Two Cities: Andrea Breth and Phyllida Lloyd." *WES*. 1995-96 Win; 7(3): 35-44. Lang.: Eng.
Germany: Berlin. UK-England: London. 1995. Histories-sources. ▪Interview with directors Andrea Breth of Berlin and Phyllida Lloyd of London.

2083 Wallis, Mick. "Feeling Structures: a Production Method for Schiller's *Mary Stuart*." *STP*. 1993 Dec.; 8: 36-62. Notes. Lang.: Eng.
Germany: Weimar. UK-England: Loughborough. 1800-1992. Histories-sources. ▪The author's own production of *Mary Stuart* at the University of Loughborough, exploring the 'structure of feeling' (Raymond Williams) by inviting his performers to develop adequate 'gestural codes' to elucidate the themes of the play.

2084 Walz, Ruth, photo. "[Untitled Photo Collage of Peter Stein's Work at Schaubühne]." *THeute*. 1996; 12: 7-9. Illus.: Photo. B&W. 26. Lang.: Ger.
Germany: Berlin. 1969-1996. Histories-sources. ▪Photographs of stagings by Peter Stein at Berliner Schaubühne by theatre photographer and documentarist Ruth Walz.

2085 Wesemann, Arnd. "Politisches Theater an den Grenzen der Medienkunst." (Political Theatre at the Boundary of Media Art.) *TZ*. 1996; 2: 46-48. Illus.: Photo. B&W. 3. Lang.: Ger.
Germany. 1996. Critical studies. ▪Political theatre productions of Hans-Werner Kroesinger, including *Stille Abteilung (Silent Section)* and *Adolf Eichmann—Questions and Answers*, described as non-didactic yet beyond 'fun' culture.

2086 Wille, Franz. "Sorins Gesetz." (Sorin's Law.) *THeute*. 1996; 2: 54-57. Illus.: Photo. B&W. 3. Lang.: Ger.
Germany: Berlin. 1996. Critical studies. ▪Andrea Breth's production of *Čajka (The Seagull)*, her first Čechov play, and its marketing at Berliner Schaubühne.

2087 Wille, Franz. "Der Untergangsdirigent." (The Conductor of Doom.) *THeute*. 1996; 4: 6-13. Illus.: Photo. B&W. 4. Lang.: Ger.
Germany: Berlin. 1996. Historical studies. ▪The aesthetics of Einar Schleef's much-criticized production of Brecht's *Herr Puntila* at Berliner Ensemble.

2088 Wille, Franz. "Scherz lass nach!" (Take it Easy with the Joke!) *THeute*. 1996; 10: 27-28. Illus.: Photo. B&W. 2. Lang.: Ger.
Germany: Berlin. 1996. Historical studies. ▪Comparison of stagings of plays by Heiner Müller: *Der Bau (The Construction Site)* directed by Thomas Heise and *Der Auftrag (The Mission)* directed by Frank Castorf at Berliner Ensemble and *Zement (Cement)* directed by Andreas Kriegenburg at Volksbühne.

2089 Wille, Franz. "Das Drama und Lebensfragen." (Drama and the Questions of Life.) *THeute*. 1996; 11: 28-34. Illus.: Photo. B&W. 7. Lang.: Ger.
Germany. Switzerland. Austria. 1996. Reviews of performances. ▪Covers performances of *Carleton* by Thomas Hürlimann, directed by Volker Hesse at Theater Neumarkt and directed by Hartmut Wickert at Niedersächsische Staatstheater Hannover Schauspiel, *Der Schatten eines Fluges (The Shadow of a Flight)* by Wolfgang Maria Bauer directed by Hans Gratzer at Burgtheater Vienna, *Der graue Engel (The Grey Angel)*

DRAMA: —Performance/production

by Moritz Rinke, directed by Anne-Marie Blanc at Schauspielhaus Zurich, *Der Zimmerspringbrunnen (The Room Fountain)* by Jens Sparschuh directed by Ulrich Anschütz at Maxim Gorki Theater, *Das zwischen den Augen ... den Schläfen (That Between the Eyes ... the Temples)* by Ulrich Zieger directed by Ernst M. Binder at Mecklenburgisches Staatstheater, Kammerbühne.

2090   Wille, Franz. "Hamburgische Dramaturgien, Konkurrenz der Giganten." (Hamburg's Dramaturgies: Competition of Giants.) *THeute.* 1996; 12: 10-19. Illus.: Photo. B&W. 9. Lang.: Ger.

Germany: Hamburg. 1996. Reviews of performances. ■Productions of the two leading theatres of Hamburg. *Kaspar* by Peter Handke, directed by Jossi Wieler, *Woyzeck* by Georg Büchner, directed by Franz Xaver Kroetz, and *As You Like It* by William Shakespeare, directed by Karin Beier, all at Deutsches Schauspielhaus, and *Antigone* by Sophocles, directed by Jürgen Flimm at Thalia Theater.

2091   Wirsing, Sibylle. "Das Ende der Geschichte." (The End of the Story.) *THeute.* 1996; 8: 34-37. Illus.: Photo. B&W. 4. Lang.: Ger.

Germany: Bochum, Berlin. 1996. Critical studies. ■Comparison of two productions of *Germania 3* by Heiner Müller, directed by Leander Haussmann at Bochumer Schauspielhaus shortly after the author's death, and by Martin Wuttke with the Berliner Ensemble.

2092   Taxidou, Olga. "Women and War: An Exercise in Intercultural Production." *STP.* 1993 June; 7: 34-46. Notes. Lang.: Eng.

Greece: Athens. UK-Scotland. 1993. Critical studies. ■Report on a collaboration between a group of women performers in Greece and John McGrath and John Bett to adapt Euripides' *Troádes (The Trojan Women)*, exploring the relationship between women and war.

2093   Albert, Pál. "Rondó az avignoni hídról—Nádas franciául." (Rondo About the Bridge of Avignon—Péter Nádas In French.) *Sz.* 1996; 29(8): 41-42. Lang.: Hun.

Hungary. France: Paris. 1996. Reviews of performances. ■Analysis of Pierre Tabard's production of Péter Nádas' *Találkozás (The Encounter)* at Théâtre du Rond-Point. Sound effects, which are integral to the play, were designed by László Vidovszky.

2094   Bérczes, László; Temesi, Zsolt, photo. "Túl a korlátokon—Beszélgetés Csiky Andrással." (Beyond the Bounds—An Interview with András Csiky.) *Sz.* 1996; 29(2): 32-35. Illus.: Photo. B&W. 4. Lang.: Hun.

Hungary. Romania: Cluj-Napoca. 1953-1996. Histories-sources. ■A conversation with the actor, one of the pillars of Hungarian theatre in Transylvania (Romania) on his 40-year career and teaching.

2095   Bérczes, László. "A másik könyv—Tompa Miklós (1910-1996)." (The Other Book—Miklós Tompa, 1910-1996.) *Sz.* 1996; 29(9): 1. Illus.: Photo. B&W. 1. Lang.: Hun.

Hungary. Romania. 1910-1996. Biographical studies. ■Commemorating one of the significant personalities of Hungarian ethnic minority theatre in Romania, director Miklós Tompa, founder of Székely Színház in Marosvásárhely/Tîrgu Mureş, deceased recently.

2096   Bérczes, László; Koncz, Zsuzsa, photo. "A dolgok rendje—Beszélgetés Cserhalmi Györggyel." (The Order of Things—An Interview with György Cserhalmi.) *Sz.* 1996; 29(11): 29-32. Illus.: Photo. B&W. 4. Lang.: Hun.

Hungary. 1957-1996. Histories-sources. ■A conversation with the actor on his life and career, and his work at Új Színház.

2097   Böhm, Edit. "Déryné naplója mint a biedermeier regény jellegzetes alkotása." (Déry's Diary as a Characteristic Piece of the 'Biedermeier' Novel.) *SzSz.* 1996; 30/31: 30-38. Notes. Lang.: Hun.

Hungary. 1869-1955. Critical studies. ■Study of the memoir of Róza Déry-Széppataki (1793-1872) as a literary work based on the editions of 1879, 1900, and 1955.

2098   Darvay Nagy, Adrienne; Koncz, Zsuzsa, photo. "Jókedvűen görgetni a követ—Szatmári beszélgetés Czintos Józseffel." ('Rolling the Stone' Merrily—An Interview with József Czintos at Szatmár/Satu-Mare.) *Sz.* 1996; 29 (1): 27-29. Illus.: Photo. B&W. 9. Lang.: Hun.

Hungary: Budapest. Romania: Satu-Mare. 1969-1995. Histories-sources. ■A talk to an actor of Hungarian theatre in Transylvania on the occasion of the 'joint venture' of Budapest Merlin Theatre and György Harag Company of Szatmár/Satu-Mare (Romania) presenting Harold Pinter's *The Caretaker* in Budapest.

2099   Dömötör, Adrienne; Koncz, Zsuzsa, photo. "Van egy hely, a színpad—Beszélgetés Kulka Jánossal." (There Is a Place: the Stage—An Interview with János Kulka.) *Sz.* 1996; 29(3): 31-34. Illus.: Photo. B&W. 4. Lang.: Hun.

Hungary. 1990-1996. Histories-sources. ■A conversation with actor János Kulka on his performances of the recent past.

2100   Dömötör, Adrienne; Koncz, Zsuzsa, photo. "Itt a helyem—Beszélgetés Bán Jánossal." (My Place Is Here—Interview with János Bán.) *Sz.* 1996; 29(7): 34-35. Illus.: Photo. B&W. 4. Lang.: Hun.

Hungary. 1986-1996. Histories-sources. ■A conversation with actor János Bán of Katona József Theatre on his career of the past ten years.

2101   Gábor, Miklós. "Naplót olvasva—Részletek egy készülő könyvből." (While Reading a Diary—Details from a Book Yet Unpublished.) *Sz.* 1996; 29(9): 8-10. Illus.: Dwg. B&W. 6. Lang.: Hun.

Hungary. 1954-1955. Histories-sources. ■Excerpt from the memoirs of actor Miklós Gábor, working title: *Naplót olvasva.*

2102   Gajdó, Tamás. "Egy Nyugat-matiné története. Balázs Béla: *A kékszakállú herceg vára.*" (History of a 'Nyugat'-Matinée, Béla Balázs: *Bluebeard's Castle.*) *SzSz.* 1996; 30/31: 196-200. Notes. Lang.: Hun.

Hungary: Budapest. 1910-1913. Historical studies. ■Balázs' mystery play as directed by Artúr Bárdos in a production sponsored by the literary revue *Nyugat.*

2103   Jákfalvi, Magdolna. "Ha mesél a színház." (Tales from the Theatre.) *Sz.* 1996; 29(5): 27-32. Illus.: Photo. B&W. 4. Lang.: Hun.

Hungary. 1961-1996. Critical studies. ■Analysis of dramaturgical problems in staging of Tankred Dorst's *Merlin* at Budapest New Theatre (Új Színház) directed by Iván Hargitai with survey of some monumental productions of world theatre from the 1960s based on epic and mythic works, especially trilogies of world drama.

2104   Koltai, Tamás. "Millecentenary Escapades." *HQ.* 1996 Fall; 37(143): 155-160. Lang.: Eng.

Hungary: Budapest. 1995-1996. Reviews of performances. ■Reflections of the 1100th anniversary of the Magyar Conquest and the centenary of the millennium (1896) on Budapest stages: Gergely Csiky's *A nagymama (The Grandmother)* dir István Iglódi, and the stage version of Menyhért Lengyel's filmscript To Be or Not To Be by Jürgen Hofmann, dir Géza Bodolay, both at Nemzeti Színház. Albert Szirmai's *Mágnás Miska (Magnate Mishka)* dir János Mohácsi, and Dezső Szomory's *Hermelin (Ermine)* dir Gábor Máté, both at Vígszínház. Ernő Szép's *Lila ákác (Lilac Acacias)* dir Árpád Árkosi, and György Spiró and János Másik's *Ahogy tesszük (As We Do It)* dir Erzsébet Gaál, both at Várszínház. Ferenc Molnár's *Nászinduló (Wedding March)* dir Lajos Balázsovits, Játékszín. Lajos Parti Nagy's *Mauzóleum (Mausoleum)* dir Gábor Máté, and Péter Halász's *Pillanatragasztó (Super Glue)*, dir by the author, both at Katona József Színház, Kamra.

2105   Koltai, Tamás. "Intellectual Impulses." *HQ.* 1996 Win; 37(144): 143-148. Lang.: Eng.

Hungary. 1995-1996. Reviews of performances. ■Six Budapest productions: József Katona's *Bánk bán* under the title *Bánk bán '96* dir József Ruszt, Budapesti Kamarszínház. *Dobardan (Good Day)* dir István Horvai, Vígszínház, and *Vircsaft (Hunky Business)*, dir Pál Mácsai, József Attila Színház, both by György Spiró. Shakespeare's *Measure for Measure* dir Gábor Máté, and Kaiser's *Der Mitmacher (The Follower)* dir Andor Lukáts, both at Katona József Színház. Dürrenmatt's *David und Goliath* dir Géza Bodolay, Nemzeti Színház.

2106   Kovács, Ferenc; Szalóky, Melinda, transl. *Olvasópróba előtt: Ibsen, H.: John Gabriel Borkman című drámájának színpadi elemzése.* (Before the Rehearsal: A Staging Plan of Ibsen's *Johan Gabriel Borkman.*) Budapest: Országos Színháztörténeti Múzeum és Intézet; 1996. 72 pp. (Skenotheke 1.) Illus.: Photo. B&W. 6. Lang.: Hun, Eng.

DRAMA: —Performance/production

Hungary: Budapest. 1898-1993. Critical studies. ■Analysis of the synopsis, characters, treatment, dramaturgy with the stage career of the drama in Hungary and list of translations.

2107   Magyar, Judit Katalin; Koncz, Zsuzsa, photo. "Csapatjátékos vagyok—Beszélgetés Mertz Tiborral.". (I Am a Team Player—An Interview with Tibor Mertz.) *Sz.* 1996; 29(12): 34-36. Illus.: Photo. B&W. 3. Lang.: Hun.
Hungary. 1985-1996. Histories-sources. ■A talk with actor Tibor Mertz on some interesting productions of the past seasons and his recent leading part in Milán Füst's *A lázadó (The Rebel)* presented at the Budapest Chamber Theatre directed by Csaba Tasnádi.

2108   Máriássy, Judit; Kürti, László. "Egykorú csörte—Vita Halász Péter drámájáról." (A One-Time Polemic—A Discussion on Péter Halász' Play.) *Sz.* 1996; 29(9): 11-15. Illus.: Photo. B&W. 4. Lang.: Hun.
Hungary. 1955. Reviews of performances. ■Quotation of three highly controversial reviews of *Vihar után (After the Tempest)* by Péter Halász as typical writings of the dogmatic criticism of the fifties.

2109   Nánay, István; Csomafáy, Ferenc, photo. "Más az értékrendem—Beszélgetés Orosz Lujzával." (My Scale of Values Is Different—An Interview with Lujza Orosz.) *Sz.* 1996; 29(5): 33-36. Illus.: Photo. B&W. 4. Lang.: Hun.
Hungary. Romania: Cluj-Napoca. 1926-1990. Histories-sources. ■A conversation with one of the leading actresses of post-war Hungarian theatre of Kolozsvár/Cluj-Napoca.

2110   Nyerges, András. "Félönarckép, retus nélkül—Gábor Miklós: Egy csinos zseni." (Unretouched Half Self-Portrait—Miklós Gábor: A Handsome Genius.) *Sz.* 1996; 29(9): 16-20. Illus.: Photo. B&W. 5. Lang.: Hun.
Hungary. 1954. Critical studies. ■Praises the actor's autobiography *Egy csinos zseni* (Budapest: Magvető, 1995).

2111   Páll, Árpád. "Shakespeare-drámák jelentésváltozásai." (Changes of Interpretations of Shakespeare's Plays.) 71-83 in Kántor, Lajos, ed. *Kolozsvár magyar színháza 1792-1992.* Kolozsvár (Cluj-Napoca): Kolozsvári Állami Magyar Színház; 1992. 141 pp. Notes. Lang.: Hun.
Hungary: Kolozsvár. Romania: Cluj-Napoca. 1794-1987. Historical studies. ■Summarizing the performances of Shakespeare's plays in the program of Hungarian theatre of Kolozsvár/Cluj-Napoca from the beginnings in 1794 to the end of the 1980s.

2112   Sándor, L. István; Ilovszky, Béla, photo. "Kettéhasadt előadások Beatrice Bleont zsámbéki rendezései." (Performances Split in Two—Beatrice Bleont Stagings at Zsámbék.) *Sz.* 1996; 29(11): 43-44. Illus.: Photo. B&W. 2. Lang.: Hun.
Hungary: Zsámbék. Romania. 1996. Reviews of performances. ■Romanian director Beatrice Bleont's staging of Bulgakov's *Master i Margarita (The Master and Margarita)* and *Antik tragédia (Antique Tragedy)*, based on Aeschylus' *Oresteia* and Euripides' *Troádes (The Trojan Women)*, using a mixed Hungarian and Romanian company in the ruins of the Roman church of Zsámbék.

2113   Bouvier, Hélène. "The Scenarist's Composition in a Madurese Popular Theatre." *TA.* 1995; 48: 84-96. Notes. Illus.: Photo. B&W. Lang.: Eng.
Indonesia: Madura. 1986-1995. Critical studies. ■A view of the modern *loddrok* troupes of Madura, their performance venues and the role of scenarist in development of their shows.

2114   Pauka, Kirstin. "A Flower of Martial Arts: The *Randai* Folk Theatre of the Minangkabau in West Sumatra." *ATJ.* 1996 Fall; 13(2): 167-191. Notes. Biblio. Illus.: Photo. Sketches. Graphs. Sketches. B&W. 15. Lang.: Eng.
Indonesia. 1891-1996. Historical studies. ■Form of West-Sumatran folk theatre *randai*: origins, troupe compositions, performance techniques. Relationship of the martial art *silek* to the dance and movement of *randai*.

2115   Barth, Diana. "The Steward of Christendom at Dublin's Gate." *WES.* 1996 Fall; 8(3): 83-84. Lang.: Eng.
Ireland: Dublin. 1996. Historical studies. ■Description of Max Stafford's successful production of *The Steward of Christendom* by Sebastian Barry at the Gate Theaatre, soon to tour the U.S. Includes discussion of the performance of Donal McCann.

2116   Barth, Diana. "Interview with Donal McCann." *WES.* 1996 Fall; 8(3): 85-90. Illus.: Photo. 1. Lang.: Eng.
Ireland: Dublin. 1996. Histories-sources. ■Interview with actor Donal McCann, currently appearing in Sebastian Barry's *The Steward of Christendom* at the Gate Theatre. Interview covers current production and past career.

2117   Barth, Diana. "Report from Dublin." *WES.* 1996 Fall; 8(3): 77-81. Illus.: Photo. 2. Lang.: Eng.
Ireland: Dublin. 1996. Historical studies. ■Recent theatre events in Dublin including *Portia Coughlan* by Marina Carr, directed by Garry Hynes at the Abbey's second stage, the Peacock, Pirandello's *Six Characters in Search of an Author (Sei personaggi in cerca d'autore)* on the main stage of the Abbey, directed by John Crowley, Tivoli Theatre's *The Woman in Black*, adapted by Stephen Mallatratt from a novel by Susan Hill, directed by Michael Scott, *Frugal Comforts* by Eamonn Kelly at the Andrews Lane Theatre, directed by David Quinn, and Alan Bennett's *A Chip in the Sugar*, at Oriental Café's 'lunch theatre,' directed by Bairbre Ni Chaoimh.

2118   Ben-Zvi, Linda. "Rina Yerushalmi." 373-382 in Ben-Zvi, Linda, ed. *Theater In Israel.* Ann Arbor, MI: Univ. of Michigan P; 1996. 450 pp. Lang.: Eng.
Israel. 1988-1993. Histories-sources. ■Interview with Rina Yerushalmi actor, director, choreographer on her work as director of *Hamlet* at the Itim Ensemble.

2119   Puzo, Madeline. "Who was Jud Süss?" *AmTh.* 1996 Dec.; 13(10): 16-18, 61. Illus.: Photo. Sketches. B&W. 6. Lang.: Eng.
Israel: Beersheba. 1931-1996. Critical studies. ■Collaboration of director Robert Woodruff, artistic director of Beersheba Municipal Theatre Gadi Roll, and actor Doron Tavory on Paul Kornfeld's play *Jud Süss (The Jew Suess)* about Josef Süss Oppenheimer. Historical background, structure, Woodruff's techniques in staging.

2120   Rosenberg, Tiina. "Uppenbarelsen i Tel Aviv." (The Apocalypse at Tel Aviv.) *Tningen.* 1996; 20(79): 17-19. Illus.: Photo. B&W. Lang.: Swe.
Israel: Tel Aviv. 1989. Historical studies. ■A report from Itim Theatre Ensemble and its project of staging Bible stories under the direction of Rina Yerushalmi.

2121   Shaked, Gershon. "Actors as Reflections of Their Generation: Cultural Interactions between Israeli Actors, Playwrights, Directors, and Theaters." 85-100 in Ben-Zvi, Linda, ed. *Theater In Israel.* Ann Arbor, MI: Univ. of Michigan P; 1996. 450 pp. Notes. Lang.: Eng.
Israel. 1996. Critical studies. ■Argues that stage actors embody the cultural and artistic norms of their society, and that their interaction with playwrights and directors create a semiotic system that can reveal the cultural character of the period. Applies this method to Israeli actors and cultural life.

2122   D'Aponte, Mimi Gisolfi. "Franca Rame, Woman of 20th-Century Theatre Par Excellence." *WES.* 1995-96 Win; 7(3): 81-82. Illus.: Photo. 1. Lang.: Eng.
Italy. 1995. Historical studies. ■Career of actress Franca Rame, and her recent performance of the diary of her deceased son. Directed by her husband, Dario Fo, it celebrated World AIDS Day.

2123   D'Aponte, Mimi Gisolfi. "Fusion in the Theatre of Graziella Martinoli." *WES.* 1995-96 Win; 7(3): 83-84. Lang.: Eng.
Italy: Genoa. 1995. Histories-sources. ■Interview with Graziella Martinoli, actress and director with the La Pinguicola Sulle Vigne theatre company.

2124   Féral, Josette. "Strehler le magicien." (Strehler the Magician.) *JCT.* 1991; 60: 7-16. Notes. Illus.: Photo. B&W. 2. Lang.: Fre.
Italy: Milan. 1947-1991. Historical studies. ■Historical influences on Giorgio Strehler and his approach to directing Eduardo De Filippo's *La Grande Magia (Grand Magic)*.

2125   Ferguson, Marcia L. "To America: Ronconi's Sturm und Drang at the Teatro Argentina." *WES.* 1996 Spr; 8(2): 5-8. Illus.: Photo. 1. Lang.: Eng.

DRAMA: —Performance/production

Italy: Rome. 1995. Reviews of productions. ■Luca Ronconi's production of Maximilian Klinger's *Sturm und Drang* (1776) at Teatro Argentina. Only the second production of this play in Italy in this century.

2126 Geraci, Stefano. "Il contrario del coraggio. Edoardo Ferravilla tra gli artisti, i ribelli e i teatri del suo tempo." (The Opposite of Courage: Edoardo Ferravilla Among the Artists, Rebels and Theatre of His Time.) *TeatroS*. 1996; 11(18): 305-331. Notes. Lang.: Ita.
Italy: Milan. 1846-1916. Biographical studies. ■Edoardo Ferravilla was a great actor of the Milanese dialect theatre. The tragicomic images of Ferravilla's characters result from the metamorphosis of the types of the mid-nineteenth century dialect theatre.

2127 Granatella, Laura. "A proposito del 'Sogno di un tramonto d'autunno' di D'Annunzio." (With Regard to 'Dream of an Autumn Sunset' by D'Annunzio.) *IlCast*. 1996; 9(25): 5-16. Notes. Lang.: Ita.
Italy: Rome. 1905. Historical studies. ■Mario Fumagalli's production at Teatro Costanzi, and contemporary indications that D'Annunzio's intentions for the play were not respected.

2128 Grande, Maurizio. "Schiavi e padroni nell'isola di Strehler." (Slaves and Masters in Strehler's Island.) *IlCast*. 1996; 9(25): 103-106. Notes. Biblio. Lang.: Ita.
Italy: Milan. 1995. Reviews of performances. ■Giorgio Strehler's Piccolo Teatro production of *L'Île des esclaves (Island of Slaves)* by Marivaux, originally written for the Comédie-Italienne.

2129 Kezich, Tullio. *De Lullo o il teatro empirico. Ricordando un maestro dello spettacolo italiano.* (De Lullo or Empirical Theatre: Remembering a Master of Italian Entertainment.) Venice: Marsilio; 1996. 177 pp. (Gli specchi dello spettacolo.) Filmography. Lang.: Ita.
Italy: Rome. 1921-1981. Biographies. ■The life and works of the Italian actor and director Giorgio De Lullo, including his career as an actor with directors Visconti and Strehler and his own productions with the Compagnia dei Giovani (The Young Company).

2130 Lapini, Lia. "Carlo Cecchi rappresenta Beckett: un incontro teatrale inevitabile." (Carlo Cecchi Performs Beckett: An Inevitable Theatrical Meeting.) *IlCast*. 1996; 9(25): 107-113. Notes. Illus.: Photo. B&W. Lang.: Ita.
Italy. 1996. Reviews of performances. ■Carlo Cecchi's production of Beckett's *Fin de partie (Endgame)*, with emphasis on his respect for the author's cues and stage directions.

2131 Patterson, Michael. "Reconstructing the Fragments: a Staging of Büchner's *Woyzeck* at Schloss Prösels in the South Tyrol." *STP*. 1994 June; 9: 16-21. Lang.: Eng.
Italy: Völs. Germany. 1837-1987. Histories-sources. ■The author's own site-specific production of *Woyzeck* with a group of German students in a medieval castle in the South Tyrol. By staging nearly all the scenes simultaneously in different parts of the castle, thus reinforcing the fragmentary nature of the original, the production not only explored the use of a non-theatrical venue but also attempted to 'generate a new aesthetic of theatre'.

2132 Zana, Danielle. "Giorgio Strehler, poète et serviteur de deux maîtres: le théâtre et la vie." (Giorgio Strehler, Poet and Servant of Two Masters: Theatre and Life.) *JCT*. 1991; 60: 17-21. Notes. Illus.: Photo. B&W. 2. Lang.: Fre.
Italy: Milan. 1947-1991. Biographical studies. ■Career of Giorgio Strehler, influences of other directors and his text-first approach to directing.

2133 Androvskaja, Ol'ga N.; Šingareva, E. "Japonskij dnevnik." (Japanese Diary.) *TeatZ*. 1996; 3: 38-44. Lang.: Rus.
Japan. 1958-1959. Histories-sources. ■The actress's notes on her tour of Asia with the Moscow Art Theatre.

2134 Sawada, Keiji. "The Japanese Version of the Floating World: A Cross-Cultural Event Between Japan and Australia." *ADS*. 1996 Apr.; 28: 3-19. Notes. Illus.: Photo. B&W. 1. Lang.: Eng.
Japan. Australia. 1995. Critical studies. ■Comparison of a Japanese production of Australian playwright John Romeril's *The Floating World* and an Australian production of Japanese playwright Chikao Tanaka's *Maria no kubi (The Head of Mary)* each performed in the playwright's native country, with an eye toward audience reception.

2135 Schmidhuber de la Mora, Guillermo. "Postmodernismo y teatro hispanoamericano: dos ensayos y una desiderata." (Postmodernism and Hispanic-American Theatre: Two Rehearsals and a Desideratum.) *Cjo*. 1996 Jan-June; 102: 15-20. Notes. Illus.: Photo. 4. Lang.: Spa.
Latin America. 1980-1996. Historical studies. ■Postmodernism as seen in recent performances in Latin America: *Historia de una bala de plata* by Enrique Buenaventura by Teatro Experimental in Cali, and others.

2136 Ljuga, A. "Ljubov' i smert' v Verone." (Love and Death in Verona.) *TeatZ*. 1996; 9: 40-41. Lang.: Rus.
Latvia: Vilnius. 1982. Historical studies. ■Eimuntas Nekrošius' production of *Ljubov' i smert' v Verone (Love and Death in Verona)*, an adaptation of Shakespeare's *Romeo and Juliet*, with Vilnius Youth Theatre.

2137 Lehmann, Barbara. "Ein System habe ich nicht." (I Have No Method.) *DB*. 1996; 8: 15-17. Illus.: Photo. B&W. 2. Lang.: Ger.
Lithuania. 1996. Histories-sources. ■Interview with director Eimuntas Nekrošius about his life, work, and political changes in his native Lithuania.

2138 Rojtman, Jurij. "Vid na zitel'stvo." (Certificate of Occupancy.) *TeatZ*. 1996; 5: 14-15. Lang.: Rus.
Lithuania: Vilnius. 1996. Critical studies. ■Russian theatre in Vilnius, with emphasis on Maksim Kuročkin's production of *Za nami—Nju-Jork! (Behind Us—New York)* by Maks Kurro.

2139 Ruprecht, Alvina. "Staging Aimé Césaire's *Une Tempête*: Anti-Colonial Theatre in the Counter-Culture Continuum." *ET*. 1996; 15(1): 59-68. Notes. Biblio. Lang.: Eng.
Martinique: Fort-de-France. 1992. Critical studies. ■Analysis of Elie Pennont's staging of *Une Tempête (A Tempest)* by Aimé Césaire at the Centre Dramatique Régional.

2140 Akerman, Anthony. "*The Road to Mecca* in Mexico." *SATJ*. 1995 Sep.; 9(2): 117-135. Illus.: Photo. B&W. 3. Lang.: Eng.
Mexico: Mexico City. 1995. Histories-sources. ■Diary kept by Akerman while directing the Mexican production of Athol Fugard's play.

2141 Duess, Bart. *Waarheid of doen? Handleiding voor intercultureel-theater met jongeren voorzien van regels, voorbeelden en foto's.* (Truth or Dare? Guideline for Intercultural Theatre for Youth, With Rules, Examples, and Photos.) Amsterdam: Stichting Artisjok/Nultwintig; 1996. 70 pp. Illus.: Photo. B&W. 36. Lang.: Dut.
Netherlands. 1994-1995. Instructional materials. ■The production methods of the theatre group Nultwintig, with emphasis on training and performing with young amateur actors.

2142 Hoff, Marlies. *Johanna Cornelia Ziesenis-Wattier (1762-1827): 'De grootste actrice van Europa'.* (Johanna Cornelia Ziesenis-Wattier, 1762-1827: 'The Greatest Actress of Europe'.) Leiden: Astraea; 1996. 185 pp. Notes. Biblio. Index. Illus.: Photo. B&W. 15. Lang.: Dut.
Netherlands. 1760-1830. Biographies. ■The life of the principal Dutch actress of her time.

2143 Berg, Thoralf. "Women Directors in Norway: Edith Roger and Catrine Telle." *WES*. 1995-96 Win; 7(3): 107-110. Illus.: Photo. 3. Lang.: Eng.
Norway: Oslo. 1995. Historical studies. ■Careers of two important female directors in Norway, Edith Roger at the Nationaltheatret, and Catrine Telle with the Nationaltheatret, the Norsk Dramatikfestival, Det Norske Teatret, and the Trondelag Teater.

2144 Muinzer, Louis. "Erasmus Montanus at the National Theatre, Oslo." *WES*. 1996 Fall; 8(3): 57-58. Lang.: Eng.
Norway: Oslo. 1996. Historical studies. ■The Norwegian National Theatre's production of Holberg's *Erasmus Montanus*, directed by Catrine Telle.

2145 "Bradecki on Topor." *TP*. 1996 Apr.; 38(2): 42-44. Illus.: Photo. Color. B&W. 3. Lang.: Eng, Fre.
Poland: Warsaw. 1996. Histories-sources. ■Interview with director Tadeusz Bradecki prior to the Polish premiere of Roland Topor's *L'Hiver sous la table (Winter Under the Table)* at Teatr Studio, regarding the difficulties of the project.

DRAMA: —Performance/production

2146 Baniewicz, Elżbieta; Dutkiewicz, Joanna, transl. "Theatre's Lean Years in Free Poland." *TJ.* 1996 Dec.; 48(4): 461-478. Notes. Biblio. Illus.: Photo. 5. Lang.: Eng.
Poland. 1989-1995. Historical studies. ▪Argues that democracy, instituted in 1989, has been destructive to Polish theatre. Analyzes recent productions including Andrzej Wajda's *Hamlet* (1989) and Rudolf Ziolo's *A Midsummer Night's Dream* (1992), both at the Stary Teatr.

2147 Baniewicz, Elżbieta. "*The Ambassador*—Years Later." *TP.* 1995 Oct.; 37(4): 25-30. Illus.: Photo. B&W. Color. 4. Lang.: Eng, Fre.
Poland: Warsaw. 1995. Reviews of performances. ▪Review of *Ambasador (The Ambassador)* by Sławomir Mrożek directed by Erwin Axer at the Teatr Współczesny.

2148 Bołtuć, Irena. "Theatre and Drama: Tradition Versus Opposition." *TP.* 1996 Oct.; 38(4): 24-27. Illus.: Photo. B&W. 2. Lang.: Eng, Fre.
Poland. 1901-1996. Historical studies. ▪Production history of Poland's principal Romantic drama *Dziady (Forefathers' Eve)* by Adam Mickiewicz. Among the directors who tackled the piece are Leon Schiller, Jerzy Grotowski, Kazimierz Dejmek, and Jerzy Grzegorzewski.

2149 Drewniak, Łukasz. "Nowy, parszywy świat." (Rotten New World.) *DialogW.* 1996; 8: 78-89. Lang.: Pol.
Poland: Cracow. 1994-1996. Critical studies. ▪Recent work of director Rudolf Ziolo.

2150 Dziewulska, Małgorzata. "The Heritage of Konrad Swinarksi." *TP.* 1995 July; 37(3): 3-7. Illus.: Photo. B&W. 3. Lang.: Eng, Fre.
Poland. 1929-1975. Biographical studies. ▪Career and philosophy of Polish director Konrad Swinarski.

2151 Dziewulska, Małgorzata. "In Unequal Battle with Myth." *TP.* 1995 Oct.; 37(4): 10-13. Illus.: Photo. B&W. 2. Lang.: Eng, Fre.
Poland: Poznań. 1994. Critical studies. ▪Analysis of Teatr Ósmego Dnia's production of *Tańcz, póki możesz (Dance as Long as You Can)*, a collectively developed piece.

2152 Fik, Marta. "Shakespeare in Poland, 1918-1989." *ThR.* 1996; 21(2): 147-156. Notes. Illus.: Photo. B&W. 8. Lang.: Eng.
Poland. 1918-1989. Historical studies. ▪Overview of significant or memorable productions of Shakespeare on twentieth-century Polish stage.

2153 Gruszczyński, Piotr. "New Productions: In the Polish Creche." *TP.* 1996 Jan.; 38(1): 32-37. Illus.: Dwg. B&W. Color. 6. Lang.: Eng, Fre.
Poland: Warsaw. 1995. Reviews of performances. ▪Review of the revival of Stanisław Wyspiański's play *Wesele (The Wedding)* directed by Krzysztof Nazar at the Teatr Powszechny.

2154 Gruszczyński, Piotr. "*The Misanthrope* is Right." *TP.* 1996 Apr.; 38(2): 32-35. Illus.: Photo. B&W. 3. Lang.: Eng, Fre.
Poland: Warsaw. 1995. Reviews of performances. ▪Review of Molière's *Le Misanthrope* directed by Ewa Bułhak at Teatr Studio.

2155 Gruszczyński, Piotr. "The Mystery and the Mundane." *TP.* 1995 July; 37(3): 27-33. Illus.: Photo. Color. B&W. 5. Lang.: Eng, Fre.
Poland: Warsaw. 1994. Reviews of performances. ▪Review of the sixteenth-century drama *Historia o chwalebnym Zmartwychwstaniu Pańskim (The History of the Lord's Glorious Resurrection)* by Mikołaj of Wilkowiecko, directed by Piotr Cieplak at Teatr Dramatyczny.

2156 Guczalska, Beata. "Investing in Art." *TP.* 1995 Oct.; 37(4): 3-9. Illus.: Photo. Color. B&W. 2. Lang.: Eng, Fre.
Poland. 1946-1995. Histories-sources. ▪Interview with stage, film and television actor Andrzej Seweryn, discussing his career.

2157 Hasselberg, Viola. "Auf der Suche nach postmodernen Mythen." (In Search of Post-Modern Myths.) *TZ.* 1996; 4: 48-50. Illus.: Photo. B&W. 5. Lang.: Ger.
Poland: Cracow. 1996. Historical studies. ▪Director Krystian Lupa of Stary Teatr and his work within the Polish theatre tradition.

2158 Kłossowicz, Jan. "Changing of the Guard." *TP.* 1996 Jan.; 38(1): 22-24. Illus.: Dwg. B&W. 2. Lang.: Eng, Fre.
Poland: Cracow. Belgium: Brussels. 1995. Historical studies. ▪Overview of events commemorating the fifth anniversary of the death of Tadeusz Kantor, beginning with an exhibition of memorobilia from past productions of Cricot 2 at the Maison du Spectacle in Brussels.

2159 Kłossowicz, Jan. "Hard to Say." *TP.* 1995 July; 37(3): 8-10. Illus.: Photo. B&W. 1. Lang.: Eng, Fre.
Poland. 1975-1995. Critical studies. ▪Reappraisal of the place of the late director Konrad Swinarski in the annals of late twentieth-century Polish theatre.

2160 Kłossowicz, Jan. "The Polish Theatre in the World." *TP.* 1995 Apr.; 37(2): 3-8. Illus.: Photo. Color. B&W. 4. Lang.: Eng, Fre.
Poland. 1995. Critical studies. ▪Reasons for the steady decline of the Polish theatre in the world's estimation.

2161 Kosicka, Jadwiga. "The Emergence of a New Genre in Polish Drama: Plays of Juvenile Crime." *SEEP.* 1996 Win; 16(1): 36-38 . Biblio. Lang.: Eng.
Poland. 1995. Historical studies. ▪The popularity of 'angry young people' on the contemporary Polish stage, including Osborne's *Look Back in Anger* (1956), and Hall and Waterhouse's *Billy Liar* (1960), and new Polish plays, such as *Mloda śmierć (Young Death)* by Grzegorz Nawrocki.

2162 Krakowska, Joanna. "Shakespeare's Paradoxical Victory: the 1990s." *ThR.* 1996; 21(2): 164-170. Notes. Illus.: Photo. B&W. 4. Lang.: Eng.
Poland. 1989-1996. Historical studies. ▪Overview of productions of Shakespeare in Poland, with reference to new translations by Stanisław Barańczak.

2163 Kristoffersson, Birgitta; Hanneberg, Peter. "Dramatiskt gästspel i Kraków." (A Dramatic Guest Visit at Cracow.) *Dramat.* 1996; 4(2): 46-47. Illus.: Photo. Color. Lang.: Swe.
Poland: Cracow. 1996. Critical studies. ▪A report from the Royal Dramatic Theatre's visit at Cracow with Ingmar Bergman's staging of Gombrowicz' *Iwona, Księzniczka Burgundia (Princess Yvonne)*.

2164 Krzyżan, Katarzyna. "Witkacy in Andrzej Dziuk's Theatre." *TP.* 1996 Jan.; 38(1): 25-31. Illus.: Dwg. B&W. Color. 4. Lang.: Eng, Fre.
Poland: Zakopane. 1984-1995. Historical studies. ▪Andrzej Dziuk's concepts for Witkiewicz's plays *Pragmatyści (The Pragmatists), Sonata b, Katzenjammer, Nowe Wyzwolenie (The New Deliverance), Matka (The Mother)*, and *OL 12-7 Steg, Wien (The Crazy Locomotive)* for the Teatr Witkacego.

2165 Kubikowski, Tomasz. "*Roberto Zucco* in Poznań." *TP.* 1996 Apr.; 38(2): 28-31. Illus.: Photo. B&W. 3. Lang.: Eng, Fre.
Poland: Poznań. 1995. Reviews of performances. ▪Review of *Roberto Zucco* by Bernard-Marie Koltès, directed by Krzysztof Warlikowski at Teatr Nowy.

2166 Kubikowski, Tomasz. "'Deck My National Stage...'." *TP.* 1995 July; 37(3): 34-39. Illus.: Photo. B&W. 3. Lang.: Eng, Fre.
Poland: Warsaw. 1995. Reviews of performances. ▪Review of *La Bohème*, a pastiche of texts and motifs by Stanisław Wyspiański, selected and directed by Jerzy Grzegorzewski at Teatr Studio.

2167 Kubikowski, Tomasz. "Each Goes His Own Way." *TP.* 1996 Oct.; 38(4): 28-34. Illus.: Photo. B&W. 5. Lang.: Eng, Fre.
Poland: Cracow. 1995. Reviews of performances. ▪Review of *Dziady—Dwanaście improwizacji (Forefathers' Eve—Twelve Improvisations)* adapted and directed by Jerzy Grzegorzewski, from Adam Mickiewicz's original *Dziady*, at Stary Teatr.

2168 Kubikowski, Tomasz. "Days of Yore, the Dream and Lovers." *TP.* 1995 Apr.; 37(2): 26-33. Illus.: Photo. Color. B&W. 8. Lang.: Eng, Fre.
Poland: Wrocław. 1994. Reviews of performances. ▪Review of Teatr Polski's production of Heinrich von Kleist's *Käthchen von Heilbronn*, translated by Jacek Buras, and directed by Jerzy Jarocki at the Swiebodzki Train Station.

2169 Niziołek, Grzegorz. "New Perspective." *TP.* 1995 Oct.; 37(4): 14-20. Illus.: Photo. Color. B&W. 3. Lang.: Eng, Fre.

DRAMA: —Performance/production

Poland: Cracow. 1995. Reviews of performances. ■Review of *Lunatycy (The Sleepwalkers)*, written and directed by Krystian Lupa, based on the work of Hermann Broch, at the Stary Teatr.

2170 Niziolek, Grzegorz. "Krystian Lupa: Teatr na granicy teatru." (Krystian Lupa: Theatre on the Verge of Theatre.) *DialogW*. 1996; 5-6: 205-222. Lang.: Pol.
Poland. 1943-1996. Critical studies. ■The work of director Krystian Lupa.

2171 Osterloff, Barbara. "A Showcase for Actresses." *TP*. 1996 Apr.; 38(2): 36-41. Illus.: Photo. Color. B&W. 5. Lang.: Eng, Fre.
Poland: Warsaw. 1995. Reviews of performances. ■Reviews of Eugène Ionesco's *Les Chaises (The Chairs)* directed by Maciej Prus at Teatr Polski, and *Happy Days* by Samuel Beckett, directed by Antoni Libera at Teatr Dramatyczny.

2172 Osterloff, Barbara. "*The Curse* and the Fundamental Questions." *TP*. 1995 Apr.; 37(2): 34-40. Illus.: Photo. B&W. 5. Lang.: Eng, Fre.
Poland: Warsaw. 1994. Reviews of performances. ■Review of *Klątwa (The Curse)* by Stanisław Wyspiański, adapted and directed by Piotr Tomaszuk at Towarzystwo Teatralne Wierszalin.

2173 Ouaknine, Serge. "Les Sorcières et le diable de l'an ... 2000." (Witches and the Devil and the Year ... 2000.) *JCT*. 1989; 50: 57-64. Illus.: Dwg. 20. Lang.: Fre.
Poland: Wroclaw. 1966. Historical studies. ■Annotation of twenty sketches recording improvisation on theme of 'witches' in preparation for Jerzy Grotowski's *Apocalypsis cum figuris*.

2174 Raczak, Lech. "Two Avant-Gardes." *TP*. 1995 July; 37(3): 22-26. Illus.: Photo. B&W. 1. Lang.: Eng, Fre.
Poland. 1970-1995. Critical studies. ■Examines divisions in the Polish avant-garde movement since the 1970s, with consideration of the definition of avant-garde.

2175 Rostworowski, Marek. "They Danced on the Bridge a Whole Century Through." *TP*. 1996 Jan.; 38(1): 10-17. Illus.: Photo. B&W. 4. Lang.: Eng, Fre.
Poland: Cracow. 1995. Historical studies. ■Essay by the curator of the exhibition of the theatre of Tadeusz Kantor held in Cracow, June-August 1995.

2176 Stafiej, Anna. "Authenticity is the Hope of Our Theatre." *TP*. 1995 Apr.; 37(2): 10-17. Illus.: Photo. Dwg. B&W. 2. Lang.: Eng, Fre.
Poland: Cracow. 1995. Histories-sources. ■Interview with actor, director and rector of the State Theatre Academy of Cracow, Jerzy Stuhr, on the future of drama in Poland.

2177 Walaszek, Joanna. "Konrad Swinarski's *Midsummer Night's Dream*." *ThR*. 1996; 21(2): 157-163. Notes. Illus.: Photo. B&W. 2. Lang.: Eng.
Poland: Cracow. 1970. Historical studies. ■Account of production of *A Midsummer Night's Dream* by Konrad Swinarski (Stary Teatr, 1970).

2178 Wanat, Andrej. "Sketches from Hermann Broch's *The Sleepwalkers*." *TP*. 1995 Oct.; 37(4): 20-24. Illus.: Photo. B&W. 4. Lang.: Eng, Fre.
Poland: Cracow. 1995. Critical studies. ■Analysis of Krystian Lupa's stage interpretation of Hermann Broch's *Lunatycy (The Sleepwalkers)* in social and political context.

2179 Wojtyszko, Maciej. "The Korczak Festival." *TP*. 1996 July; 38(3): 7-8. Illus.: Photo. B&W. 1. Lang.: Eng, Fre.
Poland: Warsaw. 1996. Critical studies. ■Ruminations on the appropriateness of a children's theatre festival being named after Janusz Korczak, writer of children's stories.

2180 Zielińska, Maryla; Rembowska, Aleksandra. "International Meetings." *TP*. 1995 Oct.; 37(4): 31-41. Illus.: Photo. B&W. Color. 8. Lang.: Eng, Fre.
Poland: Toruń, Radom, Poznań. 1995. Historical studies. ■Reports on the 1995 KONTAKT Festival in Toruń, the Second Gombrowicz Festival in Radom, and the Fifth Malta International Theatre Festival in Poznań.

2181 Kuligowska, Anna. "Józef Szajna's *Restos*." *TP*. 1995 Oct.; 37(4): 42-46. Illus.: Photo. Sketches. B&W. Color. 3. Lang.: Eng, Fre.
Portugal: Lisbon, Almada. 1995. Critical studies. ■World premiere of *Restos (The Remains)*, directed, designed and written by Szajna, performed at the International Theatre Festival at Almada. Szajna later spoke at conference addressing the difference between contemporary and Greek tragedy.

2182 Strianese, Maria. "Teatro e cinema: un esperimento a Madeira nel 1913." (Theatre and Cinema: An Experiment in Madeira in 1913.) *IlCast*. 1996; 9(25): 69-81. Notes. Lang.: Ita.
Portugal-Madeira: Funchal. 1913. Critical studies. ■João dos Reis Gomez's use of film to represent a battle scene in the production of his play *Guimor Texeira*, Teatro Municipal do Funchal.

2183 Jancsó, Adrienn. *Újra és újra: Életpályám.* (Again and Again: My Life.) Budapest: Nap; 1996. 365 pp. (Alarcok.) Illus.: Photo. B&W. 49. Lang.: Hun.
Romania. Hungary. 1921-1995. Histories-sources. ■Documents of a career compiled by actress Adrienn Jancsó, solo artist of the stage as elocutionist, on the occasion of her 75th birthday.

2184 Margitházi, Bela. "Északnyugaton a helyzet—Két szatmári bemutató." (The Situation in the North-West... Two Premieres at Satu-Mare.) *Sz*. 1996; 29(12): 21-23. Illus.: Photo. B&W. 4. Lang.: Hun.
Romania: Satu-Mare. 1995-1996. Reviews of performances. ■Schiller's *Kabale und liebe (Intrigue and Love)*, directed by István Kövesdi and Strindberg's *Dödsdansen (Dance of Death)* directed by Miklós Tóth.

2185 McKeown, Roberta. "Ionesco in Transylvania." *STP*. 1993 Dec.; 8: 76-79. Notes. Lang.: Eng.
Romania: Cluj. 1989-1993. Critical studies. ■The enthusiasm for and political resonances of Ionesco's work in post-Ceauşescu Romania, especially exemplified in productions of *La Leçon (The Lesson)* and of *La Cantatrice chauve (The Bald Soprano)* in Cluj.

2186 Akimov, Nikolaj P. "Čertik na pružine'." (Little Devil on a Spring.) *TeatZ*. 1996; 4: 20-23. Lang.: Rus.
Russia: St. Petersburg. 1920-1939. Histories-sources. ■Director describes his work with Andrej Lavrentjėv, senior director of the Bolšoj Drama Theatre.

2187 Alekseeva, E. "Teni vstrečajutsja tol'ko svetlye." (We Meet Only Bright Shadows.) *TeatZ*. 1996; 10: 21-23. Lang.: Rus.
Russia: St. Petersburg. 1996. Histories-sources. ■Interview with director Aleksand'r Galibin about his work at Aleksandrinskij Theatre (now Puškin Academic Drama Theatre).

2188 Amaspjurjanc, Abri. *Princessa Turandot—93.* Moscow: Folium; 1996. 148 pp. Lang.: Rus.
Russia: Moscow. 1993. Historical studies. ■Vachtangov Theatre's efforts to revive *Princessa Turandot* by Vachtangov, directed by Reuben Simonov.

2189 Ardašnikova, Ariadna. "'I budeta oba v plot' edinu'." (And Both Will Be One Flesh.) *TeatZ*. 1996; 2: 36-43. Lang.: Rus.
Russia: Moscow. 1990-1996. Histories-sources. ■Actress discusses her work in the Jérmolova Theatre, her views on the problems of contemporary dramaturgy and the meaning of the acting profession.

2190 Bagration-Muhraneli, Irina. "Mjusse i russkaja drama." (Musset and Russian Drama.) *SovD*. 1996; 3: 207-216. Lang.: Rus.
Russia: Moscow. 1995. Critical studies. ■Mark Vajl's production of *On ne badine pas avec l'amour (No Trifling With Love)* by Alfred de Musset, at the Mossovét Theatre.

2191 Bartoševič, A. "Ardenskij les v stalinskoj Rossii." (The Ardennes Forest in Stalin's Russia.) *TeatZ*. 1996; 9: 51-52. Lang.: Rus.
Russia. 1930-1939. Historical studies. ■Shakespeare's comedies in the Soviet theatre of the 1930s.

2192 Borovskij, D. "Desjat' dnej s Leonid Viktorovič Varpachovskij." (Ten Days with Leonid Viktorovič Varpachovskij.) *TeatZ*. 1996; 8: 53-55. Lang.: Rus.

DRAMA: —Performance / production

Russia: Moscow. 1908-1972. Histories-sources. ■Memoirs about the Jermolova Theatre director and producer.

2193   Cunskij, I. "Cel'igry—igra." (The Goal of the Game Is the Game Itself.) *SovD.* 1996; 1: 158-168. Lang.: Rus.

Russia: Moscow. 1996. Reviews of productions. ■The premiere of *Toibele i ee demon (Teibele and Her Demon)* by I.B. Singer and Eve Friedman, directed by Vjačeslav Dolgačev at the Čechov Moscow Art Theatre.

2194   Dmitrievskaja, M. "Den' sčast'ja." (A Day of Happiness.) *PTZ.* 1996; 9: 11-18. Lang.: Rus.

Russia: St. Petersburg. 1995. Historical studies. ■Aleksandrinskij Theatre's production of *Moj bednyj Marat (The Promise)* by Aleksej Arbuzov, directed by Anatolij Praudin.

2195   Dmitrievskaja, M. "Ljubov' i demonizm v processe voploščenija." (Love and Evil in a Process of Evolution.) *PTZ.* 1996; 9: 50-51. Lang.: Rus.

Russia. 1900-1996. Historical studies. ■The work of director Vladislav Pazi.

2196   Dürr, Carola. "Stanislawskis Enkel." (Stanislavskij's Grandchildren.) *DB.* 1996; 9: 40-43. Illus.: Photo. B&W. 5. Lang.: Ger.

Russia: Moscow. 1996. Critical studies. ■A new generation of directors seeking their own styles: Anatolij Leduchovskij, Sergej Ženovač, Aleksand'r Galibin, and Vladimir Mašckov.

2197   Eberth, Michael. "Das Wunder von Omsk." (The Miracle of Omsk.) *TZ.* 1996; 3: 68-72. Illus.: Photo. B&W. 4. Lang.: Ger.

Russia: Omsk. 1996. Histories-sources. ■A dramaturg reports his experiences in Omsk during a twelve-day cultural exchange with Omskij Akademičéskij Teat'r Dramy, directed by Vladimir Petrov.

2198   Freedman, John. "Big Names Keep Moscow Moving: The 1995-1996 Season." *SEEP.* 1996 Fall; 16(3): 19-30. Illus.: Photo. 5. Lang.: Eng.

Russia: Moscow. 1995-1996. Historical studies. ■Focus on Jurij Ljubimov at the Taganka, Roman Viktjuk at the Čechov Moscow Art Theatre and Konstantin Rajkin at Satirikon.

2199   Freedman, John. "The Second Anton Chekhov International Theatre Festival." *SEEP.* 1996 Fall; 16(3): 45-55. Notes. Illus.: Photo. 4. Lang.: Eng.

Russia. 1996. Historical studies. ■Includes *Uncle Vanya (Diadia Vania)*, directed by Peter Stern for Teatro di Parma and Teatro di Roma, *Three Sisters (Tri sestry)*, directed by Eimuntas Nekrošius, *Medea* by Euripides and Heiner Müller, dir by Theodoros Terzopoulos, co-produced by Theatre A (Moscow) and Attis Theatro (Athens), *The Seagull (Čajka)*, directed by Petr Lébl, for Divadlo na Zábradlí (Prague), and *Platonov*, directed by Anatolij Ivanov, by the Koltsov Drama Theatre (Teat'r Dramy im. A. Kol'cova) in Voronezh.

2200   Freedman, John. "Moscow Buoyed by Touring Companies." *SEEP.* 1996 Win; 16(1): 39-50. Notes. Illus.: Photo. 5. Lang.: Eng.

Russia: Moscow. 1995. Historical studies. ■Current theatre in Moscow centered on three festivals, the Baltic States Theatre Festival, the tour of St. Petersburg's Maly Drama Theatre, and the Theatrical Omsk Festival, all sponsored by the Theatre of Nations, a Russian production entity which arranges and conducts festivals throughout Russia, while supporting Russian projects abroad.

2201   Fridštejn, Ju. "Ženitba' v zazerkal'e." (*The Marriage* in a Surreal World.) *TeatZ.* 1996; 8: 33-35. Lang.: Rus.

Russia: Moscow. 1996. Critical studies. ■Sergej Arcybašev's production of Gogol's play at Teat'r na Pokrovke.

2202   Garon, L. "Ljubimyj obgryzannyj i karandaš, kuličiki iz peska i nemnogo mistiki." (Favorite Bitten Pencil, Sand Pretzels, and a Bit of Mystique.) *TeatZ.* 1996; 4: 9-10. Lang.: Rus.

Russia: Moscow. 1996. Historical studies. ■Vitalij Lanskoj, senior director of the Stanislavskij Theatre.

2203   Ginkas, Kama. "'Bezdny mračnoj na kraju...'." (On the Edge of the Dark Void.) *TeatZ.* 1996; 9: 42-45. Lang.: Rus.

Russia. 1970-1996. Histories-sources. ■Director reflects on the role of Shakespeare in his career.

2204   Gould, Bonnie. "Stanislavsky Meets Shepard at the Shchepkin." 43-57 in Oliva, Judy Lee, ed. *New Theatre Vistas: Modern Movements in International Theatre.* New York, NY/London: Garland; 1996. 219 pp. (Studies in Modern Drama 7.) Notes. Lang.: Eng.

Russia: Moscow. 1992. Histories-sources. ■Educational theatre exchange between Russia and the US. Author recounts her experiences directing Sam Shepard's *Curse of the Starving Class* at the Shchepkin Institute, the conservatory training program of the Maly Theatre in Moscow.

2205   Gribkova, N. "Jevgenij Knjazev." *MoskNab.* 1996; 5-6: 17-19. Lang.: Rus.

Russia: Moscow. 1990-1996. Historical studies. ■Actor Jevgenij Knjazev and his work at Vachtangov Theatre.

2206   Gvozdickij, V. "Proživaet ne zdes' i vernetsja ne sejčas." (Not Living Here, Will Not Return.) *MoskNab.* 1996; 3-4: 60-64. Lang.: Rus.

Russia: Moscow. 1980-1996. Biographical studies. ■Director Michajl Z. Levitin and his work at Teat'r Ermitaž.

2207   Injachin, A. "Zvezdy na pasmurnom nebe." (Stars in a Cloudy Sky.) *TeatZ.* 1996; 11-12: 6-8. Lang.: Rus.

Russia: Moscow. 1990-1996. Historical studies. ■Actors Elizaveta Nikiščichina, Vladimir Korenev, and Pětr Glebov of the Stanislavskij Theatre.

2208   Islantjeva, A.; Marinova, Ju.; Šejko, N. "Cjužet dlja bol'šogo romana." (Story Line for a Big Novel.) *TeatZ.* 1996; 2: 24-29. Lang.: Rus.

Russia. 1869-1956. Histories-sources. ■Memories of director Aleksand'r Sanin and his work in the Aleksandrinskij Theatre.

2209   Jakubova, N. "Pionerskaja propast' absurda: Novyj prizyv 'fomenok'." (A Pit of Absurdity for Pioneers: A New Version of Pětr Fomenko's Workshop.) *MoskNab.* 1996; 1-2: 32-35. Lang.: Rus.

Russia: Moscow. 1995. Critical studies. ■Artistic successes of the Masterskaja Petra Fomenko (Pětr Fomenko Workshop): Konstantin Vaginov's *Garpagoniana (Harpagoniana)* directed by Venjamin Sal'nikov.

2210   Kinkul'kina, N. "Borisov Oleg: Glava iz rukopisi 'Oleg Borisov'." (Borisov, Oleg: Chapter from his Manuscript *Oleg Borisov*.) *Avrora.* 1996; 9-10: 157-165. Lang.: Rus.

Russia: Moscow. 1929-1994. Biographical studies. ■Career path of actor Oleg I. Borisov.

2211   Kjuchel'garten, G. "Cheese!: 'Chlestakov' po 'Revizoru' N. V. Gogolja. Teat'r im. Stanislavskogo. Režisser V. Mirzoev." (Cheese! *Chlestakov*, based on Gogol's *The Inspector General*, Directed by Vladimir Mirzoev at Stanislavskij Drama Theatre.) *MoskNab.* 1996; 3-4: 39-43. Lang.: Rus.

Russia: Moscow. 1995. Critical studies. ■Analysis of Mirzoev's production.

2212   Kolesova, N. "'Nyet, ja ne German, ja—drugoj...'." (No, I Am Not German, I Am—Someone Else.) *TeatZ.* 1996; 1: 5-7. Lang.: Rus.

Russia: Moscow. 1995. Histories-sources. ■Interview with Mark Zacharov, senior director of the 'Lenkom' theatre.

2213   Kolosova, G. "Metamorfozy šekspirovskogo prostranstva." (Metamorphoses of Shakespearean Art.) *TeatZ.* 1996; 6: 46-47 . Lang.: Rus.

Russia: Rostov-na-Donu. 1990-1996. Histories-sources. ■Interview with scholar Aleksej Bartoševič about Vladimir Čigiėv's production of *Hamlet* with the young people's theatre of Rostov.

2214   Kovalevskij, V.M. *Ot zamysla—k voploščeniju: Učebnoe posobie.* (From an Idea to Reality: Study Guide.) St. Petersburg: Sankt-Peterburgskij Gosudarstvénnyj akademija kultur; 1996. 86 pp. Lang.: Rus.

Russia. 1990-1996. Critical studies. ■Modern problems in theatre, including the underlying meaning of a play, its atmosphere, and the actor-director relationship.

2215   Kravcov, A. "Meždu grustnym i smešnym." (Between Sad and Funny.) *Smena.* 1996; 10: 106-113. Lang.: Rus.

DRAMA: —Performance/production

Russia: Moscow. 1896-1984. Biographical studies. ■Creative methods and acting style of actress Faina Ranevskaja, with a few episodes from her life.

2216   Krymova, N. "V svoem krugu." (In My Own Circle.) *TeatZ.* 1996; 6: 3-5. Lang.: Rus.

Russia: Moscow. 1990-1996. Historical studies. ■Pëtr Fomenko's production of Ostrovskij's *Bez viny vinovatjë (Guilty Though Innocent).*

2217   L'vov-Anochin, Boris. "Tragičéskie aforizmy Serafimy Birman." (Tragic Aphorisms of Serafima Birman.) *TeatZ.* 1996; 5: 30-33. Lang.: Rus.

Russia. 1890-1976. Biographical studies. ■Director discusses the career of the actress with the Komsomol Theatre and others.

2218   Lebedina, L. "Propadi vse propadom—ja leču na Lunu!" (To Hell with Everything, I'm Going to the Moon.) *TeatZ.* 1996; 1: 46-49. Lang.: Rus.

Russia: Moscow. 1996. Histories-sources. ■Interview with director Mark Rozovskij.

2219   Levinskaja, E. "Ljubov' k iskusstvu i kotletam." (Love for Art and Beef Patties.) *TeatZ.* 1996; 2: 6-7. Lang.: Rus.

Russia: Moscow. 1990-1996. Critical studies. ■The contemporary relevance of the plays of Shakespeare, with reference to productions of the Vachtangov Theatre, Čechov Theatre (Moscow Art Theatre), and others.

2220   Levinskaja, E. "Kto sumasšedšij? 'Maskarad' v Chudožestvennom teatre imeni Čechova." (Who Is Crazy? *Masquerade* at the Čechov Art Theatre.) *MoskNab.* 1996; 1-2: 36-38. Lang.: Rus.

Russia: Moscow. 1990-1996. Critical studies. ■Lermontov's *Maskarad (Masquerade)* directed by Nikolaj Šejko at Chudožestvénnyj Teat'r im. A.P. Čechova.

2221   Lyndina, E. "Čest' i dostoinstvo." (Pride and Honor.) *Ekran.* 1996; 2: 40-43. Lang.: Rus.

Russia: Moscow. 1940-1996. Biographical studies. ■Scenarist and actor Vladimir M. Zel'din, with emphasis on his successes in Moscow Theatre of Transport in the 1940s.

2222   Maksimova, V. "Simbol very: (Vachtangov i krasota)." (Symbol of Faith: Vachtangov and Beauty.) *TeatZ.* 1996; 6: 16-17. Lang.: Rus.

Russia: Moscow. 1883-1922. Historical studies. ■The directorial work of Jėvgenij Vachtangov: beauty as method.

2223   Maksimova, V. "Pochval'noe slovo konservatizmu: Malyj teat'r i ego aktery." (In Praise of Conservatism: Malyj Theatre and Its Actors.) *MoskNab.* 1996; 1-2: 47-57. Lang.: Rus.

Russia: Moscow. 1980-1996. Historical studies. ■On actors of the Malyj Theatre: Jurij Solomin, Aleksand'r Michajlov, Nelli Kornienko, Jevgenija Glušenko, Viktor Koršunov.

2224   Maksimova, V. "Ritmy tragedii: Ol'ga Jakovleva v spektakle 'Poslednije'." (Tragic Rhythms: Ol'ga Jakovleva in *The Last Ones.*) *MoskNab.* 1996; 3-4: 56-57. Lang.: Rus.

Russia: Moscow. 1995. Historical studies. ■Adol'f Šapiro's production of *Poslednije* by Maksim Gorkij for the theatre of Oleg Tabakov, with reference to actress Ol'ga Jakovleva.

2225   Marčenko, T. "Pamjati Grigorija Gaja." (In Memory of Grigorij Gaj.) *PTZ.* 1996; 9: 97-100. Lang.: Rus.

Russia: St. Petersburg. 1949-1995. Biographical studies. ■The life of actor Grigorij Gaj, including his best roles and details on his work.

2226   Mašukova, E. "O čem stoit igrat': 'Torikos' iz Gelendžika." (What Is Worth Playing: 'Torikos' from Gelendzik.) *MoskNab.* 1996; 1-2: 77-79. Lang.: Rus.

Russia. 1995. Historical studies. ■The Moscow tour of Torikos Drama Theatre, Anatolij Sljusarenko, artistic director.

2227   Michaleva, A. "Po obe storony okeana." (On Both Sides of the Ocean.) *SovD.* 1996; 1: 194-199. Lang.: Rus.

Russia: Moscow. 1994-1995. Histories-sources. ■Interview with director Vladimir Mirzoev about his 1994 production of Gogol's *Ženitba (The Marriage)* at the Stanislavskij Theatre.

2228   Mišarin, A. "Tajna javnogo." (Secret of the Obvious.) *NovRos.* 1996; 1: 98-101. Lang.: Rus.

Russia: Moscow. 1925-1994. Biographical studies. ■The career of actor Innokentij Smoktunovskij.

2229   Naumov, A. "Bez tajnych kompleksov." (Without Secret Complexes.) *TeatZ.* 1996; 5: 20-22. Lang.: Rus.

Russia: Rostov. 1995-1996. Historical studies. ■The work of director Aleksand'r Slavutskij and scenographer Aleksand'r Patrakov at Rostovskij Akademičéskij Teat'r within Bolšoj Dramatičéskij Teat'r im. G. Kamala.

2230   Novikova, L. "Alla Demidova, vypavšaja iz gnezda, ili aktrisa, nikogda ne igravšaja sobja." (Alla Demidova, Fallen from the Nest, or The Actress Who Never Played Herself.) *TeatZ.* 1996; 11-12: 46-49. Lang.: Rus.

Russia: Moscow. 1960-1996. Biographical studies. ■Creative portrait of the Taganka Theatre actress.

2231   Omblet, Ju. "Deti podzemel'ja." (Children of the Underground.) *TeatZ.* 1996; 9: 22-24. Lang.: Rus.

Russia: Moscow. 1995. Critical studies. ■Jurij Pogrebničko's staging of *Hamlet* at Teat'r Okolo Doma Stanislavskogo (Theatre Near Stanislavskij's House).

2232   Orechanova, G. "'Ja, russkaja aktrisa...'." (I, a Russian Actress.) *NasSovr.* 1996; 3: 197-204. Lang.: Rus.

Russia: Moscow. 1996. Histories-sources. ■Interview with actress Tatjana Doronina of the Gorkij Academic Theatre about the theatre's future, directors, and the status of the actor in modern society.

2233   Pčelkin, L. "Moi vstreči so Smoktunovskim." (My Meetings with Smoktunovskij.) *Ekran.* 1996 Sep.; 6: 33-35. Lang.: Rus.

Russia: Moscow. 1980-1996. Histories-sources. ■Third in a series of memoirs relating to actor Innokentij Smoktunovskij. Emphasis on actor-audience relationship.

2234   Popov, L. "'Deti knižnych bogov'." (Children of the Book Gods.) *TeatZ.* 1996; 2: 32-34. Lang.: Rus.

Russia: St. Petersburg. 1995. Critical studies. ■Analysis of Boris Cejtlin's production of Shakespeare's *Romeo and Juliet* at Baltiskij Dom.

2235   Popov, L. "Skvernyj anekdot." (An Awful Anecdote.) *PTZ.* 1996; 9: 22-23. Lang.: Rus.

Russia: St. Petersburg. 1996. Historical studies. ■Aleksand'r Isakov's production of *Čonkin* by Vladimir Vojnovič at Baltiskij Dom.

2236   Popov, L. "Soldatami ne roždajutsja." (One Cannot Be Born a Soldier.) *PTZ.* 1996; 9: 34-37. Lang.: Rus.

Russia: St. Petersburg. 1996. Historical studies. ■Otkritij Teat'r's St. Petersburg production of *Esli prozivy leto... (If I Live Through the Summer)* by Gennadij Trostjaneckij, directed by Svetlana Aleksjevič.

2237   Popov, L. "Régtajm: Ob artiste Anatolij Petrove." (Ragtime: On Actor Anatolij Petrov.) *MoskNab.* 1996; 1-2: 58-61. Lang.: Rus.

Russia: Moscow. 1996. Critical studies. ■Petrov's portrayal of tragic characters, with emphasis on his work in *Tango* by Sławomir Mrożek, directed by Semyon Spivak for St. Petersburg Youth Theatre.

2238   Rjuntju, Ju.M. *Roman Viktjuk: recept dlja genija.* (Roman Viktjuk: Recipe for Genius.) Moscow: SP; 1996. 256 pp. Lang.: Rus.

Russia: Moscow. 1990-1996. Biographies. ■Anecdotes from the life of director Roman Viktjuk.

2239   Šachmatova, E. "'Želtaja kofta' Aleksandra Tairova." (*Yellow Jacket* by Aleksand'r Tairov.) *MoskNab.* 1996; 1-2: 90-95. Lang.: Rus.

Russia: Moscow. 1933. Historical studies. ■Aleksand'r Tairov's production of *The Yellow Jacket* by George C. Hazelton and J.H. Benrimo at the Svobodnyj Teat'r (Free Theatre).

2240   Sal'nikova, E. "Prostranstvo ljudej i salatov: 'Tanja-Tanja' v 'Masterskoj Petra Fomenko'." (People and Salads: Pëtr Fomenko Workshop's *Tanja-Tanja.*) *MoskNab.* 1996; 3-4: 19-21. Lang.: Rus.

Russia: Moscow. 1995-1996. Historical studies. ■The workshop's experimental interpretation of contemporary drama: Ol'ga Muchina's *Tanja-Tanja* directed by Andrej Prichod'ko, Ivan Popovskij, and Pëtr Fomenko.

DRAMA: —Performance / production

2241 Sal'nikova, E. "Ljudmila Maksakova." *MoskNab*. 1996; 5-6: 13-16. Lang.: Rus.
Russia: Moscow. 1980-1996. Historical studies. ■Analysis of the traditions of the Vachtangov Theatre through the work of actress Ljudmila Maksakova.

2242 Salnikova, E. "Tradicionno-avangardistskaja scena." (The Traditional-Avant-Garde Stage.) *TeatZ*. 1996; 11-12: 2-5. Lang.: Rus.
Russia: Moscow. 1995-1996. Reviews of performances. ■Productions at the Stanislavskij Theatre: *Cyrano de Bergerac*, adapted and directed by Boris Morozov (based on the original play by Rostand). *Fortynbras się upił (Fortinbras Got Drunk)* by Głowacki, directed by Dmitrij Brusnikin. *Černyj čelovek (Black Person)*, based on Puškin's *Mocart i Saljeri (Mozart and Salieri)*, directed by Vitalij Lanskoj.

2243 Ščeglov, A. "'Očen' skučno mne bez tebja...'." (I Am So Blue Without You.) *TeatZ*. 1996; 4: 30-34. Lang.: Rus.
Russia. 1896-1984. Biographical studies. ■Memories of actress Faina Ranevskaja.

2244 Ščeglov, Aleksej V. *O Faine Georgievne Ranevskoj.* (About Faina Georgievna Ranevskaja.) Moscow: Rossija; 1996. 78 pp. Lang.: Rus.
Russia: Moscow. 1896-1984. Biographical studies. ■The life of actress Faina Ranevskaja, including memoirs, letters, and photographs.

2245 Semenovskij, V. "Grafinja i plebej." (The Countess and the Slave.) *MoskNab*. 1996; 5-6: 7-10. Lang.: Rus.
Russia: Moscow. 1980-1996. Critical studies. ■Thoughts on the directorial work of Pëtr Fomenko: analysis of his creative methods and stage approach.

2246 Šitenburg, L. "Sekret vinodelija: Teat'r Roberta Sturua." (The Secret of Wine-Making: The Theatre of Robert Sturua.) *PTZ*. 1996; 9: 5-10. Lang.: Rus.
Russia: St. Petersburg. 1996. Historical studies. ■The work of Robert Sturua, artistic director of Teat'r im. Šato Rustaveli, on tour from Georgia to St. Petersburg.

2247 Šitenburg, L. "Smert' ej k licy." (Death Becomes Her.) *PTZ*. 1996; 9: 113-114. Lang.: Rus.
Russia: Moscow. 1996. Historical studies. ■Jurij Ljubimov's production of Euripides' *Medea*, Taganka Theatre.

2248 Sizenko, E. "Grafinja i drugie..." (The Countess and Others.) *TeatZ*. 1996; 6: 35-38. Lang.: Rus.
Russia: Moscow. 1995. Historical studies. ■Pëtr Fomenko's staging of *Pikovaja Dama (Queen of Spades)* by Puškin.

2249 Sokolanskij, A. "Oleg Tabakov igraet Kolomijceva." (Oleg Tabakov in the Role of Kolomijcev.) *MoskNab*. 1996; 1-2: 66-68. Lang.: Rus.
Russia: Moscow. 1960-1996. Biographical studies. ■Creative portrait of the actor and the characteristics of his work.

2250 Sokolinskij, E. "Ol'ga Antonova." *PTZ*. 1996; 9: 58-61. Lang.: Rus.
Russia: St. Petersburg, Moscow. 1980-1996. Biographical studies. ■The actress's work at the Vachtangov and Comedy theatres and with director Pëtr Fomenko.

2251 Stanislavskij, Konstantin Sergejévič; Malcovati, Franco, ed.; Martinelli, Milli, transl. *Le mie regie (2): Zio Vanja.* (My Productions (2): Uncle Vanya.) Milan: Ubulibri; 1996. 149 pp. Illus.: Sketches. B&W. Lang.: Ita.
Russia. 1899. Histories-sources. ■Stanislavskij's notations about his production of *Diadia Vania (Uncle Vanya)* by Čechov and the text itself.

2252 Starosel'skaja, N. "Romeo, Džul'etta i svet." (Romeo, Juliet, and Society.) *TeatZ*. 1996; 9: 36-39. Lang.: Rus.
Russia: Moscow. 1990-1996. Historical studies. ■Productions of Shakespeare's *Romeo and Juliet* on Moscow stages.

2253 Stukalov, B. "Pamjati Michajla Danilova." (In Memory of Michajl Danilov.) *PTZ*. 1996; 9: 93-96. Lang.: Rus.
Russia: St. Petersburg. 1973-1995. Biographical studies. ■The actor's life and work at the Tovstonogov Drama Theatre.

2254 Svobodin, A. "'Neobchodimo legkoe dychanie!'." (Light Breathing Is Necessary.) *TeatZ*. 1996; 6: 39-42. Lang.: Rus.
Russia: Moscow. 1980-1996. Histories-sources. ■Interview with director Pëtr Fomenko.

2255 Tolubeev, A. "Pamjati Vladislava Stržel'čika." (In Memory of Vladislav Strželčik.) *PTZ*. 1996; 9: 88-92. Lang.: Rus.
Russia: St. Petersburg. 1921-1995. Biographical studies. ■The actor's career with the Tovstonogov Dramatic Theatre.

2256 Ukolova, Ju. "Marina Šitova." *PTZ*. 1996; 10: 37-40. Lang.: Rus.
Russia: St. Petersburg. 1990-1996. Biographical studies. ■The actress' repertoire and her work with Litejnyj Theatre.

2257 Vasilinina, I. "Lico étogo teatra—režisser." (The Face of this Theatre: Its Director.) *TeatZ*. 1996; 4: 45-47. Lang.: Rus.
Russia: Moscow. 1990-1996. Historical studies. ■The work of Boris L'vov-Anochin, director of Novyj Teat'r.

2258 Vergasova, I. "Nezavisimyj talant Aleksandra Mezenceva." (The Independent Talent of Aleksand'r Mezencev.) *TeatZ*. 1996; 8: 23-25. Lang.: Rus.
Russia: Cheljabinsk. 1990-1996. Biographical studies. ■Profile of the Cheljabinsk Drama Theatre actor.

2259 Vestergol'm, E. "Ol'ga Samošina." *PTZ*. 1996; 9: 74-79. Lang.: Rus.
Russia: St. Petersburg. 1990-1996. Historical studies. ■Artistic portrait of actress with Tovstonogov Drama Theatre.

2260 Zabavskich, E. "Dmitrij Pevcov." *Selmol*. 1996 Jan.: 48-50. Lang.: Rus.
Russia: Moscow. 1980-1996. Histories-sources. ■Interview with the actor about his work in Taganka, Satire, and Lenkom theatres.

2261 Bérczes, László; Nemcoková, Jana, photo. "A csoda esélyei: Eszenyi—Pozsony—*Ahogy tetszik*." (Chances of Wonder: Eszenyi—Bratislava—*As You Like It*.) *Sz*. 1996; 29(12): 2-3. Illus.: Photo. B&W. 3. Lang.: Hun.
Slovakia: Bratislava. 1996. Critical studies. ■Enikő Eszenyi, actress-director of Budapest Comedy Theatre, staged Shakespeare's play at Slovak National Theatre in Pozsony/Bratislava.

2262 Gombač, Branko. *Ves ta svet je oder.* (All the World's a Stage.) Slovenska Bistrica: The Municipality; 1996. 583 pp. Illus.: Photo. B&W. Lang.: Slo.
Slovenia: Celje. Italy: Trieste. 1945-1996. Histories-sources. ■Slovene actor and director on his work developing the Celje national theatre, originally an amateur theatre.

2263 Predan, Vasja. "Sled odrskih senc—gledališki dnevnik 1995-1996." (The Trail of Stage Shadows—a Theatre Diary, 1995-1996.) *Sodob*. 1996; 44(1-7): 116, 131, 280-290, 383-396, 542-557. Lang.: Slo.
Slovenia. 1995-1996. Histories-sources. ■Diary of Slovene theatres and productions of the season.

2264 Ricklef, Sven. "Opulente Mythenspiele." (Lavish Myth Plays.) *TZ*. 1996; 3: 40-41. Illus.: Photo. B&W. 2. Lang.: Ger.
Slovenia: Maribor. 1996. Critical studies. ■Tomaž Pandur's production *Babylon*.

2265 Bain, Keith. "The Standard Bank National Arts Festival." *SATJ*. 1996 Sep.; 10(2): 135-147. Biblio. Illus.: Photo. B&W. 2. Lang.: Eng.
South Africa, Republic of: Grahamstown. 1996. Historical studies. ■Report on the 1996 National Arts Festival held in Grahamstown.

2266 Hauptfleisch, Gaerin; Toerien, François. "Klein Karoo Nasionale Kunstefees." (Little Karoo National Festival of the Arts.) *SATJ*. 1996 May; 10(1): 101-106. Biblio. Illus.: Photo. B&W. 2. Lang.: Afr.
South Africa, Republic of: Oudtshoorn. 1996. Historical studies. ■Report on the Klein Karoo Nasionale Kunstefees, a largely Afrikaans arts festival which is growing in popularity yearly.

2267 Larlham, Peter. "Journey to Grahamstown: 1995 Standard Bank National Arts Festival." *SATJ*. 1995 Sep.; 9(2): 103-116. Illus.: Photo. B&W. 4. Lang.: Eng.
South Africa, Republic of: Grahamstown. 1995. Critical studies. ■Report on the 1995 Standard Bank National Arts Festival.

DRAMA: —Performance/production

2268 Omotoso, Kole. "Whose Culture is the Culture of the Global Village?" *SATJ.* 1996 May; 10(1): 85-88. [Address at the 1996 Fleur du Cap awards for drama.] Lang.: Eng.
South Africa, Republic of. 1996. Histories-sources. ■Address on the state of African drama, and its place in the culture of the global village, from one of South Africa's prominent men of theatre, Kole Omotoso.

2269 Tomkins, Joanne. "'One Point of Sanity': An Interview with Barney Simon." *SATJ.* 1995 Sep.; 9(2): 83-96. Lang.: Eng.
South Africa, Republic of: Johannesburg. 1994. Histories-sources. ■Interview with director Barney Simon discussing the Market Theatre and an upcoming production of *The First Day of Christmas* which was workshopped by Simon and his cast.

2270 Wertheim, Albert. "The 1995 Grahamstown Festival." *SATJ.* 1996 May; 10(1): 94-100. Notes. Lang.: Eng.
South Africa, Republic of: Grahamstown. 1995. Historical studies. ■Report on the annual National Arts Festival in Grahamstown.

2271 Holt, Marion P. "Madrid, a Season of Diversity: American and Catalán Productions Among the Highlights." *WES.* 1996 Fall; 8(3): 53-56. Illus.: Photo. 2. Lang.: Eng.
Spain: Madrid. 1996. Historical studies. ■Current season in Madrid: the Festival de Otoño (Fall Festival), including Zorrilla's *Don Juan Tenorio*, Lope de Vega's *La discreta enamorada*, *El acero de Madrid*, and *El maestro de danzar*, directed by Angel Gutiérrez at the Teatro de Cámara. The season also included a number of foreign plays, such as McNally's *Love! Valour! Compassion!*, directed by Angel García Moreno at the Teatro Marquina, Albee's *Three Tall Women* and Cocteau's *Les Parents terribles* (seen on Broadway last year as *Indiscretions*), both directed by Jaime Chávarri at the Teatro Lara.

2272 Villegas, Juan. "Festival de festivales: Décimo Festival Iberoamericano de Teatro de Cádiz 1995." (Festival of Festivals: Tenth Festival of Spanish-American Theatre, Cadiz 1995.) *Gestos.* 1996 Apr.; 11(21): 176-192. Illus.: Photo. B&W. 7. Lang.: Eng.
Spain: Cádiz. 1995. Historical studies. ■Report on the Tenth Festival of Spanish American theatre held in Cádiz.

2273 Zatlin, Phyllis. "Women Directors: A Growing Presence on the Spanish Stage." *WES.* 1995-96 Win; 7(3): 89-92. Illus.: Photo. 1. Lang.: Eng.
Spain. 1995. Historical studies. ■The growing numbers of directors on the Spanish stage signals a new strength for women. Includes discussion of female directors Josefina Molina, María Ruiz, Carme Portaceli, Mara Recatero, and Helena Pimenta.

2274 Andersson, Bibi. "Bibi om Bergman." (Bibi About Bergman.) *Dramat.* 1996; 4(3): 30-34. Illus.: Photo. B&W. Lang.: Swe.
Sweden: Malmö, Stockholm. 1950. Historical studies. ■A personal survey of all the years Bibi Andersson has known Ingmar Bergman, with reference to her part in *Long Day's Journey Into Night* by O'Neill.

2275 Carlson, Harry G. "Salesman in a Time Warp." *WES.* 1996 Spr; 8(2): 63-66. Illus.: Photo. 3. Lang.: Eng.
Sweden: Stockholm. 1995. Historical studies. ■Swedish production of Miller's *Death of a Salesman* at the experimental Plazateatern, directed by Thorsten Flinck.

2276 Carlson, Harry G. "Suzanne Osten and the Unga Klara Group." *WES.* 1995-96 Win; 7(3): 93-98. Illus.: Photo. 2. Lang.: Eng.
Sweden. 1995. Histories-sources. ■Interview with Suzanne Osten of the Unga Klara improvisational theatre group within the Stockholm Municipal Theatre. Osten is interviewed on her career, the role of feminism in her work, and her latest production of *Hamlet* using *commedia dell'arte* traditions.

2277 Hoogland, Rikard. "Ner i kloakerna." (Down Into the Sewers.) *Tningen.* 1996; 20(79): 34-35. Illus.: Photo. B&W. Lang.: Swe.
Sweden: Gothenburg. 1996. Histories-sources. ■An interview with the director Björn Melander about his production of Lars Norén's *Blod (Blood)* for Göteborgs Stadsteater.

2278 Kronlund, Dag. "Skådespelarna och Georg Pauli." (The Actors and Georg Pauli.) *Dramat.* 1996; 4(2): 45-47. Illus.: Photo. Color. Lang.: Swe.
Sweden: Stockholm. 1840-1879. Historical studies. ■Historical background on the mural paintings by Georg and Hanna Pauli in the Royal Dramatic Theatre, in which numerous Swedish actors of the mid-nineteenth century are portrayed.

2279 Lagercrantz, Ylva; Mörk, Lennart, illus. "Spöken." (Ghosts.) *Dramat.* 1996; 4(3): 42-43. Illus.: Sketches. Color. Lang.: Swe.
Sweden: Stockholm. 1996. Critical studies. ■A presentation of the children's theatre project: Staffan Roos' *Spöken* staged by himself at the Royal Dramatic Theatre.

2280 Lagercrantz, Ylva. "Kristina Adolphson—40 år på Dramaten." (Kristina Adophson—40 Years at Dramaten.) *Dramat.* 1996; 4(1): 6. Illus.: Photo. B&W. Lang.: Swe.
Sweden: Stockholm. 1955. Biographical studies. ■A short survey of the career of actress Kristina Adolphson.

2281 Lagerlöf, Malin. "Skevt och spretigt." (Warped and Straggly.) *Tningen.* 1996; 20(79): 4-5. Illus.: Photo. Color. Lang.: Swe.
Sweden: Stockholm. 1980. Histories-sources. ■An interview with the actress Ingela Olsson, with reference to her involvement in Teater Galeasen.

2282 Lahger, Håkan. "Thommy Berggren i en klass för sig." (Thommy Berggren In a Class By Himself.) *Dramat.* 1996; 4 (1): 8-14. Illus.: Photo. B&W. Color. Lang.: Swe.
Sweden: Gothenburg, Stockholm. 1955. Histories-sources. ■An interview with Thommy Berggren about his staging of Molière's *Les Précieuses Ridicules* at The Royal Dramatic Theatre, with references to his career as actor and his cooperation with Kent Andersson, both actor and author of *Fint Folk (Fashionable People)*.

2283 Lahger, Håkan. "Kristina Lugns engelska helvete." (The English Hell of Kristina Lugn.) *Dramat.* 1996; 4(2): 30-32. Illus.: Photo. B&W. Lang.: Swe.
Sweden: Stockholm. 1993. Histories-sources. ■An interview with poet Kristina Lugn, who has turned to playwriting and directing at the Royal Dramatic Theatre, with references to her cooperation with the actor and director Thorsten Flinck and her staging of Anna Reynolds' *Red*.

2284 Lahger, Håkan. "Progrocken äntrar dramaten." (The Prog Rock Boards the Dramaten.) *Dramat.* 1996; 4(3): 45-47. Illus.: Photo. Color. Lang.: Swe.
Sweden: Stockholm. 1991. Critical studies. ■Thorsten Flinck's Dramaten production of Brecht's *Herr Puntila* using rock music by Ulf Dageby, which is performed by real rock musicians who are involved in the action as well.

2285 Lahger, Håkan. "En skådespelares val." (An Actor's Choice.) *Dramat.* 1996; 4(4): 20-21. Illus.: Photo. B&W. Lang.: Swe.
Sweden: Stockholm. 1970. Histories-sources. ■An interview with the actress Karin Bjurström about her parts at Stockholms Stadsteater, the Royal Dramatic Theatre and in soap operas as well as her interest in playwriting.

2286 Lahger, Håkan. "Se dig om i lust." (Look Back In Delight.) *Dramat.* 1996; 4(3): 10-14. Illus.: Photo. Color. Lang.: Swe.
Sweden: Gothenburg, Stockholm. 1984. Histories-sources. ■An interview with the actor Reine Brynolfsson about his background and career, with reference to his parts in plays by Lars Norén and films by Colin Nutley.

2287 Marker, Lise-Lone; Marker, Frederick J. *Ingmar Bergman. Tutto il teatro.* (Ingmar Bergman: Complete Theatre.) Milan: Ubulibri; 1996. 315 pp. (I libri bianchi.) Illus.: Photo. Sketches. B&W. Lang.: Ita.
Sweden. Germany. 1918-1996. Historical studies. ■Italian translation of *Ingmar Bergman: A Life in the Theatre* (Cambridge/New York, NY, Cambridge UP, 2d ed., 1992). Covers Bergman's activity as a theatre director, with attention to Molière, Strindberg, and Ibsen. Includes a chronology of his work from 1944 to 1996.

2288 Rosenberg, Göran; Hjortensjö, Petra; Wahlbeck, Peter; Björk, Nina. "4 reflektioner kring Backanterna." (Four Reflections on the Bacchae.) *Dramat.* 1996; 4(2): 20-23. Illus.: Photo. B&W. Lang.: Swe.

CLASSED ENTRIES

DRAMA: —Performance/production

Sweden: Stockholm. 1996. Histories-sources. ▪A journalist, a student, an actor and an author speak about their impressions of Ingmar Bergman's staging of Euripides' *Bákchai* at the Royal Dramatic Theatre.

2289 Sörenson, Elisabeth. "Björn Melander: Att berätta en historia." (Björn Melander: To Tell a Story.) *Dramat.* 1996; 4(1): 30-33. Illus.: Photo. B&W. Lang.: Swe.

Sweden: Gothenburg, Stockholm. 1991. Histories-sources. ▪An interview with the director Björn Melander about his 'method', his staging of Arthur Miller's *The Last Yankee* with comments by the actor Reine Brynolfsson.

2290 Sörenson, Elisabeth. "En skådespelare, tre regissörer." (One Actor, Three Directors.) *Dramat.* 1996; 4(2): 34-38. Illus.: Photo. Color. Lang.: Swe.

Sweden: Stockholm. 1989. Histories-sources. ▪An interview with the actor Börje Ahlstedt about the many ways to rehearse a play, with references to his cooperations with Ingmar Bergman, Björn Melander and now in Thorsten Flinck's staging of Brecht's *Herr Puntila und sein Knecht Matti*.

2291 Sörenson, Elisabeth. "Skådespelerska i 200 år." (An Actress For 200 Years.) *Dramat.* 1996; 4(4): 40. Illus.: Photo. Color. Lang.: Swe.

Sweden: Stockholm. 1996. Historical studies. ▪A presentation of Staffan Roos's production *Spöken* where the Royal Dramatic Theatre itself has the leading part.

2292 Tiselius, Henric. "Inre eld." (An Inner Fire.) *Tningen.* 1996; 20(76-77): 5-6. Illus.: Photo. B&W. Lang.: Swe.

Sweden: Malmö. 1996. Histories-sources. ▪An interview with the actress Lena Nylén, with reference to her interpretation of Medea in Euripides' play directed by Sven Ahlström at Malmös Unga Ensembleteater.

2293 Tiselius, Henric. "Synonym med det unga." (Synonymous With Youth.) *Tningen.* 1996; 20(79): 32-33. Illus.: Photo. B&W. Lang.: Swe.

Sweden: Gothenburg. 1985. Histories-sources. ▪An interview with the young actor Shanti Roney about his roles at Göteborgs Stadsteater.

2294 Wanselius, Bengt, photo. "Repetition Puntila." (Puntila Rehearsal.) *Dramat.* 1996; 4(3): 48-51. Illus.: Photo. Color. Lang.: Swe.

Sweden: Stockholm. 1996. Historical studies. ▪A photographic report from the rehearsals of Bertolt Brecht's *Herr Puntila und sein Knecht Matti*, staged by Thorsten Flinck.

2295 Werkelid, Carl Otto; Krekin, Irmelie, photo. "Salen där vi är oss själva." (The Ward Where We Are Ourselves.) *Dramat.* 1996; 4(1): 22-25. Illus.: Photo. B&W. Lang.: Swe.

Sweden: Stockholm. 1989. Historical studies. ▪A presentation of Katarina Frostenson's new play *Sal P (Ward P)* about the women's asylum of La Salpêtrière, and the staging of Pia Forsgren with the actress Agneta Ekmanner at the Royal Dramatic Theatre.

2296 Werkelid, Carl Otto. "Erland Josephson—på ett lågmält sätt på bettet." (Erland Josephson—In Good Form, in a Low Voice.) *Dramat.* 1996; 4(4): 32-36. Illus.: Photo. Color. Lang.: Swe.

Sweden: Stockholm. 1946. Histories-sources. ▪An interview with Erland Josephson about his view of himself as actor and writer, the Royal Dramatic Theatre and the changing role of the theatre today as part of the society.

2297 Wigardt, Gaby. "Glasmenageriet på turné." (The Glass Menagerie on Tour.) *Dramat.* 1996; 4(1): 26-28. Illus.: Photo. Color. Lang.: Swe.

Sweden. 1996. Historical studies. ▪A report from the actors of the Royal Dramatic Theatre who are touring all around Sweden with *The Glass Menagerie* in a joint production with Svenska Riksteatern, with glimpses of the everyday events of a touring company.

2298 Wigardt, Gaby. "Dramatenfolk." (People at Dramaten.) *Dramat.* 1996; 4(3): 6. Illus.: Photo. B&W. Lang.: Swe.

Sweden: Stockholm. 1966. Histories-sources. ▪A short interview with Gunilla Nyroos about her thirty years as an actress.

2299 Wigardt, Gaby. "Improvisation till verkligheten." (Improvisation on Reality.) *Dramat.* 1996; 4(4): 16-19. Illus.: Photo. Color. Lang.: Swe.

Sweden: Stockholm. 1996. Historical studies. ▪A presentation of how *Mottagningen (The Medical Center)* by Bengt Bratt was staged by Gunilla Nyroos through half a year's improvisation at the Royal Dramatic Theatre.

2300 Richard, Christine. "Augen auf und durch!" (Open Your Eyes and Endure!) *THeute.* 1996; 11: 25-28. Illus.: Photo. B&W. 4. Lang.: Ger.

Switzerland: Basel. 1996. Reviews of performances. ▪Director Michael Schindhelm has started the season of Basler Theater with: *Baal* by Brecht, directed by Michael Heicks, *Herakleida* by Euripides, directed by Hans-Dieter Jendreyko, *Der Snob (The Snob)* by Carl Sternheim, directed by Andreas von Studnitz, *Vinny* by Klaus Pohl, directed by Hermann Schmidt-Rahmer.

2301 Bobkoff, Ned. "After the Visit, the Ruins." 135-147 in Oliva, Judy Lee, ed. *New Theatre Vistas: Modern Movements in International Theatre.* New York, NY/London: Garland; 1996. 219 pp. (Studies in Modern Drama 7.) Notes. Lang.: Eng.

Turkey: Eskisehir. 1993. Histories-sources. ▪Directing Dürrenmatt's *The Visit* in Turkey at the Konservatuvari, the National Institute for Music and the Performing Arts at Anadolu University.

2302 The Open University/BBC and Women's Playhouse Trust. *The Rover.* London: Routledge; 1996. 200 mins. [Video format.] Lang.: Eng.

UK-England. 1994. Histories-sources. ▪Videotape of a 1994 production of Aphra Behn's *The Rover*, directed by Tony Coe, and performed by the Women's Playhouse Trust. The production was taped in a studio, not a live stage performance.

2303 The Open University/BBC and Women's Playhouse Trust. *As You Like It.* London: Routledge; 1996. 120 mins. [Video format.] Lang.: Eng.

UK-England. 1994. Histories-sources. ▪Videotape of directors and actors discussing the process by which Shakespeare's *As You Like It* becomes a performance. Directors Peter Sellars, Annie Castledine, and Deborah Warner, and actors Fiona Shaw and Juliet Stevenson discuss how interpretations are derived. Also includes a section on Cheek by Jowl's all-male production of the play, directed by Declan Donnellan, featuring Adrian Lester as Rosalind.

2304 "Reviews of Productions." *LTR.* 1996; 16(4): 218-222. Lang.: Eng.

UK-England: London. 1996. ▪*Journey West* by Ivan Heng and Chantal Rosas Cobian, dir by Lim Kay Sui at BAC 1: rev by Bassett, McPherson. *A Doll's House (Et Dukkehjem)* by Henrik Ibsen, transl. by Mark Sparrow, dir by Indhu Rubasingham at the Young Vic Studio: rev by Edwardes, Michaels, Stratton. *Serving It Up* by David Eldridge, dir by Jonathan Lloyd at the Bush: rev by Bayley, Billington, Coveney, Curtis, Edwardes, Gore-Langton, Kingston, Nathan, Peter, Shuttleworth, Tinker, Woddis.

2305 "Reviews of Productions." *LTR.* 1996; 16(1): 7-17. Lang.: Eng.

UK-England: London. 1996. ▪*The Duchess of Malfi* by John Webster, dir Declan Donnellan at Wyndham's: rev by Billington, Butler, Christopher, Coveney, de Jongh, Gross, Hirschhorn, Hughes, Macaulay, Morley, Nathan, Nightingale, Paton, Peter, Smith, Spencer, Taylor, Usher. *The Blood Knot* by Athol Fugard, dir Jonathan Lloyd at the Gate: rev by Christopher, Gardner, Hassell, Kingston, Murray, Peter, Spencer. *Dancing Attendance* and *Under Surveillance* by Brian Rostron, dir by Ali Robertson at the Finborough: rev by Edwardes.

2306 "Reviews of Productions." *LTR.* 1996; 16(2): 86-88. Lang.: Eng.

UK-England: London. 1996. ▪*Comic Cuts* by Jack Shepherd, dir by Jonathan Church at the Lyric Studio: rev by Billington, Curtis, Hirshhorn, Kingston, Marlowe, Paton, Stratton. *D.H. Lawrence—Son and Lover* by Patricia Doyle and Peter Needham from the works of D.H. Lawrence, dir by Martin Lloyd Evans at the Wimbledon Studio: rev by McPherson. *Fred and Ginger* by Tracy Hitchen, at the Baron's Court: rev by Godfrey-Faussett, McPherson.

2307 "Reviews of Productions." *LTR.* 1996; 16(1): 18-25. Lang.: Eng.

DRAMA: —Performance/production

UK-England: London. 1996. ■*Fav'rite Nation* by Robin Brooks, dir by Andrew Holmes at the Lyric Studio: rev by Bayley, Butler, Christopher, Curtis, Foss, Gardner, Hemming, Nathan, Nightingale, Sierz. *Swingers* by Ashmeed Sohoye, dir by Brian Croucher at the Grace: rev by Gardner, Tushingham. *Saltimbanco* by Cirque du Soleil, dir by Franco Dragone at the Royal Albert Hall: rev by Barker, Bayley, Crisp, Dougill, Dromgoole, Edwardes, Gardner, Gore-Langton, Hirschhorn, Hughes, Nightingale, Paton, Sacks, Smith, Tinker.

2308   "Reviews of Productions." *LTR*. 1996; 16(1): 25-30. Lang.: Eng.

UK-England: London. 1996. ■*Liar Liar* by Ned Cox, dir by Lisa Goldman at the Red Room: rev by Smith, Stratton. *Damn Yankees* by Douglass Wallop, music and lyrics by Richard Adler and Jerry Ross, dir by Carol Metcalfe at the Bridewell: rev by Benedict, Billington, Butler, Coveney, Curtis, Darvell, Grace, Hirschhorn, Hughes, Macaulay, Morley, Nathan, Nightingale, Peter, Spencer, Tinker, Tushingham. *Doomsday* by Inder Manocha, dir by Michael Kingsbury at the Southwark Playhouse: rev by Murray, Reade.

2309   "Reviews of Productions." *LTR*. 1996; 16(1): 31-36. Lang.: Eng.

UK-England: London. 1996. ■*Erections Ejaculations Exhibitions* and *The Fuck Machine* by Michael Werner and Michael Schaldemose, adapted from the work of Charles Bukowski, dir by Werner at the Old Red Lion: rev by Christopher, Kingston, Marlowe, Spencer, Taylor. *Daphne's Vase* by John Parker, dir by Fiona Banks at the Canal Cafe: rev by Hemblade. *Goldhawk Road* by Simon Bent, dir by Paul Miller at the Bush: rev by Billington, Butler, Coveney, Curtis, Edwardes, Gross, Hirschhorn, Hughes, Morley, Nathan, Nightingale, Peter, Sierz, Smith, Spencer, Taylor, Tinker.

2310   "Reviews of Productions." *LTR*. 1996; 16(2): 88-89. Lang.: Eng.

UK-England: London. 1996. ■*Two* by Jim Cartwright, dir by John Forgeham at the Fox: rev by Neumark. *Screwed* by Geoffrey Parkinson, based on an idea by Lucy Irving, dir by Irving at the Finborough: rev by Foss, Reade. *The Greek Amphibian* by Dimitris Potamitis, dir by Potamitis at Theatro Technis rev by Hajaj.

2311   "Reviews of Productions." *LTR*. 1996; 16(1): 37-41. Lang.: Eng.

UK-England: London. 1996. ■*A Doll's House (Et Dukkehjem)* by Henrik Ibsen, transl. by Christopher Hampton, dir by Alison Brown at BAC: rev by Bassett, Bayley, Curtis, Gale, Macaulay. *The Miracle People* by Maeve Murphy, dir by Murphy at the Etcetera: rev by Abdulla, Bayley. *Betjemania* by David Benedictus and John Gould, dir by Richard Syms at the King's Head: rev by Creamer, Curtis, Edwardes, Gross, Hughes, Kellaway, Morley, Nathan, Nightingale, Peter, Shuttleworth, Spencer, Taylor, Tinker.

2312   "Reviews of Productions." *LTR*. 1996; 16(1): 42-46. Lang.: Eng.

UK-England: London. 1996. ■*A Strange Bit of History* by Annabel Knight and *Short, Fat Kebab-Shop Owner's Son* by Omid Djalili, dir by Knight at the Riverside: rev by Games, Kingston, McPherson, Tushingham. *Romeo and Juliet* by William Shakespeare, dir by Simon Parry at the New End: rev by Abdulla, Bassett, Hutera, Tinker. *Voyage in the Dark* by Joan Wiles, adapted from the novel by Jean Rhys, dir by Sue Parrish at the Young Vic: rev by Bayley, Butler, Curtis, Foss, Gardner, Greer, Gross, Kellaway, Kingston, Nathan, Reade.

2313   "Reviews of Productions." *LTR*. 1996; 16(1): 46,53. Lang.: Eng.

UK-England: London. UK-Scotland: Edinburgh. 1996. ■*Contested Will* by Olly Figg, dir by David Cottis at the Etcetera: rev by Abdulla, Foss, Shuttleworth. *The Steamie* by Tony Roper, music by David Anderson, dir by Caroline Hall at the Royal Lyceum (Edinburgh): rev by Donald, Fisher, Millar, *Sunday Times* (no byline).

2314   "Reviews of Productions." *LTR*. 1996; 16(2): 65-70. Lang.: Eng.

UK-England: London. 1996. ■*Macbeth* by William Shakespeare, dir by Stephen Unwin at the Lyric Hammersmith: rev by Butler, Curtis, Edwardes, Gross, Hughes, Macaulay, Morley, Murray, Nathan, Nightingale, Paton, Peter, Tinker. *Sykes and Nancy* from the work of Charles Dickens, dir by John Mowat at the Jackson's Lane: rev by Abdulla, Sim-

pkins. *Flesh Fly* by Trevor Lloyd, adapted from *Volpone* by Ben Jonson, dir by Ewan Marshall at the Oval House: rev by Christopher, Curtis, Gardner, Hutera, Kellaway, Spencer, Taylor.

2315   "Reviews of Productions." *LTR*. 1996; 16(2): 71-79. Lang.: Eng.

UK-England: London. 1996. ■*An Ideal Husband* by Oscar Wilde, dir by Peter Hall at the Theatre Royal, Haymarket: rev by Billington, Butler, Christopher, de Jongh, Gross, Hassell, Hirschhorn, Hughes, Kellaway, Macaulay, Morley, Nathan, Nightingale, Paton, Peter, Spencer, Taylor, Tinker. *Charlie's Angel* by Ron Ceji, dir by Tim Schuler at the Baron's Court: rev by Foss. *Night of the Fox* by Peter Briffa, dir by Sam Shammas at the Lilian Baylis: rev by Bassett, Bayley, Nathan.

2316   "Reviews of Productions." *LTR*. 1996; 16(2): 80-85. Lang.: Eng.

UK-England: London. 1996. ■*The Misanthrope* by Molière, transl. by John Edmunds, dir by Pamela Merrick at the Pentameters: rev by Curtis, Foss, Hemblade. *Slaughter City* by Naomi Wallace, dir by Ron Daniels for the RSC at The Pit: rev by Billington, Butler, de Jongh, Edwardes, Gross, Hewison, Hirschhorn, Hughes, Kellaway, Macaulay, Nathan, Nightingale, Sierz, Smith, Spencer, Taylor, Tinker. *Struck Off and Die* by Phil Hammond and Tony Gardner, at the Bloomsbury: rev by Ramptom.

2317   "Reviews of Productions." *LTR*. 1996; 16(2): 90-93. Lang.: Eng.

UK-England: London. 1996. ■London International Mime Festival 1996: Overall rev by Bayler, Gardner, Gilbert, Hemming. *Twin Houses* by Nicole Mossoux, dir by Patrick Bonté, for Compagnie Mossoux-Bonté, at the Purcell Room: rev by Billington, Craine, Hemming. *Musical Scenes* by the Clod Ensemble at BAC, Studio 2: rev by Stratton.

2318   "Reviews of Productions." *LTR*. 1996; 16(4): 200-214. Lang.: Eng.

UK-England: London. 1996. ■*The Misanthrope* by Molière, transl. by Martin Crimp, dir by Lindsay Posner at the Young Vic: rev by Billington, Butler, Coveney, de Jongh, Edwardes, Gross, Morley, Nathan, Nightingale, Paton, Peter, Sierz, Smith, Spencer, Taylor. *1953* by Craig Raine, dir by Patrick Marber at the Almeida: rev by Billington, Butler, Coveney, Davé, de Jongh, Edwardes, Gross, Hughes, Morley, Nathan, Nightingale, Paton, Peter, Sherrin, Spencer, Taylor, Tinker. *On the Playing Fields after Rejection* by Jyll Bradley, dir by Sue Golding at the Drill Hall: rev by Curtis, Dowden, Stratton.

2319   "Reviews of Productions." *LTR*. 1996; 16(4): 215-218. Lang.: Eng.

UK-England: London. 1996. ■*The Gorilla Hunters* by Ben Benison, dir by Benison at the Courtyard: rev by Abdulla, Spencer. *The Summit* conceived and performed by Jonathan and Barnaby Stone, for Ralf Ralf at BAC Main: rev by Christopher, Gale, Hawkins. *Twelfth Night* by William Shakespeare, dir by Ian Judge for the RSC at the Barbican: rev by Bassett, Foss, Hemming, Hughes, Peter, Reade, Spencer, Tinker.

2320   "Reviews of Productions." *LTR*. 1996; 16(4): 223-232. Lang.: Eng.

UK-England: London. 1996. ■*Chapter Two* by Neil Simon, dir by David Gilmore at the Gielgud: rev by Billington, Coveney, Darvell, Gross, Hanks, Hughes, Macauley, Morley, Nathan, Nightingale, Peter, Preston, Sherrin, Spencer, Stratton, Tinker. *Skylight* by David Hare, dir by Richard Eyre at Wyndham's: rev by Billington, Clark, Coveney, de Jongh, Edwardes, Gross, Hughes, Macauley, Morley, Nightingale, Preston, Sherrin, Spencer. *Snowshow* by Slava Polunin at Hackney Empire: rev by Bayley, Foss, Gardner, Gore-Langton, Kellaway, Read.

2321   "Reviews of Productions." *LTR*. 1996; 16(4): 240-246. Lang.: Eng.

UK-England: London. 1996. ■*Markurell* by Hjalmar Bergman, transl. by Eivor Martinus, dir by Derek Martinus at Chelsea Centre: rev by Godfrey-Faussett, Kingston. *Dead White Males* by David Williamson, dir by Patrick Sandford at Nuffield: rev by Billington, Butler, Hemming, Kingston, Spencer, Taylor. *Frogs (Batrakhoi)* by Aristophanes, transl. by Fiona Laird, dir by Laird at Gardner Centre, Brighton: rev by Bassett, Coveney, Curtis, Gardner, Hughes, Macauley, Shuttleworth, Spencer, Taylor, Tinker.

2322   "Reviews of Productions." *LTR*. 1996; 16(4): 232-236. Lang.: Eng.

DRAMA: —Performance/production

UK-England: London. 1996. ∎*Joined at the Head* by Catherine Butterfield, dir by Jacqui Somerville at Man in the Moon: rev by Hajaj, McPherson. *Slump*, an opera by Stephen McNeff, words by Andy Rashleigh, based on cartoon strip by Will Self, dir by Richard Williams at the Lyric Studio: rev by Bassett, Curtis, Darvell, Reade. *Gulp Fiction* by Trish Cooke, from an idea by Martin Glynn, dir by Cooke, musical dir by Felix Cross at the Theatre Royal, Stratford East: rev by Abdulla, Bayley, Billington, Curtis, Foss, Hemming, Nathan, Nightingale, Peter, Tinker.

2323   "Reviews of Productions." *LTR*. 1996; 16(4): 236-240.
        Lang.: Eng.

UK-England: London. 1996. ∎*The Return of the Soldier* by Anthony Psaila, from the novel by Rebecca West, dir by Andrea Brooks at the White Bear: rev by Butler, Foss, Godfrey-Faussett. *The End of the World Romance* by Sean Dixon, dir by Andrea Montgomery at the Lilian Baylis: rev by Gardner, Higginson, Marlowe, Peter. *Laughing Wild* by Christopher Durang, dir by Henry Goodman at Riverside 3: rev by Billington, Christopher, Curtis, Gross, Hanks, Hewison, Hutera, Macauley, Morley, Nathan, Nightingale.

2324   "Reviews of Productions." *LTR*. 1996; 16(5): 288-293.
        Lang.: Eng.

UK-England: London. 1996. ∎*The Beauty Queen of Leenane* by Martin McDonagh, dir by Garry Hynes at Theatre Upstairs: rev by Billington, Butler, Christopher, Coveney, Curtis, Gross, Hassell, Hemming, Kingston, Nathan, Peter, Spencer, Taylor, Usher. *Passion Plays* by Simon Blake, dir by Blake at BAC 2: rev by Godfrey-Faussett, Spencer. *Heaven* by Jane Buckley, dir by Phillip MacKenzie at BAC Main: rev by Adams, Bassett, Brennan, Farrell, Foster, Stratton.

2325   "Reviews of Productions." *LTR*. 1996; 16(4): 263-266.
        Lang.: Eng.

UK-England: London. 1996. ∎*Joseph and the Amazing Technicolor Dreamcoat* by Tim Rice and Andrew Lloyd Webber, dir by Steven Pimlott at the Apollo: rev by Abdulla, Butler, Curtis, Kingston, Morgan, Sherrin, Smith. *The Body Trade* by Deborah Lavin, dir by Lisa Goldman at the Red Room, NW5: rev by Marlowe, Tushingham. *Sisters, Brothers (Systrar, bröder)* by Stig Larsson, transl by Frank Gabriel Perry, dir by David Farr, and *The Oginski Polonaise (Polonez Oginskogo)* by Nikolaj Koljada, transl. by Peter Tegel, dir by Pat Kiernan at the Gate: rev by Bassett, Billington, Christopher, Curtis, Hanks, Marlowe.

2326   "Reviews of Productions." *LTR*. 1996; 16(4): 269-276.
        Lang.: Eng.

UK-England: London. 1996. ∎*Present Laughter* by Noël Coward, dir by Richard Olivier at the Aldwych: rev by Billington, Butler, Coveney, de Jongh, Dowden, Edwardes, Gross, Hughes, Macauley, Morley, Nathan, Nightingale, Peter, Preston, Spencer, Taylor, Tinker. *A Talent to Amuse* words and music of Noël Coward, performed by Peter Greenwell, at the Vaudeville: rev by Butler, Coveney, Darvell, de Jongh, Godfrey-Faussett, Gross, Hughes, Morley, Nathan, Nightingale, Sherrin, Spencer, Tinker. *Flowerpot, Superglue and Judy* by Gregory Williams, at the Finborough: rev by Abdulla.

2327   "Reviews of Productions." *LTR*. 1996; 16(4): 277-282.
        Lang.: Eng.

UK-England: London. 1996. ∎*The Ends of the Earth* by David Lan, dir by Andrei Serban at the Cottesloe: rev by Billington, Butler, Christopher, Coveney, de Jongh, Foss, Gross, Macauley, Morley, Nathan, Nightingale, Peter, Spencer, Taylor, Tinker. *Breaking Bread Together* by Robert Shearman, dir by Shearman at Etcetera: rev by Stratton. *The Lady from the Sea (Fruen fra havet)* by Henrik Ibsen, dir by Sue Lefton at the Bridewell: rev by Curtis, Peter, Simpkins, Tushingham.

2328   "Reviews of Productions." *LTR*. 1996; 16(5): 283-287.
        Lang.: Eng.

UK-England: London. 1996. ∎*20-52* by Jeremy Weller, dir by Weller at the Tricycle: rev by Curtis, Gardner, Hutera, Kingston, Nathan, Sierz, Stratton, Taylor. *The King of Prussia* by Nick Darke, dir by Mike Shepherd at Donmar Warehouse: rev by Billington, Butler, Coveney, de Jongh, Hemming, Morley, Nightingale, Spencer, Taylor, Usher. *A Play for Jimmy Baldwin* by P.K. Addo, dir by Olusola Oyeleye at the Oval House: rev by Bartholomew, Higginson.

2329   "Reviews of Productions." *LTR*. 1996; 16(12): 725-726.
        Lang.: Eng.

UK-England: London. 1996. ∎*The Road to Mecca* by Athol Fugard, dir by David Prescott at the Lookout: rev by Higginson. *Appetite*, devised and performed by Club Swing at the Riverside: rev by Abdulla, McPherson. *As You Like It* by William Shakespeare, dir by Peter Brewis at BAC Main and *Wicked Bastard of Venus*, an adaptation of *As You Like It* by Julie-Anne Robinson, dir by Robinson at Southwark Playhouse: rev by Hutera, O'Mahoney, Reade, Taylor.

2330   "Reviews of Productions." *LTR*. 1996; 16(12): 727-730.
        Lang.: Eng.

UK-England: London. 1996. ∎*The Sins of Dalia Baumgarten* by Ryan Craig, dir by Craig at the Etcetera: rev by Seligman, Simpkins. *Camelot* by Alan Jay Lerner, music by Frederick Loewe, dir by Frank Dunlop at Freemason's Hall: rev by Curtis, Gore-Langton, Hughes, Kingston, Morley, Seckerson. *Hanging Hanratty* by Michael Burnham, dir by David Taylor at the Bird's Nest: rev by Higginson.

2331   "Reviews of Productions." *LTR*. 1996; 16(5): 293-300.
        Lang.: Eng.

UK-England: London. 1996. ∎*Little White Lies* by Daniel Jamieson, dir by Nikki Sved at the Warehouse, Croydon: rev by Bassett, Gale, Greer. *Tommy* by Pete Townshend, book by Townshend and Des McAnuff, dir by McAnuff at the Shaftesbury: rev by Butler, Coveney, de Jongh, Edwardes, Fanshawe, Gilbey, Glaister, Gross, Hibbet, Hirschhorn, Lister, Morley, Nathan, Nightingale, Paton, Peter, Shuttleworth, Smith, Spencer, Tinker. *Fool for Love* by Sam Shepard, dir by Eric Richard at the Grace: rev by Abdulla, Simpkins.

2332   "Reviews of Productions." *LTR*. 1996; 16(5): 301-302.
        Lang.: Eng.

UK-England: London. 1996. ∎*The London Merchant* by George Lillo, dir by Mehmet Ergen at the Southwark Playhouse: rev by Christopher, Hutera. *Ecstasy* by Mike Leigh, dir by Patrick Davey at the New End: rev by Abdulla, Marlowe. *Moonlight Serenade* by Jez Simons and Jyoti Patel, dir by Topher Campbell at the Lyric Studio: rev by McPherson, Reade.

2333   "Reviews of Productions." *LTR*. 1996; 16(5): 302-308.
        Lang.: Eng.

UK-England: London. 1996. ∎*Morphine* by Michajl Bulgakov, adapt by Victor Sobchak, dir by Sobchak at the Courtyard: rev by Bassett, Higgonson. *Observe the Sons of Ulster Marching Towards the Somme* by Frank McGuinness, dir by Patrick Mason at the Barbican: rev by Butler, Daily Express, de Jongh, Edwardes, Gore-Langton, Gross, Hirshhorn, Morley, Nightingale, Shuttleworth, Smith, Tinker. *The Complete Works of William Shakespeare (Abridged)* by the Reduced Shakespeare Company, dir by Adam Long at the Criterion: rev by Curtis, Foss, Hirshhorn, Hughes, Morley, Nathan, Nightingale, Peter, Rampton, Shuttleworth, Spencer, Tinker, Tushingham.

2334   "Reviews of Productions." *LTR*. 1996; 16(6): 331-338.
        Lang.: Eng.

UK-England: London. 1996. ∎*Buddleia* by Paul Mercier, dir by Mercier at the Donmar Warehouse: rev by Billington, Coveney, Curtis, Hemming, Kingston. *What Did You Say?* by Jim Hawkins, dir by Rupert Creed at Chelsea Centre: rev by Spencer. *The Shoe Horn Sonata* by John Misto, dir by Dan Crawford at the King's Head: rev by Billington, Christopher, Coveney, de Jongh, Foss, Gross, Hemming, Hirshhorn, Hughes, Morley, Nathan, Nightingale, Paton, Peter, Spencer, Tinker.

2335   "Reviews of Productions." *LTR*. 1996; 16(6): 338-342.
        Lang.: Eng.

UK-England: London. 1996. ∎*The Complete History of America—Abridged* by the Reduced Shakespeare Company, dir by Adam Long at the Criterion: rev by Edwardes, Nightingale, Paton, Shuttleworth. *Company* by Stephen Sondheim, book by George Furth, dir by Sam Mendes at the Albery: rev by Benedict, Butler, Christopher, Darvell, de Jongh, Hemming, Hirshhorn, Hughes, Kingston, Morley, Nathan, Paton, Peter, Tinker. *Obsession Is not a Perfume* by Emma Lucia, dir by Lindsey McAlister at the Finborough: rev by Godfrey-Faussett, Paton.

2336   "Reviews of Productions." *LTR*. 1996; 16(6): 343-346.
        Lang.: Eng.

UK-England: London. 1996. ∎*Watch My Lips* by Nigel Charnock, dir by Charnock at the Drill Hall: rev by Bayley, Butler, Coveney, de Jongh, Dromgoole, Harpe, Hewison, Hutera, Kingston, Reade, Spencer. *Trainspotting* by Harry Gibson, from the novel by Irvine Welsh, dir by Gibson

DRAMA: —Performance/production

at Whitehall: rev by Marlowe, Nightingale. *Happy Families* by Deborah Lavin, dir by Judith Roberts at Man in the Moon: rev by Gale, Higginson.

2337   "Reviews of Productions." *LTR*. 1996; 16(6): 346-350. Lang.: Eng.

UK-England: London. 1996. ■*Just a Matter of Time* by Derek Parkes, dir by Sam Shammas at Wimbledon Studio: rev by McPherson. *The Undertaking* by Philip Osment, dir by James Neale-Kennerly at the Albany: rev by Coveney, de Jongh, Gardner, Kingston, Taylor, Tinker, Tushingham, Woddis. *Baby Jean* by Dermot Bolger, dir by Jim O'Hanlon at BAC: rev by Bassett, Dowden, Edwardes, Shuttleworth, Stratton.

2338   "Reviews of Productions." *LTR*. 1996; 16(6): 350-354. Lang.: Eng.

UK-England: London. 1996. ■*In High Germany* by Dermot Bolger, dir by Miles Plant at BAC: rev by Spencer. *The Soldier's Song* by Brian James Ryder, dir by John Dove at the Theatre Royal, Stratford East: rev by Billington, Butler, Coveney, de Jongh, Edwardes, Foss, Morley, Nathan, Nightingale, Peter, Shuttleworth, Sierz, Spencer, Taylor. *Frogs (Batrakhoi)* by Aristophanes, musically adapted by Fiona Laird, dir by Laird at the Cottesloe: rev by Morley, Nightingale, Stratton.

2339   "Reviews of Productions." *LTR*. 1996; 16(3): 131-134. Lang.: Eng.

UK-England: London. 1996. ■*The Lottery Ticket* by Roddy McDevitt, dir by Yvon McDevitt at the Red Room: rev by Curtis, Davé, Reade. *Sweetheart* by Nick Grosso, dir by Roxanna Silbert at the Theatre Upstairs: rev by Christopher, Coveney, Curtis, Hassell, Kingston, Murray, Nathan, Peter, Sierz, Taylor. *The Kissing Game* by Dale Smith, dir by Tim Crook at the Tristan Bates: rev by Reade.

2340   "Reviews of Productions." *LTR*. 1996; 16(2): 98-99. Lang.: Eng.

UK-England: London. 1996. ■*Acts Without Words I & II (Acte sans paroles I & II)* by Samuel Beckett, dir by Andy Lavender at BAC: rev by Nightingale. *Le Fou de Bassan* by circus company Rasposo, at the Queen Elizabeth Hall: rev by Billington. *Paper Walls* by Scarlett Theatre, dir by Alice Power and Alice Purcell at the Purcell Room: rev by Nightingale.

2341   "Reviews of Productions." *LTR*. 1996; 16(7): 387-393. Lang.: Eng.

UK-England: London. 1996. ■*Brothers of the Brush* by Jimmy Murphy, dir by Lynne Parker at the Arts: rev by Billington, Butler, de Jongh, Hewison, Murray, Nathan, Nightingale, Paton, Sierz, Spencer, Taylor, Tinker, Tushingham, Woddis. *The Bells* by Leopold Lewis, dir by David Oldman at the White Bear: rev by Reade, Simpkins. *Byrne and Brother* by Eamon Morrissey at the Tricycle: rev by Curtis, Foss, Godfrey-Faussett, Hemming.

2342   "Reviews of Productions." *LTR*. 1996; 16(3): 113-131. Lang.: Eng.

UK-England: London. 1996. ■*Two Trains Running* by August Wilson, dir by Paulette Randall at the Tricycle: rev by Billington, Butler, Coveney, Curtis, Grant, Gross, Hewison, Hughes, Macaulay, Michaels, Morley, Nathan, Nightingale, Sierz, Spencer, Taylor, Tinker. *Les Enfants du Paradis* by Simon Callow, based on film by Jacques Prévert, dir by Callow at the Barbican: rev by Billington, Butler, de Jongh, Edwardes, Gross, Hirschhorn, Hughes, Macaulay, Morley, Nathan, Nightingale, Paton, Peter, Smith, Spencer, Taylor, Tinker. *Stanley* by Pam Gems, dir by John Caird at the Cottesloe: rev by Benedict, Billington, Butler, Coveney, de Jongh, Edwardes, Feaver, Gross, Macaulay, Morley, Nathan, Nightingale, Peter, Sherrin, Smith, Spencer, Taylor, Tinker.

2343   "Reviews of Productions." *LTR*. 1996; 16(3): 132-144. Lang.: Eng.

UK-England: London. 1996. ■*The Fields of Ambrosia* by Joel Higgins, lyrics by Higgins, music by Martin Silvestri, dir by Gregory S. Hurst at the Aldwych: rev by Butler, Campbell, Christopher, Coveney, Darvell, de Jongh, Gardner, Gross, Hirschhorn, Hughes, Macaulay, Morley, Nathan, Nightingale, Paton, Peter, Spencer, Taylor, Tinker. *The Bitter Tears of Petra von Kant (Die Bitteren Tränen der Petra von Kant)* by Rainer Werner Fassbinder, transl. by Anthony Vivis, dir by Alex Krokidas at the Etcetera: rev by Hajaj. *The Art of Random Whistling* by Mark

Jenkinson, dir by Rufus Norris at the Young Vic Studio: rev by Bayley, Curtis, Gardner, Greer, Spencer.

2344   "Reviews of Productions." *LTR*. 1996; 16(3): 144-147. Lang.: Eng.

UK-England: London. 1996. ■*Erasmus Montanus* by Ludvig Holberg, adapted by Julian Forsyth, dir by Forsyth and Margarete Forsyth at BAC: rev by Bassett, Curtis. *Cat and Mouse (Sheep)* by Gregory Motton, dir by Motton and Ramin Gray, and *Services* by Elfriede Jelinek, transl. by Nick Grindell, dir by Annie Siddons at the Gate: rev by Bassett, Bayley, Billington, Curtis, Foss, Hemming, Stratton. *Don Juan*, devised by Commotion Theatre Company, dir by John Wright at BAC: rev by Abdulla, Gale.

2345   "Reviews of Productions." *LTR*. 1996; 16(4): 201-204. Lang.: Eng.

UK-England: London. 1996. ■*East Lynne* by Lisa Evans, from the novel by Mrs. Henry Wood, dir by Philip Franks at the Greenwich: rev by Coveney, de Jongh, Gross, Hanks, Nathan, Nightingale, Silvester-Carr, Tushingham. *Heaven by Storm* by The Umbilical Brothers (Shane Dundas and Dave Collins), at the Arts: rev by Armitstead, Games, Hay, Kingston, Michaels, Rampton. *The Crime* by Doug Rollins, dir by Rollins at the Man in the Moon: rev by Godfrey-Faussett.

2346   "Reviews of Productions." *LTR*. 1996; 16(6): 355-356. Lang.: Eng.

UK-England: London. 1996. ■*Nunsense* by Dan Goggin, dir by Graham Ashe at the Jermyn Street: rev by Foss, Hughes, Stratton. *Turpin* by Barry Purchese, dir by John Price at the Old Red Lion: rev by Michaels, Stratton. *Modern Problems in Science*, devised and performed by Dick Costolo, Phil Granchi and Rich Fulcher, at the Bloomsbury: rev by Kingston, Rampton, Yates.

2347   "Reviews of Productions." *LTR*. 1996; 16(6): 357-361. Lang.: Eng.

UK-England: London. 1996. ■*Disgracefully Yours* by Richard O'Brien, dir by Christopher Malcolm at the Comedy: rev by Bell, Butler, Edwardes, Gardner, Gross, Hagerty, Hughes, Macaulay, Nathan, Nightingale, Paton, Peter, Rampton, Smith, Spencer, Usher. *Flesh* by Spencer Hazel, dir by Frantic Assembly at the Warehouse: rev by Bayley, Brennan, Godfrey-Faussett, Kingston, McPherson. *Skirmishes* by Neil Biswas, dir by Robert Pepper at the Etcetera: rev by Abdulla, Marlowe.

2348   "Reviews of Productions." *LTR*. 1996; 16(3): 159-163. Lang.: Eng.

UK-England: London. 1996. ■*Artemisia* by Anne-Marie Casey, dir by Joy Perino at the Turtle Key: rev by Bassett, Curtis, Greer, Simpkins. *Lee Evans* at the Lyric and Apollo: rev by Games, Hawkins, Nightingale, Sherrin, Shuttleworth, Smith, Taylor, Thompson, Tinker. *Time Out*, Wareham, Yates. *It Took More than One Man* by Ivan Cartwright, dir by Robin Baker at the Southwark Playhouse: rev by Abdulla, Hutera.

2349   "Reviews of Productions." *LTR*. 1996; 16(6): 362-368. Lang.: Eng.

UK-England: London. 1996. ■*Mary Stuart (Maria Stuart)* by Friedrich Schiller, transl. by Jeremy Sams, dir by Howard Davies at the Lyttelton: rev by Billington, Butler, Coveney, de Jongh, Grant, Gross, Hagerty, Hirschhorn, Hughes, Macaulay, Morley, Nathan, Nightingale, Paton, Peter, Smith, Spencer, Taylor, Tinker. *Song from a Forgotten City* by Edward Thomas, dir by Thomas at the Donmar Warehouse: rev by de Jongh, Nightingale. *The Strangest Meeting* by Jean Robinson and John Sinclair, dir by Seamus Newham at the Baron's Court: rev by Bassett.

2350   "Reviews of Productions." *LTR*. 1996; 16(6): 369-370. Lang.: Eng.

UK-England: London. 1996. ■*Corpsing* by Peter Barnes, dir by Diana Fairfax at the Tristan Bates: rev by Foss, Reade. *More Than Kisses*, written and dir by Clare Basel and Graeme Messer, at the Riverside: rev by Abdulla, Hutera. *Clowns* by Christina Reid, dir by Natasha Betteridge at the Orange Tree Room: rev by Gale, Gardner, Tushingham.

2351   "Reviews of Productions." *LTR*. 1996; 16(3): 148-153. Lang.: Eng.

UK-England: London. 1996. ■*The Long and the Short and the Tall* by Willis Hall, dir by Paul Jerricho at the Albery: rev by Abdulla, Butler, Coveney, de Jongh, Dowden, Gardner, Gilbert, Gross, Hewison, Kingston, Paton, Spencer, Tinker. *Ben Hur* by Rob Ballard, dir by Patrick Bramwells at the Croydon Warehouse: rev by Bassett, Curtis, Foss,

DRAMA: —Performance/production

Tushingham. *The Goodwoman of Setzuan (Der Gute Mensch von Sezuan)* by Bertolt Brecht, transl. by Eric Bentley, collaborators Ruth Berlau and Margarete Steffin, dir by Sam Walters at the Orange Tree: rev by Curtis, Kingston, Marlowe, Murray, Stratton.

2352   "Reviews of Productions." *LTR*. 1996; 16(3): 153-158. Lang.: Eng.

UK-England: London. 1996. ■*Samuel Beckett Season (Breath, Rockaby, Footfalls, Not I, Come and Go)*, five plays by Samuel Beckett, dir by Ilan Reichel at the Etcetera: rev by Foss. *Valley Song* by Athol Fugard, dir by Fugard at the Royal Court: rev by Billington, Butler, Coveney, de Jongh, Edwardes, Gross, Hassell, Hughes, Macaulay, Morley, Nathan, Nightingale, Paton, Peter, Reade, Sherrin, Sierz, Spencer, Taylor, Tinker. *Immaterial Witness* by Ron Aldridge, dir by Richard Bridge at the Grace: rev by Godfrey-Faussett.

2353   "Reviews of Productions." *LTR*. 1996; 16(3): 172-176. Lang.: Eng.

UK-England: London. 1996. ■*Sweet Panic* by Stephen Poliakoff, dir by Poliakoff at the Hampstead: rev by Billington, Butler, Coveney, de Jongh, Grant, Gross, Hughes, Macaulay, Morley, Nathan, Nightingale, Peter, Sierz, Smith, Spencer, Taylor. *Twentieth Century* by Andrew Scott, dir by Kate Bligh at the New End: rev by Hemblade, Marlowe.

2354   "Reviews of Productions." *LTR*. 1996; 16(3): 164-171. Lang.: Eng.

UK-England: London. 1996. ■*Down Among the Mini-Beasts* by Bryony Lavery, dir by Roman Stefanski at the Polka: rev by Bassett, Gardner, Haydon, Taylor. *The Changing Room* by David Storey, dir by James Macdonald at the Duke of York's: rev by Billington, Butler, Christopher, Coveney, Darvell, de Jongh, Gross, Macaulay, Morley, Nathan, Nightingale, Paton, Peter, Sherrin, Spencer, Taylor, Tinker. *O Isabella! You Bad, Bad Girl*, conceived by Alison Andrews, text by Lavinia Murray, dir by Andrews and Claire Thacker at BAC: rev by Edwardes, Kingston.

2355   "Reviews of Productions." *LTR*. 1996; 16(7): 394-401. Lang.: Eng.

UK-England: London. 1996. ■*Bondagers* by Sue Glover, dir by Ian Brown at the Donmar Warehouse: rev by Curtis, Foss, Grant, Gross, Kingston, Murray, Woddis. *Sex and Sadness* by Ronald Selwyn Phillips, from fiction by Guy de Maupassant, dir by Katherine Shannon at the Etcetera: rev by Higginson. *Passion*, a musical by Stephen Sondheim, book by James Lapine, dir by Jeremy Sams at the Queen's: rev by Barnsley, Billington, Butler, Coveney, de Jongh, Grant, Gross, Hirschhorn, Hughes, Macaulay, Morley, Nathan, Nightingale, Peter, Seckerson, Smith, Taylor, Tinker.

2356   "Reviews of Productions." *LTR*. 1996; 16(8): 487-489. Lang.: Eng.

UK-England: London. 1996. ■*Oedipus Needs Help* by Jonathan Neale, dir by Fay Barratt at the Diorama, NW1: rev by Godfrey-Faussett, Hutera. *Nothing Lasts Forever* by Huw Chadbourn, dir by Chadbourn at BAC 1: rev by Bassett, Curtis, Gardner, Marlowe, Reade. *Bitter Lemon (La Piel del limón)* by Jaime Salom, transl. by Patricia W. O'Connor, dir by James Brining at the Orange Tree Room: rev by Godfrey-Faussett, McPherson.

2357   "Reviews of Productions." *LTR*. 1996; 16(7): 402-412. Lang.: Eng.

UK-England: London. 1996. ■*Harry and Me* by Nigel Williams, dir by James Macdonald at the Royal Court: rev by Barnsley, Billington, Butler, Christopher, Coveney, de Jongh, Gross, Hemming, Hirschhorn, Hughes, Morley, Nathan, Nightingale, Paton, Peter, Sierz, Smith, Spencer, Taylor, Usher. *The Last Romantics* by Nigel Williams, dir by Matthew Francis at the Greenwich: rev by Billington, Butler, de Jongh, Gross, Hanks, Hemming, Hirschhorn, Nathan, Nightingale, Peter, Reade, Spencer, Usher, Woddis. *Tap Dogs* by Dein Perry, dir by Nigel Triffit at the Lyric: rev by Barnsley, Brown, Gross, Marlowe, Robertson, Sacks, Taylor.

2358   "Reviews of Productions." *LTR*. 1996; 18(10): 1063-1066. Lang.: Eng.

UK-England: London. 1996. ■*A Midsummer Night's Dream* by William Shakespeare, dir by Yukio Ninagawa at the Mermaid: rev by Butler, Coveney, Curtis, Foss, Gross, Logan, Macauley, Nightingale, Peter, Spencer, Stratton, Taylor, Usher. *A Midsummer Night's Dream* by William Shakespeare, dir by Lucy Gordon-Clark at the Chelsea Centre: rev by Logan.

2359   "Reviews of Productions." *LTR*. 1996; 16(7): 412-415. Lang.: Eng.

UK-England: London. 1996. ■*Immaculate Deception*, a musical by David Young, book by Lynn Kilcourse, dir by Gail Lowe at the Wimbledon Studio: rev by McPherson. *Lady Into Fox* by Neil Bartlett, from the novel by David Garnett, dir by Leah Hausman at the Lyric: rev by Bayley, Coveney, Gardner, Godfrey-Faussett, Gross, Hutera, Nathan, Nightingale, Peter, Reade, Spencer. *Vagina Dentata* by Paul Davies, with additional material by Anton Čechov, dir by Davies at the Riverside: rev by Abdulla, Foss.

2360   "Reviews of Productions." *LTR*. 1996; 16(8): 467-469. Lang.: Eng.

UK-England: London. 1996. ■*Lady Chatterley* by Marshall Gould, adapted from the novel by D.H. Lawrence, dir by Clare Davidson at the Cockpit: rev by Curtis, Foss, Marmion, Nightingale, Turpin. *Downtown Paradise* by Mark Jenkins, dir by Sarah Esdaile at the Finborough: rev by Godfrey-Faussett, Kingston, Simpkins. *Emilia Galotti* by Gotthold Ephraim Lessing, transl by Mary Luckhurst, dir by Christopher Hynes at the Courtyard, N1: rev by Higginson, Kingston, Reade.

2361   "Reviews of Productions." *LTR*. 1996; 16(7): 416-420. Lang.: Eng.

UK-England: London. 1996. ■*Sugar Dollies* by Klaus Chatten, transl. by Anthony Vivis, dir by Indhu Rubasingham, and *After the Rain* by Sergi Belbel, transl. by Xavier Rodriguez Rosell, David George and John London, dir by Gaynor Macfarlane at the Gate: rev by Billington, Spencer, Tushingham. *Roberto Calvi Is Alive and Well* by Roy Smiles, dir by Smiles at the Hen & Chickens: rev by Higginson, Stevens. *Miss Julie (Fröken Julie)* by August Strindberg, transl. by Meredith Oakes, dir by Polly Teale at the Young Vic: rev by Bassett, Bayley, Christopher, Gardner, Gross, Hughes, Kellaway, Macaulay, Morley, Paton, Peter, Smith, Spencer.

2362   "Reviews of Productions." *LTR*. 1996; 16(7): 420-423. Lang.: Eng.

UK-England: London. 1996. ■*A Dream Play (Ett Drömspel)* by August Strindberg, transl by Jonas Finlay, dir by Finlay at the Bridewell: rev by Driver, Michaels, Reade. *The Verge* by Susan Glaspell, dir by Sam Walters at the Orange Tree: rev by Abdulla, Billington, Curtis, Darvell, Gore-Langton, Hewison, Kingston. *The Three Penny Opera (Die Dreigroschenoper)* by Bertolt Brecht and Kurt Weill, dir by Mark Pattenden at the Lyric Hammersmith: rev by Milnes.

2363   "Reviews of Productions." *LTR*. 1996; 16(7): 438-439. Lang.: Eng.

UK-England: London. 1996. ■*Binary Dreamers* by Robert Shearman, dir by David Craik at the Man in the Moon: rev by Marlowe, Marmion. *An Insect Aside* by Somervell Scott, dir by Philip D'Orleans and *Stealing Souls* by Judy Upton, dir by Shabnam Shabazi at the Red Room: rev by Gardner, Godfrey-Faussett, Stevens.

2364   "Reviews of Productions." *LTR*. 1996; 16(7): 424-432. Lang.: Eng.

UK-England: London. 1996. ■*Clocks and Whistles* by Samuel Adamson, dir by Dominic Dromgoole at the Bush: rev by Billington, Butler, Christopher, Curtis, Hirshhorn, Kellaway, Macauley, Morley, Peter, Sierz, Smith, Spencer, Taylor, Tinker. *The Thickness of Skin* by Clare McIntyre, dir by Hettie MacDonald at Theatre Upstairs: rev by Billington, Butler, Christopher, de Jongh, Foss, Gross, Hemming, Kellaway, Morley, Nathan, Nightingale, Peter, Spencer, Taylor, Tinker. *The Fruit Has Turned to Jam in the Fields* by Jyll Bradley, dir by Grainne Byrne and Emma Byrne at the Young Vic Studio: rev by Bassett, Hutera, Turpin, Tushingham.

2365   "Reviews of Productions." *LTR*. 1996; 16(7): 435-438. Lang.: Eng.

UK-England: London. 1996. ■*A Week's Worth* by Irene Worth, dir by Worth at the Almeida: rev by Billington, Cavendish, de Jongh, Kellaway, Macauley, Morley. *Dirty Boggers* by Ray Kilby, Carolina Giametta and Abi Cohen, dir by Kilby at the Grace: Abdulla, McPherson. *Victoriana* by David Hart, dir by Jon Harris at the New End: rev by Abdulla, Church, Driver, Kingston, Nathan, Smith.

2366   "Reviews of Productions." *LTR*. 1996; 16(7): 451-458. Lang.: Eng.

DRAMA: —Performance/production

UK-England: London. 1996. ■*La Dolce Vita* by David Glass and Paul Sand, music by Nino Rota, lyrics by Sand, adapted from movie by Federico Fellini, dir by Glass at the Lyric Hammersmith: rev by Barnsley, Bassett, Billington, Christopher, Coveney, Gilbert, Gross, Hanks, Hughes, Hutera, Kingston, Nathan, Shuttleworth, Spencer, Stratton. *Bravely Fought the Queen* by Mahesh Dattani, dir by Dattani and Michael Walling at the BAC 2: rev by Shuttleworth, Spencer, Tushingham. *Mandy Patinkin in Concert* with Paul Ford at piano at the Almeida: rev by Davis, Jones, Kellaway, O'Connor, Seckerson, Sweeting.

2367   "Reviews of Productions." *LTR*. 1996; 16(8): 458-461. Lang.: Eng.

UK-England: London. 1996. ■*The Return of the Soldier* by Anthony Psaila, from the novel by Rebecca West, dir by Andrea Brooks at the Old Red Lion: rev by Kingston. *The Taming of the Shrew* by William Shakespeare, presented by the Royal Shakespeare Company, dir by Gale Edwards at the Barbican: rev by Curtis, Gore-Langton, Hanks, Hassell, Kellaway, Morley, Nightingale, Paton, Stratton. *The School for Wives (L'École des femmes)* by Molière, transl by Neil Bartlett, dir by Kate Hall at the Etcetera: rev by Godfrey-Faussett.

2368   "Reviews of Productions." *LTR*. 1996; 16(8): 462-466. Lang.: Eng.

UK-England: London. 1996. ■*Definitely Doris* by Leo Carusone and Patty Carver, dir by Larry Pellegrini at the King's Head: rev by Barnsley, Curtis, Gardner, Gross, Hemblade, Hughes, Hutera, Lyttle, Nathan, Nightingale, Peter, Spencer, Tinker. *Ground Zero* by Adam Kimmel, dir by Lucy Pitman-Wallace at the Southwark Playhouse: rev by Hutera, Tushingham. *The Relapse* by Sir John Vanbrugh, presented by the Royal Shakespeare Company, dir by Ian Judge at The Pit: rev by Curtis, Hirshhorn, Hughes, Kingston, Marlowe, Murray, Paton, Stratton.

2369   "Reviews of Productions." *LTR*. 1996; 16(8): 470-478. Lang.: Eng.

UK-England: London. 1996. ■*Some Sunny Day* by Martin Sherman, dir by Roger Michell at the Hampstead: rev by Barnsley, Benedict, Billington, Christopher, de Jongh, Gross, Hanks, Hirshhorn, Hughes, Kellaway, Morley, Murray, Nathan, Nightingale, Paton, Peter, Sierz, Tinker, Woddis. *The Boys in the Bar* by Toby Collins, dir by Lynn Tilden at the White Bear: rev by Foss. *Miss Julie (Fröken Julie)* by August Strindberg, transl by Gregory Motton, dir by Nick Philippou at the Gate: rev by Butler, Edwardes, Hassell, Hewison, Massey, Nightingale, Shuttleworth, Sierz, Spencer, Taylor.

2370   "Reviews of Productions." *LTR*. 1996; 16(8): 478-487. Lang.: Eng.

UK-England: London. 1996. ■*Angels* by Mary Considine, dir by Considine at the Man in the Moon: rev by Abdulla, Stevens. *Elvis—The Musical* by Jack Good and Ray Cooney, dir by Keith Strachan and Carole Todd at the Prince of Wales: rev by Christopher, de Jongh, Gross, Hagerty, Hibbert, McPherson, Morley, Nightingale, Paton, Smith, Spencer, Sullivan, Thorncroft, Tinker. *Endgame (Fin de partie)* by Samuel Beckett, dir by Katie Mitchell at the Donmar Warehouse: rev by Billington, Butler, Coveney, Curtis, Edwardes, Gross, Hagerty, Macauley, Morley, Nightingale, Paton, Peter, Smith, Spencer, Taylor.

2371   "Reviews of Productions." *LTR*. 1996; 16(19): 1198. Lang.: Eng.

UK-England: London. 1996. ■*Sunspots* by Judy Upton, dir by Lisa Goldman at the BAC 1: rev by Bassett, Williams. *City of Love* by Toby Mitchell, dir by Olivia Jacobs at the Etcetera: rev by Barton, Whitebrook.

2372   "Reviews of Productions." *LTR*. 1996; 16(8): 490-500. Lang.: Eng.

UK-England: London. 1996. ■*Salad Days*, book and lyrics by Dorothy Reynolds and Julian Slade, music by Slade, dir by Ned Sherrin at the Vaudeville: rev by Abdulla, Benedict, Billington, Bradshaw, Coveney, Curtis, Foss, Gross, Hagerty, Hughes, Kingston, Macauley, Morley, Nathan, Paton, Peter. *The Prince's Play* by Victor Hugo, new verse adaptation of *Le Roi s'amuse* by Tony Harrison, dir by Richard Eyre at the Olivier: rev by Billington, Butler, Coveney, Curtis, Edwardes, Gross, Hughes, Macauley, Morley, Nathan, Nightingale, Peter, Smith, Spencer, Taylor. *The Shattered Vessel (Der zerbruchene Krug)* by Heinrich von Kleist, dir by Tim Merchant at the Riverside: rev by Abdulla, Bassett, Shuttleworth, Stevens. *Two Gentlemen of Soho* by Josh Lacey, dir by Ali-

son Rigden at the Warehouse, Croydon: rev by Bassett, Higgonson, McPherson, Stratton.

2373   "Reviews of Productions." *LTR*. 1996; 16(8): 519-528. Lang.: Eng.

UK-England: London. 1996. ■*Twelve Angry Men* by Reginald Rose, dir by Harold Pinter at the Comedy: rev by Billington, Butler, Coveney, Curtis, Grant, Gross, Hagerty, Hirshhorn, Hughes, Macauley, Morley, Nathan, Nightingale, Peter, Sierz, Smith, Spencer, Taylor, Tinker. *Penn and Teller* at the Sadler's Wells: rev by Bassett, Games, Preston, Shuttleworth. *Romeo and Juliet* by William Shakespeare presented by the Royal Shakespeare Company, dir by Adrian Noble at the Barbican: rev by Abdulla, Bassett, Gore-Langton, Hassell, Murray, Stratton.

2374   "Reviews of Productions." *LTR*. 1996; 16(8): 529-534. Lang.: Eng.

UK-England: London. 1996. ■*The Devil Is an Ass* by Ben Jonson, presented by The Royal Shakespeare Company, dir by Matthew Warchus at The Pit: rev by Curtis, Hemming, Hirshhorn, Kingston, Smith, Stratton. *Dealt With* by Tony Marchant, dir by Tim Stark at Chelsea Centre: rev by Tushingham, Woddis. *Tartuffe* by Molière, transl. by Richard Wilbur, dir by Jonathan Kent at the Almeida: rev by Benedict, Butler, Christopher, Coveney, Curtis, Gardner, Gore-Langton, Gross, Kingston, Macauley, Morley, Peter, Smith.

2375   "Reviews of Productions." *LTR*. 1996; 16(8): 534-536. Lang.: Eng.

UK-England: London. 1996. ■*Sweetest Gift* by Matthew Campling, dir by Campling at the Hen & Chickens: rev by Bassett, Stevens, Stratton. *What a Bleedin' Liberty* by Tom Kempinski, dir by Philip Hedley at Theatre Royal, Stratford East: rev by Abdulla, Curtis, Foss, Kingston, Morgan, Turpin. *Tales of the Lost Formicans* by Constance Congdon, dir by Caroline Hunt at Brixton Shaw: rev by Foss, Godfrey-Faussett.

2376   "Reviews of Productions." *LTR*. 1996; 16(9): 537-542. Lang.: Eng.

UK-England: London. 1996. ■*The Designated Mourner* by Wallace Shawn, dir by David Hare at the Cottesloe: rev by Billington, Butler, Coveney, de Jongh, Edwardes, Gross, Hagerty, Hirshhorn, Macauley, Morley, Nathan, Nightingale, Paton, Peter, Smith, Spencer, Taylor, Tinker. *Epilogue of the Raindrops* adapted from the novel by Einer Mar Gudmundson by the Gargoyle Theatre Company (Reykjavik) dir by Franziska Schutz at the Duke of Cambridge: rev by Hutera, Stratton. *Breaking the Mould* devised by Strathcona Theatre Company, dir by Anne Cleary and Ian McCurrach at the Young Vic Studio: rev by Reade, Simpkins.

2377   "Reviews of Productions." *LTR*. 1996; 16(9): 543-547. Lang.: Eng.

UK-England: London. 1996. ■*Foe* by Mark Wheatley, adapted from the novel by J.M. Coetzee, dir by Annie Castledine and Marcello Magni at the Young Vic: rev by Curtis, Edwardes, Kingston, Marlowe. *Haven* by Deborah Catesby, dir by Pat O'Toole at the Bridewell: rev by Bassett, Curtis, Reade. *Mules* by Winsome Pinnock, dir by Roxanna Silbert at Theatre Upstairs: rev by Bayley, Coveney, Curtis, Edwardes, Gore-Langton, Gross, Hewison, Kingston, Michaels, Murray, Nathan.

2378   "Reviews of Productions." *LTR*. 1996; 18(9): 1049-1050. Lang.: Eng.

UK-England: London. 1996. ■*They Shoot Horses, Don't They?* by Ray Hermann, from the novel by Horace McCoy, dir by Edward Wilson at the Bloomsbury: rev by Bassett, Cavendish, Dowden. *A Plague on Both Your Houses* by Pete Brooks, from the work of William Shakespeare, dir by Brooks at The Place: rev by Curtis, Stratton. *Othello* by William Shakespeare, dir by Edward Wilson at the Bloomsbury: rev by Reade, Skelton.

2379   "Reviews of Productions." *LTR*. 1996; 18(9): 1051-1061. Lang.: Eng.

UK-England: London. 1996. ■*The Heidi Chronicles* by Wendy Wasserstein, dir by David Taylor at the Greenwich: rev by de Jongh, Edwardes, Gardner, Gross, Hagerty, Morley, Nathan, Sierz, Smith, Spencer, Taylor. *When We Dead Awaken (Når vi døde vågner)* by Henrik Ibsen, adapted by Ajay Chowdhury, dir by Chowdhury at the Etcetera: rev by Marmio. *Blinded by the Sun* by Stephen Poliakoff, dir by Ron Daniels at the Cottesloe: rev by Butler, Christopher, Clark, Coveney, Curtis, Edwardes,

DRAMA: —Performance/production

Gardner, Gross, Hagerty, Hughes, Macauley, Morley, Nathan, Nightingale, Peter, Smith, Spencer, Taylor, Tinker.

2380 "Reviews of Productions." *LTR.* 1996; 18(9): 1061-1062. Lang.: Eng.

UK-England: London. 1996. ■*The Tailor-Made Man* by Claudio Macor, dir by Macor at the Cockpit: rev by Abdulla, Morley. *Into the Woods*, musical by Stephen Sondheim, book by James Lapine, dir by Caterina Loriggio at the Landor: rev by Cavendish, Foss. *A Midsummer Night's Dream* by William Shakespeare, dir by Barrie Rutter at Shakespeare's Globe: rev by Cavendish.

2381 "Reviews of Productions." *LTR.* 1996; 18(10): 1081-1088. Lang.: Eng.

UK-England: London. 1996. ■*L'splendida vergonya del fet mal fet (The Splendid Shame of the Deed Badly Done)* by Carles Santos, dir by Santos at the King's: rev by Billington, Christiansen, Fisher, Hoyle, Kingston, Lockerbie, Peter, Turpin. *Time and the Room (Die Zeit und das Zimmer)* by Botho Strauss, transl. by Jeremy Sams, dir by Martin Duncan at the Royal Lyceum: rev by Benedict, Billington, Christiansen, Coveney, Donald, Fisher, Kingston, Peter, Shuttleworth. *Uncle Vanya (Diadia Vania)* by Anton Čechov, Italian transl by Milli Martinelle and Peter Stein, dir by Stein at the King's: rev by Butler, Couling, Coveney, Fisher, Lockerbie, Macauley, Nightingale, O'Connor.

2382 "Reviews of Productions." *LTR.* 1996; 18(10): 1119-1120. Lang.: Eng.

UK-England: London. 1996. ■*Restless Farewell* by William George Q, dir by Tim Crook and *Free Fall* by Elizabeth Berry, dir by Richard Shannon at BAC 2: rev by Tushingham, Walsh. *Great Things* by Nigel Smith, dir by Richard Bridge at the Grace: rev by Cavendish, McPherson. *Entertaining Angels* by Nicola McCartney and Lucy McLellan, dir by McCartney at Warehouse, Croydon: rev by Billington, Cooper, Farrell, Fisher, Lockerbie.

2383 "Reviews of Productions." *LTR.* 1996; 18(10): 1121-1127. Lang.: Eng.

UK-England: London. 1996. ■*Bartleby* by Larry Lane, from novella *Bartleby the Scrivener* by Herman Melville, dir by Jonathan Hollaway at Pleasance London: rev by Bruce, Kingston, Lockerbie, Logan, Shuttleworth, Spencer, Stratton. *Pentecost* by Stewart Parker, dir by Lynne Parker at Donmar Warehouse: rev by Benedict, Curtis, Edwardes, Gardner, Gross, Macauley, Nightingale, Peter, Sierz, Smith, Spencer, Tinker. *Judith* by Howard Barker, dir by Barker at BAC Main: rev by Cooper, Coveney, Curtis, Fisher, Gardner, Marlowe, Marmion, Peter.

2384 "Reviews of Productions." *LTR.* 1996; 16(18): 1127-1128. Lang.: Eng.

UK-England: London. 1996. ■*The Lives of the Saints* by Sebastian Baczkiewicz, dir by Patrick Kealey at the Old Red Lion: rev by Abdulla, Allan, Bassett. *Carbon Miranda* by Robert Young, dir by Dawn Lintern at the Southwark Playhouse: rev by Abdulla, Simpkins. *Three Girls in Blue (Tri devuški v golubom)* by Ludmila Petruševskaya, transl by Stephen Mulrine, dir by Wils Wilson at the White Bear: rev by Barton, Marmion.

2385 "Reviews of Productions." *LTR.* 1996; 16(19): 1180-1182. Lang.: Eng.

UK-England: London. 1996. ■*Fine* by Christine Entwisle, dir by Entwisle at the Young Vic Studio: rev by Barten, Stratton. *Close to You* by Stella Duffy, songs by Karen Carpenter, dir by Martyn Duffy at Hen & Chickens: rev by Marmion, Stevens. *Sarrasine* by Neil Bartlett, from story by Honoré de Balzac, dir by Bartlett at the Lyric Hammersmith: rev by Coveney, Curtis, Hewison, Kingston, Logan, Macauley, McPherson, Morley, Nathan, Taylor.

2386 "Reviews of Productions." *LTR.* 1996; 16(19): 1147-1154. Lang.: Eng.

UK-England: London. 1996. ■*Kindertransport* by Diane Samuels, dir by Abigail Morris at the Vaudeville: rev by Butler, Coveney, Curtis, Edwardes, Gardner, Gore-Langton, Gross, Hagerty, Hughes, Kingston, Macauley, McPherson, Morley, Round, Sierz, Spencer, Usher. *Portrait of an Unknown Woman* by Andrew Merkler, dir by Simon Parry at New End: rev by Nathan, Reade. *The Flight Into Egypt* by Julian Garner, dir by John Dove at the Hampstead: rev by Billington, Butler, Coveney, Curtis, Edwardes, Foss, Gross, Kingston, Morley, Nathan, Peter, Spencer, Taylor.

2387 "Reviews of Productions." *LTR.* 1996; 16(19): 1155-1156. Lang.: Eng.

UK-England: London. 1996. ■*Damon and Pythias* by Richard Edwards, dir by Gaynor Macfarlane at Shakespeare's Globe: rev by Gardner, Woddis. *If I Should Fall* by Bret Allen, dir by Adam Fahey at the Off Broadway: rev by Godfrey-Faussett. *Rhona Cameron*, a solo show by Cameron at the Drill Hall: rev by Bassett, Dessau, Foss, Games, Rampton.

2388 "Reviews of Productions." *LTR.* 1996; 16(19): 1159-1164. Lang.: Eng.

UK-England: London. 1996. ■*A Midsummer Night's Dream* by William Shakespeare, presented by the RSC, dir by Adrian Noble at the Barbican: rev by Bassett, Butler, Christopher, Curtis, Macauley, Nathan, Stevens, Stratton. *Swan Lake* by Čajkovskij, choreographed by Matthew Bourne for Adventures In Motion Pictures at the Piccadilly: rev by Brown, Craine, Crisp, Dromgoole, Gilbert, Kyle, Mackrell, Morley, Parry, Robertson, Sacks, Smith, Usher. *The Ruffian on the Stair* by Joe Orton at the Man in the Moon: rev by Hemblade.

2389 "Reviews of Productions." *LTR.* 1996; 16(19): 1165-1168. Lang.: Eng.

UK-England: London. 1996. ■*Faust* by Goethe, adapted by Howard Brenton from a literal transl by Christa Weisman, dir Michael Bogdanov for the RSC at The Pit: rev by Curtis, Logan, Kingston, Macauley, Smith. *King Lear* by Shakespeare, dir by Harry Meacher at Pentameters: rev by Abdulla. *The Little Comedy* and *SummerShare*, two one-act musicals by Keith Herrmann, book and lyrics by Barry Harmlan, dir by Steven Dexter at the Bridewell: rev by Abdulla, Bassett, Darvell, Hagerty, Morley, Nathan, Usher.

2390 "Reviews of Productions." *LTR.* 1996; 16(19): 1168-1179. Lang.: Eng.

UK-England: London. 1996. ■*Passionfish* by Joff Chafer and Toby Wilsher, dir by Chafer and Wilsher at the Purcell Room: rev by Affleck, Bassett, Brennan. *Oedipus the King (Oidípous Týrannos)* and *Oedipus at Colonus (Oidípous epì Kolonō)* by Sophocles, transl by Ranjit Bolt, dir by Peter Hall at the Olivier: rev by Billington, Butler, Christopher, Coveney, Curtis, de Jongh, Edwardes, Gore-Langton, Gross, Hagerty, Hassell, Hughes, Macauley, Morley, Murray, Nathan, Nightingale, Peters, Spencer, Stothard, Taylor, Whitley. *Uncle Vanya (Diadia Vania)* by Anton Čechov, transl by Mike Poulton, dir by Bill Bryden at the Albery: rev by Curtis, Gardner, Smith, Stratton.

2391 "Reviews of Productions." *LTR.* 1996; 16(19): 1183-1191. Lang.: Eng.

UK-England: London. 1996. ■*Ashes to Ashes* by Harold Pinter, dir by Pinter at the Theatre Upstairs (Ambassador's Circle): rev by Billington, Brown, Butler, Coveney, de Jongh, Edwardes, Gore-Langton, Gross, Haggerty, Macauley, Morley, Nathan, Nightingale, Peter, Sierz, Smith, Spencer, Taylor, Tinker. *Bug* by Tracy Letts, dir by Wilson Milam at the Gate: rev by Bassett, de Jongh, Gardner, Peter, Shuttleworth, Smith, Spencer, Turpin, Tushingham. *Gulp Fiction* by Trish Cooke, dir by Indhu Rubasingham at Theatre Royal, Stratford East: rev by Stratton.

2392 "Reviews of Productions." *LTR.* 1996; 16(19): 1197. Lang.: Eng.

UK-England: London. 1996. ■*The Fall of the House of Usherettes* by Penny Saunders, Chris Britton and Tim Britton, dir by John Tellett at the Lyric Studio: rev by Tushingham. *My Dear Emily* by Sue Emmy Jennings, dir by Andrew Wade at the Duke of Cambridge: rev by Allan. *Bluebeard's Castle (A Kékszakállú herceg vára)* by Béla Balázs, performed in Japanese by Shuji Terayama from a translation by Carol Fisher Sorgenfrei at the Riverside: rev by Kingston.

2393 "Reviews of Productions." *LTR.* 1996; 16(19): 1191-1196. Lang.: Eng.

UK-England: London. 1996. ■*Kissing Bingo* by Chris Goode, dir by Helen Rayonor at the Finborough: rev by Bassett, Skelton, Tushingham. *The Seven Streams of the River Ota (Les Sept Branches de la Rivière Ota)* by Robert Lepage and Ex Machina, dir by Lepage at Lyttelton: rev by Billington, Butler, Coveney, de Jongh, Gore-Langton, Nightingale, Shuttleworth, Smith, Spencer, Stratton, Taylor, Wardle. *The Stillness of Pleasure* by Edward Clark, Diana Harland and Martin McDougall, dir by Clark at the Turtle Key: rev by Nevett.

DRAMA: —Performance/production

2394 "Reviews of Productions." *LTR.* 1996; 16(20): 1221-1232. Lang.: Eng.

UK-England: London. 1996. ■*Cash on Delivery* by Michael Cooney, dir by Ray Cooney at the Whitehall: rev by Brown, Christopher, Darvell, de Jongh, Gardner, Gore-Langton, Gross, Hagerty, Morley, Murray, Nathan, Nightingale, Peter, Spencer, Tinker. *All Manner of Means* by Michael Kingsbury, dir by Kingsbury at BAC 2: rev by Tushingham, Woddis. *Who's Afraid of Virginia Woolf?* by Edward Albee, dir by Howard Davies at the Almeida: rev by Billington, Brown, Butler, Christopher, Coveney, de Jongh, Edwardes, Gore-Langton, Hagerty, Morley, Peter, Nightingale, Sierz, Smith, Spencer, Taylor, Tinker, Wardle.

2395 "Reviews of Productions." *LTR.* 1996; 16(20): 1233-1238. Lang.: Eng.

UK-England: London. 1996. ■*King Lear* by William Shakespeare, dir by Jack Shepherd at Southwark Playhouse: rev by Barton, Kingston, Stratton, Turpin. *When Did You Last See My Mother?* by Christopher Hampton, dir by John Burgess at BAC Main: rev by Darvell, de Jongh, Edwardes. *Blood Wedding (Bodas de sangre)* by Federico García Lorca, version by Ted Hughes, dir by Tim Supple at the Young Vic: rev by Billington, Butler, Coveney, de Jongh, Edwardes, Gross, Murray, Nathan, Nightingale, Spencer, Stevens, Taylor, Tinker.

2396 "Reviews of Productions." *LTR.* 1996; 16(20): 1251-1255. Lang.: Eng.

UK-England: London. 1996. ■*Violin Time* by Ken Campbell, dir by Colin Watkeys at the Cottesloe: rev by Coveney, Edwardes, Hanks, Nightingale, Peter, Shuttleworth, Smith, Spencer, Tinker. *Swaggers* by Mick Mahoney, dir by Mahoney at the Old Red Lion: rev by Tushingham, Williams. *When We Are Married* by J.B. Priestley, dir by Jude Kelly at the Savoy: rev by Stratton.

2397 "Reviews of Productions." *LTR.* 1996; 16(20): 1238-1243. Lang.: Eng.

UK-England: London. 1996. ■*Love, Lust and Marriage* based on four tales of Chaucer's *Canterbury Tales*, book and lyrics by Nevill Coghill and Martin Starkie, music by Richard Hill and John Hawkins, dir by Starkie and Sylvia Denning at the Arts: rev by Foss. *Variété*, music and lyrics by Carlos Miranda, book by Lindsay Kemp, dir by Kemp and Leslie Travers at the Hackney Empire: rev by Craine, Foss, Kimberly, Kyle, Mackrell, Sacks, Shuttleworth. *Temporary Rupture* by Michael Ellis, dir by Paulette Randall at the Warehouse, Croyden: rev by Bassett, Cavendish, Williams.

2398 "Reviews of Productions." *LTR.* 1996; 16(20): 1244-1249. Lang.: Eng.

UK-England: London. 1996. ■*Shopping and Fucking* by Mark Ravenhill, dir by Max Stafford-Clark at the Royal Court Upstairs Stage: rev by Billington, Brown, Butler, Christopher, Coveney, de Jongh, Edwardes, Foss, Gore-Langton, Gross, Hemming, Morley, Nightingale, Peter, Spencer, Taylor, Tinker. *The Last Yellow* by Paul Tucker, dir by Tucker at Chelsea Centre: rev by Godfrey-Faussett, McPherson. *The Public Eye* by Peter Shaffer, dir by Robbin John at the Man in the Moon: rev by Davé.

2399 "Reviews of Productions." *LTR.* 1996; 16(20): 1249-1250. Lang.: Eng.

UK-England: London. 1996. ■*Indian Summer* by Lucy Maurice, dir by Amanda Hill at Upstairs at the Landor: rev by Marmion, McPherson. *My Piece of Foreign Sky* by Lara Jane Bunting, dir by Cheryl Innes at the Link: rev by Stratton, Woddis. *Borrowed Plumes* and *Everything in the Garden* by John Cargill Thompson, dir by Andrew Stanson at the Etcetera: rev by Abdulla.

2400 "Reviews of Productions." *LTR.* 1996; 16(20): 1254-1261. Lang.: Eng.

UK-England: London. 1996. ■*Horace* by Corneille dir by Sydnee Blake at Lyric Studio: rev by Bassett, Cavendish, Foss, Taylor. *Faith and Dancing* by Lois Weaver, dir by Stormy Brandenberger and James Neale-Kennerly and *You're Just Like My Father* by Peggy Shaw, both dir by Neale-Kennerly at the Drill Hall: rev by Logan, Woddis. *Laughter on the 23rd Floor* by Neil Simon, dir by Roger Haines at the Queen's: rev by Benedict, Billington, Brown, Butler, Coveney, Gross, Hagerty, Hewison, Morley, Round, Shuttleworth, Smith, Stratton, Tinker.

2401 "Reviews of Productions." *LTR.* 1996; 16(20): 1262-1263. Lang.: Eng.

UK-England: London. 1996. ■*M.I.A.* by Bob Sherman, dir by Richard Hurst at the Grace: rev by Godfrey-Faussett, Smith. *The Kitchen of Life* a night of magic and music by Alexander Sturgis, Adam Bennett and Rachel Riggs at BAC: rev by Barton, Gardner. *The Golden Age* by Louis Nowra, dir by Lisa Carter at the Rosemary Branch: rev by Reade.

2402 "Reviews of Productions." *LTR.* 1996; 16(20): 1263-1267. Lang.: Eng.

UK-England: London. 1996. ■*Ondine* by Jean Giraudoux, adapted by Maurice Valency, dir by Sam Shammas at Brixton Shaw: rev by Marmion, Skelton. London New Play Festival: *Maison Splendide* by Laura Bridgeman, *Thinking Ahead* by Tim Blackwell and *Semper Suburbia* by Tom Minter, all dir by Sarah Frankcom, *Tongue Tied* by Sarah Clifford, dir by Shabnam Shabazi, *Hoover Bag* by Anthony Neilson, dir by Neilson, all at the Young Vic: rev by Bassett, Doughty, Edwardes, Read, Woddis. *Hard Shoulder* by John Doona, dir by Phil Setren, *An Audience with Queen* by Anita Sullivan, dir by David Prescott, *Scenes from Paradise* by Michael Wall, dir by Kate Valentine, *The Cricket Test* by James Waddington, dir by Jenny Eastop all at the Riverside: rev by Bassett, Curtis, Godfrey-Faussett, Marlowe, Skelton, Spencer.

2403 "Reviews of Productions." *LTR.* 1996; 16(21): 1287-1291. Lang.: Eng.

UK-England: London. 1996. ■*Accommodating Eva* by Sylvia Freedman, dir by Tom Dulack at the King's Head: rev by Bayley, de Jongh, Foss, Hagerty, Hewison, Morley, Reade, Spencer, Stratton, Tinker. *Closely Observed Trains* by Robin Lindsay, from the novel by Bohumil Hrabal, dir by Maggie Kinloch at the Duke of Cambridge: rev by Abdulla, Williams. *The Lodger* by Patrick Prior, from the novel by Marie Belloc Lowndes, dir by Philip Hedley at Theatre Royal, Stratford East: rev by Curtis, Darvell, Gross, Hewison, Kingston, Lubbock, Morley, Reade.

2404 "Reviews of Productions." *LTR.* 1996; 16(21): 1292-1298. Lang.: Eng.

UK-England: London. 1996. ■*Night Must Fall* by Emlyn Williams, dir by John Tydeman at Theatre Royal, Haymarket: rev by Benedict, Billington, Darvell, de Jongh, Gore-Langton, Gross, Hagerty, Hewison, Logan, Lubbock, Nathan, Nightingale, Reade, Spencer, Tinker. *The Alchemist* by Ben Jonson, dir by Bill Alexander at the Olivier: rev by Butler, de Jongh, Edwardes, Gross, Hagerty, Hemming, Kingston, Morley, Nathan, Smith. *The Woods* by David Mamet, dir by Robert Shaw at the Finborough: rev by Lavender, McPherson, Shaw, Tushingham.

2405 "Reviews of Productions." *LTR.* 1996; 16(21): 1301-1305. Lang.: Eng.

UK-England: London. 1996. ■*Fool for Love* by Sam Shepard, dir by Ian Brown at the Donmar Warehouse: rev by Billington, de Jongh, Edwardes, Gross, Hassell, Hewison, Lubbock, Macauley, Nathan, Nightingale, Spencer, Tinker. *Wallpaper* by Sophia Kingshill, dir by Joe Cushley at the Bridewell: rev by Foss, Godfrey-Faussett. *A Hand of Bridge* and *Trouble in Tahiti*, two operas by Leonard Bernstein, dir by Paul Baillie at the Southwark Playhouse: rev by Benedict, Darvell, Hemblade.

2406 "Reviews of Productions." *LTR.* 1996; 16(21): 1306-1315. Lang.: Eng.

UK-England: London. 1996. ■*What the Heart Feels* by Stephen Bill, dir by Sam Walters at the Orange Tree: rev by Bassett, Billington, Butler, McPherson, Nathan, Nightingale, Sierz, Stratton, Taylor. *I'll Be Your Dog* by Robbie McCallum, dir by Andrea Brooks at the White Bear: rev by Marmion, Woddis. *'Art'* by Yasmina Reza, transl by Christopher Hampton, dir by Matthew Warchus at Wyndham's: rev by Billington, Brown, Butler, de Jongh, Gott, Gross, Hagerty, Hampton, Hemming, Logan, Lubbock, Morley, Nathan, Nightingale, Palin, Peter, Smith, Spencer, Taylor, Usher.

2407 "Reviews of Productions." *LTR.* 1996; 16(10): 604-606. Lang.: Eng.

UK-England: London. 1996. ■*Those Colours Don't Run* and *Fist of the Dragonfly* by Gary Drabwell, dir by Drabwell at the Bird's Nest: rev by Higginson. *Beast on the Moon* by Richard Kalinoski, dir by Irina Brook at BAC Main: rev by Christopher, Coveney, Hemming, Marlowe, Taylor. *Great Pretenders*, musical by Neil Harrison, dir by David Cottis at the Etcetera: rev by Abdulla, Hutera.

DRAMA: —Performance/production

2408   "Reviews of Productions." *LTR*. 1996; 16(21): 1316-1320. Lang.: Eng.

UK-England: London. 1996. ■*Mojo* by Jez Butterworth, dir by Ian Rickson at the Royal Court Downstairs (Duke of York's): rev by Billington, Butler, de Jongh, Edwardes, Foss, Kingston, Lubbock, Macauley, Nathan, Peter, Sierz, Spencer, Taylor. *Never the Sinner* by John Logan, dir by Philip Swan at the Arts: rev by Affleck, Christopher, Curtis, Foss, Hemming, Stratton. *Abiding Passions* by Derrick Goodwin based on *Thérèse Raquin* by Emile Zola, dir by Claire Nelson at the Riverside 3: rev by Cavendish.

2409   "Reviews of Productions." *LTR*. 1996; 16(21): 1321-1323. Lang.: Eng.

UK-England: London. 1996. ■*Groping in the Dark* by James Martin Charlton, dir by Charlton at the Warehouse, Croydon: rev by Kingston, Marmion, McPherson, Turpin. *Srebrenica: 1996 The Hague War Crimes Trial*, edited and dir by Nicolas Kent at the Tricycle: rev by Benedict, Butler, Davé, Edwardes, Lubbock, Peter, Turpin. *Gin and Trickery* devised and performed by Adrian Bunting and Clea Smith at the Man in the Moon: rev by Lloyd, Reade.

2410   "Reviews of Productions." *LTR*. 1996; 16(21): 1370-1380. Lang.: Eng.

UK-England: London. 1996. ■*In the Company of Men* by Edward Bond, dir by Bond for the RSC at The Pit: rev by Billington, Butler, de Jongh, Edwardes, Foss, Gore-Langton, Gross, Kingston, Lubbock, Macauley, Nathan, Peter, Spencer, Taylor. *Talking Heads* by Alan Bennett, dir by Bennett at the Comedy: rev by Bayley, Brown, Hagerty, Macauley, Nathan, Stratton. *The Weavers (Die Weber)* by Gerhart Hauptmann, transl by Anthony Vivis at the Gate: rev by Billington, Curtis, Davé, Hanks, Hemming, Kingston, Peter, Stratton, Turpin.

2411   "Reviews of Productions." *LTR*. 1996; 16(21): 1351-1357. Lang.: Eng.

UK-England: London. 1996. ■*Mrs. Warren's Profession* by George Bernard Shaw, dir by Neil Bartlett at Lyric Hammersmith: rev by Billington, Brown, de Jongh, Kingston, Lubbock, Macauley, Morley, Nathan, Parry, Peter, Sierz, Spencer, Stratton, Taylor. *Big Al* by Bryan Goluboff, *Slam!* by Jane Nixon Willis, and *Only His Knees* by Edward L. Betz, all dir by Clare Davidson at the Man in the Moon: rev by Reade. *Hamlet* by William Shakespeare, dir by Philip Franks at the Greenwich: rev by Bassett, Billington, Butler, de Jongh, Edwardes, Kingston, Lubbock, Macauley, Peter, Smith, Taylor.

2412   "Reviews of Productions." *LTR*. 1996; 16(21): 1358-1369. Lang.: Eng.

UK-England: London. 1996. ■*The Entertainer* by John Osborne, dir by Stephen Rayne at the Hampstead: rev by Bayley, Coveney, Curtis, Edwardes, Gross, Hagerty, Hanks, Morley, Nathan, Shuttleworth, Smith, Spencer, Usher. *Death of a Salesman* by Arthur Miller, dir by David Thacker at the Lyttelton: rev by Billington, Brown, Coveney, de Jongh, Foss, Gore-Langton, Grant, Gross, Hagerty, Hanks, Morley, Nathan, Nightingale, Peter, Spencer, Taylor, Usher. *As You Like It* by William Shakespeare, dir by Steven Pimlott for the RSC at the Barbican: rev by Bayley, Gross, Hanks, Hassell, Nathan, Shuttleworth, Stratton, Thorncroft, Usher.

2413   "Reviews of Productions." *LTR*. 1996; 16(21): 1380-1386. Lang.: Eng.

UK-England: London. 1996. ■*Mrs. Freud and Mrs. Jung* by Joe Kelleher, dir by Joss Bennathan at the Pentameters: rev by Abdulla, Williams. *A Doll's House (Et Dukkehjem)* by Henrik Ibsen, version by Frank McGuinness from a literal translation by Charlotte Barslund, dir by Anthony Page at the Playhouse: rev by Butler, Christopher, de Jongh, Edwardes, Farrell, Fisher, Gross, Kingston, Lubbock, Macauley, Peter, Taylor, Usher. *Happy Days* by Samuel Beckett, dir by Karel Reisz at the Almeida: rev by Bassett, Billington, Coveney, de Jongh, Gross, Hassell, Taylor.

2414   "Reviews of Productions." *LTR*. 1996; 16(21): 1387-1390. Lang.: Eng.

UK-England: London. 1996. ■*Inside the Music* text by Christopher Durang, dir by Larry Fuller at Jermyn Street: rev by Coveney, Darvell, Gardner, Gross, Hagerty, Morley, Robertson, Thorncroft. *Sweeney Todd* by David Bridel, dir by Rhys Thomas at Bockley Jack: rev by Logan. *Buried Treasure* by David Ashton, dir by Robin Lefèvre at the Lyric Stu-

dio: rev by Benedict, Clanchy, Gardner, Hanks, Kingston, Nathan, Tushingham, Woddis.

2415   "Reviews of Productions." *LTR*. 1996; 16(10): 595-604. Lang.: Eng.

UK-England: London. 1996. ■*What Now Little Man?* by Julian Forsyth, transl by Forsyth, from the novel by Hans Fallada, dir by Margarete Forsyth at the Greenwich: rev by Christopher, Curtis, Foss, Hagerty, Hughes, Kingston, Morley, Nathan. *Nuremberg: The War Crimes Trial* by Richard Norton-Taylor, ed., and *Prologue* by Mark Penfold, *Haiti* by Keith Reddin, *Reel, Rwanda* by Femi Osofisan, and *Ex-Yu* by Goran Stefanovski all dir by Nicolas Kent at the Tricycle: rev by Billington, Butler, Coveney, Curtis, Grant, Gross, Marlowe, Morley, Nathan, Nightingale, Paton, Peter, Shuttleworth, Sierz, Spencer, Taylor, Usher. *The Sentence* by Christin Balit and Tamara Hinchco, dir by Roger Smith at the Old Red Lion: rev by Gardner, Reade, Spencer.

2416   "Reviews of Productions." *LTR*. 1996; 16(10): 606-612. Lang.: Eng.

UK-England: London. 1996. ■*The Rock Station* by Ger Fitzgibbon, dir by Annabelle Comyn at the Finborough: rev by Bassett, Hemblade, McPherson. *The Power of the Dog* by Ellen Dryden, dir by Sam Walters at the Orange Tree: rev by Abdulla, Bassett, Butler, Coveney, McPherson. *Portia Coughlan* by Marina Carr, dir by Garry Hynes for the Abbey Theatre Company at the Royal Court: rev by Billington, Butler, Coveney, de Jongh, Edwardes, Hemming, Hughes, Hutera, Morley, Nathan, Nightingale, Peter, Spencer, Taylor, Usher, Wardle.

2417   "Reviews of Productions." *LTR*. 1996; 16(10): 615-616. Lang.: Eng.

UK-England: London. 1996. ■*The Art of Success* by Nick Dear, dir by Gillian King at the Man in the Moon: rev by Higginson. *Mrs. Warren's Profession* by George Bernard Shaw, dir by Michael C. Friend at Wimbledon Studio: rev by McPherson. *Dream Time* by Sheila Goff, Cath Kilcoyne and Nick Sutton, dir by Ruth Ben-Tovim at the Young Vic Studio: rev by Michaels, Stratton.

2418   "Reviews of Productions." *LTR*. 1996; 16(10): 612-615. Lang.: Eng.

UK-England: London. 1996. ■*The Dance of Death (Dödsdansen)* by August Strindberg, transl by Matthew Telfer, dir by Telfer at the White Bear: rev by Godfrey-Faussett. *Bodas de sangre (Blood Wedding)* by Federico García Lorca, performed in Spanish, dir by Antonio Cantos at Theatro Technis: rev by Wareham. *Resurrection* by Maureen Lawrence, dir by Penny Ciniewicz at the Bush: rev by Christopher, Curtis, Gardner, Hemming, Nightingale, Peter, Spencer, Taylor, Usher, Whitebrook, Woddis.

2419   "Reviews of Productions." *LTR*. 1996; 16(10): 587-594. Lang.: Eng.

UK-England: London. 1996. ■*Mind Millie for Me (Occupe-toi d'Amélie)* by Georges Feydeau, transl by Nicki Frei and Peter Hall, dir by Hall at Theatre Royal, Haymarket: rev by Billington, Butler, Coveney, Darvell, de Jongh, Edwardes, Gross, Hagerty, Hemming, Hirshhorn, Hughes, Morley, Nathan, Nightingale, Paton, Peter, Spencer, Taylor, Tinker. *Three Sisters (Tri sestry)* by Anton Čechov, transl by Stephen Mulrine, dir by Max Stafford-Clark at the Lyric Hammersmith: rev by Christopher, de Jongh, Edwardes, Gross, Hemming, Hughes, Kingston, Simpkins, Tinker. *Fever Pitch* by Paul Hodson, from the novel by Nick Hornby, dir by Hodson at the Pleasance: rev by Godfrey-Faussett, Stevens.

2420   "Reviews of Productions." *LTR*. 1996; 16(10): 617-618. Lang.: Eng.

UK-England: London. 1996. ■*Iona Rain* by Peter Moffatt, dir by Jessica Dromgoole at Warehouse, Croydon: rev by Bassett, Foss, Marmio. *Bluff* devised by Brouhaha, dir by Andre Riot-Sarcey at BAC 2: rev by Marmion, Spencer. *Pretty Eyes, Ugly Paintings (Ojos bonitos, cuadros feos)* by Mario Vargas Llosa, transl by Brownwen Ancona, dir by Graham Watts at the Courtyard: rev by Hemblade, Stevens.

2421   "Reviews of Productions." *LTR*. 1996; 16(10): 618-619. Lang.: Eng.

UK-England: London. 1996. ■*One Hundred Years of Enchantment* by David Bridel, dir by Bridel and Rhys Thomas at the Union Chapel: rev by Stratton. *Good Bones* by Nick Cohen, from stories by Margaret Atwood, dir by Cohen at Southwark Playhouse: rev by Edwardes. *Duet*

DRAMA: —Performance/production

for One by Tom Kempinski, dir by Christopher Wren at the Riverside: rev by Curtis, Edwardes, Hagerty, Marlowe, Usher.

2422   "Reviews of Productions." *LTR*. 1996; 16(10): 619-626.
Lang.: Eng.

UK-England: London. 1996. ■*Sykes and Nancy* by John Mowat, from novels by Charles Dickens, dir by Mowat at BAC 1: rev by Bassett. *Three Hours After Marriage* by John Gay, Alexander Pope and John Arbuthnot, dir by Richard Cottrell for the RSC at the Swan, Stratford: rev by Billington, Butler, Coveney, de Jongh, Edwardes, Kingston, Peter, Shuttleworth, Taylor, Tinker, Wardle, Woddis. *Macbeth* by William Shakespeare, dir by Tim Albery for RSC at Royal Shakespeare, Stratford: rev by Billington, Butler, Coveney, Edwardes, Gross, Kingston, Nathan, Peter, Shuttleworth, Spencer, Taylor, Usher, Woddis.

2423   "Reviews of Productions." *LTR*. 1996; 16(10): 629-634.
Lang.: Eng.

UK-England: London. 1996. ■*Simply Disconnected* by Simon Gray, dir by Richard Wilson at the Minerva, Chichester: rev by Billington, Butler, Coveney, de Jongh, Hagerty, Hirshhorn, Hughes, Morley, Nightingale, Peter, Shuttleworth, Spencer, Taylor, Usher, Wardle.

2424   "Reviews of Productions." *LTR*. 1996; 16(11): 651-661.
Lang.: Eng.

UK-England: London. 1996. ■*Phaedra's Love* by Sarah Kane, dir by Kane at the Gate: rev by Bassett, Billington, Butler, Coveney, Hemming, Marlowe, Nathan, Peter, Sierz, Spencer, Stratton, Taylor, Tushingham. *Cyrano de Bergerac* by Edmond Rostand, transl by Ranjit Bolt, dir by Anna Coombs at the Bridewell: rev by Dowden, Reade. *Sylvia* by A.R. Gurney, Jr., dir by Michael Blakemore at the Apollo: rev by Butler, Coveney, Curtis, Edwardes, Gardner, Gross, Hagerty, Hanks, Hirshhorn, Hughes, Kingston, Macauley, Mitchell, Morley, Nathan, Peter, Smith, Spencer, Usher.

2425   "Reviews of Productions." *LTR*. 1996; 16(11): 661-664.
Lang.: Eng.

UK-England: London. 1996. ■*Sunspots* by Judy Upton, dir by Lisa Goldman at the Red Room: rev by Billington, Higginson, Stevens. *The Painter of Dishonor (El Pintor de su deshonra)* by Calderón, transl by David Johnston, dir by Laurence Boswell for the RSC at The Pit: rev by Christopher, Curtis, Foss, Gardner, Gore-Langton, Kingston, Shuttleworth, Tinker. *Road Movie* by Godfrey Hamilton, dir by Lorenzo Mele at the Lyric Studio: rev by Bassett, Higginson, Hutera.

2426   "Reviews of Productions." *LTR*. 1996; 16(12): 796-797.
Lang.: Eng.

UK-England: London. 1996. ■*Circus Minimus* by Charles Serio, dir by Serio at the Pigeon Loft: rev by Marmion. *Dangerous Play* by Andrew Loudon, dir by Lucille O'Flanagan at the Arts: rev by Foss, Reade. *Rags* by Joseph Stein, music by Charles Strouse, lyrics by Stephen Schwartz, dir by Raymond Wright and Barry Hooper at Spitalfields Market Opera: rev by Darvell.

2427   "Reviews of Productions." *LTR*. 1996; 16(11): 665-670.
Lang.: Eng.

UK-England: London. 1996. ■*Game Over*, Archaos, circus spectacle by Guy Carrara and Pierre Pillot, dir by Carrara at Brixton Academy: rev by Constant, Morley, Sawyer, Smith. *The Course* by Brendan O'Carroll, dir by O'Carroll and Brendan Morrissey at the Bloomsbury: rev by Spencer. *Calamity Jane* by Charles K. Freeman, Sammy Fain and Paul Frances Webster, dir by Paul Kerryson at Sadler's Wells: rev by Abdulla, Billington, Butler, Coveney, Darvell, Gross, Hagerty, Hirshhorn, Hughes, Kingston, Morley, Nathan, Paton, Peter, Spencer, Stratton, Taylor, Usher.

2428   "Reviews of Productions." *LTR*. 1996; 16(11): 671-676.
Lang.: Eng.

UK-England: London. 1996. ■*Julius Caesar* by William Shakespeare, dir by Peter Hall for the RSC at the Barbican: rev by Bassett, Curtis, Gardner, Gore-Langton, Hassell, Hirshhorn, Murray, Reade. *Fair Game (Freiwild)* by Arthur Schnitzler, transl by Michael Robinson, dir by Jonathan Banatvala at the New End: rev by Abdulla, Bassett, Nathan, Spencer. *The Comedy of Errors* by William Shakespeare, dir by Ian Talbot at the Open Air: rev by Bassett, Butler, Coveney, Curtis, Foss, Godfrey-Faussett, Gross, Hagerty, Macauley, Paton, Peter, Spencer, Taylor.

2429   "Reviews of Productions." *LTR*. 1996; 16(11): 677-681.
Lang.: Eng.

UK-England: London. 1996. ■*Dames at Sea* by George Haimsohn and Robin Miller, music by Jim Wise, dir by John Gardyne at the Ambassadors: rev by Benedict, Billington, Butler, Coveney, Darvell, de Jongh, Gross, Hagerty, Higgins, Hirshhorn, Macauley, Morley, Robertson, Spencer. *The Scourge* by Bernardo Stella, dir by Harry Meacher at Pentameters: rev by Abdulla, Hutera. *The 'No Boys' Cricket Club* by Roy Williams, dir by Indhu Rubasingham at Theatre Royal, Stratford East: rev by Bartholomew, Curtis, Edwardes, Foss.

2430   "Reviews of Productions." *LTR*. 1996; 16(13): 802-806.
Lang.: Eng.

UK-England: London. 1996. ■*Rampant in Whitehall*, Barry Humphries one man show at the Whitehall and the Albery: rev by Darvell, Games, Gore-Langton, Paton, Wareham, Yates. *A Week with Tony* by David Eldridge, dir by Mark Ravenhill at the Finborough: rev by Bassett, Butler, Edwardes, McPherson, Taylor. *The Choice* by Claire Luckham, dir by Dominic Hill at the Orange Tree: rev by Nightingale, Sierz, Taylor, Tushingham, Woddis.

2431   "Reviews of Productions." *LTR*. 1996; 16(11): 682-685.
Lang.: Eng.

UK-England: London. 1996. ■*How Dear to Me the Hour When Daylight Dies* devised by Goat Island, dir by Lin Hixson at the Greenwich Dance Agency: rev by Brennan, Donald. *Death of an Elephant* by Trevor Preston, at the Orange Tree Room, dir by Natasha Betteridge: rev by Marmion, McPherson. *Funeral Games* by Joe Orton, dir by Phil Willmott, at the Drill Hall: rev by Bassett, Butler, Darvell, de Jongh, Hagerty, Nathan, Peter, Shuttleworth, Spencer, Stratton, Taylor.

2432   "Reviews of Productions." *LTR*. 1996; 16(11): 685-688.
Lang.: Eng.

UK-England: London. 1996. ■*One Knight* by Simon Francis, dir by Gabrielle Lindemann at the Man in the Moon: rev by McPherson. *The Herbal Bed* by Peter Whelan, dir by Michael Attenborough at The Other Place, Stratford: rev by Billington, Butler, Christopher, Coveney, Gross, Kingston, Macauley, Peter, Spencer, Taylor, Woddis.

2433   "Reviews of Productions." *LTR*. 1996; 16(11): 707-709.
Lang.: Eng.

UK-England: London. 1996. ■*On the Boulevard* devised by Tommy Tune, dir by Tune at the Jermyn Street: rev by Bamigboye, Benedict, Coveney, Curtis, Darvell, Gross, Hagerty, Hemblade, Nathan, Paton, Shuttleworth, Spencer, Tinker. *Ud's Garden* by Ruth Graham, dir by Beth Wood at Wimbledon Studio: rev by Higginson. *Lonely Planet* by Steven Dietz, dir by Matt Markham at the Turtle Key: rev by Godfrey-Faussett.

2434   "Reviews of Productions." *LTR*. 1996; 16(12): 730-732.
Lang.: Eng.

UK-England: London. 1996. ■*Sins of the Mother* by David Pinner, dir by Philip Partridge at the Grace: rev by Abdulla, Walsh. *Berenice* by Racine, transl by John Cairncross, dir by Lisa Clarke at the Man in the Moon: rev by Hemblade, Macauley, Walsh. *Truth Omissions*, written and performed by Pieter-Dirk Uys, at the Tricycle: rev by Billington, Foss, Games, Kingston, Tushingham.

2435   "Reviews of Productions." *LTR*. 1996; 16(11): 710-713.
Lang.: Eng.

UK-England: London. 1996. ■*Claustrophobia (Klaustrofobicna)* based on the ideas of Vladimir Sorokin, Venedikt Verofeyev, Lyudmila Ulitskaya and Mark Kharitonov, English version by Michael Stronin, dir by Lev Dodin for Maly Drama Theatre, St. Petersburg, at the Lyric Hammersmith: rev by Bassett, Billington, Coveney, Hanks, Macauley, Peter, Spencer, Stratton, Taylor, Turpin, Wilson. *Spike Heels* by Theresa Rebeck, dir by William Marsh at Flipside Studio: rev by Marmion. *The Parable of the Blind* by Mehrdad Seyf, from the novel by Gert Hofmann, dir by Seyf at the Brixton Shaw: rev by Foss, Tushingham.

2436   "Reviews of Productions." *LTR*. 1996; 16(11): 714-725.
Lang.: Eng.

UK-England: London. 1996. ■*Habeas Corpus* by Alan Bennett, dir by Sam Mendes at Donmar Warehouse: rev by Billington, Coveney, de Jongh, Gross, Hagerty, Hanks, Hirshhorn, Macauley, Morley, Nathan, Nightingale, Paton, Peter, Sierz, Smith, Stratton, Taylor, Tinker. *Romeo and Juliet* by William Shakespeare, dir and performed in French by Babette Masson and Jean-Louis Heckel at the Purcell Room: rev by Reade. *Who Shall Be Happy...?* by Trevor Griffiths, dir by Griffiths at

DRAMA: —Performance/production

the Bush: rev by Billington, Coveney, Curtis, Foss, Edwardes, Gross, Hanks, Hemming, Nathan, Nightingale, Peter, Sierz, Taylor, Tinker.

2437   "Reviews of Productions." *LTR.* 1996; 16(12): 744-749. Lang.: Eng.

UK-England: London. 1996. ■*The Ice Pick* by John Roman Baker, dir by Baker at the BAC 2: rev by Marlowe, Marmion. *Ghosts (Gengangere)* by Ibsen, transl by Mike Poulton, dir by David Hunt at King's Head: rev by Bassett, Foss, Stratton, Turpin. *The Tempest* by William Shakespeare, dir by Patrick Garland at the Open Air: rev by Abdulla, Curtis, Gross, Hagerty, Hanks, Hassell, Hughes, Nathan, Nightingale, Peter, Spencer, Tinker.

2438   "Reviews of Productions." *LTR.* 1996; 16(12): 733-739. Lang.: Eng.

UK-England: London. 1996. ■*Sing at Sunset* by Niall Buggy, dir by Shivaun O'Casey at the Hampstead: rev by Coveney, Curtis, Edwardes, Gross, Kingston, Morley, Paton, Peter, Shuttleworth, Smith, Spencer. *Hummingbird* by Chris Lee, dir by Ken McClymont at the Old Red Lion: rev by Reade, Simpkins. *Coriolanus* by William Shakespeare, dir by Steven Berkoff at the Mermaid: rev by Benedict, Billington, Curtis, Gross, Hanks, Hirshhorn, Hughes, Morley, Nathan, Nightingale, Paton, Smith, Stratton, Tinker.

2439   "Reviews of Productions." *LTR.* 1996; 16(12): 739-744. Lang.: Eng.

UK-England: London. 1996. ■*Actor, Dog* and *The Tell Tale Heart* by Steven Berkoff, dir by Robert Dugay at the Etcetera: rev by Simpkins. *Crash* by Neil Biswas, dir by Rob Curry at the Warehouse, Croydon: rev by Curtis, Godfrey-Faussett, McPherson. *Jude the Obscure* by Mike Alfreds, from novel by Thomas Hardy, dir by Alfreds at the Lyric Hammersmith: rev by Coveney, Dowden, Edwardes, Hanks, Hemming, Kingston, Nathan, Peter, Spencer, Stratton, Taylor, Usher.

2440   "Reviews of Productions." *LTR.* 1996; 16(12): 749-756. Lang.: Eng.

UK-England: London, Chichester. 1996. ■*Little White Lies* by Daniel Jamieson, dir by Nikki Sved at BAC 1: rev by Hemming. *Mansfield Park* by Willis Hall, from novel by Jane Austen, dir by Michael Rudman at the Chichester Festival: rev by Coveney, de Jongh, Gardner, Gross, Hagerty, Hughes, Kingston, Macaulay, Peter, Spencer, Taylor, Tinker. *Beethoven's Tenth* by Peter Ustinov, dir by Joe Harmston at the Chichester Festival: rev by Coveney, de Jongh, Gore-Langton, Gross, Hughes, Nightingale, Peter, Shuttleworth.

2441   "Reviews of Productions." *LTR.* 1996; 16(12): 756-760, 787-796. Lang.: Eng.

UK-England: London. 1996. ■*Talking Heads* by Alan Bennett, dir by Bennett at the Minerva, Chichester: rev by Coveney, de Jongh, Gross, Hirschhorn, Macaulay, Morley, Nightingale, Peter, Spencer, Taylor, Tinker, Woddis. *Private Lives* by Noël Coward, dir by Mike Alfreds at the Lyric Hammersmith: rev by Benedict, Butler, Coveney, Curtis, Gross, Hagerty, Hirschhorn, Kingston, Marlowe, Morley, Nathan, Peter, Spencer, Stratton, Tinker. *The Brownings: Through Casa Guidi Windows* by Henry Grange, dir by Harry Meacher at the Pentameters: rev by Simpkins. *Flesh and Blood* by Philip Osment, dir by Mike Alfreds at the Lyric Hammersmith: rev by Billington, Butler, Coveney, Curtis, Hewison, Nathan, Nightingale, Reade, Saddler, Shuttleworth, C. Spencer, L. Spencer, Taylor, Tinker.

2442   "Reviews of Productions." *LTR.* 1996; 16(13): 798-801. Lang.: Eng.

UK-England: London. 1996. ■*(Uncle) Vanya* adapted by Howard Barker from *Diadia Vania (Uncle Vanya)* by Anton Čechov, dir by Barker at the Almeida: rev by Billington, Butler, Coveney, Fisher, Gore-Langton, Hirschhorn, Kingston, Nightingale, Peter, Reade, Shuttleworth, Stratton. *The Bear (Medved), The Proposal (Prodloženic), A Tragic Role (Tragik)* and *Smoking Is Bad for You (O vrede tabaka)* by Anton Čechov, transl by Ronald Hingley, dir by Tim Connolly at the Grace: rev by Logan, McPherson. *Creamy* by Leon London, dir by Sarah Frankcom at the Red Room: rev by Abdulla, Simpkins.

2443   "Reviews of Productions." *LTR.* 1996; 16(13): 806-817. Lang.: Eng.

UK-England: London. 1996. ■*The M.C. of a Striptease Act Doesn't Give Up (Der Ansager einer Stripteasenummer gibt nicht auf)* by Bodo Kirchhoff, transl by Patricia Benecke and Patrick Driver, dir by Benecke at the

Etcetera: rev by Marmion, Simpkins. *War and Peace*, adapt by Helen Edmundson from the novel by Leo Tolstoy, dir by Nancy Meckler and Polly Teale at the Cottesloe: rev by Billington, Butler, Coveney, Curtis, Edwardes, Gross, Hewison, Hughes, Macaulay, Morley, Nathan, Nightingale, Sierz, Smith, Spencer, Taylor, Usher. *The Odd Couple* by Neil Simon, dir by Harvey Medlinsky, at the Theatre Royal, Haymarket: rev by Benedict, Billington, Butler, Coveney, de Jongh, Foss, Grant, Gross, Hagerty, Hewison, Hirschhorn, Morley, Nathan, Nightingale, Paton, Reynolds, Shuttleworth, Spencer, Tinker.

2444   "Reviews of Productions." *LTR.* 1996; 16(13): 817-820. Lang.: Eng.

UK-England: London. 1996. ■*Celestina* by Fernando de Rojas, transl by James Mabbe, dir by Paul James at the Prince, SE 10: rev by Tushingham. *Sweeney Todd* musical by Stephen Sondheim, book by Hugh Wheeler, from an adaptation by Christopher Bond, dir by Bond at the Holland Park: rev by Benedict, Curtis, Darvell, Morley. *The Invisible Woman* by Paul Godfrey, based on *Hecyra* by Terence, dir by Godfrey and Ramin Gray at the Gate: rev by Coveney, Foss, Gardner, Gross, Hewison, Kingston, Nathan, Shuttleworth, Smith, Stratton, Taylor.

2445   "Reviews of Productions." *LTR.* 1996; 16(13): 826-829. Lang.: Eng.

UK-England: London. 1996. ■*Rain Snakes (Regnormarna)* by Per Olov Enquist, transl by Kim Dambaek, dir by Dambaek at the Young Vic Studio: rev by Abdulla, Billington, Kingston, Marlowe, Taylor. *Kicking Out* and *Angel Days* by Clifford Oliver, dir by Carole Pluckrose at the Drill Hall: rev by Edwardes, Foss, Gardner.

2446   "Reviews of Productions." *LTR.* 1996; 16(13): 820-825. Lang.: Eng.

UK-England: London. 1996. ■*The Phoenician Women (Phoinissai)* by Euripides, transl by David Thompson, dir by Katie Mitchell for the RSC at The Pit: rev by Curtis, Gardner, Gore-Langton, Kingston, Macaulay, Smith, Stratton. *Richard II* by William Shakespeare, dir by Steven Pimlott for the RSC at the Barbican: rev by de Jongh, Hagerty, Hirschhorn, Morley, Nightingale, Shuttleworth, Stratton. *Any Marks or Deviations* by Charlie Hughes-D'Aeth, dir by Judy Channing at Wimbledon Studio: rev by Abdulla, McPherson.

2447   "Reviews of Productions." *LTR.* 1996; 16(14): 843-853. Lang.: Eng.

UK-England: London. 1996. ■*The Aspern Papers* adapted by Michael Redgrave from the novel by Henry James, dir by Auriol Smith at the Wyndham's: rev by Abdulla, Benedict, Butler, Darvell, de Jongh, Gross, Hagerty, Hewison, Hirschhorn, Macaulay, Morley, Nightingale, Spencer, Tinker. *Medea in the Mirror (Medea en el espejo)* by José Triana, transl by Gwynne Edwards, dir by Yvonne Brewster at the Brixton Shaw: rev by Godfrey-Faussett, Kingston, Woddis. *By Jeeves*, musical by Andrew Lloyd Webber, book and lyrics by Alan Ayckbourn, based on stories by P.G. Wodehouse, dir by Ayckbourn at the Duke of York's: rev by Coveney, Cunningham, de Jongh, Edwardes, Gross, Hagerty, Hirschhorn, Hughes-Onslow, Lister, Macaulay, Morley, Nathan, Nightingale, Smith.

2448   "Reviews of Productions." *LTR.* 1996; 16(14): 853-857. Lang.: Eng.

UK-England: London. 1996. ■*Falling Through* by Paul Constable, dir by Brennan Street at the Riverside: rev by Godfrey-Faussett. Sam Shepard Festival: *States of Shock* by Shepard, dir by Michael Kingsbury, *A Lie of the Mind* by Shepard, dir by Toby Reisz, and *Suicide in B Flat* by Shepard, dir by Andrea Brooks at BAC: rev by Bassett, Cavendish, de Jongh, Edwardes, Hanks, Marlowe, Reade, Shuttleworth, Spencer, Woddis. *Pretty Vacant* by Paul Hodson, dir by Hodson at the Warehouse, Croydon: rev by Foss, Logan.

2449   "Reviews of Productions." *LTR.* 1996; 15(15): 924-928. Lang.: Eng.

UK-England: London. 1996. ■*Rubber* by David Hines, dir by Sian Stevenson at the Etcetera: rev by Goodwin, Logan, Simpkins. *The Memory of Water* by Shelagh Stephenson, dir by Terry Johnson at the Hampstead: rev by Billington, Butler, Coveney, de Jongh, Gross, Hagerty, Hanks, Hewison, Morley, Nathan, Nightingale, Smith, Spencer, Stratton, Tinker. *White Unto Harvest* by Mavis Howard, dir by Lisa Goldman at the Red Room: rev by Abdulla, Simpkins.

DRAMA: —Performance/production

2450   "Reviews of Productions." *LTR*. 1996; 16(14): 857-861. Lang.: Eng.

UK-England: London. 1996. ■*Duck Hunting (Utinaja ochota)* by Aleksand'r Vampilov, dir by Timothy Hughes at the Man in the Moon: rev by Simpkins. *Long Day's Journey Into Night* by Eugene O'Neill, dir by Laurence Boswell at the Young Vic: rev by Benedict, Butler, Coveney, Darvell, de Jongh, Gardner, Grant, Gross, Hewison, Macaulay, Nathan, Sierz, Tinker. *The Revenger's Tragedy* by Cyril Tourneur, dir by Sean Holmes at the Orange Tree Room: rev by Cavendish, McPherson.

2451   "Reviews of Productions." *LTR*. 1996; 14(14): 868-871. Lang.: Eng.

UK-England: London. 1996. ■*John's Maids* by Beth Wood, dir by Wood at Wimbledon Studio: rev by Kingston, Logan, McPherson. *Anoraknophobia* by Michael Norman, dir by Dawn Lintern at the Old Red Lion: rev by Kingston, Logan. *Roll with the Punches* by Chris Bond, words and music by Randy Newman, dir by Bond at the Tricycle: rev by Abdulla, Curtis, Gross, Kingston, Morley, Nathan, Shuttleworth, Spencer, Woddis.

2452   "Reviews of Productions." *LTR*. 1996; 16(14): 862-867. Lang.: Eng.

UK-England: London. 1996. ■*The Lime Tree Bower* by Conor McPherson, dir by McPherson at the Bush: rev by Billington, Coveney, Curtis, Gross, Hanks, Hassell, Hewison, Marmion, Nightingale, Shuttleworth, Spencer, Usher. *Northanger Abbey* adapted from the novel by Jane Austen by Matthew Francis, dir by Francis at the Greenwich: rev by Benedict, Cavendish, Coveney, Curtis, Foss, Gore-Langton, Nightingale, Shuttleworth. *Seascape with Sharks and Dancer* by Don Nigro, dir by Paul Miller at Southwark Playhouse: rev by Abdulla, Reade.

2453   "Reviews of Productions." *LTR*. 1996; 14(14): 871-884. Lang.: Eng.

UK-England: London. 1996. ■*The 'F' Word* by Susan Bain, Tammy Bentz, Jacqueline Dandeneau, Sharon Heath and Laura Myers and *Way Too Blonde* by Bentz, Dandeneau and Heath, dir by Micki Maunsell at the Turtle Key: rev by Logan, Spencer. *John Gabriel Borkman* by Henrik Ibsen, transl Nicholas Wright, dir by Richard Eyre for the Royal National Theatre at the Lyttelton: rev by Billington, Butler, Christopher, Coveney, de Jongh, Edwardes, Gross, Hagerty, Hewison, Hughes, Macaulay, Morley, Nathan, Nightingale, Smith, Spencer, Taylor, Tinker. *Martin Guerre*, musical with book by Alain Boublil and Claude-Michel Schönberg, music by Schönberg, lyrics by Edward Hardy, original French text by Boublil, additional lyrics by Herbert Kretzmer and Boublil, dir by Declan Donnellan at the Prince Edward: rev by Billington, Butler, Christopher, Coveney, de Jongh, Grant, Gross, Hagerty, Hewison, Hughes, Macaulay, Morley, Nathan, Nightingale, Smith, Spencer, Taylor, Tinker.

2454   "Reviews of Productions." *LTR*. 1996; 14(14): 887, 890-893. Lang.: Eng.

UK-England: London. 1996. ■*The Comedy of Errors* by William Shakespeare, dir by Tim Supple for the RSC at The Other Place, Stratford: rev by Billington, Butler, Coveney, Curtis, Gore-Langton, Macaulay, Nightingale, Taylor, Tushingham. *Uncle Vanya (Diadia Vania)* by Čechov, transl by Mike Poulton, dir by Bill Bryden at the Minerva, Chichester: rev by Billington, Butler, Coveney, Gross, Hagerty, Hughes-Onslow, Macaulay, Morley, Nathan, Nightingale, Spencer, Taylor, Tinker, Woddis.

2455   "Reviews of Productions." *LTR*. 1996; 15(15): 919-924. Lang.: Eng.

UK-England: London. 1996. ■*Birdy* by Naomi Wallace from the novel by William Wharton, dir by Kevin Knight at the Lyric Studio: rev by Benedict, Butler, Doughty, Foss, Gardner, Gross, Nightingale, Shuttleworth, Stratton, Tinker. *The Island Sea* by Paul Constable, dir by Peter Craze at the Riverside: rev by McPherson, Stratton. *Giovanni's Room* by James Baldwin, dir by Maia Guest at the Drill Hall: rev by Bassett, de Jongh, Foss, Hanks, Hemblade, Hewison, Shuttleworth, Tinker.

2456   "Reviews of Productions." *LTR*. 1996; 16(15): 929-935. Lang.: Eng.

UK-England: London. 1996. ■*Emma*, adapted by Michael Fry from novel by Jane Austen, dir by Fry at King's Head: rev by Abdulla, Gore-Langton, Nightingale, Reade, Skelton. *Kolonists* by Steven Dykes, dir by Nesta Jones at the Man in the Moon: rev by Abdulla, Bassett, Walsh. *Promises, Promises*, music and lyrics by Burt Bacharach and Hal David,

book by Neil Simon, dir by John J.D. Sheehan at the Bridewell: rev by Bassett, Butler, Darvell, Doughty, Hagerty, Hewison, Marmion, Morley, Nathan, Shuttleworth, Spencer, Tinker.

2457   "Reviews of Productions." *LTR*. 1996; 16(15): 935-943. Lang.: Eng.

UK-England: London. 1996. ■*Paint Your Wagon* musical by Frederick Loewe and Alan Jay Lerner, dir by Ian Talbot at the Open Air: rev by Benedict, Cavendish, Coveney, Curtis, Darvell, Gore-Langton, Gross, Hagerty, Hanks, Hughes, Kingston, Malins, Morley, Shuttleworth, Tinker. *The Lights* by Howard Korder, dir by Ian Rickson at the Royal Court: rev by Billington, Butler, Coveney, de Jongh, Gore-Langton, Gross, Hewison, Morley, Nathan, Nightingale, Shuttleworth, Sierz, Smith, Stratton, Taylor, Tinker. *The Yellow Wallpaper* by Judith Roberts, from the story by Charlotte Perkins Gilman, dir by Roberts at the New End: rev by Bassett, Foss, Logan.

2458   "Reviews of Productions." *LTR*. 1996; 16(15): 944-950. Lang.: Eng.

UK-England: London. 1996. ■*Voyeurz*, musical by Michael Lewis and Peter Rafelson, dir by Lewis and Rafelson at Whitehall: rev by Benedict, Butler, Cooke, de Jongh, Gross, Hagerty, Hughes, Kingston, Morley, Nathan, Reade, Shuttleworth, Smith, Spencer, Sullivan, Tinker. *Thugs* by Robert William Sherwood, dir by Brennan Street at the White Bear: rev by Marmion, McPherson. *The Decameron* by Nick Ward, adapted from stories by Boccaccio, dir by Ward at the Gate: rev by Coveney, Curtis, Dowden, Gardner, Hanks, Kingston, Shuttleworth, Stratton.

2459   "Reviews of Productions." *LTR*. 1996; 16(15): 951-958. Lang.: Eng.

UK-England: London. 1996. ■*Two Boys in a Bed on a Cold Winter's Night* by James Edwin Parker, dir by Julian Woolford at the Arts: rev by Benedict, Curtis, Dark, Kingston, Shuttleworth, Spencer, Tushingham. *Edwin* and *The Dock Brief* by John Mortimer, dir by Natasha Betteridge at the Orange Tree Room: rev by Abdulla. *Lord of the Dance* by Michael Flatley, dir by Arlene Phillips at the Coliseum: rev by Baile, Brown, Christiansen, Clancy, Crisp, Dougill, Dromgoole, Hagerty, Levene, Meisner, Sacks, Smith, Sweet, Taylor, Tinker, Watson.

2460   "Reviews of Productions." *LTR*. 1996; 16(23): 1448-1449. Lang.: Eng.

UK-England: London. 1996. ■*The Bedsit* by Paul Sellar, dir by Michael C. Friend and Andy Johnson at the Tabard: rev by Kingston, Reade. *Amerika* devised by Group K and Rob van Sickle, dir by Patrick Kealey at the Southwark Playhouse: rev by Marmion. *The Winter's Tale* by William Shakespeare, dir by Paul Burbridge at the Bridewell: rev by Cavendish, Murray.

2461   "Reviews of Productions." *LTR*. 1996; 16(15): 958-969. Lang.: Eng.

UK-England: London, Stratford. 1996. ■*The Wonderland Adventures of Alice* adapted from Lewis Carroll by Simon Corble, dir by Jonathan Petherbridge at the London Bubble: rev by Curtis, Godfrey-Faussett. *The General from America* by Richard Nelson, dir by Howard Davies for the RSC at the Swan, Stratford: rev by Billington, Butler, Coveney, de Jongh, Gore-Langton, Grant, Gross, Hewison, Hughes, Macaulay, Morley, Nathan, Nightingale, Taylor, Woddis. *Troilus and Cressida* by William Shakespeare, dir by Ian Judge for the RSC at the Royal Shakespeare, Stratford: rev by Billington, Butler, Coveney, de Jongh, Gore-Langton, Grant, Goss, Hagerty, Hewison, Hughes, Macaulay, Nathan, Nightingale, Taylor, Tinker, Woddis.

2462   "Reviews of Productions." *LTR*. 1996; 16(15): 969-972, 974-977. Lang.: Eng.

UK-England: London. 1996. ■*The Learned Ladies (Les Femmes savantes)* by Molière, transl by A. R. Waller, dir by Steven Pimlott at The Other Place, Stratford: rev by Billington, de Jongh, Gore-Langton, Grant, Hewison, Macaulay, Nightingale, Taylor. Channel 4 Sitcom Festival: 9 half-hour plays, *Kerouac* by Marcy Kahan, dir by William Burdett-Coutts, *In Exile* by Tunde Babalola, dir by Mark Williams, *Basic Instincts* by Patrick Barlow, dir by Nigel Plamer, *Last Legs* by Lenny Barker and Paul Shearer, dir by Burdett-Coutts, *The Magnificent Andersons* by David Upsher and Diana Fox, dir by Richard Georgeson, *Bleeding Hearts* by Andy Riley and Kevin Cecil, dir by Williams, *The Kidney Club* by Phil Nice and Tony Haase, dir by Jo Johnson, *The Dentons* by Merle Nygate, dir by Jonathan Lloyd, *Slap!* by Tim Dynevor at the Riverside: rev by Bassett, Edwardes, Foss, Rees, Stephen, Thompson.

DRAMA: —Performance/production

2463   "Reviews of Productions." *LTR*. 1996; 16(16-17): 985-990. Lang.: Eng.

UK-England: London. 1996. ■*Murder in the Cathedral* by T.S. Eliot, Romanian transl by Mircea Ivanescu, dir by Mihai Maniutiu at the Almeida: rev by Billington, Coveney, Curtis, Foss, Gore-Langton, Gross, Hanks, Nightingale, Shuttleworth, Stratton, Taylor, Tinker. *A Small World* by Mustapha Matura, dir by Roland Rees at Southwark Playhouse: rev by Curtis, Hewison, Kingston, Simpkins, Stratton, Taylor. *Thin Ice* by Alan Ford, dir by Ford at the Old Red Lion: rev by Bassett, Cavendish, Coveney, Simpkins.

2464   "Reviews of Productions." *LTR*. 1996; 16(16-17): 1019-1024. Lang.: Eng.

UK-England: London. 1996. ■*3 Ms Behaving* by Gillian Gregory, dir by Gregory at the Tricycle: rev by Bassett, Curtis, Edwardes, Foss, Gross, Thorncroft. *Love in a Wood* by William Wycherley, dir by Michael Cabot at the New End: rev by Doughty, Godfrey-Faussett, Gross, Kingston, Nathan, Reade, Taylor, Walsh. *Bodies* by James Saunders, dir by Dominic Hill at the Orange Tree: rev by Curtis, McPherson, Morley, Nightingale, Reade, Tushingham.

2465   "Reviews of Productions." *LTR*. 1996; 16(16-17): 991-1004. Lang.: Eng.

UK-England: London. 1996. ■*Hedda Gabler* by Henrik Ibsen, transl by Kenneth McLeish, dir by Stephen Unwin at the Donmar Warehouse, and *Hedda Gabler* by Ibsen, transl by Helen Cooper, dir by Lindy Davies at the Minerva, Chichester: rev by Billington, Butler, Christopher, Coveney, Curtis, de Jongh, Gore-Langton, Gross, Hagerty, Hughes, Hughes-Onslow, Macaulay, Morley, Nathan, Nightingale, Peter, Shuttleworth, Spencer, Stratton, Taylor, Tinker, Woddis. *Dial M for Murder* by Frederick Knott, dir by Peter Wilson at the Apollo: rev by Benedict, Campbell, Coveney, Curtis, Foss, Gross, Hagerty, Hewison, Kingston, Malins, Morley, Nathan, Spencer, Stratton, Thorncroft, Usher.

2466   "Reviews of Productions." *LTR*. 1996; 16(16-17): 1005-1010. Lang.: Eng.

UK-England: London. 1996. ■*Ferry Cross the Mersey* by Maggie Norris and Guy Picot, dir by Carole Todd at the Lyric: rev by Bassett, Curtis, Foss, Hagerty, Hewison, Morley, Spencer, Stratton, Thorncroft. *Hosanna* by Michel Tremblay, dir by Maureen Oxley, and *Serpent Kills* by Blake Brooker and Jim Milan, dir by Kate Hall at the White Bear: rev by Abdulla, Foss, McPherson, Tushingham. *The Red Balloon* by Anthony Clark from the film by Albert Lamorisse, dir by Clark at the Olivier: rev by Benedict, Coveney, Curtis, Gore-Langton, Gross, Hagerty, Hanks, Harvey (aged 13), Hewison, Hughes, Taylor.

2467   "Reviews of Productions." *LTR*. 1996; 16(16-17): 1011-1019. Lang.: Eng.

UK-England: London. 1996. ■*The Fantasticks* by Harvey Schmidt and Tom Jones, dir by Dan Crawford at the King's Head: rev by Butler, Coveney, Curtis, Darvell, Edwardes, Hagerty, Morley, Nathan, Nightingale, Taylor, Thorncroft, Tinker. *On the Twentieth Century*, musical by Cy Coleman, book and lyrics by Betty Comden and Adolph Green, dir by Carol Metcalfe at the Bridewell: rev by Abdulla, Benedict, Curtis, Darvell, Gross, Hagerty, Hewison, Kingston, Morley, Thorncroft. *Kiss the Sky* by Jim Cartwright, dir by Mike Bradwell at the Shepherd's Bush Empire: rev by Bell, Foss, Gardner, Hagerty, Hemming, Hewison, Malins, Morley, Nightingale, Sierz, Spencer, Taylor, Tushingham.

2468   "Reviews of Productions." *LTR*. 1996; 16(16-17): 1024-1030. Lang.: Eng.

UK-England: London. 1996. ■*The Taming of the Shrew* by William Shakespeare, dir by Gregory Thompson at the Lincoln's Inn Fields: rev by Reade. *The Two Gentlemen of Verona* by Shakespeare, dir by Jack Shepherd at the Globe, Bankside: rev by Billington, Butler, de Jongh, Edwardes, Gross, Hagerty, Hewison, Hughes, Macaulay, Morley, Nathan, Nightingale, Smith, Spencer, Taylor. *When I was Wee I Had a Granny Who Said...* by Tony Webb, dir by Webb at the Finborough: rev by McPherson, Tushingham.

2469   "Reviews of Productions." *LTR*. 1996; 16(16-17): 1033-1039. Lang.: Eng.

UK-England: London, Oxford. 1996. ■*When We Are Married* by J.B. Priestley, dir by Jude Kelly at the Chichester Festival: rev by Billington, Christopher, Coveney, Gore-Langton, Gross, Hagerty, Hanks, Hughes, Nathan, Nightingale, Peter, Shuttleworth, Smith, Taylor, Tinker, Watkins. *Hamlet* by William Shakespeare, dir by John Retallack and Karl

James at the Rose, Oxford: rev by Gore-Langton, Kingston, Logan, Peter, Taylor.

2470   "Reviews of Productions." *LTR*. 1996; 16(22): 1396-1399. Lang.: Eng.

UK-England: London. 1996. ■*Sherlock Holmes: The Adventure at Sir Arthur Sullivan's* by Tim Heath from the novels by Sir Arthur Conan Doyle, dir by Heath at the Warehouse, Croydon: rev by McPherson, Tushingham. Storming: The Royal Court Young Writers Festival, *The Separation* by Matty Chalk, dir by Indhu Rubasingham, *Drink, Smoking and Toking* by Stuart Swarbrick, dir by Julie-Anne Robinson, *The Future Is Betamax* by Nicholas Kelly, dir by Caroline Hall, *Business as Usual* by Michael Shaw, dir by Rubasingham, *The Call* by Lydia Prior, dir by Robinson, *Backpay* by Tamantha Hammerschlag, dir by Mary Peate at the Royal Court Upstairs: rev by Butler, Curtis, Hewison, Macaulay, Spencer, Stratton, Turpin, Williams.

2471   "Reviews of Productions." *LTR*. 1996; 16(23): 1423-1429. Lang.: Eng.

UK-England: London. 1996. ■*The Herbal Bed* by Peter Whelan, dir by Michael Attenborough for the RSC at The Pit: rev by Brown, Edwardes, Gross, Hanks, Hemming, Nathan, Nightingale, Smith, Spencer, Usher. *Macbeth* by William Shakespeare, dir by Tim Albery for the RSC at the Barbican: rev by Curtis, Dowden, Hemming, Nightingale, Stratton, Usher. *Pericles* by Shakespeare, dir by James Roose-Evans at the Riverside: rev by de Jongh, Edwardes, Hanks, Hewison, McNaughton, Nightingale, Shuttleworth.

2472   "Reviews of Productions." *LTR*. 1996; 16(23): 1436-1442. Lang.: Eng.

UK-England: London. 1996. ■*The Nun* by Julian Forsyth from the novel by Denis Diderot, dir by Margarete Forsyth at BAC 1: rev by Parry. *Martin Guerre*, music by Claude-Michel Schönberg, book by Schönberg and Alain Boublil, lyrics by Edward Hardy and Stephen Clark, original French text by Boublil, additional lyrics by Boublil and Herbert Kretzmer, dir by Declan Donnellan at the Prince Edward: rev by Billington, Brown, Butler, Clark, Coveney, Edwardes, Gore-Langton, Gross, Hagerty, Hassell, Morley, Murray, Nathan, Nightingale, Peter, Spencer, Usher. *A Quick Eternity* by Robert Hamilton, dir by Hamilton at the Man in the Moon: rev by Stratton.

2473   "Reviews of Productions." *LTR*. 1996; 16(23): 1443-1448. Lang.: Eng.

UK-England: London. 1996. ■*Scrooge* by Leslie Bricusse, dir by Tudor Davies at the Dominion: rev by Abdulla, Benedict, Butler, Davis, de Jongh, Foss, Gore-Langton, Gross, Hagerty, Morley, Nathan, Nightingale, Seckerson, Spencer, Usher. *The Razor Blade Cuckoo* by Jonathan Kemp, dir by Robert Wolstenholme at the Link: rev by Godfrey-Faussett. One Person Play Festival featuring *Twockers, Knockers and Elsie Smith* by Jean Stevens, dir by Valerie Lucas, *Poe/Play* by Mark Cole, dir by Ned Cox, *Barry Sorts it Out* by Pat Condell, dir by Condell, *Molly* by Steve Morley, dir by Tamara Hinchco, *Conversations with God* by Robin Blades, dir by Georgia Dobbs, *Still Life* by Danusia Iwaszo, dir by Mehmet Ergen, *The Uneasy Rider* by Stephen Wilson, dir by Dawn Lintern, *Lust* by Iain Heggie, dir by Liz Carruthers, *An Occasional Orchid* by Ivan Heng and Chowee Leow, dir by Heng, *After Penny* by Richard Bickley, dir by Tristan Brolly, *Miss Jessica Flynn* by Jenny Vulgar, dir by Richard Franklin, *Medicine Girl* by Laura Bridgeman, dir by Kath Mattock, *Face to the Voice* by Christopher Higgins, dir by Higgins, *Obsession* by Robert Young, dir by Lisa Goldman, *Mr. Owen's Millennium* by Mark Jenkins, dir by Steve Fisher, *Get it While You Can: A Conversation with Janis Joplin* by Roy Smiles, dir by David Cottis, *Ordinaryman* by Byron Ayanoglu, dir by Tony Yates, *Padlocked* by Gillian Plowman, dir by Arti Prasher, *Memories of a Mill Girl in a Green Shawl* by Steve McCuffen, dir by Steffyni Rigold, *The Have-Nots* by Elizabeth Handy, dir by Kate Gielgud at the Etcetera: rev by Kohil, Lavender, Marmion.

2474   "Reviews of Productions." *LTR*. 1996; 16(23): 1450-1453. Lang.: Eng.

UK-England: London. 1996. ■*Cyrano de Bergerac* by Edmond Rostand, transl by Edwin Morgan, dir by Gerry Mulgrew at the Almeida: rev by A. Donald, C. Donald, Fisher, Grant, Hanks, Kingston, Macauley, Smith, *Sunday Times*, Scotland. *The Dancing Master* by Aletta Lawson, dir by Lawson at BAC Main: rev by Benedict, Logan. *Who's Afraid of*

DRAMA: —Performance/production

Virginia Woolf? by Edward Albee, dir by Howard Davies at the Aldwych: rev by Hassell.

2475 "Reviews of Productions." *LTR.* 1996; 16(23): 1453-1458. Lang.: Eng.

UK-England: London. 1996. ■*The Jingo Drill* by Lynne Harvey, dir by Fraser Grant at the Trinity Arts: rev by Bayley, Woddis. *Shakespeare for My Father* by Lynne Redgrave, dir by John Clark at Theatre Royal, Haymarket: rev by Billington, Brown, Butler, Coveney, de Jongh, Gross, Morley, Murray, Nathan, Nightingale, Peter, Smith, Spencer, Stratton, Taylor, Usher. *Burdalane* by Judith Adams, dir by Gaynor Macfarlane: rev by Turpin, Tushingham, Woddis.

2476 "Reviews of Productions." *LTR.* 1996; 16(23): 1459-1466. Lang.: Eng.

UK-England: London, Stratford. 1996. ■*Think No Evil of Us* by David Benson, dir by Benson at the King's Head: rev by Cavendish, Curtis, Foss, Gross, Hagerty, Hewison, Kingston, Marmion, Usher. *Susan Garret* by Metin Marlow, dir by Marlow at Maison Bertaux: rev by Marmion. *Everyman* dir by Kathryn Hunter and Marcello Magni for the RSC at The Other Place, Stratford: rev by Billington, Coveney, de Jongh, Gore-Langton, Macauley, Nightingale, Peter, Spencer, Stratton, Taylor.

2477 "Reviews of Productions." *LTR.* 1996; 16(23): 1494-1496. Lang.: Eng.

UK-England: London. 1996. ■*Cold Words and Whisky Breath* by Simon Roberts, dir by Roberts at the Baron's Court: rev by Marmion. *The Belle Vue (Zur schönen Aussicht)* by Ödön von Horváth, transl by Kenneth McLeish, dir by Nick Philippou at the Lyric Studio: rev by Curtis, Kingston, Marmion, McPherson, Saddler, Shuttleworth. *The Pitchfork Disney* by Phillip Ridley, at Upstairs at the Landor: rev by Cavendish.

2478 "Reviews of Productions." *LTR.* 1996; 16(23): 1483-1494. Lang.: Eng.

UK-England: London. 1996. ■*Old Wicked Songs* by Jon Marans, dir by Elijah Moshinsky at the Gielgud: rev by Billington, Brown, Burnside, Butler, Christopher, Coveney, de Jongh, Edwardes, Gore-Langton, Gross, Hagerty, Hassell, Hemming, Morley, Nathan, Nightingale, Peter, Sierz, Spencer, Taylor, Usher. *From Morning Sun Till Dine* by Angus Graham-Campbell, dir by Graham-Campbell at the Pleasance: rev by Godfrey-Fausett, Ives. *Jesus Christ Superstar* by Andrew Lloyd Webber and Tim Rice, dir by Gale Edwards at the Lyceum: rev by Brown, Butler, Christopher, Coveney, de Jongh, Edwardes, Gardner, Gore-Langton, Gross, Hagerty, Morley, Nathan, Nightingale, Peter, Seckerson, Shuttleworth, Smith, Spencer, Usher.

2479 "Reviews of Productions." *LTR.* 1996; 16(24): 1499-1506. Lang.: Eng.

UK-England: London. 1996. ■*Fair Ladies at a Game of Poem Cards* by Peter Oswald, based on an original work by Chikamatsu Monzaemon, dir by John Crowley at the Cottesloe: rev by Brown, Coveney, Curtis, Foss, Gardner, Gross, Hemming, Hewison, Logan, Nightingale, Spencer, Taylor, Usher. *Fossil Woman* by Louise Warren, dir by Helena Uren at the Union Chapel: rev by Abdulla, Gardner, Stevens, Turpin. *Max Clapper: A Life in Pictures* a play with film by David Farr, dir by Farr (play) and Ben Hopkins (film) at the Gate at the Electric: rev by Billington, de Jongh, *Financial Times*, Hewison, Kingston, Morley, Sierz, Smith, Sweet, Turpin, Tushingham.

2480 "Reviews of Productions." *LTR.* 1996; 16(24): 1506-1511. Lang.: Eng.

UK-England: London. 1996. ■*Women and Wallace* by Jonathan Marc Sherman, dir by Ned Cox and *Cowboy Mouth* by Sam Shepard, dir by Maureen Oxley at the White Bear: rev by Godfrey-Faussett. *East Is East* by Ayub Khan-Din, dir by Kristine Landon-Smith at the Royal Court Upstairs Stage: rev by Billington, Butler, de Jongh, Foss, Nathan, Nightingale, Peter, Reade, Shuttleworth, Spencer, Taylor, Usher. *Imperfect Librarian* by Marc Von Henning, from stories by Jorgé Luis Borges, dir by Von Henning at the Young Vic Studio: rev by Christopher, Davé, Gardner, Hanks, Reade.

2481 "Reviews of Productions." *LTR.* 1996; 16(24): 1511-1516. Lang.: Eng.

UK-England: London. 1996. ■*Frankie Is OK, Peggy Is Fine and the House Is Cool* by Martin Civcak, transl by Clive Paton, dir by Civcak at the Grace: rev by McPherson. *The Cherry Orchard (Višněvyj sad)* by Anton Čechov, transl by Peter Gill, dir by Adrian Noble for the RSC at

the Albery: rev by Billington, Brown, Butler, Coveney, Darvell, de Jongh, Gore-Langton, Hagerty, Macaulay, Morley, Nathan, Nightingale, Spencer, Stratton, Usher, Wardle. *Le Cirque Invisible* devised and performed by Victoria Chaplin and Jean-Baptiste Thierrée at the Mermaid: rev by Christopher, Curtis, Hassell, Levene, Spencer, Usher.

2482 "Reviews of Productions." *LTR.* 1996; 16(24): 1517-1527. Lang.: Eng.

UK-England: London. 1996. ■*Swanwhite (Svanevit)* by August Strindberg, transl by Gregory Motton, dir by Timothy Walker at the Gate: rev by Coveney, Driver, Gardner, Kingston, Peter, Reade, Schamus. *You Haven't Embraced Me Yet*, a play devised by the company Told by an Idiot, dir by John Wright at BAC Main: rev by Benedict, Christopher, Curtis, Hemming, Smith, Stratton. *Henry VIII* by William Shakespeare, dir by Gregory Doran for the RSC at the Swan, Stratford: rev by Billington, Butler, Coveney, de Jongh, Edwardes, Gore-Langton, Hagerty, Macaulay, Nathan, Nightingale, Peter, Spencer, Usher, Wardle, Woddis.

2483 "Reviews of Productions." *LTR.* 1996; 16(24): 1527-1534. Lang.: Eng.

UK-England: London, Stratford. 1996. ■*Much Ado About Nothing* by William Shakespeare, dir by Michael Boyd for the RSC at the Royal Shakespeare, Stratford: rev by Billington, Brown, Butler, Coveney, de Jongh, Edwardes, Gore-Langton, Hagerty, Macaulay, Nathan, Nightingale, Peter, Spencer, Taylor, Usher, Wardle, Woddis. *Elsinore (Elsineur)* by Robert Lepage, dir by Lepage at the Nottingham Playhouse: rev by Bayley, Butler, Donald, Gardner, Gore-Langton, Peter, Shuttleworth, Spencer, Taylor.

2484 "Reviews of Productions." *LTR.* 1996; 16(25/26): 1551-1560. Lang.: Eng.

UK-England: London. 1996. ■*The Beauty Queen of Leenane* by Martin McDonagh, dir by Garry Hynes at the Royal Court Downstairs: rev by Bassett, Brown, Christopher, de Jongh, Foss, Gore-Langton, Gross, Hagerty, Macaulay, Nightingale, Peter, Sierz, Stratton. *I Licked a Slag's Deodorant* by Jim Cartwright, dir by Cartwright at the Royal Court Upstairs Stage (Ambassadors): rev by Billington, Butler, Christopher, Coveney, de Jongh, Edwardes, Gross, Hassell, Macaulay, Nightingale, Peter, Spencer, Taylor. *Family Circles* by Alan Ayckbourn, dir by Sam Walters at the Orange Tree: rev by Bassett, Benedict, Billington, Curtis, Gross, Kingston, Logan, Peter, Smith.

2485 "Reviews of Productions." *LTR.* 1996; 16(25/26): 1560-1569. Lang.: Eng.

UK-England: London. 1996. ■*Sympathy for the Devil* by Roy Winston, dir by Ray Harrison Graham at Oval House and the Tricycle: rev by Cavendish, Lavender, Logan, Martin, Williams. *Hamlet* by William Shakespeare, dir by John Keates at the Wimbledon Studio: rev by McPherson, Tushingham. *Plunder* by Ben Travers, dir by Peter James at the Savoy: rev by Abdulla, Billington, Brown, Butler, Christopher, Coveney, de Jongh, Gore-Langton, Gross, Hagerty, Murray, Nathan, Nightingale, Peter, Sierz, Smith, Spencer, Taylor, Usher.

2486 "Reviews of Productions." *LTR.* 1996; 16(25/26): 1569-1574. Lang.: Eng.

UK-England: London. 1996. ■*Her Aching Heart* by Bryony Lavery, dir by Jacqui Somerville at the Man in the Moon: rev by Foss, Godfrey-Faussett. *The Eleventh Commandment* by David Schneider, dir by Matthew Lloyd at the Hampstead: rev by Billington, Brown, Coveney, Curtis, Gross, Marmion, Nathan, Nightingale, Peter, Shuttleworth, Smith, Spencer, Taylor. *The Learned Ladies (Les Femmes savantes)* by Molière, transl by A.R. Waller, dir by Steven Pimlott for the RSC at The Pit: rev by Coveney, Curtis, Edwardes, Foss, Kingston, Usher.

2487 "Reviews of Productions." *LTR.* 1996; 16(25/26): 1575-1582. Lang.: Eng.

UK-England: London. 1996. ■*Troilus and Cressida* by William Shakespeare, dir by Ian Judge for the RSC at the Barbican: rev by Cavendish, de Jongh, Kingston, Murray, Nathan, Peter, Smith, Spencer, Usher. *The Servant of Two Masters (Il servitore di due padroni)* by Carlo Goldoni, transl by Ted Craig, dir by Craig and Miltos Yerolemou at the Warehouse, Croydon: rev by Foss, Stratton, Turpin. *A Midsummer Night's Dream* by Shakespeare, dir by Jonathan Miller at the Almeida: rev by Billington, Brown, Butler, Coveney, de Jongh, Gross, Hassell, Kingston, Macaulay, Morley, Nathan, Peter, Spencer, Stratton, Taylor, Usher.

DRAMA: —Performance/production

2488 "Reviews of Productions." *LTR*. 1996; 16(25/26): 1583-1587. Lang.: Eng.
UK-England: London. 1996. ■*Dylan Thomas: Return Journey* by Bob Kingdom, dir by Anthony Hopkins and *The Truman Capote Talkshow* by Kingdom, dir by Kevin Knight, in rep at the Lyric Studio: rev by Hemming, Stevens. *The Official Tribute to the Blues Brothers* a musical compilation dir by David Leland at the Apollo: rev by Bassett, Bell, Foss, Hagerty, Logan, Usher, Wareham. *Showtime* by Tim Etchells, dir by Etchells at ICA: rev by Cavendish, Edwardes, Gardner, Hewison, Sierz, Woddis.

2489 "Reviews of Productions." *LTR*. 1996; 16(25/26): 1633-1639. Lang.: Eng.
UK-England: London, Stratford. 1996. ■*Little Eyolf (Lille Eyolf)* by Henrik Ibsen, transl by Michael Meyer, dir by Adrian Noble for the RSC at the Swan, Stratford: rev by Billington, Butler, Coveney, de Jongh, Edwardes, Macaulay, Nightingale, Peter, Spencer. *The Merry Wives of Windsor* by William Shakespeare, dir by Ian Judge for the RSC at the Royal Shakespeare, Stratford: rev by Coveney, Gore-Langton, Hagerty, Macaulay, Nathan, Nightingale, Spencer, Taylor, Usher.

2490 "Reviews of Productions." *LTR*. 1996; 16(25/26): 1588-1596. Lang.: Eng.
UK-England: London. 1996. ■*Nine* by Arthur Kopit, music and lyrics by Maury Yeston, based on the film by Federico Fellini, dir by David Leveaux at the Donmar Warehouse: rev by Billington, Butler, Coveney, de Jongh, Edwardes, Gore-Langton, Gross, Hagerty, Kingston, Macaulay, Morley, Nathan, Peter, Sierz, Smith, Spencer, Taylor, Usher. *Dick Daredevil* by Phil Willmott, music by Steven Markwick, dir by Willmott at the Drill Hall: rev by Curtis, Foss, Gross, Hagerty, Lavender, Stratton, Turpin. *Listen to the Wind* by Vivian Ellis, dir by Dan Crawford at the King's Head: rev by Abdulla, Christopher, Coveney, Curtis, Darvell, Gross, Spencer, Usher.

2491 "Reviews of Productions." *LTR*. 1996; 16(25/26): 1596-1604. Lang.: Eng.
UK-England: London. 1996. ■*Starting Here, Starting Now* a musical revue with music by David Shire and lyrics by Richard Maltby, Jr., dir by Robert Miles at the Canal Cafe: rev by Marmion. *Marry Me a Little* by Craig Lucas and Norman René, based on songs by Stephen Sondheim, dir by Clive Paget at the Bridewell: rev by Benedict, Butler, Cavendish, Coveney, Curtis, Gross, Hagerty, Kingston, Nathan, Smith. *Guys and Dolls* by Jo Swerling and Abe Burrows, music and lyrics by Frank Loesser, dir by Richard Eyre at the Olivier: rev by Billington, Brown, Butler, Coveney, de Jongh, Edwardes, Gore-Langton, Gross, Hagerty, Nathan, Nightingale, Peter, Sierz, Smith, Spencer, Taylor, Usher.

2492 "Reviews of Productions." *LTR*. 1996; 16(25/26): 1604-1614. Lang.: Eng.
UK-England: London. 1996. ■*A Streetcar Named Desire* by Tennessee Williams, dir by Peter Hall at the Theatre Royal, Haymarket: rev by Billington, Brown, Butler, Christopher, Coveney, de Jongh, Edwardes, Gore-Langton, Gross, Hagerty, Macaulay, Nathan, Nightingale, Peter, Smith, Spencer, Taylor, Usher. *The Adventures of Huckleberry Finn* by Matthew Francis from the novel by Mark Twain, dir by Francis at the Greenwich: rev by Bassett, Butler, Curtis, Gardner, Gore-Langton, Hemming, Kingston, Turpin, Tushingham, Woddis. *Chloe Poems Healing Roadshow* by Jenni Potter, dir by Gerry Padden at the BAC: rev by Cavendish.

2493 "Reviews of Productions." *LTR*. 1996; 16(25/26): 1614-1619. Lang.: Eng.
UK-England: London. 1996. ■*Cold Comfort Farm* by Michael Friend from the novel by Stella Biggons, dir by Friend at the Cochrane: rev by Abdulla, Curtis, Hemming, Parry, Usher. *Obsession* by Robert Young, dir by Lisa Goldman, *Barry Sorts it Out* by Pat Condell, dir by Condell, *The Have-Nots* by Elizabeth Hand, dir by Kate Gielgud, and *An Occasional Orchid* by Ivan Heng and Chowee Low, dir by Heng at BAC 1: rev by Logan, Marlowe. *Beauty and the Beast* by Laurence Boswell, dir by Boswell at the Young Vic: rev by Butler, Christopher, Curtis, Davé, Edwardes, Gardner, Gore-Langton, Gross, Hagerty, Hewison, Kingston, O'Reilly, Spencer, Taylor, Usher.

2494 "Reviews of Productions." *LTR*. 1996; 16(25/26): 1620-1624. Lang.: Eng.
UK-England: London. 1996. ■*Beauty and the Beast* by David Cregan and Brian Protheroe, dir by Philip Hedley at the Theatre Royal, Strat-ford East: rev by Brown, Christopher, Darvell, Gardner, Godfrey-Faussett, Hemming, Sweet. *The Witches* by David Wood from the novel by Roald Dahl, dir by Wood at the Vaudeville: rev by Curtis, Gardner, Gross, Hagerty, Haydon, Hewison, Spencer, Stevens, Turpin, Usher. *Oedipus the Panto* by David Mitchell and Robert Webb, music by Mark Etherington, lyrics by Jonathan Dryden Taylor, dir by Mitchell and Webb at the Pleasance: rev by Cavendish, Games, Turpin.

2495 "Reviews of Productions." *LTR*. 1996; 16(25/26): 1624-1628. Lang.: Eng.
UK-England: London. 1996. ■*The Big Book for Girls* by Joe Richards, music by Nick Brace, dir by Iain Ormsby-Knox at the Pleasance London: rev by Foss, Godfrey-Faussett, Shuttleworth. *Phantoms of Poe* adapted from stories by Edgar Allan Poe, dir by Gari Jones at the Finborough: rev by Reade. *A Christmas Carol* by Charles Dickens, dir by Neil Bartlett at the Lyric Hammersmith: rev by Bassett, Butler, Christopher, Coveney, Curtis, Foss, Gore-Langton, Gross, Hagerty, Hewison, Murray, Nathan, Taylor, Tushingham, Usher.

2496 "Reviews of Productions." *LTR*. 1996; 16(23): 1430-1433. Lang.: Eng.
UK-England: London. 1996. ■*Derek and Shirl Dice with Death* by Julian Garner, dir by Stephen Hutton at the White Bear: rev by Cavendish, McPherson. *Life on Mars?* by Tom McCrory, dir by Stephen Gilroy at the Riverside 3: rev by Parry, Stratton. *The Colours of Living* by Camilla McGibbon, dir by Kate Matthews at the Finborough: rev by Marmion, Pearce.

2497 "Reviews of Productions." *LTR*. 1996; 16(23): 1433-1436. Lang.: Eng.
UK-England: London. 1996. ■*Still Lives* by Candida Cave, dir by Kenneth Robertson at the New End: rev by Abdulla, Williams. *Dark Tales* by Tim Arthur, dir by Karen Louise Hebden at the Arts: rev by Christopher, Davé, de Jongh, Hanks, Hemming, Kingston, Logan, Sierz. *Bingo* by P.J. Cobham, dir by Jacqueline Kelley and Cynthia Roberts at the King's Head: rev by McPherson.

2498 "Reviews of Productions." *LTR*. 1996; 16(2): 94-98. Lang.: Eng.
UK-England: London. 1996. ■*Dirty Reality II* by Black Mime Theatre, dir by Denise Wong at the Cochrane: rev by Bassett, Butler, Curtis, Dromgoole, Edwardes, Spencer, Woddis. *Peasouper* by Rejects Revenge, dir by Bim Mason at BAC: rev by Kingston. *Meinwärts* by Raimund Hoghe, dir by Hoghe at the ICA: rev by Bayley, Kingston.

2499 "Reviews of Productions." *LTR*. 1996; 16(2): 99-100. Lang.: Eng.
UK-England: London. 1996. ■*The Summit*, conceived and dir by Barnaby & Jonathan Stone for Ralf Ralf at BAC: rev by Bassett, Butler. *The House of Bernarda Alba (La Casa de Bernarda Alba)* by Lorca, dir by Nola Rae, for Manjana Theatre at the Purcell Room: rev by Kingston. *People Show 101* at the BAC: rev by Bassett.

2500 Banfield, Chris. "*Stale News* and *US*: Two Intercultural Experiments." *STP*. 1993 Dec.; 8: 19-35. Notes. Illus.: Photo. B&W. 2. Lang.: Eng.
UK-England: Birmingham. 1979-1992. Histories-sources. ■Productions of two plays by the Bengali playwright, Badal Sircar: Banfield's own production of *Stale News (Basi Khabar)* (1979), an agitprop piece dealing with an anti-colonial revolt in India in 1855, and Sircar's production of *US*, a devised political piece, both at the University of Birmingham in 1990 and 1992.

2501 Barth, Diana. "London Theatre: Highlights of the Fall Season." *WES*. 1996 Spr; 8(2): 17-22. Illus.: Photo. 4. Lang.: Eng.
UK-England: London. 1995-1996. Reviews of productions. ■London theatre season including Ronald Harwood's *Taking Sides* directed by Harold Pinter at the Criterion, Terry Johnson's *Dead Funny* at the Savoy, directed by author, *The Break of Day* by Timberlake Wertenbaker, directed by Max Stafford-Clark at the Royal Court, Alan Ayckbourn's *Communicating Doors* directed by Ayckbourn at the Gielgud, and Jonson's *Volpone* directed by Matthew Warchus at the National.

2502 Barth, Diana. "Richard Eyre." *WES*. 1996 Spr; 8(2): 31-34. Illus.: Photo. 2. Lang.: Eng.
UK-England: London. 1987-1996. Histories-sources. ■Interview with director Richard Eyre on the eve of his retirement from the National.

DRAMA: —Performance/production

2503 Barth, Diana. "Phyllida Lloyd Directs *Hysteria*." *WES*. 1995-96 Win; 7(3): 45-46. Lang.: Eng.
UK-England: London. 1995. Historical studies. ▪Account of Terry Johnson's *Hysteria*, presented at the Duke of York's Theatre as part of the first Royal Court Classics Season. Directed by Phyllida Lloyd, the play won the 1994 Olivier Award for Best Comedy.

2504 Becker, Peter von. "Howards Ende, Kyras Anfang." (Howard's End, Kyra's Beginning.) *THeute*. 1996; 6: 15-19. Illus.: Photo. Sketches. B&W. 6. Lang.: Ger.
UK-England: London. Germany: Hamburg. 1996. Reviews of performances. ▪Comparison of productions of *The Designated Mourner* by Wallace Shawn: directed by David Hare at the Cottesloe Theatre in London, and directed by Niels-Peter Rudolph at the Thalia Theater in Hamburg.

2505 Bérczes, László; Koncz, Zsuzsa, photo. "Rész vagyunk—Beszélgetés Declan Donnellannal." (We Are Part of It—An Interview with Declan Donnellan.) *Sz*. 1996; 29(4): 16-18. Illus.: Photo. B&W. 3. Lang.: Hun.
UK-England: London. Hungary: Budapest. 1996. Histories-sources. ▪A conversation with the director of the guest performance gave by the English Cheek by Jowl company at Budapest Katona József Theatre: John Webster's *The Duchess of Malfi*.

2506 Carlson, Marvin. "Katie Mitchell's The Machine Wreckers." *WES*. 1995-96 Win; 7(3): 57-58. Illus.: Photo. 1. Lang.: Eng.
UK-England: London. 1995. Historical studies. ▪Account of Toller's *The Machine Wreckers (Die Maschinenstürmer)*, directed by Katie Mitchell at the National.

2507 Charles, Peter. "A Phoenix From The Ashes, Part II." *PlPl*. 1996 Feb.: 14. Lang.: Eng.
UK-England. 1961-1996. Biographical studies. ▪Continued tribute to actor Sir Robert Stephens with references to his performances in *The Kitchen*, *Royal Hunt of the Sun* and *The Private Life of Sherlock Holmes*.

2508 Charles, Peter. "The Clergyman's Daughter." *PlPl*. 1996 Aug/Sep.: 16. Lang.: Eng.
UK-England. 1947-1996. Historical studies. ▪Tribute to actress Margaret Rawlings with references to her performance in *Salomé* by Oscar Wilde and *The Duchess of Malfi* by John Webster.

2509 Charles, Peter. "Reuters of Chiswick." *PlPl*. 1996 Apr.: 17.
UK-England. 1973-1996. Critical studies. ▪Profile of actress Margaret Courtenay with references to her performances in *Who's Afraid of Virginia Woolf?* by Edward Albee and *Relative Values* by Noël Coward.

2510 Chiba, Yoko. "Kori Torahiko and Edith Craig: A Japanese Playwright in London and Toronto." *CompD*. 1996-97 Win; 30(4): 431-451. Notes. Illus.: Photo. B&W. 1. Lang.: Eng.
UK-England: London. Canada: Toronto, ON. Japan. 1913-1924. Historical studies. ▪Experiences of expatriate Japanese playwright Kori Torahiko in both London and Toronto, and his influence on W.B. Yeats, Ezra Pound and Edith Craig, and a description of a Toronto production of his play *The Toils of Yoshitomo* in 1923.

2511 De Suinn, Colin. "Supple Futures." *PlPl*. 1996 Apr.: 27. Lang.: Eng.
UK-England: London. 1996. Critical studies. ▪Profile of director Tim Supple with references to his direction of *The Mosquito Coast* by David Glass and *Full Moon* by Caradog Pritchard. Emphasis on his affiliation with the Old Vic theatre.

2512 Dungate, Rod. "Sharing Responses." *PlPl*. 1996 May: 12-13. Illus.: Photo. B&W. 1. Lang.: Eng.
UK-England: Birmingham. 1981-1996. Critical studies. ▪Profile of director Anthony Clark with references to his productions of Rod Dungate's *Playing by the Rules*, and John Mortimer's *The Dock Brief*. Emphasis on his position as the Birmingham Repertory Theatre's Associate Director.

2513 Eddershaw, Margaret. *Performing Brecht: Forty Years of British Performances*. London/New York, NY: Routledge; 1996. 188 pp. Index. Biblio. Notes. Lang.: Eng.
UK-England. 1935-1975. Histories-specific. ▪Chronicles British production and reception of Brecht's plays, illustrating three major developments: the political rehabilitation of Brecht's plays by alternative and regional theatre companies, the 'classicizing' of Brecht at the Royal Shakespeare Company and the National Theatre, and recent efforts to free Brecht's plays from such mainstreaming.

2514 Gray, Simon. "Fat Chance (an Excerpt)." *DGQ*. 1996 Spr; 33(1): 12-17. Illus.: Photo. B&W. 1. Lang.: Eng.
UK-England: London. 1995. Histories-sources. ▪Excerpt from Simon Gray's account of his experiences during the production of his play *Cell Mates* which included the disappearance of one of his actors, Stephen Fry.

2515 Harris, Gerry. "Gender and Devising: *Europe After the Rain (no man's land)*." *STP*. 1994 June; 9: 5-15. Notes. Lang.: Eng.
UK-England: Lancaster. 1993. Critical studies. ▪The creation and performance of a devised piece, *Europe After the Rain*, at Lancaster University, based on the experiences of victims, especially women, of the conflict in the former Yugoslavia.

2516 Heywood, Liz. "Simone Benmussa's 'The Singular Life of Albert Nobbs'." *STP*. 1993 June; 7: 5-17. Notes. Illus.: Photo. B&W. 2. Lang.: Eng.
UK-England: Leeds. 1992. Histories-sources. ▪The author's own production, performed by students at the University of Leeds, of *The Singular Life of Albert Nobbs* by Simone Benmussa, based on a short story by George Moore. The text, concerning a woman disguised as a man, is said to have been used without any 'pedagogical purpose'.

2517 Jackson, Russell. "Oscar Asche: an Edwardian in Transition." *NTQ*. 1996 Aug.; 12(47): 216-228. Notes. Illus.: Photo. B&W. 6. Lang.: Eng.
UK-England: London. 1893-1932. Historical studies. ▪Outlines career of this forgotten actor-manager, emphasizing his training with Frank Benson, which led to his pictorial staging of plays by Shakespeare.

2518 Kruger, Loren. "The Dis-Play's the Thing: Gender and Public Sphere in Contemporary British Theatre." 49-77 in Keyssar, Helene, ed. *Feminist Theatre and Theory*. London: Macmillan; 1996. 288 pp. (New Casebooks.) Notes. Index. Lang.: Eng.
UK-England. 1993-1995. Critical studies. ▪The marginalization of women in the economics and institutions of theatre. Discusses plays by Caryl Churchill, the work of Women's Theatre Group, and feminist theatre's audience.

2519 Lacey, Stephen. "Naturalism, Poetic Realism, Spectacle: Wesker's *The Kitchen* in Performance." *NTQ*. 1996 Aug.; 12(47): 237-248. Notes. Illus.: Photo. B&W. 3. Lang.: Eng.
UK-England: London. 1959-1994. Critical studies. ▪Compares Stephen Daldry's revival with the original production by John Dexter, both at the Royal Court Theatre, and in particular explores their differing perceptions of naturalism and theatricality.

2520 Lebedina, L. "Neskromnoe obajanie konservatizma." (The Indiscreet Charm of Conservatism.) *TeatZ*. 1996; 9: 8-11. Lang.: Rus.
UK-England: London. 1970-1996. Critical studies. ▪Works of director Peter Hall, and the modern tendencies of English theatre.

2521 Leipold, Friedemann. "Diese verdammten Opern." (These Damned Operas.) *DB*. 1996; 2: 22-25. Illus.: Photo. B&W. 4. Lang.: Ger.
UK-England. 1947-1996. Biographical studies. ▪Portrait of director David Pountney, his reflections on theatre, his working methods and productions.

2522 Lennartz, Knut. "Hoffnung für Afrika." (Hope for Africa.) *DB*. 1996; 4: 16-17. Illus.: Photo. B&W. 2. Lang.: Ger.
UK-England: London. 1996. Critical studies. ▪The production of Athol Fugard's *Valley Song*, acted and directed by Fugard at the Royal Court Theatre.

2523 Mangan, Michael. "Theory, Practice, Theatre Praxis: Shakespeare and Practical Drama Work." *STP*. 1994 June; 9: 38-49. Notes. Lang.: Eng.
UK-England: Loughborough. 1588-1993. Historical studies. ▪Loughborough University's Shakespeare conference for school and college students of the East Midlands. Focus on the work of four groups of students on *The Tempest* and the combination of theory and practice in the workshops.

DRAMA: —Performance/production

2524 Milling, Jane. "'The Artifice': Appropriations of Intimacy." *STP*. 1993 June; 7: 47-53. Lang.: Eng.
UK-England: London, Richmond, Surrey. 1722-1993. Critical studies. ■A comparison between the original production of Susanna Centlivre's last play *The Artifice* at London's Drury Lane Theatre in 1722 and the recent revival at the Orange Tree Theatre, Richmond, Surrey. Although much of the original satirical point was lost, the piece has survived well thanks to its farcical situations.

2525 Norris, James. "Good News for the Old Vic: Sir Peter Hall Appointed." *PlPl*. 1996 Aug/Sep.; 507: 27. Lang.: Eng.
UK-England. 1996. Historical studies. ■Announces the appointment of Sir Peter Hall as the artistic director of the Old Vic Theatre Company for a five-year term beginning in January 1997.

2526 Pearce, Brian. "Granville-Barker's Production of *The Winter's Tale* (1912)." *CompD*. 1996 Fall; 30(3): 395-411. Notes. Lang.: Eng.
UK-England: London. 1912. Historical studies. ■Granville-Barker's landmark production of *The Winter's Tale*, and its influence upon the approach to staging Shakespeare in the twentieth century.

2527 Pensotti, George. "A Forgotten Hamlet." *PlPl*. 1996 June: 44. Lang.: Eng.
UK-England. 1944-1996. Critical studies. ■Brief profile of actor John Byron with emphasis on his role as Hamlet in the 1944 Stratford production.

2528 Reinelt, Janelle. "Interview with Katie Mitchell." *WES*. 1995-96 Win; 7(3): 47-54. Illus.: Photo. 1. Lang.: Eng.
UK-England: London. 1995. Histories-sources. ■Interview with director Katie Mitchell.

2529 Reinelt, Janelle. "Katie Mitchell's The Phoenician Women." *WES*. 1995-96 Win; 7(3): 55-56. Illus.: Photo. 1. Lang.: Eng.
UK-England: Stratford. 1995. Historical studies. ■Account of Euripides' *The Phoenician Women (Phoínissai)*, directed by Katie Mitchell at The Other Place.

2530 Russell, Anne. "Tragedy, Gender, Performance: Women as Tragic Heroes on the Nineteenth-Century Stage." *CompD*. 1996 Sum; 30(2): 135-157. Notes. Lang.: Eng.
UK-England. USA. 1801-1900. Historical studies. ■Occurrence of actresses, such as Ellen Tree, Fanny Kemble, and Sarah Bernhardt, performing male leads in tragedies such as Shakespeare's *Romeo and Juliet*, *Hamlet*, and *Cymbeline*, and Thomas Noon Talfourd's *Ion: A Tragedy in Five Acts*.

2531 Schafer, Elizabeth. "Census of Renaissance Drama Productions." *RORD*. 1996; 35(1): 33-51. Lang.: Eng.
UK-England. 1995. Histories-sources. ■Compilation of Renaissance dramas produced in England in 1995, with a brief description of the productions.

2532 Schoch, Richard W. "'The Homestead of History': Medievalism on the Mid-Victorian Stage." *TA*. 1995; 48: 72-83. Notes. Lang.: Eng.
UK-England: London. 1852-1859. Historical studies. ■Focuses on Charles Kean's revivals of Shakespeare's history plays *King John*, *Henry V*, *Henry VIII*, *Richard II*, and *Macbeth*, to demonstrate how his antiquarian approach constructed a model of England's medieval past with great accuracy.

2533 Shaughnessy, Robert; Otty, Nick. "*Voltaire's Brain*: Strategies for Enlightenment & Studies in the Death of the Author." *STP*. 1994 June; 9: 22-37. Notes. Illus.: Photo. B&W. 1. Lang.: Eng.
UK-England: Bristol. France. 1778-1991. Histories-sources. ■The authors' own production of a devised piece based on the last days of Voltaire, including his opium-induced dreams and a ten-minute version of Voltaire's last tragedy *Irène*, translated into English alexandrines and performed in a travesty of eighteenth-century declamatory acting style.

2534 Shenton, Mark. "Britain's Best." *TheaterW*. 1996 Mar 4; 9(31): 22-41. Illus.: Photo. B&W. 8. Lang.: Eng.
UK-England: London. 1996. Histories-sources. ■Top 100 British theatre personalities, including actors, directors, designers, theatres, playwrights, producers. Profiles, productions, strengths of these artists.

2535 Shields, Ronald E. "Voices Inside a Poet's Garden: John Masefield's Theatricals at Boar's Hill." *TextPQ*. 1996 Oct.; 16 (4): 301-320. Notes. Biblio. Illus.: Sketches. B&W. 3. Lang.: Eng.
UK-England. 1919-1932. Historical studies. ■A cultural reading of the press reports of John Masefield's theatricals at Boar's Hill, what can be garnered from them of the social and cultural debates of the time.

2536 Skasa, Michael. "Für Theater ganz brauchbar der Ibsen." (Quite Good for Theatre Use, This Ibsen.) *THeute*. 1996; 10: 14-16. Illus.: Photo. B&W. 2. Lang.: Ger.
UK-England: London. 1996. Historical studies. ■Analysis of the production of Ibsen's *John Gabriel Borkman* directed by Richard Eyre at the National, with emphasis on the acting by Paul Scofield and Vanessa Redgrave.

2537 Slater, Michael. "The Transformations of Susan: The Stage History of Douglas Jerrold's Black Eyed Susan, 1829-1994." *TN*. 1996; 50(3): 146-175. Notes. Lang.: Eng.
UK-England. 1829-1994. Historical studies. ■Adaptations of *Black Eyed Susan* throughout the nineteenth century, and its revival by community theatre groups.

2538 Smythe, Eva. "Beginners Please!" *PlPl*. 1996 July: 17. Lang.: Eng.
UK-England: London. 1996. Critical studies. ■The staging and performance of the Royal Academy of Dramatic Arts' production *The Sisterhood (Les Femmes savantes)* by Molière, directed by Nicholas Barter.

2539 Sutton, R.B. "*A Taming of the Shrew*: Adapting the Deconstruction." *STP*. 1993 Dec.; 8: 63-75. Notes. Lang.: Eng.
UK-England: Liverpool. 1992. Critical studies. ■A report on a production of Shakespeare's *The Taming of the Shrew* at John Moores University Liverpool, in which the text was deconstructed to yield a feminist reading of the play—Kate's final speech, for instance, being read from a book provided by Petruchio, which she proceeded to tear up.

2540 Trussler, Simon. "English Acting, Interactive Technology and the Elusive Quality of Englishness." *NTQ*. 1996; 12(45): 3-5. Lang.: Eng.
UK-England. 1995. Empirical research. ■Introduces a project at Goldsmiths, University of London, for using CD-ROMs to record the evidence from the past, verbal and pictorial, since 1950, and to assess its relevance to present-day acting of contemporary plays and the classical repertoire.

2541 Warner, Deborah; Cousin, Geraldine. "Exploring Space at Play: the Making of the Theatrical Event." *NTQ*. 1996 Aug.; 12 (47): 229-236. Lang.: Eng.
UK-England: London. 1980-1996. Histories-sources. ■Interview with director Deborah Warner discussing recent productions, notably *Richard II*, with Fiona Shaw, at the National Theatre, the censored *Footfalls* by Samuel Beckett at the Garrick, and her St. Pancras Project at the Midland Grand Hotel.

2542 Werner, Sarah. "Performing Shakespeare: Voice Training and the Feminist Actor." *NTQ*. 1996 Aug.; 12(47): 249-258. Notes. Biblio. Lang.: Eng.
UK-England: London. USA. 1973-1996. Critical studies. ■Argues that the cultural biases behind voice training, exemplified in the books of Cicely Berry, Kristin Linklater, and Patsy Rodenburg, limit the possibilities for feminist performances of Shakespeare, for it denies actors ways of questioning the politics of the playscripts.

2543 Žurovskij, A. "Ostrov čudes Pitera Bruka." (Peter Brook's Island of Miracles.) *TeatZ*. 1996; 9: 5-7. Lang.: Rus.
UK-England. 1991-1992. Critical studies. ■The work of director Peter Brook.

2544 Žurovskij, A. "Ésse Pitera Bruka o teatre pri nekotorom učastii Sekspira." (Peter Brook's Essay on Theatre with some Influence from Shakespeare.) *TeatZ*. 1996; 9: 21-24. Lang.: Rus.
UK-England. 1990-1996. Critical studies. ■Analysis of Brook's staging of *Hamlet*.

2545 "Reviews of Productions." *LTR*. 1996; 18(10): 1069-1081. Lang.: Eng.
UK-Scotland: Edinburgh. 1996. ■Edinburgh Festival: *Elsinore (Elsineur)* by Robert Lepage, dir by Lepage at The King's: rev by Bil-

DRAMA: —Performance/production

lington, Coveney. *Orlando* by Darryl Pinckney and Robert Wilson, from book by Virginia Woolf, dir by Wilson and Ann-Christin Rommen at the Royal Lyceum: rev by Billington, Butler, Christopher, Coveney, de Jongh, Donald, Fisher, Gross, Hagerty, Hughes, Macauley, Nightingale, Peter, Smith, Spencer, Taylor, Tinker. *A Satire of the Four Estates* by John McGrath, dir by McGrath at the Edinburgh National Conference Centre: rev by Billington, Butler, Coveney, Donald, Fisher, Hanks, Hughes, McMillan, Nightingale, Peter, Shuttleworth, Spencer.

2546   "Scots Internationalism." *Econ.* 1996 Aug 31; 340(7981): 69-70. Illus.: Photo. B&W. 1. Lang.: Eng.

UK-Scotland: Edinburgh. 1947-1996. Critical studies. ■History and success of the Edinburgh Festival, the impact of current technology on performances and highlights of this year's proceedings.

2547   Bottoms, Steve. "Towards a Rhythm Method: Exploring 'Psychological Realism' in Sam Shepard's *Buried Child.*" *STP.* 1994 Dec.; 10: 4-19. Lang.: Eng.

UK-Scotland: Glasgow. 1994. Critical studies. ■Argues that in-depth character study is still useful in approaching works by Shepard and Mamet. Based on techniques used in a University of Glasgow production of Shepard's *Buried Child.*

2548   Holderness, Graham; Loughrey, Bryan; Stott, Andrew, ed. "'Bad Quartos' in Performance: Charles Calder in Conversation." *STP.* 1996 Dec.; 14: 48-58. Lang.: Eng.

UK-Scotland: Aberdeen. 1996. Histories-sources. ■The editors of a recent reprint of the First Quarto of Shakespeare's *Henry V, The Chronicle History of Henry the fift,* interview a Lecturer in English at the University of Aberdeen about his staging with students of the 'bad quartos' of *Hamlet* and of *Henry V,* the first staging of this version since the Renaissance.

2549   "Reviews of Productions." *NYTCR.* 1996; 57(1): 4-13. Lang.: Eng.

USA: New Haven, CT, New York, NY. 1995-1996. ■*Robbers* by Lyle Kessler, dir by Marshall W. Mason at the Long Wharf: rev by Johnson, Klein, Plemmons, Ruocco, Sokol, Swift, Taylor. *Denial* by Peter Sagal, dir by Arvin Brown at the Long Wharf: rev by Flemming, Johnson, Klein, Taylor. *Paul Robeson* by Phillip Hayes Dean, dir by Harold Scott at the Longacre: rev by Barnes, Holden, Kissel, Mandell.

2550   "Reviews of Productions." *NYTCR.* 1996; 57(2): 34-49. Lang.: Eng.

USA: New York, NY. 1996. ■*The Father (Fadren)* by August Strindberg, adapt by Richard Nelson, dir by Clifford Williams at the Criterion Center Stage Right: rev by Barnes, Canby, Feingold, Franklin, Gerard, Simon, Winer. *Molly Sweeney* by Brian Friel, dir by Friel at the Roundabout's Laura Pels Theatre: rev by Barnes, Canby, Evans, Feingold, Franklin, Lyon, Simon, Winer. *The Hope Zone* by Kevin Heelan, dir by Richard Jenkins at the Circle Repertory: rev by Barnes, Brantley, Evans, Feingold, Kissel, Simon, Winer.

2551   "Reviews of Productions." *NYTCR.* 1996; 57(3): 66-77. Lang.: Eng.

USA. 1996. ■*The Rivals* by Richard Brinsley Sheridan, dir by Mark Lamos at Hartford Stage: rev by Cummings, Kissel, Matthews, Ruocco, Sokol. *Coming of the Hurricane* by Keith Glover, dir by Marion McClinton at Arena Stage: rev by Anderson, Brantley, Presley, Rose. *The Amen Corner* by James Baldwin, dir by Seret Scott at the Long Wharf: rev by Arnott, Brantley, Plemmons, Ruocco, Sokol.

2552   "Reviews of Productions." *NYTCR.* 1996; 57(2, 3): 50-65. Lang.: Eng.

USA: New York, NY. 1996. ■*Wonderful Time* by Jonathan Marc Sherman, dir by Tim Vasen at the WPA: rev by Barnes, Brantley, Feingold, Gerard, Jacobson, Kissel. *Measure for Measure* by William Shakespeare, dir by Barry Kyle for Theatre for a New Audience at St. Clements: rev by Gerard, Jacobson, Kissel, Lyons. *Mata Hari* by Jerome Coopersmith, music by Edward Thomas, lyrics by Martin Charnin, dir by Charnin at the Theatre at St. Peter's Church: rev by Evans, Holden, Jacobson, Kissel, Simon. *King Lear* by Shakespeare, dir by Adrian Hall at the Joseph Papp Public Theatre/Anspacher Theatre: rev by Brantley, Feingold, Gerard, Kissel, Lyons, Simon, Sterrit, Winer.

2553   "Reviews of Productions." *NYTCR.* 1996; 57(14): 374-380. Lang.: Eng.

USA: New York, NY, East Haddam, CT. 1996. ■*Born to Sing* book and lyrics by Vy Higgensen and Ken Wydro, music by Wesley Naylor, dir by Wydro at the Union Square: rev by Hunter, Tommasini, Waxman, Wetzstoen. *Paper Moon* by Martin Casella, music by Larry Grossman, lyrics by Ellen Fitzhugh, dir by Matt Casella at the Goodspeed Opera House: rev by Delisio, Donovan, Lucier, Mathews, Ruocco. *Valley of the Dolls* by Helen Deutsch and Dorothy Kingsley from the novel by Jacqueline Susann, dir by Tom Booker at Circle in the Square Downtown: rev by Feingold, Kissel.

2554   "Reviews of Productions." *NYTCR.* 1996; 57(15): 384-400. Lang.: Eng.

USA: New York, NY. 1996. ■*Sex and Longing* by Christopher Durang, dir by Garland Wright at Lincoln Center: rev by Barnes, Brantley, Evans, Feingold, Kissel, Lyon, Peyser, Simon. *Skylight* by David Hare, dir by Richard Eyre at the Royale: rev by Barnes, Brantley, Evans, Feingold, Lahr, Lyons, Peyser, Simon. *Edmond* by David Mamet, dir by Clark Gregg at the Atlantic Theatre: rev by Brantley, Kissel, Lyons, Simon, Waxman.

2555   "Reviews of Productions." *NYTCR.* 1996; 57(15): 400-408. Lang.: Eng.

USA: New York, NY. 1996. ■*View of the Dome* by Theresa Rebeck, dir by Michael Mayer at the New York Theatre Workshop: rev by Brantley, Evans, Feingold, Kissel, Simon. *Radio Gals* book, music and lyrics by Mike Craver and Mark Hardwick, dir by Marci Milgrom Dodge at the John Houseman: rev by Evans, Feingold, Kissel, Lyons, Simon. *Electra* by Sophocles, transl by Yorgos Heimonas, dir by Lydia Koniordou at the City Center: rev by Brantley, Evans, Feingold, Simon.

2556   "Reviews of Productions." *NYTCR.* 1996; 57(16): 412-423. Lang.: Eng.

USA: New York, NY. 1996. ■*Taking Sides* by Ronald Harwood, dir by David Jones at the Brooks Atkinson: rev by Brantley, Evans, Feingold, Franklin, Kissel, Lyons, Peyser. *Forbidden Broadway Strikes Back!* by Gerard Alessandrini, dir by Alessandrini at the Triad: rev by Barnes, Brantley, Feingold, Lyons, Waxman. *Fit to Be Tied* by Nicky Silver, dir by David Warren at Playwrights Horizons: rev by Brantley, Evans, Feingold, Franklin, Kissel.

2557   "Reviews of Productions." *NYTCR.* 1996; 57(16): 423-431. Lang.: Eng.

USA: New York, NY. 1996. ■*Missing Marisa* and *Kissing Christine* by John Patrick Shanley, dir by Shanley at Primary Stages: rev by Simon, Van Gelder, Waxman. *The Beatification of Area Boy* by Wole Soyinka, dir by Jude Kelly at the Majestic, Brooklyn: rev by Barnes, Brantley, Lyons, Simon. *Randy Newman's Faust* music and lyrics by Newman, book by Newman and David Mamet, dir by Michael Greif at the Goodman: rev by Brantley, Christiansen, Henning, Lazare, Leonard.

2558   "Reviews of Productions." *NYTCR.* 1996; 57(14). Lang.: Eng.

USA: New York, NY. 1996. ■*Hughie* by Eugene O'Neill, dir by Al Pacino at Circle in the Square: rev by Barnes, Canby, Corliss, Evans, Kissel, Lyons. *Summer and Smoke* by Tennessee Williams, dir by David Warren at Criterion Center Stage Right: rev by Barnes, Brantley, Evans, Feingold, Lahr, Lyons, Simon. *When Pigs Fly* conceived by Howard Crabtree and Mark Waldrop, music by Dick Gallagher, sketches and direction by Waldrop at the Douglas Fairbanks: rev by Canby, Evans, Feingold, Kissel, Lyons, Simon.

2559   "Reviews of Productions." *NYTCR.* 1996; 57(17): 440-450. Lang.: Eng.

USA: New York, NY. 1996. ■*Chicago* by Fred Ebb and Bob Fosse, music by John Kander, lyrics by Ebb, dir by Walter Bobbie at the Richard Rodgers: rev by Barnes, Brantley, Evans, Feingold, Peyser, Zoglin. *Present Laughter* by Noël Coward, dir by Scott Elliott at the Walter Kerr: rev by Barnes, Brantley, Evans, Kissel, Lyons. *It's a Slippery Slope* by Spalding Gray, one-person show at the Vivian Beaumont: rev by Marks.

2560   "Reviews of Productions." *NYTCR.* 1996; 57(17): 450-454. Lang.: Eng.

USA: New York, NY. 1996. ■*Into the Whirlwind (Krutoj maršrut)* by Eugenia Ginzburg, dir by Vladimir Poglazov for Moscow theatre Sovremennik at the Lunt-Fontanne: rev by Evans. *Cakewalk* by Peter Feibleman, dir by Marshall W. Mason at the Variety Arts: Barnes, Lyons. *Nine*

DRAMA: —Performance/production

Armenians by Leslie Ayvazian, dir by Lynne Meadow at the City Center Stage I: rev by Brantley, Lyons. *The Entertainer* by John Osborne, dir by David Esbjornson at CSC: rev by Marks.

2561   "Reviews of Productions." *NYTCR*. 1996; 57(18): 460-471. Lang.: Eng.

USA: New York, NY. 1996. ▪*Juan Darien: A Carnival Mass* by Julie Taymor and Elliot Goldenthal, based on a tale by Horacio Quiroga, with music and lyrics by Goldenthal, dir by Taymor at Lincoln Center: rev by Brantley, Evans, Feingold, Kissel, Lyons, Winer. *The Rehearsal (La Répétition, ou l'amour puni)* by Jean Anouilh, transl by Jeremy Sams, dir by Nicholas Martin at the Roundabout: rev by Barnes, Brantley, Evans, Feingold, Kissel, Lyons. *God Said 'Ha!'* by Julia Sweeney, dir by Beth Milles at the Lyceum: rev by Evans, Kissel, Lyons, Marks, Zoglin.

2562   "Reviews of Productions." *NYTCR*. 1996; 57(18): 471-475. Lang.: Eng.

USA: New York, NY. 1996. ▪*Golden Child* by David Henry Hwang, dir by James Lapine at the Joseph Papp Public Theatre/Newman: rev by Brantley, Feingold, Waxman. *The Waste Land* by T.S. Eliot, dir by Deborah Warner at the Liberty: rev by Brantley, Feingold.

2563   "Reviews of Productions." *NYTCR*. 1996; 57(19): 480-487. Lang.: Eng.

USA: New York, NY. 1996. ▪*David Copperfield: Dreams & Nightmares* a performance in two acts by magician David Copperfield, adapt by David Ives, creative advisor Francis Ford Coppola at the Martin Beck: rev by Barnes, Brantley, Evans, Kissel, Lyons. *The Red Devil Battery Sign* by Tennessee Williams, dir by Michael Wilson at the WPA: rev by Barnes, Brantley, Feingold, Kissel, Simon. *Permanent Brain Damage (Risk It! Risk It!)* by Richard Foreman, dir by Foreman at the Ontological Hysteric: rev by Barnes, Feingold.

2564   "Reviews of Productions." *NYTCR*. 1996; 57(19): 487-495. Lang.: Eng.

USA: New York, NY. 1996. ▪*The Seven Streams of the River Ota (Les Sept Branches de la Rivière Ota)* by Robert Lepage, dir by Lepage at the Majestic: rev by Marks. *Insurrection: Holding History* by Robert O'Hara, dir by O'Hara at the Joseph Papp Public Theatre: rev by Feingold, Marks. *Ragtime* book by Terrence McNally, music by Stephen Flaherty, lyrics by Lynn Ahrens, based on the novel by E.L. Doctorow, dir by Frank Galati, at the Ford Centre, Toronto: rev by Brantley, Coulbourn, Evans, Wagner, Winer.

2565   "Reviews of Productions." *NYTCR*. 1996; 57(20): 500-512. Lang.: Eng.

USA: New York, NY. 1996. ▪*Once Upon a Mattress* by Jay Thompson, Marshall Barer and Dean Fuller, music by Mary Rodgers, lyrics by Barer, dir by Gerald Gutierrez at the Broadhurst: rev by Brantley, Evans, Kissel, Lyons. *Henry VI* by William Shakespeare, a two-part adapt of the three plays developed by Karen Coonrod, John Dias and Henry Israeli, dir by Coonrod at the Joseph Papp Public Theatre's Martinson Hall: rev by Brantley, Evans, Feingold, Kissel, Lyons. *The Tooth of Crime (Second Dance)* by Sam Shepard, music and lyrics by T-Bone Burnett, dir by Bill Hact at Second Stage: rev by Brantley. *No Way to Treat a Lady*, book, music and lyrics by Douglas J. Cohen, based on the novel by William Goldman, dir by Scott Schwartz at St. Peter's Church, Citicorp: rev by Marks.

2566   "Reviews of Productions." *NYTCR*. 1996; 57(3): 78-79. Lang.: Eng.

USA: New York, NY. 1996. ▪*True Crimes* by Romulus Linney, dir by Linney at the Theatre for the New City: rev by Canby, Evans, Istel.

2567   "Reviews of Productions." *NYTCR*. 1996; 57(4): 83-99. Lang.: Eng.

USA: New York, NY, Houston, TX. 1996. ▪*Blue Window* by Craig Lucas, dir by Joe Mantello at City Center Stage I: rev by Canby, Gerard, Kissel, Lyons, Simon, Winer. *Rent* by Jonathan Larson, additional lyrics by Billy Aronson, dir by Michael Greif: rev by Brantley, Feingold, Gerard, Kissel, Kroll, Lahr, Simon, Winer, Zoglin. *Julius Caesar* and *Antony and Cleopatra* by William Shakespeare, dir by Vanessa Redgrave at the Alley Theatre: rev by Evans, Leydon, Scheck, Stearns, Taitte.

2568   "Reviews of Productions." *NYTCR*. 1996; 57(5): 140-144. Lang.: Eng.

USA: New York, NY. 1996. ▪*Scenes from an Execution* by Howard Barker, dir by Richard Romagnoli at the Atlantic Theatre Company: rev by Barnes, Canby, Kissel, Simon. *Dancing on Her Knees* by Nilo Cruz, dir by Graciela Daniele at Joseph Papp Public Theatre: rev by Brantley, Feingold, Simon, Winer.

2569   "Reviews of Productions." *NYTCR*. 1996; 57(5): 119-133. Lang.: Eng.

USA: New York, NY. 1996. ▪*Bus Stop* by William Inge, dir by Josephine R. Abady at the Circle in the Square: rev by Barnes, Canby, Evans, Feingold, Franklin, Kissel, Lyons, Mandell, Simon. *A Fair Country* by Jon Robin Baitz, dir by Daniel Sullivan at the Lincoln Center Theatre: rev by Barnes, Canby, Feingold, Franklin, Gerard, Kissel, Lyons, Simon, Winer. *Floyd Collins* by Tina Landau, music and lyrics by Adam Guettel, additional lyrics by Landau, dir by Landau at Playwrights Horizons: rev by Brantley, Feingold, Gerard, Kissel.

2570   "Reviews of Productions." *NYTCR*. 1996; 57(6): 158-168. Lang.: Eng.

USA: New York, NY. 1996. ▪*Seven Guitars* by August Wilson, dir by Lloyd Richards at the Walter Kerr: rev by Barnes, Canby, Gerard, Kissel, Lyons, Simon. *Below the Belt* by Richard Dresser, dir by Gloria Muzio at the John Houseman: rev by Canby, Evans, Feingold, Lyons, Musto, Simon. *Nixon's Nixon* by Russell Lees, dir by Jim Simpson at the Westside: rev by Canby, Feingold, Mandell, Talbot.

2571   "Reviews of Productions." *NYTCR*. 1996; 57(5): 133-140. Lang.: Eng.

USA: New York, NY. 1996. ▪*Entertaining Mr. Sloane* by Joe Orton, dir by David Esbjornson at the Classic Stage Company: rev by Barnes, Brantley, Evans, Feingold, Kissel, Winer. *Overtime* by A.R. Gurney, dir by Nicholas Martin at City Center, Stage II: rev by Barnes, Canby, Kissel. *In the Loneliness of the Cottonfields (Dans la solitude des champs de coton)* by Bernard-Marie Koltès, dir by Patrice Chéreau at BAM: rev by Canby, Simon.

2572   "Reviews of Productions." *NYTCR*. 1996; 57(6): 147-157. Lang.: Eng.

USA: New York, NY. 1996. ▪*Getting Away With Murder* by Stephen Sondheim and George Furth, dir by Jack O'Brien at the Broadhurst: rev by Barnes, Feingold, Gerard, Lyons, Roura, Simon. *The Night of the Iguana* by Tennessee Williams, dir by Robert Falls at the Roundabout: rev by Canby, Feingold, Gerard, Lyons, Musto, Simon. *State Fair*, music by Richard Rodgers, lyrics by Oscar Hammerstein, book by Tom Briggs and Louis Mattioli, dir by James Hammerstein and Randy Skinner at the Music Box: rev by Barnes, Gerard, Kissel, Kroll, Lyons, Simon.

2573   "Reviews of Productions." *NYTCR*. 1996; 57(6): 169-179. Lang.: Eng.

USA: New York, NY. 1996. ▪*Sabina* by Willy Holtzman, dir by Melia Bensussen at 354 West 47th Street: rev by Barnes, Feingold, Hampton, Lyons, Winer. *I Do! I Do!* by Tom Jones and Harvey Schmidt, dir by Will MacKenzie at the Lamb's: Barnes, Evans, Kissel, Simon. *The Libertine* by Stephen Jeffreys, dir by Terry Johnson for Steppenwolf: rev by Brantley, Christiansen, Henning, Lazare, Stearns, Weiss. *Working Title* by Andrew Bergman, dir by Max Mayer at the American Jewish: rev by Barnes, Brantley, Evans.

2574   "Reviews of Productions." *NYTCR*. 1996; 57(7): 183-193. Lang.: Eng.

USA: New York, NY. 1996. ▪*A Midsummer Night's Dream* by William Shakespeare, dir by Adrian Noble for the RSC at the Lunt-Fontanne: rev by Barnes, Brantley, Gerard, Kissel, Kroll, Simon. *Inherit the Wind* by Jerome Lawrence and Robert E. Lee, dir by John Tillinger at the Royale: rev by Canby, Feingold, Gerard, Kissel, Lyons, Simon. *The Apple Doesn't Fall...* by Trish Vradenburg, dir by Leonard Nimoy at the Lyceum: rev by Barnes, Canby, Gerard, Kissel.

2575   "Reviews of Productions." *NYTCR*. 1996; 57(10): 272-280. Lang.: Eng.

USA: New York, NY. 1996. ▪*The Skriker* by Caryl Churchill, dir by Mark Wing-Davey at the Joseph Papp Public/Newman Theatre: rev by Barnes, Brantley, Feingold, Gerard, Simon. *Arts & Leisure* by Steve Tesich, dir by JoAnne Akalaitis at Playwrights Horizons: rev by Canby, Feingold, Franklin, Gerard, Kissel, Lyons. *Ancient History* by David Ives, dir by John Rando at Primary Stages: rev by Barnes, Brantley, Kissel, Lyons.

DRAMA: —Performance/production

2576 "Reviews of Productions." *NYTCR*. 1996; 57(7): 193-203. Lang.: Eng.

USA: New York, NY, Washington, DC. 1996. ■*The King and I* book and lyrics by Oscar Hammerstein, music by Richard Rodgers, dir by Christopher Renshaw at the Neil Simon: rev by Barnes, Canby, Feingold, Gerard, Kissel, Kroll, Lyons, Simon. *The Dance of Death (Dödsdansen)* by August Strindberg, transl by Bill Coco and Peter Stormare, dir by JoAnne Akalaitis at the Arena Stage: rev by Anderson, Kalb, Meersman, Presley. *Cowgirls* by Betsy Howe, conceived by Mary Murfitt, music by Murfitt, dir by Eleanor Reissa at the Minetta Lane: rev by Gerard, Holden, Musto.

2577 "Reviews of Productions." *NYTCR*. 1996; 57(8): 215-228. Lang.: Eng.

USA: New York, NY. 1996. ■*A Funny Thing Happened on the Way to the Forum* by Burt Shevelove and Larry Gelbart, music and lyrics by Stephen Sondheim, dir by Jerry Zaks at the St. James: rev by Barnes, Canby, Corliss, Gerard, Kissel, Kroll, Lyons, Simon. *Bring in 'Da Noise, Bring in 'Da Funk* by Reg E. Gaines, music by Daryl Waters, Zane Mark and Ann Duquesnay, from an idea by Savion Glover and George C. Wolfe, dir by Wolfe at the Ambassador: rev by Barnes, Brantley, Duffy, Gerard, Kissel, Lyons, *New York Magazine*. *Jack—A Night on the Town with John Barrymore* by Nicol Williamson and Leslie Megahey, dir by Megahey at the Belasco: rev by Brantley, Evans, Kissel, Lyons, Simon.

2578 "Reviews of Productions." *NYTCR*. 1996; 57(8): 228-239. Lang.: Eng.

USA: New York, NY. 1996. ■*A Delicate Balance* by Edward Albee, dir by Gerald Gutierrez at Lincoln Center: rev by Barnes, Canby, Evans, Kissel, Lyons, Simon. *Antigone in New York (Antygona w Nowym Jorku)* by Janusz Głowacki, dir by Michael Mayer at the Vineyard: rev by Barnes, Bruckner, Feingold, Kissel. *Curtains* by Stephen Bill, dir by Scott Elliott at INTAR: rev by Brantley, Evans, Feingold, Kissel. *Where the Truth Lies* by Catherine Butterfield, dir by Evan Yionoulis at the Irish Repertory: rev by Brantley, Evans.

2579 "Reviews of Productions." *NYTCR*. 1996; 57(9): 244-257. Lang.: Eng.

USA: New York, NY. 1996. ■*Big* by John Weidman, music by David Shire, lyrics by Richard Maltby, dir by Mike Ockrent at the Shubert: rev by Barnes, Canby, Gerard, Kissel, Simon. *Rent* by Jonathan Larson, additional lyrics by Billy Aronson, dir by Michael Greif at the Nederlander: rev by Barnes, Brantley, Gerard, Kissel, Simon. *Buried Child*, revised version by Sam Shepard, dir by Gary Sinise at the Brooks Atkinson: rev by Barnes, Brantley, Feingold, Franklin, Gerard, Kissel, Simon, Zoglin.

2580 "Reviews of Productions." *NYTCR*. 1996; 57(9): 258-268. Lang.: Eng.

USA: New York, NY. 1996. ■*The Inconstant Lovers (La Double Inconstance)* by Marivaux, dir by Jean-Pierre Miquel for the Comédie-Française at the Majestic in Brooklyn: rev by Canby, Feingold, Kissel, Simon. *An Ideal Husband* by Oscar Wilde, dir by Peter Hall at the Ethel Barrymore: rev by Canby, Feingold, Gerard, Kissel, Simon. *Venus* by Suzan-Lori Parks, dir by Richard Foreman at Joseph Papp Public Theatre's Martinson Hall: rev by Barnes, Brantley, Feingold, Kissel, Simon, Taylor. *Papa* by John de Groot, dir by John Henry Davis at the Douglas Fairbanks: rev by Holden, Kissel.

2581 "Reviews of Productions." *NYTCR*. 1996; 57(10): 281-287. Lang.: Eng.

USA: New York, NY, Washington, DC. 1996. ■*Dark Rapture* by Eric Overmyer, dir by Scott Ellis at Second Stage: rev by Canby, Kissel, Lyons. *Tartuffe: Born Again* transl and adapt from Molière's *Tartuffe* by Freyda Thomas, dir by David Saint at Circle in the Square: rev by Brantley, Gerard, Kissel. *Candide*, adapt from Voltaire by Hugh Wheeler, music by Leonard Bernstein, lyrics by Richard Wilbur, Stephen Sondheim, and John Latouche, dir by George Fulginiti-Shakar and Darryl V. Jones at the Arena Stage: rev by Rose, Rosenthal.

2582 "Reviews of Productions." *NYTCR*. 1996; 57(11): 307-316. Lang.: Eng.

USA: New York, NY, East Haddam, CT. 1996. ■*Sweeney Todd, the Demon Barber of Fleet Street*, music and lyrics by Stephen Sondheim, book by Hugh Wheeler from an adapt by Christopher Bond, dir by Gabriel Barre at the Goodspeed Opera House: rev by Gale, Klein, Matthews, Taylor. *The Boys in the Band* by Mart Crowley, dir by Kenneth

Elliott at the WPA: rev by Brantley, Evans, Feingold, Kissel. *The Shawl* by Cynthia Ozick, dir by Sidney Lumet at Playhouse 91: rev by Brantley, Gerard, Renner.

2583 "Reviews of Productions." *NYTCR*. 1996; 57(12): 320-326, 331-334. Lang.: Eng.

USA: New York, NY, Cambridge, MA. 1996. ■*The Trojan Women: A Love Story* by Charles Mee, Jr., based on the works of Euripides and Berlioz, dir by Tina Landau at the East River Park Amphitheatre: rev by Brantley, Kissel, Lyons. *Henry V* by William Shakespeare, dir by Douglas Hughes at the Delacorte: rev by Barnes, Brantley, Feingold, Kissel, Lyons, Simon. *The Naked Eye* by Paul Rudnick, dir by Christopher Ashley at the American Repertory Theatre: rev by Brantley, Forman, Rausch, Siegal.

2584 "Reviews of Productions." *NYTCR*. 1996; 57(13): 340-346. Lang.: Eng.

USA: New York, NY. 1996. ■*A Thousand Clowns* by Herb Gardner, dir by Scott Ellis at the Roundabout/Criterion: rev by Barnes, Brantley, Evans, Kissel, Simon. *Orestes: I Murdered My Mother* by Jeff Cohen, dir by Cohen at One Dream: rev by Barnes, Brantley, Kissel. *Grace & Glorie* by Tom Ziegler, dir by Gloria Muzio at the Roundabout/Criterion: rev by Evans, Kissel, Simon, Van Gelder.

2585 "Reviews of Productions." *NYTCR*. 1996; 57(13): 347-356. Lang.: Eng.

USA: New York, NY, Chicago, IL. 1996. ■*I Love You, You're Perfect, Now Change* book and lyrics by Joe Dipietro, music by Jimmy Roberts, dir by Joel Bishoff at the Westside: rev by Barnes, Canby, Evans, Kissel. *Waiting for Godot (En attendant Godot)* by Samuel Beckett, dir by Walter Asmus for the Gate Theater at the John Jay: rev by Barnes, Canby, Evans, Kissel, Lyons. *The House of Martin Guerre* by Leslie Arden and Anna Theresa Cascio, music and lyrics by Arden, dir by David Petrarca at the Goodman Theatre: rev by Henning, Lazare, Smith, Weiss.

2586 Alexander, William. "Inside Out: From Inside Prison Out to Youth." *TDR*. 1996 Win; 40(4): 85-93. Notes. Illus.: Photo. B&W. 3. Lang.: Eng.

USA: Plymouth, MI. 1990-1996. Critical studies. ■History and productions of the Western Wayne Players, a prison theatre workshop group. Work with 'at-risk' youth, development of plays, film and video work, focus on the play/video *Inside Out*.

2587 Allen, Norman. "Mary McDonnell, Watch Her Smoke." *TheaterW*. 1996 Sep 30; 10(9): 26-30. Illus.: Photo. B&W. 2. Lang.: Eng.

USA: New York, NY. 1948-1996. Biographical studies. ■Career of film and stage actress McDonnell, her current role in Tennessee Williams' *Summer and Smoke* at the Roundabout Theatre directed by David Warren.

2588 Barnett, Dennis. "The Politics of *The Professional*: Connecting the Prose with the Passion." 89-104 in Oliva, Judy Lee, ed. *New Theatre Vistas: Modern Movements in International Theatre.* New York, NY/London: Garland; 1996. 219 pp. (Studies in Modern Drama 7.) Biblio. Notes. Lang.: Eng.

USA: Berkeley, CA. Yugoslavia. 1991. Critical studies. ■Intercultural production of Serbian playwright Dušan Kovačević's play *The Professional (Profesionalac)* by Upstart Stage, directed by Peter Craze.

2589 Barnwell, Michael. "Arthur Miller Bends the Law." *AmTh*. 1996 Oct.; 13(8): 12-14. Illus.: Photo. B&W. 3. Lang.: Eng.

USA: Williamstown, MA. 1996. Critical studies. ■Productions of Miller's *All My Sons* directed by Barry Edelstein and *The Ride Down Mount Morgan* directed by Scott Elliott at Williamstown Theatre Festival. Comparison of themes and characters.

2590 Berkowitz, Joel. "'A True Jewish Jew': Three Yiddish Shylocks." *ThS*. 1996 May; 37(1): 75-98. Notes. Biblio. Illus.: Sketches. 1. Lang.: Eng.

USA: New York, NY. 1901-1950. Historical studies. ■Three Yiddish theatre actors who performed Shylock in different productions of *The Merchant of Venice*: Jacob Adler in 1901 at the People's Theatre and several times throughout the decade, Rudolf Schildkraut in his New York debut in 1911 at the Irving Place Theatre, and Maurice Schwartz in 1947 in his own Yiddish adaptation *Shylock un zayn tokhter (Shylock and His Daughter)* at the Irving Place Theatre.

DRAMA: —Performance/production

2591 Bernardo, Melissa Rose. "Humbug for the Holidays: Tony Randall in *A Christmas Carol.*" *TheaterW.* 1996 Dec 9; 10(19): 30-33. Illus.: Photo. Sketches. B&W. 2. Lang.: Eng.
USA: New York, NY. 1996. Histories-sources. ■Interview with actor Randall on his role as Scrooge in Alan Menken's *A Christmas Carol* at Madison Square Garden, and his company The National Actors Theatre.

2592 Berson, Misha. "I Can't Believe We Staged the Whole Thing." *AmTh.* 1996 Mar.; 13(3): 6-7. Illus.: Photo. B&W. 1. Lang.: Eng.
USA: Seattle, WA. 1996. Critical studies. ■Stage adaptation of John Irving's novel *The Cider House Rules* by Peter Parnell in collaboration with Tom Hulce and Jane Jones, at Seattle Repertory. Length of the piece, themes, challenges of adapting for the stage.

2593 Blackstone, Sarah J.; McDermott, M. Joan. "White Slavery Plays of the 1910s: Fear of Victimization and the Social Control of Sexuality." *THSt.* 1996 June; 16: 141-156. Notes. Illus.: Photo. 2. Lang.: Eng.
USA. 1910-1920. Historical studies. ■The 1910 social panic over white slavery and the crucial role of white slavery melodramas, which reflected society's fears of adolescent female sexuality and attempts to control it.

2594 Bordman, Gerald. *American Theatre: A Chronicle of Comedy and Drama, 1930-1969.* New York, NY/Oxford: Oxford UP; 1996. 472 pp. Pref. Index. Lang.: Eng.
USA. 1930-1969. Histories-specific. ■Season-by-season analysis of Broadway and Off Broadway theatre.

2595 Buckley, Michael. "Rubinstein in Retrospect." *TheaterW.* 1996 Mar 18; 9(33): 28-33. Illus.: Photo. B&W. 1. Lang.: Eng.
USA: New York, NY. 1983-1996. Biographical studies. ■Award-winning actor John Rubinstein. Past roles on Broadway and in film, with focus on his lead role in *Children of a Lesser God.*

2596 Buckley, Michael. "Up for a Tony." *TheaterW.* 1996 June 3; 9(44): 54-65. Lang.: Eng.
USA: New York, NY. 1996. Histories-sources. ■Fourteen Tony nominees respond to questions regarding their experiences as a nominee and the characters they portray: Audra McDonald, Lois Smith, Viola Davis, Lewis J. Stadlen, Michele Shay, Wilson Jermain Heredia, Brett Tabisel, Scott Wise, Rosemary Harris, Martin Shaw, Crista Moore, Adam Pascal, Idina Menzel, Ann Duquesnay.

2597 Buckley, Michael. "Golden Tonys." *TheaterW.* 1996 June 17; 9(46): 28-37. Illus.: Photo. B&W. 8. Lang.: Eng.
USA: New York, NY. 1996. Historical studies. ■The fiftieth anniversary of the Tony Awards for Broadway theatre: includes comprehensive list of past winners in all performance categories.

2598 Buckley, Michael. "Q & A with Andre Braugher." *TheaterW.* 1996 July 1; 9(48): 36-38. Illus.: Photo. B&W. 1. Lang.: Eng.
USA: New York, NY. 1996. Histories-sources. ■Interview with actor Braugher on his approach to his role in *Henry V* for the New York Shakespeare Festival, directed by Douglas Hughes, and his starring role on the television series *Homicide.*

2599 Buckley, Michael. "A Perfect Balance: Rosemary Harris." *TheaterW.* 1996 July 22; 9(51): 20-24. Illus.: Photo. B&W. 6. Lang.: Eng.
USA: New York, NY. 1958-1996. Biographical studies. ■Life and career of actress Harris: past roles, career in England, current role in Edward Albee's *A Delicate Balance.*

2600 Buckley, Michael. "A Perfect Balance: George Grizzard." *TheaterW.* 1996 July 22; 9(51): 26-28. Illus.: Photo. B&W. 6. Lang.: Eng.
USA: New York, NY. 1952-1996. Biographical studies. ■Actor Grizzard discusses past roles, approaches to characters, and current role in Edward Albee's *A Delicate Balance* on Broadway.

2601 Buckley, Michael. "Outtakes from Nine Years." *TheaterW.* 1996 Aug 5; 10(1): 18-33. Illus.: Photo. B&W. 10. Lang.: Eng.
USA: New York, NY. 1985-1996. Biographical studies. ■Highlights from past interviews with performers Helen Hayes, Gwen Verdon, Chita Rivera, Robert Morse, Carol Channing, Arthur Kennedy, Dorothy Stickney, Larry Kert, Elaine Stritch.

2602 Buckley, Michael. "New York Season Preview: The Plays." *TheaterW.* 1996 Sep 9; 10(6): 22-30. Lang.: Eng.
USA: New York, NY. 1996. Histories-sources. ■New productions slated for Broadway and Off-Broadway theatres for the 1996 season. Dates, venues, directors.

2603 Buckley, Michael. "Julia Sweeney Laughs Back." *TheaterW.* 1996 Nov 18; 10(16): 31-37. Illus.: Photo. B&W. 1. Lang.: Eng.
USA: New York, NY. 1996. Biographical studies. ■Actress/comedienne Sweeney's one-woman show *God Said 'Ha'!* directed by Beth Milles on Broadway. Her career in television on *Saturday Night Live*, autobiographical sources for her show, training in comedy.

2604 Buckley, Michael. "Steve Ross: Legitimate at Last." *TheaterW.* 1996 Nov 25; 10(17): 56-59. Illus.: Photo. B&W. 1. Lang.: Eng.
USA: New York, NY. 1996. Biographical studies. ■Cabaret artist Ross appearing in the Broadway production of Noël Coward's *Present Laughter* in a small role, and playing piano during intermissions.

2605 Buckley, Michael. "Frank Langella: Man of the Moment." *TheaterW.* 1996 Dec 16; 10(20): 31-42. Illus.: Photo. B&W. 3. Lang.: Eng.
USA: New York, NY. 1939-1996. Biographical studies. ■Life and career of actor Langella: past roles, philosophy of acting, approach to his current lead role in Noël Coward's *Present Laughter* directed by Scott Elliott at the Walter Kerr Theatre.

2606 Burgoyne, Suzanne; Huston-Findley, Shirley. "Re-Visioning *The Rainmaker.*" *TextPQ.* 1996 July; 16(3): 248-269. Notes. Biblio. Illus.: Photo. B&W. 1. Lang.: Eng.
USA: Columbia, MO. 1991-1996. Histories-sources. ■The authors' feminist approach to their production of N. Richard Nash's *The Rainmaker*, their research into folklore and its reinforcement of poor female role-models, and audience reaction to their production.

2607 Camargo, Christian. "In the *Skylight* Zone: A Rehearsal Journal." *TheaterW.* 1996 Nov 4; 10(14): 38-44. Illus.: Photo. B&W. 1. Lang.: Eng.
USA: New York, NY. UK-England: London. 1996. Histories-sources. ■Transcript of daily diary describing an actor's experience in rehearsals and preparation for his Broadway debut in David Hare's *Skylight* originally directed by Richard Eyre at the Royal Theatre.

2608 Capo, Kay Ellen. "Review/Interview: Anna Deavere Smith." *TextPQ.* 1994 Jan.; 14(1): 57-76. Notes. Illus.: Photo. B&W. 1. Lang.: Eng.
USA: New York, NY. 1991-1993. Histories-sources. ■Interview with playwright/performer Anna Deavere Smith discussing her play *Fires in the Mirror: Crown Heights, Brooklyn and Other Identities* based on the 1991 riots, with a review of the piece as presented at the Public Theatre directed by Christopher Ashley.

2609 Carlisle, Barbara. "Salon Theatre: Homemade Bread." *TDR.* 1996 Win; 40(4): 56-69. Notes. Illus.: Photo. B&W. 5. Lang.: Eng.
USA. 1995. Histories-sources. ■Theatre at home as an amalgam of the court theatre and the salon. Author describes a performance of her *Paris Quartet* in her own home.

2610 Carlson, Susan. "Leaking Bodies and Fractured Texts: Representing the Female Body at the Omaha Magic Theatre." *NTQ.* 1996; 12(45): 21-29. Notes. Biblio. Illus.: Photo. B&W. 2. Lang.: Eng.
USA: Omaha, NE. 1984-1993. Critical studies. ■Considers contemporary presentation of women's bodies on stage, and discusses two productions at the Omaha Magic Theatre: *Female Leaks* and *Sound Fields*, that incorporate image, action, technology and text to engage issues of gender, identity, sexuality and the material body.

2611 Carlson, Susan. "Aphra Behn's *The Emperor of The Moon*: Staging Seventeenth-Century Farce for Twentieth-Century Tastes." *ET.* 1996; 14(2): 117-130. Notes. Biblio. Lang.: Eng.
USA: Iowa City, IA. 1992. Critical studies. ■Carol MacVey's production of Aphra Behn's *commedia dell'arte* play.

2612 Chase, Tony. "Letter from Cincinnati." *TheaterW.* 1996 Oct 21; 10(12): 38-46, 61. Illus.: Photo. B&W. 1. Lang.: Eng.

DRAMA: —Performance/production

USA: Cincinnati, OH. 1996. Critical studies. ■Vanessa Redgrave's performance in Tennessee Williams' *The Notebook of Trigorin* at the Cincinnati Playhouse in the Park, directed by Stephen Hollis. Influence of Čechov's *Čajka (The Seagull)* on Williams.

2613 Connors, Thomas. "'Happy Days' Is Here Again." *AmTh.* 1996 July/Aug.; 13(6): 10. Illus.: Photo. B&W. 1. Lang.: Eng.

USA. 1996. Historical studies. ■American productions of plays of Samuel Beckett in honor of what would have been his 90th birthday.

2614 Copeland, Roger. "David Gordon: Double Identity." *AmTh.* 1996 July/Aug.; 13(6): 44-45. Illus.: Photo. B&W. 2. Lang.: Eng.

USA. 1996. Biographical studies. ■Life and career of choreographer/director and author Gordon: past productions, techniques, approach to movement, his crossover from dance to theatre.

2615 Croyden, Margaret. "The Prime of Zoe Caldwell." *TheaterW.* 1996 Jan 15; 9(24): 26-30. Illus.: Photo. B&W. 2. Lang.: Eng.

USA: New York, NY. 1996. Biographical studies. ■Actor Caldwell's performance as Maria Callas in Terrence McNally's *Master Class* on Broadway, directed by Leonard Foglia. Research into life of Callas, interpretation of role.

2616 Croyden, Margaret. "Lepage Makes a Splash in *The River Ota.*" *TheaterW.* 1996 Dec 2; 10(18): 44-47. Illus.: Photo. B&W. 2. Lang.: Eng.

USA: New York, NY. 1996. Critical studies. ■Director Lepage and his Ex Machina theatre company's creation of *The Seven Streams of the River Ota (Les Sept Branches de la Rivière Ota)* and its performance at Brooklyn Academy of Music. Use of film, music, video and multi-theatrical techniques, political themes.

2617 Croyden, Margaret. "Rees's Theatrical Pieces." *TheaterW.* 1996 Dec 23; 10(21): 54-58. Illus.: Photo. B&W. 1. Lang.: Eng.

USA: New York, NY. UK-England: London. 1996. Biographical studies. ■Career of British-born actor Roger Rees, his current role in Roundabout Theatre's production of Jean Anouilh's *The Rehearsal (La Répétition)* directed by Nicholas Martin, translation by Jeremy Sams.

2618 Dasgupta, Gautam. "Peter Brook: The Man Who..." *PerAJ.* 1996 Jan.; 18(1): 81-88. Illus.: Photo. B&W. 3. [Number 52.] Lang.: Eng.

USA: New York, NY. 1995. Critical studies. ■Peter Brook's BAM production of *The Man Who (L'Homme qui)*, based on writings of Oliver Sacks, as a model of multicultural theatre-making.

2619 Donahue, Lester; Krajewska-Wieczorek, Anna, transl., pref. "Wspomnienie o Modjeskiej." (Recollections of Modjeska.) *PaT.* 1996; 45(3-4): 435-468. Pref. Notes. Illus.: Pntg. Photo. 8. Lang.: Pol.

USA. 1906-1912. Histories-sources. ■Unpublished recollections by an American pianist of actress Helena Modjeska.

2620 Dowd, Jim. "Distilling Hemingway." *TheaterW.* 1996 July 8; 9(49): 39-42. Illus.: Photo. B&W. 2. Lang.: Eng.

USA: New York, NY. 1996. Historical studies. ■Len Cariou's performance as Ernest Hemingway in John deGroot's *Papa* at the Douglas Fairbanks Theatre, directed by John Henry Davis. Cariou discusses research for the role, and challenges in the portrayal.

2621 Drukman, Steven. "Steel Jungle." *AmTh.* 1996 Dec.; 13(10): 4-5. Illus.: Photo. B&W. 5. Lang.: Eng.

USA: Houston, TX. 1996. Critical studies. ■Alley Theatre's 50th anniversary season featuring Brecht's *In the Jungle of Cities (Im Dickicht der Städte)* directed by Gregory Boyd.

2622 Drukman, Steven. "Campbell Scott." *AmTh.* 1996 Apr.; 13(4): 24-25. Illus.: Photo. B&W. 2. Lang.: Eng.

USA: San Diego, CA. 1990-1996. Histories-sources. ■Interview with actor Scott on his lead role in Shakespeare's *Hamlet* at the Old Globe Theatre. Personal approach to text.

2623 Elam, Harry J., Jr. "Social Urgency, Audience Participation, and the Performance of *Slave Ship* by Amiri Baraka." 13-36 in Reinelt, Janelle, ed. *Crucibles of Crisis: Performing Social Change.* Ann Arbor, MI: Univ of Michigan P; 1996. 250 pp. Notes. Illus.: Photo. 1. Lang.: Eng.

USA. 1970. Critical studies. ■Audience reaction to and interaction with the Free Southern Theatre's touring production of Amiri Baraka's *Slave Ship*, directed by Gilbert Moses.

2624 Erdman, Andrew L. "From Frank Fay to Jimmy Stewart: Broadway, Hollywood, and the Construction of Creativity." *TheatreS.* 1996; 41: 13-28. Notes. Lang.: Eng.

USA: New York, NY, Hollywood, CA. 1944-1950. Critical studies. ■Frank Fay's role in Mary Chase's *Harvey*, which later became associated with James Stewart, and his political activities in the McCarthy era.

2625 Ervin, Kathryn M.; Washington, Von H. "Impressions of Two NBTF Productions." *BlackM.* 1996 Mar/Apr.; 11(5): 14-15. Illus.: Photo. B&W. 1. Lang.: Eng.

USA: Winston-Salem, NC. 1995. Reviews of performances. ■Analysis of two productions presented at the 1995 National Black Theatre Festival: *The People Could Fly* by Deborah Adero Ferguson, from the book by Virginia Hamilton, directed by Rhonda Akanké, for the Nubian Theatre Company, and *Medea and the Doll* by Rudy Gray, directed by Dick Anthony Williams.

2626 Filichia, Peter. "Stagestruck." *TheaterW.* 1996 June 3; 9(44): 18-22. Illus.: Photo. B&W. 1. Lang.: Eng.

USA: New York, NY. 1996. Histories-sources. ■Winners of Drama Desk Awards, which are given by New York drama critics.

2627 Fuchs, Elinor. *The Death of Character: Perspectives on Theater after Modernism.* Bloomington, IN/Indianapolis, IN: Indiana UP; 1996. 224 pp. (Drama and Performance Studies.) Notes. Index. Lang.: Eng.

USA. 1979-1995. Critical studies. ■Collection of essays and review of post-modern theatre performances and theory, including performance art as well as drama.

2628 Fuchs, Elinor. "Brains in Toyland: The Season at Harvard." *PerAJ.* 1996 May; 18(2): 83-92. [Number 53.] Lang.: Eng.

USA: Cambridge, MA, Boston, MA. 1995. Historical studies. ■The author's perception of cultural indifference in Boston, with descriptions of A.R.T. productions of *Ubu Rock* by Shelley Berc and Andrei Belgrader, based on Jarry's *Ubu Roi*, and Charles Mee, Jr.'s *The Trojan Women: A Love Story* adapted from Euripides and Berlioz' *Les Troyens*, directed by Robert Woodruff. Also briefly describes a commencement address given by playwright Václav Havel.

2629 Gaffney, Perri. "Joe Seneca." *BlackM.* 1996 Nov/Dec.; 12(2): 18. Lang.: Eng.

USA. 1996. Biographical studies. ■Obituary for the actor/musician/composer/writer/dancer.

2630 Gener, Randy. "In Comic Improv, the Play's the Fling." *AmTh.* 1996 Nov.; 13(9): 72-74. Illus.: Photo. B&W. 2. Lang.: Eng.

USA. 1984-1996. Critical studies. ■Profiles of TheaterSports (founded by Keith Johnstone) and ComedySportz (founded by Dick Chudnow), two groups that use improvisational comedy performed as competition.

2631 Greene, Alexis. "Eve Ensler: Going Public." *TheaterW.* 1996 Oct 14; 10(11): 54-58. Illus.: Photo. B&W. 2. Lang.: Eng.

USA. 1970-1996. Histories-sources. ■Interview with playwright/director Ensler on her new work *The Vagina Monologues* currently performing at HERE. Her feminist politics, censorship, audience response.

2632 Haines, Chris. "Mabou Mines Lives On in Cyberspace." *AmTh.* 1996 Jan.; 13(1): 64-67. Illus.: Photo. B&W. 2. Lang.: Eng.

USA: New York, NY. 1996. Historical studies. ■Use of video-conferencing, animation and World Wide Web in the revival of Lee Breuer's *The Red Horse Animation*. Impact of computer technology on staging.

2633 Halston, Julie. "Julie Halston's One-Person Show Do's and Don't's." *DGQ.* 1996 Win; 33(4): 45-49. Illus.: Photo. B&W. 1. Lang.: Eng.

USA: New York, NY. 1996. Critical studies. ■One-person show veteran Julie Halston lists her ten do's and don'ts for anyone about to embark on performing a solo show.

DRAMA: —Performance/production

2634 Harris, John. "*Elektra*fying New York." *TheaterW.* 1996 Sep 23; 10(8): 24-28. Illus.: Photo. B&W. 4. Lang.: Eng.
USA: New York, NY. Greece. 1996. Historical studies. ■National Theatre of Greece's production of *Electra*, directed by Lydia Koniordou, touring to New York. Original production at Epidaurus, description and history of theatre space.

2635 Hatch, James V. "Josie Mae Dotson." *AInf.* 1996; 15(1): 86-99. Illus.: Photo. B&W. 1. Lang.: Eng.
USA: Los Angeles, CA. 1970. Histories-sources. ■Interview with actress and administrative director of the Inner City Cultural Center, Josie Mae Dotson. Interview was conducted in 1970, and is the first one recorded for the Hatch-Billops Collection.

2636 Hayes, Steve. "Shakespeare Goes to Prison." *AmTh.* 1996 Oct.; 13(8): 82-84. Illus.: Photo. B&W. 1. Lang.: Eng.
USA: Los Angeles, CA. 1996. Histories-sources. ■Author's diary of experiences during prison production of Shakespeare's *Henry V* directed by Joe Haj.

2637 Hendricks, Margo. "'Obscured by dreams': Race, Empire, and Shakespeare's *A Midsummer Night's Dream*." *SQ.* 1996 Spr; 47 (1): 37-60. Notes. Tables. Illus.: Photo. Dwg. B&W. 2. Lang.: Eng.
USA: Santa Cruz, CA. 1991. Critical studies. ■Using Shakespeare Santa Cruz's 1991 production of *A Midsummer Night's Dream* directed by Danny Scheie, investigates how a director's subversive approach to a text can reinforce racist and sexist attitudes instead of inverting them.

2638 Holmberg, Arthur. "Fallen Angels at Sea: Garbo, Ullman, Richardson, and the Contradictory Prostitute in *Anna Christie*." *EOR.* 1996 Spr/Fall; 20(1&2): 44-63. Biblio. Illus.: Photo. B&W. 2. Lang.: Eng.
USA: New York, NY. 1930-1993. Critical studies. ■The role of the prostitute in Romanticism and Naturalism, and O'Neill's portrait of prostitution in *Anna Christie*. Garbo's portrayal in the film version and public response, performances of Liv Ullmann in the 1977 Broadway production and Natasha Richardson in the 1993 Roundabout Theatre production.

2639 Horwitz, Simi. "Martin Shaw: Going Wilde." *TheaterW.* 1996 June 24; 9(47): 18-22. Illus.: Photo. B&W. 2. Lang.: Eng.
USA: New York, NY. 1996. Biographical studies. ■Actor Shaw on his current lead role in Oscar Wilde's *An Ideal Husband* directed by Peter Hall, originating in London. Discusses interpreting the character as a gay man. Past roles, training.

2640 Horwitz, Simi. "Rob Becker's Missing Links." *TheaterW.* 1996 July 22; 9(51): 29-34. Illus.: Photo. B&W. 1. Lang.: Eng.
USA: New York, NY. 1996. Biographical studies. ■Becker discusses his comedic monodrama *Defending the Caveman* at the Helen Hayes Theatre, the longest running solo performance in Broadway history. Relationships between men and women, structure, audience response.

2641 Horwitz, Simi. "Full Gallop's Sophisticated Lady." *TheaterW.* 1996 Oct 21; 10(12): 18-22. Illus.: Photo. B&W. 2. Lang.: Eng.
USA: New York, NY. 1996. Biographical studies. ■Actress Mary Louise Wilson's portrayal of Diana Vreeland in *Full Gallop* on Broadway, co-written by Wilson and Mark Hampton. Past acting roles, research into Vreeland's life, creation of the piece.

2642 Hutchings, William. "Everybody Gets the Blues: Blue Man Group: *Tubes*." *TextPQ.* 1994 Apr.; 14(2): 175-179. Notes. Lang.: Eng.
USA: New York, NY. 1994. Reviews of performances. ■Review of *Tubes*, devised and performed by the group at the Astor Place Theatre.

2643 Istel, John. "Emily Mann: Searching for Survivors." *AmTh.* 1996 Feb.; 13(2): 44-45. Illus.: Photo. B&W. 2. Lang.: Eng.
USA: Princeton, NJ. 1996. Critical studies. ■Director/playwright Mann discusses her process in developing documentary-style theatre pieces from interviews. Focus on her current piece *Greensboro: A Requiem* opening at the McCarter Theatre, directed by Mark Wing-Davey.

2644 Jory, Jon. "Why Directors Can't Direct." *AmTh.* 1996 Oct.; 13(8): 7. Illus.: Photo. B&W. 1. Lang.: Eng.

USA. 1996. Critical studies. ■Critical evaluation of the quality of stage directors, the training they receive and the skills they lack.

2645 Klunzinger, T.E. "Seduced & Abandoned: *Like a Brother* Gets Done in New York." *DGQ.* 1996 Win; 33(4): 18-23. Lang.: Eng.
USA: New York, NY. 1995. Histories-sources. ■Playwright Klunzinger's experience with the New York production of his play *Like a Brother*, about the sons of William the Conqueror.

2646 Kranz, Oliver. "Jenseits des Broadway." (Beyond Broadway.) *TZ.* 1996; 1: 26-31. Illus.: Photo. B&W. 3. Lang.: Ger.
USA: Minneapolis, MN. 1996. Critical studies. ■The importance of American regional theatre, with reference to the Guthrie. Productions discussed include Pinter's *Old Times* directed by Garland Wright and Frisch's *The Firebugs (Biedermann und die Brandstifter)* directed by David Gordon.

2647 Krasner, David. "Whose Role Is It Anyway?: Charles Gilpin and the Harlem Renaissance." *AfAmR.* 1995 Fall; 29(3): 483-496 . Notes. Biblio. Lang.: Eng.
USA. 1920-1930. Historical studies. ■New angle on actor Charles Gilpin. By using semiotics and cultural studies of the Harlem Renaissance, author argues against traditional historical view of Gilpin and suggests other cultural strategies to understand Gilpin's changing of O'Neill's text in *The Emperor Jones*, Gilpin's great role as an actor.

2648 Kristoffersson, Birgitta. "Misantropen—på riktigt." (Le Misanthrope—In Earnest.) *Dramat.* 1996; 4(2): 48. Illus.: Photo. B&W. Lang.: Swe.
USA: New York, NY. Sweden: Stockholm. 1995. Historical studies. ■A report about the cancelled guest performance at Brooklyn Academy of Music of Ingmar Bergman's staging of *Le Misanthrope* and the reactions.

2649 Lamont, Rosette C. "Chéreau's Metaphysical Bullfight." *TheaterW.* 1996 Feb 26; 9(30): 28-35. Illus.: Photo. B&W. 3. Lang.: Eng.
USA. 1983-1996. Histories-sources. ■Interview with director Patrice Chéreau on his stage and film productions, with focus on his approach to the plays of and collaboration with Bernard-Marie Koltès, particularly *Dans la solitude des champs de coton (In the Solitude of the Cotton Fields)*.

2650 Lamont, Rosette C. "The Return of the Comédie-Française." *TheaterW.* 1996 May 6; 9(40): 16-20. Illus.: Photo. B&W. 3. Lang.: Eng.
USA: New York, NY. France: Paris. 1979-1996. Histories-sources. ■Comédie-Française presents Molière's *Dom Juan* and Marivaux's *La Double Inconstance (The Double Inconstancy)* at, respectively, the Majestic Theatre and the Opera House at BAM. Includes interview with company administrator Jean-Pierre Miquel on productions.

2651 Lévesque, Solange; Camerlain, Lorraine, ed. "Le Chaos et la carrière: Entretien avec Richard Schechner." (Chaos and Career: Interview with Richard Schechner.) *JCT.* 1989; 50: 192-196. Illus.: Photo. B&W. 2. Lang.: Fre.
USA: New York, NY. 1989. Historical studies. ■Role of New York City in defining contemporary acting style and social role for actors.

2652 Lindfors, Bernth. "'Nothing extenuate, nor set down aught in malice': New Biographical Information on Ira Aldridge." *AfAmR.* 1994 Fall; 28(3): 457-472. Notes. Biblio. Illus.: Dwg. 1. Lang.: Eng.
USA. UK-England. 1807-1867. Biographical studies. ■New biographical information on Black American actor Ira Aldridge, concerning his years in England and the ambivalent response to his work.

2653 Lindfors, Bernth. "Ira Aldridge, 'The African Roscius'." *SATJ.* 1996 May; 10(1): 71-84. Notes. Lang.: Eng.
USA. Europe. 1825-1853. Biographical studies. ■Career of Ira Aldridge, the first important Black Shakespearean actor in Europe.

2654 Maguire, Mariangela; Mohtar, Laila Farah. "Performance and the Celebration of a Subaltern Counterpublic." *TextPQ.* 1994 July; 14(3): 238-252. Notes. Biblio. Lang.: Eng.
USA: Carbondale, IL. 1972-1994. Historical studies. ■Documents the creation of a production based on the history of the Women's Center of Carbondale, IL, focusing on difficulties of performing in celebration of an organization that exists because of the continuing abuse of women.

DRAMA: —Performance/production

2655 Mercer, Johanna; Ladouceur, Louise, transl. "Le Wooster Group, à rebours et à l'envers." (The Wooster Group, Inside Out.) *JCT.* 1991; 61: 73-83. Notes. Illus.: Photo. B&W. 11. Lang.: Fre.
USA: New York, NY. 1990-1991. Histories-sources. ■Coproducer Johanna Mercer describes rehearsals of the Wooster Group staging of Paul Schmidt's *Brace Up!*, adapted from Čechov's *Tri sestry (Three Sisters)*.

2656 Miller, Henry. "Gertrude Jeannette." *AInf.* 1996; 15(1): 122-136. Illus.: Photo. B&W. 1. Lang.: Eng.
USA. 1970. Histories-sources. ■Interview with the African-American theatre legend about her life and career.

2657 Moore, Dick. "Uta Hagen Talks About Acting and Her Career." *EN.* 1996 June; 81(5): 1, 8. Illus.: Photo. 2. Lang.: Eng.
USA: New York, NY. 1996. Histories-sources. ■Actress Uta Hagen discusses her career as an actress at an oral history videotaping for the Theatre on Film and Tape Archives of the Lincoln Center Library for the Performing Arts, sponsored by the League of Professional Theatre Women/New York. The League's project chronicles and documents the contributions of significant theatre women.

2658 Mullenix, Elizabeth Reitz. "Acting Between the Spheres: Charlotte Cushman as Androgyne." *ThS.* 1996 Nov.; 37(2): 23-66. Notes. Biblio. Illus.: Photo. 1. Lang.: Eng.
USA. 1843-1853. Historical studies. ■Actress Charlotte Cushman and the extraordinary success of her cross-gendered roles on stage. Relates her portrayals of Romeo to the androgyne, one who could construct and present a double image that was both subversive and ameliorating to audiences.

2659 Newfield, Anthony. "After the Orchard: A Journal." *AmTh.* 1996 Jan.; 13(1): 34-36, 72-78. Illus.: Photo. B&W. 6. Lang.: Eng.
USA: Pittsburgh, PA. Russia: Moscow. 1996. Histories-sources. ■Diary of student who studied with the Moscow Art Theatre as part of an exchange program with Carnegie Mellon University. Instructors Roman Kosak, Larissa Borisanna Dmitrievna, Anatolij Smeljanskij, Andrej Droznin and their methods of acting training, authors personal experiences in the theatre community of Moscow.

2660 Novak, Peter. "Jorjan Lynn Jeter." *AmTh.* 1996 Dec.; 13(10): 42. Illus.: Photo. B&W. 1. Lang.: Eng.
USA. 1996. Historical studies. ■National Theatre of the Deaf's touring production of *Curiouser and Curiouser*, an adaptation by Larry Arrick of *Through the Looking-Glass* and *Alice's Adventures in Wonderland*, staged by Adrian Blue, rendered in American Sign Language, with the lead performed by Jeter.

2661 Nunns, Stephen. "No 'Angels' on Catholic Campus." *AmTh.* 1996 Dec.; 13(10): 46-47. Illus.: Photo. B&W. 1. Lang.: Eng.
USA: Washington, DC. 1996. Critical studies. ■Controversy surrounding Catholic University's production of Tony Kushner's *Angels in America, Part I: Millennium Approaches*, directed by graduate student Christopher Bellis. Department chair Gitta Honegger discusses the play's move off-campus to Arena Stage to avoid university censorship.

2662 O'Quinn, Jim. "Getting Closer to America." *AmTh.* 1996 Oct.; 13(8): 18-20. Illus.: Photo. B&W. 1. Lang.: Eng.
USA: Washington, DC. 1996. Histories-sources. ■Interview with solo performer Anna Deavere Smith on her newest work, an as-yet untitled one-person show about the press and the presidency. Her research, interviews conducted.

2663 Olivenbaum, David. "On the Interactive Circuit." *DGQ.* 1996 Win; 33(4): 34-39. Illus.: Photo. B&W. 1. Lang.: Eng.
USA: New York, NY. 1996. Critical studies. ■Speculation on the future of interactive theatre pieces such as *Grandma Sylvia's Funeral* and *Tony 'n' Tina's Wedding*: suggests possible alternation between interactive and fourth wall techniques within a single show.

2664 Orzechowski, Emil. "Amerykańscy poeci ku czci Heleny Modrzejewskiej." (American Poets in Praise of Helena Modjeska.) *PaT.* 1996; 1-2(144): 144-181. Pref. Notes. Illus.: Photo. B&W. Lang.: Pol.
USA. 1877-1909. Histories-sources. ■Accounts of U.S. performances by actress Helena Modjeska.

2665 Pace, David. "'Angels' in Utah." *AmTh.* 1996 Mar.; 13(3): 49-50. Illus.: Photo. B&W. 1. Lang.: Eng.
USA: Salt Lake City, UT. 1996. Critical studies. ■Production of Tony Kushner's *Angels in America* at Salt Lake Acting Company directed by Allen Nevins and the impact of its themes on the Mormon community.

2666 Paran, Janice. "Mary Lou Rosato." *AmTh.* 1996 May/June; 13(5): 36-37. Illus.: Photo. B&W. 4. Lang.: Eng.
USA. 1996. Biographical studies. ■Profile of actress Rosato: her roles and training in classical theatre, her move into directing.

2667 Potter, Lois. "*The Two Noble Kinsmen* in 1993-94." *SQ.* 1996 Sum; 47(2): 197-203. Lang.: Eng.
USA: New York, NY, Ashland, OR, Philadelphia, PA. 1993-1994. Critical studies. ■Critique of three productions of *The Two Noble Kinsmen*, one directed at Theatre Row Studios by Beth Milles, one presented by the Red Heel Theatre Company, and Nagle Jackson's production at the Oregon Shakespeare Festival, with discussion of the reasons for infrequency of modern productions.

2668 Pourchot, Eric. "Performing Arts of Romania at the New York Public Library for the Performing Arts." *SEEP.* 1996 Win; 16 (1): 14-20. Notes. Lang.: Eng.
USA: New York, NY. Romania. 1995-1996. Historical studies. ■Account of the 1995/96 festival of Performing Arts of Romania held at the New York Public Library for the Performing Arts, including a lecture by director Liviu Ciulei and a new touring company, Masca, founded in 1990 by Mihai Mălaimare and Anca Dana Florea, that concentrates on the actor's body as communication.

2669 Raymond, Gerard. "Vanessa Redgrave: Deep in the Art of Texas." *TheaterW.* 1996 Jan 29; 9(26): 22-24. Illus.: Photo. B&W. 3. Lang.: Eng.
USA: Houston, TX. 1996. Biographical studies. ■Redgrave's appearance in Shakespeare's *Antony and Cleopatra*, directed by Corin Redgrave, at the Alley Theatre. Production originated at the Redgraves' Moving Theatre Company in London.

2670 Raymond, Gerard. "Tennessee's Tropical Night." *TheaterW.* 1996 Mar 25; 9(34): 22-26. Illus.: Photo. B&W. 1. Lang.: Eng.
USA: New York, NY. 1960-1996. Critical studies. ■Tennessee Williams' *The Night of the Iguana*: characters, themes, current production at the Roundabout Theatre starring Cherry Jones directed by Robert Falls. Falls' approach to the text, what draws him to the play.

2671 Raymond, Gerard. "Sex, Dreams, and Wonder with the RSC." *TheaterW.* 1996 Apr 8; 9(36): 24-26. Illus.: Photo. B&W. 1. Lang.: Eng.
USA: New York, NY. UK-England: Stratford-upon-Avon. 1996. Critical studies. ■Royal Shakespeare Company's production of *A Midsummer Night's Dream* directed by Adrian Noble touring to Broadway. Interpretation, production elements.

2672 Raymond, Gerard. "Love at First Site: Tina Landau Directs *Trojan Women*." *TheaterW.* 1996 July 1; 9(48): 14-19. Illus.: Photo. B&W. 3. Lang.: Eng.
USA: New York, NY. 1996. Histories-sources. ■Interview with director Landau on her site-specific production of Charles L. Mee Jr.'s *The Trojan Women: A Love Story* for En Garde Arts (artistic director Anne Hamburger). Influences of Euripides' *Troádes (The Trojan Women)*, its staging at the East River Amphitheatre, directing site-specific theatre.

2673 Raymond, Gerard. "Director in Demand: Scott Elliott." *TheaterW.* 1996 July 15; 9(50): 18-23. Illus.: Photo. B&W. 4. Lang.: Eng.
USA: New York, NY. 1995-1996. Histories-sources. ■Interview with director Elliott discussing his theatre company The New Group, his productions of Mike Leigh's *Ecstasy* and Stephen Bill's *Curtains*, how he works with actors, themes of the plays.

2674 Raymond, Gerard. "Setting the Scene: Tony Walton Turns Director." *TheaterW.* 1996 Nov 11; 10(15): 50-52. Lang.: Eng.
USA: New York, NY. 1996. Historical studies. ■Set designer Walton's direction of Oscar Wilde's *The Importance of Being Earnest* at Irish Repertory Theatre.

DRAMA: —Performance/production

2675 Richardson, Brian. "Genre, Transgression, and the Struggle for (Self) Representation in U.S. Ethnic Drama." *JADT*. 1996 Fall; 8(3): 1-18. Notes. Lang.: Eng.
USA. 1967-1990. Historical studies. ■The use of the montage structure in American plays by ethnic minorities: Amiri Baraka's *Slave Ship* (1967), Leslie Lee's *Colored People's Time: A History Play* (1982), George C. Wolfe's *The Colored Museum* (1988), *Foghorn* by Hanay Geiogamah (1973), *Voz de la mujer (A Woman's Voice)* (1981) by Women in Teatro, Luis Valdez's *Los Vendidos (The Sellouts)* (1967) and Ping Chong's *Nuit Blanche: A Select View of Earthlings* (1990).

2676 Rose, Heidi M. "'Novelizing' Brian Friel's *Lovers*." *TextPQ*. 1996 Jan.; 16(1): 83-91. Notes. Biblio. Lang.: Eng.
USA: Philadelphia, PA. 1995. Reviews of performances. ■Analysis of the Arden Theatre Company production of Brian Friel's *Lovers* directed by Adam Posner, in which just the 'Winners' section of the play was staged.

2677 Salter, Denis. "Blood ... Sex ... Death ... Birth: Paula de Vasconcelos's 'Le Making of de Macbeth': An Interview." *ADS*. 1996 Oct.; 29: 66-83. Notes. Illus.: Photo. B&W. 3. Lang.: Eng.
USA: Montreal, PQ. 1996. Histories-sources. ■Interview with Théâtre Pigeons International co-founder Paula de Vasconcelos discussing the company's production of *Le Making of de Macbeth*, a bilingual production about the making of a play with scenes from the Shakespearean text interspersed.

2678 Scasserra, Michael P. "Olympia Dukakis in *The Hope Zone*." *TheaterW*. 1996 Jan 8; 9(23): 20-25. Illus.: Photo. B&W. 2. Lang.: Eng.
USA: New York, NY. 1960-1996. Biographical studies. ■Dukakis' role in Kevin Heelan's play at Circle Repertory, directed by Richard Jenkins. Origins of play, approach to the role, her acting career on stage, in television and film.

2679 Sellar, Tom. "Suzan-Lori Parks's *Venus*: The Shape of the Past." *TheatreF*. 1996 Sum/Fall; 9: 35-36. Lang.: Eng.
USA. 1996. Historical studies. ■Background essay on Suzan-Lori Parks's play *Venus*, first presented at Yale Repertory Theatre and later at the Public Theater/New York Shakespeare Festival, both directed by Richard Foreman.

2680 Shaughnessy, Edward L. "Brutus in the Heartland: *The Emperor Jones* in Indianapolis, 1921." *EOR*. 1996 Spr/Fall; 20 (1&2): 36-42. Biblio. Lang.: Eng.
USA: Indianapolis, IN. 1921-1922. Historical studies. ■Production of O'Neill's play in 1922 at the Little Theatre of Indianapolis: its experimental nature, controversial racial subject matter, the amateur actor who performed the lead role, Arthur T. Long. Includes excerpts from play reviews.

2681 Sheehy, Catherine. "Platinum Paradox: The Difficulties, Not to Say Impossibilities of Resuscitating the Best American Play Ever Written." *ThM*. 1996; 26(3): 85-94. Illus.: Dwg. Sketches. B&W. 4. Lang.: Eng.
USA. 1932-1996. Historical studies. ■Difficulties in reviving interest in the long-neglected Ben Hecht-Gene Fowler play *The Great Magoo*, with an account of the play's original production presented by Billy Rose.

2682 Shenton, Mark. "Fiona Shaw Enters The Waste Land." *TheaterW*. 1996 Dec 2; 10(18): 38-43. Illus.: Photo. B&W. 1. Lang.: Eng.
USA: New York, NY. UK-England: London. 1922-1996. Histories-sources. ■Life and career of actress Shaw: past roles, collaborations, and current performance in T.S. Eliot's poem *The Waste Land* at the Liberty Theatre, directed by Deborah Warner.

2683 Taylor, Kelly S. "Exploiting the Medium: Anna Cora Mowatt's Creation of Self Through Performance." *TextPQ*. 1996 Oct.; 16(4): 321-335. Notes. Biblio. Lang.: Eng.
USA. 1841-1881. Historical studies. ■Performer and playwright Anna Cora Mowatt's use of her involvement with mesmerism to enable her to create an alternate persona, 'the Gypsy', as a means of expressing her dissatisfaction with the repressive codes of upper-class feminine behavior in the mid-nineteenth century, within her solo performances.

2684 Thebus, Jessica. "Dreaming *S/M*: An Interview with Mary Zimmerman." *TextPQ*. 1996 Oct.; 16(4): 359-366. Biblio. Illus.: Photo. B&W. 1. Lang.: Eng.
USA: Chicago, IL. 1996. Histories-sources. ■Interview with director Mary Zimmerman regarding her fourth collaboration with Lookingglass Theatre Company, the production of her *S/M: A Dream Biography*.

2685 Trott, Karen. "First Person: Karen Trott: 'There's No Such Thing As a One-Person Show'." *TheaterW*. 1996 Dec 23; 10(21): 60-61, 63. Illus.: Photo. B&W. 1. Lang.: Eng.
USA: New York, NY. 1996. Histories-sources. ■Author discusses her one-woman show *The Springhill Singing Disaster*.

2686 Villeneuve, Isabelle. "Tchekhov revisité: 'Brace Up!' the Entertainment (Sketches from 'Three Sisters')." (Cechov Revisited: 'Brace Up!' the Entertainment (Sketches from 'Three Sisters').) *JCT*. 1991; 61: 84-88. Notes. Illus.: Photo. B&W. 2. Lang.: Fre.
USA: New York, NY. 1991. Critical studies. ■Wooster Group's staging of Paul Schmidt's *Brace Up!*, adaptation of Čechov's *Tri sestry (Three Sisters)*, transgresses theatrical conventions to destabilize the spectator.

2687 Watson, Jamantha Williams. "Ernie McClintock and His Harlem Homecoming." *BlackM*. 1996 Aug/Sep.; 12(1): 9,15. Illus.: Photo. Design. B&W. 1. Lang.: Eng.
USA: New York, NY. 1958-1996. Biographical studies. ■Return of theatre director and educator to his boyhood home, and the resonance it holds for him.

2688 West, Ron. "Others, Adults, Censored: The Federal Theatre Project's Black *Lysistrata* Cancellation." *ThS*. 1996 Nov.; 37(2): 93-114. Notes. Biblio. Illus.: Photo. 2. Lang.: Eng.
USA: Seattle, WA. 1936-1939. Historical studies. ■Censorship of the Federal Theatre Project's 1936 *Lysistrata*, produced and performed by the Seattle Negro Repertory Company. Article explores the connections between localized theatrical actions and a wider network of socially, politically, and racially repressive forces.

2689 Yarbro-Bejarano, Yvonne. "Chicanas' Experience in Collective Theatre: Ideology and Form." 213-227 in Keyssar, Helene, ed. *Feminist Theatre and Theory*. London: Macmillan; 1996. 288 pp. (New Casebooks.) Notes. Index. Lang.: Eng.
USA. 1968-1995. Critical studies. ■History and process of feminism and politics in the Chicana-Chicano political movement. Contrasts the objectification of the Chicana woman in traditional Chicano theatre productions to the alternatives created in the mid-eighties by Chicanas working in a much more collaborative manner.

2690 Yawney, Michael. "Obscene Eloquence: Assurbanipal Babilla's *Othello*." *TheaterW*. 1996 Sep 30; 10(9): 32-35. Illus.: Photo. B&W. 3. Lang.: Eng.
USA: New York, NY. 1996. Critical studies. ■Playwright/director Babilla's and Purgatorio Ink's production *Othello and the Circumcised Turk* at the Vineyard Theatre. Personal life and career of Babilla, previous work on Shakespeare, influences of roohozie, a type of Iranian theatre.

2691 Zinman, Toby Silverman. "Irene Worth." *AmTh*. 1996 Feb.; 13(2): 13-17. Illus.: Photo. B&W. 6. Lang.: Eng.
USA: New York, NY. 1916-1996. Histories-sources. ■Interview with actress Worth on long acting career and current solo performance in *Portrait of Edith Wharton* which she adapted from Wharton's writings.

2692 Efros, Anatolij; Krymova, N., ed. "Ustno i pis'menno." (Orally and in Writing.) *MoskNab*. 1996; 3-4: 49-55. Lang.: Rus.
USSR: Moscow. 1971-1987. Histories-sources. ■Excerpts from letters and presentations of director Anatolij Efros, including his 1971 address at the Puškin Museum.

2693 Konovalova, Galina. "Mne minulo semnadcat' let..." (I Turned Seventeen.) *TeatZ*. 1996; 7: 46-47. Lang.: Rus.
USSR: Moscow. 1950-1979. Histories-sources. ■Actress Galina Konovalova recalls her work at Vachtangov Theatre.

2694 Leach, Robert. "*I Want a Baby* Three Times." *STP*. 1993 Dec.; 8: 5-18. Notes. Lang.: Eng.
USSR: Moscow. UK-England: Birmingham. Germany: Berlin. 1927-1993. Histories-sources. ■Four productions of *Choču Rebenka (I Want*

DRAMA: —Performance/production

A Baby), three of them directed by the author of the article (in 1989, 1990, and 1993) and one performed by the Berliner Ensemble in 1989, with attention to the use of Eisenstein's and Mejerchol'd's techniques in the 1993 production.

2695 Levsin, Alexander Ivanovic. "La messinscena del 'Saggio' di Ejzenstein al Teatro del Proletkul't." (Eisenstein's Staging of *The Wise Man* at the Proletkult Theatre.) *TeatroS.* 1996; 11(18): 141-165. Notes. Lang.: Ita.
USSR. 1923. Histories-sources. ■Levsin, an actor in the production, describes Eisenstein's methods as a theatre director.

2696 Muza, Anna. "Meyerhold at Rehearsal: New Materials on Meyerhold's Work with Actors." *TTop.* 1996 Mar.; 6(1): 15-30. Biblio. Lang.: Eng.
USSR. 1925-1938. Historical studies. ■Examination of rehearsal records for productions of Gogol's *Revizor (The Inspector General)* and *33 Swoons*, composed of three one-act comedies by Čechov.

2697 Piette, Alain. "Crommelynck and Meyerhold: Two Geniuses Meet on the Stage." *MD.* 1996 Fall; 39(3): 436-447. Notes. Lang.: Eng.
USSR. 1917-1922. Historical studies. ■Moscow Art Theatre production of *The Magnanimous Cuckold* directed by Mejerchol'd. Revolutionary staging, scenic elements, rehearsal techniques and use of biomechanics.

2698 Sirota, Roza. "'Idiot' Smoktunovskogo." (Smoktunovskij's *Idiot*.) *PTZ.* 1996; 9: 80-83. Lang.: Rus.
USSR: St. Petersburg. 1956-1957. Historical studies. ■Analysis of Innokentij Smoktunovskij's performance as Prince Myshkin in *Idiot*, based on the novel by Dostojévskij, performed at Tovstonogov Drama Theatre, directed by Tovstonogov.

2699 Stanislavskij, Konstantin Sergejévič; Morcsányi, Géza, transl.; Fodor, Géza, intro. "Sztaniszlavszkij noteszeiből." (From Stanislavskij's Notebooks.) *Sz.* 1996; 29(5): 37-42. Notes. Illus.: Dwg. Photo. B&W. 7. Lang.: Hun.
USSR: Moscow. 1919-1938. Histories-sources. ■Introducing and publishing a selection of Stanislavskij's notebooks from the 1920s and 1930s.

2700 Moravec, Dušan. *Slovenski gledališki kvartet (z gostom).* (The Slovene Theatre Quartet with Guest.) Ljubljana: SGFM; 1996. 307 pp. Biblio. Illus.: Photo. B&W. Lang.: Slo.
Yugoslavia: Ljubljana. 1918-1941. Historical studies. ■The work of four Slovene directors (Osip Šest, Ciril Debevec, Bratko Kreft, Bojan Stupica) and the guest (Branko Gavella) who worked at the National Drama Theatre in Ljubljana between the two World Wars. With an English summary and a bibliography of directed productions.

2701 Kerr, David. "Giving Voice to the Silent War: An Essay Review of *Simuka Zimbabwe!* by Zambuko/Izibuko." *SATJ.* 1996 May ; 10(1): 107-112. Illus.: Photo. B&W. 1. Lang.: Afr.
Zimbabwe: Harare. 1994-1996. Critical studies. ■Review of the Zambuko/Izibuko theatre group's collectively written and directed *Simuka Zimbabwe! (Zimbabwe Arise!)*, against the changing political background of southern Africa.

Plays/librettos/scripts

2702 Bruhm, Steven. "Blond Ambition: Tennessee Williams's Homographesis." *ET.* 1996; 14(2): 97-105. Notes. Biblio. Lang.: Eng.
USA. 1958. Critical studies. ■Explores Williams's self-representation through the character of the dead Sebastian in *Suddenly Last Summer*.

2703 Élson, D. "Predlagaju éksperiment." (I Offer an Experiment.) *TeatZ.* 1996; 9: 2-4. Lang.: Rus.
1996. Critical studies. ■Shakespeare's dramaturgy in the context of modern theatre.

2704 Fortier, Mark. "Two-Voiced, Delicate Monster: *The Tempest*, Romance, and Post-Colonialism." *ET.* 1996; 15(1): 91-101. Notes. Biblio. Lang.: Eng.
1957-1993. Critical studies. ■Analysis of Shakespeare's *The Tempest* as both romance and 'post-colonial' text.

2705 Harner, James L., ed. *The World Shakespeare Bibliography on CD-ROM, 1990-1993.* New York, NY: Cambridge UP; 1996. [CD-ROM format.] Lang.: Eng.

1990-1993. Bibliographical studies. ■Publications on Shakespeare and his works from around the world collected on CD-ROM format.

2706 Lazaridès, Alexandre. "Voix croisées de la francophonie: collections 'Théâtre en Tête' et 'Théâtre à vif.'" (Varied Voices of the French-Speaking World: The 'Théâtre en Tête' and 'Théâtre à vif' Collections.) *JCT.* 1991; 61: 102-107. Illus.: Photo. B&W. 6. Lang.: Fre.
1975-1991. Historical studies. ■Éditions Promotion (recently become Éditions Lansman) publishes two collections, 'Théâtre en Tête' and 'Théâtre à vif' which give voice to playwrights throughout the French-speaking world.

2707 Nelson, Jeanne-Andrée. "So Close to Closure: The Selling of Desire in *Glengarry Glen Ross*." *ET.* 1996; 14(2): 107-116. Notes. Biblio. Lang.: Eng.
USA. 1984. Critical studies. ■An analysis of Mamet's 1984 Pulitzer Prize winning play, *Glengarry Glen Ross*.

2708 Piannaci, Rómulo E. "Antígona: o la vectorización del deseo." (Antigone: Or the Vectorization of Desire.) *Cjo.* 1996 Jan-June; 102: 28-36. Illus.: Sketches. 7. Lang.: Spa.
441 B.C.-1986 A.D. Critical studies. ■The legend of Antigone as dramatized by Sophocles, Jean Cocteau, Jean Anouilh, and Bertolt Brecht, with emphasis on Spanish-language versions by Argentinians Leopoldo Marechal (*Antígona Vélez*, 1951) and Griselda Gambaro (*Antígona Furiosa*, 1980) and Puerto Rican Luis Rafael Sánchez, (*La pasión según Antígona Pérez*, 1968).

2709 Ženovač, S. "Ego možno počuvstvovat' tol'ko čerez igru." (It Is Possible to Feel Him Only Through Acting.) *TeatZ.* 1996; 9: 46-47. Lang.: Rus.
1564-1996. Critical studies. ■The role of Shakespeare's plays in world theatre, with an elaboration of the definition of 'Shakespeare's theatre'.

2710 Arnott, Peter D.; Walton, J. Michael. *Menander and the Making of Comedy.* Westport, CT/London: Greenwood; 1996. 161 pp. (Contributions in Drama and Theatre Studies 67.) Append. Biblio. Index. Pref. Illus.: Photo. 12. Lang.: Eng.
Ancient Greece. 342-292 B.C. Histories-specific. ■Historical account of Menander's life and works. Covers the comic tradition of Ancient Greece out of which Menander emerged, his particular time and social/cultural conditions, and his plays and their unique characters.

2711 Emery, Sarah Watson. *Plato's Euthyphro, Apology, and Crito: Arranged for Dramatic Presentation from the Jowett Translation with Choruses.* Lanham, MD/New York, NY/London: UP of America; 1996. 79 pp. Pref. Lang.: Eng.
Ancient Greece. 427-347 B.C. Critical studies. ■Three dialogues of Plato, *Euthyphro*, *Apology*, and *Crito*, presented in dramatic form, adapted by the author.

2712 deMoor, Magda Castellví. "Entrevista a Beatriz Mosquera: A través de las máscaras." (Interview with Beatriz Mosquera: Through the Masks.) *LATR.* 1996 Fall; 30(1): 105-110. Notes. Lang.: Spa.
Argentina. 1994. Histories-sources. ■Interview with Argentinian playwright Beatriz Mosquera. Discusses her dramaturgical style, the individual and his relationship with the Marxist Argentinian regime of the past and the recent democracy, as well as how women are represented in Argentinian drama, and differences between male and female playwrights in their depictions of women.

2713 Gambaro, Griselda; Mitra, Saoli; Sarumpaet, Ratna; Sigurdardóttir, Thorunn. "New Stories From Old." *AFS.* 1995 Fall; 21: 55-66. Lang.: Eng.
Argentina. Indonesia. Iceland. 1879-1995. Histories-sources. ■Four playwrights discuss their reworkings of old tales at the International Women Playwrights Conference: retellings of *Antigone* by Ratna Sarumpaet and by Griselda Gambaro (*Antígona Furiosa*), of the Mahabharata by Saoli Mitra (*Naathabati Anaathabat*), and of Icelandic sagas by Thorunn Sigurdadóttir.

2714 Molinaro, Nina L. "Discipline and Drama: Panoptic Theatre and Griselda Gambaro's *El campo*." *LATR.* 1996 Spr; 29(2): 29-42. Notes. Biblio. Lang.: Eng.
Argentina: Buenos Aires. 1967-1968. Critical studies. ■Explores the connections between Griselda Gambaro's *El campo* and Michel Foucault's

DRAMA: —Plays/librettos/scripts

work on power relations and discipline, and its interrogation of power and politics. *El campo*, a play about imprisonment, treats as its subject disciplinary power and foregrounds political conditions in 1960s Argentina.

2715 Nuetzel, Eric J. "Of Melons, Heads, and Blood: Psychosexual Fascism in Griselda Gambaro's *Bad Blood*." *MD*. 1996 Fall; 39(3): 467-464. Notes. Lang.: Eng.
Argentina. 1840-1996. Critical studies. ■Analysis of Gambaro's techniques used in depicting psychosexual fascism in *La Malasangre (Bitter Blood)*: violent images and misogyny.

2716 Pellettieri, Osvaldo. "El teatro de Osvaldo Dragún y las poéticas teatrales de Buenos Aires en los cincuenta." (The Theatre of Osvaldo Dragún and Theatres Poetics in 1950s Buenos Aires.) *LATR*. 1996 Spr; 29(2): 5-14. Notes. Biblio. Lang.: Spa.
Argentina: Buenos Aires. 1952-1957. Historical studies. ■Playwright Osvaldo Dragún and Argentinian theatre in the 1950s: influence of Brecht, Dragún's use of Brecht's dramaturgy and technique in his plays of the 1950s, such as *Historias para ser contadas (Stories to Be Told)* and *Historia de mi esquina (Story of My Neighborhood)* as 'social melodramas'.

2717 Salgado, María A. "Reflejos de espejos cóncavos: El teatro clásico en las 'farsas pirotécnicas' de Alfonsina Storni." (Reflections in a Concave Mirror: Classical Theatre in the 'Pyrotechnical Farces' of Alfonsina Storni.) *LATR*. 1996 Fall; 30(1): 21-32. Lang.: Spa.
Argentina. 1892-1938. Critical studies. ■Analysis of *Dos farsas pirotécnicas (Two Pyrotechnical Farces)*, consisting of *Cimbelina en 1900 y pico*, an adaptation of Shakespeare's *Cymbeline*, and *Polixena y la cocinerita*, an adaptation of Euripides' *Hecuba*.

2718 Taylor, Diana. "Theater and Terrorism: Griselda Gambaro's *Information for Foreigners*." 207-230 in Reinelt, Janelle, ed. *Crucibles of Crisis: Performing Social Change.* Ann Arbor, MI: Univ of Michigan P; 1996. 250 pp. Notes. Illus.: Photo. 3. Lang.: Eng.
Argentina. 1963-1995. Critical studies. ■Themes of persecution and criminal violence (terrorism, torture, fascism, misogyny, anti-Semitism, and racism) in the plays of Griselda Gambaro, especially *El Campo* and *Información por extranjeros (Information for Foreigners)*.

2719 Toro, Alfonso de. "Das postmoderne Theater von Eduardo Pavlovsky." (The Postmodern Theatre of Eduardo Pavlovsky.) *MuK*. 1996; 1: 69-94. Notes. Lang.: Ger.
Argentina. 1957-1994. Biographical studies. ■The life and work of playwright, actor, director, and psychiatrist Eduardo Pavlovsky.

2720 Croft, Susan. "A Lost Australian Playwright: 'A Lady', c. 1850." *ADS*. 1996 Apr.; 28: 99-105. Notes. Lang.: Eng.
Australia: Melbourne. 1850-1996. Critical studies. ■Examination of *A Dialogue Between a Stump Orator and a Noted Squatter* as a means to identify authorship other than that of 'A Lady'.

2721 Davison, Rémy. "Outside Looking In: An Interview with Ray Mooney." *ADS*. 1996 Apr.; 28: 53-62. Notes. Biblio. Illus.: Photo. 1. Lang.: Eng.
Australia. 1975-1996. Histories-sources. ■Interview with playwright Ray Mooney discussing his time spent in prison, his first play *The Blue Freckle* performed by the prison's Players Anonymous, as well as his novel *A Green Light*.

2722 Gardner, Anita. "The Land Never Forgets." *FAR*. 1995; 10(2): 14-15. Illus.: Photo. B&W. 1. Lang.: Eng.
Australia: Perth. 1994-1995. Histories-sources. ■Interview with Andrea Lemon, who is half of the creative duo Snakehouse (Sarah Cathcart is the performing half) about their piece *Tiger Country* done cooperatively with the Deckchair Theatre.

2723 Hanson, Beverly; Imlah, Cherie; Kon, Stella; Matthie, Pauline; Laughton, Verity, ed. "Writing in New Englishes." *AFS*. 1995 Fall; 21: 79-91. Illus.: Photo. B&W. 2. Lang.: Eng.
Australia. 1995. Histories-sources. ■The experience of writing in a language imposed on a culture by colonialism: discusses Kon's *Emily of Emerald Hill*, Hanson's *Bellywoman Bangarang* and Imlah's *The Dormitory*.

2724 O'Loughlin, Iris. "The Production of Australian Women's Plays." *AWBR*. 1994 June; 6(2): 26-27. Illus.: Photo. B&W. 1. Lang.: Eng.
Australia. 1928-1994. Critical studies. ■The dearth of professional productions of women playwrights with discussion of *The Touch of Silk* by Betty Roland (1928) which, although produced on the amateur stage and on radio for years, did not receive a legitimate stage production until 1984. Also, points to alternative venues for women playwrights.

2725 Pickett, Carolyn. "'The past is here': An Interview with Tes Lyssiotis." *ADS*. 1996 Apr.; 28: 79-85. Lang.: Eng.
Australia. 1980-1995. Histories-sources. ■Interview with Greek-Australian playwright Lyssiotis, one of the first playwrights to produce bilingual works for the Australian theatre.

2726 Tompkins, Joanne. "Re-Citing Shakespeare in Post-Colonial Drama." *ET*. 1996; 15(1): 15-22. Notes. Biblio. Lang.: Eng.
Australia. Canada. 1969-1990. Critical studies. ■Post-colonial plays that place Shakespeare in the literary mainstream of the author's country. Considers Louis Nowra's *The Golden Age*, Dorothy Hewett's *The Man from Mukinupin*, and Ann-Marie MacDonald's *Goodnight Desdemona (Good Morning Juliet)*.

2727 Archipov, Ju. "Samaja skandal'naja pjesa mirovogo repertuara." (The Most Scandalous Play in the World's Repertoire.) *SovD*. 1996; 2: 208-211. Lang.: Rus.
Austria. 1893. Critical studies. ■Analysis of Arthur Schnitzler's *Reigen (Round)*.

2728 Hede, Mikkel. "Faekaliedramaer." (Fecal Drama.) *TE*. 1996 Feb.; 77: 4-6. Illus.: Photo. B&W. 1. Lang.: Dan.
Austria. Netherlands: Amsterdam. 1958-1994. Critical studies. ■Analysis of plays by Werner Schwab developed with De Trust: *De Presidentes (The Female Presidents)* and *Volksvernietiging of mijn lever is zinloos (Genocide or My Liver Is Meaningless)*, as well as a consideration of his life and works.

2729 Rosenberg, Tiina. "Brutalitet och politik." (Brutality and Politics.) *Tningen*. 1996; 20(75): 38-41. Illus.: Photo. B&W. Lang.: Swe.
Austria. 1946. Critical studies. ■A presentation of Elfriede Jelinek and her plays, with reference to *Krankheit oder Moderne Frauen (Illness or Modern Women)*.

2730 Svobodin, A. "O Fridriche Gorenštejne." (About Friedrich Gorenstein.) *TeatZ*. 1996; 1: 20-23. Lang.: Rus.
Austria. 1980-1996. Critical studies. ■Analysis of plays written by the Russian-born director and producer, including *Valemir, Dom s bašenkoj (House with a Tower)* and *Detoubijca (Child Killer)*.

2731 Taborski, Roman. "Dramaty Tadeusza Rittnera na wiedeńskich scenach." (Drama of Tadeusz Rittner on the Viennese Stage.) *PaT*. 1996; 45(3-4): 469-486. Notes. Illus.: Photo. B&W. 2. Lang.: Pol.
Austria: Vienna. 1904-1961. Historical studies. ■Viennese reception of plays by the Polish dramatist Tadeusz Rittner, who worked both in German and in Polish.

2732 Tureček, Dalibor. "Jazyk Vídně a jazyk Prahy (O jazyku českých obrozeneckých adaptací rakouského Volksstücku)." (The Language of Vienna and of Prague: The Language of Czech Adaptations of Austrian *Volksstück* in the Revivalist Period.) *DivR*. 1996; 7(4): 3-11. Lang.: Cze.
Austro-Hungarian Empire: Prague, Vienna. 1825-1847. Historical studies. ■Changes in the language of the plays when transposed to the Prague stage.

2733 Lansman, Émile. "Moi, éditeur belge..." (Me, A Belgian Publisher.) *JCT*. 1996; 80: 96-101. Illus.: Photo. B&W. 12. Lang.: Fre.
Belgium. 1985-1996. Histories-sources. ■The author describes his work publishing francophone theatre at Éditions Lansman.

2734 Just, Vladimír. "Oráč, Mastičkář a Smrt–to celé z Čech (Poznámky ke kulturní jednotě v mnohosti)." (The Ploughman, the Quack and Death: They All Came From Bohemia—Multifaceted Cultural Unity?) *DivR*. 1996 ; 7(4): 12-16. Illus.: Photo. B&W. 2. Lang.: Cze.

DRAMA: —Plays/librettos/scripts

Bohemia. 1400. Historical studies. ■Analysis of the medieval dialogue *Oráč a Smrt (The Ploughman and Death)* written in 1400 by Jan z Žatec (Johannes von Saaz).

2735 Ravetti, Graciela; Rojo, Sara. "María Adelaide Amaral ou a Crise da Classe Média Brasileira." (María Adelaide Amaral ou a Crisis of the Brazilian Middle Class.) *LATR*. 1996 Fall; 30(1): 43-54. Lang.: Por.
Brazil. 1985-1995. Critical studies. ■A cultural study of middle-class families in five plays by María Adelaide Amaral: *Bodas de Papel (Paper Wedding)*, *Querida Mamãe (Dear Mommy)*, *De Braços Abertos (With Open Arms)*, *Intensa Magia (Intense magic)*, and *Para tão Largo Amor (For Such Great Love)*.

2736 Miller, Judith G. "Werewere Liking: Pan/Artist and Pan-Africanism in the Theatre." *ThR*. 1996; 21(3): 229-238. Notes. Illus.: Photo. B&W. 5. Lang.: Eng.
Cameroon. Ivory Coast. 1976-1996. Critical studies. ■Analysis of plays and performances by Werewere Liking and the Ki-Yi M'Bock company, with evaluation of her attempts to create a theatrical Pan-Africanism.

2737 Sanko, Hélène. "Considering Molière in Oyônô-Mbia's *Three Suitors: One Husband*." *ThR*. 1996; 21(3) : 239-244. Notes. Lang.: Eng.
Cameroon. 1667-1996. Critical studies. ■Intercultural and post-colonial themes of *Trois prétendants ... un mari*, as well as Guillaume Oyônô-Mbia's borrowings from Molière. Includes analysis of linguistic and cultural aspects of contemporary African francophone theatre.

2738 Ackerman, Marianne; Vaïs, Michel, transl. "Hôtel Montréal: On y dort bien, mais ne préfériez-vous pas y vivre?" (Hotel Montreal: You Sleep Well There, But Wouldn't You Rather Live There?)*JCT*. 1991; 58: 17-23. Notes. Illus.: Photo. B&W. 5. Lang.: Fre.
Canada: Montreal, PQ. 1980-1990. Critical studies. ■Anglo-Quebec drama, with emphasis on the work of playwrights David Fennario and Vittorio Rossi, and the companies Theatre Centaur, Imago, and Black Theatre Workshop.

2739 Allen, Michelle. "Derrière le flou féerique ('le Songe d'une nuit d'été', T.N.M., 1989)." (Behind the Fairy Haze: *A Midsummer Night's Dream*, Théâtre du Nouveau Monde, 1989.) *JCT*. 1990; 56: 78-81. Illus.: Photo. B&W. 3. Lang.: Fre.
Canada: Montreal, PQ. 1990. Histories-sources. ■Michelle Allen reflects on process of translating Shakespeare's *A Midsummer Night's Dream*. Includes parallel reprints of extract from original text along with translations by François-Victor Hugo and Michelle Allen.

2740 Allen, Michelle. "Entre le porc-épic et la cathédral de Gaudí." (Between the Porcupine and the Cathedral of Gaudí.) *JCT*. 1989; 50: 186-187. Illus.: Pntg. 1. Lang.: Fre.
Canada. 1989. Histories-sources. ■Playwright and translator Michelle Allen describes tensions in translation among author, translator and actor.

2741 Archambault, François. "Ma façon de marcher." (My Way of Walking.) *JCT*. 1996; 78: 12-17. Biblio. Illus.: Photo. B&W. Lang.: Fre.
Canada: Montreal, PQ. 1992-1996. Histories-sources. ■François Archambault's writing process and notes on the creation of his plays *Cul sec (Dry Ass)*, *Les Gagnants (The Winners)* and *Si la tendance se maintient—chronique référendaire (If the Trend Continues—Referendum Chronicle)*.

2742 Aubry, Suzanne. "Les trois coups de théâtre de Marcel Dubé." (Marcel Dubé's Three Hits.) *JCT*. 1992; 65: 108-111. Illus.: Photo. B&W. 6. Lang.: Fre.
Canada: Montreal, PQ, Quebec, PQ. 1958-1993. Critical studies. ■Themes and characters of Marcel Dubé's *Les Beaux Dimanches*, *Le Temps des lilas* and *Florence* justifying their recent revivals at Théâtre du Nouveau Monde, Théâtre du Rideau Vert and Théâtre du Trident, respectively.

2743 Bélisle, Rosemarie. "Une Question de niveau de langue." (A Question of Level of Language.) *JCT*. 1990; 56: 18-23. Notes. Illus.: Maps. Photo. B&W. 3. Lang.: Fre.
Canada. France. 1990. Critical studies. ■Variations in spoken French in France and Quebec, with implications for theatrical translation.

2744 Belzil, Patricia. "Jean-Frédéric Messier: Maux et mots d'amour." (Jean-Frédéric Messier: Pains and Words of Love.) *JCT*. 1991; 61: 29-31. Notes. Illus.: Photo. B&W. 2. Lang.: Fre.
Canada: Montreal, PQ. 1987-1991. Critical studies. ■Existential themes of self and love in playwright-director Jean-Frédéric Messier's *Le Dernier Délire permis (Death, Delirium and Desire)* and *Aussi creux que le Grand Canyon (As Empty as the Grand Canyon)*.

2745 Bienvenue, Yvan; Caron, Jean-François. "Dialogue de relevants." (Dialogue of the Up-and-Coming.) *JCT*. 1996; 78: 69-72. Notes. Illus.: Photo. B&W. Lang.: Fre.
Canada: Montreal, PQ. 1993-1996. Histories-sources. ■Yvan Bienvenue and Jean-François Caron express, in the form of personal correspondence, fears and hopes related to becoming professional playwrights.

2746 Bird, Kym. "Leaping Into the Breeches: Liberal Feminism and Cross-Dressing in Sarah Ann Curzon's *The Sweet Girl Graduate*." *ADS*. 1996 Oct.; 29: 168-179. Notes. Lang.: Eng.
Canada. 1882. Critical studies. ■Cross-dressing and liberal feminist politics in Sarah Anne Curzon's *The Sweet Girl Graduate* in which a woman masquerades as a man in order to attend college.

2747 Boucher, Serge. "Le tragique quotidien." (Everyday Tragedy.) *JCT*. 1996; 78: 30-32. Biblio. Illus.: Photo. B&W. 1. Lang.: Fre.
Canada: Montreal, PQ. 1993-1996. Histories-sources. ■Everyday life of characters is central feature of Serge Boucher's plays *Natures mortes (Still Lives)* and *Motel Hélène*.

2748 Brisset, Annie. "Tremblay, traducteur lauréat." (Tremblay, Prizewinning Translator.) *JCT*. 1990; 56: 103-107. Notes. Illus.: Photo. B&W. 2. Lang.: Fre.
Canada: Montreal, PQ. 1968-1990. Histories-sources. ■Excerpt from *Sociocritique de la traduction: théâtre et altérité au Québec, 1968-1988* (Montreal: Le Préambule, 1990). Analysis of translations by playwright Michel Tremblay and the extent to which these translations are presented as original works. Discussion of Aristophanes' *Lysistrata*, Zindel's *The Effect of Gamma Rays on Man-in-the-Moon Marigolds (L'Effet des rayons gamma sur les vieux-garçons)*, and Gogol's *Revizor (The Inspector General)*, translated as *Le Gars de Québec*.

2749 Brisset, Annie. "Shakespeare, l'afficheur qui hurle." (Shakespeare, the Shouting Billposter.) *JCT*. 1990; 56: 108-119. Notes. Illus.: TA. Photo. B&W. 4. Lang.: Fre.
Canada. 1969-1978. Critical studies. ■Excerpt from *Sociocritique de la traduction: théâtre et altérité au Québec, 1968-1988* (Montreal: Le Préambule, 1990). Analysis of Quebec nationalist discourse in Michel Garneau's translation of Shakespeare's *Macbeth* IV:iii.

2750 Brisset, Annie. "Traduire pour s'inventer." (Translating to Invent Oneself.) *JCT*. 1990; 56: 55-60. Notes. Illus.: Dwg. Photo. B&W. 3. Lang.: Fre.
Canada. 1968-1990. Critical studies. ■Quebecois nationalism's influence on translation and adaptation.

2751 Brisset, Annie. "L''Action parlée'." (The 'Speech Act'.) *JCT*. 1989; 50: 188-189. Illus.: Photo. B&W. 1. Lang.: Fre.
Canada. 1989. Critical studies. ■Inscription of social context and theatrical codes of receiving culture in translations.

2752 Burgoyne, Lynda. "Théâtre et homosexualité féminine: Un Continent invisible." (Theatre and Female Homosexuality: An Invisible Continent.) *JCT*. 1990; 54: 114-118. Notes. Illus.: Photo. B&W. 3. Lang.: Fre.
Canada: Montreal, PQ. 1976-1990. Historical studies. ■Lesbianism in Quebecois society and drama, with particular attention to works by Jovette Marchessault and Pol Pelletier.

2753 Burgoyne, Lynda. "Au Nom du père." (In the Name of the Father.) *JCT*. 1991; 58: 115-118. Notes. Illus.: Photo. B&W. 2. Lang.: Fre.
Canada: Montreal, PQ. 1990. Critical studies. ■Father figures in Tremblay's *La Maison suspendue (The House Among the Stars)*.

2754 Burgoyne, Lynda. "D'une sorcière à l'autre." (From One Witch to Another.) *JCT*. 1992; 66: 29-37. Notes. Illus.: Dwg. Photo. B&W. 5. Lang.: Fre.
Canada. 1968-1993. Critical studies. ■Witches as a metaphor for women defying traditional stereotypes in Quebecois feminist plays.

DRAMA: —Plays/librettos/scripts

2755 Burgoyne, Lynda. "Biographie et théâtre chez Jovette Marchessault: du 'mentir-vrai'." (Biography and the Theatre of Jovette Marchessault: 'Lying True.') *JCT*. 1991; 60: 111-120. Notes. Illus.: Photo. B&W. 6. Lang.: Fre.
Canada: Montreal, PQ. 1970-1991. Biographical studies. ■The playwright's uses of biography and the confrontation of reality with fiction to examine women's identities and culture. Particular attention to her play *Le Voyage magnifique d'Emily Carr*.

2756 Burgoyne, Lynda. "Les mots... sous la surface de la peau: Entretien avec Larry Tremblay." (Words... Under the Surface of the Skin: Interview with Larry Tremblay.) *JCT*. 1992; 65: 8-12. Illus.: Photo. B&W. 3. Lang.: Fre.
Canada: Montreal, PQ. 1992. Histories-sources. ■Playwright-actor Larry Tremblay's character-oriented approach to writing the one-woman play *Leçon d'anatomie (Anatomy Lesson)*.

2757 Burgoyne, Lynda. "Carole Fréchette: Le blues d'un chant intérieur." (Carole Fréchette: The Blues of an Inner Song.) *JCT*. 1991; 61: 22-26. Notes. Illus.: Photo. B&W. 2. Lang.: Fre.
Canada: Montreal, PQ. 1983-1991. Critical studies. ■Carole Fréchette's plays *Baby Blues* and *Les Quatre Morts de Marie (The Four Deaths of Marie)* express a personal and poetic femininity without feminism.

2758 Cadieux, Anne-Marie. "La mémoire du corps." (Body Memory.) *JCT*. 1996; 78: 26-29. Biblio. Illus.: Photo. B&W. 2. Lang.: Fre.
Canada: Montreal, PQ. 1992-1996. Histories-sources. ■Actor-playwright Anne-Marie Cadieux finds traces of subconscious preoccupations in her plays *La Nuit (Night)* and *Le Point Aveugle (The Blind Spot)*.

2759 Camerlain, Lorraine; David, Gilbert; Godin, Jean Cléo; Lavoie, Pierre; Lazaridès, Alexandre; Lépine, Stéphane; Lévesque, Solange; Pavlovic, Diane; Richard, Hélène; Vaïs, Michel. "Séminaire (1re séance)." (Seminar: First Session.) *JCT*. 1990; 54: 43-81. Notes. Illus.: Photo. B&W. 20. Lang.: Fre.
Canada. 1960-1990. Critical studies. ■Psychology and sociology of homosexuality and of gay playwriting.

2760 Camerlain, Lorraine. "'Théâtre et homosexualité'." ('Theatre and Homosexuality'.) *JCT*. 1990; 54: 5-7. Notes. Lang.: Fre.
Canada: Montreal, PQ. 1987-1990. Historical studies. ■Public debate in Montreal over perceived preponderance of gay plays in Quebec theatres.

2761 Camerlain, Lorraine. "Le Récit des origines." (The Story of Origins.) *JCT*. 1991; 58: 119-125. Notes. Illus.: Photo. B&W. 3. Lang.: Fre.
Canada: Montreal, PQ. 1990. Critical studies. ■Representations of storytelling and the juncture of fiction with reality in Michel Tremblay's *La Maison suspendue (The House Among the Stars)*.

2762 Camerlain, Lorraine. "Jean-François Caron: Une histoire qui s'écrit." (Jean-François Caron: A Story through Writing.) *JCT*. 1991; 61: 12-14. Notes. Illus.: Photo. B&W. 2. Lang.: Fre.
Canada: Montreal, PQ. 1986-1991. Critical studies. ■Generational conflicts and the representation of writing as recurring themes in plays by Jean-François Caron: *Donut, Rio, J'écrirai bientôt une pièce sur les nègres (Soon I'll Write a Play about the Negroes)* and *Le Scalpel du diable (The Devil's Scalpel)*.

2763 Camerlain, Lorraine, ed.; Vigeant, Louise. "'Gil': Du Roman à la scene, de l'adulte à l'enfant: Entretien avec Suzanne Lebeau." ('Gil': From the Novel to the Stage, From Adult to Child: Interview with Suzanne Lebeau.) *JCT*. 1989; 53: 50-56. Illus.: Photo. B&W. 7. Lang.: Fre.
Canada. 1987-1988. Histories-sources. ■Playwright Suzanne Lebeau describes adapting Howard Buten's novel *Quand j'avais cinq ans, je m'ai tué (When I was Five, I Killed Myself)* as children's play *Gil*.

2764 Canac-Marquis, Normand. "Au sud de Dieu." (South of God.) *JCT*. 1991; 61: 10-11. Illus.: Photo. B&W. 1. Lang.: Fre.
Canada: Montreal, PQ. 1988-1991. Histories-sources. ■For playwright Normand Canac-Marquis, writing is impulsive creation rather than conscious discourse.

2765 Caron, Jean-François. "Mon jardin, mon enfance, ma vie." (My Garden, My Childhood, My Life.) *JCT*. 1991; 61: 15-16. Illus.: Photo. B&W. 1. Lang.: Fre.
Canada: Montreal, PQ. 1986-1991. Histories-sources. ■Jean-François Caron strives to give significance to his plays by inscribing his life experience in them.

2766 Champagne, Dominic. "Ce qu'il reste au rêveur." (What Is Left for the Dreamer.) *JCT*. 1991; 61: 19-21. Illus.: Photo. B&W. 2. Lang.: Fre.
Canada: Montreal, PQ. 1988-1991. Histories-sources. ■Dominic Champagne's writing is motivated by preoccupations with recurring characters and themes, and by the desire to create theatre.

2767 Charest, Rémy. "Les bonnes réponses aux bonnes questions: une façon d'écrire pour André Morency et Lili Pichet." (The Right Answers to the Right Questions: A Way of Writing for André Morency and Lili Pichet.) *JCT*. 1996; 81: 112-116. Notes. Illus.: Photo. B&W. 2. Lang.: Fre.
Canada: Montreal, PQ. 1995-1996. Critical studies. ■Collaborative methods and dramatic structure of André Morency and Lili Pichet's play *Le Piège: Terre des hommes (The Trap: World of Men)*.

2768 Chassay, Jean-François. "Lettre ouverte à Réjean Ducharme." (Open Letter to Réjean Ducharme.) *JCT*. 1989; 51: 49-52. Illus.: Photo. B&W. 5. Lang.: Fre.
Canada: Montreal, PQ. 1989. Historical studies. ■Reflections on novels of Réjean Ducharme prompted by stage adaptation of his *À quelle heure on meurt? (What Time Do We Die?)* directed by Martin Faucher.

2769 Danis, Louison; Gingras, René; Ladouceur, Louise; Lefebvre, Paul; Turp, Gilbert; Denis, Jean-Luc; Camerlain, Lorraine, ed. "Le Statut du québécois comme langue de traduction: Table ronde animé par Jean-Luc Denis." (The Status of Quebecois French as Language of Translation: Roundtable Discussion Moderated by Jean-Luc Denis.) *JCT*. 1990; 56: 25-37. Illus.: Photo. B&W. 4. Lang.: Fre.
Canada. 1980-1990. Histories-sources. ■Quebecois translators discuss: existence of a Quebecois language suitable for theatrical translation, evolution of translation practice, faithful translation versus creativity, and techniques of theatrical translation.

2770 Denis, Jean-Luc. "Traduire le théâtre en contexte québécois: Essai de caractérisation d'une pratique." (Translating Theatre in a Quebecois Context: Attempted Characterization of a Practice.) *JCT*. 1990; 56: 9-17. Notes. Illus.: Photo. B&W. 2. Lang.: Fre.
Canada. 1990. Histories-sources. ■Translator Jean-Luc Denis argues need for Quebecois translations to employ regional dialect without changing action to a Quebec setting.

2771 Denis, Jean-Luc; Lavoie, Pierre; Camerlain, Lorraine, ed. "Shakespeare ... en québécois?: Entretien avec Jean-Louis Roux." (Shakespeare ... in Quebecois French?: Interview with Jean-Louis Roux.) *JCT*. 1990; 56: 38-43. Illus.: Poster. Photo. B&W. 3. Lang.: Fre.
Canada. 1970-1990. Histories-sources. ■Jean-Louis Roux on translation versus adaptation in Quebec, and his own work translating Shakespeare into French.

2772 Doré, Isabelle. "L'ombre et la lumière." (Shadow and Light.) *JCT*. 1996; 78: 33-37. Notes. Biblio. Illus.: Photo. B&W. 3. Lang.: Fre.
Canada: Montreal, PQ. 1962-1996. Histories-sources. ■Isabelle Dorée traces her playwriting career.

2773 Downton, Dawn Rae. "Words, Words & Moving Pictures." *ArtsAtl*. 1996; 14(2): 42-43. Illus.: Photo. B&W. 2. Lang.: Eng.
Canada: Glace Bay, NS. 1984-1996. Critical studies. ■Comparison of the story, film and play of *The Glace Bay Miners' Museum* by Sheldon Currie.

2774 Eruli, Brunella. "Les Attracteurs étranges." (Strange Attractors.) *JCT*. 1990; 55: 29-34. Notes. Illus.: Photo. B&W. 5. Lang.: Fre.

CLASSED ENTRIES

DRAMA: —Plays/librettos/scripts

Canada. 1990. Critical studies. ■Search for meaning in plays of Tadeusz Kantor: *Umarła klasa (The Dead Class), Où sont les neiges d'antan (Where Are the Snows of Yesteryear?), Wielopole Wielopole, Niech sczezną artyści (Let the Artists Die)* and *Nigdy tu już nie powrócę (I Shall Never Return).*

2775 Farfan, Penny. "Women Playwrights in Regina." *CTR.* 1996 Sum; 87: 55. Lang.: Eng.
Canada: Regina, SK. 1996. Histories-sources. ■A panel discussion moderated by Penny Farfan, with Kelly Jo Burke, Connie Gault, Rachael Van Fossen and Dianne Warren discussing theatre opportunities in Regina and the economic and social issues facing female playwrights.

2776 Filewod, Alan. "The Comintern and the Canon: Workers' Theatre, *Eight Men Speak* and the Genealogy of Mise-en-Scène." *ADS.* 1996 Oct.; 29: 16-32. Notes. Illus.: Photo. B&W. 1. Lang.: Eng.
Canada: Toronto, ON. 1933. Historical studies. ■Agit-prop play *Eight Men Speak* by Oscar Ryan, Ed Cecil-Smith and Frank Love, its workers' theatre production, political climate of the time, and possible reasons for its fade into obscurity.

2777 Forgues, Michel. "Le Scaphandrier." (The Scubadiver.) *JCT.* 1989; 53: 47-49. Illus.: Photo. B&W. 2. Lang.: Fre.
Canada: Montreal, PQ. 1977-1989. Histories-sources. ■Director Michel Forgues describes his experience creating collages based on non-dramatic texts.

2778 Fréchette, Carole. "Questions et confidences." (Questions and Secrets.) *JCT.* 1991; 61: 27-28. Illus.: Photo. B&W. 1. Lang.: Fre.
Canada: Montreal, PQ. 1983-1991. Histories-sources. ■For Carole Fréchette, writing expresses personal stories, not a political agenda or a feminist ideal.

2779 Fréchette, Carole. "Parmi les milliards de mots." (Among the Billions of Words.) *JCT.* 1996; 78: 8-11. Biblio. Illus.: Photo. B&W. 2. Lang.: Fre.
Canada: Montreal, PQ. 1989-1996. Histories-sources. ■Playwright Carole Fréchette describes her writing methods and thematic preoccupations such as the body and numbers.

2780 Fréchette, Carole. "Pour donner une forme à la vie." (To Give a Shape to Life.) *JCT.* 1996; 80: 227-229. Illus.: Photo. B&W. 2. Lang.: Fre.
Canada. 1996. Histories-sources. ■Playwright Carole Fréchette on her motivations for writing plays.

2781 Gaboriau, Linda. "Traduire le génie de l'auteur." (Translating the Genius of the Author.) *JCT.* 1990; 56: 43-48. Illus.: Poster. 3. Lang.: Fre.
Canada: Montreal, PQ. 1960-1990. Histories-sources. ■Translator Linda Gaboriau retraces her career path and reflects on techniques and difficulties of translating Quebecois French plays into English.

2782 Gauthier, Richard. "'Don Juan revient de guerre'." *JCT.* 1992; 63: 74-76. Notes. Illus.: Photo. B&W. 1. Lang.: Fre.
Canada: Montreal, PQ. Austria. 1625-1991. Historical studies. ■Proliferation of Don Juan adaptations, both historically in Europe and presently in Montreal, and specific case of Ödön von Horváth's *Don Juan kommt aus dem Krieg (Don Juan Comes Back from the War)* produced in 1991 by Théâtre de la Récidive, directed by Jean-Claude Côté.

2783 Gilbert, Reid. "'Shine on us, Grandmother Moon': Coding in Canadian First Nations Drama." *ThR.* 1996; 21(1): 24-32. Notes. Illus.: Photo. B&W. 2. Lang.: Eng.
Canada. 1987-1996. Critical studies. ■The layering of myth and iconography in productions by First Nations Canadians from an intercultural perspective, with reference to Clements' *Age of Iron*, Favel's *Requiem*, and Baumander's production of *The Tempest.*

2784 Godin, Diane. "La laideur, le bruit et la fureur: Sur les traces de nouvelles voies." (Ugliness, Sound and Fury: On the Traces of New Paths.) *JCT.* 1996; 78: 73-78. Illus.: Photo. B&W. 4. Lang.: Fre.
Canada: Montreal, PQ. 1993-1995. Critical studies. ■The aesthetic of harsh realism in contemporary Quebecois plays such as Anne-Marie Cadieux's *La Nuit (Night)*, Yvan Bienvenue's diptych *Histoires à mourir d'amour (Stories to Die of Love)* and François Archambault's *Cul sec (Dry Ass).*

2785 Godin, Diane. "Une mythologie du désastre." (A Mythology of Disaster.) *JCT.* 1996; 79: 21-24. Notes. Illus.: Photo. B&W. 2. Lang.: Fre.
Canada: Montreal, PQ. Germany. 1980-1996. Critical studies. ■Themes of disaster and death in Heiner Müller's *Quartett* with Brigitte Haentjen's 1996 staging at Espace GO.

2786 Godin, Jean Cléo. "Qu'est-ce qu'un 'Dragonfly'." (What is a 'Dragonfly.) *JCT.* 1996; 78: 90-95. Notes. Illus.: Photo. B&W. 3. Lang.: Fre.
Canada: Montreal, PQ. 1995. Critical studies. ■Associates use of English in Larry Tremblay's *The Dragonfly of Chicoutimi* with ambiguities of gender, sexuality and identity.

2787 Gravel, Pierre. "Traduire ('Antigone' de Sophocle)." (To Translate: Sophocles' *Antigone.*) *JCT.* 1990; 56: 75-77. Illus.: Photo. B&W. 1. Lang.: Fre.
Canada. France. 1967-1986. Histories-sources. ■Comparison of Gravel's own translation of the opening of Sophocles' *Antigone* to the version in Gilbert Kahn's translation of Martin Heidegger's *Introduction à la métaphysique (Introduction to Metaphysics).*

2788 Gravel, Pierre. "Antigone aujourd'hui." (Antigone Today.) *JCT.* 1989; 50: 74-76. Illus.: Photo. B&W. 1. Lang.: Fre.
Canada. 1989. Critical studies. ■Analogies for Antigone's struggle in contemporary Quebec.

2789 Gurik, Robert. "L'eczéma de l'ingénieur." (The Engineer's Eczema.) *JCT.* 1996; 80: 136-137. Illus.: Photo. B&W. 2. Lang.: Fre.
Canada: Montreal, PQ. 1963. Histories-sources. ■Robert Gurik describes circumstances of writing his first play, *Le Sang du poète (The Blood of the Poet).*

2790 Holder, Heidi J. "Broken Toys: The Destruction of the National Hero in the Early Plays of Sharon Pollock." *ET.* 1996; 14 (2): 131-145. Notes. Biblio. Lang.: Eng.
Canada. 1973-1976. Critical studies. ■Analysis of *The Komagata Maru Incident* and *Walsh*, two of Pollock's early historical plays which deal with the failure of the heroic.

2791 Hunt, Nigel; Vaïs, Michel. "Offrir une résistance à l'unité nationale: L'Oeuvre de quelques dramaturges anglo-canadiens récents." (Resisting National Unity: The Work of Some Recent Anglo-Canadian Playwrights.) *JCT.* 1991; 58: 24-34. Biblio. Notes. Illus.: Photo. B&W. 9. Lang.: Fre.
Canada. 1970-1990. Historical studies. ■Overview of English-language Canadian playwrights, with brief discussions of French, Cook, Murrell, Pollock, Lambert Griffiths, Reaney, Walker, Thompson, Krizanc, Clark, MacDonald, Mighton, Lill, Gault, Fraser, Fulford, Liitoja.

2792 Joubert, Ingrid. "Le Passé a-t-il de l'avenir devant lui? Bilan du théâtre francophone de l'Ouest canadien." (Does the Past Have a Future? French-Language Theatre in Western Canada.) *ThR.* 1996; 21(3): 208-218. Notes. Illus.: Photo. B&W. 2. Lang.: Fre.
Canada. 1886-1986. Historical studies. ■Manitoban history in dramatizations of the legend of Louis Riel. Discussion centers mainly on John Coulter's *Riel: A Play in Two Parts*, Marcel Ferland's *Au temps de la prairie* and Elzéar Paquin's *Riel.*

2793 Kerr, Rosalind. "Once Were Lesbians...: Re/Negotiating Re/Presentations in *The Catherine Wheel* and *Difference of Latitude.*" *MD.* 1996 Spr; 39(1): 177-189. Notes. Lang.: Eng.
Canada. 1710-1996. Critical studies. ■Depiction of emerging lesbians as women who challenged accepted gender roles in *The Catherine Wheel* by Ingrid MacDonald and *Difference of Latitude* by Lisa Walter.

2794 Kerr, Rosalind. "With(holding) the Knife: Representing the Unrepresentable (Wo)man in *Anna.*" *MD.* 1996 Win; 39(4): 566-573. Notes. Lang.: Eng.
Canada: Toronto, ON. 1994. Historical studies. ■Analysis of *Anna* by April Hubért and the production by Company of Sirens for which she served as dramaturg. Discussion of violence against women, male characters, and the effect of men playing female roles.

2795 Knowles, Richard Paul. "The Theatre of Form and the Production of Meaning: Contemporary Canadian Dramaturgies." *ADS.* 1996 Oct.; 29: 43-56. Notes. Lang.: Eng.

DRAMA: —Plays/librettos/scripts

Canada. 1972-1996. Critical studies. ■Form, negotiation of cultural values, and cultural affirmation and intervention in contemporary English-language Canadian theatre. Examples from *Jakob's Wake* by Michael Cook and *Leaving Home* and *Of the Fields, Lately* by David French.

2796 Labbé, Jérôme. "Détournement d'auteur." (Author's Detour.) *JCT.* 1996; 78: 41-43. Biblio. Illus.: Photo. B&W. 2. Lang.: Fre.
Canada: Montreal, PQ. 1987-1996. Histories-sources. ■Jérôme Labbé describes his playwriting process and his academic research into the structure of dialogue.

2797 Lavigne, Louis-Dominique. "Les Purs." (The Innocents.) *JCT.* 1996; 80: 123-125. Illus.: Photo. B&W. 2. Lang.: Fre.
Canada: Montreal, PQ. 1985-1986. Histories-sources. ■Playwright describes his autobiographical play *Les Purs* and its reception.

2798 Lavoie, Pierre. "La dernière réplique de l'auteur." (The Author's Last Line.) *JCT.* 1996; 80: 212-226. Illus.: Photo. B&W. 4. Lang.: Fre.
Canada. 1996. Histories-sources. ■Thirty Quebecois playwrights answer question: 'If you had to write your last play, what would be the last line?'.

2799 Lavoie, Pierre. "La Famille morte." (The Dead Family.) *JCT.* 1991; 58: 104-106. Illus.: Photo. B&W. 2. Lang.: Fre.
Canada: Montreal, PQ. 1990. Critical studies. ■Themes of reconciliation and anti-intellectualism in Michel Tremblay's *La Maison suspendue (The House Among the Stars)*, and relation of that play to other Tremblay works.

2800 Lavoie, Pierre. "Normand Canac-Marquis: Vivre pour mourir." (Normand Canac-Marquis: Living for Dying.) *JCT.* 1991; 61: 8-10. Notes. Illus.: Photo. B&W. 1. Lang.: Fre.
Canada: Montreal, PQ. 1988-1991. Critical studies. ■Nightmare and death characterize Normand Canac-Marquis' plays *Le Syndrome de Cézanne* and *Jumeaux d'Uritania*.

2801 Lavoie, Pierre. "Marie, Simon, Carole et les autres." (Marie, Simon, Carole and the Others.) *JCT.* 1996; 79: 105-107. Notes. Illus.: Photo. B&W. 1. Lang.: Fre.
Canada: Montreal, PQ. 1995. Historical studies. ■Suffering and humor in Carole Fréchette's plays *Les Quatre Morts de Marie (The Four Deaths of Marie)* and *Les Sept Jours de Simon Labrosse—Si la vie vous intéresse! (The Seven Days of Simon Labrosse—If His Life Interests You!)*.

2802 Lazaridès, Alexandre. "Revue de la production dramatique de 1989." (Review of Drama Production of 1989.) *JCT.* 1990; 54: 141-150. Illus.: TA. Photo. B&W. 19. Lang.: Fre.
Canada: Montreal, PQ. 1979-1989. Historical studies. ■Statistical analysis of roles and thematic trends in Quebec plays published in 1989.

2803 Lazaridès, Alexandre. "Notes sur la 'biographie dramatisée'." (Notes on 'Dramatized Biography'.) *JCT.* 1991; 60: 101-106. Notes. Illus.: Photo. B&W. 5. Lang.: Fre.
Canada: Montreal, PQ. 1986-1991. Critical studies. ■General discussion of the problems of writing biographical drama.

2804 Legris, Pierre. "Un Problème de choix ('Glengarry Glen Ross', Théâtre de la Manufacture 1989)." (A Problem of Choice: 'Glengarry Glen Ross', Théâtre de la Manufacture 1989.) *JCT.* 1990; 56: 92-96. Notes. Illus.: Photo. B&W. 2. Lang.: Fre.
Canada: Montreal, PQ. 1989. Histories-sources. ■Legris' intentions and methods for producing a new, Quebec French translation of David Mamet's *Glengarry Glen Ross*. Parallel reprints of an extract of Legris' translation and the translation by Pierre Laville.

2805 Lesage, Marie-Christine. "Archipels de mémoire: L'oeuvre de Daniel Danis." (Archipelagos of Memory: The Works of Daniel Danis.) *JCT.* 1996; 78: 79-89. Notes. Illus.: Photo. B&W. 5. Lang.: Fre.
Canada: Montreal, PQ. 1993. Critical studies. ■Fragmentation of memory and the relation of form to content in Daniel Danis' plays *Celle-là (That One)* and *Cendres de cailloux (Ashes of Stone)*.

2806 Lévesque, Solange. "Du Roman au théâtre: 'Le Grand Cahier' et 'la Preuve': Entretien avec Odette Guimond et Jacques Rossi." (From Novel to Theatre: *The Big Book* and *The Proof*.) *JCT.* 1989; 53: 61-68. Illus.: Poster. Photo. B&W. 5. Lang.: Fre.
Canada: Montreal, PQ. 1988-1989. Histories-sources. ■Co-directors Odette Guimond and Jacques Rossi describe process of writing *Le Grand Cahier (The Big Book)* and *La Preuve (The Proof)*, adaptations for the stage of novels by Agota Kristof.

2807 Lévesque, Solange. "'La Terre paternelle'." ('The Fatherland'.) *JCT.* 1991; 58: 107-111. Illus.: Photo. B&W. 2. Lang.: Fre.
Canada: Montreal, PQ. 1990. Critical studies. ■Strengths and weaknesses of Michel Tremblay's *La Maison suspendue* as drama and as documentation of Quebec's history.

2808 Lévesque, Solange. "'Broue': La foire des anti-héros." ('Scum': The Anti-Heroes' Fair.) *JCT.* 1993; 66: 130-134. Notes. Illus.: Dwg. Photo. B&W. 3. Lang.: Fre.
Canada. 1979-1992. Critical studies. ■Character construction and competence of acting as reasons for longevity and popular success of *Broue (Scum)*, collective creation of Marc Messier, Michel Côté and Marcel Gauthier.

2809 Lévesque, Solange. "Cher François." (Dear François.) *JCT.* 1996; 81: 140-142. Illus.: Photo. B&W. 3. Lang.: Fre.
Canada: Montreal, PQ. 1996. Historical studies. ■Representations of Saint Francis of Assisi in Éloi Leclerc's *Exil et Tendresse (Exile and Tenderness)*, Christian Bobin's *Le Très-Bas (The Lowly)* and Joseph Delteil's *François d'Assise (Francis of Assisi)*. Includes brief reviews of their Montreal stagings.

2810 Martin, Alexis. "Un vide plein d'attentes..." (A Void Full of Expectations.) *JCT.* 1996; 78: 38-40. Biblio. Illus.: Photo. B&W. 3. Lang.: Fre.
Canada: Montreal, PQ. 1992-1996. Histories-sources. ■Playwright Alexis Martin views playwriting as a means to bridge the gap between himself and the world.

2811 Mercure, Marthe. "Le gliss de la voix (*glissando*)." (The Gliss of the Voice *glissando*.) *JCT.* 1996; 80: 151. Illus.: Photo. B&W. 1. Lang.: Fre.
Canada. 1996. Histories-sources. ■Poem on weightlessness, voice and body, presented as 'Prelude' to an upcoming play entitled: *How is your spine, Roberta Bondar? ou la tragédie de l'apesanteur*.

2812 Messier, Jean-Frédéric. "Une écriture nourrie par le jeu." (Writing Nourished by Acting.) *JCT.* 1991; 61: 32-33. Notes. Illus.: Photo. B&W. 1. Lang.: Fre.
Canada: Montreal, PQ. 1987-1991. Histories-sources. ■Jean-Frédéric Messier explains his method of writing in collaboration with actors who co-create.

2813 Micone, Marco. "Speak What." *JCT.* 1989; 50: 83-85. Illus.: Photo. B&W. 1. Lang.: Fre.
Canada: Montreal, PQ. 1989. Histories-sources. ■Playwright Marco Micone explains his social intentions writing as an immigrant in Quebec. In poetic form.

2814 Monmart, Francis. "Réflexions d'un cordonnier ému." (Reflections of a Deeply Moved Cobbler.) *JCT.* 1996; 78: 22-25. Biblio. Illus.: Photo. B&W. 3. Lang.: Fre.
Canada: Montreal, PQ. 1981-1996. Histories-sources. ■Francis Monmart's love of the theatre and the creative process behind his play *L'Ange et le Corbeau (The Angel and the Crow)*.

2815 Moss, Jane. "Québécois Theatre: Michel Tremblay and Marie Laberge." *ThR.* 1996; 21(3): 196-207. Notes. Illus.: Photo. B&W. 3. Lang.: Eng.
Canada: Quebec, PQ. 1964-1992. Historical studies. ■Careers of playwright Michel Tremblay and playwright and actress Marie Laberge, with evaluation of their contribution to the development of a distinctive Quebecois theatre.

2816 Mouawad, Wajdi. "Acte de foi." (Act of Faith.) *JCT.* 1996; 78: 18-21. Notes. Biblio. Illus.: Photo. B&W. 3. Lang.: Fre.
Canada: Montreal, PQ. 1991-1996. Histories-sources. ■Playwright Wajdi Mouawad gives ninety-two reasons for refusing to explain his writing process.

CLASSED ENTRIES

DRAMA: —Plays/librettos/scripts

2817 Nyman, Ed. "Out with the Queers: Moral Triage and George F. Walker's *Theatre of the Film Noir*." *ADS*. 1996 Oct.; 29: 57-65. Notes. Lang.: Eng.
Canada. 1981. Critical studies. ■Reconfiguration of male and female identities and desecration of the film noir sensibility in his *Theatre of the Film Noir*.

2818 Ouaknine, Serge. "Ces textes que je n'ai pas écrits?" (Those Texts I Didn't Write?)*JCT*. 1989; 53: 83-90. Illus.: Pntg. Photo. B&W. 3. Lang.: Fre.
Canada: Montreal, PQ. 1971-1989. Histories-sources. ■Director Serge Ouaknine on decline of textual authority and preponderance of collages and borrowed texts, in general and in his own work.

2819 Parenteau-Lebeuf, Dominick. "Graffitis." *JCT*. 1996; 80: 128-133. Illus.: Photo. B&W. 4. Lang.: Fre.
Canada: Montreal, PQ. 1996. Histories-sources. ■Plays as walls and lines as graffiti, in autobiographical poem of playwright Dominick Parenteau-Lebeuf.

2820 Parenteau-Lebeuf, Dominick. "Histoire d'une jeune femme piquée d'héroïnes et de son double qui écrit pour elle." (The Story of a Young Woman Fascinated by Heroines and Her Double Who Writes for Her.) *JCT*. 1992; 66: 19-22. Illus.: Photo. B&W. 3. Lang.: Fre.
Canada. 1975-1993. Critical studies. ■Playwriting student Dominick Parenteau-Lebeuf gives new generation's perspective on Quebecois feminist playwriting of the 1970s.

2821 Pavlovic, Diane; Corneau, Guy; Krysinski, Wladimir; Mavrikakis, Catherine; Camerlain, Lorraine, ed. "Théâtre et littérature à la Veillée." (Theatre and Literature at la Veillée.) *JCT*. 1989; 53: 57-60. Illus.: Photo. B&W. 6. Lang.: Fre.
Canada: Montreal, PQ. 1981-1990. Historical studies. ■Reprints of critical commentaries on stage adaptations of novels by Montreal's Groupe de la Veillée. Theatrography of la Veillée adaptations.

2822 Pedneault, Hélène. "Du soliloque au théâtre." (On Soliloquy in Theatre.) *JCT*. 1991; 61: 36-38. Illus.: Photo. B&W. 2. Lang.: Fre.
Canada: Montreal, PQ. 1988-1991. Histories-sources. ■The place of the soliloquy in Hélène Pedneault's development as a writer.

2823 Poissant, Claude. "Adapter: le choix de trahir." (To Adapt: The Choice to Betray.) *JCT*. 1990; 56: 69-72. Illus.: Photo. B&W. 2. Lang.: Fre.
Canada: Montreal, PQ. France: Limoges. 1988. Histories-sources. ■Director Claude Poissant gives opinions on adaptions, both in writing and in staging, based on experiences principally at series of workshops 'Pièces en transit (Plays in Transit)' at Limoges' Festival international des francophonies.

2824 Purkhardt, Brigitte. "Le mythe du cygne et sa représentation." (The Swan Myth and Its Representation.) *JCT*. 1996; 81: 117-125. Notes. Illus.: Dwg. Photo. B&W. 6. Lang.: Fre.
Canada: Montreal, PQ. USA. 1990-1996. Critical studies. ■Symbolism of swan in Elizabeth Egloff's *The Swan* and in subsequent 1996 staging of Louise Bombardier's translation *Le Cygne* at Montreal's Espace GO.

2825 Rabillard, Sheila. "The Seductions of Theatricality: Mamet, Tremblay and Political Drama." *ADS*. 1996 Oct.; 29: 33-42. Notes. Illus.: Photo. B&W. 1. Lang.: Eng.
Canada. USA. 1972-1996. Critical studies. ■Theatricality as political or social commentary, as reflected in David Mamet's *American Buffalo* and Michel Tremblay's *Les Belles-soeurs*.

2826 Richard, Hélène. "Le Théâtre gai québécois: Conjoncture sociale et sentiment de filiation." (Quebecois Gay Theatre: Social Situation and Sense of Connection.) *JCT*. 1990; 54: 15-23. Notes. Illus.: Photo. B&W. 4. Lang.: Fre.
Canada: Montreal, PQ. 1990. Critical studies. ■Social and psychological reasons for pertinence of Quebec gay dramaturgy, such as Michel-Marc Bouchard's *Les Feluettes (Lilies)*, René-Daniel Dubois' *Being at home with Claude* and Hervé Dupuis' *Fugues pour un cheval et un piano (Fugues for Horse and Piano)*.

2827 Ringuet, Louise. "La peste enjambe les frontières ('Comme chez les Grecs' de Steven Berkoff, U.Q.A.M. 1989)." (The Plague Straddles Borders: *Greek* by Steven Berkoff, Université du Québec à Montréal 1989.) *JCT*. 1990; 56: 97-101. Notes. Illus.: Photo. B&W. 2. Lang.: Fre.
Canada: Montreal, PQ. 1989-1990. Histories-sources. ■Problems of language and cultural references in Ringuet's translation/adaptation of Steven Berkoff's *Greek* to a version set in Montreal. Line-by-line comparisons of original text to French translation by Geoffrey Dyson and Antoinette Monod and Ringuet's adaptation.

2828 Ronfard, Alice. "Traduire: Un Travail sur l'irrespect ('la Tempête', T.E.F. 1988)." (Translating: A Work in Disrespect—*The Tempest*, Théâtre Expérimental des Femmes 1988.) *JCT*. 1990; 56: 85-91. Illus.: Photo. B&W. 2. Lang.: Fre.
Canada: Montreal, PQ. 1988. Histories-sources. ■Ronfard describes process of translating *The Tempest* with Marie Cardinal for 1988 Théâtre Expérimental des Femmes production, directed by Ronfard. Includes parallel reprints of selections from Cardinal/Ronfard translation and translation by Christine and René Lalou.

2829 Ronfard, Jean-Pierre. "Une Culture biodégradable." (A Biodegradable Culture.) *JCT*. 1989; 50: 216-218. Illus.: Pntg. Photo. B&W. 2. Lang.: Fre.
Canada: Montreal, PQ. 1989. Histories-sources. ■Importance of 'pillaging' classic literature and myths in theatre of Jean-Pierre Ronfard.

2830 Ronfard, Jean-Pierre. "Le Triomphe du mélo." (The Triumph of Melodrama.) *JCT*. 1989; 51: 32-34. Lang.: Fre.
Canada. 1989. Critical studies. ■Melodramatic cliches in themes and language of contemporary Quebecois drama.

2831 Roux, Jean-Louis. "Traduire Shakespeare: Ravissement et cauchemar ('Hamlet', T.N.M. 1990)." (Translating Shakespeare: Wonder and Nightmare—*Hamlet*, Théâtre du Nouveau Monde 1990.) *JCT*. 1990; 56: 82-84. Illus.: Photo. B&W. 1. Lang.: Fre.
Canada: Montreal, PQ. England. 1990. Histories-sources. ■Shakespeare's use of iambic pentameter and Jean-Louis Roux's attempt to render it into French. Includes parallel reprints of an extract of Roux's translation and translation by Yves Bonnefoy.

2832 Shantz, Valerie. "Colonising Yvette Nolan: The Making of an Aboriginal Playwright." *ADS*. 1996 Oct.; 29: 99-111. Notes. Lang.: Eng.
Canada. 1990-1996. Critical studies. ■Introduction to Manitoban feminist playwright Nolan's *Child*, with a few career details touched upon including her first play *Blade*.

2833 Simon, Sherry. "'Corilan' 'la Tempête': Shakespeare/Garneau." (*Coriolanus, The Tempest*: Shakespeare/Garneau.) *JCT*. 1990; 56: 120-122. Illus.: Photo. B&W. 2. Lang.: Fre.
Canada. 1989. Critical studies. ■Transformations in Michel Garneau's translations of Shakespeare's *Coriolanus* and *The Tempest*.

2834 Spickler, Robert. "Le trop-plein et le vide." (Excess and Void.) *JCT*. 1996; 78: 104-115. Notes. Illus.: Photo. B&W. 9. Lang.: Fre.
Canada. 1943-1996. Critical studies. ■Place and identity in Quebec drama, with reference to Gélinas, Dubé, Loranger, Michel Tremblay, and Germain, and speculation on the future.

2835 Tremblay, Larry. "Miss Beaths et les autres." (Miss Beaths and the Rest.) *JCT*. 1996; 78: 44-67. Illus.: Photo. B&W. 8. Lang.: Fre.
Canada: Montreal, PQ. 1981-1996. Histories-sources. ■Larry Tremblay explains his approach to playwriting in the form of a script uniting characters from his plays *Leçon d'anatomie*, *Le Déclic du destin* and *The Dragonfly of Chicoutimi*.

2836 Vaïs, Michel; Fréchette, Carole. "Questions sur un malaise." (Questions about an Uneasiness.) *JCT*. 1990; 54: 9-14. Notes. Illus.: Photo. B&W. 2. Lang.: Fre.
Canada. 1990. Critical studies. ■Gay dramaturgy in Quebec considered from point of view of critics, theatre artists, and society at large.

2837 Vaïs, Michel. "Des Personnages en suspens." (Characters in Suspension.) *JCT*. 1991; 58: 112-114. Illus.: Photo. B&W. 2. Lang.: Fre.

DRAMA: —Plays/librettos/scripts

Canada: Montreal, PQ. 1990. Critical studies. ■Describes characters in Michel Tremblay's *La Maison suspendue (The House Among the Stars)* as being 'suspended' or not fully developed.

2838 Vaïs, Michel. "Dominic Champagne: Les copains, d'abord." (Dominic Champagne: Friends First.) *JCT*. 1991; 61: 17-18. Notes. Illus.: Photo. B&W. 1. Lang.: Fre.
Canada: Montreal, PQ. 1988-1991. Critical studies. ■Friendship and adversity as defining traits in Dominic Champagne's plays: *Import-Export, La Répétition (The Rehearsal)* and *La Cité interdite (The Forbidden City)*.

2839 Vigeant, Louise. "Du Réalisme à l'expressionnisme: La Dramaturgie québécoise récente à grands traits." (From Realism to Expressionism: Broad Lines of Quebecois Drama.) *JCT*. 1991; 58: 7-16. Notes. Illus.: Photo. B&W. 8. Lang.: Fre.
Canada: Montreal, PQ. 1980-1990. Historical studies. ■Thematic and formal trends in Quebecois drama of the 1980s.

2840 Vigeant, Louise; Camerlain, Lorraine, ed. "'Madame Louis 14': Solo périlleux: Entretien avec Lorraine Pintal." ('Madame Louis 14': Perilous Solo: Interview with Lorraine Pintal.) *JCT*. 1989; 53: 73-82. Illus.: Maps. Photo. B&W. 5. Lang.: Fre.
Canada: Montreal, PQ. 1980-1989. Histories-sources. ■Actor/director Lorraine Pintal describes adapting Françoise Chandernagor's *l'Allée du roi (The King's Path)* as solo performance *Madame Louis 14*.

2841 Vigeant, Louise. "Le Ducharme de Faucher: Des romans au spectacle: Un Même univers." (Faucher's Ducharme: From Novels to Shows: A Single World.) *JCT*. 1989; 51: 35-43. Notes. Illus.: Photo. B&W. 7. Lang.: Fre.
Canada: Montreal, PQ. 1988. Historical studies. ■Techniques used by director Martin Faucher in adapting Réjean Ducharme's novel *A quelle heure on meurt? (What Time Do We Die?)* for Productions Branle-Bas staging, 1988.

2842 Vigeant, Louise. "Des Lettres écrites, jouées, filmées: Entretien avec Denys Arcand." (Letters Written, Performed, Filmed: Interview with Denys Arcand.) *JCT*. 1991; 60: 93-99. Notes. Illus.: Photo. B&W. 2. Lang.: Fre.
Canada: Montreal, PQ. 1990. Histories-sources. ■Denys Arcand describes his first theatre experience directing his adaptation *Les Lettres de la religieuse portugaise (Letters from the Portuguese Nun)* based on *Lettres portugaises*, attributed to Guilleragues.

2843 Vigeant, Louise. "Clin d'oeil et coup de chapeau: 'La Répétition' de Dominic Champagne." (A Wink and a Tip of the Hat: *The Rehearsal* by Dominic Champagne.) *JCT*. 1992; 64: 95-101. Notes. Illus.: Dwg. Photo. B&W. 4. Lang.: Fre.
Canada: Montreal, PQ. France. Ireland. 1953-1990. Critical studies. ■Intertextuality and citations of Samuel Beckett's *En attendant Godot* in the characters and structure of Dominic Champagne's *La Répétition*.

2844 Vigeant, Louise. "Hélène Pedneault: Histoire de haine et d'amour." (Hélène Pedneault: A Story of Hate and Love.) *JCT*. 1991; 61: 34-35. Notes. Illus.: Photo. B&W. 1. Lang.: Fre.
Canada: Montreal, PQ. 1988. Critical studies. ■Themes of love, hate and search for self in Hélène Pedneault's *La Déposition*.

2845 Vigeant, Louise. "L'implacable intelligence: Des 'Liaisons dangereuses' à 'Quartett'." (Implacable Intelligence: From 'Les Liaisons dangereuses' to 'Quartett'.) *JCT*. 1996; 79: 8-14. Notes. Illus.: Photo. B&W. 3. Lang.: Fre.
Canada: Montreal, PQ. Germany. 1980-1996. Critical studies. ■Analysis of Heiner Müller's *Quartett (Quartet)*, an adaptation of the novel *Les Liaisons Dangereuses* by Laclos, with reference to a production by Brigitte Haentjens at Espace GO.

2846 Vincent, Julie. "Écrire pour fabriquer de la réalité." (Writing to Create Reality.) *JCT*. 1991; 61: 45-46. Illus.: Photo. B&W. 1. Lang.: Fre.
Canada: Montreal, PQ. 1988-1991. Histories-sources. ■Actor Julie Vincent explains attraction playwriting holds for her.

2847 Walker, Craig Stewart. "James Reaney's *The Donnellys* and the Recovery of 'the Ceremonies of Innocence'." *ADS*. 1996 Oct.; 29: 187-196. Notes. Illus.: Photo. B&W. 1. Lang.: Eng.

Canada. 1973-1975. Critical studies. ■Examines James Reaney's *The Donnellys* trilogy, which includes *Sticks and Stones*, *The St. Nicholas Hotel* and *Handcuffs*, considered by many to be the most important Canadian dramatic accomplishment to date.

2848 Wallace, Robert; Godin, Jean Cléo, transl. "Homo création: Pour une poétique du théâtre gai." (Homo Creation: Towards a Poetics of Gay Theatre.) *JCT*. 1990; 54: 24-42. Notes. Illus.: Photo. B&W. 9. Lang.: Fre.
Canada. USA. 1960-1990. Critical studies. ■Impact of playwrights' homosexuality on writing and interpretation of plays.

2849 Wasserman, Jerry. "Confessions of a Vile Canonist: Anthologising Canadian Drama." *ADS*. 1996 Oct.; 29: 197-205. Notes. Lang.: Eng.
Canada. 1996. Critical studies. ■Argues for the importance of anthologizing Canadian drama.

2850 Wilson, Ann. "Border Crossing: The Technology of Identity in *Fronteras Americanas*." *ADS*. 1996 Oct.; 29: 7-15. Notes. Lang.: Eng.
Canada. 1993. Critical studies. ■Examination of Argentine emigre playwright Guillermo Verdecchia's *Fronteras Americanas* as well as his own performance of it, highlighting Anglo-Saxon perception of Latinos as one group instead of the diversity of the many cultures.

2851 Bravo-Elizondo, Pedro. "Una entrevista con Inés Margarita Stranger (Chile) y sus personajes femeninos." (An Interview with Inés Margarita Stranger (Chile) and Her Female Characters.) *LATR*. 1996 Fall; 30(1): 89-95. Lang.: Spa.
Chile. 1990-1993. Histories-sources. ■Interview with Chilean playwright Inés Margarita Stranger. She discusses her plays, female characters, and feminist approach to playwriting.

2852 Díaz-Ortiz, Oscar A. "Marco Antonio de la Parra: *Matatangos* y la resemantización de su causa ausente." (Marco Antonio de la Parra's *Kill Tangos* and the Re-Semanticization of its Absent Cause.) *LATR*. 1996 Spr; 29(2): 43-60. Biblio. Lang.: Spa.
Chile. 1979. Critical studies. ■Analysis of de la Parra's *Matatangos (Kill Tangos)* with attention to gender, sexuality, and unconscious political narrative.

2853 Gregory, Stephen. "Ariel Dorfman and Harold Pinter: Politics of the Periphery and Theatre of the Metropolis." *CompD*. 1996 Fall; 30(3): 325-345. Notes. Lang.: Eng.
Chile. UK-England. 1957-1996. Critical studies. ■Personal, professional and political relationship between Harold Pinter and Chilean playwright Ariel Dorfman.

2854 Lei, Daphne Pi-Wei. "Wang Zhaojun on the Border: Gender and Intercultural Conflicts in Premodern Chinese Drama." *ATJ*. 1996 Fall; 13(2): 229-237. Notes. Biblio. Lang.: Eng.
China. 1700-1900. Historical studies. ■Analysis of dramas about the heroine Wang Zhaojun.

2855 Yan, Haiping. "Male Ideology and Female Identity: Images of Women in Four Modern Chinese Historical Plays." 251-274 in Keyssar, Helene, ed. *Feminist Theatre and Theory*. London: Macmillan; 1996. 288 pp. (New Casebooks.) Notes. Index. Lang.: Eng.
China. 1923-1995. Critical studies. ■Analysis of *Wang Zhao-jun* by Cao Yu, *The Song of the Wind* by Chen Baichen, and *Cai Wen-ji* and *Zhuo Wen-jun* by Guo Moruo. Argues that these male authors achieve self-criticism through positive portrayals of women.

2856 Salter, Denis. "Survival in China—Open Secrets: Mou Sen's *File Zero*." *CTR*. 1996 Fall; 88: 44-48. Notes. Illus.: Photo. B&W. 8. Lang.: Eng.
China, People's Republic of: Beijing. 1993-1996. Critical studies. ■Mou Sen, artistic director of Xi Ju Che Jian, and his production *Ling Dang An (File 0)*, with emphasis on its political content.

2857 Kuhnheim, Jill S. "Set in Haiti: The Construction of Race in *Historia de una bala de plata*." *LATR*. 1996 Spr; 29(2): 95-110. Notes. Biblio. Lang.: Eng.
Colombia. 1979. Critical studies. ■Haiti and its slave rebellion as reflected in Enrique Buenaventura's play *Historia de una bala de plata (Story of a Silver Bullet)*. Relations between race and colonialism and the use of Brechtian techniques.

CLASSED ENTRIES

DRAMA: —Plays/librettos/scripts

2858 Rizk, Beatriz J. "La Asociación de Colombianistas y el teatro en Colombia." (The Association for Colombian Studies and Colombian Theatre.) *LATR*. 1996 Spr; 29(2): 165-172. Notes. Biblio. Lang.: Spa.
Colombia: Bogotá. 1995. Critical studies. ■Annual conference of the North-American Association for Colombian Studies covering dramaturgy, directors as critics, women in theatre, and featuring performances by Colombian theatre groups such as La Candelaria and Mapa Teatro.

2859 Yewah, Emmanuel. "Congolese Playwrights as Cultural Revisionists." *ThR*. 1996; 21(3): 219-228. Notes. Lang.: Eng.
Congo. 1960-1996. Critical studies. ■Analysis of strategies adopted by Congolese playwrights since 1960 in plays dealing with issues of colonialism, post-colonial dictatorships and cultural identities.

2860 Dubravka, Vrgoč. "Croatian Theatre During the Recent War (1990-1995)." *SEEP*. 1996 Win; 16(1): 21-27. Illus.: Photo. 3. Lang.: Eng.
Croatia. 1990-1995. Historical studies. ■The problem of identity in the new dramaturgy of Croatia as seen in the plays of Ivan Vidić, Asja Srnec-Todorović, Pavo Marinković, Lada Kaštelan, and Mislav Brumec.

2861 del Campo, Alicia. "A manera de prólogo: preguntas a Víctor Varela." (By Way of a Prologue: Interview with Víctor Varela.) *Gestos*. 1996 Nov.; 11(22): 123-132. Notes. Illus.: Photo. B&W. 1. Lang.: Spa.
Cuba. 1996. Histories-sources. ■Interview with playwright Víctor Varela, conducted through the mail, regarding the breadth of his work.

2862 Kent, Assunta Bartolomucci. *Maria Irene Fornes and Her Critics*. Westport, CT/London: Greenwood; 1996. 230 pp. (Contributions in Drama and Theatre Studies 70.) Index. Notes. Biblio. Append. Illus.: Photo. B&W. 1. Lang.: Eng.
Cuba. USA. 1930-1990. Biographies. ■Critical biography of playwright Maria Irene Fornes, with analysis of her career and works, as well as their critical, theoretical, and historical contexts.

2863 Martínez Tabares, Vivian; Winks, Christopher, transl. "*Manteca*: Catharsis and Absurdity." *TDR*. 1996 Spr; 40(1): 44-48. [Originally published as 'Manteca: Catarsis y Absurdo' in *Conjunto* Oct. 1993-Mar. 1994: 98-101.] Lang.: Eng.
Cuba. 1993. Critical studies. ■Analysis of structure, plot, characters and themes of Alberto Pedro Torriente's play.

2864 Morales, Ed. "Havana Affair." *AmTh*. 1996 Dec.; 13(10): 6-7. Illus.: Photo. B&W. 1. Lang.: Eng.
Cuba: Havana. USA: New York, NY. 1993-1996. Critical studies. ■Performance of *Vagos Rumores (Vague Rumors)* by Teatro Hubert de Blanck, directed and written by Abelardo Estorino.

2865 Muguercia, Magaly; Winks, Christopher, transl. "The Gift Of Precariousness: Alberto Pedro Torriente's *Manteca*." *TDR*. 1996 Spr; 40(1): 49-60. Notes. Biblio. Lang.: Eng.
Cuba. 1993. Critical studies. ■Analysis of the play in the context of Cuban politics and society.

2866 Seda, Laurietz. "Coloquio Internacional en Cuba." (International Colloquium in Cuba.) *LATR*. 1996 Fall; 30(1): 133-134. Lang.: Spa.
Cuba. 1996. Historical studies. ■An international conference on new frontiers in theatrical texts held in Cuba, concentrating on new plays by controversial postmodern playwrights, women playwrights, and new dramaturgical approaches.

2867 Seda, Laurietz. "Ruptura y Caos en *Timeball* de Joel Cano." (Rupture and Chaos in Joel Cano's *Timeball*.) *LATR*. 1996 Fall; 30(1): 5-20. Notes. Biblio. Illus.: Sketches. 2. Lang.: Spa.
Cuba. 1990. Critical studies. ■How the play uses chaos theory to criticize any system based on rules.

2868 Hořínek, Zdeněk. "Man within the System and Outside it/ L'homme dans le système et hors du système." *DTh*. 1996; 12: 14-24. Illus.: Photo. B&W. 14. Lang.: Eng, Fre.
Czech Republic. 1963-1996. Critical studies. ■Analysis of characters in the plays of Václav Havel.

2869 Vojtková, Milena. "Karel Steigerwald (Pokus o analýzu autorského stylu)." (Karel Steigerwald: An Attempt at an Analysis of the Author's Style.) *DivR*. 1996; 7(4): 31-40. Lang.: Cze.
Czech Republic. 1979-1994. Critical studies. ■Analysis of plays by Steigerwald.

2870 Albertová, Helena; Vaïs, Michel, transl. "Qui est Václav Havel." (Who Is Václav Havel.) *JCT*. 1993; 66: 96-100. Notes. Illus.: Photo. B&W. 1. Lang.: Fre.
Czechoslovakia. 1936-1993. Biographical studies. ■Václav Havel's life as dissident, nationalist and playwright.

2871 Burian, Jarka M. "Václav Havel's Notable Encounters in His Early Theatrical Career." *SEEP*. 1996 Spr; 16(2): 13-29. Notes. Illus.: Photo. 7. Lang.: Eng.
Czechoslovakia. 1956-1965. Historical studies. ■Václav Havel's early experiences with other important Czech theatre figures during the first post-Stalinist decade of loosening controls and creative energies. Figures include actor/director Otomar Krejča and director Alfred Radok of the National Theatre, designer Josef Svoboda and critic Jan Grossman of Theatre on the Balustrade.

2872 Müller, Péter, P. *Central European Playwrights within and without the Absurd: Václav Havel, Sławomir Mrożek and István Örkény*. Pécs: JPTE TK Kiadói Iroda; 1996. 114 pp. Append. Biblio. Index. Lang.: Eng.
Czechoslovakia. Hungary. Poland. 1950-1980. Critical studies. ■Study in the dramatic oeuvres of the most significant playwrights of post-war Central Europe representing the grotesque, ironic and absurdist point of view in their plays. (Appendix: Central European drama on the British stage 1964-1992).

2873 Andreasen, John. "Community Plays—A Search for Identity." *ThR*. 1996; 21(1): 72-78. Notes. Illus.: Photo. B&W. 3. Lang.: Eng.
Denmark. 1970-1996. Historical studies. ■Overview of Danish amateur community play tradition since 1970, with discussion of the 1983 *Aarhus Play*, Hansens's *Teglvaerksspillet (The Brickworks' Play)*, and Iversen's Viking trilogy.

2874 Sadgrove, P.C. *The Egyptian Theatre in the Nineteenth Century (1799-1882)*. Berkshire: Centre for Middle Eastern and Islamic Studies, Univ of Durham/Ithaca P; 1996. 214 pp. Pref. Biblio. Index. Notes. Append. Lang.: Eng.
Egypt. 1799-1882. Histories-specific. ■Includes discussion of Arabic drama both traditional and experimental, Syrian Arab theatre, and European theatre, primarily Italian and French, in Cairo and Alexandria.

2875 Astington, John H. "Three Shakespearean Prints." *SQ*. 1996 Sum; 47(2): 178-189. Notes. Illus.: Dwg. B&W. 4. Lang.: Eng.
England. 1529-1614. Critical studies. ■Influence of three contemporary emblems of the day on the work of Shakespeare, exemplified in *Love's Labour's Lost, Romeo and Juliet* and *Hamlet*.

2876 Baldo, Jonathan. "Wars of Memory in *Henry V*." *SQ*. 1996 Sum; 47(2): 132-159. Notes. Lang.: Eng.
England. 1590-1600. Critical studies. ■Battle over memory of an important event, such as war, and its importance to the formation and strength of a sovereign national state in Shakespeare's *Henry V*.

2877 Bancroft, Vicky. "Mrs. Midnight, Mrs. Mandrake, and the Serious Presentation of the 'Drag Role' in The Twin-Rivals." *Restor*. 1996 Sum; 11(1): 22-31. Notes. Lang.: Eng.
England. 1697-1702. Critical studies. ■Character of Mrs. Midnight, changed from Mandrake, in George Farquhar's *The Twin Rivals*. Significance of character's occupation as a midwife, serious elements of the drag role.

2878 Barish, Jonas. "Remembering and Forgetting in Shakespeare." 214-221 in Parker, R.B., ed.; Zitner, S.P., ed. *Elizabethan Theater: Essays in Honor of S. Schoenbaum*. Newark, DE/London: Univ of Delaware P; 1996. 324 pp. Notes. Lang.: Eng.
England. 1608. Critical studies. ■Argues that the title character's memory lapse in *Coriolanus* indicates repression, and that the moral dimension of Shakespeare's plays is conveyed through the themes of memory and forgetting.

DRAMA: —Plays/librettos/scripts

2879 Bawcutt, N.W., ed. *The Control and Censorship of Caroline Drama: The Records of Sir Henry Herbert, Master of the Revels 1623-73.* Oxford: Clarendon; 1996. 350 pp. Notes. Append. Index. Lang.: Eng.

England. 1623-1673. Critical studies. ■Examination of the private papers of Sir Henry Herbert, London's Master of the Revels. Includes several additional items in the collection, such as office-books, play licenses, records from the Lord Chamberlain's office, records of lawsuits, and provincial records.

2880 Bécsy, Tamás. "Triptichon a *Téli regé-ről.*" (Triptych on Shakespeare's *The Winter's Tale.*) *SzSz.* 1996; 30/31: 69-86. Notes. Lang.: Hun.

England. 1610. Critical studies. ■Analysis of Shakespeare's drama from three aspects: genre, the 'happy ending' and love, on art as an ars poetica.

2881 Berger, Harry, Jr. "Impertinent Trifling: Desdemona's Handkerchief." *SQ.* 1996 Fall; 47(3): 235-250. Notes. Lang.: Eng.

England. 1603. Critical studies. ■The actual size of Desdemona's handkerchief and its symbolism in Shakespeare's *Othello.*

2882 Betcher, Gloria J. "Place Names and Political Patronage in the Cornish *Ordinalia.*" *RORD.* 1996; 35(1): 111-131. Notes. Lang.: Eng.

England: Cornwall. 1300-1419. Historical studies. ■Focuses on the dramatic context in which Cornish place names appear, considering audience interpretation of the names and the relation to the patronage of powerful men, in the *Ordinalia.*

2883 Bly, Mary. "Bawdy Puns and Lustful Virgins: The Legacy of Juliet's Desire in Comedies of the Early 1600s." *ShS.* 1996; 49: 97-109. Notes. Lang.: Eng.

England. 1594-1607. Critical studies. ■Influence of *Romeo and Juliet* upon later comedies, such as Henry Porter's *The Two Angry Women of Abington,* Thomas Dekker's *Blurt, Master Constable* and *The Puritan* (anon).

2884 Bobker, Danielle. "Behn: Auth-WHORE OR WrITer? Authorship and Identity in The Rover." *Restor.* 1996 Sum; 11(1): 32-39. Notes. Biblio. Lang.: Eng.

England. 1677. Critical studies. ■Playwright Aphra Behn's author-persona in connection to female characters in her play *The Rover.* Relies heavily on Janet Todd's introduction to *The Sign of Angellica* and an essay by Catherine Gallagher.

2885 Boling, Ronald J. "Stage Images of Cressida's Betrayal." *ET.* 1996; 14(2): 147-158. Notes. Biblio. Lang.: Eng.

England. 1601. Critical studies. ■Analysis of the stage imagery which exemplifies the role of Cressida in Shakespeare's *Troilus and Cressida.*

2886 Brannen, Anne L. "Parish Play Accounts in Context: Interpreting the Bassingbourn St. George Play." *RORD.* 1996; 35(1): 55-72. Notes. Lang.: Eng.

England: Bassingbourn. 1498-1518. Histories-reconstruction. ■Reconstructs the significance of the no longer extant St. George play to the community through contemporary accounts and analogous texts from the continent.

2887 Candido, Joseph. "'Women & fooles break off your conference': Pope's Degradations and the Form of *King John.*" 90-109 in Velz, John W., ed. *Shakespeare's English Histories: A Quest for Form and Genre.* Binghamton, NY: Medieval and Renaissance Texts and Studies; 1996. 267 pp. Index. Notes. Biblio. Lang.: Eng.

England. 1590-1725. Critical studies. ■Analysis of Alexander Pope's eighteenth-century critical edition of Shakespeare's *King John.* Argues that examination of critical biases of Pope's reworking of the play provides insights into its form.

2888 Cervantes, Xavier. "Playwright Henry Fielding: Enemy or Connoisseur of Italian Opera?" *THSt.* 1996 June; 16: 157-172. Notes. Lang.: Eng.

England. 1705-1735. Historical studies. ■A new assessment of Fielding's attitude towards the Italian opera 'invasion' of London, as reflected in his plays of the period. Plays examined include *The Intriguing Chambermaid* (1734), *The Tragedy of Tragedies* (1733), and *The Author's Farce* (1730).

2889 Counsell, Colin. "Traversing the Unknown: Spatiality and the Gaze in Pre and Post Renaissance Theatre." *JDTC.* 1996 Fall ; 11(1): 19-34. Notes. Illus.: Sketches. 1. Lang.: Eng.

England. 1425-1700. Critical studies. ■Spatial codes and the conceptual frames of English Renaissance theatre. Concentrates on the anonymous *The Castle of Perseverance* (1425) and Congreve's *The Way of the World* (1700).

2890 Cox, John D. "Devils and Vices in English Non-Cycle Plays: Sacrament and Social Body." *CompD.* 1996 Sum; 30(2): 188-219. Notes. Lang.: Eng.

England. 1300-1500. Critical studies. ■Parallels in the treatment of devils and vice in liturgical representation and English mystery plays such as *The Castle of Perseverance,* the *N-town Plays, Wisdom,* the Digby *Mary Magdalen* and *St. Paul,* Henry Medwall's *Nature,* and John Skelton's *Magnyfycence.*

2891 Dash, Irene G. "Single-Sex Retreats in Two Early Modern Dramas: *Love's Labor's Lost* and *The Convent of Pleasure.*" *SQ.* 1996 Win; 47(4): 387-395. Notes. Illus.: Photo. B&W. 2. Lang.: Eng.

England. 1590-1668. Critical studies. ■Female independence in a society hostile to such notions, and a comparison of Margaret Cavendish's *The Convent of Pleasure* and Shakespeare's *Love's Labour's Lost.*

2892 Davis, Lloyd. "'Death-Marked Love': Desire and Presence in *Romeo and Juliet.*" *ShS.* 1996; 49: 57-67. Notes. Lang.: Eng.

England. 1592-1594. Critical studies. ■The meanings of desire in Shakespeare's play.

2893 Davis, Philip. *Sudden Shakespeare: The Shaping of Shakespeare's Creative Thought.* London: Athlone; 1996. 259 pp. Index. Notes. Biblio. Lang.: Eng.

England. 1590-1613. Critical studies. ■Shakespeare's joining of time and space is said to result in a 'sudden mental performance' by the reader or spectator as Shakespeare follows the dramatic form of creative thinking.

2894 Deise, Kyle R. "Detecting the Victorian Stage: The Ticket-of-Leave Man and the New Stage Detective." *TheatreS.* 1996; 41 : 5-12. Notes. Lang.: Eng.

England: London. 1863. Critical studies. ■Tracing the first appearance of a crime-solving detective in a play to the character Hawkshaw in Tom Taylor's *The Ticket-of-Leave Man,* and its impact upon the Victorian stage.

2895 Desai, R.W. "'What means Sicilia? He something seems unsettled': Sicily, Russia and Bohemia in *The Winter's Tale.*" *CompD.* 1996 Fall; 30(3): 311-324. Notes. Lang.: Eng.

England. 1547-1619. Historical studies. ■Views on race and ethnic differentiation during Shakespeare's time, and their reflection in *The Winter's Tale.*

2896 DiGangi, Mario. "Queering the Shakespearean Family." *SQ.* 1996 Fall; 47(3): 269-290. Notes. Lang.: Eng.

England. 1580-1620. Critical studies. ■Homosexuality and its relation to family, sex and marriage in the Shakespearean era, and its reflection in plays such as *As You Like It* and John Mason's *The Turk.*

2897 Donaldson, Ian. "Jonson and the Tother Youth." 111-129 in Parker, R.B., ed.; Zitner, S.P., ed. *Elizabethan Theater: Essays in Honor of S. Schoenbaum.* Newark, DE/London: Univ of Delaware P; 1996. 324 pp. Notes. Lang.: Eng.

England. 1609. Critical studies. ■Author argues that the 'tother youth' referred to in Jonson's *Epicoene, or The Silent Woman* is Shakespeare, and that the comparison between the two has encouraged reconstruction of their lives, in turn affecting the reading and interpretation of their works.

2898 Dutton, Richard. "The Birth of the Author." 71-92 in Parker, R.B., ed.; Zitner, S.P., ed. *Elizabethan Theater: Essays in Honor of S. Schoenbaum.* Newark, DE/London: Univ of Delaware P; 1996. 324 pp. Notes. Lang.: Eng.

England. 1590-1640. Critical studies. ■Argues that Shakespeare's apparent lack of interest in publishing his plays reflects the conditions of licensing and performance: since the license to perform a play was specific to a single company, violations of performance rights were rare.

DRAMA: —Plays/librettos/scripts

2899 Elam, Keir. "As They Did in the Golden World: Romantic Rapture and Semantic Rupture in *As You Like It*." 163-176 in Hart, Jonathan, ed. *Reading the Renaissance: Culture, Poetics, and Drama*. New York, NY/London: Garland; 1996. 290 pp. (Garland Studies in the Renaissance.) Notes. Biblio. Index. Lang.: Eng.
England. 1598-1601. Critical studies. ■Shakespeare's treatment of the literary styles of romance and pastoral in creating symbols of a lost world in *As You Like It*, as seen in the play's literary allusions.

2900 Elam, Keir. "The Fertile Eunuch: *Twelfth Night*, Early Modern Intercourse, and the Fruits of Castration." *SQ*. 1996 Spr ; 47(1): 1-36. Notes. Tables. Lang.: Eng.
England. 1600-1614. Critical studies. ■The representation of social and sexual contact in Shakespeare's *Twelfth Night* in the context of early modern codes of behavior.

2901 Emck, Katy. "Female Transvestism and Male Self-Fashioning in *As You Like It* and *La vida es sueño*." 75-88 in Hart, Jonathan, ed. *Reading the Renaissance: Culture, Poetics, and Drama*. New York, NY/London: Garland; 1996. 290 pp. (Garland Studies in the Renaissance.) Notes. Biblio. Index. Lang.: Eng.
England. Spain. 1599-1635. Critical studies. ■Female transvestism, a symbol of female insurgency, power and deceptiveness, as male social identities under construction. In Shakespeare's *As You Like It* and Calderón's *La vida es sueño*, the transvestism of the female characters is central to the development of the male subjects, and thus reflects anxiety about self-fashioned male identity.

2902 Farley-Hills, David. "The 'Bad' Quarto of *Romeo and Juliet*." *ShS*. 1996; 49: 27-44. Notes. Lang.: Eng.
England. 1597. Textual studies. ■Argues that the first 'bad' quarto of *Romeo and Juliet* is a shortened version of Shakespeare's original prepared for provincial performance.

2903 Finkelpearl, Philip J. "Two Distincts, Division None: Shakespeare and Fletcher's *The Two Noble Kinsmen* of 1613." 184-199 in Parker, R.B., ed.; Zitner, S.P., ed. *Elizabethan Theater: Essays in Honor of S. Schoenbaum*. Newark, DE/London: Univ of Delaware P; 1996. 324 pp. Notes. Lang.: Eng.
England. 1613. Critical studies. ■Links Fletcher and Shakespeare's *The Two Noble Kinsmen* to the marriage of Princess Elizabeth and other topical matters of the year.

2904 Foakes, R.A. "King Lear: Monarch or Senior Citizen?" 271-289 in Parker, R.B., ed.; Zitner, S.P., ed. *Elizabethan Theater: Essays in Honor of S. Schoenbaum*. Newark, DE/London: Univ of Delaware P; 1996. 324 pp. Notes. Illus.: Photo. 3. Lang.: Eng.
England. 1605-1996. Critical studies. ■The body of the king in Shakespeare's *King Lear*, with references to the representation of the title character in production.

2905 Foakes, R.A. "French Leave, or Lear and the King of France." *ShS*. 1996; 49: 217-223. Notes. Lang.: Eng.
England. 1600. Textual studies. ■Analysis of Kent's speech in the quarto and folio editions of *King Lear* II.iv.

2906 Forker, Charles R. "Marlowe's *Edward II* and its Shakespearean Relatives: the Emergence of a Genre." 55-90 in Velz, John W., ed. *Shakespeare's English Histories: A Quest for Form and Genre*. Binghamton, NY: Medieval and Renaissance Texts and Studies; 1996. 267 pp. Index. Notes. Biblio. Lang.: Eng.
England. 1590-1592. Critical studies. ■Shakespeare's influence on Christopher Marlowe, as seen in Marlowe's *Edward II*. Compares Marlowe's play and Shakespeare's *Richard II*, *King John*, *Henry VI*, and *Romeo and Juliet*.

2907 Fowler, Patsy S. "Rejecting the Status Quo: The Attempts of Mary Pix & Susanna Centlivre to Reform Society's Patriarchal Attitudes." *Restor*. 1996 Win; 11(2): 49-59. Biblio. Lang.: Eng.
England. 1700-1800. Critical studies. ■Attempts of Centlivre's *The Basset Table* and *The Busybody* and Pix's *The Beau Defeated* to reform society's attitudes toward women and attitudes concerning accepted behavior toward and the control of women.

2908 Gibbons, Brian. "Jonson and Reflection." 50-67 in Parker, R.B., ed.; Zitner, S.P., ed. *Elizabethan Theater: Essays in Honor of S. Schoenbaum*. Newark, DE/London: Univ of Delaware P; 1996. 324 pp. Notes. Lang.: Eng.
England. 1600-1616. Critical studies. ■The authorial presence in the plays and poetry of Ben Jonson.

2909 Gul'čenko, V. "Samopoznanie Lira, ili Vkus soli." (Lear's Self-Discovery, or the Taste of Salt.) *TeatZ*. 1996; 9: 14-16. Lang.: Rus.
England. 1605. Critical studies. ■Analysis of Shakespeare's *King Lear*.

2910 Happé, Peter. "Staging Folly in the Early Sixteenth Century: Heywood, Lindsay, and Others." 73-111 in Davidson, Clifford, ed. *Fools and Folly*. Kalamazoo, MI: Medieval Institute Publications; 1996. 176 pp. (Early Drama, Art, and Music Monograph Series 22.) Notes. Lang.: Eng.
England. 1047-1548. Historical studies. ■The depiction of the fool in early Tudor theatre with focus on the plays of John Heywood (particularly *Witty and Witless*) and Sir David Lindsay (*Ane Satire of the Thrie Estaitis*). Explores reasons for rise in popularity of the fool character.

2911 Hawkins, Barrie. "The Country Wife: Metaphor Manifest." *Restor*. 1996 Sum; 11(1): 40-63. Notes. Lang.: Eng.
England. 1675. Critical studies. ■Relationship of metaphoric density to its action and visual groupings in the treatment of women by men, and metaphoric use of stage and theatre space itself in Wycherley's play.

2912 Holmer, Joan Ozark. "The Poetics of Paradox: Shakespeare's versus Zeffirelli's Cultures of Violence." *ShS*. 1996; 49: 163-179. Notes. Lang.: Eng.
England. Italy. 1594-1968. Critical studies. ■Contrasts Shakespeare's improvement on his source for *Romeo and Juliet* by complicating and heightening Romeo's role with Zeffirelli's oversimplication of the tragic texture of his source in the film version.

2913 Hopkins, Lisa. "'Dead Shepherd, now I find thy saw of might': *Tamburlaine* and Pastoral." *RORD*. 1996; 35(1): 1-16. Notes. Lang.: Eng.
England. 1587-1588. Critical studies. ■Analyzes the title character in Marlowe's play, from the angle of his original profession of shepherd, the connection with the Elizabethan pastoral in the context of social mobility, religion, warfare and colonialism.

2914 Hughes, Derek. *English Drama, 1660-1700*. Oxford: Clarendon; 1996. 503 pp. Index. Notes. Biblio. Pref. Lang.: Eng.
England. 1660-1700. Critical studies. ■A study of all surviving plays which were professionally premiered; analyzes individual texts, examines the social, political, and philosophical influence which shaped the dramatists' work, as well as tracing recurring and interacting motifs.

2915 Hunt, Maurice. "Predestination and the Heresy of Merit in *Othello*." *CompD*. 1996 Fall; 30(3): 346-376. Notes. Lang.: Eng.
England. 1604. Critical studies. ■Calvinism and the doctrine of predestination in Shakespeare's *Othello*.

2916 Hunter, G.K. "Notes on the Genre of the History Play." 229-240 in Velz, John W., ed. *Shakespeare's English Histories: A Quest for Form and Genre*. Binghamton, NY: Medieval and Renaissance Texts and Studies; 1996. 267 pp. Index. Notes. Biblio. Lang.: Eng.
England. 1588-1613. Critical studies. ■The interaction of event and meaning in Shakespeare's history plays, examining truth and fiction in history.

2917 Hunter, George K. "Theatrical Politics and Shakespeare's Comedies, 1590-1600." 241-251 in Parker, R.B., ed.; Zitner, S.P., ed. *Elizabethan Theater: Essays in Honor of S. Schoenbaum*. Newark, DE/London: Univ of Delaware P; 1996. 324 pp. Notes. Lang.: Eng.
England. 1590-1600. Critical studies. ■The effects of theatrical politics in London on the kinds of plays that were performed in particular theatres.

DRAMA: —Plays/librettos/scripts

2918   Kaufman, Anthony. "'The Perils of Florinda': Aphra Behn, Rape, and the Subversion of Libertinism in *The Rover, Part II*." *Restor.* 1996 Win; 11(2): 1-21. Notes. Lang.: Eng.
England. 1660-1700. Critical studies. ■Female empowerment and feminism in the plays of Behn. Use of rape to define male characters and male/female relationships.

2919   Kiefer, Frederick. *Writing on the Renaissance Stage: Written Words, Printed Pages, Metaphoric Books.* Newark, DE/ London: Univ of Delaware P/Associated Univ Presses; 1996. 377 pp. Index. Notes. Biblio. Append. Illus.: Handbill. Photo. Sketches. B&W. 17. Lang.: Eng.
England. 1450-1600. Critical studies. ■The role of writing and printing in Renaissance culture, the English stage as a site of contention over reading and writing, the proliferation on stage of metaphors involving writing or printing and the cultural assumptions underlying such metaphoric language. Also examines specific forms of reading and writing used by playwrights for theatrical effect.

2920   Kiernan, Pauline. *Shakespeare's Theory of Drama.* Cambridge: Cambridge UP; 1996. 218 pp. Biblio. Index. Notes. Lang.: Eng.
England. 1589-1613. Critical studies. ■Argues that Shakespeare developed a new theory of drama for his dramaturgy, repudiating literary and historiographical representations of truth. He relied upon his version of dramatic illusion, or 'fictitious truth,' to challenge the conventions of his day.

2921   Kinney, Arthur F. "Speculating Shakespeare, 1605-1606." 252-270 in Parker, R.B., ed.; Zitner, S.P., ed. *Elizabethan Theater: Essays in Honor of S. Schoenbaum.* Newark, DE/ London: Univ of Delaware P; 1996. 324 pp. Notes. Lang.: Eng.
England. 1605-1606. Critical studies. ■Analysis of *Macbeth* for clues about Shakespeare's activities and concerns during a little-known period of his life.

2922   Knowles, Ronald. "Carnival and Death in *Romeo and Juliet*: A Bakhtinian Reading." *ShS.* 1996; 49: 69-85. Notes. Illus.: Dwg. B&W. 6. Lang.: Eng.
England. 1594. Critical studies. ■Argues, through the theories of Mikhail Bakhtin, that Shakespeare's inheritance of carnival or festival culture finds expression in *Romeo and Juliet*.

2923   Korda, Natasha. "Household Kates: Domesticating Commodities in *The Taming of the Shrew*." *SQ.* 1996 Sum; 47(2): 109-131 . Notes. Lang.: Eng.
England. 1590-1604. Critical studies. ■Maintains that *The Taming of the Shrew* recasts the traditional medieval shrew tale by reflecting the new market-value system of Shakespeare's time, and its infiltration and reorganization of the household economy of the early modern period.

2924   Kurland, Stuart M. "'The care ... of subjects' good': *Pericles*, James I, and the Neglect of Good Government." *CompD.* 1996 Sum; 30(2): 220-224. Notes. Lang.: Eng.
England. 1606. Historical studies. ■Examines the similarities between Shakespeare's title character of Pericles and the English monarch at the time of the play's production, James I.

2925   Lamb, Susan. "The Popular Theatre of Samuel Foote and British National Identity." *CompD.* 1996 Sum; 30(2): 245-265. Notes. Lang.: Eng.
England. 1752-1800. Historical studies. ■Re-evaluation of the work of playwright Samuel Foote, through the lens of the jingoistic era in which they were written, citing *The Minor*, *The Nabob*, *A Trip to Calais*, and the *The Capuchin* as good examples of the fare required by Foote's contemporaries.

2926   Leggatt, Alexander. "The Presence of the Playwright, 1580-1640." 130-146 in Parker, R.B., ed.; Zitner, S.P., ed. *Elizabethan Theater: Essays in Honor of S. Schoenbaum.* Newark, DE/London: Univ of Delaware P; 1996. 324 pp. Notes. Lang.: Eng.
England. 1580-1640. Critical studies. ■The shift in attitudes toward playwrights that occurred around 1600, when printed plays prominently displayed authors' names, compared to the earlier emphasis on the performances.

2927   Leggatt, Alexander. "The Death of John Talbot." 11-30 in Velz, John W., ed. *Shakespeare's English Histories: A Quest for Form and Genre.* Binghamton, NY: Medieval and Renaissance Texts and Studies; 1996. 267 pp. Index. Notes. Biblio. Lang.: Eng.
England. 1589-1594. Critical studies. ■Argues that Shakespeare's *Henry VI, Part 1* is an intersection of two forms, tragedy and history, each one shaping and affecting the other. The death of Talbot is examined as an archetype of this relationship.

2928   Levenson, Jill L. "Shakespeare's *Romeo and Juliet*: The Places of Invention." *ShS.* 1996; 49: 45-55. Notes. Lang.: Eng.
England. 1559-1594. Critical studies. ■Rhetorical strategies in the play, compared to its sources.

2929   Levin, Harry. "Two Tents on Bosworth Field: *Richard III* V.iii, iv, v." 145-162 in Hart, Jonathan, ed. *Reading the Renaissance: Culture, Poetics, and Drama.* New York, NY/ London: Garland; 1996. 290 pp. (Garland Studies in the Renaissance.) Notes. Biblio. Index. Lang.: Eng.
England. 1591-1594. Critical studies. ■The convergence of the heroic epic, narrative and historical styles/genres in Shakespeare's *Richard III*.

2930   Liebler, Naomi Conn. "King of the Hill: Ritual and Play in the Shaping of *3 Henry VI*." 31-54 in Velz, John W., ed. *Shakespeare's English Histories: A Quest for Form and Genre.* Binghamton, NY: Medieval and Renaissance Texts and Studies; 1996. 267 pp. Index. Notes. Biblio. Lang.: Eng.
England. 1589-1594. Critical studies. ■Government and war as games in Shakespeare's *Henry VI, Part 3*. Suggests Shakespeare was experimenting with ways of shaping his historical drama by drawing upon familiar forms of rituals and games.

2931   Lindley, Arthur. *Hyperion and the Hobbyhorse: Studies in Carnivalesque Subversion.* Newark, DL/London: Univ of Delaware P/Associated Univ Presses; 1996. 197 pp. Index. Notes. Biblio. Pref. Illus.: Photo. 1. Lang.: Eng.
England. 1300-1607. Critical studies. ■Argues that carnivalesque elements in literary and dramatic texts reveal English assumptions about carnality and the multiplicity of the self. Examines 'The Wife of Bath's Prologue and Tale', *Sir Gawain and the Green Knight*, the plays of Christopher Marlowe, *Hamlet* and the genre of revenge tragedy, and Shakespeare's *Antony and Cleopatra*.

2932   Mann, David D.; Mann, Susan Garland. *Women Playwrights in England, Ireland, and Scotland, 1660-1823.* Bloomington/ Indianapolis, IN: Indiana UP; 1996. 417 pp. Pref. Append. Lang.: Eng.
England. Ireland. Scotland. 1660-1823. Bibliographical studies. ■Listing of all English drama texts by women. Includes plot synopses, playwright biographies, and production histories.

2933   Milowicki, Edward; Wilson, Robert Rawdon. "*Troilus and Cressida*: Voices in the Darkness of Troy." 129-144 in Hart, Jonathan, ed. *Reading the Renaissance: Culture, Poetics, and Drama.* New York, NY/London: Garland; 1996. 290 pp. (Garland Studies in the Renaissance.) Notes. Biblio. Index. Lang.: Eng.
England. 1601-1602. Critical studies. ■The genres of the heroic epic and romance in Shakespeare's *Troilus and Cressida*. Author argues that the play explores and redefines both love and honor, in the process dissecting the rhetoric of epic and of romance.

2934   Morrison, Paul. "Noble Deeds and the Secret Singularity: *Hamlet* and *Phèdre*." 179-202 in Hart, Jonathan, ed. *Reading the Renaissance: Culture, Poetics, and Drama.* New York, NY/London: Garland; 1996. 290 pp. (Garland Studies in the Renaissance.) Notes. Biblio. Index. Lang.: Eng.
England. France. 1599-1677. Critical studies. ■Compares Shakespeare's *Hamlet* to Racine's *Phèdre* through analysis of individual texts with the history of literary forms, and the history of the social construction of subjectivity.

2935   Moulton, Ian Frederick. "'A Monster Great Deformed': The Unruly Masculinity of *Richard III*." *SQ.* 1996 Fall; 47(3): 251-268. Notes. Lang.: Eng.

DRAMA: —Plays/librettos/scripts

England. 1598. Critical studies. ■Independent masculine aggression as a tragedy, in which an unruly, singular protagonist is inevitably destroyed by larger social forces in *Richard III*.

2936   Mowat, Barbara A. "Constructing the Author." 93-110 in Parker, R.B., ed.; Zitner, S.P., ed. *Elizabethan Theater: Essays in Honor of S. Schoenbaum*. Newark, DE/London: Univ of Delaware P; 1996. 324 pp. Notes. Lang.: Eng.
England. 1400-1710. Critical studies. ■The parameters of the author category as it was constructed in England during the early modern period, which saw a change from the medieval *auctor* to the modern proprietary author.

2937   Mukherji, Subha. "'Lawful Deed': Consummation, Custom, and Law in *All's Well That Ends Well*." *ShS*. 1996; 49: 181-200. Notes. Lang.: Eng.
England. 1587-1600. Critical studies. ■Background on legal aspects of the play with respect to the marriage of Bertram and Helena: legal and church definitions of the consummation of a marriage.

2938   Naumann, Anna C. "Der Witz der Rosalind." (Rosalind's Wit.) *SJW*. 1996; 132: 93-102. Append. Lang.: Ger.
England. 1599. Critical studies. ■The language of Rosalind in Shakespeare's *As You Like It*, especially in relation to the language of Shakespearean fools. Argues that Rosalind uses the provocative power of ridicule to establish her individuality within the game of social roles.

2939   Neill, Michael. "The World Beyond: Shakespeare and the Tropes of Translation." 290-308 in Parker, R.B., ed.; Zitner, S.P., ed. *Elizabethan Theater: Essays in Honor of S. Schoenbaum*. Newark, DE/London: Univ of Delaware P; 1996. 324 pp. Notes. Lang.: Eng.
England. 1595-1611. Critical studies. ■The New World and the Other in *Henry V*, *A Midsummer Night's Dream*, and *The Tempest*.

2940   Newlyn, Evelyn S. "The *Middle Cornish Interlude*: Genre and Tradition." *CompD*. 1996 Sum; 30(2): 266-281. Notes. Lang.: Eng.
England. 1340-1578. Histories-reconstruction. ■Attempts to date and interpret the earliest extant piece of literature in the Middle Cornish language, the *Middle Cornish Interlude*, using other contemporary work such as *The Ordinalia* as a measuring stick.

2941   Nordlund, Anna. "Som ni vill ha det och vad du vill!" (As You Like It and What You Will!)*Tningen*. 1996; 20(76-77): 15-19. Illus.: Photo. B&W. Lang.: Swe.
England. 1599. Critical studies. ■An analysis of Shakespeare's *Twelfth Night* and *As You Like It*, and their portrayal of free and latent passions.

2942   Patterson, Annabel. "'All Is True': Negotiating the Past in *Henry VIII*." 147-166 in Parker, R.B., ed.; Zitner, S.P., ed. *Elizabethan Theater: Essays in Honor of S. Schoenbaum*. Newark, DE/London: Univ of Delaware P; 1996. 324 pp. Notes. Lang.: Eng.
England. 1611. Critical studies. ■The relationship between the Holinshed *Chronicles* and Shakespeare's *Henry VIII*. Argues that Shakespeare was playing with the nature of historical truth in the play, in order to prove the difficulty of historical objectivity.

2943   Pechter, Edward. "'Have you not read of some such thing?': Sex and Sexual Stories in *Othello*." *ShS*. 1996; 49: 201-216 . Notes. Lang.: Eng.
England. 1600. Critical studies. ■Sex and the effect of innuendo on Othello, Iago, and Desdemona in Shakespeare's tragedy.

2944   Perdue, Danielle. "The Male Masochist in Restoration Drama." *Restor*. 1996 Sum; 11(1): 10-21. Notes. Biblio. Lang.: Eng.
England. 1550. Critical studies. ■Exploration of male masochist figures in Thomas Shadwell's *The Virtuoso*, and Thomas Otway's *The Orphan* and *Venice Preserv'd*. How authors used cultural mechanisms of oppression to further the agenda of empowered males.

2945   Pugliatti, Paola. *Shakespeare the Historian*. New York, NY: St. Martin's; 1996. 265 pp. Index. Notes. Lang.: Eng.
England. 1592-1613. Critical studies. ■Argues that Shakespeare's idea of history is crucial to his styles of writing, particularly his use of perspectivism, or polyphony.

2946   Ray, J. Karen. "'The Yielding Moment': A Woman's View of Amorous Females and Fallen Women." *Restor*. 1996 Win; 11(2): 39-48. Biblio. Lang.: Eng.
England: London. 1660-1750. Critical studies. ■Female dramatists in Restoration theatre and their sympathetic portrayals of fallen women and female sexuality. *The Rover* by Aphra Behn, *Love At A Loss* by Mary Pix, and *The Spanish Wives* by Catharine Trotter.

2947   Reid, Robert L. "Humoral Psychology in Shakespeare's *Henriad*." *CompD*. 1996-97 Win; 30(4): 471-502. Notes. Illus.: Sketches. B&W. 4. Lang.: Eng.
England. 1590-1613. Critical studies. ■Shakespeare's use of Galen's psychology of humors.

2948   Richmond, Hugh M. "The Resurrection of an Expired Form: *Henry VIII* as Sequel to *Richard III*." 205-228 in Velz, John W., ed. *Shakespeare's English Histories: A Quest for Form and Genre*. Binghamton, NY: Medieval and Renaissance Texts and Studies; 1996. 267 pp. Index. Notes. Biblio. Illus.: TA. 1. Lang.: Eng.
England. 1613. Critical studies. ■Argues that Shakespeare attempted, in his last complete play, to fuse the more gracious mood of his previous romances with the harsh facts of English political history, as portrayed in his earlier histories.

2949   Robinson, Marsha S. "Mythoi of Brotherhood: Generic Emplotment in *Henry V*." 143-170 in Velz, John W., ed. *Shakespeare's English Histories: A Quest for Form and Genre*. Binghamton, NY: Medieval and Renaissance Texts and Studies; 1996. 267 pp. Index. Notes. Biblio. Lang.: Eng.
England. 1599. Critical studies. ■Shakespeare's repeated allusions to brotherhood, fraternal strife and reconciliation not only articulate historical symbols but shape the historical genre as well. Examines *Richard II* and *Henry V* using White's theories of historical narratives.

2950   Ross, A. Elizabeth. "Hand-me-Down-Heroics: Shakespeare's Retrospective of Popular Elizabethan Heroical Drama in *Henry V*." 171-203 in Velz, John W., ed. *Shakespeare's English Histories: A Quest for Form and Genre*. Binghamton, NY: Medieval and Renaissance Texts and Studies; 1996. 267 pp. Index. Notes. Biblio. Lang.: Eng.
England. 1599. Critical studies. ■The relation between Marlowe's *Tamburlaine* and Shakespeare's *Henry V*. Argues that Shakespeare manipulates the traditional heroic genre of *Tamburlaine* in order to question the cultural significance of the heroic genre and its traditions.

2951   Rumrich, John P. "Shakespeare's Walking Plays: Image and Form in *1 and 2 Henry IV*." 111-141 in Velz, John W., ed. *Shakespeare's English Histories: A Quest for Form and Genre*. Binghamton, NY: Medieval and Renaissance Texts and Studies; 1996. 267 pp. Index. Notes. Biblio. Lang.: Eng.
England. 1596-1597. Critical studies. ■Images of constant movement or walking as a primary element of meaning and form in Shakespeare's *Henry IV* plays and as a metaphoric link between *Richard II* and *Henry V*.

2952   Schulz, David. "Redressing Oscar: Performance and the Trials of Oscar Wilde." *TDR*. 1996 Sum; 40(2): 37-59. Notes. Biblio. Illus.: Photo. Sketches. B&W. 3. Lang.: Eng.
England. 1890-1996. Historical studies. ■Playwright Wilde's criminal trial for indecency, his function as a role model for homosexuals and how he defined a homosexual social identity. Includes transcript of exchange between Wilde and counsel Edward Carson debating impropriety in his work.

2953   Snyder, Susan. "'The Norwegians Are Coming!' Shakespearean Misleadings." 200-213 in Parker, R.B., ed.; Zitner, S.P., ed. *Elizabethan Theater: Essays in Honor of S. Schoenbaum*. Newark, DE/London: Univ of Delaware P; 1996. 324 pp. Notes. Lang.: Eng.
England. 1600-1604. Critical studies. ■Structural analysis of two battles in Shakespeare's *Othello* and *Hamlet* reveals deeper dramaturgical strategies used to address contemporary concerns.

2954   Snyder, Susan. "Ideology and the Feud in *Romeo and Juliet*." *ShS*. 1996; 49: 87-96. Notes. Lang.: Eng.
England. 1594. Critical studies. ■The Capulet-Montague feud as emblematic of ideological structures in Shakespeare's play.

CLASSED ENTRIES

DRAMA: —Plays/librettos/scripts

2955 Spencer, Janet M. "Princes, Pirates, and Pigs: Criminalizing Wars of Conquest in *Henry V*." *SQ*. 1996 Sum; 47(2): 160-177. Notes. Lang.: Eng.
England. 1419-1609. Critical studies. ■Conqueror as figure of legal excess, and efforts to legitimize war's necessary criminality in Shakespeare's *Henry V*.

2956 Štejn, A.L. *Uil'jam Šekspir: Žizn' i tvorčestvo*. (William Shakespeare: Life and Work.) Moscow: Institut inostrannich jaz'kov; 1996. 268 pp. Lang.: Rus.
England: London. 1564-1616. Critical studies. ■Analysis of Shakespeare's works, with biographical information pertinent to the 'Shakespeare question'.

2957 Stirm, Jan. "'For solace a twinne-like sister': Teaching Themes of Sisterhood in *As You Like It* and Beyond." *SQ*. 1996 Win; 47(4): 374-386. Notes. Illus.: Photo. B&W. 1. Lang.: Eng.
England. 1590. Critical studies. ■Feminist analysis of sisterhood in Shakespeare's play, with description of a classroom approach to the text.

2958 Twycross, Meg. "The York Mercers' 'Lewent Bride' and the Hanseatic Trade." *MET*. 1995; 17: 96-119. Notes. [Cover title: *Using Early Drama Records*.] Lang.: Eng.
England: York. 1433. Historical studies. ■Considers the meaning of 'Lewent Bride' which appears in the York Mercers' indenture of stage properties and costumes for their play *Doomsday* in connection with hangings for the pageant wagon, and adds evidence from contemporary commercial records.

2959 Urkowitz, Steven. "Two Versions of *Romeo and Juliet* 2.6 and *Merry Wives of Windsor* 5.5.215-45: An Invitation to the Pleasures of Textual/Sexual Di(Per)versity." 222-238 in Parker, R.B., ed.; Zitner, S.P., ed. *Elizabethan Theater: Essays in Honor of S. Schoenbaum*. Newark, DE/London: Univ of Delaware P; 1996. 324 pp. Notes. Lang.: Eng.
England. 1595-1600. Critical studies. ■Analysis of early versions of *Romeo and Juliet* and *The Merry Wives of Windsor* that suggest new ways of imaging gender in Shakespeare.

2960 Videbaek, Bente A. *The Stage Clown in Shakespeare's Theatre*. Westport, CT/London: Greenwood; 1996. 215 pp. (Contributions in Drama and Theatre Studies 69.) Append. Biblio. Index. Lang.: Eng.
England. 1590-1613. Critical studies. ■The expanded role and importance of clown characters in Shakespeare's plays. Argues that Shakespeare used the clown to guide the viewer through the play and also as a forum for improvisation for talented actors.

2961 Wells, Stanley. "The Challenge of *Romeo and Juliet*." *ShS*. 1996; 49: 1-14. Notes. Lang.: Eng.
England. 1597-1996. Critical studies. ■Concentrates on the text of *Romeo and Juliet*, and some of the challenges faced by directors who try to translate the text into terms of modern theatre.

2962 Whigham, Frank. *Seizures of the Will in Early Modern English Drama*. Cambridge: Cambridge UP; 1996. 299 pp. (Cambridge Studies in Renaissance Literature and Culture 11.) Index. Notes. Biblio. Lang.: Eng.
England. 1580-1613. Critical studies. ■Gesture and moments of self-construction in early modern English drama, including Kyd's *The Spanish Tragedy*, Webster's *The Duchess of Malfi*, and the anonymous *Arden of Faversham*.

2963 Yachnin, Paul. "Magical Properties: Vision, Possession, and Wonder in *Othello*." *TJ*. 1996 May; 48(2): 197-208. Notes. Biblio. Lang.: Eng.
England. 1604. Critical studies. ■New historicist evaluation of operations of wonder in Shakespeare's *Othello*, specifically the fetishizing of theatrical properties such as the fabric of the handkerchief and the body of the boy actor who played Desdemona.

2964 Zupančič, Mirko. *Teoretske osnove meščanske drame v 18. stoletju: Lillo, Diderot, Lessing*. (The Theoretical Bases of Bourgeois Drama in the 18th Century: Lillo, Diderot, Lessing.) Ljubljana: Študenska organizacija Univerze; 1996. 50 pp. Lang.: Slo.
England. France. Germany. 1731-1779. Critical studies. ■European bourgeois drama and the break with classical tradition.

2965 *Épochalnje rubeži v istorii iskusstva Zapada*. (Periods in the History of Western Art.) Moscow: Gosudarstvennyj institut iskusstvoznanija; 1996. 192 pp. Lang.: Rus.
Europe. 1800-1996. Critical studies. ■Collection of articles on the dramatic genre, with attention to realism, symbolism, and English theatre.

2966 De Gregorio, Maria Paola. "Sofonisba: dalla storia al mito, dalla vita al teatro." (Sophonisba: From History to Myth, from Life to Theatre.) *Ariel*. 1996; 11(1): 43-71. Notes. Lang.: Ita.
Europe. 1515-1805. Critical studies. ■Plays about the historical figure Sophonisba, including *Sofonisba* by Trissino (1515), *The Wonder of Women or the Tragedy of Sophonisba* by Marston (1606), and *Sophonisbe* by Mairet (1634).

2967 Egri, Péter. *Modern Games with Renaissance Forms: from Leonardo and Shakespeare to Warhol and Stoppard*. Budapest: Akadémiai; 1996. 114 pp. (Studies in Modern Philology 12.) Notes. Lang.: Eng.
Europe. 1800-1990. Critical studies. ■Nineteenth- and twentieth-century approaches to Shakespearean characters and themes in plays of Gogol, Beckett, Dürrenmatt, and especially Tom Stoppard.

2968 Harbeck, James. "The Quaintness—and Usefulness—of the Old Chinese Traditions: *The Yellow Jacket* and *Lady Precious Stream*." *ATJ*. 1996 Fall; 13(2): 238-247. Notes. Biblio. Illus.: Photo. B&W. 1. Lang.: Eng.
Europe. China, People's Republic of. 1912-1996. Critical studies. ■Examination of *The Yellow Jacket* by George C. Hazelton and J. Harry Benrimo, and *Lady Precious Stream* by S.I. Hsiung, and their roles in introducing Chinese theatre concepts to Western audiences.

2969 Hart, Jonathan. "The Ends of Renaissance Comedy." 91-127 in Hart, Jonathan, ed. *Reading the Renaissance: Culture, Poetics, and Drama*. New York, NY/London: Garland; 1996. 290 pp. (Garland Studies in the Renaissance.) Notes. Biblio. Index. Lang.: Eng.
Europe. 1590-1664. Critical studies. ■The structural development of comedy in the European Renaissance, with emphasis on their ambivalent endings, and generic mixing. Discusses Shakespeare's *As You Like It* and *Twelfth Night*, Guarini's *Il Pastor Fido*, and Calderón's *No hay burlas con el amor* (romantic pastoral comedies) and Jonson's *Volpone* and Molière's *Tartuffe* (satirical comedies).

2970 Kempinski, Tom. "Playwrights Are Madder Than Poets." *PlPl*. 1996 Oct.; 508: 16-18. Lang.: Eng.
Europe. 1996. Critical studies. ■Essay on psychological development and manifestation in playwrights, as seen in the topic of 'madness'.

2971 Klaić, Dragan. "Playwriting in Europe: A View from the Other Side." *ThM*. 1996; 26(3): 95-98. Lang.: Eng.
Europe. 1996. Critical studies. ■Difficulties faced by contemporary European playwrights, particularly those who do not write in English, French, or German, in getting their work produced.

2972 Mész, Lászlóné. *Színterek. Drámaértelmezések*. (Stages: Interpretations of Drama.) Budapest: Korona; 1995. 454 pp. Notes. Lang.: Hun.
Europe. 1590-1980. Critical studies. ■Analysis of twenty-five plays of world drama from Shakespeare to Péter Nádas.

2973 Ramanathan, Geetha. *Sexual Politics and the Male Playwright: The Portrayal of Women in Ten Contemporary Plays*. Jefferson, NC/London: McFarland; 1996. 190 pp. Index. Biblio. Pref. Lang.: Eng.
Europe. 1836-1978. Critical studies. ■Marginality, sexuality, ideology and form in Büchner's *Woyzeck* (1836), Strindberg's *Fadren (The Father)* (1887), Pirandello's *Enrico IV (Henry IV)* (1922), Weiss's *Marat/Sade* (1964), Brecht's *Gute Mensch von Sezuan (The Good Person of Szechwan)* (1939), Dürrenmatt's *Die Physiker (The Physicists)* (1962), Hare's *Plenty* (1978), Barnes's *The Ruling Class* (1968), Pinter's *The Hothouse* (1958), and Orton's *What the Butler Saw* (1969).

2974 Szondi, Péter. *Saggio sul tragico*. (Essay on the Tragic.) Turin: Einaudi; 1996. 163 pp. (Piccola Biblioteca Einaudi 631.) Pref. Index. Lang.: Ita.
Europe. Critical studies. ■Italian translation of *Versuch über das Tragische* (Insel Verlag, 1964). Analysis of the essence of tragic, not only as a literary genre but in the context of Aristotelian poetics.

DRAMA: —Plays/librettos/scripts

2975 Tansi, Sony Labou. "L'Ouragan du corps." (The Hurricane of the Body.) *JCT*. 1989; 50: 89-90. Illus.: Photo. B&W. 1. Lang.: Fre.
Europe. Congo. 1989. Histories-sources. ■Relative values of soul and body in Europe and Africa and consequences on Sony Labou Tansi's plays.

2976 Wells, Stanley. "Shakespeare's Lives: 1991-1994." 15-29 in Parker, R.B., ed.; Zitner, S.P., ed. *Elizabethan Theater: Essays in Honor of S. Schoenbaum*. Newark, DE/London: Univ of Delaware P; 1996. 324 pp. Notes. Lang.: Eng.
Europe. USA. 1991-1994. Critical studies. ■Summarizes and discusses some of the more conspicuous contributions to Shakespearean biography from brief notes to learned journals. Concerned mainly with original documents and fresh contributions to Shakespeare's life and works.

2977 Zumthor, Paul. "Corps et mémoire." (Body and Memory.) *JCT*. 1989; 50: 219-221. Illus.: Photo. B&W. 1. Lang.: Fre.
Europe. USA. 1300-1989. Historical studies. ■Emergence of literary hegemony in Renaissance dramatic form, and rediscovery of spontaneous corporal expression in contemporary theatre.

2978 Artioli, Umberto. "Artaud e la semplificazione antropologica." (Artaud and Anthropological Simplification.) *IlCast*. 1996; 9(27): 5-29. Notes. Lang.: Ita.
France. 1922-1947. Critical studies. ■Artaud's confrontation with the problem of evil and his search for salvation in the rituals of ancient cultures.

2979 Becker, Peter von. "Die Kunst des Erfolgs." (The Art of Success.) *THeute*. 1996; 3: 40-44. Illus.: Photo. B&W. 11. Lang.: Ger.
France: Paris. 1996. Biographical studies. ■Portrait of writer Yasmina Reza and her frequently-performed plays.

2980 Brown, Erella. "The Lake of Seduction: Body Acting and Voice in Hélène Cixous's *Portait de Dora*." *MD*. 1996 Win; 39(4): 626-649. Notes. Lang.: Eng.
France. 1900-1995. Critical studies. ■Feminist theatre elements in Cixous's play, based on Freud's *Dora: An Analysis of a Case of Hysteria*.

2981 Burgoyne, Lynda. "Eugène Durif: poète dramatique." (Eugène Durif: Dramatic Poet.) *JCT*. 1992; 65: 101-103. Notes. Biblio. Illus.: Photo. B&W. 1. Lang.: Fre.
France. 1981-1992. Critical studies. ■Importance of poetic language in plays of Eugène Durif such as *l'Arbre de Jonas*, *Petit Bois* and *Les Petites Heures*.

2982 Collingwood, Sharon. *Market Pledge and Gender Bargain: Commercial Relations in French Farce, 1450-1550*. New York, NY: Peter Lang; 1996. 209 pp. (Studies in the Humanities, 23.) Index. Notes. Biblio. Append. Lang.: Eng.
France. 1450-1550. Critical studies. ■The importance of commerce and monetary systems, commercial language, mercantile customs and practices, and gender bargain-making practices, such as betrothal customs and ritual actions and gifts for seduction, as reflected in French farces of the period.

2983 De Nuccio, Fernando. "Tutti si sono creati il proprio Artaud." (Everyone Has Created His Own Artaud.) *TeatroS*. 1996; 11 (18): 25-34. Lang.: Ita.
France. 1915-1951. Histories-sources. ■Interview with Rolande Ibrahim-Delguste, widow of poet Jacques Prevel, a close friend of Antonin Artaud.

2984 Des Landes, Claude. "États généraux de la création théâtrale francophone: France 1989." (The Estates General of Francophone Theatrical Creation: France 1989.) *JCT*. 1990; 54: 151-153. Lang.: Fre.
France: Limoges. 1989. Historical studies. ■Conference focused on function of playwriting in French-speaking countries, rights of playwright, and French-African tensions.

2985 Djušen, I. "Vspominaja Ionesko." (Ionesco Remembers.) *AT*. 1996; 3: 169-174. Lang.: Rus.
France. 1909-1994. Critical studies. ■Problematics of the absurdist comedies of Eugène Ionesco.

2986 Godin, Diane. "'C'est toute l'humanité'." ('It's All of Humanity'.) *JCT*. 1992; 66: 27-28. Notes. Illus.: Photo. B&W. 1. Lang.: Fre.
France. 1952. Critical studies. ■Universality and gender specificity as exemplified in Samuel Beckett's *En attendant Godot*.

2987 Godin, Diane. "Albert Camus: le bonheur et la révolte." (Albert Camus: Happiness and Revolt.) *JCT*. 1992; 65: 104-107. Notes. Illus.: Photo. B&W. 2. Lang.: Fre.
France. 1938-1948. Critical studies. ■Absurdism as tragedy of the everyday and the absence of truth in Camus' *Le Malentendu* and *Caligula*.

2988 Hébert, Lorraine. "'Pièces en transit': Limoges, octobre 1988." (Plays in Transit: Limoges, October 1988.) *JCT*. 1990; 56: 62-68. Notes. Illus.: Poster. Photo. B&W. 3. Lang.: Fre.
France: Limoges. Belgium. Canada. Mali. 1988. Historical studies. ■Series of workshops 'Pièces in transit (Plays in transit)', at the Festival international des francophonies at Limoges, allowed plays from France, Belgium, Mali and Quebec to be subjected to presentation in contexts differing from their origins.

2989 Hellot, Marie-Christiane. "La corde et le pantalon: Du clown comme Héros tragique." (The Rope and the Pants: Of the Clown as a Tragic Hero.) *JCT*. 1992; 64: 57-64. Notes. Illus.: Photo. B&W. 4. Lang.: Fre.
France. 1952. Critical studies. ■Influence of clowning in the characters of Samuel Beckett's *En attendant Godot*.

2990 Jákfalvi, Magdolna. "'Éljen Übü apó!'—Századik születésnapi kicsiny biográfia." ('Vivat Ubu roi!'—A Brief Biography on the 100th Birthday.) *Sz*. 1996; 29(12): 43-48. Illus.: Photo. Design. B&W. 5. Lang.: Hun.
France. 1896. Historical studies. ■Essay on the genesis of Alfred Jarry's trail-blazing *Ubu Roi (King Ubu)* on the occasion of its centenary.

2991 Kiernander, Adrian. "Paris Was Always Burning: (Drag) Queens and Kings in Two Early Plays by Alexandre Dumas père." *ET*. 1996; 14(2): 159-173. Notes. Biblio. Illus.: Photo. Dwg. B&W. 4. Lang.: Eng.
France. 1820-1829. Critical studies. ■Explores the theme of transvestism and homosexuality, and speculates on approaches to staging *Henri III et sa Cour (Henry III and His Court)*.

2992 KIossowicz, Jan. "French Presence." *TP*. 1996 Apr.; 38(2): 3-7. Lang.: Eng, Fre.
France. Poland. 1600-1996. Historical studies. ■Influence of French drama on the Polish theatre since the seventeenth century.

2993 Kuligowska, Anna. "Molière Our Contemporary." *TP*. 1996 Apr.; 38(2): 8-13. Illus.: Photo. B&W. 4. Lang.: Eng, Fre.
France. Cracow. 1948-1992. Historical studies. ■Timeliness of Bohdan Korzeniewski's translations into Polish of the plays of Molière, focusing on his own 1962 production of *Dom Juan* at the J. Słowacki Theatre, and Krzysztof Nazar's 1992 production of Korzeniewski's translation of *Le Misanthrope* at Stary Teatr.

2994 Lahaye, Louise. "Deux écrivains de langue allemande au festival d'automne à Paris." (Two German-speaking Playwrights at Paris' Festival d'automne.) *JCT*. 1989; 51: 64-66. Lang.: Fre.
France: Paris. 1988. Historical studies. ■Théâtre de la Ville's two productions of German plays in translation at Paris' Festival d'automne: Thomas Bernhard's *Vor dem Ruhestand (Eve of Retirement)* and Peter Handke's *Über die Dörfer (Above the Villages)*.

2995 Lavoie, Pierre. "Cultures in transit." (Cultures in Transit.) *JCT*. 1990; 56: 61. Lang.: Fre.
France: Limoges. 1988. Historical studies. ■Project 'Pièces en transit (Plays in Transit)' at Limoges' 1990 Festival international des francophonies helped understanding effects of producing plays in contexts different from their origin.

2996 Lavoie, Pierre. "'Quatre ateliers/laboratoires: le pari de la diffusion d'une pièce francophone dans une autre francophonie'." (Four Workshops/Laboratories: The Wager of Producing a French Play in a Different French-speaking Community.) *JCT*. 1990; 56: 73-74. Notes. Lang.: Fre.
France: Limoges. 1988. Historical studies. ■Lessons from workshops of 'Pièces en transit (Plays in transit)' at Limoges' Festival international des

DRAMA: —Plays/librettos/scripts

francophonies, especially that of Madeleine Laïc's *Les Voyageurs (The Travelers)*, directed by Claude Poissant.

2997 Lazaridès, Alexandre. "Dans l'outre de Dionysos." (In the Wineskin of Dionysus.) *JCT.* 1989; 53: 32-37. Illus.: Photo. B&W. 2. Lang.: Fre.
France. 1801-1989. Historical studies. ■Adaptation and interrelation of playwriting with other written forms.

2998 Lazaridès, Alexandre. "Actualité d'"OEdipe roi'." (Contemporary Relevance of 'Oedipus Rex'.) *JCT.* 1996; 78: 167-173. Notes. Illus.: Photo. B&W. 5. Lang.: Fre.
France. 1993-1995. Critical studies. ■Recent rebirth of interest in tragedy, particularly Sophocles' *Oidípous Týrannos*, demonstrated by Jean Bollack's re-interpretations in *La Naissance d'OEdipe. Traduction et commentaires d''OEdipe roi'.*

2999 Lépine, Stéphane. "Éléments de bibliographie." (Elements of a Bibliographie.) *JCT.* 1992; 64: 112-122. Lang.: Fre.
France. 1938-1992. Bibliographical studies. ■164 works in French by and about Samuel Beckett, including plays, bibliographies, biographies, and critical works.

3000 Lépine, Stéphane. "L'ombilic." (The Navel.) *JCT.* 1992; 64: 65-80. Notes. Illus.: Photo. B&W. 8. Lang.: Fre.
France. 1938-1992. Critical studies. ■Themes of void, silence and non-existence in the works of Samuel Beckett.

3001 Miller, Judith. "Contemporary Women's Voices in French Theatre." 228-250 in Keyssar, Helene, ed. *Feminist Theatre and Theory.* London: Macmillan; 1996. 288 pp. (New Casebooks.) Notes. Index. Lang.: Eng.
France. 1975-1995. Critical studies. ■The emergence of feminist theatre in France, with discussion of the work of Michèle Foucher, Chantal Chawaf, Marguerite Duras, and the Mnouchkine-Cixous collaboration.

3002 Péraldi, François. "La Part de l'autre." (The Place of the Other.) *JCT.* 1990; 56: 49-54. Notes. Illus.: Dwg. Photo. B&W. 3. Lang.: Fre.
France. Germany. 1990. Critical studies. ■Translation interpreted through psychoanalytic and philosophical concepts of Lacan and Heidegger.

3003 Pfister, Eva. "Die Kunst der Yasmina Reza." (The Art of Yasmina Reza.) *DB.* 1996; 2: 40-43. Illus.: Photo. B&W. 6. Lang.: Ger.
France. 1987-1996. Critical studies. ■Portrait of playwright Yasmina Reza, with discussion of several productions of her play *'Art'*: her success, the subjects of her plays, and being misunderstood as the author of light plays.

3004 Sadowska-Guillon, Irène. "La Révolution dans tous ses états." (Revolution in All Its States.) *JCT.* 1989; 53 : 112-118. Notes. Illus.: Dwg. 4. Lang.: Fre.
France. 1789-1989. Historical studies. ■Theatrical legacy of French revolution, and treatment of revolution in contemporary plays.

3005 Sadowska-Guillon, Irène. "Forme bâtarde ou légitime? L'Adaptation, cet obscur objet de théâtre." (Bastardization or Legitimate Form? Adaptation, That Obscure Object of Theatre.) *JCT.* 1989; 53: 91-94. Illus.: Photo. B&W. 2. Lang.: Fre.
France. 1980-1989. Historical studies. ■Motivations and methods of adaptation, with case studies *Le Désespoir tout blanc (Pure White Despair)* by Clarisse Nicoïdsky, *La Nuit des chats (The Night of the Cats)* by Jean-Claude Grumberg, *Monstre aimé (Beloved Monster)* by Javier Tomeo and *Nacimiento (Birth)*, Françoise Coupat's adaptation of *Bâtisseur de ruines (Builder of Ruins)* by Clarice Lispector.

3006 Savona, Jeannelle Laillou. "Lesbians on the French Stage: From Homosexuality to Monique Wittig's Lesbianization of the Theatre." *MD.* 1996 Spr; 39(1): 132-156. Notes. Illus.: Photo. B&W. 4. Lang.: Eng.
France. 1933-1995. Critical studies. ■Lesbians on the French stage, with comparison of *Gertrude morte cet après-midi (Gertrude Died This Afternoon)* by Monick Lepeu and *Le Voyage sans fin (The Constant Journey)* by Monique Wittig.

3007 Sugiera, Malgorzata. "Artaud dramatopisarz." (Artaud the Playwright.) *DialogW.* 1996; 4: 164-176. Lang.: Pol.

France. 1926-1935. Critical studies. ■Analysis of plays by Antonin Artaud.

3008 Tremblay, Jean-Louis; Vaïs, Michel, ed. "Le Jeune auteur français: Issu du sérail." (The Young French Author: Born to the Harem.) *JCT.* 1991; 58: 62-63. [Extracts from an interview of Jean-Louis Tremblay with Jean-Jacques Samary for 'En scène', Radio-Canada FM broadcast December 3, 1990, material selected by Michel Vaïs.] Lang.: Fre.
France. 1990. Historical studies. ■Status of playwriting and creation of new plays in France.

3009 Vaïs, Michel; Vigeant, Louise. "Un auteur vivant de sa plume, en France: Entretien avec Pierre Laville." (An Author Living by His Pen, in France: Interview with Pierre Laville.) *JCT.* 1996; 81: 100-111. Illus.: Poster. Photo. B&W. 7. Lang.: Fre.
France. 1950-1996. Histories-sources. ■Career of playwright Pierre Laville, and Laville's views on the state of French theatre.

3010 Vigeant, Louise. "Bernard-Marie Koltès: Les Contours infranchissables de la solitude." (Bernard-Marie Koltès: The Impenetrable Contours of Solitude.) *JCT.* 1990; 57: 35-40. Notes. Biblio. Illus.: Photo. B&W. 2. Lang.: Fre.
France. 1977-1989. Historical studies. ■Characteristics of language, location and theme in plays of Bernard-Marie Koltès. Brief list of bibliographical material.

3011 Vigeant, Louise. "Ubu chez Dubé." (Ubu at Dubés'.) *JCT.* 1993; 66: 118-123. Notes. Illus.: Photo. B&W. 3. Lang.: Fre.
France. 1985-1993. Critical studies. ■Playwright-director Joël Dragutin's *Trilogie des tables (La Baie de Naples, Eau de Cologne* and *Le Chant des signes)* uses clichéd language to criticize the state of communications and independent thinking in consumer society.

3012 Wittig, Monique. "*The Constant Journey*: An Introduction and a Prefatory Note." *MD.* 1996 Spr; 39(1): 156-159. Notes. Lang.: Eng.
France: Paris. 1985. Histories-sources. ■Introduction by author of *Le Voyage sans fin*, originally printed in program for Paris production at Théâtre du Petit Rond-Point, directed by Wittig and Sande Zeig. Prefatory note originally published in supplement to *Vlasta*, 4 (June 1985), 5-6.

3013 Cereteli, V. "Prišelcy iz drugich mirov." (Visitors from Other Worlds.) *TeatZ.* 1996; 9: 30-32. Lang.: Rus.
Georgia. 1900-1996. Historical studies. ■The influence of Shakespeare on Georgian theatre.

3014 "Heiner Müller." *Econ.* 1996 Jan 20; 338(7949): 90. Illus.: Photo. B&W. 1. Lang.: Eng.
Germany. 1996. Biographical studies. ■Obituary of playwright Heiner Müller, discussing how politics impacted on his plays and how they reflected the bleakness of the political scene. Influence of Brecht on his work.

3015 Becker, Peter von. "Der Streit ums gute Werk." (The Conflict over Good Work.) *THeute.* 1996; 10: 29. Illus.: Photo. B&W. 1. Lang.: Ger.
Germany. 1996. Historical studies. ■The dispute over copyright between Heiner Müller's widow and his former publisher Rotbuch.

3016 Becker, Peter von. "Gespenster am toten Mann." (Ghosts Are after a Dead Man.) *THeute.* 1996; YB: 108-111. Illus.: Photo. B&W. 6. Lang.: Ger.
Germany: Berlin, Bochum. 1996. Historical studies. ■Heiner Müller's work and its reception on stage after his death.

3017 Clemons, Leigh. "An Identity With 'Honorable Intent': Ernst Toller's Autobiographical (Re)constructions." *THSt.* 1996 June; 16: 105-116. Notes. Lang.: Eng.
Germany. 1919-1923. Historical studies. ■Complex critical analysis of life and early works of Ernst Toller, based on Foucaultian principles of author and discourse, rather than on his works as a whole. Plays analyzed are *Die Wandlung (Transfiguration)*, *Masse-Mensch (Masses and Man)*, *Die Maschinenstürmer (The Machine Wreckers)*, and *Hinkemann*.

3018 Fangauf, Henning. "Ameley, Dilldapp und der Erfolg." (Ameley, Dilldapp, and Success.) *DB.* 1996; 1: 38-40. Illus.: Photo. B&W. 4. Lang.: Ger.

DRAMA: —Plays/librettos/scripts

Germany. 1982-1996. Biographical studies. ■Portrait of playwright Tankred Dorst, with emphasis on the popularity of his plays for young audiences, including *Wie Dilldapp nach dem Riesen ging (How Dilldapp Went After the Giant)*, *Ameley, der Biber und der König auf dem Dach (Ameley, the Beaver and the King on the Roof)*, *Merlin*, *Grindkopf*, and *Parzival*.

3019 Forgách, András. "Heiner Müller (1929-1995)." *Sz*. 1996; 29(3): 2. Illus.: Photo. B&W. 1. Lang.: Hun.
Germany. 1929-1995. Biographical studies. ■A Hungarian playwright commemorates the recently deceased German playwright.

3020 Gerland, Oliver. "'An Icy Hand Has Set Me Loose!': Max Weber Reads Ibsen's *John Gabriel Borkman*." *JDTC*. 1996 Fall; 11 (1): 3-18. Notes. Lang.: Eng.
Germany. Norway. 1896-1930. Critical studies. ■Influence of Ibsen's *Johan Gabriel Borkman* on German sociologist Max Weber. Argues that the protagonist's struggle mirrors Weber's own struggles reflected in his later works, which examine capitalism, charisma, and aesthetics.

3021 Grange, William. *Comedy in the Weimar Republic: A Chronicle of Incongruous Laughter*. Westport, CT/London: Greenwood P; 1996. 166 pp. (Contributions in Drama and Theatre Studies, 74.) Append. Biblio. Index. Pref. Lang.: Eng.
Germany. 1918-1933. Histories-specific. ■Study of comedy, comic playwrights, and comedy production in Germany during the Weimar Republic. Covers reasons for popularity, authors, performers, cultural and historical significance.

3022 Györgyey, Clara. "Ellenportré." (Counter-Portrait.) *Sz*. 1996; 29(3): 3-5. Illus.: Photo. B&W. 3. Lang.: Hun.
Germany. 1929-1995. Histories-sources. ■The author, a critic and scholar, describes several meetings with playwright Heiner Müller at conferences and a premiere of one of his plays.

3023 Hart, Gail K. *Tragedy in Paradise: Family and Gender Politics in German Bourgeois Tragedy, 1750-1850*. Columbia, SC: Camden House; 1996. 136 pp. (Studies in German Literature, Linguistics, and Culture.) Index. Biblio. Lang.: Eng.
Germany. 1750-1850. Critical studies. ■The absence or removal of women, said to be central to German bourgeois tragedy, analyzed as a response to the perceived threat of domestic instability and disorder on the part of an emerging middle class.

3024 Herzinger, Richard. "Die Heimkehr der romantischen Moderne." (The Return of the Romantic Modern.) *THeute*. 1996; 8: 6-13 . Illus.: Photo. B&W. 5. Lang.: Ger.
Germany. 1996. Critical studies. ■Analysis of *Ithaka* by Botho Strauss.

3025 Kalb, Jonathan. "On the Becoming Death of Poor H.M." *ThM*. 1996; 27(1): 65-73. Illus.: Photo. B&W. 4. Lang.: Eng.
Germany: Berlin. USA. 1929-1996. Biographical studies. ■Reflection on the life and career of playwright/director Heiner Müller upon his death, and searches for reasons on why his passing was barely reported in the US.

3026 Kleist, Heinrich von; Forgách, András, transl. "Színházi írások." (Writings on Theatre.) *Sz*. 1996 ; 29(9): 34-38. Illus.: Dwg. B&W. 7. Lang.: Hun.
Germany. 1810. Critical studies. ■Presentation and publication of Kleist's theatre-related writing: reviews, commentaries, theoretical notes.

3027 Kluncker, Heinz. "Original Ton und Ironie." (Original Tone and Irony.) *DB*. 1996; 1: 12-15. Illus.: Photo. B&W. 7. Lang.: Ger.
Germany: Berlin. 1995. Critical studies. ■Reflections on Klaus Pohl's *Wartesaal Deutschland StimmenReich (Waiting Room Germany)*, drama and politics, the relationship of former East and West Germans, and German drama criticism, said to be too modest.

3028 Kuhn, Juliane. "Theater braucht Tragödien." (Theatre Needs Tragedies.) *DB*. 1996; 5: 30-33. Illus.: Photo. B&W. 3. Lang.: Ger.
Germany. 1964-1996. Biographical studies. ■Profile of playwright Rea Loher. Includes an interview with her about the meaning and social relevance of theatre.

3029 Kuhns, David F. "Palimpsestus: Frank Wedekind's Theatre of Self-Performance." *NTQ*. 1996; 12(45): 50-64. Notes. Illus.: Photo. B&W. 3. Lang.: Eng.

Germany. 1891-1918. Critical studies. ■Argues that Wedekind's notorious public persona became inseparable from his self-perceived identity: it was both the real subject of his dramatic art, and the essential character he performed.

3030 Lennartz, Knut. "Sterben kann ein Idiot." (Even an Idiot Can Die.) *DB*. 1996; 2: 12-17. Append. Illus.: Photo. B&W. 10. Lang.: Ger.
Germany. 1960-1996. Biographical studies. ■Portrait of the late playwright and director Heiner Müller and his performances in East Germany.

3031 Malkin, Jeanette R. "Mourning and the Body: Heiner Müller's Fathers and *The Foundling* Son." *MD*. 1996 Fall; 39(3): 490-506. Notes. Lang.: Eng.
Germany. 1929-1995. Historical studies. ■Social and political influences on the work of Müller with close analysis of his quasi-autobiographical play *Der Findling (The Foundling)*. Parallels to German history, its placement as last part of cycle of performance texts *Volokolamsk Highway (Wolokolamsker Chaussee)*.

3032 Manacorda, Giorgio. *La tragedia del ridicolo. Testo e teatralità nel Novecento tedesco.* (The Tragedy of the Absurd: Theatre and Theatricality in Twentieth-Century Germany.) Milan: Ubulibri; 1996. (La collanina 16.) Pref. Notes. Lang.: Ita.
Germany. 1900-1996. Critical studies. ■The tragic or its absence in works of Wedekind, Brecht, Weiss, Müller, Handke, Fassbinder.

3033 Massoutre, Guylaine. "Müller ou Comment mettre des corps aux prises avec des idées." (Müller, or How to Set Bodies Against Minds.) *JCT*. 1996; 79: 15-20. Notes. Illus.: Photo. B&W. 3. Lang.: Fre.
Germany. 1980-1996. Critical studies. ■Political and sexual themes in Heiner Müller's *Quartett*, and challenges of staging his texts.

3034 Mayer, Hans. "Rede über Heiner Müller." (Speech about Heiner Müller.) *THeute*. 1996; YB: 128-149. Illus.: Photo. B&W. 12. Lang.: Ger.
Germany. 1929-1996. Biographical studies. ■Intimate portrait of Heiner Müller by a literary scholar and professor.

3035 Molinari, Cesare. *Bertolt Brecht.* Rome/Bari: Laterza; 1996. 218 pp. (Biblioteca Universale Laterza 448.) Pref. Notes. Biblio. Illus.: Photo. B&W. Lang.: Ita.
Germany. 1898-1956. Critical studies. ■A critical portrait, an anthology of texts and an up-to-date bibliography of the German dramatist Bertolt Brecht, theorist of epic theatre. His coherent idea of theatre and his method with actors and direction.

3036 Müller, Heiner; Weber, Carl, transl. "*Dreamtext: The Night of the Directors*." *PerAJ*. 1996 Jan.; 18(1): 31-33. [Number 52.] Lang.: Eng.
Germany. 1994. Histories-sources. ■Complete text of Heiner Müller's dream narrative.

3037 Nordmann, Alfred. "Blotting and the Line of Beauty: On Performances by Botho Strauss and Peter Handke." *MD*. 1996 Win; 39(4): 680-697. Notes. Illus.: Pntg. B&W. 5. Lang.: Eng.
Germany. 1745-1991. Critical studies. ■Comparison of the aesthetics of the two playwrights using parallels with eighteenth-century painters.

3038 Oberholzer, Rosmarie. "Coup d'oeil: La dramaturgie allemande depuis la deuxième guerre mondiale." (German Playwriting Since the Second World War.) *JCT*. 1991; 61: 54-63. Notes. Biblio. Illus.: Photo. B&W. 8. Lang.: Fre.
Germany. 1945-1991. Historical studies. ■Trends in German playwriting since World War II, with sections on Heiner Müller, Thomas Bernhard, Peter Handke, Botho Strauss, Rainer Werner Fassbinder and Franz Xaver Kroetz.

3039 Raddatz, Frank M. "Im Jenseits ist jetzt mehr los." (In the Next World There Is Something More Happening Now.) *TZ*. 1996 ; 2: 8-11. Illus.: Photo. B&W. 6. Lang.: Ger.
Germany. Histories-sources. ■The author's personal memories of collaboration and contacts with Heiner Müller.

3040 Reddatz, Frank M. "Mythos Nation." (Myth Nation.) *TZ*. 1996; 1: 16-19. Illus.: Sketches. B&W. 2. Lang.: Ger.

DRAMA: —Plays/librettos/scripts

Germany. 1996. Histories-sources. ■Conversation with playwright Heiner Müller about the metaphysical.

3041 Rossi, Doc. "Brecht on Shakespeare: A Revaluation." *CompD.* 1996 Sum; 30(2): 158-187. Notes. Lang.: Eng.
Germany. 1917-1985. Critical studies. ■Explores how much, and in what way, Shakespeare influenced the plays and the theatrical approach of Bertolt Brecht.

3042 Ruffini, Franco. "A Little More Healthy Sport! Bertolt Brecht and Objective Boxing." *MimeJ.* 1996; 18(1): 3-15. Notes. Biblio. Illus.: Dwg. B&W. 1. Lang.: Eng.
Germany: Berlin. 1922-1926. Critical studies. ■Analysis of Brecht's use of boxing as a metaphor in *A Man's a Man (Mann ist Mann)* and *In the Jungle of Cities (Im Dickicht der Städte)*.

3043 Rühle, Günther. "Am Abgrund des Jahrhunderts." (At the Abyss of the Century.) *THeute.* 1996; 2: 6-11. Illus.: Photo. B&W. 2. Lang.: Ger.
Germany: Berlin. 1929-1995. Biographical studies. ■The life and work of Heiner Müller.

3044 Rühle, Günther. "Was sollen wir tun?" (What Shall We Do?)*THeute.* 1996; YB: 114-127. Illus.: Photo. B&W. 11. Lang.: Ger.
Germany. 1945-1996. Historical studies. ■Postwar drama in both East and West Germany.

3045 Sadowska-Guillon, Irène. "La Fatalité de l'histoire: entretien avec Heiner Müller." (The Fatality of History: Interview with Heiner Müller.) *JCT.* 1989; 53: 95-103. Illus.: Pntg. Photo. B&W. 5. Lang.: Fre.
Germany. 1929-1989. Histories-sources. ■Life of Heiner Müller and his work as playwright and director with respect to theatrical practice and social context.

3046 Sieg, Katrin. "Subjectivity and Socialism: Feminist Discourses in East Germany." 79-106 in Reinelt, Janelle, ed. *Crucibles of Crisis: Performing Social Change.* Ann Arbor, MI: Univ of Michigan P; 1996. 250 pp. Notes. Lang.: Eng.
Germany. 1978-1994. Critical studies. ■The position of women and feminist theatre in Germany before and after its reunification, with discussion of Doris Paschiller's *One Great Family (Eine grosse Familie)* and Monika Maron's *Ada and Evald*, as well as writings from women in theatre.

3047 Stammen, Silvia. "Vom Fussball zum Theater." (From Football to Theatre.) *DB.* 1996; 12: 36-39. Append. Illus.: Photo. B&W. 3. Lang.: Ger.
Germany. Austria. 1963-1996. Biographical studies. ■Portrait of playwright, actor, and director Wolfgang Bauer.

3048 Tabori, George; Wood, Kevin S. "*The Kiss.*" *ThM.* 1996; 27(1): 74. Lang.: Eng.
Germany: Berlin. 1995. Histories-sources. ■Poem composed by George Tabori in response to the passing of Heiner Müller.

3049 Vigeant, Louise. "Franz Xaver Kroetz: Le Degré zéro du réel." (Franz Xaver Kroetz: The Zero Degree of Reality.) *JCT.* 1990; 57: 45-50. Notes. Illus.: Photo. B&W. 1. Lang.: Fre.
Germany. 1968-1990. Biographical studies. ■Playwright Franz Xaver Kroetz employs a hyperrealistic style to depict characters lacking discursive capacity to understand and rectify their social dilemmas.

3050 Weber, Carl. "A Dream Play by Heiner Müller." *PerAJ.* 1996 Jan.; 18(1): 29-30. [Number 52.] Lang.: Eng.
Germany: Berlin. 1994. Critical studies. ■Introduction to a piece by Heiner Müller, *Dreamtext: The Night of the Directors*, trying to capture dreams in the form of narrative.

3051 Wellman, Mac. "Edges of Language." *ThM.* 1996; 26(3): 25-26. Lang.: Eng.
Germany: Hamburg. 1996. Histories-sources. ■Interview with playwright Paul Schmidt on his collaboration with director Robert Wilson on *Alice*, an adaptation of Lewis Carroll's original for a production at the Thalia Theatre, with music and lyrics by Tom Waits and Kathleen Brennan.

3052 Wille, Franz. "Morgensterns Abendrot." (Morgenstern's Sunset.) *THeute.* 1996; 5: 5-8. Illus.: Photo. B&W. 5. Lang.: Ger.
Germany: Munich. Austria: Vienna. 1968-1996. Historical studies. ■Analysis of *Die Ballade vom Wiener Schnitzel (The Ballad of the Wiener Schnitzel)* by George Tabori, and a comparison with the earlier play *Die Kannibalen (The Cannibals)*, first produced in Munich in 1968.

3053 Wille, Franz. "Klar bin ich ein Ostler." (Of Course I Am from the East.) *THeute.* 1996; 9: 37-40. Illus.: Photo. B&W. 3. Lang.: Ger.
Germany: Berlin. 1996. Critical studies. ■Portrait of playwright Oliver Bukowski.

3054 Massoutre, Guylaine. "Heiner Müller sous les projecteurs." (Heiner Müller Under the Lights.) *JCT.* 1991; 61: 64-71. Notes. Illus.: Photo. B&W. 3. Lang.: Fre.
Germany, East. France: Avignon. 1957-1991. Critical studies. ■Aesthetic properties of Heiner Müller's plays, their inscription in the East German sociopolitical context, and stagings at the 1991 Avignon Festival.

3055 Bonelli, Guido. "Le libere donne del Citerone. Fenomenologia delle pulsioni delle 'Baccanti' di Euripide." (The Free Women of Cyterion: Phenomenology of Emotions in the *Bákchai* of Euripides.) *IlCast.* 1996; 9(26): 5-26. Notes. Lang.: Ita.
Greece. 406 B.C. Critical studies. ■The conflict between nature and culture in Euripides' *Bákchai (The Bacchae)*.

3056 Dunn, Francis M. *Tragedy's End: Closure and Innovation in Euripidean Drama.* New York, NY/Oxford: Oxford UP; 1996. 252 pp. Index. Notes. Biblio. Pref. Lang.: Eng.
Greece. 440-400 B.C. Critical studies. ■Closure and generic innovation in Euripidean drama. Argues that the issues of formal closure and of generic innovation are interrelated.

3057 Josephson, Erland. "Att kastas i tidens brunn." (To Throw Oneself into the Source of Time.) *Dramat.* 1996; 4(4): 38-39. Illus.: Photo. Color. Lang.: Swe.
Greece. Sweden. 404 B.C.-1996 A.D. Histories-sources. ■Some thoughts about Kadmos' part in Euripides' *Bákchai* as played in ancient Athens and in Stockholm of today.

3058 Lesky, Albin. *La poesia tragica dei greci.* (The Tragic Poetry of the Greeks.) Bologna: Il Mulino; 1996. 824 pp. Lang.: Ita.
Greece. 500-400 B.C. Critical studies. ■Italian translation of *Die tragische Dichtung der Hellenen* (Göttingen: Vandendoeck & Ruprecht, 1972).

3059 Páll, Árpád. "Arisztophanész, avagy a komédia születése." (Aristophanes or the Birth of Comedy.) *SzSz.* 1996; 30/31: 130-140. Lang.: Hun.
Greece. 450-380 B.C. Critical studies. ■Study on the works of Aristophanes, 'father' of Greek comedy.

3060 Romilly, Jacqueline de. *La tragedia greca.* (Greek Tragedy.) Bologna: Il Mulino; 1996. 171 pp. Biblio. Append. Lang.: Ita.
Greece. 500-400 B.C. Historical studies. ■Italian translation of *La tragédie grecque* (Paris: Presses Universitaires de France, 1970).

3061 Sommerstein, Alan H. *Aeschylean Tragedy.* Bari: Levante Editori; 1996. 544 pp. (Collana di Studi e Testi 15.) Notes. Append. Index. Pref. Biblio. Lang.: Eng.
Greece. 525-456 B.C. Critical studies. ■Begins with a study of Greek society and theatre, and situates the plays within a cultural, political, and historical framework.

3062 Vrečko, Janez. "Značaj in tragično pri Aristotelu." (Character and the Tragic in Aristotle.) *Novr.* 1996; 15 (170-171): 158-172. Lang.: Slo.
Greece. 500-400 B.C. Critical studies. ■Aristotle's *Poetics* and his interpretation of the tragic in drama.

3063 Vrečko, Janez. "Sofoklov Filoktet." (Sophocles' *Philoctetes.*) *Dialogi.* 1996; 32(1/2): 10-55. Lang.: Slo.
Greece. 409 B.C. Critical studies. ■An interpretation of Sophocles' tragedy *Philoctetes*.

3064 Durán-Cogan, Mercedes F. "Instancias de poder en *El Corazón del Espantapájaros* de Hugo Carrillo." (Instances of Power in Hugo Carrillo's *The Heart of the Scarecrow.*) *Ges-*

CLASSED ENTRIES

DRAMA: —Plays/librettos/scripts

tos. 1996 Nov.; 11(22): 87-104. Notes. Biblio. Append. Illus.: Graphs. 1. Lang.: Spa.
Guatemala. 1962. Critical studies. ■The impotence of the individual in the face of tyrannical power in Carrillo's play, and the play's relevance to the present situation in Latin America.

3065 Adamson, Ginette. "L'engagement dans le théâtre haïtien: l'oeuvre dramatique de Jean Métellus." (Engagement in Haitien Theatre: The Dramatic Work of Jean Métellus.) *ThR.* 1996; 21(3): 245-255. Notes. Lang.: Fre.
Haiti. 1986-1992. Critical studies. ■Analysis of dramatizations of the genocide of Haiti's indigenous Indian population in Jean Métellus's *Anacoana* and *Colomb*, situating the plays in the context of Antillean theatrical tradition.

3066 Coates, Carrol F. "Folklore in the Theatre of Franck Fouché." *ThR.* 1996; 21(3): 256-261. Notes. Biblio. Lang.: Eng.
Haiti. 1953-1981. Critical studies. ■Analysis of role of Haitian popular culture in plays by Franck Fouché, referring mainly to *Bouki nan paradi (Bouki in Paradise)* and *Général Baron-la-Croix*, and concentrating on folklore and language.

3067 Hüsken, W.N.M. "The Fool as Social Critic: The Case of Dutch Rhetoricians' Drama." 112-145 in Davidson, Clifford, ed. *Fools and Folly.* Kalamazoo, MI: Medieval Institute Publications; 1996. 176 pp. (Early Drama, Art, and Music Monograph Series 22.) Notes. Lang.: Eng.
Holland. 1395-1596. Historical studies. ■Depiction and role of fools in Dutch rhetoricians' drama and their reflection of society. Focus on *Van Nyeuvont, Loosheit ende Practike: hoe sij Vrou Lortse verheffen (Of New Findings, Cunning, and Slyness, how they exalt Lady Fraud)*.

3068 De Costa, Elena M. "Nationhood-as-Community: Teatro La Fragua's Liberating Honduran Theatre for the People and by the People." *LATR.* 1996 Spr; 29(2): 111-130. Notes. Biblio. Lang.: Eng.
Honduras: El Progreso. 1979-1996. Critical studies. ■The function of community theatre Teatro La Fragua, founded in 1979 by Jack Warner, to popularize, revitalize and re-evaluate Honduran culture. Also, use of visual-oral narrative in its religious cycle plays and folk plays.

3069 Bécsy, Tamás. *Kalandok a drámával: magyar drámák 1945-1989.* (Adventures in Drama: Hungarian Dramas, 1945-1989.) Budapest: Balassi; 1996. 169 pp. Lang.: Hun.
Hungary. 1945-1989. Critical studies. ■Analysis of plays by Csurka, Gáspár, Görgey, Hernádi, Hubay, Illyés, Kamondi, Karinthy, Kertész, Kornis, Mészöly, Nádas, Nagy, Németh, Örkény, Páskándi, Sarkadi, Spiró, and Szakonyi.

3070 Csáki, Judit. "A zavar bősége—Bécsy Tamás: Kalandok a drámával." (The Abundance of Confusion—Tamás Bécsy: *Adventures Around the Drama*.) *Sz.* 1996; 29(11): 47-48. Illus.: Photo. B&W. 1. Lang.: Hun.
Hungary. 1945-1990. Critical studies. ■Review of a theoretical volume by a theatre researcher on post-war Hungarian drama (Budapest: Balassi, 1996).

3071 Györgyey, Clara. "Merely a Player? Mátyás Sárközi: Színház az egész világ. Molnár Ferenc regényes élete (Osiris-Századvég, 1995)." (Merely a Player? Mátyás Sárközi: *All the World's a Stage: The Fantastic Life of Ferenc Molnár* (Osiris-Századvég, 1995).) *HQ.* 1996 Fall; 37(143): 117-122. Lang.: Eng.
Hungary. USA: New York, NY. 1878-1952. Critical studies. ■Review essay of a biography of playwright Ferenc Molnár, written by his grandson Mátyás Sárközi, a writer, critic, translator, and director of the Humanities in Medicine at Yale University.

3072 Kerényi, Ferenc. "Az erdélyi magyar drámairodalom kezdetei." (The Beginnings of Hungarian Drama in Transylvania.) 7-18 in Kántor, Lajos, ed. *Kolozsvár magyar színháza 1792-1992.* Kolozsvár (Cluj-Napoca): Kolozsvári Állami Magyar Színház; 1992. 141 pp. Lang.: Hun.
Hungary: Kolozsvár. 1693-1820. Histories-specific. ■Study in the first chapter of theatre history in Transylvania: drama literature, writers, actor-translators, adaptations and original plays of the program.

3073 Lázok, János. "A második bűn. Kísérlet Sütő András *Káin és Ábel* című drámájának értelmezésére." (The Second Sin: Attempt at an Interpretation of András Sütő's *Cain and Abel.*) *SzSz.* 1996; 30/31: 100-129. Notes. Lang.: Hun.
Hungary. 1977. Critical studies. ■A polemic analysis of András Sütő's play concerning Tamás Bécsy's interpretation.

3074 Sándor, L. István. "A játékszíni költőmesterség—Kortárs magyar drámák." (The Profession of the Dramatist—Contemporary Hungarian Dramas.) *Sz.* 1996; 29(9): 2-7. Illus.: Photo. B&W. 7. Lang.: Hun.
Hungary. 1995-1996. Critical studies. ■A theoretical essay on the season's new Hungarian plays transcending mere criticism: chief tendencies in the dramaturgy, the structure and the portrayal of characters. Focus on works of Garaczi, Kárpáti, Németh, Parti Nagy, and Sultz.

3075 Székely, György. "Az átmenet dramaturgiája. Korai dramatikus emlékeink dilemmái." (Dramaturgy of a Transitional Period: Problems of Early Dramatic Remains.) *SzSz.* 1996; 30/31: 87-99. Notes. Lang.: Hun.
Hungary. 1516-1698. Critical studies. ■Essay on the medieval Christian and humanist dramaturgy of Western European theatre traditions in the plays of Mihály Sztárai and Péter Bornemisza's *Elektra*.

3076 Atkinson, William. "J.M. Synge's Vagrant Aesthetic." 169-181 in Gonzalez, Alexander G., ed. *Assessing the Achievement of J.M. Synge.* Westport, CT/London: Greenwood; 1996. 197 pp. (Contributions in Drama and Theatre Studies 73.) Biblio. Index. Pref. Notes. Lang.: Eng.
Ireland. 1902-1909. Historical studies. ■Attempts to articulate Synge's aesthetic and place it in its political context.

3077 Casey, Dan. "Of Holy Wells and Sacred Spells: Strange Comedy at the Abbey." 75-83 in Gonzalez, Alexander G., ed. *Assessing the Achievement of J.M. Synge.* Westport, CT/London: Greenwood; 1996. 197 pp. (Contributions in Drama and Theatre Studies 73.) Biblio. Index. Pref. Lang.: Eng.
Ireland. 1905. Historical studies. ■Analysis of Synge's first full-length play *The Well of the Saints* and some possible explanations for the public's hostility at its premiere.

3078 Davy, Daniely. "Tragic Self-Referral in *Riders to the Sea*." 38-50 in Gonzalez, Alexander G., ed. *Assessing the Achievement of J.M. Synge.* Westport, CT/London: Greenwood; 1996. 197 pp. (Contributions in Drama and Theatre Studies 73.) Biblio. Index. Pref. Lang.: Eng.
Ireland. 1904. Historical studies. ■The nature of the tragic experience in Synge's *Riders to the Sea*. Analyzes elements of character, structure and theme to reveal play's complexities in the apparently simple organization.

3079 Doll, Eileen J. "Synge's *Deirdre of the Sorrows*: Defamiliarizing the Myth." 130-138 in Gonzalez, Alexander G., ed. *Assessing the Achievement of J.M. Synge.* Westport, CT/London: Greenwood; 1996. 197 pp. (Contributions in Drama and Theatre Studies 73.) Biblio. Index. Pref. Notes. Lang.: Eng.
Ireland. 1909. Historical studies. ■Analysis of Synge's last play, the unfinished *Deirdre of the Sorrows*.

3080 Elkins, Jane Duke. "'Cute Thinking Women': The Language of Synge's Female Vagrants." 118-129 in Gonzalez, Alexander G., ed. *Assessing the Achievement of J.M. Synge.* Westport, CT/London: Greenwood; 1996. 197 pp. (Contributions in Drama and Theatre Studies 73.) Biblio. Index. Pref. Notes. Lang.: Eng.
Ireland. 1902-1905. Historical studies. ■Examines the female vagrant characters in Synge's plays *The Shadow of the Glen*, *The Well of the Saints*, and *The Tinker's Wedding*. Argues that Synge liberates these women from contemporary social constraints of behavior and place, yet binds them to their male traveling companions.

3081 Fitzgerald-Hoyt, Mary. "Death and the Colleen: *The Shadow of the Glen*." 51-56 in Gonzalez, Alexander G., ed. *Assessing the Achievement of J.M. Synge.* Westport, CT/London: Greenwood; 1996. 197 pp. (Contributions in Drama and Theatre Studies 73.) Biblio. Index. Pref. Lang.: Eng.

DRAMA: —Plays/librettos/scripts

Ireland. 1903. Historical studies. ■Feminist analysis of the character of Nora in Synge's one-act play *The Shadow of the Glen.*

3082 Grove, Robin. "Samuel Beckett at Verbum's Brink: Words and Space." *CritRev.* 1995; 35: 95-105. Notes. Lang.: Eng.

Ireland. France. 1953-1957. Critical studies. ■Beckett's use of language, action and themes in *Fin de partie (Endgame)* and *En attendant Godot (Waiting for Godot).*

3083 Harris, Susan C. "Blow the Witches Out: Gender Construction and the Subversion of Nationalism in Yeats's *Cathleen ni Houlihan* and *On Baile's Strand.*" *MD.* 1996 Fall; 39(3): 475-489. Notes. Lang.: Eng.

Ireland. 1903-1910. Critical studies. ■Nationalism and evolution of the use of female figures in plays of Yeats. Influence of Synge on Yeats's writing, public response to his plays.

3084 Hawkins, Maureen S.G. "Schizophrenia and the Politics of Experience in Three Plays by Brian Friel." *MD.* 1996 Fall; 39 (3): 465-474. Notes. Lang.: Eng.

Ireland. UK-Ireland. 1972-1988. Critical studies. ■Projection of dual personalities in *Philadelphia, Here I Come!, The Freedom of the City,* and *Translations.* Political division in Ireland, high rate of schizophrenia in the population, and metaphoric representation of this in plays.

3085 Holder, Heidi J. "'Stimulating stories of our own land': 'History Making' and the Work of J.M. Synge." 139-150 in Gonzalez, Alexander G., ed. *Assessing the Achievement of J.M. Synge.* Westport, CT/London: Greenwood; 1996. 197 pp. (Contributions in Drama and Theatre Studies 73.) Biblio. Index. Pref. Notes. Lang.: Eng.

Ireland. 1903-1909. Historical studies. ■Irish history in the plays of J.M. Synge. Argues that while Synge fully participated in the movement of his day to link an understanding of the past with the political and cultural circumstances of the moment, his work transcends the realm of practical and local politics.

3086 Mathews, Carolyn L. "'Passing the gap': Reading the Betwixt and Between of Liminality in J.M. Synge's *The Well of the Saints.*" 84-96 in Gonzalez, Alexander G., ed. *Assessing the Achievement of J.M. Synge.* Westport, CT/London: Greenwood; 1996. 197 pp. (Contributions in Drama and Theatre Studies 73.) Biblio. Index. Pref. Notes. Lang.: Eng.

Ireland. 1905. Historical studies. ■Language and the meaning of reality in Synge's *The Well of the Saints.* Author uses anthropologist Victor Turner's concept of liminality to explore social and cultural norms in the play.

3087 Owens, Cóilín D. "The Wooing of Étaín: Celtic Myth and *The Shadow of the Glen.*" 57-74 in Gonzalez, Alexander G., ed. *Assessing the Achievement of J.M. Synge.* Westport, CT/London: Greenwood; 1996. 197 pp. (Contributions in Drama and Theatre Studies 73.) Biblio. Index. Pref. Lang.: Eng.

Ireland. 1903. Historical studies. ■Argues that Synge used Celtic myth in *The Shadow of the Glen* and refutes the realistic stereotype that has been applied to the play.

3088 Pew, Katherine. "Beckett at the Gate." *TheaterW.* 1996 July 29; 9(52): 34-35. Illus.: Photo. B&W. 1. Lang.: Eng.

Ireland: Dublin. 1991-1996. Historical studies. ■Michael Colgan, artistic director of the Gate Theatre, discusses playwright Samuel Beckett and his plays, and his negotiations with the playwright to produce all nineteen of his plays together.

3089 Rhodes, Robert E. "'More Matter for a May Morning': J.M. Synge's *The Tinker's Wedding.*" 97-117 in Gonzalez, Alexander G., ed. *Assessing the Achievement of J.M. Synge.* Westport, CT/London: Greenwood; 1996. 197 pp. (Contributions in Drama and Theatre Studies 73.) Biblio. Index. Pref. Lang.: Eng.

Ireland. 1902. Historical studies. ■Analysis of the least successful comedy of Synge's career, focusing on the characters of the priest and the tinker.

3090 Stengel, Ellen Powers. "A Young Man's Ghost: J.M. Synge, *The Playboy of the Western World,* and W.B. Yeats's *A Vision.*" 24-37 in Gonzalez, Alexander G., ed. *Assessing the Achievement of J.M. Synge.* Westport, CT/London: Greenwood; 1996. 197 pp. (Contributions in Drama and Theatre

Studies 73.) Biblio. Index. Pref. Notes. Append. Illus.: Diagram. 1. Lang.: Eng.

Ireland. 1907. Historical studies. ■The influence of Synge's play on Yeats's writings on the occult.

3091 Strand, Ginger. "*The Playboy,* Critics, and the Enduring Problem of the Audience." 10-23 in Gonzalez, Alexander G., ed. *Assessing the Achievement of J.M. Synge.* Westport, CT/London: Greenwood; 1996. 197 pp. (Contributions in Drama and Theatre Studies 73.) Biblio. Index. Pref. Lang.: Eng.

Ireland. 1907. Historical studies. ■The complex role of the audience in Synge's *The Playboy of the Western World.* Both the reaction of the villagers in the play, who serve as an audience for the main action, and the initial violent reaction of the first public audiences in Dublin at its premiere reveal the cultural politics that shaped both.

3092 Swiontkowski, Gale Schricker. "The Devil and Auld Mahoun: Exposing the Trickster Archetype in Synge's Christy Mahon by Way of Rushdie's Muhammad/Mahound." 151-168 in Gonzalez, Alexander G., ed. *Assessing the Achievement of J.M. Synge.* Westport, CT/London: Greenwood; 1996. 197 pp. (Contributions in Drama and Theatre Studies 73.) Biblio. Index. Pref. Notes. Lang.: Eng.

Ireland. 1907. Historical studies. ■Compares Synge's use of the trickster archetype in *The Playboy of the Western World* to that of novelist Salman Rushdie in his novel *The Satanic Verses.*

3093 Alkalay-Gut, Karen. "Danny Horowitz." 349-354 in Ben-Zvi, Linda, ed. *Theater In Israel.* Ann Arbor, MI: Univ. of Michigan P; 1996. 450 pp. Lang.: Eng.

Israel. 1969-1995. Histories-sources. ■Interview with Israeli playwright Danny Horowitz on themes in his plays.

3094 Avigal, Shosh. "Patterns and Trends in Israeli Drama and Theater, 1948 to Present." 9-50 in Ben-Zvi, Linda, ed. *Theater In Israel.* Ann Arbor, MI: Univ. of Michigan P; 1996. 450 pp. Notes. Lang.: Eng.

Israel. 1948-1996. Historical studies. ■The shift in Israeli theatre from the political to the personal, from ideological content to an awareness of aesthetics and theatrical craftsmanship. Considers themes of self-fulfillment, survival dilemmas, the Holocaust, doubt and questioning of national actions, and coexistence in a heterogeneous society.

3095 Avigal, Shosh. "Liberated Women in Israeli Theater." 303-308 in Ben-Zvi, Linda, ed. *Theater In Israel.* Ann Arbor, MI: Univ. of Michigan P; 1996. 450 pp. Notes. Lang.: Eng.

Israel. 1970-1995. Critical studies. ■The depiction of women in Israeli drama, as well as the progress of women, both Israeli and Palestinian, in a theatre world dominated by men.

3096 Avigal, Shosh. "Miriam Kainy." 355-360 in Ben-Zvi, Linda, ed. *Theater In Israel.* Ann Arbor, MI: Univ. of Michigan P; 1996. 450 pp. Lang.: Eng.

Israel. 1950-1992. Histories-sources. ■Interview with Israeli playwright Miriam Kainy on themes in her plays.

3097 Ben-Zvi, Linda. "Katya Sosonsky." 399-402 in Ben-Zvi, Linda, ed. *Theater In Israel.* Ann Arbor, MI: Univ. of Michigan P; 1996. 450 pp. Lang.: Eng.

Israel: Yaffo. 1991. Histories-sources. ■Interview with Katya Sosonsky, founding member and dramaturg of the Gesher Theatre, a company composed entirely of Russian emigres in Yaffo.

3098 Brown, Erella. "Politics of Desire: Brechtian 'Epic Theater' in Hanoch Levin's Postmodern Satire." 173-199 in Ben-Zvi, Linda, ed. *Theater In Israel.* Ann Arbor, MI: Univ. of Michigan P; 1996. 450 pp. Notes. Lang.: Eng.

Israel. 1968-1990. Critical studies. ■Avant-garde Brechtian elements in the early satires and later plays of Hanoch Levin.

3099 Feingold, Ben-Ami. "Hebrew Holocaust Drama as a Modern Morality Play." 269-283 in Ben-Zvi, Linda, ed. *Theater In Israel.* Ann Arbor, MI: Univ. of Michigan P; 1996. 450 pp. Notes. Lang.: Eng.

Israel. 1950-1984. Critical studies. ■Holocaust drama as a modern morality play in that it insists on the immediate and continuous engagement of the audience's personal, moral, and ethical involvement. Author argues that playwrights can use certain elements of mysteries and moral-

DRAMA: —Plays/librettos/scripts

ity plays as devices for creating more sophisticated and spiritually weightier plays. Plays analyzed include: Sobol's *Geto (Ghetto)*, *Cheshbon Chadash (Stocktaking)* by Natan Shacham, Moshe Shamir's *Hayoresh (The Heir)*, Leah Goldberg's *Baalat Haarmon (Lady of the Castle)* and Ben-Zion Tomer's *Yaldei Hatzel (Children of the Shadow)*.

3100 Moscati-Steindler, Gabriella; Paltrinieri, Lorella, transl. "Yehoshua Sobol." 361-365 in Ben-Zvi, Linda, ed. *Theater In Israel.* Ann Arbor, MI: Univ. of Michigan P; 1996. 450 pp. Lang.: Eng.
Israel. 1982-1993. Histories-sources. ■Interview with Israeli playwright Yehoshua Sobol on the role of women and the 'other' in his plays.

3101 Rokem, Freddie. "Hebrew Theater from 1889 to 1948." 51-84 in Ben-Zvi, Linda, ed. *Theater In Israel.* Ann Arbor, MI: Univ. of Michigan P; 1996. 450 pp. Notes. Lang.: Eng.
Israel. 1889-1948. Historical studies. ■Historical account of Israeli theatrical tradition, focusing on questions of repertoire and the establishment of theatrical institutions that formed the basis for Israeli theatre today.

3102 Rokem, Freddie. "Yehoshua Sobol—Between History and the Arts: A Study of *Ghetto* and *Shooting Magda (The Palestinian Woman)*." 201-224 in Ben-Zvi, Linda, ed. *Theater In Israel.* Ann Arbor, MI: Univ. of Michigan P; 1996. 450 pp. Notes. Lang.: Eng.
Israel. 1939-1995. Critical studies. ■Analysis of *Ha-Palistinait* and *Geto* by Yehoshua Sobol.

3103 Rozik, Eli. "Isaac Sacrifices Abraham in *The American Princess*." 133-150 in Ben-Zvi, Linda, ed. *Theater In Israel.* Ann Arbor, MI: Univ. of Michigan P; 1996. 450 pp. Notes. Lang.: Eng.
Israel. 1920-1995. Critical studies. ■The use of mythic allusions in the absurdist drama *Haneshica Haamerikait (The American Princess)* by Nissim Aloni.

3104 Shoham, Chaim. "The Drama and Theater of Nissim Aloni." 119-131 in Ben-Zvi, Linda, ed. *Theater In Israel.* Ann Arbor, MI: Univ. of Michigan P; 1996. 450 pp. Notes. Biblio. Lang.: Eng.
Israel. 1926-1995. Critical studies. ■Themes in the plays of Nissim Aloni.

3105 Vill, Susanne. "Erinnerungsrituale und intermediäre Dramaturgie in Joshua Sobol's 'Die Palästinenserin'." (Rituals of Remembrance and Intermediary Dramaturgy in Yehoshua Sobol's *The Palestinian Woman*.) *FMT.* 1996; 1: 82-93. Notes. Lang.: Ger.
Israel. 1985. Critical studies. ■Analysis of *Ha-Palistinait*, with emphasis on the complex relationships between realities and fictions, changes of perspective and roles.

3106 Weitz, Shoshana. "From Combative to Bourgeois Theater: Public Theater in Israel in 1990." 101-116 in Ben-Zvi, Linda, ed. *Theater In Israel.* Ann Arbor, MI: Univ. of Michigan P; 1996. 450 pp. Notes. Tables. Lang.: Eng.
Israel. 1990. Empirical studies. ■The role of Israeli public theatre in communicating social norms. Includes tables of sociodemographic characteristics of the protagonists as well as the themes of plays presented by the public theatres in 1990.

3107 Yaari, Nurit. "Life as a Lost Battle: The Theater of Hanoch Levin." 151-171 in Ben-Zvi, Linda, ed. *Theater In Israel.* Ann Arbor, MI: Univ. of Michigan P; 1996. 450 pp. Notes. Lang.: Eng.
Israel. 1944-1995. Critical studies. ■Anti-war themes in the plays of Hanoch Levin, with reference to the heroic tradition of Israeli drama.

3108 *I libri in maschera: Luigi Pirandello e le biblioteche.* (The Masked Books: Luigi Pirandello and Libraries.) Rome: De Luca; 1996. 166 pp. Pref. Index. Illus.: Photo. Pntg. Dwg. Sketches. Color. B&W. Lang.: Ita.
Italy. 1867-1936. Histories-sources. ■Catalogue of an exhibition on Pirandello's own library, his reading and his relationship with books. The exhibition was held in Rome at the Teatro dei Dioscuri from 7 November to 31 December.

3109 Alberti, Carmelo, ed.; Herry, Ginette, ed. *Tra libro e scena: Carlo Goldoni.* (Between Book and Stage: Carlo Goldoni.) Venice: Il Cardo; 1996. 259 pp. Biblio. Index. Lang.: Ita.

Italy. 1707-1793. Critical studies. ■Collection of essays on Carlo Goldoni published on the bicentenary of his death and reflecting renewed interest in his works with new productions and translations in various languages. Includes bibliography of Goldoni's works, translations and critical essays from 1978 to 1995.

3110 Alonge, Roberto. "Microappunti per 'Emma B. vedova Giocasta'." (Micro-Notes for *Emma B., Widow Jocasta*.) *IlCast.* 1996 ; 9(27): 79-86. Notes. Lang.: Ita.
Italy. 1891-1952. Critical studies. ■The central sequence of the monologue by Alberto Savinio (Andrea De Chirico), with emphasis on mother-son incest as the regaining of an Edenic state.

3111 Bartolazzi, Marita. "Pirandello tra disegni, schizzi e caricature." (Pirandello in Drawings, Sketches and Caricatures.) *Ariel.* 1996; 11(1): 197-203. Notes. Lang.: Ita.
Italy. 1924-1938. Biographical studies. ■An analysis and bibliographical indications of the caricatures of Luigi Pirandello published in contemporary periodicals: *Almanco Letterario, Bertoldo* and *Il becco giallo.*

3112 Budor, Dominique. "Ipertesto e gioco dei segni nella 'Didone abbandonata'." (Hyper-text and the Play of Signs in Alberto Savinio's *Dido Abandoned.*) *IlCast.* 1996; 9(27): 87-96. Notes. Lang.: Ita.
Italy. 1942. Critical studies. ■Analysis of *Didone abbandonata (Dido Abandoned)* by Alberto Savinio (Andrea De Chirico).

3113 Carchia, Gianni. "Michele Perreira: un tragico postmoderno." (Michele Perreira: A Post-Modern Tragedian.) *IlCast.* 1996 ; 9(27): 139-140. Lang.: Ita.
Italy. 1994. Critical studies. ■Dramatic work of Michele Perreira.

3114 Collura, Matteo. *Il maestro di Regalpetra. Vita di Leonardo Sciascia.* (The Master of Regalpetra: The Life of Leonardo Sciascia.) Milan: Longanesi; 1996. 390 pp. (Il Cammeo 319.) Notes. Biblio. Illus.: Photo. B&W. 28. Lang.: Ita.
Italy. 1921-1989. Biographies. ■The biography of the Sicilian writer Leonardo Sciascia.

3115 Cope, Jackson I. *Secret Sharers in Italian Comedy: From Machiavelli to Goldoni.* Durham, NC/London: Duke UP; 1996. 221 pp. Notes. Index. Lang.: Eng.
Italy. 1522-1793. Critical studies. ■Secrecy as a plot device in Italian Renaissance comedy, with discussion of plays by Ruzzante, the 'Rozzi dramatists', Machiavelli, Cecchi, Grazzini, Fagiuoli, Maggi and Goldoni.

3116 Corsinovi, Graziella. *Diego Fabbri tra seduzione e rivelazione. Antologia teatrale.* (Diego Fabbri Between Revelation and Seduction.) Cinisiello Balsamo: San Pãolo; 1996. 190 pp. (Pinnacoli 5.) Biblio. Lang.: Ita.
Italy. 1911-1980. Critical studies. ■Brief study on the Italian Catholic dramatist Diego Fabbri, with a chronology of his life and works.

3117 Falco, Angela. "A proposito della prima rappresentazione della 'Figlia di Iorio'. Osservazioni sul gusto romanzesco negli studi teatrali." (The First Performance of *Iorio's Daughter*: Remark on Novelistic Sensibility in Theatrical Studies.) *IlCast.* 1996; 9(25): 29-40. Notes. Lang.: Ita.
Italy. 1904-1995. Histories-reconstruction. ■Challenges Valentina Valentini's reconstruction of the first performance of D'Annunzio's play on the grounds that her novelistic sensibility is misplaced in the analysis of documentation.

3118 Ferguson, Marcia L. "At Least 'They Are There': Dacia Maraini and Contemporary Italian Theatre." *WES.* 1995-96 Win; 7(3) : 85-87. Lang.: Eng.
Italy. 1995. Historical studies. ■Career of director/playwright Dacia Maraini.

3119 Ferrone, Siro; Bougé, Réjane, transl. "La Dramaturgie italienne de la fin du siècle." (Italian Playwriting at the End of the Century.) *JCT.* 1991; 59: 95-101. Illus.: Photo. B&W. 3. Lang.: Fre.
Italy. 1980-1991. Historical studies. ■Trends in Italy's most remarkable contemporary plays and playwrights.

3120 Gedda, Lido. "Alcesti di Samuele, il ventre che risucchia ed espelle." (*Alcesti di Samuele*: The Womb that Swallows Up

DRAMA: —Plays/librettos/scripts

and Discharges.) *IlCast.* 1996; 9(27): 61-78. Notes. Lang.: Ita.

Italy. 1891-1952. Critical studies. ■Analysis of the play by Alberto Savinio (Andrea De Chirico), with reference to its classical source, its avant-garde structure, and the author's response to femininity.

3121 Giani, Roberta. "Il teatro di Malaparte e la sua fortuna scenica." (Malaparte's Theatre and its Scenic Fortune.) *Ariel.* 1996; 11(1): 91-130. Notes. Lang.: Ita.

Italy. 1948-1954. Critical studies. ■Analysis of plays by Curzio Malaparte: *Du côté de chez Proust (Proust's Way)* and *Das Kapital*, both in French, and *Anche le donne hanno perso la guerra (Women Also Lost the War)*.

3122 Gramsci, Antonio; Mitchell, Tony, transl., intro. "Gramsci on Theatre." *NTQ.* 1996 Aug.; 12(47): 259-265. Notes. Lang.: Eng.

Italy. 1917-1932. Historical studies. ■Continues the series on early Marxist theatre criticism with two essays by the Italian philosopher Gramsci: a review of Ibsen's *Et Dukkehjem (A Doll's House,* 1917) and a discussion of Pirandello whose use of the power of abstract thought made him a potentially revolutionary playwright.

3123 Isotti Rosowsky, Giuditta. "Dittico 'Capitano Ulisse—a casa inspirata'." (The Diptych 'Captain Ulysse and *The Inspired House*.) *IlCast.* 1996; 9(27): 31-60. Notes. Lang.: Ita.

Italy. 1822-1852. Critical studies. ■Analysis of *Capitano Ulisse* and *Casa ispirata* by Alberto Savinio.

3124 Leslie, Robert W. "Sforza Oddi and the *Commedia Grave*: Setting the Stage for Shakespeare." *CompD.* 1996-97 Win; 30(4): 525-551. Notes. Lang.: Eng.

Italy. England. 1521. Critical studies. ■'Serious comedy' playwright and Renaissance humanist Sforza Oddi as a literary antecedent of Shakespeare, parallels between Oddi's *Erofilomachia* and *Love's Labour's Lost.*

3125 Luppichini, Francesca. "L'opera di Svevo sulla scena." (Svevo's Work on the Stage.) *Ariel.* 1996; 11(1): 139-187. Notes. Biblio. Lang.: Ita.

Italy. 1927-1996. Historical studies. ■The scenic fortune and misfortune of the theatrical works of the Italian writer Italo Svevo, a chronology of the Italian production and a bibliography of the reviews of every production.

3126 Mazzaro, Jerome. "Pirandello's *Sei Personaggi* and Expressive Form." *CompD.* 1996-97 Win; 30(4): 503-524. Notes. Lang.: Eng.

Italy. 1921. Critical studies. ■Author as disaffected God in Pirandello's approach to his *Sei personaggi in cerca d'autore (Six Characters in Search of an Author).*

3127 Mollica, Susanna. "Alberto Savinio e il teatro: una conferenza inedita." (Alberto Savinio and the Theatre: An Unpublished Lecture.) *IlCast.* 1996; 9(27): 119-136. Notes. Lang.: Ita.

Italy. 1926. Critical studies. ■Introduction to and analysis of an unpublished text by Alberto Savinio (Andrea De Chirico), with emphasis on the importance of theatre in Savinio's many artistic activities.

3128 Ortolani, Benito, transl., ed. *Pirandello's Love Letters to Marta Abba.* Princeton, NJ: Princeton UP; 1994. 371. Index. Biblio. Illus.: Photo. B&W. 31. Lang.: Eng.

Italy. 1925-1936. Histories-sources. ■Translation of a selection of Pirandello's letters to the actress, from *Lettere a Marta Abba,* ed. Ortolani (Milan: Mondadori, 1995).

3129 Perreira, Michele. "L'invisibile e la caducità." (The Invisible and Transiency.) *IlCast.* 1996; 9(27): 141-147. Lang.: Ita.

Italy. 1994. Histories-sources. ■Playwright reflects on the significance of writing for live theatre within a society of consumerism and performance.

3130 Pizza, Maria. *Il gesto, la parola, l'azione. Poetica, drammaturgia e storia dei monologhi di Dario Fo.* (Gesture, Word, Action. The Poetics, Dramaturgy, and History of Dario Fo's Monologues.) Rome: Bulzoni; 1996. 471 pp. (Biblioteca teatrale 90.) Pref. Index. Biblio. Discography. Illus.: Photo. B&W. Lang.: Ita.

Italy. 1926-1995. Critical studies. ■A study on the monologues written and acted by the Italian author-actor Dario Fo.

3131 Plaisance, Michel. "Su *La Mandragola* di Niccolò Machiavelli." (Some Notes about *The Mandrake* by Niccolò Machiavelli.) *IlCast.* 1996; 9(26): 27-35. Notes. Lang.: Ita.

Italy. 1518-1521. Critical studies. ■Argues for a later date of composition for the play, based on the author's anti-Savonarola stance, said to be reflected in the character Timoteo.

3132 Richard, Hélène. "Apparence de folie chez Pirandello." (Appearance of Madness in Pirandello.) *JCT.* 1991; 60: 23-29. Notes. Illus.: Photo. B&W. 3. Lang.: Fre.

Italy. 1903-1924. Critical studies. ■Various meanings of madness in plays of Luigi Pirandello, especially *Enrico IV (Henry IV).*

3133 Schächter, Elizabeth, ed. *Yearbook, nos. 15/16.* Canterbury: Univ. of Kent, for the Society for Pirandello Studies; 1996. 149 pp. Pref. Biblio. Notes. Illus.: Photo. B&W. 2. Lang.: Eng.

Italy. 1889-1995. Critical studies. ■Two articles in Italian reflect on the links between the Taviani brothers' film *Káos* and the short stories which inspired them, and examine the artistic relationship between Alberto Savinio (Andrea De Chirico) and Pirandello. Articles in English consider his correspondence with Marta Abba, female age and aging, adultery in the earlier plays, his approach to Buddhism, and a recent production of *All'uscita* by the Irish Chaos Company.

3134 Schmid, Julie. "Mina Loy's Futurist Theatre." *PerAJ.* 1996 Jan.; 18(1): 1-7. Notes. [Number 52.] Lang.: Eng.

Italy: Florence. 1905-1916. Critical studies. ■Career of avant-garde poet and playwright Mina Loy, with emphasis on the influence of Italian futurism during her stay in Florence.

3135 Scuderi, Antonio. "Framing and Improvisation in Dario Fo's *Johan Padan.*" *TA.* 1996; 49: 76-91. Lang.: Eng.

Italy. 1940-1996. Critical studies. ■Dario Fo's rejection of Aristotelian aesthetics in writing and performance, as reflected in his play *Johan Padan e la scoperta dell'America (Johan Padan and the Discovery of America).*

3136 Scuderi, Antonio. "Subverting Religious Authority: Dario Fo And Folk Laughter." *TextPQ.* 1996 July; 16(3): 216-232. Notes. Biblio. Illus.: Photo. B&W. 1. Lang.: Eng.

Italy. 1970-1995. Critical studies. ■Fo's use of folk tales and humor as a means of questioning and subverting the Catholic Church in his plays *Johan Padan* and *Il Papa e la strega (The Pope and the Witch).*

3137 Sinisi, Silvana. "L'ora, i luoghi, le stagioni nella 'Figlia di Iorio'." (Time, Place and Seasons in 'Iorio's Daughter'.) *IlCast.* 1996; 9(25): 17-27. Notes. Lang.: Ita.

Italy. 1904. Critical studies. ■The significance of the vernal and autumnal equinoxes that begin and end D'Annunzio's play.

3138 Tinterri, Alessandro. "Savinio e Ibsen." (Savinio and Ibsen.) *IlCast.* 1996; 9(27): 109-118. Notes. Lang.: Ita.

Italy. Norway. 1828-1952. Critical studies. ■The influence of Ibsen on Alberto Savinio (Andrea De Chirico), who wrote a critical biography of the Norwegian playwright.

3139 Toro, Alfonso de. "Die Tradition der 'Tragedia Con Fine Lieto' und der spanischen Tragikomödie bei Corneilles 'Le Cid,' 'Horace' und Cinna'." (The Tradition of 'Tragedy with a Happy Ending' and Spanish Tragicomedy in Corneille's *Le Cid, Horace,* and *Cinna*.) *MuK.* 1996; 2-4: 9-23. Notes. Lang.: Ger.

Italy. Spain. France. 1600-1641. Critical studies. ■A historical and systematic type pattern for mixed genres.

3140 Chang, Lan-joo. "Yeonkuksoge Duronan Kwolyeoge Hyoungtae." (Depiction of Power in Drama.) *KTR.* 1996 Feb.; 21(2): 30-32. Illus.: Photo. B&W. 7. Lang.: Kor.

Korea: Seoul. 1996. Critical studies. ■Analysis of *Nan, Keocheoleom Sagosipji Anta (I Don't Want to Live Like a Dog)* by theatre collective Kihwaengman Company and *Uliegenun Ddodarun Chungbuga Itda (There is Another Government for Us)* by Ulikuk Yeonguso Company in view of power structure. Discusses power structure via sex and money.

3141 Rizk, Beatriz J. "Post-estructuralismo y discurso teatral en la América Latina." (Poststructuralism and Theatrical Discourse in Latin America.) *Cjo.* 1996 Jan-June; 102: 22-27. Notes. Illus.: Photo. 8. Lang.: Spa.

DRAMA: —Plays/librettos/scripts

Latin America. 1985-1995. Critical studies. ■Elements of poststructuralism in Latin American plays of the last decade such as Antunes Filho's *Nova velha estoria (New Old Story)*, Mauricio Celedón's *Malasangre o las mil y una noches del poeta (Bitter Blood or The Thousand and One Nights of the Poet)*, Marco Antonio de la Parra's *Dédalo en el vientre de la bestia (In the Belly of the Beast)*, and La Candelaria's *El paso (The Pass)*.

3142　Seda, Laurietz. "De Conquistadores a Superheroes: Breve panorama del teatro postmoderno en Latinoamérica." (From Conquistadors to Superheroes: A Brief Overview of Postmodern Theatre in Latin America.) *Cjo.* 1996 Jan-June; 102: 9-14. Illus.: Sketches. 1. Lang.: Spa.
Latin America. 1994-1996. Critical studies. ■Postmodernism in today's Latin American theatre including playwrights Marco Antonio de la Parra of Chile, Rodolfo Santana of Venezuela, Joel Cano of Cuba, Roberto Ramos-Perea of Puerto Rico, Mauricio Kartun, Susana Torres Molina, and Diana Raznovich of Argentina, Sabina Berman of Mexico, and Consuelo de Castro of Brazil.

3143　Valdez, Pedro Antonio. "En busca del dramaturgo perdido." (In Search of the Lost Playwright.) *Cjo.* 1996 Jan-June; 102: 58-60. Illus.: Photo. 1. Lang.: Spa.
Latin America. 1995. Critical studies. ■A young playwright critiques the 'new' dramaturgy.

3144　Beardsell, Peter. "Crossing the Border in Three Plays by Hugo Salcedo." *LATR.* 1996 Spr; 29(2): 71-84. Notes. Biblio. Lang.: Eng.
Mexico. 1987-1990. Critical studies. ■Analysis of *El viaje de los cantores*, *Arde el desierto con los vientos que llegan del sur*, and *Sinfonía en una botella* by Hugo Salcedo. Their treatment of the crossing of the Mexican/U.S. border as exploration of identity—personal, cultural, and national.

3145　Magnarelli, Sharon. "Tea for Two: Performing History and Desire in Sabina Berman's *Entre Villa y una mujer desnuda*." *LATR.* 1996 Fall; 30(1): 55-74. Lang.: Eng.
Mexico. 1993. Critical studies. ■Analysis of Sabina Berman's play *Entre Villa y una mujer desnuda (Between Villa and a Naked Woman)* as demonstrating that gendered identity is a product of historical, gendered circumstances. Uses theoretical work of feminist critic Judith Butler to examine performance and citation, especially in the ritualistic serving and drinking of tea in one scene of the play.

3146　de Baar, Peter-Paul. "Herman Heijermans. Kamertjeszonde en getto-bestaan." (Herman Heijermans: Backroom Sins and Ghetto Life.) *OnsA.* 1996; 48(6): 160-165. Illus.: Photo. Color. 13. Lang.: Dut.
Netherlands: Amsterdam. 1892-1924. Biographical studies. ■Author Herman Heijermans, for whom the city of Amsterdam was a source of inspiration both as playwright and as journalist.

3147　Goedkoop, Hans. *Geluk. Het leven van Herman Heijermans.* (Happiness: The Life of Herman Heijermans.) Amsterdam/Antwerp: Arbeiderspers; 1996. 556 pp. Biblio. Index. Lang.: Dut.
Netherlands. 1864-1924. Biographies. ■The life of a major Dutch playwright and representative of social engagement in the theatre.

3148　Horwitz, Simi. "Wole Soyinka: Playwright/Provocateur." *TheaterW.* 1996 Oct 14; 10(11): 40-52. Illus.: Photo. B&W. 3. Lang.: Eng.
Nigeria. 1960-1996. Biographical studies. ■Profile and career of author Soyinka: American response to his work, socio-political influences on his writing, personal background.

3149　Jones, Joni L. "The Self as Other: Creating the Role of Joni the Ethnographer for *Broken Circles*." *TextPQ.* 1996 Apr.; 16(2): 131-145. Notes. Biblio. Illus.: Photo. B&W. 3. Lang.: Eng.
Nigeria: Osogbo. USA: Austin, TX. 1993-1994. Histories-sources. ■The development of the author's play based on her attendance at the Osum Festival in Osogbo: how performance gave her the distance to gain perspective on her conflicting feelings.

3150　Layiwola, Dele. "The Philosophy of Wole Soyinka's Art." *JDTC.* 1996 Spr; 10(2): 19-42. Notes. Illus.: Sketches. 2. Lang.: Eng.

Nigeria. 1960-1975. Critical studies. ■Soyinka's use of African aesthetics, found in ritual and festival dances, in his plays and poetry. Critically examines his epic poem *Idanre* as well as his plays *A Dance of the Forests* (1963), *Death and the King's Horseman* (1975), *The Road* (1965), and *The Bacchae of Euripides* (1973).

3151　Richards, Sandra. *Ancient Songs Set Ablaze: The Theatre of Femi Osofisan.* Washington, DC: Howard UP; 1996. 203 pp. Notes. Biblio. Index. Lang.: Eng.
Nigeria. 1960-1995. Critical studies. ■Examines Osofisan's major works and attempts to delineate major constructs of a theory of contemporary African theatre. Discusses *Farewell to a Cannibal Rage*, *Once Upon Four Robbers*, *A Restless Run of Locusts*, *Red Is the Freedom Road*, *No More the Wasted Breed*, *The Oriki of a Grasshopper*, and *Who's Afraid of Solarin*.

3152　Ukala, Sam. "'Folkism': Towards a National Aesthetic Principle for Nigerian Dramaturgy." *NTQ.* 1996 Aug.; 12(47): 279-287. Notes. Biblio. Lang.: Eng.
Nigeria. 1963-1996. Critical studies. ■Considers objections raised to English-language Nigerian plays and proposes the concept of 'folkism' as a national aesthetic principle—a way of reconciling the use of a common language with the distinctive and often disparate needs of the multilingual Nigerian people.

3153　Alter, Nora M. *Vietnam Protest Theatre: The Television War on Stage.* Bloomington, IN/Indianapolis, IN: Indiana UP; 1996. 225 pp. (Drama and Performance Studies.) Notes. Index. Append. Lang.: Eng.
North America. Europe. 1965-1971. Critical studies. ■Analysis of stage plays written and performed during the War in Vietnam that protest the war.

3154　Dévényi, Jutka. *Metonymy and Drama.* Lewisburg, VA/London: Bucknell UP/Associated Univ Presses; 1996. 120 pp. Index. Notes. Biblio. Lang.: Eng.
North America. Europe. 1600-1996. Critical studies. ■The impact of metonymy on the subject position of the main character in a drama with respect to the body on stage, the text and the overall dramaturgy. Examines four plays from four different periods: Webster's *The Duchess of Malfi*, Racine's *Phèdre*, Büchner's *Dantons Tod (Danton's Death)*, and Shakespeare's *Troilus and Cressida*.

3155　Andersen, Merete Morken. "At føde et barn og glemme det igen på vejen." (To Give Birth to a Child and Then Forget It.) *TE.* 1996 Sep.; 80: 14-15. Illus.: Photo. B&W. 1. Lang.: Dan.
Norway. 1995. ■An interview with playwright Cecilie Løveid about her work.

3156　Lépine, Stéphane. "Henrik Ibsen: La Révolte morale." (Henrik Ibsen: The Moral Revolt.) *JCT.* 1990; 57: 41-44 . Biblio. Illus.: Photo. B&W. 2. Lang.: Fre.
Norway. 1863-1899. Biographical studies. ■Overview of Ibsen's life and reflection of his political views in his plays.

3157　Petersen, Nils Holger. "'Diverse Galskaber' in Ibsen's *The Wild Duck*." *CompD.* 1996 Spr; 30(1): 41-71. Notes. Lang.: Eng.
Norway. 1884. Critical studies. ■Judeo-Christian symbolism in the conflicting personages of Gregers Werle and Dr. Relling, and the significance of the wild duck in Henrik Ibsen's *Vildanden*.

3158　Baniewicz, Elżbieta. "Polish Plays in the Post-Communist Countries." *TP.* 1995 Apr.; 37(2): 22-25. Illus.: Photo. B&W. 2. Lang.: Eng, Fre.
Poland. Czech Republic. Russia. 1989-1995. Critical studies. ■Popularity of Polish plays in Eastern Bloc countries after the fall of Communism.

3159　Błoński, Jan. *Wszystkie sztuki Sławomira Mrożka.* (All of Sławomir Mrożek's Plays.) Cracow: Wydawnictwo Literackie; 1995. 286 pp. Index. Notes. Biblio. Append. Lang.: Pol.
Poland. 1994. Critical studies. ■Analysis of Mrożek's dramatic work and its relationships with plays of Gombrowicz and Witkiewicz. Includes discussion of Mrożek and censorship.

3160　Filipowicz, Halina. "Textualizing Trauma: From Valesa to Kościuszko in Polish Theatre of the 1980s." *TJ.* 1996 Dec.; 48(4): 443-460. Notes. Biblio. Lang.: Eng.

DRAMA: —Plays/librettos/scripts

Poland. 1980-1989. Historical studies. ■Conflicting tendencies in Polish cultural mythology during the 1980s: the nature of defeat in Polish drama as seen in three plays, *Walesa (Valesa)* by Kazimierz Braun, *Alfa (Alpha)* by Sławomir Mrożek, and *Lekcja polskiego (A Polish Lesson)* by Anna Bojarska, all of which are responses to the defeat of the Solidarity movement in 1981.

3161 Grota, Marcin. "Różewicz, Kafka, Anonim." (Różewicz, Kafka, Anonymous.) *DialogW*. 1996; 10: 117-125. Lang.: Pol.

Poland. 1996. Critical studies. ■Motifs in Różewicz's work relating to Kafka.

3162 Hernik-Spalińska, Jagoda. "Rodzaju żeńskiego." (Feminine Gender.) *DialogW*. 1996; 3: 150-158. Lang.: Pol.

Poland. 1932-1938. Critical studies. ■Women's and feminist plays and reactions of male critics: discusses *Sprawa Moniki (Monica's Case)* by Maria Morozowicz-Szczepkowska, *Dom kobiet (Women's House)* by Zofia Nałkowska, and *Milcząca siła (Silent Power)* by Marcelina Grabowska.

3163 Komorowski, Jarosław. "Shakespeare and the Birth of Polish Romanticism: Vilna, 1786-1846." *ThR*. 1996; 21(2): 141-146. Notes. Lang.: Eng.

Poland. 1786-1846. Historical studies. ■The reception of Shakespeare in Poland up to mid-nineteenth century, highlighting influence on emergence of Polish Romanticism in Vilna. Discusses translations and includes some performance information.

3164 Komorowski, Jarosław. "'The Graves of Verona': Two Hundred Years of Polish Shakespeare." *TP*. 1996 Oct.; 38(4): 42-46. Illus.: Photo. B&W. 2. Lang.: Eng, Fre.

Poland. 1796-1868. Historical studies. ■Analysis of Louis-Sébastian Mercier's adaptation of Shakespeare's *Romeo and Juliet, Les Tombeaux de Verona (The Graves of Verona)*. This French version was performed on the Polish stage from 1796 until 1868 when the first English-to-Polish translation of the actual text appeared, penned by Leon Rudkiewicz.

3165 Krajewska, Anna. "Dramat niemożliwego dramatu." (The Drama of the Impossible Drama.) 64-80 in Wąchocka, Ewa, ed. *Od symbolizmu do post-teatru*. Warsaw: Fundacja Astronomii Polskiej; 1996. 256 pp. Lang.: Pol.

Poland. 1960-1996. Critical studies. ■Analysis of experimental theatre techniques of Tadeusz Kantor, Bogusław Schaeffer, and Tadeusz Różewicz.

3166 Krajewska, Anna. *Dramat i teatr absurdu w Polsce.* (The Theatre and Drama of the Absurd in Poland.) Poznań: Wydawnictwo Naukowe Uniwersytetu im A. Mickiewicza; Pref. Notes. Index. Append. Lang.: Pol.

Poland. 1920-1990. Critical studies. ■The origin and evolution of the theatre of the absurd in Poland in the context of twentieth-century culture. Discusses work of Witkiewicz, Gombrowicz, Białoszewski, Różewicz, and Mrożek.

3167 Lewko, Marian. *Obecność Skandynawów w polskiej kulturze teatralnej w latach 1876-1918.* (Scandinavian Literature in Polish Theatrical Culture, 1876-1918.) Lublin: Redakcja Wydawnictw Katolickiego Uniwersytetu Lubelskiego; 1996. 848 pp. Pref. Notes. Biblio. Index. Tables. Lang.: Pol.

Poland. Scandinavia. 1876-1918. Histories-specific. ■The Polish reception and staging of Scandinavian drama and its impact on Polish theatre, literature, and consciousness.

3168 Owxczarek, Wojciech. *Diabeł w dramacie polskim. Z dziejów motywu.* (The Devil in Polish Drama: From the History of the Motif.) Gdańsk: Wydawnictwo Uniwersytetu Gdańskiego; 1996. 115 pp. Biblio. Lang.: Pol.

Poland. 1832-1957. Critical studies. ■The devil in plays of Adam Mickiewicz, Zygmunt Krasiński, Juliusz Słowacki, Tadeusz Miciński, Stanisław Ignacy Witkiewicz, and Witold Gombrowicz.

3169 Rudziński, Zbigniew. "Five Proposals for the Children's Theatre." *TP*. 1996 July; 38(3): 38-43. Illus.: Photo. Color. B&W. 2. Lang.: Eng, Fre.

Poland. 1996. Critical studies. ■Five suggested play scenarios for a children's theatre to perform: *Mama-Nic (Mum-Nothing)* by Andrzej Maleszka, *Rycerz niezłomny (The Indomitable Knight)* by Maciej Wojtyszko, *Pokój do wynajęcia (A Room to Let)* by Anna Onichimowska,

Wszyscy kochamy Barbie (We All Love Barbie) by Jerzy Niemczuk, and *Baśń o złym śmiechu (A Tale of Evil Laughter)* by Liliana Bardijewska.

3170 Sadowska-Guillon, Irène. "Le Théâtre subversif de Witold Gombrowicz." (The Subversive Theatre of Witold Gombrowicz.) *JCT*. 1989; 53: 7-12. Illus.: Photo. B&W. 2. Lang.: Fre.

Poland. France. Argentina. 1904-1989. Biographical studies. ■Life of Witold Gombrowicz, thematic and formal characteristics of his plays, and posthumous productions of his work.

3171 Sieradzki, Jacek. "New Polish Plays." *TP*. 1995 Oct.; 37(4): 49-52. Illus.: Photo. B&W. 1. Lang.: Eng, Fre.

Poland. 1995. Critical studies. ■Very brief analysis of five new plays: Anna Strońska's *Nocne życie (Night Life)*, Asja Lamtiugina's *Pies (A Dog)*, Jan Krzysztofcyk's *Święcone na pół (Easter)*, Rafał Maciąg's *Blazen (The Fool)*, and *Młoda śmierć (Young Death)* by Grzegorz Nawrocki.

3172 Sieradzki, Jacek. "Janusz Krasiński: *The Burning Bush*." *TP*. 1996 Jan.; 38(1): 44-45. Lang.: Eng, Fre.

Poland. 1995. Critical studies. ■Brief analysis of Janusz Krasiński's play *Krzak gorejacy (The Burning Bush)*.

3173 Sieradzki, Jacek. "New Polish Plays." *TP*. 1996 Apr.; 38(2): 45-49. Illus.: Photo. B&W. 2. Lang.: Eng, Fre.

Poland. 1996. Critical studies. ■Analysis of *Cud na Greenpoincie (A Greenpoint Miracle)* by Edward Redliński, and *Semiramida* by Maciej Wojtyszko.

3174 Sieradzki, Jacek. "Ewa Lachnit: *Man from the Garbage Dump*." *TP*. 1996 Oct.; 38(4): 52-53. Lang.: Eng, Fre.

Poland. 1996. Critical studies. ■Analysis of Ewa Lichnit's debut play *Człowiek ze śmieci (Man from the Garbage Dump)*.

3175 Sieradzki, Jacek. "New Polish Plays." *TP*. 1995 Apr.; 37(2): 40-43. Illus.: Photo. B&W. 1. Lang.: Eng, Fre.

Poland. 1995. Critical studies. ■Analyses of two new Polish plays, Paweł Huelle's *Kto Mówi O Czekaniu (Who's Talking About Waiting?)* and Marek Biszczanik's *Goguly*.

3176 Sieradzki, Jacek. "New Polish Plays." *TP*. 1995 July; 37(3): 40-41. Lang.: Eng, Fre.

Poland. 1995. Critical studies. ■Analysis of Władysław Terlecki's new play *Mateczka (Little Mother)*.

3177 Sugiera, Małgorzata. *Dramaturgia Sławomira Mrożka.* (The Dramaturgy of Sławomir Mrożek.) Cracow: Universitas; 1996. 295 pp. Pref. Notes. Biblio. Index. Append. Lang.: Pol.

Poland. 1994. Critical studies. ■Analysis of Mrożek's plays in the context of European theatre of the absurd and contemporary Eastern drama.

3178 Montañez, Carmen L. "Un aparte con Roberto Ramos-Perea." (An Aside with Roberto Ramos-Perea.) *LATR*. 1996 Fall; 30 (1): 97-104. Lang.: Spa.

Puerto Rico. 1991-1992. Histories-sources. ■Interview with Puerto Rican playwright Roberto Ramos-Perea on his plays, their place in the dramaturgy of Hispanic America and the difficulty of having his plays produced in the United States.

3179 Seda, Laurietz. "Modernidad y postmodernidad en *Mistiblú* de Roberto Ramos-Perea." (Modernism and Postmodernism in Roberto Ramos-Perea's *Mistiblú*.) *Gestos*. 1996 Nov.; 11(22): 105-122. Notes. Biblio. Illus.: Photo. B&W. 2. Lang.: Spa.

Puerto Rico. 1990. Critical studies. ■Modernism and postmodernism in Ramos-Perea's theatrical *roman à clef*, with each 'ism' represented by various figures in history.

3180 Berry, Jon M. "The Dramatic Incarnation of Will in Seneca's *Medea*." *JDTC*. 1996 Spr; 10(2): 3-18. Notes. Lang.: Eng.

Roman Empire. 30-60. Critical studies. ■Reevaluation of the play through the hypothesis of a highly physicalized staging that allows the play its full voice.

3181 Munk, Erika. "Word Migrations." *ThM*. 1996; 26(3): 51-52. Lang.: Eng.

Romania. USA. 1990-1996. Histories-sources. ■Interview with Romanian playwright Oana Hock Cajal regarding the political climate for theatre post-Ceauşescu, and her first English-language play *Berlin/Berlin*.

DRAMA: —Plays/librettos/scripts

3182 Al', D.N. *Osnovy dramaturgii: Učebnoe posobie dlja studentov vozov kul'tury i iskusstv.* (Fundamentals of Dramaturgy: Study Book for Students in Colleges of Art and Culture.) St. Petersburg: Gosudarstvennaja Akademija kul'tury; 1995. 64 pp. Lang.: Rus.
Russia. 1995. Instructional materials. ■Textbook on the problems of dramaturgy: a contemporary view of dramaturgy as art, analysis of the characteristics of the genre.

3183 Binevič, E. "Neždannaja nachodka." (An Unexpected Find.) *SovD.* 1996; 3: 220-224. Lang.: Rus.
Russia: St. Petersburg. 1886-1958. Critical studies. ■Theatrical works of Jévgenij L. Švarc.

3184 Binevič, E. "Na puti k 'Drakonu'." (The Way to the Dragon.) *Neva.* 1996; 10: 171-181. Lang.: Rus.
Russia: St. Petersburg. 1896-1958. Critical studies. ■Career path of dramatist Jévgenij Švarc.

3185 Bogomolova, O. "Kukol'nyj dom." (A Doll's House.) *SovD.* 1996; 3: 201-206. Lang.: Rus.
Russia: Moscow. 1990-1996. Critical studies. ■Analysis of plays by Michajl Ugarov.

3186 Cekinovskij, B. "'My pretenduem na to, čtoby nazyvat'sja professionalami'." (We Demand to Be Called Professionals.) *TeatZ.* 1996; 8: 48-52. Lang.: Rus.
Russia: Moscow. 1990-1996. Histories-sources. ■Interview with young playwrights including Elena Kuznecova, Jurij Andrejčuk, and Vladimir D'jačenko about their work.

3187 Dmitrievskij, V. "Zerkalo dlja geroja." (Mirror for a Hero.) *SovD.* 1996; 3: 178-187. Lang.: Rus.
Russia. 1980-1996. Critical studies. ■The reflection of recent political processes in contemporary Russian dramaturgy.

3188 Érnandez, Elena. "Eres' ljubvi." (Gibberish of Love.) *SovD.* 1996; 1: 169-174. Lang.: Rus.
Russia. 1990-1996. Critical studies. ■Analysis of plays by Marija Arbatova, including *Vsatije Bastilii (The Taking of the Bastille)* and *Uravnenije s dvumja neizvestnimi (Equation with Two Unknowns).*

3189 Gorfunkel', E. "Žil-byl Saša Popov." (Once Upon a Time There Lived Saša Popov.) *SovD.* 1996; 2: 173-180. Lang.: Rus.
Russia: St. Petersburg. 1951-1995. Biographical studies. ■Career of dramatist Aleksand'r Popov, author of *Nasledstvo (Inheritance)* in 1973 and *Carstvo (Kingdom)* in 1993.

3190 Kolesnikov, A. "Rossiej interesuetes'?" (Are You Interested in Russia?) *TeatZ.* 1996; 8: 36-37. Lang.: Rus.
Russia: Moscow. 1990-1996. Critical studies. ■Analysis of *Usmirenye Badadoškina (The Taming of Badodoshkin)* by Leonid Leonov.

3191 Lehmann, Barbara. "Pop-Art, Soz-Art, Sorokin." *DB.* 1996; 2: 30-33. Illus.: Photo. B&W. 4. Lang.: Ger.
Russia. Germany. 1955-1996. Biographical studies. ■Portrait of playwright Vladimir Sorokin and his status as a cult figure in Germany, where his plays are frequently performed.

3192 Moskvina, T. "I mužčiny ljubit' umejut (O ljubvi v pjesach A.N. Ostrovskogo)." (And Men Can Love: On Love in the Plays of Ostrovskij.) *TeatZ.* 1996; 2: 8-9. Lang.: Rus.
Russia. 1823-1886. Critical studies. ■Analysis of works of A.N. Ostrovskij, with reference to problem statements in his plays.

3193 Moskvina, T. "Istoričeskij moralizm A.N. Ostrovskogo." (Historical Moralism of A.N. Ostrovskij.) *PTZ.* 1996; 10: 62-72. Lang.: Rus.
Russia. 1823-1886. Critical studies. ■Analysis of national consciousness in Ostrovskij's plays.

3194 Pavlinov, S.A. *Tajnopis' Gogolja: 'Revizor'.* (Gogol's Secret Manuscript: *The Inspector General*.) Moscow: n.p.; 1996. 64 pp. Lang.: Rus.
Russia: Moscow. 1835-1836. Historical studies. ■Analysis of Gogol's comedy.

3195 Perkins, Owen. "Beyond Perestroika." *DGQ.* 1996 Fall; 33(3): 16-23. Lang.: Eng.
Russia. 1996. Histories-sources. ■Interview with Russian playwright Aleksand'r Galin about his work and the future of Russian theatre.

3196 Pokrovskaja, E. "Cikličeskie processy v dramaturgii Novogo i novejšego vremeni." (Cyclical Processes in the Dramaturgy of the New and Newer Times.) *SovD.* 1996; 1: 186-190. Lang.: Rus.
Russia. 1500-1996. Critical studies. ■Comparative analysis of the dynamics of dramatic elements as a method for learning the history of dramaturgy. Continued in *SovD* 2 (1996), 181-185, with discussion of the history theory of drama since the Renaissance.

3197 Poplavskij, V. "Struktura dramatičeskogo konflikta i akterskie amplua." (The Structure of Dramatic Conflict and Actors' Specialties.) *SovD.* 1996; 4: 188-199. Lang.: Rus.
Russia: Moscow. 1996. Critical studies. ■Analysis of the system of characters in dramaturgy, the aesthetic requirements of a play, the story line, and the building of a play on stage.

3198 Ptuškina, Nadežda. "Sveči, zažženje v teatre Stanislavskogo." (Candles Lit in the Stanislavskij Theatre.) *TeatZ.* 1996; 11-12: 14-17. Lang.: Rus.
Russia: Moscow. 1980-1996. Histories-sources. ■Dramatist discusses her plays and career.

3199 Rassadin, S. "Dela famil'nye." (Familiar Matters.) *TeatZ.* 1996; 5: 3-6. Lang.: Rus.
Russia: Moscow. 1996. Critical studies. ■Theatre as a school for the Russian language: analysis of the language of A.N. Ostrovskij.

3200 Rudnev, P. "Doroga v žutkoe prostranstvo." (A Road into a Horrible Space.) *SovD.* 1996; 4: 200-211. Lang.: Rus.
Russia: Moscow. 1921. Critical studies. ■Analysis of Sergej Esenin's *Pugačev.*

3201 Sal'nikova, E. "Uslovnyj bezyslovnyj mir." (Conditional Unconditional World.) *SovD.* 1996; 3: 188-200. Lang.: Rus.
Russia. 1990-1996. Critical studies. ■Survey of the dramaturgy of the 1990s.

3202 Šavrygin, S.M. *Tvorčestvo A.A. Šachovskogo v istoriko-literaturnom processe 1800-1840-ch godov.* (A.A. Šachovskij's Work on the Historical Literary Process, 1800-1840.) St. Petersburg: RAN; 1996. 180 pp. Lang.: Rus.
Russia. 1777-1846. Critical studies. ■Analysis of works by writer and dramatist Aleksand'r A. Šachovskij, comparison with those of Gribojédov, Gogol, and Puškin.

3203 Sokolov, B.V. *Bulgakovskaja énciklopedija.* (The Bulgakov Encyclopedia.) Moscow: Lorid/Mif; 1996. 592 pp. Lang.: Rus.
Russia: Moscow. 1891-1940. Biographies. ■The life of the writer and his unpublished play *Synovja Mully (The Sons of Mulla).*

3204 Starosel'skaja, N. "V bezdnach skryvaetsja novoe dno..." (In the Depths a New Bottom Is Hidden.) *TeatZ.* 1996; 8: 13-17. Lang.: Rus.
Russia: Moscow. 1996. Critical studies. ■The characters of A.N. Ostrovskij in contemporary theatre life.

3205 Starosel'skaja, N. "Osvetitel' spektaklja žizni." (Lighting Specialist for the Play of Life.) *VLit.* 1996; 5: 36-55. Lang.: Rus.
Russia. 1854-1958. Critical studies. ■The influence of A.V. Suchovo-Kobylin on playwright Michajl Zoščenko.

3206 Višnevskaja, I. *Aplodismenty v prošloe. A.P. Sumarokov i ego tragedii.* (Applause for the Past: A.P. Sumarokov and His Tragedies.) Moscow: Izdatel'stvo Literaturnogo instituta im. A.M. Gorkogo; 1996. 262 pp. Lang.: Rus.
Russia: St. Petersburg. 1717-1777. Historical studies. ■Research on the dramaturgy of Aleksand'r P. Sumarokov.

3207 Zlobina, A. "Platoničeskij teat'r." (Platonic Theatre.) *NovyjMir.* 1996; 8: 209-213. Lang.: Rus.
Russia: Moscow. 1970-1996. Critical studies. ■Analysis of the plays of Michajl Uvarov.

3208 Čokl, Sonja. *Šolske ure z Antigono Dominika Smoleta—za učence.* (School Lessons with Dominik Smole's *Antigona*—for Students.) Ljubljana: Zavod Republike Slovenije za Šolstvo in sport; 1996. 98 pp. Lang.: Slo.

DRAMA: —Plays/librettos/scripts

Slovenia. 1996. Instructional materials. ■A method for understanding modern Slovene drama classics and for creative home and school analysis and interpretation, using Smole's *Antigona*. Intended for students.

3209 Čokl, Sonja. *Šolske ure z Antigono Dominika Smoleta—za učitelje.* (School Lessons with Dominik Smole's *Antigona*—for School Teachers.) Ljubljana: Zavod Republike Slovenije za Šolstvo in sport; 1996. 129 pp. Lang.: Slo.
Slovenia. 1996. Instructional materials. ■A method for understanding modern Slovene drama classics and for creative home and school analysis and interpretation using Smole's *Antigona*. Intended for teachers.

3210 Jovanović, Dušan. *Paberki.* (Gleanings.) Ljubljana: Mestno gledališče ljubljansko; 1996. 220 pp. (The Ljubljana City Theatre Library 123.) Lang.: Slo.
Slovenia. 1986-1996. Histories-sources. ■Reflections of a playwright and director on recent Slovene drama and theatre.

3211 Jovanović, Dušan, et al.; Svetina, Ivo, ed. *Dominik Smole.* Ljubljana: Nova Revija; 1996. 291 pp. Biblio. Illus.: Photo. B&W. Lang.: Slo.
Slovenia. 1959-1995. Critical studies. ■Collection of articles by scholars and theatre professionals about the work of playwright Dominik Smole.

3212 Kermauner, Taras. *Blagor blata.* (Welfare of Mud.) Ljubljana: SGFM; 1996. 318 pp., 259 pp. [2 vols.] Lang.: Slo.
Slovenia. 1900-1996. Critical studies. ■Analysis of plays by Marko Kremžar, Ivan Cankar, Dušan Jovanović, and Ivan Mrak in Volume I, *Rdeči brat (The Red Brother)*, and by Boris A. Novak in Volume II, *Rdeče zlata zgodovina (Red Golden History)*.

3213 Kermauner, Taras. *Od bratovščine k bratomoru II, Zbogom zvezde.* (From Brotherhood to Fratricide II: Goodbye Stars.) Ljubljana: SGFM; 1996. 359 pp. Lang.: Slo.
Slovenia. 1900-1996. Critical studies. ■Analysis of dramatic works of Jože Javoršek, Tone Partljič, Borivoj Wudler, Bojan Stih, Anton Tomaž Linhart, Dominik Smole and France Bevk. With summaries of twenty-five dramatic works by Alenka Goljevšček.

3214 Lado. "Dve drami o prvi svetovni vojni." (Two Dramas about the First World War.) *PrimK.* 1996; 19(1): 95-105. Lang.: Slo.
Slovenia. Germany. 1918-1922. Critical studies. ■Comparison of *Seeschlacht (Sea Battle)* by Reinhard Goering and *V globini (In the Deep)* by France Bevk.

3215 Novak, Boris A., ed. *Dane Zajc.* Ljubljana: Nova revija; 1995. 233 pp. Biblio. Illus.: Photo. B&W. Lang.: Slo.
Slovenia. 1958-1995. Critical studies. ■Collection of articles by scholars and theatre professionals on the work of poet and playwright Dane Zajc.

3216 Poniž, Denis, ed. *Žrtve, rablji in ... popotovanje po deželi Strniševih Ljudožercev.* (Victims, Hangmen and ... a Journey through Strniša's Land of Cannibals.) Ljubljana: AGRFT; 1996. 131 pp. Illus.: Photo. B&W. Lang.: Slo.
Slovenia. 1996. Critical studies. ■A collection of dramaturgical analyses of the dramatic work *Ljudožerci (The Cannibals)* G. Strniša's performed as a collective project by students of Ljubljana's Academy at the Seminar of the Slovene drama history.

3217 Saksida, Igor. "Vrste mladinske dramatike in mladinske gledališke igre." (Types of Youth Drama and the Youth Play.) *Oik.* 1996; 41(1, 2): 5-25, 5-24. Lang.: Slo.
Slovenia. 1872-1996. Historical studies. ■History of the Slovene youth play, with establishment of theoretical terminology and analysis of playtexts published in books and magazines for youth.

3218 Saksida, Igor. "Začetki slovenske mladinske dramatike—od prvih besedil (1872) do J. Stritarja." (The Beginnings of the Slovene Youth Dramatics—from the First Texts (1872) to J. Stritar.) *SlavR.* 1996; 44(2): 179-192. Biblio. Lang.: Slo.
Slovenia. 1872-1929. Historical studies. ■Early Slovene youth theatre, including ethical and educational plays by F. Fralj, F.S. Finžgar, and J. Stritar.

3219 Bosch, Barbara. "Powerspeak in Rezá de Wet's *Diepe Grond.*" *SATJ.* 1995 May; 9(1): 79-88. Notes. Biblio. Lang.: Eng.
South Africa, Republic of. 1988. Critical studies. ■Linguistic analysis of the play illustrating gender relations in the text.

3220 Colleran, Jeanne. "Re-Situating Fugard: Re-Thinking Revolutionary Theatre." *SATJ.* 1995 Sep.; 9(2): 39-49. Biblio. Lang.: Eng.
South Africa, Republic of. 1948-1994. Critical studies. ■Examination of Athol Fugard's *Statements after an Arrest under the Immorality Act*, with the focus on the place of revolutionary theatre after the revolution.

3221 Huismans, Anja; Finestone, Juanita. "Interview: Rezá de Wet." *SATJ.* 1995 May; 9(1): 89-95. Lang.: Eng.
South Africa, Republic of. 1988-1995. Histories-sources. ■Interview with playwright, actress, director Rezá de Wet about her experiences and her play *Diepe grond (Deep Ground)*.

3222 Kruger, Loren. "New African Drama and National Representation in South Africa: Notes from the 1930s to the Present Moment." 123-141 in Reinelt, Janelle, ed. *Crucibles of Crisis: Performing Social Change.* Ann Arbor, MI: Univ of Michigan P; 1996. 250 pp. Notes. Lang.: Eng.
South Africa, Republic of. 1930-1995. Critical studies. ■The revival of plays by Herbert Dhlomo, a pioneer of modern Black drama, including *The Girl Who Killed to Save, Cetshwayo, The Workers* and *The Pass.*

3223 Loots, Lliane. "'The Personal is Political': Gender in the Context of Apartheid South Africa: A Look at Two Women Playwrights." *SATJ.* 1996 May; 10(1): 63-70. Notes. Biblio. Lang.: Eng.
South Africa, Republic of. 1945-1996. Critical studies. ■Gender oppression under apartheid in *Have You Seen Zandile?* by Gcina Mhlophe and *Curl Up and Dye* by Sue Pam-Grant.

3224 O'Brien, Anthony. "Staging Whiteness: Beckett, Havel, Maponya." 143-164 in Reinelt, Janelle, ed. *Crucibles of Crisis: Performing Social Change.* Ann Arbor, MI: Univ of Michigan P; 1996. 250 pp. Notes. Lang.: Eng.
South Africa, Republic of. 1930-1995. Critical studies. ■Maishe Maponya's use of Beckett's *Catastrophe* and Havel's *Chyba (Mistake)* in his play *Gangsters* as a strategy of postcolonial theatre.

3225 Worthen, W.B. "Convicted Reading: *The Island*, Hybridity, Performance." 165-184 in Reinelt, Janelle, ed. *Crucibles of Crisis: Performing Social Change.* Ann Arbor, MI: Univ of Michigan P; 1996. 250 pp. Notes. Lang.: Eng.
South Africa, Republic of. 1968-1974. Critical studies. ■The use of absurdism in *The Island* by Athol Fugard, in collaboration with the actors who helped create the piece, John Kani and Winston Ntshona, to illustrate the dehumanizing experience of prison life.

3226 Abraham, James T. "The Other Speaks: Tirso de Molina's *Amazonas en las Indias.*" 143-161 in Simerka, Barbara, ed. *El arte nuevo de estudiar comedias: Literary Theory and Spanish Golden Age Drama.* London: Associated Univ. Presses; 1996. 260 pp. Notes. Index. Biblio. Lang.: Eng.
Spain. 1635. Critical studies. ■Semiotic analysis of Tirso de Molina's *Amazonas en las Indias (Amazons in the Indies)* as a reflection of Spanish colonialism.

3227 Allinson, M.E. *Metatheatre in Spain (1900-1936): Theatre within Theatre and Theatre about Theatre in the Work of Valle-Inclán and García Lorca.* Ph.D. thesis, *Index to theses*, 45-6136. Leeds: Univ. of Leeds; 1994. Notes. Biblio. Lang.: Eng.
Spain. 1900-1936. Critical studies. ■Aims to bring twentieth-century Spanish theatre into the wider context of European modernism by showing how it exemplifies 'self-reliance', i.e., metatheatre.

3228 Burton, Grace M. "Deconstruction and the *Comedia*: The Case for *Peribáñez.*" 21-35 in Simerka, Barbara, ed. *El arte nuevo de estudiar comedias: Literary Theory and Spanish Golden Age Drama.* London: Associated Univ. Presses; 1996. 260 pp. Notes. Index. Biblio. Lang.: Eng.
Spain. 1580-1680. Critical studies. ■A deconstructionist analysis of Lope de Vega's *Peribáñez y el Comendador de Ocaña.*

3229 de Armas, Frederick A. "Painting and Graffiti: (Sub) Versions of History in Golden Age Theatre (Notes on Cervantes and Claramonte)." *Gestos.* 1996 Apr.; 11(21): 83-101. Notes. Biblio. Lang.: Eng.
Spain. 1492-1650. Historical studies. ■Political and social function of painting and graffiti in Cervantes' *El Cerco de Numancia (The Siege of*

DRAMA: —Plays/librettos/scripts

Numancia) and Claramonte's *El Infante de Aragón (The Prince of Aragón).*

3230 de Armas, Frederick A. "The Necromancy of Imitation: Lucan and Cervantes's *La Numancia.*" 246-258 in Simerka, Barbara, ed. *El arte nuevo de estudiar comedias: Literary Theory and Spanish Golden Age Drama.* London: Associated Univ. Presses; 1996. 260 pp. Notes. Index. Biblio. Lang.: Eng.

Spain. 1580-1590. Critical studies. ■Mythical substructures and the imitation of the classics can be found in Cervantes' *El Cerco de Numancia,* in which he imitates Lucan.

3231 Feldman, Sharon G. "*Los gatos (The Cats):* Gómez-Arco's Spectacle of Sacrifice." *Estreno.* 1995; 21(1): 38-44. Illus.: Photo. B&W. 3. Lang.: Eng.

Spain: Madrid. 1965-1993. Critical studies. ■Agustín Gómez-Arco's *Los gatos (The Cats)* as a post-civil war allegory, with attention to the internalization of oppressive authority and Georges Bataille's connection of death and sensuality. Discusses a 1993 production at the Festival de Octubre.

3232 Fernández Insuela, Antonio. "Un peculiar drama histórico de Rodríguez Méndez: *Isabelita tiene ángel.*" (A Peculiar Historic Drama by Rodríguez Méndez: *Isabelita Has an Angel.*) *Estreno.* 1994; 20(1): 7-9. Lang.: Spa.

Spain. 1976. Critical studies. ■Analysis of *Isabelita tiene Ángel (Isabelita Has an Angel)* by José María Rodríguez Méndez with attention to the humanizing effect of the fantasized angel on the character of Queen Isabella.

3233 Fischer, Susan L. "Reader Response, Iser, and *La estrella de Sevilla.*" 86-104 in Simerka, Barbara, ed. *El arte nuevo de estudiar comedias: Literary Theory and Spanish Golden Age Drama.* London: Associated Univ. Presses; 1996. 260 pp. Notes. Index. Biblio. Lang.: Eng.

Spain. 1600-1620. Critical studies. ■Intratextual readings 'performed' by three characters in the anonymous *La estrella de Sevilla* reveal ways in which the reading process itself might function as a textual strategy through which the subversive nature of the play may emerge.

3234 Fox, Dian. "The Literary Use of History: *El médico de su honra* in Context." 206-232 in Simerka, Barbara, ed. *El arte nuevo de estudiar comedias: Literary Theory and Spanish Golden Age Drama.* London: Associated Univ. Presses; 1996. 260 pp. Notes. Index. Biblio. Lang.: Eng.

Spain. 1622. Critical studies. ■Analysis of Calderón's *El médico de su honra (Physician to His Own Honour)* in its historical context.

3235 Friedman, Edward H. "Theater Semiotics and Lope de Vega's *El caballero de Olmedo.*" 66-85 in Simerka, Barbara, ed. *El arte nuevo de estudiar comedias: Literary Theory and Spanish Golden Age Drama.* London: Associated Univ. Presses; 1996. 260 pp. Notes. Index. Biblio. Lang.: Eng.

Spain. 1620-1625. Critical studies. ■Semiotics and the analysis of Lope de Vega's *El caballero de Olmedo (The Knight of Olmedo).*

3236 Gabriele, John P. "Breve encuentro con Manuel Martínez Mediero." (Brief Encounter with Manuel Martínez Mediero.) *Estreno.* 1995; 21(1): 45-47. Illus.: Photo. B&W. 1. Lang.: Spa.

Spain. 1939-1993. Histories-sources. ■1993 interview with playwright Martínez Mediero about his reasons for writing plays and his efforts to make theatre coincide with social change. Refers to his plays *El bébé furioso (The Furious Baby)* and *Las hermanas de Búfalo Bill (Buffalo Bill's Sisters).*

3237 García Verdugo, Julia. "Temática y forma en el teatro de las mujeres de España." (Theme and Form in Spanish Women's Theatre.) *Estreno.* 1995; 21(1): 17-18, 23. Lang.: Spa.

Spain. 1983-1990. Critical studies. ■The development of women's theatre in Spain, with analysis of María Manuelo Reina's 1984 *La libertad esclava (Enslaved Liberty),* Maribel Lázaro's 1985 *Humo de beleño (Henbane Smoke),* Paloma Pedrero's 1988 *Invierno de luna alegre (Happy Moon Winter)* and Pilar Pombo's *No nos escribos más canciones (Don't Write Us Any More Songs)* from 1990.

3238 González, Bernardo Antonio. "Teatro Nacional Popular: Sobre la Teoría y Práctica de José María Rodríguez Méndez." (Popular National Theatre: On the Theory and Practice of José María Rodríguez Méndez.) *Estreno.* 1994; 20(1): 29-34. Illus.: Photo. B&W. 2. Lang.: Spa.

Spain. 1965. Critical studies. ■Analyzes works of José María Rodríguez Méndez as portraying the political transition marked by Francisco Franco's death. Details the playwright's attempt to unite theory and practice and his belief that a national theatre must be essentially Marxist.

3239 Halsey, Martha T. "José María Rodríguez Méndez: Bibliografía selecta." (José María Rodríguez Méndez: Select Bibliography.) *Estreno.* 1994; 20(1): 35-37, 52. Lang.: Spa.

Spain. 1946. Bibliographical studies. ■Bibliography, including works and critical material.

3240 Harris, Carolyn J. "La perspectiva femenina en Escena: *Allá Él* de Concha Romero." (The Feminine Perspective in Performance: Concha Romero's *It's Up to Him.*) *Estreno.* 1994; 20(1): 5-6. Lang.: Spa.

Spain. 1989. Critical studies. ■Contrasts the masculine monologue of Romero Pineda's unproduced *¿Tengo razón o no? (Am I Right or Not?)* with the feminine counterpart in *Allá él (It's Up to Him)* in order to explore the playwright's interest in personal identity as determined and shaped by gender roles.

3241 Harris, Carolyn J. "Concha Romero: Bibliografía Selecta." (Concha Romero: Select Bibliography.) *Estreno.* 1994; 20(1) : 7. Lang.: Spa.

Spain. 1989-1994. Bibliographical studies. ■Bibliography of Concha Romero (Concha Romero Pineda), including dramatic works and criticism.

3242 Larson, Catherine. "The Visible and the Hidden: Speech Act Theory and Cervantes's *El retablo de las maravillas.*" 52-65 in Simerka, Barbara, ed. *El arte nuevo de estudiar comedias: Literary Theory and Spanish Golden Age Drama.* London: Associated Univ. Presses; 1996. 260 pp. Notes. Index. Biblio. Lang.: Eng.

Spain. 1615. Critical studies. ■Speech act theory in Cervantes's *El retablo de las maravillas:* the characters' linguistic behavior plays a significant role in determining their fates.

3243 Leonard, Candyce. "Role-Playing in Concha Romero's *A Damn Kiss (Un maldito beso).*" *Estreno.* 1994; 20(1): 15-17. Lang.: Eng.

Spain. 1989. Critical studies. ■The problem of maintaining personal identity within the context of socially constructed marriage roles in Concha Romero Pineda's *Un maldito beso (A Damn Kiss).*

3244 Makris, Mary. "Metadrama, Creation, Reception and Interpretation: The Role of Art in Paloma Pedrero's *El color de agosto (The Color of August).*" *Estreno.* 1995; 21(1): 19-23. Lang.: Eng.

Spain. 1982. Critical studies. ■Analyzes the play as simultaneously challenging the traditional use of women's bodies for art objects and questioning the reception of all texts, whether literary or artistic. Asserts that, as the two women transform their bodies into visual texts, they emphasize the possibilities for interpretation, misinterpretation and reworking.

3245 Meléndez, Priscilla. "Silencios y ausencias en *Historia de nadie* de Jorge Díaz." (Silences and Absences in Jorge Díaz's *Nobody's Story.*) *Estreno.* 1995; 21(1): 11-13. Lang.: Spa.

Spain. France. Chile. 1966. Critical studies. ■The absurdist vision in plays of Díaz, a Chilean exile, with respect to the failure of communication and the isolation and alienation of the individual. Comparison of his *Historia de nadie (Nobody's Story)* with works of Samuel Beckett.

3246 Mukhopadhyay, Atandra. "La mujer y la Guerra: Reincarnaciones de Hécuba en *La llanura* de Martín Recuerda y en *Historia de unos cuantos* de Rodríguez Méndez." (Woman and War: Reincarnations of Hecuba in Martín Recuerda's *The Plain* and Rodríguez Méndez's *Story of a Few.*) *Estreno.* 1994; 20(1): 38-39. Lang.: Spa.

Spain. 1947-1971. Critical studies. ■Women's suffering as mothers and wives as consequence of war in José Martín Recuerda's *The Plain (La llanura)* which deals with victimization caused by civil war, and in

DRAMA: —Plays/librettos/scripts

Rodríguez Méndez's *Story of a Few (Historia de unos cuantos)*, following the idea from colonialism to the post-war era.

3247 Newberry, Wilma. "Dionysus Triumphant: José Luis Alonso de Santos's Metatheatrical Farce *Fuero de juício (Out of His Mind)*." *Estreno*. 1995; 21(1): 28-31. Illus.: Photo. B&W. 1. Lang.: Eng.
Spain. 1977. Critical studies. ∎Use of the setting of a mental asylum to represent a corrupt external society using TV and other entertainment media as perception-dulling drugs.

3248 Nicholas, Robert L. "Benavente y Buero, dos dramaturgos ante un siglo." (Benavente y Buero, Two Playwrights Leading a Century.) *Estreno*. 1994; 20(1): 33-37. Illus.: Photo. B&W. 2. Lang.: Spa.
Spain. 1946. Critical studies. ∎Argues that Jacinto Benavente and Antonio Buero Vallejo have dominated Spanish theatre for the past one hundred years, compares and contrasts their works.

3249 Nieva de la Paz, Pilar. "Recreación y transformación de un mito: *La nieta de Fedra*, drama de Halma Angélico." (Recreation and Transformation of a Myth: *Phaedra's Niece* a Play by Halma Angélico.) *Estreno*. 1994; 20(1): 18-22. Lang.: Spa.
Spain. 1929. Critical studies. ∎The improvement of women's social condition in pre-war plays of Halma Angélico, with particular attention to *La nieta de Fedra (Phaedra's Niece)*, said to be an attempt to free women from artificial social constraints throught the use of myth.

3250 O'Connor, Patricia W. "¿La 'verdadera fórmula socialista'? A Conversation with Antonio Buero Vallejo." (The 'True Socialist Formula'? A Conversation with Antonio Buero Vallejo.) *Estreno*. 1994; 20(1): 23-27. Lang.: Spa.
Spain. 1993. Histories-sources. ∎Interview with Antonio Buero Vallejo, in which the playwright discusses the factors influencing his political evolution and his utopian socialist ideas as typified in his 1966 *El tragaluz (The Skylight)*.

3251 Oriel, Charles. "The Play of Presence and Absence: Writing and Supplementarity in the *Comedias de privanza*." 36-51 in Simerka, Barbara, ed. *El arte nuevo de estudiar comedias: Literary Theory and Spanish Golden Age Drama*. London: Associated Univ. Presses; 1996. 260 pp. Notes. Index. Biblio. Lang.: Eng.
Spain. 1604-1624. Critical studies. ∎The transition from oral tradition to literacy in Spanish Golden Age drama as seen through the role of written documents in *comedias de privanza* (dramas that deal with the rise and fall of court favorites). Focuses on *La adversa fortuna de Ruy López de Avalos (The Ill Fortune of Ruy López de Avalos)*, 1604, and *La adversa fortuna de don Alvaro de Luna (The Ill Fortune of Don Alvaro de Luna)*, 1624.

3252 Parr, James A. "On Canonization and Canonicity: *El burlador de Sevilla y convidado de piedra* (Or, a Rake's Progress and Pride of Place)." 235-245 in Simerka, Barbara, ed. *El arte nuevo de estudiar comedias: Literary Theory and Spanish Golden Age Drama*. London: Associated Univ. Presses; 1996. 260 pp. Notes. Index. Biblio. Lang.: Eng.
Spain. 1622. Critical studies. ∎Using Tirso de Molina's *Burlador de Sevilla* as a paradigm, examines the creation of canons and argues that canonization fulfills needs of commonality and consensus, but that the shared process of questioning, confirming or denying canonicity may be just as important.

3253 Piskunova, S. "Teat'r zolotogo veka kak takovoj." (Theatre of the Golden Age.) *VLit*. 1996; 4: 348-357. Lang.: Rus.
Spain. 1500-1700. Critical studies. ∎Review of a recent work by Vitas Siljunas on Spanish theatre of the sixteenth and seventeenth centuries (*Ispanskij teat'r XVI-XVII v.*).

3254 Podol, Peter L.; Vicente, Arie. "El drama Español del siglo XX: bibliografía selecta del año 1992." (20th Century Spanish Drama: Select Bibliography for 1992.) *Estreno*. 1994; 20(1): 38. Lang.: Spa.
Spain. 1992. Bibliographical studies. ∎Annual bibliography for 1992, including playtexts and critical works relating to artist and figures.

3255 Ríos, Juan A. "Un reencuentro crítico con Arniches." (A Critical Reencounter with Arniches.) *Estreno*. 1994; 20(1) : 40-43, 53. Illus.: Photo. B&W. 1. Lang.: Spa.
Spain. 1916-1943. Critical studies. ∎Urges a reevaluation of prolific playwright Carlos Arniches, with emphasis on *La Señorita de Trevélez (The Woman from Trevélez)*.

3256 Ruiz, Victor Garcia. "El Joven Jardiel en su contexto: Los compañeros y la crítica." (The Young Jardiel in His Context: Contemporaries and Critics.) *Estreno*. 1995; 21(1): 32-37. Lang.: Spa.
Spain. 1901-1952. Critical studies. ∎Urges a reading of Enrique Jardiel Poncela that acknowledges his limitations, yet recognizes his work as a substantive departure from tradition. Emphasizes the playwright's exploration of the boundaries of comedic possibility through his absurdist works.

3257 Sadowska-Guillon, Irène. "De la parole enchaînée au geste libre: La Dramaturgie espagnole contemporaine depuis 1945." (Flowing Speech to Free Gestures: Contemporary Spanish Drama Since 1945.) *JCT*. 1991; 58: 44-54. Notes. Illus.: Photo. B&W. 12. Lang.: Fre.
Spain. 1945-1991. Historical studies. ∎Works of important contemporary Spanish playwrights such as Alfonso Sastre, Antonio Buero Vallejo, Jaime Salom, Miguel Romero Esteo, Francisco Nieva, José Sanchis Sinisterra, and Sergi Belbel.

3258 Sadowska-Guillon, Irène. "José Sanchis Sinisterra: Explorateur des nouveaux mondes du théâtre." (José Sanchis Sinisterra: Explorer of New Worlds of Theatre.) *JCT*. 1991; 61: 47-53. Illus.: Photo. B&W. 3. Lang.: Fre.
Spain. 1960-1991. Histories-sources. ∎Playwright José Sanchis Sinisterra discusses influences of Bertolt Brecht and Samuel Beckett on his writing.

3259 Sáez, Victoria Sotomayor. "Villanea: La aportación de Arniches a la Imaginería Provinciana de la literatura Española." (Villanea: Arniche's Contribution to Provincial Imagery in Spanish Literature.) *Estreno*. 1994; 20(1): 44-46. Lang.: Spa.
Spain. 1912-1921. Critical studies. ∎The imaginary village of Villanea, created by playwright Carlos Arniches in several of his plays, said to be emblematic of Spain's duality, combining liberal vitality with reactionary mediocrity.

3260 Siljunas, V. "Auto Kal'derona, ili Triumf dramaturga." (Auto Calderón, or Triumph of a Dramatist.) *SovD*. 1996; 1: 228-238. Lang.: Rus.
Spain. 1600-1681. Critical studies. ∎Outlook on Calderón and the Spanish theatre of the seventeenth century.

3261 Simerka, Barbara. "Dramatic and Discursive Genres: *La verdad sospechosa* as Problem Comedy and Marriage Treatise." 187-205 in Simerka, Barbara, ed. *El arte nuevo de estudiar comedias: Literary Theory and Spanish Golden Age Drama*. London: Associated Univ. Presses; 1996. 260 pp. Notes. Index. Biblio. Lang.: Eng.
Spain. 1628. Critical studies. ∎A genre theory study of Juan Ruiz de Alarcón's *La verdad sospechosa (Suspicious Truth)*. Includes an overview of the development of genre theory, and how this plays relates to other forms of cultural discourse.

3262 Soufas, C. Christopher. *Audience and Authority in the Modernist Theater of Federico García Lorca*. Tuscaloosa, AL: Univ of Alabama P; 1996. 192 pp. Notes. Biblio. Index. Lang.: Eng.
Spain. 1920-1936. Critical studies. ∎Theoretical critique of the work of García Lorca. Focuses on the audience's role in the theatrical event and his underestimated contribution to Modernism and to European drama.

3263 Soufas, Teresa S. "A Feminist Approach to a Golden Age *Dramaturga*'s Play." 127-142 in Simerka, Barbara, ed. *El arte nuevo de estudiar comedias: Literary Theory and Spanish Golden Age Drama*. London: Associated Univ. Presses; 1996. 260 pp. Notes. Index. Biblio. Lang.: Eng.
Spain. 1625-1672. Critical studies. ∎Feminist analysis of the work of Ana Caro Mallén de Soto, one of the few female Golden Age dramatists. Argues that her work challenged social institutions in which the women she depicts position themselves in compliance with or against the expectations of their society.

DRAMA: —Plays/librettos/scripts

3264	Stern, Charlotte. *The Medieval Theater in Castile.* Binghamton, NY: Medieval and Renaissance Texts and Studies; 1996. 321 pp. Index. Pref. Biblio. Lang.: Eng.
Spain. 1100-1400. Histories-specific. ■Early Spanish theatre, as seen in historical materials and critical accounts never before examined, such as municipal records.

3265	Stroud, Matthew D. *The Play in the Mirror: Lacanian Perspectives on Spanish Baroque Theater.* Lewisburg, PA/London: Bucknell UP/Associated Univ Presses; 1996. 242 pp. Index. Biblio. Notes. Illus.: Diagram. Sketches. B&W. 9. Lang.: Eng.
Spain. 1580-1680. Critical studies. ■Lacanian critial theory applied to plays of Lope de Vega, Calderón, and others, with discussion of the structure of the subject, female sexuality, the 'lack,' and Otherness.

3266	Sullivan, Henry W. "Jacques Lacan and the Golden Age Drama." 105-124 in Simerka, Barbara, ed. *El arte nuevo de estudiar comedias: Literary Theory and Spanish Golden Age Drama.* London: Associated Univ. Presses; 1996. 260 pp. Notes. Index. Biblio. Lang.: Eng.
Spain. 1635. Critical studies. ■A reassessment of the *comedia* in light of recent psychoanalytic theory of Jacques Lacan. Analyzes Calderón's *El médico de su honra (Physician to His Own Honour)* and *La vida es sueño (Life Is a Dream).*

3267	Weimer, Christopher B. "Desire, Crisis, and Violence in *Fuenteovejuna*: A Girardian Perspective." 162-186 in Simerka, Barbara, ed. *El arte nuevo de estudiar comedias: Literary Theory and Spanish Golden Age Drama.* London: Associated Univ. Presses; 1996. 260 pp. Notes. Index. Biblio. Lang.: Eng.
Spain. 1612-1614. Critical studies. ■Author applies several theories of René Girard to Lope de Vega's *Fuente ovejuna*: the nature of mimetic desire, which leads to conflict that is mediated, and the resulting violence that perpetuates itself through mimesis (offense and retaliation).

3268	Weiner, Christopher. "Logocentrism in Crisis: Buero Vallejo's *El sueño de la razón (The Sleep of Reason)* as Post-Structuralist Text." *Estreno.* 1994; 20(1): 28-32. Lang.: Eng.
Spain. 1969. Critical studies. ■Derridean analysis of the play suggesting that the conflict between Goya and Ferdinand VII is used as a metaphor of Spain under Franco.

3269	Young, Richard A. "Narrative and Theatre: From Manuel Puig to Lope de Vega." 203-217 in Hart, Jonathan, ed. *Reading the Renaissance: Culture, Poetics, and Drama.* New York, NY/London: Garland; 1996. 290 pp. (Garland Studies in the Renaissance.) Notes. Biblio. Index. Lang.: Eng.
Spain. 1500-1990. Critical studies. ■The narrative and theatrical modes in Spanish Renaissance drama.

3270	Yudin, Mary F. "'Nunca he tenido tiempo para ser ... yo (I've Never had Time to be ... Me)': A Study of the Protagonists in Two Monodramas by Pilar Pombo." *Estreno.* 1995; 21(1): 24-27. Illus.: Photo. B&W. 1. Lang.: Eng.
Spain. 1987. Critical studies. ■Analysis of two monologues by Pilar Pombo, *Isabella* (1987) and *Remedios* (1988), with attention to women's lack of economic independence and the subversion of patriarchal stereotypes.

3271	Florin, Magnus. "Ordet og Scenen." (The Word and the Stage.) *TE.* 1996 Sep.; 80: 4-7. Illus.: Photo. B&W. 3. Lang.: Dan.
Sweden. 1950-1996. Critical studies. ■A dramaturg's work with plays of Lars Norén, Lars Forssell, Katarina Frostenson, Stig Larsson, and Kristina Lugn. Discusses the connection between poetry and drama.

3272	Hoogland, Rikard. "Finns det någon framtid för svenska dramatiker?" (Is There Any Future For Swedish Playwrights?)*Tningen.* 1996; 20(78): 15. Lang.: Swe.
Sweden. 1996. Critical studies. ■The present status of playwriting in Swedish.

3273	Lagerlöf, Malin. "Man är mer sin egen när man skriver." (You Are More On Your Own When You Write.) *Tningen.* 1996; 20(76-77): 40. Illus.: Photo. B&W. Lang.: Swe.

Sweden: Gothenburg. 1989. Histories-sources. ■An interview with the young actor and playwright Mattias Andersson, with reference to his play *Våning 12 (The Twelfth Floor).*

3274	Löfgren, Lars; Danielsson, Ronny; Sandström, Gugge; Degerlund, Rolf; Svensson, Lars. "5 teaterchefer om svensk dramatik." (Five Theatre Managers on Swedish Drama.) *Tningen.* 1996; 20(78): 18-19. Lang.: Swe.
Sweden. 1996. Historical studies. ■A presentation of the Swedish theatre's attitude towards the Swedish playwrights.

3275	Olzon, Janna. "Jag känner något svirr bakom alla trivialiteter." (I Feel Some Spree Behind All the Trivialities.) *Tningen.* 1996; 20(79): 6-10. Illus.: Photo. B&W. Color. Lang.: Swe.
Sweden: Luleå, Stockholm. 1944. Histories-sources. ■A presentation and an interview with the playwright and actor Staffan Göthe, with references to his children's plays and the current situation of Swedish drama.

3276	Stockenström, Göran. "Strindberg's Cosmos in *A Dream Play*: Medieval or Modern." *CompD.* 1996 Spr; 30(1): 72-105. Notes. Lang.: Eng.
Sweden. 1902. Critical studies. ■Argues that Strindberg's view of the cosmic order of the universe is essentially a medieval one, with an eye to the future, illustrating the position in *Ett Drömspel.*

3277	Strindberg, August; Robinson, Michael, ed., transl. *Selected Essays: August Strindberg.* Cambridge/New York, NY: Cambridge UP; 1996. 295 pp. Notes. Index. Biblio. Lang.: Eng.
Sweden. 1870-1912. Critical studies. ■New critical edition/translation of essays by Swedish playwright August Strindberg.

3278	Chanzafarov, N.G. *Tatarskaja komedija.* (Tatar Comedy.) Kazan: FEN; 1996. 268 pp. Lang.: Rus.
Tatarstan. 1900-1996. Histories-specific. ■The problems of twentieth-century Tatar comic drama.

3279	Aston, Elaine; Clarke, Ian. "The Dangerous Woman of Melvillean Drama." *NTQ.* 1996; 12(45): 30-42. Notes. Biblio. Illus.: Photo. Dwg. B&W. 3. Lang.: Eng.
UK-England: London. 1899-1918. Historical studies. ■Analysis of strong female roles in plays such as Walter Melville's melodramatic *The Worst Woman in London* as acting vehicles and as embodiments of male fears and fantasies.

3280	Bartlett, Laurence. *William Congreve: An Annotated Bibliography, 1978-1994.* Lanham, MD/London: Scarecrow; 1996. 109 pp. (Scarecrow Author Bibliographies 97.) Index. Biblio. Pref. Lang.: Eng.
UK-England. USA. 1978-1994. Bibliographical studies. ■Bibliography of contemporary works on playwright William Congreve including a short introduction on recent critical styles. Includes materials found online, as well as in printed form.

3281	Barzun, Jacques. "Berlioz and Shaw: An Affinity." *ShawR.* 1996; 16(1): 67-87. Notes. Illus.: Photo. 1. Lang.: Eng.
UK-England. 1880. Critical studies. ■Entries in playwright George Bernard Shaw's diaries concerning the influence of composer Hector Berlioz. Also examines an early unpublished manuscript on Shaw, 'A Reminiscence of Hector Berlioz'.

3282	Bennett, Susan. "Rehearsing *The Tempest*, Directing the Post-Colonial Body: Disjunctive Identity in Philip Osment's *This Island's Mine.*" *ET.* 1996; 15(1): 35-44. Notes. Biblio. Illus.: Photo. B&W. 2. Lang.: Eng.
UK-England: London. 1988-1996. Critical studies. ■Examination of Osment's post-colonial play *This Island's Mine*, which has its roots in *The Tempest.*

3283	Berst, Charles A. "Superman Theater: Gusts, Galumphs, and Grumps." *ShawR.* 1996; 16(1): 195-220. Notes. Lang.: Eng.
UK-England. 1901-1912. Critical studies. ■Three previously unpublished dramatic manuscripts by George Bernard Shaw: 'The Superman, or Don Juan's great grandson's grandson,' a scenario for his play *Man and Superman*, and two playlets, *The Man Who Stands No Nonsense: A Drama* (1904) and *The Trinity v Jackson* (1912).

DRAMA: —Plays/librettos/scripts

3284   Creighton, Al. "The Metaphor of the Theatre in *The Four Banks of the River of Space.*" *Callaloo.* 1995 Win; 18(1): 71-82. Notes. Illus.: Photo. B&W. 2. Lang.: Eng.
UK-England. 1954-1990. Critical studies. ■Examines novelist Wilson Harris' short verse play *Canje (The River of Ocean)*, written in 1954, for themes of journeys, later found in Harris' novels of the 1980s and 1990s. Also examines Harris' use of theatrical metaphors and masks in the play.

3285   Davis, Philip. "Nineteenth-Century Juliet." *ShS.* 1996; 49: 131-140. Notes. Lang.: Eng.
UK-England. 1800-1899. Critical studies. ■Nineteenth-century views of Shakespeare's heroine, with emphasis on Hazlitt.

3286   Davis, Tracy C. "*Extremities* and *Masterpieces.*" 137-154 in Keyssar, Helene, ed. *Feminist Theatre and Theory.* London: Macmillan; 1996. 288 pp. (New Casebooks.) Notes. Index. Lang.: Eng.
UK-England. USA. 1991-1995. Critical studies. ■Representations of violence and power in *Masterpieces* by Sarah Daniels and *Extremities* by William Mastrosimone. Describes Daniels' play as feminist and Mastrosimone's as non-feminist.

3287   Demastes, William W., ed.; Kelly, Katherine E., ed. *British Playwrights, 1880-1956: A Research and Production Sourcebook.* Westport, CT/London: Greenwood; 1996. 457 pp. Biblio. Index. Lang.: Eng.
UK-England. 1880-1956. Bibliographical studies. ■Dictionary entries on major British playwrights who initiated, developed or resisted English dramatic modernism.

3288   Demastes, William W., ed. *British Playwrights, 1956-1995: A Research and Production Sourcebook.* London/Westport, CT: Greenwood; 1996. 502 pp. Pref. Biblio. Lang.: Eng.
UK-England. 1956-1995. Bibliographical studies. ■Sourcebook of information on British playwrights and their plays. Includes biographical information, major plays, assessment of playwright's career, archival sources and bibliographies.

3289   Donesky, Finlay. *David Hare: Moral and Historical Perspectives.* Westport, CT/London: Greenwood; 1996. 214 pp. (Contributions in Drama and Theatre Studies 75.) Notes. Index. Biblio. Lang.: Eng.
UK-England. 1971-1995. Histories-specific. ■Analyzes moral absence in the plays of David Hare. Examines *Knuckle, Teeth 'n' Smiles, Fanshen, Plenty, Dreams of Leaving,* and *Skylight.*

3290   Eltis, Sos. *Revising Wilde: Society and Subversion in the Plays of Oscar Wilde.* Oxford: Clarendon; 1996. 226 pp. (Oxford English Monographs.) Notes. Biblio. Index. Lang.: Eng.
UK-England. 1880-1900. Critical studies. ■The plays of Oscar Wilde in the context of contemporary theatre, as well as nineteenth-century society, demonstrating how the plays enter into contemporary debates on sexual roles and the position of women, individual duty and morality, and the dangers of social revolution and unrest. Plays examined are *Vera, or, The Nihilists, Lady Windermere's Fan, A Woman of No Importance, An Ideal Husband,* and *The Importance of Being Earnest.*

3291   Fowler, James. "Picturing *Romeo and Juliet.*" *ShS.* 1996; 49: 111-129. Notes. Illus.: Dwg. B&W. 7. Lang.: Eng.
UK-England. 1679-1996. Critical studies. ■Examines the great number of paintings and illustrations *Romeo and Juliet* has generated over the last 300 years.

3292   Garfinkel, Sharon. "The Chief Prosecutor." *PlPl.* 1996 Aug/Sep; 507: 21. Lang.: Eng.
UK-England. 1945-1996. Histories-sources. ■Interview with playwright Richard Norton-Taylor on his play *Nuremberg: The War Crimes Trial.* Also speaks with Lord Hartley Shawcross, Nuremberg's Chief Prosecutor, soliciting his opinion of the play.

3293   Garner, Stanton B., Jr. "Politics over the Gulf: Trevor Griffiths in the Nineties." *MD.* 1996 Fall; 39(3): 381-391. Notes. Lang.: Eng.
UK-England. 1980-1996. Historical studies. ■Political and historical influences on work of playwright Griffiths. His plays *Piano, The Gulf Between Us or The Truth and Other Fictions.*

3294   Goodman, Lizbeth. "Who's Looking at Who(m)?: Reviewing Medusa." *MD.* 1996 Spr; 39(1): 190-210. Notes. Illus.: Photo. B&W. 5. Lang.: Eng.
UK-England. Canada. 1995. Critical studies. ■Considering the figure, and configuration, of Medusa as a metaphorical presence in Nina Rapu's *Ithaka,* Dorothea Smartt's one-woman show *Medusa,* and performance installation *Holding.../waiting for ecstasy* designed and directed by Beau Coleman. Queer theory, politics and lesbian theatre.

3295   Härtinger, Heribert. "Elemente des epischen Theaters in 'The War Plays' von Edward Bond." (Elements of Epic Theatre in *The War Plays* of Edward Bond.) *FMT.* 1996; 1: 70-81. Notes. Lang.: Ger.
UK-England. 1985. Critical studies. ■The influence of Brecht's alienation effect on Bond's play.

3296   Herbert, Ian; Vaïs, Michel, transl. "La Dramaturgie anglaise contemporaine." (Contemporary English Drama.) *JCT.* 1991 ; 58: 65-70. Notes. Illus.: Photo. B&W. 4. Lang.: Fre.
UK-England. 1956-1990. Historical studies. ■Thematic and stylistic characteristics of plays by Howard Barker, Caryl Churchill, Howard Brenton, David Edgar, Alan Ayckbourn, and David Hare.

3297   Lacey, Stephen. *British Realist Theatre: The New Wave in its Context, 1956-1965.* London/New York, NY: Routledge; 1996. 206 pp. Index. Biblio. Notes. Lang.: Eng.
UK-England. 1956-1965. Critical studies. ■Argues that British 'New Wave' drama, as exemplified by Osborne and Wesker, embodied British conflicts between hegemonic and counterhegemonic socioeconomic forces.

3298   Laurence, Dan H. "Approaching the Challenge." *ShawR.* 1996; 16(1): 17-34. Notes. Lang.: Eng.
UK-England. 1878-1889. Critical studies. ■Social influences of Charles Dickens on the young playwright George Bernard Shaw, as revealed in some of his early unpublished writings.

3299   Liebman, Herbert. *The Dramatic Art of David Storey: The Journey of a Playwright.* Westport, CT/London: Greenwood; 1996. 183 pp. (Contributions in Drama and Theatre Studies 71.) Index. Biblio. Lang.: Eng.
UK-England. 1966-1992. Critical studies. ■Critical examination of Storey's plays with discussion of the development of Storey's technique as a dramatist and his understanding of his thematic material.

3300   Margaroni, Maria. "Storey's 'Snare of Doubling'." *MD.* 1996 Fall; 39(3): 507-517. Notes. Illus.: Pntg. B&W. 3. Lang.: Eng.
UK-England. 1960-1995. Critical studies. ■Self-repetition in novels and plays of David Storey: rewriting and reworking of plots and characters, challenges critical dismissal of this tendency to repeat.

3301   Megson, Chris. "Mandegal." (Mancrazy.) *TE.* 1996 Feb.; 77: 7-9. Illus.: Photo. B&W. 2. Lang.: Dan.
UK-England. 1970-1996. Critical studies. ■Theatre in England with emphasis on new plays, especially with homosexuality as topic. *Mojo* by Jez Butterworth, *Burning Blue* by DMW Greer and *Rupert Street Lonely Hearts Club* by Jonathan Harvey are used as examples.

3302   Musolf, Peter. "Bunburying and the Art of Kabuki: or, Wilde, Mishima, and the Importance of Being a Sardine Seller." *NTQ.* 1996 Nov.; 12(48): 333-339. Lang.: Eng.
UK-England. Japan. 1895-1954. Critical studies. ■Compares Oscar Wilde's *The Importance of Being Earnest* with Yukio Mishima's *kabuki* play *Iwashiuri Koi no Hikiami (The Sardine Seller)*, showing that they shared the sovreignty of illusion over fact.

3303   Nickson, Richard. "Shaw as Poetaster: In Fyttes and Starts." *ShawR.* 1996; 16(1): 7-15. Notes. Lang.: Eng.
UK-England. 1876-1877. Critical studies. ■Examines an early literary effort of playwright George Bernard Shaw, an untitled, unpublished narrative poem in heroic couplets written by Shaw after his arrival in London.

3304   Obrazcova, A. "Oskar Uajl'd ob iskusstve i chudožestvennoj kritike." (Oscar Wilde on Art and Artistic Criticism.) *AT.* 1996; 3: 70-93. Lang.: Rus.
UK-England. 1856-1900. Historical studies. ■Wilde's reaction to reviews of his works, his view of the art of the play.

DRAMA: —Plays/librettos/scripts

3305 Peters, Sally. "Shaw and the Seamy Side of the Ring." *ShawR.* 1996; 16(1): 155-163. Notes. Lang.: Eng.
UK-England. 1888. Critical studies. ■Playwright George Bernard Shaw's adventures and interest in pugilism as revealed in his unpublished manuscript 'A Prizefighter on Prizefighting: The Seamy Side of the Ring'.

3306 Raymond, Gerard. "Scenes From Howard Barker." *TheaterW.* 1996 Mar 4; 9(31): 42-43. Illus.: Photo. B&W. 1. Lang.: Eng.
UK-England: London. 1990-1996. Biographical studies. ■Profile of author Barker with special focus on his play *Scenes from an Execution.* Themes of his work, influences, methodology.

3307 Raymond, Gerard. "Through the *Skylight* with David Hare and Richard Eyre." *TheaterW.* 1996 Oct 7; 10(10): 18-24. Illus.: Photo. B&W. 3. Lang.: Eng.
UK-England: London. 1968-1996. Histories-sources. ■Interview with playwright Hare on his new work *Skylight* opening at the Royale Theatre, and its director Eyre. Discuss past and current collaboration, origins and direction of *Skylight.*

3308 Ritchie, Martha. "Almost 'Better to be Nobody': Feminist Subjectivity, the Thatcher Years, and Timberlake Wertenbaker's *The Grace of Mary Traverse.*" *MD.* 1996 Fall; 39(3): 404-420. Notes. Lang.: Eng.
UK-England. 1985-1996. Critical studies. ■Analysis of Wertenbaker's play: characters, forms of feminism and influence of Thatcherism.

3309 Rogal, Samuel J., comp. *A Companion to the Characters in the Fiction and Drama of W. Somerset Maugham.* Westport, CT/London: Greenwood; 1996. 468 pp. Index. Biblio. Lang.: Eng.
UK-England. 1874-1965. Histories-sources. ■Alphabetical guide to the characters in the plays and novels of W. Somerset Maugham.

3310 Sakellaridou, Elizabeth. "Awakening the Dead: Teaching Restoration Comedy to Contemporary Cross-Cultural Audiences." *STP.* 1996 June; 13: 5-16. Notes. Biblio. Lang.: Eng.
UK-England. 1660-1996. Critical studies. ■The relevance of Restoration drama to contemporary society, in spite of resistance in educational institutions. With discussion of Timberlake Wertenbaker's use of Farquhar in *Our Country's Good,* and feminist analysis of the plays of Aphra Behn.

3311 Scarr, Richard. "Alan Bennett: Political Playwright." *NTQ.* 1996 Nov.; 12(48): 309-322. Notes. Lang.: Eng.
UK-England. 1968-1996. Critical studies. ■Bennett is normally regarded as an apolitical, popular dramatist, but this article argues that his work is in fact politically contentious, his ideological viewpoint changing as his career progressed.

3312 Sellar, Tom. "Truth and Dare: Sarah Kane's *Blasted.*" *ThM.* 1996; 27(1): 29-34. Illus.: Photo. B&W. 2. Lang.: Eng.
UK-England. 1950-1996. Critical studies. ■Sarah Kane's *Blasted* is examined as a dramatic descendant of John Osborne and Edward Bond, and reflects the terror and social decay of the late 1990s.

3313 Sierz, Alex. "John Osborne and the Myth of Anger." *NTQ.* 1996; 12(46): 136-146. Notes. Lang.: Eng.
UK-England. 1956-1994. Historical studies. ■Examines mythic status of *Look Back in Anger* and shows how the author and his anti-hero became fused in the public mind into a symbolic figure, the Angry Young Man.

3314 Sinfield, Alan. "'The Moment of Submission': Neil Bartlett in Conversation." *MD.* 1996 Spr; 39(1): 211-221. Notes. Lang.: Eng.
UK-England. 1948-1995. Histories-sources. ■Interview with gay writer/director/producer Bartlett: views on gay theatre vs. mainstream, audience response, representation of homosexuality in theatre.

3315 Spong, Andrew. "Bad Habits, 'Bad' Quartos, and the Myth of Origin in the Editing of Shakespeare." *NTQ.* 1996; 12(45): 65-70. Notes. Lang.: Eng.
UK-England. 1592-1995. Textual studies. ■Continues debate on editing Shakespeare, and defends 'Shakespearean Originals' project of Graham Holderness and Bryan Loughrey.

3316 Stearns, David Patrick. "Furtwängler, on Trial: Ronald Harwood's London Hit *Taking Sides* about the Conductor's Denazification Hearings, Comes to Broadway." *OpN.* 1996 Nov.; 61(5): 18-20. Illus.: Photo. B&W. 1. Lang.: Eng.
UK-England. 1934-1995. Critical studies. ■Discussion of *Taking Sides,* a play by Ronald Harwood on the denazification hearings of German conductor Wilhelm Furtwängler (1886-1954). Daniel Massey plays Furtwängler, and Ed Harris, his fictional nemesis.

3317 Stevenson, Melanie A. "Prospero Back Home in Milan: Bond's *Lear* as Paradigm for Post-Imperial Britain." *ET.* 1996; 15 (1): 23-34. Notes. Biblio. Lang.: Eng.
UK-England. 1971-1990. Critical studies. ■Examines the historical and theatrical context of Bond's *Lear* as a comment on post-imperialist Britain's political system.

3318 Cordones-Cook, Juanamaría. "El teatro negro uruguayo de Andrés Castillo." (The Black Uruguayan Theatre of Andrés Castillo.) *LATR.* 1996 Spr; 29(2): 85-94. Notes. Biblio. Lang.: Spa.
Uruguay: Montevideo. 1995-1996. Critical studies. ■African influences in the work of playwright Andrés Castillo and El Teatro Negro Independiente (Independent Black Theatre).

3319 Irigoyen, Emilio. "Gestualidad neoclásica y tradicionalismo en Uruguay: Sobre una recuperada loa de 1831." (Neoclassical Gestures and Traditionalism in Uruguay: On a Rediscovered *Loa* of 1831.) *Gestos.* 1996 Apr.; 11(21): 103-126. Notes. Biblio. Lang.: Eng.
Uruguay. 1831. Historical studies. ■Political and social analysis of two of playwright/director Joaquín Culebras' plays *La Contienda de los Dioses por el Estado Oriental* and *Loa al General Manuel Belgrano* which heralded Uruguay's acceptance of a new constitution.

3320 "Forging New Myths for New Realities." *AmTh.* 1996 May/June; 13(5): 42-45. Illus.: Photo. B&W. 4. Lang.: Eng.
USA: Los Angeles, CA. 1995-1996. Histories-sources. ■Excerpt from symposium panel discussions of Blacksmyths, the Black playwrights project of the Mark Taper Forum. Tim Bond, artistic director of Seattle's Group Theatre, Sheldon Epps, associate artistic director of the Old Globe Theatre, actor/producer Michele Shay, actor/writer Shabaka, Negro Ensemble Company founder Douglas Turner Ward, playwright Robert Alexander, actor/director Shirley Jo Finney, playwright/director Robert O'Hara.

3321 Abel, Sam. "The Death of Queens: *The Lisbon Traviata* Controversy and Gay Male Representation in Mainstream Theatre." *THSt.* 1996 June; 16: 91-104. Notes. Lang.: Eng.
USA: New York, NY. 1989-1996. Historical studies. ■Terrence McNally's play *The Lisbon Traviata* and its impact on gay male identity on the American stage. The conflict between McNally's portrayal of gay men and critical reception led to a renegotiation of the relationship between 'gay drama' and the critics' definition of 'mainstream' commercial theatre.

3322 Adler, Thomas P. "The Legacy of Eugene O'Neill According to Stark Young." *EOR.* 1996 Spr/Fall; 20(1&2): 64-71. Biblio. Lang.: Eng.
USA. 1922-1996. Critical studies. ■Drama critic and author Young's friendship with O'Neill and his critical response to his plays. Young's analysis of O'Neill's use of language, myth, and expression of emotions.

3323 Adler, Thomas P. "Tennessee Williams's 'Personal Lyricism': Toward an Androgynous Form." 172-188 in Demastes, William W., ed. *Realism and the American Dramatic Tradition.* Tuscaloosa, AL/London: Univ of Alabama P; 1996. 290 pp. Index. Notes. Biblio. Pref. Lang.: Eng.
USA. 1944-1973. Critical studies. ■Argues that Williams situates realistically conceived and handled characters within a nonrealistic, poeticized stage space, allowing him to unlock integral aspects of human existence that audiences of the time generally demanded remain closeted. Plays analyzed are: *The Glass Menagerie, A Streetcar Named Desire, Out Cry,* and *Battle of Angels* (later rewritten as *Orpheus Descending*).

3324 Anthony, Susan. "Made in America: Adaptations of British Gothic Plays for the American Stage: 1790-1820." *JADT.* 1996 Fall; 8(3): 19-34. Notes. Lang.: Eng.
USA. 1790-1820. Historical studies. ■Four early American plays imitating the Gothic form popular in English theatre of the time: *The Forest of Rosenwald* by John Stokes, *The Wood Daemon* by John Turnbull, *Fon-*

DRAMA: —Plays/librettos/scripts

tainville Abbey and *Bluebeard* by William Dunlap (*Bluebeard* adapted from play of same title by George Colman the Younger). Differences between the American and English form.

3325 Appler, Keith. "Multicultural Theatre and the White Physician." *AmerD.* 1996 Spr; 5(2): 57-75. Notes. Biblio. Lang.: Eng.
USA. 1985. Critical studies. ■Character interaction between white and Black medical professionals in David Feldshuh's play *Miss Evers' Boys*, based on the 'Tuskegee Study of Untreated Syphilis in the Negro Male' experiments in the 1930s and 1940s.

3326 Backalenick, Irene. "Suzan-Lori Parks: The Joy of Playwrighting." *TheaterW.* 1996 Apr 8; 9(36): 27-28. Illus.: Photo. B&W. 1. Lang.: Eng.
USA: New York, NY. 1996. Biographical studies. ■Life and career of playwright Parks. Her experiences as an African-American writer, past productions, and collaboration with director Liz Diamond.

3327 Bak, John S. "Eugene O'Neill and John Reed: Recording the Body Politic, 1913-1922." *EOR.* 1996 Spr/Fall; 20(1&2): 17-33. Notes. Biblio. Lang.: Eng.
USA: New York, NY. 1913-1922. Critical studies. ■How the two writers recorded their societies' responses to the world around them, and their work with the Provincetown Players. O'Neill's *Anna Christie, The Personal Equation* and *The Hairy Ape*, and Reed's *Moondown*, stories and essays.

3328 Barlow, Judith E. "Into the Foxhole: Feminism, Realism, and Lillian Hellman." 156-171 in Demastes, William W., ed. *Realism and the American Dramatic Tradition.* Tuscaloosa, AL/London: Univ of Alabama P; 1996. 290 pp. Pref. Biblio. Index. Notes. Lang.: Eng.
USA. 1939. Critical studies. ■Feminist analysis of realism's power and limitations in plays of American women, with focus on *The Little Foxes* by Lillian Hellman.

3329 Barnett, Claudia. "'This Fundamental Challenge to Identity': Reproduction and Representation in the Drama of Adrienne Kennedy." *TJ.* 1996 May; 48(2): 141-156. Notes. Biblio. Lang.: Eng.
USA. 1988. Critical studies. ■ The subtext of pregnancy in Adrienne Kennedy's plays, using Kristeva's model of woman's reproductive experience as a theatrical metaphor. Plays examined include *Funnyhouse of a Negro, A Movie Star Has to Star in Black and White*, and others.

3330 Barnett, Claudia. "Adrienne Kennedy and Shakespeare's Sister." *AmerD.* 1996 Spr; 5(2): 44-56. Notes. Biblio. Lang.: Eng.
USA. 1996. Critical studies. ■Discusses various influences on the work of playwright Adrienne Kennedy reflected in her plays *Funnyhouse of a Negro* and *The Owl Answers*.

3331 Bassiri, Amadou. "Aspects of Africanness in August Wilson's Drama: Reading *The Piano Lesson* through Wole Soyinka's Drama." *AfAmR.* 1996 Spr; 30(1): 99-113. Notes. Biblio. Lang.: Eng.
USA. Africa. 1990-1996. Critical studies. ■Elements of Africanness in Wilson's *The Piano Lesson* using Wole Soyinka's dramatic ideas as a lens.

3332 Bechtel, Roger. "P.C. Power Play: Language and Representation in David Mamet's *Oleanna*." *TheatreS.* 1996; 41: 29-48. Notes. Lang.: Eng.
USA. 1992. Critical studies. ■'Political correctness' and harassment, language as action, and the battle between men and women in Mamet's play.

3333 Bennett, Elizabeth. "Egloff Riffs Russian." *AmTh.* 1996 Mar.; 13(3): 8-9. Illus.: Sketches. Photo. B&W. 1. Lang.: Eng.
USA. 1854-1996. Critical studies. ■Playwright Elizabeth Egloff and her play *The Lover* adapted from Turgenjëv's novel *On the Eve*.

3334 Bergesen, Eric; Demastes, William W. "The Limits of African-American Political Realism: Baraka's *Dutchman* and Wilson's *Ma Rainey's Black Bottom*." 218-234 in Demastes, William W., ed. *Realism and the American Dramatic Tradition.* Tuscaloosa, AL/London: Univ of Alabama P; 1996. 290 pp. Index. Notes. Biblio. Pref. Lang.: Eng.

USA. 1964-1984. Critical studies. ■The strengths and weaknesses of realism in the political agenda of *Dutchman* by LeRoi Jones (Amiri Baraka) as compared to the aestheticism of *Ma Rainey's Black Bottom* by August Wilson.

3335 Berson, Misha. "Have You Reached a Verdict?" *AmTh.* 1996 Apr.; 13(4): 6-7. Illus.: Photo. B&W. 2. Lang.: Eng.
USA. 1995-1996. Critical studies. ■Joe Sutton's play *Voir Dire*: its themes and their potential impact in light of current events and celebrity trials.

3336 Black, Stephen A. "O'Neill's Early Recklessness." *EOR.* 1996 Spr/Fall; 20(1&2): 11-16. Lang.: Eng.
USA. 1913. Critical studies. ■The process of self-psychoanalysis carried out by O'Neill in an early, and as yet unperformed, play titled *Recklessness*. Comparison of plot and themes to his personal life.

3337 Blank, Martin. "Thornton Wilder's Early Work in the Theatre." *JADT.* 1996 Win; 8(1): 18-37. Notes. Lang.: Eng.
USA. 1914-1937. Historical studies. ■Playwright Thornton Wilder's early plays, novels, and criticism, from one-acts written in high school to his first full-length play *The Trumpet Shall Sound* as an undergraduate. Also covers his novels *The Bridge of San Luis Rey* and *The Woman from Andros*, as well as his first published collection of one-act plays, including *The Long Christmas Dinner, The Happy Journey to Trenton and Camden*, and *Pullman Car Hiawatha*.

3338 Bloom, Steven F. "The Lingering (Comic?) Legacy of Eugene O'Neill." *EOR.* 1996 Spr/Fall; 20(1&2): 139-146. Lang.: Eng.
USA. 1949-1989. Critical studies. ■Tracing O'Neill's writing legacy in the works of American comic writers, particularly in the work of Neil Simon. Examines characters in Simon's trilogy (*Brighton Beach Memoirs, Biloxi Blues* and *Broadway Bound*) and comparing them to the characters in O'Neill's *Long Day's Journey Into Night*.

3339 Bottoms, Stephen J. "Re-Staging Roy: Citizen Cohn and the Search for Xanadu." *TJ.* 1996 May; 48(2): 157-184. Notes. Biblio. Illus.: Photo. 5. Lang.: Eng.
USA. 1986-1994. Critical studies. ■Controversial lawyer Roy Cohn and his portrayal in American plays since his death in 1986, including Tony Kushner's *Angels in America, We Got a Date* by Chicago-based physical theatre group Goat Island, and *Roy Cohn/Jack Smith*, a pair of complementary monologues devised by Ron Vawter of the Wooster Group.

3340 Brunn, Elena. "Richard Nelson: A Career in Two Countries." *DGQ.* 1996 Win; 33(4): 7-17. Illus.: Photo. B&W. 2. Lang.: Eng.
USA. UK-England. 1995. Histories-sources. ■Interview with American playwright Nelson discussing his success in both England and the U.S., his plays *New England* and *The General from America*, and his adaptation of Strindberg's *Fadren (The Father)*.

3341 Burke, Sally. *American Feminist Playwrights: A Critical History.* New York, NY: Twayne; 1996. 270 pp. (Twayne's Critical History of American Drama.) Pref. Notes. Biblio. Index. Illus.: Photo. 15. Lang.: Eng.
USA. 1785-1995. Histories-specific. ■Feminist and proto-feminist playwriting from colonial times to the present, including suffrage drama, the nineteenth-century women's movement, and twentieth-century feminism.

3342 Cardullo, Bert. "Whose Town Is It, Anyway? An Historico-Aesthetic Inquiry into *Our Town*." *JADT.* 1996 Win; 8(1): 38-49. Notes. Lang.: Eng.
USA. 1938. Critical studies. ■Contrasts the avant-garde structure of Wilder's play with its conventional characters, which results in a 'conventionally unconventional' theatre experience.

3343 Centola, Steven R. "'How to Contain the Impulse of Betrayal': A Sartrean Reading of *The Ride Down Mount Morgan*." *AmerD.* 1996 Spr; 6(1): 14-28. Notes. Biblio. Lang.: Eng.
USA. 1991-1996. Critical studies. ■Existentialist analysis of Arthur Miller's *The Ride Down Mount Morgan*.

3344 Champagne, Lenora. "Ellen McLaughlin." *AmTh.* 1996 Nov.; 13(9): 58. Illus.: Photo. B&W. 1. Lang.: Eng.
USA: New York, NY. 1996. Biographical studies. ■Profile of actress/playwright McLaughlin: use of flight imagery in her plays, influence of classic Greek plays on her writing.

DRAMA: —Plays/librettos/scripts

3345 Cless, Downing. "Ecology vs. Economy in Robert Schenk-kan's *The Kentucky Cycle*." *JADT*. 1996 Spr; 8(2): 59-72. Notes. Lang.: Eng.
USA. 1992. Historical studies. ■The theme of conflict between ecology and economy reflected in Robert Schenkkan's *The Kentucky Cycle*.

3346 Cless, Downing. "Eco-Theatre, USA: The Grassroots Is Greener." *TDR*. 1996 Sum; 40(2): 79-102. Notes. Biblio. Illus.: Photo. B&W. 11. Lang.: Eng.
USA. 1988-1996. Critical studies. ■Plays with environmental themes developed and produced by grassroots theatres. Focus on *upROOTED* developed by Ukiah Players Theatre, *Heroes and Saints* by Cherríe Moraga and *La Quinceañera* by Teatro Nuestro, *Standing on Fishes* developed by Martha Bocsing for the Environmental Action Theatre Project, *The Christopher Columbus Follies: An Eco-Cabaret* and *InTOXICating: An Eco-Cabaret* by Underground Railway Theatre.

3347 Clum, John M. "From *Summer and Smoke* to *Eccentricities of a Nightingale*: The Evolution of the Queer Alma." *MD*. 1996 Spr; 39(1): 31-50. Notes. Lang.: Eng.
USA. 1945. Critical studies. ■Gay connotations in Williams' second dramatization of the conversion of the character Alma in *Eccentricities of a Nightingale* and how they move toward a prescient exploration of queer politics.

3348 Coen, Stephanie. "Nixon's Last Tango." *AmTh*. 1996 Mar.; 13(3): 4-5. Illus.: Photo. B&W. 1. Lang.: Eng.
USA: New York, NY. 1994-1996. Critical studies. ■Playwright Russell Lee's *Nixon's Nixon* at the MCC Theatre: political and historical influences, characterizations. Includes sample of dialogue from play.

3349 Cohen, Frumi. "A View from the Closet: A Playwright for Youth Speaks." *DGQ*. 1996 Win; 33(4): 30-33. Lang.: Eng.
USA. 1996. Histories-sources. ■Youth playwright Frumi Cohen laments the obscurity of the toiler in the category of playwright for youth.

3350 Combs, Robert. "O'Neill's (and Others') Characters *as* Others." *EOR*. 1996 Spr/Fall; 20(1&2): 119-125. Lang.: Eng.
USA. 1911-1953. Critical studies. ■The concept of the Other in the plays of Eugene O'Neill.

3351 Croal, N'Gai. "Rebellion With a Cause: Insurrection at The Public." *TheaterW*. 1996 Dec 2; 10(18): 30-37. Illus.: Photo. B&W. 2. Lang.: Eng.
USA: New York, NY. 1831-1996. Critical studies. ■Robert O'Hara's play *Insurrection: Holding History* at the Public Theatre, which he also directs. Plot and themes, research for play, experiences as a Black, gay artist.

3352 Cronacher, Karen. "Unmasking the Minstrel Mask's Black Magic in Ntozake Shange's *spell #7*." 189-212 in Keyssar, Helene, ed. *Feminist Theatre and Theory*. London: Macmillan; 1996. 288 pp. (New Casebooks.) Notes. Index. Lang.: Eng.
USA. 1979-1995. Critical studies. ■The minstrel mask as a sign in Shange's play, based on feminist interpretation of psychoanalysis and African-American history.

3353 Croyden, Margaret. "The Writer as Wild Beast: A Profile of Cynthia Ozick." *TheaterW*. 1996 June 24; 9(47): 24-25. Illus.: Photo. B&W. 1. Lang.: Eng.
USA: New York, NY. 1996. Biographical studies. ■Profile of writer Ozick, including her recent adaptation of her novel *The Shawl* for the stage. Originally performed at Bay Street Theatre under the title *Blue Light*, its current New York production returns to the original name of the novel.

3354 Cunningham, Frank R. "Eugene O'Neill and Reality in America." 107-122 in Demastes, William W., ed. *Realism and the American Dramatic Tradition*. Tuscaloosa, AL/London: Univ of Alabama P; 1996. 290 pp. Pref. Biblio. Index. Notes. Lang.: Eng.
USA. 1915-1948. Critical studies. ■Argues that O'Neill forged a new humane, imaginative realism merged with a spiritual quest which exposes his characters as both victims of and responsible for the increasingly coarsened conditions of their culture.

3355 Demastes, William W.; Vanden Heuvel, Michael. "The Hurlyburly Lies of the Causalist Mind: Chaos and the Realism of Rabe and Shepard." 255-274 in Demastes, William W.,

ed. *Realism and the American Dramatic Tradition*. Tuscaloosa, AL/London: Univ of Alabama P; 1996. 290 pp. Index. Notes. Biblio. Pref. Lang.: Eng.
USA. 1976-1991. Critical studies. ■Analysis of *Streamers* and *Hurlyburly* by David Rabe, and *A Lie of the Mind* and *States of Shock* by Sam Shepard. Argues that their 'chaos-informed' realism challenges the dominant linear ideology inherent in traditional realism.

3356 Denison, Patricia D. "The Legacy of James A. Herne: American Realities and Realisms." 18-36 in Demastes, William W., ed. *Realism and the American Dramatic Tradition*. Tuscaloosa, AL/London: Univ of Alabama P; 1996. 290 pp. Pref. Biblio. Index. Notes. Lang.: Eng.
USA. 1890-1930. Critical studies. ■The relationship of theatrical melodrama, social realism, and cultural configurations as reflected in the work of playwright James A. Herne, known as the 'American Ibsen.' Herne's 1897 manifesto 'Art for Truth's Sake in the Drama' and his controversial play *Margaret Fleming* illustrate the mingling of aestheticism with culture, the dramatic agenda with the social agenda, and aesthetic theory with social practice.

3357 Denisov, V. "Made in USA: 'projdennoe' i propuščennoe." (Made in the USA: 'Covered' and Skipped.) *SovD*. 1996; 1 : 175-185. Lang.: Rus.
USA. Russia. 1900-1996. Critical studies. ■American dramaturgy and its influence on Russian theatre.

3358 Denneny, Michael. "Turning...Turning *The Boys in the Band*." *TheaterW*. 1996 June 17; 9(46): 24-27. Illus.: Photo. B&W. 5. Lang.: Eng.
USA. 1968-1996. Critical studies. ■Analysis of characters in Mart Crowley's play about gay men. Relationships, themes, relevance to contemporary culture.

3359 DeRose, David J. "Cherríe Moraga." *AmTh*. 1996 Oct.; 13(8): 76-78. Illus.: Photo. B&W. 1. Lang.: Eng.
USA. 1996. Biographical studies. ■Work of playwright Moraga: sources for her work, interviews and videotaped oral histories used, and focus on her newest work *Watsonville: Some Place Not Here*.

3360 Diamond, Liz; Ladouceur, Louise, transl. "Mort et vie du langage: Trois nouvelles voix américaines." (Death and Life of Language: Three New American Voices.) *JCT*. 1991; 58: 35-43. Notes. Illus.: Photo. B&W. 6. Lang.: Fre.
USA: New York, NY. 1991. Historical studies. ■Language use and dominant themes in alternative 'downtown theatre' of Jeffrey M. Jones, Mac Wellman and Suzan-Lori Parks.

3361 Dillon, John. "Three Places in Asia." *AmTh*. 1996 Mar.; 13(3): 19-22. Illus.: Photo. B&W. 5. Lang.: Eng.
USA: New York, NY. 1990-1996. Biographical studies. ■Profile of experimental playwright/director Ping Chong, his acting company, and his works *Deshima* and *Chinoiserie* co-written with Michael Matthews. Themes, style of performance, historical events that shaped the plays, staging and touring.

3362 Drukman, Steven. "A Show Business Tale/Tail." *AmTh*. 1996 May/June; 13(5): 4-5. Illus.: Photo. B&W. 2. Lang.: Eng.
USA: New Haven, CT. 1996. Critical studies. ■Suzan-Lori Parks' new play *Venus* at Yale Repertory, directed by Richard Foreman. Historical sources for the play, themes and performance.

3363 Duffy, Susan. *American Labor on Stage: Dramatic Interpretations of the Steel and Textile Industries in the 1930s*. Westport, CT/London: Greenwood; 1996. 156 pp. (Contributions in Drama and Theatre Studies 72.) Index. Biblio. Lang.: Eng.
USA. 1930-1940. Histories-specific. ■Study of propaganda plays that dramatized the plight of labor: *Strike Song* (1930) by J.O. and Loretta Carroll Bailey, *Strike!* (1931), adapted by William Dorsey Blake from Mary Heaton Vorse's novel, *Steel* (1937) by John Wexley, and *Altars of Steel* (1936) by Thomas Hall Rogers.

3364 Eaton, Richard; Smith, Madeline. "Harold DePolo: Pulp Fiction's Dark Horse." *EOR*. 1996 Spr/Fall; 20(1&2): 80-87. Biblio. Lang.: Eng.
USA. 1929-1958. Biographical studies. ■Eugene O'Neill biographer Louis Sheaffer's interviews with DePolo, a friend of O'Neill's in his

DRAMA: —Plays/librettos/scripts

younger days. Personal recollections of those in O'Neill's circle, DePolo's career as a writer of pulp fiction, excerpts from the interviews.

3365 Elam, Harry J., Jr. "*Ma Rainey's Black Bottom*: Singing Wilson's Blues." *AmerD*. 1996 Spr; 5(2): 76-99. Notes. Biblio. Lang.: Eng.
USA. 1982-1996. Critical studies. ▪Blues music as a tool of self-accentuation, as well as collective cultural memory in August Wilson's play *Ma Rainey's Black Bottom*.

3366 Farabough, Laura. "Bay Area Playwrights Festival." *TheatreF*. 1996 Sum/Fall; 9: 73-82. Lang.: Eng.
USA: San Francisco, CA. 1995. Histories-sources. ▪Interviews with three playwrights from the Bay Area Playwrights Festival of new plays: Erin Cressida Wilson, author of *Hurricane*, directed by Mary Coleman, Elena Penga, author of *Gorky's Wife*, directed by Antigone Trimis, and Brighde Mullins, author of *Fire Eater*, directed by Jayne Wenger.

3367 Field, Brad. "Characterization in O'Neill: Self-doubt as Aid to Art." *EOR*. 1996 Spr/Fall; 20(1&2): 126-131. Biblio. Lang.: Eng.
USA. 1911-1953. Critical studies. ▪Elements of characterization in O'Neill's plays: evolution of characterization techniques from early to later plays, autobiographical elements.

3368 Filichia, Peter. "Stagestruck." *TheaterW*. 1996 June 17; 9(46): 8-11. Illus.: Photo. B&W. 3. Lang.: Eng.
USA: New York, NY. 1960-1996. Historical studies. ▪Playwright Mart Crowley discusses current revival of his play *The Boys in the Band*, past audience reception for its depiction of openly gay male characters.

3369 Fleche, Anne. "The Lesbian Rule: Lillian Hellman and the Measures of Realism." *MD*. 1996 Spr; 39(1): 16-30. Notes. Lang.: Eng.
USA. 1930-1996. Critical studies. ▪Lesbian representation and feminist theory in Hellman's *The Children's Hour* in the context of its style of realism.

3370 Forte, Jeanie. "Realism, Narrative, and the Feminist Playwright—A Problem of Reception." 19-34 in Keyssar, Helene, ed. *Feminist Theatre and Theory*. London: Macmillan; 1996. 288 pp. (New Casebooks.) Notes. Index. Lang.: Eng.
USA. 1993-1995. Critical studies. ▪Feminist playwriting and realism.

3371 Frick, John W. "'Odets, Where Is Thy Sting?': Reassessing the 'Playwright of the Proletariat'." 123-138 in Demastes, William W., ed. *Realism and the American Dramatic Tradition*. Tuscaloosa, AL/London: Univ of Alabama P; 1996. 290 pp. Pref. Biblio. Index. Notes. Lang.: Eng.
USA. 1930-1945. Critical studies. ▪Argues that realism in Clifford Odets's plays was intended to reflect the average American's hunger for humane community, ultimately free of any formal leftist or political agenda.

3372 Funke, Christoph. "Sanfter Horror, schöne Schrecken im Leben wie in Märchen." (Tender Horror, Beautiful Nightmares in Life as in Fairy Tales.) *THeute*. 1996; 4: 38-40. Illus.: Photo. B&W. 4. Lang.: Ger.
USA. Germany: Munich. 1996. Critical studies. ▪Comic playwright Nicky Silver and his plays, on the occasion of the first German production of his *Pterodactyls*, directed by Gerd Heinz at Cuvilliés Theatre.

3373 Gainor, J. Ellen. "The Provincetown Players' Experiments with Realism." 53-70 in Demastes, William W., ed. *Realism and the American Dramatic Tradition*. Tuscaloosa, AL/London: Univ of Alabama P; 1996. 290 pp. Pref. Biblio. Index. Notes. Lang.: Eng.
USA: New York, NY. 1915-1922. Critical studies. ▪Challenges to realism at Provincetown Players, with discussion of Susan Glaspell's *Trifles* and *Inheritors*, and Theodore Dreiser's *The Hand of the Potter*. Includes discussion of the relations between realism and the feminist agenda, and the Brechtian critique of realism.

3374 Gardner, Lyn. "The Mythic and the Marxist." *AmTh*. 1996 Apr.; 13(4): 4-5. Illus.: Photo. B&W. 1. Lang.: Eng.
USA: Cambridge, MA. 1996. Critical studies. ▪Debut of Naomi Wallace's *Slaughter City* at American Repertory Theatre, directed by Ron Daniels. Influences on her writing, themes of the play.

3375 Gehman, Geoff. "Every Letter Is a Soapbox." *AmTh*. 1996 Sep.; 13(7): 68-69. Illus.: Photo. B&W. 2. Lang.: Eng.
USA: Bloomsburg, PA. 1996. Historical studies. ▪Bloomsburg Theatre Ensemble's *Letters to the Editor*, comprised of missives appearing in newspapers in northeastern Pennsylvania spanning 200 years. Rehearsal and development process.

3376 Geis, Deborah R. "Wordscapes of the Body: Performative Language as *Gestus* in Maria Irene Fornes's Plays." 168-188 in Keyssar, Helene, ed. *Feminist Theatre and Theory*. London: Macmillan; 1996. 288 pp. (New Casebooks.) Notes. Index. Lang.: Eng.
USA. 1981-1995. Critical studies. ▪Brechtian/feminist analysis of Fornes' plays, illustrating the power of Brechtian devices in plays by and for women.

3377 Gener, Randy. "Eduardo Muchado: The Playwright as Romantic, Exile, and Punk." *DGQ*. 1996 Spr; 33(1): 18-27. Illus.: Photo. B&W. 1. Lang.: Eng.
USA: New York, NY. Cuba. 1953-1996. Histories-sources. ▪Interview with playwright Muchado, covering his life and work with special attention to his plays *Stevie Wants to Play the Blues* and *Across a Crowded Room*.

3378 Giles, Freda Scott. "Willis Richardson and Eulalie Spence: Dramatic Voices of the Harlem Renaissance." *AmerD*. 1996 Spr; 5(2): 1-22. Notes. Biblio. Lang.: Eng.
USA: New York, NY. 1920-1930. Historical studies. ▪Examines the work of African-American playwrights Willis Richardson and Eulalie Spence during the Harlem Renaissance, looking specifically at Richardson's *The Chip Woman's Fortune* and Spence's *Fool's Errand*.

3379 Gillilan, Cinda. "*Tracers*: This Is Our Parade: A First Look at an Understudied Vietnam Drama." *JADT*. 1996 Fall; 8(3): 50-78. Notes. Lang.: Eng.
USA. 1980-1994. Historical studies. ▪Essay on the structure of John DiFusco's play *Tracers* and its critical reception. Examines the history of the play, including changes by author in 1980 and 1994.

3380 Gilman Bower, Martha. "Upstairs/Downstairs: Dueling Triangles in *A Touch of the Poet*." *EOR*. 1996 Spr/Fall; 20(1&2): 96-101. Biblio. Lang.: Eng.
USA. 1935-1942. Critical studies. ▪Evolution of O'Neill's *A Touch of the Poet*: his plans for the cycle of plays in which it would be included, character and relationship development.

3381 Grant, Nathan L. "Men, Women, and Culture: A Conversation with August Wilson." *AmerD*. 1996 Spr; 5(2): 100-122. Lang.: Eng.
USA. 1996. Histories-sources. ▪Interview with playwright August Wilson.

3382 Gross, Robert F. "Servant of Three Masters: Realism, Idealism, and 'Hokum' in American High Comedy." 71-90 in Demastes, William W., ed. *Realism and the American Dramatic Tradition*. Tuscaloosa, AL/London: Univ of Alabama P; 1996. 290 pp. Pref. Biblio. Index. Notes. Lang.: Eng.
USA. 1920-1940. Critical studies. ▪Realism in the high-society comedies of Philip Barry, S.N. Behrman, and Robert Sherwood. Plays examined are Behrman's *Brief Moment*, Barry's *In a Garden*, and Sherwood's *Reunion in Vienna*.

3383 Gunter, Gregory. "Creating *Skin*: Naomi Iizuka." *TheatreF*. 1996 Win/Spr; 8: 40-41. Illus.: Photo. 1. Lang.: Eng.
USA: Dallas, TX. 1995-1996. Histories-sources. ▪Interview with playwright Naomi Iizuka on her current production *Skin* at Dallas Theatre Center, directed by Matthew Wilder.

3384 Haedicke, Janet V. "Margins in the Mainstream: Contemporary Women Playwrights." 203-217 in Demastes, William W., ed. *Realism and the American Dramatic Tradition*. Tuscaloosa, AL/London: Univ of Alabama P; 1996. 290 pp. Index. Notes. Biblio. Pref. Lang.: Eng.
USA. 1981-1989. Critical studies. ▪The compatibility of realism and the feminist agenda: analysis of plays by Beth Henley, Tina Howe, Marsha Norman, and Wendy Wasserstein.

3385 Hamlin, Scott. "Out of Danger." *ThM*. 1996; 27(1): 99-101. Lang.: Eng.

DRAMA: —Plays/librettos/scripts

USA: Princeton, NJ. 1996. Histories-sources. ■Interview with playwright/director Emily Mann on what effect she would like her play *Greensboro: A Requiem*, produced by the McCarter Theatre, to have.

3386 Hanson, Philip. "*The Emperor Jones*: Naturalistic Tragedy in Hemispheric Perspective." *AmerD*. 1996 Spr; 5(2): 23-43. Notes. Biblio. Lang.: Eng.
USA. Haiti. 1898-1920. Historical studies. ■Analyzes O'Neill's *The Emperor Jones* from its historical perspective, citing political and military events in the years preceding its first production.

3387 Harris, Will. "Early Black Women Playwrights and the Dual Liberation Motif." *AfAmR*. 1994 Sum; 28(2): 205-221. Notes. Biblio. Lang.: Eng.
USA. 1915-1930. Critical studies. ■Examines the theme of 'dual liberation' (strong Black women, traditional white male hegemony) in the plays of early Black women playwrights, such as Zora Neale Hurston, Shirley Graham, Mary P. Burrill, Angelina W. Grimké, May Miller, Marita Bonner, Eulalie Spence, and Georgia Douglas Johnson.

3388 Helfer, Richard. "*The Drag*: Mae West and the Gay World." *JADT*. 1996 Win; 8(1): 50-66. Notes. Lang.: Eng.
USA. 1927. Historical studies. ■Actress Mae West and her play on homosexual themes, *The Drag*. Author traces the historical context of the play: West's familiarity with gay life, her use of tabloids to titillate the public about the play. Argues that West's motives were not box-office greed, but defends play as a breakthrough in representations of gay people.

3389 Horwitz, Simi. "Nixon's Playwright Russell Lees." *TheaterW*. 1996 Apr 8; 9(36): 30-32. Illus.: Photo. B&W. 1. Lang.: Eng.
USA: New York, NY. 1996. Biographical studies. ■Life and career of Lees, author of *Nixon's Nixon*, currently being presented at West Side Arts. Historical influences on play, themes.

3390 Jacobs, Dorothy H. "Mamet's Inland Sea." *JADT*. 1996 Spr; 8(2): 41-47. Notes. Lang.: Eng.
USA. 1972-1980. Critical studies. ■The theme of the inland sea, with its own set of rigid rules and idiosyncratic rituals, in three plays of David Mamet: *Duck Variations* (1972), *The Water Engine* (1977), and *Lakeboat* (1980).

3391 Jacobson, Lynn. "Y York." *AmTh*. 1996 Jan.; 13(1): 44-45. Illus.: Photo. B&W. 2. Lang.: Eng.
USA. 1996. Biographical studies. ■Career of playwright York, her move to writing for children's theatre, includes sample of dialogue from her play *The Secret Wife*.

3392 Jones, Chris. "The Emperor Garvey." *AmTh*. 1996 Feb.; 13(2): 6-7. Illus.: Photo. B&W. 1. Lang.: Eng.
USA: Chicago, IL. 1996. Historical studies. ■Playwright Charles Smith researches life of controversial figure Marcus Garvey, founder of United Negro Improvement Association, for his new play *Black Star Line* at the Goodman Theatre.

3393 Keene, John. "Rita Dove's *The Darker Face of the Earth*: An Introductory Note." *Callaloo*. 1994 Sum; 17(2): 371-373. Lang.: Eng.
USA. 1994. Critical studies. ■Introductory essay to the verse play by Rita Dove, a retelling of the story of Oedipus in the antebellum southern U.S.

3394 Kerr, Berrilla; Robertson, Lanie, ed. "Berrilla Kerr, Playwright." *DGQ*. 1996 Fall; 33(3): 4-7. Lang.: Eng.
USA. 1910-1985. Histories-sources. ■Notes from playwright Kerr's unpublished memoir, *My Life*.

3395 Keyssar, Helene. "Drama and the Dialogic Imagination: *The Heidi Chronicles* and *Fefu and Her Friends*." 109-136 in Keyssar, Helene, ed. *Feminist Theatre and Theory*. London: Macmillan; 1996. 288 pp. (New Casebooks.) Notes. Index. Lang.: Eng.
USA. 1991-1995. Critical studies. ■Feminist drama as dialogic (in the Bakhtinian sense), with analysis of plays by Wendy Wasserstein and Maria Irene Fornes.

3396 Kolin, Philip C. "Orpheus Descending: Music, Race and Gender in Adrienne Kennedy's *She Talks to Beethoven*." *AfAmR*. 1994 Sum; 28(2): 293-304. Biblio. Lang.: Eng.

USA. 1989-1993. Critical studies. ■Music, race, memory, and issues of gender in Adrienne Kennedy's recent play *She Talks to Beethoven*, said to represent a new direction for her work.

3397 Kolin, Philip C., ed.; Kullman, Colby H., ed. *Speaking on Stage: Interviews with Contemporary American Playwrights*. Tuscaloosa, AL/London: Univ. of Alabama P; 1996. 425 pp. Index. Illus.: Photo. 1. Lang.: Eng.
USA. 1945-1995. Histories-sources. ■Interviews with major American playwrights.

3398 Kramm, Maggi. "The Artist in Us All." *AmTh*. 1996 May/June; 13(5): 24-27, 61. Illus.: Photo. Sketches. B&W. 2. Lang.: Eng.
USA. 1996. Critical studies. ■Argues that the cultural significance of Shakespeare's works lies in his invention of a language that helps us order our perceptions more clearly. Article includes listing of U.S. Shakespeare festivals.

3399 Langworthy, Douglas. "Sternheim's Comic Masks." *AmTh*. 1996 Feb.; 13(2): 10-11. Illus.: Sketches. B&W. 1. Lang.: Eng.
USA: Dallas, TX. Germany. 1911-1996. Critical studies. ■Director of Dallas Theatre Center Richard Hamburger discusses his production of Carl Sternheim's comedies *The Unmentionables (Die Hose)* and *The Snob (Der Snob)* adapted by Paul Lambert and Kate Sullivan. Characters, story, public response.

3400 Lapisardi, Frederick S. "Not-so-Random Notes on Masks in Yeats & O'Neill." *EOR*. 1996 Spr/Fall; 20(1&2): 132-137. Biblio. Lang.: Eng.
USA. 1911-1953. Critical studies. ■Parallels between Yeats's and O'Neill's theories and stage use of masks: philosophical concepts, mutual influences.

3401 London, Todd. "Mamet vs. Mamet." *AmTh*. 1996 July/Aug.; 13(6): 18-20, 62. Illus.: Photo. Sketches. B&W. 2. Lang.: Eng.
USA. 1975-1996. Biographical studies. ■Playwright, director, theorist Mamet: analysis of his recent plays *Oleanna* and *The Cryptogram*, language and themes in his work, view of Mamet as a director of his own work.

3402 Luczak, Raymond. "PlayOps: A New Blessing for Playwrights." *TheaterW*. 1996 June 17; 9(46): 43. Lang.: Eng.
USA: New York, NY. 1996. Technical studies. ■Playwright-specific computer program which creates databases to aid playwrights in tracking their submissions.

3403 Malpede, Karen. "Theatre of Witness: Passage into a New Millenium." *NTQ*. 1996 Aug.; 12(47): 266-278. Notes. Lang.: Eng.
USA. Croatia. 1991-1996. Histories-sources. ■Explains the origins of her monologue 'Baghdad Bunker' later the centerpiece in her play *Going to Iraq*, and her subsequent play *The Beekeeper's Daughter*, and compares them with *Schlangenhaut (Snakeskin)* by the dissident Croatian playwright Slobodan Snajder. In each the witnessing imagination affirms connections based upon the human capacity to experience empathy with the historical events witnessed.

3404 Manheim, Michael. "At Home with the Harfords." *EOR*. 1996 Spr/Fall; 20(1&2): 102-109. Biblio. Lang.: Eng.
USA. 1930. Critical studies. ■Patterns of emotional reversal in Eugene O'Neill's dialogue and characters, with emphasis on *More Stately Mansions*.

3405 Martin, Robert A. "Arthur Miller's *After the Fall*." *AmerD*. 1996 Fall; 6(1): 73-88. Biblio.
USA. 1964. Critical studies. ■The relationship of God and man, after man's fall, as a way to self-knowledge in Arthur Miller's *After the Fall*.

3406 McNamara, Brooks. "Owen Davis and the Shubert Brothers." *PasShow*. 1995 Spr; 18(1): 2-6. Biblio. Illus.: Handbill. Photo. Poster. B&W. 8.
USA: New York, NY. 1874-1956. Biographical studies. ■Playwright Owen Davis and his relationship with the Shuberts. Discusses his plays *Paging Mr. Cupid* and *The Detour*, as well as *Icebound*, which was produced by Sam Harris and won the Pulitzer Prize.

CLASSED ENTRIES

DRAMA: —Plays/librettos/scripts

3407 McNulty, Charles. "*Angels in America*: Tony Kushner's Theses on the Philosophy of History." *MD.* 1996 Spr; 39(1): 84-96 . Notes. Lang.: Eng.
USA. 1940-1996. Critical studies. ■Historical, philosophical and political influences on Kushner's play. Political vision and presentation of the experience of gay men and AIDS in Parts I and II.

3408 Mitchell, Karen S. "Ever After: Reading the Women Who Read (and Re-Write) Romances." *TTop.* 1996 Mar.; 6(1): 51-69. Notes. Biblio. Illus.: Photo. B&W. 1. Lang.: Eng.
USA. 1990-1996. Histories-sources. ■Discussion of the research, performance concept and adaptation of the novel *The Rainbow Season* for the production *The Rainbow Season: Romancing the Romance* by playwright Karen S. Mitchell.

3409 Murphy, Brenda. "Arthur Miller: Revisioning Realism." 189-202 in Demastes, William W., ed. *Realism and the American Dramatic Tradition.* Tuscaloosa, AL/London: Univ of Alabama P; 1996. 290 pp. Index. Notes. Biblio. Pref. Lang.: Eng.
USA. 1949-1992. Critical studies. ■The development of realism throughout Miller's career, revealing his interest in dramatizing the individual both as experiential subject and as citizen.

3410 Murphy, Brenda. "*The Man Who Had All the Luck*: Miller's Answer to *The Master Builder*." *AmerD.* 1996 Spr; 6(1): 29-41 . Notes. Biblio. Lang.: Eng.
USA. Norway. 1886-1996. Critical studies. ■Comparison and examination of Ibsen's *Bygmester Solness (The Master Builder)* as the source for Arthur Miller's *The Man Who Had All the Luck.*

3411 Müry, Andres. "Der Wahnsinnige und die Ignoranten." (The Lunatic and the Ignoramuses.) *THeute.* 1996; 10: 30-32. Illus.: Photo. B&W. 3. Lang.: Ger.
USA: New York, NY. 1996. Critical studies. ■Analysis of *Master Class* by Terrence McNally, with reference to Zoe Caldwell's role in the Broadway production.

3412 Neff, D.S. "Horse vs. Crow: Sam Shepard, Ted Hughes, and *The Tooth of Crime*." *JADT.* 1996 Fall; 8(3): 35-49. Notes. Lang.: Eng.
USA. 1971-1972. Historical studies. ■The influence of Ted Hughes' book of poetry *Crow: From the Life and Songs of the Crow* (1970) on playwright Sam Shepard's rock 'n' roll play *The Tooth of Crime.*

3413 Otten, Terry. "Historical Drama and the Dimensions of Tragedy: *A Man For All Seasons* and *The Crucible*." *AmerD.* 1996 Spr; 6(1): 42-60. Notes. Biblio. Lang.: Eng.
USA. UK-England. 1953-1966. Critical studies. ■Comparison of Robert Bolt's *A Man For All Seasons* and Arthur Miller's *The Crucible* in the context of both historical determinism and individual choice.

3414 Parker, Brian. "A Developmental Stemma for Drafts and Revisions of Tennessee Williams's *Camino Real*." *MD.* 1996 Sum; 39(2): 331-341. Notes. Lang.: Eng.
USA. 1946-1995. Bibliographical studies. ■Stemma cataloguing drafts and revisions to the play with introduction discussing difficulties in collating bibliographic material on Williams from many sources.

3415 Parker, Scott. "Robert Schenkkan: Pulitzer Prize-winner Shares Insight on Business of Playwriting." *SoTh.* 1996 Spr; 37 (2): 18-22. Illus.: Photo. B&W. 1. Lang.: Eng.
USA. 1996. Histories-sources. ■Interview with playwright Robert Schenkkan focusing on his career (notably his play *The Kentucky Cycle*) and the business aspects of playwriting.

3416 Parks, Suzan-Lori. "Playing with Indeterminacy." *ThM.* 1996; 26(3): 9-10. Notes. Lang.: Eng.
USA: New York, NY. 1996. Histories-sources. ■Interview with playwright Thalia Field, discussing her ideas of 'interdeterminate' theatre, and her new piece *Hey-Stop-That.*

3417 Pearce, Michele. "The Trouble with Cobb County." *AmTh.* 1996 Sep.; 13(7): 58-59. Illus.: Photo. B&W. 1. Lang.: Eng.
USA: Atlanta, GA. 1996. Critical studies. ■Barbara Lebow's community play *Cobb County Stories*, inspired by anti-gay and anti-arts legislation, directed by Frank Wittow at Theatre in the Square. It was developed with members of the community. Includes sidebar article by Stephen Nunns on production of plays with gay-related themes.

3418 Peterson, William M. "O'Neill's Divided Agonists." *EOR.* 1996 Spr/Fall; 20(1&2): 110-118. Biblio. Lang.: Eng.
USA. 1920-1943. Critical studies. ■Progression of O'Neill's heroes from his early to later plays: progression of starkly polarized emotions and divided characters to fully developed studies of complex characters.

3419 Plunka, Gene A. "Buddhism on the Contemporary American Stage: Jean-Claude Van Itallie's *The Tibetan Book of the Dead*." *JADT.* 1996 Spr; 8(2): 26-40. Notes. Lang.: Eng.
USA. India. 1968-1983. Historical studies. ■From his first experience with Buddhism in the late 1960s, Van Itallie has integrated the religion into several of his plays, including *Bag Lady* (1979), *Struck Dumb* (1988) and *The Tibetan Book of the Dead or How Not to Do It Again*, which is analyzed in this article.

3420 Porter, Thomas E. "Strong Gods and Sexuality: Guilt and Responsibility in the Later Plays of Arthur Miller." *AmerD.* 1996 Fall; 6(1): 89-112. Notes. Biblio.
USA. 1964-1996. Critical studies. ■Relationship of God and sexuality in *Creation, After the Fall, Ride, The Ride Down Mount Morgan*, and *The Archbishop's Ceiling.*

3421 Quinn, John R. "*Corpus Juris Tertium*: Redemptive Jurisprudence in *Angels in America*." *TJ.* 1996 Mar.; 48(1): 79-90. Notes. Biblio. Lang.: Eng.
USA. 1993. Critical studies. ■The law as a theme in Tony Kushner's *Angels in America.* Suggests that the law contributes to the play's messages about spirituality and apocalypse and ultimately acquires the characteristics of a secular religion in the play.

3422 Quinn, Michael L. "Anti-theatricality and American Ideology: Mamet's Performative Realism." 235-254 in Demastes, William W., ed. *Realism and the American Dramatic Tradition.* Tuscaloosa, AL/London: Univ of Alabama P; 1996. 290 pp. Index. Notes. Biblio. Pref. Lang.: Eng.
USA. 1972-1992. Critical studies. ■Argues that Mamet's plays are not representative but expressive, focusing on performed actions rather than mimesis.

3423 Raymond, Gerard. "Christopher Durang: On Sex, Politics, and Comedy." *DGQ.* 1996 Fall; 33(3): 8-11. Illus.: Photo. B&W. 1. Lang.: Eng.
USA. 1996. Histories-sources. ■Interview with Christopher Durang discussing his play *Sex and Longing.*

3424 Raymond, Gerard. "Mart Crowley: Where the Boys Are Now." *DGQ.* 1996 Sum; 33(2): 25-28. Illus.: Photo. B&W. 1. Lang.: Eng.
USA: New York, NY. 1996. Histories-sources. ■Interview with playwright Crowley regarding his plays *The Boys in the Band, Remote Asylum* and *A Breeze from the Gulf*, as well as discussing the recent revival of *The Boys in the Band* at the WPA Theatre.

3425 Reinelt, Janelle. "The Hybrid Cultures of *Gospel at Colonus* and the Politics of Representation." *TA.* 1994; 47: 97-109 . Notes. Lang.: Eng.
USA. 1987. Critical studies. ■Critique of *The Gospel at Colonus* by Lee Breuer and Bob Telson, focusing on the problems of intercultural representation at the heart of contemporary attempts to represent and interweave disparate cultural practices.

3426 Richardson, Brian. "Introduction: The Struggle for the Real—Interpretive Conflict, Dramatic Method, and the Paradox of Realism." 1-17 in Demastes, William W., ed. *Realism and the American Dramatic Tradition.* Tuscaloosa, AL/London: Univ of Alabama P; 1996. 290 pp. Pref. Biblio. Index. Notes. Lang.: Eng.
USA. 1890-1994. Critical studies. ■Theoretical and practical paradoxes of realism: it can help refute idealistic or romantic worldviews, but its own alternative vision can never be definitely established.

3427 Rosen, Carol. "Make it Strange: An Interview with Craig Lucas." *TheaterW.* 1996 Feb 12; 9(28): 24-33. Illus.: Photo. B&W. 1. Lang.: Eng.
USA: New York, NY. 1984-1996. Histories-sources. ■Interview with playwright Lucas discussing revival of his play *Blue Window* at Manhattan Theatre Club, directed by Joe Mantello. Origins of play, collaboration with director, techniques of playwriting, and past productions of other works.

DRAMA: —Plays/librettos/scripts

3428 Rosen, Carol. "August Wilson: Bard of the Blues." *TheaterW.* 1996 May 27; 9(43): 18-35. Illus.: Photo. B&W. 4. Lang.: Eng.
USA: New York, NY. 1952-1996. Histories-sources. ∎Profile of and interview with playwright Wilson on his current play *Seven Guitars* (currently on Broadway), influence of music on his writing, relationship with director Lloyd Richards, and past plays *Joe Turner's Come and Gone, Fences, The Piano Lesson.*

3429 Rosen, Carol. "Signature Presents Shepard." *TheaterW.* 1996 Sep 9; 10(6): 16-20. Illus.: Photo. B&W. 1. Lang.: Eng.
USA. 1960-1996. Biographical studies. ∎Career of playwright Sam Shepard, and his selection as featured author for Signature Theatre Company's current season, influence of director Joe Chaikin on his work. Artistic director James Houghton describes company's mission and goals, working with Shepard.

3430 Rosen, Carol. "Edward Albee." *DGQ.* 1996 Fall; 33(3): 27-39. Illus.: Photo. B&W. 1. Lang.: Eng.
USA: New York, NY. 1996. Histories-sources. ∎Interview with playwright Edward Albee discussing the influence of Samuel Beckett on his work, and his plays *Zoo Story, Tiny Alice, Who's Afraid of Virginia Woolf?* as well as the recent production of *A Delicate Balance.*

3431 Roudané, Matthew C. *American Drama Since 1960: A Critical History.* New York, NY: Twayne; 1996. 298 pp. (Twayne's Critical History of American Drama.) Pref. Biblio. Index. Notes. Illus.: Photo. B&W. 8. Lang.: Eng.
USA. 1960-1995. Histories-specific. ∎Critical history of American drama concentrating on twenty-four major dramatists and the cultural movements, historical events, and literary milieu that shaped their work. Includes sections on women's and African-American drama.

3432 Roudané, Matthew C. "Arthur Miller and His Influence on Contemporary American Drama." *AmerD.* 1996 Spr; 6(1): 1-13. Biblio. Lang.: Eng.
USA. 1930-1996. Critical studies. ∎Explores playwright Arthur Miller's continuing influence on modern American drama in the work Edward Albee, Sam Shepard and David Rabe.

3433 Ryan, Kate Moira. "Adapting Biography for the Stage." *DGQ.* 1996 Win; 33(4): 24-29. Illus.: Photo. B&W. 1. Lang.: Eng.
USA. 1996. Histories-sources. ∎Interview with playwright Doug Wright regarding his play *Quills*: its focus on the character of the Marquis de Sade, and its upcoming New York production.

3434 Ryan, Steven. "*Oleanna*: David Mamet's Power Play." *MD.* 1996 Fall; 39(3): 392-403. Notes. Lang.: Eng.
USA. 1990-1996. Critical studies. ∎Analysis of Mamet's play in terms of power struggle vs. sexual harassment between the male and female character. Characters, language, audience response.

3435 Ryen, Dag. "Humana: 20th Festival Characterized by Excellent Writing, Creative Staging and Lack of Daring." *SoTh.* 1996 Sum; 37(3): 22-23, 32. Illus.: Photo. B&W. 2. Lang.: Eng.
USA: Louisville, KY. 1996. Critical studies. ∎A critical summary of the offerings at the 1996 Humana Festival of new plays at the Actors Theatre of Louisville.

3436 Sandoval, Alberto; Sternbach, Nancy Saporta. "Rehearsing in Front of the Mirror: Marga Gomez's Lesbian Subjectivity as a Work-in-Progress." *WPerf.* 1996; 8(2): 205-223. Notes. Biblio. [Issue 16.] Lang.: Eng.
USA. 1990-1995. Critical studies. ∎Latina lesbian subjectivity in three performance pieces by Marga Gomez: *Memory Tricks* and *Marga Gomez Is Pretty, Witty and Gay* (both 1990), and *A Line Around the Block* (1994).

3437 Scasserra, Michael P. "Steve Tesich Reviews the American Character." *TheaterW.* 1996 May 27; 9(43): 42-44. Illus.: Photo. B&W. 1. Lang.: Eng.
USA: New York, NY. 1996. Historical studies. ∎Playwright Tesich discusses characters and themes in his new play *Arts & Leisure* currently performing at Playwrights Horizons.

3438 Scasserra, Michael P. "Wrestling with Angels." *TheaterW.* 1996 Oct 21; 10(12): 24-30. Illus.: Photo. B&W. 1. Lang.: Eng.
USA: New York, NY. 1996. Histories-sources. ∎Interview with playwright Bill C. Davis on his new work *Avow*, themes and characters, influence of Catholicism on his writing.

3439 Schroeder, Patricia R. "Locked Behind the Proscenium: Feminist Strategies in *Getting Out* and *My Sister in This House.*" 155-167 in Keyssar, Helene, ed. *Feminist Theatre and Theory.* London: Macmillan; 1996. 288 pp. (New Casebooks.) Notes. Index. Lang.: Eng.
USA. 1991-1995. Critical studies. ∎Modified realism in feminist drama: Marsha Norman's *Getting Out* and Wendy Kesselman's *My Sister in This House.*

3440 Schroeder, Patricia R. "Remembering the Disremembered: Feminist Realists of the Harlem Renaissance." 91-106 in Demastes, William W., ed. *Realism and the American Dramatic Tradition.* Tuscaloosa, AL/London: Univ of Alabama P; 1996. 290 pp. Pref. Biblio. Index. Notes. Lang.: Eng.
USA. 1916-1930. Critical studies. ∎Women of the Harlem Renaissance used realism to protest the social oppression of African-Americans, to replace demeaning stereotypes of African-American women with fully human, female characters, and to recover the lost history of African-American women in America. Analyzes Angelina Weld Grimké's *Rachel*, Mary P. Burrill's *They That Sit in Darkness*, Georgia Douglas Johnson's *Safe*, and Shirley Graham's *It's Morning.*

3441 Schroeder, Patricia R. *The Feminist Possibilities of Dramatic Realism.* Madison, NJ/London: Fairleigh Dickinson UP/Associated Univ Presses; 1996. 185 pp. Notes. Biblio. Index. Pref. Lang.: Eng.
USA. 1900-1988. Critical studies. ∎The place of realism in American feminist drama. Examines plays by Rachel Crothers, Zona Gale, Georgia Douglas Johnson, Shirley Graham, Alice Childress, Marsha Norman, Wendy Kesselman, and Barbara Lebow.

3442 Schroeder, Patricia R. "Transforming Images of Blackness: Dramatic Representation, Women Playwrights, and the Harlem Renaissance." 107-122 in Reinelt, Janelle, ed. *Crucibles of Crisis: Performing Social Change.* Ann Arbor, MI: Univ of Michigan P; 1996. 250 pp. Notes. Lang.: Eng.
USA: New York, NY. 1916-1930. Critical studies. ∎Black women's struggle with representation and access, with focus on Angelina Weld Grimké's *Rachel* and Shirley Graham's *It's Morning.*

3443 Seldes, Marian. "Albee and Me." *AmTh.* 1996 Sep.; 13(7): 24-26, 74. Illus.: Photo. B&W. 3. Lang.: Eng.
USA. 1996. Histories-sources. ∎Actress Seldes discusses her personal experiences working with playwright Edward Albee, with special focus on *Three Tall Women.* Discusses Albee's past collaborators, his relationship to his characters.

3444 Sellar, Tom. "Making History: Suzan-Lori Parks." *TheatreF.* 1996 Sum/Fall; 9: 37-39. Lang.: Eng.
USA. 1996. Histories-sources. ∎Interview with Suzan-Lori Parks on her career and especially her new play *Venus.*

3445 Shafer, Yvonne. "Whose Realism? Rachel Crothers's Power Struggle in the American Theatre." 37-52 in Demastes, William W., ed. *Realism and the American Dramatic Tradition.* Tuscaloosa, AL/London: Univ of Alabama P; 1996. 290 pp. Pref. Biblio. Index. Notes. Lang.: Eng.
USA. 1910-1920. Critical studies. ∎Compares Rachel Crothers's *A Man's World* with Augustus Thomas's rebuttal of Crothers, *As a Man Thinks*, concluding that Crothers's play contributes to both social and theatrical advancement while Thomas's work is reactionary.

3446 Sherwood, Topper. "The Arms of the Octopus." *AmTh.* 1996 July/Aug.; 13(6): 9. Lang.: Eng.
USA. 1996. Historical studies. ∎Playwright Jon Klein discusses the political source material for his play *Octopus* being produced at Contemporary American Theatre Festival, directed by Ed Herendeen.

3447 Shout, John D. "The Idiosyncratic Theatre of John Howard Lawson." *JADT.* 1996 Win; 8(1): 67-77. Notes. Lang.: Eng.
USA. 1922-1929. Historical studies. ∎Five forgotten plays by John Howard Lawson, better known as a dramaturg and critic: *Roger Bloomer, Processional, Nirvana, Loud Speaker*, and *The International.*

3448 Smith, Caroline Jackson. "From Drama to Literature: The Unparalleled Vision of Adrienne Kennedy." *BlackM.* 1996

DRAMA: —Plays/librettos/scripts

Aug/Sep. ; 12(1): 5-6, 14-15. Illus.: Photo. B&W. 2. Lang.: Eng.

USA. 1965-1996. Biographical studies. ■Career of playwright Adrienne Kennedy, focusing on her plays *Funnyhouse of a Negro, June and Jean: A Concert,* and *Sleep Deprivation Chamber.*

3449 Stockdale, Joe. "Tallahassee! San Rafael! Kalamazoo!" *TheaterW.* 1996 June 24; 9(47): 26-32. Lang.: Eng.

USA. 1996. Histories-sources. ■Author's personal experience having his play *Taking Tennessee to Hart* produced in regional and university theatres. Playwright/director relationship, playwright's role in the rehearsal process.

3450 Sweet, Jeffrey. "Improvisation as a Playwriting Tool." *DGQ.* 1996 Spr; 33(1): 28-36. Lang.: Eng.

USA. 1996. Critical studies. ■Champions the use of improvisational techniques as a tool to be used by the playwright to develop a script.

3451 Sweet, Jeffrey. "How I Publish My Plays." *DGQ.* 1996 Fall; 33(3): 24-26. Lang.: Eng.

USA: New York, NY. 1996. Instructional materials. ■Playwright Jeffrey Sweet on how to publish your own early edition using a computer program.

3452 Taylor, Regina. "that's why they call it the Blues." *AmTh.* 1996 Apr.; 13(4): 18-23. Illus.: Photo. B&W. 6. Lang.: Eng.

USA. 1996. Critical studies. ■Influence of blues music on the plays of August Wilson, special focus on *Seven Guitars, Ma Rainey's Black Bottom.* Includes sidebar interview with Wilson conducted by Susan Johann.

3453 Thompson, Deborah. "Blackface, Rape, and Beyond: Rehearsing Interracial Dialogue in *Sally's Rape*." *TJ.* 1996 May; 48 (2): 123-140. Notes. Biblio. Lang.: Eng.

USA. 1993-1994. Critical studies. ■Author examines how Robbie McCauley's *Sally's Rape* intervenes in the historical stages of blackface minstrelsy and interracial rape and how the play uses the theatrical stage to create more productive, positive paradigms of interracial dialogue.

3454 Turner, Beth. "August Wilson: A Blues-Driven Journey to Broadway." *BlackM.* 1996 May/June; 11(6): 5-8. Illus.: Photo. B&W. 1. Lang.: Eng.

USA. 1945-1996. Biographical studies. ■Background and career of playwright August Wilson, prior to the opening of his play *Seven Guitars* on Broadway.

3455 Turner, Beth. "Lonnie Elder III." *BlackM.* 1996 Nov/Dec.; 12(2): 9. Lang.: Eng.

USA. 1996. Biographical studies. ■Obituary for playwright Lonnie Elder III.

3456 Tuttle, Jon. "The Efficacy of Work: Arthur Miller and Albert Camus' 'The Myth of Sisyphus'." *AmerD.* 1996 Fall; 6(1): 61-72. Biblio.

USA. 1950-1996. Critical studies. ■Albert Camus' philosophy that 'the struggle itself ... is enough to fill a man's heart', and how it is reflected in such Miller works as *The Price, A View From the Bridge,* and *A Memory of Two Mondays.*

3457 Urist, Rachel Feldbin. "On the Meaning of Meeting Athol Fugard." *DGQ.* 1996 Spr; 33(1): 45-49. Lang.: Eng.

USA: New York, NY. 1980-1989. Histories-sources. ■Author's meeting with playwright Athol Fugard in 1980, and its effect on her over the subsequent nine years before seeing him again during a production of *The Road to Mecca.*

3458 Vera, Yvonne. "Observations as System in Eugene O'Neill's *The Iceman Cometh*." *MD.* 1996 Fall; 39(3): 448-456. Notes. Lang.: Eng.

USA. 1995. Critical studies. ■Impact of observation among characters in O'Neill's play and how these observations motivate their action.

3459 Vetere, Richard. "A Playwright on Television." *DGQ.* 1996 Win; 33(4): 40-44. Lang.: Eng.

USA. 1996. Critical studies. ■Possible reasons for the flight of playwrights to film and television, primarily financial.

3460 Vorlicky, Robert H. "O'Neill's First Play: *A Wife for a Life*." *EOR.* 1996 Spr/Fall; 20(1&2): 5-10. Biblio. Lang.: Eng.

USA. 1913. Critical studies. ■Analysis of O'Neill's first play: its treatment of male characters who interact amid the absence of women, structural elements that are more fully realized in his later plays.

3461 Wang, Qun. "Towards a Poeticization of the 'Field of Manners'." *AfAmR.* 1995 Win; 29(4): 605-613. Notes. Biblio. Lang.: Eng.

USA. 1995. Critical studies. ■Analysis of African-American language and cultural metaphors in their historical context, and the celebration of African-American heritage in the plays of August Wilson: *The Piano Lesson, Ma Rainey's Black Bottom, Fences, Joe Turner's Come and Gone* and *Two Trains Running.*

3462 Wheatley, Christopher J. "Thornton Wilder, the Real, and Theatrical Realism." 139-155 in Demastes, William W., ed. *Realism and the American Dramatic Tradition.* Tuscaloosa, AL/London: Univ of Alabama P; 1996. 290 pp. Pref. Biblio. Index. Notes. Lang.: Eng.

USA. 1931-1962. Critical studies. ■Argues that Thornton Wilder rejected realism in his plays because of its insistence on the probable and its emphasis on causality, which he felt insulated the audience from vital dramatic action.

3463 Wilder, Matthew. "From Büchner's Skin to Naomi's *Skin* or Things I Was Wrong About When I Directed a Play." *TheatreF.* 1996 Win/Spr; 8: 38-39. Illus.: Photo. 3. Lang.: Eng.

USA: Dallas, TX. 1995-1996. Histories-sources. ■Director Matthew Wilder writes about his experiences directing Naomi Iizuka's *Skin* at the Dallas Theatre Center. Iizuka's play centers on a character based on the playwright Georg Büchner.

3464 Williams, John. "Hip-Hop Homer." *AmTh.* 1996 May/June; 13(5): 6-7. Illus.: Photo. B&W. 1. Lang.: Eng.

USA: San Francisco, CA. 1996. Critical studies. ■Ifa Bayeza's political satire *Homer G. and the Rhapsodies in the Fall of Detroit* debuting at the Lorraine Hansberry Theatre. Development of script, themes of play, brief biographical background of Bayeza.

3465 Wright, Steven K. "The Betrayer's Art: Translating Medieval Drama for Modern Readers." *RORD.* 1996; 35(1): 85-96. Notes. Lang.: Eng.

USA. 1996. Critical studies. ■Discusses the many compromises, deceptions and other difficulties that arise for the translator of medieval texts for the modern reader.

3466 Kazimirovskaja, Natalia. "Varje lidande gör oss medvetna om livet." (Each Suffering Makes Us Conscious of Life.) *Tningen.* 1996; 20(75): 35-37. Illus.: Photo. B&W. Lang.: Swe.

USSR. 1983. Histories-sources. ■An interview with the Russian playwright Ljudmila Rasumovskaja.

3467 Rodríguez Sosa, Fernando. "Sortilegio de Carpentier." (Carpentier's Spell.) *Cjo.* 1996 July/Dec.; 103: 94-96. Notes. Illus.: Photo. 2. Lang.: Spa.

Venezuela: Caracas. Cuba. 1945-1959. Historical studies. ■Cuban writer Alejo Carpentier's rich, productive output during his stay in Venezuela and the theatrical effects in and South American influences on his novels.

3468 Romero, Pilar. "José Ignacio Cabrujas: de la dramaturgia venezolana del compromiso (antiponencia)." (José Ignacio Cabrujas: On the Venezuelan Dramaturgy of Compromise—Antispeech.) *Cjo.* 1996 Jan-June; 102: 61-66. Illus.: Photo. 4. Lang.: Spa.

Venezuela. 1995. Critical studies. ■Essay on the dramaturgical style of Venezuelan playwright José Ignacio Cabrujas, quoting extensively from his play *El día que me quieras (The Day You'll Love Me).*

3469 Kermauner, Taras. *Slovensko perspektivovstvo.* (Slovene 'Perspectivism'.) Ljubljana: Drustvo za preučevanje zgodovine, literature in antropologije, Znanstveno in publicistično središče; 1996. 415 pp. Lang.: Slo.

Yugoslavia. 1950-1969. Critical studies. ■Proceedings of a conference on perspectivism in Slovene drama of the 1950s and '60s.

3470 Wille, Franz. "Vielleicht ist irgendetwas im Wasser." (Perhaps There Is Something in the Water.) *THeute.* 1996; 7: 41-44 . Illus.: Photo. B&W. 6. Lang.: Ger.

DRAMA: —Plays/librettos/scripts

Yugoslavia: Belgrade. 1994-1996. Critical studies. ■Political implications and language in *Bure barut (The Powder Keg)* by Rejan Dukovski.

Reference materials

3471 Balassa, Anna, et al. *77 híres dráma.* (77 Famous Dramas.) Budapest: Móra; 1996. 445,[7] pp. Index. [3rd ed.] Lang.: Hun.
500 B.C.-1970 A.D. ■Brief content of important plays as a guide to world dramatic literature from Aeschylus to Mrożek.

3472 Lavoie, Pierre; Lépine, Stéphane. "Théâtrographie." (Theatrography.) *JCT.* 1990; 54: 127-133. Illus.: Photo. B&W. 2. Lang.: Fre.
Canada: Montreal, PQ. 1966-1989. ■Performance and bibliographic information on gay and lesbian plays by Quebec playwrights and collectives.

3473 "Western European Stages Index, vols 6-7." *WES.* 1996 Spr; 8(2): 39-58. Lang.: Eng.
Europe. 1994-1995. ■Index to 1994 and 1995 (vols 6-7) *Western European Stages.*

3474 Beach, Cecilia, comp. *French Women Playwrights of the Twentieth Century: A Checklist.* Westport, CT/London: Greenwood; 1996. 515 pp. (Bibliographies and Indexes in Women's Studies 24.) Index. Biblio. Pref. Lang.: Eng.
France. 1900-1990. Bibliographical studies. ■Comprehensive list of works by French women playwrights. Playwrights are listed alphabetically, with plays listed chronologically under authors' names.

3475 *Teatry Rossii (Dramatičeskie teatry): Spravočnik. Č.I.* (Russia's Theatres: Drama Theatres—Directory, Part 1.) Moscow: Ministerstvo kul'tury Rossii; 1996. 282 pp. Lang.: Rus.
Russia. 1980-1996. Histories-sources. ■Includes information on theatres, their repertoire and most famous participants.

3476 Greenfield, Peter H. "Census of Medieval Drama Productions." *RORD.* 1996; 35(1): 133-152. Lang.: Eng.
USA. Canada. UK-Scotland. 1995. Historical studies. ■Compilation of productions of medieval dramas in the US, Canada, and Scotland, with a description of the productions.

Relation to other fields

3477 Gill, Christopher. *Personality in Greek Epic, Tragedy, and Philosophy: The Self in Dialogue.* Oxford: Clarendon; 1996. 510 pp. Biblio. Index. Lang.: Eng.
Ancient Greece. 525-405 B.C. Critical studies. ■Ancient Greek thinking about personality and selfhood as presented in epic, tragedy and philosophy. Includes analysis of Euripides' *Medea.*

3478 Fischer, Gerhard. "The Australian-German Intercultural Dramaturgy: On Mudrooroo's Play." 225-244 in Jurgensen, Manfred, ed. *German-Australian Cultural Relations Since 1945.* Volume 9. Berne: Peter Lang; 1995. 345 pp. Notes. Lang.: Eng.
Australia. Germany. 1945-1995. Historical studies. ■German-Australian theatrical exchange since the end of World War II, focusing on *The Mudrooroo/Müller project* of 1991, a co-created piece by Aboriginal author Mudrooroo (Colin Johnson) and Heiner Müller.

3479 Shurbanov, Alexander; Sokolova, Boika. "Shakespeare in the Bulgarian School." *RDE.* 1996; 1(1): 11-21. Biblio. Lang.: Eng.
Bulgaria. 1950-1989. Historical studies. ■Examines the place of Shakespeare in Bulgarian education during Communism, exploring how his works, especially *Hamlet* and *Macbeth,* were interpreted in ways that supported the dominant ideology.

3480 Belzil, Patricia; Burgoyne, Lynda; Camerlain, Lorraine; David, Gilbert; Godin, Jean Cléo; Lavoie, Pierre; Lazaridès, Alexandre; Lévesque, Solange; Richard, Hélène; Vaïs, Michel; Vigeant, Louise. "Seminaire (2e séance)." (Seminar (Second Session).) *JCT.* 1990; 54: 91-113. Illus.: Dwg. Photo. B&W. 14. Lang.: Fre.
Canada. 1960-1990. Critical studies. ■Societal attitudes towards homosexuality and gay theatre in contemporary Quebec.

3481 David, Gilbert. "Ce qui est resté dans le placard." (What Stayed in the Closet.) *JCT.* 1990; 54: 119-122. Notes. Biblio. Lang.: Fre.
Canada. 1960-1990. Historical studies. ■Homosexuality in Quebecois society and theatre.

3482 Gilman, Marvin. "Fennario and Ryga: Canadian Political Playwrights." *ADS.* 1996 Oct.; 29: 180-186. Lang.: Eng.
Canada. 1932-1996. Critical studies. ■Political influences on Canadian playwrights George Ryga and David Fennario, their backgrounds and other details.

3483 Larue, Monique. "Abscisse et ordonnée de la vie." (Abscissa and Ordinate of Life.) *JCT.* 1989; 50: 224-225. Illus.: Photo. B&W. 1. Lang.: Fre.
Canada. 1950-1989. Critical studies. ■Refutes suggestion that novels and theatre deal with different types of memory. Individual and collective memory in Quebec novels and plays.

3484 Lasnier, Marie. "Des Coups de coeur d'ici." (Lovestruck for Here.) *JCT.* 1989; 50: 226-227. Illus.: Photo. B&W. 1. Lang.: Fre.
Canada. 1989. Critical studies. ■Colonial mentality in Quebec and need to encourage cultural autonomy through teaching Quebecois theatre history.

3485 Lévesque, Solange. "Passage." *JCT.* 1989; 50: 124-129. Notes. Illus.: Pntg. Photo. B&W. 3. Lang.: Fre.
Canada. 1900-1989. Critical studies. ■Traces origin of psychological usage of French word 'pulsion' ('urge') to Freud. Importance of urges in Quebec drama.

3486 Micone, Marco. "Le palimpseste impossible." (The Impossible Palimpsest.) *JCT.* 1996; 80: 20-22. Notes. Illus.: Dwg. Photo. B&W. 2. Lang.: Fre.
Canada: Montreal, PQ. Histories-sources. ■Immigrant playwright Marco Micone's perspective on multiculturalism and cultural assimilation.

3487 Roberts, Diane; Mojica, Monique; Lushington, Kate; Obokata, Dawn. "Dramaturgy: A Nightwood Conversation." *CTR.* 1996 Sum ; 87: 22-24. Lang.: Eng.
Canada: Toronto, ON. 1996. Histories-sources. ■Feminism, the importance of women's performance and the role of dramaturgy at Nightwood Theatre.

3488 Breitenberg, Mark. *Anxious Masculinity in Early Modern England.* Cambridge: Cambridge UP; 1996. 225 pp. Index. Pref. Biblio. Lang.: Eng.
England. 1580-1620. Historical studies. ■Masculine anxiety in texts and performances, including Shakespeare's *Love's Labour's Lost.*

3489 Dubrow, Heather. "'Incertainties now crown themselves assur'd': The Politics of Plotting Shakespeare's Sonnets." *SQ.* 1996 Fall; 47(3): 291-305. Notes. Lang.: Eng.
England. 1590-1609. Critical studies. ■Reexamines assumptions about the structure and 'plot' of Shakespeare's sonnets and for whom they were intended.

3490 Hopkins, Lisa. "Judith Shakespeare's Reading: Teaching *The Concealed Fancies.*" *SQ.* 1996 Win; 47(4): 396-406. Notes. Illus.: Photo. B&W. 1. Lang.: Eng.
England. 1645. Critical studies. ■Feminist classroom approach to *The Concealed Fancies* by Lady Jane Cavendish and Lady Elizabeth Brackley.

3491 Roberts, Josephine, A. "'Thou maist have thy Will': The Sonnets of Shakespeare and His Stepsisters." *SQ.* 1996 Win; 47 (4): 407-423. Notes. Lang.: Eng.
England. 1590-1621. Critical studies. ■Teaching the sonnets of Shakespeare in conjunction with lyrics by contemporary women poets such as Aemilia Lanyer and Lady Mary Wroth to show their differing treatments of conventional motifs.

3492 Teague, Frances. "Judith Shakespeare Reading." *SQ.* 1996 Win; 47(4): 361-373. Notes. Illus.: Dwg. B&W. Lang.: Eng.
England. 1510-1621. Historical studies. ■Literacy among women in Shakespeare's age, and his treatment of this subject in such plays as *The Merry Wives of Windsor, Troilus and Cressida* and *Twelfth Night.* Masculine attitudes toward the necessity of feminine education.

CLASSED ENTRIES

DRAMA: —Relation to other fields

3493 Wilson, Jean. "The Grave Shall Have a Living Monument." *AtG.* 1996 Win: 14-16. Illus.: Photo. Color. 6. Lang.: Eng.
England: London. 1599-1631. Historical studies. ■Influence of Shakespeare's plays on the funerary and decorative sculptors of the Southwark section of London.

3494 Tindermans, Klaas; Jean-Marie Piemme, transl. "Le Théâtre et la Loi." (Theatre and the Law.) *JCT.* 1989; 50: 76-79. Illus.: Photo. B&W. 2. Lang.: Fre.
Europe. 500 B.C.-1989 A.D. Critical studies. ■From unity of drama and law in ancient Greece to irreconcilable differences between drama and the state in contemporary Europe.

3495 Tiner, Elza. "English Law in the York Trial Plays." *EDAM.* 1996 Spr; 18(2): 103-112. Lang.: Eng.
Europe. 1400-1600. Historical studies. ■English plays of the Passion in the medieval civic cycles need to be seen against the background of English legal practice. In the case of the York plays dramatizing the trial of Christ, legal errors are rampant.

3496 Lambert, Josée. "Les vivantes." (The Living.) *JCT.* 1996; 80: 23-24. Notes. Illus.: Photo. B&W. 2. Lang.: Fre.
France: Paris. Lebanon. 1940-1996. Historical studies. ■Compares Claudia, the deported acting student in Brigitte Jaques' *Elvire Jouvet 40*, with a contemporary political prisoner in Lebanon.

3497 Lévesque, Claude. "Des Paroles colossales." (Colossal Words.) *JCT.* 1989; 50: 133-135. Illus.: Photo. B&W. 2. Lang.: Fre.
France. Germany. 1989. Critical studies. ■Postmodern possibilities of meaning in theatre, drawing on philosophies of Friedrich Nietzsche and Jacques Lacan.

3498 Popovic, Pierre. "Fausse fiction en l'honneur de Marie Dorval." (False Fiction in Honor of Marie Dorval.) *JCT.* 1996; 80 : 166-168. Illus.: Photo. B&W. 2. Lang.: Fre.
France: Paris. 1835-1996. Historical studies. ■Overview of assumptions regarding relationship of theatre to literature, followed by fictional account of Marie Dorval preparing to perform in the premier of Vigny's *Chatterton* at the Comédie-Française, 1835.

3499 Hallberg, Marie Clahr. "Dionysus och det gudomliga vansinnet." (Dionysus and the Divine Madness.) *Dramat.* 1996; 4(1): 42-45. Illus.: Photo. Color. Lang.: Swe.
Greece. 407 B.C. Critical studies. ■An essay about the god Dionysus and the cult around him in relation to Euripides' play *Bákchai* and modern psychology.

3500 Urian, Dan. "The Image of the Arab on the Israeli Stage." 227-268 in Ben-Zvi, Linda, ed. *Theater In Israel.* Ann Arbor, MI: Univ. of Michigan P; 1996. 450 pp. Notes. Lang.: Eng.
Israel. 1912-1990. Critical studies. ■The evolution of the Arab character on the Israeli stage, both in Israeli plays and in Israeli productions of European plays in which characters are interpreted as Arabs and Jews.

3501 Beauchamp, Hélène. "Un théâtre de résistance dans une culture en quête d'elle-même: Festival du théâtre japonais pour la jeunesse, Tokyo 20 juillet au 5 août 1995." (A Theatre of Resistance in a Culture in Search of Itself: Festival of Japanese Children's Theatre, Tokyo, June 20 to August 5, 1995.) *JCT.* 1996; 78: 152-166. Notes. Illus.: Dwg. Photo. B&W. 11. Lang.: Fre.
Japan: Tokyo. 1995. Historical studies. ■Account of Tokyo's 1995 Festival of Japanese Children's Theatre, identifying social and aesthetic trends.

3502 Seo, Yoo-Jin. "Jinan kyoul, Chongsonyoni Polmana dun Yeonkukdul." (The Plays for Teenagers From Last Winter.) *KTR.* 1996 Mar.; 21(3): 26-28. Illus.: Photo. B&W. 4. Lang.: Kor.
Korea: Seoul. 1995-1996. Critical studies. ■Analysis of three plays created by theatre collectives for teenagers. Discusses need for government support for educational theatre: *Ne muddero haela (Do What You Want)* by Anol, *Blue Saigon* by Mosinun Salamdu, and *Blue Guitar* by Teacher's Theatre.

3503 Pees, Matthias. "Nie wieder Moskau." (Never Again Moscow.) *TZ.* 1996; 3: 42-43. Illus.: Photo. B&W. 1. Lang.: Ger.

Lithuania. 1996. Historical studies. ■Eimuntas Nekrošius' production of *Tri sestry (Three Sisters)* by Čechov in the context of political changes in Lithuania.

3504 Stangret, Lech. "Wandering with Kantor." *TP.* 1996 Jan.; 38(1): 18-21. Illus.: Dwg. B&W. 2. Lang.: Eng, Fre.
Poland: Cracow. 1995. Historical studies. ■The Tadeusz Kantor Gallery, where Kantor's artworks are exhibited.

3505 Węgrzyniak, Rafal. "Ferdynand Goetel—ideolog i dramatopisarz." (Ferdynand Goetel, Ideologue and Playwright.) *DialogW.* 1996; 3: 99-106. Lang.: Pol.
Poland. 1890-1989. Biographical studies. ■Profile of Goetel, an ideologue with ties to the Piłsudski movement then in power. He later developed fascist leanings and emigrated to London after World War II.

3506 Wille, Franz. "Kunst, Sex und Politik." (Art, Sex, and Politics.) *THeute.* 1996; 1: 8-12. Illus.: Photo. B&W. Color. 6. Lang.: Ger.
Russia: Moscow. Germany: Berlin. 1995. Historical studies. ■Playwright Vladimir Sorokin in the context of socialist society, on the occasion of the performance of his *Hochzeitsreise (Honeymoon)* at Volksbühne.

3507 Cohen, Dan Baron. "Resistance to Liberation: Decolonizing the Mindful-Body." *PerfR.* 1996 Sum; 1(2): 60-74. Notes. Illus.: Photo. B&W. 3. [Text of a plenary presentation to the Young People's Theatre Education Trust conference 'Drama-action: strategies for the future', Johannesburg, December 1995.] Lang.: Eng.
South Africa, Republic of. UK-Ireland: Derry. UK-England: Manchester. 1980-1996. Historical studies. ■The potential of drama to contribute to political liberation, after external oppression has been removed. Draws on the writer's experiences with Manchester Frontline and Derry Frontline. Provides non-verbal exercises which could form the basis of a drama workshop designed to free individuals from the political past.

3508 Johnson, David. *Shakespeare and South Africa.* Oxford: Clarendon; 1996. 276 pp. Notes. Biblio. Index. Lang.: Eng.
South Africa, Republic of. 1800-1995. Critical studies. ■The political mission of English studies in South Africa, its historical context, and speculations on future development.

3509 Orkin, Martin. "Possessing the Book and Peopling the Text." *ET.* 1996; 15(1): 45-57. Notes. Biblio. Lang.: Eng.
South Africa, Republic of. 1994-1996. Critical studies. ■Explores the relevance of Shakespeare in modern day South Africa, especially in education.

3510 Baker, Stuart E. "On Politics." *ShawR.* 1996; 16(1): 125-144. Notes. Lang.: Eng.
UK-England. 1885-1929. Critical studies. ■Glimpses of the Fabian politician in playwright George Bernard Shaw's unpublished oratorical essays 'Open Air Meetings,' 'Ten Reasons Why Women Should Support the Progressives at the Borough Council Election,' and 'Lady Day Speech'.

3511 Bertolini, John A. "Shaw Family Values." *ShawR.* 1996; 16(1): 145-154. Notes. Lang.: Eng.
UK-England. 1886. Critical studies. ■Playwright George Bernard Shaw's unpublished manuscript on family issues, 'Socialism and the Family'.

3512 Gibson, Rex. "'O, what learning is!': Pedagogy and the Afterlife of *Romeo and Juliet*." *ShS.* 1996; 49: 141-152. Notes. Lang.: Eng.
UK-England. 1996. Critical studies. ■Emphasizes the importance of schools teaching children under the age of nineteen *Romeo and Juliet* as one reason for the strong popularity of the play, and reasons that teachers often reinforce interpretive misconceptions because of indifference.

3513 Kennedy, Judith M. "Bottom Transformed by the Sketching Society." *SQ.* 1996 Fall; 47(3): 308-318. Notes. Illus.: Dwg. Sketches. 8. Lang.: Eng.
UK-England: London. 1831. Historical studies. ■Analysis of sketches done by the 'Sketching Society' of Bottom's appearance to the rustics in ass's head in *A Midsummer Night's Dream*.

3514 Peters, Margot. "Shaw's True Gentleman." *ShawR.* 1996; 16(1): 59-66. Notes. Lang.: Eng.

DRAMA: —Relation to other fields

UK-England. 1879. Critical studies. ■Examines an early unpublished article by playwright George Bernard Shaw, 'On the True Signification of the Term Gentleman'.

3515 Turco, Alfred, Jr. "On War and Peace." *ShawR.* 1996; 16(1): 165-193. Notes. Lang.: Eng.

UK-England. 1899-1950. Critical studies. ■Examines playwright George Bernard Shaw's unpublished writings on war, revealing his views on warfare and peace.

3516 Donawerth, Jane. "Teaching Shakespeare in the Context of Renaissance Women's Culture." *SQ.* 1996 Win; 47(4): 476-489. Notes. Illus.: Dwg. B&W. 1. Lang.: Eng.

USA. 1991-1996. Histories-sources. ■The author's attempts to build a feminist course on 'Shakespeare in the Context of Renaissance Women's Culture' in which students take responsibility for their own learning.

3517 Gutierrez, Nancy. "Why William and Judith Both Need Their Own Rooms." *SQ.* 1996 Win; 47(4): 424-432. Notes. Lang.: Eng.

USA. 1995. Histories-sources. ■Record of author's experience teaching Elizabeth Cary's *The Tragedy of Mariam* with Shakespeare's *The Winter's Tale* in a graduate seminar on Shakespeare at Arizona State University.

3518 Hall, Kim F. "Beauty and the Beast of Whiteness: Teaching Race and Gender." *SQ.* 1996 Win; 47(4): 461-475. Notes. Illus.: Photo. Dwg. B&W. 3. Lang.: Eng.

USA. 1996. Critical studies. ■Use of Elizabeth Cary's *The Tragedy of Mariam*, Shakespeare's *Othello*, and Aphra Behn's *Oroonoko* to crystallize for students of the Renaissance some of the dynamics of race and gender.

3519 Kemp, Theresa D. "The Family is a Little Commonwealth': Teaching *Mariam* and *Othello* in a Special-Topics Course on Domestic England." *SQ.* 1996 Win; 47(4): 451-460. Notes. Illus.: Photo. B&W. 1. Lang.: Eng.

USA. 1995. Histories-sources. ■The author's experience teaching a special-topics course on domestic England in the early modern period, and her use of Shakespeare's *Othello* and Elizabeth Cary's *The Tragedy of Mariam* to convey how private issues are inextricably connected to the public and political.

3520 Matchinske, Megan. "Credible Consorts: What Happens When Shakespeare's Sisters Enter the Syllabus?" *SQ.* 1996 Win; 47(4) : 433-450. Notes. Illus.: Photo. B&W. 1. Lang.: Eng.

USA. 1996. Critical studies. ■Argues that Shakespeare must be taught in conjunction with his contemporary female writers such as Aemilia Lanyer, Elizabeth Cary and Dorothy Leigh in order to give students a comparative, issue-oriented, culture-based, and gender-aware study.

3521 Nesmith, Eugene. "What's Race Got to Do with It?" *AmTh.* 1996 Mar.; 13(3): 12-17. Illus.: Photo. B&W. 12. Lang.: Eng.

USA. 1926-1996. Critical studies. ■African-American cultural renaissance in American theatre. History of cultural representation, Afrocentric view that Blacks must have their own theatres, multiculturalism in regional theatres.

3522 Weales, Gerald. "Awake and Paint!" *AmTh.* 1996 Sep.; 13(7): 56-57. Illus.: Photo. B&W. 3. Lang.: Eng.

USA: New York, NY. 1940-1996. Critical studies. ■The paintings of playwright Clifford Odets on the occasion of a showing at J.B. Neumann's gallery in New York. Includes sidebar article written by Edward Karam on Joanne Woodward's direction of Odets' *Golden Boy* for the Blue Light Theatre Company.

3523 Becker, Peter von. "Handke und der Krieg." (Handke and the War.) *THeute.* 1996; 4: 1, 4-5. Illus.: Photo. B&W. 3. Lang.: Ger.

Yugoslavia. 1996. Histories-sources. ■Interview with playwright Slobodan Šnajder about the relationships between intellectuals and politics, author Peter Handke, and the war in the former Yugoslavia.

Research/historiography

3524 Wyatt, Diana. "*REED* and the *Oxford English Dictionary*." *MET.* 1995; 17: 120-131. Notes. [Cover title: *Using Early Drama Records.*] Lang.: Eng.

England. 970-1535. Textual studies. ■Reports on the use of texts from *Records of Early English Drama*, which modify, whether in dating, status, or meaning, the range of vocabulary in the second edition of the *OED*.

3525 Runnals, Graham A. "Records of Early French Drama: Archival Research on the Medieval French Theatre." *MET.* 1995; 17: 5-19. Pref. Index. [Cover title: *Using Early Drama Records.*] Lang.: Eng.

France. 1160-1520. Bibliographical studies. ■Provides general guidance for non-French scholars who need to research in French libraries and archives. Describes the archive system, its organization, inventories, and access, as well as selected libraries, and the Institut de recherche et d'histoire des textes.

3526 Orzechowski, Emil. "Our Theatre Studies." *TP.* 1995 July; 37(3): 11-16. Illus.: Photo. Color. 1. Lang.: Eng, Fre.

Poland. 1995. Critical studies. ■Stresses the need for coordination in developing Poland's nascent discipline of theatre studies among theatres, academics and other parties involved in safeguarding the nation's theatre heritage.

3527 Pleśniarowicz, Krzysztof. "Kantor's Living Museum." *TP.* 1996 Jan.; 38(1): 3-9. Illus.: Photo. B&W. 3. Lang.: Eng, Pol.

Poland: Cracow. 1980-1995. Historical studies. ■A look at what is contained in the Cricoteka, a living archive of Tadeusz Kantor's theatre legacy, includes manuscripts, drawings, set pieces from Kantor's productions, as well as costumes.

3528 Banham, Martin. "Feedback Statement from RAE Drama, Dance and Performing Arts Panel to Submitting Institutions." *STP.* 1996 Dec.; 14: 64-66. Lang.: Eng.

UK. 1991-1996. Histories-sources. ■The Chair of the Research Assessment Exercise panel for Drama etc reports on the means by which the grades for research were awarded to British university theatre departments in the 1996 Research Assessment Exercise (RAE).

3529 King, Pamela M.; Twycross, Meg. "Beyond *REED*? The York *Doomsday* Project." *MET.* 1995; 17: 132-148. Notes. [Cover title: *Using Early Drama Records.*] Lang.: Eng.

UK-England: York. 1995. Historical studies. ■Description of the creation of a machine-readable archive of material pertinent to the York Mercers' *Doomsday* play, including sound, video, 3-D reconstructions, visual images (contemporary iconography, recent productions), and cataloguing data and transcription of texts.

3530 King, Pamela M. "*Records of Early English Drama*: Reflections of a Hardened User." *MET.* 1995; 17: 52-57. Notes. [Cover title: *Using Early Drama Records.*] Lang.: Eng.

UK-England. 1978-1995. Bibliographical studies. ■Argues that, despite its defects, *REED* complements other scholarly approaches by providing hard evidence and reinforcing the habit of reading playscripts.

3531 Walker, Greg. "A Broken Reed?: Early Drama Records, Politics, and the Old Historicism." *MET.* 1995; 17: 42-51. Notes. [Cover title: *Using Early Drama Records.*] Lang.: Eng.

UK-England. 1978-1995. Critical studies. ■Considers utility and validity of studying the archival records of early drama, with special reference to the *REED* project, as well as the broader implications of such a debate for the future.

Theory/criticism

3532 Zupančič, Alenka. "Mesto tragedije v psihoanalizi: Ojdip in Synge." (The Place of Tragedy in Psychoanalysis: Oedipus and Synge.) 171-237 in Zupančič, Alenka. *Claudel z Lacanom.* Ljubljana: Društvo za teoretsko psihoanalizo; 1996. 237 pp. (Analecta.) Lang.: Slo.

Critical studies. ■A psychoanalytical approach to the problem of tragic ethic in classical and modern drama.

3533 Burgoyne, Lynda. "Critique théâtrale et pouvoir androcentrique: Réception critique de 'Leçon d'anatomie' et de 'Joie'." (Theatre Criticism and Androcentric Power: Critical Reception of *Anatomy Lesson* and *Joy*.) *JCT.* 1992; 65: 46-53 . Notes. Illus.: Photo. B&W. 2. Lang.: Fre.

Canada: Montreal, PQ. 1992. Critical studies. ■Hegemony of antifeminist male perspective in theatre criticism of the printed press, illustrated by reviews of Larry Tremblay's *Leçon d'anatomie* and Pol Pelle-

DRAMA: —Theory/criticism

tier's *Joie* (both Théâtre d'Aujourd'hui, 1992) in Montreal's French dailies: *Le Devoir, La Presse* and *Le Journal de Montréal*.

3534 Salter, Denis. "Introduction: The End(s) of Shakespeare." *ET.* 1996; 15(1): 3-14. Biblio. Lang.: Eng.
Canada. 1878-1996. Critical studies. ■Introduction to a special issue in the post-colonial criticism of Shakespeare, with special reference to *The Tempest.*

3535 Vaïs, Michel. "L'été: Aller au théâtre 'pour rire'." (Summer: Going to the Theatre 'for Laughs'.) *JCT.* 1990; 55: 116-117. Notes. Illus.: Photo. B&W. 2. Lang.: Fre.
Canada. 1990. Critical studies. ■Reasons why summer stock theatre is not worthy of serious criticism.

3536 Wallace, Robert; Denis, Jean-Luc. "Relativité et subversion." (Relativity and Subversion.) *JCT.* 1989; 50: 106-109. Notes. Illus.: Photo. B&W. 2. Lang.: Fre.
Canada. 1891-1989. Critical studies. ■Sentimentality in theatre.

3537 Douglas, Krystan V. *Guide to British Drama Explication.* New York, NY: G.K. Hall; 1996. 275 pp. (A Reference Publication in Literature.) Pref. Biblio. [Volume 1: Beginnings to 1640s.] Lang.: Eng.
England. 1200-1640. Bibliographies. ■First of two volumes focusing on English language explication of British drama. Deals primarily with drama written in the British Isles up to the closing of the theatres in 1640.

3538 Freedman, Barbara. "Frame-Up: Feminism, Psychoanalysis, Theatre." 78-108 in Keyssar, Helene, ed. *Feminist Theatre and Theory.* London: Macmillan; 1996. 288 pp. (New Casebooks.) Notes. Index. Lang.: Eng.
Europe. 1995. Critical studies. ■The potential of theatre to revise representations of gender difference on the stage. Presents an approach to feminist theatre drawn from philosophical French feminism and feminist film criticism.

3539 Sponsler, Clive. "Producing the Past: Modern Performances of Medieval Drama." *TA.* 1995; 48: 60-71. Notes. Lang.: Eng.
Europe. USA. 1995. Critical studies. ■Investigates approaches to reviving medieval drama for the contemporary stage: as an experiment to recreate the feel and spirit of an actual medieval production or to reinterpret the text to give it more cogency for a modern audience.

3540 Vogel, Viveka. "Männens makt." (The Power of the Men.) *Dramat.* 1996; 4(2): 14-20. Illus.: Photo. B&W. Lang.: Swe.
Europe. 400 B.C.-1996 A.D. Critical studies. ■Theatre and feminism: Tiina Rosenberg's research on the theatre and the dominance of the men in all roles, and a discussion with actresses of two different generations: Anita Björk and Marie Richardson.

3541 Wille, Franz. "Vorsicht! Sie verlassen den politisch-korrekten Sektor!" (Warning: You Are Leaving the PC Sector.) *THeute.* 1996; YB: 59-60. Illus.: Photo. B&W. 1. Lang.: Ger.
Germany: Berlin. 1996. Historical studies. ■Critical reaction to Einar Schleef's Berliner Ensemble production of Brecht's *Herr Puntila.*

3542 Linzer, Martin. "Wechselvoller Umgang mit einem Autor." (Various Dealings with an Author.) *TZ.* 1996; 2: 12-15. Illus.: Photo. B&W. 3. Lang.: Ger.
Germany, East. 1957-1989. Historical studies. ■Documents the relationship between this periodical and the playwright Heiner Müller, including the publication of his plays and reviews.

3543 Lazaridès, Alexandre. "Sisyphe le pathétique." (Sisyphus the Pathetic.) *JCT.* 1989; 50: 100-104. Illus.: Pntg. Photo. B&W. 3. Lang.: Fre.
Greece: Athens. France. 500 B.C.-1989 A.D. Critical studies. ■Transition from tragedy to pathos in Greek myth and drama. Pathos examined through views of French philosophers.

3544 Levy, Shimon. "Heroes of Their Consciousness: Self-Referential Elements in Contemporary Israeli Drama." 311-319 in Ben-Zvi, Linda, ed. *Theater In Israel.* Ann Arbor, MI: Univ. of Michigan P; 1996. 450 pp. Biblio. Lang.: Eng.
Israel. 1948-1995. Critical studies. ■Self-reflection and self-reference in Israeli theatre, with respect to both social and political aspects on one hand and artistic, psychological, or spiritual aspects on the other.

3545 Fridštejn, Ju. "Piršestvo dlja čtenija." (A Feast for Reading.) *TeatZ.* 1996; 9: 55-56. Lang.: Rus.
Russia: Moscow. 1980-1996. Critical studies. ■Analysis of the works of Shakespearean scholar Aleksej Bartoševič.

3546 Sal'nikova, E. "Živaja énergija renessansa." (The Live Energy of the Renaissance.) *TeatZ.* 1996; 9: 53-54. Lang.: Rus.
Russia. 1990-1996. Critical studies. ■The 'laws' of contemporary Shakespearean theatre.

3547 Sell, Mike. "Gluttonous Cyborgs, Industrial-Strength Jugglers and Meyerhold's 'Constructivist' Theatre." *JDTC.* 1996 Spr ; 10(2): 43-60. Notes. Lang.: Eng.
Russia. 1917-1928. Critical studies. ■Analysis of criticism, including contemporaneous reactions, of productions of Vs. E. Mejerchol'd.

3548 Kos, Janko. "K vprašanju o bistvu tragedije." (On the Question of the Essence of Tragedy.) *PrimK.* 1996; 19(1): 1-16 . Lang.: Slo.
Slovenia. 1996. Critical studies. ■Tragedy in Slovene literary theory.

3549 Poniž, Denis. *Anatomija dramskega besedila.* (Anatomy of the Dramatic Text.) Ljubljana: Znanstveno in publicistično središče; 1996. 122 pp. Lang.: Slo.
Slovenia. 1996. Instructional materials. ■An introduction to the basic elements of classical and modern dramatics and a presentation of analytical methodologies.

3550 Zlobec, Ciril. "Vasja Predan: intervju." (Vasja Predan: Interview.) *Sodob.* 1996; 44(8/9): 629-639. Lang.: Slo.
Slovenia. 1952-1996. Histories-sources. ■Interview with theatre and literary critic Vasja Predan about the historical and present situation of theatre criticism in Slovenia.

3551 Kruger, Loren. "New Africans, Neocolonial Theatre and 'An African National Dramatic Movement'." *SATJ.* 1995 May; 9(1): 29-51. Notes. Biblio. Lang.: Eng.
South Africa, Republic of. 1933. Critical studies. ■Argues that African playwrights can best be true to themselves as Africans by putting artistic concerns over political ones. Refers to Herbert Dhlomo's 1933 essay 'The Importance of African Drama'.

3552 Thomson, Peter. "Humanism and Catastrophe: a Note on Howard Barker's Polarities." *STP.* 1994 Dec.; 10: 39. Lang.: Eng.
UK. 1993. Critical studies. ■Analysis of the 'humanist theatre' and the 'catastrophic theatre' as defined by Howard Barker in *Arguments for a Theatre.*

3553 Farfan, Penny. "From *Hedda Gabler* to *Votes for Women*: Elizabeth Robins's Early Feminist Critique of Ibsen." *TJ.* 1996 Mar.; 48(1): 59-78. Notes. Biblio. Illus.: Sketches. 2. Lang.: Eng.
UK-England. 1890-1928. Critical studies. ■The development of actress/director Elizabeth Robins's feminist critique of Ibsen, her assessment of Ibsen's contribution to actresses, and his non-contribution to the emancipation of women. Draws on Robins's critiques of the Ibsen plays in which she appeared, including the 1889 Janet Achurch production of *A Doll's House* and the English-language premiere of *Hedda Gabler*, as well as her own 1907 play *Votes for Women.*

3554 Jenckes, Norma. "A Spring-Cleaning for the Arts." *ShawR.* 1996; 16(1): 89-97. Notes. Lang.: Eng.
UK-England. 1880. Critical studies. ■Examines playwright George Bernard Shaw's unpublished treatise on the current state of the arts, 'Exhausted Arts'.

3555 Reinelt, Janelle. "Beyond Brecht: Britain's New Feminist Drama." 35-48 in Keyssar, Helene, ed. *Feminist Theatre and Theory.* London: Macmillan; 1996. 288 pp. (New Casebooks.) Notes. Index. Lang.: Eng.
UK-England. 1993-1995. Critical studies. ■Brechtian elements in British feminist drama that examine the relationships among class, gender, labor, and capital. Focus on Red Ladder Theatre Company's production of *Strike While the Iron Is Hot.*

3556 Shellard, Dominic. "The Actor as Artist: Harold Hobson's Shakespearean Theatre Criticism." *ShS.* 1996; 49: 225-223. Notes. Lang.: Eng.

DRAMA: —Theory/criticism

UK-England: London. 1930-1977. Biographical studies. ■Career of London *Times* theatre critic Harold Hobson, with emphasis on his belief that the actor was the pre-eminent member of the actor—director—playwright triumvirate as seen in his reviews of performances of Shakespeare.

3557   Shellard, Dominic. "A Magnificent Obsession: Harold Hobson and Waiting for Godot." *TN.* 1996; 50(2): 68-77. Notes. Lang.: Eng.

UK-England. 1955. Critical studies. ■Describes Hobson's critical reaction to the play and sets it in the context of the blank incomprehension which greeted its first appearance.

3558   Skura, Meredith. "Is There a Shakespeare after the *New* New Bibliography?" 169-183 in Parker, R.B., ed.; Zitner, S.P., ed. *Elizabethan Theater: Essays in Honor of S. Schoenbaum.* Newark, DE/London: Univ of Delaware P; 1996. 324 pp. Notes. Lang.: Eng.

UK-England. 1994. Critical studies. ■Criticizes the move to replace the author with the historical voices of the material text especially in Shakespeare.

3559   Tyson, Brian. "Enter the Literary Critic." *ShawR.* 1996; 16(1): 99-123. Notes. Lang.: Eng.

UK-England. 1880-1887. Critical studies. ■Playwright George Bernard Shaw's early unpublished literary criticism: analysis of reviews of George Vanbrugh's *Mistake* (1880), *The Future of Marriage: An Eirenikon for a Question of Today. By a Respectable Woman* (1885), and *Landon Deecroft* by Laon Ramsey (1886).

3560   Wisenthal, J.L. "Music: Laying Down the Law." *ShawR.* 1996; 16(1): 35-58. Notes. Lang.: Eng.

UK-England. 1879. Critical studies. ■Early unpublished writings by playwright George Bernard Shaw on music criticism: 'Conductors and Organists,' and 'Unconscionable Abuses'.

3561   Connolly, Thomas F. "Was Good Old Nathan Reliable?" *EOR.* 1996 Spr/Fall; 20(1&2): 72-79. Biblio. Lang.: Eng.

USA. 1908-1958. Critical studies. ■Drama critic George Jean Nathan: his friendship with Eugene O'Neill, his presentation of a public image of O'Neill that contrasted with his popular image, personal background and upbringing.

3562   Freeman, Elizabeth. "'The We of Me': *The Member of the Wedding*'s Novel Alliances." *WPerf.* 1996; 8(2): 111-135. Notes. Biblio. [Issue 16.] Lang.: Eng.

USA. 1946-1996. Critical studies. ■Queer theory analysis of Carson McCullers's novel and play *The Member of the Wedding.* Frankie's yearning to be part of the bridal couple could also operate as a lesbian 'coming of age' story, fantasizing about gay marriage.

3563   Gill, Glenda. "Rosamond Gilder: Influential Talisman for African-American Performers." *ThS.* 1996 May; 37(1): 99-117. Notes. Biblio. Illus.: Photo. 3. Lang.: Eng.

USA. 1891-1986. Historical studies. ■Theatre critic Rosamond Gilder's contributions to American Black theatre. More than any other critic, she helped the careers of African-American performers and playwrights.

3564   Miller, Eileen. "The Turks on O'Neill: Putting the Iceman on Ice." *EOR.* 1996 Spr/Fall; 20(1&2): 88-96. Biblio. Lang.: Eng.

USA: New York, NY. 1946. Critical studies. ■Analysis of Mary McCarthy and Eric Bentley's negative criticism of the Broadway production of O'Neill's *The Iceman Cometh*, and why these drama critics may have disliked the play.

3565   Parker, Andrew. "Praxis and Performativity." *WPerf.* 1996; 8(2): 265-273. Notes. Biblio. [Issue 16.] Lang.: Eng.

USA. 1996. Critical studies. ■The place of practice and performativity in Marxism, using the theoretical writings of Spivak, Butler, Derrida, Baliban and Rancière.

3566   Reinelt, Janelle. "Staging the Invisible: The Crisis of Visibility in Theatrical Representation." *TextPQ.* 1994 Apr.; 14 (2): 97-107. Notes. Lang.: Eng.

USA. 1994. Critical studies. ■Appreciation and critique of the positions of performance theorists Judith Butler and Peggy Phelan regarding possibilities for productive cultural subversion, and of their underplaying of the materiality and historicity of cultural production in the context of live theatrical performance.

MEDIA

General

Administration

3567   Moore, Dick. "AFTRA and SAG Presidents Report to Council on Status of Merger." *EN.* 1996 Oct.; 81(8): 1-2, 8. Illus.: Photo. 1. Lang.: Eng.

USA: New York, NY. 1996. Historical studies. ■Shelby Scott, president of American Federation of Television and Radio Artists, and Richard Masur, president of Screen Actors' Guild, are guests of Actors' Equity President Ron Silver at a meeting called to update Equity on the status of the prospective merger of their unions.

3568   Moore, Dick. "AFTRA, SAG Boards Approve Merger Plan." *EN.* 1996 Dec.; 81(10): 8. Lang.: Eng.

USA: New York, NY. 1996. Historical studies. ■The merger of two unions, American Federation of Television and Radio Artists and Screen Actors' Guild.

Performance/production

3569   Rohloff, Thomas. "Fernsehen—die verpasste Chance?" (TV: A Wasted Opportunity?)*PInfo.* 1996; 74(1): 21-24. Append. Illus.: Photo. B&W. 5. Lang.: Ger.

Germany. USA. 1996. Histories-sources. ■Professional puppeteer assesses job prospects in TV and film in Germany and the U.S.

Reference materials

3570   Culley, Sarah A., ed. *Blue Book of British Broadcasting 1996.* London: Tellex Monitors; 1996. 656 pp. Pref. Index. [22nd ed.] Lang.: Eng.

UK. 1995-1996. Histories-sources. ■Lists names and addresses for all sections of BBC and independent radio and television, with indexes to names, programs, stations, and associations.

Relation to other fields

3571   Claasen, George. "News as Vaudeville: Dramatic Image, News Diffusion and Demise of Cultural Literacy Through Show Business." *SATJ.* 1996 Sep.; 10(2): 101-115. Notes. Biblio. Lang.: Eng.

USA. 1945-1996. Critical studies. ■A critique of the trend toward giving amusement priority over news presentation, and toward gearing the themes of film to younger viewers, said to be 'culturally handicapped'.

3572   Zurbrugg, Nicholas. "Baudrillard and the Ambiguities of Radical Illusion." *PerfR.* 1996 Fall; 1(3): 1-5. Notes. Lang.: Eng.

USA. 1964-1996. Critical studies. ■Critique of Baudrillard's attack, in *The Perfect Crime*, of media and industrial culture, with references to performance artists Bill Viola and John Giorno.

Audio forms

Design/technology

3573   Camner, James. "Wizards of Sound: Through Their Art, Transfer Engineers Bring Us Closer and Closer to Performances of the Past." *OpN.* 1996 Oct.; 61(4): 32-35. Illus.: Photo. Color. B&W. 4. Lang.: Eng.

USA. 1996. Technical studies. ■The work of such audio-transfer engineers as Ward Marston, Seth Winner, Dan Hladik, and Mark Obert-Thorn.

Institutions

3574   Vilmányi, Zita. "Egy magyar zenei szerkesztő Amerikában." (A Hungarian Music Editor in America.) *OperaL.* 1996; 5(1): 26-27. Illus.: Photo. B&W. 1. Lang.: Hun.

USA: New York, NY. 1937-1995. Histories-sources. ■Interview with Hungarian-born George Jellinek, formerly music director of classical music radio station WQXR, regarding his contributions to American musical life.

MEDIA: Audio forms

Performance/production

3575 Benedetti, Amedeo. *Il comportamento radiofonico.* (Radio Behavior.) Genoa: Regione Liguria; 1996. 84 pp. Pref. Lang.: Ita.
Europe. 1996. Instructional materials. ■A handbook for people and associations that need to communicate by radio.

3576 Hamilton, David. "Knights of the Grail: The Association for Recorded Sound Collections Is Devoted to Safeguarding the Sounds of the Past." *OpN.* 1996 Oct.; 61(4): 26-28. Illus.: Photo. Color. 2. Lang.: Eng.
Europe. 1996. Historical studies. ■The work of the Association of Recorded Sound Collections: their efforts to preserve musical works across the spectrum.

3577 Norris, James. "What Price the Classics?" *PlPl.* 1996 Aug/ Sep.; 507: 23. Lang.: Eng.
UK-England. 1996. Historical studies. ■Report on the current state of classical music recordings sales worldwide. Outlines some new strategies for improving sales.

3578 Jellinek, George. "The Vocal Scene." *OQ.* 1996/97 Win; 13(2): 5-11. Illus.: Photo. B&W. 2. Lang.: Eng.
USA: New York, NY. 1968-1996. Histories-sources. ■Jellinek's first-person account of his involvement with his syndicated radio program *The Vocal Scene*, originating on WQXR, which is exclusively dedicated to the art of the singer.

Plays/librettos/scripts

3579 Villeneuve, Raymond. "Suspense théâtral contre suspense radiophonique." (Theatrical Suspense Versus Radio Suspense.) *JCT.* 1991; 61: 42-43. Illus.: Photo. B&W. 1. Lang.: Fre.
Canada: Montreal, PQ. 1987-1991. Histories-sources. ■Specificities of a purely aural form and Raymond Villeneuve's techniques for writing radio dramas.

3580 Becket, Joachim. "Klangkörper und Mentalchöre—Becketts Hörspiele und das Dramatische Werk." (Bodies of Sound and Mental Choirs: Beckett's Radio Plays and the Dramatic Work.) *FMT.* 1996; 2: 170-180. Notes. Lang.: Ger.
Europe. 1955-1980. Critical studies. ■How the radio plays of Samuel Beckett stimulate the theatre in the mind of the listener, who is said to become the subject of both radio and stage plays.

3581 Miers, M.E. *British Radio Drama: A Critical Analysis of its Development as a Distinctive Aesthetic Form.* Ph.D. thesis, *Index to theses*, 45-156. Hertfordshire: Hatfield; 1994. Notes. Biblio. Lang.: Eng.
UK-England. 1920-1990. Historical studies. ■Radio drama as a specialized form of poetic drama exhibiting structuring relationships resembling those of poetry. Discusses experimental drama of the 20s and 30s, the work of poets of the 40s and 70s, and playwrights who have made a distinctive artistic contribution.

3582 Goldfarb, Alvin. "The Holocaust on the Air: The Radio Plays of the Writers' War Board." *JADT.* 1996 Spr; 8(2): 48-58. Notes. Lang.: Eng.
USA. 1942-1944. Historical studies. ■A series of radio scripts distributed by the Writers' War Board that reflects Allied knowledge of the Third Reich's extermination of Jews. How this information was mediated in the scripts, which included *They Burned the Books* by Stephen Vincent Benét, Morton Wishengrad's *The Battle of the Warsaw Ghetto*, Max Ehrlich's *Der Fuehrer (and the Great Lie He Borrowed)*, Richard P. McDonagh's *War Criminals and Punishment*, and William K. Clarke's *The Promise Versus the Deed*.

3583 Guralnick, Elissa S. *Sight Unseen: Beckett, Pinter, Stoppard, and Other Contemporary Dramatists on Radio.* Athens, OH: Ohio UP; 1996. 238 pp. Pref. Notes. Biblio. Index. Lang.: Eng.
USA. UK-England. 1972-1984. Critical studies. ■Examines stage plays performed on radio, with attention to playwrights' use of the form. Discussion of Howard Barker's *Scenes from an Execution*, Tom Stoppard's *Artist Descending a Staircase*, Robert Ferguson's *Transfigured Night*, Arthur Kopit's *Wings*, Harold Pinter's *A Slight Ache*, David Rudkin's

Cries from Casement as His Bones Are Brought to Dublin, and John Arden's *Pearl* and *The Bagman*.

Theory/criticism

3584 Weiss, Allen S., ed. "Experimental Sound & Radio." *TDR.* 1996 Fall; 40(3): 9-191. Notes. Biblio. Illus.: Photo. B&W. 52. Lang.: Eng.
USA. 1932-1996. Critical studies. ■Special issue of *TDR* dedicated to exploring various topics in the area of experimental radio and sound. Includes *Mendicant Erotics (Sydney)*, a performance for radio by Ellen Zweig, and excerpt from *Hotel Radio* by Richard Foreman.

Film

Administration

3585 Noonan, Karen Colizzi. "The Golden Era of J. Myer and Louis W. Schine." *MarqJTHS.* 1996 2nd Qtr; 28(2): 20-27. Notes. Illus.: Photo. B&W. 7. [First Place 1994 Jeffrey Weiss Literary Competition.] Lang.: Eng.
USA: Gloversville, NY. 1914-1965. Historical studies. ■History of Schine Circuit Theatres, a chain of some 150 venues in New York, Pennsylvania, Delaware, Maryland, Ohio, and Kentucky.

Basic theatrical documents

3586 Linders, Jan. "Molière & Müller." *PerfR.* 1996 Sum; 1(2): 93-104. Notes. Illus.: Photo. B&W. 15. Lang.: Eng.
Germany. France. 1991-1996. Histories-sources. ■A revised English translation of the text and illustrative stills from a video of *La Mort de Molière (The Death of Molière)*, Heiner Müller's final collaboration with Robert Wilson and Jan Linders. The film was scored by Philip Glass. Includes an introduction by Linders.

Design/technology

3587 Litson, Jo. "*Così*: Kennedy and Schofield Create Opera in a Madhouse." *TCI.* 1996 Mar.; 30(3): 42-43. Illus.: Photo. Color. 3. Lang.: Eng.
Australia. 1996. Technical studies. ■Scene designer Chris Kennedy and costume designer Tess Schofield's concept for filming the opera scene from Mozart's *Così fan tutte*, in the film *Così*.

3588 Calhoun, John. "Wigs of Steel." *TCI.* 1996 Dec.; 30(10): 7. Illus.: Photo. Color. 1. Lang.: Eng.
France. 1996. Technical studies. ■The incorporation of steel wool to build the wigs for Patrice Leconte's film *Ridicule*, by hairdresser John Nollet.

3589 Calhoun, John. "*Carrington*: The Face as a Canvas." *TCI.* 1996 Jan.; 30(1): 38. Illus.: Photo. Color. 7. Lang.: Eng.
UK-England. 1995. Technical studies. ■Make-up and hair designer Chrissie Beveridge's approach to the period make-up and hair styles needed in Christopher Hampton's film *Carrington*.

3590 Calhoun, John. "The Young Poisoner's Handbook." *TCI.* 1996 Feb.; 30(2): 8. Illus.: Photo. Color. 1. Lang.: Eng.
UK-England. 1995. Technical studies. ■Color schemes employed by production designer Maria Djurkovic to contribute to the movie's vision.

3591 Calhoun, John. "*Beautiful Thing*." *TCI.* 1996 Nov.; 30(9): 13-15. Illus.: Photo. Color. 1. Lang.: Eng.
UK-England: London. 1995-1996. Technical studies. ■Mark Stevenson's production design and choice of an outdoor location for the film version of Jonathan Harvey's *Beautiful Thing* directed by Hettie MacDonald.

3592 Calhoun, John. "*Restoration*." *TCI.* 1996 Mar.; 30(3): 44-46. Illus.: Photo. Color. 6. Lang.: Eng.
UK-England: London. 1996. Technical studies. ■Designer Eugenio Zanetti's sets for the film *Restoration*, directed by Michael Hoffman.

3593 Calhoun, John. "*Richard III*." *TCI.* 1996 Apr.; 30(4): 34-37. Illus.: Photo. Color. 13. Lang.: Eng.
UK-England: London. 1991-1996. Technical studies. ■Fascist 1930s style of set designs by Tony Burroughs and costumes by Shuna Harwood for Shakespeare's *Richard III*, adapted for the screen by director Richard Loncraine and star Ian McKellen based on Richard Eyre's 1991 stage production.

MEDIA: Film—Design/technology

3594 Calhoun, John. "In Memoriam: Dorothy Jeakins." *TCI.* 1996 Feb.; 30(2): 10. Lang.: Eng.
USA: Santa Barbara, CA. 1995. Biographical studies. ■Obituary for movie costumer Dorothy Jeakins.

3595 Calhoun, John. "*Toy Story*: Pixar Animation Studios Fills a Virtual World with Virtual Light." *TCI.* 1996 Feb.; 30(2): 34-37. Illus.: Photo. Color. 6. Lang.: Eng.
USA: Hollywood, CA. 1995. Technical studies. ■Sharon Calahan and Galyn Susman, lighting supervisors for the computer-animated film *Toy Story*, and their techniques.

3596 Calhoun, John. "In Memoriam: Richard Hornung." *TCI.* 1996 Mar.; 30(3): 10. Lang.: Eng.
USA: Los Angeles, CA. 1995. Biographical studies. ■Obituary of film and theatre costume designer Richard Hornung.

3597 Calhoun, John. "Recreating Stonewall." *TCI.* 1996 Aug/Sep.; 30(7): 7-8. Illus.: Photo. Color. 1. Lang.: Eng.
USA: New York, NY. 1996. Technical studies. ■Designer Michael Clancy's costumes for Nigel Finch's film, *Stonewall*, which are aimed at recreating '60s style drag.

3598 Calhoun, John. "States of Grace." *TCI.* 1996 Nov.; 30(9): 8. Illus.: Photo. Color. 1. Lang.: Eng.
USA: New York, NY. 1996. Technical studies. ■Susan Bertram's evocative costumes for Allison Anders' film *Grace of My Heart* which carry the film from the 1950s to the 1970s.

3599 Calhoun, John. "*12 Monkeys*." *TCI.* 1996 Mar.; 30(3): 34-37. Illus.: Photo. Color. 8. Lang.: Eng.
USA: Philadelphia, PA. 1996. Technical studies. ■Jeffrey Beecroft's scene design for Terry Gilliam's film *12 Monkeys*.

3600 Lampert-Gréaux, Ellen. "Making It in Hollywood." *TCI.* 1996 Feb.; 30(2): 30-31. Illus.: Photo. Color. 2. Lang.: Eng.
USA: Hollywood, CA. 1982-1996. Historical studies. ■History of Scenery West, a custom fabricator of scenery and props for film, founded by Ron Antone.

3601 Litson, Jo. "*Romeo and Juliet*." *TCI.* 1996 Nov.; 30(9): 46-49. Illus.: Photo. Color. 9. Lang.: Eng.
USA: Miami, FL. 1996. Technical studies. ■Director Baz Luhrmann and longtime collaborator production designer Catherine Martin's design concept for Luhrmann's filming of Shakespeare's *Romeo and Juliet*.

Institutions

3602 Kotychov, V. "Francuzskij 'desant'." (French 'Landing'.) *Balet.* 1996; 2: 18-20. Lang.: Rus.
Russia: Moscow. 1995. Historical studies. ■The Dance on Screen film festival, showing the correlation between modern ballet and cinema.

Performance spaces

3603 Dombowsky, Philip. "Theatres of the 1966 Conclave." *MarqJTHS.* 1996 1st Qtr; 28(1): 1, 7-28, 32. Illus.: Photo. Dwg. Handbill. B&W. Architec. 50. Lang.: Eng.
Canada: Montreal, PQ, Quebec, PQ. 1884-1966. Historical studies. ■Guide to theatres to be visited on the Theatre Historical Society's 1966 tour of Canada. Includes brief histories and photos of twenty-two venues on the group's itinerary and histories of eight theatres that have been destroyed or significantly altered.

3604 Dombowsky, Philip. "Emmanuel Briffa: Canada's Outstanding Theatre Decorator." *MarqJTHS.* 1996 3rd Qtr; 28(3): 4-13, 32. Notes. Illus.: Photo. Sketches. B&W. 13. Lang.: Eng.
Canada: Montreal, PQ. USA: Detroit, MI. 1875-1941. Biographical studies. ■Life of the Maltese-born decorator—his education in Italy, move to Detroit in 1912, and theatre work with Theodore Jagman in Montreal after 1924.

3605 Lanken, Dane. "Theatres of Montreal: An Introduction." *MarqJTHS.* 1996 1st Qtr; 28(1): 4-6. Illus.: Photo. B&W. 3. [An introduction to the Conclave issue.] Lang.: Eng.
Canada: Montreal, PQ. 1922-1934. Historical studies. ■A history of the cinema in Montreal from its beginnings in 1895 until the present time. Discusses the leading management chains, designers and decorators and other individuals involved in the history of the city's cinema. A number of specific theatres, both remaining and lost, are described and discussed.

3606 DuciBella, Joseph. "Belmont, Chicago—Revisited." *MarqJTHS.* 1996 3rd Qtr; 28(3): 1, 3, 20-28. Notes. Illus.: Photo. Dwg. B&W. Architec. 16. Lang.: Eng.
USA: Chicago, IL. 1926-1996. Historical studies. ■History of the Belmont Theatre (3,244 seats), which was converted to a bowling alley in the 1950s and later to an apartment building. Includes illustrations of the theatre as built.

3607 Fowler, Brother Andrew. "Diagonal Floor Plan Seating: What ... Why? ... Where?" *MarqJTHS.* 1996 2nd Qtr; 28(2): 1, 4-15. Notes. Illus.: Photo. Plan. Dwg. B&W. Grd.Plan. 25. Lang.: Eng.
USA: New York, NY. 1916-1929. Historical studies. ■Description of eight legitimate and film theatres built with the seats placed in a diagonal pattern from one corner of the building to the other to provide the largest number of seats across the center area.

3608 Levin, Steve. "Granada San Francisco." *MarqJTHS.* 1996 2nd Qtr; 28(2): 16-19, 32. Notes. Illus.: Photo. B&W. 13. [Photo Feature.] Lang.: Eng.
USA: San Francisco, CA. 1921-1965. Historical studies. ■History of the Granada Theatre, later the Paramount, which was demolished in 1965.

3609 Levin, Steve. "Orpheum Los Angeles California." *MarqJTHS.* 1996 3rd Qtr; 28(3): 14-17. Illus.: Photo. B&W. 5. [Photo Feature.] Lang.: Eng.
USA: Los Angeles, CA. 1926-1996. Historical studies. ■History of the Orpheum, designed by Lansburg, opened in 1926 and still in operation.

3610 Levin, Steve. "Selections from the Terry Helgesen Collection." *MarqJTHS.* 1996 4th Qtr; 28(4): 1, 3-29, 32. Pref. Illus.: Photo. Plan. Dwg. B&W. Architec. 47. [Photographs and plans from the THS Archives.] Lang.: Eng.
USA: New York, NY. UK-England: London. 1882-1996. Historical studies. ■The Terry Helgesen Collection of 26 albums of photos and other items recently became part of the THS Archives. Some of the albums are devoted to a single architect or firm, some to a single theatre, and some to an assortment of regional theatres. This issue is devoted to representative theatre photographs from the albums.

3611 Levin, Steve, ed.; Longstreth, Richard; Owen, Tom. "Grauman's Metropolitan Theatre Los Angeles, California—William Woollett, Architect." *MarqJTHS.* 1996 Annual; A23: 1-36. Notes. Illus.: Photo. Design. Dwg. Plan. B&W. Architec. Grd.Plan. Fr.Elev. 54. [Theatre Historical Society Annual No 23—1966.] Lang.: Eng.
USA: Los Angeles, CA. 1926-1960. Historical studies. ■History of the Metropolitan Theatre, which was destroyed in 1960. Includes photographs, plans, excerpts from writings of the architect (William Lee Woollett), and promotional materials.

3612 Markham, Steve. "Los Angeles Theatres: Ups and Downs, Part II, The Orpheum." *MarqJTHS.* 1996 3rd Qtr; 28(3): 18-19. Illus.: Photo. B&W. 1. Lang.: Eng.
USA: Los Angeles, CA. 1926-1996. Historical studies. ■History of the Orpheum Theatre, which has been used for film, vaudeville, dance, concerts, and theatre.

Performance/production

3613 Ábel, Péter, ed. *Hungarian Society of Cinematographers 1996.* Budapest: Hungarian Society of Cinematographers; 1996. 186 pp. Pref. Lang.: Eng.
Biographical studies. ■Handbook of the artists of today's Hungarian film living in Hungary and honorary members living abroad (entry: name, address, agent, awards, major works).

3614 Poirier, Anne-Claire. "Cinéma mémoire, cinéma d'archives." (Memory Film, Archival Film.) *JCT.* 1989; 50: 214-215. Illus.: Photo. B&W. 1. Lang.: Fre.
Canada: Stratford, ON. 1962-1989. Histories-sources. ■Film director Anne-Claire Poirier describes her experience of filming theatre, such as *Trente minutes, Mr. Plummer (Thirty Minutes, Mr. Plummer)*.

3615 Birringer, Johannes; Cambiasso, Gabriela M., transl. "Homosexuality and the Nation: An Interview with Jorge Perugorría." *TDR.* 1996 Spr; 40(1): 61-76. Biblio. Illus.: Photo. B&W. 5. Lang.: Eng.

MEDIA: Film—Performance/production

Cuba. 1994-1996. Histories-sources. ■Actor Perugorría discusses his career and his role as a gay man in the film *Fresa y Chocolate (Strawberries and Chocolate)* directed by Tomás Gutiérrez Alea and Juan Carlos Tabío. Cuban perception of homosexuality, political influence on art in Cuba.

3616   Nemeskürty, István. "Janovics Jenő, a művészi igényű magyar filmgyártás megteremtője." (Jenő Janovics, Creator of the Hungarian Art Film.) *SzSz.* 1996; 30/31: 17-18. Lang.: Hun.

Hungary: Kolozsvár. 1894-1915. Historical studies. ■Career of theatre director Jenő Janovics, founder of Hungarian film.

3617   "Kiyoshi Atsumi." *Econ.* 1996 Aug 17; 340(7979): 71. Illus.: Photo. B&W. 1. Lang.: Eng.

Japan. 1968-1996. Biographical studies. ■Obituary of popular comic actor Atsumi Kiyoshi, his career including forty-eight films featuring his popular character Tora-san, audience popularity and his early days in music halls and television.

3618   Degler, Janusz. "Witkacy i kino." (Witkacy and Cinema.) *DialogW.* 1996; 3: 131-138. Lang.: Pol.

Poland. USA. 1919-1996. Biographical studies. ■The little-known attempt of Stanisław Ignacy Witkiewicz to become a film actor, his views on cinema, and film adaptations of his plays.

3619   Goldfarb, David. "Revelation and Camouflage: Polish Cinema from 1930 to the Present—A Symposium." *SEEP.* 1996 Spr; 16(2) : 40-43. Notes. Lang.: Eng.

Poland. USA: New York, NY. 1930-1996. Historical studies. ■As part of the month-long festival of Polish cinema by the Film Society of New York, this two-day symposium examines Polish cinema prior to martial law and Polish cinema today. Participants included director Andrzej Wajda, playwright/screenwriter Janusz Głowacki, and American film critic Stanley Kauffmann.

3620   Liebman, Stuart. "Wanda Jakubowska's *The Last Stop (Ostatni Etap).*" *SEEP.* 1996 Fall; 16(3): 56-63. Notes. Illus.: Photo. 2. Lang.: Eng.

Poland. 1947-1948. Historical studies. ■Jakubowska's film, written by Gerda Schneider, was about the women's concentration camp at Auschwitz-Birkenau. It was filmed on site two years after the end of World War II and used former inmates as extras.

3621   *Aktery sovětskogo kino: Spravočnik T. III.* (Actors of the Soviet Cinema: Directory. Volume 3.) Moscow: Niva Rossii; 1995. 376 pp. Lang.: Rus.

Russia. 1920-1996. Histories-sources. ■Part of a series commemorating the one hundredth anniversary of Russian cinema, the book gives biographies and filmographies of Russian film actors.

3622   Novikova, L. "'Iskusstva vne sfery ideal'nogo prosto ne byvaet'." (Art Does Not Exist Outside a Sphere of Idealism.) *TeatZ.* 1996; 1: 9-13. Lang.: Rus.

Russia: Moscow. 1996. Histories-sources. ■Interview with film director and producer Sergej Solovjév.

3623   Guldimann, Colette. "The (Black) Male Gaze: Mbongeni Ngema's *Sarafina!*" *SATJ.* 1996 Sep.; 10(2): 85-99. Notes. Biblio. Filmography. Lang.: Eng.

South Africa, Republic of. 1992. Critical studies. ■Examines the attempt made to set up female icons alongside the prominent male activists against apartheid in the film of Mbongeni Ngema's *Sarafina!* directed by Darrell Roodt.

3624   Hees, Edwin. "Foregrounding the Background: Landscape and Ideology in South African Films." *SATJ.* 1996 Sep.; 10(2): 63-84. Notes. Biblio. Filmography. Illus.: Photo. B&W. 4. Lang.: Eng.

South Africa, Republic of. 1949-1996. Critical studies. ■The symbolic use of space in South African films as an expression of white South African perceptions of the position, status, culture, and identity of Black people.

3625   Prinsloo, Jeanne. "South African Films in Flux: Thoughts on Changes in the Politics of Identity in Recent Film Productions." *SATJ.* 1996 Sep.; 10(2): 31-49. Notes. Biblio. Filmography. Lang.: Eng.

South Africa, Republic of. 1987-1996. Critical studies. ■Changes in the politics of identity, notions of nationhood, and relations of power in South African society, as reflected in Richard Attenborough's *Cry Freedom*, Elizabeth Proctor's *On the Wire*, and Darrell Roodt's *Cry, the Beloved Country*.

3626   Eagleton, Julie. "Eagleton's Angle." *PlPl.* 1996 June: 8-9. Lang.: Eng.

UK-England. 1996. Histories-sources. ■Interview with actor Richard E. Grant discussing his roles in films *The Player* and *Pret A Porter*, his performance diaries and his performance in *Withnail and I*.

3627   Mayer, David. "Changing Horses in Mid-Ocean: *The Whip* in Britain and America." 220-235 in Booth, Michael R., ed.; Kaplan, Joel H., ed. *The Edwardian Theatre: Essays on Performance and the Stage.* Cambridge: Cambridge UP; 1996. 243 pp. Notes. Index. Illus.: Photo. 2. Lang.: Eng.

UK-England. 1916. Histories-sources. ■Maurice Tourneur's 1916 cinematic adaptation of Henry Hamilton and Cecil Raleigh's 1909 Drury Lane melodrama *The Whip*.

3628   Raymond, Gerard. "Screening Room." *TheaterW.* 1996 Jan 15; 9(24): 19-25. Illus.: Photo. B&W. 2. Lang.: Eng.

UK-England. 1996. Histories-sources. ■Interview with actor Ian McKellen: discusses his adaptation of Shakespeare's *Richard III* for film and his performance of the lead role. Film directed by Richard Eyre, who also directed the National Theatre production.

3629   "A Tribute to Gene Kelly." *TheaterW.* 1996 Feb 19; 9(29): 56-57. Illus.: Photo. B&W. 10. Lang.: Eng.

USA. 1940-1996. Biographical studies. ■Photo essay of actor, dancer and choreographer Gene Kelly, on the occasion of his death.

3630   Belzil, Patricia. "Les faibles, les méchants et Al Pacino." (The Weak, The Wicked and Al Pacino.) *JCT.* 1993; 67: 148-152. Notes. Illus.: Photo. B&W. 3. Lang.: Fre.

USA. 1992. Critical studies. ■The effect of Hollywood's star system on James Foley's film adaptation of David Mamet's *Glengarry Glen Ross* and Al Pacino as Roma.

3631   Davies, Anthony. "The Film Versions of *Romeo and Juliet.*" *ShS.* 1996; 49: 153-162. Notes. Lang.: Eng.

USA. UK-England. Italy. 1936-1978. Critical studies. ■Examines films of *Romeo and Juliet* by George Cukor, Renato Castellani, and Franco Zeffirelli, and one television production directed by Alvin Rakoff, tracing changing attitudes and approaches to faithfulness to the text and spirit of the play.

3632   Hillegas, Don. "Butterfly McQueen." *AInf.* 1996; 15(1): 64-84. Illus.: Photo. B&W. 2. Lang.: Eng.

USA. 1911-1995. Histories-sources. ■Interview with the film actress conducted in 1972, includes an introduction with a sketch of her life and career between the interview and her death in 1995.

3633   Hough, Coleman. "Gaze Anatomy." *AmTh.* 1996 Nov.; 13(9): 70-71. Illus.: Photo. B&W. 1. Lang.: Eng.

USA. 1996. Critical studies. ■Filming of Spalding Gray's solo performance piece *Gray's Anatomy* directed by Steven Soderbergh. Themes, transference from stage to film.

3634   Howard, Jessica H. "*Hallelujah!*: Transformation in Film." *AfAmR.* 1996 Fall; 30(3): 441-451. Notes. Biblio. Illus.: Photo. 4. Lang.: Eng.

USA. 1929. Critical studies. ■Transformation as a theme and a dynamic in *Hallelujah!*, and its role in the genre of film musical.

3635   Langworthy, Douglas. "Kim Hunter." *AmTh.* 1996 Sep.; 13(7): 50-52. Illus.: Photo. B&W. 1. Lang.: Eng.

USA. 1951-1996. Histories-sources. ■Interview with actress Hunter discussing her career, work in film and experience performing in *A Streetcar Named Desire* directed by Elia Kazan.

3636   Mandelbaum, Ken. "Review: Evita." *TheaterW.* 1996 Dec 30; 10(22): 22-28. Illus.: Photo. B&W. 2. Lang.: Eng.

USA. 1979-1996. Historical studies. ■Making of the film version of the musical *Evita* directed by Alan Parker starring Madonna, Jonathan Pryce and Antonio Banderas. Comparison to the stage version, changes in musical score, budget.

3637   Marx, Lesley. "Underworld RSA." *SATJ.* 1996 Sep.; 10(2): 11-30. Notes. Biblio. Filmography. Lang.: Eng.

USA: Hollywood, CA. South Africa, Republic of. 1930-1996. Critical studies. ■Ambiguity of the character of the gangster in Hollywood films such as Michael Curtiz' *Angels With Dirty Faces*, Samuel Fuller's *Pickup on South Street*, and Elia Kazan's *On the Waterfront*, and their influence on South African films like Oliver Schmitz and Thomas Mogotlane's *Mapantsula* and Michael Hammon's *Wheels and Deals*. Explores the reigning vigilantic attitude of present South African society, and how the media approaches this issue.

3638 Portantiere, Michael. "Jazz Babies: Julie Andrews and Carol Channing Recall *Thoroughly Modern Millie*." *TheaterW*. 1996 Feb 26; 9(30): 36-41. Illus.: Photo. B&W. 5. Lang.: Eng.

USA. 1967. Histories-sources. ■Actresses share experiences while making the musical film *Thoroughly Modern Millie*, produced by Ross Hunter and directed by George Roy Hill. Casting choices, approaches to the roles. Film is currently being screened as a benefit for the Actors' Fund of America.

3639 Stoddard, Sylvia. "Oh What a Circus: *Evita*'s Long Journey to the Screen." *ShowM*. 1996/97 Win; 12(4): 29-36, 61-62. Illus.: Photo. B&W. 29. Lang.: Eng.

USA. UK-England. 1974-1995. Historical studies. ■The history of the filming of *Evita* and the casting of the title role for the film, tracing fact and rumor from the 1970s to the actual filming of the musical in the mid-1990s.

Plays/librettos/scripts

3640 Belzil, Patricia. "Le Théâtre dans 'Jésus de Montréal'." (Theatre in *Jesus of Montreal*.) *JCT*. 1989; 52: 160-163. Notes. Illus.: Photo. B&W. 3. Lang.: Fre.

Canada: Montreal, PQ. 1989. Critical studies. ■Representation of theatre and problems facing artists in Denys Arcand's *Jésus de Montréal (Jesus of Montreal)*.

3641 Belzil, Patricia. "L'instant et l'éternité." (The Instant and Eternity.) *JCT*. 1993; 66: 141-144. Notes. Illus.: Photo. B&W. 2. Lang.: Fre.

Canada: Quebec, PQ. 1991. Critical studies. ■Different relationships to time of theatre and film, and difficulties in Peter Mettler's film adaptation of Robert Lepage's *Plaques tectoniques*.

3642 Belzil, Patricia. "Du *fatum* au Zeus des vues." (From *fatum* to All-Seeing Zeus.) *JCT*. 1996; 79: 120-124. . Illus.: Photo. B&W. 1. Lang.: Fre.

Canada. USA. 1993-1996. Critical studies. ■Representation of theatre and relation of fiction to reality in Jane Campion's *The Piano*, Gilles Noël's *Erreur sur la personne* and Woody Allen's *Mighty Aphrodite*.

3643 Letourneur, Micheline. "La 20e édition du Festival international du nouveau cinéma et de la vidéo de Montréal." (The 20th Edition of Montreal's Festival of New Cinema and Video.) *JCT*. 1992; 63: 90-93. Notes. Illus.: Handbill. Photo. B&W. 3. Lang.: Fre.

Canada: Montreal, PQ. 1991. Critical studies. ■Film and video adaptations of theatrical texts at the festival, with attention to Beckett's *En attendant Godot (Waiting for Godot)* by La Sept, and *Umarła klasa (The Dead Class)* by Tadeusz Kantor.

3644 Lépine, Stéphane. "Une Saison de théâtre au cinéma." (A Season of Theatre in the Cinema.) *JCT*. 1989 ; 51: 14-31. Notes. Illus.: Photo. B&W. 13. Lang.: Fre.

Europe. 1988-1989. Historical studies. ■European film adaptations of plays, in 1988-89 season.

3645 Bernardi, Auro. "Alberto Savinio e il cinema, utopia visibile." (Alberto Savinio and Cinema: A Visible Utopia.) *IlCast*. 1996; 9(27): 97-107. Notes. Lang.: Ita.

Italy. 1891-1952. Critical studies. ■The remarkable contribution of Savinio to the history and aesthetics of cinema, often undervalued or even ignored. Examines connections to the art of cinema as a witness to Savinio's interest in its means of expression.

3646 Mishler, William. "*The Virgin Spring* and *The Seventh Seal*: A Girardian Reading." *CompD*. 1996 Spr; 30(1): 106-134. Notes. Illus.: Photo. B&W. 1. Lang.: Eng.

Sweden. 1956-1959. Critical studies. ■Analysis of Ingmar Bergman's films *Jungfrukällen* and *Det Sjunge inseglet* using the work of anthropologist and critic René Girard as its point of reference.

3647 Dukore, Bernard F. "'Responsibility to Another'?: Graham Greene's Screen Version of Bernard Shaw's *Saint Joan*." *THSt*. 1996 June; 16: 3-14. Notes. Illus.: Photo. 1. Lang.: Eng.

UK-England. 1957. Historical studies. ■Analysis of Graham Greene's film treatment of Bernard Shaw's *Saint Joan*, directed by Otto Preminger: substantive changes made by Greene, in light of his Catholicism.

3648 Belzil, Patricia. "*The Crucible*: le héros lumineux de Daniel Day-Lewis." (*The Crucible*: The Radiant Hero of Daniel Day-Lewis.) *JCT*. 1996; 81: 147-151. Notes. Illus.: Photo. B&W. 4. Lang.: Fre.

USA. 1996. Historical studies. ■Transformation of character John Proctor in Nicholas Hytner's screen adaptation of *The Crucible*, portrayed by Daniel Day-Lewis.

3649 McMullen, Wayne J.; Solomon, Martha. "The Politics of Adaptations: Steven Spielberg's Appropriation of *The Color Purple*." *TextPQ*. 1994 Apr.; 14(2): 158-174. Notes. Lang.: Eng.

USA. 1982-1986. Critical studies. ■Potential political and social implications of corruptive film adaptations, using Steven Spielberg's screen version of Alice Walker's novel *The Color Purple* as an example.

Relation to other fields

3650 Rijsdijk, Ian-Malcolm. "Black Film and Power Dynamics in Contemporary American Culture." *SATJ*. 1996 Sep.; 10(2): 117-133. Notes. Biblio. Lang.: Eng.

USA. 1985-1996. Critical studies. ■Problems of Black directors within the studio system, with attention to ideology and social structre.

Theory/criticism

3651 Noël, Gilles. "Le faux-vrai et le vrai-faux." (The True-False and the False-True.) *JCT*. 1996; 80: 164-165. Illus.: Photo. B&W. 1. Lang.: Fre.

Canada: Montreal, PQ. 1991. Histories-sources. ■Film director Gilles Noël's concepts of reality and artifice in film and theatre, and the functions of film and theatre in his personal life.

3652 Chin, Daryl. "As Time Goes By: A Century of Cinema." *PerAJ*. 1996 Sep.; 18(3): 26-40. Illus.: Photo. B&W. 4. [Number 54.] Lang.: Eng.

USA: New York, NY. 1996. Critical studies. ■Reflections on the place of film within culture, what the arts mean, and where they are now, as emphasized in two film retrospectives at Museum of Modern Art (MOMA) whose subjects are the actress Asta Nielsen and the American independent filmmaker Gregory J. Markopoulos.

Training

3653 Rostockij, A. "'Ego interesovala licnost'." (He Was Interested in Personality.) *ISK*. 1996; 8: 140-142. Lang.: Rus.

Russia: Moscow. 1970-1996. Historical studies. ■Sergej Bondarčuk's work as a teacher at the State Institute of Cinematography.

Mixed media

Institutions

3654 Arbo-Cyber, théâtre (?). "Interrogations." (Questionings.) *JCT*. 1989; 52: 141-146. Notes. Illus.: Photo. B&W. 5. Lang.: Fre.

Canada: Quebec, PQ. 1989. Histories-sources. ■Arbo-Cyber, théâtre (?)'s experiments intended to redefine theatre in age of mass communication.

3655 Forced Entertainment. "A Decade of Forced Entertainment." *PerfR*. 1996 Spr; 1(1): 73-88. Illus.: Photo. Dwg. B&W. 41. Lang.: Eng.

UK-England: Sheffield. 1984-1994. Histories-sources. ■An indirect and often oblique account of the first ten years of the work of Forced Entertainment, written and illustrated by members of the company. References are made to their work in theatres, galleries and unusual sites, in an account described as part autobiography, part archive, part historical meditation and part theoretical speculation.

MEDIA: Mixed media

Performance/production

3656 Phillips, Andrea. "Accounting for Absence." *PerfR.* 1996 Spr; 1(1): 70-72. Notes. Lang.: Eng.
UK-England: London. 1995. Critical studies. ■An analytical review of *Self-Storage*, an exhibition by Brian Eno, Laurie Anderson and students from the Royal College of Art in the spaces of a storage warehouse in Wembley. Discusses responses to the exhibition and critiques the enthusiasm for constructing 'ordinary' buildings as performers, and for the strangeness of the everyday.

3657 Young, Lisa Jaye. "Electronic Verses: Reading the Body vs. Touching the Text." *PerAJ.* 1996 Jan.; 18(1): 36-43. Illus.: Photo. B&W. 5. [Number 52.] Lang.: Eng.
USA: New York, NY. 1995. Critical studies. ■The articulation of textual and visual memory, in the video/sculpture work of Gary Hill.

Relation to other fields

3658 Morgan, Robert C. "Moving Images." *PerAJ.* 1996 May; 18(2): 53-63. Illus.: Photo. B&W. 5. [Number 53.] Lang.: Eng.
France: Lyon. 1995-1996. Historical studies. ■Report on the third Biennale de Lyon, at the Musée d'art contemporain, which highlighted the diversity of media currently being used to represent the moving image in art.

Video forms

Administration

3659 Buckley, Michael. "Gary Smith: Getting the Tonys On (Off)." *TheaterW.* 1996 June 3; 9(44): 69-70. Lang.: Eng.
USA: New York, NY. 1996. Technical studies. ■Technical challenges in producing the Tony Awards for television. Executive producer Smith describes problems with stars, production numbers, timing for the network.

Basic theatrical documents

3660 Paterson, Andrew James. "Performance: A Performance." *CTR.* 1996 Spr; 86: 15-18. Illus.: Photo. B&W. 12.
Canada. 1996. ■Script excerpt from the video *Performance.*

3661 Johnson, Charles. "*The Green Belt*: A Play for Television." *AfAmR.* 1996 Win; 30(4): 559-578. Lang.: Eng.
USA. 1982. ■Complete text of Johnson's 1982 teleplay.

Design/technology

3662 Riisgaard, Helle-Vibeke. "Fablen om en Brygger og hans familie." (The Tale of a Brewer and His Family.) *TE.* 1996 Dec.; 81-82: 20-22. Illus.: Dwg. 1. Lang.: Dan.
Denmark. 1995-1996. Histories-sources. ■An interview with the costume designer Søren Breum on his work creating costumes for a new Danish TV-series, *Bryggeren (The Brewer)* directed by Kaspar Rostrup.

3663 Calhoun, John. "Lighting Letterman." *LDim.* 1996 Sep.; 20(7): 76-83. Illus.: Photo. Lighting. Color. 4. Lang.: Eng.
USA: New York, NY. 1996. Technical studies. ■Equipment and designs used by lighting designer Steven Brill and set designer Kathleen Ankers on David Letterman's *Late Show.* Differentiating look of musical performances, lighting for audience, architectural lighting for theatre.

3664 Calhoun, John. "The Master of Ceremonies." *LDim.* 1996 Nov.; 20(9): 68-73, 177-182. Illus.: Photo. Color. B&W. 8. Lang.: Eng.
USA: Atlanta, GA. 1996. Technical studies. ■Television lighting designer Bob Dickinson's work for the Opening Ceremonies for the 1996 Summer Olympics. Challenges in lighting variety of performers and dancers, equipment used, budget. Includes selected designology for his career.

3665 Cashill, Robert. "Cinema Services: A Family Portrait." *TCI.* 1996 Jan.; 30(1): 22-23. Illus.: Photo. Color. 1. Lang.: Eng.
USA: Las Vegas, NV. 1995. Technical studies. ■Contribution of the family run Cinema Services of Las Vegas, Inc. to the $60 million video extravaganza *EFX* playing at the MGM Grand Hotel.

3666 McHugh, Catherine. "The 1995 MTV Video Music Awards: Another Allen Branton and Roy Bennett Design Extrava-ganza." *TCI.* 1996 Jan.; 30(1): 26-29. Illus.: Photo. Dwg. B&W. Color. 7. Lang.: Eng.
USA: New York, NY. 1995. Technical studies. ■Production design for the awards held at Radio City Music Hall, with a focus on lights including an instrument breakdown.

3667 Rorke, Robert. "Building a Better City." *TCI.* 1996 Apr.; 30(4): 8. Illus.: Photo. Color. 2. Lang.: Eng.
USA: New York, NY. 1996. Technical studies. ■Designer Boyd Dumrose's loft design that changes into ten separate sets for the television soap opera *The City.*

Performance/production

3668 Schwartzberg, Shlomo. "The Accidental Actress." *PAC.* 1996; 30(1): 4-5. Illus.: Photo. B&W. 1. Lang.: Eng.
Canada. 1996. Critical studies. ■Tina Keeper, a Cree actress who began her career in *North of 60* which has attracted a large Canadian following, both native and white.

3669 Merschmeier, Michael; Wille, Franz. "'Wir wagen es wieder!'." (We Risk It Again.) *THeute.* 1996; 4: 35-37. Illus.: Photo. B&W. 4. Lang.: Ger.
Germany: Berlin. 1996. Histories-sources. ■Interview with Walter Konrad and Wolfgang Bergmann, program managers at television station SAT 3, about a new beginning for the relationship between television and theatre.

3670 Benedetti, Amedeo. *Il comportamento televisivo.* (Television Behavior.) Genoa: Regione Liguria; 1996. 178 pp. Pref. Gloss. Illus.: Photo. B&W. Lang.: Ita.
Italy. 1996. Instructional materials. ■Handbook for non-actors who must appear on television or in a televised conference.

3671 Majcherek, Wojciech. "French Drama in the TV Theatre." *TP.* 1996 Apr.; 38(2): 14-18. Illus.: Photo. Color. B&W. 2. Lang.: Eng, Fre.
Poland. France. 1955-1996. Historical studies. ■Influence of French drama on the repertoire of the Polish Television Theatre, an institution which produces over one hundred plays a year for television, and has done so for over forty years.

3672 Höglund, Christina. "Var finns dansen i svensk musik-video?" (Where Is Dance in the Swedish Music Video?) *Danst.* 1996 ; 6(4): 14-15. Illus.: Photo. B&W. Lang.: Swe.
Sweden. USA. 1996. Historical studies. ■Discussion among choreographers Jens Östberg and Jan Åström and video producer Martin Persson about the poor showing of dance in Swedish music videos compared to American ones.

3673 Wrange, Ann-Marie. "Birgit & TV." (Birgit & TV.) *Danst.* 1996; 6(3): 14. Illus.: Photo. B&W. Lang.: Swe.
Sweden. 1968-1990. Historical studies. ■A survey of the pioneering works for TV by Birgit Cullberg and her cooperation with the producer Måns Reutersvärd.

3674 Berghaus, Günter; Slater, Ben. "Video Performance: An Electronic Theatre of (Dis-)Illusion." *STP.* 1996 Dec.; 14: 4-19. Notes. Biblio. Illus.: Design. Photo. B&W. Grd.Plan. 3. Lang.: Eng.
UK-England: Bristol. 1980-1995. Reviews of performances. ■Description of the video performance *Degraded* with students from Bristol University at the Vandyke Gallery, Bristol, 1995. Drawing on imagery familiar from spy films, the video performance used the technique of re-recording videos several times over and thus degrading the image as a reflection of the degradation of meaning in an unsolvable mystery.

3675 Will Vinton Studios. "'Home Improvement' Goes Animated: Tool Man Turns 'Toon Man'." *PuJ.* 1996 Win; 48(2): 15. Illus.: Photo. 1. Lang.: Eng.
USA: Los Angeles, CA. 1995-1996. Historical studies. ■For the first time in sit-com history, a stop-motion animation segment will be aired on a prime-time situation comedy. Produced by Will Vinton Studios, the four-minute dream sequence segment took three months to complete.

3676 Daniel, Douglass K. *Lou Grant: The Making of TV's Top Newspaper Drama.* Syracuse, NY: Syracuse UP; 1996. 269 pp. Notes. Index. Biblio. Append. Illus.: Photo. 10. Lang.: Eng.

MEDIA: Video forms—Performance/production

USA. 1977-1982. Histories-specific. ■History of the television series *Lou Grant*, with discussion of the genre of newspaper drama. Includes a season-by-season chronology of the episodes.

3677 Kaplan, E. Ann. "Feminism(s)/Postmodernism(s): MTV and Alternate Women's Videos and Performance Art." 82-103 in Campbell, Patrick, ed. *Analysing Performance: A Critical Reader*. Manchester/New York, NY: Manchester UP; 1996. 307 pp. Notes. Biblio. Index. Illus.: Photo. 6. Lang.: Eng.

USA. 1990-1995. Critical studies. ■Explores connections among postmodernism, video/computer technology, and feminism.

3678 London, Barbara. "Video Spaces." *PerAJ*. 1996 Sep.; 18(3): 14-19. Illus.: Photo. B&W. 4. [Number 54.] Lang.: Eng.

USA: New York, NY. 1995. Critical studies. ■Sampling of video installations that were on view at New York's Museum of Modern Art during the summer of 1995.

3679 Qualls, Larry. "Five Video Artists." *PerAJ*. 1996 Sep.; 18(3): 1-13. Illus.: Photo. B&W. 5. [Number 54.] Lang.: Eng.

USA. 1996. Critical studies. ■Appraisal of the work of five active video artists: Dawn Dedeaux, Krzysztof Wodiczko, Diana Thater, Jocelyn Taylor and Janet Biggs.

3680 Reinelt, Janelle. "Performing Race: Anna Deavere Smith's *Fires in the Mirror*." *MD*. 1996 Win; 39(4): 609-617. Notes. Illus.: Photo. B&W. 1. Lang.: Eng.

USA. 1991. Critical studies. ■Video performances of Smith's solo work, *Fires in the Mirror: Crown Heights, Brooklyn and Other Identities*: background material, structure, themes and differences between television and stage as a medium for the piece.

3681 Robin, Kerry. "Mystery Science Theater 3000: The Flamingos Still Stand." *PuJ*. 1996 Spr; 47(3): 2-3. Illus.: Photo. 2. Lang.: Eng.

USA: Hollywood, CA. 1990-1996. Historical studies. ■Focuses on the work of *Mystery Science Theatre 3000*, a popular cable show on Comedy Central featuring one human and two puppet robots critiquing 'B' movies. The show was created by Joel Hodgson and performed by Trace Beaulieu, Kevin Murphy and Mike Nelson.

3682 Watts, Mark. "Electrifying Fragments: Madonna and Postmodern Performance." *NTQ*. 1996; 12(46): 99-107. Notes. Illus.: Photo. B&W. 1. Lang.: Eng.

USA. 1990-1993. Critical studies. ■Analyzes the appeal of the singer-actress Madonna in terms of the concept of *punctum*, defined by Barthes (in opposition to the rational, linear understanding of *studium*) as the electrifying fragment that seizes and ravishes the imagination.

Plays/librettos/scripts

3683 Anyanwu, Joseph Chika. "TV Drama in Papua New Guinea: A Case Study in National Identity Versus Economic Strangulation." *NTQ*. 1996; 12(45): 79-84. Notes. Lang.: Eng.

Papua New Guinea. 1975-1995. Historical studies. ■The lack of significant national interest in most of the programs transmitted typifies the development of television in the Third World, as traditional cultures give way before the easy attraction of homogenized imports.

3684 Sumser, John. *Morality and Social Order in Television Crime Drama*. Jefferson, NC/London: McFarland; 192 pp. Pref. Notes. Biblio. Index. Lang.: Eng.

USA. 1968-1991. Critical studies. ■How narrative language blends moral and intellectual aspects of mystery dramas, specifically the television crime drama. Uses poststructuralist theory to examine this supposedly contextless media form and how it functions to reveal social boundaries and conventions of real life.

Reference materials

3685 Grasso, Aldo, ed. *Enciclopedia della televisione Garzanti*. (The Garzanti Television Encyclopedia.) Milan: Garzanti; 1996. 970 pp. (Le Garzantine.) Biblio. Illus.: Photo. B&W. Lang.: Ita.

Italy. 1954-1996. ■An encyclopedia of Italian television from its beginnings til now: programs, genres, authors, actors and showmen, technology, technical terms, etc.

Relation to other fields

3686 Dodge, Helen. "The Role of South African Television as an Agent of 'Truth and Reconciliation'." *SATJ*. 1996 Sep.; 10(2): 148-154. Notes. Lang.: Eng.

South Africa, Republic of. 1996. Critical studies. ■South African television after twenty years: its political impact, the responsibility of the industry.

3687 Tomaselli, Keyan; Shepperson, Arnold. "Misreading Theory, Sloganising Analysis: The Development of South African Media and Film Policy." *SATJ*. 1996 Sep.; 10(2): 161-175. Notes. Biblio. [Revised version of a paper presented at the Conference on Development Support Communication HSRC, UNESCO, CCMS, and UNISA 28-31 August, 1996 Pretoria, RSA.] Lang.: Eng.

South Africa, Republic of. 1980-1996. Historical studies. ■Media policy in South Africa: the debates of the 1980s and early 1990s, the shift in the basis of its engagement with the state in response to political developments since 1990.

MIME

General

Training

3688 Leabhart, Thomas. "L'Homme de Sport: Sport, Statuary and the Recovery of the Pre-Cartesian Body in Etienne Decroux's Corporeal Mime." *MimeJ*. 1996; 18(1): 31-65. Notes. Biblio. Illus.: Photo. Dwg. Diagram. B&W. 33. Lang.: Eng.

France: Paris. 1918-1996. Critical studies. ■Analysis of mime teacher Etienne Decroux's theory of corporeal mime, and his influences, from vocal theorist François Delsarte, dancers Ruth St. Denis and Ted Shawn, to athletes, laborers and classical statues, with explicative diagrams.

3689 Risum, Janne. "The Sporting Acrobat: Meyerhold's Biomechanics." *MimeJ*. 1996; 18(1): 67-111. Notes. Biblio. Lang.: Eng.

Russia. 1896-1996. Critical studies. ■Mejerchol'd's theory of biomechanics and its application as both a training and performance tool, and his influence on Etienne Decroux and Jacques Copeau.

3690 Rudlin, John. "Play's the Thing." *MimeJ*. 1996; 18(1): 17-29. Notes. Illus.: Photo. B&W. 2. Lang.: Eng.

USA: New York, NY. France: Paris. 1918-1996. Historical studies. ■Development of Jacques Copeau's theory of mimesis while in New York, his return to Paris, and his formation of L'École du Vieux-Colombier with collaborator Suzanne Bing.

Pantomime

Performance/production

3691 Klechot, Rajmund. "*The Overcoat* in Dramatic Pantomime: Reflections on My Life and Art." *SEEP*. 1996 Fall; 16(3): 31-40 . Illus.: Photo. 3. Lang.: Eng.

Poland: Wrocław. USA: Dayton, OH. 1945-1996. Histories-sources. ■Polish pantomimist Rajmund Klechot discusses his artistic life and career as a mime in the theatre world of Wrocław, including the Wrocław Pantomime Theatre. Includes his work on Gogol's short story *The Overcoat* as a 'dramatic pantomime' produced in Dayton, Ohio, with students from a local community college.

Plays/librettos/scripts

3692 Rainer, Werner. "'Es könnte einem nicht närrischer träumen'." (One Could Not Dream a More Foolish Dream.) *MuK*. 1996; 2-4: 155-231. Notes. Illus.: Photo. Plan. B&W. 4. Lang.: Ger.

Austria: Salzburg. 1766-1767. Historical studies. ■Florian Reichssiegel's pantomime theatre, its connections with university theatre, and notes on Michael Haydn's 'Dream' pantomime.

3693 Lantagne, Suzanne. "L'Adaptation théâtrale: 'Le Festin chez la comtesse Fritouille' de Gombrowicz." (Theatrical

MIME: Pantomime—Plays/librettos/scripts

Adaptation: Gombrowicz' *Countess Fritouille's Feast*.) *JCT*. 1989; 53: 44-46. Illus.: Photo. B&W. 3. Lang.: Fre.

Canada: Montreal, PQ. 1928-1989. Histories-sources. ■Director Suzanne Lantagne describes creation of a mime adaptation of Witold Gombrowicz' short story *Le Festin chez la comtesse Fritouille (Countess Fritouille's Feast)*.

3694 Vigeant, Louise; Camerlain, Lorraine, ed. "Le Texte chez les 'dramaturges du mouvement': Entretien avec Jean Asselin." (Text in the Hands of 'Playwrights of Movement': Interview with Jean Asselin.) *JCT*. 1989; 53: 38-43. Illus.: Photo. B&W. 4. Lang.: Fre.

Canada: Montreal, PQ. 1982-1989. Histories-sources. ■Director Jean Asselin describes his process of adapting non-theatrical texts to mime productions with his troupe Omnibus.

MIXED ENTERTAINMENT

General

Design/technology

3695 Ouaknine, Serge. "De lumière et de feu, mettre en scène le ciel." (Of Light and Fire, Staging the Sky.) *JCT*. 1996; 80: 116-120. Notes. Illus.: Maps. Photo. B&W. 4. Lang.: Fre.

France: Paris. 1992-1995. Histories-sources. ■Ouaknine's experience as painter/designer of two fireworks shows for Parc de la Villette's Fête de la musique (1992 and 1995) and relation to his work as painter and stage director.

3696 McHugh, Catherine. "Oh, Sugar." *TCI*. 1996 Feb.; 30(2): 23. Illus.: Sketches. B&W. 1. Lang.: Eng.

Italy. 1996. Technical studies. ■Theatrical set and lighting designer Vince Foster's experience designing a 'change-of-image' show for Italian rock star Zucchero.

3697 Barbour, David. "Lighting a Restaurant Out of Control." *LDim*. 1996 Jan/Feb.; 20(1): 38-42. Illus.: Photo. Lighting. Color. 4. Lang.: Eng.

USA: New York, NY. 1996. Technical studies. ■Jason Kantrowitz's lighting design for cabaret/circus/theme entertainment production *Pomp Duck and Circumstance* created by Hans Peter Wodarz. Challenges of lighting in a tent.

3698 Lampert-Gréaux, Ellen. "Hail Caesar." *TCI*. 1996 Mar.; 30(3): 8-9. Illus.: Photo. Color. 1. Lang.: Eng.

USA: Las Vegas, NV. 1996. Technical studies. ■Design of the new Caesar's Magical Empire, an addition to Caesar's Palace casino.

3699 Lampert-Gréaux, Ellen. "Horsing Around." *TCI*. 1996 Oct.; 30(8): 9-10. Illus.: Photo. Color. 1. Lang.: Eng.

USA: New York, NY. France. 1996. Technical studies. ■Difficulty in transporting actors, sets, horses and costumes across the ocean for the American debut of Zingaro Equestrian Theatre's *Chimère* at BAM's Next Wave Festival.

3700 McHugh, Catherine. "The Cure." *TCI*. 1996 Nov.; 30(9): 42-45. Illus.: Photo. Color. 8. Lang.: Eng.

USA. 1996. Technical studies. ■Light and production design conceived by LeRoy Bennett and Gary Westcott for The Cure's recent U.S. tour.

3701 McHugh, Catherine. "*Quadrophenia* Takes Manhattan." *TCI*. 1996 Oct.; 30(8): 6-7. Illus.: Photo. Color. 1. Lang.: Eng.

USA: New York, NY. 1996. Technical studies. ■Production team of LeRoy Bennett on lights, Tom McPhillips on set with video director Aubrey Powell and production manager Mick Double were brought together to create The Who's special performance of *Quadrophenia*.

Institutions

3702 Litvinceva, G. "'Znakom'tes', provincija!'." (Please Meet the Countryside.) *Vstreča*. 1996; 9: 17-19. Lang.: Rus.

Russia: Kiev. 1995-1996. Historical studies. ■Festival of arts variety theatres.

Performance spaces

3703 Kaye, Nick. "Site/Intermedia." *PerfR*. 1996 Spr; 1(1): 63-69. Biblio. Illus.: Photo. B&W. 4. Lang.: Eng.

UK-England: Sheffield, London. UK-Wales. USA: New York, NY. 1965-1995. Critical studies. ■Contemporary and post-modern performance and the blurring of the distinction between performers and audience. Considers Forced Entertainment's *Nights in the City*, Brith Grof's site-specific *Haearn*, and Fiona Templeton's *You—The City*.

3704 Phillips, Andrea. "Review of *Hidden Cities*: Mobile Events." *PerfR*. 1996 Sum; 1(2): 111-115. Notes. Lang.: Eng.

UK-England. 1995. Critical studies. ■Review of four mobile events collectively titled *Hidden Cities*, in which artists were commissioned by the Laboratory of the Ruskin School of Drawing and Fine Art to conduct guided tours of British cities with the intent of 'uncovering the gloss of national heritage'. Includes broad theoretical and conceptual discussion of the events.

Performance/production

3705 Doré, Marc. "ABRACADABRA." *JCT*. 1996; 80: 145-147. Illus.: Photo. B&W. 1. Lang.: Fre.

Canada: Quebec, PQ. 1969-1976. Histories-sources. ■Marc Doré, co-founder of Théâtre Euh! clown troupe, describes a typical street performance.

3706 Lai, Sheila. "So You Want to Be a Comedian, eh?" *PAC*. 1996; 30(1): 17-19. Illus.: Photo. B&W. 3. Lang.: Eng.

Canada. 1973-1996. Historical studies. ■Assessment of the careers of three Canadian comics: Marla Lukofsky, Kedar Brown, and Frank Van Keeken. Difficulty in breaking through, and how this is often achieved only by going to the U.S.

3707 Serreau, Nicolas. "L'Art d'improviser sous le masque." (The Art of Improvising Under the Mask.) *JCT*. 1990; 57: 63-70. Notes. Illus.: Dwg. Photo. B&W. 6. Lang.: Fre.

Canada. 1989. Histories-sources. ■Text of Serreau's lecture at the University of Quebec/Montreal on mask-based improvisation and creating characters with masks.

3708 Vaïs, Michel. "La Mode derrière la modernité: Entretien avec Michel Lemieux." (The Style Behind Modernity: Interview with Michel Lemieux.) *JCT*. 1989; 50: 166-168. Illus.: Photo. B&W. 1. Lang.: Fre.

Canada. 1982-1989. Histories-sources. ■Artifice and modernity of multidisciplinary creations of Michel Lemieux.

3709 Christoffersen, Erik Exe. "Hotel Pro Forma: Exposing Reality as a Visual Illusion." *PerfR*. 1996 Fall; 1(3): 77-89. Illus.: Photo. B&W. 9. Lang.: Eng.

Denmark: Copenhagen. 1986-1995. Historical studies. ■Analysis of a series of performances/exhibitions by Hotel Pro Forma, focusing on their concerns with form, with the withholding of meaning and refusal of narrative, with altering audience perceptions and perspectives, and with art as art.

3710 Knudsen, Eva Rask; Christoffersen, Erik Exe. "Die Wirklichkeit als Fata Morgana." (Reality as Fata Morgana.) *Flamb*. 1996; 4: 55-84. Illus.: Photo. B&W. 6. Lang.: Ger.

Denmark: Copenhagen. 1985-1996. Histories-sources. ■Portrait of the avant-garde troupe Hotel Pro Forma, including an interview with director Kirsten Rehlhom.

3711 Theil, Per. "Fru Delholms sans for drama." (Mrs. Delholm's Sense of Drama.) *TE*. 1996 Dec.; 81-82: 56-57. Illus.: Photo. B&W. 2. Lang.: Dan.

Denmark: Copenhagen. 1996. Reviews of performances. ■*Monkey Business Class—en memorial musical* produced by Hotel Pro Forma and directed and created by Kirsten Delholm is a mix between performance art and musical theatre.

3712 Chajčenko, E.G. *Vlikie romantičeskie zrelisca. Anglijskaja melodrama, burlesk, ėkstravaganca, pantomima*. (Great Romantic Productions: English Melodrama, Burlesque, Extravaganza, and Pantomime.) Moscow: GITIS; 1996. 150 pp. Lang.: Rus.

England. 1700-1899. Histories-specific. ■English theatrical genres in the context of eighteenth- and nineteenth-century culture. Includes discussion of the influence of popular culture on novelist Charles Dickens.

MIXED ENTERTAINMENT: General—Performance/production

3713 Zaerr, Linda Marie. "*Cil d'aval et cil d'amont*: Borderlands and the Woman *Jogleor* in *Aucassin et Nicolette*." *TextPQ*. 1994 Jan.; 14(1): 46-56. Notes. Biblio. Lang.: Eng.
France. 1200-1994. Critical studies. ■Suggests that the anonymous thirteenth-century *chantefable*, *Aucassin et Nicolette*, could have been performed by a woman, and that when this theory is tested in contemporary performance the piece conveys many reversals of ideas not evident in the text alone.

3714 Haupt, Adam. "Stifled Noise in the South African Music Box: Prophets of da City and the Struggle for Public Space." *SATJ*. 1996 Sep.; 10(2): 51-61. Notes. Biblio. Filmography. Discography. Lang.: Eng.
South Africa, Republic of: Cape Town. 1990-1996. Historical studies. ■Explores the ways the Cape Town rap group Prophets of da City articulated their resistance to the repression and oppression of apartheid, focusing on Black artists' struggles to obtain a public space, as well as self-representation and expression.

3715 Falke, Christoph. "Den Puls der Zeit nehmen." (A Finger on the Pulse of Time.) *Flamb*. 1996; 4: 9-33. Illus.: Photo. B&W. 7. Lang.: Ger.
UK-England: Sheffield. 1984-1996. Historical studies. ■Portrait of the avant-garde group Forced Entertainment.

3716 Kift, Dagmar; Kift, Roy, transl. *The Victorian Music Hall: Culture, Class and Conflict*. Cambridge/New York, NY: Cambridge UP; 1996. 254 pp. Index. Biblio. Notes. Illus.: Photo. 11. Lang.: Eng.
UK-England. 1830-1890. Histories-specific. ■History of Victorian music halls and examination of their programs and the composition of their audiences. Deals with specific conflicts of class and culture.

3717 B, Mats; Birnbaum, Anja; Reich, Carina; Szyber, Bogdan. "... och behäftad med hjärnan." (... and Marred By the Brains.) *Danst*. 1996; 6(1): 6-9. Illus.: Photo. B&W. Lang.: Swe.
USA: New York, NY. Sweden: Stockholm. 1995. Critical studies. ■A discussion about movement and the different attitudes towards acting, dance and performance in the avant-garde.

3718 Bell, John. "The Sioux War Panorama and American Mythic History." *TJ*. 1996 Oct.; 48(3): 279-300. Notes. Biblio. Illus.: Sketches. Pntg. Handbill. 8. Lang.: Eng.
USA. 1860-1879. Historical studies. ■Essay on the Sioux War Panorama, which toured the American Midwest. Created by John Stevens, this mechanical picture screen consisting of a wooden frame with painted canvas, backlit with oil lamps, was popular with settlers. Author suggests this was due to the panorama's narrative appeal of white innocence and Indian savagery as they interacted in American mythic history.

3719 Graham, Jomo Kale. "Another Dream Deferred: Tupac Shakur (1971-1996)." *BlackM*. 1996 Nov/Dec.; 12(2): 17. Lang.: Eng.
USA. 1971-1996. Biographical studies. ■Obituary for the murdered 'gangsta' rapper and actor.

3720 Horwitz, Simi. "The Bartabas Mystique." *TheaterW*. 1996 Sep 16; 10(6): 38-43. Lang.: Eng.
USA: New York, NY. France: Paris. 1996. Historical studies. ■Founder and creator Bartabas discusses history of his Paris-based company Zingaro, which creates equestrian theatre with music. Current production of *Chimère* appearing at Brooklyn Academy of Music.

3721 Shalom, Jack. "The Ira Aldridge Troupe: Early Black Minstrelsy in Philadelphia." *AfAmR*. 1994 Win; 28(4): 653-658. Notes. Biblio. Lang.: Eng.
USA: Philadelphia, PA. 1863. Historical studies. ■Account of the Ira Aldridge Troupe, a Black-controlled troupe of Black minstrel performers. Argues for troupe's subversive interpretation of traditional minstrel fare, directed at a majority Black audience, receptive to the message.

3722 Streb, Elizabeth. "Pop-Action." *PerAJ*. 1996 May; 18(2): 72-76. Illus.: Photo. B&W. 2. [Number 53.] Lang.: Eng.
USA: New York, NY. 1996. Histories-sources. ■Choreographer describes the work of her company Ringside.

Theory/criticism

3723 Harris, Gerry. "Regarding History: Some Narratives Concerning the Café-Concert, Le Music Hall, and the Feminist Academic." *TDR*. 1996 Win; 40(4): 70-84. Notes. Illus.: Photo. B&W. 5. Lang.: Eng.
France: Paris. 1848-1996. Critical studies. ■Critical perceptions of French popular theatre genres.

Cabaret

Administration

3724 Moore, Dick. "Equity, AGVA Sign Joint Agreement." *EN*. 1996 July/Aug.; 81(6): 3. Lang.: Eng.
USA: Washington, DC. 1996. Historical studies. ■Actors' Equity and the American Guild of Variety Artists (AGVA) share jurisdiction over a series of cabaret shows presented at the Kennedy Center.

Audience

3725 Kun, Eva. "'Als obs ein leben wär....' Gedanken über die Beziehungen zwischen Darstellern und Publikum in Theresienstadt." (As if It Were Life: Thoughts on the Relationship between Actors and Audience in Theresienstadt.) *FMT*. 1996; 2: 156-169. Notes. Illus.: Dwg. B&W. 2. Lang.: Ger.
Czechoslovakia: Terezin. 1941-1942. Historical studies. ■The conditions and reception of cabaret performances in the Theresienstadt concentration camp.

Design/technology

3726 Hogan, Jane. "Pennies from Heckman." *TCI*. 1996 Oct.; 30(8): 9. Illus.: Photo. Color. 1. Lang.: Eng.
USA: New York, NY. 1996. Technical studies. ■Philip Heckman's costume design for Varla Jean Merman's drag extravaganza *I, Who Have Nothing*.

Performance/production

3727 Lévesque, Solange. "Dis-moi de qui tu ris." (Tell Me Who Makes You Laugh.) *JCT*. 1990; 55: 65-71. Illus.: Photo. B&W. 4. Lang.: Fre.
Canada. 1980-1996. Critical studies. ■Expressions of collective identity in Quebec comic monologues. Decline in authenticity of comic characters since 1980 referendum on Quebec sovereignty.

3728 Schlewitt, Carena. "Wir haben es zu etwas gebracht." (We Got Somewhere.) *TZ*. 1996; 1: 38-40. Illus.: Photo. Sketches. B&W. 4. Lang.: Ger.
Germany. 1986-1996. Historical studies. ■The experimental one-man show of artist and designer Wolfgang Krause Zwieback.

3729 Hanenberg, Patrick van den; Verhallen, Frank. *Het is weer tijd om te bepalen waar het allemaal op slaat. Nederlands cabaret 1970–1995*. (Once Again, It's Time to Find Out What's the Scoop: Dutch Cabaret, 1970-1995.) Amsterdam: Nijgh & Van Ditmar; 1996. 356 pp. Biblio. Discography. Index. Illus.: Photo. B&W. 108. Lang.: Dut.
Netherlands. 1970-1995. Historical studies. ■Summary of the main developments of the flourishing Dutch cabaret genre. Includes interviews with the most important artists, discography, program outline, awards.

3730 McMurtry, Mervyn. "Adam Leslie and His Contribution to Satire in Intimate Revue in South African Theatre." *SATJ*. 1995 May; 9(1): 3-27. Notes. Biblio. Illus.: Photo. B&W. 4. Lang.: Eng.
South Africa, Republic of: Johannesburg. 1956-1979. Biographical studies. ■Career of Adam Leslie, pioneer of intimate revue in South Africa, and driving force behind the Adam Leslie Theatre, for which he has devised and directed such satirical revues as *Two's Company*.

3731 "Inside Cabaret." *TheaterW*. 1996 Mar 11; 9(32): 16-17. Illus.: Photo. B&W. 8. Lang.: Eng.
USA: New York, NY. 1996. Histories-sources. ■Pictorial essay featuring cabaret artists in the New York area.

3732 "And the Nominees Are..." *TheaterW*. 1996 Mar 18; 9(33): 44-47. Illus.: Photo. B&W. 19. Lang.: Eng.

MIXED ENTERTAINMENT: Cabaret—Performance/production

USA: New York, NY. 1996. Histories-sources. ■1996 nominees for the 10th annual MAC awards (Manhattan Association of Cabarets and Clubs).

3733 Blake, Leslie (Hoban). "London Cabaret." *TheaterW*. 1996 Mar 11; 9(32): 36-41. Illus.: Photo. B&W. 13. Lang.: Eng.

USA: New York, NY. 1961-1996. Historical studies. ■Absence of native cabaret artists in London, and experience of American artists touring there to perform. Native London artists training in small venues.

3734 Blake, Leslie (Hoban). "Choicest Voices: Cabaret." *TheaterW*. 1996 July 29; 9(52): 28-34. Illus.: Photo. B&W. 5. Lang.: Eng.

USA: New York, NY. 1996. Biographical studies. ■Profiles of cabaret singers Tom Andersen, Charles Cermele, Baby Jane Dexter, Karen Mason, Thos Shipley, Phillip Officer. Performance careers, vocal training, recordings, current cabaret performances.

3735 Horwitz, Simi. "The Sisters Callaway: Nightclub Knockout." *TheaterW*. 1996 Mar 11; 9(32): 18-28. Illus.: Photo. B&W. 3. Lang.: Eng.

USA: New York, NY. 1996. Biographical studies. ■Profile of cabaret singers Ann Hampton Callaway and Liz Callaway. Previous roles in musical theatre, current performance of their musical work *Sibling Revelry*. Autobiographical elements in their work, and challenges of family working together.

3736 Moore, Dick. "The Celebration Concluded on Monday, February 26 with Cafe Afrocentric, A Cabaret Marathon in the Club at La Mama, E.T.C." *EN*. 1996 May; 81(4): 5. Illus.: Photo. 20. Lang.: Eng.

USA: New York, NY. 1996. Histories-sources. ■Photo montage of Cafe Afrocentric, a cabaret marathon held at La MaMa to celebrate Black History Month.

3737 Portantiere, Michael. "Color Him Barbra." *TheaterW*. 1996 Apr 8; 9(36): 33-34. Illus.: Photo. B&W. 2. Lang.: Eng.

USA: New York, NY. 1993-1996. Biographical studies. ■Performer Steven Brinberg's portrayal of Barbra Streisand in *Simply Barbra* at Don't Tell Mama cabaret. Creating the role, audience response.

3738 Portantiere, Michael. "Nancy LaMott: An Appreciation." *TheaterW*. 1996 Jan 1; 9(22): 16-17. Illus.: Photo. B&W. 1. Lang.: Eng.

USA: New York, NY. 1952-1996. Biographical studies. ■Obituary for cabaret singer LaMott. Overview of her career and collaborators.

Plays/librettos/scripts

3739 Blumer, Arnold. "Die Duitse Kabaret: 'n Beknopte oorsigi." (German Cabaret: A Concise Survey.) *SATJ*. 1995 May; 9(1): 53-68. Append. Lang.: Eng.

Germany. 1929-1989. Historical studies. ■Survey of German cabaret from its beginning to the present-day 'Liedermacher', emphasizing the supremacy of the word in all true cabarets which intend to criticize mediocrity and complacency. Includes examples of German cabaret songs translated into Afrikaans.

Relation to other fields

3740 Kift, Roy. "Comedy in the Holocaust: the Theresienstadt Cabaret." *NTQ*. 1996 Nov.; 12(48): 299-308. Notes. Illus.: Dwg. B&W. 1. [Paper presented at conference 'The Shoah and Performance', University of Glasgow, in September 1995.] Lang.: Eng.

Czechoslovakia: Terezin. 1944. Historical studies. ■Concentration camp in Theresienstadt was used by the Nazis as a flagship ghetto to deceive the world about the fate of the Jews. It featured a cabaret 'Karussel (Carousel)', run by Kurt Gerron, and article shows how his songs and sketches confronted the harsh realities of camp existence or attempted to avoid them by promoting illusions.

3741 Berghaus, Günter. "Oppositional Cabaret in Nazi Germany, or: Walking a Political Tightrope over the Abyss." *PerfR*. 1996 Sum; 1(2): 57-59. Lang.: Eng.

Germany. 1929-1945. Biographical studies. ■Using material drawn from his 1972 autobiography, the article traces the career of Werner Flinck, whose satirical cabaret became more political—if more subtle—as Nazi power increased. Discusses Flinck's work in a concentration camp as well as after the war.

3742 Bean, Annemarie. "Presenting the Prima Donna: Black Femininity and Performance in Nineteenth-Century American Blackface Minstrelsy." *PerfR*. 1996 Fall; 1(3): 23-30. Notes. Illus.: Photo. Handbill. B&W. 4. Lang.: Eng.

USA. 1820-1890. Historical studies. ■Political and sexual implications of the popularity of impersonation of Black women by white male performers in nineteenth-century American minstrel tradition. Refers in detail to significant artists, notably Francis Leon, within a general survey.

Carnival

Performance/production

3743 Wiles, David. "The Lewes Bonfire Festival." *NTQ*. 1996; 12(46): 177-191. Notes. Illus.: Photo. Maps. B&W. 8. Lang.: Eng.

UK-England: Lewes, East Sussex. 1846-1994. Historical studies. ■Every year costumed participants, watched by many spectators, take over the streets and burn effigies of contemporary politicians and the Pope during six hours of carnivalesque rule.

Relation to other fields

3744 Hall, Christine. "The Carnival Yearning." *NTQ*. 1996 Aug.; 12(47): 288-289. [*NTQ* Reports and Announcements.] Lang.: Eng.

Canary Islands: Santa Cruz de Tenerife. 1949-1996. Historical studies. ■The modern version of carnival in Santa Cruz de Tenerife originated with the anti-fascist politician Antonio Cubillo, as such gatherings were prohibited at the time. It is still seen as an important political forum and an opportunity to regain the personal freedom which is suppressed throughout the year.

3745 Breiner, Matthias. "Der Stickfighter—Traditionelle Karnevalsmasken in Trinidad." (Stickfighter: Traditional Trinidadian Carnival Masks.) *MuK*. 1996; 1: 95-113. Notes. Illus.: Dwg. Photo. B&W. 9. Lang.: Ger.

Trinidad. 1790-1996. Historical studies. ■The history and social context of stickfighting in Trinidadian carnival.

Circus

Design/technology

3746 Johnson, David. "Cirque du Soleil's *Quidam*." *TCI*. 1996 Oct.; 30(8): 30-33. Illus.: Photo. Plan. Color. 7. Lang.: Eng.

Canada: Montreal, PQ. 1996. Technical studies. ■The challenge sound designer François Bergeron faced in wiring Cirque du Soleil's *Quidam* in a big top tent.

3747 Sudakevič, A.A. "Portret moej sud'by." (Portrait of My Destiny.) *ISK*. 1996; 5: 93-105. Lang.: Rus.

Russia. 1996. Histories-sources. ■Circus and variety show performer describes how she became a senior designer in the Soviet circus.

3748 Lampert-Gréaux, Ellen. "Jazz Babies." *TCI*. 1996 Feb.; 30(2): 6. Illus.: Photo. Color. 1. Lang.: Eng.

USA: New York, NY. 1996. Technical studies. ■Costume designer David Belugou's 1920s-style costumes for the Big Apple Circus' presentation *Jazzmatazz*.

Institutions

3749 Beauchamp, Hélène. "Dix ans! Ça se fête: Cirque, circus, dynamo." (Ten Years! It's to be Celebrated: Cirque, Circus, Dynamo.) *JCT*. 1991; 59: 127-133. Notes. Illus.: Photo. B&W. 4. Lang.: Fre.

Canada: Montreal, PQ. 1980-1991. Historical studies. ■History of Circus' (now Dynamo Théâtre) attempts to create theatre using gymnastics and circus techniques. Review of their 1991 production of Gilbert Dupuis' *Déséquilibre (Instability)*, directed by Alain Fournier.

3750 Lévesque, Solange. "Tour de pistes." (Tour of the Rings.) *JCT*. 1989; 53: 13-16. Notes. Illus.: Dwg. Photo. B&W. 2. Lang.: Fre.

Canada: Montreal, PQ. 1981-1989. Historical studies. ■Creation and development of École nationale de cirque. Montreal productions of Shanghai Circus and Moscow Circus.

MIXED ENTERTAINMENT: Circus

Performance spaces

3751 Kwint, M.S. *Astley's Amphitheatre and the Early Circus in England, 1768-1830.* D.Phil. thesis, *Index to theses,* 45-6141. Oxford: Univ. of Oxford; 1994. Notes. Biblio. Lang.: Eng.
England. 1768-1830. Historical studies. ■Charts formative years of the institution and its contribution to a popular genre previously neglected by systematic historical analysis. Discusses artistic development, stagecraft, and its various ingredients from high, low, and possibly archaic cultures.

Performance/production

3752 Tait, Peta. "Danger Delights: Text of Gender and Race in Aerial Performance." *NTQ.* 1996; 12(45): 43-49. Notes. Illus.: Photo. B&W. 1. Lang.: Eng.
Australia. 1900-1961. Critical studies. ■Analyzes the careers of Aboriginal wire-walkers Con Colleano and Dawn de Ramirez, and shows how circus artists transgress and reconstruct the boundaries of racial and gender identity as part of their routine.

3753 Lacombe, Denis. "La Comédie visuelle, démystification." (Visual Comedy, Demystification.) *JCT.* 1990; 55: 112-113. Notes. Illus.: Photo. B&W. 2. Lang.: Fre.
Canada. 1990. Histories-sources. ■Peculiarities of performing visual comedy described by Cirque du Soleil clown Denis Lacombe.

3754 Olsson-Forsberg, Marito. "Cirkus—en egen värld." (Circus—a World of Its Own.) *Danst.* 1996; 6(2): 21-22. Illus.: Photo. B&W. Lang.: Swe.
Canada: Montreal, PQ. 1980. Critical studies. ■A survey of the new concept of circus, where ballet, theatre and design are combined to a total effect, with reference to Cirque du Soleil and the choreographer Debra Brown.

3755 Dmitriev, Ju.A. *Prekrasnoe iskusstvo cirka.* (The Beautiful Art of the Circus.) Moscow: Iskusstvo; 1996. 528 pp. Lang.: Rus.
Russia. 1800-1996. Histories-specific. ■The birth and development of circus art in Russia, with reference to the work of Jurij Nikulin, Oleg Popov, and Irina Bugrimova.

3756 Olofsson, Marie. "Varandras spegelbilder." (Each Other's Reflections.) *Danst.* 1996; 6(2): 23. Illus.: Photo. B&W. Lang.: Swe.
Sweden. 1996. Historical studies. ■A presentation of the Steben Sisters, and their lyrical trapeze act.

3757 McGill, Stewart. "Smart Move." *PlPl.* 1996 Dec/1997 Jan.; 510: 31. Lang.: Eng.
UK-England. 1996. Historical studies. ■Account of circus manager Gary Smart's decision to bring his family's circus back to England, touring all over the country, after being away for twenty-one years.

Theory/criticism

3758 Tait, Peta. "Feminine Free Fall: A Fantasy of Freedom." *TJ.* 1996 Mar.; 48(1): 27-34. Notes. Biblio. Lang.: Eng.
Australia. 1850-1929. Critical studies. ■Performance studies critique of women performers in the circus. Author suggests that the circus provided an arena for public displays of female bodies that defied social conventions and allowed women performers to explore a freedom of movement that was prohibited elsewhere in late nineteenth-century Australian society.

Commedia dell'arte

Administration

3759 "Neue Wege der Forschung über Commedia dell'arte." (New Avenues of Research on *Commedia dell'arte.*) *MuK.* 1996; 1: 7-16. Notes. Lang.: Ger.
Italy. France. 1576-1654. Historical studies. ■Director, author, and reformer Giovan Battista Andreini at the beginning of professional theatre.

Design/technology

3760 Lampert-Gréaux, Ellen. "Green Bird Soars." *TCI.* 1996 May; 30(5): 8-9. Illus.: Photo. Color. 1. Lang.: Eng.

USA: New York, NY. 1996. Technical studies. ■Challenge of designing an eighteenth-century philosophical play that satirizes the French Enlightenment via *commedia dell'arte*, and the collaboration of director Julie Taymor, costumer Constance Hoffman, set designer Christine Jones and light designer Donald Holder on the New Victory Theatre production of Carlo Gozzi's *The Green Bird (L'augellino belverde),* with emphasis on Hoffman's costumes.

Institutions

3761 Martinelli, Marco. "Ravenna Teatrets tredie år: mod et pirat teater." (The Third Season of the Ravenna Theatre: Toward a Pirate Theatre.) *TE.* 1996 June; 79: 22-24. Illus.: Photo. B&W. 1. Lang.: Dan.
Italy: Ravenna. 1991-1996. Histories-sources. ■Marco Martinelli, whose theatre company took over two city theatres in Ravenna, the Alighieri and the Rasi, in 1991, recalls his thoughts prior to the take-over.

Performance/production

3762 Schindler, Otto G. "Kasperl, der Hausherr in der Narrengasse." (Punch, Head of the Household in 'Narrengasse'.) *KSGT.* 1996; YB: 177-201. Notes. Illus.: Design. B&W. 7. Lang.: Ger.
Austria: Vienna. 1700-1799. Historical studies. ■*Commedia dell'arte* in the Viennese *Volkstheater.*

3763 Schindler, Otto G. "'Mio compadre Imperatore'. Comici dell'arte an der Höfen der Habsburger." ('Mio compadre Imperatore': Actors of the *Commedia dell'arte* at the Courts of the Habsburgs.) *MuK.* 1996; 2-4: 25-154. Notes. Illus.: Graphs. Handbill. Dwg. B&W. 36. Lang.: Ger.
Austria: Vienna. 1500-1599. Historical studies. ■Guest appearances of Italian touring troupes and their specific performance style.

3764 Artoni, Ambrogio. "Poeti mercenari e comici virtuosi." (Mercenary Poets and Virtuoso Actors.) *IlCast.* 1996; 9(26): 37-110. Notes. Lang.: Ita.
Italy. 1500-1700. Histories-specific. ■The origins of *commedia dell'arte* with emphasis on the art of medieval jesters, the theatricality of feasts, and the popular ritualism of carnival.

3765 Guardenti, Renzo. "Il ritorno di Scaramouche: intervista a Leo De Bernardis." (The Return of Scaramouche: An Interview with Leo De Bernardis.) *IlCast.* 1996; 9(26): 123-131. Lang.: Ita.
Italy: Scandicci. 1650-1996. Histories-sources. ■Actor discusses his staging of *Il ritorno di Scaramouche (The Return of Scaramouche)* at Teatro Studio in Scandicci near Florence.

3766 Guardenti, Renzo. "Leo, il corpo vivente dell'attore." (Leo, the Living Body of the Actor.) *IlCast.* 1996; 9(26): 135-141. Lang.: Ita.
Italy: Scandicci. 1996. Reviews of performances. ■Actor Leo De Bernardis' staging of *Il ritorno di Scaramouche (The Return of Scaramouche)* at Teatro Studio in Scandicci, freely adapted from the work of Tiberio Fiorilli who originally created the character.

3767 Katritzky, M.A. "Eight Portraits of Gelosi Actors in 1589." *ThR.* 1996; 21(2): 108-120. Notes. Illus.: Sketches. B&W. 10. Lang.: Eng.
Italy. 1568-1589. Historical studies. ■Identifies depictions of stock comic types in a dated print of 1589 as portraits of actors associated with Gelosi troupe. Includes a short history of the troupe.

Plays/librettos/scripts

3768 Cuppone, Roberto. "Il sogno teatrale di Maurice Sand." (Maurice Sand's Theatrical Dream.) *TeatroS.* 1996; 11(18): 241-304. Notes. Biblio. Lang.: Ita.
France. 1846-1863. Critical studies. ■Actor and scenographer Maurice Sand, son of George Sand, and his attempts to revive the *commedia dell'arte.*

Relation to other fields

3769 Kirk, Thomas. "Magnifici e Zanni: la metafora dei ruoli dell'Arte nel dibattito politico genovese del Cinquecento." (Magnifici and Zanni: The Metaphor of Commedia dell'Arte

MIXED ENTERTAINMENT: *Commedia dell'arte*—Relation to other fields

Roles in the Genoese Political Debate of the Sixteenth Century.) *IlCast.* 1996; 9(26): 111-119. Notes. Lang.: Ita.
Italy: Genoa. 1528-1586. Historical studies. ■The incorporation of imagery from the *commedia dell'arte* into the language of the ruling class of the Genoese Republic.

Court entertainment

Performance/production

3770   Franke, Birgit. "'D'un mets à entre mets.' Tafelspiele am Burgunderhof." ('D'un mets à entre mets': Table Plays at the Burgundian Court.) *KSGT.* 1996; YB: 119-137. Notes. Illus.: Dwg. Photo. B&W. 5. Lang.: Ger.
Burgundy. 1468. Historical studies. ■Analysis of the plays presented in the context of the ten-day wedding celebration of Karl the Bold and Margaret of York.

3771   Hasche, Christa. "Köningin Luise von Preussen als erste Darstellerin in den Inszenierungen des Hofes." (Queen Luise of Prussia as the First Actress in Court Performances.) 69-77 in Fiebach, Joachim, ed.; Mühl-Benninghaus, Wolfgang, ed. *Spektakel des Moderne.* Berlin: Humboldt-Universität: Institut für Theaterwissenschaft/Kulturelle Kommunikation; 1996. (Berliner Theaterwissenschaft 2.) Notes. Lang.: Ger.
Prussia. 1790-1810. Historical studies. ■The queen's performance and style at court, and the change from courtly to bourgeois representation.

Relation to other fields

3772   Costola, Sergio. "Storia di un pellegrinaggio. Momenti fra il sacro e il profano nella vita culturale ferrarese ai tempi di Ercole I d'Este." (The Story of a Pilgrimage: Between Sacred and Profane in the Cultural Life of Ferrara in the Times of Ercole I d'Este.) *TeatroS.* 1996; 11(18): 205-240. Notes. Lang.: Ita.
Italy: Ferrara. 1476-1487. Historical studies. ■A performance of *Santo Jacopo* and the subsequent 'performances' of Ercole's vow to make the pilgrimage to Compostela and his later departure, enacted in the public square.

English pantomime

Plays/librettos/scripts

3773   Davis, Jim. "Imperial Transgressions: the Ideology of Drury Lane Pantomime in the Late Nineteenth Century." *NTQ.* 1996; 12(46): 147-155. Notes. Illus.: Dwg. B&W. 6. Lang.: Eng.
UK-England: London. 1880-1900. Historical studies. ■Considers how the spectacular pantomimes, in which the original text gave way to scenic effects, music-hall songs and comedians' ad-libitum material, treated issues of patriotism, class, race, gender, and contemporary morals, while subverting the respectable middle class audiences which attended them.

Pageants/parades

Design/technology

3774   Butterworth, Philip. "Royal Firework Theater: The Fort Holding, Part II." *RORD.* 1996; 35(1): 17-31. Notes. Illus.: Photo. B&W. 3. Lang.: Eng.
England: Warwick, Bristol. 1572-1574. Historical studies. ■Second part of a description of the form, and machines used, in a 'fort holding'—a military pageant in which a mock siege was staged, focusing on two that were held for Queen Elizabeth in Warwick and Bristol.

3775   Davidson, Clifford. *Technology, Guilds, and Early English Drama.* Kalamazoo, MI: Medieval Institute Publications; 1996. 128 pp. Index. Pref. Biblio. Illus.: Photo. 102. Lang.: Eng.
England. 1300-1500. Historical studies. ■Explores evidence of various early craft technologies used and displayed in pageants and parades.

Performance/production

3776   Johnson, Odai. "Pope-Burning Pageants: Performing the Exclusion Crisis." *ThS.* 1996 May; 37(1): 35-58. Notes. Biblio. Illus.: Photo. 1. Lang.: Eng.
England: London. 1677. Historical studies. ■A pageant designed by playwright Elkanah Settle and sponsored by the current political party, effigies of the Pope, devils, etc., were carried in a mock papal procession through the city and burned. Argues that this form of street entertainment represents an expansion of the theatrical marketplace.

3777   Wyatt, Diana. "The English Pater Noster Play: Evidence and Extrapolations." *CompD.* 1996-97 Win; 30(4): 452-470. Notes. Append. Illus.: Maps. B&W. 1. Lang.: Eng.
England: Beverly. 1378-1577. Historical studies. ■Attempts to classify the Pater Noster play in a genre given the extant evidence of performance, particularly from the Beverly Pater Noster records.

3778   Engarås, Ingrid. "Technofest för fred och kärlek." (A Techno-Party For Peace and Love.) *Danst.* 1996; 6(4): 7. Illus.: Photo. B&W. Lang.: Swe.
Germany: Berlin. 1989. Historical studies. ■Report from a *Love Parade* dance party.

3779   Mason, Jeffrey D. "Street Fairs: Social Space, Social Performance." *TJ.* 1996 Oct.; 48(3): 301-320. Notes. Biblio. Illus.: Photo. 4. Lang.: Eng.
USA: Nevada City, CA. 1995. Historical studies. ■Performance analysis of events and audience behavior at the Hot Summer Nights Street Festival that concludes that the street fair serves as a means of community affirmation and cultural exhibition.

3780   Rigal, Laura. "'Raising the Roof': Authors, Spectators, and Artisans in the Grand Federal Procession of 1788." *TJ.* 1996 Oct.; 48(3): 253-278. Notes. Biblio. Illus.: Photo. Sketches. Pntg. 3. Lang.: Eng.
USA: Philadelphia, PA. 1788. Historical studies. ■Critical essay on the structure and meaning of the 1788 Grand Processional, a street parade celebrating the ratification of the US Constitution. It served not only to control, but to produce pleasure as reflected in Rousseau's theories on republicanism and the state.

Relation to other fields

3781   Cowling, Jane. "The Wood Eaves." *MET.* 1995; 17: 20-28. Notes. [Cover title: *Using Early Drama Records.*] Lang.: Eng.
England. 1567-1621. Historical studies. ■Presents excerpts form the *Ligger Book*, from the Isle of Wight, which refer to a woodland ceremony, an aspect of folk customs and gentry entertainment: suggests that the cessation of May-games stems from clerical disapproval combined with socioeconomic and political influences.

3782   Humphrey, Chris. "'To Make a New King': Seasonal Drama and Local Politics in Norwich, 1443." *MET.* 1995; 17: 29-41. Notes. [Cover title: *Using Early Drama Records.*] Lang.: Eng.
England: Norwich. 1443. Historical studies. ■Considers two disparate reports of 'Gladman's Insurrection', an incident in which a merchant John Gladman rode through the streets of Norwich dressed as a king, possibly as part of a Shrovetide procession, and which assumed political significance for the local community.

3783   Knight, Alan E. "Beyond Misrule: Theatre and the Socialization of Youth in Lille." *RORD.* 1996; 35(1): 73-84. Notes. Lang.: Eng.
France: Lille. 1270-1499. Historical studies. ■Local authorities' attempts to keep the young men of the community under control by overseeing and writing the plays they were to perform for the city procession which often ended in a brawl.

Performance art

Audience

3784   Liliefeldt, Louis Ethel. "Confessions of a Performance Artist." *CTR.* 1996 Spr; 86: 29-31. Illus.: Photo. B&W. 4. Lang.: Eng.
Canada. 1996. Histories-sources. ■Performance artist Louis Ethel Liliefeldt discusses the function of her body in her performance art, the psychological interaction between performer and spectator during

MIXED ENTERTAINMENT: Performance art—Audience

performance and the importance of space in performance art. References to her performance art piece *Frida*.

3785 Vaïs, Michel. "Sexy Sprinkle." *JCT*. 1993; 67: 118-124. Illus.: Handbill. Dwg. 2. Lang.: Fre.
Canada: Montreal, PQ. 1993. Historical studies. ■Repercussions of Annie Sprinkle's *Post-Post Porn Modernist* and *The Sluts and Goddesses Video Workshop: Or How To Be a Sex Goddess In 101 Easy Steps* among critics and city officials.

3786 Madsen, Steen. "Om oprindelig oplevelse og non-verbal dramaturgi." (The Genuine Experience and Non-Verbal Dramaturgy.) *TE*. 1996 Sep.; 80: 10-13. Illus.: Photo. B&W. 4. Lang.: Dan.
Denmark. 1995-1996. Critical studies. ■Analysis of a performance by French dancer and performance artist Jérôme Bel in which the audience was obliged to participate. The author, who is the leader of the performance group Kom De Bagfra, discusses how theatre can approach the audience through the five senses and the options of theatre without words.

Basic theatrical documents

3787 Block, Elizabeth; Levinthal, David, photo. "*Exposing We*." *TDR*. 1996 Sum; 40(2): 71-78. Notes. Illus.: Photo. B&W. 4. Lang.: Eng.
USA. 1996. ■Complete text of performance art piece, including notes on photographic inspiration for the work.

Design/technology

3788 Mars, Tanya. "Personal Reflections on *Blood Bath*." *CTR*. 1996 Spr; 86: 5-8. Notes. Lang.: Eng.
Canada. 1996. Histories-sources. ■Performance artist Tanya Mars' personal response to the computer game *Blood Bath*. Emphasis on the violent nature of the game.

Performance/production

3789 Büscher, Barbara. "Ich sehe was, was Du nich sehest..." (I See Things You Do Not See.) *TZ*. 1996; 2: 52-55. Illus.: Photo. B&W. 4. Lang.: Ger.
Germany: Cologne. 1985-1996. Historical studies. ■The work of performance artist and director Angie Hiesl, including her work with amateurs and her confrontation with urban spaces.

3790 Plata, Tomasz. "Ariergarda Awangardy." (Rearguard of the Avant-Garde.) *DialogW*. 1996; 9: 165-171. Lang.: Pol.
Poland: Znin. 1996. Critical studies. ■Performances of the Albert Tisson Theatre (Teatr im. Alberta Tisson), a new alternative theatre group, with emphasis on its attempt to develop a language to express issues of concern to contemporary Poles and its awkward position between neo-avant-garde and postmodernist aesthetics.

3791 Rozik, Eli. "Theatre at One of Its Borderlines: Reflections on *Suz o Suz* by La Fura dels Baus." *TA*. 1996; 49: 92-104. Notes. Lang.: Eng.
Spain: Barcelona. 1996. Critical studies. ■Analysis of the production using performance precepts of Richard Schechner.

3792 Bergvall, Caroline. "Éclat sites 1-10." *PerfR*. 1996 Fall; 1(3): unnumbered between pp. 70-71 (9 pages). Illus.: Photo. B&W. 6. Lang.: Eng.
UK-England: London. 1996. ■Documentation and translation through text, illustrations and fragments of a commissioned performance presented at the Institution of Rot as part of a series of site-specific works under the collective title of *Four Humours*, dedicated to E.M. Cioran. Bergvall's work used multiple audio-tapes to guide audiences through actual and fictive spaces.

3793 English, Rose; Fleming, Martha. "Breast Heart—a trailer for *Rosita Clavel*—a horse opera by Rose English and Ian Hill." *PerfR*. 1996 Fall; 1(3): between pp 76 and 77 (4 pages). Illus.: Photo. B&W. 4. Lang.: Eng.
UK-England. 1997. Histories-sources. ■A photomontage of horses and places by Rose English and Martha Fleming, described as a 'premonition' of English's forthcoming 'horse opera' *Rosita Clavel*.

3794 MacRitchie, Lynn. "Rose English: A Perilous Profession." *PerfR*. 1996 Fall; 1(3): 58-70. Notes. Illus.: Photo. B&W. 6. Lang.: Eng.

UK-England. 1996. Historical studies. ■The development of English's career, her changing concerns with the nature of performance, illusion, relationships with audience, and magic. Focuses on her interest in spectacle, design and visual imagery.

3795 Wessendorf, Markus. "Szenen ans einen rauhen Leben." (Scenes from a Harsh Life.) *TZ*. 1996; 1: 22-25. Illus.: Photo. B&W. 5. Lang.: Ger.
UK-England: London. USA: Los Angeles, CA. 1995-1996. Historical studies. ■Analysis of the performance aesthetics of Ron Athey.

3796 Herbert, Simon. "Come Back to Life: An Interview with André Stitt." *PerfR*. 1996 Fall; 1(3): 40-45. Illus.: Photo. B&W. 2. Lang.: Eng.
UK-Ireland. 1976-1995. Histories-sources. ■Interview with performance artist André Stitt in which he discusses the personal and psychological contexts of his work, his views on art, the importance of risk and confrontation, and his relationship to audience expectations.

3797 Baldwyn, Lucy. "Blending In: The Immaterial Art of Bobby Baker's Culinary Events." *TDR*. 1996 Win; 40(4): 37-55. Notes. Illus.: Photo. B&W. 7. Lang.: Eng.
USA. 1996. Critical studies. ■Performance artist Bobby Baker and her use of domestic and culinary imagery and actions in her work. Focus on her plays *Kitchen Show*, *Drawing on a Mother's Experience* and her work as a painter.

3798 Basting, Anne Davis. "Amnesia Interrupted: Re-Membering the Living Past in Feminist Theory and Suzanne Lacy's *Crystal Quilt*." *JDTC*. 1996 Fall; 11(1): 55-80. Notes. Illus.: Photo. 2. Lang.: Eng.
USA: Minneapolis, MN. 1984-1987. Critical studies. ■Suzanne Lacy's performance art piece *The Crystal Quilt*, which was part of a larger project called Whisper Minnesota, designed to empower older women as active citizens.

3799 Drukman, Steven. "Holly Hughes." *DGQ*. 1996 Sum; 33(2): 33-43. Lang.: Eng.
USA: New York, NY. 1983-1996. Histories-sources. ■Interview with playwright and performance artist Hughes, dealing with her work, NEA troubles and her recent book *Clit Notes: A Sapphic Sampler*.

3800 Epstein, Marcy J. "Consuming Performances: Eating Acts and Feminist Embodiment." *TDR*. 1996 Win; 40(4): 20-36. Notes. Illus.: Photo. B&W. 6. Lang.: Eng.
USA. 1994-1996. Critical studies. ■Acts of eating and feminist embodiment in performance. Focus on actress Hilary Ramsden in *Kentucky Fried*, Holly Hughes' *World Without End*.

3801 Export, Valie; Stelarc; Acconci, Vito; Hsieh, Tenching; Arnold, Skip; Colo, Papo; Montano, Linda; Marioni, Tom; Abramovic, Marina. "Endurance Art." *PerAJ*. 1996 Sep.; 18(3): 66-70. Illus.: Photo. B&W. 8. [Number 54.] Lang.: Eng.
USA: New York, NY. 1996. Histories-sources. ■Texts of artists' statements that were featured alongside the photographs of the performers' feats of endurance in exhibition at Exit Art, New York.

3802 Gentile, John S. "'The Sissy as Hero': Paul Bonin-Rodriguez Performing the Gay Male Body In *The Texas Trinity*." *TextPQ*. 1996 July; 16(3): 290-299. Notes. Biblio. Illus.: Photo. B&W. 1. Lang.: Eng.
USA. 1992-1996. Critical studies. ■Analysis of Bonin-Rodriguez's acting style when performing his solo pieces *Talk of the Town, The Bible Belt and Other Accessories*, and *Love in the Time of College*, which make up his *Texas Trinity*.

3803 Langworthy, Douglas. "Deb Margolin: Take Back Your Proscenium." *AmTh*. 1996 May/June; 13(5): 38-40. Illus.: Photo. B&W. 1. Lang.: Eng.
USA: New York, NY. 1996. Histories-sources. ■Interview with performance artist Margolin: her techniques, influences, style, work as a solo artist.

3804 Marowitz, Charles. "Asides." *TheaterW*. 1996 June 24; 9(47): 42-43. Lang.: Eng.
USA. 1996. Biographical studies. ■Performance artist Rachel Rosenthal and her latest original work, *Tohubohu*. Her imagery, sources of inspiration, audience response.

MIXED ENTERTAINMENT: Performance art—Performance/production

3805 Schneider, Rebecca. "After Us the Savage Goddess: Feminist Performance Art of the Explicit Body Staged, Uneasily, Across Modernist Dreamscapes." 155-176 in Diamond, Elin, ed. *Performance and Cultural Politics.* London/New York, NY: Routledge; 1996. 282 pp. Notes. Index. Illus.: Photo. 2. Lang.: Eng.

USA. 1989-1994. Critical studies. ■Explicitly erotic feminist performance and its embodiment of horror, 'savagery,' and the marked body as seen in the work of Annie Sprinkle, Carolee Schneemann and others.

3806 Shields, Ronald E.; Kepke, Allen N. "Prolegomenon to Gallery Theatre: Staging/Performing Fusing, Shifting and Contrasting Horizons." *TTop.* 1996 Mar.; 6(1): 70-90. Biblio. Notes. Illus.: Photo. B&W. 1. Lang.: Eng.

USA. 1996. Critical studies. ■Description of 'gallery theatre' as 'site-specific, environmental stagings of multiple texts within the collage tradition'. Describes Shield's *Ohio Tower* as an example.

3807 Simard, Claude. "The Web of Memory." *PerAJ.* 1996 May; 18(2): 40-43. Illus.: Photo. B&W. 3. [Number 53.] Lang.: Eng.

USA. 1996. Histories-sources. ■Performance artist Simard's belief that an artist cannot escape his memories and they are always reflected in his performances.

3808 Tierney, Hanne. "Hannah Wilke: The Intra-Venus Photographs." *PerAJ.* 1996 Jan.; 18(1): 44-49. Illus.: Photo. B&W. 6. [Number 52.] Lang.: Eng.

USA: New York, NY. 1993-1995. Critical studies. ■Discusses exhibition of photographs taken by performance artist Hannah Wilke of herself recording the effects of chemotherapy on her body.

3809 MacRitchie, Lynn. "Marina Abramovic: Exchanging Energies." *PerfR.* 1996 Sum; 1(2): 27-34. Biblio. Illus.: Photo. B&W. 2. Lang.: Eng.

Yugoslavia. 1946-1995. Biographical studies. ■Career of performance artist Marina Abramovic, one of the few performers from the 1970s who still subject their bodies to pain and danger through performance. Chronicles specific performances, her collaboration with Ulay, her creation of objects from natural materials.

Plays/librettos/scripts

3810 Derome, Nathalie. "Avancer à reculons." (Going Forward by Going Backward.) *JCT.* 1989; 50: 136. Illus.: Photo. B&W. 5. Lang.: Fre.

Canada: Montreal, PQ. 1989. Histories-sources. ■Performance artist Nathalie Derome free-associates about life and identity based on a song from her show *Canada errant (Wandering Canada).*

3811 Simonsen, Majbrit. "Banke, Banke på!" (Knock, Knock!)*TE.* 1996 Feb.; 77: 15-17. Illus.: Photo. B&W. 2. Lang.: Dan.

Denmark. 1995. Histories-sources. ■Account of a seminar titled *Body, Ritualmanipulation* held in Copenhagen, with discussion of the participation of Ron Athey, Fakir Musafar and Stuart Lynch, as well as two performances: *Amleto* by Societas Raffaello Sanzio and *Paradance Fable* by Stuart Lynch.

3812 Goat Island. "Illusiontext." *PerfR.* 1996 Fall; 1(3): 6-10. Illus.: Photo. B&W. 2. Lang.: Eng.

USA: Chicago, IL. 1996. Histories-sources. ■The process of creating *How Dear to Me the Hour When Daylight Dies*, and responses to it, while also demonstrating the uses of illusion in exceeding the real.

3813 Goulish, Matthew. "Five Microlectures." *PerfR.* 1996 Fall; 1(3): 94-99. Notes. Illus.: Photo. B&W. 1. [Delivered at symposium on Performance Writing at Dartington College of Arts, Totnes, Devon, April 1996.] Lang.: Eng.

USA: Chicago, IL. 1996. Histories-sources. ■Reflections of the author, a member of Goat Island, on writing for performance, with particular attention to the boundaries between repetition and difference.

Relation to other fields

3814 Most, Henrik. "Kroppen som forvandlingsnummer." (The Body as a Quick-Change Turn.) *TE.* 1996 Feb.; 77: 12-14. Lang.: Dan.

1980-1996. Critical studies. ■The changes in the nature of performance art in the 1990s, as the body becomes the main object of performance. Includes brief discussion of work by Ron Athey and Annie Sprinkle.

3815 Roepstorff, Sylvester. "Bodyart set igennem teologiske briller." (A Theological View of Body Art.) *TE.* 1996 Feb.; 77: 20-21. Illus.: Pntg. 1. Lang.: Dan.

1995-1996. Critical studies. ■The connection between Christianity and body art, such as that of Ron Athey and Fakir Musafar, with emphasis on the use of Christian iconography in spite of the performers' rejection of Christian duality, and the theme of the resurrection of the body.

3816 Letarte, Geneviève. "La Plaie." (The Wound.) *JCT.* 1989; 50: 143-144. Illus.: Photo. B&W. 1. Lang.: Fre.

Canada. 1988. Histories-sources. ■Performance-art poet Geneviève Letarte expresses views on social problems and role of the artist to address them.

3817 Gómez-Peña, Guillermo; Winks, Christopher, transl. "The Artist as Criminal." *TDR.* 1996 Spr; 40(1): 112-118. Notes. Illus.: Photo. B&W. 4. Lang.: Eng.

Mexico. 1996. Critical studies. ■Inherent risks for political performance artists. Focus on street artist Hugo Sánchez who was deported for political statements made during an artistic performance.

3818 "Temper of the Times: A Correspondence." *PerfR.* 1996 Spr; 1(1): 1-4, 89-95. Illus.: Photo. B&W. 2. Lang.: Eng.

UK-England: London. 1995. Histories-sources. ■Responses by performance artists and writers when invited to comment on the current concerns in their work, and how these relate to the times in which they live. All define their work—often obliquely—within political and personal/political contexts. The respondents are Misha Glenny, Kirsten Lavers, Jude Wolton, Jill Orr, Johannes Birringer, Brigid McLeer, Alastair MacLennan, Michael McMillan, Eugenio Barba, Peter Hulton, Josette Féral, Brigitte Kaquet, Margaret Trail, Rachel Rosenthal, Janne Risum, Katie Duck, Mike Pearson, Caroline Bergvall, and Richard Schechner.

3819 Etchells, Tim; Glendinning, Hugo, photo. "Looking Forwards." *PerfR.* 1996 Spr; 1(1): 26-31 (unnumbered). Illus.: Photo. B&W. 6. Lang.: Eng.

UK-England: Sheffield. 1995-1996. Empirical research. ■A series of photographs of people described as real life counterparts to the fictional figures who have often haunted Forced Entertainment's work, and who are supposedly shown contemplating the future. Readers are also invited to consider how we ascribe meaning to portraits, and to imagine ourselves within them.

3820 Warr, Tracey. "Sleeper." *PerfR.* 1996 Sum; 1(2): 1-19. Notes. Biblio. Illus.: Photo. B&W. 30. Lang.: Eng.

UK-England. 1959-1996. Critical studies. ■The relationship between risk and performance, with reference to artists such as Nitsch, Brus, Burnden, Orlan and Pane, who have used their own bodies—often violently—as the site and focus of their art. Discusses experiments by Paul Gilchrist with the use of sleep and dreams within live performances, and his use of advanced technology to allow communication through electric shocks between sleeping and waking participants and spectators.

3821 Birringer, Johannes. "This is the Theatre that Was to Be Expected and Foreseen." *PerfR.* 1996 Spr; 1(1): 32-46. Illus.: Photo. B&W. 8. Lang.: Eng.

USA. Yugoslavia. 1968-1995. Critical studies. ■The place of theatre and performance in the West today, and the relationship between forms and lived realities. Responses of the avant-garde to economic, social and political crises, and to the dominant culture. Includes discussion of works by Slobodan Snajder, Goran Stefanovski, Robert Wilson, Bill T. Jones, and Reza Abdoh.

3822 Brodin, Lisbeth. "De uforenelige forskelle—et interview med Richard Schechner." (Irreconcilable Differences: An Interview with Richard Schechner.) *TE.* 1996 June; 79: 20-21. Illus.: Photo. B&W. 1. Lang.: Dan.

USA. 1967-1996. Histories-sources. ■Schechner, a professor of Performance Studies at Tisch School of Arts (New York University) who was in Denmark to talk about intercultural theatre, discusses his own performance art and American performance art in general.

3823 Davidian, Blanche. "The Performance of Patriotism: Infiltration and Identity at the End of the World." *ThM.* 1996; 27(1) : 7-28. Illus.: Photo. B&W. 5. Lang.: Eng.

CLASSED ENTRIES

MIXED ENTERTAINMENT: Performance art—Relation to other fields

USA. 1995-1996. Histories-sources. ▪Performance artist Blanche Davidian recounts, through diary excerpts, her experience joining as many right-wing extremist groups as she could, and hoping it would deepen her conviction in her art.

3824 Iles, Chrissie. "An Interview with Marina Abramovic." *PerfR.* 1996 Sum; 1(2): 20-26. Notes. Illus.: Photo. B&W. 3. Lang.: Eng.

Yugoslavia. 1974-1996. Histories-sources. ▪Performance artist Marina Abramovic explains that her performances have become more theatrical and less dependent on immediate physical dangers, which she now sees as only one way of taking risks, and discusses the implications of the recreation of her earlier works by herself or by others, of employing video recordings, and of involving audiences in the processes of recreation.

Theory/criticism

3825 Quick, Andrew. "Approaching the Real: Reality Effects and the Play of Fiction." *PerfR.* 1996 Fall; 1(3): 12-22. Notes. Illus.: Photo. B&W. 5. Lang.: Eng.

UK-England. 1978-1994. Critical studies. ▪Questions the designation of live art events as essentially 'real', and analyses the work of Impact Theatre, Peter Brook and Claire MacDonald within a Lacanian perspective on the gap between fiction and reality.

3826 Toepfer, Karl. "Nudity and Textuality in Postmodern Performance." *PerAJ.* 1996 Sep.; 18(3): 76-91. Biblio. Illus.: Photo. B&W. 4. [Number 54.] Lang.: Eng.

USA. 1960-1996. Critical studies. ▪Through the work of artists Karen Finley, Carolee Schneemann, Hermann Nitsch, Otto Mühl, Annie Sprinkle, and Hannah Wilke, an attempt is made to define true nudity (vulnerability) beyond the naked body, and its effect on artist and audience in performance.

Variety acts

Administration

3827 Rozon, Gilbert. "Faire rire: Une Recette? Le Point de vue d'un producteur." (Getting Laughs: A Recipe? The Point of View of a Producer.) *JCT.* 1990; 55: 118-119. Illus.: Dwg. 1. Lang.: Fre.

Canada: Montreal, PQ. 1990. Histories-sources. ▪Gilbert Rozon shares secrets of producing comedy shows.

Audience

3828 Gamache, Chantale. "Liberté et contraintes ou le rire familier du théâtre des variétés." (Freedom and Constraint or the Familiar Laugh of the Théâtre des Variétés.) *JCT.* 1990; 55: 95-100. Notes. Illus.: Photo. B&W. 3. Lang.: Fre.

Canada: Montreal, PQ. 1990. Critical studies. ▪Laughter at Montreal's Théâtre des Variétés as expression of popular culture.

3829 Anderson, Lisa M. "From Blackface to 'Genuine Negroes': Nineteenth-Century Minstrelsy and the Icon of the 'Negro'." *ThR.* 1996; 21(1): 17-23. Notes. Illus.: Handbill. B&W. 5. Lang.: Eng.

USA. 1822-1898. Historical studies. ▪The development of nineteenth-century minstrelsy, arguing that audience expectation of how Black actors should perform Black roles was conditioned by iconised images of the 'Negro' created by white minstrels.

Design/technology

3830 Bergen, Jim van. "Nickelodeon on Tour." *TCI.* 1996 Apr.; 30(4): 25. Illus.: Photo. B&W. 2. Lang.: Eng.

USA: New York, NY. 1996. Technical studies. ▪System and equipment employed by sound designer Simon Nathan for the Nickelodeon tour, based on the television channel of the same name.

3831 McHugh, Catherine. "Reba McEntire." *TCI.* 1996 Aug/Sep.; 30(7): 32-35. Illus.: Photo. Plan. Color. 8. Lang.: Eng.

USA. 1996. Technical studies. ▪Theatricality of the production design for country singer McEntire's 1996 road tour, that combines Hollywood glamour and Broadway pretentions.

Performance/production

3832 Villeneuve, Lucie. "Le *Stand up* comique: Le Rire à tout prix?" (Stand-up Comedy: Laughter at All Costs?)*JCT.* 1990 ; 55: 106-107. Illus.: Photo. B&W. 1. Lang.: Fre.

Canada. USA. 1990. Critical studies. ▪American-style stand-up comedians' need to provoke laughter contrasted with character-driven comedy of traditional Quebecois humorists.

3833 Charitonov, N.N.; Pozdeev, P., ed. *'Zvezdy v provincii' Kn. I.* ('Stars in the Countryside' Book I.) Archangelsk: n.p.; 1996. 544 pp. Lang.: Rus.

Russia: St. Petersburg. 1900-1996. Historical studies. ▪Articles and notes about variety performer Jurij Ševčuk and his group DDT.

3834 Kruger, Loren. "Acting Africa." *ThR.* 1996; 21(2): 132-140. Notes. Illus.: Photo. B&W. 4. Lang.: Eng.

South Africa, Republic of. 1900-1985. Historical studies. ▪Post-apartheid re-examination of theatrical traditions in South Africa, focusing on variety entertainers seen as a paradigm for a folk culture which escapes the dichotomy between European civilization and the colonial objectification of 'savage' Africa.

3835 Bratton, J.S. "Beating the Bounds: Gender Play and Role Reversal in the Edwardian Music Hall." 86-110 in Booth, Michael R., ed.; Kaplan, Joel H., ed. *The Edwardian Theatre: Essays on Performance and the Stage.* Cambridge: Cambridge UP; 1996. 243 pp. Notes. Index. Illus.: Photo. 6. Lang.: Eng.

UK-England. 1900-1914. Historical studies. ▪Variety transvestism as a response to the misogyny of the music halls. Uses carnival tropes as well as gender theory to analyze the relationship of cross-dressing to specific periods of cultural crisis. The careers of female music-hall performers such as Hetty King, Bessie Wentworth and Vesta Tilley are used as examples.

3836 Russell, Dave. "Varieties of Life: the Making of the Edwardian Music Hall." 61-85 in Booth, Michael R., ed.; Kaplan, Joel H., ed. *The Edwardian Theatre: Essays on Performance and the Stage.* Cambridge: Cambridge UP; 1996. 243 pp. Notes. Index. Lang.: Eng.

UK-England. 1890-1914. Historical studies. ▪A new examination of Edwardian music hall genre, arguing that a resilient response to new business practices and altered patterns of audience attendance transformed an institution dominated by comic song into one characterized by a collection of hybrid variety acts.

3837 Mazer, Sharon. "'She's So Fat...': Facing the Fat Lady at Coney Island's Sideshows by the Seashore." *TA.* 1994; 47: 11-28. Notes. Illus.: Photo. B&W. 3. Lang.: Eng.

USA: Brooklyn, NY. 1992-1994. Critical studies. ▪The act of Katy Dierlam, who appears as Helen Melon the fat lady of the Coney Island Sideshow: her singing, persona and audience reaction to her.

3838 Shalom, Jack. "Finding the Red Card: The Performance of Three-Card Monte." *TA.* 1994; 47: 61-70. Notes. Lang.: Eng.

USA. 1856-1994. Critical studies. ▪Intricacies of performing three-card monte, a sleight-of-hand confidence game often seen on urban streets, and its roots in theatre and magic.

3839 Warnke, Nina. "Immigrant Popular Culture as a Contested Sphere: Yiddish Music Halls, the Yiddish Press, and the Processes of Americanization, 1900-1910." *TJ.* 1996 Oct.; 48(3): 321-336. Biblio. Lang.: Eng.

USA. 1900-1910. Historical studies. ▪The controversy between the Yiddish press and Yiddish community over Yiddish music halls and variety entertainment. Author suggests that the subtext for controversy was cultural identity, as reflected in a fear of assimilation, or 'Americanization,' and the hypocrisy of the press as it used the controversy to increase readership.

Plays/librettos/scripts

3840 "Is He a Jolly Good Fellow? Gentiles as Jews on the American Variety Stage of the 1870's." *TA.* 1994; 47: 28-46. Notes. Illus.: Handbill. Dwg. B&W. 3. Lang.: Eng.

MIXED ENTERTAINMENT: Variety acts—Plays/librettos/scripts

USA. 1870-1880. Critical studies. ■Jews as portrayed on the American stage, including Milton Nobles' Jewish character Moses Solomons in his variety play *The Phoenix* and Frank Bush's variety act.

Relation to other fields

3841 Eigtved, Michael. "Varietéens genfødsel." (The Rebirth of the Variety.) *TE.* 1996 Apr.; 78: 14-16. Illus.: Photo. B&W. 1. Lang.: Dan.
Germany. 1900-1996. Historical studies. ■The history of the variety in Germany. The sociologist Georg Simmel and the philosopher Walter Benjamin used as theoretical background.

3842 Featherson, Simon. "E Dunno Where'E Are: Coster Comedy and Politics of Music Hall." *NCT.* 1996 Sum; 24(1): 7-33. Notes. Illus.: Photo. Poster. B&W. 4. Lang.: Eng.
UK-England: London. 1914-1970. Historical studies. ■The use of the coster, or street-seller, character in music hall performances with reference to British politics and society.

Vaudeville

Institutions

3843 Bell, Karen. "The Four-A-Day." *PAC.* 1996; 30(1): 23-25. Illus.: Photo. B&W. 3. Lang.: Eng.
Canada: Toronto, ON. 1925-1996. Historical studies. ■A memorial performance to recall the long success of the Casino Theatre which presented vaudeville-type shows from the 1930s until the early 1960s.

MUSIC-DRAMA

General

Administration

3844 Dmitrievskaja, M. "O prirode ljubovnogo dueta." (On the Nature of the Love Duet.) *PTZ.* 1996; 10: 17-19. Lang.: Rus.
Russia: St. Petersburg. 1996. Histories-sources. ■Interview with Jurij Švarckopf, former director of the Mariinskij Theatre, about the management of the theatre.

Basic theatrical documents

3845 Schmidt, Paul. "*Alice.*" *ThM.* 1996; 26(3): 27-50. Illus.: Photo. B&W. 4. Lang.: Eng.
Germany: Hamburg. 1996. ■Text of Schmidt's *Alice*, with lyrics and music by Tom Waits and Kathleen Brennan.

Institutions

3846 Reissinger, Marianne. "Stück-Werk." (Unfinished Work.) *DB.* 1996; 6: 20-21. Illus.: Photo. B&W. 2. Lang.: Ger.
Germany: Munich. 1996. Historical studies. ■New plans of Münchner Biennale, the festival of new music theatre, directed by Hans Werner Henze.

3847 László, Ferenc. "A kilencedik, a legnagyobb (A Kolozsvári Magyar Opera)." (The Ninth, the Biggest: The Kolozsvár Hungarian Opera.) 109-120 in Kántor, Lajos, ed. *Kolozsvár magyar színháza 1792-1992.* Kolozsvár (Cluj-Napoca): Kolozsvári Állami Magyar Színház; 1992. 141 pp. Lang.: Hun.
Hungary. Romania: Cluj-Napoca. 1948-1990. Historical studies. ■History of Hungarian ethnic minority musical stage of Kolozsvár/Cluj-Napoca, Romania: opera, operetta and ballet performances of four decades.

3848 Rónai, István. "Az utolsó negyvennégy a kétszázból (Egy vázlat vázlata)." (The Last Forty-Four of Two Hundred Years: An Outline of a Draft.) 121-123 in Kántor, Lajos, ed. *Kolozsvár magyar színháza 1792-1992.* Kolozsvár (Cluj-Napoca): Kolozsvári Állami Magyar Színház; 1992. 141 pp. Lang.: Hun.
Hungary. Romania: Cluj-Napoca. 1948-1992. Historical studies. ■The program policy of the musical stage of Kolozsvár's Hungarian ethnic minority theatre with respect to politics, fashions, gala performances and ceremonies.

3849 Čurova, M. "Saratov slušaet 'Chovanščinu'." (Saratov Hears *Chovanščina.*) *MuZizn.* 1996; 5-6: 19-20. Lang.: Rus.
Russia: Saratov. 1996. Historical studies. ■Profile of the Saratov Opera and Ballet Theatre, its repertoire and future plans.

3850 Vasiljév, Vladimir. "'Naš' teat'r—teat'r akademičéskij'." (Our Theatre: Academic Theatre.) *Balet.* 1996; 1: 6-7. Lang.: Rus.
Russia: Moscow. 1990-1996. Histories-sources. ■Artistic director of the Bolšoj Opera and Ballet explains the theatre's goals.

Performance spaces

3851 Weathersby, William, Jr. "Teatro de los Insurgentes, Mexico City." *TCI.* 1996 May; 30(5): 44-47. Illus.: Photo. Color. 4. Lang.: Eng.
Mexico: Mexico City. 1996. Historical studies. ■Report on the recently completed renovation of Teatro de los Insurgentes for the purpose of presenting musical productions.

3852 "The Shubert Theatre Shines Anew." *PasShow.* 1996 Spr/Sum; 19(1): 16-18. Illus.: Photo. B&W. 4.
USA: New York, NY. 1996. Historical studies. ■Description of the newly renovated Shubert Theatre, with a list of shows that opened there before its facelift.

Performance/production

3853 Kennedy, Michael. "Circle of Friends: Schubert and His Creative Coterie Represented the Romantic Period at Its Brilliant Best—and Hyperion's Schubert Edition, Spearheaded by Pianist Graham Johnson, Recaptures the Era." *OpN.* 1996 Aug.; 61(2): 26-30. Illus.: Photo. B&W. Color. 6. Lang.: Eng.
1996. Critical studies. ■The Hyperion recording company's project to record all Schubert *Lieder* on compact disc under the direction of pianist Graham Johnson and director Ted Perry.

3854 Sørensen, Lilo. "Kvinden med de maerkelige rum." (The Woman with the Strange Spaces.) *TE.* 1996 Dec.; 81-82: 16-19. Illus.: Photo. B&W. 2. Lang.: Dan.
Denmark. UK-England. 1994-1996. Histories-sources. ■An interview with set designer Louise Beck on her training at Wimbledon School of Art and on a music theatre project titled *Gudruns 4. Sang (Gudrun's Fourth Song)*, directed by Lucy Bailey and staged in a dry dock in Copenhagen.

3855 Mills, David. "Music and Musicians in Chester: a Summary Account." *MET.* 1995; 17: 58-75. Notes. [Cover title: *Using Early Drama Records.*] Lang.: Eng.
England: Chester. 1518-1642. Historical studies. ■Presents extracts from the drama records of the county of Cheshire which demonstrate the pervasive nature of music. Sections cover: Church music, the Minstrel Court, the Waits, ensembles, itinerant and other musicians.

3856 Collins, Fletcher, Jr. "*The Play of Daniel* in Modern Performance." 63-75 in Ogden, Dunbar H., ed. *The Play of Daniel: Critical Essays.* Kalamazoo, MI: Medieval Institute Publications; 1996. 132 pp. (Early Drama, Art, and Music Monograph Series 24.) Notes. Lang.: Eng.
Europe. USA. 1140-1984. Historical studies. ■The staging choices of modern productions of *Ludus Danielis*, the first of its repertory to be revived.

3857 Davidson, Audrey Ekdahl. "Music in the Beauvais *Ludus Danielis.*" 77-86 in Ogden, Dunbar H., ed. *The Play of Daniel: Critical Essays.* Kalamazoo, MI: Medieval Institute Publications; 1996. 132 pp. (Early Drama, Art, and Music Monograph Series 24.) Notes. B&W. 5. Lang.: Eng.
France. 1140. Critical studies. ■Examines the musical characteristics, especially the singular mixture of ecclesiastical and secular music that distinguishes the play. Analyzes musical impact on an audience.

3858 Ogden, Dunbar H. "The Staging of *The Play of Daniel* in the Twelfth Century." 11-32 in Ogden, Dunbar H., ed. *The Play of Daniel: Critical Essays.* Kalamazoo, MI: Medieval Institute Publications; 1996. 132 pp. (Early Drama, Art, and Music Monograph Series 24.) Notes. Lang.: Eng.
France: Beauvais. 1140-1975. Historical studies. ■Examines the evidence concerning the probable conditions at Beauvais Cathedral for the origi-

MUSIC-DRAMA: General—Performance/production

nal production: architecture, liturgical calendar and the scholastic community. Includes a brief discussion of a twentieth-century staging.

3859 Keller, James M. "The Essential Fischer-Dieskau." *OpN.* 1996 Aug.; 61(2): 32-35. Illus.: Photo. B&W. Color. 3. Lang.: Eng.
Germany. 1950-1985. Critical studies. ■Evaluation of Dietrich Fischer-Dieskau's recordings of Schubert *Lieder.*

3860 Benkő, András. "Énekesjátéktól—az operáig (A kolozsvári zenés színpad fejlődése 1948 decemberéig)." (From the Musical Play—to the Opera: The Development of Musical Stage at Kolozsvár to December 1948.) 85-107 in Kántor, Lajos, ed. *Kolozsvár magyar színháza 1792-1992.* Kolozsvár (Cluj-Napoca): Kolozsvári Állami Magyar Színház; 1992. 141 pp. Notes. Append. Lang.: Hun.
Hungary: Kolozsvár. Romania: Cluj-Napoca. 1793-1948. Historical studies. ■History of the musical stage of Kolozsvár theatre from its beginnings in 1793 to the 1950s: survey of the various genres of musical plays in the repertory of the seasons (opera, operetta, ballet etc.) with complete collection of data on the program and artists.

3861 Buchau, Stephanie von. "New from the Studios: A Selective Listing of this Season's Releases." *OpN.* 1996 Oct.; 61(4): 20, 22, 24. Illus.: Diagram. Lang.: Eng.
North America. 1996. Histories-sources. ■Listing of new audio and video recordings of musical materials: reissues and abridged, recitals, solo albums, miscellaneous, and video.

3862 Bardadym, V.P. *Aleksand'r Vertinskij bez grima.* (Aleksand'r Vertinskij Without Make-Up.) Krasnodar: Sovetskaja Kuban; 1996. 208 pp. Lang.: Rus.
Russia: Moscow. 1957-1996. Biographies. ■The life and work of singer Aleksand'r Vertinskij.

3863 Bernaskoni, E. "Slavjanka s persidskimi glazami." (Slavic Girl with Persian Eyes.) *EchoP.* 1996; 35: 20-25. Lang.: Rus.
Russia. 1960-1996. Biographical studies. ■Profile of singer Alla Bajanova: creative distinctions, problems and successes of her stage career.

3864 Morozova, T. "'Poju—sebe ne prinadležu...'." (When I Sing, I Do Not Belong to Myself.) *OSZ.* 1996; 6: 54-55. Lang.: Rus.
Russia: Moscow. 1996. Historical studies. ■Ljudmila Rjumina, honored with the designation 'national' singer.

3865 Zajceva, T. "Vlad Staševskij: 'Naprasno sebja rastračivaju'." (Vlad Staševskij: Too Bad, I'm Not Spending Myself.) *My.* 1996; 7: 162-169. Lang.: Rus.
Russia: Moscow. 1990-1996. Biographical studies. ■Career of pop singer Vlad Staševskij.

3866 Lagercrantz, Ylva. "Romeo & Julia Kören—en musikalisk resa genom kriget." (Romeo & Julia Choir—a Musical Journey Through the War.) *Dramat.* 1996; 4(3): 16-17. Illus.: Photo. B&W. Lang.: Swe.
Sweden: Stockholm. Slovenia. Croatia. 1991. Historical studies. ■A presentation of the Romeo & Julia Kören, which after the first appearance as part of a production of *Romeo and Juliet* at the Royal Dramatic Theatre, has produced performances of their own, with mostly Renaissance songs and references to several tours in former Yugoslavia.

3867 Fuller, Sophie. "New Perspectives: Feminism and Music." 70-81 in Campbell, Patrick, ed. *Analysing Performance: A Critical Reader.* Manchester/New York, NY: Manchester UP; 1996. 307 pp. Notes. Biblio. Index. Lang.: Eng.
UK-England. 1990-1995. Critical studies. ■The current state of feminist criticism in music, as well as new directions for challenge and insight.

3868 O'Brien, Lucy. "'Sexing the Cherry': High or Low Art? Distinctions in Performance." 234-243 in Campbell, Patrick, ed. *Analysing Performance: A Critical Reader.* Manchester/New York, NY: Manchester UP; 1996. 307 pp. Index. Notes. Biblio. Lang.: Eng.
UK-England. USA. 1990-1995. Critical studies. ■The distinction between high and low culture in contemporary popular music, and the marginality of female artists.

3869 Hampson, Thomas. "Lexicon of Song: German Romantic Lieder and Its Symbols." *OpN.* 1996 Aug.; 61(2): 35-39. Illus.: Photo. Color. 1. Lang.: Eng.
USA. 1996. Critical studies. ■American baritone Thomas Hampson discusses the background and symbolism of German *Lieder.*

3870 Rorem, Ned. "The American Art Song: Dead or Alive." *OpN.* 1996 Aug.; 61(2): 14-16, 18, 21, 30. Illus.: Photo. B&W. Color. 9. Lang.: Eng.
USA. 1996. Critical studies. ■Composers and performers of the American art song.

3871 Sperry, Paul. "Tenor Paul Sperry Salutes the Great American Songbook." *OpN.* 1996 Aug.; 61(2): 22-25. Illus.: Photo. B&W. Color. 4. Lang.: Eng.
USA. 1996. Histories-sources. ■The author's exploration of the American art song repertory.

Plays/librettos/scripts

3872 Emmerson, Richard K. "Divine Judgement and Local Ideology in the Beauvais *Ludu Danielis.*" 33-61 in Ogden, Dunbar H., ed. *The Play of Daniel: Critical Essays.* Kalamazoo, MI: Medieval Institute Publications; 1996. 132 pp. (Early Drama, Art, and Music Monograph Series 24.) Notes. Lang.: Eng.
France: Beauvais. 1099-1233. Historical studies. ■The contexts of the Beauvais *Ludus Danielis (The Play of Daniel)* beyond its liturgical setting, including discussion of its exegetical, historical, and cultural contexts and its place in local ideology.

3873 Ogden, Dunbar H., ed. *The Play of Daniel: Critical Essays.* Kalamazoo, MI: Medieval Institute Publications; 1996. 132 pp. (Early Drama, Art, and Music Monograph Series 24.) Notes. Illus.: Photo. B&W. 27. Lang.: Eng.
France: Beauvais. 1140-1975. Critical studies. ■Essays on the analysis, staging, and cultural and ecclesiastical context of the music and text of *The Play of Daniel.*

3874 Kobialka, Michal. *"Corpus Mysticum et Representationem:* Hildegard of Bingen's *Scivias* and *Ordo Virtutum.*" *ThS.* 1996 May; 37(1): 1-22. Notes. Biblio. Lang.: Eng.
Germany: Bingen. 1120-1179. Historical studies. ■Uses representational practice of Hildegard's works to refer to the shifting relationship among theological, historical, and metaphysical formulations in historical constructions.

Relation to other fields

3875 Greenfield, Peter H. "Using Dramatic Records: History, Theory, Southampton's Musicians." *MET.* 1995; 17: 76-95. Notes. [Cover title: *Using Early Drama Records.*] Lang.: Eng.
England: Southampton. 1577-1640. Historical studies. ■Through a detailed account of the civic musicians in Southampton shows the importance of ceremonial display and the theatricality of power.

Theory/criticism

3876 Pioquinto, Ceres. "Dangdut at Sekaten: Female Representations in Live Performance." *RevIM.* 1995 Win/Sum; 29: 59-89. Notes. Biblio. Illus.: Photo. B&W. 2. Lang.: Eng.
Indonesia: Java. 1995. Critical studies. ■Analysis of live performances of *dangdut* that accompany major religious festivals in terms of relationship between gender and performance, specifically how gender is socially and culturally constructed and transformed in performance.

Chinese opera

Design/technology

3877 Wei, Li. "Linear Decoration in the Stage Design of Traditional Chinese Operas." *TD&T.* 1996 Spr; 32(2): 25-33. Illus.: Dwg. 24. Lang.: Eng.
China. 1850-1995. Historical studies. ■History and development of linear decoration in Chinese opera set design, seen especially in the stage curtains used to form the main body of the stage design.

Performance/production

3878 Chen, Zongbao. "Stylisation et symbolisation dans le théâtre traditionnel chinois." (Stylization and Symbolization in Tra-

system CLASSED ENTRIES

MUSIC-DRAMA: Chinese opera—Performance/production

ditional Chinese Theatre.) *JCT.* 1990; 57: 71-79. Biblio. Illus.: Dwg. 6. Lang.: Fre.
China. 221 B.C.-1990 A.D. Historical studies. ■Brief history of Chinese opera, and symbolism and style in design and performance techniques.

3879 Sun, Mei. "Performances of *Nanxi*." *ATJ.* 1996 Fall; 13(2): 142-166. Notes. Biblio. Lang.: Eng.
China. 1368-1996. Historical studies. ■Scholarship and what is known of *nanxi*, the earliest example of Chinese theatre forms known as *xiqu*. Includes its music, prosody, role types, acting, make-up and props.

Musical theatre

Administration

3880 Bloom, Ken. "The Decline and Fall of the Entire World as Seen Through the Eyes of Ben Bagley." *ShowM.* 1996 Fall; 12(3): 42-46, 68. Illus.: Photo. B&W. 9. Lang.: Eng.
USA: New York, NY. 1949-1996. Historical studies. ■Profile of the career of theatre and record producer Ben Bagley, with extensive narrative from Bagley, focusing on his early revues, notably the *Shoestring Revues*, their history, and the then-unknown talents they introduced.

3881 Grode, Eric. "Signs of the Time." *ShowM.* 1996 Fall; 12(3): 19-23. Illus.: Photo. Poster. B&W. 14. Lang.: Eng.
USA: New York, NY. 1892-1996. Historical studies. ■A survey of the art of poster design for Broadway musicals, with comments from contemporary poster designers, among them Paul Davis, James McMullan, Bob King, and Robin Wagner.

3882 Moore, Dick. "Equity Beans Non-Union Shows in Boston, Orlando." *EN.* 1996 July/Aug.; 81(6): 2. Illus.: Photo. 3. Lang.: Eng.
USA: Boston, MA. 1996. Historical studies. ■Equity pickets the Wang Center for the Performing Arts, protesting the presentation of a non-union production of *42nd Street.*

3883 Sherman, Howard. "Cultivating Broadway's Field of Dreams: The Cast Album Business is a Labor of Love and Money." *ShowM.* 1996 Fall; 12(3): 39-40, 65-66. Lang.: Eng.
USA. 1996. Historical studies. ■An examination of the business of producing original cast albums of musicals—economics, selection criteria, CD reissues—with comments from major record-company producers.

3884 Wolfe, Donald H. "Co-Production: Community Theatres Share Cost of *Annie*." *SoTh.* 1996 Win; 37(1): 12-13. Illus.: Photo. B&W. 2. Lang.: Eng.
USA: Winston-Salem, NC. 1995. Historical studies. ■An account of the experience of two North Carolina community theatres, the Little Theatre of Winston-Salem and the Hickory Community Theatre, in co-producing the musical *Annie.*

Design/technology

3885 Litson, Jo. "*The King & I*: Brian Thomson." *TCI.* 1996 Aug/Sep.; 30(7): 26-31. Illus.: Photo. Color. B&W. 20. Lang.: Eng.
Australia. USA: New York, NY. 1971-1996. Technical studies. ■Career of Australian scene designer Brian Thomson, with emphasis on his Tony-winning set for *The King and I*, and with a chronological list of the shows and films he has designed.

3886 Ruling, Karl G. "Beastly Hydraulics." *TCI.* 1996 Nov.; 30(9): 15-17. Lang.: Eng.
Australia: Melbourne, Sydney. 1996. Technical studies. ■Hydraulic system employed for the Australian production of *Beauty and the Beast*, that makes the scene changes much quieter than the productions in the U.S.

3887 Krzeszowiak, Tadeusz. "Licht für 'Die Schöne und das Biest'." (Lighting for *Beauty and the Beast*.) *BtR.* 1996 ; 3: 58-63. Illus.: Design. Photo. B&W. Color. 12. Lang.: Ger.
Austria: Vienna. 1995. Histories-sources. ■The lighting for the German-language production of Disney's *Beauty and the Beast* at the Raimund Theater.

3888 Thor, Harald B. "Disney's 'Die Schöne und das Biest'." (Disney's *Beauty and the Beast*.) *BtR.* 1996; 1: 10-15. Append. Illus.: Design. Photo. B&W. Color. 30. Lang.: Ger.

Austria: Vienna. 1995. Histories-sources. ■Production manager of scenery describes technical aspects of the first German-language production of *Beauty and the Beast* performed at Raimund Theater.

3889 Iakala, Kimmo; Pääkkönen, Susanna, transl. "Rörelse i ett ovänligt landskap." (Movement in a Rude Landscape.) *ProScen.* 1996; 20(Extra): 5-7. Illus.: Photo. Color. Lang.: Swe, Eng.
Finland: Helsinki. 1996. Histories-sources. ■An interview with the scenographer Kati Lukka, about her concept of scenery for *West Side Story* set in the nineties and using computer animation as well as videoforms at Helsingin Kaupunginteatteri.

3890 Barbour, David. "*Martin Guerre* Faces the Music." *LDim.* 1996 Sep.; 20(7): 12-13. Illus.: Photo. Color. 1. Lang.: Eng.
UK-England: London. 1996. Technical studies. ■Lighting design and systems used for *Martin Guerre* by Alain Boublil and Claude-Michel Schönberg, designed by Nick Ormerod and directed by Declan Donnellan, and for *The House of Martin Guerre* by Leslie Arden and Anna Theresa Cascio, at the Goodman Theatre, lighting design by Jim Ingalls, directed by David Petrarca.

3891 Halliday, Robert. "Bring in 'da Dogs." *TCI.* 1996 Oct.; 30(8): 12-13. Illus.: Photo. Color. 1. Lang.: Eng.
UK-England: London. Ireland: Dublin. 1996. Technical studies. ■Designer Rick Fisher's use of moving lights for the London and Dublin productions of Dein Perry's *Tap Dogs* with programming assistance from Andrew Voller.

3892 Loney, Glenn. "NYMT on Tour." *TCI.* 1996 Feb.; 30(2): 18-19. Illus.: Photo. Color. 1. Lang.: Eng.
UK-England. USA: New York, NY. 1995. Technical studies. ■Alison Darke's production design for the National Youth Music Theatre of Great Britain's *Pendragon* by Jeremy James Taylor, Frank Whatley, Peter Allwood and Joanna Horton, seen at City Center.

3893 Moles, Steve. "Pinball Wizardry." *LDim.* 1996 May; 20(4): 32-34. Illus.: Photo. Color. 1. Lang.: Eng.
UK-England: London. USA: New York, NY. 1996. Technical studies. ■Associate lighting designer of the musical *The Who's Tommy*, David Grill, discusses differences in equipment and design between Broadway and West End productions. Use of video and projections.

3894 Barbour, David. "Two-Part Invention." *TCI.* 1996 Dec.; 30(10): 12-14. Illus.: Photo. Color. 1. Lang.: Eng.
USA: New York, NY. 1996. Technical studies. ■Collaboration of lighting designer Howard Werner and set designer Markas Henry to bring a naturalistic look to the Promenade Theatre's production of Jon Marans' *Old Wicked Songs* directed by Seth Barrish.

3895 Barbour, David. "*Rent*." *LDim.* 1996 Apr.; 20(3): 44-48, 50. Illus.: Photo. Lighting. Color. 6. Lang.: Eng.
USA: New York, NY. 1996. Technical studies. ■Blake Burba's lighting design for the musical *Rent* by Jonathan Larson. Themes of the show, collaboration with scenic designers, his work at New York Theatre Workshop and adapting his design for the show when it moved to Broadway.

3896 Barbour, David. "Razzle Dazzle." *LDim.* 1996 Nov.; 20(9): 76-79, 154-156. Illus.: Photo. Lighting. Color. B&W. 5. Lang.: Eng.
USA: New York, NY. 1996. Technical studies. ■Lighting designer Ken Billington's work on the Broadway musical *Chicago* by John Kander and Fred Ebb, directed by Walter Bobbie. Includes sidebar article by Leanne Boepple on the successful ad campaign used.

3897 Barbour, David. "Alvin Colt." *TCI.* 1996 Nov.; 30(9): 30. Illus.: Photo. B&W. 3. Lang.: Eng.
USA: New York, NY. 1944-1996. Biographical studies. ■The long career of costume designer Alvin Colt, who is presently working on the design for *Forbidden Broadway Strikes Back.*

3898 Barbour, David. "Tony Meola." *TCI.* 1996 Oct.; 30(8): 38. Illus.: Photo. Color. B&W. 2. Lang.: Eng.
USA: New York, NY. 1985-1996. Biographical studies. ■Profile of Broadway sound designer Tony Meola whose work includes *A Funny Thing Happened on the Way to the Forum* and *Smokey Joe's Cafe.*

3899 Johnson, David. "Scharff Weisberg." *TCI.* 1996 Nov.; 30(9): 28. Illus.: Photo. Color. 3. Lang.: Eng.

MUSIC-DRAMA: Musical theatre—Design/technology

USA: New York, NY. 1996. Historical studies. ■Profile of Scharff Weisberg, the company which made its Broadway debut providing the video equipment for *The Who's Tommy.*

3900 Lampert-Gréaux, Ellen. "*Carousel* Goes Around." *LDim.* 1996 Dec.; 20(10): 26. Lang.: Eng.

USA. 1996. Technical studies. ■Lighting design for touring production of *Carousel*, original design by Paul Pyant, associate designer Christina Giannelli. Changes in design to accomodate tour, moving the equipment safely.

3901 Lampert-Gréaux, Ellen. "20-Ton House Tour." *TCI.* 1996 Nov.; 30(9): 9. Illus.: Photo. Color. 1. Lang.: Eng.

USA: New York, NY. 1996. Technical studies. ■Re-design of Andrew Lloyd Webber's *Sunset Boulevard* by associate designer Ray Huessy for its national tour.

3902 Napoleon, Davi. "How Big is *Big?*" *TheaterW.* 1996 Apr 22; 9(38): 28-33. Illus.: Photo. B&W. 1. Lang.: Eng.

USA: Detroit, MI. 1996. Technical studies. ■Technical challenges facing designers of musical *Big* during its out of town tryout. Gregory Meeh, special effects artist, discusses coordinating effects with artists, and costume designer William Ivey Long describes inspiration for his designs.

3903 Napoleon, Davi. "Shlemiels on Wheels." *TCI.* 1996 Nov.; 30(9): 15. Illus.: Photo. Color. 1. Lang.: Eng.

USA: Cambridge, MA, Philadelphia, PA. 1996. Technical studies. ■Robert Israel's sets and Catherine Zuber's costumes for the American Repertory Company/American Music Theatre Festival co-production of Robert Brustein's adaptation of Isaac B. Singer's *Shlemiel the First.*

3904 Phillips, Michael. "Babe Army." *TCI.* 1996 May; 30(5): 7. Illus.: Photo. Color. 1. Lang.: Eng.

USA: Minneapolis, MN. 1996. Technical studies. ■John Arnone's set designs for Rodgers and Hart's *Babes in Arms*, adapted by librettist Ken LaZebnik and directed by Garland Wright at the Guthrie Theatre.

3905 Sandla, Robert. "Victor/Victoria." *TCI.* 1996 Jan.; 30(1): 34-37. Lang.: Eng.

USA: New York, NY. 1995. Technical studies. ■Scenic designer Robin Wagner's sets for the musical *Victor/Victoria.*

Institutions

3906 Stenzl, Jurg. "A Report on the 1995 Jeunesse Festival." *KWN.* 1996 Spr; 14(1): 7-9. Illus.: Photo. Poster. B&W. 2. Lang.: Eng.

Austria: Vienna. 1995. Reviews of performances. ■Kurt Weill's work at the 1995 Festival of Jeunesse (Musikalische Jügend Österreichs). Special attention is paid to *Der Silbersee, Aufstieg und Fall der Stadt Mahagonny* and *Der Lindberghflug.* Argues that Weill is a more complex personality and thus composer than currently realized.

3907 Kämpfer, Frank. "Motor ohne Öl." (Motor without Oil.) *DB.* 1996; 4: 32-33. Illus.: Photo. B&W. 2. Lang.: Ger.

Germany. 1970-1996. Historical studies. ■The merger of Theater Greifswald and Theater Stralsund into Theater Vorpommern, and its plans and successes in contemporary musical theatre.

3908 Weiss, Bonnie. "Keepers of the Flame: Bay Area Musical Lovers Unite." *TheaterW.* 1996 July 15; 9(50): 30-35. Illus.: Photo. B&W. 8. Lang.: Eng.

USA: San Francisco, CA. 1996. Historical studies. ■Focus on two organizations dedicated to preserving the legacy of the musical: The Center for the American Musical and Musical Theater Lovers United.

Performance spaces

3909 Sonntag-Kunst, Helga. "Rendezvous im Ronacher Theater mit dem Musical 'Sie liebt mich'." (Meeting at Ronacher Theater, with the Musical *She Loves Me.*) *BtR.* 1996; 6: 24-31. Illus.: Design. Lighting. Photo. B&W. Color. 15. Lang.: Ger.

Austria: Vienna. 1872-1996. Historical studies. ■Profile of the Ronacher and its technical possibilities, its production of the musical *She Loves Me*, and its history before the new era of Stella GmbH, a professional production business.

3910 Sonntag-Kunst, Helga. "Technische Details von 'Broadway an der Ruhr': Neubau Musicaltheater Duisberg." (Technical Details of 'Broadway on the Ruhr': Duisberg's New Musical

Theatre Building.) *BtR.* 1996; 3: 8-18. Illus.: Design. Photo. B&W. Color. 17. Lang.: Ger.

Germany: Duisberg. 1996. Historical studies. ■Architectural and technical aspects of the Musical Theater Duisburg's new building and its opening performance of *Les Misérables.*

Performance/production

3911 Johnson, Reed. "Songs for Salvation." *AmTh.* 1996 Feb.; 13(2): 18-21. Illus.: Photo. B&W. 7. Lang.: Eng.

1996. Critical studies. ■Themes and characters of African-American gospel musicals. Promotion and tours of shows, audience response, sociological influences, examines charges that these shows promote stereotypes.

3912 Chase, Tony. "Diahann Carroll Becomes Norma Desmond." *TheaterW.* 1996 Jan 8; 9(23): 26-33. Illus.: Photo. B&W. 6. Lang.: Eng.

Canada: Toronto, ON. 1950-1996. Biographical studies. ■Carroll's role in Andrew Lloyd Webber's *Sunset Boulevard* at the Ford Centre for the Performing Arts. Her past roles on stage and in film, and challenges she has faced as an African-American artist.

3913 Greenberg, Joel. "Montreal/Toronto ... But Our Own?" *CTR.* 1996 Spr; 86: 49-50. Lang.: Eng.

Canada: Toronto, ON, Montreal, PQ. 1996. Critical studies. ■Examination of musical theatre's coming of age in Canada with emphasis on the production models employed for mounting *Napoleon* by Timothy Williams and Andrew Sabiston, score arranged by David Cullen, directed by John Wood at the North York Centre for the Performing Arts and *Jeanne*, script by Vincent de Tourdonnot, music by Peter Sipos, directed by Roger Peace, at the Saidye Bronfman Centre in Montreal.

3914 "Schmaltzy Days Are Here Again." *Econ.* 1996 Nov 30; 341(7994): 87-89. Illus.: Photo. B&W. 4. Lang.: Eng.

Germany. Austria. 1928-1996. Historical studies. ■Resurgence in popularity of operettas and musical theatre on German and Austrian stages. Current revivals, popularity of Gilbert and Sullivan, impact of Nazi politics on Jewish authors, and the lack of productions of their work.

3915 Delekat, Thomas. "Musicals, Musicals, zu viele Musicals." (Musicals, Musicals, Too Many Musicals.) *DB.* 1996; 1: 26-29. Append. Illus.: Photo. B&W. 4. Lang.: Ger.

Germany. 1996. Critical studies. ■Survey of the musical theatre scene in Germany, its successes and limitations, following the opening of a new musical theatre, Rhein-Main-Theater, in Niedernhausen with *Sunset Boulevard.*

3916 Farneth, David. "Norbert Gingold Remembers Die Dreigroschenoper." *KWN.* 1996 Spr; 14(1): 4-6. Illus.: Photo. Poster. B&W. 2. Lang.: Eng.

Germany: Berlin. Austria: Vienna. 1928-1929. Histories-sources. ■Edited oral history interview with Norbert Gingold who prepared the piano-vocal score for *Die Dreigroschenoper* and conducted the Vienna production in 1929 with Harold Paulsen as Macheath. Interview also touches on his preparation of the piano-vocal score for *Aufstieg und Fall der Stadt Mahagonny* and the relationship of Weill and Brecht.

3917 Goebbels, Heiner. "Opening up the Text." *PerfR.* 1996 Spr; 1(1): 52-58. Illus.: Photo. B&W. 2. Lang.: Eng.

Germany: Berlin. UK-England: London. 1995. Histories-sources. ■Text from a discussion following the performance of *Murx*, between its director Heiner Goebbels, the company's dramaturg, performance critics and audience, preceded by a talk by Goebbels. Discussion centers on the relationships between music and text, speaking and singing voices, audiences and performers, semantics and rhythm. Goebbels argues against political performance where meaning resides in the words alone, and insists on complexity within performance.

3918 Sutton, Douglas. "Robert Wilson and Lou Reed Make Music in Hamburg." *AmTh.* 1996 Sep.; 13(7): 70. Illus.: Photo. B&W. 1. Lang.: Eng.

Germany: Hamburg. 1996. Critical studies. ■Collaboration of director Wilson and musician Reed on *Time Rocker*, the last of a trilogy which includes *The Black Rider* and *Alice* (collaborations between Wilson and musician Tom Waits) at the Thalia Theater.

3919 Jákfalvi, Magdolna; Ilovszky, Béla, photo. "Képzelt riport egy képzelt színdarabról." (Imaginary Report on an Imagi-

MUSIC-DRAMA: Musical theatre—Performance/production

nary Play.) *Sz.* 1996; 29(3): 26-30. Illus.: Photo. B&W. 6. Lang.: Hun.

Hungary. 1973-1995. Critical studies. ■Three 1995 revivals of the first Hungarian pop musical (1973), *Képzelt riport egy amerikai popfesztiválról (Imaginary Report on an American Pop Festival)*, by Sándor Pós, Anna Adamis, and Gábor Presser, based on a novel by Tibor Déry, at Hevesi Sándor Színház (Zalaegerszeg), directed and choreographed by György Krámer, at Békés Megyei Jókai Színház (Békéscsaba), directed by István Szőke, and at Petőfi Színház (Veszprém), directed by László Vándorfi: a new text successfully updated the musical and saved the music, said to be the best part of the show.

3920 Machlina, S.T. *Kul'tura na poroge III tysjačeletija: Materialy III Meždunarodnogo seminara v St.-Peterburge. 6-7 maja 1996 goda.* (Culture at the Gates of the Third Millennium: Materials from the Third International Seminar, St. Petersburg, May 6-7, 1996.) St. Petersburg: Gosudarstvennaja Akademija kul'tury; 1996. 308 pp. Lang.: Rus.

Russia. 1996. Critical studies. ■Articles on culture, including 'cosmic' musical theatre.

3921 Sörenson, Margareta. "Karl Dyall." *Danst.* 1996; 6(5): 20. Illus.: Photo. Color. Lang.: Swe.

Sweden: Stockholm. 1980. Biographical studies. ■A presentation of the street dancer Karl Dyall's career from the streets to an all-round artist of musicals.

3922 Bailey, Peter. "'Naughty but nice': Musical Comedy and the Rhetoric of the Girl, 1892-1914." 36-60 in Booth, Michael R., ed.; Kaplan, Joel H., ed. *The Edwardian Theatre: Essays on Performance and the Stage.* Cambridge: Cambridge UP; 1996. 243 pp. Notes. Index. Illus.: Photo. 2. Lang.: Eng.

UK-England. 1892-1914. Historical studies. ■Edwardian eroticism and its place in the popular theatre genre of the musical comedy. Introduces the figure of the girl-heroine and explores the implications of this figure in Edwardian formulations of sexuality and gender.

3923 Charles, Peter. "Never Too Old." *PlPl.* 1996 Apr.: 18-19. Lang.: Eng.

UK-England. 1918-1996. Critical studies. ■Profile of musical theatre performer Evelyn Laye with references to her performances in *Cinderella*, *The Sleeping Beauty*, *Peter Pan* and *Wedding In Paris*.

3924 Eagleton, Julie. "Eagleton's Angle: Tony Newley Talks to Julie Eagleton." *PlPl.* 1996 Dec/1997 Jan.; 510: 8-9. Lang.: Eng.

UK-England. 1935-1996. Histories-sources. ■Interview with musical actor Anthony Newley on his career in stage, film, cabaret and television.

3925 Ford, Piers. "A Page Turn." *ShowM.* 1996 Sum; 12(2): 18-22, 68. Illus.: Photo. B&W. 10. Lang.: Eng.

UK-England: London. USA: New York, NY. 1968-1996. Historical studies. ■Profile of the career of British singer/actress Elaine Page, creator of the title role in *Evita*, on the eve of her Broadway debut as Norma Desmond in *Sunset Boulevard*.

3926 Kaán, Zsuzsa. "Crazy For Original, avagy Seregi és a *Crazy For You*—Gershwin zenés játéka a Fővárosi Operett Színházban." (Crazy For Original, or László Seregi and *Crazy For You*—Gershwin's Musical at the Municipal Operetta Theatre.) *Tanc.* 1995; 26(7/9): 26-29. Illus.: Photo. B&W. Color. 7. Lang.: Hun.

UK-England: London. Hungary: Budapest. 1993-1995. Reviews of performances. ■A comparison between the performances of *Crazy For You* in London and Budapest, with focus on the Hungarian choreography by László Seregi supported by Béla Kanyó's photo report of the premiere at Budapest Operetta Theatre.

3927 Shenton, Mark. "Bob Hoskins Gets Wicked." *TheaterW.* 1996 Nov 18; 10(16): 18-30. Illus.: Photo. B&W. 3. Lang.: Eng.

UK-England. 1968-1996. Biographical studies. ■Life and career of film and stage actor Hoskins, his work in Great Britain and his current appearance in *Old Wicked Songs* by Jon Marans, directed by Elijah Moshinsky.

3928 Allen, Norman. "Donna McKechnie: Back on Broadway." *TheaterW.* 1996 Mar 25; 9(34): 28-31. Illus.: Photo. B&W. 2. Lang.: Eng.

USA: New York, NY. 1996. Biographical studies. ■Life and career of dancer/singer McKechnie. Past roles in *A Chorus Line*, collaboration with choreographer and directors Michael Bennett and Bob Fosse, current performance on Broadway in *State Fair*.

3929 Angelo, Gregory. "Brian Stokes Mitchell: Riding on the Wheels of a Dream." *ShowM.* 1996/97 Win; 12(4): 15-17. Illus.: Photo. B&W. 6. Lang.: Eng.

USA. Canada. 1988-1996. Historical studies. ■Brief profile of the career of actor/singer Brian Stokes Mitchell as he is playing the leading role in the pre-Broadway production of *Ragtime*.

3930 Bernardo, Melissa Rose. "Big Songwriters Maltby & Shire." *TheaterW.* 1996 Apr 22; 9(38): 22-27. Illus.: Photo. B&W. 2. Lang.: Eng.

USA: New York, NY. 1973-1996. Biographical studies. ■Collaborative team of composer David Shire and lyricist Richard Maltby, Jr. Past collaborations, collaborative techniques, and current work on the Broadway musical *Big*.

3931 Bernardo, Melissa Rose. "The *Misérable*zation of Ricky Martin." *TheaterW.* 1996 Aug 12; 10(2): 30-31. Illus.: Photo. B&W. 1. Lang.: Eng.

USA: New York, NY. 1996. Biographical studies. ■Actor Martin appearing in the Broadway musical *Les Misérables*. Crossover from pop music and soap operas, approach to the role.

3932 Berson, Misha. "The Bosnia Blues." *AmTh.* 1996 Jan.; 13(1): 14-18. Illus.: Photo. B&W. 6. Lang.: Eng.

USA: Seattle, WA. 1991-1996. Critical studies. ■Production of rock-musical *Sarajevo: Behind God's Back* performed by Amir Beso and Srdjan Yevjdevich and written by performers with playwright Talvin Wilks, staged by Tim Bond at the Group Theatre. Political influences and themes of the piece, American audience response.

3933 Bird, Dorothy; Greenberg, Joyce. "A Bird's-Eye View of *Hooray For What!*." *PasShow.* 1995 Spr; 18(1): 6-14. Illus.: Handbill. Photo. Poster. B&W. 8.

USA: New York, NY. 1937. Histories-sources. ■Dancer Dorothy Bird's reminiscence of being in the original Broadway production of *Hooray For What!*, music by Harold Arlen, lyrics by E.Y. Harburg, book by Howard Lindsay and Russel Crouse, starring Ed Wynn.

3934 Buckley, Michael. "Encores! Encores!" *TheaterW.* 1996 Feb 12; 9(28): 30-37. Illus.: Photo. B&W. 1. Lang.: Eng.

USA: New York, NY. 1994-1996. Historical studies. ■Musical concert series which focuses on workshop revivals of older musicals, Judith E. Daykin executive director, Walter Bobbie artistic director, and Rob Fisher musical director. Team discusses how they select musicals, casting, past and upcoming productions.

3935 Buckley, Michael. "John Cullum: Broadway Exposure." *TheaterW.* 1996 Mar 25; 9(34): 32-34. Illus.: Photo. B&W. 1. Lang.: Eng.

USA: New York, NY. 1965-1996. Biographical studies. ■Life and career of singer/actor John Cullum. Past roles on Broadway, in film and on television, current lead role on Broadway in *Show Boat*, book and lyrics by Oscar Hammerstein II, music by Jerome Kern, based on the novel by Edna Ferber, directed by Harold Prince.

3936 Buckley, Michael. "Leslie Uggams: Madam's Adams." *TheaterW.* 1996 Apr 1; 9(35): 24-30. Illus.: Photo. B&W. 1. Lang.: Eng.

USA: New York, NY. 1967-1996. Biographical studies. ■Life and career of singer/actress Leslie Uggams. Past roles on Broadway and on television, current role in Irving Berlin's *Call Me Madam* at the Paper Mill Playhouse.

3937 Buckley, Michael. "Tall Story: Daniel Jenkins." *TheaterW.* 1996 Apr 22; 9(38): 18-20. Illus.: Photo. B&W. 1. Lang.: Eng.

USA: New York, NY. 1988-1996. Biographical studies. ■Life and career of actor Jenkins, and his current lead role in the new Broadway musical *Big*, an adaptation of the 1988 film. Sidebar article on actor Patrick Levis who portrays the lead character as a child.

3938 Buckley, Michael. "A Day in the Life of Lou Diamond Phillips." *TheaterW.* 1996 July 1; 9(48): 20-37. Illus.: Photo. B&W. 4. Lang.: Eng.

MUSIC-DRAMA: Musical theatre—Performance/production

USA: New York, NY. 1996. Biographical studies. ■A detailed chronology of the actor's day in preparation for and performance of his starring role in Rodgers and Hammerstein's *The King and I* on Broadway. Personal life, past roles, work in film and research for the role of the King.

3939 Buckley, Michael. "*Chicago* on Broadway." *TheaterW*. 1996 Nov 11; 10(15): 34-47. Illus.: Photo. B&W. 7. Lang.: Eng.
USA: New York, NY. 1975-1996. Historical studies. ■Revival of the Kander and Ebb, Bob Fosse musical *Chicago* on Broadway, directed by Walter Bobbie, starring Ann Reinking, Bebe Neuwirth, James Naughton, Marcia Lewis, and Joel Grey. Actors discuss their background and experiences with the show.

3940 Buckley, Michael. "Choicest Voices: Broadway." *TheaterW*. 1996 July 29; 9(52): 16-27. Lang.: Eng.
USA: New York, NY. 1996. Biographical studies. ■Profiles of singers Adam Pascal, Lonette McKee, Davis Gaines, Taewon Kim, Jay Hunter Morris. Their past training and roles, and current roles in Broadway productions.

3941 Buckley, Michael. "Kander & Ebb: Color Them Happy." *TheaterW*. 1996 Nov 11; 10(15): 18-32. Illus.: Photo. B&W. 4. Lang.: Eng.
USA: New York, NY. 1996. Histories-sources. ■Interview with writing team John Kander and Fred Ebb discussing their past collaborations including *Cabaret* and *Flora, the Red Menace*, and their upcoming productions of *Chicago* and *Steel Pier*.

3942 Buckley, Michael. "Sarah Jessica Parker: Princess with a Capital Pea." *TheaterW*. 1996 Dec 23; 10(21): 28-31. Illus.: Photo. B&W. 2. Lang.: Eng.
USA: New York, NY. 1976-1996. Biographical studies. ■Actress Parker discusses her current role in the Broadway production of *Once Upon a Mattress* directed by Gerald Gutierrez at the Broadhurst Theatre, past roles on stage and in film.

3943 Buckley, Michael. "Gerald Gutierrez: Mattress Maker." *TheaterW*. 1996 Dec 23; 10(21): 32-38. Illus.: Photo. B&W. 1. Lang.: Eng.
USA: New York, NY. 1959-1996. Biographical studies. ■Director Gutierrez discusses his career, with specific focus on his work for *Once Upon a Mattress*. Sidebar article on history of the musical including original Broadway cast information, television adaptations and cast.

3944 Buckley, Michael. "Evita! Evita! Evita!: Comments from a Theater Trio." *TheaterW*. 1996 Dec 30; 10(22): 30-36. Illus.: Photo. B&W. 3. Lang.: Eng.
USA. 1996. Histories-sources. ■Reminiscences of actresses Elaine Page, Florence Lacey and Patti LuPone on their portrayals of the lead role in Lloyd Webber's *Evita*.

3945 Chase, Tony. "John Davidson's Return." *TheaterW*. 1996 May 27; 9(43): 36-40. Illus.: Photo. B&W. 3. Lang.: Eng.
USA: New York, NY. 1964-1996. Biographical studies. ■Profile and career of actor/singer Davidson and his current role in the Broadway musical *State Fair* by Rodgers and Hammerstein. Past roles in theatre and on television.

3946 Dahlin, Robert. "It's Always Tomorrow: Andrea McArdle Today." *ShowM*. 1996 Sum; 12(2): 45-48. Illus.: Photo. B&W. 6. Lang.: Eng.
USA. 1976-1996. Historical studies. ■Career of actress/singer Andrea McArdle since her creation of the title role in *Annie*, on the occasion of her return to Broadway in *State Fair*.

3947 Davis, Lee. "Where Have All the Girls and Gags Gone: The Rise and Fall of the Broadway Revue, Part I." *ShowM*. 1996 Spr; 12(1): 34-38, 68-70. Illus.: Photo. B&W. 9. Lang.: Eng.
USA: New York, NY. 1866-1996. Historical studies. ■Overview of the Broadway musical revue. Continued in *ShowM* 12:2 (1996 Sum), 40-44, 71-73.

3948 Filichia, Peter. "Stagestruck." *TheaterW*. 1996 Feb 5; 9(27): 28-37. Illus.: Photo. B&W. 1. Lang.: Eng.
USA: New York, NY. 1967-1996. Historical studies. ■History of Jerome Coopersmith, Edward Thomas and Martin Charnin's musical *Mata Hari* currently being revived. Its poor audience reception, production problems, casting.

3949 Filichia, Peter. "Stagestruck." *TheaterW*. 1996 Feb 26; 9(30): 10-12. Illus.: Photo. B&W. 1. Lang.: Eng.
USA: New York, NY. 1970-1996. Biographical studies. ■Profile of singer/actress Janie Sell, her career work outside of performing, and current return to the theatre as Carol Burnett's standby in *Moon Over Buffalo*.

3950 Finkle, David. "Take Two: The New Off-Broadway Musical Revisited." *TheaterW*. 1996 May 6; 9(40): 22-27. Illus.: Photo. B&W. 4. Lang.: Eng.
USA: New York, NY. 1996. Historical studies. ■Profiles of musicals *Bring in 'Da Noise, Bring in 'Da Funk* conceived and co-created by George C. Wolfe, Savion Glover and Reg E. Gaines, *Floyd Collins* by Tina Landau and Adam Guettel, *Bed and Sofa* by Polly Pen, Laurence Klavan, *Cowgirls* by Beth Howie, music and lyrics by Mary Murfitt, directed by Eleanor Reissa. Origins of plays, characters, audience reception, trends in developing musicals.

3951 Fricker, Karen. "George C. Wolfe: Examining American History Through Rhythm." *DGQ*. 1996 Sum; 33(2): 6-9. Lang.: Eng.
USA: New York, NY. 1989. Histories-sources. ■Interview with *Bring in 'Da Noise, Bring in 'Da Funk* director George C. Wolfe about the creation of the show, and how tap and rhythm are employed to tell the story and convey emotion.

3952 Grode, Eric. "Five Minutes with Ann Reinking." *ShowM*. 1996/97 Win; 12(4): 23-24. Illus.: Photo. B&W. 2. Lang.: Eng.
USA. 1996. Histories-sources. ■Tongue-in-cheek account of having only five minutes to interview Ann Reinking, currently both choreographer and star of *Chicago* on Broadway.

3953 Grode, Eric. "A Forum with Jerry Zaks." *ShowM*. 1996 Spr; 12(1): 14-17, 63. Illus.: Photo. B&W. 8. Lang.: Eng.
USA: New York, NY. 1980-1996. Historical studies. ■A survey of the career of director Jerry Zaks, focusing on his work in musical theatre, as he prepares for his upcoming Broadway revival of Stephen Sondheim and Larry Gelbart's *A Funny Thing Happened on the Way to the Forum*.

3954 Grode, Eric. "Comin' Uptown: Off-Broadway Makes Noise in the High Rent District." *ShowM*. 1996 Sum; 12(2): 23-25, 70. Illus.: Photo. B&W. 4. Lang.: Eng.
USA: New York, NY. 1975-1996. Historical studies. ■Discusses the transfers of *Rent* and *Bring in 'Da Noise, Bring in 'Da Funk* from Off-Broadway to Broadway, with consideration of other smaller musicals that have transferred to Broadway.

3955 Horwitz, Simi. "The John Stamos Story." *TheaterW*. 1996 Jan 1; 9(22): 18-22. Illus.: Photo. B&W. 1. Lang.: Eng.
USA: New York, NY. 1996. Biographical studies. ■Career of television actor Stamos and his upcoming work as replacement for lead actor Matthew Broderick in the Broadway musical *How to Succeed in Business Without Really Trying*.

3956 Horwitz, Simi. "A Visit with Sally Struthers." *TheaterW*. 1996 Aug 26; 10(4): 32-41. Illus.: Photo. B&W. 1. Lang.: Eng.
USA: New York, NY. 1996. Biographical studies. ■Career of actress Struthers: past work on television in the series *All in the Family*, her current role in the Broadway musical *Grease*, her commitment to charitable institutions, personal background.

3957 Horwitz, Simi. "Pointer Sisters Misbehavin'." *TheaterW*. 1996 Feb 26; 9(30): 22-27. Illus.: Photo. B&W. 3. Lang.: Eng.
USA. 1973-1996. Biographical studies. ■Pop singers the Pointer Sisters starring in national tour of *Ain't Misbehavin'*. Overview of their career in pop music, challenges faced in approaching a theatrical production, their perceptions of African-American music.

3958 Horwitz, Simi. "Rent: The Musical Theater's New Lease on Life." *TheaterW*. 1996 Apr 29; 9(39): 20-25. Illus.: Photo. B&W. 3. Lang.: Eng.
USA: New York, NY. 1996. Historical studies. ■Profile of new Broadway musical *Rent*, directed by Michael Greif, written and composed by Jonathan Larson. Influence of *La Bohème* on the play's development through New York Theatre Workshop and its artistic director James Nicola. Brief biography of Larson, who died shortly before play's opening.

MUSIC-DRAMA: Musical theatre—Performance/production

3959 Horwitz, Simi. "McGrath Goes *Cocoanuts.*" *TheaterW.* 1996 Aug 12; 10(2): 18-21. Illus.: Photo. B&W. 2. Lang.: Eng.
USA: New York, NY. 1920-1996. Biographical studies. ■Actor Michael McGrath as comedian Groucho Marx in a revival of the George S. Kaufman/Irving Berlin musical *The Cocoanuts* at the American Place Theatre directed by Richard Sabellico. Approach to the role, revisions made to piece, personal background.

3960 Horwitz, Simi. "The Biggest Little Show in Town." *TheaterW.* 1996 Oct 14; 10(11): 26-30. Illus.: Photo. B&W. 2. Lang.: Eng.
USA: New York, NY. 1996. Critical studies. ■Howard Crabtree's *When Pigs Fly* at the Douglas Fairbanks Theatre, directed by Mark Waldrop. Gay content, collaboration between Waldrop and Crabtree.

3961 Istel, John. "'Rent Check'." *AmTh.* 1996 July/Aug.; 13(6): 12-17, 62. Illus.: Photo. B&W. 6. Lang.: Eng.
USA: New York, NY. 1996. Historical studies. ■Jonathan Larson's musical *Rent*: origins and workshop, production at New York Theatre Workshop, audience response, themes and influences. Includes sidebar interview with Larson, and sidebar article by Stephanie Coen on New York Theatre Workshop and artistic director James Nicola's decision to develop and produce *Rent*.

3962 Jones, Chad S. "Jason Graae: Fully Dressed." *ShowM.* 1996 Fall; 12(3): 24-26, 65. Illus.: Photo. B&W. 6. Lang.: Eng.
USA. 1980-1996. Historical studies. ■Overview of the career of singer/actor Jason Graae, focusing on his work as a recording artist as well as his work in stage musicals.

3963 Kahn, Sheryl. "Melba Moore Battles Back." *TheaterW.* 1996 Jan 22; 9(25): 11-16. Illus.: Photo. B&W. 3. Lang.: Eng.
USA: New York, NY. 1970-1996. Biographical studies. ■Personal and professional life of singer Moore, and her current role as Fantine in Broadway's *Les Misérables*.

3964 Kahn, Sheryl. "Big Shoes to Fill." *TheaterW.* 1996 Apr 22; 9(38): 34-35. Illus.: Photo. B&W. 3. Lang.: Eng.
USA: New York, NY. 1996. Biographical studies. ■Personal and professional relationship of choreographer Susan Stroman and director Mike Ockrent, who collaborated on the musical *Big*.

3965 Krasner, David. "'The Mirror Up to Nature': Modernist Aesthetics and Racial Authenticity in African American Theatre, 1895-1900." *THSt.* 1996 June; 16: 117-140. Notes. Illus.: Photo. Sketches. 3. Lang.: Eng.
USA. 1895-1900. Historical studies. ■Cultural study of the two forms of Black musical theatre emerging at the end of the nineteenth century: one engineered by white producers interested in cashing in on new forms of racial representation, and the other created by Blacks who sought to challenge that very representation.

3966 Krasner, David. "Parody and Double Consciousness in the Language of Early Black Musical Theatre." *AfAmR.* 1995 Spr; 29 (2): 317-323. Notes. Biblio. Lang.: Eng.
USA. 1900-1925. Historical studies. ■Examines the role of parody as a performative subversion in the work of early Black musical theatre performers, writers and musicians. By parodying racism, they undermined and destabilized racial stereotypes. Also examines the sense of double consciousness (American and Negro) in the lyrics of Black musical theatre songs.

3967 Lynch, Richard C. "For the Record: Ben Vereen." *ShowM.* 1996 Sum; 12(2): 37-39. Discography. Illus.: Photo. B&W. 6. Lang.: Eng.
USA. 1965-1995. Historical studies. ■A brief profile of the career of actor/singer Ben Vereen, with a discography of his recordings of theatre and film music.

3968 Lynch, Richard C. "For the Record: Patti LuPone." *ShowM.* 1996 Spr; 12(1): 31-33, 64. Discography. Illus.: Photo. Dwg. B&W. 7. Lang.: Eng.
USA. England. 1972-1995. Historical studies. ■A survey of the performing and recording career of actress/singer Patti LuPone, with a discography of all of her theatre-music recordings.

3969 Lynch, Richard C. "For the Record: Daniel Massey." *ShowM.* 1996/97 Win; 12(4): 37-39. Discography. Illus.: Photo. Dwg. B&W. 7. Lang.: Eng.
USA. UK-England. 1942-1995. Historical studies. ■Brief profile of the career of actor/singer Daniel Massey, with a discography of his theatre-music recordings.

3970 Lynch, Richard C. "For the Record: Tommy Tune." *ShowM.* 1996 Fall; 12(3): 35-38. Discography. Illus.: Photo. Dwg. B&W. 7. Lang.: Eng.
USA. 1965-1996. Historical studies. ■Brief profile of the career of actor/singer/dancer/director/ choreographer Tommy Tune, with a discography of his recordings of theatre-music.

3971 McKinley, Jesse. "A-Train to Illyria." *AmTh.* 1996 Nov.; 13(9): 8-9. Illus.: Photo. B&W. 2. Lang.: Eng.
USA: San Diego, CA. 1993-1996. Critical studies. ■Old Globe Theatre production of *Play On!*, a musical adaptation of Shakespeare's *Twelfth Night*, directed and conceived by Sheldon Epps, book by Cheryl L. West. Development of script, influence of jazz.

3972 McNamara, Brooks. "The Shuberts and 'The Gladiola Girl'." *PasShow.* 1996 Spr/Sum; 19(1): 14-16. Illus.: Photo. B&W. 4. Lang.: Eng.
USA: New York, NY. 1948-1949. Historical studies. ■Background of the 1948 Shubert-produced revue *Lend an Ear*, which contained a sketch, 'The Gladiola Girl', that parodied the Shuberts' own outmoded production tastes.

3973 Moore, Dick. "Carol Channing Closes in on Performance Record." *EN.* 1996 Jan/Feb.; 81(1): 2. Lang.: Eng.
USA: New York, NY. 1996. Historical studies. ■The occasion of Carol Channing's 4,500th performance in the title role of *Hello, Dolly!* at the Lunt-Fontanne Theatre.

3974 Nachman, Gerald. "42nd St. Moon Shines on Bay Area." *TheaterW.* 1996 July 15; 9(50): 24-28. Illus.: Photo. B&W. 4. Lang.: Eng.
USA: San Francisco, CA. 1989-1996. Historical studies. ■Artistic directors of 42nd St. Moon theatre Greg MacKellan and Stephanie Rhoads discuss the company's success and its dedication to reviving musicals rarely produced.

3975 Ostrow, Stuart. "Best Assistant Choreographer: Remembering the Original *Chicago.*" *TheaterW.* 1996 Nov 11; 10(15): 48-49. Illus.: Photo. B&W. 1. Lang.: Eng.
USA: New York, NY. 1975. Histories-sources. ■Excerpt from Ostrow's forthcoming book *The Broadway Musical Canon: Mid-Century to the Millenium* (Praeger). Author's experience in assisting Bob Fosse with original production.

3976 Pesner, Ben. "Reg E. Gaines: The Text as Tap Dancing's Evil Twin." *DGQ.* 1996 Sum; 33(2): 10-14. Lang.: Eng.
USA: New York, NY. 1996. Histories-sources. ■Interview with Gaines, text writer of *Bring in 'Da Noise, Bring in 'Da Funk*, discussing the problem of balancing text with dancing.

3977 Pigarev, A. "Chrustal'nye tufel'ki dlja Zoluški." (Glass Slippers for Cinderella.) *My.* 1996; 6: 128-134. Lang.: Rus.
USA: New York, NY. 1970-1996. Biographical studies. ■Pop star Mariah Carey.

3978 Scott, Andrue. "Sandra Church: Knowing When to Leave." *ShowM.* 1996/97 Win; 12(4): 40-42, 58-59. Illus.: Photo. B&W. 6. Lang.: Eng.
USA. 1954-1964. Historical studies. ■Profile of the career of actor/singer/dancer Sandra Church, covering her training and early career, her creation of the title role in *Gypsy*, and her subsequent stage and film career and retirement from acting in 1964.

3979 Shenton, Mark. "At Long Last Elaine." *TheaterW.* 1996 Sep 16; 10(6): 18-20. Illus.: Photo. B&W. 1. Lang.: Eng.
USA: New York, NY. UK-England: London. 1996. Biographical studies. ■Actress/singer Elaine Page, who created the majority of the female leads in Andrew Lloyd Webber's musicals, comes to Broadway to appear in Lloyd Webber's *Sunset Boulevard*.

3980 Sherman, Howard. "The Rock and Show Tune Hall of (Little-Known) Fame." *ShowM.* 1996 Spr; 12(1): 19-22. Illus.: Photo. Dwg. B&W. 7. Lang.: Eng.
USA. England. 1967-1992. Historical studies. ■A survey of show-tunes recorded by rock singers for popular release.

MUSIC-DRAMA: Musical theatre—Performance/production

3981 Viagas, Robert. "Something Wonderful: Donna Murphy becomes Mrs. Anna." *ShowM*. 1996 Spr; 12(1): 39-42. Illus.: Photo. B&W. 6. Lang.: Eng.
USA. 1991-1996. Historical studies. ■A profile of the career of actress/singer Donna Murphy, with an emphasis on her leading role in the upcoming Broadway revival of Rodgers and Hammerstein's *The King and I*.

3982 Warren, Charmaine Patricia. "Henry Le Tang: Seven Decades of Tap and Still Counting." *BlackM*. 1996 Nov/Dec.; 12(2): 7-8, 18. Illus.: Photo. Design. B&W. 1. Lang.: Eng.
USA: New York, NY. 1915-1996. Biographical studies. ■Career of veteran tap-dancer Henry Le Tang.

Plays/librettos/scripts

3983 Makeham, Paul. "Singing the Landscape: Bran Nue Dae." *ADS*. 1996 Apr.; 28: 117-132. Notes. Lang.: Eng.
Australia. 1995. Critical studies. ■The musical drama *Bran Nue Dae* by Jimmy Chi and the band 'Kuckles': its celebration of the Aborigines' survival of and resistance to the white culture.

3984 Anderson, Robert. "The Muses of Chaos and Destruction of *Arena conta Zumbi*." *LATR*. 1996 Spr; 29(2): 15-28. Notes. Biblio. Lang.: Eng.
Brazil: São Paulo. 1965-1967. Historical studies. ■Explains the success of the epic musical *Arena conta Zumbi (Arena Tells Zumbi's Story)*, an early production by Augusto Boal, Gianfrancesco Guarnieri, and Teatro Arena, in spite of what some critics term its 'fragility.' It was successful in producing chaos in the theatre, in the Boalian sense of destroying existing theatrical codes.

3985 Chang, Lan-joo. "Musical Sooip, Udduge Padadlil Kusinga." (How to Deal With Import of Musicals.) *KTR*. 1996 Mar.; 21(3): 30-33. Illus.: Photo. B&W. 5. Lang.: Kor.
Korea: Seoul. 1996. Critical studies. ■The importation of American musicals such as *Annie* and *The Phantom of the Opera* into Korea, the need to adapt the storyline and words for Korean culture, and the special technical requirements for administration and crews.

3986 Backalenick, Irene. "*By Jeeves!* They've Finally Got It. An Interview with Alan Ayckbourn." *TheaterW*. 1996 Nov 4; 10 (14): 25-32. Illus.: Photo. B&W. 4. Lang.: Eng.
UK-England: London. 1996. Historical studies. ■Playwright Ayckbourn discusses his collaboration with Andrew Lloyd Webber and the development and eventual production of their musical *By Jeeves*, based on stories by P.G. Wodehouse.

3987 Coen, Stephanie. "How to Make a Musical." *AmTh*. 1996 Jan.; 13(1): 26-29. Illus.: Photo. B&W. 6. Lang.: Eng.
USA: New York, NY, Denver, CO. 1996. Historical studies. ■The Harold Prince Musical Theatre Program, an alliance between the Directors Company of New York and Denver Center for the Performing Arts, and its goal of developing new musicals for the American stage by involving the director early in the collaborative process. Workshop and training techniques, participation of designers.

3988 Davis, Lee. "Bring on the Reprises." *ShowM*. 1996/97 Win; 12(4): 18-22. Illus.: Photo. B&W. 6. Lang.: Eng.
USA: New York, NY. 1996. Critical studies. ■Proposes ten musicals for revival: *Annie Get Your Gun, One Touch of Venus, Finian's Rainbow, On the Town, Kiss Me, Kate, A Connecticut Yankee, Lady in the Dark, Very Warm for May, Fiorello!*, and *Follies*.

3989 Frankel, Haskel; Kreuger, Miles; Gershwin, Ira; McClung, Bruce D. "Ira Gershwin—100 Years." *KWN*. 1996 Fall; 14(2): 4-12 . Notes. MU. Illus.: Photo. Dwg. B&W. 10. Lang.: Eng.
USA. 1937-1945. Historical studies. ■A series of short essays detailing Ira Gershwin's work with Kurt Weill on theatre and film projects.

3990 Horwitz, Simi. "Cowgirls Creator Mary Murfitt." *TheaterW*. 1996 June 10; 9(45): 24-31. Illus.: Photo. B&W. 3. Lang.: Eng.
USA: New York, NY. 1996. Biographical studies. ■Composer/lyricist of country-western musical *Cowgirls* discusses the show (directed by Eleanor Reissa), influences on her writing, casting of the production, audience response.

3991 Jones, Chris. "C'est Les Guerres." *AmTh*. 1996 Oct.; 13(8): 10-11. Illus.: Photo. B&W. 2. Lang.: Eng.
USA. 1996. Critical studies. ■Adaptations of the 16th-century French tale of Martin Guerre: *Martin Guerre*, music, book and lyrics by Laura Harrington, music by Roger Ames, *Martin Guerre*, by Alain Boublil and Claude-Michel Schönberg, and *The House of Martin Guerre* music and lyrics by Leslie Arden, book co-authored by Anna Theresa Cascio.

3992 Marans, Jon. "Playwright Jon Marans Talks About *Old Wicked Songs*." *TheaterW*. 1996 Nov 18; 10(16): 53-54. Illus.: Photo. B&W. 1. Lang.: Eng.
USA: New York, NY. 1996. Histories-sources. ■Author discusses his sources for his musical *Old Wicked Songs* directed by Seth Barrish.

3993 Mates, Julian. "Experiments on the American Musical Stage in the Twenties." *JADT*. 1996 Spr; 8(2): 12-25. Notes. Lang.: Eng.
USA. 1920-1929. Historical studies. ■The musical theatre world of the 1920s: female playwrights such as Anne Caldwell and Fanny Todd Mitchell, lyricists Dorothy Fields and Dorothy Donnell, Black theatre such as Sissle and Blake's *Shuffle Along*, and revues, vaudeville and burlesque. Important experiments in the musical theatre form include Kern's *Show Boat*.

3994 McNicholl, BT. "The Invisible Tracks of Michael Stewart, Part II." *ShowM*. 1996 Spr; 12(1): 43-48, 65-66. Illus.: Photo. B&W. 8. Lang.: Eng.
USA. UK-England. 1970-1987. Historical studies. ■Continuation of a two-part overview of the career of librettist/lyricist Michael Stewart, covering the years and the shows between 1970 and his death in 1987.

3995 Swarbrick, Carol. "Apples, Oranges and Theatre: An Interview with Albert Hague." *EN*. 1996 Nov.; 81(9): 3, 8. Illus.: Photo. 1. Lang.: Eng.
USA: New York, NY. 1960-1996. Histories-sources. ■Interview with musical theatre composer, actor and teacher Albert Hague on his career in theatre, and his views and advice on the audition process.

3996 Toomer, Jeanette. "Vy Higgensen: Let the Music Play Gospel." *BlackM*. 1996 Nov/Dec.; 12(2): 5-6, 19. Illus.: Photo. Design. B&W. 2. Lang.: Eng.
USA: New York, NY. 1970-1996. Biographical studies. ■Career of playwright/lyricist Vy Higgensen, and her plays *Mama, I Want to Sing* and *Born to Sing*.

3997 Viagas, Robert. "Chasing a Rainbow: The Determination of Larry Grossman." *ShowM*. 1996 Sum; 12(2): 27-30. Illus.: Photo. B&W. 6. Lang.: Eng.
USA. 1970-1996. Historical studies. ■Profile of the career of composer Larry Grossman, discussing his techniques in writing theatre music and the contrast between his failures in the theatre and his successes in television and film.

3998 Viagas, Robert. "The Fantastick Career of Jones & Schmidt." *ShowM*. 1996 Fall; 12(3): 12-18, 69-70. Illus.: Photo. B&W. 10. Lang.: Eng.
USA. 1960-1996. Historical studies. ■A profile of the later career of the team of composer Harvey Schmidt and lyricist/librettist Tom Jones, focusing on their less-known work since 1970, primarily *Colette Collage, Grover's Corners*, and their current *Mirette*.

3999 Wallach, Allan. "A League of Her Own: Mary Rodgers Strikes Back." *TheaterW*. 1996 Dec 9; 10(19): 45-47. Illus.: Photo. B&W. 1. Lang.: Eng.
USA: New York, NY. 1959-1996. Biographical studies. ■Musical author Rodgers discusses relationship with her father, (musical author Richard Rodgers) and current revival of her musical *Once Upon a Mattress*, book by Jay Thompson, Marshall Barer and Dean Fuller, on Broadway.

4000 Wolf, Stacy. "The Queer Pleasures of Mary Martin and Broadway: *The Sound of Music* as a Lesbian Musical." *MD*. 1996 Spr ; 39(1): 51-63. Notes. Lang.: Eng.
USA. 1938-1959. Critical studies. ■Feminist and lesbian reading of the role of Maria in *The Sound of Music*, and of the personal life and career of actress Martin.

MUSIC-DRAMA: Musical theatre

Relation to other fields

4001   Markiewicz, Lily. "*Murx*: Berliner Volksbühne." *PerfR*. 1996 Spr; 1(1): 47-51. Notes. Illus.: Photo. B&W. 1. Lang.: Eng.
Germany: Berlin. UK-England: London. 1992-1995. Critical studies. ■The political implications of Christoph Marthaler's *Murx*, directed by Heiner Goebbels: the use of folk songs and Nazi imagery said to point to fascism in German culture. With discussion of problems of translation, relation of music and text.

Theory/criticism

4002   Smart, Jeffrey. "Labels Are Not Characters: Critical Misrepresentation of *Falsettoland*." *JDTC*. 1996 Spr; 10(2): 61-74 . Notes. Lang.: Eng.
USA. 1990. Critical studies. ■Criticism of William Finn and James Lapine's musical *Falsettoland*. Argues that critics have failed to examine the characters, instead relying on stereotypes of homosexuality.

Opera

Administration

4003   Kandel, Jonathan. "New Beat in Buenos Aires: With Argentina's Economy Back on Track, Business is Booming at the Teatro Colón." *OpN*. 1996 Sep.; 61(3): 56-57. Illus.: Photo. Color. 2. Lang.: Eng.
Argentina: Buenos Aires. 1989-1996. Biographical studies. ■The career of Sergio Renán as general manager and artistic director of the Teatro Colón, Buenos Aires.

4004   Citron, Paula. "Debut: Ken Freeman." *OC*. 1996 Spr; 37(1): 11. Illus.: Photo. B&W. 7. Lang.: Eng.
Canada: Hamilton, ON. 1970-1996. Critical studies. ■Profile of Opera Hamilton's general director Ken Freeman. Emphasis on his involvement with Opera Ontario, his prior position with the Virginia Opera and the importance of attracting a wider opera audience.

4005   McGeary, Thomas. "The Opera Accounts of Sir Robert Walpole." *Restor*. 1996 Sum; 11(1): 1-9. Notes. Append. Lang.: Eng.
England: London. 1719-1734. Historical studies. ■Household account book of shareholder in Royal Academy of Music detailing attendance and patronage of Italian opera in England. Includes appendix listing excerpts from account book itself.

4006   Waleson, Heidi. "Charting the Classics: The First Flush of CD Enthusiasm Is Giving Way to More Realistic Market Expectations." *OpN*. 1996 Oct.; 61(4): 16-19, 64. Illus.: Photo. Color. 7. Lang.: Eng.
Europe. North America. 1996. Historical studies. ■The marketing approaches of CD companies, with emphasis on their operatic offerings. Includes comments on and by marketing directors of major record companies.

4007   Brug, Manuel; Zimmermann, Monika. "Künstler, im Machtkampf." (Artists in Power Struggle.) *DB*. 1996; 6: 22-25. Append. Illus.: Photo. B&W. 3. Lang.: Ger.
Germany: Berlin. 1996. Histories-sources. ■Interview with conductor Christian Thielemann, new music director of Deutsche Oper, about his plans and the public accusations regarding his political opinions.

4008   Kranz, Dieter. "Kunst unterm Rohstift." (Art under Dramatic Cutbacks.) *DB*. 1996; 11: 10-13. Illus.: Photo. B&W. Color. 2. Lang.: Ger.
Germany: Berlin. 1996. Historical studies. ■Effect of budget cuts on Berlin opera houses: Deutsche Oper, Deutsche Staatsoper, Komische Oper.

4009   Steensen, Steen Christian. "Den tyske operascene." (The German Opera Scene.) *TE*. 1996 Apr.; 78: 7-9. Illus.: Photo. B&W. 1. Lang.: Dan.
Germany. 1993-1996. Historical studies. ■The cultural crisis of opera in the face of competition from other forms and the media.

4010   Szomory, György. "Leköszönő főigazgató: Ütő Endre." (Resigning Director: Endre Ütő.) *OperaL*. 1996; 5(3): 2-3. Illus.: Photo. B&W. 1. Lang.: Hun.
Hungary: Budapest. 1990-1995. Histories-sources. ■A conversation with bass Endre Ütő surveying his five and a half years' activity as director of the Budapest Opera House.

4011   Szomory, György. "Főigazgató: Szinetár Miklós." (Director: Miklós Szinetár.) *OperaL*. 1996; 5(4): 3-5. Illus.: Photo. B&W. 1. Lang.: Hun.
Hungary: Budapest. 1996. Histories-sources. ■Conversation with the newly appointed director of the Budapest Opera House.

4012   Eriksson, Torbjörn. "In memoria." *MuD*. 1996; 18(1): 43. Lang.: Swe.
Sweden. 1950-1996. Biographical studies. ■Two brief portraits of the producer Gertrud Sivall, one of the creators of Stockholms MusikDramatiska Ensemble, and the musicologist Gisela Tamsen, specialist on German operatic life.

Design/technology

4013   Lampert-Gréaux, Ellen. "Silver Screen, Golden West." *TCI*. 1996 Aug/Sep.; 30(7): 9. Illus.: Photo. Color. 1. Lang.: Eng.
Belgium: Antwerp. 1996. Technical studies. ■Designer Paul Steinberg's golden-era cinema style sets for the Flemish National Opera's production of Puccini's *La Fanciulla del West* directed by Robert Carsen.

4014   Hogan, Jane. "Shaker Heights." *TCI*. 1996 Feb.; 30(2): 20. Illus.: Sketches. B&W. 1. Lang.: Eng.
Canada: Toronto, ON. 1996. Technical studies. ■Allen Moyer's set and costume design for the Canadian Opera Company's production of Wagner's *Der Fliegende Holländer* at the O'Keefe Centre.

4015   Sørensen, Lilo. "'Jeg kan godt lide opera'—publikummets kontante afregning...." ('I like opera': The Immediate Reaction of the Audience.) *TE*. 1996 Dec.; 81-82: 4-7. Illus.: Photo. B&W. 2. Lang.: Dan.
Denmark: Copenhagen. 1996. Histories-sources. ■An interview with Nina Flagstad on her set design for Alban Berg's opera *Lulu* staged at Christiansborg Ridehus in the summer of 1996.

4016   Butzmann, Volker. "Die Soldaten." (The Soldiers.) *BtR*. 1996; 1: 29-32. Append. Illus.: Design. Photo. B&W. Color. 14. Lang.: Ger.
Germany: Dresden. 1995-1996. Histories-sources. ■Technical director for Bernd Alois Zimmermann's *Die Soldaten*, directed by Willy Decker, at Semper Oper describes the problems of an overly large orchestra on stage and the sound and space requirements.

4017   Hase, Thomas. "Designing with 'Team Toelstede'." *LDim*. 1996 Nov.; 20(9): 92-97. Illus.: Photo. Color. B&W. 6. Lang.: Eng.
Germany: Cologne. 1996. Technical studies. ■Career of lighting designer Hans Toelstede: training, his work for Cologne Opera, techniques.

4018   Loney, Glenn. "Munich Festival Modernism." *TCI*. 1996 Jan.; 30(1): 19-20. Illus.: Photo. Color. 3. Lang.: Eng.
Germany: Munich. 1995. Technical studies. ■Post-modernist look created for *Don Giovanni* by designer Bob Crowley at the 1995 Munich Festival, and other designs on display there.

4019   Loney, Glenn. "Unfaithful *Fidelio*." *TCI*. 1996 May; 30(5): 31-32. Illus.: Photo. Color. B&W. 2. Lang.: Eng.
Germany: Bregenz. 1996. Technical studies. ■Massive scenic elements employed in director David Pountney and set designer Stefanos Lazarides' controversial production of Beethoven's *Fidelio* at the Bregenz Festival.

4020   Kelemen, László H. "Ötven esztendő az Operaházban." (Fifty Years with the Opera House.) *OperaL*. 1996; 5(4): 22-24. Illus.: Photo. B&W. 1. Lang.: Hun.
Hungary. 1942-1996. Biographical studies. ■Portrait of the chief stage-inspector György Földvári who has been member of the Budapest Opera House for fifty years.

4021   Szomory, György. "'...vizuálisan is felépíteni a zenei folyamat ívét!' - Díszlettervező: Csikós Attila." ('To Construct the Arch of the Musical Process in a Visual Way'—Stage Designer: Attila Csikós.) *OperaL*. 1996; 5(3): 15-19. Illus.: Photo. Sketches. B&W. 2. Lang.: Hun.
Hungary: Budapest. 1969-1996. Histories-sources. ■The renowned stage designer has been working at the Budapest Opera House—with a short interruption—for 27 years and its leading stage designer since 1989.

MUSIC-DRAMA: Opera—Design/technology

4022 Clark, Mike. "In the Verona Arena." *LDim.* 1996 Mar.; 20(2): 67-69, 72. Illus.: Photo. Color. 6. Lang.: Eng.
Italy: Verona. 1996. Technical studies. ■Paolo Mazzon's lighting design for operas in the ancient Verona Arena. Challenges of lighting in the outdoor venue, his background and training, working with the music.

4023 Vanečkina, I.L. "O svetovoj scenografii opery B. Bartoka 'Zamok gercoga Sinjaja Boroda'." (Lighting for Bartók's Opera *Bluebeard's Castle*.) 71-73 in *Elektronika, muzyka, svet.* Kazan: FEN; 1996. 299 pp. Lang.: Rus.
Russia. 1990-1996. Historical studies. ■Stage lighting for a production of *A Kékszakállú herceg vára* by Béla Bartók.

4024 Hogan, Jane. "Protecting a Lost World." *LDim.* 1996 Jan.; 20(1): 12-13. Illus.: Photo. Color. 2. Lang.: Eng.
USA. 1996. Technical studies. ■Set and projection designer John Boesche's work for Austin Lyric Opera's production of Wagner's *Tannhäuser*.

4025 Lampert-Gréaux, Ellen. "Command Performance." *LDim.* 1996 Oct.; 20(8): 32-33. Illus.: Lighting. B&W. 1. Lang.: Eng.
USA: New York, NY. 1996. Technical studies. ■Renovation of the Metropolitan Opera House's lighting system. Includes equipment list.

4026 Lampert-Gréaux, Ellen. "Revolutionary Opera." *TCI.* 1996 Oct.; 30(8): 8-9. Illus.: Photo. Color. 1. Lang.: Eng.
USA: New York, NY. 1996. Technical studies. ■Minimalist set and costumes by designer Hubert Monloup for the Metropolitan Opera's 1996-1997 season opener, Umberto Giordano's *Andrea Chénier*.

4027 Lampert-Gréaux, Ellen. "Baby Doe Re Mi." *TCI.* 1996 Nov.; 30(9): 9-11. Illus.: Photo. Color. 1. Lang.: Eng.
USA: Central City, CO. 1996. Technical studies. ■Designer Michael Anania's sets for the Central City Opera's fortieth anniversary production of *The Ballad of Baby Doe* by Douglas Moore.

4028 Loney, Glenn. "Valhalla on a Budget." *LDim.* 1996 Sep.; 20(7): 27. Illus.: Photo. Color. 1. Lang.: Eng.
USA: Flagstaff, AZ. 1996. Technical studies. ■Wagner's *Ring Cycle* presented by Arizona Opera, set design by Amy Shock, lighting design by Russell Stagg. Collaboration with director Henry Holt, colors and images used.

4029 Stearns, David Patrick. "New Cues: What to Look for in This Season's Met Productions." *OpN.* 1996 Sep.; 61(3): 20-22. Illus.: Dwg. Lang.: Eng.
USA: New York, NY. 1996. Historical studies. ■New approaches to opera design at the Metropolitan Opera: to ensure financial returns, the company is looking for 'progressive but not radical' productions.

Institutions

4030 Koltai, Tamás. "Fesztiválopera—Bregenz, Salzburg, Bayreuth." (Festival Opera—Bregenz, Salzburg, Bayreuth.) *Sz.* 1996; 29(11): 10-15. Illus.: Photo. B&W. 8. Lang.: Hun.
Austria: Bregenz, Salzburg. Germany: Bayreuth. 1996. Critical studies. ■An account of the summer opera festivals in Europe.

4031 Loney, Glenn. "Freedom: From Fidelio to Porgy in Bregenz." *WES.* 1996 Spr; 8(2): 81-86. Illus.: Photo. 2. Lang.: Eng.
Austria: Bregenz. 1995. Historical studies. ■Account of the Bregenz Festival and its production of Beethoven's *Fidelio* directed by David Pountney and an advance peek at the 1997 production, Gershwin's *Porgy and Bess*.

4032 Bernstein, Tamara. "Opera on The Cutting Edge." *OC.* 1996 Sum; 37(2): 20-23. Illus.: Photo. B&W. 1. Lang.: Eng.
Canada: Toronto, ON. 1994-1996. Critical studies. ■Profile of Autumn Leaf Performance, with emphasis on founder and director Thom Sokolowski and the company's dedication to the development of innovative Canadian opera.

4033 Citron, Paula. "Tuning a New Generation." *OC.* 1996 Sum; 37(2): 12-16. Illus.: Photo. B&W. 7. Lang.: Eng.
Canada. 1996. Historical studies. ■Children's programs organized by opera companies in an effort to build a new audience, including the Canadian Opera Company's Create An Opera program, the Adopt-A-School program and the Canadian Children's Opera Chorus.

4034 Jordan, Robert. "Victoria Victorious." *OC.* 1996 Win; 37(4): 14-17. Illus.: Photo. B&W. 4. Lang.: Eng.

Canada: Victoria, BC. 1980-1996. Critical studies. ■Profile of the Pacific Opera Victoria. Emphasis on the artistic director Timothy Vernon's directorial vision, the company's financial restraints, and its premiere productions of Benjamin Britten's *A Midsummer Night's Dream* and Italo Montemezzi's *L'Amore dei Tre Re.*

4035 Klett, Renate. "Glauben heisst hoffen." (To Believe Means to Hope.) *THeute.* 1996; 5: 33-34. Illus.: Photo. B&W. 1. Lang.: Ger.
China, People's Republic of: Hong Kong. 1996. Historical studies. ■The Canadian Opera Company's production of *Bluebeard's Castle (A kékszakállú herceg vára)* and *Erwartung*, directed by Robert Lepage, described as the highlight of the Hong Kong Arts Festival.

4036 Pistone, Danièle; Glasow, E. Thomas, transl. "Opera in Paris During the Roaring Twenties." *OQ.* 1996/97 Win; 13(2): 55-67. Notes. Lang.: Eng.
France: Paris. 1920-1929. Historical studies. ■The emphasis on opera in Parisian theatres, with a chronology of the operas performed at the Opéra-Comique and Paris Opéra.

4037 Reilly, Patricia. "City of Music." *OpN.* 1996 May; 60(16): 23. Illus.: Photo. Color. 1. Lang.: Eng.
France: Paris. 1996. Historical studies. ■The Cité de la Musique, newly opened at the Parc de la Villette, a low-income area, aims to attract a varied audience. Comments on its first year and future plans.

4038 Sevilla-Gonzaga, Marylis. "The Boss: In the Past Thirty Years, the Paris Opera Has Had More Than Twenty Administrations. Will Hugues Gall Succeed in Implementing a Coherent Policy?" *OpN.* 1996 May; 60(16): 17-20. Illus.: Photo. B&W. Color. 10. Lang.: Eng.
France: Paris. 1996. Histories-sources. ■Interview with Hugues Gall, new director of the restructured Opéra National de Paris, consisting of the Opéra Bastille and the Palais Garnier. American James Conlon is the new principal conductor, and Christine Bullin supervisor of the Centre de Formation Lyrique, the young artists program.

4039 Zalesova-Doktorova, L. "Dva večera v opere." (Two Nights at the Opera.) *Zvezda.* 1996; 10: 234-235. Lang.: Rus.
France: Paris. 1862-1996. Historical studies. ■Notes on the history of the Paris Grand Opera.

4040 Balogh, Anikó. "Bayreuth '96." *OperaL.* 1996; 5(5): 21-24. Illus.: Photo. B&W. 3. Lang.: Hun.
Germany: Bayreuth. 1996. Reviews of performances. ■A short review about the novelty of the festival.

4041 Brandenburg, Detlef. "Tristan und der Träumer." (Tristan and the Dreamer.) *DB.* 1996; 12: 25-28. Illus.: Pntg. Photo. B&W. 4. Lang.: Ger.
Germany: Munich. 1996. Historical studies. ■The reopening of the Prinzregententheater with Wagner's *Tristan und Isolde*, with emphasis on director August Everding's success in raising funds for the production.

4042 Hegedorn, Volker. "Zwei stolze Schwestern." (Two Proud Sisters.) *DB.* 1996; 8: 28-30. Illus.: Photo. B&W. 2. Lang.: Ger.
Germany: Dresden, Leipzig. 1996. Historical studies. ■The competition between opera theatres Oper Leipzig and Sächsische Staatsoper in Dresden.

4043 Cenner, Mihály. "A száműzöttek színházáról–Az OMIKE Művészakció (1939-1944) I." (The Theatre of the Exiled: The OMIKE Artists' Enterprise, 1939-1944.) *OperaL.* 1996; 5(4): 26-32. Illus.: Photo. Handbill. Dwg. B&W. 9. Lang.: Hun.
Hungary: Budapest. 1939-1944. Historical studies. ■The OMIKE Artists' Enterprise, under the aegis of the already existing Hungarian Jewish Cultural Association, provided work and livelihood for Jewish artists and administrative and technical staff dismissed from the Budapest Opera as a result of racial laws in 1939. Performances were given in Goldmark Hall until the occupation of Hungary. Continued in *OperaL* 5:5 (1996), 26-31.

4044 Hollósi, Zsolt. "Új zeneigazgató Szegeden." (A New Musical Director at Szeged.) *OperaL.* 1996; 5(3): 28-30. Illus.: Photo. B&W. 1. Lang.: Hun.

MUSIC-DRAMA: Opera—Institutions

Hungary: Szeged. 1975-1996. Histories-sources. ■Interview with Tamás Pál, newly appointed musical director of Szeged National Theatre, a post he held 1975 to 1983.

4045 Németh, Amadé. "Volt egyszer egy Gördülő Opera." (Once Upon a Time There Was an 'Opera on Rails'.) *OperaL.* 1996; 5(3): 24-27. Illus.: Photo. B&W. 3. Lang.: Hun.
Hungary: Budapest. 1945-1954. Historical studies. ■History of a touring operatic company, Gördülő Opera, that brought opera productions to provincial towns before the development of regional opera ensembles. Continued in *OperaL* 5:4 (1996), 14-17 and 5:5 (1996), 13-16.

4046 Szomory, György. "Megbízott főigazgató: Dr. Venczel Sándor." (Commissioned Director: Dr. Sándor Venczel.) *OperaL.* 1996; 5(2): 3-4. Illus.: Photo. B&W. 1. Lang.: Hun.
Hungary: Budapest. 1996. Histories-sources. ■Interview with the newly appointed director *pro tem* of the Budapest Opera House on the financial and structural problems and future plans.

4047 Larsson, Henry. "Wexford—mot alla odds." (Wexford—Against All Odds.) *MuD.* 1996; 18(5): 22-24. Illus.: Photo. B&W. Lang.: Swe.
Ireland: Wexford. 1951-1996. Historical studies. ■A presentation of the opera festival at Wexford, with references to Zdenek Fibich's *Sarka* staged by Inga Levant, and Meyerbeer's *L'étoile du Nord* staged by Giovanni di Cicco.

4048 Bruls, Willem. *Fotojaarboek seizoen 1995-1996. De Nederlandse Opera.* (Photo Yearbook 1995-1996: De Nederlandse Opera.) Amsterdam: De Nederlandse Opera; 1996. 96 pp. Illus.: Photo. Poster. Color. B&W. 80. Lang.: Dut.
Netherlands: Amsterdam. 1995-1996. Histories-sources. ■Photos of the Netherlands Opera season.

4049 Honig, Piet Hein. *Annalen van de operagezelschappen in Nederland, 1886-1995.* (Annals of the Opera Companies of the Netherlands, 1886-1995.) Amsterdam: Theater Instituut Nederland/De Nederlandse Opera; 1996. 1276 pp. Illus.: Design. Graphs. Handbill. Graphs. Dwg. Poster. Photo. B&W. 840. Lang.: Dut.
Netherlands. 1886-1995. Histories-specific. ■History of Dutch opera companies.

4050 Mansell, Wendy. "Opera on Vacation." *OC.* 1996 Spr; 37(1): 14-15. Lang.: Eng.
North America. Europe. 1996. Histories-sources. ■International guide to 1996 summer opera festivals.

4051 Tranberg, Sören. "Bjørn med Manifest." (Bjørn with the Manifesto.) *MuD.* 1996; 18(3): 14-17. Illus.: Photo. B&W. Lang.: Swe.
Norway: Oslo. 1984. Histories-sources. ■An interview with Bjørn Simensen, the new theatre manager at Den Norske Opera, about his ideas to vitalize the Norwegian opera.

4052 Lagina, N. "Ljubov' vo vlasti t'my: 'Aida' v 'Gelikonopere'." (Love in the Power of Darkness: *Aida* at Gelikonopera.) *MuZizn.* 1996; 3-4: 7-9. Lang.: Rus.
Russia: Moscow. 1990-1996. Historical studies. ■Profile of the new Gelikonopera, Dmitrij Bertman, artistic director.

4053 Petrov, I.; Kurcman, A., ed. "Vernut' tradicii v Bolšoj teat'r." (To Return Traditions to the Bolšoj Theatre.) *MuZizn.* 1996; 3-4: 24-25. Lang.: Rus.
Russia: Moscow. 1995-1996. Critical studies. ■Thoughts on the future of the Bolšoj Opera.

4054 Rojtman, Jurij. "'Ne vnemlja kritike surovoj...'." (Not Paying Attention to Harsh Criticism.) *TeatZ.* 1996; 11-12: 36-39 . Lang.: Rus.
Russia: Moscow. 1990-1996. Historical studies. ■Profile of the Moscow municipal theatre Novaja Opera, directed by Jévgenij Kolobov.

4055 Bergström, Gunnel. "Det har hänt något vidunderligt på Stockholmsoperan." (Something Marvelous Has Happened at the Stockholm Opera.) *MuD.* 1996; 18(3): 26-27. Illus.: Photo. B&W. Lang.: Swe.
Sweden: Stockholm. 1996. Historical studies. ■A survey of the repertory of Kungliga Teatern, the Royal Swedish Opera, with reference to the suc-

cessful staging by Ann-Margret Pettersson of *Die Tote Stadt* by Erich Wolfgang Korngold, and to the new artistic manager Walton Grönroos.

4056 Bergström, Gunnel. "Opera på låtsas eller i grym samtid." (Opera as Make Believe or as Cruel Contemporary History.) *MuD.* 1996; 18(5): 30-32. Illus.: Photo. B&W. Color. Lang.: Swe.
Sweden: Stockholm. 1996. Critical studies. ■A critical view of the Royal Swedish Opera compared to Folkoperan's musically and scenically striking performances, with references to *Boris Godunov* staged by Knut Henriksen and Staffan Valdemar Holm's staging of *Carmen*.

4057 Feltzin, Per; Graune, Erik; Lundberg, Camilla; Ericson, Barbro; Bergström, Gunnel. "Operan—för vem?" (The Operan—for Whom?)*MuD.* 1996; 18(4): 7-10, 47. Illus.: Photo. Dwg. B&W. Lang.: Swe.
Sweden: Stockholm. 1976. Histories-sources. ■Journalists, singers, directors give their views of Kungliga Teatern (The Royal Swedish Opera) today compared with twenty years ago.

4058 Tiselius, Henric. "Barock multimedia." (Baroque Multi Media.) *Tningen.* 1996; 20(79): 42-43. Illus.: Photo. Color. Lang.: Swe.
Sweden: Gothenburg. 1990. Historical studies. ■A presentation of Utomjordiska Barockbolaget, and their founders Mikael Paulsson and Johann Nordqvist, with reference to their new production of Monteverdi's madrigals *Joystick*.

4059 Ramsden, Timothy. "Buxton Festival 96." *PlPl.* 1996 Aug/Sep.: 43. Lang.: Eng.
UK-England: Buxton. 1996. Critical studies. ■Profile of the 1996 Buxton Festival with references to the Dublin Opera Theatre Company's production of Handel's *Amadigi* and the Ensemble of the Golden Age recital.

4060 Albright, William. "Southwest Passage: Dallas Opera Celebrates Its Fortieth Anniversary." *OpN.* 1996 Nov.; 61(5): 36-38. Illus.: Photo. B&W. Color. 4. Lang.: Eng.
USA: Dallas, TX. 1957-1996. Historical studies. ■History of the Dallas Opera (known as the Dallas Civic Opera until 1982) with special mention of Maria Callas, Lawrence Kelly, Nicola Rescigno, and Plato Karyanis, its general director since 1977.

4061 Di Virgilio, Nicholas. "Director's Notebook: Y.O.P.E.: Youth Opera Preparation and Education." *OJ.* 1996 Dec.; 29(4): 43-48. Lang.: Eng.
USA. 1991-1995. Histories-sources. ■Nicholas Di Virgilio, the artistic director of YOPE, or Youth Opera Preparation and Education, headquartered at the University of Ilinois. A traveling workshop in opera production, singing styles, make-up and pantomime, YOPE educates students on opera in both elementary and secondary schools.

4062 Duncan, Scott. "The A-List: In Its First Decade, Los Angeles Music Center Opera Has Become a Major Force in the City's Cultural Life." *OpN.* 1996 Mar 30; 60(14): 20-23. Illus.: Photo. Color. 7. Lang.: Eng.
USA: Los Angeles, CA. 1986-1996. Historical studies. ■The development of the Los Angeles Music Center Opera. Its relationship to the Hollywood community, its repertory, and the involvement of Plácido Domingo as singer, conductor and advisor.

4063 Glasow, E. Thomas. "From Under a Green Eyeshade." *OQ.* 1996 Fall; 13(1): 1-4. Lang.: Eng.
USA. 1996. Histories-sources. ■Reaffirmation of the *Opera Quarterly's* mission to provide a variety of informative and entertaining texts, and a critique of new recording technology and its effect on the future of opera.

4064 Kellow, Brian. "Portland's Progress: Opera in Oregon's Coming of Age." *OpN.* 1996 Nov.; 61(5): 40-41. Illus.: Photo. Color. 3. Lang.: Eng.
USA: Portland, OR. 1982-1996. Historical studies. ■The Portland Opera, now in its thirty-second season, has an adventurous repertoire under the direction of Robert Bailey, who succeeded Stefan Minde.

4065 Kennicott, Philip. "Motown Miracle: Against All Odds, Detroit's Michigan Opera Theatre Is Opening a New Opera House This April." *OpN.* 1996 Mar 30; 60(14): 32-33. Illus.: Photo. Color. 4. Lang.: Eng.

MUSIC-DRAMA: Opera—Institutions

USA: Detroit, MI. 1970-1995. Historical studies. ■The Michigan Opera of Detroit is building a new house, the Michigan Opera Theatre, under General Director David DiChiera.

4066   Ruling, Karl G. "Opera Company of Philadelphia." *TCI.* 1996 Mar.; 30(3): 28-29. Illus.: Photo. Dwg. Color. 2. Lang.: Eng.

USA: Philadelphia, PA. 1990-1995. Technical studies. ■The company's creation of its own scene shop as part of efforts to achieve financial stability.

Performance spaces

4067   Edström, Per Simon. "Om akustik för musikteater och särskilt då om akustik för en utomhus flytande operateater." (A Lecture On Acoustics In Theatres For Musical Performances, In Particular Acoustics In a Floating Open Air Opera.) *ProScen.* 1996; 20(1): 8-12. Illus.: Dwg. B&W. Lang.: Swe, Eng.

Finland: Kastelholm. 1996. Historical studies. ■A proposal for a floating open-air theatre for operatic performances, to be placed just beside Kastelholm, built on the same principle as musical instruments.

4068   Brandenburg, Dieter. "Luxusliner für Hanseaten." (Luxury Liner for Hanseatic People.) *DB.* 1996; 6: 26-29. Illus.: Photo. B&W. 3. Lang.: Ger.

Germany: Lübeck. 1906-1996. Historical studies. ■The reopening of Theater Lübeck, built in the art nouveau style by Martin Dülfer, with a performance of Wagner's *Die Meistersinger.* Discusses the effects of the new architecture and technology.

4069   Reissinger, Marianne. "Prinze und Tristan." ('Prinze' and Tristan.) *DB.* 1996; 4: 24-25. Illus.: Photo. B&W. 2. Lang.: Ger.

Germany: Munich. 1901-1996. Historical studies. ■The reopening of the Prinzregententheater, or Prinze: its structural history and use, and the role of August Everding, former director of Bayerisches Staatsoper.

4070   Weathersby, William, Jr. "Venice Opera House Destroyed by Fire." *TCI.* 1996 Apr.; 30(4): 18. Lang.: Eng.

Italy: Venice. 1996. Historical studies. ■Report on the destruction by fire of Teatro La Fenice in Venice.

4071   Rosenberg, Ulf. "Akustik för musikteater." (An Acoustic For the Music Theatre.) *ProScen.* 1996; 20(3): 14-15. Lang.: Swe.

Sweden. 1996. Historical studies. ■A reply to Per Simon Edström's article on acoustics in *ProScen* 20:1 (1996), 8-12.

Performance/production

4072   Baker, Dennis J. "Problem Child: The Dilemma of Finding an Ideal Salome." *OpN.* 1996 Mar 30; 60(14): 14-17, 43. Illus.: Photo. B&W. Color. 3: cd. Lang.: Eng.

1905-1996. Historical studies. ■The perennial difficulty of casting a suitable soprano for the role of Salome in the eponymous opera by Richard Strauss.

4073   Rosenfeld, Lorraine. "Opera News International Opera Forecast, 1996-1997." *OpN.* 1996 Sep.; 61(3): 30-32, 34-37, 39-40, 42-44, 46, 48-55. Lang.: Eng.

1996-1997. Histories-sources. ■List of 1996-1997 worldwide scheduled opera performances.

4074   Flieder, Paul. "Oper im Land der Skipetaren." (Opera in the Land of the Skipetarians.) *DB.* 1996; 7: 32-35. Illus.: Photo. B&W. 6. Lang.: Ger.

Albania: Tirana. 1996. Histories-sources. ■Director's diary of rehearsals for Mozart's *Don Giovanni* in Tirana, with discussion of the effects of Albania's changing society on everyday life at the opera house. Continued in *DB* 8 (1996), 31-35 and 9 (1996), 32-35.

4075   Colón, Teatro. "Lyrical Season 1996." *OpN.* 1996 June; 60(17): 23. [*Don Carlo, Roméo et Juliette, L'Incoronazione di Poppea, Andrea Chénier, Aida, Die Zauberflöte, Die Walküre, The Artist and Four Maidens, Renard, Doña Francisquita, Saverio el Cruel.*] Lang.: Eng.

Argentina: Buenos Aires. 1996. Histories-sources. ■Program, principals, conductors, and directors for the 1996 opera season at the Teatro Colón.

4076   Jakovenko, S. *Volšebnaja Zara Doluchanova: Tvorčeskaja biografija. Tajna interpretacii. Vokal'naja škola. Ocenki sovremennikov.* (The Magical Zara Doluchanova: Biography of Her Works, Secret of Her Interpretation, Vocal School and Scores by Her Contemporaries.) Moscow: Kompozitor; 1996. 332 pp. Lang.: Rus.

Armenia. 1970-1996. Biographies. ■Monograph devoted to singer Zara Doluchanova, with thoughts on music and vocal style.

4077   Sevilla-Gonzaga, Marylis. "Voices of Summer: *Opera News* Picks the Highlights of Summer Festivals Abroad." *OpN.* 1996 Jan 6; 60(8): 40-42, 44-53. Illus.: Photo. Color. 9. Lang.: Eng.

Asia. 1996. Histories-sources. ■List of summer 1995 opera festivals in Europe, Scandinavia, Russia, Turkey.

4078   "De Mortier, nil nisi bonum." *Econ.* 1996 Sep 7; 340(7982): 82-83. Illus.: Photo. B&W. 1. Lang.: Eng.

Austria: Salzburg. 1996. Critical studies. ■Operatic highlights of the Salzburg Festival, including a semi-staged version of Beethoven's *Leonore,* an early version of his *Fidelio.*

4079   Bene, Kálmán. "Egy tanulságos balsiker története. Erkel Ferenc: *Hunyadi László*-jának külföldi bemutatójáról." (History of An Instructive Failure: The Premiere of Ferenc Erkel's *László Hunyadi* Abroad.) *SzSz.* 1996; 30/31: 153-161. Notes. Lang.: Hun.

Austria: Vienna. Hungary. 1856. Historical studies. ■The premiere of Ferenc Erkel's opera at Theater an der Wien on August 14, 1856, during a 3-day guest performance by a Hungarian theatrical company.

4080   Brandenburg, Detlef. "'Faul war ich nicht...'." (I Have Not Been Lazy.) *DB.* 1996; 9: 20-23. Illus.: Photo. B&W. 3. Lang.: Ger.

Austria. 1944-1996. Histories-sources. ■Interview with composer Gottfried von Einem about his life, opera, musical traditions and influences.

4081   Gidwitz, Patricia Lewy. "Mozart's Fiordiligi: Adriana Ferrarese del Bene." *COJ.* 1996; 8(3): 199-214. Notes. Tables. Lang.: Eng.

Austria: Vienna. 1780-1790. Biographical studies. ■Considers Adriana Ferrarese del Bene's largely undistinguished career in both comic opera and *opera seria* and the ways in which Mozart turned this to his advantage in composing the role of Fiordiligi for her.

4082   Kuger, Reinhard; Stammen, Silvia. "Salzburger Glanzlichter." (Salzburg Highlights.) *DB.* 1996; 10: 16-18. Illus.: Photo. B&W. 3. Lang.: Ger.

Austria: Salzburg. 1996. Reviews of performances. ■Productions of the Salzburg Festival: Beethoven's *Fidelio* directed by Herbert Wernicke and Schoenberg's *Pierrot Lunaire* and Messiaen's *Quatuor pour la fin du temps* directed by Christoph Marthaler.

4083   Freeman, John W. "City Father: New York City Opera's Founding Father, Laszlo Halasz, Looks Back." *OpN.* 1996 Sep.; 61(3): 28-29. Illus.: Photo. B&W. 1. Lang.: Eng.

Austro-Hungarian Empire: Debrecen. 1905-1996. Histories-sources. ■Interview with Hungarian-born first conductor of the New York City Opera on his career and early days of the company.

4084   Gurewitsch, Matthew. "This Summer, Lincoln Center Festival Offers a Study in Contrasts: *Fidelio* and the Opera's Earlier Version, *Lenore*: ... the Metamorphosis of Beethoven's Only Opera." *OpN.* 1996 July; 61(1): 42-46. Illus.: Dwg. 1. Lang.: Eng.

Austro-Hungarian Empire: Vienna. 1805-1814. Critical studies. ■Comparison and discussion of Beethoven's *Fidelio* and its earlier version, *Lenore.*

4085   Citron, Paula. "Grand Tradition." *OC.* 1996 Fall; 37(3): 9-10. Illus.: Photo. B&W. 1. Lang.: Eng.

Canada. 1939-1991. Biographical studies. ■Profile of lyric soprano Lilian Sukis with references to her performances in Healey Wilan's opera *Deirdre* and the Stratford Festival production of *Le Nozze di Figaro.*

4086   Citron, Paula. "Debut: Tenor Gary Rideout Steps Up to Take the Leads." *OC.* 1996 Win; 37(4): 9. Illus.: Photo. B&W. 1. Lang.: Eng.

Canada. 1983-1996. Biographical studies. ■Profile of tenor Gary Rideout. Emphasis on his involvement with the Canadian Opera Company and his performance in the San Francisco Opera's production of *Phantom of the Opera*.

4087 Eatock, Colin. "Debut: Maria Popescu." *OC*. 1996 Fall; 37(3): 11. Illus.: Photo. B&W. 1. Lang.: Eng.

Canada: Montreal, PQ. 1996. Biographical studies. ■Profile of mezzosoprano Maria Popescu with references to her training at McGill University and her performances in *Falstaff*, *Les Troyens* and *Don Giovanni*.

4088 Eatock, Colin. "Debut: John Haley-Relyea." *OC*. 1996 Sum; 37(2): 11. Illus.: Photo. B&W. 1. Lang.: Eng.

Canada. 1973-1996. Biographical studies. ■Profile of bass baritone John Haley-Relyea with emphasis on his training at the Curtis Institute, his performance in Puccini's *La Bohème* and as Antonio in *Le Nozze di Figaro*.

4089 Eatock, Colin. "Glitter and Gay." *OC*. 1996 Win; 37(4): 10-13. Illus.: Photo. B&W. 1. Lang.: Eng.

Canada. 1995-1996. Biographical studies. ■Coloratura soprano Tracy Dahl's repertoire, with emphasis on her performances in comic roles.

4090 Gooding, Wayne. "From A Coffee Shop To The Met." *OC*. 1996 Fall; 77(3): 12-14. Illus.: Photo. B&W. 1. Lang.: Eng.

Canada. 1970-1996. Biographical studies. ■Profile of tenor Richard Margison with references to his training at the Victoria Conservatory of Music, his performance as Pinkerton in *Madama Butterfly* and his performance in *Faust* at Covent Garden.

4091 Hamilton, Stuart. "Learning Their Parts." *OC*. 1996 Sum; 37(2): 17-19. Illus.: Photo. B&W. 1. Lang.: Eng.

Canada. 1996. Critical studies. ■How singers prepare their roles.

4092 Lazaridès, Alexandre. "Musique pour un livret iconoclaste." (Music for an Iconoclastic Libretto.) *JCT*. 1996; 81: 8-14. Notes. Illus.: Photo. B&W. 5. Lang.: Fre.

Canada: Montreal, PQ. 1949-1996. Critical studies. ■Possibilities and problems of creating music for Claude Gauvreau's libretto *Le Vampire et la Nymphomane*, and qualities of score by Serge Provost.

4093 Mansell, Wendy. "Close Collaborators." *OC*. 1996 Fall; 77(3): 18-24. Illus.: Photo. B&W. 5. Lang.: Eng.

Canada. USA. 1996. Histories-sources. ■Accompanists and vocal coaches Dixie Ross Neill, Bliss Johnston, Stephen Ralls, John Greer and Mark Morash reflect on the importance of the accompanist in preparing the singer for the staging of an opera. Emphasis on the rapport between singer and accompanist.

4094 Mansell, Wendy. "Grand Tradition: Eva Gauthier." *OC*. 1996 Sum; 37(2): 9-10. Illus.: Photo. B&W. 1. Lang.: Eng.

Canada. 1885-1958. Biographical studies. ■Profile of contralto Eva Gauthier with references to her training at the Paris Conservatory, her debut in Bizet's *Carmen* and her career as a vaudeville entertainer.

4095 Massoutre, Guylaine. "Réinventer l'opéra: chant lyrique à la Licorne." (Reinventing Opera: Lyric Song at la Licorne.) *JCT*. 1991; 61: 127-132. Illus.: Photo. B&W. 2. Lang.: Fre.

Canada: Montreal, PQ. 1991. Critical studies. ■Effects of adding a musical score by Alain Thibault to René-Daniel Dubois' text *Ne blâmez jamais les Bédouins (Don't Blame the Bedouins)* for the 1991 Chants Libres staging, directed by Joseph Saint-Gelais and featuring Pauline Vaillancourt.

4096 So, Joseph. "Grand Tradition: Lois Marshall." *OC*. 1996 Spr; 37(1): 9-10. Illus.: Photo. B&W. 1. Lang.: Eng.

Canada: Toronto, ON. 1940-1980. Biographical studies. ■Profile of soprano Lois Marshall with references to her training at the Royal Conservatory of Music and performance in *La Bohème*.

4097 Turp, Richard. "The Friendly Invasion." *OC*. 1996 Fall; 77(3): 15-17. Illus.: Photo. B&W. 8. Lang.: Eng.

Canada. USA. 1917-1996. Biographical studies. ■Profile of Eastern European singers Valerij Aleksejév, Igor Emeljanov, Aleksand'r Ševčenko, Marina Meščerjakova, and Sergei Leiferkus who have recently made their debuts on Western stages.

4098 Turp, Richard. "Grand Tradition: Joseph Saucier 1869-1941." *OC*. 1996 Win; 37(4): 8. Illus.: Photo. B&W. 1. Lang.: Eng.

Canada: Montreal, PQ. 1869-1941. Biographical studies. ■Profile of choirmaster and baritone soloist Joseph Saucier.

4099 Vaïs, Michel. "Vampire sur scène ou l'impossible pari." (Vampire on the Stage or The Impossible Bet.) *JCT*. 1996; 81: 15-18. Notes. Illus.: Photo. B&W. 3. Lang.: Fre.

Canada: Montreal, PQ. 1996. Historical studies. ■Lorraine Pintal's directorial solutions to highly problematic opera, Claude Gauvreau's *Le Vampire et la Nymphomane*, score by Serge Provost.

4100 Danilova, I. "I ljetsja golos vdochnovennyj." (And a Magical Voice Is Spreading Around.) *LikC*. 1996; 3-4: 111-113. Lang.: Rus.

Chuvashia. 1990-1996. Biographical studies. ■Creative portrait of opera singer Valentina Smirnova.

4101 Loomis, George W. "Before the Nightmare: Hans Krása created *Verlobung im Traum (Betrothal in a Dream)* Just Before the Rise of the Third Reich." *OpN*. 1996 Jan 20; 60(9): 16-19. Illus.: Photo. Color. 2. Lang.: Eng.

Czech Republic: Prague. 1994-1996. Historical studies. ■Historical and musical introduction to the work of Czech composer Hans Krása, libretto by Rudolf Thomas and Rudolf Fuchs, from *Uncle's Dream*, a short story by Fëdor Michajlovič Dostojévskij. It receives its American premiere this year at the Washington Opera, with staging borrowed from the 1994-1995 production at the Mannheimer Nationalteater.

4102 Teachout, Terry. "An Affair to Remember: Janáček's Musical Originality Makes *The Makropulos Case* Memorable." *OpN*. 1996 Jan 20; 60(9): 8-11. Illus.: Photo. B&W. Color. 4. Lang.: Eng.

Czechoslovakia: Prague. 1926-1996. Critical studies. ■Discussion of the plot/libretto of *Věc Makropulos*, rarely performed in the U.S. Libretto adapted by the composer Leoš Janáček from the play by Karel Čapek.

4103 Larsson, Henry. "Den första Lulu är en riktig Trollflöjt." (The First Lulu Is a Real Magic Flute.) *MuD*. 1996; 18(2): 38-41. Illus.: Dwg. B&W. Lang.: Swe.

Denmark: Copenhagen. 1786-1832. Historical studies. ■A survey of the composer Friedrich Kuhlau's life and his opera *Lulu*.

4104 Freitas, Roger. "Singing Handel: How Changing Tastes Have Dictated Performance Style." *OpN*. 1996 July; 61(1): 14-17. Illus.: Photo. B&W. Color. 3. Lang.: Eng.

England. 1685-1759. Historical studies. ■The reasons for changed performance practices and audience taste in Baroque music (particularly opera), with background examples from art, architecture, and singing technique, emphasizing the importance of the *castrato* singer.

4105 Rosand, Ellen. "It Bears Repeating; Or, Desiring the Da Capo." *OpN*. 1996 July; 61(1): 18-20. Illus.: Photo. B&W. Color. 3. Lang.: Eng.

England. 1600-1800. Historical studies. ■The development of the *da capo* aria in *opera seria*, to demonstrate the singers' skill, emphasizing the work of G.F. Handel.

4106 Pappel, Kristel. "Mozarts Opern in Tallinn (Reval) vor 200 Jahren." (Mozart's Operas in Tallinn Two Hundred Years Ago.) *KSGT*. 1996; YB: 139-145. Notes. Lang.: Ger.

Estonia: Tallinn. 1795. Historical studies. ■Performances of the touring company of Madame Tilly and the mixed reaction of the audiences.

4107 Bergeron, Katherine. "The Castrato as History." *COJ*. 1996; 8(2): 167-184. Notes. Lang.: Eng.

Europe. 1707-1994. Historical studies. ■The sound of the *castrato* voice, sexual connotations, and the *castrato*'s social position, as seen in Gérard Corbiau's film *Farinelli, Il Castrato*, the writings of Dr. Charles Burney in the eighteenth century, and recordings of Alessandro Moreschi, the 'last *castrato*' in the early twentieth century.

4108 Björkstén, Ingmar. "Maria Callas—ett brinnande liv." (Maria Callas—a Burning Life.) *Dramat*. 1996; 4(4): 22-25. Illus.: Photo. B&W. Lang.: Swe.

Europe. USA. 1950. Historical studies. ■A survey of Maria Callas' career with references to Terrence McNally's play *Master Class*.

4109 Glass, Herbert. "Romany Life: What Is the Gypsy Tradition?" *OpN*. 1996 Mar 16; 60(13): 18-19, 52. Illus.: Photo. B&W. 3. Lang.: Eng.

Europe. 1996. Historical studies. ■European Gypsies in fact and fiction: their musical talents and physical appearance in opera plots.

CLASSED ENTRIES

MUSIC-DRAMA: Opera—Performance/production

4110 Guinther, Louise T. "Conquistador: After Three Decades, There's Still No Stopping Plácido Domingo." *OpN*. 1996 Mar 16; 60(13): 8-11, 47. Illus.: Photo. Color. 5. Lang.: Eng.
Europe. North America. 1941-1996. Histories-sources. ∎Profile, interview with tenor Plácido Domingo, whose career now embraces conducting and opera administration in the United States and elsewhere.

4111 Kerner, Leighton. "That Was Then: A Look Back at the New Operas of the 1946-47 Season." *OpN*. 1996 Dec 28; 61(7): 10-12. Illus.: Photo. B&W. 7. Lang.: Eng.
Europe. 1946-1947. Histories-sources. ∎Brief account of *The Mother of Us All* and *Four Saints in Three Acts* by Gertrude Stein and Virgil Thomson, *The Trial of Lucullus* and *Montezuma* by Roger Sessions, *Albert Herring* and *The Rape of Lucretia* by Benjamin Britten, *Les Mamelles de Tirésias* by François Poulenc, *Street Scene* by Kurt Weill with Elmer Rice and Langston Hughes. Includes a list of other premieres by Gottfried von Einem, John Eaton, Bernard Rogers, Julia Smith, Boris Blacher, Ildebrando Pizzetti, and Carl Orff. Also suggests the revival of operas by Menotti.

4112 Levi, Erik. "Towards an Aesthetic of Fascist Opera." 260-276 in Berghaus, Günter, ed. *Fascism and Theatre: Comparative Studies on the Aesthetics and Politics of Performance in Europe, 1925-1945*. Oxford: Berghahn Books; 1996. 315 pp. Notes. Index. Biblio. Illus.: Photo. 24. Lang.: Eng.
Europe. 1933-1944. Historical studies. ∎General features common to opera repertoire during the war years, especially in Germany and Italy, the extent to which operas of the fascist era represented a reaction against the immediate past, and whether performing traditions, reception and taste altered as a result of political influence.

4113 Mekras, Mikael. "Tenorissimi. Efter de tre tenorerna—de fyra musketörerna på väg att ta över." (Tenorissimi: After the Three Tenors—the Four Musketeers Are on Their Way to Take Over.) *MuD*. 1996; 18(1): 24-25. Illus.: Photo. B&W. Color. Lang.: Swe.
Europe. USA. 1990. Critical studies. ∎A presentation of the next generation of tenors, with references to Roberto Alagna, Jerry Hadley, Ben Heppner, Fernando de La Moras and Peter Seiffert.

4114 Phillips-Matz, Mary Jane. "Hooked on the Orient Express: ... an Operatic Journey on the World's Most Elegant Train." *OpN*. 1996 June; 60(17): 20-21, 46. Illus.: Photo. Color. 7. Lang.: Eng.
Europe. 1995. Biographical studies. ∎An opera critic combines love of opera and of luxury trains on a musical odyssey from London through Europe and back on the Orient Express.

4115 Smith, Terry Donovan. "Shifting Through Space-Time: A Chronotopic Analysis of Peter Sellars' *Don Giovanni*." *MD*. 1996 Win; 39(4): 668-679. Notes. Lang.: Eng.
Europe. 1980-1996. Critical studies. ∎Structures of time and place in Sellars' production of the Mozart opera.

4116 Hagman, Bertil. "(Finsk) baskunskap." ((Finnish) Bass Knowledge.) *MuD*. 1996; 18(2): 23-25. Illus.: Photo. B&W. Lang.: Swe.
Finland. Sweden. 1919. Biographical studies. ∎A presentation of Kim Borg's career as singer and pedagogue, with reference to his recordings.

4117 "Staging a Revolution: Jochen Bereiholz Speaks with Nicolas Joël, Director of the Met's New *Andrea Chénier*." *OpN*. 1996 Apr 13; 60(15): 38-40. Illus.: Photo. Color. 4. Lang.: Eng.
France. Germany. 1942-1996. Histories-sources. ∎Interview with Nicolas Joël, director of the new Metropolitan Opera production of *Andrea Chénier*. Includes comments on his work with Jean-Pierre Ponnelle and Patrice Chéreau, especially on *Der Ring des Nibelungen*.

4118 Biron, Michel. "Une soirée pas comme les autres, au centre de la terre..." (A Night Unlike Any Other, at the Center of the Earth...)*JCT*. 1989; 51: 53-54. Lang.: Fre.
France: Liège. 1989. Critical studies. ∎Framing techniques designate Festival musical de Liège's staging of R. Murray Schafer's *Le Théâtre noir* as extraordinary event.

4119 d'Alberty (Bertie-Marriott, Clément); Illo, John, transl. "American Divas in Paris: 1880's Press Interviews by d'Alberty." *OQ*. 1996 Spr; 12(3): 45-57. Notes. Lang.: Eng.

France: Paris. 1880-1889. Histories-sources. ∎Interviews conducted by the French journalist d'Alberty of three U.S.-based opera divas living and performing in Paris during the 1880s: Adelina Patti, Emma Nevada, and Marie Van Zandt.

4120 Eckert, Nora. "Schönberg en vogue." (Schoenberg in Vogue.) *TZ*. 1996; 1: 46-48. Illus.: Photo. B&W. 4. Lang.: Ger.
France: Paris. Belgium: Brussels. 1996. Reviews of performances. ∎Describes expectations on and choreography of productions of Schoenberg's operas, including *Moses und Aron*, directed by Herbert Wernicke at Théâtre du Châtelet, *Erwartung* by Klaus Michael Grüber, *Verklärte Nacht*, choreographed by Anne Teresa De Keersmaeker at Théâtre de la Monnaie. Includes discussion of the significance of Schoenberg.

4121 Gounod, Charles; Kelkel, Manfred, intro.; Ashbrook, William, transl. "An Article by Gounod: 'Composers as Conductors'." *OQ*. 1996 Sum; 12(4): 5-17. Notes. Lang.: Eng.
France. 1873. Critical studies. ∎The relationship between composer and conductor, and the feasibility of a composer conducting his own work. First time published in the USA with an introduction.

4122 Heed, Sven-Åke. "Vad ska vi med festivaler?" (What Is the Use of Festivals?) *MuD*. 1996; 18(4): 34-36. Illus.: Photo. Color. Lang.: Swe.
France: Avignon, Aix-en-Provence. 1996. Historical studies. ∎A critical survey of the festivals, and the conventional repertory.

4123 Heed, Sven-Åke. "En modernistisk mardröm." (A Modernistic Nightmare.) *MuD*. 1996; 18(5): 12-15. Illus.: Photo. B&W. Color. Lang.: Swe.
France: Paris. 1996. Historical studies. ∎A presentation of Peter Sellars' staging of Igor Stravinskij's *The Rake's Progress* set in an American prison of today.

4124 Innaurato, Albert. "Anatomy of Seduction: ... the Appeal of French Vocal Style." *OpN*. 1996 May; 60(16): 24-26, 28-29. Illus.: Photo. B&W. 5. Lang.: Eng.
France. 1996. Historical studies. ∎Playwright operaphile Innaurato discusses French vocalism and its artists, notably Marthe Angelici, Pierre Berbac, Germaine Cernay, Suzanne Cesbron-Viseur, Régine Crespin, Reynaldo Hahn, Raoul Jobin, Jean Lasalle, Germaine Lubin, José Luccioni, Charles Panzéra, Pol Plançon, Gabriel Soulacroix, Gérard Souzay, Ninon Vallin. Also discusses reissues of *L'Enfant et les Sortilèges*, by Maurice Ravel, conducted by Maurice Bour, *Carmen*, by Georges Bizet, conducted by André Cluytens, *Les Pêcheurs de perles*, by Georges Bizet, and tenor works sung by Paul Franz.

4125 Innaurato, Albert. "To Live: Régine Crespin's Life Experiences Are Reflected in Her Art." *OpN*. 1996 May; 60(16): 35-38. Illus.: Photo. B&W. Color. 7. Lang.: Eng.
France. 1927-1996. Histories-sources. ∎Interview, profile of Régine Crespin, whose life experiences are reflected in her art and autobiography *La Vie et l'Amour d'une Femme* (1982).

4126 Macdonald, Hugh. "Comique Touch: ... the Traditions of Opéra Comique." *OpN*. 1996 May; 60(16): 30-33. Illus.: Photo. Color. 6. Lang.: Eng.
France: Paris. 1750-1972. Historical studies. ∎History of *opéra comique*, the development of its conventions, its institutionalization at the Opéra-Comique, Paris, which closed in 1972. Discusses the *opéra comique* repertoire, with stock characters, and frequent parody, along with official limitations on the genre.

4127 Pistone, Danièle; Glasow, E. Thomas, transl. "Emmanuel Chabrier, Opera Composer." *OQ*. 1996 Spr; 12(3): 17-25. Notes. Lang.: Eng.
France: Paris. 1863-1894. Biographical studies. ∎Concentrates on the work produced by composer Emmanuel Chabrier, during an era of flux on the opera stages of France. Looks at his operas *L'étoile, Une éducation manquée, Gwendoline* and *Le roi malgré lui*.

4128 Sevilla-Gonzaga, Marylis. "Advantage Alagna: ... the Newest Star Tenor." *OpN*. 1996 May; 60(16): 12-14. Illus.: Photo. Color. 3. Lang.: Eng.
France. 1932-1996. Histories-sources. ∎Profile, interview with autodidact tenor Roberto Alagna, with reference to Russian soprano Angela Gheorghiu.

MUSIC-DRAMA: Opera—Performance/production

4129   Steiner, George. "Lévi-Strauss *with* Music: The Classic *Tristes Tropiques* Becomes an Opera." *OpN*. 1996 Dec 28; 61(7): 50-51. Lang.: Eng.
France: Strasbourg. 1996. Critical studies. ■Review, analysis, and plot summary of the world premiere of *Tristes Tropiques*, an opera with an Amerindian theme, based on the anthropological work by Claude Lévi-Strauss, libretto by Catherine Clément, music by Georges Aperghis, at the Festival des Musiques d'Aujourd'hui, Strasbourg, September 29, 1996.

4130   Wood, Caroline. *Music and Drama in the* Tragédie en Musique, *1673-1715: Jean-Baptiste Lully and His Successors.* New York, NY/London: Garland; 1996. 391 pp. (Outstanding Dissertations in Music from British Universities.) Pref. Notes. Index. Biblio. Append. Lang.: Eng.
France. 1673-1715. Histories-specific. ■The first forty years of French opera, with emphasis on the works of Jean-Baptiste Lully and his influence on the early development of opera in France.

4131   "Twilight of the Passions." *Econ*. 1996 Nov 9; 341(7991): 104. Illus.: Photo. B&W. 1. Lang.: Eng.
Germany. 1970-1996. Critical studies. ■Staging in post-modernist productions of Wagner, especially *The Ring*, and the attempts to make its world view relevant, de-emphasizing and reworking the mythic content.

4132   Baker, Evan. "The Assistant: When Staging the First *Ring* Cycle, Wagner Came to Depend on His Solid Right-Hand Man, Richard Fricke." *OpN*. 1996 Apr 13; 60(15): 34-37. Illus.: Photo. Dwg. B&W. 3. Lang.: Eng.
Germany: Bayreuth. 1818-1903. Historical studies. ■Brief biography of Richard Fricke, assistant stage director for the first performance of *Der Ring des Nibelungen* (1876). His diary of the production was published in 1906 as *Bayreuth Thirty Years Ago: Memories of Wahnfried and from the Festival Theater (Bayreuth vor dreissig Jahren)*.

4133   Brandenburg, Detlef. "Hüter des Hügels." (Guardian of the Hill.) *DB*. 1996; 9: 10-12. Append. Illus.: Photo. B&W. 3. Lang.: Ger.
Germany: Bayreuth. 1996. Reviews of performances. ■Impressions of the 85th Bayreuther Festspiele, including the opening work, Wagner's *Die Meistersinger*, directed and designed by Wolfgang Wagner.

4134   Brandenburg, Detlef; Regler, Bellinger, Brigitte. "Verzaubert im Zelt." (Enchanted in a Marquee.) *DB*. 1996; 12: 12-17. Illus.: Photo. B&W. 4. Lang.: Ger.
Germany: Cologne. 1996. Critical studies. ■A children's opera, *Nattergalen (The Nightingale)* based on story by Hans Christian Andersen, composer Igor Stravinskij, directed by Christian Schuller at Bühnen der Stadt Köln. Considers the question of how opera affects children.

4135   Cerf, Steven R. "Too Grimm for Words: Taming *Hänsel und Gretel* for Opera." *OpN*. 1996 Dec 28; 61(7): 14-17. Illus.: Photo. B&W. 3. Lang.: Eng.
Germany. 1893-1996. Critical studies. ■Problems of adapting the violence of the Wilhelm and Jacob Grimm fairy tale from *Kinder- und Hausmärchen* to the operatic stage were partially solved by the bowdlerizing of Ludwig Bechstein.

4136   Delekat, Thomas. "Die Herrin der Zeichen." (The Lady Ruler of Signs.) *DB*. 1996; 3: 10-11. Illus.: Photo. B&W. 1. Lang.: Ger.
Germany. 1981-1996. Biographical studies. ■Portrait of opera director Ruth Berghaus, her influence on other opera directors, and her early work with choreography at the Palucca School.

4137   Delekat, Thomas. "Hilflosigkeit, Langeweile." (Helplessness, Boredom.) *DB*. 1996; 3: 18-21. Illus.: Photo. B&W. 5. Lang.: Ger.
Germany. 1996. Histories-sources. ■Interview with composer Heiner Goebbels about contemporary aesthetic forms and subjects of opera, the relationship between music and language, and his own operas.

4138   Delekat, Thomas. "Mister Universal." *DB*. 1996; 4: 10-14. Illus.: Photo. B&W. 7. Lang.: Ger.
Germany. 1975-1996. Biographical studies. ■Portrait of Peter Mussbach, director and set designer: his productions and reliance on teamwork.

4139   Delekat, Thomas. "Der Mann aus der Reihe." (The Man of the Line.) *DB*. 1996; 5: 18-21. Illus.: Photo. B&W. 2. Lang.: Ger.

Germany. 1996. Historical studies. ■Portrait of opera chorus member Stefan Kohnke.

4140   Honig, Joel. "Seasons of Schwarzkopf: A New Biography Revives Time-Honored Questions." *OpN*. 1996 Aug.; 61(2): 40-41, 52 . Illus.: Photo. B&W. 1. Lang.: Eng.
Germany. UK-England. 1915-1996. Critical studies. ■A new biography by Alan Jefferson examines Dame Elisabeth Schwarzkopf's relationship to the Nazis in World War II.

4141   Kämpfer, Frank. "Körper, Tod und Utopia." (Body, Death, and Utopia.) *TZ*. 1996; 4: 18-21. Illus.: Photo. B&W. 4. Lang.: Ger.
Germany. 1996. Histories-sources. ■A conversation with opera director Peter Konwitschny about his experiences directing works of Verdi and Wagner.

4142   Lilo, Sørensen. "Morgendagens Musikteater." (The Music Theatre of Tomorrow.) *TE*. 1996 Apr.; 78: 9-11. Illus.: Photo. B&W. 3. Lang.: Dan.
Germany: Berlin. 1996. Histories-sources. ■Interview with Götz Friedrich of Deutsche Oper on the future direction of opera.

4143   Loney, Glenn. "Orff at 100." *TCI*. 1996 Feb.; 30(2): 12-13. Illus.: Photo. Color. 1. Lang.: Eng.
Germany. 1996. Technical studies. ■Review of performance and technical aspects of the Bavarian State Opera's production of Carl Orff's *Carmina Burana*.

4144   Midgette, Anne. "Wilhelmine's Bayreuth: How a Prussian Princess Transformed a Backwater Town into a Cultural Center." *OpN*. 1996 Apr 13; 60(15): 26, 28, 30. Illus.: Photo. B&W. Color. 5. Lang.: Eng.
Germany: Bayreuth. 1709-1758. Historical studies. ■How Wilhelmine, Margravine of Bayreuth, sister of Frederick the Great, transformed the town into a musical center. References to the building of the Markgräffliche Opernhaus, performers Faustina Bordoni, Johann Adolf Hesse, Giacomo Zaghini. the premiere of *L'Uomo* by Andrea Bernasconi, and her own opera *Argenore*.

4145   Tranberg, Sören. "Bas-kultur." (Bass Culture.) *MD*. 1996; 18(2): 26-27, 37. Illus.: Photo. Color. Lang.: Swe.
Germany. Finland. 1966. Histories-sources. ■An interview with Matti Salminen about his singing career.

4146   Zimmermann, Gero. "Neuinszenierung *Die Meistersinger von Nürnberg* bei den Bayreuther Festspielen." (A New Staging of *Die Meistersinger* at the Bayreuth Festival.) *BtR*. 1996; 5: 31-36. Illus.: Design. Photo. B&W. Color. 18. Lang.: Ger.
Germany: Bayreuth. 1996. Histories-sources. ■The technical realization of almost abstract scenery using dome horizon and projections, designed by the director of the production, Wolfgang Wagner.

4147   Huldin-Halldin, Marga. "Vorpommern åter 'svenskt'." (Vorpomerania 'Swedish' Again.) *MuD*. 1996; 18(5): 6-7. Illus.: Photo. B&W. Lang.: Swe.
Germany, East: Greifswald, Stralsund. 1984. Histories-sources. ■An interview with the Swedish conductor Per Borin about his successful career in Germany and Theater Vorpommern, and the singer Katarina Nilsson, with reference to their cooperation on Verdi's *La Traviata*.

4148   Boros, Attila. "Száz éve született Pataky Kálmán." (Kálmán Pataky Was Born One Hundred Years Ago.) *OperaL*. 1996; 5(5): 4-6. Illus.: Photo. B&W. 2. Lang.: Hun.
Hungary. 1896-1996. Biographical studies. ■Tribute to the tenor Kálmán Pataky.

4149   Csák, P. Judit. "Lírai tenorból hős tenor: Bándi János." (How a Lyric Tenor Became a Heroic Tenor: János Bándi.) *OperaL*. 1996; 5(2): 20-22. Illus.: Photo. B&W. 2. Lang.: Hun.
Hungary. 1953-1990. Histories-sources. ■Career of tenor János Bándi, interrupted in 1987 by vocal problems and successfully resumed thereafter.

4150   Dalos, László. "Domahidy László (1920-1996)." (László Domahidy, 1920-1996.) *OperaL*. 1996; 5(5): 33. Illus.: Photo. B&W. 1. Lang.: Hun.

MUSIC-DRAMA: Opera—Performance/production

Hungary. 1920-1996. Biographical studies. ■Profile of the late bass with the Budapest Opera House.

4151   Dalos, László. "'A-S-D-F-köz'—Múltidézés Czanik Zsófiával." ('A-S-D-F-Interval'—Reminiscences of the Past—The Career of Zsófia Czanik.) *OperaL.* 1996; 5(1): 17-19. Illus.: Photo. B&W. 2. Lang.: Hun.

Hungary. 1947-1969. Histories-sources. ■Interview with the retired dramatic soprano of the Hungarian State Opera House on her career.

4152   Dalos, László. "'Mélyen lehajtom a fejem'—Életút-vázlatféle Vadas Kiss Lászlóról." ('I Bow My Head Humbly'—A Biographical Sketch of László Vadas Kiss.) *OperaL.* 1996; 5(2): 27-31. Illus.: Photo. B&W. 4. Lang.: Hun.

Hungary. 1926-1990. Biographical studies. ■Life and career of the outstanding tenor László Vadas Kiss, who sang at the Szeged National Theatre and at the Budapest Opera House.

4153   Dalos, László. "Négy évtized néhány pillanata—Látogatás Orosz Júliánál." (Four Decades: Flashbacks—A Visit with Júlia Orosz.) *OperaL.* 1996; 5(3): 4-8. Illus.: Photo. B&W. 5. Lang.: Hun.

Hungary. 1929-1990. Histories-sources. ■Interview with the retired soprano, life member of the Budapest Opera House.

4154   Dalos, László. "Királylány, királyné, királynő—Látogatóban Palánkay Kláránál." (Royal Princess, Queen Consort, Reigning Queen—A Visit with Klára Palánkay.) *OperaL.* 1996; 5(4): 18-22. Illus.: Photo. B&W. 4. Lang.: Hun.

Hungary. 1944-1990. Histories-sources. ■Interview with the former mezzo-soprano of the Budapest Opera House, retired in 1970, who spent a quarter of a century on the opera stage appearing in thirty roles. She is a life member of the Hungarian State Opera House.

4155   Huszár, Klára. "Személyes portré Birkás Lilianról." (An Intimate Portrait of Lilian Birkás.) *OperaL.* 1996; 5(5): 36-38. Illus.: Photo. B&W. 3. Lang.: Hun.

Hungary. 1916-1990. Biographical studies. ■Career of the retired soprano of the Budapest Opera.

4156   Kerényi, Ferenc. "'A magyar Catalani?' A primadonna mint társadalmi jelenség a reformkorban." ('The Hungarian Catalani?' The Primadonna as a Society Personality in the Age of Reform.) *SzSz.* 1996; 30/31: 39-43. Lang.: Hun.

Hungary. 1823-1847. Historical studies. ■Career of actress Róza Déry-Széppataki (1793-1872) in musical plays as the first primadonna of the Hungarian theatre history.

4157   Kerényi, Mária. "'Mi leszel, kislány?'—Portré Zempléni Máriáról." ('What Are You Going to Be, Little Girl?'—A Portrait of Mária Zempléni.) *OperaL.* 1996; 5(3): 30-33. Illus.: Photo. B&W. Color. 3. Lang.: Hun.

Hungary. 1971-1996. Biographical studies. ■Career of the soprano of the Budapest Opera House.

4158   Kerényi, Mária. "Magyar énekiskolák IV.—Kutrucz Éva." (Hungarian Schools of Singing—Part 4: Éva Kutrucz.) *OperaL.* 1996; 5(2): 7-8. Illus.: Photo. B&W. 1. Lang.: Hun.

Hungary. 1948-1996. Histories-sources. ■Profile of Éva Kutrucz, a singing teacher at the Liszt Ferenc Zeneakadémia for 34 years.

4159   Kerényi, Mária. "Az Operaház örökös tagjai: László Margit." (Life Members of the Opera House: Margit László.) *OperaL.* 1996; 5(2): 22-25. Illus.: Photo. B&W. 5. Lang.: Hun.

Hungary. 1931-1996. Histories-sources. ■Interview with soprano Margit László of the Budapest Opera House, who has also performed in operetta and musical theatre, and as a singer of chamber music, oratorio, and song.

4160   Kertész, Iván. "Némethy Ella emlékezete." (In Remembrance of Ella Némethy.) *OperaL.* 1996; 5(2): 4-6 . Illus.: Photo. B&W. 4. Lang.: Hun.

Hungary. 1895-1961. Biographical studies. ■Recollections of soprano and mezzo-soprano Ella Némethy, who performed with the Budapest Opera and abroad in the first half of the twentieth century.

4161   László, Péter. "Parpignoltól a Siegfriedig—Portré Molnár Andrásról." (From Parpignol to Siegfried—A Portrait of

András Molnár.) *OperaL.* 1996; 5(4): 6-13. Illus.: Photo. B&W. 6. Lang.: Hun.

Hungary. 1963-1996. Biographical studies. ■The tenor's roles in operas by Mozart and Wagner at the Hungarian State Opera House.

4162   Mátai, Györgyi; Kanyó, Béla, photo.; Mezey, Béla, photo. "Egy igazi partnerkapcsolat: Rujsz Edit-Nagyszentpéteri Miklós." (A Real Partnership: Edit Rujsz-Miklós Nagyszentpéteri.) *Tanc.* 1995; 26(10/12): 12-13. Illus.: Photo. B&W. 3. Lang.: Hun.

Hungary. 1994-1995. Histories-sources. ■Interview with the soloists of the Budapest Opera House, who have worked together in numerous performances.

4163   Mátai, Györgyi. "'A pénz markában eszközzé silányul a művészet!' Pályakép Bokor Juttáról." ('Art Degenerates Into a Mere Means in the Hands of Money'—The Career of Jutta Bokor.) *OperaL.* 1996; 5 (5): 17-20. Illus.: Photo. B&W. 3. Lang.: Hun.

Hungary. 1955-1996. Histories-sources. ■Career of mezzo-soprano Jutta Bokor.

4164   Mátai, Györgyi. "'A sikerhez vezető út számomra tartalmasabb, mint maga a siker'—Pályakép Tóth Jánosról." ('The Road Leading to Success Is More Important than Success Itself'—The Career of János Tóth.) *OperaL.* 1996; 5(3): 20-23. Illus.: Photo. Dwg. B&W. 4. Lang.: Hun.

Hungary. 1955-1996. Histories-sources. ■Life and career of Hungarian State Opera baritone and opera director János Tóth.

4165   Mátai, Györgyi. "Pályakép Mészöly Katalinról." (Katalin Mészöly—A Career.) *OperaL.* 1996; 5(2): 16-19. Illus.: Photo. B&W. Lang.: Hun.

Hungary. 1949-1990. Histories-sources. ■Mezzo-soprano of the Budapest Opera House speaks about her life and career.

4166   Mészáros, Szilvia. "'Lelkileg, technikailag éretten'—Portré Rozsos Istvánról." ('An Artist Mature both Mentally and Technically'—A Portrait of István Rozsos.) *OperaL.* 1996; 5(1): 22-25. Illus.: Photo. B&W. 4. Lang.: Hun.

Hungary. 1944-1995. Histories-sources. ■The tenor celebrated a twofold jubilee recently: his 50th birthday and a 25-year career at the Budapest Opera House.

4167   Szeghalmi, Elemér. "Találkozás Pálos Imrével." (Meeting Imre Pálos.) *OperaL.* 1996; 5(1): 28-30. Illus.: Photo. B&W. 3. Lang.: Hun.

Hungary. 1956-1980. Histories-sources. ■Interview with *heldentenor* Imre Pálos of the Hungarian State Opera.

4168   Szomory, György. "Pillanatfelvétel Szilfai Mártáról." (A Snapshot of Márta Szilfai.) *OperaL.* 1996; 5(5): 7-9. Illus.: Photo. B&W. 4. Lang.: Hun.

Hungary. 1970-1996. Histories-sources. ■The young dramatic soprano of the Budapest Opera House speaks about her career and future plans.

4169   Szomory, György. "'A hanggal teremteni kell'—Látogatóban Gregor Józsefnél." ('You Have to Create with Your Voice'—Visiting József Gregor.) *OperaL.* 1996; 5(1): 4-9. Illus.: Photo. Color. 6. Lang.: Hun.

Hungary. 1957-1995. Histories-sources. ■Interview with József Gregor on his life and career.

4170   Szomory, György. "Beszélgetés a *Faust* rendezőjével." (Mephisto Reborn—Gábor Miklós Kerényi on *Faust.*) *OperaL.* 1996; 5(2): 13-15. Lang.: Hun.

Hungary: Budapest. 1996. Histories-sources. ■The stage director on his concept for the revival of Gounod's *Faust* at Budapest Erkel Theatre.

4171   Till, Géza. "Szerep és hang IV." (Role and Voice—Part 4.) *OperaL.* 1996; 5(1): 13-16. Lang.: Hun.

Hungary. 1930-1940. Critical studies. ■Analysis of the bass voices from the technical and artistic point of view surveying the bass parts of the repertoires at the great opera houses ranging from Mozart to Richard Strauss. Includes profiles of Hungarian singers Oszkár Kálmán, Endre Kóréh, and Mihály Székely.

4172   Abel, Sam. "The World Cup of Opera, Or a Sale of Three Tenors." *TA.* 1996; 48: 1-13. Notes. Lang.: Eng.

CLASSED ENTRIES

MUSIC-DRAMA: Opera—Performance/production

Italy: Rome. USA: Los Angeles, CA. 1990-1994. Critical studies. ■Critique of the operatic and sporting elements inherent in the two concerts involving the three tenors Luciano Pavarotti, Plácido Domingo, and José Carreras.

4173 Baxter, Robert. "The Last Tenore Lirico: Ferruccio Tagliavini (1913-1995)." *OQ.* 1996 Fall; 13(1): 29-36. Notes. Illus.: Photo. B&W. 1. Lang.: Eng.
Italy. 1913-1995. Biographical studies. ■Obituary for Italian opera singer Ferruccio Tagliavini, with notes on his life and career.

4174 Bernardoni, Virgili, ed. *Puccini.* Bologna: Il Mulino; 1996. 390 pp. (Polifonie. Musica e Spettacolo nella storia.) Notes. Biblio. Lang.: Ita.
Italy. 1858-1924. Critical studies. ■A new critical approach to the works of the Italian composer Giacomo Puccini in a collection of essays translated in Italian for the first time.

4175 Borovskij, D. "Vynuzdennje 'memuary'." (Forced 'Memories'.) *TeatZ.* 1996; 3: 27-30. Lang.: Rus.
Italy: Milan. 1970-1980. Historical studies. ■Jurij Ljubimov's opera productions at La Scala, including Berg's *Lulu* and Prokofjév's *Ljubov k Trem Apelsinam (Love for Three Oranges).*

4176 Bosisio, Paolo. "La regia degli spettacoli scaligeri nel periodo della sovrintendenza Grassi (1972-1977)." (Opera Production at La Scala Under the Superintendance of Grassi, 1972-77.) *Ariel.* 1996; 11(1): 73-90. Notes. Lang.: Ita.
Italy: Milan. 1972-1977. Historical studies. ■The staging of operas under the direction of Paolo Grassi.

4177 Csák, P. Judit. "Magyar énekesek Ricciarelli mesteriskoláján." (Hungarian Singers at the Master Course of Ricciarelli.) *OperaL.* 1996; 5(5): 24-25. Illus.: Photo. B&W. 1. Lang.: Hun.
Italy. Hungary. 1995. Histories-sources. ■Interview with two young Hungarian singers, Kornélia Pérchy and Andrea Szántó who participated in the course last summer at a five-week master course organized annually by Katia Ricciarelli at the village Desenzano del Garda.

4178 Dalos, László. "Giuseppe Taddei 80 éves." (Giuseppe Taddei—80 Years Old.) *OperaL.* 1996; 5(4): 37. Illus.: Photo. B&W. 1. Lang.: Hun.
Italy. Hungary. 1916-1996. Biographical studies. ■Greeting the Italian baritone on his birthday, recalling his guest performances in Budapest.

4179 Hastings, Stephen. "The Art of Luciano: ... an In-Depth Look at What Makes Pavarotti Pavarotti." *OpN.* 1996 Apr 13; 60 (15): 18-20. Illus.: Photo. Color. 7. Lang.: Eng.
Italy. 1935-1996. Critical studies. ■Critical analysis of the art of Luciano Pavarotti, said to be perhaps the greatest of post-World War II tenors. Offers comparison with Plácido Domingo, Jussi Björling, Carlo Bergonzi, Beniamino Gigli, Giuseppe di Stefano and others. Praises his gift of spontaneity.

4180 Innaurato, Albert. "First Impression: Mezzo Sonia Ganassi's Sensational New York Debut in Opera Orchestra of New York's *Norma.*" *OpN.* 1996 Mar 30; 60(14): 34. Illus.: Photo. B&W. 1. Lang.: Eng.
Italy: Parma. 1996. Histories-sources. ■The New York debut of Italian mezzo-soprano Sonia Ganassi, as Adalgisa in *Norma* for Opera Orchestra of New York, conducted by Eve Queler.

4181 Jacobson, Bernard; Earle, John, photo. "Opera's Deconstructionist: Luciano Berio, Whose *Un Re in Ascolto* opens at Lyric Opera of Chicago This Month Has Spent His Career Overturning Expectations." *OpN.* 1996 Nov.; 61(5): 22-25. Illus.: Photo. Color. 2. Lang.: Eng.
Italy. 1925-1996. Critical studies. ■Italian composer Luciano Berio specializes in deconstructing the genre of opera in such works as *Opera, Un Re in Ascolto, Orfeo ed Euridice, Armide, Allez-Hop, Theme (Omaggio a Joyce), La Vera Storia, Outis, Passaggio, Laborintus II.* The actual genre of some of these works is debatable.

4182 Kirillina, L.V. *Italjanskaja opera pervoj poloviny XX veka.* (Italian Opera of the Early Twentieth Century.) Moscow: Gosudarstvénnyj institut iskusstvoznanija; 1996. 232 pp. Lang.: Rus.
Italy. 1900-1950. Histories-specific. ■Operatic works of Busoni, Respighi, Casella, and others.

4183 Martin, George. "Verdi's *Stiffelio*: Lost, Found, Misunderstood." *OQ.* 1996 Fall; 13(1): 11-19. Notes. Lang.: Eng.
Italy. UK-England: London. USA: New York, NY. 1850-1996. Historical studies. ■The history of Verdi's fifteenth opera *Stiffelio*, lost only to be recovered. After productions in London, New York, and Los Angeles, most audiences experienced disappointment.

4184 Most, Henrik. "Vox Humanum XXL." *TE.* 1996 Apr.; 78: 4-6. Illus.: Dwg. Dwg. 2. Lang.: Dan.
Italy. 1600-1996. Historical studies. ■The era of the *castrato*, with mention of Carlo Broschi and Alessandro Moreschi, inspired by the film *Farinelli* directed by Gérard Corbiau.

4185 Nyblom, Sofia. "Berio—besatt." (Berio—Possessed.) *MuD.* 1996; 18(5): 26-29. Illus.: Photo. B&W. Color. Lang.: Swe.
Italy: Milan. 1996. Critical studies. ■A presentation of Luciano Berio and his new opera *Outis* staged by Graham Vick at Teatro alla Scala.

4186 Phillips-Matz, Mary Jane. "Verdi's Heir: How the Composer's Mantle Was Passed on to Puccini." *OpN.* 1996 Mar 2; 60(12): 12-15, 23. Illus.: Photo. B&W. Color. 6. Lang.: Eng.
Italy. 1858-1924. Historical studies. ■An account of the way Giuseppe Verdi's career and work influenced his successor, Giacomo Puccini, to become Italy's most respected operatic composer, with comments on Puccini's teachers, conductors.

4187 Porter, Andrew. "Grand Canvas: In *La Forza del Destino*, Verdi Etched a Broad Picture of Humanity." *OpN.* 1996 Mar 16; 60(13): 12-17. MU. Illus.: Photo. B&W. Color. 7. Lang.: Eng.
Italy. 1862-1996. Historical studies. ■Discussion of the musical and plot development of *La Forza del Destino*, by Giuseppe Verdi.

4188 Rehorovszky, Béla. "Pillantás a Veronai Arénára." (A Snapshot of the Arena of Verona.) *OperaL.* 1996; 5 (1): 20-21. Illus.: Photo. B&W. 3. Lang.: Hun.
Italy: Verona. 1913-1995. Historical studies. ■Brief survey of the festival's 73 seasons with statistical data recalling the stars of the opera world appeared on its stage.

4189 Schmid, Patric; White, Don. "The Mysterious Case of *Ermione.*" *OQ.* 1996 Spr; 12(3): 7-15. Notes. Lang.: Eng.
Italy. 1819. Historical studies. ■Explores possible reasons for the failure of Rossini's opera *Ermione*, which was closed by Rossini and Teatro San Carlo impresario Domenico Barbaja after only one performance.

4190 Stratton, John. "Francesco Tamagno, the Extraordinary." *OQ.* 1996 Sum; 12(4): 61-73. Notes. Tables. Illus.: Photo. B&W. 2. Lang.: Eng.
Italy. 1850-1905. Critical studies. ■Assessment of the extant recordings of the Italian dramatic tenor Francesco Tamagno, with a table of recommended pitch adjustments for each track of the CD.

4191 Zucker, Stefan. "Corelli: Tenore del Mondo." *OpN.* 1996 Feb 3; 60(10): 16-19, 45. Illus.: Photo. Color. B&W. 9. Lang.: Eng.
Italy. 1921. Histories-sources. ■Excerpts from radio interviews with tenor Franco Corelli.

4192 Myers, Eric. "Sweet and Low: The Case of the Missing Contralto." *OpN.* 1996 Dec 28; 61(7): 18-21. Illus.: Photo. B&W. Color. 8. Lang.: Eng.
North America. 1813-1996. Historical studies. ■The lack of true contralto voices in opera today, with comments on great voices of the past. Today few contraltos are being trained and they may be eclipsed by counternors. Includes discussion of numerous contraltos of the past and their repertoire.

4193 Tranberg, Sören. "Tenoren som förändrade sitt liv." (The Tenor Who Changed His Life.) *MuD.* 1996; 18(4): 18-20. Illus.: Photo. Color. Lang.: Swe.
Norway. Finland. 1979. Histories-sources. ■An interview with the Norwegian tenor Arild Helleland, who turned to character-tenor.

4194 Wypych-Gawrońska, Anna. "Zespół śpewsaków lwowskiej sceny operowej (1872-1918)." (The Ensemble of Singers of the Lvov Opera Stage, 1872-1918.) *PaT.* 1996; 1-2(29): 29-60. Illus.: Photo. B&W. Lang.: Pol.
Poland: Lvov. 1872-1918. Historical studies. ■Activity of the Polish opera in Lvov after the Austrian theatre was closed and before Poland

MUSIC-DRAMA: Opera—Performance/production

regained its independence, with emphasis on engaging soloists, educating singers, and promoting the Polish language in performance.

4195 Baeva, A. "Poetičeskij mir turgenevskich geroev." (The Poetic World of Turgenjév's Heroes.) *MA*. 1996; 1: 150-154. Lang.: Rus.
Russia. 1990-1996. Historical studies. ■V. Rebikov's opera *Dvorjanskoje Gnezdo (Aristocratic Nest)*, adapted from the work of Ivan Turgenjev, produced and directed by Boris Pokrovskij at Kamernyj Muzikal'nyj Teat'r.

4196 Bjalik, M. "Épičeskaja opera—kak ee stavit'?" (Epic Opera: How Is It Done?)*MA*. 1996; 1: 144-150. Lang.: Rus.
Russia. 1990-1996. Historical studies. ■The specifics of staging an epic opera.

4197 Buev, I. "Moreplavatel' ponevole." (Sailor in Spite of Himself.) *Neva*. 1996; 6: 232-238. Lang.: Rus.
Russia. 1844-1908. Biographical studies. ■Rimskij-Korsakov's development as a composer.

4198 Chripin, A. "'Železnyj' Lejferkus." (Leiferkus: Made of Steel.) *MuZizn*. 1996; 7-8: 10-14. Lang.: Rus.
Russia: Moscow. 1990-1996. Biographical studies. ■Profile of opera singer Sergei Leiferkus.

4199 Fattachova, K. "Narod bezmolvstvuet." (The Crowds Are Silent.) *PTZ*. 1996; 10: 30-33. Lang.: Rus.
Russia: St. Petersburg. 1995-1996. Historical studies. ■Jurij Aleksandrov's production of Mussorgskij's *Boris Godunov* at the St. Petersburg Opera.

4200 Groševa, E. "Poslednie iz mogikan." (The Last of the Mohicans.) *MA*. 1996; 1: 155-166. Lang.: Rus.
Russia. 1895-1995. Biographical studies. ■Opera singers Mark Rejzen (1895-1992) and Natalija Špiller (1909-1995).

4201 Isaakjan, G. "Opera v otsutstvie ljubvi i smerti." (Opera in the Absence of Love and Death.) *MA*. 1996; 1: 139-144. Lang.: Rus.
Russia. 1990-1996. Critical studies. ■The interpretation of opera classics and the ideology of the operatic genre.

4202 Ivanov, V.L. *Amiko Šaljapo ... ili Putesestvie F.I. Šaljapina v Afriku.* (Amico Šaljapo: Fédor Šaljapin's Trip to Africa.) Moscow: Rerich; 1996. 146 pp. Lang.: Rus.
Russia. 1873-1938. Biographical studies. ■The opera singer's life and career, including his travels throughout Europe, Asia, and Africa.

4203 Kornakova, M. "'Skorpiony—éto te, kto vozroždajutsja, kak feniksy iz pepla'." (Scorpions Are Those Who Are Reborn Like the Phoenix from Its Ashes.) *PTZ*. 1996; 10: 20-27. Lang.: Rus.
Russia: St. Petersburg. 1996. Histories-sources. ■Interview with director Aleksand'r Petrov on his work in opera.

4204 Kuznecov, I. "Pokolenie 'semidesjatych'—večno vtorye?" (The Generation of the Seventies: Always Second?)*MA*. 1996; 1 : 129-131. Lang.: Rus.
Russia: Moscow. 1990-1996. Historical studies. ■Operatic works of composer Leonid Bobylev, including *Grigorij Melechov*, libretto by Aleksand'r Medvedev, and *Propastčaja ochota (The Lost Hunt)*, text by Viktor Astafjev.

4205 Potapova, N. "O čem voždeleet Salomeja." (What Salome Dreams About.) *PTZ*. 1996; 10: 15-17. Lang.: Rus.
Russia: St. Petersburg. 1996. Historical studies. ■Account of a new production of Strauss's *Salome* directed by Julie Taylor at the Mariinskij Theatre.

4206 Sedov, Ma. "Rycar' opery." (Knight of the Opera.) *MuZizn*. 1996; 7-8: 16-17. Lang.: Rus.
Russia: Moscow. 1990-1996. Biographical studies. ■The work of opera composer Aleksand'r Cholminov.

4207 Širinskij, N. "Solisty ego Veličestva." (Soloists for Her Majesty.) *OSZ*. 1996; 10: 9-12. Lang.: Rus.
Russia: St. Petersburg. 1880-1910. Biographical studies. ■Opera singers Nikolaj N. Figner and Medeja I. Mej of the Mariinskij Theatre.

4208 Šleev, V. "Sergej Lifar' o Fëdore Šaljapine." (Sergej Lifar' on Fëdor Šaljapin.) *Balet*. 1996; 1: 43-44. Lang.: Rus.

Russia. 1873-1938. Historical studies. ■Lifar's recollections of the great singer.

4209 Smeljanskij, A. "Jeremija s Povarskoj." (Jeremiah of Povarskaja.) *MoskNab*. 1996; 3-4: 10-15. Lang.: Rus.
Russia: Moscow. 1995-1996. Historical studies. ■Production of *Plach Jeremii*, music by Vladimir Martynov, by the School of Dramatic Art of Anatolij Vasiljév.

4210 Šochman, G. "V poiskach smysla." (In Search of Meaning.) *MA*. 1996; 1: 135-138. Lang.: Rus.
Russia: Moscow. 1996. Historical studies. ■On the profession of opera director and its requirements.

4211 Tret'jakova, E. "Rok-n-roll s petlej na šee—P.T. Žurn." (Rock 'n' Roll with a Rope around the Neck: PTZ.) *PTZ*. 1996; 9: 52-55. Lang.: Rus.
Russia: St. Petersburg. 1996. Historical studies. ■Sergej Spivak's work with the Fontanka Youth Theatre, including a production of Brecht and Weill's *Dreigroschenoper (Three Penny Opera)*.

4212 Tret'jakova, E. "Pis'mo v 2050-j god." (Letter to the Year 2050.) *PTZ*. 1996; 10: 11-14. Lang.: Rus.
Russia: St. Petersburg. 1996. Historical studies. ■The dynamics of opera production at the Mariinskij Theatre.

4213 Innaurato, Albert. "The Strange Case of Conchita Supervia." *OpN*. 1996 Mar 16; 60(13): 22-27. Illus.: Photo. B&W. 7. Lang.: Eng.
Spain: Barcelona. 1895-1936. Biographical studies. ■Evaluation of the life and career of Spanish mezzo-soprano Conchita Supervia.

4214 Bergström, Gunnel. "Professor Wiklund: Besjälad är ordet!" (Professor Wiklund: Inspired Is the Word!)*MuD*. 1996; 18(2): 10-12. Illus.: Photo. B&W. Lang.: Swe.
Sweden: Gothenburg, Vadstena. 1980. Histories-sources. ■An interview with Anders Wiklund, musicologist, conductor, and director of Vadstena akademien, about his research on forgotten operas, his views on the training of young singers and the planning of the Swedish opera houses, with references to Göteborgs Operan and Vadstena Akademien.

4215 Bergström, Gunnel. "'Opera—den mest fantastiska psykoterapin'." ('Opera—the Most Fantastic Psychotherapy'.) *MuD*. 1996; 18(4): 15-17. Illus.: Photo. Color. Lang.: Swe.
Sweden. 1989. Histories-sources. ■Interview with Wagnerian tenor Thomas Sunnegårdh about this work with text, song and scenic expression.

4216 Hammarlund, Jan. "Hjördis Schymberg: Entusiasm och vemod, vrede och förtjusning..." (Hjördis Schymberg: Enthusiasm and Sadness, Wrath and Enchantment.) *MuD*. 1996; 18(2): 14-19. Illus.: Photo. B&W. Lang.: Swe.
Sweden. 1909-1992. Biographical studies. ■A survey of Hjördis Schymberg's career at Kungliga Teatern and abroad, with references to her many roles and recordings.

4217 Karlsson, Seth. "När Hitler kom till Wien bröt hon operakontraktet." (When Hitler Arrived at Vienna She Broke Off the Opera Contract.) *MuD*. 1996; 18(4): 22-24. Illus.: Photo. B&W. Lang.: Swe.
Sweden. Austria. 1896. Biographical studies. ■A survey of Kerstin Thorborg's international career.

4218 Keller, James M. "Papageno Comes of Age: At Fifty Håkan Hagegård Sees Some of His Artistic Goals Fulfilled." *OpN*. 1996 Jan 20; 60(9): 20-23. Illus.: Photo. B&W. Color. 7. Lang.: Eng.
Sweden. 1940-1996. Histories-sources. ■Profile, interview with Swedish baritone Håkan Hagegård.

4219 Lundman, Tony. "En djupdykning i det inre." (A Deep Dying in the Inner Man.) *MuD*. 1996; 18(3): 5-6. Illus.: Photo. B&W. Lang.: Swe.
Sweden: Vadstena. 1996. Critical studies. ■A presentation of Carl Unander-Scharin's new opera *Tokfursten (The Foolish Prince)* staged by Nils Spangenberg at Vadstena Akademien.

4220 Tranberg, Sören. "Världens vackraste operasångerska." (The World's Most Beautiful Opera Singer.) *MuD*. 1996; 18(5): 18-21. Illus.: Photo. B&W. Color. Lang.: Swe.

MUSIC-DRAMA: Opera—Performance/production

Sweden. 1965. Histories-sources. ■An interview with the Swedish mezzo-soprano Marie-Louise Hasselgren about her career at Stora Teatern and Göteborgs Operan.

4221 Tranberg, Sören. "'Opera är ingen livsstil för mig'." (For Me, Opera Is Not a Life Style.) *MuD*. 1996; 18(1) : 10-12. Illus.: Photo. B&W. Lang.: Swe.

Sweden: Gothenburg. Czech Republic: Prague. 1990. Histories-sources. ■David Radok in an interview about opera, and his cooperation with the scenographer Tazeena Firth, with reference to his staging of *Jenůfa* by Janáček.

4222 Kellow, Brian. "The Road to Istanbul: At the Yapi Kredi International Leyla Gencer Voice Competition." *OpN*. 1996 Mar 16 ; 60(13): 36-39. Illus.: Photo. B&W. Color. 8. Lang.: Eng.

Turkey. 1924-1996. Histories-sources. ■Profile, interview with Turkish soprano Leyla Gencer.

4223 Sutcliffe, Tom. "British Journal." *OpN*. 1996 Dec 14; 61(6): 71. Illus.: Photo. B&W. 1. Lang.: Eng.

UK. 1996. Histories-sources. ■Accounts of performances at the Royal Opera House, Covent Garden, the English National Opera, the Welsh National Opera, and Glyndebourne.

4224 Aiello, Peter. "Children of Covent Garden." *OQ*. 1996 Sum; 12(4): 75-78. Lang.: Eng.

UK-England: London. 1959-1960. Histories-sources. ■Author's experiences attending opera performances at Covent Garden while teaching at a secondary school.

4225 Dervan, Michael. "Midsummer Magic: ... the Musical Idioms of Britten's Most Bewitching Opera." *OpN*. 1996 Dec 14; 61(6): 35-36, 38. Illus.: Dwg. Photo. B&W. 4. Lang.: Eng.

UK-England. 1960-1996. Critical studies. ■Discussion of the musical and performance values and plot summary of *A Midsummer Night's Dream* by Benjamin Britten, based on the play by William Shakespeare.

4226 Driscoll, F. Paul. "Hit Singles: Famous Handel Arias and Their Interpreters, 1900-50." *OpN*. 1996 July; 61(1): 38-41. Discography. Illus.: Photo. B&W. 5. Lang.: Eng.

UK-England. 1900-1950. Historical studies. ■Discography of Handel arias performed by British singers.

4227 Duffie, Bruce. "Conversation Piece: Kathryn Harries." *OJ*. 1996 Mar.; 29(1): 47-55. Lang.: Eng.

UK-England. 1985-1996. Histories-sources. ■Interview with opera singer Kathryn Harries on her career, repertoire, interpretations, and family life.

4228 Graeme, Roland. "'So Fair the Game, So Rich the Sport': *Dido and Aneas* on Record." *OQ*. 1996 Fall; 13(1): 55-70. Notes. Discography. Lang.: Eng.

UK-England. 1996. Critical studies. ■Rating the recordings of Henry Purcell's *Dido and Aeneas*, with discography and cast list of each disc.

4229 Larson, Martin. "Peter Grimes—från Suffolk till Stockholm." (Peter Grimes—from Suffolk to Stockholm.) *MuD*. 1996; 18 (3): 20-24. Illus.: Photo. B&W. Lang.: Swe.

UK-England. Sweden: Stockholm. 1945-1980. Critical studies. ■A presentation of Benjamin Britten's opera *Peter Grimes*, and the first productions in England staged by Eric Crozier at Sadler's Wells and in Sweden staged by Harald André at Kungliga Teatern.

4230 Larsson, Martin. "Hjärtat i rösten är engelskt." (The Heart of the Voice is English.) *MuD*. 196; 18(1): 7-9: ia. Illus.: Photo. B&W. Lang.: Swe.

UK-England. 1939. Histories-sources. ■An interview with the tenor Philip Langridge about his career.

4231 Lewis, Wilbur Watkin. "Gilbert and Sullivan Repertoire for the Voice Studio and Workshop." *OJ*. 1996 Sep.; 29(3): 17-37. Notes. Biblio. Lang.: Eng.

UK-England. 1872-1900. Critical studies. ■The solo and ensemble literature of Sullivan and Gilbert for use in the voice studio and opera workshop to build technique and stagecraft. Pieces have been catalogued from the piano vocal scores of the twelve operettas.

4232 Pleasants, Henry. "A Reactionary View of Modern Opera (1814-1823)." *OQ*. 1996 Fall; 13(1): 5-10. Notes. Lang.: Eng.

UK-England. 1814-1823. Critical studies. ■Analysis of Richard, Earl of Mount-Edgecumbe's book *Musical Reminiscences*, focusing on the section dealing with years 1814-23, using his observation as a gauge of opera tastes during that era, and his admiration of the *castrato* Gasparo Pachierotti.

4233 Sutcliffe, Tom. "British Journal." *OpN*. 1996 Jan 6; 60(8): 40-41. Illus.: Photo. Color. 1. Lang.: Eng.

UK-England. 1995. Critical studies. ■Review of the preceding season in Great Britain.

4234 Sutcliffe, Tom. "British Journal." *OpN*. 1996 Feb 17; 60(11): 44-45. Illus.: Photo. B&W. 1. Lang.: Eng.

UK-England: London, Leeds, Lewes. 1995-1996. Critical studies. ■Review of 1995 productions at the Royal Opera House, Covent Garden, Opera North (Leeds), and the Glyndebourne Opera touring company.

4235 Teachout, Terry. "A Little *Night* Music." *OpN*. 1996 Dec 14; 61(6): 20-22. Illus.: Photo. B&W. 5. Lang.: Eng.

UK-England. 1960-1996. Critical studies. ■General treatment of *A Midsummer Night's Dream*, by Benjamin Britten, based on the play by William Shakespeare. Includes stills from the Covent Garden production and the 1961 San Francisco production, as well as stills from the 1935 Max Reinhardt film with James Cagney, Mickey Rooney, Anita Louise and Victor Jory, with Hal Mohr's Academy Award-winning photography.

4236 White, Michael J. "The *Norma* Conquest: Bellini's Heroine Has Shot Jane Eaglen to the Top." *OpN*. 1996 Jan 6; 60(8): 18-21. Illus.: Photo. Color. B&W. 3. Lang.: Eng.

UK-England. 1996. Histories-sources. ■Profile, interview with English dramatic/bel canto soprano Jane Eaglen of the English National Opera.

4237 Ramsden, Timothy. "Puccini On Stage." *PlPl*. 1996 Aug/Sep.: 42. Lang.: Eng.

UK-Wales: Cardiff. UK-England: Leeds. 1996. Critical studies. ■Discussion of recent productions of Puccini operas. References to the Welsh National Opera's production of *La Bohème* and Opera North's production of *Madama Butterfly*.

4238 Egrafov, Ju. "Oživajut obrazy Kievskoj Rusi." (Images of Kiev's Rus Are Coming Alive.) *Balet*. 1996; 1: 22-23. Lang.: Rus.

Ukraine: Kiev. 1990-1996. Historical studies. ■The Ukrainian national opera, with emphasis on composer Valerij Kita, choreographer Jurij Puzakov, and conductor Vladimir Kozuchar'.

4239 "The Levine Years: A Chronology ... To Be Continued." *OpN*. 1996 Apr 13; 60(15): 12-14, 16. Illus.: Photo. B&W. Color. 6. Lang.: Eng.

USA. 1943-1996. Histories-sources. ■Chronological and numerical listing of all operas conducted by James Levine, principal conductor and artistic director at the Metropolitan Opera, New York, 1971-1996, for a current total of 1,538 performances.

4240 "Telecast Performance." *OpN*. 1996, Mar 16; 60(13): 48. Illus.: Photo. B&W. [*The Merry Widow* (*Die Lustige Witwe*).] Lang.: Eng.

USA: New York, NY. 1996. Histories-sources. ■Photograph, list of principals, conductor, production staff, telecast performance.

4241 "Metropolitan Opera: Telecast Performances." *OpN*. 1996; 61. Illus.: Design. Diagram. Dwg. Photo. Color. B&W. [*La Forza del Destino* (Sep): 69, *Così fan tutte* (Dec 14): 73.] Lang.: Eng.

USA: New York, NY. 1996. Histories-sources. ■Photograph, list of principals, conductor, production staff, telecast performance.

4242 "Music Makers Devalued." *Econ*. 1996 Feb 17; 338(7953): 80-82. Illus.: Photo. B&W. 1. Lang.: Eng.

USA. 1996. Critical studies. ■Direction and staging in contemporary opera production. Updated productions, radical interpretations and how they affect librettos.

4243 "A Bucolic Chorus." *Econ*. 1996 Aug 24; 340(7980): 69-70. Illus.: Photo. B&W. 1. Lang.: Eng.

USA: Cooperstown, NY. 1995-1996. Historical studies. ■Profile of Glimmerglass Opera, production highlights, artistic director Paul Kellogg, and a comparison with the festival in Glyndebourne.

MUSIC-DRAMA: Opera—Performance/production

4244 "Lyric Opera of Chicago: Radio Broadcast Performances." *OpN.* 1996; 60. Discography. Illus.: Design. Diagram. Dwg. Photo. Color. B&W. [*Simon Boccanegra* (May): 35, *Xerxes* (May): 55, *Faust* (May): 56, *The Ghosts of Versailles* (May), 56, *Don Pasquale* (June): 40, *Don Giovanni* (June): 40, *The Makropulos Affair [Věc Makropulos]* (June): 42, *Andrea Chénier* (June): 42.] Lang.: Eng.
USA: Chicago, IL. 1996. Histories-sources. ■Photographs, lists of principals, conductors, production staff, Lyric Opera of Chicago radio broadcast performances.

4245 Barker, John W. "Handel Harvest: ... The Flourishing Handel Discography." *OpN.* 1996 July; 61(1): 32-37, 46. Discography. Illus.: Photo. B&W. Color. 7. Lang.: Eng.
USA. Europe. 1996. Critical studies. ■Descriptive and evaluative discography of Handel operas available on CD.

4246 Bernheimer, Martin. "*Altmeister*: At Seventy-Five, Julius Rudel Looks Back on His Rich Career." *OpN.* 1996 Mar 2; 60 (12): 16-19. Illus.: Photo. Color. B&W. 8. Lang.: Eng.
USA: New York, NY. 1921-1996. Histories-sources. ■Interview, profile and assessment of the career of conductor Julius Rudel, who joined the New York City Opera in 1943 and was artistic director 1957-79.

4247 Betley, Marge. "John Moran: Composing the Sounds for His Own Magic Kingdom." *AmTh.* 1996 Mar.; 13(3): 42-43. Illus.: Photo. B&W. 1. Lang.: Eng.
USA. 1996. Biographical studies. ■Composer Moran discusses his techniques, influences, collaboration with director Bob McGrath, and work on his opera *Mathew in the School of Life.*

4248 Björling, Anna-Lisa; Farkas, Andrew. "Jussi Björling's Debut at the Met." *OQ.* 1996/97 Win; 13(2): 75-88. Notes. Lang.: Eng.
USA: New York, NY. 1937. Histories-sources. ■Events surrounding Swedish tenor Jussi Björling's maiden performance at the Metropolitan Opera House.

4249 Blier, Steven. "Time after Time: Throughout her Long Career, Leontyne Price Has Inspired Fans and a New Generation of Singers." *OpN.* 1996 Oct.; 61(4): 10-12, 14, 64. Discography. Illus.: Photo. B&W. Color. 13. Lang.: Eng.
USA. 1927-1996. Critical studies. ■Detailed review of the eleven-disc CD retrospective *The Essential Leontyne Price,* covering approximately twenty-five years of her career.

4250 Blier, Steven. "Stand and Deliver: ... the Appeal of Concert Opera." *OpN.* 1996 June; 60(17): 14-19. Illus.: Photo. B&W. Color. 5. Lang.: Eng.
USA: New York, NY. 1952-1996. Historical studies. ■The tradition, conventions, and development of concert opera in New York, particularly by the American Opera Society of New York, under Allen Sven Oxenburg, and the Opera Orchestra of New York under Eve Queler.

4251 Daines, Matthew. "An Interview with John Adams." *OQ.* 1996 Fall; 13(1): 37-54. Notes. Illus.: Photo. B&W. 1. Lang.: Eng.
USA: Berkeley, CA. 1994. Histories-sources. ■Interview with composer John Adams discussing his opera *Nixon in China.*

4252 Davidson, Erika; Elbers, Johan; Bergman, Beth; Klotz, Winnie; Schiller, Beatriz. "Metropolitan Opera: Radio Broadcast Performances." *OpN.* 1996; 60. Discography. Illus.: Design. Diagram. Dwg. Photo. Color. B&W. [*La Bohème* (Jan 6): 30-33, *Don Giovanni* (Jan 6): 34-37, *The Makropulos Case (Věc Makropulos)* (Jan 20): 24-27, *Il Barbiere di Siviglia* (Jan 20): 28-31, *Falstaff* (Feb 3): 28-31, *Otello* (Feb 3): 32-35, *Turandot* (Feb 17): 32-35, *Così fan tutte* (Feb 17): 36-39, *Aida* (Mar 2): 30-33, *Madama Butterfly* (Mar 2): 34-37, *La Forza del Destino* (Mar 16): 28-31, *Carmen* (Mar 16): 32-35, *Salome* (Mar 30): 24-27, *The Voyage* (Mar 30): 28-31, *Andrea Chénier* (Apr 13): 44-47, *Die Walküre* (Apr 13): 48-51, *L'Élisir d'Amore* (Dec 14): 40-43, *Midsummer Night's Dream* (Dec 14): 44-47, *Hansel and Gretel* (Dec 28): 28-31, *Tosca* (Dec 28): 32-35.] Lang.: Eng.
USA: New York, NY. 1996. Histories-sources. ■Photographs, lists of principals, conductors, production staff, biographies, synopses, discographies, radio broadcast performances.

4253 Davidson, Justin. "Hellcat: Denyce Graves Has Made a Career Out of *Carmen.*" *OpN.* 1996 Mar 16; 60(13): 20-21. Illus.: Photo. B&W. Color. 2. Lang.: Eng.
USA. 1966-1996. Histories-sources. ■Profile, interview with Denyce Graves who has built her career on the role of Carmen.

4254 Davidson, Justin. "Dorian Mode: Lowell Liebermann's Version of the Oscar Wilde Classic Bows This Month in Monte Carlo." *OpN.* 1996 May; 60(16): 57, 69. Illus.: Photo. Color. 1. Lang.: Eng.
USA: New York, NY. Monaco: Monte Carlo. 1961-1996. Histories-sources. ■Profile, interview with Lowell Liebermann, composer of the opera *The Picture of Dorian Gray,* based on the novella by Oscar Wilde, with the help of John Cox, textual reviser, and John Mordler, director of Opéra de Monte Carlo. A co-production of Opéra de Monte Carlo and Opera Pacific (Costa Mesa, CA).

4255 Dibbern, Mary. "Coach's Notebook: From Germany." *OJ.* 1996 Sep.; 29(3): 38-45. Lang.: Eng.
USA. Europe. 1985-1995. Histories-sources. ■Interview with opera conductor Mary Chun on her musical education, career progress, and the difficulties and challenges for a woman in a traditionally male occupation.

4256 Driscoll, F. Paul. "Going to the Opera ... with Pat Carroll." *OpN.* 1996 Sep.; 61(3): 25-27, 72. Illus.: Photo. B&W. 2. Lang.: Eng.
USA: New York, NY. 1996. Histories-sources. ■Interview with TV performer/stage actress Pat Carroll on *Falstaff,* by Giuseppe Verdi, libretto by Arrigo Boito. She is probably the only woman to perform Falstaff in *The Merry Wives of Windsor,* by William Shakespeare. Gives her comments on the Metropolitan Opera's production of *Falstaff.*

4257 Driscoll, F. Paul. "Going to the Opera ... with Tama Janowitz: *La Forza del Destino.*" *OpN.* 1996 Nov.; 61(5): 26, 28-29, 65. Illus.: Photo. B&W. Color. 3. Lang.: Eng.
USA: New York, NY. 1996. Biographical studies. ■An evening at the Metropolitan Opera with author Tama Janowitz for *La Forza del Destino,* by Giuseppe Verdi. Includes her reactions to the house itself and comments on the Met titles.

4258 Duffie, Bruce. "Conversation Piece: Eric Halfvarson." *OJ.* 1996 Sep.; 29(3): 52-59. Lang.: Eng.
USA. Europe. 1985-1995. Histories-sources. ■Interview with opera singer Eric Halfvarson on his career and singing technique.

4259 Graune, Erik. "Bland tenorer och Metropolitaner." (Among Tenors and Metropolitans.) *MuD.* 1996; 18(4): 44-45, 47. Lang.: Swe.
USA: New York, NY. 1996. Historical studies. ■A report from a week in April at the Metropolitan, culminating in James Levine's 25th jubilee.

4260 Guinther, Louise T. "Sing Low: Onetime Tenor Dwayne Croft Has Found His True Voice in the Baritone Repertory." *OpN.* 1996 Feb 17; 60(11): 28-31. Illus.: Photo. Color. 4. Lang.: Eng.
USA: Cooperstown, NY. 1962-1996. Histories-sources. ■Profile, interview with American baritone Dwayne Croft.

4261 Gurewitsch, Matthew. "Thriller: Powerhouse Mezzo Dolora Zajick Always Delivers." *OpN.* 1996 Mar 2; 60(12): 8-11. Illus.: Photo. Color. 8. Lang.: Eng.
USA. 1996. Histories-sources. ■Profile, interview with dramatic mezzo-soprano Dolora Zajick with particular emphasis on her clinical approach to style and vocal production.

4262 Innaurato, Albert. "Coda: Middle Voices." *OpN.* 1996 Apr 13; 60(15): 70. Illus.: Photo. B&W. 3. Lang.: Eng.
USA. 1996. Historical studies. ■Comments on the mezzo soprano vocal range, including notes on Kerstin Thorborg, Bruna Castagna, Cloe Elmo, Sonia Ganassi.

4263 James, Jamie. "American Opera Today: A Gloomy Scenario." *OpN.* 1996 Sep.; 61(3): 18, 69-71. Illus.: Photo. Color. 1. Lang.: Eng.
USA. 1946-1996. Critical studies. ■A pessimistic view of American opera today, despite *The Voyage* by Philip Glass, *The Ghosts of Versailles* by John Corigliano, and *Nixon in China* by John Adams. Lists a number of operas given only one production.

CLASSED ENTRIES

MUSIC-DRAMA: Opera—Performance/production

4264   Kálmán, Péter. "Villáminterjú Samuel Ramey-vel." (A Short Interview with Samuel Ramey.) *OperaL.* 1996; 5(4): 24-26. Illus.: Photo. B&W. 1. Lang.: Hun.
USA. 1970-1996. Histories-sources. ■Interview at the Vienna Staatsoper following a performance of *Don Carlos.*

4265   Kellow, Brian. "Notebook." *OpN.* 1996 Dec 28; 61(7): 8. Illus.: Photo. B&W. 2. Lang.: Eng.
USA. 1996. Histories-sources. ■Assessment of the career of soprano Alessandra Marc.

4266   Kellow, Brian. "Sound Bites: Amy Burton." *OpN.* 1996 Dec 28; 61(7): 26-27. Illus.: Photo. Color. 1. Lang.: Eng.
USA. 1996. Biographical studies. ■Brief profile, interview with lyric soprano Amy Burton.

4267   Kennicott, Philip. "Family Affair: Tobias Picker's *Emmeline* Transplants the Oedipus Myth to a New England Setting." *OpN.* 1996 June; 60(17): 24-25. Illus.: Photo. B&W. 1. Lang.: Eng.
USA: Santa Fe, NM. 1996. Historical studies. ■*Emmeline*, a new opera by Tobias Picker, libretto by J.D. McClatchy, based on the novel by Judith Rossner.

4268   Kestner, Joseph A. "Music First: Tulsa Opera Artistic Director Carol I. Crawford Brings Missionary Zeal and Wide-Ranging Talents to Her Work." *OpN.* 1996 Mar 30; 60(14): 18-19, 45. Illus.: Photo. B&W. Color. 4. Lang.: Eng.
USA: Tulsa, OK. 1995. Biographical studies. ■Profile of Carol I. Crawford, new artistic director of the Tulsa Opera.

4269   Kimball, Carol. "Lunch with a Young American Artist: Herbert Perry." *OJ.* 1996 Sep.; 29(3): 46-50. Lang.: Eng.
USA. Europe. 1985-1995. Histories-sources. ■Interview with opera singer Herbert Perry on his career, training, and future engagements.

4270   Kramer, Leighton; Heleotis, Harry, photo. "Wilson's Prism: In Houston *Four Saints in Three Acts* Will Be Transformed by One of Today's Most Imaginative Director-Designers." *OpN.* 1996 Jan 6; 60(8): 10-13. Illus.: Photo. Color. 6. Lang.: Eng.
USA: Houston, TX. 1996. Historical studies. ■Avant-garde director-designer Robert Wilson's new production for the Houston Grand Opera of *Four Saints in Three Acts* by Virgil Thomson, libretto by Gertrude Stein, and the history of its earlier performances, including scenario by Maurice Grosser and a production by Rouben Ter-Artunian. Notes the convention of using an all-Black cast.

4271   Larson, Susan. "Homeless in Boston: ... The Dilemma of Presenting Opera in Beantown." *OpN.* 1996 Sep.; 61(3): 12-14, 17. Illus.: Photo. B&W. Color. 7. Lang.: Eng.
USA: Boston, MA. 1909-1996. Historical studies. ■The history of opera in Boston and its need for a permanent home. Special attention is given to the work of Sarah Caldwell and her Boston Opera Company.

4272   Loomis, George W. "Choice Cuts: The Art of Abridging Handel's Operas." *OpN.* 1996 July; 61(1): 26, 28-30. Illus.: Photo. B&W. Color. 3. Lang.: Eng.
USA. 1920-1996. Historical studies. ■Cutting and editing of Handel operas, particularly in the United States. Emphasis on Lyric Opera of Chicago, Metropolitan Opera, and Glimmerglass Opera.

4273   Marranca, Bonnie. "Hymns of Repetition." *PerAJ.* 1996 Sep.; 18(3): 42-47. Illus.: Photo. B&W. 2. [Number 54.] Lang.: Eng.
USA: New York, NY. 1996. Reviews of performances. ■Robert Wilson's production of Gertrude Stein and Virgil Thomson's *Four Saints in Three Acts* at the Lincoln Center Festival '96.

4274   McKee, David. "Boutique Artist: Patricia Racette Continues to Hone Her Repertory." *OpN.* 1996 Feb 3; 60(10): 27, 49. Illus.: Photo. Color. 1. Lang.: Eng.
USA. 1996. Histories-sources. ■Profile, interview with Patricia Racette.

4275   Melick, Jennifer. "Who is Sylvia?" *OpN.* 1996 Dec 14; 61(6): 12-14, 16, 18. Illus.: Photo. B&W. Color. 4. Lang.: Eng.
USA. 1996. Histories-sources. ■Profile, interview with soprano Sylvia McNair.

4276   Morgan, Kenneth. "Fritz Reiner as Opera Conductor in the 1930s." *OQ.* 1996 Spr; 12(3): 59-77. Notes. Lang.: Eng.
USA: Philadelphia, PA, San Francisco, CA. UK-England: London. 1931-1941. Biographical studies. ■Reiner's work with the Philadelphia Orchestra, San Francisco Opera, and the Royal Opera.

4277   Page, Tim. "Return Trip: The Met Revival of Philip Glass' *The Voyage.*" *OpN.* 1996 Mar 30; 60(14): 8-9. Illus.: Photo. Color. 1. Lang.: Eng.
USA: New York, NY. 1992-1996. Critical studies. ■The genesis and initial performances of *The Voyage*, an opera by Philip Glass commissioned to commemorate the 500th anniversary of the voyage of Christopher Columbus to the New World.

4278   Parsons, Charles H. "The Money Pit: How Did Kentucky Opera Solve Its Rising-Cost Dilemma? By Substituting a Synthesized Orchestra for Real Musicians." *OpN.* 1996 Mar 2; 60(12): 20-22. Illus.: Photo. B&W. Color. 3. Lang.: Eng.
USA: Louisville, KY. 1995. Historical studies. ■Discussion and evaluation of the use of a synthesizer instead of the Louisville Orchestra for the Kentucky Opera's 1995 production of *Hänsel und Gretel.* Use of digital music as a dehumanization of opera.

4279   Rhein, John von. "Truth or Dare: Catherine Malfitano Has Made a Career out of Taking Risks." *OpN.* 1996 June; 60(17): 12-15. Illus.: Photo. Color. B&W. 6. Lang.: Eng.
USA. 1996. Histories-sources. ■Profile, interview with soprano singing-actress Catherine Malfitano concerning her many and varied roles.

4280   Roman, Zoltan. "Mahler and Opera in America." *OQ.* 1996/97 Win; 13(2): 39-54. Notes. Tables. [Revised version of a paper delivered at the Carnegie Hall symposium 'Mahler in America' in November 1994.] Lang.: Eng.
USA: New York, NY. Austria: Vienna. 1907-1911. Historical studies. ■Artistic reverberations felt in American opera when Gustav Mahler agreed to a contract to be a conductor of opera and concerts for the Metropolitan Opera.

4281   Rosenfeld, Lorraine. "All Summer Long: ... From Oregon to Rhode Island—a Guide to Festival Opera in the U.S." *OpN.* 1996 June; 60(17): 31-37. Illus.: Photo. Color. B&W. 10. Lang.: Eng.
USA. Canada. 1996. Histories-sources. ■List of summer 1996 opera festivals.

4282   S[mith], P[atrick] J. "An Era Ends." *OpN.* 1996 Dec 28; 61(7): 4. Lang.: Eng.
USA: New York, NY. 1996. Histories-sources. ■Retirement of Edward Downes as Metropolitan Opera Saturday afternoon broadcast quizmaster.

4283   Sandla, Robert. "A Little Bit Country: Nashville Composer Mike Reid Tackles Opera in *Different Fields.*" *OpN.* 1996 Feb 3; 60(10): 20. Illus.: Photo. B&W. 1. Lang.: Eng.
USA: Nashville, TN. 1996. Historical studies. ■*Different Fields*, a new opera by composer Mike Reid (a former football star) and librettist Sarah Schlesinger, treats American worship of football. This is the third in the Metropolitan Opera Guild's New Opera for New Audiences commissioning program, and is co-commissioned with Opera Memphis.

4284   Schwarz, K. Robert. "Knowing the Score: Conductor Dennis Russell Davies, Long a Champion of New Music, Makes His Met Debut with *The Voyage.*" *OpN.* 1996 Mar 30; 60(14): 10-13. Illus.: Photo. B&W. Color. 2. Lang.: Eng.
USA: Toledo, OH. 1945-1996. Histories-sources. ■Profile, interview with American conductor Dennis Russell Davies making his Metropolitan Opera debut with *The Voyage* by Philip Glass.

4285   Scott, Michael. "American Legend: A Centennial Tribute to Lawrence Tibbett." *OpN.* 1996 Nov.; 61(5): 30-33. Illus.: Photo. B&W. 3. Lang.: Eng.
USA. 1896-1960. Biographical studies. ■The career of American baritone Tibbett, with comments on his performance in new American operas as well as the standard repertory.

4286   Smith, Patrick J. "The Bottom Line." *OpN.* 1996 Mar 2; 60(12): 21. Lang.: Eng.
USA: Louisville, KY. 1996. Critical studies. ■Computerized music instead of an orchestra for operatic performances, with reference to Kentucky Opera. Technology versus live performance—an evaluation.

MUSIC-DRAMA: Opera—Performance/production

4287 Tabachnik, Robin. "Character Studies: The Importance of the Comprimario Singer." *OpN.* 1996 Apr 13; 60(15): 42-43. Illus.: Photo. Color. 3. Lang.: Eng.
USA: New York, NY. 1996. Histories-sources. ■Comments on changes in the comprimario system at the Metropolitan Opera by assistant artistic director, Lenore Rosenberg, language coach Nico Castel, and singers Heidi Grant Murphy, Charles Anthony, Jane Shaulis, Anthony Laciura, Diane Kesling, Betsy Norden, Ariel Bybee, Shirley Love, Andrea Velis. The new system uses participants in the Young Artist Development as a cost-saving device.

4288 Thomason, Paul; Needham, Steven Mark. "More than Mozart: Carol Vaness' Repertory Has Expanded to Include Verdi, Puccini and—Maybe—Bellini." *OpN.* 1996 Feb 17; 60(11): 14-17. Illus.: Photo. Color. B&W. 6. Lang.: Eng.
USA. 1996. Histories-sources. ■Interview with American soprano Carol Vaness.

4289 Tosic, Ljubisa. "Tränen und schlaflose Nächte." (Tears and Sleepless Nights.) *DB.* 1996; 4: 18-21. Append. Illus.: Photo. B&W. 2. Lang.: Ger.
USA. 1975-1996. Biographical studies. ■Portrait of tenor Neil Shicoff, described as expressive but unpredictable.

4290 Van Sant, James A. "Miss Margaret's Way: Veteran Met Diva Margaret Harshaw Shares Her Ideas on Singing." *OpN.* 1996 Mar 2; 60(12): 26-29. Illus.: Photo. B&W. 5. Lang.: Eng.
USA. 1910-1996. Histories-sources. ■Profile, interview with soprano Margaret Harshaw, who spent part of her career as a mezzo-soprano.

4291 Wadsworth, Stephen. "Wild at Heart: How Does a Director Harness a Talent like Lorraine Hunt's?" *OpN.* 1996 Nov.; 61(5): 12-13, 17, 65. Illus.: Photo. B&W. Color. 4. Lang.: Eng.
USA. 1995-1996. Histories-sources. ■Critical evaluation and interviews with soprano Lorraine Hunt and director Peter Sellars. Praises her actorly and vocal interpretations.

4292 Walseon, Heidi. "High and Mighty: David Daniels Is Redefining Boundaries for Countertenors." *OpN.* 1996 July; 61(1): 22-25. Illus.: Photo. Color. 5. Lang.: Eng.
USA. 1966-1996. Biographical studies. ■Profile, interview, and assessment of American countenor David Daniels.

4293 Warburton, Thomas. "Eleanor Everest Freer and the American Opera Movement." *OJ.* 1996 Dec.; 29(4): 2-11. Notes. Chart. 1. Lang.: Eng.
USA. 1864-1940. Historical studies. ■Career of opera impresario, patroness, fundraiser, and composer Eleanor Everest Freer, especially her interest in encouraging the development of American opera in English.

4294 Ward, Robert. "American Opera Today: A Second Chance." *OpN.* 1996 Sep.; 61(3): 19, 71, 74. Lang.: Eng.
USA. 1966-1996. Critical studies. ■Cross-fertilization of opera and musical comedy, as well as grants for development of new operas and revivals of underperformed works, sometimes by regional companies, offer hope for American opera.

4295 Wilcox, Dean. "Political Allegory or Multimedia Extravaganza? A Historical Reconstruction of the Opera Company of Boston's *Intolleranza*." *ThS.* 1996 Nov.; 37(2): 115-134. Notes. Biblio. Illus.: Photo. 5. Lang.: Eng.
USA: Boston, MA. 1965. Historical studies. ■Reconstruction of scenographer Josef Svoboda's designs for the Opera Company of Boston's production of Luigi Nono's *Intolleranza*, directed by Sarah Caldwell. Describes the controversy that surrounded the production.

4296 Wolff, Matt. "*Dream Team*." *OpN.* 1996 Dec 14; 61(6): 24-26. Color. B&W. 4. Lang.: Eng.
USA: New York, NY. 1996. Histories-sources. ■Profile, interview with Tim Albery and Antony McDonald, director and designer of the production of *A Midsummer Night's Dream* by Benjamin Britten, at the Metropolitan Opera, 1996.

4297 Zakariasen, Bill. "Stagecoach Valhalla: Hang on Tight—Glynn Ross Is Bringing Arizona Opera Its First Ever *Ring* Cycle." *OpN.* 1996 June; 60(17): 26-27. Illus.: Photo. Color. 3. Lang.: Eng.

USA: Flagstaff, AZ. 1914-1996. Historical studies. ■Glynn Ross, formerly general director of the Seattle Opera and since 1983 director of the Arizona Opera is presenting the *Ring* in the Ardrey Auditorium, a copy of the Bayreuther Festspielhaus.

Plays/librettos/scripts

4298 Halliwell, Michael. "'The Space Between': Postcolonial Opera?—The Meale/Malouf Adaptation of Voss." *ADS.* 1996 Apr.; 28: 86-98. Notes. Illus.: Photo. B&W. 1. Lang.: Eng.
Australia. 1978-1996. Historical studies. ■Difficulties faced, and liberties taken, by librettist David Malouf and composer Richard Meale in their adaptation of the Patrick White novel, *Voss*.

4299 Shevtsova, Maria. "Greek-Australian Odysseys in a Multicultural World." *PerAJ.* 1996 Jan.; 18(1): 64-70. Notes. Illus.: Photo. B&W. 2. [Number 52.] Lang.: Eng.
Australia: Hobart. 1992-1995. Critical studies. ■IHOS Opera co-founder, composer Constantine Koukias: influence of his background on his work, his multicultural bent, and his pieces *Days and Nights with Christ* and *To Traverse Water*.

4300 Barry, Barbara R. "The Spider's Strategem: The Motif of Masking in *Don Giovanni*." *OJ.* 1996 June; 29(2): 38-55. Lang.: Eng.
Austria. 1786-1789. Critical studies. ■The use of masking in Mozart's *Don Giovanni*, commissioned by the city of Prague (libretto by Lorenzo Da Ponte).

4301 Brown, Bruce Alan; Rice, John A. "Salieri's *Così fan tutte*." *COJ.* 1996; 8(1): 17-43. Notes. Lang.: Eng.
Austria: Vienna. 1731-1837. Historical studies. ■Evidence that Antonio Salieri was Da Ponte's first choice as the composer for his libretto *La scola degli amanti*, which became *Così fan tutte* composed by Mozart.

4302 Cerf, Steven R. "Mixed Doubles: How Should Lovers Match Up?" *OpN.* 1996 Feb 17; 60(11): 10-12. Illus.: Photo. B&W. Color. 3. Lang.: Eng.
Austria: Vienna. 1790-1996. Critical studies. ■Changing views and interpretations of *Così fan tutte* by Wolfgang Amadeus Mozart, his last collaboration with librettist Lorenzo Da Ponte. Suggests that the real challenge to its audiences is its 'trenchant intellectualism, chromatic melancholia, multivalent psychology'.

4303 Platoff, John. "Myths and Realities about Tonal Planning in Mozart's Operas." *COJ.* 1996; 8(1): 3-15. Notes. Lang.: Eng.
Austria: Vienna. 1769-1792. Critical studies. ■Considers tonal structure of Mozart's operas, especially *Le Nozze di Figaro*. Concludes that there is no proof Mozart used tonal planning in his compositions. However, he did associate certain character types with particular keys.

4304 Baker, David J. "Hoffmann's Night with Donna Anna." *OpN.* 1996 Jan 6; 60(8): 22-25. Illus.: Photo. B&W. Color. 5. Lang.: Eng.
Austro-Hungarian Empire: Vienna. 1787-1813. Historical studies. ■An apparent critique of Mozart's *Don Giovanni* in a short story by E.T.A. Hoffmann (*Don Juan: A Fantastical Occurrence*, 1813), with emphasis on the seduction of Donna Anna.

4305 Gurewitsch, Matthew. "How Old is Despina?" *OpN.* 1996 Feb 17; 60(11): 18-21. Illus.: Photo. B&W. 7. Lang.: Eng.
Austro-Hungarian Empire: Vienna. 1790. Critical studies. ■The age and background of Despina in *Così fan tutte* by Wolfgang Amadeus Mozart, developed through close study of the libretto by Lorenzo Da Ponte.

4306 Loomis, George W. "Master List: *Don Giovanni*'s Catalog Aria." *OpN.* 1996 Jan 6; 60(8): 14-17. Illus.: Photo. Color. B&W. 7. Lang.: Eng.
Austro-Hungarian Empire: Vienna. 1787-1996. Historical studies. ■Analysis of the catalog aria 'Madamina' sung by Leporello, in *Don Giovanni* by Wolfgang Amadeus Mozart. Notes the borrowings by librettist Lorenzo Da Ponte, from the opera *Don Juan Tenorio o sia Il Convertato di Pietra* of Giuseppe Gazzaniga, libretto by Giovanni Bertati. Includes photographs of notable interpreters: Salvatore Baccaloni, Walter Berry, Fernando Corena, Geraint Evans, Erich Kunz, Paul Plishka, and Bryn Terfel.

4307 Bolt, Carol. "One Word at a Time." *OC.* 1996 Spr; 37(1): 12-13. Illus.: Photo. B&W. 3. Lang.: Eng.

MUSIC-DRAMA: Opera—Plays/librettos/scripts

Canada. 1996. Histories-sources. ▪Playwright Carol Bolt reflects on the art of becoming an opera librettist. Emphasis on the adaptation of her play *Red Emma* into an opera.

4308 Massoutre, Guylaine. "La musique au théâtre: Entretien avec Alain Thibault." (Music in the Theatre: Interview with Alain Thibault.) *JCT.* 1991; 61: 120-126. Illus.: Photo. B&W. 3. Lang.: Fre.

Canada: Montreal, PQ. 1985-1991. Histories-sources. ▪Alain Thibault describes composing a score for René-Daniel Dubois' text *Ne blâmez jamais les Bédouins*, and his other work in theatrical composition.

4309 Dorsey, Sarah B. "Janáček's *Cunning Little Vixen.*" *OJ.* 1996 Dec.; 29(4): 28-41. Notes. Chart. 4. Lang.: Eng.

Czechoslovakia. 1900-1920. Critical studies. ▪Rural and country influences on Janáček's most best-known opera *Příhody lišky bystroušky*.

4310 Simon, John. "The End of Immortality: ...Love and Death Themes in Janáček's *The Makropulos Case.*" *OpN.* 1996 Jan 20; 60(9): 12-15, 45. Illus.: Photo. Dwg. B&W. 5. Lang.: Eng.

Czechoslovakia: Prague. 1926-1996. Critical studies. ▪Themes of love and death in *Věc Makropulos*, emphasizing the contribution of Czech playwright Karel Čapek, whose comic work Leoš Janáček adapted for his libretto.

4311 Payne, Linda R. "'Setting Shakespear A-Quavering': Characterization and Lyrics in Garrick's Shakespearean Operas of the 1750s." *Restor.* 1996 Win; 11(2): 22-38. Notes. Lang.: Eng.

England. 1712-1756. Historical studies. ▪David Garrick's brief career as a librettist for Shakespearean opera and his work with composer Johann Christoph Schmidt on *The Fairies*, adapted from *A Midsummer Night's Dream* and *The Tempest*.

4312 Hamilton, Kenneth. "Not With a Bang but a Whimper: The Death of Liszt's *Sardanapale.*" *COJ.* 1996; 8(1): 45-58. Notes. Tables. Lang.: Eng.

Europe. 1821-1850. Biographical studies. ▪Considers the reasons for Liszt's failure as an operatic composer with *Le Corsaire* and *Sardanapale* following the relative success of *Don Sanche ou le Château d'Amour*, composed at the age of thirteen.

4313 Lehrman, Leonard J. "Composer's Notebook: What Is Jewish Opera?" *OJ.* 1996 June; 29(2): 56-61. Lang.: Eng.

Europe. USA. 1834-1995. Critical studies. ▪Essay on what constitutes a Jewish repertory in opera, with examination of many operas and operettas from the mid-nineteenth century on.

4314 Armstrong, Alan. "Gilbert-Louis Duprez and Gustave Roger in the Composition of Meyerbeer's *Le Prophète.*" *COJ.* 1996; 8(2): 147-165. Notes. Lang.: Eng.

France: Paris. 1831-1849. Historical studies. ▪Studies the changes made to the role of Jean in the libretto and score of *Le Prophète* between its original composition for singer Gilbert-Louis Duprez in 1841 and its 1848 revision for Gustave Roger.

4315 Cronin, Charles P.D.; Klier, Betje Black. "Théodore Pavie's 'Les babouches du Brahmane' and the Story of Delibes's *Lakmé.*" *OQ.* 1996 Sum; 12(4): 19-23. Notes. Illus.: Photo. Dwg. 4. Lang.: Eng.

France. 1884-1896. Critical studies. ▪Argues that writings of French linguist and orientalist Théodore Pavie were the actual source for Léo Delibes opera *Lakmé*, and not Pierre Loti's quasi-autobiographical *Rarahu, ou le mariage de Loti*.

4316 Everist, Mark. "Meyerbeer's *Il crociato in Egitto*: Melodrama, Opera, Orientalism." *COJ.* 1996; 8(3): 215-250. Notes. Tables. Lang.: Eng.

France. Italy: Venice. 1744-1840. Critical studies. ▪Similarities and differences between Rossi's libretto for *Il crociato* and *Les Chevaliers de Malte* on which it is based, oriental influences on the text, the general interest in exoticism and their reflection in the music of Meyerbeer and his contemporaries.

4317 Habachy, Nimet Saba. "Last Illusion: The Poet André Chénier Penned a Final Poetic Tribute to an 'Aristotart'." *OpN.* 1996 Apr 13; 60(15): 32-33. Illus.: Photo. B&W. 1. Lang.: Eng.

France: Paris. 1750-1820. Biographical studies. ▪The life and loves of Anne-Françoise Aimée de Franquetot de Coigny, a notorious debauchée

of the Napoleonic era, to whom André Chénier gave his poem 'La Jeune Captive.' She is the original of the heroine Maddalena de Coigny in the opera *Andrea Chénier* by Umberto Giordano.

4318 Harwood, Gregory W. "Musical and Literary Parody in Ravel's *L'Enfant et les sortilèges.*" *OJ.* 1996 Mar.; 29(1): 2-16. Notes. Illus.: TA. Photo. 3. Lang.: Eng.

France. 1920-1925. Critical studies. ▪Satire and fantasy in Ravel's second opera *L'Enfant et les Sortilèges*, libretto by Colette. Argues that by viewing the opera as a succession of miniature satires, one can understand the composer's juxtaposition of disparate musical styles.

4319 "Second-Rank Soldiers." *Econ.* 1996 Dec 14; 341(7996): 85-86. Illus.: Photo. B&W. 2. Lang.: Eng.

Germany. 1958-1960. Critical studies. ▪Analysis of characters and music of *Die Soldaten* by Bernd Alois Zimmermann, based on a play by Jakob Lenz, and influence of Berg's *Wozzeck* and Wedekind's *Lulu*.

4320 Buller, Jeffrey L. "The Messianic Hero in Wagner's *Ring.*" *OQ.* 1996/97 Win; 13(2): 21-38. Notes. Lang.: Eng.

Germany. 1996. Critical studies. ▪Wagner's view of Jesus as social revolutionary and that view's reflection in the heroes of his *Ring* cycle.

4321 Ditzler, Kirk. "Influences of Heinrich Marschner's *Der Vampyr* on Richard Wagner's *Der fliegende Holländer.*" *OJ.* 1996 June; 29(2): 2-13. Lang.: Eng.

Germany. 1827-1843. Critical studies. ▪Influence of composer Heinrich Marschner's *Der Vampyr* on Richard Wagner's *Der fliegende Holländer*.

4322 Hannum, Hunter G. "Artist and Audience in *Die Meistersinger von Nürnberg* and *Ariadne auf Naxos.*" *OQ.* 1996 Sum; 12(4): 35-46. Notes. Lang.: Eng.

Germany. Austria. 1849-1913. Critical studies. ▪Self-contained musical composition as a central element of the plot, much like a play within a play, in Wagner's *Die Meistersinger von Nürnberg* and Richard Strauss' *Ariadne auf Naxos*, and how the characters working on their pieces within the opera present it to their onstage audience.

4323 Nelson, Byron. "Weibertotenlieder: German Musical Narratives of Women's Deaths, from Kundry to Schoenberg's *Waldtaube.*" *OQ.* 1996 Sum; 12(4): 47-59. Notes. Lang.: Eng.

Germany. Austria: Vienna. 1842-1911. Critical studies. ▪Examines Wagner's *Parsifal*, Strauss' *Salome* and Schoenberg's *Gurrelieder* in which doomed love results in the death of the woman. The composers' emphasis on the theme of love that is stronger than death.

4324 Peterson, Hans-Gunnar. "Henze, tonsättaren som tänder gnistor." (Henze, the Composer Who Is the Spark That Set It All Off.) *MuD.* 1996; 18(5): 10, 52. Illus.: Photo. B&W. Lang.: Swe.

Germany. Italy. 1926. Biographical studies. ▪A short survey of Hans Werner Henze's career, with references to his operas.

4325 Zoppelli, Luca. "The Twilight of the True Gods: *Cristoforo Colombo*, *I Medici* and the Construction of Italian History." *COJ.* 1996; 8(3): 251-269. Notes. Tables. Lang.: Eng.

Germany. Italy. 1840-1923. Critical studies. ▪Looks at thematic links between *Cristoforo Colombo* by Alberto Franchetti, libretto by Luigi Illica, and *I Medici* by Leoncavallo and at their common ideal of kindling a sense of Italian nationalism through the recreation of historic events. Considers how this 'historical verismo' adversely affected the structure of the two operas.

4326 Baranyi, Ferenc. *Operaszövegek. Szavakkal a zene szolgálatában.* (Librettos: The Text in the Service of Music.) Horpács: Mikszáth; 1996. 206 pp. (Metál könyvek.) Index. Lang.: Hun.

Hungary. 1793-1976. Critical studies. ▪Analysis of the libretti of Hungarian opera.

4327 Sólyom, György. "Mítosz-zenedráma-világdráma: A *Nibelung gyűrűje* felújítása elé IV. Második nap: *Siegfried.*" (Myth, Musical Drama, World Drama—The Revival of *The Ring of the Nibelungen*—Part 4—Second Day: *Siegfried*.) *OperaL.* 1996; 5(3): 13-14. Lang.: Hun.

Hungary: Budapest. 1996. Critical studies. ▪Introduction to the musical drama by Wagner which will be staged by the Budapest Opera House in June, thus continuing the revival of the Ring Tetralogy which was begun three years ago.

CLASSED ENTRIES

MUSIC-DRAMA: Opera—Plays/librettos/scripts

4328 Ashbrook, William. "Whatever Happened to the Cabaletta?" *OQ.* 1996 Spr; 12(3): 35-44. Notes. Lang.: Eng.
Italy. 1700-1799. Critical studies. ■The dramatic use and form of the double-aria form *cabaletta*, much used in 18th-century Italian opera and virtually non-existent today.

4329 Baker, David J. "Passé Composé: In *Andrea Chénier*, Giordano Fashioned His Own Version of the French Revolution." *OpN.* 1996 Apr 13; 60(15): 22-25. MU. Illus.: Photo. Color. 4. Lang.: Eng.
Italy. 1896. Critical studies. ■Musical and factual analysis of the *verismo* opera *Andrea Chénier* composed by Umberto Giordano.

4330 Burton, Deborah. "The Creation of *Tosca*: Toward a Clearer View." *OQ.* 1996 Spr; 12(3): 27-34. Notes. Illus.: Handbill. B&W. 1. Lang.: Eng.
Italy: Milan. 1891-1899. Historical studies. ■Clarifies misconceptions regarding the development of *Tosca*, with attention to Puccini's acquisition of the rights to Sardou's play *La Tosca*, how those rights passed to composer Alberto Franchetti, and then back to Puccini, and how publisher Giulio Ricordi felt about the third act.

4331 Edwards, Geoffrey; Edwards, Ryan. "Images of What Might Have Been: Drama and Dramaturgy in Mercadante's *Il Giuramento*." *OJ.* 1996 Sep.; 29(3): 2-16. Notes. Biblio. Lang.: Eng.
Italy. 1837. Critical studies. ■Examination of the 'failed' opera *Il Giuramento* composed by Saverio Mercadante, libretto by Gaetano Rossi. Author argues that the failure of the opera rests with its misguided libretto.

4332 Kerner, Leighton. "Verdi's Green-Eyed Monster: Jealousy Themes in *Otello* and *Falstaff*." *OpN.* 1996 Feb 3; 60(10): 12-14. Illus.: Photo. B&W. 5. Lang.: Eng.
Italy. 1887-1893. Critical studies. ■Musical and dramatic analysis of jealousy as treated by Giuseppe Verdi and his librettist, Arrigo Boito, in *Otello* and *Falstaff*, adaptations of *Othello* and *The Merry Wives of Windsor*, by William Shakespeare. Includes photographs of Lawrence Tibbett, Sherrill Milnes, and Antonio Scotto as Iago, plus Tibbett and Richard Stilwell as Master Ford.

4333 Phillips-Matz, Mary Jane. "The Venetian Goth and the 'Adorable Bear' of Sant'Agata." *OQ.* 1996/97 Win; 13(2): 13-20. Notes. Illus.: Pntg. B&W. 1. Lang.: Eng.
Italy: Venice, Milan. 1843-1867. Historical studies. ■Relationship between Giuseppe Verdi and his librettist Francesco Maria Piave.

4334 Roccatagliati, Alessandro. "Felice Romani, Librettist by Trade." *COJ.* 1996; 8(2): 113-145. Notes. Lang.: Eng.
Italy. 1810-1850. Biographical studies. ■Analyses the demands made on Romani by the theatrical institutions that employed him. Studies the collaborative process between Romani and different composers, including Meyerbeer and Bellini, and the degree to which he could influence the composition of an opera.

4335 Sommariva, Andrea, ed. *Felice Romani. Melodrammi. Poesie. Documenti.* (Felice Romani: Music Dramas. Poems. Documents.) Florence: Olschki; 1996. 363 pp. (Historiae Musicae Cultures. Biblioteca 77.) Pref. Index. Notes. Lang.: Ita.
Italy. 1788-1865. Critical studies. ■A collection of essays on the Italian librettist Felice Romani. His librettos for Simone Mayr, Gaetano Donizetti and Vincenzo Bellini.

4336 Marczyński, Jacek. "World's Shame at the Opera." *TP.* 1996 Oct.; 38(4): 35-41. Illus.: Photo. Color. 4. Lang.: Eng, Fre.
Poland. 1995. Critical studies. ■Comparison of the work of composers Elżbieta Sikora and Joanna Bruzdowicz, focusing on Sikora's opera *Wyrywacz serc* and Bruzdowicz's opera *Kolonia karna*.

4337 Malm, Anna Stina. "Boris Godunov—skrämmande aktuell." (Boris Godunov—Frighteningly Up-to-Date.) *MuD.* 1996; 18(4): 12-14. Illus.: Photo. B&W. Lang.: Swe.
Russia. 1874. Historical studies. ■A short survey of the historical person Boris Godunov, and Puškin's and Mussorgskij's interpretations.

4338 Quraishi, Ibrahim. "*Kitezh* and the Russian Notion of Oriental Despotism." *OQ.* 1996/97 Win; 13(2): 69-74. Notes. Lang.: Eng.

Russia. 1907. Critical studies. ■The popularity of Rimskij-Korsakov's *The Legend of the Invisible City of Kitezh* from the perspective of Russia's fear of the 'restless heathens' of the orient, and from the fallout of the Russo-Japanese, Crimean and Russo-Turkish Wars.

4339 Peterson, Hans-Gunnar. "Rucklarens väg, svensk text: Östen Sjöstrand." (The Rake's Progress, Swedish Version: Östen Sjöstrand.) *MuD.* 1996; 18(5): 16-17. Illus.: Photo. B&W. Lang.: Swe.
Sweden. 1953-1974. Biographical studies. ■A presentation of the Swedish poet Östen Sjöstrand, who translated W.H. Auden's libretto to *The Rake's Progress* for the Swedish version staged by Ingmar Bergman in 1961, with references to his own libretto *Gästabudet (The Banquet)* and his cooperation with the composers György Ligeti and Sven Erik Bäck.

4340 Ganz, Arthur. "*Don Giovanni* Shavianized: *Man and Superman* as Mozartean Commentary." *OQ.* 1996 Fall; 13(1): 21-28. Notes. Lang.: Eng.
UK-England. 1905. Critical studies. ■Argues that Shaw wrote *Man and Superman* as a commentary on Mozart's *Don Giovanni*.

4341 McClatchie, Stephen. "Benjamin Britten, *Owen Wingrave* and the Politics of the Closet, or, 'He Shall Be Straightened Out at Paramore'." *COJ.* 1996; 8(1): 59-75. Notes. Lang.: Eng.
UK-England. 1930-1971. Critical studies. ■Analyses *Owen Wingrave* as a reflection of the main issues in Britten's life—pacifism and homosexual love. Considers the constant conflicts for both Britten and Wingrave between secrecy and disclosure, militarism and pacifism.

4342 Smillie, Thomson. "Britten's *Albert Herring*: A Glossary of Unfamiliar Words and Phrases." *OJ.* 1996 June; 29(2): 14-37 . Lang.: Eng.
UK-England. 1947-1996. Instructional materials. ■Glossary of the comic opera *Albert Herring* by composer Benjamin Britten and librettist Eric Crozier, compiled for use in Kentucky Opera's 1996 production at the Bomhard Theatre, directed by Peter Hemmings.

4343 Tommasini, Anthony. "In Britten's Complex 'Dream,' a Balance of Light and Dark." *New York Times.* 1996 Nov 24(Sect 2): 31, 33. Illus.: Photo. B&W. 1. Lang.: Eng.
UK-England. 1960-1996. Historical studies. ■Analysis of the opera *A Midsummer Night's Dream* by Benjamin Britten, with comments by Tim Albery, stage director of the Metropolitan Opera's premiere production of the work. The dark underside of the opera and its relation to the composer's life are examined, with notes on the music and plot adaptation of the play by William Shakespeare.

4344 National Opera Association. "Transcript of the Symposium on Marc Blitzstein's Unfinished Opera *Sacco and Vanzetti*." *OJ.* 1996 Mar.; 29(1): 26-46. Lang.: Eng.
USA: Cambridge, MA. 1996. Histories-sources. ■Transcript of a conference symposium held by the National Opera Association (publishers of *Opera Journal*) on Blitzstein's opera *Sacco and Vanzetti* in January 1996.

4345 Gainer, Rosemary. "*Natoma*, by Victor Herbert: An American 'Grand' Opera?" *OJ.* 1996 Dec.; 29(4): 12-27. Notes. Chart. 4. Lang.: Eng.
USA. 1900-1920. Historical studies. ■Early opera in America as seen in Victor Herbert's first full-length opera *Natoma*, libretto by Joseph Deign Redding.

4346 Kellow, Brian. "Notebook." *OpN.* 1996 July; 61(1): 12. Illus.: Photo. B&W. Color. Lang.: Eng.
USA. 1996. Critical studies. ■Brief notes on operas by American composer Jack Beeson, *Hello Out There, The Sweet Bye and Bye, My Heart's in the Highlands, Captain Jinks of the Horse Marines, Dr. Heidegger's Fountain of Youth, Sorry, Wrong Number* (story by Lucille Fletcher), and especially *Lizzie Borden*, with libretto by Kenward Elmslie and scenario by Richard Plant. Has comments on the Columbia Opera Workshop and its production of such works as *Paul Bunyan* by Benjamin Britten, *The Mother of Us All* by Virgil Thomson and Gertrude Stein, *Evangeline* by Otto Luening, and *The Medium* by Giancarlo Menotti.

4347 Wynne, Peter. "Return of the Native: David Carlson's *Dreamkeepers* Revives a Once-Popular American Opera Theme." *OpN.* 1996 Jan 6; 60(8): 28-29. Illus.: Photo. B&W. Color. 3. Lang.: Eng.

MUSIC-DRAMA: Opera—Plays/librettos/scripts

USA: Salt Lake City, UT. 1996. Histories-sources. ■The new opera *Dreamkeepers* by David Carlson, libretto by Aden Ross, focuses on the Ute Indians, who inhabited eastern Utah for thousands of years before the arrival of white settlers. Commissioned by the Utah Opera to commemorate the centennial of Utah's statehood. Traditional Ute musical material and instruments are included.

4348 Moss, Linell Gray. "Rhythm and Text in the Music of Igor Stravinsky: A Study of Three Neoclassical Operatic Works." *OJ.* 1996 Mar.; 29(1): 17-25. Notes. Chart. 3. Lang.: Eng.
USSR. 1926-1951. Critical studies. ■The unification of text and music in three Stravinsky operas: *Oedipus Rex* (libretto by Cocteau), *Perséphone* (libretto by André Gide), and *The Rake's Progress* (libretto by W.H. Auden and Chester Kallman). Specifically, the author examines the influences on the works, the characteristics of Stravinsky's rhythmic style in the operas, and his perspectives on drama and text.

Reference materials

4349 Gooding, Wayne. "Opera On-Line." *OC.* 1996 Spr; 37(1): 16-19. Lang.: Eng.
Canada. 1996. Historical studies. ■Information on various opera web sites, how to search for opera information on the internet and how to subscribe to electronic opera mailing lists.

4350 Gelli, Piero, ed. *Dizionario dell'opera.* (Dictionary of Opera.) Milan: Baldini & Castoldi; 1996. 1429 pp. Index. Lang.: Ita.
Europe. 1500-1996. ■A dictionary of operas with a brief summary of the plot and information about the premiere.

4351 Milnes, Rodney, ed. *Opera Index 1996.* London: Opera; 1996. 93 pp. Lang.: Eng.
UK-England. USA. 1996. Histories-sources. ■General subject index to volume 47 of *Opera*, with additional separate indexes, artists and contributors.

Relation to other fields

4352 Castelvecchi, Stefano. "From *Nina* to *Nina*: Psychodrama, Absorption and Sentiment in the 1780s." *COJ.* 1996; 8(2): 91-112. Notes. MU. Illus.: Dwg. B&W. 2. Lang.: Eng.
France: Paris. 1750-1794. Historical studies. ■The interrelationship between melodrama in Paisiello's *Nina* and psychodramatic cures practiced by psychiatrists of the day. Analyzes the way Nina's disturbed mental state is portrayed in Paisiello's music.

4353 Žižek, Slavoj. "Ni spolnega razmerja—Wagner kot Lacanovec." (No Sexual Relationship: Wagner as Lacanian.) 7-42 in Zupančič, Alenka, ed. *Filozofija v operi 2. Simptom Wagner.* Ljubljana: Društvo za teretsko analizo; 1996. 93 pp. Lang.: Slo.
Germany. 1840-1882. Critical studies. ■A psychoanalytical approach to the sexual theme in Wagner's operas.

4354 Dell'Antonio, Andrew. "*Il divino Claudio*: Monteverdi and Lyric Nostalgia in Fascist Italy." *COJ.* 1996; 8(3): 271-284. Notes. Lang.: Eng.
Italy. 1901-1947. Historical studies. ■How historical evidence was adjusted by Italian scholars and critics in accordance with the mood for 'lyric nostalgia' generated by the fascist regime. This 'adjustment' created Monteverdi as the 'father of opera' following the death of Verdi.

4355 Crory, Neil. "Crossover Art." *OC.* 1996 Win; 37(4): 18-21. Illus.: Photo. B&W. 5. Lang.: Eng.
USA. Canada. 1950-1996. Critical studies. ■Examination of opera in popular culture. Emphasis on the use of opera in advertising and in films.

Research/historiography

4356 Langer, Arne. "Zur Aufzeichnung der Operainszenierung." (Toward a Record of Opera Productions.) *KSGT.* 1996; YB: 103-118 . Illus.: Graphs. Handbill. Dwg. B&W. 10. Lang.: Ger.
Germany. 1700-1799. Historical studies. ■Analytical approaches to the performance of roles and busy scenes in records of operatic performance.

Theory/criticism

4357 Peterson, Hans-Gunnar. "Musikens universum heter Kundera." (The Universe of Music Is Named Kundera.) *MuD.* 1996; 18(1): 15. Illus.: Photo. B&W. Lang.: Swe.

Europe. 1995. Critical studies. ■A presentation of Milan Kundera's book *Les testaments trahis* with reference to music and Leoš Janáček.

4358 Pompe, Gregor. "Rojstvo in smrt tragedije ali kako sta se združili apolinična in dionizična sila." (Birth and Death of Tragedy or How the Apollonian and Dionysian Forces Were United.) *Dialogi.* 1996; 32(7-8): 18-25. Lang.: Slo.
Germany. 1840-1882. Historical studies. ■Nietzsche's view of Greek tragic art applied to Wagnerian opera, interpreted as a fusion of the Apollonian and the Dionysian.

4359 Reinäcker, Gerd. "Asyl des schönen Scheins." (Asylum of Nice Appearance.) *TZ.* 1996; 6: 52-55. Illus.: Photo. B&W. 1. Lang.: Ger.
Germany. 1900. Historical studies. ■Analysis of the opera criticism of Eduard Hanslick.

4360 Malmborg, Lars af; Huldin-Halldin, Marga. "En aldrig stillad nyfikenhet." (A Never Appeased Curiosity.) *MuD.* 1996; 18 (3): 8-13. Illus.: Photo. B&W. Lang.: Swe.
Sweden. 1996. Histories-sources. ■A conversation about the opera today, the training of the singers, and the staging policy, with references to Walter Felsenstein.

Training

4361 Ackermann, Renate. "Stimme, Körper." (Voice, Body.) *DB.* 1996; 6: 34-35. Lang.: Ger.
1996. Histories-sources. ■The author, an opera director and teacher, on the education of the body as well as the voice of opera singers.

4362 Thöming, Anja-Rosa. "Übungsplatz für Opernsänger." (Training Ground for Opera Singers.) *DB.* 1996; 11: 47-49. Illus.: Photo. B&W. 3. Lang.: Ger.
Germany: Hamburg. 1994-1996. Historical studies. ■An experiment of the Hamburger Staatsoper, offering a studio where graduates of colleges of music, or individuals on grants, have a chance to act and sing.

Operetta

Performance spaces

4363 Scharferberg, Chrisfried. "Die Staatsoperette Dresden." (The Dresden State Operetta.) *BtR.* 1996; Special issue: 56-62. Illus.: Design. Lighting. Photo. B&W. Color. 12. Lang.: Ger.
Germany: Dresden. 1925-1996. Historical studies. ■The technical director of the theatre describes its use as a ballroom before the founding of the Staatsoperette in 1947.

Performance/production

4364 Nagy, Ildikó. "Adalékok a magyar századforduló mentalitástörténetéhez Kacsóh-Heltai-Bakonyi: *János vitéz* és Lehár-Leon-Stein: *A víg özvegy* alapján." (A Contribution to the Turn-of-the-Century History of Mentality in Hungary Based on Pongrác Kacsóh-Jenő Heltai-Károly Bakonyi: *John, the Brave* and Ferenc Lehár-Victor Leon-Leo Stein: *The Merry Widow (Die Lustige Witwe).)* *SzSz.* 1996; 30/31: 162-171. Notes. Lang.: Hun.
Austro-Hungarian Empire. 1904-1906. Historical studies. ■A comparative analysis of the two operettas as a popular genre in the Austro-Hungarian Monarchy.

4365 Bredschneyder, Fred. *Meer dan een eeuw operette in Nederland.* (More than a Century of Operetta in the Netherlands.) Naarden: Stengholt; 1995. 14 pp. Biblio. Index. Illus.: Photo. B&W. Color. 42. Lang.: Dut.
Netherlands. 1890-1995. Histories-specific. ■History of the genre in the Netherlands.

PUPPETRY
General

Administration

4366 Rebehn, Lars. "Plakate für das Puppentheater." (Posters for the Puppet Theatre.) *PInfo.* 1996; 74(1): 41-46. Illus.: Poster. B&W. 9. Lang.: Ger.
Germany. 1800-1996. Historical studies. ■History of advertising materials for puppet theatre, from seventeenth-century handbills to contemporary posters.

Design/technology

4367 Gschandtner, Doris. "Genächte Puppen aus Trikot." (Sewn Puppets from Cotton Jersey.) *PInfo.* 1996; 74(2): 36-39. Illus.: Design. Photo. B&W. 10. Lang.: Ger.
Germany. 1996. Histories-sources. ■Report on a workshop in which puppets were made from cotton jersey. Includes instructions for construction.

4368 Bóta, Gábor. "Intellektuális sziget volt a bábszínház." (The Puppet Theatre Was an 'Intellectual Island'.) *Sz.* 1996; 29(6): 8-10. Illus.: Photo. B&W. 2. Lang.: Hun.
Hungary: Budapest. France: Paris. 1947-1996. Histories-sources. ■A talk with Vera Bródy, a leading puppet designer of the Hungarian State Puppet Theatre since 1951, now living in Paris.

4369 Hogan, Jane. "A Puppet Regime." *TCI.* 1996 Aug/Sep.; 30(7): 9. Illus.: Photo. Color. 1. Lang.: Eng.
USA: Storrs, CT. 1996. Technical studies. ■Joyce L. Fritz designed more than 200 puppets, including costumes, for a production of Mark Twain's *A Connecticut Yankee in King Arthur's Court* for the Connecticut Repertory Theatre.

4370 Johnson, Iver. "Finding the Right Tool." *PuJ.* 1996 Sum; 47(4): 16-17. Illus.: Photo. Dwg. 4. Lang.: Eng.
USA. 1996. Technical studies. ■How to choose the correct tool for the job. Covers hand and power tools for sculpting, puppet making, woodcarving, and where to order tool supplies.

4371 Rixford, Ellen. "'Extra Terrestrials Do Winter': Rockefeller Plaza Holiday Windows." *PuJ.* 1996 Spr; 47(3): 12-13. Illus.: Photo. 5. Lang.: Eng.
USA: New York, NY. 1995-1996. Historical studies. ■Puppetry designs for store Christmas windows in New York City, created by students at the School of Visual Arts.

Institutions

4372 Ábrahám, Eszter; Koncz, Zsuzsa, photo.; Révész, Róbert, photo. "Jan Dvorak és a Drak." (Jan Dvorak and the Drak.) *Sz.* 1996; 29(6): 15-17. Illus.: Photo. B&W. 3. Lang.: Hun.
Czechoslovakia: Prague. 1948-1990. Histories-sources. ■An interview with Czech artist Jan Dvořak, founder of the renowned Divadlo Drak of Prague on structure, financial operation, designing and training with survey of outstanding performances.

4373 Vaïs, Michel. "Le Pouls des marionnettes du monde entier: Le Huitième Festival mondial de marionnettes de Charleville-Mézières: 23 septembre - 2 octobre 1988." (The Pulse of Puppets of the Entire World: The Eighth World Puppetry Festival of Charleville-Mézières: September 23-October 2, 1988.) *JCT.* 1989; 51: 117-131. Notes. Illus.: Dwg. Photo. B&W. 14. Lang.: Fre.
France: Charleville-Mézières. Spain. 1988. Historical studies. ■Background and impressions of productions at 1988 festival, including important Spanish representation and theatre of animated objects.

4374 Fuchs, Barbara. "Mut zur Konsequenz." (Courage to Take the Consequences.) *TZ.* 1996; 4: 65-67. Illus.: Photo. B&W. 2. Lang.: Ger.
Germany: Bochum. 1996. Reviews of performances. ■Report on Fidena 1996, an international puppetry festival held in Bochum, and its program.

4375 Nieguth, Elke. "11. Internationale Festwoche im FITS." (Eleventh International 'Festwoche' in FITS.) *PInfo.* 1996; 74(1) : 14-17. Illus.: Photo. B&W. 5. Lang.: Ger.
Germany: Stuttgart. 1996. Reviews of performances. ■Survey of the international puppetry festival in Stuttgart.

4376 Reach, Wilfried; Toen, Ulrich, pref. "Der X. Versuch: die alte Kunst des Puppenspiels in der alten Stadt Leipzig zu etablieren." (The Nth Attempt to Establish the Old Art of Puppetry in the Old Town of Leipzig.) *PInfo.* 1996; 74(1): 29-32. Pref. Illus.: Photo. B&W. 4. Lang.: Ger.
Germany: Leipzig. 1989-1996. Histories-sources. ■Reach describes how his puppetry became part of Theater der Jungen Welt in the 1991-92 season.

4377 Schoppan, Marianne; Weindorf, Anne. "Das Bühnenportrait: Puppentheater Knorzkopp." (The Portrait of a Theatre Group: Knorzkopp Puppet Theatre.) *PInfo.* 1996; 74(2): 28-30. Illus.: Photo. B&W. 5. Lang.: Ger.
Germany: Kassel. 1984-1996. Histories-sources. ■The authors' table theatre for children ages six to ten, and their method of cooperation.

4378 Balogh, Géza. "Elfogult jóslatok." (Biased Prophecies.) *Sz.* 1996; 29(6): 21-23. Illus.: Photo. B&W. 3. Lang.: Hun.
Hungary: Budapest. 1996. Histories-sources. ■Director Géza Balogh succinctly introduces the companies and individual artists invited to the UNIMA festival, and outlines also his expectations concerning the artistic balance of the event.

4379 Bóta, Gábor. "Bábvilág Magyarországon." (World of Puppetry in Hungary.) *Sz.* 1996; 29(6): 6-8. Illus.: Photo. B&W. 5. Lang.: Hun.
Hungary. 1950-1990. Historical studies. ■Presenting a general survey of the Hungarian puppet stage with focus on the internationally known Hungarian State Puppet Theatre (Állami Bábszínház), Budapest.

4380 Busse, Christiane. "'Kommission für déjà vus'." (Commission For Déjà Vu.) *PInfo.* 1996; 74(2): 4-8. Illus.: Photo. Poster. B&W. 6. Lang.: Ger.
Hungary: Budapest. 1996. Reviews of performances. ■Survey of the seventeenth congress and world festival of UNIMA.

4381 Mészáros, Emőke. "Élettelen tárgyak élő múzeuma." (Living Museum of Lifeless Objects.) *Sz.* 1996; 29(6): 12-15. Illus.: Photo. B&W. 6. Lang.: Hun.
Hungary: Budapest. 1969-1996. Historical studies. ■An introduction to the puppetry collection of the Hungarian Theatre Museum and Institute by the head of the department with special accent on Hedvig Belitska-Scholtz's activity in collecting and creating the special division in 1969.

4382 Székely, György. "A bábok világünnepe." (World Festival of Puppets.) *Sz.* 1996; 29(6): 1. Illus.: Photo. B&W. 1. Lang.: Hun.
Hungary: Budapest. 1996. Historical studies. ■A brief historical survey on the history of puppet art on the occasion of the 17th Festival of UNIMA (International Association of Puppetry) held in Budapest June 23-30, where, with exception of Africa, each continent was richly represented within the framework of an official and an 'off' program.

4383 Trefalt, Uroš. "Lutkovni festival Klemenčičevi dnevi, Novo mesto." (Klemenčič Days Puppet Festival in Novo mesto.) *Lutka.* 1996; 52: 1-20. Illus.: Photo. B&W. Lang.: Slo.
Slovenia: Novo mesto. 1996. Historical studies. ■Program of the second Puppetry Biennial in Novo mesto.

4384 Varl, Breda. *Letopis Lutkovnega gledališča Maribor.* (Maribor Puppet Theatre Chronicle.) Maribor: Lutkovno gledališče; 1995. 80 pp. Biblio. Illus.: Photo. Color. Lang.: Slo.
Slovenia: Maribor. 1974-1995. Historical studies. ■The production history of the Maribor Puppet Theatre.

4385 Latshaw, Pat. "A Magic Weekend in Atlanta." *PuJ.* 1996 Win; 48(2): 16-17. Illus.: Photo. Sketches. 3. Lang.: Eng.
USA: Atlanta, GA. 1995. Historical studies. ■Gala opening ceremony for Center of Puppetry Arts' new west wing and a one-day Puppetry Arts Festival. Describes the new wing and activities to be conducted there. The Festival highlighted the role of civic participation in the arts, with its emphasis on corporate, volunteer, and private involvement.

4386 Trefalt, Uroš. "Iskanje izgubljenega časa." (In Search of Lost Time.) *Lutka.* 1996; 51: 18-22. Biblio. Illus.: Photo. B&W. Lang.: Slo.
Yugoslavia: Primskovo. 1931-1958. Historical studies. ■History of the Primskovo puppet theatre, Lutkovno gledališče Primskovo, founded by the Czech A. V. Ševcu. Continued in *Lutka* 52, 71-74, and 53, 1120.

PUPPETRY: General

Performance spaces

4387 Flechsig, Horst. "Marionetten als Messeattraktion." (Marionettes as Fairground Attractions.) *Mimos.* 1996; 1/2: 23-25. Notes. Lang.: Ger.
Germany: Leipzig. 1600-1799. Historical studies. ■New knowledge about the history of puppeteers in the seventeenth and eighteenth centuries, including their expulsion from the fairgrounds.

Performance/production

4388 Adam, Marthe. "Le Théâtre de marionnettes actuel: Ambiguïté, provocation, recherche." (Contemporary Puppet Theatre: Ambiguity, Provocation, Searching.) *JCT.* 1989; 51: 70-89. Notes. Illus.: TA. Dwg. Photo. B&W. 16. Lang.: Fre.
Canada. 1989. Historical studies. ■Sources of inspiration and contemporary trends in Quebec's puppet and marionette theatres.

4389 Blanchette, Diane. "Le Moi et la marionnette: Témoignage." (The Self and the Puppet: Testimony.) *JCT.* 1989; 51: 104-107. Illus.: Photo. B&W. 1. Lang.: Fre.
Canada: Montreal, PQ. 1985-1989. Histories-sources. ■Actor-puppeteer Diane Blanchette compares tasks of puppetry and acting.

4390 Fréchette, Michel. "La Marionnette au Québec: Histoire et réalité." (Puppetry in Quebec: History and Reality.) *JCT.* 1989; 51: 90-103. Notes. Biblio. Illus.: Poster. Dwg. Photo. B&W. 7. Lang.: Fre.
Canada. 1655-1989. Historical studies. ■Use of puppets and marionettes in Quebec from first records of Amerindian practice to present day.

4391 Vaïs, Michel. "Renaissance et déclin en Chine: Entretien avec Jean-Luc Penso." (Renaissance and Decline in China: Interview with Jean-Luc Penso.) *JCT.* 1989; 51: 145-147. Illus.: Photo. B&W. 1. Lang.: Fre.
China. Taiwan. 1975-1989. Histories-sources. ■French puppeteer Jean-Luc Penso describes studying and performing in Taiwan, and condition of puppet theatre in Taiwan and China.

4392 Malíková, Nina. "Stars Appearing in the Puppeteers' Sky/ Les étoiles montantes du théâtre de marionnettes tchèque." *DTh.* 1996; 12: 65-73. Illus.: Photo. B&W. 11. Lang.: Eng, Fre.
Czech Republic: Cheb, Vodňany. 1996. Critical studies. ■The young puppet theatre groups Buchty a loutky and Divadlo Continuo.

4393 Vaïs, Michel. "La Descente du sphinx: Entretien avec Brunella Eruli." (Descent of the Sphinx: Interview with Brunella Eruli.) *JCT.* 1989; 51: 111-116. Illus.: Photo. B&W. 3. Lang.: Fre.
France. Italy. Poland. 1960. Historical studies. ■Uses and limits of puppets in theatrical exploration by established European directors.

4394 Lieser, Stefan. "Vom Menschen und Puppen." (Of Men and Puppets.) *DB.* 1996; 7: 50-51. Illus.: Photo. B&W. 2. Lang.: Ger.
Germany: Bochum. 1996. Reviews of performances. ■The 37th annual Fidena festival of puppetry.

4395 Spillmann, Uwe. "Kaspers Drekorgel-Theater." (Punch's Hurdy-Gurdy Theatre.) *PInfo.* 1996; 74(1): 25-28. Illus.: Photo. B&W. 6. Lang.: Ger.
Germany. 1996. Histories-sources. ■Author describes his own form of puppet theatre, involving street theatre and 'open acting' to encourage audience participation.

4396 Recoing, Alain. "Gilgamesh en Indonésie: Tradition et modernité." (Gilgamesh in Indonesia: Tradition and Modernity.) *JCT.* 1989; 51: 137-144. Illus.: Photo. B&W. 7. Lang.: Fre.
Indonesia. France. 1988. Histories-sources. ■Problems and solutions of co-production between French company Théâtre aux Mains Nues, led by Alain Recoing, and Indonesian *dalang* artists of Seni Karawitan de Solo, resulting in *Le Voyage spirituel de Gilgamesh (The Spiritual Voyage of Gilgamesh).*

4397 Bardijewska, Liliana. "The Magic World of Janusz Ryl-Krystianowski." *TP.* 1996 July; 38(3): 27-31. Illus.: Photo. Color. B&W. 4. Lang.: Eng, Fre.
Poland: Poznań. 1994-1995. Reviews of performances. ■Review of two Teatr Animacji productions directed by Janusz Ryl-Krystianowski, *Ribidi rabidi knoll*, scenario by Katarzyna Grajewska and Tadeusz Pajdala, opened in 1994, and *Bajka o księciu Pipo (A Tale of Prince Pipo)* by Pierre Gripari, adapted by Pajdala, opened in 1995.

4398 Pászt, Patrícia; Koncz, Zsuzsa, photo. "Színház-forma-művészet: Beszélgetés Henryk Jurkowski-val." (Theatre—Form—Art: An Interview with Henryk Jurkowski.) *Sz.* 1996; 29(10): 27-28. Illus.: Photo. B&W. 3. Lang.: Hun.
Poland. 1950-1990. Histories-sources. ■A talk with professor Henryk Jurkowski, honorary chairman of UNIMA, on tendencies of the Polish puppet theatre during the past four decades.

4399 Rogacki, Henryk Izydor. "The Odyssey of Orpheus." *TP.* 1996 July; 38(3): 32-37. Illus.: Photo. Color. B&W. 5. Lang.: Eng, Fre.
Poland: Warsaw. 1995. Reviews of performances. ■Review of the puppet play *Orfeusz (Orpheus)* written and directed by Zygmunt Smandzik at Teatr Lalka.

4400 Waszkiel, Marek. "Theatre for Children—The Puppet Theatre." *TP.* 1996 July; 38(3): 15-22. Illus.: Photo. Dwg. Color. B&W. 8. Lang.: Eng, Fre.
Poland. 1945-1996. Historical studies. ■Comparison of the puppetry performance styles of Jan Dorman and Jan Wilkowski, with attention to Dorman's school of actor-audience interaction and Wilkowski's Brechtian philosophy of alienation.

4401 Wolanski, Valdemer. "Puppetry in Poland." *PuJ.* 1996 Sum; 47(4): 6-7. Illus.: Photo. Dwg. Sketches. 5. [Part 1.] Lang.: Eng.
Poland. 1500-1945. Historical studies. ■History of puppetry in Poland from early medieval wandering juggling troupes to World War II.

4402 Kovács, Ildikó. "A mágia színháza." (Theatre of Magic.) *Sz.* 1996; 29(6): 10-12. Illus.: Photo. B&W. 3. Lang.: Hun.
Romania: Cluj-Napoca. 1928-1996. Histories-sources. ■The eminent personality of Hungarian puppetry in Transylvania writes about the experiences of her rich career.

4403 Ljandzberg, Ol'ga. "Ovacii, perechodjašćie v lu..." (Ovation, Turning into Puddles.) *PTZ.* 1996; 6: 19-21. Lang.: Rus.
Russia: Leningrad. 1940-1945. Histories-sources. ■Recollections of the founding of Kukolnyj Teat'r Skazki during the siege of Leningrad, by its founder.

4404 Vychodceva, L.A. *Teat'r kukol: Metodičeskie rekomendacii.* (Puppet Theatre: Recommendations on Methodology.) Magnitogorsk: Magnitogorskij Ped. In-t; 1995. 29 pp. Lang.: Rus.
Russia. 1995. Instructional materials. ■Manual for organizing puppet theatre, including illustrations of puppet theatre characters.

4405 Gysin, Gustav. "Das aktuelle Puppentheater in der Schweiz." (Current Puppetry in Switzerland.) *Mimos.* 1996; 1/2: 3-8. Illus.: Photo. B&W. 6. Lang.: Ger.
Switzerland. 1996. Historical studies. ■Survey of Swiss puppetry, including organizations, reception, performance methods and competence, and the special importance of small forms in Switzerland.

4406 Disney Studios. "James and the Giant Peach." *PuJ.* 1996 Sum; 47(4): 4-5. Illus.: Photo. 2. Lang.: Eng.
USA: Hollywood, CA. 1993-1995. Historical studies. ■Puppets and three dimensional animation in the film *James and the Giant Peach*, directed by Henry Selick, produced by Jake Eberts and Disney Studios, adapted from a story by Roald Dahl. Puppets by Lane Smith and Shelley Daniels, animation by Paul Berry.

4407 Abrams, Steve; Evans, Annie; Gunderson, Greta; Harms, Carl; Killmer, Ted; Kurten, Allelu; Latshaw, George; Levenson, Mark; Lobdell, Peter; McCarthy, Kerry; Periale, Andrew; Young, Rod. "The Jim Henson International Festival." *PuJ.* 1996 Win; 48(2): 2-8 . Illus.: Dwg. 8. Lang.: Eng.
USA: New York, NY. 1995. Historical studies. ■Puppetry performances at the Jim Henson International Festival, held at the Public Theatre in New York City in September 1995. Includes performance of *Erotec: The Human Life of Machines* by Alice Farley and Henry Threadgill, *The Repugnant Story of Clotario Demoniax (La Historia repugnante de Clo-*

PUPPETRY: General—Performance/production

tario Demoniax) by Mexico City's Teatro Tinglado, written by Hugo Hiriart, *Piskanderdula* by Czech puppeteers Vera Ricarova and Frantisek Vitek, *Evidence of Floods* by Janie Gelser and Company, Mabou Mines's *Peter and Wendy* adapted by Lee Breuer and Liza Lorwin, Basil Twist's *The Araneidae Show*, Seattle's Warner Blake's *Soup Talk I and II*, Maine's Figures of Speech Theatre's *Nightingale* by Carol Farrell, *Sunjata* co-produced by Luc Amoros and Michèle Augustin of France and Théâtre Ki-Yi M'Bock from Ivory Coast, written and directed by Werewere Liking and Amoros, Wales's Green Ginger's *Frank Einstein* by Terry Lee, and Germany's Theater Laku Paka *Rapunzel*, directed and written by Günter Staniewski.

4408   Costine, Deborah. "Boston's First Puppet Slam." *PuJ.* 1996 Win; 48(2): 14. Lang.: Eng.
USA: Boston, MA. 1996. Historical studies. ■Boston area puppeteers present a 'slam,' a variety of short performance pieces designed to provide area puppeteers with an opportunity for trying out new ideas in front of adult audiences.

4409   Gibson, Norman. "It Can't Happen to Me!... Can It?" *PuJ.* 1996 Spr; 47(3): 13-14. Illus.: Sketches. 1. Lang.: Eng.
USA: New York, NY. 1996. Histories-sources. ■Call for anecdotal stories from puppeteers for a collection of puppeteer stories.

4410   Gross, Kenneth; Katz, Leslie. "Pinokio." *SATJ.* 1995 May; 9(1): 69-77. Notes. Biblio. Illus.: Photo. B&W. 4. Lang.: Eng.
USA: New York, NY. 1992. Critical studies. ■The 1992 Theatre Drak version of *Pinokio* presented at the Joseph Papp Public Theatre during the First International Festival of Puppet theatre directed by Josef Krofta.

4411   Handelman, Elise; Nathanson, Bob. "Lenny's Place." *PuJ.* 1996 Sum; 47(4): 14-15. Illus.: Photo. 2. Lang.: Eng.
USA: New York, NY. 1980-1996. Historical studies. ■Tribute to Lenny Suib, director and founder of the Puppet Playhouse, on his retirement.

4412   Kurten, Allelu. "A Connecticut Yankee in King Arthur's Court: A Look at a Writer/Puppet Collaboration." *PuJ.* 1996 Sum; 47(4): 10-11. Illus.: Photo. 2. Lang.: Eng.
USA: Hartford, CT. 1996. Historical studies. ■University of Connecticut's Puppet Arts Program presents a master's thesis production of *A Connecticut Yankee in King Arthur's Court.* Production was directed by Jerry Krasser and adapted by Brad Korbesmeyer from a story by Mark Twain. Puppets designed by Joyce Fritz.

4413   Meltzer, Steven. "Paul Winchell: Getting the Dummy Off the Knee." *PuJ.* 1996 Spr; 47(3): 6-7. Illus.: Photo. 5. Lang.: Eng.
USA. 1937-1978. Historical studies. ■Ventriloquist Paul Winchell's career in early television. Winchell discovered new ways to adapt ventriloquism to television's visual medium. His importance to and influence on later puppetry.

4414   Putz, Fred. "Chicago Lyric Opera's *Ring*." *PuJ.* 1996 Sum; 47(4): 2-3. Illus.: Photo. 3. Lang.: Eng.
USA: Chicago, IL. 1996. Historical studies. ■Puppets used in Lyric Opera of Chicago's production of *Der Ring des Nibelungen.* Lisa Aimee Sturz is puppetmaster.

4415   Putz, Fred. "Compagnie Philippe Genty: 'Voyageur Immobile'." *PuJ.* 1996 Sum; 47(4): 11-12. Illus.: Photo. 1. Lang.: Eng.
USA: Chicago, IL. France: Paris. 1961-1965. Historical studies. ■Based on his travels around the world, director Philippe Genty created *Voyageur Immobile (Motionless Traveler)* using puppets, human movement, and dance. Though based in Paris, Genty's company, Compagnie Philippe Genty, presented this production at the Athenaeum Theatre under the auspices of Performing Arts Chicago.

4416   Ross, Molly; Thebus, Jessica. "Redmoon Theatre Winter Festival." *PuJ.* 1996 Sum; 47(4): 12-14. Illus.: Photo. 3. Lang.: Eng.
USA: Chicago, IL. 1995. Historical studies. ■Redmoon Theatre's fourth annual Winter Pageant, dependent on audience participation, at Logan Square auditorium. Employs puppetry, masks, storytelling, stilts, and music. Involved senior citizens from the local senior citizens center.

4417   Smith, Nancy. "Peter Pan: The Trilogy." *PuJ.* 1996 Spr; 47(3): 3-6. Illus.: Photo. 4. Lang.: Eng.

USA: Phoenix, AZ. 1993-1995. Historical studies. ■Great Arizona Puppet Theatre's production of *Peter Pan*, created by Nancy Smith and Ken Bonar, performed in three installments. Gives particulars and history of production, as well as how puppets were made.

4418   Spelvin, George. "Disney Dives Into Puppetry." *PuJ.* 1996 Win; 48(2): 9-12. Illus.: Photo. 6. Lang.: Eng.
USA: Orlando, FL. 1995. Historical studies. ■Puppetry at Walt Disney's World Resort, training a staff of 130 in complex, skilled puppetry routines. Reviews technical requirements of three puppet shows on view at Disney World: *Legend of the Lion King, Voyage of the Little Mermaid,* and *The Hunchback of Notre Dame.* Includes notes on the traveling Disney puppet troupe, The Disney Crew, and puppetry's role in the parades around the park.

4419   Taylor, Charles W. "Remembering Forman Brown." *PuJ.* 1996 Win; 48(2): 12-14. Illus.: Photo. 1. Lang.: Eng.
USA. 1901-1996. Historical studies. ■Career of and tribute to Forman Brown, the last surviving member of the Yale Puppeteers, a famous puppetry troupe consisting of Brown, Harry Burnett, and Richard Brandon. The troupe worked all over the country from the 1920s to the early 1960s.

4420   Tömöry, Márta. "A vietnámi vízibábszínház." (Water Puppet Theatre of Vietnam.) *Sz.* 1996; 29(6): 17-21. Illus.: Photo. B&W. 5. Lang.: Hun.
Vietnam. 1996. Reviews of performances. ■The roots and the practice of one of the UNIMA Festival's highlights, the Water Puppet Theatre of Vietnam.

4421   Trefalt, Miha. "O času, ki je še verjel lutki." (The Time when Puppets were Believed In.) *Lutka.* 1996; 51: 14-17. Illus.: Photo. B&W. Lang.: Slo.
Yugoslavia. 1948-1964. Historical studies. ■The development of Slovene puppetry and the important role of Jože Pengov.

4422   Peltonen, Leila. "In Search of Zambian Puppetry." *PuJ.* 1996 Spr; 47(3): 8-11. Illus.: Photo. 7. Lang.: Eng.
Zambia. 1992-1994. Historical studies. ■Author's experience as a puppeteer in Zambia, performing with her Travelcase Theatre and giving workshops. In addition, the influence of strong Zambian traditions of masks and puppets on her work.

Plays/librettos/scripts

4423   Weinkauff, Gina. "Affinität und Diskrepanz." (Affinity and Discrepancy.) *Mimos.* 1996; 1/2: 35-40. Illus.: Design. Graphs. Handbill. Dwg. Photo. B&W. 5. Lang.: Ger.
1809-1996. Critical studies. ■First thoughts about historical aspects of literary texts in puppetry.

4424   Voisard, Claire. "Écrire pour la marionnette." (Writing for Puppets.) *JCT.* 1989; 51: 108-110. Illus.: Photo. B&W. 1. Lang.: Fre.
Canada: Montreal, PQ. 1979-1989. Histories-sources. ■Playwright Claire Voisard describes peculiarities of writing for puppet theatre, using as examples her adaptations of *Gilgamesh* as *Pré en bulles (Meadow of Bubbles)*, and Antoine de Saint-Exupéry's *Le Petit Prince (The Little Prince)*.

4425   Waszkiel, Marek. "Kinetozograficzny teatr Kuparenki." (Kuparenko's Kinetographic Theatre.) *PaT.* 1996; 1-2(88): 88-112. Append. Illus.: Graphs. Pntg. Poster. Photo. B&W. 18. Lang.: Pol.
Poland. Russia. 1816-1842. Historical studies. ■The life and activities of Jordaki Kuparenko (1784-1844), author of panoramas, dioramas, theatrum mundi, and puppet mechanical theatre.

Reference materials

4426   Fréchette, Michel; Fortin, Liette. "Les Différents aspects de la marionnette." (Different Aspects of Puppetry.) *JCT.* 1989; 51: 163-168. Biblio. Lang.: Fre.
Canada: Montreal, PQ. 1938-1989. ■Classified bibliography of various aspects of puppetry. Lists libraries in Montreal with works on puppetry.

4427   "Annex." *TP.* 1996 July; 38(3): 57-59. Append. Lang.: Eng, Fre.
Poland. 1996. Instructional materials. ■Appendix with directory of puppet theatres in Poland, listing of the major professional and amateur children's theatre festivals held in the country, and the winners of Jan

PUPPETRY: General—Reference materials

Dorman Prize for innovation in theatre for young audiences since the award's inception in 1990.

Relation to other fields

4428 Vaïs, Michel. "Marionnette et thérapie: Entretien avec Madeleine Lions." (Puppets and Therapy: Interview with Madeleine Lions.) *JCT.* 1989; 51: 135-136. Illus.: Dwg. 1. Lang.: Fre.
France: Paris, Charleville-Mézières. 1988. Histories-sources. ■Madeleine Lions explains her technique using puppet creation as therapy for patients with physical injuries or psychosis tendencies.

Research/historiography

4429 Krafka, Elke. "Puppentheater als Quelle der Theaterhistoriographie." (Puppet Theatre as a Source for Theatre Historiography.) *Mimos.* 1996; 1/2: 20-23. Notes. Illus.: Photo. Dwg. B&W. 3. Lang.: Ger.
Critical studies. ■The use of puppet stages, costumes, paper theatres, and puppets for a general theatre historiography.

4430 Des Rosiers, Renée. "Patrimoine et conservation." (Heritage and Preservation.) *JCT.* 1989; 51: 148-152. Biblio. Lang.: Fre.
Canada. 1988. Historical studies. ■Identifies important marionette collections in Canada, and explains methods of preservation used by museums.

4431 Tanke, Gerd. "Theatralität und Materialität." (Theatricality and Materiality.) *Mimos.* 1996; 1/2: 13-19. Notes. Biblio. Append. Illus.: Photo. B&W. 9. Lang.: Ger.
Germany. 1850-1996. Historical studies. ■The treatment of puppetry by German studies, folklore, and theatre studies since the mid-nineteenth century, and the possibility of a relevant interdisciplinary historiography.

Theory/criticism

4432 Jurkowski, Henryk; Pászt, Patrícia, transl.; Révész, Róbert, photo.; Kádár, Kata, photo. "Bábok, tárgyak és emberek." (Puppets, Objects and People.) *Sz.* 1996; 29(6): 2-5. Illus.: Photo. B&W. 6. Lang.: Hun.
Europe. 1800-1992. Critical studies. ■Polish aesthetician Henryk Jurkowski analyzes puppetry as a very special art.

4433 Weibe, Richard E. "Der künstliche Akteur als Denkmodell." (The Artificial Protagonist as a Model for a Theory.) *Mimos.* 1996; 1/2: 40-44. Illus.: Photo. B&W. 2. Lang.: Ger.
Germany. 1810-1817. Critical studies. ■The utility value of the artificial protagonist conceived as a model for a theory, with reference to *Der Sandman* by E.T.A. Hoffmann and *Über das Marionettentheater* by Kleist.

Training

4434 Vaïs, Michel. "Deux voies de formation: Entretien avec Margareta Niculescu." (Two Paths for Training: Interview with Margareta Niculescu.) *JCT.* 1989; 51: 132-134. Illus.: Photo. B&W. 2. Lang.: Fre.
France: Charleville-Mézières. 1988. Histories-sources. ■Possibilities for training in puppetry offered by Institut international de marionnette and the École nationale supérieure des arts de la marionnette, under the direction of Margareta Niculescu.

4435 Steinmann, P.K. "Seminare und Inszenierungen mit Laien." (Seminars and Productions with Amateurs.) *PInfo.* 1996; 74(2): 40-43. Lang.: Ger.
Switzerland. 1975-1996. Histories-sources. ■Interview with professional puppeteer Hanspeter Bleischaus about his work with students and amateurs.

Marionettes

Audience

4436 Rebehn, Lars. "Das Stadttheater des Kleinen Mannes." (The Municipal Theatre for the Common Man.) *Mimos.* 1996; 1/2: 25-27. Illus.: Dwg. B&W. 2. Lang.: Ger.
Germany: Hamburg. 1800-1899. Historical studies. ■The situation of the marionette theatre in Hamburg, its social importance, and its relationship with the citizens.

Design/technology

4437 Varl, Breda. *Lutke na nitkah.* (Hanging Puppets.) Šentilj: Aristej; 1995. 36 pp. Illus.: Photo. Dwg. B&W. Color. Lang.: Slo.
Slovenia. 1996. Instructional materials. ■A basic handbook of technical methods used to make hanging puppets. For amateur puppeteers and school teachers.

Institutions

4438 Tremblay, Micheline. "La Marionnette en liesse: Semaine mondiale de la marionnette à Jonquière." (Celebrating Marionettes: Marionette Festival in Jonquière.) *JCT.* 1990; 57: 123-127. Notes. Illus.: Photo. B&W. 5. Lang.: Fre.
Canada: Jonquière, PQ. 1990. Historical studies. ■Productions for the public mixed with workshops for professional puppeteers at World Marionette Week. Descriptions of individual productions.

Performance/production

4439 Bell, Karen. "Talking Heads With Something to Say." *PAC.* 1996; 30(1): 10-11. Illus.: Photo. B&W. 3. Lang.: Eng.
Canada: Toronto, ON. 1994-1995. Historical studies. ■Traces the career of outspoken Ronnie Burkett, who uses his marionettes to air his political views.

Rod puppets

Design/technology

4440 Varl, Breda. *Lutke na palici.* (Rod Puppets.) Šentilj: Aristej; 1995. 36 pp. Illus.: Photo. Dwg. B&W. Color. Lang.: Slo.
Slovenia. 1996. Instructional materials. ■A basic handbook of technical methods used to make rod puppets. For amateur puppeteers and school teachers.

4441 Ford, Hobey. "Rod Puppet Mechanisms." *PuJ.* 1996 Win; 48(2): 19-20. Illus.: Sketches. 4. Lang.: Eng.
USA. 1996. Technical studies. ■How to make a rod puppet.

Performance/production

4442 Čeplak Mencin, Rolf. "Indonezijske lutke v Sloveniji." (Indonesian Puppets in Slovenia.) *Lutka.* 1996; 53: 111-116. Biblio. Illus.: Photo. B&W. Lang.: Slo.
Slovenia. Indonesia. 1996. Historical studies. ■Performances of traditional Indonesian puppet plays by Indonesian students at the Slovenian ethnographic museum, using the puppet collection of the former Yugoslav ambassador.

Shadow puppets

Performance/production

4443 Roos, Ajda. "Senčno lutkarstvo na Slovenskem." (Slovene Shadow Puppetry.) *Lutka.* 1996; 53: 104-110. Biblio. Illus.: Photo. B&W. Lang.: Slo.
Slovenia. 1938-1996. Historical studies. ■History of shadow puppetry in Slovenia since the first production by Niko Kuret. Includes bibliography of performances and texts.

4444 Putz, Fred. "Redmoon Theatre's *Frankenstein.*" *PuJ.* 1996 Sum; 47(4): 7-9. Illus.: Photo. 5. Lang.: Eng.
USA: Chicago, IL. 1996. Historical studies. ■Redmoon Theatre's production of *Frankenstein* combines live actors and puppets (including shadow puppets). Production conceived, directed and designed by Jim Lasko and Blair Thomas, puppets by Christopher Barbar, Stephanie Brash, Molly Ross, Doug O'Connell, and Kristen Mylander. Production staged at Chicago's Steppenwolf Theatre.

Relation to other fields

4445 Sears, Laurie J. *Shadows of Empire: Colonial Discourse and Javanese Tales.* Durham, NC/London: Duke UP; 1996. 349 pp. Index. Biblio. Notes. Illus.: Photo. 5. Lang.: Eng.
Indonesia. 1935-1975. Historical studies. ■Colonial discourse in the *wayang purwa*, shadow puppet plays based on the *Rāmāyana* and *Mahābhārata* epics. How various rulers of Java used the *wayang* as a political tool of government, and how Javanese puppeteers used the puppet performance as a form of resistance against colonial rule and colonial myths.

SUBJECT INDEX

Acting — cont'd

Acting — cont'd

Portrait of actress Jacqueline Macauley. UK-England: London. 1967-1996. Lang.: Ger. 991

Child performers in the Victorian theatre. UK-England. 1835-1865. Lang.: Eng. 999

Report on Mejerchol'd symposium. UK-Wales: Aberystwyth. 1995. Lang.: Eng. 1000

Director Michajl Reznikovič on the theatrical professions. Ukraine: Kiev. 1990-1996. Lang.: Rus. 1003

Myths regarding physical disabilities that exclude the handicapped from acting. USA. 1996. Lang.: Eng. 1008

Holiday memories of Broadway actors. USA: New York, NY. 1996. Lang.: Eng. 1013

Comparison of the relationship between illusion and reality in shamanic/ritual practice and the Western acting tradition. USA. 1959-1995. Lang.: Eng. 1018

History and current state of autobiographical solo performance. USA. 1276-1995. Lang.: Eng. 1020

Actress Bea Arthur. USA: Beverly Hills, CA. 1996. Lang.: Eng. 1024

Account of actresses' scrapbook that sheds light on working conditions. USA: New York, NY. 1895-1910. Lang.: Eng. 1032

The Moscow Art Theatre's Boston season. USA: Boston, MA. 1923. Lang.: Eng. 1036

Stage physicality in acting. USA. 1996. Lang.: Eng. 1038

Physical centers as an aspect of characterization in acting. USA. 1970-1996. Lang.: Eng. 1043

Preparation and use of a 'period movement score'. USA. 1996. Lang.: Eng. 1045

Account of Method acting seminar by Anna Strasberg. USA. 1995. Lang.: Eng. 1046

Fundraising of Broadway Cares/Equity Fights AIDS. USA: New York, NY. 1987-1996. Lang.: Eng. 1052

Call for actors to enroll in Non-Traditional Casting Project registry. USA: New York, NY. 1996. Lang.: Eng. 1053

Ruben Santiago-Hudson and Lisa Gay Hamilton, winners of the Derwent Award. USA: New York, NY. 1996. Lang.: Eng. 1054

Successful nontraditional casting. USA: New York, NY. 1996. Lang.: Eng. 1055

Actor Al Krulick's candidacy for Congress. USA: Orlando, FL. 1996. Lang.: Eng. 1056

Methods of teaching stage combat. USA. 1996. Lang.: Eng. 1058

Biography of actor Fredric March. USA. 1897-1975. Lang.: Eng. 1059

Interview with actor Jeff Trachta. USA: New York, NY. 1994-1996. Lang.: Eng. 1060

Profile of Joseph Chaikin, with emphasis on *1969 Terminal 1996*. USA: New York, NY. 1969-1996. Lang.: Eng. 1065

Equity and the 1919 actors' strike. USA: New York, NY. 1919. Lang.: Eng. 1072

Gender in performances of actress Mary Martin. USA. 1922-1994. Lang.: Eng. 1074

Profile of New World Performance Laboratory. USA: Cleveland, OH. 1987-1995. Lang.: Eng. 1075

Memoirs of Aleksand'r Beniaminov of Leningrad Comedy Theatre. USSR: Leningrad. 1937-1969. Lang.: Rus. 1076

History of the Russian school of acting. Uzbekistan: Tashkent. 1996. Lang.: Rus. 1078

Dancer and actor Niklas Ek. Sweden: Stockholm. 1968. Lang.: Swe. 1443

Social boundaries and the transformation of the cakewalk. USA. 1900-1918. Lang.: Eng. 1448

Analysis of traditional African masked performance. Nigeria. Sierra Leone. 1968-1993. Lang.: Eng. 1547

The performance of female temple servants in religious rituals. India: Kerala. 1300-1996. Lang.: Eng. 1610

Gender, character, and direction. 1996. Lang.: Ger. 1895

Antonin Artaud's work as actor, director, and theorist. 1886-1948. Lang.: Ita. 1896

Theatre seminar featuring performance of works by Arthur Miller. Austria: Salzburg. 1996. Lang.: Eng. 1903

The premiere of the first German translation of Wyspiański's *Wesele (The Wedding)*. Austria: Salzburg. 1992. Lang.: Eng, Fre. 1904

The acting in Peter Zadek's production of *The Cherry Orchard* at Burgtheater. Austria: Vienna. 1996. Lang.: Ger. 1906

Gyula Ecsedi Kovács' staging of *Tigris és hiéna*. Austro-Hungarian Empire: Kolozsvár. 1876-1883. Lang.: Hun. 1910

Christopher Plummer's one-man show *Barrymore*. Canada: Stratford, ON. 1996. Lang.: Eng. 1918

Leslie Nielsen's one-man show *Clarence Darrow for the Defense*. Canada. 1996. Lang.: Eng. 1919

Multiple roles of Tom Wood and Nicola Cavendish in *Later Life*. Canada. 1996. Lang.: Eng. 1920

Interview with actors Normand Chouinard and Rémy Girard. Canada: Montreal, PQ. 1992. Lang.: Fre. 1922

Interview with actors Jean-Louis Millette and Alexis Martin. Canada: Montreal, PQ. 1992. Lang.: Fre. 1923

Marie Brassard of Théâtre Repère. Canada: Quebec, PQ. 1985-1989. Lang.: Fre. 1924

Actress Lorraine Côté. Canada: Quebec, PQ. 1978-1989. Lang.: Fre. 1926

Actor Martin Drainville and his background in comedy. Canada. 1970-1990. Lang.: Fre. 1930

Actress Sylvie Drapeau on the acting advice of Louis Jouvet. Canada: Montreal, PQ. 1989. Lang.: Fre. 1931

Sylvia Drapeau on playing Winnie in Beckett's *Happy Days*. Canada: Montreal, PQ. 1990. Lang.: Fre. 1932

Interview with actress Anne Dorval. Canada: Montreal, PQ. 1990. Lang.: Fre. 1933

Françoise Faucher on playing Winnie in Beckett's *Happy Days*. Canada: Montreal, PQ. 1981. Lang.: Fre. 1934

Pol Pelletier's actor training methods. Canada: Montreal, PQ. 1992. Lang.: Fre. 1935

Manon Gauthier's one-woman adaptation of a Michel Tremblay novel. Canada: Montreal, PQ. 1980-1986. Lang.: Fre. 1936

Rationalism and the realist school of acting. Canada. USA. UK-England. 1989. Lang.: Fre. 1938

Anne-Marie Cadieux's performance in Müller's *Quartett* at Espace GO. Canada: Montreal, PQ. 1996. Lang.: Fre. 1939

Interview with actress Hélène Loiselle. Canada: Montreal, PQ. 1950-1992. Lang.: Fre. 1946

Patricia MacGeachy on performing in Beckett's *Not I*. Canada: Montreal, PQ. 1991-1992. Lang.: Fre. 1949

Actor Michèle Magny's favorite lines. Canada: Montreal, PQ. 1976-1995. Lang.: Fre. 1950

Actor André Montmorency's interpretation of Sandra in *Damnée Manon, sacrée Sandrá (Damned Manon, Cursed Sandra)* by Michel Tremblay. Canada: Montreal, PQ. 1976. Lang.: Fre. 1952

Danièle Panneton on performing in Beckett's *Not I*. Canada: Montreal, PQ. 1990. Lang.: Fre. 1953

Interview with actor Yves Jacques. Canada: Montreal, PQ. 1989. Lang.: Fre. 1954

Anecdote of Jack Robitaille's role in a production of Pirandello's *Questa sera si recita a soggetto (Tonight We Improvise)*. Canada: Quebec, PQ. 1994. Lang.: Fre. 1957

Interview with director André Brassard. Canada: Montreal, PQ. 1992. Lang.: Fre. 1963

Interview with actor Marc Béland. Canada: Montreal, PQ. 1992-1993. Lang.: Fre. 1964

The contemporary actor and the classical text. Canada. 1989. Lang.: Fre. 1971

Interview with actress Patricia Ariza of Teatro La Candelaria. Colombia. 1994. Lang.: Ita. 1974

Actor's description of voice training. Denmark. UK-England. 1996. Lang.: Dan. 1985

Tragic actresses Siddons, Rachel, and Ristori. England. France. Italy. 1755-1906. Lang.: Eng. 1986

History and technique of the English acting tradition. England. 1590-1995. Lang.: Eng. 1988

Diary evidence of David Garrick's interpretation of Hamlet. England. 1755. Lang.: Eng. 1994

Assembling an international cast for a production of *A Midsummer Night's Dream*. Europe. 1995. Lang.: Ger. 2001

Peter Brook's *Qui est là (Who Is There)*. France: Paris. 1996. Lang.: Ger. 2011

Acting — cont'd

Interview with director Ariane Mnouchkine. France: Paris. 1988. Lang.: Fre. 2017

Ariane Mnouchkine's acting workshop. France: Paris. 1988. Lang.: Fre. 2018

Interview with Sophie Moscoso of Théâtre du Soleil. France: Paris. 1988. Lang.: Fre. 2019

Gender construction and two performances of *Orlando*. France: Paris. Switzerland: Lausanne. Germany: Berlin. 1990-1996. Lang.: Ger. 2020

Jean Genet's staging and acting indications. France. 1950-1996. Lang.: Fre. 2021

Anecdote concerning Jacques Galipeau's role in *Tartuffe*, Théâtre du Nouveau Monde. France: Paris. 1971. Lang.: Fre. 2022

Portrait of Sven-Eric Bechtolf, actor and director at Thalia Theater. Germany: Hamburg. 1957-1996. Lang.: Ger. 2060

Actor Udo Samel. Germany. 1996. Lang.: Ger. 2072

Portrait of actor Martin Schwab. Germany. Austria. 1979-1996. Lang.: Ger. 2077

A student production of Schiller's *Mary Stuart*. Germany: Weimar. UK-England: Loughborough. 1800-1992. Lang.: Eng. 2083

Interview with actor András Csiky. Hungary. Romania: Cluj-Napoca. 1953-1996. Lang.: Hun. 2094

Interview with actor György Cserhalmi. Hungary. 1957-1996. Lang.: Hun. 2096

Literary analysis of the diary of actress Róza Déry-Széppataki. Hungary. 1869-1955. Lang.: Hun. 2097

Interview with actor József Czintos. Hungary: Budapest. Romania: Satu-Mare. 1969-1995. Lang.: Hun. 2098

Interview with actor János Kulka. Hungary. 1990-1996. Lang.: Hun. 2099

Interview with actor János Bán. Hungary. 1986-1996. Lang.: Hun. 2100

Excerpt from diaries of Miklós Gábor. Hungary. 1954-1955. Lang.: Hun. 2101

Interview with actor Tibor Mertz. Hungary. 1985-1996. Lang.: Hun. 2107

Interview with actress Lujza Orosz. Hungary. Romania: Cluj-Napoca. 1926-1990. Lang.: Hun. 2109

Review of the autobiography of actor Miklós Gábor. Hungary. 1954. Lang.: Hun. 2110

Interpretations of Shakespeare in Hungarian theatre in Transylvania. Hungary: Kolozsvár. Romania: Cluj-Napoca. 1794-1987. Lang.: Hun. 2111

Interview with Rina Yerushalmi of Itim. Israel. 1988-1993. Lang.: Eng. 2118

Israeli theatre and Israel's changing cultural life. Israel. 1996. Lang.: Eng. 2121

Actress Franca Rame. Italy. 1995. Lang.: Eng. 2122

Interview with Graziella Martinoli of La Pinguicola Sulle Vigne. Italy: Genoa. 1995. Lang.: Eng. 2123

Edoardo Ferravilla of the Milanese dialect theatre. Italy: Milan. 1846-1916. Lang.: Ita. 2126

Actor-director Giorgio De Lullo. Italy: Rome. 1921-1981. Lang.: Ita. 2129

Actress Ol'ga Androvskaja's notes on Asian tour of Moscow Art Theatre. Japan. 1958-1959. Lang.: Rus. 2133

Use of young amateur actors by Nultwintig. Netherlands. 1994-1995. Lang.: Dut. 2141

Biography of actress Johanna Cornelia Ziesenis-Wattier. Netherlands. 1760-1830. Lang.: Dut. 2142

Interview with actor Andrzej Seweryn. Poland. 1946-1995. Lang.: Eng, Fre. 2156

The two branches of Polish avant-garde theatre. Poland. 1970-1995. Lang.: Eng, Fre. 2174

Interview with actor and director Jerzy Stuhr. Poland: Cracow. 1995. Lang.: Eng, Fre. 2176

Actress Adrienn Jancsó. Romania. Hungary. 1921-1995. Lang.: Hun. 2183

Actress Ariadna Ardašnikova. Russia: Moscow. 1990-1996. Lang.: Rus. 2189

Actor Jevgenij Knjazev of the Vachtangov Theatre. Russia: Moscow. 1990-1996. Lang.: Rus. 2205

Actors of the Stanislavskij Theatre. Russia: Moscow. 1990-1996. Lang.: Rus. 2207

Actor Oleg Borisov. Russia: Moscow. 1929-1994. Lang.: Rus. 2210

Modern problems in theatre. Russia. 1990-1996. Lang.: Rus. 2214

Actress Faina Ranevskaja. Russia: Moscow. 1896-1984. Lang.: Rus. 2215

Career of actress Serafima Birman. Russia. 1890-1976. Lang.: Rus. 2217

Scenarist and actor Vladimir M. Zel'din. Russia: Moscow. 1940-1996. Lang.: Rus. 2221

Actors of the Malyj Theatre. Russia: Moscow. 1980-1996. Lang.: Rus. 2223

Actor Grigorij Gaj. Russia: St. Petersburg. 1949-1995. Lang.: Rus. 2225

Actor Innokentij Smoktunovskij. Russia: Moscow. 1925-1994. Lang.: Rus. 2228

Actress Alla Demidova of Taganka Theatre. Russia: Moscow. 1960-1996. Lang.: Rus. 2230

Interview with actress Tatjana Doronina. Russia: Moscow. 1996. Lang.: Rus. 2232

Memoirs relating to actor Innokentij Smoktunovskij. Russia: Moscow. 1980-1996. Lang.: Rus. 2233

Actor Anatolij Petrov. Russia: Moscow. 1996. Lang.: Rus. 2237

Actress Ljudmila Maksakova and the traditions of the Vachtangov Theatre. Russia: Moscow. 1980-1996. Lang.: Rus. 2241

Memories of actress Faina Ranevskaja. Russia. 1896-1984. Lang.: Rus. 2243

Actress Faina Ranevskaja. Russia: Moscow. 1896-1984. Lang.: Rus. 2244

Actor Oleg Tabakov. Russia: Moscow. 1960-1996. Lang.: Rus. 2249

Actress Ol'ga Antonova. Russia: St. Petersburg, Moscow. 1980-1996. Lang.: Rus. 2250

Actor Michajl Danilov. Russia: St. Petersburg. 1973-1995. Lang.: Rus. 2253

Actor Vladislav Stржelčik. Russia: St. Petersburg. 1921-1995. Lang.: Rus. 2255

Actress Marina Šitova. Russia: St. Petersburg. 1990-1996. Lang.: Rus. 2256

Profile of actor Aleksand'r Mezencev. Russia: Cheljabinsk. 1990-1996. Lang.: Rus. 2258

Actress Ol'ga Samošina. Russia: St. Petersburg. 1990-1996. Lang.: Rus. 2259

Interview with actor Dmitrij Pevcov. Russia: Moscow. 1980-1996. Lang.: Rus. 2260

Memoirs of actor-director Branko Gombač. Slovenia: Celje. Italy: Trieste. 1945-1996. Lang.: Slo. 2262

Actress Bibi Andersson's work with Ingmar Bergman. Sweden: Malmö, Stockholm. 1950. Lang.: Swe. 2274

Portraits of nineteenth-century actors in mural art of the Royal Dramatic Theatre. Sweden: Stockholm. 1840-1879. Lang.: Swe. 2278

Actress Kristina Adolphson. Sweden: Stockholm. 1955. Lang.: Swe. 2280

Interview with actress Ingela Olsson. Sweden: Stockholm. 1980. Lang.: Swe. 2281

Interview with director Thommy Berggren. Sweden: Gothenburg, Stockholm. 1955. Lang.: Swe. 2282

Interview with Kristina Lugn, poet, playwright, and director. Sweden: Stockholm. 1993. Lang.: Swe. 2283

Interview with actress Karin Bjurström. Sweden: Stockholm. 1970. Lang.: Swe. 2285

Interview with actor Reine Brynolfsson. Sweden: Gothenburg, Stockholm. 1984. Lang.: Swe. 2286

Interview with actor Börje Ahlstedt about working with different directors. Sweden: Stockholm. 1989. Lang.: Swe. 2290

Interview with actress Lena Nylén. Sweden: Malmö. 1996. Lang.: Swe. 2292

Interview with actor Shanti Roney. Sweden: Gothenburg. 1985. Lang.: Swe. 2293

Interview with actor Erland Josephson. Sweden: Stockholm. 1946. Lang.: Swe. 2296

Interview with actress Gunilla Nyroos. Sweden: Stockholm. 1966. Lang.: Swe. 2298

Acting — cont'd

Acting — cont'd

The career of performance artist Rose English. UK-England. 1996. Lang.: Eng. 3794

The performance aesthetics of Ron Athey. UK-England: London. USA: Los Angeles, CA. 1995-1996. Lang.: Ger. 3795

Performance artist Paul Bonin-Rodriguez. USA. 1992-1996. Lang.: Eng. 3802

Performance artist Deb Margolin. USA: New York, NY. 1996. Lang.: Eng. 3803

Comparison of American and Canadian comic styles. Canada. USA. 1990. Lang.: Fre. 3832

The variety entertainment tradition in South African theatre. South Africa, Republic of. 1900-1985. Lang.: Eng. 3834

The act of the fat lady at the sideshow of Coney Island. USA: Brooklyn, NY. 1992-1994. Lang.: Eng. 3837

Symbolism and style in Chinese opera. China. 221 B.C.-1990 A.D. Lang.: Fre. 3878

Performance of *nanxi*. China. 1368-1996. Lang.: Eng. 3879

Diahann Carroll's role in *Sunset Boulevard* at the Ford Centre. Canada: Toronto, ON. 1950-1996. Lang.: Eng. 3912

Musical theatre performer Evelyn Laye. UK-England. 1918-1996. Lang.: Eng. 3923

Interview with musical theatre actor Anthony Newley. UK-England. 1935-1996. Lang.: Eng. 3924

Singer/actress Elaine Page. UK-England: London. USA: New York, NY. 1968-1996. Lang.: Eng. 3925

Actor Bob Hoskins. UK-England. 1968-1996. Lang.: Eng. 3927

Actor/singer Brian Stokes Mitchell. USA. Canada. 1988-1996. Lang.: Eng. 3929

Ricky Martin's role in *Les Misérables*. USA: New York, NY. 1996. Lang.: Eng. 3931

Singer/actor John Cullum. USA: New York, NY. 1965-1996. Lang.: Eng. 3935

Actor Daniel Jenkins. USA: New York, NY. 1988-1996. Lang.: Eng. 3937

Lou Diamond Phillips' role in *The King and I*. USA: New York, NY. 1996. Lang.: Eng. 3938

Sarah Jessica Parker's role in *Once Upon a Mattress*. USA: New York, NY. 1976-1996. Lang.: Eng. 3942

Actor/singer John Davidson. USA: New York, NY. 1964-1996. Lang.: Eng. 3945

Actress/singer Andrea McArdle. USA. 1976-1996. Lang.: Eng. 3946

Singer/actress Janie Sell. USA: New York, NY. 1970-1996. Lang.: Eng. 3949

Actor John Stamos. USA: New York, NY. 1996. Lang.: Eng. 3955

Parody in the work of early African-American musical theatre performers. USA. 1900-1925. Lang.: Eng. 3966

Actor/singer/dancer Sandra Church. USA. 1954-1964. Lang.: Eng. 3978

Actress/singer Donna Murphy. USA. 1991-1996. Lang.: Eng. 3981

Interview with actress Pat Carroll on Verdi's *Falstaff*. USA: New York, NY. 1996. Lang.: Eng. 4256

Comparison of acting and puppetry. Canada: Montreal, PQ. 1985-1989. Lang.: Fre. 4389

Plays/librettos/scripts

Technical and thematic changes in Korean theatre. Korea: Seoul. 1987-1996. Lang.: Kor. 1099

History of early Ukrainian theatre. Ukraine. 1600-1799. Lang.: Rus. 1108

Playwright, actor, director, and psychiatrist Eduardo Pavlovsky. Argentina. 1957-1994. Lang.: Ger. 2719

Analysis of *Broue (Scum)* by Marc Messier, Michel Côté, and Marcel Gauthier. Canada. 1979-1992. Lang.: Fre. 2808

The role and importance of Shakespeare's clowns. England. 1590-1613. Lang.: Eng. 2960

Portrait of playwright, actor, and director Wolfgang Bauer. Germany. Austria. 1963-1996. Lang.: Ger. 3047

Actor Erland Josephson on the role of Kadmos in Euripides' *Bákchai (The Bacchae)*. Greece. Sweden. 404 B.C.-1996 A.D. Lang.: Swe. 3057

Dario Fo's rejection of Aristotelian aesthetics in *Johan Padan*. Italy. 1940-1996. Lang.: Eng. 3135

Interview with actor and playwright Mattias Andersson. Sweden: Gothenburg. 1989. Lang.: Swe. 3273

Children's plays of Staffan Göthe. Sweden: Luleå, Stockholm. 1944. Lang.: Swe. 3275

Actress/playwright Ellen McLaughlin. USA: New York, NY. 1996. Lang.: Eng. 3344

Daniel Day-Lewis' role in Nicholas Hytner's film version of *The Crucible* by Arthur Miller. USA. 1996. Lang.: Fre. 3648

Interview with Albert Hague, musical theatre professional. USA: New York, NY. 1960-1996. Lang.: Eng. 3995

Reference materials

Primary sources in English on European Naturalist and Symbolist theatre. Europe. 1850-1918. Lang.: Eng. 1120

Relation to other fields

The social function of theatrical practice. Canada: Quebec, PQ. 1950-1996. Lang.: Fre. 1152

Garrick, painting, and a shift in theatre aesthetics. England. 1700-1799. Lang.: Ger. 1170

East German actresses' reactions to social changes after the fall of the Berlin wall. Germany, East: Berlin, East. 1990-1991. Lang.: Ger. 1195

Actress Georgina Weldon's use of theatrical techniques to avoid incarceration for lunacy. UK-England: London. 1875-1885. Lang.: Eng. 1243

Actress Mira Furlan on refusing to take sides in ethnic conflict. Yugoslavia. 1991. Lang.: Eng. 1288

The risks inherent in political performance art: the example of Hugo Sánchez. Mexico. 1996. Lang.: Eng. 3817

Theory/criticism

Reprint of a 1958 interview with the late critic Walter Kerr. USA: New York, NY. 1958. Lang.: Eng. 1383

Swedish actresses and feminist research on the dominance of men in the theatre. Europe. 400 B.C.-1996 A.D. Lang.: Swe. 3540

Feminist criticism of Ibsen in the work of Elizabeth Robins. UK-England. 1890-1928. Lang.: Eng. 3553

Critic Harold Hobson of the *Times*. UK-England: London. 1930-1977. Lang.: Eng. 3556

Acton, David
Performance/production
Staging *Richard III* at the Panasonic Globe Theatre. Japan: Tokyo. 1996. Lang.: Eng. 871

Actor
Performance/production
Collection of newspaper reviews by London theatre critics. UK-England: London. 1996. Lang.: Eng. 2439

Actor-managers
Performance/production
Actor-manager Oscar Asche. UK-England: London. 1893-1932. Lang.: Eng. 2517

Actor's Express (Atlanta, GA)
Institutions
Atlanta Theatre offerings for Olympic Arts Festival. USA: Atlanta, GA. 1990-1996. Lang.: Eng. 585

Actor's Nightmare, The
Design/technology
Using a flash camera for theatrical lighting effects. USA. 1996. Lang.: Eng. 287
Performance/production
Directing at the English Language Theatre of Gdańsk University. Poland: Gdańsk. 1984-1988. Lang.: Eng. 892

Actors' Charitable Trust (London)
Institutions
Denville Hall, a retirement home for actors. UK-England: Northwood. 1926-1996. Lang.: Eng. 552

Actors' Equity Association (Canada)
Administration
US and Canadian Equity associations discuss actor transfers in a production of *Show Boat*. USA: New York, NY. Canada. 1996. Lang.: Eng. 87

Actors' Equity Association (UK)
Administration
Actor exchanges between British and American Equity associations. USA: New York, NY. 1995-1996. Lang.: Eng. 76

Actors' Equity Association (USA)
Administration
Annual Congress of International Federation of Actors. Denmark: Copenhagen. 1996. Lang.: Eng. 14

Contract negotiations for League of Resident Theatres. USA: New York, NY. 1996. Lang.: Eng. 69

Adams, Judith
Performance/production
Collection of newspaper reviews by London theatre critics. UK-England: London. 1996. Lang.: Eng.　2475

Adamson, Samuel
Performance/production
Collection of newspaper reviews by London theatre critics. UK-England: London. 1996. Lang.: Eng.　2364

Adaptations
Performance/production
Commentary on the trend of producing non-dramatic texts. Canada. 1989. Lang.: Fre.　751

Operatic and ballet adaptations of Shakespearean plays reviewed. Switzerland. 1994-1995. Lang.: Ger.　956

Graciela Daniele's dance adaptation of *Chronicle of a Death Foretold* by Gabriel García Márquez. USA: New York, NY. 1981-1996. Lang.: Eng.　1446

Analysis of dance interpretations of Shakespearean plays. Europe. 1809-1994. Lang.: Hun.　1500

Manon Gauthier's one-woman adaptation of a Michel Tremblay novel. Canada: Montreal, PQ. 1980-1986. Lang.: Fre.　1936

Director Laura Jäntti. Finland: Turku. 1995. Lang.: Eng.　2005

Robert Lepage's Shakespearean adaptations at the Odéon. France: Paris. 1996. Lang.: Ger.　2034

An intercultural adaptation of Euripides' *Troádes (The Trojan Women)*. Greece: Athens. UK-Scotland. 1993. Lang.: Eng.　2092

Hungarian productions by Romanian director Beatrice Bleont. Hungary: Zsámbék. Romania. 1996. Lang.: Hun.　2112

Student production of *The Singular Life of Albert Nobbs* by Simone Benmussa. UK-England: Leeds. 1992. Lang.: Eng.　2516

Stage history of *Black Eyed Susan* by Douglas Jerrold. UK-England. 1829-1994. Lang.: Eng.　2537

Stage adaptation of John Irving's *The Cider House Rules*, Seattle Repertory. USA: Seattle, WA. 1996. Lang.: Eng.　2592

Rehearsals of Wooster Group's adaptation of Čechov, *Brace Up!*. USA: New York, NY. 1990-1991. Lang.: Fre.　2655

Jorjan Lynn Jeter's role in *Curiouser and Curiouser* by National Theatre of the Deaf. USA. 1996. Lang.: Eng.　2660

Interview with Tina Landau, director of *The Trojan Women: A Love Story*. USA: New York, NY. 1996. Lang.: Eng.　2672

Wooster Group's production of *Brace Up!*, an adaptation of Čechov's *Tri sestry (Three Sisters)*. USA: New York, NY. 1991. Lang.: Fre.　2686

Assurbanipal Babilla's *Othello and the Circumcised Turk*, Purgatorio Ink. USA: New York, NY. 1996. Lang.: Eng.　2690

Witkacy and cinema. Poland. USA. 1919-1996. Lang.: Pol.　3618

Ian McKellen's role in his own adaptation of Shakespeare's *Richard III*. UK-England. 1996. Lang.: Eng.　3628

Al Pacino's role in the film version of David Mamet's *Glengarry Glen Ross*. USA. 1992. Lang.: Fre.　3630

Review of the film version of the musical *Evita*. USA. 1979-1996. Lang.: Eng.　3636

Play On!, a musical adaptation of Shakespeare's *Twelfth Night*. USA: San Diego, CA. 1993-1996. Lang.: Eng.　3971

The adaptation of Grimm's fairy tale in Humperdinck's opera *Hänsel und Gretel*. Germany. 1893-1996. Lang.: Eng.　4135

Background on Benjamin Britten's treatment of Shakespeare's *A Midsummer Night's Dream*. UK-England. 1960-1996. Lang.: Eng.　4235

Work of Tim Albery and Antony McDonald on Met production of Britten's *A Midsummer Night's Dream* by Britten. USA: New York, NY. 1996. Lang.: Eng.　4296

Puppet production of *A Connecticut Yankee in King Arthur's Court*. USA: Hartford, CT. 1996. Lang.: Eng.　4412

Plays/librettos/scripts
Evolution of the Beast character in treatments of the fairy tale *Beauty and the Beast*. UK-England. 1945-1996. Lang.: Eng.　1106

Adaptations of *The Strange Case of Dr. Jekyll and Mr. Hyde* by Robert Louis Stevenson. USA. 1887-1990. Lang.: Eng.　1113

Dramatic adaptations of dialogues by Plato. Ancient Greece. 427-347 B.C. Lang.: Eng.　2711

Analysis of plays by Alfonsina Storni. Argentina. 1892-1938. Lang.: Spa.　2717

The language of Austrian *volksstück* on the Prague stage. Austro-Hungarian Empire: Prague, Vienna. 1825-1847. Lang.: Cze.　2732

The translation of Shakespeare's *A Midsummer Night's Dream* for Théâtre du Nouveau Monde. Canada: Montreal, PQ. 1990. Lang.: Fre.　2739

Tensions among playwright, translator, and actor. Canada. 1989. Lang.: Fre.　2740

Translations by playwright Michel Tremblay. Canada: Montreal, PQ. 1968-1990. Lang.: Fre.　2748

Quebec nationalism in Garneau's translation of *Macbeth*. Canada. 1969-1978. Lang.: Fre.　2749

Quebec nationalism in translation and adaptation. Canada. 1968-1990. Lang.: Fre.　2750

Translation and social context. Canada. 1989. Lang.: Fre.　2751

Suzanne Lebeau's play for children, *Gil*. Canada. 1987-1988. Lang.: Fre.　2763

Réjean Ducharme's novel *À quelle heure on meurt? (What Time Do We Die?)*, adapted for the stage by Martin Faucher. Canada: Montreal, PQ. 1989. Lang.: Fre.　2768

Interview with translator Jean-Louis Roux. Canada. 1970-1990. Lang.: Fre.　2771

Michel Forgues' 'collages' based on non-dramatic texts. Canada: Montreal, PQ. 1977-1989. Lang.: Fre.　2777

The recent proliferation of Don Juan adaptations. Canada: Montreal, PQ. Austria. 1625-1991. Lang.: Fre.　2782

Comparison of translations of the opening of Sophocles' *Antigone*. Canada. France. 1967-1986. Lang.: Fre.　2787

Pierre Legris' translation and production of David Mamet's *Glengarry Glen Ross*. Canada: Montreal, PQ. 1989. Lang.: Fre.　2804

Odette Guimond and Jacques Rossi's stage adaptations of novels by Agota Kristof. Canada: Montreal, PQ. 1988-1989. Lang.: Fre.　2806

Director Serge Ouaknine on the decline of textual authority. Canada: Montreal, PQ. 1971-1989. Lang.: Fre.　2818

Reprints of commentary on productions by Groupe de la Veillée. Canada: Montreal, PQ. 1981-1990. Lang.: Fre.　2821

Problems of translating Steven Berkoff's *Greek*. Canada: Montreal, PQ. 1989-1990. Lang.: Fre.　2827

Alice Ronfard's translation of *The Tempest* for Théâtre Expérimental des Femmes. Canada: Montreal, PQ. 1988. Lang.: Fre.　2828

Jean-Pierre Ronfard's use of classic literature and myths. Canada: Montreal, PQ. 1989. Lang.: Fre.　2829

Jean-Louis Roux's translation of *Hamlet* for Théâtre du Nouveau Monde. Canada: Montreal, PQ. England. 1990. Lang.: Fre.　2831

Analysis of Michel Garneau's translations of Shakespearean plays. Canada. 1989. Lang.: Fre.　2833

Lorraine Pintal's solo performance *Madame Louis 14*. Canada: Montreal, PQ. 1980-1989. Lang.: Fre.　2840

Martin Faucher's adaptation of *À quelle heure on meurt? (What Time Do We Die?)* by Réjean Ducharme. Canada: Montreal, PQ. 1988. Lang.: Fre.　2841

Interview with director Denys Arcand. Canada: Montreal, PQ. 1990. Lang.: Fre.　2842

Romeo and Juliet—how Shakespeare and Zeffirelli used their sources. England. Italy. 1594-1968. Lang.: Eng.　2912

Profile of the 'plays in transit' workshops at the Festival international des francophonies. France: Limoges. Belgium. Canada. Mali. 1988. Lang.: Fre.　2988

Francophone plays in new contexts at Francophone theatre festival. France: Limoges. 1988. Lang.: Fre.　2995

Claude Poissant's production of *Les Voyageurs* by Madeleine Laïc at Festival internationale des francophonies. France: Limoges. 1988. Lang.: Fre.　2996

Playwriting, adaptation, and other forms. France. 1801-1989. Lang.: Fre.　2997

Psychoanalytic and philosophical analysis of translation. France. Germany. 1990. Lang.: Fre.　3002

The methods and objectives of theatrical adaptation. France. 1980-1989. Lang.: Fre.　3005

Interview with playwright Paul Schmidt. Germany: Hamburg. 1996. Lang.: Eng.　3051

Shakespeare and Polish Romanticism. Poland. 1786-1846. Lang.: Eng.　3163

A French adaptation of *Romeo and Juliet* on the Polish stage. Poland. 1796-1868. Lang.: Eng, Fre.　3164

Adaptations — cont'd

Elizabeth Egloff's *The Lover*, adapted from Turgenjév. USA. 1854-1996. Lang.: Eng. 3333

Profile of writer Cynthia Ozick and her stage adaptation of her novel *The Shawl*. USA: New York, NY. 1996. Lang.: Eng. 3353

Karen S. Mitchell's *The Rainbow Season: Romancing the Romance*. USA. 1990-1996. Lang.: Eng. 3408

Problems of translating medieval texts. USA. 1996. Lang.: Eng. 3465

Stage plays performed on radio. USA. UK-England. 1972-1984. Lang.: Eng. 3583

The film and stage versions of *Plaques tectoniques (Tectonic Plates)* by Robert Lepage. Canada: Quebec, PQ. 1991. Lang.: Fre. 3641

Filmed theatre at festival of new cinema and video. Canada: Montreal, PQ. 1991. Lang.: Fre. 3643

Recent European film adaptations of stage plays. Europe. 1988-1989. Lang.: Fre. 3644

Graham Greene's screen adaptation of Shaw's *Saint Joan*. UK-England. 1957. Lang.: Eng. 3647

Critique of Steven Spielberg's film adaptation of *The Color Purple* by Alice Walker. USA. 1982-1986. Lang.: Eng. 3649

Suzanne Lantagne's mime adaptation of a short story by Gombrowicz. Canada: Montreal, PQ. 1928-1989. Lang.: Fre. 3693

Interview with director Jean Asselin of Omnibus. Canada: Montreal, PQ. 1982-1989. Lang.: Fre. 3694

Alan Ayckbourn on his collaboration with Andrew Lloyd Webber, *By Jeeves*. UK-England: London. 1996. Lang.: Eng. 3986

The operatic adaptation of Patrick White's novel *Voss*. Australia. 1978-1996. Lang.: Eng. 4298

Playwright Carol Bolt on becoming an opera librettist. Canada. 1996. Lang.: Eng. 4307

Analysis of Britten's opera *A Midsummer Night's Dream*. UK-England. 1960-1996. Lang.: Eng. 4343

Writing for puppet theatre. Canada: Montreal, PQ. 1979-1989. Lang.: Fre. 4424

Adding Machine, The
Design/technology
Virtual reality in a production of *The Adding Machine* by Elmer Rice. USA: Lawrence, KS. 1996. Lang.: Eng. 310

Use of computer-generated projections in a University of Kansas production of *The Adding Machine*. USA: Lawrence, KS. 1996. Lang.: Eng. 1744

Addison, Adele
Performance/production
Composers and performers of the American art song. USA. 1996. Lang.: Eng. 3870

Addo, P.K.
Performance/production
Collection of newspaper reviews by London theatre critics. UK-England: London. 1996. Lang.: Eng. 2328

Aden, Laura
Institutions
Theatre in New Jersey, with emphasis on New Jersey Shakespeare Festival. USA: Madison, NJ. 1996. Lang.: Eng. 582

Adler, Jacob
Performance/production
Three actors of Yiddish theatre as Shylock. USA: New York, NY. 1901-1950. Lang.: Eng. 2590

Adler, Peter Herman
Performance/production
Composers and performers of the American art song. USA. 1996. Lang.: Eng. 3870

Adler, Richard
Performance/production
Collection of newspaper reviews by London theatre critics. UK-England: London. 1996. Lang.: Eng. 2308

Administration
SEE ALSO
Classed Entries.
Institutions
Claes Peter Hellwig's year as manager of Östgötateatern and his view of its troubles. Sweden: Norrköping. 1995. Lang.: Swe. 538

Ronny Danielsson, the new manager of Göteborgs Stadsteater. Sweden: Gothenburg. 1996. Lang.: Swe. 540

Profile of Broadway Initiatives Working Group. USA: New York, NY. 1996. Lang.: Eng. 596

Politics and the placing of Tanzwerk under the administration of Städtische Bühnen's Opernhaus. Germany: Nuremberg. 1996. Lang.: Ger. 1408

Interview with Lars Löfgren, manager of the Royal Dramatic Theatre. Sweden: Stockholm. 1985-1996. Lang.: Swe. 1852
Performance/production
Generational change among directors at German-language theatres. Germany. Austria. Switzerland. 1996. Lang.: Ger. 819
Relation to other fields
Problems of Black directors within the studio system. USA. 1985-1996. Lang.: Eng. 3650

Adolf Eichmann—Questions and Answers
Performance/production
Political theatre of Hans-Werner Kroesinger. Germany. 1996. Lang.: Ger. 2085

Adolphson, Kristina
Performance/production
Actress Kristina Adolphson. Sweden: Stockholm. 1955. Lang.: Swe. 2280

Adventures In Motion Pictures (London)
Performance/production
Collection of newspaper reviews by London theatre critics. UK-England: London. 1996. Lang.: Eng. 2388

Adventures of Huckleberry Finn, The
Performance/production
Collection of newspaper reviews by London theatre critics. UK-England: London. 1996. Lang.: Eng. 2492

Adversa fortuna de don Alvaro de Luna, La (Ill Fortune of Don Alvaro de Luna, The)
Plays/librettos/scripts
Written documents in Spanish plays of the Golden Age. Spain. 1604-1624. Lang.: Eng. 3251

Adversa fortuna de Ruy López de Avalos, La (Ill Fortune of Ruy López de Avalos, The)
Plays/librettos/scripts
Written documents in Spanish plays of the Golden Age. Spain. 1604-1624. Lang.: Eng. 3251

Advertising
Administration
Cracow theatre posters. Poland: Cracow. 1781-1893. Lang.: Pol. 41

Commercial art for Broadway theatre. USA: New York, NY. 1996. Lang.: Eng. 60

The 'Golden Jubilee of Light' and the development of public relations. USA: Dearborn, MI. 1929. Lang.: Eng. 61

Graphic design and poster artwork for theatre promotion. USA. 1996. Lang.: Eng. 67

Survey of poster design for Broadway musicals. USA: New York, NY. 1892-1996. Lang.: Eng. 3881

History of advertising for puppet theatre. Germany. 1800-1996. Lang.: Ger. 4366
Design/technology
John Alvin's posters for film and Broadway theatre. USA. 1996. Lang.: Eng. 236
Performance/production
The use of well-known actors in advertising and PR campaigns. Sweden. 1950. Lang.: Swe. 950

AE (Russell, George)
Institutions
Profile of Irish women's nationalist group Inghinidhe na h'Eireann. Ireland: Dublin. 1900-1902. Lang.: Eng. 1814

Aerialists
Performance/production
Gender and race in the work of Aboriginal aerialists Con Colleano and Dawn de Ramirez. Australia. 1900-1961. Lang.: Eng. 3752

Aeschylus
Performance/production
The fiftieth Avignon Festival. France: Avignon. 1996. Lang.: Eng. 805

Productions by returned expatriate directors. Romania. 1994-1996. Lang.: Hun. 896

Analysis of *Les Atrides* by Ariane Mnouchkine's Théâtre du Soleil. France: Paris. 1992. Lang.: Eng. 2010

Politics and the actor's body in productions by Théâtre du Soleil. France. 1990-1995. Lang.: Eng. 2036

Hungarian productions by Romanian director Beatrice Bleont. Hungary: Zsámbék. Romania. 1996. Lang.: Hun. 2112
Plays/librettos/scripts
Aeschylean tragedy in its sociopolitical context. Greece. 525-456 B.C. Lang.: Eng. 3061

Aeschylus — cont'd

Relation to other fields
Theatre and law. Europe. 500 B.C.-1989 A.D. Lang.: Fre. 3494

Aesop
Performance/production
Analysis of Vanbrugh's *Aesop*. England. 1696-1759. Lang.: Eng. 1995

Aesthetics
Institutions
Comparison of Carbone 14 and Nouveau Théâtre Expérimental. Canada: Montreal, PQ. 1989. Lang.: Fre. 1778
Performance/production
Principal trends in Argentinian theatre. Argentina. 1975-1990. Lang.: Fre. 682
Slowed or frozen images in Quebec theatre. Canada. 1989. Lang.: Fre. 711
The work of director Jévgenij Vachtangov. Russia: Moscow. 1883-1922. Lang.: Rus. 2222
Plays/librettos/scripts
Harsh realism in contemporary Quebec plays. Canada: Montreal, PQ. 1993-1995. Lang.: Fre. 2784
Trends in recent Quebec drama. Canada: Montreal, PQ. 1980-1990. Lang.: Fre. 2839
Traditional African aesthetics in the plays of Wole Soyinka. Nigeria. 1960-1975. Lang.: Eng. 3150
Relation to other fields
Modernism as closed to innovation. Canada. 1989. Lang.: Fre. 1142
Garrick, painting, and a shift in theatre aesthetics. England. 1700-1799. Lang.: Ger. 1170
The fascist aesthetic in speeches and manifestos. Italy. 1925-1943. Lang.: Eng. 1205
Teaching theatre in general aesthetics classes. Russia: Moscow. 1996. Lang.: Rus. 1225
Social and aesthetic trends in Japanese children's theatre festival. Japan: Tokyo. 1995. Lang.: Fre. 3501
Political implications of Christoph Marthaler's *Murx*, directed by Heiner Goebbels. Germany: Berlin. UK-England: London. 1992-1995. Lang.: Eng. 4001
Theory/criticism
Aesthetic and ideological characteristics of experimental theatre. Canada. 1968-1989. Lang.: Fre. 1320
Theatre tradition in competition with media technology. Canada. 1989. Lang.: Fre. 1324
The evolution of Les Cahiers de Théâtre *Jeu*. Canada: Montreal, PQ. 1976-1989. Lang.: Fre. 1326
Anti-intellectualism in Quebec theatre criticism. Canada. 1993. Lang.: Fre. 1327
Argument that theatre's value is in excitement generated, not production values. Canada. 1950-1996. Lang.: Fre. 1329
The historical meaning of Symbolist theatre. Europe. 1900. Lang.: Ger. 1338
Systems theory and theatre historiography. Europe. 1700-1799. Lang.: Ger. 1339
Pathos and kitsch in art. Europe. 1791-1989. Lang.: Fre. 1341
Critical reception of productions by Robert Lepage at the Festival d'Automne. France: Paris. 1992. Lang.: Fre. 1345
Analysis of Diderot's *Paradoxe sur le comédien*. France. 1773. Lang.: Ger. 1346
The question of art in indigenous aesthetics. North America. 1996. Lang.: Eng. 1354
Optical theatre, an emerging form. Russia. 1990-1996. Lang.: Rus. 1359
Falangist theatre aesthetics. Spain. 1935-1945. Lang.: Eng. 1363
The origins and evolution of physical theatre. UK-England. Germany. 1900-1996. Lang.: Eng. 1368
Interview with dance scholar Iván Vitányi. Hungary. 1943-1995. Lang.: Hun. 1549
Sylvie Laliberté on the aesthetics of postmodern dance. Canada: Montreal, PQ. 1991. Lang.: Fre. 1603
Antifeminism in Montreal theatre criticism. Canada: Montreal, PQ. 1992. Lang.: Fre. 3533
Sentimentality in theatre. Canada. 1891-1989. Lang.: Fre. 3536
Contemporary approaches to the revival of medieval drama. Europe. USA. 1995. Lang.: Eng. 3539
Tragedy, pathos, and French philosophy. Greece: Athens. France. 500 B.C.-1989 A.D. Lang.: Fre. 3543

Art, politics, and the African playwright. South Africa, Republic of. 1933. Lang.: Eng. 3551
Howard Barker's 'humanist' and 'catastrophic' theatres. UK. 1993. Lang.: Eng. 3552
Director Gilles Noël—reality and artifice in theatre and film. Canada: Montreal, PQ. 1996. Lang.: Fre. 3651
Film retrospectives of actress Asta Nielsen and filmmaker Gregory J. Markopoulos. USA: New York, NY. 1996. Lang.: Eng. 3652
Novelist Milan Kundera's ideas on music and Janáček. Europe. 1995. Lang.: Swe. 4357
Aesthetic analysis of puppetry. Europe. 1800-1992. Lang.: Hun. 4432

Affamée (Starving)
Relation to other fields
Interview with Jo Lechay and Eugene Lion, creators of *Affamée (Starving)*. Canada: Montreal, PQ. 1990. Lang.: Fre. 1595

Afonin, Boris
Performance/production
Moscow theatre life of the twenties and thirties. USSR: Moscow. 1927-1931. Lang.: Rus. 1077

African-American theatre
SEE ALSO
Black theatre.
Administration
Equity observance of African-American Heritage Month. USA: New York, NY. 1996. Lang.: Eng. 59
Basic theatrical documents
Anthology of unknown plays of the Harlem Renaissance. USA: New York, NY. 1920-1940. Lang.: Eng. 1694
Institutions
Community theatres arising from the reform movement and settlement houses. USA: Chicago, IL, Cleveland, OH, New York, NY. 1896-1930. Lang.: Eng. 570
Robert Brustein's response to August Wilson's call for separation of Black and white theatre. USA. 1996. Lang.: Eng. 573
The Federal Theatre Project's plans for numerous Black theatres. USA. 1935-1939. Lang.: Eng. 577
Obituary for Vivian Robinson of AUDELCO. USA: New York, NY. 1996. Lang.: Eng. 586
George C. Wolfe receives Equity's Paul Robeson Award. USA: New York, NY. 1996. Lang.: Eng. 595
Sydné Mahone, director of play development, Crossroads Theatre. USA: New Brunswick, NJ. 1980-1996. Lang.: Eng. 604
August Wilson's address on the separation of white and Black theatre. USA: Princeton, NJ. 1996. Lang.: Eng. 607
Performance/production
Account of National Black Theatre Festival. USA: Winston-Salem, NC. 1995. Lang.: Eng. 1026
Social boundaries and the transformation of the cakewalk. USA. 1900-1918. Lang.: Eng. 1448
Two productions of the National Black Theatre Festival. USA: Winston-Salem, NC. 1995. Lang.: Eng. 2625
A new view of actor Charles Gilpin. USA. 1920-1930. Lang.: Eng. 2647
Biographical information on actor Ira Aldridge. USA. UK-England. 1807-1867. Lang.: Eng. 2652
Interview with actress Gertrude Jeannette. USA. 1970. Lang.: Eng. 2656
Production of O'Neill's *The Emperor Jones* at the Little Theatre of Indianapolis. USA: Indianapolis, IN. 1921-1922. Lang.: Eng. 2680
Censorship of Federal Theatre Project's *Lysistrata* performed by Seattle Negro Repertory Company. USA: Seattle, WA. 1936-1939. Lang.: Eng. 2688
The career of actress Butterfly McQueen. USA. 1911-1995. Lang.: Eng. 3632
Subversive minstrelsy of the Ira Aldridge Troupe. USA: Philadelphia, PA. 1863. Lang.: Eng. 3721
Photos of Cafe Afrocentric at La MaMa, celebrating Black History Month. USA: New York, NY. 1996. Lang.: Eng. 3736
African-American gospel musicals. 1996. Lang.: Eng. 3911
Diahann Carroll's role in *Sunset Boulevard* at the Ford Centre. Canada: Toronto, ON. 1950-1996. Lang.: Eng. 3912
The Pointer Sisters in *Ain't Misbehavin'*. USA. 1973-1996. Lang.: Eng. 3957
Two forms of late nineteenth-century Black musical theatre. USA. 1895-1900. Lang.: Eng. 3965

Albery Theatre (London) — cont'd

Collection of newspaper reviews by London theatre critics. UK-England: London. 1996. Lang.: Eng.   2430

Collection of newspaper reviews by London theatre critics. UK-England: London. 1996. Lang.: Eng.   2481

Albery, Tim
Design/technology
The director-designer relationship. UK. 1912-1995. Lang.: Eng.   221

New approaches to opera design at the Metropolitan Opera. USA: New York, NY. 1996. Lang.: Eng.   4029
Performance/production
Collection of newspaper reviews by London theatre critics. UK-England: London. 1996. Lang.: Eng.   2422

Collection of newspaper reviews by London theatre critics. UK-England: London. 1996. Lang.: Eng.   2471

Work of Tim Albery and Antony McDonald on Met production of Britten's *A Midsummer Night's Dream* by Britten. USA: New York, NY. 1996. Lang.: Eng.   4296
Plays/librettos/scripts
Analysis of Britten's opera *A Midsummer Night's Dream*. UK-England. 1960-1996. Lang.: Eng.   4343

Alcesti di Samuele
Plays/librettos/scripts
Analysis of *Alcesti di Samuele* by Alberto Savinio (Andrea De Chirico). Italy. 1891-1952. Lang.: Ita.   3120

Alchemist, The
Performance/production
Collection of newspaper reviews by London theatre critics. UK-England: London. 1996. Lang.: Eng.   2404

Aldridge, Ira
Performance/production
Biographical information on actor Ira Aldridge. USA. UK-England. 1807-1867. Lang.: Eng.   2652

Black Shakespearean actor Ira Aldridge. USA. Europe. 1825-1853. Lang.: Eng.   2653

Subversive minstrelsy of the Ira Aldridge Troupe. USA: Philadelphia, PA. 1863. Lang.: Eng.   3721

Aldridge, Ron
Performance/production
Collection of newspaper reviews by London theatre critics. UK-England: London. 1996. Lang.: Eng.   2352

Aldwych Theatre (London)
Performance/production
Collection of newspaper reviews by London theatre critics. UK-England: London. 1996. Lang.: Eng.   2326

Collection of newspaper reviews by London theatre critics. UK-England: London. 1996. Lang.: Eng.   2343

Collection of newspaper reviews by London theatre critics. UK-England: London. 1996. Lang.: Eng.   2474

Aleksandrinskij Teat'r (St. Petersburg)
Performance/production
Arbuzov's *Moj bednyj Marat (The Promise)* directed by Anatolij Praudin, Aleksandrinskij Theatre. Russia: St. Petersburg. 1995. Lang.: Rus.   2194

Aleksandrov, Jurij
Performance/production
Jurij Aleksandrov's production of Mussorgskij's *Boris Godunov*, St. Petersburg Opera. Russia: St. Petersburg. 1995-1996. Lang.: Rus.   4199

Aleksejév, Valerij
Performance/production
Canadian debuts of singers from Eastern Europe. Canada. USA. 1917-1996. Lang.: Eng.   4097

Aleksjevič, Svetlana
Performance/production
Trostjaneckij's *Esli proživy leto... (If I Live Through the Summer)* performed by Otkritij Teat'r. Russia: St. Petersburg. 1996.Lang.: Rus.   2236

Alessandrini, Gerard
Performance/production
Collection of newspaper reviews by New York theatre critics. USA: New York, NY. 1996. Lang.: Eng.   2556

Alexander, Bill
Performance/production
The production of meaning in interpretations of Shakespeare's *The Merchant of Venice*. Europe. 1740-1987. Lang.: Eng.   2002

Collection of newspaper reviews by London theatre critics. UK-England: London. 1996. Lang.: Eng.   2404

Alexander, Robert
Plays/librettos/scripts
Blacksmyths, Black playwrights project—excerpt from symposium panel discussion. USA: Los Angeles, CA. 1995-1996. Lang.: Eng.   3320

Alexis, Agathe
Performance/production
Actress/director Agathe Alexis. France. 1995. Lang.: Eng.   2031

Alfa (Alpha)
Plays/librettos/scripts
Responses to the defeat of Solidarity in Polish drama. Poland. 1980-1989. Lang.: Eng.   3160

Alfarda, La (Tithe, The)
Basic theatrical documents
Anthology of Argentine Jewish theatre. Argentina. 1926-1988. Lang.: Eng.   1639

Alföldi, Róbert
Performance/production
English plays and subjects on the Hungarian stage. Hungary. 1995-1996. Lang.: Eng.   847

Alfreds, Mike
Performance/production
Collection of newspaper reviews by London theatre critics. UK-England: London. 1996. Lang.: Eng.   2439

Collection of newspaper reviews by London theatre critics. UK-England: London. 1996. Lang.: Eng.   2441

Alice
Basic theatrical documents
Text of *Alice* by Paul Schmidt, Tom Waits, and Kathleen Brennan. Germany: Hamburg. 1996. Lang.: Eng.   3845
Plays/librettos/scripts
Interview with playwright Paul Schmidt. Germany: Hamburg. 1996. Lang.: Eng.   3051

Alice in Wonderland
Plays/librettos/scripts
Interview with playwright Paul Schmidt. Germany: Hamburg. 1996. Lang.: Eng.   3051

All Manner of Means
Performance/production
Collection of newspaper reviews by London theatre critics. UK-England: London. 1996. Lang.: Eng.   2394

All My Sons
Performance/production
Plays by Arthur Miller at the Williamstown Theatre Festival. USA: Williamstown, MA. 1996. Lang.: Eng.   2589

All's Well That Ends Well
Plays/librettos/scripts
Legal aspects of Shakespeare's *All's Well That Ends Well*. England. 1587-1600. Lang.: Eng.   2937

All'uscita (At the Exit)
Plays/librettos/scripts
Pirandello Society Yearbook. Italy. 1889-1995. Lang.: Eng.   3133

Allá él (It's Up to Him)
Basic theatrical documents
Text of *Allá él (It's Up to Him)* by Concha Romero. Spain. 1994. Lang.: Spa.   1680
Plays/librettos/scripts
Gender roles in plays of Concha Romero. Spain. 1989. Lang.: Spa. 3240

Állami Bábszínház (Budapest)
Design/technology
Interview with puppet designer Vera Bródy. Hungary: Budapest. France: Paris. 1947-1996. Lang.: Hun.   4368
Institutions
Survey of Hungarian puppetry. Hungary. 1950-1990. Lang.: Hun.   4379

Állami Balettintézet (Budapest)
Performance/production
Tribute to dancer Zsuzsa Kún of the Hungarian Ballet Institute. Hungary: Budapest. 1950-1994. Lang.: Hun.   1503

Állami Magyar Opera (Cluj-Napoca)
Institutions
Hungarian ballet, opera and operetta in Cluj-Napoca. Hungary. Romania: Cluj-Napoca. 1948-1990. Lang.: Hun.   3847

Programming of the musical stages of the Hungarian ethnic minority of Kolozsvár (Cluj-Napoca). Hungary. Romania: Cluj-Napoca.1948-1992. Lang.: Hun.   3848
Performance/production
Music theatre in Hungarian theatre in Transylvania. Hungary: Kolozsvár. Romania: Cluj-Napoca. 1793-1948. Lang.: Hun.   3860

Állami Magyar Színház (Budapest)
Relation to other fields
Hungarian theatre life in the 1950s. Hungary. 1910-1956. Lang.: Hun.   1197

Állami Magyar Színház (Cluj-Napoca)
Institutions
György Harag and Hungarian theatre in Romania. Hungary. Romania: Cluj-Napoca. 1944-1992. Lang.: Hun.   472

SUBJECT INDEX

Alternative theatre — cont'd

Institutions
History of Canadian fringe festivals. Canada. 1985-1991. Lang.: Fre. 373

Profile of Teatret Cantabile 2. Denmark: Vordingsborg. 1980-1996. Lang.: Swe. 400

The fiftieth Avignon festival. France: Avignon. 1996. Lang.: Ger. 407

Alternative theatre at the Theater der Welt festival. Germany: Dresden. 1996. Lang.: Ger. 434

History of Hungarian alternative theatre. Hungary. 1945-1989. Lang.: Hun. 465

Retrospective on festivals of studio theatres. Hungary: Gödöllő. 1986-1996. Lang.: Hun. 480

Profile of the Kana alternative theatre group. Poland: Szczecin. 1996. Lang.: Pol. 507

Polish alternative theatre during the time of transition. Poland. 1989-1994. Lang.: Eng. 511

Performance/production
Alternative and regional Colombian theatre. Colombia. 1995. Lang.: Spa. 762

Review of Irvine Welsh's *Trainspotting* directed by János Csányi. Hungary: Budapest. 1995. Lang.: Hun. 840

Forty years of Polish alternative theatre. Poland. 1956-1996. Lang.: Ger. 891

Alternative theatre group Teatr im. Alberta Tisson. Poland: Znin. 1996. Lang.: Pol. 3790

Plays/librettos/scripts
The dearth of professional productions of plays by Australian women. Australia. 1928-1994. Lang.: Eng. 2724

Work of playwrights Jeffrey M. Jones, Mac Wellman, and Suzan-Lori Parks. USA: New York, NY. 1991. Lang.: Fre. 3360

Reference materials
Guide to non-mainstream theatre. UK. USA: New York, NY. 1996. Lang.: Eng. 1129

Alvin, John
Design/technology
John Alvin's posters for film and Broadway theatre. USA. 1996. Lang.: Eng. 236

Amadigi
Institutions
Some performances at the Buxton opera festival. UK-England: Buxton. 1996. Lang.: Eng. 4059

Amaral, María Adelaide
Plays/librettos/scripts
Analysis of plays by María Adelaide Amaral. Brazil. 1985-1995. Lang.: Por. 2735

AMAS Musical Theatre Company (New York, NY)
Administration
Tributes to various theatre people. USA: New York, NY. 1996. Lang.: Eng. 85

Amateur theatre
Audience
The audience for school theatre. Germany. 1996. Lang.: Ger. 137
Design/technology
Design in amateur theatre of Scottish Rite Freemasons. USA. 1896-1929. Lang.: Eng. 332
Institutions
The Montreal amateur theatre festival. Canada: Montreal, PQ. 1992. Lang.: Fre. 372

History of amateur theatre in Békéscsaba. Hungary: Békéscsaba. 1845-1944. Lang.: Hun. 482

Profile of Societas Raffaello Sanzio. Italy: Cesena. 1981-1996. Lang.: Ger. 491

History of amateur theatre Šentjakobsko gledališce. Slovenia: Ljubljana. 1921-1996. Lang.: Slo. 1844
Performance/production
Rudolf Mirbt and children's, school, and amateur theatre. Germany. 1896-1974. Lang.: Ger. 814

Recollections of actor, director, and teacher István Keleti. Hungary: Budapest. 1950-1990. Lang.: Hun. 848

The training of directors of amateur theatre. Russia. 1996. Lang.: Rus. 899

Use of young amateur actors by Nultwintig. Netherlands. 1994-1995. Lang.: Dut. 2141
Plays/librettos/scripts
The Danish community play tradition. Denmark. 1970-1996. Lang.: Eng. 2873

Reference materials
Directory of Polish puppet and children's theatre, festivals, and awards. Poland. 1996. Lang.: Eng, Fre. 4427
Relation to other fields
Amateur political theatre of the National Socialist period. Germany. 1900-1945. Lang.: Ger. 1194
Training
Puppeteer Hanspeter Bleisehaus' work with students and amateurs. Switzerland. 1975-1996. Lang.: Ger. 4435

Amazonas en las Indias (Amazons in the Indies)
Plays/librettos/scripts
Analysis of *Amazonas en las Indias (Amazons in the Indies)* by Tirso de Molina. Spain. 1635. Lang.: Eng. 3226

Ambasador (Ambassador, The)
Performance/production
Mrożek's *Ambasador (The Ambassador)*, directed by Erwin Axer, Teatr Wspólczesny. Poland: Warsaw. 1995. Lang.: Eng, Fre. 2147

Ambassador Theatre (New York, NY)
Performance/production
Collection of newspaper reviews by New York theatre critics. USA: New York, NY. 1996. Lang.: Eng. 2577

Ambassadors Theatre (London)
Institutions
Impact of architectural restructuring on the mission of the Royal Court Theatre. UK-England: London. 1996. Lang.: Eng. 1858
Performance/production
Collection of newspaper reviews by London theatre critics. UK-England: London. 1996. Lang.: Eng. 2429

Collection of newspaper reviews by London theatre critics. UK-England: London. 1996. Lang.: Eng. 2484

Ameley, der Biber und der König auf dem Dach (Ameley, the Beaver and the King on the Roof)
Plays/librettos/scripts
Children's plays of Tankred Dorst. Germany. 1982-1996. Lang.: Ger. 3018

Amen Corner, The
Performance/production
Collection of newspaper reviews by New York theatre critics. USA. 1996. Lang.: Eng. 2551

American Ballet Theatre (New York, NY)
Performance/production
Dancer and choreographer Twyla Tharp. USA. 1973-1994. Lang.: Hun. 1451

Obituary for ballet dancer Aleksand'r Godunov. USSR. USA. 1949-1995. Lang.: Hun. 1540

American Buffalo
Plays/librettos/scripts
Theatricality as sociopolitical commentary in plays of Mamet and Tremblay. Canada. USA. 1972-1996. Lang.: Eng. 2825

American Conservatory Theatre (San Francisco, CA)
Design/technology
Scott Bradley's set design for *Seven Guitars* by August Wilson. USA: Pittsburgh, PA, New York, NY. 1996. Lang.: Eng. 1731
Performance spaces
Restoration of the Geary Theatre. USA: San Francisco, CA. 1996. Lang.: Eng. 668

American Federation of Television and Radio Artists (New York, NY)
Administration
Report on possible merger of SAG and AFTRA. USA: New York, NY. 1996. Lang.: Eng. 3567

The merger of SAG and AFTRA. USA: New York, NY. 1996. Lang.: Eng. 3568

American Guild of Variety Artists (New York, NY)
Administration
Equity and AGVA agreement on cabaret shows at the Kennedy Center. USA: Washington, DC. 1996. Lang.: Eng. 3724

American Jewish Theatre (New York, NY)
Performance/production
Collection of newspaper reviews by New York theatre critics. USA: New York, NY. 1996. Lang.: Eng. 2573

American Music Theatre Festival (Philadelphia, PA)
Design/technology
Set and costume design for *Shlemiel the First*, ART/American Music Theatre Festival. USA: Cambridge, MA, Philadelphia, PA. 1996.Lang.: Eng. 3903

American Opera Society (New York, NY)
Performance/production
Concert opera in New York. USA: New York, NY. 1952-1996. Lang.: Eng. 4250

André, Harald
  Performance/production
    Britten's *Peter Grimes*: productions by Eric Crozier and Harald André. UK-England. Sweden: Stockholm. 1945-1980. Lang.: Swe.   4229
André, J.P.
  Performance/production
    Report on the Avignon fringe festival. France: Avignon. 1996. Lang.: Eng.   796
Andrea Chénier
  Design/technology
    Hubert Monloup's set and costume designs for *Andrea Chénier*, Metropolitan Opera. USA: New York, NY. 1996. Lang.: Eng.   4026
  Performance/production
    Background information on Teatro Colón season. Argentina: Buenos Aires. 1996. Lang.: Eng.   4075
    Interview with opera director Nicolas Joël. France. Germany. 1942-1996. Lang.: Eng.   4117
    Background material on Lyric Opera of Chicago radio broadcast performances. USA: Chicago, IL. 1996. Lang.: Eng.   4244
    Background material on Metropolitan Opera radio broadcast performances. USA: New York, NY. 1996. Lang.: Eng.   4252
  Plays/librettos/scripts
    Historical background of Giordano's opera *Andrea Chénier*. France: Paris. 1750-1820. Lang.: Eng.   4317
    Analysis of *Andrea Chénier* by Umberto Giordano. Italy. 1896. Lang.: Eng.   4329
Andrea, Guillermo de
  Performance/production
    Analysis of five Shakespearean productions in Quebec. Canada: Montreal, PQ, Quebec, PQ. Romania: Craiova. 1993. Lang.: Fre.   1947
Andreini, Francesco
  Performance/production
    Portraits of actors of the Gelosi company. Italy. 1568-1589. Lang.: Eng.   3767
Andreini, Giovan Battista
  Administration
    Giovan Battista Andreini at the beginning of professional theatre. Italy. France. 1576-1654. Lang.: Ger.   3759
Andreini, Isabella
  Performance/production
    Portraits of actors of the Gelosi company. Italy. 1568-1589. Lang.: Eng.   3767
Andrejčuk, Jurij
  Plays/librettos/scripts
    Interview with young playwrights. Russia: Moscow. 1990-1996. Lang.: Rus.   3186
Andrejév, Leonid Nikolajévič
  Institutions
    Festival in honor of playwright Leonid Andrejév. Russia: Orel. 1996. Lang.: Rus.   1822
Andrews Lane Theatre (Dublin)
  Performance/production
    Current Dublin productions. Ireland: Dublin. 1996. Lang.: Eng.   2117
Andrews, Alison
  Performance/production
    Collection of newspaper reviews by London theatre critics. UK-England: London. 1996. Lang.: Eng.   2354
Andrews, Julie
  Administration
    Inductions into the theatrical Hall of Fame. USA: New York, NY. 1996. Lang.: Eng.   99
  Performance/production
    Former Broadway stars and their careers in television and film. USA: New York, NY. 1996. Lang.: Eng.   1057
    Recollections of making the musical film *Thoroughly Modern Millie*. USA. 1967. Lang.: Eng.   3638
Androvskaja, Ol'ga N.
  Performance/production
    Actress Ol'ga Androvskaja's notes on Asian tour of Moscow Art Theatre. Japan. 1958-1959. Lang.: Rus.   2133
Ange et le Corbeau, L' (Angel and the Crow, The)
  Performance/production
    Alliance of text and acting in three French-language productions. Canada: Montreal, PQ. Switzerland: Geneva. 1985-1995. Lang.: Fre.   722
  Plays/librettos/scripts
    Playwright Francis Monmart discusses his craft. Canada: Montreal, PQ. 1981-1996. Lang.: Fre.   2814

Angel Days
  Performance/production
    Collection of newspaper reviews by London theatre critics. UK-England: London. 1996. Lang.: Eng.   2445
Angelici, Marthe
  Performance/production
    French vocalism and its artists. France. 1996. Lang.: Eng.   4124
Angélico, Halma
  Plays/librettos/scripts
    Analysis of *La nieta de Fedra (Phaedra's Niece)* by Halma Angélico. Spain. 1929. Lang.: Spa.   3249
Angels
  Performance/production
    Collection of newspaper reviews by London theatre critics. UK-England: London. 1996. Lang.: Eng.   2370
Angels in America
  Performance/production
    Intercultural theatre exchange at the American University in Bulgaria. Bulgaria: Blagoevgrad. 1993. Lang.: Eng.   1915
    Production of Kushner's *Angels in America* by Salt Lake Acting Company. USA: Salt Lake City, UT. 1996. Lang.: Eng.   2665
  Plays/librettos/scripts
    Plays about politician Roy Cohn. USA. 1986-1994. Lang.: Eng.   3339
    Law in *Angels in America* by Tony Kushner. USA. 1993. Lang.: Eng.   3421
Angels in America, Part I: Millennium Approaches
  Administration
    Angels in America and local ordinances prohibiting public nudity. USA: Charlotte, NC. 1996. Lang.: Eng.   1622
  Performance/production
    Angels in America and censorship at Catholic University. USA: Washington, DC. 1996. Lang.: Eng.   2661
  Plays/librettos/scripts
    Influences on Tony Kushner's *Angels in America*. USA. 1940-1996. Lang.: Eng.   3407
Angels in America, Part II: Perestroika
  Plays/librettos/scripts
    Influences on Tony Kushner's *Angels in America*. USA. 1940-1996. Lang.: Eng.   3407
Angels With Dirty Faces
  Performance/production
    Influence of Hollywood gangster films on South African cinema. USA: Hollywood, CA. South Africa, Republic of. 1930-1996. Lang.: Eng. 3637
Angeredsteatern (Gothenburg)
  Institutions
    Niklas Hjulström, new manager of Angeredsteatern. Sweden. 1996. Lang.: Swe.   1849
Anima (Her Soul)
  Basic theatrical documents
    International anthology of modern drama by women. 1880-1940. Lang.: Eng.   1637
Animation
  Design/technology
    Lighting effects for the animated film *Toy Story*. USA: Hollywood, CA. 1995. Lang.: Eng.   3595
  Performance/production
    Description of a stop-motion animation segment used in a prime-time situation comedy. USA: Los Angeles, CA. 1995-1996. Lang.: Eng.   3675
    Puppets and 3-D animation in Disney's *James and the Giant Peach*. USA: Hollywood, CA. 1993-1995. Lang.: Eng.   4406
  Plays/librettos/scripts
    Evolution of the Beast character in treatments of the fairy tale *Beauty and the Beast*. UK-England. 1945-1996. Lang.: Eng.   1106
Ankers, Kathleen
  Design/technology
    Television lighting design by Steven Brill and Kathleen Ankers. USA: New York, NY. 1996. Lang.: Eng.   3663
Anna
  Plays/librettos/scripts
    Analysis of *Anna* by April Hubért. Canada: Toronto, ON. 1994. Lang.: Eng.   2794
Anna Christie
  Performance/production
    Portrayals of Eugene O'Neill's *Anna Christie*. USA: New York, NY. 1930-1993. Lang.: Eng.   2638
  Plays/librettos/scripts
    Comparison of writings by Eugene O'Neill and John Reed. USA: New York, NY. 1913-1922. Lang.: Eng.   3327
Annie
  Performance/production
    Actress/singer Andrea McArdle. USA. 1976-1996. Lang.: Eng.   3946

Architecture — cont'd

Audience reactions/comments — cont'd

Relation to other fields
Survey of American attitudes toward the arts. USA. 1996. Lang.: Eng.
1256

Theory/criticism
Argument that theatre's value is in excitement generated, not production values. Canada. 1950-1996. Lang.: Fre. 1329

Audience with Queen, An
Performance/production
Collection of newspaper reviews by London theatre critics. UK-England: London. 1996. Lang.: Eng. 2402

Audience-performer relationship

Audience
A new definition of theatre in the age of technological interaction. 1996. Lang.: Ger. 127

Poems on the fleeting contact between actor and audience. Canada. 1989. Lang.: Fre. 130

The actor-audience relationship and the culture of performance. Europe. 1700-1799. Lang.: Ger. 135

Israeli theatre and its audience. Israel. 1990-1991. Lang.: Eng. 139

Audience participation in avant-garde theatre. USA: New York, NY. 1960-1969. Lang.: Ger. 141

Laughter and the development of community among spectators. Canada. 1990. Lang.: Fre. 1627

Brecht and the actor-audience relationship. Russia: Moscow. Germany: Berlin. 1898-1956. Lang.: Rus. 1634

The Elizabethan experience at the reconstructed Globe theatre. UK-England: London. 1996. Lang.: Eng. 1636

Cabaret performances in Theresienstadt concentration camp. Czechoslovakia: Terezin. 1941-1942. Lang.: Ger. 3725

Performance artist Louis Ethel Liliefeldt. Canada. 1996. Lang.: Eng. 3784

Audience participation in a performance of dancer Jérôme Bel. Denmark. 1995-1996. Lang.: Dan. 3786

The role of white minstrels in creating the stereotype of the Black minstrel. USA. 1822-1898. Lang.: Eng. 3829

The social importance of the Hamburg marionnette theatre. Germany: Hamburg. 1800-1899. Lang.: Ger. 4436

Institutions
Grupo Teatro Escambray's communication with its audience. Cuba: La Macagua. 1968-1996. Lang.: Eng. 388

Performance spaces
Montreal's adjustable-stage theatres. Canada: Montreal, PQ. 1996. Lang.: Fre. 626

Profile of Shakespeare's Globe Theatre and the International Shakespeare Globe Centre. UK-England: London. 1985-1996. Lang.: Swe. 659

Historic theatre structures—implications for scenography, audience-performer relationship. Europe. 600 B.C.-1996 A.D. Lang.: Fre. 1886

Performance/production
The social function of comedy and laughter. Canada: Montreal, PQ. 1990. Lang.: Fre. 742

The ban on Grand Théâtre Émotif du Québec's *Nudité (Nudity)*. Canada: Montreal, PQ. 1996. Lang.: Fre. 749

The seductive nature of theatre. Europe. 1989. Lang.: Fre. 792

History and current state of autobiographical solo performance. USA. 1276-1995. Lang.: Eng. 1020

Analysis of traditional African masked performance. Nigeria. Sierre Leone. 1968-1993. Lang.: Eng. 1547

Memoirs relating to actor Innokentij Smoktunovskij. Russia: Moscow. 1980-1996. Lang.: Rus. 2233

The career of performance artist Rose English. UK-England. 1996. Lang.: Eng. 3794

The career of performance artist Marina Abramovic. Yugoslavia. 1946-1995. Lang.: Eng. 3809

The act of the fat lady at the sideshow of Coney Island. USA: Brooklyn, NY. 1992-1994. Lang.: Eng. 3837

Discussion surrounding a performance of *Murx* by Christoph Marthaler. Germany: Berlin. UK-England: London. 1995. Lang.: Eng. 3917

Uwe Spillmann's street puppet theatre. Germany. 1996. Lang.: Ger. 4395

Plays/librettos/scripts
Reflections on categorization of interactive theatre pieces. USA: New York, NY. 1996. Lang.: Eng. 1114

Relation to other fields
Description and analysis of *Arbeit macht frei* by Akko Theatre Center. Germany. Israel. 1991-1995. Lang.: Eng. 1191

Interview with performance artist Marina Abramovic. Yugoslavia. 1974-1996. Lang.: Eng. 3824

Theory/criticism
The origins and evolution of physical theatre. UK-England. Germany. 1900-1996. Lang.: Eng. 1368

Sentimentality in theatre. Canada. 1891-1989. Lang.: Fre. 3536

Nudity and vulnerability in performance art. USA. 1960-1996. Lang.: Eng. 3826

Audio forms

SEE ALSO
Classed Entries under MEDIA—Audio forms.

Administration
The business of producing original cast albums of major musicals. USA. 1996. Lang.: Eng. 3883

Marketing of operatic offerings. Europe. North America. 1996. Lang.: Eng. 4006

Design/technology
Technical elements of Silver Legacy Resort and Casino. USA: Reno, NV. 1995. Lang.: Eng. 265

Performance/production
Biography of actor Fredric March. USA. 1897-1975. Lang.: Eng. 1059

Listing of new audio and video recordings of musical materials.. North America. 1996. Lang.: Eng. 3861

Recordings of dramatic tenor Francesco Tamagno. Italy. 1850-1905. Lang.: Eng. 4190

Assessment of recordings of *Dido and Aeneas* by Henry Purcell. UK-England. 1996. Lang.: Eng. 4228

CD retrospective of the recordings of Leontyne Price. USA. 1927-1996. Lang.: Eng. 4249

Retirement of Edward Downes as Metropolitan Opera broadcast quizmaster. USA: New York, NY. 1996. Lang.: Eng. 4282

Reference materials
Directory of British broadcasting. UK. 1995-1996. Lang.: Eng. 3570

Auditions

Administration
Member and non-member auditions in new Equity-LORT contract. USA: New York, NY. 1996. Lang.: Eng. 73

Performance/production
Critique of audition system for actor-training institutions. Australia. 1993. Lang.: Eng. 686

Plays/librettos/scripts
Interview with Albert Hague, musical theatre professional. USA: New York, NY. 1960-1996. Lang.: Eng. 3995

Auditorium

Performance spaces
Proposal to restore original lighting equipment in the auditorium of a retirement home. Sweden: Stockholm. 1920. Lang.: Swe. 656

Acoustics for music theatre. Sweden. 1996. Lang.: Swe. 4071

Aufhaltsame Aufstieg des Arturo Ui, Der (Resistible Rise of Arturo Ui, The)
Performance/production
Konstanze Lauterbach's production of *Der aufhaltsame Aufstieg des Arturo Ui (The Resistible Rise of Arturo Ui)* by Bertolt Brecht. Germany: Klagenfurt. 1995. Lang.: Eng. 2048

Aufstieg und Fall der Stadt Mahagonny (Rise and Fall of the City of Mahagonny)
Institutions
Jeunesse's festival of works by Kurt Weill. Austria: Vienna. 1995. Lang.: Eng. 3906

Performance/production
Interview with Norbert Gingold regarding score preparation and conducting of *The Three Penny Opera*. Germany: Berlin. Austria: Vienna. 1928-1929. Lang.: Eng. 3916

Auftrag, Der (Mission, The)
Performance/production
The use of Müller's *Der Auftrag (The Mission)* in *The Aboriginal Protesters* by Mudrooroo. Australia: Sydney. 1996. Lang.: Ger. 1898

Theatre in Leipzig since reunification. Germany: Leipzig. 1996. Lang.: Eng. 2061

Comparison of productions of Müller's *Der Auftrag (The Mission)*. Germany: Leipzig, Berlin. 1996. Lang.: Ger. 2069

Productions of plays by Heiner Müller at Berliner Ensemble and Volksbühne. Germany: Berlin. 1996. Lang.: Ger. 2088

Augellino belverde, L' (Green Bird, The)
Design/technology
Design for Gozzi's *The Green Bird (L'augellino belverde)* at the New Victory Theatre. USA: New York, NY. 1996. Lang.: Eng. 3760

Augellino belverde, L' (Green Bird, The) — cont'd

Performance/production
Alliance of text and acting in three French-language productions.
Canada: Montreal, PQ. Switzerland: Geneva. 1985-1995. Lang.: Fre.
722

Augustin, Michèle
Performance/production
Performances of the Jim Henson International Festival. USA: New
York, NY. 1995. Lang.: Eng. 4407

Aurélie, ma soeur (My Sister, Aurélie)
Plays/librettos/scripts
Careers of playwrights Michel Tremblay and Marie Laberge. Canada:
Quebec, PQ. 1964-1992. Lang.: Eng. 2815

Aussi creux que le Grand Canyon (As Empty as the Grand Canyon)
Plays/librettos/scripts
Analysis of plays by Jean-Frédéric Messier. Canada: Montreal, PQ.
1987-1991. Lang.: Fre. 2744

Austen, Jane
Performance/production
Collection of newspaper reviews by London theatre critics. UK-England:
London, Chichester. 1996. Lang.: Eng. 2440

Collection of newspaper reviews by London theatre critics. UK-England:
London. 1996. Lang.: Eng. 2452

Collection of newspaper reviews by London theatre critics. UK-England:
London. 1996. Lang.: Eng. 2456

Australian-Macedonian Drama Group (Melbourne)
Institutions
Profile of the Australian-Macedonian Drama Group. Australia:
Melbourne. 1983-1994. Lang.: Eng. 1749

Austrian Federal Theatres
SEE
Österreichische Bundestheater.

Author's Farce, The
Plays/librettos/scripts
Italian opera in plays of Henry Fielding. England. 1705-1735. Lang.:
Eng. 2888

Autumn Leaf Performance (Toronto, ON)
Institutions
Profile of opera company Autumn Leaf Performance. Canada: Toronto,
ON. 1994-1996. Lang.: Eng. 4032

Auzely, Yvan
Performance/production
Dancer and actor Yvan Auzely. France. Sweden: Stockholm. 1965-1995.
Lang.: Swe. 1502

Avant-garde theatre
SEE ALSO
Experimental theatre.

Alternative theatre.

Shōgekijō undō.

Audience
Audience participation in avant-garde theatre. USA: New York, NY.
1960-1969. Lang.: Ger. 141

Basic theatrical documents
English translation of the manuscript of *La Mort de Molière (The Death
of Molière)* by Heiner Müller. Germany. France. 1991-1996. Lang.: Eng.
3586

Institutions
Profile of Societas Raffaello Sanzio. Italy: Cesena. 1981-1996. Lang.:
Ger. 491

Theatre of the 8th Day's return from exile. Poland: Poznań. 1989-1995.
Lang.: Eng. 506

Avant-garde theatre at the Steirischer Herbst Festival. Austria: Graz.
1996. Lang.: Ger. 1753

The Chicago Theatre Society and its work. USA: Chicago, IL. 1909-
1915. Lang.: Eng. 1875

Forced Entertainment's own account of its first decade of performance.
UK-England: Sheffield. 1984-1994. Lang.: Eng. 3655

Performance spaces
Post-modern performance: Forced Entertainment, Brith Grof, Fiona
Templeton. UK-England: Sheffield, London. UK-Wales. USA: New
York, NY. 1965-1995. Lang.: Eng. 3703

The artist-led guided tours known as *Hidden Cities*. UK-England. 1995.
Lang.: Eng. 3704

Performance/production
The decline of experimental theatre in Quebec. Canada. USA. 1982-
1989. Lang.: Fre. 712

Tendencies in avant-garde theatre. Canada. USA. 1980-1989. Lang.:
Fre. 723

Life and work of Ritsaert ten Cate, founder of the Mickery Theater.
Netherlands. 1930-1995. Lang.: Eng. 885

Włodzimierz Staniewski and the Gardzienice Theatre Associaton.
Poland: Gardzienice. 1977-1996. Lang.: Ger. 893

The two branches of Polish avant-garde theatre. Poland. 1970-1995.
Lang.: Eng, Fre. 2174

Computer technology in *The Red Horse Animation* by Lee Breuer. USA:
New York, NY. 1996. Lang.: Eng. 2632

Review of the installation *Self-Storage* by Laurie Anderson, Bruce Eno,
and others. UK-England: London. 1995. Lang.: Eng. 3656

Portrait of Hotel Pro Forma. Denmark: Copenhagen. 1985-1996. Lang.:
Ger. 3710

Movement in the avant-garde. USA: New York, NY. Sweden:
Stockholm. 1995. Lang.: Swe. 3717

Discussion surrounding a performance of *Murx* by Christoph Marthaler.
Germany: Berlin. UK-England: London. 1995. Lang.: Eng. 3917

Plays/librettos/scripts
Futurism and writer Mina Loy. Italy: Florence. 1905-1916. Lang.: Eng.
3134

Relation to other fields
Description and analysis of *Arbeit macht frei* by Akko Theatre Center.
Germany. Israel. 1991-1995. Lang.: Eng. 1191

Performance artists and writers comment on political concerns in their
work. UK-England: London. 1995. Lang.: Eng. 3818

Sleep and dreams in performances of Paul Gilchrist. UK-England. 1959-
1996. Lang.: Eng. 3820

Theory/criticism
Similarities between African vernacular performance and avant-garde
theatre. North America. Togo. Europe. 1970-1994. Lang.: Eng. 1355

The origins and evolution of physical theatre. UK-England. Germany.
1900-1996. Lang.: Eng. 1368

Avare, L' (Miser, The)
Plays/librettos/scripts
Analysis of Oyônô-Mbia's *Trois prétendants ... un mari (Three Suitors:
One Husband).* Cameroon. 1667-1996. Lang.: Eng. 2737

Avas Táncegyüttes (Miskolc)
Institutions
History of folk dance group Avas Táncegyüttes. Hungary: Miskolc.
1951-1996. Lang.: Hun. 1544

Avec l'hiver qui s'en vient (With Winter as it Goes)
Plays/librettos/scripts
Careers of playwrights Michel Tremblay and Marie Laberge. Canada:
Quebec, PQ. 1964-1992. Lang.: Eng. 2815

Avow
Plays/librettos/scripts
Interview with playwright Bill C. Davis. USA: New York, NY. 1996.
Lang.: Eng. 3438

Awards
Administration
Tributes to various theatre people. USA: New York, NY. 1996. Lang.:
Eng. 85

Scholarships awarded by Actors' Work Program sponsored by Equity.
USA: New York, NY. 1996. Lang.: Eng. 97

Ellen Stewart of La MaMa receives Rosetta LeNoire award for
nontraditional casting. USA: New York, NY. 1996. Lang.: Eng. 1623

Design/technology
Winners of the 1996 USITT Architecture Awards. USA. 1996. Lang.:
Eng. 284

Institutions
Prix d'Europe honors Robert Wilson, Théâtre de Complicité, and Carte
Blanche-Compagnia della Fortezza. Italy: Taormina. 1971-1996. Lang.:
Fre. 492

George C. Wolfe receives Equity's Paul Robeson Award. USA: New
York, NY. 1996. Lang.: Eng. 595

Choreographer Imre Eck. Hungary. 1930-1995. Lang.: Hun. 1482

Performance/production
Peter Stein on Fritz Kortner's understanding of theatre. Germany:
Hamburg. 1996. Lang.: Ger. 830

Recipients of the annual theatre critics' awards. Hungary. 1995-1996.
Lang.: Hun. 846

Winners of the Helen Hayes Awards. USA: Washington, DC. 1996.
Lang.: Eng. 1005

The annual OBIE Awards for Off Broadway and Off-off Broadway
theatre. USA: New York, NY. 1996. Lang.: Eng. 1009

Ruben Santiago-Hudson and Lisa Gay Hamilton, winners of the
Derwent Award. USA: New York, NY. 1996. Lang.: Eng. 1054

Barbican Theatre (London) — cont'd

Collection of newspaper reviews by London theatre critics. UK-England: London. 1996. Lang.: Eng. 2388

Collection of newspaper reviews by London theatre critics. UK-England: London. 1996. Lang.: Eng. 2412

Collection of newspaper reviews by London theatre critics. UK-England: London. 1996. Lang.: Eng. 2446

Collection of newspaper reviews by London theatre critics. UK-England: London. 1996. Lang.: Eng. 2471

Collection of newspaper reviews by London theatre critics. UK-England: London. 1996. Lang.: Eng. 2487

Barbiere di Siviglia, Il
Performance/production
Background material on Metropolitan Opera radio broadcast performances. USA: New York, NY. 1996. Lang.: Eng. 4252

Bardijewska, Liliana
Plays/librettos/scripts
Suggested texts for children's theatre. Poland. 1996. Lang.: Eng, Fre. 3169

Bárdos, Artúr
Performance/production
Artúr Bárdos' production of *A kékszakállú herceg vára (Bluebeard's Castle)* by Béla Balázs. Hungary: Budapest. 1910-1913. Lang.: Hun. 2102

Bárdy, Margit
Design/technology
The work of Hungarian-born costume designer Margit Bárdy. Hungary. Germany. 1929-1996. Lang.: Hun. 180

Barer, Marshall
Performance/production
Collection of newspaper reviews by New York theatre critics. USA: New York, NY. 1996. Lang.: Eng. 2565

Sarah Jessica Parker's role in *Once Upon a Mattress*. USA: New York, NY. 1976-1996. Lang.: Eng. 3942

Plays/librettos/scripts
Musical author Mary Rodgers. USA: New York, NY. 1959-1996. Lang.: Eng. 3999

Barker, Howard
Performance/production
Collection of newspaper reviews by London theatre critics. UK-England: London. 1996. Lang.: Eng. 2383

Collection of newspaper reviews by London theatre critics. UK-England: London. 1996. Lang.: Eng. 2442

Collection of newspaper reviews by New York theatre critics. USA: New York, NY. 1996. Lang.: Eng. 2568

Plays/librettos/scripts
Contemporary English drama. UK-England. 1956-1990. Lang.: Fre. 3296

Playwright Howard Barker. UK-England: London. 1990-1996. Lang.: Eng. 3306

Stage plays performed on radio. USA. UK-England. 1972-1984. Lang.: Eng. 3583

Theory/criticism
Howard Barker's 'humanist' and 'catastrophic' theatres. UK. 1993. Lang.: Eng. 3552

Barker, Lenny
Performance/production
Collection of newspaper reviews by London theatre critics. UK-England: London. 1996. Lang.: Eng. 2462

Barlacchia (Barlacchi, Domenico)
Performance/production
Renaissance actors Cherea and Barlacchia. Italy. 1500-1600. Lang.: Ita. 865

Barlow, Patrick
Performance/production
Collection of newspaper reviews by London theatre critics. UK-England: London. 1996. Lang.: Eng. 2462

Barnes, Djuna
Basic theatrical documents
International anthology of modern drama by women. 1880-1940. Lang.: Eng. 1637

Institutions
Report on the Dutch Theatre Festival. Netherlands: Amsterdam. 1996. Lang.: Eng. 1816

Barnes, Peter
Performance/production
Collection of newspaper reviews by London theatre critics. UK-England: London. 1996. Lang.: Eng. 2350

Plays/librettos/scripts
Portrayals of women in works of ten male playwrights. Europe. 1836-1978. Lang.: Eng. 2973

Barnes, Richard
Institutions
Profile of Market Theatre, the institution and the building. South Africa, Republic of: Johannesburg. 1976. Lang.: Swe. 1846

Barnum
Plays/librettos/scripts
Librettist/lyricist Michael Stewart. USA. UK-England. 1970-1987. Lang.: Eng. 3994

Baron's Court Theatre (London)
Performance/production
Collection of newspaper reviews by London theatre critics. UK-England: London. 1996. Lang.: Eng. 2306

Collection of newspaper reviews by London theatre critics. UK-England: London. 1996. Lang.: Eng. 2315

Collection of newspaper reviews by London theatre critics. UK-England: London. 1996. Lang.: Eng. 2349

Collection of newspaper reviews by London theatre critics. UK-England: London. 1996. Lang.: Eng. 2477

Baroque opera
Performance/production
Performance practices and audience tastes in Baroque music, particularly opera. England. 1685-1759. Lang.: Eng. 4104

Jean-Baptiste Lully and early French opera. France. 1673-1715. Lang.: Eng. 4130

Plays/librettos/scripts
The double aria, or *cabaletta* of Baroque opera. Italy. 1700-1799. Lang.: Eng. 4328

Baroque theatre
SEE
Geographical-Chronological Index under Europe, and other European countries, 1594-1702.

Barr, Margaret
Research/historiography
Description of theatre and dance-related holdings of the Darlington Hall Trust archives. UK-England: Totnes, Devon. 1920-1995. Lang.: Eng. 1305

Barratt, Fay
Performance/production
Collection of newspaper reviews by London theatre critics. UK-England: London. 1996. Lang.: Eng. 2356

Barre, Gabriel
Performance/production
Collection of newspaper reviews by New York theatre critics. USA: New York, NY, East Haddam, CT. 1996. Lang.: Eng. 2582

Barrett, Michael
Performance/production
Composers and performers of the American art song. USA. 1996. Lang.: Eng. 3870

Barrish, Seth
Design/technology
Set and lighting design for *Old Wicked Songs*, Promenade Theatre. USA: New York, NY. 1996. Lang.: Eng. 3894

Plays/librettos/scripts
Jon Marans on his musical *Old Wicked Songs*. USA: New York, NY. 1996. Lang.: Eng. 3992

Barry Sorts it Out
Performance/production
Collection of newspaper reviews by London theatre critics. UK-England: London. 1996. Lang.: Eng. 2473

Collection of newspaper reviews by London theatre critics. UK-England: London. 1996. Lang.: Eng. 2493

Barry, Philip
Plays/librettos/scripts
Realism in the high-society comedies of Philip Barry, S.N. Behrman, and Robert Sherwood. USA. 1920-1940. Lang.: Eng. 3382

Barry, Sebastian
Performance/production
Sebastian Barry's *The Steward of Christendom* directed by Max Stafford-Clark at the Gate. Ireland: Dublin. 1996. Lang.: Eng. 2115

Interview with actor Donal McCann. Ireland: Dublin. 1996. Lang.: Eng. 2116

Barrymore
Performance/production
Christopher Plummer's one-man show *Barrymore*. Canada: Stratford, ON. 1996. Lang.: Eng. 1918

Barrymore, Ethel
  Performance/production
    Equity and the 1919 actors' strike. USA: New York, NY. 1919. Lang.:
    Eng. 1072
Barslund, Charlotte
  Performance/production
    Collection of newspaper reviews by London theatre critics. UK-England:
    London. 1996. Lang.: Eng. 2413
Bartabas
  Performance/production
    The equestrian theatre of Zingaro, appearing at BAM. USA: New York,
    NY. France: Paris. 1996. Lang.: Eng. 3720
Barter, Nicholas
  Performance/production
    Nicholas Barter's production of *Les Femmes savantes* by Molière,
    RADA. UK-England: London. 1996. Lang.: Eng. 2538
Bartered Bride, The
  SEE
    Prodana Nevěsta.
Bartis, Ricardo
  Performance/production
    Political significance of two productions of *Telarañas (Cobwebs)* by
    Eduardo Pavlovsky. Argentina: Buenos Aires. 1976-1985. Lang.: Eng.
    1897
Bartleby
  Performance/production
    Collection of newspaper reviews by London theatre critics. UK-England:
    London. 1996. Lang.: Eng. 2383
Bartlett, Neil
  Performance/production
    Collection of newspaper reviews by London theatre critics. UK-England:
    London. 1996. Lang.: Eng. 2359
    Collection of newspaper reviews by London theatre critics. UK-England:
    London. 1996. Lang.: Eng. 2367
    Collection of newspaper reviews by London theatre critics. UK-England:
    London. 1996. Lang.: Eng. 2385
    Collection of newspaper reviews by London theatre critics. UK-England:
    London. 1996. Lang.: Eng. 2411
    Collection of newspaper reviews by London theatre critics. UK-England:
    London. 1996. Lang.: Eng. 2495
  Plays/librettos/scripts
    Interview with Neil Bartlett, playwright, director, and producer. UK-
    England. 1948-1995. Lang.: Eng. 3314
Bartók, Béla
  Design/technology
    Stage lighting for a production of *A Kékszakállú herceg vára* by Béla
    Bartók. Russia. 1990-1996. Lang.: Rus. 4023
  Institutions
    Canadian Opera Company's *Erwartung* and *Bluebeard's Castle* at the
    Hong Kong Arts Festival. China, People's Republic of: Hong Kong.
    1996. Lang.: Ger. 4035
  Performance/production
    Interview with dancer Ferenc Havas. Hungary. 1935-1995. Lang.: Hun.
    1509
    Artúr Bárdos' production of *A kékszakállú herceg vára (Bluebeard's
    Castle)* by Béla Balázs. Hungary: Budapest. 1910-1913. Lang.: Hun.
    2102
Basel, Clare
  Performance/production
    Collection of newspaper reviews by London theatre critics. UK-England:
    London. 1996. Lang.: Eng. 2350
Basi Khabar (Stale News)
  Performance/production
    Productions of plays by Badal Sircar. UK-England: Birmingham. 1979-
    1992. Lang.: Eng. 2500
Basic Instincts
  Performance/production
    Collection of newspaper reviews by London theatre critics. UK-England:
    London. 1996. Lang.: Eng. 2462
Basic Training of Pavlo Hummel, The
  Plays/librettos/scripts
    Vietnam War protest plays. North America. Europe. 1965-1971. Lang.:
    Eng. 3153
Basler Theater (Basel)
  Institutions
    Basler Theater under Michael Schindhelm. Switzerland: Basel. 1996.
    Lang.: Ger. 548
    Interview with Michael Schindhelm of Basler Theater. Switzerland:
    Basel. 1996. Lang.: Ger. 550

  Performance/production
    Operatic and ballet adaptations of Shakespearean plays reviewed.
    Switzerland. 1994-1995. Lang.: Ger. 956
    Productions of Basler Theater. Switzerland: Basel. 1996. Lang.: Ger.
    2300
Baśń o złym śmiechu (Tale of Evil Laughter, A)
  Plays/librettos/scripts
    Suggested texts for children's theatre. Poland. 1996. Lang.: Eng, Fre.
    3169
Basset Table, The
  Plays/librettos/scripts
    Reformist goals of plays by Susanna Centlivre and Mary Pix. England.
    1700-1800. Lang.: Eng. 2907
Basson, Marthinus
  Institutions
    Report on the Grahamstown Festival. South Africa, Republic of:
    Grahamstown. 1996. Lang.: Eng. 532
Bastien, Jean-Luc
  Performance/production
    Three directors publicly direct actors in scenes from Racine's *Phèdre.*
    Canada: Montreal, PQ. 1996. Lang.: Fre. 1965
Bataille, Nicolas
  Institutions
    Profile of Théâtre de la Huchette, which produces the plays of Ionesco.
    France: Paris. 1950-1996. Lang.: Swe. 1792
Batalov, Aleksej
  Performance/production
    Comparison of film and theatre acting. Russia: Moscow. 1980-1996.
    Lang.: Rus. 921
Bateman, Edgar
  Relation to other fields
    Politics, society, and the street-seller character in the music-hall
    performances. UK-England: London. 1914-1970. Lang.: Eng. 3842
Batman Forever
  Design/technology
    John Alvin's posters for film and Broadway theatre. USA. 1996. Lang.:
    Eng. 236
Batrakhoi (Frogs)
  Performance/production
    Collection of newspaper reviews by London theatre critics. UK-England:
    London. 1996. Lang.: Eng. 2321
    Collection of newspaper reviews by London theatre critics. UK-England:
    London. 1996. Lang.: Eng. 2338
Batsheva Dance Company (Tel Aviv)
  Performance/production
    Israeli productions at the Hamburg summer theatre festival. Germany:
    Hamburg. Israel: Tel Aviv. 1996. Lang.: Ger. 811
Battersea Arts Centre (London)
  Performance/production
    Collection of newspaper reviews by London theatre critics. UK-England:
    London. 1996. Lang.: Eng. 2304
    Collection of newspaper reviews by London theatre critics. UK-England:
    London. 1996. Lang.: Eng. 2311
    Collection of newspaper reviews by London theatre critics. UK-England:
    London. 1996. Lang.: Eng. 2317
    Collection of newspaper reviews by London theatre critics. UK-England:
    London. 1996. Lang.: Eng. 2319
    Collection of newspaper reviews by London theatre critics. UK-England:
    London. 1996. Lang.: Eng. 2324
    Collection of newspaper reviews by London theatre critics. UK-England:
    London. 1996. Lang.: Eng. 2329
    Collection of newspaper reviews by London theatre critics. UK-England:
    London. 1996. Lang.: Eng. 2337
    Collection of newspaper reviews by London theatre critics. UK-England:
    London. 1996. Lang.: Eng. 2338
    Collection of newspaper reviews by London theatre critics. UK-England:
    London. 1996. Lang.: Eng. 2340
    Collection of newspaper reviews by London theatre critics. UK-England:
    London. 1996. Lang.: Eng. 2344
    Collection of newspaper reviews by London theatre critics. UK-England:
    London. 1996. Lang.: Eng. 2354
    Collection of newspaper reviews by London theatre critics. UK-England:
    London. 1996. Lang.: Eng. 2356
    Collection of newspaper reviews by London theatre critics. UK-England:
    London. 1996. Lang.: Eng. 2366

Battersea Arts Centre (London) — cont'd

Collection of newspaper reviews by London theatre critics. UK-England: London. 1996. Lang.: Eng.   2371

Collection of newspaper reviews by London theatre critics. UK-England: London. 1996. Lang.: Eng.   2382

Collection of newspaper reviews by London theatre critics. UK-England: London. 1996. Lang.: Eng.   2383

Collection of newspaper reviews by London theatre critics. UK-England: London. 1996. Lang.: Eng.   2394

Collection of newspaper reviews by London theatre critics. UK-England: London. 1996. Lang.: Eng.   2395

Collection of newspaper reviews by London theatre critics. UK-England: London. 1996. Lang.: Eng.   2401

Collection of newspaper reviews by London theatre critics. UK-England: London. 1996. Lang.: Eng.   2407

Collection of newspaper reviews by London theatre critics. UK-England: London. 1996. Lang.: Eng.   2420

Collection of newspaper reviews by London theatre critics. UK-England: London. 1996. Lang.: Eng.   2422

Collection of newspaper reviews by London theatre critics. UK-England: London. 1996. Lang.: Eng.   2437

Collection of newspaper reviews by London theatre critics. UK-England: London, Chichester. 1996. Lang.: Eng.   2440

Collection of newspaper reviews by London theatre critics. UK-England: London. 1996. Lang.: Eng.   2448

Collection of newspaper reviews by London theatre critics. UK-England: London. 1996. Lang.: Eng.   2472

Collection of newspaper reviews by London theatre critics. UK-England: London. 1996. Lang.: Eng.   2474

Collection of newspaper reviews by London theatre critics. UK-England: London. 1996. Lang.: Eng.   2482

Collection of newspaper reviews by London theatre critics. UK-England: London. 1996. Lang.: Eng.   2492

Collection of newspaper reviews by London theatre critics. UK-England: London. 1996. Lang.: Eng.   2493

Collection of newspaper reviews by London theatre critics. UK-England: London. 1996. Lang.: Eng.   2498

Collection of newspaper reviews by London theatre critics. UK-England: London. 1996. Lang.: Eng.   2499

Battersea Latchmere Theatre (London)
SEE
Latchmere Theatre (London).

Battle of Angels
Plays/librettos/scripts
Realistic characterization and poeticized stage space in plays of Tennessee Williams. USA. 1944-1973. Lang.: Eng.   3323

Battle of the Warsaw Ghetto, The
Plays/librettos/scripts
Radio plays of the Writers' War Board. USA. 1942-1944. Lang.: Eng.   3582

Bau, Der (Construction Site, The)
Performance/production
Productions of plays by Heiner Müller at Berliner Ensemble and Volksbühne. Germany: Berlin. 1996. Lang.: Ger.   2088

Bauer, Wolfgang
Institutions
Avant-garde theatre at the Steirischer Herbst Festival. Austria: Graz. 1996. Lang.: Ger.   1753
Plays/librettos/scripts
Portrait of playwright, actor, and director Wolfgang Bauer. Germany. Austria. 1963-1996. Lang.: Ger.   3047

Bauer, Wolfgang Maria
Basic theatrical documents
Text of *Spät (Late)* by Wolfgang Maria Bauer. Germany. 1996. Lang.: Ger.   1657
Performance/production
Reviews of German-language productions. Germany. Switzerland. Austria. 1996. Lang.: Ger.   2089

Baumander, Louis
Plays/librettos/scripts
Myth and iconography in Native Canadian theatre. Canada. 1987-1996. Lang.: Eng.   2783

Baumbauer, Frank
Relation to other fields
Interview with Frank Baumbauer, director of Deutsches Schauspielhaus. Germany: Hamburg. 1996. Lang.: Ger.   1183

Bausch, Pina
Institutions
Productions of the Edinburgh Festival. UK-Scotland: Edinburgh. 1996. Lang.: Ger.   561
Performance/production
Tanztheater Wuppertal's Copenhagen guest performance. Denmark: Copenhagen. 1996. Lang.: Swe.   1573

Press conference with dancer and choreographer Pina Bausch. Germany: Wuppertal. 1995. Lang.: Eng.   1576

Reviews of dance performances by Pina Bausch, Mats Ek, and Joachim Schlömer. Germany. 1996. Lang.: Ger.   1578
Theory/criticism
The origins and evolution of physical theatre. UK-England. Germany. 1900-1996. Lang.: Eng.   1368

Bavarian State Opera
SEE
Bayerische Staatsoper im Nationaltheater.

Bawtree, Michael
Institutions
The Atlantic Theatre Festival. Canada: Wolfville, NS. 1991-1996. Lang.: Eng.   1757

Profile of Atlantic Theatre Festival. Canada: Wolfville, NS. 1993-1996. Lang.: Eng.   1774

Baxter, Virginia
Plays/librettos/scripts
Conversation between playwrights Virginia Baxter and Clare Grant. Australia. 1978-1995. Lang.: Eng.   1082

Bayerische Staatsoper im Nationaltheater (Munich)
Performance/production
Performance and technical aspects of Orff's *Carmina Burana* at the Bavarian State Opera. Germany. 1996. Lang.: Eng.   4143

Bayerisches Staatsschauspiel, Residenztheater (Munich)
Institutions
Highlights of the Wiener Festwochen festival. Austria: Vienna. 1996. Lang.: Ger.   1752

Bayeza, Ifa
Plays/librettos/scripts
Ifa Bayeza's *Homer G. and the Rhapsodies in the Fall of Detroit*. USA: San Francisco, CA. 1996. Lang.: Eng.   3464

Bayreuther Festspiele (Bayreuth)
Design/technology
Conference on hydraulic and electronic stage technology. Germany: Lohr am Main. 1996. Lang.: Swe.   174
Institutions
Iván Markó's role as ballet director at the Bayreuth Festival. Germany: Bayreuth. Hungary. 1985-1995. Lang.: Hun.   1480

Review of the Bayreuth Festival. Germany: Bayreuth. 1996. Lang.: Hun.   4040
Performance/production
Interview with opera director Nicolas Joël. France. Germany. 1942-1996. Lang.: Eng.   4117

Wolfgang Wagner's production of *Die Meistersinger* at Bayreuther Festspiele. Germany: Bayreuth. 1996. Lang.: Ger.   4133

Wolfgang Wagner's scenery and direction of *Die Meistersinger* at the Bayreuth Festival. Germany: Bayreuth. 1996. Lang.: Ger.   4146

BDT
SEE
Bolšoj Dramatičéskij Teat'r.

Beast on the Moon
Performance/production
Collection of newspaper reviews by London theatre critics. UK-England: London. 1996. Lang.: Eng.   2407

Beatification of Area Boy, The
Performance/production
Collection of newspaper reviews by New York theatre critics. USA: New York, NY. 1996. Lang.: Eng.   2557

Beau Defeated, The
Plays/librettos/scripts
Reformist goals of plays by Susanna Centlivre and Mary Pix. England. 1700-1800. Lang.: Eng.   2907

Beaulieu, Michel
Performance/production
Scenography of Beckett's *Waiting for Godot* directed by André Brassard, TNM. Canada: Montreal, PQ. 1992. Lang.: Fre.   1937

Beaulieu, Trace
Performance/production
Puppetry on *Mystery Science Theatre 3000*. USA: Hollywood, CA. 1990-1996. Lang.: Eng.   3681

Beaulne, Martine
 Performance/production
 Actor and director Martine Beaulne. Canada. 1976-1996. Lang.: Fre.
 700

 Interview with director Martine Beaulne. Canada. 1970-1993. Lang.:
 Fre. 733

 Directors Martine Beaulne and Lorraine Pintal. Canada: Montreal, PQ.
 1996. Lang.: Eng. 1917

Beausoleil, Claude
 Relation to other fields
 Memory and the uncertainty of the future in theatre. Canada. 1989.
 Lang.: Fre. 1138

Beautiful Thing
 Design/technology
 Work of designer Mark Stevenson on the film *Beautiful Thing*. UK-
 England: London. 1995-1996. Lang.: Eng. 3591

Beauty and the Beast
 Basic theatrical documents
 Anthology of works by Split Britches. USA. 1985-1995. Lang.: Eng.
 1685

 Design/technology
 Quiet hydraulic system used for scene changes in Australian production
 of *Beauty and the Beast*. Australia: Melbourne, Sydney. 1996. Lang.:
 Eng. 3886

 Lighting for the German-language production of Disney's *Beauty and
 the Beast*. Austria: Vienna. 1995. Lang.: Ger. 3887

 Technical aspects of a German-language production of Disney's *Beauty
 and the Beast*. Austria: Vienna. 1995. Lang.: Ger. 3888

 Performance/production
 Stage and film treatments of the fairy tale *Beauty and the Beast*. Europe.
 USA. Canada. 1946-1996. Lang.: Eng. 793

 Collection of newspaper reviews by London theatre critics. UK-England:
 London. 1996. Lang.: Eng. 2493

 Collection of newspaper reviews by London theatre critics. UK-England:
 London. 1996. Lang.: Eng. 2494

 Plays/librettos/scripts
 Evolution of the Beast character in treatments of the fairy tale *Beauty
 and the Beast*. UK-England. 1945-1996. Lang.: Eng. 1106

Beauty Queen of Leenane, The
 Performance/production
 Collection of newspaper reviews by London theatre critics. UK-England:
 London. 1996. Lang.: Eng. 2324

 Collection of newspaper reviews by London theatre critics. UK-England:
 London. 1996. Lang.: Eng. 2484

Beaux Dimanches, Les (Beautiful Sundays, The)
 Plays/librettos/scripts
 Analysis of plays by Marcel Dubé. Canada: Montreal, PQ, Quebec, PQ.
 1958-1993. Lang.: Fre. 2742

Bébé furioso, El (Furious Baby, The)
 Plays/librettos/scripts
 Interview with playwright Manuel Martínez Mediero. Spain. 1939-1993.
 Lang.: Spa. 3236

Becher, Ulrich
 Relation to other fields
 Ideological uses of theatre during the National Socialist period.
 Germany. 1933-1945. Lang.: Ger. 1186

Bechstein, Ludwig
 Performance/production
 The adaptation of Grimm's fairy tale in Humperdinck's opera *Hänsel
 und Gretel*. Germany. 1893-1996. Lang.: Eng. 4135

Bechtolf, Sven-Eric
 Performance/production
 Portrait of Sven-Eric Bechtolf, actor and director at Thalia Theater.
 Germany: Hamburg. 1957-1996. Lang.: Ger. 2060

Beck-Friis, Regina
 Performance/production
 The Royal Swedish Ballet and the eighteenth-century tradition. Sweden:
 Stockholm. 1773-1996. Lang.: Swe. 1533

Beck, Louise
 Design/technology
 The skills needed by young set designers: interview with professionals.
 Denmark: Copenhagen. 1995-1996. Lang.: Dan. 164

 Performance/production
 Interview with set designer Louise Beck. Denmark. UK-England. 1994-
 1996. Lang.: Dan. 3854

Becker, Hans-Ulrich
 Performance/production
 Performances of Shakespeare's plays in southern Germany. Germany:
 Munich, Mannheim. 1994-1995. Lang.: Ger. 2055

Becker, Rob
 Performance/production
 Rob Becker and his solo performance *Defending the Caveman*. USA:
 New York, NY. 1996. Lang.: Eng. 2640

Beckett, Samuel
 Institutions
 Productions of the month-long Beckett festival. France: Strasbourg.
 1996. Lang.: Eng. 408

 Productions of the Carrefour theatre festival. Canada: Quebec, PQ.
 1979-1996. Lang.: Eng. 1760

 Performance/production
 Intercultural work of Noho Theatre Group. Japan: Kyoto. 1981-1994.
 Lang.: Eng. 875

 Comparison of productions of *Waiting for Godot* for stage and video.
 Canada: Montreal, PQ. 1988-1992. Lang.: Fre. 1921

 Interview with actors Normand Chouinard and Rémy Girard. Canada:
 Montreal, PQ. 1992. Lang.: Fre. 1922

 Interview with actors Jean-Louis Millette and Alexis Martin. Canada:
 Montreal, PQ. 1992. Lang.: Fre. 1923

 Sylvia Drapeau on playing Winnie in Beckett's *Happy Days*. Canada:
 Montreal, PQ. 1990. Lang.: Fre. 1932

 Françoise Faucher on playing Winnie in Beckett's *Happy Days*. Canada:
 Montreal, PQ. 1981. Lang.: Fre. 1934

 Scenography of Beckett's *Waiting for Godot* directed by André Brassard,
 TNM. Canada: Montreal, PQ. 1992. Lang.: Fre. 1937

 Photos of a 1971 production of Beckett's *En attendant Godot (Waiting
 for Godot)* directed by André Brassard. Canada: Montreal, PQ. 1971.
 Lang.: Fre. 1943

 Patricia MacGeachy on performing in Beckett's *Not I*. Canada:
 Montreal, PQ. 1991-1992. Lang.: Fre. 1949

 Danièle Panneton on performing in Beckett's *Not I*. Canada: Montreal,
 PQ. 1990. Lang.: Fre. 1953

 Interview with director André Brassard. Canada: Montreal, PQ. 1992.
 Lang.: Fre. 1963

 Chronology of Beckett productions. Canada: Ottawa, ON, Montreal,
 PQ, Quebec, PQ. 1956-1992. Lang.: Fre. 1969

 Paris productions of the fall season. France: Paris. 1996. Lang.: Eng.
 2032

 Carlo Cecchi's production of *Fin de partie (Endgame)* by Samuel
 Beckett. Italy. 1996. Lang.: Ita. 2130

 Productions of plays by Beckett and Ionesco. Poland: Warsaw. 1995.
 Lang.: Eng, Eng. 2171

 Collection of newspaper reviews by London theatre critics. UK-England:
 London. 1996. Lang.: Eng. 2340

 Collection of newspaper reviews by London theatre critics. UK-England:
 London. 1996. Lang.: Eng. 2352

 Collection of newspaper reviews by London theatre critics. UK-England:
 London. 1996. Lang.: Eng. 2370

 Collection of newspaper reviews by London theatre critics. UK-England:
 London. 1996. Lang.: Eng. 2413

 Interview with director Deborah Warner. UK-England: London. 1980-
 1996. Lang.: Eng. 2541

 Collection of newspaper reviews by New York theatre critics. USA:
 New York, NY, Chicago, IL. 1996. Lang.: Eng. 2585

 Productions of Beckett plays on the ninetieth anniversary of his birth.
 USA. 1996. Lang.: Eng. 2613

 Plays/librettos/scripts
 The influence of Samuel Beckett on Carole Nadeau's one-woman show
 Chaos K.O. Chaos. Canada: Quebec, PQ. 1992. Lang.: Fre. 1089

 Dominic Champagne's *La Répétition (The Rehearsal)* and its relation to
 Beckett's *En attendant Godot (Waiting for Godot)*. Canada: Montreal,
 PQ. France. Ireland. 1953-1990. Lang.: Fre. 2843

 Modern adaptations of Shakespeare. Europe. 1800-1990. Lang.: Eng.
 2967

 Universality and gender in Beckett's *Waiting for Godot*. France. 1952.
 Lang.: Fre. 2986

 The influence of clowning on Beckett's *En attendant Godot (Waiting for
 Godot)*. France. 1952. Lang.: Fre. 2989

 Bibliography of works in French by and about Samuel Beckett. France.
 1938-1992. Lang.: Fre. 2999

 The void, silence, and non-existence in the works of Samuel Beckett.
 France. 1938-1992. Lang.: Fre. 3000

Beckett, Samuel — cont'd

Analysis of *Fin de partie* and *En attendant Godot* by Samuel Beckett. Ireland. France. 1953-1957. Lang.: Eng.   3082

Michael Colgan's plan to produce all of Samuel Beckett's plays at the Gate Theatre. Ireland: Dublin. 1991-1996. Lang.: Eng.   3088

Analysis of *Gangsters* by Maishe Maponya. South Africa, Republic of. 1930-1995. Lang.: Eng.   3224

Jorge Díaz's *Historia de nadie (Nobody's Story)* compared to Beckett's *En attendant Godot (Waiting for Godot)*. Spain. France. Chile. 1966. Lang.: Spa.   3245

Interview with playwright José Sanchis Sinisterra. Spain. 1960-1991. Lang.: Fre.   3258

Interview with playwright Edward Albee. USA: New York, NY. 1996. Lang.: Eng.   3430

Analysis of the radio plays of Samuel Beckett. Europe. 1955-1980. Lang.: Ger.   3580

Filmed theatre at festival of new cinema and video. Canada: Montreal, PQ. 1991. Lang.: Fre.   3643

Theory/criticism

Harold Hobson's response to Beckett's *Waiting for Godot*. UK-England. 1955. Lang.: Eng.   3557

Bed and Sofa

Performance/production

Profile of recent Broadway musicals. USA: New York, NY. 1996. Lang.: Eng.   3950

Bed Language

Institutions

The 1995 Saskatoon Fringe Festival. Canada: Saskatoon, SK. 1995. Lang.: Eng.   1768

Bédard, Réjean

Performance/production

Comic actors of Théâtre Parminou. Canada. 1990. Lang.: Fre.   701

Bedford, Brian

Administration

Inductions into the theatrical Hall of Fame. USA: New York, NY. 1996. Lang.: Eng.   99

Bedsit, The

Performance/production

Collection of newspaper reviews by London theatre critics. UK-England: London. 1996. Lang.: Eng.   2460

Beecroft, Jeffrey

Design/technology

Jeffrey Beecroft's scene design for Terry Gilliam's film *12 Monkeys*. USA: Philadelphia, PA. 1996. Lang.: Eng.   3599

Beekeeper's Daughter, The

Plays/librettos/scripts

Political theatre of Karen Malpede and Slobodan Snajder. USA. Croatia. 1991-1996. Lang.: Eng.   3403

Beelitz, Günther

Institutions

Interview with Günther Beelitz of Deutsches Nationaltheater. Germany: Weimar. 1996. Lang.: Ger.   462

Beeson, Jack

Plays/librettos/scripts

The operas of Jack Beeson and the Columbia Opera Workshop. USA. 1996. Lang.: Eng.   4346

Beethoven, Ludwig van

Design/technology

Stefanos Lazarides' scene design for *Fidelio*, directed by David Pountney at the Bregenz Festival. Germany: Bregenz. 1996. Lang.: Eng.   4019

Institutions

Opera at the Bregenz festival. Austria: Bregenz. 1995. Lang.: Eng.   4031

Performance/production

Beethoven's *Lenore* at Salzburger Festspiele. Austria: Salzburg. 1996. Lang.: Eng.   4078

Performances of the Salzburg festival. Austria: Salzburg. 1996. Lang.: Ger.   4082

Beethoven's *Fidelio* and its earlier version, *Lenore*. Austro-Hungarian Empire: Vienna. 1805-1814. Lang.: Eng.   4084

Beethoven's Tenth

Performance/production

Collection of newspaper reviews by London theatre critics. UK-England: London, Chichester. 1996. Lang.: Eng.   2440

Bèg (Flight)

Performance/production

Productions by returned expatriate directors. Romania. 1994-1996. Lang.: Hun.   896

Behind the Curtain

Design/technology

Stage designer Christian Thee's children's book about a theatre performance of *Hansel and Gretel*. USA. 1996. Lang.: Eng.   336

Behn, Aphra

Performance/production

Videotape of Aphra Behn's *The Rover* performed by Women's Playhouse Trust. UK-England. 1994. Lang.: Eng.   2302

Carol MacVey's production of *The Emperor of the Moon* by Aphra Behn. USA: Iowa City, IA. 1992. Lang.: Eng.   2611

Plays/librettos/scripts

Authorship and identity in *The Rover* by Aphra Behn. England. 1677. Lang.: Eng.   2884

Feminism and female empowerment in plays of Aphra Behn. England. 1660-1700. Lang.: Eng.   2918

Women and sexuality in plays of Aphra Behn, Mary Pix, and Catharine Trotter. England: London. 1660-1750. Lang.: Eng.   2946

The continuing relevance of Restoration theatre. UK-England. 1660-1996. Lang.: Eng.   3310

Relation to other fields

Teaching race and gender in plays of Cary, Shakespeare, and Behn. USA. 1996. Lang.: Eng.   3518

Behrman, S.N.

Plays/librettos/scripts

Realism in the high-society comedies of Philip Barry, S.N. Behrman, and Robert Sherwood. USA. 1920-1940. Lang.: Eng.   3382

Beier, Karin

Performance/production

Assembling an international cast for a production of *A Midsummer Night's Dream*. Europe. 1995. Lang.: Ger.   2001

Theatre in the Ruhr Valley. Germany. 1995. Lang.: Eng.   2043

Karin Beier's productions of *A Midsummer Night's Dream* and *Les Chaises (The Chairs)*. Germany: Düsseldorf. 1995. Lang.: Eng.   2045

Two productions of Gombrowicz's *Iwona, Księzniczka Burgundia (Princess Yvonne)*. Germany: Hamburg, Leipzig. 1996. Lang.: Ger.   2064

Director Karin Beier. Germany: Düsseldorf. 1990-1996. Lang.: Ger.   2073

Productions of Thalia Theater and Deutsches Schauspielhaus. Germany: Hamburg. 1996. Lang.: Ger.   2090

Beijing opera

SEE ALSO

Chinese opera.

Beil, Hermann

Administration

Dramaturg Hermann Beil's work with Claus Peymann at Burgtheater. Austria: Vienna. 1974-1996. Lang.: Ger.   5

Being at Home with Claude

Plays/librettos/scripts

Social context of Quebec's gay theatre. Canada: Montreal, PQ. 1990. Lang.: Fre.   2826

Békés Megyei Jókai Színház (Békéscsaba)

Performance/production

Revivals of the Hungarian pop musical *Képzelt riport egy amerikai popfesztiválról (Imaginary Report on an American Pop Festival)*. Hungary. 1973-1995. Lang.: Hun.   3919

Békés, Pál

Performance/production

Recipients of the annual theatre critics' awards. Hungary. 1995-1996. Lang.: Hun.   846

English plays and subjects on the Hungarian stage. Hungary. 1995-1996. Lang.: Eng.   847

Bel, Jérôme

Audience

Audience participation in a performance of dancer Jérôme Bel. Denmark. 1995-1996. Lang.: Dan.   3786

Relation to other fields

Reflections of social trends in international modern dance festival. Denmark: Copenhagen. 1996. Lang.: Dan.   1596

Béland, Luc J.

Performance/production

Scenography of Beckett's *Waiting for Godot* directed by André Brassard, TNM. Canada: Montreal, PQ. 1992. Lang.: Fre.   1937

Béland, Marc

Performance/production

Interview with actor Marc Béland. Canada: Montreal, PQ. 1992-1993. Lang.: Fre.   1964

Belasco Theatre (New York, NY)

Performance/production

Actor Beryl Reid. UK-England. 1919-1996. Lang.: Eng.   967

Belasco Theatre (New York, NY) — cont'd

Collection of newspaper reviews by New York theatre critics. USA: New York, NY. 1996. Lang.: Eng. 2577

Belbel, Sergi
Basic theatrical documents
Dutch translations of plays by Belbel, Cabal, and Sanchis Sinisterra. Spain. 1990-1995. Lang.: Dut. 1677
Performance/production
Collection of newspaper reviews by London theatre critics. UK-England: London. 1996. Lang.: Eng. 2361
Plays/librettos/scripts
Overview of contemporary Spanish playwriting. Spain. 1945-1991. Lang.: Fre. 3257

Belden, Ursula
Design/technology
Exhibitors at the USITT design exhibition on scenery, lighting, and costuming. USA. 1996. Lang.: Eng. 335

Belden, Wendy
Design/technology
Elizabeth Fried's costumes for *Crocodiles in the Potomac* by Wendy Belden. USA: New York, NY. 1996. Lang.: Eng. 1723

Belgrader, Andrei
Performance/production
Impressions of the Boston theatre scene. USA: Cambridge, MA, Boston, MA. 1995. Lang.: Eng. 2628

Bell, Mike
Institutions
The 1995 Winnipeg Fringe Festival. Canada: Winnipeg, MB. 1995. Lang.: Eng. 348

Bell, Zandra
Institutions
The 1995 Edmonton Fringe Festival. Canada: Edmonton, AB. 1995. Lang.: Eng. 1775

Belle et la Bête, La (Beauty and the Beast)
Performance/production
Stage and film treatments of the fairy tale *Beauty and the Beast*. Europe. USA. Canada. 1946-1996. Lang.: Eng. 793
Plays/librettos/scripts
Evolution of the Beast character in treatments of the fairy tale *Beauty and the Beast*. UK-England. 1945-1996. Lang.: Eng. 1106

Belle Reprieve
Basic theatrical documents
Anthology of works by Split Britches. USA. 1985-1995. Lang.: Eng. 1685

Belles-soeurs, Les (Sisters-in-Law, The)
Plays/librettos/scripts
Careers of playwrights Michel Tremblay and Marie Laberge. Canada: Quebec, PQ. 1964-1992. Lang.: Eng. 2815
Theatricality as sociopolitical commentary in plays of Mamet and Tremblay. Canada. USA. 1972-1996. Lang.: Eng. 2825

Bellini, Vincenzo
Plays/librettos/scripts
Librettist Felice Romani. Italy. 1810-1850. Lang.: Eng. 4334
Essays on librettist Felice Romani. Italy. 1788-1865. Lang.: Ita. 4335

Bellis, Christopher
Performance/production
Angels in America and censorship at Catholic University. USA: Washington, DC. 1996. Lang.: Eng. 2661

Bells, The
Performance/production
Collection of newspaper reviews by London theatre critics. UK-England: London. 1996. Lang.: Eng. 2341

Bellywoman Bangarang
Plays/librettos/scripts
Women writers in postcolonial English. Australia. 1995. Lang.: Eng. 2723

Belmont Theatre (Chicago, IL)
Performance spaces
History of the Belmont Theatre. USA: Chicago, IL. 1926-1996. Lang.: Eng. 3606

Below the Belt
Basic theatrical documents
Collection of plays from the Humana Festival. USA. 1986-1995. Lang.: Eng. 1687
Design/technology
Stephen Olson's design for Dresser's *Below the Belt*, John Houseman Theatre. USA: New York, NY. 1996. Lang.: Eng. 1719
Performance/production
Collection of newspaper reviews by New York theatre critics. USA: New York, NY. 1996. Lang.: Eng. 2570

Belugou, David
Design/technology
David Belugou's costumes for the Big Apple Circus. USA: New York, NY. 1996. Lang.: Eng. 3748

Bemba, Sylvain
Plays/librettos/scripts
Colonialism, post-colonial dictatorships, and cultural identity in the work of Congolese playwrights. Congo. 1960-1996. Lang.: Eng. 2859

Ben Hur
Performance/production
Collection of newspaper reviews by London theatre critics. UK-England: London. 1996. Lang.: Eng. 2351

Ben-Tovim, Ruth
Performance/production
Collection of newspaper reviews by London theatre critics. UK-England: London. 1996. Lang.: Eng. 2417

Benavente, Jacinto
Plays/librettos/scripts
Jacinto Benavente and Antonio Buero Vallejo as the leading Spanish playwrights of the century. Spain. 1946. Lang.: Spa. 3248

Benecke, Patricia
Performance/production
Collection of newspaper reviews by London theatre critics. UK-England: London. 1996. Lang.: Eng. 2443

Benedetto, André
Plays/librettos/scripts
Vietnam War protest plays. North America. Europe. 1965-1971. Lang.: Eng. 3153

Benedictus, David
Performance/production
Collection of newspaper reviews by London theatre critics. UK-England: London. 1996. Lang.: Eng. 2311

Benefit performances
Administration
Tributes to various theatre people. USA: New York, NY. 1996. Lang.: Eng. 85
Performance/production
Equity and the 1919 actors' strike. USA: New York, NY. 1919. Lang.: Eng. 1072

Benét, Stephen Vincent
Plays/librettos/scripts
Radio plays of the Writers' War Board. USA. 1942-1944. Lang.: Eng. 3582

Beniaminov, Aleksand'r D.
Performance/production
Memoirs of Aleksand'r Beniaminov of Leningrad Comedy Theatre. USSR: Leningrad. 1937-1969. Lang.: Rus. 1076

Benison, Ben
Performance/production
Collection of newspaper reviews by London theatre critics. UK-England: London. 1996. Lang.: Eng. 2319

Benmussa, Simone
Performance/production
Student production of *The Singular Life of Albert Nobbs* by Simone Benmussa. UK-England: Leeds. 1992. Lang.: Eng. 2516

Bennathan, Joss
Performance/production
Collection of newspaper reviews by London theatre critics. UK-England: London. 1996. Lang.: Eng. 2413

Bennent, Anne
Performance/production
Portrait of actress Anne Bennent. Europe. 1963-1996. Lang.: Ger. 780

Bennett, Adam
Performance/production
Collection of newspaper reviews by London theatre critics. UK-England: London. 1996. Lang.: Eng. 2401

Bennett, Alan
Performance/production
Current Dublin productions. Ireland: Dublin. 1996. Lang.: Eng. 2117
Collection of newspaper reviews by London theatre critics. UK-England: London. 1996. Lang.: Eng. 2410
Collection of newspaper reviews by London theatre critics. UK-England: London. 1996. Lang.: Eng. 2436
Collection of newspaper reviews by London theatre critics. UK-England: London. 1996. Lang.: Eng. 2441
Plays/librettos/scripts
Politics in the plays of Alan Bennett. UK-England. 1968-1996. Lang.: Eng. 3311

Bienvenue, Yvan — cont'd

Harsh realism in contemporary Quebec plays. Canada: Montreal, PQ. 1993-1995. Lang.: Fre. 2784

Bierbichler, Josef
 Performance/production
 Actor of the year Josef Bierbichler: profile and interview. Germany. Austria. 1948-1996. Lang.: Ger. 828

 The acting in Peter Zadek's production of *The Cherry Orchard* at Burgtheater. Austria: Vienna. 1996. Lang.: Ger. 1906

Big
 Design/technology
 Design for the musical *Big*. USA: Detroit, MI. 1996. Lang.: Eng. 3902
 Performance/production
 Collection of newspaper reviews by New York theatre critics. USA: New York, NY. 1996. Lang.: Eng. 2579

 Composer David Shire and lyricist Richard Maltby, Jr. USA: New York, NY. 1973-1996. Lang.: Eng. 3930

 Actor Daniel Jenkins. USA: New York, NY. 1988-1996. Lang.: Eng. 3937

 Work of choreographer Susan Stroman and director Mike Ockrent on the musical *Big*. USA: New York, NY. 1996. Lang.: Eng. 3964

Big Al
 Performance/production
 Collection of newspaper reviews by London theatre critics. UK-England: London. 1996. Lang.: Eng. 2411

Big Apple Circus (New York, NY)
 Design/technology
 David Belugou's costumes for the Big Apple Circus. USA: New York, NY. 1996. Lang.: Eng. 3748

Big Book for Girls, The
 Performance/production
 Collection of newspaper reviews by London theatre critics. UK-England: London. 1996. Lang.: Eng. 2495

Big Idea (Perth)
 Performance/production
 Big Idea's environmental theatre. Australia: Perth. 1994. Lang.: Eng. 1900

Biggons, Stella
 Performance/production
 Collection of newspaper reviews by London theatre critics. UK-England: London. 1996. Lang.: Eng. 2493

Biggs, Janet
 Performance/production
 Analysis of the work of video artists. USA. 1996. Lang.: Eng. 3679

Bilderschnur (String of Pictures, A)
 Institutions
 Review of children's theatre performances. Europe. 1996. Lang.: Ger. 403

Bill, Stephen
 Performance/production
 Collection of newspaper reviews by London theatre critics. UK-England: London. 1996. Lang.: Eng. 2406

 Collection of newspaper reviews by New York theatre critics. USA: New York, NY. 1996. Lang.: Eng. 2578

 Interview with director Scott Elliott. USA: New York, NY. 1995-1996. Lang.: Eng. 2673

Billington, Ken
 Design/technology
 Lighting designer Ken Billington. USA: New York, NY. 1970-1996. Lang.: Eng. 274

 Lighting designs for Broadway musical *Chicago* by Ken Billington. USA: New York, NY. 1996. Lang.: Eng. 3896

Billy Liar
 Performance/production
 The angry young man on the Polish stage. Poland. 1995. Lang.: Eng. 2161

Biloxi Blues
 Plays/librettos/scripts
 The influence of Eugene O'Neill on playwright Neil Simon. USA. 1949-1989. Lang.: Eng. 3338

Binary Dreamers
 Performance/production
 Collection of newspaper reviews by London theatre critics. UK-England: London. 1996. Lang.: Eng. 2363

Binder, Ernst M.
 Performance/production
 Reviews of German-language productions. Germany. Switzerland. Austria. 1996. Lang.: Ger. 2089

Bing, Suzanne
 Training
 Jacques Copeau, Suzanne Bing, and the founding of L'École du Vieux-Colombier. USA: New York, NY. France: Paris. 1918-1996. Lang.: Eng. 3690

Bingo
 Performance/production
 Collection of newspaper reviews by London theatre critics. UK-England: London. 1996. Lang.: Eng. 2497

Binnie, John
 Institutions
 The work of Clyde Unity Theatre. UK-Scotland: Glasgow. 1986-1995. Lang.: Eng. 1859

Biofästet (Stockholm)
 Performance spaces
 Proposal to restore original lighting equipment in the auditorium of a retirement home. Sweden: Stockholm. 1920. Lang.: Swe. 656

Bird, Dorothy
 Performance/production
 Dancer Dorothy Bird recalls the original Broadway production of *Hooray For What!*. USA: New York, NY. 1937. 3933

Bird's Nest Theatre (London)
 Performance/production
 Collection of newspaper reviews by London theatre critics. UK-England: London. 1996. Lang.: Eng. 2330

 Collection of newspaper reviews by London theatre critics. UK-England: London. 1996. Lang.: Eng. 2407

Birdy
 Performance/production
 Collection of newspaper reviews by London theatre critics. UK-England: London. 1996. Lang.: Eng. 2455

Birkás, Lilian
 Performance/production
 Career of soprano Lilian Birkás. Hungary. 1916-1990. Lang.: Hun. 4155

Birman, Serafima
 Performance/production
 Career of actress Serafima Birman. Russia. 1890-1976. Lang.: Rus. 2217

Birmingham Repertory Theatre
 Performance/production
 Director Anthony Clark. UK-England: Birmingham. 1981-1996. Lang.: Eng. 2512

Birringer, Johannes
 Relation to other fields
 Performance artists and writers comment on political concerns in their work. UK-England: London. 1995. Lang.: Eng. 3818

Birtwhistle, Harrison
 Design/technology
 Computer animation in a production of Birtwhistle's *The Second Mrs. Kong*. Germany: Heidelberg. 1996. Lang.: Ger. 176

Bishoff, Joel
 Performance/production
 Collection of newspaper reviews by New York theatre critics. USA: New York, NY, Chicago, IL. 1996. Lang.: Eng. 2585

Biswas, Neil
 Performance/production
 Collection of newspaper reviews by London theatre critics. UK-England: London. 1996. Lang.: Eng. 2347

 Collection of newspaper reviews by London theatre critics. UK-England: London. 1996. Lang.: Eng. 2439

Biszczanik, Marek
 Plays/librettos/scripts
 Analysis of new plays by Pawel Huelle and Marek Biszczanik. Poland. 1995. Lang.: Eng, Fre. 3175

Bitteren Tränen der Petra von Kant, Die (Bitter Tears of Petra von Kant, The)
 Performance/production
 Collection of newspaper reviews by London theatre critics. UK-England: London. 1996. Lang.: Eng. 2343

Biwa-kei (Tokyo)
 Performance/production
 Japanese performances of Japanese themes at Toronto Theatre Festival. Japan. Canada: Toronto, ON. 1996. Lang.: Eng. 874

Bizet, Georges
 Institutions
 The Royal Swedish Opera compared unfavorably to Folkoperan. Sweden: Stockholm. 1996. Lang.: Swe. 4056
 Performance/production
 Contralto Eva Gauthier. Canada. 1885-1958. Lang.: Eng. 4094

Brecht, Bertolt — cont'd

Einar Schleef's production of *Herr Puntila* by Brecht, Berliner Ensemble. Germany: Berlin. 1996. Lang.: Ger. 2042

Konstanze Lauterbach's production of *Der aufhaltsame Aufstieg des Arturo Ui (The Resistible Rise of Arturo Ui)* by Bertolt Brecht. Germany: Klagenfurt. 1995. Lang.: Eng. 2048

Productions at Frankfurter Schauspielhaus in light of recent budget cuts. Germany: Frankfurt am Main. 1995. Lang.: Ger. 2051

Freiburger Theater under the leadership of Hans J. Amman. Germany: Freiburg. 1995. Lang.: Ger. 2059

Two productions of Brecht's *Herr Puntila*. Germany: Hamburg, Halle. 1996. Lang.: Ger. 2079

Einar Schleef's production of Brecht's *Herr Puntila*. Germany: Berlin. 1996. Lang.: Ger. 2087

Thorsten Flinck's staging of Brecht's *Herr Puntila* using rock music. Sweden: Stockholm. 1991. Lang.: Swe. 2284

Interview with actor Börje Ahlstedt about working with different directors. Sweden: Stockholm. 1989. Lang.: Swe. 2290

Photos of rehearsals for Thorsten Flinck's production of *Herr Puntila* at Royal Dramatic Theatre. Sweden: Stockholm. 1996. Lang.: Swe. 2294

Productions of Basler Theater. Switzerland: Basel. 1996. Lang.: Ger. 2300

Collection of newspaper reviews by London theatre critics. UK-England: London. 1996. Lang.: Eng. 2351

Collection of newspaper reviews by London theatre critics. UK-England: London. 1996. Lang.: Eng. 2362

British production and reception of the plays of Bertolt Brecht. UK-England. 1935-1975. Lang.: Eng. 2513

Brecht's *In the Jungle of Cities* at Alley Theatre. USA: Houston, TX. 1996. Lang.: Eng. 2621

Productions of Tretjakov's *Choču Rebenka (I Want a Baby)*. USSR: Moscow. UK-England: Birmingham. Germany: Berlin. 1927-1993.Lang.: Eng. 2694

Interview with Norbert Gingold regarding score preparation and conducting of *The Three Penny Opera*. Germany: Berlin. Austria: Vienna. 1928-1929. Lang.: Eng. 3916

The Three Penny Opera at Fontanka Youth Theatre. Russia: St. Petersburg. 1996. Lang.: Rus. 4211

Plays/librettos/scripts
Versions of the legend of Antigone. 441 B.C.-1986 A.D. Lang.: Spa. 2708

Playwright Osvaldo Dragún and Argentinian theatre. Argentina: Buenos Aires. 1952-1957. Lang.: Spa. 2716

Portrayals of women in works of ten male playwrights. Europe. 1836-1978. Lang.: Eng. 2973

Obituary of playwright Heiner Müller. Germany. 1996. Lang.: Eng. 3014

Twentieth-century German theatre and the tragic. Germany. 1900-1996. Lang.: Ita. 3032

Critical portrait and bibliography on Bertolt Brecht. Germany. 1898-1956. Lang.: Ita. 3035

Shakespeare's influence on Brecht reevaluated. Germany. 1917-1985. Lang.: Eng. 3041

Boxing as metaphor in plays of Brecht. Germany: Berlin. 1922-1926. Lang.: Eng. 3042

Interview with playwright José Sanchis Sinisterra. Spain. 1960-1991. Lang.: Fre. 3258

Elements of epic theatre in *The War Plays* by Edward Bond. UK-England. 1985. Lang.: Ger. 3295

Survey of German cabaret. Germany. 1929-1989. Lang.: Eng. 3739

Relation to other fields
Ideological uses of theatre during the National Socialist period. Germany. 1933-1945. Lang.: Ger. 1186

Theory/criticism
The origins and evolution of physical theatre. UK-England. Germany. 1900-1996. Lang.: Eng. 1368

The Alienation effect in the Rodney King beating trial. USA: Los Angeles, CA. 1991-1994. Lang.: Eng. 1379

Critical reaction to Einar Schleef's Berliner Ensemble production of Brecht's *Herr Puntila*. Germany: Berlin. 1996. Lang.: Ger. 3541

Breeze from the Gulf, A

Plays/librettos/scripts
Interview with playwright Mart Crowley. USA: New York, NY. 1996. Lang.: Eng. 3424

Bremer Schauspielhaus (Bremen)

Performance/production
Reviews of Shakespearean and other productions. Germany. 1994-1995. Lang.: Ger. 2058

Bremer Shakespeare Company (Bremen)

Institutions
Interview with Norbert Kentrup of Bremer Shakespeare Company. Germany: Bremen. 1996. Lang.: Ger. 1798

Competition between Theater der Freien Hansestadt and Bremer Shakespeare Company. Germany: Bremen. 1986-1996. Lang.: Ger. 1807

Performance/production
Reviews of Shakespearean and other productions. Germany. 1994-1995. Lang.: Ger. 2058

Bremer Shakespearetheater (Bremen)

Performance/production
Bremer Shakespearetheater and the advantages of directing Shakespeare in translation. Germany: Bremen. UK-England: London. 1993. Lang.: Eng. 2071

Bremer Theater (Bremen)

Institutions
The difficult second season Bremer Theater. Germany: Bremen. 1996. Lang.: Ger. 435

Bremner Theater (Bremen)

Institutions
Profile of Bremner Theater personnel. Germany: Bremen. 1996. Lang.: Ger. 426

Brennan, Kathleen

Basic theatrical documents
Text of *Alice* by Paul Schmidt, Tom Waits, and Kathleen Brennan. Germany: Hamburg. 1996. Lang.: Eng. 3845

Plays/librettos/scripts
Interview with playwright Paul Schmidt. Germany: Hamburg. 1996. Lang.: Eng. 3051

Brenton, Howard

Performance/production
Collection of newspaper reviews by London theatre critics. UK-England: London. 1996. Lang.: Eng. 2389

Plays/librettos/scripts
Contemporary English drama. UK-England. 1956-1990. Lang.: Fre. 3296

Breth, Andrea

Performance/production
Schaubühne's production of *Hedda Gabler* at Toronto conference and theatre festival. Canada: Toronto, ON. 1996. Lang.: Eng. 1940

Andrea Breth's production of Ibsen's *Hedda Gabler*. Germany: Berlin. 1995. Lang.: Eng. 2044

Interview with directors Andrea Breth and Phyllida Lloyd. Germany: Berlin. UK-England: London. 1995. Lang.: Eng. 2082

Andrea Breth's production of *The Seagull* and its marketing. Germany: Berlin. 1996. Lang.: Ger. 2086

Breuer, Lee

Performance/production
Computer technology in *The Red Horse Animation* by Lee Breuer. USA: New York, NY. 1996. Lang.: Eng. 2632

Performances of the Jim Henson International Festival. USA: New York, NY. 1995. Lang.: Eng. 4407

Plays/librettos/scripts
Telson and Breuer's *The Gospel at Colonus* and the problems of multiculturalism. USA. 1987. Lang.: Eng. 3425

Breum, Søren

Design/technology
Interview with costume designer Søren Breum. Denmark. 1995-1996. Lang.: Dan. 3662

Brewis, Peter

Performance/production
Collection of newspaper reviews by London theatre critics. UK-England: London. 1996. Lang.: Eng. 2329

Brewster, Yvonne

Performance/production
Collection of newspaper reviews by London theatre critics. UK-England: London. 1996. Lang.: Eng. 2447

Bricusse, Leslie

Performance/production
Collection of newspaper reviews by London theatre critics. UK-England: London. 1996. Lang.: Eng. 2473

Bridel, David

Performance/production
Collection of newspaper reviews by London theatre critics. UK-England: London. 1996. Lang.: Eng. 2414

Broadway theatre — cont'd

Interview with actor Jeff Trachta. USA: New York, NY. 1994-1996. Lang.: Eng. 1060

Actress and director Antoinette Perry. USA: New York, NY. 1889-1996. Lang.: Eng. 1073

Graciela Daniele's dance adaptation of *Chronicle of a Death Foretold* by Gabriel García Márquez. USA: New York, NY. 1981-1996. Lang.: Eng. 1446

Season-by-season analysis of Broadway and Off Broadway theatre. USA. 1930-1969. Lang.: Eng. 2594

Interviews with Tony Award nominees. USA: New York, NY. 1996. Lang.: Eng. 2596

The fiftieth anniversary of the Tony Awards. USA: New York, NY. 1996. Lang.: Eng. 2597

Actress Rosemary Harris. USA: New York, NY. 1958-1996. Lang.: Eng. 2599

Actor George Grizzard. USA: New York, NY. 1952-1996. Lang.: Eng. 2600

Highlights of interviews with Broadway stars. USA: New York, NY. 1985-1996. Lang.: Eng. 2601

Preview of Broadway and Off Broadway productions. USA: New York, NY. 1996. Lang.: Eng. 2602

Julia Sweeney's one-woman show *God Said 'Ha!'*. USA: New York, NY. 1996. Lang.: Eng. 2603

Actor Frank Langella. USA: New York, NY. 1939-1996. Lang.: Eng. 2605

Actor's diary of Broadway debut in David Hare's *Skylight*. USA: New York, NY. UK-England: London. 1996. Lang.: Eng. 2607

Zoe Caldwell's role in *Master Class*, directed by Leonard Foglia. USA: New York, NY. 1996. Lang.: Eng. 2615

Rob Becker and his solo performance *Defending the Caveman*. USA: New York, NY. 1996. Lang.: Eng. 2640

Singer/actress Elaine Page. UK-England: London. USA: New York, NY. 1968-1996. Lang.: Eng. 3925

Singer/dancer Donna McKechnie. USA: New York, NY. 1996. Lang.: Eng. 3928

Ricky Martin's role in *Les Misérables*. USA: New York, NY. 1996. Lang.: Eng. 3931

Revivals of musicals by Encores. USA: New York, NY. 1994-1996. Lang.: Eng. 3934

Singer/actress Leslie Uggams. USA: New York, NY. 1967-1996. Lang.: Eng. 3936

Actor Daniel Jenkins. USA: New York, NY. 1988-1996. Lang.: Eng. 3937

Lou Diamond Phillips' role in *The King and I*. USA: New York, NY. 1996. Lang.: Eng. 3938

The Broadway revival of the musical *Chicago*. USA: New York, NY. 1975-1996. Lang.: Eng. 3939

Profiles of singers in current Broadway musicals. USA: New York, NY. 1996. Lang.: Eng. 3940

Sarah Jessica Parker's role in *Once Upon a Mattress*. USA: New York, NY. 1976-1996. Lang.: Eng. 3942

Actor/singer John Davidson. USA: New York, NY. 1964-1996. Lang.: Eng. 3945

Overview of the Broadway musical revue. USA: New York, NY. 1866-1996. Lang.: Eng. 3947

Singer/actress Janie Sell. USA: New York, NY. 1970-1996. Lang.: Eng. 3949

Profile of recent Broadway musicals. USA: New York, NY. 1996. Lang.: Eng. 3950

Musical theatre director Jerry Zaks. USA: New York, NY. 1980-1996. Lang.: Eng. 3953

Off-Broadway musicals and their transfer to Broadway. USA: New York, NY. 1975-1996. Lang.: Eng. 3954

Actor John Stamos. USA: New York, NY. 1996. Lang.: Eng. 3955

Jonathan Larson's Broadway musical *Rent*. USA: New York, NY. 1996. Lang.: Eng. 3958

Melba Moore's role in *Les Misérables*. USA: New York, NY. 1970-1996. Lang.: Eng. 3963

Carol Channing's 4,500th performance in the title role of *Hello, Dolly!*. USA: New York, NY. 1996. Lang.: Eng. 3973

Stuart Ostrow's experience assisting Bob Fosse in original choreography for *Chicago*. USA: New York, NY. 1975. Lang.: Eng. 3975

Elaine Page's role in *Sunset Boulevard*. USA: New York, NY. UK-England: London. 1996. Lang.: Eng. 3979

Plays/librettos/scripts

Analysis of *Master Class* by Terrence McNally. USA: New York, NY. 1996. Lang.: Ger. 3411

Profile of playwright August Wilson. USA. 1945-1996. Lang.: Eng. 3454

Musicals proposed for revival. USA: New York, NY. 1996. Lang.: Eng. 3988

Experiments in musical theatre in the twenties. USA. 1920-1929. Lang.: Eng. 3993

Musical author Mary Rodgers. USA: New York, NY. 1959-1996. Lang.: Eng. 3999

Broch, Hermann
Performance/production
Krystian Lupa's *Lunatycy (The Sleepwalkers)* at Stary Teatr. Poland: Cracow. 1995. Lang.: Eng, Fre. 2169

Analysis of Krystian Lupa's *Lunatycy (The Sleepwalkers)*, based on writing of Hermann Broch. Poland: Cracow. 1995. Lang.: Eng, Fre. 2178

Brockman, Bruce
Design/technology
Exhibitors at the USITT design exhibition on scenery, lighting, and costuming. USA. 1996. Lang.: Eng. 335

Broderick, Matthew
Performance/production
Actor John Stamos. USA: New York, NY. 1996. Lang.: Eng. 3955

Brodsky, Joseph
Basic theatrical documents
Text of Act II of *Demokratija (Democracy!)* by Joseph Brodsky. Russia. USA. 1996. Lang.: Eng. 1675

Bródy, Vera
Design/technology
Interview with puppet designer Vera Bródy. Hungary: Budapest. France: Paris. 1947-1996. Lang.: Hun. 4368

Broken Circles: A Journey Through Africa and the Self
Plays/librettos/scripts
Performance and the development of *Broken Circles* by Joni L. Jones. Nigeria: Osogbo. USA: Austin, TX. 1993-1994. Lang.: Eng. 3149

Broken Glass
Plays/librettos/scripts
Realism and the plays of Arthur Miller. USA. 1949-1992. Lang.: Eng. 3409

Brolly, Tristan
Performance/production
Collection of newspaper reviews by London theatre critics. UK-England: London. 1996. Lang.: Eng. 2473

Bronner, Michajl
Performance/production
Dramatic music of Michajl Bronner. Russia: Moscow. 1990-1996. Lang.: Rus. 1440

Brook, Irina
Performance/production
Collection of newspaper reviews by London theatre critics. UK-England: London. 1996. Lang.: Eng. 2407

Brook, Peter
Institutions
Productions of the Carrefour theatre festival. Canada: Quebec, PQ. 1979-1996. Lang.: Eng. 1760
Performance/production
Russian translation of *The Shifting Point* by Peter Brook. Europe. 1946-1987. Lang.: Rus. 782

Responses to the RSC's Theatre of Cruelty experiments. UK-England: London. 1964. Lang.: Eng. 961

Peter Brook's *Qui est là (Who Is There)*. France: Paris. 1996. Lang.: Ger. 2011

Paris productions of the fall season. France: Paris. 1996. Lang.: Eng. 2032

Review of recent Paris productions. France: Paris. 1996. Lang.: Ger. 2033

The work of director Peter Brook. UK-England. 1991-1992. Lang.: Rus. 2543

Peter Brook's staging of Shakespeare's *Hamlet*. UK-England. 1990-1996. Lang.: Rus. 2544

Peter Brook's *L'homme qui (The Man Who)* as a model of multicultural theatre. USA: New York, NY. 1995. Lang.: Eng. 2618

Burlesque — cont'd

Performance/production

Notorious appearances of prostitutes on stage. England: London. 1673-1864. Lang.: Eng.   777

Interview with actors Normand Chouinard and Rémy Girard. Canada: Montreal, PQ. 1992. Lang.: Fre.   1922

Interview with actors Jean-Louis Millette and Alexis Martin. Canada: Montreal, PQ. 1992. Lang.: Fre.   1923

Interview with director André Brassard. Canada: Montreal, PQ. 1992. Lang.: Fre.   1963

Popular theatrical genres in their cultural context. England. 1700-1899. Lang.: Rus.   3712

Plays/librettos/scripts

Experiments in musical theatre in the twenties. USA. 1920-1929. Lang.: Eng.   3993

Burnden, Chris

Relation to other fields

Sleep and dreams in performances of Paul Gilchrist. UK-England. 1959-1996. Lang.: Eng.   3820

Interview with performance artist Marina Abramovic. Yugoslavia. 1974-1996. Lang.: Eng.   3824

Burnett, Harry

Performance/production

Forman Brown of Yale Puppeteers. USA. 1901-1996. Lang.: Eng.   4419

Burnett, T-Bone

Performance/production

Collection of newspaper reviews by New York theatre critics. USA: New York, NY. 1996. Lang.: Eng.   2565

Burnham, Michael

Performance/production

Collection of newspaper reviews by London theatre critics. UK-England: London. 1996. Lang.: Eng.   2330

Burning Blue

Plays/librettos/scripts

Analysis of English plays with homosexual content. UK-England. 1970-1996. Lang.: Dan.   3301

Burrill, Mary P.

Plays/librettos/scripts

The dual liberation motif in early Black women playwrights. USA. 1915-1930. Lang.: Eng.   3387

Feminist realism in African-American theatre. USA. 1916-1930. Lang.: Eng.   3440

Burris, Andrew M.

Basic theatrical documents

Anthology of unknown plays of the Harlem Renaissance. USA: New York, NY. 1920-1940. Lang.: Eng.   1694

Burroughs, Tony

Design/technology

Design for film adaptation of Shakespeare's *Richard III* by Shuna Harwood and Tony Burroughs. UK-England: London. 1991-1996. Lang.: Eng.   3593

Burrows, Abe

Performance/production

Collection of newspaper reviews by London theatre critics. UK-England: London. 1996. Lang.: Eng.   2491

Actor John Stamos. USA: New York, NY. 1996. Lang.: Eng.   3955

Burton, Amy

Performance/production

Lyric soprano Amy Burton. USA. 1996. Lang.: Eng.   4266

Burton, Richard

Plays/librettos/scripts

Black or white actors in the role of Othello. UK-England. 1956-1996. Lang.: Eng.   1107

Bus Stop

Performance/production

Collection of newspaper reviews by New York theatre critics. USA: New York, NY. 1996. Lang.: Eng.   2569

Bush Theatre (London)

Institutions

Profile of Bush and Almeida theatres. UK-England: London. 1996. Lang.: Ger.   1857

Performance/production

Collection of newspaper reviews by London theatre critics. UK-England: London. 1996. Lang.: Eng.   2304

Collection of newspaper reviews by London theatre critics. UK-England: London. 1996. Lang.: Eng.   2309

Collection of newspaper reviews by London theatre critics. UK-England: London. 1996. Lang.: Eng.   2364

Collection of newspaper reviews by London theatre critics. UK-England: London. 1996. Lang.: Eng.   2418

Collection of newspaper reviews by London theatre critics. UK-England: London. 1996. Lang.: Eng.   2436

Collection of newspaper reviews by London theatre critics. UK-England: London. 1996. Lang.: Eng.   2452

Bush, Frank

Plays/librettos/scripts

The representation of Jews on the American stage. USA. 1870-1880. Lang.: Eng.   3840

Business as Usual

Performance/production

Collection of newspaper reviews by London theatre critics. UK-England: London. 1996. Lang.: Eng.   2470

Busoni, Ferruccio

Performance/production

Operatic works of Busoni, Respighi, Casella, and others. Italy. 1900-1950. Lang.: Rus.   4182

Bussani, Dorothea

Plays/librettos/scripts

The age and background of Despina in Mozart's *Così fan tutte*. Austro-Hungarian Empire: Vienna. 1790. Lang.: Eng.   4305

Busybody, The

Plays/librettos/scripts

Reformist goals of plays by Susanna Centlivre and Mary Pix. England. 1700-1800. Lang.: Eng.   2907

Buten, Howard

Plays/librettos/scripts

Suzanne Lebeau's play for children, *Gil*. Canada. 1987-1988. Lang.: Fre.   2763

Butō

Performance/production

Japanese performances of Japanese themes at Toronto Theatre Festival. Japan. Canada: Toronto, ON. 1996. Lang.: Eng.   874

Interview with dancer Jocelyne Montpetit. Canada: Montreal, PQ. Japan. 1980-1990. Lang.: Fre.   1569

Butterfield, Catherine

Performance/production

Collection of newspaper reviews by London theatre critics. UK-England: London. 1996. Lang.: Eng.   2322

Collection of newspaper reviews by New York theatre critics. USA: New York, NY. 1996. Lang.: Eng.   2578

Butterworth, Jez

Performance/production

Collection of newspaper reviews by London theatre critics. UK-England: London. 1996. Lang.: Eng.   2408

Plays/librettos/scripts

Analysis of English plays with homosexual content. UK-England. 1970-1996. Lang.: Dan.   3301

Buttons on Broadway

Design/technology

Lighting designer Ken Billington. USA: New York, NY. 1970-1996. Lang.: Eng.   274

Buzoianu, Cătălina

Performance/production

Productions by returned expatriate directors. Romania. 1994-1996. Lang.: Hun.   896

By Jeeves

Performance/production

Collection of newspaper reviews by London theatre critics. UK-England: London. 1996. Lang.: Eng.   2447

Plays/librettos/scripts

Alan Ayckbourn on his collaboration with Andrew Lloyd Webber, *By Jeeves*. UK-England: London. 1996. Lang.: Eng.   3986

Bybee, Ariel

Performance/production

Changes in the comprimario system at the Metropolitan Opera. USA: New York, NY. 1996. Lang.: Eng.   4287

Bygmester Solness (Master Builder, The)

Plays/librettos/scripts

Influence of Ibsen's *Bygmester Solness (The Master Builder)* on *The Man Who Had All the Luck* by Arthur Miller. USA. Norway. 1886-1996. Lang.: Eng.   3410

Byrne and Brother

Performance/production

Collection of newspaper reviews by London theatre critics. UK-England: London. 1996. Lang.: Eng.   2341

Byrne, Emma

Performance/production

Collection of newspaper reviews by London theatre critics. UK-England: London. 1996. Lang.: Eng.   2364

Canac-Marquis, Normand
Plays/librettos/scripts
Playwright Normand Canac-Marquis on his work. Canada: Montreal, PQ. 1988-1991. Lang.: Fre. 2764

Analysis of plays by Normand Canac-Marquis. Canada: Montreal, PQ. 1988-1991. Lang.: Fre. 2800

Canada errant (Wandering Canada)
Plays/librettos/scripts
Performance artist Nathalie Derome. Canada: Montreal, PQ. 1989. Lang.: Fre. 3810

Canadian Children's Opera Chorus (Toronto, ON)
Institutions
Children's programs of opera companies. Canada. 1996. Lang.: Eng. 4033

Canadian Opera Company (Toronto, ON)
Design/technology
Design for *Der Fliegende Holländer*, Canadian Opera Company, by Allen Moyer. Canada: Toronto, ON. 1996. Lang.: Eng. 4014
Institutions
Children's programs of opera companies. Canada. 1996. Lang.: Eng. 4033

Canadian Opera Company's *Erwartung* and *Bluebeard's Castle* at the Hong Kong Arts Festival. China, People's Republic of: Hong Kong. 1996. Lang.: Ger. 4035
Performance/production
Profile of tenor Gary Rideout. Canada. 1983-1996. Lang.: Eng. 4086

Canadian Stage Company (Toronto, ON)
Performance/production
Multiple roles of Tom Wood and Nicola Cavendish in *Later Life*. Canada. 1996. Lang.: Eng. 1920

Canal Cafe (London)
Performance/production
Collection of newspaper reviews by London theatre critics. UK-England: London. 1996. Lang.: Eng. 2309

Collection of newspaper reviews by London theatre critics. UK-England: London. 1996. Lang.: Eng. 2491

Canaris, Volker
Institutions
Interview with Volker Canaris, managing director of Düsseldorfer Schauspielhaus. Germany: Düsseldorf. 1986-1996. Lang.: Ger. 1801

Candelaria, La (Bogotá)
SEE
Teatro La Candelaria.

Candide
Performance/production
Collection of newspaper reviews by New York theatre critics. USA: New York, NY, Washington, DC. 1996. Lang.: Eng. 2581

Canje (The River of Ocean)
Plays/librettos/scripts
Theatrical metaphors in prose and dramatic works of Wilson Harris. UK-England. 1954-1990. Lang.: Eng. 3284

Cankar, Ivan
Plays/librettos/scripts
Analysis of plays by major Slovene dramatists. Slovenia. 1900-1996. Lang.: Slo. 3212

Cano, Joel
Plays/librettos/scripts
Chaos theory in *Timeball* by Joel Cano. Cuba. 1990. Lang.: Spa. 2867

Postmodernism in Latin American theatre. Latin America. 1994-1996. Lang.: Spa. 3142

Cantatrice chauve, La (Bald Soprano, The)
Institutions
Profile of Théâtre de la Huchette, which produces the plays of Ionesco. France: Paris. 1950-1996. Lang.: Swe. 1792
Performance/production
Plays of Ionesco in Romania after Ceauşescu. Romania: Cluj. 1989-1993. Lang.: Eng. 2185

Cantos, Antonio
Performance/production
Collection of newspaper reviews by London theatre critics. UK-England: London. 1996. Lang.: Eng. 2418

Cao, Yu
Plays/librettos/scripts
Images of women in modern Chinese historical plays. China. 1923-1995. Lang.: Eng. 2855

Cap with Bells, The
SEE
Berretto a sonagli, Il.

Cape Playhouse (Dennis, MA)
Administration
Theatres withdraw from Council of Stock Theatres collective bargaining unit. USA. 1996. Lang.: Eng. 81

Čapek, Karel
Performance/production
The plot of Janáček's opera *Věc Makropulos*. Czechoslovakia: Prague. 1926-1996. Lang.: Eng. 4102
Plays/librettos/scripts
Love and death in Janáček's opera *Věc Makropulos*. Czechoslovakia: Prague. 1926-1996. Lang.: Eng. 4310

Capitano Ulisse (Captain Ulysse)
Plays/librettos/scripts
Analysis of *Capitano Ulisse* and *Casa inspirata* by Alberto Savinio. Italy. 1822-1852. Lang.: Ita. 3123

Cappucino Strip
Performance/production
Deckchair Theatre's *Cappucino Strip* directed by Angela Chaplin. Australia: Fremantle. 1995. Lang.: Eng. 687

Caprioli, Cristina
Performance/production
Christina Caprioli's dance work *L'Invisibile canto del camminare*. Sweden: Stockholm. 1996. Lang.: Swe. 1589

Captain Jinks of the Horse Marines
Plays/librettos/scripts
The operas of Jack Beeson and the Columbia Opera Workshop. USA. 1996. Lang.: Eng. 4346

Capuchin, The
Plays/librettos/scripts
Nationalism and the plays of Samuel Foote. England. 1752-1800. Lang.: Eng. 2925

Carbon Miranda
Performance/production
Collection of newspaper reviews by London theatre critics. UK-England: London. 1996. Lang.: Eng. 2384

Carbone 14 (Montreal, PQ)
Design/technology
Scenography of Gilles Maheu for Carbone 14. Canada: Montreal, PQ. 1980-1992. Lang.: Fre. 152
Institutions
Comparison of Carbone 14 and Nouveau Théâtre Expérimental. Canada: Montreal, PQ. 1989. Lang.: Fre. 1778

Card Index
SEE
Kartoteka.

Cardinal, Marie
Plays/librettos/scripts
Alice Ronfard's translation of *The Tempest* for Théâtre Expérimental des Femmes. Canada: Montreal, PQ. 1988. Lang.: Fre. 2828

Caretaker, The
Performance/production
Interview with actor József Czintos. Hungary: Budapest. Romania: Satu-Mare. 1969-1995. Lang.: Hun. 2098

Carey, Mariah
Performance/production
Pop star Mariah Carey. USA: New York, NY. 1970-1996. Lang.: Rus. 3977

Carin Ari Biblioteket (Stockholm)
Administration
Bengt Häger's career in dance production, training, and research. Sweden: Stockholm. 1916. Lang.: Swe. 1402

Cariou, Len
Performance/production
Len Cariou's role in *Papa* directed by John Henry Davis. USA: New York, NY. 1996. Lang.: Eng. 2620

Carleton
Performance/production
Reviews of German-language productions. Germany. Switzerland. Austria. 1996. Lang.: Ger. 2089

Carleton, John
Relation to other fields
National and regional identities in Canadian theatre companies. Canada. 1860-1994. Lang.: Eng. 1157

Carlisle, Barbara
Performance/production
Barbara Carlisle's at-home production of *Paris Quartet*. USA. 1995. Lang.: Eng. 2609

Carlson, David
Plays/librettos/scripts
David Carlson's opera *Dreamkeepers*, which uses traditional Ute music and instruments. USA: Salt Lake City, UT. 1996. Lang.: Eng. 4347

Cary, Elizabeth
  Relation to other fields
    Teaching *The Winter's Tale* and Elizabeth Cary's *The Tragedy of
    Mariam*. USA. 1995. Lang.: Eng.   3517
    Teaching race and gender in plays of Cary, Shakespeare, and Behn.
    USA. 1996. Lang.: Eng.   3518
    Teaching plays of Shakespeare and Cary in a course on domestic
    England in the early modern period. USA. 1995. Lang.: Eng.   3519
    Argument in favor of teaching Shakespeare in conjunction with his
    female contemporaries. USA. 1996. Lang.: Eng.   3520
Casa de Bernarda Alba, La (House of Bernarda Alba, The)
  Performance/production
    Collection of newspaper reviews by London theatre critics. UK-England:
    London. 1996. Lang.: Eng.   2499
Casa del Teatro (Medellín)
  Institutions
    Colombian National Theatre Festival. Colombia: Cali. 1996. Lang.: Spa.
                                                                        386
Casa inspirata (Inspired House)
  Plays/librettos/scripts
    Analysis of *Capitano Ulisse* and *Casa inspirata* by Alberto Savinio. Italy.
    1822-1852. Lang.: Ita.   3123
Casa via Magia (Rio de Janeiro)
  Institutions
    Account of Spanish-American theatre festival. Spain: Cádiz. 1995.
    Lang.: Spa.   534
Cascio, Anna Theresa
  Design/technology
    Lighting design for plays about Martin Guerre. UK-England: London.
    1996. Lang.: Eng.   3890
  Performance/production
    Collection of newspaper reviews by New York theatre critics. USA:
    New York, NY, Chicago, IL. 1996. Lang.: Eng.   2585
  Plays/librettos/scripts
    Musical adaptations of the story of Martin Guerre. USA. 1996. Lang.:
    Eng.   3991
Casella, Alfredo
  Performance/production
    Operatic works of Busoni, Respighi, Casella, and others. Italy. 1900-
    1950. Lang.: Rus.   4182
Casella, Martin
  Performance/production
    Collection of newspaper reviews by New York theatre critics. USA:
    New York, NY, East Haddam, CT. 1996. Lang.: Eng.   2553
Casella, Matt
  Performance/production
    Collection of newspaper reviews by New York theatre critics. USA:
    New York, NY, East Haddam, CT. 1996. Lang.: Eng.   2553
Casey, Anne-Marie
  Performance/production
    Collection of newspaper reviews by London theatre critics. UK-England:
    London. 1996. Lang.: Eng.   2348
Casey, Warren
  Performance/production
    Interview with actor Jeff Trachta. USA: New York, NY. 1994-1996.
    Lang.: Eng.   1060
Cash on Delivery
  Performance/production
    Collection of newspaper reviews by London theatre critics. UK-England:
    London. 1996. Lang.: Eng.   2394
Casino Theatre (Toronto, ON)
  Institutions
    Vaudeville shows at the Casino Theatre. Canada: Toronto, ON. 1925-
    1996. Lang.: Eng.   3843
Castagna, Bruna
  Performance/production
    Comments on the mezzo soprano vocal range, including notes on
    specific singers. USA. 1996. Lang.: Eng.   4262
Castel, Nico
  Performance/production
    Changes in the comprimario system at the Metropolitan Opera. USA:
    New York, NY. 1996. Lang.: Eng.   4287
Castellani, Renato
  Performance/production
    Analysis of film and video versions of *Romeo and Juliet*. USA. UK-
    England. Italy. 1936-1978. Lang.: Eng.   3631
Castillo, Andrés
  Plays/librettos/scripts
    Andrés Castillo and El Teatro Negro Independiente. Uruguay:
    Montevideo. 1995-1996. Lang.: Spa.   3318

Castillos en el aire (Castles in the Air)
  Basic theatrical documents
    Dutch translations of plays by Belbel, Cabal, and Sanchis Sinisterra.
    Spain. 1990-1995. Lang.: Dut.   1677
Casting
  Administration
    Ellen Stewart of La MaMa receives Rosetta LeNoire award for
    nontraditional casting. USA: New York, NY. 1996. Lang.: Eng.   1623
  Performance/production
    Performance-based productions for predominantly female student
    groups. UK-England: Hull. 1891-1990. Lang.: Eng.   969
    Call for actors to enroll in Non-Traditional Casting Project registry.
    USA: New York, NY. 1996. Lang.: Eng.   1053
    Successful nontraditional casting. USA: New York, NY. 1996. Lang.:
    Eng.   1055
  Plays/librettos/scripts
    Black or white actors in the role of Othello. UK-England. 1956-1996.
    Lang.: Eng.   1107
Casting No. 7, Structure No. 7
  Relation to other fields
    Avant-garde representations of the human body. Canada. 1996. Lang.:
    Eng.   1145
Castle of Perseverance, The
  Performance/production
    The staging of French and English mystery plays. France. England.
    1400-1600. Lang.: Eng.   2027
  Plays/librettos/scripts
    Spatial codes and English Renaissance theatre. England. 1425-1700.
    Lang.: Eng.   2889
    Representation of devils and vices in English liturgy and theatre.
    England. 1300-1500. Lang.: Eng.   2890
Castle Theatre (Budapest)
  SEE
    Várszinház.
Castle Theatre (Gyula)
  SEE
    Gyulai Várszinház.
Castle Theatre (Kisvárda)
  SEE
    Kisvárdai Várszinház.
Castle Theatre (Kőszeg)
  SEE
    Kőszegi Várszinház.
Castledine, Annie
  Performance/production
    Videotape on interpreting and performing Shakespeare's *As You Like It*.
    UK-England. 1994. Lang.: Eng.   2303
    Collection of newspaper reviews by London theatre critics. UK-England:
    London. 1996. Lang.: Eng.   2377
Castorf, Frank
  Performance/production
    Frank Castorf's production of Zuckmayer's *Der Teufels General (The
    Devil's General)*, Volksbühne. Germany: Berlin. 1996. Lang.: Ger.   2068
    Comparison of productions of Müller's *Der Auftrag (The Mission)*.
    Germany: Leipzig, Berlin. 1996. Lang.: Ger.   2069
    Two productions of Brecht's *Herr Puntila*. Germany: Hamburg, Halle.
    1996. Lang.: Ger.   2079
    Productions of plays by Heiner Müller at Berliner Ensemble and
    Volksbühne. Germany: Berlin. 1996. Lang.: Ger.   2088
  Relation to other fields
    Berlin theatre in the current German intellectual debate. Germany:
    Berlin. 1991-1996. Lang.: Eng.   1192
Castrati
  Performance/production
    Performance practices and audience tastes in Baroque music, particularly
    opera. England. 1685-1759. Lang.: Eng.   4104
    The *castrato* voice, with emphasis on the film *Farinelli*. Europe. 1707-
    1994. Lang.: Eng.   4107
    Historical view of *castrati* inspired by the film *Farinelli*. Italy. 1600-
    1996. Lang.: Dan.   4184
    Opera tastes of the early nineteenth-century. UK-England. 1814-1823.
    Lang.: Eng.   4232
Castro, Alfredo
  Relation to other fields
    Theatre, aesthetics, and resistance in the southern part of South
    America. Chile. Argentina. Uruguay. 1970-1996. Lang.: Ger.   1163
Cat and Mouse (Sheep)
  Performance/production
    Collection of newspaper reviews by London theatre critics. UK-England:
    London. 1996. Lang.: Eng.   2344

Català, Víctor
  SEE
    Albert, Caterina.
Catalogues
  Reference materials
    Review of catalogue of German theatre in Pest-Buda. Hungary.
    Germany. 1770-1850. Lang.: Hun.   1122
Catastrophe
  Plays/librettos/scripts
    Analysis of *Gangsters* by Maishe Maponya. South Africa, Republic of.
    1930-1995. Lang.: Eng.   3224
Cate, Ritsaert ten
  Performance/production
    Life and work of Ritsaert ten Cate, founder of the Mickery Theater.
    Netherlands. 1930-1995. Lang.: Eng.   885
Catesby, Deborah
  Performance/production
    Collection of newspaper reviews by London theatre critics. UK-England:
    London. 1996. Lang.: Eng.   2377
Cathcart, Sarah
  Plays/librettos/scripts
    Presentations by story-tellers at women playwrights conference.
    Australia. USA. Philippines. 1981-1995. Lang.: Eng.   1083
    Interview with playwright Andrea Lemon of Snakehouse. Australia:
    Perth. 1994-1995. Lang.: Eng.   2722
Catherine Wheel, The
  Plays/librettos/scripts
    Analysis of two new lesbian-themed Canadian plays. Canada. 1710-
    1996. Lang.: Eng.   2793
Cathleen ni Houlihan
  Plays/librettos/scripts
    Nationalism and the female figure in plays of Yeats. Ireland. 1903-1910.
    Lang.: Eng.   3083
Catling, Brian
  Performance spaces
    The artist-led guided tours known as *Hidden Cities*. UK-England. 1995.
    Lang.: Eng.   3704
Caucasian Chalk Circle, The
  SEE
    Kaukasische Kreidekreis, Der.
Cavalcade
  Design/technology
    Scene designer Cameron Porteous. Canada: Niagara-on-the-Lake, ON.
    1980-1995. Lang.: Eng.   1707
Cave, Candida
  Performance/production
    Collection of newspaper reviews by London theatre critics. UK-England:
    London. 1996. Lang.: Eng.   2497
Cavendish, Lady Jane
  Relation to other fields
    Feminist classroom approach to *The Concealed Fancies* by Cavendish
    and Brackley. England. 1645. Lang.: Eng.   3490
Cavendish, Margaret
  Plays/librettos/scripts
    Women's retreats in plays of Shakespeare and Margaret Cavendish.
    England. 1590-1668. Lang.: Eng.   2891
Cavendish, Nicola
  Performance/production
    Multiple roles of Tom Wood and Nicola Cavendish in *Later Life*.
    Canada. 1996. Lang.: Eng.   1920
Čcheidze, Temur
  Institutions
    St. Petersburg's theatres, directors, and repertory. Russia: St. Petersburg.
    1995-1996. Lang.: Swe.   518
    Profile of Bolšoj Dramatičéskij Teat'r im. G.A. Tovstonogova. Russia:
    St. Petersburg. 1990-1996. Lang.: Rus.   1825
Ce tellement 'cute' des enfants (Kids Are So Cute)
  Performance/production
    Marie-Francine Hébert of Théâtre des Deux Mondes, formerly Théâtre
    de la Marmaille. Canada: Montreal, PQ. 1975. Lang.: Fre.   724
Cecchi, Carlo
  Performance/production
    Carlo Cecchi's production of *Fin de partie (Endgame)* by Samuel
    Beckett. Italy. 1996. Lang.: Ita.   2130
Cecchi, Giovan Maria
  Plays/librettos/scripts
    Secrecy in Italian Renaissance comedy. Italy. 1522-1793. Lang.: Eng.
                                                                       3115

Čechov, Anton Pavlovič
  Design/technology
    Candice Donnelly's costumes for Tennessee Williams' *The Notebook of
    Trigorin*, Cincinnati Playhouse. USA: Cincinnati, OH. 1996.Lang.: Eng.
                                                                       1728
  Institutions
    Productions of the Edinburgh Festival. UK-Scotland: Edinburgh. 1996.
    Lang.: Ger.   561
    Productions of the Ruhrfestspiele festival. Germany: Recklinghausen.
    1996. Lang.: Eng.   1797
    Report on the second international Čechov theatre festival. Russia:
    Moscow. 1995-1996. Lang.: Rus.   1823
    Report on the second international Čechov festival. Russia: Moscow.
    1996. Lang.: Rus.   1829
  Performance/production
    The fiftieth Avignon Festival. France: Avignon. 1996. Lang.: Eng.   805
    Peter Zadek's production of Čechov's *The Cherry Orchard* at
    Burgtheater. Austria: Vienna. 1996. Lang.: Ger.   1902
    The acting in Peter Zadek's production of *The Cherry Orchard* at
    Burgtheater. Austria: Vienna. 1996. Lang.: Ger.   1906
    Two productions of Čechov's *Ivanov*. Germany: Seifenberg, Gera. 1996.
    Lang.: Ger.   2081
    Andrea Breth's production of *The Seagull* and its marketing. Germany:
    Berlin. 1996. Lang.: Ger.   2086
    Account of Čechov International Theatre Festival. Russia. 1996. Lang.:
    Eng.   2199
    Italian translation of Stanislavskij's notes on directing *Diadia Vania
    (Uncle Vanya)*. Russia. 1899. Lang.: Ita.   2251
    Collection of newspaper reviews by London theatre critics. UK-England:
    London. 1996. Lang.: Eng.   2359
    Collection of newspaper reviews by London theatre critics. UK-England:
    London. 1996. Lang.: Eng.   2381
    Collection of newspaper reviews by London theatre critics. UK-England:
    London. 1996. Lang.: Eng.   2390
    Collection of newspaper reviews by London theatre critics. UK-England:
    London. 1996. Lang.: Eng.   2419
    Collection of newspaper reviews by London theatre critics. UK-England:
    London. 1996. Lang.: Eng.   2442
    Collection of newspaper reviews by London theatre critics. UK-England:
    London. 1996. Lang.: Eng.   2454
    Collection of newspaper reviews by London theatre critics. UK-England:
    London. 1996. Lang.: Eng.   2481
    Vanessa Redgrave's role in *The Notebook of Trigorin* by Tennessee
    Williams. USA: Cincinnati, OH. 1996. Lang.: Eng.   2612
    Rehearsals of Wooster Group's adaptation of Čechov, *Brace Up!*. USA:
    New York, NY. 1990-1991. Lang.: Fre.   2655
    Wooster Group's production of *Brace Up!*, an adaptation of Čechov's
    Tri sestry (Three Sisters). USA: New York, NY. 1991. Lang.: Fre. 2686
    Newly discovered records of Mejerchol'd rehearsals. USSR. 1925-1938.
    Lang.: Eng.   2696
  Relation to other fields
    The political context of Nekrošius' production of Čechov's *Three Sisters*.
    Lithuania. 1996. Lang.: Ger.   3503
Čechov, Michajl A.
  Performance/production
    Moscow theatre life of the twenties and thirties. USSR: Moscow. 1927-
    1931. Lang.: Rus.   1077
  Research/historiography
    Description of theatre and dance-related holdings of the Darlington Hall
    Trust archives. UK-England: Totnes, Devon. 1920-1995. Lang.: Eng.
                                                                       1305
Cecil-Smith, Ed
  Plays/librettos/scripts
    The workers' theatre play *Eight Men Speak*. Canada: Toronto, ON.
    1933. Lang.: Eng.   2776
Cecil, Kevin
  Performance/production
    Collection of newspaper reviews by London theatre critics. UK-England:
    London. 1996. Lang.: Eng.   2462
Ceji, Ron
  Performance/production
    Collection of newspaper reviews by London theatre critics. UK-England:
    London. 1996. Lang.: Eng.   2315
Cejtlin, Boris
  Performance/production
    Boris Cejtlin's production of *Romeo and Juliet*, Baltiskij Dom. Russia:
    St. Petersburg. 1995. Lang.: Rus.   2234

Chaplin, Victoria
Performance/production
Collection of newspaper reviews by London theatre critics. UK-England: London. 1996. Lang.: Eng. 2481

Chapman, George
Basic theatrical documents
Text of plays by Fletcher and his collaborators. England. 1609-1613. Lang.: Eng. 1655

Chapter Two
Performance/production
Collection of newspaper reviews by London theatre critics. UK-England: London. 1996. Lang.: Eng. 2320

Characters/roles
Performance/production
The portrayal of female characters in Büchner's *Dantons Tod (Danton's Death)*. Germany. 1902-1994. Lang.: Eng. 2053
Plays/librettos/scripts
The fool in *commedia dell'arte* and in Jonson's *Every Man in His Humour*. England. Italy. 1465-1601. Lang.: Eng. 1093
Essays on the representation of the fool. Europe. 1047-1673. Lang.: Eng. 1094
Witches in Quebecois feminist plays. Canada. 1968-1993. Lang.: Fre. 2754
The depiction of the fool in early Tudor theatre. England. 1047-1548. Lang.: Eng. 2910
The role and importance of Shakespeare's clowns. England. 1590-1613. Lang.: Eng. 2960
The devil in Polish drama. Poland. 1832-1957. Lang.: Pol. 3168
Strong female roles in turn-of-the-century drama. UK-England: London. 1899-1918. Lang.: Eng. 3279

Charlie's Angel
Performance/production
Collection of newspaper reviews by London theatre critics. UK-England: London. 1996. Lang.: Eng. 2315

Charlotte Repertory (Charlotte, NC)
Administration
Angels in America and local ordinances prohibiting public nudity. USA: Charlotte, NC. 1996. Lang.: Eng. 1622

Charlton, James Martin
Performance/production
Collection of newspaper reviews by London theatre critics. UK-England: London. 1996. Lang.: Eng. 2409

Charms, Daniel
Performance/production
Documents relating to Jévrejnov, Charms, and Foregger. Russia. 1910-1929. Lang.: Rus. 908

Charney, Melvin
Relation to other fields
Interview with sculptor and architect Melvin Charney. Canada. 1982-1989. Lang.: Fre. 1160

Charnin, Martin
Performance/production
Collection of newspaper reviews by New York theatre critics. USA: New York, NY. 1996. Lang.: Eng. 2552
The musical *Mata Hari* by Jerome Coopersmith, Edward Thomas, and Martin Charnin. USA: New York, NY. 1967-1996. Lang.: Eng. 3948

Charnock, Nigel
Performance/production
Collection of newspaper reviews by London theatre critics. UK-England: London. 1996. Lang.: Eng. 2336

Chase, Mary
Performance/production
Political activities of actor Frank Fay. USA: New York, NY, Hollywood, CA. 1944-1950. Lang.: Eng. 2624

Chat with Mrs. Chicky, A
Performance/production
Margaret Metcalf's *Playing for Power*, based on drama of the Actresses' Franchise League. UK-England. 1908-1993. Lang.: Eng. 987

Chatten, Klaus
Performance/production
Collection of newspaper reviews by London theatre critics. UK-England: London. 1996. Lang.: Eng. 2361

Chatterton
Relation to other fields
Assumptions about the relationship between theatre and literature. France: Paris. 1835-1996. Lang.: Fre. 3498

Chaucer, Geoffrey
Performance/production
Collection of newspaper reviews by London theatre critics. UK-England: London. 1996. Lang.: Eng. 2397

Plays/librettos/scripts
Carnivalesque subversion of literary and dramatic texts. England. 1300-1607. Lang.: Eng. 2931

Chaurette, Normand
Performance/production
Norman Chaurette's *Provincetown Playhouse...* staged by Alice Ronfard, Espace GO. Canada: Montreal, PQ. 1981-1992. Lang.: Fre. 1929
Staging *Le Passage de l'Indiana (The Crossing of the Indiana)* by Normand Chaurette. Canada: Montreal, PQ. 1996. Lang.: Fre. 1944
Gabriel Garran's Paris productions of plays by Quebec authors. Canada. France: Paris. 1975-1990. Lang.: Fre. 1959
Alice Ronfard's staging of *Provincetown Playhouse...* by Normand Chaurette. Canada: Montreal, PQ. 1981-1992. Lang.: Fre. 1968
Critical reception of productions by Théâtre UBU at the Avignon festival. France: Avignon. 1996. Lang.: Fre. 2016

Chávarri, Jaime
Performance/production
The Madrid theatre season. Spain: Madrid. 1996. Lang.: Eng. 2271

Chawaf, Chantal
Plays/librettos/scripts
The emergence of French feminist theatre. France. 1975-1995. Lang.: Eng. 3001

Cheek by Jowl (London)
Performance/production
English plays and subjects on the Hungarian stage. Hungary. 1995-1996. Lang.: Eng. 847
Videotape on interpreting and performing Shakespeare's *As You Like It*. UK-England. 1994. Lang.: Eng. 2303
Interview with director Declan Donnellan. UK-England: London. Hungary: Budapest. 1996. Lang.: Hun. 2505

Chekhov, Anton
SEE
Čechov, Anton Pavlovič.

Chekhov, Michael
SEE
Čechov, Michajl A.

Chelsea Centre (London)
Performance/production
Collection of newspaper reviews by London theatre critics. UK-England: London. 1996. Lang.: Eng. 2321
Collection of newspaper reviews by London theatre critics. UK-England: London. 1996. Lang.: Eng. 2334
Collection of newspaper reviews by London theatre critics. UK-England: London. 1996. Lang.: Eng. 2358
Collection of newspaper reviews by London theatre critics. UK-England: London. 1996. Lang.: Eng. 2374
Collection of newspaper reviews by London theatre critics. UK-England: London. 1996. Lang.: Eng. 2398

Chen, Bai-chen
Plays/librettos/scripts
Images of women in modern Chinese historical plays. China. 1923-1995. Lang.: Eng. 2855

Cherea (de' Nobili, Francesco)
Performance/production
Renaissance actors Cherea and Barlacchia. Italy. 1500-1600. Lang.: Ita. 865

Chéreau, Patrice
Performance/production
Interview with director Patrice Chéreau. France. 1996. Lang.: Eng. 2013
Patrice Chéreau's productions of plays by Bernard-Marie Koltès. France. 1964-1996. Lang.: Dan. 2039
Collection of newspaper reviews by New York theatre critics. USA: New York, NY. 1996. Lang.: Eng. 2571
Interview with director Patrice Chéreau. USA. 1983-1996. Lang.: Eng. 2649
Interview with opera director Nicolas Joël. France. Germany. 1942-1996. Lang.: Eng. 4117

Cherli Ka Cherli
Audience
Israeli theatre and its audience. Israel. 1990-1991. Lang.: Eng. 139

Cherry Orchard, The
SEE
Višněvyj sad.

Cheshbon Chadash (Stocktaking)
Plays/librettos/scripts
Analysis of Israeli Holocaust drama. Israel. 1950-1984. Lang.: Eng. 3099

Children's theatre — cont'd

The inclusion of puppetry in the repertoire of Theater der Jungen Welt. Germany: Leipzig. 1989-1996. Lang.: Ger. 4376

Portrait of Puppentheater Knorzkopp by its two members. Germany: Kassel. 1984-1996. Lang.: Ger. 4377

Performance spaces
History of Theater der Jungen Generation. Germany: Dresden. 1949. Lang.: Ger. 636

Performance/production
Productions of children's theatre festival Coups de théâtre. Canada: Montreal, PQ. 1996. Lang.: Fre. 703

Interview with Serge Marois of children's theatre company Arrière-Scène. Canada: Montreal, PQ. 1976-1993. Lang.: Fre. 719

Marie-Francine Hébert of Théâtre des Deux Mondes, formerly Théâtre de la Marmaille. Canada: Montreal, PQ. 1975. Lang.: Fre. 724

Stage and film treatments of the fairy tale *Beauty and the Beast*. Europe. USA. Canada. 1946-1996. Lang.: Eng. 793

Rudolf Mirbt and children's, school, and amateur theatre. Germany. 1896-1974. Lang.: Ger. 814

Kama Ginkas' work in youth theatre. Russia: Moscow. 1996. Lang.: Rus. 904

Children's theatre actor Valerij D'jačenko. Russia: St. Petersburg. 1980-1996. Lang.: Rus. 924

Handbook of acting exercises for children. Slovenia. 1996. Lang.: Slo. 939

Appeal for maintaining quality children's theatre in spite of reduced funding. Sweden. 1995. Lang.: Swe. 953

Use of young amateur actors by Nultwintig. Netherlands. 1994-1995. Lang.: Dut. 2141

The Janusz Korczak festival of children's theatre. Poland: Warsaw. 1996. Lang.: Eng, Fre. 2179

Vladimir Čigiév's production of *Hamlet* with Teat'r Junogo Zritelja. Russia: Rostov-na-Donu. 1990-1996. Lang.: Rus. 2213

Actor Anatolij Petrov. Russia: Moscow. 1996. Lang.: Rus. 2237

Staffan Roos's children's theatre project *Spöken (Ghosts)* at Royal Dramatic Theatre. Sweden: Stockholm. 1996. Lang.: Swe. 2279

Kungliga Dramatiska Teatern and Staffan Roos's children's production *Spöken (Ghosts)*. Sweden: Stockholm. 1996. Lang.: Swe. 2291

Production of Stravinskij's opera for children, *Nattergalen*. Germany: Cologne. 1996. Lang.: Ger. 4134

The Three Penny Opera at Fontanka Youth Theatre. Russia: St. Petersburg. 1996. Lang.: Rus. 4211

Puppetry performance styles of Jan Dorman and Jan Wilkowski. Poland. 1945-1996. Lang.: Eng, Fre. 4400

Plays/librettos/scripts
Suzanne Lebeau's play for children, *Gil*. Canada. 1987-1988. Lang.: Fre. 2763

Children's plays of Tankred Dorst. Germany. 1982-1996. Lang.: Ger. 3018

Slovene youth drama. Slovenia. 1872-1996. Lang.: Slo. 3217

Early Slovene theatre for youth. Slovenia. 1872-1929. Lang.: Slo. 3218

Children's plays of Staffan Göthe. Sweden: Luleå, Stockholm. 1944. Lang.: Swe. 3275

The obscurity of playwrights for youth. USA. 1996. Lang.: Eng. 3349

Playwright Y York. USA. 1996. Lang.: Eng. 3391

Reference materials
Directory of Polish puppet and children's theatre, festivals, and awards. Poland. 1996. Lang.: Eng, Fre. 4427

Relation to other fields
The touring company Arrière-Scène. Canada. 1972-1992. Lang.: Fre. 1153

Interview with theatre teacher Werner Schulte. Germany: Berlin. 1989-1996. Lang.: Ger. 1180

The importance of theatre education in Polish schools. Poland. 1996. Lang.: Eng, Fre. 1220

Teaching theatre in general aesthetics classes. Russia: Moscow. 1996. Lang.: Rus. 1225

Blah, Blah, Blah's fusion of performance art and educational theatre. UK-England. 1995. Lang.: Eng. 1247

Erna Grönlund, professor of dance therapy. Sweden: Stockholm. 1942. Lang.: Swe. 1458

Social and aesthetic trends in Japanese children's theatre festival. Japan: Tokyo. 1995. Lang.: Fre. 3501

Plays for youth created by Seoul theatre collectives. Korea: Seoul. 1995-1996. Lang.: Kor. 3502

Research/historiography
Walter Röhler's paper theatre collection. Germany: Darmstadt. 1800-1996. Lang.: Ger. 1297

Training
Profile of Compania Infantil de Danza. Spain: Palma de Mallorca. 1980. Lang.: Swe. 1470

Childress, Alice
Plays/librettos/scripts
Contemporary American drama. USA. 1960-1995. Lang.: Eng. 3431

Realism in American feminist drama. USA. 1900-1988. Lang.: Eng. 3441

Chilton, Nola
Performance/production
Interview with director Nola Chilton. Israel. 1960-1995. Lang.: Eng. 854

Chiment, Marie Anne
Design/technology
Marie Anne Chiment's costume designs for *The Winter's Tale*, Oregon Shakespeare Festival. USA: Ashland, OR. 1996. Lang.: Eng. 1720

Chimère
Design/technology
Transport problems of Zingaro, an equestrian theatre group. USA: New York, NY. France. 1996. Lang.: Eng. 3699

Performance/production
The equestrian theatre of Zingaro, appearing at BAM. USA: New York, NY. France: Paris. 1996. Lang.: Eng. 3720

Chinese opera
SEE ALSO
Classed Entries under MUSIC-DRAMA—Chinese opera.
Performance/production
A Swedish guest performance of *A Midsummer Night's Dream* in Shanghai. Sweden: Stockholm. China, People's Republic of: Shanghai. 1996. Lang.: Swe. 954

Collaboration of directors Peter Oskarson and Ma Ke at Orionteatern. Sweden: Stockholm. China, People's Republic of. 1989. Lang.:Swe. 955

Chinoiserie
Plays/librettos/scripts
Experimental playwright and director Ping Chong. USA: New York, NY. 1990-1996. Lang.: Eng. 3361

Chip in the Sugar, A
Performance/production
Current Dublin productions. Ireland: Dublin. 1996. Lang.: Eng. 2117

Chip Woman's Fortune, The
Plays/librettos/scripts
Harlem Renaissance playwrights Willis Richardson and Eulalie Spence. USA: New York, NY. 1920-1930. Lang.: Eng. 3378

Chlestakov
Performance/production
Mirzoev's production of *Chlestakov*, based on Gogol's *The Inspector General*, Stanislavskij Theatre. Russia: Moscow. 1995. Lang.: Rus. 2211

Chloe Poems Healing Roadshow
Performance/production
Collection of newspaper reviews by London theatre critics. UK-England: London. 1996. Lang.: Eng. 2492

Choču Rebenka (I Want a Baby)
Performance/production
Productions of Tretjakov's *Choču Rebenka (I Want a Baby)*. USSR: Moscow. UK-England: Birmingham. Germany: Berlin. 1927-1993.Lang.: Eng. 2694

Choephoroi (Libation Bearers, The)
Performance/production
Analysis of *Les Atrides* by Ariane Mnouchkine's Théâtre du Soleil. France: Paris. 1992. Lang.: Eng. 2010

Politics and the actor's body in productions by Théâtre du Soleil. France. 1990-1995. Lang.: Eng. 2036

Choi, Joohee
Performance/production
Profiles of new actors on Broadway. USA: New York, NY. 1996. Lang.: Eng. 1012

Choice, The
Performance/production
Collection of newspaper reviews by London theatre critics. UK-England: London. 1996. Lang.: Eng. 2430

Chōji midare (Wavering Traces)
Basic theatrical documents
International anthology of modern drama by women. 1880-1940. Lang.: Eng. 1637

Cid, Le (Cid, The)
Plays/librettos/scripts
Analysis of tragicomedies and tragedies with happy endings. Italy. Spain. France. 1600-1641. Lang.: Ger. 3139

Cider House Rules, The
Performance/production
Stage adaptation of John Irving's *The Cider House Rules*, Seattle Repertory. USA: Seattle, WA. 1996. Lang.: Eng. 2592

Cieplak, Piotr
Performance/production
Piotr Cieplak's production of a sixteenth-century mystery play at Teatr Dramatyczny. Poland: Warsaw. 1994. Lang.: Eng, Fre. 2155

Ciepliński, Jan
Institutions
History of Balet Jana Cieplińskiego. Poland. 1922-1925. Lang.: Pol. 1484

Cieslak, Dirk
Relation to other fields
The crisis of independent theatre. Germany: Berlin. 1996. Lang.: Ger. 1188

Čigiév, Vladimir
Performance/production
Vladimir Čigiév's production of *Hamlet* with Teat'r Junogo Zritelja. Russia: Rostov-na-Donu. 1990-1996. Lang.: Rus. 2213

Cimbelina en 1900 y pico (Cymbeline in 1900 or So)
Plays/librettos/scripts
Analysis of plays by Alfonsina Storni. Argentina. 1892-1938. Lang.: Spa. 2717

Cincinnati Playhouse in the Park (Cincinnati, OH)
Design/technology
Candice Donnelly's costumes for Tennessee Williams' *The Notebook of Trigorin*, Cincinnati Playhouse. USA: Cincinnati, OH. 1996.Lang.: Eng. 1728

Performance/production
Vanessa Redgrave's role in *The Notebook of Trigorin* by Tennessee Williams. USA: Cincinnati, OH. 1996. Lang.: Eng. 2612

Cinderella
Performance/production
Musical theatre performer Evelyn Laye. UK-England. 1918-1996. Lang.: Eng. 3923

Cinderella by Kalmár
SEE
Hamupipőke.

Cine Mexico (Chicago, IL)
SEE
Congress Theatre.

Ciniewicz, Penny
Performance/production
Collection of newspaper reviews by London theatre critics. UK-England: London. 1996. Lang.: Eng. 2418

Cinna
Plays/librettos/scripts
Analysis of tragicomedies and tragedies with happy endings. Italy. Spain. France. 1600-1641. Lang.: Ger. 3139

Cinzio
SEE
Giraldi Cinthio, Giovanbattista.

Cioffi, Frank
Performance/production
Directing at the English Language Theatre of Gdańsk University. Poland: Gdańsk. 1984-1988. Lang.: Eng. 892

Circle in the Square (New York, NY)
Design/technology
Don Holder's lighting design for O'Neill's *Hughie* directed by Al Pacino. USA: New York, NY, New Haven, CT. 1996. Lang.: Eng. 1722
Set and lighting design for *Holiday* in the round at Circle in the Square. USA: New York, NY. 1996. Lang.: Eng. 1746
Institutions
Josephine Abady, the new artistic director of Circle in the Square. USA: New York, NY. 1991-1996. Lang.: Eng. 1861
Performance/production
Collection of newspaper reviews by New York theatre critics. USA: New York, NY, East Haddam, CT. 1996. Lang.: Eng. 2553
Collection of newspaper reviews by New York theatre critics. USA: New York, NY. 1996. Lang.: Eng. 2558
Collection of newspaper reviews by New York theatre critics. USA: New York, NY. 1996. Lang.: Eng. 2569

Collection of newspaper reviews by New York theatre critics. USA: New York, NY, Washington, DC. 1996. Lang.: Eng. 2581

Circle Repertory (New York, NY)
Institutions
Jeff Daniels' experience acting in *Fifth of July* at Circle Rep. USA: New York, NY. 1978-1996. Lang.: Eng. 1864
Performance/production
Collection of newspaper reviews by New York theatre critics. USA: New York, NY. 1996. Lang.: Eng. 2550
Olympia Dukakis' role in *The Hope Zone* by Kevin Heelan at Circle Rep. USA: New York, NY. 1960-1996. Lang.: Eng. 2678

Circle Theatre (Budapest)
SEE
Körszinház.

Circus
SEE ALSO
Classed Entries under MIXED ENTERTAINMENT—Circus.
Design/technology
Technical challenges of international Musical Circus. Japan: Tokyo. 1996. Lang.: Eng. 186
Performance/production
Analysis of *Appetite* by Club Swing, directed by Gail Kelly. Australia: Melbourne. 1996. Lang.: Eng. 689
The influence of painter Marc Chagall on O Vertige and Cirque du Soleil. Canada: Montreal, PQ. 1988-1989. Lang.: Fre. 730

Circus (Montreal, PQ)
Institutions
The work of Dynamo Théâtre, formerly Circus. Canada: Montreal, PQ. 1980-1991. Lang.: Fre. 3749

Circus Minimus
Performance/production
Collection of newspaper reviews by London theatre critics. UK-England: London. 1996. Lang.: Eng. 2426

Cirque du Soleil (Montreal, PQ)
Design/technology
Sound design for Cirque du Soleil's *Quidam*. Canada: Montreal, PQ. 1996. Lang.: Eng. 3746
Performance/production
The influence of painter Marc Chagall on O Vertige and Cirque du Soleil. Canada: Montreal, PQ. 1988-1989. Lang.: Fre. 730
Collection of newspaper reviews by London theatre critics. UK-England: London. 1996. Lang.: Eng. 2307
Cirque du Soleil clown Denis Lacombe on visual comedy. Canada. 1990. Lang.: Fre. 3753
The new concept of circus. Canada: Montreal, PQ. 1980. Lang.: Swe. 3754

Cirque Invisible, Le (Invisible Circus, The)
Performance/production
Collection of newspaper reviews by London theatre critics. UK-England: London. 1996. Lang.: Eng. 2481

Ciskaridze, Nikolaj
Performance/production
Dancer Nikolaj Ciskaridze. Russia: Moscow. 1990-1996. Lang.: Rus. 1522

Cité de la Musique (Paris)
Institutions
The first season of the Cité de la Musique. France: Paris. 1996. Lang.: Eng. 4037

Cité interdite, La (Forbidden City, The)
Plays/librettos/scripts
Analysis of plays by Dominic Champagne. Canada: Montreal, PQ. 1988-1991. Lang.: Fre. 2838

Cittàbapini
Basic theatrical documents
Text of futurist plays by Mina Loy. Italy. 1915. Lang.: Eng. 1668

City Center (New York, NY)
Performance/production
Collection of newspaper reviews by New York theatre critics. USA: New York, NY. 1996. Lang.: Eng. 2571

City Center Theatre (New York, NY)
SEE ALSO
Manhattan Theatre Club.
Performance/production
Collection of newspaper reviews by New York theatre critics. USA: New York, NY. 1996. Lang.: Eng. 2555
Collection of newspaper reviews by New York theatre critics. USA: New York, NY, Houston, TX. 1996. Lang.: Eng. 2567

Comedy — cont'd

Careers of three comedians. Canada. 1973-1996. Lang.: Eng. 3706

Expressions of collective identity in Quebec comic monologues. Canada. 1980-1990. Lang.: Fre. 3727

Cirque du Soleil clown Denis Lacombe on visual comedy. Canada. 1990. Lang.: Fre. 3753

Comparison of American and Canadian comic styles. Canada. USA. 1990. Lang.: Fre. 3832

Plays/librettos/scripts
Humor in French-Canadian theatre. Canada. 1606-1990. Lang.: Fre. 1088

The fool in *commedia dell'arte* and in Jonson's *Every Man in His Humour*. England. Italy. 1465-1601. Lang.: Eng. 1093

Comedy as a weapon against apartheid. South Africa, Republic of. 1980-1990. Lang.: Ita. 1102

Menander's life and works. Ancient Greece. 342-292 B.C. Lang.: Eng. 2710

The structural development of comedy in the Renaissance. Europe. 1590-1664. Lang.: Eng. 2969

Problematics of the absurdist comedies of Eugène Ionesco. France. 1909-1994. Lang.: Rus. 2985

Study of Aristophanes' comedies. Greece. 450-380 B.C. Lang.: Hun. 3059

Secrecy in Italian Renaissance comedy. Italy. 1522-1793. Lang.: Eng. 3115

Analysis of the plays of Sławomir Mrożek. Poland. 1994. Lang.: Pol. 3159

The plays of Sławomir Mrożek in the context of Eastern drama and the theatre of the absurd. Poland. 1994. Lang.: Pol. 3177

Tatar comedy. Tatarstan. 1900-1996. Lang.: Rus. 3278

The influence of Eugene O'Neill on playwright Neil Simon. USA. 1949-1989. Lang.: Eng. 3338

Realism in the high-society comedies of Philip Barry, S.N. Behrman, and Robert Sherwood. USA. 1920-1940. Lang.: Eng. 3382

Reference materials
Lexicon of comedy. North America. Europe. 1990. Lang.: Fre. 1124

Comedy of Errors, The
Performance/production
Collection of newspaper reviews by London theatre critics. UK-England: London. 1996. Lang.: Eng. 2428

Collection of newspaper reviews by London theatre critics. UK-England: London. 1996. Lang.: Eng. 2454

Comedy Theatre (Budapest)
SEE
Vigszinház.

Comedy Theatre (London)
Performance/production
Collection of newspaper reviews by London theatre critics. UK-England: London. 1996. Lang.: Eng. 2347

Collection of newspaper reviews by London theatre critics. UK-England: London. 1996. Lang.: Eng. 2373

Collection of newspaper reviews by London theatre critics. UK-England: London. 1996. Lang.: Eng. 2410

ComedySportz (Milwaukee, WI)
Performance/production
Profiles of groups using improvisational comedy competitions. USA. 1984-1996. Lang.: Eng. 2630

Comic Cuts
Performance/production
Collection of newspaper reviews by London theatre critics. UK-England: London. 1996. Lang.: Eng. 2306

Coming of the Hurricane, The
Performance/production
Collection of newspaper reviews by New York theatre critics. USA. 1996. Lang.: Eng. 2551

Commander Carrigan
Plays/librettos/scripts
Vietnam War protest plays. North America. Europe. 1965-1971. Lang.: Eng. 3153

Commedia dell'arte
SEE ALSO
Classed Entries under MIXED ENTERTAINMENT—*Commedia dell'arte.*
Performance/production
Interview with Suzanne Osten of Unga Klara. Sweden. 1995. Lang.: Eng. 2276

Carol MacVey's production of *The Emperor of the Moon* by Aphra Behn. USA: Iowa City, IA. 1992. Lang.: Eng. 2611
Plays/librettos/scripts
The fool in *commedia dell'arte* and in Jonson's *Every Man in His Humour*. England. Italy. 1465-1601. Lang.: Eng. 1093

Commentaires d'Habacuc, Les (Commentaries of Habakuk)
Performance/production
The fiftieth Avignon Festival. France: Avignon. 1996. Lang.: Eng. 805

Common Weal Productions (Regina, SK)
Audience
Common Weal Productions' community play *A North Side Story or Two*. Canada: Regina, SK. 1993-1995. Lang.: Eng. 1629
Performance/production
The community play *A North Side Story or Two*. Canada: Regina, SK. 1995-1996. Lang.: Eng. 1925

Commotion Theatre Company (London)
Performance/production
Collection of newspaper reviews by London theatre critics. UK-England: London. 1996. Lang.: Eng. 2344

Communicating Doors
Performance/production
The London theatre season—fall. UK-England: London. 1995-1996. Lang.: Eng. 2501

Community relations
Administration
Translator Linda Gaboriau on promoting Quebec drama. Canada: Montreal, PQ, Toronto, ON. 1983-1988. Lang.: Fre. 1613

Crisis on the German opera scene. Germany. 1993-1996. Lang.: Dan. 4009

Community theatre
Administration
Account of a co-production of *Annie* by two community theatres. USA: Winston-Salem, NC. 1995. Lang.: Eng. 3884
Audience
Common Weal Productions' community play *A North Side Story or Two*. Canada: Regina, SK. 1993-1995. Lang.: Eng. 1629
Institutions
Community theatres arising from the reform movement and settlement houses. USA: Chicago, IL, Cleveland, OH, New York, NY. 1896-1930. Lang.: Eng. 570

Profile of Cornerstone Theatre. USA. 1986-1996. Lang.: Eng. 1870
Performance/production
The community play *A North Side Story or Two*. Canada: Regina, SK. 1995-1996. Lang.: Eng. 1925

Stage history of *Black Eyed Susan* by Douglas Jerrold. UK-England. 1829-1994. Lang.: Eng. 2537
Plays/librettos/scripts
The Danish community play tradition. Denmark. 1970-1996. Lang.: Eng. 2873

Profile of community theatre Teatro La Fragua. Honduras: El Progreso. 1979-1996. Lang.: Eng. 3068

Barbara Lebow's community play *Cobb County Stories*. USA: Atlanta, GA. 1996. Lang.: Eng. 3417
Relation to other fields
Non-formal education in Nigerian Theatre for Development. Nigeria. 1972-1996. Lang.: Eng. 1215

The relevance of Theatre for Development to Britain. UK. 1976-1995. Lang.: Eng. 1237

Women, reform, and performance at the Marionette Club. USA: Chicago, IL. 1890-1915. Lang.: Eng. 1260

Drama's role in political liberation after the external oppressor has been removed. South Africa, Republic of. UK-Ireland: Derry.UK-England: Manchester. 1980-1996. Lang.: Eng. 3507
Theory/criticism
The current state of South African theatre historiography and theory. South Africa, Republic of. 1900-1996. Lang.: Eng. 1360

Compagnia dei Giovani (Rome)
Institutions
The Compagnia dei Giovani. Italy. 1954-1973. Lang.: Ita. 490
Performance/production
Actor-director Giorgio De Lullo. Italy: Rome. 1921-1981. Lang.: Ita. 2129

Compagnie Jean-Duceppe (Montreal, PQ)
Performance/production
Production notes for Tremblay's *La Maison suspendue* by Compagnie Jean-Duceppe. Canada: Montreal, PQ. 1990. Lang.: Fre. 1916

Themes and structures of Tremblay's *La Maison suspendue* as directed by Brassard. Canada: Montreal, PQ. 1990. Lang.: Fre. 1966

Costuming — cont'd

Elizabeth Fried's costumes for *Crocodiles in the Potomac* by Wendy Belden. USA: New York, NY. 1996. Lang.: Eng. 1723

Michael Krass's costume design for *Full Gallop* by Mary Louise Wilson and Mark Hampton. USA: New York, NY. 1996. Lang.: Eng. 1727

Candice Donnelly's costumes for Tennessee Williams' *The Notebook of Trigorin*, Cincinnati Playhouse. USA: Cincinnati, OH. 1996.Lang.: Eng. 1728

Set and costume research consultant Peter Dervis. USA: New York, NY. 1996. Lang.: Eng. 1730

Contemporary costuming by designer Jane Greenwood. USA: New York, NY. 1996. Lang.: Eng. 1738

Technical aspects of *The Libertine* directed by Terry Johnson for Steppenwolf. USA: Chicago, IL. 1996. Lang.: Eng. 1740

Career of set and costume designer Felix E. Cochren. USA: New York, NY. 1980-1996. Lang.: Eng. 1742

Design for an opera segment in the film *Così*. Australia. 1996. Lang.: Eng. 3587

Design for film adaptation of Shakespeare's *Richard III* by Shuna Harwood and Tony Burroughs. UK-England: London. 1991-1996. Lang.: Eng. 3593

Obituary for movie costumer Dorothy Jeakins. USA: Santa Barbara, CA. 1995. Lang.: Eng. 3594

Obituary for costume designer Richard Hornung. USA: Los Angeles, CA. 1995. Lang.: Eng. 3596

Michael Clancy's costume designs for Nigel Finch's film *Stonewall*. USA: New York, NY. 1996. Lang.: Eng. 3597

Susan Bertram's costume design for the film *Grace of My Heart*. USA: New York, NY. 1996. Lang.: Eng. 3598

Production design for Baz Luhrmann's film *Romeo and Juliet*. USA: Miami, FL. 1996. Lang.: Eng. 3601

Interview with costume designer Søren Breum. Denmark. 1995-1996. Lang.: Dan. 3662

Transport problems of Zingaro, an equestrian theatre group. USA: New York, NY. France. 1996. Lang.: Eng. 3699

Costume design for drag artist Varla Jean Merman by Philip Heckman. USA: New York, NY. 1996. Lang.: Eng. 3726

David Belugou's costumes for the Big Apple Circus. USA: New York, NY. 1996. Lang.: Eng. 3748

Design for Gozzi's *The Green Bird (L'augellino belverde)* at the New Victory Theatre. USA: New York, NY. 1996. Lang.: Eng. 3760

Scene designer Brian Thomson. Australia. USA: New York, NY. 1971-1996. Lang.: Eng. 3885

Technical aspects of a German-language production of Disney's *Beauty and the Beast*. Austria: Vienna. 1995. Lang.: Ger. 3888

Alison Darke's production design for *Pendragon* by the National Youth Music Theatre of Great Britain. UK-England. USA: New York,NY. 1995. Lang.: Eng. 3892

Costume designer Alvin Colt. USA: New York, NY. 1944-1996. Lang.: Eng. 3897

Design for the musical *Big*. USA: Detroit, MI. 1996. Lang.: Eng. 3902

Set and costume design for *Shlemiel the First*, ART/American Music Theatre Festival. USA: Cambridge, MA, Philadelphia, PA. 1996.Lang.: Eng. 3903

Design for *Der Fliegende Holländer*, Canadian Opera Company, by Allen Moyer. Canada: Toronto, ON. 1996. Lang.: Eng. 4014

Hubert Monloup's set and costume designs for *Andrea Chénier*, Metropolitan Opera. USA: New York, NY. 1996. Lang.: Eng. 4026

Joyce L. Fritz's design of puppets and costumes for *A Connecticut Yankee in King Arthur's Court*, Connecticut Repertory Theatre.USA: Storrs, CT. 1996. Lang.: Eng. 4369

Institutions

Theatre-related disciplines at the Hochschule für Bildende Künste. Germany: Dresden. 1996. Lang.: Swe. 433

Performance/production

Symbolism and style in Chinese opera. China. 221 B.C.-1990 A.D. Lang.: Fre. 3878

Performance and technical aspects of Orff's *Carmina Burana* at the Bavarian State Opera. Germany. 1996. Lang.: Eng. 4143

Reference materials

Primary sources in English on European Naturalist and Symbolist theatre. Europe. 1850-1918. Lang.: Eng. 1120

Côté, Jean-Claude

Plays/librettos/scripts

The recent proliferation of Don Juan adaptations. Canada: Montreal, PQ. Austria. 1625-1991. Lang.: Fre. 2782

Côté, Lorraine

Performance/production

Actress Lorraine Côté. Canada: Quebec, PQ. 1978-1989. Lang.: Fre. 1926

Côté, Michel

Plays/librettos/scripts

Analysis of *Broue (Scum)* by Marc Messier, Michel Côté, and Marcel Gauthier. Canada. 1979-1992. Lang.: Fre. 2808

Cotter, Joseph Seamon, Jr.

Basic theatrical documents

Anthology of unknown plays of the Harlem Renaissance. USA: New York, NY. 1920-1940. Lang.: Eng. 1694

Cottesloe Theatre (London)

SEE ALSO

National Theatre (London).

Performance/production

Collection of newspaper reviews by London theatre critics. UK-England: London. 1996. Lang.: Eng. 2327

Collection of newspaper reviews by London theatre critics. UK-England: London. 1996. Lang.: Eng. 2338

Collection of newspaper reviews by London theatre critics. UK-England: London. 1996. Lang.: Eng. 2342

Collection of newspaper reviews by London theatre critics. UK-England: London. 1996. Lang.: Eng. 2376

Collection of newspaper reviews by London theatre critics. UK-England: London. 1996. Lang.: Eng. 2379

Collection of newspaper reviews by London theatre critics. UK-England: London. 1996. Lang.: Eng. 2396

Collection of newspaper reviews by London theatre critics. UK-England: London. 1996. Lang.: Eng. 2443

Collection of newspaper reviews by London theatre critics. UK-England: London. 1996. Lang.: Eng. 2479

Two productions of *The Designated Mourner* by Wallace Shawn. UK-England: London. Germany: Hamburg. 1996. Lang.: Ger. 2504

Cottis, David

Performance/production

Collection of newspaper reviews by London theatre critics. UK-England: London. UK-Scotland: Edinburgh. 1996. Lang.: Eng. 2313

Collection of newspaper reviews by London theatre critics. UK-England: London. 1996. Lang.: Eng. 2407

Collection of newspaper reviews by London theatre critics. UK-England: London. 1996. Lang.: Eng. 2473

Cottrell, Richard

Performance/production

Collection of newspaper reviews by London theatre critics. UK-England: London. 1996. Lang.: Eng. 2422

Coulter, John

Performance/production

Postcolonial drama in theory and performance. 1880-1950. Lang.: Eng. 1893

Plays/librettos/scripts

Plays about Louis Riel. Canada. 1886-1986. Lang.: Fre. 2792

Council of Stock Theatres (COST, New York, NY)

Administration

Details of Council of Stock Theatres' new three-year agreement. USA: New York, NY. 1996. Lang.: Eng. 80

Theatres withdraw from Council of Stock Theatres collective bargaining unit. USA. 1996. Lang.: Eng. 81

Country Wife, The

Plays/librettos/scripts

Metaphor in *The Country Wife* by William Wycherley. England. 1675. Lang.: Eng. 2911

Coupat, Françoise

Plays/librettos/scripts

The methods and objectives of theatrical adaptation. France. 1980-1989. Lang.: Fre. 3005

Course, The

Performance/production

Collection of newspaper reviews by London theatre critics. UK-England: London. 1996. Lang.: Eng. 2427

Court entertainment

SEE ALSO

Classed Entries under MIXED ENTERTAINMENT—Court entertainment.

Performance/production

References to performers and entertainment in medieval Scandinavian literature. Norway. Sweden. Iceland. 793-1400. Lang.: Eng. 888

Crowley, Mart — cont'd

The revival of Mart Crowley's *The Boys in the Band*. USA: New York, NY. 1960-1996. Lang.: Eng. 3368

Interview with playwright Mart Crowley. USA: New York, NY. 1996. Lang.: Eng. 3424

Croydon Warehouse (London)
Performance/production
Collection of newspaper reviews by London theatre critics. UK-England: London. 1996. Lang.: Eng. 2331

Collection of newspaper reviews by London theatre critics. UK-England: London. 1996. Lang.: Eng. 2351

Collection of newspaper reviews by London theatre critics. UK-England: London. 1996. Lang.: Eng. 2372

Collection of newspaper reviews by London theatre critics. UK-England: London. 1996. Lang.: Eng. 2382

Collection of newspaper reviews by London theatre critics. UK-England: London. 1996. Lang.: Eng. 2397

Collection of newspaper reviews by London theatre critics. UK-England: London. 1996. Lang.: Eng. 2409

Collection of newspaper reviews by London theatre critics. UK-England: London. 1996. Lang.: Eng. 2420

Collection of newspaper reviews by London theatre critics. UK-England: London. 1996. Lang.: Eng. 2439

Collection of newspaper reviews by London theatre critics. UK-England: London. 1996. Lang.: Eng. 2448

Collection of newspaper reviews by London theatre critics. UK-England: London. 1996. Lang.: Eng. 2470

Collection of newspaper reviews by London theatre critics. UK-England: London. 1996. Lang.: Eng. 2487

Crozier, Eric
Performance/production
Britten's *Peter Grimes*: productions by Eric Crozier and Harald André. UK-England. Sweden: Stockholm. 1945-1980. Lang.: Swe. 4229
Plays/librettos/scripts
Glossary for Benjamin Britten's *Albert Herring* intended for American singers. UK-England. 1947-1996. Lang.: Eng. 4342

Crucible, The
Performance/production
Suzanne Burgoyne's experiments in intercultural performance. Belgium: Brussels. USA: Omaha, NE. 1986-1987. Lang.: Eng. 1911

Intercultural theatre exchange at the American University in Bulgaria. Bulgaria: Blagoevgrad. 1993. Lang.: Eng. 1915
Plays/librettos/scripts
Comparison of historical dramas by Robert Bolt and Arthur Miller. USA. UK-England. 1953-1966. Lang.: Eng. 3413

Daniel Day-Lewis' role in Nicholas Hytner's film version of *The Crucible* by Arthur Miller. USA. 1996. Lang.: Fre. 3648

Crutcher, Julie
Basic theatrical documents
Collection of southern plays from Actors' Theatre of Louisville. USA. 1984-1992. Lang.: Eng. 1688

Cruz González, José
Institutions
Chicano theatre groups. USA: Los Angeles, CA. 1986-1996. Lang.: Eng. 1880

Cruz, Nilo
Design/technology
Peggy Eisenhauer's lighting design for *Dancing on Her Knees*, Public Theatre. USA: New York, NY. 1996. Lang.: Eng. 1718

Scene designer Robert Brill. USA: New York, NY. 1996. Lang.: Eng. 1724
Performance/production
Collection of newspaper reviews by New York theatre critics. USA: New York, NY. 1996. Lang.: Eng. 2568

Cry Freedom
Performance/production
Political changes reflected in recent South African films. South Africa, Republic of. 1987-1996. Lang.: Eng. 3625

Cry, the Beloved Country
Performance/production
Political changes reflected in recent South African films. South Africa, Republic of. 1987-1996. Lang.: Eng. 3625

Cryptogram, The
Plays/librettos/scripts
Analysis of *Oleanna* and *The Cryptogram* by David Mamet. USA. 1975-1996. Lang.: Eng. 3401

Crystal Quilt, The
Performance/production
Analysis of Suzanne Lacy's *The Crystal Quilt*. USA: Minneapolis, MN. 1984-1987. Lang.: Eng. 3798

Csányi, János
Performance/production
Review of Irvine Welsh's *Trainspotting* directed by János Csányi. Hungary: Budapest. 1995. Lang.: Hun. 840

CSC Repertory (New York, NY)
Design/technology
Scenic designer Narelle Sissons. USA: New York, NY. 1996. Lang.: Eng. 250
Performance/production
Collection of newspaper reviews by New York theatre critics. USA: New York, NY. 1996. Lang.: Eng. 2560

Collection of newspaper reviews by New York theatre critics. USA: New York, NY. 1996. Lang.: Eng. 2571

Cserhalmi, György
Performance/production
Interview with actor György Cserhalmi. Hungary. 1957-1996. Lang.: Hun. 2096

Csikós, Attila
Design/technology
Budapest Opera's stage designer Attila Csikós. Hungary: Budapest. 1969-1996. Lang.: Hun. 4021

Csiky Gergely Színház (Timişoara)
Institutions
History of Hungarian ethnic theatre in Romania. Hungary. Romania. 1919-1992. Lang.: Hun. 473
Performance/production
Survey of ethnic Hungarian theatre in neighboring countries. Romania. Slovakia: Kosiče. Ukraine: Beregovo. 1995-1996. Lang.: Hun. 897

Csiky, András
Performance/production
Interview with actor András Csiky. Hungary. Romania: Cluj-Napoca. 1953-1996. Lang.: Hun. 2094

Csiky, Gergely
Performance/production
Budapest productions of the millicentenary season. Hungary: Budapest. 1995-1996. Lang.: Eng. 2104

Csizmadia, Tibor
Performance/production
English plays and subjects on the Hungarian stage. Hungary. 1995-1996. Lang.: Eng. 847

Csodálatos mandarin, A (Miraculous Mandarin, The)
Performance/production
Interview with dancer Ferenc Havas. Hungary. 1935-1995. Lang.: Hun. 1509

Csomós, Mari
Performance/production
Recipients of the annual theatre critics' awards. Hungary. 1995-1996. Lang.: Hun. 846

Csurka, István
Plays/librettos/scripts
Postwar Hungarian drama. Hungary. 1945-1989. Lang.: Hun. 3069

Čubarova, Alena
Performance/production
Actress Alena Čubarova on work in Erotičéskij Teat'r. Russia: Moscow. 1996. Lang.: Rus. 903

Cud na Greenpoincie (Greenpoint Miracle, A)
Plays/librettos/scripts
Analysis of new plays by Edward Redliński and Maciej Wojtyszko. Poland. 1996. Lang.: Eng, Fre. 3173

Cukor, George
Performance/production
Analysis of film and video versions of *Romeo and Juliet*. USA. UK-England. Italy. 1936-1978. Lang.: Eng. 3631

Cul sec (Dry Ass)
Plays/librettos/scripts
Playwright François Archambault discusses his craft. Canada: Montreal, PQ. 1992-1996. Lang.: Fre. 2741

Harsh realism in contemporary Quebec plays. Canada: Montreal, PQ. 1993-1995. Lang.: Fre. 2784

Culbert, John
Design/technology
Exhibitors at the USITT design exhibition on scenery, lighting, and costuming. USA. 1996. Lang.: Eng. 335

Culebras, Joaquín
Plays/librettos/scripts
Analysis of plays by Joaquín Culebras. Uruguay. 1831. Lang.: Eng. 3319

Dancing — cont'd

Dance partners Edit Rujsz and Miklós Nagyszentpéteri of the Budapest Opera ballet company. Hungary. 1994-1995. Lang.: Hun. 4162

Puppets, Human Movement, and dance in Philippe Genty's *Voyageur Immobile (Motionless Traveler)*. USA: Chicago, IL. France: Paris. 1961-1965. Lang.: Eng. 4415

Relation to other fields
Rhythm as a form of social discourse. USA. 1994. Lang.: Eng. 1275

Theory/criticism
Essay on theatre and simulation. Europe. 1000-1996. Lang.: Ger. 1340

Gender constructions and dance and movement education. South Africa, Republic of. 1995. Lang.: Eng. 1361

The origins and evolution of physical theatre. UK-England. Germany. 1900-1996. Lang.: Eng. 1368

The concept of dance as a universal language. 1996. Lang.: Ger. 1464

Dance criticism of Birgit Cullberg. Sweden. UK-England. France. 1946-1953. Lang.: Swe. 1467

Gender construction in ritual performance of *dangdut*. Indonesia: Java. 1995. Lang.: Eng. 3876

Training
Etienne Decroux's theory of corporeal mime. France: Paris. 1918-1996. Lang.: Eng. 3688

Dancing Attendance
Performance/production
Collection of newspaper reviews by London theatre critics. UK-England: London. 1996. Lang.: Eng. 2305

Dancing Master, The
Performance/production
Collection of newspaper reviews by London theatre critics. UK-England: London. 1996. Lang.: Eng. 2474

Dancing on Her Knees
Design/technology
Peggy Eisenhauer's lighting design for *Dancing on Her Knees*, Public Theatre. USA: New York, NY. 1996. Lang.: Eng. 1718

Performance/production
Collection of newspaper reviews by New York theatre critics. USA: New York, NY. 1996. Lang.: Eng. 2568

Dandeneau, Jacqueline
Performance/production
Collection of newspaper reviews by London theatre critics. UK-England: London. 1996. Lang.: Eng. 2453

Dangdut
Performance/production
Articles on Indonesian performing arts. Indonesia. 1995. Lang.: Eng. 853

Theory/criticism
Gender construction in ritual performance of *dangdut*. Indonesia: Java. 1995. Lang.: Eng. 3876

Dangerous Play
Performance/production
Collection of newspaper reviews by London theatre critics. UK-England: London. 1996. Lang.: Eng. 2426

Daniele, Graciela
Design/technology
Peggy Eisenhauer's lighting design for *Dancing on Her Knees*, Public Theatre. USA: New York, NY. 1996. Lang.: Eng. 1718

Performance/production
Graciela Daniele's dance adaptation of *Chronicle of a Death Foretold* by Gabriel García Márquez. USA: New York, NY. 1981-1996. Lang.: Eng. 1446

Collection of newspaper reviews by New York theatre critics. USA: New York, NY. 1996. Lang.: Eng. 2568

Daniels, David
Performance/production
Countenor David Daniels. USA. 1966-1996. Lang.: Eng. 4292

Daniels, Jeff
Institutions
Jeff Daniels' experience acting in *Fifth of July* at Circle Rep. USA: New York, NY. 1978-1996. Lang.: Eng. 1864

Theatre companies devoted to new plays: BoarsHead and Purple Rose. USA: Chelsea, MI. 1966-1996. Lang.: Eng. 1869

Daniels, Ron
Performance/production
Collection of newspaper reviews by London theatre critics. UK-England: London. 1996. Lang.: Eng. 2316

Collection of newspaper reviews by London theatre critics. UK-England: London. 1996. Lang.: Eng. 2379

Plays/librettos/scripts
Naomi Wallace's *Slaughter City* at American Rep. USA: Cambridge, MA. 1996. Lang.: Eng. 3374

Daniels, Sarah
Plays/librettos/scripts
Violence and power in plays of Sarah Daniels and William Mastrosimone. UK-England. USA. 1991-1995. Lang.: Eng. 3286

Daniels, Shelley
Performance/production
Puppets and 3-D animation in Disney's *James and the Giant Peach*. USA: Hollywood, CA. 1993-1995. Lang.: Eng. 4406

Danielsson, Ronny
Institutions
Ronny Danielsson, the new manager of Göteborgs Stadsteater. Sweden: Gothenburg. 1996. Lang.: Swe. 540

Danilov, Michajl
Performance/production
Actor Michajl Danilov. Russia: St. Petersburg. 1973-1995. Lang.: Rus. 2253

Danis, Daniel
Plays/librettos/scripts
Analysis of plays by Daniel Danis. Canada: Montreal, PQ. 1993. Lang.: Fre. 2805

Danis, Louison
Plays/librettos/scripts
Round-table discussion of Quebec translators. Canada. 1980-1990. Lang.: Fre. 2769

Dans la solitude des champs de coton (In the Solitude of the Cotton Fields)
Performance/production
Interview with director Patrice Chéreau. France. 1996. Lang.: Eng. 2013

Patrice Chéreau's productions of plays by Bernard-Marie Koltès. France. 1964-1996. Lang.: Dan. 2039

Collection of newspaper reviews by New York theatre critics. USA: New York, NY. 1996. Lang.: Eng. 2571

Interview with director Patrice Chéreau. USA. 1983-1996. Lang.: Eng. 2649

Dansereau, Luc
Performance/production
Mécanique Générale's *Méchant Motel (Mean Motel)* directed by Luc Dansereau. Canada: Montreal, PQ. 1992. Lang.: Fre. 710

Dansmuseet (Stockholm)
Administration
Bengt Häger's career in dance production, training, and research. Sweden: Stockholm. 1916. Lang.: Swe. 1402

Dantons Tod (Danton's Death)
Plays/librettos/scripts
Metonymy and drama. North America. Europe. 1600-1996. Lang.: Eng. 3154

Performance/production
The portrayal of female characters in Büchner's *Dantons Tod (Danton's Death)*. Germany. 1902-1994. Lang.: Eng. 2053

Daphne's Vase
Performance/production
Collection of newspaper reviews by London theatre critics. UK-England: London. 1996. Lang.: Eng. 2309

Darden, Norma Jean
Administration
Equity observance of African-American Heritage Month. USA: New York, NY. 1996. Lang.: Eng. 59

Dark Fruit
Theory/criticism
Identity and representation in *Dark Fruit* by Pomo Afro Homos. USA: San Francisco, CA. 1990-1996. Lang.: Eng. 1387

Dark Rapture
Performance/production
Collection of newspaper reviews by New York theatre critics. USA: New York, NY, Washington, DC. 1996. Lang.: Eng. 2581

Dark Tales
Performance/production
Collection of newspaper reviews by London theatre critics. UK-England: London. 1996. Lang.: Eng. 2497

Darke, Alison
Design/technology
Alison Darke's production design for *Pendragon* by the National Youth Music Theatre of Great Britain. UK-England. USA: New York,NY. 1995. Lang.: Eng. 3892

Darke, Nick
Performance/production
Collection of newspaper reviews by London theatre critics. UK-England: London. 1996. Lang.: Eng. 2328

Decker, Willy
Design/technology
Technical problems of producing *Die Soldaten* at Semper Oper.
Germany: Dresden. 1995-1996. Lang.: Ger. 4016

Déclic du destin, Le (Ticking of Destiny, The)
Plays/librettos/scripts
Playwright Larry Tremblay discusses his work. Canada: Montreal, PQ.
1981-1996. Lang.: Fre. 2835

Decodex
Institutions
Account of Dancin' City '96 festival. Denmark: Copenhagen. 1996.
Lang.: Dan. 1406

Deconstruction
Performance/production
Gender construction and two performances of *Orlando*. France: Paris.
Switzerland: Lausanne. Germany: Berlin. 1990-1996. Lang.: Ger. 2020

A feminist student production of Shakespeare's *The Taming of the
Shrew*. UK-England: Liverpool. 1992. Lang.: Eng. 2539

Review of the installation *Self-Storage* by Laurie Anderson, Bruce Eno,
and others. UK-England: London. 1995. Lang.: Eng. 3656

Theory/criticism
Introduction to an *ET* issue devoted to post-colonial Shakespearean
criticism. Canada. 1878-1996. Lang.: Eng. 3534

The designation of live art events as essentially 'real'. UK-England.
1978-1994. Lang.: Eng. 3825

Decouflé, Philippe
Institutions
Account of Dancin' City '96 festival. Denmark: Copenhagen. 1996.
Lang.: Dan. 1406

Decroux, Etienne
Performance/production
Theories of acting and performance. Latin America. 1910-1995. Lang.:
Spa. 879

Training
Etienne Decroux's theory of corporeal mime. France: Paris. 1918-1996.
Lang.: Eng. 3688

Mejerchol'd's theory of biomechanics and its application to training and
performance. Russia. 1896-1996. Lang.: Eng. 3689

Dédalo en el vientre de la bestia (In the Belly of the Beast)
Plays/librettos/scripts
Poststructuralism in Latin American plays. Latin America. 1985-1995.
Lang.: Spa. 3141

Dedeaux, Dawn
Performance/production
Analysis of the work of video artists. USA. 1996. Lang.: Eng. 3679

Dedecius, Karl
Performance/production
The premiere of the first German translation of Wyspiański's *Wesele
(The Wedding)*. Austria: Salzburg. 1992. Lang.: Eng, Fre. 1904

Defending the Caveman
Performance/production
Rob Becker and his solo performance *Defending the Caveman*. USA:
New York, NY. 1996. Lang.: Eng. 2640

Definitely Doris
Performance/production
Collection of newspaper reviews by London theatre critics. UK-England:
London. 1996. Lang.: Eng. 2368

Degraded
Performance/production
Description of the video performance *Degraded* by students of Bristol
University. UK-England: Bristol. 1980-1995. Lang.: Eng. 3674

deGroot, John
Performance/production
Len Cariou's role in *Papa* directed by John Henry Davis. USA: New
York, NY. 1996. Lang.: Eng. 2620

Deirdre
Institutions
Profile of Irish women's nationalist group Inghinidhe na h'Eireann.
Ireland: Dublin. 1900-1902. Lang.: Eng. 1814
Performance/production
Lyric soprano Lilian Sukis. Canada. 1939-1991. Lang.: Eng. 4085

Deirdre of the Sorrows
Plays/librettos/scripts
Analysis of the unfinished *Deirdre of the Sorrows* by John Millington
Synge. Ireland. 1909. Lang.: Eng. 3079

Deirdre's Cause
Institutions
The 1995 Saskatoon Fringe Festival. Canada: Saskatoon, SK. 1995.
Lang.: Eng. 1768

Dejmek, Kazimierz
Institutions
The work of directors Osterwa, Horzyca, and Dejmek at Teatr
Narodowy. Poland: Warsaw. 1923-1996. Lang.: Eng, Fre. 1821
Performance/production
Production history of *Dziady (Forefathers' Eve)* by Adam Mickiewicz.
Poland. 1901-1996. Lang.: Eng, Fre. 2148
Relation to other fields
Theatre artists of the Communist period. Poland. 1924. Lang.: Pol. 1219

Dekker, Keso
Design/technology
Set designer Keso Dekker's work with choreographer Hans von Manen.
Netherlands. 1946-1996. Lang.: Ger. 1403

Dekker, Thomas
Plays/librettos/scripts
The influence of *Romeo and Juliet* on later English comedies. England.
1594-1607. Lang.: Eng. 2883

Del Valle-Inclán, Ramón
SEE
Valle-Inclán, Ramón María del.

Delacorte Theatre (New York, NY)
Design/technology
Paul Gallo's lighting design for *The Tempest* directed by George C.
Wolfe. USA: New York, NY. 1996. Lang.: Eng. 1737
Performance/production
Collection of newspaper reviews by New York theatre critics. USA:
New York, NY, Cambridge, MA. 1996. Lang.: Eng. 2583

Delbée, Anne
Performance/production
Interview with director Anne Delbée. France: Avignon. 1996. Lang.:
Eng. 799

Review of recent Paris productions. France: Paris. 1996. Lang.: Ger.
2033

Delholm, Kirsten
Performance/production
Review of *Monkey Business Class* by Hotel Pro Forma. Denmark:
Copenhagen. 1996. Lang.: Dan. 3711

Delibes, Léo
Plays/librettos/scripts
A possible source for Delibes' opera *Lakmé*. France. 1884-1896. Lang.:
Eng. 4315

Delić, Džemila
Performance/production
Refugee performers Savić and Džemila Delić. Bosnia: Sarajevo. 1992-
1995. Lang.: Eng. 697

Delić, Savić
Performance/production
Refugee performers Savić and Džemila Delić. Bosnia: Sarajevo. 1992-
1995. Lang.: Eng. 697

Delicate Balance, A
Design/technology
Contemporary costuming by designer Jane Greenwood. USA: New
York, NY. 1996. Lang.: Eng. 1738
Performance/production
Collection of newspaper reviews by New York theatre critics. USA:
New York, NY. 1996. Lang.: Eng. 2578

Actress Rosemary Harris. USA: New York, NY. 1958-1996. Lang.: Eng.
2599

Actor George Grizzard. USA: New York, NY. 1952-1996. Lang.: Eng.
2600
Plays/librettos/scripts
Interview with playwright Edward Albee. USA: New York, NY. 1996.
Lang.: Eng. 3430

Delsarte, François
Training
Etienne Decroux's theory of corporeal mime. France: Paris. 1918-1996.
Lang.: Eng. 3688

Delteil, Joseph
Plays/librettos/scripts
Representations of Saint Francis in plays of Leclerc, Bobin, and Delteil.
Canada: Montreal, PQ. 1996. Lang.: Fre. 2809

Demidov, Aleksand'r
Performance/production
Actress Alena Čubarova on work in Erotičeskij Teat'r. Russia: Moscow.
1996. Lang.: Rus. 903

Demidova, Alla S.
Performance/production
Actress Alla Demidova of Taganka Theatre. Russia: Moscow. 1960-
1996. Lang.: Rus. 2230

Directing — cont'd

Interview with Russian directors. Russia. 1990-1996. Lang.: Rus. 925

Interview with director Jasenko Selimović. Sweden: Stockholm. Bosnia and Herzegovina: Sarajevo. 1993. Lang.: Swe. 948

The creative and the interpretive in theatre. UK-England. 1996. Lang.: Eng. 984

The roles of actor and director in television as compared to the stage. UK-England. 1995-1996. Lang.: Eng. 989

Report on Mejerchol'd symposium. UK-Wales: Aberystwyth. 1995. Lang.: Eng. 1000

Opera and stage director Marcus Stern. USA: New York, NY. 1996. Lang.: Eng. 1039

Actress and director Antoinette Perry. USA: New York, NY. 1889-1996. Lang.: Eng. 1073

Comparison of frozen stage images with photography. Canada: Montreal, PQ. 1989. Lang.: Fre. 1417

Graciela Daniele's dance adaptation of *Chronicle of a Death Foretold* by Gabriel García Márquez. USA: New York, NY. 1981-1996. Lang.: Eng. 1446

Press conference with dancer and choreographer Pina Bausch. Germany: Wuppertal. 1995. Lang.: Eng. 1576

Gender, character, and direction. 1996. Lang.: Ger. 1895

Antonin Artaud's work as actor, director, and theorist. 1886-1948. Lang.: Ita. 1896

Two productions of *Déryné ifjasszony (Mrs. Déry)* by Ferenc Herczeg. Austria-Hungary. Hungary: Budapest. 1907-1928.Lang.: Hun. 1908

Suzanne Burgoyne's experiments in intercultural performance. Belgium: Brussels. USA: Omaha, NE. 1986-1987. Lang.: Eng. 1911

Directors Martine Beaulne and Lorraine Pintal. Canada: Montreal, PQ. 1996. Lang.: Eng. 1917

Scenography of Beckett's *Waiting for Godot* directed by André Brassard, TNM. Canada: Montreal, PQ. 1992. Lang.: Fre. 1937

Interview with director René Richard Cyr. Canada: Montreal, PQ. 1980-1990. Lang.: Fre. 1945

Difficulties of staging plays of Marivaux in Quebec. Canada. 1996. Lang.: Fre. 1951

Gabriel Garran's Paris productions of plays by Quebec authors. Canada. France: Paris. 1975-1990. Lang.: Fre. 1959

Interview with Jacques Lessard of Théâtre Repère. Canada: Quebec, PQ. 1968-1989. Lang.: Fre. 1960

René Richard Cyr's production of Molière's *L'Ecole des Femmes (The School for Wives)*. Canada: Montreal, PQ. 1990. Lang.: Fre. 1961

Interview with director André Brassard. Canada: Montreal, PQ. 1992. Lang.: Fre. 1963

Themes and structures of Tremblay's *La Maison suspendue* as directed by Brassard. Canada: Montreal, PQ. 1990. Lang.: Fre. 1966

Individualism and sexuality as traits of the Quebecois directing approach. Canada: Montreal, PQ. 1993-1996. Lang.: Fre. 1967

Interview with director Mati Unt of Tallinn Drama Theatre. Estonia. 1996. Lang.: Rus. 1997

Director Laura Jäntti. Finland: Turku. 1995. Lang.: Eng. 2005

Analysis of *Gibiers du Temps (Spoils of Time)* by Didier-Georges Gabily. France: Gennevilliers. 1996. Lang.: Hun. 2008

Productions of Molière and Shakespeare directed by Daniel Mesguich. France: Lille. 1996. Lang.: Eng. 2014

Interview with director Ariane Mnouchkine. France: Paris. 1988. Lang.: Fre. 2017

Jean Genet's staging and acting indications. France. 1950-1996. Lang.: Fre. 2021

Interview with director Ewa Lewinson. France. 1995. Lang.: Eng. 2026

Ariane Mnouchkine's production of Molière's *Tartuffe*. France. 1995. Lang.: Eng. 2030

Interview with director/playwright Ariane Mnouchkine. France. 1995. Lang.: Eng. 2035

Interview with director Stéphane Braunschweig. France. 1980-1992. Lang.: Fre. 2038

Director Robert Sturua. Georgia. 1980-1996. Lang.: Rus. 2040

Andrea Breth's production of Ibsen's *Hedda Gabler*. Germany: Berlin. 1995. Lang.: Eng. 2044

Karin Beier's productions of *A Midsummer Night's Dream* and *Les Chaises (The Chairs)*. Germany: Düsseldorf. 1995. Lang.: Eng. 2045

Obituary for director Ruth Berghaus. Germany. 1928-1996. Lang.: Ger. 2047

Konstanze Lauterbach's production of *Der aufhaltsame Aufstieg des Arturo Ui (The Resistible Rise of Arturo Ui)* by Bertolt Brecht. Germany: Klagenfurt. 1995. Lang.: Eng. 2048

The portrayal of female characters in Büchner's *Dantons Tod (Danton's Death)*. Germany. 1902-1994. Lang.: Eng. 2053

Interview with director Oliver Reese. Germany: Berlin. 1995. Lang.: Eng. 2057

Portrait of Sven-Eric Bechtolf, actor and director at Thalia Theater. Germany: Hamburg. 1957-1996. Lang.: Ger. 2060

Director Jurij Ljubimov on his work in Berlin. Germany: Berlin. 1988. Lang.: Rus. 2070

Director Karin Beier. Germany: Düsseldorf. 1990-1996. Lang.: Ger. 2073

Heiner Müller—his commemoration by Berliner Ensemble, his East German productions. Germany: Berlin. 1996. Lang.: Ger. 2076

Interview with directors Andrea Breth and Phyllida Lloyd. Germany: Berlin. UK-England: London. 1995. Lang.: Eng. 2082

Photographs of Peter Stein's work at Schaubühne. Germany: Berlin. 1969-1996. Lang.: Ger. 2084

Andrea Breth's production of *The Seagull* and its marketing. Germany: Berlin. 1996. Lang.: Ger. 2086

Pierre Tabard's production of *Találkozás (The Encounter)* by Péter Nádas and László Vidovszky. Hungary. France: Paris. 1996. Lang.: Hun. 2093

Profile of Miklós Tompa, founder of Székely Színház. Hungary. Romania. 1910-1996. Lang.: Hun. 2095

Hungarian productions by Romanian director Beatrice Bleont. Hungary: Zsámbék. Romania. 1996. Lang.: Hun. 2112

Interview with Rina Yerushalmi of Itim. Israel. 1988-1993. Lang.: Eng. 2118

Production of *Jud Süss (The Jew Suess)* at BeerSheba Municipal Theatre. Israel: Beersheba. 1931-1996. Lang.: Eng. 2119

Interview with Graziella Martinoli of La Pinguicola Sulle Vigne. Italy: Genoa. 1995. Lang.: Eng. 2123

Strehler's direction of *La Grande Magia (Grand Magic)* by Eduardo De Filippo. Italy: Milan. 1947-1991. Lang.: Fre. 2124

Actor-director Giorgio De Lullo. Italy: Rome. 1921-1981. Lang.: Ita. 2129

Director Giorgio Strehler. Italy: Milan. 1947-1991. Lang.: Fre. 2132

Interview with director Eimuntas Nekrošius. Lithuania. 1996. Lang.: Ger. 2137

Director Anthony Akerman's diary of a production of *The Road to Mecca* by Athol Fugard. Mexico: Mexico City. 1995. Lang.: Eng. 2140

Directors Edith Roger and Catrine Telle. Norway: Oslo. 1995. Lang.: Eng. 2143

Director Konrad Swinarski. Poland. 1929-1975. Lang.: Eng, Fre. 2150

Director Krystian Lupa. Poland: Cracow. 1996. Lang.: Ger. 2157

Director Konrad Swinarski and his place in Polish theatre. Poland. 1975-1995. Lang.: Eng, Fre. 2159

Interview with actor and director Jerzy Stuhr. Poland: Cracow. 1995. Lang.: Eng, Fre. 2176

Interview with director Aleksand'r Galibin. Russia: St. Petersburg. 1996. Lang.: Rus. 2187

The new generation of Russian directors. Russia: Moscow. 1996. Lang.: Ger. 2196

Vitalij Lanskoj of Stanislavkij Theatre. Russia: Moscow. 1996. Lang.: Rus. 2202

Director Michajl Levitin of Teat'r Ermitaž. Russia: Moscow. 1980-1996. Lang.: Rus. 2206

Memories of director Aleksand'r Sanin. Russia. 1869-1956. Lang.: Rus. 2208

Interview with director Mark Rozovskij. Russia: Moscow. 1996. Lang.: Rus. 2218

Italian translation of Stanislavskij's notes on directing *Diadia Vania (Uncle Vania)*. Russia. 1899. Lang.: Ita. 2251

The work of Boris L'vov-Anochin, director of Novyj Teat'r. Russia: Moscow. 1990-1996. Lang.: Rus. 2257

Enikő Eszenyi's production of Shakespeare's *As You Like It* at Slovenske Narodni Divadlo. Slovakia: Bratislava. 1996. Lang.:Hun. 2261

Directing — cont'd

Plays/librettos/scripts

Directing — cont'd

The life and career of the late playwright/director Heiner Müller. Germany: Berlin. USA. 1929-1996. Lang.: Eng. 3025

Portrait of playwright and director Heiner Müller. Germany. 1929-1996. Lang.: Ger. 3034

Memories of working with Heiner Müller. Germany. Lang.: Ger. 3039

Shakespeare's influence on Brecht reevaluated. Germany. 1917-1985. Lang.: Eng. 3041

The life and work of Heiner Müller. Germany: Berlin. 1929-1995. Lang.: Ger. 3043

Interview with playwright and director Heiner Müller. Germany. 1929-1989. Lang.: Fre. 3045

Portrait of playwright, actor, and director Wolfgang Bauer. Germany. Austria. 1963-1996. Lang.: Ger. 3047

Director/playwright Dacia Maraini. Italy. 1995. Lang.: Eng. 3118

Interview with playwright David Hare and director Richard Eyre. UK-England: London. 1968-1996. Lang.: Eng. 3307

Interview with playwright Craig Lucas. USA: New York, NY. 1984-1996. Lang.: Eng. 3427

Suzanne Lantagne's mime adaptation of a short story by Gombrowicz. Canada: Montreal, PQ. 1928-1989. Lang.: Fre. 3693

Interview with director Jean Asselin of Omnibus. Canada: Montreal, PQ. 1982-1989. Lang.: Fre. 3694

Relation to other fields

The meeting of cultures in work of Peter Brook and Ariane Mnouchkine. France. UK-England. 1970-1996. Lang.: Dan. 1179

Theatre artists of the Communist period. Poland. 1924. Lang.: Pol. 1219

Theory/criticism

Feminist criticism of Ibsen in the work of Elizabeth Robins. UK-England. 1890-1928. Lang.: Eng. 3553

Directories

Administration

Discontinuation of *Players' Guide*, a talent directory. USA: New York, NY. 1942-1996. Lang.: Eng. 93

Performance/production

Directory of Hungarian film actors. Lang.: Eng. 3613

Directory of Russian film actors. Russia. 1920-1996. Lang.: Rus. 3621

Reference materials

Yearbook of European performing arts. Europe. 1996-1997. Lang.: Eng. 1119

Yearbook of British performing arts. UK. 1996-1997. Lang.: Eng. 1127

British theatre directory. UK. 1995-1996. Lang.: Eng. 1128

Guide to non-mainstream theatre. UK. USA: New York, NY. 1996. Lang.: Eng. 1129

Directory of Hungarian dance art. Hungary. 1990-1995. Lang.: Hun. 1452

Directory of Russian drama theatres. Russia. 1980-1996. Lang.: Rus. 3475

Directory of British broadcasting. UK. 1995-1996. Lang.: Eng. 3570

Directory of Polish puppet and children's theatre, festivals, and awards. Poland. 1996. Lang.: Eng, Fre. 4427

Directors Company (New York, NY)

Plays/librettos/scripts

Profile of the Harold Prince Musical Theatre Program. USA: New York, NY, Denver, CO. 1996. Lang.: Eng. 3987

Dirty Boggers

Performance/production

Collection of newspaper reviews by London theatre critics. UK-England: London. 1996. Lang.: Eng. 2365

Dirty Reality II

Performance/production

Collection of newspaper reviews by London theatre critics. UK-England: London. 1996. Lang.: Eng. 2498

Discographies

Performance/production

Career of actor/singer Ben Vereen. USA. 1965-1995. Lang.: Eng. 3967

The performing and recording career of Patti LuPone. USA. England. 1972-1995. Lang.: Eng. 3968

Actor/singer Daniel Massey. USA. UK-England. 1942-1995. Lang.: Eng. 3969

Tommy Tune's career in musical theatre. USA. 1965-1996. Lang.: Eng. 3970

Discreta enamorada, La (Clever Girl in Love, The)

Performance/production

The Madrid theatre season. Spain: Madrid. 1996. Lang.: Eng. 2271

Disgracefully Yours

Performance/production

Collection of newspaper reviews by London theatre critics. UK-England: London. 1996. Lang.: Eng. 2347

Disney Corporation (Hollywood, CA)

Design/technology

Lighting for the German-language production of Disney's *Beauty and the Beast*. Austria: Vienna. 1995. Lang.: Ger. 3887

Technical aspects of a German-language production of Disney's *Beauty and the Beast*. Austria: Vienna. 1995. Lang.: Ger. 3888

Performance spaces

Renovation and reconstruction of Broadway theatres. USA: New York, NY. 1920-1996. Lang.: Eng. 665

Performance/production

Stage and film treatments of the fairy tale *Beauty and the Beast*. Europe. USA. Canada. 1946-1996. Lang.: Eng. 793

Actor Al Krulick's candidacy for Congress. USA: Orlando, FL. 1996. Lang.: Eng. 1056

Puppets and 3-D animation in Disney's *James and the Giant Peach*. USA: Hollywood, CA. 1993-1995. Lang.: Eng. 4406

Disney Productions and puppetry. USA: Orlando, FL. 1995. Lang.: Eng. 4418

Plays/librettos/scripts

Evolution of the Beast character in treatments of the fairy tale *Beauty and the Beast*. UK-England. 1945-1996. Lang.: Eng. 1106

District of Centuries, The

Basic theatrical documents

Text of *The District of Centuries* by Sean Dixon. Canada. 1996. Lang.: Eng. 1645

Divadlo Continuo (Vodňany)

Performance/production

Profile of new Czech puppet theatre groups. Czech Republic: Cheb, Vodňany. 1996. Lang.: Eng, Fre. 4392

Divadlo Drak (Prague)

Institutions

Interview with Jan Dvořak of Divadlo Drak. Czechoslovakia: Prague. 1948-1990. Lang.: Hun. 4372

Performance/production

Divadlo Drak's *Pinokio* at Public Theatre's puppetry festival. USA: New York, NY. 1992. Lang.: Eng. 4410

Divadlo Husa na Provázku (Brno)

Institutions

History of Divadlo Husa na Provázku. Czechoslovakia. 1968-1995. Lang.: Eng. 395

Divadlo Jokai (Komarno)

SEE

Jókai Színház.

Divadlo na Vinohradech (Prague)

Performance/production

Jiří Menzel's production of *Jacobowsky und der Oberst (Jacobowsky and the Colonel)* by Franz Werfel. Czech Republic: Prague. 1996. Lang.: Cze. 764

Divadlo na Zábradlí (Prague)

Performance/production

Aspects of puppetry in productions by Pétr Lebl. Czech Republic: Prague. 1996. Lang.: Cze. 1976

Account of Čechov International Theatre Festival. Russia. 1996. Lang.: Eng. 2199

Plays/librettos/scripts

The early theatrical career of Václav Havel. Czechoslovakia. 1956-1965. Lang.: Eng. 2871

Divadlo Petra Bezruce (Opava)

Design/technology

Set and costume designer Marta Roszkopfová. Czech Republic. 1974-1996. Lang.: Eng, Fre. 159

Dixon, Sean

Basic theatrical documents

Text of *The District of Centuries* by Sean Dixon. Canada. 1996. Lang.: Eng. 1645

Performance/production

Collection of newspaper reviews by London theatre critics. UK-England: London. 1996. Lang.: Eng. 2323

Djalili, Omid

Performance/production

Collection of newspaper reviews by London theatre critics. UK-England: London. 1996. Lang.: Eng. 2312

Djurgårdsteatern (Stockholm)

Performance spaces

Proposal to reconstruct the Djurgårdsteatern. Sweden: Stockholm. 1801. Lang.: Swe. 655

Djurkovic, Maria
Design/technology
Maria Djurkovic's production design for the film *The Young Poisoner's Handbook*. UK-England. 1995. Lang.: Eng. 3590

Dmitrievna, Larissa Borisanna
Performance/production
Moscow Art Theatre's exchange program with Carnegie Mellon University. USA: Pittsburgh, PA. Russia: Moscow. 1996. Lang.: Eng. 2659

Dobardan (Good Day)
Performance/production
Review of some Budapest productions. Hungary. 1995-1996. Lang.: Eng. 2105

Dobbs, Georgia
Performance/production
Collection of newspaper reviews by London theatre critics. UK-England: London. 1996. Lang.: Eng. 2473

Dock Brief, The
Performance/production
Collection of newspaper reviews by London theatre critics. UK-England: London. 1996. Lang.: Eng. 2459

Director Anthony Clark. UK-England: Birmingham. 1981-1996. Lang.: Eng. 2512

Doctor Faustus
Performance/production
Magic in Elizabethan theatre and society. England: London. 1590-1642. Lang.: Eng. 773

Doctor Faustus Lights the Lights
Performance/production
Beauty and death in Montreal productions by Robert Wilson. Canada: Montreal, PQ. 1980-1993. Lang.: Fre. 753

Doctorow, E.L.
Performance/production
Collection of newspaper reviews by New York theatre critics. USA: New York, NY. 1996. Lang.: Eng. 2564

Documentary theatre
Performance/production
Emily Mann's creation of documentary-style theatre based on interviews. USA: Princeton, NJ. 1996. Lang.: Eng. 2643
Plays/librettos/scripts
Interview with playwright/director Emily Mann. USA: Princeton, NJ. 1996. Lang.: Eng. 3385

Dodge, Marci Milgrom
Performance/production
Collection of newspaper reviews by New York theatre critics. USA: New York, NY. 1996. Lang.: Eng. 2555

Dodin, Lev Abramovič
Institutions
St. Petersburg's theatres, directors, and repertory. Russia: St. Petersburg. 1995-1996. Lang.: Swe. 518

Productions of Malyj Drama Theatre, Lev Dodin, artistic director. Russia: St. Petersburg. 1990-1996. Lang.: Rus. 1838
Performance/production
Collection of newspaper reviews by London theatre critics. UK-England: London. 1996. Lang.: Eng. 2435

Dödsdansen (Dance of Death, The)
Performance/production
Productions of works by Schiller and Strindberg by the Hungarian theatre of Satu Mare/Szatmárnémeti. Romania: Satu-Mare. 1995-1996. Lang.: Hun. 2184

Collection of newspaper reviews by London theatre critics. UK-England: London. 1996. Lang.: Eng. 2418

Collection of newspaper reviews by New York theatre critics. USA: New York, NY, Washington, DC. 1996. Lang.: Eng. 2576

Dog
Performance/production
Collection of newspaper reviews by London theatre critics. UK-England: London. 1996. Lang.: Eng. 2439

Dog in the Manger, The
SEE
Perro del hortelano, El.

Doktor Dragan
Basic theatrical documents
Texts of plays by Josip Vošnjak and Anton Funtek. Slovenia. 1834-1932. Lang.: Slo. 1676

Dolan, Jill
Institutions
The production of knowledge and the institutionalization of performance studies. USA. 1996. Lang.: Eng. 575

Theory/criticism
Gay and lesbian studies, performance, and criticism. USA: New York, NY. 1960-1996. Lang.: Eng. 1377

Dolce Vita, La
Performance/production
Collection of newspaper reviews by London theatre critics. UK-England: London. 1996. Lang.: Eng. 2366

Dolgačev, Vjačeslav
Performance/production
Vjačeslav Dolgačev's production of *Toibele i ee demon (Teibele and Her Demon)* by I.B. Singer and Eve Friedman. Russia: Moscow. 1996. Lang.: Rus. 2193

Dolgušin, Nikita
Performance/production
Dancer Nikita Dolgušin. Russia. USA. 1995. Lang.: Rus. 1525

Doll's House, A
SEE
Dukkehjem, Et.

Dollmatch
Performance/production
Productions of new plays by Elfriede Müller and Jens Roselt. Germany: Saarbrücken, Mainz. 1996. Lang.: Ger. 2052

Doluchanova, Zara
Performance/production
Opera singer Zara Doluchanova. Armenia. 1970-1996. Lang.: Rus. 4076

Dom Juan (Don Juan)
Performance/production
Critical reception of Jerzy Grzegorzewski's production of Molière's *Dom Juan*. France: Paris. 1994-1995. Lang.: Eng, Fre. 2006

Productions of Molière and Shakespeare directed by Daniel Mesguich. France: Lille. 1996. Lang.: Eng. 2014

Productions of the Comédie-Française at Brooklyn Academy of Music. USA: New York, NY. France: Paris. 1979-1996. Lang.: Eng. 2650
Plays/librettos/scripts
Recent Polish translations and productions of the plays of Molière. France. Poland: Cracow. 1948-1992. Lang.: Eng, Fre. 2993

Dom kobiet (Women's House)
Plays/librettos/scripts
Reactions of male critics to Polish feminist drama. Poland. 1932-1938. Lang.: Pol. 3162

Domahidy, László
Performance/production
Bass László Domahidy. Hungary. 1920-1996. Lang.: Hun. 4150

Domingo, Plácido
Institutions
The development of the Los Angeles Music Center Opera. USA: Los Angeles, CA. 1986-1996. Lang.: Eng. 4062
Performance/production
Profile, interview with tenor Plácido Domingo. Europe. North America. 1941-1996. Lang.: Eng. 4110

Operatic and sporting elements in the 'three tenors' concerts. Italy: Rome. USA: Los Angeles, CA. 1990-1994. Lang.: Eng. 4172

Critical analysis of the art of tenor Luciano Pavarotti. Italy. 1935-1996. Lang.: Eng. 4179

Dominion Theatre (London)
Performance/production
Collection of newspaper reviews by London theatre critics. UK-England: London. 1996. Lang.: Eng. 2473

Don Carlo
Performance/production
Background information on Teatro Colón season. Argentina: Buenos Aires. 1996. Lang.: Eng. 4075

Don Giovanni
Design/technology
Post-modern design at the Munich Festival. Germany: Munich. 1995. Lang.: Eng. 4018
Performance/production
Director Paul Flieder's diary of rehearsals for Mozart's *Don Giovanni*. Albania: Tirana. 1996. Lang.: Ger. 4074

Mezzo-soprano Maria Popescu. Canada: Montreal, PQ. 1996. Lang.: Eng. 4087

Peter Sellars' interpretation of Mozart's *Don Giovanni*. Europe. 1980-1996. Lang.: Eng. 4115

Background material on Lyric Opera of Chicago radio broadcast performances. USA: Chicago, IL. 1996. Lang.: Eng. 4244

Background material on Metropolitan Opera radio broadcast performances. USA: New York, NY. 1996. Lang.: Eng. 4252

Don Giovanni — cont'd

Plays/librettos/scripts
The mask in Mozart's *Don Giovanni*. Austria. 1786-1789. Lang.: Eng.
4300

E.T.A. Hoffmann's critique of Mozart's *Don Giovanni*. Austro-Hungarian Empire: Vienna. 1787-1813. Lang.: Eng.
4304

Leporello's aria 'Madamina' in Mozart's *Don Giovanni*. Austro-Hungarian Empire: Vienna. 1787-1996. Lang.: Eng.
4306

Shaw's *Man and Superman* as a commentary on Mozart's *Don Giovanni*. UK-England. 1905. Lang.: Eng.
4340

Don Juan

Performance/production
Collection of newspaper reviews by London theatre critics. UK-England: London. 1996. Lang.: Eng.
2344

Don Juan by Molière
SEE
Dom Juan.

Don Juan by Tirso de Molina
SEE
Burlador de Sevilla, El.

Don Juan kommt aus dem Krieg (Don Juan Comes Back from the War)

Institutions
Productions of Carrefour 92. Canada: Quebec, PQ. 1992. Lang.: Fre.
376

Plays/librettos/scripts
The recent proliferation of Don Juan adaptations. Canada: Montreal, PQ. Austria. 1625-1991. Lang.: Fre.
2782

Don Juan Tenorio

Performance/production
The Madrid theatre season. Spain: Madrid. 1996. Lang.: Eng.
2271

Don Juan Tenorio o sia Il Convertato di Pietra

Plays/librettos/scripts
Leporello's aria 'Madamina' in Mozart's *Don Giovanni*. Austro-Hungarian Empire: Vienna. 1787-1996. Lang.: Eng.
4306

Don Pasquale

Performance/production
Background material on Lyric Opera of Chicago radio broadcast performances. USA: Chicago, IL. 1996. Lang.: Eng.
4244

Don Sanche, ou le Château d'Amour

Plays/librettos/scripts
Franz Liszt's failure as an operatic composer. Europe. 1821-1850. Lang.: Eng.
4312

Don't Tell Mama (New York, NY)

Performance/production
Steven Brinberg's cabaret performance as Barbra Streisand. USA: New York, NY. 1993-1996. Lang.: Eng.
3737

Doña Francisquita

Performance/production
Background information on Teatro Colón season. Argentina: Buenos Aires. 1996. Lang.: Eng.
4075

Doña Rosita la soltera (Doña Rosita Remains Single)

Performance/production
Productions of Schauspielhaus Bonn. Germany: Bonn. 1996. Lang.: Ger.
2075

Donizetti, Gaetano

Performance/production
Background material on Lyric Opera of Chicago radio broadcast performances. USA: Chicago, IL. 1996. Lang.: Eng.
4244

Background material on Metropolitan Opera radio broadcast performances. USA: New York, NY. 1996. Lang.: Eng.
4252

Plays/librettos/scripts
Essays on librettist Felice Romani. Italy. 1788-1865. Lang.: Ita.
4335

Donkerland

Institutions
Report on the Grahamstown Festival. South Africa, Republic of: Grahamstown. 1996. Lang.: Eng.
532

Donmar Warehouse (London)

Performance/production
Collection of newspaper reviews by London theatre critics. UK-England: London. 1996. Lang.: Eng.
2328

Collection of newspaper reviews by London theatre critics. UK-England: London. 1996. Lang.: Eng.
2334

Collection of newspaper reviews by London theatre critics. UK-England: London. 1996. Lang.: Eng.
2349

Collection of newspaper reviews by London theatre critics. UK-England: London. 1996. Lang.: Eng.
2355

Collection of newspaper reviews by London theatre critics. UK-England: London. 1996. Lang.: Eng.
2370

Collection of newspaper reviews by London theatre critics. UK-England: London. 1996. Lang.: Eng.
2383

Collection of newspaper reviews by London theatre critics. UK-England: London. 1996. Lang.: Eng.
2405

Collection of newspaper reviews by London theatre critics. UK-England: London. 1996. Lang.: Eng.
2436

Collection of newspaper reviews by London theatre critics. UK-England: London. 1996. Lang.: Eng.
2465

Collection of newspaper reviews by London theatre critics. UK-England: London. 1996. Lang.: Eng.
2490

Donnell, Dorothy

Plays/librettos/scripts
Experiments in musical theatre in the twenties. USA. 1920-1929. Lang.: Eng.
3993

Donnellan, Declan

Design/technology
Lighting design for plays about Martin Guerre. UK-England: London. 1996. Lang.: Eng.
3890

Performance/production
Videotape on interpreting and performing Shakespeare's *As You Like It*. UK-England. 1994. Lang.: Eng.
2303

Collection of newspaper reviews by London theatre critics. UK-England: London. 1996. Lang.: Eng.
2305

Collection of newspaper reviews by London theatre critics. UK-England: London. 1996. Lang.: Eng.
2453

Collection of newspaper reviews by London theatre critics. UK-England: London. 1996. Lang.: Eng.
2472

Interview with director Declan Donnellan. UK-England: London. Hungary: Budapest. 1996. Lang.: Hun.
2505

Donnelly, Candice

Design/technology
Candice Donnelly's costumes for Tennessee Williams' *The Notebook of Trigorin*, Cincinnati Playhouse. USA: Cincinnati, OH. 1996.Lang.: Eng.
1728

Donnellys, The

Plays/librettos/scripts
Analysis of *The Donnellys* by James Reaney. Canada. 1973-1975. Lang.: Eng.
2847

Donut

Plays/librettos/scripts
Analysis of plays by Jean-François Caron. Canada: Montreal, PQ. 1986-1991. Lang.: Fre.
2762

Doomsday

Performance/production
Collection of newspaper reviews by London theatre critics. UK-England: London. 1996. Lang.: Eng.
2308
Plays/librettos/scripts
Meaning of 'lewent bride' in the York *Doomsday* play. England: York. 1433. Lang.: Eng.
2958
Research/historiography
Description of the Archive database of the York *Doomsday*. UK-England: York. 1995. Lang.: Eng.
3529

Doona, John

Performance/production
Collection of newspaper reviews by London theatre critics. UK-England: London. 1996. Lang.: Eng.
2402

Doran, Gregory

Performance/production
Collection of newspaper reviews by London theatre critics. UK-England: London. 1996. Lang.: Eng.
2482

Doré, Isabelle

Plays/librettos/scripts
Playwright Isabelle Doré on her career. Canada: Montreal, PQ. 1962-1996. Lang.: Fre.
2772

Doré, Marc

Performance/production
Street performances of Théâtre Euh!. Canada: Quebec, PQ. 1969-1976. Lang.: Fre.
3705

Dorfman, Ariel

Performance/production
Productions of Schauspielhaus Bonn. Germany: Bonn. 1996. Lang.: Ger.
2075
Plays/librettos/scripts
Playwrights Harold Pinter and Ariel Dorfman. Chile. UK-England. 1957-1996. Lang.: Eng.
2853

Dorge, Claude

Plays/librettos/scripts
Plays about Louis Riel. Canada. 1886-1986. Lang.: Fre.
2792

Dorman, Jan
Performance/production
Puppetry performance styles of Jan Dorman and Jan Wilkowski.
Poland. 1945-1996. Lang.: Eng, Fre.   4400

Dormitory, The
Plays/librettos/scripts
Women writers in postcolonial English. Australia. 1995. Lang.: Eng.
2723

Dorn, Dieter
Performance/production
Politics and Botho Strauss's *Ithaka* at Münchner Kammerspiele.
Germany: Munich. 1996. Lang.: Ger.   2067

Dornröschen (Sleeping Beauty, The)
Performance/production
Mats Ek's ballet version of *The Sleeping Beauty*. Germany: Hamburg.
1996. Lang.: Swe.   1580

Doronina, Tatjana
Performance/production
Interview with actress Tatjana Doronina. Russia: Moscow. 1996. Lang.:
Rus.   2232

Dorst, Tankred
Performance/production
Iván Hargitai's production of Dorst's *Merlin* for Új Színház. Hungary.
1961-1996. Lang.: Hun.   2103
Plays/librettos/scripts
Children's plays of Tankred Dorst. Germany. 1982-1996. Lang.: Ger.
3018

Dortmunder Schauspielhaus (Dortmund)
Performance/production
Theatre in the Ruhr Valley. Germany. 1995. Lang.: Eng.   2043

Dorval, Anne
Performance/production
Interview with actress Anne Dorval. Canada: Montreal, PQ. 1990.
Lang.: Fre.   1933

Dorval, Marie
Relation to other fields
Assumptions about the relationship between theatre and literature.
France: Paris. 1835-1996. Lang.: Fre.   3498

Dostojévskij, Fëdor Michajlovič
Performance/production
Analysis of *Une Femme Douce (The Meek Girl)* by Robert Wilson and
Wolfgang Wiens. France. 1994. Lang.: Eng.   2012
Three Parisian performances of productions from Quebec. France: Paris.
1988. Lang.: Fre.   2028
Innokentij Smoktunovskij's role in *Idiot*, Tovstonogov Bolšoj Drama
Theatre. USSR: St. Petersburg. 1956-1957. Lang.: Rus.   2698
Hans Krása's opera *Verlobung im Traum*. Czech Republic: Prague.
1994-1996. Lang.: Eng.   4101
Relation to other fields
Portrayal of character and theatricality in the work of Dostojévskij.
Russia. 1880. Lang.: Fre.   1228

Dostoyevsky, Fyodor
SEE
Dostojévskij, Fëdor Michajlovič.

Dotson, Josie Mae
Performance/production
Interview with actress and administrator Josie Mae Dotson. USA: Los
Angeles, CA. 1970. Lang.: Eng.   2635

Double Inconstance, La (Double Inconstancy, The)
Performance/production
Collection of newspaper reviews by New York theatre critics. USA:
New York, NY. 1996. Lang.: Eng.   2580
Productions of the Comédie-Française at Brooklyn Academy of Music.
USA: New York, NY. France: Paris. 1979-1996. Lang.: Eng.   2650

Double Wedding, The
Performance/production
The career of performance artist Rose English. UK-England. 1996.
Lang.: Eng.   3794

Double, Mick
Design/technology
The production team for The Who's *Quadrophenia*. USA: New York,
NY. 1996. Lang.: Eng.   3701

Douglas Fairbanks Theatre (New York, NY)
Performance/production
Collection of newspaper reviews by New York theatre critics. USA:
New York, NY. 1996. Lang.: Eng.   2558
Collection of newspaper reviews by New York theatre critics. USA:
New York, NY. 1996. Lang.: Eng.   2580

Len Cariou's role in *Papa* directed by John Henry Davis. USA: New
York, NY. 1996. Lang.: Eng.   2620
Howard Crabtree's *When Pigs Fly* directed by Mark Waldrop, Douglas
Fairbanks Theatre. USA: New York, NY. 1996. Lang.: Eng.   3960

Dove, John
Performance/production
Collection of newspaper reviews by London theatre critics. UK-England:
London. 1996. Lang.: Eng.   2338
Collection of newspaper reviews by London theatre critics. UK-England:
London. 1996. Lang.: Eng.   2386

Dove, Rita
Basic theatrical documents
Excerpt from *The Darker Face of the Earth* by Rita Dove. USA. 1994.
Lang.: Eng.   1689
Text of *The Darker Face of the Earth* by Rita Dove. USA. 1996. Lang.:
Eng.   1690
Plays/librettos/scripts
Introduction to *The Darker Face of the Earth* by Rita Dove. USA. 1994.
Lang.: Eng.   3393

Dove, The
Basic theatrical documents
International anthology of modern drama by women. 1880-1940. Lang.:
Eng.   1637

Down Among the Mini-Beasts
Performance/production
Collection of newspaper reviews by London theatre critics. UK-England:
London. 1996. Lang.: Eng.   2354

Downes, Edward
Performance/production
Retirement of Edward Downes as Metropolitan Opera broadcast
quizmaster. USA: New York, NY. 1996. Lang.: Eng.   4282

Downtown Paradise
Performance/production
Collection of newspaper reviews by London theatre critics. UK-England:
London. 1996. Lang.: Eng.   2360

Doyle, Patricia
Performance/production
Collection of newspaper reviews by London theatre critics. UK-England:
London. 1996. Lang.: Eng.   2306

Dr. Heidegger's Fountain of Youth
Plays/librettos/scripts
The operas of Jack Beeson and the Columbia Opera Workshop. USA.
1996. Lang.: Eng.   4346

Drabinsky, Garth
Performance spaces
Livent Realty's plan to renovate the Lyric and Apollo theatres. USA:
New York, NY. 1996. Lang.: Eng.   673

Drabwell, Gary
Performance/production
Collection of newspaper reviews by London theatre critics. UK-England:
London. 1996. Lang.: Eng.   2407

Drag, The
Plays/librettos/scripts
Mae West's gay play *The Drag*. USA. 1927. Lang.: Eng.   3388

Dragone, Franco
Performance/production
Collection of newspaper reviews by London theatre critics. UK-England:
London. 1996. Lang.: Eng.   2307

Dragonfly of Chicoutimi, The
Plays/librettos/scripts
Analysis of *The Dragonfly of Chicoutimi* by Larry Tremblay. Canada:
Montreal, PQ. 1995. Lang.: Fre.   2786
Playwright Larry Tremblay discusses his work. Canada: Montreal, PQ.
1981-1996. Lang.: Fre.   2835

Dragún, Osvaldo
Basic theatrical documents
Anthology of Argentine Jewish theatre. Argentina. 1926-1988. Lang.:
Eng.   1639
Plays/librettos/scripts
Playwright Osvaldo Dragún and Argentinian theatre. Argentina: Buenos
Aires. 1952-1957. Lang.: Spa.   2716

Dragutin, Joël
Plays/librettos/scripts
Analysis of *Trilogie des tables (Trilogy of the Tables)* by Joël Dragutin.
France. 1985-1993. Lang.: Fre.   3011

Drainville, Martin
Performance/production
Actor Martin Drainville and his background in comedy. Canada. 1970-
1990. Lang.: Fre.   1930

Economics — cont'd

Performance spaces
The multidisciplinary cultural complex, Place des Arts. Canada:
Montreal, PQ. 1996. Lang.: Fre.   622
Performance/production
Theatre as a Falangist propaganda tool. Spain. 1935-1945. Lang.: Eng.
                                                                   942
Shakespeare and Elizabethan cultural politics: *A Midsummer Night's
Dream.* England. 1590-1620. Lang.: Eng.   1990
Plays/librettos/scripts
Place and identity in Quebecois drama. Canada. 1943-1996. Lang.: Fre.
                                                                   2834
Renaissance economics as reflected in Shakespeare's *The Taming of the
Shrew.* England. 1590-1604. Lang.: Eng.   2923
Status of playwriting in Swedish. Sweden. 1996. Lang.: Swe.   3272
Relation to other fields
Crisis and the performing arts. Canada. USA.. 1966-1996. Lang.: Fre.
                                                                   1147
Experimental theatre in the contexts of scientific advancement and
commercialism. France. 1850-1989. Lang.: Fre.   1177
Government involvement in Israeli arts. Israel. 1920-1996. Lang.: Eng.
                                                                   1202
Current financial difficulties of Polish theatres. Poland. 1994. Lang.:
Eng.   1221
Report on 1995 event of the Magdalena Project. UK-Wales: Cardiff.
1995. Lang.: Eng.   1251

Ecsedi Kovács, Gyula

Performance/production
Gyula Ecsedi Kovács' staging of *Tigris és hiéna.* Austro-Hungarian
Empire: Kolozsvár. 1876-1883. Lang.: Hun.   1910

Ecstasy

Performance/production
Collection of newspaper reviews by London theatre critics. UK-England:
London. 1996. Lang.: Eng.   2332
Interview with director Scott Elliott. USA: New York, NY. 1995-1996.
Lang.: Eng.   2673

Edelstein, Barry

Performance/production
Plays by Arthur Miller at the Williamstown Theatre Festival. USA:
Williamstown, MA. 1996. Lang.: Eng.   2589

Edgar, David

Plays/librettos/scripts
Contemporary English drama. UK-England. 1956-1990. Lang.: Fre.
                                                                   3296

Edinburgh Festival

Design/technology
Technical aspects of Abbey Theatre production at the Edinburgh
Festival. UK-Scotland: Edinburgh. 1995. Lang.: Eng.   1715
Institutions
The music program of the Edinburgh Festival. UK-Scotland: Edinburgh.
1996. Lang.: Ger.   560
Productions of the Edinburgh Festival. UK-Scotland: Edinburgh. 1996.
Lang.: Ger.   561
Productions of the Edinburgh Festival. UK-Scotland: Edinburgh. 1996.
Lang.: Eng.   562
Guide to the Edinburgh Festival. UK-Scotland: Edinburgh. 1996. Lang.:
Eng.   563
Review of productions at Edinburgh Festival. UK-Scotland: Edinburgh.
1994. Lang.: Eng.   564
Evolving *Les Sept Branches de la Rivière Ota (The Seven Streams of the
River Ota)* by Robert Lepage. Canada: Quebec, PQ. 1995. Lang.: Eng.
                                                                   1779
Performance/production
Interview with director Patrice Chéreau. France. 1996. Lang.: Eng. 2013
Collection of newspaper reviews by London theatre critics. UK-
Scotland: Edinburgh. 1996. Lang.: Eng.   2545
The Edinburgh Festival: history, success, technology. UK-Scotland:
Edinburgh. 1947-1996. Lang.: Eng.   2546

Edinburgh National Conference Centre

Performance/production
Collection of newspaper reviews by London theatre critics. UK-
Scotland: Edinburgh. 1996. Lang.: Eng.   2545

Editions

Performance/production
Staging the 'bad quartos' of Shakespeare's *Hamlet* and *Henry V.* UK-
Scotland: Aberdeen. 1996. Lang.: Eng.   2548
Plays/librettos/scripts
Recent publication of plays and theatre essays. France. 1949-1991.
Lang.: Fre.   1097

Analysis of Pope's edition of Shakespeare's *King John.* England. 1590-
1725. Lang.: Eng.   2887
Analysis of the 'bad' quarto of Shakespeare's *Romeo and Juliet.*
England. 1597. Lang.: Eng.   2902
Analysis of a speech in the quarto and folio editions of *King Lear.*
England. 1600. Lang.: Eng.   2905
The continuing debate on editing Shakespeare: defense of the
Shakespearean originals project. UK-England. 1592-1995. Lang.: Eng.
                                                                   3315

Edmond

Performance/production
Collection of newspaper reviews by New York theatre critics. USA:
New York, NY. 1996. Lang.: Eng.   2554

Edmundson, Helen

Performance/production
Collection of newspaper reviews by London theatre critics. UK-England:
London. 1996. Lang.: Eng.   2443

Edstrom, Per Simon

Design/technology
Sven Olof Ehrén's *Va nu då (What Now),* set in an ice stadium. Sweden:
Stockholm. 1907-1961. Lang.: Swe, Eng.   1711

Education

Audience
Effect of classroom drama and theatre attendance on children's
interpretation of theatre. USA: Tempe, AZ. 1984-1991. Lang.: Eng. 143
Institutions
Montreal theatres' role in education and the preparation of future
audiences. Canada: Montreal, PQ. 1992. Lang.: Fre.   361
Problems of children's theatre companies touring Quebec schools.
Canada. 1991. Lang.: Fre.   374
The production of knowledge and the institutionalization of performance
studies. USA. 1996. Lang.: Eng.   575
The conversion of Fort Ord into a university multi-use facility. USA:
Monterey Bay, CA. 1996. Lang.: Eng.   580
Collaboration between Cleveland Play House and the theatre
department of Case Western Reserve University. USA: Cleveland, OH.
1996. Lang.: Eng.   599
Children's programs of opera companies. Canada. 1996. Lang.: Eng.
                                                                   4033
Performance/production
The *carri di tespi* as a theatrical propaganda tool. Italy. 1925-1943.
Lang.: Eng.   870
Contemporary Philippine theatre and the formation of cultural identity.
Philippines: Manila. 1565-1996. Lang.: Eng.   889
Director, teacher, and scholar Konstantin Nikolajévič Deržavin. Russia:
St. Petersburg. 1903-1956. Lang.: Rus.   900
Performance-based productions for predominantly female student
groups. UK-England: Hull. 1891-1990. Lang.: Eng.   969
History of the London Speech Festival. UK-England. 1928-1939. Lang.:
Eng.   995
The relationship of teacher to student in Indian classical dance. India.
1949-1996. Lang.: Eng.   1433
Theory and practice at Loughborough University's Shakespeare
conference for students. UK-England: Loughborough. 1588-1993. Lang.
:Eng.   2523
Angels in America and censorship at Catholic University. USA:
Washington, DC. 1996. Lang.: Eng.   2661
Plays/librettos/scripts
Sisterhood in *As You Like It* by Shakespeare. England. 1590. Lang.:
Eng.   2957
Handbook of Slovenenian drama for students. Slovenia. 1996. Lang.:
Slo.   3208
Teacher's handbook of Slovenia drama. Slovenia. 1996. Lang.: Slo. 3209
The continuing relevance of Restoration theatre. UK-England. 1660-
1996. Lang.: Eng.   3310
Relation to other fields
Drama in Jesuit schools. 1551-1773. Lang.: Eng.   1130
Personalities and motivations of adolescents active in theatre. Canada.
1989-1990. Lang.: Fre.   1137
Study of teacher perceptions of the value and status of drama in
education. Canada: St. Catharine's, ON. 1995-1996. Lang.: Eng.   1146
An example of college-level theatre education in Quebec. Canada:
Rouyn, PQ. 1972-1992. Lang.: Fre.   1151
The social function of theatrical practice. Canada: Quebec, PQ. 1950-
1996. Lang.: Fre.   1152

Education — cont'd

The touring company Arrière-Scène. Canada. 1972-1992. Lang.: Fre.
1153

Theatre education in Quebec. Canada. 1992. Lang.: Fre. 1161

Examples of college and secondary-school theatre in Quebec. Canada: Montreal, PQ, Outremont, PQ, Saint-Laurent, PQ. 1991-1992. Lang.: Fre. 1162

Report on tenth symposium of the International School of Theatre Anthropology. Denmark: Copenhagen. 1996. Lang.: Eng. 1169

Interview with theatre teacher Werner Schulte. Germany: Berlin. 1989-1996. Lang.: Ger. 1180

Jewish/Arab encounters in drama projects. Israel. 1977-1995. Lang.: Eng. 1203

New developments in Theatre for Development. Lesotho. 1970-1994. Lang.: Eng. 1210

Non-formal education in Nigerian Theatre for Development. Nigeria. 1972-1996. Lang.: Eng. 1215

The importance of theatre education in Polish schools. Poland. 1996. Lang.: Eng, Fre. 1220

Interview with theatre anthropologist Zbigniew Osiński. Poland. 1995. Lang.: Eng, Fre. 1222

Teaching theatre in general aesthetics classes. Russia: Moscow. 1996. Lang.: Rus. 1225

Methodology of a course on Russian theatre and film. Russia. 1996. Lang.: Rus. 1227

Theatre in AIDS education. Uganda. 1989-1991. Lang.: Eng. 1234

List of taught MA courses in theatre and drama in British universities. UK. 1994. Lang.: Eng. 1235

Humorous piece on the challenges of keeping up-to-date with computer technology. UK. 1996. Lang.: Eng. 1236

The relevance of Theatre for Development to Britain. UK. 1976-1995. Lang.: Eng. 1237

The history of Theatre-in-Education. UK. 1965-1996. Lang.: Ger. 1238

The body as representation—implications for drama education. UK-England. 1979-1995. Lang.: Eng. 1241

Problems of teachers required to stage plays with student groups. UK-England. 1996. Lang.: Eng. 1245

The Teaching Quality Assessment of British university theatre departments. UK-England. 1996. Lang.: Eng. 1246

Blah, Blah, Blah's fusion of performance art and educational theatre. UK-England. 1995. Lang.: Eng. 1247

Drama as an agent for changing behavior. UK-England. 1978-1995. Lang.: Eng. 1248

Study of how elementary-school teachers implement a drama curriculum. USA. 1996. Lang.: Eng. 1258

Educational programming of the National Black Theatre Festival. USA: Winston-Salem, NC. 1995. Lang.: Eng. 1266

Intercollegiate performance festivals and their influence on performance. USA. 1945-1994. Lang.: Eng. 1270

Reflections on the donation of archival materials to a university library. USA: Columbus, OH. 1996. Lang.: Eng. 1272

Camille Paglia on teaching as performance art. USA. 1996. Lang.: Eng. 1273

Account of a course in dance therapy. UK-England: Chichester. 1996. Lang.: Eng. 1460

Shakespeare and the dominant ideology in Bulgarian education. Bulgaria. 1950-1989. Lang.: Eng. 3479

The need for education in Quebec theatre history. Canada. 1989. Lang.: Fre. 3484

Feminist classroom approach to *The Concealed Fancies* by Cavendish and Brackley. England. 1645. Lang.: Eng. 3490

Teaching lyrics of women poets alongside those of Shakespeare. England. 1590-1621. Lang.: Eng. 3491

Plays for youth created by Seoul theatre collectives. Korea: Seoul. 1995-1996. Lang.: Kor. 3502

Shakespeare in South African education. South Africa, Republic of. 1994-1996. Lang.: Eng. 3509

Shakespeare's *Romeo and Juliet* and pedagogy. UK-England. 1996. Lang.: Eng. 3512

Teaching Shakespeare in the context of Renaissance women's culture. USA. 1991-1996. Lang.: Eng. 3516

Teaching *The Winter's Tale* and Elizabeth Cary's *The Tragedy of Mariam.* USA. 1995. Lang.: Eng. 3517

Teaching race and gender in plays of Cary, Shakespeare, and Behn. USA. 1996. Lang.: Eng. 3518

Teaching plays of Shakespeare and Cary in a course on domestic England in the early modern period. USA. 1995. Lang.: Eng. 3519

Argument in favor of teaching Shakespeare in conjunction with his female contemporaries. USA. 1996. Lang.: Eng. 3520

South African media and film policy. South Africa, Republic of. 1980-1996. Lang.: Eng. 3687

Research/historiography
Research on drama and theatre in education. South Africa, Republic of. 1995. Lang.: Eng. 1302

The need for coordination in the new Polish discipline of theatre studies. Poland. 1995. Lang.: Eng, Fre. 3526

Training
Using practical drama to teach critical practice. UK-England: Reading. 1994. Lang.: Eng. 1397

The impact of media on theatrical actor training. USA. 1996. Lang.: Eng. 1399

Music and theatre programs at Syracuse University and the University of Arizona. USA. 1996. Lang.: Eng. 1400

Éducation manquée, Une
Performance/production
Operas of Emmanuel Chabrier. France: Paris. 1863-1894. Lang.: Eng. 4127

Educational theatre
Audience
The audience for school theatre. Germany. 1996. Lang.: Ger. 137
Performance/production
Rudolf Mirbt and children's, school, and amateur theatre. Germany. 1896-1974. Lang.: Ger. 814

Student production of *The Singular Life of Albert Nobbs* by Simone Benmussa. UK-England: Leeds. 1992. Lang.: Eng. 2516
Relation to other fields
Interview with theatre teacher Werner Schulte. Germany: Berlin. 1989-1996. Lang.: Ger. 1180

The importance of theatre education in Polish schools. Poland. 1996. Lang.: Eng, Fre. 1220

Teaching theatre in general aesthetics classes. Russia: Moscow. 1996. Lang.: Rus. 1225

Edward II
Performance/production
The fiftieth Avignon Festival. France: Avignon. 1996. Lang.: Eng. 805
Plays/librettos/scripts
Shakespeare's influence on Marlowe's *Edward II.* England. 1590-1592. Lang.: Eng. 2906

Edwards, Gale
Performance/production
Collection of newspaper reviews by London theatre critics. UK-England: London. 1996. Lang.: Eng. 2367

Collection of newspaper reviews by London theatre critics. UK-England: London. 1996. Lang.: Eng. 2478

Edwards, Gwynne
Performance/production
Collection of newspaper reviews by London theatre critics. UK-England: London. 1996. Lang.: Eng. 2447

Edwards, Nettie
Design/technology
The director-designer relationship. UK. 1912-1995. Lang.: Eng. 221

Edwards, Richard
Performance/production
Collection of newspaper reviews by London theatre critics. UK-England: London. 1996. Lang.: Eng. 2387

Edwin
Performance/production
Collection of newspaper reviews by London theatre critics. UK-England: London. 1996. Lang.: Eng. 2459

Effect of Gamma Rays on Man-in-the-Moon Marigolds, The
Plays/librettos/scripts
Translations by playwright Michel Tremblay. Canada: Montreal, PQ. 1968-1990. Lang.: Fre. 2748

Efremov, Oleg
SEE
Jefremov, Oleg.

Efros, Anatolij
Performance/production
Excerpts from speeches and letters of director Anatolij Efros. USSR: Moscow. 1971-1987. Lang.: Rus. 2692

Elizabethan theatre — cont'd

Shakespeare, publishing, and performing rights. England. 1590-1640.
Lang.: Eng.   2898

Historical background of *The Two Noble Kinsmen* by Shakespeare and
Fletcher. England. 1613. Lang.: Eng.   2903

The body of the king in Shakespeare's *King Lear*. England. 1605-1996.
Lang.: Eng.   2904

Marlowe's *Tamburlaine the Great* and the pastoral. England. 1587-1588.
Lang.: Eng.   2913

Theatrical politics and Shakespearean comedy. England. 1590-1600.
Lang.: Eng.   2917

Speculation on Shakespeare's life at the time of the writing of *Macbeth*.
England. 1605-1606. Lang.: Eng.   2921

Changing attitudes regarding plays and playwrights. England. 1580-
1640. Lang.: Eng.   2926

Construction of the author in the early modern period. England. 1400-
1710. Lang.: Eng.   2936

Shakespeare's *Henry VIII* and its source, Holinshed's chronicles.
England. 1611. Lang.: Eng.   2942

The reflection of contemporary concerns in Shakespeare's *Hamlet* and
Othello. England. 1600-1604. Lang.: Eng.   2953

Theory/criticism
Argument against criticism that devalues the author. UK-England. 1994.
Lang.: Eng.   3558

Elizarjev, Valerij
Performance/production
The premiere of the ballet *Strasti (Rogneda)* by Andrej Mdivani and
Valerij Elizarjev. Belorus: Minsk. 1995. Lang.: Rus.   1496

Elliott, Kenneth
Performance/production
Collection of newspaper reviews by New York theatre critics. USA:
New York, NY, East Haddam, CT. 1996. Lang.: Eng.   2582

Elliott, Scott
Performance/production
Collection of newspaper reviews by New York theatre critics. USA:
New York, NY. 1996. Lang.: Eng.   2559

Collection of newspaper reviews by New York theatre critics. USA:
New York, NY. 1996. Lang.: Eng.   2578

Plays by Arthur Miller at the Williamstown Theatre Festival. USA:
Williamstown, MA. 1996. Lang.: Eng.   2589

Steve Ross's role in *Present Laughter* on Broadway. USA: New York,
NY. 1996. Lang.: Eng.   2604

Actor Frank Langella. USA: New York, NY. 1939-1996. Lang.: Eng.
                                                                  2605

Interview with director Scott Elliott. USA: New York, NY. 1995-1996.
Lang.: Eng.   2673

Ellis, Michael
Performance/production
Collection of newspaper reviews by London theatre critics. UK-England:
London. 1996. Lang.: Eng.   2397

Ellis, Scott
Performance/production
Collection of newspaper reviews by New York theatre critics. USA:
New York, NY, Washington, DC. 1996. Lang.: Eng.   2581

Collection of newspaper reviews by New York theatre critics. USA:
New York, NY. 1996. Lang.: Eng.   2584

Ellis, Vivian
Performance/production
Collection of newspaper reviews by London theatre critics. UK-England:
London. 1996. Lang.: Eng.   2490

Elmo, Cloe
Performance/production
Comments on the mezzo soprano vocal range, including notes on
specific singers. USA. 1996. Lang.: Eng.   4262

Elmslie, Kenward
Plays/librettos/scripts
The operas of Jack Beeson and the Columbia Opera Workshop. USA.
1996. Lang.: Eng.   4346

Elsineur (Elsinore)
Performance/production
Robert Lepage's performances in Denmark of *Hiroshima* and *Elsineur
(Elsinore)*. Denmark. Canada. 1996. Lang.: Dan.   1984

Robert Lepage's Shakespearean adaptations at the Odéon. France:
Paris. 1996. Lang.: Ger.   2034

Collection of newspaper reviews by London theatre critics. UK-England:
London, Stratford. 1996. Lang.: Eng.   2483

Collection of newspaper reviews by London theatre critics. UK-
Scotland: Edinburgh. 1996. Lang.: Eng.   2545

Elssler, Fanny
Performance/production
Articles on Western European ballet theatre and its artists. Europe.
1800-1900. Lang.: Rus.   1499

Elvire Jouvet 40
Relation to other fields
Brigitte Jaques' *Elvire Jouvet 40*, and the continuing reality of political
detention and torture. France: Paris. Lebanon. 1940-1996. Lang.: Fre.
                                                                  3496

Elvis—The Musical
Performance/production
Collection of newspaper reviews by London theatre critics. UK-England:
London. 1996. Lang.: Eng.   2370

Em-Fuehrer Jones, The
Basic theatrical documents
Anthology of unknown plays of the Harlem Renaissance. USA: New
York, NY. 1920-1940. Lang.: Eng.   1694

Emeljanov, Igor
Performance/production
Canadian debuts of singers from Eastern Europe. Canada. USA. 1917-
1996. Lang.: Eng.   4097

Emig-Könning, Christine
Performance/production
New directorial interpretations of Kroetz's *Der Drang (The Crowd)*.
Germany: Hamburg, Leipzig. 1996. Lang.: Ger.   2063

Emilia Galotti
Performance/production
Collection of newspaper reviews by London theatre critics. UK-England:
London. 1996. Lang.: Eng.   2360

Emily of Emerald Hill
Plays/librettos/scripts
Women writers in postcolonial English. Australia. 1995. Lang.: Eng.
                                                                  2723

Emma
Performance/production
Collection of newspaper reviews by London theatre critics. UK-England:
London. 1996. Lang.: Eng.   2456

Emma B. vedova Giocasta (Emma B., Widow Jocasta)
Plays/librettos/scripts
Analysis of *Emma B. vedova Giocasta (Emma B., Widow Jocasta)* by
Alberto Savinio (Andrea De Chirico). Italy. 1891-1952. Lang.: Ita. 3110

Emmeline
Performance/production
Tobias Picker's new opera *Emmeline*. USA: Santa Fe, NM. 1996. Lang.:
Eng.   4267

Emmes, David
Institutions
South Coast Repertory, Martin Benson and David Emmes, artistic
directors. USA: Costa Mesa, CA. 1996. Lang.: Eng.   567

Emmons, Beverly
Design/technology
Lighting designer Beverly Emmons, artistic director of Lincoln Center
Institute. USA: New York, NY. 1996. Lang.: Eng.   301

Emperor Jones, The
Performance/production
A new view of actor Charles Gilpin. USA. 1920-1930. Lang.: Eng. 2647

Production of O'Neill's *The Emperor Jones* at the Little Theatre of
Indianapolis. USA: Indianapolis, IN. 1921-1922. Lang.: Eng.   2680
Plays/librettos/scripts
Political and military context of O'Neill's *The Emperor Jones*. USA.
Haiti. 1898-1920. Lang.: Eng.   3386

Emperor of the Moon, The
Performance/production
Carol MacVey's production of *The Emperor of the Moon* by Aphra
Behn. USA: Iowa City, IA. 1992. Lang.: Eng.   2611

Emperor Regrets, The
Basic theatrical documents
Text of *The Emperor Regrets* by Thérèse Radic. Australia. 1994. Lang.:
Eng.   1642

Emu Plains Theatre (Australia)
Relation to other fields
Theatre and the normalization of the New South Wales penal colony.
Australia. 1789-1830. Lang.: Eng.   1133

En attendant Godot (Waiting for Godot)
Performance/production
Comparison of productions of *Waiting for Godot* for stage and video.
Canada: Montreal, PQ. 1988-1992. Lang.: Fre.   1921

Enström, Rolf
Performance/production
Report from conference on music in theatre and theatre in music. Sweden: Västerås. 1996. Lang.: Swe. 945

Entertainer, The
Performance/production
Collection of newspaper reviews by London theatre critics. UK-England: London. 1996. Lang.: Eng. 2412

Collection of newspaper reviews by New York theatre critics. USA: New York, NY. 1996. Lang.: Eng. 2560

Entertaining Angels
Performance/production
Collection of newspaper reviews by London theatre critics. UK-England: London. 1996. Lang.: Eng. 2382

Entertaining Mr. Sloane
Design/technology
Scenic designer Narelle Sissons. USA: New York, NY. 1996. Lang.: Eng. 250
Performance/production
Collection of newspaper reviews by New York theatre critics. USA: New York, NY. 1996. Lang.: Eng. 2571

Entre Villa y una mujer desnuda (Between Villa and a Naked Woman)
Plays/librettos/scripts
Analysis of *Entre Villa y una mujer desnuda (Between Villa and a Naked Woman)* by Sabina Berman. Mexico. 1993. Lang.: Eng. 3145

Entwisle, Christine
Performance/production
Collection of newspaper reviews by London theatre critics. UK-England: London. 1996. Lang.: Eng. 2385

Environment
Basic theatrical documents
Anthology of unknown plays of the Harlem Renaissance. USA: New York, NY. 1920-1940. Lang.: Eng. 1694

Environmental Action Theatre Project (Minneapolis, MN)
Plays/librettos/scripts
Grassroots theatres' productions of plays with environmental themes. USA. 1988-1996. Lang.: Eng. 3346

Environmental theatre
Audience
Israeli theatre and its audience. Israel. 1990-1991. Lang.: Eng. 139
Institutions
Gorilla Rep's free park performances of Shakespeare. USA: New York, NY. 1996. Lang.: Eng. 1865
Performance spaces
Post-modern performance: Forced Entertainment, Brith Grof, Fiona Templeton. UK-England: Sheffield, London. UK-Wales. USA: New York, NY. 1965-1995. Lang.: Eng. 3703
Performance/production
Deckchair Theatre's *Cappucino Strip* directed by Angela Chaplin. Australia: Fremantle. 1995. Lang.: Eng. 687

Pavolini and Blasetti's fascist spectacle *18BL*. Italy: Florence. 1933. Lang.: Eng. 867

Big Idea's environmental theatre. Australia: Perth. 1994. Lang.: Eng. 1900

Some Copenhagen theatre events. Denmark: Copenhagen. 1996. Lang.: Eng. 1982

Copenhagen performing arts events. Denmark: Copenhagen. 1996. Lang.: Eng. 1983

Simultaneous staging of scenes from Büchner's *Woyzeck* in a medieval castle. Italy: Völs. Germany. 1837-1987. Lang.: Eng. 2131

Barbara Carlisle's at-home production of *Paris Quartet*. USA. 1995. Lang.: Eng. 2609

Interview with Tina Landau, director of *The Trojan Women: A Love Story*. USA: New York, NY. 1996. Lang.: Eng. 2672

The concept of 'gallery theatre'. USA. 1996. Lang.: Eng. 3806

Epicoene
Plays/librettos/scripts
Epicoene, Jonson, and Shakespeare. England. 1609. Lang.: Eng. 2897

Epilogue of the Raindrops
Performance/production
Collection of newspaper reviews by London theatre critics. UK-England: London. 1996. Lang.: Eng. 2376

Epps, Sheldon
Performance/production
Play On!, a musical adaptation of Shakespeare's *Twelfth Night*. USA: San Diego, CA. 1993-1996. Lang.: Eng. 3971

Plays/librettos/scripts
Blacksmyths, Black playwrights project—excerpt from symposium panel discussion. USA: Los Angeles, CA. 1995-1996. Lang.: Eng. 3320

Epstein, Alvin
Institutions
Productions of the month-long Beckett festival. France: Strasbourg. 1996. Lang.: Eng. 408

Equestrian acts
Design/technology
Transport problems of Zingaro, an equestrian theatre group. USA: New York, NY. France. 1996. Lang.: Eng. 3699
Performance/production
The equestrian theatre of Zingaro, appearing at BAM. USA: New York, NY. France: Paris. 1996. Lang.: Eng. 3720

Equinoxes
Performance/production
Interview with choreographer Alain Populaire. Canada: Montreal, PQ. Belgium. 1996. Lang.: Fre. 1416

Equipment
Uses of the internet for theatre fans or practitioners. USA: New York, NY. 1996. Lang.: Eng. 4
Design/technology
The Entech theatre technology trade show. Australia: Sydney. 1996. Lang.: Eng. 144

Survey of SIEL trade show. France: Paris. 1996. Lang.: Eng. 166

Technical equipment of Bühnen Lübeck. Germany: Lübeck. 1996. Lang.: Ger. 171

Renewal of the sound system at Staatstheater. Germany: Darmstadt. 1996. Lang.: Ger. 172

Conference on hydraulic and electronic stage technology. Germany: Lohr am Main. 1996. Lang.: Swe. 174

Report on SIB trade show. Italy: Rimini. 1996. Lang.: Eng. 183

Technical challenges of international Musical Circus. Japan: Tokyo. 1996. Lang.: Eng. 186

Description of a bench-built cable tester. North America. 1996. Lang.: Eng. 187

Procedure for patching scrim with glue. North America. 1996. Lang.: Eng. 188

How to extend the life of strip-lights. North America. 1996. Lang.: Eng. 194

Instructions for constructing pneumatic tab turner and controls. North America. 1996. Lang.: Eng. 195

Report on PLASA trade show. UK-England: London. 1996. Lang.: Eng. 223

Maris Ensing, developer of lighting-control software. UK-England: Kent. Netherlands: Rotterdam. 1984-1996. Lang.: Eng. 226

Report on ABTT trade show. UK-England. 1996. Lang.: Eng. 229

Survey of ABTT trade shows. UK-England: London. 1996. Lang.: Eng. 230

Profile of *Lighting Dimensions* trade show. USA: Miami, FL. 1996. Lang.: Eng. 234

Guide to industry resources for technical theatre. USA. 1996. Lang.: Eng. 237

Guide to manufacturers and equipment for theatre technology. USA. 1996. Lang.: Eng. 238

Issue of *LDim* devoted to lighting industry resources. USA. 1996. Lang.: Eng. 240

Square-section metal tubes in scene construction. USA. 1950-1996. Lang.: Eng. 241

Patent infringement suits between two theatrical lighting companies. USA. 1996. Lang.: Eng. 251

The use of air-lift casters in scenery. USA. 1996. Lang.: Eng. 253

Sound equipment for the papal visit. USA. 1995. Lang.: Eng. 255

Report on lighting and sound trade shows. USA: Miami Beach, FL, New York, NY. 1995. Lang.: Eng. 256

Assessment of several high-quality microphones. USA: New York, NY. 1996. Lang.: Eng. 257

Digital technology at ShowBiz Expo. USA: Los Angeles, CA. 1996. Lang.: Eng. 263

New products at National Association of Broadcasters trade show. USA: Las Vegas, NV. 1996. Lang.: Eng. 264

Technical elements of Silver Legacy Resort and Casino. USA: Reno, NV. 1995. Lang.: Eng. 265

Equipment — cont'd

Sound equipment of Electro-Voice. USA: New York, NY, Buchanan, MI. 1996. Lang.: Eng.   267

Profile of BRC Imagination Arts, creator of educational attractions. USA: Burbank, CA. 1996. Lang.: Eng.   268

Software choices of professional sound designers. USA. 1996. Lang.: Eng.   269

Analysis of new lighting unit by High End. USA. 1996. Lang.: Eng.   271

Building a treadmill for a production of *The Mystery of Edwin Drood*. USA. 1996. Lang.: Eng.   273

Method of sewing pipe pockets. USA. 1996. Lang.: Eng.   282

Digital technology at the Crosswaves festival. USA: Philadelphia, PA. 1996. Lang.: Eng.   283

Using a flash camera for theatrical lighting effects. USA. 1996. Lang.: Eng.   287

Description of lighting instrument's color-mixing system. USA. 1996. Lang.: Eng.   292

Lighting manufacturers High End Systems. USA: Austin, TX. 1996. Lang.: Eng.   293

Profile of Electronic Theatre Controls. USA: Madison, WI. 1996. Lang.: Eng.   295

Review of new lighting products. USA. 1995. Lang.: Eng.   297

Control of heat in lighting systems. USA. 1996. Lang.: Eng.   299

Description of pneumatic debris cannon used for explosion effects. USA. 1996. Lang.: Eng.   303

Protection against falls in arena shows. USA. 1996. Lang.: Eng.   305

The Olio Roll Drop. USA. 1996. Lang.: Eng.   309

Profile of Jands Hog lighting control consoles. USA. 1996. Lang.: Eng.   312

Analysis of new lighting instrument, Strand Lekolite Zoom 25150. USA: New York, NY. 1996. Lang.: Eng.   313

Description of techniques for sound control and monitoring. USA. 1996. Lang.: Eng.   314

Description of the Altman Shakespeare 600 lighting instrument. USA. 1996. Lang.: Eng.   315

Description of Light Shop V2.3 lighting software. USA. 1996. Lang.: Eng.   316

Survey of USITT conference and trade show. USA: Fort Worth, TX. 1996. Lang.: Eng.   317

Hudson Scenic's computerized theatrical motion control system. USA: New York, NY. 1996. Lang.: Eng.   318

National System Contractors Association trade show. USA: St. Louis, MO. 1996. Lang.: Eng.   319

Advantages to using grounded neutral wye power systems. USA. 1996. Lang.: Eng.   320

Report on Strand lighting consoles. USA. 1996. Lang.: Eng.   321

The replacement of DMX512 by Ethernet for controlling moving lights and other stage devices. USA. 1996. Lang.: Eng.   322

Health effects of glycol-based stage fog. USA. 1996. Lang.: Eng.   323

Assessment of computer-generated scenic design. USA. 1996. Lang.: Eng.   325

New techniques for theatrical sound design. USA. 1996. Lang.: Eng.   329

Advantages of virtual reality in theatre. USA. 1996. Lang.: Eng.   331

Lightfair International trade exhibition. USA: San Francisco, CA. 1996. Lang.: Eng.   333

Peggy Eisenhauer's lighting design for *Dancing on Her Knees*, Public Theatre. USA: New York, NY. 1996. Lang.: Eng.   1718

Television lighting design by Steven Brill and Kathleen Ankers. USA: New York, NY. 1996. Lang.: Eng.   3663

Bob Dickinson's TV lighting designs for the summer Olympics. USA: Atlanta, GA. 1996. Lang.: Eng.   3664

Design of MTV video music awards ceremony. USA: New York, NY. 1995. Lang.: Eng.   3666

Transport problems of Zingaro, an equestrian theatre group. USA: New York, NY. France. 1996. Lang.: Eng.   3699

Sound design for Cirque du Soleil's *Quidam*. Canada: Montreal, PQ. 1996. Lang.: Eng.   3746

Description of the mock siege or 'fort holding'. England: Warwick, Bristol. 1572-1574. Lang.: Eng.   3774

Performance artist Tanya Mars and the computer game *Blood Bath*. Canada. 1996. Lang.: Eng.   3788

Sound equipment and design for the Nickelodeon tour. USA: New York, NY. 1996. Lang.: Eng.   3830

Production design for tour of country singer Reba McEntire. USA. 1996. Lang.: Eng.   3831

Quiet hydraulic system used for scene changes in Australian production of *Beauty and the Beast*. Australia: Melbourne, Sydney. 1996. Lang.: Eng.   3886

Technical differences between Broadway and West End productions of *The Who's Tommy*. UK-England: London. USA: New York, NY. 1996. Lang.: Eng.   3893

Scharff Weisberg, purveyor of video equipment for *The Who's Tommy*. USA: New York, NY. 1996. Lang.: Eng.   3899

Renovation of Metropolitan Opera lighting system. USA: New York, NY. 1996. Lang.: Eng.   4025

Performance spaces
The restoration of the Hawaii Theatre Center. USA: Honolulu, HI. 1996. Lang.: Eng.   670

Equipo Teatro Payro (Buenos Aires)
Institutions
Account of Spanish-American theatre festival. Spain: Cádiz. 1995. Lang.: Spa.   534

Erasmus Montanus
Performance/production
Catrine Telle directs Holberg's *Erasmus Montanus*, Nationaltheatret. Norway: Oslo. 1996. Lang.: Eng.   2144

Collection of newspaper reviews by London theatre critics. UK-England: London. 1996. Lang.: Eng.   2344

Erdélyi Magyar Színjátszó (Kolozsvár)
Institutions
Early professional acting in Hungary and Transylvania. Hungary. 1696-1809. Lang.: Hun.   475

Erdős, Irma
Institutions
Artists of Allami Székely Színház. Hungary. Romania: Tîrgu Mureş. 1946-1995. Lang.: Hun.   477

Erections Ejaculations Exhibitions
Performance/production
Collection of newspaper reviews by London theatre critics. UK-England: London. 1996. Lang.: Eng.   2309

Ergen, Mehmet
Performance/production
Collection of newspaper reviews by London theatre critics. UK-England: London. 1996. Lang.: Eng.   2332

Collection of newspaper reviews by London theatre critics. UK-England: London. 1996. Lang.: Eng.   2473

ERIC
SEE
Educational Resources Information Center.

Erkel Színház (Budapest)
Performance/production
Miklós Gábor Kerényi's concept for a revival of Gounod's *Faust*. Hungary: Budapest. 1996. Lang.: Hun.   4170

Erkel, Ferenc
Performance/production
The Vienna premiere of Erkel's *Hunyadi László*. Austria: Vienna. Hungary. 1856. Lang.: Hun.   4079

Ermione
Performance/production
The failure of Rossini's opera *Ermione*. Italy. 1819. Lang.: Eng.   4189

Ermitažnyj Teat'r (St. Petersburg)
Institutions
History of the Hermitage Theatre, Teat'r Ermitažnyj. Russia: St. Petersburg. 1785-1996. Lang.: Rus.   519

Erofilomachia
Plays/librettos/scripts
Sforza Oddi, a literary antecedent of Shakespeare. Italy. England. 1521. Lang.: Eng.   3124

Erotec: The Human Life of Machines
Performance/production
Performances of the Jim Henson International Festival. USA: New York, NY. 1995. Lang.: Eng.   4407

Erotičéskij Teat'r (Moscow)
Performance/production
Actress Alena Čubarova on work in Erotičéskij Teat'r. Russia: Moscow. 1996. Lang.: Rus.   903

Erreur sur la personne (Mistaken Identity)
Plays/librettos/scripts
Representation of theatre and relation of fiction to reality in film. Canada. USA. 1993-1996. Lang.: Fre.   3642

Euripides — cont'd

Actor Erland Josephson on the role of Kadmos in Euripides' *Bákchai (The Bacchae)*. Greece. Sweden. 404 B.C.-1996 A.D. Lang.: Swe.   3057

Relation to other fields

Personality and selfhood in the writings of the ancient Greeks. Ancient Greece. 525-405 B.C. Lang.: Eng.   3477

The Dionysian cult as reflected in *Bákchai (The Bacchae)* of Euripides. Greece. 407 B.C. Lang.: Swe.   3499

Europäische Theaterakademie Konrad Ekhof (Hamburg)

Performance/production

The present state of German actor training. Germany. 1996. Lang.: Ger.   817

Europe After the Rain

Performance/production

Creation and production of a devised piece on the former Yugoslavia at Lancaster University. UK-England: Lancaster. 1993. Lang.: Eng.   2515

European Directors School (Leeds)

Institutions

The European Directors School at West Yorkshire Playhouse. UK-England: Leeds. 1996. Lang.: Eng.   558

European Scenography Centre (London)

Design/technology

Account of Scenofest at London's European Scenography Centre. UK-England: London. 1994-1995. Lang.: Eng.   231

Euthyphro

Plays/librettos/scripts

Dramatic adaptations of dialogues by Plato. Ancient Greece. 427-347 B.C. Lang.: Eng.   2711

Evangheliṣti (Evangelists, The)

Basic theatrical documents

English translation of *Evangheliṣti (The Evangelists)* by Alina Mungiu Pippidi. Romania. 1996. Lang.: Eng.   1673

Evans, Geraint

Plays/librettos/scripts

Leporello's aria 'Madamina' in Mozart's *Don Giovanni*. Austro-Hungarian Empire: Vienna. 1787-1996. Lang.: Eng.   4306

Evans, Lee

Performance/production

Collection of newspaper reviews by London theatre critics. UK-England: London. 1996. Lang.: Eng.   2348

Evans, Lisa

Performance/production

Collection of newspaper reviews by London theatre critics. UK-England: London. 1996. Lang.: Eng.   2345

Everding, August

Institutions

The reopening of the Prinzregententheater with Wagner's *Tristan und Isolde*. Germany: Munich. 1996. Lang.: Ger.   4041

Performance spaces

The reopening of the Prinzregententheater. Germany: Munich. 1901-1996. Lang.: Ger.   4069

Every Man in His Humor

Plays/librettos/scripts

The fool in *commedia dell'arte* and in Jonson's *Every Man in His Humour*. England. Italy. 1465-1601. Lang.: Eng.   1093

Everyman

Performance/production

Collection of newspaper reviews by London theatre critics. UK-England: London, Stratford. 1996. Lang.: Eng.   2476

Everyman Players (New Orleans, LA)

Design/technology

Costume designer Irene Corey of the Everyman Players. USA: New Orleans, LA. 1980-1995. Lang.: Eng.   275

Everything in the Garden

Performance/production

Collection of newspaper reviews by London theatre critics. UK-England: London. 1996. Lang.: Eng.   2399

Evidence of Floods

Performance/production

Performances of the Jim Henson International Festival. USA: New York, NY. 1995. Lang.: Eng.   4407

Evita

Performance/production

Review of the film version of the musical *Evita*. USA. 1979-1996. Lang.: Eng.   3636

History of the filming of *Evita*. USA. UK-England. 1974-1995. Lang.: Eng.   3639

Singer/actress Elaine Page. UK-England: London. USA: New York, NY. 1968-1996. Lang.: Eng.   3925

Actresses recall playing the lead role in the musical *Evita*. USA. 1996. Lang.: Eng.   3944

Evreinov, Nikolaj Nikolajévič

SEE

Jévrejnov, Nikolaj Nikolajévič.

Ex Machina (Montreal, PQ)

Institutions

Productions of the Carrefour theatre festival. Canada: Quebec, PQ. 1979-1996. Lang.: Eng.   1760

Evolving *Les Sept Branches de la Rivière Ota (The Seven Streams of the River Ota)* by Robert Lepage. Canada: Quebec, PQ. 1995. Lang.: Eng.   1779

Performance/production

Japanese performances of Japanese themes at Toronto Theatre Festival. Japan. Canada: Toronto, ON. 1996. Lang.: Eng.   874

Collection of newspaper reviews by London theatre critics. UK-England: London. 1996. Lang.: Eng.   2393

Robert Lepage's *The Seven Streams of the River Ota* at BAM. USA: New York, NY. 1996. Lang.: Eng.   2616

Ex-Yu

Performance/production

Collection of newspaper reviews by London theatre critics. UK-England: London. 1996. Lang.: Eng.   2415

Exhibitions

Design/technology

Report on Prague Quadrennial. Czech Republic: Prague. 1995. Lang.: Hun.   160

Scenographer Mátyás Varga. Hungary: Budapest, Szeged. 1910-1995. Lang.: Hun.   179

Introduction to exhibition of designs by Mátyás Varga. Hungary. 1910-1995. Lang.: Hun.   181

Exhibit of theatrical painting at Dom Aktera. Russia: Moscow. 1995-1996. Lang.: Rus.   198

Professional Lighting and Sound Association exhibitors. UK-England: London. 1996. Lang.: Eng.   222

Report of Show Biz Expo. USA: New York, NY. 1996. Lang.: Eng.   262

Lightfair International trade exhibition. USA: San Francisco, CA. 1996. Lang.: Eng.   333

Exil et Tendresse (Exile and Tenderness)

Plays/librettos/scripts

Representations of Saint Francis in plays of Leclerc, Bobin, and Delteil. Canada: Montreal, PQ. 1996. Lang.: Fre.   2809

Experimental theatre

SEE ALSO

Avant-garde theatre.

Alternative theatre.

Administration

Théâtre Petit à Petit: managing experimental theatre. Canada: Montreal, PQ. 1989. Lang.: Fre.   7

Basic theatrical documents

Text of *Luna Park Eclipses* with an introduction by its author Peter Barnes. UK-England: London. 1995. Lang.: Eng.   1683

Institutions

Overview of Saskatoon Fringe Festival. Canada: Montreal, PQ. 1990. Lang.: Fre.   357

Changing meanings of the term 'experimental theatre'. Canada. 1970-1989. Lang.: Fre.   363

Théâtre Parminou's experimental popular theatre. Canada. 1978-1989. Lang.: Fre.   364

Jean-Pierre Ronfard on his Nouveau Théâtre Expérimental. Canada: Montreal, PQ. 1975-1989. Lang.: Fre.   367

Nouveau Théâtre Expérimental and the systematic testing of theatrical principles. Canada: Montreal, PQ. 1989. Lang.: Fre.   368

Report on Cairo International Theatre Festival. Egypt: Cairo. 1995. Lang.: Eng.   401

Community theatres arising from the reform movement and settlement houses. USA: Chicago, IL, Cleveland, OH, New York, NY. 1896-1930. Lang.: Eng.   570

Tangente's contribution to experimental dance. Canada: Montreal, PQ. 1980-1991. Lang.: Fre.   1554

Comparison of Carbone 14 and Nouveau Théâtre Expérimental. Canada: Montreal, PQ. 1989. Lang.: Fre.   1778

Interview with Ellen Stewart of La MaMa Experimental Theatre Club. USA: New York, NY. 1960-1996. Lang.: Eng.   1871

SUBJECT INDEX

Festivals — cont'd

Festival of arts variety theatres. Russia: Kiev. 1995-1996. Lang.: Rus.
3702

Profile of Münchner Biennale, festival of new music theatre. Germany: Munich. 1996. Lang.: Ger.
3846

Jeunesse's festival of works by Kurt Weill. Austria: Vienna. 1995. Lang.: Eng.
3906

Account of major European opera festivals. Austria: Bregenz, Salzburg. Germany: Bayreuth. 1996. Lang.: Hun.
4030

Opera at the Bregenz festival. Austria: Bregenz. 1995. Lang.: Eng. 4031

Canadian Opera Company's *Erwartung* and *Bluebeard's Castle* at the Hong Kong Arts Festival. China, People's Republic of: Hong Kong. 1996. Lang.: Ger.
4035

The Wexford opera festival. Ireland: Wexford. 1951-1996. Lang.: Swe.
4047

Guide to summer opera festivals. North America. Europe. 1996. Lang.: Eng.
4050

Some performances at the Buxton opera festival. UK-England: Buxton. 1996. Lang.: Eng.
4059

Productions of world puppetry festival. France: Charleville-Mézières. Spain. 1988. Lang.: Fre.
4373

Report on Fidena 1996 international puppetry festival. Germany: Bochum. 1996. Lang.: Ger.
4374

Review of international puppetry festival. Germany: Stuttgart. 1996. Lang.: Ger.
4375

Introduction to the UNIMA puppetry festival by its director. Hungary: Budapest. 1996. Lang.: Hun.
4378

Review of the UNIMA festival and conference. Hungary: Budapest. 1996. Lang.: Ger.
4380

Report on UNIMA puppetry festival. Hungary: Budapest. 1996. Lang.: Hun.
4382

Program of biennial puppetry festival. Slovenia: Novo mesto. 1996. Lang.: Slo.
4383

Opening ceremony of new wing at Center of Puppetry Arts. USA: Atlanta, GA. 1995. Lang.: Eng.
4385

Account of puppetry festival. Canada: Jonquière, PQ. 1990. Lang.: Fre.
4438

Performance/production
Criticism of the Cordoba theatre festival. Argentina: Cordoba. 1996. Lang.: Spa.
680

Cultural difference and the Cordoba festival of Latin American theatre. Argentina: Cordoba. 1996. Lang.: Spa.
681

Productions of children's theatre festival Coups de théâtre. Canada: Montreal, PQ. 1996. Lang.: Fre.
703

The experimental theatre festival Vingt jours de théâtre à risque. Canada: Montreal, PQ. 1989-1996. Lang.: Fre.
721

Impressions of Festival de Théâtre des Amériques productions. Canada: Montreal, PQ. 1989. Lang.: Fre.
725

Report on multi-disciplinary expo, Today's Japan. Canada: Toronto, ON. Japan. 1995. Lang.: Eng.
741

Memories of a story-telling festival. Canada: Montreal, PQ. 1992. Lang.: Fre.
754

Interview with Octavio Arbeláez, director of the Manizales festival. Colombia: Manizales. 1984-1996. Lang.: Spa.
760

History of Havana's Latin American theatre festival. Cuba: Havana. 1981-1996. Lang.: Spa.
763

Report on the Avignon fringe festival. France: Avignon. 1996. Lang.: Eng.
796

Israeli productions at the Hamburg summer theatre festival. Germany: Hamburg. Israel: Tel Aviv. 1996. Lang.: Ger.
811

Tadashi Suzuki's plan for an international Theatre Olympics. Japan: Toga-Mura. 1960-1996. Lang.: Eng.
873

Japanese performances of Japanese themes at Toronto Theatre Festival. Japan. Canada: Toronto, ON. 1996. Lang.: Eng.
874

History of Latin American theatre festivals. Latin America. 1936-1996. Lang.: Spa.
876

The theatre festival as a valuable resource. Latin America. 1936-1996. Lang.: Spa.
877

Defense of theatre festivals. Latin America. 1996. Lang.: Spa. 878

Reasons for the continued interest in theatre festivals. Latin America. 1968-1996. Lang.: Spa.
880

Profile of Asian-oriented Singaporean theatre festival. Singapore. 1994-1996. Lang.: Eng.
938

Distinctive characteristics of theatre festivals. South America. 1996. Lang.: Spa.
941

Observations of the London theatre season. UK-England: London. 1996. Lang.: Ger.
986

History of the London Speech Festival. UK-England. 1928-1939. Lang.: Eng.
995

Festival of plays by Eduardo Pavlovsky. USA: Hollywood, CA. Argentina. 1995-1996. Lang.: Eng.
1021

Account of National Black Theatre Festival. USA: Winston-Salem, NC. 1995. Lang.: Eng.
1026

'The Cultural Olympiad' linking sports and the arts. USA: Atlanta, GA. 1996. Lang.: Eng.
1034

American fringe theatre festivals. USA. 1996. Lang.: Eng. 1040

Account of *Compression 100* by Tess de Quincey and Stuart Lynch. Denmark: Copenhagen. Australia. 1996. Lang.: Dan.
1420

Characteristics of Montreal choreography as seen at the Festival International de la Nouvelle Danse. Canada: Montreal, PQ. 1992. Lang.: Fre.
1565

Modern dance festival Spring Collection. UK-England: London. 1996. Lang.: Swe.
1592

The premiere of the first German translation of Wyspiański's *Wesele (The Wedding)*. Austria: Salzburg. 1992. Lang.: Eng, Fre. 1904

Report on the Shanghai International Shakespeare Festival. China, People's Republic of: Shanghai. 1994. Lang.: Eng.
1972

German-language production of *Splendid's* by Jean Genet, directed by Klaus Michael Grüber. France: Paris. 1995. Lang.: Eng.
2023

Paris productions of the fall season. France: Paris. 1996. Lang.: Eng.
2032

Konstanze Lauterbach's production of *Der aufhaltsame Aufstieg des Arturo Ui (The Resistible Rise of Arturo Ui)* by Bertolt Brecht. Germany: Klagenfurt. 1995. Lang.: Eng.
2048

The Janusz Korczak festival of children's theatre. Poland: Warsaw. 1996. Lang.: Eng, Fre.
2179

Reports from Polish theatre festivals. Poland: Toruń, Radom, Poznań. 1995. Lang.: Eng, Fre.
2180

Józef Szajna's *Restos (The Remains)*. Portugal: Lisbon, Almada. 1995. Lang.: Eng, Fre.
2181

Account of Čechov International Theatre Festival. Russia. 1996. Lang.: Eng.
2199

Current Moscow theatre, with emphasis on festivals. Russia: Moscow. 1995. Lang.: Eng.
2200

Report on the National Arts Festival. South Africa, Republic of: Grahamstown. 1996. Lang.: Eng.
2265

Report on Klein Karoo arts festival. South Africa, Republic of: Oudtshoorn. 1996. Lang.: Afr.
2266

Report on the national arts festival. South Africa, Republic of: Grahamstown. 1995. Lang.: Eng.
2267

Report on annual National Arts Festival. South Africa, Republic of: Grahamstown. 1995. Lang.: Eng.
2270

The Madrid theatre season. Spain: Madrid. 1996. Lang.: Eng. 2271

Report on festival of Spanish American theatre. Spain: Cádiz. 1995. Lang.: Eng.
2272

Collection of newspaper reviews by London theatre critics. UK-England: London. 1996. Lang.: Eng.
2317

Collection of newspaper reviews by London theatre critics. UK-England: London. 1996. Lang.: Eng.
2498

Two productions of the National Black Theatre Festival. USA: Winston-Salem, NC. 1995. Lang.: Eng.
2625

Account of a symposium on Polish cinema. Poland. USA: New York, NY. 1930-1996. Lang.: Eng.
3619

Carnival events of the Lewes Bonfire Festival. UK-England: Lewes, East Sussex. 1846-1994. Lang.: Eng.
3743

List of summer 1995 opera festivals in Europe, Scandinavia, Russia, Turkey.. Asia. 1996. Lang.: Eng.
4077

R. Murray Schafer's opera *Le Théâtre noir* at the Festival musical de Liège. France: Liège. 1989. Lang.: Fre.
4118

Critical survey of opera festivals and their conventional repertory. France: Avignon, Aix-en-Provence. 1996. Lang.: Swe.
4122

The opera festival at Verona's open-air arena. Italy: Verona. 1913-1995. Lang.: Hun.
4188

Figurative arts — cont'd

Portraits of nineteenth-century actors in mural art of the Royal Dramatic Theatre. Sweden: Stockholm. 1840-1879. Lang.: Swe. 2278

Video-sculptural performances of Gary Hill. USA: New York, NY. 1995. Lang.: Eng. 3657

Plays/librettos/scripts
The influence of contemporary emblems on plays by Shakespeare. England. 1529-1614. Lang.: Eng. 2875

Analysis of the aesthetics of plays by Handke and Strauss. Germany. 1745-1991. Lang.: Eng. 3037

Analysis of caricatures of Pirandello. Italy. 1924-1938. Lang.: Ita. 3111

Artists' renderings of scenes from Shakespeare's *Romeo and Juliet*. UK-England. 1679-1996. Lang.: Eng. 3291

Medusa as a metaphorical presence in some contemporary productions. UK-England. Canada. 1995. Lang.: Eng. 3294

Relation to other fields
Postmodernism and formal conventions of performance. Canada. USA. 1950-1996. Lang.: Fre. 1136

Avant-garde representations of the human body. Canada. 1996. Lang.: Eng. 1145

Interview with sculptor and architect Melvin Charney. Canada. 1982-1989. Lang.: Fre. 1160

Garrick, painting, and a shift in theatre aesthetics. England. 1700-1799. Lang.: Ger. 1170

Description of the portraits in the lobby of the Stadsschouwburg. Netherlands: Amsterdam. 1895-1995. Lang.: Dut. 1212

Spanish theatre and photography. Spain. 1956-1996. Lang.: Eng. 1232

Theatricality in the painting *Las meninas* by Velázquez. Spain. 1400-1996. Lang.: Eng. 1233

The rediscovery of artworks that formerly hung in the Shubert Theatre. USA: New York, NY. 1925-1995. 1257

Labeling artworks to create broader audience appeal. USA. 1996. Lang.: Eng. 1280

Narrative structure in museum exhibits. USA. 1996. Lang.: Eng. 1281

Social status and the *tableau vivant*. USA: New York, NY. 1850-1900. Lang.: Eng. 1282

Dramatic compositions in the photographs of Roger Witkin. USA: New York, NY. 1996. Lang.: Eng. 1283

Report on the Carnegie International Festival. USA: Pittsburgh, PA. 1995. Lang.: Eng. 1284

Shakespeare's influence on sculpture in Southwark. England: London. 1599-1631. Lang.: Eng. 3493

Profile of the Tadeusz Kantor Gallery-Studio, which houses Kantor's artworks. Poland: Cracow. 1995. Lang.: Eng, Fre. 3504

The Sketching Society's drawings of Bottom with ass's head in Shakespeare's *A Midsummer Night's Dream*. UK-England: London. 1831. Lang.: Eng. 3513

Paintings by Clifford Odets and a production of his *Golden Boy*. USA: New York, NY. 1940-1996. Lang.: Eng. 3522

Theory/criticism
Theatre practitioners on the ethics of theatrical collaboration. Australia: Perth. 1994. Lang.: Eng. 1319

Nudity and vulnerability in performance art. USA. 1960-1996. Lang.: Eng. 3826

Training
Etienne Decroux's theory of corporeal mime. France: Paris. 1918-1996. Lang.: Eng. 3688

Figures of Speech (Portland, ME)
Performance/production
Performances of the Jim Henson International Festival. USA: New York, NY. 1995. Lang.: Eng. 4407

Filatov, Leonid
Performance/production
Comparison of film and theatre acting. Russia: Moscow. 1980-1996. Lang.: Rus. 921

Filho, Antunes
Plays/librettos/scripts
Poststructuralism in Latin American plays. Latin America. 1985-1995. Lang.: Spa. 3141

Filiatrault, Denise
Performance/production
Interview with comedian Denise Filiatrault. Canada. 1970-1990. Lang.: Fre. 731

Film
Reflections on the difference between theatre and film. 1995-1996. Lang.: Fre. 1

SEE ALSO
Classed Entries under MEDIA—Film.
Administration
Revivals on Broadway and on film. USA. 1937-1996. Lang.: Eng. 53

Interview with city officials about Broadway Initiatives. USA: New York, NY. 1996. Lang.: Eng. 100
Audience
Unexpected reactions to films and plays. Canada: Montreal, PQ. 1950-1989. Lang.: Fre. 129

Perception of women in theatre and film. Canada. 1989. Lang.: Fre. 132

Reactions to Montreal performances of Annie Sprinkle. Canada: Montreal, PQ. 1993. Lang.: Fre. 3785
Design/technology
John Alvin's posters for film and Broadway theatre. USA. 1996. Lang.: Eng. 236

Digital technology at ShowBiz Expo. USA: Los Angeles, CA. 1996. Lang.: Eng. 263

Set and costume research consultant Peter Dervis. USA: New York, NY. 1996. Lang.: Eng. 1730

Scene designer Brian Thomson. Australia. USA: New York, NY. 1971-1996. Lang.: Eng. 3885
Institutions
Account of Broadway Cares/Equity Fights Aids fundraising events. USA: New York, NY. 1996. Lang.: Eng. 597
Performance spaces
Chronology of Hippodrome performances. USA: New York, NY. 1905-1939. Lang.: Eng. 662
Performance/production
Actor, cabaret artist, and playwright Josef Hader and his play *Indien (India)*. Austria: Vienna. 1996. Lang.: Ger. 693

Comparison of acting for theatre, television and film. Canada. USA. 1996. Lang.: Fre. 743

Interview with director Robert Lepage. Denmark. Canada. 1996. Lang.: Dan. 768

Stage and film treatments of the fairy tale *Beauty and the Beast*. Europe. USA. Canada. 1946-1996. Lang.: Eng. 793

Expressionism and acting on stage and screen. Germany. 1918-1929. Lang.: Eng. 829

Articles on Indonesian performing arts. Indonesia. 1995. Lang.: Eng. 853

Interview with actor Sergej Makoveckij. Russia: Moscow. 1990-1996. Lang.: Rus. 901

Interview with actor Valerij Garkalin. Russia: Moscow. 1996. Lang.: Rus. 906

Interview with actor and directors who left theatre for film. Russia: Moscow. 1960-1996. Lang.: Rus. 907

Actor Beryl Reid. UK-England. 1919-1996. Lang.: Eng. 967

The reader and postmodern performance. UK-England. 1994-1995. Lang.: Eng. 983

Former Broadway stars and their careers in television and film. USA: New York, NY. 1996. Lang.: Eng. 1057

Biography of actor Fredric March. USA. 1897-1975. Lang.: Eng. 1059

The present state of ballet theatre. Russia: Moscow. 1996. Lang.: Rus. 1521

Patricia MacGeachy on performing in Beckett's *Not I*. Canada: Montreal, PQ. 1991-1992. Lang.: Fre. 1949

Postmodern 'nostalgia' and recent Shakespearean performances. Europe. North America. 1985-1995. Lang.: Eng. 1998

Interview with actor Andrzej Seweryn. Poland. 1946-1995. Lang.: Eng, Fre. 2156

Political activities of actor Frank Fay. USA: New York, NY, Hollywood, CA. 1944-1950. Lang.: Eng. 2624

Puppetry-related job prospects in TV and film. Germany. USA. 1996. Lang.: Ger. 3569

Ian McKellen's role in his own adaptation of Shakespeare's *Richard III*. UK-England. 1996. Lang.: Eng. 3628

Video installation at the Museum of Modern Art. USA: New York, NY. 1995. Lang.: Eng. 3678

Analysis of the work of video artists. USA. 1996. Lang.: Eng. 3679

Interview with musical theatre actor Anthony Newley. UK-England. 1935-1996. Lang.: Eng. 3924

Actor Bob Hoskins. UK-England. 1968-1996. Lang.: Eng. 3927

Lou Diamond Phillips' role in *The King and I*. USA: New York, NY. 1996. Lang.: Eng. 3938

Funnyhouse of a Negro — cont'd

Career of playwright Adrienne Kennedy. USA. 1965-1996. Lang.: Eng.
3448

Funtek, Anton
Basic theatrical documents
Texts of plays by Josip Vošnjak and Anton Funtek. Slovenia. 1834-1932. Lang.: Slo.
1676

Fura dels Baus, La (Barcelona)
Performance/production
Productions of the Festival de Théâtre des Amériques. Canada: Montreal, PQ. 1989. Lang.: Fre.
702

Analysis of *Suz o Suz* by La Fura dels Baus. Spain: Barcelona. 1996. Lang.: Eng.
3791

Furious
Basic theatrical documents
Collection of Australian gay and lesbian plays. Australia. 1970-1996. Lang.: Eng.
1641

Furlan, Mira
Relation to other fields
Actress Mira Furlan on refusing to take sides in ethnic conflict. Yugoslavia. 1991. Lang.: Eng.
1288

Furth, George
Performance/production
Collection of newspaper reviews by London theatre critics. UK-England: London. 1996. Lang.: Eng.
2335

Collection of newspaper reviews by New York theatre critics. USA: New York, NY. 1996. Lang.: Eng.
2572

Furtwängler, Wilhelm
Plays/librettos/scripts
Analysis of *Taking Sides* by Ronald Harwood. UK-England. 1934-1995. Lang.: Eng.
3316

Furu
Plays/librettos/scripts
Korean influence on *Furu*, attributed to Zeami. Japan. Korea. 1183-1420. Lang.: Eng.
1612

Furuhashi, Teiji
Performance/production
Japanese performances of Japanese themes at Toronto Theatre Festival. Japan. Canada: Toronto, ON. 1996. Lang.: Eng.
874

Fusco, Coco
Theory/criticism
Performance and self-representation of Hispanic artists. USA. 1992-1996. Lang.: Eng.
1375

Füst, Milán
Performance/production
Interview with actor Tibor Mertz. Hungary. 1985-1996. Lang.: Hun.
2107

Future Is Betamax, The
Performance/production
Collection of newspaper reviews by London theatre critics. UK-England: London. 1996. Lang.: Eng.
2470

Futurism
Basic theatrical documents
Text of futurist plays by Mina Loy. Italy. 1915. Lang.: Eng.
1668
Plays/librettos/scripts
Futurism and writer Mina Loy. Italy: Florence. 1905-1916. Lang.: Eng.
3134
Theory/criticism
Hungarian translation of Marinetti's Futurist manifesto. Italy. 1913-1921. Lang.: Hun.
1353

Gaál, Erzsébet
Performance/production
Budapest productions of the millicentenary season. Hungary: Budapest. 1995-1996. Lang.: Eng.
2104

Gabily, Didier-Georges
Performance/production
Analysis of *Gibiers du Temps (Spoils of Time)* by Didier-Georges Gabily. France: Gennevilliers. 1996. Lang.: Hun.
2008

Gábor, Miklós
Performance/production
Excerpt from diaries of Miklós Gábor. Hungary. 1954-1955. Lang.: Hun.
2101

Review of the autobiography of actor Miklós Gábor. Hungary. 1954. Lang.: Hun.
2110

Gaboriau, Linda
Administration
Translator Linda Gaboriau on promoting Quebec drama. Canada: Montreal, PQ, Toronto, ON. 1983-1988. Lang.: Fre.
1613
Plays/librettos/scripts
Translator Linda Gaboriau. Canada: Montreal, PQ. 1960-1990. Lang.: Fre.
2781

Gadd, Ulf
Performance/production
Interview with choreographer Ulf Gadd about attitudes toward dance. Sweden. Indonesia. 1985. Lang.: Swe.
1442

Gagnants, Les (Winners, The)
Plays/librettos/scripts
Playwright François Archambault discusses his craft. Canada: Montreal, PQ. 1992-1996. Lang.: Fre.
2741

Gaiety Theatre (Budapest)
SEE
Vígszínház.

Gaines, Davis
Performance/production
Profiles of singers in current Broadway musicals. USA: New York, NY. 1996. Lang.: Eng.
3940

Gaines, Reg E.
Performance/production
Collection of newspaper reviews by New York theatre critics. USA: New York, NY. 1996. Lang.: Eng.
2577

Profile of recent Broadway musicals. USA: New York, NY. 1996. Lang.: Eng.
3950

Interview with Reg E. Gaines, who wrote the text for *Bring in 'Da Noise, Bring in 'Da Funk*. USA: New York, NY. 1996. Lang.: Eng. 3976

Gaj, Grigorij
Performance/production
Actor Grigorij Gaj. Russia: St. Petersburg. 1949-1995. Lang.: Rus. 2225

Galati, Frank
Performance/production
Collection of newspaper reviews by New York theatre critics. USA: New York, NY. 1996. Lang.: Eng.
2564

Gale, Zona
Plays/librettos/scripts
Realism in American feminist drama. USA. 1900-1988. Lang.: Eng.
3441

Galefyrsten (Crazy Prince, The)
Institutions
Report from Danish theatre festival. Denmark: Odense. 1995. Lang.: Dan.
1784

Galibin, Aleksand'r
Performance/production
Interview with director Aleksand'r Galibin. Russia: St. Petersburg. 1996. Lang.: Rus.
2187

The new generation of Russian directors. Russia: Moscow. 1996. Lang.: Ger.
2196

Galin, Aleksand'r
Plays/librettos/scripts
Interview with playwright Aleksand'r Galin. Russia. 1996. Lang.: Eng.
3195

Galipeau, Jacques
Performance/production
Anecdote concerning Jacques Galipeau's role in *Tartuffe*, Théâtre du Nouveau Monde. France: Paris. 1971. Lang.: Fre.
2022

Gall, Hugues
Institutions
Interview with Hugues Gall, new director of the restructured Opéra National de Paris. France: Paris. 1996. Lang.: Eng.
4038

Gallagher, Dick
Performance/production
Collection of newspaper reviews by New York theatre critics. USA: New York, NY. 1996. Lang.: Eng.
2558

Gallert, Hans
Institutions
History of Theater der Jugend. Germany: Leipzig. 1946-1996. Lang.: Ger.
455

Galletti, Andrea
Performance/production
The development of Bayreuth as a cultural center. Germany: Bayreuth. 1709-1758. Lang.: Eng.
4144

Gallo, Paul
Design/technology
Paul Gallo's lighting design for *The Tempest* directed by George C. Wolfe. USA: New York, NY. 1996. Lang.: Eng.
1737

Gallotta, Jean-Claude
Performance/production
Choreography of Jean-Claude Gallotta. France: Grenoble. 1989. Lang.: Fre.
1423

Gambaro, Griselda
Plays/librettos/scripts
Versions of the legend of Antigone. 441 B.C.-1986 A.D. Lang.: Spa.
2708

Gambaro, Griselda — cont'd

Women's reinterpretations of traditional stories. Argentina. Indonesia. Iceland. 1879-1995. Lang.: Eng.   2713

Analysis of *El campo (The Camp)* by Griselda Gambaro. Argentina: Buenos Aires. 1967-1968. Lang.: Eng.   2714

Psychosexual fascism in *La Malasangre (Bitter Blood)* by Griselda Gambaro. Argentina. 1840-1996. Lang.: Eng.   2715

Persecution and criminal violence in plays of Griselda Gambaro. Argentina. 1963-1995. Lang.: Eng.   2718

Game Over
Performance/production
Collection of newspaper reviews by London theatre critics. UK-England: London. 1996. Lang.: Eng.   2427

Ganassi, Sonia
Performance/production
The New York debut of Italian mezzo-soprano Sonia Ganassi. Italy: Parma. 1996. Lang.: Eng.   4180

Comments on the mezzo soprano vocal range, including notes on specific singers. USA. 1996. Lang.: Eng.   4262

Gangsters
Plays/librettos/scripts
Analysis of *Gangsters* by Maishe Maponya. South Africa, Republic of. 1930-1995. Lang.: Eng.   3224

Garaczi, László
Plays/librettos/scripts
Theoretical essay on recent Hungarian drama. Hungary. 1995-1996. Lang.: Hun.   3074

Garbo, Greta
Performance/production
Portrayals of Eugene O'Neill's *Anna Christie*. USA: New York, NY. 1930-1993. Lang.: Eng.   2638

García Lorca, Federico
Performance/production
Productions of Schauspielhaus Bonn. Germany: Bonn. 1996. Lang.: Ger.   2075

Collection of newspaper reviews by London theatre critics. UK-England: London. 1996. Lang.: Eng.   2395

Collection of newspaper reviews by London theatre critics. UK-England: London. 1996. Lang.: Eng.   2418

Collection of newspaper reviews by London theatre critics. UK-England: London. 1996. Lang.: Eng.   2499

Plays/librettos/scripts
Metatheatre in the works of Lorca and Valle-Inclán. Spain. 1900-1936. Lang.: Eng.   3227

Playwright Federico García Lorca and Modernism. Spain. 1920-1936. Lang.: Eng.   3262

García Márquez, Gabriel
Performance/production
Graciela Daniele's dance adaptation of *Chronicle of a Death Foretold* by Gabriel García Márquez. USA: New York, NY. 1981-1996. Lang.: Eng.   1446

García Moreno, Angel
Performance/production
The Madrid theatre season. Spain: Madrid. 1996. Lang.: Eng.   2271

García, Rodrigo
Basic theatrical documents
Text of *Obras cómicas (Comic Works)* by Rodrigo García. Spain: Madrid. 1996. Lang.: Eng.   1679

Gardner Centre (Brighton)
Performance/production
Collection of newspaper reviews by London theatre critics. UK-England: London. 1996. Lang.: Eng.   2321

Gardner, Herb
Performance/production
Collection of newspaper reviews by New York theatre critics. USA: New York, NY. 1996. Lang.: Eng.   2584

Gardner, Tony
Performance/production
Collection of newspaper reviews by London theatre critics. UK-England: London. 1996. Lang.: Eng.   2316

Gardyne, John
Performance/production
Collection of newspaper reviews by London theatre critics. UK-England: London. 1996. Lang.: Eng.   2429

Gardzienice Theatre Association (Poland)
SEE
Ośrodek Praktyk Teatralnych.

Gargoyle Theatre Company (Reykjavik)
Performance/production
Collection of newspaper reviews by London theatre critics. UK-England: London. 1996. Lang.: Eng.   2376

Garkalin, Valerij
Performance/production
Interview with actor Valerij Garkalin. Russia: Moscow. 1996. Lang.: Rus.   906

Garland, Hamlin
Institutions
The Chicago Theatre Society and its work. USA: Chicago, IL. 1909-1915. Lang.: Eng.   1875

Garland, Patrick
Performance/production
Collection of newspaper reviews by London theatre critics. UK-England: London. 1996. Lang.: Eng.   2437

Garneau, Michel
Performance/production
Gabriel Garran's Paris productions of plays by Quebec authors. Canada. France: Paris. 1975-1990. Lang.: Fre.   1959

Plays/librettos/scripts
Quebec nationalism in Garneau's translation of *Macbeth*. Canada. 1969-1978. Lang.: Fre.   2749

Analysis of Michel Garneau's translations of Shakespearean plays. Canada. 1989. Lang.: Fre.   2833

Theory/criticism
Critical reception of productions by Robert Lepage at the Festival d'Automne. France: Paris. 1992. Lang.: Fre.   1345

Garner, Julian
Performance/production
Collection of newspaper reviews by London theatre critics. UK-England: London. 1996. Lang.: Eng.   2386

Collection of newspaper reviews by London theatre critics. UK-England: London. 1996. Lang.: Eng.   2496

Garnett, David
Performance/production
Collection of newspaper reviews by London theatre critics. UK-England: London. 1996. Lang.: Eng.   2359

Garpagoniana (Harpagoniana)
Performance/production
Vaginov's *Harpagoniana* directed by Venjamin Sal'nikov at Masterskaja Petra Fomenko. Russia: Moscow. 1995. Lang.: Rus.   2209

Garran, Gabriel
Performance/production
Gabriel Garran's Paris productions of plays by Quebec authors. Canada. France: Paris. 1975-1990. Lang.: Fre.   1959

Garrick, David
Performance/production
Diary evidence of David Garrick's interpretation of Hamlet. England. 1755. Lang.: Eng.   1994

Plays/librettos/scripts
David Garrick's librettos for Shakespearean opera. England. 1712-1756. Lang.: Eng.   4311

Relation to other fields
Garrick, painting, and a shift in theatre aesthetics. England. 1700-1799. Lang.: Ger.   1170

Garson, Barbara
Plays/librettos/scripts
Vietnam War protest plays. North America. Europe. 1965-1971. Lang.: Eng.   3153

Gáspár, Margit
Plays/librettos/scripts
Postwar Hungarian drama. Hungary. 1945-1989. Lang.: Hun.   3069

Gassman, Vittorio
Performance/production
Vittorio Gassman's correspondence with writer Giorgio Soavi. Italy. 1995-1996. Lang.: Ita.   862

Gästabudet (Banquet, The)
Plays/librettos/scripts
Librettist and poet Östen Sjöstrand. Sweden. 1953-1974. Lang.: Swe.   4339

Gate Theatre (Dublin)
Performance/production
Sebastian Barry's *The Steward of Christendom* directed by Max Stafford-Clark at the Gate. Ireland: Dublin. 1996. Lang.: Eng.   2115

Interview with actor Donal McCann. Ireland: Dublin. 1996. Lang.: Eng.   2116

Collection of newspaper reviews by New York theatre critics. USA: New York, NY, Chicago, IL. 1996. Lang.: Eng.   2585

Plays/librettos/scripts
Michael Colgan's plan to produce all of Samuel Beckett's plays at the Gate Theatre. Ireland: Dublin. 1991-1996. Lang.: Eng.   3088

Gay theatre — cont'd

Interview with playwright Mart Crowley. USA: New York, NY. 1996. Lang.: Eng.   3424

Interview with playwright Bill C. Davis. USA: New York, NY. 1996. Lang.: Eng.   3438

Reference materials
Information on gay and lesbian plays by Quebecois. Canada: Montreal, PQ. 1966-1989. Lang.: Fre.   3472

Relation to other fields
Attitudes toward gay theatre in Quebec. Canada. 1960-1990. Lang.: Fre.   3480

Homosexuality in Quebecois society and theatre. Canada. 1960-1990. Lang.: Fre.   3481

Theory/criticism
Charles Ludlam's Ridiculous Theatrical Company, and gay and lesbian politics. USA: New York, NY. 1967-1987. Lang.: Eng.   1376

Gay and lesbian studies, performance, and criticism. USA: New York, NY. 1960-1996. Lang.: Eng.   1377

The question of proof in performance studies. USA. 1996. Lang.: Eng.   1384

Identity and representation in *Dark Fruit* by Pomo Afro Homos. USA: San Francisco, CA. 1990-1996. Lang.: Eng.   1387

Performance theory and *My Queer Body* by Tim Miller. USA. 1992-1996. Lang.: Eng.   1392

Critical misrepresentation of *Falsettoland* by William Finn and James Lapine. USA. 1990. Lang.: Eng.   4002

Gay theory

Performance/production
Gender in performances of actress Mary Martin. USA. 1922-1994. Lang.: Eng.   1074

Plays/librettos/scripts
Analysis of works by Paul Bonin-Rodriguez. USA. 1992-1994. Lang.: Eng.   1109

Feminist/lesbian reading of *The Sound of Music*, and its star Mary Martin. USA. 1938-1959. Lang.: Eng.   4000

Theory/criticism
Lesbian interpretation of *The Member of the Wedding* by Carson McCullers. USA. 1946-1996. Lang.: Eng.   3562

Gay, John

Performance/production
Collection of newspaper reviews by London theatre critics. UK-England: London. 1996. Lang.: Eng.   2422

Gazzaniga, Giuseppe

Plays/librettos/scripts
Leporello's aria 'Madamina' in Mozart's *Don Giovanni*. Austro-Hungarian Empire: Vienna. 1787-1996. Lang.: Eng.   4306

Geary Theatre (San Francisco, CA)

Performance spaces
Restoration of the Geary Theatre. USA: San Francisco, CA. 1996. Lang.: Eng.   668

Geer, Richard Owen

Institutions
Community plays of Swamp Gravy. USA: Colquitt, GA. 1987-1996. Lang.: Eng.   578

Geiogamah, Hanay

Performance/production
Montage structure in plays of American ethnic minorities. USA. 1967-1990. Lang.: Eng.   2675

Gélas, Gérard

Performance/production
Report on the Avignon fringe festival. France: Avignon. 1996. Lang.: Eng.   796

Gelbart, Larry

Performance/production
Profiles of new actors on Broadway. USA: New York, NY. 1996. Lang.: Eng.   1012

Collection of newspaper reviews by New York theatre critics. USA: New York, NY. 1996. Lang.: Eng.   2577

Gelber, Jack

Plays/librettos/scripts
Interviews with American playwrights. USA. 1945-1995. Lang.: Eng.   3397

Contemporary American drama. USA. 1960-1995. Lang.: Eng.   3431

Gelikonopera (Moscow)

Institutions
Profile of Gelikonopera, Dmitrij Bertman, artistic director. Russia: Moscow. 1990-1996. Lang.: Rus.   4052

Gélinas, Aline

Performance/production
Representation of the body in choreographies of Aline Gélinas. Canada: Montreal, PQ. 1992. Lang.: Fre.   1415

Gélinas, Gratien

Plays/librettos/scripts
Place and identity in Quebecois drama. Canada. 1943-1996. Lang.: Fre.   2834

Gelosi, I (Italy)

Performance/production
Portraits of actors of the Gelosi company. Italy. 1568-1589. Lang.: Eng.   3767

Gelser, Janie

Performance/production
Performances of the Jim Henson International Festival. USA: New York, NY. 1995. Lang.: Eng.   4407

Gems, Pam

Performance/production
Collection of newspaper reviews by London theatre critics. UK-England: London. 1996. Lang.: Eng.   2342

Gencer, Leyla

Performance/production
Profile, interview with Turkish soprano Leyla Gencer. Turkey. 1924-1996. Lang.: Eng.   4222

Gender studies

Institutions
Profile of the Greater Toronto Drag King Society. Canada: Toronto, ON. 1996. Lang.: Eng.   370

Performance/production
Performance artist Stelarc on performance, gender, and cyberspace. Australia. 1996. Lang.: Eng.   688

The performance of gender on the Elizabethan stage. England. 1589-1613. Lang.: Eng.   774

Orientalism and sexual identity. France: Paris. 1898-1905. Lang.: Eng.   795

Theatrical sign-systems and the feminist spectator. UK-England. 1990-1995. Lang.: Eng.   960

Concepts of masculinity in the libel trial of playwright Oscar Wilde. UK-England: London. 1895-1896. Lang.: Eng.   970

Women playwrights and performers on the London stage. UK-England: London. 1918-1962. Lang.: Eng.   977

AIDS and performance work. UK-England. 1990-1995. Lang.: Eng. 979

Secular rituals of New Orleans culture. USA: New Orleans, LA. 1874-1995. Lang.: Eng.   1063

Gender in performances of actress Mary Martin. USA. 1922-1994. Lang.: Eng.   1074

Social boundaries and the transformation of the cakewalk. USA. 1900-1918. Lang.: Eng.   1448

Gender, character, and direction. 1996. Lang.: Ger.   1895

Shakespeare and Elizabethan cultural politics: *A Midsummer Night's Dream*. England. 1590-1620. Lang.: Eng.   1990

Gender construction and two performances of *Orlando*. France: Paris. Switzerland: Lausanne. Germany: Berlin. 1990-1996. Lang.: Ger.   2020

An intercultural adaptation of Euripides' *Troádes (The Trojan Women)*. Greece: Athens. UK-Scotland. 1993. Lang.: Eng.   2092

Videotape on interpreting and performing Shakespeare's *As You Like It*. UK-England. 1994. Lang.: Eng.   2303

Actresses in the roles of tragic heroes on the English-speaking stage. UK-England. USA. 1801-1900. Lang.: Eng.   2530

Androgynous characteristics of actress Charlotte Cushman. USA. 1843-1853. Lang.: Eng.   2658

Female anti-apartheid activists in *Sarafina!* by Mbongeni Ngema. South Africa, Republic of. 1992. Lang.: Eng.   3623

The use of a female performer for the Old French *chantefable, Aucassin et Nicolette*. France. 1200-1994. Lang.: Eng.   3713

Gender and race in the work of Aboriginal aerialists Con Colleano and Dawn de Ramirez. Australia. 1900-1961. Lang.: Eng.   3752

Transvestism in the Edwardian music hall. UK-England. 1900-1914. Lang.: Eng.   3835

Eroticism in Edwardian musical comedy. UK-England. 1892-1914. Lang.: Eng.   3922

Plays/librettos/scripts
Transvestism and feminism in *The Sweet Girl Graduate* by Sarah Anne Curzon. Canada. 1882. Lang.: Eng.   2746

Analysis of *Theatre of the Film Noir* by George F. Walker. Canada. 1981. Lang.: Eng.   2817

Analysis of dramas about the heroine Wang Zhaojun. China. 1700-1900. Lang.: Eng.   2854

Gender studies — cont'd

Early versions of Shakespeare's *Romeo and Juliet* and *The Merry Wives of Windsor*. England. 1595-1600. Lang.: Eng. 2959

Gender and the marketplace in French farce. France. 1450-1550. Lang.: Eng. 2982

Universality and gender in Beckett's *Waiting for Godot*. France. 1952. Lang.: Fre. 2986

Women in Israeli theatre. Israel. 1970-1995. Lang.: Eng. 3095

Analysis of *Entre Villa y una mujer desnuda (Between Villa and a Naked Woman)* by Sabina Berman. Mexico. 1993. Lang.: Eng. 3145

Playwrights Gcina Mhlophe and Sue Pam-Grant. South Africa, Republic of. 1945-1996. Lang.: Eng. 3223

The dual liberation motif in early Black women playwrights. USA. 1915-1930. Lang.: Eng. 3387

Analysis of *A Wife for a Life* by Eugene O'Neill. USA. 1913. Lang.: Eng. 3460

Relation to other fields

Performance in the work of novelist Virginia Woolf. UK-England. 1941. Lang.: Eng. 1240

Actress Georgina Weldon's use of theatrical techniques to avoid incarceration for lunacy. UK-England: London. 1875-1885. Lang.: Eng. 1243

Profile of a lesbian 'marriage' in the theatre community. USA: New York, NY. 1886-1933. Lang.: Eng. 1264

Masculine anxiety in early modern writings. England. 1580-1620. Lang.: Eng. 3488

Female education in Shakespeare's time and plays. England. 1510-1621. Lang.: Eng. 3492

Teaching race and gender in plays of Cary, Shakespeare, and Behn. USA. 1996. Lang.: Eng. 3518

Teaching plays of Shakespeare and Cary in a course on domestic England in the early modern period. USA. 1995. Lang.: Eng. 3519

Argument in favor of teaching Shakespeare in conjunction with his female contemporaries. USA. 1996. Lang.: Eng. 3520

Theory/criticism

Gender constructions and dance and movement education. South Africa, Republic of. 1995. Lang.: Eng. 1361

Gender construction in ritual performance of *dangdut*. Indonesia: Java. 1995. Lang.: Eng. 3876

Training

Ballet training and the male body. USA: Pasadena, CA. 1994. Lang.: Eng. 1542

Général Baron-la-Croix

Plays/librettos/scripts

Haitian popular culture in plays by Franck Fouché. Haiti. 1953-1981. Lang.: Eng. 3066

General from America, The

Institutions

Recent RSC openings. UK-England: London, Stratford. 1996. Lang.: Eng. 1856

Performance/production

Collection of newspaper reviews by London theatre critics. UK-England: London, Stratford. 1996. Lang.: Eng. 2461

Plays/librettos/scripts

Interview with playwright Richard Nelson. USA. UK-England. 1995. Lang.: Eng. 3340

Genet, Jean

Institutions

Prix d'Europe honors Robert Wilson, Théâtre de Complicité, and Carte Blanche-Compagnia della Fortezza. Italy: Taormina. 1971-1996. Lang.: Fre. 492

Performance/production

Jean Genet's staging and acting indications. France. 1950-1996. Lang.: Fre. 2021

German-language production of *Splendid's* by Jean Genet, directed by Klaus Michael Grüber. France: Paris. 1995. Lang.: Eng. 2023

Gengangere (Ghosts)

Performance/production

Collection of newspaper reviews by London theatre critics. UK-England: London. 1996. Lang.: Eng. 2437

Genio buono e il genio cattivo, Il (Good Genius and the Bad Genius, The)

Performance/production

Paris productions of the fall season. France: Paris. 1996. Lang.: Eng. 2032

Genres

Performance/production

Essay on the status of the word in theatre. Denmark. 1996. Lang.: Dan. 767

Cultural and theatrical history of English drama. England. 1500-1994. Lang.: Eng. 1992

Plays/librettos/scripts

Problems of writing biographical plays. Canada: Montreal, PQ. 1986-1991. Lang.: Fre. 2803

Trends in recent Quebec drama. Canada: Montreal, PQ. 1980-1990. Lang.: Fre. 2839

The influence of the detective in Tom Taylor's *The Ticket-of-Leave Man* on Victorian theatre. England: London. 1863. Lang.: Eng. 2894

Romance and pastoral in Shakespeare's *As You Like It*. England. 1598-1601. Lang.: Eng. 2899

Shakespeare's *Henry IV, Part I* as a blending of genres. England. 1589-1594. Lang.: Eng. 2927

Heroic epic, narrative, and history in Shakespeare's *Richard III*. England. 1591-1594. Lang.: Eng. 2929

Carnivalesque subversion of literary and dramatic texts. England. 1300-1607. Lang.: Eng. 2931

Epic and romance in Shakespeare's *Troilus and Cressida*. England. 1601-1602. Lang.: Eng. 2933

Analysis of tragicomedies and tragedies with happy endings. Italy. Spain. France. 1600-1641. Lang.: Ger. 3139

Analysis of *La verdad sospechosa (Suspicious Truth)* by Juan Ruiz de Alarcón. Spain. 1628. Lang.: Eng. 3261

Theory/criticism

Critical perceptions of French popular theatre genres. France: Paris. 1848-1996. Lang.: Eng. 3723

Genty, Philippe

Performance/production

Puppets, Human Movement, and dance in Philippe Genty's *Voyageur Immobile (Motionless Traveler)*. USA: Chicago, IL. France: Paris. 1961-1965. Lang.: Eng. 4415

George Coates Productions (San Francisco, CA)

Performance/production

Interactive internet interview with performer George Coates. USA: San Francisco, CA. 1996. Lang.: Eng. 1068

George, David

Performance/production

Collection of newspaper reviews by London theatre critics. UK-England: London. 1996. Lang.: Eng. 2361

Theory/criticism

Theatre practitioners on the ethics of theatrical collaboration. Australia: Perth. 1994. Lang.: Eng. 1319

Georgeson, Richard

Performance/production

Collection of newspaper reviews by London theatre critics. UK-England: London. 1996. Lang.: Eng. 2462

Georgian Academic Theatre (Tbilisi)

SEE

Gruzinskij Akademičéskij Teat'r im. Kote Mordžanišvili.

Germain, Jean-Claude

Plays/librettos/scripts

Place and identity in Quebecois drama. Canada. 1943-1996. Lang.: Fre. 2834

Germania 3

Performance/production

Two productions of Müller's *Germania 3*. Germany: Berlin, Bochum. 1996. Lang.: Ger. 2056

Leander Haussmann's production of Heiner Müller's last play *Germania 3*. Germany: Bochum. 1996. Lang.: Ger. 2062

Two productions of Heiner Müller's *Germania 3*. Germany: Bochum, Berlin. 1996. Lang.: Ger. 2091

Gerrard-Pinker, Chris

Performance/production

The gay male body in *Strains* by Rumble Productions. Canada: Vancouver, BC. 1949-1996. Lang.: Eng. 720

Gerron, Kurt

Relation to other fields

The cabaret of the Theresienstadt concentration camp. Czechoslovakia: Terezin. 1944. Lang.: Eng. 3740

Gershwin Theatre (New York, NY)

Performance/production

The twenty-fifth anniversary of the Theatre Hall of Fame. USA: New York, NY. 1971-1996. Lang.: Eng. 1051

Gershwin, George

Institutions

Opera at the Bregenz festival. Austria: Bregenz. 1995. Lang.: Eng. 4031

Goodman Theatre (Chicago, IL) — cont'd

Collection of newspaper reviews by New York theatre critics. USA: New York, NY, Chicago, IL. 1996. Lang.: Eng.　　2585

Plays/librettos/scripts
Charles Smith's play about Marcus Garvey, *Black Star Line*. USA: Chicago, IL. 1996. Lang.: Eng.　　3392

Goodman, Henry
Performance/production
Collection of newspaper reviews by London theatre critics. UK-England: London. 1996. Lang.: Eng.　　2323

Goodman, Lizbeth
Performance/production
The emerging South African feminist theatres. UK. USA. South Africa, Republic of: Cape Town. 1968-1994. Lang.: Eng.　　959

Goodman, Rob
Design/technology
Danila Korogodsky's dinosaur costumes for First Stage Milwaukee. USA: Milwaukee, WI. 1994-1995. Lang.: Eng.　　298

Goodnight Desdemona (Good Morning Juliet)
Plays/librettos/scripts
Shakespeare in post-colonial drama. Australia. Canada. 1969-1990. Lang.: Eng.　　2726

Goodspeed Opera House (East Haddam, CT)
Performance/production
Collection of newspaper reviews by New York theatre critics. USA: New York, NY, East Haddam, CT. 1996. Lang.: Eng.　　2553

Collection of newspaper reviews by New York theatre critics. USA: New York, NY, East Haddam, CT. 1996. Lang.: Eng.　　2582

Goodwin, Derrick
Performance/production
Collection of newspaper reviews by London theatre critics. UK-England: London. 1996. Lang.: Eng.　　2408

Gordon-Clark, Lucy
Performance/production
Collection of newspaper reviews by London theatre critics. UK-England: London. 1996. Lang.: Eng.　　2358

Gordon, David
Performance/production
Choreographer and director David Gordon. USA. 1996. Lang.: Eng.　　2614

The importance of American regional theatre, with reference to the Guthrie. USA: Minneapolis, MN. 1996. Lang.: Ger.　　2646

Gordon, Gary
Performance/production
Interview with choreographer Gary Gordon. South Africa, Republic of: Grahamstown. 1994. Lang.: Eng.　　1586

Gordon, Sally
Institutions
Chicano theatre groups. USA: Los Angeles, CA. 1986-1996. Lang.: Eng.　　1880

Gordone, Charles
Plays/librettos/scripts
Interviews with American playwrights. USA. 1945-1995. Lang.: Eng.　　3397

Gördülő Opera (Budapest)
Institutions
History of Gördülő Opera, Opera on Rails. Hungary: Budapest. 1945-1954. Lang.: Hun.　　4045

Gorenstein, Friedrich
Plays/librettos/scripts
Valemir, Dom s bašenkoj (House with a Tower) and *Detoubijca (Child Killer)* by Friedrich Gorenstein. Austria. 1980-1996. Lang.: Rus.　　2730

Görgey, Gábor
Basic theatrical documents
English translation of *Népfürdő (Public Bath)* by Gábor Görgey. Hungary. 1996. Lang.: Eng.　　1664

Plays/librettos/scripts
Postwar Hungarian drama. Hungary. 1945-1989. Lang.: Hun.　　3069

Gorilla Hunters, The
Performance/production
Collection of newspaper reviews by London theatre critics. UK-England: London. 1996. Lang.: Eng.　　2319

Gorilla Rep (New York, NY)
Institutions
Gorilla Rep's free park performances of Shakespeare. USA: New York, NY. 1996. Lang.: Eng.　　1865

Gorkij, Maksim
Performance/production
Adol'f Šapiro's production of *Poslednije* by Maksim Gorkij. Russia: Moscow. 1995. Lang.: Rus.　　2224

Gorky's Wife
Plays/librettos/scripts
Interviews with playwrights Erin Cressida Wilson, Elena Penga, and Brighde Mullins. USA: San Francisco, CA. 1995. Lang.: Eng.　　3366

Gorman, Clem
Basic theatrical documents
Collection of Australian gay and lesbian plays. Australia. 1970-1996. Lang.: Eng.　　1641

Görme, Matthias
Performance/production
The recording of Schubert's *Lieder* on CD. 1996. Lang.: Eng.　　3853

Gospel at Colonus, The
Plays/librettos/scripts
Telson and Breuer's *The Gospel at Colonus* and the problems of multiculturalism. USA. 1987. Lang.: Eng.　　3425

Gosudarstvénnyj Akademičéskij Bolšoj Teat'r (Moscow)
Performance/production
Obituary for ballet dancer Aleksand'r Godunov. USSR. USA. 1949-1995. Lang.: Hun.　　1540

Gosudarstvénnyj Institut Teatral'nogo Iskusstva im. A.V. Lunačarskogo (GITIS, Moscow)
SEE ALSO
Rossiskaja Akademija Teatral'nogo Iskusstva.

Gosudarstvénnyj Teat'r Družby Narodov (Moscow)
SEE ALSO
Teat'r Nacij.

Gosudarstvénnyj Teat'r Nacij.

Gotanda, Philip Kan
Basic theatrical documents
Text of *Ballad of Yachiyo* by Philip Kan Gotanda. USA. 1996. Lang.: Eng.　　1693

Göteborgs Operan (Gothenburg)
Design/technology
Conference on hydraulic and electronic stage technology. Germany: Lohr am Main. 1996. Lang.: Swe.　　174

Performance/production
Dancer Mia Johansson. Sweden: Gothenburg. 1988. Lang.: Swe.　　1530

Interview with Anders Wiklund, director of Vadstena Akademien. Sweden: Gothenburg, Vadstena. 1980. Lang.: Swe.　　4214

Interview with mezzo soprano Marie-Luise Hasselgren. Sweden. 1965. Lang.: Swe.　　4220

Interview with director David Radok. Sweden: Gothenburg. Czech Republic: Prague. 1990. Lang.: Swe.　　4221

Göteborgs Stadsteatern (Gothenburg)
Institutions
Ronny Danielsson, the new manager of Göteborgs Stadsteater. Sweden: Gothenburg. 1996. Lang.: Swe.　　540

Góth, Sándor
Performance/production
Two productions of *Déryné ifjasszony (Mrs. Déry)* by Ferenc Herczeg. Austria-Hungary. Hungary: Budapest. 1907-1928.Lang.: Hun.　　1908

Gothár, Péter
Performance/production
Recipients of the annual theatre critics' awards. Hungary. 1995-1996. Lang.: Hun.　　846

Göthe, Staffan
Plays/librettos/scripts
Children's plays of Staffan Göthe. Sweden: Luleå, Stockholm. 1944. Lang.: Swe.　　3275

Götterdämmerung
Performance/production
Review of 1995 British opera productions. UK-England: London, Leeds, Lewes. 1995-1996. Lang.: Eng.　　4234

Plays/librettos/scripts
The Messianic hero in Wagner's *Ring*. Germany. 1996. Lang.: Eng.　　4320

Gottlieb, Jon
Design/technology
Software choices of professional sound designers. USA. 1996. Lang.: Eng.　　269

Gould, John
Performance/production
Collection of newspaper reviews by London theatre critics. UK-England: London. 1996. Lang.: Eng.　　2311

Gould, Marshall
Performance/production
Collection of newspaper reviews by London theatre critics. UK-England: London. 1996. Lang.: Eng.　　2360

SUBJECT INDEX

Gounod, Charles
  Performance/production
    Background information on Teatro Colón season. Argentina: Buenos
    Aires. 1996. Lang.: Eng.   4075

    Tenor Richard Margison. Canada. 1970-1996. Lang.: Eng.   4090

    Translation of composer Charles Gounod's essay on the conductor/
    composer relationship. France. 1873. Lang.: Eng.   4121

    Miklós Gábor Kerényi's concept for a revival of Gounod's *Faust*.
    Hungary: Budapest. 1996. Lang.: Hun.   4170

    Background material on Lyric Opera of Chicago radio broadcast
    performances. USA: Chicago, IL. 1996. Lang.: Eng.   4244

Government Inspector, The
  SEE
    Revizor.

Government subsidies
  SEE
    Funding, government.

Gow, Michael
  Basic theatrical documents
    Collection of Australian gay and lesbian plays. Australia. 1970-1996.
    Lang.: Eng.   1641

Goyette, Claude
  Design/technology
    Scene designer Claude Goyette. Canada: Montreal, PQ. 1996. Lang.:
    Fre.   149

Gozzi, Carlo
  Design/technology
    Design for Gozzi's *The Green Bird (L'augellino belverde)* at the New
    Victory Theatre. USA: New York, NY. 1996. Lang.: Eng.   3760
  Performance/production
    Alliance of text and acting in three French-language productions.
    Canada: Montreal, PQ. Switzerland: Geneva. 1985-1995. Lang.: Fre.
    722

    Viktor Fülöp's choreography for *Il re cervo (King Stag)* by Carlo Gozzi.
    Hungary: Budapest. 1995. Lang.: Hun.   1432

Graae, Jason
  Performance/production
    Singer/actor Jason Graae. USA. 1980-1996. Lang.: Eng.   3962

Grabowska, Marcelina
  Plays/librettos/scripts
    Reactions of male critics to Polish feminist drama. Poland. 1932-1938.
    Lang.: Pol.   3162

Grace & Glorie
  Design/technology
    Edward Gianfrancesco's set design for *Grace and Glorie*. USA: New
    York, NY. 1996. Lang.: Eng.   1716
  Performance/production
    Collection of newspaper reviews by New York theatre critics. USA:
    New York, NY. 1996. Lang.: Eng.   2584

Grace of Mary Traverse, The
  Plays/librettos/scripts
    The influence of Thatcherism on *The Grace of Mary Traverse* by
    Timberlake Wertenbaker. UK-England. 1985-1996. Lang.: Eng.   3308

Grace of My Heart
  Design/technology
    Susan Bertram's costume design for the film *Grace of My Heart*. USA:
    New York, NY. 1996. Lang.: Eng.   3598

Grace Theatre (London)
  SEE ALSO
    Latchmere Theatre.
  Performance/production
    Collection of newspaper reviews by London theatre critics. UK-England:
    London. 1996. Lang.: Eng.   2307

    Collection of newspaper reviews by London theatre critics. UK-England:
    London. 1996. Lang.: Eng.   2331

    Collection of newspaper reviews by London theatre critics. UK-England:
    London. 1996. Lang.: Eng.   2352

    Collection of newspaper reviews by London theatre critics. UK-England:
    London. 1996. Lang.: Eng.   2365

    Collection of newspaper reviews by London theatre critics. UK-England:
    London. 1996. Lang.: Eng.   2382

    Collection of newspaper reviews by London theatre critics. UK-England:
    London. 1996. Lang.: Eng.   2401

    Collection of newspaper reviews by London theatre critics. UK-England:
    London. 1996. Lang.: Eng.   2434

    Collection of newspaper reviews by London theatre critics. UK-England:
    London. 1996. Lang.: Eng.   2442

Collection of newspaper reviews by London theatre critics. UK-England:
London. 1996. Lang.: Eng.   2481

Graeae Theatre Company (London)
  Performance/production
    Survey of theatre with and of the handicapped. Germany. UK. 1980-
    1996. Lang.: Ger.   812

Graham-Campbell, Angus
  Performance/production
    Collection of newspaper reviews by London theatre critics. UK-England:
    London. 1996. Lang.: Eng.   2478

Graham, Martha
  Performance/production
    The career of choreographer Birgit Cullberg. Sweden: Stockholm. 1920.
    Lang.: Swe.   1531
  Relation to other fields
    The Socialist agenda and modern dance. USA. 1931-1938. Lang.: Eng.
    1600
  Research/historiography
    Description of theatre and dance-related holdings of the Darlington Hall
    Trust archives. UK-England: Totnes, Devon. 1920-1995. Lang.: Eng.
    1305
  Theory/criticism
    Dance and its relationship to written definitions and reconstructions.
    North America. Europe. 1960-1996. Lang.: Eng.   1465

Graham, Ray Harrison
  Performance/production
    Collection of newspaper reviews by London theatre critics. UK-England:
    London. 1996. Lang.: Eng.   2485

Graham, Ruth
  Performance/production
    Collection of newspaper reviews by London theatre critics. UK-England:
    London. 1996. Lang.: Eng.   2433

Graham, Shirley
  Basic theatrical documents
    Anthology of unknown plays of the Harlem Renaissance. USA: New
    York, NY. 1920-1940. Lang.: Eng.   1694
  Plays/librettos/scripts
    The dual liberation motif in early Black women playwrights. USA.
    1915-1930. Lang.: Eng.   3387

    Feminist realism in African-American theatre. USA. 1916-1930. Lang.:
    Eng.   3440

    Realism in American feminist drama. USA. 1900-1988. Lang.: Eng.
    3441

    Black women playwrights of the Harlem Renaissance. USA: New York,
    NY. 1916-1930. Lang.: Eng.   3442

Grajewska, Katarzyna
  Performance/production
    Review of puppetry performances by Teatr Animacji. Poland: Poznań.
    1994-1995. Lang.: Eng, Fre.   4397

Gramm, Donald
  Performance/production
    Composers and performers of the American art song. USA. 1996. Lang.:
    Eng.   3870

Granada Theatre (San Francisco, CA)
  Performance spaces
    Photos of the Granada Theatre, later the Paramount. USA: San
    Francisco, CA. 1921-1965. Lang.: Eng.   3608

Granche, Pierre
  Design/technology
    Scene design by sculptor Pierre Granche. Canada: Montreal, PQ. 1982-
    1992. Lang.: Fre.   151

Granchi, Phil
  Performance/production
    Collection of newspaper reviews by London theatre critics. UK-England:
    London. 1996. Lang.: Eng.   2346

Grand Cahier, Le (Big Book, The)
  Plays/librettos/scripts
    Odette Guimond and Jacques Rossi's stage adaptations of novels by
    Agota Kristof. Canada: Montreal, PQ. 1988-1989. Lang.: Fre.   2806

Grand Cirque Ordinaire (Montreal, PQ)
  Performance/production
    The influence of Living Theatre on Raymond Cloutier of Grand Cirque
    Ordinaire. France: Grenoble. Canada: Montreal, PQ. 1968. Lang.: Fre.
    2015

Grand Théâtre Émotif du Québec (Montreal, PQ)
  Performance/production
    Experimental productions of Grand Théâtre Émotif. Canada: Montreal,
    PQ. 1996. Lang.: Fre.   739

Grand Théâtre Émotif du Québec (Montreal, PQ) — cont'd

The ban on Grand Théâtre Émotif du Québec's *Nudité (Nudity)*.
Canada: Montreal, PQ. 1996. Lang.: Fre.   749

Grand Tour, The
  Plays/librettos/scripts
    Librettist/lyricist Michael Stewart. USA. UK-England. 1970-1987.
    Lang.: Eng.   3994

Grand-Opéra (Paris)
  Institutions
    Notes on the Paris Grand Opera. France: Paris. 1862-1996. Lang.: Rus.
    4039

Grande Magia, La (Grand Magic)
  Performance/production
    Strehler's direction of *La Grande Magia (Grand Magic)* by Eduardo De
    Filippo. Italy: Milan. 1947-1991. Lang.: Fre.   2124

Grandma Sylvia's Funeral
  Performance/production
    Speculation on the future of interactive theatre. USA: New York, NY.
    1996. Lang.: Eng.   2663
  Plays/librettos/scripts
    Reflections on categorization of interactive theatre pieces. USA: New
    York, NY. 1996. Lang.: Eng.   1114

Grange, Henry
  Performance/production
    Collection of newspaper reviews by London theatre critics. UK-England:
    London. 1996. Lang.: Eng.   2441

Grant, Clare
  Plays/librettos/scripts
    Conversation between playwrights Virginia Baxter and Clare Grant.
    Australia. 1978-1995. Lang.: Eng.   1082

Grant, Fraser
  Performance/production
    Collection of newspaper reviews by London theatre critics. UK-England:
    London. 1996. Lang.: Eng.   2475

Grant, Richard E.
  Performance/production
    Interview with actor Richard E. Grant. UK-England. 1996. Lang.: Eng.
    3626

Granville-Barker, Harley
  Performance/production
    The influence of Shakespeare's *The Winter's Tale* directed by Harley
    Granville-Barker. UK-England: London. 1912. Lang.: Eng.   2526

Grassi, Paolo
  Performance/production
    Opera production at La Scala under Paolo Grassi. Italy: Milan. 1972-
    1977. Lang.: Ita.   4176

Gratzer, Hans
  Institutions
    Highlights of the Wiener Festwochen festival. Austria: Vienna. 1996.
    Lang.: Ger.   1752
  Performance/production
    Reviews of German-language productions. Germany. Switzerland.
    Austria. 1996. Lang.: Ger.   2089

Graue Engel, Der (Grey Angel, The)
  Performance/production
    Reviews of German-language productions. Germany. Switzerland.
    Austria. 1996. Lang.: Ger.   2089

Graun, Carl Heinrich
  Performance/production
    The development of Bayreuth as a cultural center. Germany: Bayreuth.
    1709-1758. Lang.: Eng.   4144

Gravel, Pierre
  Plays/librettos/scripts
    Comparison of translations of the opening of Sophocles' *Antigone*.
    Canada. France. 1967-1986. Lang.: Fre.   2787

Gravel, Robert
  Performance/production
    The ban on Grand Théâtre Émotif du Québec's *Nudité (Nudity)*.
    Canada: Montreal, PQ. 1996. Lang.: Fre.   749

Graves, Denyce
  Performance/production
    Profile, interview with soprano Denyce Graves. USA. 1966-1996. Lang.:
    Eng.   4253

Graves, Rupert
  Design/technology
    Building a treadmill for a production of *The Mystery of Edwin Drood*.
    USA. 1996. Lang.: Eng.   273

Gray, Nicholas Stuart
  Performance/production
    Stage and film treatments of the fairy tale *Beauty and the Beast*. Europe.
    USA. Canada. 1946-1996. Lang.: Eng.   793

  Plays/librettos/scripts
    Evolution of the Beast character in treatments of the fairy tale *Beauty
    and the Beast*. UK-England. 1945-1996. Lang.: Eng.   1106

Gray, Oriel
  Plays/librettos/scripts
    The work of Australian women playwrights. Australia. 1930-1970.
    Lang.: Eng.   1084

Gray, Ramin
  Performance/production
    Collection of newspaper reviews by London theatre critics. UK-England:
    London. 1996. Lang.: Eng.   2344
    Collection of newspaper reviews by London theatre critics. UK-England:
    London. 1996. Lang.: Eng.   2444

Gray, Rudy
  Performance/production
    Two productions of the National Black Theatre Festival. USA: Winston-
    Salem, NC. 1995. Lang.: Eng.   2625

Gray, Simon
  Performance/production
    Collection of newspaper reviews by London theatre critics. UK-England:
    London. 1996. Lang.: Eng.   2423
    Simon Gray's experiences during the production of his play *Cell Mates*.
    UK-England: London. 1995. Lang.: Eng.   2514

Gray, Spalding
  Performance/production
    Collection of newspaper reviews by New York theatre critics. USA:
    New York, NY. 1996. Lang.: Eng.   2559
    The filming of Spalding Gray's solo piece *Gray's Anatomy*. USA. 1996.
    Lang.: Eng.   3633

Gray, Terence
  Administration
    Terence Gray and the Cambridge Festival Theatre. UK-England:
    Cambridge. 1926-1932. Lang.: Eng.   1620

Gray's Anatomy
  Performance/production
    The filming of Spalding Gray's solo piece *Gray's Anatomy*. USA. 1996.
    Lang.: Eng.   3633

Grazzini, Antonfrancesco
  Plays/librettos/scripts
    The fool in *commedia dell'arte* and in Jonson's *Every Man in His
    Humour*. England. Italy. 1465-1601. Lang.: Eng.   1093
    Secrecy in Italian Renaissance comedy. Italy. 1522-1793. Lang.: Eng.
    3115

Grease
  Performance/production
    Interview with actor Jeff Trachta. USA: New York, NY. 1994-1996.
    Lang.: Eng.   1060
    Actress Sally Struthers. USA: New York, NY. 1996. Lang.: Eng.   3956

Great Arizona Puppet Theatre (Phoenix, AZ)
  Performance/production
    Great Arizona Puppet Theatre's production of *Peter Pan*. USA:
    Phoenix, AZ. 1993-1995. Lang.: Eng.   4417

Great Divide, The
  Performance/production
    Banner Theatre Company and English alternative theatre. UK-England.
    1960-1996. Lang.: Eng.   992

Great Magoo, The
  Performance/production
    The first production of *The Great Magoo* by Ben Hecht and Gene
    Fowler. USA. 1932-1996. Lang.: Eng.   2681

Great Pretenders
  Performance/production
    Collection of newspaper reviews by London theatre critics. UK-England:
    London. 1996. Lang.: Eng.   2407

Great Things
  Performance/production
    Collection of newspaper reviews by London theatre critics. UK-England:
    London. 1996. Lang.: Eng.   2382

Greater Toronto Drag King Society (Toronto, ON)
  Institutions
    Profile of the Greater Toronto Drag King Society. Canada: Toronto,
    ON. 1996. Lang.: Eng.   370

Greco, Loretta
  Design/technology
    Scene designer Robert Brill. USA: New York, NY. 1996. Lang.: Eng.
    1724

Greek
  Plays/librettos/scripts
    Problems of translating Steven Berkoff's *Greek*. Canada: Montreal, PQ.
    1989-1990. Lang.: Fre.   2827

Greek Amphibian, The
Performance/production
Collection of newspaper reviews by London theatre critics. UK-England: London. 1996. Lang.: Eng. 2310

Green Belt, The
Basic theatrical documents
Text of *The Green Belt* by Charles Johnson. USA. 1982. Lang.: Eng. 3661

Green Ginger (Tenby)
Performance/production
Performances of the Jim Henson International Festival. USA: New York, NY. 1995. Lang.: Eng. 4407

Green, Adolph
Performance/production
Collection of newspaper reviews by London theatre critics. UK-England: London. 1996. Lang.: Eng. 2467

Green, Julien
Performance/production
Productions at Frankfurter Schauspielhaus in light of recent budget cuts. Germany: Frankfurt am Main. 1995. Lang.: Ger. 2051

Greene, Graham
Plays/librettos/scripts
Graham Greene's screen adaptation of Shaw's *Saint Joan*. UK-England. 1957. Lang.: Eng. 3647

Greensboro: A Requiem
Design/technology
Robert Brill's sets for Emily Mann's *Greensboro* using projections by John Boesche. USA: Princeton, NJ. 1996. Lang.: Eng. 1729
Performance/production
Emily Mann's creation of documentary-style theatre based on interviews. USA: Princeton, NJ. 1996. Lang.: Eng. 2643
Plays/librettos/scripts
Interview with playwright/director Emily Mann. USA: Princeton, NJ. 1996. Lang.: Eng. 3385

Greenwell, Peter
Performance/production
Collection of newspaper reviews by London theatre critics. UK-England: London. 1996. Lang.: Eng. 2326

Greenwich Dance Agency (London)
Performance/production
Collection of newspaper reviews by London theatre critics. UK-England: London. 1996. Lang.: Eng. 2431

Greenwich Theatre (London)
Performance/production
Collection of newspaper reviews by London theatre critics. UK-England: London. 1996. Lang.: Eng. 2345

Collection of newspaper reviews by London theatre critics. UK-England: London. 1996. Lang.: Eng. 2357

Collection of newspaper reviews by London theatre critics. UK-England: London. 1996. Lang.: Eng. 2379

Collection of newspaper reviews by London theatre critics. UK-England: London. 1996. Lang.: Eng. 2411

Collection of newspaper reviews by London theatre critics. UK-England: London. 1996. Lang.: Eng. 2415

Collection of newspaper reviews by London theatre critics. UK-England: London. 1996. Lang.: Eng. 2452

Collection of newspaper reviews by London theatre critics. UK-England: London. 1996. Lang.: Eng. 2492

Greenwood, Jane
Design/technology
Contemporary costuming by designer Jane Greenwood. USA: New York, NY. 1996. Lang.: Eng. 1738

Greer, David M.W.
Plays/librettos/scripts
Analysis of English plays with homosexual content. UK-England. 1970-1996. Lang.: Dan. 3301

Greer, John
Performance/production
The role of the accompanist in an opera singer's preparation of a role. Canada. USA. 1996. Lang.: Eng. 4093

Gregg, Clark
Performance/production
Collection of newspaper reviews by New York theatre critics. USA: New York, NY. 1996. Lang.: Eng. 2554

Gregor, József
Performance/production
Interview with József Gregor. Hungary. 1957-1995. Lang.: Hun. 4169

Gregory, Augusta Isabella, Lady
Institutions
Profile of Irish women's nationalist group Inghinidhe na h'Eireann. Ireland: Dublin. 1900-1902. Lang.: Eng. 1814

Gregory, Gillian
Performance/production
Collection of newspaper reviews by London theatre critics. UK-England: London. 1996. Lang.: Eng. 2464

Greif, Michael
Design/technology
Jim Youmans' set design for *Randy Newman's Faust* at La Jolla Playhouse. USA: La Jolla, CA. 1995. Lang.: Eng. 276
Performance/production
Profiles of new actors on Broadway. USA: New York, NY. 1996. Lang.: Eng. 1012

Collection of newspaper reviews by New York theatre critics. USA: New York, NY. 1996. Lang.: Eng. 2557

Collection of newspaper reviews by New York theatre critics. USA: New York, NY, Houston, TX. 1996. Lang.: Eng. 2567

Collection of newspaper reviews by New York theatre critics. USA: New York, NY. 1996. Lang.: Eng. 2579

Jonathan Larson's Broadway musical *Rent*. USA: New York, NY. 1996. Lang.: Eng. 3958

Greig, David
Institutions
Productions of the Edinburgh Festival. UK-Scotland: Edinburgh. 1996. Lang.: Eng. 562

Grein, J.T.
Institutions
History of the People's National Theatre. UK-England: London. 1930-1940. Lang.: Eng. 557

Grey, Joel
Performance/production
The Broadway revival of the musical *Chicago*. USA: New York, NY. 1975-1996. Lang.: Eng. 3939

Gribojédov, Aleksand'r Sergejévič
Plays/librettos/scripts
Writer and dramatist Aleksand'r A. Šachovskij. Russia. 1777-1846. Lang.: Rus. 3202

Griffiths, Linda
Plays/librettos/scripts
Overview of Anglophone Canadian playwriting. Canada. 1970-1990. Lang.: Fre. 2791

Griffiths, Trevor
Performance/production
Collection of newspaper reviews by London theatre critics. UK-England: London. 1996. Lang.: Eng. 2436
Plays/librettos/scripts
Political and historical influences on plays of Trevor Griffiths. UK-England. 1980-1996. Lang.: Eng. 3293

Grigorij Melechov
Performance/production
Operatic works of composer Leonid Bobylev. Russia: Moscow. 1990-1996. Lang.: Rus. 4204

Grill, David
Design/technology
Technical differences between Broadway and West End productions of *The Who's Tommy*. UK-England: London. USA: New York, NY. 1996. Lang.: Eng. 3893

Grillo Theater (Essen)
Performance/production
Theatre in the Ruhr Valley. Germany. 1995. Lang.: Eng. 2043

Grimké, Angelina Weld
Plays/librettos/scripts
The dual liberation motif in early Black women playwrights. USA. 1915-1930. Lang.: Eng. 3387

Feminist realism in African-American theatre. USA. 1916-1930. Lang.: Eng. 3440

Black women playwrights of the Harlem Renaissance. USA: New York, NY. 1916-1930. Lang.: Eng. 3442

Grindkopf
Plays/librettos/scripts
Children's plays of Tankred Dorst. Germany. 1982-1996. Lang.: Ger. 3018

Gripari, Pierre
Performance/production
Review of puppetry performances by Teatr Animacji. Poland: Poznań. 1994-1995. Lang.: Eng, Fre. 4397

Gysin, Margrit
  Institutions
    Review of children's theatre performances. Europe. 1996. Lang.: Ger.
    403
HA ha!...
  Theory/criticism
    Excerpts from criticism of *HA ha!* by Réjean Ducharme. Canada: Montreal, PQ. 1990. Lang.: Fre.
    1322
Ha-Palistinait (Palestinian Woman, The)
  Plays/librettos/scripts
    Analysis of plays by Yehoshua Sobol. Israel. 1939-1995. Lang.: Eng.
    3102
    Analysis of *Ha-Palistinait (The Palestinian Woman)* by Yehoshua Sobol. Israel. 1985. Lang.: Ger.
    3105
Haase, Tony
  Performance/production
    Collection of newspaper reviews by London theatre critics. UK-England: London. 1996. Lang.: Eng.
    2462
Habeas Corpus
  Performance/production
    Collection of newspaper reviews by London theatre critics. UK-England: London. 1996. Lang.: Eng.
    2436
Habert, Horst Gerhard
  Administration
    Interviews with directors of two regional theatres. Germany: Schwerin. Austria: Graz. 1996. Lang.: Ger.
    20
Hackett, Peter
  Institutions
    Collaboration between Cleveland Play House and the theatre department of Case Western Reserve University. USA: Cleveland, OH. 1996. Lang.: Eng.
    599
Hackl, Karl-Heinz
  Performance/production
    Austrian productions of Shakespearean plays and operas. Austria. 1994-1995. Lang.: Ger.
    691
Hackney Empire Theatre (London)
  Performance/production
    Collection of newspaper reviews by London theatre critics. UK-England: London. 1996. Lang.: Eng.
    2320
    Collection of newspaper reviews by London theatre critics. UK-England: London. 1996. Lang.: Eng.
    2397
Hact, Bill
  Performance/production
    Collection of newspaper reviews by New York theatre critics. USA: New York, NY. 1996. Lang.: Eng.
    2565
Hader, Josef
  Performance/production
    Actor, cabaret artist, and playwright Josef Hader and his play *Indien (India)*. Austria: Vienna. 1996. Lang.: Ger.
    693
Hadley, Jerry
  Performance/production
    The new generation of tenors. Europe. USA. 1990. Lang.: Swe. 4113
Haearn
  Performance spaces
    Post-modern performance: Forced Entertainment, Brith Grof, Fiona Templeton. UK-England: Sheffield, London. UK-Wales. USA: New York, NY. 1965-1995. Lang.: Eng.
    3703
Haentjens, Brigitte
  Institutions
    Montreal theatres' role in education and the preparation of future audiences. Canada: Montreal, PQ. 1992. Lang.: Fre.
    361
  Performance/production
    Sylvia Drapeau on playing Winnie in Beckett's *Happy Days*. Canada: Montreal, PQ. 1990. Lang.: Fre.
    1932
    Anne-Marie Cadieùx's performance in Müller's *Quartett* at Espace GO. Canada: Montreal, PQ. 1996. Lang.: Fre.
    1939
  Plays/librettos/scripts
    Disaster and death in Heiner Müller's *Quartett*, staged at Espace GO by Brigitte Haentjens. Canada: Montreal, PQ. Germany. 1980-1996. Lang.: Fre.
    2785
    Themes of Heiner Müller's *Quartett* presented at Espace GO. Canada: Montreal, PQ. Germany. 1980-1996. Lang.: Fre.
    2845
Haffenden, Audley
  Institutions
    Profile of Stage One Productions of Bermuda. Bermuda: Hamilton. 1996. Lang.: Eng.
    1755
Hafner, Dorinda
  Plays/librettos/scripts
    Influence of story-telling traditions on women playwrights. Ghana. Australia. Sri Lanka. 1988-1995. Lang.: Eng.
    1098

Hagegård, Håkan
  Performance/production
    Baritone Håkan Hagegård—profile and interview. Sweden. 1940-1996. Lang.: Eng.
    4218
Hagen, Uta
  Performance/production
    Account of a videotaped archive interview with actress Uta Hagen. USA: New York, NY. 1996. Lang.: Eng.
    2657
Häger, Bengt
  Administration
    Bengt Häger's career in dance production, training, and research. Sweden: Stockholm. 1916. Lang.: Swe.
    1402
Hague, Albert
  Plays/librettos/scripts
    Interview with Albert Hague, musical theatre professional. USA: New York, NY. 1960-1996. Lang.: Eng.
    3995
Hahn, Reynaldo
  Performance/production
    French vocalism and its artists. France. 1996. Lang.: Eng. 4124
Haifa Municipal Theatre
  SEE
    Teatron HaIroni (Haifa).
Haimsohn, George
  Performance/production
    Collection of newspaper reviews by London theatre critics. UK-England: London. 1996. Lang.: Eng.
    2429
Haines, Roger
  Performance/production
    Collection of newspaper reviews by London theatre critics. UK-England: London. 1996. Lang.: Eng.
    2400
Haiti
  Performance/production
    Collection of newspaper reviews by London theatre critics. UK-England: London. 1996. Lang.: Eng.
    2415
Haj, Joe
  Performance/production
    Joe Haj's experience directing Shakespeare in prison. USA: Los Angeles, CA. 1996. Lang.: Eng.
    2636
Halac, Ricardo
  Basic theatrical documents
    Anthology of Argentine Jewish theatre. Argentina. 1926-1988. Lang.: Eng.
    1639
Halasz, Laszlo
  Performance/production
    Interview with Laszlo Halasz, first conductor of the New York City Opera Company. Austro-Hungarian Empire: Debrecen. 1905-1996. Lang.: Eng.
    4083
Halász, Péter
  Performance/production
    Budapest productions of the millicentenary season. Hungary: Budapest. 1995-1996. Lang.: Eng.
    2104
    Contemporary reviews of *Vihar után (After the Tempest)* by Péter Halász. Hungary. 1955. Lang.: Hun.
    2108
Haley-Relyea, John
  Performance/production
    Bass baritone John Haley-Relyea. Canada. 1973-1996. Lang.: Eng. 4088
Halfvarson, Eric
  Performance/production
    Interview with opera singer Eric Halfvarson. USA. Europe. 1985-1995. Lang.: Eng.
    4258
Hall, Adrian
  Performance/production
    Collection of newspaper reviews by New York theatre critics. USA: New York, NY. 1996. Lang.: Eng.
    2552
Hall, Caroline
  Performance/production
    Collection of newspaper reviews by London theatre critics. UK-England: London. UK-Scotland: Edinburgh. 1996. Lang.: Eng.
    2313
    Collection of newspaper reviews by London theatre critics. UK-England: London. 1996. Lang.: Eng.
    2470
Hall, Edward
  Performance/production
    Staging *Richard III* at the Panasonic Globe Theatre. Japan: Tokyo. 1996. Lang.: Eng.
    871
Hall, Kate
  Performance/production
    Collection of newspaper reviews by London theatre critics. UK-England: London. 1996. Lang.: Eng.
    2367

Harlan, Thomas Christoph
Institutions
Productions of the Ruhrfestspiele festival. Germany: Recklinghausen.
1996. Lang.: Eng. 1797
Harland, Diana
Performance/production
Collection of newspaper reviews by London theatre critics. UK-England:
London. 1996. Lang.: Eng. 2393
Harmlan, Barry
Performance/production
Collection of newspaper reviews by London theatre critics. UK-England:
London. 1996. Lang.: Eng. 2389
Harms, Kirsten
Performance/production
Directors Kirsten Harms, Emmanuel Bohn, and Nikolaus Büdel.
Germany: Kiel. 1995-1996. Lang.: Ger. 810
Harmston, Joe
Performance/production
Collection of newspaper reviews by London theatre critics. UK-England:
London, Chichester. 1996. Lang.: Eng. 2440
Harries, Kathryn
Performance/production
Interview with opera singer Kathryn Harries. UK-England. 1985-1996.
Lang.: Eng. 4227
Harrigan 'n' Hart
Plays/librettos/scripts
Librettist/lyricist Michael Stewart. USA. UK-England. 1970-1987.
Lang.: Eng. 3994
Harrington, Laura
Plays/librettos/scripts
Musical adaptations of the story of Martin Guerre. USA. 1996. Lang.:
Eng. 3991
Harris, Ed
Plays/librettos/scripts
Analysis of *Taking Sides* by Ronald Harwood. UK-England. 1934-1995.
Lang.: Eng. 3316
Harris, Jon
Performance/production
Collection of newspaper reviews by London theatre critics. UK-England:
London. 1996. Lang.: Eng. 2365
Harris, Julie
Performance/production
Theatre production in Florida. USA: Boca Raton, FL. 1977-1996. Lang.:
Eng. 1023
Harris, Rosemary
Performance/production
Interviews with Tony Award nominees. USA: New York, NY. 1996.
Lang.: Eng. 2596
Actress Rosemary Harris. USA: New York, NY. 1958-1996. Lang.: Eng.
2599
Harris, Sam
Plays/librettos/scripts
Playwright Owen Davis. USA: New York, NY. 1874-1956. 3406
Harris, Wilson
Plays/librettos/scripts
Theatrical metaphors in prose and dramatic works of Wilson Harris.
UK-England. 1954-1990. Lang.: Eng. 3284
Harrison, Kathleen
Performance/production
Actress Kathleen Harrison. UK-England. 1927-1996. Lang.: Eng. 968
Harrison, Neil
Performance/production
Collection of newspaper reviews by London theatre critics. UK-England:
London. 1996. Lang.: Eng. 2407
Harrison, Tony
Performance/production
Collection of newspaper reviews by London theatre critics. UK-England:
London. 1996. Lang.: Eng. 2372
Harrop, John
Research/historiography
Obituary for teacher, actor, and director John Harrop. UK-England.
USA. 1931-1995. Lang.: Eng. 1306
Harry and Me
Performance/production
Collection of newspaper reviews by London theatre critics. UK-England:
London. 1996. Lang.: Eng. 2357
Harshaw, Margaret
Performance/production
Profile, interview with soprano Margaret Harshaw, who spent part of
her career as a mezzo-soprano. USA. 1910-1996. Lang.: Eng. 4290

Hart, David
Performance/production
Collection of newspaper reviews by London theatre critics. UK-England:
London. 1996. Lang.: Eng. 2365
Hart, Lorenz
Design/technology
John Arnone's set design for the revival of *Babes in Arms* at the
Guthrie. USA: Minneapolis, MN. 1996. Lang.: Eng. 3904
Hart, Moss
Plays/librettos/scripts
Ira Gershwin's work with Kurt Weill. USA. 1937-1945. Lang.: Eng.
3989
Hartford Stage Company (Hartford, CT)
Performance/production
Collection of newspaper reviews by New York theatre critics. USA.
1996. Lang.: Eng. 2551
Harvey
Performance/production
Political activities of actor Frank Fay. USA: New York, NY,
Hollywood, CA. 1944-1950. Lang.: Eng. 2624
Harvey, Jonathan
Design/technology
Work of designer Mark Stevenson on the film *Beautiful Thing*. UK-
England: London. 1995-1996. Lang.: Eng. 3591
Plays/librettos/scripts
Analysis of English plays with homosexual content. UK-England. 1970-
1996. Lang.: Dan. 3301
Harvey, Lynne
Performance/production
Collection of newspaper reviews by London theatre critics. UK-England:
London. 1996. Lang.: Eng. 2475
Harwood, Ronald
Performance/production
The London theatre season—fall. UK-England: London. 1995-1996.
Lang.: Eng. 2501
Collection of newspaper reviews by New York theatre critics. USA:
New York, NY. 1996. Lang.: Eng. 2556
Plays/librettos/scripts
Impressions from a trip through the European theatre landscape. UK-
England. Germany. Slovakia. 1996. Lang.: Dan. 1103
Analysis of *Taking Sides* by Ronald Harwood. UK-England. 1934-1995.
Lang.: Eng. 3316
Harwood, Shuna
Design/technology
Design for film adaptation of Shakespeare's *Richard III* by Shuna
Harwood and Tony Burroughs. UK-England: London. 1991-1996.
Lang.: Eng. 3593
Hasselgren, Marie-Louise
Performance/production
Interview with mezzo soprano Marie-Luise Hasselgren. Sweden. 1965.
Lang.: Swe. 4220
Hästen och tranan (Horse and the Crane, The)
Performance/production
Theatre musician Ale Möller. Sweden. 1970. Lang.: Swe. 946
Hauptmann, Gerhart
Performance/production
Collection of newspaper reviews by London theatre critics. UK-England:
London. 1996. Lang.: Eng. 2410
Hausman, Leah
Performance/production
Collection of newspaper reviews by London theatre critics. UK-England:
London. 1996. Lang.: Eng. 2359
Hausmann, Andrès
Performance/production
Patricia MacGeachy on performing in Beckett's *Not I*. Canada:
Montreal, PQ. 1991-1992. Lang.: Fre. 1949
Haussmann, Leander
Institutions
Productions of the Salzburger Festspiele. Austria: Salzburg. 1996. Lang.:
Ger. 345
Leander Haussmann, new director of Bochumer Schauspielhaus.
Germany: Bochum. 1995-1996. Lang.: Ger. 1800
Bochumer Schauspielhaus under the directorship of Leander
Haussmann. Germany: Bochum. 1995-1996. Lang.: Ger. 1804
Performance/production
Theatre in the Ruhr Valley. Germany. 1995. Lang.: Eng. 2043
Two productions of Müller's *Germania 3*. Germany: Berlin, Bochum.
1996. Lang.: Ger. 2056

Hochschule der Schauspielkunst Ernst Busch (Berlin) — cont'd

Performance/production
Profile of students at the Hochschule der Schauspielkunst Ernst Busch. Germany: Berlin. 1996. Lang.: Ger. 831

Hochschule für Bildende Künste (Dresden)
Institutions
Theatre-related disciplines at the Hochschule für Bildende Künste. Germany: Dresden. 1996. Lang.: Swe. 433

Hochschule für Musik und Theater Felix Mendelssohn Bartholdy (Leipzig)
Institutions
Portrait of Hochschule für Musik und Theater Felix Mendelssohn Bartholdy. Germany: Leipzig. 1996. Lang.: Ger. 429

Hochschwab
Institutions
Highlights of the Wiener Festwochen festival. Austria: Vienna. 1996. Lang.: Ger. 1752

Hochzeitsreise (Honeymoon)
Relation to other fields
Playwright Vladimir Sorokin in the context of socialist society. Russia: Moscow. Germany: Berlin. 1995. Lang.: Ger. 3506

Hodgson, Joel
Performance/production
Puppetry on *Mystery Science Theatre 3000*. USA: Hollywood, CA. 1990-1996. Lang.: Eng. 3681

Hodson, Paul
Performance/production
Collection of newspaper reviews by London theatre critics. UK-England: London. 1996. Lang.: Eng. 2419

Collection of newspaper reviews by London theatre critics. UK-England: London. 1996. Lang.: Eng. 2448

Hoffman, Constance
Design/technology
Design for Gozzi's *The Green Bird (L'augellino belverde)* at the New Victory Theatre. USA: New York, NY. 1996. Lang.: Eng. 3760

Hoffman, Dan
Design/technology
Theatrical components of the Jekyll & Hyde Restaurant. USA: New York, NY. 1996. Lang.: Eng. 266

Hoffman, Dustin
Performance/production
Physical centers as an aspect of characterization in acting. USA. 1970-1996. Lang.: Eng. 1043

Hoffman, Michael
Design/technology
Eugenio Zanetti's sets for Michael Hoffman's film *Restoration*. UK-England: London. 1996. Lang.: Eng. 3592

Hoffman, William M.
Performance/production
A pessimistic view of contemporary American opera. USA. 1946-1996. Lang.: Eng. 4263

Hoffmann, E.T.A.
Plays/librettos/scripts
E.T.A. Hoffmann's critique of Mozart's *Don Giovanni*. Austro-Hungarian Empire: Vienna. 1787-1813. Lang.: Eng. 4304
Theory/criticism
The artificial protagonist as a theoretical model. Germany. 1810-1817. Lang.: Ger. 4433

Hoffmann, Frank
Performance/production
Reviews of Shakespearean and other productions. Germany. 1994-1995. Lang.: Ger. 2058

Productions of Schauspielhaus Bonn. Germany: Bonn. 1996. Lang.: Ger. 2075

Hoffmeyer, Klaus
Performance/production
Essay on the status of the word in theatre. Denmark. 1996. Lang.: Dan. 767

Hofmann, Gert
Performance/production
Collection of newspaper reviews by London theatre critics. UK-England: London. 1996. Lang.: Eng. 2435

Hofmann, Jürgen
Performance/production
Budapest productions of the millicentenary season. Hungary: Budapest. 1995-1996. Lang.: Eng. 2104

Hoghe, Raimund
Performance/production
Collection of newspaper reviews by London theatre critics. UK-England: London. 1996. Lang.: Eng. 2498

Holberg, Ludvig
Performance/production
Catrine Telle directs Holberg's *Erasmus Montanus*, Nationaltheatret. Norway: Oslo. 1996. Lang.: Eng. 2144

Collection of newspaper reviews by London theatre critics. UK-England: London. 1996. Lang.: Eng. 2344

Holder, Donald
Design/technology
Don Holder's lighting design for O'Neill's *Hughie* directed by Al Pacino. USA: New York, NY, New Haven, CT. 1996. Lang.: Eng. 1722

Set and lighting design for *Holiday* in the round at Circle in the Square. USA: New York, NY. 1996. Lang.: Eng. 1746

Design for Gozzi's *The Green Bird (L'augellino belverde)* at the New Victory Theatre. USA: New York, NY. 1996. Lang.: Eng. 3760

Holding.../waiting for ecstasy
Plays/librettos/scripts
Medusa as a metaphorical presence in some contemporary productions. UK-England. Canada. 1995. Lang.: Eng. 3294

Holdt, Walter
Performance/production
Expressionist mask dancers Lavinia Schulz and Walter Holdt. Germany: Hamburg. 1918-1924. Lang.: Ger. 1606

Holiday
Design/technology
Set and lighting design for *Holiday* in the round at Circle in the Square. USA: New York, NY. 1996. Lang.: Eng. 1746

Holl, István
Performance/production
Recipients of the annual theatre critics' awards. Hungary. 1995-1996. Lang.: Hun. 846

Holland Park Theatre (London)
Performance/production
Collection of newspaper reviews by London theatre critics. UK-England: London. 1996. Lang.: Eng. 2444

Hollandia (Amsterdam)
Basic theatrical documents
Annotated Dutch translation of Euripides' *Phoinissai (The Phoenician Women)* as produced by Hollandia. Greece. Netherlands. 409 B.C.-1996 A.D. Lang.: Dut. 1662

Hollaway, Jonathan
Performance/production
Collection of newspaper reviews by London theatre critics. UK-England: London. 1996. Lang.: Eng. 2383

Holm, Staffan Valdemar
Institutions
The Royal Swedish Opera compared unfavorably to Folkoperan. Sweden: Stockholm. 1996. Lang.: Swe. 4056

Holmes, Andrew
Performance/production
Collection of newspaper reviews by London theatre critics. UK-England: London. 1996. Lang.: Eng. 2307

Holmes, Sean
Performance/production
Collection of newspaper reviews by London theatre critics. UK-England: London. 1996. Lang.: Eng. 2450

Holoubek, Gustaw
Performance/production
Polish productions of Shakespeare. Poland. 1989-1996. Lang.: Eng. 2162

Holt, Henry
Design/technology
Technical aspects of Wagner's *Ring* cycle, Arizona Opera. USA: Flagstaff, AZ. 1996. Lang.: Eng. 4028

Holtzman, Willy
Performance/production
Collection of newspaper reviews by New York theatre critics. USA: New York, NY. 1996. Lang.: Eng. 2573

Holzwarth, Pit
Performance/production
Reviews of Shakespearean and other productions. Germany. 1994-1995. Lang.: Ger. 2058

Bremer Shakespearetheater and the advantages of directing Shakespeare in translation. Germany: Bremen. UK-England: London. 1993. Lang.: Eng. 2071

Home
Plays/librettos/scripts
Analysis of the plays of David Storey. UK-England. 1966-1992. Lang.: Eng. 3299

Homer G. and the Rhapsodies in the Fall of Detroit
Plays/librettos/scripts
Ifa Bayeza's *Homer G. and the Rhapsodies in the Fall of Detroit*. USA: San Francisco, CA. 1996. Lang.: Eng. 3464

Jardin des amours enchantées, Le (Garden of Enchanted Lovers, The)
Performance/production
Paris productions of the fall season. France: Paris. 1996. Lang.: Eng.
2032

Jarocki, Jerzy
Performance/production
Teatr Polski's production of Kleist's *Käthchen von Heilbronn*, directed by Jerzy Jarocki. Poland: Wrocław. 1994. Lang.: Eng, Fre.
2168

Jarry, Alfred
Performance/production
Impressions of the Boston theatre scene. USA: Cambridge, MA, Boston, MA. 1995. Lang.: Eng.
2628
Plays/librettos/scripts
The genesis of Jarry's *Ubu Roi (King Ubu)*. France. 1896. Lang.: Hun.
2990

Jaschik, Álmos
Performance/production
Scene design and the work of director Antal Németh. Hungary. 1929-1944. Lang.: Hun.
843

Jasmin, le héros (Jasmin the Hero)
Plays/librettos/scripts
Analysis of stage and radio plays by Raymond Villeneuve. Canada: Montreal, PQ. 1987-1991. Lang.: Fre.
1090

Játékszín (Budapest)
SEE
Magyar Játékszín.

Javoršek, Jože
Plays/librettos/scripts
Analysis of works by significant Slovene playwrights. Slovenia. 1900-1996. Lang.: Slo.
3213

Jazzmatazz
Design/technology
David Belugou's costumes for the Big Apple Circus. USA: New York, NY. 1996. Lang.: Eng.
3748

Jeakins, Dorothy
Design/technology
Obituary for movie costumer Dorothy Jeakins. USA: Santa Barbara, CA. 1995. Lang.: Eng.
3594

Jeanne
Performance/production
Canadian musical theatre. Canada: Toronto, ON, Montreal, PQ. 1996. Lang.: Eng.
3913

Jeannette, Gertrude
Performance/production
Interview with actress Gertrude Jeannette. USA. 1970. Lang.: Eng. 2656

Jeffreys, Stephen
Design/technology
Technical aspects of *The Libertine* directed by Terry Johnson for Steppenwolf. USA: Chicago, IL. 1996. Lang.: Eng.
1740
Performance/production
Collection of newspaper reviews by New York theatre critics. USA: New York, NY. 1996. Lang.: Eng.
2573

Jelinek, Elfriede
Performance/production
Gender, character, and direction. 1996. Lang.: Ger.
1895
Thirza Bruncken's production of *Stecken, Stab und Stangl (Stick, Rod, and Pole)* by Elfriede Jelinek. Germany: Hamburg. 1996. Lang.: Ger.
2074
Collection of newspaper reviews by London theatre critics. UK-England: London. 1996. Lang.: Eng.
2344
Plays/librettos/scripts
Playwright Elfriede Jelinek, author of *Krankheit oder Moderne Frauen (Illness or Modern Women)*. Austria. 1946. Lang.: Swe.
2729

Jellinek, George
Institutions
Interview with George Jellinek, reviewer and producer of classical music. USA: New York, NY. 1937-1995. Lang.: Hun.
3574
Performance/production
George Jellinek's radio show *The Vocal Scene*. USA: New York, NY. 1968-1996. Lang.: Eng.
3578

Jendreyko, Hans-Dieter
Performance/production
Productions of Basler Theater. Switzerland: Basel. 1996. Lang.: Ger.
2300

Jenisch, Jakob
Institutions
Changes in theatre training of the 1970s. Germany: Essen. 1970-1979. Lang.: Ger.
451

Jenkins, Daniel
Performance/production
Actor Daniel Jenkins. USA: New York, NY. 1988-1996. Lang.: Eng.
3937

Jenkins, David
Design/technology
The use of programmable logic controllers at the Simon Edison Center. USA: San Diego, CA. 1990. Lang.: Eng.
1747

Jenkins, Mark
Performance/production
Collection of newspaper reviews by London theatre critics. UK-England: London. 1996. Lang.: Eng.
2360
Collection of newspaper reviews by London theatre critics. UK-England: London. 1996. Lang.: Eng.
2473

Jenkins, Richard
Performance/production
Collection of newspaper reviews by New York theatre critics. USA: New York, NY. 1996. Lang.: Eng.
2550
Olympia Dukakis' role in *The Hope Zone* by Kevin Heelan at Circle Rep. USA: New York, NY. 1960-1996. Lang.: Eng.
2678

Jenkinson, Mark
Performance/production
Collection of newspaper reviews by London theatre critics. UK-England: London. 1996. Lang.: Eng.
2343

Jenner, Caryl
Institutions
Unicorn Theatre, England's oldest professional children's theatre company. UK-England: London. 1926-1996. Lang.: Eng.
556

Jennings, Sue Emmy
Performance/production
Collection of newspaper reviews by London theatre critics. UK-England: London. 1996. Lang.: Eng.
2392

Jenůfa
Performance/production
Interview with director David Radok. Sweden: Gothenburg. Czech Republic: Prague. 1990. Lang.: Swe.
4221
Review of 1995 British opera productions. UK-England: London, Leeds, Lewes. 1995-1996. Lang.: Eng.
4234

Jermyn Street Theatre (London)
Performance/production
Collection of newspaper reviews by London theatre critics. UK-England: London. 1996. Lang.: Eng.
2346
Collection of newspaper reviews by London theatre critics. UK-England: London. 1996. Lang.: Eng.
2414
Collection of newspaper reviews by London theatre critics. UK-England: London. 1996. Lang.: Eng.
2433

Jerricho, Paul
Performance/production
Collection of newspaper reviews by London theatre critics. UK-England: London. 1996. Lang.: Eng.
2351

Jerrold, Douglas
Performance/production
Stage history of *Black Eyed Susan* by Douglas Jerrold. UK-England. 1829-1994. Lang.: Eng.
2537
Theory/criticism
Analysis of *The Mutiny at the Nore* intended to refute the 'new historical' approach. UK-England: London. 1797-1830. Lang.: Eng.
1366

Jesse Jones Hall (Houston, TX)
Design/technology
The history of multiple-use theatre design. USA. 1966-1996. Lang.: Eng.
291

Jessner, Leopold
Institutions
Leopold Jessner's acting studios at Hochschule der Künste. Germany: Berlin. 1925-1931. Lang.: Ger.
452
Relation to other fields
Ideological uses of theatre during the National Socialist period. Germany. 1933-1945. Lang.: Ger.
1186

Jesus Christ Superstar
Performance/production
Collection of newspaper reviews by London theatre critics. UK-England: London. 1996. Lang.: Eng.
2478

Jésus de Montréal (Jesus of Montreal)
Plays/librettos/scripts
Representations of theatre in Denys Arcand's film *Jésus de Montréal*. Canada: Montreal, PQ. 1989. Lang.: Fre.
3640

Jeter, Jorjan Lynn
Performance/production
Jorjan Lynn Jeter's role in *Curiouser and Curiouser* by National Theatre of the Deaf. USA. 1996. Lang.: Eng.
2660

Kecskés, András M.
Performance/production
Interview with dancer-mime András Kecskés. Hungary. 1974-1995.
Lang.: Hun. 1429
Keeper, Tina
Performance/production
Cree actress Tina Keeper. Canada. 1996. Lang.: Eng. 3668
Kékszakállú herceg vára, A
Design/technology
Stage lighting for a production of *A Kékszakállú herceg vára* by Béla
Bartók. Russia. 1990-1996. Lang.: Rus. 4023
Institutions
Canadian Opera Company's *Erwartung* and *Bluebeard's Castle* at the
Hong Kong Arts Festival. China, People's Republic of: Hong Kong.
1996. Lang.: Ger. 4035
Kékszakállú herceg vára, A (Bluebeard's Castle)
Performance/production
Artúr Bárdos' production of *A kékszakállú herceg vára (Bluebeard's
Castle)* by Béla Balázs. Hungary: Budapest. 1910-1913. Lang.: Hun.
2102
Collection of newspaper reviews by London theatre critics. UK-England:
London. 1996. Lang.: Eng. 2392
Kelemen, László
Administration
Résumé of writings on theatre manager, actor, and director László
Kelemen. Hungary. 1792-1990. Lang.: Hun. 32
Institutions
László Kelemen and the first professional Hungarian theatre company.
Hungary. 1790-1890. Lang.: Hun. 467
Performance/production
The family of actor-director László Kelemen. Hungary. 1730-1812.
Lang.: Hun. 852
Kelleher, Joe
Performance/production
Collection of newspaper reviews by London theatre critics. UK-England:
London. 1996. Lang.: Eng. 2413
Kelley, Jacqueline
Performance/production
Collection of newspaper reviews by London theatre critics. UK-England:
London. 1996. Lang.: Eng. 2497
Kelling, Petra
Relation to other fields
East German actresses' reactions to social changes after the fall of the
Berlin wall. Germany, East: Berlin, East. 1990-1991. Lang.: Ger. 1195
Kellogg, Paul
Performance/production
Profile of Glimmerglass Opera. USA: Cooperstown, NY. 1995-1996.
Lang.: Eng. 4243
Kelly, Eamonn
Performance/production
Current Dublin productions. Ireland: Dublin. 1996. Lang.: Eng. 2117
Kelly, Gail
Performance/production
Analysis of *Appetite* by Club Swing, directed by Gail Kelly. Australia:
Melbourne. 1996. Lang.: Eng. 689
Kelly, Gene
Performance/production
Photo essay on the late Gene Kelly, actor, dancer, and choreographer.
USA. 1940-1996. Lang.: Eng. 3629
Kelly, Jude
Performance/production
Collection of newspaper reviews by London theatre critics. UK-England:
London. 1996. Lang.: Eng. 2396
Collection of newspaper reviews by London theatre critics. UK-England:
London, Oxford. 1996. Lang.: Eng. 2469
Collection of newspaper reviews by New York theatre critics. USA:
New York, NY. 1996. Lang.: Eng. 2557
Kelly, Lawrence
Institutions
History of the Dallas Opera. USA: Dallas, TX. 1957-1996. Lang.: Eng.
4060
Kelly, Nicholas
Performance/production
Collection of newspaper reviews by London theatre critics. UK-England:
London. 1996. Lang.: Eng. 2470
Kemble, Fanny
Performance/production
Actresses in the roles of tragic heroes on the English-speaking stage.
UK-England. USA. 1801-1900. Lang.: Eng. 2530

Kemp, Jonathan
Performance/production
Collection of newspaper reviews by London theatre critics. UK-England:
London. 1996. Lang.: Eng. 2473
Kemp, Lindsay
Performance/production
Collection of newspaper reviews by London theatre critics. UK-England:
London. 1996. Lang.: Eng. 2397
Kempe, Will
Performance/production
The replacement of Will Kempe by Robert Armin in the Lord
Chamberlain's Men. England: London. 1599. Lang.: Eng. 776
Kempinski, Tom
Performance/production
Collection of newspaper reviews by London theatre critics. UK-England:
London. 1996. Lang.: Eng. 2375
Collection of newspaper reviews by London theatre critics. UK-England:
London. 1996. Lang.: Eng. 2421
Plays/librettos/scripts
Playwright Tom Kempinksi: the distinction between creative and
interpretive artists. UK-England. 1996. Lang.: Eng. 1104
Kenn, Dana
Design/technology
Interviews with associate designers. USA: New York, NY. 1996. Lang.:
Eng. 277
Kenna, Peter
Basic theatrical documents
Collection of Australian gay and lesbian plays. Australia. 1970-1996.
Lang.: Eng. 1641
Kennedy Center for the Performing Arts (Washington, DC)
Administration
Equity and AGVA agreement on cabaret shows at the Kennedy Center.
USA: Washington, DC. 1996. Lang.: Eng. 3724
Institutions
Modern ballet in the Kennedy Center's jubilee season. USA:
Washington, DC. 1970-1995. Lang.: Hun. 1494
Kennedy, Adrienne
Plays/librettos/scripts
Pregnancy in plays of Adrienne Kennedy. USA. 1988. Lang.: Eng. 3329
Influences on the plays of Adrienne Kennedy. USA. 1996. Lang.: Eng.
3330
Analysis of *She Talks to Beethoven* by Adrienne Kennedy. USA. 1989-
1993. Lang.: Eng. 3396
Interviews with American playwrights. USA. 1945-1995. Lang.: Eng.
3397
Contemporary American drama. USA. 1960-1995. Lang.: Eng. 3431
Career of playwright Adrienne Kennedy. USA. 1965-1996. Lang.: Eng.
3448
Kennedy, Arthur
Performance/production
Highlights of interviews with Broadway stars. USA: New York, NY.
1985-1996. Lang.: Eng. 2601
Kennedy, Chris
Design/technology
Design for an opera segment in the film *Così*. Australia. 1996. Lang.:
Eng. 3587
Kent, Jonathan
Performance/production
The London theatre season—winter. UK-England: London. 1996. Lang.:
Eng. 973
Collection of newspaper reviews by London theatre critics. UK-England:
London. 1996. Lang.: Eng. 2374
Kent, Nicolas
Performance/production
Collection of newspaper reviews by London theatre critics. UK-England:
London. 1996. Lang.: Eng. 2409
Collection of newspaper reviews by London theatre critics. UK-England:
London. 1996. Lang.: Eng. 2415
Kentrup, Norbert
Institutions
Interview with Norbert Kentrup of Bremer Shakespeare Company.
Germany: Bremen. 1996. Lang.: Ger. 1798
Kentucky Cycle, The
Plays/librettos/scripts
Ecology and economy in *The Kentucky Cycle* by Robert Schenkkan.
USA. 1992. Lang.: Eng. 3345
Interview with playwright Robert Schenkkan. USA. 1996. Lang.: Eng.
3415

Kokotović, Nada
Performance/production
Dancer and choreographer Nada Kokotović. Germany: Konstanz. 1996.
Lang.: Ger.   1575

Koljada, Nikolaj V.
Performance/production
Collection of newspaper reviews by London theatre critics. UK-England:
London. 1996. Lang.: Eng.   2325

Kolobov, Jévgenij
Institutions
Profile of Novaja Opera Theatre. Russia: Moscow. 1990-1996. Lang.:
Rus.   4054

Kolonia karna
Plays/librettos/scripts
Analysis of contemporary Polish opera. Poland. 1995. Lang.: Eng, Fre.
                                                                               4336

Kolonists
Performance/production
Collection of newspaper reviews by London theatre critics. UK-England:
London. 1996. Lang.: Eng.   2456

Kolozsvár State Theatre
SEE
Állami Magyar Szinház (Cluj).

Kolozsvári Állami Magyar Opera (Cluj-Napoca)
Institutions
Hungarian ballet, opera and operetta in Cluj-Napoca. Hungary.
Romania: Cluj-Napoca. 1948-1990. Lang.: Hun.   3847

Programming of the musical stages of the Hungarian ethnic minority of
Kolozsvár (Cluj-Napoca). Hungary. Romania: Cluj-Napoca.1948-1992.
Lang.: Hun.   3848
Performance/production
Music theatre in Hungarian theatre in Transylvania. Hungary:
Kolozsvár. Romania: Cluj-Napoca. 1793-1948. Lang.: Hun.   3860

Kolozsvári Állami Színház
SEE
Állami Magyar Szinház (Cluj-Napoca).

Kolozsvári Bábszínház (Cluj-Napoca)
Performance/production
Puppeteer Ildikó Kovács on her career. Romania: Cluj-Napoca. 1928-
1996. Lang.: Hun.   4402

Kolozsvári Magyar Színház (Cluj-Napoca)
Performance/production
Guest performances of the Hungarian theatre of Kolozsvár. Hungary.
Romania: Bucharest. 1925. Lang.: Hun.   841

Kolozsvári Nemzeti Színház (Cluj)
Performance/production
Music theatre in Hungarian theatre in Transylvania. Hungary:
Kolozsvár. Romania: Cluj-Napoca. 1793-1948. Lang.: Hun.   3860

Kolozsvári Nemzeti Színház (Cluj-Napoca)
Institutions
Hungarian theatre in Romania between the wars. Hungary. Romania:
Cluj-Napoca. 1919-1944. Lang.: Hun.   476

Kolozsvári Nemzeti Színház (Kolozsvár)
Institutions
History of Kolozsvári Nemzeti Szinház. Hungary: Kolozsvár. 1821-1919.
Lang.: Hun.   468

Koltès, Bernard-Marie
Institutions
Change of direction at Stadttheater Heidelberg. Germany: Heidelberg.
1996. Lang.: Ger.   1795
Performance/production
Interview with director Patrice Chéreau. France. 1996. Lang.: Eng. 2013
Patrice Chéreau's productions of plays by Bernard-Marie Koltès. France.
1964-1996. Lang.: Dan.   2039
Review of Koltès' *Roberto Zucco*, directed by Krzysztof Warlikowski,
Teatr Nowy. Poland: Poznań. 1995. Lang.: Eng, Fre.   2165
Collection of newspaper reviews by New York theatre critics. USA:
New York, NY. 1996. Lang.: Eng.   2571
Interview with director Patrice Chéreau. USA. 1983-1996. Lang.: Eng.
                                                                               2649
Plays/librettos/scripts
Analysis of plays by Bernard-Marie Koltès. France. 1977-1989. Lang.:
Fre.   3010

Kom De Bagfra (Copenhagen)
Audience
Audience participation in a performance of dancer Jérôme Bel.
Denmark. 1995-1996. Lang.: Dan.   3786

Komagata Maru Incident, The
Plays/librettos/scripts
Analysis of *Walsh* and *The Komagata Maru Incident* by Sharon Pollock.
Canada. 1973-1976. Lang.: Eng.   2790

Komische Oper (Berlin)
Administration
Effect of budget cuts on Berlin opera houses. Germany: Berlin. 1996.
Lang.: Ger.   4008
Institutions
The dance company of the Komische Oper. Germany: Berlin. 1996.
Lang.: Ger.   1407

Komissarževskij, Fëdor Fëdorovič
Performance/production
The production of meaning in interpretations of Shakespeare's *The
Merchant of Venice*. Europe. 1740-1987. Lang.: Eng.   2002

Komorous, Rudolph
Performance/production
Japanese performances of Japanese themes at Toronto Theatre Festival.
Japan. Canada: Toronto, ON. 1996. Lang.: Eng.   874

Kompanijcev, Aleksand'r
Institutions
Profile of Rostov's Theatre for Youth. Russia: Rostov-na-Donu. 1996.
Lang.: Rus.   527

Komsomol Theatre (USSR)
SEE
Teat'r im. Leninskogo Komsomola.

Kon, Stella
Performance/production
Women playwrights of the Pacific Rim. Australia. Asia. 1994. Lang.:
Eng.   1899
Plays/librettos/scripts
Women writers in postcolonial English. Australia. 1995. Lang.: Eng.
                                                                               2723

Konenkov, Vladimir I.
Design/technology
Artists of the Vachtangov Theatre. Russia: Moscow. 1990-1996. Lang.:
Rus.   205

Kongelige Danske Ballett (Copenhagen)
Administration
Critique of the use of dancers at the Royal Danish Ballet. Denmark.
1951-1996. Lang.: Dan.   1473
Maina Gielgud, new ballet mistress of the Royal Danish Ballet.
Denmark. 1992-1996. Lang.: Dan.   1474

Kongelige Teater (Copenhagen)
Design/technology
Scenography at Kongelige Teater. Denmark: Copenhagen. 1830-1871.
Lang.: Dan.   1475
Institutions
Interview with Birgitte Price, drama director of Kongelige Teater.
Denmark: Copenhagen. 1995. Lang.: Eng.   1785
Performance spaces
The possible rebuilding of Kongelige Teater, the royal theatre.
Denmark: Copenhagen. 1996. Lang.: Ger.   628
Performance/production
Essay on the status of the word in theatre. Denmark. 1996. Lang.: Dan.
                                                                               767
Copenhagen performing arts events. Denmark: Copenhagen. 1996.
Lang.: Eng.   1983

Koniordou, Lydia
Performance/production
Collection of newspaper reviews by New York theatre critics. USA:
New York, NY. 1996. Lang.: Eng.   2555
Sophocles' *Electra* as performed by the National Theatre of Greece.
USA: New York, NY. Greece. 1996. Lang.: Eng.   2634

Konold, Wulf
Institutions
Wulf Konold, general director of Städtische Bühnen. Germany:
Nuremberg. 1996. Lang.: Ger.   457

Konovalov, Pavel M.
Institutions
Problems of youth theatre. Russia. 1990-1996. Lang.: Rus.   516

Konovalova, Galina
Performance/production
Actress Galina Konovalova recalls her work at Vachtangov Theatre.
USSR: Moscow. 1950-1979. Lang.: Rus.   2693

Konrad, Walter
Performance/production
Interview with program managers at TV station SAT 3. Germany:
Berlin. 1996. Lang.: Ger.   3669

Konstantinov, Vladimir
Performance/production
Interview with Russian directors. Russia. 1990-1996. Lang.: Rus.   925

Kungliga Dramatiska Teatern (Stockholm) — cont'd

Actor Robert Gustafsson. Sweden: Stockholm. 1996. Lang.: Swe. 951

Dramaten guest performance in Cracow. Poland: Cracow. 1996. Lang.: Swe. 2163

Portraits of nineteenth-century actors in mural art of the Royal Dramatic Theatre. Sweden: Stockholm. 1840-1879. Lang.: Swe. 2278

Staffan Roos's children's theatre project *Spöken (Ghosts)* at Royal Dramatic Theatre. Sweden: Stockholm. 1996. Lang.: Swe. 2279

Actress Kristina Adolphson. Sweden: Stockholm. 1955. Lang.: Swe. 2280

Interview with director Thommy Berggren. Sweden: Gothenburg, Stockholm. 1955. Lang.: Swe. 2282

Interview with Kristina Lugn, poet, playwright, and director. Sweden: Stockholm. 1993. Lang.: Swe. 2283

Thorsten Flinck's staging of Brecht's *Herr Puntila* using rock music. Sweden: Stockholm. 1991. Lang.: Swe. 2284

Interview with actress Karin Bjurström. Sweden: Stockholm. 1970. Lang.: Swe. 2285

Audience reaction to Ingmar Bergman's staging of Euripides' *Bákchai (The Bacchae)*. Sweden: Stockholm. 1996. Lang.: Swe. 2288

Interview with director Björn Melander. Sweden: Gothenburg, Stockholm. 1991. Lang.: Swe. 2289

Kungliga Dramatiska Teatern and Staffan Roos's children's production *Spöken (Ghosts)*. Sweden: Stockholm. 1996. Lang.: Swe. 2291

Photos of rehearsals for Thorsten Flinck's production of *Herr Puntila* at Royal Dramatic Theatre. Sweden: Stockholm. 1996. Lang.: Swe. 2294

Pia Forsgren's production of *Sal P (Ward P)* by Katarina Frostenson. Sweden: Stockholm. 1989. Lang.: Swe. 2295

Interview with actor Erland Josephson. Sweden: Stockholm. 1946. Lang.: Swe. 2296

The Glass Menagerie in a touring coproduction of Kungliga Dramatiska Teatern and Svenska Riksteatern. Sweden. 1996. Lang.: Swe. 2297

The development of Bengt Bratt's *Mottagningen (The Medical Center)* by improvisation. Sweden: Stockholm. 1996. Lang.: Swe. 2299

The cancelled guest performance of Bergman's *Misanthrope* at BAM. USA: New York, NY. Sweden: Stockholm. 1995. Lang.: Swe. 2648

Profile of the Romeo & Julia Choir. Sweden: Stockholm. Slovenia. Croatia. 1991. Lang.: Swe. 3866

Plays/librettos/scripts

Actor Erland Josephson on the role of Kadmos in Euripides' *Bákchai (The Bacchae)*. Greece. Sweden. 404 B.C.-1996 A.D. Lang.: Swe. 3057

Kungliga Teatern (Stockholm)
Institutions

Recent developments at the Royal Swedish Opera. Sweden: Stockholm. 1996. Lang.: Swe. 4055

The Royal Swedish Opera compared unfavorably to Folkoperan. Sweden: Stockholm. 1996. Lang.: Swe. 4056

Views on the Royal Swedish Opera. Sweden: Stockholm. 1976. Lang.: Swe. 4057

Performance spaces

New scene and costume shops of Dramaten and Operan. Sweden: Stockholm. 1995-1996. Lang.: Swe. 657

Performance/production

Britten's *Peter Grimes*: productions by Eric Crozier and Harald André. UK-England. Sweden: Stockholm. 1945-1980. Lang.: Swe. 4229

Kungliga Teaterns Balett (Stockholm)
Performance/production

The Royal Swedish Ballet and the eighteenth-century tradition. Sweden: Stockholm. 1773-1996. Lang.: Swe. 1533

Kungliga Tekniska Högskolan (Stockholm)
Performance spaces

Ideas for a new theatre building from students of Kungliga Tekniska Högskolan. Sweden: Gustavsberg. 1995. Lang.: Swe. 658

Kunz, Erich
Plays/librettos/scripts

Leporello's aria 'Madamina' in Mozart's *Don Giovanni*. Austro-Hungarian Empire: Vienna. 1787-1996. Lang.: Eng. 4306

Kuparenko, Jordaki
Plays/librettos/scripts

Puppet playwright Jordaki Kuparenko. Poland. Russia. 1816-1842. Lang.: Pol. 4425

Kupferberg, Tuli
Plays/librettos/scripts

Vietnam War protest plays. North America. Europe. 1965-1971. Lang.: Eng. 3153

Kuret, Niko
Performance/production

Slovene shadow puppetry. Slovenia. 1938-1996. Lang.: Slo. 4443

Kuročkin, Maksim
Performance/production

Russian theatre in Vilnius. Lithuania: Vilnius. 1996. Lang.: Rus. 2138

Kurosawa, Akira
Audience

Unexpected reactions to films and plays. Canada: Montreal, PQ. 1950-1989. Lang.: Fre. 129

Kurro, Maks
Performance/production

Russian theatre in Vilnius. Lithuania: Vilnius. 1996. Lang.: Rus. 2138

Kusenberg, Klaus
Institutions

Interview with Klaus Kusenberg, artistic director of Städtische Bühnen. Germany: Osnabruck. 1990-1996. Lang.: Ger. 1806

Kushner, Tony
Administration

Angels in America and local ordinances prohibiting public nudity. USA: Charlotte, NC. 1996. Lang.: Eng. 1622

Performance/production

Intercultural theatre exchange at the American University in Bulgaria. Bulgaria: Blagoevgrad. 1993. Lang.: Eng. 1915

Angels in America and censorship at Catholic University. USA: Washington, DC. 1996. Lang.: Eng. 2661

Production of Kushner's *Angels in America* by Salt Lake Acting Company. USA: Salt Lake City, UT. 1996. Lang.: Eng. 2665

Plays/librettos/scripts

Plays about politician Roy Cohn. USA. 1986-1994. Lang.: Eng. 3339

Interviews with American playwrights. USA. 1945-1995. Lang.: Eng. 3397

Influences on Tony Kushner's *Angels in America*. USA. 1940-1996. Lang.: Eng. 3407

Law in *Angels in America* by Tony Kushner. USA. 1993. Lang.: Eng. 3421

Kūtiyāttam
Basic theatrical documents

Translated excerpt from *Tapafi-Samvaranam* by Kulaśekhara Varman. India: Kerala. 1100-1996. Lang.: Eng. 1609

Performance/production

The performance of female temple servants in religious rituals. India: Kerala. 1300-1996. Lang.: Eng. 1610

Kutrucz, Éva
Performance/production

Singing teacher Éva Kutrucz. Hungary. 1948-1996. Lang.: Hun. 4158

Kuznecova, Elena
Plays/librettos/scripts

Interview with young playwrights. Russia: Moscow. 1990-1996. Lang.: Rus. 3186

Kvarnström, Kenneth
Design/technology

The partnership of set designer Carouschka and lighting designer Jens Sethzman. Sweden. 1996. Lang.: Dan. 212

Kyd, Thomas
Plays/librettos/scripts

Gesture and self-construction in early modern English drama. England. 1580-1613. Lang.: Eng. 2962

Kyle, Barry
Performance/production

Collection of newspaper reviews by New York theatre critics. USA: New York, NY. 1996. Lang.: Eng. 2552

Kyle, Christopher
Basic theatrical documents

Text of *The Monogamist* by Christopher Kyle. USA. 1992-1996. Lang.: Eng. 1697

Kyotopolis
Basic theatrical documents

Plays by Canadian natives and people of color. Canada. 1995-1996. Lang.: Eng. 1650

Kyrlja, Jyvan
Performance/production

The work of actor Jyvan Kyrlja. Mari El Republic: Yoshkar-Ola. 1898-1942. Lang.: Rus. 881

L.S.D. (...Just the High Points...)
Relation to other fields

Performance and theatre in the politics of postindustrial societies. UK-Scotland: Glasgow. USA: New York, NY. 1994-1995. Lang.: Eng. 1249

L'vov-Anochin, Boris
Institutions

Novyj Teat'r, Boris L'vov-Anochin, director. Russia: Moscow. 1980-1996. Lang.: Rus. 1826

Langham, Michael
Institutions
The Atlantic Theatre Festival. Canada: Wolfville, NS. 1991-1996. Lang.:
Eng.   1757

Profile of Atlantic Theatre Festival. Canada: Wolfville, NS. 1993-1996.
Lang.: Eng.   1774
Langhoff, Matthias
Performance/production
Review of recent Paris productions. France: Paris. 1996. Lang.: Ger.
                                                                             2033
Langridge, Philip
Performance/production
Interview with tenor Philip Langridge. UK-England. 1939. Lang.: Swe.
                                                                             4230
Lanskoj, Vitalij
Institutions
The season's productions of Stanislavskij Theatre. Russia: Moscow.
1996. Lang.: Rus.   1837
Performance/production
Vitalij Lanskoj of Stanislavkij Theatre. Russia: Moscow. 1996. Lang.:
Rus.   2202

Productions of the Stanislavskij Theatre. Russia: Moscow. 1995-1996.
Lang.: Rus.   2242
Lansman, Émile
Plays/librettos/scripts
Émile Lansman's career in theatrical publishing. Belgium. 1985-1996.
Lang.: Fre.   2733
Lantagne, Suzanne
Plays/librettos/scripts
Suzanne Lantagne's mime adaptation of a short story by Gombrowicz.
Canada: Montreal, PQ. 1928-1989. Lang.: Fre.   3693
Lanyer, Aemilia
Relation to other fields
Teaching lyrics of women poets alongside those of Shakespeare.
England. 1590-1621. Lang.: Eng.   3491

Argument in favor of teaching Shakespeare in conjunction with his
female contemporaries. USA. 1996. Lang.: Eng.   3520
Łapicki, Andrzej
Relation to other fields
Theatre artists of the Communist period. Poland. 1924. Lang.: Pol. 1219
Lapine, James
Performance/production
Collection of newspaper reviews by London theatre critics. UK-England:
London. 1996. Lang.: Eng.   2355

Collection of newspaper reviews by London theatre critics. UK-England:
London. 1996. Lang.: Eng.   2380

Collection of newspaper reviews by New York theatre critics. USA:
New York, NY. 1996. Lang.: Eng.   2562
Theory/criticism
Critical misrepresentation of *Falsettoland* by William Finn and James
Lapine. USA. 1990. Lang.: Eng.   4002
Laprise, Antoine
Performance/production
Recent trends in Quebec theatre production. Canada: Quebec, PQ.
1992-1993. Lang.: Fre.   728
Larocque, Pierre-A.
Performance/production
Publication of an interview with the late director Pierre-A. Larocque.
Canada: Montreal, PQ. 1971-1989. Lang.: Fre.   729
Larson, Jonathan
Design/technology
Blake Burba's lighting design for *Rent*, New York Theatre Workshop.
USA: New York, NY. 1996. Lang.: Eng.   3895
Performance/production
Profiles of new actors on Broadway. USA: New York, NY. 1996. Lang.:
Eng.   1012

Collection of newspaper reviews by New York theatre critics. USA:
New York, NY, Houston, TX. 1996. Lang.: Eng.   2567

Collection of newspaper reviews by New York theatre critics. USA:
New York, NY. 1996. Lang.: Eng.   2579

Jonathan Larson's Broadway musical *Rent*. USA: New York, NY. 1996.
Lang.: Eng.   3958

Jonathan Larson's musical *Rent*. USA: New York, NY. 1996. Lang.:
Eng.   3961
Larson, Larry
Basic theatrical documents
Collection of plays from the Humana Festival. USA. 1986-1995. Lang.:
Eng.   1687

Collection of southern plays from Actors' Theatre of Louisville. USA.
1984-1992. Lang.: Eng.   1688
Larsson, Stig
Performance/production
Collection of newspaper reviews by London theatre critics. UK-England:
London. 1996. Lang.: Eng.   2325
Plays/librettos/scripts
Poetry and drama in the work of Swedish playwrights. Sweden. 1950-
1996. Lang.: Dan.   3271
Lasalle, Jean
Performance/production
French vocalism and its artists. France. 1996. Lang.: Eng.   4124
Lasko, Jim
Performance/production
Puppet production of *Frankenstein* by Redmoon Theatre. USA:
Chicago, IL. 1996. Lang.: Eng.   4444
Last Legs
Performance/production
Collection of newspaper reviews by London theatre critics. UK-England:
London. 1996. Lang.: Eng.   2462
Last Romantics, The
Performance/production
Collection of newspaper reviews by London theatre critics. UK-England:
London. 1996. Lang.: Eng.   2357
Last Yankee, The
Performance/production
Interview with director Björn Melander. Sweden: Gothenburg,
Stockholm. 1991. Lang.: Swe.   2289
Plays/librettos/scripts
Realism and the plays of Arthur Miller. USA. 1949-1992. Lang.: Eng.
                                                                             3409
Last Yellow, The
Performance/production
Collection of newspaper reviews by London theatre critics. UK-England:
London. 1996. Lang.: Eng.   2398
László, Margit
Performance/production
Interview with soprano Margit László. Hungary. 1931-1996. Lang.: Hun.
                                                                             4159
Latchmere Theatre (London)
SEE ALSO
Grace Theatre.
Later Life
Performance/production
Multiple roles of Tom Wood and Nicola Cavendish in *Later Life*.
Canada. 1996. Lang.: Eng.   1920
Latouche, John
Performance/production
Collection of newspaper reviews by New York theatre critics. USA:
New York, NY, Washington, DC. 1996. Lang.: Eng.   2581
Laughing Wild
Performance/production
Collection of newspaper reviews by London theatre critics. UK-England:
London. 1996. Lang.: Eng.   2323
Laughter on the 23rd Floor
Performance/production
Collection of newspaper reviews by London theatre critics. UK-England:
London. 1996. Lang.: Eng.   2400
Laura Pels Theatre (New York, NY)
Design/technology
Edward Gianfrancesco's set design for *Grace and Glorie*. USA: New
York, NY. 1996. Lang.: Eng.   1716
Performance spaces
Roundabout Theatre Company's new Laura Pels Theatre. USA: New
York, NY. 1994-1995. Lang.: Eng.   669
Laurin, Ginette
Performance/production
Character in modern dance choreography. Canada: Montreal, PQ. 1976-
1991. Lang.: Fre.   1568
Lauterbach, Konstanze
Institutions
Profile of Bremner Theater personnel. Germany: Bremen. 1996. Lang.:
Ger.   426
Performance/production
Konstanze Lauterbach's production of *Der aufhaltsame Aufstieg des
Arturo Ui (The Resistible Rise of Arturo Ui)* by Bertolt Brecht.
Germany: Klagenfurt. 1995. Lang.: Eng.   2048

Theatre in Leipzig since reunification. Germany: Leipzig. 1996. Lang.:
Eng.   2061

Learning, Walter
  Institutions
    Interview with Walter Learning of Theatre New Brunswick. Canada:
    Fredericton, NB. 1961-1996. Lang.: Eng.   1758
Leaving Home
  Plays/librettos/scripts
    Form and meaning in contemporary English-language theatre. Canada.
    1972-1996. Lang.: Eng.   2795
Lebeau, Suzanne
  Plays/librettos/scripts
    Suzanne Lebeau's play for children, *Gil*. Canada. 1987-1988. Lang.: Fre.
                                                                      2763
Lebedinoje osero (Swan Lake)
  Design/technology
    Interview with painter and scenographer Per Kirkeby. Denmark:
    Copenhagen. 1996. Lang.: Dan.   1476
Leben des Galilei (Life of Galileo, The)
  Performance/production
    Jean-Guy Sabourin's production of Brecht's *Leben des Galilei (The Life
    of Galileo)*, Théâtre de la Grande Réplique. Canada: Montreal, PQ.
    1980. Lang.: Fre.   1958
Lébl, Petr
  Performance/production
    Aspects of puppetry in productions by Pétr Lebl. Czech Republic:
    Prague. 1996. Lang.: Cze.   1976
    Account of Čechov International Theatre Festival. Russia. 1996. Lang.:
    Eng.   2199
Lebow, Barbara
  Plays/librettos/scripts
    Barbara Lebow's community play *Cobb County Stories*. USA: Atlanta,
    GA. 1996. Lang.: Eng.   3417
    Realism in American feminist drama. USA. 1900-1988. Lang.: Eng.
                                                                      3441
Lechay, Jo
  Relation to other fields
    Interview with Jo Lechay and Eugene Lion, creators of *Affamée
    (Starving)*. Canada: Montreal, PQ. 1990. Lang.: Fre.   1595
Leclerc, Éloi
  Plays/librettos/scripts
    Representations of Saint Francis in plays of Leclerc, Bobin, and Delteil.
    Canada: Montreal, PQ. 1996. Lang.: Fre.   2809
Leçon d'anatomie (Anatomy Lesson)
  Performance/production
    Interview with actress Hélène Loiselle. Canada: Montreal, PQ. 1950-
    1992. Lang.: Fre.   1946
  Plays/librettos/scripts
    Interview with playwright Larry Tremblay. Canada: Montreal, PQ.
    1992. Lang.: Fre.   2756
    Playwright Larry Tremblay discusses his work. Canada: Montreal, PQ.
    1981-1996. Lang.: Fre.   2835
  Theory/criticism
    Antifeminism in Montreal theatre criticism. Canada: Montreal, PQ.
    1992. Lang.: Fre.   3533
Leçon, La (Lesson, The)
  Institutions
    Profile of Théâtre de la Huchette, which produces the plays of Ionesco.
    France: Paris. 1950-1996. Lang.: Swe.   1792
  Performance/production
    Actor Robert Gustafsson. Sweden: Stockholm. 1996. Lang.: Swe.   951
    Plays of Ionesco in Romania after Ceauşescu. Romania: Cluj. 1989-
    1993. Lang.: Eng.   2185
Leconte, Patrice
  Design/technology
    John Nollet's wigs for the film *Ridicule* by Patrice Leconte. France.
    1996. Lang.: Eng.   3588
Lector (Reader, The)
  Performance/production
    Productions of Schauspielhaus Bonn. Germany: Bonn. 1996. Lang.: Ger.
                                                                      2075
Leduchovskij, Anatolij
  Performance/production
    The new generation of Russian directors. Russia: Moscow. 1996. Lang.:
    Ger.   2196
Lee, Chris
  Performance/production
    Collection of newspaper reviews by London theatre critics. UK-England:
    London. 1996. Lang.: Eng.   2438
Lee, Don L.
  SEE
    Madhubuti, Haki R.

Lee, Leslie
  Performance/production
    Montage structure in plays of American ethnic minorities. USA. 1967-
    1990. Lang.: Eng.   2675
Lee, Levi
  Basic theatrical documents
    Collection of plays from the Humana Festival. USA. 1986-1995. Lang.:
    Eng.   1687
    Collection of southern plays from Actors' Theatre of Louisville. USA.
    1984-1992. Lang.: Eng.   1688
Lee, Robert E.
  Performance/production
    Collection of newspaper reviews by New York theatre critics. USA:
    New York, NY. 1996. Lang.: Eng.   2574
  Plays/librettos/scripts
    Interviews with American playwrights. USA. 1945-1995. Lang.: Eng.
                                                                      3397
Lee, Russell
  Plays/librettos/scripts
    Russell Lee's *Nixon's Nixon*. USA: New York, NY. 1994-1996. Lang.:
    Eng.   3348
Lee, Terry
  Performance/production
    Performances of the Jim Henson International Festival. USA: New
    York, NY. 1995. Lang.: Eng.   4407
Lees, Russell
  Performance/production
    Collection of newspaper reviews by New York theatre critics. USA:
    New York, NY. 1996. Lang.: Eng.   2570
  Plays/librettos/scripts
    Playwright Russell Lees. USA: New York, NY. 1996. Lang.: Eng.   3389
Lefebvre, Paul
  Institutions
    Montreal theatres' role in education and the preparation of future
    audiences. Canada: Montreal, PQ. 1992. Lang.: Fre.   361
  Plays/librettos/scripts
    Round-table discussion of Quebec translators. Canada. 1980-1990.
    Lang.: Fre.   2769
Lefèvre, Robin
  Performance/production
    Collection of newspaper reviews by London theatre critics. UK-England:
    London. 1996. Lang.: Eng.   2414
Leffler Edgren, Anne Charlotte
  Basic theatrical documents
    International anthology of modern drama by women. 1880-1940. Lang.:
    Eng.   1637
Lefton, Sue
  Performance/production
    Collection of newspaper reviews by London theatre critics. UK-England:
    London. 1996. Lang.: Eng.   2327
Legal aspects
  Administration
    Analysis of contract discussions. Germany. 1995-1996. Lang.: Ger.   19
    Censorship in Pécs theatre. Hungary: Pécs. 1850-1863. Lang.: Hun.   33
    Fundraising and the restricted gift. USA. 1996. Lang.: Eng.   58
    Not-for-profit institutions and participation in politics. USA:
    Washington, DC. 1996. Lang.: Eng.   105
    Copyright law and the internet. USA. 1996. Lang.: Eng.   122
    German copyright law for choreography. Germany. 1996. Lang.: Ger.
                                                                      1401
    Víctor Ruiz Iriarte's *Los pájaros ciegos (The Blind Birds)* and censorship
    in the Franco regime. Spain. 1939-1975. Lang.:Eng.   1618
    Directors' property rights and the Joe Mantello case. USA: New York,
    NY. 1996. Lang.: Eng.   1621
    Angels in America and local ordinances prohibiting public nudity. USA:
    Charlotte, NC. 1996. Lang.: Eng.   1622
    Directors' rights: Joe Mantello's lawsuit regarding his staging of *Love!
    Valour! Compassion!*. USA: New York, NY. 1996. Lang.: Eng.   1624
  Design/technology
    Patent infringement suits between two theatrical lighting companies.
    USA. 1996. Lang.: Eng.   251
  Institutions
    The establishment of theatres in Bohemia. Czech Republic: Prague.
    1700-1996. Lang.: Cze.   391
  Plays/librettos/scripts
    Shakespeare, publishing, and performing rights. England. 1590-1640.
    Lang.: Eng.   2898

Lighting — cont'd

Lighting design for Peter Sagal's *Denial* at the Long Wharf Theatre. USA: New Haven, CT. 1996. Lang.: Eng. 1745

Set and lighting design for *Holiday* in the round at Circle in the Square. USA: New York, NY. 1996. Lang.: Eng. 1746

Lighting effects for the animated film *Toy Story*. USA: Hollywood, CA. 1995. Lang.: Eng. 3595

Television lighting design by Steven Brill and Kathleen Ankers. USA: New York, NY. 1996. Lang.: Eng. 3663

Bob Dickinson's TV lighting designs for the summer Olympics. USA: Atlanta, GA. 1996. Lang.: Eng. 3664

Cinema Services and the video spectacle *EFX*. USA: Las Vegas, NV. 1995. Lang.: Eng. 3665

Design of MTV video music awards ceremony. USA: New York, NY. 1995. Lang.: Eng. 3666

Vince Foster's design for rock star Zucchero. Italy. 1996. Lang.: Eng. 3696

Jason Kantrowitz's lighting design for *Pomp Duck and Circumstance*. USA: New York, NY. 1996. Lang.: Eng. 3697

Transport problems of Zingaro, an equestrian theatre group. USA: New York, NY. France. 1996. Lang.: Eng. 3699

Design for the U.S. tour of rock group The Cure. USA. 1996. Lang.: Eng. 3700

The production team for The Who's *Quadrophenia*. USA: New York, NY. 1996. Lang.: Eng. 3701

Design for Gozzi's *The Green Bird (L'augellino belverde)* at the New Victory Theatre. USA: New York, NY. 1996. Lang.: Eng. 3760

Production design for tour of country singer Reba McEntire. USA. 1996. Lang.: Eng. 3831

Lighting for the German-language production of Disney's *Beauty and the Beast*. Austria: Vienna. 1995. Lang.: Ger. 3887

Technical aspects of a German-language production of Disney's *Beauty and the Beast*. Austria: Vienna. 1995. Lang.: Ger. 3888

Lighting design for plays about Martin Guerre. UK-England: London. 1996. Lang.: Eng. 3890

Lighting for London and Dublin productions of *Tap Dogs*. UK-England: London. Ireland: Dublin. 1996. Lang.: Eng. 3891

Alison Darke's production design for *Pendragon* by the National Youth Music Theatre of Great Britain. UK-England. USA: New York,NY. 1995. Lang.: Eng. 3892

Technical differences between Broadway and West End productions of *The Who's Tommy*. UK-England: London. USA: New York, NY. 1996. Lang.: Eng. 3893

Set and lighting design for *Old Wicked Songs*, Promenade Theatre. USA: New York, NY. 1996. Lang.: Eng. 3894

Blake Burba's lighting design for *Rent*, New York Theatre Workshop. USA: New York, NY. 1996. Lang.: Eng. 3895

Lighting designs for Broadway musical *Chicago* by Ken Billington. USA: New York, NY. 1996. Lang.: Eng. 3896

Lighting design for a touring production of *Carousel*. USA. 1996. Lang.: Eng. 3900

Lighting designer Hans Toelstede of Cologne Opera. Germany: Cologne. 1996. Lang.: Eng. 4017

Paolo Mazzon's lighting designs for Verona's amphitheatre. Italy: Verona. 1996. Lang.: Eng. 4022

Stage lighting for a production of *A Kékszakállú herceg vára* by Béla Bartók. Russia. 1990-1996. Lang.: Rus. 4023

John Boesche's lighting design for *Tannhäuser*, Austin Lyric Opera. USA. 1996. Lang.: Eng. 4024

Renovation of Metropolitan Opera lighting system. USA: New York, NY. 1996. Lang.: Eng. 4025

Technical aspects of Wagner's *Ring* cycle, Arizona Opera. USA: Flagstaff, AZ. 1996. Lang.: Eng. 4028

Performance spaces

Proposal to restore original lighting equipment in the auditorium of a retirement home. Sweden: Stockholm. 1920. Lang.: Swe. 656

Lights, The

Performance/production

Collection of newspaper reviews by London theatre critics. UK-England: London. 1996. Lang.: Eng. 2457

Ligue Nationale d'Improvisation (Montreal, PQ)

Institutions

The principles of the Ligue Nationale de l'Improvisation. Canada. 1988-1990. Lang.: Fre. 359

Liitoja, Hillar

Plays/librettos/scripts

Overview of Anglophone Canadian playwriting. Canada. 1970-1990. Lang.: Fre. 2791

Liitooma Project (Zambia)

Performance/production

Imipashi (The Spirits): a touring production of the national Liitooma Project. Zambia. 1995-1996. Lang.: Eng. 1080

Like a Brother

Performance/production

The production of *Like a Brother* by T.E. Klunzinger. USA: New York, NY. 1995. Lang.: Eng. 2645

Liking, Werewere

Institutions

Profile of international festival of Francophone theatre. France. 1984-1991. Lang.: Fre. 410

Performance/production

Performances of the Jim Henson International Festival. USA: New York, NY. 1995. Lang.: Eng. 4407

Plays/librettos/scripts

Pan-Africanism in the theatre of Werewere Liking. Cameroon. Ivory Coast. 1976-1996. Lang.: Eng. 2736

Lila ákác (Lilac Acacias)

Performance/production

Budapest productions of the millicentenary season. Hungary: Budapest. 1995-1996. Lang.: Eng. 2104

Lilian Baylis Theatre (London)

Performance/production

Collection of newspaper reviews by London theatre critics. UK-England: London. 1996. Lang.: Eng. 2315

Collection of newspaper reviews by London theatre critics. UK-England: London. 1996. Lang.: Eng. 2323

Liliefeldt, Louis Ethel

Audience

Performance artist Louis Ethel Liliefeldt. Canada. 1996. Lang.: Eng. 3784

Lill, Wendy

Basic theatrical documents

Text of *The Glace Bay Miners' Museum* by Wendy Lill. Canada. 1996. Lang.: Eng. 1647

Plays/librettos/scripts

Overview of Anglophone Canadian playwriting. Canada. 1970-1990. Lang.: Fre. 2791

Lille Eyolf (Little Eyolf)

Performance/production

Collection of newspaper reviews by London theatre critics. UK-England: London, Stratford. 1996. Lang.: Eng. 2489

Lillo, George

Performance/production

Collection of newspaper reviews by London theatre critics. UK-England: London. 1996. Lang.: Eng. 2332

Plays/librettos/scripts

European bourgeois drama and the break with classical tradition. England. France. Germany. 1731-1779. Lang.: Slo. 2964

Lime Tree Bower, The

Performance/production

Collection of newspaper reviews by London theatre critics. UK-England: London. 1996. Lang.: Eng. 2452

Lina Bögli

Institutions

Productions of the Welt in Basel festival. Switzerland: Basel. 1996. Lang.: Ger. 549

Lincoln Center Institute (New York, NY)

Design/technology

Lighting designer Beverly Emmons, artistic director of Lincoln Center Institute. USA: New York, NY. 1996. Lang.: Eng. 301

Relation to other fields

Programs for teachers' professional development in theatre. USA. 1994-1996. Lang.: Eng. 1261

Lincoln Center Library for the Performing Arts (New York, NY)

Performance/production

Account of a videotaped archive interview with actress Uta Hagen. USA: New York, NY. 1996. Lang.: Eng. 2657

Lincoln Center Repertory Theatre (New York, NY)

Design/technology

John Arnone's set for *Sex and Longing* by Christopher Durang. USA: New York, NY. 1996. Lang.: Eng. 1725

Performance/production

Collection of newspaper reviews by New York theatre critics. USA: New York, NY. 1996. Lang.: Eng. 2554

Lunt-Fontanne Theatre (New York, NY) — cont'd

Collection of newspaper reviews by New York theatre critics. USA: New York, NY. 1996. Lang.: Eng.   2574

Carol Channing's 4,500th performance in the title role of *Hello, Dolly!*. USA: New York, NY. 1996. Lang.: Eng.   3973

Lupa, Krystian
  Performance/production
Director Krystian Lupa. Poland: Cracow. 1996. Lang.: Ger.   2157

Krystian Lupa's *Lunatycy (The Sleepwalkers)* at Stary Teatr. Poland: Cracow. 1995. Lang.: Eng, Fre.   2169

The work of director Krystian Lupa. Poland. 1943-1996. Lang.: Pol.   2170

Analysis of Krystian Lupa's *Lunatycy (The Sleepwalkers)*, based on writing of Hermann Broch. Poland: Cracow. 1995. Lang.: Eng, Fre.
                                2178

Lupo
  Basic theatrical documents
Text of *Lupo* by Elfriede Müller. Germany. 1996. Lang.: Ger.   1660

LuPone, Patti
  Performance/production
Actresses recall playing the lead role in the musical *Evita*. USA. 1996. Lang.: Eng.   3944

The performing and recording career of Patti LuPone. USA. England. 1972-1995. Lang.: Eng.   3968

Lust
  Performance/production
Collection of newspaper reviews by London theatre critics. UK-England: London. 1996. Lang.: Eng.   2473

Lust and Comfort
  Basic theatrical documents
Anthology of works by Split Britches. USA. 1985-1995. Lang.: Eng.
                                1685

Lustige Witwe, Die
  Performance/production
Background material on New York City Opera telecast performance of *The Merry Widow*. USA: New York, NY. 1996. Lang.: Eng.   4240

Analysis of two popular operettas *János vitéz* and *Die lustige Witwe*. Austro-Hungarian Empire. 1904-1906. Lang.: Hun.   4364

Lustigen Weiber von Windsor, Die
  Performance/production
Austrian productions of Shakespearean plays and operas. Austria. 1994-1995. Lang.: Ger.   691

Luther
  Performance/production
Comparison of productions about Martin Luther. Germany: Wittenberg, Magdeburg. 1996. Lang.: Ger.   2065

Luther Rufen (Calling Luther)
  Performance/production
Comparison of productions about Martin Luther. Germany: Wittenberg, Magdeburg. 1996. Lang.: Ger.   2065

Lutkovno gledališče (Maribor)
  Institutions
Production history of Maribor Puppet Theatre. Slovenia: Maribor. 1974-1995. Lang.: Slo.   4384

Lutkovno gledališče Primskovo
  Institutions
History of Lutkovno gledališče Primskovo, Primskovo Puppet Theatre. Yugoslavia: Primskovo. 1931-1958. Lang.: Slo.   4386

Luzzati, Emanuele
  Design/technology
Illustrations of scenographer Emanuele Luzzati. Italy: Genoa. 1921-1996. Lang.: Ita.   182

Lyceum Theatre (Edinburgh)
  SEE
Royal Lyceum Theatre.

Lyceum Theatre (London)
  Performance/production
Collection of newspaper reviews by London theatre critics. UK-England: London. 1996. Lang.: Eng.   2478

Lyceum Theatre (New York, NY)
  Performance/production
Collection of newspaper reviews by New York theatre critics. USA: New York, NY. 1996. Lang.: Eng.   2561

Collection of newspaper reviews by New York theatre critics. USA: New York, NY. 1996. Lang.: Eng.   2574

Lynch, Stuart
  Performance/production
Account of *Compression 100* by Tess de Quincey and Stuart Lynch. Denmark: Copenhagen. Australia. 1996. Lang.: Dan.   1420

Plays/librettos/scripts
Performance art at a Copenhagen seminar on the body and ritual manipulation. Denmark. 1995. Lang.: Dan.   3811
Lyric Hammersmith (London)
  Performance/production
Collection of newspaper reviews by London theatre critics. UK-England: London. 1996. Lang.: Eng.   2314

Collection of newspaper reviews by London theatre critics. UK-England: London. 1996. Lang.: Eng.   2362

Collection of newspaper reviews by London theatre critics. UK-England: London. 1996. Lang.: Eng.   2366

Collection of newspaper reviews by London theatre critics. UK-England: London. 1996. Lang.: Eng.   2385

Collection of newspaper reviews by London theatre critics. UK-England: London. 1996. Lang.: Eng.   2411

Collection of newspaper reviews by London theatre critics. UK-England: London. 1996. Lang.: Eng.   2419

Collection of newspaper reviews by London theatre critics. UK-England: London. 1996. Lang.: Eng.   2435

Collection of newspaper reviews by London theatre critics. UK-England: London. 1996. Lang.: Eng.   2439

Collection of newspaper reviews by London theatre critics. UK-England: London. 1996. Lang.: Eng.   2441

Collection of newspaper reviews by London theatre critics. UK-England: London. 1996. Lang.: Eng.   2495

Lyric Opera of Chicago (Chicago, IL)
  Performance/production
Background material on Lyric Opera of Chicago radio broadcast performances. USA: Chicago, IL. 1996. Lang.: Eng.   4244

Cutting and editing of Handel operas. USA. 1920-1996. Lang.: Eng.
                                4272

Puppets in Wagner's *Ring* at Lyric Opera of Chicago. USA: Chicago, IL. 1996. Lang.: Eng.   4414
Lyric Studio (London)
  Performance/production
Collection of newspaper reviews by London theatre critics. UK-England: London. 1996. Lang.: Eng.   2306

Collection of newspaper reviews by London theatre critics. UK-England: London. 1996. Lang.: Eng.   2307

Collection of newspaper reviews by London theatre critics. UK-England: London. 1996. Lang.: Eng.   2322

Collection of newspaper reviews by London theatre critics. UK-England: London. 1996. Lang.: Eng.   2332

Collection of newspaper reviews by London theatre critics. UK-England: London. 1996. Lang.: Eng.   2348

Collection of newspaper reviews by London theatre critics. UK-England: London. 1996. Lang.: Eng.   2357

Collection of newspaper reviews by London theatre critics. UK-England: London. 1996. Lang.: Eng.   2359

Collection of newspaper reviews by London theatre critics. UK-England: London. 1996. Lang.: Eng.   2392

Collection of newspaper reviews by London theatre critics. UK-England: London. 1996. Lang.: Eng.   2400

Collection of newspaper reviews by London theatre critics. UK-England: London. 1996. Lang.: Eng.   2414

Collection of newspaper reviews by London theatre critics. UK-England: London. 1996. Lang.: Eng.   2425

Collection of newspaper reviews by London theatre critics. UK-England: London. 1996. Lang.: Eng.   2455

Collection of newspaper reviews by London theatre critics. UK-England: London. 1996. Lang.: Eng.   2466

Collection of newspaper reviews by London theatre critics. UK-England: London. 1996. Lang.: Eng.   2477

Collection of newspaper reviews by London theatre critics. UK-England: London. 1996. Lang.: Eng.   2488

Lyric Theatre (New York, NY)
  Performance spaces
Livent Realty's plan to renovate the Lyric and Apollo theatres. USA: New York, NY. 1996. Lang.: Eng.   673
Lysistrata
  Performance/production
Censorship of Federal Theatre Project's *Lysistrata* performed by Seattle Negro Repertory Company. USA: Seattle, WA. 1936-1939. Lang.: Eng.
                                2688

Manhattan Theatre Club (New York, NY)
Design/technology
Brian MacDevitt's lighting design for *Blue Window*, Manhattan Theatre Club. USA: New York, NY. 1996. Lang.: Eng. 1721
Institutions
Annual fundraising event for Manhattan Theatre Club. USA: New York, NY. 1996. Lang.: Eng. 584
Lynne Meadow and Barry Grove on Manhattan Theatre Club's twenty-fifth anniversary. USA: New York, NY. 1972-1996. Lang.: Eng. 1868
Performance/production
Collection of newspaper reviews by New York theatre critics. USA: New York, NY. 1996. Lang.: Eng. 2555
Collection of newspaper reviews by New York theatre critics. USA: New York, NY. 1996. Lang.: Eng. 2560
Collection of newspaper reviews by New York theatre critics. USA: New York, NY, Houston, TX. 1996. Lang.: Eng. 2567
Collection of newspaper reviews by New York theatre critics. USA: New York, NY. 1996. Lang.: Eng. 2571
Plays/librettos/scripts
Interview with playwright Craig Lucas. USA: New York, NY. 1984-1996. Lang.: Eng. 3427

Manitoba Theatre Centre (Winnipeg, MB)
Administration
Canadian theatres' response to funding cuts. Canada. 1994-1996. Lang.: Eng. 11

Maniutiu, Mihai
Performance/production
Collection of newspaper reviews by London theatre critics. UK-England: London. 1996. Lang.: Eng. 2463

Manjana Theatre (Stockholm)
Performance/production
Collection of newspaper reviews by London theatre critics. UK-England: London. 1996. Lang.: Eng. 2499

Manker, Paulus
Institutions
Highlights of the Wiener Festwochen festival. Austria: Vienna. 1996. Lang.: Ger. 1752

Mann ist Mann (Man's a Man, A)
Plays/librettos/scripts
Boxing as metaphor in plays of Brecht. Germany: Berlin. 1922-1926. Lang.: Eng. 3042

Mann, Emily
Design/technology
Robert Brill's sets for Emily Mann's *Greensboro* using projections by John Boesche. USA: Princeton, NJ. 1996. Lang.: Eng. 1729
Performance/production
Emily Mann's creation of documentary-style theatre based on interviews. USA: Princeton, NJ. 1996. Lang.: Eng. 2643
Plays/librettos/scripts
Interview with playwright/director Emily Mann. USA: Princeton, NJ. 1996. Lang.: Eng. 3385
Interviews with American playwrights. USA. 1945-1995. Lang.: Eng. 3397

Mannheimer Nationalteater (Mannheim)
Performance/production
Hans Krása's opera *Verlobung im Traum*. Czech Republic: Prague. 1994-1996. Lang.: Eng. 4101

Manning, Frank
Performance/production
Profile of dancer Frank Manning. USA: New York, NY. 1926. Lang.: Swe. 1450

Manning, Peter
Plays/librettos/scripts
Producer Peter Manning of New York Stage and Film. USA: Poughkeepsie, NY. 1996. Lang.: Eng. 1111

Manocha, Inder
Performance/production
Collection of newspaper reviews by London theatre critics. UK-England: London. 1996. Lang.: Eng. 2308

Manochin, Valentin
Performance/production
Interview with choreographer Valentin Manochin. Russia: Moscow. 1990-1996. Lang.: Rus. 1441

Manoel Theatre (Malta)
Performance spaces
Censorship at the Manoel Theatre. Malta. 1741-1996. Lang.: Swe. 649

Mansfield Park
Performance/production
Collection of newspaper reviews by London theatre critics. UK-England: London, Chichester. 1996. Lang.: Eng. 2440

Manteca
Basic theatrical documents
English translation of *Manteca* by Alberto Pedro Torriente. Cuba. 1993. Lang.: Eng. 1653
Plays/librettos/scripts
Analysis of *Manteca* by Alberto Pedro Torriente. Cuba. 1993. Lang.: Eng. 2863
Alberto Pedro Torriente's *Manteca* in the context of Cuban politics and society. Cuba. 1993. Lang.: Eng. 2865

Mantello, Joe
Administration
Directors' property rights and the Joe Mantello case. USA: New York, NY. 1996. Lang.: Eng. 1621
Directors' rights: Joe Mantello's lawsuit regarding his staging of *Love! Valour! Compassion!*. USA: New York, NY. 1996. Lang.: Eng. 1624
Performance/production
Collection of newspaper reviews by New York theatre critics. USA: New York, NY, Houston, TX. 1996. Lang.: Eng. 2567
Plays/librettos/scripts
Interview with playwright Craig Lucas. USA: New York, NY. 1984-1996. Lang.: Eng. 3427

Manual of Trench Warfare, A
Basic theatrical documents
Collection of Australian gay and lesbian plays. Australia. 1970-1996. Lang.: Eng. 1641

Mapa Teatro (Bogotá)
Plays/librettos/scripts
Report on Colombian studies conference. Colombia: Bogotá. 1995. Lang.: Spa. 2858

Mapantsula
Performance/production
Influence of Hollywood gangster films on South African cinema. USA: Hollywood, CA. South Africa, Republic of. 1930-1996. Lang.: Eng. 3637

Maponya, Maishe
Plays/librettos/scripts
Analysis of *Gangsters* by Maishe Maponya. South Africa, Republic of. 1930-1995. Lang.: Eng. 3224

Maraden, Marti
Design/technology
Mechanized sets for *The Merchant of Venice* at Stratford Festival. Canada: Stratford, ON. 1996. Lang.: Eng. 1706

Maraini, Dacia
Plays/librettos/scripts
Director/playwright Dacia Maraini. Italy. 1995. Lang.: Eng. 3118

Marais, Jean
Performance/production
Stage and film treatments of the fairy tale *Beauty and the Beast*. Europe. USA. Canada. 1946-1996. Lang.: Eng. 793

Marans, Jon
Design/technology
Set and lighting design for *Old Wicked Songs*, Promenade Theatre. USA: New York, NY. 1996. Lang.: Eng. 3894
Performance/production
Collection of newspaper reviews by London theatre critics. UK-England: London. 1996. Lang.: Eng. 2478
Actor Bob Hoskins. UK-England: London. 1968-1996. Lang.: Eng. 3927
Plays/librettos/scripts
Jon Marans on his musical *Old Wicked Songs*. USA: New York, NY. 1996. Lang.: Eng. 3992

Marat/Sade
Plays/librettos/scripts
Portrayals of women in works of ten male playwrights. Europe. 1836-1978. Lang.: Eng. 2973

Marber, Patrick
Performance/production
Collection of newspaper reviews by London theatre critics. UK-England: London. 1996. Lang.: Eng. 2318

Marbury, Elisabeth
Relation to other fields
Profile of a lesbian 'marriage' in the theatre community. USA: New York, NY. 1886-1933. Lang.: Eng. 1264

Marc, Alessandra
Performance/production
The career of soprano Alessandra Marc. USA. 1996. Lang.: Eng. 4265

Marčello, Boris
Performance/production
Marčello's ballet *Prizračnyj Bal (Ghostly Ball)* directed by Dmitrij Brjancev, Teat'r Kamernogo Baleta. Russia: St. Petersburg. 1995. Lang.: Rus. 1515

Marthaler, Christoph — cont'd

Performance/production
Work of director Christoph Marthaler. Germany. Switzerland. 1996.
Lang.: Ger. 835

Physical theatre in guest performances by Robert Lepage, Volksbühne,
and Théâtre de Complicité. Sweden: Stockholm. 1994. Lang.: Swe. 949

Discussion surrounding a performance of *Murx* by Christoph Marthaler.
Germany: Berlin. UK-England: London. 1995. Lang.: Eng. 3917

Performances of the Salzburg festival. Austria: Salzburg. 1996. Lang.:
Ger. 4082

Relation to other fields
Political implications of Christoph Marthaler's *Murx*, directed by Heiner
Goebbels. Germany: Berlin. UK-England: London. 1992-1995. Lang.:
Eng. 4001

Martin Beck Theatre (New York, NY)
Performance/production
Collection of newspaper reviews by New York theatre critics. USA:
New York, NY. 1996. Lang.: Eng. 2563

Martin Guerre
Design/technology
Lighting design for plays about Martin Guerre. UK-England: London.
1996. Lang.: Eng. 3890

Performance/production
Collection of newspaper reviews by London theatre critics. UK-England:
London. 1996. Lang.: Eng. 2453

Collection of newspaper reviews by London theatre critics. UK-England:
London. 1996. Lang.: Eng. 2472

Plays/librettos/scripts
Musical adaptations of the story of Martin Guerre. USA. 1996. Lang.:
Eng. 3991

Martín Recuerda, José
Plays/librettos/scripts
Women and war in plays of José Martín Recuerda and José María
Rodríguez Méndez. Spain. 1947-1971. Lang.: Spa. 3246

Martin-Harvey, John
Administration
A chapter in the history of theatre unionization. UK-England. 1920-
1935. Lang.: Eng. 51

Martin, Alexis
Performance/production
The ban on Grand Théâtre Émotif du Québec's *Nudité (Nudity)*.
Canada: Montreal, PQ. 1996. Lang.: Fre. 749

Interview with actors Jean-Louis Millette and Alexis Martin. Canada:
Montreal, PQ. 1992. Lang.: Fre. 1923

Plays/librettos/scripts
Playwright Alexis Martin on his work. Canada: Montreal, PQ. 1992-
1996. Lang.: Fre. 2810

Martin, Andrea
Design/technology
Contemporary costuming by designer Jane Greenwood. USA: New
York, NY. 1996. Lang.: Eng. 1738

Martin, Catherine
Design/technology
Production design for Baz Luhrmann's film *Romeo and Juliet*. USA:
Miami, FL. 1996. Lang.: Eng. 3601

Martin, Jane
Basic theatrical documents
Collection of plays from the Humana Festival. USA. 1986-1995. Lang.:
Eng. 1687

Martin, Mary
Performance/production
Gender in performances of actress Mary Martin. USA. 1922-1994.
Lang.: Eng. 1074

Plays/librettos/scripts
Feminist/lesbian reading of *The Sound of Music*, and its star Mary
Martin. USA. 1938-1959. Lang.: Eng. 4000

Martin, Nicholas
Performance/production
Collection of newspaper reviews by New York theatre critics. USA:
New York, NY. 1996. Lang.: Eng. 2561

Collection of newspaper reviews by New York theatre critics. USA:
New York, NY. 1996. Lang.: Eng. 2571

Roger Rees's role in *The Rehearsal* by Anouilh, Roundabout Theatre
Company. USA: New York, NY. UK-England: London. 1996. Lang.:
Eng. 2617

Martin, Ricky
Performance/production
Ricky Martin's role in *Les Misérables*. USA: New York, NY. 1996.
Lang.: Eng. 3931

Martin, Steve
Design/technology
Scott Bradley's set design for three productions of *Picasso at the Lapin
Agile* by Steve Martin. USA: New York, NY. 1996. Lang.:Eng. 1717

Martineau, Maureen
Performance/production
Comic actors of Théâtre Parminou. Canada. 1990. Lang.: Fre. 701

Martinelli, Marco
Institutions
Marco Martinelli's Teatro Ravenna. Italy: Ravenna. 1991-1996. Lang.:
Dan. 3761

Martínez Mediero, Manuel
Plays/librettos/scripts
Interview with playwright Manuel Martínez Mediero. Spain. 1939-1993.
Lang.: Spa. 3236

Martinoli, Graziella
Performance/production
Interview with Graziella Martinoli of La Pinguicola Sulle Vigne. Italy:
Genoa. 1995. Lang.: Eng. 2123

Martins, Peter
Design/technology
Interview with painter and scenographer Per Kirkeby. Denmark:
Copenhagen. 1996. Lang.: Dan. 1476

Martinus, Derek
Performance/production
Collection of newspaper reviews by London theatre critics. UK-England:
London. 1996. Lang.: Eng. 2321

Marton, László
Performance/production
English plays and subjects on the Hungarian stage. Hungary. 1995-1996.
Lang.: Eng. 847

Martynov, Vladimir
Performance/production
Martynov's *Plach Jeremii* staged by Vasiljėv's School of Dramatic Art.
Russia: Moscow. 1995-1996. Lang.: Rus. 4209

Marx Brothers
Performance/production
Michael McGrath's role in *The Cocoanuts* directed by Richard Sabellico.
USA: New York, NY. 1920-1996. Lang.: Eng. 3959

Marxist criticism
Plays/librettos/scripts
English translation of two essays by Gramsci. Italy. 1917-1932. Lang.:
Eng. 3122

Theory/criticism
Practice and performativity in Marxism. USA. 1996. Lang.: Eng. 3565

Mary Magdalen
Plays/librettos/scripts
Representation of devils and vices in English liturgy and theatre.
England. 1300-1500. Lang.: Eng. 2890

Maryland Stage Company (Baltimore, MD)
Institutions
Productions of the month-long Beckett festival. France: Strasbourg.
1996. Lang.: Eng. 408

Masca (Bucharest)
Performance/production
Account of festival of Romanian performing arts. USA: New York, NY.
Romania. 1995-1996. Lang.: Eng. 2668

Maschinenstürmer, Die (Machine Wreckers, The)
Performance/production
Katie Mitchell's production of *The Machine Wreckers (Die
Maschinenstürmer)* by Ernst Toller. UK-England: London. 1995. Lang.:
Eng. 2506

Plays/librettos/scripts
The life and early plays of Ernst Toller. Germany. 1919-1923. Lang.:
Eng. 3017

Maščkov, Vladimir
Performance/production
The new generation of Russian directors. Russia: Moscow. 1996. Lang.:
Ger. 2196

Masefield, John
Performance/production
John Masefield's theatricals. UK-England. 1919-1932. Lang.: Eng. 2535

Másik, János
Performance/production
Budapest productions of the millicentenary season. Hungary: Budapest.
1995-1996. Lang.: Eng. 2104

Maskarad (Masquerade)
Performance/production
Nikolaj Šejko directs Lermontov's *Maskarad (Masquerade)* at Čechov
Art Theatre. Russia: Moscow. 1990-1996. Lang.: Rus. 2220

Méduse (Montreal, PQ) — cont'd

Performance/production
Recent trends in Quebec theatre production. Canada: Quebec, PQ. 1992-1993. Lang.: Fre. 728

Medved (Bear, The)
Performance/production
Collection of newspaper reviews by London theatre critics. UK-England: London. 1996. Lang.: Eng. 2442

Medvedev, Aleksand'r
Performance/production
Operatic works of composer Leonid Bobylev. Russia: Moscow. 1990-1996. Lang.: Rus. 4204

Medwall, Henry
Plays/librettos/scripts
Representation of devils and vices in English liturgy and theatre. England. 1300-1500. Lang.: Eng. 2890

Mee, Charles L., Jr.
Design/technology
Lighting design for amphitheatre production of *The Trojan Women: A Love Story*. USA: New York, NY. 1996. Lang.: Eng. 1733
Performance/production
Collection of newspaper reviews by New York theatre critics. USA: New York, NY, Cambridge, MA. 1996. Lang.: Eng. 2583
Impressions of the Boston theatre scene. USA: Cambridge, MA, Boston, MA. 1995. Lang.: Eng. 2628
Interview with Tina Landau, director of *The Trojan Women: A Love Story*. USA: New York, NY. 1996. Lang.: Eng. 2672
Theory/criticism
American participation in international theatre. USA. 1950-1995. Lang.: Eng. 1382

Meeh, Gregory
Design/technology
Design for the musical *Big*. USA: Detroit, MI. 1996. Lang.: Eng. 3902

Megahey, Leslie
Performance/production
Collection of newspaper reviews by New York theatre critics. USA: New York, NY. 1996. Lang.: Eng. 2577

Megged, Aharon
Basic theatrical documents
Israeli Holocaust drama. Israel. 1955-1989. Lang.: Eng. 1667

Mehta, Xerxes
Institutions
Productions of the month-long Beckett festival. France: Strasbourg. 1996. Lang.: Eng. 408

Meinwärts
Performance/production
Collection of newspaper reviews by London theatre critics. UK-England: London. 1996. Lang.: Eng. 2498

Meirelles, Marcio
Performance/production
The creation of *Zumbi* by Bando de Teatro Olodum and the Black Theatre Co-operative. Brazil: Salvador. UK-England: London. 1995-1996. Lang.: Eng. 1914

Meistersinger von Nürnberg, Die
Performance spaces
The reopening of Theater Lübeck. Germany: Lübeck. 1906-1996. Lang.: Ger. 4068
Performance/production
Wolfgang Wagner's production of *Die Meistersinger* at Bayreuther Festspiele. Germany: Bayreuth. 1996. Lang.: Ger. 4133
Wolfgang Wagner's scenery and direction of *Die Meistersinger* at the Bayreuth Festival. Germany: Bayreuth. 1996. Lang.: Ger. 4146
Plays/librettos/scripts
Self-contained musical compositions in operas of Wagner and Richard Strauss. Germany. Austria. 1849-1913. Lang.: Eng. 4322

Mej, Medeja I.
Performance/production
Opera singers Nikolaj N. Figner and Medeja I. Mej of the Mariinskij Theatre. Russia: St. Petersburg. 1880-1910. Lang.: Rus. 4207

Mejerchol'd, Vsevolod Emiljévič
Performance/production
Theories of acting and performance. Latin America. 1910-1995. Lang.: Spa. 879
Anecdotes about Šaljapin and Mejerchol'd. Russia. 1900-1938. Lang.: Rus. 902
Mejerchol'd's work in acting. Russia. 1874-1940. Lang.: Ita. 922
Report on Mejerchol'd symposium. UK-Wales: Aberystwyth. 1995. Lang.: Eng. 1000
Otrabanda's production of *The Fairground Booth (Balagančik)* by Blok at La MaMa E.T.C.. USA: New York, NY. 1996. Lang.: Eng. 1006

Productions of Tretjakov's *Choču Rebenka (I Want a Baby)*. USSR: Moscow. UK-England: Birmingham. Germany: Berlin. 1927-1993.Lang.: Eng. 2694
Newly discovered records of Mejerchol'd rehearsals. USSR. 1925-1938. Lang.: Eng. 2696
Mejerchol'd's production of *Le cocu magnifique (The Magnificent Cuckold)* by Crommelynck. USSR. 1917-1922. Lang.: Eng. 2697
Theory/criticism
Memoirs of theatre critic A.P. Mackin. Russia. 1906-1996. Lang.: Rus. 1357
Criticism of Mejerchol'd productions. Russia. 1917-1928. Lang.: Eng. 3547
Training
Mejerchol'd's theory of biomechanics and its application to training and performance. Russia. 1896-1996. Lang.: Eng. 3689

Melander, Björn
Performance/production
Interview with director Björn Melander. Sweden: Gothenburg. 1996. Lang.: Swe. 2277
Interview with director Björn Melander. Sweden: Gothenburg, Stockholm. 1991. Lang.: Swe. 2289
Interview with actor Börje Ahlstedt about working with different directors. Sweden: Stockholm. 1989. Lang.: Swe. 2290

Melbourne Women's Theatre Group (Melbourne)
Institutions
The Melbourne Women's Theatre Group. Australia: Melbourne. 1974-1977. Lang.: Eng. 1750

Mele, Lorenzo
Performance/production
Collection of newspaper reviews by London theatre critics. UK-England: London. 1996. Lang.: Eng. 2425

Melodrama
Performance/production
Facial characteristics of the Victorian stage villain. UK-England. 1830-1900. Lang.: Eng. 981
Cultural and theatrical history of English drama. England. 1500-1994. Lang.: Eng. 1992
Analysis of plays about white slavery. USA. 1910-1920. Lang.: Eng. 2593
Cinematic adaptation of *The Whip*. UK-England. 1916. Lang.: Eng. 3627
Popular theatrical genres in their cultural context. England. 1700-1899. Lang.: Rus. 3712
Plays/librettos/scripts
Melodramatic aspects of contemporary Quebecois drama. Canada. 1989. Lang.: Fre. 2830
Strong female roles in turn-of-the-century drama. UK-England: London. 1899-1918. Lang.: Eng. 3279
American adaptations of English Gothic plays. USA. 1790-1820. Lang.: Eng. 3324
Social realism and the work of James A. Herne. USA. 1890-1930. Lang.: Eng. 3356
Theory/criticism
Analysis of *The Mutiny at the Nore* intended to refute the 'new historical' approach. UK-England: London. 1797-1830. Lang.: Eng. 1366

Melville, Herman
Performance/production
Collection of newspaper reviews by London theatre critics. UK-England: London. 1996. Lang.: Eng. 2383

Melville, Walter
Plays/librettos/scripts
Strong female roles in turn-of-the-century drama. UK-England: London. 1899-1918. Lang.: Eng. 3279

Member of the Wedding, The
Theory/criticism
Lesbian interpretation of *The Member of the Wedding* by Carson McCullers. USA. 1946-1996. Lang.: Eng. 3562

Memories of a Mill Girl in a Green Shawl
Performance/production
Collection of newspaper reviews by London theatre critics. UK-England: London. 1996. Lang.: Eng. 2473

Memory of Two Mondays, A
Plays/librettos/scripts
Influence of Albert Camus on plays of Arthur Miller. USA. 1950-1996. 3456

Interview with actress Pat Carroll on Verdi's *Falstaff*. USA: New York, NY. 1996. Lang.: Eng. 4256

Plays/librettos/scripts
Humoral psychology in Shakespeare's Henriad. England. 1590-1613. Lang.: Eng. 2947

Early versions of Shakespeare's *Romeo and Juliet* and *The Merry Wives of Windsor*. England. 1595-1600. Lang.: Eng. 2959

Jealousy in *Otello* and *Falstaff* by Giuseppe Verdi. Italy. 1887-1893. Lang.: Eng. 4332

Relation to other fields
Female education in Shakespeare's time and plays. England. 1510-1621. Lang.: Eng. 3492

Mertz, Tibor
Performance/production
Interview with actor Tibor Mertz. Hungary. 1985-1996. Lang.: Hun. 2107

Meščerjakova, Marina
Performance/production
Canadian debuts of singers from Eastern Europe. Canada. USA. 1917-1996. Lang.: Eng. 4097

Mesguich, Daniel
Performance/production
Productions of Molière and Shakespeare directed by Daniel Mesguich. France: Lille. 1996. Lang.: Eng. 2014

Messer, Graeme
Performance/production
Collection of newspaper reviews by London theatre critics. UK-England: London. 1996. Lang.: Eng. 2350

Messerer, Sulamif'
Performance/production
Ballerina Sulamif' Messerer of the Bol'šoj Ballet. Russia: Moscow. 1980-1989. Lang.: Rus. 1524

Messier, Jean-Frédéric
Plays/librettos/scripts
Analysis of plays by Jean-Frédéric Messier. Canada: Montreal, PQ. 1987-1991. Lang.: Fre. 2744

Playwright Jean-Frédéric Messier on his work. Canada: Montreal, PQ. 1987-1991. Lang.: Fre. 2812

Messier, Marc
Plays/librettos/scripts
Analysis of *Broue (Scum)* by Marc Messier, Michel Côté, and Marcel Gauthier. Canada. 1979-1992. Lang.: Fre. 2808

Mészöly, Katalin
Performance/production
Interview with mezzo-soprano Katalin Mészöly. Hungary. 1949-1990. Lang.: Hun. 4165

Mészöly, Miklós
Plays/librettos/scripts
Postwar Hungarian drama. Hungary. 1945-1989. Lang.: Hun. 3069

Métaphore, La (Lille)
Performance/production
Productions of Molière and Shakespeare directed by Daniel Mesguich. France: Lille. 1996. Lang.: Eng. 2014

Metatheatre
Plays/librettos/scripts
Metatheatre in the works of Lorca and Valle-Inclán. Spain. 1900-1936. Lang.: Eng. 3227

The continuing relevance of Restoration theatre. UK-England. 1660-1996. Lang.: Eng. 3310

Metcalf, Margaret
Performance/production
Margaret Metcalf's *Playing for Power*, based on drama of the Actresses' Franchise League. UK-England. 1908-1993. Lang.: Eng. 987

Metcalfe, Carol
Performance/production
Collection of newspaper reviews by London theatre critics. UK-England: London. 1996. Lang.: Eng. 2308

Collection of newspaper reviews by London theatre critics. UK-England: London. 1996. Lang.: Eng. 2467

Métellus, Jean
Plays/librettos/scripts
Analysis of plays by Jean Métellus. Haiti. 1986-1992. Lang.: Fre. 3065

Methodology
Administration
Archival evidence of the activities of the German touring company. Estonia: Tallinn. 1630-1692. Lang.: Ger. 15

Research/historiography
Critique of theatre historiography. Lang.: Ger. 1292

Contemporary theatre criticism and scholarship. 1900-1995. Lang.: Pol. 1294

Düsseldorf's theatre historiography. Germany: Düsseldorf. 1996. Lang.: Ger. 1298

Research on drama and theatre in education. South Africa, Republic of. 1995. Lang.: Eng. 1302

Obituary for teacher, actor, and director John Harrop. UK-England. USA. 1931-1995. Lang.: Eng. 1306

Essay on academic theatre historiography. USA. 1996. Lang.: Eng. 1310

History and theory of orchestics movement system. France: Paris. Hungary: Budapest. 1908-1994. Lang.: Hun. 1601

Interview with dance scholar Gedeon Dienes. Hungary. 1914-1995. Lang.: Hun. 1602

Defense of the *Records of Early English Drama* project. UK-England. 1978-1995. Lang.: Eng. 3530

Evaluation of the *Records of Early English Drama* project. UK-England. 1978-1995. Lang.: Eng. 3531

Eighteenth-century records of operatic performances. Germany. 1700-1799. Lang.: Ger. 4356

The relevance of puppetry to theatre historiography. Lang.: Ger. 4429

Marionette collections and preservation. Canada. 1988. Lang.: Fre. 4430

The historiography of German puppetry. Germany. 1850-1996. Lang.: Ger. 4431

Theory/criticism
Theory of studies of theatricality, including cultural and sociopolitical communication. 1996. Lang.: Ger. 1311

Systems theory and theatre historiography. Europe. 1700-1799. Lang.: Ger. 1339

Critic and researcher Sally Banes. USA: New York, NY. 1960. Lang.: Swe. 1604

Metro Theatre Company (St. Louis, MO)
Relation to other fields
Programs for teachers' professional development in theatre. USA. 1994-1996. Lang.: Eng. 1261

Metropolitan Opera (New York, NY)
Design/technology
Renovation of Metropolitan Opera lighting system. USA: New York, NY. 1996. Lang.: Eng. 4025

Hubert Monloup's set and costume designs for *Andrea Chénier*, Metropolitan Opera. USA: New York, NY. 1996. Lang.: Eng. 4026

New approaches to opera design at the Metropolitan Opera. USA: New York, NY. 1996. Lang.: Eng. 4029

Performance/production
Interview with opera director Nicolas Joël. France. Germany. 1942-1996. Lang.: Eng. 4117

Operas conducted by James Levine. USA. 1943-1996. Lang.: Eng. 4239

Background material on Metropolitan Opera telecast performances. USA: New York, NY. 1996. Lang.: Eng. 4241

Jussi Björling's Metropolitan Opera debut. USA: New York, NY. 1937. Lang.: Eng. 4248

Background material on Metropolitan Opera radio broadcast performances. USA: New York, NY. 1996. Lang.: Eng. 4252

Interview with actress Pat Carroll on Verdi's *Falstaff*. USA: New York, NY. 1996. Lang.: Eng. 4256

An evening at the Metropolitan Opera with author Tama Janowitz. USA: New York, NY. 1996. Lang.: Eng. 4257

Report from a week at the Metropolitan Opera. USA: New York, NY. 1996. Lang.: Swe. 4259

Cutting and editing of Handel operas. USA. 1920-1996. Lang.: Eng. 4272

The revival of *The Voyage* by Philip Glass at the Metropolitan Opera. USA: New York, NY. 1992-1996. Lang.: Eng. 4277

Gustav Mahler, the Metropolitan, and opera in America. USA: New York, NY. Austria: Vienna. 1907-1911. Lang.: Eng. 4280

Retirement of Edward Downes as Metropolitan Opera broadcast quizmaster. USA: New York, NY. 1996. Lang.: Eng. 4282

Conductor Dennis Russell Davies—profile and interview. USA: Toledo, OH. 1945-1996. Lang.: Eng. 4284

Changes in the comprimario system at the Metropolitan Opera. USA: New York, NY. 1996. Lang.: Eng. 4287

Profile, interview with soprano Margaret Harshaw, who spent part of her career as a mezzo-soprano. USA. 1910-1996. Lang.: Eng. 4290

Metropolitan Opera (New York, NY) — cont'd

Work of Tim Albery and Antony McDonald on Met production of Britten's *A Midsummer Night's Dream* by Britten. USA: New York, NY. 1996. Lang.: Eng. 4296

Plays/librettos/scripts
Analysis of Britten's opera *A Midsummer Night's Dream*. UK-England. 1960-1996. Lang.: Eng. 4343

Metropolitan Opera Guild (New York, NY)
Performance/production
Mike Reid's new opera *Different Fields*. USA: Nashville, TN. 1996. Lang.: Eng. 4283

Metropolitan Theatre (Los Angeles, CA)
Performance spaces
History of the Metropolitan Theatre. USA: Los Angeles, CA. 1926-1960. Lang.: Eng. 3611

Mettler, Peter
Plays/librettos/scripts
The film and stage versions of *Plaques tectoniques (Tectonic Plates)* by Robert Lepage. Canada: Quebec, PQ. 1991. Lang.: Fre. 3641

Meyerbeer, Giacomo
Institutions
The Wexford opera festival. Ireland: Wexford. 1951-1996. Lang.: Swe. 4047

Plays/librettos/scripts
Singers Gilbert-Louis Duprez and Gustave Roger and the creation of Meyerbeer's opera *Le Prophète*. France: Paris. 1831-1849.Lang.: Eng. 4314

Melodrama and orientalism in *Il crociato in Egitto* by Meyerbeer. France. Italy: Venice. 1744-1840. Lang.: Eng. 4316

Librettist Felice Romani. Italy. 1810-1850. Lang.: Eng. 4334

Meyerhold, V.E.
SEE
Mejerchol'd, Vsevolod Emiljévič.

Mezencev, Aleksand'r
Performance/production
Profile of actor Aleksand'r Mezencev. Russia: Cheljabinsk. 1990-1996. Lang.: Rus. 2258

MGM Grand Hotel (Las Vegas, NV)
Design/technology
Cinema Services and the video spectacle *EFX*. USA: Las Vegas, NV. 1995. Lang.: Eng. 3665

Mhlophe, Gcina
Plays/librettos/scripts
Playwrights Gcina Mhlophe and Sue Pam-Grant. South Africa, Republic of. 1945-1996. Lang.: Eng. 3223

Miami City Ballet (Miami, FL)
Performance/production
Edward Villella, director of Miami City Ballet. USA: Miami, FL. 1936-1995. Lang.: Hun. 1538

Miceli, Grace
Design/technology
Obituary for costumer Grace Miceli. USA: New York, NY. 1995. Lang.: Eng. 246

Michaels, Brian
Institutions
Productions of the Ruhrfestspiele festival. Germany: Recklinghausen. 1996. Lang.: Eng. 1797

Michajlov, Aleksand'r
Performance/production
Actors of the Malyj Theatre. Russia: Moscow. 1980-1996. Lang.: Rus. 2223

Michell, Roger
Performance/production
Collection of newspaper reviews by London theatre critics. UK-England: London. 1996. Lang.: Eng. 2369

Michigan Opera Theatre (Detroit, MI)
Institutions
The Michigan Opera of Detroit's new house. USA: Detroit, MI. 1970-1995. Lang.: Eng. 4065

Michoo (Seoul)
Institutions
Profile of four Seoul theatre companies. Korea: Seoul. 1986-1996. Lang.: Kor. 494

Michoue, Sylvain
Performance/production
Milène Roy and Sylvain Michoue of Voxtrot. Canada: Montreal, PQ. 1989. Lang.: Fre. 745

Miciński, Tadeusz
Plays/librettos/scripts
The devil in Polish drama. Poland. 1832-1957. Lang.: Pol. 3168

Mickery Theater (Amsterdam)
Performance/production
Life and work of Ritsaert ten Cate, founder of the Mickery Theater. Netherlands. 1930-1995. Lang.: Eng. 885

Mickiewicz, Adam
Performance/production
Dziady—Dwanaście improwizacji (Forefathers'Eve—Twelve Improvisations) : Grzegorzewski's adaptation of the Mickiewicz classic. Poland: Cracow. 1995. Lang.: Eng, Fre. 2167

Plays/librettos/scripts
The devil in Polish drama. Poland. 1832-1957. Lang.: Pol. 3168

Micone, Marco
Plays/librettos/scripts
Poetic essay by playwright Marco Micone. Canada: Montreal, PQ. 1989. Lang.: Fre. 2813

Relation to other fields
Immigrant playwright Marco Micone on multiculturalism and cultural assimilation. Canada: Montreal, PQ. Lang.: Fre. 3486

Microscope Stage (Budapest)
SEE
Mikroszkóp Szinpad.

Mid-South California Arts Project (Northridge, CA)
Relation to other fields
Programs for teachers' professional development in theatre. USA. 1994-1996. Lang.: Eng. 1261

Middleton, Thomas
Performance/production
English plays and subjects on the Hungarian stage. Hungary. 1995-1996. Lang.: Eng. 847

Midsummer Night's Dream, A
Institutions
Productions of the Salzburger Festspiele. Austria: Salzburg. 1996. Lang.: Ger. 345

Performance/production
A Swedish guest performance of *A Midsummer Night's Dream* in Shanghai. Sweden: Stockholm. China, People's Republic of: Shanghai. 1996. Lang.: Swe. 954

Collaboration of directors Peter Oskarson and Ma Ke at Orionteatern. Sweden: Stockholm. China, People's Republic of. 1989. Lang.:Swe. 955

Operatic and ballet adaptations of Shakespearean plays reviewed. Switzerland. 1994-1995. Lang.: Ger. 956

Nele Paxinou and Les Baladins du Miroir. Belgium. 1995. Lang.: Eng. 1912

Shakespeare and Elizabethan cultural politics: *A Midsummer Night's Dream*. England. 1590-1620. Lang.: Eng. 1990

Assembling an international cast for a production of *A Midsummer Night's Dream*. Europe. 1995. Lang.: Eng. 2001

Karin Beier's productions of *A Midsummer Night's Dream* and *Les Chaises (The Chairs)*. Germany: Düsseldorf. 1995. Lang.: Eng. 2045

Reviews of Shakespearean and other productions. Germany. 1994-1995. Lang.: Ger. 2058

The negative impact of democracy on Polish theatre. Poland. 1989-1995. Lang.: Eng. 2146

Significant Polish productions of Shakespearean plays. Poland. 1918-1989. Lang.: Eng. 2152

Polish productions of Shakespeare. Poland. 1989-1996. Lang.: Eng. 2162

Swinarski's production of *A Midsummer Night's Dream*, Stary Teatr. Poland: Cracow. 1970. Lang.: Eng. 2177

Collection of newspaper reviews by London theatre critics. UK-England: London. 1996. Lang.: Eng. 2358

Collection of newspaper reviews by London theatre critics. UK-England: London. 1996. Lang.: Eng. 2380

Collection of newspaper reviews by London theatre critics. UK-England: London. 1996. Lang.: Eng. 2388

Collection of newspaper reviews by London theatre critics. UK-England: London. 1996. Lang.: Eng. 2487

Collection of newspaper reviews by New York theatre critics. USA: New York, NY. 1996. Lang.: Eng. 2574

Racism and sexism in *A Midsummer Night's Dream* at Shakespeare Santa Cruz, directed by Danny Scheie. USA: Santa Cruz, CA. 1991. Lang.: Eng. 2637

Adrian Noble's RSC production of *A Midsummer Night's Dream*. USA: New York, NY. UK-England: Stratford-upon-Avon. 1996. Lang.: Eng. 2671

Work of Tim Albery and Antony McDonald on Met production of Britten's *A Midsummer Night's Dream* by Britten. USA: New York, NY. 1996. Lang.: Eng. 4296

SUBJECT INDEX

Molivar, Carlo Felipe
Basic theatrical documents
French adaptation of a scene from *Carnes Frescas (Fresh Meat)* by
Carlo Felipe Molivar. Canada: Montreal, PQ. Spain: Madrid. 1995-
1996. Lang.: Fre. 1648

Möller, Ale
Performance/production
Theatre musician Ale Möller. Sweden. 1970. Lang.: Swe. 946

Mollerup, Asta
Performance/production
Modern dancer and teacher Asta Mollerup. Denmark: Copenhagen.
1881-1945. Lang.: Dan. 1572

Molly
Performance/production
Collection of newspaper reviews by London theatre critics. UK-England:
London. 1996. Lang.: Eng. 2473

Molly Sweeney
Performance/production
Collection of newspaper reviews by New York theatre critics. USA:
New York, NY. 1996. Lang.: Eng. 2550

Molnár, András
Performance/production
Tenor András Molnár. Hungary. 1963-1996. Lang.: Hun. 4161

Molnár, Ferenc
Institutions
Highlights of the Wiener Festwochen festival. Austria: Vienna. 1996.
Lang.: Ger. 1752
Performance/production
Budapest productions of the millicentenary season. Hungary: Budapest.
1995-1996. Lang.: Eng. 2104
Plays/librettos/scripts
Review of a biography of playwright Ferenc Molnár. Hungary. USA:
New York, NY. 1878-1952. Lang.: Eng. 3071

Molodežnyj Teat'r (St. Petersburg)
Performance/production
Actor Anatolij Petrov. Russia: Moscow. 1996. Lang.: Rus. 2237

Molodežnyj Teat'r (Vilnius)
Performance/production
Eimuntas Nekrošius' youth theatre production of an adaptation of
Shakespeare's *Romeo and Juliet*. Latvia: Vilnius. 1982. Lang.: Rus. 2136

Molodežnyj Teat'r na Fontankė (St. Petersburg)
Performance/production
Actress Nina Usatova of Fontanka Youth Theatre. Russia: St.
Petersburg. 1990-1996. Lang.: Rus. 931
The Three Penny Opera at Fontanka Youth Theatre. Russia: St.
Petersburg. 1996. Lang.: Rus. 4211

Monette, Richard
Institutions
The change of artistic director at the Stratford Festival. Canada:
Stratford, ON. 1992. Lang.: Fre. 1756
Profile and evaluation of the 1995 Stratford Festival season. Canada:
Stratford, ON. 1995. Lang.: Eng. 1765
Performance/production
Productions of *Hamlet* by Richard Monette and Henry Woronicz.
Canada: Stratford, ON. USA: Ashland, OR. 1994. Lang.: Eng. 1927

Monk, Meredith
Performance/production
Essays on contemporary performance. Europe. USA. 1980-1995. Lang.:
Eng. 790

Monkey Business Class—en memorial musical
Performance/production
Review of *Monkey Business Class* by Hotel Pro Forma. Denmark:
Copenhagen. 1996. Lang.: Dan. 3711

Monloup, Hubert
Design/technology
Hubert Monloup's set and costume designs for *Andrea Chénier*,
Metropolitan Opera. USA: New York, NY. 1996. Lang.: Eng. 4026

Monmart, Francis
Performance/production
Alliance of text and acting in three French-language productions.
Canada: Montreal, PQ. Switzerland: Geneva. 1985-1995. Lang.: Fre.
722
Plays/librettos/scripts
Playwright Francis Monmart discusses his craft. Canada: Montreal, PQ.
1981-1996. Lang.: Fre. 2814

Monodrama
Performance/production
Acting, directing, and writing work of Julie Vincent. Canada: Montreal,
PQ. 1988-1991. Lang.: Fre. 734

Essay on the status of the word in theatre. Denmark. 1996. Lang.: Dan.
767
Recently recovered information on playwright/performers Elizabeth
Macauley and Jane Scott. UK-England. 1800-1835. Lang.: Eng. 962
Margaret Metcalf's *Playing for Power*, based on drama of the Actresses'
Franchise League. UK-England. 1908-1993. Lang.: Eng. 987
History and current state of autobiographical solo performance. USA.
1276-1995. Lang.: Eng. 1020
Text and movement in *Une cloche à vache suspendue à mon âme (A
Cowbell Hung on My Soul)* by Milène Roy. Canada: Montreal, PQ.
1996. Lang.: Fre. 1412
Christopher Plummer's one-man show *Barrymore*. Canada: Stratford,
ON. 1996. Lang.: Eng. 1918
Leslie Nielsen's one-man show *Clarence Darrow for the Defense*.
Canada. 1996. Lang.: Eng. 1919
Manon Gauthier's one-woman adaptation of a Michel Tremblay novel.
Canada: Montreal, PQ. 1980-1986. Lang.: Fre. 1936
Pol Pelletier's one-woman show *Joie (Joy)*. Canada: Montreal, PQ.
1975-1992. Lang.: Fre. 1941
Interview with actress Hélène Loiselle. Canada: Montreal, PQ. 1950-
1992. Lang.: Fre. 1946
Pol Pelletier on her one-woman show *Joie (Joy)*. Canada: Montreal, PQ.
1990-1992. Lang.: Fre. 1955
Julia Sweeney's one-woman show *God Said 'Ha!'*. USA: New York,
NY. 1996. Lang.: Eng. 2603
Interview with playwright/performer Anna Deavere Smith, and review
of her *Fires in the Mirror*. USA: New York, NY. 1991-1993. Lang.:
Eng. 2608
Interview with playwright/director Eve Ensler on *The Vagina
Monologues*. USA. 1970-1996. Lang.: Eng. 2631
Performer Julie Halston's advice on one-person shows. USA: New York,
NY. 1996. Lang.: Eng. 2633
Rob Becker and his solo performance *Defending the Caveman*. USA:
New York, NY. 1996. Lang.: Eng. 2640
Mary Louise Wilson's role in *Full Gallop*. USA: New York, NY. 1996.
Lang.: Eng. 2641
Interview with solo performer Anna Deavere Smith. USA: Washington,
DC. 1996. Lang.: Eng. 2662
Social significance of solo performances by Anna Cora Mowatt. USA.
1841-1881. Lang.: Eng. 2683
Karen Trott's one-woman show *The Springhill Singing Disaster*. USA:
New York, NY. 1996. Lang.: Eng. 2685
Interview with actress Irene Worth on her *Portrait of Edith Wharton*.
USA: New York, NY. 1916-1996. Lang.: Eng. 2691
The filming of Spalding Gray's solo piece *Gray's Anatomy*. USA. 1996.
Lang.: Eng. 3633
Video performances of *Fires in the Mirror* by Anna Deavere Smith.
USA. 1991. Lang.: Eng. 3680
The experimental one-man show of artist and designer Wolfgang
Krause Zwieback. Germany. 1986-1996. Lang.: Ger. 3728
Performance artist Paul Bonin-Rodriguez. USA. 1992-1996. Lang.: Eng.
3802

Plays/librettos/scripts
The influence of Samuel Beckett on Carole Nadeau's one-woman show
Chaos K.O. Chaos. Canada: Quebec, PQ. 1992. Lang.: Fre. 1089
Interview with playwright Andrea Lemon of Snakehouse. Australia:
Perth. 1994-1995. Lang.: Eng. 2722
Interview with playwright Larry Tremblay. Canada: Montreal, PQ.
1992. Lang.: Fre. 2756
Lorraine Pintal's solo performance *Madame Louis 14*. Canada:
Montreal, PQ. 1980-1989. Lang.: Fre. 2840
Analysis of *Emma B. vedova Giocasta (Emma B., Widow Jocasta)* by
Alberto Savinio (Andrea De Chirico). Italy. 1891-1952. Lang.: Ita. 3110
The monologues of Dario Fo. Italy. 1926-1995. Lang.: Ita. 3130
Medusa as a metaphorical presence in some contemporary productions.
UK-England. Canada. 1995. Lang.: Eng. 3294
Latina lesbian subjectivity in works of Marga Gomez. USA. 1990-1995.
Lang.: Eng. 3436
Theory/criticism
Performance theory and *My Queer Body* by Tim Miller. USA. 1992-
1996. Lang.: Eng. 1392

Mrożek, Sławomir
Performance/production
Mrożek's *Ambasador (The Ambassador)*, directed by Erwin Axer, Teatr Współczesny. Poland: Warsaw. 1995. Lang.: Eng, Fre.   2147

Actor Anatolij Petrov. Russia: Moscow. 1996. Lang.: Rus.   2237
Plays/librettos/scripts
Analysis of plays by Havel, Mrożek, and Örkény. Czechoslovakia. Hungary. Poland. 1950-1980. Lang.: Eng.   2872

Analysis of the plays of Sławomir Mrożek. Poland. 1994. Lang.: Pol.   3159

Responses to the defeat of Solidarity in Polish drama. Poland. 1980-1989. Lang.: Eng.   3160

Polish theatre of the absurd. Poland. 1920-1990. Lang.: Pol.   3166

The plays of Sławomir Mrożek in the context of Eastern drama and the theatre of the absurd. Poland. 1994. Lang.: Pol.   3177

Mrs. Freud and Mrs. Jung
Performance/production
Collection of newspaper reviews by London theatre critics. UK-England: London. 1996. Lang.: Eng.   2413

Mrs. Thursday
Performance/production
Actress Kathleen Harrison. UK-England. 1927-1996. Lang.: Eng.   968

Mrs. Warren's Profession
Performance/production
Collection of newspaper reviews by London theatre critics. UK-England: London. 1996. Lang.: Eng.   2411

Collection of newspaper reviews by London theatre critics. UK-England: London. 1996. Lang.: Eng.   2417

Mtetwa Zulu Players (South Africa)
Performance/production
The variety entertainment tradition in South African theatre. South Africa, Republic of. 1900-1985. Lang.: Eng.   3834

Mtwa, Percy
Performance/production
Postcolonial drama in theory and performance. 1880-1950. Lang.: Eng.   1893

Much Ado About Nothing
Audience
Audience and critical reaction to a line in Shakespeare's *Much Ado About Nothing*. England. 1599-1990. Lang.: Eng.   1631
Performance/production
Operatic and ballet adaptations of Shakespearean plays reviewed. Switzerland. 1994-1995. Lang.: Ger.   956

Collection of newspaper reviews by London theatre critics. UK-England: London, Stratford. 1996. Lang.: Eng.   2483

Muchado, Eduardo
Plays/librettos/scripts
Interview with playwright Eduardo Muchado. USA: New York, NY. Cuba. 1953-1996. Lang.: Eng.   3377

Muchina, Ol'ga
Performance/production
Ol'ga Muchina's *Tanja-Tanja* staged by Masterskaja Petra Fomenko. Russia: Moscow. 1995-1996. Lang.: Rus.   2240

Mud
Performance/production
Freiburger Theater under the leadership of Hans J. Amman. Germany: Freiburg. 1995. Lang.: Ger.   2059

Mudrooroo (Johnson, Colin)
Performance/production
The use of Müller's *Der Auftrag (The Mission)* in *The Aboriginal Protesters* by Mudrooroo. Australia: Sydney. 1996. Lang.: Ger.   1898
Relation to other fields
German-Australian theatrical exchange. Australia. Germany. 1945-1995. Lang.: Eng.   3478

Mudrooroo/Müller project, The
Relation to other fields
German-Australian theatrical exchange. Australia. Germany. 1945-1995. Lang.: Eng.   3478

Muerte y la doncella, La (Death and the Maiden)
Plays/librettos/scripts
Playwrights Harold Pinter and Ariel Dorfman. Chile. UK-England. 1957-1996. Lang.: Eng.   2853

Mühl, Otto
Theory/criticism
Nudity and vulnerability in performance art. USA. 1960-1996. Lang.: Eng.   3826

Muitos (Seoul)
Design/technology
Projections and multimedia in Korean theatre productions. Korea: Seoul. 1996. Lang.: Kor.   1708

Mulchong (Water Gun, The)
Design/technology
Projections and multimedia in Korean theatre productions. Korea: Seoul. 1996. Lang.: Kor.   1708

Mules
Performance/production
Collection of newspaper reviews by London theatre critics. UK-England: London. 1996. Lang.: Eng.   2377

Mulgrew, Gerard
Performance/production
Collection of newspaper reviews by London theatre critics. UK-England: London. 1996. Lang.: Eng.   2474

Müller, Elfriede
Basic theatrical documents
Text of *Lupo* by Elfriede Müller. Germany. 1996. Lang.: Ger.   1660
Performance/production
Productions of new plays by Elfriede Müller and Jens Roselt. Germany: Saarbrücken, Mainz. 1996. Lang.: Ger.   2052

Müller, Harald
Performance/production
Comparison of productions about Martin Luther. Germany: Wittenberg, Magdeburg. 1996. Lang.: Ger.   2065

Müller, Heiner
Basic theatrical documents
English translation of the manuscript of *La Mort de Molière (The Death of Molière)* by Heiner Müller. Germany. France. 1991-1996. Lang.: Eng.   3586
Performance/production
Essays on contemporary performance. Europe. USA. 1980-1995. Lang.: Eng.   790

Interview with actor Gert Voss. Germany. Austria. 1940-1996. Lang.: Ger.   808

Theodoros Terzopoulos of Theatre Attis. Greece: Athens. 1986-1996. Lang.: Eng.   836

The use of Müller's *Der Auftrag (The Mission)* in *The Aboriginal Protesters* by Mudrooroo. Australia: Sydney. 1996. Lang.: Ger.   1898

Anne-Marie Cadieux's performance in Müller's *Quartett* at Espace GO. Canada: Montreal, PQ. 1996. Lang.: Fre.   1939

Psychoanalysis and theatricality. Europe. 1990-1995. Lang.: Eng.   2003

Tribute to deceased theatre artist Heiner Müller. Germany. Latin America. 1929-1994. Lang.: Spa.   2049

Two productions of Müller's *Germania 3*. Germany: Berlin, Bochum. 1996. Lang.: Ger.   2056

Theatre in Leipzig since reunification. Germany: Leipzig. 1996. Lang.: Eng.   2061

Leander Haussmann's production of Heiner Müller's last play *Germania 3*. Germany: Bochum. 1996. Lang.: Ger.   2062

Comparison of productions of Müller's *Der Auftrag (The Mission)*. Germany: Leipzig, Berlin. 1996. Lang.: Ger.   2069

Heiner Müller—his commemoration by Berliner Ensemble, his East German productions. Germany: Berlin. 1996. Lang.: Ger.   2076

Productions of plays by Heiner Müller at Berliner Ensemble and Volksbühne. Germany: Berlin. 1996. Lang.: Ger.   2088

Two productions of Heiner Müller's *Germania 3*. Germany: Bochum, Berlin. 1996. Lang.: Ger.   2091

Account of Čechov International Theatre Festival. Russia. 1996. Lang.: Eng.   2199

Discussion surrounding a performance of *Murx* by Christoph Marthaler. Germany: Berlin. UK-England: London. 1995. Lang.: Eng.   3917
Plays/librettos/scripts
Disaster and death in Heiner Müller's *Quartett*, staged at Espace GO by Brigitte Haentjens. Canada: Montreal, PQ. Germany. 1980-1996. Lang.: Fre.   2785

Themes of Heiner Müller's *Quartett* presented at Espace GO. Canada: Montreal, PQ. Germany. 1980-1996. Lang.: Fre.   2845

Obituary of playwright Heiner Müller. Germany. 1996. Lang.: Eng. 3014

Copyright dispute in Heiner Müller's estate. Germany. 1996. Lang.: Ger.   3015

Heiner Müller's work and its reception on stage after his death. Germany: Berlin, Bochum. 1996. Lang.: Ger.   3016

Commemoration of playwright Heiner Müller. Germany. 1929-1995. Lang.: Hun.   3019

Recollections of playwright Heiner Müller. Germany. 1929-1995. Lang.: Hun.   3022

Murphy, Donna — cont'd

Actress/singer Donna Murphy. USA. 1991-1996. Lang.: Eng.   3981

Murphy, Heidi Grant

Performance/production

Changes in the comprimario system at the Metropolitan Opera. USA: New York, NY. 1996. Lang.: Eng.   4287

Murphy, Jimmy

Performance/production

Collection of newspaper reviews by London theatre critics. UK-England: London. 1996. Lang.: Eng.   2341

Murphy, Kevin

Performance/production

Puppetry on *Mystery Science Theatre 3000*. USA: Hollywood, CA. 1990-1996. Lang.: Eng.   3681

Murphy, Maeve

Performance/production

Collection of newspaper reviews by London theatre critics. UK-England: London. 1996. Lang.: Eng.   2311

Murray Theatre (Highland Park, IL)

Design/technology

USITT architectural awards. USA. 1994. Lang.: Eng.   285

Murray, Anne

Performance/production

The recording of Schubert's *Lieder* on CD. 1996. Lang.: Eng.   3853

Murray, Lavinia

Performance/production

Collection of newspaper reviews by London theatre critics. UK-England: London. 1996. Lang.: Eng.   2354

Murrell, John

Plays/librettos/scripts

Overview of Anglophone Canadian playwriting. Canada. 1970-1990. Lang.: Fre.   2791

Murrow, Jessica

Design/technology

Sound design for Inge's *Picnic* at National Technical Institute of the Deaf. USA: Rochester, NY. 1996. Lang.: Eng.   1743

Murx

Performance/production

Physical theatre in guest performances by Robert Lepage, Volksbühne, and Théâtre de Complicité. Sweden: Stockholm. 1994. Lang.: Swe.   949

Discussion surrounding a performance of *Murx* by Christoph Marthaler. Germany: Berlin. UK-England: London. 1995. Lang.: Eng.   3917

Relation to other fields

Political implications of Christoph Marthaler's *Murx*, directed by Heiner Goebbels. Germany: Berlin. UK-England: London. 1992-1995. Lang.: Eng.   4001

Musafar, Fakir

Plays/librettos/scripts

Performance art at a Copenhagen seminar on the body and ritual manipulation. Denmark. 1995. Lang.: Dan.   3811

Relation to other fields

Christianity and body art. 1995-1996. Lang.: Dan.   3815

Musée d'art contemporain (Montreal, PQ)

Design/technology

Scene design by sculptor Pierre Granche. Canada: Montreal, PQ. 1982-1992. Lang.: Fre.   151

Museums

Institutions

Problems of theatre museums. Germany: Düsseldorf. 1996. Lang.: Ger.   454

Theatre in the Center for Contemporary Art. Poland: Warsaw. 1995. Lang.: Eng, Fre.   512

The puppetry collection of the Hungarian Theatre Museum. Hungary: Budapest. 1969-1996. Lang.: Hun.   4381

Performance/production

Problems of performing arts exhibition Resetting the Stage. USA: Chicago, IL. 1960-1990. Lang.: Eng.   1014

The use of Native American performance in museums. USA. 1994. Lang.: Eng.   1033

Events commemorating the fifth anniversary of the death of Tadeusz Kantor. Poland: Cracow. Belgium: Brussels. 1995. Lang.: Eng, Fre. 2158

Essay on a museum exhibition dedicated to the theatre of Tadeusz Kantor. Poland: Cracow. 1995. Lang.: Eng, Fre.   2175

Relation to other fields

Performance of the Holocaust in American museums. USA: Washington, DC, Los Angeles, CA. 1994-1995. Lang.: Eng.   1271

Labeling artworks to create broader audience appeal. USA. 1996. Lang.: Eng.   1280

Narrative structure in museum exhibits. USA. 1996. Lang.: Eng.   1281

Profile of the Tadeusz Kantor Gallery-Studio, which houses Kantor's artworks. Poland: Cracow. 1995. Lang.: Eng, Fre.   3504

Research/historiography

Marionette collections and preservation. Canada. 1988. Lang.: Fre. 4430

Music

Audience

Fundraising strategies of the American Symphony Orchestra. USA: New York, NY. 1996. Lang.: Eng.   142

Design/technology

Vince Foster's design for rock star Zucchero. Italy. 1996. Lang.: Eng.   3696

Production design for tour of country singer Reba McEntire. USA. 1996. Lang.: Eng.   3831

Institutions

The music program of the Edinburgh Festival. UK-Scotland: Edinburgh. 1996. Lang.: Ger.   560

Performance/production

Mejerchol'd's work in acting. Russia. 1874-1940. Lang.: Ita.   922

Report from conference on music in theatre and theatre in music. Sweden: Västerås. 1996. Lang.: Swe.   945

Recently-discovered fragment of a *Visitatio sepulchri*. Sweden: Stockholm. 1201-1300. Lang.: Eng.   952

Feminist performance and theory. USA. UK-England. 1968-1995. Lang.: Eng.   1015

Opera and stage director Marcus Stern. USA: New York, NY. 1996. Lang.: Eng.   1039

Dramatic music of Michajl Bronner. Russia: Moscow. 1990-1996. Lang.: Rus.   1440

Thorsten Flinck's staging of Brecht's *Herr Puntila* using rock music. Sweden: Stockholm. 1991. Lang.: Swe.   2284

Steve Ross's role in *Present Laughter* on Broadway. USA: New York, NY. 1996. Lang.: Eng.   2604

Status of sales of classical-music recordings. UK-England. 1996. Lang.: Eng.   3577

MTV, postmodernism, and feminism. USA. 1990-1995. Lang.: Eng.   3677

Anti-apartheid message of rap group Prophets of da City. South Africa, Republic of: Cape Town. 1990-1996. Lang.: Eng.   3714

Modern productions of *Ludus Danielis (The Play of Daniel)*. Europe. USA. 1140-1984. Lang.: Eng.   3856

Music in the Beauvais *Ludus Danielis (The Play of Daniel)*. France. 1140. Lang.: Eng.   3857

Production conditions for *Ludus Danielis (The Play of Daniel)* at Beauvais Cathedral. France: Beauvais. 1140-1975. Lang.: Eng.   3858

Feminist music criticism. UK-England. 1990-1995. Lang.: Eng.   3867

High and low culture in contemporary music. UK-England. USA. 1990-1995. Lang.: Eng.   3868

Performance of *nanxi*. China. 1368-1996. Lang.: Eng.   3879

Interview with writing team John Kander and Fred Ebb. USA: New York, NY. 1996. Lang.: Eng.   3941

Parody in the work of early African-American musical theatre performers. USA. 1900-1925. Lang.: Eng.   3966

Serge Provost's score for *Le Vampire et la Nymphomane* by Claude Gauvreau. Canada: Montreal, PQ. 1949-1996. Lang.: Fre.   4092

Alain Thibault's musical score for *Ne blâmez jamais les Bédouins (Don't Blame the Bedouins)* by René-Daniel Dubois. Canada: Montreal, PQ. 1991. Lang.: Fre.   4095

Kentucky Opera's use of a synthesizer in place of a live orchestra. USA: Louisville, KY. 1995. Lang.: Eng.   4278

The use of synthesized rather than live music in opera. USA: Louisville, KY. 1996. Lang.: Eng.   4286

Redmoon Theatre's Winter Pageant. USA: Chicago, IL. 1995. Lang.: Eng.   4416

Plays/librettos/scripts

The influence of composer Hector Berlioz on George Bernard Shaw. UK-England. 1880. Lang.: Eng.   3281

Blues music in *Ma Rainey's Black Bottom* by August Wilson. USA. 1982-1996. Lang.: Eng.   3365

Playwright August Wilson. USA: New York, NY. 1952-1996. Lang.: Eng.   3428

The influence of blues music on the plays of August Wilson. USA. 1996. Lang.: Eng.   3452

Neilson, Anthony
Performance/production
Collection of newspaper reviews by London theatre critics. UK-England:
London. 1996. Lang.: Eng.   2402
Nekrošius, Eimuntas
Performance/production
Eimuntas Nekrošius' youth theatre production of an adaptation of
Shakespeare's *Romeo and Juliet*. Latvia: Vilnius. 1982. Lang.: Rus. 2136
Interview with director Eimuntas Nekrošius. Lithuania. 1996. Lang.:
Ger.   2137
Account of Čechov International Theatre Festival. Russia. 1996. Lang.:
Eng.   2199
Relation to other fields
The political context of Nekrošius' production of Čechov's *Three Sisters*.
Lithuania. 1996. Lang.: Ger.   3503
Nelken (Carnations)
Performance/production
Tanztheater Wuppertal's Copenhagen guest performance. Denmark:
Copenhagen. 1996. Lang.: Swe.   1573
Press conference with dancer and choreographer Pina Bausch. Germany:
Wuppertal. 1995. Lang.: Eng.   1576
Nelson, Claire
Performance/production
Collection of newspaper reviews by London theatre critics. UK-England:
London. 1996. Lang.: Eng.   2408
Nelson, Mike
Performance/production
Puppetry on *Mystery Science Theatre 3000*. USA: Hollywood, CA.
1990-1996. Lang.: Eng.   3681
Nelson, Richard
Design/technology
Lighting design for Peter Sagal's *Denial* at the Long Wharf Theatre.
USA: New Haven, CT. 1996. Lang.: Eng.   1745
Institutions
Recent RSC openings. UK-England: London, Stratford. 1996. Lang.:
Eng.   1856
Performance/production
Collection of newspaper reviews by London theatre critics. UK-England:
London, Stratford. 1996. Lang.: Eng.   2461
Collection of newspaper reviews by New York theatre critics. USA:
New York, NY. 1996. Lang.: Eng.   2550
Plays/librettos/scripts
Interview with playwright Richard Nelson. USA. UK-England. 1995.
Lang.: Eng.   3340
Nelson, Tracy
Performance/production
Holiday memories of Broadway actors. USA: New York, NY. 1996.
Lang.: Eng.   1013
Német Színház-Deutsche Bühne (Szekszárd)
Performance spaces
Creation of a German-language theatre in a former cinema. Hungary:
Szekszárd. 1913-1994. Lang.: Hun.   646
Németh, Ákos
Plays/librettos/scripts
Theoretical essay on recent Hungarian drama. Hungary. 1995-1996.
Lang.: Hun.   3074
Németh, Antal
Performance/production
Scene design and the work of director Antal Németh. Hungary. 1929-
1944. Lang.: Hun.   843
Németh, László
Plays/librettos/scripts
Postwar Hungarian drama. Hungary. 1945-1989. Lang.: Hun.   3069
Némethy, Ella
Performance/production
Soprano Ella Némethy. Hungary. 1895-1961. Lang.: Hun.   4160
Nemirovič-Dančenko, Vladimir Ivanovič
Performance/production
The Moscow Art Theatre's Boston season. USA: Boston, MA. 1923.
Lang.: Eng.   1036
Nemzeti Játékszíni Társaság (Pest-Buda)
Institutions
László Kelemen and the first professional Hungarian theatre company.
Hungary. 1790-1890. Lang.: Hun.   467
Research/historiography
János Endrődy, the first Hungarian theatre historian. Hungary. 1790-
1793. Lang.: Hun.   1300
Nemzeti Színház (Budapest)
Performance/production
Scene design and the work of director Antal Németh. Hungary. 1929-
1944. Lang.: Hun.   843

Two productions of *Déryné ifjasszony (Mrs. Déry)* by Ferenc Herczeg.
Austria-Hungary. Hungary: Budapest. 1907-1928.Lang.: Hun.   1908
Budapest productions of the millicentenary season. Hungary: Budapest.
1995-1996. Lang.: Eng.   2104
Review of some Budapest productions. Hungary. 1995-1996. Lang.: Eng.
                                                                        2105
Nemzeti Színház (Miskolc)
SEE
Miskolci Nemzeti Színház.
Nemzeti Színház (Pécs)
SEE
Pécsi Nemzeti Színház.
Nemzeti Színház (Pest)
SEE
Pesti Nemzeti Színház.
Nemzeti Színház (Szeged)
SEE
Szegedi Nemzeti Színház.
Nemzeti Színjátszó Társaság (Kolozsvár)
Performance/production
Early professional acting on the Hungarian stage in Transylvania.
Hungary: Kolozsvár. 1792-1821. Lang.: Hun.   842
Neoclassicism
SEE ALSO
Geographical-Chronological Index under Europe 1540-1660, France
1629-1660, Italy 1540-1576.
Népfürdő (Public Bath)
Basic theatrical documents
English translation of *Népfürdő (Public Bath)* by Gábor Görgey.
Hungary. 1996. Lang.: Hun.   1664
Népszínház (Budapest)
Performance/production
The stage history of *Ezer év (A Thousand Years)* by György Verő.
Austria-Hungary: Budapest. 1896-1926. Lang.: Hun.   1909
Népszínház (Topolya)
Institutions
Hungarian theatre in Voivodship. Hungary. Yugoslavia. 1949-1959.
Lang.: Hun.   464
Népszínház (Zombor)
Institutions
Hungarian theatre in Voivodship. Hungary. Yugoslavia. 1949-1959.
Lang.: Hun.   464
Népszínház (Zrenjanin)
Institutions
Hungarian theatre in Voivodship. Hungary. Yugoslavia. 1949-1959.
Lang.: Hun.   464
Neptune Theatre (Halifax, NS)
Relation to other fields
National and regional identities in Canadian theatre companies. Canada.
1860-1994. Lang.: Eng.   1157
Neue Bühne (Seifenberg)
Performance/production
Two productions of Čechov's *Ivanov*. Germany: Seifenberg, Gera. 1996.
Lang.: Ger.   2081
Neuenfels, Hans
Institutions
Highlights of the Wiener Festwochen festival. Austria: Vienna. 1996.
Lang.: Ger.   1752
Neuer Tanz (Düsseldorf)
Institutions
Profile of dance theatre group Neuer Tanz. Germany: Düsseldorf. 1992-
1996. Lang.: Ger.   1558
Neues Theater, Schauspiel Halle
Performance/production
Two productions of Brecht's *Herr Puntila*. Germany: Hamburg, Halle.
1996. Lang.: Ger.   2079
Neuwirth, Bebe
Performance/production
The Broadway revival of the musical *Chicago*. USA: New York, NY.
1975-1996. Lang.: Eng.   3939
Nevada, Emma
Performance/production
Translation of interviews with opera divas Adelina Patti, Emma
Nevada, and Marie Van Zandt. France: Paris. 1880-1889. Lang.: Eng.
                                                                        4119
Never the Sinner
Performance/production
Collection of newspaper reviews by London theatre critics. UK-England:
London. 1996. Lang.: Eng.   2408

Novosadsko Pozorište (Novi Sad)
SEE
Újvidéki Színház.
Novyj Teat'r (Moscow)
Institutions
Novyj Teat'r, Boris L'vov-Anochin, director. Russia: Moscow. 1980-
1996. Lang.: Rus. 1826
Performance/production
The work of Boris L'vov-Anochin, director of Novyj Teat'r. Russia:
Moscow. 1990-1996. Lang.: Rus. 2257
Nowe Wyzwolenie (New Deliverance, The)
Performance/production
Andrzej Dziuk's productions of plays by Witkacy. Poland: Zakopane.
1984-1995. Lang.: Eng, Fre. 2164
Nowra, Louis
Performance/production
Collection of newspaper reviews by London theatre critics. UK-England:
London. 1996. Lang.: Eng. 2401
Plays/librettos/scripts
Shakespeare in post-colonial drama. Australia. Canada. 1969-1990.
Lang.: Eng. 2726
Nozze di Figaro, Le
Performance/production
Lyric soprano Lilian Sukis. Canada. 1939-1991. Lang.: Eng. 4085
Bass baritone John Haley-Relyea. Canada. 1973-1996. Lang.: Eng. 4088
Plays/librettos/scripts
Tonal planning in Mozart's operas. Austria: Vienna. 1769-1792. Lang.:
Eng. 4303
Ntshona, Winston
Plays/librettos/scripts
The use of absurdism in Fugard's *The Island*. South Africa, Republic of.
1968-1974. Lang.: Eng. 3225
Nubian Theatre Company (Memphis, TN)
Performance/production
Two productions of the National Black Theatre Festival. USA: Winston-
Salem, NC. 1995. Lang.: Eng. 2625
Nude Nude Totally Nude
Design/technology
Contemporary costuming by designer Jane Greenwood. USA: New
York, NY. 1996. Lang.: Eng. 1738
Nudité (Nudity)
Performance/production
The ban on Grand Théâtre Émotif du Québec's *Nudité (Nudity)*.
Canada: Montreal, PQ. 1996. Lang.: Fre. 749
Nuffield Theatre (Southampton)
Performance/production
Collection of newspaper reviews by London theatre critics. UK-England:
London. 1996. Lang.: Eng. 2321
Nuit Blanche: A Select View of Earthlings
Performance/production
Montage structure in plays of American ethnic minorities. USA. 1967-
1990. Lang.: Eng. 2675
Nuit des chats, La (Night of the Cats, The)
Plays/librettos/scripts
The methods and objectives of theatrical adaptation. France. 1980-1989.
Lang.: Fre. 3005
Nuit, La (Night)
Institutions
Some productions of the Festival de Théâtre des Amériques. Canada:
Montreal, PQ. 1996. 1773
Plays/librettos/scripts
Playwright Anne-Marie Cadieux discusses her craft. Canada: Montreal,
PQ. 1992-1996. Lang.: Fre. 2758
Harsh realism in contemporary Quebec plays. Canada: Montreal, PQ.
1993-1995. Lang.: Fre. 2784
Nultwintig (Amsterdam)
Performance/production
Use of young amateur actors by Nultwintig. Netherlands. 1994-1995.
Lang.: Dut. 2141
Nun, The
Performance/production
Collection of newspaper reviews by London theatre critics. UK-England:
London. 1996. Lang.: Eng. 2472
Nunn, Trevor
Performance/production
Ricky Martin's role in *Les Misérables*. USA: New York, NY. 1996.
Lang.: Eng. 3931
Melba Moore's role in *Les Misérables*. USA: New York, NY. 1970-
1996. Lang.: Eng. 3963

Elaine Page's role in *Sunset Boulevard*. USA: New York, NY. UK-
England: London. 1996. Lang.: Eng. 3979
Nunsense
Performance/production
Collection of newspaper reviews by London theatre critics. UK-England:
London. 1996. Lang.: Eng. 2346
Nuremberg: The War Crimes Trial
Audience
The chief prosecutor of the Nuremberg trial reactions to *Nuremberg:
The War Crimes Trial* by Richard Norton-Taylor. UK-England:
London. 1996. Lang.: Eng. 1635
Performance/production
Collection of newspaper reviews by London theatre critics. UK-England:
London. 1996. Lang.: Eng. 2415
Plays/librettos/scripts
Interview with playwright Richard Norton-Taylor. UK-England. 1945-
1996. Lang.: Eng. 3292
Nureyev, Rudolf
Performance/production
Kirov Ballet master Faruch Ruzimatov. Russia: St. Petersburg. 1990-
1996. Lang.: Rus. 1518
Nutcracker, The
SEE
Sčelkunčik.
Nutley, Colin
Performance/production
Interview with actor Reine Brynolfsson. Sweden: Gothenburg,
Stockholm. 1984. Lang.: Swe. 2286
Nygate, Merle
Performance/production
Collection of newspaper reviews by London theatre critics. UK-England:
London. 1996. Lang.: Eng. 2462
Nylén, Lena
Performance/production
Interview with actress Lena Nylén. Sweden: Malmö. 1996. Lang.: Swe.
2292
Nyroos, Gunilla
Performance/production
Interview with actress Gunilla Nyroos. Sweden: Stockholm. 1966. Lang.:
Swe. 2298
The development of Bengt Bratt's *Mottagningen (The Medical Center)*
by improvisation. Sweden: Stockholm. 1996. Lang.: Swe. 2299
Ô Délire (Quebec, PQ)
Performance/production
Recent trends in Quebec theatre production. Canada: Quebec, PQ.
1992-1993. Lang.: Fre. 728
O Isabella! You Bad, Bad Girl
Performance/production
Collection of newspaper reviews by London theatre critics. UK-England:
London. 1996. Lang.: Eng. 2354
O Vertige (Montreal, PQ)
Performance/production
The influence of painter Marc Chagall on O Vertige and Cirque du
Soleil. Canada: Montreal, PQ. 1988-1989. Lang.: Fre. 730
O vrede tabaka (On the Harmfulness of Tobacco)
Performance/production
Collection of newspaper reviews by London theatre critics. UK-England:
London. 1996. Lang.: Eng. 2442
O'Brien, Jack
Performance/production
Collection of newspaper reviews by New York theatre critics. USA:
New York, NY. 1996. Lang.: Eng. 2572
O'Brien, Richard
Performance/production
Collection of newspaper reviews by London theatre critics. UK-England:
London. 1996. Lang.: Eng. 2347
O'Carroll, Brendan
Performance/production
Collection of newspaper reviews by London theatre critics. UK-England:
London. 1996. Lang.: Eng. 2427
O'Casey, Shivaun
Performance/production
Collection of newspaper reviews by London theatre critics. UK-England:
London. 1996. Lang.: Eng. 2438
O'Connell, Doug
Performance/production
Puppet production of *Frankenstein* by Redmoon Theatre. USA:
Chicago, IL. 1996. Lang.: Eng. 4444

Osborne, John — cont'd

Collection of newspaper reviews by New York theatre critics. USA: New York, NY. 1996. Lang.: Eng. 2560

Plays/librettos/scripts
Political ramifications of British realist theatre. UK-England. 1956-1965. Lang.: Eng. 3297

John Osborne's *Look Back in Anger* and the symbolic figure of the Angry Young Man. UK-England. 1956-1994. Lang.: Eng. 3313

Osiński, Zbigniew
Relation to other fields
Interview with theatre anthropologist Zbigniew Osiński. Poland. 1995. Lang.: Eng, Fre. 1222

Oskarson, Peter
Performance/production
Theatre musician Ale Möller. Sweden. 1970. Lang.: Swe. 946

Collaboration of directors Peter Oskarson and Ma Ke at Orionteatern. Sweden: Stockholm. China, People's Republic of. 1989. Lang.:Swe. 955

Osment, Philip
Performance/production
Collection of newspaper reviews by London theatre critics. UK-England: London. 1996. Lang.: Eng. 2337

Collection of newspaper reviews by London theatre critics. UK-England: London. 1996. Lang.: Eng. 2441

Plays/librettos/scripts
Analysis of *This Island's Mine* by Philip Osment. UK-England: London. 1988-1996. Lang.: Eng. 3282

Osofisan, Femi
Performance/production
Collection of newspaper reviews by London theatre critics. UK-England: London. 1996. Lang.: Eng. 2415

Plays/librettos/scripts
The plays of Femi Osofisan. Nigeria. 1960-1995. Lang.: Eng. 3151

Ośrodek Praktyk Teatralnych (Gardzienice)
Performance/production
Włodzimierz Staniewski and the Gardzienice Theatre Associaton. Poland: Gardzienice. 1977-1996. Lang.: Ger. 893

Ostatni etap (Last Stop, The)
Performance/production
Account of *Ostatni etap (Last Stop)*, a film directed by Wanda Jakubowska. Poland. 1947-1948. Lang.: Eng. 3620

Östberg, Jens
Performance/production
Choreographers and video producers on dance in Swedish music videos. Sweden. USA. 1996. Lang.: Swe. 3672

Osten, Suzanne
Performance/production
Interview with Suzanne Osten of Unga Klara. Sweden. 1995. Lang.: Eng. 2276

Osterwa, Juliusz
Institutions
The work of directors Osterwa, Horzyca, and Dejmek at Teatr Narodowy. Poland: Warsaw. 1923-1996. Lang.: Eng, Fre. 1821

Östgötateatern (Norrköping)
Institutions
Claes Peter Hellwig's year as manager of Östgötateatern and his view of its troubles. Sweden: Norrköping. 1995. Lang.: Swe. 538

Ostrovskij, Aleksand'r Nikolajevič
Institutions
Moscow Art Theatre and Russian tradition. Russia: Moscow. 1990-1996. Lang.: Rus. 1831

Performance/production
Pëtr Fomenko's production of Ostrovskij's *Bez viny vinovatje (Guilty Though Innocent)*. Russia: Moscow. 1990-1996. Lang.: Rus. 2216

Plays/librettos/scripts
Love in the plays of Ostrovskij. Russia. 1823-1886. Lang.: Rus. 3192

National consciousness in the plays of A.N. Ostrovskij. Russia. 1823-1886. Lang.: Rus. 3193

The language of playwright A.N. Nikolajević. Russia: Moscow. 1996. Lang.: Rus. 3199

Ostrovskij's characters on the contemporary stage. Russia: Moscow. 1996. Lang.: Rus. 3204

Ostrow, Stuart
Performance/production
Stuart Ostrow's experience assisting Bob Fosse in original choreography for *Chicago*. USA: New York, NY. 1975. Lang.: Eng. 3975

Osvobozené divadlo V. & W. (Prague)
Institutions
Profile of Osvobozené divadlo (Liberated Theatre of V & W). Czechoslovakia: Prague. 1925-1938. Lang.: Fre. 396

Oswald, Peter
Performance/production
Collection of newspaper reviews by London theatre critics. UK-England: London. 1996. Lang.: Eng. 2479

Otello
Performance/production
Background material on Metropolitan Opera radio broadcast performances. USA: New York, NY. 1996. Lang.: Eng. 4252

Plays/librettos/scripts
Jealousy in *Otello* and *Falstaff* by Giuseppe Verdi. Italy. 1887-1893. Lang.: Eng. 4332

Othello
Performance/production
English plays and subjects on the Hungarian stage. Hungary. 1995-1996. Lang.: Eng. 847

Analysis of dance interpretations of Shakespearean plays. Europe. 1809-1994. Lang.: Hun. 1500

Reviews of Shakespearean and other productions. Germany. 1994-1995. Lang.: Ger. 2058

Collection of newspaper reviews by London theatre critics. UK-England: London. 1996. Lang.: Eng. 2378

Plays/librettos/scripts
Black or white actors in the role of Othello. UK-England. 1956-1996. Lang.: Eng. 1107

Study of Desdemona's handkerchief in Shakespeare's *Othello*. England. 1603. Lang.: Eng. 2881

Calvinism in Shakespeare's *Othello*. England. 1604. Lang.: Eng. 2915

Sex and innuendo in Shakespeare's *Othello*. England. 1600. Lang.: Eng. 2943

The reflection of contemporary concerns in Shakespeare's *Hamlet* and *Othello*. England. 1600-1604. Lang.: Eng. 2953

Wonder in Shakespeare's *Othello*. England. 1604. Lang.: Eng. 2963

Shakespeare and Polish Romanticism. Poland. 1786-1846. Lang.: Eng. 3163

Jealousy in *Otello* and *Falstaff* by Giuseppe Verdi. Italy. 1887-1893. Lang.: Eng. 4332

Relation to other fields
Teaching race and gender in plays of Cary, Shakespeare, and Behn. USA. 1996. Lang.: Eng. 3518

Teaching plays of Shakespeare and Cary in a course on domestic England in the early modern period. USA. 1995. Lang.: Eng. 3519

Othello and the Circumcised Turk
Performance/production
Assurbanipal Babilla's *Othello and the Circumcised Turk*, Purgatorio Ink. USA: New York, NY. 1996. Lang.: Eng. 2690

Other Place, The (Stratford)
SEE ALSO
Royal Shakespeare Company.
Performance/production
Collection of newspaper reviews by London theatre critics. UK-England: London. 1996. Lang.: Eng. 2432

Collection of newspaper reviews by London theatre critics. UK-England: London. 1996. Lang.: Eng. 2454

Collection of newspaper reviews by London theatre critics. UK-England: London. 1996. Lang.: Eng. 2462

Collection of newspaper reviews by London theatre critics. UK-England: London, Stratford. 1996. Lang.: Eng. 2476

Katie Mitchell's production of *The Phoenician Women (Phoinissai)* by Euripides. UK-England: Stratford. 1995. Lang.: Eng. 2529

Other Weapon, The
Performance/production
Feminist playwright and performer Robbie McCauley. USA. 1990-1995. Lang.: Eng. 1047

Otkritij Teat'r (St. Petersburg)
Performance/production
Interview with director Vladislav Pazi of Otkritij Teat'r. Russia: St. Petersburg. 1990-1996. Lang.: Rus. 935

Trostjaneckij's *Esli prozivy leto... (If I Live Through the Summer)* performed by Otkritij Teat'r. Russia: St. Petersburg. 1996.Lang.: Rus. 2236

Otrabanda (New York, NY)
Performance/production
Otrabanda's production of *The Fairground Booth (Balagančik)* by Blok at La MaMa E.T.C.. USA: New York, NY. 1996. Lang.: Eng. 1006

Otway, Thomas
Plays/librettos/scripts
The 'male masochist' role in plays of Otway and Shadwell. England. 1550. Lang.: Eng. 2944

Paradance Fable
Plays/librettos/scripts
Performance art at a Copenhagen seminar on the body and ritual manipulation. Denmark. 1995. Lang.: Dan. 3811
Parades
SEE
Pageants/parades.
Paradise Now
Audience
Comparison of riots by audiences of Abbey Theatre and Living Theatre. Ireland: Dublin. USA: Berkeley, CA. 1907-1968. Lang.: Eng. 1632
Parenteau-Lebeuf, Dominick
Plays/librettos/scripts
Text of a poem by playwright Dominick Parenteau-Lebeuf. Canada: Montreal, PQ. 1996. Lang.: Fre. 2819
Parents terribles, Les (Intimate Relations)
Performance/production
The Madrid theatre season. Spain: Madrid. 1996. Lang.: Eng. 2271
Paris Quartet
Performance/production
Barbara Carlisle's at-home production of *Paris Quartet*. USA. 1995. Lang.: Eng. 2609
Park in Our Own House, A
Design/technology
Scene designer Robert Brill. USA: New York, NY. 1996. Lang.: Eng. 1724
Park Theatre (London)
SEE
Battersea Park Theatre.
Parker, Alan
Performance/production
Review of the film version of the musical *Evita*. USA. 1979-1996. Lang.: Eng. 3636
Parker, Charles
Performance/production
Banner Theatre Company and English alternative theatre. UK-England. 1960-1996. Lang.: Eng. 992
Parker, James Edwin
Performance/production
Collection of newspaper reviews by London theatre critics. UK-England: London. 1996. Lang.: Eng. 2459
Parker, John
Performance/production
Collection of newspaper reviews by London theatre critics. UK-England: London. 1996. Lang.: Eng. 2309
Parker, Lynne
Performance/production
Collection of newspaper reviews by London theatre critics. UK-England: London. 1996. Lang.: Eng. 2341
Collection of newspaper reviews by London theatre critics. UK-England: London. 1996. Lang.: Eng. 2383
Parker, Sarah Jessica
Performance/production
Sarah Jessica Parker's role in *Once Upon a Mattress*. USA: New York, NY. 1976-1996. Lang.: Eng. 3942
Parker, Stewart
Performance/production
Collection of newspaper reviews by London theatre critics. UK-England: London. 1996. Lang.: Eng. 2383
Parkes, Derek
Performance/production
Collection of newspaper reviews by London theatre critics. UK-England: London. 1996. Lang.: Eng. 2337
Parkinson, Brian
Institutions
How musical summer theatre finances serious productions at New West Theatre Company. Canada: Lethbridge, AB. 1983-1996. Lang.: Eng. 365
Parkinson, Geoffrey
Performance/production
Collection of newspaper reviews by London theatre critics. UK-England: London. 1996. Lang.: Eng. 2310
Parks, Suzan-Lori
Basic theatrical documents
Text of *Venus* by Suzan-Lori Parks. USA. 1996. Lang.: Eng. 1699
Performance/production
Collection of newspaper reviews by New York theatre critics. USA: New York, NY. 1996. Lang.: Eng. 2580
Background on *Venus* by Suzan-Lori Parks. USA. 1996. Lang.: Eng. 2679

Plays/librettos/scripts
Playwright Suzan-Lori Parks. USA: New York, NY. 1996. Lang.: Eng. 3326
Work of playwrights Jeffrey M. Jones, Mac Wellman, and Suzan-Lori Parks. USA: New York, NY. 1991. Lang.: Fre. 3360
Suzan-Lori Parks' *Venus* at Yale Rep. USA: New Haven, CT. 1996. Lang.: Eng. 3362
Interview with playwright Suzan-Lori Parks. USA. 1996. Lang.: Eng. 3444
Parkteatern (Stockholm)
Institutions
Interview with Benny Fredriksson, artistic director of Stockholms Parkteater. Sweden: Stockholm. 1996. Lang.: Swe. 546
Parnell, Feliks
Institutions
Feliks Parnell's Balet Polski. Poland: Warsaw. 1935-1939. Lang.: Pol. 1485
Parnell, Peter
Performance/production
Stage adaptation of John Irving's *The Cider House Rules*, Seattle Repertory. USA: Seattle, WA. 1996. Lang.: Eng. 2592
Parrish, Sue
Performance/production
Collection of newspaper reviews by London theatre critics. UK-England: London. 1996. Lang.: Eng. 2312
Parry, Lorae
Performance/production
Women writers and performers of comedy. Australia. 1992-1995. Lang.: Eng. 685
Women playwrights of the Pacific Rim. Australia. Asia. 1994. Lang.: Eng. 1899
Parry, Simon
Performance/production
Collection of newspaper reviews by London theatre critics. UK-England: London. 1996. Lang.: Eng. 2312
Collection of newspaper reviews by London theatre critics. UK-England: London. 1996. Lang.: Eng. 2386
Parsifal
Plays/librettos/scripts
Love and the death of women in works of Wagner, Strauss, and Schoenberg. Germany. Austria: Vienna. 1842-1911. Lang.: Eng. 4323
Partage de midi (Break of Noon)
Audience
Unexpected reactions to films and plays. Canada: Montreal, PQ. 1950-1989. Lang.: Fre. 129
Parti Nagy, Lajos
Performance/production
Recipients of the annual theatre critics' awards. Hungary. 1995-1996. Lang.: Hun. 846
Budapest productions of the millicentenary season. Hungary: Budapest. 1995-1996. Lang.: Eng. 2104
Plays/librettos/scripts
Theoretical essay on recent Hungarian drama. Hungary. 1995-1996. Lang.: Hun. 3074
Partljič, Tone
Plays/librettos/scripts
Analysis of works by significant Slovene playwrights. Slovenia. 1900-1996. Lang.: Slo. 3213
Partridge, Philip
Performance/production
Collection of newspaper reviews by London theatre critics. UK-England: London. 1996. Lang.: Eng. 2434
Parzival
Plays/librettos/scripts
Children's plays of Tankred Dorst. Germany. 1982-1996. Lang.: Ger. 3018
Pasadena Dance Theatre (Pasadena, CA)
Training
Ballet training and the male body. USA: Pasadena, CA. 1994. Lang.: Eng. 1542
Pascal, Adam
Performance/production
Interviews with Tony Award nominees. USA: New York, NY. 1996. Lang.: Eng. 2596
Profiles of singers in current Broadway musicals. USA: New York, NY. 1996. Lang.: Eng. 3940
Paschiller, Doris
Plays/librettos/scripts
German feminist theatre before and after reunification. Germany. 1978-1994. Lang.: Eng. 3046

People's Theatre (New York, NY)
  Performance/production
    Three actors of Yiddish theatre as Shylock. USA: New York, NY. 1901-1950. Lang.: Eng.   2590
Pepper, Robert
  Performance/production
    Collection of newspaper reviews by London theatre critics. UK-England: London. 1996. Lang.: Eng.   2347
Pérchy, Kornélia
  Performance/production
    Hungarian singers at Katia Ricciarelli's master course. Italy. Hungary. 1995. Lang.: Hun.   4177
Percy, Edward
  Performance/production
    Theatre production in Florida. USA: Boca Raton, FL. 1977-1996. Lang.: Eng.   1023
Perez Peña, Carlos
  Institutions
    History of Grupo Teatro Escambray. Cuba: La Macagua. 1959-1996. Lang.: Eng.   389
Perfect Crime, The
  Relation to other fields
    Critique of attacks on media and industrial culture, with references to performance art. USA. 1964-1996. Lang.: Eng.   3572
Perfect Moment
  Performance/production
    Politics, feminism, and postmodern dance. UK-England: London. 1992. Lang.: Eng.   1444
Performance
  Basic theatrical documents
    Excerpt from the video script *Performance* by Andrew James Paterson. Canada. 1996.   3660
Performance art
  SEE ALSO
    Classed Entries under MIXED ENTERTAINMENT—Performance art.
  Institutions
    Forced Entertainment's own account of its first decade of performance. UK-England: Sheffield. 1984-1994. Lang.: Eng.   3655
  Performance/production
    Theatre, stand-up comedy, and performance art in Daniel MacIvor's *House*, directed by Daniel Brooks. Canada: Toronto, ON. 1992. Lang.: Fre.   705
    Excerpts from conference papers on ritual, theatre, and performance art. Japan. USA: New York, NY. 1977-1995. Lang.: Eng.   872
    Women's performance art and theatre. USA. 1970-1979. Lang.: Eng.   1017
    History and current state of autobiographical solo performance. USA. 1276-1995. Lang.: Eng.   1020
    Performance art in the choreography of Per Jonsson. Sweden: Stockholm. 1996. Lang.: Swe.   1590
    Interview with choreographer Margaretha Åsberg. USA: New York, NY. Sweden: Stockholm. 1960. Lang.: Swe.   1594
    Latin American and Hispanic performance. Cuba. Mexico. 1994. Lang.: Eng.   1975
    Essays and reviews of post-modern theatre. USA. 1979-1995. Lang.: Eng.   2627
    Video-sculptural performances of Gary Hill. USA: New York, NY. 1995. Lang.: Eng.   3657
    MTV, postmodernism, and feminism. USA. 1990-1995. Lang.: Eng.   3677
  Relation to other fields
    Blah, Blah, Blah's fusion of performance art and educational theatre. UK-England. 1995. Lang.: Eng.   1247
    Camille Paglia on teaching as performance art. USA. 1996. Lang.: Eng.   1273
  Theory/criticism
    Signs and bodies in the media age. 1996. Lang.: Ger.   1313
    Interview with critic Camille Paglia. USA. 1990-1996. Lang.: Eng.   1388
Performance Space (Sydney)
  Performance/production
    The use of Müller's *Der Auftrag (The Mission)* in *The Aboriginal Protesters* by Mudrooroo. Australia: Sydney. 1996. Lang.: Ger.   1898
Performance spaces
  SEE ALSO
    Classed Entries.
  Audience
    The influence of space on audience perception and appreciation. Netherlands. 1650-1995. Lang.: Dut.   140

Performance artist Louis Ethel Liliefeldt. Canada. 1996. Lang.: Eng.
                                                                                3784
Design/technology
    Protection against falls in arena shows. USA. 1996. Lang.: Eng.   305
    Jason Kantrowitz's lighting design for *Pomp Duck and Circumstance*. USA: New York, NY. 1996. Lang.: Eng.   3697
Institutions
    Performance spaces of Montreal's cultural centers. Canada: Montreal, PQ. 1996. Lang.: Fre.   354
    Kanata Theatre, housing local theatre groups. Canada: Kanata, ON. 1968-1996. Lang.: Eng.   383
    Dena Davida of Tangente describes the difficulty of finding a home for the company. Canada: Montreal, PQ. 1977-1991. Lang.: Fre.   1553
    Forced Entertainment's own account of its first decade of performance. UK-England: Sheffield. 1984-1994. Lang.: Eng.   3655
Performance/production
    The use of space and the meaning of scenic structure. 500 B.C.-1996 A.D. Lang.: Ita.   675
    Survey of the independent theatre scene. Germany: Berlin. 1996. Lang.: Ger.   818
    Review of Irvine Welsh's *Trainspotting* directed by János Csányi. Hungary: Budapest. 1995. Lang.: Hun.   840
    Myths regarding physical disabilities that exclude the handicapped from acting. USA. 1996. Lang.: Eng.   1008
    Barbara Carlisle's at-home production of *Paris Quartet*. USA. 1995. Lang.: Eng.   2609
Plays/librettos/scripts
    Technical and thematic changes in Korean theatre. Korea: Seoul. 1987-1996. Lang.: Kor.   1099
Performance studies
  Institutions
    The production of knowledge and the institutionalization of performance studies. USA. 1996. Lang.: Eng.   575
  Performance/production
    The modern concept of performance. Europe. North America. 1960-1995. Lang.: Eng.   783
    Essays on contemporary performance. Europe. USA. 1980-1995. Lang.: Eng.   790
    Gender in performances of actress Mary Martin. USA. 1922-1994. Lang.: Eng.   1074
    Performance analysis of a street fair. USA: Nevada City, CA. 1995. Lang.: Eng.   3779
  Plays/librettos/scripts
    Analysis of works by Paul Bonin-Rodriguez. USA. 1992-1994. Lang.: Eng.   1109
    Latina lesbian subjectivity in works of Marga Gomez. USA. 1990-1995. Lang.: Eng.   3436
  Relation to other fields
    Performance and sexuality as observed in an Irish pub. Ireland: Dublin. 1996. Lang.: Eng.   1201
    Theatricality in Latin America and its historical impact. Latin America. 1996. Lang.: Eng.   1209
    Performance in the work of novelist Virginia Woolf. UK-England. 1941. Lang.: Eng.   1240
    Performance aspects of Faulkner's novel *As I Lay Dying*. USA. 1930. Lang.: Eng.   1252
    Camille Paglia on teaching as performance art. USA. 1996. Lang.: Eng.
                                                                                1273
    Rhythm as a form of social discourse. USA. 1994. Lang.: Eng.   1275
    Stylistic features of American Sign Language theatre. USA. 1994. Lang.: Eng.   1276
    Ritual performance in the Charismatic religious movement. USA. 1994. Lang.: Eng.   1279
  Theory/criticism
    Space, time, and action in the analysis of performance. France. 1996. Lang.: Eng.   1347
    Similarities between African vernacular performance and avant-garde theatre. North America. Togo. Europe. 1970-1994. Lang.: Eng.   1355
    Carnivalesque aspects of British football songs. UK-England. 1994. Lang.: Eng.   1365
    Narrative and phenomenology. USA. 1994. Lang.: Eng.   1371
    Performance analysis of public announcements by flight attendants. USA. 1994. Lang.: Eng.   1374
    The Alienation effect in the Rodney King beating trial. USA: Los Angeles, CA. 1991-1994. Lang.: Eng.   1379

Performance studies — cont'd

The question of proof in performance studies. USA. 1996. Lang.: Eng.
1384

Essay on the meaning and nature of performance. USA. 1996. Lang.:
Eng. 1391

Performance analysis of Los Angeles riots. USA: Los Angeles, CA.
1970-1992. Lang.: Eng. 1393

Practice and performativity in Marxism. USA. 1996. Lang.: Eng. 3565

Performance theory and cultural subversion. USA. 1994. Lang.: Eng.
3566

Female circus performers and social convention. Australia. 1850-1929.
Lang.: Eng. 3758

Performing Arts Chicago (Chicago, IL)
Performance/production
Puppets, Human Movement, and dance in Philippe Genty's *Voyageur
Immobile (Motionless Traveler)*. USA: Chicago, IL. France: Paris. 1961-
1965. Lang.: Eng. 4415

**Peribáñez y el Comendador de Ocaña (Peribáñez and the Knight of
Ocaña)**
Plays/librettos/scripts
Analysis of *Peribáñez y el Comendador de Ocaña* by Lope de Vega.
Spain. 1580-1680. Lang.: Eng. 3228

Pericles
Performance/production
Reviews of Shakespearean and other productions. Germany. 1994-1995.
Lang.: Ger. 2058

Collection of newspaper reviews by London theatre critics. UK-England:
London. 1996. Lang.: Eng. 2471
Plays/librettos/scripts
Shakespeare's Pericles compared to James I. England. 1606. Lang.: Eng.
2924

Perino, Joy
Performance/production
Collection of newspaper reviews by London theatre critics. UK-England:
London. 1996. Lang.: Eng. 2348

Permanent Brain Damage (Risk It! Risk It!)
Performance/production
Collection of newspaper reviews by New York theatre critics. USA:
New York, NY. 1996. Lang.: Eng. 2563

Permskogo Teat'r Opery i Baleta im. P.I. Čajkovskogo (Perm)
Institutions
History of the ballet troupe of the Perm opera and ballet theatre.
Russia: Perm. 1925-1996. Lang.: Rus. 1486

Perrault, Jean-Pierre
Performance/production
Character in modern dance choreography. Canada: Montreal, PQ. 1976-
1991. Lang.: Fre. 1568

Modern dance in Francophone Canada. Canada: Montreal, PQ. 1995.
Lang.: Swe. 1570

Perreira, Michele
Plays/librettos/scripts
Dramatic work of Michele Perreira. Italy. 1994. Lang.: Ita. 3113

Playwright Michele Perreira. Italy. 1994. Lang.: Ita. 3129

Perrot, Jules
Performance/production
Articles on Western European ballet theatre and its artists. Europe.
1800-1900. Lang.: Rus. 1499

Perry, Antoinette
Performance/production
Actress and director Antoinette Perry. USA: New York, NY. 1889-1996.
Lang.: Eng. 1073

Perry, Dein
Design/technology
Lighting for London and Dublin productions of *Tap Dogs*. UK-
England: London. Ireland: Dublin. 1996. Lang.: Eng. 3891
Performance/production
Collection of newspaper reviews by London theatre critics. UK-England:
London. 1996. Lang.: Eng. 2357

Perry, Herbert
Performance/production
Interview with opera singer Herbert Perry. USA. Europe. 1985-1995.
Lang.: Eng. 4269

Perry, Jeff
Institutions
Profile of Steppenwolf Theatre Company. USA: Chicago, IL. 1974-1996.
Lang.: Eng. 1862

Perry, Ted
Performance/production
The recording of Schubert's *Lieder* on CD. 1996. Lang.: Eng. 3853

Perséphone
Plays/librettos/scripts
Analysis of operas by Igor Stravinskij. USSR. 1926-1951. Lang.: Eng.
4348

Persephone
Institutions
Prix d'Europe honors Robert Wilson, Théâtre de Complicité, and Carte
Blanche-Compagnia della Fortezza. Italy: Taormina. 1971-1996. Lang.:
Fre. 492

Personal Equation, The
Plays/librettos/scripts
Comparison of writings by Eugene O'Neill and John Reed. USA: New
York, NY. 1913-1922. Lang.: Eng. 3327

Personnel
Administration
A chapter in the history of theatre unionization. UK-England. 1920-
1935. Lang.: Eng. 51

Equity health insurance for domestic partners. USA: New York, NY.
1996. Lang.: Eng. 71

Account of membership vote on Equity-LORT contract. USA: New
York, NY. 1996. Lang.: Eng. 77

Critique of the use of dancers at the Royal Danish Ballet. Denmark.
1951-1996. Lang.: Dan. 1473

Maina Gielgud, new ballet mistress of the Royal Danish Ballet.
Denmark. 1992-1996. Lang.: Dan. 1474
Institutions
Open enrollment period for Equity health insurance. USA: New York,
NY. 1996. Lang.: Eng. 591

Problems of maintaining a resident company, with emphasis on
American Repertory Theatre. USA: Cambridge, MA. 1996. Lang.: Eng.
1874

Opera Company of Philadelphia's creation of its own scene shop. USA:
Philadelphia, PA. 1990-1995. Lang.: Eng. 4066

Persson, Martin
Performance/production
Choreographers and video producers on dance in Swedish music videos.
Sweden. USA. 1996. Lang.: Swe. 3672

Perugorría, Jorge
Performance/production
Interview with actor Jorge Perugorría. Cuba. 1994-1996. Lang.: Eng.
3615

Pesti Színház (Budapest)
Performance/production
Recipients of the annual theatre critics' awards. Hungary. 1995-1996.
Lang.: Hun. 846

English plays and subjects on the Hungarian stage. Hungary. 1995-1996.
Lang.: Eng. 847

Peter and Wendy
Performance/production
Performances of the Jim Henson International Festival. USA: New
York, NY. 1995. Lang.: Eng. 4407

Peter Grimes
Performance/production
Britten's *Peter Grimes*: productions by Eric Crozier and Harald André.
UK-England. Sweden: Stockholm. 1945-1980. Lang.: Swe. 4229

Peter Pan
Performance/production
Musical theatre performer Evelyn Laye. UK-England. 1918-1996. Lang.:
Eng. 3923

Great Arizona Puppet Theatre's production of *Peter Pan*. USA:
Phoenix, AZ. 1993-1995. Lang.: Eng. 4417

Petherbridge, Jonathan
Performance/production
Collection of newspaper reviews by London theatre critics. UK-England:
London, Stratford. 1996. Lang.: Eng. 2461

Petipa, Marius
Performance/production
Memoirs of Marius Petipa. Russia. 1822-1900. Lang.: Rus. 1513

Petit Bois (Kindling)
Plays/librettos/scripts
Analysis of plays by Eugène Durif. France. 1981-1992. Lang.: Fre. 2981

Petit Prince, Le (Little Prince, The)
Plays/librettos/scripts
Writing for puppet theatre. Canada: Montreal, PQ. 1979-1989. Lang.:
Fre. 4424

Petites Heures, Les (Small Hours, The)
Plays/librettos/scripts
Analysis of plays by Eugène Durif. France. 1981-1992. Lang.: Fre. 2981

Petőfi Színház (Veszprém)
Performance/production
Revivals of the Hungarian pop musical *Képzelt riport egy amerikai popfesztiválról (Imaginary Report on an American Pop Festival)*. Hungary. 1973-1995. Lang.: Hun.   3919

Petőfi, Sándor
Performance/production
Gyula Ecsedi Kovács' staging of *Tigris és hiéna*. Austro-Hungarian Empire: Kolozsvár. 1876-1883. Lang.: Hun.   1910

Petrarca, David
Design/technology
Lighting design for plays about Martin Guerre. UK-England: London. 1996. Lang.: Eng.   3890
Performance/production
Collection of newspaper reviews by New York theatre critics. USA: New York, NY, Chicago, IL. 1996. Lang.: Eng.   2585

Petrolini, Ettore
Performance/production
Letters to Silvio D'Amico from Petrolini, Copeau, and Costa. Italy. 1899-1955. Lang.: Ita.   860

Petrov, Aleksand'r
Performance/production
Interview with director Aleksand'r Petrov on his work in opera. Russia: St. Petersburg. 1996. Lang.: Rus.   4203

Petrov, Anatolij
Performance/production
Actor Anatolij Petrov. Russia: Moscow. 1996. Lang.: Rus.   2237

Petrov, Andrej
Performance/production
Choreographer Andrej Petrov. Russia: Moscow. 1990-1996. Lang.: Rus.   1514

Petrov, Vladimir
Performance/production
Account of a cultural-exchange visit to Omskij Akademičéskij Teat'r Dramy. Russia: Omsk. 1996. Lang.: Ger.   2197

Petrozavodsk Teat'r Junogo Zritelja
Institutions
Problems of youth theatre. Russia. 1990-1996. Lang.: Rus.   516

Petruševskaja, Ljudmila
Performance/production
Collection of newspaper reviews by London theatre critics. UK-England: London. 1996. Lang.: Eng.   2384

Pettersson, Allan
Performance/production
Birgit Cullberg's ballet *Rapport*. Sweden: Stockholm. 1977. Lang.: Swe.   1529

Pettersson, Ann-Margret
Institutions
Recent developments at the Royal Swedish Opera. Sweden: Stockholm. 1996. Lang.: Swe.   4055

Pevcov, Dmitrij
Performance/production
Interview with actor Dmitrij Pevcov. Russia: Moscow. 1980-1996. Lang.: Rus.   2260

Peymann, Claus
Administration
Dramaturg Hermann Beil's work with Claus Peymann at Burgtheater. Austria: Vienna. 1974-1996. Lang.: Ger.   5
Performance/production
Claus Peymann's *Ingeborg Bachmann Wer? (Ingeborg Bachmann Who?)* at Burgtheater. Austria: Vienna. 1996. Lang.: Ger.   1905

Pfalztheater (Kaiserslautern)
Administration
Wolfgang Quetes, artistic director-designate of Pfalztheater. Germany: Kaiserslautern. 1996. Lang.: Ger.   30
Institutions
The opening of Pfalztheater. Germany: Kaiserslautern. 1995. Lang.: Ger.   419

pH
Performance/production
Japanese performances of Japanese themes at Toronto Theatre Festival. Japan. Canada: Toronto, ON. 1996. Lang.: Eng.   874

Phaedra's Love
Performance/production
Collection of newspaper reviews by London theatre critics. UK-England: London. 1996. Lang.: Eng.   2424

Phantom of the Opera, The
Performance/production
Profile of tenor Gary Rideout. Canada. 1983-1996. Lang.: Eng.   4086

Plays/librettos/scripts
The adaptation of American musicals for a Korean public. Korea: Seoul. 1996. Lang.: Kor.   3985

Phantoms of Poe
Performance/production
Collection of newspaper reviews by London theatre critics. UK-England: London. 1996. Lang.: Eng.   2495

Phèdre
Performance/production
Three directors publicly direct actors in scenes from Racine's *Phèdre*. Canada: Montreal, PQ. 1996. Lang.: Fre.   1965
Review of recent Paris productions. France: Paris. 1996. Lang.: Ger.   2033
Plays/librettos/scripts
Comparison of Shakespeare's *Hamlet* and Racine's *Phèdre*. England. France. 1599-1677. Lang.: Eng.   2934
Metonymy and drama. North America. Europe. 1600-1996. Lang.: Eng.   3154

Phelan, Peggy
Performance/production
Excerpts from conference papers on ritual, theatre, and performance art. Japan. USA: New York, NY. 1977-1995. Lang.: Eng.   872

Phenomenology
Theory/criticism
A phenomenological methodology for analyzing performance. Europe. 1995. Lang.: Eng.   1337
Essay on theatre and simulation. Europe. 1000-1996. Lang.: Ger.   1340
Narrative and phenomenology. USA. 1994. Lang.: Eng.   1371
The concept of dance as a universal language. 1996. Lang.: Ger.   1464
Self-referentiality in Israeli theatre. Israel. 1948-1995. Lang.: Eng.   3544

Philadelphia Orchestra (Philadelphia, PA)
Performance/production
Fritz Reiner's work as a conductor of opera. USA: Philadelphia, PA, San Francisco, CA. UK-England: London. 1931-1941. Lang.: Eng.   4276

Philadelphia, Here I Come!
Plays/librettos/scripts
Dual personalities in plays of Brian Friel. Ireland. UK-Ireland. 1972-1988. Lang.: Eng.   3084

Philippine Educational Theatre Association (PETA, Manila)
Performance/production
Contemporary Philippine theatre and the formation of cultural identity. Philippines: Manila. 1565-1996. Lang.: Eng.   889

Philippou, Nick
Performance/production
Collection of newspaper reviews by London theatre critics. UK-England: London. 1996. Lang.: Eng.   2369
Collection of newspaper reviews by London theatre critics. UK-England: London. 1996. Lang.: Eng.   2477

Phillips, Andy
Design/technology
Design for RSC production of *A Patriot for Me* by John Osborne. UK-England: London. 1996. Lang.: Eng.   1713

Phillips, Arlene
Performance/production
Interview with dancer Michael Flatley. USA: Chicago, IL. 1958-1996. Lang.: Eng.   1548
Collection of newspaper reviews by London theatre critics. UK-England: London. 1996. Lang.: Eng.   2459

Phillips, Lou Diamond
Performance/production
Holiday memories of Broadway actors. USA: New York, NY. 1996. Lang.: Eng.   1013
Lou Diamond Phillips' role in *The King and I*. USA: New York, NY. 1996. Lang.: Eng.   3938

Phillips, Ronald Selwyn
Performance/production
Collection of newspaper reviews by London theatre critics. UK-England: London. 1996. Lang.: Eng.   2355

Philoctetes
Plays/librettos/scripts
Analysis of Sophocles' *Philoctetes*. Greece. 409 B.C. Lang.: Slo.   3063

Philosophy
Performance/production
Rationalism and the realist school of acting. Canada. USA. UK-England. 1989. Lang.: Fre.   1938
Account of a devised piece on the death of Voltaire. UK-England: Bristol. France. 1778-1991. Lang.: Eng.   2533

Playtexts — cont'd

Text of *Lakoma* by Oliver Bukowski. Germany. 1996. Lang.: Ger. 1658

Text of *Triumph der Schauspielkunst (Triumph of Acting)* by Thomas Jonigk. Germany. 1996. Lang.: Ger. 1659

Text of *Lupo* by Elfriede Müller. Germany. 1996. Lang.: Ger. 1660

Text of *Aschenputtels (Cinderellas)* by Paul Scheller. Germany. 1996. Lang.: Ger. 1661

Annotated Dutch translation of Euripides' *Phoinissai (The Phoenician Women)* as produced by Hollandia. Greece. Netherlands. 409 B.C.-1996 A.D. Lang.: Dut. 1662

English translation of *The Four Legs of the Table* by Iákovos Kampanéllis. Greece. 1996. Lang.: Eng. 1663

English translation of *Népfürdö (Public Bath)* by Gábor Görgey. Hungary. 1996. Lang.: Eng. 1664

English translation of *Árnyékban (In Shadow)* by Géza Páskándi. Hungary. 1996. Lang.: Eng. 1665

English translation of *Kalauz nélkül (No Conductor)* by Géza Páskándi. Hungary. 1996. Lang.: Eng. 1666

Israeli Holocaust drama. Israel. 1955-1989. Lang.: Eng. 1667

Text of futurist plays by Mina Loy. Italy. 1915. Lang.: Eng. 1668

Text of *The Pamperers* by Mina Loy. Italy. 1916. Lang.: Eng. 1669

Collection of plays by Don Duyns. Netherlands. 1989-1996. Lang.: Dut. 1670

Text of *Berlin/Berlin* by Oana Hock Cajal. Romania. 1996. Lang.: Eng. 1672

English translation of *Evanghelişti (The Evangelists)* by Alina Mungiu Pippidi. Romania. 1996. Lang.: Eng. 1673

English translation of *Joc de şah (Chessgame)* by Sergiu Viorel Urma. Romania. 1996. Lang.: Eng. 1674

Text of Act II of *Demokratija (Democracy!)* by Joseph Brodsky. Russia. USA. 1996. Lang.: Eng. 1675

Texts of plays by Josip Vošnjak and Anton Funtek. Slovenia. 1834-1932. Lang.: Slo. 1676

Dutch translations of plays by Belbel, Cabal, and Sanchis Sinisterra. Spain. 1990-1995. Lang.: Dut. 1677

Text of *Historia de nadie (Nobody's Story)* by Jorge Díaz. Spain. 1995. Lang.: Spa. 1678

Text of *Obras cómicas (Comic Works)* by Rodrigo García. Spain: Madrid. 1996. Lang.: Eng. 1679

Text of *Allá él (It's Up to Him)* by Concha Romero. Spain. 1994. Lang.: Spa. 1680

Text of *Isabelita tiene ángel (Isabelita Has an Angel)* by José María Rodríguez Méndez. Spain. 1976. Lang.: Spa. 1681

English translation of *¡Ay, Carmela!* by José Sanchis Sinisterra. Spain. 1996. Lang.: Eng. 1682

Text of *Luna Park Eclipses* with an introduction by its author Peter Barnes. UK-England: London. 1995. Lang.: Eng. 1683

Text of *Blasted* by Sarah Kane. UK-England. 1994. Lang.: Eng. 1684

Anthology of works by Split Britches. USA. 1985-1995. Lang.: Eng. 1685

Text of *Blues for an Alabama Sky* by Pearl Cleage. USA. 1996. Lang.: Eng. 1686

Collection of plays from the Humana Festival. USA. 1986-1995. Lang.: Eng. 1687

Collection of southern plays from Actors' Theatre of Louisville. USA. 1984-1992. Lang.: Eng. 1688

Excerpt from *The Darker Face of the Earth* by Rita Dove. USA. 1994. Lang.: Eng. 1689

Text of *The Darker Face of the Earth* by Rita Dove. USA. 1996. Lang.: Eng. 1690

Text of *Real Original Thinker* by Volker Schachenmayr and Laura Farabough. USA. 1995-1996. Lang.: Eng. 1691

Text of *Hey-Stop-That* by Thalia Field. USA. 1996. Lang.: Eng. 1692

Text of *Ballad of Yachiyo* by Philip Kan Gotanda. USA. 1996. Lang.: Eng. 1693

Anthology of unknown plays of the Harlem Renaissance. USA: New York, NY. 1920-1940. Lang.: Eng. 1694

Text of *Trying to Find Chinatown* by David Henry Hwang. USA. 1996. Lang.: Eng. 1695

Text of *Skin* by Naomi Iizuka. USA. 1995-1996. Lang.: Eng. 1696

Text of *The Monogamist* by Christopher Kyle. USA. 1992-1996. Lang.: Eng. 1697

The work of writer Louise McCord. USA: Charleston, SC. 1810-1879. Lang.: Eng. 1698

Text of *Venus* by Suzan-Lori Parks. USA. 1996. Lang.: Eng. 1699

Text of *Savage Wilds* by Ishmael Reed. USA. 1988. Lang.: Eng. 1700

Text of *Maricela de la Luz Lights the World* by José Rivera. USA. 1996. Lang.: Eng. 1701

Text of *Atomic Field* by Kenneth Robbins. USA. 1996. Lang.: Eng. 1702

Revised text of *Buried Child* by Sam Shepard. USA. 1978-1996. Lang.: Eng. 1703

Text of *Under the Knife* by Theodora Skipitares. USA: New York, NY. 1996. Lang.: Eng. 1704

Excerpt from the video script *Performance* by Andrew James Paterson. Canada. 1996. 3660

Text of *The Green Belt* by Charles Johnson. USA. 1982. Lang.: Eng. 3661

Text of *Exposing We* by Elizabeth Block. USA. 1996. Lang.: Eng. 3787

Text of *Alice* by Paul Schmidt, Tom Waits, and Kathleen Brennan. Germany: Hamburg. 1996. Lang.: Eng. 3845

Playwrights Horizons (New York, NY)
Performance/production
Collection of newspaper reviews by New York theatre critics. USA: New York, NY. 1996. Lang.: Eng. 2556

Collection of newspaper reviews by New York theatre critics. USA: New York, NY. 1996. Lang.: Eng. 2569

Collection of newspaper reviews by New York theatre critics. USA: New York, NY. 1996. Lang.: Eng. 2575

Plays/librettos/scripts
Steve Tesich's *Arts and Leisure*. USA: New York, NY. 1996. Lang.: Eng. 3437

Playwrights' Workshop (Montreal, PQ)
Institutions
Profile of Playwrights' Workshop. Canada: Montreal, PQ. 1996. Lang.: Eng. 1776

Playwriting
Institutions
Interview with personnel of the Centre des Auteurs Dramatiques. Canada: Montreal, PQ. 1965-1991. Lang.: Fre. 1762

Theatre New Brunswick's development of new and regional plays. Canada: Fredericton, NB. 1996. Lang.: Eng. 1771

Profile of Playwrights' Workshop. Canada: Montreal, PQ. 1996. Lang.: Eng. 1776

Theatre companies devoted to new plays: BoarsHead and Purple Rose. USA: Chelsea, MI. 1966-1996. Lang.: Eng. 1869

Plays/librettos/scripts
Playwright François Archambault discusses his craft. Canada: Montreal, PQ. 1992-1996. Lang.: Fre. 2741

Playwright Anne-Marie Cadieux discusses her craft. Canada: Montreal, PQ. 1992-1996. Lang.: Fre. 2758

Playwright Normand Canac-Marquis on his work. Canada: Montreal, PQ. 1988-1991. Lang.: Fre. 2764

Playwright Jean-François Caron on his work. Canada: Montreal, PQ. 1986-1991. Lang.: Fre. 2765

Playwright Dominic Champagne on his work. Canada: Montreal, PQ. 1988-1991. Lang.: Fre. 2766

Playwright Isabelle Doré on her career. Canada: Montreal, PQ. 1962-1996. Lang.: Fre. 2772

Playwright Carole Fréchette on her work. Canada: Montreal, PQ. 1983-1991. Lang.: Fre. 2778

Playwright Carole Fréchette discusses her craft. Canada: Montreal, PQ. 1989-1996. Lang.: Fre. 2779

Robert Gurik on his first play *Le Sang du poète (The Blood of the Poet)*. Canada: Montreal, PQ. 1963. Lang.: Fre. 2789

Playwright Jérôme Labbé discusses his craft. Canada: Montreal, PQ. 1987-1996. Lang.: Fre. 2796

Playwrights imagine writing the last line of their last play. Canada. 1996. Lang.: Fre. 2798

Playwright Alexis Martin on his work. Canada: Montreal, PQ. 1992-1996. Lang.: Fre. 2810

Playwright Jean-Frédéric Messier on his work. Canada: Montreal, PQ. 1987-1991. Lang.: Fre. 2812

Poissant, Claude — cont'd

Claude Poissant's production of *Les Voyageurs* by Madeleine Laïc at Festival internationale des francophonies. France: Limoges. 1988. Lang.: Fre. 2996

Pokój do wynajęcia (Room to Let, A)
Plays/librettos/scripts
Suggested texts for children's theatre. Poland. 1996. Lang.: Eng, Fre. 3169

Pokrovskij, Boris Aleksandrovič
Performance/production
Boris Pokrovskij's production of the opera *Dvorjanskoje Gnezdo* by V. Rebikov, based on work of Turgenjev. Russia. 1990-1996. Lang.: Rus. 4195

Poliakoff, Stephen
Performance/production
Collection of newspaper reviews by London theatre critics. UK-England: London. 1996. Lang.: Eng. 2353

Collection of newspaper reviews by London theatre critics. UK-England: London. 1996. Lang.: Eng. 2379

Polic, Radko
Relation to other fields
Interview with actor Radko Polic on the Slovenian political situation. Slovenia. 1995. Lang.: Eng. 1231

Political theatre
Audience
The chief prosecutor of the Nuremberg trial reactions to *Nuremberg: The War Crimes Trial* by Richard Norton-Taylor. UK-England: London. 1996. Lang.: Eng. 1635

Institutions
Grupo Teatro Escambray's communication with its audience. Cuba: La Macagua. 1968-1996. Lang.: Eng. 388

History of Grupo Teatro Escambray. Cuba: La Macagua. 1959-1996. Lang.: Eng. 389

History of Divadlo Husa na Provázku. Czechoslovakia. 1968-1995. Lang.: Eng. 395

The history of Squat Theatre. Hungary: Budapest. USA: New York, NY. 1969-1981. Lang.: Eng. 485

Report on the Grahamstown Festival. South Africa, Republic of: Grahamstown. 1996. Lang.: Eng. 532

History of Teatro de la Esperanza. USA: Santa Barbara, CA. 1965-1994. Lang.: Eng. 576

Forced Entertainment's own account of its first decade of performance. UK-England: Sheffield. 1984-1994. Lang.: Eng. 3655

Performance/production
Interview with Mou Sen, artistic director, and Wu Wenguang, actor, of Xi Ju Che Jian (Garage Theatre). China, People's Republic of. 1996. Lang.: Eng. 759

Contemporary Philippine theatre and the formation of cultural identity. Philippines: Manila. 1565-1996. Lang.: Eng. 889

Thomas Riccio's experience of street theatre in Natal. South Africa, Republic of: Durban. 1993-1996. Lang.: Eng. 940

AIDS and performance work. UK-England. 1990-1995. Lang.: Eng. 979

Belgrade's political theatre activities. Yugoslavia: Belgrade. 1978-1995. Lang.: Eng. 1079

Defense of Bill T. Jones's dance piece *Still/Here*. USA. 1996. Lang.: Eng. 1593

The use of Müller's *Der Auftrag (The Mission)* in *The Aboriginal Protesters* by Mudrooroo. Australia: Sydney. 1996. Lang.: Ger. 1898

Interview with director/playwright Ariane Mnouchkine. France. 1995. Lang.: Eng. 2035

Political theatre of Hans-Werner Kroesinger. Germany. 1996. Lang.: Ger. 2085

Productions of plays by Badal Sircar. UK-England: Birmingham. 1979-1992. Lang.: Eng. 2500

Robert Lepage's *The Seven Streams of the River Ota* at BAM. USA: New York, NY. 1996. Lang.: Eng. 2616

Angels in America and censorship at Catholic University. USA: Washington, DC. 1996. Lang.: Eng. 2661

Interview with solo performer Anna Deavere Smith. USA: Washington, DC. 1996. Lang.: Eng. 2662

Productions of Tretjakov's *Choču Rebenka (I Want a Baby)*. USSR: Moscow. UK-England: Birmingham. Germany: Berlin. 1927-1993.Lang.: Eng. 2694

Review of *Simuka Zimbabwe! (Zimbabwe Arise!)* by Zambuko/Izibuko. Zimbabwe: Harare. 1994-1996. Lang.: Afr. 2701

Political street entertainments as theatre. England: London. 1677. Lang.: Eng. 3776

Discussion surrounding a performance of *Murx* by Christoph Marthaler. Germany: Berlin. UK-England: London. 1995. Lang.: Eng. 3917

The rock musical *Sarajevo: Behind God's Back* at Group Theatre. USA: Seattle, WA. 1991-1996. Lang.: Eng. 3932

Plays/librettos/scripts
Evaluation of workers' drama in historical context. USA. 1929-1995. Lang.: Eng. 1112

The workers' theatre play *Eight Men Speak*. Canada: Toronto, ON. 1933. Lang.: Eng. 2776

Mou Sen and the political theatre of Xi Ju Che Jian. China, People's Republic of: Beijing. 1993-1996. Lang.: Eng. 2856

Teatro Hubert de Blanck's *Vagos Rumores (Vague Rumors)*. Cuba: Havana. USA: New York, NY. 1993-1996. Lang.: Eng. 2864

Obituary of playwright Heiner Müller. Germany. 1996. Lang.: Eng. 3014

Analysis of *Der Findling (The Foundling)* by Heiner Müller. Germany. 1929-1995. Lang.: Eng. 3031

Nationalism and the female figure in plays of Yeats. Ireland. 1903-1910. Lang.: Eng. 3083

Analysis of Israeli Holocaust drama. Israel. 1950-1984. Lang.: Eng. 3099

Athol Fugard and the role of revolutionary theatre after the revolution. South Africa, Republic of. 1948-1994. Lang.: Eng. 3220

Politics in the plays of Alan Bennett. UK-England. 1968-1996. Lang.: Eng. 3311

Plays about politician Roy Cohn. USA. 1986-1994. Lang.: Eng. 3339

Russell Lee's *Nixon's Nixon*. USA: New York, NY. 1994-1996. Lang.: Eng. 3348

Propaganda plays about the steel and textile industries. USA. 1930-1940. Lang.: Eng. 3363

Charles Smith's play about Marcus Garvey, *Black Star Line*. USA: Chicago, IL. 1996. Lang.: Eng. 3392

Shakespeare and the language of perception. USA. 1996. Lang.: Eng. 3398

Political theatre of Karen Malpede and Slobodan Snajder. USA. Croatia. 1991-1996. Lang.: Eng. 3403

Influences on Tony Kushner's *Angels in America*. USA. 1940-1996. Lang.: Eng. 3407

Barbara Lebow's community play *Cobb County Stories*. USA: Atlanta, GA. 1996. Lang.: Eng. 3417

Analysis of David Mamet's *Oleanna*. USA. 1990-1996. Lang.: Eng. 3434

Jon Klein's *Octopus* directed by Ed Herendeen. USA. 1996. Lang.: Eng. 3446

Ifa Bayeza's *Homer G. and the Rhapsodies in the Fall of Detroit*. USA: San Francisco, CA. 1996. Lang.: Eng. 3464

Relation to other fields
Interview with Patricia Ariza on theatre work with the poor and dispossessed. Colombia: Bogotá. 1975-1995. Lang.: Eng. 1165

Description and analysis of *Arbeit macht frei* by Akko Theatre Center. Germany. Israel. 1991-1995. Lang.: Eng. 1191

Amateur political theatre of the National Socialist period. Germany. 1900-1945. Lang.: Ger. 1194

Theatre in Romania after Ceauşescu. Romania. 1965-1995. Lang.: Eng. 1223

Scottish political theatre. UK-Scotland. 1979-1990. Lang.: Eng. 1250

Theatrical productions in the vicinity of the Republican National Convention. USA: San Diego, CA. 1996. Lang.: Eng. 1259

Contemporary dance as a democratic counter-movement to classical ballet. Europe. 1995. Lang.: Eng. 1597

Creating dances of political resistance. UK-England. 1995. Lang.: Eng. 1599

Drama's role in political liberation after the external oppressor has been removed. South Africa, Republic of. UK-Ireland: Derry.UK-England: Manchester. 1980-1996. Lang.: Eng. 3507

The cabaret of the Theresienstadt concentration camp. Czechoslovakia: Terezin. 1944. Lang.: Eng. 3740

The risks inherent in political performance art: the example of Hugo Sánchez. Mexico. 1996. Lang.: Eng. 3817

Performance artists and writers comment on political concerns in their work. UK-England: London. 1995. Lang.: Eng. 3818

Political implications of Christoph Marthaler's *Murx*, directed by Heiner Goebbels. Germany: Berlin. UK-England: London. 1992-1995. Lang.: Eng. 4001

Politics — cont'd

SUBJECT INDEX

Politics — cont'd

Comparison of writings by Eugene O'Neill and John Reed. USA: New York, NY. 1913-1922. Lang.: Eng. 3327

Analysis of David Mamet's *Oleanna*. USA. 1992. Lang.: Eng. 3332

Plays about politician Roy Cohn. USA. 1986-1994. Lang.: Eng. 3339

Insurrection: Holding History, written and directed by Robert O'Hara at the Public Theatre. USA: New York, NY. 1831-1996. Lang.: Eng. 3351

Political and military context of O'Neill's *The Emperor Jones*. USA. Haiti. 1898-1920. Lang.: Eng. 3386

Comparison of historical dramas by Robert Bolt and Arthur Miller. USA. UK-England. 1953-1966. Lang.: Eng. 3413

Radio plays of the Writers' War Board. USA. 1942-1944. Lang.: Eng. 3582

Critique of Steven Spielberg's film adaptation of *The Color Purple* by Alice Walker. USA. 1982-1986. Lang.: Eng. 3649

Relation to other fields

Asian stereotypes on the Australian stage. Australia. 1850-1993. Lang.: Eng. 1131

Theatre and the normalization of the New South Wales penal colony. Australia. 1789-1830. Lang.: Eng. 1133

Social and political context of contemporary Australian theatre. Australia: Sydney. 1995. Lang.: Eng. 1134

Prague and German *Nationaltheater*. Bohemia: Prague. 1783-1938. Lang.: Ger. 1135

Theatre's lack of influence as a source of strength and independence. Canada. 1989. Lang.: Fre. 1143

Report on international conference on government cultural policy. Canada: Montreal, PQ. 1991. Lang.: Fre. 1144

Tension between the arts and political and religious power. Canada. 1970-1989. Lang.: Fre. 1149

National and regional identities in Canadian theatre companies. Canada. 1860-1994. Lang.: Eng. 1157

Theatre, aesthetics, and resistance in the southern part of South America. Chile. Argentina. Uruguay. 1970-1996. Lang.: Ger. 1163

American musicals and plays in China. China, People's Republic of. 1984-1996. Lang.: Eng. 1164

Interview with Patricia Ariza on theatre work with the poor and dispossessed. Colombia: Bogotá. 1975-1995. Lang.: Eng. 1165

Václav Havel's acceptance of an honorary degree from the Academy of Performing Arts. Czech Republic: Prague. 1996. Lang.: Eng, Fre. 1166

Social and political conditions in Czech theatre. Czechoslovakia. 1989-1992. Lang.: Fre. 1167

Review of art installation about the fall of the Soviet empire. Denmark: Copenhagen. 1996. Lang.: Eng. 1168

Intellectual property rights in the 'postmodern' world. Europe. North America. 1996. Lang.: Eng. 1174

Reception of alien cultures in Western theatre. Europe. 1600-1996. Lang.: Ger. 1176

Report on first European Theatre Forum. France: St. Etienne. 1996. Lang.: Ger. 1178

Interview with Frank Baumbauer, director of Deutsches Schauspielhaus. Germany: Hamburg. 1996. Lang.: Ger. 1183

Remarks about German cultural policy by the president of the republic. Germany. 1996. Lang.: Ger. 1184

Life and theatre in Chemnitz. Germany: Chemnitz. 1996. Lang.: Ger. 1185

Ideological uses of theatre during the National Socialist period. Germany. 1933-1945. Lang.: Ger. 1186

Reaction to the closing of part of the Bremen theatre. Germany: Bremen. 1995. Lang.: Ger. 1187

The crisis of independent theatre. Germany: Berlin. 1996. Lang.: Ger. 1188

The influence of social movements and changes on German theatre. Germany. 1968-1989. Lang.: Ger. 1189

Interview with Jürgen Kruse, director of Schauspielhaus Bochum. Germany: Bochum. 1996. Lang.: Ger. 1190

Berlin theatre in the current German intellectual debate. Germany: Berlin. 1991-1996. Lang.: Eng. 1192

Amateur political theatre of the National Socialist period. Germany. 1900-1945. Lang.: Ger. 1194

East German actresses' reactions to social changes after the fall of the Berlin wall. Germany, East: Berlin, East. 1990-1991. Lang.: Ger. 1195

Hungarian theatre life in the 1950s. Hungary. 1910-1956. Lang.: Hun. 1197

Archival documents on Hungarian theatre in Romania. Hungary. Romania. 1918-1940. Lang.: Hun. 1198

Archival documents on Hungarian theatre. Hungary. 1950-1956. Lang.: Hun. 1199

Government involvement in Israeli arts. Israel. 1920-1996. Lang.: Eng. 1202

Jewish/Arab encounters in drama projects. Israel. 1977-1995. Lang.: Eng. 1203

The fascist aesthetic in speeches and manifestos. Italy. 1925-1943. Lang.: Eng. 1205

Interview with director and author Cesare Lievi. Italy. 1996. Lang.: Ger. 1206

The dramatization of Fascist politics. Italy. 1925-1945. Lang.: Eng. 1207

Theatricality in Latin America and its historical impact. Latin America. 1996. Lang.: Eng. 1209

New developments in Theatre for Development. Lesotho. 1970-1994. Lang.: Eng. 1210

Religious spectacle as political propaganda in Chiapas. Mexico. 1904-1994. Lang.: Eng. 1211

Essays on multiculturalism by members of the Scarabes Foundation. Netherlands. 1988-1996. Lang.: Dut. 1213

Polish theatre in its social and political context. Poland. 1939-1989. Lang.: Eng. 1217

Post-communist repertory of Polish theatre companies. Poland. 1989-1996. Lang.: Pol. 1218

Theatre artists of the Communist period. Poland. 1924. Lang.: Pol. 1219

Current financial difficulties of Polish theatres. Poland. 1994. Lang.: Eng. 1221

Theatre in Romania after Ceauşescu. Romania. 1965-1995. Lang.: Eng. 1223

Russian cultural policy and theatre economy. Russia. 1996. Lang.: Ger. 1226

Interview with actor Radko Polic on the Slovenian political situation. Slovenia. 1995. Lang.: Eng. 1231

Spanish theatre and photography. Spain. 1956-1996. Lang.: Eng. 1232

The relevance of Theatre for Development to Britain. UK. 1976-1995. Lang.: Eng. 1237

Theatre of the organized working class. UK-England. 1830-1930. Lang.: Eng. 1242

Performance and theatre in the politics of postindustrial societies. UK-Scotland: Glasgow. USA: New York, NY. 1994-1995. Lang.: Eng. 1249

Scottish political theatre. UK-Scotland. 1979-1990. Lang.: Eng. 1250

Report on 1995 event of the Magdalena Project. UK-Wales: Cardiff. 1995. Lang.: Eng. 1251

Theatre riots as an expression of class conflict. USA. 1754-1849. Lang.: Eng. 1253

Theatrical productions in the vicinity of the Republican National Convention. USA: San Diego, CA. 1996. Lang.: Eng. 1259

The situation of Black theatre groups. USA. 1996. Lang.: Eng. 1263

Presidential candidate Bob Dole's attacks on the arts and entertainment industry. USA: Washington, DC. 1996. Lang.: Eng. 1267

American Arts Alliance's salute to retiring members of Congress. USA: Washington, DC. 1996. Lang.: Eng. 1268

Performance of the Holocaust in American museums. USA: Washington, DC, Los Angeles, CA. 1994-1995. Lang.: Eng. 1271

Materials on the inquiry on Witold Wandurski. USSR. 1933. Lang.: Pol. 1285

Artists of the former Yugoslavia discuss the impact of the political situation on their art. Yugoslavia. 1996. Lang.: Ger. 1287

Actress Mira Furlan on refusing to take sides in ethnic conflict. Yugoslavia. 1991. Lang.: Eng. 1288

Nationalism as paranoia, even in the arts. Yugoslavia. 1978. Lang.: Eng. 1289

Interview with theatre scholar who gave up her position at the University of Belgrade. Yugoslavia: Belgrade. 1992-1995. Lang.: Eng. 1290

Theatre and the disintegration of Yugoslavia. Yugoslavia. 1996. Lang.: Eng. 1291

International Bibliography of Theatre: 1996   489

Politics — cont'd

The role of the Ministry of Cultural Affairs in Quebec dance. Canada. 1991. Lang.: Fre. 1453

Conference on dance and politics. Germany: Cologne. 1996. Lang.: Ger. 1454

Interview with Jo Lechay and Eugene Lion, creators of *Affamée (Starving)*. Canada: Montreal, PQ. 1990. Lang.: Fre. 1595

Contemporary dance as a democratic counter-movement to classical ballet. Europe. 1995. Lang.: Eng. 1597

Multiculturalism and contemporary British dance. UK-England. 1995. Lang.: Eng. 1598

Creating dances of political resistance. UK-England. 1995. Lang.: Eng. 1599

The Socialist agenda and modern dance. USA. 1931-1938. Lang.: Eng. 1600

German-Australian theatrical exchange. Australia. Germany. 1945-1995. Lang.: Eng. 3478

Shakespeare and the dominant ideology in Bulgarian education. Bulgaria. 1950-1989. Lang.: Eng. 3479

Political influences on playwrights David Fennario and George Ryga. Canada. 1932-1996. Lang.: Eng. 3482

Theatre and law. Europe. 500 B.C.-1989 A.D. Lang.: Fre. 3494

Brigitte Jaques' *Elvire Jouvet 40*, and the continuing reality of political detention and torture. France: Paris. Lebanon. 1940-1996. Lang.: Fre. 3496

The Arab on the Israeli stage. Israel. 1912-1990. Lang.: Eng. 3500

The political context of Nekrošius' production of Čechov's *Three Sisters*. Lithuania. 1996. Lang.: Ger. 3503

Political playwright Ferdynand Goetel. Poland. 1890-1989. Lang.: Pol. 3505

Playwright Vladimir Sorokin in the context of socialist society. Russia: Moscow. Germany: Berlin. 1995. Lang.: Ger. 3506

Drama's role in political liberation after the external oppressor has been removed. South Africa, Republic of. UK-Ireland: Derry.UK-England: Manchester. 1980-1996. Lang.: Eng. 3507

The political mission of South African English studies, with emphasis on Shakespeare. South Africa, Republic of. 1800-1995. Lang.: Eng. 3508

Unpublished political essays by George Bernard Shaw. UK-England. 1885-1929. Lang.: Eng. 3510

Analysis of Shaw's essay on socialism and the family. UK-England. 1886. Lang.: Eng. 3511

Shaw's views on war and peace in his unpublished manuscripts. UK-England. 1899-1950. Lang.: Eng. 3515

Teaching plays of Shakespeare and Cary in a course on domestic England in the early modern period. USA. 1995. Lang.: Eng. 3519

Interview with playwright Slobodan Šnajder about intellectuals and the war in the former Yugoslavia. Yugoslavia. 1996. Lang.:Ger. 3523

Political and ethical considerations regarding South African television. South Africa, Republic of. 1996. Lang.: Eng. 3686

South African media and film policy. South Africa, Republic of. 1980-1996. Lang.: Eng. 3687

The cabaret of the Theresienstadt concentration camp. Czechoslovakia: Terezin. 1944. Lang.: Eng. 3740

Werner Flinck's career in political cabaret. Germany. 1929-1945. Lang.: Eng. 3741

The impersonation of Black women by white male performers. USA. 1820-1890. Lang.: Eng. 3742

History and profile of Santa Cruz's carnival. Canary Islands: Santa Cruz de Tenerife. 1949-1996. Lang.: Eng. 3744

The history and social context of stickfighting in Trinidadian carnival. Trinidad. 1790-1996. Lang.: Ger. 3745

The *commedia dell'arte* in the language of the Genoese ruling class. Italy: Genoa. 1528-1586. Lang.: Ita. 3769

Analysis of excerpts from a woodland ceremony in the *Ligger Book*. England. 1567-1621. Lang.: Eng. 3781

Accounts of the quasi-theatrical event known as Gladman's Insurrection. England: Norwich. 1443. Lang.: Eng. 3782

The risks inherent in political performance art: the example of Hugo Sánchez. Mexico. 1996. Lang.: Eng. 3817

Performance artists and writers comment on political concerns in their work. UK-England: London. 1995. Lang.: Eng. 3818

Responses of theatre and performance to social and political conditions. USA. Yugoslavia. 1968-1995. Lang.: Eng. 3821

Performance artist Blanche Davidian's infiltration of right-wing extremist groups. USA. 1995-1996. Lang.: Eng. 3823

Interview with performance artist Marina Abramovic. Yugoslavia. 1974-1996. Lang.: Eng. 3824

Politics, society, and the street-seller character in the music-hall performances. UK-England: London. 1914-1970. Lang.: Eng. 3842

Political implications of Christoph Marthaler's *Murx*, directed by Heiner Goebbels. Germany: Berlin. UK-England: London. 1992-1995. Lang.: Eng. 4001

Claudio Monteverdi and Italian fascism. Italy. 1901-1947. Lang.: Eng. 4354

Colonial discourse in Javanese puppetry. Indonesia. 1935-1975. Lang.: Eng. 4445

Research/historiography

Nationalism in Uruguayan theatre historiography. Uruguay. 1910-1990. Lang.: Spa. 1307

Theory/criticism

Theory of studies of theatricality, including cultural and sociopolitical communication. 1996. Lang.: Ger. 1311

Aesthetic and ideological characteristics of experimental theatre. Canada. 1968-1989. Lang.: Fre. 1320

The evolution of Les Cahiers de Théâtre *Jeu*. Canada: Montreal, PQ. 1976-1989. Lang.: Fre. 1326

War diary of critic and theatre historian Silvio D'Amico. Italy. 1916-1917. Lang.: Ita. 1351

Falangist theatre aesthetics. Spain. 1935-1945. Lang.: Eng. 1363

Theatre criticism in suffrage newspapers. UK-England. 1912-1914. Lang.: Eng. 1370

Charles Ludlam's Ridiculous Theatrical Company, and gay and lesbian politics. USA: New York, NY. 1967-1987. Lang.: Eng. 1376

Interview with dance scholar Iván Vitányi. Hungary. 1943-1995. Lang.: Hun. 1549

Art, politics, and the African playwright. South Africa, Republic of. 1933. Lang.: Eng. 3551

Practice and performativity in Marxism. USA. 1996. Lang.: Eng. 3565

Polixena y la cocinerita (Polyxena and the Scullery Maid)
Plays/librettos/scripts

Analysis of plays by Alfonsina Storni. Argentina. 1892-1938. Lang.: Spa. 2717

Polka Theatre (London)
Performance/production

Collection of newspaper reviews by London theatre critics. UK-England: London. 1996. Lang.: Eng. 2354

Pollock, Sharon
Plays/librettos/scripts

Analysis of *Walsh* and *The Komagata Maru Incident* by Sharon Pollock. Canada. 1973-1976. Lang.: Eng. 2790

Overview of Anglophone Canadian playwriting. Canada. 1970-1990. Lang.: Fre. 2791

Polonez (Polonaise)
Performance/production

Galina Sinel'nikova's *Polonez* at Belorussian Opera and Ballet Theatre. Belorus: Minsk. 1995. Lang.: Rus. 1495

Polonez Oginskogo (Oginskij Polonaise, The)
Performance/production

Collection of newspaper reviews by London theatre critics. UK-England: London. 1996. Lang.: Eng. 2325

Polunin, Slava
Performance/production

Collection of newspaper reviews by London theatre critics. UK-England: London. 1996. Lang.: Eng. 2320

Polygraphe (Polygraph)
Theory/criticism

Critical reception of productions by Robert Lepage at the Festival d'Automne. France: Paris. 1992. Lang.: Fre. 1345

Pombo, Pilar
Plays/librettos/scripts

Spanish women's theatre. Spain. 1983-1990. Lang.: Spa. 3237

Analysis of plays by Pilar Pombo. Spain. 1987. Lang.: Eng. 3270

Pomo Afro Homos (San Francisco, CA)
Theory/criticism

Identity and representation in *Dark Fruit* by Pomo Afro Homos. USA: San Francisco, CA. 1990-1996. Lang.: Eng. 1387

Provost, Serge — cont'd

Lorraine Pintal's direction of *Le Vampire et la Nymphomane* by Claude Gauvreau and Serge Provost. Canada: Montreal, PQ. 1996. Lang.: Fre.
4099

Prus, Maciej
Performance/production
Productions of plays by Beckett and Ionesco. Poland: Warsaw. 1995. Lang.: Eng, Fre.
2171

Pryce, Jonathan
Performance/production
Review of the film version of the musical *Evita*. USA. 1979-1996. Lang.: Eng.
3636

Psaila, Anthony
Performance/production
Collection of newspaper reviews by London theatre critics. UK-England: London. 1996. Lang.: Eng.
2323

Collection of newspaper reviews by London theatre critics. UK-England: London. 1996. Lang.: Eng.
2367

Psychology
Audience
The influence of space on audience perception and appreciation. Netherlands. 1650-1995. Lang.: Dut.
140
Institutions
Conference of theatre artists and scientists. France: Saintes. 1989. Lang.: Fre.
412
Performance/production
Psychoanalysis and theatricality. Europe. 1990-1995. Lang.: Eng. 2003

Social significance of solo performances by Anna Cora Mowatt. USA. 1841-1881. Lang.: Eng.
2683

Influence of Hollywood gangster films on South African cinema. USA: Hollywood, CA. South Africa, Republic of. 1930-1996. Lang.: Eng. 3637
Plays/librettos/scripts
Playwright, actor, director, and psychiatrist Eduardo Pavlovsky. Argentina. 1957-1994. Lang.: Ger.
2719

The psychology and sociology of gay theatre. Canada. 1960-1990. Lang.: Fre.
2759

Sex and innuendo in Shakespeare's *Othello*. England. 1600. Lang.: Eng.
2943

Humoral psychology in Shakespeare's Henriad. England. 1590-1613. Lang.: Eng.
2947

Playwrights and madness. Europe. 1996. Lang.: Eng. 2970

Feminism in *Portrait de Dora (Portrait of Dora)* by Hélène Cixous. France. 1900-1995. Lang.: Eng.
2980

Psychoanalytic and philosophical analysis of translation. France. Germany. 1990. Lang.: Fre.
3002

Dual personalities in plays of Brian Friel. Ireland. UK-Ireland. 1972-1988. Lang.: Eng.
3084

Self-psychoanalysis in Eugene O'Neill's *Recklessness*. USA. 1913. Lang.: Eng.
3336

Analysis of *spell #7* by Ntozake Shange. USA. 1979-1995. Lang.: Eng.
3352

Recollections of meetings with playwright Athol Fugard. USA: New York, NY. 1980-1989. Lang.: Eng.
3457
Relation to other fields
Personalities and motivations of adolescents active in theatre. Canada. 1989-1990. Lang.: Fre.
1137

The role of memory in perceptions of theatre. Canada. 1989. Lang.: Fre.
1159

Theatre, asylums, and therapy. Germany. France. 1800-1966. Lang.: Ger.
1182

Actress Georgina Weldon's use of theatrical techniques to avoid incarceration for lunacy. UK-England: London. 1875-1885. Lang.: Eng.
1243

Drama as an agent for changing behavior. UK-England. 1978-1995. Lang.: Eng.
1248

Blackface performances in the early nineteenth century. USA. 1800-1844. Lang.: Eng.
1254

Bondage in Black writing, including plays of Soyinka. USA. Africa. 1996. Lang.: Eng.
1255

Dancer and dance therapist Karin Thulin. Sweden: Stockholm. 1967. Lang.: Swe.
1457

Erna Grönlund, professor of dance therapy. Sweden: Stockholm. 1942. Lang.: Swe.
1458

Account of a course in dance therapy. UK-England: Chichester. 1996. Lang.: Eng.
1460

Account of a dance therapy workshop. USA: San Francisco, CA. 1996. Lang.: Ger.
1461

Personality and selfhood in the writings of the ancient Greeks. Ancient Greece. 525-405 B.C. Lang.: Eng.
3477

Impulse in Quebec drama. Canada. 1900-1989. Lang.: Fre. 3485

Masculine anxiety in early modern writings. England. 1580-1620. Lang.: Eng.
3488

The Dionysian cult as reflected in *Bákchai (The Bacchae)* of Euripides. Greece. 407 B.C. Lang.: Swe.
3499

Photographs by Hugo Glendinning of Forced Entertainment. UK-England: Sheffield. 1995-1996. Lang.: Eng.
3819

Sleep and dreams in performances of Paul Gilchrist. UK-England. 1959-1996. Lang.: Eng.
3820

Psychodrama in Paisiello's *Nina*. France: Paris. 1750-1794. Lang.: Eng.
4352

Psychoanalytical analysis of Wagnerian opera. Germany. 1840-1882. Lang.: Slo.
4353

Use of puppetry in psychotherapy. France: Paris, Charleville-Mézières. 1988. Lang.: Fre.
4428
Theory/criticism
Public punishment and execution as a theatrical event. Colonial America: New York. 1741. Lang.: Eng.
1334

Theoretic analysis of acting. Europe. 1800-1990. Lang.: Hun. 1344

Hungarian translation of Freud's essay on psychopathology on stage. Germany. 1905-1906. Lang.: Hun.
1348

Sentimentality in theatre. Canada. 1891-1989. Lang.: Fre. 3536

An approach to feminist theatre based on French philosophy and film criticism. Europe. 1995. Lang.: Eng.
3538
Training
Theatre training for self-discovery and healing. Canada: Vancouver, BC. 1996. Lang.: Eng.
1395

The training of dance therapists. Sweden: Stockholm. Finland: Helsinki. 1991. Lang.: Swe.
1471

Jacques Copeau, Suzanne Bing, and the founding of L'École du Vieux-Colombier. USA: New York, NY. France: Paris. 1918-1996. Lang.: Eng.
3690

Pterodactyls
Plays/librettos/scripts
The plays of Nicky Silver and the first German production of his *Pterodactyls*. USA. Germany: Munich. 1996. Lang.: Ger.
3372

Ptuškina, Nadežda
Plays/librettos/scripts
Playwright Nadežda Ptuškina. Russia: Moscow. 1980-1996. Lang.: Rus.
3198

Public Eye, The
Performance/production
Collection of newspaper reviews by London theatre critics. UK-England: London. 1996. Lang.: Eng.
2398

Public relations
Drama Desk luncheon meeting on the future of Broadway theatre. USA: New York, NY. 1996. Lang.: Eng.
3
Administration
Account of a theatre marketing project. Netherlands. 1990-1995. Lang.: Dut.
37

Cracow theatre programs. Poland: Cracow. 1871-1939. Lang.: Pol. 39

Cracow theatre posters. Poland: Cracow. 1781-1893. Lang.: Pol. 41

Interview with theatre merchandiser George Fenmore. USA: New York, NY. 1927-1996. Lang.: Eng.
56

The 'Golden Jubilee of Light' and the development of public relations. USA: Dearborn, MI. 1929. Lang.: Eng.
61

Graphic design and poster artwork for theatre promotion. USA. 1996. Lang.: Eng.
67

Press agent Merle Debuskey. USA: New York, NY. 1996. Lang.: Eng.
119

Translator Linda Gaboriau on promoting Quebec drama. Canada: Montreal, PQ, Toronto, ON. 1983-1988. Lang.: Fre.
1613

Survey of poster design for Broadway musicals. USA: New York, NY. 1892-1996. Lang.: Eng.
3881

Marketing of operatic offerings. Europe. North America. 1996. Lang.: Eng.
4006

Crisis on the German opera scene. Germany. 1993-1996. Lang.: Dan.
4009

History of advertising for puppet theatre. Germany. 1800-1996. Lang.: Ger.
4366

Purcell Room (London) — cont'd

Collection of newspaper reviews by London theatre critics. UK-England: London. 1996. Lang.: Eng. 2340

Collection of newspaper reviews by London theatre critics. UK-England: London. 1996. Lang.: Eng. 2390

Collection of newspaper reviews by London theatre critics. UK-England: London. 1996. Lang.: Eng. 2436

Collection of newspaper reviews by London theatre critics. UK-England: London. 1996. Lang.: Eng. 2499

Purcell, Alice
Performance/production
Collection of newspaper reviews by London theatre critics. UK-England: London. 1996. Lang.: Eng. 2340

Purcell, Henry
Performance/production
Assessment of recordings of *Dido and Aeneas* by Henry Purcell. UK-England. 1996. Lang.: Eng. 4228

Purchese, Barry
Performance/production
Collection of newspaper reviews by London theatre critics. UK-England: London. 1996. Lang.: Eng. 2346

Purgatorio Ink (New York, NY)
Performance/production
Assurbanipal Babilla's *Othello and the Circumcised Turk*, Purgatorio Ink. USA: New York, NY. 1996. Lang.: Eng. 2690

Puritan, The
Plays/librettos/scripts
The influence of *Romeo and Juliet* on later English comedies. England. 1594-1607. Lang.: Eng. 2883

Purple Flower, The
Basic theatrical documents
International anthology of modern drama by women. 1880-1940. Lang.: Eng. 1637

Purple Rose Theatre Company (Chelsea, MI)
Institutions
Theatre companies devoted to new plays: BoarsHead and Purple Rose. USA: Chelsea, MI. 1966-1996. Lang.: Eng. 1869

Purs, Les (Innocents, The)
Plays/librettos/scripts
Reception of *Les Purs (The Innocents)* by Louis-Dominique Lavigne. Canada: Montreal, PQ. 1985-1986. Lang.: Fre. 2797

Pushkin Theatre (Leningrad)
SEE
Akademičéskij Teat'r Dramy im. A.S. Puškina.

Puškin, Aleksand'r I.
Training
Aleksand'r I. Puškin, classical ballet teacher. Russia: St. Petersburg. 1932-1970. Lang.: Rus. 1541

Puškin, Aleksand'r Sergejévič
Performance/production
Productions of the Stanislavskij Theatre. Russia: Moscow. 1995-1996. Lang.: Rus. 2242

Pëtr Fomenko's staging of *Pikovaja Dama (Queen of Spades)* by Puškin. Russia: Moscow. 1995. Lang.: Rus. 2248

Plays/librettos/scripts
Writer and dramatist Aleksand'r A. Šachovskij. Russia. 1777-1846. Lang.: Rus. 3202

Historical background of Mussorgskij's *Boris Godunov*. Russia. 1874. Lang.: Swe. 4337

Puzakov, Jurij
Performance/production
Ukrainian opera. Ukraine: Kiev. 1990-1996. Lang.: Rus. 4238

PWST im. L. Solskiego (Cracow)
Institutions
History of the Cracow Theatre School. Poland: Cracow. 1945-1995. Lang.: Pol. 510

Py, Olivier
Performance/production
Paris productions of the fall season. France: Paris. 1996. Lang.: Eng. 2032

Pyant, Paul
Design/technology
Lighting design for a touring production of *Carousel*. USA. 1996. Lang.: Eng. 3900

Pyeokwagulinun Namja (Man Painting on the Wall, The)
Design/technology
Projections and multimedia in Korean theatre productions. Korea: Seoul. 1996. Lang.: Kor. 1708

Pygmalion
Design/technology
Scene designer Cameron Porteous. Canada: Niagara-on-the-Lake, ON. 1980-1995. Lang.: Eng. 1707
Performance/production
Choreographic realizations of the story of Pygmalion. France. 1734-1847. Lang.: Eng. 1422

Q, William George
Performance/production
Collection of newspaper reviews by London theatre critics. UK-England: London. 1996. Lang.: Eng. 2382

Qu'ils crèvent les artistes
SEE
Niech sczezną artyści.

Quartett (Quartet)
Performance/production
Anne-Marie Cadieux's performance in Müller's *Quartett* at Espace GO. Canada: Montreal, PQ. 1996. Lang.: Fre. 1939
Plays/librettos/scripts
Disaster and death in Heiner Müller's *Quartett*, staged at Espace GO by Brigitte Haentjens. Canada: Montreal, PQ. Germany. 1980-1996. Lang.: Fre. 2785

Themes of Heiner Müller's *Quartett* presented at Espace GO. Canada: Montreal, PQ. Germany. 1980-1996. Lang.: Fre. 2845

Themes of *Quartett* by Heiner Müller. Germany. 1980-1996. Lang.: Fre. 3033

Quatre Morts de Marie, Les (Four Deaths of Marie, The)
Plays/librettos/scripts
Analysis of plays by Carole Fréchette. Canada: Montreal, PQ. 1983-1991. Lang.: Fre. 2757

Study of plays by Carole Fréchette. Canada: Montreal, PQ. 1995. Lang.: Fre. 2801

Queen Elizabeth Hall (London)
Performance/production
Collection of newspaper reviews by London theatre critics. UK-England: London. 1996. Lang.: Eng. 2340

Queen of Spades (opera)
SEE
Pique Dame.

Queen of Spades by Puškin
SEE
Pikovaja Dama.

Queen's Cavern Theatre (Orissa)
Performance spaces
Profile of the Queen's Cavern Theatre. India: Orissa. 1600-1996. Lang.: Eng. 647

Queen's Theatre (London)
Performance/production
Collection of newspaper reviews by London theatre critics. UK-England: London. 1996. Lang.: Eng. 2355

Collection of newspaper reviews by London theatre critics. UK-England: London. 1996. Lang.: Eng. 2400

Queler, Eve
Performance/production
The New York debut of Italian mezzo-soprano Sonia Ganassi. Italy: Parma. 1996. Lang.: Eng. 4180

Concert opera in New York. USA: New York, NY. 1952-1996. Lang.: Eng. 4250

Querida Mamãe (Dear Mommy)
Plays/librettos/scripts
Analysis of plays by Maria Adelaide Amaral. Brazil. 1985-1995. Lang.: Por. 2735

Questa sera si recita a soggetto (Tonight We Improvise)
Performance/production
Anecdote of Jack Robitaille's role in a production of Pirandello's *Questa sera si recita a soggetto (Tonight We Improvise)*. Canada: Quebec, PQ. 1994. Lang.: Fre. 1957

Quetes, Wolfgang
Administration
Wolfgang Quetes, artistic director-designate of Pfalztheater. Germany: Kaiserslautern. 1996. Lang.: Ger. 30

Qui est là? (Who Is There?)
Performance/production
Review of recent Paris productions. France: Paris. 1996. Lang.: Ger. 2033

Quick Eternity, A
Performance/production
Collection of newspaper reviews by London theatre critics. UK-England: London. 1996. Lang.: Eng. 2472

Religion — cont'd

Profile of community theatre Teatro La Fragua. Honduras: El Progreso. 1979-1996. Lang.: Eng. 3068

Influence of Synge's *The Playboy of the Western World* on work of Yeats. Ireland. 1907. Lang.: Eng. 3090

Judeo-Christian symbolism in Ibsen's *Vildanden (The Wild Duck)*. Norway. 1884. Lang.: Eng. 3157

God and man in Arthur Miller's *After the Fall*. USA. 1964. 3405

The influence of Buddhism on playwright Jean-Claude Van Itallie. USA. India. 1968-1983. Lang.: Eng. 3419

Guilt and responsibility in later plays of Arthur Miller. USA. 1964-1996. 3420

Graham Greene's screen adaptation of Shaw's *Saint Joan*. UK-England. 1957. Lang.: Eng. 3647

The Messianic hero in Wagner's *Ring*. Germany. 1996. Lang.: Eng. 4320

Relation to other fields
Tension between the arts and political and religious power. Canada. 1970-1989. Lang.: Fre. 1149

Intellectual property rights in the 'postmodern' world. Europe. North America. 1996. Lang.: Eng. 1174

Ritual in the theatre of Grotowski, Barba, and Brook. Europe. 1996. Lang.: Pol. 1175

The architecture of theatres and churches in northern Germany. Germany. 1700-1799. Lang.: Ger. 1193

Religious spectacle as political propaganda in Chiapas. Mexico. 1904-1994. Lang.: Eng. 1211

Ritual performance in the Charismatic religious movement. USA. 1994. Lang.: Eng. 1279

Theatricality of rituals devoted to María Lionza. Venezuela: Yaracuy. 1996. Lang.: Eng. 1286

The public performance of vows and pilgrimages. Italy: Ferrara. 1476-1487. Lang.: Ita. 3772

Christianity and body art. 1995-1996. Lang.: Dan. 3815

Religious theatre
Plays/librettos/scripts
Representational practice in works of Hildegard of Bingen. Germany: Bingen. 1120-1179. Lang.: Eng. 3874
Relation to other fields
The significance of the mermaid in the Cornish *Ordinalia*. England: Cornwall. 1400-1600. Lang.: Eng. 1171

Florentine art and drama. Italy: Florence. 1400-1600. Lang.: Eng. 1208

Remedios
Plays/librettos/scripts
Analysis of plays by Pilar Pombo. Spain. 1987. Lang.: Eng. 3270

Remote Asylum
Plays/librettos/scripts
Interview with playwright Mart Crowley. USA: New York, NY. 1996. Lang.: Eng. 3424

Remotigue, Fe
Performance/production
Women playwrights of the Pacific Rim. Australia. Asia. 1994. Lang.: Eng. 1899
Relation to other fields
Female identity as seen through culture. Philippines: Mindanao. India: New Delhi. 1986-1995. Lang.: Eng. 1216

Renaissance Theater (Berlin)
Institutions
Horst H. Filohn, director of Renaissance Theater. Germany: Berlin. 1995-1996. Lang.: Ger. 443

Renaissance theatre
SEE ALSO
Geographical-Chronological Index under Europe 1400-1600, France 1500-1700, Italy 1400-1600, Spain 1400-1600.
Performance/production
Renaissance actors Cherea and Barlacchia. Italy. 1500-1600. Lang.: Ita. 865

Cultural and theatrical history of English drama. England. 1500-1994. Lang.: Eng. 1992

Census of productions of Renaissance drama. UK-England. 1995. Lang.: Eng. 2531
Plays/librettos/scripts
Homosexuality in Renaissance drama. England. 1580-1620. Lang.: Eng. 2896

The written and printed word on the English Renaissance stage. England. 1450-1600. Lang.: Eng. 2919

Renán, Sergio
Administration
Sergio Renán of Teatro Colón. Argentina: Buenos Aires. 1989-1996. Lang.: Eng. 4003

Renard
Performance/production
Background information on Teatro Colón season. Argentina: Buenos Aires. 1996. Lang.: Eng. 4075

René, Norman
Performance/production
Collection of newspaper reviews by London theatre critics. UK-England: London. 1996. Lang.: Eng. 2491

Renée
Performance/production
Women playwrights of the Pacific Rim. Australia. Asia. 1994. Lang.: Eng. 1899

Renovation, theatre
Design/technology
USITT architectural awards. USA. 1994. Lang.: Eng. 285

Renovation of Metropolitan Opera lighting system. USA: New York, NY. 1996. Lang.: Eng. 4025
Institutions
Impact of architectural restructuring on the mission of the Royal Court Theatre. UK-England: London. 1996. Lang.: Eng. 1858

Work of Third Eye, Alpha and Omega, and Gilgamesh theatre companies. USA: New York, NY. 1996. Lang.: Eng. 1860
Performance spaces
Transformation of buildings into performance spaces in the Plateau neighborhood. Canada: Montreal, PQ. 1985-1996. Lang.: Fre. 624

The renovation and extension of the Theater Carré. Netherlands: Amsterdam. 1887-1995. Lang.: Dut. 651

Renovation and reconstruction of Broadway theatres. USA: New York, NY. 1920-1996. Lang.: Eng. 665

The renovation of Appalachian State University's Volberg Theatre. USA: Boone, NC. 1938-1994. Lang.: Eng. 667

Livent Realty's plan to renovate the Lyric and Apollo theatres. USA: New York, NY. 1996. Lang.: Eng. 673

Profile of the renovated New Victory Theatre. USA: New York, NY. 1996. Lang.: Eng. 674

The renovation and expansion of Actors' Theatre of Louisville. USA: Louisville, KY. 1964-1995. Lang.: Eng. 1892

The newly renovated Teatro de los Insurgentes. Mexico: Mexico City. 1996. Lang.: Eng. 3851

Renshaw, Christopher
Performance/production
Profiles of new actors on Broadway. USA: New York, NY. 1996. Lang.: Eng. 1012

Collection of newspaper reviews by New York theatre critics. USA: New York, NY, Washington, DC. 1996. Lang.: Eng. 2576

Rent
Design/technology
Blake Burba's lighting design for *Rent*, New York Theatre Workshop. USA: New York, NY. 1996. Lang.: Eng. 3895
Performance/production
Profiles of new actors on Broadway. USA: New York, NY. 1996. Lang.: Eng. 1012

Collection of newspaper reviews by New York theatre critics. USA: New York, NY, Houston, TX. 1996. Lang.: Eng. 2567

Collection of newspaper reviews by New York theatre critics. USA: New York, NY. 1996. Lang.: Eng. 2579

Off-Broadway musicals and their transfer to Broadway. USA: New York, NY. 1975-1996. Lang.: Eng. 3954

Jonathan Larson's Broadway musical *Rent*. USA: New York, NY. 1996. Lang.: Eng. 3958

Jonathan Larson's musical *Rent*. USA: New York, NY. 1996. Lang.: Eng. 3961

Renz, Frederick
Performance/production
Ensemble for Early Music's performance of the St. Martial *Sponsus* at The Cloisters. USA: New York, NY. 1996. Lang.: Eng. 1019

Répétition, La (Rehearsal, The) by Champagne
Plays/librettos/scripts
Analysis of plays by Dominic Champagne. Canada: Montreal, PQ. 1988-1991. Lang.: Fre. 2838

Dominic Champagne's *La Répétition (The Rehearsal)* and its relation to Beckett's *En attendant Godot (Waiting for Godot)*. Canada: Montreal, PQ. France. Ireland. 1953-1990. Lang.: Fre. 2843

Riverside Theatre (London) — cont'd

Collection of newspaper reviews by London theatre critics. UK-England: London. 1996. Lang.: Eng.   2392

Collection of newspaper reviews by London theatre critics. UK-England: London. 1996. Lang.: Eng.   2402

Collection of newspaper reviews by London theatre critics. UK-England: London. 1996. Lang.: Eng.   2421

Collection of newspaper reviews by London theatre critics. UK-England: London. 1996. Lang.: Eng.   2448

Collection of newspaper reviews by London theatre critics. UK-England: London. 1996. Lang.: Eng.   2455

Collection of newspaper reviews by London theatre critics. UK-England: London. 1996. Lang.: Eng.   2462

Collection of newspaper reviews by London theatre critics. UK-England: London. 1996. Lang.: Eng.   2471

Collection of newspaper reviews by London theatre critics. UK-England: London. 1996. Lang.: Eng.   2496

Rjumina, Ljudmila
Performance/production
National singer Ljudmila Rjumina. Russia: Moscow. 1996. Lang.: Rus.
                                                                   3864

Road Movie
Performance/production
Collection of newspaper reviews by London theatre critics. UK-England: London. 1996. Lang.: Eng.   2425

Road to Mecca, The
Performance/production
Director Anthony Akerman's diary of a production of *The Road to Mecca* by Athol Fugard. Mexico: Mexico City. 1995. Lang.: Eng.   2140

Collection of newspaper reviews by London theatre critics. UK-England: London. 1996. Lang.: Eng.   2329
Plays/librettos/scripts
Recollections of meetings with playwright Athol Fugard. USA: New York, NY. 1980-1989. Lang.: Eng.   3457

Road to Nirvana
Basic theatrical documents
Collection of plays from the Humana Festival. USA. 1986-1995. Lang.: Eng.   1687

Road, The
Plays/librettos/scripts
Traditional African aesthetics in the plays of Wole Soyinka. Nigeria. 1960-1975. Lang.: Eng.   3150

Robbers
Performance/production
Collection of newspaper reviews by New York theatre critics. USA: New Haven, CT, New York, NY. 1995-1996. Lang.: Eng.   2549

Robbins, Kenneth
Basic theatrical documents
Text of *Atomic Field* by Kenneth Robbins. USA. 1996. Lang.: Eng. 1702

Roberto Calvi Is Alive and Well
Performance/production
Collection of newspaper reviews by London theatre critics. UK-England: London. 1996. Lang.: Eng.   2361

Roberto Zucco
Performance/production
Review of Koltès' *Roberto Zucco*, directed by Krzysztof Warlikowski, Teatr Nowy. Poland: Poznań. 1995. Lang: Eng, Fre.   2165

Roberts, Cynthia
Performance/production
Collection of newspaper reviews by London theatre critics. UK-England: London. 1996. Lang.: Eng.   2497

Roberts, Jimmy
Performance/production
Collection of newspaper reviews by New York theatre critics. USA: New York, NY, Chicago, IL. 1996. Lang.: Eng.   2585

Roberts, Judith
Performance/production
Collection of newspaper reviews by London theatre critics. UK-England: London. 1996. Lang.: Eng.   2336

Collection of newspaper reviews by London theatre critics. UK-England: London. 1996. Lang.: Eng.   2457

Roberts, Simon
Performance/production
Collection of newspaper reviews by London theatre critics. UK-England: London. 1996. Lang.: Eng.   2477

Robertson, Ali
Performance/production
Collection of newspaper reviews by London theatre critics. UK-England: London. 1996. Lang.: Eng.   2305

Robertson, Donald
Institutions
The Chicago Theatre Society and its work. USA: Chicago, IL. 1909-1915. Lang.: Eng.   1875
Robertson, Kenneth
Performance/production
Collection of newspaper reviews by London theatre critics. UK-England: London. 1996. Lang.: Eng.   2497
Robertson, Tim
Institutions
Tim Robertson on his work at the Pram Factory. Australia: Melbourne. 1968-1978. Lang.: Eng.   342
Robins, Elizabeth
Basic theatrical documents
International anthology of modern drama by women. 1880-1940. Lang.: Eng.   1637
Theory/criticism
Feminist criticism of Ibsen in the work of Elizabeth Robins. UK-England. 1890-1928. Lang.: Eng.   3553
Robinson, Jean
Performance/production
Collection of newspaper reviews by London theatre critics. UK-England: London. 1996. Lang.: Eng.   2349
Robinson, Julie-Anne
Performance/production
Collection of newspaper reviews by London theatre critics. UK-England: London. 1996. Lang.: Eng.   2329

Collection of newspaper reviews by London theatre critics. UK-England: London. 1996. Lang.: Eng.   2470
Robinson, Vivian
Institutions
Obituary for Vivian Robinson of AUDELCO. USA: New York, NY. 1996. Lang.: Eng.   586
Robitaille, Jack
Performance/production
Anecdote of Jack Robitaille's role in a production of Pirandello's *Questa sera si recita a soggetto (Tonight We Improvise)*. Canada: Quebec, PQ. 1994. Lang.: Fre.   1957
Robitaille, Pierrette
Performance/production
The social function of comedy and laughter. Canada: Montreal, PQ. 1990. Lang.: Fre.   742
Rochaix, François
Design/technology
Design for *Tartuffe* at American Repertory Theatre. USA: Cambridge, MA. 1996. Lang.: Eng.   1735
Rock music
Design/technology
Lighting and structural design of the Rock & Roll Hall of Fame. USA: Cleveland, OH. 1996. Lang.: Eng.   334

Vince Foster's design for rock star Zucchero. Italy. 1996. Lang.: Eng.
                                                                   3696

Design for the U.S. tour of rock group The Cure. USA. 1996. Lang.: Eng.   3700
Performance/production
Analysis of the appeal of the singer-actress Madonna. USA. 1990-1993. Lang.: Eng.   3682

The rock musical *Sarajevo: Behind God's Back* at Group Theatre. USA: Seattle, WA. 1991-1996. Lang.: Eng.   3932

Show tunes recorded by rock singers. USA. England. 1967-1992. Lang.: Eng.   3980
Rock Odüsszeia (Rock Odyssey)
Performance/production
Interview with dancer Pál Solymos. Hungary. 1972-1995. Lang.: Hun.
                                                                   1430

Rock Station, The
Performance/production
Collection of newspaper reviews by London theatre critics. UK-England: London. 1996. Lang.: Eng.   2416
Rock Színház (Budapest)
Performance/production
Interview with dancer Pál Solymos. Hungary. 1972-1995. Lang.: Hun.
                                                                   1430
Rockaby
Performance/production
Collection of newspaper reviews by London theatre critics. UK-England: London. 1996. Lang.: Eng.   2352
Rodenburg, Patsy
Performance/production
Cultural bias in vocal training and feminist performances of Shakespeare. UK-England: London. USA. 1973-1996. Lang.: Eng. 2542

Rodgers, Mary
Performance/production
Collection of newspaper reviews by New York theatre critics. USA: New York, NY. 1996. Lang.: Eng.   2565

Sarah Jessica Parker's role in *Once Upon a Mattress*. USA: New York, NY. 1976-1996. Lang.: Eng.   3942
Plays/librettos/scripts
Musical author Mary Rodgers. USA: New York, NY. 1959-1996. Lang.: Eng.   3999
Rodgers, Richard
Design/technology
Scene designer Brian Thomson. Australia. USA: New York, NY. 1971-1996. Lang.: Eng.   3885

Lighting design for a touring production of *Carousel*. USA. 1996. Lang.: Eng.   3900

John Arnone's set design for the revival of *Babes in Arms* at the Guthrie. USA: Minneapolis, MN. 1996. Lang.: Eng.   3904
Performance/production
Profiles of new actors on Broadway. USA: New York, NY. 1996. Lang.: Eng.   1012

Collection of newspaper reviews by New York theatre critics. USA: New York, NY. 1996. Lang.: Eng.   2572

Collection of newspaper reviews by New York theatre critics. USA: New York, NY, Washington, DC. 1996. Lang.: Eng.   2576

Lou Diamond Phillips' role in *The King and I*. USA: New York, NY. 1996. Lang.: Eng.   3938

Actor/singer John Davidson. USA: New York, NY. 1964-1996. Lang.: Eng.   3945
Plays/librettos/scripts
Musical author Mary Rodgers. USA: New York, NY. 1959-1996. Lang.: Eng.   3999
Rodrigues, Nelson
Performance/production
The work of director-designer Gerald Thomas. Brazil. 1985-1996. Lang.: Eng.   699
Rodríguez Méndez, José María
Basic theatrical documents
Text of *Isabelita tiene ángel (Isabelita Has an Angel)* by José María Rodríguez Méndez. Spain. 1976. Lang.: Spa.   1681
Plays/librettos/scripts
Analysis of *Isabelita tiene ángel (Isabelita Has an Angel)* by José María Rodríguez Méndez. Spain. 1976. Lang.: Spa.   3232

Theory and practice in the Marxist theatre of José María Rodríguez Méndez. Spain. 1965. Lang.: Spa.   3238

Bibliography of playwright José María Rodríguez Méndez. Spain. 1946. Lang.: Spa.   3239

Women and war in plays of José Martín Recuerda and José María Rodríguez Méndez. Spain. 1947-1971. Lang.: Spa.   3246
Roger Bloomer
Plays/librettos/scripts
The plays of John Howard Lawson. USA. 1922-1929. Lang.: Eng.   3447
Roger, Edith
Performance/production
Directors Edith Roger and Catrine Telle. Norway: Oslo. 1995. Lang.: Eng.   2143
Roger, Gustave
Plays/librettos/scripts
Singers Gilbert-Louis Duprez and Gustave Roger and the creation of Meyerbeer's opera *Le Prophète*. France: Paris. 1831-1849.Lang.: Eng.   4314
Rogers, Richard
Design/technology
Comparison of U.S. and European tech directors' duties. USA: Milwaukee, WI. Germany. 1996. Lang.: Eng.   286
Rogers, Thomas Hall
Plays/librettos/scripts
Propaganda plays about the steel and textile industries. USA. 1930-1940. Lang.: Eng.   3363
Roi Lear (King Lear)
Performance/production
Robert Lepage's Shakespearean adaptations at the Odéon. France: Paris. 1996. Lang.: Ger.   2034
Roi malgré lui, Le
Performance/production
Operas of Emmanuel Chabrier. France: Paris. 1863-1894. Lang.: Eng.   4127
Roi s'amuse, Le (King Amuses Himself, The)
Performance/production
Collection of newspaper reviews by London theatre critics. UK-England: London. 1996. Lang.: Eng.   2372

Roitelet, Le (Kinglet, The)
Plays/librettos/scripts
Plays about Louis Riel. Canada. 1886-1986. Lang.: Fre.   2792
Roland, Betty
Plays/librettos/scripts
The work of Australian women playwrights. Australia. 1930-1970. Lang.: Eng.   1084

The dearth of professional productions of plays by Australian women. Australia. 1928-1994. Lang.: Eng.   2724
Roles
SEE
Characters/roles.
Rolfe Johnson, Anthony
Performance/production
The recording of Schubert's *Lieder* on CD. 1996. Lang.: Eng.   3853
Roll with the Punches
Performance/production
Collection of newspaper reviews by London theatre critics. UK-England: London. 1996. Lang.: Eng.   2451
Roll, Gadi
Performance/production
Production of *Jud Süss (The Jew Suess)* at BeerSheba Municipal Theatre. Israel: Beersheba. 1931-1996. Lang.: Eng.   2119
Rollins, Doug
Performance/production
Collection of newspaper reviews by London theatre critics. UK-England: London. 1996. Lang.: Eng.   2345
Rollo
Basic theatrical documents
Text of plays by Fletcher and his collaborators. England. 1609-1613. Lang.: Eng.   1655
Roma Theater Pralipe (Mülheim)
Institutions
Productions of the Ruhrfestspiele festival. Germany: Recklinghausen. 1996. Lang.: Eng.   1797
Performance/production
Reviews of Shakespearean productions. Germany. 1994-1995. Lang.: Ger.   2046
Romagnoli, Richard
Performance/production
Collection of newspaper reviews by New York theatre critics. USA: New York, NY. 1996. Lang.: Eng.   2568
Romani, Felice
Plays/librettos/scripts
Librettist Felice Romani. Italy. 1810-1850. Lang.: Eng.   4334

Essays on librettist Felice Romani. Italy. 1788-1865. Lang.: Ita.   4335
Romanticism
SEE ALSO
Geographical-Chronological Index under Europe 1800-1850, France 1810-1857, Germany 1798-1830, Italy 1815-1876, UK 1801-1850.
Romeo & Julia Kören (Stockholm)
Performance/production
Profile of the Romeo & Julia Choir. Sweden: Stockholm. Slovenia. Croatia. 1991. Lang.: Swe.   3866
Romeo and Juliet
Design/technology
Production design for Baz Luhrmann's film *Romeo and Juliet*. USA: Miami, FL. 1996. Lang.: Eng.   3601
Institutions
Productions of the Ruhrfestspiele festival. Germany: Recklinghausen. 1996. Lang.: Eng.   1797
Performance/production
Austrian productions of Shakespearean plays and operas. Austria. 1994-1995. Lang.: Ger.   691

Operatic and ballet adaptations of Shakespearean plays reviewed. Switzerland. 1994-1995. Lang.: Ger.   956

Analysis of dance interpretations of Shakespearean plays. Europe. 1809-1994. Lang.: Hun.   1500

Technical-theatre aspects of dating the first performance of Shakespeare's *Romeo and Juliet*. England: London. 1592-1599. Lang.:Eng.   1987

Report on Paris productions. France: Paris. 1995-1996. Lang.: Eng. 2029

Reviews of Shakespearean productions. Germany. 1994-1995. Lang.: Ger.   2046

Eimuntas Nekrošius' youth theatre production of an adaptation of Shakespeare's *Romeo and Juliet*. Latvia: Vilnius. 1982. Lang.: Rus. 2136

Significant Polish productions of Shakespearean plays. Poland. 1918-1989. Lang.: Eng.   2152

Rose Theatre (London) — cont'd

Performance/production
Technical-theatre aspects of dating the first performance of Shakespeare's *Romeo and Juliet*. England: London. 1592-1599. Lang. :Eng. 1987
Relation to other fields
Performance theory and the excavation of the Rose Theatre. UK-England: London. 1989. Lang.: Eng. 1244

Rose Theatre (Oxford)
Performance/production
Collection of newspaper reviews by London theatre critics. UK-England: London, Oxford. 1996. Lang.: Eng. 2469

Rose, Billy
Performance/production
The first production of *The Great Magoo* by Ben Hecht and Gene Fowler. USA. 1932-1996. Lang.: Eng. 2681

Rose, Reginald
Performance/production
Collection of newspaper reviews by London theatre critics. UK-England: London. 1996. Lang.: Eng. 2373

Roselt, Jens
Performance/production
Productions of new plays by Elfriede Müller and Jens Roselt. Germany: Saarbrücken, Mainz. 1996. Lang.: Ger. 2052

Rosemary Branch Theatre (London)
Performance/production
Collection of newspaper reviews by London theatre critics. UK-England: London. 1996. Lang.: Eng. 2401

Rosenberg, Lenore
Performance/production
Changes in the comprimario system at the Metropolitan Opera. USA: New York, NY. 1996. Lang.: Eng. 4287

Rosenberg, Marc
Design/technology
Theatrical lighting designer Marc Rosenberg's move to architectural lighting design. USA: Las Vegas, NV. 1996. Lang.: Eng. 278

Rosenberg, Tiina
Theory/criticism
Swedish actresses and feminist research on the dominance of men in the theatre. Europe. 400 B.C.-1996 A.D. Lang.: Swe. 3540

Rosenthal, Rachel
Performance/production
Essays on contemporary performance. Europe. USA. 1980-1995. Lang.: Eng. 790
Performance artist Rachel Rosenthal's *Tohubohu*. USA. 1996. Lang.: Eng. 3804
Relation to other fields
Performance artists and writers comment on political concerns in their work. UK-England: London. 1995. Lang.: Eng. 3818

Rosita Clavel
Performance/production
Illustrations for Rose English's *Rosita Clavel*. UK-England. 1997. Lang.: Eng. 3793

Rosmer, Ernst (Bernstein, Elsa)
Basic theatrical documents
International anthology of modern drama by women. 1880-1940. Lang.: Eng. 1637

Ross, Aden
Plays/librettos/scripts
David Carlson's opera *Dreamkeepers*, which uses traditional Ute music and instruments. USA: Salt Lake City, UT. 1996. Lang.: Eng. 4347

Ross, Glynn
Performance/production
The Arizona Opera's first *Ring des Nibelungen*. USA: Flagstaff, AZ. 1914-1996. Lang.: Eng. 4297

Ross, Jerry
Performance/production
Collection of newspaper reviews by London theatre critics. UK-England: London. 1996. Lang.: Eng. 2308

Ross, Molly
Performance/production
Puppet production of *Frankenstein* by Redmoon Theatre. USA: Chicago, IL. 1996. Lang.: Eng. 4444

Ross, Steve
Performance/production
Steve Ross's role in *Present Laughter* on Broadway. USA: New York, NY. 1996. Lang.: Eng. 2604

Rosselli, Amelia
Basic theatrical documents
International anthology of modern drama by women. 1880-1940. Lang.: Eng. 1637

Rossi, Gaetano
Plays/librettos/scripts
Melodrama and orientalism in *Il crociato in Egitto* by Meyerbeer. France. Italy: Venice. 1744-1840. Lang.: Eng. 4316
Analysis of Mercadante's opera *Il Giuramento*. Italy. 1837. Lang.: Eng. 4331

Rossi, Jacques
Plays/librettos/scripts
Odette Guimond and Jacques Rossi's stage adaptations of novels by Agota Kristof. Canada: Montreal, PQ. 1988-1989. Lang.: Fre. 2806

Rossi, Vittorio
Plays/librettos/scripts
Profile of Anglo-Quebec theatre. Canada: Montreal, PQ. 1980-1990. Lang.: Fre. 2738

Rossignol, Michelle
Relation to other fields
Report on international conference on government cultural policy. Canada: Montreal, PQ. 1991. Lang.: Fre. 1144

Rossini, Gioacchino
Performance/production
The failure of Rossini's opera *Ermione*. Italy. 1819. Lang.: Eng. 4189
Background material on Metropolitan Opera radio broadcast performances. USA: New York, NY. 1996. Lang.: Eng. 4252

Rossiskaja Akademija Teatral'nogo Iskusstva (RATI, Moscow)
SEE ALSO
Gosudarstvénnyj Institut Teatral'nogo Iskusstva im. A.V. Lunačarskogo (Moscow).

Rossner, Judith
Performance/production
Tobias Picker's new opera *Emmeline*. USA: Santa Fe, NM. 1996. Lang.: Eng. 4267

Rostand, Edmond
Design/technology
Scene designer Cameron Porteous. Canada: Niagara-on-the-Lake, ON. 1980-1995. Lang.: Eng. 1707
Performance/production
Productions of the Stanislavskij Theatre. Russia: Moscow. 1995-1996. Lang.: Rus. 2242
Collection of newspaper reviews by London theatre critics. UK-England: London. 1996. Lang.: Eng. 2424
Collection of newspaper reviews by London theatre critics. UK-England: London. 1996. Lang.: Eng. 2474

Rostovskij Akademičéskij Teat'r (Rostov)
Performance/production
Director A. Slavutskij and scenographer A. Patrakov of Rostovskij Akademičéskij Teat'r. Russia: Rostov. 1995-1996. Lang.:Rus. 2229

Rostron, Brian
Performance/production
Collection of newspaper reviews by London theatre critics. UK-England: London. 1996. Lang.: Eng. 2305

Rostrup, Kaspar
Design/technology
Interview with costume designer Søren Breum. Denmark. 1995-1996. Lang.: Dan. 3662

Roszkopfová, Marta
Design/technology
Set and costume designer Marta Roszkopfová. Czech Republic. 1974-1996. Lang.: Eng, Fre. 159
Scenery and costume designs of Marta Roszkopfová and Jana Zbořilová. Czechoslovakia. 1980-1995. Lang.: Eng. 162

Rota, Nino
Performance/production
Collection of newspaper reviews by London theatre critics. UK-England: London. 1996. Lang.: Eng. 2366

Roth, Robert Jess
Performance/production
Stage and film treatments of the fairy tale *Beauty and the Beast*. Europe. USA. Canada. 1946-1996. Lang.: Eng. 793

Rouland, Joelle
Institutions
Review of children's theatre performances. Europe. 1996. Lang.: Ger. 403

Roundabout Theatre Company (New York, NY)
Performance spaces
Roundabout Theatre Company's new Laura Pels Theatre. USA: New York, NY. 1994-1995. Lang.: Eng. 669
Performance/production
Collection of newspaper reviews by New York theatre critics. USA: New York, NY. 1996. Lang.: Eng. 2550

Roundabout Theatre Company (New York, NY) — cont'd

Collection of newspaper reviews by New York theatre critics. USA:
New York, NY. 1996. Lang.: Eng.   2558

Collection of newspaper reviews by New York theatre critics. USA:
New York, NY. 1996. Lang.: Eng.   2561

Collection of newspaper reviews by New York theatre critics. USA:
New York, NY. 1996. Lang.: Eng.   2572

Collection of newspaper reviews by New York theatre critics. USA:
New York, NY. 1996. Lang.: Eng.   2584

Actress Mary McDonnell. USA: New York, NY. 1948-1996. Lang.: Eng.
                                                                       2587

Roger Rees's role in *The Rehearsal* by Anouilh, Roundabout Theatre
Company. USA: New York, NY. UK-England: London. 1996. Lang.:
Eng.   2617

Robert Falls' production of *The Night of the Iguana* by Tennessee
Williams, Roundabout Theatre Company. USA: New York, NY. 1960-
1996. Lang.: Eng.   2670

Roux, Jean-Louis
Plays/librettos/scripts
Interview with translator Jean-Louis Roux. Canada. 1970-1990. Lang.:
Fre.   2771

Jean-Louis Roux's translation of *Hamlet* for Théâtre du Nouveau
Monde. Canada: Montreal, PQ. England. 1990. Lang.: Fre.   2831

Rover, The
Performance/production
Videotape of Aphra Behn's *The Rover* performed by Women's
Playhouse Trust. UK-England. 1994. Lang.: Eng.   2302
Plays/librettos/scripts
Authorship and identity in *The Rover* by Aphra Behn. England. 1677.
Lang.: Eng.   2884

Feminism and female empowerment in plays of Aphra Behn. England.
1660-1700. Lang.: Eng.   2918

Women and sexuality in plays of Aphra Behn, Mary Pix, and Catharine
Trotter. England: London. 1660-1750. Lang.: Eng.   2946

Rowley, William
Performance/production
English plays and subjects on the Hungarian stage. Hungary. 1995-1996.
Lang.: Eng.   847

Roy Cohn/Jack Smith
Plays/librettos/scripts
Plays about politician Roy Cohn. USA. 1986-1994. Lang.: Eng.   3339
Roy, Lise
Performance/production
Actress Lise Roy. Canada: Montreal, PQ, Quebec, PQ. 1976-1996.
Lang.: Fre.   744

Roy, Milène
Performance/production
Milène Roy and Sylvain Michoue of Voxtrot. Canada: Montreal, PQ.
1989. Lang.: Fre.   745

Text and movement in *Une cloche à vache suspendue à mon âme (A
Cowbell Hung on My Soul)* by Milène Roy. Canada: Montreal, PQ.
1996. Lang.: Fre.   1412

Roy, Stéphane
Design/technology
Set designer Stéphane Roy. Canada: Montreal, PQ. 1988-1992. Lang.:
Fre.   150
Performance/production
Scenography of Beckett's *Waiting for Godot* directed by André Brassard,
TNM. Canada: Montreal, PQ. 1992. Lang.: Fre.   1937

Royal Academy of Dramatic Art (RADA, London)
Performance/production
Actor training in London. UK-England: London. 1963-1996. Lang.:
Eng.   980

Nicholas Barter's production of *Les Femmes savantes* by Molière,
RADA. UK-England: London. 1996. Lang.: Eng.   2538
Royal Academy of Music (London)
Administration
Italian opera in England: a Royal Academy of Music shareholder's
account book. England: London. 1719-1734. Lang.: Eng.   4005
Royal Albert Hall (London)
Design/technology
Flawed lighting design for Yanni show at Royal Albert Hall. UK-
England: London. 1995. Lang.: Eng.   228
Performance/production
Collection of newspaper reviews by London theatre critics. UK-England:
London. 1996. Lang.: Eng.   2307
Royal Ballet (London)
Institutions
Contemporary dance works in the Royal Ballet repertoire. UK-England:
London. 1963-1994. Lang.: Hun.   1492

Notes on Royal Ballet productions. UK-England: London. 1993-1995.
Lang.: Hun.   1493
Performance/production
London performances of musicals and ballet. UK-England: London.
1992-1995. Lang.: Hun.   982

Interview with ballet dancer Zoltán Solymosi. Hungary. UK-England:
London. 1992-1995. Lang.: Hun.   1510
Royal Coburg Theatre (London)
Theory/criticism
Analysis of *The Mutiny at the Nore* intended to refute the 'new
historical' approach. UK-England: London. 1797-1830. Lang.: Eng.
                                                                       1366

Royal Conservatory of Music (Toronto, ON)
Performance/production
Soprano Lois Marshall. Canada: Toronto, ON. 1940-1980. Lang.: Eng.
                                                                       4096

Royal Court Downstairs (London)
Performance/production
Collection of newspaper reviews by London theatre critics. UK-England:
London. 1996. Lang.: Eng.   2484
Royal Court Theatre (London)
SEE ALSO
English Stage Company.
Design/technology
Interview with scenographer Jocelyn Herbert. UK-England: London.
1956-1994. Lang.: Eng.   232
Institutions
Impact of architectural restructuring on the mission of the Royal Court
Theatre. UK-England: London. 1996. Lang.: Eng.   1858
Performance/production
Collection of newspaper reviews by London theatre critics. UK-England:
London. 1996. Lang.: Eng.   2352

Collection of newspaper reviews by London theatre critics. UK-England:
London. 1996. Lang.: Eng.   2357

Collection of newspaper reviews by London theatre critics. UK-England:
London. 1996. Lang.: Eng.   2416

Collection of newspaper reviews by London theatre critics. UK-England:
London. 1996. Lang.: Eng.   2457

Collection of newspaper reviews by London theatre critics. UK-England:
London. 1996. Lang.: Eng.   2470

The London theatre season—fall. UK-England: London. 1995-1996.
Lang.: Eng.   2501

Phyllida Lloyd's production of *Hysteria* by Terry Johnson. UK-England:
London. 1995. Lang.: Eng.   2503

Productions of Arnold Wesker's *The Kitchen* by Stephen Daldry and
John Dexter. UK-England: London. 1959-1994. Lang.: Eng.   2519

Athol Fugard in his own *Valley Song* at the Royal Court. UK-England:
London. 1996. Lang.: Ger.   2522
Royal Court Upstairs Stage (London)
Performance/production
Collection of newspaper reviews by London theatre critics. UK-England:
London. 1996. Lang.: Eng.   2398

Collection of newspaper reviews by London theatre critics. UK-England:
London. 1996. Lang.: Eng.   2480
Royal Dramatic Theatre of Stockholm
SEE
Kungliga Dramatiska Teatern.
Royal Hunt of the Sun, The
Institutions
The collaboration of Diablomundo and the Clarence Brown Theatre
Company. USA: Knoxville, TN. Argentina: Buenos Aires. 1994. Lang.:
Eng.   1876
Performance/production
Tribute to actor Robert Stephens. UK-England. 1961-1996. Lang.: Eng.
                                                                       2507

Royal Lyceum Theatre (Edinburgh)
Performance/production
Collection of newspaper reviews by London theatre critics. UK-England:
London. UK-Scotland: Edinburgh. 1996. Lang.: Eng.   2313

Collection of newspaper reviews by London theatre critics. UK-England:
London. 1996. Lang.: Eng.   2381

Collection of newspaper reviews by London theatre critics. UK-
Scotland: Edinburgh. 1996. Lang.: Eng.   2545
Royal National Theatre (London)
SEE
National Theatre.

Royal National Theatre Studio (London)
Institutions
The Royal National Theatre Studio, directed by Sue Higgins. UK-England: London. 1990. Lang.: Swe. 555

Royal Opera (London)
Performance/production
Fritz Reiner's work as a conductor of opera. USA: Philadelphia, PA, San Francisco, CA. UK-England: London. 1931-1941. Lang.: Eng. 4276

Royal Opera House (Stockholm)
SEE
Kungliga Teatern.

Royal Opera House, Covent Garden (London)
Performance/production
Tenor Richard Margison. Canada. 1970-1996. Lang.: Eng. 4090

Brief reviews of British opera performances. UK. 1996. Lang.: Eng. 4223

Recollections of opera performances at Covent Garden. UK-England: London. 1959-1960. Lang.: Eng. 4224

Review of 1995 British opera productions. UK-England: London, Leeds, Lewes. 1995-1996. Lang.: Eng. 4234

Background on Benjamin Britten's treatment of Shakespeare's *A Midsummer Night's Dream*. UK-England. 1960-1996. Lang.: Eng. 4235

Royal Shakespeare Company (RSC, Stratford & London)
Design/technology
Simon Corder's lighting design for *Les Enfants du Paradis*, RSC. UK-England: London. 1996. Lang.: Eng. 1712

Design for RSC production of *A Patriot for Me* by John Osborne. UK-England: London. 1996. Lang.: Eng. 1713

Institutions
The RSC's 96-97 season. UK-England: Stratford. 1996. Lang.: Eng. 1855

Recent RSC openings. UK-England: London, Stratford. 1996. Lang.: Eng. 1856

Performance/production
Responses to the RSC's Theatre of Cruelty experiments. UK-England: London. 1964. Lang.: Eng. 961

Collection of newspaper reviews by London theatre critics. UK-England: London. 1996. Lang.: Eng. 2316

Collection of newspaper reviews by London theatre critics. UK-England: London. 1996. Lang.: Eng. 2319

Collection of newspaper reviews by London theatre critics. UK-England: London. 1996. Lang.: Eng. 2367

Collection of newspaper reviews by London theatre critics. UK-England: London. 1996. Lang.: Eng. 2368

Collection of newspaper reviews by London theatre critics. UK-England: London. 1996. Lang.: Eng. 2373

Collection of newspaper reviews by London theatre critics. UK-England: London. 1996. Lang.: Eng. 2374

Collection of newspaper reviews by London theatre critics. UK-England: London. 1996. Lang.: Eng. 2388

Collection of newspaper reviews by London theatre critics. UK-England: London. 1996. Lang.: Eng. 2389

Collection of newspaper reviews by London theatre critics. UK-England: London. 1996. Lang.: Eng. 2410

Collection of newspaper reviews by London theatre critics. UK-England: London. 1996. Lang.: Eng. 2412

Collection of newspaper reviews by London theatre critics. UK-England: London. 1996. Lang.: Eng. 2422

Collection of newspaper reviews by London theatre critics. UK-England: London. 1996. Lang.: Eng. 2425

Collection of newspaper reviews by London theatre critics. UK-England: London. 1996. Lang.: Eng. 2428

Collection of newspaper reviews by London theatre critics. UK-England: London. 1996. Lang.: Eng. 2446

Collection of newspaper reviews by London theatre critics. UK-England: London. 1996. Lang.: Eng. 2454

Collection of newspaper reviews by London theatre critics. UK-England: London, Stratford. 1996. Lang.: Eng. 2461

Collection of newspaper reviews by London theatre critics. UK-England: London. 1996. Lang.: Eng. 2471

Collection of newspaper reviews by London theatre critics. UK-England: London, Stratford. 1996. Lang.: Eng. 2476

Collection of newspaper reviews by London theatre critics. UK-England: London. 1996. Lang.: Eng. 2481

Collection of newspaper reviews by London theatre critics. UK-England: London. 1996. Lang.: Eng. 2482

Collection of newspaper reviews by London theatre critics. UK-England: London, Stratford. 1996. Lang.: Eng. 2483

Collection of newspaper reviews by London theatre critics. UK-England: London. 1996. Lang.: Eng. 2486

Collection of newspaper reviews by London theatre critics. UK-England: London. 1996. Lang.: Eng. 2487

Collection of newspaper reviews by London theatre critics. UK-England: London, Stratford. 1996. Lang.: Eng. 2489

Actor John Byron. UK-England. 1944-1996. Lang.: Eng. 2527

Collection of newspaper reviews by New York theatre critics. USA: New York, NY. 1996. Lang.: Eng. 2574

Adrian Noble's RSC production of *A Midsummer Night's Dream*. USA: New York, NY. UK-England: Stratford-upon-Avon. 1996. Lang.: Eng. 2671

Royal Shakespeare Theatre (Stratford)
Performance/production
Collection of newspaper reviews by London theatre critics. UK-England: London. 1996. Lang.: Eng. 2422

Collection of newspaper reviews by London theatre critics. UK-England: London, Stratford. 1996. Lang.: Eng. 2461

Collection of newspaper reviews by London theatre critics. UK-England: London, Stratford. 1996. Lang.: Eng. 2489

Royal Swedish Ballet
SEE
Kungliga Teaterns Balett.

Royal Swedish Opera
SEE
Kungliga Teatern.

Royal Theatre (London)
Performance/production
Actor's diary of Broadway debut in David Hare's *Skylight*. USA: New York, NY. UK-England: London. 1996. Lang.: Eng. 2607

Royale Theatre (New York, NY)
Performance/production
Collection of newspaper reviews by New York theatre critics. USA: New York, NY. 1996. Lang.: Eng. 2554

Collection of newspaper reviews by New York theatre critics. USA: New York, NY. 1996. Lang.: Eng. 2574

Rozenmacher, Germán
Basic theatrical documents
Anthology of Argentine Jewish theatre. Argentina. 1926-1988. Lang.: Eng. 1639

Różewicz, Tadeusz
Plays/librettos/scripts
Motifs in Różewicz's work relating to Kafka. Poland. 1996. Lang.: Pol. 3161

Experimental theatre of Kantor, Schaeffer, and Różewicz. Poland. 1960-1996. Lang.: Pol. 3165

Polish theatre of the absurd. Poland. 1920-1990. Lang.: Pol. 3166

Rozon, Gilbert
Administration
Producing comedy shows. Canada: Montreal, PQ. 1990. Lang.: Fre. 3827

Rozovskij, Mark
Performance/production
Interview with director Mark Rozovskij. Russia: Moscow. 1996. Lang.: Rus. 2218

Rozsos, István
Performance/production
Tenor István Rozsos. Hungary. 1944-1995. Lang.: Hun. 4166

Rubasingham, Indhu
Performance/production
Collection of newspaper reviews by London theatre critics. UK-England: London. 1996. Lang.: Eng. 2304

Collection of newspaper reviews by London theatre critics. UK-England: London. 1996. Lang.: Eng. 2361

Collection of newspaper reviews by London theatre critics. UK-England: London. 1996. Lang.: Eng. 2391

Collection of newspaper reviews by London theatre critics. UK-England: London. 1996. Lang.: Eng. 2429

Collection of newspaper reviews by London theatre critics. UK-England: London. 1996. Lang.: Eng. 2470

Rubber
Performance/production
Collection of newspaper reviews by London theatre critics. UK-England: London. 1996. Lang.: Eng. 2449

Sabina
Performance/production
Collection of newspaper reviews by New York theatre critics. USA: New York, NY. 1996. Lang.: Eng. 2573

Sabourin, Gabriel
Performance/production
Experimental productions of Grand Théâtre Émotif. Canada: Montreal, PQ. 1996. Lang.: Fre. 739

Sabourin, Jean-Guy
Performance/production
Jean-Guy Sabourin's production of Brecht's *Leben des Galilei (The Life of Galilei)*, Théâtre de la Grande Réplique. Canada: Montreal, PQ. 1980. Lang.: Fre. 1958

Sacco and Vanzetti
Plays/librettos/scripts
Symposium on Marc Blitzstein's opera *Sacco and Vanzetti*. USA: Cambridge, MA. 1996. Lang.: Eng. 4344

Sacharova, Ljudmila P.
Performance/production
Profile of Ljudmila P. Sacharova, artistic director of Perm's school of choreography. Russia: Perm. 1970-1996. Lang.: Rus. 1523
Work of choreographer Ljudmila P. Sacharova. Russia: Perm. 1970-1996. Lang.: Rus. 1526

Šachovskij, Aleksand'r A.
Plays/librettos/scripts
Writer and dramatist Aleksand'r A. Šachovskij. Russia. 1777-1846. Lang.: Rus. 3202

Sacks, Oliver
Performance/production
Peter Brook's *L'homme qui (The Man Who)* as a model of multicultural theatre. USA: New York, NY. 1995. Lang.: Eng. 2618

Sacre du Printemps, Le
SEE
Vesna svjaščennaja.

Sacri rappresentazioni
Relation to other fields
Florentine art and drama. Italy: Florence. 1400-1600. Lang.: Eng. 1208

Sada, Yacco
SEE
Kawakami, Sadayacco.

Sadler's Wells Theatre (London)
Performance/production
Collection of newspaper reviews by London theatre critics. UK-England: London. 1996. Lang.: Eng. 2373
Collection of newspaper reviews by London theatre critics. UK-England: London. 1996. Lang.: Eng. 2427
Britten's *Peter Grimes*: productions by Eric Crozier and Harald André. UK-England. Sweden: Stockholm. 1945-1980. Lang.: Swe. 4229

Safe
Plays/librettos/scripts
Feminist realism in African-American theatre. USA. 1916-1930. Lang.: Eng. 3440

Safety
SEE
Health/safety.

Sagal, Peter
Design/technology
Lighting design for Peter Sagal's *Denial* at the Long Wharf Theatre. USA: New Haven, CT. 1996. Lang.: Eng. 1745
Performance/production
Collection of newspaper reviews by New York theatre critics. USA: New Haven, CT, New York, NY. 1995-1996. Lang.: Eng. 2549

Saidpour, Massoud
Performance/production
Profile of New World Performance Laboratory. USA: Cleveland, OH. 1987-1995. Lang.: Eng. 1075

Saidye Bronfman Centre (Montreal, PQ)
Performance/production
Canadian musical theatre. Canada: Toronto, ON, Montreal, PQ. 1996. Lang.: Eng. 3913

Saint Joan
Design/technology
Scene designer Cameron Porteous. Canada: Niagara-on-the-Lake, ON. 1980-1995. Lang.: Eng. 1707
Plays/librettos/scripts
Graham Greene's screen adaptation of Shaw's *Saint Joan*. UK-England. 1957. Lang.: Eng. 3647

Saint-Exupéry, Antoine de
Plays/librettos/scripts
Writing for puppet theatre. Canada: Montreal, PQ. 1979-1989. Lang.: Fre. 4424

Saint-Gelais, Joseph
Performance/production
Alain Thibault's musical score for *Ne blâmez jamais les Bédouins (Don't Blame the Bedouins)* by René-Daniel Dubois. Canada: Montreal, PQ. 1991. Lang.: Fre. 4095

Saint, David
Performance/production
Collection of newspaper reviews by New York theatre critics. USA: New York, NY, Washington, DC. 1996. Lang.: Eng. 2581

Saks, Gene
Performance/production
Christopher Plummer's one-man show *Barrymore*. Canada: Stratford, ON. 1996. Lang.: Eng. 1918

Sal P (Ward P)
Performance/production
Pia Forsgren's production of *Sal P (Ward P)* by Katarina Frostenson. Sweden: Stockholm. 1989. Lang.: Swe. 2295

Sal'nikov, Venjamin
Performance/production
Vaginov's *Harpagoniana* directed by Venjamin Sal'nikov at Masterskaja Petra Fomenko. Russia: Moscow. 1995. Lang.: Rus. 2209

Salad Days
Performance/production
Collection of newspaper reviews by London theatre critics. UK-England: London. 1996. Lang.: Eng. 2372

Salcedo, Hugo
Plays/librettos/scripts
Analysis of plays by Hugo Salcedo. Mexico. 1987-1990. Lang.: Eng. 3144

Salieri, Antonio
Plays/librettos/scripts
Antonio Salieri—Da Ponte's first choice to compose the music for *Così fan tutte*. Austria: Vienna. 1731-1837. Lang.: Eng. 4301

Šaljapin, Fëdor Ivanovič
Performance/production
Anecdotes about Šaljapin and Mejerchol'd. Russia. 1900-1938. Lang.: Rus. 902
Life and travels of singer Fëdor Šaljapin. Russia. 1873-1938. Lang.: Rus. 4202
Serge Lifar's recollections of opera singer Fëdor Šaljapin. Russia. 1873-1938. Lang.: Rus. 4208

Salle Fred-Barry (Montreal, PQ)
Institutions
Montreal theatres' role in education and the preparation of future audiences. Canada: Montreal, PQ. 1992. Lang.: Fre. 361

Sallé, Marie
Performance/production
Choreographic realizations of the story of Pygmalion. France. 1734-1847. Lang.: Eng. 1422

Sallin, Gisèle
Performance/production
Pol Pelletier's one-woman show *Joie (Joy)*. Canada: Montreal, PQ. 1975-1992. Lang.: Fre. 1941

Sally's Rape
Plays/librettos/scripts
Analysis of *Sally's Rape* by Robbie McCauley. USA. 1993-1994. Lang.: Eng. 3453

Salminen, Matti
Performance/production
Interview with opera singer Matti Salminen. Germany. Finland. 1966. Lang.: Swe. 4145

Salom, Jaime
Performance/production
Collection of newspaper reviews by London theatre critics. UK-England: London. 1996. Lang.: Eng. 2356
Plays/librettos/scripts
Overview of contemporary Spanish playwriting. Spain. 1945-1991. Lang.: Fre. 3257

Salome
Performance/production
Problems of casting the lead role in Strauss's *Salome*. 1905-1996. Lang.: Eng. 4072
Strauss's *Salome* at the Mariinskij Theatre. Russia: St. Petersburg. 1996. Lang.: Rus. 4205
Background material on Metropolitan Opera radio broadcast performances. USA: New York, NY. 1996. Lang.: Eng. 4252
Plays/librettos/scripts
Love and the death of women in works of Wagner, Strauss, and Schoenberg. Germany. Austria: Vienna. 1842-1911. Lang.: Eng. 4323

Scenery — cont'd

Scenery — cont'd

Design for *Tartuffe* at American Repertory Theatre. USA: Cambridge, MA. 1996. Lang.: Eng. 1735

Description of rotating doors on a stage set. USA. 1996. Lang.: Eng. 1736

Scene designer Riccardo Hernández. USA. 1996. Lang.: Eng. 1739

Technical aspects of *The Libertine* directed by Terry Johnson for Steppenwolf. USA: Chicago, IL. 1996. Lang.: Eng. 1740

Career of set and costume designer Felix E. Cochren. USA: New York, NY. 1980-1996. Lang.: Eng. 1742

Use of computer-generated projections in a University of Kansas production of *The Adding Machine*. USA: Lawrence, KS. 1996. Lang.: Eng. 1744

Set and lighting design for *Holiday* in the round at Circle in the Square. USA: New York, NY. 1996. Lang.: Eng. 1746

The use of programmable logic controllers at the Simon Edison Center. USA: San Diego, CA. 1990. Lang.: Eng. 1747

Design for an opera segment in the film *Così*. Australia. 1996. Lang.: Eng. 3587

Work of designer Mark Stevenson on the film *Beautiful Thing*. UK-England: London. 1995-1996. Lang.: Eng. 3591

Eugenio Zanetti's sets for Michael Hoffman's film *Restoration*. UK-England: London. 1996. Lang.: Eng. 3592

Design for film adaptation of Shakespeare's *Richard III* by Shuna Harwood and Tony Burroughs. UK-England: London. 1991-1996. Lang.: Eng. 3593

Jeffrey Beecroft's scene design for Terry Gilliam's film *12 Monkeys*. USA: Philadelphia, PA. 1996. Lang.: Eng. 3599

Scenery West, custom set and prop makers. USA: Hollywood, CA. 1982-1996. Lang.: Eng. 3600

Production design for Baz Luhrmann's film *Romeo and Juliet*. USA: Miami, FL. 1996. Lang.: Eng. 3601

Boyd Dumrose's sets for the TV show *The City*. USA: New York, NY. 1996. Lang.: Eng. 3667

Vince Foster's design for rock star Zucchero. Italy. 1996. Lang.: Eng. 3696

Design for the U.S. tour of rock group The Cure. USA. 1996. Lang.: Eng. 3700

The production team for The Who's *Quadrophenia*. USA: New York, NY. 1996. Lang.: Eng. 3701

Circus performer and scene designer A.A. Sudakevič. Russia. 1996. Lang.: Rus. 3747

Design for Gozzi's *The Green Bird (L'augellino belverde)* at the New Victory Theatre. USA: New York, NY. 1996. Lang.: Eng. 3760

Production design for tour of country singer Reba McEntire. USA. 1996. Lang.: Eng. 3831

Linear decoration in set design for Chinese opera. China. 1850-1995. Lang.: Eng. 3877

Scene designer Brian Thomson. Australia. USA: New York, NY. 1971-1996. Lang.: Eng. 3885

Quiet hydraulic system used for scene changes in Australian production of *Beauty and the Beast*. Australia: Melbourne, Sydney. 1996. Lang.: Eng. 3886

Technical aspects of a German-language production of Disney's *Beauty and the Beast*. Austria: Vienna. 1995. Lang.: Ger. 3888

Interview with scenographer Kati Lukka. Finland: Helsinki. 1996. Lang.: Swe, Eng. 3889

Alison Darke's production design for *Pendragon* by the National Youth Music Theatre of Great Britain. UK-England. USA: New York,NY. 1995. Lang.: Eng. 3892

Set and lighting design for *Old Wicked Songs*, Promenade Theatre. USA: New York, NY. 1996. Lang.: Eng. 3894

Scharff Weisberg, purveyor of video equipment for *The Who's Tommy*. USA: New York, NY. 1996. Lang.: Eng. 3899

Ray Huessy's re-design of *Sunset Boulevard* for its tour. USA: New York, NY. 1996. Lang.: Eng. 3901

Set and costume design for *Shlemiel the First*, ART/American Music Theatre Festival. USA: Cambridge, MA, Philadelphia, PA. 1996.Lang.: Eng. 3903

John Arnone's set design for the revival of *Babes in Arms* at the Guthrie. USA: Minneapolis, MN. 1996. Lang.: Eng. 3904

Robin Wagner's sets for *Victor/Victoria*. USA: New York, NY. 1995. Lang.: Eng. 3905

Paul Steinberg's cinematic design for a production of Puccini's *La Fanciulla del West*, Flemish National Opera. Belgium: Antwerp. 1996. Lang.: Eng. 4013

Design for *Der Fliegende Holländer*, Canadian Opera Company, by Allen Moyer. Canada: Toronto, ON. 1996. Lang.: Eng. 4014

Nina Flagstad's set design for Berg's *Lulu* at Christiansborg Ridehus. Denmark: Copenhagen. 1996. Lang.: Dan. 4015

Technical problems of producing *Die Soldaten* at Semper Oper. Germany: Dresden. 1995-1996. Lang.: Ger. 4016

Post-modern design at the Munich Festival. Germany: Munich. 1995. Lang.: Eng. 4018

Stefanos Lazarides' scene design for *Fidelio*, directed by David Pountney at the Bregenz Festival. Germany: Bregenz. 1996. Lang.: Eng. 4019

Budapest Opera's stage designer Attila Csikós. Hungary: Budapest. 1969-1996. Lang.: Hun. 4021

Hubert Monloup's set and costume designs for *Andrea Chénier*, Metropolitan Opera. USA: New York, NY. 1996. Lang.: Eng. 4026

Michael Anania's sets for *The Ballad of Baby Doe*, Central City Opera. USA: Central City, CO. 1996. Lang.: Eng. 4027

Technical aspects of Wagner's *Ring* cycle, Arizona Opera. USA: Flagstaff, AZ. 1996. Lang.: Eng. 4028

New approaches to opera design at the Metropolitan Opera. USA: New York, NY. 1996. Lang.: Eng. 4029

Institutions

Theatre-related disciplines at the Hochschule für Bildende Künste. Germany: Dresden. 1996. Lang.: Swe. 433

Performance spaces

Montreal's adjustable-stage theatres. Canada: Montreal, PQ. 1996. Lang.: Fre. 626

Historic theatre structures—implications for scenography, audience-performer relationship. Europe. 600 B.C.-1996 A.D. Lang.: Fre. 1886

Performance/production

Director and scenographer Eva Tálská. Czech Republic: Brno. 1996. Lang.: Eng, Fre. 765

Scene design and the work of director Antal Németh. Hungary. 1929-1944. Lang.: Hun. 843

The creative and the interpretive in theatre. UK-England. 1996. Lang.: Eng. 984

Design for *The Nutcracker* at the National Ballet of Canada. Canada: Toronto, ON. 1995. Lang.: Eng. 1498

Director A. Slavutskij and scenographer A. Patrakov of Rostovskij Akademičéskij Teat'r. Russia: Rostov. 1995-1996. Lang.:Rus. 2229

Symbolism and style in Chinese opera. China. 221 B.C.-1990 A.D. Lang.: Fre. 3878

Peter Mussbach, opera director and set designer. Germany. 1975-1996. Lang.: Ger. 4138

Performance and technical aspects of Orff's *Carmina Burana* at the Bavarian State Opera. Germany. 1996. Lang.: Eng. 4143

Wolfgang Wagner's scenery and direction of *Die Meistersinger* at the Bayreuth Festival. Germany: Bayreuth. 1996. Lang.: Ger. 4146

Opera Company of Boston's *Intolleranza* by Nono—directed by Sarah Caldwell, designed by Josef Svoboda. USA: Boston, MA. 1965. Lang.: Eng. 4295

Reference materials

Primary sources in English on European Naturalist and Symbolist theatre. Europe. 1850-1918. Lang.: Eng. 1120

Relation to other fields

Profile of a lesbian 'marriage' in the theatre community. USA: New York, NY. 1886-1933. Lang.: Eng. 1264

Scenery West (Hollywood, CA)

Design/technology

Scenery West, custom set and prop makers. USA: Hollywood, CA. 1982-1996. Lang.: Eng. 3600

Scenes from an Execution

Performance/production

Collection of newspaper reviews by New York theatre critics. USA: New York, NY. 1996. Lang.: Eng. 2568

Plays/librettos/scripts

Playwright Howard Barker. UK-England: London. 1990-1996. Lang.: Eng. 3306

Stage plays performed on radio. USA. UK-England. 1972-1984. Lang.: Eng. 3583

Scenes from Paradise

Performance/production

Collection of newspaper reviews by London theatre critics. UK-England: London. 1996. Lang.: Eng. 2402

Shakespeare, William — cont'd

Productions of *Hamlet* by Richard Monette and Henry Woronicz. Canada: Stratford, ON. USA: Ashland, OR. 1994. Lang.: Eng. 1927

Analysis of five Shakespearean productions in Quebec. Canada: Montreal, PQ, Quebec, PQ. Romania: Craiova. 1993. Lang.: Fre. 1947

Report on the Shanghai International Shakespeare Festival. China, People's Republic of: Shanghai. 1994. Lang.: Eng. 1972

Some Copenhagen theatre events. Denmark: Copenhagen. 1996. Lang.: Eng. 1982

Actor's description of voice training. Denmark. UK-England. 1996. Lang.: Dan. 1985

Technical-theatre aspects of dating the first performance of Shakespeare's *Romeo and Juliet*. England: London. 1592-1599. Lang.:Eng. 1987

Shakespeare and Elizabethan cultural politics: *A Midsummer Night's Dream*. England. 1590-1620. Lang.: Eng. 1990

'Review' of 'The Murder of Gonzago' in Shakespeare's *Hamlet*. England. 1600-1601. Lang.: Eng. 1991

History of English drama in performance. England. 1300-1990. Lang.: Eng. 1993

Diary evidence of David Garrick's interpretation of Hamlet. England. 1755. Lang.: Eng. 1994

Postmodern 'nostalgia' and recent Shakespearean performances. Europe. North America. 1985-1995. Lang.: Eng. 1998

Assembling an international cast for a production of *A Midsummer Night's Dream*. Europe. 1995. Lang.: Ger. 2001

The production of meaning in interpretations of Shakespeare's *The Merchant of Venice*. Europe. 1740-1987. Lang.: Eng. 2002

Peter Brook's *Qui est là (Who Is There)*. France: Paris. 1996. Lang.: Ger. 2011

Productions of Molière and Shakespeare directed by Daniel Mesguich. France: Lille. 1996. Lang.: Eng. 2014

Report on Paris productions. France: Paris. 1995-1996. Lang.: Eng. 2029

Review of recent Paris productions. France: Paris. 1996. Lang.: Ger. 2033

Robert Lepage's Shakespearean adaptations at the Odéon. France: Paris. 1996. Lang.: Ger. 2034

Director Robert Sturua. Georgia. 1980-1996. Lang.: Rus. 2040

Karin Beier's productions of *A Midsummer Night's Dream* and *Les Chaises (The Chairs)*. Germany: Düsseldorf. 1995. Lang.: Eng. 2045

Reviews of Shakespearean productions. Germany. 1994-1995. Lang.: Ger. 2046

Shakespearean productions by directors from Israel and England. Germany: Weimar, Erfurt. 1994-1995. Lang.: Ger. 2054

Performances of Shakespeare's plays in southern Germany. Germany: Munich, Mannheim. 1994-1995. Lang.: Ger. 2055

Reviews of Shakespearean and other productions. Germany. 1994-1995. Lang.: Ger. 2058

Bremer Shakespearetheater and the advantages of directing Shakespeare in translation. Germany: Bremen. UK-England: London. 1993. Lang.: Eng. 2071

Director Karin Beier. Germany: Düsseldorf. 1990-1996. Lang.: Ger. 2073

Productions of Schauspielhaus Bonn. Germany: Bonn. 1996. Lang.: Ger. 2075

Productions of Thalia Theater and Deutsches Schauspielhaus. Germany: Hamburg. 1996. Lang.: Ger. 2090

Review of some Budapest productions. Hungary. 1995-1996. Lang.: Eng. 2105

Interpretations of Shakespeare in Hungarian theatre in Transylvania. Hungary: Kolozsvár. Romania: Cluj-Napoca. 1794-1987. Lang.: Hun. 2111

Interview with Rina Yerushalmi of Itim. Israel. 1988-1993. Lang.: Eng. 2118

Eimuntas Nekrošius' youth theatre production of an adaptation of Shakespeare's *Romeo and Juliet*. Latvia: Vilnius. 1982. Lang.: Rus. 2136

Elie Pennont's staging of *Une Tempête (A Tempest)* by Aimé Césaire. Martinique: Fort-de-France. 1992. Lang.: Eng. 2139

The negative impact of democracy on Polish theatre. Poland. 1989-1995. Lang.: Eng. 2146

Significant Polish productions of Shakespearean plays. Poland. 1918-1989. Lang.: Eng. 2152

Polish productions of Shakespeare. Poland. 1989-1996. Lang.: Eng. 2162

Swinarski's production of *A Midsummer Night's Dream*, Stary Teatr. Poland: Cracow. 1970. Lang.: Eng. 2177

Shakespeare's comedies in the Soviet theatre. Russia. 1930-1939. Lang.: Rus. 2191

The importance of Shakespeare in the career of director Kama Ginkas. Russia. 1970-1996. Lang.: Rus. 2203

Vladimir Čigiév's production of *Hamlet* with Teat'r Junogo Zritelja. Russia: Rostov-na-Donu. 1990-1996. Lang.: Rus. 2213

Shakespearean productions on Moscow stages. Russia: Moscow. 1990-1996. Lang.: Rus. 2219

Jurij Pogrebničko's staging of Shakespeare's *Hamlet*. Russia: Moscow. 1995. Lang.: Rus. 2231

Boris Cejtlin's production of *Romeo and Juliet*, Baltiskij Dom. Russia: St. Petersburg. 1995. Lang.: Rus. 2234

Productions of Shakespeare's *Romeo and Juliet* on Moscow stages. Russia: Moscow. 1990-1996. Lang.: Rus. 2252

Enikő Eszenyi's production of Shakespeare's *As You Like It* at Slovenske Narodni Divadlo. Slovakia: Bratislava. 1996. Lang.:Hun. 2261

Interview with Suzanne Osten of Unga Klara. Sweden. 1995. Lang.: Eng. 2276

Collection of newspaper reviews by London theatre critics. UK-England: London. 1996. Lang.: Eng. 2312

Collection of newspaper reviews by London theatre critics. UK-England: London. 1996. Lang.: Eng. 2314

Collection of newspaper reviews by London theatre critics. UK-England: London. 1996. Lang.: Eng. 2319

Collection of newspaper reviews by London theatre critics. UK-England: London. 1996. Lang.: Eng. 2329

Collection of newspaper reviews by London theatre critics. UK-England: London. 1996. Lang.: Eng. 2358

Collection of newspaper reviews by London theatre critics. UK-England: London. 1996. Lang.: Eng. 2367

Collection of newspaper reviews by London theatre critics. UK-England: London. 1996. Lang.: Eng. 2373

Collection of newspaper reviews by London theatre critics. UK-England: London. 1996. Lang.: Eng. 2378

Collection of newspaper reviews by London theatre critics. UK-England: London. 1996. Lang.: Eng. 2380

Collection of newspaper reviews by London theatre critics. UK-England: London. 1996. Lang.: Eng. 2388

Collection of newspaper reviews by London theatre critics. UK-England: London. 1996. Lang.: Eng. 2389

Collection of newspaper reviews by London theatre critics. UK-England: London. 1996. Lang.: Eng. 2395

Collection of newspaper reviews by London theatre critics. UK-England: London. 1996. Lang.: Eng. 2411

Collection of newspaper reviews by London theatre critics. UK-England: London. 1996. Lang.: Eng. 2412

Collection of newspaper reviews by London theatre critics. UK-England: London. 1996. Lang.: Eng. 2422

Collection of newspaper reviews by London theatre critics. UK-England: London. 1996. Lang.: Eng. 2428

Collection of newspaper reviews by London theatre critics. UK-England: London. 1996. Lang.: Eng. 2436

Collection of newspaper reviews by London theatre critics. UK-England: London. 1996. Lang.: Eng. 2437

Collection of newspaper reviews by London theatre critics. UK-England: London. 1996. Lang.: Eng. 2438

Collection of newspaper reviews by London theatre critics. UK-England: London. 1996. Lang.: Eng. 2446

Collection of newspaper reviews by London theatre critics. UK-England: London. 1996. Lang.: Eng. 2454

Collection of newspaper reviews by London theatre critics. UK-England: London. 1996. Lang.: Eng. 2460

Collection of newspaper reviews by London theatre critics. UK-England: London, Stratford. 1996. Lang.: Eng. 2461

Collection of newspaper reviews by London theatre critics. UK-England: London. 1996. Lang.: Eng. 2468

Collection of newspaper reviews by London theatre critics. UK-England: London, Oxford. 1996. Lang.: Eng. 2469

Shakespeare, William — cont'd

Female transvestism in Shakespeare's *As You Like It* and Calderon's *La Vida es sueño*. England. Spain. 1599-1635. Lang.: Eng. 2901

Analysis of the 'bad' quarto of Shakespeare's *Romeo and Juliet*. England. 1597. Lang.: Eng. 2902

Historical background of *The Two Noble Kinsmen* by Shakespeare and Fletcher. England. 1613. Lang.: Eng. 2903

The body of the king in Shakespeare's *King Lear*. England. 1605-1996. Lang.: Eng. 2904

Analysis of a speech in the quarto and folio editions of *King Lear*. England. 1600. Lang.: Eng. 2905

Shakespeare's influence on Marlowe's *Edward II*. England. 1590-1592. Lang.: Eng. 2906

Analysis of Shakespeare's *King Lear*. England. 1605. Lang.: Rus. 2909

Romeo and Juliet—how Shakespeare and Zeffirelli used their sources. England. Italy. 1594-1968. Lang.: Eng. 2912

Calvinism in Shakespeare's *Othello*. England. 1604. Lang.: Eng. 2915

Event and meaning in Shakespeare's history plays. England. 1588-1613. Lang.: Eng. 2916

Theatrical politics and Shakespearean comedy. England. 1590-1600. Lang.: Eng. 2917

Shakespeare's theory of drama. England. 1589-1613. Lang.: Eng. 2920

Speculation on Shakespeare's life at the time of the writing of *Macbeth*. England. 1605-1606. Lang.: Eng. 2921

The carnivalesque in Shakespeare's *Romeo and Juliet*. England. 1594. Lang.: Eng. 2922

Renaissance economics as reflected in Shakespeare's *The Taming of the Shrew*. England. 1590-1604. Lang.: Eng. 2923

Shakespeare's Pericles compared to James I. England. 1606. Lang.: Eng. 2924

Shakespeare's *Henry IV, Part I* as a blending of genres. England. 1589-1594. Lang.: Eng. 2927

Rhetoric in Shakespeare's *Romeo and Juliet*. England. 1559-1594. Lang.: Eng. 2928

Heroic epic, narrative, and history in Shakespeare's *Richard III*. England. 1591-1594. Lang.: Eng. 2929

Ritual and play in *Henry IV, Part 3* by Shakespeare. England. 1589-1594. Lang.: Eng. 2930

Carnivalesque subversion of literary and dramatic texts. England. 1300-1607. Lang.: Eng. 2931

Epic and romance in Shakespeare's *Troilus and Cressida*. England. 1601-1602. Lang.: Eng. 2933

Comparison of Shakespeare's *Hamlet* and Racine's *Phèdre*. England. France. 1599-1677. Lang.: Eng. 2934

Masculine aggression in Shakespeare's *Richard III*. England. 1598. Lang.: Eng. 2935

Legal aspects of Shakespeare's *All's Well That Ends Well*. England. 1587-1600. Lang.: Eng. 2937

Rosalind's language and individuality in Shakespeare's *As You Like It*. England. 1599. Lang.: Ger. 2938

The New World and the Other in plays of Shakespeare. England. 1595-1611. Lang.: Eng. 2939

Passions in Shakespeare's *Twelfth Night* and *As You Like It*. England. 1599. Lang.: Swe. 2941

Shakespeare's *Henry VIII* and its source, Holinshed's chronicles. England. 1611. Lang.: Eng. 2942

Sex and innuendo in Shakespeare's *Othello*. England. 1600. Lang.: Eng. 2943

Shakespeare's use of history. England. 1592-1613. Lang.: Eng. 2945

Humoral psychology in Shakespeare's Henriad. England. 1590-1613. Lang.: Eng. 2947

The form of Shakespeare's *Henry VIII*. England. 1613. Lang.: Eng. 2948

Brotherhood and fraternal strife in Shakespeare's *Henry V* and *Richard II*. England. 1599. Lang.: Eng. 2949

Shakespeare's *Henry V* as a response to Marlowe's *Tamburlaine*. England. 1599. Lang.: Eng. 2950

Images of constant motion in Shakespeare's *Henry IV* and *Richard II*. England. 1596-1597. Lang.: Eng. 2951

The reflection of contemporary concerns in Shakespeare's *Hamlet* and *Othello*. England. 1600-1604. Lang.: Eng. 2953

Ideology and the feud in Shakespeare's *Romeo and Juliet*. England. 1594. Lang.: Eng. 2954

Criminality and wars of conquest in Shakespeare's *Henry V*. England. 1419-1609. Lang.: Eng. 2955

Shakespeare's life and work. England: London. 1564-1616. Lang.: Rus. 2956

Sisterhood in *As You Like It* by Shakespeare. England. 1590. Lang.: Eng. 2957

Early versions of Shakespeare's *Romeo and Juliet* and *The Merry Wives of Windsor*. England. 1595-1600. Lang.: Eng. 2959

The role and importance of Shakespeare's clowns. England. 1590-1613. Lang.: Eng. 2960

Challenges for modern productions of the text of *Romeo and Juliet*. England. 1597-1996. Lang.: Eng. 2961

Wonder in Shakespeare's *Othello*. England. 1604. Lang.: Eng. 2963

Modern adaptations of Shakespeare. Europe. 1800-1990. Lang.: Eng. 2967

The structural development of comedy in the Renaissance. Europe. 1590-1664. Lang.: Eng. 2969

Significant contributions to Shakespearean biography. Europe. USA. 1991-1994. Lang.: Eng. 2976

The influence of Shakespeare on Georgian theatre. Georgia. 1900-1996. Lang.: Rus. 3013

Shakespeare's influence on Brecht reevaluated. Germany. 1917-1985. Lang.: Eng. 3041

Sforza Oddi, a literary antecedent of Shakespeare. Italy. England. 1521. Lang.: Eng. 3124

Metonymy and drama. North America. Europe. 1600-1996. Lang.: Eng. 3154

Shakespeare and Polish Romanticism. Poland. 1786-1846. Lang.: Eng. 3163

A French adaptation of *Romeo and Juliet* on the Polish stage. Poland. 1796-1868. Lang.: Eng, Fre. 3164

Analysis of *This Island's Mine* by Philip Osment. UK-England: London. 1988-1996. Lang.: Eng. 3282

Nineteenth-century critical views of Shakespeare's Juliet. UK-England. 1800-1899. Lang.: Eng. 3285

Artists' renderings of scenes from Shakespeare's *Romeo and Juliet*. UK-England. 1679-1996. Lang.: Eng. 3291

The continuing debate on editing Shakespeare: defense of the Shakespearean originals project. UK-England. 1592-1995. Lang.: Eng. 3315

The historical and theatrical context of Edward Bond's *Lear*. UK-England. 1971-1990. Lang.: Eng. 3317

Shakespeare and the language of perception. USA. 1996. Lang.: Eng. 3398

David Garrick's librettos for Shakespearean opera. England. 1712-1756. Lang.: Eng. 4311

Jealousy in *Otello* and *Falstaff* by Giuseppe Verdi. Italy. 1887-1893. Lang.: Eng. 4332

Analysis of Britten's opera *A Midsummer Night's Dream*. UK-England. 1960-1996. Lang.: Eng. 4343

Relation to other fields

Shakespeare and the dominant ideology in Bulgarian education. Bulgaria. 1950-1989. Lang.: Eng. 3479

Masculine anxiety in early modern writings. England. 1580-1620. Lang.: Eng. 3488

Reexaminations of assumptions about Shakespeare's sonnets. England. 1590-1609. Lang.: Eng. 3489

Teaching lyrics of women poets alongside those of Shakespeare. England. 1590-1621. Lang.: Eng. 3491

Female education in Shakespeare's time and plays. England. 1510-1621. Lang.: Eng. 3492

Shakespeare's influence on sculpture in Southwark. England: London. 1599-1631. Lang.: Eng. 3493

The political mission of South African English studies, with emphasis on Shakespeare. South Africa, Republic of. 1800-1995. Lang.: Eng. 3508

Shakespeare in South African education. South Africa, Republic of. 1994-1996. Lang.: Eng. 3509

Shakespeare's *Romeo and Juliet* and pedagogy. UK-England. 1996. Lang.: Eng. 3512

Shakespeare, William — cont'd

The Sketching Society's drawings of Bottom with ass's head in Shakespeare's *A Midsummer Night's Dream*. UK-England: London. 1831. Lang.: Eng. 3513

Teaching Shakespeare in the context of Renaissance women's culture. USA. 1991-1996. Lang.: Eng. 3516

Teaching *The Winter's Tale* and Elizabeth Cary's *The Tragedy of Mariam*. USA. 1995. Lang.: Eng. 3517

Teaching race and gender in plays of Cary, Shakespeare, and Behn. USA. 1996. Lang.: Eng. 3518

Teaching plays of Shakespeare and Cary in a course on domestic England in the early modern period. USA. 1995. Lang.: Eng. 3519

Argument in favor of teaching Shakespeare in conjunction with his female contemporaries. USA. 1996. Lang.: Eng. 3520

Theory/criticism

Introduction to an *ET* issue devoted to post-colonial Shakespearean criticism. Canada. 1878-1996. Lang.: Eng. 3534

The works of Shakespearean scholar Aleksej Bartoševič. Russia: Moscow. 1980-1996. Lang.: Rus. 3545

The 'laws' of contemporary Shakespearean theatre. Russia. 1990-1996. Lang.: Rus. 3546

Critic Harold Hobson of the *Times*. UK-England: London. 1930-1977. Lang.: Eng. 3556

Argument against criticism that devalues the author. UK-England. 1994. Lang.: Eng. 3558

Shakespeare's Globe Theatre (London)

Audience

The Elizabethan experience at the reconstructed Globe theatre. UK-England: London. 1996. Lang.: Eng. 1636

Performance spaces

Profile of Shakespeare's Globe Theatre and the International Shakespeare Globe Centre. UK-England: London. 1985-1996. Lang.: Swe. 659

The temporary *frons scenae* of Shakespeare's Globe Theatre. UK-England: London. 1996. Lang.: Eng. 1889

Performance space as a character in *The Two Gentlemen of Verona* at Shakespeare's Globe. UK-England: London. 1996. Lang.: Eng. 1890

The opening of Shakespeare's Globe. UK-England: London. 1996. Lang.: Ger. 1891

Performance/production

Bremer Shakespearetheater and the advantages of directing Shakespeare in translation. Germany: Bremen. UK-England: London. 1993. Lang.: Eng. 2071

Collection of newspaper reviews by London theatre critics. UK-England: London. 1996. Lang.: Eng. 2380

Collection of newspaper reviews by London theatre critics. UK-England: London. 1996. Lang.: Eng. 2387

Collection of newspaper reviews by London theatre critics. UK-England: London. 1996. Lang.: Eng. 2468

Shakuntala

Performance/production

The *Shakuntala* project headed by Eugenio Barba and Sanjukta Panigrahi. Italy. Denmark: Holstebro. 1993-1996. Lang.: Eng. 1437

Shakur, Tupac

Performance/production

Obituary for musician and actor Tupac Shakur. USA. 1971-1996. Lang.: Eng. 3719

Shamanism

Performance/production

Comparison of the relationship between illusion and reality in shamanic/ritual practice and the Western acting tradition. USA. 1959-1995. Lang.: Eng. 1018

Plays/librettos/scripts

Ritual in Aboriginal and shamanistic performance. Australia. Korea. 1970-1995. Lang.: Eng. 1085

Shamir, Moshe

Plays/librettos/scripts

Analysis of Israeli Holocaust drama. Israel. 1950-1984. Lang.: Eng. 3099

Shammas, Sam

Performance/production

Collection of newspaper reviews by London theatre critics. UK-England: London. 1996. Lang.: Eng. 2315

Collection of newspaper reviews by London theatre critics. UK-England: London. 1996. Lang.: Eng. 2337

Collection of newspaper reviews by London theatre critics. UK-England: London. 1996. Lang.: Eng. 2402

Shange, Ntozake

Plays/librettos/scripts

Interviews with American playwrights. USA. 1945-1995. Lang.: Eng. 3397

Contemporary American drama. USA. 1960-1995. Lang.: Eng. 3431

Shanghai Dramatic Arts Center

Institutions

Profile of Shanghai Dramatic Arts Center. China, People's Republic of: Shanghai. 1930-1996. Lang.: Eng. 1783

Shankar, Udy

Research/historiography

Description of theatre and dance-related holdings of the Darlington Hall Trust archives. UK-England: Totnes, Devon. 1920-1995. Lang.: Eng. 1305

Shanley, John Patrick

Performance/production

Collection of newspaper reviews by New York theatre critics. USA: New York, NY. 1996. Lang.: Eng. 2557

Shannon, Katherine

Performance/production

Collection of newspaper reviews by London theatre critics. UK-England: London. 1996. Lang.: Eng. 2355

Shannon, Richard

Performance/production

Collection of newspaper reviews by London theatre critics. UK-England: London. 1996. Lang.: Eng. 2382

Sharaff, Irene

Administration

Inductions into the theatrical Hall of Fame. USA: New York, NY. 1996. Lang.: Eng. 99

Sharman, Jim

Relation to other fields

Social and political context of contemporary Australian theatre. Australia: Sydney. 1995. Lang.: Eng. 1134

Sharp, William

Performance/production

Composers and performers of the American art song. USA. 1996. Lang.: Eng. 3870

Shaulis, Jane

Performance/production

Changes in the comprimario system at the Metropolitan Opera. USA: New York, NY. 1996. Lang.: Eng. 4287

Shaw Festival (Niagara-on-the-Lake, ON)

Administration

Bell Canada's sponsorship of Shaw Festival. Canada: Niagara-on-the-Lake, ON. 1972-1996. Lang.: Eng. 10

Canadian theatres' response to funding cuts. Canada. 1994-1996. Lang.: Eng. 11

Design/technology

Lighting designer Kevin Lamotte of Shaw Festival. Canada: Niagara-on-the-Lake, ON. 1996. Lang.: Eng. 1705

Scene designer Cameron Porteous. Canada: Niagara-on-the-Lake, ON. 1980-1995. Lang.: Eng. 1707

Institutions

Profile and evaluation of the 1995 Shaw Festival season. Canada: Niagara-on-the-Lake, ON. 1996. Lang.: Eng. 1764

Diversity and sponsorship at Shaw Festival. Canada: Niagara-on-the-Lake, ON. 1996. Lang.: Eng. 1770

Shaw, Fiona

Performance/production

Report on Paris productions. France: Paris. 1995-1996. Lang.: Eng. 2029

Videotape on interpreting and performing Shakespeare's *As You Like It*. UK-England. 1994. Lang.: Eng. 2303

Interview with director Deborah Warner. UK-England: London. 1980-1996. Lang.: Eng. 2541

Actress Fiona Shaw. USA: New York, NY. UK-England: London. 1922-1996. Lang.: Eng. 2682

Shaw, George Bernard

Design/technology

Scene designer Cameron Porteous. Canada: Niagara-on-the-Lake, ON. 1980-1995. Lang.: Eng. 1707

Institutions

Profile and evaluation of the 1995 Shaw Festival season. Canada: Niagara-on-the-Lake, ON. 1996. Lang.: Eng. 1764

Performance/production

History of English drama in performance. England. 1300-1990. Lang.: Eng. 1993

Shaw, George Bernard — cont'd

Collection of newspaper reviews by London theatre critics. UK-England: London. 1996. Lang.: Eng.   2411

Collection of newspaper reviews by London theatre critics. UK-England: London. 1996. Lang.: Eng.   2417

Plays/librettos/scripts

The influence of composer Hector Berlioz on George Bernard Shaw. UK-England. 1880. Lang.: Eng.   3281

Analysis of previously unpublished dramatic manuscripts by George Bernard Shaw. UK-England. 1901-1912. Lang.: Eng.   3283

Dickens' influence on George Bernard Shaw. UK-England. 1878-1889. Lang.: Eng.   3298

Analysis of an unpublished narrative poem by George Bernard Shaw. UK-England. 1876-1877. Lang.: Eng.   3303

Analysis of an unpublished manuscript by George Bernard Shaw. UK-England. 1888. Lang.: Eng.   3305

Graham Greene's screen adaptation of Shaw's *Saint Joan*. UK-England. 1957. Lang.: Eng.   3647

Shaw's *Man and Superman* as a commentary on Mozart's *Don Giovanni*. UK-England. 1905. Lang.: Eng.   4340

Relation to other fields

Unpublished political essays by George Bernard Shaw. UK-England. 1885-1929. Lang.: Eng.   3510

Analysis of Shaw's essay on socialism and the family. UK-England. 1886. Lang.: Eng.   3511

George Bernard Shaw's unpublished article on the gentleman. UK-England. 1879. Lang.: Eng.   3514

Shaw's views on war and peace in his unpublished manuscripts. UK-England. 1899-1950. Lang.: Eng.   3515

Theory/criticism

Analysis of Shaw's unpublished work on the state of the arts. UK-England. 1880. Lang.: Eng.   3554

Shaw's early literary criticism. UK-England. 1880-1887. Lang.: Eng.   3559

Music criticism of George Bernard Shaw. UK-England. 1879. Lang.: Eng.   3560

Shaw, Martin

Performance/production

Interviews with Tony Award nominees. USA: New York, NY. 1996. Lang.: Eng.   2596

Actor Martin Shaw. USA: New York, NY. 1996. Lang.: Eng.   2639

Shaw, Michael

Performance/production

Collection of newspaper reviews by London theatre critics. UK-England: London. 1996. Lang.: Eng.   2470

Shaw, Peggy

Basic theatrical documents

Anthology of works by Split Britches. USA. 1985-1995. Lang.: Eng.   1685

Performance/production

Collection of newspaper reviews by London theatre critics. UK-England: London. 1996. Lang.: Eng.   2400

Shaw, Robert

Performance/production

Collection of newspaper reviews by London theatre critics. UK-England: London. 1996. Lang.: Eng.   2404

Shawl, The

Performance/production

Collection of newspaper reviews by New York theatre critics. USA: New York, NY, East Haddam, CT. 1996. Lang.: Eng.   2582

Plays/librettos/scripts

Profile of writer Cynthia Ozick and her stage adaptation of her novel *The Shawl*. USA: New York, NY. 1996. Lang.: Eng.   3353

Shawn, Ted

Training

Etienne Decroux's theory of corporeal mime. France: Paris. 1918-1996. Lang.: Eng.   3688

Shawn, Wallace

Performance/production

Collection of newspaper reviews by London theatre critics. UK-England: London. 1996. Lang.: Eng.   2376

Two productions of *The Designated Mourner* by Wallace Shawn. UK-England: London. Germany: Hamburg. 1996. Lang.: Ger.   2504

Shay, Michele

Performance/production

Interviews with Tony Award nominees. USA: New York, NY. 1996. Lang.: Eng.   2596

Plays/librettos/scripts

Blacksmyths, Black playwrights project—excerpt from symposium panel discussion. USA: Los Angeles, CA. 1995-1996. Lang.: Eng.   3320

She Loves Me

Performance spaces

History and technical aspects of the Ronacher Theater. Austria: Vienna. 1872-1996. Lang.: Ger.   3909

She Talks to Beethoven

Plays/librettos/scripts

Analysis of *She Talks to Beethoven* by Adrienne Kennedy. USA. 1989-1993. Lang.: Eng.   3396

Shearer, Paul

Performance/production

Collection of newspaper reviews by London theatre critics. UK-England: London. 1996. Lang.: Eng.   2462

Shearman, Robert

Performance/production

Collection of newspaper reviews by London theatre critics. UK-England: London. 1996. Lang.: Eng.   2327

Collection of newspaper reviews by London theatre critics. UK-England: London. 1996. Lang.: Eng.   2363

Sheehan, John J.D.

Performance/production

Collection of newspaper reviews by London theatre critics. UK-England: London. 1996. Lang.: Eng.   2456

Shen, Hong-Guang

Performance/production

Women playwrights of the Pacific Rim. Australia. Asia. 1994. Lang.: Eng.   1899

Sheng, Yu Luo

Institutions

Profile of Shanghai Dramatic Arts Center. China, People's Republic of: Shanghai. 1930-1996. Lang.: Eng.   1783

Shepard, Sam

Basic theatrical documents

Revised text of *Buried Child* by Sam Shepard. USA. 1978-1996. Lang.: Eng.   1703

Design/technology

Scene designer Robert Brill. USA: New York, NY. 1996. Lang.: Eng.   1724

Institutions

Profile of Steppenwolf Theatre Company. USA: Chicago, IL. 1974-1996. Lang.: Eng.   1862

Performance/production

American's experience directing Shepard's *Curse of the Starving Class* at the Ščepkin Institute. Russia: Moscow. 1992. Lang.: Eng.   2204

Collection of newspaper reviews by London theatre critics. UK-England: London. 1996. Lang.: Eng.   2331

Collection of newspaper reviews by London theatre critics. UK-England: London. 1996. Lang.: Eng.   2405

Collection of newspaper reviews by London theatre critics. UK-England: London. 1996. Lang.: Eng.   2448

Collection of newspaper reviews by London theatre critics. UK-England: London. 1996. Lang.: Eng.   2480

In-depth character study in a student production of Sam Shepard's *Buried Child*. UK-Scotland: Glasgow. 1994. Lang.: Eng.   2547

Collection of newspaper reviews by New York theatre critics. USA: New York, NY. 1996. Lang.: Eng.   2565

Collection of newspaper reviews by New York theatre critics. USA: New York, NY. 1996. Lang.: Eng.   2579

Plays/librettos/scripts

'Chaos-informed' realism in the plays of David Rabe and Sam Shepard. USA. 1976-1991. Lang.: Eng.   3355

Influence of Ted Hughes' poetry on playwright Sam Shepard. USA. 1971-1972. Lang.: Eng.   3412

The Sam Shepard season at Signature Theatre company. USA. 1960-1996. Lang.: Eng.   3429

Contemporary American drama. USA. 1960-1995. Lang.: Eng.   3431

Arthur Miller's influence on playwrights Edward Albee, Sam Shepard, and David Rabe. USA. 1930-1996. Lang.: Eng.   3432

Shepherd, Jack

Performance/production

Collection of newspaper reviews by London theatre critics. UK-England: London. 1996. Lang.: Eng.   2306

Collection of newspaper reviews by London theatre critics. UK-England: London. 1996. Lang.: Eng.   2395

Shepherd, Jack — cont'd

Collection of newspaper reviews by London theatre critics. UK-England: London. 1996. Lang.: Eng. 2468

Shepherd, Mike
Performance/production
Collection of newspaper reviews by London theatre critics. UK-England: London. 1996. Lang.: Eng. 2328

Shepherd's Bush Empire Theatre (London)
Performance/production
Collection of newspaper reviews by London theatre critics. UK-England: London. 1996. Lang.: Eng. 2467

Sher, Antony
Performance/production
The production of meaning in interpretations of Shakespeare's *The Merchant of Venice*. Europe. 1740-1987. Lang.: Eng. 2002

Sheridan, Richard Brinsley
Performance/production
Collection of newspaper reviews by New York theatre critics. USA. 1996. Lang.: Eng. 2551

Sherin, Mimi Jordan
Design/technology
Production and lighting design for Shakespeare's *Timon of Athens*, New York Shakespeare Festival. USA: New York, NY. 1996. Lang.: Eng. 245

Design for *Tartuffe* at American Repertory Theatre. USA: Cambridge, MA. 1996. Lang.: Eng. 1735

Sherlock Holmes: The Adventure at Sir Arthur Sullivan's
Performance/production
Collection of newspaper reviews by London theatre critics. UK-England: London. 1996. Lang.: Eng. 2470

Sherman, Bob
Performance/production
Collection of newspaper reviews by London theatre critics. UK-England: London. 1996. Lang.: Eng. 2401

Sherman, Guy
Design/technology
Guy Sherman's sound design for Ionesco's *Rhinocéros*, Valiant Theatre Company. USA: New York, NY. 1996. Lang.: Eng. 1726

Sherman, Jonathan Marc
Performance/production
Collection of newspaper reviews by London theatre critics. UK-England: London. 1996. Lang.: Eng. 2480

Collection of newspaper reviews by New York theatre critics. USA: New York, NY. 1996. Lang.: Eng. 2552

Sherman, Martin
Performance/production
English plays and subjects on the Hungarian stage. Hungary. 1995-1996. Lang.: Eng. 847

Collection of newspaper reviews by London theatre critics. UK-England: London. 1996. Lang.: Eng. 2369

Sherrin, Ned
Performance/production
Collection of newspaper reviews by London theatre critics. UK-England: London. 1996. Lang.: Eng. 2372

Sherwood, Robert
Plays/librettos/scripts
Realism in the high-society comedies of Philip Barry, S.N. Behrman, and Robert Sherwood. USA. 1920-1940. Lang.: Eng. 3382

Sherwood, Robert William
Performance/production
Collection of newspaper reviews by London theatre critics. UK-England: London. 1996. Lang.: Eng. 2458

Shevelove, Burt
Performance/production
Profiles of new actors on Broadway. USA: New York, NY. 1996. Lang.: Eng. 1012

Collection of newspaper reviews by New York theatre critics. USA: New York, NY. 1996. Lang.: Eng. 2577

Shicoff, Neil
Performance/production
Portrait of tenor Neil Shicoff. USA. 1975-1996. Lang.: Ger. 4289

Shields, Ronald E.
Performance/production
The concept of 'gallery theatre'. USA. 1996. Lang.: Eng. 3806

Shigeyama, Akira
Performance/production
Intercultural work of Noho Theatre Group. Japan: Kyoto. 1981-1994. Lang.: Eng. 875

Shiguré, Hasegawa
Basic theatrical documents
International anthology of modern drama by women. 1880-1940. Lang.: Eng. 1637

Shinel (Overcoat, The)
Performance/production
Pantomimist Rajmund Klechot. Poland: Wrocław. USA: Dayton, OH. 1945-1996. Lang.: Eng. 3691

Shining Souls
Institutions
Productions of the Edinburgh Festival. UK-Scotland: Edinburgh. 1996. Lang.: Eng. 562

Shinjuku Ryōzanpaku (Japan)
Performance/production
Japanese performances of Japanese themes at Toronto Theatre Festival. Japan. Canada: Toronto, ON. 1996. Lang.: Eng. 874

Shipley, Thos
Performance/production
Profiles of cabaret singers. USA: New York, NY. 1996. Lang.: Eng. 3734

Shire, David
Design/technology
Design for the musical *Big*. USA: Detroit, MI. 1996. Lang.: Eng. 3902
Performance/production
Collection of newspaper reviews by London theatre critics. UK-England: London. 1996. Lang.: Eng. 2491

Collection of newspaper reviews by New York theatre critics. USA: New York, NY. 1996. Lang.: Eng. 2579

Composer David Shire and lyricist Richard Maltby, Jr. USA: New York, NY. 1973-1996. Lang.: Eng. 3930

Actor Daniel Jenkins. USA: New York, NY. 1988-1996. Lang.: Eng. 3937

Work of choreographer Susan Stroman and director Mike Ockrent on the musical *Big*. USA: New York, NY. 1996. Lang.: Eng. 3964

Shlemiel the First
Design/technology
Set and costume design for *Shlemiel the First*, ART/American Music Theatre Festival. USA: Cambridge, MA, Philadelphia, PA. 1996. Lang.: Eng. 3903

Shock, Amy
Design/technology
Technical aspects of Wagner's *Ring* cycle, Arizona Opera. USA: Flagstaff, AZ. 1996. Lang.: Eng. 4028

Shoe Horn Sonata, The
Performance/production
Collection of newspaper reviews by London theatre critics. UK-England: London. 1996. Lang.: Eng. 2334

Shoestring Revue, The
Administration
Theatre and record producer Ben Bagley. USA: New York, NY. 1949-1996. Lang.: Eng. 3880

Shōjo toshi kara no yobigoe (Cry from the City of Virgins, A)
Performance/production
Japanese performances of Japanese themes at Toronto Theatre Festival. Japan. Canada: Toronto, ON. 1996. Lang.: Eng. 874

Shooting Magda
SEE
Ha-Palistinait.

Shopping and Fucking
Performance/production
Collection of newspaper reviews by London theatre critics. UK-England: London. 1996. Lang.: Eng. 2398

Short, Fat Kebab-Shop Owner's Son
Performance/production
Collection of newspaper reviews by London theatre critics. UK-England: London. 1996. Lang.: Eng. 2312

Shostakovich, Dmitri
SEE
Šostakovič, Dmitrij.

Shotlander, Sandra
Basic theatrical documents
Collection of Australian gay and lesbian plays. Australia. 1970-1996. Lang.: Eng. 1641

Show Boat
Administration
US and Canadian Equity associations discuss actor transfers in a production of *Show Boat*. USA: New York, NY. Canada. 1996. Lang.: Eng. 87
Performance/production
Singer/actor John Cullum. USA: New York, NY. 1965-1996. Lang.: Eng. 3935
Plays/librettos/scripts
Experiments in musical theatre in the twenties. USA. 1920-1929. Lang.: Eng. 3993

Silver, Ron — cont'd

Institutions

Equity president Ron Silver reports on issues of interest to members. USA: New York, NY. 1996. Lang.: Eng. 592

Silvestri, Martin

Performance/production

Collection of newspaper reviews by London theatre critics. UK-England: London. 1996. Lang.: Eng. 2343

Simard, Claude

Performance/production

The importance of memory in the performance art of Claude Simard. USA. 1996. Lang.: Eng. 3807

Simensen, Bjørn

Institutions

Interview with Bjørn Simensen, new manager of Den Norske Opera. Norway: Oslo. 1984. Lang.: Swe. 4051

Simon Boccanegra

Performance/production

Background material on Lyric Opera of Chicago radio broadcast performances. USA: Chicago, IL. 1996. Lang.: Eng. 4244

Simon, Balázs

Performance/production

English plays and subjects on the Hungarian stage. Hungary. 1995-1996. Lang.: Eng. 847

Simon, Barney

Performance/production

Interview with director Barney Simon of Market Theatre. South Africa, Republic of: Johannesburg. 1994. Lang.: Eng. 2269

Simón, Caballero de Indias (Simón Brumelstein, Knight of the Indies)

Basic theatrical documents

Anthology of Argentine Jewish theatre. Argentina. 1926-1988. Lang.: Eng. 1639

Simon, Neil

Performance/production

Collection of newspaper reviews by London theatre critics. UK-England: London. 1996. Lang.: Eng. 2320

Collection of newspaper reviews by London theatre critics. UK-England: London. 1996. Lang.: Eng. 2400

Collection of newspaper reviews by London theatre critics. UK-England: London. 1996. Lang.: Eng. 2443

Collection of newspaper reviews by London theatre critics. UK-England: London. 1996. Lang.: Eng. 2456

Plays/librettos/scripts

The influence of Eugene O'Neill on playwright Neil Simon. USA. 1949-1989. Lang.: Eng. 3338

Interviews with American playwrights. USA. 1945-1995. Lang.: Eng. 3397

Simonov, Reuben Nikolajévič

Performance/production

Vachtangov Theatre's revival of *Princessa Turandot* by Vachtangov, directed by Reuben Simonov. Russia: Moscow. 1993. Lang.: Rus. 2188

Simons, Jez

Performance/production

Collection of newspaper reviews by London theatre critics. UK-England: London. 1996. Lang.: Eng. 2332

Simply Barbra

Performance/production

Steven Brinberg's cabaret performance as Barbra Streisand. USA: New York, NY. 1993-1996. Lang.: Eng. 3737

Simply Disconnected

Performance/production

Collection of newspaper reviews by London theatre critics. UK-England: London. 1996. Lang.: Eng. 2423

Simpson, Jim

Performance/production

Collection of newspaper reviews by New York theatre critics. USA: New York, NY. 1996. Lang.: Eng. 2570

Simuka Zimbabwe! (Zimbabwe Arise!)

Performance/production

Review of *Simuka Zimbabwe! (Zimbabwe Arise!)* by Zambuko/Izibuko. Zimbabwe: Harare. 1994-1996. Lang.: Afr. 2701

Sinclair, John

Performance/production

Collection of newspaper reviews by London theatre critics. UK-England: London. 1996. Lang.: Eng. 2349

Sinel'nikova, Galina

Performance/production

Galina Sinel'nikova's *Polonez* at Belorussian Opera and Ballet Theatre. Belorus: Minsk. 1995. Lang.: Rus. 1495

Sinfonía en una botella (Symphony in a Bottle)

Plays/librettos/scripts

Analysis of plays by Hugo Salcedo. Mexico. 1987-1990. Lang.: Eng. 3144

Sing at Sunset

Performance/production

Collection of newspaper reviews by London theatre critics. UK-England: London. 1996. Lang.: Eng. 2438

Singer, Isaac Bashevis

Design/technology

Set and costume design for *Shlemiel the First*, ART/American Music Theatre Festival. USA: Cambridge, MA, Philadelphia, PA. 1996.Lang.: Eng. 3903

Performance/production

Vjačeslav Dolgačev's production of *Toibele i ee demon (Teibele and Her Demon)* by I.B. Singer and Eve Friedman. Russia: Moscow. 1996. Lang.: Rus. 2193

Singing

Performance/production

Potential uses of song in acting. Canada. USA. Europe. 1996. Lang.: Fre. 747

Portrait of actress Anne Bennent. Europe. 1963-1996. Lang.: Ger. 780

Interview with actor/dancer Jim Dale. UK-England. 1996. Lang.: Eng. 975

Highlights of interviews with Broadway stars. USA: New York, NY. 1985-1996. Lang.: Eng. 2601

Steve Ross's role in *Present Laughter* on Broadway. USA: New York, NY. 1996. Lang.: Eng. 2604

George Jellinek's radio show *The Vocal Scene*. USA: New York, NY. 1968-1996. Lang.: Eng. 3578

Recollections of making the musical film *Thoroughly Modern Millie*. USA. 1967. Lang.: Eng. 3638

Analysis of the appeal of the singer-actress Madonna. USA. 1990-1993. Lang.: Eng. 3682

Obituary for musician and actor Tupac Shakur. USA. 1971-1996. Lang.: Eng. 3719

Pictorial essay on New York cabaret artists. USA: New York, NY. 1996. Lang.: Eng. 3731

Nominees for MAC cabaret awards. USA: New York, NY. 1996. Lang.: Eng. 3732

Cabaret in London. USA: New York, NY. 1961-1996. Lang.: Eng. 3733

Profiles of cabaret singers. USA: New York, NY. 1996. Lang.: Eng. 3734

Cabaret singers Ann Hampton Callaway and Liz Callaway. USA: New York, NY. 1996. Lang.: Eng. 3735

Cabaret singer Nancy Lamott. USA: New York, NY. 1952-1996. Lang.: Eng. 3738

The variety entertainment tradition in South African theatre. South Africa, Republic of. 1900-1985. Lang.: Eng. 3834

The act of the fat lady at the sideshow of Coney Island. USA: Brooklyn, NY. 1992-1994. Lang.: Eng. 3837

The recording of Schubert's *Lieder* on CD. 1996. Lang.: Eng. 3853

Evaluation of Dietrich Fischer-Dieskau's recordings of Schubert *Lieder*. Germany. 1950-1985. Lang.: Eng. 3859

The life and work of singer Aleksand'r Vertinskij. Russia: Moscow. 1957-1996. Lang.: Rus. 3862

Singer Alla Bajanova. Russia. 1960-1996. Lang.: Rus. 3863

National singer Ljudmila Rjumina. Russia: Moscow. 1996. Lang.: Rus. 3864

Career of pop singer Vlad Staševskij. Russia: Moscow. 1990-1996. Lang.: Rus. 3865

Baritone Thomas Hampson on the symbolism of German *Lieder*. USA. 1996. Lang.: Eng. 3869

Composers and performers of the American art song. USA. 1996. Lang.: Eng. 3870

Tenor Paul Sperry's exploration of the American art song repertory. USA. 1996. Lang.: Eng. 3871

Musical theatre performer Evelyn Laye. UK-England. 1918-1996. Lang.: Eng. 3923

Ricky Martin's role in *Les Misérables*. USA: New York, NY. 1996. Lang.: Eng. 3931

Singer/actor John Cullum. USA: New York, NY. 1965-1996. Lang.: Eng. 3935

Singing — cont'd

Society of Stage Directors and Choreographers (SSDC, New York, NY)

Administration

Directors' property rights and the Joe Mantello case. USA: New York, NY. 1996. Lang.: Eng.   1621

Directors' rights: Joe Mantello's lawsuit regarding his staging of *Love! Valour! Compassion!*. USA: New York, NY. 1996. Lang.: Eng.   1624

Sociology

Administration

Overview of government patronage in Western culture. Europe. North America. 500 B.C.-1996 A.D. Lang.: Eng.   16

Argument for a Polish cultural policy to meet today's needs. Poland. 1995. Lang.: Eng, Fre.   40

Economics, the survival of theatre, and theatre's role in society. Russia. 1980-1996. Lang.: Rus.   45

Terence Gray and the Cambridge Festival Theatre. UK-England: Cambridge. 1926-1932. Lang.: Eng.   1620

Crisis on the German opera scene. Germany. 1993-1996. Lang.: Dan.   4009

Audience

The actor-audience relationship and the culture of performance. Europe. 1700-1799. Lang.: Ger.   135

Laughter and the development of community among spectators. Canada. 1990. Lang.: Fre.   1627

Common Weal Productions' community play *A North Side Story or Two*. Canada: Regina, SK. 1993-1995. Lang.: Eng.   1629

Cabaret performances in Theresienstadt concentration camp. Czechoslovakia: Terezin. 1941-1942. Lang.: Ger.   3725

Reactions to Montreal performances of Annie Sprinkle. Canada: Montreal, PQ. 1993. Lang.: Fre.   3785

The role of white minstrels in creating the stereotype of the Black minstrel. USA. 1822-1898. Lang.: Eng.   3829

The social importance of the Hamburg marionette theatre. Germany: Hamburg. 1800-1899. Lang.: Ger.   4436

Design/technology

Design in amateur theatre of Scottish Rite Freemasons. USA. 1896-1929. Lang.: Eng.   332

Institutions

Performance spaces of Montreal's cultural centers. Canada: Montreal, PQ. 1996. Lang.: Fre.   354

Children's theatre activities of immigrant welfare agency. Germany: Munich. 1989-1996. Lang.: Ger.   420

History of Hubert Ogunde's Yoruba Travelling Theatre. Nigeria. 1944-1971. Lang.: Eng.   502

Polish alternative theatre during the time of transition. Poland. 1989-1994. Lang.: Eng.   511

Community theatres arising from the reform movement and settlement houses. USA: Chicago, IL, Cleveland, OH, New York, NY. 1896-1930. Lang.: Eng.   570

Robert Brustein's response to August Wilson's call for separation of Black and white theatre. USA. 1996. Lang.: Eng.   573

TCG National Conference, addresses by August Wilson and John Ralston Saul. USA: Princeton, NJ. 1996. Lang.: Eng.   588

August Wilson's address on the separation of white and Black theatre. USA: Princeton, NJ. 1996. Lang.: Eng.   607

Profile of the Australian-Macedonian Drama Group. Australia: Melbourne. 1983-1994. Lang.: Eng.   1749

The Melbourne Women's Theatre Group. Australia: Melbourne. 1974-1977. Lang.: Eng.   1750

The work of Clyde Unity Theatre. UK-Scotland: Glasgow. 1986-1995. Lang.: Eng.   1859

Problems of maintaining a resident company, with emphasis on American Repertory Theatre. USA: Cambridge, MA. 1996. Lang.: Eng.   1874

Performance spaces

Research on Montreal theatre culture. Canada: Montreal, PQ. 1995-1996. Lang.: Fre.   619

The need to integrate rehearsal and performance spaces in urban planning. Canada: Montreal, PQ. 1989. Lang.: Fre.   620

Transformation of buildings into performance spaces in the Plateau neighborhood. Canada: Montreal, PQ. 1985-1996. Lang.: Fre.   624

Finding and creating urban cultural spaces. Canada: Montreal, PQ. France. 1996. Lang.: Fre.   627

The artist-led guided tours known as *Hidden Cities*. UK-England. 1995. Lang.: Eng.   3704

Philip Astley's amphitheatre and the development of English circus. England. 1768-1830. Lang.: Eng.   3751

Performance/production

Critique of audition system for actor-training institutions. Australia. 1993. Lang.: Eng.   686

Theatre as play in space. Canada. Europe. 1996. Lang.: Fre.   737

The Burbage family, the theatre, and their society. England. 1573-1677. Lang.: Eng.   770

The mobility of nineteenth-century actors. Germany. 1800-1899. Lang.: Ger.   813

Generational change among directors at German-language theatres. Germany. Austria. Switzerland. 1996. Lang.: Ger.   819

Introduction to volume on performance and cultural politics. North America. Europe. 1995. Lang.: Eng.   887

References to performers and entertainment in medieval Scandinavian literature. Norway. Sweden. Iceland. 793-1400. Lang.: Eng.   888

Problems of contemporary theatre. Russia. 1990-1996. Lang.: Rus.   912

Problems of portraying love on stage. Russia: Moscow. 1990-1996. Lang.: Rus.   913

Portrayals of gypsies at Teat'r Romen. Russia. 1930-1992. Lang.: Eng.   914

Distinctive characteristics of theatre festivals. South America. 1996. Lang.: Spa.   941

Banner Theatre Company and English alternative theatre. UK-England. 1960-1996. Lang.: Eng.   992

Argument for broader representation in the performing arts. UK-England. 1994-1995. Lang.: Eng.   997

Child performers in the Victorian theatre. UK-England. 1835-1865. Lang.: Eng.   999

Women's performance art and theatre. USA. 1970-1979. Lang.: Eng.   1017

Secular rituals of New Orleans culture. USA: New Orleans, LA. 1874-1995. Lang.: Eng.   1063

Racial 'passing' as historical performance. USA: New Orleans, LA. 1896. Lang.: Eng.   1064

Interview with choreographer Ulf Gadd about attitudes toward dance. Sweden. Indonesia. 1985. Lang.: Swe.   1442

Social boundaries and the transformation of the cakewalk. USA. 1900-1918. Lang.: Eng.   1448

Individualism and sexuality as traits of the Quebecois directing approach. Canada: Montreal, PQ. 1993-1996. Lang.: Fre.   1967

History and technique of the English acting tradition. England. 1590-1995. Lang.: Eng.   1988

Shakespeare and Elizabethan cultural politics: *A Midsummer Night's Dream*. England. 1590-1620. Lang.: Eng.   1990

Impressions of Berlin theatre. Germany: Berlin. 1996. Lang.: Ger.   2078

Israeli theatre and Israel's changing cultural life. Israel. 1996. Lang.: Eng.   2121

Analysis of Krystian Lupa's *Lunatycy (The Sleepwalkers)*, based on writing of Hermann Broch. Poland: Cracow. 1995. Lang.: Eng, Fre.   2178

John Masefield's theatricals. UK-England. 1919-1932. Lang.: Eng.   2535

The Western Wayne Players prison theatre workshop group. USA: Plymouth, MI. 1990-1996. Lang.: Eng.   2586

Analysis of plays about white slavery. USA. 1910-1920. Lang.: Eng.   2593

Interview with playwright/performer Anna Deavere Smith, and review of her *Fires in the Mirror*. USA: New York, NY. 1991-1993. Lang.: Eng.   2608

Free Southern Theatre's touring production of *Slave Ship* by Amiri Baraka. USA. 1970. Lang.: Eng.   2623

Political activities of actor Frank Fay. USA: New York, NY, Hollywood, CA. 1944-1950. Lang.: Eng.   2624

Essays and reviews of post-modern theatre. USA. 1979-1995. Lang.: Eng.   2627

The creation of a production based on the history of Carbondale's Women's Center. USA: Carbondale, IL. 1972-1994. Lang.: Eng.   2654

Social significance of solo performances by Anna Cora Mowatt. USA. 1841-1881. Lang.: Eng.   2683

Sociology — cont'd

Censorship of Federal Theatre Project's *Lysistrata* performed by Seattle Negro Repertory Company. USA: Seattle, WA. 1936-1939. Lang.: Eng.
2688

Interview with actor Jorge Perugorría. Cuba. 1994-1996. Lang.: Eng.
3615

Landscape and ideology in South African films. South Africa, Republic of. 1949-1996. Lang.: Eng.
3624

Political changes reflected in recent South African films. South Africa, Republic of. 1987-1996. Lang.: Eng.
3625

Influence of Hollywood gangster films on South African cinema. USA: Hollywood, CA. South Africa, Republic of. 1930-1996. Lang.: Eng. 3637

Cree actress Tina Keeper. Canada. 1996. Lang.: Eng.
3668

Popular theatrical genres in their cultural context. England. 1700-1899. Lang.: Rus.
3712

Anti-apartheid message of rap group Prophets of da City. South Africa, Republic of: Cape Town. 1990-1996. Lang.: Eng.
3714

History of the Victorian music hall. UK-England. 1830-1890. Lang.: Eng.
3716

Expressions of collective identity in Quebec comic monologues. Canada. 1980-1990. Lang.: Fre.
3727

Origins of *commedia dell'arte*. Italy. 1500-1700. Lang.: Ita.
3764

Queen Luise of Prussia as a court actress. Prussia. 1790-1810. Lang.: Ger.
3771

Political street entertainments as theatre. England: London. 1677. Lang.: Eng.
3776

The variety entertainment tradition in South African theatre. South Africa, Republic of. 1900-1985. Lang.: Eng.
3834

African-American gospel musicals. 1996. Lang.: Eng.
3911

Two forms of late nineteenth-century Black musical theatre. USA. 1895-1900. Lang.: Eng.
3965

Plays/librettos/scripts

Adaptations of *The Strange Case of Dr. Jekyll and Mr. Hyde* by Robert Louis Stevenson. USA. 1887-1990. Lang.: Eng.
1113

Women writers in postcolonial English. Australia. 1995. Lang.: Eng.
2723

Pan-Africanism in the theatre of Werewere Liking. Cameroon. Ivory Coast. 1976-1996. Lang.: Eng.
2736

Quebec nationalism in translation and adaptation. Canada. 1968-1990. Lang.: Fre.
2750

Translation and social context. Canada. 1989. Lang.: Fre.
2751

The psychology and sociology of gay theatre. Canada. 1960-1990. Lang.: Fre.
2759

Myth and iconography in Native Canadian theatre. Canada. 1987-1996. Lang.: Eng.
2783

Form and meaning in contemporary English-language theatre. Canada. 1972-1996. Lang.: Eng.
2795

Playwriting student's reaction to feminist Quebec theatre of the 1970s. Canada. 1975-1993. Lang.: Fre.
2820

Theatricality as sociopolitical commentary in plays of Mamet and Tremblay. Canada. USA. 1972-1996. Lang.: Eng.
2825

Place and identity in Quebecois drama. Canada. 1943-1996. Lang.: Fre.
2834

Analysis of *Fronteras Americanas* by Guillermo Verdecchia. Canada. 1993. Lang.: Eng.
2850

Colonialism, post-colonial dictatorships, and cultural identity in the work of Congolese playwrights. Congo. 1960-1996. Lang.: Eng.
2859

The Danish community play tradition. Denmark. 1970-1996. Lang.: Eng.
2873

The battle over memories of past events in Shakespeare's *Henry V*. England. 1590-1600. Lang.: Eng.
2876

Place names and their significance in the Cornish *ordinalia*. England: Cornwall. 1300-1419. Lang.: Eng.
2882

Race and ethnic difference in Shakespeare's *The Winter's Tale*. England. 1547-1619. Lang.: Eng.
2895

Homosexuality in Renaissance drama. England. 1580-1620. Lang.: Eng.
2896

The representation of social and sexual contact in Shakespeare's *Twelfth Night*. England. 1600-1614. Lang.: Eng.
2900

Marlowe's *Tamburlaine the Great* and the pastoral. England. 1587-1588. Lang.: Eng.
2913

Renaissance economics as reflected in Shakespeare's *The Taming of the Shrew*. England. 1590-1604. Lang.: Eng.
2923

Oscar Wilde's trial for indecency. England. 1890-1996. Lang.: Eng. 2952

The theatrical legacy of the French Revolution. France. 1789-1989. Lang.: Fre.
3004

Analysis of *Trilogie des tables (Trilogy of the Tables)* by Joël Dragutin. France. 1985-1993. Lang.: Fre.
3011

The influence of Ibsen's *Johan Gabriel Borkman* on sociologist Max Weber. Germany. Norway. 1896-1930. Lang.: Eng.
3020

German drama, politics, and Klaus Pohl's *Wartesaal Deutschland StimmenReich (Waiting Room Germany)*. Germany: Berlin. 1995. Lang.: Ger.
3027

Trends in Israeli drama and theatre. Israel. 1948-1996. Lang.: Eng. 3094

Themes of the Israeli public theatres. Israel. 1990. Lang.: Eng.
3106

Scandinavian theatre in Polish culture. Poland. Scandinavia. 1876-1918. Lang.: Pol.
3167

Playwright Vladimir Sorokin and his popularity in Germany. Russia. Germany. 1955-1996. Lang.: Ger.
3191

Analysis of plays by major Slovene dramatists. Slovenia. 1900-1996. Lang.: Slo.
3212

Athol Fugard and the role of revolutionary theatre after the revolution. South Africa, Republic of. 1948-1994. Lang.: Eng.
3220

Painting and graffiti in plays of Cervantes and Claramonte. Spain. 1492-1650. Lang.: Eng.
3229

Status of playwriting in Swedish. Sweden. 1996. Lang.: Swe.
3272

Swedish theatres and their attitudes toward Swedish playwrights. Sweden. 1996. Lang.: Swe.
3274

Political ramifications of British realist theatre. UK-England. 1956-1965. Lang.: Eng.
3297

Analysis of plays by Joaquín Culebras. Uruguay. 1831. Lang.: Eng. 3319

Race relations and *Miss Evers' Boys* by David Feldshuh. USA. 1985. Lang.: Eng.
3325

Comparison of writings by Eugene O'Neill and John Reed. USA: New York, NY. 1913-1922. Lang.: Eng.
3327

Analysis of David Mamet's *Oleanna*. USA. 1992. Lang.: Eng.
3332

Political and military context of O'Neill's *The Emperor Jones*. USA. Haiti. 1898-1920. Lang.: Eng.
3386

Comparison of historical dramas by Robert Bolt and Arthur Miller. USA. UK-England. 1953-1966. Lang.: Eng.
3413

Guilt and responsibility in later plays of Arthur Miller. USA. 1964-1996. Lang.: Eng.
3420

Influence of Albert Camus on plays of Arthur Miller. USA. 1950-1996. Lang.: Eng.
3456

Critique of Steven Spielberg's film adaptation of *The Color Purple* by Alice Walker. USA. 1982-1986. Lang.: Eng.
3649

TV in Papua New Guinea. Papua New Guinea. 1975-1995. Lang.: Eng.
3683

The representation of Jews on the American stage. USA. 1870-1880. Lang.: Eng.
3840

The Aboriginal music drama *Bran Nue Dae*. Australia. 1995. Lang.: Eng.
3983

The adaptation of American musicals for a Korean public. Korea: Seoul. 1996. Lang.: Kor.
3985

Russian perceptions of the Orient in Rimskij-Korsakov's *Kitezh*. Russia. 1907. Lang.: Eng.
4338

Relation to other fields

Asian stereotypes on the Australian stage. Australia. 1850-1993. Lang.: Eng.
1131

Immigrant writers in Australian theatre. Australia. 1979-1995. Lang.: Eng.
1132

Theatre and the normalization of the New South Wales penal colony. Australia. 1789-1830. Lang.: Eng.
1133

Social and political context of contemporary Australian theatre. Australia: Sydney. 1995. Lang.: Eng.
1134

How the position of women in Quebec theatre has changed. Canada. 1980-1993. Lang.: Fre.
1139

Memory and Quebec theatre. Canada. 1989. Lang.: Fre.
1141

Theatre's lack of influence as a source of strength and independence. Canada. 1989. Lang.: Fre.
1143

Crisis and the performing arts. Canada. USA.. 1966-1996. Lang.: Fre.
1147

Sociology — cont'd

Theatre and collective memory in Quebec culture. Canada. 1989. Lang.: Fre.   1148

Historic and contemporary functions of the theatre critic. Canada. France. 1700-1996. Lang.: Fre.   1150

The social function of theatrical practice. Canada: Quebec, PQ. 1950-1996. Lang.: Fre.   1152

Reconsideration of feminist criticism of the early 1980s. Canada. 1975-1993. Lang.: Fre.   1154

Experimental theatre in the social context. Canada. France. 1880-1989. Lang.: Fre.   1155

The changed position of women in Quebec theatre. Canada. 1980-1993. Lang.: Fre.   1156

National and regional identities in Canadian theatre companies. Canada. 1860-1994. Lang.: Eng.   1157

The Australian perspective on Canadian theatre. Canada. Australia. 1996. Lang.: Eng.   1158

American musicals and plays in China. China, People's Republic of. 1984-1996. Lang.: Eng.   1164

Social and political conditions in Czech theatre. Czechoslovakia. 1989-1992. Lang.: Fre.   1167

Intellectual property rights in the 'postmodern' world. Europe. North America. 1996. Lang.: Eng.   1174

Reception of alien cultures in Western theatre. Europe. 1600-1996. Lang.: Ger.   1176

The meeting of cultures in work of Peter Brook and Ariane Mnouchkine. France. UK-England. 1970-1996. Lang.: Dan.   1179

French theatre at the Saarbrücken Perspectives festival. Germany: Saarbrücken. 1995. Lang.: Fre.   1181

Life and theatre in Chemnitz. Germany: Chemnitz. 1996. Lang.: Ger.   1185

Berlin theatre in the current German intellectual debate. Germany: Berlin. 1991-1996. Lang.: Eng.   1192

East German actresses' reactions to social changes after the fall of the Berlin wall. Germany, East: Berlin, East. 1990-1991. Lang.: Ger.   1195

The relevance of ancient Greek theatre to contemporary life. Greece: Athens. Sweden: Vetlanda. 404 B.C. Lang.: Swe.   1196

Rustom Bharucha's *Guindegowdana Charitre* and 'intraculturalism'. India. 1977-1995. Lang.: Eng.   1200

Performance and sexuality as observed in an Irish pub. Ireland: Dublin. 1996. Lang.: Eng.   1201

Jewish/Arab encounters in drama projects. Israel. 1977-1995. Lang.: Eng.   1203

Theatricality in Latin America and its historical impact. Latin America. 1996. Lang.: Eng.   1209

Female identity as seen through culture. Philippines: Mindanao. India: New Delhi. 1986-1995. Lang.: Eng.   1216

Transformations of Cheljabinsk's theatrical life. Russia: Cheljabinsk. 1990-1996. Lang.: Rus.   1224

The city and art, especially theatre. Russia. 1990-1996. Lang.: Rus.   1230

Spanish theatre and photography. Spain. 1956-1996. Lang.: Eng.   1232

Theatre in AIDS education. Uganda. 1989-1991. Lang.: Eng.   1234

Jatinder Verma's multicultural approach to theatre. UK. 1996. Lang.: Eng.   1239

Theatre of the organized working class. UK-England. 1830-1930. Lang.: Eng.   1242

Report on 1995 event of the Magdalena Project. UK-Wales: Cardiff. 1995. Lang.: Eng.   1251

Theatre riots as an expression of class conflict. USA. 1754-1849. Lang.: Eng.   1253

Blackface performances in the early nineteenth century. USA. 1800-1844. Lang.: Eng.   1254

Bondage in Black writing, including plays of Soyinka. USA. Africa. 1996. Lang.: Eng.   1255

Survey of American attitudes toward the arts. USA. 1996. Lang.: Eng.   1256

Theatrical productions in the vicinity of the Republican National Convention. USA: San Diego, CA. 1996. Lang.: Eng.   1259

Women, reform, and performance at the Marionette Club. USA: Chicago, IL. 1890-1915. Lang.: Eng.   1260

The political, economic, and spiritual challenges of persisting in artistic endeavors. USA. 1996. Lang.: Eng.   1262

The situation of Black theatre groups. USA. 1996. Lang.: Eng.   1263

Profile of a lesbian 'marriage' in the theatre community. USA: New York, NY. 1886-1933. Lang.: Eng.   1264

Intercollegiate performance festivals and their influence on performance. USA. 1945-1994. Lang.: Eng.   1270

Rhythm as a form of social discourse. USA. 1994. Lang.: Eng.   1275

Responses to August Wilson's call for separation of Black and white theatre. USA. 1996. Lang.: Eng.   1277

How performance festivals can give a sense of the host city. USA: Tampa, FL. 1990. Lang.: Eng.   1278

Ritual performance in the Charismatic religious movement. USA. 1994. Lang.: Eng.   1279

The present state of Hungarian artistic dance. Hungary. 1900-1990. Lang.: Hun.   1455

Appeal for a balanced view of the rave phenomenon. Sweden. 1989. Lang.: Swe.   1456

Swedish attitudes toward dance. Sweden. 1785. Lang.: Swe.   1459

Reflections of social trends in international modern dance festival. Denmark: Copenhagen. 1996. Lang.: Dan.   1596

Multiculturalism and contemporary British dance. UK-England. 1995. Lang.: Eng.   1598

The Socialist agenda and modern dance. USA. 1931-1938. Lang.: Eng.   1600

German-Australian theatrical exchange. Australia. Germany. 1945-1995. Lang.: Eng.   3478

Attitudes toward gay theatre in Quebec. Canada. 1960-1990. Lang.: Fre.   3480

Homosexuality in Quebecois society and theatre. Canada. 1960-1990. Lang.: Fre.   3481

Immigrant playwright Marco Micone on multiculturalism and cultural assimilation. Canada: Montreal, PQ. Lang.: Fre.   3486

Female education in Shakespeare's time and plays. England. 1510-1621. Lang.: Eng.   3492

The Arab on the Israeli stage. Israel. 1912-1990. Lang.: Eng.   3500

Social and aesthetic trends in Japanese children's theatre festival. Japan: Tokyo. 1995. Lang.: Fre.   3501

The political mission of South African English studies, with emphasis on Shakespeare. South Africa, Republic of. 1800-1995. Lang.: Eng.   3508

George Bernard Shaw's unpublished article on the gentleman. UK-England. 1879. Lang.: Eng.   3514

The African-American cultural renaissance in theatre. USA. 1926-1996. Lang.: Eng.   3521

The demise of cultural literacy as seen on TV and in films. USA. 1945-1996. Lang.: Eng.   3571

Problems of Black directors within the studio system. USA. 1985-1996. Lang.: Eng.   3650

Political and ethical considerations regarding South African television. South Africa, Republic of. 1996. Lang.: Eng.   3686

South African media and film policy. South Africa, Republic of. 1980-1996. Lang.: Eng.   3687

The *commedia dell'arte* in the language of the Genoese ruling class. Italy: Genoa. 1528-1586. Lang.: Ita.   3769

The public performance of vows and pilgrimages. Italy: Ferrara. 1476-1487. Lang.: Ita.   3772

Analysis of excerpts from a woodland ceremony in the *Ligger Book*. England. 1567-1621. Lang.: Eng.   3781

Drama and the control of violence in the Lille processional. France: Lille. 1270-1499. Lang.: Eng.   3783

Performance artist Geneviève Letarte. Canada. 1988. Lang.: Fre.   3816

Interview with Richard Schechner about performance art. USA. 1967-1996. Lang.: Dan.   3822

Performance artist Blanche Davidian's infiltration of right-wing extremist groups. USA. 1995-1996. Lang.: Eng.   3823

Philosophical and sociological view of German variety acts. Germany. 1900-1996. Lang.: Dan.   3841

Civic musicians and the role of ceremonial display. England: Southampton. 1577-1640. Lang.: Eng.   3875

Opera in popular culture. USA. Canada. 1950-1996. Lang.: Eng.   4355

Theory/criticism

Theory of studies of theatricality, including cultural and sociopolitical communication. 1996. Lang.: Ger.   1311

Southwark Playhouse (London) — cont'd

Collection of newspaper reviews by London theatre critics. UK-England: London. 1996. Lang.: Eng. 2368

Collection of newspaper reviews by London theatre critics. UK-England: London. 1996. Lang.: Eng. 2384

Collection of newspaper reviews by London theatre critics. UK-England: London. 1996. Lang.: Eng. 2395

Collection of newspaper reviews by London theatre critics. UK-England: London. 1996. Lang.: Eng. 2405

Collection of newspaper reviews by London theatre critics. UK-England: London. 1996. Lang.: Eng. 2421

Collection of newspaper reviews by London theatre critics. UK-England: London. 1996. Lang.: Eng. 2452

Collection of newspaper reviews by London theatre critics. UK-England: London. 1996. Lang.: Eng. 2460

Collection of newspaper reviews by London theatre critics. UK-England: London. 1996. Lang.: Eng. 2463

Souzay, Gérard
Performance/production
French vocalism and its artists. France. 1996. Lang.: Eng. 4124

Sovremennik (Moscow)
Performance/production
Collection of newspaper reviews by New York theatre critics. USA: New York, NY. 1996. Lang.: Eng. 2560

Soyinka, Wole
Performance/production
Postcolonial theatre. Europe. North America. Asia. Africa. 1880-1950. Lang.: Eng. 779

Collection of newspaper reviews by New York theatre critics. USA: New York, NY. 1996. Lang.: Eng. 2557
Plays/librettos/scripts
Wole Soyinka's work as a playwright. Nigeria. 1960-1996. Lang.: Eng. 3148

Traditional African aesthetics in the plays of Wole Soyinka. Nigeria. 1960-1975. Lang.: Eng. 3150

African aspects of the drama of August Wilson. USA. Africa. 1990-1996. Lang.: Eng. 3331
Relation to other fields
Bondage in Black writing, including plays of Soyinka. USA. Africa. 1996. Lang.: Eng. 1255

Spangenberg, Nils
Performance/production
Carl Unander-Scharin's *Tokfursten* staged at Vadstena Akademien. Sweden: Vadstena. 1996. Lang.: Swe. 4219

Spanish Curate, The
Basic theatrical documents
Text of plays by Fletcher and his collaborators. England. 1609-1613. Lang.: Eng. 1655

Spanish Tragedy, The
Plays/librettos/scripts
Gesture and self-construction in early modern English drama. England. 1580-1613. Lang.: Eng. 2962

Spanish Wives, The
Plays/librettos/scripts
Women and sexuality in plays of Aphra Behn, Mary Pix, and Catharine Trotter. England: London. 1660-1750. Lang.: Eng. 2946

Sparschuh, Jens
Performance/production
Reviews of German-language productions. Germany. Switzerland. Austria. 1996. Lang.: Ger. 2089

Spät (Late)
Basic theatrical documents
Text of *Spät (Late)* by Wolfgang Maria Bauer. Germany. 1996. Lang.: Ger. 1657

Special effects
Design/technology
Use of MIDI to create an on-stage computer. North America. 1996. Lang.: Eng. 190

Constructing a frameless scenic turntable. North America. 1996. Lang.: Eng. 192

Rigging for a flying puppet figure on stage. North America. 1996. Lang.: Eng. 193

Guide to industry resources for technical theatre. USA. 1996. Lang.: Eng. 237

Guide to manufacturers and equipment for theatre technology. USA. 1996. Lang.: Eng. 238

Design for the *Wizard of Oz* ice show. USA: New York, NY. 1996. Lang.: Eng. 239

Technical elements of Silver Legacy Resort and Casino. USA: Reno, NV. 1995. Lang.: Eng. 265

Profile of BRC Imagination Arts, creator of educational attractions. USA: Burbank, CA. 1996. Lang.: Eng. 268

Using a flash camera for theatrical lighting effects. USA. 1996. Lang.: Eng. 287

Description of pneumatic debris cannon used for explosion effects. USA. 1996. Lang.: Eng. 303

The Olio Roll Drop. USA. 1996. Lang.: Eng. 309

The replacement of DMX512 by Ethernet for controlling moving lights and other stage devices. USA. 1996. Lang.: Eng. 322

Health effects of glycol-based stage fog. USA. 1996. Lang.: Eng. 323

Lighting and special effects by Gary Fails of City Theatricals. USA: New York, NY. 1996. Lang.: Eng. 324

Cinema Services and the video spectacle *EFX*. USA: Las Vegas, NV. 1995. Lang.: Eng. 3665

Serge Ouaknine's fireworks displays—relation to his theatrical work. France: Paris. 1992-1995. Lang.: Fre. 3695

Design of Caesar's Magical Empire at Caesar's Palace casino. USA: Las Vegas, NV. 1996. Lang.: Eng. 3698

Technical aspects of a German-language production of Disney's *Beauty and the Beast*. Austria: Vienna. 1995. Lang.: Ger. 3888

Design for the musical *Big*. USA: Detroit, MI. 1996. Lang.: Eng. 3902
Performance/production
Study of adverse effects of stage smoke and fog on actors. USA: New York, NY. 1996. Lang.: Eng. 1049

Description of a stop-motion animation segment used in a prime-time situation comedy. USA: Los Angeles, CA. 1995-1996. Lang.: Eng. 3675

Speeltheater (Ghent)
Institutions
Report on the Dutch Theatre Festival. Netherlands: Amsterdam. 1996. Lang.: Eng. 1816

spell #7
Plays/librettos/scripts
Analysis of *spell #7* by Ntozake Shange. USA. 1979-1995. Lang.: Eng. 3352

Spence, Eulalie
Plays/librettos/scripts
Harlem Renaissance playwrights Willis Richardson and Eulalie Spence. USA: New York, NY. 1920-1930. Lang.: Eng. 3378

The dual liberation motif in early Black women playwrights. USA. 1915-1930. Lang.: Eng. 3387

Sperry, Paul
Performance/production
Tenor Paul Sperry's exploration of the American art song repertory. USA. 1996. Lang.: Eng. 3871

Spiderwoman Theater (New York, NY)
Plays/librettos/scripts
Presentations by story-tellers at women playwrights conference. Australia. USA. Philippines. 1981-1995. Lang.: Eng. 1083

Spielberg, Steven
Plays/librettos/scripts
Critique of Steven Spielberg's film adaptation of *The Color Purple* by Alice Walker. USA. 1982-1986. Lang.: Eng. 3649

Spike Heels
Performance/production
Collection of newspaper reviews by London theatre critics. UK-England: London. 1996. Lang.: Eng. 2435

Špiller, Natalija D.
Performance/production
Opera singers Mark Rejzen and Natalija Špiller. Russia. 1895-1995. Lang.: Rus. 4200

Spillmann, Uwe
Performance/production
Uwe Spillmann's street puppet theatre. Germany. 1996. Lang.: Ger. 4395

Spiró, György
Performance/production
Budapest productions of the millicentenary season. Hungary: Budapest. 1995-1996. Lang.: Eng. 2104

Review of some Budapest productions. Hungary. 1995-1996. Lang.: Eng. 2105
Plays/librettos/scripts
Postwar Hungarian drama. Hungary. 1945-1989. Lang.: Hun. 3069

Spitalfields Market Opera (London)
Performance/production
Collection of newspaper reviews by London theatre critics. UK-England: London. 1996. Lang.: Eng. 2426

Spivak, Semyon
Performance/production
Actor Anatolij Petrov. Russia: Moscow. 1996. Lang.: Rus. 2237

Spivak, Sergej
Performance/production
The Three Penny Opera at Fontanka Youth Theatre. Russia: St. Petersburg. 1996. Lang.: Rus. 4211

Splendid's
Performance/production
German-language production of *Splendid's* by Jean Genet, directed by Klaus Michael Grüber. France: Paris. 1995. Lang.: Eng. 2023

Splendida vergonya del fet mal fet, L' (Splendid Shame of the Deed Badly Done, The)
Performance/production
Collection of newspaper reviews by London theatre critics. UK-England: London. 1996. Lang.: Eng. 2381

Split Britches
Basic theatrical documents
Anthology of works by Split Britches. USA. 1985-1995. Lang.: Eng. 1685

Split Britches (New York, NY)
Basic theatrical documents
Anthology of works by Split Britches. USA. 1985-1995. Lang.: Eng. 1685
Performance/production
Performance at WOW Cafe. USA: New York, NY. 1980-1985. Lang.: Eng. 1071

Spöken (Ghosts)
Performance/production
Staffan Roos's children's theatre project *Spöken (Ghosts)* at Royal Dramatic Theatre. Sweden: Stockholm. 1996. Lang.: Swe. 2279
Kungliga Dramatiska Teatern and Staffan Roos's children's production *Spöken (Ghosts)*. Sweden: Stockholm. 1996. Lang.: Swe. 2291

Sponsus
Performance/production
Ensemble for Early Music's performance of the St. Martial *Sponsus* at The Cloisters. USA: New York, NY. 1996. Lang.: Eng. 1019

Sprawa Moniki (Monica's Case)
Plays/librettos/scripts
Reactions of male critics to Polish feminist drama. Poland. 1932-1938. Lang.: Pol. 3162

Springate, Michael
Institutions
The dramaturg's role at Factory Theatre. Canada: Toronto, ON. 1996. Lang.: Eng. 1777

Springhill Singing Disaster, The
Performance/production
Karen Trott's one-woman show *The Springhill Singing Disaster*. USA: New York, NY. 1996. Lang.: Eng. 2685

Sprinkle, Annie
Audience
Reactions to Montreal performances of Annie Sprinkle. Canada: Montreal, PQ. 1993. Lang.: Fre. 3785
Performance/production
Explicitly erotic feminist performance art. USA. 1989-1994. Lang.: Eng. 3805
Relation to other fields
The centrality of the body in recent performance art. 1980-1996. Lang.: Dan. 3814
Theory/criticism
Nudity and vulnerability in performance art. USA. 1960-1996. Lang.: Eng. 3826

Squat
Plays/librettos/scripts
Analysis of stage and radio plays by Raymond Villeneuve. Canada: Montreal, PQ. 1987-1991. Lang.: Fre. 1090

Squat Theatre (New York, NY)
Institutions
The history of Squat Theatre. Hungary: Budapest. USA: New York, NY. 1969-1981. Lang.: Eng. 485

Srebrenica: 1996 The Hague War Crimes Trial
Performance/production
Collection of newspaper reviews by London theatre critics. UK-England: London. 1996. Lang.: Eng. 2409

Srnec-Todorović, Asja
Plays/librettos/scripts
The problem of identity in recent Croatian drama. Croatia. 1990-1995. Lang.: Eng. 2860

St. Clements Theatre (New York, NY)
Performance/production
Collection of newspaper reviews by New York theatre critics. USA: New York, NY. 1996. Lang.: Eng. 2552

St. Denis, Ruth
Training
Etienne Decroux's theory of corporeal mime. France: Paris. 1918-1996. Lang.: Eng. 3688

St. James Theatre (New York, NY)
Performance/production
Profiles of new actors on Broadway. USA: New York, NY. 1996. Lang.: Eng. 1012
Collection of newspaper reviews by New York theatre critics. USA: New York, NY. 1996. Lang.: Eng. 2577

St. Léon, Arthur
Performance/production
Choreographic realizations of the story of Pygmalion. France. 1734-1847. Lang.: Eng. 1422

St. Nicholas Hotel, The
Plays/librettos/scripts
Analysis of *The Donnellys* by James Reaney. Canada. 1973-1975. Lang.: Eng. 2847

St. Paul
Plays/librettos/scripts
Representation of devils and vices in English liturgy and theatre. England. 1300-1500. Lang.: Eng. 2890

Staatsoper (Dresden)
SEE
Dresdner Hoftheater.

Staatsoper (Vienna)
Design/technology
Conference on hydraulic and electronic stage technology. Germany: Lohr am Main. 1996. Lang.: Swe. 174

Staatsoperette (Dresden)
Performance spaces
History of the Staatsoperette. Germany: Dresden. 1925-1996. Lang.: Ger. 4363

Staatstheater (Braunschweig)
Performance spaces
Staatstheater Braunschweig's new theatre building. Germany: Braunschweig. 1996. Lang.: Ger. 642

Staatstheater (Cottbus)
Institutions
Portrait of Staatstheater Cottbus, directed by Christoph Schroth. Germany: Cottbus. 1996. Lang.: Ger. 439

Staatstheater (Darmstadt)
Design/technology
Renewal of the sound system at Staatstheater. Germany: Darmstadt. 1996. Lang.: Ger. 172

Staatstheater (Kassel)
Performance spaces
Problems with the orchestra pit at Kassel's Staatstheater. Germany: Kassel. 1996. Lang.: Ger. 645

Staatstheater am Gärtnerplatz (Munich)
Performance/production
Current German theatre. Germany: Berlin, Trier, Munich. 1995. Lang.: Eng. 2080

Staatstheater Mainz GmbH
Performance/production
Director Michael Helle. Germany: Mainz. Germany: Düsseldorf. 1953-1996. Lang.: Ger. 809
Productions of new plays by Elfriede Müller and Jens Roselt. Germany: Saarbrücken, Mainz. 1996. Lang.: Ger. 2052

Staatstheater, Kleines Haus (Braunschweig)
Institutions
The new season at Staatstheater, Kleines Haus. Germany: Braunschweig. 1996. Lang.: Ger. 1812
Performance spaces
The architecture of the new Staatstheater, Kleines Haus. Germany: Braunschweig. 1996. Lang.: Ger. 641

Stadlen, Lewis J.
Performance/production
Interviews with Tony Award nominees. USA: New York, NY. 1996. Lang.: Eng. 2596

Stadsschouwburg (Amsterdam)
Relation to other fields
Description of the portraits in the lobby of the Stadsschouwburg. Netherlands: Amsterdam. 1895-1995. Lang.: Dut. 1212

Staging — cont'd

Staging — cont'd

Peter Brook's *L'homme qui (The Man Who)* as a model of multicultural theatre. USA: New York, NY. 1995. Lang.: Eng. 2618

Two productions of the National Black Theatre Festival. USA: Winston-Salem, NC. 1995. Lang.: Eng. 2625

Racism and sexism in *A Midsummer Night's Dream* at Shakespeare Santa Cruz, directed by Danny Scheie. USA: Santa Cruz, CA. 1991. Lang.: Eng. 2637

Review of *Tubes* by Blue Man Group. USA: New York, NY. 1994. Lang.: Eng. 2642

Jon Jory's evaluation of directing and director training. USA. 1996. Lang.: Eng. 2644

The cancelled guest performance of Bergman's *Misanthrope* at BAM. USA: New York, NY. Sweden: Stockholm. 1995. Lang.: Swe. 2648

The creation of a production based on the history of Carbondale's Women's Center. USA: Carbondale, IL. 1972-1994. Lang.: Eng. 2654

Speculation on the future of interactive theatre. USA: New York, NY. 1996. Lang.: Eng. 2663

Productions of *The Two Noble Kinsmen* by Shakespeare and Fletcher. USA: New York, NY, Ashland, OR, Philadelphia, PA. 1993-1994. Lang.: Eng. 2667

Interview with Tina Landau, director of *The Trojan Women: A Love Story.* USA: New York, NY. 1996. Lang.: Eng. 2672

Arden Theatre Company's production of *Lovers* by Brian Friel, directed by Adam Posner. USA: Philadelphia, PA. 1995. Lang.: Eng. 2676

Interview with director Mary Zimmerman. USA: Chicago, IL. 1996. Lang.: Eng. 2684

Wooster Group's production of *Brace Up!*, an adaptation of Čechov's *Tri sestry (Three Sisters).* USA: New York, NY. 1991. Lang.: Fre. 2686

Productions of Tretjakov's *Choču Rebenka (I Want a Baby).* USSR: Moscow. UK-England: Birmingham. Germany: Berlin. 1927-1993.Lang.: Eng. 2694

Eisenstein's work as a theatre director. USSR. 1923. Lang.: Ita. 2695

Mejerchol'd's production of *Le cocu magnifique (The Magnificent Cuckold)* by Crommelynck. USSR. 1917-1922. Lang.: Eng. 2697

Analysis of film and video versions of *Romeo and Juliet.* USA. UK-England. Italy. 1936-1978. Lang.: Eng. 3631

Description of the video performance *Degraded* by students of Bristol University. UK-England: Bristol. 1980-1995. Lang.: Eng. 3674

The work of Hotel Pro Forma. Denmark: Copenhagen. 1986-1995. Lang.: Eng. 3709

Review of *Monkey Business Class* by Hotel Pro Forma. Denmark: Copenhagen. 1996. Lang.: Dan. 3711

The use of a female performer for the Old French *chantefable, Aucassin et Nicolette.* France. 1200-1994. Lang.: Eng. 3713

Review of *Il ritorno di Scaramouche (The Return of Scaramouche)* directed by Leo De Bernardis. Italy: Scandicci. 1996. Lang.: Ita. 3766

Genre classification of the Pater Noster play. England: Beverly. 1378-1577. Lang.: Eng. 3777

Analysis of *Suz o Suz* by La Fura dels Baus. Spain: Barcelona. 1996. Lang.: Eng. 3791

The concept of 'gallery theatre'. USA. 1996. Lang.: Eng. 3806

Interview with set designer Louise Beck. Denmark. UK-England. 1994-1996. Lang.: Dan. 3854

Extracts from Cheshire records of music in theatre. England: Chester. 1518-1642. Lang.: Eng. 3855

Modern productions of *Ludus Danielis (The Play of Daniel).* Europe. USA. 1140-1984. Lang.: Eng. 3856

Canadian musical theatre. Canada: Toronto, ON, Montreal, PQ. 1996. Lang.: Eng. 3913

Interview with Norbert Gingold regarding score preparation and conducting of *The Three Penny Opera.* Germany: Berlin. Austria: Vienna. 1928-1929. Lang.: Eng. 3916

Discussion surrounding a performance of *Murx* by Christoph Marthaler. Germany: Berlin. UK-England: London. 1995. Lang.: Eng. 3917

Revivals of the Hungarian pop musical *Képzelt riport egy amerikai popfesztiválról (Imaginary Report on an American Pop Festival).* Hungary. 1973-1995. Lang.: Hun. 3919

Gerald Gutierrez's direction of *Once Upon a Mattress.* USA: New York, NY. 1959-1996. Lang.: Eng. 3943

Interview with director George C. Wolfe about *Bring in 'Da Noise, Bring in 'Da Funk.* USA: New York, NY. 1989. Lang.: Eng. 3951

Musical theatre director Jerry Zaks. USA: New York, NY. 1980-1996. Lang.: Eng. 3953

Alain Thibault's musical score for *Ne blâmez jamais les Bédouins (Don't Blame the Bedouins)* by René-Daniel Dubois. Canada: Montreal, PQ. 1991. Lang.: Fre. 4095

Peter Sellars' interpretation of Mozart's *Don Giovanni.* Europe. 1980-1996. Lang.: Eng. 4115

R. Murray Schafer's opera *Le Théâtre noir* at the Festival musical de Liège. France: Liège. 1989. Lang.: Fre. 4118

Peter Sellars' production of Stravinskij's *The Rake's Progress.* France: Paris. 1996. Lang.: Swe. 4123

Postmodernist stagings of Wagnerian opera. Germany. 1970-1996. Lang.: Eng. 4131

Portrait of opera director Ruth Berghaus. Germany. 1981-1996. Lang.: Ger. 4136

Peter Mussbach, opera director and set designer. Germany. 1975-1996. Lang.: Ger. 4138

Performance and technical aspects of Orff's *Carmina Burana* at the Bavarian State Opera. Germany. 1996. Lang.: Eng. 4143

Wolfgang Wagner's scenery and direction of *Die Meistersinger* at the Bayreuth Festival. Germany: Bayreuth. 1996. Lang.: Ger. 4146

Ljubimov's opera productions at La Scala. Italy: Milan. 1970-1980. Lang.: Rus. 4175

Opera production at La Scala under Paolo Grassi. Italy: Milan. 1972-1977. Lang.: Ita. 4176

Luciano Berio's *Outis* staged at La Scala by Graham Vick. Italy: Milan. 1996. Lang.: Swe. 4185

Boris Pokrovskij's production of the opera *Dvorjanskoje Gnezdo* by V. Rebikov, based on work of Turgenev. Russia. 1990-1996. Lang.: Rus. 4195

The specifics of staging an epic opera. Russia. 1990-1996. Lang.: Rus. 4196

Jurij Aleksandrov's production of Mussorgskij's *Boris Godunov*, St. Petersburg Opera. Russia: St. Petersburg. 1995-1996. Lang.: Rus. 4199

Ideology and the interpretation of opera classics. Russia. 1990-1996. Lang.: Rus. 4201

Interview with director Aleksand'r Petrov on his work in opera. Russia: St. Petersburg. 1996. Lang.: Rus. 4203

Martynov's *Plach Jeremii* staged by Vasiljév's School of Dramatic Art. Russia: Moscow. 1995-1996. Lang.: Rus. 4209

On the profession of opera director and its requirements. Russia: Moscow. 1996. Lang.: Rus. 4210

Carl Unander-Scharin's *Tokfursten* staged at Vadstena Akademien. Sweden: Vadstena. 1996. Lang.: Swe. 4219

Interview with director David Radok. Sweden: Gothenburg. Czech Republic: Prague. 1990. Lang.: Swe. 4221

Puccini operas at Opera North and Welsh National Opera. UK-Wales: Cardiff. UK-England: Leeds. 1996. Lang.: Eng. 4237

Directing and staging in contemporary opera production. USA. 1996. Lang.: Eng. 4242

Thomson and Stein's *Four Saints in Three Acts* directed by Robert Wilson. USA: New York, NY. 1996. Lang.: Eng. 4273

Work of Tim Albery and Antony McDonald on Met production of Britten's *A Midsummer Night's Dream* by Britten. USA: New York, NY. 1996. Lang.: Eng. 4296

Review of puppetry performances by Teatr Animacji. Poland: Poznań. 1994-1995. Lang.: Eng, Fre. 4397

Review of Zygmunt Smandzik's *Orfeusz (Orpheus)*, Teatr Lalka. Poland: Warsaw. 1995. Lang.: Eng, Fre. 4399

Divadlo Drak's *Pinokio* at Public Theatre's puppetry festival. USA: New York, NY. 1992. Lang.: Eng. 4410

Plays/librettos/scripts

History of early Ukrainian theatre. Ukraine. 1600-1799. Lang.: Rus. 1108

Myth and iconography in Native Canadian theatre. Canada. 1987-1996. Lang.: Eng. 2783

Reprints of commentary on productions by Groupe de la Veillée. Canada: Montreal, PQ. 1981-1990. Lang.: Fre. 2821

Symbolism in *The Swan* by Elizabeth Egloff and its French translation at Espace GO. Canada: Montreal, PQ. USA. 1990-1996. Lang.:Fre. 2824

The body of the king in Shakespeare's *King Lear.* England. 1605-1996. Lang.: Eng. 2904

Staging — cont'd

German plays in translation at the Festival d'automne. France: Paris. 1988. Lang.: Fre. 2994

Heiner Müller's work and its reception on stage after his death. Germany: Berlin, Bochum. 1996. Lang.: Ger. 3016

Portrait of playwright and director Heiner Müller. Germany. 1960-1996. Lang.: Ger. 3030

Experimental theatre of Kantor, Schaeffer, and Różewicz. Poland. 1960-1996. Lang.: Pol. 3165

Playwright and director Dušan Jovanovič on recent Slovene drama. Slovenia. 1986-1996. Lang.: Slo. 3210

Relation to other fields
Asian stereotypes on the Australian stage. Australia. 1850-1993. Lang.: Eng. 1131

Theory/criticism
Theatre practitioners on the ethics of theatrical collaboration. Australia: Perth. 1994. Lang.: Eng. 1319

Contemporary approaches to the revival of medieval drama. Europe. USA. 1995. Lang.: Eng. 3539

Swedish actresses and feminist research on the dominance of men in the theatre. Europe. 400 B.C.-1996 A.D. Lang.: Swe. 3540

The 'laws' of contemporary Shakespearean theatre. Russia. 1990-1996. Lang.: Rus. 3546

Criticism of Mejerchol'd productions. Russia. 1917-1928. Lang.: Eng. 3547

The current state of Swedish opera. Sweden. 1996. Lang.: Swe. 4360

Stamos, John
Performance/production
Actor John Stamos. USA: New York, NY. 1996. Lang.: Eng. 3955

Standing on Fishes
Plays/librettos/scripts
Grassroots theatres' productions of plays with environmental themes. USA. 1988-1996. Lang.: Eng. 3346

Stanek, Jim
Performance/production
Profiles of new actors on Broadway. USA: New York, NY. 1996. Lang.: Eng. 1012

Staniewski, Günter
Performance/production
Performances of the Jim Henson International Festival. USA: New York, NY. 1995. Lang.: Eng. 4407

Staniewski, Włodzimierz
Performance/production
Włodzimierz Staniewski and the Gardzienice Theatre Associaton. Poland: Gardzienice. 1977-1996. Lang.: Ger. 893

Stanislavskij, Konstantin Sergejěvič
Design/technology
The director-designer relationship. UK. 1912-1995. Lang.: Eng. 221
Performance/production
Theories of acting and performance. Latin America. 1910-1995. Lang.: Spa. 879

The Moscow Art Theatre's Boston season. USA: Boston, MA. 1923. Lang.: Eng. 1036

Italian translation of Stanislavskij's notes on directing *Diadia Vania (Uncle Vanya)*. Russia. 1899. Lang.: Ita. 2251

Hungarian translation of excerpts from Stanislavskij's notebooks. USSR: Moscow. 1919-1938. Lang.: Hun. 2699

Stanley
Performance/production
Collection of newspaper reviews by London theatre critics. UK-England: London. 1996. Lang.: Eng. 2342

Stanson, Andrew
Performance/production
Collection of newspaper reviews by London theatre critics. UK-England: London. 1996. Lang.: Eng. 2399

Staring at the Space
Performance/production
Interview with composer Michel van der Aa and choreographer Philippe Blanchard. Sweden: Norrköping. 1995. Lang.: Swe. 1587

Stark, Tim
Performance/production
Collection of newspaper reviews by London theatre critics. UK-England: London. 1996. Lang.: Eng. 2374

Starkie, Martin
Performance/production
Collection of newspaper reviews by London theatre critics. UK-England: London. 1996. Lang.: Eng. 2397

Starting Here, Starting Now
Performance/production
Collection of newspaper reviews by London theatre critics. UK-England: London. 1996. Lang.: Eng. 2491

Staruska
SEE
Latino, Staruska.

Stary Teatr (Cracow)
Performance/production
The negative impact of democracy on Polish theatre. Poland. 1989-1995. Lang.: Eng. 2146

Director Krystian Lupa. Poland: Cracow. 1996. Lang.: Ger. 2157

Dziady—Dwanaście improwizacji (Forefathers'Eve—Twelve Improvisations) : Grzegorzewski's adaptation of the Mickiewicz classic. Poland: Cracow. 1995. Lang.: Pol. 2167

Krystian Lupa's *Lunatycy (The Sleepwalkers)* at Stary Teatr. Poland: Cracow. 1995. Lang.: Eng, Fre. 2169

Swinarski's production of *A Midsummer Night's Dream*, Stary Teatr. Poland: Cracow. 1970. Lang.: Eng. 2177

Plays/librettos/scripts
Recent Polish translations and productions of the plays of Molière. France. Poland: Cracow. 1948-1992. Lang.: Eng, Fre. 2993

Staševskij, Vlad
Performance/production
Career of pop singer Vlad Staševskij. Russia: Moscow. 1990-1996. Lang.: Rus. 3865

State Fair
Performance/production
Profiles of new actors on Broadway. USA: New York, NY. 1996. Lang.: Eng. 1012

Collection of newspaper reviews by New York theatre critics. USA: New York, NY. 1996. Lang.: Eng. 2572

Singer/dancer Donna McKechnie. USA: New York, NY. 1996. Lang.: Eng. 3928

Actor/singer John Davidson. USA: New York, NY. 1964-1996. Lang.: Eng. 3945

Actress/singer Andrea McArdle. USA. 1976-1996. Lang.: Eng. 3946

State Puppet Theatre (Budapest)
SEE
Állami Bábszinház.

State Puppet Theatre (Moscow)
SEE
Gosudarstvénnyj Centralnyj Teat'r Kukol.

State Theatre Institute (Moscow)
SEE
Gosudarstvénnyj Institut Teatral'nogo Iskusstva.

Statements after an Arrest Under the Immorality Act
Plays/librettos/scripts
Athol Fugard and the role of revolutionary theatre after the revolution. South Africa, Republic of. 1948-1994. Lang.: Eng. 3220

States of Shock
Performance/production
Collection of newspaper reviews by London theatre critics. UK-England: London. 1996. Lang.: Eng. 2448
Plays/librettos/scripts
'Chaos-informed' realism in the plays of David Rabe and Sam Shepard. USA. 1976-1991. Lang.: Eng. 3355

Station Street Theatre (Vancouver, BC)
Performance/production
The gay male body in *Strains* by Rumble Productions. Canada: Vancouver, BC. 1949-1996. Lang.: Eng. 720

Stavisky, Claudia
Performance/production
Interview with actress/director Claudia Stavisky. France. 1995. Lang.: Eng. 2025

Stealing Souls
Performance/production
Collection of newspaper reviews by London theatre critics. UK-England: London. 1996. Lang.: Eng. 2363

Steamie, The
Performance/production
Collection of newspaper reviews by London theatre critics. UK-England: London. UK-Scotland: Edinburgh. 1996. Lang.: Eng. 2313

Steben Sisters (Sweden)
Performance/production
The trapeze act of the Steben Sisters. Sweden. 1996. Lang.: Swe. 3756

Steckel, Frank-Patrick
Performance/production
Reviews of Shakespearean productions. Germany. 1994-1995. Lang.: Ger. 2046

Steckel, Frank-Patrick — cont'd

The portrayal of female characters in Büchner's *Dantons Tod (Danton's Death)*. Germany. 1902-1994. Lang.: Eng. 2053

Stecken, Stab und Stangl (Stick, Rod, and Pole)
Performance/production
Thirza Bruncken's production of *Stecken, Stab und Stangl (Stick, Rod, and Pole)* by Elfriede Jelinek. Germany: Hamburg. 1996. Lang.: Ger. 2074

Steel Pier
Performance/production
Interview with writing team John Kander and Fred Ebb. USA: New York, NY. 1996. Lang.: Eng. 3941

Stefanovski, Goran
Performance/production
Collection of newspaper reviews by London theatre critics. UK-England: London. 1996. Lang.: Eng. 2415
Relation to other fields
Artists of the former Yugoslavia discuss the impact of the political situation on their art. Yugoslavia. 1996. Lang.: Ger. 1287
Responses of theatre and performance to social and political conditions. USA. Yugoslavia. 1968-1995. Lang.: Eng. 3821

Stefanski, Roman
Performance/production
Collection of newspaper reviews by London theatre critics. UK-England: London. 1996. Lang.: Eng. 2354

Steigerwald, Karel
Plays/librettos/scripts
Analysis of plays by Karel Steigerwald. Czech Republic. 1979-1994. Lang.: Cze. 2869

Stein, Gertrude
Institutions
Productions of the Edinburgh Festival. UK-Scotland: Edinburgh. 1996. Lang.: Ger. 561
Performance/production
Beauty and death in Montreal productions by Robert Wilson. Canada: Montreal, PQ. 1980-1993. Lang.: Fre. 753
Opera premieres of the 1946-47 season. Europe. 1946-1947. Lang.: Eng. 4111
Robert Wilson's production of *Four Saints in Three Acts* by Thomson and Stein. USA: Houston, TX. 1996. Lang.: Eng. 4270
Thomson and Stein's *Four Saints in Three Acts* directed by Robert Wilson. USA: New York, NY. 1996. Lang.: Eng. 4273

Stein, Joseph
Performance/production
Collection of newspaper reviews by London theatre critics. UK-England: London. 1996. Lang.: Eng. 2426

Stein, Leo
Performance/production
Analysis of two popular operettas *János vitéz* and *Die lustige Witwe*. Austro-Hungarian Empire. 1904-1906. Lang.: Hun. 4364

Stein, Leonie
Performance/production
Interview with Leonie Stein, director-designate of the acting section of the Bern Conservatory. Switzerland: Bern. 1996. Lang.: Ger. 958

Stein, Peter
Institutions
Productions of the Salzburger Festspiele. Austria: Salzburg. 1996. Lang.: Ger. 345
Productions of the Edinburgh Festival. UK-Scotland: Edinburgh. 1996. Lang.: Ger. 561
Performance/production
Peter Stein on Fritz Kortner's understanding of theatre. Germany: Hamburg. 1996. Lang.: Ger. 830
Photographs of Peter Stein's work at Schaubühne. Germany: Berlin. 1969-1996. Lang.: Ger. 2084
Collection of newspaper reviews by London theatre critics. UK-England: London. 1996. Lang.: Eng. 2381

Steinberg, Paul
Design/technology
Paul Steinberg's cinematic design for a production of Puccini's *La Fanciulla del West*, Flemish National Opera. Belgium: Antwerp. 1996. Lang.: Eng. 4013

Steirischer Herbst (Graz)
Administration
Interviews with directors of two regional theatres. Germany: Schwerin. Austria: Graz. 1996. Lang.: Ger. 20

Stelarc
Performance/production
Performance artist Stelarc on performance, gender, and cyberspace. Australia. 1996. Lang.: Eng. 688

Artists' statements from photo exhibition of performers' feats of endurance. USA: New York, NY. 1996. Lang.: Eng. 3801

Stella, Bernardo
Performance/production
Collection of newspaper reviews by London theatre critics. UK-England: London. 1996. Lang.: Eng. 2429

Stenskibet (Stone Ship, The)
Plays/librettos/scripts
The Danish community play tradition. Denmark. 1970-1996. Lang.: Eng. 2873

Stephens, Jenny
Institutions
Interview with Jenny Stephens, artistic director of the Swan Theatre. UK-England: Worcester. 1994-1996. Lang.: Eng. 1854

Stephens, Robert
Performance/production
Tribute to actor Robert Stephens. UK-England. 1961-1996. Lang.: Eng. 2507

Stephenson, Shelagh
Performance/production
Collection of newspaper reviews by London theatre critics. UK-England: London. 1996. Lang.: Eng. 2449

Steppenwolf Theatre Company (Chicago, IL)
Design/technology
Scott Bradley's set design for three productions of *Picasso at the Lapin Agile* by Steve Martin. USA: New York, NY. 1996. Lang.:Eng. 1717
Technical aspects of *The Libertine* directed by Terry Johnson for Steppenwolf. USA: Chicago, IL. 1996. Lang.: Eng. 1740
Institutions
Profile of Steppenwolf Theatre Company. USA: Chicago, IL. 1974-1996. Lang.: Eng. 1862
Performance/production
Collection of newspaper reviews by New York theatre critics. USA: New York, NY. 1996. Lang.: Eng. 2573
Puppet production of *Frankenstein* by Redmoon Theatre. USA: Chicago, IL. 1996. Lang.: Eng. 4444

Stern, Gerald
Relation to other fields
Interview with poet and story-teller Gerald Stern. USA. 1925-1996. Lang.: Eng. 1274

Stern, Joseph
Institutions
Profile of Matrix Theater Company, Joseph Stern, artistic director. USA: Los Angeles, CA. 1996. Lang.: Eng. 574

Stern, Marcus
Performance/production
Opera and stage director Marcus Stern. USA: New York, NY. 1996. Lang.: Eng. 1039

Stern, Peter
Performance/production
Account of Cechov International Theatre Festival. Russia. 1996. Lang.: Eng. 2199

Sternheim, Carl
Performance/production
Productions of Basler Theater. Switzerland: Basel. 1996. Lang.: Ger. 2300
Plays/librettos/scripts
Productions of plays by Carl Sternheim at Dallas Theatre Center. USA: Dallas, TX. Germany. 1911-1996. Lang.: Eng. 3399

Sterntaler
Institutions
Review of children's theatre performances. Europe. 1996. Lang.: Ger. 403

Stevens, Jean
Performance/production
Collection of newspaper reviews by London theatre critics. UK-England: London. 1996. Lang.: Eng. 2473

Stevens, John
Performance/production
The popular appeal of the Sioux War Panorama. USA. 1860-1879. Lang.: Eng. 3718

Stevenson, Jonathan
Design/technology
Work of designer Mark Stevenson on the film *Beautiful Thing*. UK-England: London. 1995-1996. Lang.: Eng. 3591

Stevenson, Juliet
Performance/production
Videotape on interpreting and performing Shakespeare's *As You Like It*. UK-England. 1994. Lang.: Eng. 2303

Storey, David — cont'd

Self-repetition in plays of David Storey. UK-England. 1960-1995. Lang.: Eng. 3300

Storm, The
SEE
Oväder.

Storni, Alfonsina
Basic theatrical documents
International anthology of modern drama by women. 1880-1940. Lang.: Eng. 1637
Plays/librettos/scripts
Analysis of plays by Alfonsina Storni. Argentina. 1892-1938. Lang.: Spa. 2717

Story-telling
Audience
The reception of story-telling as oral performance by Renaissance audiences. France. 1500-1600. Lang.: Eng. 136
Institutions
Community plays of Swamp Gravy. USA: Colquitt, GA. 1987-1996. Lang.: Eng. 578
Performance/production
Memories of a story-telling festival. Canada: Montreal, PQ. 1992. Lang.: Fre. 754
Thomas Riccio's experience of street theatre in Natal. South Africa, Republic of: Durban. 1993-1996. Lang.: Eng. 940
The use of a female performer for the Old French *chantefable, Aucassin et Nicolette.* France. 1200-1994. Lang.: Eng. 3713
Plays/librettos/scripts
Presentations by story-tellers at women playwrights conference. Australia. USA. Philippines. 1981-1995. Lang.: Eng. 1083
Ritual in Aboriginal and shamanistic performance. Australia. Korea. 1970-1995. Lang.: Eng. 1085
Influence of story-telling traditions on women playwrights. Ghana. Australia. Sri Lanka. 1988-1995. Lang.: Eng. 1098
Story-telling in *La Maison suspendue (The House Among the Stars)* by Michel Tremblay. Canada: Montreal, PQ. 1990. Lang.: Fre. 2761
Relation to other fields
Interview with poet and story-teller Gerald Stern. USA. 1925-1996. Lang.: Eng. 1274
Theory/criticism
The origins of African drama. South Africa, Republic of. Africa. 1700-1996. Lang.: Eng. 1362

Strachan, Keith
Performance/production
Collection of newspaper reviews by London theatre critics. UK-England: London. 1996. Lang.: Eng. 2370

Strains
Performance/production
The gay male body in *Strains* by Rumble Productions. Canada: Vancouver, BC. 1949-1996. Lang.: Eng. 720

Strand, Richard
Basic theatrical documents
Collection of plays from the Humana Festival. USA. 1986-1995. Lang.: Eng. 1687

Strandberg, Mikael
Institutions
Profile of the summer theatre company Skillinge Teater. Sweden: Skillinge. 1995. Lang.: Swe. 1850

Strange Bit of History, A
Performance/production
Collection of newspaper reviews by London theatre critics. UK-England: London. 1996. Lang.: Eng. 2312

Strange Sisters
Institutions
Profile of the Greater Toronto Drag King Society. Canada: Toronto, ON. 1996. Lang.: Eng. 370

Stranger, Inés Margarita
Plays/librettos/scripts
Interview with playwright Inés Margarita Stranger. Chile. 1990-1993. Lang.: Spa. 2851

Strangest Meeting, The
Performance/production
Collection of newspaper reviews by London theatre critics. UK-England: London. 1996. Lang.: Eng. 2349

Strasberg, Anna
Performance/production
Account of Method acting seminar by Anna Strasberg. USA. 1995. Lang.: Eng. 1046

Strasberg, Lee
Performance/production
Account of Method acting seminar by Anna Strasberg. USA. 1995. Lang.: Eng. 1046

Strasti (Rogneda)
Performance/production
The premiere of the ballet *Strasti (Rogneda)* by Andrej Mdivani and Valerij Elizarjev. Belorus: Minsk. 1995. Lang.: Rus. 1496

Stratford Festival (Stratford, ON)
Design/technology
Mechanized sets for *The Merchant of Venice* at Stratford Festival. Canada: Stratford, ON. 1996. Lang.: Eng. 1706
Institutions
The change of artistic director at the Stratford Festival. Canada: Stratford, ON. 1992. Lang.: Fre. 1756
History of the Saskatoon summer Shakespeare festival. Canada: Saskatoon, SK. 1953-1996. Lang.: Eng. 1763
Profile and evaluation of the 1995 Stratford Festival season. Canada: Stratford, ON. 1995. Lang.: Eng. 1765
Performance/production
Christopher Plummer's one-man show *Barrymore.* Canada: Stratford, ON. 1996. Lang.: Eng. 1918
Productions of *Hamlet* by Richard Monette and Henry Woronicz. Canada: Stratford, ON. USA: Ashland, OR. 1994. Lang.: Eng. 1927

Strathcona Theatre Company (Edmonton, AB)
Performance/production
Collection of newspaper reviews by London theatre critics. UK-England: London. 1996. Lang.: Eng. 2376

Strauss, Botho
Performance/production
Politics and Botho Strauss's *Ithaka* at Münchner Kammerspiele. Germany: Munich. 1996. Lang.: Ger. 2067
Collection of newspaper reviews by London theatre critics. UK-England: London. 1996. Lang.: Eng. 2381
Plays/librettos/scripts
Analysis of *Ithaka* by Botho Strauss. Germany. 1996. Lang.: Ger. 3024
Analysis of the aesthetics of plays by Handke and Strauss. Germany. 1745-1991. Lang.: Eng. 3037
Postwar German playwriting. Germany. 1945-1991. Lang.: Fre. 3038
Relation to other fields
Berlin theatre in the current German intellectual debate. Germany: Berlin. 1991-1996. Lang.: Eng. 1192

Strauss, Richard
Performance/production
Current German theatre productions. Germany. 1996. Lang.: Eng. 827
Problems of casting the lead role in Strauss's *Salome.* 1905-1996. Lang.: Eng. 4072
Strauss's *Salome* at the Mariinskij Theatre. Russia: St. Petersburg. 1996. Lang.: Rus. 4205
Background material on Metropolitan Opera radio broadcast performances. USA: New York, NY. 1996. Lang.: Eng. 4252
Plays/librettos/scripts
Self-contained musical compositions in operas of Wagner and Richard Strauss. Germany. Austria. 1849-1913. Lang.: Eng. 4322
Love and the death of women in works of Wagner, Strauss, and Schoenberg. Germany. Austria: Vienna. 1842-1911. Lang.: Eng. 4323

Stravinskij, Igor F.
Performance/production
Felix Mirbt's staging of *L'Histoire du Soldat,* National Arts Centre. Canada: Ottawa, ON. 1988. Lang.: Fre. 1418
Background information on Teatro Colón season. Argentina: Buenos Aires. 1996. Lang.: Eng. 4075
Peter Sellars' production of Stravinskij's *The Rake's Progress.* France: Paris. 1996. Lang.: Swe. 4123
Production of Stravinskij's opera for children, *Nattergalen.* Germany: Cologne. 1996. Lang.: Ger. 4134
Plays/librettos/scripts
Analysis of operas by Igor Stravinskij. USSR. 1926-1951. Lang.: Eng. 4348

Streamers
Plays/librettos/scripts
'Chaos-informed' realism in the plays of David Rabe and Sam Shepard. USA. 1976-1991. Lang.: Eng. 3355

Streb, Elizabeth
Performance/production
Elizabeth Streb at Ringside. USA: New York, NY. 1996. Lang.: Eng. 3722

Street Scene
Institutions
Jeunesse's festival of works by Kurt Weill. Austria: Vienna. 1995. Lang.: Eng. 3906

Sympathy for the Devil
Performance/production
Collection of newspaper reviews by London theatre critics. UK-England: London. 1996. Lang.: Eng. 2485
Syms, Richard
Performance/production
Collection of newspaper reviews by London theatre critics. UK-England: London. 1996. Lang.: Eng. 2311
Syndrome de Cézanne, Le (Cézanne Syndrome)
Plays/librettos/scripts
Analysis of plays by Normand Canac-Marquis. Canada: Montreal, PQ. 1988-1991. Lang.: Fre. 2800
Synge, John Millington
Audience
Comparison of riots by audiences of Abbey Theatre and Living Theatre. Ireland: Dublin. USA: Berkeley, CA. 1907-1968. Lang.: Eng. 1632
Performance/production
Continued interest in Synge's *The Playboy of the Western World*. Europe. North America. 1907-1995. Lang.: Eng. 2000
Plays/librettos/scripts
The aesthetics of playwright John Millington Synge. Ireland. 1902-1909. Lang.: Eng. 3076
Analysis of J.M. Synge's *The Well of the Saints*. Ireland. 1905. Lang.: Eng. 3077
Analysis of J.M. Synge's *Riders to the Sea*. Ireland. 1904. Lang.: Eng. 3078
Analysis of the unfinished *Deirdre of the Sorrows* by John Millington Synge. Ireland. 1909. Lang.: Eng. 3079
Female vagrants in plays of J.M. Synge. Ireland. 1902-1905. Lang.: Eng. 3080
Feminist analysis of *The Shadow of the Glen* by J.M. Synge. Ireland. 1903. Lang.: Eng. 3081
Nationalism and the female figure in plays of Yeats. Ireland. 1903-1910. Lang.: Eng. 3083
Irish history in the plays of J.M. Synge. Ireland. 1903-1909. Lang.: Eng. 3085
Anthropological analysis of Synge's *The Well of the Saints*. Ireland. 1905. Lang.: Eng. 3086
Celtic myth in *The Shadow of the Glen* by J.M. Synge. Ireland. 1903. Lang.: Eng. 3087
Analysis of *The Tinker's Wedding* by John Millington Synge. Ireland. 1902. Lang.: Eng. 3089
Influence of Synge's *The Playboy of the Western World* on work of Yeats. Ireland. 1907. Lang.: Eng. 3090
The audience in and of J.M. Synge's *The Playboy of the Western World*. Ireland. 1907. Lang.: Eng. 3091
The trickster in Synge's *Playboy of the Western World*. Ireland. 1907. Lang.: Eng. 3092
Synovja Mully (Sons of Mulla, The)
Plays/librettos/scripts
Bulgakov's life and his unpublished play *Synovja Mully (The Sons of Mulla)*. Russia: Moscow. 1891-1940. Lang.: Rus. 3203
Systrar, bröder (Sisters, Brothers)
Performance/production
Collection of newspaper reviews by London theatre critics. UK-England: London. 1996. Lang.: Eng. 2325
Szajna, József
Performance/production
József Szajna's *Restos (The Remains)*. Portugal: Lisbon, Almada. 1995. Lang.: Eng, Fre. 2181
Szakács, Györgyi
Performance/production
Recipients of the annual theatre critics' awards. Hungary. 1995-1996. Lang.: Hun. 846
Szakonyi, Károly
Plays/librettos/scripts
Postwar Hungarian drama. Hungary. 1945-1989. Lang.: Hun. 3069
Szántó, Andrea
Performance/production
Hungarian singers at Katia Ricciarelli's master course. Italy. Hungary. 1995. Lang.: Hun. 4177
Szatmárnémeti Északi Színház, Harag György Társulat (Satu-Mare)
Institutions
History of Hungarian ethnic theatre in Romania. Hungary. Romania. 1919-1992. Lang.: Hun. 473

Performance/production
Survey of ethnic Hungarian theatre in neighboring countries. Romania. Slovakia: Košice. Ukraine: Beregovo. 1995-1996. Lang.: Hun. 897
Interview with actor József Czintos. Hungary: Budapest. Romania: Satu-Mare. 1969-1995. Lang.: Hun. 2098
Productions of works by Schiller and Strindberg by the Hungarian theatre of Satu Mare/Szatmárnémeti. Romania: Satu-Mare. 1995-1996. Lang.: Hun. 2184
Szegedi Nemzeti Színház (Szeged)
Institutions
Interview with János Szikora, artistic director of Szegedi Nemzeti Színház. Hungary. 1980-1996. Lang.: Hun. 484
Interview with Tamás Pál, musical director of Szeged National Theatre. Hungary: Szeged. 1975-1996. Lang.: Hun. 4044
Performance/production
Tenor László Vadas Kiss. Hungary. 1926-1990. Lang.: Hun. 4152
Székely, Mihály
Performance/production
Technical and artistic analysis of the bass voice and roles. Hungary. 1930-1940. Lang.: Hun. 4171
Szentpál-Iskola (Budapest)
Performance/production
Tribute to Olga Szentpál, prominent representative of Eurhythmics. Hungary. 1895-1995. Lang.: Hun. 1583
Szentpál, Mária
Research/historiography
Dance teacher and scholar Mária Szentpál. Hungary. 1919-1995. Lang.: Hun. 1462
Szentpál, Olga
Performance/production
Tribute to Olga Szentpál, prominent representative of Eurhythmics. Hungary. 1895-1995. Lang.: Hun. 1583
Szép, Ernő
Performance/production
Budapest productions of the millicentenary season. Hungary: Budapest. 1995-1996. Lang.: Eng. 2104
Szerdahelyi, Kálmán
Performance/production
János Vajda's reviews of guest performances. Hungary: Szeged. 1855-1856. Lang.: Hun. 839
Szikora, János
Institutions
Interview with János Szikora, artistic director of Szegedi Nemzeti Színház. Hungary. 1980-1996. Lang.: Hun. 484
Szilfai, Márta
Performance/production
Interview with Márta Szilfai. Hungary. 1970-1996. Lang.: Hun. 4168
Szinetár, Miklós
Administration
Interview with Miklós Szinetár, director of Budapest Opera House. Hungary: Budapest. 1996. Lang.: Hun. 4011
Színház- és Filmművészeti Főiskola (Budapest)
Performance/production
Director Viktor Nagy recalls his teacher, László Vámos. Hungary. 1928-1996. Lang.: Hun. 850
Színművészeti Akadémia, Szentgyörgyi István Tagozat (Tîrgu Mureş)
Institutions
History of Hungarian ethnic theatre in Romania. Hungary. Romania. 1919-1992. Lang.: Hun. 473
Szirmai, Albert
Performance/production
Budapest productions of the millicentenary season. Hungary: Budapest. 1995-1996. Lang.: Eng. 2104
Szobaszínház (Budapest)
Institutions
The history of Squat Theatre. Hungary: Budapest. USA: New York, NY. 1969-1981. Lang.: Eng. 485
Szőke, István
Performance/production
Revivals of the Hungarian pop musical *Képzelt riport egy amerikai popfesztiválról (Imaginary Report on an American Pop Festival)*. Hungary. 1973-1995. Lang.: Hun. 3919
Szőke, Tibor
Institutions
History of Gördülő Opera, Opera on Rails. Hungary: Budapest. 1945-1954. Lang.: Hun. 4045
Szomory, Dezső
Performance/production
Budapest productions of the millicentenary season. Hungary: Budapest. 1995-1996. Lang.: Eng. 2104

Tartuffe — cont'd

Anecdote concerning Jacques Galipeau's role in *Tartuffe*, Théâtre du Nouveau Monde. France: Paris. 1971. Lang.: Fre. 2022

Ariane Mnouchkine's production of Molière's *Tartuffe*. France. 1995. Lang.: Eng. 2030

Collection of newspaper reviews by London theatre critics. UK-England: London. 1996. Lang.: Eng. 2374

Plays/librettos/scripts
The structural development of comedy in the Renaissance. Europe. 1590-1664. Lang.: Eng. 2969

Tartuffe: Born Again
Performance/production
Collection of newspaper reviews by New York theatre critics. USA: New York, NY, Washington, DC. 1996. Lang.: Eng. 2581

Tasnádi, Csaba
Performance/production
Interview with actor Tibor Mertz. Hungary. 1985-1996. Lang.: Hun. 2107

Premieres of *Crazy for You* in London and Budapest. UK-England: London. Hungary: Budapest. 1993-1995. Lang.: Hun. 3926

Tatai, Mária
Research/historiography
History and theory of orchestics movement system. France: Paris. Hungary: Budapest. 1908-1994. Lang.: Hun. 1601

Tatár, György
Performance/production
Interview with Hungarian-born ballet dancer György Tatár. Hungary. USA. 1940-1995. Lang.: Hun. 1582

Tatarskij Gosudarstvénnyj Akademičéskij Teat'r im. G. Kamala (Kazan)
Institutions
The Kamala Theatre and its actors. Tatarstan: Kazan. 1995. Lang.: Rus. 1853

Taviani, Paolo
Plays/librettos/scripts
Pirandello Society Yearbook. Italy. 1889-1995. Lang.: Eng. 3133

Taviani, Vittorio
Plays/librettos/scripts
Pirandello Society Yearbook. Italy. 1889-1995. Lang.: Eng. 3133

Tavory, Doron
Performance/production
Production of *Jud Süss (The Jew Suess)* at BeerSheba Municipal Theatre. Israel: Beersheba. 1931-1996. Lang.: Eng. 2119

Taylor, David
Performance/production
Collection of newspaper reviews by London theatre critics. UK-England: London. 1996. Lang.: Eng. 2330

Collection of newspaper reviews by London theatre critics. UK-England: London. 1996. Lang.: Eng. 2379

Taylor, Jeremy James
Design/technology
Alison Darke's production design for *Pendragon* by the National Youth Music Theatre of Great Britain. UK-England. USA: New York,NY. 1995. Lang.: Eng. 3892

Taylor, Jocelyn
Performance/production
Analysis of the work of video artists. USA. 1996. Lang.: Eng. 3679

Taylor, Julie
Performance/production
Strauss's *Salome* at the Mariinskij Theatre. Russia: St. Petersburg. 1996. Lang.: Rus. 4205

Taylor, Regina
Basic theatrical documents
Collection of plays from the Humana Festival. USA. 1986-1995. Lang.: Eng. 1687

Taylor, Renee
Performance/production
Actress Bea Arthur. USA: Beverly Hills, CA. 1996. Lang.: Eng. 1024

Taylor, Tom
Plays/librettos/scripts
The influence of the detective in Tom Taylor's *The Ticket-of-Leave Man* on Victorian theatre. England: London. 1863. Lang.: Eng. 2894

Taymor, Julie
Design/technology
Design for Gozzi's *The Green Bird (L'augellino belverde)* at the New Victory Theatre. USA: New York, NY. 1996. Lang.: Eng. 3760
Performance/production
Collection of newspaper reviews by New York theatre critics. USA: New York, NY. 1996. Lang.: Eng. 2561

Tchaikovsky, Peter Ilich
SEE
Čajkovskij, Pëtr Iljič.
Teacher's Theatre (Seoul)
Relation to other fields
Plays for youth created by Seoul theatre collectives. Korea: Seoul. 1995-1996. Lang.: Kor. 3502
Teaching methods
Audience
Effect of classroom drama and theatre attendance on children's interpretation of theatre. USA: Tempe, AZ. 1984-1991. Lang.: Eng. 143
Design/technology
Design and technical training at Swedish theatres. Sweden: Stockholm. 1996. Lang.: Swe. 213
Institutions
Swedish actor training. Sweden. 1965. Lang.: Swe. 544
Nora Tully MacAlvay of MacAlvay's Children's Theatre Workshop. USA: Michigan City, MI. 1900-1986. Lang.: Eng. 606
Plays/librettos/scripts
Sisterhood in *As You Like It* by Shakespeare. England. 1590. Lang.: Eng. 2957
The history of dramaturgy and dramatic theory. Russia. 1500-1996. Lang.: Rus. 3196
Relation to other fields
Drama in Jesuit schools. 1551-1773. Lang.: Eng. 1130
Study of teacher perceptions of the value and status of drama in education. Canada: St. Catharine's, ON. 1995-1996. Lang.: Eng. 1146
An example of college-level theatre education in Quebec. Canada: Rouyn, PQ. 1972-1992. Lang.: Fre. 1151
Teaching theatre in general aesthetics classes. Russia: Moscow. 1996. Lang.: Rus. 1225
Study of how elementary-school teachers implement a drama curriculum. USA. 1996. Lang.: Eng. 1258
Programs for teachers' professional development in theatre. USA. 1994-1996. Lang.: Eng. 1261
Feminist classroom approach to *The Concealed Fancies* by Cavendish and Brackley. England. 1645. Lang.: Eng. 3490
Shakespeare's *Romeo and Juliet* and pedagogy. UK-England. 1996. Lang.: Eng. 3512
Teaching Shakespeare in the context of Renaissance women's culture. USA. 1991-1996. Lang.: Eng. 3516
Teaching race and gender in plays of Cary, Shakespeare, and Behn. USA. 1996. Lang.: Eng. 3518
Teaching plays of Shakespeare and Cary in a course on domestic England in the early modern period. USA. 1995. Lang.: Eng. 3519
Argument in favor of teaching Shakespeare in conjunction with his female contemporaries. USA. 1996. Lang.: Eng. 3520
Research/historiography
Research design and practice and the conflict over research methods. USA. 1996. Lang.: Eng. 1308
Training
Survey of the training process for creative artists. Canada. 1996. Lang.: Eng. 1394
Theatre training for self-discovery and healing. Canada: Vancouver, BC. 1996. Lang.: Eng. 1395
Using practical drama to teach critical practice. UK-England: Reading. 1994. Lang.: Eng. 1397
Teaching writing in theatre courses. USA. 1996. Lang.: Eng. 1398
Etienne Decroux's theory of corporeal mime. France: Paris. 1918-1996. Lang.: Eng. 3688
Mejerchol'd's theory of biomechanics and its application to training and performance. Russia. 1896-1996. Lang.: Eng. 3689
Jacques Copeau, Suzanne Bing, and the founding of L'École du Vieux-Colombier. USA: New York, NY. France: Paris. 1918-1996. Lang.: Eng. 3690

Teale, Polly
Performance/production
Collection of newspaper reviews by London theatre critics. UK-England: London. 1996. Lang.: Eng. 2361
Collection of newspaper reviews by London theatre critics. UK-England: London. 1996. Lang.: Eng. 2443

Teat'r A (Moscow)
Performance/production
Account of Cechov International Theatre Festival. Russia. 1996. Lang.: Eng. 2199

Theory/criticism — cont'd

Analysis of dramas about the heroine Wang Zhaojun. China. 1700-1900. Lang.: Eng. 2854

Shakespeare's theory of drama. England. 1589-1613. Lang.: Eng. 2920

German drama, politics, and Klaus Pohl's *Wartesaal Deutschland StimmenReich (Waiting Room Germany)*. Germany: Berlin. 1995. Lang.: Ger. 3027

New reconstruction of the premiere of *La Figlia di Iorio (Iorio's Daughter)* by D'Annunzio. Italy. 1904-1995. Lang.: Ita. 3117

English translation of two essays by Gramsci. Italy. 1917-1932. Lang.: Eng. 3122

Poststructuralism in Latin American plays. Latin America. 1985-1995. Lang.: Spa. 3141

Reactions of male critics to Polish feminist drama. Poland. 1932-1938. Lang.: Pol. 3162

The history of dramaturgy and dramatic theory. Russia. 1500-1996. Lang.: Rus. 3196

The structure of dramatic conflict. Russia: Moscow. 1996. Lang.: Rus. 3197

Analysis of *La verdad sospechosa (Suspicious Truth)* by Juan Ruiz de Alarcón. Spain. 1628. Lang.: Eng. 3261

Lacanian analysis of Spanish Baroque drama. Spain. 1580-1680. Lang.: Eng. 3265

Nineteenth-century critical views of Shakespeare's Juliet. UK-England. 1800-1899. Lang.: Eng. 3285

Oscar Wilde's views on art and criticism. UK-England. 1856-1900. Lang.: Rus. 3304

Stark Young's appraisal of the plays of Eugene O'Neill. USA. 1922-1996. Lang.: Eng. 3322

Analysis of *Tracers* by John DiFusco and its critical reception. USA. 1980-1994. Lang.: Eng. 3379

Reference materials

Primary sources in English on European Naturalist and Symbolist theatre. Europe. 1850-1918. Lang.: Eng. 1120

Relation to other fields

The use of the word 'scandal' in theatre criticism. Canada. 1996. Lang.: Fre. 1140

Modernism as closed to innovation. Canada. 1989. Lang.: Fre. 1142

Historic and contemporary functions of the theatre critic. Canada. France. 1700-1996. Lang.: Fre. 1150

Responses to August Wilson's call for separation of Black and white theatre. USA. 1996. Lang.: Eng. 1277

Ritual performance in the Charismatic religious movement. USA. 1994. Lang.: Eng. 1279

Research/historiography

Account of a seminar on theatre and text in the 1990s. 1996. Lang.: Dan. 1293

Contemporary theatre criticism and scholarship. 1900-1995. Lang.: Pol. 1294

Seminar in honor of Antonin Artaud. France. Denmark. 1896-1996. Lang.: Dan. 1296

Theory/criticism

Theory of studies of theatricality, including cultural and sociopolitical communication. 1996. Lang.: Ger. 1311

Criticism of Mejerchol'd productions. Russia. 1917-1928. Lang.: Eng. 3547

Critical misrepresentation of *Falsettoland* by William Finn and James Lapine. USA. 1990. Lang.: Eng. 4002

Thériault, Lucie

Performance/production

Scenography of Beckett's *Waiting for Godot* directed by André Brassard, TNM. Canada: Montreal, PQ. 1992. Lang.: Fre. 1937

They Burned the Books

Plays/librettos/scripts

Radio plays of the Writers' War Board. USA. 1942-1944. Lang.: Eng. 3582

They Shoot Horses, Don't They?

Performance/production

Collection of newspaper reviews by London theatre critics. UK-England: London. 1996. Lang.: Eng. 2378

They That Sit in Darkness

Plays/librettos/scripts

Feminist realism in African-American theatre. USA. 1916-1930. Lang.: Eng. 3440

Thibault, Alain

Performance/production

Alain Thibault's musical score for *Ne blâmez jamais les Bédouins (Don't Blame the Bedouins)* by René-Daniel Dubois. Canada: Montreal, PQ. 1991. Lang.: Fre. 4095

Plays/librettos/scripts

Interview with opera composer Alain Thibault. Canada: Montreal, PQ. 1985-1991. Lang.: Fre. 4308

Thickness of Skin, The

Performance/production

Collection of newspaper reviews by London theatre critics. UK-England: London. 1996. Lang.: Eng. 2364

Thielemann, Christian

Administration

Interview with conductor Christian Thielemann, music director of Deutsche Oper. Germany: Berlin. 1996. Lang.: Ger. 4007

Thieme, Thomas

Institutions

Avant-garde theatre at the Steirischer Herbst Festival. Austria: Graz. 1996. Lang.: Ger. 1753

Thierrée, Jean-Baptiste

Performance/production

Collection of newspaper reviews by London theatre critics. UK-England: London. 1996. Lang.: Eng. 2481

Thin Ice

Performance/production

Collection of newspaper reviews by London theatre critics. UK-England: London. 1996. Lang.: Eng. 2463

Things Related to AIDS

Institutions

Chinese independent theatre: Mou Sen and Xi Ju Che Jian. China, People's Republic of: Beijing. 1995-1996. Lang.: Eng. 1782

Think No Evil of Us

Performance/production

Collection of newspaper reviews by London theatre critics. UK-England: London, Stratford. 1996. Lang.: Eng. 2476

Thinking Ahead

Performance/production

Collection of newspaper reviews by London theatre critics. UK-England: London. 1996. Lang.: Eng. 2402

Third Eye Repertory (New York, NY)

Institutions

Work of Third Eye, Alpha and Omega, and Gilgamesh theatre companies. USA: New York, NY. 1996. Lang.: Eng. 1860

Thiry, Christophe

Performance/production

Report on the Avignon fringe festival. France: Avignon. 1996. Lang.: Eng. 796

Thomas, Ambroise

Performance/production

Review of 1995 British opera productions. UK-England: London, Leeds, Lewes. 1995-1996. Lang.: Eng. 4234

Thomas, Augustus

Plays/librettos/scripts

Comparison of *A Man's World* by Rachel Crothers and *As a Man Thinks* by Augustus Thomas. USA. 1910-1920. Lang.: Eng. 3445

Thomas, Blair

Performance/production

Puppet production of *Frankenstein* by Redmoon Theatre. USA: Chicago, IL. 1996. Lang.: Eng. 4444

Thomas, Edward

Performance/production

Collection of newspaper reviews by London theatre critics. UK-England: London. 1996. Lang.: Eng. 2349

Collection of newspaper reviews by New York theatre critics. USA: New York, NY. 1996. Lang.: Eng. 2552

The musical *Mata Hari* by Jerome Coopersmith, Edward Thomas, and Martin Charnin. USA: New York, NY. 1967-1996. Lang.: Eng. 3948

Thomas, Freyda

Performance/production

Collection of newspaper reviews by New York theatre critics. USA: New York, NY, Washington, DC. 1996. Lang.: Eng. 2581

Thomas, Gerald

Performance/production

The work of director-designer Gerald Thomas. Brazil. 1985-1996. Lang.: Eng. 699

Thomas, Rhys

Performance/production

Collection of newspaper reviews by London theatre critics. UK-England: London. 1996. Lang.: Eng. 2414

Collection of newspaper reviews by London theatre critics. UK-England: London. 1996. Lang.: Eng. 2421

Thomas, Rudolf

Performance/production

Hans Krása's opera *Verlobung im Traum*. Czech Republic: Prague. 1994-1996. Lang.: Eng. 4101

Townshend, Pete — cont'd

Performance/production

Collection of newspaper reviews by London theatre critics. UK-England: London. 1996. Lang.: Eng.   2331

Toy Story
Design/technology

Lighting effects for the animated film *Toy Story*. USA: Hollywood, CA. 1995. Lang.: Eng.   3595

Tracers
Plays/librettos/scripts

Analysis of *Tracers* by John DiFusco and its critical reception. USA. 1980-1994. Lang.: Eng.   3379

Trachta, Jeff
Performance/production

Interview with actor Jeff Trachta. USA: New York, NY. 1994-1996. Lang.: Eng.   1060

Track Thirteen
Basic theatrical documents

Anthology of unknown plays of the Harlem Renaissance. USA: New York, NY. 1920-1940. Lang.: Eng.   1694

Tracy, Michael
Performance/production

Pilobolus Dance Theatre, Michael Tracy, artistic director. USA: New York, NY. 1971-1996. Lang.: Eng.   1447

Tragaluz, El (Skylight, The)
Plays/librettos/scripts

Interview with playwright Antonio Buero Vallejo. Spain. 1993. Lang.: Spa.   3250

Tragédie comique, La (Comic Tragedy, The)
Institutions

Productions of Carrefour 92. Canada: Quebec, PQ. 1992. Lang.: Fre.   376

Tragedy
Plays/librettos/scripts

Italian translation of *Versuch über das Tragische* by Péter Szondi. Europe. Lang.: Ita.   2974

Women and German bourgeois tragedy. Germany. 1750-1850. Lang.: Eng.   3023

Closure and generic innovation in Euripidean drama. Greece. 440-400 B.C. Lang.: Eng.   3056

Italian translation of *Die tragische Dichtung der Hellenen* by Albin Lesky. Greece. 500-400 B.C. Lang.: Ita.   3058

Italian translation of *La tragédie grecque* by Jacqueline de Romilly. Greece. 500-400 B.C. Lang.: Ita.   3060

Aeschylean tragedy in its sociopolitical context. Greece. 525-456 B.C. Lang.: Eng.   3061

Aristotle's interpretation of the tragic in drama. Greece. 500-400 B.C. Lang.: Slo.   3062

Analysis of J.M. Synge's *Riders to the Sea*. Ireland. 1904. Lang.: Eng.   3078

The tragedies of A.P. Sumarokov. Russia: St. Petersburg. 1717-1777. Lang.: Rus.   3206

Relation to other fields

Personality and selfhood in the writings of the ancient Greeks. Ancient Greece. 525-405 B.C. Lang.: Eng.   3477

Theory/criticism

The debate over a specifically African tragedy. Africa. 1996. Lang.: Eng.   1315

Tragedy in Slovene literary theory. Slovenia. 1996. Lang.: Slo.   3548

Tragedy of Man, The
SEE

Ember tragédiája, Az.

Tragedy of Mariam, The
Relation to other fields

Teaching *The Winter's Tale* and Elizabeth Cary's *The Tragedy of Mariam*. USA. 1995. Lang.: Eng.   3517

Teaching race and gender in plays of Cary, Shakespeare, and Behn. USA. 1996. Lang.: Eng.   3518

Teaching plays of Shakespeare and Cary in a course on domestic England in the early modern period. USA. 1995. Lang.: Eng.   3519

Tragedy of Tragedies, The
Plays/librettos/scripts

Italian opera in plays of Henry Fielding. England. 1705-1735. Lang.: Eng.   2888

Tragical History of Doctor Faustus
SEE

Doctor Faustus.

Tragik (Tragic Role, A)
Performance/production

Collection of newspaper reviews by London theatre critics. UK-England: London. 1996. Lang.: Eng.   2442

Trail, Margaret
Relation to other fields

Performance artists and writers comment on political concerns in their work. UK-England: London. 1995. Lang.: Eng.   3818

Train de nuit (Night Train)
Performance/production

Interview with Serge Marois of children's theatre company Arrière-Scène. Canada: Montreal, PQ. 1976-1993. Lang.: Fre.   719

Train 713
Performance/production

Armand Gatti describes staging his *Train 713*. USA: Rochester, NY. Lang.: Fre.   1035

Train, Le
Plays/librettos/scripts

Careers of playwrights Michel Tremblay and Marie Laberge. Canada: Quebec, PQ. 1964-1992. Lang.: Eng.   2815

Training
SEE ALSO

Classed Entries.

Design/technology

Report from OISTAT commission on education, with reference to technician training. Switzerland: Luzern. 1995. Lang.: Swe.   218

Institutions

Swedish actor training. Sweden. 1965. Lang.: Swe.   544

The production of knowledge and the institutionalization of performance studies. USA. 1996. Lang.: Eng.   575

The conversion of Fort Ord into a university multi-use facility. USA: Monterey Bay, CA. 1996. Lang.: Eng.   580

Performance/production

Recollections of actor, director, and teacher István Keleti. Hungary: Budapest. 1950-1990. Lang.: Hun.   848

Theory/criticism

The current state of Swedish opera. Sweden. 1996. Lang.: Swe.   4360

Training aids
Training

Etienne Decroux's theory of corporeal mime. France: Paris. 1918-1996. Lang.: Eng.   3688

Mejerchol'd's theory of biomechanics and its application to training and performance. Russia. 1896-1996. Lang.: Eng.   3689

Training, actor
Institutions

Critique of the University of Melbourne's performance drama program. Australia: Melbourne. 1975-1994. Lang.: Eng.   341

Music and actor training in Hamburg. Germany: Hamburg. 1996. Lang.: Ger.   418

Interview with Jurij Alšic of AKT-ZENT. Germany: Berlin. 1996. Lang.: Ger.   423

Portrait of Hochschule für Musik und Theater Felix Mendelssohn Bartholdy. Germany: Leipzig. 1996. Lang.: Ger.   429

The experience of auditioning for different drama schools. Germany: Berlin. 1996. Lang.: Ger.   440

Interview with actor Hans Schulze of the Westfälische Schauspielschule. Germany: Bochum. 1996. Lang.: Ger.   444

Hanns-Dietrich Schmidt, dramaturg and dean of the drama section of Folkwang-Hochschule. Germany: Essen. 1996. Lang.: Ger.   450

Changes in theatre training of the 1970s. Germany: Essen. 1970-1979. Lang.: Ger.   451

Leopold Jessner's acting studios at Hochschule der Künste. Germany: Berlin. 1925-1931. Lang.: Ger.   452

Profile of two actor training institutions. Germany: Berlin. 1996. Lang.: Ger.   458

Jerzy Grotowski's concept of Action. Italy: Pontedera. 1987-1996. Lang.: Eng.   493

History of the Academy of Theatre, Radio, Film, and Television. Slovenia: Ljubljana. 1946-1996. Lang.: Slo.   530

Profile of independent actors' school Sotenäs Teateratelje. Sweden: Sotenäs. 1995. Lang.: Swe.   536

Swedish actor training. Sweden. 1965. Lang.: Swe.   544

Collaboration between Cleveland Play House and the theatre department of Case Western Reserve University. USA: Cleveland, OH. 1996. Lang.: Eng.   599

Video forms — cont'd

Comparison of productions of *Waiting for Godot* for stage and video. Canada: Montreal, PQ. 1988-1992. Lang.: Fre. 1921

Postmodern 'nostalgia' and recent Shakespearean performances. Europe. North America. 1985-1995. Lang.: Eng. 1998

Interview with actor Andrzej Seweryn. Poland. 1946-1995. Lang.: Eng, Fre. 2156

Interview with actress Karin Bjurström. Sweden: Stockholm. 1970. Lang.: Swe. 2285

Videotape of Aphra Behn's *The Rover* performed by Women's Playhouse Trust. UK-England. 1994. Lang.: Eng. 2302

Videotape on interpreting and performing Shakespeare's *As You Like It.* UK-England. 1994. Lang.: Eng. 2303

Interview with actor Andre Braugher. USA: New York, NY. 1996. Lang.: Eng. 2598

Julia Sweeney's one-woman show *God Said 'Ha!'*. USA: New York, NY. 1996. Lang.: Eng. 2603

Puppetry-related job prospects in TV and film. Germany. USA. 1996. Lang.: Ger. 3569

Analysis of film and video versions of *Romeo and Juliet*. USA. UK-England. Italy. 1936-1978. Lang.: Eng. 3631

Video-sculptural performances of Gary Hill. USA: New York, NY. 1995. Lang.: Eng. 3657

Listing of new audio and video recordings of musical materials.. North America. 1996. Lang.: Eng. 3861

Interview with musical theatre actor Anthony Newley. UK-England. 1935-1996. Lang.: Eng. 3924

Actress Sally Struthers. USA: New York, NY. 1996. Lang.: Eng. 3956

Ventriloquist and puppeteer Paul Winchell. USA. 1937-1978. Lang.: Eng. 4413

Plays/librettos/scripts

The flight of playwrights to film and television. USA. 1996. Lang.: Eng. 3459

Filmed theatre at festival of new cinema and video. Canada: Montreal, PQ. 1991. Lang.: Fre. 3643

Reference materials

Directory of British broadcasting. UK. 1995-1996. Lang.: Eng. 3570

Relation to other fields

The demise of cultural literacy as seen on TV and in films. USA. 1945-1996. Lang.: Eng. 3571

Media at the Biennale de Lyon. France: Lyon. 1995-1996. Lang.: Eng. 3658

Theory/criticism

The status of live performance in a culture saturated by mass media. USA. 1994. Lang.: Eng. 1372

Vidić, Ivan

Plays/librettos/scripts

The problem of identity in recent Croatian drama. Croatia. 1990-1995. Lang.: Eng. 2860

Vidovszky, László

Performance/production

French productions of *Találkozás (The Encounter)* by Péter Nádas, sound by László Vidovszky. France: Paris. Hungary. 1979-1996. Lang.: Hun. 2037

Pierre Tabard's production of *Találkozás (The Encounter)* by Péter Nádas and László Vidovszky. Hungary. France: Paris. 1996. Lang.: Hun. 2093

Vielstich, Friderike

Institutions

Interview with Friderike Vielstich, new director of Städtische Bühne. Germany: Augsburg. 1995. Lang.: Ger. 447

Viet Rock

Plays/librettos/scripts

Vietnam War protest plays. North America. Europe. 1965-1971. Lang.: Eng. 3153

Vietnam Discourse

Plays/librettos/scripts

Vietnam War protest plays. North America. Europe. 1965-1971. Lang.: Eng. 3153

View From the Bridge, A

Plays/librettos/scripts

Influence of Albert Camus on plays of Arthur Miller. USA. 1950-1996. 3456

View of the Dome

Performance/production

Collection of newspaper reviews by New York theatre critics. USA: New York, NY. 1996. Lang.: Eng. 2555

Vigny, Alfred de

Relation to other fields

Assumptions about the relationship between theatre and literature. France: Paris. 1835-1996. Lang.: Fre. 3498

Vígszínház (Budapest)

Institutions

The 100th anniversary of the Vígszínház. Hungary: Budapest. 1896-1996. Lang.: Hun. 486

Performance/production

English plays and subjects on the Hungarian stage. Hungary. 1995-1996. Lang.: Eng. 847

Two productions of *Déryné ifjasszony (Mrs. Déry)* by Ferenc Herczeg. Austria-Hungary. Hungary: Budapest. 1907-1928.Lang.: Hun. 1908

Budapest productions of the millicentenary season. Hungary: Budapest. 1995-1996. Lang.: Eng. 2104

Review of some Budapest productions. Hungary. 1995-1996. Lang.: Eng. 2105

Vihar után (After the Tempest)

Performance/production

Contemporary reviews of *Vihar után (After the Tempest)* by Péter Halász. Hungary. 1955. Lang.: Hun. 2108

Viktjuk, Roman

Performance/production

The Moscow theatre season. Russia: Moscow. 1995-1996. Lang.: Eng. 2198

Director Roman Viktjuk. Russia: Moscow. 1990-1996. Lang.: Rus. 2238

Viktor

Performance/production

Tanztheater Wuppertal's Copenhagen guest performance. Denmark: Copenhagen. 1996. Lang.: Swe. 1573

Vildanden (Wild Duck, The)

Plays/librettos/scripts

Judeo-Christian symbolism in Ibsen's *Vildanden (The Wild Duck)*. Norway. 1884. Lang.: Eng. 3157

Ville parjure, La (Perjured City, The)

Performance/production

Politics and the actor's body in productions by Théâtre du Soleil. France. 1990-1995. Lang.: Eng. 2036

Villella, Edward

Performance/production

Edward Villella, director of Miami City Ballet. USA: Miami, FL. 1936-1995. Lang.: Hun. 1538

Villeneuve, Raymond

Plays/librettos/scripts

Analysis of stage and radio plays by Raymond Villeneuve. Canada: Montreal, PQ. 1987-1991. Lang.: Fre. 1090

Playwright Raymond Villeneuve on writing radio drama. Canada: Montreal, PQ. 1987-1991. Lang.: Fre. 3579

Vincent, Jean-Pierre

Institutions

The Théâtre Nationale de Strasbourg under the direction of Jean-Pierre Vincent. France: Strasbourg. 1975-1983. Lang.: Fre. 1787

Vincent, Julie

Performance/production

Acting, directing, and writing work of Julie Vincent. Canada: Montreal, PQ. 1988-1991. Lang.: Fre. 734

Plays/librettos/scripts

Playwright Julie Vincent on her work. Canada: Montreal, PQ. 1988-1991. Lang.: Fre. 2846

Vinegar Tom

Performance/production

Feminism and contemporary British theatre. UK-England. 1993-1995. Lang.: Eng. 2518

Vineyard Theatre (New York, NY)

Institutions

Vineyard Theatre's provision of temporary shelter for itinerant artists. USA: New York, NY. 1996. Lang.: Eng. 579

Performance/production

Collection of newspaper reviews by New York theatre critics. USA: New York, NY. 1996. Lang.: Eng. 2578

Vingoe, Mary

Performance/production

Playwright and dramaturg Mary Vingoe. Canada. 1985-1996. Lang.: Eng. 1970

Vinny

Performance/production

Productions of Basler Theater. Switzerland: Basel. 1996. Lang.: Ger. 2300

Volpone — cont'd

The London theatre season—fall. UK-England: London. 1995-1996.
Lang.: Eng.   2501
Plays/librettos/scripts
The structural development of comedy in the Renaissance. Europe.
1590-1664. Lang.: Eng.   2969
Voltaire (Arouet, François-Marie)
Performance/production
Account of a devised piece on the death of Voltaire. UK-England:
Bristol. France. 1778-1991. Lang.: Eng.   2533

Collection of newspaper reviews by New York theatre critics. USA:
New York, NY, Washington, DC. 1996. Lang.: Eng.   2581
Von Henning, Marc
Performance/production
Collection of newspaper reviews by London theatre critics. UK-England:
London. 1996. Lang.: Eng.   2480
Von Morgens bis Mitternachts (From Morn to Midnight)
Performance/production
Theatre in Leipzig since reunification. Germany: Leipzig. 1996. Lang.:
Eng.   2061
Vor dem Ruhestand (Eve of Retirement)
Plays/librettos/scripts
German plays in translation at the Festival d'automne. France: Paris.
1988. Lang.: Fre.   2994
Vorse, Mary Heaton
Plays/librettos/scripts
Propaganda plays about the steel and textile industries. USA. 1930-
1940. Lang.: Eng.   3363
Vošnjak, Josip
Basic theatrical documents
Texts of plays by Josip Vošnjak and Anton Funtek. Slovenia. 1834-
1932. Lang.: Slo.   1676
Voss
Plays/librettos/scripts
The operatic adaptation of Patrick White's novel _Voss_. Australia. 1978-
1996. Lang.: Eng.   4298
Voss, Gert
Performance/production
Interview with actor Gert Voss. Germany. Austria. 1940-1996. Lang.:
Ger.   808
Vote 'No!'
Plays/librettos/scripts
The work of Australian women playwrights. Australia. 1930-1970.
Lang.: Eng.   1084
Votes for Women
Basic theatrical documents
International anthology of modern drama by women. 1880-1940. Lang.:
Eng.   1637
Theory/criticism
Feminist criticism of Ibsen in the work of Elizabeth Robins. UK-
England. 1890-1928. Lang.: Eng.   3553
Voxtrot (Montreal, PQ)
Performance/production
Milène Roy and Sylvain Michoue of Voxtrot. Canada: Montreal, PQ.
1989. Lang.: Fre.   745
Voyage in the Dark
Performance/production
Collection of newspaper reviews by London theatre critics. UK-England:
London. 1996. Lang.: Eng.   2312
Voyage magnifique d'Emily Carr, Le (Magnificent Voyage of Emily Carr, The)
Plays/librettos/scripts
Biographical techniques in Jovette Marchessault's playwriting. Canada:
Montreal, PQ. 1970-1991. Lang.: Fre.   2755
Voyage of the Little Mermaid
Performance/production
Disney Productions and puppetry. USA: Orlando, FL. 1995. Lang.: Eng.
                                                                   4418
Voyage sans fin, Le (Constant Journey, The)
Plays/librettos/scripts
Lesbianism on the French stage. France. 1933-1995. Lang.: Eng.   3006

Monique Wittig's introduction and preface to her _Le Voyage sans fin
(The Constant Journey)_. France: Paris. 1985. Lang.: Eng.   3012
Voyage spirituel de Gilgamesh, Le (Spiritual Voyage of Gilgamesh, The)
Performance/production
Cooperation between French puppeteers and Indonesian _dalang_ artists.
Indonesia. France. 1988. Lang.: Fre.   4396
Voyage, The
Performance/production
Background material on Metropolitan Opera radio broadcast
performances. USA: New York, NY. 1996. Lang.: Eng.   4252

A pessimistic view of contemporary American opera. USA. 1946-1996.
Lang.: Eng.   4263

The revival of _The Voyage_ by Philip Glass at the Metropolitan Opera.
USA: New York, NY. 1992-1996. Lang.: Eng.   4277

Conductor Dennis Russell Davies—profile and interview. USA: Toledo,
OH. 1945-1996. Lang.: Eng.   4284
Voyageur Immobile (Motionless Traveler)
Performance/production
Puppets, Human Movement, and dance in Philippe Genty's _Voyageur
Immobile (Motionless Traveler)_. USA: Chicago, IL. France: Paris. 1961-
1965. Lang.: Eng.   4415
Voyageurs, Les (Travelers, The)
Plays/librettos/scripts
Claude Poissant's production of _Les Voyageurs_ by Madeleine Laïc at
Festival internationale des francophonies. France: Limoges. 1988. Lang.:
Fre.   2996
Voyeurz
Performance/production
Collection of newspaper reviews by London theatre critics. UK-England:
London. 1996. Lang.: Eng.   2458
Voz de la mujer (Woman's Voice, A)
Performance/production
Montage structure in plays of American ethnic minorities. USA. 1967-
1990. Lang.: Eng.   2675
Voznesénskij, Andrej
Performance/production
Creative portraits of Moscow actors. Russia: Moscow. 1996. Lang.: Rus.
                                                                   929
Vradenburg, Trish
Performance/production
Collection of newspaper reviews by New York theatre critics. USA:
New York, NY. 1996. Lang.: Eng.   2574
Vsatije Bastilii (Taking of the Bastille, The)
Plays/librettos/scripts
Analysis of plays by Marija Arbatova. Russia. 1990-1996. Lang.: Rus.
                                                                   3188
Vsesojuznyj Gosudarstvénnyj Institut Kinematografii (Moscow)
Training
Sergej Bondarčuk's work as a teacher at the State Institute of
Cinematography. Russia: Moscow. 1970-1996. Lang.: Rus.   3653
Vul'f, Irina
Performance/production
Theatre architect recalls actors. Russia: Moscow. 1900-1996. Lang.: Rus.
                                                                   926
Vulgar, Jenny
Performance/production
Collection of newspaper reviews by London theatre critics. UK-England:
London. 1996. Lang.: Eng.   2473
Vysockij, Vladimir
Institutions
Vladimir Vysockij and the Taganka Theatre. Russia: Moscow. 1964-
1996. Lang.: Rus.   1833
Wachowiak, Jutta
Relation to other fields
East German actresses' reactions to social changes after the fall of the
Berlin wall. Germany, East: Berlin, East. 1990-1991. Lang.: Ger.   1195
Wackler, Rebecca
Basic theatrical documents
Collection of southern plays from Actors' Theatre of Louisville. USA.
1984-1992. Lang.: Eng.   1688
Waddington, James
Performance/production
Collection of newspaper reviews by London theatre critics. UK-England:
London. 1996. Lang.: Eng.   2402
Wade, Andrew
Performance/production
Collection of newspaper reviews by London theatre critics. UK-England:
London. 1996. Lang.: Eng.   2392
Wagner, Chuck
Performance/production
Stage and film treatments of the fairy tale _Beauty and the Beast_. Europe.
USA. Canada. 1946-1996. Lang.: Eng.   793
Wagner, Richard
Design/technology
Design for _Der Fliegende Holländer_, Canadian Opera Company, by
Allen Moyer. Canada: Toronto, ON. 1996. Lang.: Eng.   4014

John Boesche's lighting design for _Tannhäuser_, Austin Lyric Opera.
USA. 1996. Lang.: Eng.   4024

Wagner, Richard — cont'd

Technical aspects of Wagner's *Ring* cycle, Arizona Opera. USA: Flagstaff, AZ. 1996. Lang.: Eng.   4028

Institutions
The reopening of the Prinzregententheater with Wagner's *Tristan und Isolde*. Germany: Munich. 1996. Lang.: Ger.   4041

Performance spaces
The reopening of Theater Lübeck. Germany: Lübeck. 1906-1996. Lang.: Ger.   4068

Performance/production
Background information on Teatro Colón season. Argentina: Buenos Aires. 1996. Lang.: Eng.   4075

Interview with opera director Nicolas Joël. France. Germany. 1942-1996. Lang.: Eng.   4117

Postmodernist stagings of Wagnerian opera. Germany. 1970-1996. Lang.: Eng.   4131

Richard Fricke, assistant stage director for the first performance of *Der Ring des Nibelungen*. Germany: Bayreuth. 1818-1903. Lang.: Eng.   4132

Wolfgang Wagner's production of *Die Meistersinger* at Bayreuther Festspiele. Germany: Bayreuth. 1996. Lang.: Ger.   4133

Interview with opera director Peter Konwitschny. Germany. 1996. Lang.: Ger.   4141

Wolfgang Wagner's scenery and direction of *Die Meistersinger* at the Bayreuth Festival. Germany: Bayreuth. 1996. Lang.: Ger.   4146

Review of 1995 British opera productions. UK-England: London, Leeds, Lewes. 1995-1996. Lang.: Eng.   4234

Background material on Metropolitan Opera radio broadcast performances. USA: New York, NY. 1996. Lang.: Eng.   4252

The Arizona Opera's first *Ring des Nibelungen*. USA: Flagstaff, AZ. 1914-1996. Lang.: Eng.   4297

Puppets in Wagner's *Ring* at Lyric Opera of Chicago. USA: Chicago, IL. 1996. Lang.: Eng.   4414

Plays/librettos/scripts
The Messianic hero in Wagner's *Ring*. Germany. 1996. Lang.: Eng.   4320

Musical influences on Wagner's *Der fliegende Holländer*. Germany. 1827-1843. Lang.: Eng.   4321

Self-contained musical compositions in operas of Wagner and Richard Strauss. Germany. Austria. 1849-1913. Lang.: Eng.   4322

Love and the death of women in works of Wagner, Strauss, and Schoenberg. Germany. Austria: Vienna. 1842-1911. Lang.: Eng.   4323

Background on Wagner's *Siegfried*, to be performed by Budapest Opera. Hungary: Budapest. 1996. Lang.: Hun.   4327

Relation to other fields
Psychoanalytical analysis of Wagnerian opera. Germany. 1840-1882. Lang.: Slo.   4353

Theory/criticism
Nietzschean analysis of Wagnerian opera. Germany. 1840-1882. Lang.: Slo.   4358

Wagner, Robin

Administration
Survey of poster design for Broadway musicals. USA: New York, NY. 1892-1996. Lang.: Eng.   3881

Design/technology
Robin Wagner's sets for *Victor/Victoria*. USA: New York, NY. 1995. Lang.: Eng.   3905

Wagner, Wolfgang

Performance/production
Wolfgang Wagner's production of *Die Meistersinger* at Bayreuther Festspiele. Germany: Bayreuth. 1996. Lang.: Ger.   4133

Wolfgang Wagner's scenery and direction of *Die Meistersinger* at the Bayreuth Festival. Germany: Bayreuth. 1996. Lang.: Ger.   4146

Waiting for Godot

SEE
En attendant Godot.

Waiting for Lefty

Plays/librettos/scripts
Evaluation of workers' drama in historical context. USA. 1929-1995. Lang.: Eng.   1112

Waits, Tom

Basic theatrical documents
Text of *Alice* by Paul Schmidt, Tom Waits, and Kathleen Brennan. Germany: Hamburg. 1996. Lang.: Eng.   3845

Plays/librettos/scripts
Interview with playwright Paul Schmidt. Germany: Hamburg. 1996. Lang.: Eng.   3051

Wajda, Andrzej

Performance/production
The premiere of the first German translation of Wyspiański's *Wesele (The Wedding)*. Austria: Salzburg. 1992. Lang.: Eng, Fre.   1904

The negative impact of democracy on Polish theatre. Poland. 1989-1995. Lang.: Eng.   2146

Polish productions of Shakespeare. Poland. 1989-1996. Lang.: Eng. 2162

Account of a symposium on Polish cinema. Poland. USA: New York, NY. 1930-1996. Lang.: Eng.   3619

Walcott, Derek

Performance/production
Postcolonial theatre. Europe. North America. Asia. Africa. 1880-1950. Lang.: Eng.   779

Postcolonial drama in theory and performance. 1880-1950. Lang.: Eng.   1893

Waldrop, Mark

Performance/production
Collection of newspaper reviews by New York theatre critics. USA: New York, NY. 1996. Lang.: Eng.   2558

Howard Crabtree's *When Pigs Fly* directed by Mark Waldrop, Douglas Fairbanks Theatre. USA: New York, NY. 1996. Lang.: Eng.   3960

Waleza (Valesa)

Plays/librettos/scripts
Responses to the defeat of Solidarity in Polish drama. Poland. 1980-1989. Lang.: Eng.   3160

Walker, Aida Overton

Performance/production
Social boundaries and the transformation of the cakewalk. USA. 1900-1918. Lang.: Eng.   1448

Walker, Alice

Plays/librettos/scripts
Critique of Steven Spielberg's film adaptation of *The Color Purple* by Alice Walker. USA. 1982-1986. Lang.: Eng.   3649

Walker, George F.

Plays/librettos/scripts
Overview of Anglophone Canadian playwriting. Canada. 1970-1990. Lang.: Fre.   2791

Analysis of *Theatre of the Film Noir* by George F. Walker. Canada. 1981. Lang.: Eng.   2817

Walker, Nancy

Administration
Inductions into the theatrical Hall of Fame. USA: New York, NY. 1996. Lang.: Eng.   99

Walker, Timothy

Performance/production
Collection of newspaper reviews by London theatre critics. UK-England: London. 1996. Lang.: Eng.   2482

Walks on Water

Performance/production
The career of performance artist Rose English. UK-England. 1996. Lang.: Eng.   3794

Walküre, Die

Performance/production
Background information on Teatro Colón season. Argentina: Buenos Aires. 1996. Lang.: Eng.   4075

Background material on Metropolitan Opera radio broadcast performances. USA: New York, NY. 1996. Lang.: Eng.   4252

Plays/librettos/scripts
The Messianic hero in Wagner's *Ring*. Germany. 1996. Lang.: Eng.   4320

Wall, Michael

Performance/production
Collection of newspaper reviews by London theatre critics. UK-England: London. 1996. Lang.: Eng.   2402

Wallace, Naomi

Performance/production
Collection of newspaper reviews by London theatre critics. UK-England: London. 1996. Lang.: Eng.   2316

Collection of newspaper reviews by London theatre critics. UK-England: London. 1996. Lang.: Eng.   2455

Plays/librettos/scripts
Naomi Wallace's *Slaughter City* at American Rep. USA: Cambridge, MA. 1996. Lang.: Eng.   3374

Waller, Angelika

Relation to other fields
East German actresses' reactions to social changes after the fall of the Berlin wall. Germany, East: Berlin, East. 1990-1991. Lang.: Ger.   1195

Waller, Fats

Performance/production
The Pointer Sisters in *Ain't Misbehavin'*. USA. 1973-1996. Lang.: Eng.   3957

Williams, Sita
Performance/production
The roles of actor and director in television as compared to the stage. UK-England. 1995-1996. Lang.: Eng.   989

Williams, Tennessee
Basic theatrical documents
Anthology of works by Split Britches. USA. 1985-1995. Lang.: Eng.   1685

Design/technology
Candice Donnelly's costumes for Tennessee Williams' *The Notebook of Trigorin*, Cincinnati Playhouse. USA: Cincinnati, OH. 1996.Lang.: Eng.   1728

Performance/production
Intercultural theatre exchange at the American University in Bulgaria. Bulgaria: Blagoevgrad. 1993. Lang.: Eng.   1915

The Glass Menagerie in a touring coproduction of Kungliga Dramatiska Teatern and Svenska Riksteatern. Sweden. 1996. Lang.: Swe.   2297

Collection of newspaper reviews by London theatre critics. UK-England: London. 1996. Lang.: Eng.   2492

Collection of newspaper reviews by New York theatre critics. USA: New York, NY. 1996. Lang.: Eng.   2558

Collection of newspaper reviews by New York theatre critics. USA: New York, NY. 1996. Lang.: Eng.   2563

Collection of newspaper reviews by New York theatre critics. USA: New York, NY. 1996. Lang.: Eng.   2572

Actress Mary McDonnell. USA: New York, NY. 1948-1996. Lang.: Eng.   2587

Vanessa Redgrave's role in *The Notebook of Trigorin* by Tennessee Williams. USA: Cincinnati, OH. 1996. Lang.: Eng.   2612

Robert Falls' production of *The Night of the Iguana* by Tennessee Williams, Roundabout Theatre Company. USA: New York, NY. 1960-1996. Lang.: Eng.   2670

Interview with actress Kim Hunter. USA. 1951-1996. Lang.: Eng.   3635

Plays/librettos/scripts
Analysis of *Suddenly Last Summer* by Tennessee Williams. USA. 1958. Lang.: Eng.   2702

Realistic characterization and poeticized stage space in plays of Tennessee Williams. USA. 1944-1973. Lang.: Eng.   3323

Gay connotations in *Eccentricities of a Nightingale* by Tennessee Williams. USA. 1945. Lang.: Eng.   3347

Stemma for cataloguing versions of Tennessee Williams' *Camino Real*. USA. 1946-1995. Lang.: Eng.   3414

Williamson, David
Performance/production
Collection of newspaper reviews by London theatre critics. UK-England: London. 1996. Lang.: Eng.   2321

Williamson, Nicol
Performance/production
Collection of newspaper reviews by New York theatre critics. USA: New York, NY. 1996. Lang.: Eng.   2577

Williamson, Susan
Institutions
The 1995 Saskatoon Fringe Festival. Canada: Saskatoon, SK. 1995. Lang.: Eng.   1768

Williamstown Theatre Festival (Williamstown, MA)
Performance/production
Regional theatre in the Berkshires. USA: Stockbridge, MA, Great Barrington, MA, Williamstown, MA. 1996. Lang.: Eng.   1007

Plays by Arthur Miller at the Williamstown Theatre Festival. USA: Williamstown, MA. 1996. Lang.: Eng.   2589

Willis, Jane Nixon
Performance/production
Collection of newspaper reviews by London theatre critics. UK-England: London. 1996. Lang.: Eng.   2411

Willis, Ron
Design/technology
Use of computer-generated projections in a University of Kansas production of *The Adding Machine*. USA: Lawrence, KS. 1996. Lang.: Eng.   1744

Willmott, Phil
Performance/production
Collection of newspaper reviews by London theatre critics. UK-England: London. 1996. Lang.: Eng.   2431

Collection of newspaper reviews by London theatre critics. UK-England: London. 1996. Lang.: Eng.   2490

Wilms, Bernd
Institutions
Profile of Maxim Gorki Theater, Bernd Wilms, artistic director. Germany: Berlin. 1996. Lang.: Ger.   1796

Wilsher, Toby
Performance/production
Collection of newspaper reviews by London theatre critics. UK-England: London. 1996. Lang.: Eng.   2390

Wilson, August
Design/technology
Scott Bradley's set design for *Seven Guitars* by August Wilson. USA: Pittsburgh, PA, New York, NY. 1996. Lang.: Eng.   1731
Institutions
Robert Brustein's response to August Wilson's call for separation of Black and white theatre. USA. 1996. Lang.: Eng.   573

TCG National Conference, addresses by August Wilson and John Ralston Saul. USA: Princeton, NJ. 1996. Lang.: Eng.   588

August Wilson's address on the separation of white and Black theatre. USA: Princeton, NJ. 1996. Lang.: Eng.   607

Performance/production
Postcolonial theatre. Europe. North America. Asia. Africa. 1880-1950. Lang.: Eng.   779

Collection of newspaper reviews by London theatre critics. UK-England: London. 1996. Lang.: Eng.   2342

Collection of newspaper reviews by New York theatre critics. USA: New York, NY. 1996. Lang.: Eng.   2570

Plays/librettos/scripts
African aspects of the drama of August Wilson. USA. Africa. 1990-1996. Lang.: Eng.   3331

Realism and the plays of Baraka and August Wilson. USA. 1964-1984. Lang.: Eng.   3334

Blues music in *Ma Rainey's Black Bottom* by August Wilson. USA. 1982-1996. Lang.: Eng.   3365

Interview with playwright August Wilson. USA. 1996. Lang.: Eng.   3381

Playwright August Wilson. USA: New York, NY. 1952-1996. Lang.: Eng.   3428

Contemporary American drama. USA. 1960-1995. Lang.: Eng.   3431

The influence of blues music on the plays of August Wilson. USA. 1996. Lang.: Eng.   3452

Profile of playwright August Wilson. USA. 1945-1996. Lang.: Eng. 3454

Analysis of plays by August Wilson. USA. 1995. Lang.: Eng.   3461

Relation to other fields
Responses to August Wilson's call for separation of Black and white theatre. USA. 1996. Lang.: Eng.   1277

Wilson, Carl
Design/technology
Obituaries for designers Alan Owen and Carl Wilson. USA: Plano, TX, New York, NY. 1995-1996. Lang.: Eng.   249

Wilson, Edward
Performance/production
Collection of newspaper reviews by London theatre critics. UK-England: London. 1996. Lang.: Eng.   2378

Wilson, Erin Cressida
Plays/librettos/scripts
Interviews with playwrights Erin Cressida Wilson, Elena Penga, and Brighde Mullins. USA: San Francisco, CA. 1995. Lang.: Eng.   3366

Wilson, Lanford
Institutions
Jeff Daniels' experience acting in *Fifth of July* at Circle Rep. USA: New York, NY. 1978-1996. Lang.: Eng.   1864
Plays/librettos/scripts
Contemporary American drama. USA. 1960-1995. Lang.: Eng.   3431

Wilson, Mary Louise
Design/technology
Michael Krass's costume design for *Full Gallop* by Mary Louise Wilson and Mark Hampton. USA: New York, NY. 1996. Lang.: Eng.   1727
Performance/production
Holiday memories of Broadway actors. USA: New York, NY. 1996. Lang.: Eng.   1013

Mary Louise Wilson's role in *Full Gallop*. USA: New York, NY. 1996. Lang.: Eng.   2641

Wilson, Michael
Performance/production
Collection of newspaper reviews by New York theatre critics. USA: New York, NY. 1996. Lang.: Eng.   2563

Wilson, Peter
Performance/production
Collection of newspaper reviews by London theatre critics. UK-England: London. 1996. Lang.: Eng.   2465

Wilson, Richard
Performance/production
Collection of newspaper reviews by London theatre critics. UK-England: London. 1996. Lang.: Eng.   2423

Women in theatre — cont'd

Plays/librettos/scripts

Women in theatre — cont'd

Playwright Ana Caro Mallén de Soto. Spain. 1625-1672. Lang.: Eng.
3263

Strong female roles in turn-of-the-century drama. UK-England: London. 1899-1918. Lang.: Eng.
3279

Medusa as a metaphorical presence in some contemporary productions. UK-England. Canada. 1995. Lang.: Eng.
3294

Realism and the female playwright: Lillian Hellman's *The Little Foxes*. USA. 1939. Lang.: Eng.
3328

Pregnancy in plays of Adrienne Kennedy. USA. 1988. Lang.: Eng. 3329

History of American feminist drama. USA. 1785-1995. Lang.: Eng. 3341

Realism, the feminist agenda, and recent plays by women. USA. 1981-1989. Lang.: Eng.
3384

The dual liberation motif in early Black women playwrights. USA. 1915-1930. Lang.: Eng.
3387

Political theatre of Karen Malpede and Slobodan Snajder. USA. Croatia. 1991-1996. Lang.: Eng.
3403

Realism in American feminist drama. USA. 1900-1988. Lang.: Eng.
3441

Black women playwrights of the Harlem Renaissance. USA: New York, NY. 1916-1930. Lang.: Eng.
3442

Analysis of *Sally's Rape* by Robbie McCauley. USA. 1993-1994. Lang.: Eng.
3453

Representational practice in works of Hildegard of Bingen. Germany: Bingen. 1120-1179. Lang.: Eng.
3874

Playwright Carol Bolt on becoming an opera librettist. Canada. 1996. Lang.: Eng.
4307

Reference materials

Bibliography of works by French women playwrights. France. 1900-1990. Lang.: Eng.
3474

Relation to other fields

Immigrant writers in Australian theatre. Australia. 1979-1995. Lang.: Eng.
1132

How the position of women in Quebec theatre has changed. Canada. 1980-1993. Lang.: Fre.
1139

Reconsideration of feminist criticism of the early 1980s. Canada. 1975-1993. Lang.: Fre.
1154

The changed position of women in Quebec theatre. Canada. 1980-1993. Lang.: Fre.
1156

Female identity as seen through culture. Philippines: Mindanao. India: New Delhi. 1986-1995. Lang.: Eng.
1216

Report on 1995 event of the Magdalena Project. UK-Wales: Cardiff. 1995. Lang.: Eng.
1251

Profile of a lesbian 'marriage' in the theatre community. USA: New York, NY. 1886-1933. Lang.: Eng.
1264

Feminism and dramaturgy at Nightwood Theatre. Canada: Toronto, ON. 1996. Lang.: Eng.
3487

Theory/criticism

Feminist response to alleged sexism in Montreal theatre criticism. Canada: Montreal, PQ. 1993. Lang.: Fre.
1323

Theatre criticism in suffrage newspapers. UK-England. 1912-1914. Lang.: Eng.
1370

Feminist criticism and the plays of Heiner Müller. USA. Europe. 1981. Lang.: Swe.
1389

Feminist criticism of Ibsen in the work of Elizabeth Robins. UK-England. 1890-1928. Lang.: Eng.
3553

Theatre critic Rosamond Gilder. USA. 1891-1986. Lang.: Eng. 3563

Female circus performers and social convention. Australia. 1850-1929. Lang.: Eng.
3758

Women's Playhouse Trust (London)

Performance/production

Videotape of Aphra Behn's *The Rover* performed by Women's Playhouse Trust. UK-England. 1994. Lang.: Eng.
2302

Women's Theatre and Creativity Centre (Halifax, NS)

Institutions

Workshops of the Women's Theatre and Creativity Centre. Canada: Halifax, NS. 1995-1996. Lang.: Eng.
1759

Women's Theatre Group (London)

Performance/production

Contemporary English feminist theatre. UK-England: London. 1970-1994. Lang.: Eng.
978

Feminism and contemporary British theatre. UK-England. 1993-1995. Lang.: Eng.
2518

Women's Unit (New York, NY)

Performance/production

Women's theatre and the mid-century women's movement. USA. 1960-1975. Lang.: Eng.
1062

Wonder of Women or the Tragedy of Sophonisba, The

Plays/librettos/scripts

Plays about the historical figure Sophonisba. Europe. 1515-1805. Lang.: Ita.
2966

Wonderful Time

Performance/production

Collection of newspaper reviews by New York theatre critics. USA: New York, NY. 1996. Lang.: Eng.
2552

Wonderland Adventures of Alice, The

Performance/production

Collection of newspaper reviews by London theatre critics. UK-England: London, Stratford. 1996. Lang.: Eng.
2461

Wong, Denise

Performance/production

Collection of newspaper reviews by London theatre critics. UK-England: London. 1996. Lang.: Eng.
2498

Wood Daemon, The

Plays/librettos/scripts

American adaptations of English Gothic plays. USA. 1790-1820. Lang.: Eng.
3324

Wood, Beth

Performance/production

Collection of newspaper reviews by London theatre critics. UK-England: London. 1996. Lang.: Eng.
2433

Collection of newspaper reviews by London theatre critics. UK-England: London. 1996. Lang.: Eng.
2451

Wood, David

Performance/production

Collection of newspaper reviews by London theatre critics. UK-England: London. 1996. Lang.: Eng.
2494

Wood, Mrs. Henry

Performance/production

Collection of newspaper reviews by London theatre critics. UK-England: London. 1996. Lang.: Eng.
2345

Wood, Tom

Performance/production

Multiple roles of Tom Wood and Nicola Cavendish in *Later Life*. Canada. 1996. Lang.: Eng.
1920

Wooden Prince, The

SEE

Fából faragott királyfi, A.

Woodruff, Robert

Performance/production

Production of *Jud Süss (The Jew Suess)* at BeerSheba Municipal Theatre. Israel: Beersheba. 1931-1996. Lang.: Eng.
2119

Impressions of the Boston theatre scene. USA: Cambridge, MA, Boston, MA. 1995. Lang.: Eng.
2628

Woods, The

Performance/production

Collection of newspaper reviews by London theatre critics. UK-England: London. 1996. Lang.: Eng.
2404

Woodward, Joanne

Relation to other fields

Paintings by Clifford Odets and a production of his *Golden Boy*. USA: New York, NY. 1940-1996. Lang.: Eng.
3522

Woolf, Virginia

Performance/production

Gender construction and two performances of *Orlando*. France: Paris. Switzerland: Lausanne. Germany: Berlin. 1990-1996. Lang.: Ger. 2020

Collection of newspaper reviews by London theatre critics. UK-Scotland: Edinburgh. 1996. Lang.: Eng.
2545

Relation to other fields

Performance in the work of novelist Virginia Woolf. UK-England. 1941. Lang.: Eng.
1240

Woolford, Julian

Performance/production

Collection of newspaper reviews by London theatre critics. UK-England: London. 1996. Lang.: Eng.
2459

Wooster Group (New York, NY)

Performance/production

Productions of the Festival de Théâtre des Amériques. Canada: Montreal, PQ. 1989. Lang.: Fre.
702

Tendencies in avant-garde theatre. Canada. USA. 1980-1989. Lang.: Fre.
723

Wuttke, Martin
Institutions
Interview with Martin Wuttke, new director of Berliner Ensemble. Germany: Berlin. 1996. Lang.: Ger. 1811
Performance/production
Two productions of Müller's *Germania 3*. Germany: Berlin, Bochum. 1996. Lang.: Ger. 2056

Two productions of Heiner Müller's *Germania 3*. Germany: Bochum, Berlin. 1996. Lang.: Ger. 2091
Wycherley, William
Performance/production
Collection of newspaper reviews by London theatre critics. UK-England: London. 1996. Lang.: Eng. 2464
Plays/librettos/scripts
Metaphor in *The Country Wife* by William Wycherley. England. 1675. Lang.: Eng. 2911
Wydro, Ken
Performance/production
Collection of newspaper reviews by New York theatre critics. USA: New York, NY, East Haddam, CT. 1996. Lang.: Eng. 2553
Plays/librettos/scripts
Career of playwright and lyricist Vy Higgensen. USA: New York, NY. 1970-1996. Lang.: Eng. 3996
Wyndham's Theatre (London)
Performance/production
Collection of newspaper reviews by London theatre critics. UK-England: London. 1996. Lang.: Eng. 2305

Collection of newspaper reviews by London theatre critics. UK-England: London. 1996. Lang.: Eng. 2320

Collection of newspaper reviews by London theatre critics. UK-England: London. 1996. Lang.: Eng. 2406

Collection of newspaper reviews by London theatre critics. UK-England: London. 1996. Lang.: Eng. 2447
Wynn, Ed
Performance/production
Dancer Dorothy Bird recalls the original Broadway production of *Hooray For What!*. USA: New York, NY. 1937. 3933
Wyrywacz serc
Plays/librettos/scripts
Analysis of contemporary Polish opera. Poland. 1995. Lang.: Eng, Fre. 4336
Wyspiański, Stanisław
Performance/production
The premiere of the first German translation of Wyspiański's *Wesele (The Wedding)*. Austria: Salzburg. 1992. Lang.: Eng, Fre. 1904

Krzysztof Nazar's production of Witkacy's *Wesele (The Wedding)*, Teatr Powszechny. Poland: Warsaw. 1995. Lang.: Eng, Fre. 2153

La Bohème, a pastiche of works by Wyspiański, directed by Jerzy Grzegorzewski, Teatr Studio. Poland: Warsaw. 1995. Lang.: Eng, Fre. 2166

Piotr Tomaszuk's production of Wyspiański's *Klątwa (The Curse)*. Poland: Warsaw. 1994. Lang.: Eng, Fre. 2172
Xerxes
Performance/production
Background material on Lyric Opera of Chicago radio broadcast performances. USA: Chicago, IL. 1996. Lang.: Eng. 4244
Xi Ju Che Jian (Beijing)
Basic theatrical documents
English translation of *Ling Dang An (File 0)* by Mou Sen. China, People's Republic of: Beijing. 1995-1996. Lang.: Eng. 1652
Institutions
Chinese independent theatre: Mou Sen and Xi Ju Che Jian. China, People's Republic of: Beijing. 1995-1996. Lang.: Eng. 1782
Performance/production
Interview with Mou Sen, artistic director, and Wu Wenguang, actor, of Xi Ju Che Jian (Garage Theatre). China, People's Republic of. 1996. Lang.: Eng. 759

Interview with director Mou Sen. China, People's Republic of: Beijing. 1995-1996. Lang.: Eng. 1973
Plays/librettos/scripts
Mou Sen and the political theatre of Xi Ju Che Jian. China, People's Republic of: Beijing. 1993-1996. Lang.: Eng. 2856
Xiqu
Performance/production
Performance of *nanxi*. China. 1368-1996. Lang.: Eng. 3879
XXX
Design/technology
The partnership of set designer Carouschka and lighting designer Jens Sethzman. Sweden. 1996. Lang.: Dan. 212

Yabuhara kengyō (Great Doctor Yabuhara, The)
Performance/production
Japanese performances of Japanese themes at Toronto Theatre Festival. Japan. Canada: Toronto, ON. 1996. Lang.: Eng. 874
Yaldei Hatzel (Children of the Shadow)
Basic theatrical documents
Israeli Holocaust drama. Israel. 1955-1989. Lang.: Eng. 1667
Plays/librettos/scripts
Analysis of Israeli Holocaust drama. Israel. 1950-1984. Lang.: Eng. 3099
Yale Puppeteers (Los Angeles, CA)
Performance/production
Forman Brown of Yale Puppeteers. USA. 1901-1996. Lang.: Eng. 4419
Yale Repertory Theatre (New Haven, CT)
Performance/production
Background on *Venus* by Suzan-Lori Parks. USA. 1996. Lang.: Eng. 2679
Yamada, Setsuko
Performance/production
Japanese performances of Japanese themes at Toronto Theatre Festival. Japan. Canada: Toronto, ON. 1996. Lang.: Eng. 874
Yankowitz, Susan
Performance/production
Profile of Joseph Chaikin, with emphasis on *1969 Terminal 1996*. USA: New York, NY. 1969-1996. Lang.: Eng. 1065
Yasko, Jeanne
Institutions
New possibilities for dance in Norrland. Sweden: Sundsvall, Kiruna, Härnösand. 1995. Lang.: Swe. 1409
Yates, Tony
Performance/production
Collection of newspaper reviews by London theatre critics. UK-England: London. 1996. Lang.: Eng. 2473
Year of the White Bear/The New World (B)Order, The
Theory/criticism
Performance and self-representation of Hispanic artists. USA. 1992-1996. Lang.: Eng. 1375
Yearbooks
Institutions
Photo yearbook of De Nederlandse Opera. Netherlands: Amsterdam. 1995-1996. Lang.: Dut. 4048
Reference materials
Yearbook of Italian theatre. Italy. 1996. Lang.: Ita. 1123

Yearbook of Slovene theatre. Slovenia. 1994-1995. Lang.: Slo. 1126
Yeats, William Butler
Institutions
Profile of Irish women's nationalist group Inghinidhe na h'Eireann. Ireland: Dublin. 1900-1902. Lang.: Eng. 1814
Performance/production
Intercultural work of Noho Theatre Group. Japan: Kyoto. 1981-1994. Lang.: Eng. 875

Expatriate Japanese playwright Kori Torahiko. UK-England: London. Canada: Toronto, ON. Japan. 1913-1924. Lang.: Eng. 2510
Plays/librettos/scripts
Nationalism and the female figure in plays of Yeats. Ireland. 1903-1910. Lang.: Eng. 3083

Influence of Synge's *The Playboy of the Western World* on work of Yeats. Ireland. 1907. Lang.: Eng. 3090

The mask in plays of Yeats and O'Neill. USA. 1911-1953. Lang.: Eng. 3400
Yellow Jacket, The
Performance/production
Tairov's production of *The Yellow Jacket* by George C. Hazelton and J.H. Benrimo. Russia: Moscow. 1933. Lang.: Rus. 2239
Plays/librettos/scripts
The introduction of Chinese theatre to European audiences. Europe. China, People's Republic of. 1912-1996. Lang.: Eng. 2968
Yellow Peril, The
Basic theatrical documents
Anthology of unknown plays of the Harlem Renaissance. USA: New York, NY. 1920-1940. Lang.: Eng. 1694
Yellow Wallpaper, The
Performance/production
Collection of newspaper reviews by London theatre critics. UK-England: London. 1996. Lang.: Eng. 2457
Yeonheedan Keoripae (Seoul)
Institutions
Profile of four Seoul theatre companies. Korea: Seoul. 1986-1996. Lang.: Kor. 494

GEOGRAPHICAL - CHRONOLOGICAL INDEX

Austro-Hungarian Empire — cont'd

1825-1847.   **Plays/librettos/scripts.**
The language of Austrian *volksstück* on the Prague stage.
Prague. Vienna. Lang.: Cze.   2732
1876-1883.   **Performance/production.**
Gyula Ecsedi Kovács' staging of *Tigris és hiéna*. Kolozsvár.
Lang.: Hun.   1910
1904-1906.   **Performance/production.**
Analysis of two popular operettas *János vitéz* and *Die lustige
Witwe*. Lang.: Hun.   4364
1905-1996.   **Performance/production.**
Interview with Laszlo Halasz, first conductor of the New York
City Opera Company. Debrecen. Lang.: Eng.   4083

Bashkiria
1990-1996.   **Institutions.**
Profile of Respublikanskij Russkij Dramatičéskij Teatr. Ufa.
Lang.: Rus.   1754
1995.   **Institutions.**
The Nureyev ballet festival. Ufa. Lang.: Rus.   1477

Belgium
990-1995.   .
History of Dutch and Flemish theatre. Netherlands. Flanders.
Lang.: Dut.   2
1500-1599.   **Performance/production.**
Staging the *rederijker*. Netherlands. Lang.: Eng.   1913
1985-1996.   **Plays/librettos/scripts.**
Émile Lansman's career in theatrical publishing. Lang.: Fre.
                                                               2733
1986-1987.   **Performance/production.**
Suzanne Burgoyne's experiments in intercultural performance.
Brussels. Omaha, NE. Lang.: Eng.   1911
1988.   **Plays/librettos/scripts.**
Profile of the 'plays in transit' workshops at the Festival
international des francophonies. Limoges. Canada. Mali. Lang.:
Fre.   2988
1989-1994.   **Performance/production.**
Visual artist Fabrizio Plessi and his collaboration with
choreographer Frédéric Flamand. Italy. Lang.: Ger.   1436
1995.   **Performance/production.**
Nele Paxinou and Les Baladins du Miroir. Lang.: Eng.   1912
Events commemorating the fifth anniversary of the death of
Tadeusz Kantor. Cracow. Brussels. Lang.: Eng, Fre.   2158
1996.   **Design/technology.**
Paul Steinberg's cinematic design for a production of Puccini's
La Fanciulla del West, Flemish National Opera. Antwerp.
Lang.: Eng.   4013
1996.   **Performance/production.**
Interview with choreographer Alain Populaire. Montreal, PQ.
Lang.: Fre.   1416
Review of productions of Schoenberg's operas. Paris. Brussels.
Lang.: Ger.   4120

Belorus
1995.   **Performance/production.**
Galina Sinel'nikova's *Polonez* at Belorussian Opera and Ballet
Theatre. Minsk. Lang.: Rus.   1495
The premiere of the ballet *Strasti (Rogneda)* by Andrej Mdivani
and Valerij Elizarjev. Minsk. Lang.: Rus.   1496
1996.   **Performance/production.**
Report on productions and discussions of ITI meeting. Minsk.
Lang.: Hun.   695

Bermuda
1996.   **Institutions.**
Profile of Stage One Productions of Bermuda. Hamilton. Lang.:
Eng.   1755

Bohemia
1400.   **Plays/librettos/scripts.**
Analysis of *Oráč a Smrt (Death and the Ploughman)* by
Johannes von Saaz. Lang.: Cze.   2734
1783-1938.   **Relation to other fields.**
Prague and German *Nationaltheater*. Prague. Lang.: Ger.   1135

Bolivia
1996.   **Design/technology.**
Design and technology at the Festival de Teatro de los Barrios.
Lang.: Spa.   146

Bosnia
1992-1995.   **Performance/production.**
Refugee performers Savić and Džemila Delić. Sarajevo. Lang.:
Eng.   697
1996.   **Performance/production.**
Playwright Karen Malpede's experiences with Bosnian acting
students. Sarajevo. Dubrovnik. Lang.: Eng.   696

Bosnia and Herzegovina
1993.   **Performance/production.**
Interview with director Jasenko Selimović. Stockholm. Sarajevo.
Lang.: Swe.   948

Botswana
1994.   **Performance/production.**
Traditional and modern theatrical forms. Lang.: Eng.   698

Brazil
1965-1967.   **Plays/librettos/scripts.**
The success of the epic musical *Arena conta Zumbi*. São Paulo.
Lang.: Eng.   3984
1985-1995.   **Plays/librettos/scripts.**
Analysis of plays by María Adelaide Amaral. Lang.: Por.   2735
1985-1996.   **Performance/production.**
The work of director-designer Gerald Thomas. Lang.: Eng.   699
1995-1996.   **Performance/production.**
The creation of *Zumbi* by Bando de Teatro Olodum and the
Black Theatre Co-operative. Salvador. London. Lang.: Eng.
                                                               1914
1996.   **Performance spaces.**
The new São Paulo opera house, now under construction. São
Paulo. Lang.: Eng.   617

Bulgaria
1950-1989.   **Relation to other fields.**
Shakespeare and the dominant ideology in Bulgarian education.
Lang.: Eng.   3479
1993.   **Performance/production.**
Intercultural theatre exchange at the American University in
Bulgaria. Blagoevgrad. Lang.: Eng.   1915

Burgundy
1468.   **Performance/production.**
Analysis of plays presented at a royal wedding celebration.
Lang.: Ger.   3770

Cameroon
1667-1996.   **Plays/librettos/scripts.**
Analysis of Oyônô-Mbia's *Trois prétendants ... un mari (Three
Suitors: One Husband)*. Lang.: Eng.   2737
1976-1996.   **Plays/librettos/scripts.**
Pan-Africanism in the theatre of Werewere Liking. Ivory Coast.
Lang.: Eng.   2736

Canada
                         Relation to other fields.
Immigrant playwright Marco Micone on multiculturalism and
cultural assimilation. Montreal, PQ. Lang.: Fre.   3486
1595-1996.   **Basic theatrical documents.**
Final lines of the principal characters of forty-five plays. France.
England. Lang.: Fre.   1644
1606-1990.   **Plays/librettos/scripts.**
Humor in French-Canadian theatre. Lang.: Fre.   1088
1625-1991.   **Plays/librettos/scripts.**
The recent proliferation of Don Juan adaptations. Montreal, PQ.
Austria. Lang.: Fre.   2782
1655-1989.   **Performance/production.**
The history of puppetry in Quebec. Lang.: Fre.   4390
1700-1996.   **Relation to other fields.**
Historic and contemporary functions of the theatre critic. France.
Lang.: Fre.   1150
1710-1996.   **Plays/librettos/scripts.**
Analysis of two new lesbian-themed Canadian plays. Lang.:
Eng.   2793
1860-1994.   **Relation to other fields.**
National and regional identities in Canadian theatre companies.
Lang.: Eng.   1157
1869-1941.   **Performance/production.**
Profile of baritone Joseph Saucier. Montreal, PQ. Lang.: Eng.
                                                               4098
1875-1941.   **Performance spaces.**
Theatre decorator Emmanuel Briffa. Montreal, PQ. Detroit, MI.
Lang.: Eng.   3604
1878-1996.   **Theory/criticism.**
Introduction to an *ET* issue devoted to post-colonial
Shakespearean criticism. Lang.: Eng.   3534
1880-1989.   **Relation to other fields.**
Experimental theatre in the social context. France. Lang.: Fre.
                                                               1155
1882.   **Plays/librettos/scripts.**
Transvestism and feminism in *The Sweet Girl Graduate* by
Sarah Anne Curzon. Lang.: Eng.   2746
1884-1966.   **Performance spaces.**
Guide to theatres on THS tour. Montreal, PQ. Quebec, PQ.
Lang.: Eng.   3603

Canada — cont'd

1885-1958. **Performance/production.**
Contralto Eva Gauthier. Lang.: Eng. 4094
1886-1986. **Plays/librettos/scripts.**
Plays about Louis Riel. Lang.: Fre. 2792
1891-1989. **Theory/criticism.**
Sentimentality in theatre. Lang.: Fre. 3536
1900-1989. **Relation to other fields.**
Impulse in Quebec drama. Lang.: Fre. 3485
1900-1991. **Performance/production.**
Dance notation—forms and function. USA. Lang.: Fre. 1414
1913-1924. **Performance/production.**
Expatriate Japanese playwright Kori Torahiko. London.
Toronto, ON. Japan. Lang.: Eng. 2510
1917-1996. **Performance/production.**
Canadian debuts of singers from Eastern Europe. USA. Lang.:
Eng. 4097
1921-1996. **Performance/production.**
Obituary for TV personality Fred Davis. Lang.: Eng. 738
1922-1934. **Performance spaces.**
Montreal cinemas. Montreal, PQ. Lang.: Eng. 3605
1925-1996. **Institutions.**
Vaudeville shows at the Casino Theatre. Toronto, ON. Lang.:
Eng. 3843
1928-1989. **Plays/librettos/scripts.**
Suzanne Lantagne's mime adaptation of a short story by
Gombrowicz. Montreal, PQ. Lang.: Fre. 3693
1932-1996. **Relation to other fields.**
Political influences on playwrights David Fennario and George
Ryga. Lang.: Eng. 3482
1933. **Plays/librettos/scripts.**
The workers' theatre play *Eight Men Speak*. Toronto, ON.
Lang.: Eng. 2776
1938-1989. **Reference materials.**
Bibliography of puppetry. Montreal, PQ. Lang.: Fre. 4426
1939-1991. **Performance/production.**
Lyric soprano Lilian Sukis. Lang.: Eng. 4085
1940-1980. **Performance/production.**
Soprano Lois Marshall. Toronto, ON. Lang.: Eng. 4096
1943-1996. **Plays/librettos/scripts.**
Place and identity in Quebecois drama. Lang.: Fre. 2834
1946-1996. **Performance/production.**
Stage and film treatments of the fairy tale *Beauty and the Beast*.
Europe. USA. Lang.: Eng. 793
1949-1996. **Performance/production.**
The gay male body in *Strains* by Rumble Productions.
Vancouver, BC. Lang.: Eng. 720
Serge Provost's score for *Le Vampire et la Nymphomane* by
Claude Gauvreau. Montreal, PQ. Lang.: Fre. 4092
1950-1989. **Audience.**
Unexpected reactions to films and plays. Montreal, PQ. Lang.:
Fre. 129
1950-1989. **Relation to other fields.**
Memory in Quebec novels and plays. Lang.: Fre. 3483
1950-1992. **Performance/production.**
Interview with actress Hélène Loiselle. Montreal, PQ. Lang.:
Fre. 1946
1950-1996. **Performance/production.**
Diahann Carroll's role in *Sunset Boulevard* at the Ford Centre.
Toronto, ON. Lang.: Eng. 3912
1950-1996. **Relation to other fields.**
Postmodernism and formal conventions of performance. USA.
Lang.: Eng. 1136
The social function of theatrical practice. Quebec, PQ. Lang.:
Fre. 1152
Opera in popular culture. USA. Lang.: Eng. 4355
1950-1996. **Theory/criticism.**
Argument that theatre's value is in excitement generated, not
production values. Lang.: Fre. 1329
1953-1990. **Plays/librettos/scripts.**
Dominic Champagne's *La Répétition (The Rehearsal)* and its
relation to Beckett's *En attendant Godot (Waiting for Godot)*.
Montreal, PQ. France. Ireland. Lang.: Fre. 2843
1953-1996. **Institutions.**
History of the Saskatoon summer Shakespeare festival.
Saskatoon, SK. Lang.: Eng. 1763
1956-1992. **Performance/production.**
Chronology of Beckett productions. Ottawa, ON. Montreal, PQ.
Quebec, PQ. Lang.: Fre. 1969

1958-1993. **Plays/librettos/scripts.**
Analysis of plays by Marcel Dubé. Montreal, PQ. Quebec, PQ.
Lang.: Fre. 2742
1958-1996. **Performance spaces.**
Performance spaces and conditions of Théâtre d'Aujourd'hui.
Montreal, PQ. Lang.: Fre. 1884
1960-1989. **Relation to other fields.**
Similarities between experimental theatre and scientific research.
USA. Lang.: Fre. 1269
1960-1990. **Plays/librettos/scripts.**
The psychology and sociology of gay theatre. Lang.: Fre. 2759
Translator Linda Gaboriau. Montreal, PQ. Lang.: Fre. 2781
Poetics of gay theatre. USA. Lang.: Fre. 2848
1960-1990. **Relation to other fields.**
Attitudes toward gay theatre in Quebec. Lang.: Fre. 3480
Homosexuality in Quebecois society and theatre. Lang.: Fre.
3481
1960-1991. **Performance/production.**
Interview with voice teacher Aline Caron. Lang.: Fre. 746
Theatricality in the work of Montreal choreographers. Montreal,
PQ. Lang.: Fre. 1567
1961-1996. **Institutions.**
Interview with Walter Learning of Theatre New Brunswick.
Fredericton, NB. Lang.: Eng. 1758
1962-1989. **Performance/production.**
Anne-Claire Poirier's experience of filming theatre. Stratford,
ON. Lang.: Fre. 3614
1962-1996. **Plays/librettos/scripts.**
Playwright Isabelle Doré on her career. Montreal, PQ. Lang.:
Fre. 2772
1963. **Plays/librettos/scripts.**
Robert Gurik on his first play *Le Sang du poète (The Blood of
the Poet)*. Montreal, PQ. Lang.: Fre. 2789
1964-1992. **Plays/librettos/scripts.**
Careers of playwrights Michel Tremblay and Marie Laberge.
Quebec, PQ. Lang.: Eng. 2815
1965-1991. **Institutions.**
Interview with personnel of the Centre des Auteurs
Dramatiques. Montreal, PQ. Lang.: Fre. 1762
1966-1989. **Reference materials.**
Information on gay and lesbian plays by Quebecois. Montreal,
PQ. Lang.: Fre. 3472
1966-1996. **Relation to other fields.**
Crisis and the performing arts. USA. Lang.: Fre. 1147
1967-1986. **Plays/librettos/scripts.**
Comparison of translations of the opening of Sophocles'
Antigone. France. Lang.: Fre. 2787
1967-1989. **Performance/production.**
Director Serge Marois and experimental theatre. Montreal, PQ.
Lang.: Fre. 736
1968. **Performance/production.**
The influence of Living Theatre on Raymond Cloutier of Grand
Cirque Ordinaire. Grenoble. Montreal, PQ. Lang.: Fre. 2015
1968-1989. **Performance/production.**
Interview with Jacques Lessard of Théâtre Repère. Quebec, PQ.
Lang.: Fre. 1960
1968-1989. **Theory/criticism.**
Aesthetic and ideological characteristics of experimental theatre.
Lang.: Fre. 1320
1968-1990. **Plays/librettos/scripts.**
Translations by playwright Michel Tremblay. Montreal, PQ.
Lang.: Fre. 2748
Quebec nationalism in translation and adaptation. Lang.: Fre.
2750
1968-1993. **Plays/librettos/scripts.**
Witches in Quebecois feminist plays. Lang.: Fre. 2754
1968-1996. **Institutions.**
Kanata Theatre, housing local theatre groups. Kanata, ON.
Lang.: Eng. 383
1969-1976. **Performance/production.**
Street performances of Théâtre Euh!. Quebec, PQ. Lang.: Fre.
3705
1969-1978. **Plays/librettos/scripts.**
Quebec nationalism in Garneau's translation of *Macbeth*. Lang.:
Fre. 2749
1969-1990. **Plays/librettos/scripts.**
Shakespeare in post-colonial drama. Australia. Lang.: Eng. 2726
1969-1993. **Institutions.**
Interview with Jacinthe Potvin of Théâtre du Carton. Lang.: Fre.
1772

Canada — cont'd

Writing for puppet theatre. Montreal, PQ. Lang.: Fre. 4424
1979-1992. Plays/librettos/scripts.
Analysis of *Broue (Scum)* by Marc Messier, Michel Côté, and
Marcel Gauthier. Lang.: Fre. 2808
1979-1996. Institutions.
Productions of the Carrefour theatre festival. Quebec, PQ.
Lang.: Eng. 1760
1980. Performance/production.
Jean-Guy Sabourin's production of Brecht's *Leben des Galilei
(The Life of Galileo)*, Théâtre de la Grande Réplique. Montreal,
PQ. Lang.: Fre. 1958
The new concept of circus. Montreal, PQ. Lang.: Swe. 3754
1980-1986. Performance/production.
Manon Gauthier's one-woman adaptation of a Michel Tremblay
novel. Montreal, PQ. Lang.: Fre. 1936
1980-1989. Performance/production.
Tendencies in avant-garde theatre. USA. Lang.: Fre. 723
1980-1989. Plays/librettos/scripts.
Lorraine Pintal's solo performance *Madame Louis 14*. Montreal,
PQ. Lang.: Fre. 2840
1980-1990. Performance/production.
Interview with dancer Jocelyne Montpetit. Montreal, PQ. Japan.
Lang.: Fre. 1569
Interview with director René Richard Cyr. Montreal, PQ. Lang.:
Fre. 1945
Expressions of collective identity in Quebec comic monologues.
Lang.: Fre. 3727
1980-1990. Plays/librettos/scripts.
Profile of Anglo-Quebec theatre. Montreal, PQ. Lang.: Fre.
2738
Round-table discussion of Quebec translators. Lang.: Fre. 2769
Trends in recent Quebec drama. Montreal, PQ. Lang.: Fre.
2839
1980-1991. Institutions.
Tangente's contribution to experimental dance. Montreal, PQ.
Lang.: Fre. 1554
The work of Dynamo Théâtre, formerly Circus. Montreal, PQ.
Lang.: Fre. 3749
1980-1991. Performance/production.
Interview with actress Pascale Montpetit. Montreal, PQ. Lang.:
Fre. 732
1980-1992. Design/technology.
Scenography of Gilles Maheu for Carbone 14. Montreal, PQ.
Lang.: Fre. 152
1980-1993. Performance/production.
Beauty and death in Montreal productions by Robert Wilson.
Montreal, PQ. Lang.: Fre. 753
1980-1993. Relation to other fields.
How the position of women in Quebec theatre has changed.
Lang.: Fre. 1139
The changed position of women in Quebec theatre. Lang.: Fre.
1156
1980-1995. Design/technology.
Scene designer Cameron Porteous. Niagara-on-the-Lake, ON.
Lang.: Eng. 1707
1980-1996. Institutions.
Profile of Pacific Opera Victoria. Victoria, BC. Lang.: Eng. 4034
1980-1996. Plays/librettos/scripts.
Disaster and death in Heiner Müller's *Quartett*, staged at
Espace GO by Brigitte Haentjens. Montreal, PQ. Germany.
Lang.: Fre. 2785
Themes of Heiner Müller's *Quartett* presented at Espace GO.
Montreal, PQ. Germany. Lang.: Fre. 2845
1981. Performance/production.
Françoise Faucher on playing Winnie in Beckett's *Happy Days*.
Montreal, PQ. Lang.: Fre. 1934
1981. Plays/librettos/scripts.
Analysis of *Theatre of the Film Noir* by George F. Walker.
Lang.: Eng. 2817
1981-1989. Institutions.
Circus in Montreal. Montreal, PQ. Lang.: Fre. 3750
1981-1990. Plays/librettos/scripts.
Reprints of commentary on productions by Groupe de la
Veillée. Montreal, PQ. Lang.: Fre. 2821
1981-1991. Institutions.
Chronology of works and events presented by Tangente.
Montreal, PQ. New York, NY. Lang.: Fre. 1405

1981-1992. Performance/production.
Norman Chaurette's *Provincetown Playhouse...* staged by Alice
Ronfard, Espace GO. Montreal, PQ. Lang.: Fre. 1929
Alice Ronfard's staging of *Provincetown Playhouse...* by
Normand Chaurette. Montreal, PQ. Lang.: Fre. 1968
1981-1995. Performance/production.
Notes on acting and directing in Montreal productions.
Montreal, PQ. Lang.: Fre. 735
1981-1996. Plays/librettos/scripts.
Playwright Francis Monmart discusses his craft. Montreal, PQ.
Lang.: Fre. 2814
Playwright Larry Tremblay discusses his work. Montreal, PQ.
Lang.: Fre. 2835
1982-1989. Performance/production.
The experimental theatre of Mario Boivin. Lang.: Fre. 706
The decline of experimental theatre in Quebec. USA. Lang.:
Fre. 712
Multidisciplinary creations of Michel Lemieux. Lang.: Fre. 3708
1982-1989. Plays/librettos/scripts.
Interview with director Jean Asselin of Omnibus. Montreal, PQ.
Lang.: Fre. 3694
1982-1989. Relation to other fields.
Interview with sculptor and architect Melvin Charney. Lang.:
Fre. 1160
1982-1992. Design/technology.
Scene design by sculptor Pierre Granche. Montreal, PQ. Lang.:
Fre. 151
1983-1988. Administration.
Translator Linda Gaboriau on promoting Quebec drama.
Montreal, PQ. Toronto, ON. Lang.: Fre. 1613
1983-1991. Plays/librettos/scripts.
Analysis of plays by Carole Fréchette. Montreal, PQ. Lang.: Fre.
2757
Playwright Carole Fréchette on her work. Montreal, PQ. Lang.:
Fre. 2778
1983-1993. Institutions.
Serge Denoncourt's directing at Théâtre de l'Opsis. Montreal,
PQ. Lang.: Fre. 1781
1983-1996. Institutions.
How musical summer theatre finances serious productions at
New West Theatre Company. Lethbridge, AB. Lang.: Eng. 365
1983-1996. Performance/production.
Profile of tenor Gary Rideout. Lang.: Eng. 4086
1984-1989. Performance spaces.
Experimental theatre of Productions Recto-Verso. Matane, PQ.
Lang.: Fre. 618
1984-1996. Plays/librettos/scripts.
Sheldon Currie's *The Glace Bay Miners' Museum* as story, stage
play, and film. Glace Bay, NS. Lang.: Eng. 2773
1985-1986. Plays/librettos/scripts.
Reception of *Les Purs (The Innocents)* by Louis-Dominique
Lavigne. Montreal, PQ. Lang.: Fre. 2797
1985-1989. Institutions.
European offerings at Festival de Théâtre des Amériques.
Montreal, PQ. Lang.: Fre. 360
1985-1989. Performance/production.
Marie Brassard of Théâtre Repère. Quebec, PQ. Lang.: Fre.
1924
Comparison of acting and puppetry. Montreal, PQ. Lang.: Fre.
4389
1985-1990. Administration.
Interview with Ginette Noiseux, artistic director of Espace GO.
Montreal, PQ. Lang.: Fre. 1614
1985-1991. Institutions.
History of Canadian fringe festivals. Lang.: Fre. 373
1985-1991. Plays/librettos/scripts.
Interview with opera composer Alain Thibault. Montreal, PQ.
Lang.: Fre. 4308
1985-1995. Design/technology.
Costumer Jean-Yves Cadieux. Montreal, PQ. Lang.: Fre. 154
1985-1995. Performance/production.
Alliance of text and acting in three French-language
productions. Montreal, PQ. Geneva. Lang.: Fre. 722
1985-1995. Performance spaces.
Transformation of buildings into performance spaces in the
Plateau neighborhood. Montreal, PQ. Lang.: Fre. 624
1985-1996. Performance/production.
Playwright and dramaturg Mary Vingoe. Lang.: Eng. 1970

Canada — cont'd

1986-1991.   **Plays/librettos/scripts.**
Analysis of plays by Jean-François Caron. Montreal, PQ. Lang.:
Fre.   2762

Playwright Jean-François Caron on his work. Montreal, PQ.
Lang.: Fre.   2765

Problems of writing biographical plays. Montreal, PQ. Lang.:
Fre.   2803

1987-1988.   **Plays/librettos/scripts.**
Suzanne Lebeau's play for children, *Gil.* Lang.: Fre.   2763

1987-1990.   **Plays/librettos/scripts.**
The public debate over gay theatre in Quebec. Montreal, PQ.
Lang.: Fre.   2760

1987-1991.   **Plays/librettos/scripts.**
Analysis of stage and radio plays by Raymond Villeneuve.
Montreal, PQ. Lang.: Fre.   1090

Analysis of plays by Jean-Frédéric Messier. Montreal, PQ.
Lang.: Fre.   2744

Playwright Jean-Frédéric Messier on his work. Montreal, PQ.
Lang.: Fre.   2812

Playwright Raymond Villeneuve on writing radio drama.
Montreal, PQ. Lang.: Fre.   3579

1987-1996.   **Plays/librettos/scripts.**
Myth and iconography in Native Canadian theatre. Lang.: Eng.
    2783

Playwright Jérôme Labbé discusses his craft. Montreal, PQ.
Lang.: Fre.   2796

1988.   **Audience.**
Impressions of *À quelle heure on meurt? (What Time Do We
Die?)* adapted from the novel by Réjean Ducharme. Montreal,
PQ.Lang.: Fre.   1628

1988.   **Performance/production.**
Spontaneous impulses that are not captured on stage. Montreal,
PQ. Lang.: Fre.   727

Felix Mirbt's staging of *L'Histoire du Soldat,* National Arts
Centre. Ottawa, ON. Lang.: Fre.   1418

1988.   **Plays/librettos/scripts.**
Director Claude Poissant on adaptations. Montreal, PQ.
Limoges. Lang.: Fre.   2823

Alice Ronfard's translation of *The Tempest* for Théâtre
Expérimental des Femmes. Montreal, PQ. Lang.: Fre.   2828

Martin Faucher's adaptation of *À quelle heure on meurt? (What
Time Do We Die?)* by Réjean Ducharme. Montreal, PQ. Lang.
:Fre.   2841

Analysis of *La Déposition* by Hélène Pedneault. Montreal, PQ.
Lang.: Fre.   2844

Profile of the 'plays in transit' workshops at the Festival
international des francophonies. Limoges. Belgium. Mali. Lang.:
Fre.   2988

1988.   **Relation to other fields.**
Performance artist Geneviève Letarte. Lang.: Fre.   3816

1988.   **Research/historiography.**
Marionette collections and preservation. Lang.: Fre.   4430

1988-1989.   **Performance/production.**
The influence of painter Marc Chagall on O Vertige and Cirque
du Soleil. Montreal, PQ. Lang.: Fre.   730

1988-1989.   **Plays/librettos/scripts.**
Odette Guimond and Jacques Rossi's stage adaptations of
novels by Agota Kristof. Montreal, PQ. Lang.: Fre.   2806

1988-1990.   **Institutions.**
The principles of the Ligue Nationale de l'Improvisation. Lang.:
Fre.   359

1988-1991.   **Performance/production.**
Acting, directing, and writing work of Julie Vincent. Montreal,
PQ. Lang.: Fre.   734

1988-1991.   **Plays/librettos/scripts.**
Playwright Normand Canac-Marquis on his work. Montreal,
PQ. Lang.: Fre.   2764

Playwright Dominic Champagne on his work. Montreal, PQ.
Lang.: Fre.   2766

Analysis of plays by Normand Canac-Marquis. Montreal, PQ.
Lang.: Fre.   2800

Playwright Hélène Pedneault on her work. Montreal, PQ. Lang.:
Fre.   2822

Analysis of plays by Dominic Champagne. Montreal, PQ. Lang.:
Fre.   2838

Playwright Julie Vincent on her work. Montreal, PQ. Lang.: Fre.
    2846

1988-1992.   **Design/technology.**
Set designer Stéphane Roy. Montreal, PQ. Lang.: Fre.   150

1988-1992.   **Performance/production.**
Comparison of productions of *Waiting for Godot* for stage and
video. Montreal, PQ. Lang.: Fre.   1921

1988-1995.   **Performance/production.**
Impressions of Montreal theatre productions. Montreal, PQ.
Lang.: Fre.   704

Reactions to Montreal productions. Montreal, PQ. Lang.: Fre.
    757

1988-1996.   **Performance/production.**
Actor/singer Brian Stokes Mitchell. USA. Lang.: Eng.   3929

1989.   **Administration.**
Théâtre Petit à Petit: managing experimental theatre. Montreal,
PQ. Lang.: Fre.   7

The supremacy of economics in Quebec theatre. Lang.: Fre.   9

1989.   **Audience.**
Poems on the fleeting contact between actor and audience.
Lang.: Fre.   130

The difficulty of evoking strong responses in the theatre. Lang.:
Fre.   131

Perception of women in theatre and film. Lang.: Fre.   132

Humorous quiz for Quebec theatre-goers. Lang.: Fre.   133

Incapacity of contemporary Quebec theatre to spark debate.
Lang.: Fre.   1626

1989.   **Institutions.**
Nouveau Théâtre Expérimental and the systematic testing of
theatrical principles. Montreal, PQ. Lang.: Fre.   368

Profile of the 1989 Festival internationale de la nouvelle danse.
Montreal, PQ. Lang.: Fre.   1555

Comparison of Carbone 14 and Nouveau Théâtre Expérimental.
Montreal, PQ. Lang.: Fre.   1778

Experimental theatre for the age of mass communication: Arbo-
Cyber, théâtre (?). Quebec, PQ. Lang.: Fre.   3654

1989.   **Performance spaces.**
The need to integrate rehearsal and performance spaces in
urban planning. Montreal, PQ. Lang.: Fre.   620

1989.   **Performance/production.**
Productions of the Festival de Théâtre des Amériques. Montreal,
PQ. Lang.: Fre.   702

Truth and play in acting. Montreal, PQ. Lang.: Fre.   708

Characteristics of experimental theatre. Quebec, PQ. Lang.: Fre.
    709

Slowed or frozen images in Quebec theatre. Lang.: Fre.   711

Director Jean Faucher: his hesitation to work in experimental
theatre. Montreal, PQ. Lang.: Fre.   714

Experimental theatre as scientific research. Lang.: Fre.   717

Impressions of Festival de Théâtre des Amériques productions.
Montreal, PQ. Lang.: Fre.   725

Director Claude Poissant on theatre as an emotional parade.
Montreal, PQ. Lang.: Fre.   740

Milène Roy and Sylvain Michoue of Voxtrot. Montreal, PQ.
Lang.: Fre.   745

Poses and pauses, on stage and in the audience. Lang.: Fre.   748

Commentary on the trend of producing non-dramatic texts.
Lang.: Fre.   751

Choreographer/dancer Marie Chouinard. Montreal, PQ. Lang.:
Fre.   1413

Comparison of frozen stage images with photography. Montreal,
PQ. Lang.: Fre.   1417

Dancer Martin Faucher and his work with choreographer
Daniel Léveillé. Montreal, PQ. Lang.: Fre.   1566

Actress Sylvie Drapeau on the acting advice of Louis Jouvet.
Montreal, PQ. Lang.: Fre.   1931

Rationalism and the realist school of acting. USA. UK-England.
Lang.: Fre.   1938

Interview with actor Yves Jacques. Montreal, PQ. Lang.: Fre.
    1954

The contemporary actor and the classical text. Lang.: Fre.   1971

Canada — cont'd

1994-1995.   Theory/criticism.
Press coverage of the Festival de Théâtre des Amériques.
Montreal, PQ. Lang.: Fre.   1328
1994-1996.   Administration.
Canadian theatres' response to funding cuts. Lang.: Eng.   11
1994-1996.   Institutions.
Profile of opera company Autumn Leaf Performance. Toronto,
ON. Lang.: Eng.   4032
1995.   Institutions.
The 1995 Winnipeg Fringe Festival. Winnipeg, MB. Lang.: Eng.
348
Some productions of the Why Theatre conference. Toronto, ON.
Lang.: Eng.   378
PRIMUS Theatre's Newfoundland theatre workshops. St.
John's, NF. Lang.: Eng.   380
Profile and evaluation of the 1995 Stratford Festival season.
Stratford, ON. Lang.: Eng.   1765
The 1995 Saskatoon Fringe Festival. Saskatoon, SK. Lang.: Eng.
1768
The 1995 Edmonton Fringe Festival. Edmonton, AB. Lang.:
Eng.   1775
Evolving *Les Sept Branches de la Rivière Ota (The Seven
Streams of the River Ota)* by Robert Lepage. Quebec, PQ.
Lang.: Eng.   1779
1995.   Performance/production.
Report on multi-disciplinary expo, Today's Japan. Toronto, ON.
Japan. Lang.: Eng.   741
Design for *The Nutcracker* at the National Ballet of Canada.
Toronto, ON. Lang.: Eng.   1498
Modern dance in Francophone Canada. Montreal, PQ. Lang.:
Swe.   1570
1995.   Plays/librettos/scripts.
Analysis of *The Dragonfly of Chicoutimi* by Larry Tremblay.
Montreal, PQ. Lang.: Fre.   2786
Study of plays by Carole Fréchette. Montreal, PQ. Lang.: Fre.
2801
Medusa as a metaphorical presence in some contemporary
productions. UK-England. Lang.: Eng.   3294
1995.   Reference materials.
Census of medieval drama productions. USA. UK-Scotland.
Lang.: Eng.   3476
1995-1996.   Basic theatrical documents.
French adaptation of a scene from *Carnes Frescas (Fresh Meat)*
by Carlo Felipe Molivar. Montreal, PQ. Madrid. Lang.: Fre.
1648
Plays by Canadian natives and people of color. Lang.: Eng.
1650
1995-1996.   Institutions.
Workshops of the Women's Theatre and Creativity Centre.
Halifax, NS. Lang.: Eng.   1759
1995-1996.   Performance spaces.
Research on Montreal theatre culture. Montreal, PQ. Lang.: Fre.
619
Profile of performance space Méduse. Montreal, PQ. Lang.: Fre.
621
1995-1996.   Performance/production.
The community play *A North Side Story or Two.* Regina, SK.
Lang.: Eng.   1925
Two stagings of Goldoni's *The Servant of Two Masters.*
Montreal, PQ. Lang.: Fre.   1948
Coloratura Tracy Dahl. Lang.: Eng.   4089
1995-1996.   Plays/librettos/scripts.
Analysis of *Le Piège: Terre des hommes (The Trap: World of
Men)* by Lili Pichet and André Morency. Montreal, PQ. Lang.:
Fre.   2767
1995-1996.   Relation to other fields.
Study of teacher perceptions of the value and status of drama in
education. St. Catharine's, ON. Lang.: Eng.   1146
1996.   Administration.
US and Canadian Equity associations discuss actor transfers in a
production of *Show Boat.* New York, NY. Lang.: Eng.   87
1996.   Audience.
Director Jean-Pierre Ronfard's reaction to Ariane Mnouchkine's
Méphisto. Quebec, PQ. Lang.: Fre.   1630
Performance artist Louis Ethel Liliefeldt. Lang.: Eng.   3784

1996.   Basic theatrical documents.
Text of *Out for Blood* by the Clichettes. Lang.: Eng.   1643
Text of *The District of Centuries* by Sean Dixon. Lang.: Eng.
1645
Text of *Far Away Home* by PRIMUS Theatre. Lang.: Eng.
1646
Text of *The Glace Bay Miners' Museum* by Wendy Lill. Lang.:
Eng.   1647
Text of *Child* by Yvette Nolan. Lang.: Eng.   1649
Excerpt from the video script *Performance* by Andrew James
Paterson.   3660
1996.   Design/technology.
Scene designer Claude Goyette. Montreal, PQ. Lang.: Fre.   149
Lighting designer Kevin Lamotte of Shaw Festival. Niagara-on-
the-Lake, ON. Lang.: Eng.   1705
Mechanized sets for *The Merchant of Venice* at Stratford
Festival. Stratford, ON. Lang.: Eng.   1706
Sound design for Cirque du Soleil's *Quidam.* Montreal, PQ.
Lang.: Eng.   3746
Performance artist Tanya Mars and the computer game *Blood
Bath.* Lang.: Eng.   3788
Design for *Der Fliegende Holländer,* Canadian Opera Company,
by Allen Moyer. Toronto, ON. Lang.: Eng.   4014
1996.   Institutions.
Collaborative practices at Theatre Labyrinth. Cleveland, OH.
Lang.: Eng.   350
Collaborative works of Resource Centre for the Arts. St. John's,
NF. Lang.: Eng.   351
Current difficulties for Quebec performing arts. Lang.: Eng.   352
Performance spaces of Montreal's cultural centers. Montreal,
PQ. Lang.: Fre.   354
PRIMUS Theatre's festival and symposium, Survivors of the Ice
Age. Winnipeg, MB. Lang.: Eng.   355
Summary of PRIMUS Theatre's symposium and festival
Survivors of the Ice Age. Winnipeg, MB. Lang.: Eng.   356
Anishinaable theatre group De-Ba-Jeh-Mu-Ji SUBJECT — Play
development. Manitoulin Island, ON. Lang.: Eng.   358
Assessment of the symposium portion of Survivors of the Ice
Age Festival and Symposium. Winnipeg, MB. Lang.: Eng.   369
Profile of the Greater Toronto Drag King Society. Toronto, ON.
Lang.: Eng.   370
Productions of the Carrefour international de théâtre festival.
Quebec, PQ. Lang.: Fre.   377
Savannah Walling of Vancouver Moving Theatre on indigenous
art. Vancouver, BC. Lang.: Eng.   379
New journal of master's program at UQAM. Montreal, PQ.
Lang.: Fre.   382
Profile of Dancenet. Toronto, ON. Lang.: Eng.   1404
The Walter Carsen Centre, new home of the National Ballet of
Canada. Toronto, ON. Lang.: Eng.   1478
Interview with dramaturg Urjo Kareda. Toronto, ON. Lang.:
Eng.   1761
Profile and evaluation of the 1995 Shaw Festival season.
Niagara-on-the-Lake, ON. Lang.: Eng.   1764
The role of the dramaturg at Buddies in Bad Times Theatre.
Toronto, ON. Lang.: Eng.   1767
Diversity and sponsorship at Shaw Festival. Niagara-on-the-
Lake, ON. Lang.: Eng.   1770
Theatre New Brunswick's development of new and regional
plays. Fredericton, NB. Lang.: Eng.   1771
Some productions of the Festival de Théâtre des Amériques.
Montreal, PQ.   1773
Profile of Playwrights' Workshop. Montreal, PQ. Lang.: Eng.
1776
The dramaturg's role at Factory Theatre. Toronto, ON. Lang.:
Eng.   1777
The 1996 playRites festival. Edmonton, AB. Lang.: Eng.   1780
Children's programs of opera companies. Lang.: Eng.   4033
1996.   Performance spaces.
The multidisciplinary cultural complex, Place des Arts.
Montreal, PQ. Lang.: Fre.   622

China — cont'd

1975-1989. **Performance/production.**
Interview with puppeteer Jean-Luc Penso. Taiwan. Lang.: Fre.
4391

China, People's Republic of
1912-1996. **Plays/librettos/scripts.**
The introduction of Chinese theatre to European audiences.
Europe. Lang.: Eng. 2968
1930-1996. **Institutions.**
Profile of Shanghai Dramatic Arts Center. Shanghai. Lang.:
Eng. 1783
1984-1996. **Relation to other fields.**
American musicals and plays in China. Lang.: Eng. 1164
1989. **Performance/production.**
Collaboration of directors Peter Oskarson and Ma Ke at
Orionteatern. Stockholm. Lang.: Swe. 955
1993-1995. **Design/technology.**
The performing arts in Hong Kong. Hong Kong. Lang.: Eng.
156
1993-1996. **Plays/librettos/scripts.**
Mou Sen and the political theatre of Xi Ju Che Jian. Beijing.
Lang.: Eng. 2856
1994. **Performance/production.**
Report on the Shanghai International Shakespeare Festival.
Shanghai. Lang.: Eng. 1972
1995. **Design/technology.**
Overview of USITT conference. Beijing. Lang.: Eng. 155
1995-1996. **Basic theatrical documents.**
English translation of *Ling Dang An (File 0)* by Mou Sen.
Beijing. Lang.: Eng. 1652
1995-1996. **Institutions.**
Chinese independent theatre: Mou Sen and Xi Ju Che Jian.
Beijing. Lang.: Eng. 1782
1995-1996. **Performance/production.**
Interview with director Mou Sen. Beijing. Lang.: Eng. 1973
1996. **Institutions.**
Canadian Opera Company's *Erwartung* and *Bluebeard's Castle*
at the Hong Kong Arts Festival. Hong Kong. Lang.: Ger. 4035
1996. **Performance/production.**
Interview with Mou Sen, artistic director, and Wu Wenguang,
actor, of Xi Ju Che Jian (Garage Theatre). Lang.: Eng. 759

A Swedish guest performance of *A Midsummer Night's Dream*
in Shanghai. Stockholm. Shanghai. Lang.: Swe. 954

Chuvashia
1990-1996. **Performance/production.**
Creative portrait of opera singer Valentina Smirnova. Lang.:
Rus. 4100

Colombia
1975-1995. **Relation to other fields.**
Interview with Patricia Ariza on theatre work with the poor and
dispossessed. Bogotá. Lang.: Eng. 1165
1979. **Plays/librettos/scripts.**
Analysis of *Historia de una bala de plata (Story of a Silver
Bullet)* by Enrique Buenaventura. Lang.: Eng. 2857
1984-1996. **Performance/production.**
Interview with Octavio Arbeláez, director of the Manizales
festival. Manizales. Lang.: Spa. 760
1994. **Performance/production.**
Interview with actress Patricia Ariza of Teatro La Candelaria.
Lang.: Ita. 1974
1995. **Performance/production.**
Alternative and regional Colombian theatre. Lang.: Spa. 762
1995. **Plays/librettos/scripts.**
Report on Colombian studies conference. Bogotá. Lang.: Spa.
2858
1995-1996. **Performance/production.**
Taller Investigación de la Imagen Teatral's participatory
installation at Centre for Performance Research. Bogotá. Cardiff.
Lang.: Eng. 761
1996. **Institutions.**
Account of Hispanic-American theatre festival. Bogotá. Lang.:
Spa. 385

Colombian National Theatre Festival. Cali. Lang.: Spa. 386

Performances of Colombian National Theatre Festival. Cali.
Lang.: Spa. 387

Colonial America
1741. **Theory/criticism.**
Public punishment and execution as a theatrical event. New
York. Lang.: Eng. 1334

Congo
1960-1996. **Plays/librettos/scripts.**
Colonialism, post-colonial dictatorships, and cultural identity in
the work of Congolese playwrights. Lang.: Eng. 2859
1989. **Plays/librettos/scripts.**
Playwright Sony Labou Tansi on the body in his plays. Europe.
Lang.: Fre. 2975

Croatia
1990-1995. **Plays/librettos/scripts.**
The problem of identity in recent Croatian drama. Lang.: Eng.
2860
1991. **Performance/production.**
Profile of the Romeo & Julia Choir. Stockholm. Slovenia. Lang.:
Swe. 3866
1991-1996. **Plays/librettos/scripts.**
Political theatre of Karen Malpede and Slobodan Snajder. USA.
Lang.: Eng. 3403

Cuba
1930-1990. **Plays/librettos/scripts.**
Critical biography of playwright Maria Irene Fornes. USA.
Lang.: Eng. 2862
1945-1959. **Plays/librettos/scripts.**
Cuban writer Alejo Carpentier and his work in Venezuela.
Caracas. Lang.: Spa. 3467
1953-1996. **Plays/librettos/scripts.**
Interview with playwright Eduardo Muchado. New York, NY.
Lang.: Eng. 3377
1959-1996. **Institutions.**
History of Grupo Teatro Escambray. La Macagua. Lang.: Eng.
389
1968-1996. **Institutions.**
Grupo Teatro Escambray's communication with its audience. La
Macagua. Lang.: Eng. 388
1981-1996. **Performance/production.**
History of Havana's Latin American theatre festival. Havana.
Lang.: Spa. 763
1990. **Plays/librettos/scripts.**
Chaos theory in *Timeball* by Joel Cano. Lang.: Spa. 2867
1993. **Basic theatrical documents.**
English translation of *Manteca* by Alberto Pedro Torriente.
Lang.: Eng. 1653
1993. **Plays/librettos/scripts.**
Analysis of *Manteca* by Alberto Pedro Torriente. Lang.: Eng.
2863

Alberto Pedro Torriente's *Manteca* in the context of Cuban
politics and society. Lang.: Eng. 2865
1993-1996. **Plays/librettos/scripts.**
Teatro Hubert de Blanck's *Vagos Rumores (Vague Rumors)*.
Havana. New York, NY. Lang.: Eng. 2864
1994. **Performance/production.**
Latin American and Hispanic performance. Mexico. Lang.: Eng.
1975
1994-1996. **Performance/production.**
Interview with actor Jorge Perugorría. Lang.: Eng. 3615
1996. **Basic theatrical documents.**
Text of *El Arca (The Ark)* by Víctor Varela. Lang.: Spa. 1654
1996. **Plays/librettos/scripts.**
Interview by mail with playwright Víctor Varela. Lang.: Spa.
2861

Colloquium on new frontiers in theatrical texts. Lang.: Spa.
2866

Czech Republic
1700-1996. **Institutions.**
The establishment of theatres in Bohemia. Prague. Lang.: Cze.
391
1960. **Institutions.**
Report on OISTAT conference and Prague Quadrennial.
Luzern. Prague. Lang.: Swe. 547
1963-1996. **Plays/librettos/scripts.**
Characters in the plays of Václav Havel. Lang.: Eng, Fre. 2868
1974-1996. **Design/technology.**
Set and costume designer Marta Roszkopfová. Lang.: Eng, Fre.
159
1979-1994. **Plays/librettos/scripts.**
Analysis of plays by Karel Steigerwald. Lang.: Cze. 2869
1987-1996. **Design/technology.**
Work of set designer Petr Nikl. Prague. Lang.: Eng, Fre. 158
1989-1995. **Plays/librettos/scripts.**
Popularity of Polish plays in Eastern Bloc countries after the fall
of Communism. Poland. Russia. Lang.: Eng, Fre. 3158

Europe — cont'd

France — cont'd

1599-1677.   **Plays/librettos/scripts.**
Comparison of Shakespeare's *Hamlet* and Racine's *Phèdre*.
England. Lang.: Eng.   2934
1600-1641.   **Plays/librettos/scripts.**
Analysis of tragicomedies and tragedies with happy endings.
Italy. Spain. Lang.: Ger.   3139
1600-1996.   **Plays/librettos/scripts.**
The influence of French drama on Polish theatre. Poland. Lang.:
Eng, Fre.   2992
1673-1715.   **Performance/production.**
Jean-Baptiste Lully and early French opera. Lang.: Eng.   4130
1673-1996.   **Institutions.**
History of the Comédie-Française. Paris. Lang.: Eng.   1786
1700-1996.   **Performance/production.**
Typologies of the body in French dance. Lang.: Ger.   800
1700-1996.   **Relation to other fields.**
Historic and contemporary functions of the theatre critic.
Canada. Lang.: Fre.   1150
1731-1779.   **Plays/librettos/scripts.**
European bourgeois drama and the break with classical
tradition. England. Germany. Lang.: Slo.   2964
1734-1847.   **Performance/production.**
Choreographic realizations of the story of Pygmalion. Lang.:
Eng.   1422
1744-1840.   **Plays/librettos/scripts.**
Melodrama and orientalism in *Il crociato in Egitto* by
Meyerbeer. Venice. Lang.: Eng.   4316
1750-1794.   **Relation to other fields.**
Psychodrama in Paisiello's *Nina*. Paris. Lang.: Eng.   4352
1750-1820.   **Plays/librettos/scripts.**
Historical background of Giordano's opera *Andrea Chénier*.
Paris. Lang.: Eng.   4317
1750-1972.   **Performance/production.**
History of *opéra comique*. Paris. Lang.: Eng.   4126
1755-1906.   **Performance/production.**
Tragic actresses Siddons, Rachel, and Ristori. England. Italy.
Lang.: Eng.   1986
1773.   **Theory/criticism.**
Analysis of Diderot's *Paradoxe sur le comédien*. Lang.: Ger.
                                                              1346
1778-1991.   **Performance/production.**
Account of a devised piece on the death of Voltaire. Bristol.
Lang.: Eng.   2533
1789-1799.   **Performance/production.**
Theatre in revolutionary Paris. Lang.: Eng.   801
1789-1989.   **Plays/librettos/scripts.**
The theatrical legacy of the French Revolution. Lang.: Fre.
                                                              3004
1800-1966.   **Relation to other fields.**
Theatre, asylums, and therapy. Germany. Lang.: Ger.   1182
1801-1989.   **Plays/librettos/scripts.**
Playwriting, adaptation, and other forms. Lang.: Fre.   2997
1820-1829.   **Plays/librettos/scripts.**
Transvestism and homosexuality in plays of Dumas *père*. Lang.:
Eng.   2991
1831-1849.   **Plays/librettos/scripts.**
Singers Gilbert-Louis Duprez and Gustave Roger and the
creation of Meyerbeer's opera *Le Prophète*. Paris. Lang.: Eng.
                                                              4314
1835-1996.   **Relation to other fields.**
Assumptions about the relationship between theatre and
literature. Paris. Lang.: Fre.   3498
1846-1863.   **Plays/librettos/scripts.**
Maurice Sand's efforts to revive the *commedia dell'arte*. Lang.:
Ita.   3768
1848-1996.   **Theory/criticism.**
Critical perceptions of French popular theatre genres. Paris.
Lang.: Eng.   3723
1850-1989.   **Relation to other fields.**
Experimental theatre in the contexts of scientific advancement
and commercialism. Lang.: Fre.   1177
1862-1996.   **Institutions.**
Notes on the Paris Grand Opera. Paris. Lang.: Rus.   4039
1863-1894.   **Performance/production.**
Operas of Emmanuel Chabrier. Paris. Lang.: Eng.   4127
1873.   **Performance/production.**
Translation of composer Charles Gounod's essay on the
conductor/composer relationship. Lang.: Eng.   4121
1880-1889.   **Performance/production.**
Translation of interviews with opera divas Adelina Patti, Emma
Nevada, and Marie Van Zandt. Paris. Lang.: Eng.   4119

1880-1989.   **Relation to other fields.**
Experimental theatre in the social context. Canada. Lang.: Fre.
                                                              1155
1884-1896.   **Plays/librettos/scripts.**
A possible source for Delibes' opera *Lakmé*. Lang.: Eng.   4315
1896.   **Plays/librettos/scripts.**
The genesis of Jarry's *Ubu Roi (King Ubu)*. Lang.: Hun.   2990
1896-1996.   **Research/historiography.**
Seminar in honor of Antonin Artaud. Denmark. Lang.: Dan.
                                                              1296
1898-1905.   **Performance/production.**
Orientalism and sexual identity. Paris. Lang.: Eng.   795
1900-1990.   **Reference materials.**
Bibliography of works by French women playwrights. Lang.:
Eng.   3474
1900-1995.   **Plays/librettos/scripts.**
Feminism in *Portrait de Dora (Portrait of Dora)* by Hélène
Cixous. Lang.: Eng.   2980
1904-1989.   **Plays/librettos/scripts.**
The theatre of Witold Gombrowicz and posthumous productions
of his plays. Poland. Argentina. Lang.: Fre.   3170
1906-1995.   **Administration.**
Hélène Nouguès, Parisian representative of the Shubert
Organization. Paris. New York, NY.   18
1908-1994.   **Research/historiography.**
History and theory of orchestics movement system. Paris.
Budapest. Lang.: Hun.   1601
1909-1994.   **Plays/librettos/scripts.**
Problematics of the absurdist comedies of Eugène Ionesco.
Lang.: Rus.   2985
1913-1995.   **Performance/production.**
Review of a performance at the Opéra de Paris. Paris. Lang.:
Hun.   1501
1915-1951.   **Plays/librettos/scripts.**
The friendship of Antonin Artaud with poet Jacques Prevel.
Lang.: Ita.   2983
1918-1996.   **Training.**
Etienne Decroux's theory of corporeal mime. Paris. Lang.: Eng.
                                                              3688
Jacques Copeau, Suzanne Bing, and the founding of L'École du
Vieux-Colombier. New York, NY. Paris. Lang.: Eng.   3690
1920-1925.   **Plays/librettos/scripts.**
Analysis of *L'Enfant et les Sortilèges* by Maurice Ravel. Lang.:
Eng.   4318
1920-1929.   **Institutions.**
Opera in Paris in the twenties. Paris. Lang.: Eng.   4036
1922-1947.   **Plays/librettos/scripts.**
Evil and salvation in the work of Antonin Artaud. Lang.: Ita.
                                                              2978
1926-1935.   **Plays/librettos/scripts.**
Analysis of plays by Antonin Artaud. Lang.: Pol.   3007
1927-1996.   **Performance/production.**
Interview, profile of opera singer Régine Crespin. Lang.: Eng.
                                                              4125
1931.   **Performance/production.**
Balinese theatre as seen by Artaud at the colonial exhibition.
Paris. Lang.: Ita.   804
1932-1996.   **Performance/production.**
Tenor Roberto Alagna—profile and interview. Lang.: Eng.   4128
1933-1995.   **Plays/librettos/scripts.**
Lesbianism on the French stage. Lang.: Eng.   3006
1938-1948.   **Plays/librettos/scripts.**
Analysis of plays by Albert Camus. Lang.: Fre.   2987
1938-1992.   **Plays/librettos/scripts.**
Bibliography of works in French by and about Samuel Beckett.
Lang.: Fre.   2999
The void, silence, and non-existence in the works of Samuel
Beckett. Lang.: Fre.   3000
1940-1945.   **Performance/production.**
Jacques Copeau and the Théâtre du Vieux-Colombier under the
Vichy régime. Paris. Lang.: Eng.   2007
1940-1996.   **Relation to other fields.**
Brigitte Jaques' *Elvire Jouvet 40*, and the continuing reality of
political detention and torture. Paris. Lebanon. Lang.: Fre. 3496
1942-1996.   **Performance/production.**
Interview with opera director Nicolas Joël. Germany. Lang.:
Eng.   4117
1946-1953.   **Theory/criticism.**
Dance criticism of Birgit Cullberg. Sweden. UK-England. Lang.:
Swe.   1467

France — cont'd

1947-1996. **Design/technology.**
Interview with puppet designer Vera Bródy. Budapest. Paris.
Lang.: Hun. 4368
1948-1992. **Plays/librettos/scripts.**
Recent Polish translations and productions of the plays of
Molière. Cracow. Lang.: Eng, Fre. 2993
1949-1991. **Plays/librettos/scripts.**
Recent publication of plays and theatre essays. Lang.: Fre. 1097
1950-1996. **Institutions.**
Profile of Théâtre de la Huchette, which produces the plays of
Ionesco. Paris. Lang.: Swe. 1792
1950-1996. **Performance/production.**
Jean Genet's staging and acting indications. Lang.: Fre. 2021
1950-1996. **Plays/librettos/scripts.**
Interview with playwright Pierre Laville. Lang.: Fre. 3009
1952. **Plays/librettos/scripts.**
Universality and gender in Beckett's *Waiting for Godot*. Lang.:
Fre. 2986
The influence of clowning on Beckett's *En attendant Godot
(Waiting for Godot)*. Lang.: Fre. 2989
1953-1957. **Plays/librettos/scripts.**
Analysis of *Fin de partie* and *En attendant Godot* by Samuel
Beckett. Ireland. Lang.: Eng. 3082
1953-1990. **Plays/librettos/scripts.**
Dominic Champagne's *La Répétition (The Rehearsal)* and its
relation to Beckett's *En attendant Godot (Waiting for Godot)*.
Montreal, PQ. Ireland. Lang.: Fre. 2843
1955-1996. **Performance/production.**
Influence of French drama on the repertoire of Polish Television
Theatre. Poland. Lang.: Eng, Fre. 3671
1957-1991. **Plays/librettos/scripts.**
The plays of Heiner Müller in their sociopolitical context and at
the Avignon Festival. Germany, East. Avignon. Lang.: Fre.
3054
1957-1995. **Institutions.**
Ariane Mnouchkine's Théâtre du Soleil and their production of
Molière's *Tartuffe*. Paris. Lang.: Swe. 1789
1960. **Performance/production.**
Puppets in European theatre. Italy. Poland. Lang.: Fre. 4393
1961-1965. **Performance/production.**
Puppets, Human Movement, and dance in Philippe Genty's
Voyageur Immobile (Motionless Traveler). Chicago, IL. Paris.
Lang.: Eng. 4415
1961-1992. **Design/technology.**
Interview with scenographer Guy-Claude François. Paris. Lang.:
Fre. 167
1962-1996. **Design/technology.**
Interview with scene designer Krystyna Zachwatowicz. Poland.
Lang.: Eng, Fre. 1710
1964-1996. **Performance/production.**
Patrice Chéreau's productions of plays by Bernard-Marie Koltès.
Lang.: Dan. 2039
1965-1995. **Performance/production.**
Dancer and actor Yvan Auzely. Stockholm. Lang.: Swe. 1502
1966. **Plays/librettos/scripts.**
Jorge Díaz's *Historia de nadie (Nobody's Story)* compared to
Beckett's *En attendant Godot (Waiting for Godot)*. Spain. Chile.
Lang.: Spa. 3245
1967-1986. **Plays/librettos/scripts.**
Comparison of translations of the opening of Sophocles'
Antigone. Canada. Lang.: Fre. 2787
1968. **Performance/production.**
The influence of Living Theatre on Raymond Cloutier of Grand
Cirque Ordinaire. Grenoble. Montreal, PQ. Lang.: Fre. 2015
1970-1996. **Relation to other fields.**
The meeting of cultures in work of Peter Brook and Ariane
Mnouchkine. UK-England. Lang.: Dan. 1179
1971. **Performance/production.**
Anecdote concerning Jacques Galipeau's role in *Tartuffe*,
Théâtre du Nouveau Monde. Paris. Lang.: Fre. 2022
1975-1983. **Institutions.**
The Théâtre Nationale de Strasbourg under the direction of
Jean-Pierre Vincent. Strasbourg. Lang.: Fre. 1787
1975-1990. **Performance/production.**
Gabriel Garran's Paris productions of plays by Quebec authors.
Canada. Paris. Lang.: Fre. 1959
1975-1995. **Plays/librettos/scripts.**
The emergence of French feminist theatre. Lang.: Eng. 3001
1977-1989. **Plays/librettos/scripts.**
Analysis of plays by Bernard-Marie Koltès. Lang.: Fre. 3010

1979-1996. **Performance/production.**
French productions of *Találkozás (The Encounter)* by Péter
Nádas, sound by László Vidovszky. Paris. Hungary. Lang.: Hun.
2037
Productions of the Comédie-Française at Brooklyn Academy of
Music. New York, NY. Paris. Lang.: Eng. 2650
1980-1989. **Plays/librettos/scripts.**
The methods and objectives of theatrical adaptation. Lang.: Fre.
3005
1980-1992. **Performance/production.**
Interview with director Stéphane Braunschweig. Lang.: Fre.
2038
1981-1992. **Plays/librettos/scripts.**
Analysis of plays by Eugène Durif. Lang.: Fre. 2981
1984-1991. **Institutions.**
Profile of international festival of Francophone theatre. Lang.:
Fre. 410
1985. **Plays/librettos/scripts.**
Monique Wittig's introduction and preface to her *Le Voyage
sans fin (The Constant Journey)*. Paris. Lang.: Eng. 3012
1985-1993. **Plays/librettos/scripts.**
Analysis of *Trilogie des tables (Trilogy of the Tables)* by Joël
Dragutin. Lang.: Fre. 3011
1987-1996. **Plays/librettos/scripts.**
Playwright Yasmina Reza. Lang.: Ger. 3003
1988. **Institutions.**
The overabundance of offerings at the Avignon Festival.
Avignon. Lang.: Fre. 1788
Productions of world puppetry festival. Charleville-Mézières.
Spain. Lang.: Fre. 4373
1988. **Performance/production.**
Interview with director Ariane Mnouchkine. Paris. Lang.: Fre.
2017
Ariane Mnouchkine's acting workshop. Paris. Lang.: Fre. 2018
Interview with Sophie Moscoso of Théâtre du Soleil. Paris.
Lang.: Fre. 2019
Three Parisian performances of productions from Quebec. Paris.
Lang.: Fre. 2028
Cooperation between French puppeteers and Indonesian *dalang*
artists. Indonesia. Lang.: Fre. 4396
1988. **Plays/librettos/scripts.**
Director Claude Poissant on adaptations. Montreal, PQ.
Limoges. Lang.: Fre. 2823
Profile of the 'plays in transit' workshops at the Festival
international des francophonies. Limoges. Belgium. Canada.
Mali. Lang.: Fre. 2988
German plays in translation at the Festival d'automne. Paris.
Lang.: Fre. 2994
Francophone plays in new contexts at Francophone theatre
festival. Limoges. Lang.: Fre. 2995
Claude Poissant's production of *Les Voyageurs* by Madeleine
Laïc at Festival internationale des francophonies. Limoges.
Lang.: Fre. 2996
1988. **Relation to other fields.**
Use of puppetry in psychotherapy. Paris. Charleville-Mézières.
Lang.: Fre. 4428
1988. **Training.**
Training schools for marionette art. Charleville-Mézières. Lang.:
Fre. 4434
1989. **Institutions.**
Conference of theatre artists and scientists. Saintes. Lang.: Fre.
412
The first festival of the European Theatre Convention. Lang.:
Fre. 1790
1989. **Performance/production.**
Choreography of Jean-Claude Gallotta. Grenoble. Lang.: Fre.
1423
R. Murray Schafer's opera *Le Théâtre noir* at the Festival
musical de Liège. Liège. Lang.: Fre. 4118
1989. **Plays/librettos/scripts.**
Report on Francophone theatre conference. Limoges. Lang.:
Fre. 2984
1989. **Relation to other fields.**
Postmodern possibilities of meaning in theatre. Germany. Lang.:
Fre. 3497

Germany — cont'd

1917-1985.   **Plays/librettos/scripts.**
Shakespeare's influence on Brecht reevaluated. Lang.: Eng.
    3041
1918-1922.   **Plays/librettos/scripts.**
Plays about WWI by Goering and Berk. Slovenia. Lang.: Slo.
    3214
1918-1924.   **Performance/production.**
Expressionist mask dancers Lavinia Schulz and Walter Holdt.
Hamburg. Lang.: Ger.   1606
1918-1929.   **Performance/production.**
Expressionism and acting on stage and screen. Lang.: Eng. 829
1918-1933.   **Plays/librettos/scripts.**
Comedy in the Weimar Republic. Lang.: Eng.   3021
1918-1996.   **Performance/production.**
Italian translation of *Ingmar Bergman: A Life in the Theatre.*
Sweden. Lang.: Ita.   2287
1919-1923.   **Plays/librettos/scripts.**
The life and early plays of Ernst Toller. Lang.: Eng.   3017
1922-1926.   **Plays/librettos/scripts.**
Boxing as metaphor in plays of Brecht. Berlin. Lang.: Eng. 3042
1925-1931.   **Institutions.**
Leopold Jessner's acting studios at Hochschule der Künste.
Berlin. Lang.: Ger.   452
1925-1945.   **Performance/production.**
The Stadtheater of Frankfurt under National Socialism.
Frankfurt am Main. Lang.: Eng.   826
1925-1996.   **Performance spaces.**
History of the Staatsoperette. Dresden. Lang.: Ger.   4363
1926.   **Plays/librettos/scripts.**
Composer Hans Werner Henze. Italy. Lang.: Swe.   4324
1927-1993.   **Performance/production.**
Productions of Tretjakov's *Choču Rebenka (I Want a Baby).*
Moscow. Birmingham. Berlin. Lang.: Eng.   2694
1928-1929.   **Performance/production.**
Interview with Norbert Gingold regarding score preparation and
conducting of *The Three Penny Opera.* Berlin. Vienna. Lang.:
Eng.   3916
1928-1996.   **Performance/production.**
Obituary for director Ruth Berghaus. Lang.: Ger.   2047

Operetta and musical theatre—renewed popularity. Austria.
Lang.: Eng.   3914
1929-1945.   **Relation to other fields.**
Werner Flinck's career in political cabaret. Lang.: Eng.   3741
1929-1989.   **Plays/librettos/scripts.**
Interview with playwright and director Heiner Müller. Lang.:
Fre.   3045

Survey of German cabaret. Lang.: Eng.   3739
1929-1994.   **Performance/production.**
Tribute to deceased theatre artist Heiner Müller. Latin America.
Lang.: Spa.   2049
1929-1995.   **Plays/librettos/scripts.**
Commemoration of playwright Heiner Müller. Lang.: Hun.
    3019

Recollections of playwright Heiner Müller. Lang.: Hun.   3022

Analysis of *Der Findling (The Foundling)* by Heiner Müller.
Lang.: Eng.   3031

The life and work of Heiner Müller. Berlin. Lang.: Ger.   3043
1929-1996.   **Design/technology.**
The work of Hungarian-born costume designer Margit Bárdy.
Hungary. Lang.: Hun.   180
1929-1996.   **Plays/librettos/scripts.**
The life and career of the late playwright/director Heiner
Müller. Berlin. USA. Lang.: Eng.   3025

Portrait of playwright and director Heiner Müller. Lang.: Ger.
    3034
1933-1945.   **Performance/production.**
The effect of Nazi censorship on German theatre. Lang.: Eng.
    820
1933-1945.   **Relation to other fields.**
Ideological uses of theatre during the National Socialist period.
Lang.: Ger.   1186
1935-1945.   **Performance/production.**
Analysis of Nazi rallies. Nuremberg. Lang.: Eng.   833
1935-1996.   **Performance spaces.**
History of the open-air theatre Felsenbühne. Rathen. Lang.:
Ger.   639
1940-1996.   **Performance/production.**
Interview with actor Gert Voss. Austria. Lang.: Ger.   808

1942-1996.   **Performance/production.**
Interview with opera director Nicolas Joël. France. Lang.: Eng.
    4117
1945.   **Performance/production.**
Report from conference on the development of Tanztheater.
Sweden. Lang.: Swe.   1579
1945-1991.   **Plays/librettos/scripts.**
Postwar German playwriting. Lang.: Fre.   3038
1945-1995.   **Relation to other fields.**
German-Australian theatrical exchange. Australia. Lang.: Eng.
    3478
1945-1996.   **Plays/librettos/scripts.**
Postwar drama in both East and West Germany. Lang.: Ger.
    3044
1946-1996.   **Institutions.**
Profile of drama, opera, and open-air theatre Landesbühne
Sachsen. Rathen. Lang.: Ger.   436

History of Theater der Jugend. Leipzig. Lang.: Ger.   455
1948-1996.   **Performance/production.**
Actor of the year Josef Bierbichler: profile and interview.
Austria. Lang.: Ger.   828
1949.   **Performance spaces.**
History of Theater der Jungen Generation. Dresden. Lang.: Ger.
    636
1950-1985.   **Performance/production.**
Evaluation of Dietrich Fischer-Dieskau's recordings of Schubert
Lieder. Lang.: Eng.   3859
1953-1996.   **Performance/production.**
Director Michael Helle. Mainz. Düsseldorf. Lang.: Ger.   809
1955-1996.   **Plays/librettos/scripts.**
Playwright Vladimir Sorokin and his popularity in Germany.
Russia. Lang.: Ger.   3191
1957-1996.   **Performance/production.**
Interview with actress Imogen Kogge. Lang.: Ger.   822

Portrait of Sven-Eric Bechtolf, actor and director at Thalia
Theater. Hamburg. Lang.: Ger.   2060
1958-1960.   **Plays/librettos/scripts.**
Analysis of *Die Soldaten* by Bernd Alois Zimmermann. Lang.:
Eng.   4319
1958-1996.   **Performance/production.**
Choreographer Richard Wheelock. Hagen. UK-England. Lang.:
Ger.   1426
1960-1996.   **Plays/librettos/scripts.**
Portrait of playwright and director Heiner Müller. Lang.: Ger.
    3030
1963-1996.   **Plays/librettos/scripts.**
Portrait of playwright, actor, and director Wolfgang Bauer.
Austria. Lang.: Ger.   3047
1964-1996.   **Plays/librettos/scripts.**
Playwright Rea Loher. Lang.: Ger.   3028
1966.   **Performance/production.**
Interview with opera singer Matti Salminen. Finland. Lang.:
Swe.   4145
1968-1989.   **Relation to other fields.**
The influence of social movements and changes on German
theatre. Lang.: Ger.   1189
1968-1990.   **Plays/librettos/scripts.**
Analysis of the work of playwright Franz Xaver Kroetz. Lang.:
Fre.   3049
1968-1996.   **Plays/librettos/scripts.**
Analysis of *Die Ballade vom Wiener Schnitzel (The Ballad of the
Wiener Schnitzel)* by George Tabori. Munich. Vienna. Lang.:
Ger.   3052
1969-1995.   **Performance/production.**
Director Klaus Michael Grüber. Lang.: Ger.   807
1969-1996.   **Performance/production.**
Photographs of Peter Stein's work at Schaubühne. Berlin. Lang.:
Ger.   2084
1970-1979.   **Institutions.**
Changes in theatre training of the 1970s. Essen. Lang.: Ger. 451
1970-1996.   **Institutions.**
The merger of Theater Greifswald and Theater Stralsund into
Theater Vorpommern. Lang.: Ger.   3907
1970-1996.   **Performance/production.**
Interview with emigré director Alejandro Quintana. Chile.
Lang.: Ger.   758

Postmodernist stagings of Wagnerian opera. Lang.: Eng.   4131
1975-1996.   **Performance/production.**
Peter Mussbach, opera director and set designer. Lang.: Ger.
    4138

Germany — cont'd

Comparison of productions of Müller's *Der Auftrag (The Mission)*. Leipzig. Berlin. Lang.: Ger. 2069

Actor Udo Samel. Lang.: Ger. 2072

Thirza Bruncken's production of *Stecken, Stab und Stangl (Stick, Rod, and Pole)* by Elfriede Jelinek. Hamburg. Lang.: Ger. 2074

Productions of Schauspielhaus Bonn. Bonn. Lang.: Ger. 2075

Heiner Müller—his commemoration by Berliner Ensemble, his East German productions. Berlin. Lang.: Ger. 2076

Impressions of Berlin theatre. Berlin. Lang.: Ger. 2078

Two productions of Brecht's *Herr Puntila*. Hamburg. Halle. Lang.: Ger. 2079

Two productions of Čechov's *Ivanov*. Seifenberg. Gera. Lang.: Ger. 2081

Political theatre of Hans-Werner Kroesinger. Lang.: Ger. 2085

Andrea Breth's production of *The Seagull* and its marketing. Berlin. Lang.: Ger. 2086

Einar Schleef's production of Brecht's *Herr Puntila*. Berlin. Lang.: Ger. 2087

Productions of plays by Heiner Müller at Berliner Ensemble and Volksbühne. Berlin. Lang.: Ger. 2088

Reviews of German-language productions. Switzerland. Austria. Lang.: Ger. 2089

Productions of Thalia Theater and Deutsches Schauspielhaus. Hamburg. Lang.: Ger. 2090

Two productions of Heiner Müller's *Germania 3*. Bochum. Berlin. Lang.: Ger. 2091

Two productions of *The Designated Mourner* by Wallace Shawn. London. Hamburg. Lang.: Ger. 2504

Puppetry-related job prospects in TV and film. USA. Lang.: Ger. 3569

Interview with program managers at TV station SAT 3. Berlin. Lang.: Ger. 3669

Survey of the German musical theatre scene. Lang.: Ger. 3915

Account of *Time Rocker* by Robert Wilson and Lou Reed. Hamburg. Lang.: Eng. 3918

Wolfgang Wagner's production of *Die Meistersinger* at Bayreuther Festspiele. Bayreuth. Lang.: Ger. 4133

Production of Stravinskij's opera for children, *Nattergalen*. Cologne. Lang.: Ger. 4134

Interview with composer Heiner Goebbels. Lang.: Ger. 4137

Portrait of opera chorus member Stefan Kohnke. Lang.: Ger. 4139

Interview with opera director Peter Konwitschny. Lang.: Ger. 4141

Interview with Götz Friedrich of Deutsche Oper. Berlin. Lang.: Dan. 4142

Performance and technical aspects of Orff's *Carmina Burana* at the Bavarian State Opera. Lang.: Eng. 4143

Wolfgang Wagner's scenery and direction of *Die Meistersinger* at the Bayreuth Festival. Bayreuth. Lang.: Ger. 4146

The 37th annual Fidena festival of puppetry. Bochum. Lang.: Ger. 4394

Uwe Spillmann's street puppet theatre. Lang.: Ger. 4395

1996. Plays/librettos/scripts.

Impressions from a trip through the European theatre landscape. UK-England. Slovakia. Lang.: Dan. 1103

Obituary of playwright Heiner Müller. Lang.: Eng. 3014

Copyright dispute in Heiner Müller's estate. Lang.: Ger. 3015

Heiner Müller's work and its reception on stage after his death. Berlin. Bochum. Lang.: Ger. 3016

Analysis of *Ithaka* by Botho Strauss. Lang.: Ger. 3024

Interview with playwright Heiner Müller. Lang.: Ger. 3040

Interview with playwright Paul Schmidt. Hamburg. Lang.: Eng. 3051

Playwright Oliver Bukowski. Berlin. Lang.: Ger. 3053

The plays of Nicky Silver and the first German production of his *Pterodactyls*. USA. Munich. Lang.: Ger. 3372

The Messianic hero in Wagner's *Ring*. Lang.: Eng. 4320

1996. Relation to other fields.

Interview with Frank Baumbauer, director of Deutsches Schauspielhaus. Hamburg. Lang.: Ger. 1183

Remarks about German cultural policy by the president of the republic. Lang.: Ger. 1184

Life and theatre in Chemnitz. Chemnitz. Lang.: Ger. 1185

The crisis of independent theatre. Berlin. Lang.: Ger. 1188

Interview with Jürgen Kruse, director of Schauspielhaus Bochum. Bochum. Lang.: Ger. 1190

Conference on dance and politics. Cologne. Lang.: Ger. 1454

1996. Research/historiography.

Düsseldorf's theatre historiography. Düsseldorf. Lang.: Ger. 1298

1996. Theory/criticism.

Critical reaction to Einar Schleef's Berliner Ensemble production of Brecht's *Herr Puntila*. Berlin. Lang.: Ger. 3541

Germany, East

1957-1989. Theory/criticism.

Heiner Müller and *Theater der Zeit*. Lang.: Ger. 3542

1957-1991. Plays/librettos/scripts.

The plays of Heiner Müller in their sociopolitical context and at the Avignon Festival. Avignon. Lang.: Fre. 3054

1970-1974. Institutions.

The work of Ruth Berghaus at Berliner Ensemble. Berlin, East. Lang.: Ger. 1813

1984. Performance/production.

Interview with conductor Per Borin and singer Katarina Nilsson of Theater Vorpommern. Greifswald. Stralsund. Lang.: Swe. 4147

1990-1991. Relation to other fields.

East German actresses' reactions to social changes after the fall of the Berlin wall. Berlin, East. Lang.: Ger. 1195

Ghana

1988-1995. Plays/librettos/scripts.

Influence of story-telling traditions on women playwrights. Australia. Sri Lanka. Lang.: Eng. 1098

Greece

525-456 B.C. Plays/librettos/scripts.

Aeschylean tragedy in its sociopolitical context. Lang.: Eng. 3061

500 B.C.-1989 A.D. Theory/criticism.

Tragedy, pathos, and French philosophy. Athens. France. Lang.: Fre. 3543

440-400 B.C. Plays/librettos/scripts.

Closure and generic innovation in Euripidean drama. Lang.: Eng. 3056

409 B.C. Plays/librettos/scripts.

Analysis of Sophocles' *Philoctetes*. Lang.: Slo. 3063

409 B.C.-1996 A.D. Basic theatrical documents.

Annotated Dutch translation of Euripides' *Phoínissai (The Phoenician Women)* as produced by Hollandia. Netherlands. Lang.: Dut. 1662

407 B.C. Relation to other fields.

The Dionysian cult as reflected in *Bákchai (The Bacchae)* of Euripides. Lang.: Swe. 3499

406 B.C. Plays/librettos/scripts.

Nature and culture in Euripides *Bákchai (The Bacchae)*. Lang.: Ita. 3055

404 B.C. Relation to other fields.

The relevance of ancient Greek theatre to contemporary life. Athens. Vetlanda. Lang.: Swe. 1196

404 B.C.-1996 A.D. Plays/librettos/scripts.

Actor Erland Josephson on the role of Kadmos in Euripides' *Bákchai (The Bacchae)*. Sweden. Lang.: Swe. 3057

450-380 B.C. Plays/librettos/scripts.

Study of Aristophanes' comedies. Lang.: Hun. 3059

500-400 B.C. Plays/librettos/scripts.

Italian translation of *Die tragische Dichtung der Hellenen* by Albin Lesky. Lang.: Ita. 3058

Italian translation of *La tragédie grecque* by Jacqueline de Romilly. Lang.: Ita. 3060

Aristotle's interpretation of the tragic in drama. Lang.: Slo. 3062

1986-1996. Performance/production.

Theodoros Terzopoulos of Theatre Attis. Athens. Lang.: Eng. 836

Greece — cont'd

1993.   Performance/production.
An intercultural adaptation of Euripides' *Troádes (The Trojan Women)*. Athens. UK-Scotland. Lang.: Eng.   2092
1996.   Basic theatrical documents.
English translation of *The Four Legs of the Table* by Iákovos Kampanéllis. Lang.: Eng.   1663
1996.   Performance/production.
Sophocles' *Electra* as performed by the National Theatre of Greece. New York, NY. Lang.: Eng.   2634
Guatemala
1900-1960.   Performance/production.
History of Guatemalan theatre. Guatemala City. Lang.: Spa.   837
1962.   Plays/librettos/scripts.
Analysis of *El Corazón del espantapájaros (The Heart of the Scarecrow)* by Hugo Carrillo. Lang.: Spa.   3064
Haiti
1898-1920.   Plays/librettos/scripts.
Political and military context of O'Neill's *The Emperor Jones*. USA. Lang.: Eng.   3386
1953-1981.   Plays/librettos/scripts.
Haitian popular culture in plays by Franck Fouché. Lang.: Eng.   3066
1986-1992.   Plays/librettos/scripts.
Analysis of plays by Jean Métellus. Lang.: Fre.   3065
Holland
ALSO.
Netherlands.   3065
1395-1596.   Plays/librettos/scripts.
Fools in the drama of Dutch rhetoricians. Lang.: Eng.   3067
Honduras
1979-1996.   Plays/librettos/scripts.
Profile of community theatre Teatro La Fragua. El Progreso. Lang.: Eng.   3068
Hungary
1516-1698.   Plays/librettos/scripts.
Analysis of plays by Mihály Sztárai and Péter Bornemisza. Lang.: Hun.   3075
1693-1820.   Plays/librettos/scripts.
Early Hungarian theatre in Transylvania. Kolozsvár. Lang.: Hun.   3072
1696-1809.   Institutions.
Early professional acting in Hungary and Transylvania. Lang.: Hun.   475
1700-1990.   Performance/production.
Introduction of ballroom dances in anticipation of the annual opera-ball. Lang.: Hun.   1431
1730-1812.   Performance/production.
The family of actor-director László Kelemen. Lang.: Hun.   852
1770-1850.   Reference materials.
Review of catalogue of German theatre in Pest-Buda. Germany. Lang.: Hun.   1122
1790-1793.   Research/historiography.
János Endrődy, the first Hungarian theatre historian. Lang.: Hun.   1300
1790-1890.   Institutions.
László Kelemen and the first professional Hungarian theatre company. Lang.: Hun.   467
1792-1821.   Performance/production.
Early professional acting on the Hungarian stage in Transylvania. Kolozsvár. Lang.: Hun.   842
1792-1990.   Administration.
Résumé of writings on theatre manager, actor, and director László Kelemen. Lang.: Hun.   32
1793-1948.   Performance/production.
Music theatre in Hungarian theatre in Transylvania. Kolozsvár. Cluj-Napoca. Lang.: Hun.   3860
1793-1976.   Plays/librettos/scripts.
Study of opera libretti. Lang.: Hun.   4326
1794-1987.   Performance/production.
Interpretations of Shakespeare in Hungarian theatre in Transylvania. Kolozsvár. Cluj-Napoca. Lang.: Hun.   2111
1798-1944.   Institutions.
Hungarian theatre in Nagyvárad/Oradea. Nagyvárad. Oradea. Lang.: Hun.   471
1803-1962.   Institutions.
Hungarian theatricals in Tîrgu Mureş. Marosvásárhely. Tîrgu Mureş. Lang.: Hun.   470
1821-1919.   Institutions.
History of Kolozsvári Nemzeti Színház. Kolozsvár. Lang.: Hun.   468

1823-1847.   Performance/production.
Actress Róza Déry-Széppataki. Lang.: Hun.   4156
1845-1944.   Institutions.
History of amateur theatre in Békéscsaba. Békéscsaba. Lang.: Hun.   482
1849-1968.   Institutions.
Documents of the Városligeti Színkör. Budapest. Lang.: Hun.   469
1850-1863.   Administration.
Censorship in Pécs theatre. Pécs. Lang.: Hun.   33
1855-1856.   Performance/production.
János Vajda's reviews of guest performances. Szeged. Lang.: Hun.   839
1856.   Performance/production.
The Vienna premiere of Erkel's *Hunyadi László*. Vienna. Lang.: Hun.   4079
1869-1955.   Performance/production.
Literary analysis of the diary of actress Róza Déry-Széppataki. Lang.: Hun.   2097
1878-1952.   Plays/librettos/scripts.
Review of a biography of playwright Ferenc Molnár. New York, NY. Lang.: Eng.   3071
1892-1895.   Research/historiography.
Retrospective view of Zoltán Ferenczi's work on Koloszvár theatre history. Lang.: Hun.   1299
1894-1915.   Performance/production.
Theatre director Jenő Janovics and Hungarian film. Kolozsvár. Lang.: Hun.   3616
1895-1961.   Performance/production.
Soprano Ella Némethy. Lang.: Hun.   4160
1895-1995.   Performance/production.
Tribute to Olga Szentpál, prominent representative of Eurhythmics. Lang.: Hun.   1583
1896-1996.   Institutions.
Centennial album of Katona József Theatre. Kecskemét. Lang.: Hun.   474
The 100th anniversary of the Vígszínház. Budapest. Lang.: Hun.   486
1896-1996.   Performance/production.
Tribute to the tenor Kálmán Pataky. Lang.: Hun.   4148
1897-1918.   Institutions.
Eleven years at Magyar Színház under László Beöthy. Budapest. Lang.: Hun.   483
1898-1993.   Performance/production.
Analysis of Ibsen's *Johan Gabriel Borkman*. Budapest. Lang.: Hun, Eng.   2106
1900-1990.   Relation to other fields.
The present state of Hungarian artistic dance. Lang.: Hun.   1455
1907-1928.   Performance/production.
Two productions of *Déryné ifjasszony (Mrs. Déry)* by Ferenc Herczeg. Austria-Hungary. Budapest. Lang.: Hun.   1908
1908-1994.   Research/historiography.
History and theory of orchestics movement system. Paris. Budapest. Lang.: Hun.   1601
1910-1913.   Performance/production.
Artúr Bárdos' production of *A kékszakállú herceg vára (Bluebeard's Castle)* by Béla Balázs. Budapest. Lang.: Hun.   2102
1910-1956.   Relation to other fields.
Hungarian theatre life in the 1950s. Lang.: Hun.   1197
1910-1995.   Design/technology.
Scenographer Mátyás Varga. Budapest. Szeged. Lang.: Hun.   179
Introduction to exhibition of designs by Mátyás Varga. Lang.: Hun.   181
1910-1996.   Performance/production.
Profile of Miklós Tompa, founder of Székely Színház. Romania. Lang.: Hun.   2095
1913-1994.   Performance spaces.
Creation of a German-language theatre in a former cinema. Szekszárd. Lang.: Hun.   646
1914-1995.   Research/historiography.
Interview with dance scholar Gedeon Dienes. Lang.: Hun.   1602
1916-1990.   Performance/production.
Career of soprano Lilian Birkás. Lang.: Hun.   4155
1916-1996.   Performance/production.
Tribute to baritone Giuseppe Taddei. Italy. Lang.: Hun.   4178
1918-1940.   Relation to other fields.
Archival documents on Hungarian theatre in Romania. Romania. Lang.: Hun.   1198

India — cont'd

1625-1996.　　　**Basic theatrical documents.**
English translation of *Kalyānasaugandhikam (The Flower of Good Fortune)* by Kottayam Tampura. Lang.: Eng.　1608
1949-1996.　　　**Performance/production.**
The relationship of teacher to student in Indian classical dance. Lang.: Eng.　1433
1968-1983.　　　**Plays/librettos/scripts.**
The influence of Buddhism on playwright Jean-Claude Van Itallie. USA. Lang.: Eng.　3419
1977-1995.　　　**Relation to other fields.**
Rustom Bharucha's *Guindegowdana Charitre* and 'intraculturalism'. Lang.: Eng.　1200
1986-1995.　　　**Relation to other fields.**
Female identity as seen through culture. Mindanao. New Delhi. Lang.: Eng.　1216
1992-1995.　　　**Training.**
Response to articles on theatre training. UK-England. USA. Lang.: Eng.　1396

Indonesia
1850-1990.　　　**Performance/production.**
Study of the Surakarta tradition of classical Javanese dance. Lang.: Eng.　1434
1879-1995.　　　**Plays/librettos/scripts.**
Women's reinterpretations of traditional stories. Argentina. Iceland. Lang.: Eng.　2713
1880-1995.　　　**Performance/production.**
Ritual, meaning, and spectacle in Southeast Asian performance. Lang.: Eng.　1435
1891-1996.　　　**Performance/production.**
Randai folk theatre. Lang.: Eng.　2114
1935-1975.　　　**Relation to other fields.**
Colonial discourse in Javanese puppetry. Lang.: Eng.　4445
1985.　　　**Performance/production.**
Interview with choreographer Ulf Gadd about attitudes toward dance. Sweden. Lang.: Swe.　1442
1986-1995.　　　**Performance/production.**
The role of the scenarist in *loddrok* performances. Madura. Lang.: Eng.　2113
1988.　　　**Performance/production.**
Cooperation between French puppeteers and Indonesian *dalang* artists. France. Lang.: Fre.　4396
1995.　　　**Performance/production.**
Articles on Indonesian performing arts. Lang.: Eng.　853
1995.　　　**Theory/criticism.**
Gender construction in ritual performance of *dangdut*. Java. Lang.: Eng.　3876
1996.　　　**Institutions.**
Performances at Asian festival of World Dance Alliance. Melbourne. Jakarta. Lang.: Ger.　1605
1996.　　　**Performance/production.**
Traditional Indonesian puppet plays at Slovenia ethnographic museum. Slovenia. Lang.: Slo.　4442

Ireland
1660-1823.　　　**Plays/librettos/scripts.**
Catalog of women's drama. England. Scotland. Lang.: Eng.　2932
1900-1902.　　　**Institutions.**
Profile of Irish women's nationalist group Inghinidhe na h'Eireann. Dublin. Lang.: Eng.　1814
1902.　　　**Plays/librettos/scripts.**
Analysis of *The Tinker's Wedding* by John Millington Synge. Lang.: Eng.　3089
1902-1905.　　　**Plays/librettos/scripts.**
Female vagrants in plays of J.M. Synge. Lang.: Eng.　3080
1902-1909.　　　**Plays/librettos/scripts.**
The aesthetics of playwright John Millington Synge. Lang.: Eng.　3076
1903.　　　**Plays/librettos/scripts.**
Feminist analysis of *The Shadow of the Glen* by J.M. Synge. Lang.: Eng.　3081
Celtic myth in *The Shadow of the Glen* by J.M. Synge. Lang.: Eng.　3087
1903-1909.　　　**Plays/librettos/scripts.**
Irish history in the plays of J.M. Synge. Lang.: Eng.　3085
1903-1910.　　　**Plays/librettos/scripts.**
Nationalism and the female figure in plays of Yeats. Lang.: Eng.　3083
1904.　　　**Plays/librettos/scripts.**
Analysis of J.M. Synge's *Riders to the Sea*. Lang.: Eng.　3078

1905.　　　**Plays/librettos/scripts.**
Analysis of J.M. Synge's *The Well of the Saints*. Lang.: Eng.　3077
Anthropological analysis of Synge's *The Well of the Saints*. Lang.: Eng.　3086
1907.　　　**Plays/librettos/scripts.**
Influence of Synge's *The Playboy of the Western World* on work of Yeats. Lang.: Eng.　3090
The audience in and of J.M. Synge's *The Playboy of the Western World*. Lang.: Eng.　3091
The trickster in Synge's *Playboy of the Western World*. Lang.: Eng.　3092
1907-1968.　　　**Audience.**
Comparison of riots by audiences of Abbey Theatre and Living Theatre. Dublin. Berkeley, CA. Lang.: Eng.　1632
1909.　　　**Plays/librettos/scripts.**
Analysis of the unfinished *Deirdre of the Sorrows* by John Millington Synge. Lang.: Eng.　3079
1951-1996.　　　**Institutions.**
The Wexford opera festival. Wexford. Lang.: Swe.　4047
1953-1957.　　　**Plays/librettos/scripts.**
Analysis of *Fin de partie* and *En attendant Godot* by Samuel Beckett. France. Lang.: Eng.　3082
1953-1990.　　　**Plays/librettos/scripts.**
Dominic Champagne's *La Répétition (The Rehearsal)* and its relation to Beckett's *En attendant Godot (Waiting for Godot)*. Montreal, PQ. France. Lang.: Fre.　2843
1972-1988.　　　**Plays/librettos/scripts.**
Dual personalities in plays of Brian Friel. UK-Ireland. Lang.: Eng.　3084
1991-1996.　　　**Plays/librettos/scripts.**
Michael Colgan's plan to produce all of Samuel Beckett's plays at the Gate Theatre. Dublin. Lang.: Eng.　3088
1996.　　　**Design/technology.**
Lighting for London and Dublin productions of *Tap Dogs*. London. Dublin. Lang.: Eng.　3891
1996.　　　**Performance/production.**
Sebastian Barry's *The Steward of Christendom* directed by Max Stafford-Clark at the Gate. Dublin. Lang.: Eng.　2115
Interview with actor Donal McCann. Dublin. Lang.: Eng.　2116
Current Dublin productions. Dublin. Lang.: Eng.　2117
1996.　　　**Relation to other fields.**
Performance and sexuality as observed in an Irish pub. Dublin. Lang.: Eng.　1201
1996.　　　**Theory/criticism.**
Analysis of the theatre critic's job. Lang.: Eng.　1350

Israel
1889-1948.　　　**Plays/librettos/scripts.**
Israeli theatrical tradition before the founding of the state of Israel. Lang.: Eng.　3101
1912-1990.　　　**Relation to other fields.**
The Arab on the Israeli stage. Lang.: Eng.　3500
1920-1995.　　　**Plays/librettos/scripts.**
Analysis of *Haneshica Haamerikait (The American Princess)* by Nissim Aloni. Lang.: Eng.　3103
1920-1996.　　　**Relation to other fields.**
Government involvement in Israeli arts. Lang.: Eng.　1202
1926-1995.　　　**Plays/librettos/scripts.**
Analysis of plays by Nissim Aloni. Lang.: Eng.　3104
1931-1996.　　　**Performance/production.**
Production of *Jud Süss (The Jew Suess)* at BeerSheba Municipal Theatre. Beersheba. Lang.: Eng.　2119
1938-1994.　　　**Performance/production.**
Interview with director Yossi Yzraely. Lang.: Eng.　856
1939-1995.　　　**Plays/librettos/scripts.**
Analysis of plays by Yehoshua Sobol. Lang.: Eng.　3102
1944-1995.　　　**Plays/librettos/scripts.**
Analysis of plays by Hanoch Levin. Lang.: Eng.　3107
1948-1995.　　　**Theory/criticism.**
Self-referentiality in Israeli theatre. Lang.: Eng.　3544
1948-1996.　　　**Plays/librettos/scripts.**
Trends in Israeli drama and theatre. Lang.: Eng.　3094
1950-1984.　　　**Plays/librettos/scripts.**
Analysis of Israeli Holocaust drama. Lang.: Eng.　3099
1950-1992.　　　**Plays/librettos/scripts.**
Interview with playwright Miriam Kainy. Lang.: Eng.　3096
1955-1989.　　　**Basic theatrical documents.**
Israeli Holocaust drama. Lang.: Eng.　1667

Latin America — cont'd

1929-1994.   **Performance/production.**
Tribute to deceased theatre artist Heiner Müller. Germany.
Lang.: Spa.   2049
1936-1996.   **Performance/production.**
History of Latin American theatre festivals. Lang.: Spa.   876

The theatre festival as a valuable resource. Lang.: Spa.   877
1968-1996.   **Institutions.**
Latin American performances at London International Festival.
London. Lang.: Spa.   554
1968-1996.   **Performance/production.**
Reasons for the continued interest in theatre festivals. Lang.:
Spa.   880
1980-1996.   **Performance/production.**
Postmodernism in Latin American performances. Lang.: Spa.
    2135
1985-1995.   **Plays/librettos/scripts.**
Poststructuralism in Latin American plays. Lang.: Spa.   3141
1988-1996.   **Institutions.**
Cultural exchange in Latin American theatre festivals. Lang.:
Spa.   495
1994-1996.   **Plays/librettos/scripts.**
Postmodernism in Latin American theatre. Lang.: Spa.   3142
1995.   **Plays/librettos/scripts.**
Playwright Pedro Antonio Valdez on the 'new dramaturgy'.
Lang.: Spa.   3143
1996.   **Institutions.**
Criticism of competitiveness at international theatre festivals.
Lang.: Spa.   496

Defense of theatre festivals. Lang.: Spa.   497
1996.   **Performance/production.**
Symposium on Latin American theatre, focus on German
collaborations. Berlin. Lang.: Spa.   821

Defense of theatre festivals. Lang.: Spa.   878
1996.   **Relation to other fields.**
Theatricality in Latin America and its historical impact. Lang.:
Eng.   1209

Latvia
1982.   **Performance/production.**
Eimuntas Nekrošius' youth theatre production of an adaptation
of Shakespeare's *Romeo and Juliet*. Vilnius. Lang.: Rus.   2136

Lebanon
1940-1996.   **Relation to other fields.**
Brigitte Jaques' *Elvire Jouvet 40*, and the continuing reality of
political detention and torture. Paris. Lang.: Fre.   3496

Lesotho
1970-1994.   **Relation to other fields.**
New developments in Theatre for Development. Lang.: Eng.
    1210

Lithuania
1996.   **Performance/production.**
Interview with director Eimuntas Nekrošius. Lang.: Ger.   2137

Russian theatre in Vilnius. Vilnius. Lang.: Rus.   2138
1996.   **Relation to other fields.**
The political context of Nekrošius' production of Čechov's
Three Sisters. Lang.: Ger.   3503

Mali
1988.   **Plays/librettos/scripts.**
Profile of the 'plays in transit' workshops at the Festival
international des francophonies. Limoges. Belgium. Canada.
Lang.: Fre.   2988

Malta
1741-1996.   **Performance spaces.**
Censorship at the Manoel Theatre. Lang.: Swe.   649

Mari El Republic
1898-1942.   **Performance/production.**
The work of actor Jyvan Kyrlja. Yoshkar-Ola. Lang.: Rus.   881
1995.   **Institutions.**
Account of festival of Russian theatres. Yoshkar-Ola. Lang.:
Rus.   498

Festival of Russian drama theatres. Yoshkar-Ola. Lang.: Rus.
    499

Martinique
1992.   **Performance/production.**
Elie Pennont's staging of *Une Tempête (A Tempest)* by Aimé
Césaire. Fort-de-France. Lang.: Eng.   2139

Mexico
1904-1994.   **Relation to other fields.**
Religious spectacle as political propaganda in Chiapas. Lang.:
Eng.   1211

1987-1990.   **Plays/librettos/scripts.**
Analysis of plays by Hugo Salcedo. Lang.: Eng.   3144
1993.   **Plays/librettos/scripts.**
Analysis of *Entre Villa y una mujer desnuda (Between Villa and
a Naked Woman)* by Sabina Berman. Lang.: Eng.   3145
1994.   **Performance/production.**
Latin American and Hispanic performance. Cuba. Lang.: Eng.
    1975
1995.   **Performance/production.**
Director Anthony Akerman's diary of a production of *The Road
to Mecca* by Athol Fugard. Mexico City. Lang.: Eng.   2140
1995-1996.   **Performance/production.**
Two summer seasons of Mexico City theatre. Mexico City.
Lang.: Eng.   882
1996.   **Performance spaces.**
Report on Mexico's National Center of the Arts. Mexico City.
Lang.: Eng.   650

The newly renovated Teatro de los Insurgentes. Mexico City.
Lang.: Eng.   3851
1996.   **Performance/production.**
Native influences on Mexican and Hispanic-American dance.
Mexico City. Irvine, CA. Lang.: Eng.   1546
1996.   **Relation to other fields.**
The risks inherent in political performance art: the example of
Hugo Sánchez. Lang.: Eng.   3817

Monaco
1961-1996.   **Performance/production.**
Lowell Liebermann, composer of the opera *The Picture of
Dorian Gray*. New York, NY. Monte Carlo. Lang.: Eng.   4254

Netherlands
409 B.C.-1996 A.D.   **Basic theatrical documents.**
Annotated Dutch translation of Euripides' *Phoínissai (The
Phoenician Women)* as produced by Hollandia. Greece. Lang.:
Dut.   1662
990-1995.   **Basic theatrical documents.**
History of Dutch and Flemish theatre. Flanders. Lang.: Dut.   2
1500-1599.   **Performance/production.**
Staging the *rederijker*. Belgium. Lang.: Eng.   1913
1650-1995.   **Audience.**
The influence of space on audience perception and appreciation.
Lang.: Dut.   140
1760-1830.   **Performance/production.**
Biography of actress Johanna Cornelia Ziesenis-Wattier. Lang.:
Dut.   2142
1813-1868.   **Performance/production.**
Influence of Parisian boulevard theatre on Amsterdam ballet.
Amsterdam. Lang.: Dut.   1512
1826-1996.   **Performance/production.**
The Huf family of actors. Amsterdam. Lang.: Dut.   886
1864-1924.   **Plays/librettos/scripts.**
Biography of playwright Herman Heijermans. Lang.: Dut.   3147
1886-1995.   **Institutions.**
History of Dutch opera companies. Lang.: Dut.   4049
1887-1995.   **Performance spaces.**
The renovation and extension of the Theater Carré. Amsterdam.
Lang.: Dut.   651
1890-1995.   **Performance/production.**
History of Dutch operetta. Lang.: Dut.   4365
1890-1996.   **Performance spaces.**
The degradation of Amsterdam's theatre district. Amsterdam.
Lang.: Dut.   653
1892-1924.   **Plays/librettos/scripts.**
Playwright Herman Heijermans. Amsterdam. Lang.: Dut.   3146
1895-1995.   **Relation to other fields.**
Description of the portraits in the lobby of the
Stadsschouwburg. Amsterdam. Lang.: Dut.   1212
1900-1990.   **Performance spaces.**
Unrealized plans for new Amsterdam theatre buildings.
Amsterdam. Lang.: Dut.   652
1920-1970.   **Performance/production.**
Cilly Wang's work as actress, dancer, and puppeteer. Lang.:
Dut.   883
1930-1995.   **Performance/production.**
Life and work of Ritsaert ten Cate, founder of the Mickery
Theater. Lang.: Eng.   885
1945-1954.   **Institutions.**
The failure of the artist club De Koepel. Amsterdam. Lang.:
Dut.   500
1946-1996.   **Design/technology.**
Set designer Keso Dekker's work with choreographer Hans von
Manen. Lang.: Ger.   1403

Norway — cont'd

1896-1930.   Plays/librettos/scripts.
The influence of Ibsen's *Johan Gabriel Borkman* on sociologist
Max Weber. Germany. Lang.: Eng.   3020
1964-1995.   Institutions.
Eugenio Barba on thirty years of Odin Teatret. Holstebro. Oslo.
Lang.: Ita.   397
1979.   Performance/production.
Interview with tenor Arild Helleland. Finland. Lang.: Swe.   4193
1984.   Institutions.
Interview with Bjørn Simensen, new manager of Den Norske
Opera. Oslo. Lang.: Swe.   4051
1995.   Performance/production.
Directors Edith Roger and Catrine Telle. Oslo. Lang.: Eng.
                                                   2143
1995.   Plays/librettos/scripts.
Interview with playwright Cecilie Løveid. Lang.: Dan.   3155
1996.   Performance/production.
Catrine Telle directs Holberg's *Erasmus Montanus*,
Nationaltheatret. Oslo. Lang.: Eng.   2144

Ottoman Empire
SEE
Turkey.

Papua New Guinea
1975-1995.   Plays/librettos/scripts.
TV in Papua New Guinea. Lang.: Eng.   3683

Paraguay
1995.   Institutions.
Profile of international theatre festival Muestra Internacional.
Montevideo. Lang.: Spa.   503

Peru
1996.   Basic theatrical documents.
Text of *Con guitarra y sin cajón (With a Guitar and Without a
Case)* by Maritza Kirchausen. Lang.: Spa.   1671

Philippines
1565-1996.   Performance/production.
Contemporary Philippine theatre and the formation of cultural
identity. Manila. Lang.: Eng.   889
1981-1995.   Plays/librettos/scripts.
Presentations by story-tellers at women playwrights conference.
Australia. USA. Lang.: Eng.   1083
1986-1995.   Relation to other fields.
Female identity as seen through culture. Mindanao. New Delhi.
Lang.: Eng.   1216

Poland
1500-1945.   Performance/production.
History of Polish puppetry. Lang.: Eng.   4401
1600-1996.   Plays/librettos/scripts.
The influence of French drama on Polish theatre. France. Lang.:
Eng, Fre.   2992
1765-1996.   Institutions.
History of Teatr Narodowy, the Polish national theatre.
Warsaw. Lang.: Eng, Fre.   1820
1781-1893.   Administration.
Cracow theatre posters. Cracow. Lang.: Pol.   41
1786-1846.   Plays/librettos/scripts.
Shakespeare and Polish Romanticism. Lang.: Eng.   3163
1796-1868.   Plays/librettos/scripts.
A French adaptation of *Romeo and Juliet* on the Polish stage.
Lang.: Eng, Fre.   3164
1816-1842.   Plays/librettos/scripts.
Puppet playwright Jordaki Kuparenko. Russia. Lang.: Pol. 4425
1832-1957.   Plays/librettos/scripts.
The devil in Polish drama. Lang.: Pol.   3168
1871-1939.   Administration.
Cracow theatre programs. Cracow. Lang.: Pol.   39
1872-1918.   Performance/production.
Activity of Lvov's Polish opera company. Lvov. Lang.: Pol.
                                                   4194
1876-1918.   Plays/librettos/scripts.
Scandinavian theatre in Polish culture. Scandinavia. Lang.: Pol.
                                                   3167
1890-1989.   Relation to other fields.
Political playwright Ferdynand Goetel. Lang.: Pol. 3505
1901-1996.   Performance/production.
Production history of *Dziady (Forefathers' Eve)* by Adam
Mickiewicz. Lang.: Eng, Fre.   2148
1904-1989.   Plays/librettos/scripts.
The theatre of Witold Gombrowicz and posthumous productions
of his plays. France. Argentina. Lang.: Fre.   3170

1918-1989.   Performance/production.
Significant Polish productions of Shakespearean plays. Lang.:
Eng.   2152
1919-1996.   Performance/production.
Witkacy and cinema. USA. Lang.: Pol.   3618
1920-1990.   Plays/librettos/scripts.
Polish theatre of the absurd. Lang.: Pol.   3166
1922-1925.   Institutions.
History of Balet Jana Cieplińskiego. Lang.: Pol.   1484
1923-1953.   Performance/production.
Collection of interviews with director Leon Schiller. Lang.: Pol.
                                                   894
1923-1996.   Institutions.
The work of directors Osterwa, Horzyca, and Dejmek at Teatr
Narodowy. Warsaw. Lang.: Eng, Fre.   1821
1924.   Relation to other fields.
Theatre artists of the Communist period. Lang.: Pol. 1219
1929-1975.   Performance/production.
Director Konrad Swinarski. Lang.: Eng, Fre.   2150
1930-1996.   Performance/production.
Account of a symposium on Polish cinema. New York, NY.
Lang.: Eng.   3619
1932-1938.   Plays/librettos/scripts.
Reactions of male critics to Polish feminist drama. Lang.: Pol.
                                                   3162
1935-1938.   Institutions.
Performances by Michał Weichert's Yiddish theatre troupe.
Cracow. Lang.: Pol.   504
1935-1939.   Institutions.
Feliks Parnell's Balet Polski. Warsaw. Lang.: Pol. 1485
1939-1989.   Relation to other fields.
Polish theatre in its social and political context. Lang.: Eng.
                                                   1217
1943-1996.   Performance/production.
The work of director Krystian Lupa. Lang.: Pol.   2170
1945-1995.   Institutions.
History of the Cracow Theatre School. Cracow. Lang.: Pol.   510
1945-1996.   Performance/production.
Pantomimist Rajmund Klechot. Wrocław. Dayton, OH. Lang.:
Eng.   3691
Puppetry performance styles of Jan Dorman and Jan Wilkowski.
Lang.: Eng, Fre.   4400
1946-1995.   Performance/production.
Interview with actor Andrzej Seweryn. Lang.: Eng, Fre.   2156
1947-1948.   Performance/production.
Account of *Ostatni etap (Last Stop)*, a film directed by Wanda
Jakubowska. Lang.: Pol.   3620
1948-1992.   Plays/librettos/scripts.
Recent Polish translations and productions of the plays of
Molière. France. Cracow. Lang.: Eng, Fre.   2993
1949-1996.   Design/technology.
Interview with Teatr Narodowy designer Łucja Kossakowska.
Warsaw. Lang.: Eng, Fre.   1709
1950-1980.   Plays/librettos/scripts.
Analysis of plays by Havel, Mrożek, and Örkény.
Czechoslovakia. Hungary. Lang.: Eng.   2872
1950-1990.   Performance/production.
Interview with Henryk Jurkowski on Polish puppetry. Lang.:
Hun.   4398
1955-1996.   Performance/production.
Influence of French drama on the repertoire of Polish Television
Theatre. France. Lang.: Eng, Fre.   3671
1956-1996.   Performance/production.
Forty years of Polish alternative theatre. Lang.: Ger.   891
1960.   Performance/production.
Puppets in European theatre. France. Italy. Lang.: Fre.   4393
1960-1996.   Plays/librettos/scripts.
Experimental theatre of Kantor, Schaeffer, and Różewicz. Lang.:
Pol.   3165
1962-1996.   Design/technology.
Interview with scene designer Krystyna Zachwatowicz. France.
Lang.: Eng, Fre.   1710
1966.   Performance/production.
Sketches documenting improvisation leading to Grotowski's
production *Apocalypsis cum figuris*. Wroclaw. Lang.: Fre.   2173
1967.   Performance/production.
Hungarian translation of an interview with Jerzy Grotowski.
Wrocław. Lang.: Hun.   890
1970.   Performance/production.
Swinarski's production of *A Midsummer Night's Dream*, Stary
Teatr. Cracow. Lang.: Eng.   2177

Russia — cont'd

Russia — cont'd

Russia — cont'd

Slovakia

1990-1995.   **Institutions.**
Account of the Slovak theatre festival. Nitra. Lang.: Hun.   528
1995-1996.   **Performance/production.**
Survey of ethnic Hungarian theatre in neighboring countries.
Romania. Košiče. Beregovo. Lang.: Hun.   897
1996.   **Institutions.**
Report on the Slovak theatre festival. Nitra. Lang.: Hun.   529
1996.   **Performance/production.**
Enikő Eszenyi's production of Shakespeare's *As You Like It* at
Slovenske Narodni Divadlo. Bratislava. Lang.: Hun.   2261
1996.   **Plays/librettos/scripts.**
Impressions from a trip through the European theatre landscape.
UK-England. Germany. Lang.: Dan.   1103

Slovenia

1650-1996.   **Institutions.**
History of Slovene dramatic theatre. Lang.: Slo.   1845
1834-1932.   **Basic theatrical documents.**
Texts of plays by Josip Vošnjak and Anton Funtek. Lang.: Slo.
  1676
1861-1941.   **Institutions.**
History of Slovenske Narodni Gledalisče. Maribor. Lang.: Slo.
  1843
1872-1929.   **Plays/librettos/scripts.**
Early Slovene theatre for youth. Lang.: Slo.   3218
1872-1996.   **Plays/librettos/scripts.**
Slovene youth drama. Lang.: Slo.   3217
1900-1996.   **Plays/librettos/scripts.**
Analysis of plays by major Slovene dramatists. Lang.: Slo.   3212
Analysis of works by significant Slovene playwrights. Lang.: Slo.
  3213
1918-1922.   **Plays/librettos/scripts.**
Plays about WWI by Goering and Berk. Germany. Lang.: Slo.
  3214
1921-1996.   **Institutions.**
History of amateur theatre Šentjakobsko gledalisče. Ljubljana.
Lang.: Slo.   1844
1938-1996.   **Performance/production.**
Slovene shadow puppetry. Lang.: Slo.   4443
1945-1995.   **Institutions.**
Survey of the productions and actors of Gledalisče Toneta
Čufarja. Jesenice. Lang.: Slo.   1841
1945-1996.   **Performance/production.**
Memoirs of actor-director Branko Gombač. Celje. Trieste. Lang.:
Slo.   2262
1946-1996.   **Institutions.**
History of the Academy of Theatre, Radio, Film, and
Television. Ljubljana. Lang.: Slo.   530
1952-1996.   **Theory/criticism.**
Interview with theatre critic Vasja Predan. Lang.: Slo.   3550
1958-1996.   **Plays/librettos/scripts.**
Collection of articles on playwright Dane Zajc. Lang.: Slo.   3215
1959-1995.   **Plays/librettos/scripts.**
Collection of articles on playwright Dominik Smole. Lang.: Slo.
  3211
1974-1995.   **Institutions.**
Production history of Maribor Puppet Theatre. Maribor. Lang.:
Slo.   4384
1986-1996.   **Plays/librettos/scripts.**
Playwright and director Dušan Jovanovič on recent Slovene
drama. Lang.: Slo.   3210
1991.   **Performance/production.**
Profile of the Romeo & Julia Choir. Stockholm. Croatia. Lang.:
Swe.   3866
1991-1994.   **Administration.**
Memoirs of Marko Sosič, former artistic director of Primorsko
dramsko gledalisče. Nova Gorica. Lang.: Slo.   1617
1991-1994.   **Design/technology.**
Catalogue of the Slovene exhibit at the Prague Quadrennial.
Lang.: Slo.   206
1994-1995.   **Reference materials.**
Yearbook of Slovene theatre. Lang.: Slo.   1126
1995.   **Relation to other fields.**
Interview with actor Radko Polic on the Slovenian political
situation. Lang.: Eng.   1231
1995-1996.   **Performance/production.**
The Slovene theatre season. Lang.: Slo.   2263
1996.   **Design/technology.**
Manual for construction of hanging puppets. Lang.: Slo.   4437

Manual for construction of rod puppets. Lang.: Slo.   4440
1996.   **Institutions.**
Programs of the international festival of performing art, Exodos.
Ljubljana. Lang.: Slo.   531
Program of the competitive theatre meeting Borštnikovo
srečanje. Lang.: Slo.   1842
Program of biennial puppetry festival. Novo mesto. Lang.: Slo.
  4383
1996.   **Performance/production.**
Handbook of acting exercises for children. Lang.: Slo.   939
Analysis of Tomaž Pandur's production *Babylon*. Maribor.
Lang.: Ger.   2264
Traditional Indonesian puppet plays at Slovenia ethnographic
museum. Indonesia. Lang.: Slo.   4442
1996.   **Plays/librettos/scripts.**
Handbook of Slovenenian drama for students. Lang.: Slo.   3208
Teacher's handbook of Slovenia drama. Lang.: Slo.   3209
Analysis of *Ljudožerci (The Cannibals)* by G. Strniša. Lang.: Slo.
  3216
1996.   **Reference materials.**
Introduction to theatre and glossary for young people. Lang.:
Slo.   1125
1996.   **Theory/criticism.**
Tragedy in Slovene literary theory. Lang.: Slo.   3548
The dramatic text and its analysis—handbook. Lang.: Slo.   3549

South Africa, Republic of

1700-1996.   **Theory/criticism.**
The origins of African drama. Africa. Lang.: Eng.   1362
1800-1995.   **Relation to other fields.**
The political mission of South African English studies, with
emphasis on Shakespeare. Lang.: Eng.   3508
1900-1985.   **Performance/production.**
The variety entertainment tradition in South African theatre.
Lang.: Eng.   3834
1900-1996.   **Theory/criticism.**
The current state of South African theatre historiography and
theory. Lang.: Eng.   1360
1930-1995.   **Plays/librettos/scripts.**
The revival of plays by Herbert Dhlomo. Lang.: Eng.   3222
Analysis of *Gangsters* by Maishe Maponya. Lang.: Eng.   3224
1930-1996.   **Performance/production.**
Influence of Hollywood gangster films on South African cinema.
Hollywood, CA. Lang.: Eng.   3637
1933.   **Theory/criticism.**
Art, politics, and the African playwright. Lang.: Eng.   3551
1945-1996.   **Plays/librettos/scripts.**
Playwrights Gcina Mhlophe and Sue Pam-Grant. Lang.: Eng.
  3223
1948-1994.   **Plays/librettos/scripts.**
Athol Fugard and the role of revolutionary theatre after the
revolution. Lang.: Eng.   3220
1949-1996.   **Performance/production.**
Landscape and ideology in South African films. Lang.: Eng.
  3624
1956-1979.   **Performance/production.**
Satirical reviews of Adam Leslie. Johannesburg. Lang.: Eng.
  3730
1968-1974.   **Plays/librettos/scripts.**
The use of absurdism in Fugard's *The Island*. Lang.: Eng.   3225
1968-1994.   **Performance/production.**
The emerging South African feminist theatres. UK. USA. Cape
Town. Lang.: Eng.   959
1976.   **Institutions.**
Profile of Market Theatre, the institution and the building.
Johannesburg. Lang.: Swe.   1846
1980-1990.   **Plays/librettos/scripts.**
Comedy as a weapon against apartheid. Lang.: Ita.   1102
1980-1996.   **Relation to other fields.**
Drama's role in political liberation after the external oppressor
has been removed. Derry. Manchester. Lang.: Eng.   3507
South African media and film policy. Lang.: Eng.   3687
1987-1996.   **Performance/production.**
Political changes reflected in recent South African films. Lang.:
Eng.   3625
1988.   **Plays/librettos/scripts.**
Linguistic analysis of *Diepe grond (Deep Ground)* by Rezá de
Wet. Lang.: Eng.   3219

South Africa, Republic of — cont'd

1988-1995. Plays/librettos/scripts.
Interview with playwright, actress, director Rezá de Wet. Lang.:
Eng. 3221
1990-1996. Performance/production.
Anti-apartheid message of rap group Prophets of da City. Cape
Town. Lang.: Eng. 3714
1991-1995. Plays/librettos/scripts.
Women and South African theatre after the 'interregnum'.
Lang.: Eng. 1101
1992. Performance/production.
Female anti-apartheid activists in *Sarafina!* by Mbongeni
Ngema. Lang.: Eng. 3623
1993-1996. Performance/production.
Thomas Riccio's experience of street theatre in Natal. Durban.
Lang.: Eng. 940
1994. Performance/production.
Interview with choreographer Gary Gordon. Grahamstown.
Lang.: Eng. 1586

Interview with director Barney Simon of Market Theatre.
Johannesburg. Lang.: Eng. 2269
1994-1996. Relation to other fields.
Shakespeare in South African education. Lang.: Eng. 3509
1995. Institutions.
Report on ATKV Toneel '95 festival. Lang.: Afr. 533
1995. Performance/production.
Report on the national arts festival. Grahamstown. Lang.: Eng.
2267

Report on annual National Arts Festival. Grahamstown. Lang.:
Eng. 2270
1995. Research/historiography.
Research on drama and theatre in education. Lang.: Eng. 1302
1995. Theory/criticism.
Gender constructions and dance and movement education.
Lang.: Eng. 1361
1996. Institutions.
Report on the Grahamstown Festival. Grahamstown. Lang.:
Eng. 532
1996. Performance/production.
Report on the National Arts Festival. Grahamstown. Lang.:
Eng. 2265

Report on Klein Karoo arts festival. Oudtshoorn. Lang.: Afr.
2266

The current state of African drama. Lang.: Eng. 2268
1996. Relation to other fields.
Political and ethical considerations regarding South African
television. Lang.: Eng. 3686
South America
1968. Institutions.
History and mission of OISTAT. Europe. North America. Lang.:
Swe. 404
1996. Performance/production.
Distinctive characteristics of theatre festivals. Lang.: Spa. 941
Spain
1100-1400. Plays/librettos/scripts.
Medieval Castilian theatre. Lang.: Eng. 3264
1400-1996. Relation to other fields.
Theatricality in the painting *Las meninas* by Velázquez. Lang.:
Eng. 1233
1492-1650. Plays/librettos/scripts.
Painting and graffiti in plays of Cervantes and Claramonte.
Lang.: Eng. 3229
1500-1700. Plays/librettos/scripts.
Review of a history of Spanish golden age theatre. Lang.: Rus.
3253
1500-1990. Plays/librettos/scripts.
The narrative and theatrical modes in Spanish Renaissance
drama. Lang.: Eng. 3269
1580-1590. Plays/librettos/scripts.
Myth and classicism in Cervantes' *El Cerco de Numancia*. Lang.:
Eng. 3230
1580-1680. Plays/librettos/scripts.
Analysis of *Peribáñez y el Comendador de Ocaña* by Lope de
Vega. Lang.: Eng. 3228
Lacanian analysis of Spanish Baroque drama. Lang.: Eng. 3265
1599-1635. Plays/librettos/scripts.
Female transvestism in Shakespeare's *As You Like It* and
Calderon's *La Vida es sueño*. England. Lang.: Eng. 2901
1600-1620. Plays/librettos/scripts.
Reading as a textual strategy in the anonymous *La estrella de
Sevilla (The Star of Seville)*. Lang.: Eng. 3233

1600-1641. Plays/librettos/scripts.
Analysis of tragicomedies and tragedies with happy endings.
Italy. France. Lang.: Ger. 3139
1600-1681. Plays/librettos/scripts.
The theatre of Calderón. Lang.: Rus. 3260
1604-1624. Plays/librettos/scripts.
Written documents in Spanish plays of the Golden Age. Lang.:
Eng. 3251
1612-1614. Plays/librettos/scripts.
Girardian analysis of *Fuente ovejuna* by Lope de Vega. Lang.:
Eng. 3267
1615. Plays/librettos/scripts.
Speech act theory in Cervantes' *El retablo de las maravillas*.
Lang.: Eng. 3242
1620-1625. Plays/librettos/scripts.
Semiotics and Lope de Vega's *El caballero de Olmedo (The
Knight of Olmedo)*. Lang.: Eng. 3235
1622. Plays/librettos/scripts.
Analysis of *El médico de su honra* by Calderón. Lang.: Eng.
3234
Tirso's *Burlador de Sevilla* and canonicity. Lang.: Eng. 3252
1625-1672. Plays/librettos/scripts.
Playwright Ana Caro Mallén de Soto. Lang.: Eng. 3263
1628. Plays/librettos/scripts.
Analysis of *La verdad sospechosa (Suspicious Truth)* by Juan
Ruiz de Alarcón. Lang.: Eng. 3261
1635. Plays/librettos/scripts.
Analysis of *Amazonas en las Indias (Amazons in the Indies)* by
Tirso de Molina. Lang.: Eng. 3226
Lacanian analysis of plays by Calderón. Lang.: Eng. 3266
1895-1936. Performance/production.
Soprano Conchita Supervia. Barcelona. Lang.: Eng. 4213
1900-1936. Plays/librettos/scripts.
Metatheatre in the works of Lorca and Valle-Inclán. Lang.: Eng.
3227
1901-1952. Plays/librettos/scripts.
The plays of Enrique Jardiel Poncela. Lang.: Spa. 3256
1912-1921. Plays/librettos/scripts.
Analysis of plays by Carlos Arniches. Lang.: Spa. 3259
1916-1943. Plays/librettos/scripts.
Reevaluation of the plays of Carlos Arniches. Lang.: Spa. 3255
1920-1936. Plays/librettos/scripts.
Playwright Federico García Lorca and Modernism. Lang.: Eng.
3262
1929. Plays/librettos/scripts.
Analysis of *La nieta de Fedra (Phaedra's Niece)* by Halma
Angélico. Lang.: Spa. 3249
1935-1945. Performance/production.
Theatre as a Falangist propaganda tool. Lang.: Eng. 942
Sport and the performance of fascism in Falangist Spain. Lang.:
Eng. 943
1935-1945. Theory/criticism.
Falangist theatre aesthetics. Lang.: Eng. 1363
1939-1975. Administration.
Víctor Ruiz Iriarte's *Los pájaros ciegos (The Blind Birds)* and
censorship in the Franco regime. Lang.: Eng. 1618
1939-1993. Plays/librettos/scripts.
Interview with playwright Manuel Martínez Mediero. Lang.:
Spa. 3236
1945-1991. Plays/librettos/scripts.
Overview of contemporary Spanish playwriting. Lang.: Fre.
3257
1946. Plays/librettos/scripts.
Bibliography of playwright José María Rodríguez Méndez.
Lang.: Spa. 3239
Jacinto Benavente and Antonio Buero Vallejo as the leading
Spanish playwrights of the century. Lang.: Spa. 3248
1947-1971. Plays/librettos/scripts.
Women and war in plays of José Martín Recuerda and José
María Rodríguez Méndez. Lang.: Spa. 3246
1956-1996. Relation to other fields.
Spanish theatre and photography. Lang.: Eng. 1232
1960-1991. Plays/librettos/scripts.
Interview with playwright José Sanchis Sinisterra. Lang.: Fre.
3258
1965. Plays/librettos/scripts.
Theory and practice in the Marxist theatre of José María
Rodríguez Méndez. Lang.: Spa. 3238

Spain — cont'd

1965-1993.   **Plays/librettos/scripts.**
Analysis of *Los gatos (The Cats)* by Austín Gómez-Arco.
Madrid. Lang.: Eng.   3231

1966.   **Plays/librettos/scripts.**
Jorge Díaz's *Historia de nadie (Nobody's Story)* compared to
Beckett's *En attendant Godot (Waiting for Godot)*. France. Chile.
Lang.: Spa.   3245

1969.   **Plays/librettos/scripts.**
Analysis of *El sueño de la razón (The Sleep of Reason)* by
Antonio Buero Vallejo. Lang.: Eng.   3268

1976.   **Basic theatrical documents.**
Text of *Isabelita tiene ángel (Isabelita Has an Angel)* by José
María Rodríguez Méndez. Lang.: Spa.   1681

1976.   **Plays/librettos/scripts.**
Analysis of *Isabelita tiene ángel (Isabelita Has an Angel)* by
José María Rodríguez Méndez. Lang.: Spa.   3232

1977.   **Plays/librettos/scripts.**
Analysis of *Fuero de juicio (Out of His Mind)* by José Luis
Alonso de Santos. Lang.: Eng.   3247

1980.   **Training.**
Profile of Compania Infantil de Danza. Palma de Mallorca.
Lang.: Swe.   1470

1982.   **Plays/librettos/scripts.**
Analysis of *El color de agosto (The Color of August)* by Paloma
Pedrero. Lang.: Eng.   3244

1983-1990.   **Plays/librettos/scripts.**
Spanish women's theatre. Lang.: Spa.   3237

1987.   **Plays/librettos/scripts.**
Analysis of plays by Pilar Pombo. Lang.: Eng.   3270

1988.   **Institutions.**
Productions of world puppetry festival. Charleville-Mézières.
Lang.: Fre.   4373

1989.   **Plays/librettos/scripts.**
Gender roles in plays of Concha Romero. Lang.: Spa.   3240
Analysis of *Un maldito beso (A Damn Kiss)* by Concha Romero.
Lang.: Eng.   3243

1989-1994.   **Plays/librettos/scripts.**
Bibliography of playwright Concha Romero Pineda. Lang.: Spa.
                                                       3241

1990-1995.   **Basic theatrical documents.**
Dutch translations of plays by Belbel, Cabal, and Sanchis
Sinisterra. Lang.: Dut.   1677

1992.   **Plays/librettos/scripts.**
Annual bibliography of Spanish drama. Lang.: Spa.   3254

1993.   **Plays/librettos/scripts.**
Interview with playwright Antonio Buero Vallejo. Lang.: Spa.
                                                       3250

1994.   **Basic theatrical documents.**
Text of *Allá él (It's Up to Him)* by Concha Romero. Lang.: Spa.
                                                       1680

1994.   **Institutions.**
The Don Quixote Festival of Hispanic Theatre. Paris. Lang.:
Spa.   411

1995.   **Basic theatrical documents.**
Text of *Historia de nadie (Nobody's Story)* by Jorge Díaz. Lang.:
Spa.   1678

1995.   **Institutions.**
Account of Spanish-American theatre festival. Cádiz. Lang.: Spa.
                                                       534

1995.   **Performance/production.**
Report on festival of Spanish American theatre. Cádiz. Lang.:
Eng.   2272
Women directors in Spanish theatre. Lang.: Eng.   2273

1995-1996.   **Basic theatrical documents.**
French adaptation of a scene from *Carnes Frescas (Fresh Meat)*
by Carlo Felipe Molivar. Montreal, PQ. Madrid. Lang.: Fre.
                                                       1648

1996.   **Basic theatrical documents.**
Text of *Obras cómicas (Comic Works)* by Rodrigo García.
Madrid. Lang.: Eng.   1679
English translation of *¡Ay, Carmela!* by José Sanchis Sinisterra.
Lang.: Eng.   1682

1996.   **Institutions.**
Profile of the Festival Internacional de Almagro. Lang.: Eng.
                                                       1847

1996.   **Performance/production.**
The Madrid theatre season. Madrid. Lang.: Eng.   2271
Analysis of *Suz o Suz* by La Fura dels Baus. Barcelona. Lang.:
Eng.   3791

Spain-Catalonia
1967-1985.   **Institutions.**
Albert Boadella's Els Joglars and the comedy of cultural politics.
Lang.: Eng.   535

Sri Lanka
1988-1995.   **Plays/librettos/scripts.**
Influence of story-telling traditions on women playwrights.
Ghana. Australia. Lang.: Eng.   1098

Sweden
404 B.C.   **Relation to other fields.**
The relevance of ancient Greek theatre to contemporary life.
Athens. Vetlanda. Lang.: Swe.   1196

404 B.C.-1996 A.D.   **Plays/librettos/scripts.**
Actor Erland Josephson on the role of Kadmos in Euripides'
Bákchai (The Bacchae). Greece. Lang.: Swe.   3057

793-1400.   **Performance/production.**
References to performers and entertainment in medieval
Scandinavian literature. Norway. Iceland. Lang.: Eng. 888

1201-1300.   **Performance/production.**
Recently-discovered fragment of a *Visitatio sepulchri*.
Stockholm. Lang.: Eng.   952

1773-1996.   **Performance/production.**
The Royal Swedish Ballet and the eighteenth-century tradition.
Stockholm. Lang.: Swe.   1533

1785.   **Relation to other fields.**
Swedish attitudes toward dance. Lang.: Swe.   1459

1801.   **Performance spaces.**
Proposal to reconstruct the Djurgårdsteatern. Stockholm. Lang.:
Swe.   655

1840-1879.   **Performance/production.**
Portraits of nineteenth-century actors in mural art of the Royal
Dramatic Theatre. Stockholm. Lang.: Swe.   2278

1870-1912.   **Plays/librettos/scripts.**
English translation of essays by playwright August Strindberg.
Lang.: Eng.   3277

1896.   **Performance/production.**
Opera singer Kerstin Thorborg. Austria. Lang.: Swe.   4217

1902.   **Plays/librettos/scripts.**
Strindberg's medieval viewpoint in *Ett Drömspel (A Dream
Play)*. Lang.: Eng.   3276

1907.   **Performance spaces.**
History of mural paintings in the Royal Dramatic Theatre.
Stockholm. Lang.: Swe.   1888

1907-1961.   **Design/technology.**
Sven Olof Ehrén's *Va nu då (What Now)*, set in an ice stadium.
Stockholm. Lang.: Swe, Eng.   1711

1909-1992.   **Performance/production.**
Opera singer Hjördis Schymberg. Lang.: Swe.   4216

1916.   **Administration.**
Bengt Häger's career in dance production, training, and
research. Stockholm. Lang.: Swe.   1402

1918-1996.   **Performance/production.**
Italian translation of *Ingmar Bergman: A Life in the Theatre*.
Germany. Lang.: Ita.   2287

1919.   **Performance/production.**
Opera singer and teacher Kim Borg. Finland. Lang.: Swe. 4116

1920.   **Performance spaces.**
Proposal to restore original lighting equipment in the auditorium
of a retirement home. Stockholm. Lang.: Swe.   656

1920.   **Performance/production.**
The career of choreographer Birgit Cullberg. Stockholm. Lang.:
Swe.   1531

1940-1970.   **Design/technology.**
The development of lighting regulation. Lang.: Swe, Eng. 209

1940-1996.   **Performance/production.**
Baritone Håkan Hagegård—profile and interview. Lang.: Eng.
                                                       4218

1942.   **Relation to other fields.**
Erna Grönlund, professor of dance therapy. Lang.:
Swe.   1458

1944.   **Plays/librettos/scripts.**
Children's plays of Staffan Göthe. Luleå. Stockholm. Lang.:
Swe.   3275

1945.   **Performance/production.**
Report from conference on the development of Tanztheater.
Germany. Lang.: Swe.   1579

1945-1980.   **Performance/production.**
Britten's *Peter Grimes*: productions by Eric Crozier and Harald
André. UK-England. Stockholm. Lang.: Swe.   4229

1912-1914.   **Theory/criticism.**
Theatre criticism in suffrage newspapers. Lang.: Eng.   1370
1912-1920.   **Performance/production.**
Rebecca West's work as a drama critic. Lang.: Eng.   996
1913-1924.   **Performance/production.**
Expatriate Japanese playwright Kori Torahiko. London.
Toronto, ON. Japan. Lang.: Eng.   2510
1914-1970.   **Relation to other fields.**
Politics, society, and the street-seller character in the music-hall
performances. London. Lang.: Eng.   3842
1915-1996.   **Performance/production.**
Discussion of new biography of opera singer Elisabeth
Schwarzkopf. Germany. Lang.: Eng.   4140
1916.   **Performance/production.**
Cinematic adaptation of *The Whip*. Lang.: Eng.   3627
1918-1962.   **Performance/production.**
Women playwrights and performers on the London stage.
London. Lang.: Eng.   977
1918-1996.   **Performance/production.**
Musical theatre performer Evelyn Laye. Lang.: Eng.   3923
1919-1932.   **Performance/production.**
John Masefield's theatricals. Lang.: Eng.   2535
1919-1996.   **Performance/production.**
Actor Beryl Reid. Lang.: Eng.   967
1920-1935.   **Administration.**
A chapter in the history of theatre unionization. Lang.: Eng.   51
1920-1990.   **Plays/librettos/scripts.**
British radio drama as a distinct aesthetic form. Lang.: Eng.
3581
1920-1995.   **Research/historiography.**
Description of theatre and dance-related holdings of the
Darlington Hall Trust archives. Totnes, Devon. Lang.: Eng.
1305
1922-1996.   **Performance/production.**
Actress Fiona Shaw. New York, NY. London. Lang.: Eng. 2682
1926-1932.   **Administration.**
Terence Gray and the Cambridge Festival Theatre. Cambridge.
Lang.: Eng.   1620
1926-1996.   **Institutions.**
Denville Hall, a retirement home for actors. Northwood. Lang.:
Eng.   552

Unicorn Theatre, England's oldest professional children's
theatre company. London. Lang.: Eng.   556
1927-1993.   **Performance/production.**
Productions of Tretjakov's *Choču Rebenka (I Want a Baby)*.
Moscow. Birmingham. Berlin. Lang.: Eng.   2694
1927-1996.   **Performance/production.**
Actress Kathleen Harrison. Lang.: Eng.   968
1928-1939.   **Performance/production.**
History of the London Speech Festival. Lang.: Eng.   995
1930-1940.   **Institutions.**
History of the People's National Theatre. London. Lang.: Eng.
557
1930-1971.   **Plays/librettos/scripts.**
Autobiographical elements in Benjamin Britten's *Owen
Wingrave*. Lang.: Eng.   4341
1930-1977.   **Theory/criticism.**
Critic Harold Hobson of the *Times*. London. Lang.: Eng. 3556
1931-1941.   **Performance/production.**
Fritz Reiner's work as a conductor of opera. Philadelphia, PA.
San Francisco, CA. London. Lang.: Eng.   4276
1931-1996.   **Research/historiography.**
Obituary for teacher, actor, and director John Harrop. USA.
Lang.: Eng.   1306
1934-1995.   **Plays/librettos/scripts.**
Analysis of *Taking Sides* by Ronald Harwood. Lang.: Eng.
3316
1935-1975.   **Performance/production.**
British production and reception of the plays of Bertolt Brecht.
Lang.: Eng.   2513
1935-1996.   **Performance/production.**
Interview with musical theatre actor Anthony Newley. Lang.:
Eng.   3924
1936-1978.   **Performance/production.**
Analysis of film and video versions of *Romeo and Juliet*. USA.
Italy. Lang.: Eng.   3631
1939.   **Performance/production.**
Interview with tenor Philip Langridge. Lang.: Swe.   4230
1941.   **Relation to other fields.**
Performance in the work of novelist Virginia Woolf. Lang.: Eng.
1240

1942-1995.   **Performance/production.**
Actor/singer Daniel Massey. USA. Lang.: Eng.   3969
1944-1996.   **Performance/production.**
Actor John Byron. Lang.: Eng.   2527
1945-1980.   **Performance/production.**
Britten's *Peter Grimes*: productions by Eric Crozier and Harald
André. Stockholm. Lang.: Swe.   4229
1945-1996.   **Plays/librettos/scripts.**
Evolution of the Beast character in treatments of the fairy tale
Beauty and the Beast. Lang.: Eng.   1106

Interview with playwright Richard Norton-Taylor. Lang.: Eng.
3292
1946-1953.   **Theory/criticism.**
Dance criticism of Birgit Cullberg. Sweden. France. Lang.: Swe.
1467
1947-1996.   **Performance/production.**
Actress Margaret Rawlings. Lang.: Eng.   2508

Director David Pountney. Lang.: Ger.   2521
1947-1996.   **Plays/librettos/scripts.**
Glossary for Benjamin Britten's *Albert Herring* intended for
American singers. Lang.: Eng.   4342
1948-1995.   **Plays/librettos/scripts.**
Interview with Neil Bartlett, playwright, director, and producer.
Lang.: Eng.   3314
1950-1996.   **Plays/librettos/scripts.**
Analysis of *Blasted* by Sarah Kane. Lang.: Eng.   3312
1953-1966.   **Plays/librettos/scripts.**
Comparison of historical dramas by Robert Bolt and Arthur
Miller. USA. Lang.: Eng.   3413
1954-1990.   **Plays/librettos/scripts.**
Theatrical metaphors in prose and dramatic works of Wilson
Harris. Lang.: Eng.   3284
1955.   **Theory/criticism.**
Harold Hobson's response to Beckett's *Waiting for Godot*.
Lang.: Eng.   3557
1956-1964.   **Performance/production.**
Absurdism in English theatre. Lang.: Eng.   990
1956-1965.   **Plays/librettos/scripts.**
Political ramifications of British realist theatre. Lang.: Eng.
3297
1956-1990.   **Plays/librettos/scripts.**
Contemporary English drama. Lang.: Fre.   3296
1956-1994.   **Design/technology.**
Interview with scenographer Jocelyn Herbert. London. Lang.:
Eng.   232
1956-1994.   **Plays/librettos/scripts.**
John Osborne's *Look Back in Anger* and the symbolic figure of
the Angry Young Man. Lang.: Eng.   3313
1956-1995.   **Plays/librettos/scripts.**
Sourcebook on British plays and playwrights. Lang.: Eng. 3288
1956-1996.   **Plays/librettos/scripts.**
Black or white actors in the role of Othello. Lang.: Eng. 1107
1957.   **Plays/librettos/scripts.**
Graham Greene's screen adaptation of Shaw's *Saint Joan*.
Lang.: Eng.   3647
1957-1996.   **Plays/librettos/scripts.**
Playwrights Harold Pinter and Ariel Dorfman. Chile. Lang.:
Eng.   2853
1958-1996.   **Performance/production.**
Choreographer Richard Wheelock. Hagen. Lang.: Ger.   1426
1959-1960.   **Performance/production.**
Recollections of opera performances at Covent Garden. London.
Lang.: Eng.   4224
1959-1994.   **Performance/production.**
Productions of Arnold Wesker's *The Kitchen* by Stephen Daldry
and John Dexter. London. Lang.: Eng.   2519
1959-1995.   **Plays/librettos/scripts.**
Sexuality and women's theatre. USA. Lang.: Eng.   1105
1959-1996.   **Relation to other fields.**
Sleep and dreams in performances of Paul Gilchrist. Lang.: Eng.
3820
1960-1995.   **Plays/librettos/scripts.**
Self-repetition in plays of David Storey. Lang.: Eng.   3300
1960-1996.   **Performance/production.**
Banner Theatre Company and English alternative theatre.
Lang.: Eng.   992

Survey of Britten's opera *A Midsummer Night's Dream*. Lang.:
Eng.   4225

Olympia Dukakis' role in *The Hope Zone* by Kevin Heelan at Circle Rep. New York, NY. Lang.: Eng. 2678

1960-1996. Plays/librettos/scripts.
The revival of Mart Crowley's *The Boys in the Band*. New York, NY. Lang.: Eng. 3368

The Sam Shepard season at Signature Theatre company. Lang.: Eng. 3429

Interview with Albert Hague, musical theatre professional. New York, NY. Lang.: Eng. 3995

The collaboration of composer Harvey Schmidt and librettist/lyricist Tom Jones. Lang.: Eng. 3998

1960-1996. Theory/criticism.
Gay and lesbian studies, performance, and criticism. New York, NY. Lang.: Eng. 1377

Nudity and vulnerability in performance art. Lang.: Eng. 3826

1961-1965. Performance/production.
Puppets, Human Movement, and dance in Philippe Genty's *Voyageur Immobile (Motionless Traveler)*. Chicago, IL. Paris. Lang.: Eng. 4415

1961-1996. Performance/production.
Cabaret in London. New York, NY. Lang.: Eng. 3733

Lowell Liebermann, composer of the opera *The Picture of Dorian Gray*. New York, NY. Monte Carlo. Lang.: Eng. 4254

1962-1996. Administration.
Broadway producer Julian Schlossberg. New York, NY. Lang.: Eng. 121

1962-1996. Performance/production.
Profile, interview with baritone Dwayne Croft. Cooperstown, NY. Lang.: Eng. 4260

1963-1996. Theory/criticism.
The use of extended previews as a means of avoiding negative reviews. Lang.: Eng. 1386

1964. Plays/librettos/scripts.
God and man in Arthur Miller's *After the Fall*. 3405

1964-1984. Plays/librettos/scripts.
Realism and the plays of Baraka and August Wilson. Lang.: Eng. 3334

1964-1995. Performance spaces.
The renovation and expansion of Actors' Theatre of Louisville. Louisville, KY. Lang.: Eng. 1892

1964-1996. Institutions.
Profile of Mill Mountain Theatre. Roanoke, VA. Lang.: Eng. 1882

1964-1996. Performance/production.
Actor/singer John Davidson. New York, NY. Lang.: Eng. 3945

1964-1996. Plays/librettos/scripts.
Guilt and responsibility in later plays of Arthur Miller. 3420

1964-1996. Relation to other fields.
Critique of attacks on media and industrial culture, with references to performance art. Lang.: Eng. 3572

1965. Performance/production.
Opera Company of Boston's *Intolleranza* by Nono—directed by Sarah Caldwell, designed by Josef Svoboda. Boston, MA. Lang.: Eng. 4295

1965-1994. Institutions.
History of Teatro de la Esperanza. Santa Barbara, CA. Lang.: Eng. 576

1965-1995. Performance spaces.
Post-modern performance: Forced Entertainment, Brith Grof, Fiona Templeton. Sheffield. London. UK-Wales. New York, NY. Lang.: Eng. 3703

1965-1995. Performance/production.
Career of actor/singer Ben Vereen. Lang.: Eng. 3967

1965-1996. Performance/production.
Singer/actor John Cullum. New York, NY. Lang.: Eng. 3935

Tommy Tune's career in musical theatre. Lang.: Eng. 3970

1965-1996. Plays/librettos/scripts.
Career of playwright Adrienne Kennedy. Lang.: Eng. 3448

1966-1996. Institutions.
Thirtieth anniversary of *TCI* and the NY Public Library for the Performing Arts. New York, NY. Lang.: Eng. 568

Theatre companies devoted to new plays: BoarsHead and Purple Rose. Chelsea, MI. Lang.: Eng. 1869

1966-1996. Performance/production.
Profile, interview with soprano Denyce Graves. Lang.: Eng. 4253

Countenor David Daniels. Lang.: Eng. 4292

The cross-fertilization of opera and musical comedy. Lang.: Eng. 4294

1966-1996. Relation to other fields.
Crisis and the performing arts. Canada. Lang.: Fre. 1147

1967. Performance/production.
Recollections of making the musical film *Thoroughly Modern Millie*. Lang.: Eng. 3638

1967-1987. Theory/criticism.
Charles Ludlam's Ridiculous Theatrical Company, and gay and lesbian politics. New York, NY. Lang.: Eng. 1376

1967-1990. Performance/production.
Montage structure in plays of American ethnic minorities. Lang.: Eng. 2675

1967-1992. Performance/production.
Show tunes recorded by rock singers. England. Lang.: Eng. 3980

1967-1996. Performance/production.
Singer/actress Leslie Uggams. New York, NY. Lang.: Eng. 3936

The musical *Mata Hari* by Jerome Coopersmith, Edward Thomas, and Martin Charnin. New York, NY. Lang.: Eng. 3948

1967-1996. Relation to other fields.
Interview with Richard Schechner about performance art. Lang.: Dan. 3822

1968-1983. Plays/librettos/scripts.
The influence of Buddhism on playwright Jean-Claude Van Itallie. India. Lang.: Eng. 3419

1968-1991. Plays/librettos/scripts.
Morality and social order in TV crime drama. Lang.: Eng. 3684

1968-1994. Performance/production.
The emerging South African feminist theatres. UK. Cape Town. Lang.: Eng. 959

1968-1995. Performance/production.
Feminism and politics in Chicana collective theatre. Lang.: Eng. 2689

1968-1995. Relation to other fields.
Responses of theatre and performance to social and political conditions. Yugoslavia. Lang.: Eng. 3821

1968-1996. Administration.
Broadway producers Michael David, Ed Strong, and Sherman Warner. New York, NY. Lang.: Eng. 102

1968-1996. Performance/production.
George Jellinek's radio show *The Vocal Scene*. New York, NY. Lang.: Eng. 3578

Singer/actress Elaine Page. London. New York, NY. Lang.: Eng. 3925

1968-1996. Plays/librettos/scripts.
The characters of *The Boys in the Band* by Mart Crowley. Lang.: Eng. 3358

1969-1981. Institutions.
The history of Squat Theatre. Budapest. New York, NY. Lang.: Eng. 485

1969-1996. Performance/production.
Profile of Joseph Chaikin, with emphasis on *1969 Terminal 1996*. New York, NY. Lang.: Eng. 1065

1970. Performance/production.
Interview with actress and administrator Josie Mae Dotson. Los Angeles, CA. Lang.: Eng. 2635

Interview with actress Gertrude Jeannette. Lang.: Eng. 2656

1970-1979. Performance/production.
Women's performance art and theatre. Lang.: Eng. 1017

1970-1987. Plays/librettos/scripts.
Librettist/lyricist Michael Stewart. UK-England. Lang.: Eng. 3994

1970-1992. Theory/criticism.
Performance analysis of Los Angeles riots. Los Angeles, CA. Lang.: Eng. 1393

1970-1995. Institutions.
Modern ballet in the Kennedy Center's jubilee season. Washington, DC. Lang.: Hun. 1494

The Michigan Opera of Detroit's new house. Detroit, MI. Lang.: Eng. 4065

1970-1996. Design/technology.
Lighting designer Ken Billington. New York, NY. Lang.: Eng. 274

1970-1996. Performance/production.
Physical centers as an aspect of characterization in acting. Lang.: Eng. 1043

Interview with playwright/director Eve Ensler on *The Vagina Monologues*. Lang.: Eng. 2631

Singer/actress Janie Sell. New York, NY. Lang.: Eng. 3949

Melba Moore's role in *Les Misérables*. New York, NY. Lang.: Eng. 3963

Pop star Mariah Carey. New York, NY. Lang.: Rus. 3977

Interview with bass Samuel Ramey. Lang.: Hun. 4264

1970-1996. **Plays/librettos/scripts.**
Career of playwright and lyricist Vy Higgensen. New York, NY. Lang.: Eng. 3996

Composer Larry Grossman. Lang.: Eng. 3997

1971-1972. **Plays/librettos/scripts.**
Influence of Ted Hughes' poetry on playwright Sam Shepard. Lang.: Eng. 3412

1971-1996. **Design/technology.**
Scene designer Brian Thomson. Australia. New York, NY. Lang.: Eng. 3885

1971-1996. **Performance/production.**
The twenty-fifth anniversary of the Theatre Hall of Fame. New York, NY. Lang.: Eng. 1051

Pilobolus Dance Theatre, Michael Tracy, artistic director. New York, NY. Lang.: Eng. 1447

Obituary for musician and actor Tupac Shakur. Lang.: Eng. 3719

1972-1980. **Plays/librettos/scripts.**
The inland sea in plays of David Mamet. Lang.: Eng. 3390

1972-1984. **Plays/librettos/scripts.**
Stage plays performed on radio. UK-England. Lang.: Eng. 3583

1972-1992. **Plays/librettos/scripts.**
The 'performative realism' of playwright David Mamet. Lang.: Eng. 3422

1972-1994. **Performance/production.**
The creation of a production based on the history of Carbondale's Women's Center. Carbondale, IL. Lang.: Eng. 2654

1972-1995. **Performance/production.**
The performing and recording career of Patti LuPone. England. Lang.: Eng. 3968

1972-1996. **Institutions.**
Lynne Meadow and Barry Grove on Manhattan Theatre Club's twenty-fifth anniversary. New York, NY. Lang.: Eng. 1868

1972-1996. **Plays/librettos/scripts.**
Theatricality as sociopolitical commentary in plays of Mamet and Tremblay. Canada. Lang.: Eng. 2825

1973-1994. **Performance/production.**
Dancer and choreographer Twyla Tharp. Lang.: Hun. 1451

1973-1996. **Performance/production.**
Cultural bias in vocal training and feminist performances of Shakespeare. London. Lang.: Eng. 2542

Composer David Shire and lyricist Richard Maltby, Jr. New York, NY. Lang.: Eng. 3930

The Pointer Sisters in *Ain't Misbehavin'*. Lang.: Eng. 3957

1974-1995. **Performance/production.**
History of the filming of *Evita*. UK-England. Lang.: Eng. 3639

1974-1996. **Institutions.**
Profile of Steppenwolf Theatre Company. Chicago, IL. Lang.: Eng. 1862

1975. **Performance/production.**
Stuart Ostrow's experience assisting Bob Fosse in original choreography for *Chicago*. New York, NY. Lang.: Eng. 3975

1975-1996. **Performance/production.**
The Broadway revival of the musical *Chicago*. New York, NY. Lang.: Eng. 3939

Off-Broadway musicals and their transfer to Broadway. New York, NY. Lang.: Eng. 3954

Portrait of tenor Neil Shicoff. Lang.: Ger. 4289

1975-1996. **Plays/librettos/scripts.**
Analysis of *Oleanna* and *The Cryptogram* by David Mamet. Lang.: Eng. 3401

1976-1991. **Plays/librettos/scripts.**
'Chaos-informed' realism in the plays of David Rabe and Sam Shepard. Lang.: Eng. 3355

1976-1992. **Research/historiography.**
Computerized dance notation and analysis. Hungary. Lang.: Hun. 1463

1976-1996. **Performance/production.**
Sarah Jessica Parker's role in *Once Upon a Mattress*. New York, NY. Lang.: Eng. 3942

Actress/singer Andrea McArdle. Lang.: Eng. 3946

1977-1982. **Performance/production.**
History of the TV series *Lou Grant*. Lang.: Eng. 3676

1977-1995. **Performance/production.**
Excerpts from conference papers on ritual, theatre, and performance art. Japan. New York, NY. Lang.: Eng. 872

1977-1996. **Design/technology.**
Set designer Linda Buchanan. Chicago, IL. Lang.: Eng. 311

1977-1996. **Performance/production.**
Theatre production in Florida. Boca Raton, FL. Lang.: Eng. 1023

1978-1994. **Plays/librettos/scripts.**
Bibliography of scholarship devoted to playwright William Congreve. UK-England. Lang.: Eng. 3280

1978-1996. **Basic theatrical documents.**
Revised text of *Buried Child* by Sam Shepard. Lang.: Eng. 1703

1978-1996. **Institutions.**
Jeff Daniels' experience acting in *Fifth of July* at Circle Rep. New York, NY. Lang.: Eng. 1864

1979-1995. **Performance/production.**
Essays and reviews of post-modern theatre. Lang.: Eng. 2627

1979-1995. **Plays/librettos/scripts.**
Analysis of *spell #7* by Ntozake Shange. Lang.: Eng. 3352

1979-1996. **Institutions.**
Profile of the International Hispanic Theatre Festival. Miami, FL. Lang.: Eng. 609

Actors' Theatre of Louisville, Jon Jory, artistic director. Louisville, KY. Lang.: Eng. 1866

1979-1996. **Performance/production.**
Productions of the Comédie-Française at Brooklyn Academy of Music. New York, NY. Paris. Lang.: Eng. 2650

Review of the film version of the musical *Evita*. Lang.: Eng. 3636

1980-1989. **Performance/production.**
Tendencies in avant-garde theatre. Canada. Lang.: Fre. 723

1980-1989. **Plays/librettos/scripts.**
Recollections of meetings with playwright Athol Fugard. New York, NY. Lang.: Eng. 3457

1980-1994. **Plays/librettos/scripts.**
Analysis of *Tracers* by John DiFusco and its critical reception. Lang.: Eng. 3379

1980-1995. **Performance/production.**
Essays on contemporary performance. Europe. Lang.: Eng. 790

1980-1996. **Design/technology.**
Set designer Van Santvoord. New York, NY. Lang.: Eng. 289

Career of set and costume designer Felix E. Cochren. New York, NY. Lang.: Eng. 1742

1980-1996. **Institutions.**
Sydné Mahone, director of play development, Crossroads Theatre. New Brunswick, NJ. Lang.: Eng. 604

1980-1996. **Performance/production.**
Musical theatre director Jerry Zaks. New York, NY. Lang.: Eng. 3953

Singer/actor Jason Graae. Lang.: Eng. 3962

Lenny Suib, director and founder of Puppet Playhouse. New York, NY. Lang.: Eng. 4411

1981. **Theory/criticism.**
Feminist criticism and the plays of Heiner Müller. Europe. Lang.: Swe. 1389

1981-1989. **Plays/librettos/scripts.**
Realism, the feminist agenda, and recent plays by women. Lang.: Eng. 3384

1981-1991. **Institutions.**
Chronology of works and events presented by Tangente. Montreal, PQ. New York, NY. Lang.: Fre. 1405

1981-1995. **Plays/librettos/scripts.**
Presentations by story-tellers at women playwrights conference. Australia. Philippines. Lang.: Eng. 1083

Brechtian/feminist analysis of plays by Maria Irene Fornes. Lang.: Eng. 3376

1981-1996. **Performance/production.**
Graciela Daniele's dance adaptation of *Chronicle of a Death Foretold* by Gabriel García Márquez. New York, NY. Lang.: Eng. 1446

1982.   **Basic theatrical documents.**
Text of *The Green Belt* by Charles Johnson. Lang.: Eng.   3661
1982-1986.   **Plays/librettos/scripts.**
Critique of Steven Spielberg's film adaptation of *The Color Purple* by Alice Walker. Lang.: Eng.   3649
1982-1989.   **Performance/production.**
The decline of experimental theatre in Quebec. Canada. Lang.: Fre.   712
1982-1996.   **Design/technology.**
Scenery West, custom set and prop makers. Hollywood, CA. Lang.: Eng.   3600
1982-1996.   **Institutions.**
The adventurous repertoire of the Portland Opera. Portland, OR. Lang.: Eng.   4064
1982-1996.   **Plays/librettos/scripts.**
Blues music in *Ma Rainey's Black Bottom* by August Wilson. Lang.: Eng.   3365
1983-1996.   **Institutions.**
Northern Kentucky University's 'Y.E.S.' Festival of new plays. Highland Heights, KY. Lang.: Eng.   1883
1983-1996.   **Performance/production.**
Actor John Rubinstein. New York, NY. Lang.: Eng.   2595
Interview with director Patrice Chéreau. Lang.: Eng.   2649
Interview with performance artist Holly Hughes. New York, NY. Lang.: Eng.   3799
1984-1987.   **Performance/production.**
Analysis of Suzanne Lacy's *The Crystal Quilt*. Minneapolis, MN. Lang.: Eng.   3798
1984-1991.   **Audience.**
Effect of classroom drama and theatre attendance on children's interpretation of theatre. Tempe, AZ. Lang.: Eng.   143
1984-1992.   **Basic theatrical documents.**
Collection of southern plays from Actors' Theatre of Louisville. Lang.: Eng.   1688
1984-1993.   **Performance/production.**
Representation of the female body in Omaha Magic Theatre productions. Omaha, NE. Lang.: Eng.   2610
1984-1996.   **Performance/production.**
Profiles of groups using improvisational comedy competitions. Lang.: Eng.   2630
1984-1996.   **Plays/librettos/scripts.**
Interview with playwright Craig Lucas. New York, NY. Lang.: Eng.   3427
1985.   **Plays/librettos/scripts.**
Race relations and *Miss Evers' Boys* by David Feldshuh. Lang.: Eng.   3325
1985-1996.   **Design/technology.**
Lighting designer Chad McArver. New York, NY. Lang.: Eng.   288
Sound designer Tony Meola. New York, NY. Lang.: Eng.   3898
1985-1996.   **Performance/production.**
Highlights of interviews with Broadway stars. New York, NY. Lang.: Eng.   2601
1986-1987.   **Performance/production.**
Suzanne Burgoyne's experiments in intercultural performance. Brussels. Omaha, NE. Lang.: Eng.   1911
1986-1994.   **Plays/librettos/scripts.**
Plays about politician Roy Cohn. Lang.: Eng.   3339
1986-1995.   **Basic theatrical documents.**
Collection of plays from the Humana Festival. Lang.: Eng.   1687
1986-1996.   **Institutions.**
Profile of Cornerstone Theatre. Lang.: Eng.   1870
Chicano theatre groups. Los Angeles, CA. Lang.: Eng.   1880
The development of the Los Angeles Music Center Opera. Los Angeles, CA. Lang.: Eng.   4062
1987.   **Plays/librettos/scripts.**
Telson and Breuer's *The Gospel at Colonus* and the problems of multiculturalism. Lang.: Eng.   3425
1987-1995.   **Performance/production.**
Profile of New World Performance Laboratory. Cleveland, OH. Lang.: Eng.   1075
1987-1996.   **Institutions.**
Community plays of Swamp Gravy. Colquitt, GA. Lang.: Eng.   578
1987-1996.   **Performance/production.**
Fundraising of Broadway Cares/Equity Fights AIDS. New York, NY. Lang.: Eng.   1052

1988.   **Basic theatrical documents.**
Text of *Savage Wilds* by Ishmael Reed. Lang.: Eng.   1700
1988.   **Plays/librettos/scripts.**
Pregnancy in plays of Adrienne Kennedy. Lang.: Eng.   3329
1988-1996.   **Performance/production.**
Interview with street theatre artist Thomas Riccio. Lang.: Eng.   1067
Actor/singer Brian Stokes Mitchell. Canada. Lang.: Eng.   3929
Actor Daniel Jenkins. New York, NY. Lang.: Eng.   3937
1988-1996.   **Plays/librettos/scripts.**
Grassroots theatres' productions of plays with environmental themes. Lang.: Eng.   3346
1989.   **Performance/production.**
Rationalism and the realist school of acting. Canada. UK-England. Lang.: Fre.   1938
Interview with Richard Schechner. New York, NY. Lang.: Eng.   2651
Interview with director George C. Wolfe about *Bring in 'Da Noise, Bring in 'Da Funk*. New York, NY. Lang.: Eng.   3951
1989-1993.   **Plays/librettos/scripts.**
Analysis of *She Talks to Beethoven* by Adrienne Kennedy. Lang.: Eng.   3396
1989-1995.   **Performance/production.**
Dancer Margaret Illmann. Canada. Lang.: Eng.   1497
1989-1996.   **Institutions.**
Gypsy of the Year competition, a fundraiser for Broadway Cares/Equity Fights AIDS. New York, NY. Lang.: Eng.   598
1989-1996.   **Performance/production.**
Panel discussion on Romanian performing arts. New York, NY. Romania. Lang.: Eng.   1061
42nd St. Moon, Greg MacKellan and Stephanie Rhoads, artistic directors. San Francisco, CA. Lang.: Eng.   3974
1989-1996.   **Plays/librettos/scripts.**
Terrence McNally's *The Lisbon Traviata* and gay male representation in mainstream theatre. New York, NY. Lang.: Eng.   3321
1990.   **Performance/production.**
Comparison of American and Canadian comic styles. Canada. Lang.: Fre.   3832
The new generation of tenors. Europe. Lang.: Swe.   4113
1990.   **Relation to other fields.**
How performance festivals can give a sense of the host city. Tampa, FL. Lang.: Eng.   1278
1990.   **Theory/criticism.**
Critical misrepresentation of *Falsettoland* by William Finn and James Lapine. Lang.: Eng.   4002
1990-1991.   **Performance/production.**
Rehearsals of Wooster Group's adaptation of Čechov, *Brace Up!*. New York, NY. Lang.: Fre.   2655
1990-1993.   **Performance/production.**
Analysis of the appeal of the singer-actress Madonna. Lang.: Eng.   3682
1990-1994.   **Performance/production.**
Operatic and sporting elements in the 'three tenors' concerts. Rome. Los Angeles, CA. Lang.: Eng.   4172
1990-1995.   **Institutions.**
Opera Company of Philadelphia's creation of its own scene shop. Philadelphia, PA. Lang.: Eng.   4066
1990-1995.   **Plays/librettos/scripts.**
Latina lesbian subjectivity in works of Marga Gomez. Lang.: Eng.   3436
1990-1996.   **Institutions.**
Atlanta Theatre offerings for Olympic Arts Festival. Atlanta, GA. Lang.: Eng.   585
Théâtre de Complicité's U.S. tour with *The Three Lives of Lucie Cabrol*. London. Lang.: Eng.   608
1990-1996.   **Performance/production.**
Media and technology in Wooster Group's *Fish Story*. New York, NY. Lang.: Ger.   1048
The Western Wayne Players prison theatre workshop group. Plymouth, MI. Lang.: Eng.   2586
Interview with actor Campbell Scott. San Diego, CA. Lang.: Eng.   2622
Puppetry on *Mystery Science Theatre 3000*. Hollywood, CA. Lang.: Eng.   3681
1990-1996.   **Plays/librettos/scripts.**
Symbolism in *The Swan* by Elizabeth Egloff and its French translation at Espace GO. Montreal, PQ. Lang.: Fre.   2824

Venezuela
 1945-1959. **Plays/librettos/scripts.**
  Cuban writer Alejo Carpentier and his work in Venezuela.
  Caracas. Cuba. Lang.: Spa. 3467
 1971-1996. **Institutions.**
  History of Grupo Rajatabla. Caracas. Lang.: Spa. 613
 1995. **Plays/librettos/scripts.**
  Analysis of *El día que me quieras (The Day You'll Love Me)* by
  José Ignacio Cabrujas. Lang.: Spa. 3468
 1996. **Relation to other fields.**
  Theatricality of rituals devoted to María Lionza. Yaracuy.
  Lang.: Eng. 1286
Vietnam
 1996. **Performance/production.**
  Vietnamese water puppetry at UNIMA festival. Lang.: Hun.
   4420
Wales
 SEE
  UK-Wales.
Yugoslavia
 1918-1941. **Performance/production.**
  Directors at National Drama Theatre in the interwar period.
  Ljubljana. Lang.: Slo. 2700
 1931-1958. **Institutions.**
  History of Lutkovno gledališče Primskovo, Primskovo Puppet
  Theatre. Primskovo. Lang.: Slo. 4386
 1946-1995. **Performance/production.**
  The career of performance artist Marina Abramovic. Lang.: Eng.
   3809
 1948-1964. **Performance/production.**
  Jože Pengov and the history of Slovene puppetry. Lang.: Slo.
   4421
 1949-1959. **Institutions.**
  Hungarian theatre in Voivodship. Hungary. Lang.: Hun. 464
 1950-1969. **Plays/librettos/scripts.**
  Perspectivism in Slovene drama. Lang.: Slo. 3469
 1968-1995. **Relation to other fields.**
  Responses of theatre and performance to social and political
  conditions. USA. Lang.: Eng. 3821
 1974-1996. **Relation to other fields.**
  Interview with performance artist Marina Abramovic. Lang.:
  Eng. 3824

 1978. **Relation to other fields.**
  Nationalism as paranoia, even in the arts. Lang.: Eng. 1289
 1978-1995. **Performance/production.**
  Belgrade's political theatre activities. Belgrade. Lang.: Eng.
   1079
 1991. **Performance/production.**
  Upstart Stage's production of *The Professional (Profesionalac)*
  by Dušan Kovačević. Berkeley, CA. Lang.: Eng. 2588
 1991. **Relation to other fields.**
  Actress Mira Furlan on refusing to take sides in ethnic conflict.
  Lang.: Eng. 1288
 1992-1995. **Relation to other fields.**
  Interview with theatre scholar who gave up her position at the
  University of Belgrade. Lang.: Eng. 1290
 1994-1996. **Plays/librettos/scripts.**
  Analysis of *Bure barut (The Powder Keg)* by Rejan Dukovski.
  Belgrade. Lang.: Ger. 3470
 1996. **Institutions.**
  Impressions of the Bitef festival. Belgrade. Lang.: Ger. 614
 1996. **Relation to other fields.**
  Artists of the former Yugoslavia discuss the impact of the
  political situation on their art. Lang.: Ger. 1287

  Theatre and the disintegration of Yugoslavia. Lang.: Eng. 1291

  Interview with playwright Slobodan Šnajder about intellectuals
  and the war in the former Yugoslavia. Lang.: Ger. 3523
Zambia
 1992-1994. **Performance/production.**
  Leila Peltonen's puppetry work in Zambia with Travelcase
  Theatre. Lang.: Eng. 4422
 1995-1996. **Performance/production.**
  Imipashi (The Spirits): a touring production of the national
  Liitooma Project. Lang.: Eng. 1080
Zimbabwe
 1994-1996. **Performance/production.**
  Review of *Simuka Zimbabwe! (Zimbabwe Arise!)* by Zambuko/
  Izibuko. Harare. Lang.: Afr. 2701

DOCUMENT AUTHORS INDEX

Abah, Oga Steve.　1215
Ábel, Péter, ed.　3613
Abel, Sam.　3321, 4172
Åberg, Tommy.　649
Åberg, Ulla.　1848
Ábrahám, Eszter.　4372
Abraham, James T.　3226
Abramovic, Marina.　3801
Abrams, Steve.　4407
Acconci, Vito.　3801
Acker, Kathy.　55
Ackerman, Marianne.　1756, 2738
Ackermann, Renate.　4361
Acton, David.　871
Adam, Marthe.　4388
Adamson, Ginette.　3065
Added, Serge.　2007
Adler, Thomas P.　3322, 3323
Ahrends, Günter.　141
Aiello, Peter.　4224
Akerman, Anthony.　2140
Akimov, Nikolaj P.　2186
Al', D.N.　3182
Al'tšuller, A.　900
Albert, István.　838
Albert, Pál.　794, 2008, 2093
Alberti, Carmelo, ed.　3109
Albertová, Helena.　1167, 2870
Albright, William.　4060
Alekseeva, E.　2187
Alexander, William.　2586
Alfons, Gerd.　616
Alkalay-Gut, Karen.　3093
Alkema, Hanny.　883
Allen, Michelle.　2739, 2740
Allen, Norman.　1005, 2587, 3928
Allinson, M.E.　3227
Allison, John M., Jr.　1371
Alonge, Roberto.　675, 2009, 3110
Altena, Herman, transl., ed., annot.　1662
Alter, Nora M.　3153
Amaspjurjanc, Abri.　2188
Ananya.　1433
Andersen, Merete Morken.　3155
Anderson, John D.　1252
Anderson, Lisa M.　3829
Anderson, Robert.　3984
Andersson, Bibi.　1848, 2274
Andreasen, John.　2873
Andrès, Bernard.　1320
Androvskaja, Ol'ga N.　2133
Angelo, Gregory.　3929
Ångström, Anna.　1402
Anthony, Susan.　3324
Anyanwu, Joseph Chika.　3683

Appler, Keith.　3325
Apter, Emily.　795
Arbo-Cyber, théâtre (?).　3654
Arbour, Rose Marie.　1136
Archambault, François.　2741
Archipov, Ju.　2727
Ardašnikova, Ariadna.　2189
Armstrong, Alan.　4314
Arnold, Skip.　3801
Arnott, Peter D.　2710
Arrell, Doug.　348
Artioli, Umberto.　2978
Artoni, Ambrogio.　3764
Asel, Harald.　419
Ashbrook, William.　4328
Ashbrook, William, transl.　4121
Ashford, John.　1598
Astington, John H.　2875
Aston, Elaine.　960, 3279
Atkinson, William.　3076
Aubry, Suzanne.　2742
Ault, Tom.　647
Auslander, Philip.　55, 778, 1372
Aveline, Joe.　241
Avigal, Shosh.　3094, 3095, 3096
Azparren Jiménez, Leonardo.　876
B, Mats.　3717
Babb, Roger.　1006
Bablet, Denis.　890
Backalenick, Irene.　242, 1007, 3326, 3986
Bacon, Wallace A.　1373
Baeva, A.　4195
Bagration-Muhraneli, Irina.　2190
Baiardo, Enrico.　134
Bailey, Peter.　3922
Bain, Keith.　2265
Bak, John S.　3327
Baker, David J.　4304, 4329
Baker, Dennis J.　4072
Baker, Evan.　4132
Baker, Stuart E.　3510
Baku, Shango.　1914
Balassa, Anna, et al.　3471
Baldo, Jonathan.　2876
Baldridge, Charlene.　567
Baldwyn, Lucy.　3797
Balme, Christopher B.　1170
Balogh, Anikó.　4040
Balogh, Géza.　4378
Balvín, Josef.　1901
Balykina, N.　901
Bancroft, Vicky.　2877
Banfield, Chris.　779, 2500
Banham, Martin.　3528
Baniewicz, Elżbieta.　2146, 2147, 3158

Banks, Stephen P.　1374
Bános, Tibor.　1197
Banu, Georges.　648
Barácius, Zoltán.　464
Baranyi, Ferenc.　4326
Barba, Eugenio.　397, 944
Barbina, Alfredo, ed.　860
Barbour, David.　183, 186, 222, 223, 243, 244,
　　245, 246, 247, 248, 249, 250, 251, 252,
　　568, 1716, 1717, 1718, 1719, 1720, 1721,
　　1722, 1723, 1724, 1725, 1726, 1727,
　　1728, 1729, 1730, 3697, 3890, 3894,
　　3895, 3896, 3897, 3898
Barbour, Sheena, ed.　1127
Bardadym, V.P.　3862
Bardijewska, Liliana.　4397
Barish, Jonas.　2878
Barker, Clive.　961
Barker, John W.　4245
Barlow, Judith E.　3328
Barnes, Peter.　1683
Barnett, Claudia.　3329, 3330
Barnett, Dennis.　2588
Barnett, Douglas O.　1277
Barnwell, Michael.　2589
Baron, Katarzyna, transl.　891
Barranger, Milly S.　2010
Barrett, Patrick.　187
Barry, Barbara R.　4300
Barth, Claudia.　420
Barth, Diana.　2115, 2116, 2117, 2501, 2502,
　　2503
Bartha, László, photo.　478
Bartlett, Laurence.　3280
Bartolazzi, Marita.　3111
Barton, Robert.　1008
Bartošević, A.　2191
Barzun, Jacques.　3281
Bassiri, Amadou.　3331
Bassnett, Susan.　1986
Basting, Anne Davis.　3798
Bauer, Wolfgang Maria.　1657
Bawcutt, N.W., ed.　2879
Baxter, Robert.　4173
Baxter, Virginia.　1082
Beach, Cecilia, comp.　3474
Bean, Annemarie.　3742
Beard, Jane.　1018
Beardsell, Peter.　3144
Beauchamp, Hélène.　619, 1137, 1321, 1394,
　　1917, 3501, 3749
Beaulne, Martine.　700
Beausoleil, Claude.　1138
Beaven, Pat.　1404
Bechtel, Roger.　3332

FINDING LIST OF PERIODICAL TITLES WITH ACRONYMS

FINDING LIST OF PERIODICAL TITLES WITH ACRONYMS

Botteghe della Fantasia, Le ... BFant
Bouffonneries ... Bouff
Brecht Jahrbuch ... BrechtJ
Brecht Yearbook ... BY
British Performing Arts Newsletter ... BPAN
British Theatrelog ... BTlog
Broadside ... Brs
Buenos Aires Musical ... BAMu
Bühne, Die ... Buhne
Bühne Kursbuch Kultur ... Bkk
Bühne und Parkett ... BPTV
Bühnen- und Musikrecht ... BuM
Bühnengenossenschaft ... BGs
Bühnentarifrecht ... Buhnent
Bühnentechnische Rundschau ... BtR
Builder N.S. ... BNS
Bulletin ... BulS
Bulletin ... BulV
Bulletin ASSITEJ ... BASSITEJ
Bulletin de la Société Paul Claudel ... BSPC
Bulleti Magisch Plätze ... BMP
Bulletin of the Comediantes ... BCom
Bulletin of the School of Oriental & African Studies ... BSOAS
Bulletin: Van het Belgisch Centrum ITI ... BelgITI
Bundesverband Studentische Kulturarbeit ... BSK
Burlington Magazine ... BM
Cabra, La ... CRT
Cahiers Césairiens ... CahiersC
Cahiers CERT/CIRCE ... CahiersCC
Cahiers de la Bibliothèque Gaston Baty ... CBGB
Cahiers de la Maison Jean Vilar ... CMJV
Cahiers de la NCT ... CNCT
Cahiers du Rideau ... CdRideau
Cahiers du Théâtre Populaire d'Amiens ... CTPA
Cahiers Jean Cocteau ... CJC
Cahiers Jean Giraudoux ... CJG
Cahiers Renaud Barrault ... CRB
Cahiers Théâtre Louvain ... CTL
California Theatre Annual ... CTA
Californian Shavian ... CShav
Call Board ... CB
Call Boy, The ... CallB
Callahan's Irish Quarterly ... CIQ
Callaloo: A Black South Journal of Arts and Letters ... Callaloo
Callboard ... Callboard
Calliope ... Calliope
Cambridge Opera Journal ... COJ
Canada on Stage ... CS
Canadian Drama/Art Dramatique Canadien ... CDr
Canadian Literature/Littérature Canadienne ... CanL
Canadian Theatre Review (Toronto) ... CTR
Canadian Theatre Checklist ... CTCheck
Canadian Theatre Review Yearbook (Downsview) ... CTRY
Caratula ... Caratula
Carnet ... Carnet
Castelets ... Castelets
Celcit ... Celcit
Čelovek ... Cel
Central Opera Service Bulletin ... COS
Ceskoslovenski Loutkar ... CeskL
Čest'imeju ... Cesti
Chhaya Nat ... Chhaya
Children's Theatre Review ... ChTR
Chinese Literature ... ChinL
Chronico ... Chronico
Cineschedario: Letture Drammatiche ... CineLD
Circus Report ... CircusR
Circuszeitung, Die ... Cz
Cirque dans l'Univers, Le ... CU
Città Aperta ... CittaA
City Arts Monthly ... CAM
City Limits ... CityL
Classical Journal, The ... ClassJ
Claudel Studies ... ClaudelS
Clipper Studies in the American Theater ... Clip
CLSU Journal of the Arts ... CLSUJ
Club ... Club
Coleçao Teatro ... ColecaoT
College English ... CE
College Language Association Journal ... CLAJ
Columbia-VLA Journal of Law & the Arts ... ColJL&A
Comédie de l'Ouest ... CO
Comédie-Française ... CF
Comedy ... Comedy
Communications from the International Brecht Society ... ComIBS
Comparative Drama ... CompD
Confessio ... Confes
Conjunto: Revista de Teatro Latinamericano ... Cjo
Connoisseur ... Con
Contact Quarterly ... ContactQ
Contemporary French Civilization ... CFT
Contenido ... Contenido
Continuum ... Contin
CORD Dance Research Annual ... CORD
Corps écrit ... CorpsE
Costume: The Journal of the Costume Society ... Costume
Courrier Dramatique de l'Ouest ... CDO
Courrier du Centre international d'études poétiques ... CCIEP
Čovašskoe iskusstvo, Voprosy teorii istorii ... CoviVt
Creative Drama ... CreD
Crépuscule, Le ... Crepuscl
Crisis ... Crisis
Critical Arts ... CrAr
Critical Digest ... CritD
Critical Quarterly ... CritQ
Critical Review ... CritR
Critique ... CritNY
Criticism ... Criticism
CSA News: The Newsletter of the Costume Society of America ... CSAN
Cuadernos El Publico ... Cuaderno
Cue New York ... CueNY
Cue, The ... CueM
Cue International ... Cue
Cultural Post ... CuPo
Culture et Communication ... CetC
Culture ... Culture
Current Writing ... CW
C'wan t'ong Xiju Yishu/Art of Traditional Opera ... CTXY
Dabei ... DABEI
Dalnij Vostok: (Far East) ... DalVostok
Dance and Dancers ... D&D
Dance Australia ... DA
Dance Chronicle ... DnC
Dance in Canada/Danse au Canada ... DC
Dance Magazine ... Dm
Dance Research ... DRs
Dance Research Journal ... DRJ
Dance Theatre Journal ... DTJ
Dancing Times ... DTi
Danstidningen ... Danst
David Mamet Review ... DMR
Dekorativnojė Iskusstvo SSR ... DekorIsk
Detskaja Literatura ... DetLit
Deutsche Bühne, Die ... DB
Deutsche Shakespeare Gesellschaft/Deutsche Shakespeare Gesellschaft West, Jahrbuch ... DShG
Deutsche Zeitschrift für Philosophie ... DZP
Deutsches Bühnenjahrbuch ... DBj
Deutsches Institut für Puppenspiel Forschung und Lehre ... DIPFL
Devlet Tijatrolari (State Theatres) ... Devlet
Dewan Budaya ... Dewan
Diadja Vanja. Literaturnij al'manah ... DVLa
Dialog: Miesiecznik Poswiecony Dramaturgii Wspolczesnej ... DialogW
Dialog ... DialogA
Dialog ... DialogR
Dialogi ... Dialogi
Dialogue: Canadian Philosophical Review ... Dialogue
Dialogue (Tunisia) ... DialogTu
Dioniso ... Dioniso
Directors Notes ... DirNotes
Diskurs ... Diskurs
Diskurs ... DRostock
Divadelni Noviny ... DiN
Divadelní revue ... DivR
Divadlo: Theatre ... DTh
Dix-Huitième Siècle ... DHS
Dix-Septième Siècle ... DSS
Dockteatereko ... Dockt
Documentation Théâtrale ... DocTh
Documents del Centre Dramatic ... DCD
Documents of the Slovenian Theatre and Film Museum ... DSTFM
DOE ... DOE
Dokumenti Slovenskega Gledaliskega Muzeja ... DSGM
Don Saturio: Boletin Informativo de Teatro Gallego ... DSat
Dong-Guk Dramatic Art ... DongukDA
Drama and the School ... DSchool
Drama and Theater ... D&T
Drama and Theatre Newsletter ... DTN
Drama Review, The ... TDR
Drama Review ... DrRev
Drama: Nordisk dramapedagogisk tidsskrift ... DNDT
Drama: The Quarterly Theatre Review ... Drama
Drama ... DramaY
Dramat ... Dramat
Dramatherapy: SEE: Journal of Dramatherapy (JDt) ... Dtherapy
Dramatics ... DMC
Dramatists Guild Quarterly ... DGQ
Dramatists Sourcebook ... DSo
dRAMATURg ... dRAMATURg
Dramaturgi: Tedri Og Praksis ... DTOP
Dramma ... DrammaR
Dramma: Il Mensile dello Spettacolo ... DrammaT
Drammaturgia ... Drammaturgia
Dress ... Dress
Družba ... Druzba
Družba Narodov ... DruzNar
Dvatisoč 2000:časnik za mišljenje, umetnost, kulturna ... Dvat
Early Drama, Art, and Music Review, The ... EDAM
East Asian History ... EAH
Ebony ... Ebony
Echanges ... Echanges
Echo Planety ... EchoP
Economic Efficiency and the Performing Arts ... EE&PA
Economic History Review ... EHR
Economist Financial Report ... Econ
Editorial Nuevo Grupo ... ENG
Educational Theatre News ... ETN
Eire-Ireland ... Eire
Ekran ... Ekran
Elet és Irodalom: irodalmi es politkai hetilap ... ElI
Eletunk ... Elet
Elizabethan Theatre ... ETh
Empirical Research in Theatre ... ERT
Enact: monthly theatre magazine ... Enact
Encore (Australia) ... EncoreA
Encore (Georgia) ... Encore
Engekikai: Theatre World ... Egk
English Academy Review, The ... EAR
English in Africa ... EinA
English Literary Renaissance Journal ... ELR
English Studies in Africa ... ESA

FINDING LIST OF PERIODICAL TITLES WITH ACRONYMS

Title	Acronym
Korean Theatre Review	KTR
Kortárs	Kortars
Kraj smolenskij	Krajs
Kritika	Krit
Kronika	KZphK
Kulis	Kulis
Kultur-Journal	KJ
Kultura és Közösség	KesK
Kultura i Žizn (Culture and Life)	KZ
Kulturno-Prosvetitelnaja Rabota	KPR
Kultuurivihkot	Kvihkot
Kunst Bulletin	KB
Kurt Weill Newsletter	KWN
La Trobe Library Journal	LLJ
Labour History	LabH
Laientheater	Laien
Latin American Theatre Review	LATR
Lettera Dall'Italia	LettDI
Lettres Québécoises	LetQu
Letture: Libro e spettacolo	Letture
Leteraturnaja ucheba	Letuch
Light	Light
Lighting Design + Application	LD+A
Lighting Dimensions	LDim
Lik Cuvasija	LikC
Lilith:a Feminist History Journal	Lilith
Linzer Theaterzeitung	LinzerT
Lipika	Lipika
Literator: Journal of Comparative Literature and Linguistics	Literator
Literatura	Literatura
Literature & History	L&H
Literature/Film Quarterly	LFQ
Literature in North Queensland	LiNQ
Literature in Performance	LPer
Literaturnaja Gruzia	LitGruzia
Literaturnojë Obozrenijë	LO
Litva literaturnaja	Litva
Live	Live
Livres et Auteurs Québecois	LAQ
Loisir	Loisir
Lok Kala	LokK
London Theatre Record	LTR
Lowdown	Lowdown
Ludus	Ludus
Loutkar	Loutkar
Lutka	Lutka
Magazine du TNB	MdTNB
Magyar Iparművészet	MagIp
Magyar Múzeum	MagM
Maksla	Maksla
Mala Biblioteka Baletowa	MBB
Mamulengo	Mamulengo
Manadens Premiärer och Information	MPI
Manipulation	Manip
Marges, El	EIM
Marquee: The Journal of the Theatre Historical Society	MarqJTHS
Marquee	Marquee
Mask	Mask
MASKA	MASKA
Maske und Kothurn	MuK
Maske	Maske
Masque	Masque
Masterstvo	Mast
Material zum Theater	MT
Matya Prasanga	Matya
Meanjin	Meanjin
Media, Culture and Society	MC&S
Medieval and Renaissance Drama	MRenD
Medieval English Theatre	MET
Medieval Music-Drama News	MMDN
Meister des Puppenspiels	MeisterP
Meridian	Meridian
Merker, Der	Merker
Mestno gledališče Ljubljansko	MGL
Miedzynarodowny Rocznik Teatralny	MRT
Milliyet Sanat Dergisi	MSD
Mim: Revija za glumu i glumište	Mim
Mime Journal	MimeJ
Mime News	MimeN
Mimos	Mimos
Minority Voices	MV
Mitgliederzeitung	Mit
Mitteilungen der Puppentheatersammlung	MPSKD
Mitteilungen der Vereinigung	MdVO
Mobile	Mobile
Modern Austrian Literature	MAL
Modern Drama	MD
Modern International Drama	MID
Modern Language Review	MLR
Modern Philology	MP
Moja Moskva	MojM
Molodaja Gvardija	MolGvar
Molodoi Kommunist	MK
Monographs on Music, Dance and Theater in Asia	MMDTA
Monsalvat	Monsalvat
Monte Avilia	MAvilia
Monthly Diary	MoD
Monumenta Nipponica: Studies in Japanese Culture	MN
Moskovskij Nabljudatel'	MoskNab
Moskva	Mosk
Mozgó Világ	Mozgo
Mühely	Muhely
Münchener Beiträge zur Theaterwissenschaft	MBzT
Music & Letters	MLet
Music Hall	MHall
Musical Quarterly	MuQ
Musicals Das Musicalmagazin	MDM
Musical'naja Academija	MA
Musik & Teater	M&T
MusikDramatik	MuD
Musik und Gesellschaft	MusGes
Musik und Theater	MuT
Muzsika	Muzsika
Muzyka	Muzyka
Muzykal'naja akademija	MA
Muzykalnaja Žizn: (Musical Life)	MuZizn
My	My
Mykenae	Mykenae
Nadie Journal	NADIE
Näköpiiri	Nk
Naš Sovremennik	NasSovr
Nagyvilág	Nvilag
Napjaink	Napj
Narodna tvorchestvo	NTE
National Center for the Performing Arts	NCPA
Natrang	Natrang
Natya Kala	NKala
Natya Varta	NVarta
Natya	Natya
Nauka i Religija (Science and Religion)	NiR
Nauka v Rossii	NvR
Navi Prolog	NP
Naytelmauutiset	Nayt
Nederlands Theatre-en-Televisie Jaarboek	NTTJ
New Theatre Review, The	NTR
Neohelicon	Neoh
Nestroyana	Ns
Netherlands Centraal Bureau voor de Statistiek: Bezoek	NCBSBV
Netherlands Centraal Bureau voor de Statistiek: Muziek en Theater	NCBSMT
Neue Blätter des Theaters in Der Josefstadt	NBT
neue Merker, Der	neueM
Neue Musikzeitung	NMZ
Neva	Neva
New Contrasts	NC
New England Theatre Journal	NETJ
New Literatures Review	NLR
New Observations	NO
New Performance	NewPerf
New Theatre Australia	NTA
New Theatre Quarterly	NTQ
New Theatre Review	NTR
New York Onstage	NYO
New York Theatre Critics Review	NYTCR
New York Theatre Reviews	NYTR
New Yorker, The	NewY
NeWest Review	NWR
Newsletter of the ITI of the United States, Inc.	NITI
Nihon-Unima	NihonU
Nineteenth Century Music	NCM
Nineteenth Century Theatre	NCT
Nineteenth Century Theatre Research	NCTR
Nōgaku-kenkyū	NoK
Nōgaku Shiryo Shusei	NoSS
Noh	Noh
Nohgaku Times	NTimes
Nordic Theatre Studies	NTS
Notate	NIMBZ
Notes on Contemporary Literature	NConL
Nova revija	Novr
Novaja Rossija	NovRos
Novoe Vremija	NV
Novyj Mir	NovyjMir
Numero	Numero
Nya Teatertidningen	NT
Očag Semejnij Zurnal	OSZ
O'Casey Annual	OCA
Obliques	Obliques
Off-Informationen	OffI
Ogonek	Ogonek
Oktiabr	Oktiabr
Ollantay Theater Magazine	Ollan
On-Stage Studies	OSS
Ons Amsterdam	OnsA
Opal	Opal
Oper	Oper
Oper Heute	OperH
Oper und Konzert	OK
Oper & Tanz	Op&T
Opera Australia	OperaA
Opera Canada	OC
Opera Index	OperaIn
Opéra International	OI
Opera Journal	OJ
Opera News	OpN
Opera Quarterly	OQ
Opera (London)	Opera
Opera (Cape Town)	OperaCT
Opera (Milan)	OperaR
Operaélet/Operalife	OperaL
Opernglas, Das	Opern
Opernwelt	Opw
Opuscula	Opuscula
Opus Osterreichische Puppenspiel-Journalette	Opus
Organon	Organon
Orpheus Clauspeter Koscielny	Orpheus
Österreichische Dramatiker der Gegenwart	ODG
Otecestvennye arhivy	Otecest
Otrok in Knjiga	Oik
Outrage	Outrage
Overland	Over
Overture	OvA
Palócföld	Pal
Pamiętnik Teatralny	PaT
Pamir	Pamir
Pantallas y Escenarios	Pantallas
Pantuflas del Obispo	PdO
Paraules al Vent	PaV
Parergon	Parergon
Parnass	Parnass
Parnasso	Parnasso
Passing Show (Australia)	PasShowA
Passing Show: Newsletter of the Shubert Archive	PasShow

LIST OF PERIODICALS

The following list is an attempt to provide an updated and comprehensive listing of periodical literature, current and recent past, devoted to theatre and related subjects.

This Bibliography provides full coverage of materials published in periodicals marked "Full" and selected coverage of those marked "Scan".

We have not dropped periodicals that are no longer published for the sake of researchers for whom that information can be valuable. We also note and list title changes.

A&A   *The Artist. (Incorporates Art & Artists)*. Freq: 12; Lang: Eng; Subj: Related.
ISSN: 0004-3877
■The Artists' Publishing Company Ltd.; Caxton House, 63-65 High Street Tenderden, Kent TN30 6BD; UK.

A&B   *Architect & Builder*. Freq: 12; Began: 1951; Lang: Eng; Subj: Related.
ISSN: 0003-8407
■Laurie Wale (Pty) Ltd.; Box 4591; Cape Town; SOUTH AFRICA.

A&AR   *Art and Artists*. Formerly: *Art Workers News; Art Workers Newsletter*. Freq: 10; Began: 1982; Lang: Eng; Subj: Related.
ISSN: 0740-5723
■Foundation for the Community of Artists; 280 Broadway, Ste 412; New York, NY 10007; USA.

A&L   *Art and the Law*: Columbia Journal of Art and the Law. Freq: 4; Began: 1974; Ceased: 1985; Cov: Full; Lang: Eng; Subj: Related.
ISSN: 0743-5266
■Volunteer Lawyers for the Arts; 1500 Broadway; Ste. 711 New York, NY 10036; USA.

AAC   *Australian Antique Collector*. Freq: IRR; Began: 1966; Cov: Scan; Lang: Eng; Subj: Related.
■Editor, Australian Antique Collector; P.O. Box 5487; West Chatswood 2067; AUSTRALIA.

AAinNYLH   *Afro-Americans in New York Life and History*. Freq: 2; Began: 1977; Lang: Eng; Subj: Related.
ISSN: 0364-2437
■Afro-American Historical Assoc. of the, Niagara Frontier; Box 63; Buffalo, NY 14207; USA.

AATTN   *AATT News*. Freq: 11; Began: 1976; Lang: Eng; Subj: Theatre.
■Australian Assoc. for Theatre Tech.; 40 Wave Avenue Mountain; 3149 Waverly; AUSTRALIA.

Abel   *Abel Value News*. Formerly: *Abel: Panem et Circenses/Bread and Circuses*. Freq: 12; Began: 1969; Lang: Eng; Subj: Theatre.
ISSN: 0001-3153
■Abel News Agencies; 403 1st Ave.; Estherville, IA 51334-2223; USA.

AbhC   *Abhinaya*. Freq: 12; Lang: Ben; Subj: Theatre.
■Dilipa Bandyopadhyaya; 121 Harish Mukherjee Road; Calcutta; INDIA.

AbhD   *Abhinaya*. Freq: 24; Lang: Hin; Subj: Theatre.
■Yuvamanch; 4526 Amirchand Marg; Delhi; INDIA.

AbqN   *Arabesque*: A magazine of international dance. Freq: 6; Began: 1975; Cov: Scan; Lang: Eng; Subj: Related. ISSN: 0148-5865
■Ibrahim Farrah Inc.; One Sherman Square, Suite 22F; New York, NY 10023; USA.

ACH   *Australian Cultural History*. Freq: 1; Began: 1982; Cov: Scan; Lang: Eng; Subj: Related. ISSN: 0728-8433
■Faculty of Arts, Centre for Australian Studies; Deakin University; Geelong Victoria 3217; AUSTRALIA.

ACCTV   *Almanacco della Canzone e del Cinema e della TV*. Lang: Ita; Subj: Theatre.
■Viale del Vignola 105; Rome; ITALY.

ACom   *Art Com*: Contemporary Art Communication. Formerly: *Mamelle Magazine: Art Contemporary*. Available only through electronic mail 415/332-4335. Freq: 4; Began: 1975; Lang: Eng; Subj: Related. ISSN: 0732-2852
■Contemporary Arts Press; Box 3123; San Francisco, CA 94119; USA.

ACS   *Australian-Canadian Studies: an interdisciplinary social science review*. Freq: 1; Began: 1983; Cov: Scan; Lang: Eng; Subj: Related. ISSN: 0810-1906
■Department of Sociology; LaTrobe University; Bundoora Victoria 3083; AUSTRALIA.

Act   *Act*: Theatre in New Zealand. Formerly: *Theatre*. Freq: 6; Began: 1976; Ceased: 1986; Lang: Eng; Subj: Theatre. ISSN: 0010-0106
■Playmarket Inc.; Box 9767; Wellington; NEW ZEALAND.

ACTA   *Acta Classica (Proceedings of the Classical Association of South Africa)*. Freq: 1; Began: 1958; Cov: Scan; Lang: Eng.; Subj: Related. ISSN: 0065-1141
■Classical Association of South Africa; P.O. Box 392; Pretoria 0001; SOUTH AFRICA.

Acteurs   *Acteurs/Auteurs*. Formerly: *Acteurs*. Freq: 10; Began: 1982; Lang: Fre; Subj: Theatre. ISSN: 0991-949X
■Actes Sud, 18; 75006 rue de Savoie Paris; FRANCE.

ActS   *Actualité de Scénographie*. Freq: 6; Began: 1977; Lang: Fre; Subj: Theatre.
■Assoc. Belgique des Scénographes et Techniciens de Théâtre; 58 rue Servan; 75011 Paris et l'editeur; FRANCE.

ActT   *Action Théâtre*. Lang: Fre; Subj: Theatre.
■Action Culturelle de Sud-Est; 4 rue du Théâtre Français; 13001 Marseille; FRANCE.

Actualites   *Actualités*. Lang: Fre; Subj: Theatre.
■Actualités Spectacles; 1 rue Marietta Martin; 75016 Paris; FRANCE.

AD   *After Dark*. Freq: 12; Began: 1968; Ceased: 1983; Lang: Eng; Subj: Theatre.
ISSN: 0002-0702
■Dance Magazine, Inc.; 175 Fifth Avenue; New York, NY 10010; USA.

ADoc   *Arts Documentation Monthly*. Freq: 10; Began: 1978; Ceased: 1989; Last Known Address; Lang: Eng; Subj: Theatre. ISSN: 0140-6965
■The Arts Council of Great Britain Library, Information and Research Section; 105 Piccadilly; W1V OAU London; UK.

AdP   *Atti dello Psicodramma*. Freq: 1; Began: 1975; Lang: Ita; Subj: Related.
■Astrolabio-Ubaldini, Via Lungara 3, 00165 Rome; ITALY.

ADS   *Australasian Drama Studies*. Freq: 2; Began: 1982; Cov: Full; Lang: Eng; Subj: Theatre. ISSN: 0810-4123
■Australasia Drama Studies, English Dept., University of Queensland; Q 4072 St. Lucia; AUSTRALIA.

AdSpect   *Annuaire du Spectacle*. Freq: 1; Began: 1956; Lang: Fre; Subj: Theatre. ISSN: 0066-3026
■Publications Mandel L'Edison; 43 bd. Vauban 78182 St. Quentin-en-Yvelines Cedex; FRANCE.

AdT *Art du Théâtre, L'*. Freq: 3; Began: 1985; Lang: Fre; Subj: Theatre.
■Théâtre National de Chaillot; 1 Place du Trocadéro; 75116 Paris; FRANCE.

AdTI *Annuario del Teatro Italiano*. Freq: 1; Began: 1934; Lang: Ita; Subj: Theatre.
■S.I.A.E. - I.D.I.; Viale della Letteratura 30; 00100 Rome; ITALY.

AETR *AET Revista*. Lang: Spa; Subj: Theatre.
■Associación de Estudiantes de Teatro; Viamonte 1443; Buenos Aires; ARGENTINA.

AfAmArt *African American Art*. Formerly: *Black American Quarterly*. Freq: 4; Began: 1984; Cov: Scan; Lang: Eng; Subj: Related. ISSN: 1045-0920
■Museum of African American Art; Santa Monica, CA; USA.

AfAmR *African-American Review*. Freq: 4; Lang: Eng; Subj: Related.
■Department of English; Indiana State University; Terre Haute, IN 47809; USA.

Afr *Afreshiya*. Began: 1945; Last Known Address; Lang: Eng; Subj: Theatre.
■42 Commercial Buildings; Shahrah-e-Quaid-e-Azam; Lahore; PAKISTAN.

AfrA *African Arts*. Freq: 4; Began: 1967; Ceased: 1987; Cov: Scan; Lang: Eng; Subj: Related. ISSN: 0001-9933
■African Studies Center, Univ. of California, Los Angeles; 405 Hilgard Avenue; Los Angeles, CA 90024; USA.

AfricaP *Africa Perspective*. Freq: 2; Began: 1976; Lang: Eng; Subj: Related. ISSN: 0145-5311
■Students' African Studies Society, Univ. of Witwatersrand; 1 Jan Smuts Ave; 2001 Johannesburg; SOUTH AFRICA.

AFS *Australian Feminist Studies*. Freq: 2; Began: 1991; Lang: Eng; Subj: Related. ISSN: 0816-4649
■Research Centre for Women's Studies; University of Adelaide; South Australia, 5005; AUSTRALIA.

AfTR *African Theatre Review*. Freq: IRR; Began: 1985; Lang: Eng; Subj: Theatre.
■Dept. of African Literature, Fac. of Letters & Social Science; University Yaoumde, PO Box 755; Yaounde; CAMEROON.

AG *An Gael*: Irish Traditional Culture Alive in America Today. Freq: 4; Began: 1975; Lang: Eng; Subj: Related.
■An Claidheamh Soluis, The Irish Arts Center; 553 W. 51st Street; New York, NY 10019; USA.

AHA *Aha! Hispanic Arts News*. Freq: 10; Began: 1976; Lang: Eng/Spa; Subj: Related. ISSN: 0732-1643
■Association of Hispanic Arts; 200 E. 87 St.; New York, NY 10028; USA.

AHAT *Al-Hayat At-T'aqafiyya*. Lang: Ara; Subj: Theatre.
■Ministère des Affaires Culturelles; La Kasbah; Tunis; TUNISIA.

AHS *Australian Historical Studies*. Formerly: *Historical Studies*. Freq: 2 Began: 1988; Cov: Scan; Lang: Eng; Subj: Related. ISSN: 0018-2559
■Dept. of History; University of Melbourne; Parkville, Victoria 3052; AUSTRALIA.

AICRJ *American Indian Culture & Research Journal*. Freq: 4; Lang: Eng; Subj: Related.
■American Indian Studies Center; 3220 Campbell Hall; UCLA Los Angeles, CA 90095-1548; USA.

AInf *Artists and Influences*. Freq: 1; Began: 1981; Cov: Scan; Lang: Eng; Subj: Related.
■Hatch-Billops Collection, Inc.; 691 Broadway; New York, NY; USA.

AIT *Annuaire International du Théâtre*: SEE: Miedzynarodowny Rocznik Teatralny (Acro: MRT). Freq: 1; Began: 1977; Lang: Fre/Eng; Subj: Theatre.
■Warsaw; POLAND.

AIWAT *Al-Idaa Wa At-Talfaza*. Lang: Ara; Subj: Theatre.
■R.T.T.; 71 Avenue de la Liberté; Tunis; TUNISIA.

AJCS *Australian Journal of Cultural Studies*. Freq: 3; Began: 1983; Ceased: 1987; Cov: Scan; Lang: Eng; Subj: Related. ISSN: 0810-9648
■School of English; Western Australian Institute of Technology; Bentley, Western Australia 6102; AUSTRALIA.

AJChA *Australian Journal of Chinese Affairs*. Freq: 2; Began: 1979; Cov: Scan; Lang: Eng. ISSN: 0156-7365
■Contemporary China Centre, Research School of Pacific Studies, Australia National University; GPO Box 4; Canberra, ACT 2601; AUSTRALIA.

AJFS *Australian Journal of French Studies*. Freq: 3; Began: 1964; Lang: Eng; Subj: Related. ISSN: 0004-9468
■Dept. of Modern Languages; Monash University; Wellington Road, Clayton, Victoria 3168; AUSTRALIA.

AKT *AKT*: Aktuelles Theater. Freq: 12; Began: 1969; Lang: Ger; Subj: Theatre.
■Frankfurter Bund für Volksbildung GmbH; Eschersheimer Landstrasse 2; 6000 Frankfurt/1, W; GERMANY.

AL *American Literature*. Freq: 4; Began: 1929; Lang: Eng; Subj: Related. ISSN: 0002-9831
■Duke Univ. Press, Box 6697; College Station; Durham, NC 27708; USA.

Alfold *Alföld*. Freq: 12; Began: 1954; Cov: Scan; Lang: Hun; Subj: Related. ISSN: 0401-3174
■Alföld Alapítvány, Csokonai Kft.; Piac u. 26/A. I; 4024 Debrecen; HUNGARY.

Alif *Alif*. Lang: Fre; Subj: Theatre.
■24 rue Gamel Abdel-Nasser; Tunis; TUNISIA.

Alive *Alive*: The New Performance Magazine. Freq: 24; Began: 1982; Lang: Eng; Subj: Theatre.
■New York, NY; USA.

Almanach *Almanach Sceny Polskiej*. Freq: 1; Began: 1961; Lang: Pol; Subj: Theatre. ISSN: 0065-6526
■Wydawnicta Artystyczne i Filmowe; Pulawska 61; 02 595 Warsaw; POLAND.

ALS *Australian Literary Studies*. Freq: 2; Began: 1963; Cov: Scan; Lang: Eng; Subj: Related. ISSN: 0004-9697

■Univ. of Queensland, Dept. of English; Box 88; St. Lucia; Queensland 4067; AUSTRALIA.

Altaj *Altaj*. Began: 1947; Cov: Scan; Lang: Rus; Subj: Related. ISSN: 0320-7447
■Krupskaja Street, Building 91A; Barnaul City; RUSSIA.

AltR *Alternate Roots*. Lang: Eng; Subj: Related.
■1083 Austin Ave., N.E.; Atlanta, GA 30307; USA.

AltT *Alternatives Théâtrales*. Freq: 4; Began: 1979; Cov: Scan; Lang: Fre; Subj: Theatre.
■13 rue des Poissonniers, bte 15-1000 Brussels; BELGIUM.

AmatS *Amateur Stage*. Freq: 12; Began: 1946; Lang: Eng; Subj: Theatre. ISSN: 0002-6867
■Platform Publications Ltd.; 83 George Street; London W1H 5PL; UK.

AmatT *Amateur Theatre Yearbook*. Freq: 1; Began: 1988; Lang: Eng; Subj: Theatre.
■Platform Publications Ltd.; 83 George Street; London W1H 5PL; UK.

AmerD *American Drama*. Freq: 2; Began: 1991; Cov: Full; Lang: Eng; Subj: Theatre. ISSN: 1061-0057
■American Drama Institute; Department of English; ML 69, University of Cincinnati Cincinnati, OH 45221-0069; USA.

AmerM *American Music*. Freq: 4; Began: 1983; Lang: Eng; Subj: Related. ISSN: 0734-4392
■University of Illinois Press; Box 5081, Station A; Champaign, IL 61820; USA.

AMN *Arts Management Newsletter*. Freq: 5; Began: 1962; Lang: Eng; Subj: Related. ISSN: 0004-4067
■Radius Group, Inc.; 408 W. 57th Street; New York, NY 10019; USA.

AmS *Amaterska Scena*: Ochotnicke divadlo. Freq: 12; Began: 1964; Lang: Cze; Subj: Theatre. ISSN: 0002-6786
■Panorama; Halkova 1; 120 72 Prague 2; CZECH REPUBLIC.

AmTh *American Theatre*. Formerly: *Theatre Communications*. Freq: 11; Began: 1984; Cov: Full; Lang: Eng; Subj: Theatre. ISSN: 0275-5971
■Theatre Communications Group; 355 Lexington Avenue; New York, NY 10017; USA.

Amyri *Amyri*. Freq: 4; Lang: Fin; Subj: Theatre.
■Suomen Nayttelijaliitto r.y.; Arkadiankatu 12 A 18; 00100 Helsinki 10/52; FINLAND.

Anim *Animations*: Review of Puppets and Related Theatre. Freq: 6; Began: 1977; Cov: Scan; Lang: Eng; Subj: Theatre. ISSN: 0140-7740
■Puppet Centre Trust, Battersea Arts Centre; Lavender Hill; London SW11 5TN; UK.

Annuel *Annuel de Théâtre*. Freq: 1; Lang: Fre; Subj: Theatre.
■Association Loi de 1901; 30, rue de la Belgique; 92190 Meudon; FRANCE.

AnSt *Another Standard*. Freq: 6; Ceased: 1986; Cov: Scan; Lang: Eng; Subj: Related.
■PO Box 900; B70 6JP West Bromwich; UK.

AnT *Annuaire Théâtral, L'*. Freq: 1; Lang: Fre; Subj: Theatre. ISSN: 0827-0198 ■Societe d'histoire du theatre du Quebec; Montreal, PQ; CANADA.

Antipodes *Antipodes*. Freq: 1; Began: 1987; Cov: Scan; Lang: Eng; Subj: Related. ISSN: 0893-5580 ■American Association of Australian Literary Studies; 190 6th Avenue; Brooklyn, NY 11217; USA.

Antithesis *Antithesis*. Freq: 3; Began: 1987; Cov: Full; Lang: Eng; Subj: Related. ISSN: 1030-3839 ■English Department; University of Melbourne; Parkville Victoria 3052; AUSTRALIA.

ANZSC *Australian and New Zealand Studies in Canada*. Freq: 2; Began: 1989; Cov: Scan; Lang: Eng; Subj: Related. ISSN: 0843-5049 ■Dept. of English; University of Western Ontario London ON N6A 3K7 CANADA.

ANZTR *Australian and New Zealand Theatre Record*. Freq: 12; Lang: Eng; Subj: Theatre. ISSN: 1032-0091 ■Australian Theatre Studies Centre; University of New South Wales; Sydney NSW 2052; AUSTRALIA.

Apollo *Apollo*: The international magazine of art and antiques. Freq: 12; Began: 1925; Lang: Eng; Subj: Related. ISSN: 0003-6536 ■Apollo Magazine Ltd.; 45-46 Poland Street; London W1V 4AU; UK.

Apuntes *Apuntes*. Freq: 2; Began: 1960; Lang: Spa; Subj: Theatre. ISSN: 0716-4440 ■Universidad Católica de Chile, Escuela de Artes de la Comunicacion; Diagonal Oriente 3300, Casilla 114D; Santiago; CHILE.

AQ *American Quarterly*. Freq: 24; Began: 1949; Lang: Eng; Subj: Related. ISSN: 0003-0678 ■Univ. of Philadelphia; 307 College Hall; Philadelphia, PA 19104 6303; USA.

Araldo *Araldo dello Spettacolo, L'*. Lang: Ita; Subj: Theatre. ■Via Aureliana 63; Rome; ITALY.

Archivio *Archivio del Teatro Italiano*. Freq: IRR; Began: 1968; Lang: Ita; Subj: Theatre. ISSN: 0066-6661 ■Edizioni Il Polifilo; Via Borgonuovo 2; 20121 Milan; ITALY.

Arco *Arcoscenico*. Freq: 12; Began: 1945; Lang: Ita; Subj: Theatre. ■Sindacato nazionale autori drammatici; Via Ormisda 10; Rome; ITALY.

AReview *Arts Review*. Freq: 4; Began: 1983; Ceased: 1988; Lang: Eng; Subj: Related. ■National Endowment for the Arts; 1100 Pennsylvania Avenue NW; Washington, DC 20506; USA.

Ariel *Ariel*. Freq: 3; Began: 1986; Cov: Full; Lang: Ita; Subj: Theatre. ISSN: 0901-9901 ■Instituto di Studi Pirandelliani; Bulzoni Editore; Via dei Liburni n. 14; 00185 Rome; ITALY.

ArielR *Ariel:Review of International English Literature*; Began: 1970; Cov: Scan; Lang: Eng; Subj: Related. ■University of Calgary; CANADA.

Ark *Arkkitehti*: The Finnish Architectural Review. Freq: 6; Began: 1903; Cov: Scan; Lang: Fin/ Eng; Subj: Related. ISSN: 0004-2129 ■The Finnish Association of Architects; Yrjönkatu 11 A; 00120 Helsinki; FINLAND.

ArkSSSR *Arkhitektura S.S.S.R.* Freq: 6; Ceased: 1991; Cov: Scan; Lang: Rus; Subj: Related. ISSN: 0004-1939 ■Schuseva Street 7; Room 60; 103001 Moscow; RUSSIA.

ArNy *Arte Nyt*. Lang: Dut; Subj: Related. ■Hvidkildevej 64; 2400 Copenhagen NV; DENMARK.

Arrel *Arrel*. Freq: 4; Cov: Scan; Lang: Spa; Subj: Theatre. ■Disputacio de Barcelona; Placa de Sant Juame 1; 08002 Barcelona; SPAIN.

ArsU *Ars-Uomo*. Freq: 12; Began: 1975; Lang: Ita; Subj: Theatre. ■Bulzoni Editore; Via F. Cocco Ortu 120; 00139 Rome; ITALY.

Art&A *Art and Australia*. Freq: 4; Began: 1963; Cov: Scan; Lang: Eng; Subj: Related. ISSN: 0004-301x; ■Fine Arts Press Pty Ltd; P.O. Box 480; Roseville, NSW 2069; AUSTRALIA.

ArtL *Artlink*. Freq: 6; Began: 1981; Cov: Full; Lang: Eng; Subj: Theatre. ISSN: 0727-1239 ■363 The Esplanade; Henley Beach S.A. 5022; AUSTRALIA.

ArtP *Art-Press (International)*. Freq: 12; Began: 1976; Ceased: 1979; Cov: Scan; Lang: Fre; Subj: Related. ISSN: 0245-5676 ■Paris; FRANCE.

ArtsAd *Arts Advocate*. Freq: 3; Began: 1988; Lang: Eng Formerly: *In the Arts*; Subj: Theatre. ■Ohio State University College of the Arts; Office of Communications; 30 West 15th Ave. Columbus, OH 43210-1305; USA.

ArtsAtl *Arts Atlantic*: Atlantic Canada's Journal of the Arts. Freq: 4; Began: 1977; Cov: Scan; Lang: Eng; Subj: Related. ISSN: 0704-7916 ■Confederation Centre of the Arts; 145 Richmond St.; Charlottetown, PE C1A 9Z9; CANADA.

ArtsRS *Arts Reporting Service, The*. Freq: 24; Began: 1970; Ceased: 1976; Lang: Eng; Subj: Theatre. ISSN: 0196-4186 ■Charles Christopher Mark; PO Box 39008; Washington, DC 20016; USA.

ASabah *As-Sabah*. Freq: Daily; Began: 1951; Lang: Ara; Subj: Theatre. ■Avenue Du 7 Novembre; P.O. Box 441 Tunis 1004; TUNISIA.

ASamvad *Abhnaya Samvad*. Freq: 12; Lang: Hin; Subj: Theatre. ■20 Muktaram Babu Street; Calcutta; INDIA.

ASBelg *Arts du Spectacle en Belgique*. Formerly: *Centre d'Etudes Theatrales, Louvain: Annuaire*. Freq: IRR; Began: 1968; Ceased: 1991; Lang: Fre; Subj: Theatre. ISSN: 0069-1860 ■Université Catholique de Louvain, Centre d'Etudes Théâtrales; 1, place de l'Université; 1348 Louvain-la-Neuve; BELGIUM.

AScene *Autre Scène, L'*. Lang: Fre; Subj: Theatre. ■Editions Albatros; 14 rue de l'Amérique; 75015 Paris; FRANCE.

ASCFB *Annuaire du Spectacle de la Communauté Française de Belgique*. Freq: 1; Began: 1981; Lang: Fre; Subj: Theatre. ■Archives et Musée de la Littérature, ASBL; 4 Bd de l'Empereur; 1000 Brussels; BELGIUM.

ASInt *American Studies International*. Freq: 4; Began: 1975; Ceased: 1983; Cov: Scan; Lang: Eng; Subj: Related. ISSN: 0003-1321 ■American Studies Program, George Washington University; Washington, DC 20052; USA.

ASO *Avant Scène Opéra, L'*. Freq: 6; Began: 1976; Ceased: 1982; Lang: Fre; Subj: Theatre. ■27 rue St. André des Arts; 75006 Paris; FRANCE.

ASSAPHc *ASSAPH*: Section C. Studies in the Theatre. Freq: 1; Began: 1984; Cov: Full; Lang: Eng; Subj: Theatre. ISSN: 0334-5963 ■Dept. of Theatre Arts, Tel Aviv University; 69978 Ramat Aviv Tel Aviv; ISRAEL.

AST *Avant Scène Théâtre, L'*. Freq: 20; Began: 1949; Cov: Scan; Lang: Fre; Subj: Theatre. ISSN: 0045-1169 ■Editions de l'Avant Scène; 6 rue Git-le-Coeur; 75006 Paris; FRANCE.

AStage *American Stage*. Freq: 10; Began: 1979; Lang: Eng; Subj: Theatre. ■American Stage Publishing Company; 217 East 28th Street; New York, NY 10016; USA.

ASTRN *ASTR Newsletter*. Freq: 2; Began: 1972; Cov: Scan; Lang: Eng; Subj: Theatre. ISSN: 0044-7927 ■American Society for Theatre Research, C.W. Post College; Department of English; Brookvale, NY 11548; USA.

AT *Akademiceskie Tetrady*. Freq: 4; Began: 1996; Cov: Scan; Lang: Rus; Subj: Related. ■20 Ul. Povarskaja; Moscow 121069; RUSSIA.

ATAC *Aujourd'hui Tendances Art Culture*. Formerly: *Partenaires*. Lang: Fre; Subj: Related. ■FRANCE.

ATArg *Annuario del Teatro Argentino*. Freq: 1; Lang: Spa; Subj: Theatre. ■F.N.A.; Calle Alsina 673; Buenos Aires; ARGENTINA.

ATB *Annuario do Teatro Brasileiro*. Freq: 1; Began: 1976; Lang: Por; Subj: Theatre. ■Ministerio da Educacao e Cultura; Service Nacional de Teatro; Rio de Janeiro; BRAZIL.

AtG *Around the Globe*. Freq: 2; Began: 1996; Cov: Scan; Lang: Eng; Subj: Theatre. ISSN: 1366-2317 ■Shakespeare's Globe; 1 Bear Gardens; Bankside London SE1 9ED; UK.

ATJ *Asian Theatre Journal*. Formerly: *Asian Theatre Reports*. Freq: 2; Began: 1984; Cov: Full; Lang: Eng; Subj: Theatre. ISSN: 0742-5457 ■Univ. of Hawaii Press; 2840 Kolowalu Street; Honolulu, HI 96822; USA.

ATT *Amers Theatrical Times*. Freq: 12; Began: 1976; Lang: Eng; Subj: Related.

■William Amer (Pty) Ltd.; 15 Montgomery Avenue; NSW 2142 South Granville; AUSTRALIA.

Audiences *Audiences Magazine*. Freq: 12; Last Known Address; Lang: Fre; Subj: Theatre.
■55 avenue Jean Jaurés; 75019 Paris; FRANCE.

AuJCom *Australian Journal of Communication*. Freq: 2; Began: 1982; Cov: Scan; Lang: Eng; Subj: Related. ISSN: 0810-6202
■Queensland University of Technology; GPO Box 2434; Brisbane Qld 4001; AUSTRALIA.

AULLA *Journal of the Australian Universities Language & Literature Association*. Freq: 2; Began: 1953; Cov: Scan; Lang: Eng; Subj: Related. ISSN: 0001-2793
■Australasian Universities Language & Literature Association; Monash University; Clayton, Victoria 3168; AUSTRALIA.

Autor *Autor, Der*. Freq: 2; Began: 1926; Cov: Scan; Lang: Ger; Subj: Related. ISSN: 0344-7197
■Dramatiker-Union, Eckhard Schulz; Babelsberger Str. 43; D-10715 Berlin; GERMANY.

Autores *Autores*. Freq: 4; Lang: Por; Subj: Theatre.
■Sociedade Portuguesa de Autores; Av. Duque de Loule, 31; 1098 Lisbon Codex; PORTUGAL.

Avrora *Avrora*. Freq: 12; Began: 1969; Cov: Scan; Lang: Rus; Subj: Related. ISSN: 0320-6858
■4 Millionnaja Ul; St. Petersburg 191186; RUSSIA.

AWBR *Australian Women's Book Review*. Freq: 1; Began: 1988; Cov: Scan; Lang: Eng; Subj: Related. ISSB: 1033-9434
■Carole Ferrier; Dept. of English, University of Queensland; Brisbane 4072; AUSTRALIA.

Bal *Balrangmanch*. Freq: 6; Lang: Hin; Subj: Theatre.
■Post Box No. 37, G.P.O.; Lueknowy; 226001; INDIA.

Bahub *Bahubacana*. Began: 1978; Lang: Ben; Subj: Theatre.
■Bahubacana Natyagoshthi; 11/2 Jaynag Road, Bakshi Bazar; Dhaka 1; BANGLADESH.

Balet *Balet*. Freq: 6; Cov: Scan; Began: 1992; Lang: Rus; Subj: Theatre. ISSN: 0207-4788
■Tverskaja St.; Moscow 103050; RUSSIA.

BALF *Black American Literature Forum*. Formerly: *Negro American Literature*. Freq: 4; Began: 1967; Ceased: 1991; Cov: Scan; Lang: Eng; Subj: Related. ISSN: 0148-6179
■Parsons Hall 237, Indiana State Univ.; Terre Haute, IN 47809; USA.

Balkon *Balkon*. Freq: 12; Began: 1993; Cov: Scan; Lang: Hun; Subj: Related. ISSN: 1216-8890
■Enciklopédia Kiadó; Bartók Béla út 82; 1113 Budapest; HUNGARY.

Bamah *Bamah*: Educational Theatre Review. Freq: 4; Began: 1959; Cov: Full; Lang: Heb; Subj: Theatre. ISSN: 0045-138X
■Bamah Association; PO Box 7098; 910 70 Jerusalem; ISRAEL.

BAMu *Buenos Aires Musical*. Freq: IRR; Began: 1946; Lang Spa; Subj: Theatre. ISSN: 0007-3113
■Calle Alsina 912; Buenos Aires; ARGENTINA.

Band *Bandwagon*. Freq: 6; Began: 1939; Cov: Scan; Lang: Eng; Subj: Theatre. ISSN: 0005-4968
■Circus Historical Society; 2515 Dorset Road; Columbus, OH 43221; USA.

BaNe *Ballet News*. Freq: 12; Began: 1979; Lang: Eng; Subj: Related. ISSN: 0191-2690
■Metropolitan Opera Guild, Inc.; 1865 Broadway; New York, NY 10023; USA.

BANY *Black Arts New York*. Freq: 10; Cov: Scan; Lang: Eng; Subj: Related. ISSN: 1057-4239
■215 West 125th St. Dr. Martin Luther King, Jr. Blvd; 4th Floor New York, NY 10027; USA.

BASSITEJ *Bulletin ASSITEJ*. Formerly: *Bulletin d'Information ASSITEJ*. Freq: 3; Began: 1966; Ceased: 1994; Lang: Fre/Eng/Rus; Subj: Theatre.
■ASSITEJ; Celetna 17; 110 01 Prague 1; CZECH REPUBLIC.

BCl *Beckett Circle/Cercle de Beckett*. Freq: 2; Began: 1978; Lang: Eng/Fre; Subj: Theatre. ISSN: 0732-2224
■Samuel Beckett Society; University of California at Los Angeles; Los Angeles, CA 90024; USA.

BCom *Bulletin of the Comediantes*. Freq: 2; Began: 1949; Lang: Eng/ Spa; Subj: Theatre. ISSN: 0007-5108
■James A. Parr, Dept. of Spa. & Portuguese; University of California; Riverside, CA 92521; USA.

BelgITI *Bulletin*: Van het Belgisch Centrum ITI. Ceased; Lang: Fre; Subj: Theatre.
■Belgisch Centrum van het ITI, c/o Mark Hermans; Rudolfstraat 33; B 2000 Antwerp; BELGIUM.

Bergens *Bergens Theatermuseum Skrifter*. Began: 1970; Lang: Nor; Subj: Theatre.
■Bergens Theatermuseum, Kolstadgt 1; Box 2959 Toeyen; 6 Oslo; NORWAY.

Bericht *Bericht*. Lang: Ger; Subj: Theatre. ISSN: 0067-6047
■UMLOsterreichischer Bundestheaterverband; Goethegasse 1; A 1010 Vienna; AUSTRIA.

BFant *Botteghe della Fantasia, Le*. Last Known Address; Began: 1979; Lang: Ita; Subj: Theatre.
■Via S. Manlio 13; Milan; ITALY.

BGs *Bühnengenossenschaft*. Freq: 12; Began: 1949; Lang: Ger; Subj: Theatre. ISSN: 0007-3083
■Bühnenschriften-Vertriebs-Gesellschaft; Pf. 13 02 70; D-20102 Hamburg; GERMANY.

BGTA *Bibliographic Guide to Theatre Arts*. Freq: 1; Lang: Eng; Subj: Theatre. ISSN: 0360-2788
■G. K. Hall & Co.; 70 Lincoln Street; Boston, MA 02111; USA.

BI *Ballett International/tanz aktuell*: Aktuelle Monatszeitung für Ballett und Tanztheater. Formerly: *Ballett Info*. Freq: 12; Began: 1978; Lang: Ger; Subj: Related. ISSN: 0947-0484

■Erhard Friedrich Verlag; Im Brande 19; D-30926 Seelze; GERMANY.

BIINET *Boletin informativo del Instituto Nacional de Estudios de Teatro*. Freq: 10; Began: 1978; Lang: Spa; Subj: Theatre.
■1055 Avenida Cordoba; 1199 Buenos Aires; ARGENTINA.

Biladi *Biladi*. Lang: Ara; Subj: Theatre.
■Parti Socialiste Desourien, Maison du Parti, BP 1033; Blvd. du 9 Avril, La Kasbah; Tunis; TUNISIA.

BiT *Biblioteca Teatrale*. Freq: 4; Began: 1986; Cov: Full; Lang: Ita; Subj: Theatre. ISSN: 0045-1959
■Bulzoni Editore; 14 Via dei Liburni; 00185 Rome; ITALY.

BITIJ *Boletin Iberoamericano de Teatro para la Infancia y la Juventud*. Lang: Spa; Subj: Theatre.
■Associación Española de Teatro para la Infancia y la Juventud; Claudio Coello 141; 6 Madrid; SPAIN.

BJDT *Ballett-Journal/Das Tanzarchiv*. Freq: 5; Began: 1953; Cov: Scan; Lang: Ger; Subject: Related. ISSN 0720-3896
■Zeitung für Tanzpädagogik und Ballett-Theater; Ulrich Steiner Verlag; Obersteinbach 5 a D-51429 Bergisch Gladbach; GERMANY.

BK *Bauten der Kultur*. Freq: IRR; Began: 1976; Lang: Ger; Subj: Related. ISSN: 0323-5696
■Institut für Kulturbauten; Clara-Zetkin-Strasse 105; 1080 Berlin; GERMANY.

BKK *Bühne Kursbuch Kultur*. Freq: 2; Cov: Scan; Lang: Ger; Subj: Related.
■Orac Zeitschriftenverlag GmbH; Schönbrunner Str. 59-61; A-1010 Vienna; GERMANY.

BlackM *Black Masks*. Freq: 12; Began: 1984; Cov: Scan; Lang: Eng; Subj: Related.
■P.O. Box 2; Bronx, NY 10471; USA.

BlC *Black Collegian, The*: The National Magazine of Black College Students. Formerly: *Expressions*. Freq: IRR; Began: 1970; Cov: Scan; Lang: Eng; Subj: Related. ISSN: 0192-3757
■Black Collegiate Services, Inc.; 1240 South Broad Street; New Orleans, LA 70125; USA.

BM *Burlington Magazine*. Freq: 12; Began: 1903; Cov: Scan; Lang: Eng; Subj: Related. ISSN: 0007-6287
■Burlington Magazine Publications; 6 Bloomsbury Square; London WC1A 2LP; UK.

BMP *Bulletin Magische Plätze*. Freq: 12; Cov: Scan; Lang: Ger; Subj: Related.
■B. Kohler Verlag; Wydlerweg 17; CH-8047 Zurich; SWITZERLAND.

BMT *Biuletyn Mlodego Teatru*. Last Known Address; Began: 1978; Lang: Pol; Subj: Theatre.
■Gwido Zlatkes; Bednarska 24 m; 00 321 Warsaw; POLAND.

BNJMtd *Biblioteca Nacional José Marti*: Informacion y Documentacion de la Cultura. Serie Teatro y Danza. Freq: 12; Lang: Spa; Subj: Theatre.
■Biblioteca Nacional José Marti, Dept. Info. y Doc. de Cultura; Plaza de la Revolución; Havana; CUBA.

BNS   *Builder N.S.* Formerly: *Builder N.S.W.*. Freq: 12; Began: 1907; Cov: Scan; Lang: Eng; Subj: Related.
■Master Builders Asso. of New South Wales; Private Bag 9; Broadway; N.S.W. 2007; AUSTRALIA.Tel: 660-7188.

Bomb   *Bomb.* Freq: 4; Cov: Scan; Lang: Eng; Subj: Related.
■New Arts Publications; 594 Broadway, 10th Flr.; New York,, NY 10012; USA.

BooksC   *Books in Canada.* Freq: 9; Began: 1971; Cov: Scan; Lang: Eng/Fre; Subj: Related.   ISSN: 0045-2564
■Canadian Review of Books, Ltd.; 130 Spadina Ave.; Suite 603 Toronto, ON M5V 2L4; CANADA.

Bouff   *Bouffonneries.* Began: 1980; Lang: Fre; Subj: Theatre.   ISSN: 028-4455
■Domaine de Lestanière; 11000 Cazilhac; FRANCE.

BPAN   *British Performing Arts Newsletter.* Ceased: 1980; Lang: Eng; Subj: Related.
■London; UK.

BPM   *Black Perspective in Music.* Freq: 2; Began: 1973; Ceased: 1990; Cov: Scan; Lang: Eng; Subj: Related.   ISSN: 0090-7790
■Foundation for Research in the Afro-American Creative Arts; P.O. Drawer One; Cambria Heights, NY 11411; USA.

BPTV   *Bühne und Parkett*: Theater Journal Volksbühnen-Spiegel. Formerly: *Volksbuhnen-Spiegel.* Freq: 3; Began: 1955; Lang: Ger; Subj: Theatre.
■Verband der deutschen Volksbühne e.v.; Bismarckstrasse 17; 1000 Berlin 12; GERMANY.

BR   *Ballet Review.* Freq: 4; Began: 1965; Lang: Eng; Subj: Related. ISSN: 0522-0653
■Dance Research Foundation, Inc.; 46 Morton Street; New York, NY 10014; USA.

BrechtJ   *Brecht Jahrbuch.* Freq: 1; Began: 1971; Ceased: 1987; Lang: Ger/Eng/Fre; Subj: Theatre.
■Wayne State University; 5959 Woodward Ave.; Detroit, MI 48202; USA.

Brs   *Broadside.* Freq: 4; Began: 1940; Lang: Eng; Subj: Theatre.   ISSN: 0068-2748
■Theatre Library Assoc.; 111 Amsterdam Avenue; New York, NY 10023; USA.

BSK   *Bundesverband Studentische Kulturarbeit.* Freq: 4; Cov: Scan; Lang: Ger; Subj: Related.   ISBN: 3-927451-11-8
■BSK, Berliner Platz 31; D-53111 Bonn; GERMANY.

BSOAS   *Bulletin of the School of Oriental & African Studies.* Lang: Eng; Subj: Related.
■London; UK.

BSPC   *Bulletin de la Société Paul Claudel.* Freq: IRR; Lang: Fre; Subj: Related.
■13, rue du Pont Louis-Philippe; 75004 Paris; FRANCE.

BSSJ   *Bernard Shaw Newsletter.* Formerly: *Newsletter & Journal of the Shaw Society of London.* Freq: 1; Began: 1976; Lang: Eng; Subj: Related.
■Bernard Shaw Centre, High Orchard; 125 Markyate Road; EM8 2LB Dagenahm, Essex; UK.

BTA   *Börneteateravisen.* Freq: 4; Began: 1972; Lang: Dan; Subj: Theatre.
■Teatercentrum i Danmark; Frederiksborggade 20; 1360 Copenhagen; DENMARK.

BTlog   *British Theatrelog.* Freq: 4; Began: 1978; Ceased: 1980; Lang: Eng; Subj: Theatre.
ISSN: 0141-9056
■Associate British Centre of the ITI; 15 Hanover Sq.; London WIR 9AJ; UK.

BtR   *Bühnentechnische Rundschau*: Zeitschrift für Theatertechnik, Bühnenbau und Bühnengestaltung. Freq: 6; Began: 1907; Cov: Scan; Lang: Ger/Eng/Fre; Subj: Theatre.
ISSN: 0007-3091
■Erhard Friedrich Verlag; Im Brande 19; D-30926 Seelze; SWITZERLAND.

Buhne   *Bühne, Die.* Freq: 11; Began: 1958; Lang: Ger; Subj: Theatre.   ISSN: 0007-3075
■Orac Zeitschriftenverlag GmbH; Schönbrunner Str. 59-61; A1010 Vienna; AUSTRIA.

Buhnent   *Bühnentarifrecht.* Freq: 4; Cov: Scan; Lang: Ger; Subj: Related.   ISBN: 3-7685-2731-X
■R.v. Decker's Verlag; Hüthig GmbH, Pf. 102869; D-69018 Heidelberg; GERMANY.

BulS   *Bulletin.* Freq: 10; Cov: Scan; Lang: Ger/Fre; Subj: Related.
■Schweizerischer Dachverband der Fachkräfte des künstlerischen Tanzes SDT; Dufourstr. 45; CH-3005 Bern; SWITZERLAND.

BulV   *Bulletin.* Freq: 4; Began: 1974; Cov: Scan; Lang: Ger/Fre/Ita; Subj: Related.
■Vereinigung für Künstler/innen/Theater/Veranstalter/innen; Schweiz (KTV); Pf. 3350 CH-2500 Biel 3; SWITZERLAND.

BuM   *Bühnen- und Musikrecht.* Cov: Scan; Lang: Ger; Subj: Related.
■Mykenae Verlag Rossberg KG; Ahastr. 9; D-64285 Darmstadt; GERMANY.

BY   *Brecht Yearbook.* Freq: 1; Lang: Eng; Subj: Theatre.
■German Department; 818 Van Hise Hall; University of Wisconsin Madison, WI 53706; USA.

CahiersC   *Cahiers Césairiens.* Freq: 2; Began: 1974; Lang: Eng/Fre; Subj: Theatre.
■Pennsylvania State University, Dept. of French; University Park, PA 16802; USA.

CahiersCC   *Cahiers CERT/CIRCE.* Lang: Fre; Subj: Theatre.
■Centre Etudes Recherches Théâtrale, Université de Bordeaux III; Esplanade des Antilles; 33405 Talence; FRANCE.

Callaloo   *Callaloo*: A Black South Journal of Arts and Letters. Freq: 3; Began: 1976; Cov: Scan; Lang: Eng; Subj: Related. ISSN: 0161-2492
■Department of English; 322 Bryan Hall; University of Virginia Charlottesville, VA 22903; USA.

CallB   *Call Boy, The*: Journal of the British Music Hall Society. Freq: 4; Began: 1963; Lang: Eng; Subj: Theatre.
■British Music Hall Society; 32 Hazelbourne Road; London SW12; UK.

Callboard   *Callboard.* Freq: 4; Began: 1951; Lang: Eng; Subj: Theatre.   ISSN: 0045-4044

■1809 Barrington St., Ste. 901; Halifax, NS B3J 3K8; CANADA.

Calliope   *Calliope.* Freq: 12; Began: 1968; Lang: Eng; Subj: Theatre.
■Clowns of America Inc.; 1052 Foxwood Ln.; Baltimore, MD 21221; USA.

CAM   *City Arts Monthly.* Freq: 12; Lang: Eng; Subj: Related.
■640 Natoma St.; San Francisco, CA 94103; USA.

CanL   *Canadian Literature/Littérature Canadienne*: A Quarterly of Criticism and Review. Freq: 4; Began: 1959; Cov: Scan; Lang: Eng/Fre; Subj: Related.   ISSN: 0008-4360
■University of British Columbia; 2029 West Mall; Vancouver, BC V6T 1Z2; CANADA.

Caratula   *Caratula.* Freq: 12; Last Known Address; Lang: Spa; Subj: Theatre.
■Sanchez Pacheco 83; 2 Madrid; SPAIN.

Carnet   *Carnet.* Cov: Scan; Began: 1994; Lang: Eng /Fre; Subj: Related.   ISSN: 0929-936x
■Theater Institut Nederland; Herengracht 168-1016 BP Amsterdam; NETHERLANDS.

Castelets   *Castelets.* Lang: Fre; Subj: Theatre.
■Centre Provincial de la Marionnette de Namur; Rue des Brasseurs 109; 5000 Namur; BELGIUM.

CB   *Call Board.* Formerly: *Monthly Theatre Magazine of TCCBA.* Freq: IRR; Began: 1931; Lang: Eng; Subj: Theatre.
ISSN: 0008-1701
■Theatre Bay Area; 657 Mission Street, Ste. 402; San Francisco, CA 94116; USA.

CBGB   *Cahiers de la Bibliothèque Gaston Baty.* Lang: Fre; Subj: Related.
■Paris; FRANCE.

CCIEP   *Courrier du Centre international d'études poétiques.* Freq: 4; Cov: Scan; Lang: Fre; Subj: Related.
■Archives et Musée de la Littérature; Boulevard de l'empereur, 4; 1000 Bruxelles; BELGIUM.

CDO   *Courrier Dramatique de l'Ouest.* Freq: 4; Began: 1973; Ceased; Lang: Fre; Subj: Theatre.
■Théâtre du Bout du Monde, Ctre Dramatique Natl de l'Ouest; 9B Avenue Janvier; 35100 Rennes; FRANCE.

CDr   *Canadian Drama/Art Dramatique Canadien.* Freq: 2; Began: 1975; Cov: Full; Lang: Eng/Fre; Subj: Theatre.   ISSN: 0317-9044
■Dept. of English, University of Waterloo; Waterloo, ON N2L 3G1; CANADA.

CdRideau   *Cahiers du Rideau.* Freq: 3; Began: 1976; Ceased: Lang: Fre; Subj: Theatre.
■Rideau de Bruxelles; 23 rue Ravenstein; B 1000 Bruxelles; BELGIUM.

CE   *College English.* Freq: 8; Began: 1937; Lang: Eng; Subj: Related. ISSN: 0010-0994
■National Council of Teachers of English; 1111 Kenyon Road; Urbana, IL 61801; USA.

Cel   *Čelovek.* Lang: Rus; Subj: Related.
ISSN: 0236-2007
■RUSSIA.

Celcit   *Celcit*. Lang: Spa; Subj: Theatre.
■Apartado 662; 105 Caracas; VENEZUELA.

CeskL   *Ceskoslovenski Loutkar*. SEE *Loutkar*. Began: 1951; Ceased: 1993; Lang: Cze; Subj: Theatre.
■Panorama; Mrstikova 23; 10 000 Prague 10; CZECH REPUBLIC.

Cesti   *Čest'imeju*. Freq: 12; Cov: Scan; Began: 1919; Lang: Rus; Subj: Related.
■D-7 Chorośevskoje śosse; 32-A, Building 3 Moscow 123007; RUSSIA.

CetC   *Culture et Communication*. Freq: 10; Lang: Fre; Subj: Theatre.
■Min. de la Culture et de la Documentation; 3 rue de Valois; 75001 Paris; FRANCE.

CF   *Comédie-Française*. Freq: 4; Began: 1971; Lang: Fre; Subj: Theatre. ISSN: 0759-125x
■1 Place Colette; 75001 Paris; FRANCE.

CFT   *Contemporary French Civilization*. Freq: 3; Began: 1976; Cov: Scan; Lang: Fre/Eng; Subj: Related. ISSN: 0147-9156
■Dept. of Modern Languages, Montana State University; Bozeman, MT 59717; USA.

Chhaya   *Chhaya Nat*. Freq: 4; Lang: Hin; Subj: Theatre.
■U.P. Sangeet Natak Akademi; Lucknow; INDIA.

ChinL   *Chinese Literature*. Freq: 4; Began: 1951; Lang: Eng; Subj: Related. ISSN: 0009-4617
■Bai Wan Zhuang; Beijing 100037; CHINA.

Chronico   *Chronico*. Lang: Gre; Subj: Theatre.
■ Horo'; Xenofontos 7; Athens; GREECE.

ChTR   *Children's Theatre Review*. Freq: 4; Began: 1952; Cov: Full; Ceased: 1985; Lang: Eng; Subj: Theatre. ISSN: 0009-4196
■c/o Milton W. Hamlin, Shoreline High School; 18560 1st Avenue N.E.; Seattle, WA 98155; USA.

CineLD   *Cineschedario*: Letture Drammatiche. Freq: 12; Began: 1964; Lang: Ita; Subj: Related. ISSN: 0024-1458
■Centro Salesiano dello Spettacolo; Via M. Ausiliatrice 32; Turin 10121; ITALY.

CIQ   *Callahan's Irish Quarterly*. Freq: 4; Ceased: 1983; Cov: Scan; Lang: Eng; Subj: Related.
■P.O. Box 5935; Berkeley, CA 94705; USA.

CircusR   *Circus Report*. Freq: IRR; Began: 1972; Lang: Eng; Subj: Theatre; ISSN: 0889-5996
■525 Oak St.; El Cerrito, CA 94530-3699; USA.

CittaA   *Città Aperta*. Freq: 1; Began: 1981; Lang: Ita; Subj: Theatre.
■Associazione Piccolo Teatro; Via Cesalpino 20; 52100 Arezzo; ITALY.

CityL   *City Limits*. Freq: 10; Began: 1976; Lang: Eng; Subj: Related. ISSN: 0199-0330
■City Limits, Assoc. of Neighborhood Housing Developers; 424 W. 23rd Street; New York, NY 10001; USA.

CJC   *Cahiers Jean Cocteau*. Freq: 1; Began: 1969; Lang: Fre; Subj: Theatre. ISSN: 0068-5178
■6 rue Bonaparte; 75006 Paris; FRANCE.

CJG   *Cahiers Jean Giraudoux*. Freq: 1; Began: 1972; Lang: Fre; Subj: Theatre.
■Association des Amis de Jean Giraudoux; Université F. Rabelais; 3 Rue du Tanneus 37000 TOURS; FRANCE.

Cjo   *Conjunto*: Revista de Teatro Latinamericano. Freq: 4; Began: 1964; Cov: Full; Lang: Spa; Subj: Theatre. ISSN: 0010-5937
■Departamento de Teatro Latino Americano, Casa de las Americas; Ediciones Cubanes, Obispo No. 527; Aptdo. 605, Havana; CUBA.

CLAJ   *College Language Association Journal*. Freq: 4; Began: 1957; Lang: Eng; Subj: Related. ISSN: 0007-8549
■College Language Assoc., c/o Cason Hill; Morehouse College; Atlanta, GA 30314; USA.

ClassJ   *Classical Journal, The*. Freq: 4; Lang: Eng; Subj: Theatre.
■Department of Classics; 146 New Cabell Hall; University of Virginia Charlottesville, VA 22903; USA.

ClaudelS   *Claudel Studies*. Freq: 2; Began: 1972; Lang: Eng; Subj: Related. ISSN: 0900-1237
■University of Dallas, Dept. of French; PO Box 464; Irving, TX 75060; USA.

Clip   *Clipper Studies in the American Theater*. Freq: IRR; Began: 1985; Lang: Eng; Subj: Theatre. ISSN: 0748-237X
■Borgo Press; Box 2845; San Bernardino, CA 92406; USA.

CLSUJ   *CLSU Journal of the Arts*. Freq: 1; Began: 1981; Lang: Eng/Phi; Subj: Theatre.
■Central Luzon State University, Publications House; Munoz; Nueva Ecija; PHILIPPINES.

Club   *Club*. Began: 1923; Cov: Scan; Freq: 12; Lang: Rus; Subj: Related.
■Stardca'luzzroje śosse, I; Moscow 117630; RUSSIA.

CMJV   *Cahiers de la Maison Jean Vilar*. Lang: Fre; Subj: Theatre.
■Avignon; FRANCE.

CNCT   *Cahiers de la NCT*. Freq: 3; Began: 1965; Lang: Fre; Subj: Theatre. ISSN: 1188-1461
■Nouvelle Compagnic Théâtrale; 4353 rue Ste. Catherine est.; Montreal, PQ H1V 1Y2; CANADA.

CO   *Comédie de l'Ouest*. Lang: Fre; Subj: Theatre.
■Assoc. des Amis de la Comediede l'ouest; Centre Dramatique National; Rennes; FRANCE.

COJ   *Cambridge Opera Journal*.Began: 1989;Cov: Scan;Lang: Eng Subj: Related. ISSN: 0954-5867
■Cambridge University Press; The Edinburgh Building; Shaftesbury Road, Cambridge CB2 2RU; UK

ColecaoT   *Coleçao Teatro*. Freq: IRR; Began: 1974; Lang: Por; Subj: Theatre.
■Universidade Federal do Rio Grande do Sul; Porto Alegre; BRAZIL.

ColJL&A   *Columbia-VLA Journal of Law & the Arts*. Formerly: *Art & the Law*. Freq: 4; Began: 1985; Cov: Full; Lang: Eng; Subj: Related. ISSN: 0743-5226
■Columbia University School of Law &, Volunteer Lawyers for the Arts; 435 West 116 Street; New York, NY 10027; USA.

Comedy   *Comedy*. Freq: 4; Began: 1980; Lang: Eng; Subj: Related. ISSN: 0272-7404
■Trite Explanations Ltd.; Box 505, Canal Street Station; New York, NY 10013; USA.

ComIBS   *Communications from the International Brecht Society*: The Global Brecht. Freq: 2; Began: 1970; Lang: Eng/Ger; Subj: Theatre. ISSN: 0740-8943
■Foreign Languages; Maginnes Hall #9; Lehigh University Bethlehem, PA 18015; USA.

CompD   *Comparative Drama*. Freq: 4; Began: 1967; Cov: Full; Lang: Eng; Subj: Theatre. ISSN: 0010-4078
■Department of English, Western Michigan University; Kalamazoo, MI 49008-3899; USA.

Con   *Connoisseur*. Freq: 12; Began: 1901; Lang: Eng; Subj: Related. ISSN: 0010-6275
■Hearst Magazines, Connoisseur; 250 W. 55th St.; New York, NY 10019; USA.

Confes   *Confessio*. Freq: 4; Began: 1976; Cov: Scan; Lang: Hun; Subj: Related. ISSN: 0133-8889
■Református Zsinati Iroda Sajtóosztálya; Abonyi u. 21; 1146 Budapest; HUNGARY.

ContactQ   *Contact Quarterly*. Freq: 2; Began: 1975; Lang: Eng; Subj: Related. ISSN: 0198-9634
■Contact Collaborations Inc.; Box 603; Northampton, MA 01061; USA.

Contenido   *Contenido*. Lang: Spa; Subj: Theatre.
■Centro Venezolano del ITI; Apartado 51-456; 105 Caracas; VENEZUELA.

Contin   *Continuum*. Formerly: *Continuing Higher Education Association*. Freq: 3; Began: 1977 Lang: Eng;; Subj: Related.
■National University of Continuing Education Association; 1 Dupont Circle N.W., Ste. 615; Washington, DC 20036; USA.

CORD   *CORD Dance Research Annual*. Lang: Eng; Subj: Related.
■CORD Editorial Board, NYU Dance and Dance Educ. Dept.; 35 W. 4th St., Room 675; New York, NY 10003; USA.

CorpsE   *Corps écrit*. Freq: 4; Lang: Fre; Subj: Theatre.
■Presses Universitaires de France; 12, rue Jean de Beauvais; 75005 Paris; FRANCE.

COS   *Central Opera Service Bulletin*. Freq: 4; Began: 1954; Lang: Eng; Subj: Theatre. ISSN: 0008-9508
■Metropolitan Opera Nat'l Council, Central Opera Service; Lincoln Center; New York, NY 10023; USA.

Costume   *Costume*: The Journal of the Costume Society. Freq: 1; Began: 1967; Cov: Scan; Lang: Eng; Subj: Related. ISSN: 0590-8876
■c/o Miss Anne Brogden; 3 Meadway Gate; London NW11 7LA; UK.

Covivt   *Čovaśskoe iskusstvo, Voprosy teorri i istorii*. Cov: Scan; Lang: Rus; Subj: Related. ISBN: 5-87677-003-5
■Moscow; RUSSIA.

CrAr   *Critical Arts*. Freq: IRR; Began: 1980; Cov: Scan; Lang: Eng; Subj: Related.
■Critical Arts Study Group, c/o Dept. of Journalism & Media; Rhodes University; 6140 Grahamstown; SOUTH AFRICA.

CRB   *Cahiers Renaud Barrault*. Freq: 4; Began: 1953; Lang: Fre; Subj: Theatre. ISSN: 0008-0470
- Editions Gallimard; S. Benmussa; 8 rue St. Placide; 75007 Paris; FRANCE.

CreD   *Creative Drama*. Freq: 1; Began: 1949; Lang: Eng; Subj: Theatre. ISSN: 0011-0892
- Educational Drama Association, c/o Stacey Publications; 1 Hawthorndene Road; BR2 7DZ Kent; UK.

Crepuscl   *Crépuscule, Le*. Ceased: 1979; Lang: Fre; Subj: Theatre.
- Théâtre Varia; rue du Sceptre; 78 à 1040 Bruxelles; BELGIUM.

Crisis   *Crisis*. Freq: 6; Began: 1910; Lang: Eng; Subj: Related. ISSN: 0011-1422
- Crisis Publishing Co.; 186 Remsen St.; Brooklyn, NY 11201; USA.

CritD   *Critical Digest*. Freq: 24; Began: 1948; Ceased: 1985; Lang: Eng; Subj: Theatre.
- 225 West 34th Street, Room 918; New York, NY 10001; USA.

Criticism   *Criticism*. Freq: 4; Lang: Eng; Subj: Related.
- Department of English; Wayne State University; Detroit, MI 42802; USA.

CritNY   *Critique*. Freq: 4; Began: 1976; Lang: Eng; Subj: Theatre.
- 417 Convent Avenue; New York, NY 10031; USA.

CritQ   *Critical Quarterly*. Freq: 4; Began: 1959; Lang: Eng; Subj: Related. ISSN: 0011-1562
- Blackwell Publishers; 108 Cowley Road; Oxford OX4 1JF; UK.

CritRev   *Critical Review, The*. Freq: IRR; Began: 1965; Lang: Eng; Subj: Related. ISSN: 0070-1548
- University of Melbourne; Department of English, Melbourne; AUSTRALIA.

CRT   *Cabra, La*: Revista de Teatro. Lang: Spa; Subj: Theatre.
- Mexico City; MEXICO.

CS   *Canada on Stage:The National Theatre Yearbook*. Formerly: *Canada on Stage-:Canadien Theatre Review Yearbook*. Freq: 1; Began: 1975; Lang: Eng; Subj: Theatre. ISSN: 0380-9455
- PACT Communications Centre; 64 Charles St. E.; Toronto, ON M4Y ITI; CANADA.

CSAN   *CSA News: The Newsletter of the Costume Society of America*. Formerly *Newsletter Quarterly and Dress*. Began: 1975; Lang: Eng; Subj: Related. ISSN: 0361-2112
- The Costume Society of America; 55 Edgewater Drive; P.O. Box 73 Earleville, MD 21919; USA.

CShav   *Californian Shavian*. Freq: 6; Began: 1958; Ceased: 1966; Lang: Eng; Subj: Theatre. ISSN: 0008-154X
- Shaw Society of California; 1933 S. Broadway; Los Angeles, CA 90007; USA.

CTA   *California Theatre Annual*. Ceased: 1986; Freq: 1; Lang: Eng; Subj: Theatre. ISSN: 0733-5806
- Performing Arts Network; 9025 Wilshire Blvd.; Beverly Hills, CA 90211; USA.

CTCheck   *Canadian Theatre Checklist*. Formerly: *Checklist of Canadian Theatres*. Freq: 1; Began: 1979; Ceased: 1983; Lang: Eng; Subj: Theatre. ISSN: 0226-5125
- University of Toronto Press; 63A St. George Street; Toronto, ON M5S 1A6; CANADA.

CTL   *Cahiers Théâtre Louvain*. Formerly *Cahiers Théâtre*. SEE *Etudes Théâtrales*. Freq: 4; Began: 1968; Ceased: 1991; Cov: Full; Lang: Fre; Subj: Theatre. ISSN: 0771-4653
- q. 1450 Fr. Ferme de Blocry, Place de l' Hocaille; B-1348 Louvain-La-Neuve; BELGIUM.

CTPA   *Cahiers du Théâtre Populaire d'Amiens*. Began: 1984; Lang: Fre; Subj: Theatre.
- Amiens; FRANCE.

CTR   *Canadian Theatre Review*. Freq: 4; Began: 1974; Cov: Full; Lang: Eng; Subj: Theatre. ISSN: 0315-0836
- Department of Drama; University of Guelph; Guelp, ON N1G 2WI; CANADA.

CTRY   *Canadian Theatre Review Yearbook*. Freq: 1; Began: 1974; Ceased; Lang: Eng; Subj: Theatre. ISSN: 0380-9455
- Canadian Theatre Review Publications, York University;, P.O. Box 1280 1011 Sheppard Ave. Downsview, ON M3J 1P3; CANADA.

CTXY   *C'wan t'ong Xiju Yishu/Art of Traditional Opera*. Freq: 4; Began: 1979; Lang: Chi; Subj: Theatre.
- Institute of Traditional Chinese Opera; Beijing; CHINA.

CU   *Cirque dans l'Univers, Le*. Freq: 4; Began: 1950; Lang: Fre; Subj: Theatre. ISSN: 0009-7373
- lub du Cirque; 11, rue Ch-Silvestri; 94300 Vincennes; FRANCE.

Cuaderno   *Cuadernos El Publico*. Freq: 10; Began: 1985; Ceased: 1989; Lang: Spa/Cat; Subj: Theatre. ISSN: 8602-3573
- Centro de Documentacion Teatral, Organismo Autonomo Teatros Ncnl; c/ Capitan Haya 44; 28020 Madrid; SPAIN.

Cue   *Cue International*. Formerly: *Cue: Technical Theatre Review*. Freq: 6; Began: 1979; Ceased: 1987; Cov: Full; Lang: Eng; Subj: Theatre. ISSN: 0144-6088
- Twynam Publishing Ltd.; Kitemore;, Faningdon, Oxfordshire SN7 8HR; UK.

CueM   *Cue, The*. Freq: 2; Began: 1928; Ceased; Cov: Scan; Lang: Eng; Subj: Theatre. ISSN: 0011-2666
- Theta Alpha Phi Fraternity, Dept. of Speech/ Theatre; Montclair State College; Upper Montclair, NJ 07043; USA.

CueNY   *Cue New York*. Freq: 26; Began: 1932; Ceased: 1978; Lang: Eng; Subj: Theatre. ISSN: 0011-2658
- North American Publishing Company; 545 Madison Avenue; New York, NY 10022; USA.

Culture   *Culture*. Freq: 4; Lang: Fre; Subj: Theatre.
- Maison de la Culture de La Rochelle; 11 rue Chef-de-Ville; 17000 La Rochelle; FRANCE.

CuPo   *Cultural Post*. Freq: IRR; Began: 1975; Ceased: 1983; Lang: Eng; Subj: Related.
- National Endowment for the Arts; 1100 Pennsylvania Avenue N.W.; Washington, DC 20506; USA.

CW   *Current Writing*. Freq: 2; Began: 1989; Cov: Scan; Lang: Eng; Subj: Related. ISSN 1013-929X
- English Dept.; University of Natal; King George V Ave, Durban 4001; SOUTH AFRICA.

Cz   *Circuszeitung, Die (Circus-Parade)*. Freq: 12; Began: 1955; Lang: Ger; Subj: Theatre.
- Gesellschaft für Circusfreunde; Klosterhof 10; 2308 Preetz; GERMANY.

D&D   *Dance and Dancers*. Freq: 12; Began: 1950; Lang: Eng; Subj: Related. ISSN: 0011-5983
- 214 Panther House; 38 Mount Pleasant; London WCIX OAP; UK.

D&T   *Drama and Theater*. Freq: 3; Began: 1968; Ceased: 1980; Lang: Eng; Subj: Theatre.
- Dept. of English, State University; Fredonia, NY 14063; USA.

DA   *Dance Australia*. Freq: 4; Began: 1980; Cov: Scan; Lang: Eng; Subj: Related. ISSN: 0159-6330
- Dance Australia; GPO Box 606; Sydney, NSW 2001; AUSTRALIA.

DABEI   *Dabei*. Freq: 6; Cov: Scan; Lang: Ger; Subj: Related.
- Gewerkschaft Kunst, Medien, Freie Berufe; Maria-Theresienstr. 11; A-1090 Vienna; AUSTRIA.

DalVostok   *Dalnij Vostok*: (Far East). Freq: 12; Began: 1933; Cov: Scan; Lang: Rus; Subj: Related. ISSN: 0130-3028
- Kniznoe izdatel'stvo; Khabarovsk; RUSSIA.

Danst   *Danstidningen*. Freq: 4; Began: 1991; Cov: Scan; Lang: Swe; Subj: Related. ISSN: 1102-0814
- Box 20 137; 104 60 Stockholm; SWEDEN.

DAT   *Andere Theatre, Das*. Freq: 4; Began: 1990; Lang: Ger; Subj: Theatre. ISSN: 0936-0662
- Union Internationale de la Marionette; Zentrum Brd e.V., Die Schaubude; Freifswalder Str. 81-84 D-10405 Berlin; GERMANY.

DB   *Deutsche Bühne, Die*. Freq: 12; Began: 1909; Lang: Ger; Subj: Theatre. ISSN: 0011-975X
- Erhard Friedrich Verlag; Im Brande 17; D-30926 Seelze; GERMANY.

DBj   *Deutsches Bühnenjahrbuch*. Freq: 1; Began: 1889; Lang: Ger; Subj: Theatre. ISSN: 0070-4431
- Genossenschaft Deutscher Bühnen Angehöriger; Buhnenschriften-Vertriebs Gmbh; Pf. 13 02 70; D-20102 Hamburg; GERMANY.

DC   *Dance in Canada/Danse au Canada*. Freq: 4; Began: 1973; Ceased; Lang: Eng/ Fre; Subj: Theatre. ISSN: 0317-9737
- Dance in Canada Association; 4700 Keele St.; Downsview, ON M3J 1P3; CANADA.

DCD   *Documents del Centre Dramàtic*. Freq: 4; Ceased; Lang: Spa; Subj: Theatre.
- c/o Hospital, 51, 1er; Barcelona 08001; SPAIN.

DekorIsk   *Dekorativnojè Iskusstvo SSR*. Freq: 12; Began: 1957; Cov: Scan; Lang: Rus; Subj: Related. ISSN: 0418-5153
- Soveckij Chudožnik; Moscow; RUSSIA.

DetLit *Detskaja Literatura*. Freq: 12; Began: 1932; Cov: Scan; Lang: Rus; Subj: Related. ISSN: 0130-3104 ■Moscow; RUSSIA.

Devlet *Devlet Tijatrolari (State Theatres)*. Freq: 4; Lang: Tur; Subj: Theatre. ■Genel Mudurugu; Ankara; TURKEY.

Dewan *Dewan Budaya*. Freq: 12; Began: 1979; Lang: Mal; Subj: Theatre. ISSN: 0126-8473 ■Peti Surat 803; Kuala Lumpur; MALAYSIA.

DGQ *Dramatists Guild Quarterly*. Freq: 4; Began: 1964; Cov: Full; Lang: Eng; Subj: Theatre. ISSN: 0012-6004 ■The Dramatists Guild, Inc.; 234 W. 44th St.; New York, NY 10036; USA.

DHS *Dix-Huitième Siècle*. Freq: 1; Began: 1969; Lang: Fre; Subj: Related. ISSN: 0070-6760 ■Soc. Française d'Etude du 18e Siecle; 23 Quai de Grenelle; 75015 Paris; FRANCE.

DialogA *Dialog*. Freq: 10; Began: 1973; Lang: Ger; Subj: Theatre. ISSN: 0378-6935 ■Verlag Sauerländer; Laurenzenvorstadt 89; CH 5001 Aarau; SWITZERLAND.

Dialogi *Dialogi*. Freq: 12; Began: 1965; Lang: Slo; Subj: Theatre. ISSN: 0012-2068 ■Založba Aristej d.o.o.; Dialogi, Šentilj 119a; 2212 Šentij; SLOVENIA.

DialogR *Dialog*. Freq: 12; Lang: Rus; Subj: Theatre. ISSN: 0236-0942 ■Miusskaja Square, 6; 125267 Moscow; RUSSIA.

DialogTu *Dialogue*. Lang: Fre; Subj: Theatre. ■Parti Socialiste Desourien, Maison du Parti, BP 1033; Blvd. du 9 Avril, La Kasbah; Tunis; TUNISIA.

Dialogue *Dialogue*: Canadian Philosophical Review/Revue Canadienne de Philosophie. Freq: 4; Began: 1962; Lang: Eng; Subj: Related. ISSN: 0012-2173 ■Ste. 46, 1390 Sherbrooke St. West; H3G 1K2 Montreal, PQ; CANADA.

DialogW *Dialog*: Miesiecznik Poswiecony Dramaturgii Wspolczesnej. Freq: 12; Began: 1956; Cov: Full; Lang: Pol; Subj: Theatre. ISSN: 0012-2041 ■Teatr Współczesny, ul. Mokotowska 13; 00670 Warsaw; POLAND.

DiN *Divadelni Noviny*. Freq: 26; Began: 1992; Cov: Scan; Lang: Cze; Subj: Theatre. ISSN: 0012-4141 ■Svaz Ceskoslovenskych Divadelnich a Rozhlasovych Umelcu; Valdstejnske nam. 3; Prague 1; CZECH REPUBLIC.

Dioniso *Dioniso*. Freq: 1; Began: 1929; Lang: Ita/Eng/Fre/Spa; Subj: Theatre. ■Instituto Nazionale del Dramma Antico; Corso Matteoti 29; Siracusa; ITALY.

DIPFL *Deutsches Institut für Puppenspiel Forschung und Lehre*. Freq: IRR; Began: 1964; Last Known Address; Lang: Ger; Subj: Theatre. ISSN: 0070-4490 ■Deutsches Institut für Puppenspiel; Bergstrasse 115; 4630 Bochum; GERMANY.

DirNotes *Directors Notes*. Lang: Eng; Subj: Theatre.

■American Directors Institute; 248 W. 74th St., Suite 10; New York, NY 10023; USA.

Diskurs *Diskurs*. Freq: 4; Last Known Address; Lang: Ger; Subj: Theatre. ■Schauble Verlag; Waldgurtel 5; 506 Bensberg; GERMANY.

DivR *Divadelni revue*. Freq: 4; Began: 1990; Cov: Scan; Lang: Cze; Subj: Theatre. ISSN: 0862-5409 ■Theatre Institute; Divadelni Ústav; 110 01 Prague 1 Celetna 17; CZECH REPUBLIC.

Dm *Dance Magazine*. Freq: 12; Began: 1926; Lang: Eng; Subj: Related. ISSN: 0011-6009 ■Dance Magazine, Inc.; 33 W. 60th St.; New York, NY 10023; USA.

DMC *Dramatics*. Freq: 9; Began: 1929; Lang: Eng; Subj: Theatre. ISSN: 0012-5989 ■Educational Theatre Association; 3368 Central Parkway; Cincinnati, OH 45225; USA.

DMR *David Mamet Review*. Cov: Scan; Lang: Eng ; Subj: Theatre. ■Box 455076; Las Vegas, NV 89154-5076; USA.

DnC *Dance Chronicle: Studies in Dance & the Related Arts*. Freq: 2; Began: 1978; Lang: Eng; Subj: Theatre. ISSN: 0147-2526 ■Marcel Dekker Journals; 270 Madison Avenue; New York, NY 10016; USA.

DNDT *Drama*: Nordisk dramapedagogisk tidsskrift. Freq: 4; Began: 1963; Lang: Nor/Swe/Dan; Subj: Theatre. ISSN: 0332-5296 ■Landslaget Drama i Skolen, Kongensgt. 4.; 0153 Oslo; NORWAY.

Dockt *Dockteatereko*. Freq: 4; Began: 1971; Lang: Swe; Subj: Theatre. ISSN: 0349-9944 ■Dockteaterforeningen; Sandavagen 10; 14032 Grodinge; SWEDEN.

DocTh *Documentation Théâtrale*. Began: 1974; Lang: Fre; Subj: Theatre. ■Centre d'Etudes Théâtrales, Université Paris X; 200 Avenue de la République; 92001 Nanterre Cedex; FRANCE.

DOE *DOE*. Formerly: *Speel*. Freq: 24; Began: 1951; Lang: Dut; Subj: Theatre. ISSN: 0038-7258 ■Stichting Ons Leekenspel'; Gudelalaan 2; Bussum; NETHERLANDS.

DongukDA *Dong-Guk Dramatic Art*. Freq: 1; Began: 1970; Cov: Full; Lang: Kor; Subj: Theatre. ■Department of Drama & Cinema, Dong-guk University; Seoul; SOUTH KOREA.

Drama *Drama: The Quarterly Theatre Review*: Third Series. Formerly: *Drama*. Freq: 4; Began: 1919; Ceased: 1989; Cov: Scan; Lang: Eng; Subj: Theatre. ISSN: 0012-5946 ■Cranbourne Mansions; Cranbourne Street; London WC2H 7AG; UK.

Dramat *Dramat*. Freq: 4 Began: 1993; Cov: Full; Lang: Swe; Subj: Theatre. ISSN: 1104-2885 ■Kungliga Dramatiska Teatern; Nybrogatan2; P.O. Box 5037 S-102 41 Stockholm; SWEDEN.

DrammaR *Dramma*. Freq: 12; Began: 1925; Cov: Scan; Lang: Ita; Subj: Theatre. ISSN: 0012-6004 ■Romana Teatri s.r.l.; Via Torino 29; 00184 Rome; ITALY.

DrammaT *Dramma*: Il Mensile dello Spettacolo. Freq: 12; Lang: Ita; Subj: Theatre. ■I.L.T.E.; Corso Bramante 20; Turin; ITALY.

dRAMATURg *dRAMATURg*. Freq: 2; Began: 1970; Cov: Scan; Lang: Ger; Subj: Theatre. ■Nachrichtenbrief; Dramaturgische Gesellschaft e.V.; Tempelherrenstr. 4 D-10961 Berlin; GERMANY.

Drammaturgia *Drammaturgia*. Freq: 2; Cov: Scan; Began: 1994; Lang: Ita; Subj: Theatre. ISSN: 1122-9365; ■Salerno Editrice Via di Donna Olimpia; 20-Roma; ITALY.

DramaY *Drama*. Lang: Slo; Subj: Theatre. ■Erjavceva; Ljubljana; SLOVENIA.

Dress *Dress*. Freq: 1; Began: 1975; Lang: Eng; Subj: Related. ISSN: 0361-2112 ■Costume Society of America; 55 Edgewater Drive; P.O. Box 73 Earleville, MD 21919; USA.

DRJ *Dance Research Journal*. Freq: 2; Began: 1967; Lang: Eng; Subj: Related. ISSN: 0149-7677 ■Congress on Research in Dance, Department of Dance; State University of New York College at Brockport, Brockport, NY 14420-2939; USA.

DRostock *Diskurs*. Freq: 4; Began: 1973; Ceased: 1980; Lang: Ger; Subj: Theatre. ■Volkstheater Rostock; Patriotischer Weg 33; 25 Rostock; GERMANY.

DrRev *Drama Review*. Freq: 2; Began: 1970; Last Known Address; Lang: Kor; Subj: Theatre. ■Yonguk-pyongron-sa; 131-51 Nokbun-dong, Eunpyong-ku; 122 Seoul; SOUTH KOREA.

DRs *Dance Research*. Freq: 2; Lang: Eng; Subj: Related. ■c/o Dance Books Ltd.; 9 Cecil Court; London WC2N 4EZ; UK.

Druzba *Družba*. SEE *Rossijane*. Freq: 6; Began: 1977; Ceased: 1992; Cov: Scan; Lang: Rus/Bul; Subj: Related. ISSN: 0320-1031 ■Moscow-Sofija; RUSSIA.

DruzNar *Družba Narodov*. Freq: 12; Began: 1939; Cov: Scan; Lang: Rus; Subj: Related. ISSN: 0012-6756 ■Sovetskii pisatel; Izvestiia Sovetov narodnykh deputatov SSSR; Moscow; RUSSIA.

DSat *Don Saturio: Boletin Informativo de Teatro Gallego*. Last Known Address; Lang: Spa; Subj: Theatre. ■Coruna 70-30; Esda; SPAIN.

DSchool *Drama and the School*. Freq: 2; Began: 1948; Last Known Address; Lang: Eng; Subj: Theatre. ■Whitehall Productions; 63 Elizabeth Bay Road; NSW 2011 Elizabeth Bay; AUSTRALIA.

DSGM *Dokumenti Slovenskega Gledaliskega Muzeja*. Freq: 2; Began: 1964; Lang: Slo; Subj: Theatre. ■Slovenski Gledaliski in Filski muzej; Cankarjeva 11; Ljubljana; SLOVENIA.

DShG *Deutsche Shakespeare Gesellschaft/Deutsche Shakespeare Gesellschaft West, Jahrbuch*. Freq: 1; Began: 1993; Lang: Ger; Subj: Theatre. ISSN: 0945-5094 ■Ferdinand Kamp Verlag GmbH; Postfach 101309; 44713 Bochum; GERMANY.

DSo *Dramatists Sourcebook*. Formerly: *Information for Playwrights*. Freq: 1; Began: 1981; Cov: Scan; Lang: Eng; Subj: Theatre.
ISSN: 0733-1606
■Theatre Comm. Group, Inc; 355 Lexington Ave.; New York, NY 10017; USA.

DSS *Dix-Septième Siècle*. Freq: 4; Began: 1949; Last Known Address; Cov: Scan; Lang: Fre; Subj: Related. ISSN: 0012-4273
■Commission des Publications, c/o Collège de France; 11 Place M. Berthelot; 75005 Paris; FRANCE.

DSTFM *Documents of the Slovenian Theatre and Film Museum*. Began: 1979; Cov: Scan; Lang: Slo; Subj: Theatre.
■Slovenian Theatre and Film Museum; Ljubljana; SLOVENIA.

DTh *Divadelní ústar*. Freq: 2; Lang: Slo; Subj: Theatre.
■Celetná 17; 11001 Prague 1; CZECH REPUBLIC.

Dtherapy *Dramatherapy*. SEE: Journal of Dramatherapy (JDt). Lang: Eng; Subj: Theatre.
■The Old Mill, Tolpuddle; Dorchester; Dorset DT2 7EX; UK.

DTi *Dancing Times*. Freq: 12; Began: 1910; Lang: Eng; Subj: Theatre. ISSN: 0011-605X
■Dancing Times Ltd., Clerkenwell House; 45-47 Clerkenwell Green; London EC1R 0BE; UK.

DTJ *Dance Theatre Journal*. Freq: 4; Began: 1983; Cov: Scan; Lang: Eng; Subj: Theatre. ISSN: 02464-9160
■Laban Centre for Movement & Dance, Laurie Grove; London, SE14 6NH; UK.

DTN *Drama and Theatre Newsletter*. Freq: 4; Began: 1975; Ceased: 1982; Lang: Eng; Subj: Theatre.
■British Theatre Institute; 30 Clareville Street; London SW7 5AW; UK.

DTOP *Dramaturgi: Tedri Og Praksis*. Lang: Dan; Subj: Theatre.
■Akademisk Forlag; St. Kannikestraede 8; 1169 Copenhagen; DENMARK.

Dvat *Dvatisoč 2000: časnik za mišljenje, umetnost, kulturna*. Began: 1969; Lang: Slo; Subj: Related.
■Društvo izdajateljev časnika 2000; Ljubljana; SLOVENIA.

DVLa *Diadja Vanja. Literaturnij al'manah*. Began: 1994; Lang: Rus; Subj: Related. ISSN: 0132-8204
■Gertsen Street 50/5; Room 44; 121069 Moscow; RUSSIA.

DZP *Deutsche Zeitschrift für Philosophie*. Freq: 12; Began: 1953; Cov: Scan; Lang: Ger; Subj: Related. ISSN: 0012-1045
■VEB Deutscher Verlag der Wissenschaften; Johannes-Dieckmann-Str. 10, Postfach 1216; 1080 Berlin; GERMANY.

E&AM *Entertainment and Arts Manager*. Formerly: *Entertainment and Arts Management*. Freq: 4; Began: 1973; Ceased: 1989; Cov: Scan; Lang: Eng; Subj: Theatre. ISSN: 0143-8980
■Assoc. of Entertainment & Arts Mangement, T.G. Scott and Son Ltd.; 30-32 Southampton St., Covent Garden; London WC2E 7HR; UK.

EAH *East Asian History*. Formerly: *Papers on Far Eastern History*. Freq: 2; Began: 1991; Cov: Scan; Lang: Eng; Subj: Related. ISSN: 1036-6008
■A.C.T.: Division of Pacific and Asian History; Research School of Pacific Studies; Australian National University, Canberra; AUSTRALIA.

EAR *English Academy Review, The*. Began: 1983; Cov: Scan; Lang: Eng; Subj: Related.
■English Academy of Southern Africa, Bollater House; 35 Melle St., Braamfontein; 2001 Johannesburg; SOUTH AFRICA.

Ebony *Ebony*. Freq: 12; Began: 1945; Lang: Eng; Subj: Related. ISSN: 0012-9011
■Johnson Publishing Co., Inc.; 820 S. Michigan; Chicago, IL 60605; USA.

Echanges *Echanges*. Freq: 12; Lang: Fre; Subj: Theatre.
■Théâtre Romain-Rolland; rue Eugène Varlin; 94 Villejuif; FRANCE.

EchoP *Echo Planety*. Freq: 52; Began: 1988; Lang: Rus; Subj: Related. ISSN: 0234-1670
■Stat Unio Publishin; 103009; Tversko Boulevar 10-12; Mosco- K-9; RUSSIA.

Econ *Economist Financial Report*. Freq: 48; Began: 1976; Cov: Scan; Lang: Eng; Subj: Related. ISSN: 0013-0613
■Economist Newspaper Ltd.; 25 St. James St.; London SW1A 1HG; UK.

ECr *Esprit Créateur, L'*. Freq: 4; Began: 1961; Lang: Fre; Subj: Theatre. ISSN: 0014-0767
■John D. Erickson; Box 222; Lawrence, KS 66044; USA.

ECrit *Essays in Criticism*. Freq: 4; Began: 1951; Lang: Eng; Subj: Related. ISSN: 0014-0856
■6A Rawlinson Rd.; Oxford OX2 6UE; UK.

ECW *Essays on Canadian Writing*. Freq: IRR; Began: 1974; Cov: Scan; Lang: Eng; Subj: Related. ISSN: 0313-0300
■1980 Queen St. E.; Toronto, ON M4L 1J2; CANADA.

ED *Envers du Décor, L'*. Freq: 6; Began: 1973; Lang: Fre; Subj: Theatre. ISSN: 0319-8650
■Théâtre du Nouveau Monde; 84 Ouest, Rue Ste-Catharine; Montreal, PQ H2X 1Z6; CANADA.

EDAM *The Early Drama, Art, and Music Review*. Formerly *EDAM Newsletter*. Freq: 2; Began: 1978; Cov: Scan; Lang: Eng; Subj: Theatre. ISSN: 0196-5816
■Medieval Institute Publications; Western Michigan University; Kalamazoo, MI 49008; USA.

EE&PA *Economic Efficiency and the Performing Arts*. Lang: Eng; Subj: Theatre.
■Association for Cultural Economics, University of Akron; Akron, OH 44235; USA.

EECIT *Estudis Escenics*. Freq: 2; Began: 1979; Lang: Cat; Subj: Theatre. ISSN: 0212-3819
■Inst. del Theatre de Barcelona, c/o Nou de la Rambla; 08001 Barcelona 3; SPAIN.

Egk *Engekikai*: Theatre World. Freq: 12; Began: 1940; Lang: Jap; Subj: Theatre.
■Engeki Shuppan-sha, Chiyoda-ku; 2-11 Kanda-Jinpo-cho; Tokyo 101; JAPAN.

EHR *Economic History Review*. Freq: 4; Began: 1927; Lang: Eng; Subj: Related. ISSN: 0013-0117
■Blackwell Ltd.; 108 Cowley Rd; Oxford OX4 1JF; UK.

EiC *Estrada i cirk*. Freq: 12; Began: 1992; Cov: Scan; Lang: Rus; Subj: Theatre. ISSN: 0131-6769
■Moscow; RUSSIA.

EinA *English in Africa*. Freq: 2; Began: 1974; Cov: Scan; Lang: Eng; Subj: Related. ISSN: 0013-0117
■ISEA, Rhodes University; Grahamstown; 6140; SOUTH AFRICA.

Eire *Eire-Ireland*. Freq: 4; Began: 1966; Cov: Scan; Lang: Eng; Subj: Related. ISSN: 0013-2683
■Irish American Cultural Institute; 2115 Summit Avenue; College of St. Thomas Box 5026, St. Paul, MN 55105; USA.

EIT *Escena*: Informativo Teatral. Freq: 4; Began: 1979; Lang: Spa; Subj: Theatre.
■Universidad de Costa Rica, Teatro Universitario, Apt. 92; San Pedro de Montes de Oca; San José; COSTA RICA.

Ekran *Ekran* Formerly *Sovetski Ekran*. Freq: 4; Began: 1992; Cov: Scan; Lang: Rus; Subj: Related.
■A-319 Ul. Chasovaja 5-6; Moscow 125319; RUSSIA.

Elet *Életünk*. Freq: 12; Began: 1963; Cov: Scan; Lang: Hun; Subj: Related. ISSN: 0133-4751
■Arany János Lap- és Könyvkiadó Kft.; Forgó u. 1; 9701 Szombathely; HUNGARY.

ElI *Elet és Irodalom*: irodalmi es politikai hetilap. Freq: 52; Began: 1957; Lang: Hun; Subj: Related. ISSN: 0424-8848
■Ft. Lapkiado Vallalat; Széchenyi rkp. 1; 1054 Budapest V; HUNGARY.

ElM *Marges, El*. Freq: 4; Cov: Scan; Lang: Cat; Subj: Related. ISSN: 0210-0452
■Curial Edicions Catalanes SA; carrer del Bruc 144; 08037 Barcelona; SPAIN.

ElPu *Publico, El*: Periodico mensual de teatro. Freq: 12; Began: 1983; Lang: Spa; Subj: Theatre. ISSN: 0213-4926
■Centro de Documentación Teatral; c/ Capitán Haya, 44; 28020 Madrid; SPAIN.

ELR *English Literary Renaissance Journal*. Freq: 3; Began: 1971; Lang: Eng; Subj: Related.
■University of Massachusetts; Department of English; Amherst, MA 01003; USA.

EN *Equity News*. Freq: 12; Began: 1915; Cov: Scan; Lang: Eng; Subj: Theatre. ISSN: 0013-9890
■Actors Equity Association; 165 W. 46 St.; New York, NY 10036; USA.

Enact *Enact*: monthly theatre magazine. Freq: 12; Began: 1967; Lang: Eng; Subj: Theatre. ISSN: 0013-6980
■Paul's Press, E44-11; Okhla Industrial Area, Phase II; 110020 New Delhi; INDIA.

Encore *Encore*. Lang: Eng; Subj: Theatre.
■Fort Valley State College; Fort Valley, GA 31030; USA.

EncoreA *Encore*. Freq: 12; Began: 1976; Lang: Eng; Subj: Theatre.
■PO Box 247; NSW 2154 Castle Hill; AUSTRALIA.

ENG *Editorial Nuevo Grupo*. Lang: Spa; Subj: Theatre.
■Avenida La Colina, Prolongación Los Manolos; La Florida; 105 Caracas; VENEZUELA.

Entre *Entré*. Freq: 6; Began: 1974; Cov: Full; Lang: Swe; Subj: Theatre. ISSN: 0345-2581
■Svenska Riksteatern, Swedish National Theatre Centre; S-145 83; Norsborg; SWEDEN.

EO *Etnograjicesko obozrenie*. Freq: 6; Began: 1992; Cov: Scan; Lang: Rus; Subj: Related. ISSN: 0038-5050
■Ulica D. Uljanova 19; B 36 Moscow; RUSSIA.

EOR *Eugene O'Neill Review*. Freq: 3; Began: 1977; Cov: Full; Lang: Eng; Subj: Theatre. Formerly: *Eugene O'Neill Newsletter, The.* ISSN: 0733-0456
■Suffolk University, Department of English; Boston, MA 02114; USA.

EpicT *Epic Theatre*. Freq: 4; Lang: Ben; Subj: Theatre.
■140/24 Netaji Subhashchandra Bose Road; Calcutta; INDIA.

EquityJ *Equity Journal*. Freq: 4; Began: 1931; Lang: Eng; Subj: Theatre. ISSN: 0141-3147
■British Actor's Equity Association; Guild House, Upper St. Martin's Lane; London WC2H 9EG; UK.

ERT *Empirical Research in Theatre*. Freq: 1; Began: 1971; Ceased: 1984; Cov: Full; Lang: Eng; Subj: Theatre. ISSN: 0361-2767
■Center for Communications Research; Bowling Green State University; Bowling Green, OH 43403; USA.

ESA *English Studies in Africa: A Journal of the Humanities*. Freq: 2; Began: 1958; Cov: Scan; Lang: Eng; Subj: Related. ISSN: 0013-8398
■Witwatersrand Univ. Press; Jan Smuts Ave.; Johannesburg 2001; SOUTH AFRICA.

ESC *English Studies in Canada*. Freq: 4; Began: 1975; Cov: Scan; Lang: Eng; Subj: Related.
■Association of Canadian College and University Teachers of English; c/o Dept. of English; Carleton University Ottawa, ON K1S 5B6; CANADA.

Escena *Escena*. Lang: Spa; Subj: Theatre.
■Departamento de Publicaciones, Consejo Nacional de la Cultura; Calle Paris, Edificio Macanao 3er. Piso; 106 Caracas; VENEZUELA.

Escenica *Escénica*. Began: 1990; Lang: Spa; Subj: Theatre.
■Universidad Nacional Autónoma de México; Coordinación de Difusión Cultural; Centro Cultural Universitario Ciudad Universitaria, C.P. 04510; MEXICO.

Espill *Espill, L'*. Freq: 4; Lang: Cat; Subj: Related.
■Editorial 3 i 4, c/o Moratin 15; Porta 3; 46002 Valencia; SPAIN.

Esprit *Esprit*. Freq: 12; Began: 1932; Lang: Fre; Subj: Related. ISSN: 0014-0759
■19, rue Jacob; 75006 Paris; FRANCE.

Essence *Essence*. Freq: 12; Began: 1970; Lang: Eng; Subj: Related. ISSN: 0014-0880
■Essence Comm., Inc.; P.O. Box 53400 Boulder, CO 80322-3400; USA.

EstLit *Estafeta Literaria*: La Revista Quincenal de Libros, Artes y Espetáculos. Freq: 24; Began: 1958; Lang: Spa; Subj: Theatre. ISSN: 0014-1186
■Avda. de José Antonio, 62; 13 Madrid; SPAIN.

Estreno *Estreno*: Journal on the Contemporary Spanish Theater. Freq: 2; Began: 1975; Cov: Full; Lang: Eng/Spa; Subj: Theatre. ISSN: 0097-8663
■Penn State University; 350 N. Burrowes Bldg; University Park, PA 16802; USA.

ET *Essays in Theatre*. Freq: 2; Began: 1982; Cov: Full; Lang: Eng; Subj: Theatre. ISSN: 0821-4425
■University of Guelph, Department of Drama; Guelph, ON N1G 2W1; CANADA.

ETh *Elizabethan Theatre*. Began: 1968; Lang: Eng; Subj: Theatre. ISSN: 0071-0032
■Archon Books; 995 Sherman Avenue; Hamden, CT 06514; USA.

ETN *Educational Theatre News*. Freq: 6; Began: 1953; Lang: Eng; Subj: Theatre. ISSN: 0013-1997
■Southern California Education Theatre Association; 9811 Pounds Avenue; Whittier, CA 90603; USA.

Etoile *Etoile de la Foire*. Freq: 12; Began: 1945; Ceased: 1982; Lang: Fle/Fre; Subj: Theatre. ISSN: 0014-1895
■15 rue Vanderlinden; Brussels 3; BELGIUM.

Etudes *Etudes Theatrales* Formerly *Arts du Spectacle en Belgique*. Freq: 2; Began: 1992; Lang: Fre; Subj: Theatre. ISSN: 0778-8738
■Centre d'études théâtrales; Université catholique de Louvain; place de l'Hocaille 5 1348 Louvain-la-Neuve; BELGIUM.

Europai *Európai utas*. Lang: Rus; Subj: Related.
■Moscow; RUSSIA.

Europe *Europe*: Revue Littéraire Mensuelle. Freq: 8; Began: 1923; Lang: Fre; Subj: Related. ISSN: 0014-2751
■146, rue du Fg. Poisonnière; 75010 Paris; FRANCE.

Evento *Evento Teatrale*. Freq: 3; Began: 1975; Lang: Ita; Subj: Theatre.
■A.BE.TE.spa; Via Presentina 683; 00155 Rome; ITALY.

Exchange *Exchange*. Freq: 3; Began: 1975; Lang: Eng; Subj: Theatre.
■University of Missouri: Columbia, Dept. of Speech/Drama; 129 Fine Arts Centre; Columbia, MS 65211; USA.

FAR *Fremantle Arts Review: monthly arts digest*. Freq: 6; Began: 1986; Cov: Full; Lang: Eng; Subj: Related. ISSN: 0816-6919
■Fremantle Arts Centre; P.O. Box 891; Fremantle 6160; AUSTRALIA.

Farsa *Farsa, La*. Freq: 20; Last Known Address; Lang: Spa; Subj: Theatre.
■Pza. de los Mostenses 11; 9 Madrid; SPAIN.

FDi *Film a Divadlo*. Freq: 26; Lang: Cze; Subj: Related.
■Theatre Intitute in Bratislava; Obzor, Ceskoslovenskej Armady 35; Bratislava 815 85; SLOVAKIA.

Fds *Freedomways*: A Quarterly Review of the Freedom Movement. Freq: 4; Began: 1961; Lang: Eng; Subj: Related. ISSN: 0016-061X
■Freedomways Assoc., Inc.; 799 Broadway; New York, NY 10003 6849; USA.

FemR *Feminist Review*. Freq: 3; Began: 1979; Lang: Eng; Subj: Related. ISSN: 0141-7789
■11 Carleton Gardens, Brecknock Rd.; London N19 5AQ; UK.

FemS *Feminist Studies*. Freq: 3; Lang: Eng; Subj: Related.
■c/o Women's Studies; 2101 Woods Hall; University of Maryland College Park, MD 20742 USA.

Figura *Figura. Zeitschrift für Theater und Spiel mit Figuren*. Formerly: *Puppenspiel und Puppenspieler*. Freq: 4; Began: 1993; Cov: Scan; Lang: Ger; Subj: Related. ISSN: 1021-3244
■Brigitta Weber; Pf. 501; CH-8401 Winterthur; GERMANY.

Fikr *Al Fikr*. Lang: Ara; Subj: Theatre.
■Rue Dar Eg-gild; Tunis; TUNISIA.

FiloK *Filológiai Közlöny*. Freq: 4; Began: 1955; Cov: Scan; Lang: Hun; Subj: Related. ISSN: 0015-1785
■Akadémiai Kiadó; Amerikai út 96; 1145 Budapest V; HUNGARY.

FIRTSIB *FIRT/SIBMAS Bulletin d'information*. Freq: 4; Began: 1977; Lang: Fre/Eng; Subj: Theatre.
■Fédération Internationale pour la Recherche Théâtrale; c/o van Eeghenstraat 11311, 1071 EZ Amsterdam; NETHERLANDS.

Flam *Flamboyant. Schriften zum Theater*. Freq: 4; Began: 1995; Cov: Scan; Lang: Ger; Subj: Theatre. ISBN: 3-9804764-3-X
■Studio 7, International Theatre Ensemble e.v.; Vitalisstr. 386; D-50933 Köln; GERMANY.

FMa *Fight Master, The*. Freq: 4; Cov: Scan; Lang: Eng; Subj: Theatre.
■Society of American Fight Directors; 1834 Camp Avenue; Rockford, IL 61103; USA.

FMT *Forum Modernes Theater*. Freq: 2; Began: 1986; Cov: Scan; Lang: Ger/Eng/Fre; Subj: Theatre. ISSN: 0930-5874
■Gunter Narr Verlag; Pf. 2567 D-72015 Tübingen; GERMANY.

FN *Filologiceskije Nauki*. Freq: 6; Began: 1958; Cov: Scan; Lang: Rus; Subj: Related. ISSN: 0130-9730
■Izdatelstvo Vysšaja Škola; Prospekt Marksa 18; 103009 Moscow K-9; RUSSIA.

Fnotes *Footnotes*. Freq: 1; Began: 1975; Lang: Eng; Subj: Theatre.
■Stagestep; Box 328; Philadelphia, PA 19105; USA.

FO *Federal One*. Freq: IRR; Began: 1975; Cov: Scan; Lang: Eng; Subj: Related.
■George Mason University; 4400 University Dr.; Fairfax, VA 22030; USA.

Forras *Forrás*. Freq: 12; Began: 1969; Cov: Scan; Lang: Hun; Subj: Related. ISSN: 0133-056X
∎Petőfi Lap- és Könyvkiadó Kft.; Május 1. tér 3; 6001 Kecskemét; HUNGARY.

FR *French Review, The*. Freq: 6; Began: 1927; Lang: Fre/Eng; Subj: Related. ISSN: 0016-111X
∎American Association of Teachers of French; 57 E. Armory Ave.; Champaign, IL 61820; USA.

FranceT *France Théâtre*. Freq: 24; Began: 1957; Lang: Fre; Subj: Theatre. ISSN: 0015-9433
∎Syndicat National des Agences; 16 Avenue l'Opéra; 75001 Paris; FRANCE.

FreilD *Freilichtbühne, Die*. Freq: 2; Began: 1956; Cov: Scan; Lang: Ger; Subj: Related.
∎Verband deutscher Freilichtbühnen e.V.; Gebrüder-Funke-Weg 3; D-59073 Hamm; GERMANY.

FrF *French Forum*. Freq: 3; Began: 1976; Lang: Fre/Eng; Subj: Related. ISSN: 0098-9355
∎French Forum Publishers, Inc.; Box 5108; Lexington, KY 40505; USA.

Front *Frontiers: A Journal of Women Studies*. Freq: 3; Lang: Eng; Subj: Related. Wilso 12; Washington State University; Pullman, WA 99164-4007; USA.

FS *French Studies*: A quarterly review. Freq: 4; Began: 1947; Lang: Eng; Subj: Related. ISSN: 0016-1128
∎Society for French Studies, c/o Dr. J.M. Lewis; Dept. of French; Queen's University Belfast BT7 1NN; NORTHERN IRELAND.

FSM *Film, Szinház, Muzsika*. Freq: 52; Began: 1957; Ceased: 1990; Cov: Scan; Lang: Hun; Subj: Theatre. ISSN: 0015-1416
∎Lapkiadó Vállalat; Erzsébet körút 9-11; 1073 Budapest VII; HUNGARY.

fTep *fliegende Teppich, Der. Zeitung für Kinderkultur und Kindertheater*. Freq: 5; Cov: Scan; Lang: Ger; Subj: Theatre.
∎Verein IchduwirAnimation und Mitspieltheater für Kinder; Hockegasse 40/27; A-1180 Vienna; AUSTRIA.

Ftr *Figurentheater*. Freq: IRR; Began: 1923; Ceased; Lang: Ger; Subj: Theatre. ISSN: 0430-3873
∎Deutsches Institut für Puppenspiel; Hattingerstr. 467; D-4630 Bochum; GERMANY.

Fundarte *Fundarte*. Lang: Spa; Subj: Theatre.
∎Edificio Tajamar, P.H., Parque Central; Avenida Lecuna; 105 Caracas; VENEZUELA.

Fundevogel *Fundevogel. Kritisches Kinder-Medien-Magazin*. Freq: 4; Began: 1984; Cov: Scan; Lang: Ger; Subj: Related. ISSN: 0176-2753
∎dipa-Verlag, Nassauer Str. 1-3; D-60439 Frankfurt/M; GERMANY.

FundM *Fundraising Management*. Freq: 12; Began: 1972; Cov: Scan; Lang: Eng; Subj: Related.
∎Hoke Communications Inc.; 224 7th Street; Garden City, NY 11530-5771 USA.

Funoun *Al Funoun*: The Arts. Freq: 12; Lang: Ara; Subj: Theatre.
∎Ministry of Information, Dept. of Culture and Arts; PO Box 6140; Amman; JORDAN.

G&GBKM *Grimm & Grips. Beilage zum Kritischen Kinder-Medien Magazin-Fundevogel*. Freq: 4; Cov: Scan; Lang: Ger; Subj: Related. ISSN: 0176-2753
∎Assitej e.V. Bundesrepublik Deutschland; Schützenstr. 12; D-60311 Frankfurt/M; GERMANY.

G&GJKJ *Grimm & Grips. Jahrbuch für Kinder- und Jugendtheater*. Freq: 1; Began: 1987; Cov: Scan; Lang: Ger; Subj: Related. ISSN: 0933-4149
∎Assitej e.V. Sektion BRD; Schützenstr. 12; D-60311 Frankfurt/M; GERMANY.

Gambit *Gambit*. Freq: IRR; Began: 1963; Ceased: 1986; Cov: Scan; Lang: Eng; Subj: Theatre. ISSN: 0016-4283
∎John Calder, Ltd.; 9-15 Neal Street; London WC2H 9TU; UK.

Gap *Gap, The*. Lang: Eng; Subj: Related.
∎Washington, DC; USA.

GaR *Georgia Review*. Freq: 4; Began: 1947; Lang: Eng; Subj: Related. ISSN: 0016-8386
∎University of Georgia; Athens, GA 30602; USA.

Garcin *Garcin: Libro de Cultura*. Freq: 12; Began: 1981; Lang: Spa; Subj: Related.
∎Acali Editoria; Ituzaingo 1495; Montevideo; URUGUAY.

Gazit *Gazit*. Lang: Heb; Subj: Theatre.
∎8 Brook Street; Tel Aviv; ISRAEL.

GdBA *Gazette des Beaux Arts*. Freq: 12; Began: 1859; Lang: Fre; Subj: Related. ISSN: 0016-5530
∎Imprimerie Louis Jean, B.P. 87; Gap Cedex 05002; SWITZERLAND.

GdF *Gazette du Français*. Freq: 12; Began: 1983; Lang: Fre; Subj: Related. ISSN: 0759-1268
∎Paris; FRANCE.

GdS *Giornale dello Spettacolo*. Freq: 52; Lang: Ita; Subj: Theatre. ISSN: 0017-0232
∎Associazione Generale Italiana dello Spettacolo; Via di Villa Patrizi 10; 00161 Rome; ITALY.

GerSR *German Studies Review*. Freq: 3; Began: 1978; Cov: Scan; Lang: Ger; Subj: Related. ISSN: 0149-7952
∎German Studies Association, c/o Prof. Gerald R. Kleinfeld; Arizona State University; Tempe, AZ 85281; USA.

Gestos *Gestos*: teoria y práctica del teatro hispánico. Freq: 2; Began: 1986; Cov: Scan; Lang:Eng /Spa; Subj: Theatre. ISBN: 0-9656914-1
∎University of California, Irvine, Department of Spanish and Portuguese; Irvine, CA 92697; USA.

Gestus *Gestus*: A Quarterly Journal of Brechtian Studies. Freq: 4; Began: 1985; Cov: Full; Lang: Eng/Ger/Fre/Ita/Spa; Subj: Theatre. ISSN: 0749-7644
∎Brecht Society of America; 59 S. New St.; Dover, DE 19901; USA.

GiP *Gosudarstvo i pravo*. Freq: 12; Began: 1992; Cov: Scan; Lang: Rus; Subj: Related. ISSN: 0132-0769
∎Akad. Nauk S.S.S.R.; Inst. Gosudarstva i Prava; Izdatel'stvo Nauka; Podsosenskii Per., 21; Moscow K-62; RUSSIA.

GL&L *German Life and Letters*. Freq: 4; Began: 1936; Cov: Scan; Lang: Eng; Subj: Related. ISSN: 0016-8777
∎Basil Blackwell Publisher, Ltd.; 108 Cowley Road; Oxford 0X4 1JF; UK.

Goethe *Goethe Yearbook: Publication of the Goethe Society of North America*. Freq: IRR; Lang: Eng /Ger; Subj: Related.
∎Department of German; University of California; Irvine, CA 92717; USA.

GOS *Gazette Officielle du Spectacle*. Freq: 36; Began: 1969; Lang: Fre; Subj: Theatre.
∎Office des Nouvelles Internationales; 12 rue de Miromesnil; 75008 Paris; FRANCE.

Gosteri *Gosteri*: Performance. Freq: 12; Lang: Tur; Subj: Theatre.
∎Uluslararasi Sanat Gosterileri A.S.; Narlpbahce Sok. 15; Cagaloglu-Istanbul; TURKEY.

GQ *German Quarterly*. Freq: 4; Began: 1928; Last Known Address; Cov: Scan; Lang: Ger; Subj: Related. ISSN: 0016-8831
∎American Assoc. of Teachers of German; 523 Building, Suite 201, Rt. 38; Cherry Hill, NJ 08034; USA.

GrandR *Grande République*. Formerly: *Pratiques Théâtrales*. Freq: 3; Began: 1978; Ceased: 1981; Lang: Fre; Subj: Theatre. ISSN: 0714-8178
∎University of Québec; 200 Rue Sherbrooke Ouest; Montreal, PQ H2X 3P2; CANADA.

GrTZ *Graumann TZ*; Freq: 4; Cov: Scan; Lang: Ger; Subj: Related.
∎GraumannEigenArt, Theaterverlag Wien-Hamburg; Wipplingerstr. 34; A-1001 Vienna; AUSTRIA.

GSJ *Gilbert and Sullivan Journal*. Freq: 3; Began: 1925; Ceased: 1986; Lang: Eng; Subj: Theatre. ISSN: 0016-9951
∎Gilbert and Sullivan Society; 23 Burnside, Sawbridgeworth; Hertfordshire CM21 OEP; UK.

GSTB *George Spelvin's Theatre Book*. Freq: 3; Began: 1978; Lang: Eng; Subj: Theatre. ISSN: 0730-6431
∎Proscenium Press; Box 361; Newark, NJ 19711; USA.

GTAR *Grupo Teatral Antifaz: Revista*. Freq: 12; Lang: Spa; Subj: Theatre.
∎San Addres 146; 16 Barcelona; SPAIN.

GtE *Guidateatro: Estera*. Freq: 1; Began: 1967; Ceased; Lang: Ita; Subj: Theatre.
∎Edizione Teatron; Via Fabiola 1; 00152 Rome; ITALY.

GtI *Guidateatro: Italiana*. Freq: 1; Began: 1967; Lang: Ita; Subj: Theatre.
∎La guidateatro è venduta direttamente dall 'Théatron'; Via Fabiola 1; 00152 Rome; ITALY.

Guida *Guida dello Spettacolo*. Lang: Ita; Subj: Theatre.
∎Via Palombini 6; Rome; ITALY.

HA *Habitat Australia*. Freq: 6; Began: 1973; Lang: Eng; Subj: Related. ISSN: 0310-2939

■Australian Conservation Foundation; 340 Gore St. Fitzroy; Melbourne, Victoria; AUSTRALIA.

Harlekijn *Harlekijn*. Freq: 4; Began: 1970; Ceased; Lang: Dut; Subj: Theatre.
■Kerkdijk 11; 3615 BA Westbroek; NETHERLANDS.

Hecate *Hecate: Women's Interdisciplinary Journal*. Freq: 2; Began: 1975; Cov: Scan; Lang: Eng; Subj: Related.   ISSN: 0311-4198
■Hecate Press; English Dept., University of Queensland; P.O. Box 99 St. Lucia, Qld. 4067; AUSTRALIA.

Helik *Helikon*. Freq: 4; Began: 1955; Lang: Hun; Subj: Related.   ISSN: 0017-999X
■Argumentum Kiadó; Ménesi út 11-13 1118 Budapest; HUNGARY.

Hermes *Hermes: Zeitschrift für Klassische Philologie*. Freq: 4; Began: 1866; Lang: Eng/Ger/Fre/Ita; Subj: Related. ISSN: 0018-0777
■Franz Steiner Verlag Wiesbaden GmbH; Birkenwaldstr. 44; D-70191; Stuttgart; GERMANY.

HevN *Hevesi Napló*.Freq: 4;Began: 1991;Lang: Hun; Subj: Related. ISSN: 1217-3746
■András Farkas; Vörösmarty út 26; 3300 Eger; HUNGARY.

HgK *Higeki Kigeki*: Tragedy and Comedy. Freq: 12; Began: 1948; Lang: Jap; Subj: Theatre.
■Hayakawa-Shobo, Chiyoda-ku; 2-2 Kanda-Tacho; 101 Tokyo; JAPAN.

HispArts *Hispanic Arts*. Freq: 5; Began: 1976; Last Known Address; Lang: Spa/Eng Subj Theatre.   ISSN: 0732-1643
■Association of Hispanic Arts Inc.; 200 East 87th Street; New York, NY 10028; USA.

HisSt *Historical Studies*. Formerly: *Historical Studies: Australia and New Zealand*. SEE *Australian Historical Studies*. Freq: 2; Began: 1940; Ceased: 1988; Lang: Eng; Subj: Related.   ISSN: 0018-2559
■University of Melbourne, Dept. of History; Parkville 3052; AUSTRALIA.

HistP *Historical Performance: Journal of Early Music America*. Freq: 2; Began: 1988; Lang: Eng; Subj: Related.   ISSN: 0898-8587
■Early Music America; New York, NY; USA.

HJEAS *Hungarian Journal of English and American Studies*. Cov: Scan; Subj: Related.
■HUNGARY.

HJFTR *Historical Journal of Film, Radio and Television*. Freq: 2; Began: 1980; Lang: Eng; Subj: Related.   ISSN: 0143-9685
■Carfax Pulbishing Co.; Box 25; Abingdon OX14 3UE; UK.

Horis *Horisont*. Freq: 6; Began: 1954; Lang: Swe; Subj: Related.   ISSN: 0439-5530
■c/o Landsleapsförburden; Handelsesplanaden 23A; F 651 00 VASA; FINLAND.

HP *High Performance*. Freq: 4; Began: 1978; Lang: Eng; Subj: Related. ISSN: 0160-9769
■Astro Artz; 240 S. Broadway, 5th Floor; Los Angeles, CA 90012; USA.

HQ *Hungarian Quarterly*. Freq: 4; Began: 1959; Cov: Scan; Lang: Hun; Subj: Related.   ISSN: 0028-5390

■MTI;Naphegy tér 8;1016 Budapest; HUNGARY.

HSt *Hamlet Studies*. Freq: 2; Began: 1978; Lang: Eng; Subj: Related. ISSN: 0256-2480
■Vikas Publishing House Ltd.; 5 Ansari Road; 110 002 New Delhi; INDIA.

HTHD *Hungarian Theatre/Hungarian Drama*. Freq: 1; Began: 1981; Cov: Scan; Ceased: 1988; Lang: Eng; Subj: Theatre.
ISSN: 0230-1229
■Hungarian Theatre Institute; Krisztina körút. 57; 1016 Budapest; HUNGARY.

HTN *Hungarian Theatre News/ Ungarische Theaternachrichten*. Freq: 2; Began: 1985; Cov: Scan; Lang: Eng; Subj: Theatre.
ISSN: 0237-3963
■Hungarian Centre of the International Theatre Institute; Krisztina krt. 57; 1016 Budapest; HUNGARY.

HW *History Workshop*. Freq: 2; Began: 1976; Lang: Eng; Subj: Related. ISSN: 0309-2984
■Oxford University Press; Pinkhill House; Southfield Road Eynsham, Oxford OX8 1JJ; UK.

IA *Ibsenårboken/Ibsen Yearbook*: Contemporary Approaches to Ibsen. Freq: 1; Began: 1952; Cov: Full; Lang: Nor/Eng; Subj: Theatre.   ISSN: 0073-4365
■Universitetssorleget; Box 2959; 0608 Oslo 6; NORWAY.

IAS *Interscena/Acta Scenographica*. Freq: 2; Ceased: 1984; Lang: Eng/Fre/Ger; Subj: Theatre.
■Divadelni Ustav; Celetna 17; Prague 1; CZECH REPUBLIC.

IdS *Information du Spectacle, L'*. Freq: 11; Lang: Fre; Subj: Theatre.
■7 rue du Helder; 75009 Paris; FRANCE.

IDSelect *Irish Drama Selections*. Freq: IRR; Began: 1982; Lang: Eng; Subj: Theatre.
ISSN: 0260-7964
■Colin Smythe Ltd., Box 6; Gerrards Cross; Buckinghamshire SL9 8XA; UK.

IHoL *Irodalomtörténet*. Freq: 4; Began: 1912; Cov: Scan; Lang: Hun; Subj: Related.
ISSN: 0324-4970
■Magyar Irodalomtörténeti Társaság; Piarista köz 1. I. 59; 1052 Budapest; HUNGARY.

IHS *Irish Historical Studies*. Freq: 2; Began: 1938; Lang: Eng; Subj: Related.
ISSN: 0021-1214
■Irish Historical Society, Dept. of Modern Irish History; Arts-Commerce Bldg, University College; Dublin 4; IRELAND.

IITBI *Instituto Internacional del Teatro, Centro Espanol*: Boletin Informativo. Freq: 4; Last Known Address; Lang: Spa; Subj: Theatre.
■Paseo de Recoletos 18-60; 1 Madrid; SPAIN.

IK *Irodalomtörténeti Közlemények*. Freq: 6; Began: 1891; Cov: Scan; Lang: Hun; Subj: Related.   ISSN: 0021-1486
■Balassi Kiadó; Ménesi út 11-13; 1118 Budapest; HUNGARY.

IlCast *Il Castello di Elsinore*. Freq: 3; Began: 1988; Cov: Scan; Lang: Ita; Subj: Related.   ISSN: 0394-9389

■Rosenberg & Sellier; Via Andrea Doria, 14; 00192 Torino; ITALY.

IM *Island Magazine* Formerly: *Tasmanian Review;*. Freq: 4; Lang: Eng Cov: Scan;; Subj: Related.   ISSN: 1035-3127
■c/o Univ. of Tasmania; P.O. Box 207; Tasmania 7005; AUSTRALIA.

Impressum *Impressum*. Freq: 4; Lang: Ger; Subj: Related.
■Henschelverlag Kunst und Gesellschaft; Oranienburger Strasse 67/68; 1040 Berlin; GERMANY.

Impuls *Impuls*. Freq: 3; Cov: Scan; Lang: Ger; Subj: Related.
■Internationales Theaterinstitut; Schloss str. 48; D-12165 Berlin; GERMANY.

InArts *In the Arts*: Search, Research, and Discovery. Began: 1978; Ceased: 1988; Lang: Eng; Subj: Related.
■Ohio State University, College of the Arts; Columbus, OH 43210; USA.

INC *Ibsen News & Comments*. Freq: 1; Began: 1980; Cov: Scan; Lang: Eng; Subj: Theatre.
■Ibsen Society in America, Mellon Programs, Dekalb Hall 3; Pratt Institute; Brooklyn, NY 11205; USA.

Indonesia *Indonesia*. Freq: 2; Began: 1966; Lang: Eng; Subj: Related.   ISBN: 0-87727
■Cornell University, Southeast Asia Program Publications; East Hill Plaza; Ithaca, NY 14850; USA.

IndSh *Independent Shavian*. Freq: 3; Began: 1962; Lang: Eng; Subj: Theatre.
ISSN: 0019-3763
■The Bernard Shaw Society; Box 1159, Madison Square Station; New York, NY 10159-1159; USA.

Info *Information on New Plays*. Freq: IRR; Lang: Eng; Subj: Theatre. ISSN: 0236-6959
■Hungarian Information Service; Krisztina krt. 57; H-1016 Budapest; HUNGARY.

InoLit *Inostrannaja Literatura*: (Foreign Literature). Freq: 12; Began: 1955; Cov: Scan; Lang: Rus; Subj: Related.   ISSN: 0130-6545
■Izvestija; Moscow; RUSSIA.

ISK *Iskusstvo Kino*. Freq: 12; Cov: Scan; Lang: Rus; Subj: Related. ISSN: 0130-6405
■Moscow; RUSSIA.

Iskusstvo *Iskusstvo*. Freq: 12; Last Known Address; Began: 1918; Cov: Scan; Lang: Rus; Subj: Related.   ISSN: 0130-2523
■Tsvetnoi Bulvar 25; K 51 Moscow; RUSSIA.

Iskv *Iskusstvo v škole*. Began: 1927; Cov: Scan; Lang: Rus; Subj: Related. ISSN: 0869-4966
■State Union Publishing; Kedrov Street 8; 117804 Moscow; RUSSIA.

ISPTC *Istituto di Studi Pirandelliani e sul Teatro Contemporaneo*. Freq: 1; Began: 1967; Lang: Ita; Subj: Theatre.   ISSN: 0075-1480
■Casa Editrice Felice le Monnier; Via Scipione Ammirato 100; 50136 Florence; ITALY.

ISST *In Sachen Spiel und Theater*. Formerly *Bunte Wagen*. Freq: 6; Began: 1949; Lang: Ger; Subj: Theatre.
■Höfling Verlag, Dr. V. Mayer; Str. 18-22; 6940 Weinheim; GERMANY.

ITAN *Irish Theatre Archive's Newsletter.* Freq: 2; Began: 1993; Lang: Eng; Subj: Theatre. ■Irish Theatre Archive, Archives Division; City Hall; Dublin 2; IRELAND.

ITY *International Theatre Yearbook*: SEE: Miedzynarodowny Rocznik Teatralny (Acro: MRT). Lang: Pol; Subj: Theatre. ■Warsaw; POLAND.

IUR *Irish University Review.* Freq: 2; Began: 1970; Cov: Scan; Lang: Eng; Subj: Related. ISSN: 0021-1427 ■University College; Room K203; Arts Building; Dublin 4; IRELAND.

IW *Ireland of the Welcomes.* Freq: 6; Began: 1952; Cov: Scan; Lang: Eng; Subj: Related. ISSN: 0021-0943 ■Bord Failte - Irish Tourist Board; Baggot St. Bridge; Dublin 2; IRELAND.

JAAC *Journal of Aesthetics and Art Criticism, The.* Freq: 4; Began: 1941; Lang: Eng; Subj: Related. ISSN: 0021-8529 ■114 N. Murray St.; Madison, WI 53715; USA.

JAC *Journal of American Culture.* Freq: 4; Began: 1978; Cov: Scan; Lang: Eng; Subj: Related. ISSN: 0191-1813 ■American Culture Association, Bowling Green State University; Bowling Green, OH 43403; USA.

JADT *Journal of American Drama and Theatre, The.* Freq: 3; Began: 1989; Cov: Full; Lang: Eng; Subj: Theatre. ISSN: 1044-937X ■CASTA, Grad. School and Univ. Centre, City University of New York; 33 West 42nd Street; New York, NY 10036; USA.

JAfS *Journal of African Studies.* Freq: 4; Began: 1974; Lang: Eng; Subj: Related. ISSN: 0095-4993 ■Heldref Publications; 4000 Albemarle St, N.W.; Wasington, DC 20016; USA.

JahrfO *Jahrbuch für Opernforschung.* Cov: Scan; Lang: Ger; Subj: Related. ISSN: 0724-8156 ■Verlag Peter Lang GmbH; Eschborner Landstr. 42; D-60489 Frankfurt; GERMANY.

JahrST *Jahrbuch der Städte mit Theatergastspielen.* Freg: 1; Began: 1990; Cov: Scan; Lang: Ger; Subj: Related. ISSN: 0938-7943 ■Interessengemeinschaft der Städte mit Theatergastspielen; Mykenae-Verlag, Ahastr. 9; D-64285 Darmstadt; GERMANY.

JahrT *Jahrbuch Tanzforschung.* Freq: 1; Cov: Scan; Lang: Ger; Subj: Related. ISSN: 0940-1008 ■Florian Noetzel Verlag; Valoisstr. 11; D-29382 Wilhelmshaven; GERMANY.

JAML *Journal of Arts Management, Law and Society.* Formerly *Journal of Arts Management and Law.* Freq: 4; Began: 1969; Cov: Full; Lang: Eng; Subj: Related. ISSN: 1063-2921 ■Heldref Publications; 1319 Eighteenth Street, NW; Washington, DC 20036-1802; USA.

JAP&M *Journal of Arts Policy and Management.* Freq: 3; Began: 1984; Ceased: 1989; Cov: Full; Lang: Eng; Subj: Theatre. ISSN: 0265-0924 ■City University, Dept. of Arts Policy and Management; Level 12, Frobisher Crescent; Barbican, Silk Street; London EC2Y 8HB; UK.

JASt *Journal of Asian Studies.* Freq: 4; Began: 1941; Cov: Scan; Lang: Eng; Subj: Related. ISSN: 0021-9118 ■Association for Asian Studies, Inc., University of Michigan; One Lane Hall; Ann Arbor, MI 48109; USA.

Javisko *Javisko.* Freq: 12; Lang: Cze; Subj: Related. ISSN: 0323-2883 ■Vydavatel'stvo tosveta; Osloboditelov 21; 036-54 Martin; SLOVAKIA.

JBeckS *Journal of Beckett Studies.* Freq: 2; Began: 1976; Cov: Full; Lang: Eng; Subj: Theatre. ISSN: 0309-5207 ■John Calder Ltd.; 9-15 Neal Street; London WC2H 9TU; UK.

JCCP *Journal of Cross-Cultural Psychology.* Freq: 6; Cov: Scan; Lang: Eng; Subj: Related. ISSN: 0022-0221 ■SAGE Publications, Inc.; P.O. Box 5084; Thousand Oaks, CA 91359; USA.

JCNREC *Journal of Canadian Studies/Revue d'études canadiennes.* Freq: 4; Began: 1966; Cov: Scan; Lang: Eng/Fre; Subj: Related. ISSN: 0021-9495 ■Trent University; Box 4800; Peterborough, ON K9J 7B8; CANADA.

JCSt *Journal of Caribbean Studies.* Freq: 2; Began: 1970; Lang: Eng/Fre/Spa; Subj: Related. ISSN: 0190-2008 ■Association of Caribbean Studies; Box 248231; Coral Gables, FL 33124; USA.

JCT *Jeu*: Cahiers de Théâtre. Freq: 4; Began: 1976; Cov: Full; Lang: Fre; Subj: Theatre. ISSN: 0382-0335 ■Cahiers de Theatre Jeu Inc.; C.P. 1600 Succursale E.; Montreal, PQ H2T 3B1; CANADA.

JdCh *Journal de Chaillot.* Freq: 8; Began: 1974; Lang: Fre; Subj: Related. ■Théâtre National de Chaillot; Place du Tracadéro; 75116 Paris; FRANCE.

JDS *Jacobean Drama Studies.* Freq: IRR; Began: 1972; Ceased: 1987; Lang: Eng; Subj: Theatre. ■Universität Salzburg, Institut für Englische Sprach; Akademiestr. 24; A 5020 Salzburg; AUSTRIA.

JDSh *Jahrbuch der Deutsche Shakespeare-Gesellschaft.* SEE: *Deutsche Shakespeare Gesellschaft/Deutsche Shakespeare Gesellschaft West.* Cov: Scan; Lang: Ger; Subj: Theatre. ■Deutsche Shakespeare-Gesellschaft West; Rathaus; D 4630 Bochum; GERMANY.

JDt *Journal of Dramatherapy.* Formerly: *Dramatherapy.* Freq: 2; Began: 1977; Lang: Eng; Subj: Related. ISSN: 0263-0672 ■David Powley, British Association for Dramatherapy; PO Box 98; Kirkbymoorside YD6 6EX; UK.

JDTC *Journal of Dramatic Theory and Criticism.* Freq: 2; Began: 1986; Cov: Full; Lang: Eng; Subj: Theatre. ISSN: 0888-3203 ■University of Kansas, Dept. of Theatre and Film; 356 Murphy Hall; Lawrence, KS 66045; USA.

JEBT *JEB Théâtre.* Lang: Fre; Ceased: 1982; Subj: Theatre. ■Documentation Générale de la jeunesse, des Loisirs; Galerie Ravenstein 78; 1000 Brussels; BELGIUM.

Jelenkor *Jelenkor.* Freq: 12; Began: 1958; Cov: Scan; Lang: Hun; Subj: Related. ISSN: 0447-6425 ■Jelenkor Irodalmi és Müvészeti Kiadó; Széchenyi tér 17 7621 Pécs; HUNGARY.

JENS *Journal of the Eighteen Nineties Society.* Freq: 1; Began: 1970; Lang: Eng; Subj: Related. ISSN: 0144-008X ■28 Carlingford Rd., Hampstead; London NW3 1RQ; UK.

JFT *Journal Freie Theater.* Freq: 1; Cov: Scan; Lang: Ger; Subj: Related. ■Bundesverband Freier Theater e.V.; Mykenae-Verlag, Ahastr. 9; D-64285 Darmstadt; GERMANY.

JGG *Jahrbuch der Grillparzer-Gesellschaft.* Freq: IRR; Began: 1897; Lang: Ger; Subj: Related. ISBN: 3-273-00043-4 ■Grillparzer-Gesellschaft; Gumpendorfer Strasse 15/1; A 1060 Vienna; AUSTRIA.

JGT *Journal du Grenier de Toulouse.* Freq: 12; Lang: Fre; Subj: Theatre. ■Grenier de Toulouse; 3, rue de la Digue; 31300 Toulouse; FRANCE.

JIES *Journal of the Illuminating Engineering Society.* Freq: 1; Lang: Eng; Subj: Related. ISSN: 0099-4480 ■Illuminating Engineering Society of North America; 120 Wall Street, 17th Floor; New York, NY 10005-4001; USA.

JIL *Journal of Irish Literature.* Freq: 3; Began: 1972; Ceased: 1994; Lang: Eng; Subj: Related. ■P.O. Box 361; Newark, DE 19711; USA.

JITT *JITT.* Lang: Jap; Subj: Theatre. ■Japanese Institute for Theatre Technology; 4-437 Ikebukuro, Toshima-ku; Tokyo; JAPAN.

JJS *Journal of Japanese Studies.* Freq: 2; Began: 1974; Lang: Eng; Subj: Related. ISSN: 0095-6848 ■Society for Japanese Studies, University of Washington; Thomson Hall DR-05; Seattle, WA 98195; USA.

JLS/TLW *Journal of Literary Studies/Tydskrif vir Literatuurwetenskap.* Freq: 4; Began: 1985; Cov: Scan; Lang: Eng/Afr; Subj: Related. ISSN: 0256-4718 ■South African Society for General Literary Studies; Department of Theory of Literature Unisa P.O. Box 392 Pretoria 0001; SOUTH AFRICA.

JMH *Journal of Magic History.* Began: 1979; Lang: Eng; Subj: Related. ISSN: 0192-9917 ■Toledo, OH; USA.

JNZL *Journal of New Zealand Literature.* Lang: Eng; Subj: Related. ■Wellington; NEW ZEALAND.

JoM *Journal of Musicology.* Freq: 4; Cov: Scan; Lang: Eng; Subj: Related. ISSN: 0277-9269 ■University of California Press; 2120 Berkeley Way; Berkeley, CA 94720; USA.

JOV *Journal of Voice.* Freq: 4; Began: 1987; Cov: Scan; Lang: Eng; Subj: Related. ■Raven Press Books, Ltd.; 1185 Avenue of the Americas; New York, NY 10036; USA.

JPC   *Journal of Popular Culture.* Freq: 4; Began: 1967; Cov: Scan; Lang: Eng; Subj: Related.   ISSN: 0022-3840
■Popular Culture Association, Bowling Green State University; Bowling Green, OH 43403; USA.

JRASM   *Journal of the Royal Asiatic Society of Malaysia.* Freq: 2; Began: 1936; Lang: Eng; Subj: Related.
■Kuala Lumpur; MALAYSIA.

JRSAVP   *Journal of Research in Singing and Applied Vocal Pedagogy.* Freq: 2; Lang: Eng; Subj: Related.
■Texas Christian University; Department of Music; P.O. Box 32887 Fort Worth, TX 76129; USA.

JSDC   *Journal for Stage Directors and Choreographers.* Freq: 2; Began: 1996; Cov: Scan; Lang: Eng; Subj: Theatre.
■SDC Foundation; 1501 Broadway, Suite 1701 New York, NY 10036; USA.

JSH   *Journal of Social History.* Freq: 4; Began: 1967; Cov: Scan; Lang: Eng; Subj: Related.   ISSN: 0022-4529
■Carnegie-Mellon University Press; Schenley Park; Pittsburgh, PA 15213; USA.

JSS   *Journal of the Siam Society.* Began: 1926; Lang: Eng/Tha/Fre/Ger; Subj: Related.
■131 Soi Asoke; Sukhumvit 21 Road; Bangkok 10110; THAILAND.

JT   *Jeune Théâtre.* Began: 1970; Ceased: 1982; Lang: Fre; Subj: Theatre.   ISSN: 0315-0402
■Assoc. Québecoise du, Jeune Théâtre; 952 rue Cherrier; Montreal, PQ H2L 1H7; CANADA.

JTPR   *Journal du Théâtre Populaire Romand.* Freq: 8; Began: 1962; Lang: Fre; Subj: Theatre.
■Case Postale 80; 2301 La Chaux-de-Fonds; SWITZERLAND.

JTV   *Journal du Théâtre de la Ville.* Freq: 4; Began: 1968; Lang: Fre; Subj: Theatre.
■Theatre de la Ville; 16 quai de Gesvres; Paris; FRANCE.

Juben   *Juben:* (Playtexts). Freq: 12; Began: 1952; Lang: Chi; Subj: Theatre. ISSN: 0578-0659
■Zhongguo Xiju Chubanshe, 52; Dongsi Ba (8), Tiao 100700 Beijing; CHINA.

JugoIgre   *Jugoslovenske:* Pozorišne Igre. Began: 1962; Lang: Ser; Subj: Theatre.
■Sterijino Pozorje; Zmaj Jovina 22; Novi Sad; SERBIA.

Junkanoo   *Junkanoo.* Freq: 12; Lang: Eng; Subj: Theatre.
■Junkanoo Publications; Box N 4923; Nassau; BAHAMAS.

JWCI   *Journal of the Warburg & Courtauld Institutes.* Freq: 1; Began: 1937; Cov: Scan; Lang: Eng; Subj: Related.
■Woburn Square; London WC1H OAB; UK.

JWGT   *Jahrbuch der Wiener Gesellschaft für Theaterforschung.* Freq: 1; Lang: Ger; Subj: Related.
■Vienna; AUSTRIA.

Kabuki   *Kabuki.* Lang: Jap Cov: Scan; Lang: Jap; Subj: Theatre.
■4-12-15 Ginza; 104 Chuo-ku, Tokyo; JAPAN.

Kaekseok   *Kaekseok.* Freq: 12; Began: 1992; Cov: Scan; Lang: Kor; Subj: Related.
■58-1 Chung Jung-No 1 Ga; Jung Ku; Seoul;SOUTH KOREA.

Kalak   *Kalakalpam.* Freq: 2; Began: 1966; Lang: Eng; Subj: Theatre.
■Karyalaya Matya Kala Institute; 30-A Paddapukur Road; 20 Calcutta; INDIA.

Kalliope   *Kalliope.* Freq: 3; Began: 1995 Lang: Eng; Subj: Theatre.
■3939 Roosevelt Blvd.; Jacksonville, FL 32205; USA.

Kanava   *Kanava.* Formerly: *Aika.* Freq: 9; Began: 1932; Lang: Fin; Subj: Related. ISSN: 0355-0303
■Yhtyneet Kuvalehdet Oy; Hietalahdenranta 13; 00180 Helsinki 18; FINLAND.

KAPM   *Kassette:* Almanach für Bühne, Podium und Manege. Freq: 1; Lang: Ger; Subj: Theatre.
■Berlin; GERMANY.

Kathakali   *Kathakali.* Freq: 4; Began: 1969; Lang: Eng/Hin; Subj: Theatre.   ISSN: 0022-9326
■International Centre for Kathakali; 1-84 Rajandra Nagar; New Delhi; INDIA.

Kazal   *Kazaliste.* Freq: 26; Began: 1965; Ceased; Lang: Yug; Subj: Theatre.
■Prolaz Radoslava Bacica 1; Osijek; CROATIA.

KB   *Kunst Bulletin.* Freq: 12; Cov: Scan; Subj: Related.
■Fr. Hallwag AG; Nording 4; 4001 Bern; SWITZERLAND.

KCAB   *Korean Culture & Arts Bi-Monthly.* Freq: 6; Cov: Scan; Began: 1974; Lang: Kor; Subj: Related.
■Hankug Munhwa Yeasul Jinhyeng Won; 1-130 Chongrogu Dongsun Dong; Seoul; SOUTH KOREA.

Keshet   *Keshet.* Last Known Address; Began: 1982; Lang: Heb; Subj: Theatre.
■9 Bialik Street; Tel Aviv; ISRAEL.

KesK   *Kultúra és Közösség.* Freq: 6; Began: 1974; Ceased: 1990; Cov: Scan; Lang: Hun; Subj: Related.   ISSN: 0133-2597
■Arany János Lap- és Könyvkiadó Kft.; Corvin tér 8; 1011 Budapest; HUNGARY.

KingP   *King Pole Circus Magazine.* Freq: 4; Began: 1934; Cov: Scan; Lang: Eng; Subj: Theatre.
■Circus Fans' Assoc. of UK, c/o John Exton; 20 Foot Wood Crescent; Shawclough Rochdale, Lancaster OL12 6PB; UK.

Kino   *Kino.* Freq: 4; Cov: Scan; Lang: Eng; Subj: Theatre;
■Australian Theatre Historical Society; P.O. Box 447; Campbelltown New South Wales 2560; AUSTRALIA.

KJ   *Kultur-Journal.* Freq: 4; Lang: Ger; Subj: Related.
■Mykenae-Verlag; Ahastr. 9; D-64285 Darmstadt; GERMANY.

KJAZU   *Kronika:* Zavod za povijest hrvatske knjizevnisti. Began: 1975; Lang: Cro; Subj: Theatre.   ISSN: 0023-4929
■kazalista i glazbe Hrvatske akademije znanosti i umjetnosti; Opaticka 18; 41.000 Zagreb; CROATIA.

Klub   *Klub i Chudožestvennaja Samodejetelnost.* Freq: 26; Lang: Rus; Subj: Theatre.
■Profizdat; Ulitza Korova 13; Moscow; RUSSIA.

KMFB   *Gewerkschaft Kunst, Medien, Freie Berufe.* Freq: 11; Began: 1945; Lang: Ger; Subj: Theatre.
■UMLOsterreichischer Gewerkschaftsbund, Gewrkshft. Kunst, Medien, Freie, Berufe; Maria-Theresienstrasse 11; A 1090 Vienna; AUSTRIA.

KoJ   *Korea Journal.* Freq: 4; Began: 1961; Cov: Scan; Lang: Eng; Subj: Related.   ISSN: 0023-3900
■Korean National Commission for UNESCO; P.O. Box Central 64; Seoul; SOUTH KOREA.

Kommunist   *Kommunist.* Began: 1924; Cov: Scan; Lang: Rus; Subj: Related. ISSN: 0131-1212
■Svobodnaja mysl'; Moscow; RUSSIA.

Kont   *Kontinent.* Freq: 4; Cov: Scan; Lang: Rus; Subj: Related.   ISSN: 0934-6317
■Čistoprudnij Boulevard, 8A; 101923 Moscow; RUSSIA.

KoreanD   *Korean Drama.* Last Known Address; Lang Kor; Subj: Theatre.
■National Drama Association of Korea, Insadong, Jongno-gu; Fed. of Arts & Cult. Org. Building; 110 Seoul; SOUTH KOREA.

Kortars   *Kortárs.* Freq: 12; Began: 1957; Cov: Scan; Lang: Hun; Subj: Related.   ISSN: 0023-415X
■Magyar Irószövetség; Bajza u. 18; 1062 Budapest; HUNGARY.

KPR   *Kulturno-Prosvetitelnaja Rabota.* SEE *Vstreča.* Freq: 12; Ceased: 1990; Lang: Rus; Subj: Related.
■Sovéckaja Rossija; Bersenevskaja Naberež-naja 22; Moscow; RUSSIA.

Krajs   *Kraj smolenskij.* Began: 1996; Cov: Scan; Subj: Related.
■Dom Sovietov k. 163; Smolensk 214008; RUSSIA.

Krit   *Kritika.* Freq: 12; Began: 1963; Cov: Scan; Lang: Hun; Subj: Related.   ISSN: 0324-7775
■Népszabadság Rt; Bécsi út 122-124; 1034 Budapest; HUNGARY.

KSF   *Korean Studies Forum.* Freq: 2; Began 1976; Last Known Address; Lang: Kor; Subj: Related.   ISSN: 0147-6335
■Korean-American Educ. Commission, Garden Towers; No. 1803, 98-78 Wooni-Dong, Chongro-Ku; Seoul 110; SOUTH KOREA.

KSGT   *Kleine Schriften der Gesellschaft für Theatergeschichte.* Freq: 1; Cov: Scan; Lang: Ger; Subj: Theatre.   ISBN: 3-925191-95-X
■Gesellschaft für unterhaltende Bühnenkunst e.V. (GUBK); Hertzbergstr. 21; D-12055 Berlin; GERMANY.

KTR   *Korean Theatre Review.* Freq: 12; Lang: Kor; Cov: Scan; Subj: Theatre.
■National Theatre Association of Korea; Yechong Bldg; 1-117 Dongsoon-dong, Chongno-ku Seoul 110; SOUTH KOREA.

Kulis   *Kulis.* Freq: 12; Began: 1946; Lang: Arm; Subj: Theatre.
■H. Ayvaz; PK 83; 10 A Cagaloglu Yokusu; TURKEY.

Kvihkot   ***Kultuurivihkot***. Freq: 8; Began: 1973; Last Known Address; Lang: Fin/Swe; Subj: Theatre.
■Kultuurityontekijain Liitto; Korkeavuorenkatu 4 C 15; 00130 Helsinki; FINLAND.

KWN   ***Kurt Weill Newsletter***. Freq: 2; Began: 1983; Cov: Scan; Lang: Eng; Subj: Related.   ISSN: 0899-6407
■Weill Foundation for Music; 7 East 20th Street; New York, NY 10003-1106; USA.

KZ   ***Kultura i Žizn***. (Culture and Life). Freq: 12; Began: 1957; Cov: Scan; Lang: Rus/Eng/Ger/Fre/Spa; Subj: Related.ISSN: 0023-5199
■Sovéckaja Rossija; Projézd Sapunova 13-15; Moscow K-12; RUSSIA.

L&H   ***Literature & History***. Freq: 2; Began: 1975; Lang: Eng; Subj: Related.   ISSN: 0306-1973
■Ohio State University, Dept. of English; 421 Denney Hall; 164 W. 17th Ave. OH 43210; USA.

LabH   ***Labour History***. Freq: 2; Began: 1963; Cov: Scan; Lang: Eng; Subj: Related.   ISSN: 0023-6942
■Economic History Department; HO4, University of Sydney; NSW 2006; AUSTRALIA.

Laien   ***Laientheater***. Freq: 12; Began: 1972; Lang: Ger; Subj: Theatre.
■Schweizerischen Volkstheater; 30 Bern; SWITZERLAND.

LAQ   ***Livres et Auteurs Québecois***. Freq: 1; Began: 1969; Ceased; Lang: Fre; Subj: Related.   ISSN: 0316-2621
■Presses de l'Université Laval, Cité Universitaire; Québec, PQ G1K 7R4; CANADA.

LATR   ***Latin American Theatre Review***. Freq: 2; Began: 1967; Cov: Full; Lang: Eng/Spa/Por; Subj: Theatre.   ISSN: 0023-8813
■University of Kansas, Center of Latin American Studies; 107 Lippincott Hall; Lawrence, KS 66045; USA.

LD+A   ***Lighting Design + Application***. Freq: 12; Began: 1906; Cov: Scan; Lang: Eng; Subj: Theatre.   ISSN: 0360-6325
■Illuminating Engineering Society; 120 Wall Street; 17th Floor New York, NY 10005-4001; USA.

LDim   ***Lighting Dimensions***: For the Entertainment Lighting Industry. Freq: 6; Began: 1977; Cov: Scan; Lang: Eng; Subj: Theatre.
■Lighting Dimensions Publishing; 1590 S. Coast Highway, Suite 8; Laguna, CA 92651; USA.

LetQu   ***Lettres Québécoises***. Freq: 4; Began: 1976; Lang: Fre; Subj: Related. ISSN: 0382-084X
■Editions Jumonville; 1781 rue Saint-Hubert; Montreal, PQ, H2L 3Z1; CANADA.

LettDI   ***Lettera Dall'Italia***: Bollettino trimestrale realizzato dall'Istituto dell'Enciclopedia Italiana. Freq: 4; Began: 1985; Lang: Ita; Subj: Related. ISSN: 0393-64457
■Piazza dell'Enciclopedia Italiana, 4; 00186 Rome; ITALY.

Letture   ***Letture***: Libro e spettacolo, mensile di studi e rassegne. Freq: 10; Began: 1946; Lang: Ita; Subj: Related.   ISSN: 0024-144X
■Edizioni Letture; Piazza San Fedele 4; 20121 Milan; ITALY.

Letuch   ***Leteraturnaja ucheba***. Freq: 6; Lang: Rus; Subj: Related.   ISSN: 0203-5847
■Novodmitrovskaja Street, 5A; 125015 Moscow; RUSSIA.

LFQ   ***Literature/Film Quarterly***. Freq: 4; Began: 1973; Lang: Eng; Subj: Related.   ISSN: 0090-4260
■Salisbury State University; Salisbury, MD 21801; USA.

Light   ***Light***. Freq: 24; Began: 1921; Lang: Eng; Subj: Theatre.
■Ahmadiyya Building; Brandreth Road; Lahore; PAKISTAN.

LikC   ***Lik Čuvasija***; Freq: 6; Began: 1994; Cov: Scan; Lang: Rus; Subj: Related.
■Dom Pečaty k. 613; 13 pr. I. Jakovleva; Cheboksary 428019; CHUVASHIA.

Lilith   ***Lilith: a Feminist History Journal***. Freq: 1; Began: 1984; Cov: Scan; Lang: Eng; Subj: Related;   ISSN: 0813-8990
■Lilith Collective; P.O. Box 154; Fitzroy, Victoria 3065; AUSTRALIA.

LiNQ   ***Literature in North Queensland***. Freq: 2; Began: 1971; Cov: Scan; Lang: Eng; Subj: Related.
■Dept. of English; James Cook University of North Queensland; Townsville, 4811; AUSTRALIA.

LinzerT   ***Linzer Theaterzeitung***. Freq: 10; Began: 1955; Lang: Ger; Subj: Theatre.   ISSN: 0024-4139
■Landestheater Linz; Promenade 39; A 4010 Linz; AUSTRIA.

Lipika   ***Lipika***. Freq: 4; Began: 1972; Lang: Eng; Subj: Theatre.
■F-20 Nizzamudin West; 10013 New Delhi; INDIA.

Literator   ***Literator: Journal of Comparative Literature and Linguistics***. Freq: 3; Began: 1980; Cov: Scan; Lang: Afr/Eng; Subj: Related;   ISSN: 0258-2279
■Bureau for Scholarly Journals; Private Bag X6001; Potchefstroom 2520; REPUBLIC OF SOUTH AFRICA.

Literatura   ***Literatura***. Freq: 4; Began: 1974; Lang: Hun; Subj: Related.   ISSN: 0133-2368
■Balassi Kiadó; Ménesi út 11-13; 1118 Budapest; HUNGARY.

LitGruzia   ***Literaturnaja Gruzija***. Freq: 12; Began: 1957; Cov: Scan; Lang: Rus; Subj: Related.   ISSN: 0130-3600
■Sojuz pisatelej Gruzii; Tbilisi, Georg. SSR; GEORGIA.

Litva   ***Litva literaturnaja***. Freq: 12; Cov: Scan; Lang: Rus; Subj: Related. ISSN: 0206-296X
■Labdaryu Street, 3; 232600 Viln'yus; LITHUANIA.

Live   ***Live***. Freq: 4; Lang: Eng; Subj: Related.
■New York, NY; USA.

LLJ   ***La Trobe Library Journal***. Freq: 2; Began: 1968; Cov: Scan; Lang: Eng; Subj: Related.   ISSN: 0041-3151
■Friends of the State Library of Victoria; State Library of Victoria; Swanston Street; Melbourne, 3000; AUSTRALIA.

LO   ***Literaturnoje Obozrenijè***. Freq: 12; Began: 1973; Cov: Scan; Lang: Rus; Subj: Related.   ISSN: 0321-2904
■Sojuz Pisatelej SSSR; 9/10 ul. Dobroliubova; 127254 Moscow I-254,; RUSSIA.

Loisir   ***Loisir***. Freq: 4; Began: 1962; Lang: Fre; Subj: Theatre.
■Comédie de Caen; 120 rue St. Pierre; 1400 Caen; FRANCE.

LokK   ***Lok Kala***. Freq: 2; Ceased: 1977; Lang: Hin; Subj: Theatre.
■Bhartiya Lok kala Mandal; Udaipur 313001 Rajasthan; INDIA.

Loutkar   ***Loutkar***. Formerly Ceskoslovensky loutkar. Freq: 12; Began: 1993; Lang: Cze; Subj: Related.   ISSN: 0323-1178
■Nina Malikova, Divadelni ustav; Celetna 17; 110 01 Praha 1; CZECH REPUBLIC.

Lowdown   ***Lowdown***. Freq: 6; Began: 1979; Cov: Scan; Lang: Eng; Subj: Theatre.
■Youth Performing Arts Assoc.; 11 Jeffcott St.; Adelaide SA 5000; AUSTRALIA.

LPer   ***Literature in Performance***. SEE *Text and Performance Quarterly*. Freq: 2; Began: 1980; Ceased; Lang: Eng; Subj: Theatre.   ISSN: 0734-0796
■Inter. Div.,Speech Comm. Assoc., Dept. of Speech Communication; U. of NC, 115 Bingham Hall; Chapel Hill, NC 27514; USA.

LTR   ***London Theatre Record***. Freq: 26; Began: 1981; Cov: Full; Lang: Eng; Subj: Theatre.   ISSN: 0261-5282
■4 Cross Deep Gardens; Twickenham TW1 4QU Middlesex; UK.

Ludus   ***Ludus***: List Udruženja Dramskih Umetnika Srbije. Freq: 6; Began: 1983; Lang: Ser; Subj: Theatre.
■Udruženja Dramskih Umetnika Srbije; Terazije 26; Belgrade; SERBIA.

Lutka   ***Lutka***: Revija za lutkovno kulturo. Freq: 3; Began: 1966; Lang: Slo; Subj: Theatre.   ISSN: 0350-9303
■Zveza kulturnih organizacij Slovenije; Kidričeva 5; Ljubljana; SLOVENIA.

M&T   ***Musik & Teater***. SEE *Teater Et*. Freq: 6; Began: 1979; Ceased: 1989; Lang: Dan; Subj: Theatre.
■Bagsvard Horedgade 9914E; 2800 Bagsvard; DENMARK.

MA   ***Muzykal'naja akademija***. Freq: 6; Began: 1957; Cov: Scan; Lang: Rus; Subj: Related.   ISSN: 0869-4516
■Gadovaja Triumfal'naja uliča; #14/12;, Moscow 103006; RUSSIA.

MagIp   ***Magyar Iparművészet***. Freq: 6; Began: 1994; Cov: Scan; Lang: Hun; Subj: Related.   ISSN: 1217-839X
■Forka Tömegkommunikációs Kft.; Nádor u. 32; 1051 Budapest; HUNGARY.

MagM   ***Magyar Múzeum***. Formerly *Új Erdélyi Múzeum*. Freq: 4; Began: 1991; Lang: Hun; Subj: Related.   ISSN: 0866-4625
■Akadémiai Kiadó és a Közép-Európai Múzeum; Alapítvány; Meredek u. 25 1124 Budapest; HUNGARY.

Maksla   ***Maksla***. Began: 1959; Lang: Lat; Subj: Related.   ISSN: 0455-3772
■Riga; LATVIA.

MAL *Modern Austrian Literature*. Freq: 4; Began: 1961; Lang: Eng/Ger; Subj: Related. ISSN: 0026-7503
■Intl A. Schnitzler Research Assoc., c/o Donald G. Daviau, Ed.; Dept. of Lit. & Langs, Univ. of CA; Riverside, CA 92521; USA.

Mamulengo *Mamulengo*. Lang: Por; Subj: Theatre.
■Assoc. Brasileira de Teatro de Bonecos; Rua Barata Ribeiro; 60 C 01 Guanabara; BRAZIL.

Manip *Manipulation*. Last Known Address; Lang: Eng; Subj: Theatre.
■Mrs. Maeve Vella; 28 Macarthur Place; 3053 Carlton, Victoria; AUSTRALIA.

MarqJTHS *Marquee*: The Journal of the Theatre Historical Society. Freq: 4; Began: 1969; Cov: Scan; Lang: Eng; Subj: Theatre. ISSN: 0025-3928
■624 Wynne Rd; Springfield, PA 19064; USA.

Marquee *Marquee*. Freq: 8; Began: 1976; Last Known Address; Lang: Eng; Subj: Related. ISSN: 0700-5008
■Marquee Communications Inc.; 277 Richmond St. W.; Toronto, ON M5V 1X1; CANADA.

Mask *Mask*. Freq: 6; Began: 1967; Lang: Eng; Subj: Theatre. ISSN: 0726-9072
■Simon Pryor, Executive Officer, VADIE; 117 Bouverie Street; 3053 Carlton; AUSTRALIA.

MASKA *MASKA*. Freq: 4; Began: 1991; Lang: Slo/Eng; Subj: Theatre. ISSN: 1318-0509
■Dunajska 22; 61000 Ljubljana; SLOVENIA.

Maske *Maske*. SEE *Maska*. Began: 1985; Ceased: 1991; Lang: Slo/Eng; Subj: Theatre. ISSN: 0352-7913
■Zveza kulturnih organizacij Slovenije; Ljubljana; SLOVENIA.

Masque *Masque*. Freq: 24; Began: 1967; Lang: Eng; Subj: Theatre. ISSN: 0025-469X
■Masque Publications; Box 3504; 2001 Sydney NSW; AUSTRALIA.

Mast *Masterstvo*. Freq: 6; Lang: Ukr; Subj: Theatre.
■Pouchkineskaia Street 5; Kiev; UKRAINE.

Matya *Matya Prasanga*. Freq: 12; Lang: Ben; Subj: Theatre.
■54/1 B Patuatola Lane; Emherst Street; Calcutta; INDIA.

MAvilia *Monte Avilia*. Freq: 12; Began: 1980; Lang: Spa; Subj: Theatre.
■Apartado 70-712; 107 Caracas; VENEZUELA.

MBB *Mala Biblioteka Baletowa*. Began: 1957; Ceased: 1981; Lang: Pol; Subj: Theatre.
■Polskie Wydawnictwo Muzyczne; Al. Krasińskiego 11a; 31-111 Kraków; POLAND.

MBzT *Münchener Beiträge zur Theaterwissenschaft*. Cov: Scan; Lang: Ger; Subj: Related. ISSN: 0343-7604
■J. Kitzinger oHG, Schellingstr. 25; D-80799 Munich; GERMANY.

MC&S *Media, Culture and Society*. Freq: 4; Began: 1979; Lang: Eng; Subj: Related. ISSN: 0163-4437
■Sage Publications; 6 Bonhill Street; London EC2A 4PU; UK.

MChAT *Eżegodnik MChAT*. Freq: 1; Lang: Rus; Subj: Theatre.
■Association of Soviet Writers; Hertsen 49; Moscow; RUSSIA.

MD *Modern Drama*. Freq: 4; Began: 1958; Cov: Full; Lang: Eng; Subj: Theatre. ISSN: 0026-7694
■Univ. of Toronto Press; 5201 Dufferin Street; Downsview, ON M5T 2Z9; CANADA.

MDM *Musicals—Das Musicalmagazin*. Freq: 6; Began: 1986; Lang: Ger; Subj: Related. ISSN: 0931-8194
■Balanstr. 19; D-81669 Munich; GERMANY.

MdTNB *Magazine du TNB*. Lang: Fre; Subj: Theatre. ISSN: 1164-8600
■Theatre National De Bretagne; 1, rue St. Helier; 35008 Rennes Cedex BP 675; FRANCE.

MdVO *Mitteilungen der Vereinigung Österreichischer Bibliotheken*. Lang: Ger; Subj: Related.
■Vienna; AUSTRIA.

Meanjin *Meanjin*. Formerly: *Meanjin Quarterly* Freq: 3; Began: 1940; Cov: Scan; Lang: Eng; Subj: Related. ISSN: 0025-6293
■Meanjin Co. Ltd.; 211 Grattan Street; Parkville, Victoria 3052; AUSTRALIA.

MeisterP *Meister des Puppenspiels*. Freq: IRR; Began: 1959; Lang: Ger; Subj: Theatre. ISSN: 0076-6216
■Deutsches Institut für Puppenspiel; Hattingerstr. 467; 4630 Bochum; GERMANY.

Meridian *Meridian*. Began: 1982; Cov: Scan; Lang: Eng; Subj: Theatre. ISSN: 0728-5914
■Dept. of English, La Trobe University; Bundoora; Victoria 3083; AUSTRALIA.

Merker *Neue Merker, Der*.Oper in Wien und aller welt. Freq: 12; Lang: Ger; Subj: Theatre. ISSN: 1017-5202
■Dr. Sieglinde Pfabigan; Merker-Verein; Peitglasse 7/3/4 A 1210 Vienna; AUSTRIA.

MET *Medieval English Theatre*. Freq: 2; Began: 1979; Cov: Full; Lang: Eng; Subj: Theatre. ISSN: 0143-3784
■c/o M. Twycross, Dept. of English; University of Lancaster; Lancaster LA1 4YT; UK.

MGL *Mestno gledališče Ljubljansko*. Freq: IRR; Began: 1959; Lang: Slo; Subj: Theatre.
■Ljubljana Čopova 14; 61000; SLOVENIA.

MHall *Music Hall*. Freq: 6; Began: 1978; Lang: Eng; Subj: Theatre.
■Tony Barker; 50 Reperton Road; London SW6; UK.

MID *Modern International Drama*: Magazine for Contemporary International Drama in Translation. Freq: 2; Began: 1967; Cov: Full; Lang: Eng; Subj: Theatre. ISSN: 0026-7856
■State University of NY; P.O. Box 6000; Binghamton, NY 13902-6000; USA.

Mim *Mim: Revija za glumu i glumište*: Glasilo Udruženja dramskih umjetnika Hrvatske. Freq: 12; Began: 1984; Lang: Cro; Subj: Theatre.
■Udruž. Dramskih Umjetnika Hrvatske; Ilica 42; Zagreb; CROATIA.

MimeJ *Mime Journal*. Freq: 1; Began: 1974; Cov: Full; Lang: Eng; Subj: Theatre. ISSN: 0145-787X
■Pomona College Theater Department, Claremont Colleges; Claremont, CA 91711; USA.

MimeN *Mime News*. Freq: 5; Began: 1983; Cov: Scan; Lang: Eng; Subj: Theatre. ISSN: 0892-4910
■National Mime Association; Box 148277; Chicago, IL 60614; USA.

Mimos *Mimos*. Freq: 4; Began: 1949; Lang: Ger; Subj: Theatre. ISSN: 0026-4385
■Schweizerische Gesellschaft für Theaterkultur; Theaterkultur-Verlag; Pf. 1940 CH-4001 Basel; SWITZERLAND.

Mit *Mitgliederzeitung*. Freq: 4; Cov: Scan; Lang: Ger; Subj: Related.
■Gesellschaft für unterhaltende Bühnenkunst e.V.; Hertzbergstr. 21; D-12055 Berlin; GERMANY.

MK *Molodoi Kommunist*. SEE *Perspektiva*. Freq: 12; Began: 1918; Ceased: 1990; Cov: Scan; Lang: Rus; Subj: Related. ISSN: 0131-2278
■Izdatel'stvo Molodaya Gvardiya, Ul.; Sushevskaya, 21; Moscow A-55; RUSSIA.

MLet *Music & Letters*. Freq: 4; Began: 1920; Lang: Eng; Subj: Related. ISSN: 0027-4224
■Oxford University Press; Walton Street; Oxford OX2 6DP; UK.

MLR *Modern Language Review*. Freq: 4; Began: 1905; Lang: Eng; Subj: Related. ISSN: 0026-7937
■King's College London; Strand; London WC2 R 2LS; UK.

MMDN *Medieval Music-Drama News*. Freq: 2; Began: 1982; Ceased: 1991; Lang: Eng; Subj: Related. ISSN: 0731-0374
■Kalamazoo, MI; USA.

MMDTA *Monographs on Music, Dance and Theater in Asia*. Freq: 1; Began 1971; Last Known Address; Lang: Eng; Subj: Theatre.
■The Asia Society, Performing Arts Program; 133 East 58th Street; New York, NY 10022; USA.

MN *Monumenta Nipponica*: Studies in Japanese Culture. Freq: 4; Began: 1938; Cov: Scan; Lang: Eng; Subj: Related. ISSN: 0027-0741
■Sophia University, 7-1 Kioi-cho; Chiyoda-ku; 102 Tokyo; JAPAN.

Mobile *Mobile*. Freq: 12; Lang: Fre; Subj: Theatre.
■Maison de la Culture d'Amiens; Place Léon Gontier; 80000 Amiens; FRANCE.

MoD *Monthly Diary*. Lang: Eng; Subj: Theatre.
■Sydney; AUSTRALIA.

MojM *Moja Moskva*.Lang: Rus Subj: Related.
■ul. Tverskaja, 13 Moscow 103032 RUSSIA

MolGvar *Molodaja gvardija*. Freq: 12; Began: 1922; Cov: Scan; Lang: Rus; Subj: Related. ISSN: 0131-2257
■ Moscow; RUSSIA.

Monsalvat *Monsalvat*. Freq: 11; Began: 1973; Lang: Spa; Subj: Theatre.
■Ediciones de Nuevo Arte; Plaza Gala Placidia 1; 6 Barcelona; SPAIN.

Mosk *Moskva*. Freq: 12; Began: 1957; Cov: Scan; Lang: Rus; Subj: Related. ISSN: 0132-2382

■Chudozestvennaja Literatura; 24 Rub. Sojuz pisatelej Rossiiskoi; Moscow; RUSSIA.

MoskNab *Moskovskij Nabljudatel'*. Began: 1991; Cov: Scan; Lang: Rus; Subj: Related. ISSN: 0868-8524
■Arbat, 35; 121835 Moscow; RUSSIA.

MoskZ *Moskovskij Žurnal*. Cov: Scan; Lang: Rus; Subj: Related.
■RUSSIA.

Mozgo *Mozgó Világ*. Freq: 12; Began: 1971; Ceased; Cov: Scan; Lang: Hun; Subj: Related.
■Münnich F. u. 26; 1051 Budapest V; HUNGARY.

MP *Modern Philology*: Research in Medieval and Modern Literature. Freq: 4; Began: 1903; Cov: Scan; Lang: Eng; Subj: Related. ISSN: 0026-8232
■University of Chicago Press; 5720 S. Woodlawn Avenue; Chicago, IL 60637; USA.

MPI *Manadens Premiärer och Information*. Lang: Swe; Subj: Related.
■Svenska Teaterunionen; Svenska ITI; Nybrokajen 13 S-111 48, Stockholm; SWEDEN.

MPSKD *Mitteilungen der Puppentheatersammlung der Staatlichen Kunstsammlungen Dresde*. Freq: 32; Began: 1958; Lang: Ger; Subj: Theatre. ISSN: 0323-7567
■Puppentheatersammlung; Hohenhaus; Barkengasse 6 01445 Radebeul; GERMANY.

MRenD *Medieval and Renaissance Drama*. Lang: Eng; Began: 1984; Cov: Full; Subj: Theatre. ISSN: 0731-3403
■AMS Press; 56 E. 13th Street; New York, NY 10003; USA.

MRT *Miedzynarodowny Rocznik Teatralny*: Annuaire Intl. du Théâtre/Intl. Theatre Yearbook. Freq: 1; Began: 1977; Ceased: 1982; Lang: Pol/Fre/Eng; Subj: Theatre.
■International Association of Theatre Critics; ul. Moliera 1; 00 076 Warsaw; POLAND.

MSD *Milliyet Sanat Dergisi*. Freq: 26; Lang: Tur; Subj: Theatre.
■Aydin Dogan; Nurosmaniye Cad. 65/67; Cagaloglu-Istanbul; TURKEY.

MT *Material zum Theater*. Freq: 12; Began: 1970; Lang: Ger; Subj: Theatre.
■Verband der Theaterschaffended der DDR; Hermann-Matern-Strasse 18; 1040 Berlin; GERMANY.

MuD *MusikDramatik*. Freq: 4; Cov: Full; Lang: Swe; Subj: Theatre. ISSN: 0283-5754
■Box 4038; 5102 61 Stockholm; SWEDEN.

Muhely *Műhely*. Freq: 6; Began: 1978; Lang: Hun; Cov: Scan; Subj: Related. ISSN: 0138-922X
■Hazánk Kft.; Árpád u. 32; 9021 Győr; HUNGARY.

MuK *Maske und Kothurn*: Internationale Beiträge zur Theaterwissenschaft. Freq: 1; Began: 1955; Lang: Ger/Eng/Fre; Subj: Theatre. ISSN: 0175-1611
■Universität Wien; Institut für Theaterwissenschaft; Böhlau Verlag Sachsenplatz 4-6 A-1201 Vienna; AUSTRIA.

MuQ *Musical Quarterly*. Freq: 4; Began: 1915; Last Known Address; Lang: Eng; Subj: Related. ISSN: 0027-4631

■GoodKind Indexes, Pub.; 866 Third Avenue; New York, NY 10022; USA.

MusGes *Musik und Gesellschaft*. Freq: 12; Began: 1951; Lang: Ger; Subj: Related. ISSN: 0027-4755
■Henschelverlag Kunst und Gesellschaft; Oranienburger Str. 67/68; 1040 Berlin; GERMANY.

MuT *Musik und Theater*. Die Internationale Kulturzeitschrift. Freq: 10; Began: 1979; Lang: Ger; Subj: Theatre. ISSN: 0931-8194
■Meuli & Masüger Media GmbH; Pf. 16 80 CH-8040 Zurich; SWITZERLAND.

MuZizn *MuzykalnajaŽizn*: (Musical Life). Freq: 24; Began: 1957; Cov: Scan; Lang: Rus; Subj: Related. ISSN: 0131-2383
■Moscow; RUSSIA.

Muzsika *Muzsika*. Freq: 12; Began: 1958; Cov: Scan; Lang: Hun; Subj: Related. ISSN: 0027-5336
■Pro Musica Alapítvány; Károly krt. 7; 1075 Budapest; HUNGARY.

Muzyka *Muzyka:Bibliografičeskaja informacija*. Freq: 12; Began: 1974; Cov: Full; Lang: Rus; Subj: Related. ISSN: 0208-3086
■Gos. Biblioteka SSSR im. Lenina; NIO Informkultura; Prospekt Kalinina 101000 Moscow; RUSSIA.

MV *Minority Voices*: An Interdisciplinary Journal of Literature & Arts. Freq: 2; Began: 1977; Ceased: 1989; Lang: Eng; Subj: Theatre.
■Paul Robeson Cultural Center, 114 Walnut Bldg.; Pennsylvania State Univ.; University Park, PA 16802; USA.

My *My*. Freq: 12; Began: 1990; Cov: Scan; Lang: Rus; Subj: Related.
■B-5 ab. 1; Moscow 107005; RUSSIA.

Mykenae *Mykenae Theater-Korrespondenz*. Freq: 24; Began: 1951; Lang: Ger; Subj: Theatre.
■Der aktuelle Theaternachrichtenund Feuilletondienst; Mykenae Verlag Rossberg KG; Ahastr. 9 D-64285 Darmstadt; GERMANY.

NADIE *Nadie Journal*. Formerly: *Drama in Education*. Freq: 2; Began: 1981; Cov: Scan; Lang: Eng; Subj: Related. ISSN: 0159-6659
■National Assoc. for Drama in Education; P.O. Box 168; Carlton Victoria 3054; AUSTRALIA.

Napj *Napjaink*. Freq: 12; Began: 1962; Ceased: 1990; Cov: Scan; Lang: Hun; Subj: Related. ISSN: 0547-2075
■Borsod Megyei Lapkiadó Vállalat; Korvin Ottó u. 1; 3530 Miskolc; HUNGARY.

NasSovr *Naš sovremennik*. Freq: 12; Began: 1933; Cov: Scan; Lang: Rus; Subj: Related. ISSN: 0027-8288
■Souz pisatelej RF; Moscow; RUSSIA.

Natrang *Natrang*. Freq: 4; Lang: Hin; Subj: Theatre.
■I-47 Jangoura Extension; New Delhi; INDIA.

Natya *Natya*. Freq: 4; Began: 1969; Last Known Address; Lang: Eng; Subj: Theatre. ISSN: 0028-1115
■Bharatiya Natya Sangh; 34 New Central Market; New Delhi; INDIA.

Nayt *Näytelmäuutiset (Drama News)*. Lang: Fin; Subj: Theatre.
■Näytelmäkulma, Drama Corner; Meritullinkatu 33; 00170 Helsinki; FINLAND.

NBT *Neue Blätter des Theaters in Der Josefstadt*. Freq: 6; Began: 1953; Lang: Ger/Eng/Fre; Subj: Theatre. ISSN: 0028-3096
■Theater in der Josefstadt, Direktion; Josefstaedterstrasse 26; A 1082 Vienna; AUSTRIA.

NC *New Contrast*. Freq: 4; Cov: Scan; Lang: Eng; Subj: Related. ISSN: 1017-5415
■P.O. Box 3841; Cape Town, 8000; SOUTH AFRICA.

NCBSBV *Netherlands Centraal Bureau Voor de Statistiek*: Bezoek aan Vermakelukheidsinstellingen. Freq: 1; Began: 1940; Ceased: 1963; Lang: Dut/Eng; Subj: Related. ISSN: 0077-6688
■Centraal Bureau voor de Statistiek; Prinses Beatrixlaan 428; Voorburg; NETHERLANDS.

NCBSMT *Centraal Bureau voor de Statistiek (Statistics Netherlands)*: Muziek en theater. Formerly: *Statistiek van het Gesubsidieerde Toneel*. Freq: 1; Began: 1977; Lang: Dut; Subj: Theatre. ISSN: 0168-3519
■Statistics Netherlands; Postbox 428; 2270 AZ Voorburg; NETHERLANDS.

NCM *Nineteenth Century Music*. Freq: 3; Began: 1977; Lang: Eng; Subj: Related.
■University of California Press; 2120 Berkeley Way; Berkeley, CA 94720; USA.

NConL *Notes on Contemporary Literature*. Freq: 4; Began: 1971; Lang: Eng; Subj: Related. ISSN: 0029-4047
■English Department, West Georgia College; Carollton, GA 30118; USA.

NCPA *National Center for the Performing Arts*: Quarterly Journal. Freq: 4; Began: 1972; Lang: Eng; Subj: Related.
■Natl Ctr for the Performing Arts; Nariman Point; 400021 Bombay; INDIA.

NCT *Nineteenth Century Theatre*. Formerly: *Nineteenth Century Theatre Research*. Freq: 2; Began: 1987; Cov: Full; Lang: Eng; Subj: Theatre. ISSN: 0893-3766
■University of Massachusetts; Department of English; Amherst, MA 01003; USA.

NCTR *Nineteenth Century Theatre Research*. Freq: 2; Began: 1973; Ceased: 1986; Cov: Full; Lang: Eng; Subj: Theatre. ISSN: 0316-5329
■Department of English, University of Arizona; Tuscon, AZ 85721; USA.

Neoh *Neohelicon/Acta Comparationis Litterarum Universarum*. Freq: 2; Began: 1974; Cov: Scan; Lang: Eng /Ger /Fre; Subj: Related. ISSN: 0324-4652
■Akadémiai Kiadó; Ménesi út 11-13; 1118 Budapest; HUNGARY.

NETJ *New England Theatre Journal*. Freq: 1; Began: 1990; Lang: Eng; Subj: Theatre.
■School of Fine and Performing Arts; Roger Williams College; 1 Old Ferry Road Bristol, RI 02809-2921; USA.

neueM *neue Merker, Der*. Freq: 12; Lang: Ger; Subj: Related. ISSN: 1017-5202
■Dr. Sieglinde Pfabigan; Peitlgasse /III/4; A-1210 Vienna; AUSTRIA.

Neva *Neva*. Freq: 12; Began: 1955; Cov: Scan; Lang: Rus; Subj: Related. ISSN: 0130-741X
■3 Nevskij Pr.; St. Petersburg 191186; RUSSIA.

NewPerf *New Performance*. Freq: 4; Began: 1977; Lang: Eng; Subj: Theatre. ISSN: 0277-514X
■One 14th Street; San Francisco, CA 94103; USA.

NewY *New Yorker, The*. Freq: 50; Cov: Scan; Lang: Eng; Subj: Related. ISSN: 0028-792X
■The New Yorker Magazine, Inc.; 20 West 43rd Street; New York; NY 10036; USA.

NFT *Theatre*: News from the Finnish Theatre. Formerly: *News from the Finnish Theatre*. Freq: IRR; Began: 1958; Cov: Scan; Lang: Eng/Fre; Subj: Theatre. ISSN: 0358-3627
■Finnish Center of the ITI; Teatterikulma Meritullinkatu 33 00170 Helsinki; FINLAND.

NihonU *Nihon-Unima*. Lang: Jap; Subj: Theatre.
■Taoko Kawajiri, Puppet Theatre PUK; 2-12 Yoyogi, Shibuya; 151 Tokyo; JAPAN.

NIMBZ *Notate*: Informations-und-Mitteilungsblatt des Brecht-Zentrums der DDR. Lang: Ger; Subj: Theatre.
■Brecht Zentrum der DDR; Chausseestrasse 125; 1040 Berlin; GERMANY.

NITI *Newsletter of the International Theatre Institute of the U.S., Inc.*. Freq: 4; Began: 1988; Lang: Eng; Subj: Theatre.
■220 West 42nd Street; New York, NY 10036; USA.

NiR *Nauka i Religija*: (Science and Religion). Freq: 12; Began: 1959; Cov: Scan; Lang: Rus; Subj: Related. ISSN: 0130-7045
■Moscow; RUSSIA.

Nk *Näköpiiri*. Ceased: 1983; Lang: Fin; Subj: Theatre.
■Osuuskunta Näköpiiri; Annakatu 13 B; 00120 Helsinki 12; FINLAND.

NKala *Natya Kala*. Freq: 12; Lang: Tel; Subj: Theatre.
■Kala Bhawan; Saifabad; Hyderabad; INDIA.

NLR *New Literatures Review*. Freq: 2; Began: 1975; Cov: Scan; Lang: Eng; Subj: Related. ISSN: 0314-7495
■English Department, University of Wollongong; P.O. Box 1144; Wollongong NSW 2500; AUSTRALIA.

NMZ *Neue Musikzeitung*. Freq: 6; Began: 1951; Cov: Scan; Lang: Ger; Subj: Related. ISSN: 0944-8136
■Verlag Neue Musikzeitung GmbH; Pf. 100245; D-93047 Regensburg; GERMANY

NO *New Observations*. Freq: 10; Lang: Eng; Subj: Related.
■144 Greene Street; New York, NY 10012; USA.

Noh *Noh*. Freq: 12; Lang: Jap; Subj: Theatre.
■Ginza-Nohgakudo Building; 6-5-15 Ginza, Chuo-Ku; 104 Tokyo; JAPAN.

NoK *Nōgaku-kenkyū*. Freq: Irreg. Began: 1916; Lang: Jap; Subj: Related. ISSN: 0029-0874
■Hosei University; JAPAN.

NoSS *Nōgaku Shiryo Shusei*. Freq: Irreg. Began: 1973; Lang: Jap; Subj: Related.
■Hosei University; JAPAN.

Novr *Nova revija*: mesečnik za kulturo. Freq: 12; Began: 1982; Cov: Scan; Lang: Slo; Subj: Theatre. ISSN: 0351-9805
■ČZP Nova revija d.o.o.; Dalmatinova 1; 1001 Ljubljana; SLOVENIA.

NovRos *Novaja Rossija*. Freq: 4; Began: 1930; Lang: Rus; Subj: Related.
■GSP, 8 Moskvina K-31; Moscow 103772; RUSSIA.

NovyjMir *Novyj Mir*. Freq: 12; Began: 1925; Cov: Scan; Lang: Rus; Subj: Related. ISSN: 0130-7673
■Moscow; RUSSIA.

Ns *Nestroyana*: Blätter der Internationalen Nestroy-Gesellschaft. Freq: 4; Began: 1979; Cov: Scan; Lang: Ger; Subj: Theatre.
■Internationale Nestroy-Gesellschaft, Volkstheater; Neustiftgasse 1; A 1070 Vienna; AUSTRIA.

NT *Nya Teatertidningen*. SEE: *Teatertidningen*. Freq: 4; Began: 1977; Ceased: 1990; Cov: Full; Lang: Swe; Subj: Theatre. ISSN: 0348-0119
■Box 20137 S10460 Stockholm; SWEDEN.

NTA *New Theatre Australia*. Freq: 6; Began: 1987; Ceased: 1989; Lang: Eng; Subj: Theatre. ISSN: 1030-441X
■New Theatre Australia Publications; P.O. Box 242 Kings Cross, NSW, 2011; AUSTRALIA.

NTE *Narodna tvorchestvo*. Freq: 12; Began: 1925; Lang: Ukr; Subj: Related. ISSN: 0023-219x
■Starokaluzhskoe shosse, I. 117630; Moscow; RUSSIA.

NTimes *Nohgaku Times*. Freq: 12; Began: 1953; Lang: Jap; Subj: Theatre.
■Nohgaku Shorin Ltd.; 3-6 Kanda-Jinpo-cho, Chiyoda-ku; 101 Tokyo; JAPAN.

NTQ *New Theatre Quarterly*. Freq: 4; Began: 1985; Cov: Full; Lang: Eng; Subj: Theatre. ISSN: 0266-464X
■Cambridge University Press, Edinburgh Bldg.; Shaftesbury Rd.; Cambridge CB2 2RU; UK.

NTR *New Theatre Review*. Freq: 3; Lang: Eng; Subj: Theatre.
■Lincoln Center Theater; 150 West 65 Street; New York NY 10023; USA.

NTS *Nordic Theatre Studies*: Yearbook for Theatre Research in Scandinavia. Freq: 1; Began: 1988; Cov: Full; Lang: Eng; Subj: Theatre.
■Munksgaard; Postbox 2148; 1016 Copenhagen K; DENMARK.

NTTJ *Nederlands Theatre-en-Televisie Jaarboek*. Freq: 1; Lang: Dut; Subj: Theatre.
■Amsterdam; NETHERLANDS.

Numero *Numero*. Freq: 12; Lang: Spa; Subj: Related.
■Apt. Post. 75570; El Marques; Caracas; VENEZUELA.

NV *Novoe Vremija*. Cov: Scan; Lang: Rus; Subj: Related. ISSN: 0137-0723
■Moscow; RUSSIA.

NVarta *Natya Varta*. Freq: 12; Lang: Hin; Subj: Theatre.
■Anakima; 4 Bishop Lefroy Road; Calcutta; INDIA.

Nvilag *Nagyvilág*. Freq: 12; Began: 1956; Cov: Scan; Lang: Hun; Subj: Related. ISSN: 0547-1613
■Arany János Lap- és Könyvkiadó Kft.; Széchenyi u. 1 1054 Budapest; HUNGARY.

NvR *Nauka v Rossii*. Freq: 6; Began 1961; Cov Scan; Lang: Rus; Subj: Related.
■Maranovskij Per., 26; 117810 Moscow GSP-1; RUSSIA.

NWR *NeWest Review*: A Journal of Culture and Current Events in the West. Freq: 6; Began: 1975; Cov: Scan; Lang: Eng; Subj: Theatre. ISSN: 0380-2917
■NeWest Review Co-operative; Box 394, RPO University; Saskatoon, SK S7N 9Z9; CANADA.

NYO *New York Onstage*. Freq: 12; Lang: Eng; Subj: Theatre.
■c/o Theatre Development Fund; 1501 Broadway; Room 2110 New York, NY 10036; USA.

NYTCR *New York Theatre Critics Review*. Freq: 30; Began: 1940; Cov: Full; Lang: Eng; Subj: Theatre. ISSN: 0028-7784
■Critics Theatre Review; 52 Vanderbilt Avenue, 11th Floor; New York, NY 10017; USA.

NYTR *New York Theatre Reviews*. Began: 1977; Ceased: 1980; Lang: Eng; Subj: Theatre.
■Ira J. Bilowit; 55 West 42nd Street; New York, NY 10036; USA.

Obliques *Obliques*. Freq: 4; Last Known Address; Began: 1972; Lang: Fre; Subj: Related.
■Roger Borderie; BP1, Les Pilles; 26110 Lyons; FRANCE.

OC *Opera Canada*. Freq: 4; Began: 1960; Cov: Scan; Lang: Eng; Subj: Related. ISSN: 0030-3577
■Foundation for Coast to Coast, Opera Publication; 366 Adelaide Street E., Suite 434; Toronto, ON M5A 3X9; CANADA.

OCA *O'Casey Annual*. Freq: 1; Began: 1982; Ceased: Cov: Scan; Lang: Eng; Subj: Theatre.
■MacMillan Publishers Ltd.; Houndmills Basingstoke; Hampshire RG21 2XS; UK.

ODG *Österreichische Dramatiker der Gegenwart*. Lang: Ger; Subj: Theatre.
■Inst. für Österreichische Dramaturgie; Singerstrasse 26; A 1010 Vienna; AUSTRIA.

OffI *OFF-Informationen. Bundesverband Freier Theater e.V.*. Freq: IRR; Began: 1984; Lang: Ger; Subj: Theatre.
■Kooperative Freier Theater NRW; Günthertr. 65; D-44143 Dortmund; GERMANY.

Ogonek *Ogonek*. Cov: Scan; Lang: Rus; Subj: Related.
■RUSSIA.

OI *Opéra International*. Freq: 1; Began: 1963; Lang: Fre; Subj: Related.
■10 Galerie Vero-Dodat; 75001 Paris; FRANCE.

Oik *Otrok in knjiga*: Revija za vprašanja mladinske književnosti in knjižne vzgoje. Freq: 2; Began: 1972; Cov: Scan; Lang: Slo; Subj: Theatre. ISSN: 0351-5141
■Mariborska knjižnica; Rotovški trg 2; 2000 Maribor; SLOVENIA.

OJ *Opera Journal*. Freq: 4; Began: 1968; Cov: Scan; Lang: Eng; Subj: Theatre.
ISSN: 0030-3585
■National Opera Association, Inc., University of Mississippi; Division of Continuing Ed. and Extension; University, MS 38677; USA.

OK *Oper und Konzert*. Freq: 12; Began: 1963; Lang: Ger; Subj: Theatre.
ISSN: 0030-3518
■A. Hanuschik; Ungererstrasse 19/VI (Fuchsbau); 8000 Munich 40; GERMANY.

Oktiabr *Oktiabr*. Freq: 12; Began: 1924; Cov: Scan; Lang: Rus; Subj: Related. ISSN: 0132-0637
■Pravda; Moscow; RUSSIA.

Ollan *Ollantay Theater Magazine*. Freq: 2; Began: 1993; Cov: Scan; Lang: Eng /Spa; Subj: Theatre. ISSN: 1065-805X
■Ollantay Press; P.O. Box 449; Jackson Heights, NY 11372; USA.

OnsA *Ons Amsterdam*. Cov: Scan; Lang: Dut; Subj: Related. ISSN: 0166-1809
■Weekbladpers; Amsterdam; NETHERLANDS.

Op&T *Oper & Tanz*. Freq: 6; Lang: Ger; Subj: Related.
■Vereinigung Deutscher Opernchöre und Bühnentänzer e.V. in der DAG; Oper & Tanz GmbH, Georgstr. 2; D-50374 Erfstadt; GERMANY.

Opal *Opal*. Freq: 6; Began: 1962; Lang: Eng; Subj: Theatre. ISSN: 0030-3062
■Ontario Puppetry Association; 171 Avondale Avenue; Willowdale, ON M2N 2V4; CANADA.

Oper *Oper*. Freq: 1; Began: 1966; Lang: Ger; Subj: Theatre.
■Zurich; SWITZERLAND.

Opera *Opera*. Freq: 12; Began: 1950; Lang: Eng; Subj: Theatre. ISSN: 0030-3542
■DSB, 2a Sopwith Crescent; Hurricane Way; Shotgate Wickford, Essex SS11 8YU; UK.

OperaA *Opera Australasia*. Freq: 12; Began: 1978; Lang: Eng; Subj: Theatre.
ISSN: 1320-9299
■PO Box R361; NSW 2000 Royal Exchange; AUSTRALIA.

OperaCT *Opera*. Freq: 4; Began: 1974; Ceased; Lang: Eng/Afr; Subj: Theatre.
■Cape Performing Arts Board; POB 4107; 8000 Cape Town; SOUTH AFRICA.

OperaIn *Opera Index*. Freq: 1; Lang: Eng; Subj: Related. ISSN: 0030-3526
■Seymour Press Ltd.; Windsor House; 1270 London Road London; SW16 4DH; UK.

OperaL *Operaélet/Operalife*. Freq: 5; Began: 1992; Cov: Scan; Lang: Hun; Subj: Theatre. ISSN: 1215-6590
■Budapesti Operabarát Alapítvány; Hajós u. 19; 1065 Budapest; HUNGARY.

OperaR *Opera*. Freq: 4; Began: 1965; Last Known Address; Lang: Ita/Eng/Fre/Ger/Spa; Subj: Theatre. ISSN: 0030-3542
■Editoriale Fenarete; Via Beruto 7; Milan; ITALY.

OperH *Oper Heute*. Lang: Ger; Subj: Theatre.
■Berlin; GERMANY.

Opern *Opernglas, Das*. Freq: 11; Began: 1980; Cov: Scan; Lang: Ger; Subj: Related.
ISSN: 0935-6398
■Opernglas Verlagsgesellschaft mbH; Lappenbergsallee 45; D-20257; GERMANY.

OpN *Opera News*. Freq: 17; Began: 1936; Cov: Full; Lang: Eng; Subj: Theatre.
ISSN: 0030-3607
■Metropolitan Opera Guild, Inc.; 70 Lincoln Center Plaza; New York, NY 10023; USA.

OpuK *Oper und Konzert*. Freq: 4; Began: 1963; Cov: Scan; Lang: Ger; Subj: Related.
ISSN: 0030-3518
■Ungererstr. 19; D-80802 Munich; GERMANY.

Opus. *Opus. Osterreichische Puppenspiel-Journalette*. Freq: 4; Lang: Ger; Subj: Related.
■Österreichischer Puppenclub; Postfach; A-3130 Herzogenburg; GERMANY.

Opuscula *Opuscula*. Freq: 3; Began: 1976; Last Known Address; Lang: Dan; Subj: Theatre.
■Det Teatervidenskabelige Institot; Fredericingade 18; 1310 Copenhagen; DENMARK.

Opw *Opernwelt*. Freq: 12; Began: 1959; Lang: Ger; Subj: Theatre. ISSN: 0030-3690
■Erhar Friedric Verlag; Im Brande 19; Seelz; SWITZERLAND.

OQ *Opera Quarterly*. Freq: 4; Began: 1983; Cov: Full; Lang: Eng; Subj: Theatre.
ISSN: 0736-0053
■University of North Carolina Press; Box 2288; Chapel Hill, NC 27514; USA.

Organon *Organon*. Freq: 1; Began: 1975; Lang: Fre; Subj: Theatre.
■Ctre de Recherches Théâtrales, Univ. Lyon II; Ensemble Univ., Ave. de l'Universite; 69500 Bron; FRANCE.

Orpheus *Orpheus*. Freq: 12; Began: 1972; Lang: Ger; Subj: Related. ISSN: 0932-611
■Neue Gesellschaft für Musikinformation mbH; Livländische Str. 27; D-10715 Berlin; GERMANY.

OSS *On-Stage Studies*. Formerly: *Colorado Shakespeare Festival Annual*. Freq: 1; Began: 1976; Lang: Eng; Subj: Theatre.
ISSN: 0749-1549
■Colorado Shakespeare Festival, Campus Box 261; University of Colorado; Boulder, CO 80309 0261; USA.

OSZ *Očag. Semejnij Zurnal*. Began: 1992; Cov: Scan; Lang: Rus; Subj: Related.
ISSN: 0869-5091
■Ist Tverskaja-Tamskaja Street; Building 2, Section 1; Moscow 103006; RUSSIA.

Otecest *Otečestvennije arhivy*. Freq: 6; Began: 1992; Cov: Scan; Lang: Rus; Subj: Related. ISSN: 0869-4427
■Glavnoe Arkhivnoe Upravlenie; 119817 B. Pirogovskaja 17; Moscow G-435; RUSSIA.

Outrage *Outrage*. Freq: 12; Began: 1983; Cov: Scan; Lang: Eng; Subj: Related.
■Gay Publications Co-operative; P.O. Box 21; Carlton South Victoria 3053; AUSTRALIA.

OvA *Overture*. Freq: 12; Began: 1919; Cov: Scan; Lang: Eng; Subj: Theatre. ISSN: 0030-7556
■Los Angeles Musicians' Union, Local 47; 817 Vine Street; Los Angeles, CA 90038; USA.

Over *Overland*. Freq: 3; Began: 1954; Cov: Scan; Lang: Eng; Subj: Related. ISSN: 0043-342X
■P.O. Box 14146; Melbourne Victoria 3000; AUSTRALIA.

P&L *Philosophy and Literature*. Freq: 2; Began: 1976; Lang: Eng; Subj: Related.
ISSN: 0190-0013
■Fine Arts; University of Canterbury; Christchurch; NEW ZEALAND.

PA *Présence Africaine*. Freq: 4; Began: 1947; Lang: Fre/Eng; Subj: Related. ISSN: 0032-7638
■Nouvelle Société Presence Africaine; 25 bis rue des Ecoles; Paris 75005; FRANCE.

Pa&Pr *Past and Present*: A Journal of Historical Studies. Freq: 4; Began: 1952; Lang: Eng; Subj: Related. ISSN: 0031-2746
■Oxford University Press; Pinkhill House; Southfield Road Eynsham; Oxford OX8 1JJ; UK.

PAA *Performing Arts Annual*. SEE *Performing Arts at the Library of Congress*. Freq: 1; Began: 1986; Ceased: 1990; Cov: Full; Lang: Eng; Subj: Theatre. ISSN: 0887-8234
■Library of Congress, Performing Arts Library Resources; Dist. by G.O.P.; Washington, DC 20540; USA.

PAaLC *Performing Arts at the Library of Congress*. Formerly *Performing Arts Annual*. Freq: IRR; Began: 1990; Cov: Full; Lang: Eng; Subj: Theatre. ISSN: 0887-8234
■Library of Congress, Performing Arts Library Resources; Dist. by G.O.P.; Washington, DC 20540; USA.

PAC *Performing Arts in Canada*. SEE *Performing Arts & Entertainment in Canada*. Freq: 4; Began 1961; Ceased: 1991; Cov: Full; Lang: Eng; Subj: Theatre. ISSN: 0031-5230
■Performing Arts & Entertainment Magazine; 1100 Caledonia Road; Toronto, ON M6A 2W5; CANADA.

PAEC *Performing Arts & Entertainment in Canada*. Freq: 4; Began: 1991; Cov: Full; Lang: Eng; Subj: Theatre. ISSN: 1185-3433
■Performing Arts & Entertainment Magazine; 1100 Caledonia Road; Toronto, ON M6A 2W5; CANADA.

Pal *Palócföld*. Freq: 6; Began: 1967; Cov: Scan; Lang: Hun; Subj: Related. ISSN: 0555-8867
■Nógrád Megyei Művelődési Központ Rákóczi út 192; 310 Salgótarján HUNGARY.

Pamir *Pamir*. Freq: 12; Began: 1949; Cov: Scan; Lang: Rus; Subj: Related. ISSN: 0131-2650
■Dushanbe; TAJIKISTAN.

Pantallas *Pantallas y Escenarios*. Freq: 5; Last Known Address; Lang: Spa; Subj: Theatre.
■Maria Lostal 24; 8 Zaragoza; SPAIN.

PAR *Performing Arts Resources*. Freq: 1; Began: 1974; Cov: Scan; Lang: Eng; Subj: Theatre. ISSN: 0360-3814
■111 Amsterdam Avenue New York, NY 10023; USA.

Parergon *Parergon*. Freq: 2; Began: 1971; Cov: Scan; Lang: Eng; Subj: Related. ISSN: 0313-6221

■Dept. of English; University of Sydney; NSW 2006; AUSTRALIA.

Parnass *Parnass*: Die Österreichische Kunst- und Kulturzeitschrift. Freq: 6; Began: 1981; Lang: Ger; Subj: Theatre.
■C & E Grosser, Druckerei Verlag; Wiener Strasse 290; A 4020 Linz; AUSTRIA.

Parnasso *Parnasso*. Freq: 8; Began: 1951; Lang: Fin; Subj: Theatre. ISSN: 0031-2320
■Yhtyneet Kuvalehdet Oy; Maistraatinportti 1; 00240 Helsinki; FINLAND.

PArts *Performing Arts*: The Music and Theatre Monthly. Freq: 12; Began: 1967; Lang: Eng; Subj: Theatre. ISSN: 0031-5222
■Performing Arts Network; 3539 Motor Ave.; Los Angeles, CA 90034-4800; USA.

PArtsSF *Performing Arts Magazine*: San Francisco Music & Theatre Monthly. Freq: 12; Began: 1967; Ceased: 1987; Lang: Eng; Subj: Theatre. ISSN: 0480-0257
■Theatre Publications, Inc.; 2999 Overland Ave., Ste. 201; Los Angeles, CA 90064; USA.

PasShowA *Passing Show*. Freq: IRR; Began: 1981; Lang: Eng; Subj: Theatre. ISSN: 0706-1897
■Performing Arts Museum, Victorian Arts Centre; 1 City Rd; 3205 S. Melbourne, Victoria; AUSTRALIA.

PasShow *Passing Show: Newsletter of the Shubert Archive*. Freq: 3; Began: 1983; Cov: Full; Lang: Eng; Subj: Theatre.
■Shubert Archive, Lyceum Theatre; 149 West 45th Street; New York, NY 10026; USA.

PaT *Pamiętnik Teatralny*: Poswiecony historii i krytyce teatru. Freq: 4; Began: 1952; Cov: Full; Lang: Pol; Subj: Theatre. ISSN: 0031-0522
■Institute of the Polish Academy of Sciences; Dluga 26/28; 00950 Warsaw; POLAND.

PaV *Paraules al Vent*. Freq: 12; Lang: Spa; Subj: Related.
■Associació de Joves 'Paraules al Vent'; Casal de Sant Jordi; Sant Jordi Desvalls; SPAIN.

PAYBA *Performing Arts Year Book of Australia*. Freq: 1; Began: 1977; Lang: Eng; Subj: Theatre.
■Showcast Publications Ltd; Box 141; 2088 Spit Junction N.S.W; AUSTRALIA.

Pb *Playbill*: A National Magazine of the Theatre. Freq: 12; Began: 1982; Lang: Eng; Subj: Theatre. ISSN: 0032-146X
■Playbill Incorporated; 52 Vanderbilt Avenue; 11th Floor New York, NY 10017-3893; USA.

PCD *Premiéry československých divadel*. Freq: 12; Lang: Cze; Subj: Theatre.
■Divadelni ústav; Celetná 17; 110 01 Prague 1; CZECH REPUBLIC.

PdO *Pantuflas del Obispo*. Began: 1966; Lang: Spa; Subj: Theatre.
■Semanario Sabado; Vargas 219; Quito; ECUADOR.

Pe *Performance*. Freq: 6; Began: 1981; Lang: Eng; Subj: Related.
■Brevet Publishing Ltd.; 445 Brighton Road; South Croydon CR2 6EU; UK.

PeM *Pesti Műsor*. Freq: 52; Began: 1957; Lang: Hun; Subj: Theatre.
■Garay u.5; 1076 Budapest VII; HUNGARY.

PerAJ *Performing Arts Journal*. Freq: 3; Began: 1976; Cov: Full; Lang: Eng; Subj: Theatre. ISSN: 0735-8393
■Performing Arts Journal, Inc.; P.O. Box 260, Village Station; New York, NY 10014; USA.

PerfM *Performance-Management*. Freq: 2; Cov: Scan; Lang: Eng; Subj: Theatre.
■Brooklyn College, Dept. of Theatre; Brooklyn, NY 11210; USA.

PerfNZ *Performance: A Handbook of the Performing Arts in New Zealand*. Freq: 5; Began: 1980; Lang: Eng; Subj: Theatre. ISSN: 0112-0654
■Association of Community Theatres; P.O. 68-257; Newton, Aukland; NEW ZEALAND.

PerfR *Performance Research*. Freq: 3; Began: 1996; Cov: Scan; Lang: Eng; Subj: Theatre. ISSN: 1352-8165
■Center for Performance Research; Market Road; Canton Cardiff CF5 1QE; WALES.

Perlicko *Perlicko-Perlacko*. Began: 1950; Last Known Address; Lang: Ger; Subj: Theatre.
■Dr. Hans R. Purschke; Postfach 550135; 6000 Frankfurt; GERMANY.

Perspek *Perspektiva*. Freq: 12; Began: 1990; Cov: Scan; Lang: Rus; Subj: Related. ISSN: 0131-2278
■Izdatel'stvo Molodaya Gvardiya, Ul.; Sushevskaya, 21; Moscow A-55; RUSSIA.

Pf *Platform*. Freq: 2; Began: 1979; Ceased: 1983; Cov: Scan; Lang: Eng; Subj: Theatre.
■Dept of Literature, University of Essex; Wivenhoe Park; Colchester; UK.

PFr *Présence Francophone*. Freq: 2; Began: 1970; Ceased: 1970; Cov: Scan; Lang: Fre; Subj: Related. ISSN: 0048-5195
■Université de Sherbrooke; Sherbrooke, PQ J1K 2R1; CANADA.

PI *Plays International*. Formerly: *Plays/Plays International*. Freq: 12; Began: 1985; Cov: Scan; Lang: Eng; Subj: Theatre.
■Chancery Publications Ltd.; 55 Hatton Garden; London ECIN 8HP; UK.

PInfo *Puppenspiel-Information*. Freq: 2; Began: 1967; Lang: Ger; Subj: Theatre.
■Deutsche Puppentheater e.V.; Moorweg 1 D-21337 Lüneburg; GERMANY.

PintR *Pinter Review*. Began: 1987; Cov: Full; Lang: Eng; Subj: Theatre. ISSN: 0895-9706
■Harold Pinter Society; University of Tampa; Box 11F Tampa, FL 33606; USA.

PiP *Plays in Process*. Lang: Eng; Subj: Theatre. ISSN: 0736-0711
■Theatre Communications Group 355 Lexington Avenue; New York, NY 10017; USA.

Pja *Pipirijaina*. Freq: 6; Began: 1979; Lang: Spa; Subj: Theatre.
■c/o San Enrique 16; 20 Madrid; SPAIN.

Plateaux *Plateaux*. Formerly: *Bulletin de l'Union des Artistes*. Freq: 4; Began: 1925; Lang: Fre; Subj: Theatre.
■Syndicat Français des Artistes-Interprètes (SFA) 21 bis, rue Victor-Massé; 75009 Paris; FRANCE.

Play *Play*. Freq: 12; Began: 1974; Lang: Eng; Subj: Theatre. ISSN: 0311-4031

■Main Street; PO Box 67; 5245 Hahndorf; SOUTH AFRICA.

PlayM *Players Magazine*. Freq: 22; Began: 1924; Ceased: 1967; Lang: Eng; Subj: Theatre. ISSN: 0032-1486
■National Collegiate Players, Northern Illinois University; University Theatre; Dekalb, IL 60115; USA.

PlayN *Playmarket News*. Formerly: *Act: Theatre in New Zealand*. Freq: 2; Began: 1988; Lang: Eng; Subj: Theatre. ISSN: 0113-9703
■Level 2, 16 Cambridge Terrace; P.O. Box 9767, Te Aro; TeWhanganui-a-Tara Wellington, Aotearoa; NEW ZEALAND.

Plays *Plays*: (In 1985 became part of *Plays and Players*). Formerly: *Plays/Plays International*. Freq: 12; Began: 1983; Ceased: 1985; Cov: Scan; Lang: Eng; Subj: Theatre.
■Ocean Publications; 34 Buckingham Palace Road; London SW1; UK.

PlPl *Plays and Players*. Freq: 12; Began: 1953; Cov: Scan; Lang: Eng; Subj: Theatre. ISSN: 0032-1559
■Mineco Design Ltd.; 18 Friern Park London N12 9DA; UK.

PLUG *PLUG*: Maandelijks informatie-blad van het Cultureel Jongeren Paspoort. Freq: 12; Began: 1967; Lang: Dut; Subj: Theatre. ISSN: 0032-1621
■Cultureel Jongeren Paspoort; Kleine Gartmanplts. 10; 1017 RR Amsterdam; NETHERLANDS.

PM *Performance Magazine, The*. Freq: 6; Began: 1979; Ceased: 1992; Cov: Scan; Lang: Eng; Subj: Theatre. ISSN: 0144-5901
■Performance Magazine Ltd.; P.O. Box 717; London SW5 9BS; UK.

PMLA *PMLA*: Publications of the Modern Language Assoc. of America. Freq: 6; Began: 1929; Last Known Address; Cov: Scan; Lang: Eng; Subj: Related. ISSN: 0030-8129
■Modern Language Assoc. of America; 62 5th Avenue; New York, NY 10011; USA.

Pnpa *Peuples noirs, peuples africains*. Freq: 4; Began: 1977; Lang: Fre; Subj: Related.
■82, avenue de la Porte-des-Champs; 76000 Rouen; FRANCE.

Podium *Podiumkunsten*. Freq: 1 Began: 1987; Lang: Dut; Subj: Theatre. ISSN: 0922-1409
■Centraal Bureau voor de Statistiek (Statistics Netherlands); Postbox 428; 2270 AZ Voorburg; NETHERLANDS.

PodiumB *Podium*: Zeitschrift für Bühnenbildner und Theatertechnik. Freq: 4; Lang: Ger; Subj: Theatre.
■Abteilung Berufsbildung; Munzstrasse 21; 1020 Berlin; GERMANY.

Poppen *Poppenspelberichten*. Freq: 4; Lang: Dut; Subj: Theatre.
■Mechelen; BELGIUM.

Pozoriste *Pozorište*: Časopis za pozorišnu umjetnost. Freq: 6; Began: 1959; Lang: Cro; Subj: Theatre. ISSN: 0032-616X
■Narodno Pozorište; Matija Gupca 6; 75000 Tuzla; BOSNIA AND HERZEGOVINA.

PQ *Philological Quarterly*: Investigation of Classical & Modern Langs. and Lit. Freq: 4; Began: 1922; Cov: Scan; Lang: Eng; Subj: Related. ISSN: 0031-7977

■Editor, Philological Quarterly; University of Iowa; Iowa City, IA 52242; USA.

PQCS *Philippine Quarterly of Culture and Society*. Freq: 4; Began: 1973; Lang: Eng; Subj: Related. ISSN: 0115-0243
■San Carlos Publications; 6000 Cebu City; PHILIPPINES.

PrAc *Primer Acto*. Freq: 5; Began: 1957; Last Known Address; Lang: Spa; Subj: Theatre.
■Cervantes, 21-1 Oficina 3; 28014 Madrid; SPAIN.

Preface *Préface*. Freq: 12; Lang: Fre; Subj: Theatre.
■Centre National Nice-Côte d'Azur; Esplanade des Victoires; 06300 Nice; FRANCE.

Premiere *Première*. Lang: Ger/Fre; Subj: Related.
■Schweizerischer Bühnenverband; Pf. 9; CH-8126 Zumika; GERMANY.

Premijera *Premijera*: List Narodnog Pozorista Sombor. Lang: Ser; Subj: Theatre.
■Koste Trifkovica 2; Sombor; SERBIA.

Presg *Prešernovo gledališče*. Cov: Scan; Lang: Slo; Subj: Related.
■Glavni trg 6; 6400 Kranj; SLOVENIA.

Pretexts *Pretexts*. Began: 1989; Cov: Scan; Lang: Eng; Subj: Related. ISSN: 1015-549X
■University of Cape Town; Private Bag Rondebosch 7700; SOUTH AFRICA.

Primdg *Primorsko dramsko gledališče*. Cov: Scan; Lang: Slo; Subj: Related.
■Bevkov trg 4; 65000 Nova Gorica; SLOVENIA.

Primk *Primerjalna književnost*. Freq: 2; Began: 1978; Cov: Scan; Lang: Slo; Subj: Related. ISSN: 0351-1189
■Slovensko društvo za primerjalno književnost; Aškerčeva 2; 1000 Ljubljana; SLOVENIA.

prinz *prinzenstrasse. Hannoversche Hefte zur Theatergeschichte*. Freq: 2/3; Began: 1994; Lang: Ger; Subj: Theatre. ISSN: 0949-4049
■Theatermuseum und -archiv Hannover; Prinzenstrasse 9 (im Schasupielhaus); D-30159 Hannover; GERMANY.

Prof *Profile*: The Newsletter of the New Zealand Assoc. of Theatre Technicians. Freq: 4; Lang: Eng; Subj: Related.
■Ponsonby, Auckland; NEW ZEALAND.

Program *Program*. Began: 1925; Ceased; Lang: Cze; Subj: Theatre.
■Zemske divadlo; Dvorakova 11; Brno; CZECH REPUBLIC.

Programa *Programa*. Began: 1978; Lang: Por; Subj: Theatre.
■Grupo de Teatro de Campolide; 43, 20 D. Cde. Antas; Lisbon; PORTUGAL.

Prolog *Prolog*: Revija za dramsku umjetnost. In 1986 became Novi Prolog. Freq: 2; Began: 1968; Lang: Cro; Subj: Theatre.
■Centar za kulturnu djelatnost; Mihanoviceva 28/1; 41000 Zagreb; CROATIA.

PrologTX *Prolog*. Freq: 4; Began: 1973; Lang: Eng; Subj: Theatre. ISSN: 0271-7743
■Theatre Sources Inc., c/o Michael Firth; 104 North St. Mary; Dallas, TX 75214; USA.

Prologue *Prologue*. Freq: 4; Began: 1944; Lang: Eng; Subj: Theatre. ISSN: 0033-1007

■Arena Theater; Tufts University; Medford, MA 02155; USA.

Prompts *Prompts*. SEE *Irish Theatre Archive's Newsletter*. Freq: IRR; Began: 1981; Ceased: 1992; Lang: Eng; Subj: Theatre.
■Irish Theatre Archive, Archives Division; City Hall; 2 Dublin; IRELAND.

Propf *Pro philosophia füzetek*. Cov: Scan; Lang: Hun; Subj: Related.
■HUNGARY.

ProScen *ProScen*. Freq: 4; Began: 1986; Cov: Full; Lang: Swe; Subj: Theatre. ISSN: 0284-4346
■Svensk Teaterteknisk Förening, Section of OISTT; Mosebacke Torg 1 116 46 Stockholm; SWEDEN.

PrTh *Pratiques Théâtrales*: In 1978 became Grande République. Freq: 3; Ceased: 1978; Lang: Fre; Subj: Theatre.
■200 Ouest rue Sherbrooke; Montreal, PQ H2Y 3P2; CANADA.

Ptk *Publiekstheaterkrant*. Freq: 5; Began: 1978; Lang: Dut; Subj: Theatre.
■Publiekstheater; Marnixstraat 427; 1017 PK Amsterdam; NETHERLANDS.

PTKranj *Prešeren Theatre of Kranj*. Began: 1945; Cov: Scan; Lang: Slo; Subj: Theatre.
■Prešeren Theatre; Kranj; SLOVENIA.

PTZ *Petersburgskij Teatral'nyj Žurnal*. Began: 1992; Cov: Scan; Lang: Rus; Subj: Related.
■5 Pl. Iskusstv; kv. 56-a St. Petersburg 191011; RUSSIA.

PuJ *Puppetry Journal*. Freq: 4; Began: 1949; Cov: Full; Lang: Eng; Subj: Theatre. ISSN: 0033-443X
■Puppeteers of America; 8005 Swallow Dr.; Macedonia, OH 44056; USA.

PupM *Puppet Master*. Freq: 4; Began: 1946; Lang: Eng; Subj: Theatre.
■British Puppet and Model Theatre Guild, c/o Gordon Shapley (Hon. Sec.); 18 Maple Road, Yeading, Nr Hayes; Middlesex; UK.

Pusp *Puppenspiel und Puppenspieler*. Freq: 2; Began: 1960; Lang: Ger/Fre; Subj: Theatre. ISSN: 0033-4405
■Schweiz. Vereinigung Puppenspiel, c/o Gustav Gysin, Ed.; Roggenstr. 1; Riehen CH-4125; SWITZERLAND.

Pz *Proszenium*. Lang: Ger; Subj: Theatre.
■Zurich; SWITZERLAND.

PZOST *Premiere. Zeitschrift für Oper, Sprech- und Tanztheater*. Freq: 4; Lang: Ger; Subj: Theatre. ISSN: 0933-5390
■Andreas Berger; Berner Str. 2; D-38106 Braunschweig; GERMANY.

QQ *Queen's Quarterly*. Freq: 4; Cov: Scan; Lang: Eng; Subj: Related.
■Queen's University; Kingston, ON K7L 3N6; CANADA.

QT *Quaderni di Teatro*: Rivista Trimestrale del Teatro Regionale Toscano. Freq: 4; Began: 1978; Ceased: 1987; Cov: Full; Lang: Ita; Subj: Theatre.
■Casa Editrice Vallecchi; Viale Milton 7; 50129 Florence; ITALY.

QTST *Quaderni del Teatro Stabile di Torino*. Freq: IRR; Lang: Ita; Subj: Theatre.

■Teatro Stabile di Torino; Turin; ITALY.

Quarta *Quarta Parete*. Freq: 4; Began: 1975; Ceased: 1983; Lang: Ita; Subj: Theatre.
■Via Sant'Ottavio 15; Turin; ITALY.

QuellenT *Quellen zur Theatergeschichte*. Freq: IRR; Began: 1981; Lang: Ger; Subj: Theatre. ISSN: 0259-0786
■Verband der Wissenschaftlichen, Gesellschaften Oesterreichs; Lindengasse 37; A1070 Vienna; AUSTRIA.

Raduga *Raduga*. Freq: 12; Began: 1986; Cov: Scan; Lang: Rus; Subj: Related. ISSN: 0131-8136
■Izd-vo TSKKPE; Kiev; ESTONIA.

Raja *Rajatabla*. Lang: Spa; Subj: Theatre.
■Apartado 662; 105 Caracas; VENEZUELA.

RAL *Research in African Literature*. Freq: 4; Began: 1970; Lang: Eng; Subj: Related. ISSN: 0034-5210
■Indiana Univ. Press; 10th and Morton Sts.; Bloomington, IN 47405; USA.

Rampel *Rampelyset*. Freq: 6; Began: 1948; Lang: Dan; Subj: Theatre.
■Danske Amatør Teater Samvirke; Box 70; DK 6300 Grasten; DENMARK.

Randa *Randa*. Freq: 2; Cov: Scan; Lang: Spa; Subj: Related. ISSN: 0210-5993
■Editat per Curial Edicions Catalanes S.A.; carrer del Bruc 144; 08037 Barcelona; SPAIN.

Rangarupa *Rangarupa*. Began: 1976; Last Known Address; Lang: Ben; Subj: Theatre.
■Rangarup Natya Academy; 27/76 Central Rd.; Dhanmondi, Dacca; BANGLADESH.

Rangayan *Rangayan*. Freq: 4; Lang: Hin; Subj: Theatre.
■Bhartiya Lok kala Mandal; Udaipur 313001 Rajasthan; INDIA.

Rangyog *Rangyog*. Freq: 4; Lang: Hin; Subj: Theatre.
■Rajasthan Sangeet Natak Adademi; Paota; Jodhpur; INDIA.

Raritan *Raritan*. Freq: 4; Began: 1981; Lang: Eng; Subj: Related. ISSN: 0275-1607
■Rutgers University; 165 College Ave.; New Brunswick, NJ 08903; USA.

Rbharati *Rangbharati*. Freq: 12; Lang: Hin; Subj: Theatre.
■Bharatendu Rangmanch; Chowk;Lucknow; INDIA.

RdA *Revue de l'Art*. Freq: 4; Began: 1968; Lang: Fre; Subj: Related. ISSN: 0035-1326
■Editions du CNRS; Collège de France; 11, Place Marcelin-Berthelot 75005 Paris; FRANCE.

RdArt *Revista d'Art*. Freq: 1; Lang: Spa; Subj: Related.
■c/o Baldiri Reixac, Departament d'Historia de l'Art; Facultat de Geografia i Historia; 08028 Barcelona; SPAIN.

RdD *Rassegna di Diritto Cinematografico, Teatrale e della Televisione*. Lang: Ita; Subj: Theatre.
■Via Ennio Quirino Visconti 99; Rome; ITALY.

RDE *Research in Drama Education*. Freq: 2; Began: 1996; Cov: Full; Lang: Eng; Subj: Theatre.

■Carfax Publishing, Ltd.; P.O. Box 25; Abingdon, Oxfordshire OX14 2UE; UK.

RdS *Rassegna dello Spettacolo*. Began: 1953; Lang: Ita; Subj: Theatre. ISSN: 0033-9474
■Assoc. Gen. Italiana dello Spettacolo; Via di Villa Patrizi 10; 00161 Rome; ITALY.

RE *Revue d'esthétique*. Freq 4; Lang: Fre; Subj: Theatre.
■Privat et Cie; 14, rue des Arts; 31068 Toulouse CEDEX; FRANCE.

Recorder *Recorder, The: A Journal of the American Irish Historical Society*. Freq: 2; Began: 1985; Cov: Scan; Lang: Eng; Subj: Related.
■American Irish Historical Society; 991 Fifth Avenue; New York, NY 10028; USA.

REEDN *Records of Early English Drama Newsletter*. Freq: 2; Began: 1976; Cov: Full; Lang: Eng; Subj: Theatre. ISSN: 0070-9283
■University of Toronto, Erindale College, English Section; Mississauga, ON L5L 1C6; CANADA.

Region *Regionologia*. Began: 1992; Cov: Scan; Lang: Rus; Subj: Related. ISSN: 0131-5706
■Scientifi Researc Institut o Regionology;Proletarskaj Street 61;430000 Saransk-City RUSSIA

RenD *Renaissance Drama*. Freq: 1; Began: 1964; Cov: Full; Lang: Eng; Subj: Theatre. ISSN: 0486-3739
■Center for Renaissance Studies; Newberry Library; 60 West Walton St. Chicago, IL 60610; USA.

Renmin *Renmin Xiju*: People's Theatre. Freq: 12; Began: 1950; Lang: Chi; Subj: Theatre.
■52 Dongai Batiao; Beijing; CHINA.

RenQ *Renaissance Quarterly*. Freq: 4; Began: 1967; Lang: Eng; Subj: Related. ISSN: 0034-4338
■The Renaissance Society of America, Inc.; 24 West 12th Street; New York, NY 10011; USA.

Repliikki *Repliikki*. Freq: 4; Began: 1970; Lang: Fin; Subj: Theatre.
■Suomen Harrastajateatteriliitto; Minervankatu 1 C 21; 00100 Helsinki; FINLAND.

REsT *Revista de Estudios de Teatro*: Boletin. Freq: 3; Began: 1964; Lang: Spa; Subj: Theatre. ISSN: 0034-8171
■Instituto Nacional de Estudios de Teatro; Av. Córdoba 1199; Buenos Aires; ARGENTINA.

Restor *Restoration and Eighteenth Century Theatre Research*. Freq: 2; Began: 1962; Cov: Full; Lang: Eng; Subj: Theatre. ISSN: 0034-5822
■Loyola University of Chicago, Dept. of English; 6525 North Sheridan Road; Chicago, IL 60626; USA.

RevAS *Review: Asian Studies Association of Australia*. Freq: 3; Began: 1975; Lang: Eng; Subj: Related. ISSN: 0314-7533
■Robin Jeffrey, Dept. of Politics, La Trobe University; Bundoora; Victoria 3083; AUSTRALIA.

RevIM *Review of Indonesian and Malaysian Affairs*. Freq: 2; Began: 1962; Lang: Eng; Subj: Related. ISSN: 0034-6594

■Dept. of Indonesian & Malaysian Studies; University of Sydney; NSW 2006; AUSTRALIA.

Revue *Revue*. Freq: 6; Lang: Fre; Subj: Theatre.
■Theatre de la Commune, BP 157; 2 rue Edouard Poisson; 93304 Aubervilliers; FRANCE.

RHSTMC *Revue Roumaine d'Histoire de l'Art*: Série Théâtre, Musique, Cinéma. Freq: 4; Began: 1980; Lang: Fre; Subj: Related.
■Ed. Academiei Rep. Soc. Romania; Calea Victoriei 125; 79717 Bucharest; ROMANIA.

RHT *Revue d'Histoire du Théâtre*. Freq: 4; Began: 1948; Cov: Full; Lang: Fre; Subj: Theatre. ISSN: 0035-2373
■Société d'Histoire du Théâtre; 98 Boulevard Kellermann; 75013 Paris; FRANCE.

RIDr *Rivista Italiana di Drammaturgia*. Freq: 4; Began: 1976; Last Known Address; Lang: Ita; Subj: Theatre.
■Istituto del Dramma Italiano; Via Monte della Farina 42; Rome; ITALY.

RLC *Revue de Littérature Comparée*. Freq: 4; Began: 1921; Cov: Scan; Lang: Fre/Eng; Subj: Related. ISSN: 0035-1466
■F. Didier Erudition; 6 rue de la Sorbonne; 75005 Paris; FRANCE.

RLit *Russkaja Literatura: Istoriko-Literaturnyj Žurnal*: (Russian Literature: Historical Literary Journal). Freq: 4; Began: 1958; Cov: Scan; Lang: Rus; Subj: Related. ISSN: 0131-6095
■Inst. Russkoj Lit. Akademii Nauk SSSR, Puškinskij Dom; Nab. Makarova 4; 199164 St. Petersburg; RUSSIA.

RLtrs *Red Letters*. Freq: 3; Began: 1976; Lang: Eng; Subj: Related. ISSN: 0308-6852
■A Journal of Cultural Politics; 6 Cynthia Street; London N1 9JF; UK.

RLZ *Rossijskij Literaturovedčeskij Žurnal*. Began: 1992; Lang: Rus; Subj: Related.
■Krasikov Street 28/21; Union Ran, Literature Section; 117418 Moscow RUSSIA.

RMelo *Rassegna Melodrammatica*. Last Known Address; Lang: Ita; Subj: Theatre.
■Corso di Porta Romana 80; Milan; ITALY.

RN *Rouge et Noir*. Freq: 9; Began: 1968; Lang: Fre; Subj: Related.
■Maison de la Culture de Grenoble; BP 70-40; 38020 Grenoble; FRANCE.

Roda *Roda Lyktan*. Freq: 1; Began: 1976; Ceased: 1980; Lang: Swe; Subj: Theatre. ISSN: 0040-0750
■Skanska Teatern; Osterg 31; 26134 Landskrona; SWEDEN.

Rodina *Rodina*. Freq: 52; Began: 1989; Cov: Scan; Lang: Rus; Subj: Related. ISSN: 0235-7089
■Vozdvizenva Street, 4/7 Building; 103728 Moscow; RUSSIA.

Rossp *Rossiskaja provincija*. Cov: Scan; Lang: Rus; Subj: Related. ISSN: 0869-8376
■Moscow.; RUSSIA.

RORD *Research Opportunities in Renaissance Drama*. Freq: 1/2 yrs; Began: 1956; Cov: Full; Lang: Eng; Subj: Theatre. ISSN: 0098-647x
■Department of English; University of Kansas; Lawrence, KS 66045; USA.

RRMT *Ridotto*: Rassegna Mensile di Teatro. Freq: 12; Began: 1951; Cov: Scan; Lang: Ita; Subj: Theatre. ISSN: 0035-5186
■Società Italiana Autori Drammatici; Via Po 10; 00198 Rome; ITALY.

RSP *Rivista di Studi Pirandelliani*. Freq: 3; Began: 1978; Cov: Scan; Lang: Ita; Subj: Theatre.
■Centro Nazionale di Studi Pirandelliani; Agrigento; ITALY.

S&B *Spiel & B*04uhne (Bund Deutscher Amateurtheater)*. Freq: 3; Cov: Scan; Lang: Ger; Subj: Theatre
■Steinheimer Str. 7/1; D-89518 Heidenheim; GERMANY.

S&D *Speech & Drama*. Began: 1951; Cov: Scan; Lang: Eng; Subj: Related.
■Society of Teachers of Speech and Drama; 23 High Ash Avenue; Leeds LS17 8RS; UK.

SA *Screen Actor*. Freq: 4; Cov: Scan; Lang: Eng; Subj: Related. ISSN: 0036-956X
■Screen Actors Guild; 7065 Hollywood Boulevard; Los Angeles, CA 90028-6065; USA.

SAADYT *SAADYT Journal*. Formerly: *SAADYT Newsletter*. Began: 1979; Cov: Scan; Lang: Eng/Afr; Subj: Theatre.
■South African Assoc. for Drama and, Youth Theatre; Private Bag X41; Pretoria; SOUTH AFRICA.

SAD *Studies in American Drama, 1945-Present*. Freq: 2; Began: 1986; Cov: Full; Lang: Eng; Subj: Theatre. ISSN: 0886-7097
■Ohio State University Press; 1070 Carmack Road; Columbus, OH 43210; USA.

Sage *Sage*: A Scholarly Journal on Black Women. Freq: 2; Began: 1984; Lang: Eng; Subj: Related. ISSN: 0741-8369
■Sage Women's Educational Press, Inc.; Box 42741; Atlanta, GA 30311 0741; USA.

Sahne *Sahne (The Stage)*. Freq: 12; Began: 1981; Lang: Tur; Subj: Theatre.
■Nes'e Altiner; Cagaloglu Yokusu 2; Istanbul; TURKEY.

SAITT *SAITT Focus*. Freq: IRR; Last Known Address; Began: 1969; Lang: Eng/Afr; Subj: Theatre.
■S. African Inst. for Theatre Technology; Pretoria; SOUTH AFRICA.

SAJAL *South African Journal of African Languages*. Freq: 4; Began: 1981; Lang: Eng & Afrikaans;; Subj: Related. ISSN: 0257-2117
■African Languages Asso. of Southern Africa; Bureau for Scientific Publications; Box 1758; Pretoria 0001; SOUTH AFRICA.

SanatO *Sanat Olayi (Art Event)*. Freq: 12; Last Known Address; Lang: Tur; Subj: Theatre.
■Karacan Yayinlari; Basin Sarayi; Cagaloglu-Istanbul; TURKEY.

SATJ *South African Theatre Journal*. Freq: 2; Began: 1987; Cov: Full; Lang: Eng;; Subj: Theatre.
■SATJ School of Dramatic Art; University of Witwatersrand; WITS 2050; SOUTH AFRICA.

SCagdas *Sanajans Cagdas*. Freq: 12; Lang: Tur; Subj: Theatre.
■Istiklal Caddesi Botter Han; 475/479 Kat. 3; Istanbul; TURKEY.

Scan *Scandinavica*. Freq: 2; Lang: Eng/Dan/Ger/Fre/Swe; Subj: Related.

■University of East Anglia; Norwich; NR4 7TJ; UK.

ScCh   *Scene Changes.* Freq: 9; Began: 1973; Ceased: 1981; Cov: Scan; Lang: Eng; Subj: Theatre.   ISSN: 0381-8098
■Theatre Ontario; 8 York Street, 7th floor; Toronto, ON M5R 1J2; CANADA.

Scena   *Scena:*Časopis za pozorišnu umetnost. Freq: 6; Began: 1965; Lang: Ser; Subj: Theatre.   ISSN: 0036-5734
■Sterijino Pozorje; Zmaj Jovina 22; 21000 Novi Sad; SERBIA.

ScenaB   *Scena.* Freq: 4; Began: 1962; Lang: Ger; Subj: Theatre.   ISSN: 0036-5726
■Institut für Technologie Kultureller Einrichtung; Clara Zetkin-Str. 1205; 108 Berlin; GERMANY.

ScenaM   *Scena.* Freq: 12; Began: 1976; Lang: Ita; Subj: Theatre.
■Morrison Hotel; Via Modena 16; 20129 Milan; ITALY.

ScenaP   *Scena.* Freq: 26; Began: 1976; Ceased; Cov: Scan; Lang: Cze; Subj: Theatre.   ISSN: 0139-5386
■Scena; Valdstejnske nam. 3; Prague 1; CZECH REPUBLIC.

Scenaria   *Scenaria.* Freq: 24; Began: 1977; Cov: Scan; Lang: Eng; Subj: Theatre. ISSN: 0256-002X
■Triad Publishers Ltd.; Box 72161, Parkview 2122; Johannesburg; SOUTH AFRICA.

Scenario   *Scenario.* Freq: 4; Cov: Scan; Lang: Eng; Subj: Related.
■3200 Tower Oaks Blvd.; Rockville, MD 20852; USA.

Scenarium   *Scenarium.* Freq: 10; Began: 1879; Lang: Dut; Subj: Theatre.
■De Walburg Pres; P. O. Box 222; 7200 AE Zutphen; NETHERLANDS.

ScenaW   *Scena.* Formerly: *Poradnik Teatrow, Lirnik Wioskowy.* Freq: 48; Began: 1908; Lang: Pol; Subj: Theatre.
■Wydawnictwo Prasa ZSL; ul. Reja 9; 02 053 Warsaw; POLAND.

Scene   *Scene, De.* Freq: 10; Began: 1959; Lang: Dut; Subj: Theatre.
■Theatercentrum; Jan van Rijswijcklaan 28; B 2000 Antwerpen; BELGIUM.

Scenograf   *Scénografie.* Freq: 4; Began: 1963; Lang: Cze; Subj: Theatre.   ISSN: 0036-5815
■Divadelní ústav; Celetná 17; 110 01 Prague 1; CZECH REPUBLIC.

ScenoS   *Scen och Salong.* Freq: 12; Began: 1915; Ceased: 1990; Lang: Swe; Subj: Theatre.   ISSN: 0036-5718
■Folkparkernas Centralorganisation; Svedenborgsgatan 1; S 116 48 Stockholm; SWEDEN.

Schaus   *Schauspielfuehrer.* Der Inhalt der wichtigsten Theaterstuecke aus aller Welt. Freq: IRR; Began: 1953; Lang: Ger; Subj: Theatre.   ISSN: 0342-4553
■Anton Hiersemann Verlag, Rosenbergstr 113; 70193 Stuttgart 1; GERMANY.

SchwT   *Schweizer Theaterjahrbuch.* Freq: 1; Lang: Ger; Subj: Related.
■Gesellschaft für Theaterkultur; Theaterkultur-Verlag Postfach 1940, CH-4001 Basel; SWITZERLAND.

ScIDI   *Scena IDI, La.* Freq: 4; Began: 1971; Lang: Ita; Subj: Theatre.
■Bulzoni Editore; Via Liburni 14; 00185 Rome; ITALY.

SCN   *Seventeenth-Century News.* Freq: 4; Lang: Eng; Subj: Theatre.
■English Department; Blocker Building; Texas A & M University; College Station, TX 77843; USA.

Screen   *Screen.* Freq: 24; Began: 1959; Lang: Eng; Subj: Related.   ISSN: 0036-9543
■Oxford University Press; Pinkhill House; Southfield Road Eynsham Oxford OX8 1JJ; UK.

SCYPT   *SCYPT Journal.* Freq: 2; Began: 1977; Ceased: 1986; Cov: Scan; Lang: Eng; Subj: Theatre.
■Standing Conf. on Young People's Theatre, c/o Cockpit Theatre; Gateforth Street; London NW8; UK.

SD   *Stage Directions.* Cov: Scan; Lang: Eng; Subj: Theatre.
■SMW Communications Inc.; 3101 Poplarwood Court; Suite 310; Raleigh, NC 27604-1010; USA.

SDi   *Slovenské Divadlo.* Freq: 4; Began: 1952; Cov: Full; Lang: Slo; Subj: Theatre.   ISSN: 0037-699X
■Slovanian Acad. of Sciences; Klemensova 19; 814 30 Bratislava; SLOVAKIA.

SdO   *Serra d'Or.* Freq: 12; Began: 1959; Cov: Scan; Lang: Spa; Subj: Related. ISSN: 0037-2501
■Publicacions de l'Abadia de Montser, Ausias March 92-98; Apdo. 244; 13 Barcelona; SPAIN.

SEEA   *Slavic & East European Arts.* Freq: 2; Began: 1982; Cov: Full; Lang: Eng Subj Related.
■State Univ. of NY, Stonybrook, Dept. of Germanic & Slavic Lang.; Slavic & East European Arts; Stonybrook, NY 11794; USA.

SEEDTF   *Soviet and East European Performance: Drama Theatre Film.* Formerly: *Newsnotes on Soviet & East European Drama & Theatre.* SEE *Slavic and East European Performance.* Freq: 3; Began: 1981; Ceased: 1989; Cov: Scan; Lang: Eng; Subj: Theatre.
■Inst. for Contemporary East European and Soviet Drama and Theatre; Graduate Ctre, CUNY, 33 West 42nd St., Room 1206A; New York, NY 10036; USA.

SEEP   *Slavic and East European Performance: Drama, Theatre, Film.* Formerly: *Soviet and East-European Performance: Drama Theatre Film.* Freq: 3; Began: 1989; Cov: Scan; Lang: Eng; Subj: Theatre.
■Inst. for Contemporary East European and Soviet Drama and Theatre; Graduate Ctre, CUNY, 33 West 42nd St., Room 1206A; New York, NY 10036; USA.

Segmundo   *Segismundo.* Freq: 6; Began: 1965; Lang: Spa; Subj: Theatre.
■Consejo Superior de Investigaciones Científicas; Vitruvio 8, Apartado 14.458; Madrid 6; SPAIN.

Sehir   *Sehir Tijatrolari (City Theatre).* Freq: 12; Began: 1930; Lang: Tur; Subj: Theatre.
■Sunusi Tekiner; Basin ve Halka Iliskiler Danismanligi; Harbiye-Istanbul; TURKEY.

SEL   *SEL: Studies in English Literature, 1500-1900.* Freq: 4; Lang: Eng; Subj: Related.
■Rice University; 6100 Main Street; Houston, TX 77005-1892; USA.

Selmol   *Sel'skaja molodež.* Freq: 12; Began: 1925; Cov: Scan; Lang: Rus; Subj: Related.   ISSN: 0203-3569
■5a Novomitrovskaja ul.; Moscow 125015; RUSSIA.

Sembianza   *Sembianza.* Freq: 6; Began: 1981; Last Known Address; Lang: Ita; Subj: Theatre.
■Via Manzoni 14; 20121 Milan; ITALY.

Sentg   *Sentjakobsko gledališče.* Cov: Scan; Lang: Slo; Subj: Related.
■Mestni dom; 61000 Ljubljana; SLOVENIA.

SFN   *Shakespeare on Film Newsletter.* SEE *Shakespeare Bulletin.* Freq: 2; Began: 1977; Ceased: 1993; Cov: Scan; Lang: Eng; Subj: Related.   ISSN: 0739-6570
■Dept. of English; Nassau Community College; Garden City, NY 11530; USA.

SFo   *Szinháztechnikai Fórum.* Journal of the Section for Theatre Technology of the Hungarian Optical, Acoustic and Cinematographical Society of the Hungarian Centre of the OISTAT. Freq: 4; Began: 1974; Cov: Scan; Lang: Hun; Subj: Theatre.   ISSN: 0139-1542
■OPAKFI; Fő u. 68; 1027 Budapest; HUNGARY.

Sg   *Shingeki.* Freq: 12; Began: 1954; Lang: Jap; Subj: Theatre.
■Hakusui-sha, Chiyoda-ku; 3-24 Kanda-Ogawa-cho; 101 Tokyo; JAPAN.

SGfUB   *Schriftenreihe, Gesellschaft f*04ur Unterhaltende B*04uhnenkunst e.V..* Freq: 1; Cov: Scan; Lang: Ger; Subj: Related.
■Hertzbergstr. 21; D-12055 Berlin; GERMANY.

SGIP   *Sovetskoe Gosudarstvo i Pravo.* SEE *Gosudarstvo i pravo.* Freq: 12; Began: 1927; Ceased: 1992; Cov: Scan; Lang: Rus; Subj: Related.   ISSN: 0132-0769
■Akad. Nauk S.S.S.R.; Inst. Gosudarstva i Prava; Izdatel'stvo Nauka; Podsosenskii Per., 21; Moscow K-62; RUSSIA.

SGT   *Schriften der Gesellschaft für Theatergeschichte.* Lang: Ger; Subj: Theatre.
■Berlin; GERMANY.

SGTJ   *Schweizerische Gesellschaft für Theaterkultur Jahrbücher.* Freq: IRR; Began: 1928; Lang: Ger; Subj: Theatre.
■Swiss Association for Theatre Research, c/o Louis Naef; Postfach 180; CH-6130 Willisau; SWITZERLAND.

SGTS   *Schweizerische Gesellschaft für Theaterkultur Schriften.* Freq: IRR; Began: 1928; Ceased: 1982; Lang: Ger; Subj: Theatre.
■Swiss Association for Theatre Research, c/o Louis Naef; Postfach 180; CH-6130 Willisau; SWITZERLAND.

Shahaab   *Shahaab.* Last Known Address; Lang: Ara; Subj: Theatre.
■Hayassat Building; Cooper Road; Rawlpindi; PAKISTAN.

ShakS   *Shakespeare Studies.* Freq: 1; Lang: Eng; Subj: Theatre.   ISSN: 1067-0823
■Peter Lang Publishers; New York, NY; USA.

ShakSN   *Shakespeare Studies.* Lang: Eng; Subj: Theatre.

■Nashville, TN; USA.

Shavian *Shavian*. Freq: 2; Began: 1946; Lang: Eng; Subj: Theatre. ISSN: 0037-3346 ■Shaw Society; 6 Stanstead Grove; London SE6 4UD; UK.

ShawR *Shaw*: The Annual of Bernard Shaw Studies. Formerly: *Shaw Review (ISSN: 0037-3354)*. Freq: 1; Began: 1981; Cov: Scan; Lang: Eng; Subj: Theatre. ISSN: 0741-5842 ■Penn State Press; Barbara Building; University Park, PA 16802; USA.

ShB *Shakespeare Bulletin:A Journal of Performance Criticism and Scholarship*:Incorporating *Shakespeare on Film Newsletter*. Freq: 4; Began: 1982; Lang: Eng; Subj: Theatre. ■English Department; Lafayette College; Easton, PA 18042; USA.

ShN *Shakespeare Newsletter*. Freq: 4; Began: 1951; Lang: Eng; Subj: Theatre. ISSN: 0037-3214 ■Louis Marder, Ed. & Pub.; 1217 Ashland Ave.; Evanston, IL 60202; USA.

Show *Show*. Last Known Address; Lang: Eng; Subj: Theatre. ■9/2 Nazimabad; Karachi; PAKISTAN.

ShowM *Show Music*. Freq: 4; Began: 1981; Cov: Scan; Lang: Eng; Subj: Theatre. ■P.O. Box 466; East Haddam, CT 06423-0466; USA.

ShRA *Shakespeare and Renaissance Association: Selected Papers*. Freq: 1; Lang: Eng; Subj: Related. ■Department of English; 400 Hal Greer Blvd.; Marshall University Huntington, WV 25755-2646; USA.

ShS *Shakespeare Survey*. Freq: 1; Began: 1948; Cov: Full; Lang: Eng; Subj: Theatre. ISSN: 0080-9152 ■Cambridge University Press, The Edinburgh Building; Shaftesbury Road; Cambridge CB2 2RU; UK.

ShSA *Shakespeare in Southern Africa*. Freq: 1; Began: 1987; Cov: Full; Lang: Eng; Subj: Theatre. ■ISEA; Rhodes University; Grahamstown 6140; SOUTH AFRICA.

Silex *Silex*. Last Known Address; Lang: Fre; Subj: Theatre. ■BP 554 RP; 38013 Grenoble; FRANCE.

Sin *Sightline*: The Journal of Theatre Technology and Design. Freq: 2; Began: 1974; Ceased: 1993; Cov: Scan; Lang: Eng; Subj: Theatre. ISSN: 0265-9808 ■Assoc. of British Theatre Technicians; 4 Gt. Pulteney Street; London W1R 3DF; UK.

Sipario *Sipario*. Freq: 12; Began: 1946; Last Known Address; Lang: Ita; Subj: Theatre. ■Sipario Editrice S.R.L.; Via Flaminia 167; 00196 Milan; ITALY.

Sis *Sightlines*. Freq: 4; Began: 1965; Cov: Scan; Lang: Eng; Subj: Related. ISSN: 0065-6311 ■USITT; 10 West 19th St., Ste. 5A; New York, NY 10011; USA.

SiSo *Sight and Sound*. Freq: 4; Began: 1932; Cov: Scan; Lang: Eng; Subj: Related. ISSN: 0037-4806 ■21 Stephen Street; London W1P 1PL; UK.

SJ *Spielplan Journal*. Freq: 1; Cov: Scan; Lang: Ger; Subj: Related. ■Mykenae-Verlag, Ahastr. 9; D-64285 Darmstadt; GERMANY.

SjV *Sirp ja Vasar*. Freq: 52; Began: 1940; Lang: Est; Subj: Theatre. ■Postkast 388, Pikk t. 40; 200 001 Talin; ESTONIA.

SJW *Shakespeare Jahrbuch*. SEE: *Deutsche Shakespeare Gesellschaft/Deutsche Shakespeare Gesellschaft West, Jahrbuch*. Freq: 1; Began: 1865; Lang: Ger; Subj: Theatre. ISSN: 0080-9128 ■Deutsche Shakespeare Gesellschaft; Kamp-Kontor, Ferdinand Kamp Verlag; Widumestr. 6-8 D-44787 Bochum; GERMANY.

Skript *Skript*. Freq: 10; Last Known Address; Lang: Dut; Subj: Theatre. ■N.C.A.; Postbus 64; 3600 AB Maarssen; NETHERLANDS.

Slav *Slavjanovedenie*. Freq: 6; Began: 1992; Cov: Scan; Lang: Rus; Subj: Related. ISSN: 0132-1366 ■Izdatel'stvo Nauka; Podsosenskii Per. 21; K 62 Moscow; RUSSIA.

Slavr *Slavistična revija*:časopis za jezikoslovje in literarne vede. Freq: 4; Began: 1948; Cov: Scan; Lang: Slo; Subj: Related. ISSN: 0350-6894 ■Slavistično društvo Slovenije; Aškerčeva 2; 1000 Ljubljana; SLOVENIA.

SlovD *Slovensko narodno gledalisče-Drama*. Cov: Scan; Lang: Slo; Subj: Related. ■Erjavčeva o.1; 61000 Ljubljana; SLOVENIA.

Slovl *Slovensko ljudsko gledalisče Celje*. Cov: Scan; Lang: Slo; Subj: Related. ■Gledališki trg 5; 63000 Celje; SLOVENIA.

Slovm *Slovensko mladinsko gledalisče*. Cov: Scan; Lang: Slo; Subj: Related. ■Vilharjeva o.11; 61000 Ljubljana; SLOVENIA.

SlovO *Slovensko narodno gledalisče-Opera in balet*. Cov: Scan; Lang: Slo; Subj: Related. ■Župančičeva .1; 61000 Ljubljana; SLOVENIA.

SM *Spectacles Magazine*. Freq: 12; Lang: Fre; Subj: Theatre. ■42 Blvd. du Temple; 75011 Paris; FRANCE.

Smena *Smena*. Freq: 12; Began: 1924; Cov: Scan; Lang: Rus; Subj: Related. ISSN: 0131-6658 ■Pravda ; Moscow; RUSSIA.

SMR *SourceMonthly*: The Resource for Mimes, Clowns, Jugglers, and Puppeteers. Freq: 12; Lang: Eng; Subj: Theatre. ■Mimesource Inc.; 125 Sherman Str.; Brooklyn, NY 11218; USA.

SNJPA *Sangeet Natak*: Journal of the Performing Arts. Freq: 4; Began: 1965; Lang: Eng; Subj: Theatre. ISSN: 0036-4339 ■Sangeet Natak Akademi, Rabindra Bhavan; Ferozeshah Rd.; 110001 New Delhi; INDIA.

SobCh *Sobcota Chelovneta*. Lang: Geo; Subj: Theatre. ■Tbilisi; GEORGIA.

Sobesednik *Sobesednik*. Freq: 12; Began: 1949; Cov: Scan; Lang: Rus; Subj: Related. ISSN: 0202-3180 ■Moscow; RUSSIA.

SObzor *Scénografický Obzor*. Freq: 6; Began: 1958; Ceased: 1973; Lang: Cze; Subj: Theatre. ■Vinohradska 2; Prague 1; CZECH REPUBLIC.

SocA *Social Alternatives*. Freq: 4; Began: 1977; Cov: Scan; Lang: Eng; Subj: Related. ISSN: 0155-0306 ■c/ Department of Government, University of Queensland; St. Lucia Qld 4067; AUSTRALIA.

SocH *Social History*. Freq: 3; Began: 1976; Lang: Eng; Subj: Related. ISSN: 0307-1022 ■Routledge Ltd.; 11 New Fetter Lane; London EC4P 4EE; UK.

Sodob *Sodobnost*. Freq: 12; Began: 1953; Cov: Scan; Lang: Slo; Subj: Related. ISSN: 0038-0482 ■DZS d.d. Mestni trg 26; 1000 Ljubljana; SLOVENIA.

Sog *Soglasije*. Began: 1990; Cov: Scan; Lang: Rus; Subj: Related. ISSN: 0868-8710 ■Bakhrušin Street, 28; 113054 Moscow RUSSIA.

SogogT *Sōgō geijutsu Toshite no nō*. Freq: Irreg; Began: 1994; Lang: Jap; ISSN: 1343-1331 ■International Zeami Society, JAPAN.

SoM *Speaking of Mime*. Freq: IRR; Began: 1976; Ceased; Lang: Eng; Subj: Theatre. ISSN: 0381-9035 ■Canadian Mime Council; Niagara-on-the-Lake, ON L0S 1J0; CANADA.

Somo *Somogy*. Formerly: *Somogyi Szemle*. Freq: 6; Began: 1970; Cov: Scan; Lang: Hun; Subj: Related. ISSN: 0133-0144 ■Somogy Megyei Könyvtár; Május 1. u. 10 7400 Kaposvár; HUNGARY.

SON *Scottish Opera News*. Freq: 12; Ceased: 1987; Lang: Eng; Subj: Theatre. ISSN: 0309-7323 ■Scottish Opera Club; Elmbank Crescent; Glasgow G2 4PT; UK.

SoQ *Southern Quarterly, The*: A Journal of the Arts in the South. Freq: 4; Began: 1962; Lang: Eng; Subj: Related. ISSN: 0038-4496 ■PO Box 5078 Southern Station; Hattiesburg, MS 39406-5078; USA.

SORev *Sean O'Casey Review, The*. Freq: 2; Began: 1974; Last Known Address; Lang: Eng; Subj: Theatre. ISSN: 0365-2245 ■O'Casey Studies; PO Box 333; Holbrook, NY 11741; USA.

SoSaw *Southern Sawdust*. Freq: 4; Began: 1954; Last Known Address; Lang: Eng; Subj: Theatre. ISSN: 0038-4542 ■L. Wilson Poarch Jr.; 2965 Freeman Avenue; Sarasota, FL 33580; USA.

SoTh *Southern Theatre*. Began: 1964; Cov: Scan; Lang: Eng; Subj: Theatre. ISSN: 0584-4738 ■Southeastern Theatre Conference; University of Carolina; Box 9868 Greensboro, NC 27412-0868; USA.

SOUTHERLY *Southerly: A Review of Australian Literature*. Freq: 4; Began: 1939; Cov: Scan; Lang: Eng; Subj: Related. ISSN: 0038-3732
■Dept. of English; Univ. of Sydney; Sydney N.S.W. 2006; AUSTRALIA.

SouthR *Southern Review* Freq: 3; Began: 1963; Cov: Scan; Lang: Eng; Subj: Related. ISSN: 0038-4526
■School of Humanities and Social Sciences, Monash University; Gippsland, Chuschill VIC 3842; AUSTRALIA.

SovAr *Sovetskie Arkhivy*. SEE *Otecestvennye arhivy*. Freq: 6; Began: 1966; Ceased: 1992; Cov: Scan; Lang: Rus; Subj: Related. ISSN: 0038-5166
■Glavnoe Arkhivnoe Upravlenie; Pirogovskaya 17; Moscow G-435; RUSSIA.

SovBal *Sovetskij Balet*. SEE *Balet*. Cov: Scan; Ceased: 1992; Lang: Rus; Subj: Theatre.
■Moscow; RUSSIA.

SovD *Sovremennaja Dramaturgija*. Freq: 4; Began: 1982; Cov: Scan; Lang: Rus; Subj: Theatre. ISSN: 6207-7698
■Moscow; RUSSIA.

SovEC *Sovetskaja Estrada i Cirk*. SEE *Estrada i cirk*. Freq: 12; Ceased: 1992; Cov: Scan; Lang: Rus; Subj: Theatre. ISSN: 0131-6769
■Moscow; RUSSIA.

SovEt *Sovetskaja Ethnografia*. SEE *Etnografijceskoe obozrenie*. Freq: 6; Began: 1926; Ceased: 1992; Cov: Scan; Lang: Rus; Subj: Related. ISSN: 0038-5050
■Ulica D. Uljanova 19; B 36 Moscow; RUSSIA.

SovKult *Sovetskaja Kultura*. Cov: Scan; Lang: Rus; Subj: Related.
■Novoslobodskaja ul. 73; K 55 Moscow; RUSSIA.

SovMuzyka *Sovetskaja Muzyka*: (Soviet Music). SEE *Muzykal'naja akademija*. Freq: 12; Began: 1933; Ceased: 1992; Cov: Scan; Lang: Rus; Subj: Related. ISSN: 0131-6818
■Moscow; RUSSIA.

SovSlav *Sovetskoje Slavjanovedenje*: (Soviet Slavonic Studies). SEE *Slavjanovedenie*. Freq: 6; Began: 1965; Ceased: 1992; Cov: Scan; Lang: Rus; Subj: Related. ISSN: 0132-1366
■Izdatel'stvo Nauka; Podsosenskii Per. 21; K 62 Moscow; RUSSIA.

SovT *Sovetskij Teat'r/Soviet Theatre*. Freq: 4; Began: 1976; Cov: Scan; Lang: Rus/Ger/Eng/Fre/Spa; Subj: Theatre.
■Copyright Agency of the USSR; 6a Bolshaya Bronnaya St.; K 104 Moscow 103670; RUSSIA.

Spa *Shilpakala*. Lang: Ben; Subj: Related.
■Dacca; BANGLADESH.

SPC *Studies in Popular Culture*. Freq: 2; Began: 1977; Lang: Eng; Subj: Related.
■Popular Culture Association in the South, Florida State Univ., English Dp.; Tallahassee, FL 32306; USA.

Speak *Speak*. Began: 1977; Lang: Eng; Subj: Theatre.
■PO Box 126, Newlands; 7725 Cape Town; SOUTH AFRICA.

Spirale *Spirale: Art, letters, spectacles, sciences humaines*. Freq: 12; Began: 1979; Last Known Address; Lang: Fre; Subj: Theatre. ISSN: 0225-9004
■C.P. 98, Succ. E; Montreal, PQ; CANADA.

SpIt *Spettacolo in Italia, Lo*. Freq: 1; Began: 1951; Lang: Ita; Subj: Theatre. ISSN: 0038-738X
■S.I.A.E.; Viale della Letteratura 30; 00100 Rome; ITALY.

Spl *Spielplan, Der*. Freq: 12; Began: 1954; Lang: Ger; Subj: Theatre. ISSN: 0038-7517
■Die monatliche Theatervorschau, Hg. Löwendruck Bertram GmbH; Pf. 6202; D-38108 Braunschweig; GERMANY.

SpViag *Spettacolo Viaggiante*. Began: 1948; Lang: Ita; Subj: Theatre.
■Assoc. Naz. Eserc. Spet. Viaggianti; Via di Villa Patrizi 10; 00161 Rome; ITALY.

SQ *Shakespeare Quarterly*. Freq: 4; Began: 1950; Cov: Scan; Lang: Eng; Subj: Related. ISSN: 0037-3222
■Folger Shakespeare Library; 201 E. Capitol St. S.E.; Washington, DC 20003; USA.

SR *SIBMAS-Rundbrief, Hg. Bundesverband der Bibliotheken und Museen für Darstellende Künste e.v.*. Freq: 2; Cov: Scan; Lang: Ger; Subj: Related.
■c/o Dr. Winrich Meiszies, Theatermuseum Düsseldorf; Jägerhofstr. 1; D-40479 Düsseldorf; GERMANY.

SSSS *Szene Schweiz/Scène Suisse/Scena Svizzera*. Freq: 1; Began: 1973; Lang: Ger/Fre/Ita; Subj: Theatre.
■Swiss Association for Theatre Research; c/o Louis Naef; Postfach 180; CH-6130 Willisau; SWITZERLAND.

SSTJ *Secondary School Theater Journal*. Freq: 3; Began: 1962; Last Known Address; Lang: Eng; Subj: Theatre.
■ATHE; P.O. Box 15282; Evansville, IL 47716-0282; USA.

ST *Sovetskij Teatr*. Freq: 3; Began: 1983; Cov Scan; Lang Rus Subj Theatre.
■Vestnik; Moscow; RUSSIA.

Staff *Staffrider*. Freq: 4; Began: 1982; Cov: Scan; Lang: Eng/Afr; Subj: Related.
■Ravan Press Ltd.; Box 31134; 2017 Braamfontein; SOUTH AFRICA.

StageA *Stage of the Art*. Freq: 4; Cov: Scan; Lang: Eng; Subj: Related. ISSN: 1046-5022
■American Alliance for Theatre and Education; Tempe, AZ; USA.

StageZ *Stage*. Freq: IRR; Began: 1956; Lang: Eng; Subj: Theatre.
■Lusaka Theatre Club Ltd; Box 30615; Lusaka; ZAMBIA.

Standpunte *Standpunte*. Freq: 6; Last Known Address; Began: 1945; Cov: Scan; Lang: Afr;; Subj: Related. ISSN: 0038-9730
■Tafelberg Publishers; c/o J.C. Kannemeyer, Ed.; P.O. Box 91073; Auckland Park 2006;; SOUTH AFRICA.

Sterijino *Sterijino Pozorje*: Informativno Glasilo. Freq: IRR; Began: 1982; Lang: Ser; Subj: Theatre.
■Sterijino Pozorje; Zmaj Jovina 22; Novi Sad; SERBIA.

Stikord *Stikord*. Freq: 4; Began: 1981; Ceased; Lang: Dan; Subj: Theatre. ISSN: 0107-6582
■Foreningen Hidovre Teater; Hidovre Strandvej 70A; 2650 Hvidovre; DENMARK.

Stilet *Stilet*. Freq: 2; Began: 1989; Cov: Scan; Lang: Afr/Eng; Subj: Related.
■Serva-Uitgewers; P.O. Box 36721, Menlopark 0102; SOUTH AFRICA.

STILB *STILB*. Freq: 5; Began: 1981; Last Known Address; Lang: Ita; Subj: Theatre.
■Via della Fosse di Castello 6; 00193 Rome; ITALY.

Stol *Stolica*. Freq: 52; Began: 1990; Cov: Scan; Lang: Rus; Subj: Related. ISSN: 0868-698X
■State Union Publishing; Petrovka Street, 16 Moscow 101425; RUSSIA.

STN *Scottish Theater News*. Freq: 12; Began: 1981; Ceased: 1986; Cov: Scan; Lang: Eng; Subj: Theatre. ISSN: 0261-4057
■Scottish Society of Playwrights; 346 Sauchiehall St.; Glasgow G2 3JD; UK.

STP *Studies in Theatre Production*. Freq: 2; Cov: Full; Lang: Eng; Subj: Theatre. ISSN: 1357-5341
■Department of Drama; University of Exeter; Thornlea, New North Road Exeter, Devon EX4 4JZ; UK.

StPh *Studies in Philology*. Freq: 3; Began: 1906; Lang: Eng; Subj: Related. ISSN: 0039-3738
■University of North Carolina Press; Box 2288; Chapel Hill, NC 27514; USA.

Strind *Strindbergiana*: Meddelanden från Strindbergssällskapet. Formerly: *Meddelanden från Strindbergssällskapet*. Freq: 1; Began: 1985; Cov: Full; Lang: Swe; Subj: Theatre. ISSN: 0282-8006
■Strindbergssällskapet, c/o C. R. Smedmark; Drottninggatan 85; 111 60 Stockholm; SWEDEN.

STT *Sceniceskaja Technika i Technologija*. Freq: 6; Began: 1963; Cov: Full; Lang: Rus; Subj: Theatre. ISSN: 0131-9248
■Serebrianceskij Per. 2/5; 109028 Moscow; RUSSIA.

StudiaP *Studia i Materialy do Dziejow Teatru Polskiego*. Formerly: *Studia i Materialy z Dziejow Teatru Polskiego*. Freq: IRR; Began: 1957; Lang: Pol; Subj: Theatre. ISSN: 0208-404X
■Polish Academy of Sciences; Rynek 9; Wroclaw; POLAND.

StudiiR *Studii si Cercetari de Istoria Artei*: Seria Teatru-Muzica-Cinematografie. Freq: 1; Began: 1954; Lang: Rom; Subj: Theatre. ISSN: 0039-3991
■Academia Rep. Soc. Romania; Calea Victoriei 125; 79717 Bucharest; ROMANIA.

StudM *Studenceskij Meridian*. Freq: 12; Began: 1924; Cov: Scan; Lang: Rus; Subj: Related. ISSN: 0321-3883
■Moscow; RUSSIA.

StWAusH *Studies in Western Australian History*. Freq: IRR; Began: 1977; Cov: Scan; Lang: Eng; Subj: Related. ISSN: 0314-7525
■Department of History; University of Western Australia; Nedlands, WA 6009; AUSTRALIA.

STYol *STYolainen*. Freq: 6; Began: 1975; Lang: Fin; Subj: Theatre.
■Suomen Teatterityontekijain, Yhteisjarjesto; Maneesikatu 4c; 00170 Helsinki 17; FINLAND.

SuAS *Stratford-upon-Avon Studies*. Freq: IRR; Began: 1961; Lang: Eng; Subj: Theatre.
■Edward Arnold Ltd; 41 Bedford Square; London WC1B 3DQ; UK.

SuF *Sinn und Form: Beiträge zur Literatur*. Freq: 6; Began: 1949; Lang: Ger; Subj: Related. ISSN: 0037-5756
■Aufbau-Verlag Berlin; Französische Str. 32; 10117 Berlin; GERMANY.

Suffloren *Sufflóren*. Last Known Address; Lang: Dan; Subj: Theatre.
■Medlemsblad for Dansk Dukketeaterforening; Vestergrade 3; 1456 Copenhagen; DENMARK.

SuidAfr *Suid-Afrikaan, Die*. Began: 1985; Cov: Scan; Lang: Afr; Subj: Related.
■Die Suid-Afrikaan; P.O. Box 7010; 7610 Dalsig Stellembosch; SOUTH AFRICA.

SuT *Spiel und Theater. Zeitschrift f*04ur Amateur-, Jugend- und Schultheater*. Freq: 2; Cov: Scan; Lang: Ger; Subj: Theatre.
■Oberschleissheim u.a., Deutscher Theaterverlag; Pf. 100261; D-69442 Weinheim; GERMANY.

Svet *Svĕt a divadlo*. Began: 1990; Cov: Scan; Lang: Cze; Subj: Theatre. ISSN: 0862-7258
■Divadelni obec; Štefánikova 57; 150 43 Prague 5; CZECH REPUBLIC.

SwTS *Swedish Theater/Théâtre Suédois*. Lang: Eng/Fre; Subj: Theatre.
■Stockholm; SWEDEN.

Sz *Szinház*: (Theatre). Freq: 12; Began: 1968; Cov: Scan; Lang: Hun; Subj: Theatre. ISSN: 0039-8136
■Színház Alapítvány; Báthory u. 10; 1054 Budapest; HUNGARY.

Szab *Szabolcs-Szatmár-Beregi Szemle*. Freq: 4; Began: 1965; Cov: Scan; Lang: Hun; Subj: Theatre. ISSN: 1216-092x
■Móricz Zsigmond Könyvtár; Szabadság tér 2; 4400 Nyíregyháza; HUNGARY.

Szene *Szene*. Lang: Ger; Subj: Theatre.
■UMLOsterreichischer Bundestheaterverband; Goethegasse 1; A 1010 Vienna; AUSTRIA.

SzeneAT *Szene: Fachzeitschrift der DDR Amateur-theater, -kabarett, -puppenspiel und -ntomime*. Freq: 4; Began: 1966; Last Known Address; Cov: Scan; Lang: Ger; Subj: Theatre. ISSN: 0039-811X
■Zentralhaus für Kulturarbeit, Dittrichring 4; Postfach 1051; 7010 Leipzig; GERMANY.

SzeneS *Szene Schweiz. Eine Dokumentation des Theaterlebens in der Schweiz*. Freq: 1; Cov: Scan; Lang: Ger; Subj: Theatre.
■Hg. Schweizerische Gesellschaft für Theatrekultur; Theaterkultur-Verlag, Pf. 1940; CH-4001 Basel, Schanzenstr. 15; SWITZERLAND.

SzSz *Szinháztudományi Szemle*. Freq: 1; Began: 1977; Cov: Full; Lang: Hun; Subj: Theatre. ISSN: 0133-9907
■Országos Szinháztörténeti Múzeum és Intézet; Krisztina körut 57; 1016 Budapest; HUNGARY.

T&P *Text and Performance: Journal of the Comparative Drama Conference*. Freq: 1; Lang: Eng; Subj: Theatre.
■Department of Classics; 3-C Daver Hall; University of Florida Gainesville, FL 32611; USA.

T&R *Theatre and Religion*. Freq: IRR; Lang: Eng; Subj: Theatre.
■Box 727; Goshen College; Goshen, IN 46526; USA.

TA *Theatre Annual*. Freq: 1; Began: 1942; Cov: Full; Lang: Eng; Subj: Theatre. ISSN: 0082-3821
■Department of Theatre and Speech; College of William and Mary; Williamsburg, VA 23187; USA.

TAAm *Theater Across America*. Freq: 5; Began: 1975; Lang: Eng; Subj: Theatre.
■Theatre Sources Inc.; 104 North St. Mary; Dallas, TX 75214; USA.

Tablas *Tablas*: National Council of Performing Art's Journal. Freq: 4; Began: 1982; Lang: Spa; Subj: Theatre.
■San Ignacio #166 e/Obispo y Obrapia; Habana Vieja. C.P. 10100; CUBA.

Tabs *Tabs*. Freq: 2; Began: 1937; Ceased: 1986; Cov: Scan; Lang: Eng; Subj: Theatre. ISSN: 0306-9389
■Rank Strand Ltd., P.O. Box 51, Great West Road; Brentford; Middlesex TW8 9HR; UK.

TAD *Tiyatro Araştirmalari Dergisi (Theatre Research Magazine)*. Freq: 1; Began: 1970; Lang: Tur/Eng/Fre; Subj: Theatre.
■Tiyatro Bölümü, Ankara Universitesi; D.T.C. Fakültesi, Sihhiye; Ankara; TURKEY.

Talent *Talent Management*. Freq: 12; Began: 1981; Lang: Eng; Subj: Related.
■T M Publishing; 1501 Broadway; New York, NY 10036; USA.

Tampereen *TTT-Tampereen Työväen Teatteri*. Lang: Fin; Subj: Theatre.
■Hämeenpuisto 30-32; 33200 Tampere; FINLAND.

Tanc *Táncmũvészet*. Freq: 4; Began: 1976; Cov: Scan; Lang: Hun;; Subj: Dance. ISSN: 0134-1421
■Táncmũvészeti Alapítvány; Kerék u. 34; 1035 Budapest; HUNGARY.

Tanecni *Tanecni Listy*. Freq: 10; Began: 1963; Lang: Cze; Subj: Theatre. ISSN: 0039-937X
■Panorama; Halkova 1; 120 72 Prague 2; CZECH REPUBLIC.

TAnim *Théâtre et Animation*. Freq: 4; Began: 1976; Lang: Fre; Subj: Theatre. ISSN: 0398-0049
■Fédération National du Théâtre et d'Animation; 12 Chaussée d'Antin; 75441 Paris Cedex 09; FRANCE.

TantI *Tantsovo Izkustvo*. Freq: 12; Began: 1954; Lang: Bul; Subj: Theatre.
■Izdatelstvo Nauka i Izkustvo; 6 Rouski Blvd; Sofia; BULGARIA.

TanzA *Tanz Affiche*. Freq: 6; Cov: Scan; Lang: Ger; Subj: Related.
■Publikation für Tanz und Kultur, Hg. Affiche; Verein zur Förderung von Information und Kommunikation in künstlerischen Belangen; Eggerthgasse 10/1; A-1060 Wien; AUSTRIA.

Tanzd *Tanzdrama*. Freq: 4; Began: 1987; Cov: Scan; Lang: Ger; Subj: Theatre. ISSN: 0932-8688
■Köln/Kallmeyer'sche Verlagsbuchhandlung GmbH; Im Brande 19; D-30926 Seelze; GERMANY.

TanzG *Tanz und Gymnastik*. Freq: 4; Began: 1944; Last Known Address; Lang: Ger; Subj: Theatre.
■Schweizerischer Berufsverband für Tanz und Gymnastik; Riedbergstrasse 1; 4059 Basel; SWITZERLAND.

TArch *Teatro Archivio*. Formerly: *Bolletino del Museo Biblioteca dell'attore*. Freq: IRR; Began: 1979; Cov: Full; Lang: Ita; Subj: Theatre.
■Bulzoni Editore; Via dei Liburni n 14; 00185 Rome; ITALY.

TArsb *Teaterårsboken*. Freq: 1; Began: 1982; Cov: Scan; Lang: Swe; Subj: Theatre.
■Svenska Riksteatern; 145 83 Norsborg; SWEDEN.

Tatar *Tatarstan Republic*. Freq: 12; Began: 1920; Cov: Scan; Lang: Rus; Subj: Related. ISSN: 0130-2418
■Decabristy Street, #2; 420066 Kazan' City; RUSSIA.

Tatr *Tatr*. Freq: 4; Began: 1985; Cov: Scan; Lang: Ger/Fre; Subj: Related.
■Astej, Gessnerallee 13; CH-8001 Zurich; SWITZERLAND.

TAus *Theatre Australia*. Freq: 12; Began: 1976; Lang: Eng; Subj: Theatre.
■Pellinor Pty Ltd. A.C.N.; 001 713 319, Level 2; 44 Bridge Street NSW 2000 Sydney; AUSTRALIA.

Tbuch *Theaterbuch*. Freq: 1; Lang: Ger; Subj: Theatre.
■Munich; GERMANY.

TCB *Teatro Clásico: Boletin*. Freq: 1; Lang: Spa; Subj: Theatre.
■Teatro Clásico de México; Apartado 61-077; MEXICO.

TCGNWCP *TCG National Working Conference Proceedings*. Freq: IRR; Began: 1976; Lang: Eng; Subj: Theatre.
■Theatre Communications Group; 355 Lexington Ave; New York, NY 10017; USA.

TChicago *Theatre Chicago*. Freq: 12; Began: 1986; Last Known Address; Lang: Eng; Subj: Theatre.
■22 W Monroe, Suite 801; 60603 Chicago, IL; USA.

TCI *TCI: Theatre Crafts International*. Formerly *Theatre Crafts*. Freq: 10; Began: 1995; Cov: Full; Lang: Eng; Subj: Theatre. ISSN: 1063-9497
■Intertec Publishing Corp.; 32 West 18th Street; New York, NY 10011-4612; USA.

TCom *Theatre Communications*. Freq: 12; Began: 1979; Ceased: 1983; Lang: Eng; Subj: Theatre. ISSN: 0275-5971
■Theatre Communications Group Inc; 355 Lexington Avenue; New York, NY 10017; USA.

TCraft *Theatrecraft*. Freq: 12; Began: 1964; Lang: Eng; Subj: Theatre.
■Victorian Drama League, Fifth Floor; 17 Elizabeth Street; Melbourne 3000 Victoria; AUSTRALIA.

TCUG   *Theater Computer Users Group Notes*. Began: 1978; Lang: Eng; Subj: Theatre. ■Theatre Sources Inc.; 104 N Saint Mary; Dallas, TX 76214; USA.

TD&T   *Theatre Design and Technology*. Freq: 4; Began: 1965; Cov: Full; Lang: Eng; Subj: Theatre.   ISSN: 0040-5477 ■U.S. Institute for Theatre Technology; 966 East 1030 North; Orem, UT 84057; USA.

TDDR   *Theaterarbeit in der DDR*. Freq: 3; Began: 1979; Lang: Ger; Subj: Theatre. ■Verband der Theaterschaffended der DDR; Hermann-Matern-Strasse 18; 1040 Berlin; GERMANY.

TDonA   *Transition: Discourse on Architecture*. Freq: 4; Began: 1979; Cov: Scan; Lang: Eng; Subj: Related.   ISSN: 0157-7344 ■Faculty of Environmental Design and Construction; RMIT GPO Box 2476V Melbourne Victoria 3001; AUSTRALIA.

TDR   *Drama Review, The*. Freq: 4; Began: 1955; Cov: Full; Lang: Eng; Subj: Theatre.   ISSN: 0012-5962 ■Tisch School of the Arts; 721 Broadway, Room 626 New York, NY 10003; USA.

TE   *Teater Et*. Freq: 5; Began: 1989; Lang: Dan; Subj: Theatre. ■Købmagergade 5, 3.; Postbox 191; 1006 København K; DENMARK.

Teat   *Teatteri*. Freq: 12; Began: 1945; Last Known Address; Lang: Fin; Subj: Theatre. ■Kustannus Oy Teatteri; Vuorikatu 6 A 8; 00100 Helsinki 10; FINLAND.

TeaterD   *Teater i Danmark*: Theatre in Denmark. Freq: 1; Began: 1980; Ceased: 1987; Lang: Dan; Subj: Theatre. ISSN: 0106-7672 ■Teater i Danmark; Vesterbrogade 26, 3.; DK-1620 København V.; DENMARK.

Teaterf   *Teaterforum*. Freq: 6; Began: 1968; Cov: Full; Lang: Swe; Subj: Theatre.   ISSN: 0347-8890 ■Swedish Society for Amateur Theatres; Von Rosens väg 1 A; 737 40 Fagersta; SWEDEN.

Teatern   *Teatern*. Freq: 4; Began: 1934; Lang: Swe; Subj: Theatre. ISSN: 0040-0750 ■Riksteatern; Svenska Riksteatern; S 145 83 Norsborg; SWEDEN.

TeatL   *Teatr Lalek*. Lang: Pol; Subj: Theatre. ■Warsaw; POLAND.

TeatM   *Teatraluri Moambe*. Cov: Full; Lang: Geo; Subj: Theatre. ■Tbilisi; GEORGIA.

Teatoro   *Teatoro*. Freq: 12; Began: 1944; Lang: Jap; Subj: Theatre. ■c/o Hagiwara Building, 2-3-1 Sarugaku-cho; Chiyoda-ku; 101 Tokyo; JAPAN.

Teatras   *Teatras*. Lang: Lit; Subj: Theatre. ■Vilnius; LITHUANIA.

TeatrC   *Teatro Contemporaneo*. Freq: 3; Began: 1982; Last Known Address; Cov: Full; Lang: Ita; Subj: Theatre. ■Via Trionfale 8406; 00135 Rome; ITALY.

TeatrE   *Teatro en España*. Lang: Spa; Subj: Theatre. ■Madrid; SPAIN.

TeatrM   *Teat'r*. žurnal dramaturgii i teatra. Freq: 12; Began: 1937; Cov: Full; Lang: Rus; Subj: Theatre.   ISSN: 0131-6805 ■Izdatel'stvo Iskusstvo; Ul. Gertsena 49; Moscow 49; RUSSIA.

Teatron   *Teatron*. Began: 1962; Lang: Heb; Subj: Theatre. ■Municipal Theatre; 20 Pevsner Street; Haifa; ISRAEL.

TeatroS   *Teatro e Storia*. Began: 1986; Cov: Scan; Lang: Ita; Subj: Theatre. ISSN: 1120-9569 ■Centro per la Sperimentazione e la Ricerca Teatrale di Pontedera; Societa Editrice Il Mulino, Strada Maggiore 37 40125 Bologna; ITALY.

TeatroSM   *TeatroSM*. Began: 1980; Lang: Spa; Subj: Theatre. ■Teatro Municipal General San Martin; Ave. Corrientes 1530, 50 piso; 1042 Buenos Aires; ARGENTINA.

Teatrul   *Teatrul*. Freq: 12; Began: 1956; Lang: Rom; Subj: Theatre. ISSN: 0040-0815 ■Consiliul Culturii si Educatiei Socialiste; Calea Victoriei 174; Bucharest; ROMANIA.

TeatrW   *Teatr*. Freq: 12; Began: 1946; Cov: Scan; Lang: Pol; Subj: Theatre. ISSN: 0040-0769 ■Zarząd Glowny Związku Artystów Scen Polskich; ul. Jakubowska 14; 03-902 Warsaw; POLAND.

TeaturS   *Teatur*. Freq: 12; Began: 1946; Cov: Full; Lang: Bul; Subj: Theatre. ISSN: 0204-6253 ■Komitet za Izkustvo i Kultura; 7 Levsky St.; 1000 Sofia; BULGARIA.

TeatY   *Teatron*: Časopis za poziriśnu istoriju i teatrologiju. Freq: 4; Began: 1974; Cov: Scan; Lang: Ser; Subj: Theatre. ISSN: 0351-7500 ■Muzej Pozoriśne umetnosti Srbije; Gospodar Jevremova 19; 11000 Belgrade; SERBIA.

TeatZ   *Teatralnaja Žizn*. Freq: 24; Began: 1958; Cov: Scan; Lang: Rus; Subj: Theatre.   ISSN: 0131-6915 ■Teatral'noe obschestvo, Theatrical Workers Union; Kiselni Typik dom 1 103031 Moscow; RUSSIA.

TeC   *Teatro e Cinema*. Freq: 4; Began: 1968; Last Known Address; Lang: Ita; Subj: Theatre.   ISSN: 0040-0807 ■Silva Editore; Viale Salita Salvatore 1; 28 16128 Genoa; ITALY.

TechB   *Technical Brief*. Freq: 3; Began: 1982; Cov: Full; Lang: Eng; Subj: Theatre.   ISSN: 1053-8860 ■TD&P Dept., Yale School of Drama; 222 York St.; New Haven, CT 06520; USA.

TEJ   *Théâtre Enfance et Jeunesse*. Freq: 2; Began: 1963; Lang: Fre/Eng; Subj: Theatre.   ISSN: 0049-3597 ■Assoc. du Théâtre pour l'Enfance, et la Jeunesse; 98 Blvd. Kellermann; 75013 Paris; FRANCE.

Telerad   *Teleradioephir*. Formerly *Televidenie i Radiovešcanie*. Began: 1952; Lang: Rus; Subj: Related.   ISSN: 0869-1932 ■Pushkinskaja str. 23/8; 103009 Moscow; RUSSIA.

TEP   *Théâtre de l'Est Parisien*: TEP Actualité. Lang: Fre; Subj: Theatre. ■Paris; FRANCE.

TextPQ   *Text and Performance Quarterly*. Formerly: *Literature in Performance*. Freq: 4; Began: 1980; Lang: Eng; Subj: Theatre.   ISSN: 1046-2937 ■Speech Communication Association; 5774 Stevens; University of Maine; Orono, ME 04469-5774; USA.

Textual   *Textual*. Lang: Spa; Subj: Theatre. ■I.N.C.; Ancash; 390 Idma; PERU.

Textuel   *Textuel*. Freq: 2; Lang: Fre;; Subj: Related. ■Université de Paris VII; 2, place Jussieu; 75221 Paris CEDEX 05; FRANCE.

TF   *Teaterforum*. Freq: 2; Began: 1980; Cov: Scan; Lang: Eng/Afr; Subj: Theatre. ■University of Potchefstroom, Departement Spraakler en Drama; Potchefstroom; SOUTH AFRICA.

TF&TV   *Teater Film & TV*. Freq: 8; Began: 1974; Lang: Dan; Subj: Theatre. ■Faellesforbundet for Teater Film & TV; Ny Oestergade 12; DK 1101 Copenhagen; DENMARK.

TGDR   *Theatre in the GDR*. Lang: Ger; Subj: Theatre. ■Berlin; GERMANY.

TGlasnik   *Teatarski Glasnik*: S. Spisanic na teatrite na Republika Makedonija. Freq: 2; Began: 1977; Lang: Slo; Subj: Theatre. ■MKO, kej Dimitar Vlahov B.B.; 91000 Skopje; REPUBLIC OF MACEDONIA.

TGraz   *Theater in Graz*. Freq: 4; Began: 1952; Lang: Ger; Subj: Theatre. ■Vereinigte Bühnen Graz; Burggasse 16; A 8010 Graz; AUSTRIA.

Th   *Théâtre*. Formerly: *Théâtre du Trident*. Lang: Fre; Subj: Theatre. ■Théâtre du Trident, Edifice Palais Montcalm; 975 Place d'Youville; Quebec, PQ; CANADA.

THC   *Theatre History in Canada/Histoire du Théâtre*. Freq: 2; Began: 1980; Ceased; Cov: Full; Lang: Eng/Fre; Subj: Theatre.   ISSN: 0226-5761 ■Graduate Centre for the Study of Drama, University of Toronto; 214 College Street; Toronto, ON M5T 2Z9; CANADA.

ThCr   *Theatre Crafts*. SEE TCI. Freq: 9; Began: 1967; Ceased: 1995; Cov: Full; Lang: Eng; Subj: Theatre.   ISSN: 0040-5469 ■Theatre Crafts Associates; 135 Fifth Avenue; New York, NY 10010; USA.

ThE   *Théâtre en Europe*. Freq: 4; Began: 1984; Lang: Fre; Subj: Theatre. ■Theatre de l'Europe, 1; Place Paul Claudel; 75006 Paris; FRANCE.

TheaterW   *TheaterWeek*. Freq: 52; Began: 1987; Cov: Full; Lang: Eng; Subj: Theatre.   ISSN: 0896-1956 ■That New Magazine; 28 West 25th St., 4th Floor; New York, NY 10010; USA.

TheatreEx   *Theatre: Ex*. Freq: 3; Began: 1985; Lang: Eng; Subj: Theatre. ■104 E. 4th Street; New York, NY 10003; USA.

TheatreF   *TheatreForum*. Freq: 2; Began: 1991; Cov: Full; Lang: Eng; Subj: Theatre.
ISSN: 1060-5320
■Department of Theatre; University of California, San Diego; 9500 Gilman Dr La Jolla, CA 92093-0344; USA.

TheatreS   *Theatre Studies*. Freq: 1; Began: 1954; Cov: Full; Lang: Eng; Subj: Theatre.
ISSN: 0362-0964
■Ohio State Univ., Lawrence and Lee, Theatre Research Institute; 1430 Lincoln Tower, 1800 Cannon Drive; Columbus, OH 43210 1230; USA.

TheatreT   *Theatre Three*. Began: 1986; Ceased: 1991; Lang: Eng; Subj: Theatre.
■Carnegie Mellon, Department of Drama; Pittsburgh, PA 15213; USA.

Theatro   *Theatro*. Lang: Gre; Subj: Theatre.
■Kosta Nitsos; Christou Lada 5-7; Athens; GREECE.

Theatron   *Theatron*: Rivista quindicinale di cultura, documentazione ed informazione teatrale. Freq: 26; Began: 1961; Lang: Ita/Eng/Ger; Subj: Theatre.   ISSN: 0040-5604
■Quadrimestrale di Cultura, Documentazione e Informazione Teatrale del Centro; Via Fabiola 1; 00152 Rome; ITALY.

Theatrum   *Theatrum: A Theatre Journal*. Freq: 3; Began: 1985; Ceased: 1995; Cov: Full; Lang: Eng; Subj: Theatre.   ISSN: 0838-5696
■Theatrum; P.O. Box 688, Station C; Toronto, ON M6J 3S1; CANADA.

Theoria   *Theoria*: A Journal of Studies in the Arts, Humanities and Social Studies. Freq: 2; Began: 1947; Cov: Scan; Lang: Eng; Subj: Related.   ISSN: 0040-5817
■University of Natal Press; Box 375; Pietermaritzburg; SOUTH AFRICA.

Thespis   *Thespis*. Last Known Address; Lang: Gre; Subj: Theatre.
■Greek Centre of the ITI; Anthinou Gazi 9; Athens; GREECE.

THeute   *Theater Heute*. Freq: 12; Began: 1960; Cov: Scan; Lang: Ger; Subj: Theatre.
ISSN: 0040-5507
■Erhard Friedrich Verlag; Im Brande 19; D-30926 Seelze; SWITZERLAND.

ThIr   *Theatre Ireland*. Freq: 3; Began: 1982; Cov: Full; Lang: Eng; Subj: Theatre.
ISSN: 0263-6344
■Theatre Ireland, Ltd; 29 Main St.; Castlerock Co. Derry BT51 4RA; NORTHERN IRELAND.

ThM   *Theater Magazine*. Freq: 3; Began: 1968; Cov: Full; Lang: Eng; Subj: Theatre.
ISSN: 0161-0775
■Yale University, School of Theater; 222 York Street Yale Station; New Haven, CT 06520; USA.

ThNe   *Theatre News*. Freq: 6; Began: 1968; Ceased: 1985; Cov: Scan; Lang: Eng; Subj: Theatre.   ISSN: 0563-4040
■American Theatre Association; 1010 Wisconsin Ave., NW, Suite 620; Washington, DC 20007; USA.

ThP   *Theater Phönix*:Zeitung für dramatische Kultur. Freq: 5; Lang: Ger; Subj: Theatre.
■Verein Theater Phönix; Wiener Str. 25; A-4020 Linz; AUSTRIA.

ThPa   *Theatre Papers*. Freq: IRR; Began: 1978; Ceased: 1985; Cov: Full; Lang: Eng; Subj: Theatre.   ISSN: 0309-8036
■Documentation Unit, Dartington College of Arts; Totnes; Devon TQ9 6EJ; UK.

ThPh   *Theatrephile*. Freq: 4; Began: 1983; Ceased: 1985; Cov: Full; Lang: Eng; Subj: Theatre.   ISSN: 0265-2609
■D. Cheshire & S. McCarthy Eds. & Publ.; 5 Dryden Street, Covent Garden; London WC2E 9NW; UK.

ThPu   *Théâtre Public*. Freq: 6; Began: 1974; Lang: Fre; Subj: Theatre.   ISSN: 0335-2927
■Théâtre de Gennevilliers; 41, avenue des Gresillons; 92230 Gennevilliers; FRANCE.

Thpur   *Theater pur*. Freq: 10; Lang: Ger; Subj: Theatre.   ISSN: 0949-1481
■Pocket Verlag; Alfredstr. 58; D-45130 Essen; GERMANY.

ThR   *Theatre Research International*. Freq: 3; Began: 1958; Cov: Full; Lang: Eng; Subj: Theatre.   ISSN: 0307-8833
■Oxford University Press; Pinkhill House; Southfield Road, Eynsham, Oxford OX8 1JJ; UK.

ThS   *Theatre Survey: Journal of the American Society for Theatre Research*. Freq: 2; Began: 1960; Cov: Full; Lang: Eng; Subj: Theatre.   ISSN: 0040-5574
■Michael L. Quinn, School of Drama; DX-20 Hutchinson Hall University of Washington Seattle, WA 98195; USA.

Thsch   *Theaterschrift*. Cov: Scan; Lang: Dut; Subj: Related.
■Kaaitheater; Akenkaai 2-B 1210 Brussels; BELGIUM.

ThScot   *Theatre Scotland*. Freq: 4; Cov: Scan; Lang: Eng; Subj: Theatre; ISSN: 0968-5499
■9a Annandale Street; Edinburgh EH7 4AW; UK.

THSt   *Theatre History Studies*. Freq: 1; Began: 1981; Cov: Full; Lang: Eng; Subj: Theatre.   ISSN: 0733-2033
■Theatre Dept.; Central College; Pella, IA 50219; USA.

ThSw   *Theatre Southwest*. Freq: 3; Began: 1974; Cov: Full; Lang: Eng; Subj: Theatre.
■Oklahoma State University; 102 Seretean Center; Stillwater, OK 74078; USA.

ThToday   *Theatre Today*. Last Known Address; Lang: Eng; Subj: Theatre.
■Advanced Institute for Development, American Repertory Theatre; 245 West 52nd Street; New York, NY 10019; USA.

ThYear   *Theatre Year*. Freq: 1; Began: 1980; Ceased: 1983; Cov: Scan; Lang: Eng; Subj: Theatre.   ISSN: 0261-2348
■In (Parenthesis) Ltd.; 21 Wellington Street; London WC2E 7DN; UK.

TI   *Théâtre International*. Freq: 4; Began: 1981; Ceased: 1984; Lang: Eng/Fre; Subj: Theatre.
■British Centre of the ITI; 31 Shelton Street; London WC2H 9HT; UK.

TID   *Themes in Drama*. Freq: 1; Began: 1979; Cov: Full; Lang: Eng; Subj: Theatre.
ISSN: 0263-676X

■Cambridge Univ. Press; Edinburgh Bldg., Shaftesbury Road, Cambridge CB2 2RU; UK.

Tijatro   *Tijatro*. Freq: 12; Began: 1970; Lang: Tur; Subj: Theatre.
■PK 58; Besiktas-Istanbul; TURKEY.

TInsight   *Theatre Insight*: A Journal of Performance and Drama. Freq: 2; Began: 1988; Lang: Eng; Subj: Theatre.
■Department of Theatre and Dance, University of Texas at Austin; Austin, TX 78712-1168; USA.

TiO   *Theater in Österreich*. Freq: 1; Began: 1993; Cov: Scan; Lang: Ger; Subj: Theatre.   ISBN: 3-901126-64-3
■Jahrbuch der Wiener Gesellschaft für Theaterforschung; Edition Praesens; Umlauftgasse 3 A-1170 Vienna; AUSTRIA.

Tisz   *Tiszatáj*. Freq: 12; Began: 1947; Cov: Scan; Lang: Hun; Subj: Related.   ISSN: 0133-1167
■Tiszatáj Alapítvány Kuratóriuma; Rákóczi tér 1; 6741 Szeged; HUNGARY.

TJ   *Theatre Journal*. Formerly: *Educational Theatre Journal*. Freq: 4; Began: 1949; Cov: Full; Lang: Eng; Subj: Theatre.   ISSN: 0192-2282
■Univ./College Theatre Assoc., The Johns Hopkins Univ. Press; 701 West 40th St. Suite 275; Baltimore, MD 21211; USA.

TJV   *Teater Jaarboek voor Vlaanderen*. Lang: Dut; Subj: Theatre.
■Antwerp; BELGIUM.

Tk   *Theaterwork*. Freq: 6; Began: 1980; Ceased: 1983; Cov: Full; Lang: Eng; Subj: Theatre.   ISSN: 0735-1895
■Theaterwork; Box 8150; Sante Fe, NM 87504-8150; USA.

Tka   *Theatrika*. Freq: 52; Lang: Eng; Subj: Theatre.
■Athens; GREECE.

TkR   *TamKang Review*: Comparative Studies Between Chinese & Foreign Literature. Freq: 4; Began: 1970; Lang: Eng; Subj: Related.   ISSN: 0049-2949
■Tamkang University, Grad. Inst. of West. Langs & Lit.; Tamsui; Taipei Hsien 251; TAIWAN.

TMJ   *Theatre Movement Journal*. Lang: Eng; Subj: Theatre.
■Ohio State University, Dept. of Theatre; 1849 Cannon Drive; Columbus, OH 43210; USA.

TMK   *Teater, Musika, Kyno*. Lang: Est; Subj: Theatre.
■Talin; ESTONIA.

TN   *Theatre Notebook*: Journal of the History and Technique of the British Theatre. Freq: 3; Began: 1946; Cov: Full; Lang: Eng; Subj: Theatre.   ISSN: 0040-5523
■The Society for Theatre Research; c/o The Theatre Museum 1E Tavistock St.; London WC2E 7PA; UK.

Tningen   *Teatertidningen*. Formerly *Nya Teatertidningen*. Freq: 4; Began: 1990; Cov: Full; Lang: Swe; Subj: Theatre. ISSN: 0348-0119
■Box 20137; S10460; Stockholm; SWEDEN.

TNotes   *Theatre Notes*. SEE *Newsletter of the International Theatre Institute of The U.S., Inc.*. Freq: 10; Began: 1970; Ceased: 1984; Lang: Eng; Subj: Theatre.

■US Centre of the ITI; 1860 Broadway, Suite 1510; New York, NY 10023; USA.

TNS *Théâtre National de Strasbourg*: Actualité. Lang: Fre; Subj: Theatre.
■Théâtre National de Strasbourg; 1, rue André Malraux-BP 184/R5 67005 Strasbourg; FRANCE.

TOE *Théâtre Ouvert/Ecritures*. Freq: 4; Last Known Address; Began: 1978; Lang: Fre; Subj: Theatre. ISSN: 0181-5393
■21 rue Cassette; 75006 Paris; FRANCE.

Toneel *Toneel Teatraal*. Formerly: *Mickery Mouth and Toneel Teatraal*. Freq: 10; Began: 1879; Cov: Full; Lang: Dut; Subj: Theatre. ISSN: 0040-9170
■Nederlands Theaterinstituut; Herengracht 166-168; 1016 BP Amsterdam; NETHERLANDS.

Tournees *Tournées de Spectacles*. Freq: 12; Began: 1975; Ceased; Cov: Scan; Lang: Fre; Subj: Theatre. ISSN: 0317-5979
■Conseil des Arts du Canada; Office des Tournées; Ottawa, ON; CANADA.

TP *Theatre in Poland/Théâtre en Pologne*. Freq: 6; Began: 1958; Cov: Full; Lang: Eng/Fre; Subj: Theatre. ISSN: 0040-5493
■ITI, Polish Center; pl. Piłsudskiego 9; 00-078 Warsaw; POLAND.

TpaedB *Theaterpaedagogische Bibliothek*. Freq: IRR; Began: 1983; Lang: Ger; Subj: Theatre.
■Heinrichshofen Buecher; Valoisstrasse 11; 2940 Wilhelmshaven; GERMANY.

TProf *Théâtre Professionnel*. Lang: Fre; Subj: Theatre.
■14 rue de la Promenade; Asnieres; FRANCE.

TQ *Theatre Quarterly*: Since 1985 published as New Theatre Quarterly (NTQ). Freq: 4; Began: 1971; Ceased: 1981; Lang: Eng; Subj: Theatre. ISSN: 0049-3600
■TQ Publications, Ltd.; 44 Earlham Street; WC2 9LA London; UK.

TR *Theater Rundschau*. Freq: 12; Began: 1955; Lang: Ger; Subj: Theatre. ISSN: 0040-5442
■Bonner Talweg 10; D-53113 Bonn; GERMANY.

Traces *Traces*. Freq: 6; Lang: Fre; Subj: Theatre.
■Comédie de Rennes; Théâtre de la Parcheminerie; 35100 Rennes; FRANCE.

Tramoya *Tramoya*: Cuaderno de teatro. Freq: 4; Began: 1975; Lang: Spa; Subj: Theatre.
■Universidad Veracruzana; Zona Universitaria; Lomas del Estadio Jalapa; MEXICO.

TransA *Transforming: Art: the arts and self-knowledge*. Freq: 2; Began: 1986; Cov: Scan; Lang: Eng; Subj: Related. ISSN: 0817-2080
■Transforming Art; P.O. Box C168; Sydney, NSW 2000; AUSTRALIA.

TRC *Theatre Research in Canada/Recherches Theatrales au Canada*. Formerly: *Theatre History in Canada*. Freq: 2; Began: 1991; Cov: Scan; Lang: Eng/Fre; Subj: Theatre.
■Graduate Center for Study of Drama; University of Toronto; Toronto, ON M5T 2Z9; CANADA.

TRec *Theatre Record*. Formerly *London Theatre Record* Freq: 26; Began: 1993; Cov: Full; Lang: Eng; Subj: Theatre. ISSN: 0261-5282
■4 Cross Deep Gardens; Twickenham TW1 4QU Middlesex; UK.

Treteaux *Tréteaux*. Freq: 2; Lang: Eng; Subj: Theatre. ISSN: 0161-4479
■University of Maine at Orono Press; University of Maine; Farmington, ME 04938; USA.

Trujaman *Trujaman*. Last Known Address; Lang: Spa; Subj: Theatre.
■Casilla de Correos 3234; Buenos Aires; ARGENTINA.

TSA *Theatre S.A*: Quarterly for South African Theater. Freq: 4; Began: 1968; Lang: Eng; Subj: Theatre.
■PO Box 2153; Cape Town; SOUTH AFRICA.

TSO *Teatro del Siglo de Oro: Ediciones Criticas*. Freq: 2; Began: 1982; Lang: Eng/Spa/Fre; Subj: Theatre. ISSN: 7188-4400
■Edition Reichenberger; Pfannkuchstr. 4; D 3500 Kassel; GERMANY.

TSOL *Teatro del Siglo de Oro: Estudios de Literatura*. Freq: IRR; Began: 1984; Lang: Spa/Eng; Subj: Theatre. ISSN: 7200-9300
■Edition Reichenberger; Pfannkuchstr. 4; D 3500 Kassel; GERMANY.

TSt *Teatervidenskabelige Studier*. Freq: 1; Began: 1974; Lang: Dan; Subj: Theatre.
■Akademisk Forlag; St. Kannikestraede 8; 1169 Copenhagen; DENMARK.

TT *Theatre Times*. Formerly: *OOBA Newsletter (OOBA Guidebook to Theatre)*. Freq: 6; Began: 1982; Cov: Scan; Lang: Eng; Subj: Theatre. ISSN: 0732-300X
■Alliance of Resident Theatres; 131 Varick Street; Suite 904; New York, NY 10013-1410; USA.

TTh *Travail Théâtral*. Freq: 4; Began: 1970; Lang: Fre; Subj: Theatre. ISSN: 0049-4534
■Editions l'Age d'Homme-la Cite; Case Postale 263; 1000 Lausanne 9; SWITZERLAND.

TTop *Theatre Topics*. Freq: 2; Began: 1991; Cov: Full; Lang: Eng; Subj: Theatre. ISSN: 1054-8378
■Johns Hopkins University Press; 2715 North Charles Street; Baltimore, MD 21218-4319; USA.

TTT *Tenaz Talks Teatro*. Freq: 4; Began: 1977; Last Known Address; Lang: Eng/Spa; Subj: Theatre.
■University of California-La Jolla, Chicano Studies Program, D-009; La Jolla, CA 92093; USA.

TU *Théâtre et université*. Lang: Fre; Subj: Theatre.
■Centre Universitaire International, Form. & Recherche Dramatique; Nancy; FRANCE.

Tv *Teatervetenskap*. Freq: 2; Began: 1968; Lang: Swe/Eng; Subj: Theatre.
■Inst. för Teater & Filmvetenskap; Box 27026; S 102 Stockholm 27; SWEDEN.

TvL *Tydskri vi Letterkunde*. Freq: 4; Began: 1963; Cov: Scan; Lang: Eng & Afrikaans; Subj: Related. ISSN: 0041-476X
■Elize Botha; Posbus 1758; Pretoria;; SOUTH AFRICA.

TVOR *Tvorchestvo*. Freq: 12; Began: 1957; Cov: Scan; Lang: Rus; Subj: Related. ISSN: 0131-6877
■Izdatel'stvo Sovetskii Khudozhnik; Ul. Chernyakhovskogo; 4A; Moscow; RUSSIA.

TvT *Tijdschrift voor Theaterwetenschap*. Freq: 4; Lang: Dut; Subj: Theatre.
■Instituut voor Wetenschap, Nw.; Doelenstraat 16; 1012 CP Amsterdam; NETHERLANDS.

TvVV *Tydskrif vir Volkskunde en Volkstaal*. Freq: 3; Began: 1944; Cov: Scan; Lang: Eng. & Afrikaans; Subj: Related. ISSN: 0049-4933
■Genootskap vir Afrikaanse Volkskunde; Box 4585; Johannesburg 2000; SOUTH AFRICA.

TWI *Theaterwissenschaftlicher Informationsdienst*. Lang: Ger; Subj: Theatre.
■Theaterhochschule Hans Otto'; Sec. für Theaterwissenschaftliche Dok.; Leipzig; GERMANY.

TWNew *Tennessee Williams Review*. Formerly: *Tennessee Williams Newsletter*. Freq: 2; Began: 1980; Ceased: 1983; Lang: Eng; Subj: Theatre. ISSN: 0276-993X
■Northeastern University, Division of the Arts; 360 Huntington Ave. Boston, MA 02115; USA.

TwoT *Two Thousand (2000)*. Freq: 4; Began: 1969; Cov: Scan; Lang: Slo; Subj: Related. ISSN: 0350-8935
■Journal for Thought, Art, Cultural and Religious Issues; Association 2000 Ljubljana; SLOVENIA.

TZ *Theater der Zeit*. Freq: 6; Began: 1946; Lang: Ger; Subj: Theatre. ISSN: 0040-5418
■Interessengemeinschaft Theater der Zeit e.V., Podewil; Klosterstr. 68/70; D-10179 Berlin; GERMANY.

Tzs *Theaterzeitschrift*: Beiträge zu Theater, Medien, Kulturpolitik. Lang: Ger; Subj: Theatre.
■Verein zur Erforschung theatraler Verkehrsformen; Tzs-Wochenschau Verlag; Adolf-Damaschke Str. 103-105 6231 Schawlbach; GERMANY.

UCrow *Upstart Crow, The*. Freq: 1; Began: 1978; Last Known Address; Lang: Eng; Subj: Theatre.
■P.O. Box 740; Martin, TN 38237; USA.

UDSalaam *University of Dar es Salaam: Theatre Arts Department*: Annual Report. Freq: 1; Lang: Eng; Subj: Theatre.
■University of Dar es Salaam, Theatre Arts Department; Box 35091; Dar es Salaam; TANZANIA.

UES *Unisa English Studies: Journal of the Department of English*. Freq: 2; Began: 1963; Cov: Scan; Lang: Eng & Afr; Subj: Related. ISSN: 0041-5359
■S.G. Kossick, Ed.; Dept. of English; Univ. of South Africa; P.O. Box 392; 0001 Pretoria; SOUTH AFRICA.

Ufa *Ufahamu*: Journal of the African Activist Association. Freq: 3; Began: 1970; Cov: Scan; Lang: Eng; Subj: Related. ISSN: 0041-5715
■James S. Coleman African Studies Center; University of California; Los Angeles, CA 90024-1130; USA.

UjA   *Új Auróra*. Freq: 3; Began: 1972; Ceased: 1989; Cov: Scan; Lang: Hun; Subj: Related.   ISSN: 0133-2295
■Békéscsabai Városi Tanács; István király tér 9; 5600 Békéscsaba; HUNGARY.

UjF   *Új Forrás*. Freq: 10; Began: 1968; Cov: Scan; Lang: Hun; Subj: Related.   ISSN: 0133-5332
■Komárom-Esztergom   Megye Onkormányzata; Március 15. út 2 2800 Tatabánya; HUNGARY.

UjIras   *Új Irás*. Freq: 12; Began: 1961; Ceased; Cov: Scan; Lang: Hun; Subj: Related.   ISSN: 0041-5952
■Lapkiadó Vállalat; Erzsébet körut 9-11; 1073 Budapest; HUNGARY.

UMurcia   *Universidad de Murcia Catedra de Teatro Cuadernos*. Freq: IRR; Began: 1978; Lang: Spa; Subj: Theatre.
■Universidad de Murcia, Secretariado de Publicaciones y Intercambio Cientifico; Santo Cristo 1; 30001 Murcia; SPAIN.

UNIMA   *UNIMA France*. Freq: 4; Began: 1962; Lang: Fre; Subj: Theatre.
■Union Internationale de la Marionette, Section Française; 7 Rue du Helder; 75009 Paris; FRANCE.

Ural   *Ural*. Cov: Scan; Lang: Rus; Subj: Related.   ISSN: 130-5409
■RUSSIA.

Usbu   *Usbu Al-Masrah*. Lang: Ara; Subj: Theatre.
■Ministère des Affaires Culturelles; La Kasbah; Tunis; TUNISIA.

USITT   *USITT Newsletter*. Freq: 4; Began: 1965; Cov: Scan; Lang: Eng; Subj: Theatre.   ISSN: 0565-6311
■US Inst. for Theatre Technology; 10 West 19th Street; Ste. 5A New York, NY 10011; USA.

UTarra   *Universitas Tarraconensis*. Freq: 1; Cov: Scan; Lang: Spa; Subj: Related.
■División de Filologia; Placa Imperial Tarraco, 1; 43005 Tarragona; SPAIN.

UTeatr   *Ukrainskij Teat'r*. Lang: Ukr; Subj: Related.
■Kiev; UKRAINE.

UTQ   *University of Toronto Quarterly*. Freq: 4; Cov: Scan; Lang: Eng; Subj: Related.   ISSN: 0042-0247
■University of Toronto Press; 10 St. Mary Street; Toronto, ON M4Y 2W8; CANADA.

Uusi   *Uusi-Laulu*. Lang: Fin; Subj: Theatre.
■Uusi-Laulu-yhdistys; Eerikinkatu 14 A 9; 00100 Helsinki 10; FINLAND.

UZ   *Unterhaltungskunst*: Zeitschrift für Bühne, Podium und Manege. Freq: 12; Began: 1969; Lang: Ger; Subj: Related. ISSN: 0042-0565
■Henschelverlag Kunst und, Gesellschaft; Oranienburger Strasse 67/68; 104 Berlin; GERMANY.

Valivero   *Valiverho*. Freq: 3; Lang: Fin; Subj: Theatre.
■Helsinki; FINLAND.

Valo   *Valóság*. Freq: 12; Began: 1964; Ceased; Cov: Scan; Lang: Hun; Subj: Related.

■Kirlapkiado; Lenin krt. 5; 1073 Budapest VII; HUNGARY.

VantageP   *Vantage Point*: Issues in American Arts. Formerly: *American Arts*. Freq: 6; Began: 1984; Lang: Eng; Subj: Related. ISSN: 0194-1305
■American Council for the Arts; 1285 Ave. of the Americas, 3rd Floor; New York, NY 10019; USA.

VCA   *Voice*: Newsletter for Chorus America. Freq: 4; Cov: Scan; Lang: Eng; Subj: Related.
■Association of Professional Vocal Ensembles; 2111 Sansom Street Philadelphia, PA 19103; USA.

VFil   *Voprosy filosofii*. Freq: 12; Began: 1947; Lang: Eng/Rus;; Subj: Related. ISSN: 0042-8744
■Akademiya Nauk S.S.S.R., Institut Filosofii; Izdatel'stvo Pravda, Ul. Pravdy, 24; Moscow 125047; RUSSIA.

VHJ   *Victorian Historical Journal*. Formerly: *Journal of the Royal Historical Society*. Freq: 4; Began: 1987; Lang: Eng; Subj: Related.   ISSN: 1030-7710
■Royal Historical Society of Victoria; Royal Mint; 280 William Street Melbourne Victoria 3000; AUSTRALIA.

Vig   *Vigilia*. Freq: 12; Began: 1935; Cov: Scan; Lang: Hun; Subj: Related. ISSN: 0042-6024
■Vigilia Kiadóhivatala; Kossuth Lajos u. 1 1053 Budapest; HUNGARY.

Vilag   *Világszinház*. Formerly: *Dramaturgical News 1965-1982*. Freq: 4; Began: 1982; Cov: Scan; Lang: Hun; Subj: Theatre. ISSN: 0231-4541
■Országos Szinháztörténeti Múzeum és Intézet; Krisztina körút 57; 1016 Budapest I; HUNGARY.

VLit   *Voprosy literatury*. Freq: 6; Began: 1957; Cov: Scan; Lang: Rus; Subj: Related.   ISSN: 0042-8705
■Sojuz Pisatelej SSSR, Inst. Mirovoj Literatury; Bolšoj Gnezdnikovskij per 10; 103009 Moscow; RUSSIA.

VMGUf   *Vestnik Moskovskogo universiteta*. Freq: 6; Began: 1946; Cov: Scan; Lang: Rus; Subj: Related.   ISSN: 0201-7385
■Moscow State University; Ul. Gercena 5/7; 103009 Moscow; RUSSIA.

Volga   *Volga*. Began: 1966; Cov: Scan; Lang: Rus; Subj: Related.   ISSN: 0321-0677
■Naberežnaja Kosmonautov Street, 3; 410002 Saratov City RUSSIA.

Voprosy   *Voprosy teatra*. Freq: 1; Began: 1965; Lang: Rus; Subj: Theatre. ISSN: 0201-7482
■Teatral'noe Obshchestvo, Theatre Workers Union; Kiselni Typik doml 103031; Moscow; RUSSIA.

VoprosyK   *Voprosy istorii KPSS*: SEE Kentavr. Freq: 12; Ceased: 1991; Lang: Rus; Subj: Related.   ISSN: 0320-8907
■Vil'gel'ma Pika Street; 129256 Moscow; RUSSIA.

Vos   *Vosroždenije*. Began: 1994; Cov: Scan; Lang: Rus; Subj: Related. ISSN: 0869-7930
■Oleg Koševoj Street, 34 a; 367025 Makhačkala City; RUSSIA.

VS   *Victorian Studies*:An Interdisciplinary Journal of Social, Political and Cultural Studies. Freq: 4; Began: 1957; Cov: Scan; Lang: Eng; Subj: Related.   ISSN: 0042-5222
■Program for Victorian Studies, Indiana University; Ballantine Hall; Bloomington, IN 47405; USA.

VSov   *V sověckom teatrě*. SEE *Sovetskij Teatr*. Freq: 3; Began: 1978; Ceased: 1982; Cov: Scan; Lang: Rus; Subj: Theatre.
■Moscow; RUSSIA.

Vstreča   *Vstreča*. Freq: 12; Began: 1940; Lang: Rus; Subj: Related.
■Sovéckaja Rossija; 3 Krapirenskij per. #2; Moscow 103051; RUSSIA.

Vyakat   *Vyakat*. Freq: 4; Lang: Eng; Subj: Theatre.
■A-28 Nizamuddin West; New Delhi; INDIA.

Waiguo   *Waiguo Xiju*. Freq: 4; Began: 1962; Lang: Chi; Subj: Theatre.
■52 Dongai Ba tiao; Beijing; CHINA.

WB   *Weimarer Beiträge*: Zeitschrift für Literaturwissenschaft, Aesthetik und Kultur Wisssenschafn. Freq: 4; Began: 1955; Lang: Ger; Subj: Related.   ISSN: 0043-2199
■Passagen Verlag, Walfischgasse 15/14; A-1010 Wien; AUSTRIA.

WCP   *West Coast Plays*. Freq: 2; Began: 1977; Ceased: 1988; Lang: Eng; Subj: Theatre.   ISSN: 0147-4502
■California Theatre Council; 135 N. Grand Ave.; Los Angeles, CA 90014; USA.

WES   *Western European Stages*. Freq: 2; Began: 1989; Cov: Full; Lang: Eng; Subj: Theatre.
■Center for Advanced Study in Theatre Arts; CUNY Graduate School; 33 West 42nd Street New York, NY 10036; USA.

WEST   *Westerly*. Freq: 4; Began: 1956; Cov: Scan;; Subj: Related.   ISSN: 0043-342x
■University of Western Australia; Nedlands, WA 6009; AUSTRALIA.

WFTM   *Wiener Forschungen zur Theater und Medienwissenschaft*. Freq: IRR; Began: 1972; Lang: Ger; Subj: Theatre.
■Universitäts-Verlagsbuchhandlung Gmb; Servitengasse 5; A1092 Vienna; AUSTRIA.

WGTJ   *Wiener Gesellschaft für Theaterforschung Jahrbuch*. Freq: IRR; Began: 1944; Ceased: 1986; Lang: Ger; Subj: Theatre.
■Verband der Wissenshaftlichen, Gesellschaften Oesterreichs; Lindengasse 37; A1070 Vienna; AUSTRIA.

WIAL   *Washington International Arts Letter*. Freq: 10; Began: 1962; Last Known Address; Lang: Eng; Subj: Related.   ISSN: 0043-0609
■Box 9005; Washington, DC 20003; USA.

WijP   *WIJ Poppenspelers*. Began: 1955; Lang: Dut; Subj: Theatre.
■Wij Poppenspelers; Warmoesstraat 11 NL 2011 HN Haarlem; NETHERLANDS.

WJBS   *Western Journal of Black Studies*. Freq: 4; Began: 1977; Cov: Scan; Lang: Eng; Subj: Related.   ISSN: 0197-4327
■Washington State Univ. Press; Pullman, WA 99164 5910; USA.

WLT *World Literature Today*: a literary quarterly of the University of Oklahoma. Formerly: *Books Abroad*. Freq: 4; Began: 1927; Lang: Eng; Subj: Related. ISSN: 0196-3570
■University of Oklahoma; 110 Monnet Hall; Norman, OK 73019; USA.

WomenR *Women's Review*. Freq: 12; Began: 1985; Ceased: 1986; Cov: Scan; Lang: Eng; Subj: Related. ISSN: 0267-5080
■1-4 Christina St.; London EC2A 4PA; UK.

WonD *Writings on Dance*. Began: 1987; Cov: Scan; Lang: Eng; Subj: Related. ISSN: 0817-3710
■Elizabeth Dempster and Sally Gardner; P.O. Box 1172; Collingwood Victoria 3066; AUSTRALIA;.

WOpera *World of Opera*. Freq: 6; Lang: Eng; Subj: Theatre. ISSN: 0160-8673
■Marcel Dekker Inc.; 270 Madison Avenue; New York, NY 10016; USA.

WPerf *Women & Performance*: A Journal of Feminist Theory. Freq: 2; Began: 1983; Cov: Full; Lang: Eng; Subj: Theatre. ISSN: 0740-770X
■NYU Tisch School of the Arts, Women and Performance Project; 721 Broadway, 6th Floor; New York, NY 10003; USA.

WPIS *Working Papers in Irish Studies*. Lang: Eng; Subj: Related.
■Northeastern University; 236 Huntington Avenue; Boston, MA 02115; USA.

WPList *World Premieres Listing*. Began: 1981; Lang: Eng; Subj: Theatre.
■Hungarian Centre of the ITI; Hevesi Sandor Ter. 2; 1077 Budapest VII; HUNGARY.

WS *Women's Studies*. Freq: 4; Lang: Eng; Subj: Theatre.
■Department of English; McManus Hall; The Claremont Graduate School Claremont, CA 91711; USA.

Wsw *Wer spielte was? Werkstatistik Deutschland Österreich Schweiz*. Freq: 1; Lang: Ger; Subj: Related. ISSN: 0941-5823
■Mykenae Verlag Rossberg KG; Ahastr. 9; D-64285 Darmstadt; GERMANY.

WTops *White Tops*. Freq: 6; Began: 1927; Lang: Eng; Subj: Theatre. ISSN: 0043-499X
■Circus Fans Assoc. of America; Rt. 1, Box 6735; White Stone, VA 22578; USA.

XLunc *Xiju Luncong*: Selected Essays of Theatre. Freq: 4; Began: 1957; Lang: Chi; Subj: Theatre.
■52 Dongai Ba tiao; Beijing; CHINA.

XXuexi *Xiju Xuexi*: Theatre. Freq: 4; Began: 1957; Lang: Chi; Subj: Theatre.
■Central Institute for Modern Theatre; Jiaonan Qitiao; Beijing; CHINA.

XYanj *Xiqu Yanjiu*. Freq: 4; Began: 1980; Cov: Full; Lang: Chi; Subj: Theatre.
■Cultural and Artistic Publishing; 17 Qianhai Xijie; Beijing; CHINA.

XYishu *Xiju Yishu*: Theatre Arts. Freq: 4; Began: 1978; Cov: Full; Lang: Chi; Subj: Theatre. ISSN: 0257-943X
■Shanghai Theatre Academy; 630 Huashan Lu Road; 200040 Shanghai; CHINA.

YCT *Young Cinema & Theatre/Jeune Cinéma et Théâtre*: Cultural Magazine of the IUS. Freq: 4; Began: 1964; Lang: Eng/Fre/Spa; Subj: Theatre.
■International Union of Students; 17th November Street; 110 01 Prague 1; CZECH REPUBLIC.

Yorick *Yorick*: Revista de Teatro. Lang: Spa; Subj: Theatre.
■Via Layetana 30; 3 Barcelona; SPAIN.

YTJ *Youth Theatre Journal*. Freq: 4; Began: 1986; Cov: Full; Lang: Eng; Formerly: *Children's Theatre Review;* Subj: Theatre. ISSN: 0892-9092
■American Alliance for Theatre and Education;, Theatre Department; Arizona State University; Tempe, AZ 85287-3411; USA.

ZAA *Zeitschrift für Anglistik und Amerikanistik*. Freq: 4; Began: 1953; Lang: Ger/Eng; Subj: Related. ISSN: 0044-2305
■Verlag Enzyklopädie; Gerichtsweg 26; 7010 Leipzig; GERMANY.

ZDi *Zahranicni Divadlo*: (Theatre Abroad). Lang: Cze; Subj: Theatre.
■Prague; CZECH REPUBLIC.

ZfK *Zeitschrift für Kulturaustausch*. Freq: 4; Lang: Ger; Subj: Theatre. ISSN: 0044-2976
■Horst Erdmann Verlag für, Internationalen-Kulturaustausch; Hartmeyerstrasse 117; 7400 Tübingen 1; GERMANY.

ZG *Zeitschrift für Germanistik*. Freq: 6; Began: 1980; Last Known Address; Lang: Ger; Subj: Related. ISSN: 0323-7982
■Verlag Enzyklopädie; Gerichtsweg 26; 7010 Leipzig; GERMANY.

Znamia *Znamja*. Freq: 12; Began: 1931; Lang: Rus; Subj: Related. ISSN: 0130-1616
■Soyuz Pisatelei; Moscow; RUSSIA.

Zpravy *Zprávy DILIA*. Freq: 3; Lang: Cze/Eng; Subj: Theatre.
■Dilia; Polská 1; Prague 2 Vinohrady; CZECH REPUBLIC.

ZR *Zapad Rossii*. Cov: Scan; Lang: Rus; Subj: Related. ISSN: 0132-8166
■Soviet Prospect Street, 21; 236000 Kalingrad City; RUSSIA.

ZreIssk *Zreliščnye iskusstva* (Performing Arts). Freq: 12; Began: 1983; Cov: Full; Lang: Rus; Subj: Theatre. ISSN: 0207-9739
■Gos. Biblioteka SSSR im. Lenina, NIO Informkul'tura; Prospekt Kalinina 3; 101000 Moscow; RUSSIA.

ZS *Zeitschrift für Slawistik*. Freq: 4; Began: 1956; Lang: Ger/Eng; Subj: Related. ISSN: 0044-3506
■Akademie Verlag; Mühlenstr. 33-34; D-13187 Berlin; GERMANY.

Zvezda *Zvezda*. Freq: 12; Began: 1924; Cov: Scan; Lang: Rus; Subj: Related. ISSN: 0321-1878
■Iztadel. Chudožestvennaja Literatura; Mochovaja 20; 192028 St. Petersburg; RUSSIA.

ZZT *Zene-Zene Tánc*. Freq: 2; Began: 1994; Cov: Scan; Lang: Hun; Subj: Related. ISSN: 1218-6678
■Zene-Zene Tánc Alapítvány; Vörösmarty téri; 1051 Budapest; HUNGARY.

Photocomposition and printing services for this volume
of the *International Bibliography of Theatre* were
provided by Volt Information Sciences Inc.,

Cover Design by Irving M. Brown